"Any list of the best writers of vampire novels working today must include the dynamic duo of Barb & J. C. Hendee."
—Rambles

Dhampir

"*Dhampir* maintains a high level of excitement through interesting characters, both heroes and villains, colliding in well-written action scenes. Instead of overloading us with their world-building and the maps and glossaries typical of so much fantasy, the Hendees provide well-rounded characters that go a lot further than maps in making a lively fantasy world."
—*The Denver Post*

"An engaging adventure that is both humorous and exciting."
—*New York Times* bestselling author Kevin J. Anderson

"Take Anita Blake, vampire hunter, and drop her into a standard fantasy world and you might end up with something like this exciting first novel. . . . A well-conceived imagined world, some nasty villains, and a very engaging hero move this one into the winner's column."
—*Chronicle*

"An altogether compelling and moving work . . . these are characters and a world worthy of exploration."
—Brian Hodge, Hellnotes

"A rollicking good romp, it's *Buffy the Vampire Slayer* meets *Vampire Hunter D: Bloodlust* meets Anita Blake meets *The Vampire Lestat* in a realm reminiscent of *Dungeons and Dragons*. . . . The Hendees have taken the best of vampire pop culture and given it new un-life."
—Sequential Tart

"This Buffy-like story in a medieval setting won't disappoint vampire aficionados."
—*Booklist*

"Barb and J. C. Hendee have written a refreshingly innovative horror novel. . . . The plot is meaty and juicy with unexpected turns so that readers are anticipating the next surprise."
—*Midwest Book Review*

"This Buffy-in-medieval-Transylvania novel is fast moving and fun."
—*KLIATT*

Praise for the Noble Dead Saga

Rebel Fay

"A real page-turner."　　　　　　　　　　　*—Booklist*

"Filled with plenty of action, romance, and intrigue."
　　　　　　　　　　　—Midwest Book Review

Traitor to the Blood

"A rousing and sometimes creepy fantasy adventure . . . this is one of those books for which the term 'dark fantasy' was definitely intended."　　　　　　　　*—Chronicle*

"There is a lot of intrigue in *Traitor to the Blood*, which is one of the reasons it is so hard to put down. . . . Readers will eagerly await the next book in this terrific series."
　　　　　　　　　　　—The Best Reviews

"Winning . . . Fans of the series are sure to be pleased, while the novel stands well enough on its own to attract new readers."　　　　　　　　*—Publishers Weekly*

"A unique tale of vampires and half-vampire undead hunters set against a dark fantasy world ruled by tyrants. The personal conflicts of the heroes mirror the larger struggles in their world and provide a solid foundation for this tale of love and loyalty in a world of betrayal."
　　　　　　　　　　　—Library Journal

Sister of the Dead

"A spellbinding work that is creative and addicting."
　　　　　　　　　　　—Midwest Book Review

"A treat on the bookshelves."　　　　　　　*—SFRevu*

"[A] wonderful addition to the Noble Dead series . . . *Sister of the Dead* leads us on an amazing adventure that will keep you engrossed until the final chapter. . . . This is a series that will appeal to both horror and fantasy fans."

　　　　　　　　　　　—SF Site

continued . . .

"The Hendees continue their intelligent dark fantasy series by cleverly interweaving the sagas and personal demons of their heroes with rousing physical battles against the forces of evil. Much more than a medieval 'Buffy does the Dark Ages,' *Sister of the Dead* and its predecessors involve readers on a visceral, highly emotional level [that] fulfill[s] a craving for nifty magic, exciting action scenes, and a strong heroine who defies genre clichés."
—*Romantic Times* (4 stars)

Thief of Lives

"Readers will turn the pages of this satisfying medieval thriller with gusto."
—*Booklist*

"Fans of Anita Blake will enjoy this novel. The characters are cleverly drawn so that the several supernatural species that play key roles in the plot seem natural and real. Supernatural fantasy readers will enjoy this action-packed, strong tale because vampires, sorcerers, dhampirs, elves, fey canines, and other ilk seem real."
—*Midwest Book Review*

"*Thief of Lives* takes the whole vampire slayer mythos and moves into an entirely new setting. The world the Hendees create is . . . a mixture of pre-Victorian with a small slice of Eastern Europe flavor. . . . Magiere and Leesil are a really captivating pair. . . . [The Hendees] handle the ideas and conventions inherent in vampires really well, while, thanks to the clever setting and characters, they make it feel like a very different twist on the subject."
—*SF Site*

"The Hendees unveil new details economically and with excellent timing while maintaining a taut sexual tension between Magiere and Leesil. The multifaceted personalities of these two are what make this series so enjoyable. The mysteries . . . add texture and depth."
—*SFX Magazine*

"A great fantasy adventure, an intriguing mystery, and a chilling gothic tale, weaving a complicated but ever-alluring literary fabric. If anything, this one was even better than [*Dhampir*], which is no small feat."
—*Sequential Tart*

"A vampire story set in a high fantasy world—sound interesting? Then you would enjoy what the Hendees have created. . . . The story is complex and will keep you guessing until the end. Each character is finely crafted, like the weapons they carry. The Noble Dead series is sure to please both fantasy and horror fans. Its unique premises keep your interest level up, and nothing is rushed."
—*Sime~Gen*

REBEL
FAY

Barb & J. C. Hendee

A ROC BOOK

ROC
Published by New American Library, a division of
Penguin Group (USA) Inc., 375 Hudson Street,
New York, New York 10014, USA
Penguin Group (Canada), 90 Eglinton Avenue East, Suite 700, Toronto,
Ontario M4P 2Y3, Canada (a division of Pearson Penguin Canada Inc.)
Penguin Books Ltd., 80 Strand, London WC2R 0RL, England
Penguin Ireland, 25 St. Stephen's Green, Dublin 2,
Ireland (a division of Penguin Books Ltd.)
Penguin Group (Australia), 250 Camberwell Road, Camberwell, Victoria 3124,
Australia (a division of Pearson Australia Group Pty. Ltd.)
Penguin Books India Pvt. Ltd., 11 Community Centre, Panchsheel Park,
New Delhi - 110 017, India
Penguin Group (NZ), 67 Apollo Drive, Rosedale, North Shore 0632,
New Zealand (a division of Pearson New Zealand Ltd.)
Penguin Books (South Africa) (Pty.) Ltd., 24 Sturdee Avenue,
Rosebank, Johannesburg 2196, South Africa

Penguin Books Ltd., Registered Offices:
80 Strand, London WC2R 0RL, England

Published by Roc, an imprint of New American Library, a division of Penguin
Group (USA) Inc. Previously published in a Roc hardcover edition.

First Roc Mass Market Printing, January 2008
10 9 8 7 6 5

*In memory of Dan Hooker,
who stood by us from the start.*

The Elven Territories

Chér am an'Cróanan
Homeland (of those) of the Blood

⊙ City
◇ Clan Region
■ Major Settlement

▬▬▬ Territorial Border
••••••••• Provincial Border
▬▬▬ Major River

10 Leagues

Âlachben ◇

Ghoiyne ⊙
Ajhâjhe

Avân'núnsheach

{Âruin'nàs}

Crijheâiche ■

Hejh (the spire)

Coilehkrotall ◇

the Broken Range

the Cascade Falls

the Crown Range

Box Bay

THE WARLANDS

{Dusan}

the Blade Range

Venjetz ⊙
{Darmouth}

{Lúkina}

⊙ Soladran

STRAVINA

PROLOGUE

Eillean's heart grew heavy as she walked away from the city of Venjètz and into the night forest. Dressed in breeches, cowl, face scarf, and cloak, all dark-tinted, between night-gray and forest-green, only her movement would have betrayed her presence to any watchful eyes.

She did not care for sentiment, but lingering melancholy nagged her just the same.

Brot'ân'duivé walked silently beside her.

Tall for an elf, he stood almost a full head above her, yet he was proportioned more like a human. Both traits were common among his clan. His hair was bound back beneath his cowl, but a few silvery strands still wafted across his dark-skinned forehead. Faint lines surrounded his large amber eyes.

She had not asked him to come on this strange journey. Yet here he was.

They had traveled for nearly a moon from their homeland—what humans called the Elven Territories. Crossing the Broken Range and its western foothills, they arrived at the lake beyond Darmouth's keep. And for what? To bring a majay-hì pup to Léshil, a grandson she had only watched from afar.

Foolishness—and yet she had felt compelled.

With the pup now safely delivered to Cuirin'nên'a, her daughter, Eillean brushed her gloved hand against fir tree branches as she walked. She missed her people's verdant forest, and it was time to return home.

Brot'ân'duivé's cowl was up and a wrap covered his lower face, the same as hers. Not that it mattered. He too hid his emotions behind a passive mask. Perhaps their age and decades among their caste were responsible.

He was not that much younger than she, and she had walked this world for more than a human century. Not so old for an elf, though beyond middle-aged, but venerable for a life of service to the people. A life among the An-maglâhk was seldom a long one.

"Why do this, if it troubles you so?" Brot'ân'duivé finally asked. "Why bring the pup for Léshil? Taking a majay-hì from our land will not sit well with our people."

Always direct—his most devious approach. No matter how well Eillean hid her mood, he often sensed it. It was in part why she had taken him into her confidence shortly after Léshil's birth.

"I stopped at the enclave where I was born," she answered quietly. "There were few faces left that I remembered. A female majay-hì had borne a litter in the settlement, and this one pup was not playing with the others. I picked him up and . . ."

"Now you have doubts?"

"Léshil must be strong . . . uninfluenced by ties beyond his training. It was why Cuirin'nên'a chose to bear a son of mixed blood, an outsider to any one people. I do not wish to soften him."

"A companion does not make one soft."

Eillean scowled slightly. "You sound like his mother, and I fear Cuirin'nên'a has too much love for the boy."

"As you have for her," he answered.

She stopped walking. "You are most irritating."

His calm eyes peered down at her over his face wrap's edge. "One emotion can serve to counter another. And you are still hiding from something more."

"We labor from within the shadows," she said. "Cuirin'nên'a cannot elude the risks she faces alone. She bred Léshil in her own body and now trains him to kill an Enemy we still do not know. All we have are Most Aged Father's fears and his mad obsession with crippling the humans. I am tired of waiting for something we cannot predict."

She paused with a small snort. "So I brought my daughter a majay-hì pup for her son . . . and do not ask me why again! Perhaps it may clarify this future none of us can—"

"It might," he said.

Eillean stalled at a sudden spark of warmth in Brot'ân'duivé's eyes. How did he always know the right thing to say . . . in the fewest words possible and in the most annoying way?

Emotion had no place in an anmaglâhk's life. It clouded judgment in choice and action when both might be needed quickly and without conscious thought. That was the difference between life and death in silence and in shadows. But Brot'ân'duivé always found a way to goad her.

Eillean stepped into Brot'ân'duivé's way, bringing them both to a sudden halt.

"Swear to me that no matter what comes—no matter what you must do—you will protect Cuirin'nên'a, and that her vision will be your vision. Swear to me that all she has done will not be for nothing."

Brot'ân'duivé put his hand upon her shoulder. It slid softly down her arm to her hand.

"I swear," he whispered.

Eillean had lost her bonded mate, Cuirin'nên'a's father, long years ago. His death shattered her, and she had barely clung to life. She was too old now for such things, and still . . .

She put her free hand on Brot'ân'duivé's chest and clutched the fabric of his tunic. She did not let go so long as she felt his hand in hers.

Who among the living—even the Anmaglâhk—could claim to have never been a fool at heart?

CHAPTER ONE

Chap fought for each breath the blizzard tried to rip away, and every step sank him nearly chest-deep in the snowdrifts clinging to the cliff's path. Squinting against the wind, he flexed his paws to fight the numbing cold.

His fur and the folded blanket Magiere had tied across his body were thickly crusted, and his vision blurred if he looked up too long at the whitened sky. To his right, a deep gorge fell beyond sight, while on his left, the peak's steep face rose sharply, its upper reaches lost in the blizzard.

Lashing snow and hail had pelted his face for three days as he led his companions onward. This was the third storm since they had entered the winter-shrouded Broken Range over a moon ago. The map Wynn had procured in Soladran had guided them partway, but once beyond the Warlands' foothills, it was of little help.

Chap had crossed these mountains only once before, and in winter as well, as a pup. Leesil's grandmother, Eillean, had carried him in the company of the deceitful Brot'ân'-duivé. Here and now, so many years later, Chap tried not to think upon his failure.

He could not find a passage through to the Elven Territories.

Chap flattened his ears. Each time he raised them, pelting flakes collected in the openings and sent an icy ache into his skull. Even that pain did not quell his panic. Rather, his fear grew as he looked back down the narrow path.

A dozen paces back, a short figure trudged toward him, half-obscured by snowfall blowing in the harsh wind. It was Wynn. Beside the small sage thumped the hulking silhouette of a burdened horse, either Port or Imp. Farther behind came two more figures with the bulk of the other horse.

And three questions still plagued Chap as he waited for his companions to catch up.

Why did Aoishenis-Ahâre—Most Aged Father—seed war among the humans? Why had the dissidents among the Anmaglâhk—Leesil's mother and grandmother included—created Leesil to kill an enemy they knew nothing about? Why had Chap's own kin, the Fay, now abandoned him?

More than a season past, he had left Miiska with Magiere and Leesil. Every day and league brought more questions he could not answer. All he had wanted in the beginning was to find Magiere and keep her from the hands of the returning Enemy. And Leesil had been his instrument to accomplish this. It was—should have been—a simple task to accomplish. Perhaps this life in flesh made him foolish and naïve, stunting the awareness he had shared among his kin.

Wynn's muffled form grew distinct as she neared, one mittened hand braced against Port's shoulder. Her cloak's hood was cinched around her face, and the wool blanket tied over her cloak was caked with frozen snow. A loose corner of Port's baggage tarp snapped and cracked in the wind.

The little sage stumbled and then collapsed.

Her knees sank in the snow, but her left arm jerked straight up, as if her hand were frozen to Port's shoulder. A cord tied around her wrist disappeared beneath the tarp at the base of Port's neck. It was all that kept her from falling facedown into the drift. She dangled there, legs dragging through snow, until Port halted under the extra burden.

Chap lunged down the path and shoved his muzzle into the scrunched opening of Wynn's hood. He licked furiously at her face, but she remained limp and slack-faced, as if not seeing him.

Dark circles ringed her large brown eyes, and her olive complexion had gone pallid. Food had run low, and for the last quarter moon they traveled on half rations. Wynn's chapped lips moved slightly, but her faint words were lost beneath the wind's howl.

Chap pressed his head into her chest and shoved upward. Wynn twisted, not quite gaining her footing, and flopped against Port's shoulder. Chap braced his shoulder under her hip, ready to force her to stand.

"Get up," a voice growled. "On . . . the horse."

Magiere stood at Port's haunch with Imp's reins clutched in her gloved hand. She held her cloak closed and looked from Chap to the young sage. Like Wynn's, her appearance was one more warning of the cost of Chap's failure.

Snow clung to black locks dangling free of Magiere's hood. A crusted tendril swung across her white face, but even her steaming breath could not clear the ice. And her irises were full black.

No other sign showed of her dhampir nature. No sharpened teeth, no elongated fangs, no feral anger twisting her features. Only her eyes showed that she held her darker side half-manifested.

Chap watched her change each dawn to remain strong enough to move on and watch over Leesil and Wynn. Each dusk when she let go, her exhausted collapse grew worse, and the next morning's rise took longer. Windburn marked her face, and it was disturbing to see stains of color on her ever-pale cheeks.

Magiere dropped Imp's reins and closed on Wynn. She grabbed the sage's cloak front with both hands. Wynn lashed out wildly with her free arm, knocking Magiere's hands away.

"No—too much!" she shouted, and her voice grew weak as she sagged. "I am too much . . . Port carries . . . already carries too much."

Magiere pulled Wynn into her arms, shielding the

smaller woman from the blizzard. Around Port's far side, a third figure struggled past along the steep slope.

Leesil sidestepped across the incline, bracing one hand against Port's far shoulder. His calf-high boots were caked to their tops. At each step, the slope's white blanket cracked and chunks slid around his legs. Strands of white-blond hair blew over Leesil's face to cling to his cracked lips. He scanned the expanse over the gorge and settled angry amber eyes upon Chap.

Determination fueled Leesil in the worst of times. But since discovering his father's and grandmother's skulls displayed as trophies in Darmouth's crypt, it had become something else.

Chap had seen the warlord's death in Magiere's memories. And in Leesil's, he had felt the blade sink through the tyrant's throat to jam against the man's spine. From that moment, Leesil's determination sank into blind obsession beyond caution or reason. Any suggestion by Magiere to turn back and wait out the winter met with vehemence. Though he was as worn and weak as his companions, Leesil's fanaticism pushed all of them onward.

Somewhere in Imp's baggage, the skulls rested in a chest, where they were to remain until the moment Leesil placed them in his mother's hands. Cuirin'nên'a—Nein'a—was alive and waiting, a prisoner of her own people.

If they all lived to find her.

"Enough!" Leesil shouted at Chap, but the storm made his voice seem far away. "Find shelter . . . anything out of this wind."

Chap turned about, facing up the path and into the gale. For an instant, he forgot and lifted his ears. Snow filled them, and his head throbbed.

Where could he find shelter in these dead and barren heights?

The narrow path traced the steep mountainside, rising and falling over rock outcrops peeking above the drifts, but he had seen no worthwhile shelter or cover all day. The last place they'd stopped for the night was a half day's retreat behind them. They were too fatigued to reach it before dark.

Chap trudged up the path, wrenching chilled muscles. He rounded the next outcropping and stopped. In this lifeless place, he tried to sense Spirit from anywhere . . . anything. He reached out through the elements—Earth and frigid Air, frozen Water but no Fire, and his own Spirit. He called to his kin.

Hear me . . . come to me, for we . . . I . . . need you.

Cold seeped up his legs from stone and snow and frozen earth.

No answer. Their silence brought no more despair than he already bore, and his Spirit fired another plea.

How many times must I beg?

He tried often enough. Once before, Wynn had flinched and swallowed hard, and Chap knew the young sage sensed his efforts. Her awareness of his attempts to commune with his kin, as Wynn called it, had slowly grown.

Chap had not spoken with them since the Soladran border. He had turned from the Fay in outrage and raced to the aid of fleeing peasants. After all the times they had harassed and chided him, not once since entering these mountains had they answered his call. He looked back to three silhouettes in the storm huddled near the horses' larger shapes.

I have brought them here . . . and they will all die here!

Wind across the hidden peak above issued a mournful whistle. It ended in a strange staccato of shrill chirps. It was the only answer Chap received. He lifted his muzzle at the sound.

A horse screamed under a rumble like thunder.

The upper slope's white surface appeared to move. Every muscle in Chap's body tightened.

He lunged back down the path, struggling through the snow toward the others. Panic sharpened with each bound. He closed the distance as the rumble grew abruptly.

Leesil vanished beneath a river of cascading snow.

The slide collided into Port, pouring over him as Imp screamed and backed away. Port's rump pivoted toward the gorge's lip and caught Magiere's back. Chap lost sight of her and Wynn as the avalanche spilled around and over them.

Wind and the thundering slide smothered Chap's howl. He staggered to a halt at the slide's rushing edge. Twice he tried to wade in, only to thrash his way back before the current could drag him over the edge.

Port's head and forelegs broke through the slide, snow spraying up around the horse. It seemed impossible that the animal held its place, and Chap saw no sign of the others. Port struggled up on the precipice's edge, thrashing head and forelegs in the deep drift, but he could not pull himself up.

The river of snow slowed, and Chap lunged in before it stilled completely.

He plowed toward the horse, probing the snow with his snout as he searched for anyone not forced over the edge. His nose rammed against something.

He smelled oiled leather and wool. A metal stud grated along his left jowl. He snapped his jaws into the leather as a voice carried from the gorge below.

"Magiere!"

It was Wynn, somewhere below yet still alive. There was no time to wonder how, and Chap heaved on the leather hauberk clenched in his teeth.

A gloved hand reached out of the snow and grabbed the back of his neck.

Chap's paws scraped upon stone beneath the drift as he backed up, hauling Magiere up from where she clung to the precipice by one leg and one arm. He did not let go until she was on her knees.

"Leesil!" Wynn called out, voice filled with alarm.

Leesil rose from out of the deep snow at the path's far side with a stiletto in each gloved hand. He had somehow managed to duck in against the slope and anchor himself with his blades.

Chap darted around Magiere to peer over the edge and into the gorge.

Port's haunches hung out in midair, and Wynn clung to his baggage. She was coated in white. The cord from her wrist to the saddle horn had snapped, and she had held on to baggage lashings. She dangled against Port's rump as the horse kicked wildly at the cliff's side, trying to find footing. Wynn's eyes widened at the sight of Chap.

"Help me!" she cried and tried to pull herself farther up.

Port whinnied in panic as he slid farther over the edge. His shoulders and forelegs sank deeper in the drift. More snow shifted, tumbling around him to strike Wynn's head and shoulders. One of her hands lost its grip, as wind slapped the loosened baggage tarp into her face.

Chap leaned down, snapping his jaws, but the sage was far beyond his reach.

"Leesil, get to Wynn!" Magiere shouted and dove for Port, grabbing the horse's halter.

But Leesil scrambled the other way, toward Imp at the snow-slide's edge.

"Hold on!" he shouted. "I'll be right there."

Imp whinnied, trying to hop free of the snow that had flowed in around her legs. Leesil snatched her reins, pulled her head down, and reached under the baggage tarp. He jerked something out and lunged back toward Magiere.

"I'm coming!" he yelled.

He carried Magiere's unsheathed falchion. When he reached her, he slammed it point-down through the snow with both hands. Magiere grabbed its hilt for an anchor as the wind ripped away her blanket.

Chap peered down helplessly as Wynn coughed out snow and clawed for a grip with her free hand. He dug furiously around Port's stomach to clear footing for the animal. The horse slipped again, and Chap scrambled away before he was clubbed by a forehoof.

Wynn cried out as the horse's belly scraped across the stone and frozen earth of the path's edge.

Leesil heaved on Magiere's waist as she pulled on the embedded falchion. She swung her left leg around it and sat down to sink waist deep in snow. She braced her chest against the sword to keep from slipping toward the gorge's edge and snatched the other side of Port's halter. The falchion's hilt ground into the chest of her hauberk as the backs of Port's forelegs locked against the path's edge.

The horse's quickened snorts shot steam at Magiere. His wild eyes were as unblinking as Magiere's, but her black irises expanded rapidly. She gripped his halter tightly, trying desperately to keep him from falling.

"Get Wynn," she said through clenched teeth.

The tears that always came with her change barely reached her cheeks before the wind whipped them away. Her lips parted, and her face wrinkled in a snarl around sharpened teeth and elongated canines.

Magiere's dhampir nature rose fully, and she heaved on Port's halter. The horse's creeping slide halted.

Leesil let go of Magiere and started to rise. The falchion against her chest began to bend. He quickly sank back down, bracing his legs, and threw an arm over her shoulder, holding her tightly around the chest.

"Climb!" Leesil shouted. "Wynn, you have to climb up!"

Chap clawed the path's edge, clearing a space for himself as he barked at Wynn. The young sage looked up at him in fearful confusion.

"Climb!" Leesil shouted again.

Chap barked once for yes.

Wynn grabbed the next lashing within reach. She pulled herself up and braced one booted foot against Port's rump. The horse kicked again at the cliff's face, and the strap in Wynn's first grip snapped.

She spun like a tassel in the wind and twisted over Port's side. Her back and head slammed into the stone cliff below Chap. Her remaining grip on the baggage lashing began to slip as her hand went limp.

Chap lunged out.

One clawed forepaw ground against Port's side. He snapped his jaws closed on Wynn's wrist, and tasted blood between his teeth as it soaked through her mitten. Wynn shrieked in pain, and Port whinnied.

Chap's forepaw began to slide down the horse's side.

A heavy weight fell on him from behind and pinned him across the cliff's edge.

Leesil's panting breaths filled Chap's ear as he felt Wynn's mitten and skin tear in his teeth. Leesil squirmed and pulled on Chap. The dog's chest scraped back over the edge until his forepaws were digging into the snow.

Leesil reached over the edge and grabbed the shoulder of Wynn's cloak to pull her up. Even when she lay beside

them in the broken snow crying in pain, Chap was too terrified to release her wrist.

"Let go!" Leesil shouted.

Chap opened his jaws, and Wynn curled away from him,
grabbing her wrist.

"Let go," Leesil repeated.

But he was not looking at Chap, and Chap's gaze
flashed up.

Magiere held only Port's reins wrapped in her grip. The
horse's struggles had broken her hold on his halter. A
panic-pitched snarl twisted into growled words between
her clenched teeth.

"No . . . no . . . more . . . lost!"

One rein snapped in half.

Port jerked farther over the edge. The falchion tilted
sharply forward as Magiere was pulled hard against it. Port
struggled wildly, rolling sideways against the edge, and the
blade flattened completely.

Magiere drove her feet down through the snow to brace
herself, refusing to let go of the remaining rein. And still
she slid.

"Let go, damn you!" Leesil shouted, and thrashed in the
drift to get up.

Chap lunged at Magiere. He snapped his jaws closed on
the taut rein. The part that Magiere still held severed under
his teeth. Before he could open his jaws to release the
other half, his head wrenched sideways toward the gorge.

Chap saw white . . . the white-ringed terrified eyes of
Port vanishing over the edge . . . the white of snow in the
horse's face as he slid . . . the white blizzard air of the gorge
below him.

A hard grip closed on his rear leg and jerked him back.
Arms closed around him in a tight grip.

No sound echoed up from the gorge, at least none that
could be heard over the wind.

Held tight in Magiere's arms, Chap heard a sound in her
chest, like a low rumble smothering her whimper. He answered it with his own as he struggled about with his muzzle buried in her neck.

Somewhere above them the wind whistled across the peak. Three short bursts, sharp and quick. And then again.

Chap's ears perked and stayed there, even as the wind spiked into his skull.

He wanted to give Magiere a moment for grief. At a crunch of footsteps, he squirmed about to find Leesil half-dragging, half-carrying Wynn. Leesil lowered the sage beside Magiere.

Chap writhed free of Magiere's hold. The snow-slide had exposed part of the upper slope's face, and he climbed it for a short distance before stopping to listen.

The sound in the peak . . . it could not be the wind.

He stood there so long he wondered if he had heard anything at all, until . . .

Three short and shrill whistles of even length and spacing.

The blizzard's wind could not make such a sound—not twice. Had his kin finally answered his plea?

Chap tumbled and hopped halfway downslope, howling as he went. When Leesil looked up, Chap reversed, climbing two steps before barking loudly. He needed them to follow.

Leesil just stared at him. But when the whistles came again, his gaze rose to the heights above Chap. He scrambled to Imp and began slashing off her baggage as he shouted at Magiere.

"Get Wynn and follow Chap!"

At first Magiere did not move. Her irises were still large and black, and her teeth had not receded. She rolled onto all fours and glared upslope like a wolf searching for any member of its pack. Her black eyes found Chap, and her head swung toward the sage curled in a ball within a pocket of snow.

Magiere hoisted Wynn over one shoulder and stood up. She braced her free hand against the slope's partially exposed rock and took a step upward.

Leesil swatted Imp's bare rump, sending the unburdened horse down the way they had come. The horse could not follow them. He stepped in behind Magiere with whatever baggage he could carry.

Chap climbed toward the heights.

Magiere was near the end of her strength, even with her dhampir nature unrestrained. Wynn was injured, perhaps most by what Chap had done to save her. Even Leesil had given up driving all of them onward. A sudden doubt gripped Chap.

After a moon in these barren mountains, without one touch from his kin, why would they choose to help in this obscure way?

He grew wary of what he had heard, and what waited above in those heights. The more he pondered with each upward lunge, the more his doubt grew.

What choice was left? Either he found shelter, or those under his protection would perish.

Leesil lost sight of Chap above and stopped. Daylight was fading, and he scanned the slope, blinking against flecks of snow pelting his face. A reassuring howl and yip rolled down on the rushing wind, and Leesil turned to check on Magiere.

She still followed, one hand braced against the steep slope and the other gripping Wynn's legs where the sage hung over her shoulder. Her black irises had reduced in size, and were all that remained of her dhampir nature. She'd used up the last of both natural and unnatural strength.

Leesil tried to see through the storm to the heights. Chap had to find somewhere for them to hide, as Magiere had only moments left. He swung the small chest of skulls up on his shoulder over the saddlebags slung there. He gripped the one horse pack he had brought and dragged it upslope. A rock outcrop appeared above, and Leesil halted, panic rising.

It jutted out overhead, perpendicular to the slope. Long icicles crusted its edges. Leesil couldn't spot any passage onward but he heard Chap howl, and the sound rolled around him in the wind as he looked about.

Three paw prints showed in the snow beneath the overhang. They led to the right. The rest of the trail in the open had already vanished under snowfall. Leesil followed the way, looking upward as he passed beyond the outcrop's side.

Chap stood atop the stone protrusion and lowered his head over the edge, barking urgently. He turned a circle back from the edge and then returned.

Whatever the dog had found couldn't be seen from below. Leesil stomped down the snow, trying to make footing Magiere would need, and then heaved the chest and baggage up next to Chap. He turned back for Magiere and found her collapsed beneath the outcrop with Wynn on top of her.

"I'm done," she mouthed, and her eyes began to close.

"No, you're not!" he snapped, and heaved Wynn off of Magiere.

Wynn's whimper was barely loud enough to hear as she tried to grip her bloodied wrist and hold her head at the same time. She curled in a ball at Leesil's knees.

"A little farther," he insisted. "Chap's found something."

Magiere lay on her back with her eyes shut and mouth slack, taking long labored breaths. Each exhale sent up vapor that lingered around her white face beneath the outcrop's protection.

"Sleep . . . ," she growled at him. "Leave me alone."

Leesil's own fatigue overwhelmed him. It felt like relief, making the cold, noisy, white world seem far away. He felt warm and sleepy, ready to lie down next to her.

Chap howled from above with angry frustration.

Leesil snapped his eyes open, and the cold hurt his face once again. He leaned across Wynn and grabbed Magiere by her cloak front, catching the neck of her wool pullover as well. He jerked and nearly toppled himself as she rolled toward him.

"Get up!" he shouted. He tasted blood and knew he'd cracked his wind-parched lips.

Magiere's eyes rolled open as she glared at him. Her irises were their normal dark brown. She struggled to sit up, and then grabbed Wynn under the arms.

Leesil ducked out from beneath the outcrop. He climbed up on the ledge next to Chap and spun about to reach down. With Magiere lifting from below, they hoisted Wynn up. Chap darted away before Leesil could see where the dog went. When he turned in his crouch with Wynn slumped between his knees, he saw a narrow crack in the mountainside where the outcrop met the slope.

Chap poked his head back out of the narrow opening and barked.

Leesil grabbed Magiere's arm and pulled her up.

"I'll take Wynn," he breathed. "Get whatever baggage you can manage."

He knelt down, urging Wynn until the young sage straddled his back.

They climbed upward through the narrow crevice with Magiere in front. The footing was better, as the shielded path was reasonably bare of snow, but the tight space made the wind screech in Leesil's ears. And then a dark gash appeared in the mountainside.

Leesil couldn't see much around Magiere, until she vanished into the opening. It was jagged and ran at an awkward angle up the icy peak. The gash was far too narrow to enter with Wynn riding on his back.

Magiere reached out of the opening, and Leesil lowered Wynn so she could stand. The two of them threaded the staggering sage through the crack, and Leesil followed. Darkness swallowed them for an instant.

It took longer than expected for his half-elven eyes to adjust. Perhaps long days outside had made his eyes weary, where the world seemed brilliant white even at night. The first thing he saw was Magiere holding up Wynn against the side wall as she gazed deeper into the passage.

Its sheer walls slanted like the narrow opening, though it widened farther on, and its bottom was filled with rubble. Uneven footing at best, but the floor beyond seemed flat and manageable. Freezing winter winds and the light thaw of high summer rain had long ago loosened anything that might fall.

A strange rhythmic sound echoed softly around Leesil. It startled him until he recognized it.

Breathing.

He heard Magiere and Wynn breathing, now that they were all out of the blizzard wind. Then he heard claws scrambling over shifting stones. Light from the cave's opening caught on two crystalline eyes looking at them from down the dark passage.

Chap stepped into sight, huffed once at them, and then headed back into the dark.

Leesil rummaged through the saddlebag and horse pack but found neither of the lanterns. They must have been lost with Port. When he looked up, Wynn was trying to reach across into her left cloak pocket with her right hand.

"Crystal . . . ," she said. "I can . . . not get to it."

Magiere reached around and pulled it out for her. She removed her gloves and rubbed the crystal in her hands, but the responding light was weak.

"Too cold . . . ," Wynn added weakly. "Put it in your mouth . . . for a moment."

Magiere was too exhausted to even scowl. She slipped the crystal between her cracked lips and closed her mouth.

In the cave's darkness, her face slowly lit up. Pale features burned from within and her face became a glowing skeletal mask, too much like the skulls of Leesil's father and grandmother. The ghastly sight made him rise and reach for her.

"Take it out!" he snapped.

Magiere spit the crystal into her hand. Its light sprang up so strong that they all flinched. With the crystal in one hand, she prepared to lead the way after Chap.

"Wait," Leesil warned.

He pulled one of Magiere's extra shirts from the horse pack to fashion a sling for Wynn's arm. Then he saw the dark stains around the mitten cuff of the sage's left hand. He carefully peeled the mitten off.

Wynn's wrist wasn't bleeding anymore, but blood had smeared across her hand and up her forearm around where Chap's teeth had torn through her skin. Leesil hoped it looked worse than it truly was, but he wouldn't know until there was time to clean her up. He ripped off the shirttail for a quick bandage.

Wynn didn't flinch until he tried to tie the shirt's sleeves around her for a sling. He worried that her shoulder had been pulled from its socket, and he needed to keep her arm secured. She yelped, cringing away, and Leesil finished quickly.

"Follow Chap," he told Magiere. "We need to get away from the opening to someplace more sheltered."

Magiere scowled, as if all this were his fault, and glanced at Wynn slumped against the stone, breathing weakly. She carefully took Wynn by the waist and led the way with the crystal in her free hand.

Leesil heard Chap scrabbling ahead over the uneven floor, so he hoisted their few belongings. The deeper they went, the quieter it became, until the wind outside sounded far off. Along the way, Leesil noticed pockmarks of darkness high above that the crystal's light couldn't erase. There were smaller openings—cubbies, holes, and other natural cracks, perhaps even channels and smaller tunnels connected into the larger passage. But always at a height impossible to see into.

What at first seemed a cave at the passage's end, made from ancient shifting rock inside the mountain, became a series of subterranean pockets. One led to the next, ever inward below a connecting tangle of smaller cracks and fissures overhead. The air felt slightly warmer, or maybe it was just that they were out of the wind. The way narrowed, then widened, shortened then opened, over and over, until inside one tall cavern the crystal's light barely reached the stone ceiling overhead.

"It's so high," Leesil whispered, and then thought he heard something.

Cloth or some other soft substance dragged quickly across rough stone.

Every move they made echoed and warped off the walls, and Leesil couldn't be sure it wasn't just a trick of fatigue. He quick-stepped to catch Magiere's shoulder and called out to Chap.

"Here . . . we stop. Over by that wall there's a smooth slant of stone."

Magiere looked where he pointed and guided Wynn to their resting place. Leesil dropped their belongings beside them, but Chap remained poised at the cave's center.

The dog let out a low rumble, turning his head slowly. He scanned all around the chamber.

Something made Chap wary, and that was enough for Leesil to hesitate. He took a few steps out toward Chap, turning his own eyes upward to the hidden high places above.

"What is it?" he asked.

A long silence followed. Chap huffed three times to say he didn't know.

Leesil backed up to Magiere and Wynn, still watching all around.

Magiere had settled Wynn to lean against the horse pack. She stripped off the sage's blanket, shook away clinging snow, and laid it across the woman's legs. Leesil knelt down on Wynn's left.

"I have to look . . . feel your shoulder and upper arm," he said quietly, and pulled off his gloves.

Wynn didn't even nod. Perhaps she hadn't heard him.

Magiere sidled closer on Wynn's right, waiting tensely as Leesil unfastened the sage's cloak and short robe. He rubbed his hands together before his mouth, trying to warm them. As he pulled Wynn's shift open and slipped one hand in, Magiere slid her arm behind Wynn's back and held the sage tight against herself.

"Squeeze hard," she whispered, gripping Wynn's good hand. "Hard as you have to."

Leesil held Wynn's left arm with his free hand as he closed his fingers around the soft skin of her small shoulder. Wynn sagged and buried her face into Magiere with a soft whimper.

For all he could tell, Wynn's shoulder was sound. She had not winced when he'd first gripped her upper arm, so it was unlikely any bones had broken or cracked. He closed up Wynn's clothing and grabbed the crystal Magiere had left atop the skulls' chest. Setting it down before his knees, he unwrapped Wynn's wrist.

Once he'd rinsed away the blood with a bit of chilled water, the teeth marks in her skin didn't look so bad. He rewrapped the bandage, put the crystal back, and shook out his cloak and Magiere's.

Leesil reclined against the pack as Wynn settled and closed her eyes. With the sage between himself and Magiere, he covered all three of them with the cloaks and blanket.

Magiere watched him with something akin to a frown on her windburned face. Or was it disappointment? She finally closed her eyes.

"Go to sleep," she said, and a dull flush of shame washed through Leesil.

They were all in a desperate way, and Wynn had been injured yet again.

Leesil couldn't count the times he'd cursed at Chap for every blocked passage or dead end they'd run into. But his guilt was always outmatched by what drove him.

Somewhere beyond reach, his mother waited. As he laid his head back, his gaze fell upon the small snow-dusted chest.

Dusk fell as Chane huddled in his cloak within a makeshift tent, listening to Welstiel's incessant murmurs.

"Iced stronghold . . . show me . . . where . . ."

Chane cocked his head.

Dark hair marked with white-patched temples gave Welstiel the distinguished look of a gentleman in his forties. But over passing moons since leaving the city of Bela in Magiere's wake, the once fastidious and immaculate Welstiel had fallen into disarray.

Disheveled locks, mud-stained boots, and a cloak beginning to tatter made it hard for Chane to see the well-traveled noble he had first met.

Chane sneered. He knew that he looked no better.

"Orb . . . ," Welstiel muttered.

Chane tried to focus upon Welstiel's scattered words. He pulled the threadbare cloak tighter around his own shoulders.

Cold was a mortal concern to which he gave no thought, but he was starving. He longed for the heat of blood filling him up with life. Hunger grinding inside him made his thoughts wander.

Well past a moon ago, he and Welstiel had pursued Magiere and her companions through the Warlands and into the city of Venjètz. None of them knew Welstiel followed, and they believed Chane was gone, after Magiere had beheaded him in the dank forests of eastern Droevinka. Welstiel remained undetected, but Chane was not so certain that Magiere was unaware of his return to the world.

Welstiel purchased sturdy horses, grain for feed, and a well-worn cloak for Chane from a merchant caravan they happened upon. He also procured canvas, several daggers, and a lantern. From a distance, they followed Magiere, Leesil, Chap, and Wynn through the foothills and into the base of the Broken Range where it met with the Crown Range. On the twelfth dusk within those heights, Chane was preparing for the night's travel when Welstiel mounted and turned his horse east by southeast. Away from Magiere's path.

"We follow our own way—into the Crown Range. Magiere will find us when she has finished chasing Leesil's past among the elves."

His voice had been calm, but Chane knew better. He sensed resignation in his companion. No undead could enter the forests of the elves, or so Welstiel had once claimed.

Chane heard something that made him pause, and he urged his horse up next to Welstiel's.

Voices carried down the mountainside, not quite clear enough to understand. But his vision expanded to full range, and he caught movement far above. Magiere and her companions had set up camp below a granite spire jutting up from the mountainside. As their campfire sprang to life, Chane's grip tightened on the reins.

Wynn crouched near the sputtering flames.

Now Welstiel would have him just turn away?

Anger burned against Chane's hunger at this last glimpse of Wynn, still wearing his cloak. As far as Chane knew, Welstiel had never noticed this one telltale sign.

On the last night in Venjètz, Chane had carried Wynn from Darmouth's keep to safety. Welstiel knew as much, and Chane never denied it. Wynn remained unconscious the whole time, never seeing who carried her. But the others with her—one frail but sharp-eyed noblewoman and a strange girl child—would surely have told Wynn that he had been there.

And he had covered Wynn with his cloak.

The thought of her so far from reach, beyond his protection—especially among those bigoted elves—was unbearable. But Chane did not blame Welstiel.

He blamed Magiere.

Wynn would follow that white-skinned bitch down into every netherworld of every long-forgotten religion. Chane had once tried to dissuade her and failed. Nothing he did or said would stop Wynn. Now he had no home, nothing he truly desired, and little future other than to follow Welstiel in search of the man's fantasy—this . . . orb.

Welstiel believed some ancient artifact would free him from feeding on blood, though he was not forthcoming about how. From pieces Chane gathered, it would some-how sustain the man without "debasing" himself. But while Welstiel had once believed he could not procure the object without Magiere, he now planned to locate it himself and lure her to it, once she emerged . . . if she emerged . . . if Wynn ever left the Elven Territories.

The "orb" of Welstiel's obsession pulled Chane from the one thing that mattered most to him. Whatever source of in-formation Welstiel found in his slumber, it had begun doling out tidbits again, like a trail of bread crumbs leading a starv-ing bird into a cage. Yet the trail was incomplete. Perhaps purposefully so?

All Chane wanted was to find his way into the world of the sages, his last connection to Wynn. For that he needed Welstiel's promised letter of introduction. The man had more than once implied a past connection to that guild. So Chane followed him like a servile retainer. And then Wel-stiel turned irrationally away from Magiere . . . away from Wynn.

It made no sense, if Welstiel expected to pick up Magiere's trail later, for she would surely return—if at all—through the Broken Range. Something in Welstiel's dreams now pushed the man toward the Crown Range.

Now, Chane was starving, huddled in a makeshift tent and wrapped in a thin secondhand cloak, with no people living up this high to feed upon.

Welstiel's head rolled to the side, exposing his thick neck and throat.

The grinding hunger grew inside Chane.

Could one undead feed upon another? Steal what little life it hoarded from its own feeding?

It had been twelve days since Chane had last tasted blood. His cold skin felt like dried parchment. He could not take his eyes off Welstiel's neck.

"Wake up," he rasped.

The words grated out of his maimed throat. He slipped his hand into his cowl to rub at the scar left by Magiere's falchion.

Welstiel's eyes opened. He sat up slowly and looked about. The man always awoke disoriented.

"We are in the tent . . . again," Chane said.

Welstiel's lost expression drained away. "Pack the horses."

Chane did not move. "I must feed . . . tonight!"

He waited almost eagerly for an angry rebuke. Welstiel looked him over with something akin to concern.

"Yes, I know. We will drop into the lower elevations to find sustenance."

Chane's anger caught in his throat. Welstiel had agreed too easily. His surprise must have shown, for Welstiel's voice hardened.

"You are no good to me if you become incapacitated."

Welstiel's self-interest did not matter, so long as the prospect of human blood—and the life it carried—was real. Chane slapped open the tent's canvas and stood up beneath spindly branches of mountain fir trees. Welstiel followed him out.

Half a head taller than his companion, Chane appeared over a decade younger. Jaggedly cut red-brown hair hung just long enough to tuck behind his ears.

Snow drifted around him in light flurries across a landscape barren and rocky except for the scattered trees leaning slightly north from relentless winds. Chane hated this monotonous, hungry existence. For a moment he closed his eyes, submerging in a waking dream of nights in Bela at the sages' guild.

Warmly lit rooms were filled with books and scrolls. Simple stools and tables were the only furniture, though often covered in so many curiosities it was hard to know where to begin the night's journey into unknown pasts and places far away or long lost. The scent of mint tea suddenly filled the room, and Wynn appeared, greeting him with a welcoming smile.

Chane surfaced from memory and turned dumbly to saddling the horses.

Both were sturdy mountain stock but showed signs of exhaustion and the lack of food. Chane had begun rationing their grain as the supply dwindled.

Géorn-metade . . .

Wynn's Numanese greeting stuck in Chane's thoughts. She spoke many languages, and this was the tongue of her homeland. Chane glanced sidelong at Welstiel with a strange thought.

He knew next to nothing of Welstiel's past, but several times the man had said things . . . comments that implied the places Welstiel had traveled. How could the man have a connection to the Guild of Sagecraft abroad without the ability to converse with them?

"Géorn-metade," Chane said.

"Well met? What do you mean?" Welstiel stepped closer. "Where did you hear that greeting?"

Chane ignored the question. "You've traveled in the Numan lands?"

Welstiel lost interest and reached for his horse's bridle. "You are well aware that I have."

"You speak the language."

"Of course."

"Fluently?"

Welstiel held the bridle in midair as he turned on Chane. "What is brewing in that head of yours?"

Chane hefted the saddle onto his horse. "You will teach me Numanese while we travel. If I'm to seek out the sages' guild in that land, I'll need to communicate with its people."

Snowflakes grew larger, and the wind picked up. Welstiel stared into the growing darkness, but he finally nodded.

"It will pass the time. But be warned, the conjugations are often irregular, and the idioms so—"

He stopped as Chane whirled to the left, head high, sniffing the air.

"What is it?" Welstiel asked.

"I smell life."

*   *   *

Chap slowly paced the cavern, watching its dark heights. He smelled something.

Like a bird, but with a strange difference he could not place.

Perhaps a hawk or eagle took refuge here against the storm. The crystal's light did not reach high enough for even his eyes to see into the dark holes above. He approached the far wall, peering upward.

A thrumming snap echoed through the cavern.

An arrow struck in front of him and clattered on the stone.

Chap backpedaled, twisting about in search of its origin. He braced on all fours with ears perked and remained poised to lunge aside at any sound. About to bark a warning to his companions, he heard another sound high to his right.

Something soft . . . pliant . . . smooth that dragged on stone, followed by a brief and careless scrape of wood. Then silence.

Chap growled.

"Come back here!" Leesil called in a hushed voice.

Chap remained where he was but heard nothing further. Whatever hid above and had called to him amid the storm, it did not care for anyone coming too close. And he no longer believed it had anything to do with his kin.

He inched forward, sniffing carefully at the small, plain arrow.

The strange bird scent was strong on it, especially on the mottled gray feathers mounted at its notched end. The shaft was no longer than his own head, and ended in a sharpened point rather than a metal head. He gripped it with his teeth, and the light-colored wood was harder than expected. It tasted faintly sweet, not unlike the scent of jasmine, and maybe cinnamon, reminding him of spiced tea Magiere served at the Sea Lion Tavern.

Memory. How strange the things that came to him—and the things that would not. Things he must have once known among the Fay.

Chap looked up to the cavern heights. Instinct and intellect told him there was likely no danger, so long as they left their hidden benefactor well enough alone. Still, he did not care for a skulker watching them from the dark. He loped back to his companions with the small arrow in his teeth.

He dropped it upon the edge of the layered blankets and cloaks, prepared to nudge Leesil.

Wynn rolled her head and half-opened her eyes. Chap stepped as close as he could, sniffing at her loosely bandaged wrist, the one he had injured trying to save her.

He peered at Wynn's round face by the waning light of the crystal atop the chest. She settled her hand clumsily on his head. It slid over his ear, down his face, and dropped limply against her side as her eyes closed again.

"It is all right," she said, and even weaker, like a child on the edge of sleep, "thank you."

Chap turned a circle and curled up at Wynn's feet.

He laid his head upon his paws, trying to keep his eyes open, and watched the heights of the cavern. He never knew whether fatigue or the waning crystal finally pulled him down into darkness.

CHAPTER TWO

Welstiel urged his horse through the dark, keeping up with Chane amid the scattered trees of the rocky mountainside. Occasionally, Chane slowed to sniff the night breeze.

Disdain tainted Welstiel's grudging respect for Chane's hunting instincts. He had suppressed such long ago, but given their present situation, the need for life to feed upon grew desperate even for him.

Since leaving Venjètz, Chane had reverted to the resourceful companion he had been in Magiere's homeland of Droevinka, securing supplies, setting proper camps before dawn, and hunting. Even his ambition to seek out the sages had renewed. Welstiel was pleasantly relieved, at least in part.

"Are we close?" he asked quietly.

Chane did not answer. He wheeled his horse aside, sniffed the air like a wolf, and then kicked his panting mount forward.

Welstiel followed with a frown. When they pushed through thin trees tilted by decades of wind, he caught a whiff of smoke. Chane's starvation might drive him to lunge the instant they found prey, but Welstiel had other plans.

"Stop!" he whispered sharply.

"What?" Chane rasped. He reined his horse in, his long features half-feral around eyes drained of color.

"Whoever we find, I will question them first." Welstiel pulled up beside Chane. "Then you may do as you please."

The sides of Chane's upper lips drew back, but his self-control held. He pointed between two small boulder knolls.

"Through there."

Welstiel smoothed back his hair. Despite his threadbare cloak, he still had the haughty manner of a noble. It was near midnight, and as Welstiel rounded a rocky hillock he saw a small flickering campfire. Two figures sat beyond its ring of scavenged stones.

"Hallo," he called out politely.

Their faces lifted. The flames lit up the ruddy dark features of an aging Móndyalítko couple. Unbound black hair hung past the old woman's shoulders with thin streaks of gray turning white in the firelight. She was layered in motley fabrics, from her quilted jacket to her broomstick skirt. The man tensed and reached behind where he sat. Dressed in as many layers as his mate, he wore a thick sheepskin hat with flaps over his ears.

Behind them stood a lean mule tied to a small enclosed cart not nearly so large as these wanderers usually lived in. What were they doing up here all alone? Welstiel smiled with a genteel nod and urged his horse to the clearing's edge.

"Could we share your refuge and perhaps some tea?" he asked, gesturing to a silent Chane. "We had trouble finding a place out of the wind. We can pay for the imposition."

The man stood up, an age-stained machete in his grip. His manner eased as he eyed the night visitors, who were clearly not roving bandits.

"Coin's not much good up here," he replied in Belaskian with a guttural accent. "Perhaps a trade?"

"Our food supply is low," Welstiel lied, as he had no food. "But we have grain to spare for your mule."

The old man glanced at his beast, which looked like it had not eaten properly in some time. With a satisfied nod, he waved the night visitors in.

"We have spiced tea brewing. Are you lost?"

"Not yet," Welstiel answered wryly. "We are cartographers . . . for the sages' guild in Bela."

The old man raised one bushy gray eyebrow.

"I know . . . mapmakers, wandering about in the dark," Welstiel replied. "We stayed in the upper peaks too long. Our supplies dwindled faster than anticipated."

The woman snorted and reached for the blackened teapot resting in the fire's outer coals.

"Hope these sages—whatever they are—pay good coin to track ways that few ever travel."

Chane remained silent as he settled by the fire. Welstiel knew these pleasantries were difficult for him at such close range, but Chane would have to hold out a little longer.

"And what are you two doing up here in winter?" Welstiel asked.

"Stole cows from the wrong baron," the man said without the slightest shame. "We know these ways, but the baron's men don't."

This blatant honesty surprised Welstiel, and it must have shown on his face.

The old man laughed. "If you were the baron's hired men, you'd hardly have waited for an invite."

Likely true. Welstiel glanced at Chane and noticed his hands were shaking. In the camp's flickering light, Chane's skin looked dry like parchment beginning to show its age. Neither Móndyalítko took notice of Chane's odd silence.

Welstiel hurried things along. He returned to their horses, took a grain sack hanging from Chane's saddlebag, and dropped it beside the fire.

"Take what you need," he said. "At dawn, we head down for supplies."

"We thank you," the old man said with a casual shrug, though it did not hide the eager widening of his eyes.

"Our employers asked us to locate any structures or settlements," Welstiel went on. "Way stations, villages, even old ruins . . . any strongholds high up. Do you know of any we should seek out when we come back?"

The woman handed him a chipped mug of tea. "There's

Hoar's Hollow Keep. A lonely old place trapped where the snow and ice last most year 'round."

Welstiel paused in midsip, then finished slowly. *Locked in snow and ice.*

"You're certain? How many towers does it have?"

The woman frowned, as if trying to remember. "Towers? I don't know. Haven't seen it since I was a girl."

She stepped around the ring of stones and poured Chane a mug of tea. He took it but did not drink.

"Can you tell us the best route?" Welstiel asked.

"You'd do better to wait for the thaw," the old man answered. "It's a ways, and at least then most of the path would be clear."

"Yes, but where?" Welstiel's grip tightened on the mug, and he struggled to relax his fingers.

"Thirty leagues . . . or likely more, into the Crown Range," the woman answered.

Chane let out a hissing sigh.

"Hard going, so it'll seem longer," said the man.

"Just head southeast until you reach a large ravine," his wife continued. "Like a giant gouge in the mountainside. It stretches into the range, so you can't miss it. The passage is marked by flat granite slabs. Come to think, they might not be easy to spot in the snow. Once down through the passage, you'll see your stronghold, but it'll be blocked away by winter now."

Welstiel stayed silent. It was the only way he could contain a rising relief that had waited for decades. A chance meeting with two Móndyalítko thieves put the end of his suffering in sight.

Elation faded like the vapor of hot tea in a cold breeze. Was it chance?

Perhaps his dream patron relented from years of teasing hints. Perhaps those massive coils in his slumber took a more active role in his favor.

A season had passed since he had trailed Magiere into Droevinka, the land of her birth. Before her birth, in his own living days, Welstiel had resided there. Ubâd, his father's retainer, had waited there all Magiere's life for her to return within his reach. When she came and then re-jected him, the mad necromancer had called out to some-thing by a name.

il'Samar.

In hiding amid Apudâlsat's dank forest, Welstiel watched dark spaces between the trees undulate with spec-tral black coils taller than a mounted rider. The same coils of his dreams—his own patron—or so it seemed. And it abandoned Ubâd in his moment of need. Welstiel had watched as Chap tore out the old conjuror's throat.

He turned the warm mug in his hands as he studied the Móndyalítko couple. What he had seen in that dank forest left him wondering.

Were this il'Samar and his patron one and the same? If indeed his patron could reach beyond wherever it rested—beyond dreams and into this world—had it done so here and now? Should he trust such fortune appearing when he desired it most?

He had learned all he could from the old couple. He rose and leaned over on the pretense of opening the grain sack. The old man stood as well.

Welstiel drove his elbow back into the man's chest just below his sternum.

The old man buckled, gagging for air. Before Chane's mug hit the frigid earth, his fingers closed on the old woman's throat.

"Wait!" Welstiel shouted. He whirled and smashed his fist into the man's temple, and the aged Móndyalítko dropped limp, face buried in the grain sack.

The pulsing life force of the woman in his hands drove Chane half-mad. He jerked her head back until it seemed her neck might snap, opening his jaws and exposing elon-gated canine teeth.

She gasped in fear, but couldn't draw enough breath to scream. He bit down hard below her jawline, drinking in-ward the instant he broke her skin, desperate to draw blood into his body.

Welstiel rushed in and back-fisted Chane across the cheek.

Chane stumbled away. His grip tore from the woman's throat. She screeched once as his fingernails scraped bleeding lines across her neck.

He spun with his teeth bared as Welstiel struck the woman down and she crumpled next to her mate.

"I said wait!" Welstiel shouted.

Chane closed in slowly, enraged enough to rip his companion's throat out instead.

"There is a better way," Welstiel stated. "Watch."

Something in his voice cut through Chane's hunger, and he paused warily.

Welstiel held up both hands, palms outward. "Stay there."

He hurried to his horse and retrieved an ornate walnut box from his pack. Chane had never seen it before. Kneeling by the unconscious old woman, Welstiel opened the box and glanced up.

"There are ways to make the life we consume last longer."

Chane crouched and crept forward, forcing himself to hold off from savaging the woman as he looked into the walnut box.

Resting in burgundy padding were three hand-length iron rods, a teacup-sized brass bowl, and a stout bottle of white ceramic with an obsidian stopper. Welstiel removed the rods, each with a loop in its midsection, and intertwined them into a tripod stand. He placed the brass cup upon it and lifted out the white bottle.

"This contains thrice-purified water, boiled in a prepared vessel," he said. "We will replenish the fluid later."

He pulled the stopper and filled half the cup, then rolled the woman onto her back. Chane pressed both hands against the ground and fought the urge to lunge for her throat.

"Bloodletting is a wasteful way to feed," Welstiel said, his voice sounding far away. "It is not blood that matters but the leak of life caused by its loss. Observe."

He drew his dagger and dipped its point into the blood trailing from the woman's nostrils. When the steel point held a tiny red puddle, he carefully tilted the blade over the cup. One drop struck the water.

Blood thinned and diffused beneath the water's dying ripples, and Welstiel began to chant. It started slowly at first, and Chane saw no effect.

Then the woman's skin began to dry and shrivel. Her eyelids sank inward and her cheekbones jutted beneath withering skin. Her body dried inward, shrunken to a husk as her life drained away. When Chane heard her heart stop beating, Welstiel ceased his chant.

The fluid in the cup brimmed near its lip, so dark it appeared black.

Welstiel lifted the small brass vessel and offered it to Chane. "Drink only half. The rest is for me."

Chane blinked. He reached out for the cup, lifted it, and gulped in a mouthful.

"Brace yourself," Welstiel warned and tilted his head back to pour the remaining liquid down his throat.

For a moment, Chane only tasted dregs of ground metal and salt. Then a shock of pain in his gut wrenched a gag from him.

So much life taken in pure form . . . it burst inside him and rushed through his dead flesh.

It burned, and his head filled with its heat. He waited with jaws and eyes clenched. When the worst passed, he opened his eyes with effort. Welstiel crouched on all fours, gagging and choking.

Chane's convulsions finally eased.

"This is how you feed?" he asked.

For a moment Welstiel didn't answer, then his body stopped shaking. "Yes . . . and it will be some time before we need to do so again, perhaps half a moon or more."

He crawled to the unconscious old man and repeated the process. But this time, instead of drinking, Welstiel poured the black fluid into the emptied white bottle and sealed the stopper.

"It will keep for a while," he said. "We may need it, with so little life in these peaks."

For the first time in many nights, the painful ache of hunger eased from Chane's body. He rose up, his mind clearing. He felt more . . . like himself again, but he turned toward Welstiel with growing suspicion.

"How did you learn this?"

"A good deal of experimentation." Welstiel paused. "I do not share your bloodlust."

A cryptic answer—with a thinly veiled insult.

Welstiel picked up the abandoned kettle and poured tea into two mugs. He held out one to Chane. "Drink this. All of it."

"Why?"

"Does your flesh still feel brittle like dried parchment?"

Chane frowned and absently rubbed at his scarred throat. "Yes . . . for several nights past."

"Our bodies need fluid to remain supple and functional. Otherwise, even one of our kind can succumb to slow desiccation. Drink."

Chane took the mug and sipped the contents, annoyed that Welstiel lectured him like a child. But as the liquid flowed down his throat, the ease in his body increased. He retrieved the grain sack, but also untied the donkey and let it go.

Welstiel watched this last act with a confused shake of his head.

Chane kicked the fire apart to kill its flames and headed for his horse, glancing once at Welstiel as if noticing him for the first time.

They mounted up, and Chane led the way southeast until dawn's glow drove them once more into the tent and another day of hiding from the sun. He thought he knew most of Welstiel's secrets—or at least hints of them. What else of import did his companion hide?

Eyes closed in half sleep, Magiere rolled and reached out across Wynn for Leesil. Her fingers touched hard stone beneath a flattened blanket. She sat up too quickly, and Wynn rolled away, grasping the cloaks and blankets with a grumble.

"Leesil?" Magiere called in a hushed voice.

She teetered with exhaustion and her head swam in the dark. She tried to force her dhampir nature to rise and expand her senses.

No feral hunger heated her insides or rose in her throat.

She'd held her dhampir nature in part for too many days, and now it wouldn't come in her exhaustion.

Magiere crawled around Wynn, feeling along the cave's rough floor until her fingers struck sharply against the side of the skulls' chest. She cursed, shook her hand, and followed the chest's contours until she touched the cold lamp crystal atop it. She rubbed it briskly, and it sparked into life between her palms.

Wynn slept rolled in Chane's old cloak beneath Magiere's own and the blanket. The makeshift sling had slipped off the sage's arm. She seemed in no serious pain or she would've fully awoken. There was no sign of Leesil—or Chap—anywhere in the slanted cavern.

Magiere's gaze fell upon something that made her tense, and she shifted to the bottom edge of their makeshift bed. Amid clinging strands of Chap's fur lay a small arrow. She picked it up, glancing warily about the cave.

Its light yellow shaft was too short for any bow and too thin for a crossbow quarrel. Tiny featherings bound at its notched end were a strange mottled white and almost downy at the forward ends. In place of a metal head, it ended in a sharpened point—or would have if it weren't blunted. Its last flight must have dashed it against something hard.

And it lay in Chap's resting place. Where had he found it?

Magiere tucked it in the back of her belt and rose to head up the way they'd come. The crystal's light spread wider and caught on something else.

Beside where she'd slept was a small mat of green leaves, each as large as her opened hand. They held a pile of what appeared to be grapes. Magiere dropped back to one knee.

Each fruit was the size of a shil coin, and dark burgundy in color, but they were not grapes. A green leafy ring as on a strawberry remained where each had been plucked from a stem. They looked more like bloated blueberries. There were more than she could quickly count, enough to overfill a cupped hand.

Magiere looked about, wondering how anyone could have approached while they slept, especially with Chap present. Then she spotted another pile near where Leesil had rested.

Where had they come from in these winter mountains?

Magiere checked Wynn one last time to be sure she rested peacefully. She considered waking the sage to eat or to ask what she knew of the berries. Instead she quietly picked up her falchion and headed for the opening to the path back outside.

She called out softly when she reached the next smaller pocket along the way. "Leesil? Chap?"

A rustling echo carried up the passage from behind her.

"Leesil?" came a voice, and it grew louder in panic. "Magiere . . . Chap, where are you?"

Wynn had awoken. Magiere hesitated between calling out and turning back, and finally retreated to the cavern so that Wynn saw she wasn't alone.

"Here," she said, "I'm here."

A distinct scrape and padding footfalls sounded from the passage behind her. She looked back to see two sparks in the dark passage that became crystal blue-white eyes.

Chap trotted out, silver-gray fur rustling and his tail high, as if he'd been out for a morning run. Leesil followed, carrying a torn horse pack and another set of saddlebags. His cloak's hood had fallen, and white-blond hair swung loose around his dark face to his shoulders. His oblong, slightly pointed ears showed clearly.

"Where in the seven hells have you been?" Magiere growled at him.

Leesil stopped, looked at her in bewilderment, and then held up the saddlebags. "Where do you think? I climbed back down and gathered what was left."

She paused, slightly embarrassed. Of course that was what he would do, but he might have thought enough to let her know.

"Next time, you wake me before you disappear! I told you—"

"That I'm not to leave your side," Leesil finished for her, "or you'll club me down before the second step."

For three slow blinks, his amber eyes glowered in cold silence. Magiere's anger melted toward the edge of despair. Was there anything left of the man she'd once resisted falling in love with? Or had he too been murdered in Darmouth's family crypt?

The barest smile pulled the corners of Leesil's mouth. Not quite the mocking grin he used to flash at her, but still . . .

"Were you worried sick about me?" he asked. "Afraid I'd been packed off by some prowling cave beast?"

A hint of the old Leesil reappeared—the one who'd teased her so often. The one she'd known before this journey of unwanted answers, their own dark natures, and too much death.

Leesil's smile vanished, as if he'd read her thoughts and couldn't face them.

"We should take stock of what's left," he said, and stepped past, heading for Wynn.

Magiere followed, feeling bruised inside. "How's the shoulder?"

"It is stiff, and it aches," Wynn answered, shifting her arm back into its sling. "But I can move it without sharp pain."

Wynn pulled back her hood, running fingers through her tangled, light-brown hair, and then winced.

"What's wrong?" Magiere asked too sharply.

"Nothing," she answered. "I have a lump like a . . . I banged my head when I hit the cliff, but I will be fine."

Wispy tufts of hair stuck out above Wynn's forehead. Chap circled around Leesil, sniffing at her wrist.

Magiere set the cold lamp crystal on the chest and crouched. She unwrapped Wynn's bandage to inspect her wounded wrist. Chap whined softly, and Wynn settled her good hand upon his head.

"That's good to hear," Leesil said. "Shouldn't be long before—"

"Did you find Imp?" Wynn asked.

Another long silence, and Magiere waited for it to end.

"No," Leesil answered. "I sent her down the path before we carried you here. It's still dark out, but the storm has faded. Hopefully she'll make it to the foothills."

Magiere dropped from her crouch to one knee.

They were only animals, Port and Imp, but they'd been with her for the better part of a long journey. She barely hung on to what she had left of herself—what was left of the Leesil she wanted. Anything more she lost sliced away another piece of her.

Chap licked at Wynn's cheek, and his ears perked. He turned around to sniff the cave floor beyond the blankets. Magiere was too lost to give him much notice.

She wanted to say something comforting to Wynn but couldn't think of anything. They had survival to attend to, and this place might offer hidden threats beneath its guise of sanctuary.

Chap barked sharply, shifting about until he faced all of them with his nose to the ground. Magiere realized what the dog had found. She grabbed the crystal and held its light up.

"Bisselberries?" Wynn whispered. "But . . . where? I have not seen such since . . . How did you find—"

"How do you know these?" Leesil dropped onto his haunches before the pile.

"These are bisselberries," Wynn repeated, then picked up one plump fruit, dropped it in the hand with the bandaged wrist, and tried to split its skin with a fingernail. "That is what my people call them, or roughly that in your language. We buy them at market to make puddings and jams for the harvest festival or special occasions. But they have to be—"

"Stop jabbering!" Magiere snapped. "How could they grow in winter mountains?"

Wynn scowled at her, still trying to split the berry's skin.

"They do not grow here. They only come from . . ."

Wynn's big brown eyes widened as she looked up at Magiere; then her breath quickened, and her voice vibrated with nervous excitement. "Elves . . . they only grow in the elven lands south of my country!"

Leesil spun to his feet, pulling stilettos from his sleeves. Magiere snatched her falchion and jerked it free of its sheath, as he turned about, searching the shadows.

Chap's rapid chain of barks echoed around the cavern.

Magiere spotted him off near the far right wall, opposite the opening they had come through.

"Stay with Wynn," Magiere told Leesil, and trotted toward the dog.

Chap dropped his head as she joined him. At his forepaws was a small hollow where the floor met the wall. She couldn't see far into it, but it seemed another passage below headed deeper into the mountain's belly. Chap huffed at her, head still low.

Another pile of berries lay on a mat of leaves near the hollow's far edge.

"No, don't!" Leesil snapped.

Magiere twisted about to see Leesil slap away a berry that Wynn tried to pop into her mouth. The sage looked up at him with shock.

"We are starving, you idiot!"

"Better than dead!" he countered. "We're not eating anything left by one of them."

"It's not elves," Magiere said as she returned. "Not that I can guess. Look at this."

She pulled the small arrow out, and Leesil's brow wrinkled.

"I found it on our blankets when I awoke," she added, "along with the berries near my head. Chap found more of those over there by another opening."

Leesil took the shaft, turning it in his hand. "Too thin for a crossbow . . . too short for any bow I know of, and it looks newly fletched. That other opening must be how . . . whoever got in here. Maybe another passage out to the mountainside."

Chap thumped Leesil's leg with his head, then stepped out a ways to the cave and looked upward. Magiere picked up the crystal, rubbed it harshly, and held up its brightening light.

Above them in the ragged slanting walls were other openings scattered about. Their irregular positions, sizes, and shapes suggested they were natural and hadn't been dug. Leesil headed for the far wall, eyes raised to one larger opening.

Chap rushed into his way with a snarl of warning.

"You found the arrow," Magiere said. "It came from up there? Did you see it hit?"

Chap huffed once for "yes."

"Wynn, dig out the talking hide," she called.

"She can't," Leesil said.

Wynn was already pawing one-handed through the pile of saddlebags, packs, and bundles that Leesil had scavenged. Her frown deepened.

"Where is my pack?"

Magiere knew the answer. She'd been the one to pack the horses the previous morning.

"It must've been on Port," Leesil answered. "Everything I could find . . . this is all we have left."

The little sage's eyes widened further, then narrowed at Leesil. "What? All my journals were in that pack, my quills and parchments . . . Chap's talking hide!"

Leesil turned away and wouldn't look at her.

"You sent most of your journals to Domin Tilswith," Magiere said, anxious to calm Wynn. "Before we left Soladran. You can rewrite anything of importance, and there's been nothing worth noting since we left the Warlands. The Elven Territories are still ahead, and that's what you've been waiting for most. We'll find parchment or paper—and I've seen you make ink."

"Of course," Leesil put in. "Soon as we're through these mountains . . . and a feather to cut a new—"

"If we get through!" Wynn shouted at him, and her words echoed about the high cavern. "If Chap finds a way. If we do not starve. If we do not die of exposure or walk blindly over a cliff into a chasm . . . because you could not wait for winter to pass!"

Any defense Magiere might have offered for Leesil was smothered in her own rising guilt.

They all knew from the beginning that if Leesil's mother still lived, she was imprisoned by her people. The elves wouldn't kill her, it seemed, so she would still be there no matter how long it took to find her. But from the moment Leesil discovered the skulls of his father and grandmother, he'd stopped listening to reason.

Magiere had argued with him, time and again, over waiting out winter. In the end, she always relented, and he pushed them onward. Now here they were without horses or adequate food, and beaten down with fatigue and injury. Wynn's words were aimed at Leesil, but they struck Magiere into silence.

"What about Chap's talking hide?" Wynn continued. "How is he to talk efficiently with me, now that it is gone?"

The talking hide was a large square of tanned leather upon which Wynn had inked rows of Elvish symbols, words, and phrases. Both she and Chap could read it, and Chap pawed out responses beyond his one, two, or three barks.

Chap shook himself and barked once for "yes," then poked his nose into Wynn's shoulder.

"He can still talk with us a bit," Magiere offered.

Wynn didn't answer. She took another berry, fumbling to peel its skin with her thumbnail.

Magiere was about to stop her, for Leesil's suspicion was half-right. They had no idea where this gift of food had come from or why. She glanced at Chap, ready to ask if the berries smelled safe. He huffed a "yes" before she spoke and headed off across the cavern floor.

With a sigh, Magiere set the crystal aside and took up a bisselberry of her own, pulling back the fruit's skin.

Leesil wandered off to the cave's far side and crouched to gaze blankly down into the hole Chap had found. He was so driven to keep moving, to reach the Elven Territories and find his mother. But Magiere knew they'd be lucky to even find their way back out of the range. She looked toward the hole he inspected and saw a flash of silver fur.

"Leesil, where is Chap?"

Magiere snatched up the crystal and her falchion as the tip of Chap's tail disappeared down the hole.

"Get back here, you misguided mutt!"

Chap crawled over the hole's lip and hopped down into a sloped tunnel, heading deeper inside the mountain. In the darkness he barely made out the passage, but scent guided him more than sight. He smelled something familiar. As much as that made his instincts cry a warning, he had to be certain of what he suspected.

The passage was rough and its ceiling so low that his ears scraped if he raised them. A few sliding paces downward, it dropped again a short way to the floor of a wider tunnel. The scent was strong, and Chap jumped down. His nose bumped a pile of plump fruits that tumbled apart, rolling off their platter of fresh leaves.

Bisselberries, Wynn had called them. What the elves of this continent called *réicheach sghiahean*—bitter shields—for their edible skin was as unpleasant as the inside was sweet.

He pushed on down the tunnel, and when it seemed he had gone too far without encountering another pile, he paused and sniffed the air. It took a moment to separate the scent behind him from anything ahead, but they were there, somewhere down in the dark.

More bisselberries.

Someone . . . something . . . had laid a trail for them into the belly of the mountain. This was too mundane to be the working of his kin. He could not determine the direction in which the passage ran—forward or back or even to the side through the so-called Broken Range. Where would they end up, even if the trail led out of the mountain at all?

Entombed in stone, a manifestation of the element of Earth, Chap called out through his Spirit one last time.

In this dark place, the silence of his kin made him sag. He stiffened and rumbled with outrage.

They would not come to him, and the survival of his companions—his charges—now depended on skulkers who would not reveal themselves. Behind the scent of fresh fruit and their green leaves, behind grime and dust kicked up by his own paws, was the other scent he had smelled upon first entering this place.

Like a bird and yet not. Faint but everywhere in the dark beneath the mountain.

Chap turned back, stopping long enough to pick up several bisselberries in his mouth to show the others. Hopefully it would not take long to make them understand. There was only one path to take, if they were to avoid starving or succumbing to winter.

Someone was trying to lead them through the inside of

this mountain. Someone had called them in from the storm to find shelter.

Chap headed back toward his companions. He had to convince them to follow him into this passage . . . to trust his judgment once more.

CHAPTER THREE

Aoishenis-Ahâre—a title, a heritage, and an obligation. "Most Aged Father" waited within the massive oak at Crijheäiche—Origin-Heart. As the centermost community of what humans called the Elven Territories, it was also home to the Anmaglâhk, a caste apart from the clans of his people. He had lived so long that even the elders of the twenty-seven clans no longer remembered scant tales of where he came from or why he had led his followers into seclusion in this far corner of the world.

The massive and ancient oak that was his home had lived almost as long as he. A dozen or more men with outstretched arms could not have encompassed its girth. One of the eldest in the forest, the hollowed chamber within its heart-root had been carefully nurtured from the living wood since its earliest days. It sustained him to fulfill future needs for his people's sake. And its long roots reached more deeply and widely than any other in the land.

Wise in the way of trees, Most Aged Father no longer walked among his people. His withered body clung to life by the great forest's efforts that sustained him through the oak. But he was still founder and leader of the Anmaglâhk.

They in turn were the guardians of the an'Cróan—(Those) of the Blood, as the people properly called themselves.

Through the oak's deep roots, he reached out with his awareness through branches and leaves to wander and watch within his people's land. Through slivers of "word-wood" taken from his oak and placed against any living tree, he heard and spoke with his Anmaglâhk in far lands.

Now he waited beneath the earth in his root chamber. He waited for his most trusted servant, Fréthfâre— Watcher of the Woods—who lived by her namesake. He sensed her approach as she pressed apart the curtains across the doorway above, at ground level.

"Father?" she called. "May I come down?"

All anmaglâhk called him Father, for they were the children of his vision and his strength.

"Come," he answered weakly. "I am awake."

Her step light as a thrush, he still heard her descend the steps molded from the tree's living wood. She entered the earthen chamber around the heart-root and appeared at its opening into his resting place.

The hood of her gray-green cloak was thrown back, revealing long wheat-blond hair. Most of the people possessed hair as straight as corn silk, but Fréthfâre's tumbled past her narrow shoulders in gentle waves when she did not bind it back. Today it hung loose and tucked behind her peaked ears.

Her large amber eyes were unusually narrow, and her lips thin. An overly slender build gave her the illusion of height, though she was not tall compared to others. She was Covârleasa—Trusted Adviser—and thereby highly honored among the Anmaglâhk.

"You are well?" she asked, always concerned for his comfort.

Most Aged Father lifted a frail, bony hand with effort and gestured to the stacked cushions before his bower.

"Yes. Sit."

Fréthfâre crossed her legs as she settled. "Has there been sign of the human interlopers? Has Sgäilsheilleache sent word?"

"No, but they come. Sgäilsheilleache will bring Léshil to us."

He had sent Sgäilsheilleache—Willow's Shade—to lead a small band of anmaglâhk to intercept Léshil before that abomination entered their land unescorted. But there were more important things to discuss.

"You will assist me in presenting Léshil an offer," he continued. "One which no other should know."

Fréthfâre arched her feathery eyebrows. "Of course, Father, but what bargain could you make with such a creature? He is not one of us . . . and has polluted blood."

When Most Aged Father smiled, responding warmth flooded her eyes. She never saw him as the withered husk he knew himself to be. His dry white hair, too thin for his pale scalp, and the shriveled skin stretched over his long bones never troubled her.

"True enough," he acknowledged. "Léshil has human blood, and any human is not to be trusted. But he comes for his traitor mother—Cuirin'nên'a—and that is the reason I give him safe passage. Cuirin'nên'a could not have acted alone in her treachery, and we must find her conspirators. We will promise Léshil anything, even his mother, in exchange for his service. With such an offering, we secure his fidelity for as long as we need it."

Cuirin'nên'a's subversion pained Most Aged Father like an ache in his sunken chest. In the end, it had done her little good. After years of delay, Darmouth was finally dead. His province would rip itself apart, and the other tyrants of the Warlands would be at one another's throats trying to claim the spoils.

Since the birth of the Anmaglâhk in forgotten times, their service was revered by the people. Cuirin'nên'a seeded doubt and deception among their caste. It must be rooted out before it spread, even unto the elders of the caste. Or had it already done so? One more name lingered in his mind with that concern.

Brot'ân'duivé—Dog in the Dark—friend of the fallen Eillean, one of their greatest.

Eillean had stood for Fréthfâre when she had first come as a girl, barely past her name taking, to beg admittance to the Anmaglâhk. It seemed impossible that Eillean could be in question, but she had borne Cuirin'nên'a, a treacherous daughter, and lost her life in retrieving that wayward offspring. In turn, Cuirin'nên'a had borne a half-blood son.

Between these two women of their caste—faithful Eillean and deceitful Cuirin'nên'a—which way did Brot'ân'-duivé lean?

Fréthfâre showed open surprise and pursed her thin lips. "Promise him anything, Father? Very well, but why depend on the half-blood? We have our own to uncover subversion—"

Most Aged Father raised one finger ending in a yellowed nail. "For our people . . . and their survival in fearful times to come, we must follow this path. Upon Léshil's arrival, escort him to me. Reveal nothing of what I have said. You are my hand outside of this oak . . . now I must rest."

Fréthfâre stood with a daughter's affection in her eyes. "I will bring food and tea later."

As she stepped to the opening of his heart-root chamber, she looked back at him. A gentle bow of her head accompanied the whispered litany of her caste.

"In silence and in shadows, Father."

He lowered his eyelids in place of bowing a head too heavy for his weariness.

"In silence and in shadows," he answered.

Most Aged Father slipped his awareness into the oak. He watched Fréthfâre step out through the curtained doorway and into the daily life of Crijheäiche.

A true daughter of his own blood would not have filled him with greater pride.

But he valued his caste and the clans of his people more. It was why he had brought them to this land so long ago. Here they remained safe, shutting out the humans with their flawed blood, ignorant minds, and weak spirits.

Most Aged Father took a heavy breath to smother ancient fear.

Yet the fear still coursed through him.

Lost were the track of years, decades, and centuries, but not the sharpest memories of a war that had swallowed his world. Nor memories of an unseen adversary called by many names. It had whispered in the dark to its puppets and minions, the perverted, the weak-willed, and those hungry for power without caring for its price. And in death and defeat, it merely slumbered.

It would return.

He knew this, believed in it with a horrified faith. He felt it like a worm burrowing its twisted way through the earth's depths. It had only to waken and show itself, in whatever ways it would, to wage a renewed assault.

This time, it would not have the human horde as one of its engines of war. Despite any ill-conceived deception by Cuirin'nên'a and her confederates, he would see to it. He would remove all instruments of this Ancient Enemy and leave it raging helplessly in hiding. His wisdom, his will, and his Anmaglâhk would shield their people.

Most Aged Father drifted into sleep—but, as always, a fitful one. Among all other dreams, one had come each night for centuries.

Broken corpses lay strewn across a bloodied land as far as he could see. Numb in heart and mind, he stood unmoving until the sight was slowly swallowed by dusk. Only then he turned away, stained spear dragging in his grip and his quiver empty.

Somewhere in the growing dark, he thought he heard something struggling to get up.

Wynn flinched each time Leesil mimicked any Elvish word she pronounced.

He would never become conversant by the time they reached the elves—if they reached the elves—but he insisted that she teach him. And she had agreed. A bad decision, upon reflection.

At least it passed the time, as they climbed ever downward through the mountain toward an uncertain destination. Chap had convinced them to follow him, and as they walked, Wynn suffered through the attempt to assist Leesil with his Elvish. What started as distraction from doubts and fears became a lesson in futility rather than language.

"Soob!" Leesil said again.

Wynn cringed.

"No." She tried not to sigh. "The ending is like the V in your language, but the lips close on its termination, like a B."

"So which is it?" Leesil snapped. "B or V?"

"Just"—Wynn started to snap—"listen carefully . . . *suv'*."

"That's not your Elvish word for your bisselberries," Leesil sniped.

Wynn gritted her teeth. "It is a general reference for any type of berry."

She carried his pack slung over her good shoulder. He paused ahead of her without turning and shifted the lashings holding the chest of skulls to his back, trying to resettle his burden.

Wynn did not like that vessel constantly before her eyes.

"Everything in Elvish," she continued, "has its root word to be transformed to noun, verb, adjective, adverb—and so on. But there are general terms for things of like kind."

"So, 'eat a berry' is . . . ," Leesil mumbled, trying to remember. "La-hong-ah-jah-va . . . soob?"

Wynn clenched her teeth. "Only if the berry is eating you!"

"Leesil, please," Magiere growled behind Wynn. "Enough! You're not going to learn it like this. Just leave the talking to Wynn, if . . . when we find the elves."

He glanced over his shoulder with the cold lamp crystal held high like a torch. Its light turned his glower into a misshapen mask that would frighten small children. Wynn did not care.

They had traveled downward for more than a day, perhaps two. And yet they had stopped only three times. She was cold and hungry all the way.

Leesil sidestepped a twisted angle in the passage, and a jagged outcrop caught his shoulder.

"*Valhachkasej'â!*" he barked.

Wynn stiffened, then grabbed the shoulder flap of his hauberk and jerked him about.

"Do not ever say that around an elf!" she snapped at him. "Or is profanity the only thing you can pronounce correctly?"

Leesil blinked. "It's something my mother said. You've heard me use it before."

"Your mother?" Wynn's voice rose to a squeak.

The last thing they needed was Leesil's ignorant expletives offending someone, especially one of those blood-thirsty Anmaglâhk.

"Smuân'thij arthane!" Wynn snapped at him. She pushed past as Leesil wrinkled his brow in confusion.

Chap waited out in front and stared at her with his ears ridged in surprise. He cocked his head, glanced at Leesil, then huffed once in apparent agreement with her outburst.

Wynn was too miffed to even feel embarrassed that Chap understood exactly what she had called Leesil . . . though it hadn't been half as offensive as his own utterance.

"Time for another rest," Magiere said.

"No," Leesil said, his expression cold and pitiless. "We keep moving."

She ignored him and unstrapped her pack to drop it with the saddlebags she carried.

In their early days, Wynn had never seen such a look on Leesil's face. Lately she had seen it too often. Hardness overwhelmed him from within whenever he was pushed any way he did not want to go. And he did not wish to stop this journey for anything.

Chap padded back up the tunnel and plopped down. Clearly outvoted, Leesil sighed and lowered the chest off his back.

Wynn dropped too quickly in exhaustion and got a sharp pain for it in the seat of her pants. She let Leesil's pack slide off her shoulder in a heap as Magiere dug out what remained of their rations. The last of the bisselberries were nearly gone, and they had discovered no more such gifts along the way. Magiere held a few crumbling biscuits and a handful of venison jerky strips.

"That cannot be all of it," Wynn said.

Magiere uncorked a water flask and dropped down beside her. "We'll find more once we're out of this mountain."

Wynn divided the biscuits and tossed a jerky strip to Chap. He caught it with a clack of his jaws. Leesil muttered to himself as he inspected the chest's rigging. Wynn turned her eyes from the grisly vessel.

"What was that Elvish you just said?" Magiere whispered.

"It was . . . nothing," Wynn whispered back. "I was tired and irritated."

"Yes, I got that." Magiere rolled her eyes and bit into half of a dry biscuit, still waiting for a better answer.

Wynn dropped her head, voice hushed even more. "It means something like . . . 'thoughts of stone.' "

Magiere coughed up crumbs and covered her mouth. "Rock-head? You called him a rock-head?"

A flush of shame heated Wynn's cheeks, but the look on Magiere's face cooled it with surprise. She knew Magiere well enough to gauge her dark moods and acidic nature. The tall woman was often caustic even at her friendliest. But this expression was almost something new.

Was Magiere trying not to grin?

"I'll remember that one," Magiere whispered back.

"I heard that," Leesil growled.

He sat on the chest with his back turned to them, like some monstrous guardian statue perched the wrong way upon a castle parapet.

Wynn quietly ate her half biscuit and two berries. She pulled a tin cup out of Magiere's pack and poured some water for Chap. When she set the water flask down, it teetered on the tunnel's uneven surface, and she made a grab for it. She tried to settle it more firmly, but something grated beneath its bottom.

She felt the tunnel floor beneath the flask, and something soft shifted beneath her fingertips. When she took hold with a pinch, it felt light as a feather. She lifted it up into the light. . . .

It was a feather.

Mottled gray, it was longer than her outstretched hand,

with downy frills at its base. It seemed familiar, and that was unsettling, for she could not think why.

Where had she seen it before?

Chap's rumble startled her. He glared intently at the feather and then lifted his muzzle high to gaze about overhead. Wynn cast her own gaze upward and saw nothing but the uneven tunnel roof.

"There's a quill in the making," Magiere said, and reclined on the cold stone. "All you need now are ink and paper. Get some rest while you can."

She rolled onto her side, eyes open, watching Leesil perched upon the chest.

Wynn lay back as well with Leesil's pack as a pillow. She rolled over to face away from him and Magiere. Chap lay with his head on his paws, but he was not trying to sleep either. He studied the feather in her hand, but without the talking hide, she could not ask him why.

Cuirin'nên'a . . . Nein'a . . . Mother . . .

Memories flickered through Leesil's thoughts as he followed the others down the passage. He hadn't slept during their last pause, even after the crystal waned and went out. How long did he sit in the dark before waking the others to move on? It had been hard to meet Magiere's eyes when he finally shook her by the shoulder.

She might see him for what he really was. It hadn't been long since he'd realized it himself.

Guilt for long ago abandoning his parents didn't drive him anymore. Nor was it just sorrow in returning the remains of his father to his mother. Longing was still part of it, remembering a mother's gentle touch and firm lilting voice, and how these made his first life bearable for a while. But it had taken the memories that Chap stole from Brot'an in Darmouth's family crypt to make Leesil face much of the truth.

Darmouth had used him. And Brot'an had wielded him like the bone knife Leesil gouged deep into Darmouth's throat. If that moment had been the end of it, he might have put those bloody events behind him. He'd done it before.

But he began to see the pattern of his life, to understand the reason for his existence.

His life had been engraved by the scheme of a grand-mother he never knew—Eillean. Even his own father must have had a hand in it, for Gavril had gone along with Nein'a's insistence. Leesil couldn't escape what he was—what his mother had made him.

A weapon.

He wanted to look her in the eyes and know the reasons for all she'd done to him, everything she'd trained him to be.

Wynn stumbled along in front of him. Beyond her, Magiere now led the way with the renewed crystal in hand. Somewhere farther on, Chap tried to sniff their way out, for the trail of berries had ended far behind them. Too far to turn back with no food left. Leesil hoped they had made the right decision following Chap.

The tunnel forked again.

Chap shifted anxiously between the mouths of the two passages. He sniffed the stone floor, staring down each in turn. The dog stood silent for so long that Leesil came out of his own dark thoughts, and then Chap trotted off down the right fork without looking back.

"I hope he knows what he's doing," Magiere muttered.

They moved on, and time dragged in this place without day or night. Leesil's shoulders ached from the chest's ropes biting into them. He'd sunk into himself once more when Chap suddenly stopped.

"What now?" Leesil asked, and peered around a too-silent Wynn.

Magiere felt cold inside standing behind Chap in tense silence. But it wasn't from the tunnel's chill. She resisted looking back at Leesil. He'd driven them hard with his desperation, but he drove himself even harder.

Their food was gone, and they'd been on half rations for longer than she could reckon. Their situation was dire, and they all knew it.

Chap lowered his head with a growl.

Magiere dropped her pack to the tunnel floor. She

reached over her right shoulder and gripped the falchion's hilt where she'd strapped it to her back.

"What is it?" Leesil demanded in a hushed voice.

Chap let out a whine, then snorted as if some scent in the air had clogged his nose.

"Chap?" she whispered.

His ears pricked up, and he whined again, but it sounded more disgruntled than alarmed.

A light scratching carried up the tunnel from below.

"We are not alone," Wynn whispered.

Magiere drew her falchion, holding the crystal out with her other hand.

Beyond the light's reach, a pair of shimmers appeared in the dark. They bobbed up and down as the soft sound of claws on stone came nearer. The paired shimmers rose slightly from the floor. The dark shape of a small creature formed around them.

No larger than a house cat, its body was elongated like a weasel or ferret. A stubby tail, darker than its bark-colored fur, twitched erratically as it sat up on its hindquarters.

Around its eyes and down its pug muzzle spread a black mask of fur. Wide ears perked up with small tufts of white hairs on their points. Its strangest features were its tiny forepaws. Less like paws and more like small hands, they ended in stubby little fingers with short claws.

"Oh no!" Wynn breathed out.

Magiere had to look back. The astonishment on Wynn's features melted to loathing.

Chap shifted to the tunnel's side opposite the little beast.

"What is that?" Magiere asked.

"*Tâshgâlh!*" Wynn said. "And Leesil can swear at it all he wants!"

"Is it poisonous or something?" Magiere asked.

Wynn wrinkled her nose. "No, it's not—"

Chap growled, but he didn't close on the creature. He snapped his jaws threateningly and it dashed straight up the tunnel's side wall to the ceiling.

Magiere shoved Wynn back and held out her blade at the animal.

It clung there as if standing upside down on the tunnel's

craggy roof. With one quick hiss at Chap, it turned its attention back toward Magiere. It began to coo at her, like a dove, and swayed slightly as its head bobbed with excitement.

Magiere carefully aimed the cold lamp crystal for a better look, and its black, glassy eyes followed the movement.

"Oh no, not on your mangy little life!" Wynn yelled, and ducked around Magiere to snatch the crystal. Then she scooped up a loose stone and threw it at the creature. "That is mine!"

Chap scurried back as the stone went wide, bouncing from one tunnel wall to the other.

The *tâshgâlh* hopped sideways across the ceiling, trying to regain sight of the crystal. Wynn pulled the glowing stone behind her back with a groan.

"We will never get rid of the little beast."

"What is it?" Magiere demanded.

"Its name means 'finder of lost things,'" Wynn answered. "A rather polite wording. They are nothing but incorrigible little thieves. It will follow us and dig through our belongings the moment we are asleep . . . now that it has seen something pretty that it fancies."

Chap jumped at the *tâshgâlh,* his barks filling the tunnel with echoes.

"You see?" Wynn shouted over the noise. "Chap knows the trouble they make."

"Quiet down, Chap," Leesil yelled.

The *tâshgâlh* darted back and forth across the ceiling, trying to stay out of reach but maintain sight of its coveted item. Chap kept barking as he lunged up one wall or the other. The little creature screeched at him, then raced along an arc down the tunnel wall and back the way it had come.

"How many of these things could be in the tunnels?" Leesil demanded. "And how do you know this animal? Magiere, will you shut that dog up!"

Magiere shot him an angry glance. When she turned to do as he'd asked, all she saw of Chap was his swishing tail as he took off after the fleeing animal.

"They do not live in caves," Wynn said. "They live in . . ."

Wynn spun about, staring wide-eyed down the tunnel. Before Magiere could demand a better answer, Wynn took off in a headlong rush after Chap.

"Wait! What are you doing?" Magiere called.

"They do not live in caves," Wynn shouted back. "They live in forests."

Magiere grabbed up her pack and slung it over one shoulder, preparing to run Wynn down before the sage added to her injuries in some stumbling fall.

"Forests?" Leesil repeated.

Magiere stared down the tunnel. The bobbing light of Wynn's crystal grew smaller as her voice echoed back up the passage.

"Elven forests!"

Chap raced after the *tâshgâlh*. The dark tunnel made it almost impossible to see his quarry, and he followed mostly by sound. The instant he had seen the little creature, he knew what its presence meant, but he had no way to tell the others. All he could do was terrify it enough to flee for its life.

The *tâshgâlh* went silent, and Chap skidded to a stop, listening. Then he heard its paws scraping on stone ahead.

He had seen its like twice when he was a pup in the elven lands. Majay-hì did not hunt *tâshgâlh,* for the little pests were a clever breed and easier prey was available. He could smell its fear of him, knew it wondered why he came after it, but this pursuit could not be helped. He knew it would run for the familiar safety of the forest.

Another scent filled his nose over the animal's musky fear and the passage's stale odor.

Pine . . . and wet earth . . . and warm, humid air.

Somewhere behind him, clumsy feet kicked rocks down the passage in haste. The *tâshgâlh* raced away ahead of him. Chap chased onward, and the scent of the forest grew stronger.

He could see the animal's stiff tail and pumping rear legs. And then light beyond it. An opening appeared, curtained by branches, but not enough to blot out the light of the sun.

The *tâshgâlh* jumped as it reached the passage's end, grabbing a tree limb. As the branch recoiled upward under the creature's weight, it swung out of sight.

Chap slowed to a halt just shy of the exit and stared at wet green pine needles glistening in sunlight.

It was still winter, but in the Elven Territories, the snow touched only the higher ranges.

He waited there, almost not believing that he had found his way through. For a moment he could not bring himself to step out into the world.

Chap breathed deep and filled his head with all the subtle scents of his days as a pup among his siblings. He was home once again, or at least the place where he had chosen to be born in flesh.

Wynn came scrambling up behind him. Her round eyes and olive-skinned face filled with relief at the sight of branches overhanging the opening.

"Oh, Chap," she said.

He stepped out with the young sage close upon his tail. Somewhere above in the trees, the *tâshgâlh* squawked derisively.

Morning had broken, with the sun just cresting the eastern horizon. But the trees still obscured the view down the mountainside. Chap pushed his way through the foliage dotting the small plateau onto which they emerged. When the last branch dragged across his back, he stood upon a rocky slope still partway up the mountain.

"We're on the eastern side of the Broken Range," Leesil whispered.

He and Magiere had finally caught up, but Chap did not turn his eyes from the vision spread out before him.

Down the sparsely forested ridge and stretching as far as he could see lay a vast forestland. Not as in Belaskia or Stravina, with spots of open plains and fields, nor the dank and dull green of Droevinka's moss-strewn fir and spruce trees.

It was vivid glowing green of multiple hues, even though winter was upon it and it lay nearly at the northernmost end of the continent. Multiple rivers flowed away from the range through the heart of a vast land, each a shimmering blue ribbon across a verdant fabric that rolled here and there with the hills beneath its surface.

The forest stretched as far as Chap could see. Somewhere beyond it to the northeast were the eastern ocean and the gulf bay no foreign ship had ever berthed in. He did not remember how large the Elven Territories truly were. But then he had not seen much of them as a pup before he was taken away.

"It seems to go on forever," Wynn said.

At the mountain's base, stepped slopes dropped gradually, and the sparse growth of the plateau built quickly to warm, bright foliage that reached for uncountable leagues.

Magiere stepped up beside Chap, but of them all, she appeared the least touched by the sight.

"Yes, so large it looks closer than it is," she said. "We're out of food, and we still have to make it down this mountain."

Chap looked up at her pale features marred by exhaustion. Where Wynn's showed relief and overwhelmed awe, in Magiere's face he saw some hint of fallen resignation. Then he glanced at Leesil, whose amber eyes sparked in the sunlight but were chill with determination.

A human, a dhampir, and a half-blood. He had brought them into a place where the word "unwelcome" was but a polite term for what awaited them.

Wynn's lips had parted to speak when a high-pitched chirp sounded above them. Chap looked up, but the sky was empty except for dark billowing clouds trapped upon the mountain peaks. The sound trailed into a string of slurred notes, erratic but strangely lyrical, and then it faded in the light breeze.

Wynn fished in her coat pocket. She pulled out the feather she had found. In the sunlight, it was mottled white.

"Where did you get that?" Leesil asked, as he had not seen the feather until now.

"I found it at our last stop in the tunnels."

Leesil took his pack off her shoulder and dug through it until he pulled out the small arrow. The trimmed feathers on its notched end matched the one in Wynn's hand.

Magiere only glanced at the feathers and then down the slope. "We need to get moving."

Chap turned along the plateau to find them a path. He barked for the others to follow him. For a moment, Wynn looked up into the empty sky then back toward the mountain's passage, hidden behind the trees. The feather was still in her hand.

CHAPTER FOUR

Descending the rocky mountainside took most of the day. As the sun passed to the west above the Broken Range, the forest surrounded Chap and his companions. He returned to the land of his birth.

Whenever a break appeared in the green canopy of needles and leaves, Wynn's gaze wandered to the mountain behind them. She insisted that the *tâshgâlh* might still follow them. Chap neither heard nor smelled it, but she was likely right. Those little bandits were persistent.

Chap nudged Wynn aside before she stumbled into a tangle of poison ivy clinging to an oak. She slowed, wavering on her feet, and Chap paused when he noticed that Leesil had halted as well.

Leesil glanced about as if searching for his bearings. With a shrug, he took a deep breath, prepared to move on, but Chap saw Wynn swallow hard with panic on her smudged face.

"You all right?" Magiere asked.

The question startled Wynn. "No . . . yes, I am fine, just . . . it is nothing."

Wynn shook her head and continued onward, but Chap watched her with concern. Now and then she stared through the forest, her wonder mixed with worry.

Chap stayed close as they moved deeper into the trees. He expected Wynn's normally incessant babbling to begin over all the subtle strange differences the forest held compared to those of the human lands. Her sage's curiosity was the main reason she had forced her own inclusion in this journey long moons ago back in Bela. But she remained silent and watchful, and more than once started at the sight of even the most mundane foliage or tree.

Chap had been just a pup when Eillean had carried him away from this place. Lush, oversized leaves and enormous red and yellow hyacinths hung from the vines in one grove. They all stopped briefly to replenish their water at a crystal-clear brook winding through scattered azalea bushes. A small flight of bees thrummed between the flowers until a hawk-wasp chased them off.

"It is almost warm here," Wynn said. "How is that possible?"

For once, Chap was relieved that the talking hide was lost. He did not wish for conversation now. He simply wanted to breathe the air and to *feel* the forest's life. Just for one more moment to forget the danger that lay ahead.

It was still winter, even here, but far warmer than the Broken Range or its chill labyrinth of caves and tunnels they had traveled. Here, winter would feel like early autumn to outsiders. He did not know why. Perhaps the elves had lived here for so long that the region itself responded to their nurturing presence and returned it in kind.

He hopped another brook. Wynn scurried to catch up and dug her fingers into the fur between his shoulders. She gripped him too tightly until he complained with a whine. She need not worry about losing him.

A wandering line of elms, silver birch, and willows led to a small open slope. On its far side rose an old cedar, its trunk stout and wide as a grain wagon.

"It's enormous," Magiere said. "I've never seen its like, even in the depths of Droevinka."

Chap sniffed the scent of clean loam on the breeze.

"We're here," Leesil half-whispered. "We actually found it."

They had all suffered for it. Now Leesil walked a vast

foreign territory, with little notion what to do next or where to look for his mother. In truth, Chap was little better off.

He shrugged free of Wynn's grip, though she was reluctant to let go, and drifted back to lick Leesil's hand with a whine. Leesil was only half-elven, but could he feel the life that pulsed around them? If he let its current run through him, perhaps it would cleanse some of his burdens.

Leesil scratched lightly behind Chap's ear but did not look down.

Chap called up one of Leesil's distant memories of Nein'a leading a ten-year-old half-elf through the forest outside of Venjètz. The two moved in sync through the trees.

Leesil breathed deeply. "I know. We have to go deeper."

Magiere stepped close on Leesil's far side, brushing her shoulder to his.

"Almost a dream of sorts . . . wasn't it? As if we'd never really find it."

He did not respond at first, but finally hooked his tan fingers into her white ones.

"Yes . . . no matter how hard we looked."

"But we're here," Magiere added.

"Have you learned to read minds now?"

The jest held only a hint of Leesil's old mocking humor, but Magiere still smiled and pulled him forward.

"Let's find your mother," she said.

He followed but turned his head both ways, as if looking for something, and then frowned.

Wynn looked back at Chap over and over, to make sure he was still there. He trotted ahead to catch up to her. Her eyes wandered, but even as she passed black-stemmed amethyst flowers sprouting from dank tree branches, her wonderment was brief. Tiny hummingbirds of brashly mixed colors darted in and out of the large blooms.

Chap led them deeper into the trees, and the world shifted completely to rich hues pulsing in the somber light filtering down through the forest canopy. He pondered calling a rest while he hunted for food on his own; his companions were fatigued and hungry, but at the same time, he was wary of letting them out of his watchful sight.

"Did we pass those trees before?" Wynn asked, grasping his fur again.

Chap barked twice for "no" and took another step. He led them true with certainty. Within a day he hoped to reach the nearest river sighted from up the mountain.

Wynn's grip tightened and pulled him to a stop.

"I don't think so," Leesil answered, and glanced back at the cluster of elms.

Magiere released his hand, looking back along their path.

"We're lost!" Wynn whispered sharply.

"No, we're not." Magiere pointed to the old hulking cedar by the clearing slope, still within sight. "You can just see the line of trees back to the brook we crossed."

Her gesture pulled Chap's attention, and Leesil followed it as well, but his brow wrinkled with uncertainty.

"Yes . . . that's right," he finally agreed.

"No, it is not," Wynn said.

She turned a full circle, switching hands to keep hold of Chap. Twice she looked to where Magiere pointed, but her gaze flicked quickly about in confusion.

"It is not the same," Wynn whispered, and shook her head.

Chap was baffled. Even without scent he could backtrack their exact route by sight.

"Not the same?" Magiere asked. "Not like . . . the elven lands near your home?"

"No!" Wynn snapped. "I know those flowers— *blhäcraova*—and the birds feeding upon them are *vänranas,* but . . . but they are not where I saw them last."

Chap stared at the purple tree-flowers and garish hummingbirds. They were exactly where he had passed them.

"It changes," Leesil said quietly. "Sometimes . . . I think. The forest changes."

Magiere grabbed his arm. "Nothing's changed."

"I see where we came through." Leesil's uncertain gaze drifted back the way they had come. "But if . . . it's like I'm not sure until I look hard. And even then . . ."

Chap studied all of them. In his youth, he had encountered no elf with memories of humans in this land. The mere thought raised fear, even among the Anmaglâhk, who walked secretly within the human nations. He knew some of the forest's natural safeguards, such as the majay-hì, but was there something more? Perhaps there was a reason no outsider ever returned from searching for this place.

It seemed the impassible mountains were not the only barrier to entering the Elven Territories.

Chap studied the forest's depths. Something here addled the minds of his companions. It rejected those foreign to it, and each of his charges had human blood.

"What about you?" Leesil asked.

Magiere shook her head. "It all looks as it was."

A question occurred to Chap an instant before Leesil asked it.

"And why is that?"

Chap eyed Magiere, wondering at this strange inconsistency. Magiere looked to him, and he huffed twice, for he had no answer.

Leesil's lesser confusion, compared to Wynn's, could be attributed to his half-elven blood, but Magiere was as human as the sage. The only difference was her dhampir nature. But Chap could not see how that would make her immune. And if it did . . . such a twist left him deeply disturbed.

Dusk thickened among the trees and undergrowth.

"We must camp," Wynn said too quickly. "I do not want to walk this place at night."

Chap agreed. Before he barked approval, a flash of movement back near the massive cedar caught his eye. He growled.

"What?" Wynn asked too loudly.

Leesil jerked loose the holding straps of his punching blades as Magiere drew her falchion. Chap pulled free of Wynn's grip and inched back the way they had come.

From a distance, two of the cedar's branches seemed to move.

They separated from the others, drifting around the cedar's far side and into the clearing. Below them came a long equine head that turned toward the interlopers.

Large crystalline eyes like Chap's own peered through the forest.

A deer would have been dainty next to this massive beast, though this was the closest comparison that came to Chap. Silver-gray in hue, its coat was long and shaggy. Two curved horns sprouted high from its head—smooth, without prongs, but as long as Chap's whole body.

He had never seen such a creature near the elven enclave where he was born.

Leesil pulled the crossbow off his back and quietly cocked its string, as Magiere handed him a quarrel from the quiver strapped to her pack.

The enormous silver animal stood motionless, staring at them through the forest. It slowly stepped an arc along the clearing's slope. Its crystal eyes never blinked, never strayed from watching them. It had no fear. Perhaps it did not know it was in danger.

Chap turned cold inside.

In the wild elven lands, this creature did not know of being hunted. He barked twice, as loudly as he could.

"Quiet!" Leesil ordered in a whisper. "We need food."

The animal did not start at the sound of Chap's voice. Whatever this creature might be, it appeared that neither elf nor even majay-hì hunted its kind. If they had, it would have fled at the sight of Chap himself, if not the others. And its eyes . . . the hue of its fur . . . so similar to his own.

Chap whirled about and lunged at Leesil with snapping jaws. Again, he barked twice for "no."

"Leesil, stop!" Wynn hissed. "Chap says no!"

"I heard him," Leesil answered, but remained poised with the crossbow aimed through the trees.

"Leesil . . . ," Magiere said.

He simply held the crossbow in place, fingers wrapped around the stock upon its firing lever.

Then the animal pawed the earth once, lifted its muzzle skyward, and a deafening bellow filled the air.

The sound rose up from its wide chest and out its open mouth and rolled through the forest.

Wynn sucked in a sharp breath, and even Magiere backed up a step.

Chap froze where he stood, not knowing what this meant. Then he bolted toward the creature, weaving through bushes and underbrush, until he slowed to stand beneath the cedar's branches.

The deer ceased its bellow, muzzle dropping from the air, and it studied him in stillness.

The scent of musk and something sweet like lilacs filled Chap's head.

It began wandering off the way it had come, but in a few steps it stopped. With long horns tilted to touch its own back, it lifted its muzzle high and bellowed again.

Chap ducked behind the cedar and raced back to his companions. A third bellow rang in his ears as he reached Leesil.

Leesil turned with the crossbow still raised, following the deer's passage. His eyes shifted once toward Magiere.

"That thing is making a lot of noise. And it would still make a decent supper."

Chap snarled at him.

Wynn stepped in front of the crossbow. "Put it away."

"He's joking," Magiere said, but cast Leesil a warning glance. "He's not going to shoot it."

The deer vanished into the forest's depths, but another bellow carried from farther off as Leesil lowered the crossbow.

"Let's put some distance between ourselves and that loudmouth."

Chap searched for any recollection of this strange being but found nothing among his memories. The deer's continued noise unnerved him, and he agreed it was best to get away from it. He started into a trot but immediately slowed so Wynn could take hold of him. He pushed the pace as fast as the little sage could manage.

Daylight was nearly gone. Somewhere behind them, the deer bellowed again—and again. No matter how far or fast Chap went, the next tone was no farther behind them. The deer was following.

A flash of steel gray darted through a teal-leafed bush ahead.

Chap dug his forepaws into mossy earth, and Wynn stumbled as he jerked to a halt.

The movement vanished in the deepening dusk behind a cluster of pale pines.

Not the deer, for it was too quick and low, and the ground did not tremble beneath large hooves. Chap heard claws cutting the earth as it flashed by.

He sidestepped, herding Wynn to the nearest tree. He settled himself, ready to charge anything that might rush from hiding.

Undergrowth rustled, and his head snapped to the left. Another movement flickered in the right corner of his vision, then another ahead. This time he caught a glimpse of fur, four legs, and glittering eyes. A scent drifted to his nose, but too thin as yet to recognize. A canine?

Chap slowly turned, watching darting forms circling around, out in the forest.

Across the way, Leesil half-crouched and blindly aimed the crossbow out into the trees. He jerked it quickly to the right. Magiere stood behind him with her falchion drawn.

"Light the damn crystal!" he snapped. "Now, Wynn!"

A head peeked out from behind a fir tree.

Chap growled before he could stop himself. He sniffed the air as Wynn's crystal lit up the narrow clearing. Something pushed its way through the teal-leafed bush into clear view.

Chap's tension melted in shock as he heard Magiere exhale.

"Majay-hì!" Wynn whispered.

Crystalline irises like sky-tinted gems stared at Chap from a long face covered in silver-blue fur. Its ears rose up to match his own, and Chap's breath caught.

At least five more circled in the forest around the intruders, weaving in and out of the vegetation. Like himself, they were long-legged, long-faced, and tall as hounds. Two were a darker shade of steel-gray, nearly as alike as twins. And one more was darker still.

His dark color, like ink brushed into his thick coat, made his eyes float in the dusk-shadowed space beneath a fir tree. He loped an arc to another overhang of branches, and the crystal's light caught the gray peppering in his muzzle.

The one peeking out from the teal-leafed bush dipped

his nose, head cocked in puzzlement. He looked from Leesil to Wynn and wrinkled his jowls to expose teeth.

Chap answered with a low rumble and exposed his own fangs.

Leesil backed toward Magiere, crossbow still raised. "Chap?"

He had no answer, even if he could have given one. He had no idea what these majay-hì wanted or why they closed in. A glimmer of white darted from around the tree where the black-furred elder stood watching.

The female's coat was so pale it looked cream-white in the crystal's glow. A hint of yellow sparked in her irises. She was delicate and narrow-boned, and stepped so lightly that Chap wondered if her paws even left prints in the loam.

"Look," Wynn murmured, and the sight of the white majay-hì seemed to blot away her panic. "Like a water lily . . . I never thought others would vary so much from Chap."

"Don't get any ideas," Magiere warned. "They're not Chap . . . and I don't think they want us here."

Chap knew they were not like him, and not only in the way Magiere meant. They were only majay-hì—distant descendants of born-Fay from long ago and guardians of this wild land. They were like his mother and his siblings of childhood.

"Their faces . . . ," Wynn said, the edge in her voice returning, "the way they move. I do not think any are inhabited by a Fay. But can they still understand us at all?"

Chap took two steps toward the silver-blue before him. It backed into the brush, sniffing the air. A growl pulled Chap's attention to the dark elder beneath the fir tree.

A steel-gray and the white female circled him. As they passed each other, they touched or rubbed heads, one to the next. Chap reached out, trying to snatch any surfacing memory passing through their thoughts.

Jumbled images assaulted him, one after the other. Some repeated and the order disjointed further. He fought to grasp and sort them, but there were so many coming so fast. He caught only pieces. . . .

The strange massive deer, and its urgent voice.

Racing toward its distant bellow.

A glimpse of an anmaglâhk in forest-gray attire.

Himself . . .

In the last flash that Chap grasped before it was buried in another cascade of sights, sounds, and scents, he saw himself through their eyes.

And these pieces of memory echoed from one among the touching trio to another.

Chap watched the majay-hì brush heads as the white and gray circled about the black elder.

Memories passed each time they touched. Not the random, scant surfacings of humans, but images passed willfully, one to the other.

Chap withdrew his awareness, shutting out the kaleidoscope that filled him with vertigo. It was too much to take in. But one image lingered as the silver-gray in the bush stepped forward.

An anmaglâhk in forest gray.

Chap backed away, looking again to the trio beneath the tree.

His eyes locked with the white female's. There were indeed flecks of gold within her chill-blue irises.

Chap's inaction left Leesil dumbfounded. He didn't know how much threat these dogs posed, and he expected some kind of lead from Chap.

All the majay-hì froze under another thrumming bellow in the forest.

Far out in the trees Leesil spotted the dim shape of the large silver deer. It stood posed upon a deep green hillock.

The majay-hì circled away into the forest like smoke thinning into the dark.

Chap stood rigid, ears pricked forward.

"Why are they are leaving?" Wynn asked.

Leesil had no answer. "We need to get out of here . . . find a place to camp."

Magiere's gaze remained on the trees where the majay-hì had vanished.

"What about food?" Wynn added.

Leesil had no idea where or how to find food, let alone what might be edible. This forest played with his wits, and even in daylight he had to concentrate just to see which way he had come.

"Camp first," Magiere said. "Then maybe Chap can come up with something."

Leesil sidestepped toward Chap, still watching the trees, and laid a hand on the dog's back. Chap was trembling.

"Can you find us another clearing?" Leesil asked.

Chap shook himself. He glanced about, circled around for Wynn to take hold, and padded off away from the sound of the deer.

A long arrow pierced the earth in front of Chap.

Leesil grabbed Wynn and jerked her back.

"Find cover!" he yelled.

With Wynn tucked behind him, he backed toward a moss-covered old log to his right. He heard a knock as something struck wood.

Wynn gasped. "Leesil!"

Another long arrow shuddered where it stood, embedded in the log. The shining metal head was familiar enough, like the bright-bladed stilettos his mother had once given him.

"Smother the crystal," he whispered.

Wynn closed the crystal in her fist, stuffed it into her coat pocket, and its light vanished.

Leesil couldn't see anything up in the branches, but he didn't wish to give their attackers the advantage of light. He heard something strike the earth to his rear, and then Magiere's voice.

"Damn it!"

Leesil didn't need to look for the arrow that had cut her off. "Get up against that tree, and don't move until we see them. We're open targets down here."

Chap rumbled from somewhere out in the darkness.

Leesil knew the dog was trying to sniff out their assailants. None of the three shafts had struck them but rather blocked any attempt at escape. He reached under with his left hand and undid the catch-strap of the stiletto on his right wrist.

A dark form dropped through the branches of the fir tree ahead of him.

Leesil heard another to his right, and then again to the rear.

One came forward out of the shadows.

Leesil aimed the crossbow at its center mass, ready to fire and then drop it to pull his blades or stilettos. Figures took shape as they approached with quiet footsteps.

"I've got two," Magiere whispered behind him.

A rustle of brush pulled his glance. A fourth figure rose from behind the old log. The one in front stepped into plain sight.

Each tall and slender figure wore a wrap across the lower half of its face. They'd tied the trailing corners of their cloaks across their waists. All of their attire was a dark blend of gray and forest green. Two carried short bows with metal grips as bright as the arrowhead in the log.

Anmaglâhk.

Desperation filled Leesil. Four assassins had intercepted him and his companions before they'd finished one day's travel into this immense land. How could the Anmaglâhk have known, let alone found him so quickly?

He slowly twisted the ball of his foot on the earth, rooting himself for an ugly fight, one that he and Magiere probably couldn't win against four of them.

"Wynn!" he whispered. "Run!"

Leesil swung the crossbow one-handed, over Wynn's head to his right, and fired. The gray-green figure behind the log twisted away to the earth as the quarrel hissed by.

He released the crossbow from his right hand and snapped it like a whip. The hilt of the unclasped stiletto slid sharply across his palm. He snatched the blade's tip as it passed, his arm cocked back to throw.

"Léshil, stop!" A deep and lyrical voice spoke in clear Belaskian. "No harm will come to you and yours!"

Leesil halted in midthrow. The lead anmaglâhk raised empty gloved hands, palms out to him, and quickly spread them wide toward his companions.

"Bârtva'na!"

The one to Leesil's left cautiously lowered his bow, but

kept his arrow drawn and ready. As the leader lifted one hand to his cowl, Leesil spotted Chap behind the elf. The dog crept in low and silent beneath the very tree the man had dropped from.

Leesil shook his head slightly, and Chap halted.

"We mean no threat to you," the leader said as he pulled back his cowl and, with one finger, lowered the wrap across his face.

Leesil sucked air through gritted teeth.

The man's narrow, deeply tanned face was unmistakable. His dark amber eyes were so slanted that their outer corners reached his temples. His nose was straight and sharp, like his cheekbones. He wore his thick, white-blond hair tied back at the nape of his neck, exposing his pointed ears. Everything about his appearance seemed elongated . . . and foreign.

"Sgäile," Leesil whispered.

Just last autumn, this one had come to Bela with an order to kill him, and then changed his mind. Sgäile was the one who'd first hinted that Leesil's mother might still be alive.

Before anyone spoke, Sgäile motioned to his companions. All removed their cowls and face wraps. Chap rushed in snarling, and Sgäile spun away, startled.

Chap circled around, placing himself between Sgäile and Leesil. Sgäile's companions' eyes went wide.

"He remembers you," Leesil spit out.

Sgäile glanced once at Leesil, then kept his amber eyes steadily on Chap.

Among Sgäile's companions were two men and one young woman with glowing white hair. She didn't linger as long as the others in studying Chap and turned her attention upon Leesil. While the others were still shocked by the dog's action, this female's feather eyebrows cinched together and open hatred wrinkled her angular features.

Leesil had never seen an elven woman besides his mother.

In spite of this one's expression, he couldn't take his eyes off of her. She didn't look anything like Nein'a. Her skin was darker and her features were almost gaunt in their narrow construction. He made out a prominent scar hiding beneath the feathering of her left eyebrow. Still, her white silky hair and peaked ears made his heart pound as he thought of his mother.

One of the men looked about middle-aged, perhaps even older than Sgäile, though how many human years that meant was beyond Leesil to guess. Though taller than Leesil, he was the shortest of the males, with a rough complexion compared to the others.

The fourth was even taller than Sgäile and young. He looked no more than twenty by human standards and was the most stricken by Chap's savage entrance.

Light erupted behind Leesil.

Wynn stepped close beside him, her expression awash with fascination as she held up the crystal.

"What do you want?" Magiere demanded.

"Lower your weapons," Sgäile said, slow and soft. "Please, put them away."

The elven woman stepped closer to him but didn't sheathe her stilettos. They were longer of blade than any Leesil had seen, perhaps a third the length of a sword. She gestured with one toward Magiere and Wynn.

"Lhâgshuilean . . . schi chér âyâg," she hissed, and then pointed the blade toward Leesil. *"Ag'us so trú, mish meas—"*

"Tosajij!" Sgäile returned sharply.

She never looked at him but hissed and fell silent, her eyes still locked on Leesil.

Leesil didn't understand what either had said. Except for one word so close to what he'd heard from a young anmaglâhk in Darmouth's crypt.

Trú . . . Trué . . . traitor. He'd never have trouble understanding that.

Sgäile's half hints were the reason he'd come here. The reason he'd dragged Magiere and Wynn and Chap halfway across the continent. He wanted answers, and he kept his stiletto at ready. His own anger sharpened, and he stepped closer.

"We're not putting anything away," he said right into Sgäile's face, "until you tell us why you've come . . . and where my mother is."

The younger male had circumvented Magiere, coming up near Sgäile. His expression changed to nearly visible surprise at either Leesil's words or his tone, possibly both. He wasn't carrying a bow, but a boning knife appeared in his hand. From behind Leesil. Wynn spoke out in a long string of Elvish.

All four anmaglâhk turned full attention upon the sage with guarded surprise.

"You speak our language," Sgäile replied in Belaskian. "Yet strangely."

"Bithâ," Wynn answered.

The young female hissed something in Sgäile's ear.

"Do not let your grief breach our ways," said the older male with the rough face.

He stood off to the left but clearly spoke to the woman. She turned on him, but fell silent.

Leesil wondered what grief the elder elf spoke of.

"Where did you learn our language?" Sgäile asked, refusing to speak to Wynn in his own tongue.

"On my own continent," she answered. "There are elves south of the Numan countries."

"Liar!" the female snapped. "Deceitful, like all humans."

These were the first non-Elvish words she'd spoken. Magiere had kept her eyes on the older anmaglâhk to the left, but her attention shifted to the woman, and her voice crackled low like Chap's growl.

"How rich . . . coming from the likes of you."

She swung her falchion slowly around toward the woman. Sgäile raised an arm in front of his comrade, but it wasn't clear exactly who he protected or restrained.

Leesil was getting tired of all this. "You aren't going to keep us out of this forest. Where is my mother? Is she still alive?"

Sgäile's expression remained guarded, but a flicker of discomfort crossed his narrow face. "Cuirin'nên'a lives, I assure you."

Leesil quivered in sudden weakness, and the chest's rope halter seemed to bite deeper into his shoulders.

"We would never kill one of our own," Sgäile continued. "But she is a great distance off, and the forest will not long tolerate your companions . . . or perhaps even you. We were sent to guide and protect you."

"And we're supposed to trust you?" Magiere asked.

"No," Sgäile answered politely. "I offer guardianship . . . and the safe passage of Aoishenis-Ahâre himself." His gaze shifted back to Leesil. "Do you accept?"

Leesil's anger got the better of him. "Not by every dead deity that I can—"

"We accept your guardianship," Wynn cut in, "and that of your . . . great-grandfather?"

Leesil turned bewildered outrage on Wynn. She remained calm and composed, facing only Sgäile as he returned a gracious nod.

"Wynn!" Magiere hissed. "What do you think you're doing?"

"What you brought me for," she answered flatly. "You do not understand what is happening, and there is no time to explain it all now."

"My caste is trusted by all of our clans," Sgäile added. "I will not allow harm upon you, so long as you are under my guardianship . . . and how else will you find Cuirin'nên'a but through us? She was once one of our caste."

Those last words taunted Leesil. Who else among the elves but the Anmaglâhk would know his mother's location? They had imprisoned her as a traitor, and it seemed this "great-grandfather" had authority over the whole caste.

"If she's still alive," Leesil asked bitterly, "did you leave her suffering in some cell all these years?"

The thought made him ill, for he blamed himself as much as the Anmaglâhk—as much as Sgäile. Nein'a had twisted Leesil's life to a hidden purpose, but he was the one who'd abandoned his parents eight years ago.

Sgäile's features twisted in revulsion, and his eyes flashed with anger.

"I did not leave Cuirin'nên'a anywhere! She is safe and well—and that is all I may tell you. I am a messenger and your assigned guardian. Aoishenis-Ahâre"—he glanced at Wynn—"Most Aged Father will answer your questions."

Leesil turned to Magiere; her white skin glowed in the crystal's light.

"I don't think we have a choice," he said quietly.

Magiere let out a derisive snort. "They're only concerned for themselves and their own goals! Every one of them we've met . . . they're all butchers who use the truth like a lie. They'll twist you around, Leesil, until you wouldn't know your own choice from theirs . . . until it's too late!"

Leesil flinched at her thinly veiled reference. Brot'an had tricked him into murdering Darmouth to start a war among the Warlands' provinces. But he still saw no alternative.

"Then believe in guardianship," Wynn said. "They would put their lives at stake to fulfill it. If you cannot trust them, then trust what I tell you. The way of guardianship is an old tradition and a serious matter."

Chap had remained silent and still all this time. His eyes held uncertainty and the quiver of his jowls echoed Magiere's distrust. As he crept around next to Wynn, he huffed sharply once in agreement.

"All right then," Leesil said with restraint. "As Wynn said, we accept . . . for now."

Sgäile nodded. "We will set camp through those trees. I will bring food and fresh water."

Wynn appeared to sag at those words, letting out all her fatigue.

Leesil sheathed his stiletto but had to nudge Magiere. She glared at him before doing likewise with her falchion, and then took Wynn by the arm with a frown at Chap.

"You two better be right."

Chap huffed three times for "maybe."

Magiere stopped short and her jaw clenched. "Oh, that's comforting."

She moved on with Wynn after Sgäile.

Leesil fell silent. They'd just placed their lives in the hands of the Anmaglâhk. He hoisted the pack Wynn left behind, retrieved the crossbow, and followed, his eyes on Sgäile's exposed back.

In a short time and distance, Magiere sat upon a toppled tree stump before a small fire. She settled Wynn on the ground in front of her and covered the sage with a blanket. Wynn leaned back to rest against Magiere's legs.

The four anmaglâhk didn't appear to carry anything besides their bows and stilettos. She watched two of them disassemble the bows, unstringing first and then pulling the wood arms out of the metal grips. They stored the parts behind their backs beneath their tied-up cloaks. While Magiere was distracted by this, one of them had struck a fire, though she wasn't certain how this was accomplished so quickly.

Chap settled beside Wynn, his eyes always upon the elves, who moved off to gather by a far oak and argue in low voices. Leesil piled their packs and saddlebags with the chest of skulls and paced about the fire before crouching on Wynn's other side.

"Can you hear what they're saying?" he whispered.

Wynn nodded. "Bits and pieces—enough to catch the essence of contention. Their dialect is strange . . . older, I think, than the one I know."

Although no food had been provided yet, the chance to rest in warmth had revived the young sage a bit.

"I cannot quite determine their hierarchy," Wynn said with a shake of her head. "Sgäile is the leader, but perhaps only based on the mission he was given. They do not seem to use rank titles that I can pick out. The rough-skinned man is clearly the eldest, though I would guess Sgäile is perhaps fifty to sixty years old."

"Sixty years?" Magiere said too loudly, then lowered her voice. "He doesn't look more than thirty."

She knew most people would find Sgäile strikingly handsome—although she'd die before admitting that aloud. His white-blond hair was thicker than that of most elves, and he wore it neatly tied back. His face was narrow and smooth, with skin slightly darker than Leesil's.

"They live longer than we do," Wynn replied. "One hundred and fifty is a common age. Some live to be two hundred."

Magiere glanced sidelong at Leesil, who watched the conclave of assassins with fixed interest. By how many years would Leesil outlive her?

"The others are questioning Sgäile," Wynn continued. "Especially the angry woman."

"What about?" Magiere asked.

"They are unsettled by the task they were given, though the elder male supports Sgäile's adherence to the custom of guardianship. It seems safe passage for humans is unprecedented. None of them have even seen a human set foot in these lands."

Wynn cocked her head, still listening. "They are hesitant to question what this Most Aged Father has asked of them . . . but they are to take Leesil to him."

"I knew it," Magiere whispered. "Leesil, they're up to more than taking you to your mother."

He didn't answer. He didn't even look at her.

"I do not think Sgäile is lying to us," Wynn argued. "And this patriarch of their caste may have been the one to order Nein'a's imprisonment. If so, he is the one we need to see."

She tilted her head up to look at Magiere.

"The elder and the woman do not wish you or me to be taken farther. They do not want"—she stopped, eyes widening—"any 'weakbloods' in their homeland."

Wynn fell silent for a moment, listening.

"Sgäile refuses. He gave his word to Most Aged Father to offer guardianship to all with Leesil and deliver us to a place called Crijheäiche . . . 'Origin Heart' . . . I think." Then she sucked in a long breath of air. "Oh, Leesil, you are considered dangerous, even by Sgäile . . . a criminal."

Magiere tensed. They'd had more than one run-in with these murdering elves in gray, who always found some way to put Leesil under suspicion.

The elves' debate ended as Sgäile stood up. He and the younger male disappeared into the forest. Magiere watched the two who stayed behind. They remained at a distance, and the woman turned her back, leaving only the elder man gazing stoically at the invaders gathered about the fire.

Sgäile returned sooner than Magiere would've guessed. He was alone and carried a bunched cloth of lightweight tan fabric. He approached and opened the cloth for Leesil. Within were more bisselberries mixed with bits of strangely wrinkled gray lumps.

"This will keep you until Osha returns from the stream." He turned toward Chap. "He will bring fish to roast."

Sgäile neither spoke nor looked at Magiere or Wynn. Leesil didn't appear to notice and took the offered food. He poked suspiciously at one gray lump.

"Muhkgean," Sgäile explained, then paused thoughtfully. "The heads of flower-mushrooms."

With a grimace, Leesil took a few berries and held the rest out to Magiere and Wynn.

Wynn snatched one mushroom head, popped it in her mouth, and chewed quickly with a deep sigh of satisfaction. Magiere took only berries.

"Osha . . . is this the young man's name?" Wynn asked.

Sgäile didn't answer.

"It means . . . 'Sudden Breeze,' " Wynn explained with her mouth still full. "A good name."

She yawned and drooped so heavily that Magiere had to separate her knees so Wynn leaned against the stump.

Sgäile remained silent. Regardless of this guardianship oath he'd taken, it was clear to Magiere that he was no more comfortable with the arrangement than his comrades were. Magiere placed a hand on Wynn's soft hair, thinking the sage grew weary beyond good sense.

"Soon as you've had some fish, you're going to sleep."

"Mmm-hmm," was all that came from Wynn, and she popped a peeled berry and another mushroom together into her mouth.

"Where did you find these?" Leesil asked, picking up the cloth of the berries and mushrooms. "We saw nothing like them in the forest."

Sgäile's thin white eyebrows arched. "The forest provides."

Leesil again offered the cloth bundle to Magiere. She shook her head. She wasn't about to touch one of the wrinkled gray lumps, and peeling berries seemed like too much trouble. And she didn't feel hungry.

This made no sense, considering she'd gone without food for as long as the others. Strangely, she wasn't even tired.

Sgäile walked back out into the forest, only to return moments later carrying six sharpened and forked sticks.

He stuck three into the earth around the fire, so their forked ends slanted upward above the low flames.

Osha melted out of the trees. He carried three large trout hooked by their gills upon his fingers. He half-smiled at Sgäile and dropped to his knees by the fire.

The two elves' flurry of busy preparation was almost more than Magiere could follow. Three more sticks appeared, pointed on both ends. Osha skewered each fish from mouth to tail, then balanced the ends in the forked sticks Sgäile had planted. Soon, the trout began to sizzle above the flames.

Wynn murmured sleepily, closing her eyes, "*Am'alhtahk âr tú*, Osha."

Osha jerked his head up to look at her, studying Wynn's round face and wispy brown hair, but his expression held no malice. He went back to fanning the fire, then he sprinkled some powdered spice over the fish and a savory smell filled the air.

Chap sat up and whined. Magiere hoped he'd wait until the fish finished cooking before helping himself.

The other two elves finally approached, carrying large leaves, which they handed to Osha. All was quiet but for the crackling fire, and then Wynn's eyes popped open.

"Do all Anmaglâhk speak Belaskian?" she blurted out.

Leesil looked to Sgäile. "Well, do they?"

Sgäile frowned. "Some. . . . Osha is learning at present."

Groggy and exhausted, Wynn still seemed unaware that Sgäile avoided speaking to her.

"Wynn," the sage said to Osha, pointing to herself, and then to the others in turn. "Magiere . . . Leesil . . . Chap."

Osha blinked, glancing tentatively at Sgäile, then bowed his head briefly to Wynn.

"You placed a name upon a majay-hì?" Sgäile asked.

All the elves appeared unsettled by this. The woman hissed something Magiere didn't catch and turned away.

"Wynn, that's enough," Magiere warned.

"Should we not be introduced," Wynn asked, "if we are to travel together?"

Sgäile stood up in discomfort. Again, Osha glanced at him, clearly uncertain if he should speak. Then he pointed to the elven woman off among the trees with her back turned.

"Én'nish," he said.

"Én'nish . . . ," Wynn repeated sleepily, "the wild, open field."

Osha pointed to the elder man. "Urhkarasiférin."

"Shot or cast . . . truly?" Wynn tried to translate.

Osha scrunched one eye and looked up to Sgäile, who nodded.

"And Sgäile," Wynn added.

"Sgäilsheilleache," he corrected, the first words he'd spoken to any but Leesil since their earlier standoff.

"Willow . . . shade . . . ," Wynn murmured.

"Sgäile it is, then," muttered Leesil.

Magiere tried to retain the names. Hopefully, shortened ones wouldn't cause offense, not that she cared much if they did. To her relief, Osha finally lifted one trout off the fire, and all attention was diverted as he deftly slid it onto a large leaf.

He boned the fish, cut the fillets into pieces, and, using smaller leaves as plates, passed them around in no particular order. Sgäile worked on the next trout. He fanned a full fillet to cool it before placing it on a leaf for Chap. Urhkar picked up two servings and joined Én'nish off in the trees.

Magiere took small bites. She still wasn't hungry, even after three mouthfuls that smelled and tasted better than any fish she could remember. She continued to nibble rather than have Leesil or even Wynn make a fuss about her not eating. Once her own companions finished, she put a hand on Wynn's shoulder.

"Lie down and sleep."

The sage didn't argue. She scooted over to lie on the ground, but she stopped halfway.

"Oh, Sgäile, whoever keeps watch should take care. We encountered a *tâshgâlh* this morning. I have not seen it again, but you would know what they are like."

To Magiere's surprise, Sgäile spoke directly to Wynn with concern.

"A *tâshgâlh*? Where?"

"That little rodent?" Leesil asked. "We found it in a cave on the mountain. It didn't seem dangerous."

"But troublesome," Sgäile answered carefully, and gestured out into the dark. "The majay-hì should warn us, and Osha will stand first watch."

Magiere looked where he pointed. Here and there a shadow moved. She saw the shapes of the dogs among the far trees, some near enough that their eyes glimmered from the firelight.

Wynn lay down and pulled her blanket up, and Chap curled in next to her as always.

Both Sgäile and Osha stared with differing degrees of astonishment. Osha's mouth opened slightly as Leesil spread his cloak out on the ground and reached for Magiere. She lay down on her side.

Osha turned quickly and walked away. Sgäile followed without a word.

Magiere put her back against Leesil's chest. He pulled the blanket up and placed his palm on her temple, slowly stroking her head and hair.

"This isn't what I expected," he whispered.

What had he expected?

"We'll find Nein'a," she whispered back.

"I know. Go to sleep."

Magiere heard his breathing grow steady and deep. Once certain he'd drifted off, she reached over him for her falchion left leaning against the stump. She tucked it under the blanket next to herself with her hand on its hilt.

She lay awake for a long time, not tired enough to sleep, strange as that was. She listened but couldn't hear the elves above the forest's soft sounds.

Magiere finally closed her eyes and tried to drift off. . . .

She suddenly found herself walking the forest in darkness, alone, wondering how she had gotten so far from the camp.

Pieces of the night moved around her between the trees.

Here and there, half-seen shapes shadowed her. Their colorless and glittering eyes watched her, as if waiting for her to do something.

These were not majay-hì. They walked on two legs. And

in her belly she felt their hunger. She smelled it, like blood on the damp breeze, and her own hunger rose up in answer.

The forest began to wither around her, until the stench of rot made her choke.

Magiere snapped her eyes open with every muscle ridged from the nightmare. It felt disturbingly familiar, as if she'd seen such a vision before. Lifting her head, she found the fire was now little more than glowing embers.

She didn't sleep for the rest of the night.

CHAPTER FIVE

By midmorning, Wynn's fear of becoming lost succumbed to awe as she walked the elven forest. Patchy lime-colored moss cushioned her footfalls as she followed the others. With all her ink and journals gone, it was heartbreaking to witness such diverse flora without a way to take notes.

Fresh food and a night's rest had revived her, and the pain in her shoulder had dwindled to an intermittent twinge, but her improved mood still wavered. This was a desperate search for Leesil's mother, and their guides were now the Anmaglâhk. These elven assassins were manifested dark shadows of the Leesil that Wynn had come to know in the Warlands.

Yet, she found them fascinating. Their ways were so different from the elves on her continent. She tried to mentally note everything about them for later records. Once she returned to her guild in Bela, she would write extensive work comparing the two elven cultures of the world as she knew them. And how stark the contrasts were or might yet be, for she had not met any elves here besides Sgäile's caste.

A temperate breeze rustled the foliage, and she pushed Chane's cloak back over her shoulders.

What would he think of this place? His interests lay in distant times back to the Forgotten History, and how societies evolved from unknown beginnings in the aftermath of the great war. He was always more interested in studying the past than the present.

Wynn pushed aside thoughts of Chane. He was part of her own past.

Sgäile led the way with his comrades following behind their guests. The pace was too slow for him, as he often paused after stepping too far ahead, but he made no complaint.

Wynn avoided looking back at Én'nish walking at the procession's rear. The woman was no less angry than in their first meeting. Silent and stoic Urhkar walked in front of his bitter comrade, and Osha came directly behind Wynn.

All four elves left their cowls and face wraps down. There was some significance in this, as secrecy seemed paramount to their ways. Perhaps they simply felt at ease in their homeland.

Leesil and Magiere walked ahead, behind Sgäile, and Chap trotted beside Wynn with his head turning at every new sight. His nose worked all the time, and Wynn often heard him sniffing as his muzzle bobbed in the air. She looked about at the lush flora, and more than once her boot toe caught on a root, stone, or depression when she was not paying attention to the trail.

Of all their escorts, Osha betrayed the most curiosity about the interlopers. He was so tall that when he stepped close, Wynn had to tilt her head back to see up to his chin. She felt awkward and rather too short. His hair was white-blond like Leesil's and hung loose to the center of his back. His somewhat horselike face was not nearly so handsome as Sgäile's, but it was pleasant. Although quiet, he was certainly the most polite of their guides.

They passed a large weeping willow with vivid orange fungus growing up its trunk's northern side. The color was so eye-catching that Wynn wandered absently toward the tree. Chap rumbled at her, following partway, but she ignored him in her rapt fascination.

"Osha, what is this?" she asked in Elvish, and pointed to the shelves of fungus. "The edges look like seashells."

Osha hesitated, looking to Sgäile as if awaiting instructions. He finally joined her.

"It is called woodridge," he answered in Elvish, and he put his hand against the fungus, closed his eyes for an instant, and then broke off a small piece to offer her. "It is safe to eat, though pungent until properly cooked."

His strange conjugations and declinations took time to comprehend. It reminded her of the oldest texts she had been permitted to browse at the elven branch of the guild on her own continent. It made some sense, for these elves had lived in isolation for centuries, while their counterparts of her world interacted with other races more freely.

Wynn put the orange lump near her lips and breathed in its scent. It smelled of wet earth. She snipped it with her teeth. A sweet sensation flowed over her tongue.

"Very good."

The taste thickened suddenly, bitter and pastelike. She swallowed, trying not to grimace, and smiled. Osha nodded in approval with perhaps a little surprise.

"Wynn, what are you doing?" Magiere called. "Did you just eat that?"

"Osha said it is safe."

Chap stood stiff and silent, watching the tall young elf, and then cast a glare Wynn's way.

She knew that look on his furry face. She did not care for his parental disapproval.

Wynn stuffed the hunk of woodridge in her pocket and hurried to catch up, as both Magiere and Leesil looked uncomfortable. She stepped back into the traveling line with the others.

Since Osha was the most amiable among his group, she continued questioning him in Elvish. His answers were short, but at least he answered—with occasional glances toward Sgäile, as if expecting admonishment. Sgäile remained silent, not once looking back.

Wynn kept her questions to the world around them,

though she wanted to ask of the people here. Intuition told her not to do so. A few times Osha paused after an answer, about to say something in turn. Perhaps he had questions of his own. He seemed intensely puzzled or startled by the way she acted and spoke, but he never asked. They passed an oak so large that its trunk was far wider than Osha's height.

Wynn stared at it a bit too long. "How old is this one?"

"As old as the forest perhaps," Osha answered. "The trees are the bones and blood of its body."

At this, Sgäile looked back sternly. Osha fell silent, dropping his eyes as he stepped out ahead of Wynn.

She was uncertain whether to be disappointed or worried. Clearly Sgäile thought the conversation had gone on long enough. Hopefully she had not gotten Osha into trouble.

Leesil slowed, his irritation far plainer than Sgäile's.

"What is wrong?" she asked.

"How could anything be wrong?" he muttered. "I haven't understood a word all morning."

"Leesil . . . you brought me because I speak Elvish—and you do not."

He sighed, grudgingly. "I know, I know . . . but I didn't think it would be like this—not understanding anything that anybody said."

Wynn was not sure which would be worse—a Leesil completely inept with the language or one able to proficiently express his ire in Elvish. He remained silent a moment, then looked up thoughtfully at Osha in a way that made Wynn nervous.

"I'll ask him if he knows how far away my mother is."

Before Wynn could grab him, Leesil quick-stepped up beside Osha.

"A-hair-a too bith-a ka-naw, too brah?"

Osha's mouth gaped.

All four elves came to a sudden halt. Any tentative curiosity in Osha's long face turned to horror. He glared at Leesil, and a stiletto appeared in his hand.

Magiere dropped a hand to her falchion's hilt. Before she could do anything stupid, Wynn scurried in between

Osha and Leesil. She turned on Leesil angrily but never got out a word before Én'nish thrust her heel into his tailbone.

Leesil sprawled forward as Én'nish drew her long stilettos. Wynn floundered out of Leesil's way, stumbling back into Osha, who caught her under the arms. She flinched at the sight of his blade appearing in front of her.

Leesil tried to roll, but the chest on his back hindered him. Even Urhkar was caught off guard as Én'nish rushed in. Leesil pulled his own stiletto as he spun around on his knees.

"*Bârtva'na!*" Sgäile barked at Én'nish and grabbed the back of Magiere's pack. "Stop this now! He does not know our tongue."

Én'nish slapped away Urhkar's attempted grasp and slashed at Leesil's face. He ducked and spun on one knee, swinging a stiletto on his pivot. Én'nish bent rearward at her midsection like a willow branch, and the blade tip cleared her stomach. She tried again to close on Leesil.

Chap rushed in and snatched her cloak from behind. He bolted around her side, twisting her in its cloth. In the same instant, Wynn lunged from Osha's support. Én'nish, intent with fury and shocked at a majay-hì hobbling her, did not see the sage coming.

Wynn swung, and her palm cracked loudly against Én'nish's cheek.

"This is your oath at its best?" she shouted in Elvish, and then gripped her throbbing hand. It was a challenge to Én'nish, and even to her comrades, for this violent breach of guardianship.

Én'nish turned upon the sage. When she raised one of her blades, Urhkar angrily grabbed her wrist. She held her place without resisting him.

Wynn shook with sudden fear as she turned and found Sgäile on guard beyond the tip of Magiere's falchion.

"Is this what the oath of guardianship is worth among your people?" Wynn asked.

"No!" he answered flatly, and his hard gaze turned on Én'nish. "You have our deep regret for this shame. . . . It will not occur again."

Osha still looked offended, but his expression melted into shame as Wynn glared at him.

"Leesil does not know what he said," she explained. "It was a mistake, not an insult."

Osha nodded and sheathed his blade as Leesil did the same.

"Please . . . put up your weapon," Sgäile said. With an open hand he cautiously tilted Magiere's falchion aside and then closed on Én'nish. *"Ajhâjhva ag'us äicheva!"*

Én'nish spun away and stalked past all of them into the lead. Osha followed her with his eyes lowered as he passed Sgäile. Leesil stood baffled.

"What just happened?" Magiere asked.

Wynn ignored her, turning all her fear-fed anger on Leesil. "What did I tell you?"

"All I asked was how far to—"

"No, you did not!" Wynn clenched her fists. "You said his mother is 'nowhere,' and that he knew it . . . and you said it wrong, even at that. You called his mother an outcast!"

Magiere let out a deep sigh.

"Wait . . . ," Leesil started. "I didn't mean—"

"Shut your mouth!" Wynn shouted. "And never again speak Elvish to an elf!"

Leesil blinked. He looked down at Chap for help, but the dog just licked his nose with a huff.

"That would be best," Sgäile added quietly.

"Don't blame him," Magiere warned. "However he bungled his words, it had nothing to do with Én'nish."

"Yes . . . and no," Sgäile replied. "Én'nish is the daughter of Osha's mother's sister by bonding . . . similar to what you call marriage."

"So she takes it on herself to step in?" Magiere asked. "Because she's his cousin by marriage?"

"No, not precisely," Wynn added. "Relations are a serious matter among elves—and more complex than Sgäile can state in your language."

Magiere shifted toward Sgäile. "That had nothing to do with kin."

"She is . . . was . . . the *bóijt'äna* of Grôyt'ashia," Sgäile said pointedly. "The closest term you would know is a 'betrothed.' "

The name was unfamiliar to Wynn. She was about to ask when Sgäile turned sharply away to follow Osha.

Brief puzzlement passed quickly from Magiere's face and her gaze dropped as her dark eyes slowly closed. Wynn heard the creak of leather as Magiere squeezed the falchion's hilt.

"Who is Grôyt'ashia?" Wynn asked.

When no answer came, she looked down at Chap, but the dog's eyes remained on Leesil. Without acknowledgment, Chap quickly trotted after Sgäile.

Magiere wouldn't look up. She sheathed her falchion and strode after the others.

Leesil just stood there in cold silence.

"What did you do?" Wynn asked, not certain she wanted to know.

Grôyt . . . Grôyt'ashia.

Magiere had heard the name once before. It echoed in her head with Brot'an's voice as he had shouted it in Darmouth's crypt. She'd turned to see Brot'an's young accomplice and Leesil trying to kill each other. It ended with Leesil soaked in blood—again—as it spilled from Grôyt's split throat.

It hadn't been Leesil's fault. Not that death. But Magiere couldn't stop from wondering. How many women—or men—in Leesil's life path waited for someone who would never return?

It wasn't his fault. Not for what Darmouth had made Leesil do to survive . . . do for his parents' lives, and all because of what Nein'a made him. Magiere closed on Sgäile from behind.

"It was self-defense," she said quietly, so the others couldn't hear.

"I am aware of the events involved," he answered without stopping.

"You knew . . . and you let Én'nish come with you?"

"It was not my choice to make."

"No more dodging!" Magiere snapped, too loudly, and grabbed Sgäile's shoulder.

He spun about, jerking free before she could get a true grip. "You know nothing of an'Cróan ways," he warned, "with your simple-minded human . . ."

He stopped himself as his eyes wandered across her face and hair.

Magiere didn't understand the term he'd used, but she grew unsettled under his scrutiny.

She wondered if he noticed her appearance, maybe how it differed from other humans'. Or had Brot'an spoken to his kind of what he'd seen of her during their fight in the crypt? How much did Sgäile know?

"Then tell me a little," she said. "Make it simple for a . . . human, if you wish."

"You were offered guardianship because of Léshil," Sgäile said, once more composed and formally polite. "That will be honored at all cost. How the events in Venjètz are seen in the end will depend on what status Léshil truly has with our people . . . and perhaps our caste. It is not my place to speak. You will wait until he has spoken with Most Aged Father."

With visible restraint, Sgäile turned and stepped on-ward.

Magiere bit back another demand. Regardless of Sgäile's personal feelings, it seemed he would stand by his words and strange customs, obeying his superiors and doing what had been asked of him.

"And what are these an'Cróan?" she asked instead.

Sgäile slowed. "It is the proper name of our people, ver-sus your human labels. Your short companion would say . . . Those of the Blood."

Magiere's stomach turned. Everything concerning Leesil came back to blood.

Chap walked behind Magiere as she argued with Sgäile. He reached for any memory surfacing in the man's thoughts.

Flashes of human faces surfaced in Sgäile's mind. He was well traveled, from what Chap caught. It was as if the elf searched for a comparison to Magiere's pale skin and red-stained black hair. Nothing came close, and Sgäile remained perplexed. He did not know what Magiere was and saw her only as some oddly pale human.

There remained the issue of blood. Blood of heritage, of people, and blood spilled.

It was a tangle that even Chap found himself trapped within. Whether it unsnarled or cinched tight to strangle them all depended on how Leesil was viewed by his mother's people.

No matter how many memory fragments Chap gleaned from Sgäile, he could not clearly piece together all concerning this issue and the consequences of killing an anmaglâhk. But Chap felt certain that Sgäile would follow his people's ways with as much conformity and integrity as he could.

Én'nish was another matter.

Her thoughts were clouded with memories of Grôyt'ashia. They shared a like fire that had burned hot in their separate natures. She smelled of blinding anguish and hatred, even from a distance.

Another scent reached Chap as he trotted watchfully behind Magiere. Movement in the trees caught his eye—a flash of silver-gray.

All other thoughts vanished when he saw the majay-hì skirting the path. He watched for them—for one of them— as they wove among the trees, drifting in and out of sight.

The silver-white female appeared briefly and then vanished.

"It is all right, Chap," Wynn said. "Go run with them, if you like."

He had not even realized he had slowed to fall back beside her. He peered into the forest with rapt attention but remained at Wynn's side. A high-pitched chirp made his ears perk up.

It trailed into a song, like someone whistling too perfectly, and then faded. He had never heard any such bird in his infancy among the elves.

Wynn lifted her gaze, searching for what had made the sound.

"What kind of bird was that?" she asked, and turned toward Urhkar at the rear.

Urhkar stopped for a long pause, and Chap did so as well, as the man looked back the way they had come. When the elder elf turned around, his expression was astonished.

He did not answer Wynn's question. And when Chap reached for any memory surfacing in Urhkar's thoughts, he caught only a vanishing glimpse of full black eyes and wings of mottled white feathers.

Six days more, and Leesil still didn't know how far Sgäile intended them to travel. They encountered no other elves and few animals besides the majay-hì among the trees. He once had to pull Wynn back from going after a multihued dragonfly and a cloud of shimmering moths. There were a few common squirrels in the trees, and ones colored something like a mink.

And the infrequent song of some bird out of sight.

Wynn's warning about the *tâshgâlh* had unfortunately proven valid. They hadn't seen it, but small things were missing from their packs. Including a flint stone, the last tin of Wynn's tea leaves, and several coins, as they'd found their purse spilled on the ground one morning. Leesil took to sleeping with the chest of skulls near his head.

Clear streams were plentiful, and the Anmaglâhk produced two decent meals a day for them with little effort. One of them simply disappeared into the forest and returned shortly with necessities for breakfast or dinner. Fruits, nuts, and more ugly little mushrooms served as a light midday meal while they walked.

Every time Leesil thought of Wynn, he felt small and petty. She annoyed him, and he couldn't help it. She might be fluent in Elvish, as she often reminded him, but what good was it? Sgäile barely acknowledged she existed; so the only elf Wynn spoke with at length was Osha, who didn't strike Leesil as particularly bright.

Each day was new torture as Leesil pictured his mother in some elven prison, though shame or anguish always mixed with resentment. Every time he asked Sgäile how many more leagues, the only answer he got was "More days . . . we will travel more days."

Leesil grew tired of it.

Magiere walked beside him, plainly uncomfortable and as distrusting as always. But more so now with the Anmaglâhk. She looked well enough, her black hair shimmering with lines of red in the sunlight, but he'd noticed how sparingly she ate, and at night she had difficulty sleeping. Each day she grew more tense, a nervous energy building in her.

He'd always viewed Magiere as someone who preferred the night—who felt out of place in the sun—but here, she'd changed somehow.

Leesil tried to remember the last time they'd been truly alone. Too long. Each night, guilt mixed with longing as he crawled beneath the blanket with her and pressed his face into the back of her neck. It was one moment when he forgot why he had come here and what he'd done to achieve it.

On this sixth day, Sgäile put his hand up, and everyone stopped.

"We near my home enclave, where we will spend the night with my family." His features tightened thoughtfully until he pointed to Magiere's falchion. "You are hu . . . outsiders, and bearing weapons might produce a dangerous reaction. I will carry them for you until we leave tomorrow."

"Not if I were already dead," Magiere growled at him.

Sgäile sighed, gesturing to Leesil's winged punching blades. "You have my word. We enter among my people, my clan. None have ever seen a human in this land. They will not take kindly to your presence. Less so, if you are armed."

"No," Magiere said flatly.

Én'nish backtracked to stand behind Sgäile. The corner of her left eye twitched.

"Savages!" she whispered to Sgäile, though she spoke in Belaskian for all to understand.

Leesil's eyes shifted quickly to Magiere, prepared for the inevitable flare of anger, but she was so quiet that it made him even more wary.

"Why did they send you?" he asked Sgäile. "Out of all of your kind, why you?"

Sgäile slowly swung his arm back until Én'nish retreated. "Because I am the only one you might trust . . . enough."

Leesil would never admit it to Magiere, but a part of him had begun to trust Sgäile—or at least the man's word.

"What if we keep our weapons out of sight?" he asked.

Magiere shook her head in disbelief. "You're not seriously considering what he asks?"

"They have their customs," Wynn warned. "And we are guests here."

Magiere turned to spit out a retort, but she didn't.

"No one else will touch your blades," Sgäile repeated. "And no one will touch you."

Én'nish uttered something under her breath. Leesil didn't care for her tone, let alone whatever she'd said. Sgäile held up his hand for silence and waited upon Leesil's reply.

For all Sgäile's calm manner, it was clear that unless Leesil and his companions agreed, they were not going one step farther. Leesil unlashed the sheaths of his winged blades from his thighs. Osha crept closer. Even silent Urhkar stepped around to a better vantage point. Én'nish kept her distance, though she watched intently.

Leesil handed his blades to Sgäile and followed with his two remaining stilettos, but he kept his wrist sheaths.

"What use?" Osha asked in clipped Belaskian, pointing to one winged blade.

Before Leesil answered, Sgäile uttered a short stream of Elvish with a lift of his chin toward Magiere as well. Osha's eyes widened.

"No," he said, then looked to Leesil. "It is . . . is truth?"

Sgäile fell back into Belaskian. "Pardon . . . I told Osha of your hunt for undead beneath your city."

Leesil remembered it clearly. He'd been half-crazed to take Ratboy's head. From Sgäile's perspective, it must have seemed bizarre indeed, considering why he'd tracked Leesil into those sewers beneath Bela. The Anmaglâhk hunted in silence . . . hunted the living.

The thought gave Leesil pause. In that, he saw himself—
his past—once again halfway between worlds.

"May I?" Sgäile asked, gesturing to the strange weapon.

Leesil nodded, and Sgäile unsheathed one winged blade
with a firm grip on its crosswise handle. He held it up,
slowly rotating the weapon in plain sight.

Its front end was shaped like a flattened spade, tapering
smoothly from its forward point along sharpened arcs that
ended to either side of the crosswise grip. The grip was
formed by an oval cut into the back of the spade's base.
The handle was wrapped tightly in a leather strapping. The
blade's outside edge continued in a long wing of a forearm's length, like a narrow and short saber that ended at
one's elbow. Where the wing would have protruded a
touch beyond Leesil's elbow, it was slightly short next to
Sgäile's forearm.

In place of Sgäile's studious inspection, Osha looked
suddenly confused.

"This dead-not . . . dead-not-dead," he said with effort.
"We see . . . hear . . . not here, but hear stories small of
other place . . . places. How you kill, if is dead?"

This talkative turn took Leesil by surprise, but it made
sense. An unusual weapon captured attention from a caste
of killers, even one as young as Osha. Where some humans
might think of undeads as only myth and superstition,
Sgäile had stated the issue so plainly. The others accepted
his word as fact.

Vampires might be rare enough in human lands, but
Osha hinted at something else.

"What does he mean by 'not here'?" Leesil asked. "You
have no tales or myths of undead?"

Sgäile seemed to consider his reply with great care. "No
undead has been known to walk this land."

A direct though polite response, but Leesil caught the
implication.

The undead—noble or otherwise—could not enter this
forest.

"How kill not-dead . . . un . . . dead?" Osha repeated.

Leesil was lost in thought. "What?"

Magiere clasped her falchion's hilt, which made the

young elf tense, but she didn't pull it. With her other hand she drew a slow, scything arc of fingertips across her throat.

Wynn sighed in disgust. "Oh, Magiere."

"Throat?" Osha asked.

Urhkar startled Leesil with a reply. "Not throat—neck. They take heads."

Osha's face paled through his dark complexion. Further off, Én'nish hissed under her breath. Sgäile spoke quickly to Osha. The young elf nodded.

"Forgive his reaction," Sgäile said. "Dismemberment of the departed is repulsive to us . . . but we understand the necessity."

"Have we finished with our debate over slaughter?" Wynn asked, disdain coloring her face.

Sgäile raised an eyebrow. He sheathed Leesil's blade and turned to Magiere, waiting.

Magiere didn't move a muscle.

"I don't like it any more than you," Leesil said. "But Wynn is right. It's their world . . . their way."

"All right!" she said. "Only because I can't see another way to find your mother. But don't get stupid on me. They're guards, not escorts, and they serve their own goals first."

Her blunt accusation jolted Leesil. In essence, she was right. The Anmaglâhk might look and even act somewhat like his mother, but he was a stranger here and didn't understand their customs, let alone the way they thought. But it changed nothing.

Magiere finally unbuckled her sword and held it out to Sgäile. He accepted it, and one feathery eyebrow rose a bit at its weight. He looked at her as if not quite believing she could wield it.

Wynn handed him the crossbow and quiver off Leesil's back. Sgäile gave these last items to Urhkar, who slung them over his shoulder. It made sense, as there were more arms than one person could carry efficiently, and Sgäile had promised to guard the blades.

Leesil took his rolled cloak off the pack that Wynn carried and handed it to Sgäile.

"Use this to bundle them . . . easier to carry and keep out of sight."

Sgäile nodded agreement. He was about to turn and lead on.

"Magiere!" Wynn said.

The little sage folded her arms and stared at Magiere's back. Stranger still, Chap gave Wynn a rumble, a displeased sneer, and a lick of his nose. She ignored him.

Leesil was lost. They'd handed over the crossbow, his blades and stilettos, Magiere's falchion . . .

For an instant Leesil considered saying nothing, but Wynn had already drawn too much attention.

"Give it up—now," he told Magiere.

How one woman could deliver so much spite from the corner of her eye still worried Leesil at times. It made him think of long-lost days in the Sea Lion Tavern, when she grew fed up with his antics.

Magiere reached behind her back and beneath her pack. She drew out the long-bladed dagger acquired before they'd headed into the Warlands.

Sgäile just opened the cloak bundle of weapons and waited. Leesil thought he caught a hint of humor in the man's eyes. Magiere tossed the dagger into the cloak.

"Come," Sgäile said, and gestured to his own companions. "The majay-hì may walk where he pleases, but you must stay inside our circle. Our people may become unsettled at the sight of you."

Én'nish remained in front, while Sgäile and Osha spread to the sides, with Urhkar at the rear behind Wynn.

They traveled only a short ways. Leesil caught odd changes in the trees when they passed through an area of dense undergrowth. Wild brush grew higher than his head. There were more oaks and cedars than other trees, with trunks wider than any he'd seen before.

Ivy ran up into their lowest branches, which were just within reach if he'd stretched upward with one hand. Their trunks bulged in odd ways that didn't seem natural, yet he saw no sign of disease. Foliage grew lush, thick and green overhead. In the spaces between trees, the underbrush gave way to open areas carpeted in lime-colored moss. Someone stepped out and turned away as if emerging like a spirit from the bloated trunk of a redwood.

As Leesil drew closer, he saw thickened ivy hanging from its branches. The vines shaped an entryway into the tree's wide opening between the ridges of its earthbound roots.

"Dwellings?" Wynn asked, but no one answered.

Osha fidgeted nervously. Sgäile was as tensely watchful as the first night he'd appeared in the forest. And both made Leesil worry.

They passed more dwelling trees with openings and flora-marked entryways. A tall elf peered through a bordering arch of primroses around the dark hollow in an oak. Leesil couldn't make out more than that he was male and would have to duck his head to come out. The large clay dome of an oven sat in an open lawn, smoke rising from its top opening. Several women and two men standing near it stopped, touched their companions, and turned one by one to stare.

Among them was the one Leesil first thought had walked straight out of a tree. He recognized her strange hair. She stood off from the others upon the moss lawn, and a break in the canopy captured her in a shaft of sunlight.

Soft creases in her skin, darker brown than Leesil's own, marked the corners of her large eyes and small mouth. She was slender and tall like his memory of Nein'a, but this woman's hair was like aspen bark, shot with gray that looked dark amid the white blond. Advanced age on an elf seemed strange.

Her narrow jaw ended in a pointed chin tilted down to a slender and lined throat as she fingered through whatever was in her basket. She hadn't yet spotted the new arrivals, but other elves began to gather.

They appeared at openings in the living dwellings or stepped through ivy curtains and around arches of vines and bramble plants shaped to divide and define the community's spaces. A teenage boy in nothing but breeches crouched overhead in an oak's limbs, his brown torso smooth and perfect.

Some faces looked calm and welcoming at first, until they spotted the outsiders walking between the Anmaglâhk. Others froze immediately, and fear was tinged with something more dangerous. All stared at Wynn and Magiere. Some even looked at Leesil uncertainly.

Unlike in the human lands, no one here would long mistake him for one of their own. He was short by comparison, his amber eyes smaller, and, though beardless, his wedged chin was too blunt and wide. And his clothing was nothing like theirs.

Chap pushed in to walk close to Wynn.

In a few more steps, their small group was surrounded by people at all sides of the community's center green. A lean man about Sgäile's age stepped out. Én'nish halted, but the man wasn't looking at her.

"Sgäilsheilleache!" he spit out.

Leesil couldn't catch the stream of Elvish that followed, but Osha stepped back, positioning himself closer to Wynn. Leesil didn't find this comforting as he studied the growing crowd of elves. Their dress differed noticeably from the Anmaglâhks'.

A few wore their hair bound in tails upon the crowns of their heads by polished wood rings. Their clothing was dyed mostly in shades of deep russet and yellow. They wore quilted and plain tunics and vests, and shirts of lighter fabric, some white, which shimmered where sunlight struck it. Tangled embroidered patterns marked collars and loose sleeves on a few. Though some women wore long skirts of rich dark tints, just as many had loose tan breeches and the soft calf-high boots favored by the men. Besides the one boy, no other children were visible. No one carried tools or anything Leesil counted as a weapon.

As conspicuous as he'd felt among humans, here it felt worse that he looked like an elf at all.

Stunned, frightened, or angry, several of the village elves were now spitting words at Sgäile. The air filled with their noise, until the clamor made it hard to hear Sgäile's replies.

"Wynn," Leesil whispered, "what are they saying?"

"They accuse Sgäile of breaking sacred law," she whispered back. "He assures them he acts for Most Aged Father, that we are under guardianship."

Osha put a finger to his lips and shook his head in warning. Wynn fell silent, and Leesil listened carefully, though he picked out few words.

When Sgäile mentioned Aoishenis-Ahâre, half those who argued with him fell silent, some in shock, but their initial anger returned quickly enough.

Leesil took a step forward, watching their faces. He hadn't expected Sgäile to be challenged this aggressively. Part of the reason he'd agreed to follow was so that Magiere and Wynn would have protection in this land. Now he questioned how far this guardianship custom could reach. Gradually, the voices lowered, and Sgäile appeared to convince the others to back away and let him through.

Leesil heard and felt something grate along the chest on his back.

The chest toppled away behind him as severed harness ropes fell down his front.

He whirled to find Én'nish behind him, a long stiletto in her hand as she grabbed for the chest's latch. So intent in watching and listening, Leesil hadn't noticed her slip around behind him.

Magiere saw the chest fall from Leesil's back. Én'nish dropped to a crouch, fighting with the latch.

"No!" Magiere shouted, and made a lunge for the chest.

Én'nish's hand shot out, flat-palming the inside of her knee.

Magiere crumpled before getting a grip on the chest, and Én'nish flipped the chest's lid before Leesil could pull it away.

The cloth bundle within tumbled across the ground, and the two skulls rolled into plain sight.

Someone gasped.

Exclamations followed that Magiere didn't understand. Pain flooded her leg and her heart quickened. Too many things happened at once. She watched helplessly as Leesil rushed for the skulls, to hide these last remains of his father and grandmother from prying eyes.

Én'nish kicked into the side of his abdomen. Leesil stumbled beyond reach, gasping for breath, and Én'nish began shouting in Elvish.

Wynn screamed out, "*Nâ*—no! *Na-bithâ* . . . it is not true!"

Osha pulled both blades, but he stood in confusion, as if uncertain who to attack or who to defend.

Magiere ignored the pain in her leg and scrambled up to rush Én'nish from behind.

A grip like a manacle encircled her wrist, and she was heaved backward. She swung hard at whoever had grabbed her and caught a glimpse of Urhkar's face as he ducked the blow.

He swept one leg against the back of her knees, dropping her instantly, and pinned her to the ground. Anger gave way to shock as she fought to get free. Urhkar bent her wrist hard, with her arm twisted around his grounded leg, and she was pinned facedown on the village green. He remained crouched over her.

"Stay," he said calmly.

"Get off!" she ordered.

He didn't even respond. Anxiety stronger than rage filled Magiere.

With one cheek against the moss, she tried to look for Leesil.

Chap darted in front of Én'nish, snarling and snapping. She backed away, and Wynn made a dive for the skulls.

"Én'nish told them you came to hunt elves!" she shouted to Leesil. "For trophies!"

Magiere's stomach clenched.

Leesil either didn't understand or didn't care as he grabbed Gavril's skull. Wynn beat him to his grandmother's and placed her hand on it. She burst into Elvish, voice full of fear as she shouted to Sgäile. The only word Magiere caught was "Eillean."

Leesil dropped to his knees, clutching at his grandmother's skull in Wynn's arms.

"Stop!" Wynn cried. "Be still, or they will kill you!"

Magiere bucked again, trying to pitch off Urhkar, but he was like a stone statue above her, unmovable.

* * *

Wynn's words didn't matter to Leesil—only the skull. He wrenched it from her, crouching with the remains of a father and grandmother wrapped in his arms.

Sgäile's eyes were wide, and Leesil thought he saw his own torments mirrored in those amber irises.

"Eillean?" Sgäile whispered, pointing to the elven skull.

Leesil quickly pulled it aside.

A woman in breeches and an old man in a robe stepped from the crowd, their expressions hard. Chap snarled and rushed out with wild howling barks, and they stumbled back in a startled retreat. The dog cut a wide circle around the green before all those gathered, rumbling with menace. Elven villagers were bewildered—a majay-hì turning on them to defend an outsider.

The village glen grew quiet but for uncertain whispers. The ring of onlookers cast confused glances from Chap to Sgäile and then back to Leesil. His skin crawled with their fixed attention.

"You took her remains from the keep's crypt?" Sgäile asked.

It sounded strange in Leesil's ears—a fervent statement hinted within a question. Sgäile said something loudly in Elvish, and the words carried the same tone and inflection. Reactions from those around the clearing changed little. Some became wary and startled, while others glowered in disbelief.

"You brought her home to her people . . . yes?" Sgäile added.

The words barely registered. Leesil didn't care what they wanted. His dead were no one's business but his own.

"Answer him!" Wynn insisted. "He is trying to save your life . . . and ours!"

Én'nish growled something, and her voice rose to a near screech. Leesil twisted about.

Urgent anticipation twisted her sharp features, as if she'd finally cornered some animal long hunted. Fury rose in Leesil, but he remained still.

Tears began to run down Én'nish's eager face and drip from the wedge of her chin. Urhkar barked at her in

Elvish. She snapped around at him, and twisted hope vanished from her face.

Urhkar had Magiere pinned, but his expression remained passively stoic. Magiere was barely able to lift her head from the ground, and her dark eyes locked on Leesil.

How long before he saw those irises blacken and her teeth elongate? He wanted it to happen, to see her tear into the elf.

Urhkar leaned down and spoke softly to Magiere. She ceased struggling, and he glanced beyond Leesil. The elder elf nodded sharply once to someone, and then leaped backward, releasing Magiere. She scrambled about, facing him as she rose, then backed slowly to Leesil.

"It's all right," Magiere whispered, crouching with one hand braced against the earth. "No one will take them . . . I won't let anyone take them from you."

The roar of rushing blood in Leesil's ears began to ease under her voice.

"Please," Sgäile pleaded, "tell them all . . . tell my people I speak the truth."

Leesil saw pain on the anmaglâhk's face—and fear.

"Érin'n," Sgäile whispered, " 'truth' . . . say it!"

Leesil didn't understand, but Sgäile's urgency crept into his muddled mind.

"Ay-rin-en . . . ," he said once, and then again with force. Sgäile sagged in relief.

Magiere reached for the fallen cloth, but Sgäile picked it up first. He opened it, draping it over his open hands like an offering.

"You shame me," he said quietly, and dropped his gaze to Eillean's skull. "You should have told me. I would have . . . begged to carry her. Even for a little of the way."

Sgäile hesitated at the sight of Gavril's skull, but then he held out the draped cloth. Magiere snatched it away and laid it carefully over the skulls in Leesil's arms.

He quickly wrapped them, hiding them from all prying eyes and stood up only when Magiere coaxed him.

Some of the elves gathered around still looked angry, but others lowered their heads in rising sorrow. Leesil didn't understand why his grandmother's return and one Elvish word had caused such a change.

Magiere slid her arm around his shoulders, but she looked behind him toward Én'nish.

"You touch him again," she said coldly, "and I won't need a sword to take your head."

Leesil heard no answer from Én'nish, but she came into sight around his right side, circling wide as she approached Sgäile. Urhkar strode into Leesil's view and cut her off.

Without the slightest emotion on his face, the elder anmaglâhk raised an empty hand, palm outward. He waved it between them, as if brushing some annoyance from the air.

Anger drained from Én'nish's face. She flinched as if struck suddenly by someone she cared for. She backed away from Urhkar, turned, and fled from the clearing.

Wynn climbed to her feet as Osha tucked away his stilettos and hurried to assist her. When he offered his hand, the sage pulled away and wouldn't look at him.

"We should get out of sight immediately," Wynn said.

Chap still paced before the elves, glancing every so often at Leesil.

An elderly man in a quilted russet shirt pushed through the crowd. His unruly hair was darker than the others' and shot with steel gray. Chap turned on him with a snarl. The old man froze just inside the ring of onlookers but would not retreat.

"Sgäilsheilleache?" he called.

In an unguarded moment, relief flashed across Sgäile's narrow features. *"Foirreach-ahâre!"*

"Chap, stop! Leave him be," Wynn called; then she whispered to Magiere, "Sgäile called that man his grandfather."

Chap turned a hesitant circle back toward Wynn, his eyes still on the new arrival. The older man approached, eying the dog. He didn't appear angry or frightened, only a bit startled and worried.

Sgäile spoke rapidly in Elvish, and his grandfather's answers carried a tone of polite admonishment. Leesil wondered at what was said and looked to Wynn. The sage followed their words with fixed attention but offered no translation. Sgäile gestured Leesil forward and kept his voice low.

"Hurry. Come to my home. You will be safe there."

Leesil bit his tongue to keep from snapping. Sgäile had made this promise before, and his assurance had proved false. Leesil wondered how much worse things could get.

CHAPTER SIX

Wynn gasped softly as she stepped through a wool curtain and into an oak tree as wide as a small cottage.

Moss from outside flowed inward across the chamber's floor, though she could not fathom how it remained a vibrant yellow-green without sunlight. The oak's interior had grown into a large rounded room with naturally curving doorways and walls. The walls were bark-covered like its outside, but in some places bare wood showed through. Not as if the bark had been stripped, but rather that the oak had grown this way yet still lived and thrived. Tawny-grained wood shaped arches to other curtained spaces. Steps rose upward around the left wall and through an opening in the low ceiling, perhaps leading to further rooms above.

Ledges at the height of seating places were adorned with saffron-colored cushions covered in floral patterns of a lighter yellow. Through one archway Wynn saw a smaller chamber with stuffed mattresses laid out upon the moss carpet. Soft pillows and green wool blankets graced those resting places.

She ran fingertips lightly across the bark wall as Osha stepped in.

After what had happened in the village green, she no longer felt certain he could be trusted. He drew blades at the sight of the skulls, but not to protect those under guardianship.

Magiere swept aside the doorway curtain and looked about with little interest in the surroundings. Her study of the place was more a wary search for potential threats or perhaps other ways out. She finally stepped in, holding aside the curtain.

Leesil entered, still gripping the bundled skulls, and behind him came Chap, who surveyed their surroundings much the same way as Magiere had. Sgäile carried the skulls' chest under one arm. Beneath the other he held the cloak-wrapped weapons. Last came Sgäile's soft-spoken grandfather, and yet there was room for all.

Osha stared at the bundle in Leesil's arms. He took a long breath, held it for a moment, and then exhaled.

"It is a blessing you speak our language," he said to Wynn. "When I saw those . . . and heard Én'nish . . ."

He did not look at her. Wynn assumed he was shamed by yet another violent breach of guardianship. And he should be.

Sgäile gently set the chest at the room's far side.

"I should not have been so quick in my thoughts," Osha added.

Wynn didn't answer. Sgäile laid the cloak-bundled weapons beside the chest and turned a hard gaze upon Osha.

"The day has been long," he said. "The remaining journey will be longer. You may take leave for food and rest."

A polite dismissal, but Sgäile's dissatisfaction was plain. Én'nish had been a growing threat, but Wynn had come to expect better from Osha.

Osha looked down at her, as if to say something more, but he quickly headed for the doorway. He gave a brief nod of respect to Sgäile's grandfather and left.

Magiere turned on Sgäile. "You gave us your word that we'd be safe, and it meant nothing."

"Please sit and rest," Sgäile's grandfather interceded. "Be at ease in my home, for none will trouble you here."

Beneath his thick elven accent, his Belaskian was perfect. Wynn stepped in, hoping to divert further conflict.

"You are not Anmaglâhk," she said to the elder elf. "How did you learn Belaskian?"

"He is a Shaper—specifically a healer," Sgäile explained. "And a clan elder. He has twice been on envoy, sailing to the human coastal countries. He also serves enclaves many leagues apart, including Crijheäiche, the housing place of the Anmaglâhk. I have taught him more of the language, at his request."

Sgäile stepped back and held his palm out. "This is my grandfather, Gleannéohkân'thva."

Wynn turned the long name in her head—Reposed within the Glen. Even she would have trouble saying it properly, and she hesitated to try. Enough offense had already been given on this journey by a slip of the tongue.

"Gleann?" she said hesitantly.

Dark flecks of brown within his amber irises gave them a strange allure. The thin, soft creases around his mouth made Wynn think of an old owl. Unlike Sgäile and his comrades, Gleann looked Wynn straight in the eyes, sternly.

A faint curl grew at the corners of his mouth. He placed one hand over his heart with a nod, but as he turned to Sgäile, one feathery eyebrow rose.

"What have you done?"

Sgäile fidgeted like a boy caught in mischief. "I must report on our progress. Would you ask Leanâlhâm to bring food for our guests?"

As the words left his lips, the doorway's curtain flipped wildly aside. A pretty elven girl nearly fell into the room in a rush, panting out Elvish.

"Grandfather? . . . Uncle! What has happened? I heard you brought—"

She sucked in a breath so quickly that it choked her and backed against the wall beside the door. She stared fearfully at Magiere.

Wynn guessed the girl at about sixteen by human or elven standards, for the early years of either's development were much the same. Leanâlhâm's hair was almost dark enough for light brown rather than the varied blonds of her people. Her eyes, with their large irises . . .

Wynn blinked and looked more carefully.

Leanâlhâm's irises were not amber—they were topaz, with a touch of green.

Two thin braids down the sides of her triangular face held back the rest of her hair. On second look, her narrow ears were ever so blunted at the tips, though not as much as Leesil's.

Wynn's gaze slipped once to Leesil, the only half-blood she had ever seen or heard of. But she knew this girl was not a full elf.

Sgäile took Leanâlhâm in his arms, pulling her into his chest as he whispered in her ear. Wynn would never have imagined such affection from the reserved leader of their escort.

"It is all right, Leanâlhâm," Gleann said, keeping to Belaskian, which suggested the girl spoke it as well. "Your cousin brought unexpected guests for dinner."

Wynn took a cautious step toward the girl. "I am Wynn . . . and pleased to meet you."

Only one of Leanâlhâm's strange eyes peered around Sgäile's shoulder. It shifted quickly from Wynn to Magiere, paused briefly upon Chap, and then held on Leesil. He returned her gaze, pivoting to face her.

"Leesil," he said, and then nodded toward Magiere, saying her name.

Leanâlhâm remained apprehensive, though she pulled back from Sgäile enough to study all the strange visitors. Sgäile released her and headed for the doorway.

"I will return. Please see to their needs." He paused and dropped back into Elvish. "Make a bath for them and find spare clothing while theirs are washed. The smell grows worse each day."

Smell? Wynn's jaw dropped. At least neither Magiere nor Leesil understood. None of them had bathed or washed their clothes in weeks. Sgäile left, and an uncomfortable silence followed.

"Food first," Gleann said in Belaskian. "Then baths.

Leanâlhâm, go to the communal oven and see what is left. Try to bring meat or fish for the majay-hì. I will find our guests some clean attire."

Chap barked once at the mention of food.

"What's this about baths?" Leesil asked.

Sgäile restrained himself from running. Once out of the village and into the forest, he broke into a jog. He fought to quiet his thoughts, to regain stillness and clarity, but his mind churned against his will.

Finding a young pine, he dropped to his knees. He waited for his breathing to ease and took an elongated oval of pale word-wood from inside his cloak. He reached for the pine's trunk, the word-wood couched in his palm, but then paused and lowered his hand.

He needed a moment more.

Regret was not an emotion he tolerated. There was no room for it in the life of service he had sworn to his people. But no one had ever been asked to escort humans through their land.

Of those few who ever made it through the mountains, skirted the northern peninsula by sea, or came up the eastern coast from the south, even fewer lived to tell of it to their own kind. But Sgäile needed to know how his people would react before he brought Léshil to Crijheäiche—to Aoishenis-Ahâre, Most Aged Father.

Word would travel swiftly, and he had thought this best rather than to appear suddenly in Crijheäiche with two humans and a half-blood. And selfishly, he had wanted Leanâlhâm to see Léshil, to know she was not the only one of mixed heritage in this world. Just one moment in which she did not feel alone among her own kind.

He thought his own clan would respect his mission and stand behind him, even in this unprecedented task. He was Anmaglâhk. His caste was unquestioned. And his own clan honored by his service.

Pride . . . Like some youthful supplicant first accepted to the caste, he had let pride—and sentiment—cloud his judgment. He should have bypassed his home and never brought Léshil among his own clan.

He should not have jeopardized his mission for personal reasons. Yet every time he dwelled on Léshil, everything became unclear, not unlike that moment in the human city of Bela, when he held an unaware Léshil in the sight of his bow. How could any one person be so stained in contradictions as Léshil?

Murderer, son of a traitor, with no connection to his heritage . . . who willingly slept beside a human woman.

Léshil, grandson of Eillean, who took great risk in returning her last remains to her people.

And just how had he breached the Broken Range and walked into this land?

Sgäile had refrained from asking, no matter how the question nagged him. It would be viewed as interrogation. Gaining trust from Léshil was far more important—and Léshil had shown trust in relinquishing his weapons.

The last thing Sgäile had wanted was to force the issue in a fight between Léshil and his own Anmaglâhk. It would have ended in bloodshed, perhaps on both sides, and this was not what Most Aged Father requested. So he allowed Léshil time to travel with him and hopefully trust in his word. He had waited until the last possible moment to ask for those weapons.

No blood was spilled, though entering among his people had been far more dangerous than Sgäile had imagined. He had thought only the humans would rouse anger and fear among his people.

Én'nish had nearly cost him everything. And when Urhkarasiférin dismissed her from his tutelage, she fled in shame.

The revelation of Eillean's remains—or rather the way it had occurred—nearly ruined all Sgäile's silent efforts. What little trust he had gained from Léshil had been shaken.

Then there was the majay-hì. The one the humans forced a name upon—perhaps the one who had found a way through the mountains.

One of the old ones . . . the first ones . . . imbued by the Fay.

Sgäile knew the first time he looked upon the dog from

a distant rooftop in Bela. It was why he had stayed his arrow from killing Léshil.

Awareness of the Spirit side of existence was not shared by many of his people. Those born with it, as he had been, most often became Shapers or Makers. Humans would call them "thaumaturges," a grotesque term for humans who worked magics of the physical side of existence. In Sgäile's youth, his grandfather encouraged him to follow the way of Shapers, whose careful ministrations guided trees and other living things into domiciles, or encouraged the healing of the sick and injured. He had not the patience for it, and no interest in the Maker's arts of imbuing and fashioning inert materials, such as stone and metal and harvested wood. His heart turned toward a greater calling.

Anmaglâhk.

His own Spirit awareness did not fade as it did in many who went untrained. It stayed with him through the years. He could feel the power of Spirit within the trees and flowers of the forest, if he stopped long enough to focus. What he sensed within the creature that ran beside the half-blood was so strong he knew it without effort.

No majay-hì had ever been seen outside elven lands. And none born in generations had left Sgäile so stricken upon first sight.

And such a one had joined Léshil.

Sgäile could not fathom why, but it was not to be ignored. It had meaning, even if he could not immediately understand.

He grew calm, more focused.

Among his people there were twenty-seven clans. People were born into one, and sometimes bonded—married—into another. Then there was the Anmaglâhk. Not a clan, but a caste of protectors among the people, they followed a founder from the ancient days. No one was born an anmaglâhk, and not all who sought admittance were accepted.

Sgäile had never doubted where he belonged. Never doubted he would walk in a life of service.

His breaths deepened, grew even. He lifted the word-wood to place it against the pine's bark and closed his eyes.

"Father?" he whispered, and then waited.

Most Aged Father's voice entered his thoughts. *Sgäil-sheilleache.*

"I am here, Father, at the prime enclave of my clan. We are on our way to Crijheäiche."

And Léshil comes willingly?

"Yes . . ." He did not wish Most Aged Father to know that he was troubled. "And two human companions. He would not come without them."

They are of no concern.

"Our welcome here . . . was worse than I anticipated. The presence of the humans . . . or even human blood did not sit well. And another matter that worsened the—"

That is of no consequence. Bring Léshil to me. But perhaps keep clear of our people when possible. Yes?

"Yes, Father."

Sgäile hesitated, wondering if he should say more. . . .

The short human female understood all their words. The white-skinned one had strange black hair that simmered like fire-coals in the sun. Léshil carried the remains of the great Eillean. And they all traveled with a majay-hì like no other—except in the oldest of tales, remembered only in fables for children.

"Soon, Father," he said.

He hesitated once more. He would not call it doubt, as there was no place for such in anything that he did.

"In silence and in shadows," he added respectfully, and lifted the word-wood from the pine, stood up, and turned back toward the village.

Chap's restlessness grew with the dusk. Time spent with Gleann and Leanâlhâm over dinner had gone quickly, and he found them pleasant. Perhaps trustworthy enough that his charges might sleep safely for the night. Leanâlhâm brought him a rich broth with portioned chunks of roasted rabbit, and he licked the bowl clean.

Gleann's voice carried from beyond a curtained doorway at the rear of the main room.

"No, it is a natural hot spring guided through earth channels by our Makers. It can be closed off, like this.

When finished, lift the center stone in the bottom. The water will drain slowly away and nourish our oak."

"Makers?" Magiere asked, with her usual bite of suspicion.

A moment followed before Gleann answered. "Let us leave that until you are clean and comfortable."

Chap worried Magiere might aggravate their unusually friendly host. He trotted over and poked his head through the shimmering wool curtain.

He had seen bathing rooms before. Not all domicile trees had such. The enclave where he was born had warm springs nearby in the forest. Raspberry and ivy vines were nurtured into dividers, providing a half dozen private spaces there.

In this small room was something akin to a tub hollowed out of the moss and earth floor. It was lined in polished black stones tightly fitted together. Sunk into the mossy floor next to the tub was a helmet-sized metal basin. Its lip met with the tub's edge via a shallow trough the width of a paw.

Wynn took hold of a wide metal peg standing upright in the basin's center. When she pulled it, steaming water welled in the basin. As it reached the lip, it spilled through the trough into the tub.

"A miracle," she said smiling.

"It may be too hot," Gleann warned. "Mix in the cooler rainwater we keep in those vessels."

At the far wall sat several cask-sized containers. But these were solid wood, with smooth grain and round edges, not slats held together with iron bands. Each appeared molded from one piece of wood.

Gleann gestured to a pile of russet and yellow clothing on a ledge. "Dress when you are finished, and I will show you where to rest for the night."

He headed for the doorway, glancing at Chap as he passed through the curtain.

Magiere inspected the clothing with uncertainty, but Wynn pulled off her cloak.

"Magiere . . . what did Urhkar say before he released you?"

"It was in Droevinkan," she answered. "He said stop resisting . . . that I had to help Sgäile with Leesil."

"Urhkar speaks Droevinkan?"

"Too well," Magiere added, "for what's happening in my homeland."

Wynn didn't reply, but Chap understood where her thoughts wandered.

In the Warlands, two anmaglâhk—Brot'ân'duivé and the deceased Grôyt'ashia—had come to assassinate Darmouth in a time of unrest. Before this, in Soladran, he and Wynn had heard word that civil war erupted in Droevinka. In turn, Magiere feared for the life of her aunt Bieja, who still lived there. And so Magiere and Wynn wondered about an elf who spoke Droevinkan fluently—as did Chap.

But it was impossible that Urhkar had gone there and returned before Chap and his charges found their way here. Still, there were other anmaglâhk to consider.

Wynn stopped short of popping the first button of her old short-robe and frowned at Chap.

"Get out," she said.

Chap backed out with a snort. She had little left to hide after this long journey together.

In the outer room, Gleann collected polished wood bowls and platters from the felt mat where they had all gathered to eat. Leesil sat against the wall next to the chest. The bundled skulls were gone, so he had likely returned them to the vessel. He had remained silent during supper, shifting uncomfortably under Leanâlhâm's furtive glances. The girl was nowhere about, though Chap wondered at the existence of another mixed-blood besides Leesil.

The outer door's curtain lifted, and Sgäile entered. He paused, looking at Chap.

Chap twitched his jowl, though he tried to remain the courteous guest in this home. Sgäile dropped to one knee, giving Chap a start.

The man's eyes held quiet sadness.

Chap had tried in the passing days to catch any memory surfacing within Sgäile, but he had gleaned little. This one did not dwell often on even the very recent past, but an image flashed briefly before Chap's awareness. As if Chap himself reached out with a "hand" to the trunk of a young pine tree. He heard the word "Father."

Chap tried to grasp Sgäile's passing memory for more of the conversation, but it faded.

"Your companions should stay inside," Sgäile said to him, and it was easier to understand than the dialect that Wynn spoke. "You are free to go where you wish, as all majay-hì do."

Sgäile stood up and pulled back the doorway's wool curtain. Chap looked uncertainly to Leesil.

"They will be safe here," Sgäile said.

A part of Chap wanted to go, to lope through the forest of his youth and all it offered to soothe his senses.

"Don't be long," Leesil said.

Chap trusted Sgäile's word, but not his purpose. He crept past the anmaglâhk with a low rumble, and loped outside among the elven dwellings.

Most of the people had retired and only a thin line of smoke drifted up from the communal oven. A howl drifted in from a distance. Chap gazed out into the forest beyond the domicile trees.

He hungered for soft earth beneath his paws and wild grass whipping his legs as he ran.

All of Leesil's grief, Magiere's anger and doubt, and even little Wynn's fears were too much at times. Uncertainty wore upon him, for he no longer saw what the future might bring for any of them. If only he could put down his burdens and forget for a little while, but he could not afford one instant of thoughtlessness. He was alone.

Where were his kin? Why so silent? Why not chide him again, if he acted now in spite of their disapproval?

Memory of existence among the Fay had faded over the years. Perhaps it had never been complete at all. The flesh he wore could not house the wide awareness he had shared with them. But flesh had its advantages, or so he believed.

Chap's instinct cried out that Most Aged Father was poisonous, and Leesil should not be allowed anywhere near him. And yet . . . how else could they find and free Nein'a?

Leesil would not turn from this purpose. And if truth be told, neither could Chap.

He stepped between the house trees, hearing voices within, and cleared the last one to stand upon the fringe of the wild. The eerie cry came again, closer this time. A shimmer darted through the trees. And then another.

Two majay-hì burst from the brush and stopped at the sight of him. Both were dark steel gray with crystalline eyes, so alike in look they were nearly twins. One whined and then both darted back into the underbrush.

Chap took a few steps.

They spoke in memories. He had caught such the first day the pack circled in at the silver deer's call.

Was their way of communing . . . communicating . . . where his own memory play came from? Was this, mingled with his born Fay essence, what gave him such ability? Could they give him one memory not so dark and heavy as his own?

A piece of night moved beneath a shaggy old cedar, and a pair of eyes glittered at him.

The grizzled pack elder took shape as he stepped out. Other majay-hì circled among the trees, and with them came a flash of white. She turned around a bramble and stopped, one forepaw poised above the ground as she looked at Chap.

Wynn had called the female's color that of a lily. The light touch of yellow in the female's eyes reminded Chap of the pistils of that flower.

She came close and sniffed his nose, and her own scent was laced with rich earth and damp leaves. Chap felt her nose trace up along his shoulder, his neck, below his ear. Then her head pressed in against the side of his.

A silver female shining in moonlight flashed in his mind.

A mother . . . the white female showed him a memory of her mother.

Chap recalled running with his siblings on the moss of an elven clearing.

Another memory not his own flashed. Cubs wrestled over who could stay atop an old downed tree, half-covered in lichen that flaked under their tumbling little bodies.

She had heard his memory, and answered in kind.

To speak like this without effort, to share memory instead of only seeing those of others . . . It was as if he found his voice for the first time and heard those of others after a lifetime in silence.

Chap had never known this as a pup. Perhaps he had not stayed long enough to learn it before Eillean took him away to a young Leesil. Maybe it was a skill, like human speech, that came with maturity. His thoughts rushed to memories of Nein'a and her half-elven son trapped within the city of Venjètz.

The white female pulled back. She knew nothing of human cities and ways, and the image must have been unsettling. He whined and licked her face.

She did not appear disturbed. She yipped at him, wheeled about, and bolted partway into the forest. She stopped, looking back.

Chap released all but the earth beneath his paws and the rich scent of her fur and followed.

The dreamer rolled in slumber. Within his dream, wind rushed over his body and ripped at his dark cloak. He flew high over rocky cliffs painted in snow and ice.

He had never traveled like this before in his slumber.

In a deep canyon valley between mountain ridges like teeth rested a six-towered castle. Each of the tall towers was topped with a conical spire fringed with a curtain of ice suspended from its roof's lower edge. He wanted to pass over its outer wall and reach the courtyard, but did not. Instead, he lighted upon the crusted snow outside and sank deep as it broke beneath his feet.

Twin gates of ornate iron curls joined together at their high tops in an arched point. Mottled with rust, the gates were still sound in their place. Far beyond them, the castle's matching iron doors waited atop a wide cascade of stone steps.

Something moved upon those steps.

At first she seemed dressed in form-fitting white, with hair as cleanly black. As she took a first step down the stairs, it was clear she was naked. A shadow appeared to flutter above her right shoulder. It coalesced into a raven, which rustled its wings as it settled next to her head.

Her face was so pale it was almost translucent around strangely shaped eyes that . . .

The image vanished.

The dreamer stood in a stone hall with shelves all around filled with scrolls, books, and bound sheaves. Upon a table of gray-aged wood lay a black feather quill next to a squat bottle half-filled with ink.

At the hall's far end, another set of heavy doors were sealed shut with a solid iron beam too massive to lift.

The dreamer lost his aching hunger. His body desired nothing.

It is here . . . , his patron whispered all around him, though he saw no massive coils of black scales, . . . *the orb . . . the sister of the dead will lead you.*

He was wrenched from sleep and back into the cold world of the awakened.

"No!"

Welstiel's eyes opened fully to find Chane crouched within the tent, staring, his narrow face intense.

The sister of the dead will lead you.

A bitter promise. Welstiel had heard it one too many times.

"What's wrong?" Chane asked. "Why are you shouting?"

Welstiel sat up without answering.

They had ridden night after night, and their mounts grew thin and slow from dwindling grain. He feared that soon they would be on foot and wished to get every last step from the horses before the beasts collapsed and died.

"Pack up," he said.

Lingering bitterness faded. His patron showed him much more than ever before, but again in small pieces that did not quite fit together. He had seen an inhabitant of the fortress—perhaps one of the ancients? And he had felt the calm from the close presence of what he sought.

Welstiel's hunger to feed had died in that place within his dream, and now his hunger for what he sought grew in its place. So why did he feel so bitter upon waking?

The sister of the dead will lead you.

Magiere was the crux. Whatever his patron showed him, it was never quite enough to be certain of his destination—and always with the reminder that Magiere was necessary. Yet she was far off on another deviation with Leesil. Welstiel would find a time and place to bring her back under his control.

He smoothed his dark hair back. He would have to trust in his patron but also in himself, and practice a mix of effort and reserve. He stepped out as Chane began pulling down the tent.

"Why were you shouting?" Chane asked again. "You have never shouted quite like that before."

Welstiel's suspicion rose. "What do you mean?"

"You talk in your dormancy."

Welstiel remained passive, hiding anxiety. How long had this gone on, and why did Chane choose this moment to reveal such?

"What do you hear while I am dormant?"

"Nothing comprehensible, but never such an outcry." Chane became hesitant and changed the subject. "I wish to continue my lessons in Numanese as we ride."

Chane finished saddling his bony horse and swung up.

Welstiel followed suit. "Where did we leave off? I believe it was the common irregular verbs in past tense."

"Yes."

Lessons continued as they rode, but Welstiel's thoughts drifted often to the icebound castle, to the new scroll-filled hall, and to the calm stillness he had felt as he looked upon the iron-barred doors.

He started from his wandering thoughts, as he thought he heard a whisper on the cold wind.

The sister of the dead will lead you.

CHAPTER SEVEN

Hot baths were almost a vague memory, until Magiere slipped into one beside Wynn, listening to the sage's embarrassing groans of pleasure as they washed. Once finished, Magiere pulled on the elven clothing made of felt and raw-spun cotton. Her skin smelled of honey and fennel from the soap. Leesil had his turn, complete with grumbling about soapy water that hadn't drained completely for his own fresh bath.

Magiere spent the rest of the evening sitting cross-legged in the outer room with her hosts. Leesil sat on her left with young Leanâlhâm on his far side. The girl studied Leesil with brief glances, thinking she went unnoticed, peering at his ears, eyes, and the shape of his face—until suddenly aware of Magiere watching her. Magiere didn't really mind the girl's interest in Leesil, or shouldn't have.

Leanâlhâm was overwhelmed that someone else in this world shared her differences from her own people. Magiere understood being different, constantly reminded of it when anyone looked closely at her.

Still, Leanâlhâm kept staring at Leesil.

How had this mixed-blood girl survived in a land where

Leesil wasn't even welcome? And how could she possibly be related to Sgäile?

Magiere turned her attention elsewhere, seeking any distraction.

"Tell us about these Shapers," she heard Wynn say to Gleann.

"Some of our people are born with a heightened awareness," Gleann began, and his gaze slipped once to Sgäile. "They sense what you call the Spirit element of things. Given time and training, they can become Makers or Shapers . . . and a few healers."

It seemed Makers worked lifeless materials. When Wynn called them thaumaturges, Gleann made an effort not to grimace. They called Spirit into inert substance where they sensed accepting emptiness, making wood, stone, and metal pliable for fashioning by will, hand, and tool. Not in pieces but as a whole, like the rainwater barrels in the washroom.

Shapers took a separate path, plying living things that still held their natural Spirit at its fullest. They guided, nurtured, and altered living growth, like the trees and other plants shaped over years into useful things. Some learned to make a tree or plant grow part of itself into a separate piece that still lived. Patience seemed an absolute for a Shaper. And among them were the few like Gleann, who turned to the care of the sick and injured. Flesh as well as living wood could be guided by those with enough skill and training, and healers learned herb lore, medicines, and more common skills as well.

Magiere followed most of this, though some of Wynn's questions left her baffled. Gleann often answered the sage in Elvish, and then returned to Belaskian with a less lengthy reply.

Gleann spoke Belaskian well, despite his strong accent, and he'd taught Leanâlhâm in turn. Strangest of all was that Leanâlhâm was a quarter human. His strong love of the girl was surprising, as their people despised and feared anything foreign.

"You called Sgäile your uncle," Wynn said to Leanâlhâm. "But your grandfather referred to him as your cousin?"

Leanâlhâm grew shy, mustering a response, but Gleann answered in her place.

"Her grandmother was my sister by bonding, having married my elder brother. I believe, by your culture, this makes her Sgäilsheilleache's . . . second cousin? But he is a generation older than her, so . . ." He shook his head in resignation. "Our familial titles and relations do not translate well into your language."

"But would not her maternal grandmother be human?" Wynn asked bluntly. "I do not understand how her mother was half-human. And what of her mother—and her father?"

Gleann's expression grew tight and closed. "It is a family matter we do not discuss often."

Magiere glanced at Leanâlhâm and suspicions began to form. A marriage didn't mean both parents were involved in the making of a child. Nor that the mother was a willing participant. Magiere's own mother had been given no choice in her conception.

"Tell us of crossing the Broken Range," Gleann asked quickly.

"It took nearly a whole moon," Wynn began, "before we found a way . . ."

Sgäile lifted his eyes from pouring herb tea and fixed on the sage. All Magiere's senses sharpened in warning.

"In a blizzard, we were caught in a snow-slide . . . ," Wynn continued.

Leesil shifted uncomfortably, bumping shoulders with Magiere. He too spotted Sgäile's rapt interest, and yet Wynn kept babbling.

". . . we lost nearly everything, and then Chap—"

"That's enough for now," Leesil cut in, a blink before Magiere did so herself. "It's getting late."

Sgäile's narrowing eyes shifted to Leesil. It was only a brief instant, but enough for Magiere to catch his too-eager interest.

How they'd found the Elven Territories was a story best kept to themselves. To Magiere's knowledge, no one before had ever returned from such a journey. Should they have a chance to use a way out of this land, she didn't want the Anmaglâhk to know it.

"Maybe some tea first?" Wynn suggested. "To cut the weight of fatigue."

Gleann gazed among his guests with concern before returning to Wynn. "At least I can assist with your scholarly losses."

He rose and climbed the stairs to the upper level, disappearing from sight. Sgäile held out a baked-clay cup of herb tea to Magiere. She shook her head, and he passed it on to Leesil.

She didn't care for this herbal stuff, too different from the true tea that Wynn had lost to a skulking *tâshgâlh*. And she trembled inside, as though she'd already had too much real tea.

Gleann returned with a drawstring bag of olive-colored suede. He settled on the felt rug and opened it as Wynn curiously leaned his way.

Out came a roll of off-white single sheets with mottled grain from whatever plant fibers were used to make them. Next were pearl-white ceramic vials, which Gleann explained were filled with black, red, and green ink. Last came a strange form of quill.

Its dark wood shaft was long and narrow, but the bottom widened bulbously above the head. The quill tip was made of a metal Magiere recognized immediately. It had the same brilliant sheen of Leesil's old stilettos and those of the Anmaglâhk.

"No," Wynn protested, studying the gifts with painful eagerness. "This is too much."

"Take them," Gleann insisted with a chuckle. "Beneath the quill's head is a pocket of sponge-weed fibers. It will draw ink deeply, and needs to be replenished less often."

Wynn was still politely reluctant, but eyed the quill's bright metal head. "Such a stylus . . . I have nothing to trade for something so dear."

Gleann rolled his large elven eyes. "How else will you record your travels and what you learn?"

"Grandfather!" Sgäile's expression darkened in alarm. "I do not think that wise. Some might not want—"

"By 'some' you mean your Most Aged Father." Gleann

snorted, but then paused before turning back to Wynn. "Be discreet and save these for when you have privacy."

Sgäile spoke low to Gleann, but the old man flicked the words away with his hand, and patted Sgäile's shoulder like a patronizing grandfather. Sgäile swallowed any further argument as Gleann slid the pile of gifts in front of Wynn.

"Thank you . . . ," Wynn said, "so much."

Any spell of the evening's lingering ease broke as Sgäile stood up abruptly.

"Now to rest," Gleann said. "Thank you for a most pleasant chat."

The outer doorway's curtain rumpled and its hem dragged across Chap's back as he stalked in. Grass seed and strands stuck out in his fur, and his paws were filthy. He glanced about, movements sharp and manic in a way that magnified Magiere's own nagging nervous energy. And still she didn't know why she felt this way.

"Look at yourself!" Wynn said, and wrinkled her small nose at the dog. "What have you been doing? You will not crawl onto my bed in such a state."

Chap's eyes cleared as he fixed upon her. He barked twice for "no" and, startled by his own voice, whined and repeated himself more softly. He circled around to curl up beside the bundled weapons and the chest. Magiere wondered what he'd been up to.

Gleann showed them to the adjacent room of floor mats. As he said good night, Leanâlhâm nodded to them, but her eyes were on Leesil. She turned quickly away and hurried up the stairs.

As Leesil pulled the room's curtain closed, Magiere saw Sgäile sit down against the wall near the front door. Leesil remained poised, as if about to leave the sleeping quarters. Magiere sighed, understanding.

"The chest is safe," she said.

Wynn sat on one of the three beds. "Sgäile would not let anyone touch them, I think."

Leesil let go of the curtain and settled on the bed nearest the doorway. Magiere knelt on the one in the center.

The soft mattress smelled of wild grass, and the pillow's strange fabric felt like silk. She dreaded the rest of the night, fearful that sleep wouldn't find her or that worse might come if it did. Her only relief was in being away from so many strange faces, though Leanâlhâm surfaced in her thoughts.

"How does she bear it?" Magiere said. "Living among people who will always see her as different?"

Wynn, halfway into her bed, pulled up a blanket. "Who . . . oh, Leanâlhâm? Perhaps . . ." She shook her head sadly and lay down. "I do not know. But her name means 'Child of Misfortune.' "

Magiere's ire rose, smothering her edgy state. She had her own meaning for such a label. Magelia, her mother, had been forced to give birth, and had died shortly after. What could be more unfortunate than that in bearing children?

And though Leanâlhâm had her grandfather and, oddly enough, Sgäile, the girl was branded with a name that marked her for life. Like Leesil's own mother, how much cruelty could these people heap upon their children?

Magiere lay beneath her blanket a long while. She heard Wynn's breathing slow and deepen. She watched Leesil until certain he'd drifted into fitful sleep, then closed her own eyes, trying to rest. The night became endless under the persistent quiver in her body.

She found herself standing in the dark amid the forest; then she saw a shadow shift among the trees, coming closer.

It stepped so softly that footfalls came and went beneath the rustle of branches and underbrush in the light breeze. When she looked about, she saw no other dark shapes that had shadowed her through the night so many times before.

Magiere heard and felt something skitter across her foot.

Leaning against her boot was a freshly fallen oak leaf, still green and satin. She stooped and reached for it. At the touch of her finger, a brown spot appeared on it.

The dry color spread through the leaf's veins as its tissue faded and dried until fully wilted. Decay set in.

She jerked her hand away, rising up. The leaf rotted, then crumbled and came apart. Its fragments scattered across the ground in the night breeze.

A deeply shadowed figure stood quiet and still in the dark between two oaks. Something glinted in its hand . . . a stiletto. Even at night her eyes picked up a sheen brighter than silver. The glimmer of elven eyes showed within the figure's raised cowl.

Magiere reached for her falchion, gripping the hilt without taking her eyes off the anmaglâhk, but she hesitated. Was it an anmaglâhk? His forearm was bare—except for a wrist sheath. At his shoulder, she saw the hint of leather . . . of a hauberk?

She froze before the silent figure facing her in the dark. Rings of metal were bound in a weave of leather straps on the hauberk's front.

"Leesil?" Magiere whispered.

The figure didn't answer. Only the blade's tip tilted slowly up at her.

She pulled the falchion, backing away. "Leesil!"

Magiere half-awoke from the dream and thrashed the blanket aside. She scrambled across the pillow and backed against the small room's wall, looking about in terror. Her dhampir nature rose and widened her senses.

Leesil shifted in his slumber, rolling over with a mumble. Wynn didn't stir.

Magiere felt the rough bark through the elven felt jerkin she wore. Its touch made her back muscles spasm. Her shudders settled inward and grew to a hum in her flesh.

She fell forward onto hands and knees, and then collapsed in a heap when her shaking arms wouldn't hold. She curled in a ball upon her bed. The tremors slowly subsided. She wanted to reach for Leesil, to wake him.

But it had only been a dream . . . one more nightmare that plagued her sleep since they'd come into this forest. And for all she'd endured, Leesil's burden seemed far greater here.

Magiere turned about to put her head upon the pillow. Try though she might, she couldn't rest quietly, nor think clearly. Her muscles would not unclench.

Leesil roused slowly the next morning from a restless sleep filled with unwanted dreams—of his mother, and of a young anmaglâhk's split throat, the man's blood soaking into his breeches. When he stepped out into the main room, Magiere was already up.

She sat on the moss next to the chest, with Chap sprawled out beside her as she stared blankly at nothing. A clay cup of steaming tea sat next to her, but it looked untouched. Their cloak-bundled weapons were gone.

Leesil looked about and found the bundle stacked by the outer doorway with the rest of their gear. There was also an extra pack of dark canvas he didn't recognize.

He should have known Magiere would hardly be sitting quietly if her falchion were missing. Before he was ready to deal with the day, their hosts were up and about, taking away any private chance to learn what troubled Magiere.

Leanâlhâm descended the stairs without a sound. She saw him, and this time smiled slightly before slipping out the front doorway. Sgäile crouched to tuck something in the new pack. Gleann came down and followed his grandniece outside, but the two quickly returned as Wynn came out rubbing her face with a yawn.

Leanâlhâm and Gleann each returned with a wooden platter of food. Sgäile took some as they passed and returned to fussing with the gear. Leesil didn't like him digging about in their stuff.

Gleann unrolled a felt rug upon the moss, and breakfast was served: wheat biscuits with nuts, more bisselberries, smoked fish, and a thickened hot porridge smelling of cinnamon.

While Leesil satisfied himself on the latter, Magiere sat quietly beside him and touched none of the food. He nudged her several times, but she shook her head. She didn't even react when Chap snuck in and snatched a whole fillet of smoked fish before anyone could stop him. Wynn scolded the dog, brushing off dried mud he'd left on the felt spread. She loaded a plate to set behind herself, just for him.

As everyone finished, Magiere stood. Sgäile looked her up and down. Whether he studied her or the new clothes she wore, Leesil didn't care for it.

"Your own clothes are clean," Sgäile said, "and packed.

It would be best for all of you to wear what you have on for the journey."

What was he up to?

"Where's my armor?" Magiere asked sharply. "If you think I'm walking about without protection, waiting for another of yours to jump us . . . think again."

Sgäile held up his hands with a frustrated sigh.

"Your protection is my concern," he said. "From afar at least, your present attire will draw less attention."

Leesil just frowned. Magiere didn't look any less foreign in loose brown elven pants and a yellow jerkin. She might be tall for a woman, but she wasn't built like an elf. And he was pretty sure Wynn wore the clothing of an elvish youth, but the bottoms of her drawstring pants were rolled up to keep from dragging. Her clothes were too long for her short stature.

"I do not mind," Wynn offered. "These are quite comfortable, but I will take my own cloak."

Osha stuck his head in through the doorway curtain, long white-blond hair hanging across his shoulders.

"Prepared?" he asked in Belaskian.

Leesil didn't have time to wonder where the young anmaglâhk and Urhkar had been all night. No one answered before Sgäile continued.

"There is much to carry, and we travel with haste. If you would allow, one of mine can carry your blades. They will all be at hand if needed."

"What?" Magiere spit back. "We disarmed for coming into your village—and little good it did! You keeping our weapons wasn't part of the arrangement."

Leesil agreed, though he grudgingly wondered if Sgäile made a valid point.

"Let's leave it be," he told her, "at least until we're out of this place."

Magiere turned her nervous glare on him. She shuddered suddenly and then turned away.

"I think Urhkar would be best to carry them," Wynn added.

"No," Magiere said flatly. "Sgäile will carry them."

Her choice baffled Leesil, but only for a moment. The

way she looked at Sgäile, she was almost daring him to agree. If it came to taking their arms by force . . .

Leesil understood Magiere's choice and grew nervous at what it meant.

Sgäile wouldn't let inexperienced Osha stand against them. If they came fast at the younger elf, he probably couldn't stop them both. Urhkar was another matter, from what Magiere had experienced last evening at his hands. But Sgäile himself?

Magiere hadn't forgotten why the man had come to Bela. If she came at him, she wouldn't be reserved in how she took from Sgäile what was hers.

Sgäile gave her a pronounced nod. "I will carry them. You have my word."

Leesil put a hand on Magiere's arm, then noticed Osha standing silently inside the doorway with his eyes on Wynn. The young anmaglâhk dropped his gaze with the barest hint of hurt on his long face. She hadn't suggested him as the bearer of arms.

Strangest of all, Chap hadn't moved or spoken up. He lay quietly behind Wynn, his eyes equally on Magiere and Sgäile. The dog had been the first to turn vicious at the sight of Sgäile appearing with the other anmaglâhk, but now he was merely watchful.

Leesil took a slow breath. Things were growing more tense by the day.

Leanâlhâm returned from taking away platters and bowls. She stopped in the doorway but didn't seem to note the mood in the room. She remained in place, blocking anyone's exit.

"I come with you, Uncle," she said.

Sgäile's expression flattened, and then turned incredulous. Leesil had never seen so much unguarded emotion on the man's face. Before Sgäile could speak, Leanâlhâm rushed on.

"We need beeswax and seed oil—for the candles and lanterns—and we are almost out of cinnamon. . . ."

"Such things are available in closer reach," Sgäile said, his voice rising a bit too much. "Closer than where we are headed."

"It is a year since you took me to Crijheäiche. There are many craftspeople who gather there, and it is the heart of our land, is it not? Please, Uncle."

Sgäile's jaw twitched. He switched to Elvish, speaking sharply to the girl. Leesil didn't have to know the language to get the gist of it. He suspected Leanâlhâm's request had nothing to do with cinnamon or beeswax.

Gleann jumped in with a few words, and Sgäile's open frustration mounted. This festival of emotion on his usually passive face was almost amusing. But Leesil found himself agreeing. He didn't need some infatuated girl tagging along.

"Let her come," Magiere said suddenly. "We'll look out for her."

"Then it is settled," Gleann said.

"It is not settled!" Sgäile replied. "Grandfather, you do not understand what—"

"I will prepare you a list, Leanâlhâm," Gleann said. "Your uncle will help you find everything."

Sgäile gestured at Magiere and Wynn, speaking Elvish again in short, clipped words.

"That is no reason your cousin cannot accompany you," Gleann replied in plain Belaskian. "How could she not be safe traveling with two others of your own caste? Leanâlhâm, get your things, as everyone is now waiting on you."

Sgäile almost threw up his hands.

Leesil remembered Wynn's scant comments from their first night within the forest. The Anmaglâhk didn't have rank like soldiers. Seniority of experience aside, they obeyed the one chosen to lead a particular mission. It seemed family hierarchies were another matter, even among mature adults. Gleann was the household elder and had the last word.

Leanâlhâm rushed past Sgäile and up the stairs. By the time Sgäile uttered two more frustrated phrases to Gleann, the girl scrambled back down with a hastily cinched canvas bundle slung over her narrow shoulder.

Leesil groaned softly as he grabbed the skulls' chest and Magiere picked up her pack. Sgäile hauled the rest of the baggage out the door in silence, where Urhkar awaited.

Others of the village were already out and about. Most paused to watch from between domicile trees or across the village's mossy center space. Once loaded up, Sgäile led their procession quickly back out the way they'd come. Leesil didn't look about to see the reaction of those watching, but he noticed that Gleann followed along.

Once out of sight of the village, Gleann caught up to Leesil and stopped Magiere as well. He shooed the stoic Urhkar on ahead. Urhkar might have frowned, though it was hard to tell as he walked on.

Leesil offered his hand to Gleann. "Thanks for the welcome stay."

Gleann studied this gesture in puzzlement and slowly lifted his hand. Leesil had to take it in his own before the man smiled with understanding of the parting gesture.

"Perhaps we'll see you again someday," Magiere added.

Gleann turned serious, almost hard. "I do not hope so. For if so, I fear events will have turned against you. Finish what you must in our land . . . then leave quickly."

He looked warily beyond Magiere at Sgäile and the others before he faced her again.

"My grandson has a true if misguided heart," he said, "so trust his word, but not always his judgment."

Magiere slowly held out her own hand. Gleann took it with a smile as if he'd said nothing at all—as if she were no more human than he. He walked back toward the village, with Leesil watching him in silence.

When Leesil turned away, he found Sgäile waving to them, so he tugged Magiere's sleeve as he moved on. No sooner had they rejoined the others than Leanâlhâm took up walking close behind on his right. The rest stepped ahead except for Urhkar, who trailed at the rear.

From far behind, Leesil heard the strange high-pitched song of a bird as on other days of their journey. And just as before, when he searched for it, he saw nothing.

As they crossed a grass field beyond the village enclosure, Chap veered off, looking into the trees. Leesil spotted movement as a rush of silver-gray scurried by on all fours. Then another, as the majay-hì appeared one by one out in the forest. None came closer.

Wynn stepped up behind Chap, and then something shook the leaves of a bush. A blur of silver-white burst into sight.

The white female hopped forward and stopped. She yipped and darted at Chap, then quickly dodged away.

"Go on," Wynn said to Chap.

Chap didn't look at her but rather toward Sgäile's back, and then he trotted off.

Unlike the other majay-hì, Chap always remained within sight. More often than the others, Leesil spotted the white dog roaming near him.

CHAPTER EIGHT

Four days passed without incident. The forest's monotonous sounds droned in Leesil's ears, but his mother was never far from his thoughts.

Their routine was little more than breaking camp at dawn, trudging all day, and stopping only when dusk ended and night settled upon them. Every time Leesil asked how much farther they would travel, Sgäile only answered, "Days . . . more days."

Chap ran with the majay-hì, returning often to pace close to the procession, at which point Leesil noticed the other dogs vanished. But the last time this happened, the white female stayed in sight among the trees.

Osha tried steadily in broken Belaskian to coax Wynn into talking, as she ignored him completely when he spoke Elvish. Little by little she relented. If their conversation carried on too long, Sgäile halted it with a single look. But today, he was less vigilant, and the two continued, often slipping into Elvish. The longer Leesil listened to them shifting between tongues, the more he picked out words here and there. He wasn't certain what was a verb or noun, but perhaps one of two "root words," as Wynn called them, began to sound familiar.

"Wynn," he called out, "none of our stuff has gone missing since we left Sgäile's village. Ask Osha if he thinks we've lost that *tâshgâlh*."

She craned her head around at him, slightly troubled. "I already have. He said it may have found something more interesting in the enclave. The Coilehkrotall will not thank us."

"The Co-il-ee . . . the what?"

"Sgäile and Gleann's clan . . . people of the 'Lichen Woods.' "

"Well, they can't blame us. We didn't invite that overgrown squirrel along."

Though Sgäile didn't turn, Leesil saw the man shake his head as he continued onward.

"Osha, what are these?" Wynn asked as she pointed to a large clear space between two silver birches.

Leesil stopped beside her and leaned over to examine a strange patch of flowers. Normally, Wynn's fascination with plants bored him, but he had to admit these were odd.

The pearl-colored petals—or leaves by their shape—looked fuzzy like velvet. They seemed to glow under the bright sun filling the small space. Their stems and base were a dark green, nearly black where sunlight didn't touch them. Leesil crouched down as Wynn reached for one.

Soft booted feet appeared beside Leesil, and a dark-skinned hand grabbed Wynn's wrist. Leesil rose quickly, nearly knocking over Leanâlhâm standing too close behind him.

Osha shook his head, releasing Wynn. "No."

Leanâlhâm took Leesil's arm, trying to pull him away.

Magiere came up behind them. "What's all this about?"

Sgäile hurried over and looked down at the flowers. "You cannot touch these. They are sacred," he said pointedly. "Osha should have explained before you tried to approach."

Osha's jaw clenched. Clearly he was growing tired of being blamed whenever one of their charges broke some unknown rule.

"Sacred?" Wynn asked.

Questioning Sgäile was futile from Leesil's perspective, but it seemed an especially bad idea whenever he looked displeased.

"They are sacred," Sgäile repeated. "Do not disturb them."

He motioned everyone to start moving again.

For the first time, Leesil had some idea what it must feel like to be Wynn. Maybe he was sick of Sgäile's evasiveness, or maybe he just wanted a real answer for once. The notion was interrupted by a burst of chittering overhead that sounded oddly like laughter. To Leesil's surprise, the elves all looked up with brightened expressions. Wynn tilted her head back so far that Leesil thought she might topple right over.

"Now what?" Magiere asked.

The trees seemed to come alive with movement as small creatures jumped from one branch to the next, making the leafy limbs shudder as if they too were laughing.

"Good fortune," Osha said in Belaskian, his lilting accent so thick the words were barely recognizable. He called Wynn over with the wave of one finger, pointing above as he spoke to her in Elvish.

The little creatures tumbling and hopping among the leaves had arms and tails longer than their thin furry bodies. Their heads had flat snouts and wide mouths between rounded ears, making them look almost human. Soft cream-colored bellies and faces broke their overall rusty coloring and matched the tuft of light hair springing from the ends of their long, curling tails. Oddest of all, they had feet like long hands.

"*Fra'cise!*" Wynn smiled widely. "Osha says they are filled with the playful spirits of the forest and bring good luck to those they follow. They are similar to a type of monkey."

"A type of what?" Leesil asked, as he'd never heard of such a creature.

Wynn started to reply, then simply shook her head and went back to watching the antics among the branches. One *fra'cise* hung upside down by its feet and swung so wildly back and forth that Leesil started to get queasy.

"They don't look fortunate to me," Magiere said. "More like a *tâshgâlh* that's been sneaking someone's ale."

Leanâlhâm put her hand over her mouth to hide her smile. "These are not thieves, just playful ones of our forest."

The *fra'cise* didn't come closer. They continued to swing and chatter overhead. Then as quickly as they appeared, they were gone, lunging from one tree to the next and off into the forest.

Wynn's barrage of Elvish erupted so fast that Osha looked overwhelmed.

The appearance of these idiotic little animals seemed to cut away Leanâlhâm's wary shyness. She dashed out into the forest, following them and pointing ahead to the branches above. Wynn jogged after the girl, a little less gracefully in her oversized clothes, and they slipped from sight among the tree trunks.

Magiere took two steps after them. "Both of you get back here!"

From somewhere in the brush, Leanâlhâm cried out, "Sgäilsheilleache!"

Leesil lunged off the path behind Magiere. Then he remembered they were unarmed. He ran on with the chest slamming against his back. Magiere dropped her pack, trying to keep up with him.

Sgäile was already five paces ahead, running through the trees, smashing his way through underbrush around stout cedars and oaks.

Far off to the left, Urhkar outdistanced all of them. Osha came up quick on Leesil's heels as they broke the edge of a bare ground clearing with patches of long-leafed yellow grass.

Wynn and Leanâlhâm knelt at the center before two adolescent elven males, bare to the waist . . . or were they elves?

They were shorter than even Wynn, if she were standing. Their bodies and faces were marked with strange symbols in blue-black ink or paint.

They had the pointed ears, triangular faces, and amber eyes of elves but wore no shirts or boots—only loose breeches of rough natural fabric frayed off below the knees. Their wooden spears with blackened and sharpened ends were pointed at the women on the ground. One had an ivy vine wreath around his neck, and he stared at Wynn in horror. When he lifted his gaze to Magiere entering the clearing, his reaction grew to trembling outrage.

Sgäile froze at the clearing's edge. He raised a quick hand for his own comrades to halt. When Magiere didn't stop, he grabbed her by the arm. She turned on him, but he shook his head.

"Please stay," Osha whispered behind Leesil.

And more of these short elves appeared from behind all the trees around the clearing.

Some carried bows with arrows drawn. Like the spears, these ended in sharpened points without heads. A few carried cudgels of polished wood shaped as if made from gnarled tree roots. Most had wild hair pleated back or bound with cords of twisted wild grass.

Chap burst from the brush at the clearing's far right.

Two of the small newcomers leaped out of his path. One more ran up the side of a tree trunk and clung to its lower branches. None appeared worried by the dog's snarling, only startled as they watched him.

Chap worked his way toward Wynn, still rumbling with teeth exposed.

Urhkar stepped forward with both hands open and empty at his sides. He crossed the space slowly and placed himself before Wynn and Leanâlhâm. The first savage short one stepped back, and the second lifted his spear.

Sgäile barked one word of Elvish, and Chap stopped growling.

One of the pair facing Urhkar snapped something at him, nearly shouting, and Wynn cringed back, pulling at Leanâlhâm. The girl looked as frightened as the sage, but her eyes turned toward her uncle in confusion, as if she had no idea what was happening.

"Sgäile . . . ," Leesil whispered harshly, "do something, damn you."

Sgäile's eyes never left the scene before him. He rapidly placed a finger to his lips and that was all.

Leesil's frustration vanished in dull surprise—Sgäile was afraid.

Sgäile had too many people to protect, a mission to complete, and now Wynn had made things even worse. He could not allow violence to break out here but hesitated to speak.

Although Sgäile had authority over this mission, Urhkarasiférin was clearly the eldest among them. Such distinction was all that these people—the old race of this land—would respect as authority. Sgäile let him take the lead.

Then Chap glanced his way.

A memory of grief-enraged Én'nish rose suddenly in Sgäile's mind. He did not know why this came to him now, and he pushed it aside.

One of the diminutive pair before Urhkarasiférin was called Rujh. Sgäile had seen him before as a messenger sent to the an'Cróan by the man's own people—the Äruin'nas. They had been in this land long before Sgäile's people, or so it was said.

Rujh spat an accusation at Urhkarasiférin. "You break faith with the trees!"

The elder elf shook his head with steady calm. "No. We are in guardianship of these humans and act on behalf of Most Aged Father."

His words had no impact on Rujh. "Your aged leader has no right to such a choice. We do not answer to him or your kind. The forest's own law is above his wishes—and yours."

"We escort these humans to him for questioning," Urhkarasiférin explained. "We must know how they entered this land . . . before others follow in their path."

"The forest has its way to deal with such!" Rujh nearly shouted. "It has no need of your assistance. You defile it with no remorse, and it is offensive enough that we now find mixed-bloods walking here."

He gestured to Leanâlhâm and then to Léshil. Sgäile crept slowly inward, blocking Leanâlhâm from Rujh's sight.

"They have the blood in them," Sgäile insisted. "And the forest has not seen fit to reject them."

Rujh turned his head toward Sgäile, and frustrated reluctance filled his angry face.

"We accept those who have blood that should not be spilled, but the other two . . ." He pointed to Wynn and then Magiere. "If you will not kill them, then we will do it."

"Do not attempt to violate guardianship," Urhkarasiférin warned.

Rujh tilted his spear slightly toward Urhkarasiférin, but the elder elf did not move or flinch.

Sgäile's stomach began to tighten. No doubt Urhkarasiférin and Osha would follow his orders if violence broke out, but it was the last thing he wanted. They could escape Rujh's numbers, but getting Léshil and his companions out would be a harder fight.

Én'nish's face flashed again in Sgäile's thoughts. He pushed the image away. Why did he keep thinking of her? Then came a memory of Rujh appearing out of the forest at Crijheäiche.

It startled Sgäile. He could not clearly remember which occasion this memory came from or why he thought of it now. But it made him study the short man.

Rujh had spotted Léshil too quickly as half-blooded. Had he known before Léshil appeared?

A flash of Én'nish came again. It flickered in and out with the memory of Rujh appearing from the forest. Sgäile felt dizzy, and then he realized . . .

There were too many Äruin'nas here at once. Not a hunting party or even an envoy to one of the elven clans. They lived to the northwest, where the forest thickened against the range. How had Rujh known to come here?

Someone had sought out the Äruin'nas, or sent word to them.

Én'nish's blind anguish and hunger for vengeance went further than Sgäile had thought possible. Perhaps Urhkarasiférin should not have dismissed her from his tutelage but kept her close and watched.

Urhkarasiférin sharply backhanded Rujh's spear aside. "You are not a judge of the forest's natural law."

"Neither can your Most Aged Father take exceptions upon himself," Rujh answered.

"You will do nothing without the will of all blood," Urhkarasiférin warned, "that of your people and of mine."

"Have your clan elders agreed to allow humans to walk among the trees?"

A ray of hope grew inside Sgäile. "Nor have they agreed to execute them."

"Speak when spoken to!" Urhkarasiférin snapped, and Sgäile clenched his jaw.

He watched Rujh's face. Only clan leaders decided such weighty issues for Sgäile's people. Rujh knew this, for it was much the same among his kind. The small man scowled.

"There is a judgment to be made," he said, and turned away. "We will meet at Crijheäiche . . . where all will hear of this matter."

Sgäile quickly reached down and pulled Leanâlhâm to her feet, her innocent face still full of fear.

"Up," he said to Wynn. "Everyone return to our path."

Magiere grabbed Wynn's arm and turned back with Leesil close behind. Urhkarasiférin took the lead as Sgäile pulled Leanâlhâm along. Not one of the Äruin'nas remained among the trees. They had all vanished from sight.

What fuel of lies had Én'nish used to kindle this fire in her hunger for vengeance?

"Do not stop and do not look back," Sgäile said to the others.

He knew where Én'nish would head next. The same place he must take his own group in order to shorten the journey. Traveling alone and unburdened, she would beat him to the river and passage down to Crijheäiche. Leanâlhâm's hand trembled in his grip.

"You are safe," he whispered, pulling her close.

An anmaglâhk's duty, by life oath, was to protect his people. Sgäile had one failing in this. Leanâlhâm's safety came before all others.

Chap trotted beside Wynn, longing for the lost talking hide and the privacy to use it.

He needed to speak with Leesil, and he did not know how else this could be done.

Chap had never met the Äruin'nas—had never even heard the word until it rose from Sgäile's memories. But now, Chap had things to tell . . . things he'd seen in Rujh's memories.

Én'nish, for one.

The instant he realized what the female anmaglâhk had done, he pulled upon Sgäile's memories, until he felt Sgäile reach a realization. But Chap could not shake off his puzzlement over the tone Rujh used when speaking of Most Aged Father.

In youth, Chap had known but a few of the Anmaglâhk. Most Aged Father was no elder of a clan, for Anmaglâhk were a caste apart and servants to their people, but their patriarch was still held in high esteem. His word carried the weight of a clan elder, if not its authority. His word held power among the elves. Was that now changing?

Brot'an and Eillean had believed they took great risks in defying Most Aged Father. The patriarch believed an Ancient Enemy would return, as did Chap's kin. It was the reason they had sent him to Magiere—to keep her from falling into the hands of those who searched for her.

But what of Leesil?

His own mother and grandmother had conspired to create him, to train him, in order to kill this same enemy Most Aged Father feared. The thought rankled Chap, and he growled.

Leesil was no one's tool. Why had Nein'a wanted a half-blood for the plans of her dissidents? And what did Most Aged Father really want with Leesil?

Chap steeled himself for what would come at Crijheäiche, and what he might have to do to protect Leesil, Magiere, and Wynn from all sides.

His thoughts were broken as the white majay-hì loped toward him from the trees. Wynn had once compared her to a water "lily."

Chap agreed.

Lily kept her distance, glancing hesitantly at those walking with Chap along a wide-open way through the forest. Whenever the breeze shifted Chap's way, he caught her earthy scent.

His thoughts tumbled through memories passed between them in the night outside the elven enclave. He wanted more of this—more of her. He wanted to run with Lily among the pack. Or without them.

Was this what passed between Magiere and Leesil? A depth of longing he had not felt since Eillean had taken him from his siblings?

Lily yipped once in a standing pause, watching him. He did not need touch, as the other majay-hì did, to see her memories. Images of leaves and brush and grass and trees whipping by in the night filled his head. He caught a flash of silver gray running beside her.

A memory of him.

Chap remained beside Wynn, but he often turned his eyes to Lily.

Past nightfall, Leesil sat staring into the campfire that Magiere stoked with more wood. Wynn sat on the ground and struggled with a hay-bristle brush Leanâlhâm provided. But try as the sage might, she couldn't get the last mat out of Chap's coat. The dog's restless fidgeting didn't make it any easier.

At a light footfall, he turned to find Leanâlhâm approaching. She crouched near him, her expression uneasy. Perhaps the encounter with the Äruin'nas still troubled the girl. It certainly troubled Leesil.

Leanâlhâm watched Wynn's efforts and Chap's scant tolerance with fascination. The girl obviously hadn't known what the sage intended with the brush.

Osha had gone in search of food, and Sgäile stood at the clearing's far side, speaking in low tones with Urhkar.

"Magiere, come and hold him down," Wynn called, and Chap tried to belly-crawl out of reach. "He is a mess, but he will not let me finish."

"You hold him, and I'll do it," Magiere said.

Chap saw her coming. With a rumble, he licked his nose.

"I saw that," Magiere warned.

"You lose again," Leesil said to Chap. This resulted in another tongue-and-nose gesture just for him.

Leanâlhâm leaned forward. "Why are you talking to the majay-hì?"

Before Leesil could think up an answer, Wynn pounced on Chap and grabbed his neck with both arms. Magiere dropped on her knees, pinning the dog's hindquarters as she took up the brush.

"Oh . . . you stink!" Wynn said, wrinkling up her face.

The sight of the two women wrestling the dog into submission, and getting as dirty as he, was almost amusing enough for Leesil to forget the day's troubles.

"No! Do not treat him that way!"

Leanâlhâm's thick accent made her words hard to catch, and she jumped to her feet indignantly before Leesil understood. She grabbed for the back of Wynn's coat, and Leesil shoved his arm in her way.

"He is a guardian of our forest," the girl shouted. "Let him go!"

Both Magiere and Wynn froze and stared at Leanâlhâm.

Chap's ears perked as he ceased struggling. He rolled crystalline eyes and huffed once in agreement with Leanâlhâm's outrage. It sounded a bit too pompous to Leesil.

A way off, Sgäile and Urhkar looked on, and neither appeared pleased.

"It's all right," Leesil said, pulling Leanâlhâm down on the log. "Chap's a bit of a pig. If we don't clean him, he gets unbearable . . . and he knows it."

Chap growled at him.

"Oh, be quiet!" Wynn snapped, and clamped the dog's snout in her little fingers. "Magiere, finish it."

"And if he didn't really like it," Leesil added, "he wouldn't make it so easy for them."

Leanâlhâm's face filled with hesitant wonder. "He . . . understands?"

Chap shook his snout with a grunt, nearly toppling Wynn forward into the dirt.

Leesil sighed. They couldn't hide Chap's unusual intelligence forever, but perhaps it was best not to answer too many questions.

"Done," Magiere said and got up. "It might have gone quicker if you'd kept your butt still!"

Chap wrinkled a jowl at her and slunk off to the clearing's far side. He flopped down to clean himself. Wynn picked herself up, brushing dirt from her breeches.

Leanâlhâm was still watching Chap.

Leesil studied her face. A small loop of her light brown hair was pulled through a wooden ring and held there over a crosswise wood peg. From there, her hair fell down her back in a tail. Her skin was a bit lighter in tone than his, which was strange considering he had more human blood. She turned to warm her hands by the fire, her expression suddenly too serious.

"You all right?" he asked.

She only nodded.

"If elves don't spill the blood of their own," he asked, "why did you cry out?"

"I have only seen the Äruin'nas a few times," she answered, "but never so many at once . . . and so angry."

This was the most Leesil had heard the girl say to anyone but Sgäile or Gleann.

"They wanted to kill your companions," she added, "humans, but . . . they hated me the same way . . . and you. The words they spoke . . . terrible things . . . before my uncle came."

Leanâlhâm went silent, staring into the fire.

"People say terrible things about me all the time," Leesil answered. "Don't let it bother you."

He heard a hiss, and looked up. For an instant, he thought Magiere's vicious expression was aimed at the girl. She stepped slow and steady in front of him, until she stood beside Leanâlhâm while facing away from the fire. Leesil couldn't see her face.

Magiere's fingertips gently touched Leanâlhâm's shoulder. The girl jumped slightly, but Magiere headed off across the clearing toward Sgäile and Urhkar.

What was she doing? Leesil was about to go after her before she stirred up another conflict.

"You are fortunate to have the right hair and eyes," Leanâlhâm said.

"What?"

"Your hair is light," she said. "And your eyes are amber. You look more like our people than I do, and you are half human. I am . . . I wish I had hair and eyes like yours."

Her words were sickeningly ironic. Leesil wanted to tell her that in his world, growing up, his hair and eyes cut him off from everyone but his parents.

"There's nothing wrong with who you are, Leanâlhâm," Wynn replied. She sat on a folded blanket at the fire's far side, fingers laced around her pulled-up knees.

"Leanâlhâm," Leesil asked slowly, "how did you come to be here?"

"I wanted to tell you that first night you came to our home, but my grandfather and uncle are always worried."

She watched the fire for a while, and Leesil waited in silence until she spoke.

"My grandmother was not only bond-mate to my true grandfather, the brother of Gleannéohkân'thva—or Gleann, as you call him. She was also under Gleann's tutelage to become a healer. I call him grandfather because he is the one who raised me. It is the closest word in your tongue for the title.

"My grandmother traveled with Gleann as needed, helping those who had no healer among their own enclave. Illness spread through another clan's settlements to the southeast, and they went to assist. Grandmother was gathering *basha* weed in the hills near the shore, which helps lower fevers. She was attacked . . . by human men."

Leanâlhâm paused and did not look at Leesil. "Do you understand?"

"Yes," Wynn whispered.

"She was badly hurt when Gleann found her and brought her home. In another moon, they knew she was with child. My grandparents did all they could to make certain their coming child would not be treated as an outsider."

Leanâlhâm's voice broke with a painful breath. Firelight glistened in the tears running down to the edge of her triangular jaw.

Leesil understood. Even if Leanâlhâm's grandparents had accepted and shielded their half-blood child, some among their people still wouldn't accept it.

"Grandmother died the night my mother was born," Leanâlhâm went on. "Grandfather was broken inside, as happens among many who are bonded. He left my mother for Gleann to raise. No one saw him again.

"My mother was . . . not right in her mind. She wept often and seldom left the enclave's dwelling trees. Except at night, when she might sit alone in the forest. It was difficult for Gleann, as he never found a way to make her feel like one of the people.

"By the time my mother was of age, Gleann was a most respected healer. A young man with the Spirit awareness came from clan Chiurr to ask that she bond with him— but only if Gleann took him under tutelage as a healer. I think Grandfather was desperate to see my mother have a normal life. He agreed to the bargain. But my parents' bonding was short and then broken by my father, as my mother did not change. He left after I was born and returned to his own clan. By then it was clear that he had never truly loved her, or he would not have been able to leave."

Leesil knew better. Love didn't always last—and sometimes it wasn't enough.

"Not long after," Leanâlhâm continued, "my mother disappeared one night. Some in the southwest say a woman was seen heading for the mountains. She evaded all who approached. Perhaps she found a place among humans."

Leesil waited for more, but Leanâlhâm went silent.

"You grew up alone with Gleann?" he asked.

She nodded. "Except for Sgäile, but not until after my mother left . . . and his last testing to be Anmaglâhk. He was then free to see family again and to live where he wished, though most of his caste live in Crijheäiche."

Leanâlhâm turned to face Leesil fully.

"Sgäile's grandfather was bond-brother of my grandmother's father, though he calls Gleann his grandfather in respect. Sgäile and I share blood. He is often away, but his acceptance of me weighed greatly. Sgäile never knew my mother, but he stood for me among our clan, and he is An-maglâhk."

She nodded slowly, as if remembering something.

"He has traveled many lands, but other mixed-bloods are unknown. So you are the first half-blood he has ever met."

Osha stepped from the trees with two gutted and cleaned rabbits ready for roasting. He also carried a bulging square of canvas tied up by its corners. Leanâlhâm took a long breath and stood up.

"I should help prepare the meal, as it grows late and we are all hungry . . . yes?"

Leesil nodded to her. He had no notion what else to say, no matter how much they shared. Words would weigh nothing against the life she had led and the one he had lived. He glanced across the clearing to where Magiere faced Sgäile engaged in some talk he couldn't quite hear. Chap was with them as well. Leesil couldn't help studying Sgäile for a moment.

The man must have more immediate relatives than Leanâlhâm and Gleann. Yet he chose to call the dwelling of a mixed-blood girl and an eccentric old healer his "home" and these two people his "family."

Leesil didn't believe he would ever understand Sgäile.

Magiere approached in quick pounding strides. Sgäile's tension rose and he broke off his discussion with Urhkarasiférin.

After their confrontation with the Äruin'nas, it had taken a long and heated argument with this woman to keep her and Léshil from reclaiming their weapons. Apparently that debate was not yet settled.

"No more," Magiere growled at him. "Give me our arms . . . now!"

Sgäile took a long breath. "I understand your concern, but if you had been armed today, we might not have talked our way out. I gave you my word. You will be protected."

"You can't," Magiere insisted. "We saw that today. What if those people hadn't listened? I won't risk those I care for, whether I believe you or not. It's not about your word or keeping it. . . . It's about failing, regardless."

Sgäile was not certain how much insult hid beneath her words. He had his ways and customs to follow with faith, and his oath of guardianship to fulfill, and arming this human woman would make neither easy to accomplish.

"You couldn't even keep Leanâlhâm safe," Magiere whispered.

Sgäile fought down rising anger. Her voice carried no malice, but his frustration made it seem so.

"Get me my weapon, or I'll get it myself," Magiere threatened. "Choose!"

Sgäile hesitated too long, and Magiere took a step toward him. A snarl rose up, and she halted.

Chap stood between them, braced in Magiere's path against her legs, but his crystalline eyes looked up at Sgäile.

"Get out of the way!" Magiere snapped.

The majay-hì only growled and would not move.

Sgäile felt a moment's relief that this Fay-touched creature shared his concerns. Then the dog trotted around him, skirting Urhkarasiférin, and headed straight for the bundle and pack that held the weapons and armor. Sgäile went cold inside as the dog sat down next to the arms and stared at him.

Did Chap not understand anything he had tried to make this ill-tempered human accept? Now the majay-hì appeared to side with her.

Ever since the time Sgäile went to kill a half-blood marked as a traitor, this unique being's presence had shaken all he believed concerning the ways of his people.

A memory surfaced in Sgäile's thoughts, of Magiere, her white face aglow, standing by her companions in the forest the night he and his brethren had come to take them. Sword out, she stood ready to defend them from whatever came.

The memory snapped away, replaced with one of a terrified Leanâlhâm huddled next to Wynn amid the Äruin'nas.

The majay-hì lifted its paw and shoved the pack over.

Urhkarasiférin whispered in Elvish. "What is it doing?"

Still Sgäile hesitated and glanced at Magiere. She folded her arms, waiting, as if the dog's action required no explanation.

How could Sgäile explain to Urhkarasiférin what he saw and felt? How could he justify relenting to the majay-hì's request?

Sgäile was bitterly forced to admit that Magiere might speak the truth.

They had escaped the rightful anger of the Äruin'nas, but it had come too close to bloodshed. Leanâlhâm had suffered for it, despite the final outcome.

Sgäile knelt before Chap with uncertainty. He unbound Magiere's heavy blade and lifted it with the rest of the arms still in the pack. He held out the sheathed sword, and Magiere wrapped her hand solidly around it.

Sgäile did not let go. His gaze drifted across the clearing to Leanâlhâm. The girl was assisting Osha in spitting rabbits to cook over the flames.

Magiere followed his glance and then turned her hard eyes back on him.

"No one will touch her," she said. "That's my word."

Sgäile released Magiere's sword.

CHAPTER NINE

Wynn walked beside Osha with Leanâlhâm nearby as they passed through an aspen grove filled with low grass and patches of dandelions. Magiere trudged ahead in her studded hauberk, the falchion strapped on her hip. Leesil was fitted with his weapons and hauberk covered in steel rings. Wynn was still uncertain how Magiere had managed all this, but part of her was relieved when she saw the two gearing up that morning, until Magiere forced Wynn to strap on the battle dagger over her short robe.

The last time Wynn tried to use a weapon she had been beaten to near unconsciousness by two of Darmouth's soldiers. The sheathed blade thumping against her side was an unpleasant reminder. She tilted back her head and saw a thousand green leaves haloed by the bright sun. Ahead, she heard the sound of running water.

"We have reached the river people," Leanâlhâm said. "Our journey will be easier."

"Why is that?" Wynn asked.

Leanâlhâm smiled. "You will see. Sgäile will arrange passage down the Hâjh."

"The . . . 'spine'?"

"Yes. The river passes by Crijheäiche, the settlement of the Anmaglâhk, on its way to the northeast bay."

Wynn admitted that traveling by boat was more convenient, but it offered less of an opportunity to see this world up close. Still, she might get a thorough overview from the river's open way.

"Chap!" she called, scanning the trees. "Come back here, unless you wish to swim the rest of the way."

Sgäile turned his head with a warning frown, and Wynn fell quiet.

It was not hard to fathom his worry. Soon Sgäile would face another encounter with his people. Anmaglâhk he might be, but his social skills were as stunted as Magiere's. Unlike Magiere, this shortcoming appeared to concern him.

"Gather," he called out in Elvish.

Osha and Urhkar took parallel positions at the procession's sides. As the aspen grove thinned, Wynn drew a long breath. Through the trees she saw three broad vessels slipping past upon the wide Hâjh River.

The barges looked like massive flat-bottomed canoes as opposed to their square and flat human counterparts. Laden with twine-bound bundles and smooth, slatless barrels, they rode lightly like leaves in a stream. Two headed downriver, while the other passed on its way up.

Each had a central mast of polished yellow wood. Their sails were furled, but the bound fabric was brilliant white in the bright sun. Where their raised sides turned inward at the pointed bow and stern, single tines sprouted to either side of their hulls like straight, bare branches on a tree's trunk. Wynn could not guess what these were for.

Elves front and rear in the barges held long poles but seldom dipped these. The downstream vessels moved on the current, and although the one headed upstream traveled as smoothly as the others, behind its stern, river water churned softly, like the slow thrashing of a giant fish just below the surface.

"Wynn! Get up here!"

Leesil's harsh shout broke Wynn's enchantment. She had unwittingly stopped while staring at the barges. Leanâlhâm pulled on Wynn's sleeve, while everyone else stood waiting. Their entire procession had halted and not one of them looked pleased with Wynn.

She hurried to catch up as Leanâlhâm outdistanced her. Magiere firmly pushed Wynn out ahead of herself, and Osha sighed some exclamation under his breath.

Chap charged through the aspens, the white female on his heels. Wynn saw no sign of the majay-hì pack, and Chap's companion stopped short, hanging back to shift uncertainly among the trees. Before Wynn tried coaxing her closer, Sgäile urged all of them onward. Just ahead lay a settlement more diverse than that of Sgäile's clan.

A few domiciles were made of stout aspens bent toward each other overhead, with vines of spadelike leaves woven into walls between them. In the upper branches of an elm, wood platforms supported partitions of anchored fabrics as well as shaped vines. One tall building was made of planked wood, grayed with age and weather. Thin smoke rose into the air from somewhere hidden at the settlement's far end.

The elves worked at varied tasks, mostly to do with goods near the docks. Their clothing had more hide and leather than the people of Sgäile's home wore. Many wore their hair cut midlength or even short to the scalp. Dockworkers picked among barrels and bundles, taking stock of goods arriving or awaiting departure.

Few noticed the newcomers at first, but by ones and twos they paused and called or gestured to companions. Wynn saw displeasure and even hatred, as in Sgäile's enclave, but none showed initial shock upon seeing humans. This made her more anxious.

"Is this a center of commerce?" Wynn asked.

"Commerce?" Leanâlhâm said. "I do not understand this word."

"The way you purchase . . . acquire with money."

Leanâlhâm blinked twice. "Money?"

"The people trade," Osha explained in Elvish, "all knowing the value of a thing, by its make and the time and effort involved. We barter, but we do not have . . ." He stumbled and switched to Belaskian: "Money. And Anmaglâhk do not trade."

"Why not the Anmaglâhk?" Wynn asked, still baffled.

"Quiet," Sgäile said.

A darker-skinned elf in matching leather breeches and tunic-style shirt rose at the head of one dock from inspecting bales of cattail heads. He appeared neither hostile nor surprised, and Wynn suspected all here somehow knew they were coming.

Leesil and Magiere hung back as Sgäile approached, but Wynn crept a little closer to listen.

The leather-clad man scanned them all, with an especially close study of Leesil and then Magiere. His blond hair was cropped semishort and stuck out in bristles. Soft lines creased his brow as if he frowned too often, and his tan skin glistened with sweat.

"Sgäilsheilleache," he said. "You are always welcome."

"My thanks, Ghuvésheane," Sgäile answered.

It took Wynn some thought to discern the man's name—Black Cockerel. It matched his demeanor if not his appearance.

"I need passage to Crijheäiche," Sgäile said, "for seven and one majay-hì."

Ghuvésheane shifted his weight to settle on the other foot. "I cannot ask this of any bargemaster. Not even for you."

Sgäile's expression hardened. "Has one of my caste passed this way?"

Ghuvésheane nodded sharply. "Three days ago. A woman, traveling fast. She took passage on Hionnahk's barge, headed downriver."

"You must try for us," Sgäile insisted. "By request of Most Aged Father."

Ghuvésheane's eyes narrowed, and he closed them.

"Ask them," Sgäile said flatly. "Ask in the name of Most Aged Father. Who among you would refuse the Anmaglâhk?"

"Assisting your caste is not at issue," Ghuvésheane returned, eyes still closed. "As you well know."

Several elves down the docks stopped in their labors. Two came up behind Ghuvésheane, dressed akin to him. But they looked far more offended, as if Sgäile had asked something shameful—something he should not have asked at all.

"Is it not enough that you bring humans among us"—Ghuvésheane finally opened his eyes, his steady gaze shifting toward Leesil—"let alone a murderer and traitor?"

Wynn bit her lip against a blurted denial. Osha remained passive, but an echo of the dockworkers' embarrassment filled his expression.

Urhkar licked his lips as if they had gone dry. "That charge has not been validated."

Ghuvésheane remained unconvinced. "Perhaps not, but you still ask too much, and my answer is the same."

Neither Leesil nor Magiere understood what was said, but Wynn wondered what would happen if Sgäile was unable to procure passage.

A young and thin-muscled elf came up the shoreline. "I will take you," he said, ignoring Ghuvésheane. "No one need ask me." He glanced at Leanâlhâm, as if he knew her. "We are still loading, but there is space near the front."

Dressed in leather breeches, he wore a goatskin vest with the leather side out and no shirt beneath it. He was barefoot and gestured to a small half-loaded barge down at the end of the next dock.

Ghuvésheane turned away with an exhale tainted with disdain.

Sgäile's jaw twitched as he nodded to the young bargemaster.

The exchange was peaceful enough, yet Wynn felt that it cost Sgäile more than all the rest of the journey combined. Much of their passage seemed to have taxed the anmaglâhk's pride.

They were shown to a space near the barge's front where cushions and fur hides were laid out. Wynn made more seats out of their blankets. By the time the barge pulled into the river, everyone was situated, and the settlement slipped away behind them.

Their host's name was Kânte—Spoken Word. Though the young bargemaster seldom issued commands to his crew, two of four elves always stood post, one rear and one forward, while the other pair rested at the barge's stern, away from the passengers.

They floated down the Hâjh both day and night, and Wynn passed the time watching a strange world drift by on the shores.

Trees of various make, flowers of wild color, a small waterfall, a bright flock of birds never ceased to pull her attention this way and that. Two *fra'cise* drank at the river's edge, until they saw the barge and began jumping and splashing in foolish antics. Parts of the forest grew dense and dim. Then the barge would pass a large meadow spilling its vivid green to the river's shore, where a herd of speckled antelope grazed. Once, Wynn caught a glimpse of a large silver deer with tineless antlers, the same as had bellowed at them the first evening in the forest.

But eventually she grew frustrated and then weary.

All the wondrous sights passed beyond her reach. Landfall was rare. They ate cold meals, with no fire but for the large lantern hung at the bow each night. The simple fare was plentiful—fresh or dried fruit and smoked fish. The river provided clean water for drinking and basic washing. But as Wynn continued to watch the shore slip past, she began to feel slightly dizzy.

Osha remained good-natured, though he sat day after day in the same position.

He explained that this barge was loaded with raw materials. Kânte would unload some in Crijheäiche, trading with skilled craftsmen in the community. He would then fill his barge with other materials or goods—pottery, spices, tools, fabric, clothing, and more—for the journey to the bay. Some would be traded with the people of the city there called Ghoivne Ajhâjhe—Front of the Deep—while the rest would be bartered with ships bringing goods and materials to and from other coastal communities.

While they spoke, a high-pitched yip carried along the riverside, and Chap looked over, whining softly.

The entire majay-hì pack bolted out of the forest to run along the reedy shore, paws splashing through the shallow water. Shades of silver-blue, steel, and inky gray moved in circles along the bank.

"Magiere, look!" Wynn said. "They are following us."

The white female barked once at Chap. He whined again, and Magiere reached down to scratch his head.

And still they floated onward four more days and nights.

Then as they passed an enormous sycamore with large roots reaching from the bank into the river, Wynn saw an archway in the base of its trunk. She almost missed it, mistaking its gray curtain for part of its bark.

"We are close to Crijheäiche," Leanâlhâm said.

Wynn went numb. She did not know what to feel—relief or anxiety?

"How close?" Leesil asked, craning his head around.

Leanâlhâm pointed to two broad elms.

Wynn saw more doorways as the barge drifted by. Soon, every other oak, cedar, and fir was larger than the last, and the spaces between them broadened.

Sgäile stood up when five long docks appeared on the shore ahead, with barges and smaller boats moored along them. Wynn caught a hint of joy on his face.

From what she understood, they would enter one of the largest communities in all the Elven Territories. But Sgäile did not appear nervous. Was he not worried about their reception?

He put two fingers in this mouth and let out a long whistle.

Kânte stood in the barge's prow and dipped his pole into the water. All four of his crew around the vessel did likewise, and the barge turned smoothly toward the docks. Where the docks met land, no trees blocked the view, and Wynn took her first glimpse of Crijheäiche.

The doorways in these trees were larger than those she'd seen elsewhere, and some trunks bulged to impossible size at their bases. She saw stalls of planked wood and shaped flora and colored fabrics. Inside these, occupants were busy at many kinds of work. One place appeared dedicated to the purification of beeswax. She heard rhythmic metallic clanks but could not spot anything like a smithy. There were fishmongers nearer the river, or the elven equivalent of such.

As the barge slowed in order to make harbor, a wild tangle of aromas filled Wynn's head. Beneath the scent of baked and roasted foods were rich spices and the powerful scent of herbs she had only known in the gardens of her guild on another continent.

For all the industry here, everything was still interwoven with the natural world.

Kânte set his pole to stop the barge as four anmaglâhk trotted through the open bazaar and down the dock. Their long hair of sandy to white blond blew free in the breeze. None wore his or her cloak tied the way the few Wynn had seen beyond this land.

At first, only a few other elves turned and stared at the new arrivals, for barges landing here would be a common sight. From a distance, Leesil and even Magiere appeared to escape scrutiny. Perhaps their elven clothing obscured their true nature until an onlooker peered more closely. But a few eyes widened at Chap. Apparently, a majay-hì riding a barge was not a common sight.

The first of the four anmaglâhk to reach the barge's side was young, with blunt but prominent cheekbones.

"Sgäilsheilleache, well met," he said in Elvish. "Fréthfâre hoped you would arrive by today."

He did not look at Wynn or Magiere. In fact, he seemed determined to cast his eyes anywhere but in their direction.

"Where is she?" Sgäile asked without greeting.

"With Most Aged Father," the young one answered. "I will tell her you have arrived."

"Has anyone seen Én'nish?" Urhkar added.

The young anmaglâhk became rigidly formal at the sight of him and bowed his head in a reverent fashion.

"Yes, Greimasg'äh. She arrived two nights ago."

That one strange word eluded Wynn. A "holder" of something? Perhaps a title, as it certainly was not part of Urhkar's full name.

Sgäile nodded. "Have the quarters been prepared?"

"Yes, of course," the young elf answered.

Sgäile turned to Leesil, switching to Belaskian. "My caste has prepared a comfortable place for all of you. Please follow, but first . . . you must relinquish your weapons once more."

Leesil snorted. "You want to get us out of sight? Then where is my mother?"

"In truth, I cannot say," Sgäile answered and looked away. "You will soon speak to Most Aged Father, and he will answer in good faith. Now please, your weapons."

Wynn unbuckled the dagger, uncertain whether or not she was relieved to be rid of it. She was about to hand it to Sgäile, but turned instead to Osha. He took it with surprise and bowed his head as he tucked it in his belt.

"All right," Leesil said, unstrapping his punching blades. "But I want to see this leader of yours, and soon. Today."

He held out his blades and his stilettos. Sgäile took them with a hint of relief in his eyes. Once again, Magiere was last to relinquish her falchion, but she handed it over without a word. Leesil placed his hand on the back of her neck, combing his fingers through her dangling black hair.

Throughout the community up the slope, and across the other docks, numerous elves in bright clothing went about their business. Wynn noticed the Anmaglâhk among them. They stood out like dark pebbles in a clear stream's bed.

Kânte picked up Leanâlhâm's bundle before she could do so and held it out to her. The gesture made the girl fidget nervously, and she would not look him in the eyes.

"You have my thanks . . . ," Sgäile said to the bargemaster, but trailed off, unable to say more.

Kânte raised a hand in polite dismissal. "No need. You always have my service."

He offered his hand to Leanâlhâm. This made the girl even more uneasy, but she took it as he helped her onto the dock. Leesil lifted the chest of skulls and slipped his arms into its rope harness. Osha and Urhkar handed baggage off to their newly arrived comrades.

As Wynn stepped from the barge behind the others, the first young anmaglâhk glared at Leesil and pointed insistently to the chest. When Leesil returned only a silent stare, the young one's expression hardened. Two of his companions dropped their baggage and closed in as he reached out.

Before Leesil could strike, Magiere stepped in front of

him, shielding him from any assault. Sgäile shifted instantly between her and the others.

"No!" he snapped. "Move on!"

The young anmaglâhk looked at Sgäile as if he had committed some violation. Osha, who had always kept silent behind his elders, startled Wynn with his harsh tone.

"He is bearer of the dead," Osha said in Elvish to the others. "Léshil, descendant of Eillean."

The young anmaglâhk before Sgäile blinked twice. He glanced once at Leesil and Magiere, both still poised for a fight.

"I beg forgiveness," he said.

"Attend your duty," Urhkar added flatly.

The four anmaglâhk quickly took up the baggage. Not one of them said anything more.

Solid wood of the dock and then sound earth beneath Wynn's feet were quite welcome, but Sgäile rushed them all onward. Perhaps he was not so confident of their reception; or he neared the end of his mission and longed for it to be over.

Wynn wanted to study this new place, to poke about the stalls and observe how exchanges were made, but she found herself jogging half the time just to keep up. All around them, elves paused at the sight of Magiere's dark hair and pale skin—and Wynn's own short stature and round olive-toned face. The four anmaglâhk with the baggage split into twos, a pair walking at each side of their passage. No one questioned or challenged them for bringing humans into this place.

A way past the shoreside bazaar, Sgäile halted before an enormous elm. He pulled aside the door hanging and motioned them inside. Only Wynn, Magiere, Leesil, and Chap entered, and Sgäile remained in the doorway.

"Be comfortable," he said. "You are safe and my caste will make certain of it. But do not leave this dwelling without Osha or another I designate. I will send food and drink as quickly as possible."

Leesil stepped toward him, and his mouth was taut in anger. Before he uttered a word, Sgäile cut him off.

"Soon," he said, and his expression seemed troubled.

"You will speak to Most Aged Father soon. But heed me, Léshil. Do not leave this dwelling until I come for you."

He released the curtain and was gone.

Magiere put her hand on Leesil's shoulder, then began pulling the chest off his back.

Wynn believed that Sgäile would keep his word, though Leesil's impatience was mounting. No words of comfort from her would do any good, so she looked about their new quarters.

The elm's interior was one room, though larger than the family space in Gleann's home. Soft cushions were stacked to one side along with a rolled-up felt carpet of cerulean blue. The floor was bare earth instead of moss. There were ledges growing from the tree walls for beds or seats with cream blankets of downy wool folded upon each. A wide curtain of gray-green, like the clothes of the Anmaglâhk, hung from a mounted oak rod across the room's back. Wynn pulled it aside and found a small stone tub akin to Gleann's.

"Our guest house has been well prepared," she said.

Leesil's amber eyes flashed as he turned on her. "It's a cell."

By early evening, Leesil paced the tree's interior, berating himself for his stupidity.

Magiere and Wynn were captives, and he had no one to blame but himself. A wooden tray piled with fruit and a water pitcher had been brought, but he didn't touch any of it. There was also a glass lantern, prelit, that sent an aroma of pine needles through their cell. Some of their baggage had been delivered—but not their weapons.

To make matters worse, Magiere watched him with that same silent tension on her face that she'd worn throughout their time in Venjètz. She sat vigil on him, waiting to see if he would lose himself again.

Chap was the only one who could walk out if he wished. No elf so far had interfered with the comings and goings of the majay-hì. But the dog just lay on the floor with his head on his paws.

Though Leesil seethed over their situation, it was mostly

frustration. At least one of his companions might suggest something helpful. Were they any closer at all to finding Nein'a?

"What do you think happens next?" Magiere asked.

She sat on a wall shelf with one leg pulled up, and Leesil's frustration faded.

Magiere was just worried about him—about them all. She looked paler than usual, and the sleeves of her dark-yellow elven shirt were lightly marred from the journey. With her head tipped forward, black hair hung around her cheeks. He reached down and hooked her hand with two of his fingers.

"I don't know," he answered honestly. "Whatever comes, it'll depend on what this leader of theirs wants . . . this Most Aged Father. He put Sgäile through a great deal to bring us here, so I'd assume this meeting won't wait long."

"He wants something from you," Magiere whispered.

Leesil saw the vicious narrowing of her eyes and wondered if her irises flickered to black for an instant.

"Of course he does," he answered.

She watched him, probably wondering what reckless notion he had in his head.

"And that means he'll pay for it," Leesil added. "Perhaps he wants it badly enough to release my mother. It's been so many days since we left the mountains. I thought surely I'd find her by now . . . seen for myself that she's all right."

Magiere stood up suddenly, and Leesil flinched, expecting another tongue-lashing.

She slipped her arms around his waist. The studs of her hauberk clicked against the rings on his.

Chap got up with a warning rumble, and the doorway curtain swung aside as Sgäile stepped in.

"Come, Léshil," he said. "It is time."

"Alone?" Magiere said. "I don't think so."

The curtain lifted once more, and another anmaglâhk stood in the doorway without entering. Something about her put Leesil on edge.

She was slender like a willow, with thin lips and a narrow face, but her features were otherwise pure elven. Her hair was like the color of sun-bleached wheat and hung in slight waves.

This one wasn't as adept as Urhkar, or even Sgäile, at hiding her feelings. Her loathing of him was plain to the eyes. Leesil nearly felt it crawl on his skin like dry heat from a weaponer's forge.

It was different from Én'nish's personal and manic hatred. This woman took in the sight of Magiere touching him, and Wynn sitting on the ledge next to Chap, as if she would burn this long-nurtured tree just to cleanse it of any human taint.

"You will come," she said in Belaskian. "Now."

"He's not going anywhere," Magiere answered. "Your leader can come here to speak to him."

The look in the woman's eyes almost made Leesil back up and pull Magiere away. She said something to Sgäile in Elvish.

Sgäile stepped close to Leesil, leaning in and speaking softly. "Léshil, you must come. This is Fréthfâre, the hand of Most Aged Father. He cannot come to you, so Fréthfâre carries his . . . request that you come to him—as a courtesy. All will be made clear."

Leesil only half-trusted anything Sgäile said, for one could bend one's word without breaking it.

"And then I see my mother?" he asked.

Sgäile hesitated. "I cannot say. That is for Most Aged Father to decide."

Chap crossed the room in silence. He stared at this woman, Fréth, for so long that she finally looked down at him. A bit of uncertainty broke through her revulsion.

Chap lifted his head toward Leesil and barked once.

"All right," Leesil said. He ran his hand down Magiere's back. "Stay here and look out for Wynn."

Magiere grabbed his arm so tight it hurt. "No."

"Chap is coming with me," he said. "They won't . . . can't stop him from doing what he wants. I'll be back when I learn what this is all about."

She was frightened, and a scared Magiere was dangerous. Her fear pulled at him, but he couldn't stop now. If he let her keep arguing, fear would quickly shift to anger. He peeled her fingers from his arm and held her hand for a moment.

Fréth backed out through the curtain as if the sight disgusted her.

Sgäile pulled the curtain back again, waiting. As Leesil turned to leave, Magiere tightened her grip.

"You owe me a promise for a promise," she warned.

Leesil wondered what it meant until he glanced back to find that Magiere's eyes weren't on him. They were on Sgäile.

Sgäile glanced at Leesil and nodded firmly to her. "Always."

Magiere finally released Leesil's hand.

"I'll be back soon," he said, and slipped out.

He emerged on the outskirts of Crijheäiche again. Fréth had already moved off, and Sgäile urged him to follow. He couldn't help but notice how fluidly Fréth moved—just like his mother. She turned in the waning daylight to look down at Chap.

"Majay-hì?" she said. "In Crijheäiche?"

Sgäile spoke something brief in Elvish. Fréth's lips were pursed. His answer did not seem to satisfy her, but she walked on.

Leesil looked about, but there were no other dogs in sight. The majay-hì pack that followed the barge had only appeared now and then, always hesitant to come too close. Perhaps they had lived so long in a land where humans weren't tolerated that they were confused by those who walked with elves. But still, Fréth's question was odd.

Fréth led them away from the riverside, but they continued to pass through populated areas. Many amber eyes watched their passing. Some whispers reached Leesil's ears. He thought he heard someone say "Cuirin'nên'a." His gaze wandered so much that, when they came upon it, the oak tree seemed to rise out of nowhere in front of them.

Sitting in a wide mossy clearing, it was ringed by other domiciles a stone's throw away. Any one of them would have matched Gleann's home, but compared to the oak at the clearing's center, they appeared small and stunted. Its roots made the earth rise in ridges spreading out from its base. Its breadth would have matched six men laid end to end. It seemed impossible that it even existed. And its mass of branches and leaves rose beyond sight, nearly blotting out the sky.

Five anmaglâhk stood near it, and one stepped out, exposing himself to full view.

He was taller than Sgäile, with broad shoulders and a build that seemed too heavy for an elf. To Leesil, he looked rather like a human stretched to a height not of his race. But the man was purely elvish, from hair streaked with silver-gray among the whitish-blond to large amber eyes in a triangular face with—

Leesil stopped and planted himself firmly. Anger made his throat go dry.

Four scar lines angled down the man's forehead, jumping his right eye to continue through his cheek to the back of his jaw.

"Brot'an," Leesil whispered to himself. Memories burned inside his head.

In Darmouth's family crypt, Brot'an had whispered to him; he'd told him that the one elven skull among the warlord's bone trophies was his own mother's. Leesil had rushed Darmouth, ramming his curved bone knife through the warlord's throat, and then watched as the tyrant drowned in the blood flooding his lungs.

Brot'an had done it with nothing but Leesil's own guilt, turning it to anguish with a simple lie. Leesil had finished what this anmaglâhk had come to do—assassinate Lord Darmouth and start a bloodbath in the Warlands.

Leesil had taken one more life, just like the weapon he was. The one Brot'an had used.

Chap's rage mounted until it overwhelmed what he sensed from Leesil. Ears flattened, he pulled back his jowls and opened his jaws.

Brot'ân'duivé—Dog in the Dark. Deceiver!

Chap shook under taut muscles with fur rising across his neck.

Brot'an's white eyebrows knitted, bending the scars on his face.

It did not matter to Chap whether this one shared any feeling for Eillean. Brot'an had used Leesil like a tool and brought Nein'a back to be condemned and caged. This much and more Chap had learned when he had dipped into the tall elf's surfacing memories in Darmouth's crypt.

He should have never listened to Magiere—never let this man leave that place alive. He should have torn off Brot'an's scared face, there and then.

And now, here was Brot'an, waiting as Leesil came to the patriarch of the Anmaglâhk. How much had this assassin told his own kind of Leesil and Magiere?

The others near Brot'an moved a few steps toward Chap in surprise. One of them said, "Majay-hì?"

Chap reached out quickly from one to the next, searching for any surfacing memory. All he caught were images of majay-hì in the forest mingled with a few from various inhabited settlements.

He had learned from the memories of Lily and her pack that the majay-hì occasionally bore their young among elven communities. They wanted their children to be aware of and accustomed to the elves before they returned to life in the forest. Chap was uncertain why these four and even Brot'an found his presence here so baffling.

Then it struck him. Of all the forest packs these anmaglâhk had witnessed, none had ever seen a majay-hì in this place—in Crijheäiche.

Why?

He heard Fréthfâre's sharp voice but did not catch her words—all his attention returned to Brot'an.

Let instinct take all reason from him. Here and now, all he wanted was to tear into Brot'an.

But Chap held his ground. Where would that leave Leesil?

Brot'an stood his place with only a puzzled frown on his long, marred features. The four behind him took hesitant steps forward, two shifting to either side of Chap and just out of his lunging reach.

"Greimasg'äh?" one said, looking to Brot'an, but the elder elf gave no reply.

Chap had heard this word, though he did not know its meaning. At the docks, it had been used for Urhkar as well.

Sgäile dropped to one knee before Chap, holding his palms out.

"No," he said in Elvish. "No . . . violence . . . here."

He spoke with slow emphasis, as if to make certain Chap understood.

"Léshil, make him understand!" Sgäile added in Belaskian.

Brot'an's eyes shifted with keen interest at this strange demand. Chap held his ground.

"Is this the real reason you took my weapons?" Leesil asked, but it sounded more like an accusation.

"No," Sgäile answered. "But it is now just as good a reason. This is neither the place nor the way for whatever grievance you and the majay-hì have with Brot'ân'duivé."

Reluctantly, Chap agreed. He circled back around Leesil's legs, coming up beside him to face the others. Let the deceiver breathe for now.

As far as Chap was concerned, Brot'ân'duivé was dead, though the man did not yet know it.

An exclamation erupted from one of the other anmaglâhk. Chap followed the man's astonished gaze out between the domicile trees at the clearing's edge.

A white blur darted from one tree to another, reappearing halfway around the next trunk.

Lily peered out at Chap and looked hesitantly at the others.

Chap's rage softened at the sight of her. Without thinking, he yipped, hoping she would join him.

Lily shifted nervously. She took two steps toward him but then backed away, half-hiding behind a domicile tree.

Chap knew her reluctance to be near humans and often sensed her concern and puzzlement that he did so. But as he reached for any memories surfacing within her, an image of the central oak appeared in his mind.

Its doorway was but a dark hollow he could not see into, and the sight of it was coated in Lily's fear.

He turned his attention back to the Anmaglâhk as

Brot'an raised an arm toward the tree and stepped out of the way.

"Go inside, Fréthfâre," he said in Belaskian. "Most Aged Father awaits." His face took on a more pleased expression. "Well met, Sgäilsheilleache. Your journey was swifter than expected. Come and tell me of it."

Sgäile hesitated. "I have taken guardianship for Léshil and his companions."

"And my word holds all others to your purpose," Brot'an said. "No one will touch him or his. You will come with me."

Sgäile seemed only half-satisfied, but relented. "Yes, Greimasg'äh."

Events were not playing out to Chap's liking, but he saw nothing he could do. He and Leesil were surrounded by their enemies for now. Fréthfâre headed for the behemoth tree, and he nudged Leesil forward, keeping himself between his companion and Brot'an.

Brot'an's head turned sharply and fixed upon a point at Chap's rear. Something sharp clamped on Chap's right hind leg. He whirled to snap but quickly stopped.

Lily held his leg firmly in her jaws. She tugged, trying to pull him, then let go and began barking wildly as she backed across the clearing.

Chap saw the center oak and its black hollow doorway in her thoughts. She wanted him to leave this place, but why? And how could he tell her that he could not do as she asked?

He barked twice at her and trotted toward the oak. Lily did not follow.

Fréthfâre pulled the doorway curtain aside, and Chap entered first into a large empty space within. The only fixture was a wide stairway of living wood to one side, but it led downward into the earth, not up as in Gleann's home.

Chap descended watchfully and emerged into a large earthen chamber. He stood in a hollow space below the massive oak. Thick roots arched down all its sides to support walls of packed dirt lined with embedded stones for strength. Glass lanterns hung from above, filling the space with yellowed twilight. In the chamber's middle was the tree's vast center root. As large as a normal oak, it reached from ceiling to floor and into the earth.

Leesil stepped down beside Chap, his tan face paled by the sickly light. Leesil hated not having control, as did Chap, and they had long since lost hold of their own path.

Fréthfâre descended behind them as a thin voice filled the earthen chamber.

"Come to me . . . here."

It came from the wide center root.

Chap stepped through the earthen chamber, around the center root, and found an oval opening that at first had been too hard to spot in its earth-stained wood. Leesil hesitated, but Chap inched forward to peer within. He froze at what awaited them.

The oak's vast center root held a smaller room more dimly lit than the outer chamber surrounding it. And its inner walls appeared alive even in its stillness.

Hundreds of tinier root tendrils ran through its curved walls like taupe-colored veins in dark flesh. The walls curved smoothly into a floor of the same make, and Chap was reluctant to even place his paw on its surface. Soft teal cushions rested before a pedestal flowing out of the floor's living wood. The back wall's midpoint flowed inward as well to support it.

Wall and floor protrusions melded together into a bower . . . or was it more a crude cradle? Among the clumps of fresh moss therein, two eyes stared out from a decrepit form.

Once he would have been tall, but he now curled fetal with his head twisted toward his visitors.

Thin, dry white hair trailed from his pale scalp around a neck and shoulders barely more than shriveled skin draped over frail bones. His triangular elven face was little more than jutting angles of bone beneath skin grayed by want of daylight. Deep cracks covered features around eyes sunken deeply into their large slanted sockets. His amber irises had lost nearly all color. All that remained was a milky yellow tint surrounded by whites with thread-thin red blood vessels. Cracked and yellowed fingernails jutted from the shriveled and receding skin of his skeletal fingers. His once peaked ears were reduced to wilted remnants.

"Father," Fréthfâre said.

She stood away from Leesil, bowing to the ancient elf. The old one ignored her and studied Chap and Leesil.

"Majay-hì," he said in a reedy voice. "I have not had such a visit in long years." He raised a hand to Leesil with slow effort. "Come closer . . . my son. Let me see you."

Chap reached for the memories of Most Aged Father.

He saw nothing. Not one image rose in the old one's mind. Chap remained poised and focused as he entered behind Leesil, and Fréthfâre followed.

Leesil tensed beside Chap as he took his first clear look at their host.

"I see your mother in you," said Most Aged Father. "And I know she trained you in the ways of our caste. You are Anmaglâhk."

"Not in your oldest dreams," Leesil croaked, finding his voice. "Where is she?"

At that question, Chap caught the flicker of a glade in Most Aged Father's mind. Before it vanished, he saw a tall elven woman seated upon the grass. Beside her was a basket of moth cocoons, which she had been using to spin strands for raw *shéot'a* cloth.

Chap swallowed. Nein'a. But he caught no hint of where she was held.

"She is with us," Most Aged Father said, and lowered his hand. "She is a traitor to her people . . . to your people, Léshil. You are Anmaglâhk, so I have brought you here to help her."

"Stop saying that!" Leesil answered. "I am not your son. You're nothing to me. Release her, and I'll take her far from here, where she'll never trouble you again."

Most Aged Father nodded, his head rubbing the moss on which he lay. A stale scent like dust flooded Chap's nostrils.

"In good time," he said. "First you must do a service for your people. . . . Yes, you are of the people, and you would not turn your back on your own. Not on your kin and blood."

Leesil's voice rose. "Make some sense, old man! What do you want from me?"

Fréthfâre spun toward Leesil, as if she wished to strike him down. Most Aged Father remained calm and unaffected.

"There are others like your mother." A long silence followed before he went on. "She was misled—misguided—so she could not have acted alone. Your birth was a violation of our ways, but that is no fault of yours. But the idea of . . . a half-blood child . . . it could not have come from her. No, she was misled . . . yes?"

Chap saw a flash in Most Aged Father's mind—another woman, an anmaglâhk. The resemblance to Nein'a would be clear to anyone, though her face was harder, her eyes colder.

Eillean.

"My sole concern is to protect our people," Most Aged Father continued. "Now you are honored to serve them as well. Most of the Anmaglâhk are true in their hearts. But a few . . . just a few have fallen from our way, like your mother. They will see you as the son of Cuirin'nên'a. They will seek you out. Find them, Léshil—help me shield our people—and I will release Cuirin'nên'a to you."

Chap could not help looking up at Leesil. This offer was nothing more than a trade of flesh, the dissidents for Leesil's mother.

Sweat now matted Leesil's blond hairs to the sides of his face, but his expression was guarded.

"Let me see her first."

"No," Most Aged Father answered softly.

"Then you get nothing from me. I talk to her first . . . then you and I might come to an arrangement."

Chap could not believe what he heard.

Most Aged Father seeded violence among humans. Did the Fay know of this ancient elf hidden in this shielded land? And if so, why had they never spoken of him? So concerned with keeping Magiere from the enemy's reach, had they no interest in why Leesil had been born and trained?

And now Most Aged Father sought to use Leesil for his own purpose, and Leesil had half-agreed.

Chap stifled a growl.

"We are not bargaining here," Most Aged Father said. "But there is no need for haste. I have given you so much to think on. I understand that you need time to consider. In the end you will do what is correct for your people . . . as I do. Go now. I will call for you again soon."

"I'm not going anywhere." Leesil's voice rose with every word. "My mother couldn't possibly be a threat to you now. Your Anmaglâhk . . . they may look at you like some saint, but I'm not one of them. And with all those like Sgäile, following you blindly . . . what could you possibly fear from a few dissenters?"

As these words left Leesil's lips, a rapid barrage of memories emerged in Most Aged Father's mind and assaulted Chap's awareness. The room went dark before his eyes.

Out of the darkness came black scaled coils—circling and writhing.

Chap's legs began to buckle.

He heard screams as the battlefield took focus.

Bodies of elves and dwarves and humans of varied race lay mingled among those of other creatures that walked on two or four legs. All mutilated and left to rot beneath a dying sun.

Two seas of the living had crashed together on this open plain of rolling hills. The battle's remains were so mangled and mixed that Chap could not tell which direction either had come from. Broken armor and lances and every other thing were spattered in blood that had already begun to dry or soak into the earth. There were so many . . .

So many that Chap saw not a blade of grass for as far as his sight could reach.

The growing stench thickened until it choked him.

On the ground at his feet—for he saw elven boots of forest green suede, and not his own paws—lay the broken body of what the humans called a goblin. Two-thirds a man's height, these pack animals walked on two legs with cunning enough to use a weapon as well as their teeth and claws.

Wild spotted fur covered its apish body and caninelike head of shortened snout and muzzle. It had clothed itself in motley pieces of armor, likely stolen from the dead in previous battles. Foam-matted jaws hung open, and its tongue sagged in the dirt. Dead eyes with sickening yellow irises stared unblinking at Chap's feet.

A jagged rent in its throat exposed the ends of its severed windpipe.

Perhaps one of its own had turned on it in their frenzy for slaughter. There was strangely too little blood on the ground beneath it.

Dusk rapidly closed in on Chap.

At first he noticed stars along the horizon. Then they moved.

Not stars, but glints from some light . . . on black scales that writhed all around him . . .

"Chap!"

Strong hands gripped his shoulders until his forepaws almost lifted from the floor. Leesil knelt before him, glistening face wary and awash in concern.

"Chap, what's wrong?"

Chap lifted his head, his legs still shuddering, and looked over Leesil's shoulder. Most Aged Father watched him in suspicion. He whined and pushed his head into Leesil's chest.

"You are dismissed," Most Aged Father said. "Leave now. We will talk again."

Leesil carefully released Chap and stood up. "Until I see Nein'a . . . don't bother sending for me."

He turned and, with a brush of fingertips across Chap's neck, strode out for the stairs, not waiting for Fréthfâre to usher him out. Chap did not look back to the old elf as he followed on unsteady paws.

The great war was but a myth to some. What he had seen and felt in that flash of the old elf's memory left him shaken.

The humans called it the Forgotten History . . . or just the Forgotten. Some believed this war had covered the known world.

And Most Aged Father had been there.

Most Aged Father settled in his moss-padded bower, neither worried nor distressed. The meeting with Léshil had progressed as expected. After so long a life, there was little he could not easily anticipate.

Léshil would struggle in anger and denial, until he realized no other choice remained. He could not leave this land without permission. He could not stay indefinitely. He could not find his mother without assistance.

He would realize the truth soon enough and accept it.

Most Aged Father was patient. The names of the dissenters would be uncovered. They would join Nein'a, each in his or her own separate solitude unto the end of their days. And he would turn his full attention to the human masses once again.

Only one thing troubled him. He had not anticipated the majay-hì.

None of its kind ever came here. He knew their history better than anyone, for in the end days he had fought beside a few of the born-Fay, who had come into flesh in the war against the Enemy. But their descendants never neared this place. He felt no blame toward them. No matter their ancestry, they did not understand why he clung to life for so long.

The Enemy only slumbered and would return.

It would always return.

But this majay-hì with Léshil had walked into his dwelling and looked him in the eyes.

Most Aged Father would learn more of this one. He did not care for being in the dark on such matters. In his long years, he'd learned that nothing ever happened without purpose.

But the conversation with Léshil had exhausted him. He placed withered hands against the wood of his home, his life's blood. Slowly, the forest's life flowed toward him. In recent years, it took more to sustain him another day. His moments of strength and vitality shortened ever so slightly.

His Anmaglâhk thought him omniscient and eternal. They honored his sacrifice for remaining among them rather than joining their ancestors in rest. They believed his presence could reach to all living things that thrived and grew from the earth. But this was no longer true.

He could reach out through the trees and hear words

spoken anywhere in this land, but long distances now took great effort. And remaining aware of just one place at a time was all he managed. It drained him quickly.

Today it was necessary. Today he must hear what was said between Léshil and his companions.

Some time had passed, and likely Fréthfâre had returned Léshil to the quarters prepared for him and his companions. Comfortable quarters but lacking in any luxury or pleasing distraction that might make waiting easier. Lacking enough to keep Léshil always on edge and wanting to leave.

Most Aged Father closed his eyes, his feeble hands still resting upon the bower's living wood, and reached out through the roots of the trees. Through the wood and leaves of a domicile elm, he heard Léshil's voice.

CHAPTER TEN

Magiere watched the light wane below the doorway curtain's hem as dusk settled in. All she could do was wait and listen, but she heard no footfalls outside.

Where was Leesil?

She paced their one-room quarters, glancing at the curtain each time she drew near it. Even if she got by Osha or whoever stood post outside, she had little chance of finding Leesil. And she no longer had her falchion or even the dagger she'd made Wynn carry.

The strange vibration in her bones returned. It had faded to an almost unnoticeable level once they'd boarded the barge. Here in this place of the Anmaglâhk, it built in her flesh once again. It made her even more anxious to take Leesil and run from this land by any passage they could find.

She finally sat and watched Wynn writing out one enlarged Elvish letter after another upon a piece of Gleann's paper.

"This will not be as quick as the talking hide," Wynn said with frustration. "Chap will have to spell out every word. Another hide would be better, or something less fragile than paper."

"At least we can to talk to him," Magiere said.

For once she took comfort in Wynn's sudden bursts of chatter. Wynn carefully scribed and blew dry two pages of symbols and pulled out another blank sheet.

"I did not expect their dialect to be so different," Wynn said, "until I heard these elves speak. It is no wonder Chap and I have problems communicating . . . beyond his frustration with language. If only I could dip into that messy head of his, in the same way he sees and uses other people's memories."

Magiere didn't answer. No one had come to their quarters after Sgäile took Leesil away. She hardly considered him or his companions to be friends, but it was strange that not even Leanâlhâm had looked in on them.

"Do not start pacing again," Wynn said. "If the elves wanted Leesil dead, none of us would have made it this far . . . nor would Sgäile have gone through so much to guard us. Our bodies would have vanished like any other curious human who came looking for this land."

How blunt the little scholar had become. A far cry from the soft-spoken sage Magiere had met back in Bela.

"I know," Magiere said. "It's just that lately Leesil has been so—"

"Erratic, pigheaded, idiotic, obsessive—"

"Yes, yes, all right," Magiere interrupted. A far cry indeed.

Wynn smirked slightly, her strange new stylus scratching out the next symbol. Just how many letters were there in Elvish?

Magiere hadn't bathed, wanting to be ready the instant Leesil and Chap returned. But she did change her clothing, tossing aside the elven attire for a pair of dark breeches and a loose white shirt. It was warm enough to leave off the wool pullover, but she had strapped on her hauberk again. It made her feel more secure—more like herself.

She closed her eyes. When all of this was over and done, perhaps Leesil might find his old self again. The one she'd fallen in love with so reluctantly at first. And if he didn't—she still couldn't see any day ahead of her without him.

The doorway curtain wafted inward, bulging up from the ground, and Chap slipped in under its hem. The curtain swung aside, and Leesil entered right behind the dog. Magiere was on her feet before the fabric settled into place.

"Are you all right? Did you see your mother?"

One look at his face answered both questions.

"What happened?" Wynn asked, and set aside paper and quill.

"He wants a bargain with me," Leesil answered flatly, and Chap issued a low rumble. "Most Aged Father wants the names of every anmaglâhk who might have a connection to my mother. If I get him those names, he'll release her."

Of all unsettling possibilities, this wasn't among the imagined worries that had run through Magiere's head.

"What makes him think any of his butchers would talk to you?"

"Because I'm Nein'a's son." He looked up, eyes sad and distant. "But he's lying. No matter what I do, I don't believe he'll release Nein'a—or us. You should've seen him. . . ."

His eyes squinted and his mouth tightened as though he'd tasted something stale and bitter.

"Why go to such lengths?" Wynn asked. "By bringing you here, he has clearly alienated his people, even some of his caste. He must be desperate."

"Who better to hide from the Anmaglâhk than an anmaglâhk?" Leesil retorted. "I think he's already exhausted his own means. I'm guessing my mother's refused to tell him anything in all these years. And I think he suspected my grandmother, but she's beyond his reach now."

"Chap, careful!" Wynn snapped. "I am not done. . . . You are slobbering all over the pages!"

Chap was pulling Wynn's papers off the ledge seat, and Wynn couldn't keep up with him. He dropped them on the ground, separating the sheets with his nose, and began pawing the Elvish symbols.

"Ancient Enemy," Wynn translated.

They'd heard this from him before outside of Venjètz,

when he'd tried to explain that it was Eillean's skull, not Nein'a's, that Leesil carried. And that Neina, Eillean, and perhaps even Brot'an had some hand in a conspiracy surrounding Leesil's birth and training.

Chap continued, and Wynn shook her head in puzzlement. "He spelled out . . . 'il'Samar' . . . or as close as he could."

The name snapped a memory in Magiere's head.

She and Chap had closed on Ubâd within a forest clearing near the abandoned village of Apudâlsat. Enormous spectral coils of black scales had appeared in the dark between the wet, moss-laden trees.

"That's the name Ubâd cried out before . . ." Magiere couldn't finish.

Looking at Chap with that memory in her head made her shiver. The dog had gone into a frenzy at the sight of those coils, which had seemingly come to Ubâd's plea. They didn't answer the old man, but instead spoke to her, Magiere, in a whispering hiss of a voice.

Sister of the dead . . . lead on.

And then Chap had torn out the necromancer's throat.

"What do you know about this?" Magiere asked of Wynn.

"It is definitely Sumanese. 'Samar' is obscure, meaning 'conversation in the dark,' or something secretly passed. And 'il' is a prefix for a proper noun . . . a title or name."

Wynn shook her head with uncertainty and perhaps a taint of fright.

"Back in Bela, Domin Tilswith showed me and Chane . . . a copy of an ancient parchment believed to be from the Forgotten. I cannot remember the exact Sumanese wording, but it mentioned something called 'the night voice.' Perhaps . . . from what you told us of Ubâd in that clearing . . ."

Magiere wasn't listening anymore. The name that Ubâd had cried out echoed in her mind. And then came a piece of the vision that her mother's ghost had shown to her.

Her so-called half brother, Welstiel, walked alone in the courtyard of their father's keep. As Magelia came upon him, he whispered to himself in the dark . . . or in answer to a voice no one else heard.

*   *   *

Chap struggled with how much he should tell them—and how to manage complex ideas with only a few sheets of large Elvish letters. The idea that Most Aged Father had been alive during the ancient war seemed too much for the moment. There was no telling what Leesil, or even Magiere or Wynn, might do in this strained moment if they knew.

Leesil and Wynn were little help with their tangled debate and speculations, and Magiere seemed lost within her own thoughts. For now, it was enough that they learned of an enemy that was known by many names in many places—and that Magiere was never as far from its reach as she might assume. Chap knew better.

As he was about to bark for their attention, the room blurred slightly before his eyes. It was more like a waver in the living wood of the wall. Then it was gone an instant before he fixed upon it.

Chap shook his head and looked about. Nothing had changed, yet he had felt something. Elation and then anxiety rose in him.

Had his kin finally come? But surely not in the presence of others, especially those in his charge?

They would not reveal themselves so explicitly to mortals. He sensed no echo within his own spirit that marked their presence and shook off the strange sensation. There was nothing here, and he was being foolish. Even so, the disruption left him restless. He padded to the outer doorway and stuck his head through its curtain.

Osha looked down curiously at him from the doorway's far side. Chap ignored him, and searched the trees.

There was no sign of Lily, and she had not been waiting when he emerged from Most Aged Father's home. Something about this place—and that one great tree—frightened her. It frightened all the majay-hì, and they would not come near. Lily had only come to try to drag him from it.

He heard a soft whine and raised his ears.

The barest hint of creamy white showed beneath a bush of lilacs beyond one domicile tree. Between its lower branches, two crystalline eyes stared back across the open space at Chap.

Lily hid where she might not be noticed. For all her fear of this place, she had come back and silently watched for him.

Chap glanced up at Osha, but the young elf had not noticed her. He wanted to run beside Lily through the wild forest and let nature's ebb help him decide what course to follow.

He knew he should stay and help his companions consider this shackling bargain with which Most Aged Father tried to bind Leesil. Magiere and Wynn were also in danger here as unwanted outsiders. And in some way, great or small, this was all bound together by the hidden whereabouts of Nein'a. Chap's companions desperately needed to gain some element of power here.

Nein'a's location was the crux of it all.

If they only knew where she was imprisoned, that would remove a good deal of Most Aged Father's hold on Leesil.

Chap heard Wynn half-shout behind him, "This is futile! We will not figure this all out tonight."

"It's all we have to work with," Leesil growled back. "And I'm tired of waiting."

"Stop it, both of you," Magiere said. "Leesil, come take a bath and let it rest for now. I can't even think anymore."

Chap looked out to Lily hiding among the white lilacs. He caught her memories of the two of them running with the pack—and alone by themselves.

Unlike her, Chap could read and even recall and use another's memories within line of sight, but he could not send Lily his own without touching her. There was something he must tell her . . . something she and her pack needed to help him do.

He had no time to tell his companions and have them argue over it.

Osha still watched him, so Chap turned away from Lily as he slipped out.

He trotted down toward the riverside bazaar, hoping she would circle through the forest and follow. When he cut between a canvas pavilion and a stall made of ivy walls, she was waiting for him.

Lily slid her muzzle along his, until they each rested their head upon the other's neck.

Chap rolled his face into her fur and recalled Lily's own memories of her time with her siblings under the watchful eyes of her mother. He sent his memory of tall Nein'a and a young Leesil together.

He was not as adept as her kind with this memory speech, and his limitation was frustrating. He had "listened" in as Lily and one of the steel-gray twins did this. Memories came and went in such a quick cascade. Whenever she spoke to him, the images were slow and gentle in simple sights, sounds, and scents. She understood he needed time to learn their ways and always showed him patience.

Chap repeated the parallel memories of mother and child. This time, when he called the one of Nein'a and young Leesil, he pulled away Leesil's image, leaving Nein'a alone. He then recalled Lily's memories of her pack hunting in the forest, and did his best to mingle it with his own memory of the tall elven woman.

The last image he sent was one stolen from Most Aged Father—a memory that had now become his own. Cuirin'nên'a, in a shimmering *shéot'a* wrap, sat in a glade clearing beside a basket of cocoons.

Lily grew still beside him. She sent him no memory-talk. She nudged his muzzle with her own and took off, out of the settlement and into the forest.

Chap raced after as Lily cut loose a howl. Somewhere in the distant trees, the pack answered.

"Where's Chap?" Wynn called out.

She sat alone on her ledge bed with the occasional splash coming from the bath area at the room's rear.

"At least one of us can get out of here for a stretch," Magiere grumbled from behind the curtain.

Wynn was a bit uncomfortable with Magiere and Leesil back there together, with only that gray-green fabric providing privacy. And with all the arguing over Most Aged Father's bargain and Chap's few troubling words . . .

She climbed to her feet. "Why would Chap slip out without telling us?"

"Who knows?" Leesil called back. "Stick your head out and call him, but don't go wandering about."

Wynn left the two of them to talk—or whatever they did in there. She pulled the outer doorway curtain aside and looked out, but Chap was nowhere in sight. Neither were Sgäile or even Osha. She stepped out for a better view.

There were no elves in sight, and Chap was gone. Both worried her.

Wynn took a few more steps, looking up and down the lane of cultivated trees. To her far left she could just make out the silent and still remains of the dockside bazaar.

"Chap?" she called in a harsh whisper.

Chap rushed into a gully behind Lily. Ahead, the pack waited by a tiny stream. The black-gray elder lifted his head from lapping water gurgling over stones.

Chap had not expected the pack to be so near, but they must have gathered to wait on Lily. As he approached beside her, the majay-hì circled about with huffs and switching tails, one by one touching heads as they passed her or him.

Spry bodies surrounded him with warmth. One yearling colored much like himself charged playfully and butted Chap with his head. Chap shifted aside.

He rejoiced in their welcome, but urgency kept him from languishing. He was neither certain how they could help nor how he could ask. Lily seemed to understand but would the others? On impulse, he pressed his head to hers and again showed her the stolen memory of Nein'a's hidden prison.

Lily stayed against him, listening until he finished, then darted away.

She brushed heads with the large black elder. An instant later, the male turned and touched a passing steel-gray female, the other twin. The rest joined in, and Chap watched the swirling dance of memory-talk as it passed through the pack.

The elder's crystal blue eyes turned upon Chap.

The old one tilted his gray muzzle, and then hopped the

stream and scrambled up the gully's embankment more fleetly than his age would suggest.

Lily trotted back to Chap and pressed her head to his. He saw a memory of the two of them resting beneath a leaning cedar after a long run. It seemed he was to wait— but for what?

Chap's frustration mounted, still wondering if the pack truly understood what he needed.

A rolling, moaning howl like a bellow carried through the forest. It came from the direction where the elder had disappeared.

Lily brushed Chap's head with a memory of running as the rest of the pack charged off. He followed her up the embankment and through the woods. When he cleared the close trees, he saw the elder.

The black-gray majay-hì stood on a massive cracked boulder jutting from a hillside of sparse-leafed elms. The pack remained below, and he appeared to be waiting and watching for something. The elder glanced upslope over his shoulder, and Chap stepped back from the boulder's base to see.

Branches of a hillside elm appeared to move as if drifting through the trees. Two eyes high above the ground sparked in the half-moon's light and came downslope into clear sight.

Head high, the silver-gray deer descended, coming up beside the grizzle-jawed old majay-hì. Its tineless curved antlers rose to a height no man or elf could reach. The shimmer of its long-haired coat turned to pure white along its throat and belly. Its eyes were like those of the majay-hì, clear blue and crystalline.

The deer slowly lowered its head with a turn of its massive neck.

Lily nudged Chap, pushing him forward.

Chap did not understand. Was he to go to this creature?

She shoved him again and then darted around the boulder's side. She stood waiting, and Chap loped after her. Before he caught up, Lily headed upslope, and he followed. At the height where stone met the earth slope, she stood aside and lifted her muzzle toward the silver deer.

Chap hesitated. What did this have to do with finding Nein'a?

Lily pressed against him. Along with a memory echo of the tall elven woman he had first shown her, Lily showed him something more—a memory of the pack elder touching heads with one of these crystal-eyed deer.

Chap froze as the deer swung its head toward him.

He could not have imagined this creature might communicate in the same way as the pack. A tingling presence washed over him as he peered into the deer's eyes.

It felt so vague . . . like one of his kin off at a distance. And yet not quite like them.

The majay-hì were descended from the first born-Fay, born into flesh within wolves. Over many generations, the majay-hì had become the "touched" guardians of these lands.

But there were others, it seemed, as Chap had almost forgotten.

Within this deer, the trace of its ancestry was stronger than in the majay-hì, the lingering of born-Fay who had taken flesh in the form of deer and elk.

Chap crept forward to stand below the tall creature—this touched child of his own kin. It stretched out one foreleg and bent the other, until its head came low enough to reach his. Chap pressed his forehead to the deer's, smelling its heavy musk and breath marked by a meal of wild grass and sunflowers. He recalled the memories of Nein'a that he had shared with Lily.

The deer shoved Chap away, nearly knocking him off his feet. It stood silent and waiting.

What had he done wrong?

Lily slid her head in next to his, muzzle against muzzle. Images—and sounds—filled his mind.

A majay-hì howling in the dark. An elven boy calling to another. Singing birds, jabbering *fra'cise*, and the indignant screech of the *tâshgâlh* he had trailed out of the mountain tunnels.

Chap grasped the common thread. The deer wanted a sound. He approached as it lowered its head once more.

With the image of Nein'a in the clearing, Chap called

forth a memory of her voice . . . and that of any who had ever spoken her name.

Nein'a . . . Cuirin'nên'a . . . Mother . . .

Wynn scurried around a domicile tree closest to the forest's edge. She still did not know why there was no one on guard outside, and she could not find Chap anywhere. But as she turned to go back before being discovered, she heard footsteps.

She ducked low into hiding behind a tree, hoping whoever it was would just pass onward. As she leaned carefully out, she never made it far enough to see.

Wynn's vision spun blackly on a wave of nausea.

Her legs buckled, and she slumped down against the tree's base, clinging to its bulging roots as she covered her mouth and tried not to gag. Bisselberries and smoked fish rose in her throat from the evening meal, and the combined taste turned sour.

The loud buzz of an insect or crackling rustle of a leaf in the wind filled her head.

There were no insects and not even a breeze around her in the dark.

Wynn had not heard these in her mind for more than a moon. The last time was at the border of the Warlands.

Somewhere out in the forest, Chap now called to the Fay.

It had all started with a ritual in Droevinka, when she tried to make herself see the Spirit element that permeated all things. She had been trying to track an undead for Magiere, and then could not end the magic coursing through her flesh. Chap had to cleanse the mantic sight from her. But on the border at Soladran, it began to return in unexpected ways. She heard the buzz of leaf-winged insects whenever Chap communed with his kin.

Wynn swallowed her food back down, trying to quiet her gagging breaths. She braced for the onslaught of Chap's kin answering back in a chorus of leaf-wings that would make her head ache and the world whirl before her eyes.

It never came. Only one leaf-wing buzzed in her mind. The sound began to shape into . . .

Nein'a . . . Cuirin'nên'a . . . Mother . . .

A chill ran over Wynn's skin.

Words? They came in the Elvish dialect of this land. Beneath those were the same echoed in Belaskian and in her own tongue of Numanese. One voice spoke in many tongues at the same time, all words with the same meaning. Again, no chorus answered back.

Who did Chap call out to? Had he found Leesil's mother so close by? He would never try to commune with her—it would not work. To Chap's own knowledge, Wynn was the only one who had ever eavesdropped on him while communing with his kin. And she had never heard words before.

The buzz faded from her mind, leaving only a lingering ache.

But she had clearly heard those words.

There was no time to ponder another disturbing change in her unwanted gift. Chap was out in the forest, seeking Nein'a, and Wynn could not let him go on his own. How did he think he would speak with Nein'a, even if he found her prison?

Wynn braced on the tree's trunk and worked her way to her feet. She looked out into the wild and panic set in.

She could not navigate the forest without someone to lead her. It did not want her . . . a human. Even traveling with the others, it had tried to make her lost. Leesil, with his half-elven blood, had to concentrate to escape the forest's influence.

For once, Wynn wished the burden of mantic sight would come. But unpleasant as it was, it only came to her erratically. Once, it had overwhelmed her while she was alone with Chap, her fingers deep in his fur.

Wynn forced down fear until she reached calm. She closed her eyes, recalling all the sensations she had felt in that moment alone with Chap. She sank into memory until it blocked out all else.

Chap had sat before her, staring into her eyes. The room turned shadowy beneath the overlaid off-white mist just shy of blue. It permeated everything like a second view of the room on top of her normal sight, showing where the element of Spirit was strong or weak. Chap was the only thing she saw as one image, one whole shape.

His fur glistened like a million hazy threads of white silk, and his eyes scintillated like crystals held before the sun.

Wynn opened her eyes, and her food lurched up her throat once more.

Blue-white mist permeated all things of the forest. She felt so sick inside that it dampened any relief at her success.

Wynn stepped into the forest, and the trees began to look the same all around.

She turned too quickly, searching for the way she had come. The world spun in a dizzying blur. Breath pounded from her lungs when she hit the ground on her side, and she struggled up to her hands and knees.

"Only the mist . . . see only Spirit," Wynn whispered.

She tried to ignore the trees' true shapes and focus only on the permeating glimmer of Spirit in all things. Nausea sharpened, but as she turned her head, a sense of place became clearer.

Wynn saw glimmering silhouettes of trees and bushes, one overlaying the next into the distance, like silent blue-white ghosts in stillness. And beyond was a cluster of bright spots far off.

They moved, circling about each other like fireflies in the night. Three were higher above the rest, and one of those was larger than the others. A fourth glimmer separated from the largest one and shone in a sharp brilliant white.

Chap.

Wynn knew it was him. She scrambled on all fours to the nearest tree, pulled herself up, and stumbled toward him as her beacon.

Fully dressed again, Leesil pulled the bathing area's curtain aside enough to step out.

The press of Magiere's body in the hot bath still lingered on his skin. He loved her, but would she still love him when she realized he was only a thing to be used for killing? How long before she could no longer face what he really was? He would have to let her go, if that was her choice.

Knowledge of the pain yet to come felt like almost an illness in his body.

He wondered why she kept shaking slightly while immersed in the hot water.

He'd asked if she was all right. She hesitated, saying it was nothing more than all this mess they were in. Leesil knew better, but battling with Magiere was too much to face. He'd rather have one more quiet moment in her arms.

She wasn't sleeping well either, and ate too little each day. Yet she showed no more fatigue than himself, perhaps less.

"There has to be some way to get around Most Aged Father," Magiere said behind him, pulling her boots on.

Leesil wasn't really listening. Bowls of cold vegetable stew and a pitcher of water sat to one side of the room's floor. Wynn's scribbled sheets still lay on the ground where Chap had left them.

"Where's Wynn?" he asked.

"Probably at the door, looking for Chap," Magiere answered, and pulled the bath curtain fully aside. "She won't be satisfied until . . ."

Magiere looked about the empty room, lips still parted in unfinished words. Her breath drew in sharply before she snapped, "That little idiot!"

Leesil headed straight for the outer doorway. He swatted the curtain aside and looked out. There was no one on guard. Or had Osha gone with Wynn to look for Chap?

Magiere stepped past him as he looked off through the domicile trees. Then he glanced down toward the distant dockside bazaar. Among the structures there, from canvas tents entwined in briar and roses to the rising platforms in one wide walnut tree, there was no sign of Wynn or Chap.

Leesil heard footfalls coming his way.

Osha walked along with a soft smile as he studied an open cloth in his palm. Nestled in the cloth were small brown and cream lumps. He picked one and popped it in his mouth, not even looking up.

Leesil ignored the young elf and called out, "Wynn . . . Chap?"

Only then did Osha raise startled eyes.

"Stop!" he said, quickening his pace. "Stay. No leave."

"Where were you?" Leesil snapped.

Stunned at the demand, Osha quickly closed the distance to Leesil.

"I bring sweets," he began, stumbling over his Belaskian. "Honey cooked on nuts . . . for to give comfort. All you will like."

Leesil wanted to slap the nuts from the witless elf's hand. While this young whelp abandoned his post for dessert, Wynn had slipped off after Chap . . . wherever that dog had gone now.

"Get Sgäile," Magiere growled at Osha. "Wynn is gone . . . get him now!"

Osha shoved Leesil aside and peered into the tree. He turned about, panic-stricken, and pointed at Leesil as he backed away.

"Stay," he said, then turned at a run.

Leesil noticed lights all about him, spilling from doorways as curtains were pulled aside. Here and there, elves peered out at the noise. One or two even stepped from their homes.

Magiere wasn't looking at them, and Leesil saw her irises blacken. She shook visibly, though it wasn't cold, even for night. She was letting her dhampir nature rise enough to widen her night sight and search between the settlement's trees and brush.

"We have to find Wynn," she whispered, "before any of these people catch her wandering about."

"Just wait," Leesil warned. "We're no better off if we do the same as her."

"And what if she followed Chap into the forest?"

"Again, we're no better off," Leesil argued. "Even I have to think hard not to lose my way out there."

"I don't," she snapped at him.

The harsh reminder made him wonder over her strange symptoms of late.

"That's where she is," Magiere said, lifting her chin toward the open forest beyond the domicile trees. "She followed Chap . . . out there."

"She's not that stupid," Leesil replied. "Curious to a fault, maybe, but she knows she'd just get lost."

"Not if she caught Chap quickly enough." Magiere's anger intensified in her features. "He went looking for the pack . . . yes, and she just had to see the majay-hì for herself. I could kick that curiosity right out of her skull!"

A tall form came running through the wide trees.

Sgäile sprinted up, wearing a long white gown to his bare feet. Deep green oak leaf patterns were stitched around the split collar. His hair hung loose and wild around his long face, as if he'd just risen from bed. Osha came behind him, looking again like he was in serious trouble.

Accompanying them were two anmaglâhk Leesil hadn't seen before, both in the full dress of their caste.

"Do you know where your companion might have gone?" Sgäile asked immediately.

"We're not sure, but—" Leesil began.

"Get my weapons," Magiere cut in. "She's out there . . . in the forest."

Sgäile ignored her demand. "Why? A human would not last long, alone in our land. She will lose her way immediately."

All this delay frustrated Leesil. "She may have gone after Chap . . . if she thought he was headed for the other majay-hì."

Sgäile's lingering patience broke. "A pack will not tolerate a lone human wandering out there."

For an instant, Leesil was speechless.

"I kept your supervision to a minimum, wishing not to make you feel like prisoners." Sgäile glanced once at Osha, who flinched. "I trusted that all of you would have sense enough to follow my instructions. That is now finished."

Sgäile whipped about, growling at the two anmaglâhk. He turned on Osha again as the pair stepped around him, one toward Leesil and the other closing on Magiere.

"*Tâshgheâlhi Én'nish!*" he snapped. "*Mé feumasij foras äiché âyâgea.*"

Osha took off running.

"What about Én'nish?" Leesil asked.

Her name was the only word he picked out. The an-maglâhk closest to him shoved him back toward the tree's doorway, and Leesil set his footing in resistance.

"I merely wish to know her whereabouts," Sgäile answered. "Go inside and stay there!"

That instant Sgäile's other companion reached for Magiere, and the only warning Leesil got out was "Don't—"

She slammed her fist into the elf's face with such speed that he lurched over backward, one foot slipping up from the ground. As his back struck the earth, he rolled away in retreat, coming up unsteady and so shaken he nearly lost his footing again. Blood ran from one narrow nostril and the side of his mouth.

The one near Leesil shifted his weight, a stiletto already in his hand.

"We're going after Wynn," Magiere said to Sgäile, her breath coming long and hard. "With you . . . without you . . . through you. What's your word worth now?"

Leesil didn't like how she was handling this, but it was too late to stop her. All he could do was back her up. If Én'nish was loose and heard about Wynn, what might she do for vengeance if she couldn't get to him?

"You should've watched that murderous bitch," Magiere warned. "If she gets anywhere near Wynn . . ."

"It'll end any hope of agreement with your patriarch," Leesil added. "I'll have no part of the search for his dissidents."

Sgäile's attention shifted instantly to Leesil—in open confusion. Could it be that he didn't know of the bargain Most Aged Father tried to strike? Was he even aware his own caste wasn't as unified as he believed?

"We can get on with it," Leesil continued, "or we can have it out right here. But it'll cost you to keep us back . . . if you can."

Sgäile stood in angry indecision, eyes shifting between Leesil and Magiere.

Leesil slowly reached for Magiere's arm. She jerked away but settled back, waiting. He just hoped she kept her self-control, as he had one more thing to attend to.

He ducked inside and retrieved the chest containing his father's and grandmother's remains. He slipped into its rope harness and returned with it mounted on his back.

Sgäile hissed something at the bloodied anmaglâhk facing Magiere, and the man trotted off into the night.

Leesil caught two of Sgäile's words, but his thought was interrupted as Sgäile spun back and stared at the chest.

"I'm not leaving it out of my sight," Leesil said. "I won't have anyone touching them while I'm gone."

Another flash of tension rippled across Sgäile's features. Even Magiere grew quiet and still.

Of the words Sgäile had spoken to Magiere's opponent, one was Urhkar's full elven name, who still held Leesil and Magiere's weapons. At least that much had been settled, and it appeared Sgäile had sent for their arms.

But the other word Sgäile spoke, another elven name . . .

Leesil grew angrier by the moment.

Three anmaglâhk jogged down the lane between the trees. The first was Sgäile's returning messenger. The second was Urhkar, looking none too pleased, and he wasn't carrying the bundle of weapons. The third and last of the trio . . .

Leesil flushed with heat, and the air turned cold upon his skin.

Bro'tan.

The deer lifted its head from Chap and stood to full height. Its long ears rose, each turning of its own accord. After one step, its head swung northeast and it became still again. Both ears turned that same direction.

Chap followed the deer's gaze. What was it listening to?

The deer clopped off along its chosen path. The pound of its heavy hooves vibrated through the boulder. It headed into the trees.

The dark pack elder huffed to his kin and turned to follow the deer. All the other majay-hì scurried upslope around the boulder. Lily licked Chap once across the face and loped off behind them.

Chap stared after them. What was happening? Did they

know where they were going? There seemed little to do but follow, and then a voice cried out from below.

"Chap . . . wait!"

He turned as the pack froze on the hillside. He ran out to the boulder's lip and looked down.

Wynn teetered into the clearing. In the moonlight, her face glistened with a thin layer of sweat, and she dropped to her knees.

Chap lunged off the boulder's side, claws digging into the earth. What was this foolish little sage doing out alone in the forest? Somehow, she had snuck out and trailed him without getting lost. As he rounded the boulder's base, he heard a deep rolling growl.

The elder majay-hì came around the boulder's far side toward Wynn, his jowls pulled back from yellowed teeth. Snarls grew one upon the next as the pack spread around the clearing. Their crystalline eyes locked on the sage crumpled to the earth. Chap turned to face them, and the elder made an arcing inward charge to get around him.

Chap lunged around Wynn into the elder's path, snapping and snarling. The elder slowed, coming in a pace at a time with his shoulders rolling.

The pack tightened its circle.

Chap could not face all of them at once. Only Lily held back, watching from his right, and the silver yearling paced sideways in uncertainty. Lily suddenly bolted in, shoving the young one aside, and headed straight at Wynn.

Numb shock ran through Chap as he whirled to face her. He had no wish to fight Lily.

She slowed, creeping forward, and lowered her head, sniffing.

"Please . . . Chap, please," Wynn moaned. "Take it away!"

Lily shook her head, sneezed, and whined deeply.

Chap's eyes widened as Lily circled around, placing herself between Wynn and the other half of the pack. Chap backed up to Wynn, trying to think of some way to assure her that at least Lily meant no harm.

Wynn rolled on her back, squinting, and shielded her eyes from him.

"Please . . . take it," she whimpered, "from my eyes."

Her hand lowered to her mouth as she gagged. Her irises shrank at the sight of him—as if he were too bright to look upon.

Chap felt his breath turn thick and stifling in his chest. Wynn was not pleading for him to remove Lily.

Her mantic sight had risen. The little fool had somehow used it to find him and made herself sick again! He did not have his kin to call upon for aid in cleansing her.

Chap ground his paws into the clearing's floor, binding himself to the forest through Earth, Air, and his own Spirit. He leaned down and nosed Wynn's small hand aside, and ran his tongue firmly over her closed eyelids.

He could taste it. Rampant energies running like a disease still within her, which emerged to alter her sight. He swallowed them into his body, and forced them through his flesh, down into the earth . . . out with his breath to dissipate like vapor.

If only this were the end of it.

Wynn dropped her hand with a limp thud upon the ground. She sighed a long breath and swallowed hard.

The last thing Chap needed was someone to watch over in the forest. And worse still, a human wandering the territory of the majay-hì. Wynn had to go back—but would the pack wait for him to return? That was, if he could return Wynn unseen, and not end up fighting the whole pack just to get her out of this clearing.

"Where do you think you are going?" Wynn asked in a weak voice.

Chap was half-ready to snarl at her—witless girl.

Wynn sat up, and her eyes widened at Lily standing so close. She reached out her hand, but Lily backed away one step. Then Wynn noticed the pack surrounding them.

"Chap?" she said, scrambling to her knees.

He had no time to scold her. What he needed was a quick way to put the pack at ease.

Chap circled watchfully around to Lily's side. He touched his head to hers and called up a flurry of memories of every time and place he had shared with Wynn.

Lily pulled away with a grunt and shook herself. She

eyed him for a moment, and then hopped off a pace and paused to stare at Wynn. With a whine, she trotted to the steel-gray male nearby and their heads grazed.

The male jerked away with a snarl as his twin sister inched close behind him. Lily butted him in the side and growled back, then turned to his sister.

The pack began mingling, touching heads as they passed each other. Their growls became broken with huffs and whines, and Chap saw it was still not enough. Perhaps there was nothing that could balance against human interlopers.

Chap barked for Lily's attention. When she returned, he gave her memories of Wynn brushing out his coat. He clung to the sensation of the sage's small fingers running through his fur.

Lily pulled away. But she turned her long head to Wynn, stretching out to sniff at the sage. Chap ducked his head under Wynn's hand, squirming to make it slide down his neck.

"What are you doing?" she said. "Stop playing around. This is serious!"

Oh, how he wanted a voice, just to tell to her to shut her mouth. He waited with his eyes on Lily.

She inched closer, and Wynn leaned away in fear. When Lily put her nose right in front of Wynn's face, the sage lifted a hesitant hand.

Wynn lightly touched the bridge of Lily's snout and slid two fingers over Lily's head.

A deep snarl filled the clearing.

The elder glared at the three of them—a human touching two majay-hì. He turned away with a clack of his jaws and headed back up the slope. Soon all the pack drifted after him, all but the steel-gray twins, who held back a moment to study the trio curiously.

"What is happening?" Wynn asked.

Lily pulled out from under Wynn's hand and trotted a short way across the clearing. She stopped to wait. Chap grumbled and jerked Wynn's sleeve. He had little choice but to take her with him.

"I heard you," Wynn said. "I heard you calling . . . for Nein'a."

Chap looked up into her worried face.

He had called up Nein'a's name for the deer, and somehow Wynn had caught it amid her mantic state. She had mistakenly heard something unintelligible the last time he had communed with his kin. But not words.

Chap let out a deep sigh. He had no time for this.

Another aberration had surfaced from Wynn's meddling with magic and the sickness it had left within her.

How much more trouble was this little woman going to be?

Wynn ran after Chap and the majay-hì as fast as her short legs could carry her.

She guessed that Chap had somehow learned of Nein'a through the pack, but how far off was Leesil's mother? Would Most Aged Father want Nein'a close to Crijheäiche— close to other Anmaglâhk? Or would he put her where she could never interact with them or any of her people?

The inky old majay-hì in the lead was out of sight, and the others were getting well ahead. Wynn had counted seven in the pack besides Chap but now saw only three. Chap lagged behind, slowing again and again for her, and the white female hung back as well. Beyond her were the two dark gray ones identical in their markings.

Without mantic vision, Wynn had to keep one of them in sight, or she would succumb to the forest tangling up her sense of direction. But her throat was already ragged and dry. She stumbled to a halt, bending over, trying to catch her breath.

"Chap!" she panted. "Chap, wait!"

He circled back, fidgeting anxiously.

"I can . . . cannot keep this pace," she panted.

The white female let out a howl that startled even Chap. The cry faded, and she drew a breath to offer another one. The pair of steel-grays returned immediately, and the leader and the others appeared shortly after.

Wynn watched the dark old male stroll toward them with head low and lips quivering beneath a threatening glare. Chap might have convinced the white female, but the pack leader barely tolerated her. Beyond him, a young silver male made a great show of mimicking the elder's displeasure.

Chap spun toward the white dog, and they touched heads. She loped off to the elder and did the same. He jerked away and snapped viciously at her, but she curled her own lips in response and would not retreat. Chap trotted up behind her, leaving Wynn nervously alone.

A lanky silver male with a light blaze down his chest raised his head and snorted at her.

Chap remained still as the white female slid her head along his and paused. An instant later, she began to howl again.

It came out like a moaning bellow that carried through the trees. The dark elder snarled.

Chap circled back to Wynn, his glower all too familiar. Like the time she confessed to overhearing him when he was communing with his kin. He cocked his head, studying her with parental displeasure.

"I am not the one who snuck off first," she grumbled at him.

Chap let out a rolling exhale, like a growl without voice. He twisted paws into the ground as if securing his footing.

Wynn's stomach lurched.

The chattering crackle of a leaf-wing filled her head. This time the strange way it shaped was clearer than the last.

You . . . ride . . . keep up . . .

Wynn went slack-faced, even with nausea twisting her stomach. She only caught those few words, but she held her breath and blinked.

The leaf-wing vanished from her thoughts, and Chap lowered his muzzle, almost mournfully.

Perhaps neither of them truly believed she had heard him the first time. Now it was certain. It might have been a wonderful new thing if not for making her sick every time . . . if not that it was one more wild symptom of what she had foolishly done to herself in Droevinka.

Chap lifted his muzzle toward the white female, and the flutter of a leaf-wing rose again in Wynn's head.

. . . Lily . . .

Wynn remembered the first time she saw the white female as the pack surrounded them upon entering the forest. She had said the dog's color looked like a water lily.

... *Yes* ...

Wynn held a hand out to Chap's companion, and the white majay-hì remained poised and still. She carefully touched the female between her ears, and the dog lifted its nose into her palm.

"Lily," Wynn repeated.

Lily spun about, staring through the trees with raised ears.

A large silver form stalked through the underbrush and walked slowly through the pack. The dogs dispersed out of its path, but the dark leader still rumbled. Wynn felt the tall deer's thudding hooves beneath her own feet, and the vibration grew as it approached.

Chap's multitongued words rose in her head: *You will ride.*

Wynn had to tilt her head back to look up at the deer's muzzle. Its large head was crowned by two tineless antlers longer than Chap's body. The crystalline eyes above her were so large they made her cower.

"Oh no." She backed away. "No—no—no!"

The deer swung toward Lily, stretched one foreleg and bent the other, and lowered itself until the two touched heads. Then the animal folded its legs and lowered its white belly to the ground.

"You cannot be serious!" Wynn exclaimed. "What about a horse ... or pony ... anything else?"

Chap growled and huffed twice for "no." This time, it was not his voice in her head that made Wynn queasy.

"All right," she said uncertainly. "All right."

CHAPTER ELEVEN

"How long has she been gone?" Brot'an asked in Belaskian.

Leesil didn't care to answer. He didn't want Brot'an's pretended help. He didn't want the tall elf anywhere in sight—especially not trailing after them through Crijheäiche as they hurried in search of Wynn.

"We don't know," Magiere finally answered. "Not long . . . we hope."

Leesil could tell she was still spiteful that their weapons hadn't been returned.

Urhkar was already out in the forest, trying to find any trail left by the sage. Sgäile said majay-hì packs preferred to range the forest's depths in their leisure, so he was leading their search inland, away from the river. They all were in agreement that Wynn was likely far beyond the settlement's bounds. A human spotted wandering the community would have caused a disturbance.

They rounded a wide oak with a gnarled trunk, and Sgäile pulled up short. He held up his hand for everyone to stop.

A female elf, tall and impossibly thin, stood on the oak's far side before its curtained doorway. By what little light spilled out around the curtain, Leesil saw her filmy eyes as she raised one thin brow in calm puzzlement. She was elderly, dressed in a long maroon robe beneath a matching cloak. Pure white hair hung around her sunken cheeks as she leaned heavily upon a staff of rippled wood.

The old woman squinted at Leesil, studying him with silent interest.

Sgäile gave her a bow and turned away to move on.

"Who was that?" Leesil asked.

"Tosân'leag of the Avân'nûnsheach . . . the Ash River clan, known for their scholarly pursuits. They make fine paper and ink, such as my grandfather gave your companion." Sgäile hesitated, and then added, "Clan elders have been arriving for days. Word of your presence has spread. Humans have never been given passage in our land before. We must find your companion before they hear she is missing."

"And before Én'nish does," Magiere said under her breath.

Or before Wynn stumbled alone into a pack of majay-hì. Leesil only hoped Chap and the sage ran into each other first.

As they walked, Leesil saw more wide-bellied and gnarled oaks than in the few other parts of the settlement he'd seen. At night it wasn't easy to get a good look at Crijheäiche, but they'd been walking for a while and still hadn't reached its inland end. They passed many of the tree homes, but none of the canvas or otherwise handmade structures.

After a while, the domiciles thinned, and the forest ahead thickened beyond a clearing. When they stepped into the break in the trees, Leesil stood on the edge of a wide and shallow depression covered in low-trimmed grass.

The surrounding oaks weren't homes, as they had no openings, though their trunks were large enough for such. Their lowest branches were half the diameter of the trunks. They reached out level to either side and appeared grown together, forming living bridges from one tree to the next and encircling the depression. Leesil couldn't guess the purpose of this place, and Sgäile pushed on around the encompassing oaks.

A shadow moved upon one bridge-branch nearest the open forest. Sgäile slowed, and Leesil moved up beside him.

Sgäile stood in silence and watched the silhouette with narrowed eyes. The shadow dropped to the ground as two more stepped out into view. The trio approached.

All three were dressed as Anmaglâhk, but the one leading was shorter and slighter than the others.

Brot'an spoke in clear Belaskian. "Return to quarters. We have no need of your assistance."

"With respect, Greimasg'äh," the lead figure answered, "I join this pursuit at the request of the Covârleasa."

Her voice was thick with an Elvish accent.

Brot'an exhaled harshly, and Sgäile's shoulders sagged just a bit.

The trio came closer, and Leesil clearly made out the sharp features of Én'nish within her cowl. Her eyes remained on him as well.

Magiere inched forward. "What is she doing here?"

"No one can deny her," Sgäile admonished, with barely suppressed frustration in his voice.

"She acts on behalf of the Covârleasa," Brot'an added. "The 'selected and trusted adviser' of Most Aged Father . . . Fréthfâre."

"And you're going to let her come with us?" Magiere demanded.

Leesil didn't understand the bizarre command structure these Anmaglâhk followed, but he was sick of it. Were they expected to hand over the search for Wynn to this vengeance-driven woman?

Brot'an's passive gaze remained on Én'nish. "She will not interfere in a task not given to her."

Én'nish looked up at Brot'an in hesitation. In spite of his calm tone, his words sounded like a pointed reminder of her place.

"Yes, these visitors are most certainly Sgäilsheilleache's responsibility," Én'nish answered.

She nodded to Brot'an with respect. Her two companions did likewise. Whatever their twisted rules, Brot'an appeared to hold sway over all present.

"Get rid of her," Magiere demanded.

"Remember your place . . . human," Brot'an replied quietly, the last word selected with care but spoken with no malice. "You are a guest here by exception. If not for your companion's imprudence, we would all be at peace this night."

"Let it go," Leesil whispered to Magiere. "For now."

Privately, he wondered at how Fréth, and likely Most Aged Father, had learned so quickly of Wynn's disappearance, and why Én'nish was the one sent to intercept their search.

Brot'an stepped past Leesil and out ahead. Én'nish and her companions moved from his path. Sgäile followed more slowly, ushering Leesil and Magiere forward, keeping himself between them and Én'nish. They caught up to Brot'an, and Leesil looked over his shoulder as Én'nish and her followers fell in behind Osha. The young elf breathed a bit too deeply for so little exertion, and his eyes wandered nervously.

Leesil heard a chirping whistle.

They reached the far side of the tree-ringed depression, and Brot'an stood before the forest proper with his hands cupped around his mouth. He let out a birdlike series of chirps, waited a moment, and then issued another shrill call.

A longer whistling chirp answered him from the forest.

"Urhkarasiférin has found a trail," Sgäile said, as Brot'an took off at a run into the trees. "Stay close, and do not wander."

Most Aged Father lingered in that place between consciousness and slumber. He had listened to Léshil and his companions in their quarters, but the effort wore him down. He withdrew his awareness as their conversation waned and Léshil went off to bathe. But he had learned things about each—their personalities, their fumbling grasps at plans, and their nature for deception. Magiere disturbed him in particular.

She was filled with a strange agitation. She warranted more consideration and observance until he was done with Léshil. So much complication arose from humans. The world was polluted with their chaos and frailty.

Most Aged Father was so weary he did not hear Fréthfâre's footfalls until she entered his private chamber in the great oak's heart-root. She bowed. As always, he was pleased by her presence.

Until she rose up with dark concern plain on her face.

"There is trouble with the humans," she said, settling upon one teal-dyed cushion of *shéot'a* cloth. "I do not believe Sgäilsheilleache has firm control over them."

Her criticism of a fellow Anmaglâhk was disturbing. Most Aged Father valued all the Anmaglâhk, but he took greater pride in a few, such as Fréthfâre. Sgäilsheilleache was another, with his fierce devotion to his people and his strict sense of justice. Most Aged Father had known from the first time he set eyes on Sgäilsheillache that the boy was Anmaglâhk. Barely thirteen years old, he was only two moons past his name taking when he submitted himself for acceptance to the caste. He showed no fear at the prospect of training.

Taking Fréthfâre as Covârleasa had been a choice of careful consideration, and Most Aged Father valued her counsel. But he still expected good reason for her words against Sgäilsheilleache.

"One of the humans with Léshil—the small one—has gone missing," she said. "The majay-hì in their company has vanished as well. The human is believed to have gone into the forest, or so Én'nish reported. Sgäilsheilleache has gathered a hunting party to go after her, but he took Léshil and the pale woman with him. I have sent Én'nish with two others to join them."

Most Aged Father could not speak. He tried to sit up and failed, and the effort cost him.

"How long?" he demanded.

"Sometime after nightfall. I am not certain."

He was too tired for this foolishness. Of all his children, Sgäilsheilleache and Fréthfâre had done this. One unable to control the humans and the other compounding this new complication. Én'nish, who grieved the loss of her future mate, was the last who should be given any purpose involving Léshil.

Most Aged Father had been concerned when Sgäilsheilleache chose Urhkarasiférin to help escort Léshil. Én'nish was under the elder anmaglâhk's tutelage, and by caste law, the student always accompanied the teacher. Now that Urhkarasiférin had dismissed her, Én'nish was best kept far from Léshil—until Most Aged Father was done with him.

"Father?" asked Fréthfâre. He had been silent too long.

"Do not speak," Most Aged Father admonished her. "The humans are devious beyond understanding. Give me a moment to seek anomalies in the thread of life."

He had so little strength left, but it was unavoidable. He closed his eyes, worming his awareness through the forest's roots in the earth and into brush and tree and flower wherever he passed.

Nothing came to him at first, and then he felt the majay-hì. A pack loped at a fast pace behind one of the Listeners, the great silver deer, sentinels of the forest. Outrage rose in Most Aged Father.

The little human woman rode upon the deer's back.

The pack traveled purposefully, on a steady course as they wove through the forest. He followed them, slipping ahead to tree or bush whenever they outdistanced the present place of his awareness. The line they ran began to seed him with fear.

How could they know of such a destination?

Among the pack was the one majay-hì who had entered his home with Léshil.

Most Aged Father's eyes snapped open, and he tried to sit up.

"North," he cried out. "Catch Sgäilsheilleache and his charges at all costs. You will turn them back! Now!"

Fréthfâre spun up to her feet, startled by his tone.

Clan elders had been arriving for several days. Talk and rumor suggested they questioned his wisdom in allowing humans into the land for the first time. He could not let word of this wayward human's actions reach them as well.

And he could not allow any to reach the place they were headed.

"Go!" he cried out, his voice scratching the air. "None of them must reach Cuirin'nên'a's glade."

Sgäile burned with shame as he led the others through the trees. The fault was his alone.

He would never blame another serving under him—not even the naïve and immature Osha. It had been his own choice to assign the young elf as watchguard.

Osha had come later to service than most Anmaglâhk, and in the following five years, the young man had failed to attract the tutelage of a teacher among their caste. He remained a novice of only basic skills. Still, Osha wished to be of service, and Sgäile empathized with a desire that would not yield to any obstacle.

He had left Osha to watch over Léshil's quarters, and that decision resulted in the worst night of his life. Én'nish had been sent by Fréthfâre before Sgäile could resolve the crisis—which meant Most Aged Father knew everything.

It took no great feat of intelligence to guess how word had reached Most Aged Father. Én'nish must have been watching and waiting for an opportunity.

Sgäile grew sick to his stomach as they broke into a clearing where a large boulder protruded from a hillside. Halfway beyond the boulder's ledge top, Urhkarasiférin crouched upon the slope of thinly leafed elms.

"A pack was here," Brot'ân'duivé said, and Sgäile followed his gaze to the soft ground covered in paw prints. "And someone with small, human feet."

"Wynn?" Léshil asked.

Magiere stepped beyond Sgäile, pacing the ground with deep breaths.

"No blood," she said.

Sgäile was relieved, and then suspicious. Perhaps Chap had kept Wynn safe. But how, in the dark, had Magiere known no blood was spilled here? Léshil also watched her with wary concern. Én'nish hung back by the tree with her companions.

"Come," Sgäile said, and headed upslope. As he approached Urhkarasiférin, the elder anmaglâhk pointed through the elms to the northeast.

"At least seven . . . maybe eight majay-hì," he said. "Along with the woman . . . all making speed."

"And following a *clhuassas,*" Brot'ân'duivé added.

"What is that?" Magiere asked.

"One of the large silver-gray deer you have seen," Sgäile answered, and said no more. The less humans knew of such things, the better.

Leesil knelt down by the split hoof prints, larger than any deer-sign in human lands.

Sgäile rarely saw even subtle distress in Urhkarasiférin's passive expression. But the man tightened his lips with a slight scowl and breathed sharply out through his nose.

"North by northeast," he said.

Brot'ân'duivé already stared off through the trees along the path the pack had taken.

"What's out there," Léshil asked, "and why would Chap or Wynn try to follow them?"

"They are not following," Brot'ân'duivé corrected. "They are traveling with the pack . . . being taken . . . to Cuirin'nên'a."

Such a blunt statement stunned Sgäile. But if Léshil came with them, he needed to know the truth of the situation. It was only right and fair to prepare him, as the shock could cause discord later.

Léshil rose quickly from the deer tracks, his eyes on the path ahead. He took off down the trail.

"No," Brot'ân'duivé shouted, grabbing for Léshil.

Magiere slapped Brot'an's hand aside with a menacing glare and followed in Léshil's footsteps.

Sgäile was at a loss. He could not allow anyone near Cuirin'nên'a, though he understood why Brot'ân'duivé had told Léshil where the pack headed. He hoped they could catch the human woman before she and Chap reached Cuirin'nên'a.

It would be hard to turn Léshil aside, and harder still if he were in reach of his mother.

At least Brot'ân'duivé was with them—and that was

some comfort. Sgäile would need his wisdom and calm counsel.

Én'nish tried to step around and head up the trail. Before Sgäile intercepted her, Brot'ân'duivé cut her off.

"You may follow," he said, "but do not forget that guardianship belongs to Sgäilsheilleache. Do not interfere."

Urhkarasiférin, about to head onward, cast only a passing glance at the woman. But Sgäile had another concern. He reached out to stop Urhkarasiférin, touching the elder's shoulder.

"I left Leanâlhâm alone," Sgäile said. "Please stay with her, and tell her I will return when able."

Urhkarasiférin gave only the slightest cock of his head to betray his surprise. He was the elder of the two of them, yet only involved at Sgäile's request. The elder anmaglâhk nodded and headed back toward Crijheäiche.

Sgäile turned to catch up with Osha close behind him. He heard Én'nish and the other two following. For the first few steps, it struck him as odd that Fréthfâre or even Most Aged Father would send another trio of the caste to follow him in tracking down one small human.

He pushed the thought away and ran on.

Chap loped beside Lily, growing tired and sensing the same in her. At times, thickened brush between the trees made passage difficult. Wynn clung to the deer's back with nothing to grasp but the animal's coat of long hair. She bent forward against its shoulders and neck, trying to hang on.

The ink-shaded elder slowed without warning, and all of the pack pulled up around him. They dispersed among the undergrowth, and a few dropped to the ground panting, pink tongues lolling out of their mouths.

A rest had been called, and Chap was no less grateful than the others. Lily lay down on the forest floor, but Chap trotted over to Wynn and barked once. She still clung to the deer as it shifted from hoof to hoof.

Wynn looked so small upon the animal's back, no larger than a child might appear upon a full-grown horse. Her hair was tangled and her oval face smeared by clumps of kicked-up earth. She had no cloak and shivered in her light elven clothing.

Chap barked again, and Wynn lifted her head. She slid her far leg over the deer's haunches and tried to slide off its back. She ended up dropping to her rump when her feet hit the ground. Chap whined and pressed his head against her shoulder.

She was too weary and stiff to even put a hand on his head. Instead she crawled on hands and knees behind him as he returned to where Lily lay panting.

The pack lay in groups of two and three to share warmth. Wynn settled next to Lily, and Chap stretched out before both of them. Wynn reached out slowly and stroked Lily's back. Lily raised her ears once but did not object.

"She is beautiful," Wynn finally said. "All your kind are beautiful."

Chap looked into her weary face. He hoped for her sake—and his—they would not travel much farther in this manner.

"I thought that all of them would be like you—born Fay," Wynn added as she closed her eyes and lay back. "I did not know they would be so far removed—yet still like you."

He belly-crawled over to press his body against her. Winters here were far milder than beyond the mountains, yet the nights could be cool.

Chap found a strange moment of peace, considering what was at stake in this swift journey. With Wynn nestled between Lily and himself, it was good to lie on the earth of his birthplace. His eyes began to droop.

The first long baying rang through the night.

Several majay-hì stirred and got up as Chap opened his eyes. The sound rang out again, and he recognized it. The deer that had carried Wynn was still among the pack, yet this bellow came from farther off.

The deer lifted its head and issued an answering call. It turned and stalked toward the pack elder as Lily climbed to her feet. She joined them as the deer bent down to touch heads with the elder. Chap was too tired to try dipping into the exchange of memory. But when Lily returned to press her head to his, she whined in agitation. The flash of memory snapped Chap fully awake.

Gray-green-clad elves ran through the forest.

He could not see their faces clearly, for the image Lily gave him was not specific. Just anmaglâhk running in a line with purpose.

Why would she show him this? The answer came quickly to him. The Anmaglâhk were coming after them.

Wynn was still curled on the ground beside him. She had barely stirred at the deer's bellow. Chap ground his paws into the earth.

We are pursued.

Wynn thrashed over, grabbing her head. "Do not do that! Not unless I know it is coming!"

She sat up with a grimace and put a hand over her mouth. She looked at him as if he had poured a foul liquid in her mouth while she slept.

"What . . . what did you say?"

Chap repeated himself, and Wynn flinched slightly this time.

She looked back the way they had come. "How far?"

He barked three times rather than send more words to assault her. He had no idea how close the Anmaglâhk were.

He ran to the gray deer and barked once. Several of the majay-hì dashed on ahead, and if nothing else, Wynn knew they were on the move again. The deer stepped near a downed tree, and Wynn did not wait. She climbed onto its back and clutched its neck, and their race renewed. Chap took off beside Lily as the deer lunged ahead through the forest. The pace was now driven by urgency more than hope.

CHAPTER TWELVE

Wynn clung to the deer's neck, gripping its coarse hair until her fingers ached.

The majay-hì were relentless, and the pack ran all night. Wynn did her best to endure, but her legs cramped from gripping the deer's too-wide body.

She hoped dawn was not far off and kept her eyes down as much as possible. Each time she looked up, something ahead seemed as if she had just seen it behind, or to the side, or as if she'd never seen it before. Everything appeared foreign and unfamiliar in the night.

The dark forest pressed confusion into Wynn's mind. Trees flashed by like shadows. The only constants were the deer beneath her and the pack around and ahead of her. She clung to the sight of them against being overwhelmed and lost.

Wynn had no idea what they would find at the journey's end. If she and Chap came upon some elven prison, how would they gain entrance? But if—when—they reached Nein'a, Chap would definitely need her. As far as Wynn knew, Leesil's mother was unaware of Chap's true nature. Wynn would be needed to speak with her. How else could Chap relate that Leesil was among the elves and intended to free her?

She tried to shift her aching legs, but they were spread too far across the deer's wide back. Her backside was growing numb.

The black-gray pack leader slowed and the others with him. The deer's gait decreased to a steady clomp, and Chap circled back to walk below Wynn.

"Are we close?" she asked. "We must be close. It has been so long...."

When she looked ahead, the forest had thickened across their path. As the deer carried her closer, the pack spread out to the sides.

Birches of ever-peeling bark grew close together. Their branches intertwined one into the next beneath thousands of leaves. Through their tangling masses, elm and ash trees rose, exposing their tops above. Below, brambles and blackberry vines glistened with thorns and filled the spaces between the trees' trunks.

Everything was silent, without even a breeze or the vibrant creak of a cricket.

Wynn looked off to her left. The tangled woods stretched out into the darkness. When she turned the other way, the trees ahead appeared to have shifted to different positions among the strangling underbrush. When she turned left again, a clump of saw grass had sprouted through the thorny tendrils of a blackberry bush.

Had it been there, or had it appeared when she was not looking? The top of a cedar spread above the birches, dark and still, and she did not remember seeing it before. Was the forest toying with her again?

Wynn looked hopelessly about but saw no way through. Why had the pack or even the deer come this way, if this old growth barred the path? The way this wall of vegetation climbed and burrowed through itself was not natural.

The pack elder paced before the dense growth, and the other dogs trotted aimlessly about, arching necks and raising ears as they peered into it. The deer rolled its shoulders and shifted nervously beneath Wynn's thighs. It snorted and shook its antlered head.

These animals were as puzzled and disturbed as Wynn was. They had not seen this before.

The elder paced left along the wood's border and then suddenly lunged into it.

Wynn heard the rustle of leaves and bending vines from within the dense woods. The sound grew to a thunder of creaking branches and thrashing leaves. She grabbed the deer's coarse hair tightly as it back-stepped from the raucous sound.

A chokeberry bush ripped apart as the dark elder leaped out. Berries scattered in his wake like small black pellets. He stumbled, favoring one foreleg, and turned to stare back at the barrier. The rest of the pack circled hesitantly.

Lily turned right and darted for a birch of peeling bark, its lowest branches tangled in climbing blackberry vines.

"No!" Wynn cried out.

Chap went after Lily, but not before she tried thrashing her way into the thorny vines. She quickly retreated, never getting deeper than her shoulders.

Wynn shivered anxiously.

Chap remained on the barrier's edge as Lily arced around behind him. He rumbled softly in frustration. They could go back but not forward.

Wynn wondered if these woods were a safeguard, blocking trespassers from reaching Nein'a. But then how could a prisoner be fed and cared for? Or had Nein'a been left here to die, long ago? Had the elves lied to Leesil just to bring him within reach?

Chap's growl rose to a snarl and startled Wynn as nausea hit her. Soft buzzing grew like a birch leaf skittering about within her skull.

Fay . . . my kin . . . now they choose to return.

Wynn slipped from the deer's back. Nausea became vertigo, and she dropped to her knees, struggling under the chorus of leaf-wings.

The last time she had heard this was at the northern gate of Soladran as Chap communed with his kin, the Fay.

Chap quickly brushed heads with Lily and then bolted into the open forest behind them. Wynn tried to get up, hand over her mouth, to stumble after him, but Lily raced around to block her way.

Before Wynn cried out to Chap, his single leaf-winged voice crackled in her mind.

I am here . . . show yourselves, my kin . . . I demand it!

Chap ran blindly through the trees, searching. But not with eyes and ears and nose.

His Spirit expanded in rage, reaching in all directions, until he felt them as he had upon staring into the dense barrier woods.

That warped growth should not be there. He had seen this in Lily's memory flash. No majay-hì had ever encountered such a tangled mesh and it was coated with the tingle of Chap's kin.

They tried to stop the majay-hì—stop him—from reaching Nein'a.

Show yourselves! Answer me . . . now!

His coat rippled under a breeze whirling downward from the night sky. It increased to a strong wind, encircling him as it ripped up mulch. He pulled up short amid a hushed chatter of branches and turned a tight circle with a low rumble. The wind settled to a breeze once more.

Chap stood in a small clearing loosely walled by sycamores and beeches grown tall from roots sunk deep into the earth. Their branches interlaced like the limbs of sentinels holding hands, and movement within them made those limbs sway slightly.

He would not cower before them.

Why interfere now, when you have been silent . . . so useless? Why return after abandoning me for so long?

Branches behind him shook softly, and he wheeled about. Leaves rustling in the low whirling breeze shaped to a chorus of voices in his mind.

Further and further you stray from your path . . . your purpose . . . to keep the sister of the dead in ignorance and away from the Enemy.

Chap rumbled at one birch. A bend in its trunk looked too much like a figure seated in judgment. His shoulders tightened as he half-crouched to lunge.

Leesil is necessary to my task . . . our need. But his suffer-

ing serves no purpose. So why bar my way? Why can he not free his mother?

A long vine of red hyacinth rustled.

Return to your task. . . . Return to the sister of the dead. . . . Leave this land and keep her far from her maker's reach.

That was no answer. In what other place could Magiere be farther from the Enemy's reach?

The hyacinth rustled more softly.

You have told your mortal charges far too much. So much that they might well turn upon a path that would end this world. Tell them no more, and take them from this place.

Chap's rumble grew. All Leesil wanted was freedom for his last remaining family. To be with his mother once again. Yet Chap's kin became obsessed with inaction.

And why could he not remember . . . more?

Bits and pieces learned in his mortal life still did not fit together. He did not retain enough awareness from existence among his kin to bind those pieces and fill in the gaps.

The branches shuddered around him.

You have taken flesh and lost our full awareness. Trust the path . . . trust in us. In flesh, you cannot understand all things.

Chap wavered in silence. He had relinquished eternity to follow the will of his kin. Once he must have known and agreed with their purpose, but now he could not remember why.

There must have been a reason . . . one that he had forgotten.

Wynn controlled her vertigo and tried to rush around Lily. Each time, the dog shifted or barked in warning and would not let her pass.

A chorus of a thousand shuddering and crackling leaves erupted within Wynn's head.

You have taken flesh and lost our full awareness. Trust the path . . . trust in us. In flesh, you cannot understand all things.

Wynn collapsed, wracked with dry heaves. She stared

into the shifting dark trees on hands and knees, shaking uncontrollably. She heard the Fay communing with Chap.

His snarling howl rolled through the forest.

Wynn turned toward Lily. "Oh please, just get out of my way!"

Lily cocked her ears. Wynn crawled to a nearby cedar and clawed up its rough bark to her feet. The others of the pack ranged around her, but none came near. They only watched her and Lily in puzzlement.

Before Lily could react, Wynn lunged around the cedar's far side toward the sound of Chap's cry.

Chap quivered as his howl faded from his ears. Why did his kin treat him like a servant who owed blind obedience?

He had been one of them—one with them. He saw no possible harm in a son finding the mother who birthed and raised him. Nein'a did not want to see harm come to this world any more than the Fay, even though she had raised a son in her own caste's ways for her own purposes.

Chap's shudders faded, and he paced a slow circle, studying the sentinel trees. No voices came on the low rustling breeze. But they were still there—still waiting for him to acquiesce.

This had nothing to do with keeping Magiere from the enemy.

Why do you fear Leesil reaching his mother?

Chap's question rang in Wynn's head.

She spun around, lost once again with nothing to guide her. She had not taken one step. Yet if her eyes turned away for an instant, a vine, that patch of moss, or even the bare spot of earth to one side appeared to have moved.

Take the sister of the dead and leave. Go back to the human realms and never return to this land.

Wynn shut her eyes and threw her arms around an aspen trunk to keep from falling. The leaf-wing chorus drowned all other sensations. But she heard wind rustling branches not far off.

She opened her eyes, turning her face toward the sound, but Lily stood blocking her way. Wynn remembered Chap briefly touching heads with the white female. He had somehow told Lily to keep her behind.

"You must let me pass," Wynn whispered, uncertain how to make Lily understand.

Chap had communicated somehow with this dog. With Wynn's new ability to hear him and perhaps even communicate with him, she wondered if she might do the same with Lily.

She inched forward, trying to pick up any thoughts from Lily. She did not believe Chap could read her own verbal thoughts—when they communicated, she spoke aloud, and he projected words into her mind.

"Lily," she said. "Can you understand me?"

Lily stared at her intently, but the white dog seemed only to be acting as guardian, and Wynn heard nothing in her mind as she did with Chap.

Wynn closed her eyes, this time trying to reach inside Lily's mind. There must be some way to connect and express her desperate need to reach Chap! But she felt nothing and saw nothing. Lily was not like Chap.

They could not speak to each other.

Wynn grabbed for Lily. The dog hopped away and spun about to face her again. Lily's shift was in the same general direction as the sound of chattering branches.

Wynn might not be able to navigate the forest—but Lily could. The dog betrayed Chap's path in every attempt to keep Wynn from following. Wynn tottered forward and grabbed for Lily again.

This time Lily did not hop away. She turned with ears perked to look through the trees. Wynn settled her hand on Lily's back.

A shudder ran through the dog's slender body, but her attention remained fixed toward the sound they both heard.

"Chap," Wynn whispered and pushed Lily forward. Had the dog heard Wynn use that name enough to know it? Wynn repeated it, again and again.

Lily took one step, her crystalline eyes focused off into the forest, and whined.

Wynn could see Lily was afraid, but she shoved the dog forward.

Lily stepped slowly at first, weaving from tree to tree and peering around each before moving on. Wynn followed the white majay-hì as her only guide.

Chap's awareness sharpened to the presence of his kin. Within leaf and needle, branch and bark, and the air and earth, he felt their presence—their strained anticipation.

He let them wait.

Finally the breeze snapped sharply. The rustle of leaves was laced with the clatter of branches.

The elven mother is not important. Take your charges from here, and keep them in ignorance. Regain your faith in us.

Again no answer for Leesil's concern—and too much denial of Nein'a.

Even if Leesil fulfilled this blind scheme of his mother and her dissidents, why would Chap's kin not want such an Enemy to fall?

In his mind, he found no memory of his kin's concern for Leesil—only for Magiere.

From the moment of Chap's birth, he had known what to do concerning Magiere, and that a half-blood boy would be the means to that end. But he knew nothing of this hidden and evasive concern over Leesil and Nein'a.

Taking flesh was not the cause of this.

It was not the failing of his mortal mind to keep what he would have known among his own kind. Something more had happened in the infinitesimal instant between his place among his kin and being born into this world.

Why will you not speak of Leesil?

Only silence.

Why can I not remember this?

Unseen small creatures scurried among the branches and made dark spaces between them flex like mouths with lips of leaves and needles.

You are flesh, frail and faltering. Your heart and earthly senses weaken your purpose. It is little more than what we feared.

Chap cringed—but not from their admonishment. He

remembered the first part of this journey as he had tried to lead Leesil to his mother.

In the deep winter of the Broken Range, in cold and hunger, Chap's kin had ignored his pleas for aid. Only the high-pitched whistle of an unknown savior had led him and those in his care to the caves. His kin had done nothing to save them. Even with Magiere at risk among the elves, these an'Cróan, the Fay had remained silent.

Now they showed themselves only to bar Chap's way to Nein'a.

What better way to keep Magiere from the hands of the Enemy than to allow her to die?

Whether in those mountains or among a hostile people, it would simply be her fate and none of the Fay's doing.

How badly his kin wished to keep Leesil from his mother. Would they allow Leesil to die as well, so long as it served some purpose Chap could not remember?

And why could he not recall the answers? Such vital knowledge could not have just slipped from him.

Chap closed his eyes. His Spirit screamed like a wail that shook his body.

Betrayers . . . deceivers . . . you took this from me!

His own kin. They had cut his memories like a blade severing flesh and bone. They had ripped out pieces of him, tearing away any awareness they did not want him to have.

All in the moment he had chosen to be born.

Chap opened his eyes and cast his gaze about the clearing, looking for something to rend and tear.

He froze at the sight of Wynn clinging to a tree beside Lily.

The sage's olive-toned face was a mask of horror, and streams of tears ran down her cheeks as she stared at him.

Wynn heard the entire exchange. In communion with his kin, even some of Chap's inner words to himself had chattered softly in her head.

He was supposed to be one of them—a Fay.

Through him, Wynn had come to believe that whatever they truly were, they worked for a worthy purpose. Chap had been sent to save Magiere—and Leesil as well, in some way.

But the Fay had used Chap. They had left him and all those with him to die. Even her, as she dangled over that gorge, half frozen in a blizzard, while the others tried to save her.

The wind died instantly into chilling silence.

Chap's voice rose like a shout in Wynn's thoughts.

Run!

Chap bolted straight at Wynn as the air churned with growing force.

She had been listening—a mortal eavesdropping upon the Fay.

Mulch and twigs swept up to join leaves torn from above in a growing, spinning circle of wind. Debris pelted Chap from all sides, obscuring his sight. He fought to stay on his feet and keep Wynn and Lily in sight.

She is an innocent!

No answer came.

Lily snatched the leg of Wynn's breeches and pulled on the sage. Wynn toppled to the ground, shielding her face as sheared-off branches battered against her.

Chap heard an aching creak of wood and the tearing of earth. Within the crackle of snapping branches, his kin shouted in outrage.

Abomination!

He shook off their malice and then realized it was not aimed at him. A birch tree at the clearing's edge teetered toward Wynn.

Earth around its trunk heaved upward. Deep roots tore free, slinging sod and mulch in the air. The birch tipped and arced downward, ripping through the branches of other trees as it fell directly toward Wynn.

As Chap tried to run toward her, something dark and long whipped at him in the corner of his vision. He swerved and ducked.

Wynn grabbed Lily's neck and scrambled with kicking legs. Dog and sage rolled away in a tangle as the birch's trunk slammed to the earth. The impact sent a shudder through the ground. Lily yelped and Wynn cried out as both vanished beneath the tree's leaves and flailing limbs.

He charged for the downed tree with the wind's roar filling his ears.

Something heavy and hard lashed the whole side of his body. The world flashed in a painful white . . . and then black.

Chap's vision cleared, and he lay slumped on the ground. Leaves, stripped from the birch's branches in the wind, churned in a vortex that filled the clearing.

Around the downed tree's base, dark forms writhed.

Its roots moved. Wide and sluggish where they joined the huge knot at the tree's trunk, their tapering bulk bent and curled like earth-stained serpents upon the ground. Two wormed their way along the trunk and into the bulk to the birch's leaves.

Chap had so fully focused on the toppling birch that he had not seen its roots come alive. One of them must have struck him down. He squirmed on the ground, trying to get up.

Wynn screamed from somewhere beneath the birch's remaining leaves.

Wynn heard Lily struggling to escape, but she could not see the dog among the cloud of leaves and branches pinning her to the ground. She tried to roll off her back and crawl out.

Her left leg snapped straight, and her back flattened against the ground.

Something curled and twisted up Wynn's leg, and her breath began to race. It crushed inward around her calf. Wynn screamed out in pain under its grinding pressure.

Leaves dangling against her face turned blue-white as her mantic sight surged up.

Lily's howl pierced Wynn's ears, and a chorus of leaf-wings roared in her skull.

Abomination! Sick thing that spies on us. Your taint rises in your flesh.

The grip on her leg jerked hard, and Wynn slid across the ground. Leaves and branches lashed her face and arms.

The near-blue mist of Spirit permeating the leaves turned to a blur. She clutched desperately at branches only to have them bend and snap in her hands.

Wynn hooked her arm around the base of one branch and held on. The ache in her knee spiked into her hip as her whole body was pulled straight. A snarling and thrashing rose among the leaves above her.

Before Wynn's eyes, the mist of Spirit moved within the tree's bark.

It burned with a brilliance she had seen before, but only when she had looked upon Chap with her mantic sight.

Flowing blue-white wormed back and forth through the wood, as if alive and willful.

You hear us . . . listen to what is not for a mortal to know. Now you see us, yes? And you should not!

Leaves above Wynn's head split apart. A head glowing with blue-white mist shoved through at her face. Wynn almost lost her grip in fright, until she saw crystalline eyes.

One of the majay-hì snatched her tunic's shoulder with its teeth.

Chap heard Lily howl and then saw Wynn's legs emerge from the branches near the tree's base. A root was wrapped tightly around her shin and knee. Chap righted himself and staggered toward her as the pack bolted out of the forest from all sides.

Three dogs dove into the tree's bulk as the dark elder spun out in the clearing. He wove back and forth before the thrashing roots. Chap called to his kin.

Stop! You are discovered, but harming a mortal will change nothing.

Clinging dirt scattered from the roots as they rose in the air. One came down hard, rolling along the ground toward Chap.

He scuttled aside as the root lashed the earth, and mulch sprayed across his body.

The dark elder rushed in. His jaws snapped sharply over the root's narrow end and severed through it.

Chap's panic washed away in growing rage. His kin would not listen to him, and they tried to take Wynn. All because she had heard them and caught their deception, as he had. Lily hopped free from the birch's leaves, and two majay-hì followed after her.

One root rose high into the night. It lashed over backward into the mass of the downed tree. Leaves exploded upward under a clatter of snapping branches and a screeching yelp.

The root gripping Wynn coiled and jerked, and the sage spun out across the clearing. The shoulder of her tunic was torn open.

Three of the pack had gone in after Lily and Wynn, but only two had come out.

Chap rushed toward Wynn as his anger burst forth at his kin.

Now you injure your own children who took flesh long ago? It is you who have lost your way!

Wynn lay stunned as the root coiled up her leg, reaching for her torso. Its tip passed her chest, reaching for her throat, and Chap seized it, biting deep. He ripped hard, shredding it with his teeth. Another root arched upward from the tree's base, and he whirled to grip Wynn's tunic.

The root arced downward as Lily appeared beside him. She took hold of Wynn beside him, and they both lunged backward, jerking the sage away. The root cracked down on bare earth, sending a shudder up Chap's legs.

He rushed into the open clearing before the tree's exposed base. He ground his paws through the scattered leaves and rooted himself amid the whirling wind.

No more will suffer for your hidden schemes.

He felt the elemental surge of Earth and Air, the moisture of Water within them, and even Fire from the heat of his own flesh. They mingled with Spirit from his own body as he closed on his kin.

Wynn tumbled across the ground. Then a crash filled her ears and thunder shook through the earth beneath her. She rolled over to find Lily beside her and saw Chap bolt out into the clearing.

She cowered for an instant at the sight of the tree's roots

writhing in the air. Beyond Chap, the pack elder and two more majay-hì made quick darting passes as they taunted the roots. Each dog was two overlaid images in Wynn's mantic sight. Within their silver-gray forms glowed Spirit of blue-white mist. But not the tree and its roots—and not Chap.

The whiter essence of the Fay moved like shifting vapors within that dark-stained wood. And Chap was the only singular form Wynn saw.

One whole shape, glowing with brilliance. His fur glistened like luminous threads of white silk in the moonlight, and his eyes scintillated as if holding a light of their own.

And the light of him began to burn.

Wynn did not know what he was doing, but her eyes started to sting. She grabbed Lily with both hands to hold the dog back.

Trails of white mist rose from Chap like vapor in the shape of flames. Wynn squinted against the pain of his light, but could not take her eyes off of him. He stalked inward, low and tight, toward the base of the tree.

The pack elder and his companions pulled up short. They backed away with their eyes on Chap. The roots in the air quivered in hesitation, and then one cracked downward.

Wynn stopped breathing as it fell directly upon Chap.

In a burning blur, he leaped out of its path. The root hit the earth, and Wynn felt the impact beneath her. Before it could coil back again, Chap threw himself on it.

Through the white mist of his form, she thought she saw his jaws close upon the arching root.

And the light of his body flashed.

Wynn cringed as if stepping from a pitch black room into full sunlight. A thousand leaf-wings crackled inside her head. She heard only screeching blind panic and no words. Chap's lone voice rose above them.

I will tear you . . . rend you . . . I will swallow down your severed pieces into nothing!

Wynn clung to Lily as her sight slowly returned. Swirling colored blotches marred everything in the night. She barely made out Chap's muted form pacing before the birch's base.

But Chap was the only thing moving.

If you come again for me or mine . . . I will come for you!

Slowly Wynn's sight cleared more and more. Her mantic vision gone, all she saw in the moonlight was Chap standing tense and watchful.

The gnarled ball of the birch's base towered before him, but its roots extended in stillness as if the tall tree had just toppled. No hint of wind stirred the stray leaves fluttering to the ground.

Chap stood rigid, as Wynn crawled toward him on hands and knees.

His kin were gone.

Chap felt the vibrancy slowly fade from his body. He had turned on his own kind. He could taste them like blood in his mouth.

No, not his kin. Not anymore.

He wanted no more of them. They cared nothing for the lives they toyed with in silent schemes for a world they claimed was theirs. They would sacrifice those he had come to care for—all for some purpose they would not share with him.

In their vicious complacency, they cut him apart and left only those pieces that served them best.

Gentle fingers threaded through the fur on his back and up his neck.

Wynn knelt beside him, her face scratched and dirty. One abrasion on her hand and a shallow cut in the side of her forehead left smeared blood on her skin. She looked small and frail.

"I am sorry," she choked out. "I meant no harm . . . no offense. I worried for you, when I heard what they said . . . what you said."

He looked in her brown eyes. She had nothing to be sorry for. What was happening to her—her sight, the way she now heard him—was not her fault. He only wished he understood why it was happening or how to stop it.

Lily crept in, leaning around Wynn to sniff at him cautiously. The rest of the pack stayed at a distance and would not come near.

Had they seen him turn on his own kin? Did they look at him now as some being they did not recognize, which hid within a deceptively familiar form?

Only the inky black elder stalked through the open clearing. His gaze stayed on Chap until he was close, and then his grizzled muzzle lifted toward Wynn. He trotted quickly off into the branches of the fallen birch, but at least he no longer growled at the sage in disapproval.

Lily stretched out her muzzle, sniffing Chap again. He lowered his head. How would she now see him?

The warmth of her tongue slid up his jowl and across the bridge of his nose. But relief made him suddenly weary.

"You are not alone, Chap," Wynn whispered. "That will never happen."

A long mournful howl rose from the downed birch.

Chap lifted his head, and he, Lily, and Wynn looked to where the elder had slipped between the branches. When the pack had come, three had gone in after Lily and Wynn.

But only two had emerged.

CHAPTER THIRTEEN

Chane turned his horse around a jagged stone out-crop. He followed Welstiel each night southeast into the Crown Range as directed by the old Móndyalítko couple. At any moment, he expected one of their mounts to drop.

The beasts moved slower with each passing dusk. Welstiel did not appear to notice and pressed on relentlessly.

On a few evenings they had awoken trapped within the tent by heavy snowfall. Chane dug them out, but once it was so severe they spent the night inside. Not a pleasant night, for any delay aggravated Welstiel.

Tonight was cold but calm, and Chane reined in his horse as Welstiel suddenly halted to look up at the stars.

"How much farther?" Chane asked.

Welstiel shook his head. "Until we see signs of a ravine. What did the woman say—like a giant gouge in the mountainside?"

"Yes," Chane answered.

For half the journey, Welstiel seemed lost in thought. The last time Chane had heard the man talk in his sleep was the morning he awoke shouting; since then, Welstiel's dreams had grown infrequent. He had also nearly ceased any pretense of grooming. Dark hair hung lank down his forehead, and his once fine cloak continued deteriorating. Chane's was no better.

"I should look for a place to set up the tent," he said.

Welstiel just stared at the night sky.

Chane urged his mount onward, searching for natural shelter. It was some relief to be alone for a moment, as he believed Welstiel might well be going mad.

The man's state of mind grew worse each night, though at times he was as lucid as the first time Chane met him. They passed the time with Chane's lessons in Numanese, not perfectly enjoyable, but it broke the silent tension and kept Welstiel's wits from wandering. And Chane now spoke Wynn's native tongue in short but complete sentences.

Welstiel had made sure they would not starve, but feeding through his arcane methods was hardly satisfying. How a Noble Dead could settle for such bland and unpleasant sustenance was beyond Chane.

Chane's thoughts often slipped to the memory of a stimulating hunt: the taste of flesh between his teeth and blood on his tongue, and how his pleasure sharpened with the fear of his prey. Welstiel's method might last longer, and was necessary under their circumstances, but he appeared to prefer it. Chane would never understand.

He dismounted and trekked up the rocky slope to an overhang below a sheer face of granite. It would do for the day. He could tie off the canvas on the overhang's projections, weight the bottom edge with stones, and create a makeshift chamber. The extra room would be a small luxury, so he returned to his horse and began untying the rolled canvas.

He paused to scan the firs with their sparse branches and listen to the last of the night, but he heard only the coarse wind gusting across the mountainside. He dreaded another dormant day, locked in by the sun with Welstiel, only to emerge into another night of icy winds on an exhausted mount. Language lessons were his only respite.

Chane closed his eyes indulgently, his thoughts drifting forward. . . .

In Malourné, across the western ocean and the next continent, lay the founding home of the Guild of Sagecraft. Educated men and women would walk old and sound stone passages in robes of light gray. What libraries and archives they would have, tables full of scrolls, parchments, and books, all lit by the glow of cold lamp crystals.

He saw himself there.

Red-brown hair clean and combed behind his ears, he studied an ancient parchment. Not a carefully scribed copy, but the original, unearthed in some far and forgotten place.

The familiar scent of mint tea drifted into his nostrils. He looked up to see Wynn walking toward him, carrying a tray. She offered a soft smile only for him. Her wispy brown hair was woven in a braid down her back, and her olive skin glowed in the crystal's light.

She set down the tray with its two steaming cups. He wanted to smile back, but he could not. He could only drink in the sight of her face. She reached out and touched his cheek softly. The warmth of her hand made him tremble. She sat beside him, asking him questions as her eyes roved the parchment. They talked away the night, until Wynn's eyelids drooped little by little as she grew too sleepy. In that still and perfect moment, he lingered between watching her sleep and carrying her to her room.

Chane's horse neighed wildly. He opened his eyes at the first growl, and the vision of Wynn vanished.

Downslope between the wind-bent trees, wild dogs approached. He had neither heard nor smelled them while lost in wishful fantasy.

Six dogs, their eyes on him and the horse, snarled as they wove closer through the sparse foliage.

Most were black with hints of brown and slate gray, but each bore patches of bare skin where their fur thinned from starvation. Yellow eyes were glazed with hunger, and their ribs showed beneath shrunken and sagging skin.

The horse tossed its head and tried to retreat, sending stones tumbling downslope.

Chane snatched the reins and reached across the saddle for his sword slung from the saddle horn. He wondered how the dogs survived this far up with so little to eat. He closed a hand on the sword's hilt, and the two closest dogs charged for the horse's legs. Chane ducked away from the bucking mount as the lead dog sprang.

Its forelegs hooked across the horse's shoulders, and its teeth clacked wildly for a grip. The second dog charged from the front, snapping at the horse's legs. The horse screamed and reared. Before Chane could swing at either dog, another snarl sounded from behind him.

A skeletal dog was in midleap when he turned. He side-stepped and swung.

His longsword bit halfway through its neck.

The animal hit the slope and slid, smearing earth and rock with spattering blood. Another dog collided into Chane's back, and he toppled facedown.

Teeth closed on the base of his neck as his horse screamed under the growls of other dogs.

Chane released his sword and rolled, pinning the dog beneath his back, but it did not let go. He felt his skin tear as he wrenched his elbow back. The dog's jaws released with a gagging yelp at the muffled crack of its ribs. Chane turned onto his knees, pinned the dog's head, and shattered its skull with his fist.

His horse was down. Four remaining dogs tore savagely at it, and the mount's weak cries reduced to gasping whimpers.

All the dogs suddenly stopped and fell silent. Their bloodied muzzles lifted in unison.

Welstiel stood beyond them, the reins of his horse in hand. His expression was marred with livid disbelief.

"Why did you not stop them," he demanded, "instead of rolling about yourself like some rabid mongrel?"

"I was stopping . . . ," Chane answered in his nearly voiceless hiss. "There were too many to get all of them quickly enough."

"You are Noble Dead," Welstiel said with disgust. "You can control such beasts with a thought."

Chane blinked. "I do not possess that ability. Toret told me that our kind develop differing strengths—given time. That is not one of mine."

Welstiel's disgust faded, and he shook his head. His resignation made him look older.

"Yes . . . it is." He studied the dogs and then Chane's chest. "Do you still wear one of your small urns?"

Chane grasped the leather string slick with his own black fluids still running down his neck. He pulled it until a small brass urn dangled free of his shirt.

Welstiel stepped closer and the dogs remained still as he passed. "Leave one alive to take as a familiar. It can track ahead and perhaps aid in our search."

He turned away, glancing once at the dying horse with a weary sigh.

It was a sound Chane always found strange to hear from an undead, even when he did it himself. They breathed only when needing to speak, and a sigh was but a habit left over from living days.

"We'll walk and use my horse for the baggage," Welstiel said. "Collect what remains of your horse's feed, and roast its flesh to store for your new familiar."

Chane picked up his sword. It all sounded sensible and rational, but the scent of blood was thick around him. His hunger stirred, though he had no need for sustenance.

Dog and horse—lowly beasts—but the mount had served Chane, and the pack only sought to survive. He understood that, and it left him strangely disturbed as he skewered the first dog with the tip of his blade. Even at its yelp, the others just stood there, waiting to be slaughtered.

He did not pick or choose and merely killed the dogs one by one within reach, until the last stood cowering before him. He closed his eyes and imagined once more . . .

A quiet place in the world where Wynn's round face glowed by the light of a cold lamp crystal. Her eyes drooped in sleep over the parchment, and he reached out for her. . . .

Wynn returned with Chap and Lily to the barrier woods. The silver deer was gone, but the remainder of the pack ranged about.

Her face and hands stung from scratches, and her left leg ached, but she limped along. These injuries seemed paltry compared to the majay-hì found broken and dead beneath the birch's branches. The steel-gray female had come for her as the Fay tried to drag her out to her death. Now her twin brother wandered listlessly among the trees, barely in sight of the others.

Of all things Wynn had faced, from vampires to Lord Darmouth and his men, the Fay's sudden wrath terrified her most. It was so unexpected.

Before discovering Chap, she had considered the Fay to be little more than an ideological personification of the elemental forces that composed her world. In knowing Chap and coming to believe in what he was, she had thought the Fay benevolent if enigmatic, much like him.

They had killed a majay-hì because she had heard them and learned how they had used Chap.

The world now made far less sense to Wynn.

Chap stepped up to the brambles filling the trees of the barrier woods. He ground his paws into the earth. Wynn did not need mantic sight to guess what he did.

She had seen the silken vapor of spectral white fire rise around Chap as he faced his kin. When he turned on them to defend her, his body had flashed and blinded her for an instant. His kin had fled in fear.

He annoyed her so many times with his doggish behavior, slovenly and gluttonous habits that made it difficult to remember what he was. When he chomped a greasy sausage, she did not see how anything descended from the eternal could be so . . . disgusting.

But he was Fay—and now outcast. Perhaps traitor as well to his eternal kin, though they deserved no better.

Chap clamped his teeth upon a bisselberry vine, and Wynn watched in chilled fascination.

Round berries receded to flowers and then to small buds among the vine's broad leaves and long thorns. Leaves shrank in size and thorns shortened as both faded into light green stems. The vine's branching parts withdrew as they shrank in size.

Wynn watched its wild maturity turn back to infancy as the thorny plant grew younger and smaller. It receded into the earth from whatever fallow seed it had sprouted.

"You reverse the course of life?" Wynn whispered.

Chap stepped into the hollow left by the vines, and the leaf-wing whispered in Wynn's head.

Only to take my kin's touch . . . what they leave of their will upon the world . . . as I took the pieces of them reaching for you.

She had grown accustomed to picking meaning from his multitongued voice, though it still made her stomach roll. The inky elder followed Chap inward. Wynn stepped in with Lily, and the other majay-hì came behind.

Dawn grew to day as Chap led them, tunneling through the barrier woods. Wynn watched in awe as again and again he bit and licked its altered life into retreat. The sun had nearly cleared the treetops when the last bramble curled away before Chap. Wynn stepped out behind him through a patch of enormous verdant ferns with fronds reaching up taller than her head.

She emerged at a clearing's edge where the ground was covered in soft emerald grass. Here and there patches of darker moss were thick and spongy. At the center was a domicile elm as wide and massive as any oak or cedar in Crijheäiche. Beside its curtained opening sat a stool and a basket filled with white lumps. A small brook gurgled across the clearing several paces beyond the tree.

At the water's edge, a slender woman perched upon a wide saffron cushion. With her back turned, she did not notice the visitors.

Bright sunlight turned her hair nearly white, and its long glossy tresses hung forward over one caramel-colored shoulder. The folds of her shimmering wrap were pulled down, and she was naked to the waist. She washed with a square of tan felt in one narrow hand.

Wynn thought she saw lighter scars in the skin of the woman's back, as if she had been clawed by an animal long ago.

As the majay-hì wormed around Wynn and into the clearing, Chap hesitantly stepped across the green.

The woman paused and turned just a little. White-blond hair slipped from her shoulder and swung down her back almost to the cushion. She set down the felt and pulled up her wrap. Chap barked loudly and ran forward, and the woman whirled to her feet, even taller than Wynn had first guessed.

Wynn had seen elven women both here and on her continent, but none like this one.

Her face was triangular like all elves', though its long angles swept in soft curves down to a narrow jaw and chin. Her skin was flawless but for the scars Wynn had seen. White-blond eyebrows swept out and up above her temples like downy feathers upon her brow. A long delicate nose ended above a small mouth a shade darker than her skin.

Her almond-shaped eyes were large, even for her own kind.

She did not seem quite real.

"Chap?" the woman said.

He scurried to her side and rubbed into her legs a bit too hard. She crouched down and lifted an uncertain hand under his muzzle. Chap twisted his head to drag her palm and long fingers over his face.

This was Leesil's mother—Nein'a—Cuirin'nên'a, as her own people called her.

Wynn found it difficult to see her as one of the Anmaglâhk, spy and assassin, let alone a traitor to her caste or people. And Nein'a did not appear to be imprisoned.

She finally looked up at Wynn. An instant of surprise passed over her fine features before she turned with narrow-eyed suspicion to study the surrounding trees. The majay-hì spread across the green, sniffing about, and their ease in her glade seemed to calm her.

Wynn approached cautiously, uncertain how she would be received.

Nein'a stood, looking down upon the sage.

"How does a human come here?" she said in Belaskian. "And where did you find this dog?"

Beneath cold demand was an unsteady quiver in her voice.

"I came with Chap," Wynn said, "as did Leesil. He is here among your people, trying to find you . . . and free you."

Nein'a blinked once as her expression flattened. "That is

not possible. He would not be allowed among the an'Cróan . . . no more than you would, girl!"

Wynn had not expected such cold and sharp words from her, though Nein'a had been alone for a long time.

"Chap brought us through the mountains. Sgäile came to escort us by the request of Most Aged Father. I swear to . . ."

At the patriarch's name, fear washed through Nein'a's beautiful face. It was quickly replaced by something coldly vicious as she peered again into the trees around the clearing.

"Get out!" she snapped at Wynn. "Do not bring Leesil here. Take him from this land while you still can."

Wynn was shocked into silence until Chap's voice scratched in her mind.

She must come now, before pursuit catches us all.

Wynn stepped closer to Nein'a. "Come with us. Chap and I can hide you. I will get Leesil and Magiere from Crijheäiche, and we—"

"Leesil is among the Anmaglâhk?" Nein'a cut her off. "You are all fools . . . rabbits who crawl into a den of wolves! How did you even find my prison?"

Before Wynn could sort out answers, her stomach rolled at Chap's words.

No more time for this—we leave now!

Wynn swallowed down nausea under Nein'a's wary gaze and then gestured at Chap and the other majay-hì.

"He brought me . . . and they led him. They can bring us back. But you have to come. There are others pursuing us, and we do not know how close they are."

Nein'a looked away. "What makes you think I could leave . . . not having done so in the long time I have been here?"

"Of course you can leave," Wynn insisted. "There are no walls, and Chap knows the way."

He barked once as his leaf-wing voice began to rise again.

"I heard you the first time!" Wynn snapped at him. "Keep quiet for a moment!"

Nein'a frowned at them both.

Wynn had no time to explain, and all Nein'a heard was Chap's agitated bark in reply.

Nein'a shook her head. "I am cut off, girl. I can no more walk the forest than you. It rejects me. If I step beyond the clearing, I am lost . . . wandering until I am quickly retaken and returned to this place. Do you think I have not tried?"

Wynn did not understand this. Every elf she had met was at home in this great forest and none suffered the confusion it pressed upon her.

"Trust me, or at least Chap," she urged. "He can lead us back."

Lily remained close by. In two steps, Chap brushed heads with her and tossed his nose toward the tall ferns. Lily yipped and the pack elder echoed her. All the majay-hì began to gather.

Nein'a watched them, but her large eyes kept drifting warily about the clearing, as if searching for some assurance. She sighed and scratched Chap's head.

"I have nothing to lose. But not so for you, girl, when we are caught."

"Just keep your eyes on Chap and the others. The forest cannot make them shift in your mind like it does with its own flora."

Chap led the way with Nein'a following, and Wynn fell in behind with Lily as the majay-hì swarmed around them. They stepped through the giant ferns and down the channel that Chap had created in the barrier woods.

"It took us all night to reach you," Wynn said, "but Chap and the pack know where to go. We still have a long trek ahead."

Nein'a did not answer, and seemed overly disturbed by the barrier woods, as if she had never seen it before.

Wynn tried to understand what the woman must feel, trapped alone for eight years. It would take longer than a few steps for Nein'a to accept she was free.

Another patch of tall ferns appeared ahead, blocking the path. Wynn didn't remember ferns at the passage entrance, only its exit into the clearing. But she put her faith in Chap's clearer perception as they stepped through the fronds.

Wynn stood on the clearing's edge with Nein'a's domicile elm at the green lawn's center.

Nein'a huffed. "Now do you see?"

"Whenever you try to leave, you just end up back here?" Wynn asked.

"No . . . ," Nein'a answered. "I have thrice wandered, lost in the outer forest, only to be captured again. This is the first time I returned directly to my prison. But I have never before had anyone try to lead me out."

Wynn was not listening closely. She was too preoccupied, spreading the tall ferns with her hands to peer back down the passage through the tangled woods.

"I did not know the forest had thickened outside," Nein'a continued. "It has been years since I last tried to leave. Perhaps it is a new safeguard placed by Aoishenis-Ahâre . . . since my son's return."

The title caught Wynn's attention. It was not Most Aged Father but the Fay who had raised the barrier woods. And Nein'a's misconception suggested something more.

Most Aged Father had some hand in cutting the woman off from the forest, leaving her susceptible to its bewildering influence. If that were so . . .

Wynn grew more wary and mimicked Nein'a's study of the surrounding trees. How much influence did Most Aged Father wield over this land, let alone its people?

Most Aged Father wormed his awareness through the forest. He drifted from tree to bush to vine as he followed Fréthfâre. Though he watched her run hard through the night without pause, he worried that she would not catch Léshil in time.

He slipped ahead and came upon Sgäile and his procession, pushing on with just as much speed. Most Aged Father clung to his calm, watching as they ran past. His awareness caught for an instant on the one called Magiere.

Before this woman's arrival, countless decades had passed since he had looked upon any human. Of those he remembered, not one breed matched her white skin and black hair. There was something wrong about her—more than just the flawed nature of a human.

The sun had risen, glinting off the crimson shimmers in her hair.

Most Aged Father raced on, but his awareness halted in a cedar strangled by blackberry vines growing all the way up into its branches. A lingering prickle within its living wood stung his mind.

Many years had passed since a majay-hì or a *clhuassas* had come close enough to his home for him to feel their difference from the forest's mundane creatures. They shied from him, and even sensed his presence slipping through the forest's growth. But here in this tree, in these newly grown brambles, he felt it . . .

The same lingering touch as in the descendants of the born-Fay. What did this mean?

Most Aged Father drifted within the barrier woods, as if the very walls of his own home had been altered while he had slumbered. His panic mounted.

Footsteps approached in the outer forest. He slipped away, burrowing inward toward Cuirin'nên'a's clearing.

The farther north they ran, the more desperate Sgäile became.

He had never seen the prison glade of Cuirin'nên'a, though most long-standing anmaglâhk knew its location. A select few chosen only by Fréthfâre went regularly to check upon Cuirin'nên'a's needs. At the inception of her internment, some expressed concern for her well-being in isolation. Most Aged Father assured them that he would be aware of her needs—or if and when more was required for her. Fréthfâre held firm to limiting contact, and none but those she chose ever went to Cuirin'nên'a.

At the start of this pursuit, Sgäile did not believe Wynn and Chap could reach her before they were caught. The majay-hì might, but not with a small woman slowing them down. Then he had seen their tracks halt, and Wynn's boot prints vanished amid the hoof marks of a sentinel deer.

That a human rode a *clhuassas,* like some servant animal, was sickening. The sun had risen, and Sgäile knew the prison glade was not far off.

Someone called out from behind him.

Brot'ân'duivé was the first to halt and turn. As if summoned by Sgäile's heated thoughts, Fréthfâre came at a run up the path behind them.

Haggard and panting, she stopped near Én'nish and her two comrades. Fréthfâre's face dripped with sweat that matted her hair against her forehead.

"Turn back . . . by word . . . of Most Aged . . ." she gasped out, hands braced on her knees. "Do not go farther!"

Sgäile tensed in confusion. "I have oath of guardianship to fulfill, and the retrieval of a human wandering our land."

"No one goes near the traitor," Fréthfâre insisted.

This was the second time in Sgäile's life that he was ordered to violate the ways of his people. The first had been when he was sent to kill a half-blood, also marked as a traitor.

None of his people, the an'Cróan, would willingly spill the blood of their own. But the Anmaglâhk obeyed the direct wishes of Most Aged Father. Only the presence of a majay-hì and the half-blood's ignorance of his own people had justified Sgäile's disobedience.

Brot'ân'duivé spoke evenly. "Why would Most Aged Father force this upon Sgäilsheilleache and those he has chosen to share his purpose?"

"What now?" Magiere spoke up.

Through his fatigue and strain, Sgäile had forgotten that neither Léshil nor Magiere understood Elvish.

"We have been ordered to return," he answered in Belaskian, "by Most Aged Father."

Anger spread on Magiere's sweat-glistened white face. Léshil took two steps down the path toward Fréthfâre.

"I don't serve your master," he said. "Go back on your own!"

"Wait!" Brot'ân'duivé snapped, and stepped between them.

"Get out of my way!" Léshil demanded.

Magiere turned from Fréthfâre, but Sgäile was not sure if her eyes were on Léshil or Brot'ân'duivé.

"Why am I forced into shame?" Sgäile demanded, keeping to Belaskian in the hope that it might distract his angered charges a little longer. "You trap me between caste and people with no way to serve both."

"Nothing is greater than service to the caste," Fréthfâre returned. "That is our service to the people. In silence and in shadows . . . obey!"

Én'nish stepped closer to Fréthfâre, a new eagerness washing over her sharp features.

"No," Brot'ân'duivé commanded.

Én'nish's two companions—and Osha—stood with attention shifting between Brot'ân'duivé and Fréthfâre. Like Sgäile, they were at a loss as to who had the greater authority here between Most Aged Father's trusted counselor and a revered master among the Anmaglâhk. Én'nish's allegiance was clear. Fréthfâre remained certain of her position, and her words were only formally polite.

"You disagree with our father, Greimasg'äh? You question my place as Covârleasa?"

"Yes," Brot'ân'duivé answered. "When it is used against our people."

Sgäile did not know what to do when he heard this. Brot'ân'duivé had not only rejected Fréthfâre's position, he had denounced it—and that of Most Aged Father. Sgäile found himself in an untenable situation and wanted no part of this.

Fréthfâre stood to full height. "Careful, Greimasg'äh . . . you are not so highly honored as to change caste ways at your whim."

"And what purpose do those ways serve?" Brot'ân'duivé returned. "They serve our people, first and foremost. Guardianship was an old tradition before the first supplicant bent knee before Most Aged Father. Break the ways of our people, and what is left for us to protect?"

Fréthfâre remained unconvinced, but Brot'ân'duivé cut off any rebuttal.

"Take this before the elders, if you wish. Even now they gather at Crijheäiche. It is for them to decide—not you or I—if the people's ways shall be altered. Would not Most Aged Father agree, as first servant to the people?"

True as this was, Sgäile was still reluctant. Én'nish closely watched Fréthfâre's silent frustration, waiting for the Covârleasa to counter Brot'ân'duivé's words.

Brot'ân'duivé stepped to the path's side, and his passive

gaze fell upon Sgäile. The elder anmaglâhk held out a hand to the open trail ahead.

"We follow in service to your purpose."

Sgäile turned his gaze from Brot'ân'duivé to Fréthfâre and back again. He did not know which of them had put him in the worst position. He stepped past Léshil, and the others followed, including Fréthfâre.

Not long after, Sgäile paused again. Paw prints led both ahead and off into the forest on his left. Brot'ân'duivé studied the split trail. There were signs that the pack had turned into the trees and back again, but why?

"It is your purpose and your choice," Brot'ân'duivé said to him.

Sgäile took a slow breath. "We move on and leave this deviation for our return."

He headed on in silence, and a short way down the main trail he slowed in caution.

"Is this . . . ," he began in Elvish, for he did not want Léshil to hear.

"Yes," Brot'ân'duivé answered. "But it has changed."

The forest gathered upon itself in a wild and impenetrable tangle, except for one open passage that cut through the dense barrier.

"Well?" Léshil asked. "Is this it?"

Sgäile did not know how to answer, and Brot'ân'duivé had gone silent again.

"Fine!" Léshil snapped, and stepped into the path through the woods.

Sgäile followed. In spite of deep concerns over Léshil locating Cuirin'nên'a, he could not stop this search. They had to find Wynn at any cost and bring her back.

At the end of the long path, he stepped through tall ferns behind Léshil.

A pack of majay-hì bustled about a lawn of grass and dark moss surrounding a single domicile elm. There stood Chap between Wynn and a tall elven woman in a shimmering white wrap.

Despair washed through Sgäile as he met the glower of Cuirin'nên'a. Wynn had been found, and his guardianship restored, but Sgäile had failed Most Aged Father once more.

*   *   *

Leesil thrashed through the ferns and halted, rooted to the ground. He stopped breathing. Wynn and Chap stood in the clearing, but he didn't really see them.

He only saw his mother, the perfect lines of her face, her tall and lithe stature, and eyes that could swallow all his awareness. He felt as he had looking down from the mountainside upon the vast elven forest—relieved and overwhelmed all at once. He had struggled and fought—and killed—for this intangible moment.

A flicker of terror passed through his mother's eyes at the sight of him.

In Leesil's youth, she had seldom shown open fear—and never at him.

Magiere came up beside him, but Leesil couldn't take his eyes from Nein'a.

"Mother?"

Someone grabbed his shoulder

Leesil knew it wasn't Magiere. Anger rose as he glanced back to find Sgäile restraining him.

Brot'an shook his head. "We are here now, and nothing can be done for it."

Sgäile's mouth tightened, but he stepped back as the others came through the ferns. Fréth's narrowing eyes turned on Brot'an.

Leesil moved slowly forward, and Nein'a—Mother— turned her face aside. Perhaps all the years alone made her cringe with sorrow. The thought almost stopped Leesil from going on. He shrugged off the rope harness and brought the chest around into his hands.

One steel-gray majay-hì started and then lunged away from the surrounding woods. It spun about to stare into the trees, pacing.

Chap flinched and warily watched the steel-gray dog. The white female beside him hopped in closer to push at Chap with a whine. The other majay-hì grew more agitated in their movements.

It was the dogs and not Leesil that made Nein'a lift her face. Fear returned as she watched them. Her expression darkened when she peered among the trees, as if searching out some hidden threat.

Leesil slowed under the growing weight of guilt. Long imprisonment had affected his mother's mind. He kept on, stopping only when close enough to reach her.

Unbidden memories came of long hours training with her, the meals they had shared, and how she checked on him in his room when she thought he was asleep—and of a sad father who had done all this as well with unexplained reluctance.

Leesil wanted to confess his sorrow and guilt for abandoning her, for his father's death . . . for everything. But the words wouldn't come.

"Mother . . . ," he finally said, "I'm taking you out of here."

Nein'a didn't reach out to put a hand upon his cheek, as she had long ago.

"Leave," she whispered with a slow shake of her head. "Get out of this land . . . if you still can."

Leesil's voice failed. He had come all this way, risked the lives of Magiere and Wynn and Chap—and her only response was to tell him to go?

Nein'a's large eyes shifted to Brot'an as the man approached. Leesil saw pleading in her gaze, and Brot'an's passive expression softened when he looked upon her. Leesil's stunned outrage was lost in chill anger.

Nein'a briefly spoke to Brot'an in Elvish, but the name "Léshil" was easy to catch. A silent Wynn looked up in dismay at Nein'a; this was enough to tell Leesil that his mother had asked Brot'an to take him away. He couldn't bear any more of this.

Leesil dropped to one knee and flipped open the chest, lifting the cloth bundle from within. He separated the cloth's folds and thrust out the skulls like a spiteful offering.

"I took them from Darmouth," he said sharply. "I went back looking for you and Father."

Nein'a's breath turned shallow as she reached out a hand. The closer it came to the skull of Leesil's father, the more her long, slender fingers shook.

"It is him?"

"Yes," Leesil said. "And your mother . . . though I was told it was you."

He cast a hateful glance at Brot'an, daring the tall elf to even try to explain. Brot'an offered no reply by word or expression.

"It is Eillean . . . and Gavril," Leesil said. "I brought them to you . . . for whatever last rites you see fit."

Nein'a's fingers slid to her mother's skull. Leesil had rarely seen her cry, but tears dropped down her caramel cheeks in silence. They seemed to drag her down into some strange sickness, and guilt flooded through Leesil again for his harsh words.

Nein'a took the cloth with both skulls and cradled them.

"Leave here at once," she whispered. "You cannot stay."

It was a long cold moment before she looked up and saw the others behind Leesil. Low, sharp Elvish erupted from her lips. The words sounded much the same as what she'd said to Brot'an, though this time Leesil caught Sgäile's longer elven name. She wasn't making a request, but a demand.

"You're coming with me," Leesil said. "I'm not leaving without you."

"I cannot," she whispered.

"It is true," Wynn said cautiously. "The path simply returns her, and anyone with her, back to this clearing. Chap and I have tried."

The sage's face and hands were covered in small scratches and scrapes. Leesil should've been angry for all the trouble she and Chap had caused, but then, they had found his mother.

"Enough!" Sgäile commanded. "We return to Crijheäiche. Léshil, come."

"No," he whispered.

He stood within reach of his mother—and she was alive. Her insistence that he go didn't matter. If anyone thought he'd simply walk away, they were dangerously mistaken.

At quick footsteps from behind, Leesil caught the barest cinch of Brot'an's scar-cut eyebrow.

Leesil back-stepped and spun out of reach.

As Sgäile tried to close the distance, Magiere snatched his cloak at the neck. Sgäile swung back with the edge of a flattened hand. It caught Magiere across the throat, and she fell back gagging.

"Stop this," Brot'an shouted. "Both of you cease!"

Osha stiffened at Brot'an's order, but the others didn't listen. As Sgäile turned his determined attention back toward Leesil, Magiere thrashed around on the grass.

Leesil saw her irises flood black.

"No," he whispered, panic-stricken. "Not now. . . ."

Magiere kicked into the back of Sgäile's leg.

Sgäile buckled, dropping to his knee. Fréthfâre and Én'nish's two companions descended on Magiere. Leesil tried to rush in.

Én'nish dodged in his way, a long-bladed stiletto in each hand.

Anxiety overwhelmed Most Aged Father. The little human woman had reached Cuirin'nên'a. When Léshil and the others arrived, all his careful plans evaporated.

He heard Cuirin'nên'a's repeated refusals to come away with Léshil and grew even more frustrated. Her words would only make Léshil lose hope, and without that, he would become more difficult to manipulate. It was clear that Cuirin'nên'a would sacrifice any tie to her son to protect him.

Most Aged Father writhed as the means to ferret out her confederates shriveled before him. She was a cunning one. He had hoped long isolation might make her desperate enough that Léshil could be used against her. Or his attachment to his mother could be used against him.

The only relief came at Sgäilsheilleache's urgent attempt to remove Léshil from the encounter. The longer Léshil faced his mother's denial, the greater the risk he might turn from any lingering desire to free her.

The pale woman grabbed for the back of Sgäilsheilleache's cloak.

Most Aged Father's frail heart began to race.

Magiere's eyes locked on Nein'a the moment she stepped into the clearing. Less than a year past, Leesil had told her of Nein'a and Gavril. How many years before that had he drank himself to sleep, hiding from nightmares of a past he couldn't bear and a guilt he couldn't escape?

And here was Nein'a, finally, yet she offered little welcome to Leesil. Magiere barely heard what was said as she waited for the easing of Leesil's pain.

It never came.

Leesil deserved more than this. It didn't matter what he'd done. There had to be more than the denial of a cold-blooded mother.

The low thrum in Magiere's body, which she'd held down for days and nights, began to make her shake. When Sgäile closed on Leesil from behind, it lunged up her throat like hunger and filled her head.

She snatched Sgäile's cloak from behind.

Her throat clenched when he struck. She fell back and lost sight of everyone.

She hit the ground, and hunger devoured the pain in her throat. The sun blinded her for an instant when her vision widened. She writhed around to glare at Sgäile's back, his hair now brilliant white in her sight. Then she saw Leesil's glimmering amber eyes fill with anguish. He stared right at her.

Magiere kicked the back of Sgäile's knee as the first tear ran from her burning eyes.

No one was taking Leesil from here until he got what he came for.

Her jaws began to ache the instant Sgäile buckled. When she slapped her hand to the ground to get up, someone pulled it from under her. Anger mounted as her face struck the moss and she lost sight of Leesil.

Magiere twisted on the ground and a flash of gray passed above her. Chap slammed into Fréth with a snarl, and Magiere's wrist jerked free of the woman's grip. She pulled her feet under herself as one of Én'nish's companions came at her. Magiere lunged from her crouch and slammed her hand into his midsection.

Her hardened nails bit through his tunic, and she grabbed his collar with her other hand. Turning, she dragged him in an arc as she rose. Gray-green fabric tore in her grip as she flung him into the clearing's border trees.

Where was Leesil?

Urgency shivered through her and she wanted to rend anyone who touched him. The bright sun made the world burn and blur in her expanded sight. Something struck her lower back.

Moss tore under Magiere's boots as she ground her feet in resistance.

What was it—this thing that tried to stop her from finding Leesil?

Magiere turned on it.

She saw a gray-green cowl around an astonished tan face. Her anger turned manic as it backed away. She lunged at it.

Leesil twisted aside as Én'nish slashed her right blade at his face. Her left stiletto thrust instantly for his gut.

He speared his hand downward and slapped away the blade, and it passed harmlessly off his side. Her lunge brought her close. Leesil twisted sharply right, driving his left elbow at her face.

Én'nish ducked, and her parried stiletto slashed across Leesil's midsection.

He heard it skitter across the rings of his hauberk. He felt its tip catch in one laced ring at his left side.

She shifted behind the blade to thrust with all her weight, and Leesil spun quickly, trying to turn out of her path.

The tip held and tore through. Leather split.

Leesil felt no burn of pierced skin, but he heard the tinkling of metal. One of his hauberk's steel rings dangled against the round guard of Én'nish's blade.

Leesil grabbed Én'nish's wrist below that dangling ring, and his gaze caught on her amber eyes so close to his face.

Another time and place, another woman with a knife had looked at him with the same desperation. All because he'd killed someone she loved.

He raised his other arm on instinct, and Én'nish's free blade slashed his forearm.

Leesil shifted weight into his rear foot, prepared to throw a shoulder into Én'nish and take her to the ground.

His rear foot jerked from the mossy ground and a soft-booted foot struck his hip.

Without footing, Leesil flipped sideways. A grunt erupted from him as his back hit the ground. When he rolled to his feet, Brot'an stood in his path. But the scarfaced elf wasn't looking at him.

"Enough!" Brot'an ordered. "Both of you!"

He held a wide and low stance with his right palm out at arm's length. But not toward Leesil. A half dozen paces beyond Brot'an's hand lay Én'nish. She was curled on the lawn, holding her chest and gasping for breath. One of her long stilettos lay at Brot'an's feet.

Chap ground his forepaws in Fréthfâre's stomach as he snarled into her face. The woman went rigid on her back staring up at him. But Chap faltered at Magiere's hissing screech.

She lunged into one of Én'nish's companions. Tears ran from her eyes around a mouth wide with sharp teeth and fangs.

Magiere had lost all control in front of the Anmaglâhk.

She sank hardened fingernails into her target as Sgäile closed on her back.

The other majay-hì circled away from the conflict, but the pack elder lifted his grizzled muzzle. He stared intently at Magiere, and his jowls wrinkled.

Chap grew frantic. He had no more time to keep Fréthfâre pinned.

Lily paced behind the elder, looking into the trees where Magiere had flung her first opponent. That anmaglâhk had not gotten up.

Chap could not turn from Fréthfâre to touch heads with Lily. All he could do was reach for her own memories. He dipped into Lily's mind, calling up her sight of Fréthfâre standing before Most Aged Father's massive oak, and added the memory she had shown to him in fear—the dark opening in that tree. He repeated these in an alternating flurry and hoped she understood.

The pack elder charged at Magiere with an eerie howl, and Chap bolted toward Magiere and those closing on her.

*   *   *

Magiere rushed the anmaglâhk drawing his blades and drove one hand at his throat. Instead of slashing at her, he ducked into the brush beneath the closest birch. Something snagged Magiere's hair, jerking her head back. Her legs buckled under someone's whipping leg.

Her knees hit the ground. With her head pulled back, she looked up to see Sgäile, his grip tangled in her hair. He sucked a sharp breath at the sight of her face.

Magiere swung a hand upward to claw his astonished features, but Sgäile fell away beneath a snarling silver-furred bulk. Magiere toppled sideways as Sgäile's grip tore from her hair. Her hand slapped firmly against the base of the birch.

Shock ran through her and every muscle clenched tight.

A wild rush of nervous energy flooded her limbs from that brief touch and filled her up with its intensity.

Magiere jerked her hand away, rolling to her feet. Sgäile struggled under Chap's assault, but the dog wheeled around, charging the other way.

He was hunting—like her—and Magiere's hungry gaze traced the path to his target.

A dark-furred dog rushed at her, its gray-peppered jowls pulled back from yellowed teeth.

Leesil heard Magiere's feral screech as she reached for one anmaglâhk with Sgäile coming at her from behind. Chap took Sgäile down but not before Magiere toppled. When she rose, shuddering as she snatched her hand from a tree, Leesil saw her face.

Her teeth . . . the tears . . . her irises so full black they nearly blotted out the whites of her eyes. He started to run for her.

Brot'an stepped in his way, and Leesil threw himself at the tall elf.

"Leesil . . . no!" his mother shouted.

Brot'an's palm slammed against Leesil's chest, driving the air from his lungs. But it wasn't enough to stop him.

Leesil fell on Brot'an, and they both hit the ground. He tumbled away as Brot'an tried to grab him. When he reached his feet, Wynn raced by him, clutching something in her arms. She threw it, and only then Leesil saw the large, grizzled majay-hì charge Magiere.

Bits of fluffy white nodules spun from the basket Wynn had thrown. It hit the charging dog in the shoulder. The impact startled the dark majay-hì. It spun away, and Chap barreled into the dog. Both wheeled around each other in snapping growls.

Osha finally flew into motion, running after Wynn.

Leesil sidled around Brot'an, trying to reach Magiere, but he backed into someone else.

He pivoted, cutting upward with a fist at whichever anmaglâhk was behind him. He saw a flash of shimmering white before his wrist was snatched.

His mother twisted his swing aside, throwing him off balance. Leesil righted himself in panic at what he'd almost done.

Nein'a glared at him. "What have you brought among us?"

Leesil floundered in confusion until his mother raised her head. Her gaze fixed upon Magiere.

Most Aged Father's awareness flitted around the clearing from one tree to the next. Watching from within an elm, all he perceived left him overwhelmed, including the strange majay-hì assaulting his treasured Fréthfâre. Then his awareness fell upon Magiere.

Far from the glade and deep within his massive oak, Most Aged Father curled into a twitching ball. No one heard his whimper.

He saw the pale woman with her bestial face slap a hand against one tree. He felt the forest's life shudder under that touch. It hurt, as if a piece of him had been bitten away.

Ancient memory writhed in the back of his mind. In sickening fear, he slipped his awareness around the clearing toward the pale monster.

All of Magiere's rage turned on Sgäile.

"Undead!" he hissed, and a blade appeared in his hand.

She saw only one more obstacle to reaching Leesil. Her jaws widened but no words came out. A rustle of movement sounded in the brush behind her at the clearing's edge.

Sgäile held up his hand, but not at her, and he snapped some command in Elvish. He never took his eyes off her, and his horror fed Magiere's hunger.

"Stop! All of you. Stop this now!"

Brot'an's deep voice carried through the glade. Magiere twisted her head around, tensing at the threat. Behind the tall elf stood Leesil, his wrist gripped tightly in his mother's hand.

Osha had Wynn pinned in his arms.

"Magiere ... enough," the sage shouted. "Please ... get control of yourself."

Fréth knelt nearby, mouth ajar at the white majay-hì blocking her off. Just short of them, Chap crouched in the way of the larger dark dog. The rest of the pack began to circle in.

Magiere's head began to ache as the hunger shrank into the pit of her stomach. The more it receded, the more she started to shake. As if she'd swallowed too much drink ... too much of Wynn's tea ... or too much food, too much ... life.

She stumbled back, and her heel caught in a bush. She toppled, falling against a tree trunk, and slapped her hand against its bark to steady herself.

Another shock ran deep into Magiere.

The world went black before her eyes. In that sudden darkness, strange sounds and sights erupted in Magiere's head.

CHAPTER FOURTEEN

Curled in his tree's bower, Most Aged Father gaped in pain.

The pale-skinned monster touched the birch the instant his awareness slipped into it.

He felt the tree's life slipping away into her flesh. He felt it as if she touched his skin, feeding upon him, and memory welled up to wrap him in suffering.

Another like her had come for him in the dark . . . long, long ago. . . .

Sorhkafâré—Light upon the Grass. That was his true name back then.

He had dropped weary and beaten upon a stained wool blanket, filthy from moons of forced marches. He did not even care to have his wounds tended and lay in the darkness of his tent.

Only two of his commanders had survived the day. He had lost more officers upon that field than during all of the last moon. Someone called to him from outside his tent but he did not answer. Hesitantly, the voice came again.

"The human and dwarven ranks are too depleted for another engagement. They must fall back."

The enemy's condition was unknown. With his eyes

closed, Sorhkafâré saw nothing but the sea of dead he had left on the rolling plains. The fragile alliance had been outnumbered nearly five to one on this day.

Again he did not answer. He could not look at the faces of the living, and even if he opened his eyes, he couldn't stop seeing those of the dead.

The enemy's horde had pressed north along the eastern coast of the central continent. At dawn, he had received word that Bäalâle Seatt had fallen to an unknown catastrophe. The dwarven mother-city in the mountains bordering the Suman Desert had long been under siege. Scattered reports hinted that neither side had survived whatever had happened there.

The enemy's numbers seemed endless. And all that remained in the west to stop them were Sorhkafâré's forces, the last to keep the enemy from turning inland toward Aonnis Lhoin'n—First Glade—the refuge and home of his people.

He heard the footsteps outside fade away. Finally they left him alone.

Sleep would not come, and he did not want it. He still saw thousands slaughtering each other under the hot sun. He had lost all reckoning of whose cries were those of his enemies or his allies. He lost fury and even fear this day upon the plain.

Countless furred, scaled, or dark- to light-skinned faces fell before his spear and arrows, and yet they kept coming. One mutilated body blurred into another . . . except for the last rabid goblin, dead at his feet when it all ended. Its long tongue dangled from its canine mouth into the blood-soaked mud.

Sorhkafâré heard a shout and then a moan somewhere outside in the camp, and then another.

The wounded and dying were given what aid could be rendered, but they only suffered the more for it. Who would want to live another day like this one?

More shouts. Running feet. A brief clatter of steel.

Someone fumbled at the canvas flap of his tent.

"Leave me," he said tiredly and did not get up.

The tent ripped open.

Camp bonfires outside cast an orange glow around the shadowed figure of a human male. Sorhkafâré could not make out the man's face. The light glinted dully upon the edges of his steel-scaled carapace. His skin seemed dark, like that of a Suman.

Sorhkafâré's senses sharpened.

By proportions, there had been as many humans among the enemy's horde as among his alliance forces. Most with the enemy had been Suman. Had one slipped into camp unseen? He sat up quickly.

The man's arm holding aside the tent flap was severed off above the wrist. His other hand was empty.

No one walked about with such a wound. Sorhkafâré heard another cry somewhere out in the camp.

The crippled skulker rushed in with a grating hiss, guttural and full of madness.

Sorhkafâré rolled to the tent's far side and pulled his war knife. His attacker fell upon the empty bedroll. As the man turned upon the blanket, Sorhkafâré drove his blade down.

It sank through the man's dark-skinned neck above the armor's collar, and he slumped, limp.

Sorhkafâré rushed from the tent. He searched the night camp for any officer to chastise over the failure of the perimeter watch. The few remaining cries died away one by one.

The nearest fire had been doused, and only smoking embers remained. Many of the torches were gone, and darkness had thickened in the camp. The moon was not yet high enough for his elven eyes, but he thought he saw figures moving quickly from tent to tent. Now and then came strange muffled sounds or a short cry.

"Sorhkafâré . . . where were you?"

A figure approached, slow and purposeful, between the rows of tents. He knew that voice. It grated upon his nerves every time the man spoke.

Kædmon, commander of the humans among Sorhkafâré's forces—or what were left of them.

Sorhkafâré had no strength for another argument. It was always Kædmon who challenged him. He pushed his men too hard and kept demanding night strikes after his people had marched all day.

Kædmon drew closer, and Sorhkafâré saw the dark rents in the tall man's chain armor. He had not bothered to remove it, but Sorhkafâré could not blame him. There was no point in doing so, as they would only ride hard with the dawn, either in flight or to face an endless enemy once more.

Someone stepped from a tent beyond Kædmon, dragging a body.

Sorhkafâré had no more sorrow to spare for those who succumbed to wounds. But the shadowed figure dropped the body in the dirt and turned away to the next tent.

"Didn't you see them come?" Kædmon said. "Did you not hear us cry for help as the sun dropped below the hills? Or was it only your own kind . . . your wounded that you culled from the dead today?"

Sorhkafâré turned his eyes back to Kædmon. He barely made out the man's long face and square jaw below a wide mouth.

"What venom do you spit now?" he answered. "We left no one who had even a single breath in them! All were carried in, even those with no hope to see tomorrow."

The man's ugly square jaw was covered in a few days' growth of beard. Stubble on his neck looked darker still. His steel coif and its chain drape were gone, exposing lank black hair hanging around his light-skinned face. His bloodthirsty human eyes glittered.

"You didn't bring me," Kædmon hissed back and his words grew awkward as if he had difficulty speaking. "I still breathed when they crept across the dead, looking for those you forgot . . . when the sun vanished from sight."

A dark patch at Kædmon's throat glistened as he stepped to within a spear's reach.

Sorhkafâré stepped back.

A gaping wound in the side of Kædmon's neck had covered his throat in blood mixed with some black viscous fluid. His lips and teeth looked stained as well.

Kædmon's eyes were as colorless as his pallid skin.

"I can't stop myself. . . . They won't let me stop."

Kædmon shook with clenched muscles as his crystal eyes scrunched closed for an instant. He took a jerking step. All tense resistance vanished, and he charged with open hands.

Sorhkafâré set himself but did not raise his knife.

Kædmon had seen too much in these long years of battle. They all had. The man's mind finally broke under the strain. No matter their differences, he was an ally who had fought hard beside Sorhkafâré's own people. Kædmon had lost his own father when their settlement was overrun before alliance forces arrived to defend it. But still the man fought on, and his loyalty had never wavered.

Sorhkafâré sidestepped, ready to slap away Kædmon's grasp. He barely drew back his hand before Kædmon's grip latched around his throat. Too sudden and too quick for a wounded man.

Kædmon closed his fingers.

Sorhkafâré could not breathe. He tried to break the man's grip. Kædmon's features twisted in agony as his mouth opened.

"Don't fight," he whispered. "Please don't make me . . . make you suffer."

Sorhkafâré almost stopped fighting for air.

Within Kædmon's mouth he saw malformed teeth stained with blood. A human mouth with sharpened fangs like a dog or short-snouted goblin. He slashed the knife across the back of Kædmon's forearm, but the man did not even flinch.

Sorhkafâré's chest convulsed, trying to get air, and his sight began to dim. He rammed the blade into the side of Kædmon's neck.

Kædmon's head snapped sideways under the blow. He gagged once before his face turned back, now little more than a blurred oval of white in Sorhkafâré's waning sight.

"It won't help," Kædmon sobbed. "I'm sorry . . . it never does."

Air seeped in through Sorhkafâré's nose.

He heaved, filling up his lungs, then gagged and coughed as he tried to suck more air. He lay on his side upon the ground, not even knowing he had fallen. A blurred form appeared above him and reached down. Sorhkafâré twisted away in panic.

"Get up, sir!" it said, and the words were in his own Elvish tongue. "The horses have been slaughtered . . . we must run!"

Vision cleared, and Sorhkafâré saw one of his commanders. Snähacróe reached down for him, but Sorhkafâré only looked about for Kædmon.

The man lay crumpled on his side, off to the left. The shaft of an elven spear rose from his torso. Its silvery tip protruded from Kædmon's rib cage, and black fluids ran from the bright metal to the ground.

Sorhkafâré stared at the gaping wound, not truly aware of Snähacróe until his kinsman pulled at him, trying to make him follow.

Kædmon rolled onto his face and braced his hands upon the ground. He pushed up and lifted his head. Snähacróe halted in shock to look at the human.

Kædmon began to shake. Once more his whole body seemed to clench. His fingers bit into the earth as if he sought to hold on to it and keep from rising.

"Run," he whimpered.

Sorhkafâré still hesitated. The man could not be alive. The spear point dripped more black fluid from his body and the same ran from the knife wound in his neck. The broken stream of fluid vanished as it struck the earth, but Sorhkafâré heard the slow patter continue.

"Run . . . while you can!" Kædmon shouted.

Snähacróe wrenched Sorhkafâré around and they fled.

Grim silhouettes closed in behind them with pounding feet. The more that came, the more Sorhkafâré saw one here and there from the ranks of both sides that day in battle. Their faces seemed too pallid in the dark.

All around were figures with glittering eyes.

Sorhkafâré . . .

The name clung to Magiere's thoughts like her own, as she came slowly back to consciousness.

"Sgäilsheilleache, hold off!"

It was Brot'an's voice, but Magiere only saw moving

blurs around her. She felt and smelled moss against her face.

She began panting hard.

"She is unnatural," Sgäile snapped. "Undead . . . in our forest!"

"No," Brot'an barked. "She is something else. Now do as I say!"

Magiere took three rapid breaths before her thoughts cleared in realization.

Brot'an had never told the others about what he had seen of her in Darmouth's crypt. He had kept her secret.

It didn't matter anymore. She'd lost all control, and they'd all seen her.

Magiere's sight cleared slowly. She lay on her side, one hand limp upon the moss before her face. There was blood on her fingernails.

But her hand was not long-boned and tan as it had been in the dream . . . the vision . . . whatever she should call the sights and sounds that had taken her. She saw only her own pale hand, not that of the elven man she had become . . . *Sorhkafâré.*

Why? She hadn't touched the remains of any victim, trying to see through the eyes of its undead killer at the moment of death.

Magiere flopped onto her back, trying to find the faces of those around her. She looked at the birch that she'd backed into and touched before the world turned black. She began to tremble.

The tree's trunk bore the mark of her hands. Where she'd touched it, the bark had darkened and dried dead. Brittle pieces had already fallen away.

"Leesil!" she cried out.

"Here . . . I'm here!" he answered; and then, "Get out of my way!"

A wet nose grazed her neck, and Chap's head pressed into her face. She dug her fingers in his fur and hung on. Leesil dropped to his knees beside her.

Magiere latched on to him, thrashing around to bury her face in the chest of his hauberk and hide from all eyes.

"It's all right," he whispered.

She still felt the lingering shock in her body and saw in her mind the marks of her hands upon the birch. Nothing was all right anymore.

Magiere closed her fingers on Leesil's hauberk until its leather creaked in her hands and its rings bit into her palms. The name she'd been called still echoed in her head. Her . . . his allies came in the dark with colorless eyes and teeth stained with the blood of their own.

Sorhkafâré.

"I said keep back!" Leesil growled, and pulled Magiere closer. "It's over."

He knew better than to touch Magiere until she recognized him. But when she fell and cried out for him, he knew her dhampir nature had already retreated.

Brot'an stepped around to wave Sgäile off. Osha finally released Wynn.

Én'nish was on her feet but still hunkered from Brot'an's strike. Her one remaining companion aided the other that Magiere had thrown into the trees. They both emerged, but the latter man was limping badly and the front of his tunic was shredded.

Nein'a glared at Leesil in shock. Any hint of fearful and angry denials she'd cast at him were gone. There was only wary revulsion as her gaze drifted from him down to Magiere hiding in his arms.

"It is not over," Fréth said coldly, and the white majay-hì shifted silently in her way. "You have brought an undead into our midst. I do not understand how this is possible, but this thing you coddle will not remain."

Leesil's anger rose again, but he couldn't leave Magiere.

"Chap," he said quietly, "kill anyone who takes a step."

Chap didn't answer in any fashion. He simply paced around Leesil to stand before Magiere and glanced once at the white majay-hì blocking Fréth.

"Enough," Brot'an insisted. "If she were undead, the forest never would have allowed her to enter. There is nothing Léshil could have done to change that."

Leesil wasn't certain about the shift in authority taking place. Both Sgäile and Fréth were reluctant, but it seemed

Brot'an took charge. For the moment, it served to protect Magiere from the others—but still, Leesil didn't like it.

Brot'an's pale scars stood out like white slashes on his lined face. "We are all fatigued from a night of running with no food. We will rest part of the day in the outer forest."

He gestured toward the fern-curtained passage.

"Fréthfâre, please report to Most Aged Father. Tell him all is settled, that we have found the human woman and will return soon. Sgäilsheilleache, you and Osha find food, and Én'nish . . ."

Brot'an spun toward her, and now Leesil couldn't see his expression.

"You and those serving your purpose will keep well apart from Sgäile and his charges. Or you will have more to answer for upon our return."

Én'nish picked up her fallen blade as she hobbled past Brot'an. Her face dark with malice, she joined her two companions and headed out through the woods' passage.

Leesil tried to get Magiere on her feet. When Brot'an approached, Chap lunged, and his teeth clacked shut on air as Brot'an leaped away.

"No more," Sgäile said quickly to the dog. "No more fighting . . . let him pass."

Brot'an betrayed subtle surprise at Sgäile's words. "It seems there are some things you have not told me."

Sgäile sighed but didn't answer.

"It's all right, Chap," Magiere said.

Leesil's uncertainty grew. Brot'an might have pacified further conflict for the moment. But it was still Brot'an, the one who'd used him. Leesil would never sink to a hint of gratitude, but he let Magiere step forward to follow Brot'an.

Leesil looked back into the glade. Nein'a watched him, but he no longer saw anything recognizable in her cold eyes.

An abomination in his land.

Most Aged Father—who had once been Sorhkafâré—quaked in his bower.

This pallid woman with blood-stained hair had fooled even Fréthfâre.

In that long night, running beside Snähacróe and the others, he had heard the cries behind him. Each dawn that followed, fewer remained in his company.

There had been humans and dwarves as well as his own kind. The dwarves had been the first to fall. Unable to keep the pace with their short legs and heavy bodies, fewer and fewer of those stout people were present at dawn when his meager forces fell prostrate upon the ground. They foraged for water and food by day, slept what little they could in shifts, and before dusk each night they fled inland toward Aonnis Lhoin'n.

Not long past each dusk, they heard the shouts and running feet of abominations closing upon them. Each night they were closer, as he and his forces grew more weary and worn with flight. More than once he glanced back to see dozens of sparking eyes, perhaps a hundred, in the dark.

Then humans and elves began to fall behind as well, and no one could turn back for them. Along their harried passage, they found desolate and shattered towns and villages. And more than once, pale figures erupted from the dark ahead of them. They slogged their way through, but more of his fleeing band were always gone when they halted at the next dawn.

Most Aged Father could not shake the memories from his mind.

Cuirin'nên'a and her hidden dissidents no longer mattered. Long ago, he had brought his people here to safety. Now this woman—this abomination—appeared among them. A human-spawned thing. The Ancient Enemy stirred sooner than he had feared. It was the only explanation he saw to account for this new tool of bloodshed and devastation. One that could breach his people's land, the only haven that had saved them in those long lost days.

Most Aged Father lifted his wrinkled hand from the bower's wood, but his fingers would not stop shaking.

CHAPTER FIFTEEN

Fréthfâre ran from the glade with her heart pounding. She fled far into the forest before daring to find a place in which to speak with Most Aged Father. How could she tell him what had happened, what she had seen? Where would she even begin? An undead entered their land and walked freely among the people—and was now protected by Brot'ân'duivé.

She glanced up at the sun caught on the edge of drifting dark clouds. Within moments, the morning light faded. The forest darkened around her. An omen.

She dropped to her knees beneath a tall elm's branches and pressed the smooth word-wood to its bark. Her reluctance to report such disturbing events fell before her need for Most Aged Father's guidance.

"Father . . ."

I am here, daughter.

His voice in her thoughts brought some relief. "I do not know where to begin . . . I have failed—"

I know all. I was there as you faced this horror. Destroy it! Tell Brot'ân'duivé my wishes, and dispatch the smaller human woman as well. You and Sgäilsheilleache first re-

strain Léshil. Disable him if need be, but he is not to be permanently harmed.

Perhaps Most Aged Father had not seen everything.

"Brot'ân'duivé protects this undead woman," Fréthfâre answered, "and allowed Léshil to speak with Cuirin'nên'a. Even with Én'nish's assistance and those with her, I do not think we could overcome the Greimasg'äh if he refuses. And Léshil and this woman would side with Brot'ân'duivé."

The tree was silent for a long moment, and then . . .

Give Brot'ân'duivé my instructions. He will obey.

For the first time, Fréthfâre doubted Most Aged Father's wisdom. Perhaps he had not seen Brot'ân'duivé's face as the elder anmaglâhk stopped Sgäilsheilleache from going after the wild woman.

"Father, the situation is untenable. Osha is untried and in service to Sgäilsheilleache's guardianship. I do not believe they would submit even to Brot'ân'duivé in conflict with that purpose. And the Greimasg'äh is . . ."

She faltered at casting aspersions upon one of her caste's eldest.

"Brot'ân'duivé is a stranger among us. Forgive my doubts, but would it not be better to lead this undead back to Crijheäiche? With those of our caste waiting, we could take her easily, especially if Léshil is to remain unharmed."

Again the tree went silent.

Yes . . . your wise counsel gives me great pride. Bring them to Crijheäiche.

Fréth breathed easily again. "In silence and in shadows."

The morning sun slipped behind thick clouds, and the promise of a fine day vanished. The sky turned gray, and the air grew chill.

Brot'ân'duivé knew what Fréthfâre would tell Most Aged Father—what she had seen and what he had done—but it could not be helped. He needed Léshil, or all the frail plans of Cuirin'nên'a and the long lost Eillean would lead to nothing.

In the crypt of Darmouth, it was clear how much this

tainted woman, Magiere, meant to Léshil. Perhaps dangerously more than the half-blood understood. Brot'ân'-duivé could not allow her to be harmed, or Léshil would suffer and be lost from the purpose that awaited him. Brot'ân'duivé stayed close to Léshil and Magiere and made certain that Én'nish and her companions remained far off.

It had been eight years since Brot'ân'duivé had seen Cuirin'nên'a, not since the night she had been banished into permanent isolation by Most Aged Father. There was too much risk in meeting with Cuirin'nên'a—for her, for himself, and for the few who supported all that Eillean had begun long ago. But the sight of Cuirin'nên'a's face with its hints of Eillean had put him off balance.

Though he had never spoken of it, perhaps the daughter suspected how much he had loved the mother. He had sacrificed so much to keep his promise to Eillean. He had sacrificed Eillean herself. Soon he would sacrifice yet more.

Léshil had good reason to hate him. But Brot'ân'duivé had no choice in bringing Cuirin'nên'a back for judgment. One of them had to remain free of Most Aged Father's confirmed suspicions, and Cuirin'nên'a had already fallen from their leader's goodwill. It remained imperative that Brot'ân'duivé not fall with her. She understood this.

He had manipulated Léshil into finishing his own mission and assassinating Darmouth. Again, he had seen no other option. What he did, he did for his people rather than the goals of Most Aged Father.

Sgäilsheilleache and Osha returned with walnuts and berries. Sgäilsheilleache looked ill and would not raise his eyes to anyone. Brot'ân'duivé pitied him. Sworn guardianship or not, Sgäilsheilleache would not rest easy in Magiere's presence—nor would Fréthfâre.

Neither would Brot'ân'duivé.

He reached out and took walnuts and berries with both hands. "Both of you stay with Én'nish and the others. Fréthfâre will return soon."

Sgäilsheilleache finally looked up. Before he objected, Brot'ân'duivé gave his assurance.

"I will serve your guardianship as if it were my own.

Take your ease for a time. When we return to Crijheäiche, Most Aged Father will advise us wisely."

These last words stuck in his throat, but the pretense was necessary.

Sgäilsheilleache glanced toward Magiere, and a hint of revulsion resurfaced. He nodded and turned away with young Osha following.

Brot'ân'duivé stepped off through the trees toward the separate gathering of Sgäilsheilleache's charges. He had not met the small one called Wynn, who now sat against a large cedar, bare of branches at its base. She had torn a strip of cloth from some garment to make a bandage for the shallow slash on Léshil's forearm. Beside her was the majay-hì, Chap, who Sgäilsheilleache and Léshil had both spoken to in the clearing—a strange moment.

Majay-hì and human stared off through the forest, and Brot'ân'duivé caught a glimpse of the pack among the trees. Now and then, a white female ranged closer.

The fact that the pack and a *clhuassas* had aided a human in finding Cuirin'nên'a was perplexing. Against their long-standing protection of this land from outsiders, they found nothing to fear from this little one called Wynn.

Brot'ân'duivé did not believe in portents, yet it was a strange sign. The doubts he had harbored over the years for Eillean's plan lessened a little more. The touched creatures of his people's land appeared to find Most Aged Father's ways unacceptable.

Magiere lay upon the ground away from the cedar's far side, looking weary and spent from her sudden fury. Léshil now crouched beside her.

Brot'ân'duivé knelt at Magiere's feet and began splitting the walnut shells with a stiletto.

"Do not strain Sgäilsheilleache further," he said plainly to Léshil. "Your actions thus far have placed him in a difficult position. Fréthfâre will now seek any reason to execute Magiere."

Léshil stared at him. Wynn shifted around the cedar's side, followed by Chap, to listen in.

Magiere did not move. "Wynn, what were you thinking? Running off like that?"

The little human frowned. "How else would we get around Most Aged Father's coercion? Or should we just let him dangle Nein'a in front of Leesil?"

Chap nosed Wynn with a growl, and she put a hand on his head.

"I am sorry, Magiere," Wynn continued but without a hint of regret. "Chap was leaving with the majay-hì, and I . . . knew where he was going. There was no time to tell you."

Brot'ân'duivé remained silently attentive.

Most Aged Father tried to bend Léshil to his will—but for what? Aside from the custom to never spill the blood of their own, the only reason the patriarch had for keeping Cuirin'nên'a alive was to learn of any others who aided her. The purpose for Léshil's safe passage became quite clear.

Brot'ân'duivé turned to Léshil. "You cannot free your mother . . . not without Most Aged Father's consent. He holds sway over the place of her confinement. If you still wish to free her, then you must return to Crijheäiche and bargain for it."

Magiere rolled up onto one elbow with a frown.

"What do you care?" Léshil spit out. "She's here because you dragged her back!"

"If I had not," Brot'ân'duivé replied, "then another of my caste would have done so . . . or worse."

"I thought elves didn't kill their own," Magiere said.

"Their own . . . are not always a matter of blood or even race," Brot'ân'duivé returned. "I was Eillean's confidant and friend. Yes, true. So who better to assure Cuirin'nên'a was returned unharmed?"

He turned back to Léshil. "You know our word . . . *trú*?"

"It means 'traitor,' " Léshil answered coldly.

"Simplistically, yes. It also means outcast, outlawed, beyond the protection of a society. Our law against spilling the blood of our own is based in custom and tradition, not words or decrees as written down by humans."

"How convenient," Magiere said. "So much easier to twist."

Brot'ân'duivé ignored her and kept his attention on Léshil. "There are those who consider a traitor beyond the shield of custom and society—and not one of their own. As did Grôyt'ashia when he tried to take your life for interfering with my mission in Venjètz."

It was only half of the truth, but it served his purpose.

"And what about Léshil . . . Leesil?" Wynn asked. "What happens to him for killing one of yours? It was self-defense."

The young one eyed Brot'ân'duivé with a studied interest that left him wary.

"I will bear witness in Léshil's favor," he answered. "I know the truth of it, should it come to that."

"Truth?" Leesil spit. "In your mouth? Have any more sick jokes?"

"That, and the safe passage of humans in our land, is why the elders gather in Crijheäiche. Now Fréthfâre will give them something of greater concern to my people."

Brot'ân'duivé turned his eyes upon Magiere.

Magiere hurt for Leesil, despite her own pain. For all the trouble Wynn had caused, finding Nein'a had done little good.

She had lost control in front of their enemies, revealing her nature. They didn't truly understand what she was—but an explanation wouldn't gain her much. The child of a vampire would be viewed as little better than an undead.

Even worse, after all of Leesil's efforts, the loss and bloodshed, Nein'a wouldn't even speak to him.

Magiere avoided looking at the trees. Every time she did, they conjured images of the blotched dead marks her own touch had left on the birch. The ones no one else seemed to have noticed. Her vision of undead slaughtering an encampment still plagued her.

Elves, short and stout dwarves, and humans had fought side by side as allies, though it didn't seem possible. Certainly not in any part of her world. Wynn spoke at times of elves near her homeland who were far different from those here.

If it were real—if it had happened—then where and

when? And how and why had she seen it upon touching the birch?

Wynn shivered in the cooling air and clutched at Chap for warmth. Even Leesil huddled up as if chilled.

"We should start a fire," Magiere said. "Brot'an . . . help me find firewood."

"I'll go," Leesil demanded, though he kept his eyes down, unwilling to look at Brot'an. "You need rest."

Brot'an seemed about to object to either option. Magiere shook her head slightly at him, and then tilted it toward Leesil. Brot'an remained silent in puzzlement.

"Stay here," she told Leesil. "Have Wynn tell you about trying to walk Nein'a out of the clearing. Maybe there's something we've missed."

She got up and started off, and Brot'an followed. When they were far enough away not to be heard, he spoke up first.

"What is on your mind?"

"You saw me change when we fought in the crypt, but you didn't tell your . . . kind about me?"

After a pause, he replied, "It was not their concern."

"Does anyone else know that Leesil killed Darmouth?"

He stopped walking, forcing her to face him. "I reported my purpose as complete. No questions were asked, so I did not elaborate."

"Yet you did tell them he killed Grôyt?"

"A body does require explanation," Brot'an replied passively. "I returned Grôyt'ashia to his family and kin. He was Anmaglâhk, and his throat had been slashed open. Only the truth . . . only another trained in our way, was a believable explanation."

Magiere hated it when any of these butchers referred to Leesil as one of them.

"Whatever you want from Leesil, forget it," she warned. "We're leaving, and—one way or another—we're taking Leesil's mother. Your people have put him through enough. He'll live as he chooses, and I'll see to that. Understand?"

A strange weariness, or maybe sadness, washed over Brot'an's scarred face. "You have mated with Léshil."

Magiere was so taken aback that she lost her voice for

an instant. "Don't try meddling in my life. What's between Leesil and me is none of your concern."

"It is his concern, more than he may know," Brot'an answered. "I understand your intention, but you do not understand all that is involved . . . because of Léshil's heritage."

Magiere flinched at this, though she didn't understand all that Brot'an implied. Except perhaps that her connection to Leesil might be one more weight upon him in the coming days. She changed tactics.

"Then do me one favor," she said.

"If I am able."

"I need to speak with Nein'a alone . . . just for a few moments."

The wary Brot'an reappeared, and he shook his head.

"The others won't see or know," she went on. "I have questions for her before I decide what to do next. And I . . . I will owe you in return."

Being indebted to this man was almost more than Magiere could stomach, but she had to know what Leesil risked his future for. If she could go back in time and save her own mother, she would at any price. Magelia was worth the cost—but was Nein'a?

"Do not think for a moment," Brot'an warned, "that Fréthfâre will forget what she saw this day."

Brot'an's steady gaze made Magiere's persistent quiver all the more unsettling. He headed for the barrier woods, and she followed. When he stopped before the passage through those tangled trees, he held her off a moment longer.

"Remember your debt the next time I must have Léshil's cooperation for his own sake."

Magiere nodded, though it made her flush with resentment. She hoped Leesil would remain distracted by Wynn for a little while longer.

The passage through the woods had grown as dark as dusk beneath the clouded sky. As Magiere pushed aside the tall ferns and stepped into the open clearing, she wasn't certain how she would handle this meeting. She ended up waiting, lost in thought, until Nein'a appeared from around the domicile tree.

Nein'a carried the saffron cushion left beside the brook and headed toward her home. She stopped at the sight of Magiere, dropped the cushion beside the tree, and stood waiting.

As Magiere approached, Nein'a studied the two majay-hì still present. One lapped at the brook's water while the other curled upon the moss to wash. The sight seemed to bring the tall elven woman satisfaction.

"You risk the moment of peace Brot'ân'duivé created, but Sgäilsheilleache will be the one to pay if your absence is discovered."

Magiere had bargained blindly for this meeting, and now her tongue was tied as she looked upon this apparition of Leesil's past. Lovely, deadly Nein'a. Brot'an's hint at Magiere's intimacy with Leesil suddenly left her uncertain in facing Leesil's mother. Magiere wondered—out of all others, why had Leesil chosen her?

Magiere wore her emotions on her face. She had no wiles and no ways with feminine mystery.

"Don't you miss him?" she asked quietly. "Aren't you glad to see him?"

It wasn't what she'd planned to say. But if anyone had taken Leesil from her, had parted them for eight years, the sight of him again would've broken her into tears.

"You are . . . his?" Nein'a asked, though it wasn't really a question.

Neither insulting nor as bitterly sad as Brot'an's statement, and yet it intimidated Magiere.

"Yes. We own a tavern . . . in the town of Miiska on the Belaskian coast. But he has wanted to find you ever since Sgäile came at him in Bela and hinted that you might still be alive." Magiere found a touch of her own bitterness. "Even after everything you've done to him."

Nein'a stared directly into her eyes. "And what have I done to him?"

Magiere's hesitant bitterness became anger again. "You trained him—used him—forced him to murder in your footsteps. He drank himself to sleep every night just to forget the things you taught him to do."

"And would he have survived in your company without his training?" Nein'a asked.

"Survival, of course," Magiere hissed. "That is why you trained him. How unselfish!"

It was cruel, rather than just her usual bluntness. But did Nein'a bear any real love for her son?

"I know nothing of you," Nein'a returned. "Less even than you know of Léshil, who may yet serve a necessary purpose, and not just to my people alone. Only time will see if that comes to pass, and in part, I hope it does not. He must leave this land and get beyond Most Aged Father's reach. If you care for him, take him from this place."

She turned away and vanished inside the elm, not even stopping to retrieve the cushion she had dropped.

Magiere couldn't tell if it was rage or the forest's influence that made her tremble. The pieces of this game were still unclear to her.

Nein'a had trained Leesil without love—without a conscience. She had birthed him for a "purpose," as the Anmaglâhk called all their missions and dark tasks.

Chap had suggested that Nein'a and others among the Anmaglâhk wanted to thwart Most Aged Father. Or at least choose their own way to deal with some forgotten adversary their leader feared would return. For their own reasons, they wanted a half-blood for this. Perhaps they needed someone outside of their people as well as their caste. Leesil's mother had secretly trained him against the rules of her order.

Nein'a didn't love Leesil as a son, though he loved her as his mother.

Sorrow welled in Magiere as she swatted the ferns aside and strode out through the woods' passage. She would love Leesil enough to make up the difference.

Leesil glanced up as Brot'an returned with an armload of firewood and small dead branches for kindling.

"I cannot see what else to try," Wynn was saying.

"Where's Magiere?" Leesil asked Brot'an.

"Gathering more wood. She will return shortly."

Leesil rose to his feet and looked toward the elves' camp. He counted them and made certain all were present. They were, and relief from fear unleashed his anger. About to bark at Brot'an for stupidity, he held his words a moment longer. It didn't make sense that Brot'an would leave Magiere unattended.

How long had he been distracted by Wynn's experiences with Nein'a? His stomach churned each time he thought of his mother's greeting—or lack of it. He started off to find Magiere.

"She will return directly," Brot'an said. "Help me start the fire."

Leesil didn't wish to share even such a simple task with this man. But he crouched down, looking about repeatedly for any sign of Magiere.

The air grew damp, and the kindling was no better. Brot'an struck flint to a short stub of steel he produced, but it took a while to get decent flames started. Wynn fell to peeling bisselberries and cracking walnuts left beside the tree. Finally, Leesil heard footfalls crunching in the forest mulch. Magiere appeared but carried only three branches.

"Is that all you found?" Wynn asked.

Magiere didn't answer. Leesil took the branches and dropped them beside the fire.

"She's tired," he said, and pointed Magiere toward a large redwood a dozen paces off. "We're going over there to rest. Wynn, stay with Chap. Try to get some sleep."

"But you will be away from the fire," Wynn argued.

Leesil expected a challenge from Brot'an, but the man didn't even stand up.

"We should all rest," Brot'an said. "Find what comfort you can, but stay within my sight."

Leesil pushed Magiere on. Within sight, indeed. He wasn't about to leave Wynn alone in the scarred elf's company. He only wanted to be out of earshot. When he went to settle against the redwood, Magiere pulled back.

"Let's just sit in the open," she said and dropped down, waiting for him.

The forest grew darker with scant daylight, but she

didn't seem to care. So he crouched and dropped to his haunches beside her.

"This isn't what you expected, is it?" she whispered. "You thought she'd be grateful to see you after all this time—no matter what happened when you escaped from Venjètz."

Is that what made her so quiet and withdrawn—worry for him? No, there was something more. He could sense it.

"No, not what I expected," he answered. "Nothing we do turns out as we plan. It's like my childhood never happened, and she doesn't even know me."

Magiere's face grew tense and thoughtful, and she seemed reluctant to look at him. She had exposed her dhampir nature. The elves' reactions would cut her deeply, and she'd become the focus of their hatred more than he. He didn't care what she was. She was still Magiere. But was he what or who she would really want?

A thing—a tool—a weapon. She deserved more than that. Even his own mother rejected him as anything more.

"You're my blood, Leesil," Magiere whispered, "my family . . . all that I need."

Leesil's mind went blank, caught between her words and the fear of losing her. He looked at the black locks of hair hanging around her pale face.

"Marry me," she whispered, quick and sharp.

Leesil braced a hand upon the ground between his legs. He grew almost faint as the weight of the day and everything that had happened vanished and left him light-headed.

In this place, surrounded by so little hope and so many threats for the future . . .

He couldn't think straight, her two words echoing over and over in his emptied mind.

"No," he blurted out.

Magiere lifted her head, her eyes round with shock.

"Yes, I mean . . . no," he fumbled. "I mean . . ."

Any other time he'd made an ass of himself, she'd turned livid, ready to club him for his stupidity. But Magiere just sat there in startled pain.

As if he'd struck her.

Leesil grabbed Magiere's face and pressed his mouth hard to hers. She wrestled free, nearly shoving him over. Confusion mixed with a hint of her old ire.

"Yes," he said quickly. "I mean yes . . . but no, not here and not now."

Oh, how he had botched things again. But Magiere's brows softened quickly.

"Can't you see?" he rushed on, and grabbed both her hands, holding them tightly. "I don't want it like this, not among enemies. Not until we're home again with Karlin and Caleb and maybe Aunt Bieja. That's where it should happen. Where it can be the right day—a celebration. The finest day of our lives."

Two tears slid down Magiere's face. "A celebration?"

"With dancing," he added.

She slipped her arms around his neck, clutching him so hard he couldn't breathe.

Chap stayed with Wynn, eyeing Brot'an, though he knew Leesil would not move out of sight. He tried to understand Nein'a's unexpected behavior.

Unlike Leesil, Chap had never anticipated an open welcome. The Nein'a that he remembered was cunning and cautious. So much so that Chap had always had difficulty in dipping even one memory from her thoughts. Brot'an and even Eillean were much the same. All three were adept at keeping their minds clear of triggered memories that would interfere with their focus upon what must be done. But Nein'a should be doing everything in her power to help free herself. Her refusal to leave perplexed Chap.

Wynn scooted closer to the fire and tried to stuff her small hands up her tunic's opposing sleeves. Brot'an appeared to be rearranging his own attire beneath his gray-green cloak. Chap heard clinking metal and wondered what the elf was doing.

He would not trust Brot'an, but his estimation of the man grew less certain. Brot'an served his own agenda, but he had placed himself between Magiere and his caste. He had also managed to keep Leesil under control, without letting their past conflict boil into the open.

Brot'an glanced across the low flames at Wynn and stripped off his heavy cloak. The sleeves of his green tunic were pulled down, but Chap caught no signs of weapons on his wrists. Brot'an stepped around the fire and draped his cloak over the small sage. Wynn jumped slightly.

"Sleep," he told her, and he slid down to sit against the tree behind the sage.

"Thank you," Wynn said, formally polite. "I left Chane's . . . my cloak back in Crijheäiche. Will you not be cold?"

"Sleep," he repeated.

Wynn lay back and, after a moment, closed her eyes.

Chap dropped his head to his paws, still watching Brot'an.

He should rest with Wynn and keep her warm. This day had been no better for her than the others. In some ways, far worse. The Fay knew of her gift—or curse—of sensing when they manifested nearby.

A soft blur of white appeared near the edge of a far cedar. Lily poked her head around and whined.

Chap stifled his eagerness to go to her, not wanting to leave Wynn and Magiere alone and subject to so many threats. When he turned from Lily with a sigh, he found Brot'an watching him, and wrinkled his jowls at the man.

"Go," Brot'an said.

Leesil kept watch from an open space between the trees. Magiere lay with her head upon his thigh, her eyes closed. Still, Chap would not leave.

He glanced at the group of Anmaglâhk gathered at another fire off through the forest. They huddled about the flames as Fréthfâre stood over them, but he could not hear their voices clearly.

"Enough!" Sgäile said too loudly and stood up.

Chap heard no more, though it appeared Sgäile defended whatever Fréthfâre had said to all there. Én'nish turned away where she sat, and the conversation ended.

Lily came up beside Chap, surprising him with a lick on his ear. He didn't look at her but kept his eyes on the gathering of enemies.

"No one will disturb your companions," Brot'an said.

The words broke Chap's concentration as he tried to

catch any memories in the minds of the Anmaglâhk. He rumbled softly.

He did not care for so many having discovered how truly aware he was. First Sgäile—and now Brot'an spoke to him in full sentences, as if knowing he understood.

"We should all take what time is left to be with our own kind," Brot'an added.

The tall elf leaned his head back against the tree and stared into the fire's small dancing flames.

Chap got up slowly as Lily headed off. He shivered, but not from cold.

Though he was uncertain why, his thoughts slipped back to the phantasm he had suffered in the forests of Droevinka—Magiere's homeland. He had seen her, mad and feral, standing in the dark at the head of an army. Among the twisted creatures of the living walked those of the undead. He shook the memory off—it was a lie induced by sorcery.

Chap loped after Lily until she paused and circled around in a mulch-filled hollow between three close fir trees.

Her fur was warm and soft against him. He pressed into her as they turned about each other. There was relief in her gentle presence. For a little while, he was not so alone. He had kin of flesh, kin of living spirit, if not those who had betrayed him and taken his memories. And when he finally lay quiet beside her, it was with memory and not words that they spoke in whispers.

CHAPTER SIXTEEN

Leesil sat quietly with Magiere's head upon his leg. He expected rain to come, but the sky never broke open, so he saw no need to disturb Magiere and move to better cover.

Past what he guessed was noon beneath the dark clouds, Osha approached Brot'an. The young elf's gaze drifted to Wynn sleeping soundly in Brot'an's cloak.

"It is time," Brot'an called to Leesil.

At the sound of his voice, Magiere's eyes opened. She hadn't slept either and only rested.

Leesil's leg had gone numb beneath her head. He struggled to his feet, pulling Magiere up as his leg tingled with returning feeling. When Brot'an went to gather the others, Leesil left Magiere with Wynn and snuck off toward the barrier woods. Halfway there, he heard steps behind him, and turned to see Sgäile following.

"I won't be long," he said. "Unless you're fool enough to try to stop me."

"Then I will go as well," Sgäile answered. "Or you will not go at all."

Leesil was too weary to argue. He had no idea how soon another chance might come to see his mother. So he turned toward the passage through the woods with Sgäile close on his heels.

They emerged in the clearing, and Nein'a was outside her tree waiting. Leesil glanced back at Sgäile.

"Go," the man said with a sigh. "I will wait here."

Leesil had thought long on his mother while Magiere rested in his lap. Eight years in this glade, seeming so easy to leave and yet not, would drive anyone to odd ways. If he'd been thinking more clearly at their earlier meeting, he might have realized this. Stepping close before her and looking up into her calm yet disquieted face, he couldn't think of much to say besides the obvious.

"I can't free you by staying here. I'm going back to Crijheäiche to find a way to make your people listen." He lowered his voice. "Then you are leaving with me and Magiere."

She reached out and gripped his wrist. The action held no affection, and he almost pulled away.

"Forget me and leave this forest," she whispered, and then her tone grew soft, more like the lyrical voice he remembered from youth. "Please . . . my son."

All of Leesil's resentment melted in his mother's sudden warmth.

"You may trust Sgäilsheilleache's guardianship," she whispered. "But in all other things, trust only Brot'ân'duivé."

He jerked free of her grasp. "I will be back . . . and you should trust only me."

"Léshil," Sgäile called, sounding strained. "Come."

Leesil turned away from his mother.

By midafternoon, Wynn worried about keeping the pace Sgäile set. She still wore Brot'an's hopelessly oversized cloak over her baggy elven clothing, and the combined raiment was heavy and cumbersome. But she was still too cold to remove the cloak.

The few times she took her eyes from the others around her, the forest shifted in unsettling ways. With the sun hidden behind thick clouds, all the world was caught within a lingering dusk. Her spirits low, she struggled to keep up—but not only because she was exhausted and worried.

She felt cut off and alone.

Leesil and Magiere were silent except for brief glances and touches they exchanged. Wynn thought she saw Leesil smile briefly, just once, at Magiere.

Chap ranged in and out of their procession, sometimes coming back to Wynn's side. Not once did he speak into her head, and after only a short distance, he ran off into the trees once again. Even Osha rarely looked at her or Magiere. Brot'an was considerate in his actions but otherwise as distant as the rest of the Anmaglâhk.

Wynn had no one to turn to for a soft word or a look of comfort, and thoughts of Chap and her encounter with his kin returned often. This forest proved a terrible place that fed her loneliness.

Sgäile's demeanor worried her most. He had changed since witnessing Magiere's savage side. Wynn always found him daunting—occasionally frightening—but she had been certain he would protect her or Leesil or Magiere. Now his amber eyes were glazed, and any concern he showed was mechanical. Twice, he seemed about to speak to her, but then looked away.

He also appeared determined to rush them back to Crijheäiche as quickly as possible.

Somewhere behind Wynn, a strange chirp floated through the forest. She tried to slow and listen, but the procession's pace was too quick. She was left to wonder if it was the same kind of bird she had heard on their first journey in Crijheäiche.

Wynn had had enough of silence. All right, so she had brought much of this on herself. Or rather Chap had gotten her into it by running off without telling anyone. But compared to the encounter with the Fay, she should feel lucky to be alive.

She quick-stepped up behind Osha, trying to think of something to ask. Something useful—or not. Anything to break the silence for just one breath. She tugged on his cloak as she stumbled over the hem of her own.

Osha glanced over his shoulder with a frown.

"What is . . . *Greimasg'äh*?" she asked quietly. "A grasp-something? I heard the others use it to refer to Brot'an, and once for Urhkar. Some title or rank?"

Timid Osha looked ahead at Sgäile yet again. But Sgäile pressed on behind Brot'an's lead and did not appear to hear.

"Oh for goodness' sake, Osha!" Wynn snapped in a harsh whisper. "I am not trying to get some great secret out of you!"

Sgäile glanced back once.

"Shadow-grip . . . gripper . . . keeper . . . ," Osha said with difficulty, as the word seemed troublesome for his limited Belaskian. "Masters beyond our caste ways, beyond what our teachers know and teach us. Many say Greimasg'äh grip shadows, pull them in to . . . to hide them. No one see them until they want. It is great honor if Greimasg'äh accepts you for . . . to teach you. I am not lucky for this."

When Wynn looked ahead at Brot'an's back, she caught Magiere listening to Osha's words.

"There were . . . once five," Osha added. "Now are four . . . when we lose Léshil's great-mother."

For an instant, Wynn thought he meant Nein'a. "You mean 'grandmother' . . . Eillean?"

Osha nodded and went silent. Wynn was back to struggling to keep up.

"Halt for rest," Brot'an called.

Wynn expected Sgäile might argue, but he crouched by an evergreen, poised for the moment they resumed. She was grateful for any reason to pause and braced a hand on a silver birch to steady herself.

A shadow crossed Wynn, and she looked up.

Sgäile stood close enough that she could have counted the white hairs of his feathery eyebrows. His handsome face was lined with tension.

"All that happened this last day and night," he said quietly in Elvish, "was because you did not heed my words. You remain under my protection, but disobey again and I will do whatever is necessary to assure your safety . . . no matter that you will dislike my methods. Do you understand?"

Wynn bit back her retort.

If his kind had not imprisoned Nein'a, Leesil would never have needed to come here in the first place. She and Chap would not have had to break Most Aged Father's attempt at coercion. But Sgäile's tone was so serious.

"Yes," she answered stiffly.

He headed back to his resting place, and Wynn turned and found Leesil standing right behind her.

"What was that?" he asked.

"Nothing," she answered. "Just . . . nothing."

Leesil grabbed her hand and pulled her along toward where Magiere crouched. "You stay near us. And let's see if we can't tie up that cloak."

Wynn gripped down on Leesil's fingers, feeling a little less alone.

Forest scents intoxicated Chap, and still he returned often to look in on Magiere and Leesil and Wynn. The majay-hì shadowed the procession from out in the trees as they all headed toward Crijheäiche. But Chap believed the pack only made the journey because Lily stayed with him.

The dogs fell behind to sniff, and even to hunt. More than once, one of them chased down the silver yearling who had wandered off. Some ran ahead, but in the end, they always ended up back near the Anmaglâhk and Chap's companions.

He pressed his nose against Lily and drew in her warm scent. But as they returned again to the procession, he caught brief words in Leesil's memory, spoken in Magiere's hushed voice.

Marry me.

Chap paused, ears cocked.

And Leesil now dwelled in embarrassment upon his fumbled response.

How strange and surprising that it had happened in this place, in these dangerous times. But when Chap dipped Magiere's thoughts for her memory of that moment, his wonderment vanished.

He saw through her eyes the dead bark upon the tree

she had touched. He heard the name spoken in her mind as she had blacked out.

Sorhkafâré.

It was not familiar to Chap at first, until he saw tangled pieces of what Magiere experienced the moment she fell prone.

He knew the encampment, and remembered that long-ago night in an ancient elf's fearful memories. The two became one.

Sorhkafâré . . . Aoishenis-Ahâre . . . Most Aged Father.

Magiere had touched a tree. She had seen a vision she did not understand—one of Most Aged Father's oldest memories.

Chap looked wildly about the forest, wary of every quiver of leaf.

Nein'a had looked about the clearing in the same way, easing only when the majay-hì appeared peaceful and settled in their surroundings. And Lily had tried desperately to keep Chap from going into Most Aged Father's home.

Somehow the withered old elf, impossibly long in his years, had been in Nein'a's glade. He had been in the tree Magiere had touched. It was the only thing Chap could reason.

Magiere had touched a tree . . . and eaten a piece of its life without knowing it. Chap remembered his delusional vision of her at the head of an army upon the edge of a dying forest.

He paced quickly through the trees, watching Magiere from a distance as his fear rose.

He wanted no more of this. He wanted only to be alone a while longer with Lily. But he kept seeing Magiere in his own remembered delusion and the dark shapes of others waiting upon her to enter the trees.

Lily yipped as a brown hare raced out from under a bed of mammoth coleus.

Chap did not follow her.

Welstiel headed south as dusk turned to night. He led their remaining horse packed with their gear while Chane's new familiar loped ahead of them.

He noted how gaunt Chane appeared. They would need to melt snow later, perhaps use the last crumbles of tea taken from the Móndyalítko, and replenish their bodies' fluids. For the most part Chane looked tolerable, all things considered. Even in his used cloak and scuffed boots, there was still some trace of a young nobleman, tall and arrogant. No one who saw him could doubt his heritage—at least the one that Chane once had in his living days.

Welstiel feared that he could not claim so much at present. He fastened his tattered cloak more tightly, and tried to smooth his filthy hair.

He had not dreamed these past days. Why would his patron show him the castle, its inhabitant, and the very room of the orb, only to fall silent? He clung to one hope.

The Móndyalítko had been clear in their directions. It was possible that Welstiel's patron felt no further assistance was needed. Yes, that must be the case.

Barren rocks and patches of snow and ice vanished as his thoughts drifted into the future.

He wore a white silk shirt and charcoal wool tunic. He was clean and well possessed, living alone on a manor estate in isolation, perhaps somewhere on the northern peninsula of Belaski, still within reach of its capital of Bela or the shipyards of Guèshk. The manor's entire first floor was given over to a library and study, with one whole room for the practice of his arcane artificing. He could create ever more useful objects and never need to touch a mortal again. For somewhere in the cellars below, safely tucked into hiding, was the orb—his orb.

The horse tossed its head, jerking the reins in Welstiel's hand, as the animal's hoof slipped on a patch of snow-crusted stones. It righted itself, and Welstiel looked up the barren mountainside at his companion.

Chane never wavered from his desire to seek out the sages. Why—to study histories and fill his head with mountains of broken pieces culled from the past? Ridiculous.

Welstiel shook his head. Only the present was useful. Let broken days of the Forgotten History remain forgotten, once he acquired what he needed. A solitary existence with no distractions.

But still . . .

"Have you ever tried your hand at artificing?" he asked, his own voice startling in the night's silence.

Chane lifted his eyes from his trudging steps. Conjury— by ritual, spell, or artificing—always stirred Chane's interest.

"Small things," he answered. "Only temporary or passive items for my rituals. Nothing like . . . your ring or feeding cup. I once created a small orb to blind interlopers. I conjured the essence of Light—a manifestation of elemental Fire—and trapped it within a prepared globe of frosted glass. When tripped, its light erupted, and it was spent."

Welstiel hesitated. "You developed notable skill for one who had no instructor. I wonder how you would fare with a more studied guide to teach you."

Chane stopped walking, forcing Welstiel to pause.

"Have you fed without telling me?" Chane asked.

"No, why?"

"You are different tonight . . . more aware."

Welstiel ignored this bit of nonsense. A series of loud barks sounded from ahead.

Chane dropped to the ground and folded his long legs.

Welstiel struggled to be silent and wait as his companion closed his eyes.

Chane would reach out to connect—spirit to spirit, thought to thought—with the wild dog he had enslaved. He would learn through the dumb beast's senses what it had found. Far more efficient than racing after the animal and wasting remaining energies before knowing if it was worth the expenditure.

Welstiel stood tense, fighting for patience.

The castle could be just ahead. The end of his repugnant existence might be that close.

CHAPTER SEVENTEEN

Night wore on as Magiere traveled beside Leesil and kept Wynn close. She cautiously allowed her dhampir nature to rise just enough to widen her vision. It accomplished little with the moon hidden from sight.

Leesil said no more about his mother. Wynn was near physical exhaustion, so her bursts of babbling were few. All the Anmaglâhk, especially Sgäile, were withdrawn and driven by their purpose. Only in one place in the world did people accept Magiere for who, rather than what, she was—Miiska. But home was far away.

She tried to shut out the vision she'd had in Nein'a's clearing, the marks her hands left on the tree, and whatever lay ahead in Crijheäiche. She tried to focus on Leesil.

Leesil was the imaginative one, not she. After facing Nein'a's coldheartedness, all Magiere wished was to make him feel wanted—and to let him know he would at least have her for the rest of his days. He reminded her that there was a place for them in this world, where others waited to stand up with them on the day they swore their oath. Annoying as Leesil was at times, he was right.

His words painted a picture in her mind of celebration with Karlin, Caleb, little Rose, and perhaps Aunt Bieja.

Magiere imagined Leesil with his hair tied back and wearing a clean white shirt—one he hadn't mended and patched beyond its time.

Yes, she wanted this too.

The surrounding forest began to look familiar, and Magiere caught the soft glow of lanterns among the trees. They passed an enormous oak swollen into a dwelling.

"We're close," she said.

"Oh, for a bath and clean clothes," Wynn grumbled.

Fréth traveled just ahead of Leesil, but she slowed and dropped to the rear near Én'nish.

Magiere found this odd. Then she saw someone running toward them between the domicile trees, flashing in and out of pools of lantern light or the seeping glow from under a curtained doorway.

Leanâlhâm's yellow shirt stood out in the dark. She smiled and ran straight for Sgäile with her light brown ponytail swishing. Sgäile pulled her against his chest, and Leanâlhâm's eyes wandered about the group until they found Wynn.

"I am so glad you are found," she said with the relief of a lifelong friend. "Urhkarasiférin said you were lost in the forest, but I knew Sgäilsheilleache would find you."

Wynn smiled briefly over her exhaustion.

Magiere waited for Leanâlhâm's rush of questions. But when the girl tried to go to Wynn, Sgäile's arm tightened. He held her back, turning slightly away. Magiere knew it wasn't Wynn who he kept the girl from—it was herself.

Sgäile spoke harshly in Elvish to Leanâlhâm, and the girl's mouth dropped open with a flash of hurt in her eyes.

"Bârtva'na!" Sgäile half-shouted, cutting off her rising protest.

Magiere understood the word from the little Elvish that she'd heard Wynn translate. Sgäile commanded the girl to stop and obey. Leanâlhâm stared at him with open resentment.

"He ordered her back to their quarters," Wynn said quietly. "She is not to speak with us."

"What?" Leesil asked. "Why?"

It wasn't right for Sgäile to deny the girl so harshly. He

didn't want his little cousin anywhere near the unnatural thing discovered among them. But for all the man's fear, he couldn't possibly believe Magiere would harm Leanâlhâm. She'd given her word to watch over the girl whenever possible.

Sgäile's distress ran more deeply than Magiere had guessed.

She glanced carefully about at the other Anmaglâhk. Most remained expressionless, except for Én'nish's venomous glare and Fréth's smoldering silence. But Brot'an now peered about the trees with a strange uncertainty.

Magiere wanted no more confrontations with Sgäile, and hopefully Leanâlhâm would do as he asked.

Leanâlhâm backed away, her features fading in the deeper black beneath a tree in the darkness.

"Shiuvâlh!" Sgäile snapped.

That word Magiere didn't know, but his tone made her tense. A shadow appeared behind Leanâlhâm, followed by another to the right. Magiere whirled around to find more closing on the left and from behind.

"Leesil . . . ," she hissed in warning.

He turned, watching dark figures move in the night.

Osha stepped closer to Wynn. Sgäile pulled a stiletto, as did Fréth. Brot'an turned about more slowly, the puzzlement in his steady gaze becoming cold displeasure. The first shadow stepped into plain sight.

Urhkar stood calm and passive. Another anmaglâhk came in behind him, and another from beyond Sgäile, and then another. All but the elder anmaglâhk held shortbows drawn with arrows notched, their gleaming heads resting over bow handles of silver-white metal.

Magiere found herself ringed in on all sides with Leesil and Wynn by at least twenty Anmaglâhk. No wonder Sgäile pushed them all so hard, knowing what waited upon their arrival.

"You split-tongue son of . . . ," Leesil started, his gaze on Sgäile.

Magiere grabbed Leesil's wrist and squeezed hard in warning as she glanced back at Wynn. A wrinkle of the sage's brow hinted at something more beneath her fright—

a tinge of anger in the once-timid sage. Magiere saw no course of action that wouldn't end in all of their deaths.

Fréth and Sgäile faced inward toward Magiere. Sgäile kept his blade low, but Fréth did not.

"What are you doing?" Leesil demanded.

Brot'an gave Urhkar a slow shake of his head, but the other elder returned no reply.

"All of you pull back and allow us through," Brot'an called out.

Not one anmaglâhk retreated, and Fréth came straight at Magiere and Leesil.

"You will come with us."

Magiere heard Leesil's foot slip back, and the grinding of sod as he anchored it and shifted his weight. Six Anmaglâhk stepped in with bows raised. Two were aimed straight at Wynn.

"No!" Magiere whispered. "Too many for a fight."

And then Brot'an sidled into the path of the bows aimed at Wynn.

"She is correct," he said plainly. "We must wait to find another way to resolve this."

Leesil turned his head side to side, his eyes moving even quicker as he studied the spread of all those surrounding them. None of the elves lowered their weapons.

"Go!" Fréth ordered.

Uncertainly, Leesil moved up beside Magiere, and they followed Brot'an. They were swept away into the heart of Crijheäiche. Magiere grew more uncertain as they entered a wide clearing encircled by domicile trees.

Near to each tree's curtained doorway, she saw more of the Anmaglâhk. At the clearing's center rose a massive oak that dwarfed any tree she'd seen since entering these lands.

"They're taking us to Most Aged Father," Leesil whispered.

Wynn stayed close to Magiere as they faced Most Aged Father's dwelling. She looked about for any sign of Chap, but he was nowhere in sight. Neither was the pack or Lily. Sgäile pulled the doorway's curtain aside.

"Down the stairs!" Fréth ordered.

Wynn looked up anxiously at Brot'an. He nodded once and stepped through the entrance after Sgäile. Leesil went next, then Magiere, and Wynn followed with Fréth close behind her.

Inside, candle lanterns lit the wide barren chamber. A stairway of living wood along the left wall led down into the earth. Wynn reached the bottom, stepping off the last stair of embedded stone, and found herself in an earth-walled chamber. At its center was a root the size of a small domicile tree.

Glass lanterns hung from stone-packed earth walls and cast hazy yellow light upon massive roots arching through the ceiling overhead. Wynn was not certain why they were here, but this underground chamber disturbed her. No elf that she knew would choose to live this way.

"Move!" Fréth ordered and shoved Magiere from behind.

Magiere stumbled forward awkwardly, pulling her hand back from catching herself on the center root. She wobbled, and Wynn grabbed her arm, feeling the uncontrolled shudders running through Magiere.

Leesil whirled about, and Fréth raised her blade.

"You wouldn't even try," he said. "Your sickly master still needs me."

"Enough," Brot'an warned, but his eyes were turned toward Fréth.

"And Chap wouldn't let you," Leesil whispered at Fréth.

Wynn's attention was pulled in too many directions. Magiere quaked in a way Wynn had never seen before. She did not usually frighten this easily—and her fear led to fury, not weakness.

A flash of gray on the stairs caught Wynn's attention.

Chap descended, his jaws already open.

Sgäile tried to reach over the stairs and grab the dog. Leesil slammed his shoulder into Sgäile's back, shoving him aside as Chap lunged off the stairs with a rabid snarl.

Fréth barely caught sight of the dog before Chap's jaws snapped shut on her wrist. She dropped the stiletto with a startled inhale and jerked her arm free as the blade hit the chamber floor. Chap's snarls rang off the stone-packed walls as he drove Fréth backward.

Leesil snatched the fallen stiletto before Sgäile could dive for it. All Wynn could do was try to keep Magiere on her feet.

Fréth scrambled over the bottom stair, braced herself against the wall, and kicked out. Her foot struck Chap's chest, tossing him away. Chap twisted back at her so fast that Fréth gained no ground. He lunged at her, jaws opened wide.

Brot'an slipped between them, and Chap's teeth closed fast on his forearm. Chap thrashed his head and dragged Brot'an to one knee.

"Chap, stop it!" Wynn cried out.

Brot'an did not strike back. He crouched there, rigid and waiting as Chap settled to rumbling stillness.

"No more!" Brot'an said sharply.

Leesil held off Sgäile with the stiletto, but his eyes shifted toward Fréth. "There's little I wouldn't pay to kill you. Don't ever touch me or mine again."

"Chap . . . you let him go . . . now!" Wynn commanded.

Chap unclamped Brot'an's arm with clear reluctance, rumbling as he backed toward Magiere. His gaze remained fixed on the tall elf rising to his feet. Dark stains spread through the gray-green felt of Brot'an's torn sleeve.

He spotted the blade in Leesil grip, and held out his hand. "Please."

"Give it to him," Magiere whispered and straightened herself.

Leesil flipped the stiletto, catching its blade, and slapped the hilt into Brot'an's palm.

"Fréthfâre . . . ," Brot'an warned, tossing the stiletto to her, "keep your distance—and your conduct."

"And you too," Wynn said to Chap, though relieved to see him. "Where have you been?"

Chap ceased rumbling and the leaf-wing rose in Wynn's mind. *Watching.*

"This way," Sgäile said as he circled the chamber.

Wynn did not understand until she spotted the opening in the center root. Sgäile stepped through, and Wynn followed ahead of Magiere.

In the shining candlelight, Wynn at first saw only teal and saffron pillows on the floor, but her mouth went dry as she took in the rest of the small chamber.

Curled in a cradle of wood growing from the far wall and floor was the oldest elf she had ever seen. Only vague hints remained in his withered form to mark his race.

An emaciated face surrounded sunken eyes that had lost most of their amber color. Those old eyes never blinked, and patches of scalp showed through thinned hair. He shuddered with either fear or rage when he saw Magiere.

"Why are we here?" Leesil demanded.

"To be judged," Fréth snapped from the doorway.

Brot'an's broad frame stood in her way. Sgäile stepped close to the frail form in the living bower and proffered a deep, respectful nod. The old one did not even glance at him.

"Judged?" Wynn said.

Most Aged Father's thin, reedy voice filled the root chamber as he spoke in Belaskian.

"No undead will poison this forest. Destroy it at once."

Sgäile did not answer or look up.

"You'll be bleeding before anyone touches her," Leesil warned.

"She is not undead," Wynn blurted out.

"Truth," Brot'an added, and moved closer to the old one. "And this is not the way judgment is rendered . . . especially when guardianship and safe passage have already been given. Do you now break your word as well as that of Sgäilsheilleache?"

"You are Anmaglâhk," said Most Aged Father, and finally turned his attention on Brot'an. "You are sworn to protect the people. Would you leave an undead in their midst? I do not know how this one could even enter our land."

"Her heart beats," Brot'an returned. "I know little of the humans' walking dead . . . but enough to know she is not one of them."

Most Aged Father's eyes narrowed upon Brot'an.

Fréth pushed through into Wynn's sight. "Do you question Most Aged Father? Do you deny what we saw in the traitor's clearing?"

"The forest accepts her," Brot'an answered. "And the majay-hì do not hunt her."

"Until she showed herself for what she is," Fréthfâre argued.

"She is not undead," Wynn repeated straight at Most Aged Father. "She hates them as you do. She is only half of what they are, and it makes her their natural adversary."

Brot'an glanced at Wynn, as did the other elves, each with their own mix of suspicion and doubt. Magiere grabbed Wynn's hand with a sharp shake of her head.

Most Aged Father's voice screeched in Wynn's ears. "Half undead is more than enough!"

"Truly?" Brot'an asked. "Is a half-blood a human or an elf, let alone an'Cróan? And what would that make a three-quarter-blood?"

Sgäile lifted his head at the reference to Leanâlhâm, and Brot'an let the question hang. And it left Wynn wondering if the girl's status among her people was not yet determined. She watched all four elves present, waiting for someone to speak up.

They were not presenting arguments to sway Most Aged Father, for at least Fréth and Brot'an spoke from some equal authority here. It was their people's customs and cultural rule versus Anmaglâhk authority that was being called into question, as well as anyone's status of mixed heritage. In the end, Magiere's welfare alone might not be all that was at stake, though she would likely be the first weighed in the outcome.

"And still, this is not our decision," Brot'an continued. "As Most Aged Father has wisely stated, we are sworn to protect our people . . . to serve them, not to rule them or decide for them. We are not a clan."

"You overstep yourself," Fréth cut in. "Neither does a Greimasg'äh make decisions for the caste, nor define what it is."

"Yet another truth, Covârleasa," Brot'an answered agreeably. "The people determine what we are . . . have determined it. We serve them. We are defined by their will—not by ourselves or the purpose we serve. The clan elders are the voice and will of the people. They already gather to address any judgments—as is proper."

Sgäile finally spoke, in a ragged voice. "Usurp our people's ways, and there remains nothing for our caste to protect, preserve, or serve. Father . . . you would agree?"

Most Aged Father's old eyes were fixed upon Magiere. Wynn's panic rose as she realized that he wanted Fréth to murder Magiere where she stood.

"Wise as always, my son," Most Aged Father replied to Sgäile. "The elders will see this woman for what she is. But I withdraw my protection—the outsiders are no longer my guests."

Sgäile straightened and stiffened, staring at Most Aged Father as if some breach had occurred. Brot'an's features clouded. Both men were about to speak, but Most Aged Father held them silent with a frail wave of his bony hand.

"She stands formally accused," he continued, "as does Léshil for bringing her into our land, knowing what she is. All three interlopers will remain under guard. That is within the purpose and service of the Anmaglâhk. Do you not agree?"

The final question was aimed at Brot'an. Wynn waited for a denial, some argument that might get Magiere out of danger.

Brot'an nodded polite. "Yes, and I thank you for the reminder. I will escort them."

Sgäile looked ill. Perhaps he had never disagreed with Most Aged Father before.

Brot'an placed a hand on Wynn's back. "Go."

She hurried out to find Fréth waiting at the stairs, blade in hand.

Leesil hooked the doorway curtain with a finger and peered out of their living cell. Four armed anmaglâhk stood outside the domicile elm, gripping shortbows with arrows notched. Urhkar was among them, but not Osha. Leesil let the curtain fall back into place.

Magiere slumped upon one bed ledge in the tree's wall, her arms folded across her chest as if she held herself together. Wynn sat with Chap, spreading parchments of Elvish symbols on the dirt floor.

"We have to find a way out of this," Wynn said. "I do not

believe Magiere will be given a fair trial. These people are paranoid about humans, let alone a . . ."

She didn't finish, but Leesil knew what she meant. Let alone an undead, half or otherwise, though even that wasn't the truth.

"We wouldn't get six paces out the door," Leesil said in frustration. "What's this council like? What kind of trial laws do the elves have?"

"How should I know?" Wynn snapped. "I have never seen one, even in my land. Chap may know more."

Chap swung his head from side to side and huffed twice for "no." Wynn sighed, sat back, and ceased spreading out the parchments.

Magiere had hesitated upon entering their quarters and remained silent thereafter. Leesil crouched before her and placed his hands on her thighs.

"I never should have brought you here . . . any of you."

Magiere didn't answer, but Leesil felt a quiver in her legs.

"I am guilty," she finally said. "At least of what they think I might be."

"Don't talk like that!" Leesil said. "You're not some undead."

She raised only her dark eyes to him—the same look she gave him when she thought he was being thickheaded or purposefully evasive. But her face was more weary than annoyed, as if she'd already given up.

"Do not do that!" Wynn snapped. "Not unless I am expecting it. I have had enough of getting sick for one day."

Leesil pivoted to find Wynn shoving Chap away. The dog growled and then clawed at the parchments. But he wasn't tapping out symbols for Wynn to read. He just scattered them in a tantrum as the sage tried to grab the sheets away from him.

"Stop it!" Wynn shouted at the dog. "We are talking the old way, whether you like it or not."

"Keep your voice down," Leesil warned. "What's going on?"

Both of them ceased fighting over the parchments. Chap growled at the sage, barking once for "yes."

Wynn took a long breath, frowning. "I did not want to distract you from more immediate concerns."

"Spit it out," Leesil demanded, and Chap barked agreement.

Wynn rubbed her knees where she knelt, and then crawled closer to Leesil.

"I can hear Chap," she said.

"What?" Magiere asked, her voice hushed.

"And I hear when he communes with his kin," Wynn added. "Although it may never happen again. They used him—as much as anyone has used either of you."

Leesil couldn't even form a question. The more Wynn whispered of all that had happened, from hearing Chap with the silver deer to the assault of the Fay, the less he wanted to know. As the sage finished, he stared at her and the dog.

Chap watched him silently in turn.

Leesil understood being an outcast in this world. He'd been alone but for Chap, without a place of his own, until he'd stumbled into Magiere—with Chap's meddling, of course. But now it seemed the dog didn't know everything concerning his own purpose.

Chap had been played by his own kind—one more unwitting tool manipulated by the Fay. Leesil wanted to sympathize with his oldest companion, but right now the last thing he needed to hear was that Chap was almost as ignorant as the rest of them.

And Wynn could hear him?

"The mantic sight," Wynn went on, "which I invoked by ritual in Droevinka to help you track the undead sorcerer . . . it returns at times. Whatever Chap did to take it from me, something went wrong, and it is getting worse. I was able to call it at will, but then Chap had to lick it away again."

"But you still hear him, even without the sight?" Magiere asked.

Wynn nodded, and then she flinched with a gag and uttered one word. "Sorhkafâré."

Magiere's leg muscles knotted under Leesil's hands.

Wynn balled up her little fist at Chap. "I told you—not until I am ready!"

Chap ignored her and focused on Magiere, and Leesil turned his eyes on the woman he loved.

That word—or name—did it mean something to her? Magiere's pallid skin made it hard to be certain, but she looked suddenly ill.

"Where did you hear that name?" she whispered.

"Not me," Wynn said. "That was Chap."

Leesil followed Magiere's rapt attention back to Chap, as Wynn slumped in resignation, speaking for the dog and turning a bit sickly herself. For every word Chap spoke through Wynn, Leesil saw his own dread echoed in Magiere's brown eyes.

Most Aged Father had been alive during the war in what the sages called the Forgotten History. How long ago wasn't clear. Even his own people didn't remember where or when he had come from.

The sages still argued over when this war took place, and even Chap couldn't guess, for his memories didn't give him any measure of time. However long ago, Sorhkafâré had not been old. Now he was the decrepit leader of the An-maglâhk and impossibly ancient.

What Leesil heard still didn't explain the man's fanatical hatred of humans, strong enough to teach generations of his people to fear them. But how had Magiere known his long lost name?

"What else haven't you told me?" he asked her a little too harshly.

Magiere didn't answer.

Wynn flinched in fear, over and over, at the words Chap poured through her. As the tale swept on to the night following the battle, Leesil saw strange recognition in Magiere's face. More than once she mouthed a name before Wynn even spoke it aloud.

"I know them," Magiere whispered. "I was there . . . I was him that night . . . when I blacked out in Nein'a's clearing."

"How?" Leesil asked.

Magiere's voice carried none of its old bite as she glared at Chap. "You've been in my head again."

Leesil remembered the first time she'd had a vision. In

Bela, she'd held cloth from a victim's body. She had walked the place where the corpse had been found and relived the moment when an undead had slaughtered the woman, a nobleman's daughter. Nothing like that had happened in Nein'a's clearing.

Magiere slowly shook her head. "All I wanted was to kill anything that got in the way of finding you. I touched the tree, and I was there . . . inside Most Aged Father . . . or his memory, at least."

"You saw undeads?"' Wynn asked. "Vampires . . . in the form of risen soldiers?"

Magiere looked at her. "He . . . they didn't know what was happening. They just ran inland toward On-nis Lo . . . Lon . . ."

Wynn sat upright. "Aonnis Lhoin'n?"

Magiere nodded. "I don't know if they made it, though obviously Sorhkafâré . . . Most Aged Father is still alive."

"You are certain you heard it right?" Wynn demanded. "Aonnis Lhoin'n?"

Magiere lifted her head. "Why? Have you read of it somewhere?"

"No," Wynn answered. "It still exists."

The sage looked as if she'd uncovered something astonishing. Her brown eyes wandered, growing doubtful, until a scowl spread across her round face.

"Wait," Leesil said. "You've seen this place . . . and it still bears the same name?"

Wynn shook her head. "It is what the elves of my continent call the centermost place in their land—First Glade— but no one in my guild knew it was that old."

She blinked rapidly, lost for an instant somewhere other than this moment.

Leesil wasn't certain what all this meant. "Perhaps the war wasn't as long ago as the sages think."

Wynn started at his voice. "No, we have long tried to determine when the war occurred. Some do not believe it ever happened, that it is all myth and legend spun out of proportion. But I have seen old scrolls and parchments, stone carvings and other things . . . from centuries back.

Malourné, my country, goes back more than four centuries. The king's city of Calm Seatt is even older. And what we've found was much older still."

"What does that have to do with this . . . First Glade?" Leesil asked.

"Because my order has been deceived!" Wynn answered sharply. "There are three branches of the Guild of Sagecraft. The first was in my Malourné, decreed by our own kings of old. Shortly thereafter, the elves established their own to match ours. And one is in the Suman Empire along the eastern coast of my continent. It was all to help preserve civilization, present and past . . . should the worst ever come again."

Wynn turned to Magiere.

"If you heard right, a piece of what was lost has been within reach all along. Its past and history could never have been forgotten—not by the elves. It lay right before our eyes . . . and they said nothing of it!"

Leesil didn't care for this one bit. It was enough they had to deal with the secrets and lies that had tangled them among the elves of this land. How long had Wynn's far-off elven neighbors kept this to themselves, an ancient place hidden in plain sight?

"They were taken unaware, unprepared," Magiere whispered. "They didn't even know what to do . . . with what came at them in the night."

Leesil frowned until he caught up. Magiere's thoughts had turned back to her vision in the glade.

"No name," she whispered, as if searching for one, then her dark eyes settled upon him. "They didn't have a name for what they saw."

"I don't understand," Leesil said, sounding exasperated even to himself.

She grabbed his arms, fingers biting in. "Most Aged Father—Sorhkafâré—didn't have a name for what he saw. Undead, vampire, or anything in his own tongue. None of his comrades did. He didn't know . . . their own dead coming to feed upon them that night."

More disjointed pieces of a past that didn't matter here and now. None of it would help Magiere face the council of the an'Cróan.

"They had never seen or heard of an undead?" Wynn whispered. She paused, and then exclaimed, "There were no undead . . . until the war?"

"Dead history can wait!" Leesil snapped. "It's no good to us now, so enough—"

Chap snarled, and Wynn flinched as if her head ached. She looked at the dog and said, "Yes, a good question."

She held up one finger at Leesil before he could argue, and she turned to Magiere.

"I want no more secrets between us," Wynn said pointedly. "I told you, remember, as we sat at the campfire outside Venjètz? You nearly collapsed when we entered Most Aged Father's home. You tell me now—what is happening to you?"

Leesil waited tensely. Wynn had grown far less timid in the moons they'd spent together, but Magiere didn't take kindly to challenges. The last thing he needed was these two going at each other. Magiere dropped her head until Chap snarled at her again.

"I haven't slept in eight . . . maybe nine nights," she said quietly. "And not much before that . . . since we entered this land."

Leesil knew she was having trouble, but he'd had no idea it was this bad. He hadn't had many restful nights himself.

"But do I look it?" Magiere added, almost as a challenge. "I'm not tired, but I can't stop shaking. It gets worse when I'm inside these trees. I have to force myself to eat because I'm never hungry, not in any real way. Did you see the tree in Nein'a's clearing, the one I touched?"

Leesil shook his head, but Wynn sucked in a sharp breath.

"Your hands. Chap saw in your memories . . . they marked the tree."

Magiere faced Leesil. "Before I slipped into Sorhkafâré's memory, the shaking sharpened. Something ran through me as I backed into the tree, and then I was there, in his past. I didn't know what it was, and only guessed afterward, when I called for you."

She heaved a deep breath.

"I saw marks in the bark, like blight or as if part of it had died . . . shaped like my hands. I am guilty, though not for the reasons Fréth and the others think. A piece of that tree's life ripped away . . . into me. I think that's what's been happening to me . . . in this land. I'm not hungry or tired . . . because I'm . . . feeding on everything here."

"We keep this to ourselves," Leesil said quickly, hiding the panic he felt. "We can't let anyone know. Not with this council's judgment in the balance."

The doorway's hanging pulled back, and Brot'an peered in. He held a tray with several bowls and a pitcher.

"May I enter?" he asked politely.

"Do we have a choice?" Leesil answered.

"Leesil!" Wynn snapped. "Yes, Brot'an. We need to know what will happen next."

Brot'an's large form filled the entrance as he stepped in. He set down four steaming bowls of stew. He reached back through the curtain and produced four clay cups that someone handed off to him. Crouching down, he poured water for them all, including Chap. But when he offered, no one touched food or drink.

He had changed tunics, and a white cotton bandage was wrapped on his forearm.

Brot'an eyed Chap thoughtfully. "It is safe for us to speak . . . so long as your majay-hì does not sense any presence that would hear us."

Leesil understood. Magiere's stolen memory hinted that the decrepit old elf had a way of moving about the forest without leaving his home. And Leesil remembered the strange way the majay-hì pack had acted just before Magiere lost control.

Brot'an settled cross-legged on the floor. "Have you finished with my cloak, little one?"

"What? Oh . . . yes." Wynn crawled to the chamber's far side and returned with Brot'an's heavy green-gray cloak. "Thank you."

He nodded slightly and turned to Magiere. "Are you well?"

"No," she answered.

"What's going to happen?" Leesil asked, though he wished Sgäile had come instead.

"In two days there will be a gathering," Brot'an began. "It has been a long time since a majority of the clan elders came at the same time. Word of your presence spread quickly, and they began traveling here once they heard. There is concern that Most Aged Father took it upon himself to give humans safe passage. This has never happened in anyone's memory. Some believe he overstepped his position. No one outside of certain Anmaglâhk have even seen Most Aged Father in nearly fifty seasons."

"Fifty seasons?" Leesil repeated. "How is that possible?"

Brot'an paused, as if deciding how to answer. "Most Aged Father is revered as the protector of our people, and his word weights heavily with many of our leaders. But the Anmaglâhk are not a clan, and therefore Most Aged Father is not a representative of the people—he is not a clan elder. At most gatherings of the elders, he has had no reason to be present. But he will be there this time.

"He might have appeared to defend his decision in giving you safe passage, or he could have sent Fréthfâre in his place. That issue will no longer be the primary concern of the council. He is now Magiere's accuser, and a judgment must be made. He must make his claim against Magiere before the council or withdraw it entirely."

"You want them to see him, don't you?" Magiere asked.

"I wish for them to hear him," Brot'an said. "His mind . . . is not what it once was. It may work in your favor to bring his judgment into question, but in turn may show he was not of sound mind in letting humans into our land."

Leesil sat up straight. "You planned this . . . to use that old elf's accusation against Magiere as a way to alert your people?"

Brot'an shook his head. "No, I never foresaw this. Though I knew your presence would raise issues to be addressed. That is now of little advantage."

"What do you mean by that?" Leesil demanded.

"Magiere has a choice to make," Brot'an answered, ignoring Leesil entirely as he gazed only at her. "Most Aged Father will likely choose Fréthfâre as his advocate. You must choose your own for the coming proceedings."

"Wynn can do it," Leesil answered. "She's a scholar, speaks fluent Elvish, and she knows Magiere."

"Leesil, I . . . ," Wynn stammered. "I am not certain I could—"

"That is not permitted," Brot'an interrupted calmly. "As a human, her presence is still in question—and she is not an'Cróan."

Leesil flushed with rising anger. "You're saying she has to choose one of you . . . an elf? As if there's even one of you we could trust to—"

"You do it," Magiere said. "I choose you, Brot'an, for advocate . . . if you're willing."

"No!" Leesil snapped.

"It is not your decision!" Brot'an barked at him. "Only the accused can choose, unless of unsound mind."

"Then she's unsound," Leesil countered. "She's a raving madwoman! What happened in Nein'a's glade is enough to prove that. And I choose Sgäile!"

"Leesil, stop this!" Wynn shouted at him.

"That is not how mental fitness is determined," Brot'an said. "And you are suspect as much as your companions. Your involvement in any capacity would draw further suspicion and work against her."

Chap stalked over to Magiere. He sat down before her and cast a narrow-eyed sneer at Bro'tan, then lifted his snout to Magiere and barked once for "yes."

Magiere put her hand on Chap's neck.

"Can you clear me?" she asked Brot'an.

"I accept your selection as advocate," Brot'an replied. "I will serve your interests to my fullest ability. I know you are innocent . . . of the claim made against you."

Magiere fell silent, as did Wynn, but Leesil was about to explode.

Brot'an turned on him in harsh voice. "There is more at stake here than Magiere's survival. . . . There is your mother's freedom."

Leesil tensed. "You'd better start making sense."

"Most Aged Father is the one who imprisoned Cuirin'nên'a, though it was never argued before the council."

"She was never given a trial?" Wynn asked.

"The clans accepted this," Brot'an replied, "as it was a matter internal to the Anmaglâhk. The elders respect that we serve to protect the people, and anyone accused of undermining our efforts puts all of them at risk. As I have said, Most Aged Father's word carries much influence."

"They don't even know what she did," Leesil said. "They just took his word that she was a traitor."

"The elders still believe him competent," Brot'an added. "More than competent—the wisest of us all, and the eldest of our people. In placing ourselves in service, the Anmaglâhk not only answer to the laws of the people but also to the rule of our caste. We have one leader—Most Aged Father. If he is seen as having faltered in one judgment, then the elders may find reason to examine other decisions he has made. That bears directly upon Cuirin'nên'a's freedom."

Brot'an waited for further argument. When none came, he turned again to Magiere.

"Trust me."

Chap barked once.

"Yes," Magiere whispered.

As Chap watched Brot'an leave, he second-guessed his own advice.

In spite of everything Brot'an said, his flickering memories never once strayed to Magiere—only to Leesil, Nein'a, or Eillean. Chap even caught words spoken when Eillean had given him as a pup to Nein'a.

Leesil was Brot'an's true interest, not Magiere.

Still, Chap believed that Brot'an might well succeed. Exposing Most Aged Father's reasoning as questionable could dismiss his claim against Magiere, and his judgment of Nein'a as well. And Chap saw no way to accomplish either of these feats himself.

Magiere still sat shaking upon the bed ledge. He nosed her hand until she ran it across the side of his face.

"I wish you could talk . . . for yourself," she whispered. "I would have chosen you instead of Brot'an."

Chap desperately wished the same.

Leesil took up one bowl and wooden spoon and brought them to Magiere.

"Try," he said. "Not just for pretense . . . perhaps eating something might dull whatever you're suffering."

Chap agreed in sentiment. The meat smelled savory, but for once, he wasn't hungry either. Instinct and not intellect nagged him with strange notions. Somewhere in the forest beyond Crijheäiche, his Lily ran with the pack.

CHAPTER EIGHTEEN

Wynn heard footsteps approach outside the elm.

Sgäile leaned in around the doorway curtain. "It is time."

Wynn was partially relieved. Trapped inside with Magiere and Leesil for two solid days had been trying. With little to occupy them, the days crawled by, broken only by meals, Brot'an's infrequent visits, and Leesil's incessant sniping at the tall anmaglâhk.

Sgäile glanced at Magiere's attire but said nothing.

Over the previous days, Brot'an had decided upon her appearance for the hearing. Magiere argued, of course, but he won in the end, and Wynn privately agreed with Brot'an's suggestions. Appearances meant much to elves, but Magiere was still grumbling moments before Sgäile arrived. She now wore a clean, light tan elven tunic with a square-cut neck and breeches to match.

Wynn had braided Magiere's hair so that not a strand would fly free, and she looked like a simple human woman. Far less dangerous in appearance, but there was nothing to be done about her pale skin and blood-tinged black hair.

Leesil changed into his oversized muslin shirt—complete with stitched rents—chocolate-brown breeches, and his own boots. He still looked a bit ragged with his hair hanging free about his shoulders. Chap was the only one who caused no grief, sitting quietly for once as Wynn brushed out his fur.

But all of their busy preparations could not dispel Wynn's fear. If Magiere was found guilty, she would be executed, and there was nothing any of them could do to stop it.

Wynn closed her eyes for a moment, trying to push such thoughts away. But she failed, and her mind wandered in directions more morbid. How might the elves decide to kill Magiere? If they believed her undead, beheading or fire were the only options . . . and Sgäile had once expressed revulsion at the prospect of dismembering the dead.

Wynn opened her eyes and steadied herself. No, it would not come to that. They still had Brot'an.

He had explained only the barest bits of the coming proceedings. Most Aged Father had made a claim concerning Magiere's true nature. Until this was settled, there would be no direct trial before the elders. Instead, the claim must first be substantiated as a dispute between opposing parties. Wynn grasped only scant nuances, and Chap had been no help. Instead he had filled her head with questions that Brot'an never answered.

"Where is Brot'an?" she asked, for he had not returned this day to escort Magiere.

Sgäile ignored her. "It is time. Come."

Leesil headed out, and Wynn fell in behind Magiere and Chap.

Osha was among the Anmaglâhk escort waiting outside. His face filled with concern as he met Wynn's eyes. Sgäile led the way, his guards flanking and following. Chap trotted along outside their retinue.

Wynn did not see Lily or any other majay-hì. She stayed close behind Magiere as they headed inland through Crijheäiche. She had no idea where they headed, but in her mind, she pictured some mammoth oak nurtured by elven Shapers into a council hall.

Cultivated trees and brush passed by in a blur until they came to an open area and were herded between two wide oaks where many elves waited. They had reached the gathering of the elders, but there was no council hall, and the number of those gathered was greater than she had guessed.

Ancient oaks surrounded a long and gently sunken clearing covered by a lawn. Lower branches were as thick as a normal tree's trunk and grew together in bridges from one tree to the next.

Onlookers, dressed in varied attire, sat or stood upon those bridge-branches and gathered in masses between the wide trunks. Those closest turned their eyes on the newcomers, the interlopers, the humans in their midst.

One elderly woman with filmy eyes sat in a wood chair of tawny grain. All of the chair's flowing curves, from its head-high back to its armrests and legs, were made from a single piece, like the rain barrels of Gleann's home. The woman wore a maroon cloak of raw-spun cotton over a matching robe, and she held a rolled parchment on a walnut spindle in her lap. Two younger men in similar cloaks stood at her sides, and others close by shared aspects of their attire.

Their glances were more studied than others, though Wynn did not find that a relief as she stepped by them. She was gripped by an impulse to grab Magiere's hand and offer comfort, but knew she should not.

Among the crowd gathered around every inch of the clearing, many were elaborately dressed. Wynn saw hair ornaments of wood rings for tails, circlets garnished with wildflowers, sparing jewelry of polished wood and stone, and a few crystals or gems that sparked in the bright sun. Few sported metal accoutrements of any kind, although one cluster of elves wore strangely shaped broaches of copper and brass. Everywhere Wynn looked, large amber eyes watched her from within dour caramel and triangular faces.

Partway around the clearing's far side was a cluster of short figures crouched upon the grass—the Äruin'nas. Shirtless, exposing their elaborate body paintings, and with their hair shaped into spirals and curls by dried mud, two of their elders sat cross-legged on the depression's lip.

Wynn squinted, trying to make out the blue-black markings on their skin. Something about those symbols reminded her of the sigils and diagrams of thaumaturgy and conjury she had seen in the guild's library in Malourné.

Clan elders were not difficult to pick out, due to their age. Each was accompanied by attendants, though many had larger retinues.

Then she caught the yellow and russet of the Coilehkrotall, Sgäile and Leanâlhâm's clan, but she did not see an elder sitting before them.

Chap crept in beside Wynn, and there was more than one curious glance over his presence. She dropped a hand on his back, curling her fingers in his thick fur.

At either end of the clearing's floor were oval oak tables. Brot'an stood behind the nearer one, sifting through scrolls among leather-bound sheaves of paper. He looked up, his expression passive but for those severe-looking scars skipping over one eye.

Sgäile led the way downslope, and Wynn lost all self-confidence. She stepped out into full sight of the council of the an'Cróan.

"Well met," Brot'an said.

He looked solid and distinguished in his green-gray, though he wore no cloak. Without it, his shoulders seemed too broad for his tall frame. A forest-green ribbon held back his silver-streaked hair. Sgäile and his guards retreated to the slope's base.

"What are we waiting for?" Wynn whispered.

"Most Aged Father," Brot'an answered. "It should be a quietly dramatic entrance."

Wynn raised one eyebrow. Was that sarcasm?

"Who's the prosecutor?" Magiere asked in a low voice.

"The council has not chosen one," he answered, "as the claim against you must be settled first. Fréthfâre is 'advocate' for your accuser. Sgäilsheilleache serves as 'adjudicator' of proceedings."

Leesil sighed.

From the depression's upper edge and bridge-branched trees, a swarm of amber eyes looked down upon Magiere—and Leesil. Those behind Brot'an's table were close enough for Wynn to see their curiosity, anger, and baleful fascination. The elder elven woman and her companions displayed only cold interest.

As a child, Wynn had attended a livestock fair with Domin Tilswith. A calf born with three legs was on display at a center stall. Everyone stopped to stare and point. Wynn felt like that calf, though she guessed Magiere suffered far worse.

Caramel faces among the crowded turned, one by one, and then more. Wynn followed the wave of shifting focus.

Fréth came down the far slope, dressed the same as Brot'an, with her hair pulled back. Four anmaglâhk followed behind her, bearing the ends of wooden bars over their shoulders.

Between the bearers, Most Aged Father sat upon an ornate chair with rounded sides that cradled his frail body. He was wrapped in a blanket or long shawl of the gray-green, the color of his Anmaglâhk. Whispering murmurs filled the clearing at his entrance.

Most Aged Father's face was overshadowed by a fold of his wrap, but Wynn thought he squinted against the bright sun. His emaciated features and pale skin were worse to look upon than in his root chamber's dim candlelight. The bearers settled him beside Fréth's table, and he turned his head slowly, examining the crowd.

Sgäile stepped to the clearing's center and lifted his face to the gathering, calling out in clear Elvish, "I welcome the people and their clans, as represented by their elders, to hear the claim in dispute."

Not a breath passed before Fréthfâre's voice rose. "Brot'an'duivé, you are already in breach of our ways. Only the accused may stand at your side. The others will be removed immediately."

Brot'an stepped around his table past Magiere. For all his calm ways, his voice thundered across the clearing.

"Léshil is involved by implication and has a right to be present. And I choose the one called Wynn"—he pointed to her for all to take note—"to serve as Magiere's translator."

All eyes turned to Wynn, and she shrank from them, stepping halfway behind Leesil.

"The accused has the right to hear all that is said," Brot'an continued, "as it is said and not thereafter. I will not allow the accuser's advocate to complicate matters by requiring me to be Magiere's translator as well as her advocate! That would be a breach of courtesy . . . if not law."

Sgäile cut off Fréth's retort with a hand raised toward Brot'an.

"The accused's advocate is within custom and law. The advocate for the accuser"—and he turned toward Fréth-fâre—"has no further grounds for this challenge."

Fréthfâre scowled and went to crouch beside Most Aged Father.

Wynn quickly translated all that was said for Magiere and Leesil, though a few nuances of dialect frustrated her. The night before, Brot'an had advised them that proceedings were conducted in Elvish, the proper language, and few clan leaders spoke any other tongue. He told them little else, claiming there was no time to understand more. Too much preparation might work against Magiere, if Fréthfâre tried to trip her up amid rehearsed responses.

Wynn was uncertain how much of this was just Brot'an's own scheming. Undoubtedly he risked alienating Most Aged Father and his own caste in standing as Magiere's advocate.

Brot'an stepped further into the clearing. "I thank the council for being present to render judgment, but I fear your time is not well spent."

Fréthfâre stood up. Both she and Most Aged Father turned rapt attention on Brot'an as he gestured toward Magiere.

"Most Aged Father gave this woman and her companions safe passage and sent Sgäilsheilleache under oath of guardianship to escort them to Crijheäiche. Now, her own host claims that she is one of the humans' undead—something unnatural, returned from beyond death to this world. A human without a guide would have succumbed to the forest, left to wander until captured or dead. An undead could not have entered at all, as none have ever been seen in our land. Yet she walked among us for many days and in the company of a majay-hì. The claim of the accuser is shown false by Magiere's very presence."

Wynn hurried her translation, but as Brot'an paused, her gaze slipped to Most Aged Father. She unconsciously shifted back half a step at the steady hatred upon his face. The ancient elf appeared about to erupt, but Brot'an resumed in a forceful voice.

"Look upon the accused in the full light of day. Human, without doubt. For as little as we know of their kind's . . . 'undead' . . . our land and the spirits of our ancestors have never tolerated such before. By both these ancient authorities, the claim against her should be dismissed as superstition."

Wynn heard dissenting voices, high-pitched in anger, and her attention swung to their source—the Äruin'nas. One of their elders shouted to a nearby elven clan. Wynn could not follow their strange language, though its sound and cadence was akin to Elvish. Clearly they came only to see a human put to death.

Brot'an returned to his table as Wynn finished translating.

Leesil smoldered with satisfaction—perhaps surprised and pleased by the strength of Brot'an's statement. But this was only the beginning. Wynn knew the claim against Magiere could not be dispelled with words.

Most Aged Father leaned toward Fréth, whispering, and she crouched briefly to listen.

Fréth shook her head emphatically, and Most Aged Father squirmed in seething frustration. She stepped around her table, but Most Aged Father shouted out before she reached the clearing's center.

"Twister of truth!"

The wizened old elf jabbed a bony finger at Brot'an.

Brot'an dropped his eyes to the table, and Wynn faltered in her translating.

Murmurs faded among the gathering as Fréth turned in shock to Most Aged Father.

"She is undead!" he shouted weakly. "I know her kind, as the rest of you do not. My caste witnessed her change with their own eyes. Sgäilsheilleache was present, and who among you would doubt his word?"

"Do something," Leesil hissed at Brot'an.

"Be quiet," Wynn warned.

Brot'an did not look up. Neither did he seem affected by the old elf's words.

Several elders around the clearing turned to attendants and companions. Some called out to each other, while others sent companions weaving through the crowd to nearby clans. There were too many low voices for Wynn to catch anything that was said, but she noted surprise mixed with concern on many faces.

Brot'an remained placidly silent, which only made Wynn more nervous by the moment.

Fréth looked hesitantly at Sgäile, as if waiting for him rather than Brot'an to say something. She backed away as Sgäile stepped out.

"The accuser . . ." Sgäile's voice faltered. "The accuser will leave his claim in the hands of his advocate and remain silent until called upon. And as all are aware, the adjudicator is not permitted to witness for either side of a dispute."

When Brot'an lifted his head, he showed neither reluctance nor satisfaction—only cold poise.

Sgäile, standing within Most Aged Father's plain sight, was an obvious choice for support. Even Wynn understood that choice, for what she knew of Sgäile, but he had a rigid adherence to his people's customs, as well as the hidden codes of his caste.

Brot'an's blunt opening had been a goad thrust at Most Aged Father. The old one could not contain himself, and his outburst had served Brot'an. But Wynn realized still more.

If Most Aged Father's claim was proven true, then he was accountable to the elders for having given Magiere safe passage in the first place. If proven false, the elders might see him as senile and erratic for claims against one under his own protection. And either way, he might be held presumptuous for allowing humans into this land at all. The council grew unsettled by his inappropriate action.

Wynn turned a suspicious eye on Brot'an.

The tall and scarred anmaglâhk played a dangerous

game with his leader—with Magiere caught between them. Yet who better to stand against the claims of a patriarch of assassins than a master among the Anmaglâhk?

Wynn slipped her hand around Magiere's wrist and squeezed lightly.

Fréth reclaimed the clearing's center and began in a calm, clear voice.

"Do not be fooled by this woman's appearance. As Brot'ân'duivé says, we know little of the humans' undead. Who among you could swear to know one upon sight? Three days past, I saw her eyes turn black, her teeth and nails like a predator's, and her strength grow beyond any human's. She attacked my caste like a feral beast. Any acceptance by our land or the majay-hì was achieved through trickery. She is dark-begotten and must be destroyed . . ."

Fréth pointed around at the ring of clan elders. ". . . Before one of yours dies at her hands."

Wynn hesitated to translate those last words. As she did so, Leesil blew a sharp snort through his nose, but Magiere and Chap remained silent.

Sgäile stepped forward. "The accused's advocate will present first arguments."

Brot'an picked up a parchment to take the field, but a rustle among the crowd made him halt and turn. Wynn looked back as someone pushed through and descended the slope behind Brot'an's table.

Medium height and slight of build, even for an elf, he wore a cloak of dull yellow over a russet shirt. When he pulled back the hood, steel-gray hair stuck out in an unkempt mass.

Gleann of the Coilehkrotall approached Brot'an with an owlish smile. "I see I am late, but my barge only just arrived."

Magiere's wide eyes mirrored Wynn's own surprise.

"It is pleasing to see you once more," he said to them in Belaskian, then returned to Elvish. "Brot'ân'duivé, have you not stopped growing yet? How you do not knock yourself senseless on the forest's low branches is beyond me. Hmm . . . now, where am I sitting?"

Gleann gazed about but his eyes settled at the clearing's far end.

"Aoishenis-Ahâre, well met," he said and raised a hand. "And still alive, I see. Sgäilsheilleache—or adjudicator, is it—where *am* I sitting?"

His entrance brought the proceedings to a standstill, though Magiere looked relieved. Brot'an's mild frown did not hide his subtle amusement. Wynn was about to point out the other Coilehkrotall when Sgäile hurried over.

"Grandfather, why are you here?"

"Do not be dull-witted," Gleann answered. "I represent our clan. Hui'uväghas could not attend, but one of ours should hear and judge this claim."

Sgäile was openly distressed. It occurred to Wynn that Gleann had arrived a little too quickly compared to her own long journey down the river, and apparently he had more than a passing acquaintance with Brot'an. Why would a wry humored old healer have anything to do with a master assassin?

Across the clearing, Most Aged Father—who never replied to Gleann—looked both offended and anxious as he gestured Fréth to his side.

"Can we continue?" Fréth called out.

Sgäile rushed Gleann upslope to their clan. Brot'an waited politely until the elder was settled before addressing the gathering.

"I call no witnesses at present. Rather, I begin with a test, as it will require time."

Even Most Aged Father grew attentive.

"In the burial ground of our ancestors," Brot'an continued, "reserved for those first in this land, rests the ancient ash tree that began all things here—Roise Chârmune, the Seed of Sanctuary. Those who come of age seek it out and take the true name they bear for life. Most all here have done this . . . have felt the strength of hallowed ground beneath their feet . . . felt the presence of our ancestors close upon them. But Magiere is human and not allowed to attempt what I propose."

He let his pause hang until all curious eyes were cast his way.

"A proxy must go in her place to Roise Chârmune—and the ancestors—to plead for a branch."

A rumble spread quickly around the clearing. Brot'an raised his hand but had to shout over the crowd.

"What greater counsel is there than that of our first blood? No one can approach the Seed of Sanctuary without just cause, and a branch would only be given if the cause served our people. That would settle any claim against this human woman."

Wynn translated as fast as she could. Leesil stepped out before she even finished. Both she and Magiere tried to grab him before he could unwittingly commit some breach of custom, but he slipped out of their reach.

"I'll go," he demanded. "I'll do it."

"Leesil, no!" Magiere hissed, but he ignored her.

Most Aged Father crackled something at Fréth, and she called out, "Léshil does not know the way—and should not. He is not pure of blood, and he is not an'Cróan."

The crowd's rumbling grew uneven.

Brot'an's voice hammered the gathering into silence. "Do you now speak for the ancestors as well? Do you wish to raise claim concerning Léshil at this time?"

Fréth hesitated for a long moment. "He will not survive," she said finally. "He will not be allowed in, as he is not one of us."

"That is a decision for the ancestors, not you," Brot'an replied. "But if Léshil returns, and the accused takes hold of the branch without harm, then neither of them could be a threat to us. Or would you, Fréthfâre, care to tell how some 'human trick' could fool the spirits of our first blood?"

Leesil stood too far off for Wynn to tell him what was said. He looked about, at a loss, and Brot'an did not translate his words.

"What's happening?" Magiere whispered.

Wynn told her and then grabbed Magiere before she went after Leesil. "Do not say anything!"

Fréth made no reply to Brot'an's final barb. Stranger still, Most Aged Father watched the elders around the clearing with concern.

"A guide must be chosen for Léshil," Brot'an added. "Someone acceptable to the people by their elders."

Osha stepped forward. "I will take him."

"No!" Sgäile shouted, too loudly. "I am adjudicator . . . I am the impartial here . . . I will guide Léshil."

Soft murmurs grew slowly, but no voice lifted in dissent. Wynn caught a flicker of surprise on Brot'an's face before he regained stoic composure.

"Sgäilsheilleache, it shall be. As Most Aged Father said, no one would doubt his word. I ask for adjournment until he and Léshil return—or for three days as the limit."

All around, elders rose amid their clans in implied consent. The gathering broke into smaller clusters, talking among themselves in a low-voiced cacophony that filled the depression between the encircling oaks. Across the clearing, Fréth and Most Aged Father were lost in conspiratorial whispers.

As Leesil returned, Magiere grabbed his arm. "What did you do?"

"You do not know what is involved," Wynn added.

Leesil didn't answer either of them.

"Sgäilsheilleache will lead you," Brot'an said in Belaskian. "I do not know why, but he is a better choice than I had hoped for."

"Hope?" Magiere snapped. "You hoped? That's all you've got?"

"No one will doubt his word," Brot'an assured her.

Wynn tried to calm Magiere and then noticed Sgäile.

Anmaglâhk were difficult to read—except the plain-faced Osha—and Brot'an and Urhkar were the hardest of all she had met. Wynn could not take her eyes off Sgäile.

Osha approached him with open worry, but Sgäile did not react. He seemed weary, and flinched when Osha touched his shoulder. Sgäile turned his head, watching an oblivious Leesil.

Fear passed across Sgäile's narrow features.

Magiere pulled away from Wynn, closing on Brot'an like a wolf.

"What have you gotten Leesil into?"

*   *   *

"How could you blindly agree to this?" Magiere ranted.

She paced the open space of their domicile elm, watching Leesil shove the last of the grapes and a blanket into a canvas pack.

"You don't know the forest," she went on. "You don't know what you're facing!"

When Leesil looked up, Magiere went numb at his familiar expression. Cold and hard desperation suggested he would try anything without a thought for the danger.

"I'll face an ash tree," he said flatly. "What's so dangerous about that?"

"Didn't you hear Wynn? Ancestors . . . spirits! You don't know what that means." Magiere ran a hand down her face. "I can't believe I trusted Brot'an."

"Did you think this would be settled through persuasive oration?" Wynn asked. "The elders must see that you are not what Most Aged Father claims. I do not understand it, but if this branch provides disproof of the claim, then we will use it."

Magiere turned angrily on the sage, but her voice failed.

For the first time, she understood how Leesil felt in Venjètz. While she'd moved freely about, he'd remained trapped inside Byrd's Inn. But the thought of two or three more days in this tree, with him far beyond her reach, was almost more than she could bear.

Chap lay dejected on the floor, staring toward the curtained doorway.

"And you," she snapped at the dog. "Don't you have anything to say?"

He lifted his muzzle to her and then returned to his strange vigil. Magiere looked to Wynn for any response the dog offered, but the sage just shook her head with a shrug.

"Brot'an is doing better than I expected," Leesil said. "If I bring back this branch, it looks like that will settle it. Hopefully there'll be no following trial. Fréth and her withered master will have nothing left to counter."

He got up and grabbed Magiere's hand.

"This is my fault for bringing you here. It's a sick twist that Brot'an is the one to give me a way to fix this, but I'll take it anyway. It's time I woke up and did something. Please, just wish me luck."

He was desperate for her support. All Magiere could do was hang on to his fingers.

"I do," she answered, her voice breaking. "But I can't stand that you're doing this alone. I should be with you, not Sgäile."

As if called, Sgäile stuck his head through the doorway curtain. "Léshil, are you prepared? We should begin."

Leesil leaned in and kissed Magiere, quick and soft. "I'll be back in a couple days at most, and everything will be all right."

He let go and headed for the door. Chap got up to follow, but Leesil stopped him.

"No, you stay with Magiere and Wynn. We can't leave them alone among the elves."

Chap barked sharply twice in denial, and Magiere knew exactly how he felt. But the dog turned his eyes on her and then Wynn. He whined and flopped back down. There was nothing else to say, and Magiere sank to the floor beside Chap.

The curtain fell into place as Leesil left, cutting him off from her too abruptly.

CHAPTER NINETEEN

Leesil spoke little with Sgäile as they jogged through the forest. They headed northwest for the morning, but by early afternoon, Leesil grew less certain of their course. The sky clouded over. With only hazy light and no sun, the forest changed in small degrees.

There were fewer flowers and more wet moss. Patches of it clung to tree trunks and branches overhead. The trees were older and gnarled, with bark darkened by moisture thickening in the air. For a while, a drizzle pattered against the leaves.

Sgäile cast off whatever weight crushed him upon volunteering for this task. He returned to his earlier self from their first journey to Crijheäiche. Perhaps, like Leesil, Sgäile was relieved to have anything to do besides wait in frustration for others to do something.

The forest grew ancient as they traveled, its trees taller and thicker and wider, blocking out most of the sky. In the lingering false dusk beneath their leaves and needles, the forest seemed aware it had a pair of trespassers.

Leesil grew less aware of where he was—as if here the forest's manipulations pressed harder upon his wits. He often turned his head to look behind and couldn't recognize anything that he must have just passed.

Sgäile's shoulder brushed through a spider's web, glistening with dew. An eight-legged shadow scurried down the back of his cloak.

Leesil slapped it off, but when he looked down, there was nothing scurrying across the mulch into hiding. He wondered about their final destination as daylight faded even more.

Sgäile slowed and looked about. "If we keep on, we will reach the grounds well past midnight. Or we can camp and continue at dawn."

Sleeping in this dank and dark forest was less than enticing.

"Let's take rest and food," Leesil said. "Then move on."

Sgäile nodded and swung the small pack off his shoulder. "I have water, flatbread, and a little walnut oil."

"I have grapes."

They sat on a rotting log, sharing out what they'd brought. Leesil fidgeted as the damp soaked through his breeches. Sgäile removed a leather lid from a small clay pot, tore off a bit of flatbread, and dipped it in. He set the vessel between them, and Leesil did the same.

"This is good," he said, and held out the grapes. "I wanted to . . . to thank you for doing this, for trying to help Magiere."

"I care nothing for helping Magiere." Sgäile paused, shaking his head. "Pardon, I did not mean to sound . . . I do this for my caste. Brot'ân'duivé on one side and Fréthfâre on the other—this is not good. I serve my duty as adjudicator in the hope of bringing this gathering to a close, so my caste will be as one again."

Leesil kept quiet. If Sgäile really believed that ending Magiere's hearing—regardless of the outcome—would seal the rifts in his caste, he was blinder in his devotion than Leesil had first thought.

"We should focus on our task," Sgäile said, and once again his expression grew uneasy.

"Why the worry?" Leesil asked. "What's at this place with the special tree?"

Sgäile scowled at the casual reference. "The first of our people were buried there long ago. All an'Crόan are descended from them. We go there alone to seek guidance in choosing our name for life, when we come of age."

"How old is that?"

"When parents and child agree it is time."

"You did this? So you had some other name before Sgäile?"

"Sgäilsheilleache," he corrected. "It means 'In Willow Shade, or Shadow.'"

"And that's what your ancestors said you should call yourself?"

"We do not see or hear the ancestors," Sgäile answered. "It is something I saw . . . in the presence of Roise Chârmune."

"So there was a willow somewhere nearby?"

"No. It was . . . something far off, far from this land . . . in the shade of a willow."

"Then what—some kind of vision? And that's all you saw . . . just a willow tree?"

Sgäile let out a sharp sigh.

Leesil knew he was somewhere close to the mark. Superstitious nonsense—and here these elves thought themselves so much better than humans.

"So, you call yourself by whatever you see. You're stuck with whatever comes up."

It was Sgäile's turn to be disdainful. "We are free to choose any name we wish, from whatever comes—in part, in whole, or not. Though what is experienced at Roise Chârmune remains, just the same."

"Then what's got you so worried about all this with the branch?"

"As I said . . . we go alone. It is not proper for anyone else to be present. We do not even care to speak of our experience to others . . . but for the name we choose."

"I'm not going for any name, so stop dodging the question."

Sgäile covered the walnut oil and got up to tuck the jar into his pack. He stared a long while through the darkening forest before looking down at Leesil.

"You are half-blooded. None but my people go to Roise Chârmune . . . and the ancestors."

Was that it? Leesil sighed. "So they reject me, and I go back. I'll find some other way to get Magiere and my mother away from your people."

"You must first gain hallowed ground before the ancestors accept or reject your plea."

As much as Leesil preferred Sgäile over the rest, there were moments when he'd had enough.

"Oh, dead deities!" Leesil got up, weary of cryptic answers. "Just say what you mean for once."

Sgäile's jaw twitched. "I would tell you more if I knew. But unless you reach hallowed ground . . . I do not believe you will come back."

Wynn sat on the floor trying to jot down the day's events. From the customs and proceedings to what she remembered of clan distinctions, she scribbled out everything that came to her. Later, when more time permitted, she would rework it into something comprehensible.

Magiere halfheartedly groomed Chap's long fur but kept glancing toward the curtained doorway. Chap lay with his head on his paws. Wynn could think of no words of comfort for either of them.

She was thankful for the strange quill gifted her by Gleann. The bulbed grip above its silver-white head was awkward in her small hand, but in her rush, she did not have to stop as often to replenish its ink.

The doorway drape swung aside, and Leanâlhâm peeked in. "May we enter?"

"Yes, please," Magiere answered, and paused in grooming as Chap lifted his head. "Who's with you?"

"Osha," Leanâlhâm said. "No one but your advocate may see you without a guard."

Leanâlhâm carried in a tray of grilled trout with wild onions and two steaming mugs. She held a canvas bag tucked under one arm. Wynn smelled tea mingling with the scent of food. Osha stepped in behind the girl and set down a bowl of water for Chap.

Osha eyed both Wynn and Magiere, as if uncomfortable

with his formal role here. Or perhaps like others who had been in Nein'a's clearing, he believed Magiere some monster of the dead and did not care for close proximity. Either way, Wynn had no patience for it.

Leanâlhâm set down the tray and dropped to the floor before Magiere and Chap. The girl reached slowly for Chap's head. Before her touch landed, he flicked his tongue through her fingertips. She let out a startled, giggling gasp and then looked back at Osha, who fidgeted nervously.

"Oh, please," Leanâlhâm said in Elvish. "They have been alone all day. It is impolite to deliver their supper and just leave."

Osha's mouth fell open and then closed again with the barest grunt. His gray-green cloak was slightly askew on his shoulders. He crouched by the doorway and looked at Wynn.

"How do you fare?" he asked.

"I am all right," she answered and set down her quill. "Though it would be more polite to speak Belaskian among those who do not understand your language. And you need the practice."

Osha was caught somewhere between embarrassment and confusion at her tone. Or perhaps he had had enough of being chided. Wynn sighed, rolled her eyes, and forced a smile.

He relaxed sheepishly, realizing she jested. When his gaze flicked to Magiere, that hint of a smile vanished. Leanâlhâm showed no such concern.

"Sgäilsheilleache will keep Léshil safe," she said.

Magiere nodded. "Thanks . . . it's good of you to come."

"Do not worry," Leanâlhâm continued. "No matter what they face, Sgäilsheilleache never fails. Brot'ân'duivé and Grandfather will do the rest, and you will soon be free."

Osha grew uncomfortable. He understood enough of what was said, and shared another doubtful glance with Wynn.

Leanâlhâm's words rolled in Wynn's head. This was the second time she had noted some casual connection between Gleann and Brot'an. Poor Leanâlhâm was as blind as Leesil, if she thought these proceedings would end any time soon—no matter this quest's outcome. Whatever Fréth and Most Aged Father would throw at Magiere, it would be unexpected and ugly.

Wynn took the mug of tea the girl offered her. "How did Gleann arrive so quickly? It took us nearly eight days to reach Crijheäiche."

"Grandfather said that he left shortly after we did, but he did not tell me why." For the first time, Leanâlhâm hesitated and then leaned forward. "But he has the faith of our clan and our other elders. His vote will be counted, and his voice will be heard."

A simplistic view, judging by what Wynn fathomed so far.

"You should eat," Osha said, "and we should not talk of the gathering."

"Yes, Osha," Leanâlhâm answered, and did nothing to hide her exasperation.

She served trout and onions onto polished wood plates, and the savory aroma grew each time she portioned the fish.

"Here," she said, placing one plate before Chap. "A whole boned fish just for you."

Chap's tail switched the floor twice as he sniffed.

Wynn was glad to see his interest. Since facing down his kin, for her life, he had been so withdrawn.

Leanâlhâm pulled an oblong tawny box from the canvas bag, its top stained in light and dark squares.

"I brought a game we call Dreug'an. It will help pass the time."

"Dreug'an?" Osha coughed out, well past uncomfortable, and stumbled in his Belaskian. "Sgäilsheilleache question where come from. He think me lax in duty."

Leanâlhâm ignored him and removed small white and black river stones from a drawer in the box's side. "He will know exactly where it came from. It belongs to him. Grandfather brought it for me."

Osha's dark skin seemed to pale as he sagged. Then Brot'an ducked through the doorway curtain, startling everyone.

Magiere's expression hardened. She dropped her plate, and the two-tined fork clattered on it. Before she snapped a word at him, Brot'an pulled the curtain aside again. His silver hair glowed with the darkness behind him.

"I will speak with Magiere alone. Osha, you will attend Wynn outside. Leanâlhâm, return to your quarters."

Osha immediately got to his feet.

Wynn did not like having only Osha as a familiar face to look upon among the guards outside. As much as this tree was little more than a prison, it did provide limited safety. Brot'an merely stood by the doorway.

Leanâlhâm lightly touched Magiere's leg as she got up and quickly headed out. Osha stood waiting upon Wynn.

"Please," Brot'an said pointedly and looked down at Chap. "And you."

Chap rose slowly to all fours. For a moment, Wynn readied to pounce on the dog should he lunge at Brot'an. Chap turned his eyes upon Magiere.

"Go on," she said. "You stay with Wynn."

Chap trotted out. Wynn followed and found herself amid Osha and two other anmaglâhk. She wondered what Brot'an had to say to Magiere that no one else should hear. Leanâlhâm already headed off under the escort of another anmaglâhk. The girl looked back long enough to wave in parting before fading among the night trees of Crijheäiche.

Something more occurred to Wynn. When Leanâlhâm had said, "No matter what they face," she referred to Roise Chârmune.

The nametaking rite of the an'Cróan was unfamiliar to Wynn. She had never heard of such among the elves of her land. All here went to hallowed ground when they came of age to be given—or was it "to take"?—a name other than what their parents chose at birth. Leanâlhâm was about sixteen, if Wynn remembered right. Old enough to have gone herself.

But by the way the girl spoke of this sacred place, Leanâlhâm had never been there.

Leesil stopped behind Sgäile near a dank oak. The silence was wrong.

He should hear something—bugs, maybe a cricket, or even leaves shifting in a breeze. But he heard nothing, now that their own footfalls had ceased.

The forest thinned ahead, and he saw an open space screened by branches. It was so dark, the masses of leaves and trailing moss were little more than black silhouettes. Yet beyond them was soft light, like what a full moon might provide.

Leesil glanced up. He wasn't certain, with the forest canopy thick overhead, but the rest of the forest was too dark for a moon, full or not. He tried to make out what was hidden beyond in the clearing. He only caught a hint of glistening ocher limbs behind surrounding gnarled oaks draped in moss.

"Do not move," Sgäile whispered. "Do not look for it."

Leesil glanced at Sgäile, uncertain what this meant.

Something slid wetly across the forest mulch. Faint and soft, it carried from directly ahead.

Leesil did look. He saw nothing but the glow of the clearing beyond the black shapes of the oaks. Sgäile's final words after their meal echoed in Leesil's head.

Unless you reach hallowed ground . . . I do not believe you will come back.

For the first time since starting this task, fear tickled the back of Leesil's neck—not of death but of failure. What if he didn't return to Magiere? What would happen to her? He clenched one hand, ready to face whatever this place threw at him.

The sound grew subtly louder, closing off to his left, as if something circled around the clearing instead of passing through it. A wet dragging sound came between pauses in slow rhythm.

"Repeat my words," Sgäile whispered quickly, "exactly as I say them."

Leesil barely heard him, still searching for whatever came. He was prepared for a fight, not a speech. Then he glanced at Sgäile.

The elf stood frozen in place, staring straight at the silhouette trees. His eyes twitched once to the left toward the sound and then quickly turned back ahead.

"*Ahârneiv!*" Sgäile began. "*Œn päjij nävâjean'am le jhäiv . . .*"

The dark base of one oak bulged near the ground.

The swelling rolled and flowed across the forest floor toward Leesil. It turned into the path toward the half-hidden clearing.

The soft glow beyond the silhouette oaks caught on the piece of slithering darkness, and its surface glinted to iridescent green.

A long body, as thick as Leesil's own torso, was covered in fist-sized scales. Their deep green shimmered to opalescence as it came closer. Leesil caught the yellow glint of two eyes that marked its approaching head, like massive spiral-cracked crystals in an oblong boulder pushed along at a hand's-breadth above the ground.

A snake . . . no, a serpent, too large to be real.

Leesil reached slowly down his thighs, but his blades weren't there. He slid one foot back to retreat.

"No!" Sgäile whispered. "Do not move! Repeat my words . . . quickly!"

The serpent's body knotted and coiled, gathering into a mass. Its scaled and plated head rose to hover before Leesil, swaying gently. A long forked tongue whipped at his face with a hiss.

Slit irises in its yellow eyes watched him steadily.

The serpent's jaw dropped open. Fangs as long as Leesil's forearm glistened in the dark maw of its mouth. It could swallow half of him at once.

"Léshil!" Sgäile whispered. "If you would save Magiere, you must speak my words."

The serpent undulated as its head swung toward Sgäile's voice.

Leesil heard the man's shuddering breath as he felt some part of the serpent's scaled body scrape across his leg. He was still prepared to fight his way past this thing if he had to. He glanced quickly at Sgäile, and the sight was like ice pressed into his eyes, feeding its chill into his body.

Sgäile averted his gaze, anywhere but at the serpent's massive head. He closed his eyes tightly. He was shaking, his muscles rigid.

An anmaglâhk was frozen in terror, and Sgäile's fear bled rapidly into Leesil.

"I . . . I can't," Leesil whispered.

But if he died here, Magiere would die too. The serpent swung back, yellow eyes centered on him.

"I can't speak your language," he said, despair mounting. "I won't get it right."

Magiere wanted to beat answers out of Brot'an's scarred face. She had trusted him, and Leesil might pay for her mistake. Brot'an spoke before she uttered her first demand.

"There is more at stake than just your freedom. Even if Most Aged Father's claim is dismissed, neither you nor Leesil will leave this land alive. You are interlopers, humans, so do not be naïve. Am I clear so far?"

Magiere's ire held beneath her uncertainty.

"Very well," Brot'an added quietly, and settled upon the chamber floor before her. "All balances on whether Léshil steps onto hallowed ground . . . as much as whether or not he gains the branch of Roise Chârmune."

Magiere wasn't certain what this meant.

"To be elven, as you call it," Brot'an said, his voice tainted with distaste, "is not an'Cróan. We are our heritage, our blood, more than whatever race you see us as. Only as an'Cróan can Léshil plead for Cuirin'nên'a before the elders."

"If he's elven," she snapped back, "then he's got as much right as anyone, under your laws."

"No, he does not," Brot'an countered, quiet and sharp. "Do you think an outsider could demand Cuirin'nên'a's freedom? To be an'Cróan—to be of the blood—is all that matters to my people."

Magiere looked away. The last thing Leesil—or she—wanted was to be snared even deeper among these people and their ways. What arrogance, what nonsense and superstition!

"What are you talking about?"

"I mean you no malice," Brot'an said. "And only wish you to understand what is truly at stake. There was no time to waste in arguing this, so I chose not to give you that chance. The only way Léshil will be seen as one of us is if he can step onto hallowed ground. That is as important as the reason he goes there."

"If?" Magiere snapped.

"Sgäilsheilleache will guide him . . . teach him the words to ask entrance. There is no other way."

"Ask who? The ancestors?"

Brot'an shook his head. "None of us have seen what guards Roise Chârmune, as no one has gone there before but a full-blooded an'Cróan. And none have been rejected, to my knowledge. Leesil must gain entrance before he reaches it or the ancestors."

Gain entrance? What did that mean?

"What did you see at this Roi-say . . . this Seed of Sanctuary?" she demanded. "What's guarding it? Just tell me what you know."

"A sound," he answered, "something moving in the forest surrounding hallowed ground. I know no more than that. When I spoke the words my father taught me, all was silent again. I stood a long while before I tried to walk in. Even when I left, I neither saw nor heard anything more."

"What did you say?"

Brot'an hesitated. "A formal plea in my language. Nothing that would tell you more or ease your mind."

But it implied that if Leesil did not make it into the burial ground . . .

"For what it is worth," Brot'an added, "I believe Léshil will return."

"What did you . . . experience when you went for your name?" Magiere asked. She tried to remember what Wynn had said Brot'an's name meant. Something about a dog.

"That is an impudent question."

"Does it look like I care?" she hissed. "You think you'll walk out of here without answering?"

"I see that you love him," Brot'an said, "in some fashion, though I do not know if that is better or worse for him. I ask you again. Have you mated with Léshil?"

"That's still none of your business."

"No more than my naming is yours. I know the answer, but I would hear it from your own lips . . . now!"

Magiere saw Brot'an was as determined as she was to get answers.

"Yes," she said bluntly.

Brot'an slumped ever so slightly. "What do you know of Leanâlhâm's mother?"

"She was never happy or at home here. She ran off when her husband abandoned her and Leanâlhâm."

Magiere didn't care for the way Brot'an studied her.

"We have more than one word," he said, "for the degrees of what humans so casually call love. Only at its deepest do we bond . . . mate . . . for life. It is why we observe a period of *bóijt'äna* before bonding, as Én'nish did for Grôyt'ashia."

"Grôyt brought on his own death!" Magiere countered.

"I agree, though you are not following my meaning. Én'nish may look upon Léshil as the murderer of her 'betrothed,' you would say. But her obsession has taken her reason. Even Léshil's death may not end her suffering. My people bond for life."

Magiere knew of others who'd lost a loved one because of Leesil. "Grief never ends. It's just something you learn to live with."

Brot'an slowly shook his head. "Not for some . . . not for an'Crón. Mating is life—and death—and overwhelms all else. It is rare that we ever mate outside of bonding for that very reason. Do you not remember Léshil's words to me in Darmouth's crypt . . . when I stepped too close to you at the end?"

Magiere could never forget. *Touch her, and I'll kill you and everything you love.*

Brot'an went on. "It was then I first suspected what lay between the two of you."

He had purposefully chosen not to kill her that night in the crypt. Magiere now suspected the reasons were more complex than some slip of compassion.

"Leanâlhâm's mother did not flee this land," Brot'an said. "That is what the girl chose to believe. Gleannéohkân'thva and Sgäilsheilleache chose not to correct her . . . to let time bring her more slowly to the truth with the maturity to face it. Her mother ran mad into the forest.

Though her body was never found, I do not believe she survived."

Magiere tried to shut out mounting fear. "What of Leanâlhâm's father?"

"He lives," Brot'an added coldly. "Life is not always lost in such matters. The young are the most vulnerable. He did not love the girl's mother, by your definition of the word, though he will still suffer. Gleannéohkân'thva was rash in bargaining to take Leanâlhâm's father under tutelage . . . in exchange for a bonding he thought might ease the suffering of Leanâlhâm's mother."

Brot'an got up, heading for the door. "Léshil is only half-blooded, with more years than Leanâlhâm's mother had when she bonded and mated with the girl's father. Léshil knows none of what I have told you. It is important that you comprehend exactly what you have done with him."

He said this with no spite, but Magiere didn't wish to discuss her relationship with Leesil further.

"You still owe me an answer," she said quickly. "Your name . . . Wynn said something about a dog."

" 'Dog in the Dark,' in your tongue," Brot'an corrected. "Though 'mastiff' would be more precise. Not wild but domesticated, like the ones humans use in war."

"Is that what you saw when you went for your name?"

Brot'an remained halfway to the door, his back still turned to her.

"It came in silence out of the night, straight from the shadow of Roise Chârmune. It tore off its iron-spiked collar with its paws and bared its teeth, as if turning upon its master."

He finally looked back, and Magiere's own spite faltered for an instant at the discomfort in Brot'an's lined face.

"At the time, I thought it a resentful shadow of arguing with my father over what I should do with my life. He did not wish me to take up service. Then later, when I joined Eillean, I thought it an image of the coming war. But I lost my taste for omens and portents over so many years. When Eillean died, it was a name and nothing more . . . until you appeared in our land."

Brot'an turned away to the door. "And now I stand be-

fore my people to pull down Aoishenis-Ahâre for the sake
of a half-blood and a dark-tainted human woman."

He was gone, leaving Magiere alone with mounting anguish growing upon an old forgotten fear.

Her memory slipped back to a tiny inn outside of Bela. She
had waited there for Leesil. It had seemed almost better—
safer—to let him go, before he fell prey to her dhampir
side. In spite of all her fears, she wanted him too much.

What had she done to him?

Chap lay a ways off and watched the elm where Brot'an
spoke privately with Magiere. Osha tried to occupy Wynn
in learning to play Dreug'an. The sage relented but showed
little interest and watched the curtained doorway.

Try as Chap might, he could not hear what was said. And
without line of sight, he could not dip for memories surfacing in either Brot'an or Magiere. He snarled at one Anmaglâhk guard just to see the man flinch.

Chap's ears stiffened when Brot'an finally emerged and
walked on into the dark, not even stopping to tell Osha to
return Wynn to confinement.

Osha quickly packed up the Dreug'an board and pieces
and ushered Wynn off with the other two Anmaglâhk close
behind. Chap stayed a moment longer.

He reached out for Brot'an's memories.

Whatever the man discussed with Magiere had left him
unsettled, for his mind was not the blank slate Chap had
found upon other occasions. Memories flashed in his
mind so quickly that Chap had to focus hard to keep up.

A mastiff stalked out of the shadow of a strange barkless
tree amid a wet and barren clearing. It snarled silently at
Chap as he watched it through Brot'an's memory.

Brot'ân'duivé—the Dog in the Dark.

This was the moment when Brot'an had gone to the ancestors for his name.

As the memory faded, Chap saw an image of Leesil traveling in the forest. And then again the image of the dog that
appeared when Brot'an stepped onto hallowed ground.

The memory vanished. Brot'an's mind was as hidden as
before.

Chap traipsed back to the elm, trying to fathom what he had glimpsed. He turned as Brot'an's tall form slipped away between the trees.

A naming—and Leesil.

Chap stood there . . . long enough that he grasped the connection.

Leesil was traveling to the place where all an'Cróan took their true name, or so they believed. If he gained hallowed ground, it would be to plead for a branch from Roise Chârmune. But Brot'an hoped Leesil might gain more.

Why would Brot'ân'duivé want this to happen? Why did an Anmaglâhk master want to know Leesil's true name?

"I can't speak your language. I won't get it right."

Sgäile's throat closed at Léshil's panicked words. He stood shaking, and still could not open his eyes to this thing no one had ever seen, nor did they know where it came from or why it stood vigil over this hallowed ground. His people only knew it by a name and the oath that spoke of its deadly nature.

"Ahârneiv . . . ," he began again, and then faltered as he felt its hissing breath upon his face.

Would it understand in any other tongue? And if it did, would it let him live, coming here with Léshil? All who came to Roise Chârmune must come alone!

Sgäile began the litany once again, this time in words Léshil could understand.

"Father of Poison . . ."

He waited in tense silence for Léshil to repeat it.

"Father of . . . Poison . . . ," Léshil whispered.

Sgäile took a quick breath. "Who washes away our enemies with Death . . ."

Léshil echoed him again.

"Let me pass by to my ancestors, first of my blood. Give me leave to touch the Seed of Sanctuary."

As Léshil repeated his words, the serpent's breath faded from Sgäile's face, and he waited long in silence.

He heard coils grating upon the earth . . . and then the softer wet sound of mulch beneath the trees somewhere ahead. Longer he waited with his eyes shut, until the sound nearly faded altogether.

Something dropped upon Sgäile's shoulder, and he opened his eyes, breathing so quickly he grew dizzy. He kept his eyes on the dark oaks ahead, afraid to catch even one more glimpse of Ahârneiv.

It was gone.

Léshil's hand slipped off Sgäile's shoulder and fell limply at his side.

"We . . . are free . . . to go on," Sgäile whispered.

He almost did not believe the words as they came from his lips. Sgäile glanced sidelong at the half-blood—who had just changed his whole world, and perhaps that of Leanâlhâm.

For more than two years, he and his grandfather had urged Leanâlhâm to wait, to put off her name taking, though their arguments grew weaker with each passing moon. They feared that she would not return from this place, not with human blood in her.

Still, Léshil did not move.

"You have gained hallowed ground," Sgäile urged. "You are accepted as blood."

Léshil slowly turned his eyes toward Sgäile.

"I'm here for one reason," he snapped. "For Magiere, caught among your kind because of me. I don't care how you or your ghosts see me."

Léshil stepped on toward the clearing. Sgäile hung back, stunned back into silence.

Human blood, by any degree, was a baffling thing.

Leesil stood before the tree at the bare clearing's center and stared up at its wild branches filling the air above him.

It wasn't shaped like the tall and straight ash trees he had seen. Stout branches sprouting from its thick trunk curved and wound and divided up into the night. A soft glow emanated from its fine-grained wood to dimly light the clearing.

Leafless and barkless—yet somehow alive. From its wide-reaching roots lumping the earth to its thick and naked pale-yellow body and limbs, its soft rippled surface glistened beneath its own glow.

"You must touch it," Sgäile whispered from behind. "Roise Chârmune will know why you have come, and the ancestors will decide."

Leesil shivered. The night was only cool, but it had suddenly grown crisp within the clearing.

This was what he'd come for, but after passing the guardian serpent, he wavered at touching this tree. He quickly slapped his hand against its bare trunk, just to be done with it, and shivered again as the temperature dropped sharply.

"Sgäile . . . ?" he said.

The man looked anxiously about and folded his hands under his arms against the mounting cold. Whether from fear or frigid temperature, he shook where he stood.

"I do not know," Sgäile whispered.

Someone stepped around the naked tree's far side.

The figure wore the gray-green of an Anmaglâhk, cloak tied around its waist and cowl pulled forward. But it was short for an elf, no taller than Leesil himself.

Leesil began to pull back.

"Do not move!" Sgäile warned. "Do not take your hand from Roise Chârmune!"

Leesil didn't believe this was a vision. Surely one of Sgäile's caste must have followed them.

The figure raised a hand and held it up before Leesil's eyes. In that closed fist was an Anmaglâhk stiletto, silver-white blade pointed downward from its round, plain guard.

Leesil snatched the figure's wrist with his free hand.

The clearing lit up as if under a burning noon sun.

Where there had been cold, now sweltering heat choked the air in Leesil's lungs. Within the figure's cowl he saw a face . . . his face.

Leesil stared into his own reflection within that cowl.

There were the faint scars on his own cheek from where Ratboy had clawed him. His own amber eyes stared back at him, somewhat too small for an elf's, above a chin not quite tapered enough for a full-blood's.

His reflection looked older, somehow. And tears began running down his—its—face.

Leesil stood there, gripping the wrist of his reflection.

Heat made his double, his twin, or whatever it was ripple before his eyes. A shift in the land beyond the surrounding oaks tugged at his attention.

He thought he saw barren mountains beyond rolling tan hills that were too smooth and perfect. High peaks rippled in the distance as those hills radiated heat. Sgäile hissed out one word.

"Ancestors!"

Darkness filled the clearing. The cold bit again at Leesil as his gaze shifted back. His breath caught as one puff of vapor rushed from his lips.

He saw no reflection of himself anymore. His grip was closed on a slender translucent wrist that glowed like the naked ash. And he looked into . . . through . . . the transparent face of a tall elven male.

The man's eyes turned stern as he looked back at Leesil. His face was broader at the cheekbones than other elves'. An ugly scar slanted from his forehead to his right temple and another marred the left side of his jaw below his peaked ear. He had seen battle during his life; his hand around the stiletto appeared toughened and calloused.

No, not a stiletto . . . the elven warrior held a branch of naked pale wood like that of the ash tree. Long and straight overall, the wood showed gentle wavering throughout its length like any natural branch stripped of its bark.

Pale glimmers erupted in the darkness behind the branch's bearer.

Leesil remembered the ghost horde of the Apudâlsat forest, all hideously wounded in the moment of their death. These were different.

They appeared as in life, dressed as they must have been long ago, though their transparent forms held no color but that of the ash tree's wood. A third were male, the rest female, and not all appeared old. Leesil counted at least a dozen.

Their attire varied. Some were clothed no differently from the elves Leesil had seen around the council clearing. But others wore hauberks and bracers of hardened leather, either plain or covered in overlapping plates and scales of metal. Two wore helms of triple crests with scroll-work spirals engraved in their sides, as did the one Leesil still gripped.

They carried spears, some as long as pikes, and quivers and bows slung upon their backs. Not the short ones the Anmaglâhk disassembled to hide away, but longbows capable of great range. One middle-aged female with scars down her left upper arm had thick triangular war daggers on her wide studded belt. They looked more like a human weapon than those Leesil had seen among elves. The spear in her grip was shorter than her height. Its thick shaft appeared to be metal instead of wood, and its head was wide-bladed and nearly as long as a short sword.

And that one, with wild eyes full of fury, smiled at him beneath narrowing eyes.

But there were none among the spirits dressed as Anmaglâhk.

An elder woman in a robe approached behind the tall warrior holding the branch. Her face was slender and lightly lined with age. Long hair waved and floated as if she moved through water.

Take the limb of Roise Chârmune . . . and guard it as it will guard you . . . as you will guard life, Léshiârelaohk.

Leesil heard her voice, though her lips never moved.

Tell Sorhkafâré we wait for him.

A different voice. Male, tired but purposeful, like a sigh of relief after long burden.

Leesil turned his eyes back on the scarred and wide-cheeked warrior in his grip. The man's gaze shifted toward Sgäile then flickered once to Leesil. He seemed puzzled by something between the only two living people in the clearing. Then the spirit looked deep into Leesil's eyes.

Tell Sorhkafâré that Snähacróe still waits for his comrade . . . when he is finally ready to rest. Tell him . . . Léshiârelaohk.

Leesil knew the first name from Magiere's vision—the long-forgotten name of Most Aged Father. The second might be this one holding out the branch. But that final name he couldn't place, though it was close to what his mother and her people called him.

Léshil . . . Léshiârelaohk.

He wasn't sure he could repeat it aloud, but its sound vibrated in his head, as if spoken again by both the elder woman and the dour warrior.

The tall spirit opened his fingers, and the ash branch began to fall.

Leesil released his grip and snatched it from the air.

When he looked up again, the clearing was empty but for himself, Sgäile, and the soft radiance of the naked ash.

He saw no spirits. Not a one.

Leesil held up the branch of Roise Chârmune.

CHAPTER TWENTY

Midafternoon on the second day, Magiere ripped aside the elm's doorway curtain at the sound of running feet.

"Leesil?"

Six Anmaglâhk stood outside, with Osha in the front, but there was no sign of Leesil or Sgäile.

"Is time," Osha said in his thick accent.

"Where's Leesil?" she asked. "How can the elves resume proceedings without Sgäile?"

"You come," he urged.

Wynn threw on Chane's cloak as Chap rose, and they followed Magiere out.

The guards flanked them as they hurried through Crijheäiche to the council clearing. Again Magiere grew uneasy as she stepped between the bridge-branched oaks and the closest onlookers backed out of her way. She took a slow calming breath at the sight of Leesil and Sgäile standing with Brot'an behind the oak table.

Leesil held his hand out. Magiere hurried down the slope. One anmaglâhk almost grabbed for her, but Osha waved him off.

Faint dark rings surrounded Leesil's eyes, but he smiled

at her. His muslin shirt and cloak were damp and smudged. He and Sgäile had returned in half the time Brot'an had asked for, so likely they had pushed on all night. Their gear was piled beneath the table, but Leesil's punching blades rested on the surface—along with something hidden by a shimmering piece of white cloth.

"What are the blades for?" she asked.

Leesil shook his head. "They were here when I arrived. Brot'an must have sent for them."

Brot'an's hard glare told them both to be silent.

Across the clearing's depression, Fréth and Most Aged Father entered as before, his chair carried by four anmaglâhk. As he was placed beside Fréth's table, the old elf leaned forward and peered toward Leesil and Sgäile.

Wynn stepped in close to Magiere, ready to translate.

Sgäile looked as worn as Leesil as he stepped to the clearing's center. His hair was a mess, streaming down around his pointed ears in a white-blond tangle. He called out, "The review of the claim will continue. Advocate for the accused may proceed."

Brot'an stepped out as Sgäile backed away, and the crowd fell silent in anticipation. Magiere watched the faces around the clearing, and when she reached Gleann, he lifted his chin to her with a wry, subtle smile.

"I call on Osha of the Âlachben," Brot'an said.

Wynn whispered in Magiere's ear, "Osha of the Rock-Hills clan."

Osha approached, and Brot'an lifted Leesil's winged blades, still in their sheaths. He drew one, raised it for all to see, and then turned to Osha.

"Can you tell us what this is?" he asked.

"It is one of Léshil's weapons," Osha answered quietly.

Brot'an cocked his head toward those of the gathering. Osha cleared his throat and repeated with stronger voice.

"Unique blades," Brot'an continued. "Do you know where he found them?"

"I believe he designed these himself," Osha answered.

"And what are these used for?"

"To destroy undead, or so he said . . . by taking their heads."

"Irrelevant!" Fréth shouted. "Léshil is not accused and these weapons have no bearing on the claim in dispute. The accused's advocate will keep to relevant testimony."

"Relevance will be addressed," Brot'an replied calmly. "If the opposing advocate will refrain from further interruptions. As Sgäilsheilleache is not permitted to witness for either side, I have turned to another in this matter."

Magiere followed Brot'an's seeking look toward Sgäile.

"Objection noted and rejected," Sgäile proclaimed. "But the accused's advocate will be expedient in making this line of questioning relevant."

As Wynn translated, Magiere wondered about the proceeding's rules. Brot'an seemed to have some freedom in questioning, but she wasn't certain why he was concentrating on Leesil's weapons. It seemed that Sgäile's limitations as adjudicator now worked against Brot'an, for Sgäile was the most familiar of all with Leesil and herself. Sgäile had been present in Bela when they hunted undead in its streets and sewers.

Fréth whispered in Most Aged Father's ear. He glowered but kept silent.

Brot'an turned back to Osha. "How did you learn the use of these weapons?"

"Léshil told me and the others who escorted him to Crijheäiche."

"Did he work alone?"

"No, he said Magiere and the majay-hì"—he pointed to Chap—"hunted with him. Destroying undead was their vocation."

Brief and broken murmurs sifted through the crowd. Magiere remained tall and straight, with crossed arms, and tried not to meet anyone's eyes.

Brot'an held both his arms wide. "Her vocation was to destroy the undead. And why would one so-claimed undead"—he turned toward Most Aged Father—"hunt its own kind?"

"Hearsay!" Fréth shouted. "And conjecture. Your opening statements are concluded. Keep to the presentation of what is verifiable . . . or be done!"

Sgäile cut in before Brot'an could reply. "Objection upheld. What was heard by the witness from another is not direct testimony unless the original speaker is not present."

"A valid point," Brot'an replied. "Then let us hear it directly . . . I call Léshil as witness."

"He is not one of us," Fréth shouted. "He is not an'Cróan and may not speak before the council."

Brot'an paced back to his table. He ripped aside the shimmering cloth, and lifted what hid there into plain sight.

It was a smooth branch, glistening bare of bark.

"Once again, you presume to speak for the ancestors," Brot'an called to Fréth. "And yet here is a branch from Roise Chârmune. How is he not one of us . . . if he was given this?" He pointed the glistening branch at Sgäile. "I call upon the ajudicator to confirm."

Sgäile nodded slowly. "In my presence . . . the ancestors gave it freely to Léshil."

"They gave it to him directly?" Brot'an asked. "He did not procure it with their implied blessing?"

The hiss of whispered voices surrounded the clearing. Magiere looked down at Wynn in confusion, but the sage only translated the words and shook her head, looking about with uncertain worry on her round face.

"Yes," Sgäile finally answered. "They appeared to Léshil and one gave him the branch of Roise Chârmune."

Brot'an and Sgäile were the only ones who didn't look stunned. Murmurs among the elders and clans grew until the noise drowned Sgäile's shouts for silence. Across the field, Fréth stood silent. She looked back at Most Aged Father, but the old man only stared at Leesil. Even his spite was masked in surprise.

Leesil scowled with his eyes on the ground.

Magiere was so lost. If Leesil had the branch, why had Brot'an waited to reveal it like this? It seemed one more trick he played on his patriarch, perhaps to keep Fréth and the old man off balance. Magiere wished she could risk asking Leesil questions in the middle of all this.

"Not enough," Fréth called, though it lacked her usual sharp conviction. "Even among our own, only those who've taken their full place as one of us can speak before the elders when in council."

"Another true point," Brot'an answered, and Fréth looked wary, as if she'd stepped into a trap. "Blood is not enough. A name is needed to be an'Cróan . . . to be recognized as one of us."

"Léshil does not have . . . ," Fréth began, but the last of her words had no voice and were only marked by the movement of her lips.

"He does," Brot'an answered, and turned upon Leesil. "Speak your true name for all to hear and recognize your rights."

Magiere looked at Leesil.

"It doesn't mean anything," he whispered to her. "Whatever it takes to get you out of here . . . I don't care what they believe."

"The witness will refrain from speaking," Sgäile called loudly. "Except as directed by the council, an advocate, or the adjudicator."

Magiere wanted to grab Leesil and make him tell her what had happened.

Leesil took a long breath. "Leshi . . . Le . . . shi-air . . ." He sighed in frustration. "I can't pronounce it."

Sgäile frowned, the tan lines of his face creasing, and he shouted out, "Léshiârelaohk! And it was not chosen by him . . . it was given by the ancestors themselves."

All sound in the clearing faded instantly. Then a low thrum of voices grew and erupted into a deafening chaos.

Magiere spotted Gleann leaning forward upon his small stool. He was silent, staring down to the field at Leesil. But unlike the shocked disbelief or outrage of others, his expression was eager—and even excited.

Leanâlhâm stood behind him with confusion on her young face. She touched Gleann on the shoulder, whispering in his ear. He reached up and patted her hand with a satisfied smile but said nothing in return.

Whatever the name meant, either it wasn't clear or the meaning had raised disturbing questions among the council. Or maybe it was that Leesil had acquired any name at all. Magiere looked to Wynn for help.

The little sage wrinkled her nose and then whispered, "Something about 'grief' and . . . maybe 'tear'? I cannot fully decipher. Its construction seems older than even the dialect spoken here."

Brot'an stood erect with the branch gripped at his side, ardent and determined pride in his eyes as he looked upon Leesil. Clearly he knew what the name meant and it pleased him. This worried Magiere most of all.

He raised the branch, turning before the crowd, until the gathering's noise settled enough for him to be heard.

"Tell us of what happened on hallowed ground," Brot'an said to Leesil.

Fréth offered no further objection.

Leesil recounted briefly, and Brot'an translated for the gathering.

Not all of it made sense to Magiere. Leesil was reluctant and spoke simply, like the times she caught him in some foolishness and forced him to confess. By her guess, he wasn't telling everything. But he offered enough to bring all voices to full silence as the elders and others listened in rapt attention.

"And what is the use of your weapons?" Brot'an asked. "How does this use relate to the accused?"

Leesil spoke more forcefully this time, expanding upon Osha's earlier answers. He even told of their first encounter with Sgäile in Bela, and of Chap's own part in their efforts to hunt undead. The crowd listened with interest.

"Now the people may question the truth of these words," Brot'an said. "Do the elders question the naming of . . . Léshiârelaohk?"

His gaze slipped to Fréth and Most Aged Father. Neither said a word, though Fréth seethed visibly in frustration.

"The ancestors granted Léshiârelaohk's request." Brot'an lifted the branch once more. "Magiere, come forward. You may bring your translator."

She tried not to hesitate as she stepped out, and Wynn came with her, a little more cautious.

"If the accused is truly undead," Brot'an called out, "no tricks or arcane practice will serve her. This branch, gifted by the ancestors from Roise Chârmune, is their bond to our land by which no enemy of the life here could walk our forest."

He held the branch out to Magiere.

She stood frozen. Inside, she trembled—not just from the affliction the forest had pressed upon her. What if the branch did something to mark her as an undead after all? Or worse, what if it drained of all remaining life at her touch?

Magiere couldn't breathe. She reached out and grasped the branch in her bare hand.

It felt smooth but not slick or wet, as it appeared to be. At first it was cool, even cold, then it warmed gently in her grip. It felt alive, and her panic sharpened.

For some reason, her eyes met and held Sgäile's. She waited for the wooden symbol to wither or to burn her . . . or something.

Nothing happened.

"If she were undead," Brot'an called out, "this could not happen. Not one sign of rejection. No strike against her flesh by the ancestors through the very emblem of our land and bloodline of old."

Magiere began to breathe again. Brot'an walked an arc around her and around the clearing as he spoke.

"She is unusual, yes, perhaps as suited to her calling. In battle, she appears fierce . . . even predatory, as some have said, and I have seen this myself more than once. But the ancestors have not marked her as a threat to us. Whatever issues some might take with her, the current claim is false."

Brot'an waved Magiere and Wynn back to the oak table.

"I rest for now," he said, "and yield to the address of the accuser's advocate."

Magiere approached the table, watching Leesil. He reached out and grasped her pale hand. She quickly dropped the branch on the table and turned to look across the field.

Fréth remained by her table, locked in uncertainty, but Most Aged Father didn't look shaken a bit by Brot'an's presentation. Magiere quivered inside, wondering what the old man would try next.

Wynn leaned in close between Magiere and Leesil, translating quietly for them.

Fréth strode to the clearing's center, wasting no time as she addressed the gathering in a clear, light voice.

"The accused's advocate has not addressed all possibilities. This human does not merely 'appear' fierce in battle. Her body takes on more literal attributes . . . by which she turned upon the living around her. We accept the testimonies presented so far without challenge, but even her companions do not fully understand her nature."

Wynn detected the slight falterings in Fréthfâre's voice.

Not uncertainty, but more like a speech too quickly memorized, repetitious and glib. Wynn studied Most Aged Father, wondering if Fréth served as his advocate or just his mouthpiece.

Fréth strode back to her table and flicked a summoning hand at the crowd behind her. Én'nish pushed into view through a cluster of anmaglâhk and came downslope with something cupped in her hands. Fréth took it and proceeded across the clearing. As she approached Brot'an's table, Wynn saw a sacred white flower in Fréth's hand. The same as the one that Sgäile had warned her not to touch.

White velvet petals shaped like leaves gathered the sunlight that struck them and returned it in a soft glow. The base and stem of the flower were a dark green, close to black.

"We saw some of those on our way here," Leesil whispered.

Fréth held it up for the clan elders to see.

"*Anasgiah*—the Life Shield. Prepared by a healer in tea or food, it sustains the dying, so they might yet be saved from death. It is vibrant with life itself, and feeds the life of those who need it most."

Anxiety grew in Wynn's stomach. By all she had heard, the ancestors were thought to weigh and render judgment according to an'Cróan needs. This flower was an inert thing, void of such intelligent consideration—whatever its use might be in these proceedings.

"The accused will come out," Fréth ordered.

Magiere approached in an echo of Fréth's own self-confidence. Wynn trotted after, uncertain if protocol allowed it, but no one stopped her.

Without warning, Fréth slapped the white petals across Magiere's face.

Wynn gasped as Leesil tried to rush out. Brot'an pulled him back and then walked up behind Magiere.

"What is the meaning of this?" Brot'an demanded, as Sgäile moved quickly to join them.

Wynn grabbed hold of Magiere's arm, fearful of what she might do in return.

Magiere barely flinched, but her dark eyes locked on Fréth's amber ones. Then she began to shake uncontrollably. Fréth watched her with a startled satisfaction.

Wynn wrapped her arm around Magiere's waist. Fréth raised the flower for all to see.

The white petals darkened. First to dull yellow, and then ashen tan as they withered. The flower died in Fréth's hand, and crumpled petals fell away to float to the ground.

Rumbling grew among the gathering. The shrill voices of the Äruin'nas shouted above all.

"Only an undead could cause this!" Fréth cried. "*Anasgiah*'s potency is such that an undead does not have to consume the petals to consume what it offers. For that is what an undead truly feeds upon—life!"

In horror, Wynn craned her head around up at Brot'an.

His face was tight and hard, but he was caught as unaware as anyone else by this trick Fréth played. At the field's far end, Most Aged Father watched with ardent eyes, and the barest smile stretched his shriveled mouth.

Wynn tried to force calm as she held on to Magiere, but she found none. Fréth could know little more of the undead than anyone present. She could not have known how the flower would react to Magiere. This was Most Aged Father's doing.

The old one's test challenged Brot'an's—perhaps even canceled it out.

Brot'an motioned Magiere and Wynn to return to his table. Wynn walked Magiere back, steadying her until she grabbed the table's edge. Sgäile had to shout for silence again, but one of the Äruin'nas elders rose to his feet, screaming back at Sgäile in his strange tongue.

"Do not throw another demand upon these proceedings!" Sgäile replied. "No vote has been called. You will hold for deliberation."

The short old one spit one more vicious utterance. Sgäile did not answer, and stood waiting until the Äruin'nas elder settled cross-legged upon the depression's edge.

Fréth stalked back to her table as the crowd's rumble settled. She removed three stilettos and a shining garrote wire from her sleeves and belt and dropped them all upon the table.

Most Aged Father did not look at her. His ardent satisfaction remained focused across the clearing upon Magiere.

"Brot'ân'duivé sought the ancestors' judgment," Fréth cried out. "I do so as well. But words and tests will not settle this. I disarm and call for trial by combat. Let the ancestors guide my limbs in the old ways. Let them decide who speaks the truth."

The gathering's murmurs rose into a cacophony. Most Aged Father sat back in his chair, milky eyes glittering.

"Confer!" Brot'an shouted.

Sgäile nodded in discomfort and barely contained his distaste as he looked at Fréth.

Brot'an turned to Magiere as Wynn hurried to catch up in translating. She faltered and staggered as Chap shoved in beside her.

"What's happening?" Leesil asked.

"Old ways," Brot'an sighed. "All but forgotten. When a dispute cannot be settled through deliberation, trial by combat may be called, though it has never been sought in my lifetime. And it must be sanctioned by the elders. The victor must put the opponent down, or the opponent must verbally yield. It is believed that the ancestors support the victor's truth."

"That is not all she wants," Wynn said. "She goads Magiere into revealing her nature. Fréth wants them all to see Magiere transform, and if she cannot defeat Fréth without calling upon her inner nature . . ."

Either way, Magiere could lose, and she was still shaking.

Magiere's eyes shifted back and forth. "I might . . . might control it long enough . . . still win . . ."

"No," Leesil snapped. "You're not going out there!"

Magiere was barely able to speak between shudders, and Wynn knew she could not hold her dhampir half inside if a fight ensued. In Nein'a's clearing, Magiere had lost herself in this same shaken state.

"Most Aged Father told Fréth to do this," Wynn said. "She reported everything she saw in Nein'a's clearing, but only he would know how the flower would affect Magiere."

Brot'an turned hard eyes on Wynn, likely wondering how she knew this, but she gave him no chance to question her as she rushed on.

"He knows Magiere may not be able to hold back. The instant she succumbs, she will be finished. This has nothing to do with Fréth putting the outcome in the hands of her ancestors."

Magiere leaned back, half-sitting on the table's edge, and closed her arms tightly about herself. All Leesil could do was stand before her, holding her steady by the shoulders.

"A vote must still be taken," Brot'an said.

He pushed off the table and headed toward Sgäile. Fréth joined them. An unknown anmaglâhk came out as well and handed Sgäile two small baskets.

"Let us hope the vote fails," Wynn whispered as Leesil turned to watch.

"A vote on challenge is called!" Sgäile shouted.

It started slowly at first. Wynn saw stones being tossed by the elders. Black or white, they tumbled downslope or arched directly to the clearing's floor. Gleann's black one cleared the slope completely and thumped upon the turf. He gave her a smile, and Wynn understood.

Black to decline, and white in favor of combat.

Wynn did not need to look to know what color the Äru-in'nas elder threw.

Brot'an and Fréth followed as Sgäile gathered and separated the stones into the two baskets. They returned to the clearing's side, where he poured them into two piles. Both appeared equal. He began counting.

Before he shouted the results, Brot'an already headed back toward Wynn. Chap growled beside her.

"Trial by combat has been granted," Sgäile called.

Brot'an began pulling stilettos and blades from his wrist sheaths and boots, slapping them on the oak table.

"What are you doing?" Wynn asked.

He ignored her and turned to face the field. "I call the right of proxy, as the accused's advocate."

Halfway to her own table, Fréth spun about. Even from the distance, Wynn saw her eyes widen.

"No!" Most Aged Father screeched. "That would prove nothing! The human is an abomination, and you would challenge your own caste for her sake?"

Wynn grew dizzy, trying to translate amid the noise rising from the onlookers and still follow all that was happening. Nausea surged in her stomach under Chap's leaf-wing voice.

Too quick a denial! He is eager for this.

She looked down to find Chap with ears flattened, glaring across the field at Most Aged Father.

For all the old elf's accusations, and his attempt to deny Brot'an, the Anmaglâhk patriarch appeared to quiver with anticipation. Chap spoke again in Wynn's head.

Brot'an's intercession fuels the old one. He sees opportunity . . . he wants Brot'an to fight.

Most Aged Father tried to stand and failed, slumping into his chair. He lifted his frail face to all those around the clearing.

"Do you see what this thing has wrought? She has poisoned us and driven our own people to violence against each other!"

Brot'an turned to Sgäile. "By law, this is my right."

Sgäile was slow to respond. He said something Wynn could not hear over the crowd. But his answer was clearly a confirmation to Brot'an, and he hung his head.

Wynn did not know Sgäile well, but she knew where his loyalties lay. The last thing he would want was for his own caste to turn upon itself.

This is no longer just about Magiere, Chap said.

Wynn saw Most Aged Father's shouted denial for what it was—a calculated misdirection. If Brot'an won, it would shake his own caste's faith in him and might even lead to claims that he sided with enemies of the people. If he lost, though that seemed so unlikely, all that remained was the council's final judgment for what to do with Magiere. Either way, Most Aged Father would have his way in some part.

Wynn could do nothing but wait and watch.

Brot'an stood relaxed but erect upon the clearing's turf as he looked to Fréth.

"Whenever you are ready."

Chap knew Brot'an grasped for the only option he had left, but Most Aged Father spoke one truth. At any violence among the elves, Magiere would be seen as the cause. Even if found innocent in Brot'an's victory, it would only settle the immediate claim. In the end, it would weigh against all three of Chap's charges when it was time for the council to consider the human interlopers in their land.

He did not care what the Anmaglâhk did to each other, but he would not allow Magiere to be used anymore.

Chap bolted across the clearing, not caring about any attention he called.

"What are you doing?" Wynn shouted after him.

There was no time for explanations. He raced for the clearing's far slope and lunged up the incline straight at Gleann and his clan.

The old healer's jaw dropped halfway open. Chap let out a snarl. It was the only way, the safest place, to break through. Only Leanâlhâm stood transfixed with fright. Before Chap had to swerve to get around the girl, Gleann jerked her aside. The rest of his kinsman scrambled out of Chap's path.

He shot through to the open forest beyond.

Even his own presence as a majay-hì no longer counted for Magiere. He had felt the doubt and suspicion behind those who watched him from around the clearing. They saw a puzzle they could not unravel in a majay-hì who kept company with humans, and most believed that he was wrong—deviant and twisted by a life no majay-hì would choose.

They did not know how close to the truth they were—for all the wrong reasons.

If the Anmaglâhk and the elders wanted battle to find truth, he would give them one.

Chap cut through brush and trees, until he broke into a wide alley created by a deep brook. He leaped up a smooth boulder overhanging the rippling water. In the distance behind him, he heard the crowd in the clearing.

Their sounds drowned from Chap's ears as he ripped the forest's peace with a howl.

Sgäile felt as if his heart would rupture. He no longer knew what was right or wrong. He knew only the ways of his caste and of his people. He had followed both with such devotion and conscience. But since the humans' arrival, one had been continually pitted against the other. Now two of his own turned on each other over an outsider.

Brot'ân'duivé and Fréthfâre. Greimasg'äh and elder of caste against Most Aged Father's chosen Covârleasa. Two of the caste's most honored.

At its worst—if neither yielded—one would die.

Brot'ân'duivé had right of proxy for Magiere, and Sgäile could not help but agree with his decision. It was proper, for what he saw of the woman's sudden failing condition. He did not understand why the healing *Anasgiah* had done this to her, nor did he care for the manner in which it was done.

Fréthfâre's only goal appeared to be forcing Magiere to transform before the gathering. Perhaps they should see this. Perhaps Fréthfâre was not wrong either.

Sgäile's mind spun as Brot'ân'duivé stood waiting upon Fréthfâre's response.

And then Chap raced away across the clearing and through the crowd.

That instant of distraction left Sgäile uprepared. Every muscle in his body clenched as Fréthfâre rushed at Brot'ân'duivé.

All Sgäile could do was wait for one to yield—or one to die.

*   *   *

Leesil stood speechless as Chap vanished through the crowd. Then Fréth struck out at Brot'an.

Her palm strike never landed. Brot'an spun away low with a sweep of his leg. Fréth hopped back into a crouch. Before her feet touched earth, Brot'an was already up.

Leesil only cared that Brot'an won. That hope didn't even grate upon him in this moment.

Brot'an didn't close on Fréth but stood his ground, waiting as she circled. When she charged again, even Leesil was startled. It all happened before he could blink.

Fréth's lunging foot slid forward along the ground. Brot'an took a wide step left, and upon the twist of his torso, drove his right fist for her face.

She hit the ground in a hurdler's straddle, and Brot'an's strike passed over her head. She struck out for Brot'an's bent knee with her momentum. He shifted quickly onto his other leg, but the change put him into Fréth's path. She pushed off with her rear cocked leg and shot upward for his abdomen with straightened fingers.

Brot'an twisted away, dropping to his back, as Fréth rose onto her forward leg. She speared her hand downward at his exposed throat.

Leesil felt Magiere's hand close tight on his arm.

Sgäile took two quick steps forward before stopping.

Brot'an pulled his head aside, and Fréth's ridged fingers embedded in the clearing's earth.

"She's trying to kill him," Magiere hissed.

Leesil already knew this. Fréth would know she couldn't win unless she threw everything she had at Brot'an. Or maybe there was more to this than just Magiere's life—maybe a way to get around their custom of not spilling the blood of their own.

Most Aged Father watched without the slightest flinch at the way Fréth went after Brot'an. However it ended, Leesil feared that Magiere's fate would still be left dangling.

Brot'an swung his leg to the side, and the force rolled him over onto his face. As Fréth pulled soiled fingers from the earth, Brot'an's second leg shot out into her chest.

It was almost the same move Leesil used himself when trying to catch an undead from below while on the ground. Sgäile had once called it by some strange name that meant "Cat in the Grass."

Fréth wasn't fast enough to get out of the way.

Leesil heard the impact, and Fréth's body arched.

Her feet left the ground as she shot backward, headfirst. Her shoulders hit the earth a dozen steps away. Impact and momentum whipped her legs over her head. Leesil thought for certain her neck would snap under the fast folding curl.

She flattened on the ground, facedown, and then pushed herself up and got to her feet. She didn't waver, but struggled quietly to regain her breath.

For all Brot'an's size and age, he was nearly as fast as Fréth. And any slim advantage she might have in that wouldn't be enough to counter his experience.

"Yield," Brot'an demanded, circling around her.

A thin bloodied line marked the side of Brot'an's neck. Fréth had grazed him with her fingernails.

"Why is he holding back?" Wynn whispered.

Leesil swallowed any response, as Fréth went at Brot'an again.

Brot'an stamped hard against the earth with his right foot. An instant later he was turning fast in midair. His other leg whipped toward her at a downward angle.

His knee struck her forward arm, but his foot smashed her hip.

Fréth toppled under the impact. Her lighter body didn't have the mass to endure it. She slammed down sideways into the ground and somehow managed to kick out. She caught Brot'an's other foot just before it settled to the earth.

Brot'an spun sideways in the air. As he fell, he flattened one hand against the ground, but he crumpled and his right shoulder struck. He rolled away into a crouch, shaking his head. Fréth tottered as she got up, and then she stumbled to a halt as a howl echoed over the clearing.

Leesil looked about for the sound. The gathering broke

into startled cries. Elves on the forest side of the clearing scattered downslope.

Chap lunged out through the crowd, tearing up sod as he charged straight at Brot'an and Fréth.

CHAPTER TWENTY-ONE

Magiere didn't know what to think when Chap charged into the council clearing, but shock followed an instant later. He wasn't alone. An entire pack of majay-hì spilled through the crowd in his wake, including the white dog she'd seen with Chap more than once.

Chap bolted straight at Brot'an and Fréth. He cut between them with a vicious snarl and bared teeth. Without pause, he ran to Magiere. Even Wynn backed up as the dog dug in his front paws and lurched to a stop.

Majay-hì of all shades, all with crystalline eyes, ran one by one through the clearing. The white female came directly to Chap. The dark one with grayed muzzle who'd charged Magiere in Nein'a's clearing circled in on Brot'an, cutting between him and Fréth.

Fréth backed up several steps, but Brot'an looked about in open confusion. Sgäile tried to step in then froze before the maniacal snapping of a tall steel-gray dog.

Wynn grabbed Magiere's hand, pulling her forward toward Chap. "Come on! You have to go with him—now!"

"What are you doing?" Leesil asked.

"Chap says she must come," Wynn answered.

Magiere stepped out in a daze. In three breaths, all but

two majay-hì closed on her. The remaining pair paced like guardians before Brot'an, Fréth, and Sgäile. Leesil ducked around in front of Magiere to face any dog that came too close. Only the dark one with the gray muzzle growled as he approached.

More cries and shouts erupted in the crowd behind Magiere, and she looked back with Leesil and Wynn.

Another pack wormed through the gathering above. The only elf who stood her ground, watching without surprise, was the elder female in maroon holding a scroll. This second pack spread around the clearing's side slopes, pacing before the wide-eyed gathering of elves.

A third pack burst out, upslope behind Most Aged Father. These gave the old elf a wide berth as they circled around the clearing's side. As the packs met, they spread, bordering the clearing floor on all sides.

Those with Chap stayed close around Magiere, and the white female nosed her way nearer. Leesil set himself in her path, but Wynn pushed him aside as she knelt by the female.

"Stop it," she said. "Her name is Lily, and she will protect us."

Chap barked once.

Everyone, including Brot'an, Sgäile, and Fréth, looked about in shock. At least three dozen dogs ranged within the clearing, long legs trotting, long fur bouncing up and down. Four of the dogs gathered around Magiere to form some sort of vanguard. She watched them in wonder. What did it mean?

Gleann called out in Belaskian from where he stood above the dogs pacing the clearing's slope. "I think they try to tell us something." His lined face held a hint of amusement. Then he spoke in Elvish to the others around him.

"This settles nothing!" Most Aged Father shouted. "Disperse the dogs and end this interference."

"He's right," Magiere said at Wynn's translation. "We're not getting out of here this way . . . not without bloodshed."

"Stay where you are," Wynn ordered. "Chap, make that old man be quiet!"

Chap turned toward the patriarch but held his ground in front of Magiere.

Wynn flinched sharply, glanced at Chap, and then turned wide eyes upon Leesil.

"What?" Magiere asked. "What did Chap say?"

A handful of Anmaglâhk came out of the crowd in answer to Most Aged Father's demand. But any attempt to descend into the clearing was cut off by snarling dogs charging. One anmaglâhk drew a blade.

Magiere grabbed Wynn's tunic shoulder, shouting at Chap as much as the sage. "Stop this, now! It's not going to work."

"What else have we got?" Leesil argued. "I'm not letting them take you."

"Leesil, go with Chap," Wynn said suddenly. "Now . . . and when he barks once at you, only you, give Most Aged Father his message from the ancestors."

Magiere had no idea what this meant. Confusion and frustration made her shudder harder. She'd never turned from a fight. But if Leesil, or even Chap or Wynn, came under threat, she wouldn't be able to control herself in this state.

Leesil glared at Chap. "You've been in my head again!"

"Shut your mouth and do it!" Wynn snapped at him.

Magiere grabbed Leesil by the shirtfront. "This is Chap's game now. Follow his lead."

Chap stalked forward across the clearing, and Leesil followed, looking worried.

A shrill whistle like a rushing song carried above the noise of the gathering.

Chap and Leesil were only partway across the field, and even the majay-hì turned confused circles at the sound. A clan elder in a dark brown cloak raised a hand and pointed high beyond Magiere.

Leesil turned, and Chap did as well. Brot'an lost his stoic self-control for an instant as he stared beyond Magiere. She turned around.

From the upper reaches of one bridge-branched oak, something launched from the thick leaves into the air. It spread wings longer than any bird Magiere had ever seen, and spiraled downward in wild arcs. The closer it came, the more Magiere doubted its shape. The majay-hì scattered away as it landed beyond Leesil and Chap. Magiere sucked in a breath and held it.

Not a bird, for it—she—had arms and legs. She looked only at Magiere, as if she saw someone familiar.

Her wings were immense, and their combined span was at least three times her height. They folded behind a narrow and slight-boned torso of subtle curves like that of an adolescent girl. She was no taller than an Äruin'nas, and perhaps less. From pinion feathers to the downy covering on her body and face, she was a mottled off-white. Instead of hair, larger feathers combed back like a headdress and were matched by the same on the backs of her forearms and lower legs.

Two huge oval eyes dominated her face, pushed slightly to the sides by a long narrow nose that ended above a small, thin-lipped mouth. Her eyes were like polished stones, dark at first but turning as red as a dove's where they caught sunlight. She cocked her head like a crow, studying Magiere.

This frail creature stepped toward Magiere, rocking slightly upon the earth as if walking wasn't quite natural for her.

"*Úirishg*," Wynn said, the word exploding on her exhale.

Magiere couldn't take her eyes from this winged female. The majay-hì pulled farther aside to give her passage. A dry female voice from somewhere behind said, "*Séyilf!*" The word rattled in Magiere's empty mind until she heard herself try to numbly repeat it. But the closest she got out was "silf."

"The Wind-Blown," Wynn translated.

The silf drew closer and reached up with a hand of narrow fingers. She parted her lips as if to speak, and between them, in place of teeth, were ridges like the edge of a bird's beak inside her mouth. The sound that came out of her throat was somewhere between the cry of a hunting hawk and a sparrow's song.

Gleann came down and stopped beside Wynn. Most of the majay-hì descended to the clearing floor. Even Chap returned with Leesil close behind. Fréth headed for Most Aged Father, who now watched in silent suspicion. Brot'an and Sgäile approached behind Leesil.

The silf looked about, growing agitated or nervous, and flexed her wings.

Gleann waved everyone off before they came too close. From behind him, one of the Äruin'nas stepped out.

"This is Tuma'ac," Gleann said in accented Belaskian. "He may be able to translate."

Tuma'ac looked up at Magiere with a vicious twitch of his eye that made the strange markings on his sun-wrinkled face seem to dance. He nodded once to Gleann but looked to Sgäile.

Sgäile regained himself, perhaps remembering his place as adjudicator. "Yes, proceed."

Tuma'ac approached the silf, and indeed she was shorter than he. He motioned with his hands toward himself and spoke to her in his strange tongue. The odd cry erupted from the silf again, sounding much the same as before to Magiere. Tuma'ac blinked twice as he looked sidelong at Magiere, but his sudden shock faded in disgust. He barked something at Gleann.

Gleann's high eyebrows rose even higher. "He says the séyilf called you 'kin' . . . or blood of her kind."

Magiere looked to Leesil, who only shook his head, and then to Wynn.

The sage was horrified. She gave Magiere a quick shake of her head. Not in confusion but more that she couldn't speak her mind here and now.

It was enough to bring Magiere to her senses, enough to call up memories of a hidden room beneath the keep of her undead father.

One of the decayed bodies there had rotted feathers among its bones. Wynn called them Úirishg, the five mythical races, of which the elves and dwarves were the only known two. Five beings had been slaughtered in that hidden blood rite to make Magiere's birth possible.

Magiere turned cold inside, looking back into the silf's dark eyes.

It cried again, and the chain translation passed once more to Gleann.

"She says you are not to be harmed . . . her people will not tolerate any violence against one of their own."

"That cannot be true!" Most Aged Father shouted. "You translate incorrectly. And even so, how could she know?"

Again the chain of words passed, but this time Gleann stumbled and spoke one elvish word to Wynn. The sage seemed to have difficulty.

"Something like . . . ," she began and shook her head. "She is . . . a spiritual leader of some kind. 'Spirit-talker' is the closest I can think of."

Gleann turned toward Most Aged Father. "If you wish to call Tuma'ac or the séyilf a liar, then do so for yourself and not through me. Do we now reject the word of those we promised to protect and hide in our mountains?"

Wynn shifted close to Magiere with a whisper. "The feather and berries in the mountain passage. It was one of them . . . one of the séyilf."

The silf turned away. Her flurried thrash of wings sent majay-hì scattering, as she half leaped and flew to the piles of stones that Sgäile had left at the clearing's edge. She grabbed a black one and tossed it across the clearing.

It tumbled to a halt before Most Aged Father, and he shook visibly as his expression turned livid.

The silf screeched again, and Tuma'ac grunted in satisfaction before speaking to Gleann.

"She calls us to vote," Gleann said, pointing to the stone, "and gives that of her people . . . against the claim of Most Aged Father."

"Do the advocates have anything further to present?" Sgäile asked quietly.

Brot'an shook his head once. But Most Aged Father clutched at Fréth, whispering harshly. Fréth kept shaking her head in denial.

"Your answer, advocate!" Sgäile called with more force.

Fréth stood up, and her head dropped as she shook it slowly. "No . . . nothing."

Sgäile stepped to the clearing's center. "The Advocates have retired. We ask the elders to deliberate and render judgment on the claim presented."

Gleann didn't return to his clan. Instead, he simply cast a stone—black—and gave Magiere a curt bow. It was a kind gesture, but not enough to make her hopeful.

Another black stone arched out from behind her and tumbled across the ground. Magiere looked back.

The tall female in maroon stood halfway down the slope, the one Sgäile had called Tosân . . . something on the night they searched for Wynn. Her calculated study of Magiere turned suddenly upon Leesil, and then she walked back up to her chair between her like-clad attendants. How her filmy eyes saw anything was disturbing.

Magiere wasn't certain how long it would take the others, or whether a quick or protracted vote worked more in her favor. She tried not to meet the silf's steady stare, for its strange face was too difficult to read. She didn't want to think about her own past, her birth, and why this creature had mistaken her as kin.

One at a time, then in twos and threes, black and white stones fell into the clearing.

Magiere closed her eyes. She felt Leesil's arm slip around her shoulders and tighten.

She didn't watch Sgäile gather the stones, but after long moments she heard their clatter as he poured them into piles upon the ground.

Gleann's voice rose so loud it startled her, and her eyes snapped open as Wynn translated.

"As the claim against her is now dismissed, Magiere's companions cannot be held in blame either. They came here as guests of Most Aged Father and under oath of guardianship. No reason has been given to breach either. They must be released, and their property returned. Then other matters require our collected attention"—he glanced toward Most Aged Father—"concerning Anmaglâhk ways in conflict with those of the people."

"It's over," Leesil whispered.

Magiere couldn't see any difference between the stone piles at Sgäile's feet. He seemed to understand her confusion and nodded to her.

"It is over—for now," Brot'an added. "I will take you back to quarters, so you may rest."

"Not quite," Leesil returned. "I still have a claim to make for my mother."

"It will be addressed," Brot'an answered. "The rest will

be settled without either of you, and should cause you no more concern. Do not press the matter when it is not yet necessary."

Leesil glanced at Magiere, caught between concern and stubbornness.

Magiere put a hand on his chest. Both looked up as a rush of wind around Magiere whipped Leesil's loose hair wildly about.

The silf dropped upon the table behind Magiere and reached out too quickly, startling Leesil into the defensive. Magiere grabbed his wrist.

The tiny female flexed her wings and raised her hand more slowly this time. She lifted the side of Magiere's hair, letting its strands slide between narrow fingers ending in roan-colored nails that curved slightly like talons. The silf cocked her head, watching the hair fall bit by bit.

Magiere pulled back at the thrash of her wings as she lifted into the air and flapped away beyond the treetops.

Leesil exhaled. "As if we haven't had enough for one day."

"There is one more thing," Wynn said. "Brot'an, would you please wait with Magiere?"

The sage grabbed Leesil's arm, pulling him along as she followed Chap toward Most Aged Father.

Chap had no idea what this séyilf—silf—truly wanted. Like Magiere and even Wynn, he was confused as to why it mistook Magiere for kin. Somehow the small winged female sensed the blood of its own used in Magiere's conception.

He had tried reaching for its mind to catch any memories, but he found nothing besides images of himself and his charges climbing downward through the mountain. The female had been the one to leave them a trail . . . the one who had called out to him amid the blizzard. This was all he gathered from it. He was left wondering why it had twice interceded on their behalf and how long it had watched them from hiding.

Chap had planned for a fight, even wanted it in part. Or at least enough distraction to take the one person who mattered—Most Aged Father.

He had watched the an'Cróan shaken by how the majay-hì cast their "vote" in this matter. Lily had likely strained her place among the pack in convincing them for him, but they all shared some strange animosity for the leader of the Anmaglâhk, a being too old for natural life and yet making claims against Magiere as an undead.

Perhaps his rejected kin were correct—flesh and heart made him reckless. He did not care anymore.

Most Aged Father's bearers had not come for him. Even this did not matter to Chap. He wanted answers, and he would take them.

Fréthfâre stepped in his way as he closed on the old one.

"We only have a message for Most Aged Father," Wynn said.

Chap barked once, not turning his eyes from the patriarch.

"*Snaw . . . hac . . . ,*" Leesil began, then sighed in frustration.

"Snähacróe," Wynn pronounced for him.

At the name, Most Aged Father's milky eyes widened and he sat up as straight as he could.

"He said to tell you . . . ," Leesil called out clearly, "that he's waiting for his comrade to join him . . . when you're done."

Chap lunged into the old one's mind, waiting for whatever might come.

Sounds and images rose, led by the face of a tall elf with wide cheekbones. Chap let go of all else, even anger, and sank into Most Aged Father's rising memories.

Sorhkafâré stood amid the night-wrapped trees surrounding Aonnis Lhoin'n, First Glade.

It had been the longest run of his life to reach his people's land and what now seemed the only sanctuary in a blighted world. He led his dwindling group to this place hoping to find other survivors, hoping to find help. But he could still hear the grunts and weeping and madness of the night horde ranging beyond the forest's edge.

All through his flight home, every town and village, and even every keep and stronghold, was littered with bodies torn as if fed upon by animals. The few living they encountered joined them in flight from the pale predators with crystalline eyes, always in their wake.

The numbers of their pursuers grew with each fall of the sun.

Fewer than half of those who fled Sorhkafâré's encampment with him reached the forests of his people. Not one of the dwarves made it on their stout legs carrying thick heavy bodies. Thalhómêrk had been the last of their people to succumb, along with his son and daughter.

In a dead run through the dark, Sorhkafâré had heard the dwarven lord's vicious curses. He looked back as Thalhómêrk submerged under a wave of pale bodies. He shuddered at the sound of bones cracking under the dwarf's massive fists and mace. And still the horde flowed toward Sorhkafâré and over Thalhómêrk's son and daughter. He could not tell which one had screamed out, as Hoil'lhân's voice smothered it with a visceral shout. She whirled to turn back.

Her hair whipped about her long face as she swung the butt of her thick metal spear shaft. It cracked through a pale face. Splattering black fluids blotted out the creature's glittering eyes and maw of sharp teeth.

Sorhkafâré did not understand Hoil'lhân's preference for dwarven and human company, nor her restless and savage nature. Perhaps she had been killing for too long.

Hoil'lhân spun her spear without pause as three more pale figures closed on her. The spear's wide and long head split through the first's collarbone, grinding into its chest. She jerked her weapon out as the other two hesitated, and she screeched at them madly, ready to charge.

Sorhkafâré grabbed her, pulling her around as more of the horde rushed at them through the dark.

"Run," he ordered.

Even in renewed flight Hoil'lhân tried to turn on them with her metal spear. Snähacróe snatched her other arm, and they dragged her onward.

"You cannot save Thalhómêrk," Snähacróe said in a hollow voice.

The endless running took its toll. Two more of

Sorhkafâré's soldiers dropped in their tracks before any saw the forest's edge. All he could do was hope they died of exhaustion before . . .

In the clearing of First Glade, humans and elves now huddled in fear. Sorhkafâré could no longer look at their gaunt faces.

So few . . . and in the distance, beyond the forest's limits, carried the shouts and cries of dark figures with crystalline eyes. A part of him found that easier to face than to count the small number who still lived.

A small pack of the silver-gray wolves came out of the trees. They moved with eerie conscious intent. At first their presence had frightened all, but they never attempted any harm; quite the opposite. They wove among the people, sniffing about. One stopped to lick and nuzzle a small elven girl holding a human infant.

These wolves had eyes like crystals tinted with sky blue, and neither he nor his troops had ever seen such before. But during his campaigns against the enemy, Sorhkafâré had heard reports and rumors of strange wolves, deer, and other animals joining allied forces in battles in other lands. Which made these wolves a welcome sight.

The survivors in First Glade ate little and slept less. If sleep did come, they cried out in their dreams. Every night, Sorhkafâré waited for the pale horde to surge in upon them.

But they never came.

On the sixth night, he could stand it no more and walked out into the forest. Léshiâra tried to stop him.

Youngest of their council of elders, she stood in his way, soft lines of coming age on a face urgent and firm beneath her long graying hair. She pulled her maroon robe tight about herself against the night's chill.

"You cannot leave!" she whispered sharply. "These people need to see every warrior we have left ready to stand for them. You will make them think you abandon them."

"Stand against what?" he snarled at her, not caring who heard. "You do not know what is out there any more than I. And if they could come for us, why have they not done so? Leave me be!"

He stepped around her, heading into the trees, but not before he caught Snähacróe watching him with sad disappointment. In days past, his kinsman's silent reproach would have cut him, but now he felt nothing.

Sorhkafâré followed the sounds of beasts on two legs out beyond the forest, wondering why they had not come for the pitiful count of refugees. These things on two legs . . . things that would not die . . . blood-hungry with familiar faces as pale as corpses'. He heard them more clearly as the trees thinned around him, and he stopped in the night to listen.

The noise they made had changed. Screams of pain were strangled short beneath wet tearing sounds.

Sorhkafâré stumbled forward, sickened by his own curiosity.

Through a stand of border aspens before the open plain, he saw three silhouettes with sparking eyes. They rushed, one after another, upon a fourth fleeing before them.

Still, he kept on, slipping in behind one aspen.

In days past, Sorhkafâré would have leaped to defend any poor victim. But not now. It did not matter if anyone out there on the plain still lived. He peered around the aspen's trunk.

The three hunkered upon the ground with lowered heads, tearing back and forth. Beneath them, the fourth struggled wildly, its pain-pitched voice ringing in Sorhkafâré's ears.

The sound of such terrified suffering ate at him.

He lunged around the tree, running for the victim's outstretched hand. Halfway there, the figure thrashed free and scrambled across the matted grass with wide, panicked eyes. . . .

Glittering, crystalline eyes.

Sorhkafâré's feet slid upon autumn leaves as he halted.

Out on the plain, dark silhouettes chased and hunted each other with cries of fear and hunger. The moon and stars dimly lit shapes tearing into each other with fingers and teeth. With nothing else to feed upon, the pale creatures turned upon each other.

These things . . . so hungry for warm life.

One of the three lifted its head.

Sorhkafâré made out a pale face, its mouth smeared with wet black. Its eyes sparked as if gathering the waning light, and it saw him. It rose, turning toward him as the other pair chased the fourth through the grass.

Sorhkafâré heard his own breath. He retreated a few paces, just inside the forest's tree line.

This pale thing he saw . . . a man . . . was human.

His quivering lips and teeth were darkened, as if he had been drinking black ink. He sniffed the air wildly and a ravenous twist distorted his features. He began running toward Sorhkafâré.

This one smelled him, sensed his life.

Sorhkafâré jerked out his long war knife and braced himself.

The human came straight at him, its feral features pained with starvation. Perhaps it gained no sustenance in feeding on its own. But he no longer cared for anything beyond seeing these horrors gone from his world.

It ran straight at him like an animal without reason.

When it stepped between the first trees of the forest, it stopped short, hissing and gurgling in desperation. Sorhkafâré saw the man clearly now.

Young, perhaps twenty human years. His face was heavily scratched, but the marks were black lines rather than red. His flesh was white and shriveled, as if it were sinking in upon itself. The thing cried piteously at Sorhkafâré and took another hesitant step.

Why would the horde not enter the forest, if they were starved enough to turn on each other?

Sorhkafâré raised his knife and cut the back of his forearm. He swung his bloodied arm through the air.

"Hungry?" he shouted. "I am here!"

The sight of blood drove the man deeper into madness. He charged forward with a scream grating up his throat. Sorhkafâré shifted backward, feeling blindly for smooth and solid footing.

As the pale man lunged between two aspens, he grabbed his head with a strangled choke. He turned about and cried out—but not in anguished hunger. This was a sound of fear and pain as he whirled and wobbled. The man stumbled too near one aspen, and he clawed wildly at the air, as if fending off the tree.

Sorhkafâré watched in stunned confusion. A howl carried around him from within the forest.

It was like nothing Sorhkafâré had ever heard—long and desperate in warning. Two of the silver-furred wolves burst through the underbrush and out of the dark, their eyes glowing like clear crystals tinted with sky blue.

The first slammed straight into the screaming man and latched its jaws around his throat, ripping as it dragged him down. The second joined in, and their howls shifted to savage snarls as they tore at their prey.

The man's scream cut off in a wet gag, but still he thrashed and clawed.

On instinct Sorhkafâré ran in to help the wolves, but they kept snapping and tearing at the man's throat.

One of them shifted aside. It pinned the man's arm with teeth and paws. The other did the same, and they held him down as the first one looked up at Sorhkafâré.

The wolf waited for Sorhkafâré to do something—but what?

The man's throat was a dark mass shredded almost to the spine—yet still he writhed and fought to get free. Black fluids dribbled from his gaping mouth and blotted out his teeth. A mouth that either snarled or screamed with no voice.

He could not still be alive. No one could live after what these wolves had done to him . . . tearing at his neck as if . . .

Sorhkafâré dropped to his knees and snatched the man's hair with his free hand. With so little sinew left on that neck, it was easy to hold the head steady. He pressed the long knife's edge down through the mess of the man's throat until it halted against bone.

In a quick shift, he released his grip on the hair and pressed on the back of the blade with all his weight.

The blade grated and then cut down through neck bones.

The pale man ceased thrashing and fell limp as a true corpse.

Sorhkafâré sucked in air as he lifted his gaze to the first wolf, its muzzle stained with wet black like his own hands. He stared into its eyes as his mind emptied of all but two truths.

The forest would not allow the horde in. And if one got through, these wolves sensed it and came.

He climbed to his feet, still breathing hard, and crept back to the forest's edge to look out upon the rolling plain.

Dark forms rolled, ran, leaped, and crawled in the grass. Others barely moved, little more than quivering masses choking in the dark. Pale figures chased each other— slaughtered each other.

Sorhkafâré stood watching, unable to look away. Every figure that came close enough for his night eyes to see was human.

He saw not one elf. Not one dwarf. Not even a goblin, or the hulking scaled body of a reptilian locathan, or any of the other monstrosities the enemy had sent against him.

Only humans.

He turned and stumbled back toward First Glade. The wolves paced him all the way to his people.

He found Snähacróe kneeling behind an injured human youth, bracing the boy up while Léshiâra worked upon the boy's leg. In the past days, these two shared company more and more.

Léshiâra closed her eyes, and a low thrum rose from her throat. She lightly traced her fingertips around the boy's deeply bruised calf, over and over, and then went silent. She opened her eyes and rebandaged the boy's leg.

When she stood up and found Sorhkafâré watching her, she frowned.

"Come with me," he said.

Snähacróe looked worried and followed as well.

They walked into the center of the glade.

In the open space stood an immense tree like no other in this world. Its trunk was the size of a small citadel tower, and high overhead its branches reached out into the forest.

Sorhkafâré saw where those limbs stretched into the green leaves and needles of the surrounding trees and beyond. A soft glow emanated from the tree's tawny body and branches, bare of bark but still thriving with life. Massive roots like hill ridges split the clearing's turf where they emerged from the trunk to burrow deep and far into the earth.

Sorhkafâré laid a hand upon the glistening trunk of Chârmun, a name that humans would translate as "Sanctuary."

"We must take a cutting from Chârmun," he said to Léshiâra. "Can you keep it alive over a long journey?"

She grew pale and did not answer.

"What are you planning?" Snähacróe asked, moving closer to Léshiâra.

Sorhkafâré looked at his one remaining commander. "The horde turns upon itself. They have nothing else left within reach to feed upon—but it does them no good. In perhaps days, there may be few enough left for us to slip away."

"No!" someone snapped sharply.

Sorhkafâré knew the voice before he turned his head.

Hoil'lhân stood at the clearing's edge, and around her paced three of the strange tall wolves. All four were spattered and dripping in black fluids. All four watched him with equal intensity. Hoil'lhân stabbed the long, broad head of her spear into the earth, and Sorhkafâré watched more black fluid run from its sharp edges to the grass.

"Where have you been?" he demanded.

"Where do you think?" Hoil'lhân spit out at him. "The enemy's minions range upon our very borders . . . and you wish to run?"

"We cannot stay here in hiding within this blighted land," Sorhkafâré returned.

"I said no!" Hoil'lhân shouted, running a hand through her white, sweat-matted hair. "I will not let the enemy take what is ours! I will not leave any more that I cherish . . . fleeing with their screams at my back!"

"Enough," Snähacróe warned.

"It was not a request," Sorhkafâré said firmly. "I am still your commander."

Hoil'lhân breathed hard, twisting her hand around the upright shaft of her spear.

"And since when do you alone speak for our people?"

Léshiâra said quietly, stepping toward Sorhkafâré. "You do not sit in the council of First Glade, and we no longer follow the old ways of divided clans. Such decisions are the province of myself and the others of the council."

"There is no council left!" Sorhkafâré shouted at her. "You are the only one that remains . . . so do you alone choose for our people, like some human monarch?"

"That is not my meaning," she snapped back. "There are too many here who need us."

Sorhkafâré shook his head. "What if they are the very ones by which the Enemy can still reach us? Out beyond our forest . . . those dead things that move and feast . . . they were once humans, like those still among us."

"You do not know how this was done to them," Hoil'-lhân growled. "Or if the Enemy's reach could find any who shelter here!"

Snähacróe turned, staring off through the trees, as if trying to see the forest's edge. Léshiâra fell silent and closed her eyes, seeming to grow older and wearier before Sorhkafâré's eyes.

But he could not relent.

"We will take our own people. Perhaps the wolves will join us as well. We will get as far from here as we can reach. We will plant our cutting from Chârmun and create a haven for our people far from the Enemy's reach."

"Our people?" Snähacróe asked.

"Not the humans," Sorhkafâré answered.

"The outsiders are dismissed!"

Chap didn't know who spoke those words, but they jerked him to awareness. His legs trembled as he pulled free of Most Aged Father's memories.

Leesil dropped to one knee beside him, but Chap regained his own footing.

Several anmaglâhk came in around Most Aged Father. Under their threatening encouragement, Chap turned away with Leesil and Wynn. Magiere joined them as they were all ushered out of the council clearing.

Chap struggled to follow but could not stop trembling.

He looked up at Magiere's black braid swinging as she leaned against Leesil while they walked.

He knew why Most Aged Father feared Magiere so deeply, though the old man did not fully understand what she was. He saw only some new shape of those among the pale horde of his memory. She was far worse than even the old man could imagine.

Magiere was human, born of the undead. Yet she walked freely and unfettered into this land. Chap's mind raced back to his fear-spawned delusion in the Pudúrlatsat forest—of Magiere as the general at the head of an army. . . .

No, a horde—one that could not enter a shielded land without her.

If only he could tell Magiere alone, without the need of Wynn to speak for him. Magiere deserved at least that much privacy, but there was no way to achieve such.

Chap blinked but could not keep the old elf's memories from casting ghost images across all things around him. A war had devoured the living at the end of a time known only as the Forgotten . . . the Forgotten History of the world. On the plain beyond the elven forest surrounding First Glade, Most Aged Father had watched the waves of undead sent by the Enemy.

All of them—every last one—had been human.

CHAPTER TWENTY-TWO

Once Leesil had delivered the ancestors' message to Most Aged Father, they were all escorted back to quarters. Most Aged Father's claim had been dismissed, and thereby Magiere was cleared by council vote, but the elders remained to debate as they left. Leesil had no idea what would come next. The look on the old elf's face still lingered in his mind, but he felt no sympathy for the fear and festering pain he'd seen there. His mother was still imprisoned, and he'd had no chance to plead for, or demand, her freedom.

Magiere huddled on the dirt floor at the elm chamber's center, as far from the tree's inner walls as she could get. Wynn sat lost in thought upon one bed ledge with Chap sprawled at her feet. The day wore on in a lingering crawl as Leesil paced around with Magiere watching him.

She no longer visibly trembled, but her face was still weary and drawn. He finally fetched her some water, along with a few nuts and berries left for them. He reached out and stroked her black hair.

"Please," he insisted. "Try a little."

What relief he'd gained from the dismissal of Most Aged Father's claims wasn't enough. He had to get to his mother.

He had to get Magiere out of this land and away from the elven forest.

The doorway curtain bulged aside, and Brot'an stepped in. He immediately settled on the floor with a long slow breath. He looked so openly distressed, it unnerved Leesil.

Leesil would never understand this man's ever-twisting motives, but Brot'an had stood up for Magiere when no one else would or could. Grudgingly, Leesil was grateful, though he'd never say so to Brot'an's face.

"What's wrong?" Leesil asked.

"I have failed," Brot'an said flatly.

"Most Aged Father lost, and Magiere is safe," Leesil said.

"Safe?" Brot'an shook his head. "They did not even suggest replacing him, after seeing him . . . hearing him. The elders gathered to question why he allowed you safe passage, but he told them his decision was an internal matter directly related to the safety of our people."

He paused, as if not believing his own words.

"Some are still troubled that he allowed humans into our land, but they will not consider that he is unfit. Age is too much a virtue among my people."

A low throaty chuckle escaped Brot'an's lips. It sounded wrong coming from such a man.

"You mean Most Aged Father?" Magiere asked.

"All of you will be forced to leave tomorrow," Brot'an continued, running a hand over his scarred face. "Be ready by first light. At least Gleannéohkân'thva had the foresight to speak up and gain you a barge downriver to Ghoivne Ajhâjhe. From there, you will be given safe passage by sea—the first humans to step foot on one of our ships. You will not need to cross the mountains again."

Leesil crouched down. "What?"

Brot'an looked at him with a saddened expression. "The elders are resolved. The claim against Magiere may be dismissed, but your presence will no longer be tolerated."

Wynn came closer, settling near Magiere.

"We can't leave," Magiere said. "Leesil hasn't even spoken for Nein'a. If he's now recognized as one of you, he has a right to—"

The doorway curtain lifted again, and Sgäile peered inside. He looked harried and exhausted. Leesil's cloak was draped over his arm.

"Léshiârelaohk," he said. "Your property is—"

"Don't call me that," Leesil warned. "It's not my name."

Sgäile sighed. "Your property is restored. I have brought your gear and blades . . . and Magiere's sword and dagger."

"Come in," Leesil said a little less sharply.

He didn't care for how that name implied he was one of them, but Sgäile only followed custom in using it, the same as with all of his people. And Leesil wanted to hear another view on what had happened at the council. Of anyone he'd met in this land, Sgäile was the most trustworthy.

Sgäile shook his head, his tangled white-blond hair swaying. "I cannot stay. Grandfather and Leanâlhâm leave at dawn. There is much to do, but if you would, come tonight to the third oak upriver from the docks and say your farewell. Leanâlhâm has been comforted in meeting you."

Leesil chose not to press for his views on the council. Sgäile clearly believed this entire matter was finished.

"Tell Leanâlhâm that I'll try," Leesil lied.

Sgäile set the gear inside the door and was about to depart.

"Send Leanâlhâm for naming," Leesil said. "If that's something she still wants. There's no reason to keep her from it anymore. She can reach hallowed ground, if I did."

Sgäile didn't reply and slipped out. Leesil picked up his blades and began strapping them on.

"What are you doing?" Brot'an asked.

"I'm going to have a talk with Most Aged Father." He tossed Magiere her falchion. "Care to join me?"

She caught the sword and stood up.

"No more brash foolishness!" Bro'tan said. "Any threats, and you will be killed. I have been considering another tactic . . . though it may cause unpredictable changes for my caste."

"What tactic?" Wynn asked. "What more could you do?"

Brot'an's eyes shifted several times in indecision. "Remain here until I return."

"What are you up to now?" Leesil asked.

"I will speak with Most Aged Father myself. It should not take long."

Leesil locked eyes with Magiere, and she nodded at him. "All right," he agreed.

Dusk settled as Brot'ân'duivé headed for the massive oak. He did not call out for permission to enter and descended the stairs. Before he could enter the central root chamber, Fréthfâre stepped out and grew angry at the sight of him.

"Father has not sent for you."

"Leave," he whispered, stepping straight at her.

Fréthfâre's eyes narrowed.

He did not try to push past her but stopped short, waiting before the chamber's doorway so that Most Aged Father could see him.

"I would speak with you alone," Brot'ân'duivé called. "Please send your Covârleasa away."

The ancient leader reclined limply in his cradle of living wood, still shrouded in the same wrap he had worn to the gathering. His eyes were half-closed in weariness, but they opened fully at the sight of Brot'ân'duivé.

"I have no interest in the demands of a traitor," Most Aged Father said. "I will deal with you soon enough."

"Send Fréthfâre out," Brot'ân'duivé repeated. "You will have interest in what I say . . . to you alone."

Most Aged Father stared at him long, then slightly raised one hand. "Leave us, daughter."

"Father—" Fréthfâre began in alarm.

"Go!"

Fréthfâre turned a warning eye upon Brot'ân'duivé before she stepped around him. Brot'ân'duivé waited until her soft footfalls faded upon the stairs, and then he stepped into the ancient patriarch's root chamber.

"What worthless excuses do you offer for your conduct?" Most Aged Father asked, his voice cracking.

"No matter this day's outcome, the elders were disturbed by your behavior and demeanor. I expected them to replace you."

"With you, perhaps?"

Brot'ân'duivé ignored the question. "The ground you stand upon crumbles. If the elders learn what you have us do in the human countries, how long before they do as I hoped?"

"Manipulation . . . and open challenge?" Most Aged Father displayed only mock astonishment before he chuckled softly. "No surprise in this. I have long suspected you, deceiver."

Brot'ân'duivé shook his head calmly. "I serve my people, as our caste was intended from long-forgotten times . . . as all Anmaglâhk believe when they take oath of service. It is we, as well as our people, who are deceived by you. Yet we have kept faith, just the same. Turning humans upon each other serves no purpose but to salve your own fears. They are not this enemy you speak of so sparingly, whatever or whoever it might be."

Most Aged Father's hands went limp. "You had my trust, my love. . . . How long have you been a traitor among your kind?"

"I have never been a traitor to my people, though I no longer believe in your ways. And neither is Cuirin'nên'a. The elders may turn a blind eye for what you do to her, because she is one of us. They see it as an issue of the Anmaglâhk. But I would now barter for her release."

"Barter?" Most Aged Father returned. "Why, when you will soon join her?"

Brot'ân'duivé's voice grew cold. "You will release her tonight. Or I will tell the elders how you use the Anmaglâhk to set the humans on each other."

Most Aged Father's dried features stretched in mounting fury, and Brot'ân'duivé stepped closer.

"I will break my silence before the council," he said. "I will tell them all that I know of what you have done. As yet, you have nothing to hold against me. Release Cuirin'nên'a, swear to her safety . . . and I will swear my continued silence."

He watched Most Aged Father and waited.

The ancient elf would cling to power at any cost, even for just a little longer. Whatever he feared was coming would drive him to it. He would accept this bargain, and once Cuirin'nên'a was free, Léshil would leave this place and have no reason to return. If not safe, he would at least be beyond the old one's reach, until it was time for him to serve his purpose.

"I . . . accept your exchange," Most Aged Father croaked, his eyes stark with madness. "But this changes nothing. The loyal Anmaglâhk will continue to serve our people."

"Is Cuirin'nên'a released?"

Most Aged Father finally closed his eyes and placed his withered fingers against the walls of his bower for a long moment.

"She is released, so go to her, if you wish. But send Sgäilsheilleache and Fréthfâre to me at once."

Brot'ân'duivé turned away, his heart pounding.

They both knew the half-truth of all this. For now, it served Brot'ân'duivé's own ends and left him time to plan. Whether first he betrayed—or was betrayed—had yet to be seen.

But he was no traitor to his caste. He protected their future, for he still believed in the old one's fear of an enemy yet to show itself. He would do what he must to keep the Anmaglâhk whole and sound. Until they were needed no more, when it all finally ended on the stroke of the blade in Léshil's . . . in Léshiârelaohk's hand.

"In silence and in shadows," Brot'ân'duivé whispered as he left.

Magiere tried to keep Leesil calm, but he kept pacing the elm's chamber, and she finally set to cleaning her falchion. It wasn't necessary, but handling the blade kept her from snapping, between the tension of lingering and the vibrant shivers within her.

Wynn sat on the floor, writing with her quill.

"What are you recording now?" Magiere asked.

"The end of the gathering. My guild will find it of interest in comparison to elven culture elsewhere."

"I'm glad I could offer them some diversion," Magiere sniped.

"Magiere, that is not what I—"

"Sorry . . . forget it."

In Magiere's mind, she kept pondering the silf's sudden appearance, and the idea that it or one of its kind had saved them from the blizzard. Why had it chosen to appear only before the council? How long had it been following her?

The chained translation of its belief that she was somehow of its blood still haunted her. She hoped it didn't know how she'd come by such mistaken heritage.

The doorway curtain folded aside, and Brot'an stepped in. He did not look tired, but he was panting lightly.

Leesil rushed at him. "What happened?"

"Your mother is free," Brot'an answered without warning. "But she does not know it herself, so we must go to her now. I will explain the delay of your departure later and arrange for another barge."

Magiere was dumbstruck, like Leesil, but Chap lunged to his feet.

"Brot'an . . . ," Wynn began, with confusion in her eyes. "How?"

Magiere wondered the same thing, but she slammed her falchion back into its sheath as Leesil snatched up his blades and strapped them on.

"I don't care how," he said.

Chap barked once in agreement and was out the door faster than the rest of them could follow.

In the root chamber beneath the vast oak, Fréthfâre scarcely believed what Most Aged Father told her.

"Released?" she repeated.

Sgäilsheilleache stood silent beside her, his expression unreadable. She knew him better than he realized. Recent events had left him in turmoil. Today had been the worst in her life, defeat after defeat in humiliation.

"Yes, daughter," Most Aged Father said. "Cuirin'nên'a's time is served, and she is released."

"Why?"

Anger crept into his voice. "Do you question me?"

"No, Father," she answered quickly. "I only . . ."

Something was wrong. Brot'ân'duivé had demanded a

private audience, and now a traitor was released among the people.

"Will that be all, Father?" Sgäilsheilleache asked. "Do you require anything?"

Fréthfâre wondered at his calm acceptance, as if it were all part of a normal day. Sgäilsheilleache rarely questioned anything, unless faced with the unforeseen. And this was certainly unforeseen.

Most Aged Father squinted at Sgäilsheilleache, and his milky eyes grew soft. "No, my son. Do not be troubled further. Go and rest. We all need rest."

Clearly, Most Aged Father placed no blame upon Sgäilsheilleache for this day's outcome. And why should he? The blame lay with Brot'ân'duivé, and sooner or later, Fréthfâre would find the proof of it. A Greimas-g'äh had betrayed his caste, and this could not be left unattended.

Sgäilsheilleache turned and left, but Fréthfâre could not bring herself to go just yet.

"Father, pardon me, but what does this mean? Should I go to inform Cuirin'nên'a?"

He shook his ancient head. "Most likely, Brot'ân'duivé will go tonight and take Léshil with him."

The chamber seemed to grow dim around her as she tried to reason through Most Aged Father's words. Nothing made sense.

"Go now, daughter," he said.

She climbed the steps out of the earth, lost in her tumbling thoughts, and then ran outside, not stopping until she reached the elm where Léshil and his humans were kept. Before she reached the doorway, she knew the elm was empty. Still, she peered inside.

All were gone . . . gone to free Cuirin'nên'a.

Fréthfâre stood in uncertainty. Why had Most Aged Father called her in tonight to tell her this? He was exhausted, and if there was nothing for her to do, then why not leave the news until morning? Why such urgency followed by so little explanation?

She stared off through the trees as her turmoil mounted. Father had tried to tell . . . to ask her something without putting it into words. For some reason, he could not give the order himself.

Her stomach churned at the thought of Léshil, his traitorous mother, and those humans escaping. Not after they had found a way into this land. Not after all the discord they had sown among her caste. And not after what they had done to Most Aged Father.

She had been at his side for long years . . . long decades. Whatever the reason that he could not ask her outright, she knew what he expected of her.

Fréthfâre ran toward the river and the docks. In the full of night, the trees blurred by. She fled to the sixth birch upstream and fell to her knees by its doorway, pulling back the cloth hanging.

Én'nish sat alone inside on the floor. The cup of tea before her must have sat a long while, for it no longer steamed. She stared blankly ahead, and then turned her sharp face toward the doorway.

"Fréthfâre?" she said, taken back. "Are you well? What is wrong?"

"We go north immediately. Brot'ân'duivé takes Léshil and the humans to free Cuirin'nên'a. They must be stopped." She hesitated before adding, "This is the wish of Most Aged Father."

Én'nish cinched her cloak's trailing corners across her waist, and then her sudden eagerness wavered.

"I do not understand, Covârleasa," she began, respectfully. "If the Greimasg'äh is with them, why are we sent behind him?"

"Brot'ân'duivé is a traitor. You heard and saw him today." Én'nish still hesitated.

Fréthfâre was not certain how to deal with Brot'ân'-duivé, but she understood what must be done this night. A traitor escaped punishment, and humans would leave knowing the way for others to return to her people's land.

"We will not spill the blood . . . of our own," she said, firm and slow.

She let the words hang.

Longing hardened Én'nish's eyes as she understood Fréthfâre's meaning.

No, they would not spill the blood of their own, but the outsiders must be dealt with.

Én'nish blinked slowly with a deep exhale, as if finally releasing long-harbored pain. She followed Fréthfâre out like one who finally saw the salve for her wounds within reach.

Chane struggled through the heavy snow. Wind pelted his face with large flakes that clung to his hair and cloak. He could only see a few paces ahead and followed the mute shapes of Welstiel and their one remaining horse.

"We must find shelter," Chane rasped. "We cannot locate the passage until this blizzard has passed."

"No," Welstiel answered. "We keep looking. It cannot be far."

The Móndyalítko had told them to seek a passage along a deep ravine. Once they passed through, they would be able to see the castle.

Only three nights past, Chane's wild dog familiar had found the way, though calling it a ravine was an understatement. It was a deep and jagged canyon impossible to climb down, and its bottom was filled with snow-blanketed rocky crags. After its discovery, Welstiel behaved like an obsessed madman, driving them hard up through the mountains.

Chane halted. Going on was useless if they could not see. He was about to insist they pitch the tent when a long howl and yammering barks carried on the wind from somewhere ahead.

"The dog!" Welstiel shouted over the wind.

Chane was in no mood for Welstiel's premature elation. "Wait!"

He dropped to sit in the cold snow and closed his eyes, reaching out for his familiar's thoughts. When he found his way into its limited mind, he saw through the dog's eyes.

At first, his sight was obscured by snow slanting through the dark as the dog scrambled forward. Then the animal halted at the edge of a precipice. Chane looked down through its eyes into a gorge at the canyon's top end, and vertigo overwhelmed him. The dog stood on a flat rock overhang, digging through loose snow.

"What has it found?" Welstiel asked desperately.

"I do not know . . . something." He opened his eyes reluctantly and stood up. "Upward . . . ahead."

Chane took the lead, holding the dog's thoughts to sense the way. When he spotted the animal's tracks already fading under the blizzard, he released the connection and picked up his pace. Ahead he thought he saw where the canyon's upper end spiked downward into the rocky range. Upon its near side, something dug wildly in the snow.

Chane trudged quickly up and dropped beside the dog. He looked down with his own eyes to where the canyon opened into a deep gorge too wide to see its far side. He began digging by hand, clearing snow from the ledge until he exposed a piece of flat slate that did not match the ledge's basalt stone. The piece was half the length of his body and smoothly fitted to the ledge's edge—except for a hole to one side just large enough for a hand. Chane cleared the opening with his fingers and lifted the slate panel.

Welstiel hovered above him as they looked down.

Snow-covered ledges—wide steps—were carved into the gorge wall, though Chane could not be sure in the blizzard if they went all the way to the unseen bottom.

Welstiel examined the piece of slate. "This was intended to hide the passage?"

"I do not think so. More likely a marker to find it or perhaps shield the first steps from erosion. This path is used regularly by someone, for it took much work to carve it out, crude as it is. Let us hope it leads somewhere useful, though we will have to abandon the horse."

Welstiel stared into space. "The Móndyalítko said we would step out to see the castle. It has to be down there somewhere . . . it must be."

Between the darkness and the storm, Chane had no way of telling if this was true, and he was sick of blind optimism. "Do we try tonight or wait until we have more time tomorrow?"

"Now," Welstiel answered instantly, and pulled their packs from the horse. "Move on. We leave the dog as well."

Again, Chane had no voice in their decisions, and his

anger seethed quietly. But he held his tongue. Perhaps they were close to Welstiel's coveted orb, and once they found it, Chane might give Welstiel a surprise or two of his own.

Chane braced a hand against the steep rock wall and took two steps downward, peering below. He saw nothing through the blizzard—not even the gorge's bottom, nor its far side. Snowflakes slanting across the night seemed to materialize out of the dark. The lower he went, the more the wind lessened, until the snow drifted lazily downward.

Behind and above him, Chane heard Welstiel's boots scrape the steps.

Sgäile headed for the third oak upstream from the docks, eager to be with his family once more and away from all others. He pulled the doorway drape aside, and there sat his grandfather, Gleannéohkân'thva, upon an umber felt throw as he wrote with quill on parchment.

"Where is Leanâlhâm?" Sgäile asked.

"She went to find a few things for our journey," his grandfather replied. "It will be an early start. Will you come with us?"

Sinking down, Sgäile untied his cloak and lifted the clay teapot from its tray.

"I must first see Léshil and his companions safely off, then I will come home for a while. I wish to bring Osha with me—with your consent. Except for his training, I am considering a request to be relieved of duties for the remainder of winter . . . perhaps longer."

His grandfather looked up, puzzled, but merely patted his shoulder. "Osha is always welcome. And it would be good to have you home for a while."

Sgäile poured tea into one of the round cups and turned its warmth slowly between his palms.

Indeed, to have a little peace once again, even into the spring. Time to reflect on many things he had not been aware of before today. Strange animosity existed between Brot'ân'duivé and Most Aged Father—a revered Greimasg'äh and the founder of their caste. A rift that apparently had grown silently over time. Fréthfâre as well had some part in it, for her ardor in challenge had raised Sgäile's awareness in the worst of ways.

He sipped the tea slowly, but it brought him no comfort.

Leanâlhâm fell through the door, breathing hard. "Sgäil-sheilleache! Come—quickly!"

He set the cup down, grabbed her hand, and pulled her inside. "What? Are you injured?"

"No . . ." She gasped in another deep breath. "Urhkarasiférin gave me dried figs for our journey, and in returning, I saw Fréthfâre outside Én'nish's quarters. They did not see me, but I heard part of what they said. They go north after Léshil and Brot'ân'duivé."

Sgäile sat back, whispering to himself. "Léshil has gone to tell Cuirin'nên'a."

"Tell her what?" his grandfather asked.

Sgäile came back to himself. "Most Aged Father has released Cuirin'nên'a. She is forgiven. Léshil and his companions must have gone to tell her." He looked at Leanâlhâm. "Brot'ân'duivé is with them, and Fréthfâre follows after?"

"Yes," she cried. "And Én'nish. But I do not believe Brot'ân'duivé knows they follow."

Sgäile carefully set down his cup.

"They spoke of not spilling the blood . . . of their own." Leanâlhâm's voice quavered. "But why would they need to? And something in Fréthfâre's voice . . . she only mentioned Brot'ân'duivé—not Léshil or his companions! Why would she say this to Én'nish?"

Sgäile stood up, rapidly tying the corners of his cloak. His first instinct was to go directly to Most Aged Father, but if Fréthfâre acted on her own, this would only cause more discord.

"I will find Léshil first," he said. "I will uncover what is happening."

"I am coming with you," Gleannéohkân'thva said.

"No, I must run."

"Are you suggesting that I cannot keep up? Your caste is at odds with itself. You need a clan elder, and I am the closest you have." He turned to Leanâlhâm. "Do not leave our quarters, and do not tell anyone where we have gone. If asked, we have gone to gather supplies for the trip."

Leanâlhâm nodded quickly. "Hurry!"

Gleannéohkân'thva donned his cloak, not waiting for Sgäile's agreement.

"Stay behind me," he told his grandfather. Perhaps he would need the voice of an elder.

They left the oak, running along the river to the open forest, rather than through Crijheäiche.

CHAPTER TWENTY-THREE

Magiere ran beside Leesil, and a part of her still doubted such sudden good fortune. Their journey into her own past in Droevinka had uncovered horrific circumstances surrounding her birth. Their passage through the warlands and Leesil's past in Venjètz had only led to anguish and murder.

She'd hoped the journey into the Elven Territories would be different, and now it seemed Leesil would have what he wanted. The outcome was better than she had dreamed possible. Nein'a had been released with no bloodshed, and they were all promised safe passage out of the elves' lands to any destination they chose.

All they had left was the issue of Welstiel's artifact, though Magiere had little idea where to begin. Then they could go home.

Brot'an and Chap led the way, with Wynn in the center. Leesil and Magiere brought up the rear. Magiere wasn't certain how she felt about Nein'a's company, but she pushed the doubt away. Only Nein'a's freedom mattered now—or rather Leesil's relief from his long years of guilt.

"Do you know where you are going?" Wynn called to Chap and Brot'an.

Chap yipped once and tossed his head without slowing. Magiere saw a flash of white in the brush to her right, and then two more of silver-gray among the trees.

"How long have they been with us?" she called out.

No one answered, and they jogged onward at a pace meant for Wynn's short legs.

"How do you think she'll take it?" Leesil asked. "Finally being free?"

"What?"

"My mother. She's been trapped here so long . . . I wonder if she'll even believe it at first."

"Leesil—" Magiere began.

A hissing in the air broke her attention as Brot'an turned and started to duck.

A darting pale shaft struck the back of his head. He pitched forward and crashed limply to the earth.

Magiere dodged the other way, as Leesil grabbed Wynn's cloak and pulled her behind a tree. Magiere peered back the way they had come. Leesil jerked out one winged blade as she pulled her falchion.

Chap had vanished, but Magiere knew he'd be close by. She watched for movement but saw nothing in the forest.

"He's been shot," Wynn whispered, and started to crawl toward Brot'an's prone form.

Leesil pulled her back.

Magiere couldn't see Brot'an's face, but he wasn't moving. Beside him lay an arrow on the ground. It hadn't sunk in on impact—good fortune perhaps, but that didn't seem likely.

She hesitated at letting her hunger rise, but she did it. As her night sight widened, she focused upon the fallen arrow.

In place of a narrow pointed head was a blunt gray ball of metal. Whoever had fired it wanted Brot'an left alive.

"Is he breathing?" Magiere whispered.

Wynn craned her head. "Yes."

"Áruin'nas?" Magiere asked, and looked back down the path.

"I don't see anyone," Leesil answered.

A soft thud. Magiere whirled back.

A figure clad in gray-green stood between her and

Brot'an, with a stiletto in each hand. Amber eyes fixed upon Magiere. Even with the wrap across the figure's face, Magiere recognized those eyes.

Fréth charged straight for Leesil before Magiere could move.

Leesil was forced to duck into the open to get clear of the tree, and Fréth lashed out a booted foot into Wynn's head.

Magiere heard a snapping sound at the impact. "No!"

As Wynn twisted and fell into the brush, Chap leaped through the leaves above her and closed on Fréth.

In the corner of Magiere's vision, someone dropped from above behind Leesil.

Én'nish crouched with her overlong stilettos in hand.

Magiere halted in hesitation over whom to go after.

Good fortune was nothing but a fool's faith. If it wasn't the undead, it was the Anmaglâhk coming at them from the dark.

Leesil sucked in a sharp breath as Fréth's foot collided with Wynn's jaw. The little sage toppled into the brush. He heard either the crossbow or the quarrel case on her back crackle under her weight. Then Chap lunged out over the top of her, charging at Fréth as Magiere skidded to a halt, looking in his direction.

A glint of bright metal flickered in the corner of Leesil's vision. He whirled to see Én'nish coming at him from him behind.

Leesil twisted away.

Her long stiletto pierced the shoulder of his cloak. She turned sharply, her body like the handle of a twin whip. The movement drove her lead arm onward as the other came under and up. The first blade tore free of his cloak, passing his head. The second arced upward for his throat.

Leesil swept his winged blade upward, catching Én'nish's rising stiletto on its top edge. As he brushed her thrust up and away, she seemed to ride his momentum into the air.

Her foot touched a tree trunk, and she pushed off. Leesil spun around as she came down behind him, his blade on guard. Én'nish's long, narrow stiletto screeched along the wing of his punching blade.

She was sweating. Her face was twisted with rage, and the suffering in her eyes was too familiar.

He'd seen it before, as he crouched upon the frozen ground outside of Venjètz, clinging to the skulls of his father and what he'd first believed was his mother. Only the face he saw then was Hedí Progae, who sought vengeance for her father, Leesil's first kill for Darmouth.

He was tired of killing. He didn't want to be anyone's weapon anymore.

Én'nish rushed him, twisting like a cat to get inside his blade's reach and strike for his chest or throat.

Leesil spun with her, letting her lower blade skid over his hauberk as he parried the upper one. He slammed his empty hand into the side of her ribs.

Én'nish tottered off balance as she swept past, but she pivoted with a scissoring slash of both stilettos to fend him off.

Behind her, Leesil saw Chap raging and snarling after Fréth.

"No!" Magiere shouted. "Guard Wynn!"

Her voice was thick, her words awkward, and Leesil caught the black disks of her irises expanding. But he feared she might not best Fréth even in a full dhampir state.

And Én'nish stood in his way.

Leesil swallowed fear into cold dispassion, as his mother had taught him. He had to put Én'nish down to get to Magiere—and killing was what he'd been made for.

Hunger rose in Magiere's throat and rushed through her body. This time, she welcomed the ache spreading through her jaws.

Her eyes burned as her sight widened, and the night lit up before her. She swung the falchion with all the speed and force she had. Not an effective attack, unless Fréth was stupid enough to think she could block it.

Fréth quickly slid back out of the sword's arc and farther from Wynn and Brot'an. That was all Magiere wanted from her first strike.

Before Fréth could come behind the falchion's swing, Magiere reversed, bringing its dull backside straight around.

Fréth winced as it smashed into her shoulder. She bent and turned with the impact, but the falchion's tip tore through her tunic.

They both froze, eyes locked on each other.

All Magiere saw was another murdering anmaglâhk with a bloody tear across her tunic's shoulder.

Fréth flinched once at the sight of Magiere, and then her gaze fixed with determination.

"Dead thing," she hissed. "You belong in the dirt, buried and forgotten."

"You . . . don't know," Magiere grunted out, "how to deal with undead . . . and I'm much more."

Fréth darted sideways, heading for the nearest tree.

Magiere had seen Brot'an use the same move on a column in Darmouth's crypt, stepping up to spring over her head, and drop behind her.

She chopped downward as Fréth lifted a foot.

Fréth jerked her foot back in midleap, and the falchion hit the tree's trunk. Bark and wood slivers sprayed off it. Fréth extended her foot again, but it landed too high. All she could do was push off and roll back across open ground.

Magiere whirled, blade up, facing off with Fréth.

Chap charged from the other side but stopped short, planting himself between Fréth and Wynn. He had fought at Magiere's side enough to know when to attack and when to stay out of her way.

She feinted low and left, shifted right, and turned the falchion in an upward slash for Fréth's midsection. The stroke missed, but Fréth failed to get within arm's reach. They spun away from each other again.

Fréth was far enough away this time that Chap tried to close in.

Wynn groaned, and Magiere couldn't help but look. The sage rolled weakly in the brush, but the crossbow on her back caught on something.

"No!" Magiere shouted to Chap. "Guard Wynn."

The instant cost her. When her eyes shifted back, Fréth was gone.

Blinding pain shot through her side.

Chap dashed toward Wynn thrashing feebly in the brush. Blood ran from her mouth and spread through her teeth. She could not get free of the crossbow tangled in the bush. He bit into its strap, tearing at it until it snapped.

Wynn rolled onto her face, trying to push up to her hands and knees.

Load and fire! Chap shouted into her mind.

He was about to turn and pick an attack of his own, when Wynn faltered and fell to the ground again. Her olive face twisted in pain.

Chap dipped into her mind, calling up her memories of contented moments. Quiet nights sleeping by campfires or in the quilt-covered bed of an inn. Two kittens purring in her lap. Hot mint tea and spiced lentil stew. The smell of fresh parchment and the feel of a quill in her hand. Her fingers curled in his fur.

Wynn lifted her head, clutching at the crossbow.

Chap pulled an unbroken quarrel from the quiver with his teeth and dropped it beside her. She rolled onto her knees, heaving the crossbow's string back with both hands. With the string locked in place and the lever cocked, she grasped and set the quarrel.

Wynn looked up and hesitated, gaze shifting between the two conflicts.

Chap turned about.

Leesil fended off Én'nish as she slashed madly at him. He did not fight with the same quick instinct and brutality that Chap had seen in the past.

Then Magiere stumbled as Fréth stabbed her from behind. They were too close together now for Wynn's questionable aim.

Chap panicked, shouting into Wynn's thoughts: *Én'nish!*

He heard the crack of a quarrel leaving Wynn's crossbow as he charged at Fréth's exposed back.

*   *   *

Magiere felt Fréth's arm wrap around her neck and jerk tight. Then the blade slipped out of her side.

Hunger ate away the pain. She rammed her elbow back, but it never connected.

A bloodied stiletto came over her shoulder for her throat.

Magiere wouldn't release her sword. Unable to whip it back, she tried to grab Fréth's wrist before the stiletto touched her skin.

Fear should have taken Magiere as she struggled for air. Instead, rage whipped hunger into fury. She would not let Fréth win . . . or she would make her pay dearly for it.

Fréth's weight increased sharply as if her whole body lurched and slammed inward upon Magiere. The arm around Magiere's throat loosened as she toppled forward under the sound of snarls.

Magiere hit the ground face-first. Fréth's weight rolled off with an angry scream. Her voice was quickly drowned in growls and tearing cloth. Magiere spun on her hip, pulling her legs under as she twisted to a crouch.

Chap darted away from Fréth's wild slash, his teeth parted in a shuddering growl and fur bristling on his neck and shoulders. Fréth scrambled to regain her footing. The back of her cowl was shredded, and she ripped it off, side-stepping to keep her two opponents in sight.

Magiere rose up, her mind hazy with the heat welling in her body. Hunger fed on the tingling shiver the forest pressed upon her.

Instinct drove her to attack . . . to stop at nothing until Fréth was dead. This one had come at her and those she cherished, time and again, and now brought Én'nish, who served only one purpose—to kill all of them where no one would see.

Magiere held her place. A little reason remained and stirred inside her.

Each time she swung, Fréth came in behind the falchion's passing. The woman closed to advantage for her shorter blades and hampered Magiere's use of the longer and heavier weapon.

Magiere didn't need a weapon.

She could mangle this bitch with her bare hands. All she needed—wanted—was for Fréth to come in one more time. Magiere made the barest feint with the falchion's tip and then loosened her grip, ready to drop it.

Fréth's attention remained on Magiere, but she didn't come. Her left hand whipped to the side—and flung a stiletto straight at Chap.

The shudder in Magiere's body sharpened. Her grip clenched tight on the falchion. She lunged as Fréth took her first charging step.

Magiere caught Fréth's other stiletto in her free hand. She felt nothing as she wrenched the blade aside and rammed her falchion straight in. The sword didn't even jump in her hand as its tip sank into Fréth's gut.

It happened too quickly. Fréth's eyes didn't even widen until Magiere clamped her bloody hand around the woman's neck.

She squeezed until she felt Fréth choke, and then shoved hard.

Fréth's body arched backward, sliding off the falchion as Magiere jerked it loose, and Fréth hit the earth, writhing on her back.

Magiere raised the falchion to finish her.

A shout vibrated through her bones. "Stop!"

Én'nish lurched and stumbled before Leesil. A quarrel seemed to sprout suddenly from the back of her right shoulder. She didn't cry out, and only dropped one stiletto as her right arm went limp.

Leesil spotted Wynn kneeling in a flattened bush with the crossbow still against her shoulder. The little sage dropped the weapon and crumpled.

Én'nish lunged at him with her remaining blade.

Leesil slipped aside, again and again, staying beyond reach. Then he saw Fréth fling a blade at Chap, and the dog tried to duck away.

The blade missed his face and the handle clipped his ear as the weapon tumbled across his back. He snarled sharply.

The next thing Leesil saw was Fréth on the ground, holding her belly. A dark stain was spreading quickly through her tunic and between her fingers.

Magiere raised her falchion.

Én'nish lunged at Leesil again, throwing her whole weight to take him while distracted. He tried to deflect and brought up the punching blade on instinct.

Its edge sliced the back of Én'nish's hand and down her forearm, splitting her sleeve open. She cried out, jerking away, and tried to swing again.

Sgäile appeared, folding her tightly in his arms from behind and pinning her.

Sgäile ran hard toward the sounds of screeching steel and voices.

Brot'ân'duivé was on the ground, attempting to push himself up. A bludgeoning arrow lay near him. Blood dripped from Wynn's mouth down her chin. Én'nish, with a quarrel in her shoulder, still kept at Leesil.

And Magiere ran Fréth through with her sword.

Sgäile didn't hesitate. He folded his arms tightly around Én'nish from behind, pinning her up against his chest, and shouted at Magiere. "Stop!"

She wavered.

"Léshil, do not let her take Fréthfâre's life."

Léshil was already running around Magiere to stand in her way. He spoke too softly for Sgäile to hear. Magiere slowly lowered her sword.

Gleannéohkân'thva caught up, trying to get his breath. He faltered at the sight before him.

"Grandfather, see to Fréthfâre first," Sgäile blurted out.

Én'nish still struggled in his arms. He thrust his knee into the back of hers. When her leg buckled, he threw his weight on her. She dropped, and he held her down.

"Enough!" he barked, pressing hard on her until she finally lay still. "What is this? What have you done?"

"Most Aged Father ordered us to dispatch them," Én'nish snarled. "And you interfere in our purpose! They deserve to die!"

"And Brot'an as well?" Sgäile snapped. "No! Father would never . . ."

He looked at Fréthfâre, blood-stained and curled upon the earth. He did not believe Én'nish.

Sgäile had seen the way Fréthfâre went after Brot'ân'duivé before the council, all for a challenge of truth as Most Aged Father's advocate. But the patriarch of his caste would not violate his word. No, this had to be Fréthfâre's doing—and hers alone. Why else would she bring only Én'nish, in the woman's anguished state, in coming after so many with Brot'ân'duivé?

He went cold inside.

"Sgäilsheilleache!" his grandfather snapped, untying Fréth's cloak. "Question Én'nish later. Fréthfâre's wound is severe, and the others need attendance. Assist me—now!"

"I can see the bottom," Chane said.

Welstiel trembled but did not answer. After two decades and more of preparation and searching, the end was close. Never would there be another night of hunger, feeding upon the wretched and filthy masses. Only eternity filled with peace and contemplation, with the orb in his possession.

Welstiel gave silent thanks to the patron of his dreams.

He might not be able to enter the castle without Magiere. But still his patron guided his steps. He would find a way to bring Magiere to serve his need.

Welstiel was in control once more.

"Careful," Chane rasped. "These lower steps are much worn, and do not look solid."

Welstiel set his palms firmly against the gorge wall. He was still eager to lay eyes on the six-towered castle of his dreams—to see arched metal gates, the black ravens, and every detail that was engraved upon his mind.

Chane slid down the last few steps and trotted out onto the gorge's bottom filled with rough boulders and stones coated in snow. Welstiel hurried down and strode past when he reached solid footing.

At first there was nothing to see, and he scrambled recklessly over the gorge's floor, until coming upon a cleared path coated in light snow. He heard Chane behind him, but he could not wait and raced on, slipping more than once. The path turned, closing again toward the right face.

Welstiel looked about in the dark. He saw nothing but snow gathered on the craggy bottom of the gorge's expanse. He lifted his gaze, searching.

Switchbacks were carved into the gorge's more gradually sloping face, and the path led upward part of the way.

"No," he whispered, stumbling two more steps.

Chane's harsh whisper filled his ears amid the slow-falling snowflakes.

"What is wrong?"

Welstiel gazed up, unable to answer.

He looked upon a small construction chiseled out of the gorge's rock face.

A glowing torch or lantern, mounted upon a pole before its small single door, lit up wood-shuttered windows. The building seated deep into the rock face, no higher than two floors tall, was some kind of ancient and forgotten barracks or a long-lost stronghold in the middle of nowhere.

There was no castle. There were no gates. No ravens. No courtyard. No magnificent ice-fringed spires.

"No," he whispered again.

Cold numbness melted under sorrow and began to burn away in outrage. Welstiel spun around, raising his face to the dark sky.

"For this?" he shouted.

All the nights of trudging hopefully through snow and rocks and cliffs, dragging half-dead horses, and pushing Chane onward. Was his patron amused? Did it sleep, laughing, waiting for him to return to hollow dreams?

He had fallen under his own father to wake from death in a vile existence. And for more than two decades he had searched for release with only his patron's teasing whispers in his slumber. More than once he had grown weary of it, and turned to potions and arcane drugs to keep him from dormancy. But in the end, he had always relented and gone back to the scaled patron of his dreams.

This was the end of it.

He would dream no more . . . listen no more.

"Do you hear?" Welstiel called out to the stars.

They shone down upon him, distant and unconcerned. So much like an unseen light glinting upon the scales of massive coils turning in the dark.

Chane stared at him. "Who are you talking to?"

Welstiel barely heard him.

"No more!" he cried out to the sky, and grew more spiteful at the anguish in his own voice. "I am finished with you! Go back to where you hide. Find another toy . . . to cheat!"

Somewhere in the still night he heard a scrape of footsteps echo softly through the gorge.

Another small flicker of light wormed up the last switchback before the stone structure with its decrepit wood shutters. Welstiel's anger broke his self-control, and hunger widened his sight.

A figure stepped out the structure's narrow door. Dressed in a pale blue tabard over a dark robe with a full cowl, it lifted a torch high, as if calling the other light rising up the path.

That other light reached the narrow level shelf before the structure, and below it came two more figures wearing similar attire. The two met the one, and all three figures went inside.

Welstiel could not remember where he had seen such clothing before. A monastery, perhaps? It did not matter. Here was opportunity for his outrage.

How many years had he listened to his patron's mocking words?

The sister of the dead will lead you.

Very well then. But he no longer put faith in such things. She might lead, but he would not need her in the end. There would be others to serve him.

"Lock them in . . . ," he whispered. "All of them."

Chane stepped around into his sight, glancing up to the stronghold before looking into Welstiel's face. He cocked his head as if not certain of what he had heard.

"Lock them all in," Welstiel repeated. "Feed if you must, but leave them alive . . . for now."

Chane's eyes glinted in anticipation.

Welstiel just stood there.

The sister of the dead will lead you.

Yes, she would still do that. But he would not be alone when he came after her—the puppet of his deceiver.

Leesil reluctantly assisted Sgäile in holding Én'nish down. Gleann severed the quarrel's shaft and pushed the remainder through.

Fréth was more fortunate than she deserved. Magiere's falchion had not damaged any vital organs, but Most Aged Father's pet anmaglâhk would be weakened for a long while. Maybe for life, unless Gleann had tricks and skills beyond what Leesil had seen.

Magiere had taken a stiletto through the side, but Gleann claimed it wasn't serious. He scowled suspiciously at the wound, which had already stopped bleeding.

He dressed everyone's wounds with leaves and a strange lemon-yellow moss, and he hummed softly with eyes half-closed as he traced fingertips around Fréth's bandaged injury.

Wynn's jaw wasn't broken, but the inside of her mouth was cut and her gums still seeped blood. She grimaced each time she flushed her mouth with cold water, and made a sour face when Gleann forced her to chew some of the moss. She hoped that the abrasion of Fréth's boot wouldn't leave scars on her face.

Brot'an complained of dizziness and bore a large lump at the base of his skull.

Leesil waited until he was certain his own companions were well cared for, but then all he could think of was pressing onward. His mother still waited. Magiere got up, dark eyes full of understanding.

"We'll get there," she said quietly.

Leesil looked to Brot'an. "Can you still lead? If not, Chap can take us."

"No," Sgäile said. "Brot'ân'duivé and my grandfather will make a litter for Fréthfâre. Her wound must be sewn. They will take her and Én'nish back to Crijheäiche. I will take you to Cuirin'nên'a." He turned and looked down at Fréth. "Speak of this to no one outside our caste. There will be no more discord among us, and you will be dealt with accordingly, Covârleasa!"

Brot'an rose and nodded to Leesil. "Return soon. I wait to see Cuirin'nên'a as well."

Sgäile bowed slightly, and Brot'an headed off to find makings for Fréth's stretcher.

It seemed Leesil's return to his mother was finally under way again when Gleann began walking north after Sgäile.

Sgäile halted. "Grandfather, you should return with the wounded."

"There are others who can tend them upon their return," Gleann answered. "As much as it may slow him, Brot'ân'duivé is hulkish enough to drag Fréthfâre's litter by himself. And Én'nish can do no more than follow in her present state. I am coming with you."

Sensing an argument brewing, Leesil cut in. "Magiere and Wynn may still need him, as it will take us a lot longer to return."

Gleann smiled at Wynn. "Come, child. And do not remove that moss from your mouth until I tell you."

To Leesil's relief, Sgäile just grunted. They headed north once again at a slower pace.

Leesil wasn't certain of the distance, but the journey would likely take the rest of the night. They continued until the forest began to lighten with the dawn and they emerged in a shattered clearing of broken branches, torn flowers, and one large uprooted birch.

Chap stopped in sudden weariness, glanced up at Wynn, and took a few steps into the clearing. The sage joined him, placing her hand on his back. Leesil was about to call them back when Chap turned away with Wynn at his side. The dog stalked on through the trees with his head hanging.

They all moved on, and Leesil saw the edge of the barrier woods.

He wanted to run but held back, not wishing to leave Magiere or the others behind as they entered the woods' passage. When he broke through the ferns at the far end, Leesil emerged in the familiar glade.

"Mother?"

He didn't see her at first. She came around from behind her domicile elm and stopped.

"Léshil?"

The hem of her ivory wrap dragged across the grass as she walked closer. Her silken hair spilled down her shoulders and disappeared behind.

Leesil looked at her for a long moment, the sight of her washing through him.

"You're free," he said bluntly. "You're leaving with me."

He reached back for Magiere—who had stood by him and fought for him, even against his own destructive obsession. She clasped his hand.

Favoring her swollen lip, Wynn smiled as Chap trotted up to Nein'a.

Sgäile and Gleann politely remained by the ferns, but Sgäile confirmed Leesil's words.

"You have been released. Most Aged Father told me this himself."

Leesil didn't know what to expect as his mother stared at him with anxious doubt. She glanced about the clearing's border trees. For an instant Leesil saw a vicious glower spread across her elegant features.

"Free," she whispered.

Leesil wanted to take hold of his mother, but he simply stood near her. "Yes . . . finally."

"What will I do?" she asked.

There was a strange loss in her voice, as if doubt would never fade completely.

Nein'a had been a skilled assassin and spy, a wife then widow, a mother and a daughter . . . and Anmaglâhk. She had also been trapped alone in this glade for eight years. Leesil reached out slowly to take her fingers.

"Come with Magiere and me."

Anxiety grew in her large eyes.

"Into the human world again?" She shook her head. "No . . . too long, too many years there."

Leesil felt as if he'd been dropped over a precipice. Then his thoughts traced backward through what life he'd had with her.

She had been ordered to Venjètz and lived there for over twenty years, had birthed and cared for him, trained him, and all the while held Most Aged Father's bloodlust at bay.

Then imprisoned and alone, without Gavril. How long had it been since she'd lived as she wanted? As much as it hurt, Leesil tried to understand.

But what else could she do? She had no home here—only enemies. Leesil looked at Magiere in deep concern. The two of them could not stay.

Gleann stepped cautiously forward. "Cuirin'nên'a, do you remember me . . . Sgäilsheilleache's grandfather? I have a granddaughter who is . . . not unlike your Léshil. I fear she grows tired of being the only woman of the house. Our settlement is small and simple, but there is always room for one more."

Nein'a looked at him. "Gleannéohkân'thva? Yes, I remember you."

Her words came evenly, and Leesil thought he caught something more than passing recognition within them. When he glanced at Gleann, he remembered how quickly the old man had arrived for Magiere's trial before the gathering, and how familiar he'd been with Brot'an.

Brot'an and his mother—both dissidents among the Anmaglâhk, both acquainted with Gleann. Had Sgäile ever noticed this?

"Do us this honor," Gleann said to Nein'a and then turned his owlish gaze upon Leesil. "If that is agreeable to both you and Léshil."

Nein'a's serious and exquisite face twisted in pain.

It was clear to Leesil that she wanted to accept Gleann's offer of a small quiet place in her own world where she might find some normal life of her choosing. Yet a part of Leesil grew anxious at the thought of leaving her among those who'd imprisoned her . . . and perhaps others who'd plotted with her over so many years. But if he trusted anyone among those he had met in this land to help her, it would be Gleann.

Nein'a gripped Leesil's fingers, and Magiere moved up, still grasping his other hand. He stood there caught between the two women of his world.

When Leesil looked at Magiere, he thought of the wedding to come . . . someday. He would swear fealty to her before their friends and, he hoped, her aunt Bieja. Shouldn't his own mother be present as well?

"You must continue," Nein'a said. "The ancestors will guide you. Do not let anything sway you when the path becomes clear."

It never occurred to Leesil before how much she was like her people, down to their fanatical superstitions. He'd seen the ghosts at the naked tree beyond the serpent and heard them call him by a name he didn't want. But he'd seen a ghost or two in his own life. Most were somewhere between an annoyance and a threat to be banished. They weren't worth this kind of blind faith.

Leesil saw how much Gleann's offer meant to her. Perhaps she would be safe and could come back to herself—to the woman he preferred her to be, his mother.

"All right," he said. "Come back to Crijheäiche with us, and we'll talk."

"Crijheäiche?" she repeated.

"Be at ease," Gleann said. "You will not see anyone you do not wish to."

Sgäile stepped forward, stripping off his cloak. "Put this on and over your head."

Of all the things Sgäile had done, for this Leesil felt most grateful.

"Do you have things to gather?" Wynn asked in her sensible way. "Anything here you wish to bring?"

Nein'a looked about the clearing, and her eyes sparked with the smoldering anger Leesil remembered so well.

"Only what once belonged to me," she said, and turned away into the tree.

When she reemerged, she held the bundled cloth with the skulls of Gavril and Eillean.

Leesil breathed in with difficulty, as Nein'a took her first faltering steps toward the ferns. He walked beside Magiere, not knowing what more to say. She linked her arm with his as they began the journey back.

CHAPTER TWENTY-FOUR

The return to Crijheäiche left them all exhausted, even Nein'a, who looked wary of her surroundings. Sgäile settled her in a small domicile tree by the river, close to Gleann and Leanâlhâm. When he offered to sit in vigil for Nein'a, Leesil insisted upon doing this himself.

Magiere understood, and so she took Wynn and Chap back to their own quarters.

Chap had been behaving strangely since the end of the trial—from the moment he and Leesil went for a final word with Most Aged Father. His crystal blue eyes shifted continually. Magiere suspected that the strain of the past days affected him as much as any of them.

In all honesty, she'd have much preferred to sit with Leesil, but if Nein'a wished to speak to him, they would need time alone. Poor Wynn looked quite a mess with her swollen jaw and tangled hair. The young woman had been abused too much over their travels.

"You sleep now," she said, guiding Wynn to a cushioned bed ledge inside the elm. "Save the bath for when you wake up."

Chap whined loudly.

Some might think it difficult to read a canine's face. Not

so for Magiere, after all the time she'd spent with him. She could read his agitation in the bristled fur and twitch of his jowls. He prowled toward Wynn in halting steps.

Wynn rolled over on the bed ledge to sit up. With dark circles under her eyes, she glared at Chap.

"Not until I am ready!" she grumbled. "Get that through your thick head!"

Lately, her temper had grown shorter, but this was perhaps for the best.

"What now?" Magiere asked.

"He wants to talk to you," Wynn said tiredly. "As if that is all I am good for anymore. Chap, just go to sleep, and let me do the same!"

Chap stalked closer to the sage, his eyes locked into hers. Wynn let out a sigh and slid off the ledge to the chamber floor.

"He says he is afraid . . . of showing me something, but you have to know the truth, and this is the only way."

She wavered, looking small and young to Magiere.

Too many times Chap had revealed something that made Magiere wish she had a way to speak alone with the dog. Wynn might have grown hardened in the last two seasons, but there were still things the sage was not prepared to face. Things that Magiere herself didn't care to think on, and it made her dread what Chap might pass to her through Wynn.

Magiere sank down, the three of them in a huddle, and ran a hand over Chap's silver-gray ear.

"What is it?" she whispered.

The dog glanced with concern at Wynn, but then fixed his eyes on Magiere. She stared back, growing more unsettled by the moment. Until Wynn whimpered.

The sage pulled up her knees, hiding her face in her hands, and began to sob.

"Wynn?" Magiere's fear sharpened. "Chap, whatever you're doing, stop it now!"

As she reached for Wynn, the sage cringed away, then clutched Magiere's wrist tightly.

"Once we leave elven land," she said, her voice low, "never come back . . . you must never set foot here again!"

As much concern as Magiere had for Wynn, she glared at Chap. He dipped his muzzle, flinching under her watchful eyes. Whatever he said to the sage, he didn't stop. Wynn's fingers tightened on Magiere's wrist, and the sage began to whisper Chap's words.

The longer Chap spoke through Wynn, the more numb Magiere became, until all she felt was the same shudder in her flesh that grew each time she stepped within a domicile tree.

"You were made to breach these lands . . . to breach any last refuge of the living," was the last thing Wynn said.

Magiere's mind rolled in a tangled mess as Wynn crawled back into bed, hiding her face.

Magiere sat upon the chamber floor with Chap.

She kept hearing words in her head spoken in pieces. Some from the last memory Chap had stolen from Most Aged Father. And more from what she'd heard others say. The worst was the missing piece from Chap's delusion spawned by sorcery.

No undead existed . . . before the lost war of the Forgotten History.

No undead rose . . . but humans.

No undead walked elven lands . . . but her.

In the forest of Pudúrlatsat, far south in Droevinka, Chap had fallen prey to a phantasm cast by the undead sorcerer Vordana. Magiere and Leesil had suffered the same, each experiencing a delusion fed by their worst fears—and perhaps something more hidden within each of them.

Chap had never told Magiere or anyone of his delusion until now.

He had seen her with an army, its ranks filled with creatures and beasts driven by madness for slaughter. She stood at the head of those forces in black-scaled armor, fully feral with her dhampir nature cut loose. Among the horde were the shadowed and gleaming-eyed figures, as in Magiere's own delusion and nightmares. The undead waited for her to lead them into a thriving forest. Everything died in her wake . . . under their hunger.

In Most Aged Father's memory, the undead horde hadn't breached the elven forest. Those who fled to that final refuge huddled together, listening to the sounds of starving undead legions tearing each other apart.

Magiere cowered on the elm's chamber floor. She had been imbued . . . infected with the nature of a Noble Dead, and yet was still a living thing. This had been accomplished with the blood of the five races, the Úirishg. By their blood used in her conception, and the life within her, Magiere could go wherever she wished.

The undead could not breach First Glade or the forest it touched. Not until the war came again to cover the world—and Magiere was born.

This was the reason she had been made.

Chap's understanding of all these pieces, much of it hidden or stolen by his kin, was the worst thing he could have done to her.

That wasn't the end of what was grinding Magiere down. Chap knew what Leesil's strange name meant. He heard the name of the female elder in Most Aged Father's memory, the one called Léshiâra—Sorrow-Tear.

Leesil . . . Léshil . . . Léshiârelaohk . . . Sorrow-Tear's Champion.

Magiere leaned on both hands, trying to draw in breath. Chap crept in, brushing his muzzle against her face, but she barely felt it.

Nein'a and her confederates envisioned their own way to deal with this unknown enemy that Most Aged Father feared would come again. Leesil had been conceived as their instrument, made for the need of the living with the skill for killing that the Anmaglâhk knew so well.

And Magiere? She had been born tainted by the undead to breach all last refuges of life.

Each of them made for opposing sides of a war yet to come.

She couldn't stop the tears slipping from her eyes.

Small hands gripped her shoulders. Wynn knelt down, and Magiere collapsed into the sage's lap.

"I am sorry," Wynn whispered, trying to pull Magiere

closer. "For what I said . . . the way I said it. You are not what they tried to make you. You do not have to be this."

But Magiere only thought of one thing.

Outside in the dark was the half-blood she loved, made for a purpose to counter her own . . . created to be her enemy.

In two days, Magiere stood on the riverside docks beside Leesil. Of all inappropriate times, Wynn struggled with a brush to clear tangles from Chap's fur. Brot'an, Sgäile, and Leanâlhâm watched her efforts with amusement.

"Hold still!" the sage snapped in exasperation.

Osha kept his eyes on Wynn as well, but his expression held no humor.

In the middle of them all, Nein'a stood quietly distracted near Leesil, and he fell into his old habit of babbling whenever nervous or upset.

"Remember what I said—there are elven ships that sail the Belaskian coast. Just send a letter to Counselor Lanjov at the bank in Bela, and he will get it to us straight away. We have some things to finish before going home to Miiska. But you can come there just the same, whenever you wish."

Nein'a nodded, her eyes drinking in her son's face. She, Gleann, and Leanâlhâm had delayed their own departure to see the "visitors" off.

"You may have more than one task," she whispered.

Magiere hoped when they finally returned home that her aunt Bieja would be there waiting. She wondered what the blunt, gruff Bieja and the sly, watchful Nein'a might think of each other.

Gleann had handled any dissatisfaction among the elders at the delayed departure. Now they had to leave—for more reasons than just the council's decree.

The market up from the docks bustled with activity. Tall elves in bright clothing bargained over goods from smoke-cured fish to beeswax candles to bolts of the elves' strange shimmering white cloth that look much like silk or satin.

The barge arrived to take them down the river, and

pulled up to the docks. Leanâlhâm stepped out from behind Nein'a. Her face filled with alarm at the sight of it.

"Oh, Léshil . . ."

"I'll try to send word of how we fare," he said.

Most likely, that wouldn't happen, but Magiere kept
quiet. The girl would miss him, and Leesil had never been
one to write letters. Then again, he'd never had anyone to
write to, if such a letter could make it into the elven lands.

Sgäile and Brot'an boarded the barge.

"What are you doing?" Magiere asked in confusion.

"We come down the river with you," Brot'an answered.
"It is best, considering . . . It is best. We can arrange passage
for you at the coast." He gave Nein'a a long look. "Léshil
must be kept safe."

For the first time since her return, Nein'a almost smiled.

Chap whined and gazed down the riverbank. Lily
roamed there with her pack.

Wynn kneeled beside him. "Do you wish to run with
them for a while?"

He hesitated, then licked her face and bolted off.

It was time to leave, and Magiere hurt for Leesil, watching him look one last time at his mother. Magiere agreed
that Nein'a should remain here for now, to rest and gather
herself. But knowing this didn't make the parting any easier for Leesil.

Nein'a reached out with her slender tan hand to Leesil's
cheek. "Good hunting, my son."

Magiere found this an odd farewell, but Leesil just
turned and stepped onto the barge, and she followed with
Wynn.

Wynn held a hand up to Osha. She didn't speak. From
the dock, he held up his own in response, but his expression
was impossible to read.

"Good-bye," Magiere called to Gleann and Leanâlhâm.
"I won't forget you."

Gleann smiled sadly as the barge pulled away.

Wide silver birch trees and hanging vines rushed past
once again, and the docks of Crijheäiche vanished behind
them.

*　　*　　*

Eight peaceful days later, Chap stood beside Lily gazing down a gentle slope toward the coast. He clearly saw the Hâjh River and his companions' barge near its mouth spilling into a expansive gulf. An azure ocean stretched beyond it to the horizon.

After all Chap's time in the immense forest, it was strange to see a city at the far edge of these wild elven lands. Small, thatched dwellings spread around higher structures at the middle and along the shore. He was surprised that coastal elves did not live in trees like those of the inland. Lily followed as he loped down the hill through the thinning trees and headed for the city's outskirts.

As the distance closed, he saw a few shops and stalls and scattered domicile trees on the fringes. One larger structure was composed of multiple floors built around the towering trunk of a redwood. Its upper branches spread wide like a second leafy roof over the building. Judging by the windows and small specks of people about it, it appeared to be an inn or its equivalent among the an'Cróan. He kept on, looking ahead to the far docks barely visible between the shoreline structures. The barge would be tied off there soon enough.

Lily whined and stopped.

Chap spun about and pressed his head against hers, showing her memories of his companions who waited. Lily backed up. He looked into her crystalline eyes, tinted with yellow flecks.

She would not come with him.

They had left the other majay-hì beyond the last hill, for the pack would go no further. Lily pressed her head to his and showed him images of inland elven enclaves and her kin running through the forest. Perhaps her kind did not approach the coastal people.

He did not want to leave her, and barked as he bounded a few steps forward and then spun about. But she held her ground. Chap looked to the coastline with its faint white lines of waves curling into the shore.

He had broken with his kin, the Fay. He had tangled and thwarted Most Aged Father's attempt on Magiere's life and his plans to use Leesil to ferret out dissidents. And now that Brot'an had revealed himself, Chap would do whatever was necessary to keep Leesil from the man's reach.

He would resist anyone who sought to use Leesil or Magiere. He would find his own answers for what lay ahead of them all.

Chap went back and pressed his nose against Lily, breathing in the rich earthen scent of her fur. It made him feel heavy and weak with sorrow.

But Leesil and Magiere and even Wynn still needed him.

Chap turned from Lily and ran for the coast. He could not bear to look back, even when he heard her howl fade into the forest.

EPILOGUE

The dreamer fell through boundless night, frigid wind ripping past.

The night sky began to undulate.

Rippling mounds arched within the darkness like black desert dunes and then sharpened into clarity. Stars became glints of reflected light upon black reptilian scales the size of small battle shields. Those scaled dunes shifted into mammoth reptilian coils, each larger than the height of a mounted rider. They turned and writhed on all sides of the dreamer, with no beginning, no end, and no space between.

The scales vanished, but the dreamer still fell. A coastline appeared below, fringed by high snow-packed mountains.

Here, a voice whispered above the roar of rushing air. *It is here.*

The dreamer tumbled downward, until high mountain peaks of perpetual ice rose like a jagged-toothed maw on all sides. Within that snowbound canyon stood a six-towered castle bordered by stone walls. The dreamer, in rapid descent, caught only a glimpse of high arched gates.

A white snowfield beyond rushed up.

Then impact.

No pain or darkness came, only shudders of fear, as to a child lost in the wilderness. The dreamer lay in crusted snow, staring up at twin gates of ornate iron curls. They joined together at their high tops in an arched point. Mottled with rust, the gates were still sound in their place. Beyond stood the castle's matching-shaped iron doors atop a wide cascade of steps.

A carrion crow sat upon the gates, watching the dreamer expectantly.

The castle dimmed from sight into darkness. Reptilian coils rose all around, their twisting and churning increasing in speed.

The orb is yours . . . I now give it to you alone . . . take it!

The dreamer tried to scramble across the snow, but then only the black coils remained, closing in, tighter and tighter.

Sister of the dead, lead on.

Magiere's eyes snapped open, as she gasped for breath and thrashed out of the bed. She scrambled across the floor and huddled naked and shaking in one corner of the elven inn's tiny room. She tried to scream, but all that came out was a harsh whisper.

"Leesil!"

He sat up quickly in the bed.

Black coils seemed to move in every shadow of the dark room as Magiere reached out for Leesil hurrying toward her.

NEW IN HARDCOVER

OF TRUTH AND BEASTS

A Novel of the Noble Dead

by Barb & J.C. Hendee

Wynn has returned safely to the Guild of Sagecraft with her companions, the vampire Chane Andraso and Shade, an elven wolf. Though Wynn had managed to regain her seized journals, she only received a glimpse of the ancient texts penned by forgotten vampires, and once again, the volumes have slipped from her grasp. The price for her brief success may prove costly.

For the animosity of her guild superiors has grown even more fierce. This time, instead of cloistering her, they purposefully give her a mission so tedious it will keep her out of the way for as long as possible. But Wynn has her own plans...

Available wherever books are sold or at
penguin.com

R0061

National Bestselling Authors
Barb & J.C. Hendee
The Noble Dead Saga

DHAMPIR

A con artist who poses as a vampire slayer learns that she is, in fact, a true slayer—and half-vampire herself—whose actions have attracted the unwanted attention of a trio of powerful vampires seeking her blood.

THIEF OF LIVES

Magiere and Leesil are called out of their self-imposed retirement when vampires besiege the capital city of Bela.

SISTER OF THE DEAD

Magiere the dhampir and her partner, the half-elf Leesil, are on a journey to uncover the secrets of their mysterious pasts. But first their expertise as vampire hunters is required on behalf of a small village being tormented by a creature of unlimited and unimaginable power.

TRAITOR TO THE BLOOD

The saga continues as Magiere and Leesil embark on a quest to uncover the secrets of their mysterious origins—and for those responsible for orchestrating the events that brought them together.

Available wherever books are sold or at
penguin.com

R0054

National Bestselling Authors
Barb & J.C. Hendee
The Noble Dead Saga

REBEL FAY

Magiere and Leesil were brought together by the Fay to forge an alliance that might have the power to stand against the forces of dark magics. But as they uncover the truth, they discover just how close the enemy has always been...

CHILD OF A DEAD GOD

For years, Magiere and Leesil have sought a mysterious artifact that they must keep from falling into the hands of a murdering Noble Dead, Magiere's half-brother Welstiel. And now, dreams of a castle locked in ice lead her south, on a journey that has become nothing less than an obsession.

IN SHADE AND SHADOW

Wynn Hygeorht arrives at the Guild of Sagecraft, bearing texts supposedly penned by vampires. When several pages disappear and two sages are found murdered, Wynn embarks on a quest to uncover the secrets of the texts.

**Available wherever books are sold or at
penguin.com**

THE ULTIMATE IN
SCIENCE FICTION AND FANTASY!

From magical tales of distant worlds to stories of
technological advances beyond the grasp of man, Penguin has
everything you need to stretch your imagination to its limits.

penguin.com

ACE
Get the latest information on favorites like
William Gibson, Ilona Andrews, Jack Campbell,
Ursula K. Le Guin, Sharon Shinn, Charlaine Harris,
Patricia Briggs, and Marjorie M. Liu,
as well as updates on the best new authors.

ROC
Escape with Jim Butcher, Harry Turtledove, Anne Bishop,
S.M. Stirling, Simon R. Green, E.E. Knight, Kat Richardson,
Rachel Caine, and many others—plus news on the
latest and hottest in science fiction and fantasy.

DAW
Patrick Rothfuss, Seanan McGuire, Mercedes Lackey,
Kristen Britain, Tanya Huff, Tad Williams, C.J. Cherryh,
and many more—DAW has something to satisfy the
cravings of any science fiction and fantasy lover.
Also visit dawbooks.com.

*Get the best of science fiction and fantasy
at your fingertips!*

R0064-111510

arrière-pensée [arjɛrpɑ̃se] *f* (*pl* **-pensées**) mental reservation, ulterior motive

arrière-plan [arjɛrplɑ̃] *m* (*pl* **-plans**) background

arriérer [arjere] §10 *tr* to delay ‖ *ref* to fall behind (*in payment*)

arrière-train [arjɛrtrɛ̃] *m* (*pl* **-trains**) rear (*of a vehicle*); hindquarters

arrimage [arimaʒ] *m* stowage; docking (*of space vehicle*)

arrimer [arime] *tr* to stow; (aer) to dock

arrimeur [arimœr] *m* stevedore

arrivage [arivaʒ] *m* arrival (*of goods or ships*)

arrivée [arive] *f* arrival; intake; (sports) finish, goal; **arrivée en douceur** (rok) soft landing

arriver [arive] §96 *intr* (*aux:* ÉTRE) to arrive; succeed; happen; **arriver à** to attain, reach; **en arriver à** + *inf* to be reduced to + *ger*

arriviste [arivist] *mf* upstart, parvenu

arrogance [arɔgɑ̃s] *f* arrogance

arro·gant [arɔgɑ̃] **-gante** [gɑ̃t] *adj* arrogant

arroger [arɔʒe] §38 *ref* to arrogate to oneself

arrondir [arɔ̃dir] *tr* to round, round off, round out ‖ *ref* to become round

arrondissement [arɔ̃dismɑ̃] *m* district

arrosage [arozaʒ] *m* sprinkling; irrigation; (mil) heavy bombing

arroser [aroze] *tr* to sprinkle, water; irrigate; flow through (*e.g., a city*); wash down (*a meal*); (coll) to bribe; (coll) to drink to (*a success*)

arro·seur [arozœr] **-seuse** [zøz] *mf* sprinkler (*person*) ‖ *f* street sprinkler

arrosoir [arozwar] *m* sprinkling can

arse·nal [arsənal] *m* (*pl* **-naux** [no]) shipyard, navy yard; (fig) storehouse; (archaic) arsenal, armory

arsenic [arsənik] *m* arsenic

art [ar] *m* art; **arts d'agréments** music, drawing, dancing, etc.; **arts ménagers** home economics; **le huitième art** television; **les arts du spectacle** the performing arts; **le septième art** the cinema

artère [artɛr] *f* artery

arté·riel -rielle [arterjɛl] *adj* arterial

artérioscié·reux [arterjɔsklerø] **-reuse** [røz] *adj & mf* arteriosclerotic

arté·sien [artezjɛ̃] **-sienne** [zjɛn] *adj* of Artois; artesian (*well*)

arthrite [artrit] *f* arthritis

artichaut [artiʃo] *m* artichoke

article [artikl] *m* article; entry (*in a dictionary*); **à l'article de la mort** on the point of death; **article de fond** leader; editorial; **article de tête** front-page story; **articles divers** sundries

articuler [artikyle] *tr & ref* to articulate

artifice [artifis] *m* artifice; craftsmanship

artifi·ciel -cielle [artifisjɛl] *adj* artificial

artificier [artifisje] *m* fireworks maker; soldier in charge of ammunition supply

artifi·cieux [artifisjø] **-cieuse** [sjøz] *adj* artful, cunning

artillerie [artijəri] *f* artillery

artilleur [artijœr] *m* artilleryman

arti·san [artizɑ̃] **-sane** [zan] *mf* artisan, artificer ‖ *m* craftsman

artiste [artist] *adj* artistic; artist, of art, e.g., **le monde artiste** the world of art ‖ *mf* artist; actor

artistique [artistik] *adj* artistic

ar·yen [arjɛ̃] **-yenne** [jɛn] *adj* Aryan ‖ (*cap*) *mf* Aryan (*person*)

as [as] *m* ace; **as du volant** speed king ‖ [a] *v* see **avoir**

A.S. *abbr* (**assurances sociales**) social security

a/s *abbr* (**aux bons soins de**) c/o

asbeste [asbɛst] *m* asbestos

ascendance [asɑ̃dɑ̃s] *f* lineal ancestry; rising (*of air; of star*)

ascenseur [asɑ̃sœr] *m* elevator; **renvoyer l'ascenseur** to do a favor in return

ascension [asɑ̃sjɔ̃] *f* ascension; **Ascension** *f* Ascension Day

ascèse [asɛz] *f* asceticism

ascète [asɛt] *mf* ascetic

ascétique [asetik] *adj* ascetic

ascétisme [asetism] *m* asceticism

aseptique [asɛptik] *adj* aseptic

Asie [azi] *f* Asia; **Asie Mineure** Asia Minor; **l'Asie** Asia; **l'Asie Mineure** Asia Minor

asile [azil] *m* asylum, shelter, home

aspect [aspɛ] [aspɛk] *m* aspect

asperge [aspɛrʒ] *f* asparagus; **des asperges** asparagus (*stalks and tips used as food*)

asperger [aspɛrʒe] §38 *tr* to sprinkle

aspérité [asperite] *f* roughness; harshness; gruffness

aspersion [aspɛrsjɔ̃] *f* sprinkling

asphalte [asfalt] *m* asphalt

asphyxier [asfiksje] *tr* to asphyxiate ‖ *ref* to be asphyxiated

aspic [aspik] *m* asp

aspi·rant [aspirɑ̃] **-rante** [rɑ̃t] *adj* aspirant, aspiring; suction (*pump*) ‖ *mf* candidate (*for a degree*) ‖ *m* midshipman

aspirateur [aspiratœr] *m* vacuum cleaner; **aspirateur de buée** kitchen fan

aspi·ré -rée [aspire] *adj & m* (phonet) aspirate

aspirer [aspire] *tr* to inhale; suck in ‖ §96 *intr*—**aspirer à** to aspire to

aspirine [aspirin] *f* aspirin

assagir [asaʒir] *tr* to make wiser ‖ *ref* to become wiser

assail·lant [asajɑ̃] **-lante** [jɑ̃t] *adj* attacking ‖ *mf* assailant

assaillir [asajir] §69 *tr* to assail, assault

assainir [asɛnir] *tr* to purify, clean up; drain (*a swamp*)

assainissement [asɛnismɑ̃] *m* purification; draining

assaisonnement [asɛzɔnmɑ̃] *m* seasoning

assaisonner [asɛzɔne] *tr* to season, flavor

assas·sin [asasɛ̃] **-sine** [sin] *adj* murderous ‖ *m* assassin

assassinat [asasina] *m* assassination

assassiner [asasine] *tr* to assassinate; (coll) to bore to death

assaut [aso] *m* assault, attack; match, bout

assèchement [asɛʃmɑ̃] *m* drainage, drying; dryness

assécher [aseʃe] §10 *tr* to drain, dry up

assemblage [asɑ̃blaʒ] *m* assemblage; assembling (*e.g., of printed pages*); (woodworking) joint, joining

assemblée [asɑ̃ble] *f* assembly, meeting

assembler [asɑ̃ble] *tr* to assemble ‖ *ref* to assemble, convene, meet

assener [asne] §2 *tr* to land (*a blow*)

assentiment [asɑ̃timɑ̃] *m* assent, consent

asseoir [aswar] §5 *tr* to seat, sit, place; base (*an opinion*) ‖ *ref* to sit down

assermen·té -tée [asɛrmɑ̃te] *adj* under oath

assertion [asɛrsjɔ̃] *f* assertion

asser·vi -vie [asɛrvi] *adj* subservient

asservir [asɛrvir] *tr* to enslave; to subdue (*e.g., passions*) ‖ *ref* to submit (*to convention; to tyranny*)

asservissement [asɛrvismɑ̃] *m* enslavement; subservience

assesseur [asɛsœr] *adj & m* assistant; associate (*judge*)

asseyez [aseje] *v* (**assieds** [asje]) see **asseoir**

assez [ase] *adv* enough; fairly, rather; **assez de** enough; **en voilà assez!** that's enough!, cut it out!, ‖ *interj* enough!, stop!

assi·du -due [asidy] *adj* assiduous; **assidu à** attentive to

assidûment [asidymɑ̃] *adv* assiduously

assié·geant [asjeʒɑ̃] **-geante** [ʒɑ̃t] *adj* besieging ‖ *mf* besieger

assiéger [asjeʒe] §1 *tr* to besiege

assiette [asjɛt] *f* plate, dish; plateful; seat (*of a rider on horseback*); position, condition; **assiette anglaise, assiette de viandes froides** cold cuts; **assiette au beurre** (fig) gravy train; **assiette creuse** soup plate; **assiette fiscale** tax basis; **je ne suis pas dans mon assiette** I'm in low spirits

assignation [asiɲasjɔ̃] *f* assignation; subpoena, summons

assi·gné -gnée [asiɲe] *mf* appointee; **assigné à résidence** permanent appointee; **assigné intérim** temporary appointee

assigner [asiɲe] §96 *tr* to assign, allot; fix (*a date*); subpoena, summon

assimilable [asimilabl] *adj* assimilable; comparable

assimilation [asimilɑsjɔ̃] *f* assimilation

assimiler [asimile] *tr* to assimilate; compare; identify with ‖ *ref* to assimilate

as·sis [asi] **-sise** [siz] *adj* seated, sitting; firmly established ‖ *f* foundation; stratum; **assises** assizes ‖ *v* see **asseoir**

assistance [asistɑ̃s] *f* assistance; audience, persons present; presence; **assistance judiciaire** public defender; **assistance publique** welfare department; **assistance sociale** social service

assis·tant [asistɑ̃] **-tante** [tɑ̃t] *adj* assistant ‖ *mf* assistant; bystander, spectator; **assistante sociale** public health nurse; social worker

assister [asiste] *tr* to assist, help ‖ *intr*—**assister à** to attend, be present at

association [asɔsjɑsjɔ̃] *f* association; (sports) soccer; **association des spectateurs** theater club; **association sans but lucratif** nonprofit organization

asso·cié -ciée [asɔsje] *adj & mf* associate

associer [asɔsje] *tr* to associate ‖ *ref* to go into partnership

assoif·fé -fée [aswafe] *adj* thirsty

assolement [asɔlmɑ̃] *m* rotation (*of crops*)

assombrir [asɔ̃brir] *tr & ref* to darken

assom·mant [asɔmɑ̃] **-mante** [mɑ̃t] *adj* (coll) boring, fatiguing

assommer [asɔme] *tr* to kill with a heavy blow; beat up; stun; (coll) to heckle; (coll) to bore

assommoir [asɔmwar] *m* bludgeon; (coll) gin mill, dive, clip joint

Assomption [asɔ̃psjɔ̃] *f* Assumption

assonance [asɔnɑ̃s] *f* assonance

assor·ti -tie [asɔrti] *adj* assorted (*e.g., cakes*); well-matched (*couple*); stocked, supplied (*store*); to match, e.g., **une cravate assortie** a necktie to match

assortiment [asɔrtimɑ̃] *m* assortment; matching (*of colors*); set (*of dishes*); platter (*of cold cuts*)

assortir [asɔrtir] *tr* to assort, match; stock ‖ *ref* to match; harmonize; **s'assortir de** to be accompanied with

assoupir [asupir] *tr* to make drowsy, lull; deaden (*pain*) ‖ *ref* to doze off; lessen (*with time*)

assoupissement [asupismɑ̃] *m* drowsiness; lethargy

assouplir [asuplir] *tr* to make supple, flexible; break in (*a horse*) ‖ *ref* to become supple, manageable

assouplissement [asuplismɑ̃] *m* suppleness, flexibility; limbering up; relaxation (*of a rule*)

assourdir [asurdir] *tr* to deafen; tone down, muffle

assouvir [asuvir] *tr* to assuage, appease, satiate; satisfy (*e.g., a thirst for vengeance*)

assouvissement [asuvismɑ̃] *m* assuagement, appeasement, satisfying

assujet·ti -tie [asyʒɛti] *adj* fastened; subject, liable ‖ *mf* taxpayer; contributor (*e.g., to social security*)

assujettir [asyʒɛtir] *tr* to subjugate; subject; fasten, secure ‖ §96 *ref* to submit

assujettis·sant [asyʒɛtisɑ̃] **-sante** [sɑ̃t] *adj* demanding

assujettissement [asyʒɛtismɑ̃] *m* subjugation, subduing; submission (*to a stronger force*); fastening, securing

assumer [asyme] *tr* to assume, take upon oneself

assurance [asyrɑ̃s] *f* assurance; insurance; **assurances sociales** social security; **assurance incendie** fire insurance; **assurance invalidité** disability insurance; **assurance maladie-sécurité** health insurance; **assurance multirisque** comprehensive insurance

assu·ré -rée [asyre] *adj* assured, satisfied; insured ‖ *mf* insured

assurément [asyremɑ̃] *adv* assuredly

assurer [asyre] §95 *tr* to assure; secure; insure ‖ *ref* to be assured; make sure; be insured

astate [astat] *m* astatine

aster [astɛr] *m* (bot) aster

astérie [asteri] *f* starfish

astérisque [asterisk] *m* asterisk

asthénie [asteni] *f* debility

asthme [asm] *m* asthma

asticot [astiko] *m* maggot

astiquer [astike] *tr* to polish

as·tral -trale [astral] *adj* (*pl* **-traux** [tro]) astral

astre [astrə] *m* star, heavenly body; leading light; **astre de la nuit** moon; **astre du jour** sun

astreindre [astrɛ̃dr] §50 *tr* to force, compel, subject ‖ §96 *ref* to force oneself; be subjected

astrologie [astrɔlɔʒi] *f* astrology

astrologue [astrɔlɔg] *m* astrologer

astronaute [astrɔnot] *mf* astronaut

astronautique [astrɔnotik] *f* astronautics

astronef [astrɔnɛf] *m* spaceship

astronome [astrɔnɔm] *mf* astronomer

astronomie [astrɔnɔmi] *f* astronomy

astronomique [astrɔnɔmik] *adj* astronomical

astuce [astys] *f* slyness, guile; tricks (*of a trade*)

astu·cieux [astysjø] **-cieuse** [sjøz] *adj* astute, crafty

atelier [atəlje] *m* studio; workshop

atermoiement [atɛrmwamɑ̃] *m* procrastination; extension of a loan

athée [ate] *adj* atheistic ‖ *mf* atheist

athéisme [ateism] *m* atheism

Athènes [atɛn] *f* Athens

athlète [atlɛt] *mf* athlete

athlétique [atletik] *adj* athletic

athlétisme [atletism] *m* athletics

Atlantique [atlɑ̃tik] *adj* & *m* Atlantic

atlas [atlɑs] *m* atlas ‖ (*cap*) *m* Atlas

atmosphère [atmɔsfɛr] *f* atmosphere

atome [atom] *m* atom

atomique [atɔmik] *adj* atomic

atomi·sé -sée [atɔmize] *adj* afflicted with radiation sickness

atomiser [atɔmize] *tr* to atomize

atomiseur [atɔmizœr] *m* spray; atomizer

atone [atɔn] *adj* dull, expressionless; drab (*life*); (phonet) unaccented

atours [atur] *mpl* finery

atout [atu] *m* trump; **sans atout** no-trump

atrabilaire [atrabilɛr] *adj* & *mf* hypochondriac

âtre [ɑtr] *m* hearth

atroce [atrɔs] *adj* atrocious

atrocité [atrɔsite] *f* atrocity

atrophie [atrɔfi] *f* atrophy

atrophier [atrɔfje] *tr* & *ref* to atrophy

atta·chant [ataʃɑ̃] **-chante** [ʃɑ̃t] *adj* appealing, attractive

attache [ataʃ] *f* attachment, tie; paper clip; (anat) joint; **attache parisienne** paper clip

attachement [ataʃmɑ̃] *m* attachment

attacher [ataʃe] *tr* to attach; tie up ‖ *intr* (culin) to stick ‖ §96 *ref* to be fastened, tied; **s'attacher à** to stick to; become devoted to.

attaque [atak] *f* attack; (pathol) stroke; **attaque brusque** or **attaque brusquée** surprise attack; **attaque de nerfs** case of nerves

attaquer [atake] *tr* & *intr* to attack ‖ *ref*—**s'attaquer à** to attack

attar·dé -dée [atarde] *adj* retarded; behind the times; belated, delayed ‖ *mf* mentally retarded person; lover of the past

attarder [atarde] *tr* to delay, retard ‖ *ref* to be delayed; stay, remain

atteindre [atɛ̃dr] §50 *tr* to attain; reach ‖ *intr*—**atteindre à** to attain; reach; attain to

at·teint [atɛ̃] **-teinte** [tɛ̃t] *adj* stricken ‖ *f* reaching; injury; **hors d'atteinte** out of reach; **porter atteinte à** to endanger; **premières atteintes** first signs (*of illness*)

attelage [atlaʒ] *m* harnessing; coupling

atteler [atle] §34 *tr* to harness; hitch; couple (*cars on a railroad*) ‖ *ref*—**s'atteler à** (coll) to buckle down to

attelle [atɛl] *m* splint; **attelles** hames

atte·nant [atənɑ̃] **-nante** [nɑ̃t] *adj* adjoining

attendre [atɑ̃dr] §97 *tr* to wait for; await; expect ‖ *intr* to wait ‖ §96 *ref*—**s'attendre à** to expect; rely on; **s'attendre à + *inf*** to expect to + *inf*; **s'attendre à ce que + *subj*** to expect (*s.o.*) to + *inf*, e.g., **il s'attend à ce que je lui raconte toute l'affaire** he expects me to tell him the whole story; **s'y attendre** to expect it or them

attendrir [atɑ̃drir] *tr* to tenderize; soften ‖ *ref* to become tender; be deeply touched or moved

attendrissement [atɑ̃drismɑ̃] *m* softening; compassion

atten·du -due [atɑ̃dy] *adj* expected ‖ **attendus** *mpl* (law) grounds ‖ *adv*—**attendu que** whereas, inasmuch as ‖ **attendu** *prep* in view of

attentat [atɑ̃ta] *m* attempt, assault; outrage (*to decency*); offense (*against the state*)

attente [atɑ̃t] *f* wait; expectation; **en attente!** stand by!

attenter [atɑ̃te] *intr*—**attenter à** to attempt (*e.g., s.o.'s life*); **attenter à ses jours** to attempt suicide

atten·tif [atɑ̃tif] **-tive** [tiv] *adj* attentive

attention [atɑ̃sjɔ̃] *f* attention; **attentions** attention, care, consideration ‖ *interj* attention!, be careful!

attention·né -née [atɑ̃sjɔne] *adj* considerate

atténuation [atenɥasjɔ̃] *f* attenuation

atténuer [atenɥe] *tr* to subdue, soften (*color; pain; passions*); attenuate (*words;*

bacteria); extenuate (*a fault*) ‖ *ref* to soften; lessen

atterrer [atɛre] *tr* to dismay

atterrir [atɛrir] *intr* (*aux:* AVOIR or ÊTRE) to land

atterrissage [atɛrisaʒ] *m* landing; **atterrissage dur** hard landing; **atterrissage forcé** forced landing; **atterrissage sur le ventre** pancake landing

attestation [atɛstɑsjɔ̃] *f* attestation; **attestation d'études** transcript

attester [atɛste] *tr* to attest, attest to; **attester qn de q.ch.** to call s.o. to witness to s.th.

attiédir [atjedir] *tr & ref* to cool off; warm up

attifer [atife] *tr & ref* to spruce up

attirail [atiraj] *m* gear, tackle, outfit; (coll) paraphernalia

attirance [atirɑ̃s] *f* attraction, lure, attractiveness

atti·rant [atirɑ̃] **-rante** [rɑ̃t] *adj* appealing, attractive

attirer [atire] *tr* to attract ‖ *ref* to be attracted; attract each other; call forth (*criticism*)

attiser [atize] *tr* to stir, stir up, poke

atti·tré -trée [atitre] *adj* regular (*dealer*); **attitré de la cour** appointed by the court

attitude [atityd] *f* attitude

attrac·tif [atraktif] **-tive** [tiv] *adj* attractive (*force*)

attraction [atraksjɔ̃] *f* attraction; **les attractions** vaudeville

attrait [atrɛ] *m* attraction, attractiveness, appeal; **attraits** charms

attrape [atrap] *f* trap; (coll) trick, joke

attrape-mouche [atrapmuʃ] *m* (*pl* **-mouche** or **-mouches**) flypaper; Venus's-flytrap

attrape-nigaud [atrapnigo] *m* (*pl* **-nigauds**) booby trap

attraper [atrape] *tr* to catch; snare, trap; trick ‖ *ref* to trick each other; hang on

at·trayant [atrɛjɑ̃] **-trayante** [trɛjɑ̃t] *adj* attractive

attribuer [atribɥe] *tr* to ascribe, attribute; assign (*a share*) ‖ *ref* to claim, assume

attribut [atriby] *m* attribute; predicate

attribu·tif [atribytif] **-tive** [tiv] *adj* (gram) predicative

attribution [atribysjɔ̃] *f* attribution; assignment, assignation

attris·té -tée [atriste] *adj* sorrowful

attrister [atriste] *tr* to sadden ‖ §97 *ref* to become sad

attrition [atrisjɔ̃] *f* attrition

attroupement [atrupmɑ̃] *m* mob

attrouper [atrupe] *tr* to bring together in a mob ‖ *ref* to flock together in a mob

au [o] §77 to the

aubaine [obɛn] *f* windfall, godsend, bonanza

aube [ob] *f* dawn; (mach) paddle, blade, vane

aubépine [obepin] *f* hawthorn

auberge [obɛrʒ] *f* inn; **auberge de la jeunesse** youth hostel

aubergine [obɛrʒin] *f* eggplant; (Parisian slang) meter maid

aubergiste [obɛrʒist] *mf* innkeeper

auburn [obœrn] *adj invar* auburn

au·cun [okœ̃] **-cune** [kyn] *adj*—**aucun . . . ne** or **ne . . . aucun** §90 no, none, not any ‖ *pron indef*—**aucun ne** §90B no one, nobody; **d'aucuns** some, some people

aucunement [okynmɑ̃] §90 *adv*—**ne . . . aucunement** not at all, by no means

audace [odas] *f* audacity

auda·cieux [odasjø] **-cieuse** [sjøz] *adj* audacious

au-deçà [odəsa] *adv* (obs) on this side; **au-deçà de** (obs) on this side of

au-dedans [odədɑ̃] *adv* inside; **au-dedans de** inside, inside of

au-dehors [odəɔr] *adv* outside; **au-dehors de** outside, outside of

au-delà [odəla] *m*—**l'au-delà** the beyond ‖ *adv* beyond; **au-delà de** beyond

au-dessous [odəsu] *adv* below; **au-dessous de** under

au-dessus [odəsy] *adv* above; **au-dessus de** above

au-devant [odəvɑ̃] *adv*—**aller au devant de** to go to meet; anticipate (*s.o.'s wishes*); court (*defeat*)

audience [odjɑ̃s] *f* audience

audio-fréquence [odjofrekɑ̃s] *f* audio frequency

audiomètre [odjomɛtr] *m* audiometer

audio-vi·suel -suelle [odjovizɥɛl] *adj* audiovisual ‖ *m* audiovisual aids

audi·teur [oditœr] **-trice** [tris] *mf* listener; auditor (*in class*); **auditeur libre** auditor (*in class*)

audi·tif [oditif] **-tive** [tiv] *adj* auditory

audition [odisjɔ̃] *f* audition; public hearing; musical recital

auditionner [odisjone] *tr & intr* to audition

auditoire [oditwar] *m* audience; courtroom

auditorium [oditɔrjɔm] *m* auditorium; concert hall; projection room

auge [oʒ] *f* trough

augmentation [ogmɑ̃tɑsjɔ̃] *f* augmentation; raise (*in salary*)

augmenter [ogmɑ̃te] *tr* to augment; increase or supplement (*income*); raise (*prices*); raise the salary of (*an employee*) ‖ *intr* to augment, increase; **augmenter de** to increase by (*a stated amount*)

augure [ogyr] *m* augur; augury

augurer [ogyre] *tr & intr* to augur

auguste [ogyst] *adj* august

aujourd'hui [oʒurdɥi], [oʒordɥi] *m & adv* today; **d'aujourd'hui en huit** a week from today; **d'aujourd'hui en quinze** two weeks from today

aumône [omon] *f* alms; **faire l'aumône** to give alms; **faire l'aumône de** (fig) to hand out

aumônier [omonje] *m* chaplain

aune [on] *m* alder ‖ *f* ell

auparavant [oparavɑ̃] *adv* before, previously

auprès [oprɛ] *adv* close by, in the neighborhood; **auprès de** near, close to; at the side of; to, at the side of; to (*a king, a government*); with; compared with
auquel [okɛl] (*pl* **auxquels**) §78
aurai [ɔre] *v* (**auras, aura, aurons,** etc.) see **avoir**
auréole [ɔreɔl] *f* aureole, halo
auréomycine [ɔreɔmisin] *f* aureomycin
auriculaire [ɔrikylɛr] *adj* firsthand (*witness*); auricular (*confession*) ‖ *m* little finger
auricule [ɔrikyl] *f* auricle
aurifier [orifje] *tr* to fill (*a tooth*) with gold
aurore [ɔrɔr] *f* aurora, dawn
ausculter [ɔskylte] *tr* to auscultate
auspice [ospis] *m* omen; **sous les auspices de** under the auspices of
aussi [osi] *adv* also, too; therefore, and so; so; **aussi . . . que** as . . . as
aussitôt [osito] *adv* right away, immediately; **aussitôt dit, aussitôt fait** no sooner said than done; **aussitôt que** as soon as
austère [ɔstɛr] *adj* austere
austérité [ɔsterite] *f* austerity
Australie [ɔstrali] *f* Australia; **l'Australie** Australia
austra·lien [ɔstraljɛ̃] **-lienne** [ljɛn] *adj* Australian ‖ (*cap*) *mf* Australian
autant [otɑ̃] *adv* as much, as many; as far, as long; **autant de** so many; **autant que** as much as, as far as; **d'autant** by so much; **d'autant plus** all the more; **d'autant plus** (*or* **moins**) **. . . que . . . plus** (*or* **moins**) all the more (*or* less) . . . as (*or* in proportion as) . . . more (*or* less); **d'autant que** inasmuch as
autel [otɛl], [otɛl] *m* altar
auteur [otœr] *adj*—**une femme auteur** an authoress ‖ *m* author
authentifier [otɑ̃tifje] *tr* to authenticate
authentique [otɑ̃tik] *adj* authentic; genuine (*antique*); notarized
authentiquer [otɑ̃tike] *tr* to notarize
autistique [otistik] *adj* autistic
auto [oto], [oto] *f* auto
auto-allumage [otoalymaʒ] *m* preignition
autobiographie [otɔbjɔgrafi] *f* autobiography
auto-buffet [otɔbyfɛ] *m* drive-in; curb service
autobus [otɔbys] *m* bus, city bus
autocar [otɔkar] *m* interurban bus
autochenille [otɔʃənij] *f* caterpillar (*tractor*)
autochtone [otɔktɔn] *adj* & *mf* native
autoclave [otɔklav] *m* pressure cooker; autoclave, sterilizer
autocollant [otɔkɔlɑ̃] *m* bumpersticker
autocopie [otɔkɔpi] *f* duplicating, multicopying; duplicated copy
autocopier [otɔkɔpje] *tr* to run off, duplicate, ditto
auto-couchette [otɔkuʃɛt] *f*—**en auto-couchette** piggyback
autocrate [otɔkrat] *mf* autocrat
autocratique [otɔkratik] *adj* autocratic
autocritique [otɔkritik] *f* self-criticism

autocuiseur [otɔkɥizœr] *m* pressure cooker
autodétermination [otɔdetɛrminasjɔ̃] *f* self-determination
autodidacte [otɔdidakt] *adj* self-taught ‖ *mf* self-taught person
autodrome [otɔdrom] *m* race track; test strip
auto-école [otɔekɔl] *f* (*pl* **-écoles**) driving school
autogare [otɔgar] *f* bus station
autographe [otɔgraf] *adj* & *m* autograph
autographie [otɔgrafi] *f* multicopying
autographier [otɔgrafje] *tr* to duplicate
autogreffe [otɔgrɛf] *f* skin grafting
auto-grue [otɔgry] *f* (*pl* **-grues**) tow truck
autoguidage [otɔgidaʒ] *m* automatic piloting
auto-intoxication [otɔɛ̃tɔksikasjɔ̃] *f* autointoxication
automate [otomat] *m* automaton
automation [otɔmasjɔ̃] *f* automation
automatique [otɔmatik] *adj* automatic ‖ *m* dial telephone
automatisation [otɔmatizasjɔ̃] *f* automation
automatiser [otɔmatize] *tr* to automate
automitrailleuse [otɔmitrajøz] *f* armored car mounting machine guns
autom·nal -nale [otɔmnal] *adj* (*pl* **-naux** [no]) autumnal
automne [otɔn], [otɔn] *m* fall, autumn; **à l'automne, en automne** in the fall
automobile [otɔmɔbil], [otɔmɔbil] *adj* automotive ‖ *f* automobile
automobilisme [otɔmɔbilism] *m* driving, motoring
automobiliste [otɔmɔbilist] *mf* motorist
automo·teur [otɔmɔtœr] **-trice** [tris] *adj* self-propelling, automatic ‖ *m* self-propelled river barge ‖ *f* rail car
autonome [otɔnɔm] *adj* autonomous, independent; (*comp*) off line
autonomie [otɔnɔmi] *f* autonomy; cruising radius, range (*of ship, plane, or tank*)
autoplastie [otɔplasti] *f* plastic surgery
autoportrait [otɔpɔrtrɛ] *m* self-portrait
auto-propul·sé -sée [otɔpropylse] *adj* self-propelled
autopsie [otɔpsi] *f* autopsy
autopsier [otɔpsje] *tr* to perform an autopsy on
autorail [otɔraj] *m* rail car
autorisation [otɔrizasjɔ̃] *f* authorization
autoriser [otɔrize] §96, §100 *tr* to authorize ‖ *ref*—**s'autoriser de** to take as authority, to base one's opinion on
autoritaire [otɔritɛr] *adj* authoritarian, bossy
autorité [otɔrite] *f* authority
autoroute [otɔrut] *f* superhighway; **autoroute à péage** turnpike
autosable [otɔsabl] *m* dune buggy
auto-stop [otɔstɔp] *m* hitchhiking; **faire de l'auto-stop** to hitchhike
auto-stop·peur [otɔstɔpœr] **-peuse** [pøz] *mf* (*pl* **-peurs -peuses**) hitchhiker
autostrade [otɔstrad] *f* superhighway

autour [otur] *m* goshawk ‖ *adv* around; **autour de** around; about

autre [otr] *adj indef* other; **autre chose** (coll) something else; **nous autres** we, e.g., **nous autres Américains** we Americans; **vous autres** you ‖ *pron indef* other; **d'autres** others; **j'en ai vu bien d'autres** I have seen worse than that; **l'un l'autre, les uns les autres** each other, one another; **l'un et l'autre** both; **l'un ou l'autre** either; **ni l'un ni l'autre** neither; **quelqu'un d'autre** someone else; **un autre** another

autrefois [otrəfwa] *adv* formerly, of old; **d'autrefois** of yore

autrement [otrəmɑ̃] *adv* otherwise

Autriche [otriʃ] *f* Austria; **l'Autriche** Austria

autri·chien [otriʃjɛ̃] **-chienne** [ʃjɛn] *adj* Austrian ‖ (*cap*) *mf* Austrian

autruche [otryʃ] *f* ostrich

autrui [otrɥi] *pron indef* others

auvent [ovɑ̃] *m* canopy (*over door*); flap (*of tent*)

aux [o] §77 to the

auxiliaire [oksiljɛr] *adj* auxiliary, stand-by; ancillary ‖ *m* (gram) auxiliary ‖ *f* noncombatant unit

aux·quels -quelles [okɛl] §78

avachir [avaʃir] *tr* to make limp, flabby ‖ *ref* to become limp, flabby

aval [aval] *m* lower waters; **en aval** downstream; **en aval de** below ‖ *m* (*pl* **avals**) endorsement

avalanche [avalɑ̃ʃ] *f* avalanche

avaler [avale] *tr* to swallow ‖ *intr* to go downstream

ava·leur [avalœr] **-leuse** [løz] *mf* swallower; **avaleur de sabres** sword swallower

avaliser [avalize] *tr* to endorse

avance [avɑ̃s] *f* advance; **en avance** fast (*clock*)

avan·cé -cée [avɑ̃se] *adj* advanced; overripe; tainted (*meat*)

avancement [avɑ̃smɑ̃] *m* advancement

avancer [avɑ̃se] §51 *tr, intr, & ref* to advance

avanie [avani] *f* snub, insult; **essuyer une avanie** to swallow an affront

avant [avɑ̃] *adj invar* front ‖ *m* front; (aer) nose; (naut) bow; **d'avant** previous; **en avant** forward; **en avant de** in front of, ahead of ‖ *adv* before; **avant de** (with *inf*) before; **avant que** + *subj* before; **bien** (or **très**) **avant dans** late into; far into; deep into; **plus avant** farther on ‖ *prep* before; **avant Jésus-Christ (av. J.-C.)** before Christ (B.C.)

avantage [avɑ̃taʒ] *m* advantage; (tennis) add; **avantages en nature** payment in kind; **avantages sociaux** fringe benefits

avanta·geux [avɑ̃taʒø] **-geuse** [ʒøz] *adj* advantageous; bargain (*price*); becoming (*e.g., hairdo*); conceited (*manner*)

avant-bras [avɑ̃bra] *m invar* forearm

avant-cour [avɑ̃kur] *f* (*pl* **-cours**) front yard

avant-coureur [avɑ̃kurœr] (*pl* **-coureurs**) *adj masc* presaging (*signs*) ‖ *m* forerunner, precursor, harbinger

avant-goût [avɑ̃gu] *m* (*pl* **-goûts**) foretaste

avant-guerre [avɑ̃gɛr] *m & f* (*pl* **-guerres**) prewar period

avant-hier [avɑ̃tjɛr], [avɑ̃jɛr] *adv & m* the day before yesterday

avant-port [avɑ̃pɔr] *m* (*pl* **-ports**) outer harbor

avant-poste [avɑ̃pɔst] *m* (*pl* **-postes**) outpost; **avant-postes** front lines

avant-première [avɑ̃prəmjɛr] *f* (*pl* **-premières**) review (*of a play*); premiere (*for the drama critics*); preview

avant-projet [avɑ̃prɔʒɛ] *m* (*pl* **-projets**) rough draft; draft (*of a law*)

avant-propos [avɑ̃prɔpo] *m invar* foreword

avant-scène [avɑ̃sɛn] *f* (*pl* **-scènes**) forestage, proscenium

avant-toit [avɑ̃twa] *m* (*pl* **-toits**) eave

avant-train [avɑ̃trɛ̃] *m* (*pl* **-trains**) front end, front assembly (*of vehicle*)

avant-veille [avɑ̃vɛj] *f* (*pl* **-veilles**) two days before

avare [avar] *adj* avaricious, miserly; saving, economical ‖ *mf* miser

avarice [avaris] *f* avarice

avari·cieux [avarisjø] **-cieuse** [sjøz] *adj* avaricious

avarie [avari] *f* damage; breakdown; spoilage; (naut) average

avarier [avarje] *tr* to damage; spoil ‖ *ref* to spoil

avatar [avatar] *m* avatar; **avatars** vicissitudes

avec [avɛk] *adv* (coll) with it; (coll) along, with me, etc. ‖ *prep* with

aveline [avlin] *f* filbert

ave·nant [avnɑ̃] **-nante** [nɑ̃t] *adj* gracious, charming; **à l'avenant** in keeping, to match; **à l'avenant de** in accord with ‖ *m* (ins) endorsement; codicil, rider

avènement [avɛnmɑ̃] *m* Advent; accession (*to the throne*)

avenir [avnir] *m* future; **à l'avenir** in the future

Avent [avɑ̃] *m* Advent

aventure [avɑ̃tyr] *f* adventure; **à l'aventure** at random; aimlessly; **d'aventure** by chance; **la bonne aventure** fortunetelling; **par aventure** by chance

aventurer [avɑ̃tyre] *tr* to venture ‖ *ref* to take a chance; **s'aventurer à** to venture to

aventu·reux [avɑ̃tyrø] **-reuse** [røz] *adj* adventurous

aventurier [avɑ̃tyrje] *m* adventurer

aventurière [avɑ̃tyrjɛr] *f* adventuress

avenue [avny] *f* avenue

avé·ré -rée [avere] *adj* established, authenticated

avérer [avere] §10 *tr* to aver ‖ *ref* to prove to be (*e.g., difficult*)

avers [avɛr] *m* heads (*of coin*), face (*of medal*)

averse [avɛrs] *f* shower

aversion [avɛrsjɔ̃] *f* aversion

avertir [avɛrtir] §97, §99 *tr* to warn; **avertir qn de** + *inf* to warn s.o. to + *inf*
avertissement [avɛrtismɑ̃] *m* warning; notification; foreword
avertisseur [avɛrtisœr] *adj masc* warning ‖ *m* alarm; (aut) horn; (theat) callboy; **avertisseur d'incendie** fire alarm
a·veu [avø] *m* (*pl* **-veux**) avowal, confession; consent; **sans aveu** unscrupulous
aveu·glant [avœglɑ̃] **-glante** [glɑ̃t] *adj* blinding
aveugle [avœgl] *adj* blind ‖ *mf* blind person; **en aveugle** without thinking
aveuglement [avœgləmɑ̃] *m* (fig) blindness
aveuglément [avœglemɑ̃] *adv* blindly
aveugler [avœgle] *tr* to blind; dazzle; stop up, plug; board up (*a window*) ‖ *ref*—**s'aveugler sur** to shut one's eyes to
aveuglette [avœglɛt] *adv*—**à l'aveuglette** blindly
aveulir [avølir] *tr* to enervate, deaden ‖ *ref* to become limp, enervated
aveulissement [avølismɑ̃] *m* enervation
aviateur [avjatœr] *m* aviator
aviation [avjasjɔ̃] *f* aviation
aviatrice [avjatris] *f* aviatrix
avide [avid] *adj* avid, eager; greedy; voracious; **avide de** avid for
avidité [avidite] *f* avidity, eagerness; greed; voracity
avilir [avilir] *tr* to debase, dishonor; (com) to lower the price of ‖ §96 *ref* to debase oneself; (com) to deteriorate
avilis·sant [avilisɑ̃] **-sante** [sɑ̃t] *adj* debasing
avilissement [avilismɑ̃] *m* debasement; (com) depreciation
avi·né -née [avine] *adj* drunk
aviner [avine] *tr* to soak (*a new barrel*) with wine ‖ *ref* (coll) to booze
avion [avjɔ̃] *m* airplane; **avion affété, avion nolisé, avion de transport à la demande** charter (air)plane; **avion à réaction** jet; **avion de chasse** fighter plane; **avion fugitif** spy plane; **avion long-courrier** long-range plane; **en avion** by plane; **par avion** air mail
avion-cargo [avjɔ̃kargo] *m* (*pl* **avions-cargos**) cargo liner, freighter
avion-géant [avjɔ̃ʒeɑ̃] *m* jumbo jet
avion-taxi [avjɔ̃taksi] *m* (*pl* **avions-taxis**) taxiplane
aviron [avirɔ̃] *m* oar; **aviron de couple** scull
avis [avi] *m* opinion; advice; notice, warning; decision; **à mon avis** in my opinion; **avis au lecteur** note to the reader; **changer d'avis** to change one's mind
avi·sé -sée [avize] *adj* prudent, shrewd; **bien avisé** well-advised

aviser [avize] §99 *tr* to glimpse, descry; advise, inform, warn ‖ *intr* to decide; **aviser à** to think of, look into; deal with ‖ §97 *ref*—**s'aviser de** to contrive, think up; be on the look-out for; **s'aviser de** + *inf* to take it into one's head to + *inf*
aviso [avizo] *m* dispatch boat, sloop
avivage [avivaʒ] *m* brightening; polishing
aviver [avive] *tr* to revive, stir up (*fire; passions*); brighten (*colors*); (med & fig) to open (*a wound*)
av. J.-C. *abbr* (**avant Jésus-Christ**) B.C.
avo·cat [avɔka] **-cate** [kat] *mf* lawyer; advocate; barrister (Brit); **avocat du diable** devil's advocate ‖ *m* avocado
avoine [avwan] *f* oats
avoir [avwar] *m* wealth; credit side (*of ledger*) ‖ §6 *tr* to have; get; **avoir . . . ans** to be . . . years old, e.g., **mon fils a dix ans** my son is ten years old; **avoir beau** + *inf* §95 no matter how (much) (s.o.) + *v* (*expressing futility*), e.g., **j'ai beau travailler** no matter how much I work; **avoir froid** to be cold; **avoir raison** to be right ‖ *intr*—**avoir à** to have to; **en avoir à** or **contre** to be angry with ‖ *impers*—**il y a** there is, there are, e.g., **il n'y a pas d'espoir** there is no hope ‖ *aux* to have, e.g., **j'ai couru trop vite** I have run too fast
avoisiner [avwazine] *tr* to neighbor, be near
avortement [avɔrtəmɑ̃] *m* abortion; miscarriage
avorter [avɔrte] *intr* to abort; miscarry
avorton [avɔrtɔ̃] *m* runt; (biol) stunt
avoué [avwe] *m* lawyer (*doing notarial work*); solicitor (Brit)
avouer [avwe] §95 *tr* to avow, admit; claim, acknowledge authorship of ‖ *ref* to be admitted; **s'avouer vaincu** to admit defeat
avril [avril] *m* April
axe [aks] *m* axis
axénique [aksenik] *adj* germ-free
axer [akse] *tr* to set on an axis; orient
axiomatique [aksjɔmatik] *adj* axiomatic
axiome [aksjom] *m* axiom
axonge [aksɔ̃ʒ] *f* lard
ayant-droit [ɛjɑ̃drwa] *m* (*pl* **ayants-droit**) claimant; beneficiary
ayez [eje] *v* (**ayons**) see **avoir**
azalée [azale] *f* azalea
azimut or **azimuth** [azimyt] *m* azimuth
azote [azɔt] *m* nitrogen
azo·té -tée [azɔte] *adj* nitrogenous
Aztèques [aztɛk] *mpl* Aztecs
azur [azyr] *adj* & *m* azure
azyme [azim] *adj* unleavened ‖ *m* unleavened bread

B, b [be] *m invar* second letter of the French alphabet

baba [baba] *adj* (coll) flabbergasted, wide-eyed ‖ *m* baba

babeurre [babœr] *m* buttermilk

babil [babil], [babi] *m* babble, chatter; **babil enfantin** baby talk

babillage [babijaʒ] *m* babbling

babil·lard [babijar] **-larde** [jard] *adj* babbling ‖ *mf* babbler ‖ *f* (slang) letter

babiller [babije] *intr* to babble, chatter

babine [babin] *f* chop (*mouth*); **s'essuyer les babines, se lécher les babines** to lick one's chops

babiole [babjɔl] *f* (coll) bauble

bâbord [babɔr] *m* (naut) port, portside; **à bâbord** port; **bâbord armures** port sail

babouche [babuʃ] *f* babouche, slipper

babouin [babwɛ̃] *m* baboon; pimple on the lips; brat

bac [bak] *m* ferryboat; tub, vat; box, bin; tray (*for ice cubes*); drawer (*of refrigerator*); case (*of battery*); (slang) baccalaureate

baccalauréat [bakalɔrea] *m* baccalaureate, bachelor's degree

bacchanale [bakanal] *f* bacchanal

bâche [baʃ] *f* tarpaulin; hot-water tank

bache·lier [baʃəlje] **-lière** [ljɛr] *mf* bachelor (*holder of degree*) ‖ *m* (hist) bachelor (*young knight*)

bâcher [baʃe] *tr* to cover with a tarpaulin

bachique [baʃik] *adj* bacchanalian, bacchic; drinking (*song*)

bachot [baʃo] *m* dinghy, punt; (coll) baccalaureate

bachotage [baʃɔtaʒ] *m* (coll) cramming (*for an exam*)

bachoter [baʃɔte] *intr* (coll) to cram

bacille [basil] *m* bacillus

bâclage [baklaʒ] *m* blocking up (*of harbor*); (slang) botching (*of work*)

bâcle [bakl] *f* bolt (*of door*)

bâcler [bakle] *tr* to bolt (*a door*); close up (*a harbor*); (coll) to botch, to hurry through carelessly

bâ·cleur [baklœr] **-cleuse** [kløz] *mf* (coll) botcher

bacon [bakɔ̃] *m* bacon

bactéricide [bakterisid] *adj* bactericidal ‖ *m* bactericide

bactérie [bakteri] *f* bacterium; **bactéries** bacteria

bactériologie [bakterjɔlɔʒi] *f* bacteriology

ba·daud [bado] **-daude** [dod] *mf* rubberneck, gawk, idler

badauder [badode] *intr* to stand and stare

badigeon [badiʒɔ̃] *m* whitewash

badigeonner [badiʒɔne] *tr* to whitewash; (med) to paint (*e.g., the throat*)

ba·din [badɛ̃] **-dine** [din] *adj* sprightly, playful, teasing ‖ *mf* tease ‖ *m* (aer) air-speed indicator ‖ *f* cane, switch

badinage [badinaʒ] *m* banter; **badinage amoureux** necking

badiner [badine] *intr* to joke, tease; trifle, be flippant

badinerie [badinri] *f* teasing; childishness

baffe [baf] *f* (coll) slap, blow, cuff

bafouer [bafwe] *tr* to heckle, humiliate

bafouiller [bafuje] *intr* (coll) to stammer, mumble, babble

bâfrer [bafre] *tr & intr* (slang) to guzzle

bagage [bagaʒ] *m* baggage; **bagages** baggage, luggage; **bagages à main** hand baggage; **bagages non accompagnés** baggage sent on ahead; **menus bagages** hand luggage; **plier bagage** to pack one's bags; (coll) to scram; (coll) to kick the bucket

bagarre [bagar] *f* brawl, row, riot; **chercher la bagarre** (coll) to be looking for a fight

bagarrer [bagare] *intr & ref* to riot; (coll) to brawl, scrap, scuffle

bagar·reur [bagarœr] **-reuse** [røz] *mf* (coll) rioter, brawler

bagatelle [bagatɛl] *f* trifle, bagatelle; frivolity ‖ *interj* nonsense!

bagnard [baɲar] *m* convict

bagne [baɲ] *m* penitentiary, penal colony; (nav) prison ship; (slang) sweatshop

bagnole [baɲɔl] *f* (slang) jalopy

bagou [bagu] *m* (coll) gift of gab

bague [bag] *f* ring; cigar band; (mach) collar, sleeve; **bague de fiançailles** engagement ring

baguenauder [bagnode] *intr* to waste time, fool around ‖ *ref* (coll) to wander about

baguer [bage] *tr* to band (*a tree*); baste (*cloth*)

baguette [bagɛt] *f* stick, switch, rod; baton; long thin loaf of bread; chopstick; **baguette de fée** fairy wand; **baguettes de tambour** drumsticks; **mener qn à la baguette** (coll) to lead s.o. by the nose; **passer par les baguettes** to run the gauntlet

baguier [bagje] *m* jewel box

bahut [bay] *m* trunk, chest; cupboard; (slang) high school

bai baie [bɛ] *adj* bay (*horse*) ‖ *m* bay; berry; bayberry; bay window

baignade [beɲad] *m* bathing, swimming; swimming hole, bathing spot

baigner [beɲe] *tr* to bathe; wash (*the coast*) ‖ *intr* to be immersed, soak ‖ *ref* to bathe; go bathing

bai·gneur [beɲœr] **-gneuse** [ɲøz] *mf* bather; vacationist at a spa or seaside resort; bathhouse attendant ‖ *m* doll

baignoire [beɲwar] *f* bathtub; (theat) orchestra box

bail [baj] *m* (*pl* **baux** [bo]) lease; **passer un bail** to sign a lease; **prendre à bail** to lease

bâillement [bajmɑ̃] *m* yawn

bailler [baje] *tr*—**vous me la baillez belle** (coll) you're pulling my leg

bâiller [baje] *intr* to yawn; be ajar, be half open

bail·leur [bajœr] **-leresse** [jərɛs] *mf* lessor; **bailleur de fonds** lender

bailli [baji] *m* bailiff

bailliage [bajaʒ] *m* bailiwick

bâillon [bɑjɔ̃] *m* gag, muzzle

bâaillonner [bɑjɔne] *tr* to gag; (fig) to muzzle

bain [bɛ̃] *m* bath; **bain de soleil** sun bath; **bain de vapeur** steam bath; **bain moussant, bain de mousse** bubble bath; **bains** watering place, spa; bathing establishment; **être dans le bain** (coll) to be in hot water

bain·marie [bɛ̃mari] *m* (*pl* **bains-marie**) double boiler, bain-marie

baïonnette [bajɔnɛt] *f* bayonet

baiser [beze], [bɛze] *m* kiss ‖ *tr* (vulg) to have sex with; (archaic) to kiss

baisoter [bɛzɔte] *tr* (coll) to keep on kissing ‖ *ref* (coll) to bill and coo

baisse [bɛs] *f* fall; **jouer à la baisse** (com) to bear the market

baissement [bɛsmɑ̃] *m* lowering

baisser [bɛse] *m* lowering; **baisser du rideau** curtain fall ‖ *tr* to lower; take in (*sail*); dim (*headlights*) ‖ *intr* to fall, drop, sink ‖ *ref* to bend, stoop

baissier [bɛsje] *m* bear (*on the stock exchange*)

bajoue [baʒu] *f* jowl

bal [bal] *m* (*pl* **bals**) ball, dance; **bal travesti** fancy-dress ball

balade [balad] *f* stroll; **balade en auto** joy ride

balader [balade] *ref* to go for a stroll; **se balader en auto** to go joy-riding

bala·deur [baladœr] **-deuse** [døz] *adj* strolling ‖ *mf* stroller ‖ *m* gear; Walkman ‖ *f* cart (*of street vendor*); drop-cord light

baladin [baladɛ̃] *m* mountebank, showman; oaf

balafre [balɑfr] *f* gash, scar

balafrer [balafre] *tr* to gash, scar

balai [balɛ] *m* broom; **balai à laver** mop; **balai de sorcière** witches'-broom; **balai électrique** vacuum cleaner; **balai mécanique** carpet sweeper; **donner un coup de balai** to make a clean sweep of (*s.th.*); to kick (*s.o.*) out

balai-éponge [balɛepɔ̃ʒ] *m* (*pl* **balais-éponges**) mop

balance [balɑ̃s] *f* balance; scales; **faire la balance de** (bk) to balance; **la Balance** (astr, astrol) Libra

balancement [balɑ̃smɑ̃] *m* swaying, teetering; (fig) indecision, wavering; (fig) harmony (*of phrase*)

balancer [balɑ̃se] §51, §96 *tr* to balance; move (*arms or legs*) in order to balance; balance (*an account*); weigh (*the pros and cons*); swing, rock; (coll) to fire (*s.o.*); **elle est bien balancée** she is stacked (*well built*) ‖ *intr* to swing, rock; hesitate, waver ‖ *ref* to swing, seesaw; sway, rock; ride (*at anchor*)

balancier [balɑ̃sje] *m* pendulum; balance wheel; pole (*of tightrope walker*)

balançoire [balɑ̃swar] *f* swing; seesaw, teeter-totter; (slang) nonsense

balayage [balɛjaʒ] *m* sweeping; (telv) scanning

balayer [balɛje], [baleje] §49 *tr* to sweep, sweep up; sweep out; scour (*the sea*); (telv) to scan

balayeur [balɛjœr] **balayeuse** [balɛjøz] *mf* sweeper, scavenger ‖ *f* street-cleaning truck

balayures [balɛjyr] *fpl* sweepings

balbutiement [balbysimɑ̃] *m* stammering, mumbling; initial effort

balbutier [balbysje] *tr* to stammer out ‖ *intr* to stammer, mumble

balbuzard [balbyzar] *m* osprey, bald buzzard, sea eagle

balcon [balkɔ̃] *m* balcony; (theat) dress circle

baldaquin [baldakɛ̃] *m* canopy, tester

Baléares [balear] *fpl* Balearic Islands

baleine [balɛn] *f* right whale, whalebone whale; whalebone; rib (*of umbrella*); stay (*of a corset*)

baleinier [balɛnje] *m* whaling vessel

baleinière [balɛnjɛr] *f* whaleboat; lifeboat

balisage [balizaʒ] *m* (aer) ground lights; (naut) buoys

balise [baliz] *f* buoy, marker; ground light, beacon; landing signal

baliser [balize] *tr* to furnish with markers, buoys, landing lights, beacons, or radio signals

balistique [balistik] *adj* ballistic ‖ *f* ballistics

baliverne [balivɛrn] *f* nonsense, humbug

balkanique [balkanik] *adj* Balkan

ballade [balad] *f* ballade

bal·lant [balɑ̃] **-lante** [lɑ̃t] *adj* waving, swinging, dangling ‖ *m* oscillation, shaking

balle [bal] *f* ball; bullet; hull, chaff; bale; (tennis) match point; **balle traçante** tracer bullet; **prendre** or **saisir la balle au bond** to seize time by the forelock

ballerine [balrin] *f* ballerina

ballet [balɛ] *m* ballet

ballon [balɔ̃] *m* balloon; ball; football, soccer ball; round-bottom flask; rounded mountaintop; **ballon d'essai** trial balloon

ballonner [balɔne] *tr, intr,* & *ref* to balloon

ballot [balo] *m* pack; bundle; (slang) blockhead, chump

ballottage [balɔtaʒ] *m* tossing, shaking; second ballot

ballotter [balɔte] *tr* & *intr* to toss about

balnéaire [balneɛr] *adj* seaside

ba·lourd [balur] **-lourde** [lurd] *adj* awkward, lumpish ‖ *mf* blockhead, bumpkin ‖ *m* wobble

balte [balt] *adj* Baltic ‖ (*cap*) *mf* Balt

Baltique [baltik] *f* Baltic (*sea*)

balustrade [balystrad] *f* balustrade, banisters

balustre [balystr] *m* baluster, banister

bal·zan [balzɑ̃] **-zane** [zan] *adj* white-footed (*horse*) ‖ *f* white spot (*on horse's foot*)

bam·bin [bɑ̃bɛ̃] **-bine** [bin] *mf* (coll) babe
bambo·chard [bɑ̃bɔʃar] **-charde** [ʃard] *adj*
(coll) carousing ‖ *mf* (coll) carouser
bamboche [bɑ̃bɔʃ] *f* (slang) jag, bender
bambocher [bɑ̃bɔʃe] *intr* (coll) to carouse,
go on a spree
bambo·cheur [bɑ̃bɔʃœr] **-cheuse** [ʃøz] *adj*
(coll) carousing ‖ *mf* (coll) carouser
bambou [bɑ̃bu] *m* bamboo
ban [bɑ̃] *m* ban; cadenced applause; **ban de
mariage** banns; **convoquer le ban et
l'arrière-ban** to invite everyone and his
brother; **mettre au ban** to banish, ban
ba·nal -nale [banal] *adj* (*pl* **-nals -nales**)
banal, trite, commonplace ‖ *adj* (*pl* **-naux**
[no] **-nales**) (archaic) common, public, in
common
banaliser [banalize] *tr* to vulgarize, make
commonplace
banalité [banalite] *f* banality; triteness
banane [banan] *f* banana
bananier [bananje] *m* banana tree
banc [bɑ̃] *m* bench; shoal; school (*of fish*);
pew (*reserved for church officials*); (hist)
privy council; **banc de neige** snowbank;
être sur les bancs to go to high school
bancaire [bɑ̃kɛr] *adj* banking, of banks
ban·cal -cale [bɑ̃kal] *adj* (*pl* **-cals -cales**)
bowlegged, bandy-legged
bandage [bɑ̃daʒ] *m* bandage; bandaging;
truss; tire (*of metal or rubber*)
bande [bɑ̃d] *f* band; movie film; recording
tape; cushion (*in billiards*); wrapper (*of a
newspaper*); strip (*of stamps*); **bande dessinée** comic strip; **bande génératrice,
bande mère** master tape; **bande magne-
tique** recording tape; tape recording;
bande sonore or **parlante** sound track;
bande vidéo videotape; **donner de la
bande** to heel, to list; **faire bande à part**
to keep to oneself
bande-annonce [bɑ̃danɔ̃s] *f* (**bandes-
annonces**) film clip
ban·deau [bɑ̃do] *m* (*pl* **-deaux**) blindfold;
headband; bending (*of a bow*); **bandeau
royal** diadem; **bandeaux** hair parted in
the middle
bander [bɑ̃de] *tr* to band, put a band on;
bandage; blindfold; bend (*a bow*); put a
tire on; draw taut; (vulg) to have or get a
hard-on ‖ *ref* to band together; put up
resistance; **elle est bandante** (vulg) she is
a sexpot
banderole [bɑ̃derɔl] *f* pennant, streamer;
strap (*of gun*)
bandière [bɑ̃djɛr] *f* battle, e.g., **front de
bandière** battle front
bandit [bɑ̃di] *m* bandit
bandoulière [bɑ̃duljɛr] *f* shoulder strap,
sling; **en bandoulière** slung over the
shoulder
banlieue [bɑ̃ljø] *f* suburbs; **de banlieue**
suburban
banlieu·sard [bɑ̃ljøzar] **-sarde** [zard] *mf*
suburbanite (*especially of a Parisian suburb*)
banne [ban] *f* awning (*of store*)

ban·ni -nie [bani] *adj* banished, exiled ‖ *mf*
exile
bannière [banjɛr] *f* banner, flag
bannir [banir] *tr* to banish
bannissement [banismɑ̃] *m* banishment
banque [bɑ̃k] *f* bank; **banque de données**
(comp) data bank; **banque des yeux** eye
bank; **banque du sang** blood bank; **faire
sauter la banque** to break the bank
banqueroute [bɑ̃krut] *f* bankruptcy (*with
blame for negligence or fraud*)
banquerou·tier [bɑ̃krutje] **-tière** [tjɛr] *adj*
& *mf* bankrupt (*with culpability*)
banquet [bɑ̃kɛ] *m* banquet
banqueter [bɑ̃kte] §34 *intr* to banquet
banquette [bɑ̃kɛt] *f* seat (*in a train, bus,
automobile*); bank (*of earth or sand*); bunker (*in a golf course*); **banquette arrière**
back seat; **banquette de tir** (mil) emplacement for shooting; **jouer devant les
banquettes** to play to an empty house
ban·quier [bɑ̃kje] **-quière** [kjɛr] *mf* banker
banquise [bɑ̃kiz] *f* pack ice
banquiste [bɑ̃kist] *m* charlatan, quack
baptême [batɛm] *m* baptism; christening;
**baptême de la ligne, baptême des tro-
piques** or **du tropique** polliwog initiation
baptiser [batize] *tr* to baptize; christen;
(slang) to dilute (*wine*) with water
baptis·mal -male [batismal] *adj* (*pl* **-maux**
[mo]) baptismal
baptistaire [batistɛr] *adj* baptismal (*certificate*)
baptiste [batist] *mf* Baptist
baptistère [batistɛr] *m* baptistery
baquet [bakɛ] *m* wooden tub, bucket; (aut)
bucket seat
bar [bar] *m* bar; (ichth) bass, perch; **bar
payant** cash bar
baragouin [baragwɛ̃] *m* (slang) gibberish
baragouiner [baragwine] *tr* (coll) to murder
(*a language*); (coll) to stumble through (*a
speech*) ‖ *intr* (coll) to jabber
baraque [barak] *f* booth, stall; shanty, hovel
baraterie [baratri] *f* barratry
baratin [baratɛ̃] *m* (slang) blah-blah, hokum
baratte [barat] *f* churn
baratter [barate] *tr* to churn
Barbade [barbad] *f* Barbados; **la Barbade**
Barbados
barbare [barbar] *adj* barbarous, barbaric,
savage ‖ *mf* barbarian
barbaresque [barbarɛsk] *adj* of Barbary
barbarie [barbari] *f* barbarity, barbarism ‖
(*cap*) *f* Barbary
barbarisme [barbarism] *m* barbarism (*in
speech or writing*)
barbe [barb] *f* beard; bristle; whiskers (*of an
animal*); barbel; **barbes** vane (*of a
feather*); deckle edge; **faire q.ch. à la
barbe de qn** to do s.th. right under the
nose of s.o.; **rire dans sa barbe** to laugh
up one's sleeve; **se faire la barbe** to
shave ‖ *interj* **c'est la barbe!** what a
bore!; **la barbe!** shut up!
bar·beau [barbo] *m* (*pl* **-beaux**) cornflower;
(ichth) barbel; (slang) pimp

barbe·lé -lée [barbəle] *adj* barbed ‖ **barbelés** *mpl* barbed wire
bar·bet [barbɛ] **-bette** [bɛt] *mf* water spaniel
barbiche [barbiʃ] *f* goatee
barbier [barbje] *m* barber
barbillon [barbijɔ̃] *m* barb
barbiturique [barbityrik] *m* barbiturate
barbon [barbɔ̃] *m* (pej) old fogy
barboter [barbɔte] *intr* to paddle *(like ducks)*; wallow *(like pigs)*; bubble *(like carbonated water)*; (coll) to splutter; (slang) to steal
barbo·teur [barbɔtœr] **-teuse** [tøz] *mf* (slang) muddler ‖ *m* duck; wash bottle ‖ *f* rompers
barbouiller [barbuje] *tr* to smear, blur; daub; (coll) to scribble; **barbouiller le cœur à** to nauseate
barbouil·leur [barbujœr] **-leuse** [jøz] *mf* dauber; messy person; scribbler
barbouze [barbuz] *f* (slang) beard; (slang) secret agent; (slang) bodyguard
bar·bu -bue [barby] *adj* bearded
bard [bar] *m* handbarrow
bardage [bardaʒ] *m* siding *(of house)*
bardane [bardan] *f* burdock
barde [bard] *m* bard ‖ *f* blanket of bacon
bar·deau [bardo] *m (pl* **-deaux)** shingle; lath
barder [barde] *tr* to carry with a handbarrow; armor *(a horse)*; blanket *(a roast)*; **barder de** to cover with ‖ *intr* to rage
bardot [bardo] *m* hinny
barème [barɛm] *m* schedule *(of rates, taxes, etc.)*
baréter [barete] §10 *intr* to trumpet *(like an elephant)*
barge [barʒ] *f* barge; haystack; godwit, black-tailed godwit
barguigner [barɡiɲe] *intr* to shilly-shally, have trouble deciding
bargui·gneur [barɡiɲœr] **-gneuse** [ɲøz] *mf* shilly-shallyer, procrastinator
baricaut [bariko] *m* small cask, keg
baril [baril], [bari] *m* small barrel, cask, keg
barillet [barije] *m* small barrel; revolver cylinder; spring case
bariolage [barjɔlaʒ] *m* (coll) motley, mixture of colors
bario·lé -lée [barjɔle] *adj* speckled, multicolored, variegated
barioler [barjɔle] *tr* to variegate
bariolure [barjɔlyr] *f* clashing colors, motley
bar·man [barman] *m (pl* **-men** [mɛn] or **-mans)** bartender
baromètre [barɔmɛtr] *m* barometer
barométrique [barɔmetrik] *adj* barometric
baron [barɔ̃] *m* baron
baronne [barɔn] *f* baroness
baroque [barɔk] *adj* & *m* baroque
baroud [barud] *m* rumble *(gang war)*; (mil) **baroud d'honneur** gallant last stand
barque [bark] *f* boat

barrage [baraʒ] *m* dam; barrage, cordon *(of police)*; tollgate; barricade, roadblock, checkpoint; (sports) playoff
barre [bar], [bar] *f* bar; crossbar *(of a t)*; tiller, helm; bore *(tidal flood)*; **barre de contrôle** (nucl) control rod; **barre de dopage** (nucl) booster rod; **barre de justice** rod to hold shackles; **barre des témoins** witness stand; **barre du gouvernail** helm; **barres** (typ) parallels; **jouer aux barres** to play prisoner's base
bar·reau [baro] *m (pl* **-reaux)** bar, crossbar, rail, rung *(of ladder or chair)*; (law) bar
barrer [bare] *tr* to cross out, strike out, cancel; cross *(a t; a check in a British bank)*; bar *(the door; the way)*; block off *(a street)*; dam *(a stream)*; steer *(a boat)*
barrette [barɛt], [barɛt] *f* biretta; bar; slide; pin; name tag
barreur [barœr] *m* helmsman
barricade [barikad] *f* barricade
barricader [barikade] *tr* to barricade
barrière [barjɛr] *f* barrier; gate *(of a town; of a grade crossing)*; tollgate; neighborhood shopping district
barrique [barik] *f* cask; hogshead, large barrel
barrir [barir] *intr* to trumpet *(like an elephant)*
barrot [baro] *m* beam *(of a ship)*
baryton [baritɔ̃] *m* baritone; alto *(saxhorn)*
baryum [barjɔm] *m* barium
bas [ba] **basse** [bas] *adj* low; base, vile; cloudy *(weather)*; *(when standing before noun) adj* low; base, vile; early *(age)* ‖ *m* stocking; lower part, bottom; **à bas . . . !** down with . . . !; **bas de casse** (typ) lower case; **bas de laine** nest egg, savings; **en bas** at the bottom; downstairs ‖ *f* see basse ‖ **bas** *adv* softly; down, low
ba·sal -sale [bazal] *adj (pl* **-saux** [zo])** basic; basal *(metabolism)*
basalte [bazalt] *m* basalt
basa·né -née [bazane] *adj* tanned, sunburned
basaner [bazane] *tr* to tan, sunburn
bas-bleu [bablø] *m (pl* **-bleus)** bluestocking
bas-côté [bakote] *m (pl* **-côtés)** aisle *(of a church)*; footpath *(beside a road)*
bascule [baskyl] *f* scale; rocker; seesaw
basculement [baskylmɑ̃] *m* rocking, seesawing, tipping; dimming
basculer [baskyle] *tr* to tip over ‖ *intr* to tip over; seesaw, rock, swing; **faire basculer** to dim *(the headlights)*
bas-dessus [badəsy] *m* mezzo-soprano
base [baz] *f* base; basis; **à la base** at heart, to the core; **base de données** (comp) data base; **de base** basic
base-ball [bɛzbol] *m* baseball
baser [baze] *tr* to base; ground, found *(an opinion)* ‖ *ref* to be based
bas-fond [bafɔ̃] *m (pl* **-fonds)** lowland; shallows; **bas-fonds** dregs, underworld; slums
basilic [bazilik] *m* basil

basilique [bazilik] *f* basilica
basin [bazɛ̃] *m* dimity
basique [bazik] *adj* basic, alkaline
basket [baskɛt] *m* basketball
basketteur [baskɛtœr] *m* basketball player
basoche [bazɔʃ] *f* law, legal profession
basque [bask] *adj* Basque ‖ *m* Basque (*language*) ‖ *f* coattail ‖ (*cap*) *mf* Basque (*person*)
basse [bɑs] *f* shoal; tuba; (mus) bass; **basse chiffrée** (mus) figured bass
basse-contre [baskɔ̃tr] *f* (*pl* **basses-contre**) basso profundo
basse-cour [baskur] *f* (*pl* **basses-cours**) barnyard, farmyard; barnyard animals; poultry yard
bassesse [basɛs] *f* baseness; base act
bassin [basɛ̃] *m* basin; dock; artificial lake; collection plate; pelvis; **bassin à flot** tidal basin; **bassin de lit** bedpan; **bassin de radoub** dry dock; **bassin hygiénique** bedpan
bassine [basin] *f* dishpan
bassinoire [basinwar] *f* bedwarmer
basson [basɔ̃] *m* bassoon
baste [bast] *m* ace of clubs; saddle basket ‖ *interj* enough!
bastille [bastij] *f* small fortress
bastion [bastjɔ̃] *m* bastion
bastonnade [bastɔnad] *f* beating
bas-ventre [bavɑ̃tr] *m* abdomen, lower part of the belly
bât [ba] *m* packsaddle
bataclan [bataklɑ̃] *m*—**tout le bataclan** (slang) the whole caboodle
bataille [bataj], [bataj] *f* battle, fight
batailler [bataje], [bataje] *intr* to battle, fight
batail·leur [batajœr] -**leuse** [jøz] *adj* belligerent ‖ *mf* fighter
bataillon [batajɔ̃] *m* battalion
bâ·tard [batar] -**tarde** [tard] *adj & mf* mongrel; bastard ‖ *m* one-pound loaf of short-length type of bread ‖ *f* cursive handwriting
bâtar·deau [batardo] *m* (*pl* -**deaux**) cofferdam, caisson
ba·teau [bato] *m* (*pl* -**teaux**) boat; **bateau automobile** motorboat, motor launch; **bateau à vapeur** steamboat; **bateau à voiles** sailboat; **bateau de guerre** warship; **bateau de pêche** fishing boat; **bateau de sauvetage** lifeboat; **monter un bateau à qn** (slang) to pull s.o.'s leg; **par (le) bateau** by boat
bateau-citerne [batositɛrn] *m* (*pl* **bateaux-citernes**) tanker
bateau-feu [batofø] *m* (*pl* **bateaux-feux**) lightship
bateau-maison [batomezɔ̃] *m* (*pl* **bateaux-maisons**) houseboat
bateau-mouche [batomuʃ] *m* (*pl* **bateaux-mouches**) excursion boat
bateau-pompe [batopɔ̃p] *m* (*pl* **bateaux-pompes**) fireboat
batelage [batlaʒ] *m* lighterage; juggling; tumbling

batelée [batle] *f* boatload
bateler [batle] §34 *tr* to lighter ‖ *intr* to juggle; tumble
bateleur [batlœr] -**leuse** [løz] *mf* juggler; tumbler
bate·lier [batlje] -**lière** [ljɛr] *mf* skipper ‖ *m* boatman; ferryman
batellerie [batɛlri] *f* lighterage
bâter [bate] *tr* to packsaddle
bath [bat] *adj* (slang) A-one, swell
bâ·ti -tie [bati] *adj* built; **bien bâti** well-built (*person*) ‖ *m* frame; basting (*thread*); basted garment
batifoler [batifɔle] *intr* (coll) to frolic
bâtiment [batimɑ̃] *m* building; ship
bâtir [batir] *tr* to build; baste, tack ‖ *ref* to be built
bâtisse [batis] *f* masonry, construction; building, edifice; ramshackle house
bâtis·seur [batisœr] -**seuse** [søz] *mf* builder
bâton [batɔ̃] *m* stick; baton; staff, cane; rung (*of a chair*); stroke (*of a pen*); stick (*of gum*); **à bâtons rompus** by fits and starts; impromptu; (archit) with zigzag molding; **bâton de reprise** (mus) repeat bar; **bâton de rouge à lèvres** lipstick; **bâton de vieillesse** helper or nurse for the aged; **mettre des bâtons dans les roues** to throw a monkey wrench into the works
bâtonner [batɔne] *tr* to cudgel; cross out
bâtonnet [batɔnɛ] *m* rod (*in the retina*); chopstick
battage [bataʒ] *m* beating; threshing; churning; (slang) ballyhoo
bat·tant [batɑ̃] -**tante** [tɑ̃t] *adj* beating; pelting, driving; swinging (*door*) ‖ *m* flap; clapper (*of bell*); **à deux battants** double (*door*)
batte [bat] *f* mallet, beater; dasher, plunger; bench for beating clothes; wooden sword (*for slapstick comedy*); (sports) bat; **batte de l'or** goldbeating
battement [batmɑ̃] *m* beating, beat; throbbing, pulsing; clapping (*of hands*); dance step; wait (*e.g., between trains*)
batterie [batri] *f* (elec, mil, mus) battery; train service (*in one direction*); ruse, scheming; **batterie de cuisine** kitchen utensils
batteur [batœr] *m* beater; thresher; (sports) batter; **batteur de grève** beachcomber; **batteur de pieux** pile driver; **batteur électrique** electric mixer
batteuse [batøz] *f* threshing machine
battoir [batwar] *m* bat, beetle (*for washing clothes*); tennis racket
battre [batr] §7 *tr* to beat; clap (*one's hands*); flap, flutter; wink; bang; pound (*the sidewalk*); search; shuffle (*the cards*); **battre la mesure** to beat time; **battre monnaie** to mint money ‖ *intr* to beat ‖ *ref* to fight
bau [bo] *m* (*pl* **baux**) beam (*of a ship*)
baudet [bodɛ] *m* ass, donkey; stallion ass; sawhorse; (slang) jackass, idiot
baudrier [bodrije] *m* shoulder belt

bauge [boʒ] *f* lair, den; clay and straw mortar; (coll) pigsty

baume [bom] *m* balsam; (*consolation*) balm

ba·vard [bavar] **-varde** [vard] *adj* talkative, loquacious; tattletale ‖ *mf* chatterer; tattletale; gossip

bavardage [bavardaʒ] *m* chattering; gossiping

bavarder [bavarde] *intr* to chatter; gossip

bava·rois [bavarwa] **-roise** [rwaz] *adj* Bavarian ‖ (*cap*) *mf* Bavarian (*person*)

bave [bav] *f* dribble, froth, spittle; (fig) slander

baver [bave] *intr* to dribble, drool; run (*like a pen*); **baver sur** to besmirch

bavette [bavɛt] *f* bib

ba·veux [bavø] **-veuse** [vøz] *adj* drooling; tendentious, wordy; undercooked

Bavière [bavjɛr] *f* Bavaria; **la Bavière** Bavaria

bavocher [bavɔʃe] *intr* to smear

bavochure [bavɔʃyr] *f* smear

bavure [bavyr] *f* bur (*of metal*); smear

bayer [baje] §49 *intr*—**bayer aux corneilles** to gawk, stargaze

bazar [bazar] *m* bazaar; five-and-ten; **tout le bazar** (slang) the whole shebang

béant [beɑ̃] **béante** [beɑ̃t] *adj* gaping, wide-open

béat [bea] **béate** [beat] *adj* smug, complacent, sanctimonious

béatifier [beatifje] *tr* to beatify

béatitude [beatityd] *f* beatitude

beau [bo] (or **bel** [bɛl] before vowel or mute h) **belle** [bɛl] (*pl* **beaux belles**) *adj* beautiful; handsome; **bel et bien** truly, for sure; **de plus belle** more than ever; **il fait beau** it is nice out, we are having fair weather; **tout beau!** steady!, easy does it! ‖ (when standing before noun) *adj* beautiful; handsome; fine, good; considerable, large, long; fair (*weather*); odd-numbered or recto (*page*) ‖ *mf* fair one; **faire le beau, faire la belle** to strut, swagger; sit up and beg (*said of a dog*); **la belle** the deciding match; **la Belle au bois dormant** Sleeping Beauty ‖ **beau** *adv*—**il a beau parler** it is no use for him to speak ‖ **belle** *adv*—**la bailler belle** (slang) to tell a whopper; **l'échapper belle** to have a narrow escape

beaucoup [boku] §91 *adv* much, many; **beaucoup de** much, many; **de beaucoup** by far

beau-fils [bofis] *m* (*pl* **beaux-fils**) son-in-law; stepson

beau-frère [bofrɛr] *m* (*pl* **beaux-frères**) brother-in-law

beau-père [bopɛr] *m* (*pl* **beaux-pères**) father-in-law; stepfather

beau-petit-fils [bopətifis] *m* (*pl* **beaux-petits-fils**) son of a stepson or of a stepdaughter

beaupré [bopre] *m* bowsprit

beauté [bote] *f* beauty; **beauté du diable** (coll) bloom of youth; **se faire une beauté** (coll) to doll up

beaux-arts [bozar] *mpl* fine arts

beaux-parents [boparɑ̃] *mpl* in-laws

bébé [bebe] *m* baby; **bébé éprouvette** test-tube baby

bec [bɛk] *m* beak; nozzle, jet, burner; point (*of a pen*); (mus) mouthpiece; (slang) beak, face, mouth; **avoir bon bec** to be gossipy; **claquer du bec** (coll) to be hungry; **clore, clouer le bec à qn** (coll) to shut s.o. up; **tomber sur un bec** (coll) to encounter an unforeseen obstacle

bécane [bekan] *f* (coll) bike, bicycle

bécarre [bekar] *m* (mus) natural

bécasse [bekas] *f* woodcock; (slang) stupid woman

bécas·seau [bekaso] *m* (*pl* **bécas-seaux**) sandpiper

bec-de-cane [bɛkdəkan] *m* (*pl* **becs-de-cane**) door handle; flat-nosed pliers

bec-de-corbeau [bɛkdəkɔrbo] *m* (*pl* **becs-de-corbeau**) wire cutters

bec-de-corbin [bɛkdəkɔrbɛ̃] *m* (*pl* **becs-de-corbin**) crowbar

bec-de-lièvre [bɛkdəljɛvr] *m* (*pl* **becs-de-lièvre**) harelip

bêche [bɛʃ] *f* spade

bêcher [beʃe] *tr* to dig; (slang) to run (*s.th.*) down, to give (*s.o.*) a dig

bê·cheur [beʃœr] **-cheuse** [ʃøz] *mf* (coll) detractor, critic; (slang) stuffed shirt

bêchoir [beʃwar] *m* hoe

bécotage [bekotaʒ] *m* smooching, necking

bécoter [bekote] *tr* to give (*s.o.*) a peck or little kiss on the cheek

becqueter [bɛkte] §34 *tr* to peck at; (coll) to eat ‖ *ref* to bill and coo

bedaine [bədɛn] *f* paunch, beer belly

bédane [bedan] *m* cold chisel

be·deau [bədo] *m* (*pl* **-deaux**) beadle

bé·douin [bedwɛ̃] **-douine** [dwin] *adj* Bedouin ‖ (*cap*) *mf* Bedouin (*person*)

bée [be] *adj*—**bouche bée** mouth agape, flabbergasted ‖ *f* penstock

beffroi [befrwa] *m* belfry

bégaiement [begɛmɑ̃] *m* stammering, stuttering

bégayer [begeje] §49 *tr & intr* to stammer, stutter

bègue [bɛg] *adj* stammering, stuttering ‖ *mf* stammerer

bégueter [begte] §2 *intr* to bleat

bégueule [begœl] *adj* (coll) prudish ‖ *f* (coll) prudish woman

béguin [begɛ̃] *m* hood, cap; sweetheart; (coll) infatuation

béguine [begin] *f* Beguine; sanctimonious woman

beige [bɛʒ] *adj & m* beige

beignet [beɲɛ] *m* fritter

béjaune [beʒon] *m* nestling; greenhorn, novice, ninny

bel [bɛl] *adj* see **beau**

bêlement [bɛlmɑ̃] *m* bleat, bleating

bêler [bɛle] *intr* to bleat

belette [bəlɛt] *f* weasel

belge [bɛlʒ] *adj* Belgian ‖ (*cap*) *mf* Belgian (*person*)

Belgique [bɛlʒik] *f* Belgium; **la Belgique** Belgium

bélier [belje] *m* ram; battering ram; **le Bélier** (astr, astrol) Aries

bélière [beljɛr] *f* sheepbell

bélinogramme [belinɔgram] *m* Wirephoto (*trademark*)

bélinographe [belinɔgraf] *m* Wirephoto transmitter

bélître [belitr] *m* scoundrel

belladone [bɛladɔn] *f* belladonna

bellâtre [bɛlɑtr] *adj* foppish ‖ *m* fop

belle [bɛl] *adj* see **beau**

belle-dame [bɛldam] *f* belladonna

belle-de-jour [bɛldəʒur] *f* (*pl* **belles-de-jour**) morning glory

belle-de-nuit [bɛldənɥi] *f* (*pl* **belles-de-nuit**) marvel-of-Peru

belle-d'un-jour [bɛldœ̃ʒur] *f* (*pl* **belles-d'un-jour**) day lily

belle-fille [bɛlfij] *f* (*pl* **belles-filles**) daughter-in-law; stepdaughter

belle-mère [bɛlmɛr] *f* (*pl* **belles-mères**) mother-in-law; stepmother

belle-petite-fille [bɛlpətitfij] *f* (*pl* **belles-petites-filles**) daughter of a stepson or of a stepdaughter

belles-lettres [bɛllɛtr] *fpl* belles-lettres, literature

belle-sœur [bɛlsœr] *f* (*pl* **belles-sœurs**) sister-in-law

belliciste [belisist] *mf* warmonger

belligé·rant [beliʒerɑ̃] **-rante** [rɑ̃t] *adj & m* belligerent

belli-queux [belikø] **-queuse** [køz] *adj* bellicose, warlike

bel·lot [bɛlo] **-lote** [lɔt] *adj* pretty, cute; dapper

bémol [bemɔl] *adj invar & m* (mus) flat

bémoliser [bemɔlize] *tr* to flat (*a note*); provide (*a key signature*) with flats

ben [bɛ̃] *interj* (slang) well!

bénédicité [benedisite] *m* grace (*before a meal*)

bénédic·tin [benediktɛ̃] **-tine** [tin] *adj & m* Benedictine ‖ (*cap*) *f* Benedictine (liqueur)

bénédiction [benediksjɔ̃] manna from heaven

bénéfice [benefis] *m* profit; benefit; benefice; parsonage, rectory; **à bénéfice** benefit (*performance*); **sous bénéfice d'inventaire** with grave reservations

bénéficiaire [benefisjɛr] *adj* profit, e.g., **marge bénéficiaire** profit margin ‖ *mf* beneficiary

bénéficier [benefisje] *intr* to profit, benefit

benêt [bənɛ] *adj masc* simple-minded ‖ *m* simpleton, numskull

bénévolement [benevɔlmɑ̃] *adv* voluntarily, free of charge, for nothing

bé·nin [benɛ̃] **-nigne** [niɲ] *adj* benign; mild, slight; benignant, accommodating

béni-oui-oui [beniwiwi] *mpl* yes men

bénir [benir] *tr* to bless, to consecrate

bé·nit [beni] **-nite** [nit] *adj* consecrated (*bread*); holy (*water*)

bénitier [benitje] *m* font (*for holy water*)

benja·min [bɛ̃ʒamɛ̃] **-mine** [min] *mf* baby (*the youngest child*) ‖ (*cap*) *m* Benjamin

benne [bɛn] *f* bucket, bin, hopper; dumper; cage (*in mine*); **benne preneuse** (mach) scoop, jaws (*of crane*)

be·noît [bənwa] **-noîte** [nwat] *adj* indulgent; sanctimonious ‖ (*cap*) *m* Benedict

benzène [bɛ̃zɛn] *m* (chem) benzene

benzine [bɛ̃zin] *f* benzine

béquille [bekij] *f* crutch

béquiller [bekije] *intr* to walk with a crutch or crutches

bercail [bɛrkaj] *m* fold, bosom (*of church or family*)

ber·ceau [bɛrso] *m* (*pl* **-ceaux**) cradle; bower; **berceau de verdure** or **de chèvre-feuille** arbor

bercelonnette [bɛrsəlɔnɛt] *f* bassinet

bercer [bɛrse] §51 *tr* to cradle, rock; beguile; assuage (*grief, pain*) ‖ *ref* to rock, swing; delude oneself (*with vain hopes*)

ber·ceur [bɛrsœr] **-ceuse** [søz] *adj* rocking, cradling ‖ *f* rocking chair; cradle song, lullaby

béret [bere] *m* beret

berge [bɛrʒ] *f* bank, steep bank

berger [bɛrʒe] *m* shepherd; shepherd dog

bergère [bɛrʒɛr] *f* shepherdess; wing chair

bergerie [bɛrʒəri] *f* sheepfold; pastoral poem

berle [bɛrl] *f* water parsnip

Berlin [bɛrlɛ̃] *m* Berlin; **Berlin-Est** East Berlin; **Berlin-Ouest** West Berlin

berline [bɛrlin] *f* sedan (*automobile*); berlin (*carriage*)

berlingot [bɛrlɛ̃go] *m* caramel candy; milk carton

berli·nois [bɛrlinwa] **-noise** [nwaz] *adj* Berlin ‖ *mf* Berliner (*person*)

berlue [bɛrly] *f*—**avoir la berlue** (coll) to be blind to what is going on

Bermudes [bɛrmyd] *fpl*—**les Bermudes** Bermuda

bernacle [bɛrnakl] *f* (orn) anatid; (zool) barnacle

berne [bɛrn] *f* hazing; **en berne** at half-mast

berner [bɛrne] *tr* to toss in a blanket; ridicule; fool

bernique [bɛrnik] *interj* (coll) shucks!, heck!, what a shame!

berthe [bɛrt] *f* corsage; cape

béryllium [beriljɔm] *m* beryllium

besace [bəzas] *f* beggar's bag; mendicancy

besicles [bəzikl] *fpl* (archaic) spectacles; **prenez donc vos besicles!** (coll) put your specs on!

besogne [bəzɔɲe] *f* work, task; **abattre de la besogne** to accomplish a great deal of work; **aller vite en besogne** to work too hastily

besogner [bəzɔɲe] *intr* to drudge, slave

beso·gneux [bəzɔɲø] **-gneuse** [ɲøz] *adj* needy ‖ *mf* needy person

besoin [bəzwɛ̃] *m* need; poverty, distress; **au besoin** if necessary; **avoir besoin de** to need; **si besoin est** if need be

bes·son [besɔ̃] **-sonne** [sɔn] *mf* (dial) twin

bestiaire [bɛstjɛr] *m* bestiary

bes·tial -tiale [bɛstjal] (*pl* **-tiaux** [tjo]) *adj* bestial ‖ *mpl* see **bestiaux**

bestialité [bɛstjalite] *f* bestiality

bestiaux [bɛstjo] *mpl* livestock, cattle and horses

bestiole [bɛstjɔl] *f* bug, vermin

bê·ta [bɛtɑ] **-tasse** [tɑs] *adj* (coll) silly ‖ *mf* (coll) sap, dolt

bétail [betaj] *m invar* grazing animals (*on a farm*); **gros bétail** cattle and horses; **menu bétail, petit bétail** sheep, goats, pigs, etc.

bête [bɛt] *adj* stupid, foolish ‖ *f* animal; beast; **bête à bon Dieu** (ent) ladybird; **bête de charge, bête de somme** pack animal; **bonne bête** harmless fool

bêtifier [betifje], [betifje] *tr* to make stupid ‖ *intr* to play the fool, talk foolishly

bêtise [bɛtiz], [betiz] *f* foolishness, stupidity, nonsense; trifle; **faire des bêtises** to blunder, do stupid things; throw money around

béton [betɔ̃] *m* concrete; **béton armé** reinforced concrete; **béton précontraint** prestressed concrete

bétonner [betɔne] *tr* to make of concrete

bétonnière [betɔnjɛr] *f* cement mixer

bette [bɛt] *f* Swiss chard; **bette à carde** Swiss chard

betterave [bɛtrav] *f* beet; **betterave sucrière** sugar beet

beuglement [bøgləmɑ̃] *m* bellow, bellowing, lowing

beugler [bøgle], [bœgle] *tr* (slang) to bawl out (*a song*) ‖ *intr* to bellow (*like a bull*); low (*like cattle*)

beurre [bœr] *m* butter; (slang) dough; **faire son beurre** (coll) to feather one's nest

beurrée [bœre] *f* slice of bread and butter

beurrer [bœre] *tr* to butter

beur·rier -rière [jɛr] *adj* butter ‖ *m* butter dish

beuverie [bœvri] *f* drinking party

bévue [bevy] *f* blunder, slip, boner

biais [bjɛ] **biaise** [bjɛz] *adj* bias, oblique, slanting; skew (*arch*) ‖ *m* bias, slant; skew (*of an arch*); **de biais, en biais** aslant, askew

biaiser [bjɛze] *intr* to slant; (fig) to be evasive

bibelot [biblo] *m* curio, trinket, knickknack

bibeloter [biblɔte] *intr* to buy or collect curios

bibe·ron [bibrɔ̃] **-ronne** [rɔn] *adj* addicted to the bottle ‖ *mf* heavy drinker ‖ *m* nursing bottle

bibi [bibi] *m* (hum) me, yours truly

Bible [bibl] *f* Bible

bibliobus [bibliɔbys] *m* bookmobile

bibliographe [bibliɔgraf] *m* bibliographer

bibliographie [bibliɔgrafi] *f* bibliography

bibliomane [bibliɔman] *mf* book collector

bibliothécaire [bibliɔtekɛr] *mf* librarian

bibliothèque [bibliɔtɛk] *f* library; bookstand; **bibliothèque vivante** walking encyclopedia

biblique [biblik] *adj* Biblical

biceps [bisɛps] *m* biceps

biche [biʃ] *f* hind; doe; **ma biche** (coll) my darling

bicher [biʃe] *intr—***ça biche!** (slang) fine!

bichlamar [biʃlamar] *m* pidgin

bichof [biʃɔf] *m* spiced wine

bi·chon [biʃɔ̃] **-chonne** [ʃɔn] *mf* lap dog

bichonner [biʃɔne] *tr* to curl (*one's hair*); doll up ‖ *ref* to doll up

bicoque [bikɔk] *f* shack, ramshackle house

bicorne [bikɔrn] *adj* two-cornered ‖ *m* cocked hat

bicot [biko] *m* (coll) kid (*goat*); (offensive) North African, Arab

bicyclette [bisiklɛt] *f* bicycle; **aller à bicyclette** to bicycle; **bicyclette d'entraînement** exercise bicycle; **faire de la bicyclette** to go bicycling

bident [bidɑ̃] *m* two-pronged fork

bidet [bidɛ] *m* bidet; nag (*horse*)

bidon [bidɔ̃] *m* drum (*for liquids*); canteen, water bottle

bidonville [bidɔ̃vil] *m* shantytown

bidule [bidyl] *m* (slang) gadget

bief [bjɛf] *m* millrace; reach, level (*of a stream or canal*)

bielle [bjɛl] *f* connecting rod, tie rod

bien [bjɛ̃] *m* good; welfare; estate, fortune; **biens** property, possessions; **biens consomptibles** consumer goods; **biens immeubles** real estate; **biens meubles** personal property ‖ *adv* §91 well; rightly, properly, quite; indeed, certainly; fine, e.g., **je vais bien** I'm fine; **bien de** + *art* much, e.g., **bien de l'eau** much water; many, e.g., **bien des gens** many people; **bien entendu** of course; **bien que** + *subj* although; **eh bien!** so!; **si bien que** so that; **tant bien que mal** so-so, as well as possible ‖ *interj* good!; all right!; that's enough!

bien-ai·mé -mée [bjɛ̃neme] *adj & mf* beloved, darling

bien·dire [bjɛ̃dir] *m* gracious speech, eloquent delivery; **être sur son bien-dire** to be on one's best behavior

bien-di·sant [bjɛ̃dizɑ̃] **-sante** [zɑ̃t] *adj* smooth-spoken, smooth-tongued

bien-être [bjɛ̃nɛtr] *m* well-being, welfare

bienfaisance [bjɛ̃fəzɑ̃s] *f* charity, beneficence

bienfai·sant [bjɛ̃fəzɑ̃] **-sante** [zɑ̃t] *adj* charitable, beneficent

bienfait [bjɛ̃fɛ] *m* good turn, good deed, favor; **bienfaits** benefits

bienfai·teur [bjɛ̃fɛtœr] **-trice** [tris] *mf* benefactor ‖ *f* benefactress

bien-fondé [bjɛ̃fɔ̃de] *m* cogency

bien-fonds [bjɛ̃fɔ̃] *m* (*pl* **biens-fonds**) real estate

bienheu·reux [bjɛ̃nœrø] **-reuse** [røz] *adj & mf* blessed

bien·nal -nale [bjɛnnal] *adj* (*pl* -**naux** [no]) biennial ‖ *f* biennial exposition

bienséance [bjɛ̃seɑ̃s] *f* propriety

bien·séant [bjɛ̃seɑ̃] -**séante** [seɑ̃t] *adj* fitting, proper, appropriate

bientôt [bjɛ̃to] *adv* soon; **à bientôt!** so long!

bienveillance [bjɛ̃vɛjɑ̃s] *f* benevolence, kindness

bienveil·lant [bjɛ̃vɛjɑ̃] -**lante** [jɑ̃t] *adj* benevolent, kindly, kind

bienvenir [bjɛ̃vnir] *intr*—**se faire bienvenir** to make oneself welcome

bienve·nu -nue [bjɛ̃vny] *adj* welcome ‖ *m*—**soyez le bienvenu!** welcome! ‖ *f* welcome; **souhaiter la bienvenue à** to welcome

bière [bjɛr] *f* beer; coffin; **bière à la pression** draft beer

biffer [bife] *tr* to cross out, cancel, erase; (slang) to cut (*class*)

biffin [bifɛ̃] *m* (slang) ragman; (slang) doughboy, G.I. Joe

bifo·cal -cale [bifɔkal] *adj* (*pl* -**caux** [ko]) bifocal

bifteck [biftɛk] *m* beefsteak

bifurquer [bifyrke] *tr* to bifurcate, divide into two branches ‖ *intr & ref* to bifurcate, fork; branch off

bigame [bigam] *adj* bigamous ‖ *mf* bigamist

bigamie [bigami] *f* bigamy

bigar·ré -rée [bigare] *adj* mottled, variegated; motley (*crowd*)

bigar·reau [bigaro] *m* (*pl* -**reaux**) whiteheart cherry

bigarrer [bigare] *tr* to mottle, variegate, streak

bigarrure [bigaryr] *f* variegation, medley, mixture

bigle [bigl] *adj* cross-eyed

bigler [bigle] *intr* to squint; be cross-eyed

bigorne [bigɔrn] *f* two-horn anvil

bigorner [bigɔrne] *tr* to form on the anvil; (slang) to smash

bi·got [bigo] -**gote** [gɔt] *adj* sanctimonious ‖ *mf* religious bigot

bigoterie [bigɔtri] *f* religious bigotry

bigoudi [bigudi] *m* hair curler, roller

bihebdomadaire [biɛbdɔmadɛr] *adj* semiweekly

bi·jou [biʒu] *m* (*pl* -**joux**) jewel

bijouterie [biʒutri] *f* jewelry; jewelry shop; jewelry business

bijou·tier [biʒutje] -**tière** [tjɛr] *mf* jeweler

bilan [bilɑ̃] *m* balance sheet; balance; petition of bankruptcy; **bilan de santé** (med) checkup; **faire le bilan** to tabulate the results

bilboquet [bilbɔkɛ] *m* job printing

bile [bil] *f* bile; **se faire de la bile** (coll) to worry, fret

bi·lieux [biljø] -**lieuse** [ljøz] *adj* bilious; irascible, grouchy

bilingue [bilɛ̃g] *adj* bilingual

billard [bijar] *m* billiards; billiard table; billiard room

bille [bij] *f* ball; ball bearing; billiard ball; marble; log; **à bille** ball-point (*pen*)

billet [bijɛ] *m* note; ticket; bill (*currency*); **billet à ordre** promissory note; **billet d'abonnement** season ticket; **billet d'aller et retour** round-trip ticket; **billet de banque** bank note; **billet de correspondance** transfer; **billet de faire-part** announcement, notification (*of birth, wedding, death*); **billet de logement** billet; **billet doux** love letter; **billet simple** one-way ticket

billette [bijɛt] *f* billet

billetterie [bijɛtri] *f* ticketing (*at events*)

billevesée [bijvəze], [bilvəze] *f* nonsense

billion [biljɔ̃] *m* trillion (U.S.A.); billion (Brit); (obs) billion, milliard

billot [bijo] *m* block, chopping block; executioner's block

biloquer [bilɔke] *tr* to plow deeply

bimen·suel -suelle [bimɑ̃sɥɛl] *adj* semimonthly

bimes·triel -trielle [bimɛstriɛl] *adj* bimonthly (*every two months*)

bimoteur [bimɔtœr] *adj* twin-motor ‖ *m* twin-motor plane

binaire [binɛr] *adj* binary

biner [bine] *tr* to hoe; cultivate, work over (*the soil*) ‖ *intr* to say two masses the same day

binette [binɛt] *f* hoe; (hist) wig; (slang) phiz

bineur [binœr] *m* or **bineuse** [binøz] *f* cultivator (*implement*)

binocle [binɔkl] *m* pince-nez

binoculaire [binɔkylɛr] *adj & f* binocular

binôme [binom] *adj & m* binomial

binon [binɔ̃] *m* (comp) bit

biochimie [bjɔʃimi] *f* biochemistry

biographe [bjɔgraf] *mf* biographer

biographie [bjɔgrafi] *f* biography

biographique [bjɔgrafik] *adj* biographical

biologie [bjɔlɔʒi] *f* biology

biologiste [bjɔlɔʒist] *mf* biologist

biophysique [bjɔfizik] *f* biophysics

biopsie [bjɔpsi] *f* biopsy

bioxyde [bjɔksid] *m* dioxide

bip [bip] *m* (aer) blip

bipar·ti -tie [biparti] *adj* bipartite

bipartisme [bipartism] *m* bipartisanship

bipartite [bipartit] *adj* bipartite; bipartisan

bipède [bipɛd] *adj & mf* biped ‖ *m* pair of legs of a horse

biplan [biplɑ̃] *m* biplane

bique [bik] *f* nanny goat

bir·man [birmɑ̃] -**mane** [man] *adj* Burmese ‖ (*cap*) *mf* Burmese (*person*)

Birmanie [birmani] *f* Burma; **la Birmanie** Burma

bis [bi] **bise** [biz] *adj* gray-brown ‖ [bis] *m*—**un bis** an encore ‖ *f* see **bise** ‖ **bis** [bis] *adv* twice; (mus) repeat; **sept bis** seven A, seven and a half ‖ **bis** [bis] *interj* encore!

bisaïeul bisaïeule [bizajœl] *mf* great-grandparent ‖ *m* great-grandfather ‖ *f* great-grandmother

bisan·nuel -nuelle [bizanɥɛl] *adj* biennial

bisbille [bisbij] *f* (coll) squabble

biscaïen [biskajɛ̃] **biscaïenne** [biskajɛn] *adj* Biscayan ‖ (*cap*) *mf* Biscayan (*person*)
biscor·nu -nue [biskɔrny] *adj* misshapen, distorted
biscotin [biskɔtɛ̃] *m* hardtack
biscotte [biskɔt] *f* zwieback
biscuit [biskɥi] *m* hardtack; cracker; cookie; unglazed porcelain; **biscuit soda** soda cracker
bise [biz] *f* north wind; (fig) winter; (slang) kiss
bi·seau [bizo] *m* (*pl* **-seaux**) bevel, chamfer; **en biseau** beveled, chamfered
biseauter [bizote] *tr* to bevel, chamfer; to mark (*cards*)
biser [bize] *tr* to redye ‖ *intr* to blacken
bi·son [bizɔ̃] **-sonne** [zɔn] *mf* bison, buffalo
bisque [bisk] *f* bisque
bisquer [biske] *intr* (coll) to be resentful
bissac [bisak] *m* bag, sack
bisser [bise] *tr* to encore; repeat
bissextile [bisɛkstil] *adj* bissextile, leap, e.g., **année bissextile** leap year
bis·sexué -sexuée [bisɛksɥe] *adj* bisexual
bis·sexuel -sexuelle [bisɛksɥɛl] *adj* bisexual
bistouri [bisturi] *m* scalpel
bistournage [bisturnaʒ] *m* castration
bistre [bistr] *adj invar* soot-brown ‖ *m* bister, soot-brown
bis·tré -trée [bistre] *adj* swarthy
bisulfate [bisylfat] *m* bisulfate
bisulfite [bisylfit] *m* bisulfite
bitte [bit] *f* (vulg) penis
bitter [bitɛr] *m* bitters
bitume [bitym] *m* bitumen
bitumer [bityme] *tr* to asphalt
bitumi·neux [bityminø] **-neuse** [nøz] *adj* bituminous
bivouac [bivwak] *m* bivouac
bivouaquer [bivwake] *intr* to bivouac
bizarre [bizar] *adj* bizarre, strange
bizutage [bizytaʒ] *m* (slang) initiation, hazing
bizuth [bizyt] *m* (slang) freshman
blackbouler [blakbule] *tr* to blackball; (coll) to flunk
bla·fard [blafar] **-farde** [fard] *adj* pallid, pale, wan; lambent (*flame*)
blague [blag] *f* tobacco pouch; (coll) yarn, tall story, blarney; **blague à part** (coll) all joking aside; **faire une blague** (coll) to play a trick; **sale blague** (coll) dirty trick; **sans blague!** (coll) no kidding!
blaguer [blage] *tr* (coll) to kid; **blaguer qn** (coll) to pull s.o.'s leg ‖ *intr* (coll) to kid, tell tall stories
bla·gueur [blagœr] **-gueuse** [gøz] *adj* (coll) kidding, tongue-in-cheek ‖ *mf* (coll) kidder, joker
blai·reau [blɛro] *m* (*pl* **-reaux**) badger; shaving brush
blâmable [blɑmabl] *adj* blameworthy
blâme [blɑm] *m* blame; **s'attirer un blâme** to receive a reprimand
blâmer [blɑme] §97, §99 *tr* to blame; disapprove of

blanc [blɑ̃] **blanche** [blɑ̃ʃ] *adj* white; blank; clean; sleepless (*night*); expressionless (*voice*); unconsummated (*marriage*); **blanc comme un linge** white as a sheet ‖ *m* white; blank; white meat; white man; white goods; chalk; bull's-eye; **à blanc** with blank cartridges; **blanc cassé** off-white; **blanc de baleine** spermaceti; **blanc de chaux** whitewash; **en blanc** blank; **en blanc et noir** in black and white ‖ *f* white woman
blanc-bec [blɑ̃bɛk] *m* (*pl* **blancs-bécs**) (coll) greenhorn, callow youth
blanchâtre [blɑ̃ʃɑtr] *adj* whitish
blancheur [blɑ̃ʃœr] *f* whiteness
blanchir [blɑ̃ʃir] *tr* to whiten; wash or bleach; whitewash; blanch (*almonds*) ‖ *intr* to blanch, whiten; grow old
blanchissage [blɑ̃ʃisaʒ] *m* laundering; sugar refining
blanchisserie [blɑ̃ʃisri] *f* laundry
blanchis·seur [blɑ̃ʃisœr] **-seuse** [søz] *mf* launderer ‖ *m* laundryman ‖ *f* laundress, washerwoman
blanc-manger [blɑ̃mɑ̃ʒe] *m* (*pl* **blancs-manger**) blancmange
blanc-seing [blɑ̃sɛ̃] *m* (*pl* **blancs-seings**) carte blanche
bla·sé -sée [blaze] *adj* blasé, jaded
blaser [blaze] *tr* to cloy, blunt
blason [blazɔ̃] *m* (heral) blazon
blasonner [blazɔne] *tr* (heral) to blazon
blasphéma·teur [blasfematœr] **-teuse** [tøz] *adj* blasphemous, blaspheming ‖ *mf* blasphemer
blasphématoire [blasfematwar] *adj* blasphemous
blasphème [blasfɛm] *m* blasphemy
blasphémer [blasfeme] §10 *tr* & *intr* to blaspheme
blatte [blat] *f* cockroach
blé [ble] *m* wheat; (slang) dough; **blé à moudre** grist; **blé de Turquie** corn; **blé froment** wheat; **blé noir** buckwheat; **manger son blé en herbe** to spend one's money before one has it
bled [blɛd] *m* (coll) backwoods, hinterland
blême [blɛm] *adj* pale; livid, sallow, wan; ghastly
blêmir [blemir] *intr* to turn pale or livid, blanch; grow dim
blennorragie [blɛnɔraʒi] *f* gonorrhea
blèse [blɛz] *adj* lisping ‖ *mf* lisper
blèsement [blɛzmɑ̃] *m* lisping
bléser [bleze] §10 *intr* to lisp
bles·sé -sée [blɛse] *adj* wounded ‖ *mf* injured person; victim; casualty
blesser [blɛse] [blese] *tr* to wound; injure; be disagreeable to
blessure [blɛsyr] *f* wound; injury
blet blette [blɛt] *adj* overripe ‖ *f* chard
blettir [blɛtir] *intr* to overripen
bleu bleue [blø] (*pl* **bleus bleues**) *adj* blue; fairy (*stories*); violent (*anger*); rare (*meat*) ‖ *m* blue; bluing; bruise; sauce for cooking fish; telegram or pneumatic letter; (coll) raw recruit, greenhorn; **bleu bar-**

beau light blue; **bleu marine** navy blue; **bleus** coveralls, dungarees; (mil) fatigues; **passer au bleu** to avoid, elude (*a question*); **petit bleu** bad wine

bleuâtre [bløɑtr] *adj* bluish

bleuet [bløɛ] *m* bachelor's-button

bleuir [bløir] *tr & intr* to turn blue

bleu·té -tée [bløte] *adj* bluish

blindage [blɛ̃daʒ] *m* armor plate; armor plating; (elec) shield

blin·dé -dée [blɛ̃de] *adj* armored; armorplated; (elec) shielded ‖ *m* (mil) tank

blinder [blɛ̃de] *tr* to armor-plate; (elec) to shield

bloc [blɔk] *m* block; blocking; tablet, pad (*of paper*); (elec, mach) unit; brick (*of ice cream*); **à bloc** tight; **en bloc** all together, in a lump; **envoyer** or **mettre au bloc** (slang) to throw (*s.o.*) in the jug; **serrer le frein à bloc** to jam on the brakes

blocage [blɔkaʒ] *m* blockage, blocking; lumping together; rubble; freezing (*of prices; of wages*); application (*of brakes*)

blocaille [blɔkɑj] *f* rubble

bloc-diagramme [blɔkdjagram] *m* (*pl* **blocs-diagrammes**) cross section

bloc-moteur [blɔkmɔtœr] *m* (aut) motor and transmission system

bloc-notes [blɔknɔt] *m* (*pl* **blocs-notes**) scratch pad, note pad

blocus [blɔkys] *m* blockade

blond [blɔ̃] [blɔ̃d] *adj* blond ‖ *m* blond ‖ *f* see **blonde**

blondasse [blɔ̃das] *adj* washed-out blond

blonde [blɔ̃d] *f* blonde; blond lace; **blonde platinée** platinum blonde

blon·din [blɔ̃dɛ̃] **-dine** [din] *adj* fair-haired ‖ *mf* blond ‖ *m* cableway; hopper for concrete; (obs) fop

blondir [blɔ̃dir] *tr* to bleach ‖ *intr* to turn yellow, become blond

bloquer [blɔke] *tr* to blockade; block up; fill with rubble; jam on (*the brakes*); stop (*a car*) by jamming on the brakes; pocket (*a billiard ball*); run on (*two paragraphs*); tighten (*a nut or bolt*) as much as possible; freeze (*wages*)

blottir [blɔtir] *ref* to cower; curl up

blouse [bluz] *f* smock; billiard pocket

blouser [bluze] *tr* to deceive, take in ‖ *intr* to pucker around the waist ‖ *ref* to be mistaken

blouson [bluzɔ̃] *m* jacket; windbreaker

blouson-noir [bluzɔ̃war] *m* (*pl* **blousons-noirs**) juvenile delinquent; hood

blue-jean [bludʒin] *m* blue jeans

bluet [blyɛ] *m* bachelor's-button; (Canad) blueberry

bluette [blyɛt] *f* piece of light fiction; spark, flash

bluffer [blyfe] *tr & intr* to bluff

bluf·feur [blyfœr] **-feuse** [føz] *mf* bluffer

blutage [blytaʒ] *m* bolting, sifting; boltings, siftings

bluter [blyte] *tr* to bolt, sift

blutoir [blytwar] *m* bolter, sifter

B.N. *abbr* (**Bibliothèque Nationale**) National Library

boa [bɔa] *m* boa

bobard [bɔbar] *m* (coll) fish story, tall tale

bobèche [bɔbɛʃ] *f* bobeche (*disk to catch drippings of candle*)

bobine [bɔbin] *f* bobbin; spool, reel; (elec) coil; **bobine d'allumage** (aut) ignition coil

bobiner [bɔbine] *tr* to spool, wind

bobo [bobo] *m* (*language used with children*) sore; cut; **avoir bobo** to have a pain

bocage [bɔkaʒ] *m* grove

boca·ger [bɔkaʒe] **-gère** [ʒɛr] *adj* wooded

bo·cal [bɔkal] *m* (*pl* **-caux** [ko]) jar, bottle, globe; fishbowl

boche [bɔʃ] *adj & mf* (slang & pej) German

bock [bɔk] *m* beer glass (*half pint*); glass of beer; enema; douche

boëte [bwɛt] *f* fish bait

bœuf [bœf] *m* (*pl* **bœufs** [bø]) beef; head of beef; steer; ox; **bœuf en conserve** corned beef

boggie [bɔʒi] *m* (rr) truck

bogue [bɔg] *f* chestnut bur; (comp) bug

Bohême [bɔɛm] *f* Bohemia; **la Bohême** Bohemia

bohème [bɔɛm] *adj & mf* Bohemian (*artist*) ‖ *f*—**la bohème** Bohemia (*of the artistic world*)

bohé·mien [bɔɛmjɛ̃] **-mienne** [mjɛn] *adj* Bohemian; gypsy ‖ (*cap*) *mf* Bohemian; gypsy

boire [bwar] *m* drink; drinking; **le boire et le manger** food and drink ‖ §8 *tr* to drink; swallow (*an affront*) ‖ *intr* to drink; **boire à la santé de** to drink to the health of; **boire à** (**même**) to drink out of (*a bottle*); **boire comme un trou** to drink like a fish; **boire dans** to drink out of (*a glass*)

bois [bwɑ] *m* wood; woods; horns; antlers; **bois de chauffage** firewood; **bois de lit** bedstead; **bois de placage** plywood; **bois flotté** driftwood; **bois fondu** plastic wood; **les bois** (mus) the woodwinds

boisage [bwazaʒ] *m* timbering

boi·sé -sée [bwaze] *adj* wooded; paneled

boiser [bwaze] *tr* to panel, wainscot; timber (*a mine*); reforest

boiserie [bwazri] *f* woodwork, paneling, wainscoting

bois·seau [bwaso] *m* (*pl* **-seaux**) bushel

boisson [bwasɔ̃] *f* drink, beverage; **boissons hygiéniques** light wines, beer, and soft drinks

boîte [bwat] *f* box; can; canister; (slang) joint, dump; **boîte aux lettres** mailbox; **boîte chaude** (rr) hotbox; **boîte de nuit** night club; **boîte d'essieu** (mach) journal box; **boîte de vitesses** transmission-gear box; **boîte postale** post-office box; **en boîte** boxed; canned; **ferme ta boîte!** (slang) shut up!, **mettre en boîte** to box; can; (slang) to make fun of

boiter [bwate] *intr* to limp

boi·teux [bwatø] **-teuse** [tøz] *adj* lame, limping; unsteady, wobbly (*chair*) ‖ *mf* lame person

boî·tier [bwatje] **-tière** [tjɛr] *mf* boxmaker; mail collector (*from mailboxes*) ‖ *m* box, case; kit; medicine kit; (mach) housing; **boîtier de montre** watchcase

boitte [bwat] *f* fish bait

bol [bɔl] *m* bowl, basin; cud; bolus, pellet

bolchevique [bɔlʃəvik] *adj* Bolshevik ‖ (*cap*) *mf* Bolshevik

bolcheviste [bɔlʃəvist] *adj* Bolshevik ‖ (*cap*) *mf* Bolshevik

bolduc [bɔldyk] *m* colored ribbon

bolée [bɔle] *f* bowlful

bolide [bɔlid] *m* meteorite, fireball; racing car

bombance [bɔ̃bɑ̃s] *f* (coll) feast; **faire bombance** (coll) to have a blowout

bombardement [bɔ̃bardəmɑ̃] *m* bombing; bombardment; **bombardement en tapis** saturation bombing

bombarder [bɔ̃barde] *tr* to bomb; bombard; (coll) to appoint at the last minute

bombardier [bɔ̃bardje] *m* bomber; bombardier

bombe [bɔ̃b] *f* bomb; **bombe à hydrogène** hydrogen bomb; **bombe atomique** atomic bomb; **bombe glacée** molded ice cream; **bombe volante** buzz bomb; **faire la bombe** (fig) to paint the town red

bom·bé -bée [bɔ̃be] *adj* convex, bulging

bomber [bɔ̃be] *tr* to bend, arch; stick out (*one's chest*); **bomber le torse** (fig) to stick one's nose up ‖ *intr & ref* to bulge

bon [bɔ̃] **bonne** [bɔn] §91, §92 *adj* good; **à quoi bon?** what's the use?; **sentir bon** to smell good; **tenir bon** to hold fast ‖ (when standing before noun) *adj* §91 good; fast (*color*) ‖ *m* coupon; **bon de change** voucher; **bon de commande** order blank; **bon de travail** work order; **pour (tout) de bon** for good, really ‖ *f* see **bonne** ‖ **bon** *interj* good!; what!

bonace [bɔnas] *f* calm (*of the sea*)

bonasse [bɔnas] *adj* simple, naïve

bon-bec [bɔ̃bɛk] *m* (*pl* **bons-becs**) fast talker

bonbon [bɔ̃bɔ̃] *m* bonbon, piece of candy

bonbonne [bɔ̃bɔn] *f* demijohn

bonbonnière [bɔ̃bɔnjɛr] *f* candy dish; candy box

bond [bɔ̃] *m* bound, bounce; leap, jump; **faire faux bond** to miss an appointment; **faux bond** misstep

bonde [bɔ̃d] *f* plug; bunghole; sluice gate

bon·dé -dée [bɔ̃de] *adj* crammed

bondir [bɔ̃dir] *intr* to bound, bounce; leap, jump; **faire bondir** to make (*s.o.*) hit the ceiling

bondissement [bɔ̃dismɑ̃] *m* bouncing, leaping

bondon [bɔ̃dɔ̃] *m* bung

bonheur [bɔnœr] *m* happiness; good luck; **au petit bonheur** by chance, at random; **par bonheur** luckily

bonheur-du-jour [bɔnœrdyʒur] *m* (*pl* **bonheurs-du-jour**) escritoire

bonhomie [bɔnɔmi] *f* good nature; credulity

bonhomme [bɔnɔm] *adj* good-natured, simple-minded ‖ *m* (*pl* **bonshommes** [bɔ̃zɔm]) fellow, guy; old fellow; **bonhomme de neige** snowman; **Bonhomme Hiver** Jack Frost; **faux bonhomme** humbug; **petit bonhomme** little man (*child*)

boni [bɔni] *m* bonus; discount coupon; surplus (*over estimated expenses*)

bonification [bɔnifikɑsjɔ̃] *f* improvement; discount; bonus; advantage

bonifier [bɔnifje] *tr* to improve; give a discount to

boniment [bɔnimɑ̃] *m* sales talk, smooth talk

bonimenteur [bɔnimɑ̃tœr] *m* huckster, charlatan

bonjour [bɔ̃ʒur] *m* good day, good morning, good afternoon, hello

bonne [bɔn] *f* maid; **bonne à tout faire** maid of all work ‖ *adj* see **bon**

bonne-maman [bɔnmamɑ̃] *f* (*pl* **bonnes-mamans**) grandma

bonnement [bɔnmɑ̃] *adv* honestly, plainly

bonnet [bɔnɛ] *m* bonnet; stocking cap; cup (*of a brassiere*); (mil) undress hat; **bonnet d'âne** dunce cap; **bonnet de nuit** nightcap; **gros bonnet** (coll) VIP

bonneterie [bɔnətri] *f* hosiery; knitwear

bon-papa [bɔ̃papa] *m* (*pl* **bons-papas**) grandpa

bonsoir [bɔ̃swar] *m* good evening; (coll) good night

bonté [bɔ̃te] *f* goodness; kindness

boomer [bumɛr] *m* (electron) boomer

booster [bustœr] *m* (rok) booster

borborygme [bɔrbɔrigm] *m* rumbling (*in the stomach*)

bord [bɔr] *m* edge, border; rim, brim; side (*of a ship*); ship, e.g., **les porteurs du bord** the ship's porters; e.g., **les hommes du bord** the ship's company; **à bord** on board; **à pleins bords** overflowing; without hindrance; **à ras bords** full to the brim; **être du (même) bord de** to be of the same mind as; **faux bord** list (*of ship*); **jeter par-dessus bord** to throw overboard

bordage [bɔrdaʒ] *m* edging (*of dress*); planking (*of ship*)

bordé [bɔrde] *m* border, edging

bordeaux [bɔrdo] *adj invar* maroon, burgundy ‖ *m* Bordeaux (wine); **bordeaux rouge** claret

bordée [bɔrde] *f* broadside, volley; (naut) tack; **bordée de babord** port watch; **bordée de tribord** starboard watch; **courir une bordée** to go skylarking on shore leave; **tirer une bordée** to jump ship

bordel [bɔrdɛl] *m* (vulgar) brothel

borde·lais [bɔrdəlɛ] **-laise** [lɛz] *adj* of Bordeaux ‖ *f* Bordeaux cask ‖ (*cap*) *mf* native or inhabitant of Bordeaux

border [bɔrde] *tr* to border; hem; sail along (*the coast*); **border un lit** to make a bed

borde·reau [bɔrdəro] *m* (*pl* **-reaux**) itemized account, memorandum
bordure [bɔrdyr] *f* border
bore [bɔr] *m* boron
boréal boréale [bɔreal] *adj* (*pl* **boréaux** [bɔreo] or **boréals**) boreal; northern
borgne [bɔrɲ] *adj* one-eyed; blind in one eye; disreputable (*bar, house, etc.*) ǁ *mf* one-eyed person
borne [bɔrn] *f* landmark; boundary stone; milestone; (elec) binding post, terminal; (slang) kilometer; **bornes** bounds, limits
bor·né -née [bɔrne] *adj* limited, narrow; dull (*mind*)
borner [bɔrne] *tr* to mark out the boundary of; set limits to ǁ §96 *ref* to restrain oneself
bosquet [bɔskɛ] *m* grove
bosse [bɔs] *f* hump; bump; (coll) flair
bosseler [bɔsle] §34 *tr* to emboss; to dent
bossoir [bɔswar] *m* davit; bow (*of ship*)
bos·su -sue [bɔsy] *adj* hunchbacked ǁ *mf* hunchback; **rire comme un bossu** to split one's sides laughing
botanique [bɔtanik] *adj* botanical ǁ *f* botany
botte [bɔt] *f* boot; bunch (*e.g., of radishes*); sword thrust; **lécher les bottes à qn** (coll) to lick s.o.'s boots
botteler [bɔtle] §34 *tr* to tie in bunches
botter [bɔte] *tr* to boot, boot out; **cela me botte** that suits me ǁ *ref* to put on one's boots
botteur [bɔtœr] *m* (sports) kicker
bottier [bɔtje] *m* custom shoemaker
Bottin [bɔtɛ̃] *m* business directory
bottine [bɔtin] *f* high button shoe
boubouler [bubule] *intr* to hoot like an owl
bouc [buk] *m* billy goat; goatee; **bouc émissaire** scapegoat
boucan [bukɑ̃] *m* smokehouse; (coll) uproar
boucaner [bukane] *tr* to smoke (*meat*)
boucanier [bukanje] *m* buccaneer
boucharde [buʃard] *f* bushhammer
bouche [buʃ] *f* mouth; muzzle (*of gun*); door (*of oven*); entrance (*of subway*); **bouche close!** mum's the word!; **bouche d'égout** catch basin; **bouche d'incendie** fire hydrant; **bouches** mouth (*of river*); **faire la petite bouche à, faire la fine bouche devant** to turn up one's nose at
bouchée [buʃe] *f* mouthful; patty; chocolate cream (*candy*)
boucher [buʃe] *m* butcher ǁ *tr* to stop up, plug; wall up; cut off (*the view*); bung (*a barrel*); cork (*a bottle*); **bouché à l'émeri** (coll) completely dumb ǁ *ref* to be stopped up
boucherie [buʃri] *f* butcher shop; **boucherie chevaline** horsemeat butcher shop
bouche-trou [buʃtru] *m* (*pl* **-trous**) stopgap
bouchon [buʃɔ̃] *m* cork, stopper; bob (*on a fishline*); **bouchon de circulation** traffic jam; **bouchon de vapeur** vapor lock
bouclage [buklaʒ] *m* closing of circuit; (mil) encirclement
boucle [bukl] *f* buckle; earring; curl; (aer) loop; **boucler la boucle** to loop the loop

boucler [bukle] *tr* to buckle; curl (*the hair*); lock up (*prisoners*); put a nose ring on (*a bull*); **boucler son budget** (coll) to make ends meet; **la boucler** (slang) to shut up, button one's lip ǁ *intr* to curl
bouclier [buklije] *m* shield; **bouclier antithermique** heat shield; **bouclier thermique** thermal cone
bouddhisme [budism] *m* Buddhism
bouddhiste [budist] *adj* (coll) *mf* Buddhist
bouder [bude] *tr* to be distant toward ǁ *intr* to pout, sulk
bou·deur -deuse [budœr] *adj* pouting ǁ *mf* sullen person
boudin [budɛ̃] *m* blood sausage; **à boudin** spiral
boudiner [budine] *tr* to twist
boue [bu] *f* mud
bouée [bwe] *f* buoy; **bouée de sauvetage** life preserver
boueur [bwœr] *m* garbage collector; scavenger
boueux [bwø] **boueuse** [bwøz] *adj* muddy; grimy; (typ) smeary
bouf·fant [bufɑ̃] **-fante** [fɑ̃t] *adj* puffed (*sleeves*); baggy (*trousers*)
bouffe [buf] *adj* comic (*opera*) ǁ *f* (slang) grub
bouffée [bufe] *f* puff, gust
bouffer [bufe] *tr* (slang) to gobble up ǁ *intr* to puff out
bouf·fi -fie [bufi] *adj* puffed up or out
bouffir [bufir] *tr & intr* to puff up
bouffissure [bufisyr] *f* swelling
bouf·fon [bufɔ̃] **-fonne** [fɔn] *adj & m* buffoon, comic
bouffonnerie [bufɔnri] *f* buffoonery
bouge [buʒ] *m* bulge; hovel, dive
bougeoir [buʒwar] *m* flat candlestick
bougeotte [buʒɔt] *f* (coll) wanderlust
bouger [buʒe] §38 *tr—ne bougez rien!* (coll) don't move a thing! ǁ *intr* to budge, stir; (ne) **bouge pas!** don't move!
bougie [buʒi] *f* candle; candlepower; spark plug; **bougies de gâteaux d'anniversaire** birthday candles
bou·gon [bugɔ̃] **-gonne** [gɔn] *adj* grumbling ǁ *mf* grumbler
bougran [bugrɑ̃] *m* buckram
bou·gre [bugr] **-gresse** [grɛs] *mf* (slang) customer; **bougre d'âne** (slang) perfect ass ǁ *m* (slang) guy; **bon bougre** (slang) swell guy ǁ *f* (slang) wench
bougrement [bugrəmɑ̃] *adv* (slang) awfully, darned
bouillabaisse [bujabɛs] *f* bouillabaisse, fish stew, chowder
bouil·lant [bujɑ̃] **-lante** [jɑ̃t] *adj* boiling; fiery, impetuous
bouilleur [bujœr] *m* distiller (*of brandy*); boiler tube; small nuclear reactor
bouilli [buji] *m* beef stew
bouillir [bujir] §9 *tr & intr* to boil; **faire bouillir la marmite** (coll) to bring home the bacon
bouilloire [bujwar] *f* kettle

bouillon [bujɔ̃] *m* broth, bouillon; bubble; bubbling; cheap restaurant; **à gros bouillons** gushing; **boire un bouillon** (coll) to gulp water; (coll) to suffer business losses; **bouillon de culture** (bact) broth; **bouillon d'onze heures** poisoned drink; **bouillons** unsold copies, remainders

bouillonnement [bujɔnmɑ̃] *m* boiling; effervescence

bouillonner [bujɔne] *tr* to put puffs in (*a dress*) ‖ *intr* to boil up; have copies left over

bouillotte [bujɔt] *f* hot-water bottle

boulan·ger [bulɑʒe] **-gère** [ʒɛr] *mf* baker ‖ §38 *intr* to bake bread

boulangerie [bulɑʒri] *f* bakery

boule [bul] *f* ball; (slang) nut, head; **boule d'eau chaude** hot-water bottle; **boule de neige** snowball; **boule noire** blackball; **boules** bowling; **en boule** (fig) tied in a knot, on edge; **perdre la boule** (slang) to go off one's rocker; **se mettre en boule** (coll) to get mad

bou·leau [bulo] *m* (*pl* **-leaux**) birch

boule-de-neige [buldənɛʒ] *f* (*pl* **boules-de-neige**) guelder-rose; meadow mushroom

bouledogue [buldɔg] *m* bulldog

bouler [bule] *tr* to pad (*a bull's horn*) ‖ *intr* to roll like a ball; **envoyer bouler** (slang) to send (*s.o.*) packing

boulet [bulɛ] *m* cannonball; (coll) cross to bear

boulette [bulɛt] *f* ball, pellet

boulevard [bulvar] *m* boulevard; **boulevard périphérique** belt road

boulevar·dier [bulvardje] **-dière** [djɛr] *adj* fashionable ‖ *m* boulevardier, man about town

bouleversement [bulvɛrsmɑ̃] *m* upset

bouleverser [bulvɛrse] *tr* to upset; overthrow

boulier [bulje] *m* abacus (*for scoring billiards*)

bouline [bulin] *f* (naut) bowline

boulingrin [bulɛ̃grɛ̃] *m* bowling green

bouliste [bulist] *mf* bowler

boulodrome [bulɔdrɔm] *m* bowling alley

boulon [bulɔ̃] *m* bolt; **boulon à œil** eyebolt

boulonner [bulɔne] *tr* to bolt ‖ *intr* (slang) to work

bou·lot [bulo] **-lotte** [lɔt] *adj* (coll) dumpy, squat ‖ *m* (slang) cylindrical loaf of bread; (slang) work

boulotter [bulɔte] *tr* (slang) to eat

boum [bum] *interj* boom!

bouquet [bukɛ] *m* bouquet; clump (*of trees*); prawn; jack rabbit; **c'est le bouquet** (coll) it's tops; (coll) that's the last straw

bouquetière [buktjɛr] *f* flower girl

bouquin [bukɛ̃] *m* (coll) book; (coll) old book

bouquiner [bukine] *intr* to shop around for old books; (coll) to read

bouquinerie [bukinri] *f* secondhand books; secondhand bookstore

bouqui·neur [bukinœr] **-neuse** [nøz] *mf* collector of old books; browser in bookstores

bouquiniste [bukinist] *mf* secondhand bookdealer

bourbe [burb] *f* mire

bour·beux [burbø] **-beuse** [bøz] *adj* miry, muddy

bourbier [burbje] *m* quagmire

bourbillon [burbijɔ̃] *m* core (*of boil*)

bourde [burd] *f* (coll) boner

bourdon [burdɔ̃] *m* bumblebee; big bell; (mus) bourdon; **avoir le bourdon** (slang) to have the blues; **faux bourdon** drone

bourdonnement [burdɔnmɑ̃] *m* buzzing

bourdonner [burdɔne] *tr* (coll) to hum (*a tune*) ‖ *intr* to buzz

bourg [bur] *m* market town

bourgade [burgad] *f* small town

bour·geois [burʒwa] **-geoise** [ʒwaz] *adj* bourgeois, middle-class ‖ *mf* commoner, middle-class person; Philistine; **gros bourgeois** solid citizen ‖ *m* businessman; **en bourgeois** in civies ‖ *f* (slang) old woman (*wife*)

bourgeoisie [burʒwazi] *f* middle class; **haute bourgeoisie** upper middle class; **petite bourgeoisie** lower middle class

bourgeon [burʒɔ̃] *m* bud; pimple

bourgeonnement [burʒɔnmɑ̃] *m* budding

bourgeonner [burʒɔne] *intr* to bud; break out in pimples

bourgeron [burʒərɔ̃] *m* jumper, overalls; sweat shirt

bourgogne [burgɔɲ] *m* Burgundy (wine) ‖ (*cap*) *f* Burgundy (*province*); **la Bourgogne** Burgundy

bourgui·gnon [burgiɲɔ̃] **-gnonne** [ɲɔn] *adj* Burgundian ‖ *m* Burgundian (*dialect*) ‖ (*cap*) *mf* Burgundian

bourlinguer [burlɛ̃ge] *intr* to labor (*in high seas*); (coll) to travel, venture forth

bourrade [burad] *f* sharp blow; poke

bourrage [buraʒ] *m* cramming; **bourrage de crâne** (coll) ballyhoo

bourre [bur] *f* stuffing, animal hair

bour·reau [buro] *m* (*pl* **-reaux**) executioner; torturer; **bourreau des cœurs** lady-killer; **bourreau de travail** workaholic

bourrée [bure] *f* fagot of twigs

bourreler [burle] §34 *tr* to torment

bourrelet [burlɛ] *m* weather stripping; roll (*of fat*); contour pillow

bourrer [bure] *tr* to stuff, cram; **bourrer de coups** to pummel, slug ‖ *ref* to stuff

bourriche [buriʃ] *f* hamper

bourrique [burik] *f* female donkey; (coll) ass

bour·ru -rue [bury] *adj* rough; grumpy; unfermented (*wine*)

bourse [burs] *f* purse; scholarship, fellowship; stock exchange, bourse; **bourse du travail** labor union hall; **bourses** scrotum

bourse-à-pasteur [bursapastœr] *f* (*pl* **bourses-à-pasteur** [bursapastœr]) (bot) shepherd's-purse

boursicaut or **boursicot** [bursiko] *m* little purse; nest egg

boursicoter [bursikɔte] *intr* to dabble in the stock market

bour·sier [bursje] **-sière** [sjɛr] *adj* scholarship (*student*); stock-market (*operation*) ‖ *mf* scholar (*holder of scholarship*); speculator

boursoufler [bursufle] *tr* to puff up

bousculer [buskyle] *tr* to jostle

bouse [buz] *f*—**bouse de vache** cow dung

bouseux [buzø] *m* (slang) peasant

bousillage [buzijaʒ] *m* cob (*mixture of clay and straw*); (coll) botched job

bousiller [buzije] *tr* (coll) to bungle; (slang) to smash up ‖ *intr* to build with cob

boussole [busɔl] *f* compass; **perdre la boussole** (coll) to go off one's rocker

boustifaille [bustifaj] *f* (slang) feasting; (slang) good food

bout [bu] *m* end; piece, scrap, bit; head (*of a match; of a table*); **à bout** exhausted; **à bout de bras** at arm's length; **à bout portant** point-blank; **à tout bout de champ** at every turn, repeatedly; **au bout du compte** after all; **bout de fil** (telp) (coll) ring, call; **bout de l'an** watch night; **bout d'essai** screen test; **bout d'homme** wisp of a man; **bout filtre** filter tip; **de bout en bout** from start to finish; **haut bout** head (*of a table; of a lake*); **montrer le bout de l'oreille** to show one's true colors; **rire du bout des dents** to force a laugh; **sur le bout du doigt** at one's fingertips; **venir à bout de** to succeed in, to triumph over

boutade [butad] *f* sally, quip; whim

bout-dehors [budəɔr] *m* (*pl* **bouts-dehors**) (naut) boom

boute-en-train [butɑ̃trɛ̃] *m invar* life of the party, live wire

boute·feu [butfø] *m* (*pl* **-feux**) firebrand

bouteille [butɛj] *f* bottle; **bouteille isolante** vacuum bottle

bouteiller [butɛje] *m* (hist) cupbearer

bouterolle [butrɔl] *f* ward (*of lock*); rivet snap

boute-selle [butsɛl] *m* boots and saddles (*trumpet call*)

bouteur [butœr] *m* bulldozer

boutique [butik] *f* shop; stock, goods; workshop; set of tools; **boutique cadeaux, boutique de souvenirs** gift shop; **boutique de modiste** millinery shop; **boutique franche** duty-free shop; **quelle boutique!** (coll) what a hellhole!, what an awful place!

boutiquier [butikje] *m* shopkeeper

bouton [butɔ̃] *m* button; pimple; doorknob; bud; **bouton de puissance** volume control

bouton-d'argent [butɔ̃darʒɑ̃] *m* (*pl* **boutons-d'argent**) sneezewort

bouton-d'or [butɔ̃dɔr] *m* (*pl* **boutons-d'or**) buttercup

boutonner [butɔne] *tr* to button ‖ *intr* to bud

bouton·neux [butɔnø] **-neuse** [nøz] *adj* pimply

boutonnière [butɔnjɛr] *f* buttonhole

bouton-pression [butɔ̃prɛsjɔ̃] *m* (*pl* **boutons-pression**) snap (fastener)

bouture [butyr] *f* cutting (*from a plant*)

bouturer [butyre] *tr* to propagate (*plants*) by cuttings ‖ *intr* to shoot suckers

bouverie [buvri] *f* cowshed

bou·vier [buvje] **-vière** [vjɛr] *mf* cowherd

bouvillon [buvijɔ̃] *m* steer, young bullock

bouvreuil [buvrœj] *m* bullfinch; **bouvreuil cramoisi** scarlet grosbeak

box [bɔks] *m* (*pl* **-boxes**) stall

boxe [bɔks] *f* boxing

boxer [bɔksœr] *m* boxer (*dog*) ‖ [bɔkse] *tr & intr* to box

boxeur [bɔksœr] *m* (sports) boxer

boxon [bɔksɔ̃] *m* whorehouse

boy [bɔj] *m* houseboy; chorus boy

boyau [bwajo] *m* (*pl* **boyaux**) intestine, gut; inner tube; (mil) communication trench

boycottage [bɔjkɔtaʒ] *m* boycott

boycotter [bɔjkɔte] *tr* to boycott

boy-scout [bɔjskut] *m* (*pl* **-scouts**) boy scout

b. p. f. *abbr* (**bon pour francs**) value in francs

bracelet [braslɛ] *m* bracelet; wristband; **bracelet de caoutchouc** rubber band; **bracelet à breloques** charm bracelet; **bracelet de cheville** anklet

bracelet-montre [braslɛmɔ̃tr] *m* (*pl* **bracelets-montres**) wrist watch

braconnage [brakɔnaʒ] *m* poaching

braconner [brakɔne] *intr* to poach

bracon·nier [brakɔnje] **-nière** [njɛr] *mf* poacher

brader [brade] *tr* to sell off

braderie [bradəri] *f* clearance sale; garage sale

braguette [bragɛt] *f* fly (*of trousers*)

brahmane [brɑman] *m* Brahman

brai [brɛ] *m* resin, pitch

braille [brɑj] *m* braille

brailler [brɑje] *tr & intr* to bawl

brail·leur [brɑjœr] **-leuse** [jøz] *adj* loudmouthed ‖ *mf* loudmouth

braiment [brɛmɑ̃] *m* bray

braire [brɛr] §68 (usually used in: *inf; ger; pp;* 3d *sg & pl*) *intr* to bray

braise [brɛz] *f* embers, coals

braiser [brɛze] *tr* to braise

braisière [brɛzjɛr] *f* braising pan

bramer [brame] *intr* to bell

bran [brɑ̃] *m* bran; (slang) dung; **bran de scie** sawdust

brancard [brɑ̃kar] *m* stretcher; shaft (*of carriage*)

brancardier [brɑ̃kardje] *m* stretcher-bearer

branche [brɑ̃ʃ] *f* branch; blade (*of a scissors*); leg (*of a compass*); temple (*side-piece of a pair of glasses*)

brancher [brɑ̃ʃe] *tr* to branch, fork; hook up, connect; (elec) to plug in ‖ *intr* to perch

brande [brɑ̃d] *f* heather; heath

brandir [brɑ̃dir] *tr* to brandish

brandon [brɑ̃dɔ̃] *m* torch; firebrand; **brandon de discorde** mischief-maker

bran·lant [brɑ̃lɑ̃] **-lante** [lɑ̃t] *adj* shaky, tottering, unsteady

branle [brɑ̃l] *m* oscillation; impetus; **mener le branle** to lead the dance; **mettre en branle** to set in motion

branle-bas [brɑ̃ləbɑ] *m invar* call to battle stations; bustle, commotion

branler [brɑ̃le] *tr* to shake (*the head*) ‖ *intr* to shake; oscillate; be loose (*said of tooth*); **branler dans le manche** to be about to fall

braque [brak] *adj* (coll) featherbrained ‖ *mf* (coll) featherbrain ‖ *m* pointer (*dog*)

braquer [brake] *tr* to aim, point; fix (*the eyes*); turn (*a steering wheel*); **braquer contre** to turn (*e.g., an audience*) against ‖ *intr* to steer

bras [brɑ] *m* arm; handle; shaft; **à bras raccourcis** violently; **bras de mer** sound (*passage of water*); **bras de pick-up** pickup arm, tone arm; **bras dessus bras dessous** arm in arm; **en bras de chemise** in shirt sleeves; **être resté sur les bras de** to be left on the hands of; **manquer de bras** to be short-handed

braser [braze] *tr* to braze

brasero [brazero] *m* brazier

brasier [brazje] *m* glowing coals; blaze

bras-le-corps [brɑlkɔr] *m*—**à bras-le-corps** around the waist

brassage [brasaʒ] *m* brewing

brasse [brɑs], [bras] *f* fathom; breast stroke

brassée [brase] *f* armful; stroke (*in swimming*)

brasser [brase] *tr* to brew

brasserie [brasri] *f* brewery; restaurant, lunchroom

bras·seur [brasœr] **-seuse** [søz] *mf* brewer; swimmer doing the breast stroke; **brasseur d'affaires** person with many irons in the fire

brassière [brasjɛr] *f* sleeved shirt (*for an infant*); shoulder strap; **brassière de sauvetage** life preserver

bravache [bravaʃ] *adj & m* braggart

bravade [bravad] *f* bravado

brave [brav] *adj* brave ‖ (when standing before noun) *adj* worthy, honest ‖ *m* brave man

braver [brave] *tr* to brave

bravoure [bravur] *f* bravery, gallantry

break [brɛk] *m* station wagon

brebis [brəbi] *f* ewe; sheep, lamb; **brebis galeuse** black sheep

brèche [brɛʃ] *f* breach (*in a wall*); gap (*between mountains*); nick (*e.g., on china*); (fig) dent (*in a fortune*); **battre en brèche** to batter; (fig) to disparage; **mourir sur la brèche** to go down fighting

bredouille [brəduj]—**rentrer** or **revenir bredouille** to return empty-handed

bredouiller [brəduje] *tr* to stammer out (*an excuse*) ‖ *intr* to mumble

bref [brɛf] **brève** [brɛv] *adj* brief, short; curt ‖ *m* papal brief ‖ *f* short syllable;

brèves et longues dots and dashes ‖ **bref** *adv* briefly, in short

brelan [brəlɑ̃] *m* (cards) three of a kind

breloque [brəlɔk] *f* trinket, charm; **battre la breloque** to sound the all clear; keep irregular time; (coll) to have a screw loose somewhere

brème [brɛm] *f* (ichth) bream

Brésil [brezil] *m*—**le Brésil** Brazil

brési·lien [breziljɛ̃] **-lienne** [ljɛn] *adj* Brazilian ‖ (*cap*) *mf* Brazilian

Bretagne [brətaɲ] *f* Brittany; **la Bretagne** Brittany

bretelle [brətɛl] *f* strap, sling; access route; ramp; **bretelle de liaison** (aer) exit taxiway; **bretelles** suspenders

bre·ton [brətɔ̃] **-tonne** [tɔn] *adj* Breton ‖ *m* Breton (*language*) ‖ (*cap*) *mf* Breton (*person*)

bretteur [brɛtœr] *m* swashbuckler

bretzel [brɛtzɛl] *m* pretzel

breuvage [brœvaʒ] *m* beverage, drink

brevet [brəvɛ] *m* diploma; license; (mil) commission; **brevet d'invention** patent

breve·té -tée [brəvte] *adj* commissioned; patented; **non breveté** noncommissioned ‖ *m* commissioned officer

breveter [brəvte] §34 *tr* to patent

bréviaire [brevjɛr] *m* (eccl) breviary

bribe [brib] *f* hunk of bread; **bribes** scraps, leavings, fragments

bric [brik] *m*—**de bric et de broc** with odds and ends; somehow

bric-à-brac [brikabrak] *m invar* secondhand merchandise; junk shop

brick [brik] *m* brig (*kind of ship*)

bricolage [brikɔlaʒ] *m* do-it-yourself

bricole [brikɔl] *f* trifle

bricoler [brikɔle] *intr* to do odd jobs; putter around

brico·leur [brikɔlœr] **-leuse** [løz] *mf* jack-of-all-trades ‖ *m* handyman

bride [brid] *f* bridle; strap; clamp; **à toute bride** or **à bride abattue** full speed ahead

bridge [bridʒ] *m* (cards, dentistry) bridge

bridger [bridʒe] *intr* to play bridge

brid·geur [bridʒœr] **-geuse** [ʒøz] *mf* bridge player

briefing [brifiŋ] *m* briefing

brièvement [brijɛvmɑ̃] *adv* briefly

brièveté [brijɛvte] *f* brevity

brigade [brigad] *f* brigade

brigadier [brigadje] *m* corporal; police sergeant; noncom

brigand [brigɑ̃] *m* brigand

brigantin [brigɑ̃tɛ̃] *m* brigantine

brigue [brig] *f* intrigue, lobbying

briguer [brige] *tr* to influence underhandedly; lobby for (*s.th.*); court (*favor, votes*)

brigueur [brigœr] *m* schemer

bril·lant [brijɑ̃] **-lante** [jɑ̃t] *adj* brilliant, bright ‖ *m* brilliancy, luster; fingernail polish

briller [brije] *intr* to shine; sparkle; **faire briller** to show (*s.o.*) off

brimade [brimad] *f* hazing

brimborion [brɛ̃bɔrjɔ̃] *m* mere trifle

brimer [brime] *tr* to haze
brin [brɛ̃] *m* blade; sprig, shoot; staple (*of hemp, linen*); strand (*of rope*); belt (*of pulley*); (coll) (little) bit, e.g., **un brin d'air** a (little) bit of air; **ne . . . brin** §90 (archaic) not a bit, not a single; **un beau brin de fille** (coll) a fine figure of a girl
brinde [brɛ̃d] *f* (archaic) toast
brindille [brɛ̃dij] *f* twig, sprig
brioche [brijɔʃ] *f* brioche, breakfast roll
brique [brik] *f* brick
briquer [brike] *tr* (coll) to polish up, scour
briquet [brikɛ] *m* lighter
briquetage [briktaʒ] *m* brickwork
briqueter [brikte] §34 *tr* to brick (up)
briqueterie [brikətri] *f* brickyard
briqueteur [briktœr] *m* bricklayer
brisant [brizɑ̃] *m* breakers; **brisants** surf
brise [briz] *f* breeze
bri·sé -sée [brize] *adj* broken; folding (*door*) ‖ *fpl* see **brisées**
brise-bise [brizbiz] *m invar* weather stripping; café curtain
brisées [brize] *fpl* track, footsteps
brise-glace [brizglas] *m invar* (naut) icebreaker
brise-jet [brizʒɛ] *m invar* (anti)splash attachment (*for water faucet*), spray filter
brise-lames [brizlam] *m invar* breakwater
brisement [brizmɑ̃] *m* breaking
briser [brize] *tr, intr, & ref* to break
brise-tout [briztu] *m invar* (coll) butterfingers, clumsy person
bri·seur [brizœr] **-seuse** [zøz] *mf* breaker (*person*); **briseur de grève** strikebreaker
brise-vent [brizvɑ̃] *m invar* windbreak
brisque [brisk] *f* service stripe
bristol [bristɔl] *m* Bristol board, pasteboard; visiting card
brisure [brizyr] *f* break; joint
britannique [britanik] *adj* British ‖ (*cap*) *mf* Briton
broc [bro] *m* pitcher, jug
brocanter [brɔkɑ̃te] *tr* to buy, sell, or trade (*secondhand articles*) ‖ *intr* to deal in secondhand articles
brocan·teur [brɔkɑ̃tœr] **-teuse** [tøz] *mf* secondhand dealer
brocard [brɔkar] *m* lampoon, brickbat; (zool) brocket; **lancer des brocards** to make sarcastic remarks, gibe
brocart [brɔkar] *m* brocade
broche [brɔʃ] *f* brooch; pin; (culin) spit, skewer
bro·ché -chée [brɔʃe] *adj* paperback, paperbound
brocher [brɔʃe] *tr* to brocade; sew (*book bindings*); (coll) to hurry through
brochet [brɔʃɛ] *m* (ichth) pike
brochette [brɔʃɛt] *f* skewer; skewerful; string (*of decorations*)
bro·cheur [brɔʃœr] **-cheuse** [ʃøz] *mf* bookbinder ‖ *f* stapler
brochure [brɔʃyr] *f* brochure, pamphlet
brocoli [brɔkɔli] *m* broccoli
brodequin [brɔdkɛ̃] *m* buskin
broder [brɔde] *tr & intr* to embroider

broderie [brɔdri] *f* embroidery
brome [brom] *m* (chem) bromine
bromure [brɔmyr] *m* bromide
bronche [brɔ̃ʃ] *f* bronchial tube
broncher [brɔ̃ʃe] *intr* to stumble; flinch; to grumble
bronchique [brɔ̃ʃik] *adj* bronchial
bronchite [brɔ̃ʃit] *f* bronchitis
bronze [brɔ̃z] *m* bronze
bron·zé -zée [brɔ̃ze] *adj* bronze; sun-tanned
bronzer [brɔ̃ze] *tr & ref* to bronze; sun-tan
brook [bruk] *m* (turf) water jump
broquette [brɔkɛt] *f* brad, tack
brossage [brɔsaʒ] *m* brushing
brosse [brɔs] *f* brush; **brosse à cheveux** hairbrush; **brosse à dents** toothbrush; **brosse à habits** clothesbrush; **brosse de chiendent** scrubbing brush; **brosses** shrubs, bushes
brosser [brɔse] *tr* to brush; paint the broad outlines of (*a picture*); (fig) to sketch; (slang) to beat, conquer ‖ *ref* to brush one's clothes; (coll) to skimp, to scrimp
brouet [bruɛ] *m* gruel, broth
brouette [bruɛt] *f* wheelbarrow
brouetter [bruɛte] *tr* to carry in a wheelbarrow
brouhaha [bruaa] *m* (coll) babel, hubbub
brouillage [brujaʒ] *m* (rad) jamming, jam
brouillamini [brujamini] *m* (coll) mess
brouillard [brujar] *adj masc* blotting (*paper*) ‖ *m* fog, mist; (com) daybook
brouillasse [brujas] *f* (coll) drizzle
brouillasser [brujase] *intr* (coll) to drizzle
brouille [bruj] *f* discord, misunderstanding
brouiller [bruje] *tr* to mix up; jam (*a broadcast*); scramble (*eggs*); **brouiller mes** (ses, etc.) **pistes** to cover my (his, etc.) tracks ‖ *ref* to quarrel; to cloud over
brouil·lon [brujɔ̃] **-lonne** [jɔn] *adj* crackpot; blundering; at loose ends ‖ *mf* crackpot ‖ *m* scratch pad; draft; outline
broussailles [brusɑj] *fpl* underbrush, brushwood; **en broussailles** disheveled
broussail·leux [brusɑjø] **-leuse** [jøz] *adj* bushy
broussard [brusar] *m* (coll) bushman, colonist
brousse [brus] *f* veldt, bush
broutage [brutaʒ] *m* grazing (*of animal*); ratatat (*of a machine*)
brouter [brute] *intr* to browse, graze; jerk, grab (*said of clutch, cutting tool, brake*)
broutille [brutij] *f* twig; trifle, bauble
broyage [brwajaʒ] *m* grinding, crushing
broyer [brwaje] §47 *tr* to grind, crush; **broyer du noir** (coll) to be down in the dumps
broyeur [brwajœr] **broyeuse** [brwajøz] *adj* grinding, crushing ‖ *mf* grinder, crusher; **broyeur d'ordures** garbage disposal ‖ *f* (mach) grinder
bru [bry] *f* daughter-in-law
bruant [bryɑ̃] *m* (orn) bunting; **bruant jaune** yellowhammer
brucelles [brysɛl] *fpl* tweezers
brugnon [bryɲɔ̃] *m* nectarine

bruine [brчin] *f* drizzle
bruiner [brчine] *intr* to drizzle
bruire [brчir] (usually used in: *inf; 3d sg pres ind* **bruit;** 3d *sg & pl imperf ind* **bruyait** or **bruissait, bruyaient** or **bruissaient**) *intr* to rustle; to hum, buzz; to splash
bruissement [brчismᾶ] *m* rustling
bruit [brчi] *m* noise; stir, fuss; **le bruit court que** it is rumored that
bruitage [brчitaʒ] *m* sound effects
brû·lant [brylᾶ] **-lante** [lᾶt] *adj* burning; ardent; ticklish (*question*)
brû·lé -lée [bryle] *adj* burned ‖ *m* smell of burning; burned taste ‖ *f* (slang) beating
brûle-gueule [brylgœl] *m invar* (slang) short pipe (*for smoking*)
brûle-parfum [brylparfœ̃] *m invar* incense burner
brûle-pourpoint [brylpurpwɛ̃]—**à brûle-pourpoint** point-blank
brûler [bryle] §97 *tr* to burn; burn out (*a fuse*); go through (*a red light*); pass (*another car*); roast (*coffee*); distill (*liquor*); **brûler la cervelle à qn** to blow s.o.'s brains out ‖ *intr* to burn, burn up; **je brûle de vous voir** I long to see you ‖ *ref* to burn up, be burned
brû·leur [brylœr] **-leuse** [løz] *mf* arsonist; distiller ‖ *m* (mach) burner; **brûleur à café** coffee roaster
brûloir [brylwar] *m* roaster
brûlure [brylyr] *f* burn
brume [brym] *f* fog, mist
brumer [bryme] *intr* to be foggy
bru·meux [brymø] **-meuse** [møz] *adj* foggy, misty
brun [brœ̃] **brune** [bryn] *adj* brown, dark brown (*hair*); brown (*eyes; beer*); dusky, swarthy (*skin*); tanned, brown (*complexion*); dark (*tobacco*) ‖ *m* brown, dark brown; dark-haired man ‖ *f* see **brune**
brunâtre [brynɑtr] *adj* brownish
brune [bryn] *f* brunette; twilight; ale, stout
bru·net [brynɛ] **-nette** [nɛt] *adj* black-haired ‖ *m* dark-haired man, brunet ‖ *f* brunette
bru·ni -nie [bryni] *adj* burnished, polished ‖ *m* burnishment, polish
brunir [brynir] *tr* to brown; burnish, polish ‖ *intr* to turn brown
brunissoir [bryniswar] *m* (mach) buffer
brusque [brysk] *adj* brusque; sudden; surprise (*attack*); quick (*movements; decision*)
brusquement [bryskəmᾶ] *adv* brusquely; abruptly, bluntly; suddenly, quickly
brusquer [bryske] *tr* to hurry, rush through; be blunt with
brusquerie [bryskri] *f* brusqueness; suddenness
brut [bryt] **brute** [bryt] *adj* crude, unpolished, unrefined, uncivilized; uncut (*diamond*); raw (*material*); dry (*champagne*); brown (*sugar*); gross (*weight*) ‖ *f* see **brute** ‖ **brut** *adv*—**peser brut** to have a gross weight of

bru·tal -tale [brytal] (*pl* **-taux** [to]) *adj* brutal, rough; outspoken; coarse, beastly ‖ *mf* brute, bully
brutaliser [brytalize] *tr* to bully; mistreat
brutalité [brytalite] *f* brutality; **brutalité policière** police brutality
brute [bryt] *f* brute
Bruxelles [brysɛl] *f* Brussels
bruxel·lois [brysɛlwa] **-loise** [lwaz] *adj* of Brussels ‖ (*cap*) *mf* native or inhabitant of Brussels
bruyamment [brчijamᾶ] *adv* noisily
bruyant [brчijᾶ] **bruyante** [brчijᾶt] *adj* noisy
bruyère [brчijɛr] *f* heather; heath
bu bue [by] *v* see **boire**
buanderie [bчᾶdəri] *f* laundry room
buan·dier [bчᾶdje] **-dière** [djɛr] *mf* laundry worker ‖ *f* laundress
bubonique [bybɔnik] *adj* bubonic
bûche [byʃ] *f* log; (slang) dunce; **bûche de Noël** yule log; cake decorated as a yule log; **ramasser une bûche** (slang) to take a tumble
bûcher [byʃe] *m* woodshed; pyre; stake (*e.g., for burning witches*) ‖ *tr* to rough-hew; (slang) to bone up on ‖ *intr* (slang) to keep on working; slave away ‖ *ref* (slang) to fight
bûche·ron [byʃrɔ̃] **-ronne** [rɔn] *mf* woodcutter ‖ *m* lumberjack
bûchette [byʃɛt] *f* stick of wood
bû·cheur [byʃœr] **-cheuse** [ʃøz] *mf* (coll) eager beaver
budget [bydʒɛ] *m* budget; **boucler son budget** (coll) to make ends meet
budgétaire [bydʒetɛr] *adj* budgetary
buée [bye] *f* steam, mist
buffet [byfɛ] *m* buffet; snack bar; station restaurant; **buffet de salades** salad bar; **danser devant le buffet** to miss a meal
buffle [byfl] *m* buffalo; **bufflonne** [byflɔn] *mf* water buffalo; Cape buffalo
bugle [bygl] *m* (mus) saxhorn; bugle ‖ *f* (bot) bugle
building [bildiŋ] *m* large office building, skyscraper
buire [bчir] *f* ewer
buis [bчi] *m* boxwood
buisson [bчisɔ̃] *m* bush
buisson·neux [bчisɔnø] **-neuse** [nøz] *adj* bushy
buisson·nier [bчisɔnje] **-nière** [njɛr] *adj*—**faire l'école buissonnière** (coll) to play hooky
bulbe [bylb] *m* bulb
bul·beux [bylbø] **-beuse** [bøz] *adj* bulbous
bulgare [bylgar] *adj* Bulgarian ‖ *m* Bulgarian (*language*) ‖ (*cap*) *mf* Bulgarian (*person*)
Bulgarie [bylgari] *f* Bulgaria; **la Bulgarie** Bulgaria
bulle [byl] *m* wrapping paper ‖ *f* bubble; blister; (eccl) bull
bulletin [byltɛ̃] *m* bulletin; ballot; **bulletin d'adhésion** membership blank; **bulletin de bagages** baggage check; **bulletin de**

commande order blank; **bulletin de naissance** birth certificate; **bulletin scolaire** report card

bul·leux [bylø] **-leuse** [løz] *adj* blistery

bure [byr] *m* mine shaft ‖ *f* drugget, sackcloth

bu·reau [byro] *m* (*pl* **-reaux**) desk; office; **bureau à cylindre** roll-top desk; **bureau ambulant** post-office car; **bureau d'aide sociale** welfare department; **bureau de dactylos** typing pool; **bureau de l'état civil** bureau of vital statistics; **bureau de location** box office; **bureau de placement** employment agency; **bureau de poste** post office; **bureau des objets trouvés** lost-and-found department; **bureau de tabac** tobacco shop; **bureau directoire** cabinet, committee; **deuxième bureau** intelligence division

bureaucrate [byrokrat] *mf* bureaucrat

bureaucratie [byrokrasi] *f* bureaucracy

bureaucratique [byrokratik] *adj* bureaucratic

burette [byrɛt] *f* cruet; oilcan

burin [byrɛ̃] *m* engraving; burin (*tool*)

burlesque [byrlɛsk] *adj* & *m* burlesque

bus [bys] *m* city bus

busard [byzar] *m* harrier, marsh hawk

busc [bysk] *m* whalebone

buse [byz] *f* buzzard

business [biznɛs] *m* (slang) work; (slang) complicated business

bus·qué -quée [byske] *adj* arched

buste [byst] *m* bust

but [by], [byt] *m* mark, goal, target; aim, end, purpose; point (*scored in game*);

aller droit au but to come straight to the point; **de but en blanc** point-blank

bu·té -tée [byte] *adj* obstinate, headstrong ‖ *f* abutment

buter [byte] *tr* to prop up; (slang) to bump off, kill ‖ *intr*—**buter contre** to bump into, stumble on ‖ *ref*—**se buter à** to butt up against; (fig) to be dead set on

buteur [bytœr] *m* scorer

butin [bytɛ̃] *m* booty; profits, savings

butiner [bytine] *tr* to pillage; gather honey from ‖ *intr* to pillage; gather honey (*said of bees*); **butiner dans** to browse among (*books*)

butoir [bytwar] *m* buffer, stop, catch

bu·tor [bytɔr] **-torde** [tɔrd] *mf* (slang) lout, good-for-nothing

butte [byt] *f* butte, knoll; **butte de tir** butt, mound (*for target practice*); **être en butte à** to be exposed to

butter [byte] *tr* to hill (*plants*)

buttoir [bytwar] *m* (agr) hiller

buty·reux -reuse [bytirø] **-reuse** [røz] *adj* buttery

buvable [byvabl] *adj* drinkable; (pharm) to be taken by mouth

buvard [byvar] *adj* blotting (*paper*) ‖ *m* blotter

buvette [byvɛt] *f* bar, fountain

buvette-buffet [byvɛtbyfɛ] *f* (coll) snack bar

bu·veur -veuse [byvœr] **-veuse** [vøz] *mf* drinker; **buveur d'eau** abstainer; vacationist at a spa

byzan·tin [bizɑ̃tɛ̃] **-tine** [tin] *adj* Byzantine

C

C, c [se] *m invar* third letter of the French alphabet

C / *abbr* (**compte**) account

ça [sa] *pron indef* (coll) that; **ah ça non!** no indeed!; **avec ça!** tell me another!; **ça y est** that's that; that's it, that's right; **comment ça!** how so?; **et avec ça?** what else?; **où ça,** where?

çà [sa] *adv*—**ah çà!** now then! **çà et là** here and there

cabale [kabal] *f* cabal, intrigue

cabaler [kabale] *intr* to cabal, intrigue

caban [kabɑ̃] *m* (naut) peacoat

cabane [kaban] *f* cabin, hut

cabanon [kabanɔ̃] *m* hut, padded cell

cabaret [kabarɛ] *m* tavern; cabaret, night club; liquor closet

cabas [kabɑ] *m* basket; shopping bag

cabestan [kabɛstɑ̃] *m* capstan

cabillaud [kabijo] *m* haddock; (coll) fresh cod

cabine [kabin] *f* cabin (*of ship or airplane*);

bathhouse; car (*of elevator*); cab (*of locomotive or truck*); **cabine téléphonique** telephone booth

cabinet [kabinɛ] *m* cabinet (*small room; room for displaying collections; political committee; antique chest of drawers*); toilet, rest room; storeroom closet; clientele, practice; office (*of a professional person*); study (*of a scholar*); staff (*of a cabinet officer*); **cabinet d'aisance** rest room; **cabinet de débarras** storeroom closet; **cabinet de toilette** powder room; **cabinets** rest rooms

câble [kɑbl] *m* cable; **câble de démarrage** jumper cable

câbler [kɑble] *tr* & *intr* to cable

câblier [kɑblije] *m* cable ship

câblodistribution [kɑblɔdistribysjɔ̃] *f* cable television

câblogramme [kɑblɔgram] *m* cablegram

cabo·chard [kabɔʃar] **-charde** [ʃard] *adj* obstinate, pigheaded

caboche [kabɔʃ] *f* hobnail; (coll) noodle (*head*)

cabochon [kabɔʃɔ̃] *m* uncut gem; stud, upholstery nail

cabot [kabo] *m* (ichth) miller's-thumb, bullhead; (coll) ham (actor)

cabotage [kabɔtaʒ] *m* coastal navigation, coasting trade

cabo·tin [kabɔtɛ̃] **-tine** [tin] *mf* barnstormer; (coll) ham (actor); **cabotin de la politique** (coll) corny politician, political orator given to histrionics

cabotinage [kabɔtinaʒ] *m* barnstorming; (coll) ham acting

cabotiner [kabɔtine] *intr* to barnstorm; (coll) to play to the grandstand

cabrer [kabre] *tr* to make (*a horse*) rear; nose up (*a plane*) ‖ *ref* to rear; kick over the traces; (aer) to nose up

cabri [kabri] *m* (zool) kid

cabriole [kabrijɔl] *f* caper

cabrioler [kabrijɔle] *intr* to caper

caca [kaka] *m*—**caca d'oie** greenish-yellow; **faire caca** (*children's language*) to go potty

cacahouète or **cacahuète** [kakawɛt] *f* peanut

cacao [kakao] *m* cocoa; cocoa bean

cacaotier [kakaɔtje] *m* (bot) cacao

cacaoyer [kakaɔje] *m* (bot) cacao

cacarder [kakarde] *intr* to cackle

cacatoès [kakatɔɛs] or **cacatois** [kakatwa] *m* cockatoo

cachalot [kaʃalo] *m* sperm whale

cache [kaʃ] *m* masking tape ‖ *f* hiding place

cache-cache [kaʃkaʃ] *m invar* hide-and-seek

cache-col [kaʃkɔl] *m invar* scarf

cachemire [kaʃmir] *m* cashmere

cache-nez [kaʃne] *m invar* muffler

cache-poussière [kaʃpusjɛr] *m invar* duster (*overgarment*)

cacher [kaʃe] *tr* to hide; **cacher q.ch. à qn** to hide s.th. from s.o. ‖ *ref* to hide; **se cacher à** to hide from; **se cacher de q.ch.** to make a secret of s.th.

cache-radiateur [kaʃradjatœr] *m invar* radiator cover

cache-sexe [kaʃsɛks] *m invar* G-string; minimum (male) swimwear

cachet [kaʃɛ] *m* seal; postmark; fee; price of a lesson; meal ticket; (pharm, phila) cachet; (fig) seal; stylishness; **payer au cachet** to pay a set fee

cacheter [kaʃte] §34 *tr* to seal, seal up; seal with wax

cachette [kaʃɛt] *f* hiding place; **en cachette** secretly

cachot [kaʃo] *m* dungeon; prison

cacophonie [kakɔfɔni] *f* cacophony

cactier [kaktje] or **cactus** [kaktys] *m* cactus

c.-à-d. *abbr* (**c'est-à-dire**) that is

cadastre [kadastr] *m* land-survey register

cadavre [kadavr] *m* corpse, cadaver; (slang) dead soldier (*bottle*)

ca·deau [kado] *m* (*pl* **-deaux**) gift

cadenas [kadna] *m* padlock

cadenasser [kadnase] *tr* to padlock

cadence [kadɑ̃s] *f* cadence, rhythm, time; output (*of worker, of factory; etc.*); **cadence de tir** rate of firing

cadencer [kadɑ̃se] §51 *tr* to cadence ‖ *intr* to call out cadence

ca·det [kadɛ] **-dette** [dɛt] *adj* younger ‖ *mf* youngest; junior; (sports) player fifteen to eighteen years old; **le cadet de mes soucis** (coll) the least of my worries ‖ *m* caddy; (mil) cadet; younger brother; younger son ‖ *f* younger sister; younger daughter

cadmium [kadmjɔm] *m* cadmium

cadrage [kadraʒ] *m* (mov, telv) framing; (phot) centering

cadran [kadrɑ̃] *m* dial; **cadran d'appel** telephone dial; **cadran solaire** sundial; **faire le tour du cadran** to sleep around the clock

cadre [kadr] *m* frame; framework; setting; outline, framework (*of a literary work*); limits, scope (*of activities or duties*); (mil) cadre; (naut) cot; **cadres** officials; (mil) regulars; **cadres sociaux** memorable dates or events

cadrer [kadre] *tr* to frame (*film*) ‖ *intr* to conform, tally

cadreur [kadrœr] *m* (mov) cameraman

ca·duc **-duque** [kadyk] *adj* decrepit, frail; outlived (*custom*); deciduous (*leaves*); lapsed (*insurance policy*); (law) null and void

caducée [kadyse] *m* caduceus

C.A.F. *abbr* (**coût, assurance, fret**) C.I.F. (*cost, insurance, and freight*)

ca·fard [kafar] **-farde** [fard] *adj* sanctimonious ‖ *mf* hypocrite; (coll) squealer ‖ *m* (coll) cockroach; (coll) blues

café [kafe] *m* coffee; café; coffeehouse; **café au lait** coffee with hot milk; **café chantant** music hall (*with tables*); **café complet** coffee, hot milk, rolls, butter, and jam; **café crème** white coffee; **café décaféiné** decaffeinated coffee; **café en poudre** instant coffee; **café express** espresso coffee; **café filtre** drip coffee; **café instantané** instant coffee; **café liégeois** coffee ice cream topped with whipped cream; **café lyophilisé** freeze-dried coffee; **café nature, café noir** black coffee; **café vert** unroasted coffee; **café soluble** powdered coffee

café-concert [kafekɔ̃sɛr] *m* (*pl* **cafés-concerts**) music hall (*with tables*), cabaret

caféier [kafeje] *m* coffee plant

caféière [kafejɛr] *f* coffee plantation

caféine [kafein] *f* caffeine

cafétéria [kafeterja] *f* cafeteria

cafe·tier [kaftje] **-tière** [tjɛr] *mf* café owner ‖ *f* coffeepot

cafouiller [kafuje] *intr* (slang) to miss (*said of engine*); (slang) to flounder around

cage [kaʒ] *f* cage; **cage d'un ascenseur** elevator shaft; **cage d'un escalier** stairwell; **cage thoracique** thoracic cavity; **en cage** (coll) in the clink, in the pen

cageot [kaʒo] *m* crate

ca·gnard [kaɲar] -gnarde [ɲard] adj indo-lent, lazy ‖ m (coll) sunny spot
ca·gneux [kaɲø] -gneuse [ɲøz] adj knock-kneed; pigeon-toed
cagnotte [kaɲɔt] f kitty, pool
ca·got [kago] -gotte [gɔt] adj hypocritical ‖ mf hypocrite
cagoule [kagul] f cowl; hood (with eyeholes)
cahier [kaje] m notebook; cahier à feuilles mobiles loose-leaf notebook; cahier des charges (com) specifications; cahier (d'imprimerie) (bb) signature, gathering
cahin-caha [kaɛ̃kaa] adv (coll) so-so
cahot [kao] m jolt, bump
cahoter [kaɔte] tr & intr to jolt
caho·teux [kaɔtø] -teuse [tøz] adj bumpy (road)
cahute [kayt] f hut, shack
caille [kɑj] f quail
cail·lé -lée [kɑje] adj curdled ‖ m curd
caillebotis [kɑjbɔti] m boardwalk; (mil) duckboard; (naut) grating
caillebotte [kɑjbɔt] f curds
caillebotter [kɑjbɔte] tr & intr to curdle
cailler [kɑje] tr & ref to clot, curdle, curd
caillot [kɑjo] m clot; blood clot
cail·lou [kaju] m (pl -loux) pebble; (coll) bald head; caillou du Rhin rhinestone
caillou·teux [kajutø] -teuse [tøz] adj stony (road); pebbly (beach)
cailloutis [kajuti] m crushed stone, gravel
Caïn [kaɛ̃] m Cain
Caire [kɛr] m—Le Caire Cairo
caisse [kɛs] f chest, box; case (for packing; of a clock or piano); chestful, boxful; till, cash register, coffer, safe; cashier, cash-ier's window; desk (in a hotel); caisse à eau water tank; caisse claire snare drum; caisse d'épargne savings bank; caisse des écoles scholarship fund; caisse de sortie checkout counter; grosse caisse bass drum; bass drummer; petite caisse petty cash
caisson [kɛsɔ̃] m caisson; crate, box
cajoler [kaʒɔle] tr to cajole, wheedle
cajolerie [kaʒɔlri] f cajolery
cajou [kaʒu] m cashew nut
cake [kɛk] m fruit cake
cal [kal] m (pl cals) callus, callosity; cal vicieux badly knitted bone
calage [kalaʒ] m wedging, chocking; stall-ing (of motor)
calamité [kalamite] f calamity
calami·teux [kalamitø] -teuse [tøz] adj ca-lamitous
calandre [kalɑ̃dr] f mangle (for clothes); calender (for paper); grill (for car radia-tor); (ent) weevil; (orn) lark
calandrer [kalɑ̃dre] tr to calender
calcaire [kalkɛr] adj calcareous; chalky; hard (water) ‖ m limestone
calcifier [kalsifje] tr & ref to calcify
calciner [kalsine] tr & ref to burn to a cinder
calcium [kalsjɔm] m calcium
calcul [kalkyl] m calculation; (math, pathol) calculus; calcul biliaire gallstone; calcul

mental mental arithmetic; calcul rénal kidney stone
calcula·teur [kalkylatœr] -trice [tris] adj calculating ‖ mf calculator (person) ‖ m (mach) calculator ‖ f adding machine; calculatrice de poche pocket calculator
calculer [kalkyle] tr & intr to calculate
calculette [kalkylɛt] f pocket calculator
cale [kal] f wedge, chock; hold (of ship); cale de construction stocks; cale sèche dry dock
ca·lé -lée [kale] adj stalled; (coll) well-informed; (slang) involved, difficult; calé en (coll) strong in, up on
calebasse [kalbɑs] f calabash
calèche [kalɛʃ] f open carriage
caleçon [kalsɔ̃] m drawers, shorts; caleçon de bain swimming trunks
calembour [kalɑ̃bur] m pun
calendes [kalɑ̃d] fpl calends; aux calendes grecques (coll) when pigs fly
calendrier [kalɑ̃drije] m calendar
calepin [kalpɛ̃] m notebook
caler [kale] tr to wedge, chock; jam; stall; lower (sail); (naut) to draw ‖ intr to stall (said of motor); (coll) to give in ‖ ref to stall; get nicely settled
calfater [kalfate] tr to caulk
calfeutrer [kalføtre] tr to stop up ‖ ref to shut oneself up
calibre [kalibr] m caliber
calibrer [kalibre] tr to calibrate
calice [kalis] m chalice; (bot) calyx
calicot [kaliko] m calico; sign, banner; (slang) sales clerk
califat [kalifa] m caliphate
calife [kalif] m caliph
Californie [kalifɔrni] f California; la basse Californie Lower California; la Califor-nie California
califourchon [kalifurʃɔ̃] m—à califourchon astride, astraddle; s'asseoir à califour-chon to straddle
câ·lin [kɑlɛ̃] -line [lin] adj coaxing; caress-ing
câliner [kaline] tr to coax; caress
cal·leux [kalø] -leuse [løz] adj callous, cal-loused
callisthénie [kalisteni] f calisthenics
cal·mant [kalmɑ̃] -mante [mɑ̃t] adj calm-ing ‖ m sedative
calmar [kalmar] m squid
calme [kalm] adj & m calm
calmement [kalməmɑ̃] adv calmly
calmer [kalme] tr to calm ‖ ref to become calm, calm down
calmir [kalmir] intr to abate
calomnie [kalɔmni] f calumny, slander
calomnier [kalɔmnje] tr to calumniate
calorie [kalɔri] f calory
calorifère [kalɔrifɛr] adj heating, heat-conducting ‖ m heater; calorifère à air chaud hot-air heater; calorifère à eau chaude hot-water heater
calorifuge [kalɔrifyʒ] adj insulating ‖ m insulator
calorifuger [kalɔrifyʒe] §38 tr to insulate

calorique [kalɔrik] *adj* caloric
calot [kalo] *m* policeman's hat, kepi
calotte [kalɔt] *f* skullcap; dome; (coll) box on the ear; (coll) clergy; **calotte des cieux** vault of heaven; **flanquer une calotte à** (coll) to box on the ear
calotter [kalɔte] *tr* (coll) to box on the ear, cuff; (slang) to snitch
calque [kalk] *m* tracing; decal; word-for-word correspondence (*between two languages*); slavish imitation; spitting image
calquer [kalke] *tr* to trace; imitate slavishly
calumet [kalymɛ] *m* calumet; **calumet de paix** peace pipe
calvados [kalvados] *m* applejack
calvaire [kalvɛr] *m* calvary
calviniste [kalvinist] *adj & mf* Calvinist
calvitie [kalvisi] *f* baldness
camarade [kamarad] *mf* comrade; **camarade de chambre** roommate; **camarade de travail** fellow worker; **camarade d'étude** schoolmate
camaraderie [kamaradri] *f* comradeship; camaraderie, fellowship
ca·mard [kamar] **-marde** [mard] *adj* snub-nosed
cambouis [kābwi] *m* axle grease
cambrer [kābre] *tr* to curve, arch
cambrioler [kābrijɔle] *tr* to break into, burglarize
cambrio·leur [kābrijɔlœr] **-leuse** [løz] *mf* burglar
cambrure [kābryr] *f* curve, arch
cambuse [kābyz] *f* (naut) storeroom between decks
came [kam] *f* cam
ca·mé -mée [kame] *mf* drug user
camée [kame] *m* cameo
caméléon [kameleõ] *m* chameleon
camélia [kamelja] *m* camellia
camelot [kamlo] *m* cheap woolen cloth; huckster; newsboy
camelote [kamlɔt] *f* shoddy merchandise, rubbish, junk; **camelote alimentaire** junk food
caméra [kamera] *f* (mov, telv) camera
camion [kamjõ] *m* truck; paint bucket; **camion à remorque** trailer (truck); **camion à semi-remorque** semitrailer; **camion citerne** fuel truck; **camion de déménagement** moving van; **camion d'enregistrement** (mov) sound truck; **camion de remorquage** tow truck
camion-benne [kamjõbɛn] *m* (*pl* **camions-bennes**) dump truck
camion-citerne [kamjõsitɛrn] *m* (*pl* **camions-citernes**) tank truck
camion-grue [kamjõgry] *m* (*pl* **camions-grues**) tow truck
camionnage [kamjɔnaʒ] *m* trucking
camionner [kamjɔne] *tr* to truck
camionnette [kamjɔnɛt] *f* van; **camionnette de police** police wagon; **camionnette sanitaire** mobile health unit
camionneur [kamjɔnœr] *m* trucker; truck-driver, teamster

camisole [kamizɔl] *f* camisole; **camisole de force** strait jacket
camomille [kamɔmij] *f* camomile
camouflage [kamuflaʒ] *m* camouflage
camoufler [kamufle] *tr* to camouflage
camp [kā] *m* camp; **camp de base** base camp; **camp de concentration** concentration camp; **camp de vacances** resort; **changer de camp** to change sides
campa·gnard [kāpaɲar] **-gnarde** [ɲard] *adj & mf* rustic
campagne [kāpaɲ] *f* campaign; country
cam·pé -pée [kāpe] *adj* encamped; **bien campé** well-built (*man*); clearly presented (*story*); firmly fixed
campement [kāpmā] *m* encampment; camping
camper [kāpe] *tr* to camp; (coll) to clap (*e.g., one's hat on one's head*); **camper là qn** (coll) to run out on s.o. ‖ *intr & ref* to camp
cam·peur [kāpœr] **-peuse** [pøz] *mf* camper
camphre [kāfr] *m* camphor
camping [kāpiŋ] *m* campground; trailer; camping; **camping sauvage** wilderness camping
campos [kāpo] *m* (coll) vacation, day off
campus [kāpys] *m* campus
ca·mus [kamy] **-muse** [myz] *adj* snub-nosed, pug-nosed, flat-nosed
Canada [kanada] *m*—**le Canada** Canada
cana·dien [kanadjē] **-dienne** [djɛn] *adj* Canadian ‖ *f* sheepskin jacket; station wagon ‖ (*cap*) *mf* Canadian
canaille [kanɑj] *adj* vulgar, coarse ‖ *f* rabble, riffraff; scoundrel
ca·nal [kanal] *m* (*pl* **-naux** [no]) canal; tube, pipe; ditch, drain; (rad, telv) channel; **canal de Panama** Panama Canal; **canal de Suez** [sɥɛz] Suez Canal; **par le canal de** through the good offices of
canapé [kanape] *m* sofa, davenport; (culin) canapé; **canapé à deux places** settee
canapé-lit [kanapeli] *m* (*pl* **canapés-lits**) sofa bed, day bed
canard [kanar] *m* duck; sugar soaked in coffee, brandy, etc.; (mus) false note; (coll) hoax; (coll) rag, paper; **canard mâle** drake; **canard publicitaire** publicity stunt; **canard sauvage** wild duck
canarder [kanarde] *tr* to snipe at ‖ *intr* to snipe
canari [kanari] *m* canary
cancan [kākā] *m* cancan (*dance*); (coll) gossip
cancaner [kākane] *intr* to quack; (coll) to gossip
canca·nier [kākanje] **-nière** [njɛr] *adj* (coll) catty ‖ *mf* (coll) gossip
cancer [kāsɛr] *m* cancer; **le Cancer** (astr, astrol) Cancer
cancé·reux [kāserø] **-reuse** [røz] *adj* cancerous
cancérigène [kāseriʒɛn] or **cancérogène** [kāserɔʒɛn] *adj* carcinogenic ‖ *m* carcinogen

cancre [kɑ̃kr] *m* (coll) dunce, lazy student; (coll) tightwad; (zool) crab

candélabre [kɑ̃delɑbr] *m* candelabrum; espaliered fruit tree; cactus; lamppost

candeur [kɑ̃dœr] *f* naïveté; guilelessness

candi [kɑ̃di] *adj* candied (*fruit*) ‖ *m* rock candy

candi·dat [kɑ̃dida] **-date** [dat] *mf* candidate; nominee

candidature [kɑ̃didatyr] *f* candidacy

candide [kɑ̃did] *adj* naïve; ingenuous

candir [kɑ̃dir] *intr*—**faire candir** to candy, crystallize (*sugar*) ‖ *ref* to candy, crystallize

cane [kan] *f* duck, female duck

caner [kane] *intr* (slang) to chicken out

caneton [kantɔ̃] *m* duckling

canette [kanɛt] *f* female duckling; beer bottle; **canette de bière** can of beer

canevas [kanva] *m* canvas (*cloth*); outline (*of novel, story, etc.*); embroidery netting; triangulation (*in artillery, in cartography*)

canezou [kanzu] *m* sleeveless lace blouse

caniche [kaniʃ] *m* poodle

canicule [kanikyl] *f* dog days

canif [kanif] *m* penknife, pocketknife

ca·nin [kanɛ̃] **-nine** [nin] *adj* canine ‖ *f* canine (*tooth*)

canitie [kanisi] *f* grayness (*of hair*)

cani·veau [kanivo] *m* (*pl* **-veaux**) gutter; (elec) conduit

cannaie [kanɛ] *f* sugar plantation

canne [kan] *f* cane; reed; cane, walking stick; **canne à pêche** fishing rod; **canne à sucre** sugar cane

canneberge [kanberʒ] *f* cranberry

canneler [kanle] §34 *tr* to groove; corrugate; flute (*a column*)

cannelle [kanɛl] *f* cinnamon; spout

cannelure [kanlyr] *f* groove, channel; corrugation; fluting (*of column*)

canner [kane] *tr* to cane (*a chair*)

cannibale [kanibal] *adj* & *mf* cannibal

canoë [kanɔe] *m* canoe

canoéiste [kanɔeist] *mf* canoeist

canon [kanɔ̃] *m* canon; cannon; gun barrel; tube; nozzle, spout; **canon à électrons** electron gun

cañon [kaɲɔ̃] *m* canyon

cano·nial -niale [kanɔnjal] *adj* (*pl* **-niaux** [njo]) canonical

canonique [kanɔnik] *adj* canonical

canoniser [kanɔnize] *tr* to canonize

canonnade [kanɔnad] *f* cannonade

canonner [kanɔne] *tr* to cannonade

canonnier [kanɔnje] *m* cannoneer

canonnière [kanɔnjɛr] *f* gunboat; popgun

canot [kano] *m* rowboat, launch; **canot automobile** speedboat, motorboat; **canot de sauvetage** lifeboat

canotage [kanɔtaʒ] *m* boating

canoter [kanɔte] *intr* to go boating

canotier [kanɔtje] *m* rower; skimmer

cant [kɑ̃] *m* cant

cantaloup [kɑ̃talu] *m* cantaloupe

cantate [kɑ̃tat] *f* cantata

cantatrice [kɑ̃tatris] *f* singer

cantilever [kɑ̃tilevœr] *adj* & *m* cantilever

cantine [kɑ̃tin] *f* canteen (*restaurant*); **cantine d'officier** officer's kit

cantique [kɑ̃tik] *m* canticle, ode; **cantique de Noël** (eccl) Christmas carol; **Cantique des Cantiques** (Bib) Song of Songs

canton [kɑ̃tɔ̃] *m* canton, district; **Cantons de l'Est** Eastern Townships (*in Canada*)

cantonade [kɑ̃tɔnad] *f* (theat) wings; **à la cantonade** (theat) offstage; **crier à la cantonade** to yell out (*s.th.*); **parler à la cantonade** to seem to be talking to oneself; (theat) to speak toward the wings

cantonnement [kɑ̃tɔnmɑ̃] *m* billeting

cantonner [kɑ̃tɔne] *tr* to billet

cantonnier [kɑ̃tɔnje] *m* road laborer; (rr) section hand

canular [kanylar] *m* (coll) practical joke, hoax, canard

canule [kanyl] *f* nozzle (*of syringe or injection needle*)

canuler [kanyle] *tr* (slang) to bother

caoutchouc [kautʃu] *m* rubber; **caoutchouc mousse** foam rubber; **caoutchoucs** rubbers, overshoes

caoutchouter [kautʃute] *tr* to rubberize

caoutchou·teux [kautʃutø] **-teuse** [tøz] *adj* rubbery

cap [kap] *m* cape, headland; bow, head (*of ship*); **Cap de Bonne Espérance** Cape of Good Hope; **mettre le cap sur** (coll) to set a course for

capable [kapabl] §93 *adj* capable

capacité [kapasite] *f* capacity; ability

cape [kap] *f* cape; hood; derby; outer leaf, wrapper (*of cigar*); **à la cape** (naut) hove to; **de cape et d'épée** cloak-and-dagger (*novel, movie, etc.*); **rire sous cape** to laugh up one's sleeve; **vendre sous cape** (coll) to sell under the counter

C.A.P.E.S. [kapɛs] *m* (acronym) (**certificat d'aptitude au professorat de l'enseignement du second degré**) secondary-school teachers certificate

capillaire [kapillɛr] *adj* capillary ‖ *m* (bot) maidenhair (*fern*)

capitaine [kapitɛn] *m* captain; **capitaine des pompiers** fire chief

capi·tal -tale [kapital] (*pl* **-taux** [to] **-tales**) *adj* capital, principal, essential; capital (*city; punishment; crime; letter*); death (*sentence*); deadly (*sins*) ‖ *m* capital, assets; principal (*main sum*); **avec de minces capitaux** on a shoestring; **capital circulant, capital d'exploitation** working capital; **capital fixe** fixed assets; **capitaux capital**; **capitaux fébriles** (slang) hot money ‖ *f* capital (*city; letter*)

capitalisation [kapitalizasjɔ̃] *f* capitalization; hoarding (*of money*)

capitaliser [kapitalize] *tr* to capitalize (*an income*); compound (*interest*) ‖ *intr* to hoard

capitalisme [kapitalism] *m* capitalism

capitaliste [kapitalist] *adj* capitalist ‖ *mf* capitalist; investor

capi·teux [kapitø] **-teuse** [tøz] *adj* heady (*wine, champagne, etc.*); intoxicating, alluring (*beauty; woman*)

Capitole [kapitɔl] *m* Capitol

capitonner [kapitɔne] *tr* to upholster

capituler [kapityle] *intr* to capitulate; parley

ca·pon [kapɔ̃] **-ponne** [pɔn] *adj* cowardly ‖ *mf* coward; sneak; tattletale

capo·ral [kapɔral] *m* (*pl* **-raux** [ro]) corporal; shag, caporal (*tobacco*); **Caporal a dit** . . . Simon says . . .

caporalisme [kapɔralism] *m* militarism; dictatorial government

capot [kapo] *adj invar* speechless, confused; (cards) trickless ‖ *m* cover; hood (*of automobile*); (naut) hatch

capotage [kapɔtaʒ] *m* overturning

capote [kapɔt] *f* coat with a hood; hood (*of baby carriage*); **capote anglaise** condom, prophylactic; **capote rebattable** (aut) folding top

capoter [kapɔte] *intr* to capsize; overturn, upset

câpre [kɑpr] *f* (bot) caper

caprice [kapris] *m* caprice, whim

capri·cieux [kaprisjø] **-cieuse** [sjøz] *adj* capricious, whimsical

Capricorne [kaprikɔrn] *m*—**le Capricorne** (astr, astrol) Capricorn

capsule [kapsyl] *f* capsule; bottle cap; percussion cap; (bot) capsule, pod; (rok) capsule; **capsule spatiale** space capsule; **capsules surrénales** adrenal glands

capsuler [kapsyle] *tr* to cap

capter [kapte] *tr* to win over; harness (*a river*); tap (*electric current; a water supply*); (rad, telv) to receive, pick up

capteur [kaptœr] *m* (rok) sensor

cap·tieux [kapsjø] **-tieuse** [sjøz] *adj* captious, insidious; specious

cap·tif [kaptif] **-tive** [tiv] *adj & mf* captive

captiver [kaptive] *tr* to captivate

captivité [kaptivite] *f* captivity

capture [kaptyr] *f* capture

capturer [kaptyre] *tr* to capture

capuce [kapys] *m* (eccl) pointed hood

capuchon [kapyʃɔ̃] *m* hood (*of coat*); cap (*of pen*); (aut) valve cap; (eccl) cowl

capucine [kapysin] *f* nasturtium

caque [kak] *f* keg, barrel

caquet [kakɛ] *m* cackle

caqueter [kakte] §34 *intr* to cackle; gossip

car [kar] *m* bus, sightseeing bus, interurban; **car de police** patrol wagon; **car sonore** loudspeaker truck ‖ *conj* for, because

carabe [karab] *m* ground beetle

carabine [karabin] *f* carbine

carabi·né -née [karabine] *adj* (coll) violent (*wind, cold, criticism*)

caraco [karako] *m* loose blouse

caractère [karaktɛr] *m* character; **caractères gras** (typ) boldface; **caractères penchés** (typ) italics

caractériser [karakterize] *tr* to characterize

caractéristique [karakteristik] *adj & f* characteristic

carafe [karaf] *f* carafe; **rester en carafe** (slang) to be left out in the cold

carafon [karafɔ̃] *m* small carafe

caraïbe [karaib] *adj* Caribbean, Carib ‖ (*cap*) *mf* Carib (*person*)

carambolage [karɑ̃bɔlaʒ] *m* jostling; (coll) bumping (*e.g., of autos*)

caramboler [karɑ̃bɔle] *tr* (coll) to strike, bump into ‖ *intr* (billiards) to carom

caramel [karamɛl] *m* caramel

carapace [karapas] *f* turtle shell, carapace

carapater [karapate] *ref* (slang) to beat it

carat [kara] *m* carat

caravane [karavan] *f* caravan; house trailer; group (*of tourists*)

caravaning [karavaniŋ] *m* trailer camping

caravansérail [karavɑ̃seraj] *m* caravansary; (fig) world crossroads

caravelle [karavɛl] *f* caravel

carbonade [karbɔnad] *f* see **carbonnade**

carbone [karbɔn] *m* carbon

carbonique [karbɔnik] *adj* carbonic

carboniser [karbɔnize] *tr* to carbonize, char

carbonnade [karbɔnad] *f* charcoal-grilled steak (ham, etc.); beef and onion stew (*in northern France*); **à la carbonnade** charcoal-grilled

carburant [karbyrɑ̃] *m* motor fuel

carburateur [karbyratœr] *m* carburetor

carbure [karbyr] *m* carbide

carburéacteur [karbyreaktœr] *m* jet fuel

carcan [karkɑ̃] *m* pillory

carcasse [karkas] *f* skeleton; framework; (coll) carcass

cardan [kardɑ̃] *m* (mach) universal joint

carde [kard] *f* card; leaf rib; teasel head

carder [karde] *tr* to card

cardiaque [kardjak] *adj & mf* cardiac

cardi·nal -nale [kardinal] *adj & m* (*pl* **-naux** [no]) cardinal

cardiogramme [kardjɔgram] *m* cardiogram

carême [karɛm] *m* Lent; **de carême** Lenten; **faire carême** to fast during Lent

carême-prenant [karɛmprənɑ̃] *m* (*pl* **carêmes-prenants**) Shrovetide

carence [karɑ̃s] *f* lack, deficiency; failure

carène [karɛn] *f* hull

caréner [karene] §10 *tr* to streamline; (naut) to careen

caren·tiel -tielle [karɑ̃sjɛl] *adj* deficiency (*disease*)

cares·sant [karɛsɑ̃] **-sante** [sɑ̃t] *adj* caressing; lovable; nice to pet; soothing (*e.g., voice*)

caresse [karɛs] *f* caress; endearment

caresser [karɛse] *tr* to caress; pet; nourish (*a hope*)

cargaison [kargɛzɔ̃] *f* cargo

cargo [kargo] *m* freighter; **cargo mixte** freighter carrying passengers

cari [kari] *m* curry

caricature [karikatyr] *f* caricature; cartoon

caricaturer [karikatyre] *tr* to caricature

caricaturiste [karikatyrist] *mf* caricaturist; cartoonist

carie [kari] *f* caries; **carie sèche** dry rot

carillon [karijɔ̃] *m* carillon

carillonner [karijɔne] *tr* & *intr* to carillon, chime

carlingue [karlɛ̃g] *f* (aer) cockpit

carmin [karmɛ̃] *adj* & *m* carmine

carnage [karnaʒ] *m* carnage

carnas·sier [karnasje] **-sière** [sjɛr] *adj* carnivorous ‖ *m* carnivore ‖ *f* game bag

carnation [karnɑsjɔ̃] *f* flesh tint

carna·val [karnaval] *m* (*pl* **-vals**) carnival; parade dummy

car·né -née [karne] *adj* "flesh"-colored; meat (*diet*)

carnet [karnɛ] *m* notebook, address book; memo pad; book (*of tickets, checks, stamps, etc.*); **carnet à feuilles mobiles** loose-leaf notebook

carnier [karnje] *m* hunting bag

carotte [karɔt] *f* carrot; (min) core sample; **les carottes sont cuites** the die is cast; **tirer une carotte à** (coll) to cheat

carotter [karɔte] *tr* (coll) to cheat; chisel

carpe [karp] *m* (anat) wrist bones ‖ *f* carp; **être muet comme une carpe** to be still as a mouse

carpette [karpɛt] *f* rug, mat; **être une vraie carpette** to let s.o. walk all over one

carquois [karkwa] *m* quiver

carre [kar] *f* thickness (*of board*); crown (*of hat*); edge (*of ice skate*); square toe (*of shoe*); **d'une bonne carre** broadshouldered (*man*)

car·ré -rée [kare] *adj* square; forthright ‖ *m* square; landing (*of staircase*); patch (*in garden*); (cards) four of a kind; (naut) wardroom ‖ *f* (slang) room, pad

car·reau [karo] *m* (*pl* **-reaux**) tile, flagstone; windowpane; stall (*in market*); pithead (*of mine*); goose (*of tailor*); quarrel (*square-headed arrow*); (cards) diamond; (cards) diamonds; **à carreaux** checked (*design*); **rester sur le carreaux** (coll) to be left out of the running; **se garder à carreau** (coll) to be on one's guard

carrefour [karfur] *m* crossroads; square (*in a city*)

carrelage [karlaʒ] *m* tiling

carreler [karle] §34 *tr* to tile

carrément [karemɑ̃] *adv* squarely; frankly

carrer [kare] *tr* to square ‖ *ref* (coll) to plunk oneself down; (coll) to strut

carrier [karje] *m* quarryman

carrière [karjɛr] *f* career; course (*e.g., of the sun*); quarry; **donner carrière à** to give free rein to

carriole [karjɔl] *f* light cart, trap; (coll) jalopy

carrossable [karɔsabl] *adj* passable

carrosse [karɔs] *m* carriage, coach

carrosserie [karɔsri] *f* (aut) body

carrossier [karɔsje] *m* coachmaker

carrousel [karuzɛl] *m* carrousel; parade ground; tiltyard

carrure [karyr] *f* width (*of shoulders, garment, etc.*); build; **d'une belle carrure** broad-shouldered (*man*)

cartable [kartabl] *m* briefcase

cartayer [karteje] §49 *intr* to avoid the ruts

carte [kart] *f* card; map, chart; bill (*to pay*); bill of fare, menu; **carte d'abonnement** commutation ticket; season ticket; **carte de crédit** credit card; **carte de Noël** Christmas card; **carte d'entrée** pass, ticket of admission; **carte des vins** wine list; **carte d'identité** identification card; **carte grise** automobile registration; **carte perforée** punch card; **carte postale** post card; **carte routière** road map; **cartes truquées** marked cards, stacked deck; **faire une carte de France** (slang) to have a wet dream; **manger à la carte** to eat a la carte; **tirer les cartes à qn** to tell s.o.'s fortunes with cards

cartel [kartɛl] *m* cartel; wall clock; challenge (*to a duel*)

carte-lettre [kartəlɛtr] *f* (*pl* **cartes-lettres**) gummed letter-envelope

carter [kartɛr] *m* housing; bicycle chain guard; (aut) crankcase

carte-retrait [kartərətrɛ] *f* (*pl* **cartes-retrait**) bank card

cartilage [kartilaʒ] *m* cartilage, gristle

cartographe [kartɔgraf] *m* cartographer

cartomancie [kartɔmɑ̃si] *f* fortunetelling with cards

carton [kartɔ̃] *m* pasteboard, cardboard; cardboard box, carton; carton (*of cigarettes*); cartoon (*preliminary sketch*); (typ) cancel; **carton à chapeau** hatbox; **carton à dessin** portfolio for drawings and plans; **carton ondulé** corrugated cardboard

carton-pâte [kartɔ̃pat] *m* papier-mâché

cartouche [kartuʃ] *m* (archit) cartouche, tablet; inset (*in a picture*) ‖ *f* cartridge; carton (*of cigarettes*); canister (*of gas mask*); refill (*of pen*); **cartouche à blanc** blank cartridge

cartouchière [kartuʃjɛr] *f* cartridge belt, cartridge case

carvi [karvi] *m* caraway

cas [kɑ] *m* case; **cas d'espèce** individual case; **cas limite** borderline case; **cas urgent** emergency; **en aucun cas** under no circumstances; **en cas de** in the event of, in a time of; **en cas d'imprévu** in case of emergency; **en cas que, au cas que, au cas où, dans le cas où** in the event that; **faire cas de** to esteem, to make much of; **le cas échéant** should the occasion arise, if necessary; **ne jamais faire aucun cas de** to never pay any attention to; **selon le cas** as the case may be

casa·nier [kazanje] **-nière** [njɛr] *adj* homeloving ‖ *mf* homebody

casaque [kazak] *f* jockey coat; blouse; **tourner casaque** to be a turncoat

cascade [kaskad] *f* cascade; jerk; spree; **faire une cascade** (mov) to do a stunt; **prendre à la cascade** to ad-lib

cascader [kaskade] *intr* to cascade; (slang) to lead a wild life

casca·deur [kaskadœr] **-deuse** [døz] *mf* (mov) double ‖ *m* stunt man ‖ *f* stunt girl

case [kɑz] *f* compartment; pigeonhole; square (*e.g., of checkerboard or ledger*);

box (*to be filled out on a form*); hut, cabin; **case postale** post-office box; **cochez la case correspondante** check the appropriate box; **se retrouver à la case départ** (slang) to find oneself back on square one

caséine [kazein] *f* casein

caser [kaze] *tr* to put away (*e.g., in a drawer*); arrange (*e.g., a counter display in a store*); (coll) to place, find a job for ‖ *ref* (coll) to get settled

caserne [kazɛrn] *f* barracks; **caserne de pompiers** firehouse; **de caserne** off-color (*jokes*); regimented

caserner [kazɛrne] *tr & intr* to barrack

ca·sher ·shère [kaʃɛr] *adj* kosher

casier [kasje] *m* rack (*for papers, magazines, letters, bottles*); cabinet; locker; **casier à homards** lobster pot; **casier à tiroirs** music cabinet; **casier judiciaire** police record

casino [kazino] *m* casino

casque [kask] *m* helmet; earphones, headset; comb (*of rooster*); **casque à mèche** nightcap; **casque à pointe** spiked helmet; **casque blindé** crash helmet; **les Casques bleus** the U.N. peace-keeping force

casquer [kaske] *intr* to fall into a trap; (slang) to shell out

casquette [kaskɛt] *f* cap

cas·sant [kasɑ̃] **-sante** [sɑ̃t] *adj* brittle; abrupt, curt

casse [kas] *m* (slang) burglarizing ‖ *f* breakage ‖ [kas], [kɑs] *f* ladle, scoop; crucible; (bot) cassia; (pharm) senna; (typ) case; (coll) scrap heap, junk

cas·sé ·sée [kase] *adj* broken-down; shaky, weak (*voice*)

casse-cou [kasku] *m invar* (coll) daredevil; (coll) stunt man; (coll) danger spot ‖ *interj* look out!

casse-croûte [kaskrut] *m invar* snack

casse-gueule [kasgœl] *adj invar* (slang) risky ‖ *m invar* (coll) risky business

casse-langue [kaslɑ̃g] *m invar* tongue twister

casse-noisettes [kasnwazɛt] *m invar* nutcracker

casse-noix [kasnwa], [kasnwa] *m invar* nutcracker

casse-pieds [kaspje] *m invar* (coll) pain in the neck

casser [kase] *tr* to break; crack, shatter; (law) to break (*a will*); (mil) to break, bust; (coll) to split (*one's eardrums*); **casser sa pipe** (coll) to kick the bucket ‖ *ref* to break; (coll) to rack (*one's brains*); **se casser le nez** (coll) to fail

casserole [kasrɔl] *f* saucepan; (slang) jalopy; **passer à la casserole** (slang) to screw; bump off, kill

casse-tête [kastɛt] *m invar* truncheon; din; brain teaser, puzzler; **casse-tête chinois** jigsaw puzzle

cassette [kasɛt], [kasɛt] *f* strongbox, coffer; casket (*for jewels*); (phot, electron) cassette; **cassette magnétique** cassette

cassis [kasi], [kasis] *m* black currant; cassis (*liqueur*); gutter

cassolette [kasɔlɛt] *f* incense burner

cassonade [kasɔnad] *f* brown sugar

cassoulet [kasulɛ] *m* pork and beans

cassure [kasyr] *f* break; crease; rift

castagnettes [kastaɲɛt] *fpl* castanets

caste [kast] *f* caste; **hors caste** outcaste

castil·lan [kastijɑ̃] **-lane** [jan] *adj* Castilian ‖ *m* Castilian (*language*) ‖ (*cap*) *mf* Castilian (*person*)

Castille [kastij] *f* Castile; **la Castille** Castile

castor [kastɔr] *m* beaver

castrat [kastra] *m* castrato

castrer [kastre] *tr* to castrate

ca·suel ·suelle [kazɥɛl] *adj* casual; (coll) brittle ‖ *m* perquisites

cataclysme [kataklism] *m* cataclysm

catacombes [katakɔ̃b] *fpl* catacombs

catafalque [katafalk] *m* catafalque

cataire [katɛr] *f* catnip

Catalogne [katalɔɲ] *f* Catalonia; **la Catalogne** Catalonia

catalogue [katalɔg] *m* catalogue

cataloguer [katalɔge] *tr* to catalogue

catalyseur [katalizœr] *m* catalyst

cataplasme [kataplasm] *m* poultice

catapulte [katapylt] *f* catapult

catapulter [katapylte] *tr* to catapult

cataracte [katarakt] *f* cataract

catarrhe [katar] *m* catarrh; bad cold

catastrophe [katastrɔf] *f* catastrophe

catch [katʃ] *m* wrestling

catcheur [katʃœr] *m* wrestler

catéchiser [kateʃize] *tr* to catechize; reason with

catéchisme [kateʃism] *m* catechism

catégorie [kategɔri] *f* category

catégorique [kategɔrik] *adj* categorical

catgut [katgyt] *m* (surg) catgut

cathédrale [katedral] *f* cathedral

cathéter [katetɛr] *m* (med) catheter

cathode [katɔd] *f* cathode

catholicisme [katɔlisism] *m* Catholicism

catholicité [katɔlisite] *f* catholicity; Catholicism; Catholics

catholique [katɔlik] *adj* catholic; Catholic; orthodox; **pas très catholique** (coll) questionable ‖ *mf* Catholic

cati [kati] *m* glaze, gloss

catimini [katimini]—**en catimini** (coll) on the sly

catir [katir] *tr* to glaze

cauca·sien [kɔkazjɛ̃] **-sienne** [zjɛn] *adj* Caucasian ‖ (*cap*) *mf* Caucasian

caucasique [kɔkazik] *adj* Caucasian

cauchemar [koʃmar] *m* nightmare

cause [koz] *f* cause; (law) case; **à cause de** because of, on account of, for the sake of; **cause de décès** cause of death; **et pour cause** with good reason; **hors de cause** irrelevant, beside the point; **mettre q.ch. en cause** to question s.th.; **mettre qn en cause** to implicate s.o.

causer [koze] *tr* to cause ‖ *intr* to chat

causerie [kozri] *f* chat; informal lecture

causette [kozɛt] *f*—**faire la causette** (coll) to chat

cau·seur [kozœr] **-seuse** [zøz] *adj* talkative, chatty ‖ *mf* speaker, conversationalist ‖ *f* love seat

caustique [kostik] *adj* caustic

caute·leux [kotlø] **-leuse** [løz] *adj* crafty, wily; cunning (*mind*)

cautériser [koterize] *tr* to cauterize

caution [kosjɔ̃] *f* security, collateral; guarantor, bondsman; **mettre en liberté sous caution** to let out on bail; **se porter caution pour qn** to put up bail for s.o.; **sujet à caution** unreliable; **verser une caution** to make a deposit

cautionnement [kosjɔnmɑ̃] *m* surety bond, guaranty; bail; deposit

cautionner [kosjone] *tr* to bail out; guarantee

cavalcade [kavalkad] *f* cavalcade

cavalerie [kavalri] *f* cavalry

cava·lier [kavalje] **-lière** [ljɛr] *adj* cavalier; bridle (*path*) ‖ *mf* horseback rider; dance partner ‖ *m* cavalier, horseman; escort; (chess) knight; **faire cavalier seul** to go it alone ‖ *f* horsewoman

cave [kav] *adj* hollow (*cheeks*) ‖ *f* cellar; liquor cabinet; liquor store; night club; bank (*in game of chance*); stake (*in gambling*); **cave à vin** wine cellar

ca·veau [kavo] *m* (*pl* **-veaux**) small cellar; vault, crypt; rathskeller

caver [kave] *tr* to hollow out ‖ *intr* to ante ‖ *ref* to become hollow (*said of eyes*); wager

caverne [kavɛrn] *f* cave, cavern; (pathol) cavity (*e.g., in lung*)

caver·neux [kavɛrnø] **-neuse** [nøz] *adj* cavernous; hollow (*voice*)

caviar [kavjar] *m* caviar; **caviar rouge** salmon roe; **passer au caviar** to bluepencil, censor

caviarder [kavjarde] *tr* to censor

cavité [kavite] *f* cavity, hollow

caw·cher -chère [kaʃɛr] *adj* kosher

Cayes [kaj] *fpl*—**Cayes de la Floride** Florida Keys

C.C.P. *abbr* (**Compte chèques postaux**) postal banking account

ce [sə] (or **cet** [sɛt] before vowel or mute **h**) **cette** [sɛt] *adj dem* (*pl* **ces** [se]) §82A ‖ **ce** *pron* §82B, §85A4

C.E.A. *abbr* (**Commissariat à l'Énergie atomique**) Atomic Energy Commission

céans [seɑ̃] *adv* herein

ceci [sesi] *pron dem indef* this, this thing, this matter

cécité [sesite] *f* blindness

céder [sede] §10 *tr* to cede, transfer; yield; give up; **ne le céder à personne** to be second to none ‖ *intr* to yield, succumb, give way

cédille [sedij] *f* cedilla

cédrat [sedra] *m* citron

cèdre [sɛdr] *m* cedar

cédule [sedyl] *f* rate, schedule; (law) notification

C.E.E. *abbr* (**Communauté économique européenne**) Common Market

cégétiste [seʒetist] *mf* unionist

ceindre [sɛ̃dr] §50 *tr* to buckle on, gird; encircle; wreathe (*one's head*); **ceindre la couronne** to assume the crown ‖ *ref*—**se ceindre de** to gird on

ceinture [sɛ̃tyr] *f* belt; waist, waistline; sash, waistband; girdle; **ceinture de chasteté** chastity belt; **ceinture de sauvetage** life belt; **ceinture de sécurité** safety belt; **ceinture herniaire** truss; **se mettre la ceinture** or **se serrer la ceinture** to tighten one's belt

ceinturer [sɛ̃tyre] *tr* to girdle, belt; encircle, belt; (wrestling) to grip around the waist

cela [səla] *pron dem indef* that, that thing; that matter; **à cela près** with that one exception; **et avec cela?** what else?

célébrant [selebrɑ̃] *m* (eccl) celebrant

célébration [selebrasjɔ̃] *f* celebration

célèbre [selebr] *adj* famous

célébrer [selebre] §10 *tr* to celebrate

célébrité [selebrite] *f* celebrity

celer [səle] §2 *tr* to hide, conceal

céleri [selri], [sɛlri] *m* celery

céleste [selɛst] *adj* celestial

célibat [seliba] *m* celibacy

célibataire [selibatɛr] *adj* single ‖ *mf* celibate ‖ *m* bachelor ‖ *f* spinster

celle [sɛl] §83

celle-ci [sɛlsi] §84

celle-là [sɛlla] §84

cellier [selje] *m* wine cellar; fruit cellar

cellophane [selofan] *f* cellophane

cellule [selyl], [sɛlyl] *f* cell

celluloïd [selyloid] *m* celluloid

celte [sɛlt] *adj* Celtic ‖ (*cap*) *mf* Celt

celtique [sɛltik] *adj* & *m* Celtic

celui [səlɥi] **celle** [sɛl] (*pl* **ceux** [sø] **celles**) §83

celui-ci [səlɥisi] **celle-ci** [sɛlsi] (*pl* **ceux-ci** [søsi] **celles-ci**) §84

celui-là [səlɥila] **celle-là** [sɛlla] (*pl* **ceux-là** [søla] **celles-là**) §84

cémentation [semɑ̃tasjɔ̃] *f* casehardening

cendre [sɑ̃dr] *f* cinder; **cendres** ashes

cendrée [sɑ̃dre] *f* shot; buckshot; (sports) cinder track

cendrer [sɑ̃dre] *tr* to cinder

cendrier [sɑ̃drije] *m* ashtray

Cendrillon [sɑ̃drijɔ̃] *f*—**la Cendrillon** Cinderella

cène [sɛn] *f* (eccl) Holy Communion ‖ (*cap*) *f* (eccl) Last Supper

cens [sɑ̃s] *m* census; poll tax

cen·sé -sée [sɑ̃se] §95 *adj* supposed to, e.g., **je ne suis pas censé le savoir** I am not supposed to know it; reputed to be, e.g., **il est censé juge infaillible** he is reputed to be an infallible judge

censément [sɑ̃semɑ̃] *adv* supposedly, apparently, allegedly

censeur [sɑ̃sœr] *m* censor; census taker; critic; auditor; proctor

censure [sɑ̃syr] *f* censure; censorship; (psychoanal) censor

censurer [sɑ̃syre] §97 *tr* to censure; censor
cent [sɑ̃] §94 *adj & pron* (*pl* **cents** in
multiples when standing before modified
noun, e.g., **trois cents œufs** three hundred eggs) one hundred, a hundred, hundred; **cent pour cent** one hundred percent; **cent un** [sɑ̃œ̃] one hundred and one,
a hundred and one, hundred and one; **l'an
dix-neuf cent** the year nineteen hundred;
page deux cent page two hundred ‖ *m*
hundred, one hundred ‖ [sɛnt] *m* cent
centaine [sɑ̃tɛn] *f* hundred; **par centaines**
by the hundreds; **une centaine de** about a
hundred
centaure [sɑ̃tɔr] *m* centaur
centenaire [sɑ̃tnɛr] *adj* centenary ‖ *mf* centenarian ‖ *m* centennial
centen·nal -nale [sɑ̃tɛnnal] *adj* (*pl* **-naux**
[no]) centennial
centième [sɑ̃tjɛm] §94 *adj, pron* (*masc,
fem*), *& m* hundredth ‖ *f* hundredth performance
centigrade [sɑ̃tigrad] *adj & m* centigrade
centime [sɑ̃tim] *m* centime
centimètre [sɑ̃timɛtr] *m* centimeter; tape
measure
centrage [sɑ̃traʒ] *m* centering
cen·tral -trale [sɑ̃tral] *adj* (*pl* **-traux** [tro])
central; main (*office*) ‖ *m* (telp) central ‖ *f*
powerhouse; labor union; **centrale atomique** or **nucléaire** atomic generator
centralisation [sɑ̃tralizɑsjɔ̃] *f* centralization
centraliser [sɑ̃tralize] *tr & ref* to centralize
centre [sɑ̃tr] *m* center; **centre commercial**
shopping district; **centre commercial de
quartier** convenience store; **centre de
dépression** storm center; **centre de (la)
ville** center city; **centre de triage** (rr)
switchyard; **centre d'études** college; **centre de villégiature** resort; **centre social
des étudiants** student center, student
union
centrer [sɑ̃tre] *tr* to center
centrifuge [sɑ̃trifyʒ] *adj* centrifugal
centuple [sɑ̃typl] *adj & m* hundredfold; **au
centuple** hundredfold
cep [sɛp] *m* vine stock
cépage [sepaʒ] *m* (bot) vine
cèpe [sɛp] *f* cepe mushroom
cependant [səpɑ̃dɑ̃] *adv* meanwhile; however, but, still; **cependant que** while,
whereas; **et cependant** and yet
céramique [seramik] *adj* ceramic ‖ *f* (art of)
ceramics; ceramic piece; **céramiques** ceramics (*objects*)
cerbère [sɛrbɛr] *m* (coll) watchdog ‖ (*cap*)
m Cerberus
cer·ceau [sɛrso] *m* (*pl* **-ceaux**) hoop; **cer-
ceaux** pinfeathers
cercle [sɛrkl] *m* circle; circle, club, society;
clubhouse; hoop; **en cercle** in the cask
cercler [sɛrkle] *tr* to ring, encircle; to hoop
cercueil [sɛrkœj] *m* coffin
céréale [sereal] *adj & f* cereal
céré·bral -brale [serebral] *adj* (*pl* **-braux**
[bro]) cerebral

cérémo·nial -niale [seremɔnjal] *adj & m*
ceremonial
cérémonie [seremɔni] *f* ceremony; **faire des
cérémonies** to stand on ceremony
cérémo·niel -nielle [seremɔnjɛl] *adj* ceremonial
cérémo·nieux [seremɔnjø] **-nieuse** [njøz]
adj ceremonious, formal, stiff
cerf [sɛr] *m* deer, red deer; stag, buck
cerf-volant [sɛrvɔlɑ̃] *m* (*pl* **cerfs-volants**)
kite
cerisaie [sərize] *f* cherry orchard
cerise [səriz[*f* cherry
cerisier [sərizje] *m* cherry tree
cerne [sɛrn] *m* annual ring (*of tree*); ring
(*around moon, black eye, wound*)
cer·neau [sɛrno] *m* (*pl* **-neaux**) unripe nut-
meat
cerner [sɛrne] *tr* to ring, encircle; hem in,
besiege; shell (*nuts*)
cer·tain [sɛrtɛ̃] **-taine** [tɛn] §93 *adj* certain,
sure ‖ (when standing before noun) *adj*
certain, some; **certain auteur** a certain
author; **depuis un certain temps** for some
time; **d'un certain âge** middle-aged ‖
certains *pron indef pl* certain people
certainement [sɛrtɛnmɑ̃] *adv* certainly
certes [sɛrt] *adv* indeed, certainly
certificat [sɛrtifika] *m* certificate; recommendation, attestation; **certificat d'aptitude au professorat de l'enseignement
du second degré (C.A.P.E.S.)** secondary-
school teachers certificate; **certificat
d'aptitude pédagogique (C.A.P.)** teachers license; **certificat d'urbanisation** zoning permit
certifier [sɛrtifje] *tr* to certify
certitude [sɛrtityd] *f* certainty
cérumen [serymɛn] *m* earwax
céruse [seryz] *f* white lead
cer·veau [sɛrvo] *m* (*pl* **-veaux**) brain; mind;
cerveau brûlé (coll) hothead; **laver le
cerveau à** (coll) to brainwash
cerveauté [sɛrvote] *f* brain trust
cervelas [sɛrvəla] *m* salami
cervelet [sɛrvəlɛ] *m* cerebellum
cervelle [sɛrvɛl] *f* brains; **brûler la cervelle
à qn** (coll) to shoot s.o.'s brains out; **sans
cervelle** brainless
ces [se] §82A
césa·rien [sezarjɛ̃] **-rienne** [rjɛn] *adj* Caesarean ‖ *f* Caesarean section
cesse [sɛs] *f* cessation, ceasing; **sans cesse**
unceasingly, incessantly
cesser [sese] §97 *tr* to stop, cease, leave off
(*e.g., work*) ‖ *intr* to cease, stop; **cesser
de** + *inf* to stop, cease, quit + *ger*
cessez-le-feu [seselfø] *m invar* cease-fire
cession [sesjɔ̃] *f* ceding, surrender; (law)
transfer
c'est-à-dire [sɛtadir] *conj* that is, namely
césure [sezyr] *f* caesura
cet [sɛt] §82A
cette [sɛt] §82A
ceux [sø] §83
ceux-ci [søsi] §84
ceux-là [søla] §84

Ceylan [sɛlɑ̃] *m* Ceylon

C.G.T. [seʒete] *f* (letterword) (**confédération générale du travail**) national labor union ‖ *abbr* (**C**ⁱᵉ **Générale transatlantique**) French Line

cha·cal [ʃakal] *m* (*pl* -**cals**) jackal

cha·cun [ʃakœ̃] -**cune** [kyn] *pron indef* each, each one, every one; everybody, everyone; **chacun pour soi** every man for himself; **chacun son goût** every man to his own taste; **tout chacun** (coll) every Tom, Dick, and Harry

chadburn [tʃadbœrn] *m* (naut) public-address system

chadouf [ʃaduf] *m* well sweep

cha·grin [ʃagrɛ̃] -**grine** [grin] *adj* sad, downcast ‖ *m* grief, sorrow

chagriner [ʃagrine] *tr* to grieve, distress; make into shagreen leather ‖ *intr* to grieve, worry ‖ §97 *ref* to grieve

chah [ʃa] *m* shah

chahut [ʃay] *m* (coll) horseplay, row

chahuter [ʃayte] *tr* (coll) to upset; (coll) to boo, heckle ‖ *intr* (coll) to create a disturbance

chai [ʃɛ] *m* wine cellar

chaîne [ʃɛn] *f* chain; warp (*of fabric*); necklace; (archit) pier; (archit) tie; (naut) cable; (rad, telv) network; (telv) channel; **chaîne de fabrication, chaîne de montage** assembly line; **chaîne volontaire** franchise, franchising; **faire la chaîne** to form a bucket brigade; **travailler à la chaîne** to work on the assembly line

chaînon [ʃɛnɔ̃] *m* link

chair [ʃɛr] *f* flesh; pulp (*of fruits*); meat (*of animals*); **avoir la chair de poule** to have goose pimples; **chair à canon** cannon fodder; **chair de sa chair** one's flesh and blood; **chairs** (painting, sculpture) nude parts; **en chair et en os** in the flesh; **ni chair ni poisson** neither fish nor fowl

chaire [ʃɛr] *f* pulpit; lectern; chair (*held by university professor*)

chaise [ʃɛz] *f* chair; bowline knot; (mach) bracket; **chaise à bascule** rocking chair; **chaise à fond de paille** rush-bottomed chair; **chaise à porteurs** sedan chair; **chaise berceuse** rocking chair; **chaise brisée** folding chair; **chaise cannée** cane chair; **chaise d'enfant** high chair; **chaise électrique** electric chair; **chaise percée** commode, toilet; **chaise pliante** folding chair; **chaise roulante** wheelchair; **faire de la chaise longue** to relax in a deck chair; put one's feet up

cha·land [ʃalɑ̃] -**lande** [lɑ̃d] *mf* customer ‖ *m* barge; **chaland de débarquement** (mil) landing craft

châle [ʃal] *m* shawl

chalet [ʃalɛ] *m* chalet, cottage, summer home; **chalet de nécessité** public rest room

chaleur [ʃalœr] *f* heat; warmth; **les grandes chaleurs de l'été** the hot weather of summer

chaleu·reux [ʃalœrø] -**reuse** [røz] *adj* warm, heated

châlit [ʃali] *m* bedstead

chaloupe [ʃalup] *f* launch

chalu·meau [ʃalymo] *m* (*pl* -**meaux**) reed; blowtorch; (mus) pipe; **chalumeau oxhydrique, chalumeau oxyacétylénique** acetylene torch

chalut [ʃaly] *m* trawl

chalutier [ʃalytje] *m* trawler

chamade [ʃamad] *f*—**battre la chamade** to beat wildly (*said of the heart*)

chamailler [ʃamaje] *ref* to squabble

chamarrer [ʃamare] *tr* to decorate, ornament; bedizen, bedeck; (slang) to cover (*s.o.*) with ridicule

chambarder [ʃɑ̃barde] *tr* (slang) to upset, turn upside down

chambellan [ʃɑ̃bɛllɑ̃] *m* chamberlain

chambouler [ʃɑ̃bule] *tr* (slang) to upset, turn topsy-turvy

chambranle [ʃɑ̃brɑ̃l] *m* frame (*of a door or window*); mantelpiece

chambre [ʃɑ̃br] *f* chamber; room; **chambre à air** inner tube; **chambre à coucher** bedroom; **chambre d'ami** guest room; **chambre de compensation** clearing house; **chambre noire** darkroom; **chambre sourde** soundproof(ed) room

chambrée [ʃɑ̃bre] *f* dormitory, barracks; bunkmates

chambrer [ʃɑ̃bre] *tr* to keep under lock and key; keep (*wine*) at room temperature

cha·meau [ʃamo] -**melle** [mɛl] *mf* (*pl* -**meaux** camel ‖ *m* (slang) bitch (*person*)

chamois [ʃamwa] *adj & m* chamois

champ [ʃɑ̃] *m* field; **aux champs** salute (*played on trumpet or drum*); **champ clos** lists, dueling field; **champ de courses** race track; **champ de foire** fairground; **champ de repos** cemetery; **champ de tir** firing range; **champ libre** clear field; **champs Élysées** Elysian Fields; **Champs Élysées** Champs Elysées (*street*); **en champ clos** behind closed doors

champagne [ʃɑ̃paɲ] *m* champagne; **champagne brut** extra dry champagne; **champagne d'origine** vintage champagne ‖ (*cap*) *f* Champagne; **la Champagne** Champagne

champe·nois [ʃɑ̃pənwa] -**noise** [nwaz] *adj* Champagne ‖ *m* Champagne dialect ‖ (*cap*) *mf* inhabitant of Champagne

champêtre [ʃɑ̃pɛtr] *adj* rustic, rural

champignon [ʃɑ̃piɲɔ̃] *m* mushroom; fungus; (slang) accelerator pedal; **champignon de couche** cultivated mushroom; **champignon vénéneux** toadstool

champignonner [ʃɑ̃piɲɔne] *intr* to mushroom

cham·pion [ʃɑ̃pjɔ̃] -**pionne** [pjɔn] *mf* champion; best seller ‖ *f* championess

championnat [ʃɑ̃pjɔna] *m* championship

champlever [ʃɑ̃lve] §2 *tr* to chase out, gouge out

chan·çard [ʃɑ̃sar] -**çarde** [sard] *adj* (slang) in luck ‖ *mf* (slang) lucky person

chance [ʃɑ̃s] *f* luck; good luck; **avoir de la chance** to be lucky; **bonne chance!** good luck!; **chance moyenne** off chance; **chances** chances, risks, probability, possibility

chance·lant [ʃɑ̃slɑ̃] **-lante** [lɑ̃t] *adj* shaky, unsteady, tottering; delicate (*health, constitution*)

chanceler [ʃɑ̃sle] §34 *intr* to stagger, totter, teeter; waver

chancelier [ʃɑ̃səlje] *m* chancellor

chancellerie [ʃɑ̃sɛlri] *f* chancellery

chan·ceux [ʃɑ̃sø] **-ceuse** [søz] *adj* lucky; risky

chanci [ʃɑ̃si] *m* manure pile for mushroom growing

chancir [ʃɑ̃sir] *intr* to grow moldy

chancre [ʃɑ̃kr] *m* chancre; ulcer, canker

chandail [ʃɑ̃daj] *m* sweater; **chandail à col roulé** turtleneck sweater

chandeleur [ʃɑ̃dlœr] *f*—**la chandeleur** Candlemas

chandelier [ʃɑ̃dəlje] *m* candlestick; chandler

chandelle [ʃɑ̃dɛl] *f* tallow candle; prop, stay (*used in construction*); **chandelle de glace** icicle; **en chandelle** vertically; **voir trente-six chandelles** to see stars (*on account of a blow*)

chanfrein [ʃɑ̃frɛ̃] *m* forehead (*of a horse*); chamfer, beveled edge

chanfreiner [ʃɑ̃frɛne] *tr* to chamfer, bevel

change [ʃɑ̃ʒ] *m* exchange; rate of exchange; **de change** in reserve, extra; **donner le change à** to throw off the trail; **prendre le change** to let one self be duped; **rendre le change à qn** to give s.o. a taste of his own medicine

changeable [ʃɑ̃ʒabl] *adj* changeable

chan·geant [ʃɑ̃ʒɑ̃] **-geante** [ʒɑ̃t] *adj* changeable, changing, fickle; iridescent

changement [ʃɑ̃ʒmɑ̃] *m* change; shift, shifting; **changement de propriétaire** under new ownership; **changement de vitesse** gearshift

changer [ʃɑ̃ʒe] §38 *tr* to change; **changer contre** to exchange for ‖ *intr* to change; **changer d'avis** to change one's mind; **changer de place** to change one's seat; **changer de ton** (coll) to change one's tune; **changer de visage** to blush; change color ‖ *ref* to change, change clothes

chanoine [ʃanwan] *m* (eccl) canon

chanson [ʃɑ̃sɔ̃] *f* song; **chanson bachique** drinking song; **chanson de geste** medieval epic; **chanson de Noël** Christmas carol; **chanson du terroir** folk song; **chanson sentimentale** torch song

chansonner [ʃɑ̃sɔne] *tr* to lampoon in a satirical song

chansonneur [ʃɑ̃sɔnœr] *m* lampooner (*who writes satirical songs*)

chanson·nier [ʃɑ̃sɔnje] **-nière** [njɛr] *mf* songwriter ‖ *m* chansonnier; song book

chant [ʃɑ̃] *m* singing; song, chant; canto; crowing (*of rooster*); side (*e.g., of a brick*); **chant du cygne** swan song; **chant de Noël** Christmas carol; **chant national** national anthem; **chants** poetry; **de chant** on end, edgewise

chantage [ʃɑ̃taʒ] *m* blackmail

chan·tant [ʃɑ̃tɑ̃] **-tante** [tɑ̃t] *adj* singable, melodious; singsong (*accent*); musical (*evening*)

chan·teau [ʃɑ̃to] *m* (*pl* **-teaux**) chunk (*of bread*); remnant

chantepleure [ʃɑ̃tplœr] *f* wine funnel; tap (*of cask*); sprinkler; weep hole

chanter [ʃɑ̃te] *tr* to sing ‖ *intr* to sing; crow (*as a rooster*); to pay blackmail; **chanter faux** to sing out of tune; **chanter juste** to sing in tune; **faire chanter** to blackmail

chanterelle [ʃɑ̃trɛl] *f* first string (*of violin*); decoy bird; mushroom; **appuyer sur la chanterelle** (coll) to rub it in

chan·teur [ʃɑ̃tœr] **-teuse** [tøz] *adj* singing; song (*bird*) ‖ *mf* singer; **chanteur de charme** crooner; **chanteur de rythme** jazz singer

chantier [ʃɑ̃tje] *m* shipyard; stocks, slip; workshop, yard; gantry, stand (*for barrels*); (public sign) men at work; **chantier de construction** building site; **chantier de démolition** junkyard, scrap heap; **mettre en** or **sur le chantier** to start work on

chantilly [ʃɑ̃tiji] *m* whipped cream

chantonner [ʃɑ̃tɔne] *tr & intr* to hum

chantoung [ʃɑ̃tuŋ] *m* shantung

chantourner [ʃɑ̃turne] *tr* to jigsaw

chantre [ʃɑ̃tr] *m* cantor, chanter; precentor; songster; bard, poet

chanvre [ʃɑ̃vr] *m* hemp; **en chanvre** hempen; flaxen (*color*)

chan·vrier [ʃɑ̃vrije] **-vrière** [vrijɛr] *adj* hemp (*industry*) ‖ *mf* dealer in hemp; hemp dresser

chaos [kao] *m* chaos

chaotique [kaɔtik] *adj* chaotic

chaparder [ʃaparde] *tr* (coll) to pilfer, filch; gyp

chape [ʃap] *f* cover, covering; tread (*of tire*); coping (*of bridge*); frame, shell (*of pulley block*); (eccl) cope

cha·peau [ʃapo] *m* (*pl* **-peaux**) hat; head (*of mushroom*); lead (*of magazine or newspaper article*); cap (*of fountain pen; of valve*); cowl (*of chimney*); **chapeau à cornes** cocked hat; **chapeau bas** hat in hand; **chapeau bas!** hats off!; **chapeau chinois** Chinese bells; **chapeau de cotillon** little hat for New Year's Eve; **chapeau de paille** straw hat; **chapeau de roue** hubcap; **chapeau haut de forme** top hat; **chapeau melon** derby; **chapeau mou** fedora

chapeau-cloche [ʃapoklɔʃ] *m* (*pl* **chapeaux-cloches**) cloche (hat)

chapeauter [ʃapote] *tr* (coll) to put a hat on (*e.g., a child*)

chapelain [ʃaplɛ̃] *m* chaplain (*of a private chapel*)

chapeler [ʃaple] §34 *tr* to scrape the crust off of (*bread*)

chapelet [ʃaplɛ] *m* chaplet, rosary; string (*of onions; of islands; of insults*); chain (*of events; of mountains*); series (*e.g., of attacks*); (mil) stick (*of bombs*); **chapelet hydraulique** bucket conveyor; **défiler son chapelet** (coll) to speak one's mind; **dire son chapelet** to tell one's beads; **en chapelet** (elec) in series

chape·lier [ʃapəlje] `-lière** [ljɛr] *mf* hatter ‖ *f* Saratoga trunk

chapelle [ʃapɛl] *f* chapel; clique, coterie; **chapelle ardente** mortuary chamber lighted by candles; hearse

chapellerie [ʃapɛlri] *f* hatmaking; millinery; hat shop; millinery shop

chapelure [ʃaplyr] *f* bread crumbs

chaperon [ʃaprɔ̃] *m* chaperon; hood; cape with a hood; coping (*of wall*); **le Petit Chaperon rouge** Little Red Ridinghood

chaperonner [ʃaprɔne] *tr* to chaperon

chapi·teau [ʃapito] *m* (*pl* **-teaux**) capital (*of column*); circus tent

chapitre [ʃapitr] *m* chapter; **commencer un nouveau chapitre** to turn over a new leaf

chapitrer [ʃapitre] *tr* to reprimand, admonish, lecture; divide into chapters

chapon [ʃapɔ̃] *m* capon; (culin) crust rubbed with garlic

chaque [ʃak] *adj indef* each, every ‖ *pron indef* (coll) each, each one

char [ʃar] *m* chariot; float (*in parade*); (mil) tank; **char d'assaut** or **char de combat** (mil) tank; **char funèbre** hearse

charabia [ʃarabja] *m* gibberish

charançon [ʃarɑ̃sɔ̃] *m* weevil

charbon [ʃarbɔ̃] *m* coal; soft coal; charcoal; carbon (*of an electric cell or arc*); cinder (*in the eye*); **charbon ardent** live coal; **charbon de bois** charcoal; **charbon de terre** coal; **être sur les charbons ardents** to be on pins and needles

charbonnage [ʃarbɔnaʒ] *m* coal mining; coal mine

charbonner [ʃarbɔne] *tr* to char; draw (*a picture*) with charcoal ‖ *intr & ref* to char, carbonize

charbon·neux [ʃarbɔnø] **-neuse** [nøz] *adj* sooty; anthrax-carrying

charbon·nier [ʃarbɔnje] **-nière** [njɛr] *adj* coal (*e.g., industry*) ‖ *mf* coal dealer ‖ *m* charcoal burner; coaler ‖ *f* coal scuttle; charcoal kiln; (orn) coal titmouse

charcuter [ʃarkyte] *tr* to butcher, mangle

charcuterie [ʃarkytri] *f* delicatessen; pork butcher shop

charcu·tier [ʃarkytje] **-tière** [tjɛr] *mf* pork butcher; (coll) sawbones

chardon [ʃardɔ̃] *m* thistle

chardonneret [ʃardɔnrɛ] *m* (orn) goldfinch

charge [ʃarʒ] *f* charge; load, burden; caricature; public office; **à charge de** on condition of, with the proviso of; **à charge de revanche** on condition of getting the same thing in return; **charges de famille** dependents; **charge utile** payload; **être à charge à** to be dependent upon; **être à la charge**

de to be supported by; **faire la charge de** to do a takeoff of

char·gé -gée [ʃarʒe] §93 *adj* loaded; full; overcast (*sky*); registered (*letter*) ‖ *m* assistant, deputy, envoy; **chargé de cours** assistant professor

chargement [ʃarʒəmɑ̃] *m* charging; loading; cargo

charger [ʃarʒe] §38, §97, §99 *tr* to charge; drive, take (*s.o. in one's car*) ‖ *intr* (mil) to charge; (naut) to load ‖ *ref* to be loaded; **se charger de** to take charge of; take up (*a question*)

chargeur [ʃarʒœr] *m* loader; stoker; shipper; clip (*of gun*); (elec) charger

chariot [ʃarjo] *m* wagon, cart; typewriter carriage; **chariot d'enfant** walker; **chariot élévateur** fork-lift truck; **Grand Chariot, Chariot de David** Big Dipper; **Petit Chariot** Little Dipper

charitable [ʃaritabl] *adj* charitable

charité [ʃarite] *f* charity; **faire la charité** to give alms; **faites la charité de, ayez la charité de** have the goodness to; **par charité** for charity's sake

charlatan [ʃarlatɑ̃] *m* charlatan

charlemagne [ʃarləmaɲ] *m* (cards) king of hearts; **faire charlemagne** to quit while winning

char·mant [ʃarmɑ̃] **-mante** [mɑ̃t] *adj* charming

charme [ʃarm] *m* charm; (*Carpinus betulus*) hornbeam; **se porter comme un charme** to be fit as a fiddle

charmer [ʃarme] *tr* to charm

char·meur [ʃarmœr] **-meuse** [møz] *adj* charming ‖ *mf* charmer

charmille [ʃarmij] *f* bower, arbor

char·nel -nelle [ʃarnɛl] *adj* carnal

charnière [ʃarnjɛr] *f* hinge

char·nu -nue [ʃarny] *adj* fleshy; plump; pulpy

charogne [ʃarɔɲ] *f* carrion

charpentage [ʃarpɑ̃taʒ] *m* carpentry

charpente [ʃarpɑ̃t] *f* framework; scaffolding; frame, build (*of body*)

charpenter [ʃarpɑ̃te] *tr* to square (*timber*); outline, map out, plan (*a novel, speech, etc.*); **être solidement charpenté** to be well built or well constructed ‖ *intr* to carpenter

charpenterie [ʃarpɑ̃tri] *f* carpentry; structure (*of building*)

charpentier [ʃarpɑ̃tje] *m* carpenter

charpei [ʃarpi] *f* lint; **en charpie** in shreds

charrée [ʃare] *f* lye

charre·tier [ʃartje] **-tière** [tjɛr] *mf* teamster; **jurer comme un charretier** to swear like a trooper

charrette [ʃarɛt] *f* cart

charriage [ʃarjaʒ] *m* cartage; drifting (*of ice*); (slang) exaggeration

charrier [ʃarje] *tr* to cart, transport; carry away (*sand, as the river does*); (slang) to poke fun at ‖ *intr* to be full of ice (*said of river*); (slang) to exaggerate

charroi [ʃarwa], [ʃarwa] *m* cartage

charron [ʃarɔ̃], [ʃarɔ̃] *m* wheelwright, cartwright

charroyer [ʃarwaje] §47 *tr* to cart

charrue [ʃary] *f* plow; **mettre la charrue devant les bœufs** to put the cart before the horse

charte [ʃart] *f* charter; title deed; fundamental principle

chas [ʃɑ] *m* eye (*of needle*)

chasse [ʃas] *f* hunt, hunting; hunting song; chase; bag (*game caught*); **aller à la chasse** to go hunting; **chasse à courre** riding to the hounds; **chasse aux appartements** house hunting; **chasse aux fauves** big-game hunting; **chasse d'eau** flush; **chasse gardée** game preserve; **chasse réservée** (public sign) no shooting; **tirer la chasse** to pull the toilet chain

châsse [ʃɑs] *f* reliquary; frame (*e.g., for eyeglasses*) ‖ **châsses** *mpl* (slang) blinkers, eyes

chasse-ballon [ʃasbalɔ̃] *m invar* dodge ball

chasse-bestiaux [ʃasbɛstjo] *m invar* cowcatcher

chasse-clou [ʃasklu] *m* (*pl* **-clous**) punch, nail set; countersink

chassé-croisé [ʃasekrwaze] *m* (*pl* **chassés-croisées**) futile efforts; Double-Crostic

chasselas [ʃasla] *m* white table grape

chasse-mouches [ʃasmuʃ] *m invar* fly swatter; fly net

chasse-neige [ʃasnɛʒ] *m invar* snowplow; snowblower

chasse-pierres [ʃaspjɛr] *m invar* (rr) cowcatcher

chasser [ʃase] *tr* to hunt; chase; chase away, put to flight; drive (*e.g., a herd of cattle*); (coll) to fire (*e.g., a servant*) ‖ *intr* to hunt; skid; come, e.g., **le vent chasse du nord** the wind is coming from the north; **chasser de race** (coll) to be a chip off the old block

chasseresse [ʃasrɛs] *f* huntress

chas·seur [ʃasœr] **-seuse** [søz] *mf* hunter; bellhop ‖ *m* chasseur; fighter pilot; **chasseur à réaction** jet fighter; **chasseur d'assaut** fighter plane; **chasseur de chars** antitank tank; **chasseur de sous-marins** submarine chaser; **chasseur d'images** camera bug

chasseur-bombardier [ʃasœrbɔ̃bardje] *m* fighter-bomber

chassie [ʃasi] *f* gum (*on eyelids*)

chas·sieux [ʃasjø] **-sieuse** [søz] *adj* gummy (*eyelids*)

châssis [ʃasi] *m* chassis; window frame; chase (*for printing*); **châssis à demeure** or **dormant** sealed window frame; **châssis couche** (hort) hotbed; **châssis mobile** movable sash

châssis-presse [ʃasiprɛs] *m* (*pl* **-presses**) printing frame

chaste [ʃast] *adj* chaste

chasteté [ʃastəte] *f* chastity

chat [ʃa] **chatte** [ʃat] *mf* cat ‖ *m* tomcat; **à bon chat bon rat** tit for tat; **acheter chat en poche** (coll) to buy a pig in a poke;

appeler un chat un chat (coll) to call a spade a spade; **chat à neuf queues** cat-o'-nine-tails; **chat dans la gorge** (coll) frog in the throat; **chat de gouttière** alley cat; **chat fourré** (coll) judge; **chat sauvage** wildcat; **d'autres chats à fouetter** (coll) other fish to fry; **il ne faut pas réveiller le chat qui dort** let sleeping dogs lie; **le Chat botté** Puss in Boots; **mon petit chat!** darling!; **pas un chat** (coll) not a soul ‖ *f* see **chatte**

châtaigne [ʃatɛɲ] *f* chestnut

châtaignier [ʃatɛɲe] *m* chestnut tree

chataire [ʃatɛr] *f* catnip

châ·teau [ʃato] *m* (*pl* **-teaux**) chateau; palace; estate, manor; **château d'eau** water tower; **château de cartes** house of cards; **château fort** castle, fort, citadel; **château en Espagne** castles in the air; **mener une vie de château** to live like a prince

châteaubriand or **châteaubriant** [ʃatobriɑ̃] *m* filet mignon, fillet, tenderloin

châte·lain [ʃatlɛ̃] **-laine** [lɛn] *mf* proprietor of a country estate ‖ *f* wife of the lord of the manor; bracelet

châtelet [ʃatlɛ] *m* small chateau

chat-huant [ʃayɑ̃] *m* (*pl* **chats-huants** [ʃayɑ̃]) screech owl

châtier [ʃatje] *tr* to chasten, chastise; correct; purify (*style*)

chatière [ʃatjɛr] *f* ventilation hole; cathole

châtiment [ʃatimɑ̃] *m* punishment

chatoiement [ʃatwamɑ̃] *m* glisten, sparkle; sheen, shimmer; play of colors

chaton [ʃatɔ̃] *m* kitten; setting (*of ring*); (bot) catkin

chatonner [ʃatɔne] *tr* to set (*a gem*) ‖ *intr* to have kittens

chatouillement [ʃatujmɑ̃] *m* tickle; tickling sensation

chatouiller [ʃatuje] *tr* to tickle; (fig) to excite, arouse ‖ *intr* to tickle

chatouil·leux [ʃatujø] **-leuse** [jøz] *adj* ticklish; touchy

chatoyer [ʃatwaje] §47 *intr* to glisten, sparkle; shimmer

chat-pard [ʃapar] *m* (*pl* **chats-pards**) ocelot

châtrer [ʃatre] *tr* to castrate

chatte [ʃat] *adj fem* kittenish ‖ *f* cat, female cat

chatterie [ʃatri] *f* cajoling; sweets

chatterton [ʃatɛrtɔn] *m* friction tape

chaud [ʃo] **chaude** [ʃod] *adj* hot, warm; last-minute (*news flash*); **il fait chaud** it is warm (weather); **pleurer à chaudes larmes** to cry one's eyes out ‖ *m* heat, warmth; **à chaud** emergency (*operation*); (med) in the acute stage; **avoir chaud** to be warm, be hot (*said of person*); **il a eu chaud** (coll) he had a narrow escape ‖ *adv*—**coûter chaud** (coll) to cost a pretty penny; **servir chaud** to serve (*s.th.*) piping hot

chaude-pisse [ʃodpis] *f* (vulg) clap, gonorrhea

chaudière [ʃodjɛr] *f* boiler

chaudron [ʃodrɔ̃] *m* cauldron

chaudron·nier [ʃodrɔnje] **-nière** [njɛr] *mf* coppersmith; boilermaker

chauffage [ʃofaʒ] *m* heating; stoking; (coll) coaching

chauffard [ʃofar] *m* road hog, Sunday driver

chauffe [ʃof] *f* stoking; furnace

chauffe-assiettes [ʃofasjɛt] *m invar* hot plate

chauffe-bain [ʃofbɛ̃] *m* (*pl* **-bains**) bathroom water heater

chauffe-eau [ʃofo] *m invar* water heater

chauffe-lit [ʃofli] *m* (*pl* **-lits**) bed warmer

chauffe-pieds [ʃofpje] *m invar* foot warmer

chauffe-plats [ʃofpla] *m invar* chafing dish

chauffer [ʃofe] *tr* to heat; warm up; limber up; (coll) to coach; (slang) to snitch, filch ‖ *intr* to heat up; get up steam; overheat; **ça va chauffer!** (coll) watch the fur fly! ‖ *ref* to warm oneself; heat up

chaufferette [ʃofrɛt] *f* foot warmer; space heater; car heater

chauffeur [ʃofœr] *m* driver; chauffeur; (rr) stoker, fireman

chauffeuse [ʃoføz] *f* fireside chair

chaume [ʃom] *m* stubble; thatch

chaumière [ʃomjɛr] *f* thatched cottage

chaussée [ʃose] *f* pavement, road; causeway

chausse-pied [ʃospje] *m* (*pl* **-pieds**) shoehorn

chausser [ʃose] *tr* to put on (*shoes, skis, glasses, tires, etc.*); shoe; fit ‖ *intr* to fit (*said of shoe*); **chausser de** to wear (*a certain size shoe*) ‖ *ref* to put one's shoes on

chausses [ʃos] *fpl* hose (*in medieval dress*); **aux chausses de** on the heels of; **c'est elle qui porte les chausses** (coll) she wears the pants

chausse-trape [ʃostrap] *f* (*pl* **-trapes**) trap; booby trap

chaussette [ʃosɛt] *f* sock

chausseur [ʃosœr] *m* shoe salesman

chausson [ʃosɔ̃] *m* pump, slipper, savate; **chausson aux pommes** apple turnover

chaussure [ʃosyr] *f* footwear, shoes; shoe; **trouver chaussure à son pied** to find what one needs

chauve [ʃov] *adj* bald

chauve-souris [ʃovsuri] *f* (*pl* **chauves-souris**) (zool) bat

chau·vin [ʃovɛ̃] **-vine** [vin] *adj* chauvinistic ‖ *mf* chauvinist

chauvir [ʃovir] *intr*—**chauvir de l'oreille,** **chauvir des oreilles** to prick up the ears (*said of horse, mule, donkey*)

chaux [ʃo] *f* lime

chavirement [ʃavirmɑ̃] *m* capsizing, overturning

chavirer [ʃavire] *tr & intr* to tip over, capsize

chef [ʃɛf] *m* head, chief, leader; boss; scoutmaster; **au premier chef** essentially; **chef de bande** ringleader, gang leader; **chef de cuisine** chef; **chef de file** leader, standard-bearer; **chef de gare** stationmaster; **chef de l'exécutif** chief execu-

tive; **chef de musique** bandmaster; **chef de rayon** floorwalker; **chef de tribu** chieftain; **chef d'orchestre** conductor; bandleader; **de son propre chef** by one's own authority, on one's own

chef-d'œuvre [ʃɛdœvr] *m* (*pl* **chefs-d'œuvre**) masterpiece

chef-lieu [ʃɛfljø] *m* (*pl* **chefs-lieux**) county seat, capital city

cheftaine [ʃɛftɛn] *f* Girl Scout unit leader

cheik [ʃɛk] *m* sheik

chelem [ʃlɛm] *m* slam (*at bridge*); **être chelem** (cards) to be shut out

chemin [ʃmɛ̃] *m* way; road; **chemin battu** beaten path; **chemin de la Croix** (eccl) Way of the Cross; **chemin de fer** railroad; **chemin de roulement** (aer) taxiway; **chemin des écoliers** (coll) long way around; **chemin de table** table runner; **chemin de traverse** side road; shortcut; **chemin de velours** primrose path; **n'y pas aller par quatre chemins** (coll) to come straight to the point

chemi·neau [ʃmino] *m* (*pl* **-neaux**) hobo, tramp; deadbeat

cheminée [ʃmine] *f* chimney, stack, smokestack; fireplace; (naut) funnel

cheminer [ʃmine] *intr* to trudge, tramp; make headway

cheminot [ʃmino] *m* railroader

chemise [ʃmiz] *f* shirt; dust jacket (*of book*); folder, file; jacket, shell, metal casing; **chemise classeur** folder; **chemise de mailles** coat of mail; **chemise de nuit** nightgown; **chemise polo** polo shirt

chemiser [ʃmize] *tr* (mach) to case, jacket

chemiserie [ʃmizri] *f* haberdashery

chemisette [ʃmizɛt] *f* short-sleeved shirt

chemi·sier [ʃmizje] **-sière** [zjɛr] *mf* haberdasher ‖ *m* shirtwaist

che·nal [ʃnal] *m* (*pl* **-naux** [no]) channel; millrace

chenapan [ʃnapɑ̃] *m* rogue, scoundrel

chêne [ʃɛn] *m* oak

ché·neau [ʃeno] *m* (*pl* **-neaux**) rain spout

chêne-liège [ʃɛnljɛʒ] *m* (*pl* **chênes-lièges**) cork oak

chenet [ʃnɛ] *m* andiron

chènevis [ʃɛnvi] *m* hempseed, birdseed

chenil [ʃni] *m* kennel

chenille [ʃnij] *f* caterpillar; chenille; caterpillar tread

chenil·lé **-lée** [ʃnije] *adj* with a caterpillar tread

che·nu **-nue** [ʃny] *adj* hoary

cheptel [ʃɛptɛl], [ʃɛtɛl] *m* livestock; **cheptel mort** implements and buildings

chèque [ʃɛk] *m* check; **chèque certifié** certified check; **chèque de voyage** traveler's check; **chèque en blanc** blank check; **chèque en bois** bad check; **chèque prescrit** invalidated (*old*) check; **chèque sans provision** bad check

chéquier [ʃekje] *m* checkbook

cher chère [ʃɛr] *adj* expensive, dear ‖ (when standing before noun) *adj* dear, beloved ‖ *f* see **chère** ‖ **cher** *adv* dear(ly); **coûter cher** to cost a great deal

chercher [ʃɛrʃe] §96 *tr* to look for, search for, seek, hunt; try to get; **aller chercher** to go and get; **envoyer chercher** to send for ‖ *intr* to search; **chercher à** to try to, endeavor to ‖ *intr* to look for each other; feel one's way

cher·cheur [ʃɛrʃœr] **-cheuse** [ʃøz] *adj* inquiring (*mind*); homing (*device*) ‖ *mf* seeker; researcher, scholar; investigator; prospector (*for gold, uranium, etc.*)

chère [ʃɛr] *f* fare, food and drink; **faire bonne chère** to live high

chèrement [ʃɛrmɑ̃] *adv* fondly, lovingly; dearly (*bought or won*)

ché·ri -rie [ʃeri] *adj & mf* darling

chérir [ʃerir] *tr* to cherish

cherry [ʃeri] *m* cherry cordial

cherté [ʃɛrte] *f* high price; **cherté de la vie** high cost of living

chérubin [ʃerybɛ̃] *m* cherub

ché·tif [ʃetif] **-tive** [tiv] *adj* puny, sickly; poor, wretched

che·val [ʃəval] *m* (*pl* **-vaux** [vo]) horse; metric or French horsepower (*735 watts*); **à cheval** on horseback; **à cheval sur** astride; insistent upon; **cheval à bascule** rocking horse; **cheval de bât** pack horse; **cheval de bataille** charger, warhorse; (fig) main issue (*in a political campaign*); **cheval de bois** or **cheval d'arçons** horse (*for vaulting*); **cheval de course** race horse; **cheval de race** thoroughbred; **cheval de retour** (coll) jailbird; **cheval de selle** saddle horse; **cheval de trait** draft horse; **cheval de Troie** Trojan horse; **cheval entier** stallion; **cheval vapeur** horsepower; **monter sur ses grands chevaux** (fig) to get up on one's high horse

chevalement [ʃvalmɑ̃] *m* support, shoring; (min) headframe

chevaler [ʃvale] *tr* to shore up

chevaleresque [ʃvalrɛsk] *adj* knightly, chivalrous

chevalerie [ʃvalri] *f* chivalry

chevalet [ʃvalɛ] *m* easel; sawhorse; stand, frame; bridge (*of violin*)

chevalier [ʃvalje] *m* knight; (orn) sandpiper; **chevalier d'industrie** manipulator, swindler; **chevalier errant** knight-errant; **Chevaliers du taste-vin** wine-tasting club

chevalière [ʃvaljɛr] *f* signet ring

cheva·lin [ʃvalɛ̃] **-line** [lin] *adj* equine

cheval-vapeur [ʃvalvapœr] *m* (*pl* **chevaux-vapeur**) metric or French horsepower (*735 watts*)

chevauchée [ʃəvoʃe] *f* ride

chevaucher [ʃəvoʃe] *tr* to straddle ‖ *intr* to ride horseback; overlap

cheve·lu -lue [ʃəvly] *adj* hairy; long-haired

chevelure [ʃəvlyr] *f* hair, head of hair; tail (*of a comet*)

chevet [ʃəvɛ] *m* headboard; bolster; **de chevet** bedside (*lamp, table, book*)

che·veu [ʃəvø] *m* (*pl* **-veux**) hair; **avoir mal aux cheveux** (coll) to have a hangover;

cheveux hair (*of the head*); hairs; **cheveux en brosse** crew cut; **couper les cheveux en quatre** (coll) to split hairs; **en cheveux** hatless; **faire dresser les cheveux** (coll) to make one's hair stand on end; **ne tenir qu'à un cheveu** (coll) to hang by a thread; **saisir l'occasion aux cheveux** (coll) to take time by the forelock; **se faire des cheveux** (coll) to worry oneself gray; **tiré par les cheveux** (coll) far-fetched

chevillard [ʃəvijar] *m* wholesale cattle dealer or jobber

cheville [ʃəvij] *f* ankle; peg; pin; bolt; padding (*of verse*); **cheville ouvrière** (mach) kingbolt; (fig) mainspring (*of an enterprise*); **être en cheville avec** (coll) to be in cahoots with; **ne pas arriver à la cheville de qn** (coll) not to hold a candle to s.o.

chèvre [ʃɛvr] *f* goat; nanny goat

che·vreau [ʃəvro] *m* (*pl* **-vreaux**) kid

chèvrefeuille [ʃɛvrəfœj] *m* honeysuckle

chevrette [ʃəvrɛt] *f* kid; doe (*roe deer*); shrimp; tripod

chevreuil [ʃəvrœj] *m* roe deer; roebuck

chevron [ʃəvrɔ̃] *m* rafter; chevron, hash mark; **en chevron** in a herringbone pattern

chevron·né -née [ʃəvrɔne] *adj* wearing chevrons; experienced, oldest

chevronner [ʃəvrɔne] *tr* to put rafters on; give chevrons to

chevroter [ʃəvrɔte] *intr* to bleat; sing or speak in a quavering voice

chewing-gum [ʃwiŋgɔm], [tʃuwiŋgɔm] *m* chewing gum

chez [ʃe] *prep* at the house, home, office, etc., of, e.g., **chez mes amis** at my friends' house; e.g., **chez le boulanger** at the baker's; in the country of, among, e.g., **chez les Français** among the French; in the time of, e.g., **chez les anciens Grecs** in the time of the ancient Greeks; in the work of, e.g., **chez Homère** in Homer's works; with, e.g., **c'est chez lui une habitude** it's a habit with him

chez-soi [ʃeswa] *m invar* home

chialer [ʃjale] *intr* (slang) to cry

chiasse [ʃjas] *f* flyspecks; (metallurgy) dross; (coll) loose bowels

chic [ʃik] *adj invar* stylish, chic; **un chic type** (coll) a good egg ‖ *m* style; skill, knack; (coll) smartness, elegance; (slang) ovation; **de chic** from memory ‖ *interj* (coll) fine!, grand!

chicane [ʃikan] *f* chicanery; shady lawsuit; baffle, baffle plate; **chercher chicane à** to engage in a petty quarrel with; **en chicane** staggered, zigzag; curved (*tube*)

chicaner [ʃikane] *tr* to pick a fight with; **chicaner q.ch. à qn** to quibble over s.th. with s.o. ‖ *intr* to quibble

chicanerie [ʃikanri] *f* chicanery

chiche [ʃiʃ] *adj* stringy; small, dwarf ‖ *interj* (coll) I dare you!

chichi [ʃiʃi] *m* fuss; **sans chichis** informally

chicon [ʃikɔ̃] *m* (coll) romaine
chicorée [ʃikɔre] *f* chicory; **chicorée frisée** endive
chicot [ʃiko] *m* stump (*of tree*); (coll) stump, stub (*of tooth*)
chien [ʃjɛ̃] **chienne** [ʃjɛn] *mf* dog ‖ *m* hammer (*of gun*); glamour; **à la chien** (coll) with bangs; **chien couchant** setter; (slang) apple polisher; **chien d'arrêt** pointer; **chien d'aveugle** Seeing Eye dog; **chien de** or **chienne de** (coll) dickens of a; **chien de garde** watchdog; **chien de traîneau** sled dog; **chien du jardinier** (coll) dog in the manger; **chien savant** performing dog; **de chien** (coll) miserable (*weather, life, etc.*); **en chien de fusil** (coll) curled up (*e.g., to sleep*); **entre chien et loup** (coll) at dusk; **les chiens écrasés** (slang) the accident page (*of newspaper*); **petit chien** pup; **se regarder en chiens de faïence** (coll) to glare at one another ‖ *f* see **chienne**
chiendent [ʃjɛ̃dɑ̃] *m* couch grass; (coll) trouble
chienlit [ʃjɑ̃li] *mf* (vulg) person who soils his bed ‖ *m* carnival mask; masquerade, fantastic costume ‖ *f* (vulg) crap (*rowdyness, havoc*), e.g., **réforme, oui! chien-lit, non!** reform, yes! crap, no!
chien-loup [ʃjɛ̃lu] *m* (*pl* **chiens-loups**) wolfhound
chienne [ʃjɛn] *f* bitch
chienner [ʃjɛne] *intr* to whelp
chier [ʃje] *tr & intr* (vulg) to crap, defecate; **tu me fais chier!** (vulg) you're a pain in the ass!
chiffe [ʃif] *f* rag; (coll) weakling
chiffon [ʃifɔ̃] *m* rag; scrap of paper; **chiffons** (coll) fashions
chiffonnade [ʃifɔnad] *f* salad greens
chiffonner [ʃifɔne] *tr* to rumple, crumple; make (*a dress*); (coll) to ruffle (*tempers*), bother ‖ *intr* to pick rags; make dresses
chiffon·nier [ʃifɔnje] **-nière** [njɛr] *mf* scavenger, ragpicker ‖ *m* chiffonier
chiffre [ʃifr] *m* figure, number; cipher, code; sum total; combination (*of lock*); monogram; **chiffre d'affaires** turnover; **chiffres romains** roman numerals
chiffrer [ʃifre] *tr* to number; monogram; figure the cost of; cipher, code ‖ *intr* to calculate; mount up; cipher, code ‖ *ref*—**se chiffrer par** to amount to
chignole [ʃiɲɔl] *f* breast drill, hand drill; (coll) jalopy
chignon [ʃiɲɔ̃] *m* chignon, bun, knot
Chili [ʃili] *m*—**le Chili** Chile
chimère [ʃimɛr] *f* chimera; **se forger des chimères** to indulge in wishful thinking
chimie [ʃimi] *f* chemistry
chimique [ʃimik] *adj* chemical
chimiste [ʃimist] *mf* chemist
chimpanzé [ʃɛ̃pɑze] *m* chimpanzee
Chine [ʃin] *f* China; **la Chine** China; **les deux Chine** the two Chinas
chi·né -née [ʃine] *adj* mottled, figured

chiner [ʃine] *tr* to mottle (*cloth*); (coll) to make fun of
chi·nois -noise [ʃinwa] *adj* Chinese ‖ *m* Chinese (*language*) ‖ (*cap*) *mf* Chinese (*person*)
chinoiserie [ʃinwazri] *f* Chinese curio; **chinoiseries administratives** (coll) red tape
chiot [ʃjo] *m* puppy
chiourme [ʃjurm] *f* chain gang
chip [ʃip] *m* (electron) chip
chiper [ʃipe] *tr* (slang) to swipe; gyp
chipie [ʃipi] *f* (coll) shrew
chipoter [ʃipɔte] *intr* to haggle; nibble, pick at one's food
chips [ʃips] *mpl* potato chips
chique [ʃik] *f* chew, quid (*of tobacco*); (ent) chigger
chiqué [ʃike] *m* (slang) sham, bluff
chiquenaude [ʃiknod] *f* fillip, flick
chiquer [ʃike] *tr* to chew (*tobacco*) ‖ *intr* to chew tobacco
chiromancie [kirɔmɑ̃si] *f* palmistry
chiroman·cien [kirɔmɑ̃sjɛ̃] **-cienne** [sjɛn] *mf* palm reader
chiropracteur [kirɔpraktœr] *m* chiropractor
chirurgi·cal -cale [ʃiryrʒikal] *adj* (*pl* **-caux** [ko]) surgical
chirurgie [ʃiryrʒi] *f* surgery
chirur·gien [ʃiryrʒjɛ̃] **-gienne** [ʒɛn] *mf* surgeon
chirurgien-dentiste [ʃiryrʒjɛ̃dɑ̃tist] *m* (*pl* **chirurgiens-dentistes**) dental surgeon
chiure [ʃiyr] *f* flyspeck
chlamydiose [klamidjoz] *f* chlamydia
chlore [klɔr] *m* chlorine
chlo·ré -rée [klɔre] *adj* chlorinated
chlorhydrique [klɔridrik] *adj* hydrochloric
chloroforme [klɔrɔfɔrm] *m* chloroform
chloroformer [klɔrɔfɔrme] *tr* to chloroform
chlorophylle [klɔrɔfil] *f* chlorophyll
chlorure [klɔryr] *m* chloride; **chlorure de soude** sodium chloride
choc [ʃɔk] *m* shock; clash; bump; clink (*of glasses*)
chocolat [ʃɔkɔla] *adj invar & m* chocolate
chocolaterie [ʃɔkɔlatri] *f* chocolate factory
chœur [kœr] *m* choir, chorus
choir [ʃwar] (usually used only in *inf* and *pp* **chu;** sometimes used in *pres ind* **chois**, etc.; *pret* **chus**, etc; *fut* **choirai**, etc.) *intr* (*aux:* ÊTRE or AVOIR) to fall; **se laisser choir** to drop, flop
choi·si -sie [ʃwazi] *adj* choice, select; chosen; selected (*works*)
choisir [ʃwazir] §97 *tr & intr* to choose
choix [ʃwa] *m* choice; **au choix** at one's discretion; **de choix** choice
choléra [kɔlera] *m* cholera
cholérique [kɔlerik] *mf* cholera victim
cholestérol [kɔlɛsterɔl] *m* cholesterol
chômage [ʃomaʒ] *m* unemployment; **en chômage** unemployed
chô·mé -mée [ʃome] *adj* closed for business, off, e.g., **jour chômé** day off
chômer [ʃome] *tr* to take (*a day*) off; observe (*a holiday*) ‖ *intr* to take off (*from work*); be unemployed

chô·meur [ʃomœr] **-meuse** [møz] *mf* unemployed worker

chope [ʃɔp] *f* stein, beer mug

choper [ʃɔpe] *tr* (coll) to catch

chopine [ʃɔpin] *f* half-liter measure; (slang) bottle

chopper [ʃɔpe] *intr* to stumble; blunder

choquer [ʃɔke] *tr* to shock; bump; clink (*glasses*); (elec) to shock ‖ *ref* to collide; take offense

cho·ral **-rale** [kɔral] *adj* (*pl* **-raux** [ro]) choral ‖ *m* (*pl* **-rals**) chorale ‖ *f* choral society, glee club

chorégraphie [kɔregrafi] *f* choreography

choriste [kɔrist] *mf* chorister

chorus [kɔrys] *m*—**faire chorus** to repeat in unison; chime in; approve unanimously

chose [ʃoz] *adj invar* (coll) odd; **être tout chose** (coll) to feel funny ‖ *m* thingamajig; **Monsieur Chose** (coll) Mr. what's-his-name ‖ *f* thing ‖ *pron indef masc*—**autre chose** something else; **quelque chose** something

chou [ʃu] **choute** [ʃut] *mf*—**ma choute, mon chou** (coll) sweetheart ‖ *m* (*pl* **choux**) cabbage; **chou à la crème** cream puff; **chou de Bruxelles** Brussels sprouts; **de chou** (coll) of little value; **faire chou blanc** (coll) to draw a blank; **finir dans le chou** (coll) to come in last

choucas [ʃuka] *m* jackdaw

choucroute [ʃukrut] *f* sauerkraut; **choucroute garnie** sauerkraut with ham or sausage

chouette [ʃwɛt] *adj* (coll) swell; **chouette alors!** (coll) oh boy! ‖ *f* owl; (coll) radio; **chouette épervière** hawk owl

chou-fleur [ʃuflœr] *m* (*pl* **choux-fleurs**) cauliflower

chou-rave [ʃurav] *m* (*pl* **choux-raves**) kohlrabi

chow-chow [ʃuʃu] *m* (*pl* **-chows**) chow (*dog*)

choyer [ʃwaje] §47 *tr* to pamper, coddle; cherish (*a hope*); entertain (*an idea*)

chrestomatie [krɛstɔmati]. [krɛstɔmasi] *f* chrestomathy

chré·tien [kretjɛ̃] **-tienne** [tjɛn] *adj & mf* Christian

chrétiennement [kretjɛnmã] *adv* in the faith

chrétienté [kretjɛ̃te] *f* Christendom

christ [krist] *m* crucifix ‖ (*cap*) *m* Christ; **le Christ** Christ

christianiser [kristjanize] *tr* to Christianize

christianisme [kristjanism] *m* Christianity

chromatique [krɔmatik] *adj* chromatic

chrome [krom] *m* chrome, chromium

chromer [krome] *tr* to chrome

chromocodé [krɔmokɔde] *adj* (chem) color-coded

chromosome [krɔmozom] *m* chromosome

chronique [krɔnik] *adj* chronic ‖ *f* chronicle; column (*in newspaper*); **chronique financière** financial page; **chronique mondaine** society news; **chronique théâtrale** theater page

chroniqueur [krɔnikœr] *m* chronicler; columnist; **chroniqueur dramatique** drama critic

chrono [krɔno] *m*—**faire du 60 chrono** (coll) to do 60 by the clock

chronologie [krɔnɔlɔʒi] *f* chronology

chronologique [krɔnɔlɔʒik] *adj* chronological

chronomètre [krɔnɔmɛtr] *m* chronometer; stopwatch

chronométrer [krɔnɔmetre] §10 *tr* to clock, time

chronométreur [krɔnɔmetrœr] *m* timekeeper

chrysalide [krizalid] *f* chrysalis

chrysanthème [krizɑ̃tɛm] *m* chrysanthemum

chuchotement [ʃyʃɔtmɑ̃] *m* whisper, whispering

chuchoter [ʃyʃɔte] *tr & intr* to whisper

chuinter [ʃɥɛ̃te] *intr* to hoot (*said of owl*); make a swishing sound, hiss (*said of escaping gas*); pronounce [ʃ] instead of [s] and [ʒ] instead of [z]

chut [ʃyt] *interj* sh!

chute [ʃyt] *f* fall; downfall; drop (*in prices, voltage, etc.*); **chute d'eau** waterfall

chuter [ʃyte] *tr* to hush; hiss (*an actor*) ‖ *intr* (coll) to fall; (cards) to be down

Chypre [ʃipr] *f* Cyprus

ci [si] *pron indef*—**comme ci comme ça** so-so ‖ *adv*—**entre ci et là** between now and then

-ci [si] §82, §84

ci-après [siaprɛ] *adv* hereafter, below, further on

ci-bas [siba] *adv* below

cible [sibl] *f* target

ciboule [sibul] *f* chive, scallion

ciboulette [sibulɛt] *f* chive, chives

cicatrice [sikatris] *f* scar

cicatriser [sikatrize] *tr* to heal; scar ‖ *ref* to heal

Cicéron [siserɔ̃] *m* Cicero

cicérone [siseron] *m* guide

ci-contre [sikɔ̃tr] *adv* opposite, on the opposite page; in the margin

ci-dessous [sidəsu] *adv* further on, below, hereunder

ci-dessus [sidəsy] *adv* above

ci-devant [sidəvɑ̃] *mf invar* (hist) aristocrat; (coll) back number ‖ *adv* previously, formerly

cidre [sidr] *m* cider

Cie *abbr* (**Compagnie**) Co.

ciel [sjɛl] *m* (*pl* **cieux** [sjø]) sky, heavens (*firmament*); heaven (*state of great happiness*) ‖ *m* (*pl* **ciels**) heaven (*abode of the blessed*); sky (*upper atmosphere, especially with reference to meteorological conditions; representation of sky in a painting*); canopy (*of a bed*) ‖ *m* (*pl* **cieux** or **ciels**) clime, sky

cierge [sjɛrʒ] *m* wax candle; cactus; **droit comme un cierge** straight as a ramrod; **en cierge** straight up

cigale [sigal] *f* cicada, grasshopper

cigare [sigar] *m* cigar
cigarette [sigarɛt] *f* cigarette
ci·git [siʒi] see **gésir**
cigogne [sigɔɲ] *f* stork
ciguë [sigy] *f* hemlock (*herb and poison*)
ci-in·clus [siɛ̃kly] **-cluse** [klyz] *adj* enclosed ‖ **ci-inclus** *adv* enclosed
ci-joint [siʒwɛ̃] **-jointe** [jwɛ̃t] *adj* enclosed ‖ **ci-joint** *adv* enclosed
cil [sil] *m* eyelash; **cils** eyelash (*fringe of hair*)
cilice [silis] *m* hair shirt
ciller [sije] *tr* & *intr* to blink
cime [sim] *f* summit, top
ciment [simɑ̃] *m* cement; **ciment armé** reinforced concrete
cimentation [simɑ̃tɑsjɔ̃] *f* cementing
cimenter [simɑ̃te] *tr* to cement
cimeterre [simtɛr] *m* scimitar
cimetière [simtjɛr] *m* cemetery
cinéaste [sineast] *mf* film producer; movie director; scenarist; movie technician
cinégraphiste [sinegrafist] *mf* scenarist
cinéma [sinema] *m* movies; moving-picture theater; cinema; **cinéma auto** drive-in movie; **cinéma d'essai** preview theater; **cinéma muet** silent movie
cinémathèque [sinematɛk] *f* film library
cinématographique [sinematɔgrafik] *adj* motion-picture, film
ciné-park [sinepark] *m* (*pl* **ciné-parks**) drive-in (movie) theater
cinéphile [sinefil] *mf* movie fan
cinéprojecteur [sineprɔʒɛktœr] *m* motion-picture projector
ciné-roman [sinerɔmɑ̃] *m* (*pl* **-romans**) novelization (*of a film*)
cinétique [sinetik] *adj* kinetic ‖ *f* kinetics
cin·glant [sɛ̃glɑ̃] **-glante** [glɑ̃t] *adj* scathing
cin·glé -glée [sɛ̃gle] *adj* (slang) screwy ‖ *mf* (slang) screwball
cingler [sɛ̃gle] *tr* to whip; cut to the quick ‖ *intr* to go full sail
cinq [sɛ̃(k)] §94 *adj* & *pron* five; the Fifth, e.g., **Jean cinq** John the Fifth; **cinq heures** five o'clock ‖ *m* five; fifth (*in dates*); **il était moins cinq** (coll) it was a close shave
cinquantaine [sɛ̃kɑ̃tɛn] *f* about fifty; age of fifty, fifty mark, fifties
cinquante [sɛ̃kɑ̃t] §94 *adj, pron,* & *m* fifty; **cinquante et un** fifty-one; **cinquante et unième** fifty-first
cinquantième [sɛ̃kɑ̃tjɛm] §94 *adj, pron* (*masc, fem*) & *m* fiftieth
cinquième [sɛ̃kjɛm] §94 *adj, pron* (*masc, fem*) & *m* fifth
cintre [sɛ̃tr] *m* arch; coat hanger; bend; **plein cintre** semicircular arch
cin·tré -trée [sɛ̃tre] *adj* (slang) crazy
cintrer [sɛ̃tre] *tr* to arch, bend
cirage [siraʒ] *m* waxing; shoe polish; **cirage automatique des chaussures** shoeshining in an automatic machine; **dans le cirage** (coll) in the dark
circoncire [sirkɔ̃sir] §66 (*pp* **circoncis**) *tr* to circumcise

circoncision [sirkɔ̃sizjɔ̃] *f* circumcision
circonférence [sirkɔ̃ferɑ̃s] *f* circumference
circonflexe [sirkɔ̃flɛks] *adj* & *m* circumflex
circonscription [sirkɔ̃skripsjɔ̃] *f* circumscription; ward, district
circonscrire [sirkɔ̃skrir] §25 *tr* to circumscribe
circons·pect [sirkɔ̃spɛ], [sirkɔ̃spɛk(t)] **-pecte** [pɛkt] *adj* circumspect
circonstance [sirkɔ̃stɑ̃s] *f* circumstance; **circonstances et dépendances** appurtenances; **de circonstance** proper for the occasion, topical; emergency (*measure*); guest, e.g., **orateur de circonstance** guest speaker
circonstan·cié -ciée [sirkɔ̃stɑ̃sje] *adj* circumstantial, in detail
circonstan·ciel -cielle [sirkɔ̃stɑ̃sjɛl] *adj* (gram) adverbial
circonvenir [sirkɔ̃vnir] §72 *tr* to circumvent
circonvoi·sin [sirkɔ̃vwazɛ̃] **-sine** [zin] *adj* nearby, neighboring
circuit [sirkɥi] *m* circuit; circumference; detour; tour; **circuit d'attente** (aer) holding point; **circuit imprimé** printed circuit
circulaire [sirkylɛr] *adj* & *f* circular
circulation [sirkylɑsjɔ̃] *f* circulation; traffic; **circulation interdite** (public sign) no thoroughfare
circuler [sirkyle] *intr* to circulate; go, move; **circulez au pas!** walk!
cire [sir] *f* wax; **cire à cacheter** sealing wax; **cire molle** (fig) wax in one's hands
ci·ré -rée [sire] *adj* waxed ‖ *m* waterproof garment; raincoat
cirer [sire] *tr* to wax; polish
ci·reur [sirœr] **-reuse** [røz] *mf* waxer, polisher (*person*); shoeblack, bootblack ‖ *f* floor waxer (*machine*)
ci·reux [sirø] **-reuse** [røø] *adj* waxy
ciron [sirɔ̃] *m* mite
cirque [sirk] *m* circus; amphitheater
cirrhose [siroz] *f* cirrhosis
cisaille [sizɑj] *f* metal clippings, scissel; paper cutter; **cisailles** clippers, shears; pruning shears; wire cutter
cisaillement [sizɑjmɑ̃] *m* cutting, clipping, pruning; shearing off; **cisaillement du vent** wind shear
cisailler [sizɑje] *tr* to shear
ci·seau [sizo] *m* (*pl* **-seaux**) chisel; **ciseau à froid** cold chisel; **ciseaux** scissors; **ciseaux à ongles** nail scissors; **ciseaux à raisin** pruning shears; **ciseaux à tondre** sheep shears
ciseler [sizle] §2 *tr* to chisel; chase; cut, shear; prune
ciseleur [sizlœr] *m* chaser, tooler
citadelle [sitadɛl] *f* citadel
cita·din [sitadɛ̃] **-dine** [din] *adj* urban ‖ *mf* city dweller
citation [sitɑsjɔ̃] *f* citation, quotation; citation, summons
cité [site] *f* housing development; (hist) fortified city, citadel; **cité ouvrière** low-cost housing development; **cité sainte** Holy City; **cité universitaire** university dormi-

tory complex; **la Cité** the City (*district within ancient boundaries*)

cité-jardin [siteʒardɛ̃] *f* (*pl* **cités-jardins**) landscaped housing development with parks

citer [site] *tr* to cite, quote; summon, subpoena

citerne [sitɛrn] *f* cistern; tank; **citerne flottante** tanker

cithare [sitar] *f* cither, zither

citoyen [sitwajɛ̃] **citoyenne** [sitwajɛn] *mf* citizen; (coll) individual, person; **citoyens** citizenry

citoyenneté [sitwajɛnte] *f* citizenship; citizenry

citrique [sitrik] *adj* citric

citron [sitrɔ̃] *adj* & *m* lemon

citronnade [sitrɔnad] *f* lemonade

citron·né -née [sitrɔne] *adj* lemon-flavored

citronnelle [sitrɔnɛl] *f* citronella

citronner [sitrɔne] *tr* to flavor with lemon

citronnier [sitrɔnje] *m* lemon tree

citrouille [sitruj] *f* pumpkin, gourd

cive [siv] *f* chive, scallion

civet [sivɛ] *m* stew

civette [sivɛt] *f* civet; civet cat; chive, chives

civière [sivjɛr] *f* stretcher, litter

ci·vil -vile [sivil] *adj* civil; civilian; secular ‖ *m* civilian; layman; **en civil** plainclothes (*person*); in civies

civilisation [sivilizasjɔ̃] *f* civilization

civiliser [sivilize] *tr* to civilize ‖ *ref* to become civilized

civilité [sivilite] *f* civility; **civilités** kind regards; amenities

civique [sivik] *adj* civic; civil (*rights*); national (*guard*)

civisme [sivism] *m* good citizenship

clabauder [klabode] *intr* to clamor

claie [klɛ] *f* wickerwork; trellis

clair claire [klɛr] *adj* clear, bright; evident, plain; light, pale ‖ *m* light, brightness; **clair de lune** moonlight; **clairs** highlights ‖ *f* oyster bed

clairance [klɛrɑ̃s] *f* (aer) clearance

clai·ret -rette [klɛrɛ] -**rette** [rɛt] *adj* light-red; thin, high-pitched (*voice*) ‖ *m* light, red wine ‖ *f* light sparkling wine

claire-voie [klɛrvwa] *f* (*pl* **claires-voies**) latticework, slats; clerestory; **à claire-voie** with open spaces

clairière [klɛrjɛr] *f* clearing, glade

clairon [klɛrɔ̃] *m* bugle; bugler

claironner [klɛrɔne] *tr* to announce ‖ *intr* to sound the bugle

clairse·mé -mée [klɛrsəme] *adj* scattered, sparse; thin, thinned out

clairvoyance [klɛrvwajɑ̃s] *f* clear-sightedness, clairvoyance

clairvoyant [klɛrvwajɑ̃] **clairvoyante** [klɛrvwajɑ̃t] *adj* clear-sighted, clairvoyant

clamer [klame] *tr* & *intr* to cry out

clameur [klamœr] *f* clamor, outcry

clamp [klɑ̃] *m* (med) clamp

clampin [klɑ̃pɛ̃] *m* (mil) straggler

clan [klɑ̃] *m* clan, clique

clandes·tin [klɑ̃dɛstɛ̃] -**tine** [tin] *adj* clandestine

clapet [klapɛ] *m* valve; **ferme ton clapet!** (slang) shut your trap

clapier [klapje] *m* rabbit hutch

clapoter [klapɔte] *intr* to splash; be choppy

claque [klak] *m* opera hat ‖ *f* slap, smack; claque, paid applauders

cla·qué -quée [klake] *adj* dog-tired; sprained

claquement [klakmɑ̃] *m* clapping; slam (*of a door*); chattering (*of teeth*)

claquemurer [klakmyre] *tr* to shut in ‖ *ref* to shut oneself up at home

claquer [klake] *tr* to slap; clap; smack (*the lips*); slam (*the door*); crack (*the whip*); click (*the heels*); snap (*the fingers*); (coll) to tire out; (coll) to waste ‖ *intr* to clap, slap, slam; crack; (slang) to fail; (slang) to die ‖ *ref* to sprain; (slang) to work oneself to death

claquettes [klakɛt] *fpl* tap-dancing

claqueur [klakœr] *m* applauder, member of a claque

clarifier [klarifje] *tr* to clarify ‖ *ref* to become clear

clarine [klarin] *f* cowbell

clarinette [klarinɛt] *f* clarinet

clarté [klarte] *f* clarity; brightness; **clarté du soleil** sunshine

classe [klɑs] *f* class; classroom; **classe de rattrapage** refresher course (*for backward children*); **classe de travaux pratiques** lab class

clas·sé -sée [klɑse] *adj* pigeonholed, tabled; standard (*literary work*); listed; **non classé** (sports) also-ran

classer [klɑse] *tr* to class; sort out, file; pigeonhole, table ‖ *ref* to come in, rank, finish; **se classer premier** (sports) to come in first

classeur [klɑsœr] *m* file (*for letters, documents*); filing cabinet

classicisme [klasisism] *m* classicism

classification [klasifikasjɔ̃] *f* classification

classifier [klasifje] *tr* to classify; sort out

classique [klasik] *adj* classic, classical; standard (*author, work*) ‖ *mf* classicist ‖ *m* classic; standard work

claudication [klodikasjɔ̃] *f* limping

clause [kloz] *f* clause, stipulation, provision; **clause additionnelle** rider; **clause ambiguë** joker clause; **clause de style** unwritten provision; **clause d'indexation** escalator clause

claustration [klostrasjɔ̃] *f* confinement; cloistering

clavecin [klavsɛ̃] *m* harpsichord

claveciniste [klavsinist] *mf* harpsichordist

clavette [klavɛt] *f* pin, cotter pin; key

clavicule [klavikyl] *f* collarbone

clavier [klavje] *m* keyboard; key ring; range (*e.g., of the voice*); **clavier universel** standard keyboard

clayère [klɛjɛr] *f* oyster bed

clé [kle] *f* see **clef**

clef [kle] *adj invar* key ‖ *f* key; wrench; (mus) valve; (mus) clef; (wrestling) lock; **clef anglaise** monkey wrench; **clef à tube** socket wrench; **clef crocodile** alligator wrench; **clef d'allumage** ignition key; **clef de fa** bass clef; **clef des champs** vacation; **clef de sol** treble clef; **clef de voûte** keystone; **clef d'ut** tenor clef; **fausse clef** skeleton key; **sous clef** under lock and key

clémence [klemɑ̃s] *f* clemency

clé·ment [klemɑ̃] **-mente** [mɑ̃t] *adj* mild, clement

clenche [klɑ̃ʃ] *f* latch

cleptomane [klɛptɔman] *mf* kleptomaniac

clerc [klɛr] *m* cleric, clergyman; scholar; clerk

clergé [klɛrʒe] *m* clergy

clergie [klɛrʒi] *f* learning, scholarship; clergy

cléri·cal -cale [klerikal] *adj & mf* (*pl* **-caux** [ko]) clerical

cliché [kliʃe] *m* cliché; (phot) negative; (typ) plate, stereotype; **prendre un cliché** (phot) to make an exposure

clicher [kliʃe] *tr* (typ) to stereotype

client [klijɑ̃] **cliente** [klijɑ̃t] *mf* client; patient; customer; guest (*of a hotel*)

clientèle [klijɑ̃tɛl] *f* clientele; adherents

clignement [kliɲmɑ̃] *m* blinking

cligner [kliɲe] *tr* to squint (*one's eyes*) ‖ *intr* to squint, blink; **cligner de l'œil à** to wink at

cligno·tant [kliɲɔtɑ̃] **-tante** [tɑ̃t] *adj* blinking ‖ *m* (aut) directional signal

clignotement [kliɲɔtmɑ̃] *m* blinking; twinkling; flickering

clignoter [kliɲɔte] *intr* to blink; twinkle; flicker

clignoteur [kliɲɔtœr] *m* (aut) directional signal

climat [klima], [klima] *m* climate

climatisation [klimatizɑsjɔ̃] *f* air conditioning

climati·sé -sée [klimatize] *adj* air-conditioned

climatiseur [klimatizœr] *m* air conditioner

clin [klɛ̃] *m*—**à clin** (carpentry) overlapping, covering; **clin d'œil** wink; **en un clin d'œil** in the twinkling of an eye

clinicien [klinisjɛ̃] *adj masc* clinical ‖ *m* clinician

clinique [klinik] *adj* clinical ‖ *f* clinic; private hospital

clinquant [klɛ̃kɑ̃] *m* foil, tinsel; flashiness, tawdriness

clip [klip] *m* clip, brooch

clique [klik] *f* drum and bugle corps; (coll) gang; **cliques** wooden shoes

cliquet [klikɛ] *m* (mach) pawl, catch

cliqueter [klikte] §34 *intr* to click, clink, clank, jangle

cliquetis [klikti] *m* click, clink, clank, jangle

cliquette [klikɛt] *f* castanets; (fishing) sinker

clisse [klis] *f* draining rack, wicker bottle-holder

clitoris [klitɔris] *m* clitoris

clivage [klivaʒ] *m* cleavage

cliver [klive] *tr* to cleave; cut

cloaque [klɔak] *m* cesspool

clo·chard [klɔʃar] **-charde** [ʃard] *mf* beggar, tramp

cloche [klɔʃ] *adj* bell (*skirt*) ‖ *f* bell; bell; glass; blister (*on skin*); **cloche de plongeur** diving bell; **cloche de sauvetage** escape hatch (*on submarine*); **déménager à la cloche de bois** (coll) to skip out without paying; **la cloche** (slang) beggars

clochement [klɔʃmɑ̃] *m* limp, limping

cloche-pied [klɔʃpje]—**à cloche-pied** on one foot, hopping

clocher [klɔʃe] *m* steeple; belfry; parish, home town; **de clocher** local (*politics*) ‖ *intr* to limp; **quelque chose cloche** something jars, is not right

clocheton [klɔʃtɔ̃] *m* little steeple

clochette [klɔʃɛt] *f* little bell; (bot) bell-flower

cloison [klwazɔ̃] *f* partition; division, barrier (*e.g., between classes*); (anat, bot) septum, dividing membrane; (naut) bulkhead; **cloison étanche** (naut) watertight compartment

cloisonner [klwazɔne] *tr* to partition

cloître [klwatr] *m* cloister

cloîtrer [klwatre] *tr* to cloister; confine

clonage [klɔnaʒ] *m* cloning; **faire du clonage** to clone

clone [klɔn] *m* clone

clopin-clopant [klɔpɛ̃klɔpɑ̃] *adv* (coll) so-so; **aller clopin-clopant** (coll) to go hobbling along

clopiner [klɔpine] *intr* to hobble

cloque [klɔk] *f* blister

cloquer [klɔke] *tr & intr* to blister

clore [klɔr] §24 *tr & intr* to close

clos [klo] **close** [kloz] *adj* closed ‖ *m* enclosure; **clos de vigne** vineyard

clôture [klotyr] *f* fence; wall; cloistered life; closing of an account

clôturer [klotyre] *tr* to enclose, wall in; close out (*an account*); conclude (*a discussion*)

clou [klu] *m* nail; (coll) boil; (coll) jalopy; (coll) feature attraction; (slang) pawnshop; **clou de girofle** clove; **clous** pedestrian crossing; **des clous!** (slang) nothing at all!

clouer [klue] *tr* to nail; immobilize, rivet; **clouer le bec à qn** (coll) to shut s.o.'s mouth

clouter [klute] *tr* to stud; trim or border with studs, e.g., **passage clouté** pedestrian crossing (bordered with studs)

clown [klun] *m* clown; **faire le clown** to clown (around)

clownerie [klunri] *f* high jinks, clowning

club [klyb] *m* (literary) society; (political) association ‖ [klœb] *m* club (*for social and athletic purposes, etc.*); clubhouse; (golf) club; armchair

club-house [klybbaus] *m* clubhouse

clubiste [klybist] *mf* (coll) club member; (coll) joiner

clubman [klœbman] *m* club member

coaccu·sé -sée [kɔakyze] *mf* codefendant

coaguler [koagyle] *tr & ref* to coagulate

coaliser [koalize] *tr* to form into a coalition ‖ *ref* to form a coalition

coalition [koalisjɔ̃] *f* coalition

coassement [kɔasmɑ̃] *m* croak, croaking

coasser [kɔase] *intr* to croak

coasso·cié -ciée [kɔasɔsje] *mf* copartner

coauteur [kɔotœr] *m* coauthor

cobalt [kɔbalt] *m* cobalt

cobaye [kɔbaj] *m* guinea pig

Coca-Cola [kɔkakɔla] *m* (trademark) Coca-Cola

cocaïne [kɔkain] *f* cocaine

cocarde [kɔkard] *f* cockade; rosette of ribbons; **avoir sa cocarde** (coll) to be tipsy; **prendre la cocarde** (coll) to enlist

cocar·dier [kɔkardje] **-dière** [djɛr] *mf* jingoist, chauvinist

cocasse [kɔkas] *adj* (coll) funny, ridiculous

coccinelle [kɔksinɛl] *f* ladybug

coche [kɔʃ] *m* coach, stagecoach; two-door sedan; barge ‖ *f* notch, score; (zool) sow

cocher [kɔʃe] *m* coachman, driver ‖ *tr* to notch, score; check off

cochère [kɔʃɛr] *adj* carriage (*entrance*)

co·chon [kɔʃɔ̃] **-chonne** [ʃɔn] *mf* (coll) skunk, slob ‖ *m* pig, hog; **chochon de lait** suckling pig; **cochon de mer** porpoise; **cochon de phallocrate** (slang) male chauvinist pig; **cochon d'Inde** guinea pig

cochonnerie [kɔʃɔnri] *f* (slang) dirty trick; (slang) filthy speech, smut

cocker [kɔkɛr] *m* cocker spaniel

cockpit [kɔkpit] *m* (aer) cockpit

cocktail [kɔktɛl] *m* cocktail; cocktail party

coco [kɔko], [koko] *m* coconut; licorice water; **mon coco** (coll) my darling; **un joli coco** (coll) a stinker ‖ *f* (slang) cocaine

cocon [kɔkɔ̃] *m* cocoon

cocorico [kɔkɔriko] *m* cockcrow ‖ *interj* cock-a-doodle-doo!

cocotier [kɔkɔtje] *m* coconut tree

cocotte [kɔkɔt] *f* saucepan; cocotte, floozy; **ma cocotte** (coll) my little chick, my baby doll

co·cu -cue [kɔky] *adj & m* cuckold

cocufier [kɔkyfje] *tr* (slang) to cuckold

code [kɔd] *m* code; **code de la route** traffic regulations; **code pénal** criminal code; **codes** (slang) dimmers; **se mettre en code** to dip one's headlights

codex [kɔdɛks] *m* pharmacopoeia

codicille [kɔdisil] *m* codicil

codifier [kɔdifje] *tr* to codify; **codifiez vos adresses postales!** use the zip code!

coéducation [kɔedykasjɔ̃] *f* coeducation

coefficient [koefisjɑ̃] *m* coefficient; **coefficient de sécurité** (aer) safety factor

coéqui·pier [kɔekipje] **-pière** [pjɛr] *mf* teammate; running mate (*of a political candidate*)

coercition [kɔɛrsisjɔ̃] *f* coercion

cœur [kœr] *m* heart; core; courage, spirit; bosom, breast; depth (*of winter*); (cards) heart; (cards) hearts; **à cœur joie** to one's heart's content; **avoir du cœur** to be kind-hearted; **avoir du cœur au ventre** (coll) to have guts; **avoir le cœur sur la main** (coll) to be open-handed; **avoir le cœur sur les lèvres** to wear one's heart on one's sleeve; **cœur de bronze** heart of stone; **de bon cœur** willingly, heartily; **de mauvais cœur** reluctantly; **en avoir le cœur net** to get to the bottom of it; **épancher son cœur** à to open one's heart to; **fendre le cœur** à to break the heart of; **le cœur gros** with a heavy heart; **mal au cœur, mal de cœur** stomach ache; nausea; **par cœur** by heart; **prendre à cœur** to take to heart; **se ronger le cœur** to eat one's heart out; **soulever le cœur** to turn the stomach

coexistence [koegzistɑ̃s] *f* coexistence

coexister [koegziste] *intr* to coexist

coffre [kɔfr] *m* chest; coffer, bin; safe-deposit box; trunk (*of car*); buoy (*for mooring*); cofferdam

coffre-fort [kɔfrəfɔr] *m* (*pl* **coffres-forts**) safe, strongbox, vault

coffret [kɔfrɛ] *m* gift box

cognac [kɔɲak] *m* cognac

cognat [kɔɲa] *m* blood kin

cognée [kɔɲe] *f* ax, hatchet

cogner [kɔɲe] *tr, intr, & ref* to knock, bump

cohabiter [kɔabite] *intr* to cohabit

cohé·rent [kɔerɑ̃] **-rente** [rɑ̃t] *adj* coherent

cohéritier [kɔeritje] **-tière** [tjɛr] *mf* coheir

cohésion [kɔesjɔ̃] *f* cohesion

cohorte [kɔɔrt] *f* cohort

cohue [kɔy] *f* crowd, throng, mob

coi [kwa] **coite** [kwat] *adj* quiet; **demeurer coi, se tenir coi** to keep still

coiffe [kwaf] *f* cap; headdress; caul

coif·fé -fée [kwafe] *adj*—**coiffé de** wearing (*a hat*); (fig) crazy about (*a person*); **être coiffé** to be wearing a hairdo; **être né coiffé** (fig) to be lucky

coiffer [kwafe] *tr* to put a hat or cap on (*s.o.*); dress or do the hair of; to have overall responsibility for; (mil) to reach (*an objective*) ‖ *intr*—**coiffer de** to wear (*a certain size hat*) ‖ *ref* to do one's hair; **se coiffer de** (coll) to set one's cap for

coif·feur [kwafœr] **-feuse** [føz] *mf* hairdresser; barber; **coiffeur pour dames** coiffeur ‖ *f* dresser, dressing table

coiffure [kwafyr] *f* coiffure; headdress; **coiffure en brosse** crew cut

coin [kwɛ̃] *m* corner; angle; nook; wedge, coin; stamp, die (*for coining money*); (typ) quoin; **coin de détente, coin de retraite** den; **le petit coin** (coll) the powder room

coinçage [kwɛ̃saʒ] *m* wedging

coincer [kwɛ̃se] **§51** *tr* to wedge, jam; (coll) to pinch, arrest ‖ *ref* to jam

coïncidence [kɔɛ̃sidɑ̃s] *f* coincidence

coïncider [kɔɛ̃side] *intr* to coincide

coin-coin [kwɛ̃kwɛ̃] *m invar* quack (*of duck*); toot (*of horn*)
coing [kwɛ̃] *m* quince
coït [kɔit] *m* coition, coitus
coke [kɔk] *m* coke (*coal*)
cokéfier [kɔkefje] *tr & ref* to coke
col [kɔl] *m* neck (*of bottle; of womb*); collar (*of dress*); mountain pass; (coll) head (*on beer*); **col blanc** white-collar worker; **col de fourrure** neckpiece; **col roulé** turtleneck; **faux col** detachable collar
colback [kɔlbak] *m* busby
colère [kɔlɛr] *f* anger; **en colère** angry; **se mettre en colère** to become angry
colé·reux [kɔlerø] **-reuse** [røz] *adj* irascible, choleric
colérique [kɔlerik] *adj* choleric
colibri [kɔlibri] *m* hummingbird
colifichet [kɔlifiʃɛ] *m* knickknack, trinket
colimaçon [kɔlimasɔ̃] *m* snail; **en colimaçon** spiral
colin [kɔlɛ̃] *m* hake
colin-maillard [kɔlɛ̃majar] *m* blindman's buff
colique [kɔlik] *f* colic
colis [kɔli] *m* piece of baggage, package, parcel; **colis postal** parcel post
colisée [kɔlize] *m* coliseum
colis·tier [kɔlistje] **-tière** [tjɛr] *mf* (pol) running mate
collabora·teur [kɔlabɔratœr] **-trice** [tris] *mf* collaborator; contributor
collaborationniste [kɔlabɔrasjɔnist] *mf* collaborationist
collaborer [kɔlabɔre] *intr* to collaborate; **collaborer à** to contribute to
collage [kɔlaʒ] *m* pasting, mounting; collage; sizing; clarifying (*of wine*); (coll) common-law marriage
col·lant [kɔlɑ̃] **-lante** [lɑ̃t] *adj* sticky; tight, close-fitting ‖ *m* tights; panty hose
collapsus [kɔllapsys] *m* (pathol) collapse
collaté·ral -rale [kɔllateral] (*pl* **-raux** [ro]) *adj* collateral; parallel; intermediate (*points of the compass*) ‖ *mf* collateral (relative) ‖ *m* side aisle of a church
collation [kɔllasjɔ̃] *f* conferring (*of titles, degrees, etc.*); collation (*of texts*) ‖ [kɔlasjɔ̃] *f* snack
collationner [kɔllɑsjɔne] *tr* to collate, to compare; **faire collationner un télégramme** to request a copy of a telegram ‖ *intr* to have a snack
colle [kɔl] *f* paste, glue; (coll) brain teaser, stickler; (slang) detention; (slang) oral exam; (slang) flunking; **colle forte** glue; **poser une colle** (slang) to ask a hard one
collecte [kɔlɛkt] *f* collection (*for charitable cause*); (eccl) collect
collecteur [kɔlɛktœr] *adj* main, e.g., **égout collecteur** main sewer ‖ *m* collector; commutator (*of motor or dynamo*); (aut) manifold; **collecteur d'ondes** aerial
collec·tif [kɔlɛktif] **-tive** [tiv] *adj* collective
collection [kɔlɛksjɔ̃] *f* collection
collectionner [kɔlɛksjɔne] *tr* to collect

collection·neur [kɔlɛksjɔnœr] **-neuse** [nøz] *mf* collector
collège [kɔlɛʒ] *m* high school; preparatory school; college (*of cardinals, electors, etc.*); **collège universitaire** junior college
collé·gial -giale [kɔleʒjal] (*pl* **-giaux** [ʒjo]) *adj* collegiate ‖ *f* collegiate church
collé·gien [kɔleʒjɛ̃] **-gienne** [ʒjɛn] *adj* highschool ‖ *m* schoolboy ‖ *f* schoolgirl; coed
collègue [kɔllɛg] *mf* colleague
coller [kɔle] *tr* to paste, stick, glue; clarify (*wine*); mat (*e.g., with blood*); (coll) to floor, stump; (coll) to punish (*a pupil*); (coll) to flunk; (coll) to sock (*e.g., on the jaw*) ‖ *intr* to cling, fit tightly (*said of dress*); (coll) to stick close; **ça colle!** (slang) O.K.! ‖ *ref* (slang) to have a common-law marriage; **se coller contre** to stand close to; cling to
collet [kɔlɛ] *m* collar; neck (*of person; of tooth*); neck, scrag (*e.g., of mutton*); cape; snare; stalk and roots; lasso, noose; **collet monté** (coll) stuffed shirt
colleter [kɔlte] §34 *tr* to collar; ‖ *ref* to fight, scuffle
collier [kɔlje] *m* necklace; collar; dog collar; horse collar; **à collier** ring-necked; **reprendre le collier** (coll) to get back into harness
colliger [kɔlliʒe] §38 *tr* to make a collection of
colline [kɔlin] *f* hill
collision [kɔllizjɔ̃] *f* collision; **collision manquée** near collision, near miss
colloï·dal -dale [kɔllɔidal] *adj* (*pl* **-daux** [do]) colloid, colloidal
colloïde [kɔllɔid] *m* colloid
colloque [kɔllɔk] *m* colloquy, symposium
colloquer [kɔllɔke] *tr* to classify (*creditors' claims*); **colloquer q.ch. à qn** (coll) to palm off s.th. on s.o.
collusion [kɔllyzjɔ̃] *f* collusion
collyre [kɔllir] *m* (med) eyewash
Cologne [kɔlɔɲ] *f* Cologne
Colomb [kɔlɔ̃] *m* Columbus
colombe [kɔlɔ̃b] *f* dove
Colombie [kɔlɔ̃bi] *f* Columbia; **la Colombie** Colombia
colombier [kɔlɔ̃bje] *m* dovecote; large-size paper
colom·bin [kɔlɔ̃bɛ̃] **-bine** [bin] *adj* columbine ‖ *m* stock dove; lead ore ‖ *f* bird droppings; (bot) columbine
colon [kɔlɔ̃] *m* colonist; tenant farmer; summer camper
côlon [kolɔ̃] *m* (anat) colon
colonel [kɔlɔnɛl] *m* colonel
colonelle [kɔlɔnɛl] *f* colonel's wife; (theat) performance for the press
colonie [kɔlɔni] *f* colony; **colonie de déportation** penal settlement; **colonie de vacances** summer camp
coloniser [kɔlɔnize] *tr* to colonize
colonnade [kɔlɔnad] *f* colonnade
colonne [kɔlɔn] *f* column; pillar; **cinquième colonne** fifth column; **colonne vertébrale** spinal column

colophane [kɔlɔfan] *f* rosin
colophon [kɔlɔfɔ̃] *m* colophon
colo·rant [kɔlɔrɑ̃] **-rante** [rɑ̃t] *adj* coloring ‖ *m* dye, stain
colorer [kɔlɔre] *tr* & *ref* to color
colorier [kɔlɔrje] *tr* to paint, color
coloris [kɔlɔri] *m* hue; brilliance
colos·sal -sale [kɔlɔsal] *adj* (*pl* **-saux** [so]) colossal
colosse [kɔlɔs] *m* colossus
colporter [kɔlpɔrte] *tr* to peddle
colporteur [kɔlpɔrtœr] *m* peddler
coltiner [kɔltine] *tr* to lug on one's back or on one's head
coma [kɔma] *m* (pathol) coma
coma·teux [kɔmatø] **-teuse** [tøz] *adj* comatose ‖ *mf* person in a coma
combat [kɔ̃ba] *m* combat; **combat tournoyant** (aer) dogfight; **combat rapproché** (mil) close combat; **hors de combat** disabled
comba·tif [kɔ̃batif] **-tive** [tiv] *adj* combative
combat·tant [kɔ̃batɑ̃] **-tante** [tɑ̃t] *adj* & *mf* combatant; **anciens combattants** veterans
combattre [kɔ̃batr] §7 *tr* & *intr* to combat
combien [kɔ̃bjɛ̃] *adv* how much, how many; how far; how long; how, e.g., **combien il était brave!** how brave he was! ‖ *m invar*—**du combien chaussez-vous?** what size shoes do you wear?; **le combien coiffez-vous?** what size hat do you wear?; **le combien?** which one (*in a series*)?; **le combien êtes-vous?** (coll) what rank do you have?; **le combien sommes-nous?** (coll) what day of the month is it?; **tous les combien?** how often?
combinaison [kɔ̃binɛzɔ̃] *f* combination; jump suit; coveralls; slip, undergarment
combi·né -née [kɔ̃bine] *adj* combined ‖ *m* French telephone, handset; radio phonograph
combiner [kɔ̃bine] *tr* to combine; arrange, group; concoct (*a scheme*) ‖ *ref* (chem) to combine
comble [kɔ̃bl] *adj* full, packed ‖ *m* summit; roof, coping; **au comble de** at the height of; **c'est le comble!, c'est un comble!** (coll) that's the limit!, that takes the cake!; **sous les combles** in the attic
combler [kɔ̃ble] *tr* to heap up; fill to the brim; overwhelm; **combler d'honneurs** to shower honors upon
combustible [kɔ̃bystibl] *adj* & *m* combustible, fuel
combustion [kɔ̃bystjɔ̃] *f* combustion
comédie [kɔmedi] *f* comedy; play; sham
comé·dien [kɔmedjɛ̃] **-dienne** [djɛn] *mf* comedian; actor; hypocrite; **comédien ambulant** strolling player ‖ *f* comedienne; actress
comédon [kɔmedɔ̃] *m* blackhead
comestible [kɔmɛstibl] *adj* edible ‖ **comestibles** *mpl* foodstuffs
comète [kɔmɛt] *f* comet

comique [kɔmik] *adj* comic ‖ *m* comedian, comic; humorist, writer of comedies; comic aspect of the situation
comité [kɔmite] *m* committee
commandant [kɔmɑ̃dɑ̃] *m* commandant, commander; major
commande [kɔmɑ̃d] *f* order (*for goods or services*); control, command; **à la commande** (paid) down; **commande à distance** remote control; **commande postale** mail order; **commandes de vol** flight controls; **de commande** operating; **(fait) sur commande** (made) to order
commandement [kɔmɑ̃dmɑ̃] *m* command, order; commandment
commander [kɔmɑ̃de] §97, §98 *tr* to order (*goods or services*); command, order ‖ *intr* (mil) to command; **commander à** to control, have command over; **commander à qn de** + *inf* to order s.o. to + *inf* ‖ *ref* to control oneself
commanditaire [kɔmɑ̃ditɛr] *adj* sponsoring ‖ *mf* (com) sponsor, backer
commandite [kɔmɑ̃dit] *f* joint-stock company
commanditer [kɔmɑ̃dite] *tr* to back, to finance; (rad, telv) to sponsor
comme [kɔm] *adv* as; how; **comme ci comme ça** so-so ‖ *prep* as, like ‖ *conj* as; since
commémoratifs [kɔmemɔratif] *mpl* (phila) commemoratives
commémorer [kɔmmemɔre] *tr* to commemorate
commen·çant [kɔmɑ̃sɑ̃] **-çante** [sɑ̃t] *mf* beginner
commencement [kɔmɑ̃smɑ̃] *m* beginning
commencer [kɔmɑ̃se] §51, §96, §97 *tr* & *intr* to begin; **commencer à** to begin to
comment [kɔmɑ̃] *m invar* how; wherefore ‖ *adv* how; why; **mais comment donc!** by all means!; **n'importe comment** any way ‖ *interj* what!; indeed!
commentaire [kɔmɑ̃tɛr] *m* commentary; unfriendly comment
commenta·teur [kɔmɑ̃tatœr] **-trice** [tris] *mf* commentator
commenter [kɔmɑ̃te] *tr* to comment on; make a commentary on; criticize
commérage [kɔmeraʒ] *m* (coll) gossip
commer·çant [kɔmɛrsɑ̃] **-çante** [sɑ̃t] *adj* commercial, business ‖ *mf* merchant, dealer
commerce [kɔmɛrs] *m* commerce, trade; business, store; merchants
commercer [kɔmɛrse] §51 *intr* to trade
commer·cial -ciale [kɔmɛrsjal] *adj* (*pl* **-ciaux** [sjo] **-ciales**) commercial ‖ *f* station wagon
commercialisation [kɔmɛrsjalizɑsjɔ̃] *f* marketing
commercialiser [kɔmɛrsjalize] *tr* to commercialize
commère [kɔmɛr] *f* (coll) busybody, gossip
commettre [kɔmɛtr] §42 *tr* to commit; compromise ‖ *ref* to compromise oneself

commis [kɔmi] *m* clerk; **commis voyageur** traveling salesman

commisération [kɔmizerɑsjɔ̃] *f* commiseration

commissaire [kɔmisɛr] *m* commissioner; commissary

commissaire-priseur [kɔmisɛrprizœr] *m* (*pl* **commissaires-priseurs**) appraiser; auctioneer

commissariat [kɔmisarja] *m* commissariat; **commissariat de police** police station

commission [kɔmisjɔ̃] *f* commission; errand; committee

commissionnaire [kɔmisjɔnɛr] *m* agent, broker; messenger

commissionner [kɔmisjɔne] *tr* to commission

commissure [kɔmisyr] *f* corner (*of lips*)

commode [kɔmɔd] *adj* convenient; comfortable; easygoing ‖ *f* chest of drawers, bureau

commodité [kɔmɔdite] *f* comfort, accommodation; **à votre commodité** at your convenience; **commodités** comfort station; utilities

commotion [kɔmosjɔ̃] *f* commotion; concussion; shock

commotionner [kɔmosjɔne] *tr* to shake up, injure, shock

commuer [kɔmɥe] *tr* (law) to commute

com·mun [kɔmœ̃] **com·mune** [kɔmyn] *adj* common ‖ *m* common run ‖ *f* see **commune**

commu·nal -nale [kɔmynal] (*pl* **-naux** [no]) *adj* communal, common ‖ *mpl* common property, commons

communautaire [kɔmynotɛr] *adj* communal

communauté [kɔmynote] *f* community; joint estate (*of husband and wife*); **Communauté économique européenne** Common Market; **communauté familiale** extended family

commune [kɔmyn] *f* commune; **communes** Commons

commu·niant [kɔmynjɑ̃] **-niante** [njɑ̃t] *mf* communicant

communicable [kɔmynikabl] *adj* communicable

communi·cant [kɔmynikɑ̃] **-cante** [kɑ̃t] *adj* communicating

communica·teur [kɔmynikatœr] **-trice** [tris] *adj* connecting (*wire*) ‖ *m* broadcaster

communica·tif [kɔmynikatif] **-tive** [tiv] *adj* communicative; infectious (*laughter*)

communication [kɔmynikɑsjɔ̃] *f* communication; telephone call; (telp) connection; **communication avec avis d'appel** (telp) messenger call; **communication avec préavis** person-to-person call; **communication payable à l'arrivée, communication P.C.V.** collect call; **en communication** in touch; **fausse communication** (telp) wrong number; **vous avez la communication!** (telp) go ahead!

communier [kɔmynje] *intr* to take communion; have a common bond of sympathy, be in accord

communion [kɔmynjɔ̃] *f* communion

communiqué [kɔmynike] *m* communiqué

communiquer [kɔmynike] *tr* & *intr* to communicate

communi·sant [kɔmynizɑ̃] **-sante** [zɑ̃t] *adj* fellow-traveling ‖ *mf* fellow traveler

communisme [kɔmynism] *m* communism

communiste [kɔmynist] *adj* & *mf* communist

commutateur [kɔmytatœr] *m* (elec) change-over switch, two-way switch

commutation [kɔmytɑsjɔ̃] *f* commutation

commutatrice [kɔmytatris] *f* (elec) rotary converter

com·pact -pacte [kɔ̃pakt] *adj* compact

compagne [kɔ̃paɲ] *f* companion; helpmate

compagnie [kɔ̃paɲi] *f* company; **compagnie aérienne de transport régulier** scheduled airline; **de compagnie, en compagnie** together; **fausser compagnie à** to give (*s.o.*) the slip; **tenir compagnie à** to keep (*s.o.*) company

compagnon [kɔ̃paɲɔ̃] *m* companion; journeyman; **compagnon d'armes** comrade in arms; **compagnon de jeu** playmate; **compagnon de route** fellow traveler; **compagnon d'infortune** fellow sufferer; **joyeux compagnon** good fellow

comparaison [kɔ̃parɛzɔ̃] *f* comparison; **en comparaison de** compared to; **par comparaison** in comparison; **sans comparaison** beyond comparison

comparaître [kɔ̃parɛtr] §12 *intr* (law) to appear (in court)

compara·tif [kɔ̃paratif] **-tive** [tiv] *adj* & *m* comparative

compa·ré -rée [kɔ̃pare] *adj* comparative

comparer [kɔ̃pare] *tr* to compare

comparoir [kɔ̃parwar] (used only in; *inf*; *ger* **comparant**) *intr* (law) to appear in court

comparse [kɔ̃pars] *mf* (theat) walk-on; (fig) nobody, unimportant person

compartiment [kɔ̃partimɑ̃] *m* compartment

comparution [kɔ̃parysjɔ̃] *f* appearance in court

compas [kɔ̃pa] *m* compasses (*for drawing circles*); calipers; (naut) compass; **avoir le compas dans l'œil** to have a sharp eye

compas·sé -sée [kɔ̃pase] *adj* stiff, studied

compasser [kɔ̃pase] *tr* to measure out, lay off; **compasser ses discours** to speak like a book

compassion [kɔ̃pɑsjɔ̃] *f* compassion

compatibilité [kɔ̃patibilite] *f* compatibility

compatir [kɔ̃patir] *intr*—**compatir à** to take pity on, feel for; be indulgent toward; share in (*s.o.'s bereavement*); **ne pouvoir compatir** to be unable to agree

compatis·sant [kɔ̃patisɑ̃] **-sante** [sɑ̃t] *adj* compassionate, sympathetic, indulgent

compatriote [kɔ̃patrijɔt] *mf* compatriot

compensa·teur [kɔ̃pɑ̃satœr] **-trice** [tris] *adj* compensating, equalizing

compensation [kɔ̃pɑ̃sasjɔ̃] *f* compensation
compenser [kɔ̃pɑ̃se] *tr* to compensate; compensate for ‖ *ref* to balance each other
compérage [kɔ̃peraʒ] *m* complicity
compère [kɔ̃pɛr] *m* accomplice; comrade; stooge (*for a clown*)
compétence [kɔ̃petɑ̃s] *f* competence, proficiency; (law) jurisdiction
compé·tent [kɔ̃petɑ̃] **-tente** [tɑ̃t] *adj* competent, proficient; (law) having jurisdiction, expert
compéter [kɔ̃pete] §10 *intr*—**compéter à** to belong to by right; be within the competency of (*a court*)
compéti·teur [kɔ̃petitœr] **-trice** [tris] *mf* rival, competitor
compétition [kɔ̃petisjɔ̃] *f* competition
compila·teur [kɔ̃pilatœr] **-trice** [tris] *mf* plagiarist ‖ *m* (comp) compiler
compilation [kɔ̃mpilɑsjɔ̃] *f* compilation
compiler [kɔ̃pile] *tr* to compile
complainte [kɔ̃plɛ̃t] *f* sad ballad; (law) complaint
complaire [kɔ̃plɛr] §52 *intr* to please, gratify; **complaire à** to please, gratify, e.g., **les fils complaisent au père** the sons (try to) please the father ‖ §96 *ref* (*pp* **complu** *invar*)—**se complaire à** to take pleasure in
complaisance [kɔ̃plɛzɑ̃s] *f* compliance; courtesy; complacency; **auriez-vous la complaisance de . . . ?** would you be so kind as to . . . ?; **de complaisance** out of kindness
complai·sant [kɔ̃plɛzɑ̃] **-sante** [zɑ̃t] *adj* complaisant, obliging; complacent
complément [kɔ̃plemɑ̃] *m* complement; (gram) object; **complément d'attribution** (gram) indirect object
com·plet [kɔ̃plɛ] **-plète** [plɛt] *adj* complete, full; **c'est complet!** that's the last straw! ‖ *m* suit (*of clothes*); **au complet** full (*house*); **au grand complet** at full strength
complètement [kɔ̃plɛtmɑ̃] *adv* completely; right through from cover to cover
compléter [kɔ̃plete] §10 *tr* to complete ‖ *ref* to be completed; complement one another
complet-veston [kɔ̃plɛvɛstɔ̃] *m* (*pl* **complets-veston**) man's suit
complexe [kɔ̃plɛks] *adj & m* complex; **complexe de culpabilité** guilt complex
complexé complexée [kɔ̃plɛkse] *adj* (coll) timid, withdrawn ‖ *mf* person with complexes
complexion [kɔ̃plɛksjɔ̃] *f* constitution, disposition
complication [kɔ̃plikɑsjɔ̃] *f* complication
complice [kɔ̃plis] *adj* accessory, abetting ‖ *mf* accomplice; **complice d'adultère** corespondent
complicité [kɔ̃plisite] *f* complicity
compliment [kɔ̃plimɑ̃] *m* compliment
complimenter [kɔ̃plimɑ̃te] *tr* to compliment; congratulate
complimen·teur [kɔ̃plimɑ̃tœr] **-teuse** [tøz] *adj* complimentary ‖ *mf* flatterer, yes man
compli·qué -quée [kɔ̃plike] *adj* complicated

compliquer [kɔ̃plike] *tr* to complicate ‖ *ref* to become complicated; have complications
complot [kɔ̃plo] *m* plot, conspiracy
comploter [kɔ̃plɔte] *tr & intr* to plot, conspire
comploteur [kɔ̃plɔtœr] *m* conspirator
comportement [kɔ̃pɔrtəmɑ̃] *m* behavior
comporter [kɔ̃pɔrte] *tr* to permit; include ‖ *ref* to behave
compo·sant [kɔ̃pozɑ̃] **-sante** [zɑ̃t] *adj* constituent ‖ *m* (chem) component ‖ *f* (mech) component
compo·sé -sée [kɔ̃poze] *adj & m* compound
composer [kɔ̃poze] *tr* to compose; compound; dial (*a telephone number*) ‖ *intr* to take an exam; come to terms ‖ *ref*—**se composer de** to be composed of
composi·teur [kɔ̃pozitœr] **-trice** [tris] *mf* composer; compositor; **amiable compositeur** (law) arbitrator
composition [kɔ̃pozisjɔ̃] *f* composition; compound; dialing (*of telephone number*); term paper; **composition programmée** (printing) computer composition; **de bonne composition** easygoing, reasonable; **entrer en composition** to reach an agreement
composteur [kɔ̃pɔstœr] *m* composing stick; dating and numbering machine, dating stamp
compote [kɔ̃pɔt] *f* compote; **compote de pommes** applesauce
compotier [kɔ̃pɔtje] *m* compote (*dish*)
compréhensible [kɔ̃preɑ̃sibl] *adj* comprehensible
compréhen·sif [kɔ̃preɑ̃sif] **-sive** [siv] *adj* understanding; comprehensive
compréhension [kɔ̃preɑ̃sjɔ̃] *f* comprehension, understanding
comprendre [kɔ̃prɑ̃dr] §56 *tr* to understand; comprehend, include, comprise ‖ *intr* to understand ‖ *ref* to be understood; be included
compresse [kɔ̃prɛs] *f* (med) compress
compresseur [kɔ̃prɛsœr] *m* compressor
compression [kɔ̃prɛsjɔ̃] *f* compression; repression; reduction
compri·mé -mée [kɔ̃prime] *adj* compressed ‖ *m* (pharm) tablet, lozenge
comprimer [kɔ̃prime] *tr* to compress; repress
com·pris [kɔ̃pri] **-prise** [priz] *adj* understood; included, including, e.g., **la ferme comprise** or **y compris la ferme** the farm included, including the farm
compromet·tant [kɔ̃prɔmetɑ̃] **-tante** [tɑ̃t] *adj* compromising, incriminating
compromettre [kɔ̃prɔmetr] §42 *tr* to compromise ‖ *intr* to submit to arbitration ‖ *ref* to compromise oneself
compromis [kɔ̃prɔmi] *m* compromise
comptabiliser [kɔ̃tabilize] *tr* (com) to enter into the books
comptabilité [kɔ̃tabilite] *f* bookkeeping, accounting; accounting department, accounts; **comptabilité à partie double**

double-entry bookkeeping; **comptabilité simple** single-entry bookkeeping; **tenir la comptabilité** to keep the books
comptable [kɔ̃tabl] *adj* accountable, responsible; accounting (*machine*) ‖ *mf* bookkeeper; **comptable agréé** or **expert comptable** certified public accountant; **comptable contrôleur** auditor
comp·tant [kɔ̃tɑ̃] **-tante** [tɑ̃t] *adj* spot (*cash*); down, e.g., **argent comptant** cash down ‖ *m*—**au comptant** cash, for cash ‖ **comptant** *adv* cash (down), e.g., **payer comptant** to pay cash
compte [kɔ̃t] *m* account; accounting; (sports) count; **à bon compte** cheap; **à ce compte** in that case; **à compte** on account; **au bout du compte** or **en fin de compte** when all is said and done; **compte à rebours** countdown; **compte courant** current account; charge account; **compte de couverture** margin account; **compte de dépôt** checking account; **compte de profits et pertes** profit and loss statement; **compte en banque** bank account; **compte rendu** report, review; **compte rond** round numbers; **donner son compte à** to give the final paycheck to, to discharge; **être en compte à demi** to go fifty-fifty; **loin de compte** wide of the mark; **rendre compte de** to review; **se rendre compte de** to realize, to be aware of; **tenir compte de** to bear in mind
compte-fils [kɔ̃tfil] *m invar* cloth prover
compte-gouttes [kɔ̃tgut] *m invar* dropper; **au compte-gouttes** in driblets
compte-minutes [kɔ̃tminyt] *m invar* timer
compter [kɔ̃te] §95 *tr* to count; number, have; **compter** + *inf* to count on + *ger*; **sans compter** not to mention ‖ *intr* to count; **à compter de** starting from; **compter avec** to reckon with; **compter sur** to count on
compte-tours [kɔ̃tətur] *m invar* tachometer, r.p.m. counter
comp·teur [kɔ̃tœr] **-teuse** [tøz] *mf* counter, checker (*person*) ‖ *m* meter; counter; speedometer; **compteur de gaz** gas meter; **compteur de Geiger** Geiger counter; **compteur de stationnement** parking meter; **relever le compteur** to read the meter
compteur-indicateur [kɔ̃tœrɛ̃dikatœr] *m* (*pl* **compteurs-indicateurs**) speedometer
comptine [kɔ̃tin] *f* counting-out rhyme
comptoir [kɔ̃twar] *m* counter; branch bank; bank; **comptoir postal** mail-order house
compulser [kɔ̃pylse] *tr* to go through, examine (*books, papers, etc.*)
computer [kɔ̃pyte] *tr* to compute
comte [kɔ̃t] *m* count
comté [kɔ̃te] *m* county
comtesse [kɔ̃tɛs] *f* countess
con [kɔ̃] *m* (vulg) vagina; (vulg) stupid and contemptible person
concasser [kɔ̃kɑse] *tr* to crush, pound
concasseur [kɔ̃kɑsœr] *adj masc* crushing ‖ *m* (mach) crusher

concave [kɔ̃kav] *adj* concave
concéder [kɔ̃sede] §10 *tr & intr* to concede
concentration [kɔ̃sɑ̃trɑsjɔ̃] *f* concentration
concentrationnaire [kɔ̃sɑ̃trɑsjɔnɛr] *adj* concentration-camp, in concentration camps
concen·tré -trée [kɔ̃sɑ̃tre] *adj* concentrated; condensed (*milk*); reserved (*person*)
concentrer [kɔ̃sɑ̃tre] *tr* to concentrate; repress, hold back
concentrique [kɔ̃sɑ̃trik] *adj* concentric
concept [kɔ̃sɛpt] *m* concept
conception [kɔ̃sɛpsjɔ̃] *f* conception; **l'Immaculée Conception** (rel) the Immaculate Conception
concerner [kɔ̃sɛrne] *tr* to concern; **en ce qui concerne** concerning
concert [kɔ̃sɛr] *m* concert; **de concert** together, in concert
concer·tant [kɔ̃sɛrtɑ̃] **-tante** [tɑ̃t] *adj* performing together ‖ *mf* (mus) performer
concerter [kɔ̃sɛrte] *tr & ref* to concert, plan
concertiste [kɔ̃sɛrtist] *mf* concert performer
concession [kɔ̃sesjɔ̃] *f* concession
concessionnaire [kɔ̃sesjɔnɛr] *mf* grantee, licensee; dealer (*in automobiles*); agent (*for insurance*)
concetti [kɔ̃tʃeti] *mpl* conceits
concevable [kɔ̃səvabl] *adj* conceivable
concevoir [kɔ̃səvwar] §59 *tr* to conceive; compose (*a letter, telegram*)
concierge [kɔ̃sjɛrʒ] *mf* concierge, building superintendent
concile [kɔ̃sil] *m* (eccl) council
concilia·teur [kɔ̃siljatœr] **-trice** [tris] *adj* conciliating ‖ *mf* conciliator
conciliatoire [kɔ̃siljatwar] *adj* conciliatory
concilier [kɔ̃silje] *tr* to reconcile (*two parties, two ideas, etc.*); win (*e.g., favor*) ‖ *ref* to win, gain (*friendship, esteem*)
con·cis [kɔ̃si] **-cise** [siz] *adj* concise
concitoyen [kɔ̃sitwajɛ̃] **concitoyenne** [kɔ̃sitwajɛn] *mf* fellow citizen
concluant [kɔ̃klyɑ̃] **concluante** [kɔ̃klyɑ̃t] *adj* conclusive
conclure [kɔ̃klyr] §11 *tr* to conclude ‖ *intr* to conclude; **conclure à** to decide on, decide in favor of
conclusion [kɔ̃klyzjɔ̃] *f* conclusion
concombre [kɔ̃kɔ̃br] *m* cucumber
concomi·tant [kɔ̃kɔmitɑ̃] **-tante** [tɑ̃t] *adj* concomitant
concordance [kɔ̃kɔrdɑ̃s] *f* agreement; concordance (*of Bible*)
concor·dant [kɔ̃kɔrdɑ̃] **-dante** [dɑ̃t] *adj* in agreement; supporting (*evidence*)
concorde [kɔ̃kɔrd] *f* concord
concorder [kɔ̃kɔrde] *intr* to agree
concourir [kɔ̃kurir] §14, §96 *intr* to compete; cooperate; converge, concur
concours [kɔ̃kur] *m* crowd; cooperation; contest, competition, meet; competitive examination; **concours de beauté** beauty contest; **concours de créanciers** meeting of creditors; **concours hippique** horse show; **hors concours** not competing; in a class by itself

con·cret [kɔ̃krɛ] **-crète** [krɛt] *adj & m* concrete

concrétiser [kɔ̃kretize] *tr* to put in concrete form

con·çu -çue [kɔ̃sy] *v* see **concevoir**

concubine [kɔ̃kybin] *f* concubine

concurrence [kɔ̃kyrɑ̃s] *f* competition; competitors; **jusqu'à concurrence de** to the amount of; **libre concurrence** free enterprise

concurrencer [kɔ̃kyrɑ̃se] §51 *tr* to rival, compete with

concur·rent [kɔ̃kyrɑ̃] **-rente** [rɑ̃t] *adj* competitive ‖ *mf* competitor; contestant

concurren·tiel -tielle [kɔ̃kyrɑ̃sjɛl] *adj* competitive

concussion [kɔ̃kysjɔ̃] *f* extortion; embezzlement

condamnable [kɔ̃dɑnabl] *adj* blameworthy

condamnation [kɔ̃dɑnɑsjɔ̃] *f* condemnation; conviction, sentence

condam·né -née [kɔ̃dɑne] *mf* convict

condamner [kɔ̃dɑne] §96, §100 *tr* to condemn; give up (*an incurable patient*); forbid the use of; board up (*a window*); batten down (*the hatches*)

condensateur [kɔ̃dɑ̃satœr] *m* (elec) condenser

condenser [kɔ̃dɑ̃se] *tr & ref* to condense

condenseur [kɔ̃dɑ̃sœr] *m* condenser

condescendance [kɔ̃desɑ̃dɑ̃s] *f* condescension

condescen·dant [kɔ̃desɑ̃dɑ̃] **-dante** [dɑ̃t] *adj* condescending

condescendre [kɔ̃desɑ̃dr] §96 *intr* to condescend; to yield, comply

condiment [kɔ̃dimɑ̃] *m* condiment

condisciple [kɔ̃disipl] *mf* classmate

condition [kɔ̃disjɔ̃] *f* condition; **à condition, sous condition** conditionally; on approval; **à condition de, à condition que** on condition that; **dans de bonnes conditions** in good condition; **sans conditions** unconditional

condition·nel -nelle [kɔ̃disjɔnɛl] *adj & m* conditional

conditionnement [kɔ̃disjɔnmɑ̃] *m* packaging; conditioning

conditionner [kɔ̃disjɔne] *tr* to condition; (com) to package

condoléances [kɔ̃dɔleɑ̃s] *fpl* condolence

condom [kɔ̃dɔm] *m* condom, prophylactic

conduc·teur [kɔ̃dyktœr] **-trice** [tris] *adj* conducting; driving; (elec) power (*line*); (elec) lead (*wire*) ‖ *adj masc* (elec, phys) (in predicate after **être**, it may be translated by a noun) conductor, e.g., **les métaux sont bons conducteurs de l'électricité** metals are good conductors of electricity ‖ *mf* guide; leader; driver; **conducteur qui prend la fuite** hit-and-run driver ‖ *m* motorman; foreman; pressman; (elec, phys) conductor

conduire [kɔ̃dɥir] §19, §95, §96 *tr* to conduct; to lead; drive; see (*s.o. to the door*) ‖ *intr* to drive ‖ *ref* to conduct oneself

conduit [kɔ̃dɥi] *m* conduit; **conduit auditif** auditory canal; **conduits lacrymaux** tear ducts

conduite [kɔ̃dɥit] *f* conduct, behavior; management, command; driving (*of a car; of cattle*); pipe line; duct, flue; **avoir de la conduite** to be well behaved; **conduite d'eau** water main; **conduite intérieure** closed car; **faire la conduite à** to escort; **faire une conduite de Grenoble à qn** (coll) to kick s.o. out

cône [kon] *m* cone

confection [kɔ̃fɛksjɔ̃] *f* manufacture; construction (*e.g., of a machine*); ready-made clothes; **de confection** ready-made (*suit, dress, etc.*)

confectionner [kɔ̃fɛksjɔne] *tr* to manufacture; prepare (*a dish*)

confection·neur [kɔ̃fɛksjɔnœr] **-neuse** [nøz] *mf* manufacturer (*esp. of ready-made clothes*)

confédération [kɔ̃federɑsjɔ̃] *f* confederation, confederacy

confédérer [kɔ̃federe] §10 *tr & ref* to confederate

conférence [kɔ̃ferɑ̃s] *f* conference; lecture, speech; **conférence au sommet** summit conference; **conférence de presse** press conference

conféren·cier [kɔ̃ferɑ̃sje] **-cière** [sjɛr] *mf* lecturer, speaker

conférer [kɔ̃fere] §10 *tr* to confer, award; administer (*a sacrament*); collate, compare ‖ *intr* to confer

confesse [kɔ̃fɛs] *f*—**à confesse** to confession; **de confesse** from confession

confesser [kɔ̃fɛse] §95 *tr* to confess; (coll) to pump (*s.o.*) ‖ *ref* to confess

confesseur [kɔ̃fɛsœr] *m* confessor

confession [kɔ̃fɛsjɔ̃] *f* confession; (eccl) denomination

confessionnal [kɔ̃fɛsjɔnal] *m* confessional

confession·nel -nelle [kɔ̃fɛsjɔnɛl] *adj* denominational

confiance [kɔ̃fjɑ̃s] *f* confidence; **confiance en soi** self-confidence; **de confiance** reliable; confidently; **en confiance** with confidence

con·fiant [kɔ̃fjɑ̃] **-fiante** [fjɑ̃t] *adj* confident; confiding, trusting

confidence [kɔ̃fidɑ̃s] *f* confidence, secret

confi·dent [kɔ̃fidɑ̃] **-dente** [dɑ̃t] *mf* confident

confiden·tiel -tielle [kɔ̃fidɑ̃sjɛl] *adj* confidential

confier [kɔ̃fje] *tr* to entrust; confide, disclose; commit (*to memory*); consign; **confier à** to put (*seed*) in (*the ground*) ‖ *ref*—**se confier à** to confide in, to trust; **se confier en** to put one's trust in

confinement [kɔ̃finmɑ̃] *m* imprisonment; (nucl) containment (*in a reactor*)

confiner [kɔ̃fine] *tr* to confine ‖ *intr*—**confiner à** to border on, verge on ‖ *ref* to confine oneself; **se confiner dans** to confine oneself to

confins [kɔ̃fɛ̃] *mpl* confines

confire [kɔ̃fir] §66 (*pp* **confit**) *tr* to preserve; pickle; candy; can (*goose, chicken, etc.*); dip (*skins*) ‖ *ref* to become immersed (*in work, prayer, etc.*)

confirmer [kɔ̃firme] *tr* to confirm

confiscation [kɔ̃fiskɑsjɔ̃] *f* confiscation

confiserie [kɔ̃fizri] *f* confectionery

confi·seur [kɔ̃fizœr] **-seuse** [zøz] *mf* confectioner, candymaker

confisquer [kɔ̃fiske] *tr* to confiscate

con·fit [kɔ̃fi] **-fite** [fit] *adj* preserved; pickled; candied; steeped (*e.g., in piety*); incrusted (*in bigotry*) ‖ *m* canned chicken, goose, etc.

confiture [kɔ̃fityr] *f* preserves, jam

confitu·rier [kɔ̃fityrje] **-rière** [rjɛr] *mf* manufacturer of jams ‖ *m* jelly glass, jam jar

conflagration [kɔ̃flagrɑsjɔ̃] *f* conflagration, turmoil

conflit [kɔ̃fli] *m* conflict

confluer [kɔ̃flye] *intr* to meet, come together (*said of two rivers*)

confondre [kɔ̃fɔ̃dr] *tr* to confuse, mix up, mingle; confound ‖ *ref* to become bewildered, mixed up; **se confondre en excuses** to fall all over oneself apologizing

conforme [kɔ̃fɔrm] *adj* corresponding; certified, e.g., **pour copie conforme** certified copy; **conforme à** conformable to, consistent with; **conforme à l'échantillon** identical with sample; **conforme aux normes** according to specifications; **conforme aux règles** in order

confor·mé **-mée** [kɔ̃fɔrme] *adj* shaped, built; **bien conformé** well-built; **mal conformé** misshapen

conformément   [kɔ̃fɔrmemɑ̃] *adv*—**conformément à** in compliance with

conformer [kɔ̃fɔrme] *tr* & *ref* to conform

conformiste [kɔ̃fɔrmist] *mf* conformist

conformité [kɔ̃fɔrmite] *f* conformity, conformance

confort [kɔ̃fɔr] *m* comfort; convenience

confortable [kɔ̃fɔrtabl] *adj* comfortable ‖ *m* comfort; easy chair

confrère [kɔ̃frɛr] *m* confrere, colleague

confrérie [kɔ̃freri] *f* brotherhood

confronter [kɔ̃frɔ̃te] *tr* to confront; compare, collate

con·fus [kɔ̃fy] **-fuse** [fyz] *adj* confused; vague, blurred; embarrassed

confusion [kɔ̃fyzjɔ̃] *f* confusion; embarrassment

congé [kɔ̃ʒe] *m* leave; vacation; dismissal; **congé libérable** military discharge; **congé payé** vacation with pay; **donner congé à** to lay off; **donner son congé à** to give notice to; **prendre congé de** to take leave of

congédiement [kɔ̃ʒedimɑ̃] *m* dismissal, discharge; paying off (*of crew*)

congédier [kɔ̃ʒedje] *tr* to dismiss

congélateur [kɔ̃ʒelatœr] *m* freezer (*for frozen foods*)

congélation [kɔ̃ʒelɑsjɔ̃] *f* freezing

congeler [kɔ̃ʒəle] §2 *tr* & *ref* to freeze; congeal; **congeler à basse température** to deep-freeze

congénère [kɔ̃ʒenɛr] *adj* cognate (*words*); (biol) of the same species ‖ *mf* fellow creature; **lui et ses congénères** he and his like

congéni·tal **-tale** [kɔ̃ʒenital] *adj* (*pl* **-taux** [to]) congenital

congère [kɔ̃ʒer] *f* snowdrift

congestion [kɔ̃ʒɛstjɔ̃] *f* congestion; **congestion cérébrale** stroke; **congestion pulmonaire** pneumonia

congestionner [kɔ̃ʒɛstjɔne] *tr* & *ref* to congest

conglomération [kɔ̃glɔmerɑsjɔ̃] *f* conglomeration

conglomérer [kɔ̃glɔmere] §10 *tr* & *ref* to conglomerate

congratulation [kɔ̃gratylɑsjɔ̃] *f* congratulation

congratuler [kɔ̃gratyle] *tr* to congratulate

congre [kɔ̃gr] *m* conger eel

congrégation [kɔ̃gregɑsjɔ̃] *f* (eccl) congregation

congrès [kɔ̃grɛ] *m* congress, convention, meeting, conference

congressiste [kɔ̃grɛsist] *mf* delegate ‖ *m* congressman ‖ *f* congresswoman

con·gru **-grue** [kɔ̃gry] *adj* precise, suitable; scanty; (math) congruent

conifère [kɔnifer] *adj* coniferous ‖ *m* conifer

conique [kɔnik] *adj* conical ‖ *f* conic section

conjecture [kɔ̃ʒɛktyr] *f* conjecture

conjecturer [kɔ̃ʒɛktyre] *tr* & *intr* to conjecture, surmise

conjoindre [kɔ̃ʒwɛ̃dr] §35 *tr* to join in marriage

con·joint [kɔ̃ʒwɛ̃] **-jointe** [ʒwɛ̃t] *adj* united, joint ‖ *mf* spouse, consort

conjoncteur [kɔ̃ʒɔ̃ktœr] *m* automatic switch

conjonction [kɔ̃ʒɔ̃ksjɔ̃] *f* conjunction

conjoncture [kɔ̃ʒɔ̃ktyr] *f* juncture, situation; **de haute conjoncture** boom

conjugaison [kɔ̃ʒygɛzɔ̃] *f* conjugation

conju·gal **-gale** [kɔ̃ʒygal] *adj* (*pl* **-gaux** [go]) conjugal, connubial

conjuguer [kɔ̃ʒyge] *tr* to combine (*e.g., forces*); conjugate

conjuration [kɔ̃ʒyrɑsjɔ̃] *f* conjuration; conspiracy; **conjurations** entreaties

conju·ré **-rée** [kɔ̃ʒyre] *mf* conspirator

conjurer [kɔ̃ʒyre] §97 *tr* to conjure; conjure away; conjure up; conspire for, plot; **conjurer qn de** + *inf* to entreat s.o. to + *inf* ‖ *intr* to hatch a plot ‖ *ref* to plot together, conspire

connaissance [kɔnɛsɑ̃s] *f* knowledge; acquaintance; consciousness; attention; **connaissance des temps** nautical almanac; **connaissances** knowledge; **en connaissance de** with full knowledge of; **faire connaissance avec** to become acquainted with; **faire la connaissance de** to meet; **parler en connaissance de cause** to know what one is talking about; **perdre con-**

naissance to lose consciousness; **sans connaissance** unconscious

connaissement [kɔnɛsmã] *m* bill of lading

connais·seur [kɔnɛsœr] **-seuse** [søz] *mf* connoisseur; expert

connaître [kɔnɛtr] §12 *tr* to know; be acquainted with ‖ *intr*—**connaître de** (law) to have jurisdiction over ‖ *ref* to be acquainted (with); become acquainted; **se connaître à** or **en** to know a lot about; **s'y connaître** to know what one is talking about; **s'y connaître en** to know a lot about

connecter [kɔnɛkte] *tr* to connect

connerie [kɔnri] *f* stupidity; (vulg) bullshit; **faire une connerie** to foul up

connétable [kɔnetabl] *m* constable

connexe [kɔnɛks] *adj* connected

connexion [kɔnɛksjɔ̃] *f* connection

connexité [kɔnɛksite] *f* connection

con·nu -nue [kɔny] *adj* well-known ‖ *m*—**le connu** the known ‖ *v* see **connaître**

conque [kɔ̃k] *f* conch

conqué·rant [kɔ̃kerã] **-rante** [rãt] *adj* (coll) swaggering ‖ *mf* conqueror

conquérir [kɔ̃kerir] §3 *tr* to conquer

conquête [kɔ̃kɛt] *f* conquest

consa·cré -crée [kɔ̃sakre] *adj* accepted, time-honored, stock

consacrer [kɔ̃sakre] §96 *tr* to consecrate; devote, dedicate (*time, energy, effort*); give, spare (*e.g., time*); to sanction, confirm ‖ *ref*—**se consacrer à** to devote or dedicate oneself to

consan·guin [kɔ̃sãgɛ̃] **-guine** [gin] *adj* consanguineous; on the father's side ‖ *mf* blood relation

consciemment [kɔ̃sjamã] *adv* consciously

conscience [kɔ̃sjãs] *f* conscience; conscientiousness; consciousness; **avoir la conscience large** to be broad-minded; **en conscience** conscientiously

conscien·cieux [kɔ̃sjãsjø] **-cieuse** [sjøz] *adj* conscientious

cons·cient [kɔ̃sjã] **-ciente** [sjãt] §93 *adj* conscious, aware, knowing

conscription [kɔ̃skripsjɔ̃] *f* draft, conscription

conscrit [kɔ̃skri] *m* draftee, conscript

consécration [kɔ̃sekrasjɔ̃] *f* consecration; confirmation

consécu·tif [kɔ̃sekytif] **-tive** [tiv] *adj* consecutive; dependent (*clause*); **consécutif à** resulting from

conseil [kɔ̃sɛj] *m* advice, counsel; counselor; council, board, committee; **conseil d'administration** board of directors; **conseil de guerre** court-martial; staff meeting of top brass; **conseil de prud'hommes** arbitration board; **conseil de révision** draft board; **conseils** advice; **un conseil** a piece of advice

conseil·ler [kɔ̃seje] **-lère** [jɛr] *mf* councilor; counselor, adviser ‖ *f* councilor's wife; counselor's wife ‖ **conseiller** §97, §98 *tr* to advise, counsel (*s.o. or s.th.*); **conseiller q.ch. à qn** to recommend s.th. to

s.o. ‖ *intr* to advise, counsel; **conseiller à qn de** + *inf* to advise s.o. to + *inf*

conseil·leur [kɔ̃sɛjer] **-leuse** [jøz] *mf* adviser; know-it-all

consensus [kɔ̃sɛ̃sys] *m* consensus

consentement [kɔ̃sãtmã] *m* consent

consentir [kɔ̃sãtir] §41, §96 *tr* to grant, allow; accept, recognize; **consentir (à ce) que** + *subj* to permit (*s.o.*) to + *inf* ‖ *intr* to consent; **consentir à** to consent to, agree to, approve of

conséquemment [kɔ̃sekamã] *adv* consequently; consistently; **conséquemment à** as a result of

conséquence [kɔ̃sekãs] *f* consequence; consistency; **en conséquence** accordingly

consé·quent [kɔ̃sekã] **-quente** [kãt] *adj* consequent; consistent; important ‖ *m* (logic, math) consequent; **par conséquent** consequently

conserva·teur [kɔ̃sɛrvatœr] **-trice** [tris] *adj* conservative ‖ *mf* conservative; curator, keeper; warden, ranger; registrar

conservation [kɔ̃sɛrvasjɔ̃] *f* conservation, preservation; curatorship; curator's office

conservatisme [kɔ̃sɛrvatism] *m* conservatism

conservatoire [kɔ̃sɛrvatwar] *m* conservatory (*of music*); museum, academy

conserve [kɔ̃sɛrv] *f* canned food, preserves; escort, convoy; **conserves** dark glasses; **conserves au vinaigre** pickles; **mettre en conserve** to can; **voler de conserve avec** to fly alongside of

conserver [kɔ̃sɛrve] *tr* to conserve; preserve; keep (*one's health; one's equanimity; a secret*); escort, convoy (*a ship*) ‖ *ref* to stay in good shape; take care of oneself

conserverie [kɔ̃sɛrvəri] *f* canning factory; canning

considérable [kɔ̃siderabl] *adj* considerable; important; large, great

considérant [kɔ̃siderã] *m* motive, grounds; **considérant que** whereas

considération [kɔ̃siderasjɔ̃] *f* consideration

considé·ré -rée [kɔ̃sidere] respected

considérer [kɔ̃sidere] §10 *tr* to consider, examine; esteem, consider

consignataire [kɔ̃siɲatɛr] *m* consignee, trustee

consignation [kɔ̃siɲasjɔ̃] *f* consignment; **en consignation** on consignment

consigne [kɔ̃siɲ] *f* password; baggage room, checkroom; checking fee; confinement to barracks, detention; bottle deposit; (mil) orders, instructions; **consigne ordinaire** baggage check; **en consigne à la douane** held up in customs; **être de consigne** to be on duty; **manquer à la consigne** to disobey orders

consigner [kɔ̃siɲe] *tr* to consign; check (*baggage*); put down in writing, enter in the record; confine to barracks, keep (*a student*) in; put out of bounds (*e.g., for military personnel*); close (*a port*); **consigner sa** (or **la**) **porte** to be at home to no one

consistance [kɔ̃sistɑ̃s] *f* consistency; stability (*of character*); credit, reality, standing; **en consistance de** consisting of
consis·tant [kɔ̃sistɑ̃] **-tante** [tɑ̃t] *adj* consistent; stable (*character*); **consistant en** consisting of
consister [kɔ̃siste] §96 *intr*—**consister à** + *inf* to consist in + *ger;* **consister dans** or **en** to consist in; consist of
consistoire [kɔsistwar] *m* consistory
consola·teur [kɔ̃sɔlatœr] **-trice** [tris] *adj* consoling ‖ *mf* comforter
consolation [kɔ̃sɔlɑsjɔ̃] *f* consolation
console [kɔ̃sɔl] *f* console; console table; bracket
consoler [kɔ̃sɔle] §97, §99 *tr* to console
consolider [kɔ̃sɔlide] *tr* to consolidate; fund (*a debt*)
consomma·teur [kɔ̃sɔmatœr] **-trice** [tris] *mf* consumer; customer (*in a restaurant or bar*)
consommation [kɔ̃sɔmɑsjɔ̃] *f* consummation (*e.g., of a marriage*); perpetration (*e.g., of a crime*); consumption, use; drink (*e.g., in a café*)
consom·mé -mée [kɔ̃sɔme] *adj* consummate; skilled (*e.g., technician*); consumed, used up ‖ *m* consommé
consommer [kɔ̃sɔme] *tr* to consummate, complete; perpetrate (*e.g., a crime*); consume
consomp·tif [kɔ̃sɔ̃ptif] **-tive** [tiv] *adj* wasting away
consomption [kɔ̃sɔ̃psjɔ̃] *f* wasting away, decline
conso·nant [kɔ̃sɔnɑ̃] **-nante** [nɑ̃t] *adj* consonant, harmonious
consonne [kɔ̃sɔn] *f* consonant
consorts [kɔ̃sɔr] *mpl* partners, associates; (pej) confederates
conspira·teur [kɔ̃spiratœr] **-trice** [tris] *mf* conspirator
conspiration [kɔ̃spirɑsjɔ̃] *f* conspiracy
conspirer [kɔ̃spire] §96 *tr* & *intr* to conspire
conspuer [kɔ̃spɥe] *tr* to boo, hiss
constamment [kɔ̃stamɑ̃] *adv* constantly
constance [kɔ̃stɑ̃s] *f* constancy
cons·tant [kɔ̃stɑ̃] **-tante** [tɑ̃t] *adj* constant; true; established, evident ‖ *f* constant
constat [kɔ̃sta] *m* affidavit
constatation [kɔ̃statɑsjɔ̃] *f* authentication; declaration, claim
constater [kɔ̃state] *tr* to certify; find out; prove, establish
constellation [kɔ̃stɛllɑsjɔ̃] *f* constellation
consteller [kɔ̃stɛlle] *tr* to spangle
consterner [kɔ̃stɛrne] *tr* to dismay
constipation [kɔ̃stipɑsjɔ̃] *f* constipation
constiper [kɔ̃stipe] *tr* to constipate
consti·tuant [kɔ̃stitɥɑ̃] **-tuante** [tɥɑ̃t] *adj* & *m* constituent
constituer [kɔ̃stitɥe] *tr* to constitue; settle (*a dowry*); form (*a cabinet; a corporation*); empanel (*a jury*); appoint (*a lawyer*) ‖ *ref* to be formed; **se constituer prisonnier** to give oneself up

constitu·tif [kɔ̃stitytif] **-tive** [tiv] *adj* constituent
constitution [kɔ̃stitysjɔ̃] *f* constitution; settlement (*of a dowry*); **constitution en société** incorporation
construc·teur [kɔ̃stryktœr] **-trice** [tris] *adj* constructive, building ‖ *mf* constructor, builder
construc·tif [kɔ̃stryktif] **-tive** [tiv] *adj* constructive
construction [kɔ̃stryksjɔ̃] *f* construction; **construction mécanique** mechanical engineering
construire [kɔ̃strɥir] §19 *tr* to construct, build; draw (*e.g., a triangle*); (gram) to construe
consul [kɔ̃syl] *m* consul
consulaire [kɔ̃sylɛr] *adj* consular
consulat [kɔ̃syla] *m* consulate
consul·tant [kɔ̃syltɑ̃] **-tante** [tɑ̃t] *adj* consulting ‖ *mf* consultant
consulta·tif [kɔ̃syltatif] **-tive** [tiv] *adj* advisory
consultation [kɔ̃syltɑsjɔ̃] *f* consultation; **consultation externe** outpatient clinic; **consultation populaire** poll, referendum
consulte [kɔ̃sylt] *f* (eccl, law) consultation
consulter [kɔ̃sylte] *tr* to consult ‖ *intr* to consult, give consultations ‖ *ref* to deliberate
consumer [kɔ̃syme] *tr* to consume, use up, destroy ‖ §96 *ref* to burn out; waste away; fail
contact [kɔ̃takt] *m* contact; **mettre en contact** to put in touch, to connect; **prendre contact** to make contact
contacter [kɔ̃takte] *tr* (coll) to contact
conta·gieux [kɔ̃taʒiø] **-gieuse** [ʒjøz] *adj* contagious
contagion [kɔ̃taʒjɔ̃] *f* contagion
contamination [kɔ̃taminɑsjɔ̃] *f* contamination
contaminer [kɔ̃tamine] *tr* to contaminate
conte [kɔ̃t] *m* tale, story; **conte à dormir debout** cock-and-bull story, baloney; **conte de fées** fairy tale
contemplation [kɔ̃tɑ̃plɑsjɔ̃] *f* contemplation
contempler [kɔ̃tɑ̃ple] *tr* to contemplate
contempo·rain [kɔ̃tɑ̃pɔrɛ̃] **-raine** [rɛn] *adj* & *m* contemporary
contemp·teur [kɔ̃tɑ̃ptœr] **-trice** [tris] *mf* scoffer
contenance [kɔ̃tnɑ̃s] *f* capacity; area; countenance; **faire bonne contenance** to put up a bold front
conte·nant [kɔ̃tnɑ̃] **-nante** [nɑ̃t] *adj* containing ‖ *m* container
conteneur [kɔ̃tnœr] *m* container
conteneuriser [kɔ̃tnœrize] *tr* to containerize
contenir [kɔ̃tnir] §72 *tr* to contain; restrain ‖ *ref* to contain oneself, hold oneself back
con·tent [kɔ̃tɑ̃] **-tente** [tɑ̃t] §93 *adj* content; happy, glad, pleased; **content de** satisfied with ‖ *m* fill, e.g., **avoir son content** to have one's fill
contentement [kɔ̃tɑ̃tmɑ̃] *m* contentment

contenter [kɔ̃tɑ̃te] *tr* to content, satisfy ‖ §97, §99 *ref* to satisfy one's desires; **se contenter de** to be content or satisfied with

conten·tieux [kɔ̃tɑ̃sjø] **-tieuse** [sjøz] *adj* contentious ‖ *m* contention, litigation; claims department

contention [kɔ̃tɑ̃sjɔ̃] *f* application, intentness

conte·nu -nue [kɔ̃tny] *adj* contained, restrained, stifled ‖ *m* contents

conter [kɔ̃te] *tr* to relate, tell; **en conter à** (coll) to take (*s.o.*) in; **en conter (de belles)** (coll) to tell tall tales ‖ *intr* to narrate, tell a story

contestation [kɔ̃tɛstɑsjɔ̃] *f* argument, dispute; **sans contestation** without opposition

conteste [kɔ̃tɛst] *f*—**sans conteste** incontestably, unquestionably

contester [kɔ̃tɛste] *tr & intr* to contest

con·teur [kɔ̃tœr] **-teuse** [tøz] *mf* story teller, narrator

contexte [kɔ̃tɛkst] *m* context

contexture [kɔ̃tɛkstyr] *f* texture; structure, makeup

conti·gu -guë [kɔ̃tigy] *adj* contiguous; **contigue à** adjoining

continence [kɔ̃tinɑ̃s] *f* continence

conti·nent [kɔ̃tinɑ̃] **-nente** [nɑ̃t] *adj & m* continent

continen·tal -tale [kɔ̃tinɑ̃tal] *adj* (*pl* **-taux** [to]) continental

contingence [kɔtɛ̃ʒɑ̃s] *f* contingency

contin·gent [kɔ̃tɛ̃ʒɑ̃] **-gente** [ʒɑ̃t] *adj* contingent ‖ *m* contingent; quota

conti·nu -nue [kɔ̃tiny] *adj* continuous; nonstop; direct (*current*) ‖ *m* continuum

continuation [kɔ̃tinɥasjɔ̃] *f* continuation

conti·nuel -nuelle [kɔ̃tinɥɛl] *adj* continual

continuer [kɔ̃tinɥe] §96, §97 *tr* to continue; carry on (with), go on with ‖ *intr & ref* to go on, continue

continuité [kɔ̃tinɥite] *f* continuity

continûment [kɔ̃tinymɑ̃] *adv* continuously

conton·dant [kɔ̃tɔ̃dɑ̃] **-dante** [dɑ̃t] *adj* blunt

contorsion [kɔ̃tɔrsjɔ̃] *f* contortion

contour [kɔ̃tur] *m* contour

contourner [kɔ̃turne] *tr* to contour; go around, skirt; get around (*the law*); twist, distort

contrac·tant [kɔ̃traktɑ̃] **-tante** [tɑ̃t] *adj* contracting (*parties*) ‖ *mf* contracting party

contracter [kɔ̃trakte] *tr* to contract; float (*a loan*) ‖ *ref* to contract; be contracted

contraction [kɔ̃traksjɔ̃] *f* contraction

contractuelle [kɔ̃traktɥɛl] *f* meter maid

contradiction [kɔ̃tradiksjɔ̃] *f* contradiction

contradictoire [kɔ̃tradiktwar] *adj* contradictory

contraindre [kɔ̃trɛ̃dr] §15, §97 *tr* to compel, force, constrain; restrain, curb ‖ *ref* to restrain oneself

con·traint [kɔ̃trɛ̃] **-trainte** [trɛ̃t] §93 *adj* constrained, forced; stiff (*person*) ‖ *f* constraint; restraint; exigencies (*e.g., of the rhyme*)

contraire [kɔ̃trɛr] *adj* contrary; opposite (*e.g., direction*); injurious (*e.g., to health*) ‖ *m* contrary, opposite; antonym; **au contraire** on the contrary

contrairement [kɔ̃trɛrmɑ̃] *adv* contrary

contrarier [kɔ̃trarje] *tr* to thwart; vex, annoy; contrast (*e.g., colors*)

contrariété [kɔ̃trarjete] *f* vexation, annoyance; clashing (*e.g., of colors*)

contraste [kɔ̃trast] *m* contrast

contraster [kɔ̃traste] *tr & intr* to contrast

contrat [kɔ̃tra] *m* contract, agreement; **remplir son contrat** (bridge) to make one's contract

contravention [kɔ̃travɑ̃sjɔ̃] *f* infraction; **dresser une contravention** to write out a (traffic) ticket; **recevoir une contravention** to get a ticket

contre [kɔ̃tr] *m* opposite, con; (cards) double; **par contre** on the contrary ‖ *adv* against; nearby; **contre à contre** alongside ‖ *prep* against; contrary to; to, e.g., **dix contre un** ten to one; for, e.g., **échanger contre** to exchange for; e.g., **remède contre la toux** remedy for a cough; (sports) versus; **contre remboursement** (com) collect on delivery

contre-allée [kɔ̃trale] *f* (*pl* **-allées**) parallel walk

contre-amiral [kɔ̃tramiral] *m* (*pl* **-amiraux** [amiro]) rear admiral

contre-appel [kɔ̃trapɛl] *m* (*pl* **-appels**) second roll call; double-check

contre-attaque [kɔ̃tratak] *f* (*pl* **-attaques**) counterattack

contre-attaquer [kɔ̃tratake] *tr* to counterattack

contrebalancer [kɔ̃trəbalɑ̃se] §51 *tr* to counterbalance

contrebande [kɔ̃trəbɑ̃d] *f* contraband; smuggling; **faire la contrebande** to smuggle

contreban·dier [kɔ̃trəbɑ̃dje] **-dière** [djɛr] *adj* smuggled, contraband ‖ *mf* smuggler

contrebas [kɔ̃trəba]—**en contrebas** downwards

contrebasse [kɔ̃trəbas] *f* contrabass

contre-biais [kɔ̃trəbjɛ]—**à contre-biais** the wrong way, against the grain

contre-boutant [kɔ̃trəbutɑ̃] *m* (*pl* **-boutants**) shore

contrecarrer [kɔ̃trəkare] *tr* to stymie, thwart

contre-chant [kɔ̃trəʃɑ̃] *m* (*pl* **-chants**) counter melody

contrecœur [kɔ̃trəkœr] *m* smoke shelf; **à contrecœur** unwillingly

contrecoup [kɔ̃trəku] *m* rebound, recoil, backlash; repercussion

contre-courant [kɔ̃trəkurɑ̃] *m* (*pl* **courants**) countercurrent; **à contre-courant** upstream; behind the times

contredire [kɔ̃trədir] §40 *tr* to contradict ‖ *ref* to contradict oneself

contrée [kɔ̃tre] *f* region, countryside

contre-écrou [kɔ̃trekru] *m* (*pl* **-écrous**) lock nut

contre-espion [kɔ̃trɛspjɔ̃] *m* (*pl* **-espions**) counterspy

contre-espionnage [kɔ̃trɛspjɔnaʒ] *m* (*pl* **-espionnages**) counterespionage

contrefaçon [kɔ̃trəfasɔ̃] *f* infringement (*of patent or copyright*); forgery; counterfeit; plagiarism

contrefacteur [kɔ̃trəfaktœr] *m* forger; counterfeiter; plagiarist

contrefaction [kɔ̃trəfaksjɔ̃] *f* forgery; counterfeiting

contrefaire [kɔ̃trəfɛr] §29 *tr* to forge; counterfeit; imitate, mimic; disguise

contre·fait [kɔ̃trəfɛ] **-faite** [fɛt] *adj* counterfeit; deformed

contre-fenêtre [kɔ̃trəfnɛtr] *f* (*pl* **-fenêtres**) inner sash; storm window

contre-feu [kɔ̃trəfø] *m* (*pl* **-feux**) backfire (*in fire fighting*)

contreficher [kɔ̃trəfiʃe] *ref* (slang) to not give a rap

contre-fil [kɔ̃trəfil] *m* (*pl* **-fils**) opposite direction, wrong way; **à contre-fil** upstream; against the grain

contre-filet [kɔ̃trəfilɛ] *m* short loin (*club and porterhouse steaks*)

contrefort [kɔ̃trəfɔr] *m* buttress, abutment; foothills

contre-haut [kɔ̃trəo]—**en contre-haut** on a higher level; from top to bottom

contre-interrogatoire [kɔ̃trɛ̃tɛrɔgatwar] *m* cross-examination

contre-interroger [kɔ̃trɛ̃tɛrɔʒe] §38 *tr* to cross-examine

contre-jour [kɔ̃trəʒur] *m invar* backlighting; **à contre-jour** against the light

contremaî·tre [kɔ̃trəmɛtr] **-tresse** [trɛs] *mf* overseer ‖ *m* foreman; (naut) (hist) boatswain's mate; (nav) petty officer ‖ *f* forewoman

contremander [kɔ̃trəmɑ̃de] *tr* to countermand; call off

contremarche [kɔ̃trəmarʃ] *f* countermarch; riser (*of stair step*)

contremarque [kɔ̃trəmark] *f* countersign; pass-out check

contremarquer [kɔ̃trəmarke] *tr* to countersign

contre-mesure [kɔ̃trəmzyr] *f* (*pl* **-mesures**) countermeasure

contre-offensive [kɔ̃trɔfɑ̃siv] *f* (*pl* **-offensives**) counteroffensive

contrepartie [kɔ̃trəparti] *f* counterpart; (bk) duplicate entry; **en contrepartie** as against this

contre-pas [kɔ̃trəpɑ] *m invar* half step (*taken in order to get in step*)

contre-pente [kɔ̃trəpɑ̃t] *f* (*pl* **-pentes**) reverse slope

contre-performance [kɔ̃trəpɛrfɔrmɑ̃s] *f* (*pl* **-performances**) unexpected defeat

contrepèterie [kɔ̃trəpɛtri] *f* spoonerism

contre-pied [kɔ̃trəpje] *m* (*pl* **-pieds**) backtrack; opposite opinion; **à contre-pied** off balance

contre-plaqué [kɔ̃trəplake] *m* (*pl* **-plaqués**) plywood

contre-plaquer [kɔ̃trəplake] *tr* to laminate

contrepoids [kɔ̃trəpwa] *m invar* counterweight, counterbalance

contre-poil [kɔ̃trəpwal] *m* wrong way (*e.g.*, *of fur*); **à contre-poil** the wrong way; at the wrong end

contrepoint [kɔ̃trəpwɛ̃] *m* counterpoint

contre-pointe [kɔ̃trəpwɛ̃t] *f* (*pl* **-pointes**) false edge (*of sword*); tailstock (*of lathe*)

contre-pointer [kɔ̃trəpwɛ̃te] *tr* to quilt

contrepoison [kɔ̃trəpwazɔ̃] *m* antidote

contrer [kɔ̃tre] *tr & intr* (cards) to double; (coll) to counter

contreseing [kɔ̃trəsɛ̃] *m* countersignature

contresens [kɔ̃trəsɑ̃s] *m invar* misinterpretation; mistranslation; wrong way; **à contresens** in the wrong sense; in the wrong direction

contresigner [kɔ̃trəsiɲe] *tr* to countersign

contretemps [kɔ̃trətɑ̃] *m*—**à contre-temps** at the wrong moment; syncopated

contre-torpilleur [kɔ̃trətɔrpijœr] *m* (*pl* **-torpilleurs**) (nav) torpedo-boat destroyer

contreve·nant [kɔ̃trəvnɑ̃] **-nante** [nɑ̃t] *mf* lawbreaker, delinquent

contrevenir [kɔ̃trəvnir] §72 *intr*—**contrevenir à** to contravene, break (*a law*)

contrevent [kɔ̃trəvɑ̃] *m* shutter, window shutter

contre-voie [kɔ̃trəvwa] *f* (*pl* **-voies**) parallel route; **à contre-voie** in reverse (*of the usual direction*); on the side opposite the platform

contribuable [kɔ̃tribɥabl] *adj* taxpaying ‖ *mf* taxpayer

contribuer [kɔ̃tribɥe] §96 *intr* to contribute

contribution [kɔ̃tribysjɔ̃] *f* contribution; tax

contrister [kɔ̃triste] *tr* to sadden

con·trit [kɔ̃tri] **-trite** [trit] *adj* contrite

contrôlable [kɔ̃trolabl] *adj* verifiable

contrôle [kɔ̃trol] *m* inspection, verification, check; supervision, observation; auditing; inspection booth, ticket window; (mil) muster roll; **contrôle des naissances** birth control; **contrôle de soi** self-control; **contrôle par sondage** spot check

contrôler [kɔ̃trole] *tr* to inspect, verify, check; supervise, put under observation; audit; criticize ‖ *ref* to control oneself

contrô·leur [kɔ̃trolœr] **-leuse** [løz] *mf* inspector, checker; supervisor, observer; auditor, comptroller; conductor, ticket collector; **contrôleur de la navigation aérienne,** **contrôleur aérien** air-traffic controller ‖ *m* gauge; **contrôleur de vitesse** speedometer; **contrôleur de vol** flight indicator

controversable [kɔ̃trɔvɛrsabl] *adj* controversial

controverse [kɔ̃trɔvɛrs] *f* controversy

controverser [kɔ̃trɔvɛrse] *tr* to controvert

contumace [kɔ̃tymas] *f* contempt of court

con·tus [kɔ̃ty] **-tuse** [tyz] *adj* bruised

contusion [kɔ̃tyzjɔ̃] *f* contusion, bruise

contusionner [kɔ̃tyzjɔne] *tr* to bruise

convain·cant [kɔ̃vɛ̃kɑ̃] **-cante** [kɑ̃t] *adj* convincing

convaincre [kɔ̃vɛ̃kr] §70, §97, §99 *tr* to convince; to convict ‖ *ref* to be satisfied

convain·cu **-cue** [kɔ̃vɛ̃ky] *adj* convinced, dyed-in-the-wool; convicted

convalescence [kɔ̃valesɑ̃s] *f* convalescence

convales·cent [kɔ̃valesɑ̃] **-cente** [sɑ̃t] *adj & mf* convalescent

convenable [kɔ̃vnabl] *adj* suitable, proper; opportune (*moment*)

convenance [kɔ̃vnɑ̃s] *f* suitability, propriety; conformity; **convenances** conventions

convenir [kɔ̃vnir] §72, §97 *intr* to agree; **convenir à** to fit, suit, e.g., *ce travail lui convient* this work suits him; **convenir de** to admit, admit to, admit the truth of; agree on ‖ *ref* (*pp* **convenu** *invar*) to agree with one another ‖ *impers*—**il convient** it is fitting, it is appropriate

convention [kɔ̃vɑ̃sjɔ̃] *f* convention

convention·nel **-nelle** [kɔ̃vɑ̃sjɔnɛl] *adj* conventional

conve·nu **-nue** [kɔ̃vny] *adj* settled; stipulated (*price*); appointed (*time, place*); trite, stereotyped (*language*)

converger [kɔ̃vɛrʒe] §38 *intr* to converge

conversation [kɔ̃vɛrsɑsjɔ̃] *f* conversation

converser [kɔ̃vɛrse] *intr* to converse

conversion [kɔ̃vɛrsjɔ̃] *f* conversion; turning

conver·ti **-tie** [kɔ̃vɛrti] *adj* converted ‖ *mf* convert

convertible [kɔ̃vɛrtibl] *adj* convertible

convertir [kɔ̃vɛrtir] *tr* to convert ‖ *ref* to convert, be converted; change one's mind

convertissable [kɔ̃vɛrtisabl] *adj* convertible

convertisseur [kɔ̃vɛrtisœr] *m* converter; (elec) converter

convexe [kɔ̃vɛks] *adj* convex

conviction [kɔ̃viksjɔ̃] *f* conviction

convier [kɔ̃vje] §96 *tr* to invite

convive [kɔ̃viv] *mf* dinner guest; table companion

convocation [kɔ̃vɔkɑsjɔ̃] *f* convocation; summoning

convoi [kɔ̃vwa] *m* convoy; funeral procession

convoiter [kɔ̃vwate] *tr* to covet

convoi·teur [kɔ̃vwatœr] **-teuse** [tøz] *adj* covetous ‖ *mf* covetous person

convoitise [kɔ̃vwatiz] *f* covetousness, cupidity

covoquer [kɔ̃vɔke] *tr* to convoke; summon

convoyer [kɔ̃vwaje] §47 *tr* to convoy

convoyeur [kɔ̃vwajœr] *adj* convoying ‖ *m* (mach) conveyor; (nav) escort

convulser [kɔ̃vylse] *tr* to convulse

convulsion [kɔ̃vylsjɔ̃] *f* convulsion

convulsionner [kɔ̃vylsjɔne] *tr* to convulse

coopéra·tif [kɔɔperatif] **-tive** [tiv] cooperative ‖ *f*—**coopérative vinicole** cooperative winery

coopération [kɔɔperɑsjɔ̃] *f* cooperation

coopérer [kɔɔpere] *intr* to cooperate; **coopérer à** to cooperate in

coordination [kɔɔrdinɑsjɔ̃] *f* coordination

coordon·né **-née** [kɔɔrdɔne] *adj & f* coordinate; **coordonnées** address and telephone number

coordonner [kɔɔrdɔne] *tr* to coordinate

co·pain [kɔpɛ̃] **-pine** [pin] *mf* (coll) pal, chum

co·peau [kɔpo] *m* (*pl* **-peaux**) chip, shaving

copie [kɔpi] *f* copy; exercise, composition (*at school*); **copie au net** fair copy; **pour copie conforme** true copy

copier [kɔpje] *tr & intr* to copy

co·pieux [kɔpjø] **-pieuse** [pjøz] *adj* copious

copilote [kɔpilɔt] *m* copilot

copinisme [kɔpinism] *m* cronyism

copiste [kɔpist] *mf* copyist; copier

coposséder [kɔpɔsede] §10 *tr* to own jointly

copropriété [kɔprɔprijete] *f* joint ownership

copula·tif [kɔpylatif] **-tive** [tiv] *adj* (gram) coordinating

copulation [kɔpylɑsjɔ̃] *f* copulation

copule [kɔpyl] *f* (gram) copula

coq [kɔk] *adj* bantam ‖ *m* cock, rooster; (naut) cook

coq-à-l'âne [kɔkalɑn] *m invar* cock-and-bull story

coquart [kɔkar] *m* black eye, shiner

coque [kɔk] *f* shell; cocoon; hull; **à la coque** soft-boiled; **coque de noix** coconut

coquelicot [kɔkliko] *m* poppy

coqueluche [kɔklyʃ] *f* whooping cough; (coll) rage, vogue

coquemar [kɔkmar] *m* teakettle

coquerie [kɔkri] *f* (naut) galley

coqueriquer [kɔkrike] *intr* to crow

co·quet [kɔkɛ] **-quette** [ket] *adj* coquettish; stylish; considerable (*sum*)

coqueter [kɔkte] §34 *intr* to flirt

coquetier [kɔkɛtje] *m* eggcup; egg man

coquetterie [kɔkɛtri] *f* coquetry

coquillage [kɔkijaʒ] *m* shellfish; shell

coquille [kɔkij] *f* shell; typographical error (*of transposed letters*); pat (*of butter*); **coquille de noix** nutshell; **coquille Saint-Jacques** scallop

co·quin [kɔkɛ̃] **-quine** [kin] *adj* deceitful; roguish ‖ *mf* scoundrel; rogue

cor [kɔr] *m* horn; corn (*on foot*); prong (*of antler*); horn player; **à cor et à cri** with hue and cry; **cor anglais** English horn; **cor de chasse** hunting horn; **cor d'harmonie** French horn

co·rail [kɔraj] *m* (*pl* **-raux** [ro]) coral

cor·beau [kɔrbo] *m* (*pl* **-beaux**) crow, raven

corbeille [kɔrbɛj] *f* basket; flower bed; (theat) dress circle; **corbeille à papier** wastebasket; **corbeille de marriage** wedding present

corbillard [kɔrbijar] *m* hearse

corbillon [kɔrbijɔ̃] *m* small basket; word game

cordage [kɔrdaʒ] *m* cordage, rope; (naut) rigging

corde [kɔrd] *f* rope, cord; tightrope; thread (*of a carpet or cloth*); inside track; (geom) chord; (mus) string; **corde à** or **de boyau** catgut (*for, e.g., violin*); **corde à linge** wash line; **corde à nœuds** knotted rope;

corde à piano piano wire; **cordes vocales** vocal cords; **en double corde** on two strings; **être sur la corde raide** to be out on a limb; **les cordes** (mus) the strings; **toucher la corde sensible** to touch a sympathetic cord; **usé jusqu'à la corde** threadbare

cor·dé -dée [kɔrde] adj heart-shaped ǁ f cord (of wood); roped party (of mountain climbers)

cor·deau [kɔrdo] m (pl -deaux) tracing line; tracing thread; mine fuse; **tiré au cordeau** in a straight line

cordelier [kɔrdəlje] m Franciscan friar

corder [kɔrde] tr to twist; string (a tennis racket)

cor·dial -diale [kɔrdjal] adj & m (pl -diaux [djo]) cordial

cordialité [kɔrdjalite] f cordiality

cordier [kɔrdje] m ropemaker; tailpiece (of violin)

cordon [kɔrdɔ̃] m cordon; cord; latchstring; **cordon de sonnette** bellpull; **cordon de soulier** shoestring

cordon-bleu [kɔrdɔ̃blø] m (pl **cordons-bleus**) cordon bleu

cordonnerie [kɔ̃rdɔnri] f shoemaking; shoe repairing; shoe store; shoemaker's

cordon·nier [kɔrdɔnje] **-nière** [njɛr] mf shoemaker

Corée [kɔre] f Korea; **la Corée** Korea

coréen [kɔreɛ̃] **coréenne** [kɔreɛn] adj Korean ǁ m Korean (language) ǁ (cap) mf Korean (person)

coriace [kɔrjas] adj tough, leathery; (coll) stubborn

coricide [kɔrisid] m corn remover

cormoran [kɔrmɔrɑ̃] m cormorant

cornac [kɔrnak] m mahout

cor·nard [kɔrnar] **-narde** [nard] adj horned; (slang) cuckold; wheezing (of horse) ǁ m (slang) cuckold

corne [kɔrn] f horn; dog-ear (of page); hoof; shoehorn; **corne d'abondance** horn of plenty; **faire les cornes à** (coll) to make a face at

cor·né -née [kɔrne] adj horny ǁ f cornea

corneille [kɔrnɛj] f crow, rook; **corneille d'église** jackdaw

cornemuse [kɔrnəmyz] f bagpipe

cornemuseur [kɔrnəmyzœr] m bagpiper

corner [kɔrne] tr to dog-ear; give (s.o.) the horn; (coll) to trumpet (news) about ǁ intr to blow the horn, honk; ring (said of ears); (mus) to blow a horn; **cornez!** sound your horn!

cornet [kɔrnɛ] m cornet; horn; dice-box; cornetist; mouthpiece (of microphone); receiver (of telephone); **cornet acoustique** ear trumpet; **cornet à pistons** cornet; **cornet de glace** ice-cream cone

cornette [kɔrnɛt] m (mil) cornet ǁ f (headdress) cornet

cornettiste [kɔrnɛtist] mf cornetist

corniche [kɔrniʃ] f cornice

cornichon [kɔrniʃɔ̃] m pickle, gherkin; (fool) (coll) dope, drip

cor·nier [kɔrnje] **-nière** [njɛr] adj corner ǁ f valley (joining roofs); angle iron

corniste [kɔrnist] mf horn player

Cornouailles [kɔrnwaj] f Cornwall

cornouiller [kɔrnuje] m dogwood

cor·nu -nue [kɔrny] adj horned; preposterous (ideas) ǁ f (chem) retort

corollaire [kɔrɔllɛr] m corollary

coronaire [kɔrɔnɛr] adj coronary

coroner [kɔrɔnœr] m coroner

corporation [kɔrpɔrasjɔ̃] f association, guild

corpo·rel -relle [kɔrpɔrɛl] adj corporal, bodily

corps [kɔr] m body; corps; **à corps perdu** without thinking; **à mon (ton,** etc.**) corps défendant** in self-defense; reluctantly; **corps à corps** hand-to-hand; in a clinch; **corps céleste** heavenly body; **corps composé** (chem) compound; **corps de garde** guardhouse, guardroom; **corps de logis** main part of the building; **corps du délit** corpus delicti; **corps enseignant** faculty; **corps noir** (phys) black body; **corps simple** (chem) simple substance; **prendre corps** to take shape; **saisir au corps** (law) to arrest

corps-à-corps [kɔrakɔr] m hand-to-hand combat; (boxing) infighting

corpulence [kɔrpylɑ̃s] f corpulence

corpuscule [kɔrpyskyl] m (phys) corpuscle

corral [kɔral] m corral

cor·rect -recte [kɔrrɛkt] adj correct

correc·teur [kɔrrɛktœr] **-trice** [tris] mf corrector; proofreader

correc·tif [kɔrrɛktif] **-tive** [tiv] adj & m corrective

correction [kɔrrɛksjɔ̃] f correction; correctness; proofreading; punishment; **correction en course** (aer) mid-course correction

corrélation [kɔrrelasjɔ̃] f correlation

correspondance [kɔrɛspɔ̃dɑ̃s] f correspondence; transfer, connection

correspon·dant [kɔrɛspɔ̃dɑ̃] **-dante** [dɑ̃t] adj corresponding, correspondent ǁ mf correspondent; party (person who gets a telephone call)

correspondre [kɔrɛspɔ̃dr] intr to correspond; **correspondre à** to correspond to, correlate with; **correspondre avec** to correspond with (a letter writer); connect with (e.g., a train)

corridor [kɔridɔr] m corridor

corrigé [kɔriʒe] m fair copy

corriger [kɔriʒe] §38 tr to correct; proofread ǁ ref to reform

corroborer [kɔrrɔbɔre] tr to corroborate

corroder [kɔrrɔde] tr & ref to corrode; erode

corrompre [kɔrɔ̃pr] (3d sg pres ind **corrompt**) tr to corrupt; rot; bribe; seduce; spoil

corro·sif [kɔrrɔzif] **-sive** [ziv] adj & m corrosive

corrosion [kɔrrosjɔ̃] f corrosion; erosion

corroyer [kɔrwaje] §47 *tr* to weld; to plane (*wood*); to prepare (*leather*)

corruption [kɔrrypsjɔ̃] *f* corruption; bribery; seduction

corsage [kɔrsaʒ] *m* blouse; bodice, corsage, waist; (archaic) bust

corsaire [kɔrsɛr] *m* corsair; pedal pusher; **corsaire de finance** ruthless businessman, robber baron

corse [kɔrs] *adj* Corsican ‖ *m* Corsican (*language*) ‖ (*cap*) *f* Corsica; **la Corse** Corsica ‖ (*cap*) *mf* Corsican (*person*)

cor·sé -sée [kɔrse] *adj* full-bodied, heavy; spicy, racy

corser [kɔrse] *tr* to spike, give body to (*wine*); spice up (*a story*) ‖ *ref* to become serious; **ça se corse** the plot thickens

corset [kɔrsɛ] *m* corset

cortège [kɔrtɛʒ] *m* cortege; parade; **cortège funèbre** funeral procession

cortisone [kɔrtizɔn] *f* cortisone

corvée [kɔrve] *f* chore; forced labor; work party

coryphée [kɔrife] *m* coryphée; (fig) leader

cosaque [kɔzak] *adj* Cossack ‖ (*cap*) *mf* Cossack

cosmétique [kɔsmetik] *adj* cosmetic ‖ *m* cosmetic; hair set, hair spray ‖ *f* beauty culture

cosmique [kɔsmik] *adj* cosmic

cosmonaute [kɔsmɔnot] *mf* cosmonaut

cosmopolite [kɔsmɔpɔlit] *adj & mf* cosmopolitan

cosmos [kɔsmos], [kɔsmɔs] *m* cosmos; outer space

cosse [kɔs] *f* pod; **avoir la cosse** (slang) to be lazy

cos·su -sue [kɔsy] *adj* rich; well-to-do

cos·taud [kɔsto] **-taude** [tod] *adj* (slang) husky, strapping ‖ *m* (slang) muscleman

costume [kɔstym] *m* costume; suit; **costume sur mesure** custom-made or tailor-made suit; **costume tailleur** lady's tailor-made suit

costumer [kɔstyme] *tr & ref* to dress up (*for a fancy-dress ball*); **se costumer en** to come dressed as a

costu·mier [kɔstymje] **-mière** [mjɛr] *mf* costumer

cote [kɔt] *f* assessment, quota; identification mark, letter, or number; call number (*of book*); altitude (*above sea level*); bench mark; book value (*of, e.g., used cars*); racing odds; public-opinion poll; (telv) rating; **avoir la cote** (coll) to be highly thought of; **cote d'alerte** danger point; **cote d'amour** moral qualifications; **cote de la Bourse** stock-market quotations; **cote mal taillée** rough compromise

côte [kot] *f* rib; chop; coast; slope; **à côtes** ribbed, corded; **aller** or **se mettre à la côte, faire côte** to run aground; **avoir les côtes en long** (coll) to feel lazy; **côte à côte** side by side; **côte d'Azur** French Riviera; **côtes découvertes, plates côtes** spareribs; **en côte** uphill; **être à la côte** to be broke; **faire côte** to run aground

co·té -tée [kote] *adj* listed (*on the stock market*); (fig) esteemed

côté [kote] *m* side; **à côté** in the next room; near; **à côté!** a miss!; **à côté de** beside; **à côtés** fringe benefits; **côté cour** (theat) stage right; **côté jardin** (theat) stage left; **d'à côté** next-door; **de côté** sideways; sidelong; aside; **de mon côté** for my part; **donner, passer,** or **toucher à côté** to miss the mark; **du côté de** in the direction of, toward; on the side of; **d'un côté . . . de l'autre côté** or **d'un autre côté** on the one hand . . . on the other hand; **répondre à côté** to miss the point

co·teau [koto] *m* (*pl* **-teaux**) *f* knoll; slope

Côte-de-l'Or [kotdəlɔr] *f* Gold Coast

côte·lé -lée [kotle] *adj* ribbed, corded

côtelette [kotlɛt] *f* cutlet, chop; **côtelettes découvertes** spareribs

coter [kote] *tr* to assess; mark; number; esteem; (com) to quote, give a quotation on; (geog) to mark the elevations on

coterie [kotri] *f* coterie, clique

cothurne [kotyrn] *m* buskin

cô·tier [kotje] **-tière** [tjɛr] *adj* coastal

cotir [kotir] *tr* to bruise (*fruit*)

cotisation [kotizasjɔ̃] *f* dues; assessment

cotiser [kotize] *tr* to assess (*each member of a group*) ‖ *intr* to pay one's dues ‖ *ref* to club together

coton [kɔtɔ̃] *m* cotton; **c'est coton** (slang) it's difficult; **coton de verre** glass wool; **coton hydrophile** absorbent cotton; cotton batting; **élever dans le coton** to coddle; **filer un mauvais coton** (coll) to be in a bad way

cotonnade [kɔtɔnad] *f* cotton cloth

cotonner [kɔtɔne] *tr* to pad or stuff with cotton ‖ *ref* to become fluffy; become spongy or mealy

cotonnerie [kɔtɔnri] *f* cotton field; cotton mill

coton·neux [kɔtɔnø] **-neuse** [nøz] *adj* cottony; spongy, mealy

coton·nier [kɔtɔnje] **-nière** [njɛr] *adj* cotton ‖ *mf* cotton picker ‖ *m* cotton plant

côtoyer [kotwaje] §47 *tr* to skirt (*the edge*); hug (*the shore*); border on (*the truth, the ridiculous, etc.*)

cotre [kotr] *m* (naut) cutter

cotte [kɔt] *f* petticoat; peasant skirt; overalls; **cotte de mailles** coat of mail

cou [ku] *m* neck; **sauter au cou de** to throw one's arms around

couard [kwar] **couarde** [kward] *adj mf* coward

couardise [kwardiz] *f* cowardice

couchage [kuʃaʒ] *m* bedding; bed for the night

cou·chant [kuʃɑ̃] **-chante** [ʃɑ̃t] *adj* setting ‖ *m* west; decline, old age

couche [kuʃ] *f* layer, stratum; coat (*of paint*); diaper; (hort) hotbed; **couche de fond** primer, prime coat; **couches** strata; childbirth, e.g., **une femme en couches** a woman in childbirth; **fausse couche** miscarriage

coucher [kuʃe] *m* setting (*of sun*); going to bed; **coucher du soleil** sunset; **le coucher et la nourriture** room and board ‖ *tr* to put to bed; put down, lay down; bend down, flatten; mention (*in one's will*); **coucher en joue** to aim at; **coucher par écrit** to set down in writing ‖ *intr* to spend the night; **coucher avec** to sleep with (*have sex with*); (*naut*) to heel over ‖ *ref* to go to bed, lie down; set (*said of sun*); bend; **allez vous coucher!** (coll) go to blazes! **une Marie-couche-toi-là** a promiscuous woman

couchette [kuʃɛt] *f* berth; crib

couci-couça [kusikusa] or **couci-couci** [kusikusi] *adv* so-so

coucou [kuku] *m* cuckoo; cuckoo clock; (coll) marsh marigold

coude [kud] *m* elbow; angle, bend, turn; **coude à coude** shoulder to shoulder; **jouer dés coudes à travers** to elbow one's way through (*a crowd*)

coudée [kude] *f* cubit; **avoir ses coudées franches** to have a free hand; to have elbowroom

cou-de-pied [kudpje] *m* (*pl* **cous-de-pied**) instep

couder [kude] *tr* to bend like an elbow

coudoiement [kudwamã] *m* elbowing

coudoyer [kudwaje] §47 *tr* to elbow, to jostle; to rub shoulders with

coudraie [kudrɛ] *f* hazel grove

coudre [kudr] §13 *tr* & *intr* to sew

coudrier [kudrije] *m* hazel tree

couenne [kwan] *f* pigskin; rind, crackling; mole, birthmark

couette [kwɛt] *f* feather bed; (little) tail; (mach) bearing; **couette de lapin** scut; **couettes** (naut) ship

cougouar or **couguar** [kugwar] *m* cougar

couiner [kwine] *intr* to send Morse code; (coll) to squeak (*said of animal*)

coulage [kulaʒ] *m* flow; leakage; casting (*of metal*); pouring (*of concrete*); (naut) scuttling; (coll) wasting

cou·lant [kulã] **-lante** [lãt] *adj* flowing, running; permissive; accommodating (*person*) ‖ *m* sliding ring; (bot) runner

coule [kul] *f* cowl; **être à la coule** (slang) to know the ropes

cou·lé -lée [kule] *adj* cast; sunken; (coll) sunk ‖ *m* (mus) slur ‖ *f* casting; run (*of wild beasts*); **coulée volcanique** outflow of lava

couler [kule] *tr* to pour; cast (*e.g., a statue*); scuttle; pass (*e.g., many happy hours*); (mus) to slur ‖ *intr* to flow; run; leak; sink; slip (away) ‖ *ref* to slip, slide; (coll) to be done for, be sunk; **se la couler douce** (coll) to take it easy

couleur [kulœr] *f* color; policy (*of newspaper*); (cards) suit; **de couleur** colored; **les trois couleurs** the tricolor; **sous couleur de** with the pretext of, with a show of

couleuvre [kulœvr] *f* snake; **avaler des couleuvres** (coll) to swallow insults; (coll) to

be gullible; **couleuvre à collier** grass snake

coulis [kuli] *m*—**coulis de tomates** tomato sauce

coulisse [kulis] *f* groove; slide (*of trombone*); (com) curb exchange; (pol) lobby; **à coulisse** sliding; **coulisses** (theat) wings; (theat) backstage; **dans les coulisses** behind the scenes, out of sight; **travailler dans les coulisses** to pull strings

coulis·seau [kuliso] *m* (*pl* **-seaux**) slide, runner

couloir [kulwar] *m* corridor; hallway; lobby; **couloir de la mort** death row

couloire [kulwar] *f* strainer

coup [ku] *m* blow; stroke; blast (*of whistle*); jolt; move (*in a chess game*); **à coup de** with the aid of; **à coup sûr** certainly; **après coup** when it is too late; **à tout coup** each time; **boire à petits coups** to sip; **coup de bélier** water hammer (*in pipe*); **coup de chance** lucky hit; **coup de coude** nudge; **coup de dés** throw of the dice; risky business; **coup de fer** pressing, ironing; **coup de feu, coup de fusil** shot, gunshot; **coup de fion** (slang) finishing touch; **coup de foudre** thunderbolt; love at first sight; bolt from the blue; **coup de fouet** whiplash; stimulus; **coup de froid** cold snap; **coup de grâce** last straw; deathblow; **coup de Jarnac** [ʒarnak] stab in the back; **coup de patte** expert stroke (*e.g., of the brush*); (coll) dig, insult; **coup de pied** kick; **coup d'épingle** pinprick; **coup de poing** punch; **coup de pouce** final touch; help, little push; **coup de sang** (pathol) stroke; **coup de semonce** warning shot; **coup de sifflet** whistle, toot; **coup de soleil** sunburn; (coll) sunstroke; **coup de téléphone** telephone call; **coup de tête** butt; sudden impulse; **coup de théâtre** dramatic turn of events; **coup de tonnerre** thunderclap; **coup d'œil** glance, look; **coup manqué, coup raté** miss; **coup monté** put-up job, frame-up; **coups et blessures** assault and battery; **coup sur coup** one right after the other; **donner un coup de main (à)** to lend a helping hand (to); **encore un coup** once again; **en venir aux coups** to come to blows; **être dans le coup** (coll) to be in on it; **faire coup double** to kill two birds with one stone; **faire les quatre coups** (coll) to live it up, to dissipate; **faire un coup de main** to go on a raid; **manquer son coup** to miss one's chance; **se faire donner un coup de piston** (coll) to pull wires, to use influence; **sous le coup de** under the (immediate) influence of; **sur le coup** on the spot, outright; **tout à coup** suddenly; **tout d'un coup** at one shot, at once

coupable [kupabl] §93 *adj* guilty ‖ *mf* culprit

cou·pant [kupã] **-pante** [pãt] *adj* cutting, sharp ‖ *m* (cutting) edge

coup-de-poing [kudpwɛ̃] *m* (*pl* **coups-de-poing**) brass knuckles

coupe [kup] *f* champagne glass; loving cup, trophy; cup competition; cutting; cross section; wood acreage to be cut; cut (*of cloth; of clothes; of playing cards*); division (*of verse*); **coupe claire** cutover forest; **coupe de cheveux** haircut; **coupe sombre** harvested forest; **être sous la coupe de qn** (coll) to be under s.o.'s thumb; **il y a loin de la coupe aux lèvres** there is many a slip between the cup and the lip; **mettre en coupe réglée** (coll) to fleece

cou·pé -pée [kupe] *adj* cut, cut off; interrupted (*sleep*); diluted (*wine*) ‖ *m* coupé ‖ *f* gangway

coupe-circuit [kupsirkɥi] *m invar* (elec) fuse

coupe-coupe [kupkup] *m invar* machete

coupe-feu [kupfø] *m invar* firebreak

coupe-fil [kupfil] *m invar* wire cutter

coupe-file [kupfil] *m invar* police pass (*for emergency vehicles*)

coupe-gorge [kupgɔrʒ] *m invar* death trap, dangerous territory

coupe-jarret [kupʒarɛ] *m* (*pl* **-jarrets**) cutthroat

coupe-ongles [kupɔ̃gl] *m invar* nail clippers

coupe-papier [kuppapje] *m invar* paper knife, letter opener

couper [kupe] *tr* to cut; cut off; cut out; break off, interrupt; cut, water down; turn off; trump; castrate, geld; **ça te la coupe!** (coll) top that!; **couper en fin de ligne** to divide (*a word*) at the end of a line; **couper la file** (aut) to leave one's lane; **couper la parole à** to interrupt; **couper menu** to mince ‖ *intr* to cut; **couper court à** to cut (*s.o. or s.th.*) short ‖ *ref* to cut oneself; intersect; (coll) to contradict oneself; (coll) to give oneself away

couperet [kuprɛ] *m* cleaver; guillotine blade

couperose [kuproz] *f* (pathol) acne

cou·peur [kupœr] **-peuse** [pøz] *mf* cutter; **coupeur de bourses** (coll) purse snatcher; **coupeur d'oreilles** (coll) hatchet man, hired thug

couplage [kuplaʒ] *m* (mach) coupling

couple [kupl] *m* couple (*e.g., of friends, cronies, thieves, etc.; man and wife*); pair (*e.g., of pigeons*); (mech) couple, torque; **couple thermo-électrique** thermoelectric couple; **maître couple** (naut) midship frame ‖ *f* yoke (*of oxen*); couple; leash

coupler [kuple] *tr* to couple; pair

coupleur [kuplœr] *m* (mach) coupler

coupole [kupɔl] *f* cupola

coupon [kupɔ̃] *m* coupon; remnant (*of cloth*); theater ticket; **coupon date libre** open ticket

coupon—réponse [kupɔ̃repɔ̃s] *m*—**coupon-réponse international** international (postal) reply coupon; **coupon-réponse postal** return-reply post card or letter

coupure [kupyr] *f* cut, incision, slit; cut, deletion; newspaper clipping; small note;

interruption, break; drain (*e.g., through a marsh*); denomination

cour [kur] *f* court; courtyard; courtship; **bien en cour** in favor; **cour anglaise** courtyard or court (*of apartment building*); **cour d'appel** appellate court; **cour d'assises** criminal court; **cour de cassation** supreme court of appeals; **cour d'école** school playground; **faire la cour à** to court; **mal en cour** out of favor

courage [kuraʒ] *m* courage; **reprendre courage** to take heart; **travailler avec courage** to work hard ‖ *interj* buck up!, cheer up!

coura·geux [kuraʒø] **-geuse** [ʒøz] *adj* courageous; hard-working

courailler [kuraje] *intr* to gallivant

couramment [kuramɑ̃] *adv* currently; fluently, easily

cou·rant [kurɑ̃] **-rante** [rɑ̃t] *adj* current; running (*water*); present-day (*language, customs, etc.*) ‖ *m* current; flow; shift (*of opinion, population, etc.*); **courant alternatif** alternating current; **courant continu** direct current; **courant d'air** draft; **Courant du Golfe** Gulf Stream; **dans le courant du mois (de la semaine, etc.)** in the course of the month (of the week, etc.); **être au courant de** to be informed about

courant-jet [kurɑ̃ʒɛ] *m* (meteo) jet stream

courba·tu -tue [kurbaty] *adj* stiff in the joints, aching all over

courbature [kurbatyr] *f* stiffness, aching

courbaturer [kɔrbatyre] *tr* to make stiff; exhaust (*the body*)

courbe [kurb] *adj* curved ‖ *f* curve; **courbe de niveau** contour line

cour·bé -bée [kurbe] *adj* curved, bent, crooked

courber [kurbe] *tr* to bend, curve ‖ *intr & ref* to bend, curve; give in

courbure [kurbyr] *f* curve, curvature; **double courbure** S-curve

courette [kurɛt] *f* small courtyard

cou·reur [kurœr] **-reuse** [røz] *mf* runner; **coureur cycliste** bicycle racer; **coureur de cotillons** (coll) wolf; **coureur de dot** fortune hunter; **coureur de filles** Casanova, Don Juan; **coureur de girls** stage-door Johnny; **coureur de spectacles** playgoer; **coureur de vitesse** sprinter

courge [kurʒ] *f* gourd, squash

courir [kurir] §14, §95 *tr* to run; run after; roam; frequent ‖ *intr* to run; **le bruit court que** rumor has it that; **par le temps qui court** at the present time

courlis [kurli] *m* curlew

couronne [kurɔn] *f* crown; wreath; coronet; rim (*of atomic structures*)

couronnement [kurɔnmɑ̃] *m* crowning; coronation; coping

couronner [kurɔne] *tr* to crown; top, cap; reward ‖ *ref* to be crowned; be covered (*with flowers*)

courrier [kurje] *m* courier; mail; **courrier du cœur** advice to the lovelorn; **courrier**

mondain gossip column; **courrier théâtral** theater section
courriériste [kurjerist] *mf* columnist
courroie [kurwɑ] *f* strap; belt
courroucer [kuruse] §51 *tr* (lit) to anger
courroux [kuru] *m* (lit) wrath, anger
cours [kur] *m* course; current (*of river*); tree-lined walk; rate (*of exchange*); market quotation; style, vogue; **au cours de** in the course of; **avoir cours** to be in circulation; to be legal tender; to have classes; **cours d'eau** stream, river; **cours d'été** or **cours de vacances** summer school; **cours du soir** night school; **de cours** in length (*said of a river*); **de long cours** long-range; **suivre un cours** to take a course (*in school*) ‖ *v* see **courir**
course [kurs] *f* running; race; errand; trip; ride (*e.g., in a taxi*); course, path; privateering; stroke (*of a piston*); **course à pied** foot race; **course attelée** harness race; **course au trot** trotting race; **course aux armaments** arms race; **course de chevaux** horse race; **course de côte** hill climb; **course de taureaux** bullfight; **course de vitesse** sprint; **course d'obstacles** steeplechase; **courses sur route** road racing; **de course** at a run; racing (*car; track; crowd*); (mil) on the double; **en pleine course** in full swing; **faire des courses** to go shopping
cour·sier [kursje] **-sière** [sjɛr] *mf* messenger ‖ *m* errand boy; steed
coursive [kursiv] *f* (naut) alleyway, gangway (*connecting staterooms*)
court [kur] **courte** [kurt] *adj* short; brief; concise; choppy (*sea*); thick (*sauce, gravy*); close (*victory*); **à court** short; **de court** by surprise; **prendre le plus court** to take a shortcut; **tenir de court** to hold on a short leash ‖ (when standing before noun) *adj* short, brief (*interval, time, life*) ‖ *m* court (*for tennis*) ‖ **court** *adv* short; **demeurer court** to forget what one wanted to say; **tourner court** to turn sharp; to stop short, to change the subject; **tout court** simply, merely; plain ‖ **court** *v* see **courir**
courtage [kurtaʒ] *m* brokerage; broker's commission
cour·taud [kurto] **-taude** [tod] *adj* stocky, short and stocky
court-circuit [kursirkɥi] *m* (*pl* **courts-circuits**) short circuit
court-circuiter [kursirkɥite] *tr* to short-circuit
court-courrier [kurkurje] *s* (*pl* **courts-courriers**) short-range plane
courtepoint [kurtəpwɛ̃] *f* counterpane
cour·tier [kurtje] **-tière** [tjɛr] *mf* broker; agent; **courtier électoral** canvasser
courtisan [kurtizɑ̃] *m* courtier
courtisane [kurtizan] *f* courtesan
courtiser [kurtize] *tr* to court
cour·tois [kurtwa] **-toise** [twaz] *adj* courteous; courtly
courtoisie [kurtwazi] *f* courtesy

court-vê·tu -tue [kurvɛty] *adj* short-skirted
cou·ru -rue [kury] *adj* sought after, popular; **c'est couru** (coll) it's a sure thing ‖ *v* see **courir**
cou·seur [kuzœr] **-seuse** [zøz] *mf* sewer ‖ *f* seamstress; (mach) stitcher
cou·sin [kuzɛ̃] **-sine** [zin] *mf* cousin; **cousin germain** first cousin; **cousins issus de germains** first cousins once removed ‖ *m* mosquito
cousinage [kuzinaʒ] *m* cousinship; (coll) relatives
coussin [kusɛ̃] *m* cushion; **coussin gonflable** (aut) air bag
coussinet [kusinɛ] *m* little cushion; (mach) bearing
cou·su -sue [kusy] *v* see **coudre**
coût [ku] *m* cost; **coût de la vie** cost of living
cou·teau [kuto] *m* (*pl* **-teaux**) knife; **couteau à cran d'arrêt** clasp knife with safety catch; switchblade knife; **couteau à découper** carving knife; **couteau à ressort** switchblade knife; **couteau pliant, couteau de poche** jackknife
coutelas [kutlɑ] *m* cutlass; butcher knife
coutellerie [kutɛlri] *f* cutlery
coûter [kute] §96 *tr* to cost; **coûte que coûte** cost what it may; **il m'en coûte de** + *inf* it's hard for me to + *inf*
coû·teux [kutø] **-teuse** [tøz] *adj* costly, expensive
coutil [kuti] *m* duck (*cloth*); mattress ticking
coutume [kutym] *f* custom; habit; common law; **de coutume** ordinarily
coutu·mier [kutymje] **-mière** [mjɛr] *adj* customary; common (*law*); accustomed ‖ *m* book of common law
couture [kutyr] *f* needlework; sewing; seam; suture; scar; **battre qn à plate couture** (coll) to beat s.o. hollow; **examiner sur toutes les coutures** to examine inside and out or from every angle; **haute couture** fashion designing, haute couture; **sans couture** seamless
couturer [kutyre] *tr* to scar
coutu·rier [kutyrje] **-rière** [rjɛr] *mf* dressmaker ‖ *m* dress designer ‖ *f* seamstress
couvaison [kuvɛzɔ̃] *f* incubation period
couvée [kuve] *f* brood
couvent [kuvɑ̃] *m* convent; monastery; convent school
couver [kuve] *tr* to brood, hatch ‖ *intr* to brood; smolder
couvercle [kuvɛrkl] *m* cover, lid
cou·vert [kuvɛr] **-verte** [vɛrt] *adj* covered; dressed, clothed; cloudy (*weather*); wooded (*countryside*) ‖ *m* cover; setting (*of table*); service (*fork and spoon*); cover charge; room, lodging; authority (*given by a superior*); **à couvert** sheltered; **mettre le couvert** to set the table; **sous le couvert de** under cover of; **sous les couverts** under cover (*of trees*) ‖ *f* glaze
couverture [kuvɛrtyr] *f* cover; coverage; covering; wrapper; blanket; bedspread
couveuse [kuvøz] *f* brood hen; incubator

couvre-chef [kuvrəʃɛf] *m* (*pl* **-chefs**) (coll) headgear

couvre-feu [kuvrəfø] *m* (*pl* **-feux**) curfew

couvre-lit [kuvrəli] *m* (*pl* **-lits**) bedspread

couvre-livre [kuvrəlivr] *m* (*pl* **-livres**) dust jacket

couvre-oreille [kuvrɔrɛj] *m* (*pl* **-oreilles**) earmuff

couvre-pieds [kuvrəpje] *m invar* bedspread; quilt

couvre-plat [kuvrəpla] *m* (*pl* **-plats**) dish cover

couvre-théière [kuvrətejɛr] *m* (*pl* **-théières**) tea cozy

couvreur [kuvrœr] *m* roofer

couvrir [kuvrir] §65 *tr* to cover ‖ *ref* to cover; cover oneself; get cloudy; put one's hat on

co-voiturage [kɔvwatyraʒ] *m* car pool

cow-boy [kaubɔj], [kobɔj] *m* (*pl* **-boys**) cowboy

C.P. *abbr* (**case postale**) post-office box

C.R. [seɛr] *adv* (letterword) (**contre remboursement**) C.O.D.; **envoyez-le-moi C.R.** send it to me C.O.D.

crabe [krɑb] *m* crab; caterpillar (tractor)

crachat [kraʃa] *m* sputum, spit

cra·ché -chée [kraʃe] *adj* (coll) spitting (*image*)

cracher [kraʃe] *tr & intr* to spit

crachin [kraʃɛ̃] *m* light drizzle

crachoir [kraʃwar] *m* spittoon; **tenir le crachoir** (slang) to have the floor, speak

crachoter [kraʃɔte] *intr* to keep on spitting; sputter

crack [krak] *m* favorite (*the horse favored to win*); (coll) champion, ace; (coll) crackerjack

cracking [krakiŋ] *m* cracking (*of oil*)

craie [krɛ] *f* chalk; piece of chalk

craignez [krɛɲe] *v* (**craignons**) see **craindre**

crailler [krɑje] *intr* to caw

craindre [krɛ̃dr] §15, §97 *tr* to fear, be afraid of, dread; respect ‖ *intr* to be afraid

crainte [krɛ̃t] *f* fear, dread; **dans la crainte que** or **de crainte que** for fear that

crain·tif -tive [krɛ̃tif] *adj* fearful; timid

cramoi·si -sie [kramwazi] *adj & m* crimson

crampe [krɑ̃p] *f* cramp (*in a muscle*)

crampon [krɑ̃pɔ̃] *m* clamp; cleat (*on a shoe*); (coll) pest, bore

cramponner [krɑ̃pɔne] *tr* to clamp together; (coll) to pester ‖ *ref* to hold fast, hang on, cling

cran [krɑ̃] *m* notch; cog, catch, tooth; **avoir du cran** (coll) to be game (*for anything*); **baisser un cran** to come down a peg; **être à cran** (coll) to be exasperated, cross

crâne [krɑn] *adj* bold, daring ‖ *m* skull; cranium; **bourrer le crâne à qn** (coll) to hand s.o. a line

crâner [krane] *intr* (coll) to swagger

cra·neur [krɑnœr] **-neuse** [nøz] *adj* (coll) *mf* (coll) braggart

crapaud [krapo] *m* toad; baby grand; flaw (*in diamond*); low armchair; (coll) brat;

avaler un crapaud (coll) to put up with a lot

crapule [krapyl] *f* underworld, scum; bum, punk; **vivre dans la crapule** to live in debauchery

crapu·leux [krapylø] **-leuse** [løz] *adj* debauched, lewd, filthy

craquage [krakaʒ] *m* cracking (*of petroleum*)

craquement [krakmɑ̃] *m* crack, crackle

craquer [krake] *intr* to crack; burst; (coll) to crash, fail

craqueter [krakte] §34 *intr* to crackle

crash [kraʃ] *m* crash landing

crasher [kraʃe] *intr* (aer) to crash

crasse [kras] *adj* gross; crass (*ignorance*) ‖ *f* filth, squalor; avarice; dross; **faire une crasse à qn** (slang) to play a dirty trick on s.o.

cras·seux [krasø] **-seuse** [søz] *adj* filthy, squalid; (coll) stingy

crassier [krasje] *m* slag heap

cratère [kratɛr] *m* crater; ewer

cravache [kravaʃ] *f* riding whip, horsewhip

cravacher [kravaʃe] *tr* to horsewhip

cravate [kravat] *f* necktie, cravat; scarf; sling (*for unloading goods*); **cravate de chanvre** (coll) noose; **cravate de drapeau** pennant; **derrière la cravate!** down the hatch!

cravater [kravate] *tr* to tie a necktie on (*s.o.*) ‖ *intr* (slang) to tell a fish story

crawl [krol] *m* crawl (*in swimming*)

crayeux [krɛjø] **crayeuse** [krɛjøz] *adj* chalky

crayon [krɛjɔ̃] *m* pencil; **crayon à bille** ball-point pen; **crayon de pastel** wax crayon; **crayon de rouge à lèvres** lipstick

crayon-feutre [krɛjɔ̃føtr] *m* (*pl* **crayons-feutres**) magic-marker pen

crayonnages [krɛjɔnaʒ] *mpl* doodles, doodling

crayonner [krɛjɔne] *tr* to crayon, pencil, sketch

créance [kreɑ̃s] *f* belief, credence; **créances gelées** frozen assets; **créances véreuses** bad debts

créan·cier [kreɑ̃sje] **-cière** [sjɛr] *mf* creditor; **créancier hypothécaire** mortgage holder

créa·teur [kreatœr] **-trice** [tris] *adj* creative ‖ *mf* creator; originator

création [kreasjɔ̃] *f* creation

créature [kreatyr] *f* creature

crécelle [kresɛl] *f* rattle; chatterbox; **de crécelle** rasping

crèche [krɛʃ] *f* manger; crèche; day nursery

crédence [kredɑ̃s] *f* buffet, sideboard, credenza

crédibilité [kredibilite] *f* credibility

crédit [kredi] *m* credit; (govt) appropriation; **crédit bail** leasing; **crédit croisé** swap

créditer [kredite] *tr* (com) to credit

crédi·teur [kreditœr] **-trice** [tris] *adj* credit (*side, account*) ‖ *mf* creditor

credo [kredo] *m invar* credo, creed

crédule [kredyl] *adj* credulous

créer [kree] *tr* to create

crémaillère [kremajɛr] *f* pothook; rack; rack rail; **crémaillère et pignon** rack and pinion; **pendre la crémaillère** to have a housewarming

crémation [kremɑsjɔ̃] *f* cremation

crématoire [krematwar] *adj* & *m* crematory

crème [krɛm] *f* cream; **crème chantilly** whipped cream; **crème de démaquillage** cleansing cream; **crème fouettée** whipped cream; **crème glacée** ice cream

crémer [kreme] §10 *intr* to cream

crémerie [krɛmri] *f* dairy; milkhouse (*on a farm*); dairy luncheonette

cré·meux [kremø] **-meuse** [møz] *adj* creamy

crémier [kremje] *m* dairyman

crémière [kremjɛr] *f* dairymaid; cream pitcher

crémone [kremɔn] *f* casement bolt

cré·neau [kreno] *m* (*pl* **-neaux**) crenel; loophole; marked lane (*on a highway*); extra passing lane; space between two cars; **créneau temporel** time slot; **créneaux** battlements

créneler [krɛnle] §34 *tr* to crenelate; tooth (*a wheel*); mill (*a coin*)

créole [kreɔl] *adj* Creole ‖ *m* Creole (*language*) ‖ (*cap*) *mf* Creole (*person*)

crêpe [krɛp] *m* crepe ‖ *f* pancake

crépitation [krepitɑsjɔ̃] *f* crackle

crépitement [krepitmɑ̃] *m* crackling

crépiter [krepite] *intr* to crackle

cré·pu -pue [krepy] *adj* crimped, frizzly, crinkled

crépuscule [krepyskyl] *m* twilight

cresson [krɛsɔ̃] *m* cress; **cresson de fontaine** watercress

crête [krɛt] *f* crest; **crête de coq** cockscomb

Crète [krɛt] *f* Crete; **la Crète** Crete

crête-de-coq [krɛtdəkɔk] *f* (*pl* **crêtes-de-coq**) (bot) cockscomb

cré·tin -tine [kretɛ̃] **-tine** [tin] *mf* cretin; (coll) jackass, fathead

cré·tois [kretwa] **-toise** [twaz] *adj* Cretan ‖ (*cap*) *mf* Cretan

creuser [krøze] *tr* to dig, excavate; hollow out; furrow; go into thoroughly ‖ *ref*—**se creuser la tête** (coll) to rack one's brains

creuset [krøzɛ] *m* crucible

creux [krø] **creuse** [krøz] *adj* hollow; concave; sunken, deep-set; empty (*stomach*); deep (*voice*); off-peak (*hours*); **songer creux** to dream idle dreams; **sonner creux** to sound hollow ‖ *m* hollow (*of hand*); hole (*in ground*); pit (*of stomach*); trough (*of wave*); **creux de l'aisselle** armpit; **creux des reins** small of the back

crevaison [krəvɛzɔ̃] *f* blowout

crevasse [krəvas] *f* crevice; crack (*in skin*); rift (*in clouds*); flaw (*in metal*)

crevasser [krəvase] *tr* to chap ‖ *intr* & *ref* to crack, chap

crève-cœur [krɛvkœr] *m* *invar* heartbreak, keen disappointment

crever [krəve] §2 *tr* to burst; work to death (*e.g., a horse*) ‖ *intr* to burst; split; burst,

go flat (*said of a tire*); (slang) to die, kick the bucket ‖ *ref* to work oneself to death

crevette [krəvɛt] *f* shrimp; **crevette grise** shrimp; **crevette rose, crevette bouquet** prawn

C.-R.F. *abbr* (**Croix-Rouge française**) French Red Cross

cri [kri] *m* cry; shout; whine, squeal; **dernier cri** last word, latest thing

criailler [kriɑje] *intr* to honk (*said of goose*); (coll) to whine, complain, grouse; **criailler après, criailler contre** (coll) to nag at

criaillerie [kriɑjri] *f* (coll) shouting; (coll) whining, complaining; (coll) nagging

criant [krijɑ̃] **criante** [krijɑ̃t] *adj* crying (*shame*); obvious (*truth*); flagrant (*injustice*)

criard [krijar] **criarde** [krijard] *adj* complaining; shrill (*voice*); loud (*color*); pressing (*debts*) ‖ *mf* complainer ‖ *f* scold, shrew

crible [kribl] *m* sieve; **crible à gravier** gravel screen; **crible à mineral** jig; **passer au crible** to sift or screen

cri·blé -blée [krible] *adj* riddled (*with, e.g., debts*); pitted (*by, e.g., smallpox*)

cribler [krible] *tr* to sift, screen; riddle; **cribler de ridicule** to cover with ridicule

cric [krik] *m* (aut) jack ‖ *interj* crack!, snap!

cricket [krikɛt] *m* (sports) cricket

cricri [krikri] *m* (ent) cricket

crier [krije] §97, §98 *tr* to cry; cry out; shout; cry for (*revenge*); **crier misère** to complain of being poor; cry poverty (*said of clothing, furniture, etc.*) ‖ *intr* to cry; cry out; shout; creak, squeak; squeal; **crier à** to cry out against (*scandal, injustice, etc.*); cry for (*help*); **crier après** to yell at, bawl out; **crier contre** to cry out against; to rail at

crieur [krijœr] **crieuse** [krijøz] *mf* crier; hawker, peddler; **crieur public** town crier

crime [krim] *m* crime; felony

crimi·nel -nelle [kriminɛl] *adj* & *mf* criminal

crin [krɛ̃] *m* horsehair (*on mane and tail*); **à tous crins** out-and-out, hard-core (*e.g., revolutionist*)

crinière [krinjɛr] *f* mane

crique [krik] *f* cove

criquet [krikɛ] *m* locust; weak wine; (coll) shrimp (*person*)

crise [kriz] *f* crisis; **crise d'appendicite** appendicitis attack; **crise de foi** shaken faith; **crise de main-d'œuvre** labor-shortage; **crise de nerfs** fit of hysterics; **crise du foie** liver upset; **crise du logement** housing shortage; **crise économique** (com) depression

cris·pant -pante [krispɑ̃] *adj* irritating, annoying

crispation [krispɑsjɔ̃] *f* contraction, shriveling up; (coll) fidgeting

cris·pé -pée [krispe] *adj* nervous, strained, tense

crisper [krispe] *tr* to contract, clench; (coll) to make fidgety ‖ *ref* to contract, curl up

crisser [krise] *tr* to grind or grit (*one's teeth*) ‖ *intr* to grate, crunch

cris·tal [kristal] *m* (*pl* **-taux** [to]) crystal; **cristal de roche** rock crystal; **cristal taillé** cut glass; **cristaux** glassware; **cristaux de soude** washing soda

cristal·lin [kristalɛ̃] **-line** [lin] *adj* crystalline ‖ *m* crystalline lens (*of the eye*)

cristalliser [kristalize] *tr*, *intr*, & *ref* to crystallize

critère [kritɛr] *m* criterion

critérium [kriterjɔm] *m* championship game

critiquable [kritikabl] *adj* open to criticism, questionable

critique [kritik] *adj* critical ‖ *mf* critic ‖ *f* criticism; critics; **critiques** censure

critiquer [kritike] *tr* to criticize, find fault with ‖ *intr* to find fault

critiqueur [kritikœr] *m* critic, fault-finder

croassement [krɔasmɑ̃] *m* croak, caw, croaking (*of raven*)

croasser [krɔase] *intr* to croak, caw

croate [krɔat] *adj* Croatian ‖ *m* Croat, Croatian (*language*) ‖ (*cap*) *mf* Croatian (*person*)

croc [kro] *m* hook; fang (*of dog*); tusk (*of walrus*)

croc-en-jambe [krɔkɑ̃ʒɑ̃b] *m* (*pl* **crocs-en-jambes** [krɔkɑ̃ʒɑ̃b])—**faire un croc-en-jambe à qn** to trip s.o. up

croche [krɔʃ] *f* (mus) quaver

crochet [krɔʃɛ] *m* hook; fang (*of snake*); crochet work; crochet needle; picklock; **crochet radiophonique** talent show; **cro-chets** (typ) brackets; **faire un crochet** to swerve; **vivre aux crochets de** to live on or at the expense of

crocheter [krɔʃte] §2 *tr* to pick (*a lock*)

crocheteur [krɔʃtœr] *m* picklock; porter

cro·chu -chue [krɔʃy] *adj* hooked (*e.g., nose*); crooked; **avoir les mains crochues** to be light-fingered

crocodile [krɔkɔdil] *m* crocodile

crocus [krɔkys] *m* crocus

croire [krwar] §16, §95 *tr* to believe; **croire + *inf*** to think that + *ind*; **croire qn + *adj*** to believe s.o. to be + *adj*; **croire que non** to think not; **croire que oui** to think so; **je crois bien** or **je le crois bien** I should say so ‖ *intr* to believe; **croire à** to believe in; **croire en Dieu** to believe in God; **j'y crois** I believe in it ‖ *ref* to believe oneself to be

croisade [krwazad] *f* crusade

croi·sé -sée [krwaze] *adj* crossed; twilled (*cloth*); double-breasted (*suit*); alternate (*rhymes*) ‖ *m* Crusader ‖ *f* crossing, crossroads

croisement [krwazmɑ̃] *m* crossing; intersection; meeting, passing (*of two vehicles*); cross-breeding; **croisement en trèfle** cloverleaf, cloverleaf intersection

croiser [krwaze] *tr* to cross; fold over; meet, pass ‖ *intr* to fold over, lap; cruise ‖ *ref* to cross, intersect; go on a crusade

croiseur [krwazœr] *m* cruiser; **croiseur de bataille** battle cruiser

croisière [krwazjɛr] *f* cruise; **en croisière** cruising

croissance [krwasɑ̃s] *f* growth

crois·sant [krwasɑ̃] **-sante** [sɑ̃t] *adj* growing, increasing, rising ‖ *m* crescent; crescent roll; billhook

croître [krwatr] §17 *intr* to grow; to increase, to rise

croix [krwa] *f* cross; (typ) dagger; **croix de bois, croix de fer, si je mens je vais en enfer** cross my heart and hope to die; **croix gammée** swastika; **en croix** crossed, crosswise

Croix-Rouge [krwaruʒ] *f* Red Cross

cro·quant [krɔkɑ̃] **-quante** [kɑ̃t] *adj* crisp, crunchy ‖ *m* wretch

croque-mitaine [krɔkmitɛn] *m* (*pl* **-mitaines**) bugaboo, bogeyman

croque-monsieur [krɔkməsjø] *m* *invar* grilled ham-and-cheese sandwich

croque-mort [krɔkmɔr] *m* (*pl* **-morts**) (coll) funeral attendant

croquer [krɔke] *tr* to munch; sketch; dissipate (*a fortune*) ‖ *intr* to crunch

croquet [krɔkɛ] *m* croquet; almond cookie

croquis [krɔki] *m* sketch; draft, outline; **croquis coté** diagram, sketch

crosse [krɔs] *f* crosier; butt (*of gun*); hockey stick; lacrosse stick; golf club; **chercher des crosses à** (slang) to pick a fight with; **mettre la crosse en l'air** to show the white flag, to surrender

crotale [krɔtal] *m* rattlesnake

crotte [krɔt] *f* dung; mud; **crotte de chocolat** chocolate cream (candy)

crotter [krɔte] *tr* to dirty ‖ *ref* to get dirty; commit a nuisance (*said of dog*)

crottin [krɔtɛ̃] *m* horse manure

crou·lant [krulɑ̃] **-lante** [lɑ̃t] *adj* crumbling ‖ *m* (slang) old fogy

crouler [krule] *intr* to collapse

croup [krup] *m* (pathol) croup

croupe [krup] *f* croup, rump; ridge, brow; **en croupe** behind the rider

croupetons [kruptɔ̃]—**à croupetons** squatting

crou·pi -pie [krupi] *adj* stagnant

croupier [krupje] *m* croupier; financial partner

croupière [krupjɛr] *f* crupper; **tailler des croupieres à** (coll) to make it hard for

croupion [krupjɔ̃] *m* rump

croupir [krupir] *intr* to stagnate; wallow (*in vice, filth*); remain (*e.g., in ignorance*)

croustil·lant [krustijɑ̃] **-lante** [jɑ̃t] *adj* crisp, crunchy; spicy (*story*)

croustille [krustij] *f* piece of crust; snack; **croustilles** potato chips

croustiller [krustije] *intr* to munch, nibble

croustil·leux [krustijø] **-leuse** [jøz] *adj* spicy (*story*)

croûte [krut] *f* crust; pastry shell (*of meat pie*); scab (*of wound*); (coll) daub, worthless painting; **casser la croûte** (coll) to have a snack

croû·teux [krutø] **-teuse** [tøz] *adj* scabby

croûton [krutɔ̃] *m* crouton; heel (*of bread*); **vieux croûton** (coll) old dodo

croyable [krwɑjabl], [krwajabl] *adj* believable

croyance [krwajɑ̃s] *f* belief

croyant [krwajɑ̃] **croyante** [krwajɑ̃t] *adj* believing ‖ *mf* believer

C.R.S. [seerɛs] *fpl* (letterword) (**Compagnies républicaines de sécurité**) state troopers

cru crue [kry] *adj* raw, uncooked; indigestible; crude (*language; art*); glaring, harsh (*light*); hard (*water*); plain (*terms*); **à cru** directly; bareback ‖ *m* region (*in which s.th. is grown*); vineyard; vintage; **de son cru** of his own intention; **du cru** local, at the vineyard ‖ *f* see **crue** ‖ *v* see **croire**

crû crue [kry] *v* see **croître**

cruaute [kryote] *f* cruelty

cruche [kryʃ] *f* pitcher, jug

cruchon [kryʃɔ̃] *m* small pitcher or jug

cru·cial -ciale [krysjal] *adj* (*pl* **-ciaux** [sjo]) crucial; cross-shaped

crucifiement [krysifimɑ̃] *m* crucifixion

crucifier [krysifje] *tr* to crucify

crucifix [krysifi] *m* crucifix

crucifixion [krysifiksjɔ̃] *f* crucifixion

crudité [krydite] *f* crudity; indigestibility; rawness (*of food*); harshness (*of light*); hardness (*of water*); **crudités** raw fruits and vegetables; off-color remarks

crue [kry] *f* overflow (*of river*); growth

cruel cruelle [kryɛl] *adj* cruel

cruellement [kryɛlmɑ̃] *adv* cruelly; sorely

crû·ment [krymɑ̃] *adv* crudely; roughly

crustacé [krystase] *m* crustacean

crypte [kript] *f* crypt

CᵗᵉCᵗ *abbr* (**compte courant**) current account

cubage [kybaʒ] *m* volume

cu·bain [kybɛ̃] **-baine** [bɛn] *adj* Cuban ‖ (*cap*) *mf* Cuban

cube [kyb] *adj* cubic ‖ *m* cube

cuber [kybe] *tr* to cube

cubique [kybik] *adj* cubic

cueillaison [kœjɛzɔ̃] *f* picking, gathering; harvest time

cueil·leur [kœjœr] **-leuse** [jøz] *mf* picker; fruit picker

cueillir [kœjir] §18 *tr* to pick; pluck; gather; win (*laurels*); steal (*a kiss*); (coll) to nab (*a thief*); (coll) to pick up (*a friend*)

cuiller or **cuillère** [kɥijɛr] *f* spoon; ladle (*for molten metal*); scoop (*of a dredger*); **cuiller à bouche** tablespoon; **cuiller à café** teaspoon; **cuiller à pot** ladle; **cuiller à soupe** soupspoon; **cuiller et fourchette** fork and spoon

cuillerée [kɥijre] *f* spoonful

cuilleron [kɥijrɔ̃] *m* bowl (*of spoon*)

cuir [kɥir] *m* leather; hide; **cuir chevelu** scalp; **cuir verni** patent leather; **cuir vert** rawhide; **faire des cuirs** to make mistakes in liaison

cuirasse [kɥiras] *f* cuirass, breastplate; armor

cuiras·sé -sée [kɥirase] *adj* armored ‖ *m* battleship

cuirasser [kɥirase] *tr* to armor ‖ *ref* to steel oneself

cuire [kɥir] §19 *tr* to cook; ripen; **c'est du tout cuit** (coll) it's in the bag ‖ *intr* to cook; to sting, smart; **faire cuire** to cook; **il vous en cuira** you'll suffer for it

cui·sant [kɥizɑ̃] **-sante** [zɑ̃t] *adj* stinging, smarting

cuisez [kɥize] *v* (**cuisons**) see **cuire**

cuisine [kɥizin] *f* kitchen; cooking; cuisine; (coll) skulduggery; **cuisine roulante** chuck wagon, field kitchen; **faire la cuisine** to cook

cuisiner [kɥizine] *tr* to cook; (coll) to grill (*a suspect*); (coll) to fix (*an election*) ‖ *intr* to cook

cuisinette [kɥizinɛt] *f* kitchenette

cuisi·nier [kɥizinje] **-nière** [njɛr] *mf* cook ‖ *f* kitchen stove, cookstove

cuissardes [kɥisard] *fpl* hip boots

cuisse [kɥis] *f* thigh; (culin) drumstick; **cuisses de grenouille** frogs' legs; **il se croit sorti de la cuisse de Jupiter** (coll) he thinks he is the Lord God Almighty

cuis·seau [kɥiso] *m* (*pl* **-seaux**) leg of veal

cuisson [kɥisɔ̃] *f* baking, cooking; (fig) burning sensation, smarting; **en cuisson** on the stove, on the grill, in the oven

cuissot [kɥiso] *m* leg (*of game*)

cuistre [kɥistr] *m* pedant, prig

cuit [kɥi] **cuite** [kɥit] *adj* cooked; **nous sommes cuits** (coll) our goose is cooked ‖ *f* firing (*in a kiln*); **prendre une cuite** (slang) to get soused ‖ *v* see **cuire**

cuivre [kɥivr] *m* copper; **cuivre jaune** brass; **les cuivres** (mus) the brasses

cui·vré -vrée [kɥivre] *adj* copper-colored, bronzed; brassy, metallic (*sound or voice*)

cuivrer [kɥivre] *tr* to copper; bronze, tan; make (*a sound or one's voice*) brassy or metallic ‖ *ref* to become copper-colored

cui·vreux [kɥivrø] **-vreuse** [vrøz] *adj* (chem) cuprous

cul [ky] *m* bottom (*of bottle, bag*); (slang) ass, hind end, rump; **bouche en cul de poule** (slang) pursed lips; **faire cul sec** (slang) to chug-a-lug

culasse [kylas] *f* breechblock; (mach) cylinder head

cul-blanc [kyblɑ̃] *m* (*pl* **culs-blancs**) wheatear, whitetail

culbute [kylbyt] *f* somersault; tumble, bad fall; (coll) failure; (coll) fall (*of a cabinet*); **faire la culbute** to sell at double the purchase price

culbuter [kylbyte] *tr* to overthrow; overwhelm (*the enemy*) ‖ *intr* to tumble, fall backwards; somersault

culbuteur [kylbytœr] *m* (mach) rocker arm

cul-de-basse-fosse [kydbɑsfos] *m* (*pl* **culs-de-basse-fosse**) dungeon

cul-de-jatte [kydəʒat] *mf* (*pl* **culs-de-jatte**) legless person

cul-de-sac [kydəsak] *m* (*pl* **culs-de-sac**) dead end; (public sign) no outlet

culée [kyle] *f* abutment

culer [kyle] *intr* to back water

culinaire [kylinɛr] *adj* culinary

culmi·nant [kylminɑ̃] **-nante** [nɑ̃t] *adj* culminating; highest (*point*)

culmination [kylminɑsjɔ̃] *f* (astr) culmination

culminer [kylmine] *intr* to rise high, tower; (astr) to culminate

culot [kylo] *m* base, bottom; (coll) baby of the family; **avoir du culot** (slang) to have a lot of nerve

culotte [kylɔt] *f* breeches, pants; forked pipe; panties (*feminine undergarment*); (culin) rump; **culotte de golf** plus fours; **culotte de peau** (slang) old soldier; **culotte de sport** shorts; **porter la culotte** (coll) to wear the pants; **prendre une culotte** (slang) to lose one's shirt; (slang) to have a jag on

culot·té -tée [kylɔte] *adj* (coll) nervy, fresh

culotter [kylɔte] *tr* to cure (*a pipe*) ‖ *ref* to put one's pants on

culte [kylt] *m* worship; cult; divine service, ritual; religion, creed; **avoir un culte pour** to worship, adore (*e.g.*, one's parents)

cul-terreux [kytɛrø] *m* (*pl* **culs-terreux**) (coll) clodhopper, hayseed

cultivable [kyltivabl] *adj* arable, tillable

cultiva·teur [kyltivatœr] **-trice** [tris] *adj* farming ‖ *mf* farmer ‖ *m* (mach) cultivator

cultiver [kyltive] *tr* to cultivate; culture

cultu·ral -rale [kyltyral] *adj* (*pl* **-raux** [ro]) agricultural

culture [kyltyr] *f* culture; cultivation

cultu·rel -relle [kyltyrɛl] *adj* cultural

cumula·tif [kymylatif] **-tive** [tiv] *adj* cumulative

cumuler [kymyle] *intr* to moonlight

cunéiforme [kyneifɔrm] *adj* cuneiform

cupide [kypid] *adj* greedy

cupidité [kypidite] *f* cupidity

Cupidon [kypidɔ̃] *m* Cupid

curage [kyraʒ] *m* cleansing, cleaning out; unstopping (*of a drain*)

curatelle [kyratɛl] *f* guardianship, trusteeship

cura·teur [kyratœr] **-trice** [tris] *mf* guardian, trustee

cura·tif [kyratif] **-tive** [tiv] *adj* curative

cure [kyr] *f* treatment, cure; vicarage, rectory; parish; sun porch; **n'avoir cure de rien**, **n'en avoir cure** not to care

curé [kyre] *m* parish priest

cure-dent [kyrdɑ̃] *m* (*pl* **-dents**) toothpick

curée [kyre] *f* quarry (*given to the hounds*); scramble, mad race (*for gold, power, recognition, etc.*)

cure-oreille [kyrɔrɛj] *m* (*pl* **-oreilles**) earpick

cure-pipe [kyrpip] *m* (*pl* **-pipes**) pipe cleaner

curer [kyre] *tr* to clean out; dredge ‖ *ref* to pick (*one's nails, one's teeth, etc.*)

cu·rieux [kyrjø] **-rieuse** [rjøz] §93 *adj* curious

curiosité [kyrjozite] *f* curiosity; curio; connoisseurs, e.g., **le langage de la curiosité** the jargon of connoisseurs; **curiosités** sights; **visiter les curiosités** to go sightseeing

curseur [kyrsœr] *m* slide, runner

cur·sif [kyrsif] **-sive** [siv] *adj* cursory; cursive (*handwriting*) ‖ *f* cursive

cuta·né -née [kytane] *adj* cutaneous

cuticule [kytikyl] *f* cuticle

cuti-réaction [kytireaksjɔ̃] *f* skin test

cuve [kyv] *f* vat, tub, tank

cu·veau [kyvo] *m* (*pl* **-veaux**) small vat or tank

cuver [kyve] *tr* to leave to ferment; **cuver son vin** (coll) to sleep it off ‖ *intr* to ferment in a wine vat

cuvette [kyvɛt] *f* basin, pan; bulb (*of a thermometer*); (chem, phot) tray

cuvier [kyvje] *m* washtub

C.V. [seve] *m* (letterword) (**cheval-vapeur**) hp, horsepower

cyanamide [sjanamid] *f* cyanamide

cyanose [sjanoz] *f* cyanosis

cyanure [sjanyr] *m* cyanide

cyclable [siklabl] *adj* reserved for bicycles

cycle [sikl] *m* cycle

cyclique [siklik] *adj* cyclic(al)

cycliste [siklist] *mf* cyclist

cyclomoteur [siklomotœr] *m* motorbike

cyclone [siklon] *m* cyclone

cyclope [siklɔp] *m* cyclops

cyclotron [siklɔtrɔ̃] *m* cyclotron

cygne [siɲ] *m* swan

cylindrage [silɛ̃draʒ] *m* rolling (*of roads, gardens, etc.*); calendering, mangling

cylindre [silɛ̃dr] *m* cylinder; roller (*e.g.*, of rolling mill); steam roller

cylindrée [silɛ̃dre] *f* piston displacement

cylindrer [silɛ̃dre] *tr* to roll (*a road, garden, etc.*); calender, mangle

cylindrique [silɛ̃drik] *adj* cylindrical

cymbale [sɛ̃bal] *f* cymbal

cynique [sinik] *adj & m* cynic

cynisme [sinism] *m* cynicism

cyprès [siprɛ] *m* cypress

cyrillique [sirilik] *adj* Cyrillic

cytoplasme [sitoplasm] *m* cytoplasm

czar [ksar] *m* czar

czarine [ksarin] *f* czarina

D, d [de] *m invar* fourth letter of the French alphabet

d' = **de** before vowel or mute **h**

d'abord [dabɔr] see **abord**

dactylo [daktilo] *mf* (coll) typist

dactylographe [daktilɔgraf] *mf* typist

dactylographier [daktilɔgrafje] *tr* to type

dactyloscopie [daktilɔskɔpi] *f* fingerprinting

dada [dada] *m* hobby-horse; hobby, fad, pet subject; **enfourcher son dada** to ride one's hobby

dague [dag] *f* dagger; first antler; tusk

dahlia [dalja] *m* dahlia

daigner [deɲe] §95 *intr*—**daigner** + *inf* to deign to, condescend to + *inf;* **daignez** please

d'ailleurs [dajœr] see **ailleurs**

daim [dɛ̃] *m* fallow deer; suede

daine [dɛn] *f* doe

dais [dɛ] *m* canopy

dalle [dal] *f* flagstone, slab, paving block; **se rincer la dalle** (slang) to wet one's whistle

daller [dale] *tr* to pave with flagstones

dalto·nien [daltɔnjɛ̃] **-nienne** [njɛn] *adj* color-blind ‖ *mf* color-blind person

dam [dɑ̃] *m*—**au dam de** to the detriment of

damas [damɑ] *m* damask ‖ (*cap*) [damɑs] *f* Damascus

damasquiner [damaskine] *tr* to damascene

damas·sé -sée [damase] *adj & m* damask

dame [dam] *f* dame; lady; tamp, tamper; rowlock; (cards, chess) queen; (checkers) king; **aller à dame** (checkers) to crown a man king; (chess) to queen a pawn; **dame d'honneur** lady-in-waiting; **dame pipi** (slang) female toilet attendant; **dames** (public sign) ladies ‖ *interj* for heaven's sake!

damer [dame] *tr* to tamp (*the earth*); (checkers) to crown (*a checker*); (chess) to queen (*a pawn*); **damer le pion à qn** to outwit s.o.

damier [damje] *m* checkerboard

damnation [dɑnasjɔ̃] *f* damnation

dam·né -née [dane] *adj & mf* damned

damner [dane] *tr* to damn

damoi·seau [damwazo] **-selle** [zɛl] *mf* (*pl* **-seaux**) (archaic) young member of the nobility ‖ *m* lady's man ‖ *f* (archaic) damsel

dancing [dɑ̃siŋ] *m* dance hall

dandiner [dɑ̃dine] *tr* to dandle ‖ *ref* to waddle along

dandy [dɑ̃di] *m* dandy, fop

Danemark [danmark] *m*—**le Danemark** Denmark

danger [dɑ̃ʒe] *m* danger

dange·reux [dɑ̃ʒrø] **-reuse** [røz] *adj* dangerous

da·nois [danwa] **-noise** [nwaz] *adj* Danish ‖ *m* Danish (*language*) ‖ (*cap*) *mf* Dane

dans [dɑ̃] *prep* in; into; in (*at the end of*), e.g., **dans deux jours** in two days; **boire dans un verre** to drink out of a glass; **dans la suite** later

danse [dɑ̃s] *f* dance; **danse de Saint Guy** St. Vitus's dance; **danse guerrière** war dance

danser [dɑ̃se] *tr & intr* to dance; **faire danser** to mistreat

dan·seur [dɑ̃sœr] **-seuse** [søz] *mf* dancer; **danseur de corde** tightrope walker; **en danseuse** in a standing position (*taken by cyclist*)

Danube [danyb] *m* Danube

d'après [daprɛ] see **après**

dard [dar] *m* dart; sting; snake's tongue; harpoon

darder [darde] *tr* to dart, hurl

dare-dare [dardar] *adv* (coll) on the double

darse [dars] *f* wet dock

date [dat] *f* date; **de fraîche date** recent; **de longue date** of long standing; **en date de** from; **faire date** to mark an epoch; **prendre date** to make an appointment

dater [date] *tr & intr* to date; **à dater de** dating from

datif [datif] *m* dative

datte [dat] *f* date

dattier [datje] *m* date palm

daube [dob] *f* braised meat; **en daube** braised

dauber [dobe] *tr* to braise; heckle; slander; (coll) to pummel ‖ *intr* **dauber sur qn** to heckle s.o., slander s.o.

dau·beur [dobœr] **-beuse** [bøz] *mf* heckler

dauphin [dofɛ̃] *m* dolphin; dauphin

dauphine [dofin] *f* dauphiness

dauphinelle [dofinɛl] *f* delphinium

davantage [davɑ̃taʒ] §90 *adv* more; any more; any longer; **ne . . . davantage** no more; any longer; **pas davantage** no longer

de [də] §77, §78, §79 *prep* of, from; with, e.g., **frapper d'une épée** to strike with a sword; (to indicate the agent with the passive voice) by, e.g., **ils sont aimés de tous** they are loved by all; (to indicate the point of departure) from, e.g., **de Paris à Madrid** from Paris to Madrid; (to indicate the point of arrival) for, e.g., **le train de Paris** the train for Paris; (with a following infinitive after certain verbs) to, e.g., **il essaie d'écrire la lettre** he is trying to write the letter; (with a following infinitive after an adjective used with the impersonal expression **il est**) to, e.g., **il est facile de chanter cette chanson** it is easy to sing that song; (after **changer, se souvenir, avoir besoin, etc.**), e.g., **changer de vêtements** to change clothes; (after a comparative and before a numeral) than, e.g., **plus de quarante** more than forty; (to express the indefinite plural or partitive idea), e.g., **de l'eau** water, some water; (to form prepositional phrases with some adverbs), e.g., **auprès de vous** near you; (with the historical infinitive), e.g., **et chacun de pleurer** and everyone cried

dé [de] *m* die (*singular of dice*); thimble; domino; golf tee; **dés** dice

dealer [dilœr] *m* (slang) drug dealer

déambulateur [deɑ̃bylatœr] *m* walker (*used by an infirm person*)

déambuler [deɑ̃byle] *intr* to stroll

débâcle [debɑkl] *f* debacle; breakup (*of ice*)

débâcler [debɑkle] *intr* to break up (*said of ice in a river*)

déballage [debalaʒ] *m* unpacking; cut-rate merchandise (*sold by street vendor*)

déballer [debale] *tr* to unpack (*merchandise*); display (*merchandise*)

débandade [debɑ̃dad] *f* rout, stampede; **à la débandade** in confusion, helter-skelter

débander [debɑ̃de] *tr* to rout, stampede; slacken (*s.th. under tension*); unwind; **débander les yeux à qn** to take the blindfold from s.o.'s eyes ‖ *intr* to flee, stampede

débaptiser [debatize] *tr* to change the name of, rename

débarbouiller [debarbuje] *tr* to wash the face of

débarcadère [debarkadɛr] *m* wharf, dock, landing platform

débarder [debarde] *tr* to unload

débardeur [debardœr] *m* stevedore, longshoreman

débar·qué ·quée [debarke] *adj* disembarking ‖ *mf* new arrival ‖ *m* disembarkment; **au débarqué** on arrival

débarquement [debarkmɑ̃] *m* disembarkation

débarquer [debarke] *m*—**au débarquer de qn** at the moment of s.o.'s arrival ‖ *tr* to unload; lower (*a lifeboat, seaplane, etc.*); (coll) to sack (*s.o.*) ‖ *intr* to disembark, get off

débarras [debara] *m* catchall

débarrasser [debarase] *tr* to disencumber, disentangle; clear (*the table*); rid ‖ *ref*—**se débarrasser de** to get rid of

débarrasseur [debarasœr] *m* busboy

débarrer [debare] *tr* to unbar

débat [deba] *m* debate; dispute; **débats** discussion (*in a meeting*); proceedings (*in a court*)

débâter [debate] *tr* to unsaddle

débattre [debatr] §7 *tr* to debate, argue, discuss; haggle over (*a price*); question (*items in an account*) ‖ *ref* to struggle; be debated

débauche [deboʃ] *f* debauch, debauchery; riot (*e.g., of colors*); overeating; striking, quitting work

débaucher [deboʃe] *tr* to debauch; induce (*a worker*) to strike; lay off (*workers*); steal (*a worker*) from another employer ‖ *ref* to become debauched

débile [debil] *adj* weak ‖ *mf* mental defective

débilité [debilite] *f* debility

débiliter [debilite] *tr* to debilitate

débiner [debine] *tr* (slang) to run (*s.o.*) down ‖ *ref* (slang) to fly the coop

débit [debi] *m* debit; retail sale; shop; cutting up (*of wood*); output; way of speaking

débiter [debite] *tr* to debit; cut up in pieces; retail; produce; speak (*one's part*); repeat thoughtlessly

débi·teur [debitœr] **-trice** [tris] *adj* debit (*account, balance*); delivery (*spool*) ‖ *mf* debtor ‖ **-teur** [tœr] **-teuse** [tøz] *mf* gossip, talebearer; salesclerk

déblai [deblɛ] *m* excavation; **déblais** rubble, fill

déblaiement [deblɛmɑ̃] *m* clearing away

déblatérer [deblaterel] §10 *tr* to bluster or fling (*threats, abuse*) ‖ *intr*—**déblatérer contre** to rail at

déblayer [debleje] §49 *tr* to clear, clear away

débloquer [debloke] *tr* to unblock; unfreeze (*funds, credits, etc.*)

déboguer [deboge] *tr* (comp) to debug

déboire [debwar] *m* unpleasant aftertaste; disappointment

déboisement [debwazmɑ̃] *m* deforestation

déboîter [debwate] *tr* to disconnect (*pipe*); dislocate (*a shoulder*) ‖ *intr* to move into another lane (*said of automobile*); (naut) to haul (*out of line*)

débonder [debɔ̃de] *tr* to unbung

débonnaire [debɔnɛr] *adj* good-natured, easygoing; (Bib) meek

débor·dant [debɔrdɑ̃] **-dante** [dɑ̃t] *adj* overflowing

débor·de·dée [debɔrde] *adj* overwhelmed

débordement [debɔrdmɑ̃] *m* overflowing; outburst; overlap; **débordements** excesses

déborder [debɔrde] *tr* to extend beyond, jut out over; trim the border from; overwhelm; untuck (*a bed*); (mil) to outflank ‖ *intr* to overflow; (naut) to shove off

débotté [debɔte] *m*—**au débotté** immediately upon arrival, at once

débouché [debuʃe] *m* outlet; opening (*for trade; of an attack*)

déboucher [debuʃe] *tr* to free from obstruction; uncork ‖ *intr*—**déboucher dans** to empty into (*said of river*); **déboucher sur** to open onto, to emerge into

débouchoir [debuʃwar] *m* plunger

déboucler [debukle] *tr* to unbuckle; take the curls out of

débouler [debule] *tr* to fly down (*e.g., a stairway*) ‖ *intr* to run suddenly out of cover (*said of rabbits*); dash; **débouler dans** to roll down (*a stairway*)

déboulonner [debulɔne] *tr* to unbolt; (coll) to ruin, have fired; (coll) to debunk

débourber [deburbe] *tr* to clear of mud, clean

débourrer [debure] *tr* to unhair (*a hide*); remove the stuffing from (*a chair*); knock (*a pipe*) clean

débours [debur] *m* disbursement; **rentrer dans ses débours** to recover one's investment

déboursement [debursmɑ̃] *m* disbursing

débourser [deburse] *tr* to disburse

débousso·lé -lée [debusɔle] *adj* adrift, without direction, lost

debout [dəbu] *adv* upright, on end; standing; up (*out of bed*)

déboutonner [debutɔne] *tr* to unbutton; **à ventre déboutonné** immoderately ‖ *ref* (coll) to get something off one's chest

débrail·lé -lée [debrɑje] *adj* untidy, mussed up, unkempt; loose (*morals*); vulgar (*speech*) ‖ *m* untidiness

débrancher [debrɑ̃ʃe] *tr* to switch (*railroad cars*) to a siding; (elec) to disconnect

débrayage [debrɛjaʒ] *m* (aut) clutch release; (coll) walkout

débrayer [debrɛje] §49 *tr* to disengage, throw out (*the clutch*) ‖ *intr* to throw out the clutch; (coll) to walk out (*said of strikers*)

débri·dé -dée [debride] *adj* unbridled

débris [debri] *mpl* debris; remains

débrouil·lard [debrujar] **-larde** [jard] *adj* (coll) resourceful ‖ *mf* (coll) smart customer

débrouiller [debruje] *tr* to disentangle, unravel; clear up (*a mystery*); make out (*e.g., a signature*); (coll) to teach (*s.o.*) to be resourceful ‖ *ref* to clear (*said of sky*); (coll) to manage to get along, take care of oneself; (coll) to extricate oneself (*from a difficult situation*)

débucher [debyʃe] *tr* to flush out (*game*) ‖ *intr* to run out of cover (*said of game*)

débusquer [debyske] *tr* to flush out (*game; the enemy*)

début [deby] *m* debut; beginning, commencement; opening play

débu·tant [debytɑ̃] **-tante** [tɑ̃t] *adj* beginning ‖ *mf* beginner; newcomer (*e.g., to stage or screen*) ‖ *f* debutante

débuter [debyte] *intr* to make one's debut, begin; start up a business; make the opening play

deçà [dəsa] *adv*—**deçà delà** here and there; **en deçà de** on this side of

décacheter [dekaʃte] §34 *tr* to unseal

décade [dekad] *f* period of ten days; (hist, lit) decade

décadence [dekadɑ̃s] *f* decadence

déca·dent [dekadɑ̃] **-dente** [dɑ̃t] *adj* & *mf* decadent

décaféi·né -née [dekafeine] *adj* decaffeinated, caffeine-free

décagénaires [dekaʒenɛr] *mfpl* teenagers

décaisser [dekɛse] *tr* to uncrate; disburse, pay out

décalage [dekalaʒ] *m* unkeying; shift; slippage; (aer) stagger

décalcomanie [dekalkɔmani] *f* decal

décaler [dekale] *tr* to unkey; shift

décalquage [dekalkaʒ] or **décalque** [dekalk] *m* decal

décalquer [dekalke] *tr* to transfer (*a decal*) onto paper, canvas, metal, etc.; **décalquer sur** to transfer (*a decal*) onto (*e.g., paper*)

décamper [dekɑ̃pe] *intr* to decamp

décanat [dekana] *m* deanship

décanter [dekɑ̃te] *tr* to decant

décapant [dekapɑ̃] *m* scouring agent

décaper [dekape] *tr* to scour, scale

décapiter [dekapite] *tr* to behead, decapitate; top (*a tree*)

décapotable [dekapɔtabl] *adj* & *f* (aut) convertible

décapsuleur [dekapsylœr] *m* bottle opener

déca·ti -tie [dekati] *adj* haggard, worn-out, faded

décatir [dekatir] *tr* to steam (*cloth*)

décaver [dekave] *tr* (coll) to fleece

décéder [desede] §10 *intr* (*aux:* ÊTRE) to die (*said of human being*)

décèlement [desɛlmɑ̃] *m* disclosure

déceler [desle] §2 *tr* to uncover, detect; to betray (*confusion*)

décélération [deselerasjɔ̃] *f* deceleration

décembre [desɑ̃br] *m* December

décemment [desamɑ̃] *adv* decently

décennie [deseni] *f* decade

dé·cent [desɑ̃] **-cente** [sɑ̃t] *adj* decent

décentraliser [desɑ̃tralize] *tr* to decentralize

déception [desɛpsjɔ̃] *f* disappointment

décernement [desɛrnəmɑ̃] *m* awarding

décerner [desɛrne] *tr* to award (*a prize*); confer (*an honor*); issue (*a writ*)

décès [desɛ] *m* decease, demise

déce·vant [desvɑ̃] **-vante** [vɑ̃t] *adj* disappointing; deceptive

décevoir [desvwar] §59 *tr* to disappoint; deceive

déchaînement [deʃɛnmɑ̃] *m* unchaining, unleashing; outburst, wave

déchaîner [deʃɛne] *tr* to unchain, let loose ‖ *ref* to fly into a rage; break out (*said of storm*)

déchanter [deʃɑ̃te] *intr* (coll) to sing a different tune

décharge [deʃarʒ] *f* discharge; drain; rubbish heap; storeroom, shed; **à décharge** for the defense

déchargement [deʃarʒəmɑ̃] *m* unloading

décharger [deʃarʒe] §38 *tr* to discharge; unload; unburden; exculpate (*a defendant*) ‖ *ref* to vent one's anger; go off (*said of gun*); run down (*said of battery*); **se décharger de q.ch. sur qn** to shift the responsibility for s.th. on s.o.

déchargeur [deʃarʒœr] *m* porter (*e.g., in a market*); dock hand

déchar·né -née [deʃarne] *adj* emaciated, skinny, bony

décharner [deʃarne] *tr* to strip the flesh from; emaciate ‖ *ref* to waste away

déchaus·sé -sée [deʃose] *adj* barefoot

déchausser [deʃose] *tr* to take the shoes off of (*s.o.*); expose the roots of (*a tree, a tooth*) ‖ *ref* to take off one's shoes; shrink (*said of gums*)

déchéance [deʃeɑ̃s] *f* downfall; lapse, forfeiture (*of a right*); expiration, term (*of a note or loan*)

déchet [deʃɛ] *m* loss, decrease; **déchet de route** loss in transit; **déchets** waste products

décheveler [deʃəvle] §34 *tr* to dishevel, muss (*s.o.'s hair*)

déchiffonner [deʃifɔne] *tr* to iron (*wrinkled material*)

déchiffrable [deʃifrabl] *adj* legible; decipherable

déchiffrement [deʃifrəmã] *m* deciphering, decoding; sight-reading

déchiffrer [deʃifre] *tr* to decipher; sight-read (*music*)

déchif·freur [deʃifrœr] -freuse [frøz] *mf* decipherer, decoder; sight-reader

déchique·té -tée [deʃikte] *adj* jagged, torn

déchiqueter [deʃikte] §34 *tr* to cut into strips; shred; slash

déchi·rant [deʃirã] -rante [rãt] *adj* heart-rending

déchi·ré -rée [deʃire] *adj* torn; sorry

déchirer [deʃire] *tr* to tear, tear up; split (*a country; one's eardrums*); pick (*s.o.'s character*) to pieces ‖ *ref* to skin (*e.g., one's knee*)

déchirure [deʃirur] *f* tear, rent; sprain

déchoir [deʃwar] (usually used only in: *inf; pp* **déchu;** sometimes used in: *pres ind* **déchois,** etc.; *fut* **déchoirai,** etc.; *cond* **déchoirais,** etc.) *intr* (*aux:* AVOIR or ÊTRE) to fall (*from high estate*); decline, fail

dé·chu -chue [deʃy] *adj* fallen; deprived (*of rights*); expired (*insurance policy*)

décibel [desibɛl] *m* decibel

décider [deside] §97, §100 *tr* to decide, decide on; **décider qn à** + *inf* to persuade s.o. to + *inf* ‖ *intr* to decide; **décider de** to decide, determine the outcome of, e.g., **le coup a décidé de la partie** the trick decided the (outcome of the) game; **décider de** + *inf* to decide to + *inf* ‖ §96, §97 *ref* to decide, make up one's mind, resolve; **se décider à** + *inf* to decide to + *inf*

déci·mal -male [desimal] *adj* (*pl* -maux [mo]) decimal ‖ *f* decimal

décimer [desime] *tr* to decimate

déci·sif [desizif] -sive [ziv] *adj* decisive

décision [desizjɔ̃] *f* decision; decisiveness

déclama·teur [deklamatœr] -trice [tris] *adj* bombastic ‖ *mf* declaimer

déclamatoire [deklamatwar] *adj* declamatory

déclamer [deklame] *tr* to declaim ‖ *intr* to rant; **déclamer contre** to inveigh against

déclara·tif [deklaratif] -tive [tiv] *adj* declarative

déclaration [deklarasjɔ̃] *f* declaration; **déclaration de revenus** income-tax return

déclarer [deklare] §95 *tr & intr* to declare ‖ *ref* to declare oneself; arise, break out, occur

déclassement [deklasmã] *m* disarrangement; drop in social status; transfer to another class (*on ship, train, etc.*); dismantling; demoting

déclasser [deklase] *tr* to disarrange; dismantle; demote

déclenchement [deklãʃmã] *m* releasing; launching (*of an attack*)

déclencher [deklãʃe] *tr* to unlatch, disengage; release (*the shutter*); open (*fire*); launch (*an attack*)

déclencheur [deklãʃœr] *m* (mach, phot) release

déclic [deklik] *m* pawl, catch; hair trigger

déclin [deklɛ̃] *m* decline

déclinaison [deklinɛzɔ̃] *f* (astr) declination; (gram) declension

décliner [dekline] *tr & intr* to decline

déclive [dekliv] *adj* sloping ‖ *f* slope

déclivité [deklivite] *f* declivity

dé·clos [deklo] -close [kloz] *adj* in bloom

décocher [dekɔʃe] *tr* to let fly; flash (*a smile*)

décoder [dekɔde] *tr* to decode

décoiffer [dekwafe] *tr* to loosen or muss the hair of; uncap (*a bottle*) ‖ *ref* to muss one's hair; take one's hair down

décoincer [dekwɛ̃se] §51 *tr* to unwedge, loosen (*a jammed part*)

décolérer [dekɔlere] §10 *intr* to calm down

décollage [dekɔlaʒ] *m* unsticking, ungluing; takeoff (*of airplane*)

décoller [dekɔle] *tr* to unstick, detach ‖ *intr* (aer) to take off

décolletage [dekɔltaʒ] *m* low-cut neck; screw cutting; topping

décolle·té -tée [dekɔlte] *adj* décolleté ‖ *m* low-cut neckline; bare neck and shoulders

décolleter [dekɔlte] §34 *tr* to cut the neck of (*a dress*) low; bare the neck and shoulders of ‖ *ref* to wear a low-necked dress

décoloration [dekɔlɔrasjɔ̃] *f* discoloration

décolorer [dekɔlore] *tr & ref* to bleach; fade

décombres [dekɔ̃br] *mpl* debris, ruins

décommander [dekɔmãde] *tr* to cancel an order for; call off (*a dinner*); cancel the invitation to (*a guest*) ‖ *ref* to cancel a meeting

décompléter [dekɔ̃plete] §10 *tr* to break up (*a set*)

décomposer [dekɔ̃poze] *tr & ref* to decompose

décomposition [dekɔ̃pozisjɔ̃] *f* decomposition

décompresser [dekɔ̃prese] *intr* to relax

décompression [dekɔ̃presjɔ̃] *f* decompression

décomprimer [dekɔ̃prime] *tr* to decompress

décompte [dekɔ̃t] *m* itemized statement; discount (*to be deducted from total*); disappointment

décompter [dekɔ̃te] *tr* to deduct (*a sum from an account*) ‖ *intr* to strike the wrong hour

déconcerter [dekɔ̃sɛrte] *tr* to disconcert

décon·fit [dekɔ̃fi] -fite [fit] *adj* discomfited, baffled, confused

déconfiture [dekɔ̃fityr] *f* discomfiture; downfall, rout; business failure

décongeler [dekɔ̃ʒle] §2 *tr* to thaw; defrost

décongestionner [dekɔ̃ʒɛstjɔne] *tr* to relieve congestion in

déconseiller [dekɔ̃sɛje] *tr* to dissuade; **déconseiller q.ch. à qn** to advise s.o.

against s.th. ‖ *intr*—**déconseiller à qn de** + *inf* to advise s.o. against + *ger*

déconsidération [dekɔ̃siderasjɔ̃] *f* disrepute

déconsidérer [dekɔ̃sidere] §10 *tr* to bring into disrepute, discredit

déconsigner [dekɔ̃siɲe] *tr* to take (*one's baggage*) out of the checkroom; free (*soldiers*) from detention

décontenancer [dekɔ̃tnɑ̃se] §51 *tr* to discountenance, abash ‖ *ref* to lose one's self-assurance

décontrac·té -tée [dekɔ̃trakte] *adj* relaxed, at ease; indifferent

décontracter [dekɔ̃trakte] *tr* to loosen up (*one's muscles*) ‖ *intr* to stretch one's muscles; relax

déconvenue [dekɔ̃vny] *f* disappointment, mortification

décor [dekɔr] *m* décor, decoration; (theat) setting; **décor découpé** cutout; **décors** (theat) set, stage setting

décora·teur [dekɔratœr] **-trice** [tris] *mf* interior decorator; stage designer

décora·tif [dekɔratif] **-tive** [tiv] *adj* decorative, ornamental

décoration [dekɔrasjɔ̃] *f* decoration

décorum [dekɔrɔm] *m invar* decorum

découcher [dekuʃe] *intr* to sleep away from home

découdre [dekudr] §13 *tr* to unstitch, rip up; gore ‖ *intr*—**en découdre** to cross swords ‖ *ref* to come unsewn, rip at the seam

découler [dekule] *intr* to trickle; proceed, arise, be derived

découpage [dekupaʒ] *m* shooting script; **découpage des circonscriptions electorales** gerrymandering

découper [dekupe] *tr* to carve (*e.g., a turkey*); cut out (*a design*); indent (*the coast*) ‖ *ref*—**se découper sur** to stand out against (*the horizon*)

décou·plé -plée [dekuple] *adj* well-built, brawny

découpler [dekuple] *tr* to unleash

découpure [dekupyr] *f* cutting out; ornamental cutout; indentation (*in coast*)

découragement [dekuraʒmɑ̃] *m* discouragement

décourager [dekuraʒe] §38, §97, §99 *tr* to discourage ‖ *ref* to become discouraged

décours [dekur] *m* wane

décou·su -sue [dekuzy] *adj* unsewn; disjointed, unsystematic; incoherent (*words*); desultory (*remarks*) ‖ *v* see **découdre**

décou·vert [dekuvɛr] **-verte** [vɛrt] *adj* uncovered, open, exposed ‖ *m* deficit; overdraft ‖ *f* uncovering; discovery

décou·vreur [dekuvrœr] **-vreuse** [vrøz] *mf* discoverer

découvrir [dekuvrir] §65 *tr* to discover; discern (*in the distance*); pick out (*with a searchlight*); uncover ‖ *intr* to become visible (*said of rocks at low tide*) ‖ *ref* to take off one's hat; lower one's guard; clear up (*said of the sky*); say what one is thinking; come to light, be revealed

décrasser [dekrase] *tr* to clean; polish up; get the dirt out of

décré·pit [dekrepi] **-pite** [pit] *adj* decrepit

décret [dekrɛ] *m* decree; order

décrier [dekrije] *tr* to decry, disparage, run down

décrire [dekrir] §25 *tr* to describe

décrochage [dekrɔʃaʒ] *m* (aer) stall

décrocher [dekrɔʃe] *tr* to unhook, take down; (coll) to wangle; **décrocher la timbale** (coll) to hit the jackpot ‖ *intr* to withdraw, retire; (telp) to pick up the receiver ‖ *ref* to come unhooked

décrochez-moi-ça [dekrɔʃemwasa] *m invar* (coll) secondhand clothing store; (coll) hand-me-down

décroît [dekrwa] *m* last quarter (*of moon*)

décroître [dekrwatr] §17 (*pp* décru; *pres ind* décrois, etc.; *pret* décrus, etc.) *intr* to decrease; shorten (*said of days*); to fall (*said of river*)

décrotter [dekrɔte] *tr* to remove mud from; (coll) teach how to behave

décrotteur [dekrɔtœr] *m* shoeshine boy

décrottoir [dekrɔtwar] *m* doormat; scraper (*for shoes*)

décrue [dekry] *f* fall, drop, subsiding

décrypter [dekripte] *tr* to decipher

déculottage [dekylɔtaʒ] *m* undressing

déculotter [dekylɔte] *tr* to take the pants off of ‖ *ref* to take off one's pants

décuple [dekypl] *adj* & *m* tenfold

décupler [dekyple] *tr* & *intr* to increase tenfold

dédaigner [dedɛɲe] §97 *tr* to disdain; reject (*e.g., an offer*); **dédaigner de** + *inf* not to condescend to + *inf*

dédai·gneux [dedɛɲø] **-gneuse** [ɲøz] *adj* disdainful

dédain [dedɛ̃] *m* disdain

dédale [dedal] *s* maze, labyrinth

dedans [dədɑ̃] *m* inside; **en dedans** inside ‖ *adv* inside, within; **mettre dedans** (coll) to take in, to fool

dédicace [dedikas] *f* dedication

dédicacer [dedikase] §51 *tr* to dedicate, autograph

dédicatoire [dedikatwar] *adj* dedicatory

dédier [dedje] *tr* to dedicate; offer (*e.g., a collection to a museum*)

dédire [dedir] §40 *tr*—**dédire qn** to disavow s.o.'s words or actions ‖ *ref* to make a retraction, back down; **se dédire de** to go back on, fail to keep

dédit [dedi] *m* penalty (*for breaking a contract*); breach of contract

dédommagement [dedɔmaʒmɑ̃] *m* compensation, damages, indemnity

dédommager [dedɔmaʒe] §38 *tr* to compensate for a loss, indemnify

dédouaner [dedwane] *tr* to clear through customs; rehabilitate (*a politician, statesman, etc.*)

dédoublement [dedubləmɑ̃] *m* splitting; subdivision; unfolding

dédoubler [dedublə] *tr* to divide or split in two; remove the lining from; unfold; put on another section of (*a train*)

déduction [dedyksjɔ̃] *f* deduction; **déduction pour remplacement** deduction allowance (*on taxes*)

déduire [dedɥir] §19 *tr* to deduce; infer; (com) to deduct

déesse [deɛs] *f* goddess

défaillance [defajɑ̃s] *f* failure, failing; faint; lapse (*of memory*); nonappearance (*of witness*); **défaillance cardiaque** heart failure; **sans défaillance** unflinching

défail·lant [defajɑ̃] **-lante** [jɑ̃t] *adj* failing, faltering

défaillir [defajir] §69 *intr* to fail; falter, weaken, flag; faint

défaire [defɛr] §29 *tr* to undo; untie, unwrap, unpack; rearrange; let down (*one's hair*); rid; defeat, rout; wear (*s.o.*) down, tire (*s.o.*) out || *ref* to come undone; **se défaire de** to get rid of

dé·fait [defɛ] **-faite** [fɛt] *adj* undone, untied; loose; disheveled; drawn (*countenance*) || *f* defeat; disposal, turnover; (fig) loophole

défaitisme [defɛtism] *m* defeatism

défaitiste [defɛtist] *mf* defeatist

défalcation [defalkɑsjɔ̃] *f* deduction

défalquer [defalke] *tr* to deduct

défaufiler [defofile] *tr* to untack

défausser [defose] *tr* to straighten || *ref*—**se défausser (de)** to discard

défaut [defo] *m* defect, fault; lack (*of knowledge, memory, etc.*); flaw; chink (*in armor*); **à défaut de** in default of, lacking; **faire défaut à** to abandon, fail (*e.g., one's friends*); (law) to default; **mettre en défaut** to foil

défaveur [defavœr] *f* disfavor

défavorable [defavɔrabl] *adj* unfavorable

défavoriser [defavɔrize] *tr* to handicap, put at a disadvantage

défécation [defekɑsjɔ̃] *f* defecation

défec·tif [defɛktif] **-tive** [tiv] *adj* (gram) defective

défection [defɛksjɔ̃] *f* defection; **faire défection** to defect

défec·tueux [defɛktɥø] **-tueuse** [tɥøz] *adj* defective, faulty

défectuosité [defɛktɥozite] *f* imperfection

défen·deur [defɑ̃dœr] **-deresse** [drɛs] *mf* defendant

défendre [defɑ̃dr] §97, §98 *tr* to defend; protect (*e.g., against the cold*); **à son corps défendant** in self-defense; against one's will; **défendre q.ch. à qn** to forbid s.o. s.th. || *intr*—**défendre à qn de** + *inf* to forbid, s.o. to + *inf* || *ref* to defend oneself; (coll) to hold one's own; **se défendre de** to deny (*e.g., having said s.th.*); refrain from, to keep from

défen·du -due [defɑ̃dy] *adj* forbidden

défense [defɑ̃s] *f* defense; tusk; **défense passive** civil defense (*against air raids*); (public signs): **défense d'afficher** post no bills; **défense de dépasser** no passing;

défense de déposer des ordures no dumping, no littering; **défense de doubler** no passing; **défense de faire des ordures** commit no nuisance; **défense de fumer** no smoking; **défense d'entrer** private, keep out, no admittance

défenseur [defɑ̃sœr] *m* defender; lawyer for the defense; stand-by

défen·sif [defɑ̃sif] **-sive** [siv] *adj & f* defensive

déférence [deferɑ̃s] *f* deference

défé·rent [deferɑ̃] **-rente** [rɑ̃t] *adj* deferential

déférer [defere] §10 *tr* to confer, award; refer (*a case to a court*); **déférer en justice** to haul into court || *intr* to comply; **déférer à** to defer to, comply with

déferler [defɛrle] *tr* to unfurl; set (*the sails of a ship*) || *intr* to spread out (*said of a crowd*); break (*said of waves*)

défeuiller [defœje] *tr* to defoliate || *ref* to lose its leaves

défi [defi] *m* challenge, dare; **défi à l'autorité** defiance of authority; **porter un défi à** to defy; **relever un défi** to take a dare

défiance [defjɑ̃s] *f* distrust

dé·fiant [defjɑ̃] **-fiante** [fjɑ̃t] *adj* distrustful

déficeler [defisle] §34 *tr* to untie

déficience [defisjɑ̃s] *f* deficiency

défi·cient [defisjɑ̃] **-ciente** [sjɑ̃t] *adj* deficient

déficit [defisit] *m* deficit

déficitaire [defisitɛr] *adj* deficit; meager (*crop*); lean (*year*)

défier [defje] §97, §99 *tr* to challenge; defy (*death, time, etc.*); **défier qn de** to dare s.o. to || *ref*—**se défier de** to mistrust

défiger [defiʒe] §38 *tr* to liquefy

défiguration [defigyrɑsjɔ̃] *f* disfigurement; defacement

défigurer [defigyre] *tr* to disfigure; deface; distort

défilé [defile] *m* defile (*in mountains*); parade, procession, line of march; **défilé de modes** fashion parade

défilement [defilmɑ̃] *m* (mil) defilade, cover

défiler [defile] *tr* to unstring; (mil) to put under cover || *intr* to march by, parade, defile || *ref* to come unstrung; take cover; (coll) to gold-brick

défi·ni -nie [defini] *adj* definite; defined

définir [definir] *tr* to define || *ref* to be defined

définissable [definisabl] *adj* definable

défini·tif [definitif] **-tive** [tiv] *adj* definitive; standard (*edition*); **en définitive** in short, all things considered

définition [definisjɔ̃] *f* definition; **définition de fonction** job description

définitivement [definitivmɑ̃] *adv* definitively, for good, permanently

déflation [deflɑsjɔ̃] *f* deflation (*of currency*); sudden drop (*in wind*)

déflecteur [deflɛktœr] *m* vent window (*of an automobile*)

défleurir [deflœrir] *tr* to deflower, strip of flowers ‖ *intr* & *ref* to lose its flowers

déflexion [defleksjɔ̃] *f* deflection

défloraison [deflɔrezɔ̃] *f* dropping of petals

déflorer [deflɔre] *tr* to deflower

défon·cé -cée [defɔ̃se] *adj* battered, smashed, crumpled; bumpy

défoncer [defɔ̃se] §51 *tr* to batter in; stave in (*a cask*); remove the seat of (*a chair*); break up (*ground; a road*) ‖ *ref* to be broken up (*said of road*)

déformation [defɔrmɑsjɔ̃] *f* deformation, distortion; **déformation professionnelle** narrow professionalism

défor·mé -mée [defɔrme] *adj* out of shape; rough (*road*)

déformer [defɔrme] *tr* to deform, distort ‖ *ref* to become deformed

défoulement [defulmɑ̃] *m* (psychoanal) insight, recall; (coll) relief

défraî·chi -chie [defrɛʃi] *adj* dingy, faded

défraîchir [defrɛʃir] *tr* to make stale, fade

défrayer [defreje] §49 *tr* to defray the expenses of (*s.o.*); **défrayer la conversation** to be the subject of the conversation

défricher [defriʃe] *tr* to reclaim; clear up (*a puzzler*)

défricheur [defriʃœr] *m* pioneer, explorer

défriser [defrize] *tr* & *ref* to uncurl

défroncer [defrɔ̃se] §51 *tr* to remove the wrinkles from

défroque [defrɔk] *f* piece of discarded clothing

défroquer [defrɔke] *tr* to unfrock ‖ *ref* to give up the frock

dé·funt [defœ̃] **-funte** [fœ̃t] *adj* & *mf* deceased

déga·gé -gée [degaʒe] *adj* breezy, jaunty, nonchalant; free, detached

dégagement [degaʒmɑ̃] *m* disengagement; clearing, relieving of congestion; liberation (*e.g., of heat*); exit; retraction (*of promise*); redemption, taking out of hock

dégager [degaʒe] §38 *tr* to disengage; free, clear, release; draw, extract (*the moral or essential points*); give off, liberate; take back (*one's word*); redeem, take out of hock

dégaine [degɛn] *f* (coll) awkward bearing; ridiculous posture

dégainer [degɛne] *tr* to unsheathe ‖ *intr* to take up a sword

dégar·ni -nie [degarni] *adj* empty, depleted, stripped

dégarnir [degarnir] *tr* to clear (*a table*); withdraw soldiers from (*a sector*); prune ‖ *ref* to thin out

dégât [degɑ] *m* damage, havoc

dégauchir [degoʃir] *tr* to smooth out the rough edges of (*stone, wood; an inexperienced person*)

dégel [deʒɛl] *m* thaw

dégeler [deʒle] §2 *tr* to thaw, defrost; loosen up, relax ‖ *intr* to thaw out; **il dégèle** it it thawing

dégéné·ré -rée [deʒenere] *adj* & *mf* degenerate

dégénérer [deʒenere] §10 *intr* to degenerate

dégénérescence [deʒeneresɑ̃s] *f* degeneration

dégingan·dé -dée [deʒɛ̃gɑde] *adj* gangling, ungainly

dégivrage [deʒivraʒ] *m* defrosting

dégivrer [deʒivre] *tr* to defrost, deice

dégivreur [deʒivrœr] *m* defroster, deicer

déglacer [deglase] §51 *tr* to deice; remove the glaze from (*paper*)

dégommer [degɔme] *tr* to ungum; (coll) to fire (s.o.)

dégon·flé -flée [degɔ̃fle] *adj* flat (*tire*)

dégonflement [degɔ̃fləmɑ̃] *m* deflation

dégonfler [degɔ̃fle] *tr* to deflate ‖ *ref* to go flat; go down, subside (*said of swelling*); (slang) to lose one's nerve

dégorger [degɔrʒe] §38 *tr* to disgorge; unstop, open (*a pipe*); scour (*e.g., wool*) ‖ *intr* to discharge, overflow

dégour·di -die [degurdi] *adj* limbered up, lively, sharp, adroit ‖ *mf* smart aleck

dégourdir [degurdir] *tr* to remove stiffness or numbness from (*e.g., legs*); stretch (*one's limbs*); take the chill off; teach (*s.o.*) the ropes, polish (*s.o.*) ‖ *ref* to limber up

dégoût [degu] *m* distaste, dislike

dégoû·tant -tante [tɑ̃t] *adj* disgusting, distasteful

dégoû·té -tée [degute] §93 *adj* fastidious, hard to please ‖ *mf* finicky person

dégoûter [degute] §97, §99 to disgust; **dégoûter qn de** to make s.o. dislike ‖ *ref* to become fed up

dégoutter [degute] *intr* to drip, trickle

dégradation [degradɑsjɔ̃] *f* degradation; defacement; shading off, graduation; worsening (*of a situation*); (mil) demotion; **dégradation civique** loss of civil rights

dégrader [degrade] *tr* to degrade, bring down; deface; shade off, graduate; (mil) to demote, break ‖ *ref* to debase oneself; become dilapidated

dégrafer [degrafe] *tr* to unhook, unclasp

dégraissage [degresaʒ] *m* dry cleaning

dégraisser [degrese] *tr* to remove grease from; dry-clean

dégrais·seur [degresœr] **-seuse** [søz] *mf* dry cleaner, cleaner and dyer

degré [dəgre] *m* degree; step (*of stairs*); **monter d'un degré** to take a step up (*on the ladder of success*)

dégringolade [degrɛ̃gɔlad] *f* (coll) tumble; (coll) comedown, collapse, downfall

dégringoler [degrɛ̃gɔle] *tr* to bring down (*a government*) ‖ *intr* (coll) to tumble, tumble down

dégriser [degrize] *tr* & *ref* to sober up

dégrossir [degrosir] *tr* to rough-hew; make the preliminary sketches of; refine, polish (*a hick*)

déguenil·lé -lée [degənije] *adj* ragged, in tatters ‖ *mf* ragamuffin

déguerpir [degerpir] *intr* (coll) to clear out, beat it; **fair déguerpir** to evict

déguisement [degizmɑ̃] *m* disguise

déguiser [degize] *tr* to disguise

dégusta·teur [degystatœr] **-trice** [tris] *mf* winetaster

dégustation [degystɑsjɔ̃] *f* tasting, art of tasting; consumption (*of beverages*)

déguster [degyste] *tr* to taste discriminatingly; sip, drink; consume

déhancher [deɑ̃ʃe] *tr* to dislocate the hip of ‖ *intr* to swing one's hips

déharnacher [dearnaʃe] *tr* to unsaddle, unharness ‖ *ref* (coll) to throw off one's heavy clothing

dehors [dɔɔr] *m* outside; **dehors** *mpl* outward appearance; **du dehors** from without, foreign, external; **en dehors** outside; **en dehors de** outside of; beyond ‖ *adv* outside, out; out-of-doors

déification [deifikɑsjɔ̃] *f* deification

déifier [deifje] *tr* to deify

déiste [deist] *dj & mf* deist

déité [deite] *f* deity

déjà [deʒa] *adv* already; yet; before

déjanter [deʒɑ̃te] *tr* to take (*a tire*) off the rim ‖ *ref* to come off

déjection [deʒɛksjɔ̃] *f* excretion; volcanic debris

déjeter [deʒte] §34 *tr & ref* to warp, spring

déjeuner [deʒœne] *m* lunch; breakfast; breakfast set; **déjeuner d'affaires, déjeuner de travail** business lunch; **petit déjeuner** breakfast ‖ *intr* to have lunch; have breakfast

déjouer [deʒwe] *tr* to foil, thwart

déjucher [deʒyʃe] *tr* to unroost ‖ *intr* to come off the roost (*said of fowl*)

déjuger [deʒyʒe] §38 *ref* to change one's mind

delà [dəla] *adv*—**au delà de** beyond; **par delà** beyond

délabrement [delabrəmɑ̃] *m* decay, dilapidation; impairment (*of health*)

délabrer [delabre] *tr* to ruin, wreck ‖ *ref* to become dilapidated

délacer [delase] §51 *tr* to unlace

délai [delɛ] *m* term, duration, period (*of time*); postponement, extension; **à bref délai** at short notice; **dans le plus bref délai** in the shortest possible time; **dans un délai de** within; **dans un délai record** in record time; **dernier délai** deadline; **sans délai** without delay

délais·sé -sée [delɛse] *adj* forsaken, forlorn, neglected

délaissement [delɛsmɑ̃] *m* abandonment

délaisser [delɛse] *tr* to abandon, desert; relinquish (*a right*)

délassement [delɑsmɑ̃] *m* relaxation

délasser [delɑse] *tr* to rest, refresh, relax ‖ *ref* to rest up

déla·teur [delatœr] **-trice** [tris] *mf* informer

délation [delɑsjɔ̃] *f* paid informing

déla·vé -vée [delave] *adj* washed-out, weak

délayer [delɛje] §49 *tr* to add water to, dilute; **délayer un discours** to stretch out a speech

deleatur [deleatyr] *m* dele

délébile [delebil] *adj* erasable

délectable [delɛktabl] *adj* delectable

délectation [delɛktɑsjɔ̃] *f* pleasure

délecter [delɛkte] *ref*—**se délecter à** to find pleasure in

délégation [delegɑsjɔ̃] *f* delegation

délé·gué -guée [delege] *adj* delegated ‖ *mf* delegate, spokesman

déléguer [delege] §10 *tr* to delegate

délester [delɛste] *tr* to unballast; unburden, relieve

délétère [deletɛr] *adj* deleterious

délibération [deliberɑsjɔ̃] *f* deliberation

délibé·ré -rée [delibere] *adj* deliberate, firm, decided

délibérer [delibere] §10, §97 *tr & intr* to deliberate

déli·cat [delika] **-cate** [kat] *adj* delicate; fine, sensitive (*ear, mind, taste*); touchy; tactful; scrupulous, honest

délicatesse [delikatɛs] *f* delicacy; refinement, fineness; fastidiousness; fragility, weakness

délice [delis] *m* great pleasure ‖ **délices** *f pl* delights, pleasures

déli·cieux [delisjø] **-cieuse** [sjøz] *adj* delicious; delightful, charming

dé·lié -liée [delje] *adj* slender (*figure*); nimble (*mind*); fine (*handwriting*); glib (*tongue*) ‖ *m* upstroke, thin stroke

délier [delje] *tr* to untie, loosen, release ‖ *ref* to come loose

délinéament [delineamɑ̃] *m* delineation

délinéer [delinee] *tr* to delineate

délinquance [delɛ̃kɑ̃s] *f* delinquency; **délinquance juvénile** juvenile delinquency

délin·quant [delɛ̃kɑ̃] **-quante** [kɑ̃t] *adj & mf* delinquent; **délinquant primaire** first offender

déli·rant [delirɑ̃] **-rante** [rɑ̃t] *adj* delirious, raving

délire [delir] *m* delirium; **en délire** delirious, in a frenzy

délirer [delire] *intr* to be delirious, rave

délit [deli] *m* offense, wrong, crime; **en flagrant délit** in the act

délivrance [delivrɑ̃s] *f* delivrance; delivery; rescue

délivre [delivr] *m* afterbirth, placenta

délivrer [delivre] *tr* to deliver; rescue

déloger [delɔʒe] §38 *tr* to dislodge; (coll) to oust, evict ‖ *intr* to move out (*of a house*)

déloyal déloyale [delwajal] *adj* (*pl* **déloyaux** [delwajo]) disloyal; unfair, dishonest

déloyauté [delwajote] *f* disloyalty; disloyal act; dishonesty

delta [dɛlta] *m* delta

deltaplane [dɛltaplan] *m* hang glider

déluge [delyʒ] *m* deluge, flood

délu·ré -rée [delyre] *adj* smart, clever; smart-alecky, forward

délurer [delyre] *tr & ref* to wise up

délustrer [delystre] *tr* to take the gloss off of

démagnétiser [demaɲetize] *tr* to demagnetize

démagogie [demagɔʒi] *f* demagogy

démagogique [demagɔʒik] *adj* demagogic

démagogue [demagɔg] *adj* demagogic ‖ *mf* demagogue

démaigrir [demɛgrir] *tr* to thin down

démailler [demɑje] *tr* to unshackle (*a chain*); unravel (*e.g., a knitted sweater*); make a run in (*a stocking*) ‖ *ref* to run (*said of stocking*)

démailloter [demajɔte] *tr* to take the diaper off of

demain [dəmɛ̃] *adv* & *m* tomorrow; **à demain** until tomorrow; so long; **de demain en huit** a week from tomorrow; **de demain en quinze** two weeks from tomorrow; **demain matin** tomorrow morning

démancher [demɑ̃ʃe] *tr* to remove the handle of; (coll) to dislocate

demande [dəmɑ̃d] *f* request; application (*for a position*); inquiry; demand (*by buyers for goods*)

demander [dəmɑ̃de] §96, §97, §98 *tr* to ask (*a favor; one's way*); ask for (*a package; a porter*); require, need (*attention*); **demander q.ch. à qn** to ask s.o. for s.th. ‖ *intr*—**demander á** or **de** + *inf* to ask permission to + *inf*; to insist upon + *ger*; **demander après** to ask about, ask for (*s.o.*); **demander à qn de** + *inf* to ask s.o. to + *inf*; **je ne demande pas mieux** I wish I could ‖ *ref* to be needed; wonder

deman·deur [dəmɑ̃dœr] **-deuse** [døz] *mf* asker; buyer ‖ **-deur** [dœr] **-deresse** [drɛs] *mf* plaintiff

démangeaison [demɑ̃ʒezɔ̃] *f* itch

démanger [demɑ̃ʒe] §38 *tr* & *intr* to itch ‖ *intr*—**démanger à** to itch, e.g., **l'épaule lui démange** his shoulder itches, **la langue lui démange** he is itching to speak

démanteler [demɑ̃tle] §2 *tr* to dismantle (*a fort or town*); uncover (*a spy ring*)

démaquillage [demakijaʒ] *m* removal of paint or make-up

démaquillant [demakijɑ̃] *m* cleansing cream, make-up remover

démaquiller [demakije] *tr* & *ref* to take the paint or make-up off

démarcation [demarkasjɔ̃] *f* demarcation

démarchage [demarʃaʒ] *m* door-to-door selling, house-to-house selling

démarche [demarʃ] *f* gait, step, bearing; method; step, move, action

démarier [demarje] *tr* to thin out (*plants*)

démarque [demark] *f* (com) markdown

démarquer [demarke] *tr* to remove the identification marks from; plagiarize; mark down

démarrage [demaraʒ] *m* start

démarrer [demare] *tr* to unmoor ‖ *intr* to cast off (*said of ship*); start (*said of train or car*); spurt (*said of racing contestant; said of economy*); **démarrer trop tôt** to jump the gun; **faire démarrer** to start (*a car*); **ne démarrez pas!** don't stir!

démarreur [demarœr] *m* starter (*of car*)

démasquer [demaske] *tr* & *ref* to unmask

démâter [demɑte] *tr* to dismast ‖ *intr* to lose her masts (*said of ship*)

démêlé [demɛle] *m* quarrel, dispute; **avoir des démêlés avec** to be at odds with, run afoul of

démêler [demɛle] *tr* to disentangle, unravel; bring to light, uncover (*a plot*); make out, discern

démembrement [demɑ̃brəmɑ̃] *m* dismemberment

déménagement [demenaʒmɑ̃] *m* moving

déménager [demenaʒe] §38 *tr* to move (*household effects*) to another residence; move the furniture from (*a house*) ‖ *intr* to move, change one's residence; (coll) to become childish; **tu déménages!** (coll) you're out of your mind!

déménageur [demenaʒœr] *m* mover

démence [demɑ̃s] *f* madness, insanity; **en démence** demented

démener [demne] §2 *ref* to struggle, be agitated; take great pains

dé·ment [demɑ̃] **-mente** [mɑ̃t] *adj* & *mf* lunatic

démenti [demɑ̃ti] *m* contradiction, denial; proof to the contrary; (coll) shame (*on account of a failure*)

démentir [demɑ̃tir] §41 *tr* to contradict, deny; give the lie to, belie ‖ *intr* to go back on one's word; be inconsistent

démerdard [demerdar] *m* (slang) shark, sharp customer; **petit démerdard** streetwise kid

démériter [demerite] *intr* to lose esteem, become unworthy

démesure [demǝzyr] *f* lack of moderation, excess

démesu·ré -rée [demǝzyre] *adj* measureless, immense; immoderate, excessive

démettre [demetr] §42 *tr* to dismiss (*from a job or position*); dislocate (*an arm*) ‖ *ref* to resign, retire

démeubler [demœble] *tr* to remove the furniture from

demeurant [dǝmœrɑ̃]—**au demeurant** all things considered, after all

demeure [dǝmœr] *f* home, abode, dwelling; **à demeure** permanently; **dernière demeure** final resting place; **en demeure** in arrears; **mettre en demeure de** to oblige s.o. to; **sans plus longue demeure** without further delay

demeurer [dǝmœre] §96 *intr* to live, dwell ‖ *intr* (*aux:* ÊTRE) to stay, remain; **en demeurer** to leave off; **en demeurer là** to stop, rest there; leave it at that

demi [dǝmi] *m* half; (sports) center; (sports) halfback; **à demi** half; **et demi** and a half, e.g., **un centimètre et demi** a centimeter and a half; (after **midi** or **minuit**) half past, e.g., **midi et demi** half past twelve

demi-bas [dǝmiba] *m* half hose

demi-botte [dǝmibɔt] *f* (*pl* **-bottes**) half boot

demi-cercle [dǝmisɛrkl] *m* (*pl* **-cercles**) semicircle

demi-clef [dǝmikle] *f* (*pl* **-clefs**) half hitch; **demi-clef à capeler** clove hitch; **deux demi-clefs** two half hitches

demi-congé [dəmikɔ̃ʒe] *m* (*pl* -congés) half-holiday

demi-deuil [dəmidœj] *m* (*pl* -deuils) half mourning

demi-dieu [dəmidjø] *m* (*pl* -dieux) demigod

demi-douzaine [dəmiduzɛn] *f* (*pl* -douzaines) half-dozen

demie [dəmi] *f* half hour; **et demie** half past, e.g., **deux heures et demie** half past two

demi-finale [dəmifinal] *f* (*pl* -finales) semifinal

demi-frère [dəmifrɛr] *m* (*pl* -frères) half brother; stepbrother

demi-heure [dəmiœr] *f* (*pl* -heures) half-hour; **toutes les demi-heures à la demi-heure juste** every half-hour on the half-hour

demi-interligne [dəmiɛ̃terliɲ] *m*—**demi-interligne de base** half-line space (*on typewriter*)

demi-jour [dəmiʒur] *m invar* twilight, half-light

demi-journée [dəmiʒurne] *f* (*pl* -journées) half-day; **à demi-journée** half-time

démilitariser [demilitarize] *tr* to demilitarize

demi-longueur [dəmilɔ̃gœr] *f* half-length

demi-lune [dəmilyn] *f* (*pl* -lunes) half-moon

demi-mondaine [dəmimɔ̃dɛn] *f* (*pl* -mondaines) demimondaine

demi-monde [dəmimɔ̃d] *m* demimonde

demi-mot [dəmimo] *m* (*pl* -mots) understatement, euphemism; **comprendre à demi-mot** to get the drift of; to take the hint

déminer [demine] *tr* to clear of mines

demi-pause [dəmipoz] *f* (*pl* -pauses) (mus) half rest

demi-pension [dəmipɑ̃sjɔ̃] *f* (*pl* -pensions) breakfast and one meal

demi-place [dəmiplas] *f* (*pl* -places) half fare; half-price seat

demi-reliure [dəmirəljyr] *f* (*pl* -reliures) quarter binding; **demi-reliure à petits coins** half binding

demi-saison [dəmisɛzɔ̃] *f* in-between season; **de demi-saison** spring-and-fall (*coat*)

demi-sang [dəmisɑ̃] *m invar* half-bred horse

demi-sœur [dəmisœr] *f* (*pl* -sœurs) half sister; stepsister

demi-solde [dəmisɔld] *m invar* pensioned officer ‖ *f* (*pl* -soldes) army pension, half pay

demi-soupir [dəmisupir] *m* (*pl* -soupirs) (mus) eighth rest

démission [demisjɔ̃] *f* resignation

démissionnaire [demisjɔnɛr] *adj* outgoing ‖ *mf* former incumbent

démissionner [demisjɔne] *tr* (coll) to fire ‖ *intr* to resign

demi-tasse [dəmitɑs] *f* (*pl* -tasses) half-cup; small cup, demitasse

demi-teinte [dəmitɛ̃t] *f* (*pl* -teintes) halftone

demi-ton [dəmitɔ̃] *m* (*pl* -tons) (mus) half tone

demi-tour [dəmitur] *m* (*pl* -tours) about-face; half turn; **demi-tour, (à) droite!** about face!, to the rear!; **donner un demi-tour** to make a half turn; **faire demi-tour** to do an about-face; to turn back

demi-volte [dəmivɔlt] *f* U-turn

démobiliser [demɔbilize] *tr* to demobilize

démocrate [demɔkrat] *mf* democrat

démocratie [demɔkrasi] *f* democracy

démocratique [demɔkratik] *adj* democratic

démo·dé -dée [demɔde] *adj* old-fashioned, out-of-date, outmoded

démoder [demɔde] *ref* to be outmoded

demoiselle [dəmwazɛl] *f* single woman, young woman, young lady, miss; dragonfly; (slang) girl; **demoiselle de magasin** saleswoman, female salesperson; **demoiselle d'honneur** maid of honor, bridesmaid; lady-in-waiting

démolir [demɔlir] *tr* to demolish; overturn (*a cabinet or government*)

démolition [demɔlisjɔ̃] *f* demolition; **démolitions** scrap, rubble

démon [demɔ̃] *m* demon

démoniaque [demɔnjak] *adj* demonic, demoniac(al) ‖ *mf* demoniac

démonstra·teur [demɔ̃stratœr] **-trice** [tris] *mf* demonstrator

démonstra·tif [demɔ̃stratif] **-tive** [tiv] *adj* & *m* demonstrative

démontable [demɔ̃tabl] *adj* collapsible, detachable; knockdown

démonte-pneu [demɔ̃tpnø] *m* (*pl* -pneus) tire iron

démonter [demɔ̃te] *tr* to dismount; dismantle ‖ *ref* to come apart; go to pieces (*while taking an exam*)

démontrable [demɔ̃trabl] *adj* demonstrable

démontrer [demɔ̃tre] *tr* to demonstrate

démoraliser [demɔralize] *tr* to demoralize

démouler [demule] *tr* to remove from a mold

démoustication [demustikasjɔ̃] *f* mosquito control

dému·ni -nie [demyni] *adj* out of money; **démuni de** out of; devoid of

démunir [demynir] *tr* to strip, deprive; deplete (*a garrison*) ‖ *ref* to deprive oneself

démystifier [demistifje] *tr* to debunk

dénationaliser [denasjɔnalize] *tr* to denationalize

dénaturaliser [denatyralize] *tr* to denaturalize

dénatu·ré -rée [denatyre] *adj* denatured; unnatural, perverse

dénaturer [denatyre] *tr* to denature; pervert; distort

dénébulation [denebylasjɔ̃] *f* defogging

dénégation [denegasjɔ̃] *f* denial

déneigement [denɛʒmɑ̃] *m* snow removal

déni [deni] *m* refusal; (law) denial

dénicher [deniʃe] *tr* to dislodge; take out of the nest; make (*s.o.*) move; search out ‖ *intr* to leave the nest

déni·cheur [deniʃœr] **-cheuse** [ʃøz] *mf* hunter (*of rare books, antiques, etc.*); **dénicheur de vedettes** talent scout
denier [dənje] *m* (fig) penny, farthing; **denier à Dieu** gratuity; **deniers** money, funds; **de ses deniers** with his own money
dénier [denje] *tr* to deny, refuse
dénigrer [denigre] *tr* to disparage
déniveler [denivle] §34 *tr* to make uneven, change the level of
dénivellation [denivɛllɑsjɔ̃] *f* or **dénivellement** [denivɛlmɑ̃] *m* unevenness; depression, settling
dénombrement [denɔ̃brəmɑ̃] *m* census, enumeration
dénombrer [denɔ̃bre] *tr* to take a census of, enumerate
dénomination [denɔminɑsjɔ̃] *f* denomination, appellation, designation
dénommer [denɔme] *tr* to denominate, name
dénoncer [denɔ̃se] §51 *tr* to renounce; indicate, reveal ‖ *ref* to give oneself up
dénonciation [denɔ̃sjɑsjɔ̃] *f* denunciation; declaration
dénoter [denɔte] *tr* to denote
dénouement [denumɑ̃] *m* outcome, denouement; untying
dénouer [denwe] *tr* to untie; unravel
dénoyer [denwaje] §47 *tr* to pump out
denrée [dɑ̃re] *f* commodity; **denrées** provisions, products
dense [dɑ̃s] *adj* dense
densité [dɑ̃site] *f* density
dent [dɑ̃] *f* tooth; cog; scallop (*of an edge*); **dent d'éléphant** tusk; **dents de lait** baby teeth; **dents de sagesse** wisdom teeth; **sur les dents** on one's toes
dentaire [dɑ̃tɛr] *adj* dental
den·tal -tale [dɑ̃tal] *adj & f* (*pl* **-taux** [to] **-tales**) dental
dent-de-chien [dɑ̃dəʃjɛ̃] *f* (*pl* **dents-de-chien**) dogtooth violet
dent-de-lion [dɑ̃dəljɔ̃] *f* (*pl* **dents-de-lion**) dandelion
denteler [dɑ̃tle] §34 *tr* to notch, indent; perforate (*stamps*)
dentelle [dɑ̃tɛl] *f* lace; lacework
dentelure [dɑ̃tlyr] *f* notching; serration; scalloping; (phila) perforation
denter [dɑ̃te] *tr* to furnish with cogs or teeth
dentier [dɑ̃tje] *m* false teeth, denture
dentifrice [dɑ̃tifris] *m* dentifrice
dentiste [dɑ̃tist] *mf* dentist
denture [dɑ̃tyr] *f* denture; **denture artificielle** false teeth
dénuder [denyde] *tr* to strip, denude
dé·nué -nué [denɥe] §93 *adj* stripped; **dénué de** devoid of, lacking in; **dénué de tout fondement** completely unfounded
dénuement [denymɑ̃] *m* destitution
dénuer [denɥe] *tr* to deprive, strip
déodorant [deɔdɔrɑ̃] *m* deodorant
déodoriser [deɔdɔrize] *tr* to deodorize
déontologie [deɔ̃tɔlɔʒi] *f* study of ethics; **déontologie médicale** (med) code of medical ethics

dépannage [depanaʒ] *m* emergency service, repairs
dépanner [depane] *tr* to give emergency service to; (coll) to get (*s.o.*) out of a scrape
dépan·neur [depanœr] **-neuse** [nøz] *adj* repairing ‖ *m* serviceman, repairman ‖ *f* tow truck, wrecker
dépaqueter [depakte] §34 *tr* to unpack, unwrap
dépareil·lé -lée [depareje] *adj* incomplete, broken (*set*); odd (*sock*)
dépareiller [depareje] *tr* to break (*a set*)
déparer [depare] *tr* to mar, spoil the beauty of; strip of ornaments
déparier [deparje] *tr* to break, split up the pair of
départ [depar] *m* departure; beginning; division; sorting out; **départ usine** F.O.B.; **faux départ** false start
département [departəmɑ̃] *m* department, section; (govt) department
départir [departir] §64 (or sometimes like **finir**) *tr* to divide up, distribute ‖ *ref—se* **départir de** to give up; depart from
dépassement [depasmɑ̃] *m* passing
dépasser [depase] *tr* to pass, overtake; go beyond; overshoot (*the mark*); exceed; extend beyond; be longer than; (coll) to surprise ‖ *intr* to pass; stick out, overlap, show
dépayser [depeize] *tr* to take out of one's familiar surroundings; bewilder ‖ *ref* to leave one's country
dépecer [depəse] §20 *tr* to carve, cut up
dépêche [depɛʃ] *f* dispatch; telegram
dépêcher [depɛʃe] *tr* to dispatch ‖ §97 *ref* to hurry
dépeigner [depeɲe] *tr* to tousle, muss up (*the hair*)
dépeindre [depɛ̃dr] §50 *tr* to depict
dépendance [depɑ̃dɑ̃s] *f* dependence; **dépendances** outbuildings, annex; dependencies, possessions
dépen·dant [depɑ̃dɑ̃] **-dante** [dɑ̃t] *adj* dependent
dépendre [depɑ̃dr] *tr* to take down ‖ *intr* to depend; **dépendre de** to depend on; belong to; **il dépend de vous de** it is for you to
dépens [depɑ̃] *mpl* expenses, costs; **aux dépens de** at the expense of
dépense [depɑ̃s] *f* expense; pantry; dispensary (*of hospital*); flow (*of water*); consumption (*of fuel*)
dépenser [depɑ̃se] §96 *tr* to spend, expend ‖ *ref* to exert oneself, spend one's energy
dépen·sier [depɑ̃sje] **-sière** [sjɛr] *adj & mf* spendthrift
déperdition [depɛrdisjɔ̃] *f* loss; **déperdition de chaleur due au vent** wind-chill factor
dépérir [deperir] *intr* to waste away, decline
dépêtrer [depɛtre] *tr* to get (*s.o.*) out of a jam
dépeupler [depœple] *tr* to depopulate; unstock (*a pond*)

dépha·sé -sée [defaze] *adj* out of phase; out of step, out of touch

dépiauter [depjote] *tr* to skin

dépiécer [depjese] §58 *tr* to dismember

dépiler [depile] *tr* to remove the hair from

dépistage [depistaʒ] *m* tracking down; (med) screening

dépister [depiste] *tr* to track down

dépit [depi] *m* spite, resentment; **en dépit de** in spite of

dépiter [depite] *tr* to spite, vex ‖ *ref* to take offense

dépla·cé -cée [deplase] *adj* displaced (*person*); misplaced, out of place

déplacement [deplasmɑ̃] *m* displacement; movement; travel; transfer (*of an official*); shift (*in votes*); change (*in schedule*); (naut) displacement

déplacer [deplase] §51 *tr* to displace; move; **déplacer la question** to stray from the subject ‖ *ref* to move

déplaire [deplɛr] §52 *intr* to displease, e.g., **la réplique déplaît à la jeune fille** the reply displeases the young woman; to dislike, e.g., **le lait lui déplaît** he dislikes milk; **ne vous en déplaise** if you have no objection, by your leave ‖ *ref* (*pp* **déplu** *invar*) to be displeased, e.g., **ils se sont déplu** they were displeased; **se déplaire à** not to like it in, e.g., **je me déplais à la campagne** I don't like it in the country

déplai·sant -sante [deplɛzɑ̃] -sante [zɑ̃t] *adj* unpleasant, disagreeable

déplaisir [deplɛzir] *m* displeasure

déplanter [deplɑ̃te] *tr* to dig up for transplanting

déplantoir [deplɑ̃twar] *m* garden trowel

dépliant [deplijɑ̃] *m* folder, brochure

déplier [deplije] *tr* & *ref* to unfold

déplisser [deplise] *tr* to unpleat

déploiement [deplwamɑ̃] *m* unfolding, unfurling; display, array; (mil) deployment

déplorable [deplɔrabl] *adj* deplorable

déplorer [deplɔre] *tr* to deplore; grieve over

déployer [deplwaje] §47 *tr* to unfold, unfurl; display; (mil) to deploy ‖ *ref* (mil) to deploy

dé·plu -plue [deply] *v* see **déplaire**

déplumer [deplyme] *tr* to pluck (*a chicken*) ‖ *ref* (coll) to lose one's hair

dépoitrail·le -lée [depwatraje] *adj* with breast indecently exposed

dépolariser [depɔlarize] *tr* to depolarize

dépo·li -lie [depɔli] *adj* ground (*glass*)

dépolir [depɔlir] *tr* to remove the polish from; frost (*glass*)

déport [depɔr] *m* disqualifying of oneself; (com) commission; **sans déport** without delay

déportation [depɔrtasjɔ̃] *f* deportation; internment in a concentration camp

dépor·té -tée [depɔrte] *mf* deported criminal, convict; prisoner in a concentration camp

déportement [depɔrtəmɑ̃] *m* swerve; **déportements** misconduct, immoral conduct, bad habits

déporter [depɔrte] *tr* to deport; send to a concentration camp; make (*an automobile*) swerve; deflect (*an airplane*) from its course ‖ *intr* to swerve

dépo·sant [depozɑ̃] -sante [zɑ̃t] *adj* testifying; depositing ‖ *mf* deponent, witness, depositor

dépose [depoz] *f* removal

déposer [depoze] §95 *tr* to deposit; depose; drop, leave off; register (*a trademark*); lodge (*a complaint*); file (*a petition*) ‖ *intr* & *ref* to depose; settle, form a deposit

dépositaire [depozitɛr] *mf* trustee, holder; dealer

déposséder [depɔsede] §10 *tr* to dispossess

dépôt [depo] *m* deposit; depository, depot; warehouse; delivery, handing in; **dépôt d'autobus** carbarn; **dépôt de locomotives** roundhouse; **dépôt de mendicité** poorhouse; **dépôt d'épargne** savings account; **dépôt des bagages** baggage room; **dépôt d'essence** filling station; **dépôt de vivres** commissary; **dépôt d'ordures** dump

dépotoir [depɔtwar] *m* landfill, dump; garbage can; storeroom

dépouille [depuj] *f* castoff skin; hide (*taken from animal*); **dépouille mortelle** mortal remains; **dépouilles** spoils (*of war*)

dépouillement [depujmɑ̃] *m* gathering, selection, sifting; despoilment; counting (*of votes*); **dépouillement volontaire** relinquishing

dépouiller [depuje] *tr* to skin; strip; gather, select, sift; count (*votes*) ‖ *ref* to shed one's skin (*said of insects and reptiles*); strip oneself, divest oneself

dépour·vu -vue [depurvy] *adj* destitute; **au dépourvu** unaware; **dépourvu de** devoid of, lacking in

dépoussiérer [depusjere] §10 *tr* to vacuum

dépravation [depravasjɔ̃] *f* depravity

dépraver [deprave] *tr* to deprave

déprécation [deprekasjɔ̃] *f* supplication

dépréciation [depresjasjɔ̃] *f* depreciation

déprécier [depresje] *tr* & *ref* to depreciate

déprédation [depredasjɔ̃] *f* depredation; embezzlement, misappropriation

déprendre [deprɑ̃dr] §56 *ref* to detach oneself; come loose; melt

dépres·sif -sive [depresif] -sive [siv] *adj* depressive

dépression [depresjɔ̃] *f* depression

déprimer [deprime] *tr* to depress, lower ‖ *ref* to be depressed

dépriser [deprize] *tr* to undervalue

déprogrammer [deprɔgrame] *tr* to deprogram

depuis [dəpɥi] *adv* since; **depuis que** since ‖ *prep* since, for, e.g., **je suis à Paris depuis trois jours** I have been in Paris for three days; **depuis . . . jusqu'à** from . . . to

dépurer [depyre] *tr* to purify

députation [depytasjɔ̃] *f* deputation

député [depyte] *m* deputy

députer [depyte] *tr* to deputize

der [dɛr] *f*—**la der des der** (coll) the war to end all wars

déraci·né -née [derasine] *adj* uprooted ‖ *mf* uprooted person, wanderer

déraciner [derasine] *tr* to uproot, root out; eradicate

déraillement [derajmɑ̃] *m* derailment

dérailler [deraje] *intr* to jump the track; (coll) to get off the track

déraison [derɛzɔ̃] *f* unreasonableness, irrationality

déraisonnable [derɛzɔnabl] *adj* unreasonable

déraisonner [derɛzɔne] *intr* to talk nonsense

dérangement [derɑ̃ʒmɑ̃] *m* derangement; breakdown; disturbance, bother; **en dérangement** out of order

déranger [derɑ̃ʒe] §38 *tr* to derange, put out of order; disturb, trouble ‖ *ref* to move, change jobs; become disordered, upset; **ne vous dérangez pas!** don't get up!; don't bother!

déraper [derape] *intr* to skid, sideslip; weigh anchor

dératé [derate] *m*—**courir comme un dératé** to run like a jack rabbit

dératiser [deratize] *tr* to derat

derby [dɛrbi] *m* derby (*race*)

derechef [dərəʃɛf] *adv* (lit) once again

déré·glé -glée [deregle] *adj* out of order, irregular (*pulse*); disorderly, excessive

dérégler [deregle] §10 *tr* to put out of order, upset ‖ *ref* to get out of order; run wild

déridage [deridaʒ] *m* face lift

dérider [deride] *tr* to smooth, unwrinkle; cheer up ‖ *ref* to cheer up

dérision [derizjɔ̃] *f* derision

dérisoire [derizwar] *adj* derisive

dériva·tif [derivatif] **-tive** [tiv] *adj* derivative ‖ *m* diversion, distraction

dérivation [derivasjɔ̃] *f* derivation; drift; by-pass; diversion (*of river, stream, etc.*); **en dérivation** shunted (*circuit*)

dérive [deriv] *f* drift; (aer) fin; (naut) centerboard; **à la dérive** adrift

déri·vé -vée [derive] *adj* drifting; shunted (*current*) ‖ *m* derivative

dériver [derive] *tr* to derive; divert (*e.g., a river*); unrivet ‖ *intr* to derive; be derived; result; drift

dermatologie [dɛrmatɔlɔʒi] *f* dermatology

der·nier [dɛrnje] **-nière** [njɛr] §92 *adj* last; latest; latter; final; last (*just elapsed*), e.g., **la semaine dernière** last week ‖ (when standing before noun) *adj* last (*in a series*), e.g., **la dernière semaine de la guerre** the last week of the war

dernièrement [dɛrnjɛrmɑ̃] *adv* lately

dernier-né [dɛrnjene] **dernière-née** [dɛrnjɛrne] *mf* (*pl* **-nés -nées**) last-born child

dérobade [derɔbad] *f* side-stepping; cop-out; (equit) refusal

déro·bé -bée [derɔbe] *adj* secret; **à la dérobée** stealthily, on the sly

dérober [derɔbe] *tr* to steal; hide; **dérober à** to steal from; rescue from (*e.g., death*) ‖ *ref* to steal away, disappear; hide; shy away, balk; shirk; give way (*said of knees or one's footing*); **se dérober à** to slip away from, escape from

dérogation [derɔgɑsjɔ̃] *f*—**dérogation à** departure from (*custom*); waiving of (*principle*); deviation from (*instructions*); release, exemption from; **par dérogation à** notwithstanding

déroger [derɔʒe] §38 *intr*—**déroger à** to depart from (*custom*); waive (*a principle*); derogate from (*dignity; one's rank*)

dérouiller [deruje] *tr* to remove the rust from; polish (*s.o.*); (coll) to limber up; (coll) to brush up on ‖ *ref* to lose its rust; brush up; limber up

dérouler [derule] *tr* & *ref* to unroll, unfold

dérou·tant [derutɑ̃] **-tante** [tɑ̃t] *adj* baffling, misleading

déroute [derut] *f* rout, downfall

dérouter [derute] *tr* to steer off the course; reroute; disconcert, baffle ‖ *ref* to go astray; become confused

derrick [dɛrik] *m* oil derrick

derrière [dɛrjɛr] *m* rear, backside ‖ *adv* & *prep* behind

derviche [dɛrviʃ] *m* dervish

des [de] §77

dès [dɛ] *prep* by (*a certain time*); from (*a certain place*); as early as, as far back as; from, beginning with; **dès lors** from that time, ever since; **dès lors que** since, inasmuch as; **dès que** as soon as

désabonner [dezabɔne] *tr* to cancel the subscription of ‖ *ref* to cancel one's subscription

désabu·sé -sée [dezabyze] *adj* disillusioned

désabuser [dezabyze] *tr* to disabuse, disillusion ‖ *ref* to have one's eyes opened

désaccord [dezakɔr] *m* disagreement, discord

désaccorder [dezakɔrde] *tr* to put (*an instrument*) out of tune ‖ *ref* to get out of tune

désaccoupler [dezakuple] *tr* to unpair; uncouple

désaccoutumer [dezakutyme] §97 *tr* to break (*s.o.*) of a habit ‖ *ref* to break oneself of a habit

désaffecter [dezafɛkte] *tr* to turn from its intended use

désagréable [dezagreabl] *adj* disagreeable; unpleasant

désagréger [dezagreʒe] §1 *tr* to break up, dissolve, disintegrate

désagrément [dezagremɑ̃] *m* unpleasantness, annoyance

désaimanter [dezɛmɑ̃te] *tr* to demagnetize

désalté·rant [dezalterɑ̃] **-rante** [rɑ̃t] *adj* thirst-quenching, refreshing

désaltérer [dezaltere] §10 *tr* to quench the thirst of; refresh with a drink ‖ *ref* to quench one's thirst

désamorcer [dezamɔrse] §51 *tr* to deactivate, disconnect the fuse of; unprime

désappointement [dezapwɛ̃tmã] *m* disappointment

désappointer [dezapwɛ̃te] *tr* to disappoint; break the point of, blunt

désapprendre [dezaprɑ̃dr] §56, §96, §97 *tr* to unlearn, forget

désapproba·teur [dezaprɔbatœr] **-trice** [tris] *adj* disapproving ‖ *mf* critic

désapprouver [dezapruve] *tr* to disapprove of, disapprove

désarçonner [dezarsɔne] *tr* to unhorse, buck off; (coll) to dumfound

désarmement [dezarməmã] *m* disarmament; disarming; dismantling (*of ship*)

désarmer [dezarme] *tr* to disarm; deactivate; dismantle; appease ‖ *intr* to disarm; slacken, let up (*said of hostility*)

désarroi [dezarwa] *m* disorder, disarray, confusion

désarticulation [dezartikylɑsjɔ̃] *f* dislocation

désassembler [dezasɑ̃ble] *tr* to disassemble

désastre [dezastr] *m* disaster

désas·treux [dezastrø] **-treuse** [trøz] *adj* disastrous

désavantage [dezavɑ̃taʒ] *m* disadvantage

désavantager [dezavɑ̃taʒe] §38 *tr* to put at a disadvantage, to handicap

désavanta·geux [dezavɑ̃taʒø] **-geuse** [ʒøz] *adj* disadvantageous

désa·veu [dezavø] *m* (*pl* **-veux**) disavowal, denial, repudiation

désavouer [dezavwe] *tr* to disavow, deny, repudiate, disown

désaxé désaxée [dezakse] *adj* unbalanced, out of joint

desceller [desɛle] *tr* to unseal

descendance [desɑ̃dɑ̃s] *f* descent

descendeur [desɑ̃dœr] *m* ski jumper

descendre [desɑ̃dr], [dɛsɑ̃dr] §95, §96 *tr* to descend, go down (*a hill, street, stairway*); take down, to lower (*a picture*); (coll) to bring down (*an airplane; luggage*); (coll) to drop off, let off at the door ‖ *intr* (*aux:* ÊTRE) to descend; go down, go downstairs; stay, stop (*at a hotel*); **descendre** + *inf* to go down to + *inf;* stop off to + *inf;* **descendre court** to undershoot (*said of airplane*); **descendre de** to come down from (*a mountain, ladder, tree*); be descended from

descente [desɑ̃t] *f* descent; invasion, raid; stay (*at a hotel*); stop (*en route*); **descente à terre** (nav) shore leave; **descente de lit** bedside rug

descriptible [dɛskriptibl] *adj* describable

descrip·tif [dɛskriptif] **-tive** [tiv] *adj* descriptive

description [dɛskripsjɔ̃] *f* description

déségrégation [desegregɑsjɔ̃] *f* desegregation

désembrouillage [dezɑ̃brujaz] *m* (electron) descrambling

désempa·ré -rée [dezɑ̃pare] *adj* disconcerted; disabled (*ship*)

désemparer [dezɑ̃pare] *tr* to disable (*a ship*) ‖ *intr*—**sans désemparer** continuously, without intermission

désemplir [dezɑ̃plir] *intr*—**ne pas désemplir** to be always full

désenchaîner [dezɑ̃ʃɛne] *tr* to unchain

désenchantement [dezɑ̃ʃɑ̃tmã] *m* disenchantment

désenchanter [dezɑ̃ʃɑ̃te] *tr* to disenchant

désencombrer [dezɑ̃kɔ̃bre] *tr* to disencumber, clear, free

désengager [dezɑ̃gaʒe] §34 *tr* to release from a promise

désengorger [dezɑ̃gɔrʒe] §38 *tr* to unstop

désengrener [dezɑ̃grəne] §2 *tr* to disengage, throw out of gear

désenivrer [dezɑ̃nivre] *tr & intr* to sober up

désenlacer [dezɑ̃lase] §51 *tr* to unbind

désennuyer [dezɑ̃nɥije] §27 *tr* to divert, cheer up ‖ *ref* to find relief from boredom

désensabler [dezɑ̃sable] *tr* to free (*a ship*) from the sand; dredge the sand from (*a canal*)

désensibiliser [desɑ̃sibilize] *tr* to desensitize

désensorceler [desɑ̃sɔrsəle] §34 *tr* to remove the spell from

désentortiller [dezɑ̃tɔrtije] *tr* to straighten out

désenvelopper [dezɑ̃vlɔpe] *tr* to unwrap

déséquilibre [dezekilibr] *m* mental instability

déséquili·bré -brée [dezekilibre] *adj* mentally unbalanced ‖ *mf* unbalanced person

déséquilibrer [dezekilibre] *tr* to unbalance

dé·sert [dezɛr] **-serte** [zɛrt] *adj & m* desert

déserter [dezɛrte] *tr & intr* to desert

déserteur [dezɛrtœr] *m* deserter

désertion [dezɛrsjɔ̃] *f* desertion

désespérance [dezɛsperɑ̃s] *f* despair

désespé·ré -rée [dezɛspere] *adj* desperate, hopeless ‖ *mf* desperate person

désespérer [dezɛspere] §10, §97 *tr* to be the despair of ‖ *ref* to lose hope

désespoir [dezɛspwar] *m* despair; **en désespoir de cause** as a last resort

déshabillage [dezabijaz] *m* striptease

déshabillé [dezabije] *m* morning wrap

déshabiller [dezabije] *tr & ref* to undress; **déshabiller saint Pierre pour habiller saint Paul** to rob Peter to pay Paul

déshabituer [dezabitɥe] §97 *tr* to break (*s.o.*) of a habit

déshéri·té -tée [dezerite] *adj* underprivileged; **les déshérités** the underprivileged

déshériter [dezerite] *tr* to disinherit; disadvantage

déshonnête [dezɔnɛt] *adj* improper, immodest

déshonnêteté [dezɔnɛtəte] *f* impropriety, immodesty, indecency

déshonneur [dezɔnœr] *m* dishonor

déshono·rant [dezɔnɔrɑ̃] **-rante** [rɑ̃t] *adj* dishonorable, discreditable

déshonorer [dezɔnɔre] *tr* to dishonor

déshydratation [dezidratɑsjɔ̃] *f* dehydration

déshydrater [dezidrate] *tr* to dehydrate

désignation [deziɲɑsjɔ̃] *f* designation; appointment, nomination

dési·gné -gnée [desiɲe] *mf* nominee

désigner [desiɲe] *tr* to designate; indicate, point out; appoint, nominate; signify, mean; set (*the hour of an appointment*) ‖ *ref*—**se désigner à l'attention de** to bring oneself to the attention of

désillusion [dezillyzjɔ̃] *f* disillusion; disappointment

désillusionner [dezillyzjɔne] *tr* to disillusion; disappoint

désinence [dezinɑ̃s] *f* (gram) ending

désinfecter [dezɛ̃fɛkte] *tr* to disinfect

désinformation [dezɛ̃fɔrmɑsjɔ̃] *f* disinformation

désintégration [dezɛ̃tegrɑsjɔ̃] *f* disintegration

désintégrer [dezɛ̃tegre] §10 *tr* & *ref* to disintegrate

désintéres·sé -sée [dezɛ̃terɛse] *adj* disinterested, impartial; unselfish

désintéressement [dezɛ̃terɛsmɑ̃] *m* disinterestedness, impartiality; payment, satisfaction (*of a debt*); paying off (*of a creditor*)

désintéresser [dezɛ̃terɛse] *tr* to pay off; buy out ‖ *ref*—**se désintéresser de** to lose interest in

désintoxication [dezɛ̃tɔksikɑsjɔ̃] *f* treatment for alcoholism, drug addiction, or poisoning; disintoxication

désinvolte [dezɛ̃vɔlt] *adj* free and easy, casual; offhanded, impertinent

désinvolture [dezɛ̃vɔltyr] *f* free and easy manner, offhandedness; impertinence

désir [dezir] *m* desire

désirable [dezirabl] *adj* desirable

désirer [dezire] §95, §96 *tr* to desire, wish

dési·reux -reuse [dezirø] *adj* desirous

désister [deziste] *ref* to desist; withdraw from a runoff election, **se désister de** to waive (*a claim*); drop (*a lawsuit*)

désobéir [dezɔbeir] *intr* to disobey; **désobéir à** to disobey, e.g., **le fils désobéira à son père** the son will disobey his father; **être désobéi** to be disobeyed

désobli·geant -geante [dezɔbliʒɑ̃] *adj* disagreeable, ungracious

désobliger [dezɔbliʒe] §38 *tr* to offend, displease, disoblige

désodori·sant -sante [dezɔdorizɑ̃] *adj* & *m* deodorant

désodoriser [dezɔdorize] *tr* to deodorize

désœu·vré -vrée [dezœvre] *adj* idle, unoccupied, out of work; **les désœuvrés** the unemployed

désœuvrement [dezœvrəmɑ̃] *m* idleness, unemployment

déso·lant -lante [dezɔlɑ̃] *adj* distressing, sad

désolation [dezɔlɑsjɔ̃] *f* desolation; grief, distress

déso·lé -lée [dezɔle] *adj* desolate; distressed

désoler [dezɔle] *tr* to desolate, destroy; distress ‖ *ref* to be distressed

désopi·lant -lante [dezɔpilɑ̃] *adj* hilarious, sidesplitting

désordon·né -née [dezɔrdɔne] *adj* disordered; untidy; disorderly

désordonner [dezɔrdɔne] *tr* to upset, confuse

désordre [dezɔrdr] *m* disorder, confusion, moral laxity

désorganisa·teur [dezɔrganizatœr] **-trice** [tris] *adj* disorganizing ‖ *mf* troublemaker

désorganisation [dezɔrganizɑsjɔ̃] *f* disorganization

désorganiser [dezɔrganize] *tr* to disorganize

désorien·té -tée [dezɔrjɑ̃te] *adj* disoriented, bewildered

désorienter [dezɔrjɑ̃te] *tr* to disorient; mislead; disconcert ‖ *ref* to become confused; lose one's bearings

désormais [dezɔrme] *adv* henceforth

désosser [dezɔse] *tr* to bone

despote [dɛspɔt] *m* despot

despotique [dɛspɔtik] *adj* despotic

despotisme [dɛspɔtism] *m* despotism

des·quels -quelles [dekɛl] §78

dessaisir [desezir] *tr* to dispossess; let go, release ‖ *ref*—**se dessaisir de** to relinquish

dessalement [desalmɑ̃] *m* desalinization

dessaler [desale] *tr* to desalt, desalinate ‖ *ref* (coll) to wise up

dessécher [desefe] §10 *tr* to dry up, wither; drain (*a pond*); dehydrate (*the body*); sear (*the heart*) ‖ *ref* to dry up; waste away

dessein [desɛ̃] *m* design, plan, intent; **à dessein** on purpose

desseller [desele] *tr* to unsaddle

desserrer [desere] *tr* to loosen; **ne pas desserrer les dents** to keep mum

dessert [desɛr] *m* dessert, last course

desserte [desɛrt] *f* buffet, sideboard; branch (*of railroad or bus line*); ministry (*of a substituting clergyman*)

dessertir [desertir] *tr* to remove (*a gem*) from its setting

desservant [desɛrvɑ̃] *m* parish priest

desserveur [desɛrvœr] *m* busboy

desservir [desɛrvir] §63 *tr* to clear (*the table*); be of disservice to, harm; (aer, aut, rr) to stop at (*a town or station*); (aer, aut, eccl, rr) to serve (*a locality*); (elec) to supply (*a region*)

dessiller [desije] *tr*—**dessiller les yeux à qn** or **de qn** to open s.o.'s eyes, undeceive s.o.

dessin [desɛ̃] *m* drawing, sketch, design; profile (*of face*); **dessins animés** (mov) animated cartoons

dessina·teur [desinatœr] **-trice** [tris] *mf* designer; cartoonist

dessiner [desine] *tr* to draw, sketch, design; delineate, outline ‖ *ref* to stand out, be outlined

dessoûler or **dessouler** [desule] *tr* & *intr* to sober up

dessous [dəsu] *m* underpart; reverse side, wrong side; coaster (*underneath a glass*); seamy side, machinations behind the scenes; **au dessous de** below; **avoir le dessous** to get the short end of the deal;

du dessous below; **en dessous** underneath; **les dessous** lingerie, undergarments ‖ *adv & prep* under, underneath, below

dessous-de-bouteille [dəsudəbutɛj] *m invar* coaster

dessous-de-bras [dəsudəbra] *m invar* underarm pad

dessous-de-carafe [dəsudəkaraf] *m invar* coaster

dessous-de-plat [dəsudəpla] *m invar* hot pad

dessous-de-table [dəsudətabl] *m invar* under-the-counter money

dessus [dəsy] *m* upper part; back (*of the hand*); right side (*of material*); (mus) treble part; **au dessus de** beyond, above; **avoir le dessus** to have the upper hand; **le dessus du panier** the cream of the crop ‖ *adv* above ‖ *prep* on, above, over

dessus-de-cheminée [dəsydəʃmine] *m invar* mantelpiece

dessus-de-lit [dəsydəli] *m invar* bedspread

dessus-de-porte [dəsydəpɔrt] *m invar* overdoor

dessus-de-table [dəsydətabl] *m invar* table cover

destin [dɛstɛ̃] *m* destiny, fate

destinataire [dɛstinatɛr] *mf* addressee; payee; **destinataire inconnu** or **absent** (formula stamped on envelope) not at this address

destination [dɛstinasjɔ̃] *f* destination; **à destination de** to, bound for

destinée [dɛstine] *f* destiny

destiner [dɛstine] §96, §100 *tr* to destine; set aside, reserve; **destiner q.ch. à qn** to mean or intend s.th. for s.o.

destituer [dɛstitɥe] *tr* to remove from office

destitution [dɛstitysjɔ̃] *f* dismissal, removal from office

destrier [dɛstrije] *m* (hist) steed, charger

destroyer [dɛstrɔjœr] *m* (nav) destroyer

destruc·teur [dɛstryktœr] **-trice** [tris] *adj* destroying, destructive ‖ *mf* destroyer

destruc·tif [dɛstryktif] **-tive** [tiv] *adj* destructive

destruction [dɛstryksjɔ̃] *f* destruction

dé·suet [dezɥɛ] **-suète** [zɥɛt] *adj* obsolete, antiquated, out-of-date

désuétude [dezɥetyd] *f* desuetude, disuse

désu·ni -nie [dezyni] *adj* at odds, divided against itself; uncoordinated

désunion [dezynjɔ̃] *f* dissension

désunir [dezynir] *tr* to disunite, divide; estrange

déta·ché -chée [detaʃe] *adj* detached; clean; spare (*parts*); acting, temporary (*official*); staccato (*note*)

détachement [detaʃmɑ̃] *m* detachment; (mil) detail

détacher [detaʃe] *tr* to detach; let loose; clean; make (*s.th.*) stand out in relief ‖ *ref* to come loose; break loose; stand out in relief

détacheur [detaʃœr] *m* spot remover

détail [detaj] *m* detail; retail; item (*of an account*); **au détail** at retail; **en détail** detailed

détail·lant [detajɑ̃] **-lante** [jɑ̃t] *adj* retail ‖ *mf* retailer

détailler [detaje] *tr* to detail; cut up into pieces; retail; itemize (*an account*)

détartrer [detartre] *tr* to remove the scale from (*a boiler*); remove the tartar from (*teeth*)

détaxation [detaksasjɔ̃] *f* lowering or removal of taxes

détaxer [detakse] *tr* to lower or remove the tax from

détecter [detɛkte] *tr* to detect

détecteur [detɛktœr] *m* detector; **détecteur de mines** mine detector

détection [detɛksjɔ̃] *f* detection

détective [detɛktiv] *m* detective, private detective; box camera

déteindre [detɛ̃dr] §50 *tr* to fade, bleach ‖ *intr* to fade, run

dételer [detle] §34 *tr* to unharness ‖ *intr* to let up; settle down

détendre [detɑ̃dr] *tr* to relax; stretch out (*one's legs*); lower (*the gas*) ‖ *ref* to relax, enjoy oneself

déten·du -due [detɑ̃dy] *adj* relaxed; slack ‖ *v* see **détendre**

détenir [detnir] §72 *tr* to detain (*in prison*); hold, withhold; own

détente [detɑ̃t] *f* trigger; relaxation, easing (*of tension*); relaxation of tension (*in international affairs*); spring, thrust, expansion

déten·teur [detɑ̃tœr] **-trice** [tris] *mf* holder (*of stock; of a record*); keeper (*of a secret*)

détention [detɑ̃sjɔ̃] *f* detention, custody; possession; **détention préventive** pretrial imprisonment, custody

déte·nu -nue [detny] *adj* detained, imprisoned ‖ *mf* prisoner

déter·gent [detɛrʒɑ̃] **-gente** [ʒɑ̃t] *adj & m* detergent

déterger [detɛrʒe] §38 *tr* to clean

détérioration [deterjɔrasjɔ̃] *f* deterioration

détériorer [deterjɔre] *tr* to damage ‖ *intr* to deteriorate

détermination [detɛrminasjɔ̃] *f* determination

déterminer [detɛrmine] §97, §100 *tr* to determine ‖ §96 *ref* to decide

déter·ré -rée [detɛre] *adj* disinterred ‖ *mf* (fig) corpse, ghost

déterrer [detɛre] *tr* to dig up; exhume

déter·sif [detɛrsif] **-sive** [siv] *adj & m* detergent

détester [detɛste] §95, §97 *tr* to detest, hate

déto·nant [detɔnɑ̃] **-nante** [nɑ̃t] *adj & m* explosive

détoner [detɔne] *intr* to detonate, explode

détonner [detɔne] *intr* to sing or play off key; clash (*said of colors*)

détordre [detɔrdr] *tr* to untwist

détortiller [detɔrtije] *tr* to untangle

détour [detur] *m* turn, curve, bend; round-about way, detour; **sans détour** frankly, honestly

détour·né -née [deturne] *adj* off the beaten track, isolated; indirect, roundabout; twisted (*meaning*)

détournement [deturnəmɑ̃] *m* diversion, re-routing; embezzlement; hijacking (*of an airplane*); **détournement de mineur** child abuse

détourner [deturne] §97, §99 *tr* to divert; deter; embezzle; lead astray; distort, twist

détrac·teur [detraktœr] **-trice** [tris] *adj* dis-paraging ‖ *mf* detractor

détra·qué -quée [detrake] *adj* out of order; broken (*in health*); unhinged, deranged ‖ *mf* nervous wreck

détraquer [detrake] *tr* to put out of commis-sion; (coll) to upset, unhinge ‖ *ref* to break down

détrempe [detrɑ̃p] *f* distemper (*painting*); annealing (*of steel*)

détremper [detrɑ̃pe] *tr* to soak; dilute; an-neal (*steel*)

détresse [detrɛs] *f* distress

détriment [detrimɑ̃] *m* detriment

détritus [detritys] *m* debris, rubbish, refuse

détroit [detrwa] *m* strait, sound

détromper [detrɔ̃pe] *tr* to undeceive, en-lighten

détrôner [detrone] *tr* to dethrone

détrousser [detruse] *tr* to let down (*e.g., one's sleeves*); hold up (*s.o.*) in the street ‖ *ref* to let down a garment

détrousseur [detrusœr] *m* highwayman

détruire [detrɥir] §19 *tr* to destroy; put an end to ‖ *ref* (coll) to commit suicide

dette [dɛt] *f* debt; **dette active** asset; **dette passive** liability

deuil [dœj] *m* mourning; grief, sorrow; be-reavement; funeral procession; **deuil de veuve** widow's weeds; **faire son deuil de** (coll) to say good-bye to

deux [dø] §94 *adj & pron* two; the Second, e.g., **Charles deux** Charles the Second; **deux heures** two o'clock ‖ *m* two; second (*in dates*)

deuxième [døzjɛm] §94 *adj & m* second

deux-pièces [døpjɛs] *m invar* two-piece suit

deux-points [døpwɛ̃] *m invar* colon

deux-ponts [døpɔ̃] *m invar* (aer, naut) double-decker

dévaler [devale] *tr* to descend (*a slope*) ‖ *intr* to descend quickly

dévaloriser [devalɔrize] *tr* to reduce the value of, devalue, devaluate; depreciate, underrate ‖ *ref* to depreciate, fall in value

dévaluation [devalɥasjɔ̃] *f* devaluation

dévaluer [devalɥe] *tr* to devaluate

devancer [dəvɑ̃se] *tr* to get ahead; arrive ahead of; anticipate

devan·cier [dəvɑ̃sje] **-cière** [sjɛr] *mf* pre-cursor, predecessor; **nos devanciers** those who have come before us, our forefathers

devant [dəvɑ̃] *m* front; **par devant** in front; **prendre les devants** to make the first move; to get ahead; to take precautions ‖

adv before, in front ‖ *prep* before, in front of

devanture [dəvɑ̃tyr] *f* show window; dis-play; storefront

dévasta·teur [devastatœr] **-trice** [tris] *adj* devastating

dévastation [devastasjɔ̃] *f* devastation

dévaster [devaste] *tr* to devastate

déveine [devɛn] *f* bad luck

développé [devlɔpe] *m* press (*in weight lift-ing*)

développement [devlɔpmɑ̃] *m* development; unwrapping (*of package*); expansion; **dé-veloppement urbain** urban development

développer [devlɔpe] *tr* to develop; unwrap (*a package*); reveal, show (*e.g., a card*); spread out, open out; expand (*an alge-braic expression*) ‖ *ref* to develop

devenir [dəvnir] §72 *intr* (*aux:* ÊTRE) to become; **qu'est devenu Robert?** what has become of Robert?

dévergondage [devɛrgɔ̃daʒ] *m* profligacy

dévergon·dé -dée [devɛrgɔ̃de] *adj & mf* profligate

dévergonder [devɛrgɔ̃de] *ref* to become dissolute

dévernir [devɛrnir] *tr* to remove the varnish from

déverrouiller [devɛruje] *tr* to unbolt

dé·vers [devɛr] **-verse** [vɛrs] *adj* warped; out of alignment ‖ *m* inclination, slope; banking

déverser [devɛrse] *tr* to pour out; slope, bank ‖ *intr* to pour out; lean, become lopsided ‖ *ref* to empty, flow (*said of river*)

dévêtir [devɛtir] §73 *tr & ref* to undress

déviation [devjasjɔ̃] *f* deviation; detour

dévider [devide] *tr* to unwind, reel off

dévier [devje] *tr* deflect, by-pass ‖ *intr* to deviate, swerve

de·vin [dəvɛ̃] **-vineresse** [vinrɛs] *mf* fortune-teller

deviner [dəvine] *tr* to guess

devinette [dəvinɛt] *f* riddle

dévirer [devire] *tr* to turn back; bend back; feather (*an oar*)

devis [dəvi] *m* estimate

dévisager [devizaʒe] §38 *tr* to stare at, stare down

devise [dəviz] *f* motto, slogan; heraldic de-vice; name of a ship; currency; **devise forte** strong currency

deviser [dəvize] *intr* to chat

dévisser [devise] *tr* to unscrew

dévitaliser [devitalize] *tr* to kill the nerve of (*a tooth*)

dévoiler [devwale] *tr* to unveil; straighten (*e.g., a bent wheel*) ‖ *ref* to unveil; come to light

devoir [dəvwar] *m* duty; exercise, home-work; **devoirs** respects; homework ‖ §21 *tr* §95 to owe ‖ *aux* used to express 1) necessity, e.g., **il doit s'en aller** he must go away; **il devra s'en aller** he will have to go away; **il a dû s'en aller** he had to go away; 2) obligation, e.g., **il devrait s'en**

aller he ought to go away, he should go away; **il aurait dû s'en aller** he ought to have gone away, he should have gone away; 3) conjecture, e.g., **il doit être malade** he must be ill; **il a dû être malade** he must have been ill; 4) what is expected or scheduled, e.g., **que dois-je faire maintenant?** what am I to do now? **le train devait arriver à six heures** the train was to arrive at six o'clock

dévo·lu -lue [devɔly] *adj*—**dévolu à** devolving upon, vested in ‖ *m*—**jeter son dévolu sur** to fix one's choice upon

dévora·teur [devɔratœr] **-trice** [tris] *adj* devouring

dévorer [devɔre] *tr* to devour, eat up

dévo·reur [devɔrœr] **-reuse** [røz] *mf* devourer; (fig) glutton

dé·vot [devo] **-vote** [vɔt] *adj* devout, pious ‖ *mf* devout, pious person; devotee; **faux dévot** hypocrite

dévotion [devosjɔ̃] *f* devotion, devoutness; **à votre dévotion** at your service, at your disposal; **être à la dévotion de qn** to be at s.o.'s beck and call

dé·voué -vouée [devwe] *adj* devoted; **dévoué à vos ordres** (complimentary close) at your service; **votre dévoué** (complimentary close) yours truly

dévouement [devumɑ̃] *m* devotion

dévouer [devwe] *tr* §96 to sacrifice ‖ *ref*—**se dévouer à** to devote or dedicate oneself to

dévoyé dévoyée [devwaje] *adj* delinquent (*young person*) ‖ *mf* delinquent

dévoyer [devwaje] §47 *tr* to lead astray

dextérité [dɛksterite] *f* dexterity

dextrose [dɛkstroz] *m* dextrose

diabète [djabɛt] *m* diabetes

diabétique [djabetik] *adj* & *mf* diabetic

diable [djɑbl] *m* devil; hand truck, dolly; (coll) fellow; **à la diable** haphazardly; **au diable vauvert** miles from anywhere, far away; **c'est là le diable** (coll) there's the rub; **diable à ressort** jack-in-the-box; **du diable** extreme; **en diable** extremely; **faire le diable à quatre** (coll) to raise Cain; **tirer le diable par la queue** (coll) to be hard up

diablerie [djɑbləri] *f* deviltry

diabolique [djabɔlik] *adj* diabolic(al)

diaconesse [djakɔnɛs] *f* deaconess

diacre [djɑkr] *m* deacon

diacritique [djakritik] *adj* diacritical

diadème [djadɛm] *m* diadem; (*woman's headdress*) tiara, coronet

diagnose [djagnoz] *f* diagnostics, diagnosis

diagnostic [djagnɔstik] *m* diagnosis

diagnostiquer [djagnɔstike] *tr* to diagnose

diago·nal -nale [djagɔnal] *adj* & *f* (*pl* **-naux** [no] **-nales**) diagonal

diagonalement [djagɔnalmɑ̃] *adv* diagonally, cater-cornered

diagramme [djagram] *m* diagram

dialecte [djalɛkt] *m* dialect

dialogue [djalɔg] *m* dialogue; **de dialogue** (comp) conversational; **dialogue de sourds** irreconcilable argument

dialoguer [djalɔge] *tr* to dialogue, adapt (*a novel for the screen*) ‖ *intr* to carry on a dialogue

diamant [djamɑ̃] *m* diamond

diamantaire [djamɑ̃tɛr] *adj* diamond-bright ‖ *m* dealer in diamonds

diamé·tral -trale [djametral] *adj* (*pl* **-traux** [tro]) diametric(al)

diamètre [djamɛtr] *m* diameter

diane [djan] *f* reveille

diantre [djɑ̃tr] *interj* the dickens!

diapason [djapazɔ̃] *m* range (*of voice or instrument*); pitch, standard pitch; tuning fork; **être au diapason de** (fig) to be on the same wavelength as

diaphane [djafan] *adj* diaphanous

diaphragme [djafragm] *m* diaphragm

diapo [djapo] *f* (coll) slide

diapositive [djapozitiv] *f* (phot) transparency, slide

diaprer [djapre] *tr* to variegate

diarrhée [djare] *f* diarrhea

diastole [djastɔl] *f* diastole

diathermie [djatɛrmi] *f* diathermy

diatribe [djatrib] *f* diatribe

dichotomie [dikɔtɔmi] *f* dichotomy; split fee (*between physicians*)

dictaphone [diktafɔn] *m* dictaphone

dictateur [diktatœr] *m* dictator

dictature [diktatyr] *f* dictatorship

dictée [dikte] *f* dictation; **écrire sous la dictée de** to take dictation from

dicter [dikte] *tr* & *intr* to dictate

diction [diksjɔ̃] *f* diction

dictionnaire [diksjɔnɛr] *m* dictionary; **dictionnaire vivant** (coll) walking encyclopedia

dicton [diktɔ̃] *m* saying, proverb

didacticiel [didaktisjɛl] *m* (comp) instructional software

didactique [didaktik] *adj* didactic(al)

dièdre [djɛdr] *adj* & *m* dihedral

diérèse [djerɛz] *f* diaeresis

dièse [djez] *adj* & *m* (mus) sharp

diesel [dizɛl] *m* Diesel motor

diéser [djeze] §10 *tr* (mus) to sharp

diète [djɛt] *f* diet

diététi·cien [djetetisjɛ̃] **-cienne** [sjɛn] *mf* dietitian

diététique [djetetik] *adj* dietetic ‖ *f* dietetics

dieu [djø] *m* (*pl* **dieux**) god ‖ (*cap*) *m* God; **Dieu merci!** thank heavens!; **mon Dieu!** good gracious!

diffamation [difamasjɔ̃] *f* defamation

diffamer [difame] *tr* to defame

diffé·ré -rée [difere] *adj* deferred; delayed (*action*) ‖ *m* (rad, telv) prerecording; **en différé** (rad, telv) prerecorded

différemment [diferamɑ̃] *adv* differently

différence [diferɑ̃s] *f* difference; **à la différence de** unlike, contrary to

différencier [diferɑ̃sje] *tr* & *ref* to differentiate

différend [diferã] *m* dispute, disagreement, difference; **partager le différend** to split the difference

diffé·rent [diferã] **-rente** [rãt] *adj* different; **différent de** different from ‖ (when standing before noun) *adj* different, various

différen·tiel -tielle [diferãsjɛl] *adj* differential ‖ *m* (mach) differential ‖ *f* (math) differential

différer [difere] §10, §96, §97 *tr* to defer, put off ‖ *intr* to differ; disagree

difficile [difisil] §92 *adj* difficult, hard; hard to please, crotchety; **faire le difficile** to be hard to please

difficulté [difikylte] *f* difficulty

difforme [difɔrm] *adj* deformed

difformité [difɔrmite] *f* deformity

dif·fus [dify] **-fuse** [fyz] *adj* diffuse; verbose, windy

diffuser [difyze] *tr* to broadcast ‖ *ref* to diffuse

diffuseur [difyzœr] *m* spreader (*of news*); loudspeaker; nozzle

digérer [diʒere] §10 *tr* & *intr* to digest ‖ *ref* to be digested

digeste [diʒɛst] *adj* (coll) easy to digest ‖ *m* (law) digest

digestible [diʒɛstibl] *adj* digestible

diges·tif [diʒɛstif] **-tive** [tiv] *adj* digestive

digestion [diʒɛstjɔ̃] *f* digestion

digi·tal -tale [diʒital] *adj* (*pl* **-taux** [to]) digital ‖ *f* digitalis, foxglove

digitaline [diʒitalin] *f* (pharm) digitalis

digne [diɲ] §93 *adj* worthy; dignified; haughty, uppish; **digne d'éloges** praiseworthy, laudable

dignitaire [diɲitɛr] *mf* dignitary

dignité [diɲite] *f* dignity

digression [digrɛsjɔ̃] *f* digression

digue [dig] *f* dike; breakwater; (fig) barrier

dilacérer [dilasere] §10 *tr* to lacerate

dilapider [dilapide] *tr* to squander; embezzle

dilater [dilate] *tr* & *ref* to dilate

dilatoire [dilatwar] *adj* dilatory

dilemme [dilɛm] *m* dilemma

dilettante [diletãt] *mf* dilettante

diligemment [diliʒamã] *adv* diligently

diligence [diliʒãs] *f* diligence; **à la diligence de** at the request of

dili·gent [diliʒã] **-gente** [ʒãt] *adj* diligent

diluer [dilɥe] *tr* to dilute

dilution [dilysjɔ̃] *f* dilution

dimanche [dimãʃ] *m* Sunday; **du dimanche** (coll) Sunday (*driver*); (coll) amateur (*painter*); **le dimanche des Rameaux** Palm Sunday

dîme [dim] *f* tithe

dimension [dimãsjɔ̃] *f* dimension

diminuer [diminɥe] *tr* to reduce, cut down, decrease ‖ *intr* to diminish, decrease

diminu·tif [diminytif] **-tive** [tiv] *adj* & *m* diminutive

diminution [diminysjɔ̃] *f* reduction; diminishing

dinde [dɛ̃d] *f* turkey; (culin) turkey; (coll) silly girl

dindon [dɛ̃dɔ̃] *m* turkey; (coll) dupe

dindonner [dɛ̃dɔne] *tr* to dupe, take in

dîner [dine] *m* dinner; **dîner de garçons** stag dinner; **dîner prié** formal dinner ‖ *intr* to dine

dînette [dinɛt] *f* family meal; children's playtime meal

dî·neur [dinœr] **-neuse** [nøz], *mf* diner, dinner guest

dingue [dɛ̃g] *adj* (slang) crazy, nuts, nutty, goffy ‖ *mf* nutty person, goof

dinosaure [dinɔzɔr] *m* dinosaur

diocèse [djɔsɛz] *m* diocese

diode [djɔd] *f* diode

dionée [djɔne] *f* Venus's-flytrap

diphtérie [difteri] *f* diphtheria

diphtongue [diftɔ̃g] *f* diphthong

diplomate [diplɔmat] *adj* diplomatic ‖ *mf* diplomat

diplomatie [diplɔmasi] *f* diplomacy

diplomatique [diplɔmatik] *adj* diplomatic

diplôme [diplom] *m* diploma

dire [dir] §95, §97, §98 *m* statement; **au dire de** according to ‖ §22 *tr* to say, tell, relate; **à l'heure dite** at the appointed time; **à qui le dites-vous?** (coll) you're telling me!; **autrement dit** in other words; **dire que . . .** to think that; **dites-lui bien des choses de ma part** say hello for me; **tu l'as dit!** (coll) you said it! ‖ *intr* to say; **à vrai dire** to tell the truth; **cela va sans dire** it goes without saying; **c'est beaucoup dire** (coll) that's going rather far; **c'est pas peu dire** (slang) that's saying a lot; **comme on dit** as the saying goes; **dites donc!** hey!, say!; **il n'y a pas à dire** make no mistake about it ‖ *ref* to be said; to say to oneself or to each other; to claim to be, to call oneself

di·rect -recte [dirɛkt] *adj* direct ‖ *m* (boxing) solid punch; **en direct** (rad, telv) live

direc·teur [dirɛktœr] **-trice** [tris] *adj* directing, guiding; principal; driving (*rod, wheel*) ‖ *mf* director; **directeur de jeu** referee; **directeur des services municipaux** city manager ‖ *f* directress

direction [dirɛksjɔ̃] *f* direction; administration, management, board; head office; (aut) steering

direction·nel -nelle [dirɛksjɔnɛl] *adj* directional

directive [dirɛktiv] *f* directive, order

directorat [dirɛktɔra] *m* directorship

dirigeable [diriʒabl] *adj* & *m* dirigible

diri·geant [diriʒã] **-geante** [ʒãt] *adj* governing, ruling ‖ *mf* ruler, leader, head, executive

diriger [diriʒe] §38 *tr* to direct, control, manage; steer ‖ *ref* to go; **se diriger vers** to head for

dirigisme [diriʒism] *m* government economic planning and control

dis [di] *v* (**disant, disons**) see **dire**

discernable [disɛrnabl] *adj* discernible

discernement [disɛrnəmã] *m* discernment, perception

discerner [disɛrne] *tr* to discern
disciple [displ] *m* disciple
disciplinaire [disiplinɛr] *adj* disciplinary ‖ *m* military policeman
discipline [disiplin] *f* discipline; scourge
discipliner [disipline] *tr* to discipline
disconti·nu -nue [diskɔ̃tiny] *adj* discontinuous
discontinuer [diskɔ̃tine] §97 *tr* to discontinue
disconvenir [diskɔ̃vnir] §72, §97 *tr* to deny ‖ *intr*—**disconvenir à** to not suit, displease ‖ *intr (aux:* ÊTRE)—**ne pas disconvenir de** to admit, not deny
discophile [diskɔfil] *mf* record collector
discord [diskɔr] *adj masc* out of tune ‖ *m* instrument out of tune
discordance [diskɔrdɑ̃s] *f* discordance
discor·dant [diskɔrdɑ̃] **-dante** [dɑ̃t] *adj* discordant
discorde [diskɔrd] *f* discord
discorder [diskɔrde] *intr* to be discordant, jar
discothèque [diskɔtɛk] *f* record cabinet; record library; discotheque
discourir [diskurir] §14 *intr* to discourse
discours [diskur] *m* discourse; speech
discour·tois [diskurtwa] **-toise** [twaz] *adj* discourteous
discourtoisie [diskurtwazi] *f* discourtesy
discrédit [diskredi] *m* discredit
discréditer [diskredite] *tr* to discredit
dis·cret [diskrɛ] **-crète** [krɛt] *adj* discreet; discrete
discrétion [diskresjɔ̃] *f* discretion; **à discrétion** as much as one wants
discrimination [diskriminɑsjɔ̃] *f* discrimination
discriminatoire [diskriminatwar] *adj* discriminatory
discriminer [diskrimine] *tr* to discriminate
disculper [diskylpe] §97 *tr* to clear, exonerate ‖ *ref* to clear oneself
discur·sif [diskyrsif] **-sive** [siv] *adj* discursive
discussion [diskysjɔ̃] *f* discussion
discuter [diskyte] *tr & intr* to discuss; question, debate
di·sert [dizɛr] **-serte** [zɛrt] *adj* eloquent, fluent
disertement [dizɛrtəmɑ̃] *adv* eloquently, fluently
disette [dizɛt] *f* shortage, scarcity; famine
di·seur [dizœr] **-seuse** [zøz] *mf* talker, speaker; monologuist; **diseuse de bonne aventure** fortuneteller
disgrâce [disgrɑs] *f* disfavor; misfortune; surliness, gruffness
disgra·cié -ciée [disgrɑsje] *adj* out of favor; ill-favored, homely; unfortunate
disgracier [disgrɑsje] *tr* to deprive of favor
disgra·cieux [disgrɑsjø] **-cieuse** [sjøz] *adj* awkward; homely, ugly; disagreeable
disjoindre [disʒwɛ̃dr] §35 *tr* to sever, separate
disjoncteur [disʒɔ̃ktœr] *m* circuit breaker

dislocation [dislɔkɑsjɔ̃] *f* dislocation; separation; dismemberment
disloquer [dislɔke] *tr* to dislocate; disperse; dismember ‖ *ref* to break up, disperse
disparaître [disparɛtr] §12 *intr* to disappear
disparate [disparat] *adj* incongruous ‖ *f* incongruity; clash (*of colors*)
disparité [disparite] *f* disparity
disparition [disparisjɔ̃] *f* disappearance
dispa·ru -rue [dispary] *adj* disappeared; missing (*in battle*) ‖ *mf* missing person; **le disparu** the deceased ‖ *v* see **disparaître**
dispen·dieux [dispɑ̃djø] **-dieuse** [djøz] *adj* expensive
dispensaire [dispɑ̃sɛr] *m* dispensary, outpatient clinic
dispensa·teur [dispɑ̃satœr] **-trice** [tris] *mf* dispenser
dispense [dispɑ̃s] *f* dispensation, exemption
dispenser [dispɑ̃se] §97, §99 *tr* to dispense; **dispensé du timbrage** (label on envelope) mailing permit
disperser [dispɛrse] *tr & ref* to disperse
dispersion [dispɛrsjɔ̃] *f* dispersion, dissipation
disponibilité [disponibilite] *f* availability; **disponibilités** liquid assets; **en disponibilité** in the reserves
disponible [disponibl] *adj* available; vacant (*seat*); (govt, mil) subject to call
dis·pos [dispo] **-pose** [poz] *adj* alert, fit, in good condition
dispo·sé -sée [dispoze] §92 *adj* disposed; arranged; **disposé d'avance** predisposed; **peu disposé** reluctant
disposer [dispoze] §96, §100 *tr* to dispose ‖ *intr* to dispose; **disposer de** to dispose of, have use of; **disposer pour** to provide for (*e.g., the future*); **vous pouvez disposer** you may leave ‖ *ref*—**se disposer à** to be disposed to; plan on
dispositif [dispozitif] *m* apparatus, device; (mil) disposition
disposition [dispozisjɔ̃] *f* disposition; disposal; **dispositions** arrangements; aptitude; provisions (*of a legal document*)
disproportion·né -née [disprɔpɔrsjɔne] *adj* disproportionate, incompatible
dispute [dispyt] *f* dispute
disputer [dispyte] *tr* to dispute; (coll) to bawl out ‖ *ref* to dispute
disquaire [diskɛr] *m* record dealer
disqualification [diskalifikɑsjɔ̃] *f* disqualification
disqualifier [diskalifje] *tr & ref* to disqualify
disque [disk] *m* disk; record, disk; (sports) discus; **changer de disque** (coll) to change the subject; **disque de longue durée** long-playing record; **disque volant** Frisbee
disquette [diskɛt] *f* (comp) floppy disk
dissection [disɛksjɔ̃] *f* dissection
dissemblable [disɑ̃blabl] *adj* dissimilar
dissemblance [disɑ̃blɑ̃s] *f* dissimilarity
disséminer [disemine] *tr* to disseminate

dissension [disɑ̃sjɔ̃] *f* dissension
dissentiment [disɑ̃timɑ̃] *m* dissent
disséquer [diseke] §10 *tr* to dissect
dissertation [disɛrtɑsjɔ̃] *f* dissertation; (*in school*) essay, term paper
dissidence [disidɑ̃s] *f* dissent
dissi·dent [disidɑ̃] **-dente** [dɑ̃t] *adj* dissenting ‖ *mf* dissenter, dissident
dissimiler [disimile] *tr* (phonet) to dissimilate
dissimulation [disimylɑsjɔ̃] *f* dissemblance
dissimuler [disimyle] *tr* & *intr* to dissemble; **dissimuler q.ch. à qn** to conceal s.th. from s.o. ‖ *ref* to hide, skulk
dissipation [disipɑsjɔ̃] *f* dissipation
dissi·pé **-pée** [disipe] *adj* dissipated; pleasure-seeking; unruly (*schoolboy*)
dissiper [disipe] *tr* & *ref* to dissipate
dissocier [disɔsje] *tr* & *ref* to dissociate
disso·lu **-lue** [disɔly] *adj* dissolute ‖ *mf* profligate
dissolution [disɔlysjɔ̃] *f* dissolution; dissoluteness; rubber cement
dissol·vant [disɔlvɑ̃] **-vante** [vɑ̃t] *adj* & *m* solvent
dissonance [disɔnɑ̃s] *f* dissonance
dissoudre [disudr] §60 (*pp* **dissous, dissoute;** no *pret* or *imperf subj*) *tr* & *ref* to dissolve
dissuader [disɥade] §97, §99 *tr* to dissuade, deter
distance [distɑ̃s] *f* distance; **à distance** at a distance
distancer [distɑ̃se] §51 *tr* to outdistance, distance (*a race horse*)
dis·tant [distɑ̃] **-tante** [tɑ̃t] *adj* distant
distendre [distɑ̃dr] *tr* & *ref* to distend; strain (*a muscle*)
distillation [distilɑsjɔ̃] *f* distillation
distiller [distile] *tr* to distill
distillerie [distilri] *f* distillery; distilling industry
dis·tinct [distɛ̃], [distɛ̃kt] **-tincte** [tɛ̃kt] *adj* distinct
distinc·tif [distɛ̃ktif] **-tive** [tiv] *adj* distinctive
distinction [distɛ̃ksjɔ̃] *f* distinction
distin·gué -guée [distɛ̃ge] *adj* distinguished; famous; sincere, e.g., **veuillez accepter nos sentiments distingués** (complimentary close) please accept our sincere regards
distinguer [distɛ̃ge] *tr* to distinguish ‖ *ref* to be distinguished; distinguish oneself
distordre [distɔrdr] *tr* to twist, sprain
dis·tors [distɔr] **-torse** [tɔrs] *adj* twisted
distorsion [distɔrsjɔ̃] *f* sprain; convulsive twist; (electron, opt) distorsion
distraction [distrɑksjɔ̃] *f* distraction; heedlessness; lapse; embezzlement; appropriation (*of a sum of money*)
distraire [distrɛr] §68 *tr* to distract, amuse; separate, set aside (*e.g., part of one's savings*) ‖ *ref* to amuse oneself
dis·trait [distrɛ] **-traite** [trɛt] *adj* absentminded

distribuer [distribɥe] *tr* to distribute; arrange the furnishings of (*an apartment*)
distribu·teur [distribytœr] **-trice** [tris] *mf* distributor (*person*) ‖ *m* (mach) distributor; **distributeur automatique** vending machine; **distributeur de musique** jukebox
distribution [distribysjɔ̃] *f* distribution; mail delivery; supply system (*of gas, water, or electricity*); valve gear (*of steam engine*); timing gears (*of internal-combustion engine*); (theat) cast
district [distrik], [distrikt] *m* district
dit [di] **dite** [dit] *adj* agreed upon, stated ‖ *m* saying ‖ *v* see **dire**
dites [dit] *v* see **dire**
dito [dito] *adv* ditto
diva [diva] *f* diva
divaguer [divage] *intr* to ramble
divan [divɑ̃] *m* divan, sofa
diverger [divɛrʒe] §38 *intr* to diverge
di·vers [divɛr] **-verse** [vɛrs] *adj* changing, varied; miscellaneous (*expenses; remarks*); **faits divers** news items; **un fait divers** an incident ‖ **di·vers -verses** (when standing before or after noun) *adj pl* diverse, different, varied; various, several, e.g., **diverses personnes** several persons, **en diverses occasions** on various occasions
diversifier [divɛrsifje] *tr* & *ref* to diversify
diversion [divɛrsjɔ̃] *f* diversion
diversité [divɛrsite] *f* diversity
divertir [divɛrtir] §96 *tr* to divert, amuse ‖ *ref* to be diverted, amused
divertis·sant [divɛrtisɑ̃] **-sante** [sɑ̃t] *adj* entertaining, diverting, amusing
divertissement [divɛrtismɑ̃] *m* diversion, relaxation; entertainment; amusement; (mus) divertissement
dividende [dividɑ̃d] *m* dividend
di·vin [divɛ̃] **-vine** [vin] *adj* divine
divination [divinɑsjɔ̃] *f* divination
divinité [divinite] *f* divinity
diviser [divize] *tr* & *ref* to divide
diviseur [divizœr] *m* (math) divisor; (fig) troublemaker
divisible [divizibl] *adj* divisible
division [divizjɔ̃] *f* division
divisionnaire [divizjɔnɛr] *adj* divisional ‖ *m* division head
divorce [divɔrs] *m* divorce
divor·cé -cée [divɔrse] *mf* divorced person ‖ *f* divorcee
divorcer [divɔrse] §51 *tr* to divorce (*a married couple*) ‖ *intr* to divorce, get a divorce; **divorcer avec** to withdraw from (*the world*); **divorcer d'avec** to get a divorce from, be divorced from, divorce (*husband or wife*); withdraw from (*the world*)
divulguer [divylge] *tr* to divulge
dix [di(s)] §94 *adj* & *pron* ten; the Tenth, e.g., **Jean dix** John the Tenth; **dix heures** ten o'clock ‖ *m* ten; tenth (*in dates*)
dix-huit [dizɥi], [dizɥit] §94 *adj* & *pron* eighteen; the Eighteenth, e.g., **Jean dix-**

huit John the Eighteenth ‖ *m* eighteen; eighteenth (*in dates*)

dix-huitième [dizчitjɛm] §94 *adj* & *m* eighteenth

dixième [dizjɛm] §94 *adj, pron* (*masc, fem*), & *m* tenth

dix-neuf [diznœf] §94 *adj* & *pron* nineteen; the Nineteenth, e.g., **Jean dix-neuf** John the Nineteenth ‖ *m* nineteen; nineteenth (*in dates*)

dix-neuvième [diznœvjɛm] §94 *adj* & *m* nineteenth

dix-sept [dissɛt] §94 *adj* & *pron* seventeen; the Seventeenth, e.g., **Jean dix-sept** John the Seventeenth ‖ *m* seventeen; seventeenth (*in dates*)

dix-septième [dissɛtjɛm] §94 *adj* & *m* seventeenth

djinn [dʒin] *m* jinn

d° *abbr* (**dito**) do. (ditto)

docile [dɔsil] *adj* docile

dock [dɔk] *m* dock; warehouse; **dock flottant** floating dry dock

docker [dɔkɛr] *m* dock worker

docte [dɔkt] *adj* learned, scholarly ‖ *mf* scholar ‖ *m* learned man

doc·teur [dɔktœr] **-toresse** [tɔrɛs] *mf* doctor; **le docteur Marie Dupont** Dr. Mary Dupont

docto·ral -rale [dɔktɔral] *adj* (*pl* **-raux** [ro]) doctoral

doctorat [dɔktɔra] *m* doctorate

doctrine [dɔktrin] *f* doctrine

document [dɔkymã] *m* document

documentaire [dɔkymãtɛr] *adj* & *m* documentary

documentation [dɔkymãtɑsjɔ̃sasjɔ̃] *f* documentation; literature (*about a region, business, etc.*)

documenter [dɔkymãte] *tr* to document ‖ *ref* to gather documentary evidence

dodeliner [dɔdline] *tr* & *intr* to sway, rock

dodo [dɔdo] *m* (orn) dodo; **aller au dodo** (*baby talk*) to go to bed; **faire dodo** to sleep

do·du -due [dɔdy] *adj* (coll) plump

dogmatique [dɔgmatik] *adj* dogmatic ‖ *mf* dogmatic person ‖ *f* dogmatics

dogmatiser [dɔgmatize] *intr* to dogmatize

dogme [dɔgm] *m* dogma

dogue [dɔg] *m* bulldog

doigt [dwa] *m* finger; **à deux doigts de** a hairbreadth away from; **doigt annulaire** ring finger; **doigt de Dieu** hand of God; **doigt du pied** toe; **mettre le doigt dessus** to hit the nail on the head; **mon petit doigt m'a dit** (coll) a little bird told me; **montrer du doigt** to single out (*for ridicule*); to point at; **petit doigt** little finger; **se mettre le doigt dans l'œil** (coll) to fool oneself; **se mordre les doigts** to be sorry; **un doigt de vin** very little wine

doigté [dwate] *m* touch; adroitness; skillfulness; fingering

doigter [dwate] *m* fingering ‖ *tr* & *intr* to finger

doigtier [dwatje] *m* fingerstall

dois [dwa] *v* (**doit**) see **devoir**

doit [dwa] *m* debit

doléances [dɔleɑ̃s] *fpl* grievances; (pathol) symptoms

do·lent [dɔlɑ̃] **-lente** [lɑ̃t] *adj* doleful

dollar [dɔlar] *m* dollar

domaine [dɔmɛn] *m* domain

dôme [dom] *m* dome; cathedral

domestication [dɔmɛstikɑsjɔ̃] *f* domestication

domesticité [dɔmɛstisite] *f* domestication; staff of servants

domestique [dɔmɛstik] *adj* & *mf* domestic

domestiquer [dɔmɛstike] *tr* to domesticate

domicile [dɔmisil] *m* residence

domicilier [dɔmisilje] *tr* to domicile ‖ *ref* to take up residence

dominance [dɔminɑ̃s] *f* (genetics) dominance

domi·nant [dɔminɑ̃] **-nante** [nɑ̃t] *adj* dominant ‖ *f* dominating trait; (mus) dominant

domina·teur [dɔminatœr] **-trice** [tris] *adj* domineering, overbearing ‖ *mf* ruler, conqueror

domination [dɔminɑsjɔ̃] *f* domination

dominer [dɔmine] *tr* & *intr* to dominate ‖ *ref* to control oneself

domini·cal -cale [dɔminikal] *adj* (*pl* **-caux** [ko]) Sunday; dominical

domino [dɔmino] *m* domino

dommage [dɔmaʒ] *m* loss; injury; **c'est dommage!** that's too bad! **dommages et intérêts** (law) damages; **quel dommage!** what a pity!

dommageable [dɔmaʒabl] *adj* injurious

dommages-intérêts [dɔmaʒɛterɛ] *mpl* (law) damages

dompter [dɔ̃te] *tr* to tame; train (*animals*); subdue

domp·teur [dɔ̃tœr] **-teuse** [tøz] *mf* tamer, trainer; conquerer

don [dɔ̃] *m* gift; don (*Spanish title*)

donataire [dɔnatɛr] *mf* legatee

dona·teur [dɔnatœr] **-trice** [tris] *mf* (law) donor, legator

donation [dɔnɑsjɔ̃] *f* donation, gift, grant

donc [dɔ̃k], [dɔ̃] *adv* therefore, then; thus; now, of course; (often used for emphasis), e.g., **entrez donc!** do come in!

donjon [dɔ̃ʒɔ̃] *m* keep, donjon; (nav) turret

don·nant [dɔnɑ̃] **-nante** [nɑ̃t] *adj* generous, open-handed; **donnant donnant** tit for tat; cash down; **peu donnant** closefisted

donne [dɔn] *f* (cards) deal; doña (*Spanish title*); **fausse donne** misdeal

don·né -née [dɔne] *adj* given; **étant donné que** whereas, since ‖ *f* datum; **données** data, facts

donner [dɔne] §96 *tr* to give; (cards) to deal ‖ *intr* to give; **donner sur** to open onto, look out on; **donner sur les doigts** to rap one's knuckles

don·neur [dɔnœr] **-neuse** [nøz] *mf* donor; **donneur universel** type-O blood donor ‖ *m* (cards) dealer

dont [dɔ̃] §79

donzelle [dɔ̃zɛl] *f* woman of easy virtue

doper [dɔpe] *tr* to dope

doping [dɔpiŋ] *m* dope, pep pill

dorade [dɔrad] *f* gilthead

dorénavant [dɔrenavɑ̃] *adv* henceforth

dorer [dɔre] *tr* to gild; (fig) to sugar-coat

d'ores [dɔr] see **ores**

dorlotement [dɔrlɔtmɑ̃] *m* coddling

dorloter [dɔrlɔte] *tr* to coddle

dor·mant [dɔrmɑ̃] **-mante** [mɑ̃t] *adj* stagnant, immovable ‖ *m* doorframe

dor·meur [dɔrmœr] **-meuse** [møz] *adj* sleeping ‖ *mf* sleeper ‖ *f* earring

dormir [dɔrmir] §23 *intr* to sleep; lie dormant; **à dormir debout** boring, dull; **dormir debout** to sleep standing up; **dormir sur les deux oreilles** to feel secure

dors [dɔr] *v* (**dort**) see **dormir**

dortoir [dɔrtwar] *m* dormitory

dorure [dɔryr] *f* gilding; gilt; icing

dos [do] *m* back; bridge (*of nose*); **dans le dos de** behind the back of; **dos d'âne** (aut) speed bump; **en dos d'âne** saddlebacked, hog-backed; **se mettre qn à dos** to make an enemy of s.o.; **voir au dos** see other side

dosage [dozaʒ] *m* dosage

dose [doz] *f* dose; proportion, amount, share; (fig) tinge, suspicion; (slang) fix (*shot of a drug*)

doser [doze] *tr* to dose out, measure out, proportion

dossier [dosje] *m* chair back; dossier; case history

dot [dɔt] *f* dowry

dotation [dɔtasjɔ̃] *f* endowment

doter [dɔte] *tr* to endow; dower; give a dowry to

douaire [dwɛr] *m* dower

douairière [dwɛrjɛr] *f* dowager

douane [dwan] *f* customs, duty; customhouse

doua·nier [dwanje] **-nière** [njɛr] *adj* customs ‖ *m* customs officer

doublage [dublaʒ] *m* doubling; metal plating of a ship; lining (*act of lining*); dubbing (*on tape or film*)

double [dubl] *adj & adv* double; **à double face** two-faced; **se garer en double fil** to double-park ‖ *m* double; duplicate, copy; **au double** twice; **double au carbone** carbon copy; **en double** in duplicate

doublement [dubləmɑ̃] *m* doubling ‖ *adv* doubly

doubler [duble] *tr* to double; parallel, run alongside; pass (*s.o., s.th. going in the same direction*); line (*a coat*); dub (*a film*); copy, dub (*a sound tape*); replace (*an actor*); gain one lap on (*another contestant*); (coll) to cheat ‖ *intr* to double; pass (*on highway*)

doublure [dublyr] *f* lining; (theat) understudy, replacement

douce-amère [dusamɛr] *f* (*pl* **douces-amères**) (bot) bittersweet

douceâtre [dusɑtr] *adj* sweetish; mawkish

doucement [dusmɑ̃] *adv* softly; slowly ‖ *interj* easy now!, just a minute!

douce·reux [dusrø] **-reuse** [røz] *adj* unpleasantly sweet, cloying; mealy-mouthed

douceur [dusœr] *f* sweetness; softness, gentleness; **douceurs** sweets

douche [duʃ] *f* shower bath; douche; (coll) dressing down; (coll) shock, disappointment

doucher [duʃe] *tr* to give a shower bath to; (coll) reprimand; (coll) to disappoint ‖ *ref* to take a shower bath

doucir [dusir] *tr* to polish, rub

doué douée [dwe] *adj* gifted, endowed

douer [dwe] *tr* to endow; **douer de** to endow or gift (*s.o.*) with

douille [duj] *f* cartridge case; sconce (*of candlestick*); bushing; (elec) socket

douil·let [dujɛ] **-lette** [jɛt] *adj* soft, delicate; oversensitive ‖ *f* child's padded coat

douleur [dulœr] *f* pain; sorrow; soreness

doulou·reux [dulurø] **-reuse** [røz] *adj* painful; sad; sore

doute [dut] *m* doubt; **sans doute** no doubt

douter [dute] §97 *tr* to doubt, e.g., **je doute qu'il vienne** I doubt that he will come ‖ *intr* to doubt; **à n'en pas douter** beyond a doubt; **douter de** to doubt; distrust ‖ *ref*—**se douter de** to suspect; **se douter que** to suspect that

dou·teur [dutœr] **-teuse** [tøz] *adj* doubting ‖ *mf* doubter

dou·teux [dutø] **-teuse** [tøz] *adj* doubtful; dubious

Douvres [duvr] Dover

doux [du] **douce** [dus] *adj* sweet; soft; pleasing; suave; quiet; new (*wine*) fresh (*water*); gentle (*slope*); mild (*weather, climate*); **en douce** on the sly, on the q.t. ‖ **doux** *interj*—**tout doux!** easy there!

douzain [duzɛ̃] *m* twelve-line verse

douzaine [duzɛn] *f* dozen; **à la douzaine** by the dozen; **une douzaine de** a dozen

douze [duz] §94 *adj & pron* twelve; the Twelfth, e.g., **Jean douze** John the Twelfth ‖ *m* twelve; twelfth (*in dates*)

douzième [duzjɛm] §94 *adj, pron* (*masc, fem*), *& m* twelfth

doyen [dwajɛ̃] **doyenne** [dwajɛn] *mf* dean; **doyen d'âge** oldest member

doyenneté [dwajɛnte] *f* seniority

Dr *abbr* (**Docteur**) Dr.

drachme [drakm] *m* drachma; dram

dragage [dragaʒ] *m* dredging

dragée [draʒe] *f* sugar-coated almond; (pharm) pill; (coll) bitter pill; **tenir la dragée haute à qn** to make s.o. pay through the nose; be high-handed with s.o.

drageon [draʒɔ̃] *m* (bot) sucker

dragon [dragɔ̃] *m* dragon; dragoon; shrew; **dragon de vertu** prude

dragonne [dragɔn] *f* tassel, sword knot

drague [drag] *f* dredge; minesweeping apparatus

draguer [drage] *tr* to dredge, drag; sweep for mines ‖ *intr* to be on the make

dragueur [dragœr] *adj* minesweeping ‖ *m* dredger; **dragueur de mines** minesweeper

drain [drɛ̃] *m* drainpipe; (med) drain
drainage [drɛnaʒ] *m* drainage
drainer [drɛne], [drene] *tr* to drain
draisine [drɛzin] *f* (rr) handcar
dramatique [dramatik] *adj* dramatic
dramatiser [dramatize] *tr* to dramatize
dramaturge [dramatyrʒ] *mf* playwright
dramaturgie [dramatyrʒi] *f* dramatics
drame [dram] *m* drama; tragic event
drap [dra] *m* cloth; sheet; **être dans de beaux draps** to be in a pretty pickle
dra·peau [drapo] *m* (*pl* **-peaux**) flag; **au drapeau!** colors (*bugle call*)!; **drapeau parlementaire** flag of truce; **être sous les drapeaux** to be a serviceman
draper [drape] *tr* to drape ‖ *ref* to drape oneself
draperie [drapəri] *f* drapery; drygoods business; textile industry
dra·pier [drapje] **-pière** [pjɛr] *mf* draper; textile manufacturer
drastique [drastik] *adj* (med) drastic
drêche [drɛʃ] *f* draff, residue of malt
drège [drɛʒ] *f* dragnet
drelin [drəlɛ̃] *m* ting-a-ling
drépanocytose [drepanɔsitoz] *f* sickle-cell anemia
dressage [drɛsaʒ] *m* training (*of animals*); erection
dresser [drɛse] §96, §100 *tr* to raise, hold erect; train; put up, erect; set (*the table; a trap*); draw up, draft; plane, smooth; **dresser l'oreille** to prick up one's ears ‖ *ref* to stand up straight, sit up straight; **se dresser contre** to be dead set against
dressoir [drɛswar] *m* sideboard, buffet, dish closet
dribble [dribl] *m* (sports) dribble
dribbler [drible] *tr* & *intr* (sports) to dribble
drille [drij] *m*—**joyeux drille** gay blade ‖ *f* jeweler's drill brace; **drilles** rags (*for papermaking*)
drisse [dris] *f* halyard, rope
drogue [drɔg] *f* drug; chemical; nostrum; concoction; narcotic; (coll) trash, rubbish; **drogues miracles** miracle drugs
dro·gué -guée [drɔge] *mf* drug addict; **drogué du travail** workaholic
droguer [drɔge] *tr* to drug or dope (*with too much medicine*) ‖ *intr* (coll) to cool one's heels ‖ *ref* to drug or dope oneself
droguerie [drɔgri] *f* drysaltery (Brit)
droguiste [drɔgist] *mf* drysalter (Brit)
droit [drwa], [drwa] **droite** [drwat], [drwat] *adj* right; honest; sincere; fair, just ‖ *m* law; right; justice; tax; right angle; **à bon droit** with reason; **de (plein) droit** rightfully, by rights, incontestably; **droit coutumier** common law; **droit de cité** key to the city; acceptability; **droits** duties, customs; rights; **droits civils** rights to manage property; **droits civiques, droits politiques** civil rights; **droits d'auteur** royalty; **droits de reproduction réservés** copyrighted; **tous droits réservés** ,all rights reserved, copyrighted ‖ *f* right, right-hand side; right hand; straight line; **à**

droite to or on the right ‖ **droit** *adv*—**droit au but** straight to the point; **tout droit** straight ahead
droit-fil [drwafil] *m* direct tradition
droi·tier [drwatje], [drwatje] **-tière** [tjɛr] *adj* right-handed ‖ *mf* right-handed person; rightist
droiture [drwatyr], [drwatyr] *f* integrity
drolatique [drɔlatik] *adj* droll, comic
drôle [drol] *adj* droll, funny, strange; **drôle de** funny, e.g., **une drôle d'idée** a funny idea; **drôle de guerre** phony war; **drôle d'homme, de corps, de pistolet,** or **de pierrot** (coll) queer duck ‖ *mf* (coll) queer duck, strange person
drôlerie [drolri] *f* drollery
drôlesse [drolɛs] *f* wench, hussy
dromadaire [drɔmadɛr] *m* dromedary
dronte [drɔt] *m* (orn) dodo
droppage [drɔpaʒ] *m* airdrop
drosser [drɔse] *tr* to drive, carry (*as the wind drives a ship ashore*)
dru drue [dry] *adj* thick, dense; fine (*rain*) ‖ **dru** *adv* thickly, heavily
druide [drɥid] *m* druid
du [dy] §77
dû due [dy] *adj* & *m* due ‖ *v* see **devoir**
duc [dyk] *m* duke; horned owl
ducat [dyka] *m* ducat
duché [dy/e] *m* duchy, dukedom
duchesse [dy/ɛs] *f* duchess
duègne [dɥɛɲ] *f* duenna
duel [dɥɛl] *m* duel; dual number; **duel oratoire** verbal battle
duelliste [dɥelist] *m* duelist
dulcifier [dylsifje] *tr* to sweeten
dûment [dymɑ̃] *adv* duly
dune [dyn] *f* dune
dunette [dynɛt] *f* (naut) poop
Dunkerque [dœ̃kɛrk] *f* Dunkirk
duo [dɥo] *m* duet; duo; **duo d'injures** exchange of words, insults
duodénum [dɥodenɔm] *m* duodenum
dupe [dyp] *f* dupe
duper [dype] *tr* to dupe
duperie [dypri] *f* deception, trickery
duplex [dyplɛks] *adj* two-way ‖ *m* duplex apartment
duplicata [dyplikata] *m* duplicate
duplicateur [dyplikatœr] *m* duplicating machine
duplication [dyplikasjɔ̃] *f* duplication
duplicité [dyplisite] *f* duplicity
duquel [dykɛl] §78
dur dure [dyr] *adj* hard; tough; difficult; **coucher sur la dure** to sleep on the bare ground or floor; **dur à la détente** tightfisted; **dur d'oreille** hard of hearing; **élever un enfant à la dure** to give a child a strict upbringing ‖ *mf* (coll) tough customer ‖ *m* hard material, concrete ‖ **dur** *adv* hard, e.g., **travailler dur** to work hard
durable [dyrabl] *adj* durable
durant [dyrɑ̃] *prep* during; (sometimes stands after noun), e.g., **sa vie durant** during his life

durcir [dyrsir] *tr, intr & ref* to harden
durcissement [dyrsismã] *m* hardening
durée [dyre] *f* duration; wear
durer [dyre] *intr* to last, endure
dureté [dyrte] *f* hardness; cruelty
durillon [dyrijõ] *m* callus, corn
duvet [dyvɛ] *m* down, fuzz; nap (*of cloth*)
duve·té -tée [dyvte] *adj* downy
duve·teux [dyvtø] **-teuse** [tøz] *adj* fuzzy
dynamique [dinamik] *adj* dynamic ‖

f dynamics
dynamiser [dinamize] *tr* (slang) to psych out
dynamite [dinamit] *f* dynamite
dynamiter [dinamite] *tr* to dynamite
dynamo [dinamo] *f* dynamo
dynaste [dinast] *m* dynast
dynastie [dinasti] *f* dynasty
dysenterie [disãtri] *f* dysentery
dyspepsie [dispɛpsi] *f* dyspepsia

E

E, e [ə], *[ə] *m invar* fifth letter of the French alphabet
E.A.O. [eao] *m* (letterword) (**enseignement assisté par ordinateur**) CAI (*computer-assisted instruction*)
eau [o] *f* (*pl* **eaux**) water; wake (*of ship*); **à l'eau de rose** maudlin; **de la plus belle eau** of the first water; **eau calcaire** hard water; **eau de cale** bilge water; **eau de Javel** bleach; **eau dentifrice** mouthwash; **eau dormante** still water; **eau douce** soft water; fresh water; **eau dure** hard water; **eau lourde** heavy water; **eau oxygénée** hydrogen peroxide; **eau vive** running water; **eaux** waters; waterworks; **eaux d'égouts** sewage; **eaux juvéniles** mineral waters; **eaux thermales** hot springs; **eaux usées, eaux résiduelles** polluted water; **eaux vives** swift current; **être en eau** to sweat; **faire de l'eau** to take in water; **faire eau** to leak; **grandes eaux** fountains; **nager entre deux eaux** to float under the surface; to play both sides of the street; **pêcher en eau trouble** to fish in troubled waters; **porter de l'eau à la rivière** or **à la mer** to carry coals to Newcastle; **tomber à l'eau** to fizzle out
eau-de-vie [odvi] *f* (*pl* **eaux-de-vie**) brandy; spirits
eau-forte [ofɔrt] *f* (*pl* **eaux-fortes**) aqua fortis; etching
éba·hi -hie [ebai] *adj* dumfounded
ébattre [ebatr] §7 *ref* to frolic, gambol, frisk about
ébauche [eboʃ] *f* rough sketch or draft; suspicion (*of a smile*)
ébaucher [eboʃe] *tr* to sketch, make a rough draft of
ébène [ebɛn] *f* ebony
ébénier [ebenje] *m* ebony (*tree*)
ébéniste [ebenist] *m* cabinetmaker
ébénisterie [ebenistri] *f* cabinetmaking
éberluer [ebɛrlɥe] *tr* to astonish
éblouir [ebluir] *tr* to dazzle, blind
éblouissement [ebluismã] *m* dazzle; glare; (pathol) dizziness
éboueur [ebwœr] *m* street cleaner, trash man; garbage collector
ébouillanter [ebujãte] *tr* to scald

éboulement [ebulmã] *m* cave-in, landslide
ébouler [ebule] *tr & ref* to cave in
ébourif·fant [eburifã] **-fante** [fãt] *adj* (coll) astounding
ébouriffer [eburife] *tr* to ruffle; (coll) to astound
ébouter [ebute] *tr* to cut off the end of
ébranchage [ebrãʃaʒ] *m* pruning
ébrancher [ebrãʃe] *tr* to prune
ébranlement [ebrãlmã] *m* shaking; shock
ébranler [ebrãle] *tr* to shake, jar ‖ *ref* to start out; be shaken
ébrécher [ebreʃe] §10 *tr* to nick, chip; make a dent in (*e.g., a fortune*) ‖ *ref* to be nicked, chipped; break off (*a tooth*)
ébriété [ebrijete] *f* inebriation
ébrouer [ebrue] *ref* to snort (*said of horse*); splash about; shake the water off oneself
ébruiter [ebrɥite] *tr* to noise about, blab ‖ *ref* to get around (*said of news*); leak out (*said of secret*)
ébullition [ebylisjõ] *f* boiling; ebullience, ferment
ébur·né -née [ebyrne] *adj* ivory
écaille [ekɑj] *f* scale (*of fish, snake*); shell; tortoise shell
écail·ler [ekɑje] **-lère** [jɛr] *mf* oyster opener ‖ *m* oysterman ‖ *f* oysterwoman ‖ **écailler** *tr & ref* to scale
écale [ekal] *f* shell, husk, hull
écaler [ekale] *tr* to shell, husk, hull
écarlate [ekarlat] *adj & f* scarlet
écarquiller [ekarkije] *tr* (coll) to open wide, spread apart
écart [ekar] *m* swerve, side step; digression, flight (*of imagination*); difference, gap, spread; error, (*in range*); lapse (*in good conduct*); (cards) discard; **à l'écart** aside; aloof; **à l'écart de** far from; **faire le grand écart** to do the splits; **faire un écart** to shy (*said of horse*) swerve (*said of car*); step aside (*said of person*)
écartèlement [ekartɛlmã] *m* quartering
écarteler [ekartəle] §2 *tr* to quarter

écartement [ekartəmɑ̃] *m* removal, separation; spreading; space between; spark gap; gauge (*of rails*)

écarter [ekarte] *tr* to put aside; keep away; ward off; draw aside; spread; (cards) to discard ‖ *ref* to turn away; stray

ecchymose [ɛkimoz] *f* black-and-blue mark

ecclésiastique [eklezastik] *adj & m* ecclesiastic

écerve·lé -lée [esɛrvəle] *adj* scatterbrained ‖ *mf* scatterbrain

échafaud [eʃafo] *m* scaffold

échafaudage [eʃafodaʒ] *m* scaffolding

échafauder [eʃafode] *tr* to pile up; lay the ground work for ‖ *intr* to erect a scaffolding

échalasser [eʃalase] *tr* to stake

échalote [eʃalɔt] *f* shallot

échancrer [eʃɑ̃kre] *tr* to make a V-shaped cut in (*the neck of a dress*); cut (*a dress*) low in the neck; indent; to hollow out

échange [eʃɑ̃ʒ] *m* exchange

échanger [eʃɑ̃ʒe] §38 *tr* to exchange; **échanger pour** or **contre** to exchange (*s.th.*) for

échangeur [eʃɑ̃ʒœr] *m* interchange; **échangeur en trèfle** (aut) cloverleaf

échanson [eʃɑ̃sɔ̃] *m* cupbearer

échantillon [eʃɑ̃tijɔ̃] *m* sample; **comparer à l'échantillon** to spot-check

échantillonnage [eʃɑ̃tijɔnaʒ] *m* sampling; spot check

échantillonner [eʃɑ̃tijɔne] *tr* to cut samples of; spot-check; select (*a sampling to be polled*)

échappatoire [eʃapatwar] *f* loophole, way out

échap·pé -pée [eʃape] *mf* escapee ‖ *f* escape; short period; glimpse; (sports) spurt; **à l'échappée** stealthily

échappement [eʃapmɑ̃] *m* escape; leak; exhaust; escapement (*of watch*); **échappement libre** cutout

échapper [eʃape] *tr*—**l'échapper belle** to have a narrow escape ‖ *intr* to escape; **échapper à** to escape from; **échapper de** to slip out of ‖ *ref* to escape

écharde [eʃard] *f* splinter, sliver

écharpe [eʃarp] *f* scarf; sash; sling; **en écharpe** diagonally, crosswise; in a sling; across the shoulder

écharper [eʃarpe] *tr* to slash, cut up

échasse [eʃɑs] *f* stilt

échauder [eʃode] *tr* to scald; white-wash; gouge (*a customer*)

échauffement [eʃofmɑ̃] *m* heating; overexcitement

échauffer [eʃofe] *tr* to heat; warm; **échauffer les oreilles à qn** to get s.o.'s dander up ‖ *ref* to heat up; become excited

échauffourée [eʃofure] *f* skirmish; rash undertaking

éche [ɛʃ] *f* bait

échéance [eʃeɑ̃s] *f* due date, expiration; **à courte échéance** before long; **à longue échéance** in the long run

échec [eʃɛk] *m* check; chess piece, chessman; failure; **échec et mat** checkmate; **échecs** [eʃɛ] chess; chess set; **être échec** to be in check; **jouer aux échecs** to play chess; **voué à l'échec** doomed to failure

échelle [eʃɛl] *f* ladder; scale; **échelle coulisse** extension ladder; **échelle de sauvetage** fire escape; **échelle d'incendie** fire ladder; **échelle mobile** sliding scale; **échelle pliante** stepladder; **monter à l'échelle** (coll) to bite, be fooled

échelon [eʃlɔ̃] *m* echelon; rung (*of ladder*)

échelonner [eʃlɔne] *tr* to spread out, space out ‖ *ref* (aer) to stack

écheniller [eʃnije] *tr* to remove caterpillars from; exterminate (*pests*); eradicate (*corruption*)

éche·veau [eʃvo] *m* (*pl* **-veaux**) skein

écheve·lé -lée [eʃəvle] *adj* disheveled; wild (*dance, race*)

écheveler [eʃəvle] §34 *tr* to dishevel

échevin [eʃvɛ̃] *m* (hist) alderman

échine [eʃin] *f* spine, backbone; **avoir l'échine souple** (coll) to be a yes man

échiner [eʃine] *tr* to break the back of; beat, kill ‖ *ref* to tire oneself out

échiquier [eʃikje] *m* chessboard; exchequer

écho [eko] *m* echo; piece of gossip; **échos** gossip column; **faire écho** to echo

échoir [eʃwar] (usually used only in: *inf; ger* **échéant;** *pp* **échu;** 3d *sg: pres ind* **échoit;** *pret* **échut;** *fut* **échoira;** *cond* **échoirait**) *intr* (aux: AVOIR or ÊTRE) to fall, devolve; fall due

échoppe [eʃɔp] *f* burin; (com) stand, booth; workshop

échopper [eʃɔpe] *tr* to scoop out

échotier [ekɔrje] *m* gossip columnist, society editor

échouer [eʃwe] *tr* to ground, beach ‖ *intr* to sink; run aground; fail ‖ *ref* to run aground

é·chu -chue [eʃy] *adj* due, payable

écimer [esime] *tr* to top

éclaboussement [eklabusmɑ̃] *m* splash

éclabousser [eklabuse] *tr* to splash

éclair [eklɛr] *adj* lightning (*e.g., speed*); flash (*bulb*) ‖ *m* flash (*of light, of lightning, of the eyes, of wit*); (culin) éclair; **éclairs** lightning; **éclairs de chaleur** heat lightning; **éclairs en nappe** sheet lightning; **il fait des éclairs** it is lightening; **passer comme un éclair** to flash by

éclairage [eklɛraʒ] *m* lighting; **sous cet éclairage** (fig) in this light

éclaircie [eklɛrsi] *f* break, clearing; spell of good weather; glade

éclaircir [eklɛrsir] *tr* to lighten; clear up; solve; make thin ‖ *ref* to clear up; thin out

éclaircissement [eklɛrsismɑ̃] *m* explanation, clearing up

éclairement [eklɛrmɑ̃] *m* illumination

éclairer [eklɛre] *tr* to light; enlighten; **éclairer sa lanterne** (fig) to ring a bell for s.o. ‖ *intr* to light up, glitter; **il éclaire** it is lightening ‖ *ref* to be lighted

éclai·reur [eklɛrœr] **-reuse** [røz] *mf* scout ‖ *m* boy scout ‖ *f* girl scout

éclat [ekla] *m* splinter; ray (*of sunshine*); peal (*of thunder*); burst (*of laughter*); brightness, splendor

éclatement [eklatmã] *m* explosion; blowout (*of tire*); (fig) split

éclater [eklate] *intr* to splinter; sparkle, glitter; burst; break out; blow up, explode

éclateur [eklatœr] *m* spark gap (*of induction coil*)

éclectique [eklɛktik] *adj* eclectic

éclipse [eklips] *f* eclipse; **à éclipses** flashing, blinking

éclipser [eklipse] *tr* to eclipse || *ref* to be eclipsed; (coll) to vanish; (coll) to sneak off

éclisse [eklis] *f* splinter; (med) splint; (rr) fishplate

éclisser [eklise] *tr* to splint

éclo·pé -pée [eklɔpe] *adj* lame || *mf* cripple

éclore [eklɔr] §24 *intr* (*aux:* ÊTRE) to hatch; blossom out

éclosion [eklozjɔ̃] *f* hatching; blooming

écluse [eklyz] *f* lock (*of canal, river, etc.*); floodgate

écluser [eklyze] *tr* to close (*a canal*) by a lock; pass (*a boat*) through a lock

écœurer [ekœre] *tr* to sicken; dishearten

école [ekɔl] *f* school; **école à tir** artillery practice; **école d'application** model school; **école d'arts et métiers** trade school; **école dominicale, école du dimanche** Sunday School; **école libre** private school; **école maternelle** nursery school; **école mixte** co-educational school; **être à bonne école** to be in good hands; **faire école** to set a fashion; to form a school (*to set up a doctrine, gain adherents*); **faire l'école buissonnière** (coll) to play hooky

éco·lier [ekɔlje] **-lière** [ljɛr] *adj* schoolboy || *mf* pupil, scholar; novice || *m* schoolboy || *f* schoolgirl

écologie [ekɔlɔʒi] *f* ecology

éconduire [ekɔ̃dɥir] §19 *tr* to show out

économat [ekɔnɔma] *m* comptroller's office; commissary, company or co-op store; **économats** chain stores

économe [ekɔnɔm] *adj* economical || *mf* treasurer; housekeeper || *m* bursar

économie [ekɔnɔmi] *f* economy; **économie de marché** free enterprise; **économie politique** economics; **économies** savings

économique [ekɔnɔmik] *adj* economic; economical || *f* economics

économiser [ekɔnɔmize] *tr & intr* to economize, save

écope [ekɔp] *f* scoop (*for bailing*)

écoper [ekɔpe] *tr* to bail out || *intr* (coll) to get a bawling out

écorce [ekɔrs] *f* bark (*of tree*); peel, rind; crust (*of earth*)

écorcer [ekɔrse] §51 *tr* to peel, strip off; to skin

écorcher [ekɔrʃe] *tr* to peel; chafe; fleece; overcharge; grate on (*the ears*); burn (*the throat*); murder (*a language*) || *ref* to skin (*e.g., one's arm*)

écor·cheur [ekɔrʃœr] **-cheuse** [ʃøz] *mf* skinner; fleecer, swindler

écorchure [ekɔrʃyr] *f* scratch, abrasion

écorner [ekɔrne] *tr* to poll, break the horns of; dog-ear; to make a hole in (*e.g., a fortune*)

écornifler [ekɔrnifle] *tr* to cadge; **écornifler un dîner à qn** to bum a dinner off s.o.

éconi·fleur [ekɔrniflœr] **-fleuse** [fløz] *mf* sponger, moocher

écos·sais [ekɔse] **-saise** [sɛz] *adj* Scotch, Scottish || *m* Scotch, Scottish (*language*); Scotch plaid || (*cap*) *mf* Scot; **les Écossais** the Scotch || *m* Scotchman

Écosse [ekɔs] *f* Scotland; **l'Écosse** Scotland

écosser [ekɔse] *tr* to shell, hull, husk

écot [eko] *m* share; tree stump; **payer son écot** to pay one's share

écoulement [ekulmã] *m* flow; (com) sale, turnover; (pathol) discharge; **écoulement d'eau** drainage

écouler [ekule] *tr* to sell, dispose of || *ref* to run (*said, e.g., of water*); flow; drain; leak; elapse, go by

écourter [ekurte] *tr* to shorten (*a dress, coat, etc.*); crop (*the tail, ears, etc.*); cut short, curtail

écoute [ekut] *f* listening post; monitoring; (naut) sheet; **écoutes** wild boar's ears; **être aux écoutes** to eavesdrop, keep one's ears to the ground; **se mettre à l'écoute** to listen to the radio

écouter [ekute] §95 *tr* to listen to; **écouter parler** to listen to (*s.o.*) speaking || *intr* to listen; **écouter aux portes** to eavesdrop || *ref* to coddle oneself; **s'écouter parler** to be pleased with the sound of one's own voice

écou·teur [ekutœr] **-teuse** [tøz] *mf* listener; **écouteur aux portes** eavesdropper || *m* telephone receiver; earphone

écoutille [ekutij] *f* hatchway

écouvillon [ekuvijɔ̃] *m* swab, mop

écrabouiller [ekrabuje] *tr* (coll) to squash

écran [ekrã] *m* screen; (photo) filter; **écran de cheminée** fire screen; **écran de protection aérienne** air umbrella; **écran en fil de fer** window screen; **le petit écran** television screen; **porter à l'écran** to put on the screen

écra·sant [ekrazã] **-sante** [zãt] *adj* crushing

écraser [ekraze] *tr* to crush; overwhelm; run over || *ref* to be crushed; crash

écrémer [ekreme] §10 *tr* to skim; (fig) to skim the cream off

écrémeuse [ekremøz] *f* cream separator

écrevisse [ekrəvis] *f* crayfish

écrier [ekrije] *ref* to cry out, exclaim

écrin [ekrɛ̃] *m* jewel case

écrire [ekrir] §25, §97, §98 *tr* to write; spell || *intr* to write || *ref* to write to each other; be written; be spelled

é·crit [ekri] **-crite** [krit] *adj* written; **c'était écrit** it was fate || *m* writing, written word; written examination; **écrits** writings, works; **par écrit** in writing

écri·teau [ekrito] *m* (*pl* **-teaux**) sign, placard

écritoire [ekritwar] *f* desk set

écriture [ekrityr] *f* handwriting; writing (*style of writing*); **écriture de chat** scrawl; **écritures** accounts; **Écritures** Scriptures; **écritures publiques** government documents

écrivailleur [ekrivajœr] *m* (coll) scribbler, hack writer

écrivain [ekrivɛ̃] *adj*—**femme écrivain** woman writer ‖ *m* writer; **écrivain public** public letter writer

écrivasser [ekrivase] *intr* (coll) to scribble

écrou [ekru] *m* nut (*with internal thread*); register (*on police blotter*); **écrou à oreille** thumb nut

écrouer [ekrue] *tr* to jail, book

écrouler [ekrule] *ref* to collapse; crumble; flop (*in a chair*)

é·cru -crue [ekry] *adj* raw; unbleached

écu [eky] *m* shield; crown (*money*); **écus** money

écrubier [ekrybje] *m* (naut) hawsehole

écueil [ekœj] *m* reef, sandbank; stumbling block

écuelle [ekɥɛl] *f* bowl

éculer [ekyle] *tr* to wear down at the heel

écu·mant [ekymɑ̃] **-mante** [mɑ̃t] *adj* foaming; fuming (*with rage*)

écume [ekym] *f* foam; froth; lather; dross; scum (*on liquids; on metal; of society*); **écume de mer** meerschaum

écumer [ekyme] *tr* to skim, scum; pick up (*e.g., gossip*); scour (*the seas*) ‖ *intr* to foam; scum; fume (*with anger*)

écu·meur [ekymœr] **-meuse** [møz] *mf* drifter; **écumeur de marmite** hanger-on; **écumeur de mer** pirate

écu·meux [ekymø] **-meuse** [møz] *adj* foamy, frothy

écumoire [ekymwar] *f* skimmer

écurage [ekyraʒ] *m* scouring; cleaning out

écurer [ekyre] *tr* to scour; clean out

écureuil [ekyrœj] *m* squirrel

écurie [ekyri] *f* stable (*for horses, mules, etc.*); string of horses

écusson [ekysɔ̃] *m* escutcheon; bud (*for grafting*); (mil) identification tag

écuyer [ekɥije] **écuyère** [ekɥijɛr] *mf* horseback rider ‖ *m* horseman; squire; riding master ‖ *f* horsewoman

eczéma [ɛkzema], [ɛgzema] *m* eczema

edelweiss [edəlvajs], [edɛlvɛs] *m* edelweiss

éden [edɛn] *m* Eden ‖ (*cap*) *m* Garden of Eden

éden·té -tée [edɑ̃te] *adj* toothless

E.D.F. *abbr* (**Électricité de France**) French national electric company

édicter [edikte] *tr* to decree, promulgate

édicule [edikyl] *m* kiosk; street urinal

édi·fiant [edifjɑ̃] **-fiante** [fjɑ̃t] *adj* edifying

édification [edifikasjɔ̃] *f* edification; construction, building

édifice [edifis] *m* edifice, building

édifier [edifje] *tr* to edify; inform, enlighten; construct, build; found

édit [edi] *m* edict

éditer [edite] *tr* to publish; edit (*a manuscript*)

édi·teur [editœr] **-trice** [tris] *mf* publisher; editor (*of a manuscript*)

édition [edisjɔ̃] *f* edition; publishing

edito·rial -riale [editɔrjal] *adj* & *m* (*pl* **-riaux** [rjo]) editorial

édredon [edrədɔ̃] *m* eiderdown

éduca·teur [edykatœr] **-trice** [tris] *adj* educational ‖ *mf* educator

éduca·tif [edykatif] **-tive** [tiv] *adj* educational

éducation [edykɑsjɔ̃] *f* education, bringing-up, nurture

éduquer [edyke] *tr* to bring up (*children*); educate, train

éfaufiler [efofile] *tr* to unravel

effacement [efasmɑ̃] *m* effacement, erasing; self-effacement

effacer [efase] §51 *tr* to efface; erase ‖ *ref* to efface oneself; stand aside

effarement [efarmɑ̃] *m* fright, scare

effaroucher [efaruʃe] *tr* to frighten, scare off

effec·tif [efɛktif] **-tive** [tiv] *adj* actual, real ‖ *m* personnel, manpower; strength (*of military unit*); complement (*of ship*); size (*of class*)

effectivement [efɛktivmɑ̃] *adv* actually, really, sure enough, indeed

effectuer [efɛktɥe] *tr* to make, effect, perform, execute ‖ *ref* to be made; take place, go off

effémi·né -née [efemine] *adj* effeminate

efféminer [efemine] *tr* to make a sissy of; unman ‖ *ref* to become effeminate

effervescence [efɛrvesɑ̃s] *f* effervescence; excitement, ferment

efferves·cent [efɛrvesɑ̃] **-cente** [sɑ̃t] *adj* effervescent

effet [efɛ] *m* effect; (billiards) english; **à cet effet** for that purpose; **en effet** indeed, actually, sure enough; **effet de commerce** bill of exchange; **effet de serre** greenhouse effect; **effets publics** government bonds; **faire de l'effet** to be striking; **faire l'effet de** to give the impression of

effeuillage [efœjaʒ] *m* thinning of leaves; striptease

effeuillaison [efœjɛzɔ̃] *f* fall of leaves

effeuiller [efœje] *tr* to thin out the leaves of, pluck off the petals of ‖ *ref* to shed its leaves

effeuilleuse [efœjøz] *f* (coll) stripteaser

efficace [efikas] *adj* effective

efficacement [efikasmɑ̃] *adv* effectively

efficacité [efikasite] *f* efficacy, efficiency

efficience [efisjɑ̃s] *f* efficiency

effi·cient [efisjɑ̃] **-ciente** [sjɑ̃t] *adj* efficient

effigie [efiʒi] *f* effigy

effiler [efile] *tr* to unravel; taper

effilocher [efilɔʃe] *tr* to unravel

efflan·qué -quée [eflɑ̃ke] *adj* skinny

effleurer [eflœre] *tr* to graze; touch on

effluve [eflyv] *m* effluvium, emanation

effondrement [efɔ̃drəmɑ̃] *m* collapse; (pathol) breakdown

effondrer [efɔ̃dre] *tr* to break open; break (*ground*) ‖ *ref* to collapse, cave in; sink

efforcer [efɔrse] §51, §96, §97 *ref*—s'**efforcer à** or **de** to try hard to, strive to

effort [efɔr] *m* effort; (med) hernia, rupture; **effort de rupture** breaking stress; **effort de tension** torque; **faire effort sur soi-même** to get a hold of oneself

effraction [efraksjɔ̃] *f* housebreaking

effraie [efrɛ] *f* screech owl

effranger [efrɑ̃ʒe] §38 *tr & ref* to fray

ef·frayant [efrɛjɑ̃] **-frayante** [frɛjɑ̃t] *adj* frightful, dreadful

effrayer [efrɛje] §49 *tr* to frighten ‖ §97 *ref* to be frightened

effré·né -née [efrene] *adj* unbridled

effritement [efritmɑ̃] *m* crumbling

effriter [efrite] *tr & ref* to crumble

effroi [efrwɑ] *m* fright

effron·té -tée [efrɔ̃te] *adj* impudent; shameless; (slang) saucy, sassy

effronterie [efrɔ̃tri] *f* effrontery

effroyable [efrwɑjabl] *adj* frightful

effusion [efyzjɔ̃] *f* effusion; shedding (*of blood*); (fig) gushing

égailler [egɑje] *ref* to scatter

é·gal -gale [egal] (*pl* **-gaux** [go]) *adj* equal; level; (coll) indifferent; **ça m'est égal** (coll) it's all the same to me, it's all right ‖ *mf* equal; **à l'égal de** as much as, no less than

également [egalmɑ̃] *adv* equally, likewise, also

égaler [egale] *tr* to equal, match

égaliser [egalize] *tr* to equalize; equate

égalitaire [egalitɛr] *adj & mf* equalitarian

égalité [egalite] *f* equality; evenness; **égalité des chances** equality of opportunity; **être à égalité** to be tied

égard [egar] *m* respect; **à l'égard de** with regard to; **à tous (les) égards** in all respects; **eu égard à** in consideration of

éga·ré -rée [egare] *adj* stray, lost

égarement [egarmɑ̃] *m* wandering (*of mind, senses, etc.*); frenzy (*of sorrow, anger, etc.*)

égarer [egare] *tr* to mislead; misplace; bewilder ‖ *ref* to get lost, stray; be on the wrong track

égayer [egeje] §49, §96 *tr & ref* to cheer up; brighten

égide [eʒid] *f* aegis

églefin [egləfɛ̃] *m* haddock

église [egliz] *f* church

églogue [eglɔg] *f* eclogue

égoïne [egɔin] *f* handsaw

égoïsme [egɔism] *m* egoism

égoïste [egɔist] *adj* selfish ‖ *mf* egoist

égorgement [egɔrʒəmɑ̃] *m* slaughter

égorger [egɔrʒe] §38 *tr* to cut the throat of; (coll) to overcharge

égosiller [egozije] *ref* to shout oneself hoarse

égotisme [egɔtism] *m* egotism

égotiste [egɔtist] *adj* egotistical ‖ *mf* egotist

égout [egu] *m* drainage; sewer; sink, cesspool (*e.g., of iniquity*)

égoutier [egutje] *m* sewer worker

égoutter [egute] *tr* to drain; let drip ‖ *ref* to drip

égouttoir [egutwar] *m* drainboard

égrapper [egrape] *tr* to pick off from the cluster

égratigner [egratiɲe] *tr* to scratch; take a dig at, to tease

égratignure [egratiɲyr] *f* scratch; gibe, dig

égrener [egrəne]§2 *tr* to shell (*e.g., peas*); gin (*cotton*); pick off (*grapes*); unstring (*pearls*); tell (*beads*) ‖ *ref* to drop one by one; be strung out

égril·lard [egrijar] **-larde** [jard] *adj* spicy, lewd ‖ *mf* shameless, unblushing person

égrugeoir [egryʒwar] *m* mortar (*for pounding or grinding*)

égruger [egryʒe] §38 *tr* to pound (*in a mortar*)

égueuler [egœle] *tr* to break the neck of (*e.g., a bottle*)

Égypte [eʒipt] *f* Egypt; **l'Égypte** Egypt

égyp·tien [eʒipsjɛ̃] **-tienne** [sjɛn] *adj* Egyptian ‖ (*cap*) *mf* Egyptian

eh [ɛ] *interj* well!; **en bien!** well, well!; very well!

éhon·té -tée [eɔ̃te] *adj* shameless

eider [ɛjdɛr] *m* eider duck

éjaculation [eʒakylɑsjɔ̃] *f* ejaculation; (eccl) short, fervent prayer

éjaculer [eʒakyle] *tr & intr* to ejaculate

éjecter [eʒɛkte] *tr* to eject; (coll) to oust

éjection [eʒɛksjɔ̃] *f* ejection

élabo·ré -rée [elabɔre] *adj* elaborated; prepared, elaborate

élaborer [elabɔre] *tr* to elaborate; work out, develop

élaguer [elage] *tr* to prune

élan [elɑ̃] *m* dash; impulse, outburst; spirit, glow; (zool) elk, moose; **avec élan** with enthusiasm

élan·cé -cée [elɑ̃se] *adj* slender, slim

élancement [elɑ̃smɑ̃] *m* throbbing, twinge; yearning (*e.g., for God*)

élancer [elɑ̃se] §51 *intr* to throb, twinge ‖ *ref* to rush, spring, dash; spurt out

élargir [elarʒir] *tr* to widen; broaden; release (*a prisoner*) ‖ *ref* to widen; become more lax

élasticité [elastisite] *f* elasticity

élastique [elastik] *adj* elastic ‖ *m* elastic; rubber band

élec·teur [elɛktœr] **-trice** [tris] *adj* voting ‖ *mf* voter, constituent; (hist) elector; **électeurs** electorate

élec·tif [elɛktif] **-tive** [tiv] *adj* elective

élection [elɛksjɔ̃] *f* election; choice; **élection blanche** election without a valid result

électorat [elɛktɔra] *m* right to vote; (hist) electorate

électri·cien [elɛktrisjɛ̃] **-cienne** [sjɛn] *adj* electrical (*worker*) ‖ *mf* electrician

électricité [elɛktrisite] *f* electricity

électrifier [elɛktrifje] *tr* to electrify

électrique [elɛktrik] *adj* electric(al)

électriser [elɛktrize] *tr* to electrify

électro [elɛktro] *m* electromagnet

électro-aimant [elɛktrɔɛmɑ̃] *m* (*pl* -**aimants**) electromagnet

électrochoc [elɛktrɔʃɔk] *m* (med) electric shock treatment

électro-culinaire [elɛktrɔkylinɛr] *adj* electric kitchen (*appliances*)

électrocuter [elɛktrɔkyte] *tr* to electrocute

électrode [elɛktrɔd] *f* electrode

électrolyse [elɛktrɔliz] *f* electrolysis

électrolyte [elɛktrɔlit] *m* electrolyte

électromagnétique [elɛktrɔmaɲetik] *adj* electromagnetic

électroména·ger [elɛktrɔmenaʒe] -**gère** [ʒɛr] *adj* household-electric

électromo·teur [elɛktrɔmɔtœr] -**trice** [tris] *adj* electromotive ǁ *m* electric motor

électron [elɛktrɔ̃] *m* electron

électronique [elɛktrɔnik] *adj* electronic ǁ *f* electronics

électron-volt [elɛktrɔ̃vɔlt] *m* (*pl* **électrons-volts**) electron-volt

électrophone [elɛktrɔfɔn] *m* electric phonograph

électrotype [elɛktrɔtip] *m* electrotype

électrotyper [elɛktrɔtipe] *tr* to electrotype

élégamment [elegamɑ̃] *adv* elegantly

élégance [elegɑ̃s] *f* elegance

élé·gant [elegɑ̃] -**gante** [gɑ̃t] *adj* elegant

élégiaque [eleʒjak] *adj* elegiac ǁ *mf* elegist

élégie [eleʒi] *f* elegy

élément [elemɑ̃] *m* element; (*of an electric battery*) cell, element; (elec, mach) unit; **élément standard** standard part

élémentaire [elemɑ̃tɛr] *adj* elementary

éléphant [elefɑ̃] *m* elephant

éléphantesque [elefɑ̃tɛsk] *adj* (coll) gigantic, elephantine

élevage [elvaʒ], [ɛlvaʒ] *m* rearing, raising, breeding; ranch

éléva·teur [elevatœr] -**trice** [tris] *adj* lifting ǁ *m* elevator; hoist

élévation [elevasjɔ̃] *f* elevation; promotion; increase; (rok) lift-off

élève [elɛv] *mf* pupil, student; **ancien élève** alumnus; **élève externe** day student; **élève interne** boarding student ǁ *f* breeder (*animal*); (hort) seedling

éle·vé -vée [elve] *adj* high, elevated; lofty, noble; **bien élevé** well-bred; **mal élevé** ill-bred

élever [elve] §2 *tr* to raise; raise, bring up, nurture; erect ǁ *ref* to rise; arise; be built, stand

éle·veur [elvœr] -**veuse** [vøz] *mf* breeder, rancher

elfe [ɛlf] *m* elf

élider [elide] *tr* to elide

éligible [eliʒibl] *adj* eligible

élimer [elime] *tr* & *ref* to wear threadbare

éliminatoire [eliminatwar] *adj* (sports) preliminary ǁ *f* (sports) preliminaries

éliminer [elimine] *tr* to eliminate

élire [elir] §36 *tr* to elect

élision [elizjɔ̃] *f* elision

élite [elit] *f* elite

elle [ɛl] *pron disj* §85 her ǁ *pron conj* §87 she

elle-même [ɛlmɛm] §86 herself, itself

elles [ɛl] *pron disj* §85 them *pron conj* §87 they

ellipse [elips] *f* (gram) ellipsis; (math) ellipse

elliptique [eliptik] *adj* elliptic(al)

élocution [elɔkysjɔ̃] *f* elocution; choice and arrangement of words

éloge [elɔʒ] *m* eulogy; praise

élo·gieux [elɔʒjø] -**gieuse** [ʒjøz] *adj* full of praise

éloi·gné -gnée [elwaɲe] *adj* distant

éloignement [elwaɲəmɑ̃] *m* remoteness; aversion; postponement

éloigner [elwaɲe] *tr* to move away; remove; drive away; postpone ǁ *ref* to move away; digress, deviate; become estranged

élongation [elɔ̃gasjɔ̃] *f* stretching

élonger [elɔ̃ʒe] §38 *tr* to lay (*e.g., a cable*); **élonger la terre** to skirt the coast

éloquence [elɔkɑ̃s] *f* eloquence

élo·quent [elɔkɑ̃] -**quente** [kɑ̃t] *adj* eloquent

é·lu -lue [ely] *adj* elected ǁ *mf* chosen one; **les élus** the elect ǁ *v* see **élire**

élucider [elyside] *tr* to elucidate

éluder [elyde] *tr* to elude, avoid

éma·cié -ciée [emasje] *adj* emaciated

émacier [emasje] *ref* to become emaciated

é·mail [emaj] *m* (*pl* -**maux** [mo]) enamel ǁ *m* (*pl* -**mails**) nail polish; car or bicycle paint

émaillage [emajaʒ] *m* enameling

émailler [emaje] *tr* to enamel; sprinkle (*e.g., with quotations, metaphors, etc.*); dot (*e.g., the fields, as flowers do*)

émanation [emanasjɔ̃] *f* emanation; manifestation (*e.g., of authority*)

émanciper [emɑ̃sipe] *tr* to emancipate ǁ *ref* to be emancipated; (coll) to get out of hand

émaner [emane] *intr* to emanate

émarger [emarʒe] §38 *tr* to trim (*e.g., a book*); initial (*a document*) ǁ *intr* to get paid; **émarger à** to be paid from

émasculer [emaskyle] *tr* to emasculate

embâcle [ɑ̃bakl] *m* pack ice, ice floe

emballage [ɑ̃balaʒ] *m* packing, wrapping; **emballage consigné** returnable bottle; **emballage perdu** nonreturnable bottle

emballer [ɑ̃bale] *tr* to wrap up, pack; race (*a motor*); (coll) to thrill; (coll) to bawl out ǁ *ref* to bolt, run away; (mach) to race; (coll) to get worked up

embal·leur [ɑ̃balœr] -**leuse** [løz] *mf* packer

embarbouiller [ɑ̃barbuje] *tr* to besmear; (coll) to muddle, confuse ǁ *ref* (coll) to get tangled up

embarcadère [ɑ̃barkadɛr] *m* wharf; (rr) platform

embarcation [ɑ̃barkasjɔ̃] *f* small boat

embardée [ɑ̃barde] *f* lurch; (aut) swerve; (aer, naut) yaw

embarder [ɑ̃barde] *intr* (aut) to swerve; (aer, naut) to yaw

embargo [ɑ̃bargo] *m* embargo

embarquement [ɑ̃barkəmɑ̃] *m* embarkation; shipping; loading

embarquer [ɑ̃barke] *tr* to embark; ship (*a sea*); load (*in car, plane, etc.*); (coll) to put in the clink ‖ *ref* to embark; board; get into a car

embarras [ɑ̃bara] *m* embarrassment; trouble, inconvenience; encumbrance, obstruction; perplexity; financial difficulties; **embarras de voitures** traffic jam; **embarras du choix** too much to choose from; **faire des embarras** (coll) to put on airs

embarras·sé -sée [ɑ̃barase] *adj* embarrassed; awkward, ill-at-ease; confused, muddled; upset (*stomach*)

embarrasser [ɑ̃barase] *tr* to embarrass; hamper, obstruct; stump, perplex ‖ *ref*—**s'embarrasser de** to take an interest in; bother with

embaucher [ɑ̃boʃe] *tr* to hire, sign on; (coll) to entice (*soldiers*) to desert ‖ *intr* to hire; **on n'embauche pas** (*public sign*) no help wanted

embauchoir [ɑ̃boʃwar] *m* shoetree

embaumement [ɑ̃boməmɑ̃] *m* embalming; perfuming

embaumer [ɑ̃bome] *tr* to embalm; perfume ‖ *intr* to smell good

embaumeur [ɑ̃bomœr] *m* embalmer

embellir [ɑ̃bɛlir] *tr* to embellish ‖ *intr* to clear up (*said of weather*); improve in looks ‖ *ref* to grow more beautiful

embellissement [ɑ̃bɛlismɑ̃] *m* embellishment

embêtement [ɑ̃bɛtmɑ̃] *m* (coll) annoyance

embêter [ɑ̃bɛte], [ɑ̃bete] *tr* (coll) to annoy

emblave [ɑ̃blav] *f* grainfield

emblaver [ɑ̃blave] *tr* to sow

emblée [ɑ̃ble]—**d'emblée** then and there, right off; without difficulty

emblématique [ɑ̃blematik] *adj* emblematic(al)

emblème [ɑ̃blɛm] *m* emblem

embobeliner [ɑ̃bɔbline] *tr* (coll) to bamboozle

embobiner [ɑ̃bɔbine] *tr* to wind up (*e.g., on a reel*); (coll) to bamboozle

emboîter [ɑ̃bwate] *tr* to encase; nest (*boxes, boats, etc.*); (mach) to interlock, joint; **emboîter le pas** to fall into step

embolie [ɑ̃bɔli] *f* (pathol) embolism

embonpoint [ɑ̃bɔ̃pwɛ̃] *m* portliness; **prendre de l'embonpoint** to put on flesh

embouche [ɑ̃buʃ] *f* pasture

embou·ché -chée [ɑ̃buʃe] *adj*—**mal embouché** foul-mouthed

emboucher [ɑ̃buʃe] *tr* to blow, sound

embouchoir [ɑ̃buʃwar] *m* mouthpiece

embouchure [ɑ̃buʃyr] *f* mouth (*of a river*); mouthpiece

embourber [ɑ̃burbe] *tr* to stick in the mud; vilify, implicate

embout [ɑ̃bu] *m* tip, ferrule; rubber tip (*for chair*)

embouteillage [ɑ̃butɛjaʒ] *m* bottling; bottleneck, traffic jam

emboutir [ɑ̃butir] *tr* to stamp, emboss; smash (*e.g., a fender*) ‖ *ref* to bump

embranchement [ɑ̃brɑ̃ʃmɑ̃] *m* branching (off); branch; branch line; junction (*of roads, track, etc.*); **embranchement particulier** private siding

embrasement [ɑ̃brazmɑ̃] *m* conflagration; illumination, glow

embraser [ɑ̃braze] *tr* to set aflame or aglow ‖ *ref* to flame up; glow

embrassade [ɑ̃brasad] *f* embrace; kissing

embrasse [ɑ̃bras] *f* curtain tieback

embrassement [ɑ̃brasmɑ̃] *m* embrace

embrasser [ɑ̃brase] *tr* to embrace; kiss; join; undertake; take in (*at a glance*); take (*the opportunity*) ‖ *ref* to embrace; neck

embras·seur [ɑ̃brasœr] **-seuse** [søz] *mf* smoocher

embrasure [ɑ̃brazyr] *f* embrasure, loophole; opening (*for door or window*)

embrayage [ɑ̃brɛjaʒ] *m* coupling engagement; (aut) clutch

embrayer [ɑ̃brɛje], [ɑ̃breje] §49 *tr* to engage, connect; throw into gear ‖ *intr* to throw the clutch in

embrocher [ɑ̃brɔʃe] *tr* to put on a spit

embrouillage [ɑ̃brujaz] *m* (electron) scrambling

embrouiller [ɑ̃bruje] *tr* to embroil ‖ *ref* to become embroiled

embroussail·lé -lée [ɑ̃brusaje] *adj* bushy; tangled; complicated, complex

embru·mé -mée [ɑ̃bryme] *adj* foggy, misty

embruns [ɑ̃brœ̃] *mpl* spray

embryologie [ɑ̃brijɔlɔʒi] *f* embryology

embryon [ɑ̃brijɔ̃] *m* embryo

embryonnaire [ɑ̃brijɔnɛr] *adj* embryonic

em·bu -bue [ɑ̃by] *adj* lifeless, dull ‖ *m* dull tone (*of a painting*)

embûche [ɑ̃byʃ] *f* snare, trap

embuer [ɑ̃bɥe] *tr* to cloud with steam; **embué de larmes** dimmed with tears

embuscade [ɑ̃byskad] *f* ambush

embus·qué -quée [ɑ̃byske] *adj* in ambush; **se tenir embusqué** to lie in ambush ‖ *m* (mil) goldbricker, shirker

embusquer [ɑ̃byske] *tr* to ambush, trap ‖ *ref* to lie in ambush; (mil) to get a safe assignment

émé·ché -chée [emeʃe] *adj* (coll) tipsy, high

émender [emɑ̃de] *tr* to amend (*a sentence, decree, etc.*)

émeraude [ɛmrod] *f* emerald

émergence [emɛrʒɑ̃s] *f* emergence

émerger [emɛrʒe] §38 *intr* to emerge

émeri [ɛmri] *m* emery

émerillon [ɛmrijɔ̃] *m* swivel; (orn) merlin

émerillon·né -née [ɛmrijɔne] *adj* lively, gay

émérite [emerit] *adj* experienced; distinguished, remarkable; confirmed (*smoker*); (obs) retired, emeritus

émersion [emɛrsjɔ̃] *f* emersion

émerveillement [emɛrvɛjmɑ̃] *m* wonderment

émerveiller [emɛrvɛje] *tr* to astonish, amaze

émétique [emetik] *adj & m* emetic

émet·teur [emɛtœr] **-trice** [tris] *adj* issuing; transmitting ‖ *mf* maker (*of check, draft*); issuer ‖ *m* broadcasting station; (rad) transmitter

émetteur-récepteur [emɛtœrresɛptœr] *m* (*pl* **émetteurs-récepteurs**) (rad) walkietalkie

émettre [emɛtr] §42 *tr* to emit; express (*an opinion*); issue (*stamps, bank notes, etc.*); transmit (*a radio signal*) ‖ *intr* to transmit, broadcast

é·meu [emø] *m* (*pl* **-neus**) (zool) emu

émeute [emøt] *f* riot

émeutier [emøtje] *m* rioter

émietter [emjete] *tr* to crumble; break up (*an estate*)

émi·grant [emigrɑ̃] **-grante** [grɑ̃t] *adj & mf* emigrant; migrant

émi·gré -grée [emigre] *adj* emigrating ‖ *mf* emigrant; émigré

émigrer [emigre] *intr* to emigrate; migrate

émincer [emɛ̃se] §51 *tr* to cut in thin slices

éminemment [eminamɑ̃] *adv* eminently

éminence [eminɑ̃s] *f* eminence

émi·nent [eminɑ̃] **-nente** [nɑ̃t] *adj* eminent

émissaire [emisɛr] *m* emissary; outlet (*of lake, basin, etc.*)

émission [emisjɔ̃] *f* emission; utterance; issue (*of stamps, bank notes, etc.*) (rad) transmission, broadcast

emmagasiner [ɑ̃magazine] *tr* to put in storage; store up; stockpile

emmailloter [ɑ̃majɔte] *tr* to swathe; bandage

emmancher [ɑ̃mɑ̃ʃe] *tr* to put a handle on ‖ *ref* (coll) to begin; **s'emmancher bien** (coll) to get off to a good start; **s'emmancher mal** (coll) to get off to a bad start

emmêler [ɑ̃mɛle], [ɑ̃mele] *tr* to tangle up; mix up

emménagement [ɑ̃menaʒmɑ̃] *m* moving in; installation

emménager [ɑ̃menaʒe] §38 *tr & intr* to move in

emmener [ɑ̃mne] §2 *tr* to take or lead away; take out (*e.g., to dinner*); take (*on a visit*)

emmenthal [emɛtal], [emɛntal] *m* Swiss cheese

emmer·dant [ɑ̃mɛrdɑ̃] **-dante** [dɑ̃t] *adj* (slang) damned annoying, damned boring

emmerder [ɑ̃mɛrde] *tr* (slang) to annoy, bore, bug ‖ *ref* (slang) to be pissed off; (slang) to be bored stiff

emmiel·lé -lée [ɑ̃mjɛle], [ɑ̃mjele] *adj* honeyed (*e.g., words*)

emmitoufler [ɑ̃mitufle] *tr & ref* to bundle up (*in warm clothing*)

emmurer [ɑ̃myre] *tr* to wall in, immure

émoi [emwa] *m* agitation, alarm

émolument [emɔlymɑ̃] *m* share; **émoluments** emolument, fee, salary

émonder [emɔ̃de] *tr* to prune, trim

émo·tif [emɔtif] **-tive** [tiv] *adj* emotional ‖ *mf* emotional person

émotion [emosjɔ̃] *f* emotion; commotion

émotionnable [emosjɔnabl] *adj* emotional

émotion·nant [emosjɔnɑ̃] **-nante** [nɑ̃t] *adj* stirring, moving

émotionner [emosjɔne] *tr* to move deeply, thrill, affect ‖ *ref* to get excited, flustered

émoucher [emuʃe] *tr* to chase flies away from

émouchet [emuʃɛ] *m* sparrow hawk

émouchoir [emuʃwar] *m* whisk, fly swatter

émoudre [emudr] §43 *tr* to grind, sharpen

émoulage [emulaʒ] *m* grinding, sharpening

émou·lu -lue [emuly] *adj*—**frais émoulu de** (fig) fresh from, just back from

émous·sé -sée [emuse] *adj* blunt

émousser [emuse] *tr* to dull, blunt

émoustiller [emustije] *tr* (coll) to exhilarate, rouse; tantalize

émou·vant [emuvɑ̃] **-vante** [vɑ̃t] *adj* moving, touching, stirring

émouvoir [emuvwar] §45 (*pp* **ému**) *tr* to move; excite ‖ *ref* to be moved; be excited

empailler [ɑ̃pɑje] *tr* to stuff (*animals*); cane (*a chair*)

empail·leur [ɑ̃pɑjœr] **-leuse** [jøz] *mf* taxidermist; caner

empaler [ɑ̃pale] *tr* to impale

empan [ɑ̃pɑ̃] *m* span (*of hand*)

empanacher [ɑ̃panaʃe] *tr* to plume

empaquetage [ɑ̃paktaʒ] *m* packaging; package

empaqueter [ɑ̃pakte] §34 *tr* to package

emparer [ɑ̃pare] *ref*—**s'emparer de** to seize, take hold of

empâter [ɑ̃pate] *tr* to make sticky; fatten up (*chickens, turkeys, etc.*); coat (*the tongue*); (typ) to overlink ‖ *ref* to put on weight; become coated (*said of tongue*); become husky (*said of voice*)

empattement [ɑ̃patmɑ̃] *m* foundation, footing; (aut) wheelbase

empaumer [ɑ̃pome] *tr* to catch in the hand; hit with a racket; palm (*a card*); (coll) to hoodwink

empêchement [ɑ̃pɛʃmɑ̃] *m* impediment, bar; hindrance, obstacle

empêcher [ɑ̃pɛʃe] §97, §99 *tr* to hinder; **empêcher qn de** + *inf* to prevent or keep s.o. from + *ger;* **n'empêche que** all the same, e.g., **n'empêche qu'il est très poli** he's very polite all the same ‖ §97 *ref*—**ne pouvoir s'empêcher de** + *inf* not to be able to help + *ger,* e.g., **je n'ai pu m'empêcher de rire** I could not help laughing

empê·cheur [ɑ̃pɛʃœr] **-cheuse** [ʃøz] *mf*—**empêcheur de danser en rond** (coll) wet blanket

empeigne [ɑ̃pɛɲ] *f* upper (*of shoe*)

empennage [ɑ̃penaʒ] *m* feathers (*of arrow*); fins, vanes; (aer) empennage

empereur [ɑ̃prœr] *m* emperor

emperler [ɑ̃pɛrle] *tr* to ornament with pearls; cover with drops; **la sueur emper-**

lait son front his forehead was covered with beads of perspiration

empe·sé -sée [ᾱpəze] *adj* starched, stiff, wooden (*style*)

empeser [ᾱpəze] §2 *tr* to starch

empes·té -tée [ᾱpɛste] *adj* pestilential; stinking, reeking; depraved

empester [ᾱpɛste] *tr* to stink; corrupt ‖ *intr* to stink

empêtrer [ᾱpɛtre] *tr* to hamper; involve, entangle ‖ *ref* to become involved, entangled

emphase [ᾱfɑz] *f* overemphasis; bombast, pretentiousness

emphatique [ᾱfɑtik] *adj* overemphasized; bombastic, pretentious

emphysème [ᾱfizɛm] *m* emphysema

empiècement [ᾱpjɛsmᾱ] *m* yoke (*of shirt, blouse, etc.*)

empierrer [ᾱpjɛre] *tr* to pave with stones; (rr) to ballast

empiètement [ᾱpjɛtmᾱ] *m* encroachment, incursion

empiéter [ᾱpjete] §10 *intr* to encroach

empiffrer [ᾱpifre] *tr* (coll) to stuff, fatten ‖ *ref* (coll) to stuff oneself, guzzle

empiler [ᾱpile] *tr* to pile up, stack; (slang) to dupe ‖ *ref* to pile up; **se faire empiler** (slang) to be had

empire [ᾱpir] *m* empire; control, supremacy

empirer [ᾱpire] *tr* to make worse, aggravate ‖ *intr* (*aux:* AVOIR or ÊTRE) to grow worse

empirique [ᾱpirik] *adj* empiric(al) ‖ *m* empiricist; charlatan, quack

emplacement [ᾱplasmᾱ] *m* emplacement; location, site

emplâtre [ᾱplɑtr] *m* patch (*on tire*); (med) plaster; (coll) boob

emplette [ᾱplɛt] *f* purchase; **aller faire des emplettes** to go shopping

emplir [ᾱplir] *tr & ref* to fill up

emploi [ᾱplwa] *m* employment, job; employment, use; (theat) type (*of role*); **double emploi** useless duplication; **emploi du temps** schedule

em·ployé -ployée [ᾱplwaje] *mf* employee; clerk

employer [ᾱplwaje] §47, §100 *tr* to employ; to use ‖ §96 *ref* to be employed; **s'employer à** to try to, do one's best to

em·ployeur [ᾱplwajœr] **-ployeuse** [plwajøz] *mf* employer

empocher [ᾱpɔʃe] *tr* (coll) to pocket

empoi·gnant [ᾱpwaɲᾱ] **-gnante** [ɲᾱt] *adj* exciting, arresting, thrilling

empoigner [ᾱpwaɲe] *tr* to grasp; collar (*a crook*); grip, move (*an audience*)

empois [ᾱpwa] *m* starch

empoisonnement [ᾱpwazɔnmᾱ] *m* poisoning; **avoir des empoisonnements** (coll) to be annoyed

empoisonner [ᾱpwazɔne] *tr* to poison; infect (*the air*); corrupt; (coll) to bother ‖ *intr* to reek ‖ *ref* to be poisoned

empoison·neur [ᾱpwazɔnœr] **-neuse** [nøz] *adj* poisoning ‖ *mf* poisoner; corrupter

empoissonner [ᾱpwasɔne] *tr* to stock with fish

empor·té -tée [ᾱpɔrte] *adj* quick-tempered, impetuous

emportement [ᾱpɔrtəmᾱ] *m* anger, temper

emporte-pièce [ᾱpɔrtəpjɛs] *m* (*pl* **-pièces**) punch; **à l'emporte-pièce** trenchant, cutting, biting (*style, words, etc.*)

emporter [ᾱpɔrte] *tr* to take away; carry off; remove; **à emporter** to take out, to go (*e.g., said of food to take out of the restaurant*); **l'emporter sur** to have the upper hand over ‖ *ref* to be carried away; lose one's temper; run away

emporte-restes [ᾱpɔrtrɛst] *m invar* (coll) doggy bag

empo·té -tée [ᾱpɔte] *adj* (coll) clumsy ‖ *mf* (coll) butterfingers

empoter [ᾱpɔte] *tr* to pot (*a plant*)

empourprer [ᾱpurpre] *tr* to set aglow ‖ *ref* to turn crimson; flush

empoussiérer [ᾱpusjere] §10 *tr* to cover with dust

empreindre [ᾱprɛ̃dr] §50 *tr* to imprint, stamp

empreinte [ᾱprɛ̃t] *f* imprint, stamp; **empreinte des roues** wheel tracks; **empreinte digitale** fingerprint; **empreinte du pied** or **empreinte de pas** footprint

empres·sé -sée [ᾱprese] *adj* eager

empressement [ᾱpresmᾱ] *m* haste, alacrity; eagerness, readiness

empresser [ᾱprese] §96, §97 *ref* to hasten; **s'empresser à** to be anxious to; **s'empresser auprès de** to be attentive to, make a fuss over; press around; **s'empresser de** to hasten to

emprise [ᾱpriz] *f* expropriation; control, ascendancy

emprisonment [ᾱprizɔnmᾱ] *m* imprisonment

emprisonner [ᾱprizɔne] *tr* to imprison

emprunt [ᾱprœ̃] *m* loan; loan word; **d'emprunt** feigned, assumed

emprun·té -tée [ᾱprœ̃te] *adj* timid, self-conscious, awkward; feigned, sham

emprunter [ᾱprœ̃te] *tr* to borrow; take (*a road, a route*); take on (*false appearances*); **emprunter q.ch. à** to borrow s.th. from; get s.th. from

empuantir [ᾱpɥᾱtir] *tr* to stink up

empyème [ᾱpjɛm] *m* empyema

empyrée [ᾱpire] *m* empyrean

é·mu -mue [emy] *adj* moved, touched; tender (*memory*); **ému de** alarmed by ‖ *v see* **émouvoir**

émulation [emylasjɔ̃] *f* emulation, rivalry

émule [emyl] *mf* emulator, rival

émulsion [emylsjɔ̃] *f* emulsion

émulsionner [emylsjɔne] *tr* to emulsify

en [ᾱ] *pron indef & adv* §87 ‖ *prep* in; into; to, e.g., **de mal en pis** from bad to worse; at, e.g., **en mer** at sea; e.g., **en guerre** at war; on, e.g., **en congé** on leave; by, e.g., **en chemin de fer** by rail; of, made of, e.g., **en bois** (made) of wood; as, e.g., **il est mort en soldat** he died (as) a soldier

enamourer [ãnamure] *ref* to become enamored, fall in love

énarque [enark] *mf* (fig) bureaucrat

encabaner [ãkabane] *ref* (Canad) to hole up, dig in (*e.g., for the winter*)

encablure [ãkablyr] *f* cable's length (*unit of measure*)

encadrement [ãkadrəmã] *m* framing; frame: framework; window frame; doorframe; border, edge; staffing; officering (*furnishing with officers*)

encadrer [ãkadre] *tr* to frame; staff (*an organization*); officer (*troops*); incorporate (*recruits*) into a unit; train, supervise

encadreur [ãkadrœr] *m* framer (*person*)

encager [ãkaʒe] §38 *tr* to cage

encaisse [ãkɛs] *f* cash on hand, cash balance; **encaisse métallique** bullion

encais·sé -sée [ãkɛse] *adj* deeply embanked, sunken

encaissement [ãkɛsmã] *m* cashing (*e.g., of check*); boxing, crating; embankment

encaisser [ãkɛse], [ãkese] *tr* to cash; box, crate; receive (*a blow*); embank (*a river*); (coll) to put up with ‖ *ref* to be steeply embanked

encaisseur [ãkɛsœr] *m* collector; payee; cashier

encan [ãkã] *m* auction

encanailler [ãkanaje] *tr* to debase ‖ *ref* to acquire bad habits; keep low company

encapuchonner [ãkapyʃɔne] *tr* to hood

encaquer [ãkake] *tr* to barrel; pack (*sardines*); (coll) to pack in like sardines

encart [ãkar] *m* inset, insert

encarter [ãkarte] *tr* to card (*buttons, pins, etc.*); (bb) to tip in

en-cas [ãka] *m invar* snack; reserve, emergency supply

encasernement [ãkazɛrnəmã] *m*—**encasernement de conscience** thought control, regimentation

encaserner [ãkazɛrne] *tr* to quarter, barrack (*troops*)

encastrement [ãkastrəmã] *m* groove; fitting

encas·tré -trée [ãkastre] *adj* built-in

encastrer [ãkastre] *tr & ref* to fit

encaustique [ãkɔstik] *f* furniture polish; floor wax; encaustic painting

encaustiquer [ãkɔstike] *tr* to wax

encaver [ãkave] *tr* to cellar (*wine*)

enceindre [ãsɛ̃dr] §50 *tr* to enclose, encircle

enceinte [ãsɛ̃t] *adj fem* pregnant ‖ *f* enclosure; walls, ramparts; precinct, compass; (boxing) ring

encens [ãsã] *m* incense; flattery

encenser [ãsãse] *tr* to incense, perfume with incense; flatter

encensoir [ãsãswar] *m* censer

encéphalite [ãsefalit] *f* encephalitis

encercler [ãsɛrkle] *tr* to encircle

enchaînement [ãʃɛnmã] *m* chaining up; chain, sequence

enchaîner [ãʃɛne], [ãʃene], *tr* to chain; to connect ‖ *intr* to go on speaking ‖ *ref* to be connected

enchan·té -tée [ãʃãte] §93 *adj* delighted, pleased

enchantement [ãʃãtmã] *m* enchantment

enchanter [ãʃãte] *tr* to enchant

enchan·teur [ãʃãtœr] **-teresse** [trɛs] *adj* enchanting, bewitching ‖ *m* enchanter, magician ‖ *f* enchantress

enchâsser [ãʃase] *tr* to enshrine; insert; set, chase (*a gem*)

enchère [ãʃɛr] *f* bid, bidding; **folle enchère** bid that cannot be made good; folly

enchérir [ãʃerir] *tr* to bid on; raise the price of ‖ *intr* to bid; rise in price; **enchérir sur** to improve on; outbid

enchérisseur [ãʃerisœr] *m* bidder; **dernier enchérisseur** highest bidder

enchevêtrement [ãʃvɛtrəmã] *m* entanglement; network; jumble

enchevêtrer [ãʃvɛtre] *tr* to tangle up; halter (*a horse*) ‖ *ref* to become complicated or confused

enchifre·né -née [ãʃifrəne] *adj* stuffed-up (*with a cold*)

enclave [ãklav] *f* enclave

enclaver [ãklave] *tr* to enclose; dovetail

enclencher [ãklãʃe] *tr & ref* to interlock

en·clin [ãklɛ̃] **-cline** [klin] *adj* inclined, prone

encliquetage [ãkliktaʒ] *m* ratchet

encliqueter [ãklikte] §34 *tr* to cog, mesh

enclitique [ãklitik] *adj & m & f* enclitic

enclore [ãklɔr] §24 (has also 1st & 2d *pl pres ind* **enclosons, enclosez**) *tr* to close in, wall in

enclos [ãklo] *m* enclosure, close

enclume [ãklym] *f* anvil; **se trouver entre l'enclume et le marteau** (coll) to be between the devil and the deep blue sea

encoche [ãkɔʃ] *f* notch, nick; slot; thumb index

encocher [ãkɔʃe] *tr* to notch, nick; slot

encoignure [ãkɔɲyr] *f* corner; corner piece; corner cabinet

encollage [ãkɔlaʒ] *m* gluing; sizing

encoller [ãkɔle] *tr* to glue; size

encolure [ãkɔlyr] *f* collar size; neck line; neck and withers (*of horse*); **gagner par une encolure** to win by a neck

encombre [ãkɔ̃br] *m*—**sans encombre** without a hitch, without hindrance

encombrement [ãkɔ̃brəmã] *m* encumbrance, congestion

encombrer [ãkɔ̃bre] *tr* to encumber; crowd, congest; block up, jam; litter; load down ‖ *ref*—**s'encombrer de** (coll) to be saddled with

encontre [ãkɔ̃tr]—**à l'encontre de** counter to, against; contrary to

encore [ãkɔr] *adv* still, e.g., **il est encore ici** he is still here; yet, e.g., **encore mieux** better yet; e.g., **pas encore** not yet; only, e.g., **si encore vous m'en aviez parlé!** if only you had told me!; even, e.g., **il est encore plus intelligent**

que vous he is even more intelligent than you; **encore que** although; **encore une fois** once more, once again; **en voulez-vous encore?** do you want some more? ‖ *interj* again!, oh no, not again! (*expressing impatience or astonishment*)

encorner [ākɔrne] *tr* to gore, toss

encouragement [ākuraʒmā] *m* encouragement

encourager [ākuraʒe] §38, §96, §100 *tr* to encourage

encourir [ākurir] §14 *tr* to incur

encrasser [ākrase] *tr* to soil, dirty; soot (*a chimney*); foul (*a gun*) ‖ *ref* to get dirty; stop up, clog; soot up

encre [ākr] *f* ink; **encre de Chine** India ink; **encre de couleur** colored ink; **encre sympathique** invisibile ink

encrer [ākre] *tr* to ink

encreur [ākrœr] *adj* inking (*ribbon, roller*) ‖ *m* ink roller

encrier [ākrije] *m* inkwell

encroûter [ākrute] *tr* to encrust; plaster (*walls*) ‖ *ref* to become encrusted; get rusty; become hidebound, prejudiced

encyclique [āsiklik] *adj & f* encyclical

encyclopédie [āsiklɔpedi] *f* encyclopedia

encyclopédique [āsiklɔpedik] *adj* encyclopedic

endauber [ādobe] *tr* to braise

endémie [ādemi] *f* endemic

endémique [ādemik] *adj* endemic

endenter [ādāte] *tr* to tooth, cog; mesh (*gears*); **bien endenté** (coll) with plenty of teeth; (coll) with a hearty appetite

endetter [ādete] *tr & ref* to run into debt

endêver [ādeve] *intr*—**faire endêver** to bedevil, drive wild

endia·blé -blée [ādjable] *adj* devilish, reckless; full of pep

endiguement [ādigmā] *m* damming up; embankment

endiguer [ādige] *tr* to dam up

endimancher [ādimāʃe] *tr & ref* to put on Sunday clothes, dress up

endive [ādiv] *f* endive

endocrine [ādɔkrin] *adj* endocrine

endoctriner [ādɔktrine] *tr* to indoctrinate; win over

endolo·ri -rie [ādɔlɔri] *adj* painful, sore

endommagement [ādɔmaʒmā] *m* damage

endommager [ādɔmaʒe] §38 *tr* to damage ‖ *ref* to suffer damage

endor·mi -mie [ādɔrmi] *adj* asleep, sleeping; sluggish, apathetic; dormant; numb (*arm or leg*)

endormir [ādɔrmir] §23 *tr* to put to sleep; lull, put off guard ‖ *ref* to go to sleep; slack off; let down one's guard

endos [ādo] *m* endorsement

endosse [ādos] *f* responsibility

endossement [ādosmā] *m* endorsement

endosser [ādose] *tr* to endorse; take on the responsibility of

endosseur [ādosœr] *m* endorser

endroit [ādrwa], [ādrwa] *m* place, spot; right side (*of cloth*); **à l'endroit** right side

out; **à l'endroit de** with regard to; **le petit endroit** (coll) the toilet; **mettre à l'endroit** to put on right side out

enduire [ādɥir] §19 *tr* to coat, smear

enduit [ādɥi] *m* coat, coating

endurance [ādyrās] *f* endurance

endu·rant [ādyrā] **-rante** [rāt] *adj* untiring; meek, patient

endur·ci -cie [ādyrsi] *adj* hardened; tough, calloused; inveterate

endurcir [ādyrsir] *tr* to harden; inure, toughen ‖ *ref* to harden; **s'endurcir à** to become accustomed to, become inured to

endurcissement [ādyrsismā] *m* hardening

endurer [ādyre] *tr* to endure

énergétique [enɛrʒetik] *adj* energy, energy-giving, energizing ‖ *f* energetics

énergie [enɛrʒi] *f* energy

énergique [enɛrʒik] *adj* energetic

énergumène [enɛrgymɛn] *mf* ranter, wild person, nut

éner·vant [enɛrvā] **-vante** [vāt] *adj* annoying, nerve-racking

énerver [enɛrve] *tr* to enervate; unnerve ‖ *ref* to get nervous; be exasperated

enfance [āfās] *f* childhood; infancy; dotage, second childhood; **c'est l'enfance de l'art** (coll) it's child's play; **enfance délinquante** juvenile delinquents; **première enfance** infancy

enfant [āfā] *adj invar* childish, childlike; **bon enfant** good-natured ‖ *mf* child; **enfant de chœur** altar boy; **enfant de la balle** child who follows in his father's footsteps; **enfant en bas âge** infant; **enfant terrible** (fig) stormy petrel, troublemaker; **enfant trouvé** foundling; **mon enfant!** my boy!; **petit enfant** infant

enfantement [āfātmā] *m* childbirth

enfanter [āfāte] *tr* to give birth to

enfantillage [āfātijaʒ] *m* childishness

enfan·tin [āfātɛ̄] **-tine** [tin] *adj* childish, infantile

enfari·né -née [āfarine] *adj* smeared with flour

enfer [āfɛr] *m* hell; erotica (*restricted section of a library*)

enfermer [āfɛrme] *tr* to enclose; shut up, lock up ‖ *ref* to shut oneself in; closet oneself

enferrer [āfɛre] *tr* to pierce, run through ‖ *ref* to run oneself through with a sword; bite (*said of fish*); (fig) to be caught in one's own trap

enfiévrer [āfjevre] §10 *tr* to inflame, make feverish

enfilade [āfilad] *f* row, string, series; (mil) enfilade; **en enfilade** connecting, e.g., **chambres en enfilade** connecting rooms

enfile-aiguille [āfilegɥij] *m invar* threader, needle threader

enfiler [āfile] *tr* to pierce; thread (*a needle*); string (*beads*); start down (*a street*); (coll) to put on (*clothes*)

enfin [āfɛ̄] *adv* finally, at last; in short; after all, anyway

enflam·mé -mée [ãflɑme], [ãflame] *adj* flaming; bright red; inflamed

enflammer [ãflɑme], [ãflame] *tr* to inflame ‖ *ref* to be inflamed; flare up

enfler [ãfle] *tr* to swell; puff up or out; exaggerate ‖ *intr & ref* to swell, puff up

enflure [ãflyr] *f* swelling; (fig) exaggeration

enfon·cé -cée [ãfõse] *adj* sunken, deep; deep-set; broken (*ribs*); (coll) taken, had (*bested*)

enfoncement [ãfõsmã] *m* driving in; breaking open; hollow, recess

enfoncer [ãfõse] §51 *tr* to drive in; push in, break open; (coll) to get the better of ‖ *intr* to sink to the bottom ‖ *ref* to sink, plunge; give way; disappear; penetrate (*said of root, bullet, etc.*)

enforcir [ãfɔrsir] *tr* to reinforce ‖ *intr & ref* to become stronger; grow

enfouir [ãfwir] *tr* to bury; hide ‖ *ref* to burrow; bury oneself (*e.g., in an out-of-the-way locality*)

enfourcher [ãfurʃe] *tr* to stick a pitchfork into; mount, straddle

enfourchure [ãfurʃyr] *f* crotch

enfourner [ãfurne] *tr* to put in the oven; (coll) to gobble down

enfreindre [ãfrɛ̃dr] §50 *tr* to violate, break (*e.g., a law*)

enfuir [ãfɥir] §31 *ref* to run away; escape; elope

enfu·mé -mée [ãfyme] *adj* blackened; smoky (*color*)

enfumer [ãfyme] *tr* to smoke up, blacken; smoke out

enfutailler [ãfytɑje] *tr* to cask, barrel

enga·gé -gée [ãgaʒe] *adj* committed; hocked ‖ *m* (mil) enlisted man

enga·geant [ãgaʒã] **-geante** [ʒãt] *adj* winsome, charming, engaging

engagement [ãgaʒmã] *m* engagement; hocking; obligation; promise; (mil) enlistment; (mil) engagement

engager [ãgaʒe] §38, §96, §97, §100 *tr* to engage; hock; enlist, urge, involve; open, begin (*negotiations, the conversation, etc.*) ‖ *ref* to commit oneself; promise, pledge; enter a contest; become engaged to be married; (mil) to enlist; **s'engager dans** to begin (*battle; a conversation*); plunge into; fit into

engainer [ãgɛne] *tr* to sheathe, envelop

engazonner [ãgɑzɔne] *tr* to sod

engeance [ãʒɑs] *f* (pej) breed, brood

engelure [ãʒlyr] *f* chilblain

engendrer [ãʒãdre] *tr* to engender

engin [ãʒɛ̃] *m* device; **engin balistique** ballistic missile; **engin guidé, engin spécial** guided missile; **engin non-identifié** unidentified flying object; **engins de pêche** fishing tackle

englober [ãglɔbe] *tr* to put together, unite; embrace, comprise

engloutir [ãglutir] *tr* to gobble down; swallow up, engulf

engluer [ãglye] *tr* to lime (*a trap*); catch; take in, hoodwink ‖ *ref* to be caught; fall into a trap, be taken in

engommer [ãgɔme] *tr* to gum

engon·cé -cée [ãgõse] *adj* awkward, stiff (*air*)

engoncer [ãgõse] §51 *tr* to bundle up; cramp

engorgement [ãgɔrʒəmã] *m* obstruction, blocking

engorger [ãgɔrʒe] §38 *tr* to obstruct, block

engouement [ãgumã] *m* infatuation; fad; (pathol) obstruction

engouer [ãgwe] *tr* to obstruct ‖ *ref*—**s'engouer de** (coll) to be infatuated with, be wild about

engouffrer [ãgufre] *tr* to engulf; gobble up; eat up (*e.g., a fortune*) ‖ *ref* to be swallowed up; dash; surge

engour·di -die [ãgurdi] *adj* numb

engourdir [ãgurdir] *tr* to numb; dull ‖ *ref* to grow numb

engourdissement [ãgurdismã] *m* numbness; dullness, torpidity

engrais [ãgrɛ] *m* fertilizer; manure; fodder; **mettre à l'engrais** to fatten

engraisser [ãgrɛse], [ãgrese] *tr* to fatten; fertilize; enrich ‖ *intr* (*aux:* AVOIR or ÊTRE) to fatten up, get fat ‖ *ref* to become fat; become rich

engranger [ãgrãʒe] §38 *tr* to garner; get in, put in the barn

engraver [ãgrave] *tr, intr, & ref* to silt up; (naut) to run aground

engrenage [ãgrənaʒ] *m* gear; gearing; (coll) mesh, toils; **engrenage à vis sans fin** worm gear; **engrenages de distribution** timing gears

engrener [ãgrəne] §2 *tr* to feed (*a hopper, a thresher; a fowl*); put into gear, mesh ‖ *intr & ref* (mach) to mesh, engage

engrenure [ãgrənyr] *f* engaging (*of toothed wheels*)

engrosser [ãgrose] *tr* (slang) to knock up, make pregnant

engrumeler [ãgrymle] §34 *tr & ref* to clot, curdle

engueuler [ãgœle] *tr* (slang) to bawl out, to give (*s.o.*) hell

enguirlander [ãgirlãde] *tr* to garland; adorn; (coll) to bawl out

enhardir [ãardir], §96, §97 *tr* to embolden ‖ *ref*—**s'enhardir à** to be so bold as to

énième [ɛnjɛm] *adj* nth

énigmatique [enigmatik] *adj* enigmatic(al), puzzling

énigme [enigm] *f* enigma, riddle, puzzle

enivrement [ãnivrəmã] *m* intoxication

enivrer [ãnivre] *tr* to intoxicate; elate ‖ *ref* to get drunk

enjambée [ãʒãbe] *f* stride

enjambement [ãʒãbmã] *m* enjambment

enjamber [ãʒãbe] *tr* to stride over, span ‖ *intr* to stride along; run on (*said of line of poetry*); **enjamber sur** to project over; encroach on

en·jeu [ãʒø] *m* (*pl* **-jeux**) stake, bet

enjoindre [ãʒwɛ̃dr] §35, §97 *tr* to enjoin

enjôler [ɑ̃ʒole] *tr* (coll) to cajole

enjô·leur [ɑ̃ʒolœr] **-leuse** [løz] *adj* cajoling ‖ *mf* cajoler, wheedler

enjoliver [ɑ̃ʒɔlive] *tr* to embellish

enjoli·veur [ɑ̃ʒɔlivœr] **-veuse** [vøz] *mf* embellisher ‖ *m* hubcap

en·joué -jouée [ɑ̃ʒwe] *adj* sprightly

enjouement [ɑ̃ʒumɑ̃] *m* playfulness

enlacement [ɑ̃lɑsmɑ̃] *m* embrace, hug; lacing, interweaving

enlacer [ɑ̃lɑse] **§51** *tr & ref* to enlace, entwine; embrace

enlaidir [ɑ̃lɛdir], [ɑ̃ledir] *tr* to disfigure ‖ *intr* to grow ugly ‖ *ref* to disfigure oneself

enlèvement [ɑ̃lɛvmɑ̃] *m* removal; kidnaping, abduction; **enlèvement de bébé, enlèvement d'enfant** infant kidnaping

enlever [ɑ̃lve] **§2** *tr* to take away, take off, remove; carry off; lift, lift up; send up (*a balloon*); (fig) to carry away (*an audience*); **enlever le couvert** to clear the table; **enlever q.ch. à** to take s.th. from, remove s.th. from ‖ *ref* to come off, wear off; rise; boil over; (fig) to flare up

enliasser [ɑ̃ljase] *tr* to tie up in bundles

enliser [ɑ̃lize] *tr* to get (*s.th.*) stuck in the mud ‖ *ref* to get stuck

enluminer [ɑ̃lymine] *tr* to illuminate; make colorful

enluminure [ɑ̃lyminyr] *f* illuminated drawing; (painting) illumination

enneiger [ɑ̃nɛʒe], [ɑ̃neʒe] **§38** *tr* to cover with snow

enne·mi -mie [ɛnmi] *adj* hostile, inimical; enemy, e.g., **en pays ennemi** in enemy country ‖ *mf* enemy

ennoblir [ɑ̃nɔblir] *tr* to ennoble

ennui [ɑ̃nɥi] *m* ennui, boredom; nuisance, bother; worry, trouble

ennuyer [ɑ̃nɥije] **§27, §96, §97** *tr* to bore; bother ‖ *ref* to be bored

en·nuyeux [ɑ̃nɥijø] **-nuyeuse** [nɥijøz] *adj* boring, tedious; annoying, bothersome; sad, troublesome

énon·cé -cée [enɔ̃se] *m* statement; wording (*of a document*); terms (*of a theorem*)

énoncer [enɔ̃se] **§51** *tr* to state, enunciate; utter

enorgueillir [ɑ̃nɔrgœjir] *tr* to make proud or boastful ‖ **§97** *ref*—**s'enorgueillir de** to pride oneself on, boast of, glory in

énorme [enɔrm] *adj* enormous; (coll) shocking; (coll) outrageous

énormément [enɔrmemɑ̃] *adv* enormously, tremendously; (coll) awfully; **énormément de** lots of

énormité [enɔrmite] *f* enormity; (coll) nonsense; (coll) blunder

enquérir [ɑ̃kerir] **§3** *ref*—**s'enquérir de** to ask or inquire about

enquête [ɑ̃kɛt] *f* investigation, inquiry; inquest; **enquête par sondage** public-opinion poll

enquêter [ɑ̃kɛte] *intr* to conduct an investigation

enraciner [ɑ̃rasine] *tr* to root; instill ‖ *ref* to take root

enra·gé -gée [ɑ̃raʒe] *adj* enraged, hot-headed; mad (*dog*); rabid (*communist*); out-and-out (*socialist*); inveterate (*gambler*); enthusiastic (*sportsman*) ‖ *mf* enthusiast, fan; fanatic, fiend

enrager [ɑ̃raʒe] **§38, §97** *intr* to be mad; **faire enrager** to enrage

enrayer [ɑ̃rɛje], [ɑ̃reje] **§49** *tr* to put spokes to; jam, lock; stem, halt ‖ *ref* to jam

enrayure [ɑ̃rɛjyr] *f* (mach) skid, shoe

enrégimenter [ɑ̃reʒimɑ̃te] *tr* to regiment

enregistrement [ɑ̃rəʒistrəmɑ̃] *m* recording; registration; transcription; checking (*of baggage*); **enregistrement sur bande** or **sur ruban** tape recording

enregistrer [ɑ̃rəʒistre] *tr* to record; register; transcribe; check (*baggage*)

enregis·treur [ɑ̃rəʒistrœr] **-treuse** [trøz] *adj* recording ‖ *mf* recorder ‖ *m* recording machine; **enregistreur d'accident** crash recorder, black box; **enregistreur de vol** flight recorder

enrhumer [ɑ̃ryme] *tr* to give a cold to ‖ *ref* to catch cold

enrichir [ɑ̃riʃir] *tr* to enrich ‖ *ref* to become rich

enrichissement [ɑ̃riʃismɑ̃] *m* enrichment

enrober [ɑ̃rɔbe] *tr* to coat; wrap

enrôlement [ɑ̃rolmɑ̃] *m* enrollment; enlistment

enrôler [ɑ̃role] *tr & ref* to enroll, enlist

enrouement [ɑ̃rumɑ̃] *m* hoarseness, huskiness

enrouer [ɑ̃rwe] *tr* to make hoarse ‖ *ref* to become hoarse

enrouiller [ɑ̃ruje] *tr & ref* to rust

enroulement [ɑ̃rulmɑ̃] *m* coil; (archit) volute; (elec) winding

enrouler [ɑ̃rule] *tr & ref* to wind, coil; roll up

ensabler [ɑ̃sable] *tr & ref* to run aground on the sand

ensacher [ɑ̃saʃe] *tr* to bag

ensanglanter [ɑ̃sɑ̃glɑ̃te] *tr* to stain with blood; steep in blood

ensei·gnant [ɑ̃sɛɲɑ̃] **-gnante** [ɲɑ̃t] *adj* teaching ‖ *mf* teacher

enseigne [ɑ̃sɛɲ] *m* (nav) ensign ‖ *f* flag, ensign; sign (*on tavern, store*)

enseignement [ɑ̃sɛɲəmɑ̃] *m* teaching, instruction, education; **enseignement confessionnel** parochial school education; **enseignement libre** or **privé** private-school education; **enseignement mixte** coeducation; **enseignement par correspondance** correspondence courses; **enseignement programmé** computer programed courses; **enseignement public** public education; **enseignement secondaire** secondary education; **enseignement séquentiel** programed learning; **enseignement supérieur** higher education

enseigner [ɑ̃sɛɲe] **§96, §101** *tr* to teach; show; **enseigner q.ch. à qn** to teach s.o. s.th. ‖ *intr* to teach; **enseigner à qn à +** *inf* to teach s.o. to + *inf*

ensemble [ãsãbl] *m* ensemble; **avec ensemble** in harmony, with one mind; **dans son ensemble** as a whole; **d'ensemble** general, comprehensive, overall; **ensemble immobilier** housing development; **grand ensemble** housing project ‖ *adv* together

ensemencement [ãsmãsmã] *m* sowing

ensemencer [ãsmãse] §51 *tr* to seed, sow; culture (*microorganisms*)

enserrer [ãsɛre] *tr* to enclose; squeeze, clasp

ensevelir [ãsəvlir] *tr* to bury; shroud

ensevelissement [ãsəvlismã] *m* burial; shrouding

ensilage [ãsilaʒ] *m* storing in a pit or silo

ensiler [ãsile] *tr* to ensilage

ensoleiller [ãsɔlɛje] *tr* to make sunny, brighten

ensommeil·lé -lée [ãsɔmeje] *adj* drowsy

ensorceler [ãsɔrsəle] §34 *tr* to bewitch, enchant

ensorce·leur [ãsɔrsəlœr] **-leuse** [løz] *adj* bewitching, enchanting ‖ *m* sorcerer, wizard; charmer ‖ *f* witch; enchantress

ensorcellement [ãsɔrsɛlmã] *m* sorcery, enchantment; spell, charm

ensuite [ãsɥit] *adv* then, next; afterwards, after; **ensuite?** what then?, what next?; anything else?

ensuivre [ãsɥivr] §67 (used only in 3rd *sg* & *pl*) *ref* to ensue; **il s'ensuit que . . .** it follows that . . .

entacher [ãtaʃe] *tr* to blemish; **entaché de nullité** null and void

entaille [ãtaj] *f* notch, nick; gash

entailler [ãtaje] *tr* to notch; nick; gash

entame [ãtam] *f* top slice, first slice, end slice

entamer [ãtame] *tr* to cut the first slice of; begin; engage in, start (*a conversation*); make a break in (*the skin; a battle line*); cast a slur upon; open (*a bottle; negotiations; a card suit*); (coll) to make a dent in (*e.g., one's savings*)

entartrer [ãtartre] *tr* & *ref* to scale, fur

entassement [ãtasmã] *m* piling up

entasser [ãtase] *tr* & *ref* to pile up, accumulate; crowd

ente [ãt] *f* paintbrush handle; (hort) graft, scion

entendement [ãtãdmã] *m* understanding; consciousness

entendre [ãtãdr] §95 *tr* to hear; understand; mean; **entendre chanter** to hear (*s.o.*) singing, to hear (*s.o.*) sing; hear (*s.th.*) sung; **entendre dire que** to hear that; **entendre parler de** to hear of or about; **entendre raison** to listen to reason; **il entend que je le fasse** he expects me to do it, he insists that I do it ‖ *intr* to hear ‖ §96 *ref* to understand one another; get along; **s'entendre à** to be skilled in, know

enten·du -due [ãtãdy] *adj* agreed; **bien entendu** of course; **c'est entendu!** all right!

enténébrer [ãtenebre] §10 *tr* to plunge into darkness

entente [ãtãt] *f* understanding; agreement, pact; **à double entente** with a double meaning, e.g., **expression à double entente** expression with a double meaning, double entendre; **entente industrielle** (com) combine

enter [ãte] *tr* to graft; splice (*pieces of wood*)

entérinement [ãterinmã] *m* ratification

entériner [ãterine] *tr* to ratify

enterrement [ãtɛrmã] *m* burial, interment; funeral procession; funeral; funeral expenses; pigeonholing

enterrer [ãtɛre] *tr* to bury, inter; pigeonhole, sidetrack; (coll) to attend the funeral services of; **enterrer sa vie de garçon** (coll) to give a farewell stag party ‖ *ref* to bury oneself; (mil) to dig oneself in

en-tête [ãtɛt] *m* (*pl* **-têtes**) headline; chapter heading; letterhead

entê·té -tée [ãtɛte] *adj* obstinate, stubborn

entêtement [ãtɛtmã] *m* obstinacy, stubbornness

entêter [ãtɛte] *tr* to give a headache to; make giddy ‖ *intr* to go to one's head ‖ *ref* to persist

enthousiasme [ãtuzjasm] *m* enthusiasm

enthousiasmer [ãtuzjasme] *tr* & *ref* to enthuse

enthousiaste [ãtuzjast] *adj* enthusiastic ‖ *mf* enthusiast, fan, buff

entichement [ãtiʃmã] *m* infatuation

enticher [ãtiʃe] *tr* to infatuate ‖ *ref* to become infatuated

en·tier [ãtje] **-tière** [tjɛr] *adj* entire, whole, full, obstinate ‖ *m* whole, entirety; **en entier** in full

entièrement [ãtjɛrmã] *adv* entirely

entité [ãtite] *f* entity, being

entoiler [ãtwale] *tr* to put a backing on, mount

entomologie [ãtɔmɔlɔʒi] *f* entomology

entonner [ãtɔne] *tr* to barrel; intone, start off (*a song*); sing (*s.o.'s praises*) ‖ *ref* to rush up and down (*said of wind*)

entonnoir [ãtɔnwar] *m* funnel; shell hole

entorse [ãtɔrs] *f* sprain; infringement (*of a rule*); stretching (*of the truth*)

entortiller [ãtɔrtije] *tr* & *ref* to twist

entour [ãtur] *m*—**à l'entour** in the vicinity; **à l'entour de** around; **entours** surroundings

entourage [ãturaʒ] *m* setting, surroundings; entourage; (mach) casing

entourer [ãture] *tr* to surround ‖ *ref*—**s'entourer de** to surround oneself with

entourloupette [ãturlupɛt] *f* (coll) double cross; **faire une entourloupette à** (coll) to double-cross

entournure [ãturnyr] *f* armhole; **gêné dans les entournures** ill at ease

entraccuser [ãtrakyze] *ref* to accuse one another

entracte [ãtrakt] *m* intermission

entraide [ãtrɛd] *f* mutual assistance

entrailles [ɑ̃trɑj] *fpl* entrails; tenderness, pity; bowels (*of the earth*); **sans entrailles** (fig) heartless

entr'aimer [ɑ̃trɛme], [ɑ̃treme] *ref* to love each other

entrain [ɑ̃trɛ̃] *m* spirit, gusto, pep

entraînement [ɑ̃trɛnmɑ̃] *m* training; enthusiasm

entraîner [ɑ̃trɛne] §96, §100 *tr* to carry along or away, entrain; involve, entail; pull (*railroad cars*); work (*a pump*); train (*an athlete*) ‖ *ref* (sports) to train

entraîneur [ɑ̃trɛnœr] *m* trainer, coach

entraîneuse [ɑ̃trɛnøz] *f* B-girl

entr'apercevoir [ɑ̃trapɛrsəvwar] §59 *tr* to catch a glimpse of

entrave [ɑ̃trav] *f* shackle; hindrance

entra·vé -vée [ɑ̃trave] *adj* impeded, hampered; checked (*vowel*)

entraver [ɑ̃trave] *tr* to shackle; hinder, impede

entre [ɑ̃tr] *prep* between; among; in or into, e.g., **entre les mains de** in or into the hands of; **d'entre** among; from among, out of; of, e.g., **l'un d'entre eux** one of them; **entre deux eaux** under the surface of the water

entrebâillement [ɑ̃trəbɑjmɑ̃] *m* chink, slit, crack

entrebâiller [ɑ̃trəbɑje] *tr* to leave ajar

entrechat [ɑ̃trəʃfa] *m* caper; entrechat

entrechoquer [ɑ̃trəʃɔke] *tr* to bump together ‖ *ref* to clash

entrecôte [ɑ̃trəkot] *f* sirloin steak, loin of beef; top chuck roast

entrecouper [ɑ̃trəkupe] *tr* to interrupt; intersect ‖ *ref* to intersect

entrecroiser [ɑ̃trəkrwaze] *tr & ref* to interlace; intersect

entre-deux [ɑ̃trədø] *m invar* space between; interval; partition; (sports) jump ball

entre-deux-guerres [ɑ̃trədøgɛr] *m & f invar* period between the wars (*the First and Second World War*)

entrée [ɑ̃tre] *f* entrance, entry; admission, admittance; beginning; headword, entry word (*of a dictionary*); customs duty; (culin) first course; (culin) course before the main course; **avoir ses entrées à, chez,** or **dans** to have the entree into; **d'entrée** at the start, right off; **entrée de serrure** keyhole; **entrée d'un chapeau** hat size; **entrée en matière** introduction; **entrée en scène** (theat) entrance; **entrée interdite** (public sign) keep out, no admittance; **entrée libre** free admission; **entrée principale** main entrance

entrefaites [ɑ̃trəfɛt] *fpl*—**sur ces entrefaites** meanwhile

entrefer [ɑ̃trəfɛr] *m* (elec) air gap

entrefermer [ɑ̃trəfɛrme] *tr* to close part way

entrefilet [ɑ̃trəfilɛ] *m* short feature, special item

entregent [ɑ̃trəʒɑ̃] *m* tact, diplomacy, savoir-faire; **avoir de l'entregent** to be a good mixer

entrejambe [ɑ̃trəʒɑ̃b] *m* crotch

entrelacer [ɑ̃trəlase] §51 *tr & ref* to interlace, entwine, intertwine

entrelarder [ɑ̃trəlarde] *tr* to lard; interlard

entre-ligne [ɑ̃trəliɲ] *m* (*pl* -**lignes**) space (*between the lines*); insertion (*written between the lines*); **à l'entre-ligne** double-spaced

entremêler [ɑ̃trəmɛle] *tr* to mix, mingle; intersperse

entremets [ɑ̃trəmɛ] *m* side dish; dessert

entremet·teur [ɑ̃trəmɛtœr] -**teuse** [tøz] *mf* go-between ‖ *m* (pej) pimp

entremettre [ɑ̃trəmɛtr] §42 *ref* to intervene, intercede

entremise [ɑ̃trəmiz] *f* intervention; **par l'entremise de** through the medium of

entre-nuire [ɑ̃trənɥir] §19 (*pp* -**nui** *invar*) to hurt each other

entrepont [ɑ̃trəpɔ̃] *m* (naut) between-decks

entreposer [ɑ̃trəpoze] *tr* to place in a warehouse, store; bond

entrepôt [ɑ̃trəpo] *m* warehouse; **en entrepôt** in bond

entrepre·nant [ɑ̃trəprənɑ̃] -**nante** [nɑ̃t] *adj* enterprising; bold, audacious; gallant

entreprendre [ɑ̃trəprɑ̃dr] §56, §97 *tr* to undertake; contract for; enter upon; (coll) to try to win over ‖ *intr*—**entreprendre sur** to encroach upon

entrepre·neur [ɑ̃trəprənœr] -**neuse** [nøz] *mf* contractor; **entrepreneur de camionnage** trucker; **entrepreneur de pompes funèbres** undertaker

entreprise [ɑ̃trəpriz] *f* undertaking; business, firm; contract

entrer [ɑ̃tre] *tr* to introduce, bring in ‖ *intr* (*aux:* ÉTRE) to enter; go in, come in; **entrer à, dans,** or **en** to enter; enter into; begin; **entrer pour** to enter into, be an ingredient of

entre-rail [ɑ̃trəraj] *m* (rr) gauge

entre-regarder [ɑ̃trərəgarde] *ref* to exchange glances

entresol [ɑ̃trəsɔl] *m* mezzanine

entre-temps [ɑ̃trətɑ̃] *m invar* interval; **dans l'entre-temps** in the meantime ‖ *adv* meanwhile

entreteneur [ɑ̃trətnœr] *m* keeper of a mistress

entretenir [ɑ̃trətnir] §72 *tr* to maintain, keep up; carry on (*a conversation*); keep (*a mistress*); entertain, harbor ‖ *ref* to converse, talk

entrete·nu -nue [ɑ̃trətny] *adj* kept (*woman*); continuous, undamped (*waves*)

entretien [ɑ̃trətjɛ̃] *m* maintenance, upkeep; support (*of family, army, etc.*); interview; **entretien courant** servicing

entretoise [ɑ̃trətwaz] *f* strut, brace, crosspiece

entre-tuer [ɑ̃trətɥe] *ref* to kill each other, fight to the death

entre-voie [ɑ̃trəvwa] *f* (rr) gauge

entrevoir [ɑ̃trəvwar] §75 *tr* to glimpse; foresee

entre·vu **-vue** [ɑ̃trəvy] *adj* half-seen; vaguely foreseen ‖ *f* interview

entrouvrir [ɑ̃truvrir] §65 *tr* & *ref* to open part way

enture [ɑ̃tyr] *f* splice (*of pieces of wood*)

énumérer [enymere] §10 *tr* to enumerate

envahir [ɑ̃vair] *tr* to invade

envahissement [ɑ̃vaismɑ̃] *m* invasion

envaser [ɑ̃vɑze] *tr* to fill with mud; stick in the mud

enveloppe [ɑ̃vlɔp] *f* envelope; **enveloppe à fenêtre** window envelope

envelopper [ɑ̃vlɔpe] *tr* to envelop; wrap up

envenimer [ɑ̃vnime] *tr* to inflame, make sore; (fig) to envenom, embitter

envergure [ɑ̃vɛrgyr] *f* span; wingspread; spread of sail; span, scope

enverrai [ɑ̃vɛre] *v* (**enverras, enverra, enverrons,** etc.) see **envoyer**

envers [ɑ̃vɛr] *m* wrong side, reverse, back; **à l'envers** inside out; upside down; back to front; topsy-turvy; **mettre à l'envers** to put on backwards ‖ *prep* towards; with regard to; **envers et contre tous** in spite of everyone else

envi [ɑ̃vi]—**à l'envi** vying with each other; **à l'envi de** vying with

enviable [ɑ̃vjabl] *adj* enviable

envie [ɑ̃vi] *f* desire, longing; envy; birthmark; hangnail; **avoir envie de** to feel like, to have a notion to

envier [ɑ̃vje] *tr* to envy; desire; **envier q.ch. à qn** to begrudge s.o. s.th.

en·vieux [ɑ̃vjø] **-vieuse** [vjøz] *adj* envious ‖ *mf* envious person

environ [ɑ̃virɔ̃] *m* outlying section; **aux environs de** in the vicinity of; around, about; **environs** surroundings ‖ *adv* about, approximately

environnement [ɑ̃virɔnmɑ̃] *m* environment

environner [ɑ̃virɔne] *tr* to surround

envisager [ɑ̃vizaʒe] §38 *tr* to envisage ‖ *intr*—**envisager de** + *inf* to plan to + *inf*, to expect to + *inf*

envoi [ɑ̃vwa] *m* consignment; remittance; envoy (*of ballad*)

envol [ɑ̃vɔl] *m* flight; (aer) takeoff

envolée [ɑ̃vɔle] *f* flight; (aer) takeoff

envoler [ɑ̃vɔle] *ref* to fly (*said of time*); (aer) to take off

envoûtement [ɑ̃vutmɑ̃] *m* spell, voodoo

envoûter [ɑ̃vute] *tr* to cast a spell on

envoyé envoyée [ɑ̃vwaje] *mf* envoy; messenger; **envoyé spécial** special correspondent (*of newspaper*)

envoyer [ɑ̃vwaje] §26, §95 *tr* to send; send out; throw (*e.g., a stone*); give (*a kick*); **envoyer promener** to send (*s.o.*) about his business; **envoyer qn** + *inf* to send s.o. to + *inf;* **envoyer qn chercher q.ch.** or **qn** to send s.o. for s.th. or s.o. ‖ *intr*—**envoyer chercher** to send for (*s.o.* or *s.th.*) ‖ *ref* (coll) to gulp down

enzyme [ɑ̃zim] *m* & *f* enzyme

épa·gneul **-gneule** [epaɲœl] *mf* spaniel

épais [epɛ] **épaisse** [epɛs] *adj* thick ‖ **épais** *adv* thickly

épaisseur [epɛsœr] *f* thickness

épaissir [epɛsir] *tr*, *intr*, & *ref* to thicken

épanchement [epɑ̃ʃmɑ̃] *m* outpouring, effusion; (pathol) discharge

épancher [epɑ̃ʃe] *tr* to pour out; unburden (*e.g., one's feelings*) ‖ *ref* to pour out; **s'épancher auprès de** to unbosom oneself to; **s'épancher de q.ch.** to get s.th. off one's chest

épandre [epɑ̃dr] *tr* & *ref* to spread; scatter

épanouir [epanwir] *tr* to make (*flowers*) bloom; light up (*the face*) ‖ *ref* to bloom; beam (*said of face*)

épanouissement [epanwismɑ̃] *m* blossoming; brightening up (*of a face*)

épar·gnant [eparɲɑ̃] **-gnante** [ɲɑ̃t] *adj* thrifty ‖ *mf* depositor

épargne [eparɲ] *f* saving, thrift; **épargnes** savings

épargner [eparɲe] §97 *tr* to save; spare; husband

éparpillement [eparpijmɑ̃] *m* scattering

éparpiller [eparpije] *tr* to scatter; dissipate (*e.g., one's efforts*)

épars [epar] **éparse** [epars] *adj* scattered, sparse; in disorder

épa·tant [epatɑ̃] **-tante** [tɑ̃t] *adj* (coll) wonderful, terrific

épate [epat] *f*—**faire de l'épate** (slang) to make a big show, to splurge

épa·té **-tée** [epate] *adj* flattened; (slang) flabbergasted

épater [epate] *tr* (coll) to shock, amaze

épaulard [epolar] *m* killer whale

épaule [epol] *f* shoulder; **donner un coup d'épaule à qn** (coll) to give s.o. a hand; **par-dessus l'épaule** (fig) contemptuously

épaulé-jeté [epoleʒte] *m* clean and jerk (*in weight lifting*)

épaulement [epolmɑ̃] *m* breastworks

épauler [epole] *tr* to back, support ‖ *intr* to take aim

épaulette [epolɛt] *f* epaulet

épave [epav] *f* wreck; derelict, stray; **épaves** wreckage

épée [epe] *f* sword

épéiste [epeist] *m* swordsman

épeler [eple] §34 *tr* to spell, spell out; read letter by letter

épellation [epɛllasjɔ̃] *f* spelling

éper·du **-due** [epɛrdy] *adj* bewildered; desperate (*resistance*); mad (*with pain*); wild (*with joy*)

éperdument [epɛrdymɑ̃] *adv* desperately, madly, wildly

éperlan [epɛrlɑ̃] *m* smelt

éperon [eprɔ̃] *m* spur

éperonner [eprɔne] *tr* to spur

épervier [epɛrvje] *m* sparrow hawk; fish net; (pol & fig) hawk

éphémère [efemɛr] *adj* ephemeral ‖ *m* mayfly

épi [epi] *m* ear, cob, spike; cowlick; **épi de maïs** corncob

épice [epis] *f* spice

épicéa [episea] *m* Norway spruce

épicer [epise] §51 *tr* to spice

épicerie [episri] *f* grocery store; canned goods; **épicerie de dépannage** convenience store

épi·cier [episje] **-cière** [sjɛr] *mf* grocer

épidémie [epidemi] *f* epidemic

épidémiologie [epidemjɔlɔʒi] *f* epidemiology

épidémique [epidemik] *adj* epidemic; contagious (*e.g., laughter*)

épiderme [epidɛrm] *m* epidermis

épier [epje] *tr* to spy upon; be on the lookout for ‖ *intr* to ear, head

épieu [epjø] *m* (*pl* **épieux**) pike

épiglotte [epiglɔt] *f* epiglottis

épigone [epigɔn] *m* imitator, follower

épigramme [epigram] *f* epigram

épigraphe [epigraf] *f* epigraph

épilepsie [epilɛpsi] *f* epilepsy

épileptique [epilɛptik] *adj* & *mf* epileptic

épiler [epile] *tr* to pluck (*one's eyebrows*); remove hair from

épilogue [epilɔg] *m* epilogue

épiloguer [epilɔge] *intr* to split hairs; **épiloguer sur** to carp at

épinard [epinar] *m* spinach; **des épinards** spinach (*leaves used as food*)

épine [epin] *f* thorn; **épine dorsale** backbone; **épine noire** blackthorn; **être sur les épines** to be on pins and needles

épinette [epinɛt] *f* spinet; hencoop

épi·neux [epinø] **-neuse** [nøz] *adj* thorny; ticklish (*question*)

épingle [epɛ̃gl] *f* pin; **épingle à chapeau** hatpin; **épingle à cheveux** hairpin; **épingle à linge** clothespin; **épingle anglaise** safety pin; **épingle dans une meule de foin** needle in a haystack; **épingle de cravate** stickpin; **épingle de nourrice, épingle de sûreté** safety pin; **monter en épingle** (coll) to make much of; **tiré à quatre épingles** (coll) spic-and-span; (coll) all dolled up; **tirer son épingle du jeu** (coll) to get out by the skin of one's teeth

épingler [epɛ̃gle] *tr* to pin; (coll) to pin down (*s.o.*)

épinière [epinjɛr] *adj fem* spinal (*cord*)

Épiphanie [epifani] *f* Epiphany, Twelfthnight

épique [epik] *adj* epic

épisco·pal -pale [episkɔpal] (*pl* **-paux** [po]) *adj* episcopal; Episcopalian ‖ *mf* Episcopalian

épiscope [episkɔp] *m* (mil) periscope of a tank

épisode [epizɔd] *m* episode

épisodique [epizɔdik] *adj* episodic

épisser [epise] *tr* to splice

épissure [episyr] *f* splice

épistémologie [epistemɔlɔʒi] *f* epistemology; theory of knowledge

épitaphe [epitaf] *f* epitaph

épithète [epitɛt] *f* epithet

épitoge [epitɔʒ] *f* shoulder band (*worn by French lawyers and holders of French degrees*)

épitomé [epitɔme] *m* epitome

épître [epitr] *f* epistle

éplo·ré -rée [eplɔre] *adj* in tears

épluchage [eplyʃaʒ] *m* peeling; examination

éplucher [eplyʃe] *tr* to peel, pare; clean, pick; (fig) to find fault with, pick holes in

éplu·cheur [eplyʃœr] **-cheuse** [ʃøz] *mf* (coll) faultfinder ‖ *m* potato peeler, orange peeler, peeling knife ‖ *f*—**éplucheuse électrique** electric peeler

épluchure [eplyʃyr] *f* peelings; **épluchure de maïs** cornhusks

épointer [epwɛ̃te] *tr* to dull the point of

éponge [epɔ̃ʒ] *f* sponge

éponger [epɔ̃ʒe] §38 *tr* to sponge off, mop up

épopée [epɔpe] *f* epic

époque [epɔk] *f* epoch; time; period; **à l'époque de** at the time of; **d'époque** a real antique; **faire époque** to be epochmaking

épouiller [epuje] *tr* to delouse

époumoner [epumɔne] *ref* to shout oneself out of breath

épousailles [epuzaj] *fpl* wedding

épouser [epuze] *tr* to marry; espouse; **épouser la forme de** to take the exact shape of

époussetage [epustaʒ] *m* dusting

épousseter [epuste] §34 *tr* to dust

époussette [epusɛt] *f* duster

épouvantable [epuvɑ̃tabl] *adj* frightful, terrible

épouvantail [epuvɑ̃taj] *m* scarecrow

épouvante [epuvɑ̃t] *f* fright, terror

épouvanter [epuvɑ̃te] *tr* to frighten, terrify

époux [epu] **épouse** [epuz] *mf* spouse ‖ *m* husband; **les époux** husband and wife ‖ *f* wife

éprendre [eprɑ̃dr] §56 *ref*—**s'éprendre de** to fall in love with; hold fast to (*liberty, justice, etc.*)

épreuve [eprœv] *f* proof, test, trial; ordeal; examination; (phot, typ) proof; **corriger les épreuves (de)** to proofread; **épreuve de mise en pages, épreuve de pages** page proof; **épreuve en placard, épreuve sous le galet** galley proof; **épreuves** (mov) rushes

épris [épri] **éprise** [epriz] *adj* infatuated; **épris de** in love with

éprouver [epruve] *tr* to prove, test, try; experience, feel; put to the test

éprouvette [epruvɛt] *f* test tube; specimen; (med) probe

epsomite [ɛpsɔmit] *f* Epsom salts

épucer [epyse] §51 *tr* to clean of fleas, delouse

épui·sé -sée [epɥize] *adj* exhausted, tired out; sold out

épuisement [epɥizmɑ̃] *m* exhaustion; diminution, draining off

épuiser [epɥize] *tr* to exhaust, use up; wear out; tire out ‖ *ref* to run out; wear out

épuration [epyrasjɔ̃] *f* purification; refining (*e.g., of petroleum*); (pol) purge

épure [epyr] *f* working drawing

épurement [epyrmɑ̃] *m* expurgation

épurer [epyre] *tr* to purify; expurgate; weed out, purge

équanimité [ekwanimite] *f* equanimity

équarrir [ekarir] *tr* to cut up, quarter (*an animal*); square off

équateur [ekwatœr] *m* equator; **l'Équateur** Ecuador

équation [ekwɑsjɔ̃] *f* equation

équato·rial -riale [ekwatɔrjal] *adj* (*pl* **-riaux** [rjo]) equatorial

équerrage [ekɛraʒ] *m* bevel; beveling

équerre [ekɛr] *f* square (*L- or T-shaped instrument*); **d'équerre** square, true; **mettre d'équerre** to square, to true

équerrer [ekɛre] *tr* to bevel

équestre [ekɛstr] *adj* equestrian

équilaté·ral -rale [ekɥilateral] *adj* (*pl* **-raux** [ro]) equilateral

équilibre [ekilibr] *m* equilibrium, balance; equipoise

équilibrer [ekilibre] *tr* & *ref* to balance

équilibriste [ekilibrist] *mf* balancer, rope-dancer

équinoxe [ekinɔks] *m* equinox

équipage [ekipaʒ] *m* crew; retinue, suite; attire

équipe [ekip] *f* team; crew; gang, work party; (naut) train of boats; **équipe de jour** day shift; **équipe de nuit** night shift; **équipe de secours** rescue squad

équipée [ekipe] *f* escapade, lark; crazy project

équipement [ekipmɑ̃] *m* equipment; **équipement de survie** survival kit

équiper [ekipe] *tr* to equip

équi·pier -pière [ekipje] *mf* teammate; crew member

équitable [ekitabl] *adj* equitable

équitation [ekitɑsjɔ̃] *f* horseback riding

équité [ekite] *f* equity

équiva·lent -lente [ekivalɑ̃] *adj* & *m* equivalent

équivaloir [ekivalwar] §71 *intr*—**équivaloir à** to be equivalent to; be tantamount to

équivoque [ekivɔk] *adj* equivocal; questionable (*e.g., reputation*) ‖ *f* double entendre; uncertainty; **sans équivoque** without equivocation

équivoquer [ekivɔke] *intr* to equivocate, quibble; pun

érable [erabl] *m* maple; **érable à sucre** sugar maple

érafler [erɑfle] *tr* to graze, scratch

éraflure [erɑflyr] *f* graze, scratch

érail·lé -lée [erɑje] *adj* bloodshot (*eyes*); hoarse (*voice*); frayed (*rope*)

érailler [erɑje] *tr* to fray

ère [ɛr] *f* era

érection [erɛksjɔ̃] *f* erection

érein·té -tée [erɛ̃te] *adj* all in, worn out, tired out

éreinter [erɛ̃te] *tr* to exhaust, tire out; (coll) to criticize unmercifully, run down (*an author, play, etc.*) ‖ *ref* to wear oneself out; drudge

erg [ɛrg] *m* erg

ergol [ɛrgɔl] *m* (rok) propellant

ergot [ɛrgo] *m* spur (*of rooster*); **monter or se dresser sur ses ergots** (fig) to get up on a high horse

ergotage [ɛrgɔtaʒ] *m* (coll) quibbling

ergoter [ɛrgɔte] *tr* (coll) to quibble

ériger [eriʒe] §38 *tr* to erect ‖ *ref*—**s'ériger en** to set oneself up as

ermitage [ɛrmitaʒ] *m* hermitage

ermite [ɛrmit] *m* hermit

éroder [erɔde] *tr* to erode

érosion [erozjɔ̃] *f* erosion

érotique [erɔtik] *adj* erotic

érotisme [erɔtism] *m* eroticism

érotothèque [erɔtɔtɛk] *f* adult book shop

er·rant -rante [erɑ̃] *adj* wandering, stray; errant

erratique [eratik] *adj* intermittent, irregular, erratic

erre [ɛr] *f* (naut) headway; **erres** track (*e.g., of deer*)

errements [ermɑ̃] *mpl* ways, methods; (pej) erring ways, bad habits

errer [ere] *intr* to wander; err; play (*said of smile*)

erreur [erœr] *f* error, mistake; **erreur de frappe** typing error

erro·né -née [erɔne] *adj* erroneous

éructation [eryktɑsjɔ̃] *f* belch

éructer [erykte] *tr* (fig) to belch forth ‖ *intr* to belch

éru·dit -dite [erydi] [dit] *adj* erudite, learned ‖ *mf* scholar, erudite

érudition [erydisjɔ̃] *f* erudition

éruption [erypsjɔ̃] *f* eruption; blowout (*of an oil well*)

es [e] *v* see **être**

ès [ɛs] *prep* §77

esbroufe [ɛsbruf] *f* showing off; shoving

esc. *abbr* (**escompte**) discount

esca·beau [ɛskabo] *m* (*pl* **-beaux**) stool; stepladder

escadre [ɛskadr] *f* squadron; fleet

escadron [ɛskadrɔ̃] *m* (mil) squadron

escalade [ɛskalad] *f* scaling, climbing; escalation (*of a war*)

escalader [ɛskalade] *tr* to scale, climb; clamber over or up

escalator [ɛskalatɔr] *m* escalator

escale [ɛskal] *f* port of call, stop; **faire escale** to make a stop; **sans escale** nonstop

escalier [ɛskalje] *m* stairway; **escalier à vis** circular stairway; **escalier de sauvetage** fire escape; **escalier en colimaçon** spiral staircase; **escalier mécanique, escalier roulant** escalator

escalope [ɛskalɔp] *f* thin slice, escalope, scallop; **escalope de veau** veal cutlet

escamotable [ɛskamɔtabl] *adj* retractable (*e.g., landing gear*); concealable (*piece of furniture*)

escamotage [ɛskamɔtaʒ] *m* sleight of hand; side-stepping, avoiding; theft

escamoter [ɛskamɔte] *tr* to palm (*a card*); pick (*a wallet*); dodge (*a question*); slur (*a word*); hush up (*a scandal*); (aer) to retract (*landing gear*)

escamo·teur [ɛskamɔtœr] **-teuse** [tøz] *mf* prestidigitator; pickpocket

escapade [ɛskapad] *f* escapade, escape

escarbille [ɛskarbij] *f* cinder, clinker

escarbot [ɛskarbo] *m* beetle

escarboucle [ɛskarbukl] *f* (mineral) carbuncle

escargot [ɛskargo] *m* snail

escarmouche [ɛskarmuʃ] *f* skirmish

escarmoucher [ɛskarmuʃe] *intr* to skirmish

escarpe [ɛskarp] *m* ruffian, bandit ‖ *f* escarpment (*of a fort*)

escar·pé -pée [ɛskarpe] *adj* steep

escarpement [ɛskarpəmã] *m* escarpment

escarpin [ɛskarpɛ̃] *m* pump, dancing shoe

escarpolette [ɛskarpɔlɛt] *f* swing

escarre [ɛskar] *f* scab

escarrifier [ɛskarifje] *tr* to form a scab on

esche [ɛʃ] *f* bait

Eschyle [ɛsʃil] [eʃil] *m* Aeschylus

escient [ɛsjã]—**à bon escient** knowingly, wittingly; **à mon (ton,** etc.) **escient** to my (your, etc.) certain knowledge

esclaffer [ɛsklafe] *ref* to burst out laughing

esclandre [ɛsklɑ̃dr] *m* scandal

esclavage [ɛsklavaʒ] *m* slavery

esclavagiste [ɛsklavaʒist] *adj* pro-slavery ‖ *mf* advocate of slavery

esclave [ɛsklav] *adv* & *mf* slave

escompte [ɛskɔ̃t] *m* discount, rebate; **escompte de caisse** cash discount; **escompte en dehors** bank discount; **prendre à l'escompte** to discount

escompter [ɛskɔ̃te] *tr* to discount (*a premature note*); anticipate

escompteur [ɛskɔ̃tœr] *adj* discounting (*banker*) ‖ *m* discount broker

escopette [ɛskɔpɛt] *f* blunderbuss

escorte [ɛskɔrt] *f* escort

escorter [ɛskɔrte] *tr* to escort

escouade [ɛskwad] *f* infantry section; gang (*of laborers*)

escrime [ɛskrim] *f* fencing

escrimer [ɛskrime] *intr* & *ref* to fence; **s'escrimer à** to work with might and main at; **s'escrimer contre** to fence with

escri·meur [ɛskrimœr] **-meuse** [møz] *mf* fencer

escroc [ɛskro] *m* crook, swindler

escroquer [ɛskrɔke] *tr* to swindle

escroquerie [ɛskrɔkri] *f* swindling, cheating; racket, swindle

ésotérique [ezɔterik] *adj* esoteric

espace [ɛspas] *m* space; room; **espace cosmique** outer space; **espace lointain** deep space ‖ *f* (typ) space

espacement [ɛspasmã] *m* spacing

espacer [ɛspase] §51 *tr* to space

espadon [ɛspadɔ̃] *m* swordfish

espadrille [ɛspadrij] *f* tennis shoe; beach sandal; esparto sandal

Espagne [ɛspaɲ] *f* Spain; **l'Espagne** Spain

espa·gnol -gnole [ɛspaɲɔl] *adj* Spanish ‖ *m* Spanish (*language*) ‖ (*cap*) *mf* Spaniard (*person*); **les Espagnols** the Spanish

espagnolette [ɛspaɲɔlɛt] *f* espagnolette (*door fastener for French casement window*)

espalier [ɛspalje] *m* espalier

espèce [ɛspɛs] *f* species; sort, kind; **en espèces** in specie; **en l'espèce** in the matter; **espèces sonnantes** hard cash; **sale espèce** cad, bounder ‖ *mf*—**espèce de** (coll) damn, e.g., **cet espèce d'idiot** that damn fool

espérance [ɛsperãs] *f* hope; **espérance de vie** life expectancy; **espérances** expectations; prospects

espéranto [ɛsperãto] *m* Esperanto

espérer [ɛspere] §10, §95 *tr* to hope, hope for; (coll) to wait for; **espérer** + *inf* to hope to + *inf* ‖ *intr* to trust; (coll) to wait

esperluète [ɛspɛrlɥɛt] *f* ampersand

espiègle [ɛspjɛgl] *adj* mischievous ‖ *mf* rogue

espièglerie [ɛspjɛgləri] *f* mischievousness; prank

es·pion [ɛspjɔ̃] **-pionne** [pjɔn] *mf* spy ‖ *m* concealed microphone; busybody (*mirror*)

espionnage [ɛspjɔnaʒ] *m* espionage

espionner [ɛspjɔne] *tr* to spy on

espoir [ɛspwar] *m* hope; promise

esprit [ɛspri] *m* spirit; mind; intelligence; wit; spirits (*of wine*); **à l'esprit clair** clearheaded; **avoir l'esprit de l'escalier** to think of what to say too late; **bel esprit** man of letters; **esprit d'équipe** teamwork; **esprit de système** love of order; (pej) pigheadedness; **esprit fort** freethinker; **rendre l'esprit** to give up the ghost

esquif [ɛskif] *m* skiff

esqui·mau [ɛskimo] **-maude** [mod] (*pl* **-maux**) *adj* Eskimo ‖ *m* husky, Eskimo dog; Eskimo (*language*) ‖ (*cap*) *mf* Eskimo (*person*)

esquinter [ɛskɛ̃te] *tr* (coll) to tire out; (coll) to wear out; (coll) to run down, knock, criticize

esquisse [ɛskis] *f* sketch; outline, draft; beginning (*e.g., of a smile*)

esquisser [ɛskise] *tr* to sketch; outline, draft; begin

esquiver [ɛskive] *tr* to dodge, side-step; **esquiver de la tête** to duck ‖ *ref* to sneak away

essai [ɛsɛ] *m* essay; trial, test; **à l'essai** on trial; **essais** first attempts (*of artist, writer, etc.*); **faire l'essai de** to try out

essaim [ɛsɛ̃] *m* swarm

essaimer [ɛseme] *intr* to swarm

essarter [ɛsarte] *tr* to clear (*brush*)

essarts [ɛsar] *mpl* clearings

essayage [ɛsɛjaʒ] *m* fitting, trying on

essayer [ɛsɛje], [eseje] §49, §96, §97 *tr* to try on, try out; assay (*ore*) ‖ *intr* to try; **essayer de** to try to ‖ §96 *ref*—**s'essayer à** to try one's skill at

essayeur [ɛsɛjœr] **essayeuse** [ɛsɛjøz] *mf* assayer

essayiste [ɛsɛjist] *mf* essayist

esse [ɛs] *f* S-hook; sound hole (*of violin*)

essence [esɑ̃s] *f* essence; gasoline; kind, species; **par essence** by definition

essen·tiel -tielle [esɑ̃sjɛl] *adj & m* essential

essentiellement [esɑ̃sjɛlmɑ̃] *adv* essentially

esseu·lé -lée [esœle] *adj* abandoned

es·sieu [esjø] *m* (*pl* **-sieux**) axle

essor [esɔr] *m* flight; development; boom (*in business*); **donner libre essor à** to give vent to; give full scope to; **prendre son essor** to take wing

essorer [esɔre] *tr* to spin-dry; wring; centrifuge

essoreuse [esɔrøz] *f* spin-drier; wringer; centrifuge

essouf·flé -flée [esufle] *adj* breathless, out of breath

essuie-glace [esɥiglas] *m* (*pl* **-glaces**) windshield wiper

essuie-mains [esɥimɛ̃] *m invar* towel; **essuie-mains en papier** paper toweling

essuie-plume [esɥiplym] *m* (*pl* **-plumes**) penwiper

essuyer [esɥije] §27 *tr* to wipe; wipe off; wipe away; suffer, endure; undergo; weather (*a storm*); **essuyer les plâtres** (coll) to be the first to occupy a house

est [ɛst] *adj invar* east, eastern ‖ *m* east; **de l'est** eastern; **faire l'est** to steer eastward; **vers l'est** eastward ‖ [e], [ɛ] *v* see **être**

estacade [ɛstakad] *f* breakwater; pier; boom (*barrier of floating logs*); railway trestle

estafette [ɛstafɛt] *f* messenger

estaminet [ɛstaminɛ] *m* bar, café

estampe [ɛstɑ̃p] *f* print, engraving; (*tool*) stamp

estamper [ɛstɑ̃pe] *tr* to stamp (*with a design*); engrave; overcharge, fleece

estampille [ɛstɑ̃pij] *f* identification mark; trademark; hallmark

est-ce que [ɛskə] see **être**

ester [ɛstɛr] *m* ester ‖ [ɛste] *intr*—**ester en justice** to go to law, to sue

esthète [ɛstɛt] *mf* aesthete

esthéti·cien [ɛstetisjɛ̃] **-cienne** [sjɛn] *mf* aesthetician ‖ *f* beautician

esthétique [ɛstetik] *adj* aesthetic; plastic (*surgery*); ‖ *f* aesthetics

estimable [ɛstimabl] *adj* estimable

estimateur [ɛstimatœr] *m* estimator, appraiser

estimation [ɛstimasjɔ̃] *f* estimation, appraisal

estime [ɛstim] *f* esteem; **à l'estime** by guesswork; (naut) by dead reckoning

estimer [ɛstime] §95 *tr* to esteem; estimate, assess; **estimer** + *inf* to think that + *inf*. e.g., **j'estime avoir fait mon devoir** I think that I did my duty

esti·val -vale [ɛstival] *adj* (*pl* **-vaux** [vol]) summer

esti·vant [ɛstivɑ̃] **-vante** [vɑ̃t] *mf* summer vacationist, summer resident

estiver [ɛstive] *intr* to summer

estocade [ɛstɔkad] *f* thrust (*in fencing*); unexpected attack

estomac [ɛstɔma] *m* stomach

estomaquer [ɛstɔmake] *tr* (coll) to astound ‖ *ref* (coll) to be angered

estomper [ɛstɔ̃pe] *tr* to shade off, rub away (*a drawing*); blur ‖ *ref* to be blurred

estrade [ɛstrad] *f* platform

estragon [ɛstragɔ̃] *m* tarragon

estro·pié -piée [ɛstrɔpje] *adj* crippled ‖ *mf* cripple

estuaire [ɛstɥɛr] *m* estuary

estudian·tin [ɛstydjɑ̃tɛ̃] **-tine** [tin] *adj* student

esturgeon [ɛstyrʒɔ̃] *m* sturgeon

et [e] *conj* and; **et . . . et** both . . . and

Établ. *abbr* (**Établissement**) company, establishment

étable [etabl] *f* stable, cowshed

établer [etable] *tr* to stable

établi [etabli] *m* workbench

établir [etablir] *tr* to establish ‖ *ref* to settle down; set up headquarters

établissement [etablismɑ̃] *m* establishment; business; factory; **établissement d'enseignement, établissement scolaire** school; **établissements** company, firm, e.g., **les Établissements Martin** Martin & Co.

étage [etaʒ] *m* floor, story; tier, level; rank, social level; (rok) stage; **de bas étage** lower-class; **dernier étage** top floor; **premier étage** first floor above ground floor, second floor

étager [etaʒe] §38 *tr* to arrange in tiers; stagger; perform in stages

étagère [etaʒɛr] *f* rack, shelf

étai [etɛ] *m* prop, stay

étain [etɛ̃] *m* tin; pewter

étais [ete] *v* (**était, étions**) see **être**

étal [etal] *m* (*pl* **étals** or **étaux** [eto]) stall, stand; butcher's block

étalage [etalaʒ] *m* display

étalager [etalaʒe] §38 *tr* to display

étalagiste [etalaʒist] *mf* window dresser, display artist; demonstrator

étaler [etale] *tr* to display; spread out ‖ *ref* (coll) to sprawl

étalon [etalɔ̃] *m* stallion; monetary standard

étalonner [etalɔne] *tr* to verify, control; standardize; graduate, calibrate

étalon-or [etalɔ̃ɔr] *m* gold standard

étambot [etɑ̃bo] *m* (naut) sternpost

étamer [etame] *tr* to tin-plate; silver (*a mirror*)

étamine [etamin] *f*. stamen; sieve; cheese-cloth

étampe [etɑ̃p] *f* stamp, die, punch

étamper [etɑ̃pe] *tr* to stamp, punch

étanche [etɑ̃ʃ] *adj* watertight, airtight

étancher [etɑ̃ʃe] *tr* to check, stanch the flow of; quench (*one's thirst*); make watertight or airtight

étang [etɑ̃] *m* pond

étape [etap] *f* stage; stop, halt; day's march; (sports) lap; **brûler les étapes** to go straight through

état [eta] *m* state; statement, record; trade, occupation; government; (hist) estate; **en tout état de cause** at all costs; in any case; **état civil** marital status, birth and death record; **état de la technique, état présent** state of the art; **état providence** welfare state; **état tampon** buffer state; **être dans tous ses états** to stew; **être en état de** to be in a position to; **faire état de** to take into account; expect to; **hors d'état** out of order, unfit; **tenir en état** to keep in shape, repair

étatisation [etatizɑsjɔ̃] *f* nationalization

étatiser [etatize] *tr* to nationalize

étatisme [etatism] *m* statism

état-major [etamaʒɔr] *m* (*pl* **états-majors**) headquarters, staff

état-providence [etaprɔvidɑ̃s] *m* welfare state

États-Unis [etazyni] *mpl* United States

étau [eto] *m* (*pl* **étaux**) vise

étayer [eteje] §49 *tr* to prop, stay

etc. [ɛtsetera] *abbr* (**et caetera, et cetera**) etc.

et Cⁱᵉ *abbr* (**et Compagnie**) & Co.

été [ete] *m* summer; **en été** in (the) summer ‖ *v* see **être**

éteignoir [etɛɲwar] *m* candle snuffer; (coll) kill-joy, wet blanket

éteindre [etɛ̃dr] §50 *tr* to extinguish, put out; turn off; wipe out; appease (*e.g., one's thirst*); dull (*a color*) ‖ *intr* to put out the light ‖ *ref* to go out; (fig) to die, pass away

éteint [etɛ̃] **éteinte** [etɛ̃t] *adj* extinguished; exinct; dull, dim

étendard [etɑ̃dar] *m* flag, banner

étendoir [etɑ̃dwar] *m* clothesline; drying rack

étendre [etɑ̃dr] *tr* to extend, spread out ‖ *ref* to stretch out; spread

éten·du -due [etɑ̃dy] *adj* outspread; extensive; vast; diluted, adulterated ‖ *f* stretch; range, scope

éter·nel -nelle [etɛrnɛl] *adj* eternal

éterniser [etɛrnize] *tr* to perpetuate (*a name*); drag out ‖ *ref* (coll) to drag on; **s'éterniser chez qn** (coll) to overstay an invitation

éternité [etɛrnite] *f* eternity

éternuement [etɛrnymɑ̃] *m* sneeze; sneezing

éternuer [etɛrnɥe] *intr* to sneeze

étes [ɛt] *v* see **être**

étêter [etɛte] *tr* to top (*a tree*); take the head off (*a fish, nail, etc.*)

éteule [etœl] *f* stubble

éther [etɛr] *m* ether

éthé·ré -rée [etere] *adj* ethereal

Éthiopie [etjɔpi] *f* Ethiopia; **l'Éthiopie** Ethiopia

éthio·pien -pienne [etjɔpjɛ̃] **-pienne** [pjɛn] *adj* Ethiopian ‖ *m* Ethiopian (*language*) ‖ (*cap*) *mf* Ethiopian (*person*)

éthique [etik] *adj* ethical ‖ *f* ethics

ethnique [ɛtnik] *adj* ethnic(al)

ethnographie [ɛtnɔgrafi] *f* ethnography

ethnologie [ɛtnɔlɔʒi] *f* ethnology

éthyle [etil] *m* ethyl

éthylène [etilɛn] *m* ethylene

étiage [etjaʒ] *m* low-water mark

étince·lant [etɛ̃slɑ̃] **-lante** [lɑ̃t] *adj* sparkling, glittering

étinceler [etɛ̃sle] §34 *intr* to sparkle, glitter

étincelle [etɛ̃sɛl] *f* spark; (fig) flash

étiolement [etjɔlmɑ̃] *m* wilting

étioler [etjɔle] *tr & ref* to wilt

étique [etik] *adj* lean, emaciated

étiquetage [etiktaʒ] *m* labeling

étiqueter [etikte] §34 *tr* to label

étiquette [etikɛt] *f* etiquette; label; **étiquette gommée** sticker

étirer [etire] *tr* to stretch, lengthen, elongate ‖ *ref* (coll) to stretch one's limbs

étoffe [etɔf] *f* stuff; material, fabric; quality, worth

étoffer [etɔfe] *tr* to fill out; enrich; stuff (*furniture*)

étoile [etwal] *f* star; traffic circle; **à la belle étoile** out of doors; **étoile de mer** starfish; **étoile filante** shooting or falling star; **étoile polaire** polestar

étoi·lé -lée [etwale] *adj* star-spangled, starry

étole [etɔl] *f* stole

éton·nant [etɔnɑ̃] **-nante** [nɑ̃t] *adj* astonishing

étonnement [etɔnmɑ̃] *m* surprise, astonishment; fissure, crack

étonner [etɔne] *tr* to surprise, astonish; shake or crack (*masonry*) ‖ §97 *ref* to be surprised

étouf·fant [etufɑ̃] **-fante** [fɑ̃t] *adj* suffocating; sweltering

étouffée [etufe] *f* braising; **cuire à l'étouffée** to braise

étouffer [etufe] *tr, intr, & ref* to suffocate; stifle; choke

étoupe [etup] *f* oakum, tow

étourderie [eturdri] *f* thoughtlessness

étour·di -die [eturdi] *adj* scatterbrained ‖ *mf* scatterbrain

étourdir [eturdir] *tr* to stun, daze; numb; deafen (*with loud noise*) ‖ *ref* to try to forget, get in a daze

étourdissement [eturdismɑ̃] *m* dizziness; numbing

étour·neau [eturno] *m* (*pl* **-neaux**) starling

étrange [etrɑ̃ʒ] *adj* strange

étran·ger [etrɑ̃ʒe] **-gère** [ʒɛr] *adj* foreign; irrelevant; unknown, strange; **être étranger à** to be unacquainted with ‖ *mf* foreigner; stranger; **à l'étranger** abroad, in a foreign country

étrangeté [etrɑ̃ʒte] *f* strangeness

étrangler [etrɑ̃gle] *tr & intr* to strangle ‖ *ref* to choke; narrow (*said of passageway, valley, etc.*)

étran·gleur [etrɑ̃glœr] **-gleuse** [gløz] *mf* strangler

étrave [etrav] *f* (naut) stempost; **de l'étrave à l'étambot** from stem to stern

être [ɛtr] *m* being ‖ §28, §95 *intr* to be; to go to + *inf* (usually in the past tense), *e.g.,* **elle a été chanter à Paris** she went to sing in Paris, **où as-tu été passer les vacances?** Where did you go for your vacation?; **en être pour sa peine** to have nothing for one's trouble; **est-ce que** (not translated in questions), e.g., **est-ce qu'ils sont riches?** are they rich?; **être à** + *pron disj* to be + *pron poss*, e.g., **le livre est à moi** the book is mine; **n'est-ce pas** see **ne**; **s'il en fut** it surely was, to be sure; **s'il en fut jamais** if ever there was one ‖ *aux* (used with some intransitive verbs and all reflexive verbs) to have, e.g., **elles sont arrivées** they have arrived; (used to form the passive voice) to be, e.g., **il est aimé de tout le monde** he is loved by everybody

étrécir [etresir] *tr & ref* to shrink

étreindre [etrɛ̃dr] §50 *tr* to embrace; grip, seize

étreinte [etrɛ̃t] *f* embrace; hold, grasp

étrenne [etrɛn] *f* first sale of the day; **avoir l'étrenne de** to have the first use of; **étrennes** New-Year gifts

étrenner [etrɛne] *tr* to put on for the first time; be the first to wear ‖ *intr* (coll) to be the first to catch it

étrier [etrije] *m* stirrup

étrille [etrij] *f* currycomb

étriller [etrije] *tr* to curry; (coll) to thrash, tan the hide of; (coll) to overcharge, fleece

étriper [etripe] *tr* to gut, disembowel

étri·qué -quée [etrike] *adj* skimpy, tight; narrow, cramped

étriquer [etrike] *tr* to make too tight; shorten (*e.g., a speech*)

étroit [etrwa] **étroite** [etrwat] *adj* narrow; strict; tight; close; **à l'étroit** confined, cramped

étroitesse [etrwatɛs] *f* narrowness; **étroitesse d'esprit** narrow-mindedness

Ets. *abbr* **Établissements**

étude [etyd] *f* study; law office; law practice; spadework, planning; **à l'étude** under consideration; **étude de faisabilité** feasibility study; **étude des ovnis** UFOlogy; **étude sur dossier** case work; **mettre à l'étude** to study; **terminer ses études** to finish one's courses

étu·diant -diante [etydjɑ̃] -[djɑ̃t] *mf* student

étu·dié -diée [etydje] *adj* studied; set (*speech*); artificial, affected

étudier [etydje] *tr* to study; practice, rehearse; learn by heart; design ‖ *intr* to study ‖ §96 *ref* to be overly introspective; **s'étudier à** to take pains to, make a point of

étui [etɥi] *m* case, box

étuve [etyv] *f* steam bath or room; drying room; steam sterilizer; incubator (*for breeding cultures*)

étuver [etyve] *tr* to stew; steam; dry

étymologie [etimɔlɔʒi] *f* etymology

étymon [etimɔ̃] *m* etymon

eucalyptus [økaliptys] *m* eucalyptus

Eucharistie [økaristi] *f* Eucharist

eunuque [ønyk] *m* eunuch

euphémique [øfemik] *adj* euphemistic

euphémisme [øfemism] *m* euphemism

euphonie [øfɔni] *f* euphony

euphonique [øfɔnik] *adj* euphonic

euphorie [øfɔri] *f* euphoria

Europe [ørɔp] *f* Europe; **l'Europe** Europe

européen [ørɔpeɛ̃] **européenne** [ørɔpeɛn] *adj* European ‖ (*cap*) *mf* European

eus [y] *v* (**eut, eûmes,** etc.) see **avoir**

eux [ø] §85

eux-mêmes [ømɛm] §86

évacuer [evakɥe] *tr & ref* to evacuate

éva·dé -dée [evade] *mf* escapee

évader [evade] *ref* to escape, evade

évaluer [evalɥe] *tr* to evaluate, appraise; estimate

évanes·cent [evanesɑ̃] **-cente** [sɑ̃t] *adj* evanescent

évangélique [evɑ̃ʒelik] *adj* evangelic(al)

évangéliste [evɑ̃ʒelist] *m* evangelist

évangile [evɑ̃ʒil] *m* gospel

évanouir [evanwir] *ref* to faint; lose consciousness; vanish; (rad) to fade

évanouissement [evanwismɑ̃] *m* fainting; disappearance; (rad, telv) fading

évapo·ré -rée [evapɔre] *adj* flighty, fickle, giddy

évaporer [evapɔre] *tr & ref* to evaporate

évaser [evaze] *tr & ref* to widen

éva·sif -sive [evazif] -[ziv] *adj* evasive

évasion [evazjɔ̃] *f* evasion; escape; **d'évasion** escapist (*literature*)

Ève [ɛv] *f* Eve; **je ne le connais ni d'Ève ni d'Adam** (coll) I don't know him from Adam

évêché [eveʃe] *m* bishopric

éveil [evɛj] *m* awakening; alarm, warning

éveil·lé -lée [eveje] *adj* alert, lively; sharp, intelligent

éveiller [eveje] *tr & ref* to wake up

événement [evenmɑ̃], [evɛnmɑ̃] *m* event; outcome, development; **faire événement** to cause quite a stir

évent [evɑ̃] *m* vent; staleness

éventail [evɑ̃taj] *m* fan; range, spread; screen

éventaire [evɑ̃tɛr] *m* tray (*carried by flower girl, cigarette girl, etc.*); sidewalk display

éven·té -tée [evɑ̃te] *adj* stale, flat

éventer [evɑ̃te] *tr* to fan; ventilate; get wind of (*a secret*); **éventer la mèche** (coll) to let the cat out of the bag ‖ *ref* to fan oneself; fade away (*said of odor*); go stale or flat

éventrer [evɑ̃tre] *tr* to disembowel; smash open

éventualité [evɑ̃tɥalite] *f* eventuality, contingency; possibility

éven·tuel -tuelle [evɑ̃tɥɛl] *adj* possible; contingent; forthcoming ‖ *m* possibility; possibilities (*e.g., of a job*)

éventuellement [evɑ̃tɥɛlmɑ̃] *adv* possibly; if need be

évêque [evɛk] *m* bishop

évertuer [evɛrtɥe] §96 *ref*—**s'évertuer à** or **pour** + *inf* to strive to + *inf*

éviction [eviksjɔ̃] *f* eviction, removal; **éviction scolaire** quarantine

évidement [evidmɑ̃] *m* hollowing out

évidemment [evidamɑ̃] *adv* evidently

évidence [evidɑ̃s] *f* evidence, obviousness; conspicuousness; **de toute évidence** by all appearances; **se mettre en évidence** to come to the fore

évi·dent [evidɑ̃] **-dente** [dɑ̃t] *adj* evident

évider [evide] *tr* to hollow out

évier [evje] *m* sink

évincer [evɛ̃se] §51 *tr* to evict, oust; discriminate against

éviter [evite] §97 *tr* to avoid, escape

évoca·teur [evɔkatœr] **-trice** [tris] *adj* evocative, suggestive

évocation [evɔkasjɔ̃] *f* evocation

évoluer [evɔlɥe] *intr* to evolve; change one's mind

évolution [evɔlysjɔ̃] *f* evolution

évoquer [evɔke] *tr* to evoke; recall, call to mind

exact [ɛgza], [ɛgzakt] **exacte** [ɛgzakt] *adj* exact; punctual, on time

exactement [ɛgzaktəmɑ̃] *adv* exactly; on time

exactitude [ɛgzaktityd] *f* exactness; punctuality

exagération [ɛgzaʒerɑsjɔ̃] *f* exaggeration

exagérer [ɛgzaʒere] §10 *tr* to exaggerate; overdo

exal·té -tée [ɛgzalte] *adj* impassioned; high-strung, wrought-up ‖ *mf* hothead, fanatic

exalter [ɛgzalte] *tr* to exalt; excite (*e.g., the imagination*) ‖ *ref* to get excited

examen [ɛgzamɛ̃] *m* examination; **à l'examen** under consideration; on approval; **examen de fin d'études** or **examen de fin de classe** final examination; **examen de la vision** eye test; **examen de routine** routine examination; **examen probatoire** placement exam; **libre examen** free inquiry; **se présenter à, passer,** or **subir un examen** to take an examination

examina·teur [ɛgzaminatœr] **-trice** [tris] *mf* examiner

examiner [ɛgzamine] *tr* to examine

exaspération [ɛgzasperɑsjɔ̃] *f* exasperation; crisis, aggravation

exaspérer [ɛgzaspere] §10 *tr* to exasperate; make worse

exaucer [ɛgzose] §51 *tr* to answer the prayer of; fulfill (*a wish*)

excava·teur [ɛskavatœr] **-trice** [tris] *m & f* excavator, steam shovel

excaver [ɛskave] *tr* to excavate

excé·dant [ɛksedɑ̃] **-dante** [dɑ̃t] *adj* excess; tiresome

excédent [ɛksedɑ̃] *m* excess, surplus

excédentaire [ɛksedɑ̃tɛr] *adj* excess

excéder [ɛksede] §10 *tr* to exceed; tire out; overtax

excellence [ɛksɛlɑ̃s] *f* excellence; **Votre Excellence** Your Excellency

exceller [ɛksɛle] §96 *intr* to excel

excentricité [ɛksɑ̃trisite] *f* eccentricity

excentrique [ɛksɑ̃trik] *adj* eccentric; remote, outlying ‖ *mf* eccentric ‖ *m* (mach) eccentric

excep·té -tée [ɛksɛpte] *adj* excepted ‖ **excepté** *adv*—**excepté que** except that ‖ **excepté** *prep* except, except for

exception [ɛksɛpsjɔ̃] *f* exception; **à l'exception de** with the exception of

exception·nel -nelle [ɛksɛpsjɔnɛl] *adj* exceptional

exceptionnellement [ɛksɛpsjɔnɛlmɑ̃] *adv* exceptionally; as an exception

excès [ɛksɛ] *m* excess; **excès de pose** (phot) overexposure; **excès de vitesse** speeding

exces·sif [ɛksɛsif] **-sive** [siv] *adj* excessive

exciper [ɛksipe] *intr*—**exciper de** (law) to offer a plea of, allege

excitable [ɛksitabl] *adj* excitable

exci·tant [ɛksitɑ̃] **-tante** [tɑ̃t] *adj* stimulating ‖ *m* stimulant

exciter [ɛksite] §96, §100 *tr* to excite, stimulate; stir, incite; provoke (*e.g., laughter*) ‖ §96 *ref* to get excited; become (sexually) aroused

exclamation [ɛksklamɑsjɔ̃] *f* exclamation

exclamer [ɛksklame] *ref* to exclaim

exclure [ɛksklyr] §11 *tr* to exclude

exclu·sif [ɛksklyzif] **-sive** [ziv] *adj* exclusive

exclusion [ɛksklyzjɔ̃] *f* exclusion; **à l'exclusion de** exclusive of, excluding

exclusivité [ɛksklyzivite] *f* exclusiveness; exclusive rights; newsbeat; (journ) scoop; **en exclusivité** (public sign in front of a theater) exclusive showing

excommunication [ɛkskɔmynikɑsjɔ̃] *f* excommunication

excommunier [ɛkskɔmynje] *tr* to excommunicate

excorier [ɛkskɔrje] *tr* to scratch, skin

excrément [ɛkskremɑ̃] *m* excrement

excroissance [ɛkskrwasɑ̃s] *f* growth, tumor

excursion [ɛkskyrsjɔ̃] *f* excursion; tour, trip; outing

excursionner [ɛkskyrsjɔne] *intr* to go on an excursion

excusable [ɛkskyzabl] *adj* excusable

excuse [ɛkskyz] *f* excuse; **des excuses** apologies

excuser [ɛkskyze] §97, §99 *tr* to excuse ‖ *ref* to excuse oneself, apologize; **je m'excuse!** (coll) excuse me!

exécrer [ɛgzekre] §10 *tr* to execrate

exécu·tant [ɛgzekytɑ̃] **-tante** [tɑ̃t] *mf* performer

exécuter [ɛgzekyte] *tr* to execute; perform; make (*copies*) ‖ *ref* to comply

exécuteur [ɛgzekytœr] *m*—**exécuteur testamentaire** executor; **exécuteur des hautes œuvres** hangman

exécu·tif [ɛgzekytif] **-tive** [tiv] *adj & m* executive

exécution [ɛgzekysjɔ̃] *f* execution; performance; fulfillment; **mettre à exécution** to carry out

exécutrice [ɛgzekytris] *f* executrix

exemplaire [ɛgzɑ̃plɛr] *adj* exemplary ‖ *m* exemplar, model; sample, specimen; copy (*e.g., of book*); **en double exemplaire** with carbon copy; **exemplaire dédicacé**

autographed copy; **exemplaires de passe** extra copies

exemple [ɛgzɑ̃pl] *m* example; **à l'exemple de** after the example of; **par exemple** for example; **par exemple!** the idea!, well I never!; **prêcher d'exemple** to practice what one preaches; **sans exemple** unprecedented

exempt [ɛgzɑ̃] **exempte** [ɛgzɑ̃t] *adj* exempt || *m* (hist) police officer

exempter [ɛgzɑ̃te] §97, §99 *tr* to exempt

exemption [ɛgzɑ̃psjɔ̃] *f* exemption

exer·cé -cée [ɛgzɛrse] *adj* practiced, experienced

exercer [ɛgzɛrse] §51 *tr* to exercise; exert; practice (*e.g.*, *medicine*) || §96 *ref* to exercise; practice, drill

exercice [ɛgzɛrsis] *m* exercise; drill; practice; **exercice budgétaire** fiscal year

exergue [ɛgzɛrg] *m* inscription; place on a medal for an inscription, **mettre en exergue** to inscribe (*e.g.*, *a proverb*)

exhalaison [ɛgzalɛzɔ̃] *f* exhalation (*of gas, vapors, etc.*)

exhalation [ɛgzalɑsjɔ̃] *f* exhalation (*of air from lungs*)

exhaler [ɛgzale] *tr*, *intr*, *& ref* to exhale

exhaure [ɛgzɔr] *f* pumping out (*of a mine*); drain pumps

exhaussement [ɛgzosmɑ̃] *m* raising; rise

exhausser [ɛgzose] *tr* to raise, increase the height of || *ref* to rise

exhaus·tif [ɛgzostif] **-tive** [tiv] *adj* exhaustive

exhiber [ɛgzibe] *tr* to exhibit; show (*a ticket, passport, etc.*) || *ref* to make an exhibition of oneself

exhibition [ɛgzibisjɔ̃] *f* exhibition

exhorter [ɛgzɔrte] §96, §100 *tr* to exhort

exhumer [ɛgzyme] *tr* to exhume

exi·geant [ɛgziʒɑ̃] **-geante** [ʒɑ̃t] *adj* exigent, exacting; unreasonable

exigence [ɛgziʒɑ̃s] *f* demand, claim; requirement; unreasonableness; **exigences** exigencies

exiger [ɛgziʒe] §38 *tr* to demand, require, exact

exigible [ɛgziʒibl] *adj* required; due, on demand

exi·gu -guë [ɛgzigy] *adj* tiny; insufficient

exiguïté [ɛgziɡɥite] *f* smallness; insufficiency

exil [ɛgzil] *m* exile

exi·lé -lée [ɛgzile] *adj & mf* exile

exiler [ɛgzile] *tr* to exile

existence [ɛgzistɑ̃s] *f* existence

existentialisme [ɛgzistɑ̃sjalism] *m* existentialism

exister [ɛgziste] *intr* to exist

exode [ɛgzɔd] *m* exodus; flight (*of capital; of emigrants, refugees, etc.*)

exonération [ɛgzɔnerɑsjɔ̃] *f* exemption, exoneration

exonérer [ɛgzɔnere] §10 *tr* to exempt, exonerate || *ref* to pay up a debt

exorbi·tant [ɛgzɔrbitɑ̃] **-tante** [tɑ̃t] *adj* exorbitant

exorciser [ɛgzorsize] *tr* to exorcise

exorde [ɛgzɔrd] *m* introduction

exotique [ɛgzɔtik] *adj* exotic

expan·sif [ɛkspɑ̃sif] **-sive** [siv] *adj* expansive

expansion [ɛkspɑ̃sjɔ̃] *f* expansion; expansiveness; spread (*of a belief*)

expa·trié -triée [ɛkspatrije] *adj & mf* expatriate

expatrier [ɛkspatrije] *tr* to expatriate

expectorer [ɛkspɛktɔre] *tr & intr* to expectorate

expé·dient [ɛkspedjɑ̃] **-diente** [djɑ̃t] *adj* expedient || *m* expedient; (coll) makeshift; **expédient provisoire** emergency measure; **vivre d'expédients** to live by one's wits

expédier [ɛkspedje] *tr* to expedite; ship; make a certified copy of; (coll) to dash off, do hurriedly

expédi·teur [ɛkspeditœr] **-trice** [tris] *adj* forwarding (*station, agency, etc.*) || *mf* sender, shipper

expédi·tif [ɛkspeditif] **-tive** [tiv] *adj* expeditious

expédition [ɛkspedisjɔ̃] *f* expedition; shipping; shipment; certified copy

expéditionnaire [ɛkspedisjɔnɛr] *adj* expeditionary || *mf* sender; clerk

expérience [ɛksperjɑ̃s] *f* experience; experiment

expérimen·tal -tale [ɛkperimɑ̃tal] *adj* (*pl* **-taux** [to]) experimental; tentative

expérimen·té -tée [ɛksperimɑ̃te] *adj* experienced

expérimenter [ɛksperimɑ̃te] *tr* to try out, test || *intr* to conduct experiments

ex·pert [ɛkspɛr] **-perte** [pɛrt] *adj* expert || *m* expert; connoisseur; appraiser

expert-comptable [ɛkspɛrkɔ̃tabl] *m* (*pl* **experts-comptables**) certified public accountant

expertise [ɛkspɛrtiz] *f* expert appraisal

expertiser [ɛkspɛrtise] *tr* to appraise

expier [ɛkspje] *tr* to expiate, atone for

expiration [ɛkspirɑsjɔ̃] *f* expiration

expirer [ɛkspire] *tr & intr* to expire; exhale

explicable [ɛksplikabl] *adj* explicable, explainable

explica·tif [ɛksplikatif] **-tive** [tiv] *adj* explanatory

explication [ɛksplikɑsjɔ̃] *f* explanation; interpretation (*of a text*); **avoir une explication avec qn** to have it out with s.o.

explicite [ɛksplisit] *adj* explicit

expliciter [ɛksplisite] *tr* to make explicit

expliquer [ɛksplike] §98 *tr* to explain; give an interpretation of || *ref* to explain oneself; understand

exploit [ɛksplwa] *m* exploit; **exploit d'ajournement** subpoena; **signifier un exploit** to serve a summons

exploi·tant [ɛksplwatɑ̃] **-tante** [tɑ̃t] *adj* operating, working || *mf* operator (*of enterprise*); developer; cultivator; (mov) exhibitor

exploitation [εksplwatɑsjɔ̃] f exploitation; management, development, cultivation; land under cultivation

exploiter [εksplwate] tr to exploit; manage, develop, cultivate ‖ intr to serve summonses

explora·teur [εksplɔratœr] **-trice** [tris] mf explorer

exploration [εksplɔrasjɔ̃] f exploration

explorer [εksplɔre] tr to explore; (telv) to scan

exploser [εksploze] intr to explode

explosible [εksplozibl] adj explosive

explo·sif [εksplozif] **-sive** [ziv] adj & m explosive

explosion [εksplozjɔ̃] f explosion; **à explosion** internal-combustion (engine)

exporta·teur [εkspɔrtatœr] **-trice** [tris] adj exporting ‖ mf exporter

exportation [εkspɔrtɑsjɔ̃] f export; exportation

exporter [εkspɔrte] tr & intr to export

expo·sant [εkspozɑ̃] **-sante** [zɑ̃t] mf exhibitor; petitioner ‖ m (math) exponent

exposé [εkspoze] m exposition, account, statement; report (given by a student in class)

exposer [εkspoze] §96 tr to expose; explain, expound; exhibit, display

exposition [εkspozisjɔ̃] f exposition; exposure (to one of the points of the compass); introduction (of a book); lying in state; **exposition canine** dog show; **exposition d'horticulture** flower show; **exposition hippique** horse show; **exposition inter-professionelle** trade show

ex·près [εksprε] **-presse** [prεs] adj express ‖ **exprès** adj invar special-delivery (letter, package, etc.) ‖ m express; **par exprès** by special delivery ‖ **exprès** adv expressly, on purpose

express [εksprεs] adj & m express (train)

expressément [εksprεsemɑ̃] adv expressly

expres·sif [εksprεsif] **-sive** [siv] adj expressive

expression [εksprεsjɔ̃] f expression; **d'expression française** native French-speaking

exprimer [εksprime] tr to express; squeeze out

exproprier [εksprɔprije] tr to expropriate

expul·sé -sée [εkspylse] adj deported ‖ mf deportee

expulser [εkspylse] tr to expel; evict; throw out

expulsion [εkspylsjɔ̃] f expulsion

expurger [εkspyrʒe] §38 tr to expurgate

ex·quis [εkski] **-quise** [kiz] adj exquisite; sharp (pain)

exsangue [εksɑ̃g] adj bloodless, anemic

exsuder [εksyde] tr & intr to exude

extase [εkstɑz] f ecstasy

exta·sié -siée [εkstɑzje] adj enraptured, ecstatic, in ecstasy

extasier [εkstɑzje] ref to be enraptured

extatique [εkstatik] adj & mf ecstatic

extempora·né -née [εkstɑ̃pɔrane] adj (law) unpremeditated; (pharm) ready for use

exten·sif [εkstɑ̃sif] **-sive** [siv] adj wide (meaning); (mech) tensile

extension [εkstɑ̃sjɔ̃] f extension

exténuer [εkstenɥe] tr to exhaust, tire out ‖ ref to tire oneself out

exté·rieur -rieure [εksterjœr] adj exterior; external; outer, outside; foreign (policy) ‖ m exterior; outside; (mov) location shot; **à l'extérieur** outside; abroad; **en extérieur** (mov) on location

extérieurement [εksterjœrmɑ̃] adv externally; superficially; on the outside

extérioriser [εksterjɔrize] tr to reveal, show ‖ ref to open one's heart

exterminer [εkstεrmine] tr to exterminate

externat [εkstεrna] m day school

externe [εkstεrn] adj external ‖ m day student; outpatient; (med) nonresident intern

extinc·teur [εkstε̃ktœr] **-trice** [tris] adj extinguishing ‖ m fire extinguisher

extinction [εkstε̃ksjɔ̃] f exinction; extinguishing; loss (of voice); **extinction d'un traité** termination of a treaty; **l'extinction des feux** (mil) lights out, taps

extirper [εkstirpe] tr to extirpate

extorquer [εkstɔrke] tr to extort

extor·queur [εkstɔrkœr] **-queuse** [køz] mf extortionist

extorsion [εkstɔrsjɔ̃] f extortion

extra [εkstra] adj invar (coll) extraspecial, extra ‖ m invar extra

extraction [εkstraksjɔ̃] f extraction; descent, e.g., **d'extraction allemande** of German descent

extrader [εkstrade] tr to extradite

extradition [εkstradisjɔ̃] f extradition

extra·fin [εkstrafε̃] **-fine** [fin] adj high-quality

extraire [εkstrεr] §68 tr to extract; excerpt; get out ‖ ref to extricate oneself

extrait [εkstrε] m extract; excerpt; abstract; certified copy; **extrait de baptême** baptismal certificate; **extrait de naissance** birth certificate; **extraits** selections (e.g., in an anthology)

extra-muros [εkstramyros] adj invar extramural; suburban ‖ adv outside the town

extraordinaire [εkstraɔrdinεr], [εkstrɔrdinεr] adj extraordinary

extrapoler [εkstrapɔle] tr to extrapolate

extra-sensoriel -sensorielle [εkstrasɑ̃sɔrjεl] adj extrasensory

extravagance [εkstravagɑ̃s] f extravagance; excess; absurdity, wildness

extrava·gant [εkstravagɑ̃] **-gante** [gɑ̃t] adj excessive, extravagant; absurd, wild, eccentric ‖ mf eccentric, screwball

extraver·ti -tie [εkstravεrti] adj & mf extrovert

extrême [εkstrεm] adj & m extreme

extrêmement [εkstrεməmɑ̃] adv extremely

extrême-onction [εkstrεmɔ̃ksjɔ̃] f extreme unction

Extrême-Orient [εkstrεmɔrjɑ̃] m Far East

extrémiste [εkstremist] adj & mf extremist

extrémité [εkstremite] *f* extremity; **en venir à des extrémités** to resort to violence; **être à toute extrémité** to be at death's door

extrinsèque [εkstrẽsεk] *adj* extrinsic

exubé·rant [εgzyberã] **-rante** [rãt] *adj* exuberant

exulter [εgzylte] *intr* to exult

exutoire [εgzytwar] *m* outlet; means of escape; (med) exutory

ex-voto [εksvɔto] *m invar* votive inscription or tablet

F

F, f [εf], *[εf] *m invar* sixth letter of the French alphabet

F (*abbr*) (**franc**) franc

fable [fɑbl] *f* fable; laughingstock

fabri·cant [fabrikã] **-cante** [kãt] *mf* manufacturer

fabrica·teur [fabrikatœr] **-trice** [tris] *mf* fabricator (*e.g.*, *of lies*); forger; counterfeiter

fabrication [fabrikɑsjɔ̃] *f* manufacture; forging; counterfeiting

fabrique [fabrik] *f* factory; factory workers; mill hands; (obs) church trustees; (obs) church revenue; **fabrique de papier** paper mill

fabriquer [fabrike] *tr* to manufacture; fabricate; forge; counterfeit; **fabriquer en série** to mass-produce

fabu·leux [fabylø] **-leuse** [løz] *adj* fabulous

façade [fasad] *f* façade; frontage; **en façade sur** facing, overlooking

face [fas] *f* face; side (*of a diamond; of a phonograph record*); surface; heads (*of coin*); **de face** full-faced (*portrait*); **en face (de)** opposite, facing; **faire face à** to face; face up to; meet (*an obligation*); **perdre la face** to lose face; **sauver la face** to save face

face-à-main [fasamẽ] *m* (*pl* **faces-à-main**) lorgnette

facétie [fasesi] *f* off-color joke; practical joke

facé·tieux [fasesjø] **-tieuse** [sjøz] *adj* droll, funny ‖ *mf* wag

facette [fasεt] *f* facet

fâ·ché -chée [fɑʃe] *adj* angry; sorry; **fâché avec** at odds with; **fâché contre** angry with (*a person*); **fâché de** angry at (*a thing*); sorry for

fâcher [fɑʃe] *tr* to anger ‖ *ref* to get angry; be sorry

fâ·cheux [fɑʃø] **-cheuse** [ʃøz] *adj* annoying, tiresome; unfortunate ‖ *mf* nuisance, bore

fa·cial -ciale [fasjal] *adj* (*pl* **-ciaux** [sjo]) facial; face (*value*)

facile [fasil] §92 *adj* easy; easygoing; facile, glib

facilité [fasilite] *f* facility; opportunity (*e.g.*, *to meet s.o.*); **facilités de paiement** installments; easy terms

faciliter [fasilite] *tr* to facilitate

façon [fasɔ̃] *f* fashion; fashioning; way, manner; fit (*of clothes*); **à façon** job (*work; workman*); **à la façon de** like; **de façon à** so as to; **de façon que** or **de telle façon que** so that, e.g., **parlez de telle façon qu'on vous comprenne** speak so that you can be understood; **de toute façon** in any event; **façons** manners; **faire des façons** to stand on ceremony; **sans façon** informal

faconde [fakɔ̃d] *f* glibness, gift of gab

façonnage [fasɔnaʒ] *m* shaping; fashioning; manufacturing; (comp) processing

façonner [fasɔne] *tr* to fashion, shape; work (*the land*); accustom

façon·nier [fasɔnje] **-nière** [njεr] *adj* jobbing; fussy ‖ *mf* pieceworker; stuffed shirt

fac-sim [faksim] *m* (comp) hard copy

fac-similé [faksimile] *m* (*pl* **-similés**) facsimile

factage [faktaʒ] *m* delivery service; home delivery

facteur [faktœr] *m* factor; mail carrier, mailman; expressman; auctioneer (*at a market*); maker (*of musical instruments*)

factice [faktis] *adj* imitation, artificial

fac·tieux [faksjø] **-tieuse** [sjøz] *adj* factious, seditious ‖ *mf* troublemaker, agitator

faction [faksjɔ̃] *f* faction; **être de faction** to be on sentry duty

factionnaire [faksjɔnεr] *m* sentry

factorerie [faktɔrəri] *f* trading post

factotum [faktɔtɔm] *m* factotum; meddler; jack-of-all-trades

factrice [faktris] *f* woman letter carrier

factum [faktɔm] *m* political pamphlet; (law) brief

facturation [faktyrɑsjɔ̃] *f* billing, invoicing

facture [faktyr] *f* invoice; bill; workmanship; **établir une facture** to make out an invoice; **suivant facture** as per invoice

facturer [faktyre] *tr* to bill

factu·rier [faktyrje] **-rière** [rjεr] *mf* billing clerk ‖ *m* invoice book

faculta·tif [fakyltatif] **-tive** [tiv] *adj* optional

faculté [fakylte] *f* faculty; school, college (*of law, medicine, etc.*); **la Faculté** medical men

fadaise [fadεz] *f* piece of nonsense; **fadaises** drivel

fade [fad] *adj* tasteless, flat; insipid, namby-pamby

fader [fade] *tr* (coll) to beat; (coll) to share the swag with; **il est fadé** (coll) he's done for

fadeur [fadœr] *f* insipidity; pointlessness; **fadeurs** platitudes

fagot [fago] *m* fagot (*bundle of sticks*); **fagot d'épines** ill-tempered person; **sentir le fagot** to smell of heresy

fagoter [fagɔte] *tr* to tie up in bundles; fagot; (coll) to dress like a scarecrow

faible [fɛbl] *adj* feeble, weak; low (*figure; moan*); poor (*harvest*); slight (*difference*) ‖ *mf* weakling ‖ *m* weakness; foible, weak spot; **faible d'esprit** feeble-minded person

faiblesse [fɛblɛs] *f* feebleness, weakness, frailty

faiblir [feblir] *intr* to weaken; diminish

faïence [fajɑ̃s] *f* earthenware, pottery

faille [faj] *f* (geol) fault; (tex) faille; (fig) defect; (fig) rift ‖ *v* see **falloir**

fail·li -lie [faji] *adj & mf* bankrupt

faillible [fajibl] *adj* fallible

faillir [fajir] §95 *intr* to fail, go bankrupt ‖ (used only in: *inf; ger* **faillant**; *pp & compound tenses*; *pret; fut; cond*) *intr* to fail; give way; **faillir à** to fail, let (*s.o.*) down; fail in (*a duty*); fail to keep (*a promise*); **faillir à** + *inf* to fail to + *inf*; **sans faillir** without fail ‖ (used only in *pret* and *past indef*) *intr*—nearly, almost, e.g., **il a failli être écrasé** he was nearly run over

faillite [fajit] *f* bankruptcy; **faire faillite** to go bankrupt

faim [fɛ̃] *f* hunger; **avoir faim** to be hungry; **avoir une faim de loup** to be hungry as a bear; **manger à sa faim** to eat one's fill

fainéant [fɛneɑ̃] **fainéante** [fɛneɑ̃t] *adj* lazy ‖ *mf* loafer, do-nothing

fainéanter [fɛneɑ̃te] *intr* (coll) to loaf

faire [fɛr] *m* making, doing ‖ §29, §95 *tr* to make; do; give (*an order; a lecture; alms, a gift; thanks*); take (*a walk; a step*); pack (*a trunk*); clean (*the room, the shoes, etc.*); follow (*a trade*); keep (*silence*); perform (*a play; a miracle*); play the part of; charge for, e.g., **combien faites-vous ces souliers?** how much do you charge for these shoes?; to say, e.g., **oui, fit-il** yes, said he; (coll) to estimate the cost of; for expressions like **il fait chaud** it is warm, see the noun; **cela ne fait rien** it doesn't matter; **faire** + *inf* to have + *inf*, e.g., **je le ferai aller** I shall have him go; **faire** + *inf* to make + *inf*, e.g., **je le ferai parler** I will make him talk; **faire** + *inf* to have + *pp*, e.g., **je vais faire faire un complet** I am going to have a suit made; **il n'en fait pas d'autres** that's just like him; **ne faire que** + *inf* to keep on + *ger*, e.g., **il ne fait que crier** he keeps on yelling ‖ *intr* to go, e.g., **la cravate fait bien avec la chemise** the tie goes well with the shirt; to act; **comment faire?**

what shall I do?; **faire dans** to make a mess in; **ne faire que de** + *inf* to have just + *pp*, e.g., **il ne fait que d'arriver** he has just arrived ‖ *ref* to become (*a doctor, lawyer, etc.*); grow (*e.g., old*); improve; happen; pretend to be; **se faire à** to get accustomed to, adjust to; **s'en faire** to worry, e.g., **ne vous en faites pas!** don't worry!

faire-part [fɛrpar] *m invar* announcement (*of birth, marriage, death*)

faire-valoir [fɛrvalwar] *m invar* turning to account; **faire-valoir direct** farming by the owner

faisable [fəzabl] *adj* feasible

fai·san [fəzɑ̃] **-sane** [zan] or **-sande** [zɑ̃d] *mf* pheasant

faisander [fəzɑ̃de] *tr* to jerk (*game*) ‖ *intr* to become gamy, get high

fais·ceau [fɛso] *m* (*pl* **-ceaux**) bundle, cluster; beam (*of light*); pencil (*of rays*); **faisceaux** fasces; **faisceaux de preuves** cumulative evidence; **former les faisceaux** to stack or pile arms

fai·seur [fəzœr] **-seuse** [zøz] *mf*—**bon faiseur** first-rate workman; **faiseur de mariages** matchmaker; **faiseur de vers** versifier, poetaster ‖ *m* bluffer; schemer

fait [fɛ] **faite** [fɛt] *adj* well-built, shapely; full-grown; made-up (*with cosmetics*); **fait à la main** hand-made; **tout fait** ready-made ‖ *m* deed, act; fact; **dire son fait à qn** (coll) to give s.o. a piece of one's mind; **prendre fait et cause pour** to take up the cudgels for; **si fait** yes, indeed; **sur le fait** redhanded, in the act; **tout à fait** entirely ‖ [fɛt] *m*—**au fait** to the point; after all; **de fait** de facto; **du fait que** owing to the fact that; **en fait** as a matter of fact

faîtage [fɛtaʒ] *m* ridgepole; roofs; roofing

fait-divers [fɛdivɛr] *m* (*pl* **faits-divers**) news item

faîte [fɛt] *m* peak; top (*of tree*); ridge (*of roof*)

faîtière [fɛtjɛr] *adj fem* ridge ‖ *f* ridge tile; skylight

fait-tout [fɛtu] *m invar* stewpan, casserole

faix [fɛ] *m* load, burden; (archit) settling; (physiol) fetus and placenta

falaise [falɛz] *f* cliff, bluff

falla·cieux [falasjø] **-cieuse** [sjøz] *adj* fallacious

fallait [fale] *v* see **falloir**

falloir [falwar] §30, §95 *impers* to be necessary; **c'est plus qu'il n'en faut** that's more than enough; **comme il faut** proper; properly; the right kind of, e.g., **un chapeau comme il faut** the right kind of hat; **il fallait le dire!** why didn't you say so!; **il faut** + *inf* it is necessary to + *inf*, one must + *inf;* **il faut qu'il** + *subj* it is necessary that he + *subj*, it is necessary for him to + *inf;* he must + *inf* (expressing conjecture), e.g., **il n'est pas venu, il faut qu'il soit malade** he did not come, he must be sick; **il faut qu'il ne** +

subj + **pas** he must not + *inf*, e.g., **il faut qu'il ne vienne pas** he must not come; **il faut une connaissance des affaires à ce travail** the work requires business experience; **il faut une heure** it takes an hour; **il leur a fallu trois jours** it took them three days; **il leur faut** + *inf* they have to + *inf*, they must + *inf*; **il leur faut du repos** they need rest; **il leur faut sept dollars** they need seven dollars; **il ne faut pas** + *inf* one must or should not + *inf*, e.g., **il ne faut pas se fier à ce garçon** one must not trust that boy; **il ne faut pas qu'il** + *subj* he must not + *inf*; **que leur faut-il? what do they need?, que leur faut-il?**, what do they require?; **qu'il ne fallait pas** wrong, e.g., **la police a arrêté l'homme qu'il ne fallait pas** the police arrested the wrong man ‖ *ref*—**il s'en faut de beaucoup** not by a long shot, far from it, not by any means; **il s'en faut de dix dollars** there is a shortage of ten dollars; **peu m'en est fallu que** . . . it very nearly happened that . . . ; **peu s'en faut** very nearly; **tant s'en faut que** far from, e.g., **tant s'en faut qu'il soit artiste** he is far from being an artist

fallut [faly] *v* see **falloir**

fa·lot [falo] **-lotte** [lɔt] *adj* wan, colorless; quaint, droll ‖ *m* lantern

falsification [falsifikɑsjɔ̃] *f* falsification; adulteration; debasement (*of coin*)

falsifier [falsifje] *tr* to falsify; adulterate; debase (*coin*)

fa·mé -mée [fame] *adj*—**mal famé** disreputable

famélique [famelik] *adj* famished

fa·meux [famø] **-meuse** [møz] *adj* famous ‖ (when standing before noun) *adj* (coll) notorious; well-known

fami·lial -liale [familjal] *adj* (*pl* **-liaux** [ljo]) family, domestic ‖ *f* station wagon

familiariser [familjarize] *tr* to familiarize ‖ *ref* to become familiar

familiarité [familjarite] *f* familiarity

fami·lier [familje] **-lière** [ljɛr] *adj* familiar, intimate; household (*gods*); pet (*animal*) ‖ *mf* familiar, intimate; pet animal

famille [famij] *f* family; **en famille** in the family circle, at home; (Canad) pregnant

famine [famin] *f* famine

fa·nal [fanal] *m* (*pl* **-naux** [no]) lantern; (naut) running light

fanatique [fanatik] *adj* fanatic(al) ‖ *mf* fanatic; enthusiast, fan

fanatisme [fanatism] *m* fanaticism

faner [fane] *tr & ref* to fade

fanfare [fɑ̃far] *f* fanfare; brass band

fanfa·ron [fɑ̃farɔ̃] **-ronne** [rɔn] *adj* bragging ‖ *mf* braggart

fanfaronner [fɑ̃farɔne] *intr* to brag

fange [fɑ̃ʒ] *f* mire, mud; (fig) mire, gutter

fan·geux [fɑ̃ʒø] **-geuse** [ʒøz] *adj* muddy; (fig) dirty, soiled

fanion [fanjɔ̃] *m* pennant, flag

fanon [fanɔ̃] *m* dewlap (*of ox*); whalebone; fetlock; wattle

fantaisie [fɑ̃tezi] *f* imagination; fantasy; fancy, whim; **de fantaisie** fanciful; fancy, e.g., **pain de fantaisie** fancy bread

fantaisiste [fɑ̃tezist] *adj* fantastic, whimsical ‖ *mf* whimsical person; singing comedian

fantasque [fɑ̃task] *adj* fantastic; whimsical, temperamental

fantassin [fɑ̃tasɛ̃] *m* foot soldier

fantastique [fɑ̃tastik] *adj* fantastic

fantoche [fɑ̃tɔʃ] *m* puppet

fantôme [fɑ̃tom] *adj* shadow (*government*) ‖ *m* phantom, ghost

fanum [fanɔm] *m* hallowed ground

faon [fɑ̃] *m* fawn

faonner [fane] *intr* to bring forth young (*said especially of deer*)

faquin [fakɛ̃] *m* rascal

farami·neux [faraminø] **-neuse** [nøz] *adj* (coll) staggering, fantastic, astronomical

fa·raud [faro] **-raude** [rod] *adj* (coll) swanky ‖ *mf* (coll) fop, bumpkin; **faire le faraud** (coll) to show off

farce [fars] *f* farce; trick, joke; (culin) stuffing

far·ceur [farsœr] **-ceuse** [søz] *mf* practical joker; phony

farcir [farsir] *tr* to stuff

fard [far] *m* make-up; **fard à paupières** eye shadow; **parler sans fard** to speak plainly, to tell the unvarnished truth; **piquer un fard** (coll) to blush

far·deau [fardo] *m* (*pl* **-deaux**) load, burden; weight (*of years*)

farder [farde] *tr* to make up (*an actor*); disguise (*the truth*) ‖ *ref* to weigh heavily; (archit) to sink; (theat) to make up

fardier [fardje] *m* dray, cart

farfe·lu -lue [farfəly] *adj* (coll) harebrained, cockeyed, bizarre

farfouiller [farfuje] *tr* (coll) to rummage about in ‖ *intr* (coll) to rummage about; **farfouiller dans** (coll) to rummage about in

farine [farin] *f* flour, meal; **farine de froment** whole-wheat flour; **farine de riz** ground rice; **farine lactée** malted milk

fariner [farine] *tr* (culin) to flour

fari·neux [farinø] **-neuse** [nøz] *adj* white with flour; mealy; starchy

farouche [faruʃ] *adj* wild, savage; unsociable; shy; stubborn (*resistance*); fierce (*look*)

fart [fart] *m* ski wax

fascicule [fasikyl] *m* fascicle; **fascicule de mobilisation** marching orders

fascina·teur [fasinatœr] **-trice** [tris] *adj* fascinating ‖ *mf* spellbinder

fasciner [fasine] *tr* to fascinate; spellbind

fascisme [faʃism] *m* fascism

fasciste [faʃist] *adj & mf* fascist

fasse [fas] *v* (**fasses, fassions,** etc.) see **faire**

faste [fast] *adj* auspicious; feast (*day*) ‖ *m* pomp; **fastes** annals

fast food [fɛstfud] *m* fast food(s)

fasti·dieux [fastidjø] **-dieuse** [djøz] *adj* tedious, wearisome

fas·tueux [fastɥø] **-tueuse** [tɥøz] *adj* pompous, ostentatious

fat [fat] *adj masc* conceited, foppish ‖ *m* fop

fa·tal -tale [fatal] *adj* (*pl* **-tals**) fatal; fateful; inevitable

fatalement [fatalmɑ̃] *adv* inevitably

fatalisme [fatalism] *m* fatalism

fataliste [fatalist] *adj* fatalistic ‖ *mf* fatalist

fatalité [fatalite] *f* fatality; fatalism; fate; curse, misfortune

fatidique [fatidik] *adj* fateful; prophetic

fati·gant [fatigɑ̃] **-gante** [gɑ̃t] *adj* fatiguing; tiresome (*person*)

fatigue [fatig] *f* fatigue

fati·gué -guée [fatige] §93 *adj* fatigued; worn-out (*clothing*); well-thumbed (*book*)

fatiguer [fatige] *tr* to fatigue; wear out; weary ‖ *intr* to strain, labor; pull (*said of engine*); bear a heavy strain (*said of beam*) ‖ §96, §97 *ref* to get tired

fatras [fatra] *m* jumble, hodgepodge

fatuité [fatɥite] *f* conceit; foppishness

faubert [fobɛr] *m* (naut) swab

faubourg [fobur] *m* suburb; outskirts; quarter, district (*especially of Paris*)

faubou·rien [foburjɛ̃] **-rienne** [rjɛn] *adj* working-class, vulgar ‖ *mf* resident of the outskirts of a city; local inhabitant

fau·ché -chée [foʃe] *adj* (coll) broke (*without money*)

faucher [foʃe] *tr* to mow, reap; (coll) to swipe

fau·cheur [foʃœr] **-cheuse** [ʃøz] *mf* reaper ‖ *m* (ent) daddy-longlegs ‖ *f* (mach) reaper, mower

faucheux [foʃø] *m* (ent) daddy-longlegs

faucille [fosij] *f* sickle

faucon [fokɔ̃] *m* falcon

fauconnier [fokɔnje] *m* falconer

faudra [fodra] *v* see **falloir**

faufil [fofil] *m* basting thread

faufiler [fofile] *tr* to baste ‖ *ref* to thread one's way, worm one's way

faune [fon] *m* faun ‖ *f* fauna

faunesse [fonɛs] *f* female faun

faussaire [fosɛr] *mf* forger

fausser [fose] *tr* to falsify, distort; bend, twist; warp (*the judgment*); force (*a lock*); strain (*the voice*); **fausser compagnie à qn** (coll) to give s.o. the slip ‖ *intr* to sing or play out of tune ‖ *ref* to bend, buckle; crack (*said of voice*)

fausset [fosɛ] *m* falsetto; plug (*for wine barrel*)

fausseté [foste] *f* falsity; double-dealing

faut [fo] *v* see **falloir**

faute [fot] *f* fault; mistake; blame; lack, need, want; (sports) foul; (sports) error; **faire faute** to be lacking; **faute de** for want of; **faute de copiste** clerical error; **faute de frappe** typing error; **faute d'impression** misprint; **sans faute** without fail

fauter [fote] *intr* (coll) to go wrong (*said of a woman*)

fauteuil [fotœj] *m* armchair, easy chair; seat (*of member of an academy*); chair (*of presiding officer; presiding officer himself*); **fauteuil à bascule** or **à balançoire** rocking chair; **fauteuil à oreilles** wing chair; **fauteuil d'orchestre** orchestra seat; **fauteuil pliant** folding chair; **fauteuil roulant pour malade** wheelchair; **siéger au fauteuil présidentiel** to preside

fau·teur [fotœr] **-trice** [tris] *mf* instigator, agitator

fau·tif [fotif] **-tive** [tiv] *adj* faulty

fautivement [fotivmɑ̃] *adv* by mistake, in error

fauve [fov] *adj* fawn (*color*); musky (*odor*); wild (*beast*) ‖ *m* fawn color; wild beast; **fauves** big game

fauvette [fovɛt] *f* warbler

faux [fo] **fausse** [fos] (usually stands before noun) *adj* false; counterfeit; wrong, e.g., **fausse date** wrong date; e.g., **fausse note** wrong note ‖ *m* imitation; forgery; **à faux** wrongly ‖ **faux** *f* scythe ‖ **faux** *adv* out of tune, off key

faux-bourdon [foburdɔ̃] *m* (*pl* **-bourdons**) *m* (ent) drone

faux-col [fokɔl] *m* (*pl* **-cols**) collars, detachable collar

faux-filet [fofilɛ] *m* (*pl* **-filets**) sirloin

faux-fuyant [fofɥijɑ̃] *m* (*pl* **-fuyants**) subterfuge, pretext

faux-jour [foʒur] *m* (*pl* **-jours**) half-light

faux-monnayeur [fomɔnɛjœr] *m* (*pl* **-monnayeurs**) counterfeiter

faux-pas [fopɑ] *m invar* faux pas, slip, blunder

faux-semblant [fosɑ̃blɑ̃] *m* (*pl* **-semblants**) false pretense

faveur [favœr] *f* favor; **à la faveur de** under cover of; **en faveur de** in favor of; on behalf of

favorable [favɔrabl] *adj* favorable

favo·ri [favɔri] **-rite** [rit] *adj* & *mf* favorite ‖ **favoris** *mpl* sideburns ‖ *f* mistress

favoriser [favɔrize] *tr* to favor; encourage, promote

Fᶜᵒ or **fco** *abbr* (**franco**) postpaid

fébrile [febril] *adj* feverish

fèces [fɛs] *fpl* feces

fé·cond [fekɔ̃] **-conde** [kɔ̃d] *adj* fecund, fertile

féconder [fekɔ̃de] *tr* to impregnate

fécondité [fekɔ̃dite] *f* fecundity, fertility

fécule [fekyl] *f* starch; **fécule de maïs** cornstarch

fécu·lent [fekylɑ̃] **-lente** [lɑ̃t] *adj* starchy ‖ *m* starchy food

fédé·ral -rale [federal] *adj* & *m* (*pl* **-raux** [ro]) federal

fédéra·tif [federatif] **-tive** [tiv] *adj* federated, federative

fédération [federasjɔ̃] *f* federation

fédérer [federe] §10 *tr* & *ref* to federate

fée [fe] *f* fairy; **de fée** fairy; meticulous (*work*); **vieille fée** old hag

féerie [feri] *f* fairyland; fantasy

féerique [ferik] *adj* fairy, magic(al)

feindre [fɛ̃dr] §50, §97 *tr* to feign ‖ *intr* to feign; limp (*said of horse*)

feinte [fɛ̃t] *f* feint

feinter [fɛ̃te] *tr* (coll) to trick ‖ *intr* to feint
feldspath [fɛldspat], [fɛlspat] *m* feldspar
fê·lé -lée [fele] *adj* (coll) cracked, crazy
fêler [fele] *tr* to crack
félicitations [felisitasjɔ̃] *fpl* congratulations
féliciter [felisite] *tr* to congratulate; **féliciter qn de** + *inf* to congratulate s.o. for + *ger;* **féliciter qn de** or **pour** to congratulate s.o. for ‖ §97 *ref*—**se féliciter de** to congratulate oneself on, be pleased with oneself because of
fé·lon [felɔ̃] **-lonne** [lɔn] *adj* disloyal, treasonable
félonie [feloni] *f* disloyalty, treason
fêlure [felyr] *f* crack, chink
femelle [fəmɛl] *adj & f* female
fémi·nin [feminɛ̃] **-nine** [nin] *adj & m* feminine
féminisme [feminism] *m* feminism
femme [fam] *f* woman; wife; bride; **bonne femme** (coll) simple, good-natured woman; **femme agent** (*pl* **femmes agents**) policewoman; **femme auteur** (*pl* **femmes auteurs**), authoress; **femme de chambre** chambermaid; **femme de charge** housekeeper; **femme de journée** cleaning woman; **femme de ménage** cleaning woman; **femme d'intérieur** homebody; **femme docteur** woman doctor (*e.g., with Ph.D. degree*); **femme juge** woman judge; **femme médecin** woman doctor (*physician*); **femme pasteur** woman preacher; **femme porteuse** surrogate mother; **femme torero** woman bullfighter
fendiller [fɑ̃dije[*tr & ref* to crack
fendoir [fɑ̃dwar] *m* cleaver, chopper
fendre [fɑ̃dr] *tr* to crack; split (*e.g., wood*); cleave (*e.g., the air*); break (*one's heart*); elbow one's way through (*a crowd*) ‖ *ref* to crack; (escr) to lunge
fenêtre [fənɛtr] *f* window; **double fenêtre** storm window; **fenêtre à battants** casement window, French window; **fenêtre à guillotine** sash window; **fenêtre en saillie** bay window
fenil [fənil], [fəni] *m* hayloft
fenouil [fənuj] *m* fennel; **fenouil bâtard** dill
fente [fɑ̃t] *f* crack, split, fissure; notch; slot (*e.g., in a coin telephone*); (escr) lunge
féo·dal -dale [feodal] *adj* (*pl* **-daux** [do]) feudal
féodalisme [feodalism] *m* feudalism
fer [fɛr] *m* iron; head (*of tool*); point (*of weapon*); **croiser le fer avec** to cross swords with; **fer à cheval** horseshoe; **fer à friser** curling iron; **fer à marquer** or **flétrir** branding iron; **fer à repasser** iron, flatiron; **fer à souder** soldering iron; **fer de fonte** cast iron; **fer forgé** wrought iron; **fers** irons, chains, fetters; **marquer au fer** to brand; **remuer le fer dans la plaie** (coll) to rub it in
ferai [fəre], [fre] *v* see **faire**
ferblanterie [fɛrblɑ̃tri] *f* tinware; tinwork, sheet-metal work; tinsmith's shop
ferblantier [fɛrblɑ̃tje] *m* tinsmith
fé·rié -riée [ferje] *adj* feast (*day*)

férir [ferir] *tr*—**sans coup férir** without striking a blow
ferler [fɛrle] *tr* (naut) to furl
fermage [fɛrmaʒ] *m* tenant farming; rent
ferme [fɛrm] *adj* firm ‖ *f* farm, tenant farm; farmhouse ‖ *adv* firmly, fast; without parole
fer·mé -mée [fɛrme] *adj* exclusive, restricted; inscrutable (*countenance*)
ferment [fɛrmɑ̃] *m* ferment
fermenter [fɛrmɑ̃te] *intr* to ferment
fermer [fɛrme] *tr* to close, shut; turn off; **fermer à clef** to lock; **fermer au verrou** to bolt; **la ferme!** (slang) shut up!, shut your trap! ‖ *intr & ref* to close, shut
fermeté [fɛrməte] *f* firmness
fermeture [fɛrmətyr] *f* closing; fastening; **fermeture éclair, fermeture à glissière** zipper
fer·mier [fɛrmje] **-miere** [mjɛr] *adj* farming ‖ *m* farmer; tenant farmer; lessee ‖ *f* farmer's wife
fermoir [fɛrmwar] *m* snap, clasp
féroce [ferɔs] *adj* ferocious
férocité [ferɔsite] *f* ferocity
ferraille [fɛraj] *f* scrap iron; (coll) small change; **mettre à la ferraille** to junk
ferrailleur [fɛrajœr] *m* dealer in scrap iron; sword rattler
fer·ré -rée [fere] *adj* ironclad; hobnailed (*shoe*); paved (*road*); iron-tipped; **ferré sur** well versed in
ferrer [fere] *tr* to shoe (*a horse*)
ferret [fɛrɛ] *m* tag (*of shoelace*); (geol) hard core
ferronnerie [fɛrɔnri] *f* ironwork; hardware
ferron·nier [fɛrɔnje] **-nière** [njɛr] *mf* ironworker; hardware dealer
ferrotypie [fɛrɔtipi] *f* tintype
ferroviaire [fɛrɔvjɛr] *adj* railway
ferrure [fɛryr] *f* horseshoeing; **ferrures** hardware; metal trim
ferry-boat [fɛribot] *m* (*pl* **-boats**) train ferry
fertile [fɛrtil] *adj* fertile
fertiliser [fɛrtilize] *tr* to fertilize
fertilité [fɛrtilite] *f* fertility
fé·ru -rue [fery] *adj*—**féru de** wrapped up in (*an idea, an interest*)
fer·vent [fɛrvɑ̃] **-vente** [vɑ̃t] *adj* fervent ‖ *mf* devotee
ferveur [fɛrvœr] *f* fervor
fesse [fɛs] *f* buttock
fessée [fese] *f* spanking
fesse-mathieu [fɛsmatjø] *m* (*pl* **-mathieux**) usurer; skinflint
fesser [fese] *tr* to spank
fes·su -sue [fɛsy] *adj* broad-bottomed
festin [fɛstɛ̃] *m* feast, banquet
festi·val [fɛstival] *m* (*pl* **-vals**) music festival
festivité [fɛstivite] *f* festivity
feston [fɛstɔ̃] *m* festoon
festonner [fɛstɔne] *tr* to festoon; scallop
festoyer [fɛstwaye] §47 *tr* to fete, regale ‖ *intr* to feast
fê·tard [fɛtar] **-tarde** [tard] *mf* merrymaker; boisterous drinker

fête [fɛt] *f* festival; feast day, holiday; name day; party, festivity; **être à la fête** (coll) to be very pleased or gratified; **faire fête à** to receive with open arms; **faire la fête** (coll) to carouse; **fête foraine** carnival; **fête légale** or **fête nationale** legal holiday; **la fête des Mères** Mother's Day; **la fête des Morts** All Souls' Day; **la fête des Rois** Twelfth-night; **se faire une fête de** to look forward with pleasure to; **souhaiter une bonne fête à qn** to wish s.o. many happy returns

Fête-Dieu [fɛtdjø] *f* (*pl* **Fêtes-Dieu**)—**la Fête-Dieu** Corpus Christi

fêter [fɛte] *tr* to fete; celebrate (*a special event*)

fétiche [fetiʃ] *m* fetish

fétu [fety] *m* straw; trifle

feu feue [fø] *adj* (*pl* **feus**) (standing before noun) late, deceased, e.g., **la feue reine** the late queen ‖ **feu** *adj invar* (standing before article and noun) late, deceased, e.g., **feu la reine** the late queen ‖ *m* (*pl* **feux**) fire; flame; traffic light; burner (*of stove*); **à petit feu** by inches; **du feu** a light (*to ignite a cigar, etc.*); **être sous les feux de la rampe** to be in the limelight; **faire du feux** to light a fire; **faire long feu** to hang fire; to fail; (arti) to miss; **feu d'artifice** fireworks; **feu de joie** bonfire; **feu de paille** (fig) flash in the pan; **feu follet** will-o'-the-wisp; **feux de position, feux de stationnement** parking lights; **feux masqués** (mil) blackout; **mettre le feu à** to set on fire; **prendre feu** to catch fire ‖ **feu** *interj* fire! (*command to fire*); **au feu!** fire! (*warning*)

feuillage [fœjaʒ] *m* foliage; **feuillages** fallen branches

feuille [fœj] *f* leaf; sheet; form (*to be filled out*); **feuille de chou** (coll) rag (*newspaper of little value*); **feuille de présence** time sheet; **feuille d'étain** tin foil; **feuille de température** temperature chart; **feuille d'imposition, feuille d'impôt** income-tax form

feuil·lé -lée [fœje] *adj* leafy, foliaged ‖ *f* bower; **feuillées** (mil) camp latrine

feuiller [fœje] *intr* to leaf

feuille·té -tée [fœjte] *adj* foliated; in flaky layers

feuilleter [fœjte] §34 *tr* to leaf through; foliate; (culin) to roll into thin layers

feuilleton [fœjtɔ̃] *m* newspaper serial (*printed at bottom of page*); (rad, telv) serial

feuil·lu -lue [fœjy] *adj* leafy ‖ *m* foliage

feuillure [fœjyr] *f* groove

feuler [føle] *intr* to growl (*said of cat*)

feutre [føtr] *m* felt

feu·tré -trée [føtre] *adj* velvetlike; muffled (*steps*)

feutrer [føtre] *tr* to felt

fève [fɛv] *f* bean; **fève des Rois** bean or figurine baked in the Twelfth-night cake; **fèves au lard** pork and beans

février [fevrie] *m* February

fi [fi] *interj* fie!; **faire fi de** to scorn

fiabilité [fjabilite] *f* reliability

fiable [fjabl] *adj* reliable

fiacre [fjakr] *m* horse-drawn cab

fiançailles [fjɑ̃sɑj] *fpl* engagement, betrothal

fian·cé -cée [fjɑ̃se] *mf* betrothed ‖ *m* fiancé ‖ *f* fiancée

fiancer [fjɑ̃se] §51 *tr* to betroth ‖ *ref* to become engaged

fiasco [fjasko] *m* (coll) fiasco, failure; **faire fiasco** to flop, fail

fibre [fibr] *f* fiber; (fig) feeling, sensibility; **avoir la fibre sensible** to be easily moved

fi·breux -breuse [brøz] *adj* fibrous

ficeler [fisle] §34 *tr* to tie up

ficelle [fisɛl] *adj* (coll) knowing ‖ *f* string; **connaître les ficelles** (fig) to know the ropes; **tenir** or **tirer les ficelles** (fig) to pull strings; **vieille ficelle** (coll) old hand

fiche [fiʃ] *f* peg; slip, form, blank; filing card, index card; membership card; (cards) chip, counter; (elec) plug; **fiche de consolation** booby prize; **fiche femelle** (elec) jack; **fiche perforée** punch card; **fiche scolaire** report card

ficher [fiʃe] *tr* to drive in (*a stake*); take down (*information on a form*); fasten, fix, stick; **ficher qn à la porte** (coll) to kick s.o. out; **ficher une gifle à qn** (coll) to box s.o. on the ear; **fichez-moi le camp!** (slang) beat it!; **je m'en fiche!** I don't give a damn ‖ *ref*—**se ficher de** (slang) to make fun of

fichier [fiʃje] *m* card catalogue; cabinet, file (*for cards or papers*)

fichtre [fiʃtrə] *interj* (coll) gosh!

fi·chu -chue [fiʃy] *adj* (coll) wretched, ugly; **fichu de** capable of ‖ *m* scarf, shawl

fic·tif -tive [tiv] *adj* fictitious

fiction [fiksjɔ̃] *f* fiction

fidéicommis [fideikɔmi] *m* (law) trust

fidèle [fidɛl] *adj* faithful; regular ‖ *mf* supporter; **les fidèles** (eccl) the congregation, the faithful

fidèlement [fidɛlmɑ̃] *adv* faithfully; regularly

fidélité [fidelite] *f* fidelity, faithfulness; **haute fidélité** high fidelity

fief·fé [fjɛfe] *adj* (coll) downright, real, regular (*liar, coward, etc.*)

fiel [fjɛl] *m* bile; gall

fiel·leux [fjɛlø] **-leuse** [løz] *adj* galling

fiente [fjɑ̃t] *f* droppings

fier fière [fjɛr] §93 *adj* proud; haughty ‖ **fier** [fje] *tr* (archaic) to entrust ‖ *ref*—**se fier à** or **en** to trust, to have confidence in, to rely upon; **se fier à qn de** to entrust s.o. with; **s'y fier** to trust it

fier-à-bras [fjɛrabra] *m* (*pl* **fier-à-bras** or **fiers-à-bras** [fjɛrabra]) braggart

fierté [fjɛrte] *f* pride

fièvre [fjɛvr] *f* fever; **fièvre aphteuse** foot-and-mouth disease; **fièvre jaune** yellow fever

fifre [fifr] *m* fife; fife player

fi·gé -gée [fiʒe] *adj* curdled; fixed, set; frozen (*smile*); **figé sur place** rooted to the spot

figement [fiʒmɑ̃] *m* clotting, coagulation

figer [fiʒe] §38 *tr* to curdle; stop dead ‖ *ref* to curdle; set, freeze (*said, e.g., of smile*)

fignoler [fiɲɔle] *tr* to work carefully at ‖ *intr* to be finicky

figue [fig] *f* fig; **figue de Barbarie** prickly pear

figuier [figje] *m* fig tree

figu·rant [figyrɑ̃] **-rante** [rɑ̃t] *mf* (theat) supernumerary, extra

figura·tif [figyratif] **-tive** [tiv] *adj* figurative, emblematic

figure [figyr] *f* figure; face (*of a person*); face card; chess piece (other than a pawn); **faire figure** to cut a figure; **figure de proue** (naut) figurehead; **prendre figure** to take shape

figu·ré -rée [figyre] *adj* figurative; figured ‖ *m* figurative sense

figurer [figyre] *tr* to figure ‖ *intr* to figure, take part; (theat) to walk on ‖ §95 *ref* to imagine, believe

fil [fil] *m* thread; wire; edge (*e.g., of knife*); grain (*of wood*); **au fil de l'eau** with the stream; **droit fil** with the grain; **elle lui a donné du fil à retordre** (fig) she gave him more than he bargained for; **fil à plomb** plumb line; **fil de fer barbelé** barbed wire; **fil de lin** yarn; **fil d'or** spun gold; **fils de la vierge** gossamer; **passer au fil de l'épée** to put to the sword; **plein de fils** stringy; **sans fil** wireless

filage [filaʒ] *m* spinning; (telv) ghost image

filament [filamɑ̃] *m* filament

filamen·teux [filamɑ̃tø] **-teuse** [tøz] *adj* stringy

filan·dreux [filɑ̃drø] **-dreuse** [drøz] *adj* stringy (*meat*); long, drawn-out

fi·lant [filɑ̃] **-lante** [lɑ̃t] *adj* ropy (*liquid*); shooting (*star*)

filasse [filas] *f* tow, oakum

filature [filatyr] *f* manufacture of thread; spinning mill; shadowing (*of a suspect*)

fil-de-fériste [fildəferist] *mf* tightwire walker

file [fil] *f* file, row, lane; **à la file** one after another, in a row; **file d'attente** waiting line; (aer) stack; **marcher en file indienne** to walk Indian file

filer [file] *tr* to spin; pay out (*rope, cable*); prolong; shadow (*a suspect*) ‖ *intr* to ooze; smoke (*said of lamp*); (coll) to go fast; **filer à l'anglaise** (coll) to take French leave; **filer doux** (coll) to back down, to give in; **filez!** (coll) get out!

filet [filɛ] *m* net; trickle (*of water*); streak (*of light*); thread (*of screw or nut*); (culin) fillet; (typ) rule; **faux filet** sirloin; **filet à bagage** baggage rack; **filet à cheveux** hair net; **filet à provisions** string bag, mesh bag

fileter [filte] §2 *tr* to thread (*a screw*); draw (*wire*)

fi·leur [filœr] **-leuse** [løz] *mf* spinner

fi·lial -liale [filjal] *adj* (*pl* **-liaux** [ljo]) filial ‖ *f* (com) branch, subsidiary

filiation [filjasjɔ̃] *f* filiation

filière [filjɛr] *f* (mach) die; (mach) drawplate; **filière administrative** official channels; **passer par la filière** (coll) to go through channels; (coll) to work one's way up

filigrane [filigran] *m* filigree; watermark (*in paper*)

filigraner [filigrane] *tr* to filigree

filin [filɛ̃] *m* (naut) rope

fille [fij] *f* daughter; unmarried young woman or girl; servant; (pej) tart; **fille de joie, des rues,** or **de vie, fille publique** prostitute; **fille de salle** nurse's aid; **fille d'honneur** bridesmaid; **jeune fille** (unmarried) young woman; **petite fille** girl (under thirteen years of age); **vieille fille** old maid

fillette [fijɛt] *f* young girl, little lass

fil·leul -leule [fijœl] *mf* godchild ‖ *m* godson ‖ *f* goddaughter

film [film] *m* film; movie, film; (fig) train (*of events*); **film sonore** sound film

filmage [filmaʒ] *m* filming

filmer [filme] *tr* to film

filmique [filmik] *adj* film

filon [filɔ̃] *m* vein, lode; (coll) soft job; (coll) bonanza, strike; **filon guide** leader vein

filoselle [filɔzɛl] *f* floss silk

filou [filu] *m* sneak thief; cheat, sharper

filouter [filute] *tr* (coll) to swindle, cheat; **filouter q.ch.** à qn (coll) to do s.o. out of s.th. ‖ *intr* to cheat at cards

fils [fis] *m* son; (when following proper name) junior; **fils à papa** (coll) rich man's son, playboy; **fils de ses œuvres** (fig) self-made man

filtrage [filtraʒ] *m* filtering; screening; surveillance (*by the police*)

fil·trant [filtrɑ̃] **-trante** [trɑ̃t] *adj* filterable; filter, e.g., **papier filtrant** filter paper

filtre [filtrə] *m* filter

filtrer [filtre] *tr & intr* to filter

fin [fɛ̃] **fine** [fin] *adj* fine; thin; exquisite; keen, discriminating ‖ (when standing before noun) *adj* clever, sly, smart; secret, hidden; **au fin fond de** deep in the interior of; **le fin mot de l'histoire** the truth of the story ‖ *m* fine linen; smart person; **le fin du fin** the finest of the fine ‖ **fin** *f* end; **à la fin** at last; **à seule fin de** for the sole purpose of; **à toutes fins utiles** for your information; **c'est la fin des haricots** (slang) that takes the cake; **en fin de compte** in the end; to get to the point; **fin de semaine** weekend; **fins de série** (com) remnant, leftover article; **fin d'interdiction de dépasser** (*public sign*) end of no passing; **mettre fin à** to put an end to; **mot de la fin** clincher; **sans fin** endless ‖ **fin** *adv* absolutely; finely (*ground*); small, e.g., **écrire fin** to write small

fi·nal -nale [final] (*pl* **-nals** or **-naux** [no]) *adj* final ‖ *m* finale ‖ *f* last syllable or letter; (mus) keynote; (sports) finals

finalement [finalmɑ̃] *adv* finally

finaliste [finalist] *mf* finalist

finance [finɑ̃s] *f* finance

financement [finɑ̃smɑ̃] *m* financing

financer [finɑ̃se] §51 *tr* to finance

finan·cier [finɑ̃sje] **-cière** [sjɛr] *adj* financial; spicy (*sauce for vol-au-vent*) ‖ *m* financier

finasser [finase] *intr* (coll) to use finesse, finagle

finasserie [finasri] *f* shrewdness

fi·naud [fino] **-naude** [nod] *adj* wily, sly ‖ *mf* sly fox; smart aleck

finesse [finɛs] *f* finesse; fineness; **savoir les finesses** to know the fine points or niceties

fi·ni -nie [fini] *adj* finished; finite; ruined (*in health, financially, etc.*) arrant (*rogue*) ‖ *m* finish; finite

finir [finir] §97 *tr & intr* to finish; **en finir avec** to have done with; **finir de** + *inf* to finish + *ger;* **finir par** + *inf* to finish by + *inf*

finissage [finisaʒ] *m* finishing touch, final step

finition [finisjɔ̃] *f* finish; **finitions** finishing touches

finlan·dais [fɛ̃lɑ̃dɛ] **-daise** [dɛz] *adj* Finnish ‖ *m* Finnish (*language*) ‖ (*cap*) *mf* Finn

Finlande [fɛ̃lɑ̃d] *f* Finland; **la Finlande** Finland

fin·nois [finwa] **-noise** [nwaz] *adj* Finnish ‖ *m* Finnish (*language*); Finnic (*branch of Uralic*) ‖ (*cap*) *mf* Finn

fiole [fjɔl] *f* phial

fioriture [fjɔrityr] *f* flourish, curlicue

firmament [firmamɑ̃] *m* firmament

firme [firm] *f* firm, house, company

fis [fi] *v* (**fit, fîmes,** etc.) see **faire**

fisc [fisk] *m* bureau of internal revenue, tax-collection agency

fis·cal -cale [fiskal] *adj* (*pl* **-caux** [ko]) fiscal; revenue, taxation

fiscaliser [fiskalize] *tr* to subject to tax

fiscalité [fiskalite] *f* tax collections; fiscal policy

fissile [fisil] *adj* fissionable

fission [fisjɔ̃] *f* fission

fissure [fisyr] *f* fissure, crack

fissurer [fisyre] *tr & ref* to fissure

fiston [fistɔ̃] *m* (slang) sonny

fixa·teur [fiksatœr] **-trice** [tris] *adj* fixing, fixative ‖ *m* fixer; hair cream; (phot) fixing bath

fixation [fiksɑjsɔ̃] *f* fixation; fixing; **fixations** bindings (*on ski equipment*)

fixe [fiks] *adj* fixed; permanent (*ink*); glassy (*stare*); regular (*time*); set (*price*); standing (*rule*) ‖ *m* fixed income ‖*interj* (mil) eyes front!

fixe-chaussette [fiksəʃosɛt] *m* (*pl* **-chaussettes**) garter (*for men's socks*)

fixement [fiksəmɑ̃] *adv* fixedly

fixer [fikse] *tr* to fix; appoint; (coll) to stare at; **fixer son choix sur** to fix on; **pour fixer les idées** for the sake of argument ‖ *ref* to be fastened; establish residence; make up one's mind

flacon [flakɔ̃] *m* small bottle; flask

flagada [flagada] *adj* (slang) pooped

flageller [flaʒɛlle] *tr* to flagellate

flageoler [flaʒɔle] *intr* to quiver

flageolet [flaʒɔlɛ] *m* flageolet; kidney bean

flagorner [flagɔrne]*tr* to flatter

fla·grant [flagrɑ̃] **-grante** [grɑ̃t] *adj* flagrant, glaring, obvious

flair [flɛr] *m* scent, sense of smell; (*discernment*) flair, keen nose

flairer [flɛre] *tr* to smell, sniff; scent, smell out

fla·mand [flamɑ̃] **-mande** [mɑ̃d] *adj* Flemish ‖ *m* Flemish (*language*) ‖ (*cap*) *mf* Fleming (*person*)

flamant [flamɑ̃] *m* flamingo

flam·bant [flɑ̃bɑ̃] **-bante** [bɑ̃t] *adj* flaming; **flambant neuf** (coll) brand-new

flam·beau [flɑ̃bo] *m* (*pl* **-beaux**) torch; candlestick; large wax candle; (fig) light

flambée [flɑ̃be] *f* blaze; flare-up

flamber [flɑ̃be] *tr* to singe; sterilize; (culin) to flambé; **être flambé** (coll) to be all washed up, ruined ‖ *intr* to flame; burn

flamberge [flɑ̃bɛrʒ] *f* (archaic) sword, blade; **mettre flamberge au vent** to unsheathe the sword

flambeur [flɑ̃bœr] *m* high roller; big gambler

flamboiement [flɑ̃bwamɑ̃] *m* glow, flare

flamboyant [flɑ̃bwajɑ̃] **flamboyante** [flɑ̃bwajɑ̃t] *adj* flaming, blazing; (archit) flamboyant

flamboyer [flɑ̃bwaje] §47 *intr* to flame

flamme [flam] *f* flame; pennant

flammèche [flamɛʃ] *f* ember, large spark

flan [flɑ̃] *m* custard; blank (*coin, medal, record*); **à la flan** (slang) happy-go-lucky; botched (*job*); **c'est du flan** (slang) it's ridiculous

flanc [flɑ̃] *m* flank; side (*of ship, mountain, etc.*); **battre du flanc** to pant; **être sur le flanc** (coll) to be laid up; **flancs** (archaic) womb; bosom; **prêter le flanc à** to lay oneself open to; **se battre les flancs** to go to a lot of trouble for nothing; **tirer au flanc** (coll) to gold-brick, to malinger

flancher [flɑ̃ʃe] *intr* (coll) to give in; (coll) to weaken, give way

flanchet [flɑ̃ʃɛ] *m* flank (*of beef*)

Flandre [flɑ̃dr] *f* Flanders; **la Flandre** Flanders

flanelle [flanɛl] *f* flannel

flâner [flane] *intr* to stroll, saunter; loaf

flânerie [flɑnri] *f* strolling; loafing

flâ·neur [flɑnœr] **-neuse** [nøz] *mf* stroller; loafer

flanquer [flɑ̃ke] *tr* to flank; (coll) to throw, fling; **flanquer à la porte** (coll) to kick-out; **flanquer un coup à** (coll) to take a swing at

fla·pi -pie [flapi] *adj* (coll) tired out, fagged out

flaque [flak] *f* puddle, pool

flash [flaʃ] *m* (*pl* **flashes**) news flash; flash pictures; (phot) flash attachment; (phot) flash bulb

flasque [flask] *adj* flabby ‖ *m* metal trim ‖ *f* flask; powder horn

flatter [flate] *tr* to flatter; stroke; delight; cater to; delude ‖ *intr* to flatter ‖ §97 *ref*—**se flatter de** to flatter oneself on

flatterie [flatri] *f* flattery

flat·teur [flatœr] **-teuse** [tøz] *adj* flattering ‖ *mf* flatterer

flatulence [flatylɑs] *f* (pathol) flatulence

flatuosité [flatɥozite] *f* (pathol) flatulence

fléau [fleo] *m* (*pl* **fléaux**) flail; beam (*of balance*); (fig) scourge, plague

flèche [flɛʃ] *f* arrow; spire (*of church*); boom (*of crane*); flitch (*of bacon*); **en flèche** like an arrow; in tandem; **faire flèche de tout bois** to leave no stone unturned; **flèche d'eau** (bot) arrowhead

flèchette [fleʃɛt] *f* dart (*used in game*)

fléchir [fleʃir] *tr* to bend; move (*e.g., to pity*) ‖ *intr* to bend, give way; weaken, flag; go down, sag (*said of prices*)

flegmatique [flɛgmatik] *adj* phlegmatic, stolid

flegme [flɛgm] *m* phlegm

flemme [flɛm] *f* (slang) sluggishness; **tirer sa flemme** (slang) to not lift a finger

flet [flɛ] *m* flounder

flétan [fletɑ̃] *m* halibut

flétrir [fletrir] *tr* & *ref* to fade, wither; weaken

flétrissure [fletrisyr] *f* fading, withering; branding (*of criminals*); blot, stigma

fleur [flœr] *f* flower; blossom; **à fleur de** level with, even with; on the surface of; **à fleur de peau** skin-deep; **à fleur de tête** bulging (*eyes*); **elle est fleur bleue** (slang) she is a prude; **en fleur** in bloom; **en fleurs** in bloom (*said of group of different varieties*); **fleur de farine** fine white flour; **fleur de l'âge** prime of life; **fleur de lis** [flœrdəlis] fleur-de-lis; **fleur des pois** (coll) pick of the lot; **fleurs** mold (*on wine, cider, etc.*)

fleurer [flœre] *intr* to give off an odor; **fleurer bon** to smell good

fleuret [flœrɛ] *m* fencing foil

fleurette [flœrɛt] *f* little flower; **conter fleurette** to flirt

fleu·ri -rie [flœri] *adj* in bloom; flowery; florid (*complexion; style*)

fleurir [flœrir] *tr* to decorate with flowers ‖ *intr* to flower, bloom ‖ *intr* (*ger* **florissant;** *imperf* **florissais,** etc.) to flourish

fleuriste [flœrist] *mf* florist; floral gardener; maker or seller of artificial flowers

fleuron [flœrɔ̃] *m* floret; (archit) finial; **fleuron à sa couronne** feather in his cap

fleuve [flœv] *m* river (*flowing directly to the sea*); (fig) river (*of tears, blood, etc.*)

flexible [flɛksibl] *adj* flexible; (fig) pliant

flexion [flɛksjɔ̃] *f* bending, flexion; (gram) inflection

flibuster [flibyste] *tr* to rob, snitch ‖ *intr* to filibuster

flibustier [flibystje] *m* filibuster (*pirate*)

flic [flik] *m* (slang) copper, fuzz

flicaille [flikaj] *f* (slang) fuzz, cops

flic flac [flikflak] *interj* splash!

flingot [flɛ̃go] *m* (slang) rod, gat

flingue [flɛ̃g] *m* (slang) rod, gat

flipper [flipœr] *m* pinball machine ‖ [flipe] *intr* (slang) to be high; (slang) to feel low

flirt [flœrt] *m* flirt; flirtation

flirter [flœrte] *intr* to flirt

flir·teur [flœrtœr] **-teuse** [tøz] *adj* flirtatious ‖ *mf* flirt

flocon [flɔkɔ̃] *m* flake; snowflake; tuft (*e.g., of wool*); **flocons d'avoine** oatmeal; **flocons de maïs** cornflakes; **flocons de neige** snowflakes

floconner [flɔkɔne] *intr* to form flakes; become fleecy

flocon·neux [flɔkɔnø] **-neuse** [nøz] *adj* flaky; fleecy

flopée [flɔpe] *f*—(slang) **une flopée de** loads of, lots of

floraison [flɔrezɔ̃] *f* flowering, blooming

flo·ral -rale [flɔral] *adj* (*pl* **-raux** [ro]) floral

floralies [flɔrali] *fpl* flower show

flore [flɔr] *f* flora

floren·tin [flɔrɑ̃tɛ̃] **-tine** [tin] *adj* Florentine; **à la florentine** with spinach ‖ (*cap*) *mf* Florentine (*native or inhabitant of Florence*)

Floride [flɔrid] *f* Florida; **la Floride** Florida

florilège [flɔrilɛʒ] *m* anthology

floris·sant [flɔrisɑ̃] **-sante** [sɑ̃t] *adj* flourishing

floss [flɔs] *m* (coll) dental floss

flot [flo] *m* wave; tide; flood, multitude; **à flot** afloat; **à flots** in torrents, abundantly; **flots** waters (*of a lake, the sea, etc.*); **flots de** lots of

flottabilité [flɔtabilite] *f* buoyancy

flottable [flɔtabl] *adj* buoyant; navigable (*for rafts*)

flottage [flɔtaʒ] *m* log driving

flottaison [flɔtezɔ̃] *f* water line

flot·tant [flɔtɑ̃] **-tante** [tɑ̃t] *adj* floating; vacillating, undecided

flotte [flɔt] *f* fleet buoy; float (*on fishline*); (slang) water, rain

flottement [flɔtmɑ̃] *m* floating; hesitation; vacillation; undulation

flotter [flɔte] *intr* to float; waver, hesitate; fly (*said of flag*); **il flotte** (slang) it is raining

flotteur [flɔtœr] *m* log driver; float (*of fishline, carburetor, etc.*); pontoon, float (*of seaplane*)

flottille [flɔtij] *f* flotilla; **flottille de pêche** fishing fleet

flou floue [flu] *adj* blurred, hazy; fluffy (*hair*); loose-fitting (*dress*); light and soft (*tones, lines in a painting*) ‖ *m* blur, fuzziness; dressmaking

flouer [flue] *tr* to dupe, swindle; **se faire flouer** to be had
fluctuation [flyktɥɑsjɔ̃] *f* fluctuation
fluctuer [flyktɥe] *intr* to fluctuate
fluet [flyɛ] **fluette** [flyɛt] *adj* thin, slender
fluide [flɥid] *adj* & *m* fluid
fluidifier [flɥidifje] *tr* to liquefy
fluor [flyɔr] *m* fluorine
fluores·cent [flyɔresɑ̃] **-cente** [sɑ̃t] *adj* fluorescent
fluoridation [flyɔridɑsjɔ̃] *f* fluoridation
fluorider [flyɔride] *tr* & *intr* to fluoridate
fluorure [flyɔryr] *m* fluoride
flûte [flyt] *f* flute; long thin loaf of French bread; tall champagne glass; **flûte à bec** recorder; **flûte de Pan** Pan's pipes; **flûtes** (slang) legs; **grande flûte** concert flute; **jouer** or **se tirer des flûtes** (slang) to run for it; **petite flûte** piccolo ‖ *interj* shucks! rats!
flûtiste [flytist] *mf* flutist
flux [fly] *m* flow; flood tide; (cards) flush; (chem, elec, med, metallurgy) flux; **flux de caisse** cash flow; **flux de sang** flush, blush; dysentery; **flux de ventre** diarrhea; **flux et reflux** ebb and flow
fluxion [flyksjɔ̃] *f* inflammation
foc [fɔk] *m* (naut) jib
fo·cal -cale [fɔkal] *adj* (*pl* **-caux** [ko]) focal
fœtus [fetys] *m* fetus
foi [fwa] *f* faith; word (*of a gentleman*); **ajouter foi à** to give credence to; **bonne foi** good faith, sincerity; **de bonne foi** sincere; sincerely; **de mauvaise foi** dishonest; dishonestly; **en foi de quoi** in witness whereof; **faire foi de** to be evidence of; **ma foi!** upon my word!; **manquer de foi à** to break faith with; **mauvaise foi** bad faith, insincerity; **sur la foi de** on the strength of
foie [fwa] *m* liver; **avoir les foies** (slang) to be scared stiff; **foie gras** goose liver
foin [fwɛ̃] *m* hay; **avoir du foin dans ses bottes** (coll) to be well heeled; **faire du foin** (slang) to kick up a fuss
foire [fwar] *f* fair; market; (coll) chaos, mess; **faire la foire** to raise hell; **foire d'empoigne** free-for-all
foirer [fware] *intr* (slang) to flop, fail; (slang) to hang fire; (slang) to be stripped (*said of screw, nut, etc.*)
fois [fwa] *f* time, e.g., **visiter trois fois par semaine** to visit three times a week; times, e.g., **deux fois deux font quatre** two times two is four; **à la fois** at the same time, together; **deux fois** twice; twofold; **encore une fois** once more, again; **il y avait une fois** once upon a time there was; **maintes et maintes fois** time and time again; **une fois** one time, once; **une fois pour toutes** or **une bonne fois** once and for all
foison [fwazɔ̃] *f*—**à foison** in abundance
foison·nant [fwazɔnɑ̃] **-nante** [nɑ̃t] *adj* abundant, plentiful
foisonner [fwazɔne] *intr* to abound
fol *adj* see **fou**

folâtre [fɔlɑtr] *adj* frisky, playful
folâtrer [fɔlɑtre] *intr* to frolic, romp
folie [fɔli] *f* madness, insanity; folly, piece of folly; country lodge, hideaway (*for romantic trysts*); **à la folie** madly, passionately; **faire une folie** to do something crazy; **folie de la persécution** persecution complex
folio [fɔljo] *m* folio
folioter [fɔljɔte] *tr* to folio
folle [fɔl] *f* crazy woman ‖ *adj* see **fou**
follement [fɔlmɑ̃] *adv* madly
fol·let [fɔlɛ] **-lette** [lɛt] *adj* merry, playful; elfish
follicule [fɔlikyl] *m* follicle
fomenta·teur [fɔmɑ̃tatœr] **-trice** [tris] *mf* agitator, troublemaker
fomenter [fɔmɑ̃te] *tr* to foment
fon·cé -cée [fɔ̃se] *adj* dark; deep
foncer [fɔ̃se] §51 *tr* to darken; dig (*a well*); fit a bottom to (*a cask*) ‖ *intr* to charge, rush
fon·cier [fɔ̃sje] **-cière** [sjɛr] *adj* landed (*property*); property (*tax*); fundamental, natural ‖ *m* real-estate tax
foncièrement [fɔ̃sjɛrmɑ̃] *adv* fundamentally, naturally
fonction [fɔ̃ksjɔ̃] *f* function; duty; **faire fonction de** to function as; **fonction publique** government work
fonctionnaire [fɔ̃ksjɔnɛr] *mf* civil servant; officeholder
fonctionnarisme [fɔ̃ksjɔnarism] *m* bureaucracy
fonction·nel -nelle [fɔ̃ksjɔnɛl] *adj* functional
fonctionnement [fɔ̃ksjɔnmɑ̃] *m* working, functioning, operation; **bon fonctionnement** good working order
fonctionner [fɔ̃ksjɔne] *intr* to function, work
fond [fɔ̃] *m* bottom; back, far end; background; foundation; dregs; core, inner meaning, main issue; **à fond** thoroughly; **à fond de train** at full speed; **au fond, dans le fond**, or **par le fond** actually, really, basically; **de fond** fundamental, main; **de fond en comble** from top to bottom; **faire fond sur** to rely on; **fond de tarte** bottom pie crust; **fonds de placement fermé** investment trust fund; **fond sonore** background noise; **râcler les fonds du tiroir** to scrape the bottom of the barrel; **sans fond** bottomless; **y aller au fond** to go the whole way ‖ see **fonds**
fondamen·tal -tale [fɔ̃damɑ̃tal] *adj* (*pl* **-taux** [to]) fundamental, basic
fon·dant [fɔ̃dɑ̃] **-dante** [dɑ̃t] *adj* melting; juicy, luscious ‖ *m* fondant (*candy*); (metallurgy) flux
fonda·teur [fɔ̃datœr] **-trice** [tris] *mf* founder
fondation [fɔ̃dɑsjɔ̃] *f* foundation; founding; endowment
fon·dé -dée [fɔ̃de] §92 *adj* founded; justified; authorized; **bien fondé** well-founded ‖ *m*—**fondé de pouvoir** proxy, authorized agent

fondement [fɔ̃dmã] *m* foundation, basis; (coll) behind; **sans fondement** unfounded

fonder [fɔ̃de] *tr* to found

fonderie [fɔ̃dri] *f* foundry; smelting

fondeur [fɔ̃dœr] *m* founder, smelter

fondre [fɔ̃dr] *tr* to melt, dissolve; smelt; cast (*metal*); blend (*colors*); merge (*companies*) ‖ *intr* to melt; (coll) to lose weight; **fondre en larmes** to burst into tears; **fondre sur** to pounce on

fondrière [fɔ̃drijɛr] *f* quagmire; mudhole, rut, pothole

fonds [fɔ̃] *m* land (*of an estate*); business, good will; fund; **bon fonds** good nature; **fonds** *mpl* capital; **fonds de commerce** business house; **fonds de prévoyance** reserve fund; **fonds d'État** *mpl* government bonds

fon·du -due [fɔ̃dy] *adj* melted; molten ‖ *m* blending (*of colors*); (mov, telv) dissolve, fade-out ‖ *f* fondue ‖ *v* see **fondre**

fongicide [fɔ̃ʒisid] *adj* fungicidal ‖ *m* fungicide

font [fɔ̃] *v* see **faire**

fontaine [fɔ̃tɛn] *f* fountain; spring; well; cistern; **fontaine de Jouvence** Fountain of Youth; **fontaines vivantes** dancing waters

fonte [fɔ̃t] *f* melting; casting; cast iron; holster; (typ) font; **venir de fonte avec** to be cast in one piece with

fonts [fɔ̃] *mpl*—**fonts baptismaux** baptismal font

football [futbol] *m* soccer; **football américain** football

footballeur [futbolœr] *m* soccer player

footing [futiŋ] *m* walking

for [fɔr] *m*—**dans son for intérieur** in his heart of hearts; **for intérieur** conscience

forage [fɔraʒ] *m* drilling; **forage d'exploration, forage sauvage** wildcat drilling

fo·rain [fɔrɛ̃] **-raine** [rɛn] *adj* traveling, itinerant ‖ **forains** *mpl* carnival people

forban [fɔrbã] *m* pirate

forçage [fɔrsaʒ] *m* (agr) forcing

forçat [fɔrsa] *m* convict; (hist) galley slave; (fig) drudge

force [fɔrs] *f* force; strength; **à force de** by dint of, as a result of; **à toute force** at all costs; **de première force** foremost (*musician, artist, scientist, etc.*); **de toutes ses forces** with all one's might; **force de frappe** striking force; **force m'est de . . .** (lit) I am obliged to . . .; **force majeure** (law) act of God; **forces** sheep shears; **force vive** (phys) kinetic energy; **la force de l'âge** the prime of life ‖ *adj invar* (archaic) many

forcément [fɔrsemã] *adv* inevitably, necessarily

force·né -née [fɔrsəne] *adj* frenzied, frantic ‖ *m* madman ‖ *f* crazy woman

forceps [fɔrsɛps] *m* (obstet) forceps

forcer [fɔrse] §51, §96, §97, §100 *tr* to force; do violence to; bring to bay; increase (*the dose*); strain (*a muscle*); mark up (*a receipt*); **forcer la main à qn** to

force s.o.'s hand; **forcer la note** (coll) to overdo it; **forcer le respect de qn** to compel respect from s.o.; **forcer qn à** or **de** + *inf* to force s.o. to + *inf* ‖ *ref* to overdo; do violence to one's feelings

forclore [fɔrklɔr] (used only in *inf* and *pp* **forclos**) *tr* to foreclose

forclusion [fɔrklyzjɔ̃] *f* foreclosure

forer [fɔre] *tr* to drill, bore

fores·tier [fɔrɛstje] **-tière** [tjɛr] *adj* forest ‖ *m* forester

foret [fɔrɛ] *m* drill

forêt [fɔrɛ] *f* forest

fo·reur [fɔrœr] **-reuse** [røz] *adj* drilling ‖ *mf* driller ‖ *f* drill, machine drill

forfaire [fɔrfɛr] §29 (used only in *inf;* 1st, 2d, & 3d *sg pres ind;* compound tenses) *intr*—**forfaire à** to forfeit (*one's honor*); fail in (*a duty*)

forfait [fɔrfɛ] *m* heinous crime; contract; package deal; (turf) forfeit; **à forfait** for a lump sum

forfaitaire [fɔrfɛtɛr] *adj* contractual

forfaiture [fɔrfɛtyr] *f* malfeasance

forfanterie [fɔrfãtri] *f* bragging

forge [fɔrʒ] *f* forge; steel mill

forger [fɔrʒe] §38 *tr* to forge

forgeron [fɔrʒərɔ̃] *m* blacksmith

forgeur [fɔrʒœr] *m* forger, smith; coiner (*e.g., of new expressions*); fabricator (*of false stories*)

formaldéhyde [fɔrmaldeid] *m* formaldehyde

formaliser [fɔrmalize] *ref* to take offense

formaliste [fɔrmalist] *adj* formalistic, conventional ‖ *mf* formalist

formalité [fɔrmalite] *f* formality, convention

format [fɔrma] *m* size, format

formation [fɔrmasjɔ̃] *f* formation; education, training

forme [fɔrm] *f* form; **en forme** fit, in shape; **en forme, en bonne forme,** or **en bonne et due forme** in order, in due form; **pour la forme** for appearances

for·mel -melle [fɔrmɛl] *adj* explicit; strict; formal, superficial

formellement [fɔrmɛlmã] *adv* absolutely, strictly

former [fɔrme] *tr & ref* to form; educate

formidable [fɔrmidabl] *adj* formidable; (coll) tremendous, terrific

formulaire [fɔrmylɛr] *m* formulary; form (*with spaces for answers*)

formule [fɔrmyl] *f* formula; form, blank; format; **formule de politesse** complimentary close

formuler [fɔrmyle] *tr* to formulate; draw up

fort [fɔr] **forte** [fɔrt] *adj* strong; fortified (*city*); **c'est fort!** it's hard to believe! ‖ (when standing before noun) *adj* high (*fever*); large (*sum*); hard (*task*) ‖ *m* fort; strong man; forte; height (*of summer*) ‖ **fort** *adv* exceedingly; loud; hard

fort-en-thème [fɔrãtɛm] *adj* (slang) grind (*student*)

forteresse [fɔrtərɛs] *f* fortress, fort

forti·fiant [fɔrtifjɑ̃] **-fiante** [fjɑ̃t] *adj & m* tonic

fortification [fɔrtifikɑsjɔ̃] *f* fortification

fortifier [fɔrtifje] *tr* to fortify; confirm (*one's opinions*)

fortin [fɔrtɛ̃] *m* small fort

for·tuit [fɔrtɥi] **-tuite** [tɥit] *adj* fortuitous, accidental

fortune [fɔrtyn] *f* fortune; **faire fortune** to make a fortune

fortu·né -née [fɔrtyne] *adj* fortunate; rich

fosse [fos] *f* pit; grave; **fosse aux lions** lions' den; **fosse commune** pauper's grave; **fosse d'aisances** cesspool; **fossse septique** septic tank

fossé [fose] *m* ditch, trench; moat; **fossé des générations** generation gap; **sauter le fossé** to take the plunge

fossette [fosɛt] *f* dimple

fossile [fosil] *adj & m* fossil ǁ *mf* fossil (*person*)

fossoyeur [foswajœr] *m* gravedigger

fosterage [fɔsteraʒ] *m* foster parenting

fou [fu] or **fol** [fɔl] **folle** [fɔl] (*pl* **fous folles**) *adj* mad, insane; foolish; extravagant; unsteady; loose (*pulley*); (coll) tremendous (*success*); **être fou à lier** to be raving mad; **être fou de** to be wild about; to be wild with (*joy, pain, etc.*) ǁ **fou** *m* madman; fool; jester; (cards) joker; (chess) bishop ǁ *f* see **folle**

foucade [fukad] *f* whim, impulse

foudre [fudr] *m* thunderbolt (*of Zeus*); large cask; **foudre de guerre** great captain; **foudre d'éloquence** powerful orator ǁ *f* lightning; **foudres** displeasure (*e.g., of a prince*); **foudres de l'Église** excommunication

foudroyant [fudrwajɑ̃] **foudroyante** [fudrwajɑ̃t] *adj* lightning-like; crushing; overwhelming

foudroyer [fudrwaje] §47 *tr* to strike with lightning; strike suddenly; dumfound; **foudroyer d'un regard** to cast a withering glance at ǁ *intr* to hurl thunderbolts

fouet [fwɛ] *m* whip; (culin) beater

fouetter [fwɛte] *tr & intr* to whip

fougère [fuʒɛr] *f* fern

fougue [fug] *f* spirit, ardor

fou·gueux [fugø] **-gueuse** [gøz] *adj* spirited, fiery, impetuous

fouille [fuj] *f* excavation; search

fouiller [fuje] *tr* to excavate; search, comb, inspect

fouillis [fuji] *m* jumble, disorder

fouine [fwin] *f* beech marten; pitchfork; harpoon

fouiner [fwine] *intr* (coll) to pry, meddle

fouir [fwir] *tr* to dig, burrow

foulard [fular] *m* scarf, neckerchief

foule [ful] *f* crowd, mob; **en foule** in great numbers

fouler [fule] *tr* to tread on, press; sprain ǁ *ref* to sprain; (slang) to put oneself out, to tire oneself out

foulque [fulk] *f* (zool) coot

foulure [fulyr] *f* sprain

four [fur] *m* oven; kiln, furnace; (coll) flop, turkey; **faire cuire au four** to bake; to roast; **faire four** (coll) to flop; **four à briques** brickkiln; **four à chaux** limekiln; **petit four** teacake

fourbe [furb] *adj* deceiving, cheating ǁ *mf* deceiver, cheat

fourberie [furbəri] *f* deceit, cheating

fourbir [furbir] *tr* to furbish, polish

fourbissage [furbisaʒ] *m* furnishing, polishing

four·bu -bue [furby] *adj* broken-down (*horse*); (coll) dead tired, all in

fourche [furʃ] *f* fork; pitchfork; **fourche avant** front fork (*of bicycle*); **fourches patibulaires** (hist) gallows

fourcher [furʃe] *tr & intr* to fork; **la langue lui a fourché** (coll) he made a slip of the tongue

fourchette [furʃɛt] *f* fork; wishbone; **posséder une bonne fourchette** to have a hearty appetite

four·chu -chue [furʃy] *adj* forked; cloven

fourgon [furgɔ̃] *m* truck; poker; (rr) baggage car; (rr) boxcar; **fourgon bancaire** armored car; **fourgon de queue** caboose; **fourgon funèbre** hearse

fourmi [furmi] *f* ant; (slang) pusher (*of drugs*); **fourmi blanche** white ant, termite

fourmilier [furmilje] *m* anteater

fourmilière [furmiljɛr] *f* ant hill

fourmiller [furmije] *intr* to swarm; tingle (*said, e.g., of foot*); **fourmiller de** to teem with

fournaise [furnɛz] *f* furnace; (fig) oven

four·neau [furno] *m* (*pl* **-neaux**) furnace; cooking stove; **haut fourneau** blast furnace

fournée [furne] *f* batch

four·ni -nie [furni] *adj* bushy, thick; **bien fourni** well-stocked

fourniment [furnimɑ̃] *m* (mil) kit

fournir [furnir] *tr* to furnish, supply, provide; play (*a card of the same suit that has been led*); **fournir q.ch. à qn** to supply or provide s.o. with s.th. ǁ *intr* to supply (*s.o.'s needs*), e.g., **ses parents fournissent à ses besoins** his parents supply his needs; defray (*expenses*); (cards) to follow suit, e.g., **fournir à trèfle** to follow suit in clubs ǁ *ref* to grow thick; be a customer

fournissement [furnismɑ̃] *m* contribution, holdings (*of each shareholder*); statement of holdings

fournisseur [furnisœr] *m* supplier, dealer

fourniture [furnityr] *f* furnishing, supplying; (culin) seasoning; **fournitures** supplies

fourrage [furaʒ] *m* fodder

fourrager [furaʒe] §38 *tr* to forage; rummage, rummage through ǁ *intr* to rummage (about), forage

fourragère [furaʒɛr] *f* lanyard; tailboard

four·ré -rée [fure] *adj* lined with fur; furred (*tongue*); stuffed (*dates*); filled (*candies*); sham, hollow (*peace*) ‖ *m* thicket

four·reau [furo] *m* (*pl* -reaux) sheath; scabbard; tight skirt; **coucher dans son fourreau** (coll) to sleep in one's clothes

fourrer [fure] *tr* to line with fur; (coll) to cram, stuff; (coll) to shut up (*in prison*); (coll) to stick, poke ‖ *ref* (coll) to turn, go; (coll) to curl up (*in bed*); **se fourrer dans** (coll) to stick one's nose in

fourre-tout [furtu] *m invar* catchall; duffel bag; tote bag

fourreur [furœr] *m* furrier

fourrier [furje] *m* quartermaster

fourrière [furjɛr] *f* pound (*for automobiles; for stray dogs*)

fourrure [furyr] *f* fur

fourvoyer [furvwaje] §47 *tr* to lead astray

foutre [futr] §7 (*pres* **je, tu fous; il fout**) *tr* (vulg) to have sex with; (vulg) to give; **fous-le dans ta poche!** shove it in your pocket!; **fous-moi la paix!** lay off!; **fous-moi le camp!** get the hell out!; **je t'en fous!** the hell with you!; **qu'est-ce qu'il fout?** what in hell is he doing? ‖ *ref* (vulg) to be had; **je m'en fous!** to hell with it!; **se foutre de** not to give a damn about

fox [fɔks] *m* fox terrier

fox-terrier [fɔkstɛrje] *m* fox terrier

fox-trot [fɔkstrɔt] *m invar* fox trot

foyer [fwaje] *m* foyer, lobby; hearth, fireside; firebox; focus; home; greenroom; center (*of learning; of infection*); **à double foyer** bifocal; **foyer des étudiants** student center; **foyer du soldat** service club; **foyers** native land

frac [frak] *m* cutaway coat

fracas [fraka] *m* crash; roar (*of waves*); peal (*of thunder*)

fracasser [frakase] *tr & ref* to break; shatter, break to pieces

fraction [fraksjɔ̃] *f* fraction; breaking (*e.g., of bread*)

fractionnaire [fraksjɔnɛr] *adj* fractional

fractionnement [fraksjɔnmɑ̃] *m* cracking (*of petroleum*)

fractionner [fraksjɔne] *tr* to divide into fractions

fracture [fraktyr] *f* fracture; breaking open

fracturer [fraktyre] *tr* to fracture; break open

fragile [fraʒil] *adj* fragile

fragment [fragmɑ̃] *m* fragment

fragmenter [fragmɑ̃te] *tr* to fragment

frai [frɛ] *m* spawning; spawn, roe

fraîche [frɛʃ] *f* cool of the day

fraîchement [frɛʃmɑ̃] *adv* in the open air; recently; (coll) cordially

fraîcheur [frɛʃœr] *f* coolness; freshness; newness

fraîchir [fraʃir] *intr* to become cooler; freshen (*said of wind*)

frais [frɛ] **fraîche** [frɛʃ] *adj* cool; fresh; wet (*paint*); ready (*cash*); **frais et dispos, frais comme une rose** fresh as a daisy; **il**

fait frais it is cool out ‖ (when standing before noun) *adj* recent (*date*); latest (*news*) ‖ *m* cool place; fresh air; **aux frais de** at the expense of; **de frais** just, freshly; **faire les frais de la conversation** (coll) to take the lead in the conversation; be the subject of the conversation; **frais** *mpl* expenses; **frais généraux** overhead expenses; **se mettre en frais** (coll) to go to a great deal of expense or trouble ‖ *f* see **fraîche** ‖ **frais** *adv*—**boire frais** to have a cool drink ‖ **frais fraîche** *adv* (agrees with following *pp*) just, freshly, e.g., **garçon frais arrivé de l'école** boy just arrived from school; e.g., **roses fraîches cueillies** freshly gathered roses

fraise [frɛz] *f* strawberry; wattle (*of turkey*); (mach) countersink

fraiser [frɛze] *tr* (mach) to countersink

fraisier [frɛzje] *m* strawberry plant

framboise [frɑ̃bwaz] *f* raspberry

framboisier [frɑ̃bwazje] *m* raspberry bush

franc [frɑ̃] **franche** [frɑ̃ʃ] *adj* free; frank, sincere; complete ‖ (when standing before noun) *adj* arrant (*knave*); downright (*fool*) ‖ **franc franque** [frɑ̃k] *adj* Frankish ‖ *m* franc (*unit of currency*) ‖ (*cap*) *m* Frank (*medieval German*) ‖ **franc** *adv* frankly

fran·çais [frɑse] **-çaise** [sɛz] *adj* French ‖ *m* French (*language*); **en bon français** in correct French ‖ (*cap*) *m* Frenchman; **les Français** the French ‖ *f* Frenchwoman

franc-alleu [frɑ̃kalø] *m* (*pl* **francs-alleux** [frɑ̃kalø]) (hist) freehold

France [frɑ̃s] *f* France; **la France** France

franchement [frɑ̃ʃmɑ̃] *adv* frankly, sincerely; without hesitation

franchir [frɑ̃ʃir] *tr* to cross, go over or through; jump over; overcome (*an obstacle*)

franchise [frɑ̃ʃiz] *f* exemption; frankness; freedom; **franchise postale** frank

francique [frɑ̃sik] *m* Frankish

franciser [frɑ̃size] *tr* to make French

franc-maçon [frɑ̃masɔ̃] *m* (*pl* **francs-maçons**) Freemason

franc-maçonnerie [frɑ̃masɔnri] *f* Freemasonry

franco [frɑ̃ko] *adv* free, without shipping costs; **franco de bord** free on board; **franco de port** postpaid

franco-cana·dien [frɑ̃kɔkanadjɛ̃] **-dienne** [djɛn] *adj* French-Canadian ‖ **Franco-Cana·dien -dienne** *mf* French Canadian

francophone [frɑ̃kɔfɔn] *adj* French-speaking ‖ *mf* French speaker

franc-parler [frɑ̃parle] *m*—**avoir son franc-parler** to be free-spoken

franc-tireur [frɑ̃tirœr] *m* (*pl* **francs-tireurs**) free lance; sniper

frange [frɑ̃ʒ] *f* fringe; **à frange** fringed; **frange des dingues** lunatic fringe

franger [frɑ̃ʒe] §38 *tr* to fringe

franglais [frɑ̃glɛ] *m* Franglais

franquette [frɑ̃kɛt] *f*—**à la bonne franquette** (coll) simply, without fuss

frap·pant [frapɑ̃] **-pante** [pɑ̃t] *adj* striking, surprising

frappe [frap] *f* minting, striking; stamp (*on coins, medals, etc.*); touch (*in typing*); space (*in typing*), e.g., **une ligne de 65 frappes** a 65-space line

frap·pé -pée [frape] *adj* struck; iced; (slang) crazy ‖ *m* (mus) downbeat

frapper [frape] *tr* to strike, hit, knock; mint (coin); stamp (*cloth*); ice (*e.g., champagne*) ‖ *intr* to strike, hit, knock ‖ *ref* (coll) to become panic-stricken

frasque [frask] *f* escapade

frater·nel -nelle [fratɛrnɛl] *adj* fraternal, brotherly

fraterniser [fratɛrnize] *intr* to fraternize

fraternité [fratɛrnite] *f* fraternity, brotherhood

fraude [frod] *f* fraud; smuggling; **en fraude** fraudulently; **faire la fraude** to smuggle; **fraude fiscale** tax evasion

fraudu·leux [frodylø] **-leuse** [løz] *adj* fraudulent

frayer [frɛje], [freje] §49 *tr* to mark out (*a path*) ‖ *intr* to spawn; **frayer avec** to associate with

frayeur [frɛjœr] *f* fright, scare

fredaine [frədɛn] *f* (coll) escapade, prank, spree

fredon [frədɔ̃] *m* (cards) three of a kind

fredonnement [frədɔnmɑ̃] *m* hum, humming

fredonner [frədɔne] *tr & intr* to hum

frégate [fregat] *f* frigate

frein [frɛ̃] *m* bit (*of bridle*); brake (*of car*); **frein à main** hand brake; **frein à pied** foot brake; **mettre le frein** to put the brake on; **mettre un frein à** to curb, check; **ronger son frein** to champ at the bit

freiner [frɛne] *tr & intr* to brake

frelater [frəlate] *tr* to adulterate

frêle [frɛl] *adj* frail

frelon [frəlɔ̃] *m* hornet

frémir [fremir] §97 *intr* to shudder

frémissement [fremismɑ̃] *m* shudder

frêne [frɛn] *m* ash tree

frénésie [frenezi] *f* frenzy

frénétique [frenetik] *adj* frenzied

fréquemment [frekamɑ̃] *adv* frequently

fréquence [frekɑ̃s] *f* frequency; **basse fréquence** low frequency; **fréquence du pouls** pulse rate; **haute fréquence** high frequency

fré·quent [frekɑ̃] **-quente** [kɑ̃t] *adj* frequent; rapid (*pulse*)

fréquenter [frekɑ̃te] *tr* to frequent; associate with; (coll) to go steady with (*a boy or girl*)

frère [frɛr] *m* brother; **frère consanguin** half brother (*by the father*); **frère convers** (eccl) lay brother; **frère de lait** foster brother; **frère germain** whole brother; **frère jumeau** twin brother; **frères siamois** Siamese twins; **frère utérin** half brother (*by the mother*)

fresque [frɛsk] *f* fresco

fret [frɛ] *m* freight; chartering; cargo

fréter [frete] §10 *tr* to charter (*a ship*); rent (*a car*)

fréteur [fretœr] *m* shipowner

frétiller [fretije] *intr* to wriggle; quiver; **frétiller de** to wag (*its tail*)

fretin [frətɛ̃] *m*—**le menu fretin** small fry

frette [frɛt] *f* hoop, iron ring

freudisme [frødism] *m* Freudianism

freux [frø] *m* rook, crow

friand [frijɑ̃] **friande** [frijɑ̃d] *adj* tasty; fond (*of food, praise, etc.*) ‖ *m* sausage roll

friandise [frijɑ̃diz] *f* candy, sweet; delicacy, tidbit

fric [frik] *m* (slang) jack, money

fricasser [frikase] *tr* to fricassee; squander

fric-frac [frikfrak] *m* (coll) break-in

friche [friʃ] *f* fallow land; **en friche** fallow

friction [friksjɔ̃] *f* friction; massage

frictionner [friksjɔne] *tr* to rub, massage

frigide [friʒid] *adj* frigid

frigidité [friʒidite] *f* frigidity

frigorifier [frigɔrifje] *tr* to refrigerate

frigorifique [frigɔrifik] *adj* refrigerating ‖ *m* cold-storage plant

fri·leux [frilø] **-leuse** [løz] *adj* chilly, shivery

frimas [frimɑ] *m* icy mist, rime

frime [frim] *f* (coll) sham, fake, hoax

frimousse [frimus] *f* (coll) little face, cute face

fringale [frɛ̃gal] *f* (coll) mad hunger

frin·gant [frɛ̃gɑ̃] **-gante** [gɑ̃t] *adj* dashing, spirited

fringuer [frɛ̃ge] *tr* (slang) to dress ‖ *intr* (obs) to frisk about

fringues [frɛ̃g] *fpl* (slang) duds

fri·pé -pée [fripe] *adj* rumpled, mussed; worn, tired (*face*)

friper [fripe] *tr* to wrinkle, rumple

friperie [fripri] *f* secondhand clothes; secondhand furniture

fri·pier [fripje] **-pière** [pjɛr] *mf* old-clothes dealer; junk dealer

fri·pon [fripɔ̃] **-ponne** [pɔn] *adj* roguish ‖ *mf* rogue, rascal

friponnerie [fripɔnri] *f* rascality, cheating

fripouille [fripuj] *f* (slang) scoundrel

frire [frir] §22 (used in *inf; pp;* 1st, 2d, 3d *sg pres ind; sg imperv;* rarely used in *fut; cond*) *tr* to fry; deep-fry; **être frit** (coll) to be done for ‖ *intr* to fry

frise [friz] *f* frieze

friselis [frizli] *m* soft rustling; gentle lapping (*of water*)

friser [frize] *tr* to curl; border on; graze ‖ *intr* to curl

frisoir [frizwar] *m* curling iron

fri·son [frizɔ̃] **-sonne** [zɔn] *adj* Frisian ‖ *m* wave, curl; Frisian (*language*) ‖ (*cap*) *mf* Frisian

fris·quet [friskɛ] **-quette** [kɛt] *adj* (coll) chilly

frisson [frisɔ̃] *m* shiver; shudder; thrill; **frissons** shivering

frissonner [frisɔne] *intr* to shiver

frisure [frizyr] *f* curling; curls

frit [fri] **frite** [frit] *v* see **frire**
frites [frit] *fpl* French fries
frittage [fritaʒ] *m* (metallurgy) sintering
friture [frityr] *f* frying; deep fat; fried fish; (rad, telv) static
frivole [frivɔl] *adj* frivolous, trifling
froc [frɔk] *m* (eccl) frock
froid [frwɑ] **froide** [frwɑd] *adj* cold; chilly (*manner*) ‖ *m* cold; coolness (*between persons*); **avoir froid** to be cold; **il fait froid** it is cold; **jeter un froid sur** (fig) to put a damper on
froideur [frwɑdœr] *f* coldness; coolness
froissement [frwɑsmɑ̃] *m* bruising; rumpling, crumpling; clash (*of interests*); ruffling (*of feelings*)
froisser [frwɑse] *tr* to bruise; rumple, crumple ‖ *ref* to take offense
frôlement [frolmɑ̃] *m* grazing; rustle
frôler [frole] *tr* to graze, brush against; (coll) to have a narrow escape from
fromage [frɔmaʒ] *m* cheese; (coll) soft job; **fromage blanc** cream cheese; **fromage de tête** headcheese
froma·ger [frɔmaʒe] **-gère** [ʒɛr] *adj* cheese (*industry*) ‖ *m* cheesemaker; (bot) silk-cotton tree
fromagerie [frɔmaʒri] *f* cheese factory; cheese store
froment [frɔmɑ̃] *m* wheat
fronce [frɔ̃s] *f* crease, fold; **à fronces** shirred
froncement [frɔ̃smɑ̃] *m* puckering; **froncement de sourcils** frown
froncer [frɔ̃se] §51 *tr* to pucker; **froncer les sourcils** to frown, wrinkle one's brow
frondaison [frɔ̃dɛzɔ̃] *f* foliation; foliage
fronde [frɔ̃d] *f* slingshot
fronder [frɔ̃de] *tr* to scoff at
fron·deur [frɔ̃dœr] **-deuse** [døz] *adj* bantering, irreverent ‖ *mf* scoffer
front [frɔ̃] *m* forehead; impudence; brow (*of hill*); (geog, mil, pol) front; **de front** abreast; frontal; at the same time; **faire front à** to face up to; **un front froid** (meteo) a cold front
fronta·lier [frɔ̃talje] **-lière** [ljɛr] *adj* frontier ‖ *m* frontiersman ‖ *f* frontier woman
frontière [frɔ̃tjɛr] *adj & f* frontier
frontispice [frɔ̃tispis] *m* frontispiece; title page
frottement [frɔtmɑ̃] *m* rubbing, friction
frotter [frɔte] *tr* to rub; polish; strike (*a match*); **frotter les oreilles à qn** (coll) to box s.o.'s ears ‖ *ref*—**se frotter à** (coll) to attack, challenge; (coll) to rub shoulders with
froufrou [frufru] *m* rustle, swish
frousse [frus] *f* (slang) jitters
fructifier [fryktifje] *intr* to bear fruit
fruc·tueux [fryktɥø] **-tueuse** [tɥøz] *adj* fruitful, profitable
fru·gal -gale [frygal] *adj* (*pl* **-gaux** [go]) temperate; frugal (*meal*)
fruit [frɥi] *m* fruit; **des fruits** fruit; **fruits civils** income (*from rent, interest, etc.*); **fruits de mer** seafood; **fruit sec** (fig) flop, failure

fruiterie [frɥitri] *f* fruit store
frui·tier [frɥitje] **-tière** [tjɛr] *adj* fruit; fruit-bearing ‖ *mf* fruit vendor
fruste [fryst] *adj* worn; rough, uncouth
frustrer [frystre] *tr* frustrate, disappoint; cheat, defraud
f.s. *abbr* (**faux sens**) mistranslation
fuel [fjul] *m* fuel oil
fuel-oil [fjulɔl] *m* fuel oil
fugace [fygas] *adj* fleeting, evanescent
fugi·tif [fyʒitif] **-tive** [tiv] *adj & mf* fugitive
fugue [fyg] *f* sudden disappearance; (mus) fugue
fuir [fɥir] §31 *tr* to flee, run away from ‖ *intr* to flee; leak; recede (*said of forehead*)
fuite [fɥit] *f* flight; leak
fulgu·rant [fylgyrɑ̃] **-rante** [rɑ̃t] *adj* flashing; vivid; stabbing (*pain*)
fulguration [fylgyrɑsjɔ̃] *f* sheet lightning
fulgurer [fylgyre] *intr* to flash
fuligi·neux [fyliʒinø] **-neuse** [nøz] *adj* sooty
fumage [fymaʒ] *m* smoking (*of meat*); manuring (*of fields*)
fume-cigare [fymsigar] *m invar* cigar holder
fume-cigarette [fymsigarɛt] *m invar* cigarette holder
fumée [fyme] *f* smoke; steam; **fumées** fumes
fumer [fyme] *tr & intr* to smoke; fume; manure
fumerie [fymri] *f* opium den; smoking room
fumet [fyme] *m* aroma; bouquet (*of wine*)
fu·meur [fymœr] **-meuse** [møz] *mf* smoker; **fumeur à la file** chain smoker
fu·meux [fymø] **-meuse** [møz] *adj* smoky; foggy, hazy (*ideas*)
fumier [fymje] *m* manure; dunghill; (slang) skunk, scoundrel
fumiger [fymiʒe] §38 *tr* to fumigate
fumillard [fymijar] *m* smog
fumiste [fymist] *m* heater man; (coll) practical joker
fumisterie [fymistri] *f* heater work; heater shop; (coll) hooey
fumoir [fymwar] *m* smoking room; smoke-house
funambule [fynɑ̃byl] *mf* tightrope walker
funèbre [fynɛbr] *adj* funereal; funeral (*march, procession, service*)
funérailles [fynerɑj] *fpl* funeral
funéraire [fynerɛr] *adj* funeral
funeste [fynɛst] *adj* baleful, fatal
funiculaire [fynikylɛr] *adj & m* funicular
fur [fyr] *m*—**au fur et à mesure** progressively, gradually; **au fur et à mesure de** in proportion to; **au fur et à mesure que** as, in proportion as
furet [fyrɛ] *m* ferret; snoop; ring-in-the-circle (*parlor game*)
fureter [fyrte] §2 *intr* to ferret
fureur [fyrœr] *f* fury; **à la fureur** passionately; **faire fureur** to be the rage
furi·bond [fyribɔ̃] **-bonde** [bɔ̃d] *adj* furious; withering (*look*) ‖ *mf* irascible individual
furie [fyri] *f* fury; termagant

fu·rieux [fyrjø] **-rieuse** [rjøz] *adj* furious; angry (*wind*)

furoncle [fyrɔ̃kl] *m* boil

fur·tif [fyrtif] **-tive** [tiv] *adj* furtive, stealthy

fus [fy] *v* (**fut, fûmes,** etc.) see **être**

fusain [fyzɛ̃] *m* charcoal; charcoal drawing; spindle tree

fu·seau [fuzo] *m* (*pl* **-seaux**) spindle; **à fuseau** tapering; **fuseau horaire** time zone (*between two meridians*)

fusée [fyze] *f* rocket; spindleful; spindle (*of axle*); (coll) ripple, burst (*of laughter*); **fusée à retard** delayed-action fuse; **fusée d'artifice** or **fusée volante** skyrocket; **fusée éclairante, fusée de signalisation** flare; **fusée engin** rocket engine; **fusée fusante** time fuse; **fusée percutante** percussion fuse

fuselage [fyzlaʒ] *m* fuselage

fuse·lé -lée [fyzle] *adj* spindle-shaped; tapering, slender (*fingers*); streamlined

fuseler [fyzle] §34 *tr* to taper; streamline

fuser [fyze] *intr* to melt; run (*said of colors*); fizz, spurt; stream in or out (*said of light*)

fusible [fyzibl] *adj* fusible ‖ *m* fuse

fusil [fyzi] *m* gun, rifle; whetstone rifleman; **fusil à canon scié** sawed-off shotgun; **fusil à deux coups** double-barreled gun; **fusil de chasse** shot gun; **fusil mitrailleur** light machine gun; **un bon fusil** a good shot (*person*)

fusillade [fyzijad] *f* fusillade

fusiller [fyzije] *tr* to shoot, execute by a firing squad

fusion [fyzjɔ̃] *f* fusion

fusionner [fyzjɔne] *tr & intr* to blend, fuse; (com) to merge

fustiger [fystiʒe] §38 *tr* to thrash, flog; castigate

fût [fy] *m* cask, keg; barrel (*of drum*); stock (*of gun*); trunk (*of tree*); shaft (*of column*); stem (*of candelabrum*)

futaie [fytɛ] *f* stand of timber; **de haute futaie** full-grown

futaille [fytɑj] *f* cask, barrel

futaine [fytɛn] *f* fustian

fu·té -tée [fyte] *adj* (coll) cunning, shrewd ‖ *f* mastic, filler

futile [fytil] *adj* futile

futilité [fytilite] *f* futility; **futilités** trifles

fu·tur -ture [fytyr] *adj* future ‖ *m* future; husband-to-be ‖ *f* future wife

fuyant [fɥijɑ̃] **fuyante** [fɥijɑ̃t] *adj* fleeting; receding (*forehead*)

fuyard [fɥijar] **fuyarde** [fɥijard] *adj & mf* runaway

G

G, g [ʒe] *m invar* seventh letter of the French alphabet

garbardine [gabardin] *f* gabardine

gabare [gabar] *f* barge

gabarit [gabari] *m* templet; (rr) maximum structure; (coll) size

gabelle [gabɛl] *f* (hist) salt tax

gâche [gɑʃ] *f* catch (*at a door*); trowel; wooden spatula

gâcher [gɑʃe] *tr* to mix (*cement*); spoil, bungle, squander

gâchette [gɑʃɛt] *f* trigger; pawl, spring catch

gâ·cheur [gɑʃœr] **-cheuse** [ʃøz] *adj* bungling ‖ *f* bungler

gâchis [gɑʃi] *m* wet cement; mud, slush; (coll) mess, muddle

gaélique [gaelik] *adj & m* Gaelic

gaffe [gaf] *f* gaff; (coll) social blunder, faux pas

gaffer [gafe] *tr* to hook with a gaff ‖ *intr* (coll) to make a blunder

gaga [gaga] *adj* (coll) doddering ‖ *mf* (coll) dotard

gage [gaʒ] *m* pledge, pawn; forfeit (*in a game*); **gages** wage, wages; **prêter sur gages** to pawn

gager [gaʒe] §38, §97 *tr* to wager, bet; pay wages to

ga·geur [gaʒœr] **-geuse** [ʒøz] *mf* bettor

gageure [gaʒyr] *f* wager, bet

gagiste [gaʒist] *mf* pledger; wage earner; (theat) extra

ga·gnant [gaɲɑ̃] **-gnante** [ɲɑ̃t] *adj* winning ‖ *mf* winner

gagne-pain [gaɲpɛ̃] *m invar* breadwinner; livelihood, bread and butter

gagne-petit [gaɲpəti] *m invar* cheapjack, low-salaried worker

gagner [gaɲe] §96 *tr* to gain; win; earn; reach; save (*time*) ‖ *intr* to improve; gain; spread ‖ *ref* to be catching (*said of disease*)

ga·gneur [gaɲœr] **-gneuse** [ɲøz] *mf* winner; earner

gai gaie [ge] *adj* cheerful, merry, happy; (coll) tipsy

gaiement [gemɑ̃] *adv* gaily, cheerfully, merrily, happily

gaieté [gete] *f* gaiety; **de gaieté de cœur** of one's own free will

gail·lard [gajar] **-larde** [jard] *adj* healthy, hearty; merry; ribald, spicy ‖ *m* sturdy fellow; tricky fellow; **gaillard d'arrière** quarter-deck; **gaillard d'avant** forecastle ‖ *f* bold young lady; husky young woman

gaillardise [gajardiz] *f* cheerfulness; **gaillardises** spicy stories

gaîment [gemɑ̃] *adv* see **gaiement**

gain [gɛ̃] *m* gain; earnings; winning (*e.g., of bet*); **avoir gain de cause** to win one's case

gaine [gɛn] *f* sheath; case, covering; girdle (*corset*); **gaine d'aération** ventilation shaft

gainer [gɛne] *tr* to sheath, encase

gaîté [gete] *f* gaiety

gala [gala] *m* gala; state dinner

galamment [galamɑ̃] *adv* gallantly

ga·lant [galɑ̃] **-lante** [lɑ̃t] *adj* gallant; amorous; kept (*woman*) ‖ *m* gallant; **vert galant** gay old blade

galanterie [galɑ̃tri] *f* gallantry; libertinism

galaxie [galaksi] *f* galaxy

galbe [galb] *m* curve, sweep, graceful outline

gale [gal] *f* mange; (coll) backbiter, cad

galée [gale] *f* (typ) galley

galéjade [galeʒad] *f* joke, far-fetched story

galère [galɛr] *f* galley; drudgery; mason's hand truck

galerie [galri] *f* gallery; cornice, rim; baggage rack; **galerie marchande** shopping center; shopping mall

galérien [galerjɛ̃] *m* galley slave

galet [galɛ] *m* pebble; (mach) roller

galetas [galta] *m* hovel

galette [galɛt] *f* cake; buckwheat pancake; hardtack; (slang) dough, money, **galette des Rois** twelfth-cake (*eaten at Epiphany*)

ga·leux [galø] **-leuse** [løz] *adj* mangy

galimatias [galimatja] *m* nonsense, gibberish

galion [galjɔ̃] *m* galleon

Galles [gal]—**le pays de Galles** Wales; **prince de Galles** Prince of Wales

gal·lois [galwa] **gal·loise** [galwaz] *adj* Welsh ‖ *m* Welsh (*language*) ‖ (*cap*) *m* Welshman; **les Gallois** the Welsh ‖ (*cap*) *f* Welshwoman

gallon [galɔ̃] *m* gallon (*imperial or American*)

galoche [galɔʃ] *f* clog (*shoe*); **de** or **en galoche** pointed (*chin*)

galon [galɔ̃] *m* galloon, braid; (mil) stripe, chevron; **prendre du galon** to move up

galonner [galɔne] *tr* to trim with braid

galop [galo] *m* gallop; **petit galop** canter

galoper [galɔpe] *tr & intr* to gallop

galopin [galɔpɛ̃] *m* (coll) urchin

galvaniser [galvanize] *tr* to galvanize

galvanoplastie [galvãnɔplasti] *f* electroplating

galvauder [galvode] *tr* (coll) to botch; (coll) to waste (*e.g., one's talent*); (coll) to sully (*a name*) ‖ *intr* (slang) to walk the streets ‖ *ref* (slang) to go bad

gambade [gɑ̃bad] *f* gambol

gambader [gɑ̃bade] *intr* to gambol

gambit [gɑ̃bi] *m* gambit

gamelle [gamɛl] *f* mess kit

ga·min [gamɛ̃] **-mine** [min] *mf* street urchin; youngster

gaminerie [gaminri] *f* mischievousness

gamme [gam] *f* gamut, range; set (*of tools*); (mus) scale, gamut; **haut de gamme** top-of-the-line

Gand [gɑ̃] *m* Ghent

ganglion [gɑ̃glijɔ̃] *m* ganglion

gangrène [gɑ̃grɛn] *f* gangrene

gangrener [gɑ̃grəne] §2 *tr & ref* to gangrene

ganse [gɑ̃s] *f* braid, piping

gant [gɑ̃] *m* glove; **gant à laver** glove washcloth; **jeter le gant** to throw down the gauntlet; **prendre des gants pour** to put on kid gloves to; **relever le gant** to take up the gauntlet; **se donner des gants** to take all the credit

gantelet [gɑ̃tlɛ] *m* protective glove

ganter [gɑ̃te] *tr* to put gloves on (*s.o.*); fit, become (*s.o.; said of gloves*); **cela me gante** (coll) that suits me ‖ *intr*—**ganter de** to wear, take (*a certain size of glove*) ‖ *ref* to put on one's gloves

garage [garaʒ] *m* garage; turnout, passing place; service station, repair shop; used-car lot; **garage d'autobus** bus depot; **garage d'avions** hangar

garagiste [garaʒist] *m* garageman, mechanic; car dealer

ga·rant [garɑ̃] **-rante** [rɑ̃t] *adj* guaranteeing ‖ *mf* guarantor, warrantor; **se porter garant de** to guarantee ‖ *m* guarantee, warranty

garantie [garɑ̃ti] *f* guarantee, warranty

garantir [garɑ̃tir] *tr* to guarantee; vouch for; shelter, protect

garce [gars] *f* (coll) wench; (coll) bitch

garçon [garsɔ̃] *m* boy; young man; bachelor; apprentice; waiter; **être bon garçon** to be nice; **garçon de café** café waiter; **garçon de courses** errand boy; **garçon de recette** bank messenger; **garçon de salle** orderly; **garçon d'honneur** best man; **garçon manqué** tomboy; **petit garçon** boy (*two to thirteen years of age*); **vieux garçon** old bachelor

garçonne [garsɔn] *f* bachelor woman, female bachelor

garçonnet [garsɔnɛ] *m* little boy

garçon·nier [garsɔnje] **-nière** [njɛr] *adj* bachelor; tomboyish ‖ *f* bachelor apartment; tomboy

garde [gard] *m* guard, guardsman; keeper, custodian; **garde champêtre** constable; **garde de nuit** night watchman; **garde forestier** ranger ‖ *f* guard; custody; nurse; flyleaf; **de garde** on duty; **garde à vous!** (mil) attention!; **garde civique** national guard; **monter la garde** to go on guard duty; **prendre garde à** to look out for, to take notice of; **prendre garde de** to take care not to; to be careful to; **prendre garde que** to notice that; **prendre garde que . . . ne** + *subj* to be careful lest, to be careful that . . . not; **sur ses gardes** on one's guard

garde-à-vous [gardavu] *m invar* attention (*military position*)

garde-à-vue [gardavy] *f* custody, imprisonment

garde-barrière [gardəbarjɛr] *mf* (*pl* **gardes-barrière** or **gardes-barrières**) crossing guard

garde-bébé [gardəbebe] *mf* (*pl* **-bébés**) baby-sitter

garde-boue [gardəbu] *m invar* mudguard

garde-chasse [gardəʃas] *m* (*pl* **gardes-chasse** or **gardes-chasses**) gamekeeper

garde-corps [gardəkɔr] *m invar* guardrail; (naut) life line

garde-côte [gardəkot] *m* (*pl* **-côtes**) coast-guard cutter ‖ *m* (*pl* **gardes-côtes**) (obs) coastguardsman; (obs) coast guard

garde-feu [gardəfø] *m invar* fire screen

garde-fou [gardəfu] *m* (*pl* **-fous**) guardrail

garde-frein [gardəfrɛ̃] *m* (*pl* **gardes-frein** or **gardes-freins**) brakeman

garde-magasin [gardəmagazɛ̃] *m* (*pl* **gardes-magasin** or **gardes-magasins**) warehouseman

garde-malade [gardəmalad] *mf* (*pl* **gardes-malades**) nurse

garde-manger [gardəmɑ̃ʒe] *m invar* icebox; larder

garde-meuble [gardəmœbl] *m* (*pl* **-meuble** or **meubles**) furniture warehouse

garde-nappe [gardənap] *m* (*pl* **-nappe** or **nappes**) table mat, place mat

garde-pêche [gardəpɛʃ] *m* (*pl* **gardes-pêche**) fish warden ‖ *m invar* fishery service boat

garder [garde] §97 *tr* to guard; keep; **garder à vue** to hold in custody; **garder jusqu'à l'arrivée** (formula on envelope) hold for arrival; **garder la chambre** to stay in one's room; **garder la ligne** to keep one's figure ‖ *ref* to keep (*to stay free of deterioration*); **se garder de** to protect oneself from; watch out for; take care not to

garde-rats [gardəra] *m invar* rat guard

garderie [gardəri] *f* nursery; forest reserve

garde-robe [gardərɔb] *f* (*pl* **-robes**) wardrobe

gar·deur [gardœr] **-deuse** [døz] *mf* keeper, herder

garde-voie [gardəvwa] *m* (*pl* **gardes-voie** or **gardes-voies**) trackwalker

garde-vue [gardəvy] *m invar* eyeshade, visor

gar·dien [gardjɛ̃] **-dienne** [djɛn] *adj* guardian (*angel*) ‖ *mf* guard, guardian; keeper; caretaker; attendant (*at a garage*); **gardien de but** goalkeeper; **gardien de la paix** policeman

gardiennage [gardjɛnaʒ] *m* baby-sitting

gare [gar], [gar] *f* station; **gare aérienne** airport; **gare de fret** cargo terminal; **gare de triage** switchyard; **gare maritime** port, dock; **gare routière** or **gare d'autobus** bus station ‖ [gar] *interj* look out!; **sans crier gare** without warning

garer [gare] *tr* to park; put in the garage; (naut) to dock; (rr) to shunt; (coll) to secure (*e.g., a fortune*) ‖ *ref* to get out of

the way; park, park one's car; **se garer de** to look out for

gargariser [gargarize] *ref* to gargle

gargarisme [gargarism] *m* gargle

gargote [gargɔt] *f* (coll) hash house, beanery

gargouille [garguj] *f* gargoyle

gargouillement [gargujmɑ̃] *m* gurgling; rumbling (*in stomach*)

gargouiller [garguje] *intr* to gurgle

garnement [garnəmɑ̃] *m* scamp, bad boy

gar·ni -nie [garni] *adj* furnished (*room*) ‖ *m* furnished room; furnished house

garnir [garnir] *tr* to garnish, adorn; furnish; strengthen; line (*a brake*) ‖ *ref* to fill up (*said of crowded room, theater seats, etc.*)

garnison [garnizɔ̃] *f* garrison

garniture [garnityr] *f* garniture, decoration; fittings; accessories; complete set; (culin) garnish; **garniture de feu** fire irons; **garniture de lit** bedding

garrot [garo] *m* garrote (*instrument of torture*); (med) tourniquet; (zool) withers

garrotte [garɔt] *f* garrotte (*torture*)

garrotter [garɔte] *tr* to garrote; pinion

gars [ga] *m* (coll) lad; **c'est un gars!** (coll) he's a brave young man!

Gascogne [gaskɔɲ] *f* Gascony; **la Gascogne** Gascony

gasconnade [gaskɔnad] *f* gasconade; insincere invitation

gas-oil [gazwal] *m* diesel oil

Gaspésie [gaspezi] *f* Gaspé Peninsula

gaspiller [gaspije] *tr* to waste, squander

gastrique [gastrik] *adj* gastric

gastronomie [gastrɔnɔmi] *f* gastronomy

gâ·teau [gato] *adj invar* (coll) fond (*papa*); (coll) fairy (*godmother*) ‖ *m* (*pl* **-teaux**) cake; (coll) booty, loot; **gâteau de miel** honeycomb; **gâteau des Rois** twelfth-cake

gâte-métier [gatmetje] *m invar* undercutter

gâte-papier [gatpapje] *m invar* hack writer

gâter [gate] *tr* & *ref* to spoil

gâte-sauce [gatsos] *m invar* poor cook; kitchen boy

gâ·teux [gato] **-teuse** [tøz] *adj* (coll) senile ‖ *mf* (coll) dotard

gâtisme [gatism] *m* senility

gauche [goʃ] *adj* left; left-hand; crooked; awkward ‖ *f* left hand; left side; (pol) left wing; **à gauche** to the left; **à gauche, gauche!** (mil) left, face!

gauchement [goʃmɑ̃] *adv* clumsily, awkwardly

gau·cher [goʃe] **-chère** [ʃɛr] *adj* left-handed ‖ *mf* left-hander

gauchir [goʃir] *tr* & *intr* to warp

gauchiste [goʃist] *adj* & *mf* leftist

gaudriole [godrijɔl] *f* broad joke

gaufre [gofr] *f* waffle; **gaufre de miel** honeycomb

gaufrer [gofre] *tr* to emboss, figure; flute; corrugate

gaufrette [gofrɛt] *f* wafer

gaufrier [gofrije] *m* waffle iron

gaule [gol] *f* pole; **la Gaule** Gaul
gauler [gole] *tr* to bring down (*e.g., fruit*) with a pole
gau·lois [golwa] **-loise** [lwaz] *adj* Gaulish, Gallic; broad (*humor*) ‖ *m* Gaulish (*language*) ‖ (*cap*) *mf* Gaul ‖ (*cap*) *f* gauloise (*cigarette*)
gauloiserie [golwazri] *f* racy joking
gaulthèrie [goteri] *f* (bot) wintergreen
gausser [gose] *ref*—**se gausser de** (coll) to poke fun at
gaver [gave] *tr & ref* to cram
gavroche [gavrɔʃ] *mf* street urchin
gaz [gɑz] *m* gas; gaslight; gas company; **gaz d'échappement** exhaust; **gaz d'éclairage** illuminating gas; **gaz de combat** poison gas; **gaz en cylindre** bottled gas; **gaz hilarant** laughing gas; **gaz lacrimogène** tear gas; **mettre les gaz** (aut) to step on the gas
gaze [gɑz] *f* gauze; cheesecloth
ga·zé -zée [gɑze] *adj* gassed ‖ *mf* gas casualty
gazéifier [gɑzeifje] *tr* to gasify; carbonate, charge
gazelle [gɑzɛl] *f* gazelle
gazer [gɑze] *tr* to gas; cover with gauze; tone down ‖ *intr* (coll) to go full steam ahead; **ça gaze?** (coll) how goes it?
ga·zeux [gɑzø] **-zeuse** [zøz] *adj* gaseous; carbonated
ga·zier [gɑzje] **-zière** [zjɛr] *adj* gas ‖ *m* gasman; gas fitter
gazoduc [gɑzɔdyk] *m* gas pipe line
gazogène [gɑzɔʒɛn] *m* gas producer
gazoline [gɑzɔlin] *f* petroleum ether
gazomètre [gɑzɔmɛtr] *m* gasholder, gas tank
gazon [gɑzɔ̃] *m* lawn; turf, sod
gazonner [gɑzɔne] *tr* to sod
gazouiller [gazuje] *intr* to chirp, twitter; warble; babble
gazouillis [gazuji] *m* chirping; warbling; babbling
geai [ʒɛ] *m* jay
géant [ʒeɑ̃] **-géante** [ʒeɑ̃t] *adj* gigantic ‖ *m* giant ‖ *f* giantess
Gédéon [ʒedeɔ̃] *m* (Bib) Gideon
gei·gnard [ʒɛɲar] **-gnard** [ɲard] *adj* (coll) whining ‖ *mf* (coll) whiner
geignement [ʒɛɲmɑ̃] *m* whining, whimper
geindre [ʒɛ̃dr] §50 *intr* to whine, whimper; (coll) to complain
gel [ʒɛl] *m* frost, freezing; (chem) gel
gélatine [ʒelatin] *f* gelatin
gelée [ʒəle] *f* frost; (culin) jelly; **gelée blanche** hoarfrost
geler [ʒəle] §2 *tr, intr, & ref* to freeze; to congeal
gelure [ʒəlyr] *f* frostbite
Gémeaux [ʒemo] *mpl*—**les Gémeaux** (astr, astrol) Gemini
gémi·né -née [ʒemine] *adj* twin; coeducational (*school*)
gémir [ʒemir] §97 *intr* to groan, moan
gémissement [ʒemismɑ̃] *m* groaning, moaning

gemme [ʒɛm] *f* gem; bud; pine resin
gemmer [ʒɛmme] *tr* to tap for resin ‖ *intr* to bud
gê·nant [ʒɛnɑ̃] **-nante** [nɑ̃t] *adj* troublesome, embarrassing
gencive [ʒɑ̃siv] *f* (anat) gum
gendarme [ʒɑ̃darm] *m* policeman; military policeman; rock pinnacle; flaw (*of gem*); (coll) virago; (slang) red herring
gendarmerie [ʒɑ̃darmri] *f* police headquarters
gendre [ʒɑ̃dr] *m* son-in-law
gène [ʒɛn] *f* discomfort, embarrassment; **être dans la gêne** to be hard up; **être sans gêne** (coll) to be rude, casual
gène [ʒɛn] *m* (biol) gene
généalogie [ʒenealɔʒi] *f* genealogy
gêner [ʒɛne] §97 *tr* to embarrass; inconvenience; hinder; embarrass financially; pinch (*the feet*) ‖ *ref* to put oneself out, be inconvenienced; **ne vous gênez pas!** don't be disturbed; make yourself at home!
géné·ral -rale [ʒeneral] *adj & m* (*pl* **-raux** [ro]) general; **en général** in general; **général de brigade** brigadier general; **général de corps d'armée** lieutenant general; **général de division** major general ‖ *f* general's wife; (theat) opening night; **battre la générale** (mil) to sound the alarm
généralat [ʒenerala] *m* generalship
généralement [ʒeneralmɑ̃] *adv* generally
généraliser [ʒeneralize] *tr & intr* to generalize
généralissime [ʒeneralisim] *m* generalissimo
généraliste [ʒeneralist] *m* (med) general practitioner, family doctor
généralité [ʒeneralite] *f* generality; **la généralité de** the general run of
généra·teur [ʒeneratœr] **-trice** [tris] *adj* generating ‖ *m* boiler ‖ *f* generator
génération [ʒenerasjɔ̃] *f* generation; **les générations montantes** the generations to come
générer [ʒenere] §10 *tr* to generate
géné·reux [ʒenerø] **-reuse** [røz] *adj* generous; full (*bosom*); rich, full (*wine*)
générique [ʒenerik] *adj* generic ‖ *m* (mov) credit line
générosité [ʒenerozite] *f* generosity; **générosités** acts of generosity
Gênes [ʒɛn] *f* Genoa
genèse [ʒənɛz] *f* genesis
genet [ʒənɛ] *m* jennet (horse)
genêt [ʒənɛ] *m* (bot) broom; **genêt pineux** furze
génétique [ʒenetik] *adj* genetic ‖ *f* genetics
gê·neur [ʒɛnœr] **-neuse** [nøz] *mf* intruder, spoilsport
Genève [ʒənɛv] *f* Geneva
gene·vois [ʒənvwa], [ʒɛnvwa] **-voise** [vwaz] *adj* Genevan ‖ (*cap*) *mf* Genevan (*person*)
genévrier [ʒənevrije] *m* juniper
gé·nial -niale [ʒenjal] *adj* (*pl* **-niaux** [njo]) brilliant, ingenious; geniuslike, of genius

génie [ʒeni] *m* genius; bent, inclination; genie; engineer corps; **génie civil** civil engineering; **génie industriel** industrial engineering; **génie logiciel** software engineering; **génie maritime** naval construction

genièvre [ʒɛnjɛvr] *m* juniper; juniper berry; gin

génisse [ʒenis] *f* heifer

géni·tal -tale [ʒenital] *adj* (*pl* **-taux** [to]) genital

géni·teur [ʒenitœr] **-trice** [tris] *adj* engendering‖ *m* sire ‖ *f* genetrix

géni·tif [ʒenitif] **-tive** [tiv] *adj* & *m* genitive

génocide [ʒenɔsid] *m* genocide

gé·nois [ʒenwa] **-noise** [nwaz] *adj* Genoese ‖ (*cap*) *mf* Genoese

ge·nou [ʒənu] *m* (*pl* **-noux**) knee; (mach) joint

genouillère [ʒənujɛr] *f* kneecap; kneepad

genre [ʒɑr] *m* genre; genus; kind, sort; manner, way; fashion, taste; (gram) gender; **dans votre genre** like you; **de genre** (fa) genre; **faire du genre** (coll) to put on airs; **genre humain** humankind

gens [ʒɑ̃] (an immediately preceding adjective that varies in its feminine form is put in that form, and so are **certain, quel, tel,** and **tout** that precede that preceding adjective, but the noun remains masculine for pronouns that stand for it, for past participles that agree with it, and for adjectives in all other positions, e.g., **toutes ces vieilles gens sont intéressants** all these old people are interesting) *mpl* people; nations, e.g., **droit des gens** law of nations; men, e.g., **gens de lettres** men of letters; **gens d'affaires** business-people, businessmen; **gens d'Église** clergy; **gens de la presse** news persons, newsmen; **gens de mer** seamen; **gens de robe** bar; **jeunes gens** young people (*men and women*); young men

gent [ʒɑ̃] *f* (obs) nation, race

gentiane [ʒɑ̃sjan] *f* gentian

gen·til [ʒɑ̃ti] **-tille** [tij] *adj* nice, kind ‖ (*cap*) *m* pagan, gentile

gentilhomme [ʒɑ̃tijɔm] *m* (*pl* **gentils-hommes** [ʒɑ̃tizɔm]) nobleman

gentillesse [ʒɑ̃tijɛs] *f* niceness, kindness; **gentillesses** nice things, kind words

gentil·let [ʒɑ̃tijɛ] **-lette** [jɛt] *adj* rather nice

gentiment [ʒɑ̃timɑ̃] *adv* nicely; gracefully

gentleman [ʒɛntləman] *m* (*pl* **gentlemen** [ʒɛntləmɛn]) (nineteenth-century) gentleman

géographie [ʒeɔgrafi] *f* geography

geôle [ʒol] *f* jail

geô·lier [ʒolje] **-lière** [ljɛr] *mf* jailer

géologie [ʒeɔlɔʒi] *f* geology

géologique [ʒeɔlɔʒik] *adj* geologic(al)

géomé·tral -trale [ʒeɔmetral] *adj* (*pl* **-traux** [tro]) flat (*projection*)

géométrie [ʒeɔmetri] *f* geometry

géométrique [ʒeɔmetrik] *adj* geometric(al)

géophysique [ʒeɔfizik] *f* geophysics

géopolitique [ʒeɔpɔlitik] *f* geopolitics

Georges [ʒɔrʒ] *m* George

gérance [ʒerɑ̃s] *f* management; board of directors

géranium [ʒeranjɔm] *m* geranium

gé·rant [ʒerɑ̃] **-rante** [rɑ̃t] *mf* manager; **gérant d'une publication** managing editor

gerbe [ʒɛrb] *f* sheaf; spray (*of flowers; of water; of bullets*); shower (*of sparks*)

gerbée [ʒɛrbe] *f* straw

gerber [ʒɛrbe] *tr* to sheave; stack

gerce [ʒɛrs] *f* crack, split; clothes moth

gercer [ʒɛrse] §51 *tr, intr,* & *ref* to crack, chap

gerçure [ʒɛrsyr] *f* crack, chap

gérer [ʒere] §10 *tr* to manage, run

gériatrie [ʒerjatri] *f* geriatrics

ger·main [ʒɛrmɛ̃] **-maine** [mɛn] *adj* german, first (*cousin*)

germe [ʒɛrm] *m* germ

germer [ʒɛrme] *intr* to germinate

germicide [ʒɛrmisid] *adj* germicidal ‖ *m* germicide

gérondif [ʒerɔ̃dif] *m* gerund

gérontologie [ʒerɔ̃tɔlɔʒi] *f* gerontology

gésier [ʒesje] *m* gizzard

gésir [ʒezir] (used only in *inf; ger* **gisant;** 3d *sg pres ind* **git;** 1st, 2d, 3d *pl pres ind* **gisons, gisez, gisent;** *imperf ind* **gisais, gisait, gisions, gisiez, gisaient**) *intr* to lie; **ci-gît** here lies (*buried*)

gesse [ʒɛs] *f* vetch; **gesse odorante** sweet pea

gestation [ʒɛstɑsjɔ̃] *f* gestation

geste [ʒɛst] *m* gesture ‖ *f* medieval epic poem

gesticuler [ʒɛstikyle] *intr* to gesticulate

gestion [ʒɛstjɔ̃] *f* management, administration

gestionnaire [ʒɛstjɔnɛr] *adj* managing ‖ *mf* manager, administrator

geyser [ʒezɛr], [ʒejzɛr] *m* geyser

ghetto [geto], [gɛtto] *m* ghetto

gib·beux [ʒibø] **-beuse** [bøz] *adj* humped, hunchbacked

gibecière [ʒibsjɛr] *f* game bag; sack (*for papers, books, etc.*)

gibelotte [ʒiblɔt] *f* rabbit stew

gibet [ʒibɛ] *m* gibbet, gallows

gibier [ʒibje] *m* game; **gibier à plume** feathered game; **gibier de potence** gallows bird

giboulée [ʒibule] *f* shower; hailstorm

gibo·yeux [ʒibwajø] **giboyeuse** [ʒibwajøz] *adj* full of game

gibus [ʒibys] *m* opera hat

giclée [ʒikle] *f* spurt

gicler [ʒikle] *intr* to spurt

gicleur [ʒiklœr] *m* atomizer; (aut) spray nozzle (*of carburetor*)

gifle [ʒifl] *f* slap in the face

gifler [ʒifle] *tr* to slap in the face

gigantesque [ʒigɑ̃tɛsk] *adj* gigantic

gigogne [ʒigɔn] *adj*—**table gigogne** nest of tables ‖ (*cap*) *f*—**la mère Gigogne** the old woman who lived in a shoe

gigolo [ʒigɔlo] *m* (coll) gigolo

gigot [ʒigo] *m* leg of lamb, leg of mutton; **à gigot** leg-of-mutton (*sleeve*)

gigue [ʒig] *f* jig; haunch (*of venison*); (coll) leg; (slang) long-legged gawky girl

gilet [ʒilɛ] *m* vest; **gilet de sauvetage** life jacket; **gilet pare-balles** bulletproof vest; **pleurer dans le gilet de qn** (coll) to cry on s.o.'s shoulder

gimmick [gimik] *m* gadget

gingembre [ʒɛ̃ʒɑ̃br] *m* ginger

girafe [ʒiraf] *f* giraffe

giration [ʒirɑsjɔ̃] *f* gyration

girl [gœrl] *f* chorus girl

girofle [ʒirɔfl] *m* clove

giroflée [ʒirɔfle] *f* gillyflower

giron [ʒirɔ̃] *m* lap; bosom (*of the Church*)

girouette [ʒirwɛt] *f* weather vane

gisement [ʒizmɑ̃] *m* deposit; lode, seam; (naut) bearing; **gisement de pétrole** oil field

gi·tan [ʒitɑ̃] **-tane** [tan] *adj & mf* gypsy

gîte [ʒit] *m* lodging; lair, cover; deposit (*of ore*); **gîte à la noix** round steak ‖ *f* (naut) list; **donner de la gîte** to heel

gîter [ʒite] *intr* to lodge; lie, couch; perch; (naut) to list, heel ‖ *ref* to find shelter

givre [ʒivr] *m* rime, hoarfrost

givrer [ʒivre] *tr* to frost

glabre [glɑbr] *adj* beardless

glaçage [glasaʒ] *m* icing (*on cake*)

glace [glas] *f* ice; ice cream; mirror; plate glass; car window; glaze, icing; flaw (*of gem*); **être de glace** (fig) to be hard as stone; **glace au sirop** sundae; **glace panachée** Neapolitan ice cream; **rompre la glace** (fig) to break the ice

gla·cé -cée [glase] *adj* frozen; iced, chilled; icy, frosty; glazed, glossy

glacer [glase] §51 *tr* to freeze; chill; glaze; ice (*a cake*)

glacerie [glasri] *f* glass factory

glaciaire [glasjɛr] *adj* glacial

gla·cial -ciale [glasjal] *adj* (*pl* **-cials**) glacial

glacier [glasje] *m* glacier; ice-cream man

glacière [glasjɛr] *f* icehouse; icebox; freezer

glacis [glasi] *m* slope; ramp; (mil) glacis; (painting) glaze; (pol) buffer states

glaçon [glasɔ̃] *m* icicle; ice cube; ice floe; (fig) cold fish, iceberg

glaçure [glasyr] *f* (ceramics) glaze

gladiateur [gladjatœr] *m* gladiator

glaïeul [glajœl] *m* gladiola

glaire [glɛr] *f* white of egg; mucus

glaise [glɛz] *f* clay, loam

glaisière [glɛzjɛr] *f* clay pit

glaive [glɛv] *m* (lit) sword

gland [glɑ̃] *m* acorn; tassel

glande [glɑ̃d] *f* gland

glane [glan] *f* gleaning; cluster

glaner [glane] *tr* to glean

glanure [glanyr] *f* gleaning

glapir [glapir] *intr* to yelp, yap

glas [glɑ] *m* knell, tolling

glasnost [glasnɔst] *m* glasnost

glauque [glok] *adj & m* blue-green

glèbe [glɛb] *f* clod (*sod*); soil (*land*)

glène [glɛn] *f* (anat) socket; (naut) coil of rope

glissade [glisad] *f* slip; sliding; (dancing) glide; **glissade de terre** landslide; **glissade sur l'aile** (aer) sideslip; **glissade sur la queue** (aer) tail dive

glis·sant [glisɑ̃] **-sante** [sɑ̃t] *adj* slippery

glissement [glismɑ̃] *m* sliding; gliding; **glissement de terrain** landslide

glisser [glise] *tr* to slip; drop (*a word into s.o.'s ear*) ‖ *intr* to slip; slide; skid; glide ‖ *ref* to slip

glissière [glisjɛr] *f* slide, groove; **à glissière** sliding; zippered; **glissière de sécurité** guard rail

glissoire [gliswar] *f* slide (*on ice or snow*)

glo·bal -bale [glɔbal] *adj* (*pl* **-baux** [bo]) global; lump (*sum*)

globe [glɔb] *m* globe; **globe de feu** fireball; **globe de l'œil** eyeball

globule [glɔbyl] *m* globule; (physiol) corpuscle

gloire [glwar] *f* glory; pride; halo; **pour la gloire** for fun, for nothing; **se faire gloire de** to glory in

gloriette [glɔrjɛt] *f* arbor, summerhouse

glo·rieux [glɔrjø] **-rieuse** [rjøz] *adj* glorious; blessed; vain

glorifier [glɔrifje] *tr* to glorify ‖ §97 *ref*—**se glorifier de** to glory in

gloriole [glɔrjɔl] *f* vainglory

glose [gloz] *f* gloss; (coll) gossip

gloser [gloze] *intr* (coll) to gossip

glossaire [glɔsɛr] *m* glossary

glotte [glɔt] *f* glottis

glouglou [gluglu] *m* gurgle, glug; gobble-gobble; coo (*of dove*)

glouglouter [gluglute] *intr* to gurgle; gobble (*said of turkey*)

glousser [gluse] *intr* to cluck; chuckle

glou·ton [glutɔ̃] **-tonne** [tɔn] *adj* gluttonous ‖ *mf* glutton ‖ *m* (zool) glutton, wolverine

gloutonnerie [glutɔnri] *f* gluttony

glu [gly] *f* birdlime; (coll) trap

gluant [glyɑ̃] **gluante** [glyɑ̃t] *adj* sticky, gummy; (fig) tenacious

glucose [glykoz] *m* glucose

glycérine [gliserin] *f* glycerine

gnognote [ɲɔɲɔt] *f* (coll) junk

gnome [gnom] *m* gnome

gnomon [gnɔmɔ̃] *m* sundial

gnon [ɲɔ̃] *m* (slang) blow, punch

go [go]—**tout de go** (coll) straight off, at once

goal [gol] *m* goalkeeper

gobelet [gɔblɛ] *m* cup, tumbler, mug; **gobelets utilisés** (public sign) used paper drinking cups

gobe-mouches [gɔbmuʃ] *m invar* (zool) flycatcher; (fig) sucker, gull

gober [gɔbe] *tr* to gulp down, gobble; suck (*an egg*); (coll) to swallow, be a sucker for

goberger [gɔbɛrʒe] §38 *ref* (coll) to guzzle; (coll) to live in comfort

gobeter [gɔbte] §34 *tr* to plaster, fill in the cracks of

go·beur [gɔbœr] **-beuse** [bøz] *mf* (coll) sucker, gullible person

godet [gɔdɛ] *m* cup; basin; bucket (*of water wheel*); (bot) calyx; **à godets** flared

godille [gɔdij] *f* scull, oar; **à la godille** without rhyme or reason, erratically

godiller [gɔdije] *intr* to scull

godillot [gɔdijo] *m* (slang) clodhopper (*shoe*)

goéland [gɔelɑ̃] *m* seal gull

goélette [gɔelɛt] *f* (naut) schooner

goémon [gɔemɔ̃] *m* seaweed

gogo [gɔgo] *m* (coll) sucker, gull; **à gogo** (coll) galore

gogue·nard [gɔgnar] **-narde** [nard] *adj* jeering, mocking

goguenarder [gɔgnarde] *intr* to jeer

goguette [gɔgɛt] *f*—**en goguette** (coll) tipsy

goinfre [gwɛ̃fr] *m* glutton, guzzler

goitre [gwatr] *m* goiter

golf [gɔlf] *m* golf

golfe [gɔlf] *m* gulf

golfeur [gɔlfœr] *m* golfer

gomme [gɔm] *f* gum; eraser; **gomme à claquer** bubble gum; **gomme à mâcher** chewing gum; **gomme d'épinette** spruce gum; **gomme de sapin** balsam; **gomme élastique** India rubber; **mettre la gomme** (slang) to speed it up

gomme-laque [gɔmlak] *f* (*pl* **gommes-laques**) shellac

gommelaquer [gɔmlake] *tr* to shellac

gommer [gɔme] *tr* to gum; erase ‖ *intr* to stick, gum up

gond [gɔ̃] *m* hinge; **sortir de ses gonds** (coll) to fly off the handle

gondole [gɔ̃dɔl] *f* gondola

gondoler [gɔ̃dɔle] *intr & ref* to buckle up

gondolier [gɔ̃dɔlje] *m* gondolier

gonfalon [gɔ̃falɔ̃] *m* pennant

gonflement [gɔ̃fləmɑ̃] *m* swelling

gonfler [gɔ̃fle] *tr* to swell, inflate ‖ *intr* to swell up, puff up ‖ *ref* to become inflated; (coll) to swell up with pride

gonfleur [gɔ̃flœr] *m* tire pump

gong [gɔ̃g] *m* gong

gonococcie [gɔnokɔksi] *f* gonorrhea

goret [gɔrɛ] *m* piglet; (coll) slob

gorge [gɔrʒ] *f* throat; bust, breasts (*of woman*); gorge; **à pleine gorge** or **à gorge déployée** at the top of one's voice; **avoir la gorge serrée** to have a lump in one's throat; **faire des gorges chaudes de** (coll) to scoff at; to gloat over; **rendre gorge** to make restitution

gorger [gɔrʒe] §38 *tr & ref* to gorge, stuff

gorille [gɔrij] *m* gorilla; (slang) strong-arm man, bodyguard; (slang) bouncer (*in a night club*)

gosier [gozje] *m* throat, gullet; **à plein gosier** loudly, lustily; **gosier serré** with one's heart in one's mouth; **s'humecter** or **se rincer le gosier** (slang) to wet one's whistle

gosse [gɔs] *mf* (coll) kid, youngster

gothique [gɔtik] *adj* Gothic ‖ *m* Gothic (*language*); Gothic art ‖ *f* black letter, Old English

gouailler [gwɑje] *tr* to jeer at ‖ *intr* to jeer

gouape [gwap] *f* (slang) hoodlum, blackguard

gouaper [gwape] *intr* (slang) to lead a disreputable life

goudron [gudrɔ̃] *m* tar; **goudron de houille** coal tar

goudronner [gudrɔne] *tr* to tar

gouffre [gufr] *m* gulf, abyss; whirlpool

gouge [guʒ] *f* gouge; harlot

gouger [guʒe] §38 *tr* to gouge

gouine [gwin] *f* (slang) dyke (*homosexual woman*)

goujat [guʒa] *m* boor, cad

goujon [guʒɔ̃] *m* gudgeon, pin; pintle (*of hinge*); dowel; (ichth) gudgeon; **taquiner le goujon** to go fishing

goulasch [gulaʃ] *m & f* goulash

goule [gul] *f* ghoul

goulet [gulɛ] *m* narrows, sound; **goulet d'étranglement** bottleneck

goulot [gulo] *m* neck (*of bottle*); **boire au goulot** to drink right out of the bottle

gou·lu -lue [guly] *adj* gluttonous

goupil [gupi] *m* (obs) fox

goupille [gupij] *f* pin; **goupille fendue** cotter pin

goupiller [gupije] *tr* to cotter; (slang) to contrive, wangle

goupillon [gupijɔ̃] *m* bottle brush; sprinkler (*for holy water*); **goupillon nettoie-pipes** pipe cleaner

gourd [gur] **gourde** [gurd] *adj* numb (*with cold*) ‖ *adj fem* (coll) dumb ‖ *f* gourd; canteen, metal flask; (coll) dumbbell

gourdin [gurdɛ̃] *m* cudgel

gourgandine [gurgɑ̃din] *f* (hist) low-necked bodice; (coll) trollop

gour·mand [gurmɑ̃] **-mande** [mɑ̃d] *adj & mf* gourmand, gourmet

gourmander [gurmɑ̃de] *tr* to bawl out

gourmandise [gurmɑ̃diz] *f* gluttony; love of good food; **gourmandises** delicacies

gourme [gurm] *f* impetigo; **jeter sa gourme** (coll) to sow one's wild oats

gour·mé -mée [gurme] *adj* stiff, stuckup

gourmet [gurmɛ] *m* gourmet

gourmette [gurmɛt] *f* curb (*of harness*); curb watch chain

gousse [gus] *f* pod; clove (*of garlic*)

gousset [guse] *m* vest pocket; fob, watch pocket (*in trousers*)

goût [gu] *m* taste; flavor; sense of taste; **au goût du jour** up to date

goûter [gute] *m* afternoon snack ‖ *tr* to taste; sample; relish, enjoy ‖ *intr* to have a bite to eat; **goûter à** to sample, try; **goûter de** (coll) to try out (*e.g., a trade*)

goutte [gut] *f* drop; drip; (pathol) gout; **boire la goutte** (coll) to take a nip of brandy; **la goutte d'eau qui a fait déborder le vase** the straw which broke the camel's back; **ne . . . goutte** §90 (used

only with **comprendre, connaître, entendre,** and **voir**) (archaic & hum) not at all, e.g., **je n'y vois goutte** I don't see at all; **tomber goutte à goutte** to drip
goutte-à-goutte [gutagut] *m invar* (med) dropping bottle *(for intravenous drip)*; (med) I.V. stand
gouttelette [gutlɛt] *f* droplet
goutter [gute] *intr* to drip
gouttière [gutjɛr] *f* eavestrough, gutter; (med) splint
gouvernail [guvɛrnɑj] *m* rudder, helm; **gouvernail de profondeur** (aer) elevator
gouver·nant [guvɛrnɑ̃] **-nante** [nɑ̃t] *adj* governing ‖ **gouvernants** *mpl* powers that be, rulers ‖ *f* governess; housekeeper
gouverne [guvɛrn] *f* guidance; **gouvernes** (aer) controls; **pour votre gouverne** for your guidance
gouvernement [guvɛrnəmɑ̃] *m* government; **gouvernement fantoche** puppet government
gouvernemen·tal -tale [guvɛrnəmɑ̃tal] *adj* (*pl* **-taux** [to]) governmental
gouverner [guvɛrne] *tr* to govern, control; steer; manage with care ‖ *intr* to govern; (naut) to answer to the helm
gouverneur [guvɛrnœr] *m* governor; tutor; director (*e.g., of a bank*)
goyave [gɔjav] *f* guava
goyavier [gɔjavje] *m* guava tree
Graal [gral] *m* Grail
grabat [graba] *m* pallet, straw bed
grâce [grɑs] *f* grace; **de bonne grâce** willingly; **de grâce** for mercy's sake; **mauvaise grâce** unwillingly; **faire grâce à** to pardon; to spare; **faites-moi la grâce de** be kind enough to; **grâce!** mercy!; **grâce à** thanks to
gracier [grasje] *tr* to reprieve
gra·cieux [grasjø] **-cieuse** [sjøz] *adj* gracious; graceful
gracile [grasil] *adj* slender, slim
gradation [gradɑsjɔ̃] *f* gradation
grade [grad] *m* grade; rank; degree (*in school*); **en prendre pour son grade** (coll) to get called down
gra·dé -dée [grade] *adj* noncommissioned ‖ *mf* noncommissioned officer
gradient [gradjɑ̃] *m* gradient
gradin [gradɛ̃] *m* tier
graduation [gradɥasjɔ̃] *f* graduation
gra·dué -duée [gradɥe] *adj* graduated (*scale*); graded (*lessons*) ‖ *mf* graduate
gra·duel -duelle [gradɥɛl] *adj & m* gradual
graduer [gradɥe] *tr* to graduate
grailler [grɑje] *intr* to speak hoarsely; sound the horn to recall the dogs
grain [grɛ̃] *m* grain; particle, speck; bean; squall; **grain de beauté** beauty spot, mole; **grain de raisin** grape; **grains** grain, cereals; **veiller au grain** (fig) to be on one's guard
graine [grɛn] *f* seed; **graine d'anis** aniseed; **mauvaise graine** (coll) incorrigible youth; **monter en graine** to run to seed; to soon be on the shelf (*said of young girl*); (coll)

to grow; **prendre de la graine de** (coll) to follow the example of
graissage [grɛsaʒ] *m* (aut) lubrication
graisse [grɛs] *f* grease; fat; mother (*of wine*)
graisser [grɛse], [grese] *tr* to grease; lubricate; get grease stains on; **graisser la patte à qn** (coll) to grease s.o.'s palm
grais·seux [grɛsø] **-seuse** [søz] *adj* greasy
grammaire [gramɛr] *f* grammar
grammai·rien [gramɛrjɛ̃] **-rienne** [rjɛn] *mf* grammarian
grammati·cal -cale [gramatikal] *adj* (*pl* **-caux** [ko]) grammatical
gramme [gram] *m* gram
grand [grɑ̃] **grande** [grɑ̃d] *adj* tall, e.g., **un homme grand** a tall man ‖ (when standing before noun) *adj* large; great; important; tall; high (*priest; mass; society; explosive*), vain, empty (*words*); broad (*daylight*); grand (*dignitary; officer; lady*); main (*road*); long (*arms or legs*); greater, e.g., **le Grand Londres** Greater London; (fig) big (*heart*) ‖ *m* adult, grownup; grandee, noble; **en grand** life-size; on a grand scale; enlarged (*copy*); wide (*open*); **grands et petits** young and old ‖ **grand** *adv*—**voir grand** to see big, to envisage great projects
grand-chose [grɑ̃ ʃoz] *mf invar*—**pas grand-chose** (coll) nobody, person of no importance ‖ *adv*—**pas grand-chose** not much
grand-duc [grɑ̃dyk] *m* (*pl* **grands-ducs**) grand duke
grand-duché [grɑ̃dyʃe] *m* (*pl* **grands-duchés**) grand duchy
Grande-Bretagne [grɑ̃dbrətaɲ] *f* Great Britain; **la Grande-Bretagne** Great Britain
grande-duchesse [grɑ̃dədyʃɛs] *f* (*pl* **grandes-duchesses**) grand duchess
grande-let [grɑ̃dlə] **-lette** [lɛt] *adj* tall for his or her age
grandement [grɑ̃dmɑ̃] *adv* highly; handsomely; **se tromper grandement** to be very mistaken
grand-erre [grɑ̃tɛr] *adv* at full speed
gran·det [grɑ̃dɛ] **-dette** [dɛt] *adj* rather big; rather tall
grandeur [grɑ̃dœr] *f* size; height; greatness; (astr) magnitude
grandiose [grɑ̃djoz] *adj* grandiose
grandir [grɑ̃dir] *tr* to enlarge; increase ‖ *intr* to grow; grow up
grandissement [grɑ̃dismɑ̃] *m* magnification, enlargement; growth
grand-livre [grɑ̃livr] *m* (*pl* **grands-livres**) ledger
grand-maman [grɑ̃mamɑ̃] *f* (*pl* **-mamans**) grandma
grand-mère [grɑ̃mɛr] *f* (*pl* **-mères** or **grands-mères**) grandmother; (coll) old lady
grand-messe [grɑ̃mɛs] *f* (pl **-messes**) high mass
grand-oncle [grɑ̃tɔ̃kl] *m* (*pl* **grands-oncles**) granduncle
Grand-Orient [grɑ̃tɔrjɑ̃] *m* grand lodge

grand-papa [grãpapa] *m* (*pl* **grands-papas**) grandpa

grand-peine [grãpɛn]—**à grand-peine** with great difficulty

grand-père [grãpɛr] *m* (*pl* **grands-pères**) grandfather

grand-route [grãrut] *f* (*pl* **-routes**) highway

grand-rue [grãry] *f* (*pl* **-rues**) main street

Grands Lacs [grãlak] *mpl* Great Lakes

grands-parents [grãparã] *mpl* grandparents

grand-tante [grãtãt] *f* (*pl* **-tantes**) grandaunt

grange [grãʒ] *f* barn

granit [grani], [granit] *m* granite

granite [granit] *m* granite

granulaire [granylɛr] *adj* granular

granule [granyl] *m* granule

granu·lé -lée [granyle] *adj* granulated ‖ *m* little pill; medicine in granulated form

granuler [granyle] *tr* & *ref* to granulate

graphie [grafi] *f* spelling

graphique [grafik] *adj* graphic(al) ‖ *m* graph

graphite [grafit] *m* graphite

grappe [grap] *f* bunch, cluster; string (*of onions*); **une grappe humaine** a bunch of people

grappillage [grapijaʒ] *m* gleaning; (coll) graft

grappiller [grapije] *tr* & *intr* (*in vineyard*) to glean; (coll) to pilfer

grappillon [grapijõ] *m* little bunch

grappin [grapɛ̃] *m* grapnel; **jeter** or **mettre le grappin sur qn** (coll) to get one's hooks into s.o.

gras [grɑ] **grasse** [grɑs] *adj* fat; greasy; rich (*soil*); carnival (*days*); smutty (*stories*); (typ) bold-faced ‖ *m* fatty part; calf (*of leg*); foggy weather; **au gras** with meat sauce; **faire gras** to eat meat ‖ **gras** *adv*—**parler gras** to speak with uvular r; to tell smutty stories

gras-double [grɑdubl] *m* (*pl* **-doubles**) tripe

grassement [grɑsmã] *adv* comfortably; generously, handsomely

grasseyer [grɑseje] §32 *tr* to make (*one's r's*) uvular ‖ *intr* to speak with uvular r

grassouil·let [grɑsujɛ] **-lette** [jɛt] *adj* (coll) plump, chubby

gratification [gratifikɑsjõ] *f* tip, gratuity

gratifier [gratifje] *tr* to favor, reward; **gratifier qn de q.ch.** to bestow s.th. upon s.o.

gratin [gratɛ̃] *m* cooking au gratin; dish of food prepared au gratin; friction surface (*of a matchbox*); (culin) crust; (coll) upper crust; **au gratin** au gratin (*breaded and/or with grated cheese*)

gratiner [gratine] *tr* to cook au gratin ‖ *intr* to brown, crisp

gratis [gratis] *adv* gratis

gratitude [gratityd] *f* gratitude

gratte [grat] *f* scraper; (coll) graft

gratte-ciel [gratsjɛl] *m invar* skyscraper

gratte-cul [gratky] *m invar* (bot) hip

gratte-dos [gratdo] *m invar* back scratcher

gratte-papier [gratpapje] *m invar* (coll) pencil pusher, office drudge

gratte-pieds [gratpje] *m invar* shoe scraper

gratter [grate] *tr* to scratch; scratch out; scrape up, scrape together; itch; (coll) to pocket ‖ *intr* to knock gently ‖ *ref* to scratch

grattoir [gratwar] *m* scraper; knife eraser

gra·tuit [gratɥi] **-tuite** [tɥit] *adj* free of charge; gratuitous; unfounded

gratuité [gratɥite] *f* gratuity

grave [grav], [grɑv] *adj* grave; low (*frequency*); (mus) bass; (mus) flat

grave·leux [gravlø] **-leuse** [løz] *adj* gravelly, gritty; smutty, licentious

gravelle [gravɛl] *f* (pathol) gravel

graver [grave] *tr* to engrave; cut (*a phonograph record*)

graveur [gravœr] *m* engraver; etcher

gravier [gravje] *m* gravel

gravillons [gravijõ] *mpl* gravel (*on roadway*)

gravir [gravir] *tr* to climb, climb up

gravitation [gravitɑsjõ] *f* gravitation

gravité [gravite] *f* gravity

graviter [gravite] *intr* to gravitate

gravure [gravyr] *f* engraving; etching; cutting (*of phonograph record*)

gré [gre] *m* will; **à son gré** to one's liking; **bon gré mal gré** willy-nilly; **de bon gré** willingly; **de gré à gré** by mutual consent; **de gré ou de force** willy-nilly; **savoir (bon) gré de** to be grateful for; **savoir mauvais gré de** to be displeased with

grec grecque [grɛk] *adj* Greek; classic (*profile*) ‖ *m* Greek (*language*) ‖ *f* Greek fret ‖ (*cap*) *mf* Greek

Grèce [grɛs] *f* Greece; **la Grèce** Greece

gre·din [grədɛ̃] **-dine** [din] *mf* scoundrel

gréement [gremã] *m* (naut) rigging

gréer [gree] *tr* (naut) to rig

greffe [grɛf] *m* (jur) office of the court clerk ‖ *f* grafting; (hort, med) graft; **greffe du cœur** heart transplant; **greffe du rein** kidney transplant

greffer [grɛfe] *tr* to graft; add ‖ *ref* to be added

greffier [grɛfje] *m* clerk of court, recorder; court reporter

greffon [grɛfõ] *m* (hort) graft; (surg) transplant

grégaire [gregɛr] *adj* gregarious

grège [grɛʒ] *adj* raw (*silk*) ‖ *f* raw silk

grégo·rien [gregɔrjɛ̃] **-rienne** [rjɛn] *adj* Gregorian

grêle [grɛl] *adj* slender, slim; thin, high-pitched ‖ *f* hail; (fig) shower

grê·lé -lée [grɛle] *adj* pockmarked

grêler [grɛle] *tr* to damage by hail; pockmark ‖ *intr* (fig) to rain down thick; **il grêle** it is hailing

grêlon [grɛlõ] *m* hailstone

grelot [grəlo] *m* sleigh bell

grelottement [grəlɔtmã] *m* shivering, trembling; jingle, jingling

grelotter [grəlɔte] *intr* to shiver, tremble; jingle

grenade [grənad] *f* grenade; (bot) pomegranate; **grenade à main** hand grenade; **grenade éclairante** flare; **grenade lacrymogène** tear bomb; **grenade sous-marine** depth charge

grenadier [grənadje] *m* pomegranate tree; (mil) grenadier

grenadine [grənadin] *f* grenadine

grenaille [grənɑj] *f* shot; **grenaille de plomb** buckshot

grenailler [grənɑje] *tr* to granulate

grenat [grəna] *adj invar* & *m* garnet

grenier [grənje] *m* attic, loft; granary

grenouille [grənuj] *f* frog; **grenouille mugissante** or **taureau** bullfrog; **manger la grenouille** (coll) to make off with the money, to abscond

grenouillère [grənujɛr] *f* marsh

gre·nu -nue [grəny] *adj* full of grain; grainy (*leather*); granular (*marble*) ‖ *m* graininess; granularity

grès [grɛ] *m* gritstone, sandstone; stoneware; terra cotta (*for drainpipes*)

grésil [grezil] *m* sleet

grésillement [grezijmɑ̃] *m* sizzling; chirping (*of cricket*)

grésiller [grezije] *tr* to scorch, shrivel up ‖ *intr* to sizzle, sputter; **il grésille** it is sleeting

grève [grɛv] *f* beach; strike; (*armor*) greave; **faire (la) grève** to strike; **faire la grève de la faim** to go on a hunger strike; **grève avec occupation de l'usine, grève avec occupation des locaux** sitdown strike; **grève de solidarité** sympathy strike; **grève du zèle** work-to-rule action, job action (*rigid application of rules*); **grève improvisée, grève inattendue, grève surprise** walkout; **grève perlée** slowdown; **grève sauvage, grève spontanée** wildcat strike; **grève sur le tas** sitdown strike; **grève tournante** strike in one industry at a time or for several hours at a time; **se mettre en grève** to go on strike

grever [grəve] §2 *tr* to burden; assess (*property*); **grever de** to burden with

gréviste [grevist] *mf* striker

gribouillage [gribujaʒ] *m* (coll) scribble, scrawl; (coll) daub (*in painting*)

gribouiller [gribuje] *tr* (coll) to scribble off (*a note*) ‖ *intr* (coll) to scribble, scrawl; (coll) to daub

grief [grijɛf] *m* grievance, complaint; **faire grief de q.ch. à qn** to complain to s.o. about s.th.

grièvement [grijɛvmɑ̃] *adv* seriously, badly

griffe [grif] *f* claw, talon; signature stamp; (bot) tendril; (mach) hook, grip; **faire ses griffes** to sharpen its claws (*said of cat*); **griffe à papiers** paper clip; **porter la griffe de** to carry the stamp of; **tomber sous la griffe de** (coll) to fall into the clutches of

griffer [grife] *tr* to claw, scratch

griffon [grifɔ̃] *m* griffin

griffonner [grifɔne] *tr* to scrawl; (coll) to scribble off (*a letter*)

grignoter [griɲɔte] *tr* to nibble on or at; wear down (*e.g., the enemy*) ‖ *intr* (coll) to make a little profit, get a cut

gril [gril] *m* gridiron, grid, grill; (theat) upper flies; **être sur le gril** (coll) to be on tenterhooks

grillade [grijad] *f* grilled meat; broiling

grillage [grijaʒ] *m* grating, latticework, trellis; broiling; roasting; toasting; burning out (*of a light bulb*); (tex) singeing

grille [grij] *f* grille; grate, grating; bars; railing; gate; squares (*of crossword puzzle*); grid (*of storage battery and vacuum tube*); **grille d'entrée** iron gate; **grille des salaires** salary schedule

grille-pain [grijpɛ̃] *m invar* toaster

grille-pain-four [grijpɛ̃fur] *m* toaster oven

griller [grije] *tr* to grill, broil; put a grill on; roast (*coffee*); toast (*bread*); burn out (*a fuse, lamp, electric iron, etc.*); singe; scorch; nip (*a bud, as the frost does*) ‖ *intr* to grill; toast; burn out; **griller de** to long to

grilloir [grijwar] *m* roaster; (culin) broiler

grillon [grijɔ̃] *m* cricket

grimace [grimas] *f* grimace; **faire des grimaces** to make faces; smirk, simper; be full of wrinkles

grimacer [grimase] §51 *intr* to grimace; make wrong creases

grime [grim] *m* dotard, old fogey

grimer [grime] *tr* to make up (*an actor*) ‖ *ref* to make up

grimper [grɛ̃pe] *tr* to climb ‖ *intr* to climb; **grimper à** or **sur** to climb up on

grimpe·reau [grɛ̃pro] *m* (*pl* -**reaux**) (orn) tree creeper

grim·peur [grɛ̃pœr] -**peuse** [pøz] *adj* climbing ‖ *m* climber

grincement [grɛ̃smɑ̃] *m* grating

grincer [grɛ̃se] §51 *tr* to gnash, grit (*the teeth*) ‖ *intr* to grate, grind, creak; scratch (*said of pen*)

grin·cheux [grɛ̃ʃø] -**cheuse** [ʃøz] *adj* grumpy ‖ *mf* grumbler, sorehead

gringa·let [grɛ̃gale] -**lette** [lɛt] *adj* weak, puny ‖ *m* (coll) weakling, shrimp

griot [grijo] **griotte** [grijɔt] *mf* witch doctor ‖ *m* seconds (*in milling grain*) ‖ *f* sour cherry

grippe [grip] *f* grippe; **prendre en grippe** to take a dislike to

grippeminaud [gripmino] *m* (coll) smoothly, hypocrite

gripper [gripe] *tr* to snatch; (slang) to steal ‖ *intr* (mach) to jam ‖ *ref* to get stuck

grippe-sou [gripsu] *m* (*pl* -**sou** or -**sous**) (coll) tightwad, skinflint

gris [gri] **grise** [griz] *adj* gray; cloudy; brown (*paper*); (coll) tipsy

grisailler [grizɑje] *tr* to paint gray ‖ *intr* to turn gray

grisâtre [grizɑtr] *adj* grayish

griser [grize] *tr* to paint gray; (coll) to intoxicate; **les succès l'ont grisé** (coll) success has gone to his head ‖ *ref* to get tipsy; **se griser de** (coll) to revel in

griserie [grizri] *f* intoxication

grisette [grizɛt] *f* gay working girl

gris-gris [grigri] *m* lucky charm

grisonner [grizɔne] *intr* to turn gray

grisotte [grizɔt] *f* clock (*in stocking*)

grisou [grizu] *m* firedamp

grive [griv] *f* thrush; **grive mauvis** song thrush; **grive migratoire** (*Turdus migratorius*) robin

grive·lé -lée [grivle] *adj* speckled

grivèlerie [grivɛlri] *f* sneaking out without paying the check

gri·vois [grivwa] **-voise** [vwaz] *adj* spicy, off-color

grizzly [grizli] *m* grizzly bear

Groënland [grɔɛnlãd] *m*—**le Groënland** Greenland

grog [grɔg] *m* grog

gro·gnard [grɔɲar] **-gnarde** [ɲard] *adj* grumbling ‖ *mf* grumbler

grogner [grɔɲe] *intr* to grunt, growl; grumble, grouch

gro·gnon [grɔɲɔ̃] **-gnonne** [ɲɔn] *adj* grouchy, grumbling ‖ *mf* grouch, grumbler

grognonner [grɔɲɔne] *intr* to grunt; be a complainer, whine

groin [grwɛ̃] *m* snout; (coll) ugly mug

grommeler [grɔmle] §34 *tr* & *intr* to mutter, grumble; growl

grondement [grɔ̃dmã] *m* growl; rumble

gronder [grɔ̃de] §97 *tr* to scold ‖ *intr* to scold; growl; grumble

gron·deur [grɔ̃dœr] **-deuse** [døz] *adj* scolding; grumbling ‖ *mf* grumbler

groom [grum] *m* bellhop, pageboy

gros [gro] **grosse** [gros] *adj* big (*with child*); heavy (*heart*) ‖ (when standing before noun) *adj* big, large, bulky; coarse; plain (*common sense*); main (*walls*); high (*stakes*); rich (*merchant*); booming (*voice*); bad (*weather*); heavy, rough (*sea*); swear (*words*) ‖ *m* bulk, main part; **en gros** wholesale; roughly, without going into detail; **faire le gros et le détail** to deal in wholesale and retail ‖ *f* see **grosse** ‖ **gros** *adv* much, a great deal; (fig) probably

gros-bec [grobɛk] *m* (*pl* **-becs**) grosbeak

groseille [grozɛj] *f* currant; **groseille à maquereau** gooseberry

groseillier [grozɛje] *m* currant bush

Gros-Jean [groʒɑ̃] *m*—**être Gros-Jean comme devant** to be in the same fix again

gros-porteur [groportœr] *m* (*pl* **-porteurs**) (aer) jumbo jet

grosse [gros] *f* fat woman; (com) gross; (law) engrossed copy

grosserie [grosri] *f* silver dishes

grossesse [grosɛs] *f* pregnancy

grosseur [grosœr] *f* size; swelling, tumor

gros·sier [grosje] **-sière** [sjɛr] *adj* coarse; crude, rude; vulgar, ribald; glaring (*error*)

grossièrement [grosjɛrmã] *adv* grossly

grossièreté [grosjɛrte] *f* coarseness, grossness, vulgarity

grossir [grosir] *tr* to enlarge; increase ‖ *intr* to grow larger; put on weight

grossis·sant [grosisɑ̃] **-sante** [sɑ̃t] *adj* swelling; magnifying (*glasses*)

grossiste [grosist] *m* wholesaler, jobber

grotesque [grɔtɛsk] *adj* grotesque ‖ *mf* grotesque person ‖ *m* grotesque ‖ *f* grotesque (*ornament*)

grotte [grɔt] *f* grotto

grouillement [grujmã] *m* swarming; rumbling

grouiller [gruje] *intr* to swarm; **grouiller de** to teem with ‖ *ref* (slang) to get a move on

grouillot [grujo] *m* (coll) gofer, errand boy

groupe [grup] *m* group; (mach & mil) unit; **groupe de pression** lobby; **groupe d'experts** think tank; **groupe franc** (mil) commando; **groupe sanguin** blood type

groupement [grupmã] *m* grouping; organization

grouper [grupe] *tr* & *ref* to group

gruau [gryo] *m* (*pl* **gruaux**) groats; (culin) gruel; (orn) small crane

grue [gry] *f* crane; (orn) crane; (coll) tart

gruger [gryʒe] §38 *tr* to sponge on, exploit; crunch

grume [grym] *f* bark; **en grume** rough (*timber*)

gru·meau [grymo] *m* (*pl* **-meaux**) gob; curd

grumeler [grymle] §34 *intr* to curdle, clot

gruyère [gryjɛr] *m* Gruyère cheese

guatémaltèque [gwatemaltɛk] *adj* Guatemalan ‖ (*cap*) *mf* Guatemalan

gué [ge] *m* ford, crossing; **sonder le gué** (coll) to see how the land lies ‖ *interj* hurrah!

guéable [geabl] *adj* fordable

guéer [gee] *tr* to ford; water (*a horse*)

guelte [gɛlt] *f* commission, percentage

guenille [gənij] *f* ragged garment; **en guenilles** in tatters

guenon [gənɔ̃] *f* female monkey; long-tailed monkey; (coll) hag, old bag

guépard [gepar] *m* cheetah

guêpe [gɛp] *f* wasp

guère [gɛr] §90 *adv* hardly ever; **ne . . . guère** hardly, scarcely; hardly ever; not very; **ne . . . guère de** hardly any; **ne . . . guère que** hardly any but; hardly anyone but; **ne . . . plus guère** hardly ever any more; not much longer

guères [gɛr] *adv* (poetic) var of **guère**

guéret [gerɛ] *m* fallow land

guéridon [geridɔ̃] *m* pedestal table

guérilla [gerija] *f* guerrilla warfare

guérillero [gerijero] *m* guerrilla

guérir [gerir] *tr* to cure ‖ *intr* to get well; get better; heal ‖ *ref* to cure oneself; recover

guérison [gerizɔ̃] *f* cure, healing; recovery

guérissable [gerisabl] *adj* curable

guéris·seur [gerisœr] **-seuse** [søz] *mf* healer; quack

guérite [gerit] *f* sentry box; (rr) signal box; **guérite téléphonique** call box

guerre [gɛr] *f* war; **de guerre lasse** for the sake of peace and quiet; **être de bonne guerre** to be fair, to be cricket; **guerre à outrance** all-out war; **Guerre de Troie** Trojan War; **guerre d'usure** war of attrition; **guerre éclair** blitzkrieg; **guerre froide** cold war; **guerre presse-bouton** push-button war

guer·rier [gɛrje] **-rière** [rjɛr] *adj* warlike, martial ‖ *m* warrior ‖ *f* amazon

guerroyant [gɛrwajɑ̃] **guerroyante** [gɛrwajɑ̃t] *adj* warlike, bellicose

guerroyer [gɛrwaje] §47 *intr* to make war

guer·royeur [gɛrwajœr] **-royeuse** [wajøz] *adj* fighting (*spirit*) ‖ *mf* fighter

guet [gɛ] *m* watch, lookout

guet-apens [gɛtapɑ̃] *m* (*pl* **guets-apens** [gɛtapɑ̃]) ambush, trap

guêtre [gɛtr] *f* gaiter, legging

guêtrer [gɛtre] *tr* & *ref* to put gaiters on

guetter [gɛte] *tr* to watch; watch for; (coll) to lie in wait for

guetteur [gɛtœr] *m* lookout, sentinel

gueu·lard [gœlar] **-larde** [lard] *adj* (slang) loud-mouthed; (slang) fond of good eating ‖ *mf* gourmet; (slang) loud-mouth ‖ *m* mouth (*of blast furnace; of cannon*); (naut) megaphone

gueule [gœl] *f* mouth (*of animal; of furnace, cannon, etc.*); (slang) mouth, mug (*of person*); **avoir de la gueule** (coll) to have a certain air; **avoir la gueule de bois** (coll) to have a hangover; **fine gueule** (coll) gourmet; **gueule cassée** (coll) disabled veteran; **gueule noire** (coll) miner; **ta gueule!** (slang) shut up!

gueule-de-loup [gœldəlu] *f* (*pl* **gueules-de-loup**) (bot) snapdragon

gueuler [gœle] *tr* & *intr* (slang) to bellow

gueuleton [gœltɔ̃] *m* (slang) big feed

gueux [gø] **gueuse** [gøz] *adj* beggarly, wretched ‖ *mf* beggar; scamp ‖ *f* pig iron; pig (*mold*); woolen jacket; (coll) whore; **courir la gueuse** (coll) to go whoring

gugusse [gygys] *m* clown

gui [gi] *m* mistletoe; (naut) boom

guichet [giʃe] *m* window (*in post office, bank, box office, etc.*); counter (*e.g., in bank*); wicket; **guichet libre-service** automated teller

guidage [gidaʒ] *m* (rok) guidance

guide [gid] *m* guide; guidebook ‖ *f* rein; **mener la vie à grandes guides** to live extravagantly

guide-âne [gidɑn] *m* (*pl* **-âne** or **-ânes**) manual, guide

guider [gide] *tr* to guide

guidon [gidɔ̃] *m* handlebars; sight, bead (*of gun*); (naut) pennant

guigne [giɲ] *f* heart cherry; (coll) jinx

guigner [giɲe] *tr* to steal a glance at; (coll) to covet ‖ *intr* to peep

guignol [giɲɔl] *m* Punch (*puppet*); Punch and Judy show; (aer) king post

guignolet [giɲɔlɛ] *m* cherry brandy

guillaume [gijom] *m* rabbet plane; **Guillaume** William

guilledou [gijdu] *m*—**courir le guilledou** (coll) to make the rounds

guillemet [gijmɛ] *m* quotation mark; **fermer les guillemets** to close quotes; **ouvrir les guillemets** to quote

guillemeter [gijməte] §34 *tr* to put in quotes

guiller [gije] *intr* to ferment

guille·ret [gijrɛ] **-rette** [rɛt] *adj* chipper, lively, cheerful

guillotine [gijɔtin] *f* guillotine; **à guillotine** sliding; sash (*window*)

guillotiner [gijɔtine] *tr* to guillotine

guimauve [gimov] *f* (bot) marshmallow

guimbarde [gɛ̃bard] *f* (mus) jew's-harp; (coll) jalopy

guimpe [gɛ̃p] *f* wimple

guin·dé -dée [gɛ̃de] *adj* affected, stiff

guin·deau [gɛ̃do] *m* (*pl* **-deaux**) windlass

guinder [gɛ̃de] *tr* to hoist ‖ *ref* to put on airs

guinée [gine] *f* guinea (*coin*); **Guinée** Guinea (*the region*); **la Guinée** Guinea (*the region*)

guingan [gɛ̃gɑ̃] *m* gingham

guingois [gɛ̃gwa] *m*—**de guingois** askew; lopsidedly

guinguette [gɛ̃gɛt] *f* roadside inn, roadside park

guipage [gipaʒ] *m* wrapping, lapping

guiper [gipe] *tr* to wind; cover (*a wire*)

guipure [gipyr] *f* pillow lace

guirlande [girlɑ̃d] *f* garland, wreath

guirlander [girlɑ̃de] *tr* to garland

guise [giz] *f* manner; **à sa guise** as one pleases; **en guise de** by way of

guitare [gitar] *f* guitar

guitariste [gitarist] *mf* guitarist

guppy [gypi] *m* guppy

gustation [gystasjɔ̃] *f* tasting; drinking

guttu·ral -rale [gytyral] (*pl* **-raux** [ro] **-rales**) *adj* & *f* guttural

Guyane [gɥijan] *f* Guyana; **la Guyane** Guyana

gymnase [ʒimnɑz] *m* gymnasium

gymnaste [ʒimnast] *mf* gymnast

gymnote [ʒimnɔt] *m* electric eel

gynécologie [ʒinekɔlɔʒi] *f* gynecology

gypse [ʒips] *m* gypsum

gyrocompas [ʒirɔkɔ̃pa] *m* gyrocompass

gyrophare [ʒirɔfar] *m* (aut) emergency light, dome light (*flashing, revolving*)

gyroscope [ʒirɔskɔp] *m* gyroscope

H, h [aʃ], *[aʃ] m invar* eighth letter of the French alphabet

habile [abil] *adj* skillful; clever

habileté [abilte] *f* skill; cleverness

habiliter [abilite] *tr* to qualify, entitle

habillage [abijaʒ] *m* preparation; dressing; cover, outside surface; assembly; packaging and presentation; labeling and sealing; (mach) casing

habillement [abijmã] *m* clothing; clothes

habiller [abije] *tr* to dress; clothe; put together ‖ *intr* to be becoming, e.g., **robe qui habille bien** becoming dress ‖ *ref* to dress; get dressed; **s'habiller chez** to buy one's clothes at or from

habit [abi] *m* dress suit; habit, frock; **habit de cérémonie** or **soirée, habit à queue de pie, habit à queue de morue** tails; **habits** clothes

habitacle [abitakl] *m* (aer) cockpit; (naut) binnacle; (poetic) dwelling

habi·tant [abitã] **-tante** [tãt] *mf* inhabitant

habitat [abita] *m* habitat; living conditions, housing

habitation [abitɑsjɔ̃] *f* habitation; dwelling; residence; **habitation à bon marché** or **à loyer modéré** low-rent apartment

habi·té -tée [abite] *adj* inhabited; (rok) manned

habiter [abite] *tr* to live in, inhabit ‖ *intr* to live, reside

habitude [abityd] *f* habit, custom; **comme d'habitude** as usual; **d'habitude** usually

habi·tuel -tuelle [abityɛl] *adj* habitual

habituer [abitɥe] §96, §100 *tr* to accustom *ref*—**s'habituer à** to get used to

hâbler *[able] intr* to brag, to boast

hâblerie *[ablǝri] f* bragging

hâ·bleur *[ablœr] -bleuse* [bløz] *adj* boastful ‖ *mf* braggart, boaster

hache *[aʃ] f* ax, hatchet

ha·ché -chée *[aʃe] adj* ground, chopped; hachured; choppy (*sea*); jerky (*style*); dotted (*line*)

hacher *[aʃe] tr* to hack; grind, chop up; **hacher menu** to mince

hache·reau *[aʃro] m (pl -reaux)* hatchet

hachette *[aʃɛt] f* hatchet

hachis *[aʃi] m* hash, forcemeat; chopped vegetables

hachisch *[aʃiʃ] m* hashish

hachoir *[aʃwar] m* cleaver; chopping board

hachure *[aʃyr] f* shading

hachurer *[aʃyre] tr* to shade, hatch

haddock *[adɔk] m* finnan haddie

ha·gard *[agar] -garde* [gard] *adj* haggard

haie *[ɛ] f* hedge; hurdle; line, row

haïe *[aj] interj* giddap!

haillon *[ajɔ̃] m* old piece of clothing; **en haillons** in rags and tatters

haillon·neux *[ajɔnø] -neuse* [nøz] *adj* ragged, tattered

haine *[ɛn] f* hate

hai·neux *[ɛnø] -neuse* [nøz] *adj* full of hate, spiteful, malevolent

haïr *[air] §33, §96, §97 tr* to hate, detest ‖ *intr*—**haïr de** to hate to

haire *[ɛr] f* hair shirt

haïssable *[aisabl] adj* hateful

Haïti [aiti] *f* Haiti

haï·tien [aisjɛ̃] **-tienne** [sjɛn] *adj* Haitian ‖ (*cap*) *mf* Haitian

halcyon [alsjɔ̃] *m* (orn) kingfisher

hâle *[al] m* sun tan

haleine [alɛn] *f* breath; **avoir l'haleine courte** to be short-winded; (fig) to have little inspiration; **de longue haleine** hard, arduous (*work*); **en haleine** in good form; **hors d'haleine** out of breath; **perdre haleine** to get out of breath; **reprendre haleine** to catch one's breath; **tenir en haleine** to hold (*an audience*) breathless

halenée [alne] *f* whiff; strong breath

haler *[ale] tr* to haul, tow

hâler *[ale] tr* to tan

hale·tant *[altã] -tante* [tãt] *adj* breathless, panting

haleter *[alte] §2 intr* to pant, puff

hall *[ol] m* lobby; hall, auditorium

halle *[al] f* market, marketplace; exchange

hallebarde *[albard] f* halberd; **il pleut des hallebardes** (coll) it's raining cats and dogs

hallebardier [albardje] *m* halberdier

hallier *[alje] m* thicket

halluci·nant [allysinã[**-nante** [nãt] *adj* staggering, incredible

hallucination [allysinɑsjɔ̃] *f* hallucination

halo *[alo] m* halo

halogène [alɔʒɛn] *m* halogen

halte *[alt] f* halt; stop; (rr) flag stop, way station; **faire faire halte à** to halt ‖ *interj* halt!

halte-là *[altla] interj* (mil) halt!

haltère [altɛr] *m* dumbbell

haltérophile [alterɔfil] *m* weight lifter

haltérophilie [alterɔfili] *f* weight lifting

hamac *[amak] m* hammock

hamburger *[ãburgœr],* [ãbyrʒe] *m* hamburger

ha·meau *[amo] m (pl -meaux)* hamlet

hameçon [amsɔ̃] *m* hook, fishhook; (fig) bait

hammam *[ammam] m* Turkish bath

hampe *[ãp] f* staff, pole; shaft; downstroke; (culin) flank

hamster *[amstɛr] m* hamster

han *[ã],* [hã] *m* grunt

hanap *[anap] m* hanap, goblet

hanche *[ãʃ] f* hip; haunch

hancher *[ãʃe] intr* to lean on one leg ‖ *ref* (mil) to stand at ease

handball *[ãbol] m* handball

handicap *[ãdikap] m* handicap

handicaper *[ãdikape] tr* to handicap

hangar *[ãgar] m* hangar; shed

hanneton *[antɔ̃] m* June bug, chafer

hanter *[ãte] tr* to haunt

hantise *[ãtiz] f* obsession

happe *[ap] *f* crucible tongs; (carp) cramp, staple

happer *[ape] *tr* to snap up; (coll) to nab ‖ *intr* to stick

haquenée *[akne] *f* palfrey

haquet *[akɛ] *m* dray; **haquet à main** push-cart

harangue *[arɑ̃g] *f* harangue

haranguer *[arɑ̃ge] *tr* & *intr* to harangue

haras *[arɑ] *m* stud farm

harasser *[arase] *tr* to tire out

harceler *[arsəle] §2 *or* §34 *tr* to harass, harry; pester; dun

harde *[ard] *f* herd; leash; set (*of dogs*); **hardes** old clothes

har·di -die *[ardi] *adj* bold, daring; audacious, brazen ‖ **hardi** *interj* up and at them!

hardiesse *[ardjɛs] *f* boldness

hardiment *[ardimɑ̃] *adv* boldly; audaciously, brazenly

harem *[arɛm] *m* harem

hareng *[arɑ̃] *m* herring; **hareng fumé** kipper; **hareng saur** red herring; **sec comme un hareng** (coll) long and thin; **serrés comme des harengs** (coll) packed like sardines

harengère *[arɑ̃ʒɛr] *f* fishwife; (coll) shrew

harenguet *[arɑ̃gɛ] *m* sprat

hargne *[arɲ] *f* bad temper

har·gneux *[arɲø] **-gneuse** [ɲøz] *adj* bad-tempered, peevish, surly

haricot *[ariko] *m* bean; **haricot beurre** lima bean, butter bean; **haricot de Lima** lima bean; **haricot de mouton** haricot (*stew*); **haricot de Soissons** kidney bean; **haricot vert** string bean

harmonica [armɔnika] *m* mouth organ

harmonie [armɔni] *f* harmony; (mus) band

harmo·nieux [armɔnjø] **-nieuse** [njøz] *adj* harmonious

harmonique [armɔnik] *adj* harmonic

harmoniser [armɔnize] *tr* & *ref* to harmonize

harnachement *[arnaʃmɑ̃] *m* harness; harnessing

harnacher *[arnaʃe] *tr* to harness; rig out

harnais *[arnɛ] *m* harness

haro *[aro] *m*—**crier haro sur** (coll) to make a hue and cry against

harpagon [arpagɔ̃] *m* scrooge

harpe *[arp] *f* harp

harpie *[arpi] *f* harpy

harpiste *[arpist] *mf* harpist

harpon *[arpɔ̃] *m* harpoon

harponner *[arpɔne] *tr* to harpoon; (coll) to nab (*e.g., a thief*)

hart *[ar] *f* noose

hasard *[azar] *m* hazard, chance; **à tout hasard** just in case, come what may; **au hasard** at random; **par hasard** by chance

hasar·dé -dée *[azarde] *adj* hazardous

hasarder *[asarde] §96, §97 *tr* to risk, hazard, gamble ‖ §96 *ref* to venture, risk

hasar·deux *[azardø] **-deuse** [døz] *adj* risky, uncertain

hase *[ɑz] *f* doe hare

hâte *[ɑt] *f* haste; **à la hâte** hastily; **avoir hâte de** to be eager to; **en hâte, en toute hâte** posthaste

hâter *[ɑte] §97 *tr* & *ref* to hasten

hâ·tif *[ɑtif] **-tive** [tiv] *adj* premature; (hort) early

hauban *[obɑ̃] *m* (naut) shroud; (naut) guy

haubert *[obɛr] *m* coat of mail

hausse *[os] *f* rise, increase; block, wedge, prop; (mil) elevation, range; **jouer à la hausse** to bull the market

haussement *[osmɑ̃] *m* shrug

hausser *[ose] *tr* to raise, lift; shrug (*one's shoulders*) ‖ *intr* to rise

haussier *[osje] *m* bull (*on the stock exchange*)

haussière *[osjɛr] *f* (naut) hawser

haut *[o] **haute** *[ot] *adj* high; loud; high and mighty ‖ (when standing before noun) *adj* high; loud; upper, higher; extra (*pay*); early (*antiquity, Middle Ages, etc.*) ‖ *m* top; height; **de haut en bas** from top to bottom; **en haut** up; upstairs; **haut de casse** (typ) upper case; **haut des côtes** sparerib; **le prendre de haut** to get on one's high horse; **traiter de haut en bas** to high-hat ‖ *f* see **haute** ‖ **haut** *adv* high; up high; loudly; **haut les bras!** start working!; **haut les cœurs!** lift up your hearts!; **haut les mains!** hands up!

hau·tain *[otɛ̃] **-taine** [tɛn] *adj* haughty

hautbois *[obwa] *m* oboe

haut-de-chausses *[odəʃos] *m* (*pl* **hauts-de-chausses**) trunk hose, breeches

haut-de-forme *[odəfɔrm] *m* (*pl* **hauts-de-forme**) top hat

haute *[ot] *f* high society

haute-fidélité *[otfidelite] *f* high fidelity, hi-fi

hautement *[otmɑ̃] *adv* loudly; openly, clearly; highly (*qualified*); proudly

hauteur *[otœr] *f* height; hill, upland; altitude; nobility; haughtiness; (phys) pitch (*of sound*); **à la hauteur de** equal to, up to; (naut) off

haut-fond *[ofɔ̃] *m* (*pl* **hauts-fonds**) shoal, shallows

haut-le-cœur *[oləkœr] *m invar* nausea

haut-le-corps *[oləkɔr] *m invar* jump, sudden start

haut-parleur *[oparlœr] *m* (*pl* **haut-parleurs**) loudspeaker

hautu·rier *[otyrje] **-rière** [rjɛr] *adj* deep-sea

havage *[avaʒ] *m* (min) cutting

havane *[avan] *adj invar* tan, brown ‖ *m* Havana cigar ‖ (*cap*) *f*—**La Havane** Havana

hâve *[ɑv] *adj* haggard, peaked

havir *[avir] *tr* (culin) to sear

havre *[ɑvr] *m* haven, harbor

havresac *[avrəsak] *m* haversack, knapsack; tool bag

hawaïen or **hawaiien** [awajɛ̃], [avajɛ̃] **ha·waïenne** or **hawaiienne** [awajɛn], [avajɛn] *adj* Hawaiian ‖ (*cap*) *mf* Hawaiian

Hawaii [awai], [awaji] **l'île Hawaii** Hawaii; **les îles Hawaii** the Hawaiian Islands

Haye *[ɛ] *f*—**La Haye** The Hague

hayon *[ajɔ̃] *m* (aut) hatchback

H.B.M. [aʃbeɛm] *f* (letterword) (**habitation à bon marché**) low-rent apartment

he *[e], [he] *interj* hey!

heaume *[om] *m* helmet

hebdomadaire [ɛbdɔmadɛr] *adj* & *m* weekly

héberger [ebɛrʒe] §38 *tr* to lodge

hébé·té -tée [ebete] *adj* dazed

hébéter [ebete] §10 *tr* to daze, stupefy

hébraïque [ebraik] *adj* Hebrew

hébraï·sant [ebraizɑ̃] **-sante** [zɑ̃t] *mf* Hebraist

hébraïser [ebraize] *tr* & *intr* to Hebraize

hé·breu [ebrø] (*pl* **-breux**) *adj masc* Hebrew ‖ *m* Hebrew (*language*); **c'est de l'hébreu pour moi** it's Greek to me ‖ (*cap*) *m* Hebrew (*man*)

hécatombe [ekatɔ̃b] *f* hecatomb

hégire [eʒir] *f* Hegira

hein *[ɛ̃] *interj* (coll) eh!, what!

hélas [elɑs] *interj* alas!

Hélène [elɛn] *f* Helen

héler *[ele] §10 *tr* to hail, call

hélice [elis] *f* (aer) propeller; (math) helix, spiral; (naut) screw

hélicoptère [elikɔptɛr] *m* helicopter

héliport [elipɔr] *m* heliport

hélistation [elistasjɔ̃] *f* helicopter landing

hélium [eljɔm] *m* helium

hélix [eliks] *m* helix

hellène [ɛlɛn] *adj* Hellenic ‖ (*cap*) *mf* Hellene

helvétique [ɛlvetik] *adj* Swiss

hématie [emati] *f* red blood corpuscle

hémisphere [emisfɛr] *m* hemisphere

hémistiche [emistiʃ] *m* hemistich

hémoglobine [emɔglɔbin] *f* hemoglobin

hémophile [emɔfil] *adj* hemophilic ‖ *mf* hemophiliac

hémophilie [emɔfili] *f* hemophilia

hémorragie [emɔraʒi] *f* hemorrhage

hémorroïdes [emɔrɔid] *fpl* hemorrhoids

hémostatique [emɔstatik] *adj* hemostatic ‖ *m* hemostatic, hemostat

henné *[ɛnne] *m* henna

hennir *[enir] *intr* to neigh, whinny

hennissement *[enismɑ̃] *m* neigh, whinny

Henri [ɑ̃ri], *[ɑ̃ri] *m* Henry

hépatite [epatit] *f* hepatitis

héraldique [eraldik] *adj* heraldic

héraut *[ero] *m* herald

herbe [ɛrb] *f* grass; lawn; herb; **couper l'herbe sous le pied de qn** (coll) to pull the rug from under s.o.'s feet; **en herbe** unripe; budding; **fines herbes** herbs for seasoning; **herbe à la puce** (*Canad*) poison ivy; **herbe aux chats** catnip; **herbes médicinales** or **officinales** (pharm) herbs; **herbes potagères** potherbs; **mauvaise herbe** weed

her·beux [ɛrbø] **-beuse** [bøz] *adj* grassy

herbicide [ɛrbisid] *adj* herbicidal ‖ *m* weed killer

herboristerie [ɛrbɔristri] *f* herb shop

her·bu -bue [ɛrby] *adj* grassy

her·culéen [ɛrkyleɛ̃] **-culéenne** [kyleɛn] *adj* herculean

hère *[ɛr] *m* wretch

héréditaire [ereditɛr] *adj* hereditary

hérédité [eredite] *f* heredity

hérésie [erezi] *f* heresy

hérétique [eretik] *adj* & *mf* heretic

héris·sé -sée *[erise] *adj* bristly; shaggy; prickly; surly

hérisser *[erise] *tr* & *intr* to bristle

hérisson *[erisɔ̃] *m* hedgehog

héritage [eritaʒ] *m* heritage; inheritance

hériter [erite] *tr* to inherit ‖ *intr* to inherit; **hériter de** to become the heir of; inherit, come into

héri·tier [eritje] **-tière** [tjɛr] *mf* heir ‖ *f* heiress

hermétique [ɛrmetik] *adj* hermetic(al), airtight; (fig) obscure

hermine [ɛrmin] *f* ermine

herminette [ɛrminɛt] *f* adze

hernie *[ɛrni] *f* hernia

her·nieux *[ɛrnjø] **-nieuse** [njøz] *adj* ruptured

héroïne [erɔin] *f* heroine; (*drug*) heroin

héroïque [erɔik] *adj* heroic

héroïsme [erɔism] *m* heroism

héron *[erɔ̃] *m* heron

héros *[ero] *m* hero

herpès [ɛrpɛs] *m* herpes

herse [ɛrs] *f* harrow; portcullis; **les herses** (theat) stage lights

herser *[ɛrse] *tr* to harrow

hési·tant [ezitɑ̃] **-tante** [tɑ̃t] *adj* hesitant

hésitation [ezitasjɔ̃] *f* hesitation

hésiter [ezite] §96 *intr* to hesitate

hétéroclite [eterɔklit] *adj* unusual, odd

hétérodoxe [eterɔdɔks] *adj* heterodox

hétérodyne [eterɔdin] *adj* heterodyne

hétérogène [eterɔʒɛn] *adj* heterogeneous

hêtre *[ɛtr] *m* beech, beech tree

heur [œr] *m* pleasure; **heur et malheur** joys and sorrows

heure [œr] *f* hour; time (*of day*); o'clock; **à la bonne heure!** fine!; **à l'heure** on time; by the hour, per hour; **à l'heure juste, à l'heure sonnante** on the hour; **à tout à l'heure!** see you later!; **à toute heure** at any time; **de bonne heure** early; **heure d'été** daylight-saving time; **heure H** zero hour; **heure légale** twelve-month daylight time (standard time); **heure militaire** sharp, e.g., **huit heures, heure militaire** eight sharp; **heures d'affluence** rush hours; **heures de consultation** office hours; **heures de pointe** rush hours; **heures d'ouverture** business hours; **heure semestrielle** semester hour; **heures supplémentaires** overtime; **l'heure du déjeuner** lunch hour; **tout à l'heure** in a little while; a little while ago

heu·reux [œrø], [ørø] **-reuse** [røz] §93 *adj* happy, pleased; lucky, fortunate

heurt *[œr] *m* knock, bump; clash; bruise; **sans heurt** without a hitch

heur·té -tée *[œrte] *adj* clashing (*colors*); abrupt (*style*)

heurter *[œrte] *tr* to knock against, bump into; antagonize ‖ *intr*—**heurter contre** to bump into ‖ *ref* to clash, collide; **se heurter à** to come up against

heurtoir *[œrtwar] *m* door knocker; (rr) buffer

hexagone [ɛgzagɔn] *m* hexagon; **l'Hexagone (national)** (fig) France

hi *[i] *m invar*—**hi hi hi!** ho ho ho!; **pousser des hi et des ha** to sputter in amazement

hiatus [jatys], *[jatys] *m* hiatus

hiberner [ibɛrne] *intr* to hibernate

hibiscus [ibiskys] *m* hibiscus

hi·bou *[ibu] *m* (*pl* **-boux**) owl

hic *[ik] *m*—**violà le hic!** (coll) there's the rub!

hi·deux *[idø] **-deuse** [døz] *adj* hideous

hie *[i] *f* pile driver

hièble [jɛbl] *f* (bot) elder

hié·mal -male [jemal] *adj* (*pl* **-maux** [mo]) winter

hier [jɛr] *adv* & *m* yesterday; **hier soir** last evening, last night

hiérarchie *[jerarʃi] *f* hierarchy

hiéroglyphe [jerɔglif] *m* hieroglyphic

hiéroglyphique [jerɔglifik] *adj* hieroglyphic

hi-han *[iã] *interj* heehaw

hila·rant [ilarã] **-rante** [rãt] *adj* hilarious; laughing (*gas*)

hilare [ilar] *adj* hilarious

hin·dou -doue [ẽdu] *adj* Hindu ‖ (*cap*) *mf* Hindu

hippique [ipik] adj horse (*race, show*)

hippisme [ipism] *m* horse racing

hippodrome [ipɔdrom] *m* hippodrome, race track

hippopotame [ipɔpɔtam] *m* hippopotamus

hirondelle [irɔ̃dɛl] *f* (orn) swallow; (coll) bicycle cop

hispanique [ispanik] *adj* Hispanic

hispani·sant [ispanizã] **-sante** [zãt] *mf* Hispanist

hisser *[ise] *tr* to hoist, to raise

histoire [istwar] *f* history; story; **faire des histoires à** (coll) to make trouble for; **histoire à dormir debout** (coll) tall tale; **histoire de rire** (coll) just for fun; **histoire de s'informer** (coll) out of curiosity; **pas d'histoires** (coll) no fuss

histologie [istɔlɔʒi] *f* histology

histo·rien [istɔrjẽ] **-rienne** [rjɛn] *mf* historian

historier [istɔrje] *tr* to illustrate, adorn

historique [istɔrik] *adj* historic(al) ‖ *m* historical account

histrion [istrijɔ̃] *m* ham actor

hiver [ivɛr] *m* winter

hiveriser [ivɛrize] *tr* (aut) to winterize

hiver·nal -nale [ivɛrnal] *adj* (*pl* **-naux** [no]) winter

hiverner [ivɛrne] *intr* to winter

H.L.M. [aʃɛlɛm] *m* (letterword) (**habitation à loyer modéré**) low-rent apartment

ho *[o], [ho] *interj* hey there!; what!

hobe·reau *[ɔbro] *m* (*pl* **-reaux**) (orn) hobby; (coll) squire

hoche *[ɔʃ] *f* nick on a blade

hochement *[ɔʃmã] *m* shake, toss

hochepot *[ɔʃpo] *m* (culin) hotchpotch

hochequeue *[ɔʃkø] *m* (orn) wagtail

hocher *[ɔʃe] *tr* to shake; nod

hochet *[ɔʃɛ] *m* rattle (*toy*); bauble

hockey *[ɔkɛ] *m* hockey; **hockey sur glace** ice hockey

hockeyeur [ɔkɛjœr] *m* hockey player

hoirie [wari] *f* legacy

holà *[ɔla], [hɔla] *m invar*—**mettre le holà à** (coll) to put a stop to ‖ *interj* hey!; stop!

holding *[ɔldiŋ] *m* holding company

hold-up *[ɔldœp] *m invar* holdup

hollan·dais *[ɔlãdɛ] **-daise** [dɛz] *adj* Dutch ‖ *m* Dutch (*language*) ‖ (*cap*) *mf* Hollander (*person*)

hollande *[ɔlãd] *m* Edam cheese ‖ *f* Holland (*linen*) ‖ (*cap*) *f* Holland; **la Hollande** Holland

holocauste [ɔlɔkost] *m* holocaust

homard *[ɔmar] *m* lobster

home *[ɔm] *m* home

homélie [ɔmeli] *f* homily

homéopathie [ɔmeɔpati] *f* homeopathy

home-trainer [omtrɛnœr] *m* exercise bicycle

homicide [ɔmisid] *adj* homicidal ‖ *mf* homicide (*person*) ‖ *m* homicide, murder; **homicide involontaire, homicide par imprudence** manslaughter

hommage [ɔmaʒ] *m* homage; **hommage de l'auteur** (formula in presenting complimentary copies) with the compliments of the author; **hommages** respects, compliments

hommasse [ɔmas] *adj* mannish (*woman*)

homme [ɔm] *m* man; **brave homme** fine man, honest man; **être homme à** to be the man to, to be capable of; **homme à tout faire** jack-of-all-trades; handyman; **homme d'affaires** businessman; **homme d'armes** man-at-arms; **homme de droite** rightist; **homme de gauche** leftist; **homme d'église** churchman; **homme de guerre or d'épée** military man; **homme de la rue** man in the street, first comer; **homme de l'espace** spaceman; **homme de lettres** man of lettrs; **homme de paille** figurehead, stooge; **homme de peine** workingman; **homme des bois** orangutan; **homme d'État** statesman; **homme de troupe** (*pl* **hommes des troupes**) (mil) enlisted man, private; **homme d'expédition** go-getter; **homme d'intérieur** homebody; **homme du monde** man of the world; **homme galant** ladies' man; **homme orchestra** one-man band; **hommes de bien** men of good will; **honnête homme** upright man; man of culture, gentleman; **jeune homme** young man; teen-age boy; **le vieil homme** (Bib) the old Adam; **un homme à la mer!** man overboard!

homme-grenouille [ɔmgrənuj] *m* (*pl* **hommes-grenouilles**) frogman

homme-sandwich[ɔmsɑ̃dwitʃ],[ɔmsɑ̃dwiʃ] *m* (*pl* **hommes-sandwichs**) sandwich man

homogène [ɔmɔʒɛn] *adj* homogeneous

homogénéiser [ɔmɔʒeneize] *tr* to homogenize

homologation [ɔmɔlɔgɑsjɔ̃] *f* validation

homologue [ɔmɔlɔg] *adj* homologous ‖ *mf* (fig) opposite number

homologuer [ɔmɔlɔge] *tr* to confirm, endorse; probate (*e.g., a will*)

homonyme [ɔmɔnim] *adj* homonymous ‖ *m* homonym; namesake

homosexualité [ɔmɔsɛksɥalite] *f* homosexuality

homo·sexuel -sexuelle [ɔmɔsɛksɥɛl] *adj* & *mf* homosexual

hongre *[ɔ̃gr] *adj* gelded ‖ *m* gelding

hongrer *[ɔ̃gre] *tr* to geld

Hongrie *[ɔ̃gri] *f* Hungary; **la Hongrie** Hungary

hon·grois *[ɔ̃grwɑ] **-groise** [grwɑz] *adj* Hungarian ‖ *m* Hungarian (*language*) ‖ (*cap*) *mf* Hungarian (*person*)

honnête [ɔnɛt] *adj* honest, honorable

honnêteté [ɔnɛtəte] *f* honesty, uprightness

honneur [ɔnœr] *m* honor; **faire honneur à sa parole** to keep one's word

honnir *[ɔnir] *tr* to shame

honorabilité [ɔnɔrabilite] *f* respectability

honorable [ɔnɔrabl] *adj* honorable

honoraire [ɔnɔrɛr] *adj* honorary, emeritus ‖ **honoraires** *mpl* honorarium, fee

honorer [ɔnɔre] *tr* to honor ‖ *ref*—**s'honorer de** to pride oneself on

honorifique [ɔnɔrifik] *adj* honorific

honte *[ɔ̃t] *f* shame; **avoir honte** to be ashamed; **faire honte à qn** to make s.o. ashamed; **faire honte à ses parents** to be a disgrace to one's parents; **fausse honte** bashfulness; **sans honte** unashamedly

hon·teux *[ɔ̃tø], **-teuse** [tøz] *adj* ashamed; shameful; sheepish, shamefaced, bashful; venereal (*diseases*)

hop *[ɔp] *interj* go!, off with you!

hôpi·tal [ɔpital] *m* (*pl* **-taux** [to]) hospital; charity hospital

hoquet *[ɔkɛ] *m* hiccough

hoqueter *[ɔkte] §34 *intr* to hiccough

horaire [ɔrɛr] *adj* hourly, by hour ‖ *m* timetable; schedule; **horaire flottant** flex-(i)time

horde *[ɔrd] *f* horde

horion *[ɔrjɔ̃] *m* punch, clout

horizon [ɔrizɔ̃] *m* horizon

horizon·tal -tale [ɔrizɔ̃tal] (*pl* **-taux** [to] **-tales**) *adj* & *f* horizontal

horloge [ɔrlɔʒ] *f* clock; **horloge à eau, horloge d'eau** water clock; **horloge à sable, horloge de sable** hourglass; **horloge atomique, horloge moléculaire** atomic clock; **horloge comtoise, horloge normande, horloge parquet** grandfather's clock; **horloge solaire** sundial

horlo·ger [ɔrlɔʒe] **-gère** [ʒɛr] *adj* clock-making, watchmaking ‖ *mf* clockmaker, watchmaker

horlogerie [ɔrlɔʒri] *f* clockmaking, watchmaking; **d'horlogerie** clockwork

hormis *[ɔrmi] *prep* (lit) except for

hormone [ɔrmɔn] *f* hormone

horoda·té -tée [ɔrɔdate] *adj* stamped with the hour and date

horoscope [ɔrɔskɔp] *m* horoscope; **tirer l'horoscope de qn** to cast s.o.'s horoscope

horreur [ɔrœr] *f* horror; **avoir horreur de** to have a horror of; **commettre des horreurs** to commit atrocities; **dire des horreurs** to say obscene things; **dire des horreurs de** to say shocking things about

horrible [ɔribl] *adj* horrible

horrifier [ɔrifje] *tr* to horrify

horripi·lant [ɔrripilɑ̃] **-lante** [lɑ̃t] (coll) *adj* hair-raising

horripilation [ɔrripilɑsjɔ̃] *f* gooseflesh; (coll) exasperation

horripiler [ɔrripile] *tr* to give gooseflesh to; (coll) to exasperate

hors *[ɔr] *prep* out, beyond, outside; except, except for, save; **hors de** out of, outside of; **hors de soi** beside oneself, frantic; **hors d'ici!** get out!; **hors tout** overall

hors-bord *[ɔrbɔr] *m invar* outboard (*motor or motorboat*)

hors-caste *[ɔrkast] *mf invar* outcaste

hors-concours *[ɔrkɔ̃kur] *adj invar* excluded from competition ‖ *m invar* contestant excluded from competition

hors-d'œuvre *[ɔrdœvr] *m invar* hors d'œuvre; **le déjeuner commence par des hors-d'œuvre** the dinner begins with the hors d'œuvres

hors-jeu *[ɔrʒø] *m invar* offside position

hors-la-loi *[ɔrlalwa] *m invar* outlaw

hors-ligne *[ɔrliɲ] *adj invar* (coll) exceptional ‖ *m invar* roadside

hors-texte *[ɔrtɛks] *m invar* (bb) insert

hortensia [ɔrtɑ̃sja] *m* hydrangea

horticole [ɔrtikɔl] *adj* horticultural

horticulture [ɔrtikyltyr] *f* horticulture

hospice [ɔspis] *m* hospice; home (*for the old, infirm, orphaned, etc.*)

hospita·lier [ɔspitalje] **-lière** [ljɛr] *adj* hospitable; hospital ‖ *mf* hospital employee

hospitaliser [ɔspitalize] *tr* to hospitalize

hospitalité [ɔspitalite] *f* hospitality

hostie [ɔsti] *f* (eccl) Host

hostile [ɔstil] *adj* hostile

hostilité [ɔstilite] *f* hostility

hôte [ot] *mf* guest ‖ *m* host

hôtel [otɛl], [ɔtɛl] *m* hotel; mansion; **hôtel des Monnaies** mint; **hôtel des Postes** main post office; **hôtel de ville** city hall; **hôtel meublé** rooming house, residential hotel; **hôtel particulier** mansion

hôtel-Dieu [otɛldjø], [ɔtɛldjø] *m* (*pl* **hôtels-Dieu**) city hospital

hôte·lier [otəlje], [ɔtəlje] **-lière** [ljɛr] *adj* hotel (*business*) ‖ *mf* hotel manager

hôtellerie [otɛlri], [ɔtɛlri] f hotel business; fine restaurant; hostelry, hostel

hôtesse [otɛs] f hostess; **hôtesse de l'air** air hostess, stewardess

hotte *[ɔt] f basket (carried on back); hod (of mason); hood (of chimney); **hotte aspirante** exhaust hood

hou *[u] interj oh no!

houache *[waʃ] f wake (of ship)

houblon *[ublɔ̃] m hop (vine); hops (dried flowers)

houe *[u] f hoe

houer *[we] tr to hoe

houille *[uj] f coal; **houille blanche** water power; **houille bleue** tide power; **houille d'or** energy from the sun; **houille grasse** or **collante** soft coal; **houille incolore** wind power; **houille maigre** or **éclatante** hard coal; **houille rouge** energy from the heat of the earth

houil·ler *[uje] **houil·lère** *[ujɛr] adj coal-bearing, carboniferous; coal (industry) ‖ f coal mine

houilleur *[ujœr] m coal miner

houle *[ul] f swell

houlette *[ulɛt] f crook (of shepherd); (hort) trowel

hou·leux *[ulø] **-leuse** [løz] adj swelling (sea); (fig) stormy, turbulent

houp *[up], [hup] interj go to it!

houppe *[up] f tuft; crest; tassel; **houppe à poudre** powder puff

houppelande *[uplɑ̃d] f greatcoat

houppette *[upɛt] f tuft; powder puff

hourra *[ura], [hura] m—**pousser trois hourras** to give three cheers ‖ interj hurrah!

hourvari *[urvari] m call to the hounds; (coll) uproar

houspiller *[uspije] tr to jostle, knock around; to rake over the coals, to tell off

housse *[us] f slipcover; cover (e.g., for typewriter); garment bag; housing, horse-cloth; (aut) seat cover

housser *[use] tr to dust (with feather duster)

houssine *[usin] f rug beater; switch

houssoir *[uswar] m feather duster; whisk broom

houx *[u] m holly

hoyau *[wajo] m (pl hoyaux) mattock; pickax

hublot *[yblo] m porthole

huche *[yʃ] f hutch; bin

hucher *[yʃe] tr to call, shout to

hue *[y] interj gee!; gee up! **tirer à hue et à dia** (fig) to pull in opposite directions

huée *[ɥe] f hoot, boo

huer *[ɥe] tr & intr to hoot, boo

hugue·not *[ygno] **-note** [nɔt] adj Huguenot ‖ f pipkin ‖ (cap) mf Huguenot (person)

huile [ɥil] f oil; big shot; **ça baigne dans l'huile** (coll) everything is going smoothly; **d'huile** calm, e.g., **mer d'huile** calm sea; **huile de coude** elbow grease; **huile de foie de morue** cod-liver oil; **huile de freins** brake fluid; **huile de ricin** castor oil; **huile lourde** disel fuel; **huile solaire** suntan oil; **les huiles** (coll) the VIP's; **sentir l'huile** (fig) to smell of midnight oil; **verser de l'huile sur le feu** (fig) to add fuel to the fire

huiler [ɥile] tr to oil; grease

hui·leux [ɥilø] **-leuse** [løz] adj oily; greasy

huilier [ɥilje] m oil-and-vinegar cruet

huis [ɥi] m (archaic) door; **à huis clos** behind closed doors; (law) in camera; **à huis ouvert** spectators admitted ‖ *[ɥi] m—**demander le huis clos** to request a closed-door session

huisserie [ɥisri] f doorframe

huissier [ɥisje] m doorman; usher (before a person of rank); **huissier audiencier** bailiff; **huissier exploitant** process server

huit *[ɥi(t)] §94 adj & pron eight; the Eighth, e.g., **Jean huit** John the Eighth; **huit heures** eight o'clock ‖ m eight; eighth (in dates); **faire des huit** to cut figures of eight (in figure skating)

huitain *[ɥitɛ̃] m eight-line verse

huitaine *[ɥitɛn] f (grouping of) eight; week; **à huitaine** the same day next week; **une huitaine de** about eight

huitième *[ɥitjɛm] §94 adj, pron (masc, fem), & m eighth

huître [ɥitr] f oyster

huit-reflets *[ɥirəflɛ] m invar top hat

huî·trier [ɥitrije] **-trière** [trijer] adj oyster (industry) ‖ m (orn) oystercatcher ‖ f oyster bed

hulotte *[ylɔt] f hoot owl

hululer *[ylyle] intr to hoot

hum *[œm], [hœm] interj hum!

hu·main [ymɛ̃] **-maine** [mɛn] adj human; humane

humaniste [ymanist] adj & m humanist

humanitaire [ymanitɛr] adj & mf humanitarian

humanité [ymanite] f humanity; **humanités (classiques)** humanities (Greek & Latin classics); **humanités modernes** humanities, belles-letters; **humanités scientifiques** liberal studies (concerned with the observation and classification of facts)

humble [œ̃bl] adj humble

humecter [ymɛkte] tr to moisten ‖ref to become damp; **s'humecter le gosier** (slang) to wet one's whistle

humer *[yme] tr to suck, suck up; sip; inhale, breathe in

humérus [ymerys] m humerus

humeur [ymœr] f humor, body fluid; humor, mood, spirits; **avec humeur** testily; **avoir de l'humeur** to be in a bad mood; **être de bonne humeur** to be in a good humor

humide [ymid] adj humid, damp; wet

humidifier [ymidifje] tr to humidify

humidité [ymidite] f humidity

humi·liant [ymiljɑ̃] **-liante** [ljɑ̃t] adj humiliating

humiliation [ymiljɑsjɔ̃] f humiliation

humilier [ymilje] *tr* to humiliate, humble ‖ *ref* to humble oneself

humilité [ymilite] *f* humility

humoriste [ymɔrist] *adj* humorous (*writer*) ‖ *mf* humorist

humoristique [ymɔristik] *adj* humorous

humour [ymur] *m* humor; **humour noir** macabre humor, sick humor

humus [ymys] *m* humus

hune *[yn] f* (naut) top; **hune de vigie** (naut) crow's-nest

huppe *[yp] f* tuft, crest (*of bird*); (orn) hoopoe

hup·pé -pée *[ype] adj* tufted, crested; (coll) smart, stylish

hure *[yr] f* head (*of boar, salmon, etc.*); (culin) headcheese

hurlement *[yrlmɑ̃] m* howl, roar; howling, roaring (*e.g., of wind*)

hurler *[yrle] tr* to cry out, yell ‖ *intr* to howl, roar

hur·leur *[yrlœr] -leuse* [løz] *adj* howling ‖ *mf* howler ‖ *m* (zool) howler

hurluberlu [yrlybɛrly] *m* (coll) scatterbrain

hu·ron *[yrɔ̃] -ronne* [rɔn] *adj* (coll) boorish, uncouth ‖ *mf* (coll) boor

hurricane *[urikan], *[œrikɛn] m* hurricane

hutte *[yt] f* hut, cabin

hyacinthe [jasɛ̃t] *f* hyacinth (*stone*)

hya·lin [jalɛ̃] **-line** [lin] *adj* glassy

hybride [ibrid] *adj & m* hybrid

hydrate [idrat] *m* hydrate

hydrater [idrate] *tr & ref* to hydrate

hydraulique [idrolik] *adj* hydraulic ‖ *f* hydraulics

hydravion [idravjɔ̃] *m* hydroplane

hydre [idr] *f* hydra

hydrocarbure [idrɔkarbyr] *m* hydrocarbon

hydro-électrique [idrɔelɛktrik] *adj* hydro-electric

hydrofoil [idrɔfɔjl] *m* hydrofoil

hydrofuge [idrɔfyʒ] *adj* waterproof

hydrofuger [idrɔfyʒe] §38 *tr* to waterproof

hydrogène [idrɔʒɛn] *m* hydrogen

hydroglisseur [idrɔglisœr] *m* speedboat

hydromètre [idrɔmɛtr] *m* hydrometer ‖ *f* (ent) water spider

hydrophile [idrɔfil] *adj* absorbent ‖ *m*—**hydrophile brun** (ent) water devil

hydrophobie [idrɔfɔbi] *f* hydrophobia

hydropisie [idrɔpizi] *f* dropsy

hydroptère [idrɔptɛr] *m* hydrofoil

hydroscope [idrɔskɔp] *m* dowser

hydroxyde [idrɔksid] *m* hydroxide

hyène [jɛn] *f* hyena

hygiène [iʒjɛn] *f* hygiene

hygiénique [iʒjenik] *adj* hygienic

hymnaire [imnɛr] *m* hymnal

hymne [imnə], [im] *m* hymn, ode, anthem; **hymne national** national anthem ‖ *f* (eccl) hymn, canticle

hyperacidité [iperasidite] *f* hyperacidity

hyperbole [iperbɔl] *f* (math) hyperbola; (rhet) hyperbole

hypersensible [ipersɑ̃sibl] *adj* hypersensitive, supersensitive

hypersensi·tif [ipersɑ̃sitif] **-tive** [tiv] *adj* hypersensitive, supersensitive

hyper·sexué -sexuée [ipersɛksɥe] *adj* over-sexed

hypertension [ipertɑ̃sjɔ̃] *f* high blood pressure, hypertension

hypnose [ipnoz] *f* hypnosis

hypnotique [ipnɔtik] *adj & m* hypnotic

hypnotiser [ipnɔtize] *tr* to hypnotize ‖ *ref*—**s'hypnotiser sur** (fig) to be hypnotized by

hypnoti·seur [ipnɔtizœr] **-seuse** [zøz] *mf* hypnotist

hypnotisme [ipnɔtism] *m* hypnotism

hypocondriaque [ipɔkɔ̃drijak] *adj & mf* hypochondriac

hypocrisie [ipɔkrizi] *f* hypocrisy

hypocrite [ipɔkrit] *adj* hypocritical ‖ *mf* hypocrite

hypodermique [ipɔdɛrmik] *adj* hypodermic

hyposulfite [ipɔsylfit] *m* hyposulfite

hypotension [ipɔtɑ̃sjɔ̃] *f* low blood pressure

hypoténuse [ipɔtenyz] *f* hypotenuse

hypothèque [ipɔtɛk] *f* mortgage; **prendre une hypothèque sur** to put a mortgage on; **purger une hypothèque** to pay off a mortgage

hypothéquer [ipɔteke] §10 *tr* to mortgage

hypothèse [ipɔtɛz] *f* hypothesis

hypothétique [ipɔtetik] *adj* hypothetic(al)

hystérie [isteri] *f* hysteria

hystérique [isterik] *adj* hysteric(al)

I

I, i [i], *[i] m invar* ninth letter of the French alphabet

ïambique [jɑ̃bik] *adj* iambic

ibé·rien [iberjɛ̃] **-rienne** [rjɛn] *adj* Iberian ‖ (*cap*) *mf* Iberian

ibérique [iberik] *adj* Iberian

iceberg [isbɛrg] *m* iceberg

ichtyologie [iktjɔlɔʒi] *f* ichthyology

ici [isi] *adv* here; this is, e.g., **ici Paris** (rad, telv) this is Paris; e.g., **ici Robert** (telp) this is Robert; **d'ici** hereabouts; from to-day; **d'ici demain** before tomorrow; **d'ici là** between now and then, in the meantime; **d'ici peu** before long; **jusqu'ici** up to now, hitherto; **par ici** this way, through here

ici-bas [isibɑ] *adv* here below, on earth

icône [ikon] *f* icon

iconoclaste [ikɔnɔklast] *adj* iconoclastic ‖ *mf* iconoclast

iconographie [ikɔnɔgrafi] *f* iconography; pictures, pictorial material

iconoscope [ikɔnɔskɔp] *m* iconoscope

ictère [iktɛr] *m* jaundice

ictérique [ikterik] *adj* jaundiced

idéal idéale [ideal] *adj* & *m* (*pl* **idéaux** [ideo] or **idéals**) ideal

idéaliser [idealize] *tr* to idealize

idéaliste [idealist] *adj* & *mf* idealist

idée [ide] *f* idea; mind, head; opinion, esteem; (coll) shade, touch; **changer d'idée** to change one's mind

idem [idɛm] *adv* idem, the same, ditto

identification [idɑ̃tifikasjɔ̃] *f* identification

identifier [idɑ̃tifje] *tr* to identify

identique [idɑ̃tik] *adj* identic(al)

identité [idɑ̃tite] *f* identity

idéologie [ideɔlɔʒi] *f* ideology; (pej) utopianism

idéologique [ideɔlɔʒik] *adj* ideologic(al); conceptual

ides [id] *fpl* ides

idiomatique [idjɔmatik] *adj* idiomatic

idiome [idjom] *m* idiom, language

idiosyncrasie [idjɔsɛ̃krazi] *f* idiosyncrasy

i·diot [idjo] **-diote** [djɔt] *adj* idiotic ‖ *mf* idiot

idiotie [idjɔsi] *f* idiocy

idiotisme [idjɔtism] *m* idiom, idiomatic expression

idolâtrer [idɔlatre] *tr* to idolize

idolâtrie [idɔlatri] *f* idolatry

idole [idɔl] *f* idol

idylle [idil] *f* idyll; romance, love affair

idyllique [idilik] *adj* idyllic

if [if] *m* yew

IGAME [igam] *m* (acronym) (**Inspecteur Général de l'Administration en Mission Extraordinaire**) head prefect

igname [iɲam], [iɲam] *f* yam

ignare [iɲar] *adj* ignorant

ig·né -née [iɲe] *adj* igneous

ignifuge [iɲifyʒ] *adj* fireproof ‖ *m* fireproofing

ignifuger [iɲifyʒe] §38 *tr* to fireproof

ignition [iɲisjɔ̃] *f* ignition; red heat (*of metal*)

ignoble [iɲɔbl] *adj* ignoble; disgusting

ignomi·nieux [iɲɔminjø] **-nieuse** [njøz] *adj* ignominious

ignorance [iɲɔrɑ̃s] *f* ignorance

igno·rant [iɲɔrɑ̃] **-rante** [rɑ̃t] *adj* ignorant ‖ *mf* ignoramus

ignorer [iɲɔre] *tr* not to know, be ignorant of; be unacquainted with

il [il] §87, §92 *pron* he, it

île [il] *f* island, isle; **les îles Normandes** the Channel Islands

illé·gal -gale [illegal] *adj* (*pl* **-gaux** [go]) illegal

illégitime [illeʒitim] *adj* illegitimate; unjustified

illet·tré -trée [illetre] *adj* & *mf* illiterate

illicite [illisit] *adj* illicit; foul (*blow*)

illimi·té -tée [illimite] *adj* unlimited

illisible [illizibl] *adj* illegible; unreadable (*book*)

illogique [illɔʒik] *adj* illogical

illumination [illyminasjɔ̃] *f* illumination

illumi·né -née [illymine] *adj* & *mf* fanatic, visionary

illuminer [illymine] *tr* to illuminate

illusion [illyzjɔ̃] *f* illusion; **illusion de la vue** optical illusion; **se faire des illusions** to indulge in wishful thinking

illusionner [illyzjɔne] *tr* to delude ‖ *ref* to delude oneself

illusionniste [illyzjɔnist] *mf* magician

illusoire [illyzwar] *adj* illusory, illusive

illustra·teur [illystratœr] *m* illustrator

illustration [illystrasjɔ̃] *f* illustration; glorification; glory; celebrity

illustre [illystr] *adj* illustrious, renowned

illus·tré -trée [illystre] *adj* illustrated ‖ *m* illustrated magazine

illustrer [illystre] *tr* to illustrate ‖ *ref* to distinguish oneself

îlot [ilo] *m* small island, isle; block (*of houses*)

ils [il] §87 *pron* they

image [imaʒ] *f* image; picture; **images** imagery; **image de marque** name brand; **images** imagery; **images d'archives** file film; **une image vaut mieux que dix mille mots** a picture is worth a thousand words

imager [imaʒe] §38 *tr* to embellish with metaphors, to color

imagerie [imaʒri] *f*—**imagerie d'Épinal** cardboard cutouts

imaginaire [imaʒinɛr] *adj* imaginary

imagination [imaʒinasjɔ̃] *f* imagination

imaginer [imaʒine] §97 *tr* to imagine; invent ‖ *intr* to imagine; **imaginer de** + *inf* to have the idea of + *ger* ‖ §95 *ref* to imagine oneself; **imaginez-vous!** imagine!

imbattable [ɛ̃batabl] *adj* unbeatable

imbat·tu -tue [ɛ̃baty] *adj* unbeaten

imbécile [ɛ̃besil] *adj* & *mf* imbecile

imbécillité [ɛ̃besilite] *f* imbecility

imberbe [ɛ̃bɛrb] *adj* beardless

imbi·bé -bée [ɛ̃bibe] *adj* (coll) drunk, tipsy; **imbibé de** soaked with; steeped in

imbiber [ɛ̃bibe] *tr* & *ref* to soak; **s'imbiber de** to soak up; be imbued with; (coll) to imbibe (*liquor*)

imbrication [ɛ̃brikasjɔ̃] *f* overlapping

imbriquer [ɛ̃brike] *tr* to overlap; interweave; fit (*s.th.*) into ‖ *ref* to overlap; be linked; be interwoven; **ça s'imbrique l'un dans l'autre** they fit into each other; they are linked

imbrisable [ɛ̃brizabl] *adj* unbreakable

imbrûlable [ɛ̃brylabl] *adj* fireproof

im·bu -bue [ɛ̃by] *adj*—**imbu de** imbued with, steeped in

imbuvable [ɛ̃byvabl] *adj* undrinkable; unbearable, insufferable, awful

imita·teur [imitatœr] **-trice** [tris] *mf* imitator

imitation [imitasjɔ̃] *f* imitation

imiter [imite] *tr* to imitate
immacu·lé -lée [immakyle] *adj* immaculate
immangeable [ɛ̃mɑ̃ʒabl] *adj* inedible
immanquable [ɛ̃mɑ̃kabl] *adj* infallible; inevitable
immaté·riel -rielle [immaterjɛl] *adj* immaterial
immatriculation [immatrikylɑsjɔ̃] *f* registration; enrollment; **immatriculation de livraison** dealer's plate
immatriculer [immatrikyle] *tr* to register
immature [immatyr] *adj* unmatured
immé·diat [immedja] **-diate** [djat] *adj* immediate
immédiatement [immedjatmɑ̃] *adv* immediately
immémo·rial -riale [immemɔrjal] *adj* (*pl* **-riaux** [rjo]) immemorial
immense [immɑ̃s] *adj* immense
immensurable [immɑ̃syrabl] *adj* immeasurable, immensurable
immerger [immɛrʒe] §38 *tr* to immerse, dip; throw overboard; lay (*a cable*)
imméri·té -tée [immerite] *adj* undeserved
immersion [immɛrsjɔ̃] *f* immersion
immettable [ɛ̃mɛtabl] *adj* unwearable
immeuble [immœbl] *adj* real, e.g., **biens immeubles** real estate ‖ *m* building, apartment building; **immeuble à copropriété** condominium
immi·grant [immigrɑ̃] **-grante** [grɑ̃t] *adj* & *mf* immigrant
immigration [immigrɑsjɔ̃] *f* immigration
immi·gré -grée [immigre] *adj* & *mf* immigrant
immigrer [immigre] *intr* to immigrate
immi·nent [imminɑ̃] **-nente** [nɑ̃t] *adj* imminent, impending
immiscer [immise] §51 *ref*—**s'immiscer dans** to interfere with, meddle with
immixtion [immiksjɔ̃] *f* interference; **immixtions** intrusions upon privacy (*e.g., wiretapping*)
immobile [immɔbil] *adj* motionless; immobile (*resolute*); dead (*typewriter key*)
immobi·lier [immɔbilje] **-lière** [ljɛr] *adj* real-estate, property; real, e.g., **biens immobiliers** real estate
immobiliser [immɔbilize] *tr* to immobilize; tie up ‖ *ref* to come to a stop
immodé·ré -rée [immɔdere] *adj* immoderate
immonde [immɔ̃d] *adj* foul, filthy; (eccl) unclean
immondices [immɔ̃dis] *fpl* garbage, refuse
immo·ral -rale [immɔral] *adj* (*pl* **-raux** [ro]) immoral
immortaliser [immɔrtalize] *tr* to immortalize
immor·tel -telle [immɔrtɛl] *adj* & *mf* immortal ‖ *f* (bot) everlasting
immoti·vé -vée [immɔtive] *adj* groundless
immuable [immɥabl] *adj* changeless
immuniser [immynize] *tr* to immunize
immunité [immynite] *f* immunity
immunologie [imynɔlɔʒi] *f* immunology

impact [ɛ̃pakt] *m* impact; **impact résistant** unbreakable (*e.g., glasses*)
im·pair -paire [ɛ̃pɛr] *adj* odd, uneven ‖ *m* (coll) blunder
impardonnable [ɛ̃pardɔnabl] *adj* unpardonable
impar·fait [ɛ̃parfɛ] **-faite** [fɛt] *adj* & *m* imperfect
imparité [ɛ̃parite] *f* inequality, disparity
impar·tial -tiale [ɛ̃parsjal] *adj* (*pl* **-tiaux** [sjo]) impartial
impartir [ɛ̃partir] *tr* to grant
impasse [ɛ̃pɑs] *f* blind alley, dead-end street; impasse, deadlock; (cards) finesse; **faire l'impasse à** (cards) to finesse
impassible [ɛ̃pasibl] *adj* impassible; impassive (*look, face, etc.*)
impatiemment [ɛ̃pasjamɑ̃] *adv* impatiently
impatience [ɛ̃pasjɑ̃s] *f* impatience; **impatiences** (coll) attack of nerves
impa·tient -tiente [ɛ̃pasjɑ̃] [sjɑ̃t] *adj* impatient
impatienter [ɛ̃pasjɑ̃te] *tr* to make impatient ‖ §97 *ref* to lose patience
impatroniser [ɛ̃patrɔnize] *ref* to take charge; take hold
impavide [ɛ̃pavid] *adj* fearless
impayable [ɛ̃pɛjabl] *adj* (coll) priceless, very funny
im·payé -payée [ɛ̃peje] *adj* unpaid
impec [ɛ̃pɛk] *adj* (coll) impeccable
impeccable [ɛ̃pɛkabl] *adj* impeccable
impénétrable [ɛ̃penetrabl] *adj* impenetrable
impéni·tent [ɛ̃penitɑ̃] **-tente** [tɑ̃t] *adj* impenitent, obdurate, inveterate
impensable [ɛ̃pɑ̃sabl] *adj* unthinkable
imper [ɛ̃pɛr] *m* (coll) raincoat
impéra·tif [ɛ̃peratif] **-tive** [tiv] *adj* & *m* imperative
impératrice [ɛ̃peratris] *f* empress
imperceptible [ɛ̃pɛrsɛptibl] *adj* imperceptible; negligible
imperdable [ɛ̃pɛrdabl] *adj* unlosable
imperfection [ɛ̃pɛrfɛksjɔ̃] *f* imperfection, defect
impé·rial -riale [ɛ̃perjal] *adj* (*pl* **-riaux** [rjo]) imperial ‖ *f* goatee; upper deck (*of bus, coach, etc.*)
impérialiste [ɛ̃perjalist] *adj* & *mf* imperialist
impé·rieux -rieuse [ɛ̃perjø] [rjøz] *adj* imperious, haughty; imperative, urgent
impérissable [ɛ̃perisabl] *adj* imperishable
impéritie [ɛ̃perisi] *f* incompetence
imperméabiliser [ɛ̃pɛrmeabilize] *tr* to waterproof
imperméable [ɛ̃pɛrmeabl] *adj* waterproof; impervious ‖ *m* raincoat
imperson·nel -nelle [ɛ̃pɛrsɔnɛl] *adj* impersonal; commonplace; ordinary
imperti·nent [ɛ̃pɛrtinɑ̃] **-nente** [nɑ̃t] *adj* impertinent ‖ *mf* impertinent person
impesanteur [ɛ̃pəsɑ̃tœr] *f* weightlessness
impé·trant [ɛ̃petrɑ̃] **-trante** [trɑ̃t] *mf* holder (*of a title or degree*)
impé·tueux [ɛ̃petɥø] **-tueuse** [tɥøz] *adj* impetuous

impie [ɛ̃pi] *adj* impious, ungodly; blasphemous ‖ *mf* unbeliever; blasphemer

impiété [ɛ̃pjete] *f* impiety; disrespect

impitoyable [ɛ̃pitwajabl] *adj* unmerciful

implacable [ɛ̃plakabl] *adj* implacable

implanter [ɛ̃plãte] *tr* to implant; introduce ‖ *ref* to take root; **s'implanter chez** (coll) to thrust oneself upon

implication [ɛ̃plikɑsjɔ̃] *f* implication

implicite [ɛ̃plisit] *adj* implicit

impliquer [ɛ̃plike] *tr* to implicate; imply

implorer [ɛ̃plɔre] *tr* to implore

imployable [ɛ̃plwajabl] *adj* pitiless; inflexible

impo·li -lie [ɛ̃pɔli] *adj* impolite

impolitique [ɛ̃pɔlitik] *adj* ill-advised

impondérable [ɛ̃pɔ̃derabl] *adj & m* imponderable

impopulaire [ɛ̃pɔpylɛr] *adj* unpopular

impopularité [ɛ̃pɔpylarite] *f* unpopularity

importance [ɛ̃pɔrtãs] *f* importance; size; **d'importance** large, of consequence; thoroughly, very hard

impor·tant [ɛ̃pɔrtã] **-tante** [tãt] *adj* important; large, considerable ‖ *m* main thing; **faire l'important** (coll) to act big

importa·teur [ɛ̃pɔrtatœr] **-trice** [tris] *adj* importing ‖ *mf* importer

importation [ɛ̃pɔrtɑsjɔ̃] *f* importation

importer [ɛ̃pɔrte] *tr* to import ‖ *intr* to matter; be important; **n'importe** no matter, never mind; **n'importe comment** any way; **n'importe où** anywhere; **n'importe quand** anytime; **n'importe quel** . . . any . . . ; **n'importe qui** anybody; **n'importe quoi** anything; **peu m'importe** it doesn't matter to me; **qu'importe?** what does it matter?

impor·tun -tune [ɛ̃pɔrtœ̃] **-tune** [tyn] *adj* bothersome ‖ *mf* pest, nuisance

importuner [ɛ̃pɔrtyne] *tr* to importune

imposable [ɛ̃pozabl] *adj* taxable

impo·sant [ɛ̃pozã] **-sante** [zãt] *adj* imposing

impo·sé -sée [ɛ̃poze] *adj* taxed; fixed (*price*) ‖ *mf* taxpayer

imposer [ɛ̃poze] §97, §98 *tr* to impose; levy a tax on ‖ *intr*—**en imposer à** to make an impression on; impose on ‖ *ref* to assert oneself; be indispensable; **s'imposer à** to force itself upon; **s'imposer chez** to foist oneself upon

imposition [ɛ̃pozisjɔ̃] *f* imposition; taxation; laying on, levying; **niveau d'imposition** tax bracket

impossibilité [ɛ̃pɔsibilite] *f* impossibility; **être dans l'impossibilité de** to be unable to

impossible [ɛ̃pɔsibl] *adj* impossible

imposte [ɛ̃pɔst] *f* transom; (archit) impost

imposteur [ɛ̃pɔstœr] *m* impostor

imposture [ɛ̃pɔstyr] *f* imposture

impôt [ɛ̃po] *m* tax; **impôt du sang** military duty; **impôt foncier** property tax; **impôt indirecte** sales tax; **impôt retenu à la source** withholding tax; **impôt sur le revenu** income tax

impotence [ɛ̃pɔtãs] *f* lameness, infirmity

impo·tent [ɛ̃pɔtã] **-tente** [tãt] *adj* crippled; bedridden ‖ *mf* cripple

impraticable [ɛ̃pratikabl] *adj* impracticable; impassable (*e.g.*, *road*)

impré·cis [ɛ̃presi] **-cise** [siz] *adj* vague, hazy

imprégner [ɛ̃preɲe] §10 *tr* to impregnate

imprenable [ɛ̃prənabl] *adj* impregnable

impréparation [ɛ̃preparɑsjɔ̃] *f* unpreparedness

imprésario [ɛ̃presarjo] *m* impresario

impression [ɛ̃prɛsjɔ̃] *f* impression; printing; (phot) print

impression·nant [ɛ̃prɛsjɔnã] **-nante** [nãt] *adj* impressive

impressionner [ɛ̃prɛsjɔne] *tr* to impress, affect; (phot) to expose

impressionnisme [ɛ̃prɛsjɔnism] *m* (painting) impressionism

imprévisible [ɛ̃previzibl] *adj* unforeseeable

imprévision [ɛ̃previzjɔ̃] *f* lack of foresight

im·prévoyant [ɛ̃prevwajã] **-prévoyante** [prevwajãt] *adj* improvident, short-sighted

impré·vu -vue [ɛ̃prevy] *adj & m* unforeseen, unexpected; **sauf imprévu** unless something unforeseen happens

impri·mé -mée [ɛ̃prime] *adj* printed ‖ *m* print, calico; printed work, book; printing (*as opposed to script*); **imprimés** printed matter

imprimer [ɛ̃prime] *tr* to print; imprint; impress; impart (*e.g.*, *movement*)

imprimerie [ɛ̃primri] *f* printing; printing office, print shop

imprimeur [ɛ̃primœr] *m* printer

imprimeur-éditeur [ɛ̃primœreditœr] *m* (*pl* **imprimeurs-éditeurs**) printer and publisher

imprimeur-libraire [ɛ̃primœrlibrɛr] *m* (*pl* **imprimeurs-libraires**) printer and publisher

imprimeuse [ɛ̃primøz] *f* printing press

improbable [ɛ̃prɔbabl] *adj* improbable

improba·tif [ɛ̃prɔbatif] **-tive** [tiv] *adj* disapproving

improbité [ɛ̃prɔbite] *f* dishonesty

improduc·tif [ɛ̃prɔdyktif] **-tive** [tiv] *adj* unproductive

imprompt·tu -tue [ɛ̃prɔ̃pty] *adj* impromptu ‖ *m* impromptu play; (mus) impromptu ‖ **impromptu** *adv* impromptu

impropre [ɛ̃prɔpr] *adj* improper (*not right*); **impropre à** unfit for

impropriété [ɛ̃prɔprijete] *f* incorrectness

improviser [ɛ̃prɔvize] *tr & intr* to improvise

improviste [ɛ̃prɔvist]—**à l'improviste** unexpectedly, impromptu; **prendre à l'improviste** to catch napping

impru·dent [ɛ̃prydã] **-dente** [dãt] *adj* imprudent

impubère [ɛ̃pybɛr] *adj* under the age of puberty

impubliable [ɛ̃pybljabl] *adj* unpublishable, not fit to print

impu·dent [ɛ̃pydɑ̃] **-dente** [dɑ̃t] *adj* impudent

impudeur [ɛ̃pydœr] *f* immodesty

impudicité [ɛ̃pydisite] *f* indecency

impudique [ɛ̃pydik] *adj* immodest

impuissance [ɛ̃pɥisɑ̃s] *f* powerlessness, helplessness; ineffectiveness; (pathol) impotence: **être dans l'impuissance de faire q.ch.** to be incapable of doing s.th.

impuis·sant [ɛ̃pɥisɑ̃] **-sante** [sɑ̃t] *adj* impotent, powerless, helpless; (pathol) impotent

impul·sif [ɛ̃pylsif] **-sive** [siv] *adj* impulsive ‖ *mf* impulsive person

impulsion [ɛ̃pylsjɔ̃] *f* impulse; **donner l'impulsion à** to give an impetus to; **sous l'impulsion du moment** on the spur of the moment

impunément [ɛ̃pynemɑ̃] *adv* with impunity

impu·ni -nie [ɛ̃pyni] *adj* unpunished

impunité [ɛ̃pynite] *f* impunity

im·pur -pure [ɛ̃pyr] *adj* impure

impureté [ɛ̃pyrte] *f* impurity; unchastity

imputation [ɛ̃pytɑsjɔ̃] *f* imputation; (com) charge; (com) deduction

imputer [ɛ̃pyte] §97, §98 *tr* to impute, ascribe; (com) **imputer q.ch. à** to charge s.th. to

inabordable [inabɔrdabl] *adj* unapproachable, inaccessible; prohibitive (*price*)

inaccessible [inaksɛsibl] *adj* inaccessible

inaccoutu·mé -mée [inakutyme] *adj* unusual; **inaccoutumé à** unaccustomed to, unused to

inache·vé -vée [inaʃve] *adj* unfinished, uncompleted

inac·tif [inaktif] **-tive** [tiv] *adj* inactive

inaction [inaksjɔ̃] *f* inaction

inactivité [inaktivite] *f* inactivity

inadaptation [inadaptɑsjɔ̃] *f* maladjustment

inadap·té -tée [inadapte] *adj* maladjusted ‖ *mf* misfit

inadvertance [inadvɛrtɑ̃s] *f*—**par inadvertance** inadvertently

inalté·ré -rée [inaltere] *adj* unspoiled

inamovible [inamɔvibl] *adj* fixed, unmovable; not removable

inani·mé -mée [inanime] *adj* inanimate

inappréciable [inapresjabl] *adj* inappreciable, imperceptible; invaluable

inapprivoisable [inaprivwazabl] *adj* untamable

inapte [inapt] *adj* inept; **inapte à** unfit for, unsuitable for ‖ *mf* dropout, washout; **les inaptes** the unfit; the unemployable

inaptitude [inaptityd] *f* unfitness

inarticu·lé -lée [inartikyle] *adj* inarticulate

inassou·vi -vie [inasuvi] *adj* unsatisfied

inattaquable [inatakabl] *adj* unquestionable; unassailable; **inattaquable par** unaffected by, resistant to

inatten·du -due [inatɑ̃dy] *adj* unexpected

inatten·tif [inatɑ̃tif] **-tive** [tiv] *adj* inattentive; careless

inattention [inatɑ̃sjɔ̃] *f* inattentiveness, carelessness

inaudible [inodibl] *adj* inaudible

inaugu·ral -rale [inogyral] *adj* (*pl* **-raux** [ro]) inaugural

inauguration [inogyrɑsjɔ̃] *f* inauguration

inaugurer [inogyre] *tr* to inaugurate; unveil (*a statue*)

inauthentique [inotɑ̃tik] *adj* unauthentic

inavouable [inavuabl] *adj* shameful

ina·voué -vouée [inavwe] *adj* unacknowledged

inca [ɛ̃ka] *adj invar* Inca ‖ (*cap*) *m* Inca

incandes·cent [ɛ̃kɑ̃desɑ̃] **-cente** [sɑ̃t] *adj* incandescent; wild, stirred up (*crowd*)

incapable [ɛ̃kapabl] §93 *adj* incapable; (law) incompetent ‖ *mf* (law) incompetent person

incapacité [ɛ̃kapasite] *f* incapacity; disability

incarcérer [ɛ̃karsere] §10 *tr* to incarcerate

incar·nat [ɛ̃karna] **-nate** [nat] *adj* "flesh"-colored; rosy ‖ *m* "flesh" color

incarnation [ɛ̃karnɑsjɔ̃] *f* incarnation

incar·né -née [ɛ̃karne] *adj* incarnate; ingrowing (*nail*)

incarner [ɛ̃karne] *tr* to incarnate, embody ‖ *ref* to become incarnate; (pathol) to become ingrown; **s'incarner dans** to become the embodiment of

incartade [ɛ̃kartad] *f* indiscretion; prank

incassable [ɛ̃kasabl] *adj* unbreakable

incendiaire [ɛ̃sɑ̃djɛr] *adj & mf* incendiary

incendie [ɛ̃sɑ̃di] *m* fire, conflagration; **incendie volontaire** arson

incen·dié -diée [ɛ̃sɑ̃dje] *adj* burnt down ‖ *mf* fire victim

incendier [ɛ̃sɑ̃dje] *tr* to set on fire; burn down; (fig) to fire, inflame; (slang) to give a tongue-lashing to

incer·tain [ɛ̃sɛrtɛ̃] **-taine** [tɛn] *adj* uncertain; indistinct; unsettled (*weather*)

incertitude [ɛ̃sɛrtityd] *f* incertitude, uncertainty; **dans l'incertitude** in doubt

incessamment [ɛ̃sɛsamɑ̃] *adv* incessantly; without delay, at any moment

inces·sant [ɛ̃sɛsɑ̃] **-sante** [sɑ̃t] *adj* incessant

inceste [ɛ̃sɛst] *m* incest

inces·tueux [ɛ̃sɛstɥø] **-tueuse** [tɥøz] *adj* incestuous

inchan·gé -gée [ɛ̃ʃɑ̃ʒe] *adj* unchanged

incidemment [ɛ̃sidamɑ̃] *adv* incidentally

incidence [ɛ̃sidɑ̃s] *f* incidence

inci·dent [ɛ̃sidɑ̃] **-dente** [dɑ̃t] *adj & m* incident

incinérer [ɛ̃sinere] §10 *tr* to incinerate; cremate

incirconcis [ɛ̃sirkɔ̃si] *adj masc* uncircumcised

inciser [ɛ̃size] *tr* to make an incision in; tap (*a tree*); (med) to lance

inci·sif [ɛ̃sizif] **-sive** [ziv] *adj* incisive ‖ *f* incisor

incision [ɛ̃sizjɔ̃] *f* incision

incitation [ɛ̃sitɑsjɔ̃] *f* incitement

inciter [ɛ̃site] §96, §100 *tr* to incite

inci·vil -vile [ɛ̃sivil] *adj* uncivil

incivili·sé -sée [ɛ̃sivilize] *adj* uncivilized

inclassable [ɛ̃klɑsabl] *adj* unclassifiable

inclé·ment [ɛ̃klemɑ̃] **-mente** [mɑ̃t] *adj* inclement

inclinaison [ɛ̃klinɛzɔ̃] *f* inclination; slope

inclination [ɛ̃klinɑsjɔ̃] *f* inclination; bow; love, affection

incliner [ɛ̃kline] §96 *tr* & *ref* to incline; bend; bow; obey

inclure [ɛ̃klyr] §11 (*pp* **inclus**) *tr* to include; enclose

in·clus [ɛ̃kly] **-cluse** [klyz] *adj* including, e.g., **jusqu'à la page dix incluse** up to and including page ten; inclusive, e.g., **de mercredi à samedi inclus** from Wednesday to Saturday inclusive

inclu·sif [ɛ̃klyzif] **-sive** [ziv] *adj* inclusive

inclusivement [ɛ̃klyzivmɑ̃] *adv* inclusively, inclusive

incognito [ɛ̃kɔɲito] *m* & *adv* incognito

incohé·rent [ɛ̃kɔerɑ̃] **-rente** [rɑ̃t] *adj* incoherent; inconsistent, illogical

incollable [ɛ̃kɔlabl] *adj* (coll) knowing all the answers, not to be stumped

incolore [ɛ̃kɔlɔr] *adj* colorless

incomber [ɛ̃kɔ̃be] *intr*—**incomber à** to devolve on, fall upon; **il incombe à qn de** it behooves s.o. to

incombustible [ɛ̃kɔ̃bystibl] *adj* incombustible; fireproof

incommode [ɛ̃kɔmɔd] *adj* inconvenient; unwieldy

incommoder [ɛ̃kɔmɔde] *tr* to inconvenience

incommodité [ɛ̃kɔmɔdite] *f* inconvenience

incomparable [ɛ̃kɔ̃parabl] *adj* incomparable

incompatible [ɛ̃kɔ̃patibl] *adj* incompatible; conflicting

incompétence [ɛ̃kɔ̃petɑ̃s] *f* incompetence; lack of jurisdiction

incompé·tent [ɛ̃kɔ̃petɑ̃] **-tente** [tɑ̃t] *adj* incompetent; lacking jurisdiction

incom·plet [ɛ̃kɔ̃plɛ] **-plète** [plɛt] *adj* incomplete

incompréhensible [ɛ̃kɔ̃preɑ̃sibl] *adj* incomprehensible

incom·pris [kɔ̃pri] **-prise** [priz] *adj* misunderstood

inconcevable [ɛ̃kɔ̃svabl] *adj* inconceivable

inconciliable [ɛ̃kɔ̃siljabl] *adj* irreconcilable

incondition·nel -nelle [ɛ̃kɔ̃disjɔnɛl] *adj* unconditional

inconduite [ɛ̃kɔ̃dɥit] *f* misconduct

inconfort [ɛ̃kɔ̃fɔr] *m* discomfort

incon·gru -grue [ɛ̃kɔ̃gry] *adj* incongruous

incon·nu -nue [ɛ̃kɔny] *adj* unknown; **inconnu à cette adresse** address unknown || *mf* unknown (*person*) || *m* unknown (*what is not known*) || *f* (math) unknown

inconsciemment [ɛ̃kɔ̃sjamɑ̃] *adv* subconsciously; unconsciously

inconscience [ɛ̃kɔ̃sjɑ̃s] *f* unconsciousness; unawareness

incons·cient [ɛ̃kɔ̃sjɑ̃] **-ciente** [sjɑ̃t] *adj* unconscious, unaware, oblivious; thoughtless; subconscious || *mf* dazed person || *m* unconscious

inconséquence [ɛ̃kɔ̃sekɑ̃s] *f* inconsistency; thoughtlessness, inconsiderateness

inconsé·quent [ɛ̃kɔ̃sekɑ̃] **-quente** [kɑ̃t] *adj* inconsistent; thoughtless, inconsiderate

inconsidé·ré -rée [ɛ̃kɔ̃sidere] *adj* inconsiderate

inconsistance [ɛ̃kɔ̃sistɑ̃s] *f* inconsistency; flimsiness, instability

inconsis·tant [ɛ̃kɔ̃sistɑ̃] **-tante** [tɑ̃t] *adj* inconsistent; flimsy, unstable

inconsolable [ɛ̃kɔ̃sɔlabl] *adj* inconsolable

incons·tant [ɛ̃kɔ̃stɑ̃] **-tante** [tɑ̃t] *adj* inconstant

inconstitution·nel -nelle [ɛ̃kɔ̃stitysjɔnɛl] *adj* unconstitutional

incontestable [ɛ̃kɔ̃tɛstabl] *adj* incontestable, unquestionable, indisputable

inconti·nent [ɛ̃kɔ̃tinɑ̃] **-nente** [nɑ̃t] *adj* incontinent || **incontinent** *adv* at once, forthwith

incontrôlable [ɛ̃kɔ̃trolabl] *adj* unverifiable

incontrô·lé -lée [ɛ̃kɔ̃trole] *adj* unverified; unchecked, uncontrollable

inconvenance [ɛ̃kɔ̃vnɑ̃s] *f* impropriety

inconve·nant [ɛ̃kɔ̃vnɑ̃] **-nante** [nɑ̃t] *adj* improper, indecent

inconvénient [ɛ̃kɔ̃venjɑ̃] *m* inconvenience, disadvantage; **voir un inconvénient à** to have an objection to

incorporation [ɛ̃kɔrpɔrasjɔ̃] *f* incorporation; (mil) induction

incorpo·ré -rée [ɛ̃kɔrpɔre] *adj* built-in

incorpo·rel -relle [ɛ̃kɔrpɔrɛl] *adj* incorporeal; intangible (*property*)

incorporer [ɛ̃kɔrpɔre] *tr* to incorporate; (mil) to induct || *ref* to incorporate

incor·rect -recte [ɛ̃kɔrɛkt] *adj* incorrect; unfair; improper; discourteous; indecent

incorrectement [ɛ̃kɔrɛktəmɑ̃] *adv* incorrectly; improperly; discourteously; in an underhand way

incorrection [ɛ̃kɔrɛksjɔ̃] *f* impropriety; incorrectness; impolite behavior; dishonesty

incrédule [ɛ̃kredyl] *adj* incredulous; unbelieving || *mf* unbeliever, freethinker

incrédulité [ɛ̃kredylite] *f* incredulity; disbelief

incrément [ɛ̃kremɑ̃] *m* (comp) increment

incrémenter [ɛ̃kremɑ̃te] *tr* (comp) to increment

increvable [ɛ̃krəvabl] *adj* punctureproof; (slang) untiring

incriminer [ɛ̃krimine] *tr* to incriminate

incrochetable [ɛ̃krɔʃtabl] *adj* burglarproof (*lock*)

incroyable [ɛ̃krwajabl] *adj* unbelievable

in·croyant -croyante [krwajɑ̃] *adj* unbelieving || *mf* unbeliever

incrustation [ɛ̃krystasjɔ̃] *f* incrustation; inlay; (sewing) insert

incruster [ɛ̃kryste] *tr* to incrust; inlay || *ref* to take root, become ingrained

incubateur [ɛ̃kybatœr] *m* incubator

incuber [ɛ̃kybe] *tr* to incubate

inculpation [ɛ̃kylpasjɔ̃] *f* indictment; **sous l'inculpation de** on a charge of

incul·pé -pée [ɛ̃kylpe] *adj* indicted; **inculpé de** charged with, accused of || *mf* accused, defendant

inculper [ɛ̃kylpe] *tr* to indict, charge
inculquer [ɛ̃kylke] *tr* to inculcate
inculte [ɛ̃kylt] *adj* uncultivated; uncouth
incunables [ɛ̃kynabl] *mpl* incunabula
incurable [ɛ̃kyrabl] *adj & mf* incurable
incurie [ɛ̃kyri] *f* carelessness
incursion [ɛ̃kyrsjɔ̃] *f* incursion, foray
Inde [ɛ̃d] *f* India; **Indes Occidentales** West Indies; **l'Inde** India
indébrouillable [ɛ̃debrujabl] *adj* inextricable, hopelessly involved
indécence [ɛ̃desɑ̃s] *f* indecency
indé·cent [ɛ̃desɑ̃] **-cente** [sɑ̃t] *adj* indecent
indéchiffrable [ɛ̃deʃifrabl] *adj* undecipherable; incomprehensible; illegible
indé·cis [ɛ̃desi] **-cise** [siz] *adj* indecisive; uncertain, undecided; blurred
indéclinable [ɛ̃deklinabl] *adj* indeclinable
indécrottable [ɛ̃dekrɔtabl] *adj* (coll) incorrigible, hopeless
indéfectible [ɛ̃defɛktibl] *adj* everlasting; unfailing
indéfendable [ɛ̃defɑ̃dabl] *adj* indefensible
indéfi·ni -nie [ɛ̃defini] *adj* indefinite
indéfinissable [ɛ̃definisabl] *adj* indefinable
indéfrisable [ɛ̃defrizabl] *adj* permanent (*wave*) ‖ *f* permanent wave
indélébile [ɛ̃delebil] *adj* indelible
indéli·cat [ɛ̃delika] **-cate** [kat] *adj* indelicate; dishonest
indémaillable [ɛ̃demɑjabl] *adj* runproof
indemne [ɛ̃dɛmn] *adj* undamaged, unharmed
indemnisation [ɛ̃dɛmnizɑjɔ̃] *f* indemnification, compensation
indemniser [ɛ̃dɛmnize] *tr* to compensate
indemnité [ɛ̃dɛmnite] *f* indemnity; allowance, grant; compensation; **indemnité journalière** workmen's compensation; **indemnité parlementaire** salary of members (*of parliamentary body*)
indéniable [ɛ̃denjabl] *adj* undeniable
indépendamment [ɛ̃depɑ̃damɑ̃] *adv* independently; **indépendamment de** apart from; regardless of
indépendance [ɛ̃depɑ̃dɑ̃s] *f* independence
indépen·dant [ɛ̃depɑ̃dɑ̃] **-dante** [dɑ̃t] *adj & mf* independent
indéréglable [ɛ̃dereglabl] *adj* foolproof
indescriptible [ɛ̃dɛskriptibl] *adj* indescribable
indésirable [ɛ̃dezirabl] *adj* undesirable
indestructible [ɛ̃dɛstryktibl] *adj* indestructible
indétermi·né -née [ɛ̃determine] *adj* indeterminate
indétraquable [ɛ̃detrakabl] *adj* foolproof
index [ɛ̃dɛks] *m* index; forefinger; index number; **Index** (eccl) Index
indexation [ɛ̃dɛksasjɔ̃] *f*—**indexation des traitements sur le coût de la vie** consumer price index, CPI
indica·teur [ɛ̃dikatœr] **-trice** [tris] *adj* indicating ‖ *mf* informer ‖ *m* gauge; indicator, pointer; timetable; road sign; guidebook; street guide

indica·tif [ɛ̃dikatif] **-tive** [tiv] *adj* indicative, suggestive ‖ *m* (gram) indicative; (rad) station identification; **indicatif d'appel** (rad, telg) call letters or number; **indicatif postal** zip code
indication [ɛ̃dikɑsjɔ̃] *f* indication; **fausse indication** wrong piece of information; **indications** directions; **sauf indication contraire** unless otherwise directed; **sur l'indication de** at the suggestion of
indice [ɛ̃dis] *m* indication, sign; clue; **indice de pose** exposure index; **indice de refroidissement** chill factor; **indice des prix** price index; **indice d'octane** octane number; **indice du coût de la vie** cost-of-living index
indicible [ɛ̃disibl] *adj* inexpressible
in·dien [ɛ̃djɛ̃] **-dienne** [djɛn] *adj* Indian ‖ *f* calico, chintz ‖ (*cap*) *mf* Indian
indifféremment [ɛ̃diferamɑ̃] *adv* indiscriminately
indiffé·rent [ɛ̃diferɑ̃] **-rente** [rɑ̃t] *adj* indifferent; unimportant; **cela m'est indifférent** it's all the same to me
indigence [ɛ̃diʒɑ̃s] *f* indigence, poverty
indigène [ɛ̃diʒɛn] *adj* indigenous, native ‖ *mf* native
indi·gent [ɛ̃diʒɑ̃] **-gente** [ʒɑ̃t] *adj* indigent ‖ *mf* pauper; **les indigents** the poor
indigeste [ɛ̃diʒɛst] *adj* indigestible; heavy, stodgy; undigested, mixed up
indigestion [ɛ̃diʒɛstjɔ̃] *f* indigestion
indignation [ɛ̃diɲɑsjɔ̃] *f* indignation
indigne [ɛ̃diɲ] *adj* unworthy; shameful
indi·gné -gnée [ɛ̃diɲe] *adj* indignant
indigner [ɛ̃diɲe] *tr* to outrage ‖ §97 *ref* to be indignant
indignité [ɛ̃diɲite] *f* unworthiness; indignity, outrage
indigo [ɛ̃digo] *adj invar & m* indigo
indi·qué -quée [ɛ̃dike] *adj* advisable, appropriate; **être tout indiqué pour** to be just the thing for; be just the man for
indiquer [ɛ̃dike] *tr* to indicate; name; **indiquer du doigt** to point to, point out
indi·rect -recte [ɛ̃dirɛkt] *adj* indirect
indisciplinable [ɛ̃disiplinabl] *adj* unruly
indiscipline [ɛ̃disiplin] *f* lack of discipline, disobedience
indiscipli·né -née [ɛ̃disipline] *adj* undisciplined
indis·cret [ɛ̃diskrɛ] **-crète** [krɛt] *adj* indiscreet
indiscrétion [ɛ̃diskresjɔ̃] *f* indiscretion; **sans indiscrétion . . .** if I may ask . . .
indiscutable [ɛ̃diskytabl] *adj* unquestionable
indiscu·té -tée [ɛ̃diskyte] *adj* unquestioned
indispensable [ɛ̃dispɑ̃sabl] *adj & m* indispensable, essential
indisponible [ɛ̃dispɔnibl] *adj* unavailable; out of commission (*said of car, machine, etc.*)
indispo·sé -sée [ɛ̃dispoze] *adj* indisposed (*slightly ill*); ill-disposed
indisposer [ɛ̃dispoze] *tr* to indispose
indissoluble [ɛ̃disɔlybl] *adj* indissoluble

indis·tinct [ɛ̃distɛ̃], [ɛ̃distɛ̃kt] **-tincte** [tɛ̃kt] *adj* indistinct

indistinctement [ɛ̃distɛ̃ktəmɑ̃] *adv* indistinctly; indiscriminately

individu [ɛ̃dividy] *m* individual; (coll) fellow, guy

individualiser [ɛ̃dividɥalize] *tr* to individualize

individualité [ɛ̃dividɥalite] *f* individuality

indivi·duel -duelle [ɛ̃dividɥɛl] *adj* individual; separate

indi·vis [ɛ̃divi] **-vise** [viz] *adj* joint; **par indivis** jointly

indivisible [ɛ̃divizibl] *adj* indivisible

Indochine [ɛ̃dɔʃin] *f* Indochina; **l'Indochine** Indochina

indocile [ɛ̃dɔsil] *adj* rebellious, unruly

indo-européen [ɛ̃dɔørɔpeɛ̃] **-européenne** [ørɔpeɛn] *adj* Indo-European ‖ *m* Indo-European (*language*) ‖ (*cap*) *mf* Indo-European

indolemment [ɛ̃dɔlamɑ̃] *adv* indolently

indo·lent [ɛ̃dɔlɑ̃] **-lente** [lɑ̃t] *adj* indolent; apathetic; painless (*e.g.*, *tumor*) ‖ *mf* idler

indolore [ɛ̃dɔlɔr] *adj* painless

indomptable [ɛ̃dɔ̃tabl] *adj* indomitable

indomp·té -tée [ɛ̃dɔ̃te] *adj* untamed

Indonésie [ɛ̃dɔnezi] *f* Indonesia; **l'Indonésie** Indonesia

indoné·sien [ɛ̃dɔnezjɛ̃] **-sienne** [zjɛn] *adj* Indonesian ‖ *m* Indonesian (*language*) ‖ (*cap*) *mf* Indonesian (*person*)

in-douze [ɛ̃duz] *adj invar & m invar* duodecimo

in·du -due [ɛ̃dy] *adj* unseemly (*e.g.*, *hour*); undue (*haste*); unwarranted (*remark*) ‖ *m* something not due

indubitable [ɛ̃dybitabl] *adj* indubitable; **c'est indubitable** there's no doubt about it

inducteur [ɛ̃dyktœr] *m* (elec) field

induction [ɛ̃dyksjɔ̃] *f* (elec, logic) induction

induire [ɛ̃dɥir] §19, §96 *tr* to induce; **induire en** to lead into (*temptation, error, etc.*)

in·duit [ɛ̃dɥi] **-duite** [dɥit] *adj* induced ‖ *m* (elec) armature

indulgence [ɛ̃dylʒɑ̃s] *f* indulgence

indul·gent [ɛ̃dylʒɑ̃] **-gente** [ʒɑ̃t] *adj* indulgent

indûment [ɛ̃dymɑ̃] *adv* unduly

indurer [ɛ̃dyre] *tr & ref* to harden

industrialiser [ɛ̃dystrijalize] *tr* to industrialize ‖ *ref* to become industrialized

industrie [ɛ̃dystri] *f* industry; trickery; (obs) occupation, trade; **industrie du bâtiment** building industry, construction; **l'industrie du spectacle** show business

industrie-clef [ɛ̃dystrikle] *f* (*pl* **industries-clefs**) key industry

indus·triel -trielle [ɛ̃dystrijɛl] *adj* industrial ‖ *m* industrialist

indus·trieux [ɛ̃dystrijø] **-trieuse** [trijøz] *adj* industrious; skilled

inébranlable [inebrɑ̃labl] *adj* unshakable

inéchangeable [ineʃɑ̃ʒabl] *adj* unexchangeable

iné·dit [inedi] **-dite** [dit] *adj* unpublished; new, novel

inéducable [inedykabl] *adj* unteachable

ineffable [inɛfabl] *adj* ineffable

ineffaçable [inɛfasabl] *adj* indelible

inefficace [inɛfikas] *adj* ineffective, inefficient

inefficacité [inefikasite] *f* ineffectiveness, inefficiency

iné·gal -gale [inegal] *adj* (*pl* **-gaux** [go]) unequal; uneven

inégalité [inegalite] *f* inequality; unevenness

inélégamment [inelegamɑ̃] *adv* inelegantly

inéligible [ineliʒibl] *adj* ineligible

inéluctable [inelyktabl] *adj* unavoidable

inem·ployé -ployée [inɑ̃plwaje] *adj* unused

inénarrable [inenarabl] *adj* beyond words, too funny for words

inepte [inɛpt] *adj* inept, inane

ineptie [inɛpsi] *f* ineptitude, inanity; inane remark

inépuisable [inepɥizabl] *adj* inexhaustible

inerme [inɛrm] *adj* thornless

inertie [inɛrsi] *f* inertia

inescomptable [inɛskɔ̃tabl] *adj* not subject to discount

inespé·ré -rée [inɛspere] *adj* unhoped-for, unexpected

inestimable [inɛstimabl] *adj* inestimable, invaluable, priceless

inévitable [inevitabl] *adj* inevitable

inexact inexacte [inɛgzakt] *adj* inexact, inaccurate; unpunctual

inexactitude [inɛgzaktityd] *f* inexactness, inaccuracy; unpunctuality

inexau·cé -cée [inɛgzose] *adj* unfulfilled, unanswered

inexcitable [inɛksitabl] *adj* unexcitable

inexcusable [inɛkskyzabl] *adj* inexcusable

inexécutable [inɛgzekytabl] *adj* impracticable

inexécution [inɛgzekysjɔ̃] *f* nonfulfillment

inexer·cé -cée [inɛgzɛrse] *adj* untried; untrained

inexhaustible [inɛgzostibl] *adj* inexhaustible

inexigible [inɛgziʒibl] *adj* uncollectable

inexis·tant [inɛksistɑ̃] **-tante** [tɑ̃t] *adj* nonexistent

inexorable [inɛgzɔrabl] *adj* inexorable

inexpérience [inɛksperjɑ̃s] *f* inexperience

inexpérimen·té -tée [inɛksperimɑ̃te] *adj* inexperienced; untried; unskilled

inex·pié -piée [inɛkspje] *adj* unexpiated

inexplicable [inɛksplikabl] *adj* inexplicable, unexplainable

inexpli·qué -quée [inɛksplike] *adj* unexplained

inexploi·té -tée [inɛksplwate] *adj* untapped

inexplo·ré -rée [inɛksplɔre] *adj* unexplored

inexpres·sif [inɛksprɛsif] **-sive** [siv] *adj* expressionless

inexprimable [inɛksprimabl] *adj* inexpressible

inexpri·mé -mée [inɛksprime] *adj* unexpressed

inexpugnable [inɛkspygnabl] *adj* impregnable

inextinguible [inɛkstɛ̃gibl], [inɛkstɛ̃gyibl] *adj* inextinguishable; uncontrollable; unquenchable

infaillible [ɛ̃fajibl] *adj* infallible

infaisable [ɛ̃fəzabl] *adj* unfeasible

infa·mant [ɛ̃famɑ̃] **-mante** [mɑ̃t] *adj* opprobrious

infâme [ɛ̃fɑm] *adj* infamous; squalid

infamie [ɛ̃fami] *f* infamy; **dire des infamies à** to hurl insults at; **noter d'infamie** to brand as infamous

infant [ɛ̃fɑ̃] *m* infante

infante [ɛ̃fɑ̃t] *f* infanta

infanterie [ɛ̃fɑ̃tri] *f* infantry; **infanterie de l'air, infanterie aéroportée** parachute troops; **infanterie de marine** overseas troops; **infanterie portée, infanterie motorisée** motorized troops

infantile [ɛ̃fɑ̃til] *adj* infantile

infarctus [ɛ̃farktys] *m* (pathol) infarct, infarction; **infarctus du myocarde** coronary thrombosis

infatigable [ɛ̃fatigabl] *adj* indefatigable

infatuation [ɛ̃fatɥasjɔ̃] *f* conceit, false pride

infa·tué -tuée [ɛ̃fatɥe] *adj* infatuated with oneself, conceited

infé·cond [ɛ̃fekɔ̃] **-conde** [kɔ̃d] *adj* sterile, barren

in·fect -fecte [ɛ̃fɛkt] *adj* stinking; foul, vile

infecter [ɛ̃fɛkte] *tr* to infect; pollute; stink up

infec·tieux [ɛ̃fɛksjø] **-tieuse** [sjøz] *adj* infectious

infection [ɛ̃fɛksjɔ̃] *f* infection; stench

inférer [ɛ̃fere] §10 *tr* to infer, conclude

infé·rieur -rieure [ɛ̃ferjœr] *adj* lower; inferior; **inférieur à** below; less than ‖ *mf* subordinate, inferior

infériorité [ɛ̃ferjɔrite] *f* inferiority

infer·nal -nale [ɛ̃fɛrnal] *adj* (*pl* **-naux** [no]) infernal

infester [ɛ̃fɛste] *tr* to infest

infidèle [ɛ̃fidɛl] *adj* infidel; unfaithful ‖ *mf* infidel ‖ *m* unfaithful husband ‖ *f* unfaithful wife

infidélité [ɛ̃fidelite] *f* infidelity; inaccuracy, unfaithfulness

infiltration [ɛ̃filtrɑsjɔ̃] *f* infiltration

infiltrer [ɛ̃filtre] *ref* to infiltrate; seep, percolate; **s'infiltrer à travers** or **dans** to infiltrate

infime [ɛ̃fim] *adj* very small, infinitesimal; very low; trifling, negligible

infi·ni -nie [ɛ̃fini] *adj* infinite ‖ *m* infinite; (math) infinity; **à l'infini** infinitely

infiniment [ɛ̃finimɑ̃] *adv* infinitely; (coll) greatly, deeply, terribly

infinité [ɛ̃finite] *f* infinity

infini·tif [ɛ̃finitif] **-tive** [tiv] *adj* & *m* infinitive

infirme [ɛ̃firm] *adj* infirm, crippled, disabled ‖ *mf* invalid, cripple

infirmer [ɛ̃firme] *tr* (law) to invalidate

infirmerie [ɛ̃firməri] *f* infirmary; (nav) sick bay

infir·mier [ɛ̃firmje] **-mière** [mjɛr] *mf* nurse; **infirmière bénévole** volunteer nurse; **infirmière diplômée** registered nurse ‖ *m* male nurse; orderly, attendant

infirmière-major [ɛ̃firmjɛrmaʒɔr] *f* head nurse

infirmité [ɛ̃firmite] *f* infirmity

infixe [ɛ̃fiks] *m* infix

inflammable [ɛ̃flamabl] *adj* inflammable

inflammation [ɛ̃flamɑsjɔ̃] *f* inflammation

inflammatoire [ɛ̃flamatwar] *adj* inflammatory

inflation [ɛ̃flɑsjɔ̃] *f* inflation

inflationniste [ɛ̃flɑsjɔnist] *adj* inflationary

infléchir [ɛ̃fleʃir] *tr* to inflect, bend ‖ *ref* to bend, curve

inflexible [ɛ̃flɛksibl] *adj* inflexible

inflexion [ɛ̃flɛksjɔ̃] *f* inflection; change; bend, curve; metaphony

infliger [ɛ̃fliʒe] §38 *tr* to inflict; **infliger q.ch. à** to inflict s.th. on

influence [ɛ̃flyɑ̃s] *f* influence

influencer [ɛ̃flyɑ̃se] §51 *tr* to influence

in·fluent [ɛ̃flyɑ̃] **-fluente** [flyɑ̃t] *adj* influential

influenza [ɛ̃flyɑ̃za] *f* influenza

influer [ɛ̃flye] *intr*—**influer sur** to influence

in-folio [ɛ̃fɔljo] *adj* & *m* (*pl* **-folio** or **-folios**) folio

informa·teur [ɛ̃fɔrmatœr] **-trice** [tris] *mf* informant; informer

informati·cien [ɛ̃fɔrmatisjɛ̃] **-cienne** [sjɛn] *mf* informant; computer specialist

information [ɛ̃fɔrmɑsjɔ̃] *f* information; piece of information; (law) investigation; **aller aux informations** to make inquiries; **information génétique** genetic characteristics; **informations** news; information; **information de presse** press reports

informatique [ɛ̃fɔrmatik] *adj* informational; computer ‖ *f* computer science; data processing; information storage; **faire de l'informatique** to operate a computer

informatisation [ɛ̃fɔrmatizasjɔ̃] *f* computerization

informatiser [ɛ̃fɔrmatize] *tr* to computerize

informe [ɛ̃fɔrm] *adj* formless, shapeless

informer [ɛ̃fɔrme] *tr* to inform, advise ‖ *intr*—**informer contre** to inform on ‖ *ref* to inquire, keep oneself informed

infortune [ɛ̃fɔrtyn] *f* misfortune

infortu·né -née [ɛ̃fɔrtyne] *adj* unfortunate

infraction [ɛ̃fraksjɔ̃] *f* infraction

infranchissable [ɛ̃frɑ̃ʃisabl] *adj* insuperable; impassable (*e.g., mountain*)

infrarouge [ɛ̃fraruʒ] *adj* & *m* infrared

infrason [ɛ̃frasɔ̃] *m* infrasonic vibration

infrastructure [ɛ̃frastryktyr] *f* infrastructure; (rr) roadbed

infroissable [ɛ̃frwasabl] *adj* creaseless, wrinkleproof

infruc·tueux [ɛ̃fryktɥø] **-tueuse** [tɥøz] *adj* unfruitful, fruitless

in·fus -fuse [ɛ̃fy] **-fuse** [fyz] *adj* inborn, innate, intuitive

infuser [ɛ̃fyze] *tr* to infuse; brew; **infuser un sang nouveau à** to put new blood or life into ‖ *intr* to steep

infusion [ɛ̃fyzjɔ̃] *f* steeping; brew

ingambe [ɛ̃gɑ̃b] *adj* spry, nimble, alert

ingénier [ɛ̃ʒenje] §96 *ref* to strive hard

ingénierie [ɛ̃ʒeniri] or **ingéniérie** [ɛ̃ʒenjeri] *f* engineering

ingénieur [ɛ̃ʒenjœr] *m* engineer; **ingénieur des ponts et chaussées** civil engineer

ingé·nieux [ɛ̃ʒenjø] **-nieuse** [njøz] *adj* ingenious

ingéniosité [ɛ̃ʒenjozite] *f* ingenuity

ingé·nu -nue [ɛ̃ʒeny] *adj* ingenuous, artless ‖ *mf* naïve person ‖ *f* ingénue

ingénuité [ɛ̃ʒenɥite] *f* ingenuousness

ingérer [ɛ̃ʒere] §10 *tr* to ingest ‖ §97 *ref* to meddle

ingouvernable [ɛ̃guvɛrnabl] *adj* unruly, unmanageable

in·grat [ɛ̃gra] **-grate** [grat] *adj* ungrateful; disagreeable; thankless (*task*); unprofitable (*work*); barren (*soil*); awkward (*age*) ‖ *mf* ingrate

ingratitude [ɛ̃gratityd] *f* ingratitude

ingrédient [ɛ̃gredjɑ̃] *m* ingredient

inguérissable [ɛ̃gerisabl] *adj & mf* incurable

ingurgiter [ɛ̃gyrʒite] *tr* to swallow; gulp down

inhabile [inabil] §92 *adj* unfitted, unqualified; incompetent; clumsy; incapable, inefficient

inhabileté [inabilte] *f* unfitness, inability; incompetence; clumsiness; lack of skill; (law) incompetency, legal incapacity

inhabitable [inabitabl] *adj* uninhabitable

inhabi·té -tée [inabite] *adj* uninhabited

inhabi·tuel -tuelle [inabitɥel] *adj* unusual

inhaler [inale] *tr & intr* to inhale, breathe in

inhé·rent [inerɑ̃] **-rente** [rɑ̃t] *adj* inherent

inhiber [inibe] *tr* to inhibit

inhibition [inibisjɔ̃] *f* inhibition

inhospita·lier [inɔspitalje] **-lière** [ljɛr] *adj* inhospitable

inhu·main [inymɛ̃] **-maine** [mɛn] *adj* inhuman

inhumanité [inymanite] *f* inhumanity

inhumation [inymɑsjɔ̃] *f* burial

inhumer [inyme] *tr* to bury, inter

inimitable [inimitabl] *adj* inimitable

inimitié [inimitje] *f* enmity

ininflammable [inɛ̃flamabl] *adj* nonflammable, non-inflammable

inintelli·gent [inɛ̃tɛliʒɑ̃] **-gente** [ʒɑ̃t] *adj* unintelligent

inintéres·sant [inɛ̃teresɑ̃] **-sante** [sɑ̃t] *adj* uninteresting

ininterrom·pu -pue [inɛ̃terɔ̃py] *adj* uninterrupted

inique [inik] *adj* iniquitous, unjust, unfair

iniquité [inikite] *f* iniquity; unjustness, unfairness

ini·tial -tiale [inisjal] (*pl* **-tiaux** [sjo] **-tiales**) *adj & f* initial

initia·teur [inisjatœr] **-trice** [tris] *adj* initiating ‖ *mf* initiator

initiation [inisjɑsjɔ̃] *f* initiation

initiative [inisjativ] *f* initiative

initier [inisje] *tr* to initiate; introduce ‖ *ref* to become initiated

injecter [ɛ̃ʒɛkte] *tr* to inject; impregnate ‖ *ref* to become bloodshot

injec·teur [ɛ̃ʒɛktœr] **-trice** [tris] *adj* injecting ‖ *m* injector; nozzle (*in motor*)

injection [ɛ̃ʒɛksjɔ̃] *f* injection; impregnation; redness (*of eyes*); (geog) intrusion; **injection de rappel** booster shot

injonction [ɛ̃ʒɔ̃ksjɔ̃] *f* injunction, order

injouable [ɛ̃ʒwabl] *adj* unplayable

injure [ɛ̃ʒyr] *f* insult; wrong; **l'injure des ans** the ravages of time

injurier [ɛ̃ʒyrje] *tr* to insult, abuse

inju·rieux [ɛ̃ʒyrijø] **-rieuse** [rjøz] *adj* insulting, abusive; harmful, offensive

injuste [ɛ̃ʒyst] *adj* unjust

injustice [ɛ̃ʒystis] *f* injustice

injusti·fié -fiée [ɛ̃ʒystifje] *adj* unjustified

inlassable [ɛ̃lɑsabl] *adj* untiring

in·né -née [inne] *adj* innate, inborn

innocemment [inɔsamɑ̃] *adv* innocently

innocence [inɔsɑ̃s] *f* innocence

inno·cent [inɔsɑ̃] **-cente** [sɑ̃t] *adj & mf* innocent

innocenter [inɔsɑ̃te] *tr* to exonerate

innocuité [inɔkɥite] *f* innocuousness

innombrable [inɔ̃brabl] *adj* innumerable

innova·teur [inɔvatœr] **-trice** [tris] *adj* innovating ‖ *mf* innovator

innovation [inɔvɑsjɔ̃] *f* innovation

innover [inɔve] *tr & intr* to innovate

innocu·pé -pée [inɔkype] *adj* unoccupied; unemployed, idle ‖ *mf* idler

in-octavo [inɔktavo] *adj & m* (*pl* **-octavo** or **-octavos**) octavo

inoculation [inɔkylɑsjɔ̃] *f* inoculation

inoculer [inɔkyle] *tr* to inoculate

inodore [inɔdɔr] *adj* odorless

inoffen·sif [inɔfɑsif] **-sive** [siv] *adj* inoffensive

inondation [inɔ̃dɑsjɔ̃] *f* flood

inonder [inɔ̃de] *tr* to flood

inopi·né -née [inɔpine] *adj* unexpected

inoppor·tun [inɔpɔrtœ̃] **-tune** [tyn] *adj* untimely, inconvenient

inopportunité [inɔpɔrtynite] *f* untimeliness

inorganique [inɔrganik] *adj* inorganic

inorgani·sé -sée [inɔrganize] *adj* unorganized (*workers*), nonunion

inoubliable [inublijabl] *adj* unforgettable

inouï inouïe [inwi] *adj* unheard-of

inoxydable [inɔksidabl] *adj* inoxidizable, stainless, rustproof

inqualifiable [ɛ̃kalifjabl] *adj* unspeakable

in·quiet [ɛ̃kje] **-quiète** [kjɛt] *adj* anxious, worried, uneasy; restless

inquié·tant [ɛ̃kjetɑ̃] **-tante** [tɑ̃t] *adj* disquieting, worrisome

inquiéter [ɛ̃kjete] §10 *tr & intr* to worry

inquiétude [ɛ̃kjetyd] *f* uneasiness, worry

inquisi·teur [ɛ̃kizitœr] **-trice** [tris] *adj* inquisitorial; searching (*e.g., look*) ‖ *m* inquisitor; investigator

inquisition [ɛ̃kizisjɔ̃] *f* inquisition; investigation

inracontable [ɛ̃rakɔ̃tabl] *adj* untellable

insaisissable [ɛ̃sezisabl] *adj* hard to catch; elusive

insalubre [ɛ̃salybr] *adj* unhealthy

insane [ɛ̃san] *adj* insane, crazy

insanité [ɛ̃sanite] *f* insanity; piece of folly

insatiable [ɛ̃sasjabl] *adj* insatiable

insatisfaction [ɛ̃satisfaksjɔ̃] *f* dissatisfaction

inscription [ɛ̃skripsjɔ̃] *f* inscription; registration, enrollment; **inscription de** or **en faux** (law) plea of forgery; **prendre ses inscriptions** to register at a university

inscrire [ɛ̃skrir] §25 *tr* to inscribe; register; record || *ref* to register, enroll; **s'inscrire à** to join; **s'inscrire en faux contre** to deny; **s'inscrire pour** to sign up for

ins·crit [ɛ̃skri] **-crite** [krit] *adj* inscribed; registered, enrolled || *mf* registered student; (sports) entry; **inscrit maritime** naval recruit

insecte [ɛ̃sɛkt] *m* insect, bug

insecticide [ɛ̃sɛktisid] *adj* insecticidal || *m* insecticide

insen·sé -sée [ɛ̃sɑ̃se] *adj* senseless, insane, crazy || *m* madman || *f* madwoman

insensible [ɛ̃sɑ̃sibl] *adj* insensitive; imperceptible

inséparable [ɛ̃separabl] *adj* inseparable || *m* lovebird

insérer [ɛ̃sere] §10 *tr* to insert

insertion [ɛ̃sɛrsjɔ̃] *f* insertion

insi·dieux [ɛ̃sidjø] **-dieuse** [djøz] *adj* insidious

insigne [ɛ̃siɲ] *adj* signal, noteworthy; notorious || *m* badge, mark; **insignes** insignia

insigni·fiant [ɛ̃siɲifjɑ̃] **-fiante** [fjɑ̃t] *adj* insignificant

insincère [ɛ̃sɛ̃sɛr] *adj* insincere

insinuation [ɛ̃sinɥasjɔ̃] *f* insinuation

insinuer [ɛ̃sinɥe] *tr* to insinuate; hint, hint at; work in, introduce || *ref*—**s'insinuer dans** to worm one's way into

insipide [ɛ̃sipid] *adj* insipid, tasteless; insipid, dull

insister [ɛ̃siste] *intr* to insist; (coll) to continue, persevere; **insister pour** to insist on; **insister sur** to stress, emphasize

insociable [ɛ̃sɔsjabl] *adj* unsociable

insolateur [ɛ̃sɔlatœr] *m* solar heater

insolation [ɛ̃sɔlasjɔ̃] *f* exposure to the sun; sunstroke

insolence [ɛ̃sɔlɑ̃s] *f* insolence

inso·lent [ɛ̃sɔlɑ̃] **-lente** [lɑ̃t] *adj* insolent; extraordinary, unexpected

insolite [ɛ̃sɔlit] *adj* bizarre

insoluble [ɛ̃sɔlybl] *adj* insoluble

insolvabilité [ɛ̃sɔlvabilite] *f* insolvency

insolvable [ɛ̃sɔlvabl] *adj* insolvent

insomnie [ɛ̃sɔmni] *f* insomnia

insondable [ɛ̃sɔ̃dabl] *adj* unfathomable

insonore [ɛ̃sɔnɔr] *adj* soundproof; noiseless

insonoriser [ɛ̃sɔnɔrize] *tr* to soundproof

insouciance [ɛ̃susjɑ̃s] *f* carefreeness; indifference, carelessness

insou·ciant [ɛ̃susjɑ̃] **-ciante** [sjɑ̃t] *adj* carefree, unconcerned

insou·cieux [ɛ̃susjø] **-cieuse** [sjøz] *adj* carefree, unmindful

insou·mis [ɛ̃sumi] **-mise** [miz] *adj* unruly; unsubjugated || *mf* rebel || *m* (mil) A.W.O.L.

insoumission [ɛ̃sumisjɔ̃] *f* insubordination, rebellion; (mil) absence without leave

insoupçonnable [ɛ̃supsɔnabl] *adj* above suspicion

insoupçon·né -née [ɛ̃supsɔne] *adj* unsuspected

insoutenable [ɛ̃sutnabl] *adj* untenable; unbearable

inspecter [ɛ̃spɛkte] *tr* to inspect

inspec·teur [ɛ̃spɛktœr] **-trice** [tris] *mf* inspector

inspection [ɛ̃spɛksjɔ̃] *f* inspection; inspectorship

inspiration [ɛ̃spirasjɔ̃] *f* inspiration

inspirer [ɛ̃spire] §97, §98 *tr* to inspire; breathe in; **inspirer à qn de** to inspire s.o. to; **inspirer q.ch. à qn** to inspire s.o. with s.th. || *ref*—**s'inspirer de** to be inspired by

instable [ɛ̃stabl] *adj* unstable

installateur [ɛ̃stalatœr] *m* heater man; fitter, plumber

installation [ɛ̃stalɑsjɔ̃] *f* installation; equipment, outfit; appointments, fittings

installer [ɛ̃stale] *tr* to install; equip, furnish; **être bien installé** to be comfortably settled || *ref* to settle down, set up shop; **s'installer chez** to foist oneself on

instamment [ɛ̃stamɑ̃] *adv* urgently, earnestly

instance [ɛ̃stɑ̃s] *f* insistence; **avec instance** earnestly; **en instance** pending; **en instance de** on the point of; **en seconde instance** on appeal; **instances** entreaties; **introduire une instance** to start proceedings

ins·tant [ɛ̃stɑ̃] **-tante** [tɑ̃t] *adj* urgent, pressing || *m* instant, moment, **à chaque instant, à tout instant** continually; **à l'instant** at once, right away; just now; at the moment; **par instants** from time to time

instanta·né -née [ɛ̃stɑ̃tane] *adj* instantaneous || *m* snapshot

instantanément [ɛ̃stɑ̃tanemɑ̃] *adv* instantaneously; instantly

instar [ɛ̃star]—**à l'instar de** in the manner of

instauration [ɛ̃stɔrasjɔ̃] *f* establishment

instaurer [ɛ̃stɔre] *tr* to establish

instigation [ɛ̃stigasjɔ̃] *f* instigation

instiller [ɛ̃stile] *tr* to instill

instinct [ɛ̃stɛ̃] *m* instinct; **d'instinct, par instinct** by instinct

instinc·tif [ɛ̃stɛ̃ktif] **-tive** [tiv] *adj* instinctive

instituer [ɛ̃stitɥe] *tr* to found; institute (*e.g.*, *proceedings*)

institut [ɛ̃stity] *m* institute; **institut de beauté** beauty parlor; **institut de coupe** tonsorial parlor; **institut dentaire** dental school

institu·teur [ɛ̃stitytœr] **-trice** [tris] *mf* schoolteacher; founder

institution [ɛ̃stitysjɔ̃] *f* institution

instructeur [ɛ̃stryktœr] *m* instructor

instruc·tif [ɛ̃stryktif] **-tive** [tiv] *adj* instructive

instruction [ɛ̃stryksjɔ̃] *f* instruction; directive; education; (comp) statement; **instruction judiciaire** (law) preliminary investigation; **instructions** directions (*for use*); **instructions permanentes** standing orders

instruire [ɛ̃strɥir] §19, §96 *tr* to instruct; (law) to conduct the investigation of; **instruire qn de** to inform s.o. of ‖ *ref* to improve one's mind

instrument [ɛ̃strymã] *m* instrument; **instrument à anche** reed instrument; **instrument à cordes** stringed instrument; **instrument à vent** wind instrument; **instrument en bois** woodwind; **instrument en cuivre** brass

instrumen·tal -tale [ɛ̃strymãtal] *adj* (*pl* **-taux** [to]) instrumental

instrumenter [ɛ̃strymãte] *tr* to instrument

instrumentiste [ɛ̃strymãtist] *mf* instrumentalist

insu [ɛ̃sy] *m*—**à l'insu de** unknown to; **à mon insu** unknown to me

insubmersible [ɛ̃sybmɛrsibl] *adj* unsinkable

insubordon·né -née [ɛ̃sybordɔne] *adj* insubordinate

insuccès [ɛ̃syksɛ] *m* failure

insuffisamment [ɛ̃syfizamã] *adv* insufficiently

insuffi·sant [ɛ̃syfizã] **-sante** [zãt] *adj* insufficient

insulaire [ɛ̃sylɛr] *adj* insular ‖ *mf* islander

insuline [ɛ̃sylin] *f* insulin

insulte [ɛ̃sylt] *f* insult

insulter [ɛ̃sylte] *tr* to insult ‖ *intr*—**insulter à** to offend, outrage

insupportable [ɛ̃syportabl] *adj* unbearable

insur·gé -gée [ɛ̃syrʒe] *adj & mf* insurgent

insurger [ɛ̃syrʒe] §38 *ref* to revolt, rebel

insurmontable [ɛ̃syrmɔ̃tabl] *adj* insurmountable

insurrection [ɛ̃syrɛksjɔ̃] *f* insurrection

in·tact -tacte [ɛ̃takt] *adj* intact, untouched

intangible [ɛ̃tɑ̃ʒibl] *adj* intangible

intarissable [ɛ̃tarisabl] *adj* inexhaustible

inté·gral -grale [ɛ̃tegral] *adj* (*pl* **-graux** [gro]) integral; complete (*e.g., edition*); full (*e.g., payment*) ‖ *f* complete works; (math) integral

inté·grant -grante [ɛ̃tegrã] *adj* integral

intégration [ɛ̃tegrasjɔ̃] *f* integration

intègre [ɛ̃tɛgr] *adj* honest, upright

intégrer [ɛ̃tegre] §10 *tr* to integrate ‖ *ref* to form an integral part; (slang) to be accepted (*at an exclusive school*)

intégrité [ɛ̃tegrite] *f* integrity

intellect [ɛ̃telɛkt] *m* intellect

intellec·tuel -tuelle [ɛ̃telɛktɥɛl] *adj & mf* intellectual

intelligemment [ɛ̃teliʒamã] *adv* intelligently

intelligence [ɛ̃teliʒɑ̃s] *f* intelligence; intellect (*person*); **en bonne intelligence avec** on good terms with; **être d'intelligence** to be in collusion

intelli·gent [ɛ̃teliʒɑ̃] **-gente** [ʒɑ̃t] *adj* intelligent

intelligible [ɛ̃teliʒibl] *adj* intelligible

intempé·rant [ɛ̃tɑ̃perã] **-rante** [rãt] *adj* intemperate

intempéries [ɛ̃tɑ̃peri] *fpl* bad weather

intempes·tif [ɛ̃tɑ̃pɛstif] **-tive** [tiv] *adj* untimely

intenable [ɛ̃tnabl] *adj* untenable

intendance [ɛ̃tɑ̃dɑ̃s] *f* stewardship; controllership, office of bursar; **Intendance** (mil) Quartermaster Corps

inten·dant [ɛ̃tɑ̃dɑ̃] **-dante** [dɑ̃t] *mf* steward, superintendent; controller, bursar; **intendant militaire** quartermaster

intense [ɛ̃tɑ̃s] *adj* intense

inten·sif [ɛ̃tɑ̃sif] **-sive** [siv] *adj* intensive

intensifier [ɛ̃tɑ̃sifje] *tr & ref* to intensify

intensité [ɛ̃tɑ̃site] *f* intensity

intenter [ɛ̃tɑ̃te] *tr* to start (*a suit*); bring (*an action*)

intention [ɛ̃tɑ̃sjɔ̃] *f* intention, intent; **à l'intention de** for (the sake of)

intention·né -née [ɛ̃tɑ̃sjɔne] *adj* motivated; **bien intentionné** well-meaning; **mal intentionné** ill-disposed

intention·nel -nelle [ɛ̃tɑ̃sjɔnɛl] *adj* intentional

inter [ɛ̃tɛr] *m* (coll) long distance

interaction [ɛ̃tɛraksjɔ̃] *f* interaction, interplay

intercaler [ɛ̃tɛrkale] *tr* to intercalate; insert, sandwich

intercéder [ɛ̃tɛrsede] §10 *intr* to intercede

intercepter [ɛ̃tɛrsɛpte] *tr* to intercept

intercepteur [ɛ̃tɛrsɛptœr] *m* interceptor

interchangeable [ɛ̃tɛrʃɑ̃ʒabl] *adj* interchangeable

interclasse [ɛ̃tɛrklɑs] *m* (educ) break between classes

intercontinen·tal -tale [ɛ̃tɛrkɔ̃tinɑ̃tal] (*pl* **-taux** [to]) *adj* intercontinental

intercourse [ɛ̃tɛrkurs] *f* (naut) free entry

interdépen·dant [ɛ̃tɛrdepɑ̃dã] **-dante** [dãt] *adj* interdependent

interdiction [ɛ̃tɛrdiksjɔ̃] *f* interdiction; suspension; **interdiction de séjour** forbidden entry

interdire [ɛ̃tɛrdir] §40, §97, §98 *tr* to prohibit, forbid; confound, abash; interdict; suspend; **interdire q.ch. à qn** to forbid s.o. s.th.

interdisciplinaire [ɛ̃tɛrdisiplinɛr] *adj* interdisciplinary

inter·dit -dite [ɛ̃tɛrdi] [dit] *adj* prohibited, forbidden; dumfounded, abashed; deprived of rights; (mil) off limits ‖ *m* interdict

intéres·sant [ɛ̃terɛsã] **-sante** [sãt] *adj* interesting; attractive (*offer*)

intéres·sé -sée [ɛ̃terese] *adj* interested; self-seeking ‖ *mf* interested party

intéresser [ɛ̃terese] *tr* to interest; involve ‖ §96 *ref*—**s'intéresser à** or **dans** to be interested in

intérêt [ɛ̃terɛ] *m* interest; **intérêts composés** compound interest

interface [ɛ̃tɛrfas] *f* (comp) interface

interférence [ɛ̃tɛrferɑ̃s] *f* interference

interférer [ɛ̃tɛrfere] §10 *intr* (phys) to interfere ‖ *ref* to interfere with each other

inté·rieur -rieure [ɛ̃terjœr] *adj* interior; inner, inside ‖ *m* interior; inside; house, home; **à l'intérieur (de)** inside

intérieurement [ɛ̃terjœrmɑ̃] *adv* inwardly, internally; to oneself

intérim [ɛ̃terim] *m invar* interim; **dans l'intérim** in the meantime; **par intérim** acting, pro tem, interim

intérimaire [ɛ̃terimɛr] *adj* temporary, acting

interjection [ɛ̃tɛrʒɛksjɔ̃] *f* interjection

interligne [ɛ̃tɛrliɲ] *m* space between the lines; writing in the space between the lines; **à double interligne** double-spaced; **à simple interligne** single-spaced ‖ *f* lead

interligner [ɛ̃tɛrliɲe] *tr* to interline; (typ) to lead out

interlocu·teur [ɛ̃tɛrlɔkytœr] **-trice** [tris] *mf* interlocutor; intermediary; party (*with whom one is conversing*)

interlope [ɛ̃tɛrlɔp] *adj* illegal, shady ‖ *m* (naut) smuggling vessel

interloquer [ɛ̃tɛrlɔke] *tr* to disconcert

interlude [ɛ̃tɛrlyd] *m* interlude

intermède [ɛ̃tɛrmɛd] *m* (theat & fig) interlude

intermédiaire [ɛ̃tɛrmedjɛr] *adj* intermediate, intermediary ‖ *mf* intermediary ‖ *m* (com) middleman; **par l'intermédiaire de** by means of, by the medium of

interminable [ɛ̃tɛrminabl] *adj* interminable

intermit·tent [ɛ̃tɛrmitɑ̃] **-tente** [tɑ̃t] *adj* intermittent

internat [ɛ̃tɛrna] *m* boarding school; boarding-school life; (med) internship

internatio·nal -nale [ɛ̃tɛrnasjɔnal] *adj* (*pl* **-naux** [no]) international

interne [ɛ̃tɛrn] *adj* inner; (math) interior ‖ *mf* boarder (*at a school*); (med) intern

inter·né -née [ɛ̃tɛrne] *mf* internee

internement [ɛ̃tɛrnəmɑ̃] *m* internment; confinement (*of a mental patient*)

interner [ɛ̃tɛrne] *tr* to intern

interpeller [ɛ̃tɛrpele] *tr* to question, interrogate; yell at; heckle

interphone [ɛ̃tɛrfɔn] *m* intercom

interplanétaire [ɛ̃tɛrplanetɛr] *adj* interplanetary

interpoler [ɛ̃tɛrpɔle] *tr* to interpolate

interposer [ɛ̃tɛrpoze] *tr* to interpose

interprétation [ɛ̃tɛrpretasjɔ̃] *f* interpretation

interprète [ɛ̃tɛrprɛt] *mf* interpreter; spokesperson; intermediary, go-between, agent, helper; (theat) performer; **les interprètes** (theat) the cast

interpréter [ɛ̃tɛrprete] §10 *tr* to interpret; **mal interpréter** to misinterpret

interrogation [ɛ̃tɛrɔgasjɔ̃] *f* interrogation

interroger [ɛ̃tɛrɔʒe] §38 *tr* to interrogate, question

interrompre [ɛ̃tɛrɔ̃pr] (3d *sg pres ind* **interrompt** [ɛ̃tɛrɔ̃]) *tr* to interrupt; heckle ‖ §97 *ref* to break off, be interrupted

interrup·teur [ɛ̃tɛryptœr] **-trice** [tris] *adj* interrupting; circuit-breaking ‖ *m* switch; **interrupteur à couteau** knife switch; **interrupteur à culbuteur** or **à bascule** toggle switch; **interrupteur d'escalier** two-way switch; **interrupteur encastré** flush switch; **interrupteur olive** pear switch

interruption [ɛ̃tɛrypsjɔ̃] *f* interruption

intersection [ɛ̃tɛrsɛksjɔ̃] *f* intersection

intersigne [ɛ̃tɛrsiɲ] *m* omen, portent

interstellaire [ɛ̃tɛrstelɛr] *adj* interstellar

interstice [ɛ̃tɛrstis] *m* interstice

interur·bain [ɛ̃tɛryrbɛ̃] **-baine** [bɛn] *adj* interurban; (telp) long-distance ‖ *m* (telp) long distance

intervalle [ɛ̃tɛrval] *m* interval

intervenir [ɛ̃tɛrvnir] §72 (*aux:* ÊTRE) *intr* to intervene; take place, happen; (med) to operate; **faire intervenir** to call in

intervention [ɛ̃tɛrvɑ̃sjɔ̃] *f* intervention; (med) operation

intervertir [ɛ̃tɛrvɛrtir] *tr* to invert, transpose

interview [ɛ̃tɛrvju] *f* (journ) interview

interviewer [ɛ̃tɛrvjuvœr] *m* interviewer ‖ [ɛ̃tɛrvjuve] *tr* to interview

intervox [ɛ̃tɛrvɔks] *m* intercom

intestat [ɛ̃tɛsta] *adj* & *mf invar* intestate

intes·tin [ɛ̃tɛstɛ̃] **-tine** [tin] *adj* intestine, internal ‖ *m* intestine; **gros intestin** large intestine; **intestin grêle** small intestine

intimation [ɛ̃timasjɔ̃] *f* (law) summons

intime [ɛ̃tim] *adj* & *mf* intimate

inti·mé -mée [ɛ̃time] *mf* (law) defendant

intimer [ɛ̃time] *tr* to notify; give (*an order*)

intimider [ɛ̃timide] *tr* to intimidate

intimité [ɛ̃time] *f* intimacy; privacy; depths (*of one's being*)

intituler [ɛ̃tityle] *tr* to entitle

intolérable [ɛ̃tɔlerabl] *adj* intolerable

intolé·rant [ɛ̃tɔlerɑ̃] **-rante** [rɑ̃t] *adj* intolerant

intonation [ɛ̃tɔnasjɔ̃] *f* intonation

intouchable [ɛ̃tuʃabl] *adj* & *mf* untouchable

intoxication [ɛ̃tɔksikasjɔ̃] *f* poisoning

intoxiquer [ɛ̃tɔksike] *tr* to poison

intraduisible [ɛ̃tradɥizibl] *adj* untranslatable

intraitable [ɛ̃trɛtabl] *adj* intractable

intransi·geant [ɛ̃trɑ̃ziʒɑ̃] **-geante** [ʒɑ̃t] *adj* intransigent ‖ *mf* diehard, standpatter

intransi·tif [ɛ̃trɑ̃zitif] **-tive** [tiv] *adj* intransitive

intrant [ɛ̃trɑ̃] *m* input

intravei·neux [ɛ̃travɛnø] **-neuse** [nøz] *adj* intravenous

intrépide [ɛ̃trepid] *adj* intrepid; persistent

intri·gant [ɛ̃trigɑ̃] **-gante** [gɑ̃t] *adj* intriguing ‖ *mf* plotter, schemer

intrigue [ɛ̃trig] *f* intrigue, plot; love affair; **intrigues de couloir** lobbying

intriguer [ɛ̃trige] *tr & intr* to intrigue

intrinsèque [ɛ̃trɛ̃sɛk] *adj* intrinsic

introduction [ɛ̃trɔdyksjɔ̃] *f* introduction; admission

introduire [ɛ̃trɔdɥir] §19 *tr* to introduce, bring in; show in; interject (*e.g., a remark*); insert (*a coin*) ‖ *ref* to be introduced; **s'introduire dans** to slip in

intronisation [ɛ̃trɔnizɑsjɔ̃] *f* investiture, inauguration

introniser [ɛ̃trɔnize] *tr* to enthrone

introspec·tif [ɛ̃trɔspɛktif] **-tive** [tiv] *adj* introspective

introuvable [ɛ̃truvabl] *adj* unfindable

introver·ti **-tie** [ɛ̃trɔvɛrti] *adj & mf* introvert

in·trus [ɛ̃try] **-truse** [tryz] *adj* intruding ‖ *mf* intruder

intrusion [ɛ̃tryzjɔ̃] *f* intrusion

intuition [ɛ̃tɥisjɔ̃] *f* intuition

inusable [inyzabl] *adj* durable, wearproof

inusi·té **-tée** [inyzite] *adj* obsolete

inutile [inytil] *adj* useless, unnecessary

inutilement [inytilmɑ̃] *adv* in vain, uselessly; unnecessarily

inutilité [inytilite] *f* uselessness

invain·cu **-cue** [ɛ̃vɛ̃ky] *adj* unconquered

invalide [ɛ̃valid] *adj* invalid ‖ *mf* invalid, cripple; **invalide de guerre** disabled veteran

invalider [ɛ̃valide] *tr* to invalidate

invalidité [ɛ̃validite] *f* invalidity; disability

invariable [ɛ̃varjabl] *adj* invariable

invasion [ɛ̃vazjɔ̃] *f* invasion

invective [ɛ̃vɛktiv] *f* invective

invectiver [ɛ̃vɛktive] *tr* to rail at ‖ *intr* to inveigh

invendable [ɛ̃vɑ̃dabl] *adj* unsalable

inven·du **-due** [ɛ̃vɑ̃dy] *adj* unsold ‖ *m*—**les invendus** the unsold copies; the unsold articles

inventaire [ɛ̃vɑ̃tɛr] *m* inventory

inventer [ɛ̃vɑ̃te] *tr* to invent

inven·teur [ɛ̃vɑ̃tœr] **-trice** [tris] *mf* inventor; (law) finder

inven·tif [ɛ̃vɑ̃tif] **-tive** [tiv] *adj* inventive

invention [ɛ̃vɑ̃sjɔ̃] *f* invention

inventorier [ɛ̃vɑ̃tɔrje] *tr* to inventory

inversable [ɛ̃vɛrsabl] *adj* untippable, uncapsizable

inverse [ɛ̃vɛrs] *adj & m* inverse; **faire l'inverse de** to do the opposite of

inverser [ɛ̃vɛrse] *tr* to invert, reverse ‖ *intr* (elec) to reverse

inverseur [ɛ̃vɛrsœr] *m* reversing device; **inverseur des phares** (aut) dimmer

inversion [ɛ̃vɛrsjɔ̃] *f* inversion

inverté·bré **-brée** [ɛ̃vɛrtebre] *adj & m* invertebrate

inver·ti **-tie** [ɛ̃vɛrti] *mf* invert

invertir [ɛ̃vɛrtir] *tr* to invert, reverse

investiga·teur [ɛ̃vɛstigatœr] **-trice** [tris] *adj* investigative; searching ‖ *mf* investigator

investigation [ɛ̃vɛstigɑsjɔ̃] *f* investigation

investir [ɛ̃vɛstir] *tr* to invest; vest; **investir qn de sa confiance** to place one's confidence in s.o.

investissement [ɛ̃vɛstismɑ̃] *m* investment

investiture [ɛ̃vɛstityr] *f* investiture; nomination (*as a candidate for election*); primary election

invété·ré **-rée** [ɛ̃vetere] *adj* inveterate

invétérer [ɛ̃vetere] *ref* to become inveterate

invincible [ɛ̃vɛ̃sibl] *adj* invincible

invisible [ɛ̃vizibl] *adj* invisible; (coll) hiding, keeping out of sight

invitation [ɛ̃vitɑsjɔ̃] *f* invitation

invite [ɛ̃vit] *f* invitation, inducement; **répondre à l'invite de qn** (cards) to return s.o.'s lead; (fig) to respond to s.o.'s advances

invi·té **-tée** [ɛ̃vite] §92 *adj* invited ‖ *mf* guest

inviter [ɛ̃vite] §96, §100 *tr* to invite

involontaire [ɛ̃vɔlɔ̃tɛr] *adj* involuntary

invoquer [ɛ̃vɔke] *tr* to invoke

invraisemblable [ɛ̃vrɛsɑ̃blabl] *adj* improbable, unlikely, hard to believe; (coll) strange, weird

invraisemblance [ɛ̃vrɛsɑ̃blɑ̃s] *f* improbability, unlikelihood; (coll) queerness

invulnérable [ɛ̃vylnerabl] *adj* invulnerable

iode [jɔd] *m* iodine

iodure [jɔdyr] *m* iodide

ion [jɔ̃] *m* ion

ioniser [jɔnize] *tr* to ionize

iota [jɔta] *m* iota

irai [ire] *v* see **aller**

Irak [irak] *m*—**l'Irak** Iraq

ira·kien [irakjɛ̃] **-kienne** [kjɛn] *adj* Iraqi ‖ (*cap*) *mf* Iraqi

Iran [irɑ̃] *m*—**l'Iran** Iran

ira·nien [iranjɛ̃] **-nienne** [njɛn] *adj* Iranian ‖ *m* Iranian (*language*) ‖ (*cap*) *mf* Iranian (*person*)

iras [ira] *v* (**ira, irez**) see **aller**

iris [iris] *m* iris

irlan·dais [irlɑ̃dɛ] **-daise** [dɛz] *adj* Irish ‖ *m* Irish (*language*) ‖ (*cap*) *m* Irishman; **les Irlandais** the Irish ‖ (*cap*) *f* Irishwoman

Irlande [irlɑ̃d] *f* Ireland; **l'Irlande** Ireland

ironie [irɔni] *f* irony

ironique [irɔnik] *adj* ironic(al)

ironiser [irɔnize] *tr* to say ironically ‖ *intr* to speak ironically, jeer

irons [irɔ̃] *v* (**iront**) see **aller**

irradier [iradje] *tr & ref* to irradiate

irraison·né **-née** [irɛzɔne] *adj* unreasoning

irration·nel **-nelle** [irasjɔnɛl] *adj* irrational

irréalisable [irealizabl] *adj* impractical, unattainable

irréalité [irealite] *f* unreality

irrecevable [irəsvable] *adj* inadmissable (*evidence*); unacceptable (*demand*)

irrécouvrable [irekuvrabl] *adj* uncollectible

irrécupérable [irekyperabl] *adj* irretrievable

irrécusable [irekyzabl] *adj* unimpeachable, incontestable, indisputable

ir·réel **-réelle** [ireɛl] *adj* unreal

irréflé·chi -chie [irefleʃi] *adj* rash, thoughtless

irréfutable [irefytabl] *adj* irrefutable

irrégu·lier [iregylje] **-lière** [ljɛr] *adj & m* irregular

irréli·gieux [ireliʒjø] **-gieuse** [ʒjøz] *adj* irreligious

irrémédiable [iremedjabl] *adj* irremediable

irremplaçable [irɑ̃plasabl] *adj* irreplaceable

irréparable [ireparabl] *adj* irreparable; irretrievable (*loss, mistake, etc.*)

irrépressible [ireprɛsibl] *adj* irrepressible

irréprochable [ireprɔʃabl] *adj* irreproachable

irrésistible [irezistibl] *adj* irresistible

irréso·lu -lue [irezɔly] *adj* irresolute

irrespect [irɛspɛ] *m* disrespect

irrespec·tueux [irɛspɛktɥø] **-tueuse** [tɥøz] *adj* disrespectful

irrespirable [irɛspirabl] *adj* unbreathable

irresponsable [irɛspɔ̃sabl] *adj* irresponsible

irrétrécissable [iretresisabl] *adj* preshrunk, unshrinkable

irrévéren·cieux [ireverɑ̃sjø] **-cieuse** [sjøz] *adj* irreverent

irréversible [irevɛrsibl] *adj* irreversible

irrévocable [irevɔkabl] *adj* irrevocable

irrigation [irigɑsjɔ̃] *f* irrigation

irriguer [irige] *tr* to irrigate

irri·tant [iritɑ̃] **-tante** [tɑ̃t] *adj* irritating ‖ *m* irritant

irritation [iritɑsjɔ̃] *f* irritation

irriter [irite] *tr* to irritate ‖ *ref* to become irritated

irruption [irypsjɔ̃] *f* irruption; invasion; **faire irruption** to burst in

isabelle [izabɛl] *m* dun or light-bay horse ‖ (*cap*) *f* Isabel

Isaïe [izai] *m* Isaiah

Islam [islam] *m*—**l'Islam** Islam

islamique [islamik] *adj* Islamic

islan·dais [islɑ̃dɛ] **-daise** [dɛz] *adj* Icelandic ‖ *m* Icelandic (*language*) ‖ (*cap*) *mf* Icelander

Islande [islɑ̃d] *f* Iceland; **l'Islande** Iceland

isocèle [izɔsɛl] *adj* isosceles

iso·lant [izɔlɑ̃] **-lante** [lɑ̃t] *adj* insulating ‖ *m* insulator

isolation [izɔlɑsjɔ̃] *f* insulation; **isolation phonique** soundproofing

isolationniste [izɔlɑsjɔnist] *adj & mf* isolationist

iso·lé -lée [izɔle] *adj* isolated; independent; insulated

isolement [izɔlmɑ̃] *m* isolation; insulation

isolément [izɔlemɑ̃] *adv* separately, independently

isoler [izɔle] *tr* to isolate; insulate ‖ *ref* to cut oneself off

isoloir [izɔlwar] *m* polling booth

isotope [izɔtɔp] *m* isotope

Israël [israɛl] *m* Israel; **à Israël** (*to give*) to Israel; **d'Israël** of Israel, e.g., **l'état d'Israël** the state of Israel; **en Israël** in Israel; (*to go*) to Israel

israé·lien [israeljɛ̃] **-lienne** [ljɛn] *adj* Israeli ‖ (*cap*) *mf* Israeli

israélite [israelit], [izraelit] *adj* Israelite ‖ (*cap*) *mf* Israelite

is·su -sue [isy] *adj*—**issu de** descended from, born of ‖ *f* exit, way out; outlet; outcome, issue; **à l'issue de** on the way out from; at the end of; **issues** sharps, middlings (*in milling flour*); offal (*in butchering*); **sans issue** without exit; without any way out

isthme [ism] *m* isthmus

Italie [itali] *f* Italy; **l'Italie** Italy

ita·lien [italjɛ̃] **-lienne** [ljɛn] *adj* Italian ‖ *m* Italian (*language*) ‖ (*cap*) *mf* Italian (*person*)

italique [italik] *adj* Italic; (*typ*) italic ‖ *m* (*typ*) italics

item [itɛm] *m* question (*in a test*) ‖ *adv* ditto

itinéraire [itinerɛr] *adj & m* itinerary

itiné·rant [itinerɑ̃] **-rante** [rɑ̃t] *adj & mf* itinerant

itou [itu] *adv* (slang) also, likewise

I.V.G. [iveʒe] *f* (letterword) (**interruption volontaire de grossesse**) abortion

ivoire [ivwar] *m* ivory

ivraie [ivrɛ] *f* darnel, cockle; (Bib) tares

ivre [ivr] *adj* drunk, intoxicated

ivresse [ivrɛs] *f* drunkenness; ecstasy, rapture

ivrogne [ivrɔɲ] *adj* hard-drinking ‖ *m* drunkard

ivrognerie [ivrɔɲri] *f* drunkenness

ivrognesse [ivrɔɲɛs] *f* drinking woman

J

J, j [ʒi] *m invar* tenth letter of the French alphabet

jabot [ʒabo] *m* jabot; crop (*of bird*)

jabotage [ʒabɔtaʒ] *m* jabbering

jaboter [ʒabɔte] *tr & intr* to jabber

jacasse [ʒakas] *f* magpie; chatterbox

jacasser [ʒakase] *intr* to chatter, jabber

jacasserie [ʒakasri] *f* chatter, jabber

jachère [ʒaʃɛr] *f* fallow ground

jacinthe [ʒasɛ̃t] *f* hyacinth; **jacinthe des bois** bluebell

Jacques [ʒak] *m* James, Jacob; **Jacques Bonhomme** the typical Frenchman

jactance [ʒaktɑ̃s] *f* bragging

jade [ʒad] *m* jade

jadis [ʒadis] *adv* formerly of yore

jaguar [ʒagwar] *m* jaguar

jaillir [ʒajir] *intr* to gush, burst forth

jaillissement [ʒajismɑ̃] *m* gush
jais [ʒɛ] *m* jet
jalon [ʒalɔ̃] *m* stake; landmark; surveying staff
jalonner [ʒalɔne] *tr* to stake out; mark (*a way, a channel*)
jalousie [ʒaluzi] *f* jealousy; awning; Venetian blind
ja·loux [ʒalu] **-louse** [luz] *adj* jealous
jamais [ʒamɛ] *adv* ever; never; **jamais de la vie!** not on your life! **jamais plus** never again; **ne . . . jamais** §90 never; **pour jamais** forever
jambe [ʒɑ̃b] *f* leg; **à toutes jambes** as fast as possible; **prendre ses jambes à son cou** to take to one's heels
jambon [ʒɑ̃bɔ̃] *m* ham; **jambon d'York** boiled ham
jambon·neau [ʒɑ̃bɔno] *m* (*pl* **-neaux**) ham knuckle
jamboree [ʒɑ̃bɔre], [dʒambɔri] *m* jamboree
jante [ʒɑ̃t] *f* felloe; rim (*of auto wheel*)
janvier [ʒɑ̃vje] *m* January
Japon [ʒapɔ̃] *m*—**le Japon** Japan
japo·nais [ʒapɔnɛ] **-naise** [nɛz] *adj* Japanese ‖ *m* Japanese (*language*) ‖ (*cap*) *mf* Japanese (*person*)
japper [ʒape] *intr* to yap, yelp
jaquemart [ʒakmar] *m* jack (*figurine striking the time on a bell*)
jaquette [ʒakɛt] *f* coat, jacket; cut-away coat, morning coat; book jacket
jardin [ʒardɛ̃] *m* garden; **jardin d'acclimatation** zoo; **jardin d'enfants** kindergarten; **jardin d'hiver** greenhouse
jardiner [ʒardine] *tr* to clear out, trim ‖ *intr* to garden
jardi·nier [ʒardinje] **-nière** [njɛr] *adj* garden ‖ *mf* gardener ‖ *m* flower stand; mixed vegetables; spring wagon ‖ *f* kindergartner (*teacher*)
jargon [ʒargɔ̃] *m* jargon
jarre [ʒar] *f* earthenware jar
jarret [ʒarɛ] *m* hock, gambrel; shin (*of beef or veal*); back of the knee
jarretelle [ʒartɛl] *f* garter
jarretière [ʒartjɛr] *f* garter
jars [ʒar] *m* gander
jaser [ʒɑze] *intr* to babble; prattle; blab, gossip
jasmin [ʒasmɛ̃] *m* jasmine
jaspe [ʒasp] *m* jasper; (bb) marbling
jasper [ʒaspe] *tr* to marble, speckle
jatte [ʒat] *f* bowl
jauge [ʒoʒ] *f* gauge; (agr) trench; (naut) tonnage; **jauge d'huile, jauge à tige** dipstick
jauger [ʒoʒe] §38 *tr* to gauge, measure; (naut) to draw
jaunâtre [ʒonɑtr] *adj* yellowish, sallow
jaune [ʒon] *adj* yellow ‖ *mf* yellow person (*Oriental*) ‖ *m* yellow; yolk (*of egg*); scab, strikebreaker
jaunir [ʒonir] *tr & intr* to yellow
jaunisse [ʒonis] *f* jaundice
Javel [ʒavɛl] *f*—**eau de Javel** bleach

javelle [ʒavɛl] *f* swath (*of grain*); bunch (*of twigs*)
javelliser [ʒavɛlize] *tr* to chlorinate (*water*)
javelot [ʒavlo] *m* javelin
jazz [dʒaz] *m* jazz
je [ʒə] §87 I
Jean [ʒɑ̃] *m* John
Jeanne [ʒɑn] *f* Jane, Jean, Joan
jeannette [ʒanɛt] *f* gold cross (*ornament*); sleeveboard
Jeannot [ʒano] *m* (coll) Johnny, Jack
jeep [dʒip] *f* jeep
Jéhovah [ʒeɔva] *m* Jehovah
je-m'en-fichisme [ʒmɑ̃fiʃism] *m* (slang) what-the-hell attitude
je-ne-sais-quoi [ʒensekwa] *m invar* what-you-call-it
Jérôme [ʒerom] *m* Jerome
jerrycan [dʒɛrikan] *m* gasoline can
jersey [ʒɛrsɛ] *m* jersey, sweater
Jérusalem [ʒeryzalɛm] *f* Jerusalem
jésuite [ʒezɥit] *adj* Jesuit; (pej) hypocritical ‖ (*cap*) *m* Jesuit; (pej) hypocrite
Jésus [ʒezy] *m* Jesus
Jésus-Christ [ʒezykri] *m* Jesus Christ
jet [ʒɛ] *m* throw, cast; jet; spurt, gush; flash (*of light*); **du premier jet** at the first try; **jet à la mer** jettison; **jet d'eau** fountain; **jet dentaire** water pick; **jet de pierre** stone's throw
jetable [ʒetabl] *adj* disposable
jetée [ʒəte] *f* breakwater, jetty
jeter [ʒəte] §34 *tr* to throw; throw away; throw down; hurl, fling; toss; cast (*a glance*); shed (*the skin*); pour forth; utter; to drop (*anchor*); lay (*the foundations*) ‖ *intr* to sprout ‖ *ref* to throw oneself; rush; empty (*said of a river*)
jeton [ʒətɔ̃] *m* token, counter; slug
jeu [ʒø] *m* (*pl* **jeux**) play; game, sport; gambling; pack, deck (*of cards*); set (*of chess pieces; of tools*); playing, acting; execution, performance; **en jeu** in gear; at stake; **franc jeu** fair play; **gros jeu** high stakes; **jeu d'eau** dancing waters; **jeu de dames** checkers; **jeu de hasard** game of chance; **jeu de massacre** hit-the-baby (*game at fair*); **jeu de mots** pun, play on words; **jeu d'enfant** child's play; **jeu de patience** jigsaw puzzle; **jeu de puce** tiddlywinks; **jeu de société** parlor game; **jeu d'orgue** organ stop; **jouer un jeu d'enfer** to play for high stakes; **vieux jeu** old hat
jeudi [ʒødi] *m* Thursday; **jeudi saint** Maundy Thursday
jeun [ʒœ̃]—**à jeun** fasting; on an empty stomach
jeune [ʒœn] (precedes the noun it modifies) *adj* young; youthful; junior, younger ‖ *m* young man; **jeunes délinquants** juvenile delinquents; **les jeunes** young people; the young (*of an animal*)
jeûne [ʒøn] *m* fast, fasting
jeûner [ʒøne] *intr* to fast; abstain; eat sparingly

jeunesse [ʒœnɛs] *f* youth; youthfulness; boyhood, girlhood; **jeunesse dorée** young people of wealth and fashion

jeu·net [ʒœnɛ] **-nette** [nɛt] *adj* youngish

jeû·neur [ʒønœr] **-neuse** [nøz] *mf* faster

jex [ʒɛks] *m* steel wool

joaillerie [ʒɔɑjri] *f* jewelry; jewelry business; jewelry shop

joail·lier [ʒɔɑje] **-lière** [jɛr] *mf* jeweler

jobard [ʒɔbar] *m* (coll) dupe

jobarderie [ʒɔbardri] *f* gullibility

jockey [ʒɔkɛ] *m* jockey

jodler [ʒɔdle] *tr & intr* to yodel

joie [ʒwa] *f* joy; **joies** pleasures

joindre [ʒwɛ̃dr] §35 *tr* to join; add; adjoin; catch up with; **joindre les deux bouts** to make both ends meet ‖ *intr* to join ‖ *ref* to join, unite; be adjacent, come together

joint [ʒwɛ̃] **jointe** [ʒwɛ̃t] *adj* joined; joint (*effort*); **joint à** added to ‖ *m* joint; **joint de cardan** (mach) universal joint; **joint de culasse** (aut) gasket (*of cylinder head*); **joint de dilatation thermique** expansion joint; **trouver le joint** (coll) to hit on the solution ‖ *v* see **joindre**

jointure [ʒwɛ̃tyr] *f* knuckle; joint

joker [ʒɔkɛr] *m* joker

jo·li -lie [ʒɔli], [ʒɔli] (precedes the noun it modifies) *adj* pretty; tidy (*income*)

joliment [ʒɔlimɑ̃] *adv* nicely; (coll) extremely, awfully

Jonas [ʒɔnɑs], [ʒɔnɑ] *m* Jonah

jonc [ʒɔ̃] *m* rush; **jonc d'Inde** rattan

jonchée [ʒɔ̃ʃe] *f* litter (*things strewn about*); cottage cheese

joncher [ʒɔ̃ʃe] *tr* to strew; litter

jonction [ʒɔ̃ksjɔ̃] *f* junction

jongler [ʒɔ̃gle] *intr* to juggle

jonglerie [ʒɔ̃gləri] *f* jugglery

jongleur [ʒɔ̃glœr] *m* juggler; jongleur

jonque [ʒɔ̃k] *f* (naut) junk

jonquille [ʒɔ̃kij] *adj invar* pale-yellow ‖ *m* pale yellow ‖ *f* jonquil

Jordanie [ʒɔrdani] *f* Jordan; **la Jordanie** Jordan

joue [ʒu] *f* cheek; **se caler les joues** (slang) to stuff oneself

jouer [ʒwe] §96 *tr* to play; gamble away; feign; act (*a part*) ‖ *intr* to play; gamble; feign; **faire jouer** to spring (*a lock*); **jouer à** to play (*a game*); **jouer à la baisse** to bear the market; **jouer à la hausse** to bull the market; **jouer de** to play (*a musical instrument*) ‖ *ref* to frolic; **se jouer de** to make fun of; to be independent of; make light of

jouet [ʒwɛ] *m* toy, plaything

joueur [ʒwœr] **joueuse** [ʒwøz] *mf* player (*of games; of musical instruments*); gambler; **beau joueur** good sport; **joueur à la baisse** bear; **joueur à la hausse** bull; **mauvais joueur** poor sport

jouf·flu -flue [ʒufly] *adj* chubby

joug [ʒu] *m* yoke

jouir [ʒwir] §97 *intr* to enjoy oneself, enjoy life; come (*have an orgasm*); **jouir de** to enjoy

jouissance [ʒwisɑ̃s] *f* enjoyment; use, possession

jouis·seur [ʒwisœr] **-seuse** [søz] *adj* pleasure-loving ‖ *mf* pleasure lover

jou·jou [ʒuʒu] *m* (*pl* **-joux**) toy, plaything

jour [ʒur] *m* day; daylight; light, window, opening; **à jour** openwork; up to date; **de nos jours** nowadays; **du jour au lendemain** overnight, suddenly; **grand jour** broad daylight; **huit jours** a week; **il fait jour** it is getting light; **jour chômé** day off; **jour de ma fête** my birthday; **jour férié** legal holiday; **jour ouvrable** workday; **le jour de l'An** New Year's day; **le jour J** D-Day; **quinze jours** two weeks; **sous un faux jour** in a false light; **vivre au jour le jour** to live from hand to mouth

Jourdain [ʒurdɛ̃] *m* Jordan (*river*)

jour·nal [ʒurnal] *m* (*pl* **-naux** [no]) newspaper; journal; diary; (naut) logbook, journal; **journal parlé** newscast; **journal télévisé** telecast

journa·lier [ʒurnalje] **-lière** [ljɛr] *adj* daily ‖ *m* day laborer

journalisme [ʒurnalism] *m* journalism

journaliste [ʒurnalist] *mf* journalist

journée [ʒurne] *f* day; day's journey; day's pay; day's work; **journée d'accueil** open house; **toute la journée** all day long

journellement [ʒurnɛlmɑ̃] *adv* daily

joute [ʒut] *f* joust

jouter [ʒute] *intr* to joust

jo·vial -viale [ʒɔvjal] *adj* (*pl* **-vials** or **-viaux** [vjo] **-viales**) jovial, jocose

joyau [ʒwajo] *m* (*pl* **joyaux**) jewel

joyeux [ʒwajø] **joyeuse** [ʒwajøz] *adj* joyful, cheerful; jocose

jubi·lant [ʒybilɑ̃] **-lante** [lɑ̃t] *adj* jubilant

jubilé [ʒybile] *m* jubilee; golden-wedding anniversary

jucher [ʒyʃe] *tr & intr* to perch ‖ *ref* to go to roost

judaïque [ʒydaik] *adj* Jewish

judaïsme [ʒydaism] *m* Judaism

judas [ʒyda] *m* peephole ‖ (*cap*) *m* Judas

judicature [ʒydikatyr] *f* judiciary

judiciaire [ʒydisjɛr] *adj* legal, judicial

judi·cieux [ʒydisjø] **-cieuse** [sjøz] *adj* judicious, judicial

juge [ʒyʒ] *m* judge; umpire; **juge arbitre** umpire; **juge assesseur** associate judge

jugement [ʒyʒmɑ̃] *m* judgment

juger [ʒyʒe] §38, §95 *tr & intr* to judge; **juger bon de** to consider it a good thing to; **jugez de ma surprise!** imagine my surprise!; **si j'en juge par mon expérience** judging by my experience

jugulaire [ʒygylɛr] *adj* jugular ‖ *f* chin strap

juif [ʒɥif] **juive** [ʒɥiv] *adj* Jewish ‖ (*cap*) *mf* Jew

juillet [ʒɥijɛ] *m* July

juin [ʒɥɛ̃] *m* June

Jules [ʒyl] *m* Julius; (coll) Mack; (slang) pimp; (slang) chamber pot
ju·lien [ʒyljɛ̃] **-lienne** [ljɛn] *adj* Julian ‖ *f* (*soup*) julienne; (bot) rocket
ju·meau [ʒymo] **-melle** [mɛl] (*pl* **-meaux -melles**) *adj & mf* twin ‖ *f* see **jumelles**
jumelage [ʒymlaʒ] *m* twinning
jume·lé -lée [ʒymle] *adj* double; twin (*cities*); semidetached (*house*); bilingual (*text*)
jumeler [ʒymle] §34 *tr* to couple, join; pair
jumelles [ʒymɛl] *fpl* opera glasses; field glasses; **jumelles de manchettes** cuff links
jument [ʒymɑ̃] *f* mare
jungle [ʒɔ̃gl] *f* jungle
jupe [ʒyp] *f* skirt; **jupe portefeuille** wraparound skirt
jupe-culotte [ʒypkylɔt] *f* split skirt
jupon [ʒypɔ̃] *m* petticoat
juré [ʒyre] *m* juror; member of an examining board
jurer [ʒyre] §95, §97, §98 *tr* to swear ‖ *intr* to swear; clash
juridiction [ʒyridiksjɔ̃] *f* jurisdiction
juridique [ʒyridik] *adj* legal, judicial
juriste [ʒyrist] *m* writer on legal matters
juron [ʒyrɔ̃] *m* oath
jury [ʒyri] *m* jury; examining board
jus [ʒy] *m* juice; gravy; (slang) drink (*body of water*)
jusqu'au-boutiste [ʒyskobutist] *mf* (coll) bitterender, diehard

jusque [ʒysk(ə)] *adv* even; **jusqu'à** as far as, down to, up to; until; even; **jusqu'à ce que** until; **jusqu'après** until after; **jusqu'à quand** how long ‖ *prep* as far as; until; **jusques et y compris** [ʒyskəzeikɔ̃pri] up to and including; **jusqu'ici** this far; until now; **jusqu'où** how far
jusque-là [ʒyskəla] *adv* that far, until then
jusquiame [ʒyskjam] *f* henbane
juste [ʒyst] *adj* just, righteous; accurate; just enough; sharp, e.g., **à six heures justes** at six o'clock sharp; (mus) in tune, on key ‖ *adv* justly; correctly, exactly
justement [ʒystəmɑ̃] *adv* just; justly; exactly; as it happens
juste-milieu [ʒystəmiljø] *m* happy medium, golden mean
justesse [ʒystɛs] *f* justness; precision, accuracy; **de justesse** barely
justice [ʒystis] *f* justice; **faire justice de** to mete out just punishment to; to make short work of
justiciable [ʒystisjabl] *adj*—**justiciable de** accountable to; subject to
justifier [ʒystifje] *tr* to justify ‖ *intr*—**justifier de** to account for, prove ‖ *ref* to clear oneself
jute [ʒyt] *m* jute
ju·teux [ʒytø] **-teuse** [tøz] *adj* juicy
juvénile [ʒyvenil] *adj* juvenile, youthful
juxtaposer [ʒykstapoze] *tr* to juxtapose

K

K, k [kɑ] *m invar* eleventh letter of the French alphabet
kakatoès [kakatɔɛs] *m* cockatoo
kaki [kaki] *adj invar & m* khaki
kaléidoscope [kaleidɔskɔp] *m* kaleidoscope
kamikaze [kamikaze] *m* kamikaze
kangourou [kɑ̃guru] *m* kangaroo
karaté [karate] *m* karate
kascher or **kasher** [kaʃɛr] *adj* kosher; **c'est kascher** it's kosher
kayak [kajak] *m* kayak; **faire du kayak** to go canoeing
keepsake [kipsɛk] *m* giftbook, keepsake
képi [kepi] *m* kepi
kermesse [kɛrmɛs] *f* charity bazaar
kérosène [kerozɛn] *m* kerosene; **kérosène aviation** jet fuel; rocket fuel
ketchup [kɛtʃœp] *m* ketchup
khan [kɑ̃] *m* khan
kidnapper [kidnape] *tr* to kidnap
kidnap·peur [kidnapœr] **-peuse** [pøz] *mf* kidnaper
kif [kif] *m* (coll) pot, marijuana
kif-kif [kifkif] *adj invar* (coll) all the same; **c'est kif-kif** (coll) it's fifty-fifty

kilo [kilo] *m* kilo, kilogram
kilocycle [kilɔsikl] *m* kilocycle
kilogramme [kilɔgram] *m* kilogram
kilomètre [kilɔmɛtr] *m* kilometer, kilo
kilowatt [kilɔwat] *m* kilowatt
kilowatt-heure [kilɔwatœr] *m* (*pl* **kilowatts-heures**) kilowatt-hour
kilt [kilt] *m* kilt
kimono [kimɔno] *m* kimono
kinescope [kinɛskɔp] *m* kinescope
kiosque [kjɔsk] *m* newsstand; bandstand; summerhouse
kipper [kipœr], [kipɛr] *m* kipper
klaxon [klaksɔn] *m* (aut) horn
klaxonner [klaksɔne] *intr* to sound the horn
kleptomane [klɛptɔman] *adj & mf* kleptomaniac
km/h *abbr* (**kilomètres-heure, kilomètres à l'heure**) kilometers per hour
knock-out [nɔkaut], [nɔkut] *adj invar* (boxing) knocked out, groggy ‖ *m* (boxing) knockout
k.o. [kɑo] *adj* (letterword) (**knock-out**) k.o., knocked out; **mettre k.o.** to knock out ‖ *m* k.o., knockout

krach [krak] *m* crash (*e.g., on the stock market*)
kraft [kraft] *m* strong wrapping paper
krak [krak] *m* medieval castle

Kremlin [krɛmlɛ̃] *m*—**le Kremlin** the Kremlin
kyrielle [kirjɛl] *f* rigmarole, string
kyste [kist] *m* cyst

L

L, l [ɛl], *[ɛl] *m invar* twelfth letter of the French alphabet
l' = **le** or **la** before a vowel or mute *h* ‖ often untranslated, e.g., **plus que je ne l'ai fait** more than I did; never translated when used for euphony, e.g., **comme l'on** as one, **que l'on** that one, **si l'on** if one
la [la] *art* §77 the ‖ *m* (mus) la ‖ *pron* §87 her; it
là [la] *adv* there; here, e.g., **je suis là** I am here; in, e.g., **est-il là?** is he in?; **il n'était pas là** he was out; **là, là!** there, there! (*it's not as bad as that!*)
-là [la] § 82, §84
là-bas [labɑ] *adv* yonder, over there
label [labɛl] *m* union label
labeur [labœr] *m* labor, toil
la·bial -biale [labjal] (*pl* **-biaux** [bjo] **-biales**) *adj & f* labial
laboran·tin [labɔrɑ̃tɛ̃] **-tine** [tin] *mf* laboratory assistant
laboratoire [labɔratwar] *m* laboratory; **laboratoire d'analyses** pathology laboratory; **laboratoire de langues** language laboratory; **laboratoire de prothèse dentaire** dental laboratory; **laboratoire du ciel** Skylab; **laboratoire nucléaire** nuclear research laboratory
labo·rieux [labɔrj ø] **-rieuse** [rjøz] *adj* laborious; arduous; industrious; working (*classes*); **c'est laborieux!** (coll) it's endless!
labour [labur] *m* tilling, plowing
labourable [laburabl] *adj* arable, tillable
labourer [labure] *tr* to till, plow; furrow (*the brow*); scratch
laboureur [laburœr] *m* farm hand, plowman
Labrador [labradɔr] *m*—**le Labrador** Labrador
labyrinthe [labirɛ̃t] *m* labyrinth, maze
lac [lak] *m* lake; **Grands Lacs** Great Lakes
lacer [lase] §51 *tr* to lace; tie (*one's shoes*)
lacération [laserɑsjɔ̃] *f* tearing
lacérer [lasere] §10 *tr* to lacerate; tear up
lacet [lasɛ] *m* lace; snare, noose; bowstring (*for strangling*); **en lacet** winding (*road*); **lacet de soulier** shoelace
lâche [lɑʃ] *adj* slack, loose; lax, careless; cowardly ‖ *mf* coward
lâcher [lɑʃe] *tr* to loosen; let go, release; turn loose; blurt out (*a word*); fire (*a shot*); (coll) to drop (*one's friends*); **lâcher pied** to give ground; **lâcher prise** to let go
lâcheté [lɑʃte] *f* cowardice

lâ·cheur [lɑʃœr] **-cheuse** [ʃøz] *mf* fickle friend, turncoat
lacis [lɑsi] *m* network (*of threads, nerves*)
laconique [lakɔnik] *adj* laconic
lacrymogène [lakrimɔʒɛn] *adj* tear (*gas*)
lacs [lɑ] *m* noose, snare; **lacs d'amour** love knot
lac·té -tée [lakte] *adj* milky, milk (*diet*)
lacune [lakyn] *f* lacuna, gap, blank
lad [lad] *m* stableboy
là-dedans [ladədɑ̃] §85A *adv* in it, within, in that, in there
là-dessous [ladəsu] §85A *adv* under it, under that, under there
là-dessus [ladəsy] §85A *adv* on it, on that; thereupon
ladre [lɑdr] *adj* stingy, niggardly ‖ *mf* miser
ladrerie [lɑdrəri] *f* miserliness
lagon [lagɔ̃] *m* lagoon
lagune [lagyn] *f* lagoon
lai laie [lɛ] *adj* lay ‖ *m* lay (*poem*) ‖ *f* see laie
laïc laïque [laik] *adj* lay, secular ‖ *mf* layman ‖ *f* laywoman
laiche [lɛʃ] *f* (bot) sedge, reed grass
laïcisation [laisizɑsjɔ̃] *f* secularization
laïciser [laisize] *tr* to secularize
laid laide [lɛd] *adj* ugly; plain, homely; mean, low-down
laide·ron [lɛdrɔ̃] **-ronne** [rɔn] *adj* homely, ugly ‖ **laideron** *m* or *f* ugly wench
laideur [lɛdœr] *f* ugliness; meanness
laie [lɛ] *f* (zool) wild sow
lainage [lɛnaʒ] *m* woolens
laine [lɛn] *f* wool; **laine d'acier** steel wool; **manger** or **tondre la laine sur le dos à** (fig) to fleece
lainer [lɛne] *tr* to teasel, nap
lai·neux [lɛn ø] **-neuse** [nøz] *adj* wooly; downy
lai·nier [lɛnje] **-nière** [njɛr] *adj* wool (*industry*) ‖ *mf* dealer in wool; worker in wool
laïque [laik] *adj* lay, secular ‖ *mf* layman ‖ *f* laywoman
laisse [lɛs] *f* leash; foreshore
laissé-pour-compte laissée-pour-compte [lesepurkɔ̃t] *adj* returned (*merchandise*) ‖ *m* (*pl* **laissés-pour-compte**) reject; leftover merchandise
laisser [lɛse], [lese] §95, §96, §97 *tr* to leave, quit; let, allow; let go (*at a low price*); let have, e.g., **il me l'a laissé pour trois dollars** he let me have it for three dollars; **laisser** + *inf* + **qn** to let

s.o. + *inf*, e.g., **il a laissé Marie aller au théâtre** he let Mary go to the theater; e.g., **il me l'a laissé peindre** or **il m'a laissé le peindre** he let me paint it ‖ *intr*—**ne pas laisser de** to not fail to, to not stop ‖ *ref* to let oneself, e.g., **se laisser aller** to let oneself go; **se laisser aller à** to give way to

laisser-aller [leseale] *m* abandon, easygoingness; slovenliness, negligence

laisser-passer [lesepɑse] *m invar* permit, pass

lait [lɛ] *m* milk; **lait de chaux** whitewash; **lait de poule** eggnog; **lait écrémé** skim milk; **se mettre au lait** to go on a milk diet

laitage [lɛtaʒ] *m* dairy products

laitance [lɛtɑ̃s] *f* milt

laiterie [lɛtri] *f* dairy, creamery; dairy farming

lai·tier [letje] **-tière** [tjɛr] *adj* dairy; milch (*cow*) ‖ *m* milkman; (metallurgy) slag, dross ‖ *f* dairymaid; milch cow

laiton [lɛtɔ̃] *m* brass; brass wire

laitonner [letɔne] *tr* to plate with brass

laitue [lety] *f* lettuce; **laitue romaine** romaine

laïus [lajys] *m* (coll) speech, impromptu remarks; (coll) hot air

laïus·seur [lajysœr] **-seuse** [søz] *mf* (coll) windbag

laize [lɛz] *f* width (*of cloth*)

lamanage [lamanaʒ] *m* harborage

lamaneur [lamanœr] *m* harbor pilot

lam·beau [lɑ̃bo] *m* (*pl* **-beaux**) scrap, bit; rag; **en lambeaux** in tatters, in shreds

lam·bin [lɑ̃bɛ̃] **-bine** [bin] *adj* (coll) slow ‖ *mf* (coll) slowpoke

lambiner [lɑ̃bine] *intr* (coll) to dawdle

lambris [lɑ̃bri] *m* paneling, wainscoting; plaster (*of ceiling*); **lambris dorés** (fig) palatial home

lambrisser [lɑ̃brise] *tr* to panel, wainscot; plaster

lame [lam] *f* blade; slat (*of blinds*); runner (*of skate*); wave; lamina, thin plate, sword; (fig) swordsman; **lame de fond** ground swell

la·mé -mée [lame] *adj* gold-trimmed, silver-trimmed, spangled ‖ *m*—**de lamé**, e.g., **une robe de lamé** a spangled dress

lamelle [lamɛl] *f* lamella, thin strip; slide (*of microscope*)

lamentable [lamɑ̃tabl] *adj* lamentable

lamentation [lamɑ̃tɑsjɔ̃] *f* lamentation, lament

lamenter [lamɑ̃te] *intr & ref* to lament

laminer [lamine] *tr* to laminate; roll (*a metal*)

laminoir [laminwar] *m* rolling mill; calender

lampadaire [lɑ̃padɛr] *m* lamppost; floor lamp

lampe [lɑ̃p] *f* lamp; (electron) tube; **lampe à pétrole** kerosene lamp; **lampe à rayons ultraviolets** sun lamp; **lampe à souder** blowtorch; **lampe au néon** neon light; **lampe de chevet** bedlamp; **lampe de**

poche flashlight; **lampe survoltée** photoflood bulb; **s'en mettre plein la lampe** (slang) to stuff one's face

lampée [lɑ̃pe] *f* (coll) gulp, swig

lamper [lɑ̃pe] *tr* (coll) to gulp down, guzzle

lampe-tempête [lɑ̃ptɑ̃pɛt] *f* (*pl* **lampes-tempête**) hurricane lamp

lampion [lɑ̃pjɔ̃] *m* Chinese lantern; **les lampions** rhythmical call or rhythmical stamping of feet to denote impatience

lampiste [lɑ̃pist] *m* lightman; (coll) scapegoat; (coll) underling

lamproie [lɑ̃prwa] *f* lamprey

lampyre [lɑ̃pir] *m* glowworm

lance [lɑ̃s] *f* lance; nozzle (*of hose*); **rompre une lance avec** to cross swords with

lan·cé -cée [lɑ̃se] *adj* flying (*start*); in the swim

lance-bombes [lɑ̃sbɔ̃b] *m invar* trench mortar; (aer) bomb release

lancée [lɑ̃se] *f* impetus

lance-flammes [lɑ̃sflam] *m invar* flamethrower

lance-fusées [lɑ̃sfyze] *m invar* rocket launcher

lancement [lɑ̃smɑ̃] *m* launching, throwing; launching (*of ship; of new product on the market*); (aer) airdrop; (aer) release; (baseball) pitching

lance-mines [lɑ̃smin] *m invar* minelayer

lance-pierres [lɑ̃spjɛr] *m invar* slingshot

lancer [lɑ̃se] §51 *tr* to throw, fling, cast; launch (*e.g., a ship, a new product*); issue (*e.g., an appeal*); (baseball) to pitch ‖ *ref* to rush, dash; **se lancer dans** to launch out into, take up

lance-roquettes [lɑ̃srɔkɛt] *m invar* (arti) bazooka

lance-torpilles [lɑ̃stɔrpij] *m invar* torpedo tube

lancette [lɑ̃sɛt] *f* (surg) lancet

lan·ceur [lɑ̃sœr] **-ceuse** [søz] *mf* promoter; (baseball) pitcher; (sports) hurler, thrower ‖ *m* (rok) booster

lanci·nant [lɑ̃sinɑ̃] **-nante** [nɑ̃t] *adj* shooting, throbbing (*pain*); gnawing (*regret*)

lanciner [lɑ̃sine] *tr* to torment ‖ *intr* to shoot; throb

lan·dau [lɑ̃do] *m* (*pl* **-daus**) landau; baby carriage

lande [lɑ̃d] *f* moor, heath

landier [lɑ̃dje] *m* kitchen firedog with pothangers

langage [lɑ̃gaʒ] *m* language, speech; **langage de programmation** computer language

lange [lɑ̃ʒ] *m* diaper

langer [lɑ̃ʒe] §38 *tr* to swaddle, diaper

langou·reux [lɑ̃gurø] **-reuse** [røz] *adj* languorous

langouste [lɑ̃gust] *f* spiny lobster, crayfish

langous·tier [lɑ̃gustje] **-tière** [tjɛr] *m & f* lobster net ‖ *m* lobster boat

langoustine [lɑ̃gustin] *f* prawn

langue [lɑ̃g] *f* tongue; language, speech; **avoir la langue bien pendue** (coll) to have the gift of gab; **donner sa langue au**

chat (coll) to give up; **langue cible** target language; **langue d'arrivée** target language; **langue de départ** source language; **langue de terre** tongue (neck or narrow strip) of land; **langue source** source language; **langue verte** racy underworld slang; **langues vivantes** modern languages; **langue verte** slang; **mauvaise langue** backbiter, gossip; **prendre langue avec** to open up a conversation with; **tirer la langue à** to stick out one's tongue at
langue-de-chat [lãgdəʃa] f (pl **langues-de-chat**) (culin) ladyfinger
languette [lãgɛt] f tongue (e.g., of shoe); pointer (of scale); flap, strip
langueur [lãgœr] f languor
languir [lãgir] intr to languish; to pine away
languis·sant [lãgisã] **-sante** [sãt] adj languid; languishing; long-drawn-out, tiresome
lanière [lanjɛr] f strap, strip, thong
lanoline [lanɔlin] f lanolin
lanterne [lãtɛrn] f lantern; (aut) parking light; (obs) street lamp; **conter des lanternes** (coll) to talk nonsense; **lanterne d'agrandissement** (phot) enlarger; **lanterne de projection, lanterne à projections** slide projector, filmstrip projector; **lanterne rouge** (slang) tail end, last to arrive; **lanterne sourde** dark lantern; **lanterne vénitienne** Japanese lantern; **oublier d'éclairer** or **d'allumer sa lanterne** (coll) to leave out the most important point
lanterner [lãtɛrne] tr (coll) to string along, put off ‖ intr to loaf around, dawdle; **faire lanterner qn** to keep s.o. waiting
lapider [lapide] tr to stone; vilify
la·pin [lapɛ̃] **-pine** [pin] mf rabbit; **lapin de garenne** wild rabbit; **lapin russe** albino rabbit; **poser un lapin à qn** (coll) to stand s.o. up
la·pon [lapɔ̃] **-pone** [pɔn] adj Lappish ‖ m Lapp, Lappish (language) ‖ (cap) mf Lapp, Laplander (person)
Laponie [lapɔni] f Lapland; **la Laponie** Lapland
lapsus [lapsys] m slip (of tongue, pen, etc.)
laquais [lakɛ] m lackey, footman
laque [lak] m & f lacquer ‖ m lacquer ware ‖ f lac; shellac; hair spray
laquelle [lakɛl] §78
laquer [lake] tr to shellac; lacquer
larcin [larsɛ̃] m petty larceny; plagiarism
lard [lar] m bacon, side prok; (coll) fat (of a person); (slang) fat slob; **se faire du lard** (coll) to get fat
larder [larde] tr to lard; pierce, riddle
large [larʒ] adj wide, broad; generous; ample; loose-fitting ‖ (when standing before noun) adj wide, broad; generous; ample; large, e.g., **pour une large part** to a large extent ‖ m width, breadth; open sea; room, e.g. **donner du large à qn** to give s.o. room; **au large** within sight of shore; **au large de** off, e.g. **au large du Havre** off Le Havre; **de large** wide, e.g., **trois**

mètres de large three meters wide; **je suis au large dans cet habit** this suit is roomy for me; **passer au large de** to give a wide berth to; **prendre le large** (coll) to shove off ‖ adv boldly; **calculer large** to figure roughly; **habiller large** to dress in loose-fitting clothes; **il n'en mène pas large** (fig) he gets rattled in a tight spot; **voir large** (fig) to think big
largement [larʒəmã] adv widely; abundantly; fully; plenty, e.g., **vous avez largement le temps** you have plenty of time
largesse [larʒɛs] f largess
largeur [larʒœr] f width, breadth; (naut) beam; **dans les grandes largeurs** (coll) in a big way; **grande largeur** double-width (cloth); **largeur d'esprit** broadmindedness
larguer [large] tr to let go, release
larme [larm] f tear; (coll) drop; **fondre en larmes** to burst into tears; **pleurer à chaudes larmes** to shed bitter tears
lar·moyant [larmwajã] **-moyante** [mwajãt] adj tearful; watery (eyes)
larmoyer [larmwaje] §47 intr to water (said of eyes); snivel, blubber
lar·ron [larɔ̃] **lar·ronnesse** [larɔnɛs] mf thief; **s'entendre comme larrons en foire** to be as thick as thieves
larve [larv] f larva
laryn·gé -gée [larɛ̃ʒe] adj laryngeal
laryn·gien [larɛ̃ʒjɛ̃] **-gienne** [ʒjɛn] adj laryngeal
laryngite [larɛ̃ʒit] f laryngitis
laryngoscope [larɛ̃gɔskɔp] m laryngoscope
larynx [larɛ̃ks] m larynx
las [lɑ] **lasse** [lɑs] adj weary ‖ **las** [lɑs], [la] interj alas!
lascar [laskar] m character, rogue
las·cif [lasif] **las-cive** [lasiv] adj lascivious
lasciveté [lasivte] f lasciviousness
laser [lazɛr] m laser
las·sant [lɑsã] **-sante** [sãt] adj tiring, tedious
lasser [lɑse] § 96, §97 tr to tire, weary; wear out (s.o.'s patience) ‖ ref—**sans se lasser** unceasingly; **se lasser de** + inf to tire of + ger; to tire oneself out + ger
lassitude [lɑsityd] f lassitude, weariness
lasso [laso] m lasso
latence [latãs] f latency
la·tent [latã] **-tente** [tãt] adj latent
laté·ral -rale [lateral] adj (pl **-raux**) lateral
la·tin [latɛ̃] **-tine** [tin] adj Latin ‖ m Latin (language); **latin vulgaire** Vulgar Latin ‖ (cap) mf Latin (person)
latino-améri·cain [latinoamerikɛ̃] **-caine** [kɛn] (pl **-américains**) adj Latin-American ‖ (cap) mf Latin American
latitude [latityd] f latitude
latrines [latrin] fpl latrine
latte [lat] f lath; broadsword
latter [late] tr to lath
lattis [lati] m lathing, laths
laudanum [lodanɔm] m laudanum
lauda·tif [lodatif] **-tive** [tiv] adj laudatory

lau·réat [lɔrea] **-réate** [reat] *adj* laureate ‖ *mf* winner, laureate

laurier [lɔrje] *m* laurel, sweet bay; **laurier rose** rosebay; **s'endormir sur ses lauriers** to rest on one's laurels

lavable [lavabl] *adj* washable

lavabo [lavabo] *m* washbowl; washroom; **lavabos** toilet, lavatory

lavage [lavaʒ] *m* washing; **lavage de cerveau** (coll) brainwashing; **lavage des titres** wash sale; **lavage de tête** (coll) dressing down, scolding

lavallière [lavaljɛr] *f* loosely tied bow

lavande [lavɑ̃d] *f* lavender

lavandière [lavɑ̃djɛr] *f* washerwoman

lavasse [lavas] *f* (coll) dishwater

lave [lav] *f* lava

lave-glace [lavglas] *m* (*pl* **-glaces**) (aut) windshield washer

lavement [lavmɑ̃] *m* enema

laver [lave] *tr* to wash; **laver la tête à qn** (coll) to haul s.o. over the coals; **laver le cerveau à** (coll) to brainwash ‖ *intr* to wash ‖ *ref* to wash oneself, wash; **elle s'en est lavé les mains** (fig) she washed her hands of it

laverie [lavri] *f* (min) washery; **laverie automatique, laverie libre-service** self-service laundry

lavette [lavɛt] *f* dishcloth

la·veur [lavœr] **-veuse** [vøz] *mf* washer; **laveur de vaisselle** dishwasher (*person*); **laveur de vitres** window washer (*person*) ‖ *f* washerwoman; washing machine

lavoir [lavwar] *m* place for washing clothes

lavure [lavyr] *f* dishwater; (coll) swill, hogwash

laxa·tif [laksatif] **-tive** [tiv] *adj & m* laxative

layer [leje] §49 *tr* to blaze a trail through; blaze (*trees to mark a trail*)

layette [lɛjɛt] *f* layette; packing case

lazzi [lazi] *mpl* jeers

le [lə] *art* §77 the ‖ *pron* §87 him; it

leader [lidœr] *m* leader

lèche [lɛʃ] *f* (coll) thin slice (*e.g., of bread*); **faire de la lèche à qn** (slang) to lick s.o.'s boots

lèche-carreaux [lɛʃkaro] *m invar* (slang) window-shopping

lèchefrite [lɛʃfrit] *f* dripping pan

lècher [leʃe] §10 *tr* to lick; over-polish (*one's style*)

lé·cheur [leʃœr] **-cheuse** [ʃøz] *mf* (coll) bootlicker, flatterer

lèche-vitrines [lɛʃvitrin] *m invar* window-shopping; **faire du lèche-vitrines** to go window-shopping

leçon [ləsɔ̃] *f* lesson; reading (*of manuscript*); **faire la leçon à** to lecture, sermonize; prime on what to say

lec·teur [lɛktœr] **-trice** [tris] *mf* reader; lecturer (*of university rank*) ‖ *m* playback

lecture [lɛktyr] *f* reading; playback; **lecture sur les lèvres** lip reading

ledit [lədi] **ladite** [ladit] *adj* (*pl* **lesdits** [ledi] **lesdites** [ledit]) the aforesaid

lé·gal -gale [legal] *adj* (*pl* **-gaux** [go]) legal; statutory

légaliser [legalize] *tr* to legalize

légalité [legalite] *f* legality

légat [lega] *m* papal legate

légataire [legatɛr] *mf* legatee; **légataire universel** residual heir

légation [legasjɔ̃] *f* legation

légendaire [leʒɑ̃dɛr] *adj* legendary

légende [leʒɑ̃d] *f* legend; caption

lé·ger [leʒe] **-gère** [ʒɛr] §92 *adj* light; slight (*accent, difference, pain, mistake, etc.*); faint (*sound, tint, etc.*); delicate (*odor, perfume, etc.*); mild, weak (*drink*); scanty (*dress*); graceful (*figure*); empty (*stomach*); agile, active; frivolous, carefree; **à la légère** lightly; without due consideration

légèrement [leʒɛrmɑ̃] *adv* lightly; slightly; flippantly, thoughtlessly

légèreté [leʒɛrte] *f* lightness; gracefulness, frivolity; fickleness

leggings [legiŋs] *mpl & fpl* leggings

leghorn [legɔrn] *f* leghorn (*chicken*)

légiférer [leʒifere] §10 *intr* to legislate

légion [leʒjɔ̃] *f* legion

législa·teur [leʒislatœr] **-trice** [tris] *mf* legislator

législa·tif [leʒislatif] **-tive** [tiv] *adj* legislative

législation [leʒislasjɔ̃] *f* legislation

législature [leʒislatyr] *f* legislative session; legislature

légiste [leʒist] *m* jurist

légitime [leʒitim] *adj* legitimate ‖ *f* (slang) lawful spouse; **ma légitime** (slang) my better half

légitimer [leʒitime] *tr* to legitimate; justify

légitimité [leʒitimite] *f* legitimacy

legs [lɛ], [lɛg] *m* legacy

léguer [lege] §10 *tr* to bequeath

légume [legym] *m* vegetable; legume (*pod*) ‖ *f*—**grosse légume** (slang) bigwig, big wheel

légu·mier [legymje] **-mière** [mjɛr] *adj* vegetable (*garden, farming, etc.*) ‖ *m* vegetable dish

lemme [lɛm] *m* lemma

lendemain [lɑ̃dmɛ̃] *m* next day; results, outcome, e.g., **avoir d'heureux lendemains** to have happy results or a happy outcome; **au lendemain de** the day after; **le lendemain matin** the next morning; **sans lendemain** short-lived

lénifier [lenifje] *tr* (med) to soothe

lent [lɑ̃] **lente** [lɑ̃t] §92 *adj* slow ‖ *f* nit

lentement [lɑ̃tmɑ̃] *adv* slowly; deliberately

lenteur [lɑ̃tœr] *f* slowness, sluggishness; **lenteurs** delays, dilatoriness

lentille [lɑ̃tij] *f* lens; (bot) lentil; **lentilles** freckles; **lentilles cornéennes** contact lenses

léopard [leɔpar] *m* leopard

lèpre [lɛpr] *f* leprosy

lé·preux [leprø] **-preuse** [prøz] *adj* leprous ‖ *mf* leper

lequel [ləkɛl] §78

les [le] *art* §77 the ‖ *pron* §87 them ‖ *prep* near (*in place names*)

les·bien [lɛsbjɛ̃] **-bienne** [bjɛn] *adj* Lesbian ‖ *f* lesbian ‖ (*cap*) *mf* Lesbian

lèse-majesté [lɛzmaʒɛste] *f*—**crime de lèse-majesté** lese majesty, high treason

léser [leze] §10 *tr* to injure

lésine [lezin] *f* stinginess

lésiner [lezine] *intr* to haggle, be stingy

lésion [lezjɔ̃] *f* lesion; wrong, damage

les·quels -quelles [lekɛl] §78

lessivage [lesivaʒ] *m* washing; **lessivage de crâne** (coll) brainwashing

lessive [lesiv] *f* washing (*of clothes*); wash; washing soda, lye; **faire la lessive** to do the wash

lessiver [lesive] *tr* to wash; scrub (*with a cleaning agent*); (slang) to clean out (*e.g., another poker player*); **être lessivé** (slang) to be exhausted

lessiveuse [lesivøz] *f* washing machine

lest [lɛst] *m* ballast

leste [lɛst] *adj* nimble, quick; suggestive, broad; flippant

lestement [lɛstəmɑ̃] *adv* nimbly, deftly

lester [lɛste] *tr* to ballast; (coll) to fill (*one's stomach, pockets, etc.*) ‖ *ref* (coll) to stuff oneself

léthargie [letarʒi] *f* lethargy

léthargique [letarʒik] *adj* lethargic ‖ *mf* lethargic person

lettrage [lɛtraʒ] *m* lettering

lettre [lɛtr] *f* letter; **à la lettre, au pied de la lettre** to the letter; **avant la lettre** before complete development; **en toutes lettres** in full; in so many words; **lettre de change** bill of exchange; **lettre de faire-part** announcement; **lettre de voiture** bill of lading; **lettre d'imprimerie** printed letter; **lettre majuscule** capital letter; **lettre recommandée** registered letter; **lettres** letters (*literature*); **lettres numérales** roman numerals; **mettre une lettre à la poste** to mail a letter

let·tré -trée [lɛtre] *adj* lettered, literate ‖ *mf* learned person

lettre-morte [lɛtrəmɔrt] *f* letter returned to sender

lettrine [letrin] *f* catchword; initial letter

leu [lø] *m*—**à la queue leu leu** in single file

leucémie [løsemi] *f* leukemia

leucorrhée [løkɔre] *f* leucorrhea

leur [lœr] *adj poss* §88 their ‖ *pron poss* §89 theirs *pron pers* §87 them; to them

leurre [lœr] *m* lure; delusion

leurrer [lœre] *tr* to lure; trick, delude ‖ *ref* to be deceived

levain [ləvɛ̃] *m* leaven

levant [ləvɑ̃] *adj masc* rising (*sun*) ‖ *m* east ‖ (*cap*) *m* Levant

levan·tin [ləvɑ̃tɛ̃] **-tine** [tin] *adj* Levantine ‖ (*cap*) *mf* Levantine

le·vé -vée [ləve] *adj* rising (*sun*); raised (*e.g., hand*); up, e.g., **le soleil est levé** the sun is up ‖ *m* (mus) upbeat; (surv) survey ‖ *f* levee, embankment; collection (*of mail*); levying (*of troops, taxes, etc.*);

raising (*of siege*); lifting (*of embargo*); striking (*of camp*); breaking (*of seals*); upstroke (*of piston*); **faire une levée** (cards) to take a trick; **levée de boucliers** public protest, outcry; **levée d'écrou** discharge (*from prison*); **levée de séance** adjournment; **levée du corps** removal of the body; funeral service (*in front of the coffin*); **levées manquantes** (cards) undertricks

lever [ləve] *m* rising; (surv) survey; **lever du rideau** rise of the curtain; curtain raiser; **lever du soleil** sunrise ‖ §2 *tr* to lift; raise; collect, pick up (*the mail*); levy (*troops, taxes, etc.*); strike (*camp*); adjourn (*a meeting*); weigh (*anchor*); relieve (*a guard*); remit (*a punishment*); flush (*e.g., a partridge*); effect (*a survey*); break (*the seals*) ‖ *intr* to come up (*said of plants*); rise (*said of dough*) ‖ *ref* to get up; stand up; rise; heave (*said of sea*); clear up (*said of weather*)

léviathan [levjatɑ̃] *m* leviathan

levier [ləvje] *m* lever, crowbar; **être aux leviers de commande** (aer) to be at the controls; (fig) to be in control; **levier de changement de vitesse** gearshift lever; **levier d'interligne et de retour du chariot** return lever (*of a typewriter*)

lévitation [levitasjɔ̃] *f* levitation

levraut [ləvro] *m* young hare, leveret

lèvre [lɛvr] *f* lip; rim; **du bout des lèvres** half-heartedly, guardedly; **embrasser sur les lèvres** to kiss; **serrer les lèvres** to purse one's lips

lévrier [levrije] *m* greyhound

levure [ləvyr] *f* yeast, **levure anglaise** or **chimique** baking powder; **levure de bière** brewer's yeast

lexi·cal -cale [lɛksikal] *adj* (*pl* **-caux** [ko]) lexical

lexicographe [lɛksikɔgraf] *mf* lexicographer

lexicographie [lɛksikɔgrafi] *f* lexicography

lexicographique [lɛksikɔgrafik] *adj* lexicographic(al)

lexicologie [lɛksikɔlɔʒi] *f* lexicology

lexique [lɛksik] *m* lexicon, vocabulary; abridged dictionary

lez [le] *prep* near (*in place names*)

lézard [lezar] *m* lizard; **faire le lézard** (coll) to sun oneself, loaf

lézarde [lezard] *f* crack, split, crevice; gimp (*of furniture*); braid; (mil) gold braid

lézarder [lezarde] *tr & ref* to crack, split ‖ *intr* (coll) to bask in the sun

liaison [ljɛzɔ̃] *f* liaison

liant [ljɑ̃] **liante** [ljɑ̃t] *adj* flexible, supple; sociable, affable ‖ *m* flexibility; sociability; binder, binding material; **avoir du liant** to be a good mixer

liard [ljar] *m* (fig) farthing

liasse [ljas] *f* packet, bundle (*e.g., of letters*); wad (*of bank notes*)

Liban [libɑ̃] *m*—**le Liban** Lebanon

liba·nais [libanɛ] **-naise** [nɛz] *adj* Lebanese ‖ (*cap*) *mf* Lebanese

libation [libasjɔ̃] *f* libation

libelle [libɛl] *m* lampoon
libellé [libɛlle] *m* wording
libeller [libele], [libɛlle] *tr* to word; draw up (*e.g., a contract*); make out (*a check*)
libellule [libɛlyl] *f* dragonfly
libé·ral -rale [liberal] *adj* & *mf* (*pl* **-raux** [ro]) liberal
libéralisme [liberalism] *m* liberalism
libéralité [liberalite] *f* liberality
libéra·teur [liberatœr] **-trice** [tris] *adj* liberating ‖ *mf* liberator
libération [liberɑsjɔ̃] *f* liberation; freeing; **libération conditionnelle** release on parole; **libération sous caution** release on bail
libérer [libere] §10 *tr* to liberate ‖ *ref* to free oneself; pay up
liberté [libɛrte] *f* liberty, freedom; **liberté d'association** or **liberté de réunion** right of assembly; **liberté de langage** freedom of speech; **liberté de la presse** freedom of the press; **liberté de la propriété** right to own private property; **liberté du commerce et de l'industrie** free enterprise; **liberté du culte** freedom of worship
liber·tin [libɛrtɛ̃] **-tine** [tin] *adj* libertine; (archaic) freethinking ‖ *mf* libertine; (archaic) freethinker
libidi·neux [libidinø] **-neuse** [nøz] *adj* libidinous
libido [libido] *f* libido
libraire [librɛr] *mf* bookseller; publisher
libraire-éditeur [librɛreditœr] *m* (*pl* **libraires-éditeurs**) publisher and bookseller
librairie [librɛri] *f* bookstore; book trade; publishing house
libre [libr] §93 *adj* free; vacant; available; (*public sign*) not in use, empty; for hire; **je suis libre de mon temps** my time is my own; **libre arbitre** free will; **libre de** free to, at liberty to
libre-échange [libreʃɑ̃ʒ] *m* free trade
libre-échangiste [libreʃɑ̃ʒist] *m* (*pl* **-échangistes**) free trader
libre-pen·seur [librəpɑ̃sœr] **-seuse** [søz] *mf* (*pl* **libres-penseurs**) freethinker
libre-service [librəsɛrvis] *m* (*pl* **libres-services**) self-service; self-service store
lice [lis] *f* enclosure or fence (*of race track, fairground, tiltyard, etc.*); (zool) hound bitch; **de basse lice** (tex) low-warp; **de haute lice** (tex) high-warp; **entrer en lice** to enter the lists
licence [lisɑ̃s] *f* license; **licence ès lettres** advanced liberal-arts degree, master of arts; **prendre des licences avec** to take liberties with
licen·cié -ciée [lisɑ̃sje] *mf* holder of a master's degree
licenciement [lisɑ̃simɑ̃] *m* discharge, layoff
licencier [lisɑ̃sje] *tr* to discharge, lay off
licen·cieux [lisɑ̃sjø] **-cieuse** [sjøz] *adj* licentious
lichen [likɛn] *m* lichen
licher [liʃe] *tr* (slang) to gulp down
licite [lisit] *adj* lawful, licit

licorne [likɔrn] *f* unicorn
licou [liku] *m* halter
lie [li] *f* dregs, lees; (fig) dregs, scum
lie-de-vin [lidvɛ̃] *adj invar* maroon
liège [ljɛʒ] *m* cork
lien [ljɛ̃] *m* tie, bond, link
lier [lje] *tr* to tie, bind, link ‖ *ref* to bind together; make friends; **lier conversation avec** to fall into conversation with; **se lier d'amitié avec** to become friends with
lierre [ljɛr] *m* ivy
liesse [ljɛs] *f*—**en liesse** in festive mood, gay
lieu [ljø] *m* (*pl* **lieux**) place; **au lieu de** instead of, in lieu of; **avoir lieu** to take place; **avoir lieu de** to have reason to; **donner lieu à** to give rise to; **en aucun lieu** nowhere; **en dernier lieu** finally; **en haut lieu** high up, in responsible circles; **en premier lieu** first of all; **en quelque lieu que** wherever; **en tous lieux** everywhere; **il y a lieu à** there is room for; **lieu commun** commonplace; platitude; **lieu de villégiature** resort; **lieu géométrique** locus; **lieux** premises; **lieux d'aisances** rest rooms; **lieux payants** comfort station, public lavatory; **sur les lieux** on the spot; on the premises; **tenir lieu** to take place; **tenir lieu de** to take the place of
lieu-dit [ljødi] *m* (*pl* **lieux-dits**)—**le lieu-dit . . .** the place called . . .
lieue [ljø] *f* league (*unit of distance*)
lieur [ljœr] **lieuse** [ljøz] *mf* binder ‖ *f* (mach) binder
lieutenant [ljøtnɑ̃] *m* lieutenant; (merchant marine) mate; **lieutenant de port** harbor master; **lieutenant de vaisseau** (nav) lieutenant commander
lieutenant-colonel [ljøtnɑ̃kɔlɔnɛl] *m* (*pl* **lieutenants-colonels**) lieutenant colonel
lièvre [ljɛvr] *m* hare; **c'est là que gît le lièvre** there's the rub; **lever un lièvre** (fig) to raise an embarrassing question; **prendre le lièvre au gîte** (fig) to catch s.o. napping
ligament [ligamɑ̃] *m* ligament
ligature [ligatyr] *f* ligature
ligaturer [ligatyre] *tr* to tie up
lignage [liɲaʒ] *m* lineage
ligne [liɲ] *f* line; figure, waistline; (*of an automobile*) lines; **aller à la ligne** to begin a new paragraph; **avoir de la ligne** to have a good figure; **en ligne** (comp) on line; **en première ligne** of the first importance; on the firing line; **entrer en ligne de compte** to be under consideration; **garder sa ligne** to keep one's figure; **grande ligne** (rr) main line; **grandes lignes** broad outline; **hors ligne** unrivaled, outstanding; **la ligne est occupée** the line is busy, I hear the busy signal; **ligne à postes groupés** (telp) party line; **ligne brisée** dotted line; **ligne de but** goal line; **ligne de changement de date** international date line; **ligne de faille** fault line; **ligne de flottaison** water line; **ligne de mire, ligne de visée** (arti) line of sight;

ligne de partage des eaux, ligne de faîte watershed; **ligne des arbres** timber line; **ligne d'horizon** skyline; **ligne droite** straight line; **ligne partagée** (telp) party line; **ligne pointillée** or **hachée** dotted line

ligne-bloc [liɲblɔk] (*pl* **lignes-blocs**) *m* linotype slug

lignée [liɲe] *f* lineage, offspring

li·gneux [liɲø] **-gneuse** [ɲøz] *adj* woody

lignifier [liɲifje] *tr & ref* to turn into wood

ligot [ligo] *m* firewood (*in tied bundle*)

ligoter [ligɔte] *tr* to tie up, bind

ligue [lig] *f* league

liguer [lige] *tr & ref* to league

lilas [lila] *adj invar & m* lilac

li·lial -liale [liljal] *adj* (*pl* **-liaux** [ljo]) lily-white, lily-like

lillipu·tien [lilipysjɛ̃] **-tienne** [sjɛn] *adj & mf* Lilliputian

limace [limas] *f* (zool) slug; (coll) slowpoke; (slang) shirt

limaçon [limasɔ̃] *m* snail; **en limaçon** spiral

limaille [limaj] *f* filings

limbe [lɛ̃b] *m* (astr, bot) limb; **limbes** limbo

lime [lim] *f* file; (*Citrus limetta*) sweet lime; **dernier coup de lime** finishing touches; **enlever à la lime** to file off; **lime à ongles** nail file; **lime émeri** emery board

limer [lime] *tr* to file; fray; (fig) to polish

limette [limɛt] *f* (*Citrus limetta*) sweet lime

limier [limje] *m* bloodhound; (coll) sleuth

liminaire [liminɛr] *adj* preliminary

limitation [limitasjɔ̃] *f* limitation

limite [limit] *f* limit; maximum, e.g., **vitesse limite** maximum speed; **dernière limite** deadline

limiter [limite] *tr* to limit ‖ *ref* to be limited; limit oneself

limitrophe [limitrɔf] *adj* frontier; **limitrophe de** adjacent to

limogeage [limɔʒaʒ] *m* (coll) removal from office

limoger [limɔʒe] §38 *tr* (coll) to remove from office, relieve of a command

limon [limɔ̃] *m* silt; clay; mud; shaft (*of wagon*)

limonade [limɔnad] *f* lemon soda

limona·dier [limɔnadje] **-dière** [djɛr] *mf* soft-drink manufacturer; café manager

limo·neux [limɔnø] **-neuse** [nøz] *adj* silty; muddy

limousine [limuzin] *f* heavy cloak; (aut) limousine

limpide [lɛ̃pid] *adj* limpid

lin [lɛ̃] *m* flax; linen

linceul [lɛ̃sœl] *m* shroud; cover (*of snow*)

linéaire [lineɛr] *adj* linear

linéament [lineamɑ̃] *m* lineament

linge [lɛ̃ʒ] *m* linen (*sheets, tablecloths, underclothes, etc.*); piece of linen; **il faut laver son linge sale en famille** one must wash one's dirty linen in private; **laver le linge** to do the wash; **linge de corps** underclothes

lingère [lɛ̃ʒɛr] *f* linen maid; linen closet

lingerie [lɛ̃ʒri] *f* linen (*sheets, tablecloths, underclothes, etc.*); linen closet; **lingerie de dame** lingerie; **lingerie d'homme** men's underwear

lingot [lɛ̃go] *m* ingot

lin·gual -guale [lɛ̃gwal] (*pl* **-guaux** [gwo] **-guales**) *adj & f* lingual

linguiste [lɛ̃gɥist] *mf* linguist

linguistique [lɛ̃gɥistik] *adj* linguistic ‖ *f* linguistics

liniment [linimɑ̃] *m* liniment

linoléum [linɔleɔm] *m* linoleum

linon [linɔ̃] *m* lawn (*sheer linen*)

linotte [linɔt] *f* (orn) linnet

linotype [linɔtip] *f* linotype

linotypiste [linɔtipist] *mf* linotype operator

lin·teau [lɛ̃to] *m* (*pl* **-teaux**) lintel

lion [ljɔ̃] **lionne** [ljɔn] *mf* lion ‖ *m*—**le Lion** (astr, astrol) Leo ‖ *f* lioness

lion·ceau [ljɔ̃so] *m* (*pl* **-ceaux**) lion cub

lippe [lip] *f* thick lower lip, blubber lip

lip·pu -pue [lipy] *adj* thick-lipped

liquéfier [likefje] *tr* to liquefy

liqueur [likœr] *f* liqueur; liquid; (chem, pharm) liquor

liquidation [likidasjɔ̃] *f* liquidation; settlement; clearance sale

liquide [likid] *adj & m* liquid ‖ *f* liquid (*consonant*)

liquider [likide] *tr* to liquidate; settle (*a score*); wind up (*a piece of business*); (coll) to get rid of; put an end to

liquidité [likidite] *f* liquidity

liquo·reux [likɔrø] **-reuse** [røz] *adj* sweet, syrupy

lire [lir] §36 *tr & intr* to read; **lire à haute voix** to read aloud; **lire à vue** to sight-read; **lire sur les lèvres** to lip-read ‖ *ref* to read; show, e.g., **la surprise se lit sur votre visage** your face shows surprise

lis [lis] *m* lily; **lis blanc** lily; **lis jaune** day lily

Lisbonne [lizbɔn] *f* Lisbon

liseré [lizre] or **liséré** [lizere] *m* braid, border, strip

li·seur [lizœr] **-seuse** [zøz] *mf* reader ‖ *f* bookmark; reading lamp; book jacket; bed jacket

lisibilité [lizibilite] *f* legibility

lisible [lizibl] *adj* legible; readable

lisière [lisjɛr] *f* edge, border; list, selvage; **tenir en lisières** to keep in leading strings

lissage [lisaʒ] *m* face-lift

lisse [lis] *adj* smooth, polished, sleek ‖ *f* (naut) handrail

lissé [lise] *m* smoothness

lisser [lise] *tr* to smooth, polish, sleek; glaze (*paper*) ‖ *ref* to become smooth; **se lisser les plumes** to preen its feathers

lisseuse [lisøz] *f* ice resurfacer

listage [listaʒ] *m* (comp) listing

liste [list] *f* list; (comp) listing; **liste de vérification** check list

lister [liste] *tr* (comp) to list

lit [li] *m* bed; layer; stratum; **dans le lit de la marée** in the tideway; **dans le lit du vent** in the wind's eye; **du premier lit** by or of the first marriage; **lit de mort** deathbed; **lit d'époque** period bed; **lit de repos** day bed; **lit de sangle, lit de camp** folding cot, camp bed; **lit en portefeuille** applepie bed; **lit pliant, lit escamotable, lit à rabattement** foldaway bed; **lits jumeaux** twin beds; **lits superposés** bunk beds

litanie [litani] *f* litany; tale of woe

lit-cage [likaʒ] *m* (*pl* **lits-cages**) foldaway bed

lit-canapé [likanape] *m* (*pl* **lits-canapés**) sofa bed

litée [lite] *f* litter (*of animals*)

literie [litri] *f* bedding, bedclothes

lithine [litin] *f* lithia

lithium [litjɔm] *m* lithium

lithographe [litɔgraf] *mf* lithographer

lithographie [litɔgrafi] *f* lithography; lithograph

lithographier [litɔgrafje] *tr* to lithograph

litière [litjɛr] *f* litter (*bedding for animals*); **faire litière de** to trample

litige [litiʒ] *m* litigation

liti·gieux [litiʒjø] **-gieuse** [ʒjøz] *adj* litigious

litre [litr] *m* liter

littéraire [literɛr] *adj* literary ‖ *mf* teacher of literature; belletrist

litté·ral -rale [literal] *adj* (*pl* **-raux** [ro]) literal; literary, written

littérature [literatyr] *f* literature

litto·ral -rale [litɔral] *adj* (*pl* **-raux** [ro]) littoral, coastal ‖ *m* coast, coastline

liturgie [lityrʒi] *f* liturgy

liturgique [lityrʒik] *adj* liturgic(al)

livid [livid] *adj* livid

living [liviŋ] *m* living room; all-purpose room in a studio apartment

Livourne [livurn] *f* Leghorn

livrable [livrabl] *adj* ready for delivery

livraison [livrezɔ̃] *f* delivery; installment; **livraison contre remboursement** cash on delivery

livre [livr] *m* book; **à livre ouvert** at sight; **faire un livre** to write a book; (*racing*) to make book; **feuilleter un livre** to glance through a book; **grand livre** (bk) ledger; **livre broché, livre de poche** paperback; **livre de bord** (aer, naut) logbook; **livre de classe** textbook; **livre de cuisine, livre de recettes** cookbook; **livre d'or** blue book; testimonial volume; guest book; **livre jaune** white book; **petit livre** (bk) journal, day book; **porter au grand livre** (bk) to post ‖ *f* pound (*weight; currency*)

livrée [livre] *f* livery; appearances; coat (*of horse, deer, etc.*)

livrer [livre] *tr* to deliver; surrender; betray ‖ *ref*—**se livrer à** to surrender oneself to; give way to, indulge in

livresque [livrɛsk] *adj* bookish

livret [livre] *m* booklet; (mus) libretto; **livret de caisse d'épargne** bankbook; **livret de famille** marriage certificate; **livret d'instruction** instruction manual; **livret militaire** military record; **livret scolaire** transcript (*of grades*)

li·vreur [livrœr] **-vreuse** [vrøz] *mf* deliverer (*of parcels, packages, etc.*) ‖ *m* delivery-man ‖ *f* woman who makes deliveries; delivery truck

lobby [lɔbi] (*pl* **lobbies**) *m* lobby; **lobby environnementaliste** environmental-protection lobby; **lobby des marchands de revolvers** gun lobby

lobe [lɔb] *m* lobe; **lobe de l'oreille** ear lobe

lo·cal -cale [lɔkal] (*pl* **-caux** [ko]) *adj* local ‖ *m* place, premises, quarters; headquarters; **locaux** (sports) home team; **locaux commerciaux** office space

localiser [lɔkalize] *tr* to locate; localize

localité [lɔkalite] *f* locality

locataire [lɔkatɛr] *mf* tenant, renter

location [lɔkasjɔ̃] *f* rental; reservation

loch [lɔk] *m* (naut) log (*to determine speed*)

lock-out [lɔkaut] *m invar* lockout

locomotive [lɔkɔmɔtiv] *f* locomotive; (fig) mover; (fig) price leader

locuste [lɔkyst] *f* (ent) locust

locu·teur [lɔkytœr] **-trice** [tris] *mf* speaker

locution [lɔkysjɔ̃] *f* locution; phrase

lof [lɔf] *m* windward side; **aller** or **venir au lof** to sail into the wind

logarithme [lɔgaritm] *m* logarithm

loge [lɔʒ] *f* lodge; circus cage; concierge's room; chamber, cell; (theat) dressing room; (theat) box

logeabilité [lɔʒabilite] *f* spaciousness

logeable [lɔʒabl] *adj* livable, inhabitable

logement [lɔʒmɑ̃] *m* lodging, lodgings

loger [lɔʒe] §38 *tr, intr, & ref* to lodge

lo·geur [lɔʒœr] **-geuse** [ʒøz] *mf* proprietor of a boardinghouse ‖ *m* landlord ‖ *f* landlady

logiciel [lɔʒisjɛl] *m* (comp) software

logi·cien [lɔʒisjɛ̃] **-cienne** [sjɛn] *mf* logician

logique [lɔʒik] *adj* logical ‖ *f* logic

logis [lɔʒi] *m* abode

logistique [lɔʒistik] *adj* logistic(al) ‖ *f* logistics

loi [lwa] *f* law; **faire des lois** to legislate; **faire la loi** to lay down the law; **loi exceptionnelle** emergency legislation; **loi sélective du plus fort, loi du mieux adapté** survival of the fittest

loin [lwɛ̃] *adv* far; far away, far off; **au loin** in the distance; **d'aussi loin que, du plus loin que** as soon as; as far back as; **de loin** from afar; far from; far be it from (*e.g., me*); **de loin en loin** now and then; **il y a loin de** it is a far cry from; **loin des yeux, loin du cœur** out of sight, out of mind

loin·tain [lwɛ̃tɛ̃] **-taine** [tɛn] *adj* faraway, distant, remote; early (*e.g., memories*) ‖ *m* distance, background; **le lointain** (theat) upstage

loir [lwar] *m* dormouse; **dormir comme un loir** to sleep like a log

loisible [lwazibl] *adj*—**il m'est (lui est, etc.) loisible de** I am (he is, etc.) free to or entitled to, it is open for me (him, etc.) to

loisir [lwazir] *m* leisure, spare time; **à loisir** at one's convenience; **loisirs** diversions
lolo [lolo] *m* (coll) milk (*in baby talk*)
lombes [lɔ̃b] *mpl* loins
londo·nien [lɔ̃dɔnjɛ̃] **-nienne** [njɛn] *adj* London ‖ (*cap*) *mf* Londoner
Londres [lɔ̃dr] *m* London
londrès [lɔ̃drɛs] *m* Havana cigar
long [lɔ̃] **longue** [lɔ̃g] *adj* long; lengthy (*speech*); long (*syllable, vowel*); thin, weak (*sauce, gravy*); slow (*to understand, to decide*) ‖ (when standing before noun) *adj* long; **de longue main** of long standing ‖ *m* length; extent; **au long** at length; **de long** lengthwise; **de long en large** up and down, back and forth; **le long de** along; **tout au long** without forgetting anything ‖ *f* see **longue** ‖ **long** *adv* much; **en dire long** to talk a long time; to speak volumes; **en savoir long sur** to know a great deal about; **en savoir plus long** to know more about it
longanimité [lɔ̃ganimite] *f* long-suffering
long-courrier [lɔ̃kurje] (*pl* **-courriers**) *adj* long-range ‖ *m* airliner; liner, ocean liner
longe [lɔ̃ʒ] *f* tether, leash; (culin) loin
longer [lɔ̃ʒe] §38 *tr* to walk along, go beside; extend along, skirt
longeron [lɔ̃ʒrɔ̃] *m* crossbeam, girder
longévité [lɔ̃ʒevite] *f* longevity
longitude [lɔ̃ʒityd] *f* longitude
longtemps [lɔ̃tɑ̃] *m* a long time; **avant longtemps** before long; **depuis longtemps** for a long time; long since; **ne . . . plus longtemps** no . . . longer ‖ *adv* long; for a long time
longue [lɔ̃g] *f* long syllable; long vowel; long suit (*in cards*); **à la longue** in the long run
longuement [lɔ̃gmɑ̃] *adv* at length, a long time
lon·guet [lɔ̃gɛ] **-guette** [gɛt] *adj* (coll) longish, rather long
longueur [lɔ̃gœr] *f* length; lengthiness; **à longueur de journée** all day long; **de longueur, dans la longueur** lengthwise; **d'une longueur** by a length, by a head; **longueur d'onde** wavelength; **longueurs** slowness, delays; tedious passages (*e.g., of a book*); **traîner en longueur** to drag on
longue-vue [lɔ̃gvy] *f* (*pl* **longues-vues**) telescope, spyglass
looping [lupiŋ] *m* loop-the-loop
lopin [lɔpɛ̃] *m* patch of ground, plot
loquace [lɔkwas], [lɔkas] *adj* loquacious
loque [lɔk] *f* rag; **être comme une loque** to feel like a dishrag; **être en loques** to be in tatters
loquet [lɔkɛ] *m* latch
loque·teux [lɔktø] **-teuse** [tøz] *adj* in tatters ‖ *mf* tatterdemalion
lorgner [lɔrɲe] *tr* to cast a sidelong glance at; ogle; have one's eyes on (*a job, an inheritance, etc.*)
lorgnette [lɔrɲɛt] *f* opera glasses
lorgnon [lɔrɲɔ̃] *m* pince-nez; lorgnette

loriot [lɔrjo] *m* golden oriole
lorry [lɔri] *m* lorry, small flatcar
lors [lɔr] *adv*—**lors de** at the time of; **lors même que** even if
lorsque [lɔrsk] *conj* when
losange [lozɑ̃ʒ] *m* (geom) lozenge; **en losange** diamond-shaped; oval-shaped
lot [lo] *m* lot; prize (*e.g., in lottery*); **gagner le gros lot** to hit the jackpot
loterie [lɔtri] *f* lottery
lo·ti -tie [lɔti] *adj* built-up (*area*); **bien loti** well off; **mal loti** badly off
lotion [losjɔ̃] *f* lotion; **lotion capillaire** hair tonic
lotionner [losjɔne] *tr* to bathe (*a wound*)
lotir [lɔtir] *tr* to parcel out; **lotir qn de q.ch.** to allot s.th. to s.o.
lotissement [lɔtismɑ̃] *m* allotment, apportionment; building lot; (building) development
louable [lwabl] *adj* praiseworthy; for hire
louage [lwaʒ] *m* hire
louange [lwɑ̃ʒ] *f* praise; **à la louange de** in praise of
louanger [lwɑ̃ʒe] §38 *tr* to praise, extol
louan·geur [lwɑ̃ʒœr] **-geuse** [ʒøz] *adj* laudatory, flattering
loubard [lubar] *m* hood (*gangster*); punk
louche [luʃ] *adj* ambiguous; suspicious, shady; cross-eyed; cloudy (*e.g., wine*) ‖ *f* ladle; basting spoon
loucher [luʃe] *intr* to be cross-eyed, squint; **faire loucher qn de jalousie** (coll) to turn s.o. green with envy; **loucher sur** (coll) to cast longing eyes at
louchet [luʃɛ] *m* spade (*for digging*)
louer [lwe] §97 *tr* to rent, hire; to reserve (*a seat*); praise ‖ *ref* to be rented; hire oneself out; **se louer de** to be satisfied with
loueur [lwœr] **loueuse** [lwøz] *mf* operator of a rental service; flatterer
loufoque [lufɔk] *adj* (slang) cracked ‖ *m* (slang) crackpot
lougre [lugr] *m* (naut) lugger
Louisiane [lwizjan] *f* Louisiana; **la Louisiane** Louisiana
lou·lou [lulu] **-loute** [lut] *mf* (coll) darling, pet ‖ *m*—**loulou de Poméranie** Pomeranian, spitz
loup [lu] *m* wolf; mask; flaw; **avoir vu le loup** to have lost one's innocence; **crier au loup** to cry wolf; **loup de mer** (ichth) wolf eel; (coll) old salt; **mon petit loup** (coll) my pet ‖ see **louve**
loup-cervier [lusɛrvje] *m* (*pl* **loups-cerviers**) lynx
loupe [lup] *f* magnifying glass; gnarl (*on tree*); (pathol) wen
lou·pé -pée [lupe] *adj* bungled; defective ‖ *m* defect
louper [lupe] *tr* (coll) to goof up, muff; (coll) to miss (*e.g., one's train*) ‖ *intr* (coll) to fail, goof
loup-garou [lugaru] *m* (*pl* **loups-garous**) werewolf
lou·piot [lupjo] **-piotte** [pjɔt] *mf* (coll) kid, child; **loupiots** (coll) small fry

lourd [lur] **lourde** [lurd] §92 *adj* heavy; hefty; clumsy; sultry (*weather*); off-color (*joke*); dull (*mind*); (agr) hard to cultivate ‖ (when standing before noun) *adj* heavy; grave; clumsy (*e.g., compliments*); off-color (*joke*) ‖ **lourd** *adv* heavy, heavily

lour·daud [lurdo] **-daude** [dod] *adj* clumsy, loutish, dull ‖ *mf* lout, oaf

lourdement [lurdəmɑ̃] *adv* heavily; clumsily; **avancer** or **rouler lourdement** to lumber along

lourdeur [lurdœr] *f* heaviness; clumsiness; sultriness; dullness

loustic [lustik] *m* wag, clown; (coll) screwball, character

loutre [lutr] *f* otter

louve [luv] *f* she-wolf

louve·teau [luvto] *m* (*pl* **-teaux**) wolf cub; cub scout

louvoyer [luvwaje] §47 *intr* to be evasive; (naut) to tack

lovelace [lɔvlas] *m* seducer, Don Juan

lover [lɔve] *tr & refl* to coil

loyal loyale [lwajal] *adj* (*pl* **loyaux** [lwajo]) loyal; honest; fair, just

loyaliste [lwajalist] *mf* loyalist

loyauté [lwajote] *f* loyalty; honesty; fairness

loyer [lwaje] *m* rent

lu lue [ly] *v* see **lire**

lubie [lybi] *f* whim; fad

lubricité [lybrisite] *f* lubricity, lewdness

lubri·fiant [lybrifjɑ̃] **-fiante** [fjɑ̃t] *adj & m* lubricant

lubrifier [lybrifje] *tr* to lubricate

lubrique [lybrik] *adj* lecherous, lustful, lewd

lucarne [lykarn] *f* dormer window; skylight

lucide [lysid] *adj* lucid

luciole [lysjɔl] *f* firefly

lucra·tif [lykratif] **-tive** [tiv] *adj* lucrative; **sans but lucratif** nonprofit

lucre [lykr] *m* lucre

ludiciel [lydisjɛl] *m* games software

luette [lɥet] *f* uvula

lueur [lɥœr] *f* glimmer, gleam; flash, blink

luge [lyʒ] *f* sled

lugubre [lygybr] *adj* gloomy

lui [lɥi] *pron disj* §85 him ‖ *pron conj* §87 him; her; it; to him; to her; to it

lui-même [lɥimɛm] §86 himself; itself

luire [lɥir] §37 *intr* to shine; to gleam, glow, glisten; to dawn

lui·sant [lɥizɑ̃] **-sante** [zɑ̃t] *adj* shining

lulu [lyly] *m* (orn) tree pipit

lumbago [lɔ̃bago] *m* lumbago

lumière [lymjɛr] *f* light; aperture; (*person*) luminary; **avoir des lumières de** to have knowledge of; **lumière ultraviolette** ultraviolet light

lumignon [lymiɲɔ̃] *m* feeble light

luminaire [lyminɛr] *m* luminary

lumines·cent [lyminɛsɑ̃] **-cente** [sɑ̃t] *adj* luminescent

lumi·neux [lyminø] **-neuse** [nøz] *adj* luminous; light (*e.g., spot*); bright (*idea*)

lunaire [lynɛr] *adj* lunar ‖ *f* (bot) honesty

lunatique [lynatik] *adj* whimsical, eccentric ‖ *mf* whimsical person, eccentric

lunch [lœntʃ], [lœ̃ʃ] *m* buffet lunch

lundi [lœ̃di] *m* Monday

lune [lyn] *f* moon; **être dans la lune** to be daydreaming; **lune de miel** honeymoon; **lune des moissons** harvest moon; **vieilles lunes** good old days, bygone days

lu·né -née [lyne] *adj* moon-shaped; **bien luné** in a good mood; **mal luné** in a bad mood

lune·tier [lyntje] **-tière** [tjɛr] *mf* optician

lunette [lynɛt] *f* telescope, spyglass; toilet seat; hole (*in toilet seat*); wishbone (*of turkey, chicken*); (archit) lunette; (aut) rear window; **lunettes** eyeglasses, spectacles; goggles; **lunettes auditives** eyeglass hearing aid; **lunettes de lecture, lunettes pour lire** reading glasses; **lunettes de soleil** sunglasses; **lunettes noires** dark glasses

lurette [lyrɛt] *f*—**il y a belle lurette** (coll) ages ago

luron [lyrɔ̃] *m* (coll) playboy

luronne [lyrɔn] *f* (coll) hussy

lustre [lystr] *m* luster; five-year period; chandelier

lus·tré -trée [lystre] *adj* glossy, shiny

lustrine [lystrin] *f* cotton satin

lut [lyt] *m* (chem) lute

luth [lyt] *m* (mus) lute

lutherie [lytri] *f* violin making

luthé·rien [lyterjɛ̃] **-rienne** [rjɛn] *adj* Lutheran ‖ (*cap*) *mf* Lutheran

luthier [lytje] *m* violin maker

lu·tin [lytɛ̃] **-tine** [tin] *adj* impish ‖ *m* imp

lutiner [lytine] *tr* to tease

lutrin [lytrɛ̃] *m* lectern

lutte [lyt] *f* struggle, fight; wrestling; **de bonne lutte** aboveboard; **de haute lutte** by force; in open competition; hard-won; **lutte à la corde de traction** tug of war; **lutte libre** catch-as-catch-can

lutter [lyte] *intr* to fight, struggle; wrestle

lut·teur [lytœr] **-teuse** [tøz] *mf* wrestler; (fig) fighter

luxation [lyksasjɔ̃] *f* dislocation

luxe [lyks] *m* luxury; **avec un trés grand luxe** luxury (*e.g., apartment*)

Luxembourg [lyksɑ̃bur] *m*—**le Luxembourg** Luxembourg

luxer [lykse] *tr* to dislocate

lu·xueux [lyksɥø] **-xueuse** [ksɥøz] *adj* luxurious

luxure [lyksyr] *f* lechery, lust

luxu·riant [lyksyrjɑ̃] **-riante** [rjɑ̃t] *adj* luxuriant

luxu·rieux [lyksyrjø] **-rieuse** [rjøz] *adj* lecherous, lustful

luzerne [lyzɛrn] *f* alfalfa

lycée [lise] *m* high school (with academic courses); lycée

ly·céen [liseɛ̃] **-céenne** [seɛn] *mf* secondary-school student

lymphatique [lɛ̃fatik] *adj* lymphatic

lymphe [lɛ̃f] *f* lymph

lynchage [lɛ̃ʃaʒ] *m* lynching

lyncher [lɛ̃ʃe] *tr* to lynch
lynx [lɛ̃ks] *m* lynx
Lyon [ljɔ̃] *m* Lyons
lyon·nais [liɔnɛ] **-naise** [nɛz] *adj* Lyonese; **à la lyonnaise** lyonnaise
lyophilisation [ljɔfilizasjɔ̃] *f* freeze drying
lyophiliser [ljɔfilize] *tr* to freeze-dry

lyre [lir] *f* lyre
lyrique [lirik] *adj* lyric(al) ‖ *m* lyric poet ‖ *f* lyric poetry
lyrisme [lirism] *m* lyricism
lys [lis] *m* lily; **lys blanc** lily; **lys jaune** day lily
lysimaque [lizimak] *f* loosestrife

M

M, m [ɛm], *[ɛm] *m invar* thirteenth letter of the French alphabet
M. *abbr* (**Monsieur**) Mr.
m' = **me** before vowel or mute **h**
ma [ma] §88 my
ma·boul -boule [mabul] *adj* (slang) nuts, balmy ‖ *mf* (slang) nut
macabre [makɑbr] *adj* macabre
macadam [makadam] *m* macadam
macadamiser [makadamize] *tr* to macadamize
macaron [makarɔ̃] *m* macaroon; (coll) bumpersticker
macchabée [makabe] *m* (slang) stiff (*corpse*)
macédoine [masedwan] *f* macédoine, medley; **macédoine de fruits** fruit salad; **macédoine de légumes** mixed vegetables
macérer [masere] §10 *tr* to macerate; mortify (*the flesh*); soak, steep ‖ *intr* to soak, steep
mâchefer [mɑʃfɛr] *m* clinker
mâcher [mɑʃe] *tr* to chew; **mâcher la besogne à qn** to do all one's work for one; **ne pas mâcher ses mots** to not mince words
machin [maʃɛ̃] *m* (coll) what-do-you-call-it; (coll) what's-his-name, so-and-so
machi·nal -nale [maʃinal] *adj* (*pl* **-naux** [no]) mechanical
machination [maʃinɑsjɔ̃] *f* machination
machine [maʃin] *f* machine; engine; **faire machine arrière** to go into reverse; **machine à calculer** adding machine; **machine à coudre** sewing machine; **machine à écrire** typewriter; **machine à écrire portative** portable typewriter; **machine à laver** washing machine; **machine à laver la vaisselle** dishwasher; **machine à sous** slot machine; **machine à vapeur** steam engine; **machine de télégestion bancaire** automatic teller; **machines** machinery
machine-outil [maʃinuti] *f* (*pl* **machines-outils**) machine tool
machinerie [maʃinri] *f* machinery; engine room
machiniste [maʃinist] *m* (theat) stagehand
mâchoire [mɑʃwar] *f* jaw; jawbone; lower jaw
mâchonner [mɑʃɔne] *tr* to chew, munch; mumble (*e.g., the end of a sentence*)
mâchurer [mɑʃyre] *tr* to crush; smudge

maçon [masɔ̃] *m* mason
maçonner [masɔne] *tr* to mason, wall up
maçonnerie [masɔnri] *f* masonry
macule [makyl] *f* spot, blotch; inkblot; birthmark
maculer [makyle] *tr* to soil, spot; (typ) to smear
madame [madam] *f* (*pl* **mesdames** [medam]) madam; Mrs.; (not translated), e.g., **madame votre femme** your wife
Madeleine [madlɛn] *f* Madeleine, Magdalen; sponge cake; **pleurer comme une Madeleine** to weep bitterly
mademoiselle [madmwazɛl] *f* (*pl* **mesdemoiselles** [medmwazɛl]) Miss; eldest daughter; (not translated), e.g., **mademoiselle votre fille** your daughter
Madone [madɔn] *f* Madonna
ma·dré -drée [madre] *adj* sly, cagey ‖ *mf* sly one
madrier [madrije] *m* beam
mafia or **maffia** [mafja] *f* Mafia, Maffia; **la Maf(f)ia** the Mafia
maf·flu -flue [mafly] *adj* heavy-jowled
magasin [magazɛ̃] *m* store; warehouse; magazine (*of gun or camera; for munitions or powder*); **avoir en magasin** to have in stock; **grands magasins** department store; **magasin à libre service** self-service store; **magasin à prix unique** variety store; **magasin à succursales multiples** chain store; **magasin d'antiquités** antique shop; **magasin de modes** dress shop; **magasin de rabais** discount store; **magasin entrepôt** no-frills store
magasinage [magazinaʒ] *m* storage, warehousing; storage charges; (Canad) shopping
magasinier [magazinje] *m* warehouseman
magazine [magazin] *m* magazine; (mov, telv) hour, program, e.g., **magazine féminin** woman's hour
mages [maʒ] *mpl* Magi
magi·cien [maʒisjɛ̃] **-cienne** [sjɛn] *mf* magician
magie [maʒi] *f* magic
magique [maʒik] *adj* magic
magis·tral -trale [maʒistral] *adj* (*pl* **-traux** [tro]) masterful, masterly; magisterial; (pharm) magistral
magistrat [maʒistra] *m* magistrate
magnanime [maɲanim] *adj* magnanimous

magnat [magna] *m* magnate

magnésium [maɲezjɔm] *m* magnesium

magnétique [maɲetik] *adj* magnetic; hypnotic

magnétiser [maɲetize] *tr* to magnetize; hypnotize; spellbind

magnétisme [maɲetism] *m* magnetism

magnéto [maɲeto] *f* magneto

magnétophone [maɲetɔfɔn] *m* tape recorder; **magnétophone à fil d'acier** wire recorder

magnétoscope [maɲetɔskɔp] *m* videotape recorder; videocassette recorder

magnétoscopie [maɲetɔskɔpi] *f* videotape recording, videocassette recording

magnifier [magnifje] *tr* to extol, glorify

magnifique [maɲifik] *adj* magnificent; lavishly generous

magnitude [magnityd] *f* (astr) magnitude

magot [mago] *m* Barbary ape; figurine; (coll) hoard, pile (*of money*)

Mahomet [maɔmɛ] *m* Mohammad

mahomé·tan [maɔmetɑ̃] **-tane** [tan] *adj* & *m* Mohammedan

mai [mɛ] *m* May; Maypole

maie [mɛ] *f* bread bin; kneading trough

maigre [mɛgr] *adj* lean; thin; meager; meatless (*day*); **faire maigre** to abstain from meat

maigreur [mɛgrœr] *f* leanness; meagerness

maigri·chon [megriʃɔ̃] **-chonne** [ʃɔn] *adj* (coll) skinny

maigrir [megrir] *tr* to slim; make (*s.o.*) look thinner ‖ *intr* to lose weight

mail [maj] *m* mall

maille [mɑj] *f* link; stitch; mesh, loop; **avoir maille à partir avec qn** to have a bone to pick with s.o.; **mailles** mail

maillet [majɛ] *m* mallet

maillon [mɑjɔ̃] *m* link (*of a chain*)

maillot [majo] *m* swimming suit; jersey; **maillot de bain** swimming suit; **maillot de corps** undershirt; **maillot de danseur** tights; **maillot des acrobates** tights

main [mɛ̃] *f* hand; quire; **à la main** by hand; **à main levée** by show of hands; in one stroke; **avoir la haute main sur** to control; **avoir la main, être la main** (cards) to be the dealer; **battre des mains** to applaud; **de la main à la main** privately; **de longue main** carefully; for a long time; **de main à main** from one person to another; **de première main** firsthand; **donner les mains à q.ch.** to be in favor of s.th.; **en venir aux mains** to come to blows; **faire main basse sur** to grab, to steal; **haut les mains!** hands up!; **main dans la main** hand in hand; **passer la main dans le dos à qn** to soft-soap s.o.; **serrer la main à** to shake hands with; **sous main** secretly; **tout main** handmade

main-d'œuvre [mɛ̃dœvr] *f* (*pl* **mains-d'œuvre**) labor; laborers; manpower

maint [mɛ̃] **mainte** [mɛ̃t] *adj* many a; **à maintes reprises** time and again

maintenant [mɛ̃tənɑ̃] *adv* now

maintenir [mɛ̃tnir] §72 *intr* to maintain; hold up ‖ *ref* to keep on; keep up

maintien [mɛ̃tjɛ̃] *m* maintenance; bearing

maire [mɛr] *m* mayor

mairesse [mɛrɛs] *f* (coll) mayor's wife

mairie [meri] *f* town hall, city hall

mais [mɛ] *m* but ‖ *adv* why, well; **mais non** certainly not ‖ *conj* but

maïs [mais] *m* corn, maize; **maïs en épi** corn on the cob; **maïs explosé** popcorn

maison [mezɔ̃] *f* house; home; household, family; house, firm, business; **à la maison** at home, home; **fait à la maison** homemade; **la Maison Blanche** the White House; **maison centrale** state or federal prison; **maison close, borgne, publique, mal famée, de débauche, de passe, de rendez-vous, de tolérance** house of ill fame; **maison d'accouchement** lying-in hospital; **maison d'antiquités, de meubles d'époque,** or **d'originaux** antique shop; **maison de commerce** firm; **maison de confiance** (com) trustworthy firm; **maison de correction** reform school; **maison de couture** dressmaking establishment; **maison de fous** madhouse; **maison de jeux** gambling house; **maison de plaisance** or **de campagne** cottage, summer home; **maison de rapport** apartment house; **maison de repos** rest home; **maison de retraite** old-people's home; **maison de santé** nursing home; **maison jumelée** semi-detached house; **maison mère** head office; **maison mortuaire** home of the deceased; **maison religieuse** convent

maisonnée [mezɔne] *f* household

maisonnette [mezɔnɛt] *f* little house, cottage

maî·tre [mɛtr] **-tresse** [trɛs] *adj* expert, capable; basic, key; main (*beam, girder*); utter (*fool*); arrant (*knave*); high (*card*) ‖ *m* master; Mr. (*when addressing a lawyer*); (naut) mate; (naut) petty officer; **être passé maître en** to be a past master of or in; **maître chanteur** blackmailer; **maître d'armes** fencing master; **maître de chapelle** choirmaster; **maître d'école** schoolmaster; **maître de conférences** associate professor; **maître de forges** ironmaster; **maître de maison** man of the house, householder; **maître d'équipage** boatswain; **maître d'études** monitor, supervisor; **maître d'hôtel** headwaiter; butler; **maître d'œuvre** foreman; **maître Jacques** jack-of-all-trades; **maître mécanicien** chief engineer; **maître mineur** mine foreman; **maître queue** chef; **passer maître** to know one's trade ‖ *f* see **maîtresse**

maître-autel [mɛtrotɛl] *m* (*pl* **maîtres-autels**) high altar

maîtresse [mɛtrɛs] *f* mistress; **maîtresse d'école** schoolmistress; **maîtresse de maison** lady of the house

maîtrise [metriz] *f* mastery, command; master's degree; **maîtrise de soi** self-control

maîtriser [metrize] *tr* to master, control; subdue

maj. *abbr* (**majuscule**) cap.

majesté [maʒɛste] *f* majesty

majes·tueux [maʒɛstɥø] **-tueuse** [tɥøz] *adj* majestic

ma·jeur -jeure [maʒœr] *adj* & *m* major

major [maʒɔr] *m* regimental quartermaster; army doctor; **être le major de sa promotion** to be at the head of one's class

majordome [maʒɔrdɔm] *m* major-domo

majorer [maʒɔre] *tr* to increase the price of; overprice; raise (*the price*)

majoritaire [maʒɔritɛr] *adj* majority

majorité [maʒɔrite] *f* majority; time of being of full legal age

Majorque [maʒɔrk] *f* Majorca

major·quin [maʒɔrkɛ̃] **-quine** [kin] *adj* Majorcan ‖ (*cap*) *mf* Majorcan

majuscule [maʒyskyl] *adj* capital (*letter*) ‖ *f* capital letter

mal [mal] *adj*—**de mal** bad, e.g., **dire q.ch. de mal** to say s.th. bad; **pas mal** not bad, quite good-looking ‖ *m* (*pl* **maux** [mo]) evil; trouble; hurt; pain; wrong; **avoir du mal à** + *inf* to have a hard time + *ger* to have difficulty in + *ger;* **avoir mal à la tête** to have a headache; **avoir mal au cœur** to be nauseated; **avoir mal aux dents** to have a toothache; **avoir mal de gorge** to have a sore throat; **dire du mal de qn** to speak ill of s.o.; **faire mal à, faire du mal à** to hurt, to harm; **le Mal** Evil; **mal aux reins** backache; **mal blanc** whitlow; **mal de l'air** airsickness; **mal de la route** carsickness; **mal de mer** seasickness; **mal des rayons** radiation sickness; **mal du pays** homesickness; **mal du siècle** Weltschmerz, romantic melancholy; **se donner du mal** to take pains ‖ *adv* §91 badly, bad; **de mal en pis** from bad to worse; **être mal avec qn** to be on bad terms with s.o.; **pas mal** not bad; **pas mal de** a lot of, quite a few

malade [malad] *adj* sick, ill ‖ *mf* patient, sick person

maladie [maladi] *f* disease, sickness; distemper; **elle va en faire une maladie** (coll) she'll be terribly upset over it; **maladie de carence** or **par carence** deficiency disease; **maladie de cœur** heart trouble; **maladie des caissons** bends; **maladie diplomatique** malingering; **maladie sexuellement transmissible** sexually transmitted disease; **revenir de maladie** to convalesce

mala·dif [maladif] **-dive** [div] *adj* sickly; morbid

maladresse [maladrɛs] *f* awkwardness; blunder

mala·droit [maladrwa] **-droite** [drwat] *adj* clumsy, awkward

ma·lais [malɛ] **-laise** [lɛz] *adj* Malay ‖ *m* Malay (*language*) ‖ see **malaise** *m* ‖ (*cap*) *mf* Malay (*person*)

malaise [malɛz] *m* malaise, discomfort

malai·sé -sée [maleze] *adj* difficult

malap·pris [malapri] **-prise** [priz] *adj* uncouth, ill-bred ‖ *mf* ill-bred person

malard [malar] *m* (orn) mallard

malaria [malarja] *f* malaria

malavi·sé -sée [malavize] *adj* ill-advised, indiscreet

malaxer [malakse] *tr* to knead; churn (*butter*); massage

malaxeur [malaksœr] *m* churn; (mach) mixer

malchance [malʃɑ̃s] *f* bad luck; **par malchance** unluckily; **une malchance** a piece of bad luck

malchan·ceux [malʃɑ̃sø] **-ceuse** [søz] *adj* unlucky

malcommode [malkɔmɔd] *adj* inconvenient; unsuitable, impractical

maldonne [maldɔn] *f* misdeal

mâle [mal] *adj* male; energetic, virile ‖ *m* male

malédiction [malediksjɔ̃] *f* curse

maléfice [malefis] *m* evil spell

maléfique [malefik] *adj* baleful

malencon·treux [malɑ̃kɔ̃trø] **-treuse** [trøz] *adj* untimely, unfortunate

malentendu [malɑ̃tɑ̃dy] *m* misunderstanding

malfaçon [malfasɔ̃] *f* defect

malfai·sant [malfəzɑ̃] **-sante** [zɑ̃t] *adj* mischievous, harmful

malfaiteur [malfɛtœr] *m* malefactor

malfa·mé -mée [malfame] *adj* ill-famed

malgra·cieux [malgrasjø] **-cieuse** [sjøz] *adj* ungracious

malgré [malgre] *prep* in spite of; **malgré que** in spite of the fact that, although

malhabile [malabil] *adj* inexperienced, clumsy

malheur [malœr] *m* misfortune; unhappiness; bad luck; **faire un malheur** to commit an act of violence; (theat) to be a howling success; **jouer de malheur** to be unlucky

malheureusement [malœrøzmɑ̃] *adv* unfortunately

malheu·reux [malœrø] **-reuse** [røz] *adj* unfortunate; unhappy; unlucky; paltry ‖ *m* poor man, wretch; **les malheureux** the unfortunate ‖ *f* poor woman, wretch

malhonnête [malɔnɛt] *adj* dishonest; (slang) rude, uncivil

malhonnêteté [malɔnɛtte] *f* dishonesty

malice [malis] *f* mischievousness; malice; trick

mali·cieux [malisjø] **-cieuse** [sjøz] *adj* malicious, mischievous

malignité [maliɲite] *f* malignancy

ma·lin [malɛ̃] **-ligne** [liɲ] *adj* cunning, sly, smart; mischievous; malignant; **ce n'est pas malin** (coll) it's easy ‖ *mf* sly one; **Le Malin** the Evil One

malingre [malɛ̃gr] *adj* weakly, puny

malintention·né -née [malɛ̃tɑ̃sjɔne] *adj* evil-minded, ill-disposed

mal-jugé [malʒyʒe] *m* miscarriage (*of justice*)

malle [mal] *f* trunk; mailboat; **faire ses malles** to pack

malléable [maleabl] *adj* malleable; compliant, pliable

mallette [malɛt] *f* valise; case

malmener [malmǝne] §2 *tr* to rough up

malodo·rant [malɔdɔrɑ̃] **-rante** [rɑ̃t] *adj* malodorous; bad (*breath*)

malo·tru -true [malɔtry] *adj* coarse, uncouth ‖ *mf* ill-bred person, oaf

malpropre [malprɔpr] *adj* dirty; improper; crude, clumsy (*workmanship*)

mal·sain [malsɛ̃] **-saine** [sɛn] *adj* unhealthy

mal·séant [malseɑ̃] **-séante** [seɑ̃t] *adj* improper

malson·nant [malsɔnɑ̃] **-nante** [nɑ̃t] *adj* offensive, objectionable

malt [malt] *m* malt

maltraiter [maltrete] *tr* to mistreat

malveil·lant [malvɛjɑ̃] **-lante** [jɑ̃t] *adj* malevolent

malve·nu -nue [malvǝny] *adj* ill-advised, out of place; poorly developed

malversation [malvɛrsɑsjɔ̃] *f* embezzlement

maman [mamɑ̃] *f* mamma

mamelle [mamɛl] *f* breast; udder

mamelon [mamlɔ̃] *m* nipple, teat; knoll

mamie [mami] *f* (coll) my dear

mammifère [mamifɛr] *adj* mammalian ‖ *m* mammal

mammouth [mamut] *m* mammoth

mamours [mamur] *mpl* (coll) caresses

mam'selle or **mam'zelle** [mamzɛl] *f* (coll) Miss

manant [manɑ̃] *m* hick, yokel

manche [mɑ̃ʃ] *m* handle; stick, stock; neck (*of violin*); (culin) knuckle; **branler au manche** or **dans le manche** to be shaky; **manche à balai** broomstick; (aer) joy stick; **manche à gigot** holder (*for carving*) ‖ *f* sleeve; hose; channel; game, heat, round; shaft, chute; (baseball) inning; (bridge) game; (tennis) set; **en manches de chemise** in shirt sleeves; **la Manche** the English Channel; **manche à air** windsock; **manche à manche** neck and neck, even up; **manches à gigot** leg-of-mutton sleeves

manchette [mɑ̃ʃɛt] *f* cuff; (journ) headline

manchon [mɑ̃ʃɔ̃] *m* muff; mantle (*of gaslight*); (mach) casing, sleeve

man·chot [mɑ̃ʃo] **-chote** [ʃɔt] *adj* one-armed; one-handed; (coll) clumsy ‖ *mf* one-armed person; one-handed person ‖ *m* (orn) penguin

mandarine [mɑ̃darin] *f* mandarin orange

mandat [mɑ̃da] *m* mandate; term of office; money order; power of attorney; proxy; **mandat d'arrêt** warrant; **mandat de perquisition** search warrant

mandataire [mɑ̃datɛr] *mf* representative; proxy; defender

mandat-carte [mɑ̃dakart] *m* (*pl* **mandats-carte**) postal-card money order

mandat-poste [mɑ̃dapɔst] *m* (*pl* **mandats-poste**) postal money order

Mandchourie [mɑ̃tʃuri] *f* Manchuria; **la Mandchourie** Manchuria

mander [mɑ̃de] §97 *tr* to summon

mandoline [mɑ̃dɔlin] *f* mandolin

mandragore [mɑ̃dragɔr] *f* mandrake

mandrin [mɑ̃drɛ̃] *m* (mach) punch; (mach) chuck

manécanterie [manekɑ̃tri] *f* choir school

manège [manɛʒ] *m* horsemanship; riding school; trick, little game; **manège de chevaux de bois** merry-go-round

mânes [mɑn] *mpl* shades, spirits (*of ancestors*)

maneton [mantɔ̃] *m* crank handle; pin (*of crankshaft*)

manette [manɛt] *f* lever, switch

manganèse [mɑ̃ganɛz] *m* manganese

mangeable [mɑ̃ʒabl] *adj* edible; barely fit to eat

mangeaille [mɑ̃ʒɑj] *f* swill; (coll) grub, chow

mangeotter [mɑ̃ʒɔte] *tr* to pick at (*one's food*)

manger [mɑ̃ʒe] *m* food, e.g., **le boire et le manger** food and drink; (slang) meal ‖ §38 *tr* to eat; eat up; mumble (*one's words*); **manger du bout des lèvres** to nibble at ‖ *intr* to eat; **manger à la fortune du pot** to take potluck

mangerie [mɑ̃ʒri] *f* (coll) big meal

mange-tout [mɑ̃ʒtu] *m invar* sugar pea

man·geur [mɑ̃ʒœr] **-geuse** [ʒøz] *mf* eater; wastrel, spendthrift; **mangeur d'hommes** man-eater

mangouste [mɑ̃gust] *f* mongoose

maniable [manjabl] *adj* maneuverable, easy to handle, supple

maniaque [manjak] *adj* & *mf* maniac

manie [mani] *f* mania

maniement [manimɑ̃] *m* handling

manier [manje] *tr* to handle ‖ *ref* (coll) to get a move on

manière [manjɛr] *f* manner; **à la manière de** in the manner of; **de manière à** so as to; **de manière que** so that; **de toute manière** in any case; **d'une manière ou d'une autre** one way or another; **en aucune manière** by no means; **faire des manières** to pretend to be indifferent, to want to be coaxed; **manière de voir** point of view; **manières** manners

manié·ré -rée [manjere] *adj* mannered, affected

maniérisme [manjerism] *m* mannerism

ma·nieur [manjœr] **-nieuse** [njøz] *mf* handler; **grand manieur d'argent** tycoon

manifes·tant [manifɛstɑ̃] **-tante** [tɑ̃t] *mf* demonstrator

manifestation [manifɛstɑsjɔ̃] *f* demonstration, manifestation

manifeste [manifɛst] *adj* manifest ‖ *m* manifesto; (naut) manifest

manifester [manifɛste] *tr* to manifest ‖ *intr* to demonstrate ‖ *ref* to reveal oneself

manigance [manigɑ̃s] *f* trick, intrigue

manipuler [manipyle] *tr* to manipulate; handle (*e.g., packages*); arrange (*equipment*) for an experiment

manitou [manitu] *m* manitou; (coll) bigwig

manivelle [manivɛl] *f* crank

manne [man] *f* manna

mannequin [mankɛ̃] *m* model; mannequin, dummy; scarecrow

manœuvre [manœvr] *m* hand, laborer ‖ *f* maneuver; (naut) handling, maneuvering; (rr) shifting; **fausse manœuvre** wrong move; **manœuvres** rigging

manœuvrer [manœvre] *tr & intr* to maneuver; (rr) to shift

manoir [manwar] *m* manor, manor house

man·quant [mɑ̃kɑ̃] **-quante** [kɑ̃t] *adj* missing ‖ *mf* absentee ‖ *m* missing article; **manquants** shortages

manque [mɑ̃k] *m* lack; shortage; insufficiency; **manque à gagner** lost opportunity; **manque de parole** breach of faith; **par manque de** for lack of ‖ *f*—**à la manque** (coll) rotten, poor, dud

man·qué -quée [mɑ̃ke] *adj* missed, unsuccessful; broken (*engagement*); (with abilities which were not professionally developed), e.g., **le docteur est un cuisinier manqué** the doctor could have been a cook by profession

manquement [mɑ̃kmɑ̃] *m* breach, lapse

manquer [mɑ̃ke] §96, §97 *tr* to miss; flunk ‖ *intr* to misfire; be missing, e.g., **il en manque trois** three are missing; be missed, e.g., **vous lui manquez beaucoup** you are very much missed by him, he misses you very much; be short, e.g., **il lui manque cinq francs** he is five francs short; **manquer à** to break (*one's word*); disobey (*an order*); fail to observe (*a rule*); fail, e.g., **le cœur lui a manqué** his heart failed him; **manquer de** to lack, be short of, to run out of; **manquer de +** *inf* to nearly + *inf*, e.g., **il a manqué de se noyer** he nearly drowned; **sans manquer** without fail ‖ *ref* to miss each other; to fail

mansarde [mɑ̃sard] *f* mansard roof; mansard

manse [mɑ̃s] *m & f* (hist) small manor

mante [mɑ̃t] *f* mantle; **mante religieuse** (ent) praying mantis

man·teau [mɑ̃to] *m* (*pl* **-teaux** [to]) overcoat; mantle, cloak; mantelpiece; **sous le manteau** sub rosa

mantille [mɑ̃tij] *f* mantilla

manucure [manykyr] *mf* manicurist

ma·nuel -nuelle [manɥɛl] *adj* manual ‖ *mf* laborer, blue-collar worker ‖ *m* manual, handbook

manufacture [manyfaktyr] *f* factory, plant

manufacturer [manyfaktyre] *tr* to manufacture

manus·crit [manyskri] **-crite** [krit] *adj & m* manuscript

manutention [manytɑ̃sjɔ̃] *f* handling (*of goods*); stopping for unloading

manutentionner [manytɑ̃sjɔne] *tr* to handle (*merchandise*)

mappemonde [mapmɔ̃d] *f* world map; **mappemonde céleste** map of the heavens

maque·reau [makro] **-relle** [rɛl] (*pl* **-reaux -relles**) *mf* (slang) procurer ‖ *m* mackerel; (slang) pimp ‖ *f* (slang) madam (*of a brothel*)

maquette [makɛt] *f* maquette, model; dummy (*of book*); rough sketch

maquignon [makiɲɔ̃] *m* horse trader; wholesale cattle dealer; (coll) go-between

maquignonnage [makiɲɔnaʒ] *m* horse trading

maquignonner [makiɲɔne] *intr* to horse-trade

maquillage [makijaʒ] *m* make-up; fakery

maquiller [makije] *tr* to make up; fake, distort ‖ *ref* to make up

maquil·leur [makijœr] **-leuse** [jøz] *mf* make-up artist ‖ *m* make-up man

maquis [maki] *m* bush; maquis; **prendre le maquis** to go underground

maraî·cher [mareʃe] **-chère** [ʃɛr] *adj* truck-farming ‖ *mf* truck farmer

marais [marɛ] *m* marsh; truck farm; **marais salant** saltern

marasme [marasm] *m* depression; doldrums, standstill

marathon [maratɔ̃] *m* marathon

marâtre [marɑtr] *f* stepmother; cruel mother

maraude [marod] *f* marauding; **en maraude** cruising (*taxi*)

marauder [marode] *intr* to maraud; cruise (*said of taxi*)

marau·deur [marodœr] **-deuse** [døz] *adj* marauding ‖ *mf* marauder

marbre [marbr] *m* marble; (typ) stone

marbrer [marbre] *tr* to marble; mottle, vein; bruise, blotch

marc [mar] *m* mark (*old coin*); marc, pulp; **marc de café** coffee grounds; **marc de thé** tea leaves ‖ [mark] (*cap*) *m* Mark

marcassin [markasɛ̃] *m* young wild boar

mar·chand [marʃɑ̃] **-chande** [ʃɑ̃d] *adj* marketable; sale (*value*); trading (*center*); wholesale (*price*); merchant (*marine*) ‖ *mf* merchant; **marchand ambulant** peddler; **marchand clandestin** fence (*seller of stolen goods*); **marchand de canons** munitions maker; **marchand de couleurs** paint dealer, dealer in household articles; **marchand de ferraille** junk dealer; **marchand de journaux** newsdealer; **marchand des quatre-saisons** fruit vendor; **marchand en gros** wholesaler; **marchand forain** hawker ‖ *f*—**marchande d'amour** or **de plaisir** prostitute

marchandage [marʃɑ̃daʒ] *m* bargaining; haggling; deal, underhanded arrangement

marchander [marʃɑ̃de] *tr* to bargain over; haggle over; be stingy with (*e.g., one's compliments*) ‖ *intr* to haggle

marchan·deur [marʃɑ̃dœr] **-deuse** [døz] *mf* bargainer; haggler

marchandisage [marʃɑ̃dizaʒ] *m* merchandising

marchandise [marʃãdiz] *f* merchandise; **marchandises** goods

mar·chant [marʃã] **-chante** [ʃãt] *adj* marching; militant (*wing of political party*); (mil) wheeling (*flank*)

marche [marʃ] *f* march; step (*of stairway*); walking; movement; progress, course; (aut) gear; **à dix minutes de marche** ten minutes' walk from here; **attention à la marche!** watch your step!; **en marche** in motion, running, operating; **faire marche arrière** to back up; to reverse; **fermer la marche** to bring up the rear; **marche funèbre** funeral march; **ouvrir la marche** to lead off the procession

marché [marʃe] *m* market; marketing, shopping; deal, bargain; **à bon marché** cheap; cheaply; **à meilleur marché** cheaper; more cheaply; **bon marché** cheapness; cheap; cheaply; **faire bon marché de** to set little store by; **faire son marché** to do the marketing; **lancer, mettre,** or **vendre sur le marché** to market; **marché noir** black market; **par-dessus le marché** into the bargain

marchepied [marʃəpje] *m* footstool; little stepladder; running board; (fig) stepping stone

marcher [marʃe] *intr* to walk; run, operate; march; **faire marcher qn** to pull someone's leg; **marcher à grands pas** to stride; **marcher au pas** to walk in step; **marcher dans l'espace** to take a space walk; **marcher sur** to tread on, walk on; **marchez au pas** (*public sign*) drive slowly

mar·cheur [marʃœr] **-cheuse** [ʃøz] *mf* walker

mardi [mardi] *m* Tuesday; **mardi gras** Shrove Tuesday; Mardi gras

mare [mar] *f* pool, pond

marécage [mareka3] *m* marsh, swamp

maréca·geux [mareka3ø] **-geuse** [3øz] *adj* marshy, swampy

maré·chal [mareʃal] *m* (*pl* **-chaux** [ʃo]) marshal; blacksmith; **maréchal des logis** artillery or cavalry sergeant

maréchale [mareʃal] *f* marshal's wife

maréchal-ferrant [mareʃalferã] *m* (*pl* **maréchaux-ferrants**) blacksmith, farrier

marée [mare] *f* tide; fresh seafood; **marée descendante** ebb tide; **marée montante** flood tide

marelle [marɛl] *f* hopscotch

marémo·teur [maremɔtœr] **-trice** [tris] *adj* tide-driven

margarine [margarin] *f* margarine

marge [mar3] *f* margin; border, edge; leeway, room; **en marge de** on the fringe of; a footnote to; **marge bénéficiaire** margin of profit; **marge brute d'autofinancement (MBA)** cash flow; **marge de sécurité** margin of safety

margelle [mar3ɛl] *f* curb, edge (*of well, fountain, etc.*)

margeur [mar3œr] *m* margin stop

margi·nal -nale [mar3inal] *adj* (*pl* **-naux** [no]) marginal

margot [margo] *f* (coll) magpie; (coll) chatterbox; **Margot** (coll) Maggie

margotin [margɔtɛ̃] *m* kindling

margouillis [marguji] *m* (coll) rotten stinking mess

margou·lin [margulɛ̃] **-line** [lin] *mf* sharpster, shyster

marguerite [margərit] *f* daisy; **Marguerite** Margaret

marguillier [margije] *m* churchwarden

mari [mari] *m* husband

mariable [marjabl] *adj* marriageable

mariage [marja3] *m* marriage; wedding; blend, combination

Marianne [marjan] *f* Marian; Marianne (*symbol of the French Republic*)

ma·rié -riée [marje] *adj* married ‖ *m* bridegroom; **jeunes mariés** newlyweds; **les mariés** the bride and groom ‖ *f* bride

marier [marje] *tr* to marry, join in wedlock; marry off; blend, harmonize ‖ *ref* to get married; **se marier avec** to marry

marie-salope [marisalɔp] *f* (*pl* **maries-salopes**) dredger; (slang) slut

ma·rieur [marjœr] **-rieuse** [rjøz] *mf* (coll) matchmaker

marihuana [mariɥana] or **marijuana** [mari3ɥana] *f* marijuana

ma·rin [marɛ̃] **-rine** [rin] *adj* marine; seagoing; sea, e.g., **brise marine** sea breeze ‖ *m* sailor, seaman; sailor suit ‖ *f* navy; seascape; **marine marchande** merchant marine

mariner [marine] *tr & intr* to marinate

mari·nier [marinje] **-nière** [njɛr] *adj* naval; petty (*officer*); **à la marinière** cooked in gravy with onions ‖ *m* waterman ‖ *f* blouse; (swimming) sidestroke

marionnette [marjɔnɛt] *f* marionette; (fig) puppet

mari·tal -tale [marital] *adj* (*pl* **-taux** [to]) of the husband

maritime [maritim] *adj* maritime

maritorne [maritɔrn] *f* slut

marivaudage [marivoda3] *m* playful flirting; sophisticated conversation

marjolaine [mar3ɔlɛn] *f* marjoram

marlou [marlu] *m* (slang) pimp

marmaille [marmɑj] *f* (coll) brats

marmelade [marməlad] *f* marmalade; (coll) mess

marmite [marmit] *f* pot, pan; (geol) pothole; (mil) shell, heavy shell; **marmite autoclave, marmite sous pression** pressure cooker; **marmite norvégienne** double boiler

marmiton [marmitɔ̃] *m* cook's helper

marmonner [marmɔne] *tr & intr* to mumble

marmot [marmo] *m* (coll) lad; (coll) grotesque figurine (*on knocker*); **croquer le marmot** (coll) to cool one's heels; **marmots** (coll) urchins, kids

marmotte [marmɔt] *f* woodchuck; **dormir comme une marmotte** to sleep like a log; **marmotte d'Amérique** groundhog; **mar-**

motte de commis voyageur traveling salesman's sample case

marmouset [marmuzɛ] *m* grotesque figurine; little man

marner [marne] *tr* to marl ‖ *intr* (naut) to flow, rise; (coll) to drudge

Maroc [marɔk] *m*—**le Maroc** Morocco

maro·cain [marɔkɛ̃] **-caine** [kɛn] *adj* Moroccan ‖ (*cap*) *mf* Moroccan

maronner [marɔne] *intr* (coll) to grumble

maroquin [marɔkɛ̃] *m* morocco leather

maroquinerie [marɔkinri] *f* leather goods

marotte [marɔt] *f* fad; whim; dummy head (*of milliner*); jester's staff

mar·quant [markɑ̃] **-quante** [kɑ̃t] *adj* remarkable, outstanding; purple (*passages*)

marque [mark] *f* mark; brand, make; hallmark; token, sign; **à vos marques!** on your mark(s)!; **de marque** distinguished; **marque déposée** trademark

marquer [marke] *tr* to mark; brand; score; indicate, show ‖ *intr* to make a mark, leave an impression

marqueterie [markətri], [markɛtri] *f* marquetry, inlay

mar·queur [markœr] **-queuse** [køz] *mf* marker ‖ *m* scorekeeper; scorer ‖ *f* (mach) stenciler

marquis [marki] *m* marquis

marquise [markiz] *f* marchioness, marquise; marquee, awning; (rr) roof (*over platform*)

marraine [marɛn] *f* godmother, sponsor; christener; **marraine de guerre** war mother

mar·rant [marɑ̃] **-rante** [rɑ̃t] *adj* (slang) sidesplitting; (slang) funny, queer

marre [mar] *adv*—**en avoir marre** (coll) to be fed up

marrer [mare] *ref* (slang) to have a good laugh

mar·ron [marɔ̃] **-ronne** [rɔn] *adj* quack (*doctor*); shyster (*lawyer*) ‖ **marron** *adj invar* brown ‖ *m* chestnut; **marron d'Inde** horse chestnut

marronnier [marɔnje] *m* chestnut tree; **marronnier d'Inde** horse-chestnut tree

mars [mars] *m* March; Mars Mars

Marseille [marsɛj] *f* Marseilles

marsouin [marswɛ̃] *m* porpoise

marte [mart] *f* (zool) marten

mar·teau [marto] (*pl* **-teaux**) *adj* (coll) cracked; balmy ‖ *m* hammer; (ichth) hammerhead; **marteau de porte** knocker

marteau-pilon [martopilɔ̃] *m* (*pl* **marteaux-pilons**) drop hammer

marteau-piqueur [martopikœr] *m* (*pl* **marteaux-piqueurs**) pneumatic drill

marteler [martəle] §2 *tr* to hammer; hammer at; hammer out

Marthe [mart] *f* Martha

mar·tial -tiale [marsjal] *adj* (*pl* **-tiaux** [sjo]) martial

martinet [martinɛ] *m* triphammer; scourge, cat-o'-nine-tails; (orn) martin, swift

martin-pêcheur [martɛ̃pɛʃœr] *m* (*pl* **martins-pêcheurs**) (orn) kingfisher

martre [martr] *f* (zool) marten

mar·tyr -tyre [martir] *adj* & *mf* martyr ‖ **martyre** *m* martyrdom

martyriser [martirize] *tr* to martyr

marxiste [marksist] *adj* & *mf* Marxist

maryland [marilɑ̃] *m* choice tobacco ‖ (*cap*) *m*—**le Maryland** Maryland

mas [mɑ], [mɑs] *m* farmhouse or farm (*in Provence*)

mascarade [maskarad] *f* masquerade

mascaret [maskarɛ] *m* bore

mascaron [maskarɔ̃] *m* mask, mascaron

mascotte [maskɔt] *f* mascot

mascu·lin [maskylɛ̃] **-line** [lin] *adj* & *m* masculine

masque [mask] *m* mask; **masque à gaz** gas mask; **masque mortuaire** death mask

masquer [maske] *tr* & *ref* to mask

massacre [masakr] *m* massacre; botched job

massacrer [masakre] *tr* to massacre; to botch

massage [masaʒ] *m* massage

masse [mas] *f* mass; sledgehammer; mace; pool, common fund; (elec) ground (*e.g., of an automobile*); **masse d'air froid** cold front; **mettre à la masse** (elec) to ground; **une masse de** (coll) a lot of

massepain [maspɛ̃] *m* marzipan

masser [mase] *tr* to mass; massage ‖ *ref* to mass; massage oneself

massette [masɛt] *f* sledge hammer (*of stonemason*); (bot) bulrush

mas·seur [masœr] **-seuse** [søz] *mf* masseur ‖ *m* massager (*instrument*)

mas·sif [masif] **-sive** [siv] *adj* massive; heavyset; solid (*e.g., gold*) ‖ *m* massif, high plateau; clump (*of flowers, trees, etc.*)

massue [masy] *f* club, bludgeon

mastic [mastik] *m* putty

mastiquer [mastike] *tr* to masticate; putty

mastoc [mastɔk] *adj invar* heavy, massive

masturber [mastyrbe] *tr* & *ref* to masturbate

m'as-tu-vu -vue [matyvy] (*pl* **-vu -vue**) *adj* (coll) stuck-up ‖ *mf* (coll) show-off, smart aleck; (coll) bragging actor

masure [mazyr] *f* hovel, shack, shanty

mat mate [mat] *adj* dull, flat ‖ **mat** *adj invar* checkmated ‖ *m* checkmate ‖ **mat** *adv* dull

mât [mɑ] *m* mast; pole

matamore [matamɔr] *m* braggart

match [matʃ] *m* match, contest, game

matelas [matla] *m* mattress; (coll) roll (*of bills*); **matelas à eau** water bed

matelasser [matlase] *tr* to pad, cushion

matelot [matlo] *m* sailor, seaman

matelote [matlɔt] *f* fish stew in wine

mater [mate] *tr* to dull; checkmate; subdue

matérialiser [materjalize] *ref* to materialize

matérialiste [materjalist] *adj* materialistic ‖ *mf* materialist

maté·riau [materjo] *m* (*pl* **-riaux**) material

maté·riel -rielle [materjɛl] *adj* material; materialistic ‖ *m* material; equipment; (comp) hardware; (mil) material; **matériel**

roulant (rr) rolling stock ‖ *f* (slang) living
maternage [matɛrnaʒ] *m* nursing; mothering
mater·nel -nelle [matɛrnɛl] *adj* maternal ‖ *f* nursery school
maternité [matɛrnite] *f* maternity; maternity hospital
math or **maths** [mat] *fpl* (coll) math
mathémati·cien [matematisjɛ̃] **-cienne** [sjɛn] *mf* mathematician
mathématique [matematik] *adj* mathematical ‖ **mathématiques** *fpl* mathematics
matière [matjɛr] *f* matter; subject matter; material; **matière première** raw material
matin [matɛ̃] *m* morning; early part of the morning; **au petit matin** in the wee hours of the morning; **de bon matin, de grand matin** very early; **du matin** in the morning, A.M., e.g., **onze heures du matin** eleven o'clock in the morning, eleven A.M. ‖ *adv* early
mâ·tin [matɛ̃] **-tine** [tin] *mf* (coll) sly one ‖ *m* (zool) mastiff ‖ **mâtin** *adv* indeed!, well I'll be!
mati·nal -nale [matinal] *adj* (*pl* **-naux** [no]) morning; early-rising
mâti·né -née [matine] *adj* crossbred; **mâtiné de** mixed with, crossbred with
matinée [matine] *f* morning; matinée; **faire la grasse matinée** to sleep late
mâtiner [matine] *tr* to crossbreed
matines [matin] *fpl* matins
matité [matite] *f* dullness
ma·tois [matwa] **-toise** [twaz] *adj* sly, cunning ‖ *mf* sly dog
matou [matu] *m* tomcat
matraque [matrak] *f* bludgeon; club, billy
matraquer [matrake] *tr* to club, bludgeon
matriarcat [matrijarka] *m* matriarchy
matrice [matris] *f* matrix
matricide [matrisid] *mf* matricide (*person*) ‖ *m* matricide (*action*)
matricule [matrikyl] *adj* serial (*number*) ‖ *m* serial number ‖ *f* roll, register
matrimo·nial -niale [matrimɔnjal] *adj* (*pl* **-niaux** [njo]) matrimonial, marital
matrone [matrɔn] *f* matron; matriarch; old hag; midwife; abortionist
mâture [matyr] *f* masts (*of ship*)
maudire [modir] §39 *tr* to curse, damn
mau·dit [modi] **-dite** [dit] *adj* cursed
maugréer [mogree] *intr* to grumble, gripe
maure [mɔr] *adj* Moorish ‖ (*cap*) *m* Moor
mauresque [mɔrɛsk] *adj* Moorish ‖ (*cap*) *f* Moorish woman
mausolée [mozɔle] *m* mausoleum
maussade [mosad] *adj* sullen, gloomy
mau·vais [movɛ], [movɛ] **-vaise** [vɛz] (precedes the noun it modifies) §91, §92 *adj* bad; evil; wrong; **il fait mauvais** the weather is bad; **sentir mauvais** to smell bad ‖ *mf* wicked person; **le Mauvais** the Evil One ‖ *m* evil
mauve [mov] *adj* mauve ‖ *f* (bot) mallow
mauviette [movjɛt] *f* (orn) lark; (coll) milquetoast
mauvis [movi] *m* (orn) redwing

maxillaire [maksillɛr] *m* jawbone
maxime [maksim] *f* maxim
maximum [maksimɔm] *adj* & *m* maximum
mayonnaise [majɔnɛz] *f* mayonnaise
mazette [mazɛt] *f* duffer ‖ *interj* gosh!
mazout [mazut] *m* fuel oil
mazouter [mazute] *intr* to fuel up
Mᵉ *abbr* (**Maître**) Mr.
me [mə] §87 me, to me
méandre [meɑ̃dr] *m* meander
mec [mɛk] *m* (slang) guy; (slang) tough egg
mécanicien [mekanisjɛ̃] *m* mechanic; machinist; engineer (*of locomotive*)
mécanicienne [mekanisjɛn] *f* sewing-machine operator
mécanique [mekanik] *adj* mechanical ‖ *f* mechanism; mechanics
mécaniser [mekanize] *tr* to mechanize
mécanisme [mekanism] *m* mechanism
mécano [mekano] *m* (coll) mechanic
mécène [mesɛn] *m* patron, Maecenas
méchamment [meʃamɑ̃] *adv* maliciously, nastily; (coll) fantastically
méchanceté [meʃɑ̃ste] *f* malice, wickedness; nastiness
mé·chant [meʃɑ̃] **-chante** [ʃɑ̃t] *adj* malicious, wicked; nasty; naughty (*child*) ‖ *mf* mean person; **faire le méchant** to threaten; (coll) to strike back; **les méchants** the wicked; **méchant!** naughty boy!
mèche [mɛʃ] *f* wick; fuse; lock (*of hair*); bit (*of drill*); **être de mèche avec** (coll) to be in cahoots with; **éventer** or **découvrir la mèche** to discover the plot; **il n'y a pas mèche** (coll) it's no go, nothing doing; **vendre la mèche** (coll) to let the cat out of the bag
mécompte [mekɔ̃t] *m* miscalculation; disappointment
méconnaissable [mekɔnɛsabl] *adj* unrecognizable
méconnaître [mekɔnɛtr] §12 *tr* to ignore; underestimate
mécon·nu -nue (mekɔny) *adj* underestimated, misunderstood
mécon·tent [mekɔ̃tɑ̃] **-tente** [tɑ̃t] *adj* dissatisfied, displeased ‖ *mf* grumbler
mécontentement [mekɔ̃tɑ̃tmɑ̃] *m* dissatisfaction, displeasure
mécontenter [mekɔ̃tɑ̃te] *tr* to displease
Mecque [mɛk] *f*—**La Mecque** Mecca
mécréant [mekreɑ̃] **mécréante** [mekreɑ̃t] *adj* unbelieving ‖ *mf* unbeliever
médaille [medaj] *f* medal
médaillon [medajɔ̃] *m* medallion; locket; thin round slice (*e.g., of meat*); pat (*of butter*)
médecin [medsɛ̃], [mɛtsɛ̃] *m* doctor; **femme médecin** woman doctor
médecine [medsin], [mɛtsin] *f* medicine (*science and art*)
média [medja] *m* mass media
mé·dian [medjɑ̃] **-diane** [djan] *adj* & *f* median
média·teur [medjatœr] **-trice** [tris] *mf* mediator, arbitrator

médiation [medjɑsjɔ̃] *f* mediation
médi·cal -cale [medikal] *adj* (*pl* **-caux** [ko])
medical
médicament [medikamɑ̃] *m* (pharm) medicine; **médicament miracle** wonder drug
médicamenter [medikamɑ̃te] *tr* to dose
médicamen·teux [medikamɑ̃tø] **-teuse**
[tøz] *adj* medicinal
médici·nal -nale [medisinal] *adj* (*pl* **-naux**
[no]) medicinal
médié·val -vale [medjeval] *adj* (*pl* **-vaux**
[vo]) medieval
médiéviste [medjevist] *mf* medievalist
médiocre [medjɔkr] *adj* mediocre, poor,
inferior, second-rate
médiocrité [medjɔkrite] *f* mediocrity
médire [medir] §40 *intr* to backbite; **médire**
de to run down, to disparage
médisance [medizɑ̃s] *f* disparagement,
backbiting
médi·sant [medizɑ̃] **-sante** [zɑ̃t] *adj* dispar-
aging, backbiting ǁ *mf* slanderer
méditation [meditɑsjɔ̃] *f* meditation
méditer [medite] §97 *tr & intr* to meditate
méditerra·né -née [mediterane] *adj* Mediterranean; inland ǁ (*cap*) *f* Mediterranean
(Sea)
méditerranéen [mediteraneɛ̃] **méditerra-**
néenne [mediteraneɛn] *adj* Mediterranean
médium [medjɔm] *m* medium (*in spiritual-*
ism); range (*of voice*)
médiumnique [medjɔmnik] *adj* psychic
médius [medjys] *m* middle finger
méduse [medyz] *f* jellyfish, medusa ǁ (*cap*)
f Medusa
méduser [medyze] *tr* to petrify (*with terror*)
meeting [mitiŋ] *m* rally, meet, meeting
méfait [mefɛ] *m* misdeed; **méfaits** ravages
méfiance [mefjɑ̃s] *f* mistrust
mé·fiant [mefjɑ̃] **-fiante** [fjɑ̃t] *adj* mistrustful
méfier [mefje] *ref* to beware; **se méfier de**
to guard against, to mistrust
mégacycle [megasikl] *m* megacycle
mégaphone [megafɔn] *m* megaphone
mégarde [megard] *f*—**par mégarde** inadvertently
mégère [meʒɛr] *f* shrew
mégohm [megom] *m* megohm
mégot [mego] *m* butt (*of cigarette or cigar*)
meil·leur -leure [mɛjœr] (precedes the noun
it modifies) §91 *adj comp & super* better;
best; **meilleur marché** cheaper
mélancolie [melɑ̃kɔli] *f* melancholy, melancholia
mélancolique [melɑ̃kɔlik] *adj* melancholy
mélange [melɑ̃ʒ] *m* mixing, blending; mixture, blend; **mélanges** homage volume,
Festschrift
mélanger [melɑ̃ʒe] §38 *tr* to mix, blend
mélan·geur [melɑ̃ʒœr] **-geuse** [ʒøz] *m & f*
mixer
mélasse [melas] *f* molasses; **dans la mélasse**
(coll) in the soup
mê·lé -lée [mele] *adj* mixed ǁ *f* melee
mêler [mele] §97 *tr* to mix; tangle; shuffle
(*the cards*) ǁ *ref* to mix; **se mêler à** to

mingle with; join in; **se mêler de** to
meddle with, interfere with
mélèze [melɛz] *m* (bot) larch
méli-mélo [melimelo] *m* mishmash
mélodie [melɔdi] *f* melody
mélo·dieux [melɔdjø] **-dieuse** [djøz] *adj*
melodious
mélodique [melɔdik] *adj* melodic
mélodramatique [melɔdramatik] *adj* melodramatic
mélomane [melɔman] *adj* music-loving ǁ
mf music lover
melon [məlɔ̃] *m* melon; derby; **melon d'eau**
watermelon
mélopée [melɔpe] *f* singsong, chant
membrane [mɑ̃bran] *f* membrane; **mem-**
brane vibrante (elec) diaphragm
membre [mɑ̃br] *m* member; limb, member;
membre actif active member; **membre**
bienfaiteur sustaining member; **membre**
de phrase clause; **membre donateur**
contributing member; **membre perpétuel**
life member
membrure [mɑ̃bryr] *f* frame, limbs
même [mɛm] *adj indef* very, e.g., **le jour**
même on that very day ǁ (when standing
before noun) *adj indef* same, e.g., **en**
même temps at the same time ǁ *pron*
indef same, same one; **à même de** + *inf*
up to + *ger*, in a position to + *inf;* **à**
même le (la, etc.) straight out of the
(*e.g., bottle*); flush with the (*e.g., pave-*
ment); next to one's (*e.g., skin*); on the
bare (*ground, sand, etc.*) **cela revient au**
même that amounts to the same thing; **de**
même likewise; **de même que** in the
same way as; **tout de même** nevertheless
ǁ *adv* even; **même quand** even when;
même si even if
-même [mɛm] §86
mémé [meme] *f* (*children's language*)
granny
mémento [memɛ̃to] *m* memento; memo
book
mémère [memɛr] *f* (coll) granny; (coll)
blowsy dame
mémoire [memwar] *m* memorandum; statement, account; term paper; treatise; petition; **mémoires** memoirs ǁ *f* memory; **de**
mémoire from memory; **de mémoire**
d'homme within memory; **mémoire**
morte (comp) read-only memory, ROM;
mémoire vive (comp) random-access
memory, RAM; **pour mémoire** for the
record
mémorandum [memɔrɑ̃dɔm] *m* memorandum; **mémorandum de combat** battle
orders
mémo·rial [memɔrjal] *m* (*pl* **-riaux** [rjo])
memorial; (dipl) memorandum; memoirs
mena·çant [mənasɑ̃] **-çante** [sɑ̃t] *adj* menacing
menace [mənas] *f* menace, threat
menacer [mənase] § 51, §97, §99 *tr & intr*
to menace, threaten
ménage [menaʒ] *m* household; family; married couple; furniture; **de ménage** home-

made; **faire bon ménage** to get along well; **faire des ménages** to do housework (*for hire*); **faire le ménage** to do the housework; **se mettre en ménage** to set up housekeeping; (coll) to live together (*without being married*)

ménagement [menaʒmɑ̃] *m* discretion; consideration

ména·ger [menaʒe] **-gère** [ʒɛr] *adj* household; **ménager de** thrifty with ‖ *f* housewife, homemaker; silverware; silverware case ‖ **ménager** §38 *tr* to be careful with, spare; save (*money; one's strength*); husband (*one's resources, one's strength*); be considerate of, handle with kid gloves; arrange, bring about; install, provide; make (*e.g., a hole*); **ménager un espace pour** leave a space for ‖ *intr* to save ‖ *ref* to take good care of oneself

ménagerie [menaʒri] *f* menagerie

men·diant [mɑ̃djɑ̃] **-diante** [djɑ̃t] *adj & mf* beggar; **des mendiants** dessert (*of dried fruits and nuts*)

mendier [mɑ̃dje] *tr & intr* to beg

menées [məne] *fpl* intrigues, schemes

mener [məne] §2, §95 *tr* to lead; take; manage; draw (*e.g., a line*) ‖ *intr* to lead

ménestrel [menɛstrɛl] *m* wandering minstrel

ménétrier [menetrije] *m* fiddler

me·neur [mənœr] **-neuse** [nøz] *mf* leader; ringleader; **meneur de jeu** master of ceremonies; narrator; moving spirit

menotte [mənɔt] *f* tiny hand; **menottes** handcuffs; **mettre** or **passer les menottes à** to handcuff

mens [mɑ̃] *v* (**ment**) see **mentir**

mensonge [mɑ̃sɔ̃ʒ] *m* lie; **pieux mensonge** white lie

mensonger [mɑ̃sɔ̃ʒe] **-gère** [ʒɛr] *adj* lying, false; illusory, deceptive

men·struel -struelle [mɑ̃stryɛl] *adj* menstrual

menstrues [mɑ̃stry] *fpl* menses

mensualité [mɑ̃sɥalite] *f* monthly installment; monthly salary

men·suel -suelle [mɑ̃sɥɛl] *adj* monthly

men·tal -tale [mɑ̃tal] *adj* (*pl* **-taux** [to]) mental

mentalité [mɑ̃talite] *f* mentality

men·teur [mɑ̃tœr] **-teuse** [tøz] *adj* lying ‖ *mf* liar

menthe [mɑ̃t] *f* mint; **menthe poivrée** peppermint; **menthe verte** spearmint

mention [mɑ̃sjɔ̃] *f* mention; **avec mention** with honors; **biffer les mentions inutiles** to cross out the questions which do not apply; **être reçu sans mention** to receive just a passing grade

mentionner [mɑ̃sjɔne] *tr* to mention

mentir [mɑ̃tir] §41 *intr* to lie

menton [mɑ̃tɔ̃] *m* chin

mentonnière [mɑ̃tɔnjɛr] *f* chin rest; chin strap

me·nu -nue [məny] *adj* small, little; tiny, fine ‖ *m* menu; minute detail

menuet [mənɥɛ] *m* minuet

menuiserie [mənɥizri] *f* carpentry; woodwork

menuisier [mənɥizje] *m* carpenter

méprendre [meprɑ̃dr] §56 *ref* to be mistaken; **à s'y méprendre** enough to take one for the other; **il n'y a pas à s'y méprendre** there's no mistake about it

mépris [mepri] *m* contempt, scorn

méprisable [meprizabl] *adj* contemptible, despicable

mépri·sant [meprizɑ̃] **-sante** [zɑ̃t] *adj* contemptuous, scornful

méprise [mepriz] *f* mistake

mépriser [meprize] *tr* to despise, scorn

mer [mɛr] *f* sea; **basse mer** low tide; **de haute mer** seagoing; **haute mer, pleine mer** high seas; high tide; **mer des Indes** Indian Ocean; **sur mer** afloat

mercanti [mɛrkɑ̃ti] *m* profiteer

mercantile [mɛrkɑ̃til] *adj* profiteering, mercenary

mercenaire [mɛrsənɛr] *adj & mf* mercenary

mercerie [mɛrsəri] *f* notions

merci [mɛrsi] *m* thanks, thank you; **merci de** + *inf* thank you for + *ger;* **merci de** or **pour** thank you for ‖ *f*—**à la merci de** at the mercy of; **Dieu merci!** thank heavens! ‖ *interj* thanks!, thank you!; no thanks!, no thank you!

mercredi [mɛrkrədi] *m* Wednesday; **mercredi des Cendres** Ash Wednesday

mercure [mɛrkyr] *m* mercury

mercuriale [mɛrkyrjal] *f* reprimand; market quotations; mercury (*weed*)

merde [mɛrd] *f* excrement; **merde alors!** (coll) well I'll be!

mère [mɛr] *f* mother; **la mère Gigogne** the old woman who lived in a shoe

méri·dien [meridjɛ̃] **-dienne** [djɛn] *adj & m* meridian ‖ *f* meridian line; couch, sofa; siesta

méridio·nal -nale [meridjɔnal] (*pl* **-naux** [no]) *adj* meridional, southern ‖ (*cap*) *mf* inhabitant of the Midi

meringue [mərɛ̃g] *f* meringue

merise [məriz] *f* wild cherry

merisier [mərizje] *m* wild cherry (tree)

méri·tant [meritɑ̃] **-tante** [tɑ̃t] *adj* deserving, worthy

mérite [merit] *m* merit

mériter [merite] §97 *tr* to merit, deserve; win, earn ‖ *intr*—**mériter bien de** to deserve the gratitude of

méritoire [meritwar] *adj* deserving, meritorious

merlan [mɛrlɑ̃] *m* (ichth) whiting

merle [mɛrl] *m* (orn) blackbird; **merle blanc** (fig) rara avis; **vilain merle** (fig) dirty dog

merlin [mɛrlɛ̃] *m* ax; poleax; (naut) marline

merluche [mɛrlyʃ] *f* (ichth) hake, cod

merveille [mɛrvɛj] *f* marvel, wonder; **à merveille** marvelously, wonderfully

merveil·leux [mɛrvɛjø] **-leuse** [jøz] *adj* marvelous, wonderful

mes [me] §88 my

mésalliance [mezaljɑ̃s] *f* misalliance, mismatch

mésallier [mezalje] *tr* to misally ‖ *ref* to marry beneath one's station

mésange [mezɑ̃ʒ] *f* (orn) chickadee, tit-mouse

mésaventure [mezavɑ̃tyr] *f* misadventure

mesdames *fpl* see **madame**

mesdemoiselles *fpl* see **mademoiselle**

mésentente [mezɑ̃tɑ̃t] *f* misunderstanding

mésestimer [mezɛstime] *tr* to underestimate

mésintelligence [mezɛ̃teliʒɑ̃s] *f* misunderstanding, discord

mes·quin [mɛskɛ̃] **-quine** [kin] *adj* mean; stingy; petty

mess [mɛs] *m* officer's mess

message [mesaʒ] *m* message

messa·ger [mesaʒe] **-gère** [ʒɛr] *mf* messenger

messagerie [mesaʒri] *f* express; **messageries** express company; **messageries aériennes** air freight

messe [mɛs] *f* (eccl) Mass; **dire** or **faire des messes basses** (coll) to speak in an undertone; **messe basse, petite messe** Low Mass; **première messe, messe du début** early Mass

Messie [mesi] *m* Messiah

messieurs *mpl* see **monsieur**

messieurs-dames [mɛsjødam] *interj* ladies and gentlemen!

mesure [məzyr] *f* measure; measurement; (mus, poetic) measure; **à mesure** successively, one by one; **à mesure que** as; according as, proportionately as; **battre la mesure** to keep time; **dans la mesure de** insofar as; **dans une certaine mesure** to a certain extent; **être en mesure de** to be in a position to; **faire sur mesure** to make (*clothing*) to order; (fig) to tailor-make; **mesure de circonstance** emergency measure; **mesure en ruban** tape measure; **prendre des mesures de** to take measures to; **prendre la mesure de** to size up; **prendre les mesures de** to measure

mesurer [məzyre] *tr* to measure; measure off or out ‖ *ref* to measure; **se mesurer avec** to measure swords with

métairie [meteri] *f* farm (*of a sharecropper*)

mé·tal [metal] *m* (*pl* **-taux** [to]) metal

métallique [metalik] *adj* metallic

métalloïde [metalɔid] *m* nonmetal

métallurgie [metalyrʒi] *f* metallurgy

métamorphose [metamɔrfoz] *f* metamorphosis

métaphore [metafɔr] *f* metaphor

métaphorique [metafɔrik] *adj* metaphorical

métathèse [metatɛz] *f* metathesis

métayage [metejaʒ] *m* sharecropping, tenant farming

mé·tayer [meteje] **-tayère** [tejɛr] *mf* sharecropper

méteil [metɛj] *m* wheat and rye

météo [meteo] *adj invar* meteorological ‖ *m* weatherman ‖ *f* meteorology; weather bureau; weather report

météore [meteɔr] *m* meteor (*atmospheric phenomenon*)

météorite [meteɔrit] *m & f* meteorite

météorologie [meteɔrɔlɔʒi] *f* meteorology; weather bureau; weather report

métèque [metɛk] *m* (pej) foreigner

méthane [metan] *m* methane

méthode [metɔd] *f* method; **méthode insufflatoire bouche à bouche** mouth-to-mouth resuscitation

méthodique [metɔdik] *adj* methodic(al)

méthodiste [metɔdist] *adj & mf* Methodist

méticu·leux [metikylø] **-leuse** [løz] *adj* meticulous

métier [metje] *m* trade, craft; loom; **faites votre métier!** mind your own business!; **sur le métier** on the stocks

mé·tis -tisse [metis] *adj & mf* half-breed

métisser [metise] *tr* to crossbreed

métrage [metraʒ] *m* length in meters; length (*of remnant, film, etc.*); (mov) length of film in meters (*in English:* footage, *i.e., length of film in feet*); **court métrage** (mov) short subject, short; **long métrage** (mov) full-length movie, feature

mètre [mɛtr] *m* meter; **mètre à ruban** tape measure; **mètre pliant** folding rule

métrer [metre] §10 *tr* to measure out by the meter

métrique [metrik] *adj* metric(al) ‖ *f* metrics

métro [metro] *m* subway

métronome [metrɔnɔm] *m* metronome

métropole [metrɔpɔl] *f* metropolis; mother country

métropoli·tain [metrɔpɔlitɛ̃] **-taine** [tɛn] *adj* metropolitan ‖ *m* subway; (eccl) metropolitan

mets [mɛ] *m* dish, food

mettable [mɛtabl] *adj* wearable

met·teur [mɛtœr] **-teuse** [tøz]) *mf*—**metteur au point** mechanic; **metteur en œuvre** setter; (fig) promoter; **metteur en ondes** (rad) director, producer; **metteur en pages** (typ) make-up man; **metteur en scène** (mov, theat) director, producer

mettre [mɛtr] §42, §95, §96 *tr* to put, lay, place; put on (*clothes*); set (*the table*); take (*time*); **mettre à feu** (rok) to fire; **mettre au point** to carry out, complete; tune up, adjust; (opt) to focus; (rad) to tune; **mettre au rancart** to pigeonhole; **mettre en accusation** to indict; **mettre en marche** to start; **mettre en œuvre** to put into action, set off, enhance; **mettre en valeur** to develop, improve; set off, enhance; **mettre en vigueur** to enforce; **mettre feu à** to set fire to; **mettre que** (coll) to suppose that ‖ *intr*—**mettre bas** (zool) to litter ‖ §96 *ref* to sit or stand; go; **se mettre à** to begin to; **se mettre à table** to sit down to eat; (slang) to confess; **se mettre en colère** to get angry; **se mettre en route** to set out; **se mettre mal avec** to quarrel with

meuble [mœbl] *adj* uncemented; loose (*ground*); personal (*property*) ‖ *m* piece of furniture; **meubles** furniture; **meubles d'occasion** secondhand furniture

meubler [mœble] *tr* to furnish

meuglement [møgləmɑ̃] *m* lowing (*of cow*)

meugler [møgle] *intr* to low
meuh! meuh! [mœmœ] *interj* moo! moo!
meule [møl] *f* millstone; grindstone; stack (*e.g., of hay*)
meuler [møle] *tr* to grind
meu·nier [mønje] **-nière** [njɛr] *adj* milling (*e.g., industry*) ‖ *m* miller ‖ *f* miller's wife; **à la meunière** sautéed in butter
meurs [mœr] *v* (**meurt**) see **mourir**
meurt-de-faim [mœrdəfɛ̃] *mf invar* starveling; **de meurt-de-faim** starvation (*wages*)
meurtre [mœrtr] *m* manslaughter; (fig) shame, crime; **meurtre commis avec préméditation** murder
meur·trier [mœrtrije] **-trière** [trijɛr] *adj* murderous; deadly ‖ *m* murderer ‖ *f* murderess; gun slit, loophole
meurtrir [mœrtrir] *tr* to bruise
meurtrissure [mœrtrisyr] *f* bruise
meute [møt] *f* pack, band
mévente [mevɑ̃t] *f* slump (*in sales*)
mexi·cain [mɛksikɛ̃] **-caine** [kɛn] *adj* Mexican ‖ (*cap*) *mf* Mexican
Mexico [mɛksiko] Mexico City
Mexique [mɛksik] *m*—**le Mexique** Mexico
mezzanine [mɛdzanin] *m & f* (theat) mezzanine ‖ *f* mezzanine; mezzanine window
miam! miam! [mjɑ̃mjɑ̃] *interj* purr! purr!
miaou [mjau] *m* meow
miaulement [mjolmɑ̃] *m* meow; caterwauling; catcall
miauler [mjole] *intr* to meow
mi-bas [mibɑ] *m invar* half hose
mica [mika] *m* mica
miche [miʃ] *f* round loaf of bread
mi-chemin [miʃmɛ̃] *m*—**à mi-chemin** halfway
micheton [miʃtɔ̃] *m* (slang) john (*prostitute's customer*)
mi-clos [miklo] **-close** [kloz] *adj* (*pl* **-clos -closes**) half-shut
micmac [mikmak] *m* (coll) underhand dealing
mi-corps [mikɔr]—**à mi-corps** to the waist
mi-côte [mikot]—**à mi-côte** halfway up the hill
microbe [mikrɔb] *m* microbe
microbicide [mikrɔbisid] *adj & m* germicide
microbiologie [mikrɔbjɔlɔʒi] *f* microbiology
microfilm [mikrɔfilm] *m* microfilm
microfilmer [mikrɔfilme] *tr* to microfilm
micro-onde [mikrɔɔ̃d] *f* (*pl* **-ondes**) microwave
micro-ordinateur [mikrɔɔrdinatœr] *m* (*pl* **-ordinateurs**) microcomputer
microphone [mikrɔfɔn] *m* microphone
micro-plastron [mikrɔplastrɔ̃] *m* chest microphone
microscope [mikrɔskɔp] *m* microscope; **microscope électronique** electron microscope
microscopique [mikrɔskɔpik] *adj* microscopic
microsillon [mikrɔsijɔ̃] *adj & m* microgroove

midi [midi] *m* noon; south; twelve, e.g., **midi dix** ten minutes after twelve; **chercher midi à quatorze heures** (fig) to look for difficulties where there are none; **Midi** south of France
midinette [midinɛt] *f* dressmaker's assistant; working girl
mie [mi] *f* soft part, crumb; female friend; **ne . . . mie** §90 (archaic) not a crumb, not, e.g., **je n'en veux mie** I don't want any
miel [mjɛl] *m* honey
miel·leux [mjɛlø] **-leuse** [løz] *adj* honeyed, unctuous
mien [mjɛ̃] **mienne** [mjɛn] §89 mine
miette [mjɛt] *f* crumb
mieux [mjø] §91 *adv comp & super* better; **aimer mieux** to prefer; **à qui mieux mieux** trying to outdo each other; **de mieux en mieux** better and better; **être mieux, aller mieux** to feel better; **tant mieux** so much the better; **valoir mieux** to be better
mieux-être [mjøzɛtr] *m* improved wellbeing
mièvre [mjɛvr] *adj* dainty, affected
mi-figue [mifig] *f*—**mi-figue mi-raisin** half one way half the other; half in jest half in earnest
mi·gnard [miɲar] **-gnarde** [ɲard] *adj* affected, mincing
mi·gnon [miɲɔ̃] **-gnonne** [ɲɔn] *adj* cute, darling ‖ *mf* darling
mignon·net [miɲɔnɛ] **-nette** [nɛt] *adj* dainty ‖ *f* fine lace; pepper; (bot) pink
mignoter [miɲɔte] *tr* (coll) to pet (*a child*)
migraine [migrɛn] *f* migraine; headache
migratoire [migratwar] *adj* migratory
mi-jambe [miʒɑ̃b] *f*—**à mi-jambe** up to one's knee
mijoter [miʒɔte] *tr* to simmer; (coll) to cook up, brew ‖ *intr* to simmer
mijoteuse [miʒɔtøz] *f* crockpot
mil [mil] *adj* one thousand, e.g., **mil neuf cent quatorze** nineteen fourteen (*year*) ‖ *m* Indian club; millet
milan [milɑ̃] *m* (orn) kite
milice [milis] *f* militia
mi-lieu [miljø] *m* (*pl* **-lieux**) middle; milieu; **milieu de table** centerpiece
militaire [militɛr] *adj* military ‖ *m* soldier; **le militaire** the military
mili·tant [militɑ̃] **-tante** [tɑ̃t] *adj & mf* militant
militariser [militarize] *tr* to militarize
militarisme [militarism] *m* militarism
militer [milite] *intr* to militate
mille [mil] *adj & pron* thousand ‖ *m* thousand; mile; **mettre dans le mille** to hit the bull's-eye; **mille marin** international nautical mile
millefeuille [milfœj] *m* napoleon (*pastry*)
mille-feuille [milfœj] *f* (*pl* **-feuilles**) (bot) yarrow
millénaire [milenɛr] *adj* millennial ‖ *m* millennium
mille-pattes [milpat] *m invar* centipede

millésime [milezim] *m* date, vintage; year of issue

millet [mijɛ] *m* millet; birdseed

milliard [miljar] *m* billion

milliardaire [miljardɛr] *mf* billionaire

millième [miljɛm] *adj, pron (masc, fem)* thousandth ‖ *m* thousandth; mill *(thousandth part of a dollar)*

millier [milje] *m* thousand; about a thousand; **par milliers** by the thousands; **un millier de** a thousand

milligramme [miligram] *m* milligram

millimètre [milimɛtr] *m* millimeter

million [miljɔ̃] *m* million; **un million de** a million

millionième [miljɔnjɛm] *adj, pron (masc, fem)*, & *m* millionth

millionnaire [miljɔnɛr] *adj* & *m* millionaire

mime [mim] *mf* mime; mimic

mimer [mime] *tr* & *intr* to mime; mimic

mimique [mimik] *adj* sign *(language)* ‖ *f* mimicry

mi-moyen [mimwajɛ̃] *m (pl* -**moyens)** welterweight

minable [minabl] *adj* wretched, shabby; (coll) pitiful *(performance, existence, etc.)* ‖ *mf* unfortunate

minaret [minarɛ] *m* minaret

minauder [minode] *intr* to simper, smirk

minau·dier [minodje] -**dière** [djɛr] *adj* mincing

mince [mɛ̃s] *adj* thin, slim, slight; **mince!** or **mince alors!** golly!

mine [min] *f* mine; lead *(of pencil)*; look, face; looks; (fig) mine *(of information)*; **avoir bonne mine** to look well; **avoir la mine d'être** to look to be; **avoir mauvaise mine** to look badly; **faire bonne mine à** to be nice to; **faire des mines to** simper; **faire la mine à** to pout at; **faire mauvaise mine à** to be unpleasant to; **faire mine de** to make as if to

miner [mine] *tr* to mine; undermine; wear away

minerai [minrɛ] *m* ore

miné·ral -**rale** [mineral] *(pl* -**raux** [ro]) *adj* & *m* mineral

minéralogie [mineralɔʒi] *f* mineralogy

mi·net [minɛ] -**nette** [nɛt] *mf* (coll) kitty, pussy; (coll) darling

mi·neur -**neure** [minœr] *adj* & *mf* minor ‖ *m* miner

miniature [minjatyr] *f* miniature

miniaturisation [minjatyrizɑsjɔ̃] *f* miniaturization

miniaturiser [minjatyrize] *tr* to miniaturize

minijupe [miniʒyp] *f* miniskirt

mini·mal -**male** [minimal] *adj (pl* -**maux** [mo])** minimum *(temperature)*

minimarge [minimarʒ] *f* discount house

minime [minim] *adj* tiny; derisory *(salary)*

minimiser [minimize] *tr* to minimize

minimum [minimɔm] *adj* & *m* minimum; **minimum vital** minimum wage

ministère [ministɛr] *m* ministry; **ministère des affaires étrangères** ministry of foreign affairs (department of state)

ministé·riel -**rielle** [ministɛrjɛl] *adj* ministerial

ministre [ministr] *m* minister; **ministre des affaires étrangères** minister of foreign affairs (secretary of state); **premier ministre** premier, prime minister

minium [minjɔm] *m* red lead

minois [minwa] *m* (coll) pretty little face

minoritaire [minɔritɛr] *adj* minority

minorité [minɔrite] *f* minority; time of being under legal age

Minorque [minɔrk] *f* Minorca

minoterie [minɔtri] *f* flour mill; flour industry

minotier [minɔtje] *m* miller

minuit [minɥi] *m* midnight; twelve, e.g. **minuit et demi** twelve-thirty

minuscule [minyskyl] *adj* tiny; small *(letter)* ‖ *f* small letter

minus habens [minysabɛ̃s] *mf invar* (coll) moron, idiot

minutage [minytaʒ] *m* timing

minute [minyt] *f* minute; moment, instant; **à la minute** that very moment ‖ *interj* (coll) just a minute!

minuter [minyte] *tr* to itemize; time

minuterie [minytri] *f* delayed-action switch; (mach) timing mechanism

minutie [minysi] *f* minute detail; great care; **minuties** minutiae

minu·tieux [minysjø] -**tieuse** [sjøz] *adj* meticulous, thorough

mioche [mjɔʃ] *mf* (coll) brat

mi-pente [mipɑ̃t]—**à mi-pente** halfway up or halfway down

mirabilis [mirabilis] *m* (bot) marvel-of-Peru

miracle [mirakl] *m* miracle; wonder, marvel; miracle play; **crier au miracle** to go into ecstasies

miracu·leux [mirakylø] -**leuse** [løz] *adj* miraculous; wonderful, marvelous

mirador [miradɔr] *m* watchtower

mirage [miraʒ] *m* mirage

mire [mir] *f* sight *(of gun)*; surveyor's pole; (telv) test pattern

mire-œufs [mirø] *m invar* candler

mirer [mire] *tr* to candle *(eggs)* ‖ *ref* to look at oneself; be reflected

mirifique [mirifik] *adj* (coll) marvelous

mirobo·lant [mirɔbɔlɑ̃] -**lante** [lɑ̃t] *adj* (coll) astounding

miroir [mirwar] *m* mirror; **miroir à alouettes** decoy

miroiter [mirwate] *intr* to sparkle, gleam; **faire miroiter q.ch. à qn** to lure s.o. with s.th.

miroton [mirɔtɔ̃] *m* Irish stew

mis [mi] *(mis* [miz]) *v* see **mettre**

misaine [mizɛn] *f* foresail

misanthrope [mizɑ̃trɔp] *mf* misanthrope

miscellanées [miselane], [misɛllane] *fpl* miscellany

mise [miz] *f* placing, putting; dress, attire; (cards) stake, ante; **de mise** acceptable, proper; **mise à feu** firing *(e.g., of missile)*; **mise à l'eau** launching; **mise à prix** opening bid; **mise au point** carrying out, completion; tuning up, adjustment; (opt) focusing; (rad) tuning; **mise au rancart** pigeonholding; **mise bas** delivery (*of litter*); **mise de fonds** investment; **mise en accusation** indictment; **mise(s) en chantier** construction start(s); **mise en demeure** (law) injunction; **mise en marche** starting; **mise en œuvre** putting into action; **mise en plis** set; **mise en scène** (theat) direction; (theat & fig) staging; **mise en valeur** development, improvement; **mise en vigueur** enforcement; **mise sur ordinateur** computerization

miser [mize] *tr & intr* to ante; stake, bet; bid (*e.g., at auction*)

misérable [mizerabl] *adj* miserable ‖ *mf* wretch

misère [mizɛr] *f* misery, wretchedness; poverty; worry; (coll) trifle; **crier misère** to make a poor mouth; to look forsaken; **faire des misères à** to pester; **misères** woes, misfortunes

misé·reux [mizerø] **-reuse** [røz] *adj* destitute, wretched ‖ *mf* pauper

miséricorde [mizerikɔrd] *f* mercy

miséricor·dieux [mizerikɔrdjø] **-dieuse** [djøz] *adj* merciful

missel [misɛl] *m* missal

missile [misil] *m* guided missile

mission [misjɔ̃] *f* mission

missionnaire [misjɔnɛr] *adj & m* missionary

missive [misiv] *adj & f* missive

mitaine [mitɛn] *f* mitt

mite [mit] *f* (ent) mite; (ent) clothes moth

mi·té -tée [mite] *adj* moth-eaten; (coll) shabby

mi-temps [mitɑ̃] *f invar* (sports) half time; **à mi-temps** half time

miter [mite] *ref* to become moth-eaten

mi·teux [mitø] **-teuse** [tøz] *adj* shabby ‖ *mf* (coll) shabby-looking person

mitiger [mitiʒe] §38 *tr* to mitigate

mitonner [mitɔne] *tr* to simmer; pamper; (coll) to contrive, devise ‖ *intr* to simmer

mitoyen [mitwajɛ̃] **mitoyenne** [mitwajɛn] *adj* midway, intermediate, dividing; jointly owned, common

mitraille [mitrɑj] *f* scrap iron; grapeshot; artillery fire

mitrailler [mitrɑje] *tr* to machine-gun; pepper (*with gunfire, flash bulbs, etc.*)

mitraillette [mitrɑjɛt] *f* submachine gun, Tommy gun

mitrail·leur [mitrɑjœr] **-leuse** [jøz] *adj* repeating, automatic (*firearm*) ‖ *m* machine gunner ‖ *f* machine gun

mitre [mitr] *f* miter; chimney pot

mitron [mitrɔ̃] *m* baker's boy

mi-voix [mivwa]—**à mi-voix** in a low voice, under one's breath

mixer or **mixeur** [miksœr] *m* electric food mixer

mixte [mikst] *adj* mixed; coeducational; composite; joint (*e.g., commission*); (rr) freight-and-passenger

mixtion [mikstjɔ̃] *f* mixing; mixture

mixture [mikstyr] *f* mixture

M.L.F. [ɛmɛlɛf] *m* (letterword) (**mouvement de libération de la femme**) women's lib(eration movement)

Mlle *abbr* (**Mademoiselle**) Miss

MM. *abbr* (**Messieurs**) Messrs.

Mme *abbr* (**Madame**) Mrs.; Mme.

mobile [mɔbil] *adj* mobile ‖ *m* motive; (fa) mobile

mobi·lier [mɔbilje] **-lière** [ljɛr] *adj* personal ‖ *m* furniture

mobilisable [mɔbilizabl] *adj* (mil) subject to call

mobilisation [mɔbilizɑsjɔ̃] *f* mobilization

mobiliser [mɔbilize] *tr & intr* to mobilize

mobilité [mɔbilite] *f* mobility

moche [mɔʃ] *adj* (coll) ugly; (coll) lousy

modalité [mɔdalite] *f* modality, manner, method; **modalités** terms

mode [mɔd] *m* kind, method, mode; (gram) mood; (mus) mode; **mode d'emploi** directions for use; **mode dialogué** (comp) conversational mode ‖ *f* fashion; **à la mode** in style, fashionable; **à la mode de** in the manner of; **modes** fashions; millinery

modèle [mɔdɛl] *adj & m* model; sample, e.g., **villa modèle** sample home

modeler [mɔdle] §2 *tr* to model; shape, mold ‖ *ref*—**se modeler sur** to take as a model

modéliste [mɔdelist] *mf* model-airplane designer, etc.; dress designer

modéra·teur [mɔderatœr] **-trice** [tris] *adj* moderating ‖ *mf* moderator; regulator; moderator (*for slowing down neutrons*); **modérateur de son** volume control

modé·ré -rée [mɔdere] *adj* moderate

modérer [mɔdere] §10 *tr & ref* to moderate

moderne [mɔdɛrn] *adj* modern

moderniser [mɔdɛrnize] *tr* to modernize

modeste [mɔdɛst] *adj* modest

modestie [mɔdɛsti] *f* modesty

modicité [mɔdisite] *f* paucity (*of resources*); lowness (*of price*)

modifica·teur [mɔdifikatœr] **-trice** [tris] *adj* modifying ‖ *m* modifier

modifier [mɔdifje] *tr* to modify

modique [mɔdik] *adj* moderate, reasonable

modiste [mɔdist] *f* milliner

modulation [mɔdylasjɔ̃] *f* modulation; **modulation d'amplitude** amplitude modulation; **modulation de fréquence** frequency modulation

module [mɔdyl] *m* module; **module lunaire** (rok) lunar module

moduler [mɔdyle] *tr & intr* to modulate

moelle [mwal] *f* marrow; (bot) pith; **moelle épinière** spinal cord

moel·leux [mwalø] **-leuse** [løz] *adj* soft; mellow; flowing (*brush stroke*)

moellon [mwalɔ̃] *m* building stone

mœurs [mœr], [mœrs] *fpl* customs, habits; morals; **mœurs spéciales** (coll) homosexual life-style

mohair [mɔɛr] *m* mohair

moi [mwa] §85, §87 me

moignon [mwaɲɔ̃] *m* stump
moi-même [mwamɛm] §86 myself
moindre [mwɛ̃dr] (precedes the noun it modifies) §91 *adj comp & super* less; lesser; least, slightest
moine [mwan] *m* monk
moi·neau [mwano] *m* (*pl* **-neaux**) sparrow
moins [mwɛ̃] *m* less; minus; **au moins** or **du moins** at least; (**le**) **moins** (the) least; **moins de** fewer ‖ *adv comp & super* §91 less; fewer; **à moins de** + *inf* without + *ger*, unless + *ind;* **à moins que** unless; **de moins en moins** less and less; **en moins de rien** in no time at all; **moins de** (followed by numeral) less than; **moins que** less than; **rien moins que** anything but ‖ *prep* minus; to, e.g., **dix heures moins le quart** a quarter to ten
moire [mwar] *f* moire; **moire de soie** watered silk
moi·ré -rée [mware] *adj* watered (*silk*) ‖ *m* wavy sheen
mois [mwa] *m* month
Moïse [mɔiz] *m* Moses
moi·si -sie [mwazi] *adj* moldy ‖ *m* mold; **sentir le moisi** to have a musty smell
moisir [mwazir] *tr* to mold ‖ *intr* to become moldy, mold; (fig) to vegetate ‖ *ref* to mold
moisissure [mwazisyr] *f* mold
moisson [mwasɔ̃] *f* harvest
moissonner [mwasɔne] *tr* to harvest, reap
moisson·neur [mwasɔnœr] **-neuse** [nøz] *mf* reaper ‖ *f* (mach) reaper
moite [mwat] *adj* moist, damp; clammy
moiteur [mwatœr] *f* moistness, dampness; **moiteur froide** clamminess
moitié [mwatje] *f* half; (coll) better half (*wife*); **à moitié, la moitié** half; **à moitié chemin** halfway; **à moitié prix** at half price; **de moitié** by half ‖ *adv* half
moka [mɔka] *m* mocha coffee; mocha cake
mol *adj* see **mou**
molaire [mɔlɛr] *adj & f* molar
môle [mol] *m* mole, breakwater ‖ *f* (ichth) sunfish
molécule [mɔlekyl] *f* molecule
moleskine [mɔlɛskin] *f* (*fabric*) moleskin; imitation leather
molester [mɔlɛste] *tr* to molest
moleter [mɔlte] §34 *tr* to knurl, mill
mollas·son [mɔlasɔ̃] **-sonne** [sɔn] *mf* (coll) softy
molle *adj* see **mou**
mollement [mɔlmɑ̃] *adv* flabbily; listlessly
mollesse [mɔlɛs] *f* flabbiness; apathy; permissiveness; softness (*of contour*); mildness (*of climate*)
mol·let [mɔlɛ] **-lette** [lɛt] *adj* soft, downy; soft-boiled (*egg*) ‖ *m* (anat) calf
molletière [mɔltjɛr] *f* puttee, legging
molleton [mɔltɔ̃] *m* flannel
mollir [mɔlir] *intr* to weaken
mollusque [mɔlysk] *m* mollusk
molosse [mɔlɔs] *m* watchdog
molybdène [mɔlibdɛn] *m* molybdenum

môme [mom] *adj* (slang) little ‖ *mf* (coll) kid ‖ *f* (slang) babe
moment [mɔmɑ̃] *m* moment; **à aucun moment** at no time; **à ce moment-là, en ce moment-là** then, at that time; **à tout moment, à tous moments** continually; **au moment où** just when; **c'est le moment** now is the time; **d'un moment à l'autre** at any moment; **en ce moment** now; at this moment; **par moments** now and then; **sur le moment** at the very moment; **un petit moment** a little while
momenta·né -née [mɔmɑ̃tane] *adj* momentary
momerie [mɔmri] *f* mummery
momie [mɔmi] *f* mummy
mon [mɔ̃] §88 my
M^on *abbr* (**Maison**) (com) House
mona·cal -cale [mɔnakal] *adj* (*pl* **-caux** [ko]) monastic, monkish
monachisme [mɔnaʃism], [mɔnakism] *m* monasticism
monarchique [mɔnarʃik] *adj* monarchic
monarque [mɔnark] *m* monarch
monastère [mɔnastɛr] *m* monastery
monastique [mɔnastik] *adj* monastic
mon·ceau [mɔ̃so] *m* (*pl* **-ceaux**) heap, pile
mon·dain [mɔ̃dɛ̃] **-daine** [dɛn] *adj* worldly; social (*life, functions, etc.*); sophisticated ‖ *mf* worldly-minded person; socialite
mondanité [mɔ̃danite] *f* worldliness; **mondanités** social events; (journ) social news
monde [mɔ̃d] *m* world; people; **avoir du monde chez soi** to have company; **il y a du monde, il y a un monde fou** there is a big crowd; **le beau monde, le grand monde** high society, fashionable society; **mettre au monde** to give birth to; **tout le monde** everybody, everyone
monder [mɔ̃de] *tr* to hull; blanch; stone
mon·dial -diale [mɔ̃djal] *adj* (*pl* **-diaux** [djo]) world; world-wide
monétaire [mɔnetɛr] *adj* monetary
mon·gol -gole [mɔ̃gɔl] *adj* Mongol ‖ *m* Mongol (*language*) ‖ (*cap*) *mf* Mongol (*person*)
moni·teur [mɔnitœr] **-trice** [tris] *mf* coach, trainer, instructor; monitor (*at school*)
monnaie [mɔnɛ] *f* change, small change; money (*legal tender of a country*); **fausse monnaie** counterfeit money; **la Monnaie** the Mint; **monnaie forte** hard currency; **payer en monnaie de singe** to give lip service to
monnayer [mɔneje] §49 *tr* to mint, coin; convert into cash; cash in on
monnayeur [mɔnɛjœr] *m*—**faux monnayeur** counterfeiter
monocle [mɔnɔkl] *m* monocle
monogamie [mɔnɔgami] *f* monogamy
monogramme [mɔnɔgram] *m* monogram
monographie [mɔnɔgrafi] *f* monograph
monokini [mɔnɔkini] *m* topless swimsuit
monolithique [mɔnɔlitik] *adj* monolithic
monolingue [mɔnɔlɛ̃g] *adj* monolingual
monologue [mɔnɔlɔg] *m* monologue
monologuer [mɔnɔlɔge] *tr* to soliloquize

monologuiste [mɔnɔlɔgist]
mf—**monologuiste comique** stand-up comedian
monomanie [mɔnɔmani] *f* monomania
monôme [mɔnom] *m* single file (*of students*); (math) monomial
monoplan [mɔnɔplɑ̃] *m* monoplane
monopole [mɔnɔpɔl] *m* monopoly
monopoliser [mɔnɔpɔlize] *tr* to monopolize
monorail [mɔnɔrɑj] *m* monorail
monosyllabe [mɔnɔsilab] *m* monosyllable
monothéiste [mɔnɔteist] *adj & mf* monotheist
monotone [mɔnɔtɔn] *adj* monotonous
monotonie [mɔnɔtɔni] *f* monotony
monotype [mɔnɔtip] *adj* monotypic ‖ *m*
monotype ‖ *f* Monotype (*machine to set
type*)
monseigneur [mɔ̃sɛɲœr] *m* (*pl* **mes-
seigneurs** [mesɛɲœr] monseigneur
monsieur [məsjø] *m* (*pl* **messieurs** [mesjø])
gentleman; sir; mister; Mr.; (often untranslated) e.g., **oui, monsieur!** yes, of
course!, yes, I will!, etc. (*instead of "yes,
Sir!"*)
monstre [mɔ̃str] *adj* huge, monster ‖ *m*
monster; freak; **monstres sacrés** (fig) sacred cows, idols
mons·trueux [mɔ̃stryø] **-trueuse** [tryøz] *adj*
monstrous
mont [mɔ̃] *m* mount; mountain; **par monts
et par vaux** over hill and dale; **passer les
monts** to cross the Alps
montage [mɔ̃taʒ] *m* hoisting; setting up (*of
a machine*); (elec) hookup; (mov) cutting,
editing
monta·gnard [mɔ̃taɲar] **-gnarde** [ɲard] *adj*
mountain ‖ *mf* mountaineer
montagne [mɔ̃taɲ] *f* mountain; **montagnes
russes** roller coaster
monta·gneux [mɔ̃taɲø] **-gneuse** [ɲøz] *adj*
mountainous
mon·tant [mɔ̃tɑ̃] **-tante** [tɑ̃t] *adj* rising,
ascending; uphill; vertical; high-necked
(*dress*) ‖ *m* upright, riser; gatepost; total
(*sum*); allure; (culin) tang; **montants** goal
posts; (slang) pair of trousers
mont-de-piété [mɔ̃dpjete] *m* (*pl* **monts-
de-piété**) pawnshop
mon·té -tée [mɔ̃te] *adj* mounted; organized;
equipped, well-provided; worked-up, angry ‖ *f* climb; slope
monte-charge [mɔ̃tʃarʒ] *m invar* freight
elevator
monte-plats [mɔ̃tpla] *m invar* dumbwaiter
monter [mɔ̃te] §95, §96 *tr* to go up, climb;
mount; set up; carry up, take up, bring up
‖ *intr* (*aux:* ÊTRE) to go up, come up; come
upstairs; rise; come in (*said of tide*);
monter + *inf* to go up to + *inf;* **monter à**
or **en** to go up, climb, ascend, mount;
monter sur to mount (*the throne*); go on
(*the stage*) ‖ *ref*—**se monter à** to amount
to; **se monter en** to lay in a supply of; **se
monter la tête** to get excited
montre [mɔ̃tr] *f* show, display; watch; **en
montre** in the window, on display; **faire
montre de** to show off, parade; **montre à**

affichage numérique digital watch; **montre à remontoir** stem-winder; **montre à
répétition** repeater
montre-bracelet [mɔ̃trabraslɛ] *f* (*pl*
montres-bracelets) wristwatch
montrer [mɔ̃tre] §96 *tr* to show; **montrer
du doigt** to point out or at ‖ *ref* to appear;
show oneself to be (*e.g., patient*)
mon·treur [mɔ̃trœr] **-treuse** [trøz] *mf* showman, exhibitor
mon·tueux [mɔ̃tɥø] **-tueuse** [tɥøz] *adj* rolling, hilly
monture [mɔ̃tyr] *f* mounting; assembling;
mount (*e.g., horse*)
monument [mɔnymɑ̃] *m* monument; **monument aux morts** memorial monument
moquer [mɔke] §97 *tr & ref* to mock; **se
moquer de** to make fun of, laugh at
moquerie [mɔkri] *f* mockery
moquette [mɔkɛt] *f* pile carpet; wall-to-wall
carpeting
mo·ral -rale [mɔral] (*pl* **-raux** [ro]) *adj*
moral ‖ *m* morale ‖ *f* ethics; moral (*of a
fable*); **faire la morale à qn** to lecture
s.o.
moralité [mɔralite] *f* morality; moral (*e.g.,
of a fable*)
morasse [mɔras] *f* final proof (*of newspaper*)
moratoire [mɔratwar] *m* moratorium
moratorium [mɔratɔrjɔm] *m* moratorium
morbide [mɔrbid] *adj* morbid
morbleu [mɔrblø] *interj* (obs) zounds!
mor·ceau [mɔrso] *m* (*pl* **-ceaux**) piece, bit;
morsel; **bas morceaux** (culin) cheap cuts;
en morceaux in cubes (*of sugar*); **morceaux choisis** selected passages
morceler [mɔrsəle] §34 *tr* to parcel out
morcellement [mɔrsɛlmɑ̃] *m* parceling out,
division
mordancer [mɔrdɑ̃se] §51 *tr* to size
mor·dant [mɔrdɑ̃] **-dante** [dɑ̃t] *adj* mordant, caustic ‖ *m* mordant; cutting edge;
fighting spirit; (mus) mordent
mordicus [mɔrdikys] *adv* (coll) stoutly, te-
naciously
mordiller [mɔrdije] *tr & intr* to nibble; nip
mordo·ré -rée [mɔrdɔre] *adj* golden-
brown, bronze-colored
mordre [mɔrdr] *tr* to bite ‖ *intr* to bite;
mordre à to bite on; take to, find easy;
mordre dans to bite into; **mordre sur** to
encroach upon ‖ *ref* to bite; **s'en mordre
la langue** to feel like biting off one's
tongue because of it
mor·du -due [mɔrdy] *adj* bitten; smitten ‖
mf (coll) fan (*person*)
morelle [mɔrɛl] *f* nightshade
morfondre [mɔrfɔ̃dr] *tr* to chill to the bone
‖ *ref* to be bored waiting
morgue [mɔrg] *f* morgue; haughtiness
mori·caud [mɔriko] **-caude** [kod] *adj* (coll)
dark-skinned, dusky
morigéner [mɔriʒene] §10 *tr* to scold
morillon [mɔrijɔ̃] *m* rough emerald; duck;
morillon à dos blanc canvasback

mor·mon [mɔrmɔ̃] **-mone** [mɔn] *adj* & *mf* Mormon

morne [mɔrn] *adj* dismal, gloomy ‖ *m* hillock, knoll

mornifle [mɔrnifl] *f* (coll) slap

morose [mɔroz] *adj* morose

morphine [mɔrfin] *f* morphine

morphologie [mɔrfɔlɔʒi] *f* morphology

morpion [mɔrpjɔ̃] *m* tick-tack-toe; (*young-ster*) (slang) squirt; (*Phthirus pubis*) (slang) crab louse

mors [mɔr] *m* bit; jaw (*of vise*)

morse [mɔrs] *m* Morse code; walrus

morsure [mɔrsyr] *f* bite

mort [mɔr] **morte** [mɔrt] *adj* dead; spent (*bullet*); (aut) neutral; motionless, e.g., **au point mort** at a standstill ‖ *mf* dead person, corpse ‖ *m* (bridge) dummy; **faire le mort** to play dead ‖ **mort** *f* death; **attraper la mort** to catch one's death of cold ‖ *v* see **mourir**

mortadelle [mɔrtadɛl] *f* bologna

mortaise [mɔrtɛz] *f* mortise

mortaiser [mɔrteze] *tr* to mortise

mortalité [mɔrtalite] *f* mortality

mort-aux-rats [mɔrtora], [mɔrora] *f invar* rat poison

mort-bois [mɔrbwa] *m* deadwood

morte-eau [mɔrto] *f* (*pl* **mortes-eaux** [mɔrtəzo]) low tide

mor·tel -telle [mɔrtɛl] *adj* & *mf* mortal

morte-saison [mɔrtəsɛzɔ̃] *f* (*pl* **mortes-saisons**) off-season

mortier [mɔrtje] *m* mortar; round judicial cap

mortifier [mɔrtifje] *tr* to mortify; tenderize (*meat*)

mort-né -née [mɔrne] (*pl* **-nés**) *adj* stillborn ‖ *mf* stillborn child

mortuaire [mɔrtɥer] *adj* mortuary; funeral (*e.g., service*); death (*notice*)

morue [mɔry] *f* cod

morve [mɔrv] *f* snot

mor·veux [mɔrvø] **-veuse** [vøz] *adj* snotty ‖ *mf* (coll) young snot, brat, whippersnapper

mosaïque [mɔzaik] *adj* mosaic; Mosaic ‖ *f* mosaic

Moscou [mɔsku] *m* Moscow

mosquée [mɔske] *f* mosque

mot [mo] *m* word; answer (*to riddle*); **à mots couverts** guardedly; **au bas mot** at least; **avoir toujours le mot pour rire** to be always cracking jokes; **bon mot** witticism; **gros mots** foul words; **le mot à mot** the word-for-word translation; **mot à double sens** double entendre; **mot d'entrée** headword, entry word (*of a dictionary*); **mot de passe** password; **mot d'ordre** slogan; **mot pour mot** word for word; **mots croisés** crossword puzzle; **ne . . . mot** §90 (archaic) not a word, nothing; **placer un mot** to put in a word; **prendre qn au mot** to take s.o. at his word; **sans mot dire** without a word

motard [mɔtar] *m* (coll) motorcyclist; (coll) motorcycle cop

mot-clé [mokle] *m* (*pl* **mots-clés**) key word

motel [mɔtɛl] *m* motel

mo·teur [mɔtœr] **-trice** [tris] *adj* driving (*wheel*); drive (*shaft*); motive (*power*); power (*brake*); motor (*nerve*) ‖ *m* motor, engine; prime mover; instigator; **moteur à deux temps** two-cycle engine; **moteur à explosion** internal-combustion engine; **moteur à quatre temps** four-cycle engine; **moteur à réaction** jet engine; **moteur hors bord** outboard motor

moteur-fusée *m* (*pl* **moteurs-fusées**) rocket engine

motif [mɔtif] *m* motive; (fa, mus) motif

motion [mɔsjɔ̃] *f* (parl) motion

motiver [mɔtive] *tr* to state the reason for, account for, explain, justify; motivate; warrant; **motiver une décision sur** to base a decision on

moto [mɔto] *f* motorcycle

motoneige [mɔtonɛʒ] *f* snowmobile

motoriser [mɔtorize] *tr* to motorize

mot-outil [mouti] *m* (*pl* **mots-outils**) link word

mot-piège [mopjɛʒ] *m* (*pl* **mots-pièges**) tricky word

mots-croisés [mokrwaze] *mpl* crossword puzzle

mot-souche [mosuʃ] *m* (*pl* **mots-souches**) headword, entry word; (typ) catchword

motte [mɔt] *f* clod, lump; slab (*of butter*); **motte de gazon** turf, divot

motus [mɔtys] *interj* mum's the word!

mou [mu] (or **mol** [mɔl] before vowel or mute **h**) **molle** [mɔl] (*pl* **mous molles**) *adj* soft; limp, flabby, slack; spineless, listless ‖ *m* slack; lights, lungs; (coll) softy; **bourrer le mou à qn** to hand s.o. a line

mou·chard [muʃar] **-charde** [ʃard] *mf* (coll) stool pigeon, squealer

moucharder [muʃarde] *tr* (coll) to spy on; (coll) to squeal on ‖ *intr* (coll) to squeal

mouche [muʃ] *f* fly; beauty spot; **faire d'une mouche un éléphant** to make a mountain out of a molehill; **faire la mouche** to fly into a rage; **faire mouche** to hit the bull's-eye; **fine mouche** sly, cagey person; **mouche à miel** honeybee; **mouche d'Espagne** (pharm) Spanish fly; **mouche du coche** busybody

moucher [muʃe] *tr* to blow (*one's nose*); to snuff, trim; (coll) to scold ‖ *ref* to blow one's nose

moucherolle [muʃrɔl] *f* (orn) flycatcher

moucheron [muʃrɔ̃] *m* gnat; snuff (*of candle*)

moucheter [muʃte] §34 *tr* to speckle

mouchoir [muʃwar] *m* handkerchief; **mouchoirs à jeter** disposable tissues; **mouchoirs en papier** paper handkerchiefs

moudre [mudr] §43 *tr* to grind

moue [mu] *f* wry face; **faire la moue** to pout

mouette [mwɛt] *f* gull, sea gull; **mouette rieuse** black-headed gull

mouffette [mufɛt] *f* skunk

moufle [mufl] *m* & *f* pulley block ‖ *f* mitten

mouillage [mujaʒ] *m* anchorage; wetting; watering, diluting

mouil·lé -lée [muje] *adj* wet; at anchor; palatalized; liquid (*l*)

mouiller [muje] *tr* to wet; water, dilute; palatalize; drop (*anchor*) ‖ *intr* to drop anchor ‖ *ref* to get wet; water; (coll) to become involved

moulage [mulaʒ] *m* molding, casting; mold, cast; grinding, milling

moule [mul] *m* mold, form; **moule à gaufre** waffle iron ‖ *f* mussel; (slang) fleabrain; (slang) jellyfish

mouler [mule] *tr* to mold; outline, e.g., **corsage qui moule le buste** blouse which outlines the bosom

moulin [mulɛ̃] *m* mill; **moulin à café** coffee grinder; **moulin à paroles** (coll) windbag; **moulin à vent** windmill

moulinet [mulinɛ] *m* winch; reel (*of casting rod*); turnstile; pinwheel (*child's toy*); **faire le moulinet avec** to twirl

moult [mult] *adv* (obs) much, many

mou·lu -lue [muly] *adj* ground; (coll) done in ‖ *v* see **moudre**

moulure [mulyr] *f* molding

mou·rant [murɑ̃] **-rante** [rɑ̃t] *adj* dying ‖ *mf* dying person

mourir [murir] §44, §97 *intr* (*aux:* ÊTRE) to die ‖ *ref* to be dying

mouron [murɔ̃] *m* (bot) starwort, stitchwort; (bot) pimpernel

mousquetaire [muskətɛr] *m* musketeer

mousse [mus] *adj* dull ‖ *m* cabin boy ‖ *f* moss; froth, foam; lather, suds; whipped cream; (culin) mousse

mousseline [muslin] *f* muslin; **mousseline de soie** chiffon

mousser [muse] *intr* to froth, foam; lather; **faire mousser** (coll) to crack up, build up; (slang) to enrage

mous·seux [musø] **-seuse** [søz] *adj* mossy; frothy, foamy; sudsy; sparkling (*wine*)

mousson [musɔ̃] *f* monsoon

moustache [mustaʃ] *f* mustache; **moustaches** whiskers (*of, e.g., cat*); **moustaches en croc** handle-bar mustache

moustiquaire [mustikɛr] *f* mosquito net

moustique [mustik] *m* mosquito

moût [mu] *m* must; wort

moutard [mutar] *m* (slang) kid

moutarde [mutard] *f* mustard

moutier [mutje] *m* (obs) monastery

mouton [mutɔ̃] *m* sheep; mutton; (slang) stool pigeon; **doux comme un mouton** gentle as a lamb; **moutons** whitecaps; **moutons de Panurge** (fig) chameleons, yes men; **revenons à nos moutons** let's get back to our subject

mouton·né -née [mutɔne] *adj* fleecy; frothy (*sea*); mackerel (*sky*)

moutonner [mutɔne] *tr* to curl ‖ *intr* to break into whitecaps

mouton·neux [mutɔnø] **-neuse** [nøz] *adj* frothy; fleecy (*e.g., cloud*)

mouture [mutyr] *f* grinding; mixture of wheat, rye, and barley; (fig) reworking

mouvement [muvmɑ̃] *m* movement; motion; **mouvement d'horlogerie** clockwork; **mouvement d'humeur** fit of bad temper; **mouvement ondulatoire** wave motion

mouvemen·té -tée [muvmɑ̃te] *adj* lively; eventful; hilly, broken (*terrain*)

mouvementer [muvmɑ̃te] *tr* to enliven

mouvoir [muvwar] §45 *tr* to move; set in motion, drive ‖ *ref* to move, stir

moyen [mwajɛ̃] **moyenne** [mwajɛn] *adj* average; ordinary; middle, intermediate; medium ‖ *m* way, manner; **au moyen de** by means of; **moyens** means ‖ *f* average; mean; passing mark; **en moyenne** on an average

moyen-âge [mwajɛnaʒ] *m* Middle Ages

moyenâ·geux [mwajɛnaʒø] **-geuse** [ʒøz] *adj* medieval; outdated

moyen-courrier [mwajɛ̃kurje] *m* (*pl* **moyens-courriers**) medium-range plane

moyennant [mwajɛnɑ̃] *prep* in exchange for ‖ *conj* provided that

Moyen-Orient [mwajɛnɔrjɑ̃] *m* Middle East

moyeu [mwajø] *m* (*pl* **moyeux**) hub

MST [ɛmɛste] *f* (letterword) (**maladie sexuellement transmissible**) STD (*sexually transmitted disease*)

mû mue [my] *adj* (*pl* **mus mues** [my]) *adj* driven, propelled ‖ *f* see **mue** ‖ *v* see **mouvoir**

mucosité [mykozite] *f* mucus

mucus [mykys] *m* mucus

mue [my] *f* molt, shedding

muer [mɥe] *intr* to molt; shed; (*said of voice*) to break, change

muet [mɥɛ] **muette** [mɥɛt] *adj* mute; silent; non-speaking (*rôle*); blank; dead (*key*) ‖ *mf* mute ‖ *m* silent movie

mufle [myfl] *m* muzzle, snout; (coll) cad, skunk

mugir [myʒir] *intr* to bellow

mugissement [myʒismɑ̃] *m* bellow

muguet [mygɛ] *m* lily of the valley

mulâ·tre [mylɑtr] **-tresse** [trɛs] *mf* mulatto

mule [myl] *f* mule

mulet [mylɛ] *m* mule; (ichth) mullet

mule·tier [myltje] **-tière** [tjɛr] *adj* mule (*e.g., trail*) ‖ *mf* muleteer

mulette [mylɛt] *f* fresh-water clam

mulot [mylo] *m* field mouse

multilaté·ral -rale [myltilateral] *adj* (*pl* **-raux** [ro]) multilateral

multiple [myltipl] *adj* & *m* multiple

multiplet [myltiplɛ] *m* (comp) byte

multiplicité [myltiplisite] *f* multiplicity

multiplier [myltiplije] *tr* & *ref* to multiply

multiprocesseur [myltiprɔsɛsœr] *m* (comp) multiprocessor

multitraitement [myltitrɛtmɑ̃] *m* (comp) multiprocessing

multitude [myltityd] *f* multitude

munici·pal -pale [mynisipal] *adj* (*pl* **-paux** [po]) municipal

municipalité [mynisipalite] *f* municipality; city officials; city hall

munifi·cent [mynifisɑ̃] **-cente** [sɑ̃t] *adj* munificent

munir [mynir] *tr* to provide, equip ‖ *ref*—**se munir de** to provide oneself with

munitions [mynisjɔ̃] *fpl* munitions

mu·queux [mykø] **-queuse** [køz] *adj* mucous ‖ *f* mucous membrane

mur [myr] *m* wall; **mettre au pied du mur** to corner; **mur de soutènement** retaining wall; **mur sonique, mur du son** sound barrier

mûr mûre [myr] *adj* ripe, mature ‖ *f* see **mûre**

muraille [myrɑj] *f* wall, rampart

mu·ral -rale [myral] *adj* (*pl* **-raux** [ro]) mural

mûre [myr] *f* mulberry; blackberry

murer [myre] *tr* to wall up or in ‖ *ref* to shut oneself up

mûrier [myrje] *m* mulberry tree

mûrir [myrir] *tr* & *intr* to ripen, mature

murmure [myrmyr] *m* murmur

murmurer [myrmyre] *tr* & *intr* to murmur

musaraigne [myzarɛɲ] *f* (zool) shrew

musarder [myzarde] *intr* to dawdle

musc [mysk] *m* musk

muscade [myskad] *f* nutmeg; **passez muscade!** presto!

muscardin [myskardɛ̃] *m* dormouse

muscat [myska] *m* muscatel

muscle [myskl] *m* muscle

mus·clé -clée [myskle] *adj* muscular; (coll) powerful (*e.g., drama*); (slang) difficult

musculaire [myskylɛr] *adj* muscular

muscu·leux [myskylø] **-leuse** [løz] *adj* muscular

muse [myz] *f* muse; **les Muses** the Muses

mu·seau [myzo] *m* (*pl* **-seaux**) snout; (coll) mug, face

musée [myze] *m* museum

museler [myzle] §34 *tr* to muzzle

muselière [myzəljɛr] *f* muzzle

muser [myze] *intr* to dawdle

musette [myzɛt] *f* feed bag; kit bag; haversack; (mus) musette

muséum [myzeɔm] *m* museum of natural history

musi·cal -cale [myzikal] *adj* (*pl* **-caux** [ko]) musical

music-hall [myzikol] *m* (*pl* **-halls**) vaudeville; vaudeville house; music hall (Brit)

musi·cien [myzisjɛ̃] **-cienne** [sjɛn] *mf* musician

musicologie [myzikɔlɔʒi] *f* musicology

musique [myzik] *f* music; band; **musique rustique** country music; **toujours la même musique** (coll) the same old song

mus·qué -quée [myske] *adj* musk-scented

musul·man [myzylmɑ̃] **-mane** [man] *adj* & *mf* Muslim

mutation [mytɑsjɔ̃] *f* mutation; transfer; (biol) mutation, sport

muter [myte] *tr* to transfer

muti·lé -lée [mytile] *mf* disabled veteran

mutiler [mytile] *tr* to mutilate; deface; disable; garble (*e.g., the truth*)

mu·tin [mytɛ̃] **-tine** [tin] *adj* roguish ‖ *mf* mutineer

muti·né -née [mytine] *adj* mutinous ‖ *mf* mutineer

mutiner [mytine] *ref* to mutiny

mutualité [mytɥalite] *f* mutual insurance

mu·tuel -tuelle [mytɥɛl] *adj* mutual ‖ *f* mutual benefit association

myope [mjɔp] *adj* near-sighted ‖ *mf* near-sighted person

myriade [mirjad] *f* myriad

myrrhe [mir] *f* myrrh

myrte [mirt] *m* myrtle

myrtille [mirtij] *f* blueberry

mystère [mistɛr] *m* mystery

mysté·rieux [misterjø] **-rieuse** [rjøz] *adj* mysterious

mysticisme [mistisism] *m* mysticism

mystification [mistifikɑsjɔ̃] *f* mystification; hoax

mystifier [mistifje] *tr* to mystify; hoax

mystique [mistik] *adj* & *mf* mystic

mythe [mit] *m* myth

mythique [mitik] *adj* mythical

mythologie [mitɔlɔʒi] *f* mythology

mythologique [mitɔlɔʒik] *adj* mythological

N

N, n [ɛn], *[ɛn] *m invar* fourteenth letter of the French alphabet

n' = **ne** before vowel or mute **h**

na·bot [nabo] **-bote** [bɔt] *adj* dwarfish ‖ *mf* dwarf, midget

nacelle [nasɛl] *f* (aer) nacelle; (naut) wherry, skiff; (fig) boat

nacre [nakr] *f* mother-of-pearl

na·cré -crée [nacre] *adj* pearly

nage [naʒ] *f* swimming; rowing, paddling; **être (tout) en nage** to be wet with sweat; **nage à la pagaie** paddling; **nage de côté** sidestroke; **nage en couple** sculling; **nage en grenouille** breaststroke

nagée [naʒe] *f* swimming stroke

nageoire [naʒwar] *f* fin; flipper (*of seal*); float (*for swimmers*)

nager [naʒe] §38 *intr* to swim; float; row; **nager à culer** (naut) to back water; **nager debout** to tread water; to row standing up; **nager entre deux eaux** to swim under water; (fig) to carry water on both shoulders

na·geur [naʒœr] **-geuse** [ʒøz] *adj* swimming; floating ‖ *mf* swimmer; rower

naguère or **naguères** [nagɛr] *adv* lately, just now

naïf [naif] **naïve** [naiv] *adj* naïve ‖ *mf* simple-minded person

nain [nɛ̃] **naine** [nɛn] *adj* & *mf* dwarf

naissain [nɛsɛ̃] *m* seed oysters

naissance [nɛsɑ̃s] *f* birth; lineage; descent; beginning; (archit) springing line; **de basse naissance** lowborn; **de haute naissance** highborn; **de naissance** by birth; **donner naissance à** to give birth to; to give rise to; **naissance de la gorge** bosom, throat; **naissance des cheveux** hairline; **naissance du jour** daybreak; **prendre naissance** to arise, originate

nais·sant [nɛsɑ̃] **-sante** [sɑ̃t] *adj* nascent, rising, budding

naître [nɛtr] §46 *intr* (*aux*.:ÊTRE) to be born; bud; arise, originate; dawn; **faire naître** to give birth to; give rise to

naïveté [naivte] *f* naïveté; artlessness

nana [nana] *f* (slang) chick (*girl*)

nanan [nanɑ̃], [nɑ̃nɑ̃] *m* (coll) goody; **du nanan** (coll) nice

nantir [nɑ̃tir] *tr* to give security or a pledge to; **nantir de** to provide with ‖ *intr* to stock up; feather one's nest ‖ *ref*—**se nantir de** to provide oneself with

nantissement [nɑ̃tismɑ̃] *m* security

napée [nape] *f* wood nymph

napel [napɛl] *m* monkshood, wolfsbane

naphte [naft] *m* naphtha

napoléo·nien [napɔleɔnjɛ̃] **-nienne** [njɛn] *adj* Napoleonic

nappage [napaʒ] *m* table linen

nappe [nap] *f* tablecloth; sheet (*of water, flame*); net (*for fishing; for bird catching*); **mettre la nappe** to set the table; **nappe d'autel** altar cloth; **ôter la nappe** to clear the table

napperon [naprɔ̃] *m* tablecloth cover; **petit napperon** doily

narcisse [narsis] *m* narcissus; **narcisse des bois** daffodil; **Narcisse** Narcissus

narcotique [narkɔtik] *adj* & *m* narcotic

narcotiser [narkɔtize] *tr* to dope

nargue [narg] *f* scorn, contempt; **faire nargue de** to defy; **nargue de . . . !** fie on . . . !

narguer [narge] *tr* to flout, snap one's fingers at

narguilé [nargile] *m* hookah

narine [narin] *f* nostril

nar·quois [narkwa] **-quoise** [kwaz] *adj* sly, cunning; sneering

narra·teur [naratœr] **-trice** [tris] *mf* narrator, storyteller

narra·tif [naratif] **-tive** [tiv] *adj* narrative

narration [narasjɔ̃] *f* narration; narrative

narrer [nare] *tr* to narrate, relate

na·sal -sale [nazal] *adj* (*pl* **-saux** [zo]) nasal ‖ *f* nasal (*vowel*)

nasaliser [nazalize] *tr* & *intr* to nasalize

nasarde [nazard] *f* fillip on one's nose (*in contempt*); snub, insult

na·seau [nazo] *m* (*pl* **-seaux**) nostril (*of horse, etc.*); **naseaux** (coll) snout

nasil·lard [nazijar] **-larde** [jard] *adj* nasal

nasiller [nazije] *intr* to talk through one's nose; squawk, quack

nasse [nas] *f* fish trap; (sports) basket

na·tal -tale [natal] *adj* (*pl* **-tals**) natal, of birth, native

nataliste [natalist] *mf* right-to-lifer

natalité [natalite] *f* birth rate; **natalité dirigée** birth control

natation [natasjɔ̃] *f* swimming

na·tif [natif] **-tive** [tiv] *adj* & *mf* native

nation [nasjɔ̃] *f* nation; **Nations Unies** United Nations

natio·nal -nale [nasjɔnal] *adj* & *mf* (*pl* **-naux** [no] **-nales**) national

nationaliser [nasjɔnalize] *tr* to nationalize

nationalité [nasjɔnalite] *f* nationality

nativité [nativite] *f* nativity; nativity scene; **Nativité** Nativity

natte [nat] *f* mat, matting; braid

natter [nate] *tr* to weave; braid

naturalisation [natyralizasjɔ̃] *f* naturalization

naturaliser [natyralize] *tr* to naturalize

naturalisme [natyralism] *m* naturalism

naturaliste [natyralist] *adj* & *mf* naturalist

nature [natyr] *adj invar* raw; black (*coffee*) ‖ *f* nature; **nature morte** (painting) still life

natu·rel -relle [natyrɛl] *adj* natural; native ‖ *m* naturalness; native, citizen ·

naturellement [natyrɛlmɑ̃] *adv* naturally; of course

naufrage [nofraʒ] *m* shipwreck

naufra·gé -gée [nofraʒe] *adj* shipwrecked ‖ *mf* shipwrecked person; **naufragés de l'espace** persons lost in space

nauséa·bond [nozeabɔ̃] **-bonde** [bɔ̃d] *adj* nauseating

nausée [noze] *f* nausea

nau·séeux [nozeø] **-séeuse** [zeøz] *adj* nauseous

nautique [notik] *adj* nautical

nautisme [notism] *m* yachting

nauto·nier [notɔnje] **-nière** [njɛr] *mf* pilot

na·val -vale [naval] *adj* (*pl* **-vals**) naval; nautical, maritime

navel [navɛl] *f* navel orange

navet [navɛ] *m* turnip

navette [navɛt] *f* shuttle; shuttle train; **faire la navette** to shuttle, to ply back and forth; **navette spatiale** space shuttle

navigable [navigabl] *adj* navigable (*river*); seaworthy (*ship*)

naviga·teur [navigatœr] **-trice** [tris] *adj* seafaring ‖ *m* navigator

navigation [navigasjɔ̃] *f* navigation; sailing; **navigation de plaisance** (sports) sailing

naviguer [navige] *intr* to navigate, sail; **naviguer sur** to navigate, sail (*the sea*)

navire [navir] *m* ship; **navire de débarquement** landing craft; **navire marchand** merchantman

navire-citerne [navirsitɛrn] *m* (*pl* **navires-citernes**) tanker

navire-école [navirekɔl] *m* (*pl* **navires-écoles**) training ship

navire-jumeau [navirʒymo] *m* (*pl* **navires-jumeaux**) sister ship

na·vrant [navrɑ̃] **-vrante** [vrɑ̃t] *adj* distressing, heartrending

na·vré -vrée [navre] *adj* sorry, grieved

navrer [navre] *tr* to distress, grieve

nazaréen [nazareɛ̃] **nazaréenne** [nazareɛn] *adj* Nazarene ‖ (*cap*) *mf* Nazarene

na·zi -zie [nazi] *adj & mf* Nazi

N.-D. *abbr* (**Notre-Dame**) Our Lady

ne [nə] §87, §90; **n'est-ce pas?** isn't that so? La traduction précédente est généralement remplacée par diverses locutions. Si l'énoncé est négatif, la question qui équivaut à **n'est-ce pas?** sera affirmative, par ex., **Vous ne travaillez pas. N'est-ce pas?** You are not working. Are you? Si l'énoncé est affirmatif, la question sera négative, par ex., **Vous travaillez. N'est-ce pas?** You are working. Are you not? ou **Aren't** you? Si l'énoncé contient un auxiliaire, la question contiendra cet auxiliaire moins l'infinitif ou moins le participe passé, par ex., **Il arrivera demain. N'est-ce pas?** He will arrive tomorrow. Won't he?; par ex., **Paul est déjà arrivé. N'est-ce pas?** Paul has already arrived. Hasn't he? Si l'énoncé ne contient ni auxiliaire ni forme de la copule "to be," la question contiendra l'auxiliaire "do" ou "did" moins l'infinitif, par ex., **Marie parle anglais. N'est-ce pas?** Mary speaks English. Doesn't she?

né née [ne] *adj* born; by birth; **bien né** highborn; **né pour** cut out for

néanmoins [neɑ̃mwɛ̃] *adv* nevertheless

néant [neɑ̃] *m* nothing, nothingness; worthlessness; obscurity; none (*as a response on the appropriate blank of an official form*)

nébu·leux [nebylø] **-leuse** [løz] *adj* nebulous; gloomy (*facial expression*); worried (*brow*) ‖ *f* nebula

nécessaire [nesɛsɛr] *adj* necessary, needful; **nécessaire à** required for ‖ *m* necessities; kit, dressing case

nécessairement [nesɛsɛrmɑ̃] *adv* necessarily

nécessité [nesɛsite] *f* necessity; need; **nécessité préalable** prerequisite

nécessiter [nesɛsite] §96 *tr* to necessitate

nécessi·teux [nesɛsitø] **-teuse** [tøz] *adj* needy ‖ *mf* needy person; **les nécessiteux** the needy

nécrologie [nekrɔlɔʒi] *f* necrology, obituary

nectar [nɛktar] *m* nectar

néerlan·dais [neɛrlɑ̃dɛ] **-daise** [dɛz] *adj* Dutch ‖ *m* Dutch (*language*) ‖ (*cap*) *mf* Netherlander

nef [nɛf] *f* nave; (archaic) ship; **nef latérale** aisle

néfaste [nefast] *adj* ill-starred, unlucky

nèfle [nɛfl] *f* medlar

néflier [neflije] *m* medlar tree

néga·teur [negatœr] **-trice** [tris] *adj* negative

néga·tif [negatif] **-tive** [tiv] *adj* negative ‖ *m* (phot) negative ‖ *f* negative (*side of a question*)

négation [negɑsjɔ̃] *f* negation; (gram) negative

négli·gé -gée [negliʒe] *adj* careless; unadorned, unstudied ‖ *m* carelessness; negligee, dressing gown

négligeable [negliʒabl] *adj* negligible

négligence [negliʒɑ̃s] *f* negligence; (med) malpractice; **avec négligence** slovenly

négli·gent [negliʒɑ̃] **-gente** [ʒɑ̃t] *adj* negligent ‖ *mf* careless person

négliger [negliʒe] §38, §97 *tr* to neglect ‖ *ref* to neglect oneself

négoce [negɔs] *m* trade, commerce; (com) company

négociable [negɔsjabl] *adj* negotiable

négo·ciant [negɔsjɑ̃] **-ciante** [sjɑ̃t] *mf* wholesaler, dealer

négocia·teur [negɔsjatœr] **-trice** [tris] *mf* negotiator

négociation [negɔsjɑsjɔ̃] *f* negotiation

négocier [negɔsje] *tr* to negotiate ‖ *intr* to negotiate; deal

nègre [nɛgr] *adj* black (*ethnic*); dark brown ‖ *m* black (*ethnic*); ghost writer; **petit nègre** pidgin, Creole

négrerie [negrəri] *f* slave quarters

négrier [negrije] *adj masc* slave ‖ *m* slave driver; slave ship

neige [nɛʒ] *f* snow

neiger [neʒe] §38 *intr* to snow

Némésis [nemezis] *f* Nemesis

nenni [nani], [neni], [nɛni] *adv* (archaic) no, not

nénuphar [nenyfar] *m* water lily

néologisme [neɔlɔʒism] *m* neologism

néon [neɔ̃] *m* neon

néophyte [neɔfit] *mf* neophyte, convert; beginner

neptunium [nɛptynjɔm] *m* neptunium

nerf [nɛr] *m* nerve; tendon, sinew; (archit, bb) rib; (fig) backbone, sinew; **avoir du nerf** to have nerves of steel; **avoir les nerfs à fleur de peau** to be on edge; **nerf de bœuf** scourge; **porter sur les nerfs à qn** to get on s.o.'s nerves

Néron [nerɔ̃] *m* Nero

ner·veux [nɛrvø] **-veuse** [vøz] *adj* nervous; nerve; jittery; sinewy; muscular; forceful (*style*)

nervosité [nɛrvozite] *f* nervousness; irritability; agitation

nervure [nɛrvyr] *f* rib; vein, nervure

net nette [nɛt] *adj* clean; clear, sharp, distinct; net; **net d'impôt** tax-exempt ‖ *m*—**mettre au net** to make a fair copy of ‖ *adv* flatly, point-blank, outright

netteté [nɛtəte] *f* neatness; clearness, sharpness

nettoiement [nɛtwamɑ̃] *m* cleaning

nettoyage [nɛtwajaʒ] *m* cleaning; **nettoyage à sec** dry cleaning

nettoyant [nɛtwajɑ̃] *m* cleaning product

nettoyer [nɛtwaje] §47 *tr* to clean; wash up or out; **nettoyer à sec** to dry-clean ‖ *ref* to wash up, clean oneself
net·toyeur [nɛtwajœr] **-toyeuse** [twajøz] *mf* cleaner
neuf [nœf] **neuve** [nœv] §94 *adj* new; **flambant neuf, tout neuf** brand-new ‖ **neuf** *adj & pron* nine; the Ninth, e.g., **Jean neuf** John the Ninth; **neuf heures** nine o'clock ‖ *m* nine; ninth (*in dates*)
neutraliser [nøtralize] *tr* to neutralize
neutralité [nøtralite] *f* neutrality
neutre [nøtr] *adj & m* neuter; neutral
neuvième [nœvjɛm] §94 *adj, pron* (*masc, fem*), *& m* ninth
névasse [nevɑs] *f* slush
ne·veu [nəvø] *m* (*pl* **-veux**) nephew; **nos neveux** our posterity
névralgie [nevralʒi] *f* neuralgia
névrose [nevroz] *f* neurosis
névro·sé -sée [nevroze] *adj & mf* neurotic
New York [nujɔrk], [nœjɔrk] *m* New York
newyor·kais [nœjɔrkɛ] **-kaise** [kɛz] *adj* New York ‖ (*cap*) *mf* New Yorker
nez [ne] *m* nose; cape, headland; **à plein nez** entirely, really; **nez à nez** face to face; **parler du nez** to talk through one's nose
ni [ni] §90 *conj*—**ne . . . ni . . . ni** neither . . . nor, e.g., **elle n'a ni papier ni stylo** she has neither paper nor pen; **ni . . . ni** neither . . . nor; **ni . . . non plus** nor . . . either
niable [njabl] *adj* deniable
niais [njɛ] **niaise** [njɛz] *adj* foolish, silly, simple-minded ‖ *mf* fool, simpleton
niaiserie [njɛzəri] *f* foolishness, silliness, simpleness
niche [niʃ] *f* niche; alcove; prank; **niche à chien** doghouse
nichée [niʃe] *f* brood
nicher [niʃe] *tr* to niche, lodge ‖ *intr* to nestle; nest; hide ‖ *ref* to nest
nickel [nikɛl] *adj* (slang) spic and span ‖ *m* nickel
nickeler [nikle] §34 *tr* to nickel-plate
nickelure [niklyr] *f* nickel plate
nicotine [nikɔtin] *f* nicotine
nid [ni] *m* nest; **en nid d'abeilles** honeycombed; **nid de pie** crow's-nest
nid-à-feu [nidafø] *m* (*pl* **nids-à-feu**) fire trap
nid-de-poule [nidəpul] *m* (*pl* **nids-de-poule**) pothole
nièce [njɛs] *f* niece
nième [njɛm] *adj* nth
nier [nje] §97 *tr* to deny ‖ *intr* to plead not guilty
ni·gaud [nigo] **-gaude** [god] *adj* silly ‖ *mf* nincompoop
nigauderie [nigodri] *f* silliness
nihilisme [niilism] *m* nihilism
Nil [nil] *m* Nile
nimbe [nɛ̃b] *m* halo, nimbus
nimber [nɛ̃be] *tr* to halo
nimbus [nɛ̃bys] *m* (meteo) nimbus
nipper [nipe] *tr* (coll) to tog ‖ *ref* (coll) to tog oneself out

nippes [nip] *fpl* (coll) worn-out clothes; (slang) duds
nique [nik] *f*—**faire la nique à** to turn up one's nose at
nitouche [nituʃ] *f*—**de sainte nitouche** hypocritically pious
nitrate [nitrat] *m* nitrate
nitre [nitr] *m* niter, nitrate
ni·treux [nitrø] **-treuse** [trøz] *adj* nitrous
nitrière [nitrijɛr] *f* saltpeter bed
nitrique [nitrik] *adj* nitric
nitrogène [nitrɔʒɛn] *m* nitrogen
nitroglycérine [nitrɔgliserin] *f* nitroglycerin
ni·veau [nivo] *m* (*pl* **-veaux**) level; **au niveau de** on a par with; **niveau à bulle d'air** spirit level; **niveau à lunettes** surveyor's level; **niveau d'essence** gasoline gauge; **niveau de vie** standard of living; **niveau d'huile** oil gauge; **niveau mental** I.Q.
niveler [nivle] §34 *tr* to level; survey
nive·leur [nivlœr] **-leuse** [løz] *mf* leveler ‖ *m* harrow ‖ *f* (agr) leveler
nivellement [nivɛlmɑ̃] *m* leveling; surveying
N°, n° *abbr* (**numéro**) no.
noble [nɔbl] *adj & mf* noble
noblesse [nɔblɛs] *f* nobility; nobleness
noce [nɔs] *f* wedding; wedding party; **faire la noce** to go on a spree; **ne pas être à la noce** to be in trouble; **noces** wedding
no·ceur [nɔsœr] **-ceuse** [søz] *adj* (coll) bacchanalian, reveling ‖ *mf* (coll) reveler, debauchee
no·cif [nɔsif] **-cive** [siv] *adj* noxious
noctambule [nɔktɑ̃byl] *mf* nighthawk; sleepwalker
nocturne [nɔktyrn] *adj* nocturnal; night; nightly ‖ *m* (mus) nocturne ‖ *f* open night (*of store*)
nodosité [nɔdozite] *f* nodule (*of root*); node, wart
Noé [nɔe] *m* Noah
noël [nɔɛl] *m* Christmas carol; (coll) Christmas present; **Noël** Christmas
nœud [nø] *m* knot; rosette; finger joint; Adam's apple; tie, alliance; crux (*of question, plot, crisis*); node; (naut) knot; **nœud de vache** granny knot; **nœud plat** square knot; **nœuds** coils (*of snake*); **nœud vital** nerve center
noir noire [nwar] *adj* black; **noir comme poix** pitch-black ‖ *mf* black (*ethnic*) ‖ *m* black; bruise; **broyer du noir** to be blue, down in the dumps; **noir de fumée** lampblack ‖ *f* (mus) quarter note
noirâtre [nwarɑtr] *adj* blackish
noi·raud [nwaro] **-raude** [rod] *adj* swarthy
noirceur [nwarsœr] *f* blackness; black spot
noircir [nwarsir] *tr* to blacken ‖ *intr & ref* to burn black; turn dark
noircissure [nwarsisyr] *f* black spot, smudge
noise [nwaz] *f* squabble; **chercher noise à** to pick a quarrel with
noisetier [nwaztje] *m* hazelnut tree
noisette [nwazɛt] *adj invar* reddish-brown ‖ *f* hazelnut

noix [nwɑ], [nwa] *f* walnut; nut; **à la noix** (slang) trifling; **noix d'acajou, noix de cajou** cashew nut; **noix du Brésil** Brazil nut; **noix de coco** coconut; **noix de galle** nutgall; **noix de muscade** nutmeg; **noix de veau** round of veal

nolis [nɔli] *m* freight

noliser [nɔlize] *tr* to charter (*a ship*)

nom [nɔ̃] *m* name; noun; **de nom** by name; **nom à rallonges, nom à tiroirs** (coll) word made up of several parts; **nom commercial** trade name; **nom de baptême** baptismal name, Christian name; **nom de demoiselle** maiden name; **nom de Dieu!** God damn!, for Chrissakes!; **nom de famille** surname; **nom de guerre** fictitious name, assumed name; **nom de jeune fille** maiden name; **nom d'emprunt** assumed name; **nom de nom!** God damn!; **nom de théâtre** stage name; **nom marchand** trade name; **petit nom d'amitié** pet name; **sans nom** nameless; **sous le nom de** by the name of

nomade [nɔmad] *adj & mf* nomad

nombre [nɔ̃br] *m* number, quantity

nombrer [nɔ̃bre] *tr* to number

nom·breux [nɔ̃brø] **-breuse** [brøz] *adj* numerous; rhythmic, harmonious (*e.g., prose*)

nombril [nɔ̃bri] *m* navel

nomenclature [nɔmɑ̃klatyr] *f* nomenclature; vocabulary; body (*of dictionary*)

nomi·nal -nale [nɔminal] *adj* (*pl* **-naux** [no]) nominal; **appel nominal** roll call

nomina·tif [nɔminatif] **-tive** [tiv] *adj* nominative; registered (*stocks, bonds, etc.*) ‖ *m* nominative

nomination [nɔminɑsjɔ̃] *f* appointment

nom·mé -mée [nɔme] *adj* named; appointed; called ‖ *m*—**le nommé . . .** the man called . . .

nommément [nɔmenɑ̃] *adv* namely, particularly

nommer [nɔme] *tr* to name, call; appoint ‖ *ref* to be named, e.g., **je me nomme . . .** my name is . . .

non [nɔ̃] *m invar* no ‖ *adv* no, not; **non pas** not so; **non plus** neither, not, nor . . . either, e.g., **moi non plus** nor I either; **non point!** by no means!; **que non!** no indeed!

non-belligé·rant [nɔ̃bɛliʒerɑ̃] **-rante** [rɑ̃t] *adj & mf* nonbelligerent

nonce [nɔ̃s] *m* nuncio

nonchalamment [nɔ̃ʃalamɑ̃] *adv* nonchalantly

noncha·lant [nɔ̃ʃalɑ̃] **-lante** [lɑ̃t] *adj* nonchalant

non-combat·tant [nɔ̃kɔ̃batɑ̃] **-tante** [tɑ̃t] *adj & mf* noncombatant

non-conformiste [nɔ̃kɔ̃fɔrmist] *adj & mf* nonconformist

non-enga·gé -gée [nɔ̃nɑ̃gaʒe] *adj* unaligned, uncommitted

non-ingérence [nɔ̃nɛ̃ʒerɑ̃s] *f* noninterference

nonnain [nɔnɛ̃] *f* (pej) nun

nonne [nɔn] *f* nun

nonobstant [nɔnɔpstɑ̃] *adv* notwithstanding; **nonobstant que** although ‖ *prep* in spite of

non-pesanteur [nɔ̃pəzɑ̃tœr] *f* weightlessness

non-rési·dent [nɔ̃rezidɑ̃] **-dente** [dɑ̃t] *adj & mf* nonresident

non-réussite [nɔ̃reysit] *f* failure

non-sens [nɔ̃sɑ̃s] *m* absurdity, nonsense

non-usage [nɔnyzaʒ] *m* disuse

non-violence [nɔ̃vjɔlɑ̃s] *f* nonviolence

nord [nɔr] *adj invar* north, northern ‖ *m* north; **du nord** northern; **faire le nord** to steer northward; **perdre le nord** to become disoriented, not to know one's way; **vers le nord** northward

nord-est [nɔrɛst] *adj invar & m* northeast

nord-ouest [nɔrwɛst] *adj invar & m* northwest

nor·mal -male [nɔrmal] *adj* (*pl* **-maux** [mo]) normal, regular, standard; perpendicular ‖ *f* normal; perpendicular; normalcy

norma·lien [nɔrmaljɛ̃] **-lienne** [ljɛn] *mf* student at a teachers college

nor·mand [nɔrmɑ̃] **-mande** [mɑ̃d] *adj* Norman ‖ *m* Norman (*dialect*) ‖ (*cap*) *mf* Norman (*person*)

Normandie [nɔrmɑ̃di] *f* Normandy; **la Normandie** Normandy

norme [nɔrm] *f* norm; specifications

nor·rois [nɔrwa] **nor·roise** [nɔrwaz] *adj* Norse ‖ *m* Norse (*language*) ‖ (*cap*) *m* Norseman

Norvège [nɔrvɛʒ] *f* Norway; **la Norvège** Norway

norvé·gien [nɔrveʒjɛ̃] **-gienne** [ʒjɛn] *adj* Norwegian ‖ *m* Norwegian (*language*) ‖ *f* round-stemmed rowboat ‖ (*cap*) *mf* Norwegian (*person*)

nos [no] §88 our

nostalgie [nɔstalʒi] *f* nostalgia, homesickness

nostalgique [nɔstalʒik] *adj* nostalgic, homesick

nota bene [nɔtabene] *m invar* memo (*preceded by "N.B."*)

notable [nɔtabl] *adj* notable, noteworthy ‖ *m* notable

notaire [nɔtɛr] *m* notary; lawyer

notamment [nɔtamɑ̃] *adv* especially

notation [nɔtɑsjɔ̃] *f* notation

note [nɔt] *f* note; bill (*to be paid*); grade, mark (*in school*); footnote; **être dans la note** to be in the swing of things; **note de rappel** reminder; **prendre note de** to note down

noter [nɔte] *tr* to note; note down; notice; mark (*a student*); write down (*a tune*)

notice [nɔtis] *f* notice; instructions, directions; instruction manual; preface; **notice d'un livre** review of a book

notification [nɔtifikɑsjɔ̃] *f* notification, notice

notifier [nɔtifje] §97 *tr* to report on; serve (*a summons*)

notion [nosjɔ̃] *f* notion

notoire [nɔtwar] *adj* well-known
notoriété [nɔtɔrjete] *f* fame
notre [nɔtr] §88 our
nôtre [notr] §89 ours; **serez-vous des nôtres?** will you join us?
noue [nu] *f* pasture land; roof gutter
noué nouée [nwe] *adj* afflicted with rickets
nouer [nwe] *tr* to knot; tie; form; cook up (*a plot*) ‖ *ref* to form knots; be tied; (hort) to set
noueux [nwø] **noueuse** [nwøz] *adj* knotty, gnarled
nouille [nuj] *f* noodle
nounou [nunu] *f* nanny
nour·ri -rie [nuri] *adj* heavy, sustained; rich (*style*)
nourrice [nuris] *f* wet nurse; can; (aut) reserve tank
nourricerie [nurisri] *f* baby farm; stock farm; silkworm farm
nourri·cier [nurisje] **-cière** [sjɛr] *adj* nutritive; nourishing; foster
nourrir [nurir] *tr* to nourish; suckle; to feed (*a fire*); nurse (*plants; hopes*) ‖ *intr* to be nourishing ‖ *ref* to feed; thrive
nourrisseur [nurisœr] *m* stock raiser, dairyman
nourrisson [nurisɔ̃] *m* nursling, suckling; foster child
nourriture [nurityr] *f* nourishment, food; nourishing; nursing, breastfeeding; **nourriture du feu** firewood
nous [nu] §85, §87 we; us; to us; **nous autres Américains** we Americans
nous-mêmes [numɛm] §86 ourselves
nou·veau [nuvo] (or **-vel** [vɛl] before vowel or mute **h**) **-velle** [vɛl] (*pl* **-veaux -velles**) *adj* new (*recent*) ‖ (when standing before noun) *adj* new (*other, additional, different*) ‖ *m* freshman; **à nouveau** anew; **de nouveau** again; **du nouveau** something new; **le nouveau** the new ‖ *f* see **nouvelle**
nouveau-né -née [nuvone] *adj & mf* (*pl* **nés**) newborn
nouveauté [nuvote] *f* newness, novelty
nouvelle [nuvɛl] *f* piece of news; novelette, short story; **donnez-moi de vos nouvelles** let me hear from you; **nouvelles** news ‖ *adj* see **nouveau**
Nouvelle-Angleterre [nuvɛlɑ̃glətɛr] *f* New England; **la Nouvelle-Angleterre** New England
Nouvelle-Écosse [nuvɛlekɔs] *f* Nova Scotia; **la Nouvelle-Écosse** Nova Scotia
Nouvelle-Orléans [nuvɛlɔrleɑ̃] *f*—**la Nouvelle-Orléans** New Orleans
Nouvelle-Zélande [nuvɛlzelɑ̃d] *f* New Zealand; **la Nouvelle-Zélande** New Zealand
nouvelliste [nuvelist] *mf* short-story writer
nova·teur [nɔvatœr] **-trice** [tris] *adj* innovating ‖ *mf* innovator
novembre [nɔvɑ̃br] *m* November
novice [nɔvis] *adj* inexperienced, new ‖ *mf* novice, neophyte
noviciat [nɔvisja] *m* novitiate
novocaïne [nɔvɔkain] *f* novocaine
noyade [nwajad] *f* drowning

noyau [nwajo] *m* (*pl* **noyaux**) nucleus; stone, kernel; pit (*of fruit*); core (*of electromagnet*); newel; hub; (fig) cell (*of conspirators*); (fig) bunch (*of card players*), **noyau d'atome** atomic nucleus
noyautage [nwajotaʒ] *m* infiltration (*e.g., of communists*)
noyer [nwaje] *m* walnut tree; **en noyer** in walnut (*wood*) ‖ §47 *tr & ref* to drown
nu nue [ny] *adj* naked, nude; bare; barren; uncarpeted; unharnessed, unsaddled (*horse*); (aut) stripped ‖ *m* nude; **à nu** exposed; bareback ‖ *f* see **nue**
nuage [nɥaʒ] *m* cloud
nua·geux [nɥaʒø] **-geuse** [ʒøz] *adj* cloudy
nuance [nɥɑ̃s] *f* hue, shade, tone, nuance
nucléaire [nykleɛr] *adj* nuclear
nucléole [nykleɔl] *m* nucleolus
nucléon [nykleɔ̃] *m* nucleon
nudiste [nydist] *adj & mf* nudist
nudité [nydite] *f* nakedness; nudity; plainness (*of style*); nude
nue [ny] *f* clouds; sky; **mettre** or **porter aux nues** to praise to the skies
nuée [nɥe] *f* cloud, storm cloud; flock
nuire [nɥir] §19 (*pp* **nui** *invar*) *intr*—**nuire à** to harm, injure, e.g., **cette accusation lui a beaucoup nui** that accusation hurt him very much
nuisible [nɥizibl] *adj* harmful
nuit [nɥi] *f* night; **à la nuit close** after dark; **bonne nuit** good night; **cette nuit** last night; **nuit blanche** sleepless night
nuitamment [nɥitamɑ̃] *adv* at night
nu-jambes [nyʒɑ̃b] *adj invar* bare-legged
nul nulle [nyl] *adj indef* no; **ne . . . nul** or **nul . . . ne** §90 no; **nul et non avenu, nulle et non avenue** [nylenɔ̃navny] null and void ‖ *f* dummy word or letter ‖ **nul** *pron indef*—**nul ne** §90B no one, nobody
nullement [nylmɑ̃] §90 *adv* not at all
nullité [nylite] *f* nonentity, nobody; invalidity
nûment [nymɑ̃] *adv* candidly, frankly
numéraire [nymerɛr] *m* specie; **payer en numéraire** to pay in cash
numé·ral -rale [nymeral] *adj & m* (*pl* **-raux** [ro]) numeral
numération [nymerɑsjɔ̃] *f* numeration; **numération globulaire** blood count
numérique [nymerik] *adj* numerical; digital
numéro [nymero] *m* numeral; number; issue, number (*of a periodical*), e.g., **dernier numéro** current issue; e.g., **numéro ancien** back number; (slang) queer duck; **faire un numéro** to dial; **numéro de vestiaire** check (*of checkroom*); **numéro d'ordre** serial number
numéroter [nymerɔte] *tr* to number
numismatique [nymismatik] *adj* numismatic ‖ *f* numismatics
nu-pieds [nypje] *adj invar* barefooted
nup·tial -tiale [nypsjal] *adj* (*pl* **-tiaux** [sjo]) nuptial
nuque [nyk] *f* nape, scruff
nurse [nœrs] *f* children's nurse
nu-tête [nytɛt] *adj invar* bareheaded

nutri·tif [nytritif] **-tive** [tiv] *adj* nutritive; nutritious
nutrition [nytrisjɔ̃] *f* nutrition

nylon [nilɔ̃] *m* nylon
nymphe [nɛ̃f] *f* nymph; (Ent) nympha, chrysalis, pupa

O

O, o [o], *[o] *m invar* fifteenth letter of the French alphabet
oasis [ɔazis] *f* oasis
obéir [ɔbeir] *intr* to obey; yield to; be subject to; **obéir à** to obey, e.g., **je leur obéis** I obey them, **j'obéis à la loi** I obey the law; **obéir au doigt et à l'œil** to obey blindly; **vous êtes obéi** you are obeyed
obéissance [ɔbeisɑ̃s] *f* obedience
obéis·sant [ɔbeisɑ̃] **-sante** [sɑ̃t] *adj* obedient
obélisque [ɔbelisk] *m* obelisk
obérer [ɔbere] §10 *tr* to burden with debt ‖ *ref* to run into debt
obèse [ɔbez] *adj* obese
obésité [ɔbezite] *f* obesity
objecter [ɔbʒɛkte] *tr* to object, e.g., **objecter que . . .** to object that . . . ; to bring up, e.g., **objecter q.ch. à qn** to bring up s.th. against s.o.; put forward (*in opposition*), e.g., **objecter de bonnes raisons à** or **contre un argument** to put forward good reasons against an argument
objecteur [ɔbʒɛktœr] *m*—**objecteur de conscience** conscientious objector
objec·tif [ɔbʒɛktif] **-tive** [tiv] *adj* objective ‖ *m* objective; object lens; (mil) target
objection [ɔbʒɛksjɔ̃] *f* objection; **faire des objections** to object
objectivité [ɔbʒɛktivite] *f* objectivity
objet [ɔbʒɛ] *m* object; **menus objets** notions; **objet d'art** work of art; **objet de risée** laughingstock; **objets de première nécessité** articles of everyday use; **objet volant non-identifié** unidentified flying object; **remplir son objet** to attain one's end
obligation [ɔbligɑsjɔ̃] *f* obligation; (com) bond, debenture; **être dans l'obligation de** to be obliged to
obligatoire [ɔbligatwar] *adj* required, obligatory; (coll) inevitable
obli·gé -gée [ɔbliʒe] §93 *adj* obliged, compelled; necessary, indispensable; **bien obligé** much obliged; **c'est obligé** (coll) it has to be; **être obligé de** to be obliged to
obli·geant [ɔbliʒɑ̃] **-geante** [ʒɑ̃t] *adj* obliging
obliger [ɔbliʒe] §38, §96, §97, §100 *tr* to oblige ‖ §96 *ref*—**s'obliger à** + *inf* to undertake to + *inf*; **s'obliger pour qn** to stand surety for s.o.
oblique [ɔblik] *adj* oblique
oblitération [ɔbliterɑsjɔ̃] *f* obliteration; cancellation (*of postage stamp*); (pathol) occlusion

oblitérer [ɔblitere] §10 to obliterate; cancel (*a postage stamp*); obstruct (*e.g., a vein*)
o·blong [ɔblɔ̃] **-blongue** [blɔ̃g] *adj* oblong
obnubiler [ɔbnybile] *tr* to cloud, befog
obole [ɔbɔl] *f* widow's mite
obscène [ɔpsɛn] *adj* obscene
obscénité [ɔpsenite] *f* obscenity
obs·cur -cure [ɔpskyr] *adj* obscure
obscurcir [ɔpskyrsir] *tr* to obscure; dim ‖ *ref* to grow dark; grow dim
obscurité [ɔpskyrite] *f* obscurity
obséder [ɔpsede] §10 *tr* to obsess; importune, harass
obsèques [ɔpsɛk] *fpl* obsequies, funeral rites
obsé·quieux [ɔpsekjø] **-quieuse** [kjøz] *adj* obsequious
observance [ɔpsɛrvɑ̃s] *f* observance
observa·teur [ɔpsɛrvatœr] **-trice** [tris] *adj* observant ‖ *mf* observer
observation [ɔpsɛrvɑsjɔ̃] *f* observation
observatoire [ɔpsɛrvatwar] *m* observatory
observer [ɔpsɛrve] *tr* to observe ‖ *ref* to watch oneself; watch each other
obsession [ɔpsesjɔ̃] *f* obsession
obsolète [ɔpsɔlɛt] *adj* obsolete
obstacle [ɔpstakl] *m* obstacle
obstétrique [ɔpstetrik] *adj* obstetrical ‖ *f* obstetrics
obstination [ɔpstinɑsjɔ̃] *f* obstinacy
obsti·né -née [ɔpstine] *adj* obstinate
obstruction [ɔpstryksjɔ̃] *f* obstruction; (sports) blocking; **faire de l'obstruction** (pol) to filibuster; **obstruction systématique** filibustering
obstruer [ɔpstrye] *tr* to obstruct
obtempérer [ɔptɑ̃pere] §10 *intr*—**obtempérer à**) to comply with, obey
obtenir [ɔptənir] §72, §97 *tr* to obtain, get
obtention [ɔptɑ̃sjɔ̃] *f* obtaining
obtura·teur [ɔptyratœr] **-trice** [tris] *adj* stopping, closing ‖ *m* (mach) stopcock; (phot) shutter
obturation [ɔptyrɑsjɔ̃] *f* stopping up; filling (*of tooth*); **obturation des lumières** blackout
obturer [ɔptyre] *tr* to stop up; fill (*a tooth*)
ob·tus [ɔpty] **-tuse** [tyz] *adj* obtuse
obus [ɔby] *m* (mil) shell; plunger (*of tire valve*); **obus à balles** shrapnel; **obus à mitraille** shrapnel; **obus de rupture** armor-piercing shell
obvier [ɔbvje] *intr*—**obvier à** to obviate, prevent
oc [ɔk] *adv* (Old Provençal) yes
occasion [ɔkɑzjɔ̃], [ɔkazjɔ̃] *f* occasion; opportunity; bargain; **à l'occasion** on

occasion; **à l'occasion de** for (*e.g.*, *s.o.'s birthday*); **d'occasion** secondhand (*clothing*); used (*car*); **venez me voir à votre première occasion** come to see me at your first opportunity

occasion·nel -nelle [ɔkazjɔnɛl] *adj* occasional; chance (*meeting*); determining (*cause*)

occasionnellement [ɔkazjɔnɛlmɑ̃] *adv* occasionally; by chance, accidentally

occasionner [ɔkazjɔne] *tr* to occasion

occident [ɔksidɑ̃] *m* occident, west

occiden·tal -tale [ɔdsidɑ̃tal] *adj* & *mf* (*pl* **-taux** [to]) occidental

occlu·sif -sive [ɔklyzif] [ziv] *adj* & *f* occlusive

occlusion [ɔklyzjɔ̃] *f* occlusion

occulte [ɔkylt] *adj* occult

occu·pant [ɔkypɑ̃] **-pante** [pɑ̃t] *adj* occupying ‖ *mf* occupant

occupation [ɔkypasjɔ̃] *f* occupation; **occupation sauvage** sit-in

occu·pé -pée [ɔkype] *adj* occupied; **occupé** (*public sign*) in use

occuper [ɔkype] *tr* to occupy ‖ §96, §97 *ref* to find something to do; **s'occuper de** to be occupied with, be busy with; take care of, handle

occurrence [ɔkyrɑ̃s] *f* occurrence; **en l'occurrence** under the circumstances; **être en occurrence** to occur; **selon l'occurrence** as the case may be

océan [ɔseɑ̃] *m* ocean; **océan glacial arctique** Arctic Ocean; **océan Indien** Indian Ocean

océanique [ɔseanik] *adj* oceanic

ocre [ɔkr] *f* ochre

octane [ɔktan] *m* octane

octave [ɔktav] *f* octave

octa·von [ɔktavɔ̃] **-vonne** [vɔn] *mf* octoroon

octet [ɔktɛ] *m* (comp) byte (*of eight bits*)

octobre [ɔktɔbr] *m* October

octroi [ɔktrwa] *m* granting (*of a favor*); tax on provisions being brought into town

octroyer [ɔktrwaje] §47 *tr* to grant, concede; bestow

oculaire [ɔkylɛr] *adj* ocular, eye ‖ *m* ocular, eyepiece

oculariste [ɔkylarist] *mf* optician (*who specializes in glass eyes*)

oculiste [ɔkylist] *mf* oculist

ode [ɔd] *f* ode

odeur [ɔdœr] *f* odor, scent

o·dieux [ɔdjø] **-dieuse** [djøz] *adj* odious ‖ *m* odium, odiousness

odo·rant [ɔdɔrɑ̃] **-rante** [rɑ̃t] *adj* fragrant

odorat [ɔdɔra] *m* (sense of) smell

Odyssée [ɔdise] *f* Odyssey

œcuménique [ekymenik] *adj* ecumenical

œdème [edɛm] *m* (pathol) edema

Œdipe [edip] *m* Oedipus

œil [œj] *m* (*pl* **yeux** [jø] **les yeux** [lezjø]) eye; typeface, font; bud; **avoir l'œil (américain)** (coll) to be observant; **coûter les yeux de la tête** (coll) to cost a fortune; **donner de l'œil à** to give a better appearance to; **entre quatre yeux** [ɑ̃trəkatzjø]

(coll) between you and me; **faire les gros yeux à** (coll) to glare at; **faire les yeux doux à** to make eyes at; **ne pas avoir les yeux dans la poche** (coll) to keep one's eyes peeled; (coll) to be no shrinking violet; **œil au beurre noir** (coll) black eye; **œil de pie** (naut) eyelet; **œil de verre** glass eye; **œil électrique** electric eye; **pocher un œil à qn** to give s.o. a black eye; **sale œil** disapproving or dirty look; **sauter aux yeux, crever les yeux** to be obvious; **se mettre le doigt dans l'œil** (coll) to put one's foot in one's mouth; **se rincer l'œil** (slang) to get an eyeful; **taper dans l'œil à** or **de qn** (coll) to take s.o.'s fancy; **voir d'un mauvais œil** to take a dim view of

œil-de-bœuf [œjdəbœf] *m* (*pl* **œils-de-bœuf**) bull's-eye, small oval window

œil-de-chat [œjdəʃa] *m* (*pl* **œils-de-chat**) cat's-eye (*gem*)

œil-de-perdrix [œjdəpɛrdri] *m* (*pl* **œils-de-perdrix**) (pathol) soft corn

œillade [œjad] *f* glance, leer, wink; **lancer, jeter,** or **décocher une œillade à** to ogle

œillère [œjɛr] *f* eyecup; blinker; **avoir des œillères** to be biased

œillet [œjɛ] *m* eyelet; eyelet hole; carnation, clove pink; **œillet d'Inde** (*Tagetes*) marigold

œilleton [œjtɔ̃] *m* eye, bud; eyepiece; sight (*of rifle, camera, etc.*)

œillette [œjɛt] *f* opium poppy

œnologie [enɔlɔʒi] *f* science of viniculture, oenology

œsophage [ezɔfaʒ] *m* esophagus

œstres [ɛstr] *mpl* botflies, nose flies

œuf [œf] *m* (*pl* **œufs** [ø]) egg; **marcher sur des œufs** to walk on thin ice; **œuf à la coque** soft-boiled egg; **œuf à repriser** darning egg; **œuf de Colomb** ingenious, though obvious, solution to a problem; **œuf de Pâques** or **œuf rouge** Easter egg; **œuf dur** hard-boiled egg; **œuf mollet** soft-boiled egg; **œuf poché** poached egg; **œufs** spawn, roe; **œufs au lait** custard; **œufs au miroir** fried eggs; **œufs brouillés** scrambled eggs; **œuf sur le plat** fried egg; **plein comme un œuf** chock-full; **tondre un œuf** to squeeze blood out of a turnip; **tuer, écraser,** or **étouffer dans l'œuf** to nip in the bud

œuvre [œvr] *m* works (*of a painter*); **dans œuvre** inside (*measurements*); **hors d'œuvre** out of alignment; **le grand œuvre** the philosopher's stone; **le gros œuvre** (archit) the foundation, walls, and roof ‖ *f* work; piece of work; **bonnes œuvres** good works; **mettre en œuvre** to implement, to use; **mettre qn à l'œuvre** to set s.o. to work; **mettre tout en œuvre** to leave no stone unturned; **œuvres complètes** collected works; **œuvres mortes** (naut) topsides; **œuvre pie** good deed, good work; **œuvres vives** (naut) hull below water line; **se mettre à l'œuvre** to get to work

offen·sant [ɔfɑ̃sɑ̃] **-sante** [sɑ̃t] *adj* offensive
offense [ɔfɑ̃s] *f* offense; **faire offense à qn** to offend s.o.; **soit dit sans offense** with all due respect
offenser [ɔfɑ̃se] *tr* to offend ‖ *ref* to be offended
offen·sif [ɔfɑ̃sif] **-sive** [siv] *adj & f* offensive
of·fert [ɔfɛr] **-ferte** [fɛrt] *v* see **offrir**
office [ɔfis] *m* office; (eccl) office, service; **d'office** ex officio; **faire l'office de** to act as; **office d'ami** friendly turn; **remplir son office** (fig) to do its job ‖ *f* pantry
offi·ciel -cielle [ɔfisjɛl] *adj & mf* official
officier [ɔfisje] *m* officier; (naut) mate; **officier de service** (mil) officer of the day; **officier ministériel** notary public; **officier supérieur** (mil) field officer ‖ *intr* to officiate
offi·cieux [ɔfisjø] **-cieuse** [sjøz] *adj* unofficial, off-the-cuff; zealous; well-meant (*lie*); **faire l'officieux** to be officious
officine [ɔfisin] *f* pharmacy; den (*of thieves*); **officine d'intrigue** hotbed of intrigue
offrant [ɔfrɑ̃] *m*—**le plus offrant** the highest bidder
offre [ɔfr] *f* offer; **l'offre et la demande** supply and demand; **offres d'emploi** (formula in want ads) help wanted
offrir [ɔfrir] §65, §97, §98 *tr* to offer ‖ §96 *ref* to offer oneself; offer itself, occur
offset [ɔfsɛt] *m invar* offset
offusquer [ɔfyske] *tr* to obfuscate, obscure; irritate, displease ‖ *ref*—**s'offusquer de** to take offense at
ogive [ɔʒiv] *f* ogive; (rok) nose cone
ogre [ɔgr] **ogresse** [ɔgrɛs] *mf* ogre; **manger comme un ogre** (coll) to eat like a horse
ohé [ɔe] *interj* hey!; **ohé du navire!** ship ahoy!
ohm [om] *m* ohm
oie [wa] *f* goose; simpleton; **oie blanche** simple little goose (*naïve girl*); **oie sauvage** wild goose
oignon [ɔɲɔ̃] *m* onion; (hort) bulb; (pathol) bunion; (coll) turnip, pocket watch; **aux petits oignons** (coll) perfect; **ce ne sont pas mes oignons** it's no business of mine; **occupe-toi de tes oignons** (coll) mind your own business
oïl [ɔil], [ɔj] *adv* (Old French) yes
oindre [wɛ̃dr] §35 *tr* to anoint
oi·seau [wazo] *m* (*pl* **-seaux**) bird; hod (*of mason*); (coll) character; **être comme l'oiseau sur la branche** to be here today and gone tomorrow; **oiseau de paradis, oiseau des îles** bird of paradise; **oiseau des tempêtes** stormy petrel; **oiseaux domestiques, oiseaux de basse-cour** poultry
oiseau-mouche [wazomuʃ] *m* (*pl* **-mouches**) hummingbird
oiseler [wazle] §34 *tr* to train (*hawks*) ‖ *intr* to trap birds
oiselet [wazlɛ] *m* little bird
oiseleur [wazlœr] *m* fowler

oise·lier [wazəlje] **-lière** [ljɛr] *mf* bird fancier
oi·seux [wazø] **-seuse** [zøz] *adj* useless
oi·sif [wazif] **-sive** [ziv] *adj* idle ‖ *mf* idler
oisillon [wazijɔ̃] *m* fledgling
oisiveté [wazivte] *f* idleness
oison [wazɔ̃] *m* gosling; (coll) ninny
O.K. [oke] *interj* (letterword) O.K.!
oléagi·neux [ɔleaʒinø] **-neuse** [nøz] *adj* oily
oléoduc [ɔleɔdyk] *m* oil pipeline
olfac·tif [ɔlfaktif] **-tive** [tiv] *adj* olfactory
olibrius [ɔlibrijys] *m* pedant; pest; braggart (*in medieval plays*)
oligarchie [ɔligarʃi] *f* oligarchy
olivaie [ɔlivɛ] *f* olive grove
olivâtre [ɔlivɑtr] *adj* olive (*complexion*)
olive [ɔliv] *adj invar & f* olive
olivette [ɔlivɛt] *f* olive grove; plum tomato
olivier [ɔlivje] *m* olive tree; olive wood; Olivier Oliver
O.L.P. [ɔɛlpe] *f* (letterword) (**Organisation de la libération de la Palestine**) PLO
olympiade [ɔlɛ̃pjad] *f* olympiad
olym·pien [ɔlɛ̃pjɛ̃] **-pienne** [pjɛn] *adj* Olympian
olympique [ɔlɛ̃pik] *adj* Olympic
ombilic [ɔ̃bilik] *m* umbilicus
ombili·cal -cale [ɔ̃bilikal] *adj* (*pl* **-caux** [ko]) umbilical
ombrage [ɔ̃braʒ] *m* shade; **porter ombrage à** to offend; **prendre ombrage (de)** to take offense (at)
ombrager [ɔ̃braʒe] §38 *tr* to shade
ombra·geux [ɔ̃braʒø] **-geuse** [ʒøz] *adj* shy, skittish; touchy; distrustful
ombre [ɔ̃br] *f* shadow; shade; **ombres (chinoises)** shadow play, shadowgraph; **une ombre au tableau** (coll) a fly in the ointment
ombrelle [ɔ̃brɛl] *f* parasol; (aer) umbrella
ombrer [ɔ̃bre] *tr* to shade; apply eye shadow to
om·breux [ɔ̃brø] **-breuse** [brøz] *adj* shady
omelette [ɔmlɛt] *f* omelet
omettre [ɔmɛtr] §42, §97 *tr* to omit
omission [ɔmisjɔ̃] *f* omission
omnibus [ɔmnibys] *adj* omnibus; local (*train*) ‖ *m* omnibus; local (train)
omnipo·tent [ɔmnipɔtɑ̃] **-tente** [tɑ̃t] *adj* omnipotent
omnis·cient [ɔmnisjɑ̃] **-ciente** [sjɑ̃t] *adj* omniscient
omnium [ɔmnjɔm] *m* (com) holding company, general trading company; (sports) open race
omnivore [ɔmnivɔr] *adj* omnivorous
omoplate [ɔmɔplat] *f* shoulder blade
on [ɔ̃] §87 *pron indef* one, they, people; (coll) we, e.g., **y va-t-on?** are we going there?; (coll) I, e.g., **on est fatigué** I am tired; (often translated by passive forms), e.g., **on sait que** it is generally known that
once [ɔ̃s] *f* ounce
oncle [ɔ̃kl] *m* uncle
onction [ɔ̃ksjɔ̃] *f* unction; eloquence

onc·tueux [ɔ̃ktɥø] **-tueuse** [tɥøz] *adj* unctuous; greasy; bland

onde [ɔ̃d] *f* wave; watering (*of silk*); (poetic) water; **les petites ondes** (rad) shortwave; **mettre en ondes** to put on the air; **onde de choc** (aer) shock wave; **onde porteuse** (rad) carrier wave; **ondes amorties** (rad) damped waves; **ondes entretenues** (rad) continuous waves; **ondes radiophoniques** airwaves; **onde sonore** sound wave

ondée [ɔ̃de] *f* shower

on-dit [ɔ̃di] *m invar* gossip, scuttlebutt

on·doyant [ɔ̃dwajɑ̃] **-doyante** [dwajɑ̃t] *adj* undulating, wavy; wavering (*person*)

ondoyer [ɔ̃dwaje] §47 *tr* to baptize in an emergency ‖ *intr* to undulate, wave

ondulation [ɔ̃dylɑsjɔ̃] *f* undulation, waving; flowing (*e.g., of drapery*); wave (*of hair*); **à ondulations** rolling (*ground*); **ondulation permanente** permanent wave

ondu·lé -lée [ɔ̃dyle] *adj* wavy; corrugated

onduler [ɔ̃dyle] *tr* to wave (*hair*) ‖ *intr* to wave, undulate

oné·reux [ɔnerø] **-reuse** [røz] *adj* onerous

ongle [ɔ̃gl] *m* nail, fingernail; **jusqu'au bout des ongles** to or at one's fingertips; **ongle des pieds** toenail

onglée [ɔ̃gle] *f* numbness in the fingertips

onglet [ɔ̃glɛ] *m* nail hole, groove (*in blade*); thimble; **à onglets** thumb-indexed; **monter sur onglet** (bb) to insert (*a page*)

onguent [ɔ̃gɑ̃] *m* ointment, salve

ont [ɔ̃] *v* see **avoir**

O.N.U. [ɔny] (acronym) or [ɔɛny] (letterword) *f* (**Organisation des Nations Unies**) UN

onu·sien [ɔnyzjɛ̃] **-sienne** [zjɛn] *adj* UN

onyx [ɔniks] *m* onyx

onzain *[ɔ̃zɛ̃] m* eleven-line verse

onze *[ɔ̃z]* §94 *adj & pron* eleven; the Eleventh, e.g., **Jean onze** John the Eleventh; **onze heures** eleven o'clock ‖ *m* eleven; eleventh (*in dates*), e.g., **le onze mai** the eleventh of May

onzième *[ɔ̃zjɛm]* §94 *adj, pron (masc, fem), & m* eleventh

opale [ɔpal] *f* opal

opaque [ɔpak] *adj* opaque

O.P.E.P. [ɔpɛp] *f* (acronym) (**organisation des pays exportateurs de pétrole**) OPEC

opéra [ɔpera] *m* opera; opera house; **grand opéra, opéra sérieux** grand opera; **opéra bouffe** comic opera, opéra bouffe

opéra-comique [ɔperakɔmik] *m (pl* **opéras-comiques**) light opera

opéra·teur [ɔperatœr] **-trice** [tris] *mf* operator; **opérateur de permanence** operator on duty ‖ *m* cameraman

opération [ɔperɑsjɔ̃] *f* operation; **opérations à terme** (com) futures; **opération test** exploratory operation

opé·ré -rée [ɔpere] *mf* surgical patient

opérer [ɔpere] §10 *tr* to operate on; **opérer à chaud** to perform an emergency operation on (*s.o.*); **opérer qn de q.ch.** (med) to operate on s.o. for s.th. ‖ *intr* to operate; work ‖ *ref* to occur, take place

opérette [ɔperɛt] *f* operetta, musical comedy

opia·cé -cée [ɔpjase] *adj* opiate

opiner [ɔpine] *intr* to opine; **opiner du bonnet** (coll) to be a yes man

opiniâtre [ɔpinjɑtr] *adj* stubborn

opiniâtreté [ɔpinjɑtrəte] *f* stubbornness

opinion [ɔpinjɔ̃] *f* opinion; public opinion; **avoir bonne opinion de** to think highly of; **avoir une piètre opinion de** to take a dim view of

opium [ɔpjɔm] *m* opium

oponce [ɔpɔ̃s] *m* prickly pear

opossum [ɔpɔsɔm] *m* opossum

oppor·tun [ɔpɔrtœ̃] **-tune** [tyn] *adj* opportune, timely, expedient

opportuniste [ɔpɔrtynist] *adj* opportunistic *mf* opportunist

opportunité [ɔpɔrtynite] *f* opportuneness, timeliness; appropriateness

oppo·sant [ɔpozɑ̃] **-sante** [zɑ̃t] *adj* opposing ‖ *mf* opponent

oppo·sé -sée [ɔpoze] §92 *adj & m* opposite, contrary; **à l'opposé de** contrary to

opposer [ɔpoze] *tr* to raise (*an objection*); **opposer q.ch. à** to set up s.th. against; place s.th. opposite; contrast s.th. with ‖ *ref*—**s'opposer à** to oppose, object to

opposite [ɔpozit] *m*—**à l'opposite (de)** opposite

opposition [ɔpozisjɔ̃] *f* opposition; contrast

oppresser [ɔprese] *tr* to oppress; impede (*respiration*); weigh upon (*one's heart*)

oppresseur [ɔpresœr] *m* oppressor

oppres·sif [ɔpresif] **-sive** [siv] *adj* oppressive

oppression [ɔpresjɔ̃] *f* oppression; difficulty in breathing

opprimer [ɔprime] *tr* to oppress

opprobre [ɔprobr] *m* opprobrium, shame

opter [ɔpte] *intr* to opt, choose

opticien [ɔptisjɛ̃] *m* optician

optimisme [ɔptimism] *m* optimism

optimiste [ɔptimist] *adj* optimistic ‖ *mf* optimist

option [ɔpsjɔ̃] *f* option

optique [ɔptik] *adj* optic(al) ‖ *f* optics; perspective; **sous cette optique** from that point of view

opu·lent [ɔpylɑ̃] **-lente** [lɑ̃t] *adj* opulent

opuscule [ɔpyskyl] *m* opuscule, treatise; brochure, pamphlet

or [ɔr] *m* gold; **rouler sur l'or** to be rolling in money ‖ *adv* now; therefore

oracle [ɔrakl] *m* oracle

orage [ɔraʒ] *m* storm

ora·geux [ɔraʒø] **-geuse** [ʒøz] *adj* stormy

oraison [ɔrɛzɔ̃] *f* prayer; **oraison dominicale** Lord's Prayer; **oraison funèbre** funeral oration; **prononcer l'oraison funèbre de** (coll) to write off (*a custom, institution, etc.*)

o·ral -rale [ɔral] *adj (pl* **-raux** [ro]) oral

orange [ɔrɑ̃ʒ] *adj invar* orange (*color*) ‖ *m* orange (*color*) ‖ *f* orange (*fruit*)

oran·gé -gée [ɔrɑ̃ʒe] *adj & m* orange (*color*)

orangeade [ɔrɑ̃ʒad] *f* orangeade

oranger [ɔrɑ̃ʒe] *m* orange tree

orangeraie [ɔrɑ̃ʒrɛ] *f* orange grove

orangerie [ɔrɑ̃ʒri] *f* orangery; orange grove

orang-outan [ɔrɑ̃utɑ̃] *m* (*pl* **orangs-outans**) orang-outan

ora·teur [ɔratœr] **-trice** [tris] *mf* orator; speaker

oratoire [ɔratwar] *adj* oratorical ‖ *m* (eccl) oratory

oratorio [ɔratɔrjo] *m* oratorio

orbite [ɔrbit] *f* orbit; socket (*of eye*); **placer sur son orbite, mettre en orbite** to orbit; **sur orbite** in orbit

orchestre [ɔrkɛstr] *m* orchestra; band; **orchestre de typique** rumba band

orchestrer [ɔrkɛstre] *tr* to orchestrate

orchidée [ɔrkide] *f* orchid

ordalie [ɔrdali] *f* (hist) ordeal

ordinaire [ɔrdinɛr] *adj* ordinary ‖ *m* ordinary; regular bill of fare; (mil) mess; **d'ordinaire, à l'ordinaire** ordinarily

ordi·nal -nale [ɔrdinal] *adj* & *m* (*pl* **-naux** [no]) ordinal

ordinateur [ɔrdinatœr] *m* (comp) computer; **fait à l'ordinateur** computerized; **mettre sur ordinateur** to computerize; **mise sur ordinateur** computerization; **ordinateur de poche** pocket computer; **ordinateur domestique, ordinateur familial, ordinateur maison** home computer

ordination [ɔrdinasjɔ̃] *f* ordination

ordonnance [ɔrdɔnɑ̃s] *f* ordinance; order, arrangement; (pharm) prescription

ordonna·teur [ɔrdɔnatœr] **-trice** [tris] *mf* organizer; marshal; **ordonnateur des pompes funèbres** funeral director

ordon·né -née [ɔrdɔne] *adj* orderly

ordonner [ɔrdɔne] §97, §98 *tr* to arrange, put in order; order; prescribe (*e.g., medicine*); (eccl) to ordain; **ordonner à qn de** + *inf* to order s.o. to + *inf;* **ordonner q.ch. à qn** to order s.o. to do s.th.

ordre [ɔrdr] *m* order; **avoir de l'ordre** to be neat, orderly; **à vos ordres** at your service; **dans l'ordre d'entrée en scène** (theat) in order of appearance; **en ordre** in order; **jusqu'à nouvel ordre** until further notice; as things stand; **les ordres** (eccl) orders; **ordre du jour** (mil) order of the day; (parl) agenda; **ordre public** law and order; **payez à l'ordre de** (com) pay to the order of; **sous les ordres de** under the command of

ordure [ɔrdyr] *f* rubbish, filth; **ordures ménagères** garbage

ordu·rier [ɔrdyrje] **-rière** [rjɛr] *adj* lewd, filthy

orée [ɔre] *f* edge (*of a forest*)

oreille [ɔrɛj] *f* ear; **avoir l'oreille basse** to be humiliated; **dormir sur les deux oreilles** to sleep soundly; **dresser** or **tendre l'oreille** to prick up one's ears; **échauffer les oreilles à qn** to rile s.o. up; **faire la sourde oreille** to turn a deaf ear; **rompre les oreilles à qn** (coll) to talk s.o.'s head off; **se faire tirer l'oreille** (coll) to play hard to get

oreiller [ɔreje] *m* pillow

oreillette [ɔrɛjɛt] *f* earflap (*of cap*); (anat) auricle

oreillons [ɔrɛjɔ̃] *mpl* mumps

ores [ɔr] *adv*—**d'ores et déjà** [dɔrzedeʒa] from now on

Orfée [ɔrfe] *m* Orpheus

orfèvre [ɔrfɛvr] *m* goldsmith; silversmith; **être orfèvre en la matière** (coll) to know one's onions

orfèvrerie [ɔrfɛvrəri] *f* goldsmith's shop; goldsmith's trade; gold plate; gold or silver jewelry

orfraie [ɔrfrɛ] *f* osprey, fish hawk

organdi [ɔrgɑ̃di] *m* organdy

organe [ɔrgan] *m* organ; part (*of a machine*)

organique [ɔrganik] *adj* organic

organisa·teur [ɔrganizatœr] **-trice** [tris] *adj* organizing ‖ *mf* organizer

organisation [ɔrganizɑsjɔ̃] *f* organization

organiser [ɔrganize] *tr* to organize

organisme [ɔrganism] *m* organism; organization

organiste [ɔrganist] *mf* organist

orgasme [ɔrgasm] *m* orgasm

orge [ɔrʒ] *f* barley

orgelet [ɔrʒəlɛ] *m* (pathol) sty

orgie [ɔrʒi] *f* orgy

orgue [ɔrg] *m* organ; **orgue de Barbarie** hand organ; **orgue de cinéma** theater organ ‖ *f*—**les grandes orgues** the pipe organ

orgueil [ɔrgœj] *m* pride, conceit; **avoir l'orgueil de** to take pride in

orgueil·leux [ɔrgœjø] **-leuse** [jøz] *adj* proud, haughty

orient [ɔrjɑ̃] *m* orient; east; **Orient** Orient, East

orien·tal -tale [ɔrjɑ̃tal] (*pl* **-taux** [to]) *adj* oriental; eastern, east ‖ (*cap*) *mf* Oriental (*person*)

orientation [ɔrjɑ̃tɑsjɔ̃] *f* orientation; **orientation professionnelle** vocational guidance

orienter [ɔrjɑ̃te] *tr* to orient; guide ‖ *ref* to take one's bearings

orien·teur [ɔrjɑ̃tœr] **-teuse** [tøz] *mf* guidance counselor

orifice [ɔrifis] *m* orifice, hole, opening

origan [ɔrigɑ̃] *m* marjoram

originaire [ɔriʒinɛr] *adj* native; original, first

origi·nal -nale [ɔriʒinal] *adj* (*pl* **-naux** [no]) original; eccentric, peculiar ‖ *m* antique (*piece of furniture*); eccentric, card (*person*); (typ) copy, original

originalité [ɔriʒinalite] *f* originality; eccentricity

origine [ɔriʒin] *f* origin

origi·nel -nelle [ɔriʒinɛl] *adj* original (*sin; meaning*); primitive, early

ori·gnal [ɔriɲal] *m* (*pl* **-gnaux** [ɲo]) moose, elk

orillon [ɔrijɔ̃] *m* ear, handle; (archit) projection

ori·peau [ɔripo] *m* (*pl* **-peaux**) tinsel; **oripeaux** cheap finery

Orléans [ɔrleɑ̃] *f* Orléans; **la Nouvelle Orléans** New Orleans
orme [ɔrm] *m* elm; **attendez-moi sous l'orme** (coll) I won't be there
or·né -née [ɔrne] *adj* ornate
ornement [ɔrnəmɑ̃] *m* ornament
ornemen·tal -tale [ɔrnəmɑ̃tal] *adj* (*pl* **-taux** [to]) ornamental
orner [ɔrne] *tr* to ornament, adorn
ornière [ɔrnjɛr] *f* rut, groove
ornithologie [ɔrnitɔlɔʒi] *f* ornithology
orphe·lin [ɔrfəlɛ̃] **-line** [lin] *adj & mf* orphan
orphelinat [ɔrfəlina] *m* orphanage (*asylum*)
orphéon [ɔrfeɔ̃] *m* male choir, glee club; brass band
orteil [ɔrtɛj] *m* toe; **big toe**; **gros orteil** big toe
O.R.T.F. [oɛrteɛf] *m* (letterword) (**Office de radio-télévision française**) French radio and television system
orthodoxe [ɔrtɔdɔks] *adj* orthodox
orthographe [ɔrtɔgraf] *f* spelling, orthography
orthographier [ɔrtɔgrafje] *tr* to spell
ortie [ɔrti] *f* nettle
orviétan [ɔrvjetɑ̃] *m* nostrum
O.S. [oɛs] *f* (letterword) (**ouvrière spécialisée**) specialist
os [ɔs] *m* (*pl* **os** [o]) bone; **à gros os** big-boned; **os à moelle** marrowbone; **tomber sur un os** (coll) to meet up with a problem; **trempé jusqu'aux os** soaked to the skin
osciller [ɔsile] *intr* to oscillate; waver, hesitate
o·sé -sée [oze] *adj* daring, bold; risqué, off-color
oseille [ozɛj] *f* sorrel; (slang) dough
oser [oze] §95 *tr & intr* to dare
osier [ozje] *m* osier; **d'osier** wicker
osmose [ɔsmoz] *f* osmosis
ossature [ɔsatyr] *f* bone structure; framework, skeleton
ossements [ɔsmɑ̃] *mpl* bones, remains
os·seux -seuse [ɔsø] **-seuse** [søz] *adj* bony
ossifier [ɔsifje] *tr & ref* to ossify
os·su -sue [ɔsy] *adj* bony; big-boned
ostensible [ɔstɑ̃sibl] *adj* conspicuous, ostensible; ostentatious
ostensoir [ɔstɑ̃swar] *m* monstrance
ostentatoire [ɔstɑ̃tatwar] *adj* ostentatious
ostracisme [ɔstrasism] *m* ostracism
otage [ɔtaʒ] *m* hostage
otalgie [ɔtalʒi] *f* earache
O.T.A.N. or **OTAN** [ɔtan], [otan], [otɑ̃] *f* (acronym) (**Organisation du traité de l'Atlantique Nord**)—**l'O.T.A.N.** NATO
otarie [ɔtari] *f* sea lion
OTASE [ɔtaz] *f* (acronym) (**Organisation du traité de l'Asie du Sud-Est**)—**l'OTASE** SEATO
ôter [ote] *tr* to remove, take away; take off; tip (*one's hat*); **ôter q.ch. à qn** to remove or take away s.th. from s.o.; **ôter q.ch.**

de q.ch. to take s.th. away from s.th. ‖ *ref* to withdraw, get out of the way
otto·man [ɔtɔmɑ̃] **-mane** [man] *adj* Ottoman ‖ *m* ottoman (*corded fabric*) ‖ *f* ottoman (*divan*) ‖ (*cap*) *mf* Ottoman (*person*)
ou [u] *conj* or; **ou . . . ou** either . . . or
où [u] *adv* where; **d'où** from where, whence; **où que** wherever; **par où** which way ‖ *conj* where; when; **d'où** from where, whence; **par où** through which; **partout où** wherever
ouailles [waj] *fpl* (eccl) flock
ouais [wɛ] *interj* (coll) oh yeah!
ouate *[wat] f* cotton batting, wadding
ouater *[wate] tr* to pad, wad
oubli [ubli] *m* forgetfulness; omission, oversight; **tomber dans l'oubli** to fall into oblivion
oublier [ublije] §97 *tr & intr* to forget ‖ *ref* to forget oneself; be forgotten
oubliettes [ublijɛt] *fpl* dungeon of oblivion
ou·blieux [ublijø] **-blieuse** [blijøz] *adj* forgetful, oblivious, unmindful
ouche [uʃ] *f* orchard; vegetable garden
ouest [wɛst] *adj invar* west, western ‖ *m* west; **de l'ouest** western; **faire l'ouest** to steer westward; **vers l'ouest** westward
ouest-alle·mand [wɛstalmɑ̃] **-mande** [mɑ̃d] *adj* West German ‖ (*cap*) *mf* West German
ouf *[uf] interj* whew!
oui *[wi] m invar* yes; **les oui l'emportent** the ayes have it ‖ *adv* yes; **je crois que oui** I think so; **oui madame** yes ma'am; **oui monsieur** yes sir; **oui mon capitaine** (**mon général**, etc.) yes sir
ouï-dire [widir] *m invar* hearsay; **simples ouï-dire** (law) hearsay evidence
ouïe [wi] *f* hearing; **être tout ouïe** [tutwi] to be all ears; **ouïs** gills; sound holes (*of violin*) ‖ *interj* oh my!
ouïr [wir] §95 (used only in: *inf*, compound tenses with *pp* **ouï**, and 2d *pl impv* **oyez**) *tr* to hear; **oyez . . . !** hear ye . . . !
ouragan [uragɑ̃] *m* hurricane
ourdir [urdir] *tr* to warp (*cloth before weaving*); hatch (*e.g., a plot*)
ourler [urle] *tr* to hem; **ourler à jour** to hemstitch
ourlet [urlɛ] *m* hem; **ourlet de la jupe** hemline
ours [urs] *m* bear; (fig) lone wolf; **ours en peluche** teddy bear; **ours mal léché** unmannerly bear; **ours marin** (zool) seal; **vendre la peau de l'ours avant de l'avoir tué** to count one's chickens before they are hatched
ourse [urs] *f* she-bear; **la Grande Ourse** the Great Bear; **la Petite Ourse** the Little Bear
oursin [ursɛ̃] *m* sea urchin
ourson [ursɔ̃] *m* bear cub
ouste [ust] *interj* (coll) out!, out you go!
outarde [utard] *f* (orn) bustard
outil [uti] *m* tool, implement

outillage [utijaʒ] *m* tools; equipment

outil·lé -lée [utije] *adj* equipped with tools; tooled-up (*factory*)

outiller [utije] *tr* to equip with tools; tool up (*a factory*) ‖ *ref* to supply oneself with equipment; tool up

outilleur [utijœr] *m* toolmaker

outrage [utraʒ] *m* outrage, affront; ravages (*of time*); contempt of court; **faire outrage à qn** to outrage s.o.; **outrage aux bonnes mœurs** traffic in pornography; **outrage public à la pudeur** indecent exposure

outrager [utraʒe] §38 *tr* to outrage, affront

outra·geux [utraʒø] **-geuse** [ʒøz] *adj* outrageous, insulting

outrance [utrãs] *f* excess; exaggeration; **à outrance** to the limit

outran·cier [utrãsje] **-cière** [sjɛr] *adj* extreme, excessive, out-and-out ‖ *mf* extremist, out-and-outer

outre [utr] *f* goatskin canteen ‖ *adv* further; **d'outre en d'outre** right through; **en outre** besides, moreover; **passer outre à** to ignore (*e.g., an order*) ‖ *prep* in addition to, apart from; beyond

ou·tré -trée [utre] *adj* overdone, exaggerated; exasperated

outrecui·dant [utrəkɥidã] **-dante** [dãt] *adj* self-satisfied; insolent, presumptuous

outre-Manche [utrəmãʃ] *adv* across the Channel

outremer [utrəmɛr] *m* ultramarine, lapis lazuli (*color*)

outre-mer [utrəmɛr] *adv* overseas

outre-monts [utrəmɔ̃] *adv* over the mountains (*i.e., the Alps*)

outrepasser [utrəpɑse] *tr* to go beyond, to exceed

outrer [utre] *tr* to overdo, exaggerate; exasperate

outre-tombe [utrətɔ̃b] *adv*—**d'outre-tombe** posthumous

ou·vert [uvɛr] **-verte** [vɛrt] *adj* open; exposed; frank, candid; on (*said of meter, gas, etc.*); ‖ *v* see **ouvrir**

ouverture [uvɛrtyr] *f* opening; hole, gap; (mus) overture; (phot) aperture; **ouverture en fondu** (mov) fade-in

ouvrable [uvrabl] *adj* working, e.g., **jour ouvrable** working day

ouvrage [uvraʒ] *m* work, handiwork; piece of work; work, treatise

ouvrager [uvraʒe] §38 *tr* to work (*e.g., iron*); turn (*wood*)

ou·vré -vrée [uvre] *adj* worked, wrought; finished (*product*)

ouvre-boîtes [uvrəbwat] *m invar* can opener

ouvre-bouteilles [uvrəbutɛj] *m invar* bottle opener

ouvreur [uvrœr] *m* opener (*in poker*)

ouvreuse [uvrøz] *f* usher

ou·vrier [uvrije] **-vrière** [vrijɛr] *adj* working, worker; worker's, workingman's ‖ *mf* worker ‖ *m* workman, laborer; workingman ‖ *f* workingwoman

ouvrir [uvrir] §65 *tr* to open; turn on (*the light; the radio or television; the gas*); **ouvrir boutique** to set up shop ‖ *intr* to be open; open (*said of store, school, etc.; said of card player*) ‖ *ref* to open; be opened; **s'ouvrir à** to open up to, confide in

ouvroir [uvrwar] *m* workroom

ovaire [ovɛr] *m* ovary

ovale [oval] *adj & m* oval

ovation [ovasjɔ̃] *f* ovation

ovationner [ovasjone] *tr* to give an ovation to

Ovide [ovid] *m* Ovid

O.V.N.I. [ovni] *m* (acronym) (**objet volant non-identifié**) UFO

oxford [oksfor] *m* oxford cloth

oxycarbonisme [oksikarbonism] *m* carbon-monoxide poisoning

oxyde [oksid] *m* oxide

oxyder [okside] *tr & ref* to oxidize

oxygène [oksiʒɛn] *m* oxygen

oxygéner [oksiʒene] §10 *tr* to oxygenate; bleach (*hair*) ‖ *ref*—**s'oxygéner les poumons** (coll) to fill one's lungs full of ozone

oxyton [oksitɔ̃] *adj & m* oxytone

ozone [ozon] *m* ozone

P

P, p [pe] *m invar* sixteenth letter of the French alphabet

pacage [pakaʒ] *m* pasture

pacifica·teur [pasifikatœr] **-trice** [tris] *mf* pacifier

pacifier [pasifje] *tr* to pacify

pacifique [pasifik] *adj* pacific ‖ **Pacifique** *adj & m* Pacific

pacifisme [pasifism] *m* pacifism

pacifiste [pasifist] *mf* pacifist

pacotille [pakɔtij] *f* junk; **de pacotille** shoddy; junky

pacte [pakt] *m* pact, covenant

pactiser [paktize] *intr* to compromise; traffic (*with the enemy*)

paf [paf] *adj* (slang) tipsy, tight ‖ *interj* bang!

pagaie [pagɛ] *f* paddle

pagaïe or **pagaille** [pagaj] *f* disorder; **en**

pagaïe (coll) in great quantity; (coll) in a mess

paganisme [paganism] *m* paganism

pagayer [pageje] §49 *tr & intr* to paddle

page [paʒ] *m* page ‖ *f* page (*of a book*); **être à la page** to be up to date

paginer [paʒine] *tr* to page

pagne [paɲ] *m* loincloth

paie [pɛ] *f* pay, wages

paiement [pɛmɑ̃] *m* payment

païen [pajɛ̃] **païenne** [pajɛn] *adj & mf* pagan

pail·lard [pajar] **-larde** [jard] *adj* ribald ‖ *mf* debauchee

paillasse [pajas] *m* buffoon ‖ *f* straw mattress; (slang) whore

paillasson [pajasɔ̃] *m* doormat

paille [pɑj] *f* straw; flaw; (Bib) mote; **paille de fer** iron shavings

pail·lé -lée [pɑje] *adj* rush-bottomed (*chair*)

pailler [pɑje] *m* straw stack ‖ *tr* to bottom (*a chair*) with straw; mulch

pailleter [pajte] §34 *tr* to spangle

paillette [pajɛt] *f* spangle; flake (*of mica; of soap*); grain (*of gold*); flaw (*in a diamond*)

pain [pɛ̃] *m* bread; loaf (*of bread, of sugar*); cake (*of soap*); pat (*of butter*); **avoir du pain sur la planche** (coll) to have a lot to do; **pain à cacheter** sealing wafer; **pain aux raisins** raisin roll; **pain bis** brown bread; **pain complet** whole-wheat bread; **pain de fantaisie** bread sold by the loaf (*instead of by weight*); **pain de mie** sandwich bread; **pain d'épice** gingerbread; **pain grillé** toast; **pain perdu** French toast; **petit pain** roll; **se vendre comme des petits pains** (coll) to sell like hot cakes

pair paire [pɛr] *adj* even (*number*) ‖ *m* peer; equal; (com) par; **hors de pair, hors pair** unrivaled; **marcher de pair avec** to keep abreast of; **travailler au pair** (coll) to work for one's keep; **au pair** at par ‖ *f* pair; couple; brace (*of dogs, pistols, etc.*); yoke (*of oxen*)

pairesse [pɛrɛs] *f* peeress

pairie [pɛri], [peri] *f* peerage

pais [pe] *v* (**paît**) see **paître**

paisible [pezibl] *adj* peaceful

paître [pɛtr] §48 *tr & intr* to graze; **envoyer paître** (coll) to send packing

paix [pɛ] *f* peace

Pakistan [pakistɑ̃] *m*—**le Pakistan** Pakistan

pakista·nais [pakistanɛ] **-naise** [nɛz] *adj* Pakistani ‖ (*cap*) *mf* Pakistani

pal [pal] *m* (*pl* **paux** [po] or **pals**) pale, stake

palabre [palabr] *m & f* palaver

palace [palas] *m* luxury hotel

palais [palɛ] *m* palace; palate; courthouse, law courts

palan [palɑ̃] *m* block and tackle

palanque [palɑ̃k] *f* stockade

pala·tal -tale [palatal] (*pl* **-taux** [to] **-tales**) *adj & f* palatal

pale [pal] *f* blade (*of, e.g., oar*); stake; sluice gate; (eccl) pall

pâle [pɑl] *adj* pale

palefrenier [palfrənje] *m* groom; (coll) hick, oaf

palefroi [palfrwa] *m* palfrey

paleron [palrɔ̃] *m* bottom chuck roast

palet [palɛ] *m* disk, flat stone; puck

paletot [palto] *m* topcoat

palette [palɛt] *f* palette; paddle

pâleur [palœr] *f* pallor; paleness

palier [palje] *m* landing (*of stairs*); plateau (*of curve of a graph*); (mach) bearing; **en palier** on the level; **palier à billes** ball bearing; **par paliers** graduated (*e.g., tax*); in stages

pâlir [palir] *tr & intr* to pale, turn pale

palis [pali] *m* picket fence

palissade [palisad] *f* palisade; fence

palissandre [palisɑ̃dr] *m* rosewood

pallier [palje] *tr* to palliate ‖ *intr*—**pallier à** to mitigate

palmarès [palmarɛs] *m* list of winners; hit parade

palme [palm] *f* (bot) palm; **palmes** fins (*for swimming*)

palmeraie [palmərɛ] *f* palm grove

palmier [palmje] *m* palm tree

palmipède [palmipɛd] *adj* webfooted ‖ *m* webfoot

palombe [palɔ̃b] *f* ringdove

palourde [palurd] *f* clam

palpable [palpabl] *adj* palpable; plain, obvious

palper [palpe] *tr* to feel; palpate; (coll) to pocket (*money*)

palpiter [palpite] *intr* to palpitate

palsambleu [palsɑ̃blø] *interj* zounds!

paltoquet [paltɔkɛ] *m* nonentity

palu·déen [palydeɛ̃] **-déenne** [deɛn] *adj* marsh (*plant*); swamp (*fever*)

paludisme [palydism] *m* malaria

pâmer [pɑme] *ref* to swoon

pâmoison [pɑmwazɔ̃] *f* swoon

pamphlet [pɑ̃flɛ] *m* lampoon

pamplemousse [pɑ̃pləmus] *m & f* grapefruit

pan [pɑ̃] *m* tail (*of shirt or coat*); section; side, face; patch (*of sky*); **Pan** Pan ‖ *interj* bang!

panacée [panase] *f* panacea

panachage [panaʃaʒ] *m* mixing; **faire du panachage** to split one's vote

panache [panaʃ] *m* plume; wreath (*of smoke*); **aimer le panache** to be fond of show; **avoir son panache** (coll) to be tipsy; **faire panache** to somersault, turn over

pana·ché -chée [panaʃe] *adj* variegated; mixed (*salad*); motley (*crowd*)

panacher [panaʃe] *tr* to variegate; plume; split (*one's vote*) ‖ *ref* to become variegated

panais [panɛ] *m* parsnip

panama [panama] *m* panama hat; **le Panama** Panama; **Panama** Panama City

panaris [panari] *m* (pathol) whitlow, felon

pancarte [pɑ̃kart] *f* placard; poster, sign

panchromatique [pɑ̃krɔmatik] *adj* panchromatic

pancréas [pɑ̃kreas] *m* pancreas

pandémonium [pɑ̃demɔnjɔm] *m* den of iniquity; pandemonium
pa·né -née [pane] *adj* breaded
panetière [pantjɛr] *f* breadbox
panier [panje] *m* basket; hoop (*of skirt*); creel (*trap*); **être dans le même panier** to be in the same boat; **panier à ouvrage** work basket; **panier à papier** wastepaper basket; **panier à provisions** shopping basket; **panier à salade** wire salad washer; (coll) paddy wagon; **panier percé** spendthrift
panier-repas [panjerəpɑ] *m* (*pl* **paniers-repas**) box lunch
panique [panik] *adj* & *f* panic
panne [pan] *f* breakdown, trouble; plush; fat (*of pig*); peen (*of hammer*); tip (*of soldering iron*); bank (*of clouds*); purlin (*of roof*); daub; (theat) small part; **(en) panne sèche** (*public sign*) out of gas; **être dans la panne** (coll) to be hard up; **être en panne** (coll) to be unable to continue; **être en panne de** (coll) to be deprived of; **laisser en panne** to leave in the lurch; **mettre en panne** (naut) to heave to; **panne fendue** claw (*of hammer*); **rester en panne** to come to a standstill; **tomber en panne** to have a breakdown
pan·né -née [pane] *adj* (slang) hard up
pan·neau [pano] *m* (*pl* **-neaux**) panel; snare, net; **condamner les panneaux** (naut) to batten down the hatches; **donner dans le panneau** to walk into the trap; **panneau d'affichage** billboard; **panneau de tête** headboard (*of bed*); **panneaux** paneling; **panneaux de signalisation** traffic signs; **tomber** or **donner dans le panneau** to be taken in, to fall into a trap
panoplie [panɔpli] *f* panoply
panorama [panɔrama] *m* panorama
panoramiquer [panɔramike] *intr* (mov, telv) to pan
panse [pɑ̃s] *f* belly; rumen, first stomach
pansement [pɑ̃smɑ̃] *m* (surg) dressing
panser [pɑ̃se] *tr* to dress, bandage; groom (*an animal*)
pan·su -sue [pɑ̃sy] *adj* potbellied
pantalon [pɑ̃talɔ̃] *m* trousers, pair of trousers; panties; slacks; **pantalon à pattes d'éléphant** bell-bottomed trousers; **pantalon corsaire** pedal pushers; **pantalon de coutil** ducks; blue jeans; **pantalon de golf** knickers; **pantalon de ski** ski pants
pante [pɑ̃t] *m* (slang) guy
panteler [pɑ̃tle] §34 *intr* to pant
panthéisme [pɑ̃teism] *m* pantheism
panthéon [pɑ̃teɔ̃] *m* pantheon
panthère [pɑ̃tɛr] *f* panther
pantin [pɑ̃tɛ̃] *m* puppet; jumping jack; **pantin articulé** string puppet
pantois [pɑ̃twa] *adj* flabbergasted
pantomime [pɑ̃tɔmim] *f* pantomime
pantou·flard [pɑ̃tuflar] **-flarde** [flard] *mf* (coll) homebody
pantoufle [pɑ̃tufl] *f* slipper
pantoufler [pɑ̃tufle] *intr* to leave government service

paon [pɑ̃] *m* peacock, peafowl; peacock butterfly
paonne [pan] *f* peahen
papa [papa] *m* papa; **à la papa** (coll) cautiously; **de papa** (coll) outmoded; **papa gâteau** (coll) sugar daddy
papas [papɑs] *m* pope (*in Orthodox Church*)
papauté [papote] *f* papacy
pape [pap] *m* pope
pape·lard [paplar] **-larde** [lard] *adj* hypocritical ‖ *mf* hypocrite ‖ *m* scrap of paper
paperasse [papras] *f* old paper
paperasserie [paprasri] *f* red tape
paperas·sier [paprasje] **-sière** [sjɛr] *adj* fond of red tape ‖ *mf* bureaucrat
papeterie [paptri] *f* paper mill; stationery store
pape·tier [paptje] **-tière** [tjɛr] *mf* stationer
papier [papje] *m* paper; newspaper article; document; piece of paper; **être dans les petits papiers de** (coll) to be in the good graces of; **gratter du papier** to scribble; **papier à calquer, papier végétal** tracing paper; **papier à en-tête** letterhead (stationery); **papier à lettres** writing paper; **papier alu** aluminum foil; **papier à machine** typewriter paper; **papier à musique** staff paper; **papier bible, indien,** or **pelure** Bible paper, onionskin; **papier buvard** blotting paper; **papier carbone** carbon paper; **papier collant** Scotch tape; **papier d'emballage** wrapping paper; **papier de soie** tissue paper; **papier d'étain** tin foil; **papier de verre** sandpaper; **papier fort** cardboard; **papier hygiénique** toilet paper; **papier journal** newsprint; **papier kraft** cardboard (*for packing*); **papier mâché** papier-mâché; **papier ministre** foolscap; **papier paraffiné** wax paper; **papier peint** wallpaper; **papier rayé** lined paper; **papiers** (*public sign*) waste paper; **papier sensible** photographic paper; **papier tue-mouches** flypaper; **rayez cela de vos papiers!** (coll) don't count on it!
papier-filtre [papjefiltrə] *m* filter paper
papier-monnaie [papjemɔnɛ] *m* paper money
papier-pierre [papjepjɛr] *m* (*pl* **papiers-pierre**) papier-mâché
papille [papij], [papil] *f* papilla; **papille gustative** taste bud
papillon [papijɔ̃] *m* butterfly; flier, handbill; inset; form, application; thumbscrew, wing nut; butterfly valve; rider (*to document*); (coll) parking ticket; **papillon de nuit** moth; **papillons noirs** gloomy thoughts
papillonner [papijɔne] *intr* to flit about
papillote [papijɔt] *f* curlpaper; (culin) paper wrapper
papilloter [papijɔte] *intr* to blink; to flicker
papoter [papɔte] *intr* to chitchat
paprika [paprika] *m* paprika
papyrus [papirys] *m* papyrus
pâque [pɑk] *f* Passover; **la pâque russe** Russian Easter; **Pâque** Passover
paquebot [pakbo] *m* liner

pâquerette [pakrɛt] *f* white daisy

Pâques [pak] *m* Easter ‖ *fpl* Easter; **faire ses pâques** or **Pâques** to take Easter Communion; **Pâques fleuries** Palm Sunday

paquet [pakɛ] *m* packet, bundle; package; parcel; pack (*of cigarettes*); dressing down; **être un paquet d'os** [dɔs] to be nothing but skin and bones; **faire son paquet** (coll) to pack up; **mettre le paquet** (coll) to shoot the works; **paquet de mer** heavy sea; **petit paquet** parcel (*under a kilogram*); **petits paquets** parcel post; **un paquet de** a lot of

paquetage [paktaʒ] (comp) batch

par [par] *prep* by; through; out of, e.g., **par la fenêtre** out of the window; per, a, e.g., **huit dollars par jour** eight dollars per day, eight dollars a day; on, e.g., **par une belle matinée** on a beautiful morning; in, e.g., **par temps de brume** in foggy weather; **de par la loi** in the name of the law; **par avion** (*formula on envelope*) air mail; **par delà** beyond; **par derrière** at the back, the back way; **par devant** in front, before; **par exemple** for example; **par ici** this way; **par là** that way; **par où?** which way?

para [para] *m* (coll) paratrooper

parabole [parabɔl] *f* parable; (*curve*) parabola

parachever [paraʃve] §2 *tr* to finish off

parachutage [paraʃytaʒ] *m* airdrop, airdropping

parachute [paraʃyt] *m* parachute

parachuter [paraʃyte] *tr* to airdrop; (coll) to appoint in haste

parachutisme [paraʃytism] *m* parachuting; (sports) skydiving

parachutiste [paraʃytist] *mf* parachutist; (sports) skydiver ‖ *m* paratrooper

parade [parad] *f* show; parry; sudden stop (*of horse*); come-on (*in front of sideshow*); (mil) inspection, parade; **à la parade** on parade; **faire parade de** to show off, to display

parader [parade] *intr* to show off

paradis [paradi] *m* paradise; (theat) peanut gallery

parado·xal -xale [paradɔksal] *adj* (*pl* **-xaux** [kso]) paradoxical

paradoxe [paradɔks] *m* paradox

parafe [paraf] *m* flourish; initials

parafer [parafe] *tr* to initial

paraffine [parafin] *f* paraffin

paraffiner [parafine] *tr* to paraffin

parages [paraʒ] *mpl* region, vicinity; **dans ces parages** in these parts

paragraphe [paragraf] *m* paragraph

Paraguay [paragɛ] *m*—**le Paraguay** Paraguay

para·guayen [paragɛjɛ̃] **-guayenne** [gɛjɛn] *adj* Paraguayan ‖ (*cap*) *mf* Paraguayan

paraître [parɛtr] §12, §95 *intr* to appear; seem; come out; show off; **à ce qu'il paraît** from all appearances; **faire pa-** raître to publish; **vient de paraître** just out

parallèle [paralɛl] *adj* parallel ‖ *m* parallel, comparison; (geog) parallel ‖ *f* (geom) parallel

paralyser [paralize] *tr* to paralyze

paralysie [paralizi] *f* paralysis

paralytique [paralitik] *adj* & *mf* paralytic

parangon [parɑ̃gɔ̃] *m* paragon

paranoïaque [paranɔjak] *adj* & *mf* paranoiac

parapet [parapɛ] *m* railing, parapet; (mil) parapet

paraphe [paraf] *m* flourish; initials

parapher [parafe] *tr* to initial

paraphrase [parafraz] *f* circumlocution, paraphrase; commentary

paraphraser [parafraze] *tr* to paraphrase

parapluie [paraplɥi] *m* umbrella; cover, front

parasite [parazit] *adj* parasitic(al) ‖ *m* parasite; **parasites** (rad) static

parasiter [parazite] *tr* to live as a parasite on or in (*a host*); (fig) to sponge on

parasol [parasɔl] *m* parasol; beach umbrella

paratonnerre [paratɔnɛr] *m* lightning rod

parâtre [parɑtr] *m* stepfather; cruel father

paravent [paravɑ̃] *m* folding screen

parbleu [parblø] *interj* rather!, by Jove!, you bet!

parc [park] *m* park; sheepfold; corral, pen; playpen; grounds, property; (mil) supply depot; (rr) rolling stock; **parc à huîtres** oyster bed; **parc automobile** motor pool; **parc d'attractions** amusement park; **parc de stationnement** (**payant**) parking lot

parcage [parkaʒ] *m* parking

parcelle [parsɛl] *f* particle; plot

parce que [pars(ə)kə] *conj* because

parchemin [parʃəmɛ̃] *m* parchment; (coll) sheepskin (*diploma*)

parchemi·né -née [parʃəmine] *adj* wrinkled

parcheminer [parʃəmine] *tr* to parchmentize ‖ *ref* to shrivel up

par-ci [parsi] *adv*—**par-ci par-là** here and there

parcimo·nieux [parsimɔnjø] **-nieuse** [njøz] *adj* parsimonious

parcomètre [parkɔmɛtr] *m* parking meter

parcourir [parkurir] §14 *tr* to travel through, tour; wander about; cover (*a distance*); scour (*the country*); glance through

parcours [parkur] *m* run, trip; route, distance covered; round (*e.g., of golf*); stroke (*of piston*)

par-delà [pardəla] *adv* & *prep* beyond

par-derrière [pardɛrjɛr] *adv* & *prep* behind

par-dessous [pardəsu] *adv* & *prep* underneath

pardessus [pardəsy] *m* overcoat

par-dessus [pardəsy] *adv* on top, over ‖ *prep* on top of, over

par-devant [pardəvɑ̃] *adv* in front ‖ *prep* in front of, before

par-devers [pardəvɛr] *prep* in the presence of; **par-devers soi** in one's own possession

pardi [pardi] *interj* (coll) of course!

pardon [pardɔ̃] *m* pardon; Breton pilgrimage ‖ *adv* (to contradict a negative statement or question) yes, e.g., **Vous ne parlez pas français, n'est-ce pas? Pardon, je le parle très bien** You don't speak French, do you? Yes, I speak it very well ‖ *interj* pardon me!; (slang) oh boy!

pardonnable [pardɔnabl] *adj* pardonable

pardonner [pardɔne] §98 *tr* to pardon, forgive, excuse, e.g., **Marie pardonne à Robert d'avoir manqué le rendez-vous** Mary forgives Robert for missing the date; **pardonnez-moi de vous avoir dérangé** excuse me for disturbing you; **pardonnez-moi, mais . . .** excuse me, but . . . ; **pardonner q.ch. à qn** to pardon s.o. for s.th. ‖ *intr* (**à qn**) to pardon, forgive, e.g., **Marie pardonnera à Robert** Mary will forgive Robert; **ne pas pardonner** to be fatal (*said of illness, mistake, etc.*)

pare-balles [parbal] *adj invar* bulletproof

pare-boue [parbu] *m invar* mudguard

pare-brise [parbriz] *m invar* windshield

pare-chocs [parʃɔk] *m invar* (aut) bumper; **pare-chocs contre pare-chocs** bumper to bumper

pare-étincelles [paretɛ̃sɛl] *m invar* fire screen

pa·reil -reille [parɛj] *adj* identical, the same; such, such a ‖ *mf* equal, match; **sans pareil, sans pareille** without parallel, unequaled ‖ *m*—**c'est du pareil au même** (coll) it's six of one and half dozen of the other ‖ *f* same (thing); **rendre la pareille à qn** to pay s.o. back in his own coin

pareillement [parɛjmɑ̃] *adv* likewise

parement [parmɑ̃] *m* cuff; facing; trimming; (eccl) parament

pa·rent -rente [parɑ̃] *adj* like ‖ *mf* relative; parents parents; relatives; ancestors; **plus proche parent** next of kin

parenté [parɑ̃te] *f* relationship; relations

parenthèse [parɑ̃tɛz] *f* parenthesis; **entre parenthèses** in parentheses

parer [pare] *tr* to adorn; parry; prepare ‖ *intr*—**parer à** to provide for ‖ *ref* to show off

pare-soleil [parsɔlɛj] *m invar* sun visor

paresse [parɛs] *f* laziness

paresser [parese] *intr* (coll) to loaf

pares·seux -seuse [parɛsø] **-seuse** [søz] *adj* lazy ‖ *mf* lazy person, lazybones; malingerer ‖ *m* (zool) sloth

par ex. *abbr* (**par exemple**) e.g.

parfaire [parfɛr] §29 *tr* to perfect; make up (*e.g., a sum of money*)

par·fait [parfɛ] **-faite** [fɛt] *adj & m* perfect ‖ **parfait** *interj* fine!, excellent!

parfaitement [parfɛtmɑ̃] *adv* perfectly; completely; certainly, of course

parfois [parfwa] *adv* sometimes

parfum [parfœ̃] *m* perfume; aroma; bouquet (*of wines*); flavor (*of ice cream*); **au parfum** in the know

parfumer [parfyme] *tr* to perfume; flavor ‖ *ref* to use perfume

parfumerie [parfymri] *f* perfume shop; perfumery

pari [pari] *m* bet, wager

paria [parja] *m* pariah

parier [parje] §97 *tr & intr* to bet, wager

Paris [pari] *m* Paris

pari·sien [parizjɛ̃] **-sienne** [zjɛn] *adj* Parisian ‖ (*cap*) *mf* Parisian

parité [parite] *f* parity; likeness; evenness (*of numbers*)

parjure [parʒyr] *adj* perjured ‖ *mf* perjurer ‖ *m* perjury

parking [parkiŋ] *m* parking lot

par·lant [parlɑ̃] **-lante** [lɑ̃t] *adj* speaking; talking (*e.g., picture*); eloquent, expressive

parlement [parləmɑ̃] *m* parliament

parlementaire [parləmɑ̃tɛr] *adj* parliamentary ‖ *mf* peace envoy; member of a parliament, legislator

parlementer [parləmɑ̃te] *intr* to parley

parler [parle] *m* speech, way of speaking; dialect ‖ §97, §98 *tr & intr* to speak, talk; **tu parles Charles!** you don't say!

par·leur [parlœr] **-leuse** [løz] *mf*—**beau parleur** good talker; windbag

parloir [parlwar] *m* reception room

parlote [parlɔt] *f* (coll) talk, gossip, rumor

parmi [parmi] *prep* among

Parnasse [parnɑs] *m*—**le Parnasse** Parnassus (*poetry*); Mount Parnassus

parodie [parɔdi] *f* parody, travesty

parodier [parɔdje] *tr* to parody, travesty

paroi [parwa] *f* partition, wall; inner side; (anat) wall

paroisse [parwas] *f* parish

parois·sial -siale [parwasjal] *adj* (*pl* **-siaux** [sjo]) parochial, parish

parois·sien [parwasjɛ̃] **-sienne** [sjɛn] *mf* parishioner ‖ *m* prayer book; (coll) fellow

parole [parɔl] *f* word; speech; word, promise; **avoir la parole** to have the floor; **donner la parole à** to recognize, to give the floor to; **sur parole** on one's word

paro·lier [parɔlje] **-lière** [ljɛr] *mf* lyricist; librettist

parpaing [parpɛ̃] *m* concrete block; building block

parquer [parke] *tr* to park; pen in ‖ *intr* to be penned in ‖ *ref* to park

Parque [park] *f* (lit) destiny, death; **les Parques** (myth) the Fates

parquet [parkɛ] *m* parquet, floor; floor (*of stock exchange*); public prosecutor's office

parqueter [parkəte] §34 *tr* to parquet, floor

parrain [parɛ̃] *m* godfather; sponsor

parrainer [parɛne] *tr* to sponsor

parricide [parisid] *mf* parricide, patricide (*person*) ‖ *m* parricide, patricide (*act*)

parsemer [parsəme] §2 *tr* to sprinkle; spangle

part [par] *m* newborn child; dropping (*of young by animal in labor*) ‖ *f* part, share; **aller quelque part** (coll) to go to the toilet; **à part** aside; aside from; **à part entière** with full privileges; **autre part** elsewhere; **avoir part au gâteau** (coll) to have a slice of the pie; **d'autre part** besides; **de la part de** on the part of, from; **de part en part** through and through; **de toutes parts** on all sides; **d'une part . . . d'autre part** on the one hand . . . on the other hand; **faire la part de** to make allowance for; **faire part de** to announce; **faire part de q.ch. à qn** to inform s.o. of s.th.; **nulle part** nowhere; **nulle part ailleurs** nowhere else; **pour ma part** as for me, for my part; **prendre en bonne part** to take good-naturedly; **prendre en mauvaise part** to take offense at; **prendre part à** to take part in; **quelque part** somewhere

partage [partaʒ] *m* division, partition; sharing; share; tie vote; **échoir en partage à qn** to fall to s.o.'s lot; **partage de temps** (comp) time sharing

partager [partaʒe] §38 *tr* to share; divide

partance [partɑ̃s] *f* departure; **en partance** leaving; **en partance pour** bound for

partant [partɑ̃] *m* (sports) starter; **partants** departing guests, departing travelers, etc. ‖ *adv* (lit) consequently

partenaire [partənɛr] *mf* partner; sparring partner

parterre [partɛr] *m* orchestra circle; flower bed

parti [parti] *m* party; side; match, good catch; **faire un mauvais parti à** to rough up; to mistreat; **parti pris** fixed opinion; prejudice; **prendre le parti de** to decide to; **prendre le parti de qn** to take s.o.'s side; **prendre parti** to take sides; **prendre son parti** to make up one's mind; **prendre son parti de** to resign oneself to; **tirer parti de** to take advantage of

par·tial -tiale [parsjal] *adj* (*pl* **-tiaux** [sjo]) partial, biased

partici·pant [partisipɑ̃] **-pante** [pɑ̃t] *adj & mf* participant

participation [partisipɑsjɔ̃] *f* participation

participe [partisip] *m* participle

participer [partisipe] *intr*—**participer à** to participate in; **participer de** to partake of

particulariser [partikylarize] *tr* to specify ‖ *ref* to make oneself conspicuous

particularité [partikylarite] *f* peculiarity; detail

particule [partikyl] *f* particle

particu·lier [partikylje] **-lière** [ljɛr] *adj* particular; special; private ‖ *mf* private citizen; (coll) odd person ‖ *m* particular

particulièrement [partikyljɛrmɑ̃] *adv* particularly

partie [parti] *f* part; line, specialty; game; winning score; contest; party (*diversion*); (law) party; **avoir partie liée avec** to be in league with; **faire partie de** to belong to; **faire partie intégrante de** to be part

and parcel of; **partie civile** plaintiff; **partie de chasse** hunting party; **partie de plaisir** outing, picnic; **partie nulle** tie game; **prendre à partie** to take to task

par·tiel -tielle [parsjɛl] *adj* partial

partir [partir] (used only in *inf*) *tr*—**avoir maille à partir** to have a bone to pick ‖ §64, §95, §96 *intr* (*aux:* ÊTRE) to leave; go off (*said of firearm*); begin; **à partir de** from; from . . . on, e.g., **à partir de maintenant** from now on; **faire partir** to send off; remove (*a spot*); set off (*an explosive*); fire (*a gun*); **partir + inf** to leave in order to + *inf;* **partir de** to come from; start with; **partir pour** or **à** to leave for

parti·san [partizɑ̃] **-sane** [zan] *adj & mf* partisan

partition [partisjɔ̃] *f* (mus) score

partout [partu] *adv* everywhere; **partout ailleurs** anywhere else; everywhere else; **partout où** wherever; everywhere

parure [paryr] *f* ornament; set; finery; necklace

parution [parysjɔ̃] *f* appearance, publication

parvenir [parvənir] §72, §96 *intr* (*aux:* ÊTRE)—**parvenir à** to reach; **parvenir à + inf** to succeed in + *ger*

parve·nu -nue [parvəny] *adj & mf* upstart

parvis [parvi] *m* square (*in front of a church*)

pas [pɑ] *m* step; pace; footprint; footfall; pass; straits; pitch (*of screw*); **allonger le pas** to quicken one's pace; to put one's best foot forward; **à pas comptés** with measured tread; **à pas de loup, à pas feutrés** stealthily; **à pas de tortue** at a snail's pace; **à quatre pas** nearby; **au pas** at a walk; **céder le pas (à)** to stand aside (for); to keep clear (*in front of a driveway*); **de ce pas** at once; **être au pas** to be in step; **faire le premier pas** to make the first move; **faire les cent pas** to come and go; **faux pas** misstep; blunder; **marcher sur les pas de** to follow in the footsteps of; **marquer le pas** to mark time; **mauvais pas** tight squeeze, fix; **pas à pas** little by little, cautiously; **pas d'armes** passage at arms; **Pas de Calais** Straits of Dover; **pas de cheval** hoofbeat; **pas de clerc** blunder; **pas de deux** two-step; **pas de la porte** doorstep; **pas de l'oie** goosestep; **pas de porte** (com) price paid for good will; **prendre le pas sur** to get ahead of ‖ *adv*—**pas** §90 not, e.g., **je ne sais pas** I do not know; e.g., **ne pas signer** to not sign; (used with **non**), e.g., **non pas** no; (used without **ne**) (slang) not, e.g., **je fais pas de politique** I don't meddle in politics; **n'est-ce pas?** see **ne; pas?** (coll) not so?; **pas de** no; **pas du tout** not at all; **pas encore** not yet

pas·cal -cale [paskal] *adj* (*pl* **-caux** [ko]) Passover; Easter

passable [pɑsabl] *adj* passable, fair; mediocre, so-so

passade [pɑsad] *f* passing fancy

passage [pɑsaʒ] *m* passage; crossing; pass; **barrer le passage** to block the way; **du passage** in passing, in parentheses; **livrer passage à** to let through; **passage à niveau** grade crossing; **passage au-dessous de la voie, passage souterrain** underpass; **passage au-dessus de la voie** overpass; **passage clouté, passage zébré** pedestrian crossing; **passage de vitesses** gear shifting; **passage interdit** (*public sign*) do not enter; (*public sign*) no thoroughfare; **passage protégé** arterial crossing (*vehicles intersecting highway must stop*)

passa·ger [pɑsaʒe] **-gère** [ʒɛr] *adj* passing, fleeting; migratory; busy (*road*) ‖ *mf* passenger; **passager clandestin, passager de cale** stowaway; **passager d'entrepont** steerage passenger

pas·sant [pɑsɑ̃] **-sante** [sɑ̃t] *adj* busy (*street*) ‖ *mf* passer-by

passation [pɑsɑsjɔ̃] *f* handing over

passavant [pɑsavɑ̃] *m* permit; (naut) gangway

passe [pɑs] *m* master key ‖ *f* pass; channel; **être en bonne passe de** to be in a fair way to; **être en passe de** to be about to; **mauvaise passe** tight spot

pas·sé -sée [pɑse] *adj* past; faded; overripe; last (*week*) ‖ *m* past; past tense ‖ **passé** *prep* past, beyond, after

passe-bouillon [pɑsbujɔ̃] *m invar* soup strainer

passe-droit [pɑsdrwa] *m* (*pl* **-droits**) illegal favor; injustice

passe-lacet [pɑslasɛ] *m* (*pl* **-lacets**) bodkin

passe-lait [pɑslɛ] *m invar* milk strainer

passe-lettres [pɑslɛtr] *m* (*pl* **-lettres**) letter drop

passement [pɑsmɑ̃] *m* braid, trimming

passementer [pɑsmɑ̃te] *tr* to trim

passementerie [pɑsmɑ̃tri] *f* trimmings

passe-montagne [pɑsmɔ̃taɲ] *m* (*pl* **-montagnes**) storm hood, ski mask

passe-partout [pɑspartu] *m invar* master key; slip mount

passe-passe [pɑspɑs] *m invar* legerdemain; sleight of hand

passepoil [pɑspwal] *m* piping, braid

passeport [pɑspɔr] *m* passport

passer [pɑse] §96 *tr* to pass; ferry; get across (*e.g., a river*); spend, pass (*e.g., the evening*); take (*an exam*); slip on (*e.g., a dressing gown*); show (*a film*); make (*a telephone call*); go on (*one's way*); **passer q.ch. à qn** to hand or lend s.o. s.th.; forgive s.o. s.th. ‖ *intr* (*aux:* AVOIR or ÊTRE) to pass; pass away; become; **en passer par là** to knuckle under; **faire passer** to get (*e.g., a message*) through; while away (*the time*); **passer à** to pass over to; **passer chez** or **passer voir** to drop in on; **passer outre à** to override; **passer par** to pass through, go through; **passer pour** to pass for or as; **passons!** let's skip it! ‖ §97 *ref* to happen, take place; **se passer de** to do without

passe·reau [pɑsro] *m* (*pl* **-reaux**) sparrow

passerelle [pɑsrɛl] *f* footbridge; gangplank; (naut) bridge; **passerelle couverte extensible** (aer) enclosed swinging gangplank; **passerelle télescopique** telescopic corridor

passe-temps [pɑstɑ̃] *m invar* pastime, hobby

passe-thé [pɑste] *m invar* tea strainer

pas·seur [pɑsœr] **-seuse** [søz] *mf* smuggler ‖ *m* ferryman

passible [pɑsibl] *adj*—**passible de** liable for, subject to

pas·sif [pɑsif] **-sive** [siv] *adj* passive ‖ *m* passive; debts, liabilities

passiflore [pɑsiflɔr] *f* passionflower

passion [pɑsjɔ̃], [pɑsjɔ̃] *f* passion

passion·nant [pɑsjɔnɑ̃] **-nante** [nɑ̃t] *adj* thrilling, fascinating

passion·né -née [pɑsjɔne] *adj* passionate; impassioned; **passionné de** or **pour** passionately fond of ‖ *mf* enthusiast, fan

passion·nel -nelle [pɑsjɔnɛl] *adj* of passion, of jealousy

passionner [pɑsjɔne] *tr* to excite the interest of, arouse ‖ *ref*—**se passionner pour** or **à** to be passionately fond of

passoire [pɑswar] *f* colander; strainer; (fig) sieve

pastel [pɑstɛl] *m* pastel; (bot) woad

pastèque [pɑstɛk] *f* watermelon

pasteur [pɑstœr] *m* pastor, minister; shepherd

pasteuriser [pɑstœrize] *tr* to pasteurize

pastiche [pɑstiʃ] *m* pastiche; parody

pastille [pɑstij] *f* lozenge, drop; tire patch; polka dot; (comp) chip; **pastille pectorale** cough drop

pasto·ral -rale [pɑstɔral] (*pl* **-raux** [ro] **-rales**) *adj & f* pastoral

pastorat [pɑstɔra] *m* pastorate

pat [pat] *adj invar* (chess) in stalemate; **faire pat** to stalemate ‖ *m* (chess) stalemate

patache [pataʃ] *f* police boat; (coll) rattletrap

patachon [pataʃɔ̃] *m*—**mener une vie de patachon** to lead a wild life

patapouf [patapuf] *m* (coll) roly-poly ‖ *interj* flop!

pataquès [patakɛs] *m* faulty liaison; blooper, goof

patate [patat] *f* sweet potato; (coll) spud

patati [patati]—**et patati et patata** (coll) and so on and on

patatras [patatra] *interj* bang!, crash!

pa·taud [pato] **-taude** [tod] *adj* clumsy, loutish ‖ *mf* lout

pataugeoire [patoʒwar] *f* wading pool

patauger [patoʒe] §38 *intr* to splash; to wade; (coll) to flounder

pâte [pat] *f* paste; dough, batter; **en pâte** (typ) pied; **mettre la main à la pâte** to put one's shoulder to the wheel; **pâte à papier** wood pulp; **pâte brisée,** **pâte feuilletée** puff paste; **pâte dentifrice** toothpaste; **pâte molle** spineless person; **pâtes alimentaires** pastas (*macaroni,* *noodles, spaghetti, etc.*); **peindre à la pâte** to paint with a full brush; **une bonne pâte d'homme** (coll) a good sort

pâté [pɑte] *m* blot, splotch; (typ) pi; **pâté de foie gras** minced goose livers; **pâté de maisons** block of houses; **pâté en croûte** meat or fish pie; **pâté maison** chef's-special pâté

pâtée [pɑte] *f* dog food, cat food; chicken feed

pate·lin [patlɛ̃] **-line** [lin] *adj* fawning, wheedling ‖ *m* wheedler; (coll) native village

patenôtre [patnotr] *f* prayer; (archaic) mumbo jumbo

pa·tent [pɑtɑ̃] **-tente** [tɑ̃t] *adj* patent ‖ *f* license; tax; **patente (de santé)** (naut) bill of health

paten·té -tée [patɑ̃te] *adj* licensed ‖ *mf* licensed dealer

patenter [patɑ̃te] *tr* to license

Pater [patɛr] *m invar* Lord's Prayer

patère [patɛr] *f* clothes hook; curtain hook

paterne [patɛrn] *adj* mawkish, mealy-mouthed

pater·nel -nelle [patɛrnɛl] *adj* paternal; fatherly ‖ *m* (slang) pop, dad

paternité [patɛrnite] *f* paternity; fatherhood; authorship

pâ·teux [pɑtø] **-teuse** [tøz] *adj* pasty; thick; coated (*tongue*)

pathétique [patetik] *adj* pathetic ‖ *m* pathos

pathologie [patɔlɔʒi] *f* pathology

pathos [patos] *m* bathos

patibulaire [patibylɛr] *adj* hangdog (*look*)

patience [pasjɑ̃s] *f* patience

pa·tient [pasjɑ̃] **-tiente** [sjɑ̃t] *adj & mf* patient

patienter [pasjɑ̃te] *intr* to be patient

patin [patɛ̃] *m* skate; runner; sill, sleeper; (*sole*) patten; (aer) skid; (rr) base, flange (*of rails*); **patin à glace** ice skate; **patin à roulettes** roller skate; **patin de frein** brake shoe

patiner [patine] *intr* to skate; slide; skid

patinette [patinɛt] *f* scooter

pati·neur [patinœr] **-neuse** [nøz] *mf* skater

patinoire [patinwar] *f* skating rink

patio [patjo], [pasjo] *m* patio

pâtir [pɑtir] *intr*—**pâtir de** to suffer from

pâtisserie [pɑtisri] *f* pastry; pastry shop; pastry making

pâtis·sier [pɑtisje] **-sière** [sjɛr] *mf* pastry cook; proprietor of a pastry shop

patoche [patɔʃ] *f* (coll) hand, paw

patois [patwa] *m* patois; jargon, lingo

patouiller [patuje] *tr* (coll) to paw, maul ‖ *intr* (coll) to splash

patraque [patrak] *adj* in bad shape ‖ *f* (coll) turnip (*old watch*)

pâtre [pɑtr] *m* herdsman

patriarche [patrijarʃ] *m* patriarch

patrice [patris] *m* patrician; **Patrice** Patrick

patri·cien [patrisjɛ̃] **-cienne** [sjɛn] *adj & mf* patrician

patrie [patri] *f* native land, fatherland

patrimoine [patrimwan] *m* patrimony

patrio·tard [patrijɔtar] **-tarde** [tard] *adj* flag-waving, chauvinistic

patriote [patrijɔt] *adj* patriotic ‖ *mf* patriot

patriotique [patrijɔtik] *adj* patriotic

patriotisme [patrijɔtism] *m* patriotism

pa·tron [patrɔ̃] **-tronne** [trɔn] *mf* patron saint; proprietor; boss; sponsor ‖ *m* pattern, model; captain, skipper; coxswain; master, lord; medium size; **grand patron** large size; **patron à jours** stencil; **patron de thèse** thesis sponsor ‖ *f* mistress of the house; (slang) better half

patronage [patrɔnaʒ] *m* patronage, protection; sponsorship; (eccl) social center

patronat [patrɔna] *m* management

patronner [patrɔne] *tr* to patronize, protect; sponsor; stencil

patrouille [patruj] *f* patrol

patrouiller [patruje] *intr* to patrol

patte [pat] *f* paw; foot (*of bird*); leg (*of insect*); flap, tab; hook; (coll) hand, foot, or leg (*of person*); **à pattes d'éléphant** bell-bottom (*trousers*); **à quatre pattes** on all fours; **faire patte de velours** (coll) to pull in one's claws; **graisser la patte à** (coll) to grease the palm of; **patte d'épaule** shoulder strap; **pattes de mouche** (coll) scrawl

patte-d'oie [patdwa] *f* (*pl* **pattes-d'oie**) crow's-foot; crossroads; (bot) goosefoot

pattemouille [patmuj] *f* damp cloth

pâturage [pɑtyraʒ] *m* pasture; pasturage; pasture rights

pâture [pɑtyr] *f* fodder; pasture; (fig) food

paume [pom] *f* palm; (archaic) tennis

pau·mé -mée [pome] *adj* (coll) lost

paupière [popjɛr] *f* eyelid

pause [poz] *f* pause; (mus) full rest; **pause café** coffee break

pauvre [povr] *adj* poor; **pauvre de moi!** woe is me!; **pauvre d'esprit** (coll) dimwitted ‖ (when standing before noun) *adj* poor, wretched; late (*deceased*) ‖ *mf* pauper; **les pauvres** the poor

pauvreté [povrəte] *f* poverty

P.A.V. [peave] *adj* (letterword) (**payable avec préavis**) person-to-person (*telephone call*)

pavaner [pavane] *ref* to strut

pavé [pave] *m* pavement, street; paving stone; paving block; (culin) slab; **sur le pavé** pounding the streets, out of work

pavement [pavmɑ̃] *m* paving (*act*); mosaic or marble flooring

paver [pave] *tr* to pave

pavillon [pavijɔ̃] *m* pavilion; tent, canopy; lodge, one-story house; wing, pavilion; hospital ward; flag; bell (*of trumpet*); **amener son pavillon** to strike one's colors; **baisser pavillon** to knuckle under; **pavillon de chasse** hunting lodge; **pavillon des sports** field house; **pavillon noir** Jolly Roger

pavois [pavwa] *m* shield; **élever sur le pavois** to extol

pavoiser [pavwaze] *tr* to deck out with bunting, decorate

pavot [pavo] *m* poppy
payable [pɛjabl] *adj* payable
payant [pɛjɑ̃] **payante** [pɛjɑ̃t] *adj* paying
paye [pɛj] *f* pay, wages
payement [pɛjmɑ̃] *m* payment
payer [peje] §49 *tr* to pay; pay for; **payer comptant** to pay cash for; **payer de retour** to pay back; **payer q.ch. à qn** to pay s.o. for s.th.; pay for s.th. for s.o.; **payer qn de q.ch.** to pay s.o. for s.th.; **payer rubis sur l'ongle** to pay down on the nail ‖ *intr* to pay; **paye et prends** cash and carry ‖ *ref* to treat oneself to; take what is due; **pouvoir se payer** to be able to afford; **se payer de** to be satisfied with
pays [pei] *m* country; region; town; (coll) fellow countryman; **du pays** local; **le pays de** the land of; **pays de cocagne** land of milk and honey
paysage [peizaʒ] *m* landscape, scenery; (painting) landscape
paysagiste [peizaʒist] *m* landscape painter
pay·san [peizɑ̃] **-sane** [zan] *adj & mf* peasant
Pays-Bas [pɛibɑ], [pɛibɑ] *mpl*—**les Pays-Bas** The Netherlands
payse [peiz] *f* countrywoman
P.C. [pese] *m* (letterword) (**parti communiste**) Communist party; (**poste de commandement**) command post
P.c.c. *abbr* (**pour copie conforme**) certified copy
p.c.v. or **P.C.V.** [peseve] *m* (letterword) (**payable chez vous**) or (**à percevoir**)—**téléphoner en p.c.v.** to telephone collect
péage [peaʒ] *m* toll
peau [po] *f* (*pl* **peaux**) skin; pelt; hide; film (*on milk*); (slang) bag, whore; **entrer dans la peau d'un personnage** (theat) to get right inside a part; **faire peau neuve** to turn over a new leaf; **la peau!** (slang) nothing doing!; **peau d'âne** (coll) sheepskin; **peau de tambour** drumhead; **vendre la peau de l'ours avant de l'avoir tué** to count one's chickens before they are hatched
peau-rouge [poruʒ] *mf* (*pl* **peaux-rouges**) redskin
pêche [pɛʃ] *f* peach; fishing; **pêche à la mouche noyée** fly casting; **pêche au coup** fishing with hook, line, and pole; **pêche au lancer** casting; **pêche sous-marine** deep-sea fishing; **pêche sportive** fishing with a fly rod or casting rod
péché [peʃe] *m* sin
pécher [peʃe] §10 *intr* to sin
pêcher [peʃe] *m* peach tree ‖ *tr* to fish, fish for; (coll) to get ‖ *intr* to fish; **pêcher à la mouche** to fly-fish
pêcherie [pɛʃri] *f* fishery
pê·cheur [peʃœr] **-cheresse** [ʃrɛs] *mf* sinner
pê·cheur [peʃœr] **-cheuse** [ʃøz] *mf* fisher; **pêcheur de perles** pearl diver ‖ *m* fisherman
pécore [pekɔr] *f* (coll) silly goose
pecque [pɛk] *f* (coll) silly affected woman
péculat [pekyla] *m* embezzlement

pécule [pekyl] *m* nest egg
pédagogie [pedagɔʒi] *f* pedagogy, education
pédagogue [pedagɔg] *adj* pedagogical ‖ *mf* pedagogue; teacher
pédale [pedal] *f* pedal; treadle; (slang) pederast; **de la pédale** gay, homosexual; **pédale d'embrayage** (aut) clutch pedal
pédaler [pedale] *intr* to pedal; **pédaler dans la choucroute** (slang) to be mixed up
pédalier [pedalje] *m* pedal keyboard; pedal and sprocket-wheel assembly
pédalo [pedalo] *m* water bicycle
pé·dant [pedɑ̃] **-dante** [dɑ̃t] *adj* pedantic ‖ *mf* pedant
pédanterie [pedɑ̃tri] *f* pedantry
pédantesque [pedɑ̃tɛsk] *adj* pedantic
pédé [pede] *m* (slang) queer (*homosexual*)
pédéraste [pederast] *m* pederast, male homosexual
pédestre [pedɛstr] *adj* on foot
pédiatrie [pedjatri] *f* pediatrics
pédicure [pedikyr] *mf* chiropodist
pedigree [pedigri] *m* pedigree
Pégase [pegaz] *m* Pegasus
pègre [pɛgr] *f* underworld
peigne [pɛɲ] *m* comb; card (*for wool*); reed (*of loom*); (zool) scallop
peigner [peɲe] *tr* to comb; to card ‖ *ref* to comb one's hair
peignez [peɲe] *v* (**peignons**) see **peindre**; see **peigner**
peignoir [peɲwar] *m* bathrobe; dressing gown, peignoir
peindre [pɛ̃dr] §50 *tr & intr* to paint
peine [pɛn] *f* pain; trouble; difficulty; penalty; **à peine** hardly, scarcely; **en être pour sa peine** to have nothing to show for one's trouble; **faire (de la) peine à** to grieve; **faire peine à voir** to be pathetic; **peine capitale** capital punishment; **peine de cœur** heartache; **peine de mort** death penalty; **peine pécuniaire** financial distress; **purger sa peine** to serve one's sentence; **valoir la peine** to be worth while; **veuillez vous donner la peine de** please be so kind as to
peiner [pene] *tr* to pain, grieve; fatigue ‖ *intr* to labor
peint [pɛ̃] **peinte** [pɛ̃t] *v* see **peindre**
peintre [pɛ̃tr] *m* painter
peinture [pɛ̃tyr] *f* paint; painting; **attention à la peinture** (*public sign*) wet paint; **je ne peux pas le voir en peinture** (coll) I can't stand him
peinturer [pɛ̃tyre] *tr* to lay a coat of paint on; to daub
peinturlurer [pɛ̃tyrlyre] *tr* (coll) to paint in all the colors of the rainbow
péjora·tif [peʒɔratif] **-tive** [tiv] *adj & m* pejorative
pékin [pekɛ̃] *m* pekin; **en pékin** (slang) in civies; **Pékin** Peking
péki·nois [pekinwa] **-noise** [nwaz] *adj* Pekingese ‖ *m* Pekingese (*language; dog*) ‖ (*cap*) *mf* Pekingese (*inhabitant*)
pelage [pəlaʒ] *m* coat (*of animal*)
pe·lé -lée [pəle] *adj* bald; bare

pêle-mêle [pɛlmɛl] *m invar* jumble ‖ *adv* pell-mell

peler [pəle] §2 *tr, intr, & ref* to peel, peel off

pèle·rin [pɛlrɛ̃] **-rine** [rin] *mf* pilgrim ‖ *m* peregrine falcon; basking shark ‖ *f* see **pèlerine**

pèlerinage [pɛlrinaʒ] *m* pilgrimage

pèlerine [pɛlrin] *f* pelerine, cape; hooded cape

péliade [peljad] *f* adder

pélican [pelikɑ̃] *m* pelican

pellagre [pelagr] *f* pellagra

pelle [pɛl] *f* shovel; scoop; **pelle à poussière** dustpan; **pelle à vapeur** steam shovel; **pelle mécanique** power shovel; **ramasser à la pelle** to shovel, to shovel up

pelletée [pɛlte] *f* shovelful

pelleter [pɛlte] §34 *tr* to shovel

pelleterie [pɛltri] *f* fur trade; skin, pelt

pelleteuse [pɛltøz] *f* power shovel

pellicule [pelikyl] *f* film; pellicle; speck of dandruff; (phot) film; **pellicules** dandruff

pelote [plɔt] *f* ball (*of string, of snow, etc.*); **faire sa pelote** (coll) to make one's pile; **pelote basque** pelota; **pelote d'épingles** pincushion

peloter [plɔte] *tr* to wind into a ball; (fig) to flatter; (slang) to feel up, to paw ‖ *intr* to bat the ball back and forth

pelo·teur [plɔtœr] **-teuse** [tøz] *adj* flattering, ingratiating; (coll) fresh, amorous, spoony ‖ *mf* (coll) masher, spooner

peloton [plɔtɔ̃] *m* little ball (*e.g., of wool*); group (*of racers*); (mil) platoon, troop, detachment; **peloton d'exécution** firing squad

pelotonner [plɔtɔne] *tr* to wind into a ball ‖ *ref* to curl up, snuggle

pelouse [pluz] *f* lawn; (golf) green

peluche [plyʃ] *f* plush; lint

pelure [plyr] *f* peel, peeling, skin; rind; (coll) coat

pénaliser [penalize] *tr* to penalize

pénalité [penalite] *f* penalty

pe·naud [pəno] **-naude** [nod] *adj* bashful, shy; shamefaced; crestfallen

penchant [pɑ̃ʃɑ̃] *m* penchant, bent

pen·ché -chée [pɑ̃ʃe] *adj* leaning; stooping; bent over

pencher [pɑ̃ʃe] §96 *tr, intr, & ref* to lean, bend, incline; **se pencher sur** to make a close study of

pendable [pɑ̃dabl] *adj* outrageous; (archaic) hangable

pendaison [pɑ̃dɛzɔ̃] *f* hanging

pen·dant [pɑ̃dɑ̃] **-dante** [dɑ̃t] *adj* hanging; pending ‖ *m* pendant; counterpart; **pendant d'oreille** eardrop; **se faire pendant** to make a pair ‖ **pendant** *adv*—**pendant que** while ‖ **pendant** *prep* during

pendeloque [pɑ̃dlɔk] *f* pendant; jewel (*of eardrop*)

pendentif [pɑ̃dɑ̃tif] *m* pendant; eardrop; lavaliere

penderie [pɑ̃dri] *f* clothes closet

pendoir [pɑ̃dwar] *m* meat hook

pendre [pɑ̃dr] *tr* to hang; hang up; **être pendu à** to hang on (*e.g., the telephone*) ‖ *intr* to hang; hang down; sag; **ça lui pend au nez** he's got it coming to him ‖ *ref* to hang oneself; **se pendre à** to hang on to

pen·du -due [pɑ̃dy] *adj* hanging; hanged ‖ *mf* hanged person

pendule [pɑ̃dyl] *m* pendulum ‖ *f* clock; **pendule à pile** battery clock

pêne [pɛn] *m* bolt; latch

pénétration [penetrɑsjɔ̃] *f* penetration; permeation

pénétrer [penetre] §10 *tr* to penetrate, permeate ‖ *intr* to penetrate; enter ‖ *ref* to mix; **se pénétrer de** to become imbued with

pénible [penibl] *adj* hard, painful

péniche [peniʃ] *f* barge; houseboat; **péniche de débarquement** landing craft

pénicilline [penisilin] *f* penicillin

pé·nien [penjɛ̃] **-nienne** [njɛn] *adj* penile, penis

péninsulaire [penɛ̃syler] *adj* peninsular

péninsule [penɛ̃syl] *f* large peninsula

pénis [penis] *m* penis

pénitence [penitɑ̃s] *f* penitence; penalty (*in games*); punishment; **en pénitence** in disgrace; **faire pénitence** to do penance

pénitencier [penitɑ̃sje] *m* penitentiary; penal colony

péni·tent [penitɑ̃] **-tente** [tɑ̃t] *adj & mf* penitent

penne [pɛn] *f* quill, feather

Pennsylvanie [pɛnsilvani] *f* Pennsylvania; **la Pennsylvanie** Pennsylvania

pénombre [penɔ̃br] *f* penumbra; half-light; **dans la pénombre** out of the limelight

pense-bête [pɑ̃sbɛt] *m* (*pl* **-bêtes**) (coll) reminder

pensée [pɑ̃se] *f* thought; thinking; (bot) pansy

penser [pɑ̃se] §95 *tr* to think; **penser de** to think of (*to have as an opinion of*); **penser + *inf*** to intend to + *inf* ‖ *intr* to think; **penser à** to think of (*to direct one's thoughts toward*); **y penser** to think of it, e.g., **pendant que j'y pense** while I think of it

penseur [pɑ̃sœr] *m* thinker

pen·sif [pɑ̃sif] **-sive** [siv] *adj* pensive; absent-minded

pension [pɑ̃sjɔ̃] *f* pension (*annuity; room and board; boardinghouse*); **avec pension complète** with three meals; **pension alimentaire** alimony; **pension de famille** residential hotel; **pension de retraite, pension viagère** annuity; **prendre pension** to board; **sans pension** without meals

pensionnaire [pɑ̃sjɔner] *mf* boarder; guest (*in hotel*); resident student ‖ *f* naïve woman or girl

pensionnat [pɑ̃sjɔna] *m* boarding school

pension·né -née [pɑ̃sjɔne] *adj* pensioned ‖ *mf* pensioner

pensionner [pɑ̃sjɔne] *tr* to pension

pensum [pɛ̃sɔm] *m* thankless task

Pentagone [pɛ̃tagɔn] *m* Pentagon

pente [pãt] *f* slope; inclination, bent; fall (*of river*); **en pente** sloping

Pentecôte [pãtkot] *f*—**la Pentecôte** Pentecost, Whitsunday

pénultième [penyltjɛm] *adj* next to the last ‖ *f* penult

pénurie [penyri] *f* lack, shortage

pépé [pepe] *m* (slang) grandpa

pépée [pepe] *f* doll; (slang) doll

pépère [pepɛr] *adj* (coll) easygoing ‖ *m* grandpa; (coll) old duffer; (coll) overgrown boy

pépètes [pepɛt] *fpl* (slang) dough

pépie [pepi] *f* (vet) pip; **avoir le pépie** (coll) to be thirsty

pépiement [pepimã] *m* chirp

pépier [pepje] *intr* to chirp

pépin [pepɛ̃] *m* pip, seed; (coll) umbrella; **avoir un pépin** (coll) to strike a snag

pépinière [pepinjɛr] *f* (hort) nursery; (fig) training school; (fig) hotbed

pépiniériste [pepinjerist] *m* nurseryman

pépite [pepit] *f* nugget

péque·naud [pɛkno] **-naude** [nod] *adj & mf* (slang) peasant

péquenot [pɛkno] *m* (slang) peasant

perçage [pɛrsaʒ] *m* drilling, boring

per·çant [pɛrsã] **-çante** [sãt] *adj* piercing, penetrating

perce [pɛrs] *f* drill, bore; **en perce** on tap

percée [pɛrse] *f* opening, gap; clearing; breakthrough; discovery

perce-neige [pɛrsənɛʒ] *m invar* (bot) snowdrop

percepteur [pɛrsɛptœr] *m* tax collector

perceptible [pɛrsɛptibl] *adj* perceptible; collectable, payable

perception [pɛrsɛpsjɔ̃] *f* perception; tax collection; tax; tax department, bureau of internal revenue

percer [pɛrse] §51 *tr* to pierce; drill; tap (*a barrel*); break through ‖ *intr* to come through or out; burst (*said, e.g., of abscess*); to make a name for oneself

perceuse [pɛrsøz] *f* drill; machine drill

percevoir [pɛrsəvwar] §59 *tr* to perceive; collect

perche [pɛrʃ] *f* pole; (ichth) perch; (sports) pole vaulting; (coll) beanpole; **perche à sauter** vaulting pole; **perche à son** microphone stand; **tendre la perche à** to lend a helping hand to

percher [pɛrʃe] *tr* to perch ‖ *intr* to perch, roost

perchoir [pɛrʃwar] *m* perch

per·clus [pɛrkly] **-cluse** [klyz] *adj* crippled, paralyzed

percolateur [pɛrkɔlatœr] *m* large coffee maker

percuter [pɛrkyte] *tr* to strike; crash into; percuss ‖ *intr* to crash

percuteur [pɛrkytœr] *m* firing pin

per·dant [pɛrdã] **-dante** [dãt] *adj* losing ‖ *mf* loser

perdition [pɛrdisjɔ̃] *f* perdition; **en perdition** (naut) in distress

perdre [pɛrdrə] §96 *tr* to lose; ruin ‖ *intr* to lose; leak; deterioriate ‖ *ref* to get lost; disappear

per·dreau [pɛrdro] *m* (*pl* **-dreaux**) young partridge

perdrix [pɛrdri] *f* partridge

per·du -due [pɛrdy] *adj* lost; spare (*time*); stray (*bullet*); remote (*locality*); advance (*sentry*)

père [pɛr] *m* father; senior, e.g., **M. Martin père** Mr. Martin, senior; **père de famille** head of the household; **père spirituel** father confessor

péremptoire [perãptwar] *adj* peremptory

péréquation [perekwasjɔ̃] *f* equalizing

perfection [pɛrfɛksjɔ̃] *f* perfection

perfectionner [pɛrfɛksjɔne] *tr* to perfect ‖ *ref* to improve

perfide [pɛrfid] *adj* perfidious ‖ *mf* treacherous person

perfidie [pɛrfidi] *f* perfidy

perforation [pɛrfɔrasjɔ̃] *f* perforation; puncture

perforatrice [pɛrfɔratris] *f* pneumatic drill; perforator; keypunch (machine)

perforer [pɛrfɔre] *tr* to perforate; drill, bore; punch (*a card*)

performance [pɛrfɔrmãs] *f* (sports) performance

pergélisol [pɛrʒelisɔl] *m* permafrost

péricliter [periklite] *intr* to fail

péril [peril] *m* peril

péril·leux [perijø] **-leuse** [jøz] *adj* perilous

péri·mé -mée [perime] *adj* expired, elapsed; out-of-date

périmer [perime] *intr & ref* to lapse

période [perjɔd] *f* period; (phys) cycle; (phys) half-life

périodique [perjɔdik] *adj* periodic(al)

péripétie [peripesi] *f* vicissitude

périphérie [periferi] *f* periphery

périphérique [periferik] *adj* peripheral

périple [peripl] *m* journey

périr [perir] *intr* to perish

périscope [periskɔp] *m* periscope

périssable [perisabl] *adj* perishable

perle [pɛrl] *f* pearl; bead

perler [pɛrle] *tr* to pearl; do to perfection ‖ *intr* to form beads

permanence [pɛrmanãs] *f* permanence; headquarters, station; **en permanence** at all hours

perma·nent [pɛrmanã] **-nente** [nãt] *adj* permanent; standing; continuous, nonstop ‖ *f* permanent

perme [pɛrm] *f* (coll) furlough

permettre [pɛrmɛtr] §42, §97, §98 *tr* to permit; **permettre q.ch. à qn** to allow s.o. s.th. ‖ *intr*—**permettez!** excuse me!; **permettre à qn de** + *inf* to permit s.o. to or let s.o. + *inf*; **vous permettez?** may I? ‖ *ref*—**se permettre de** to take the liberty of

permis [pɛrmi] *m* permit, license; **permis de conduire** driver's license; **permis de construire** construction permit

permission [pɛrmisjɔ̃] *f* permission; (mil) furlough, leave

permissionnaire [pɛrmisjɔnɛr] *m* soldier on leave

permutation [pɛrmytɑsjɔ̃] *f* permutation; exchange of posts; transposition

permuter [pɛrmyte] *tr* to permute; exchange ‖ *intr* to change places

perni·cieux [pɛrnisjø] **-cieuse** [sjøz] *adj* pernicious

péroné [perɔne] *m* (anat) fibula

pérorer [perɔre] *intr* to hold forth

Pérou [peru] *m*—**le Pérou** Peru

peroxyde [perɔksid] *m* peroxide

perpendiculaire [pɛrpɑ̃dikylɛr] *adj & f* perpendicular

perpète [pɛrpɛt]—**à perpète** (slang) forever

perpétrer [pɛrpetre] **§10** *tr* to perpetrate

perpé·tuel -tuelle [pɛrpetɥɛl] *adj* perpetual; life (*imprisonment*); constant, continual

perpétuer [pɛrpetɥe] *tr* to perpetuate ‖ *ref* to be perpetuated

perpétuité [pɛrpetɥite] *f* perpetuity; **à perpétuité** forever; for life

perplexe [pɛrplɛks] *adj* perplexed; **rendre perplexe** to perplex

perplexité [pɛrplɛksite] *f* perplexity

perquisition [pɛrkizisjɔ̃] *f* search

perquisitionner [pɛrkizisjɔne] *intr* to make a search

perron [pɛrɔ̃] *m* front-entrance stone steps

perroquet [pɛrɔkɛ] *m* parrot

perruche [peryʃ] *f* parakeet; hen parrot

perruque [peryk] *f* wig; **vieille perruque** (coll) old fogey

per·san [pɛrsɑ̃] **-sane** [san] *adj* Persian ‖ *m* Persian (*language*) ‖ (*cap*) *mf* Persian (*person*)

perse [pɛrs] *adj* Persian ‖ (*cap*) *mf* Persian ‖ (*cap*) *f* Persia; **la Perse** Persia

persécuter [pɛrsekyte] *tr* to persecute

persécution [pɛrsekysjɔ̃] *f* persecution

persévérer [pɛrsevere] **§10, §96** *intr* to persevere

persienne [pɛrsjɛn] *f* Persian blind, slatted shutter

persil [pɛrsi] *m* parsley

persis·tant [pɛrsistɑ̃] **-tante** [tɑ̃t] *adj* persistent

persister [pɛrsiste] **§96** *intr* to persist; **persister à** to persist in

personnage [pɛrsɔnaʒ] *m* personage; (theat) character

personnalité [pɛrsɔnalite] *f* personality

personne [pɛrsɔn] *f* person; self; appearance; lady, e.g., **belle personne** beautiful lady; e.g., **jolie personne** pretty lady; **grande personne** grown-up; **par personne** per person; **payer de sa personne** to not spare one's efforts; **s'assurer de la personne de** to arrest; **une tierce personne** a third party ‖ *pron indef* no one, nobody; **personne ne or ne . . . personne §90B** no one, nobody, not anyone

person·nel -nelle [pɛrsɔnɛl] *adj* personal ‖ *m* personnel; **personnel navigant** (aer) flying personnel; **personnel de route** (rr) train crew

personnifier [pɛrsɔnifje] *tr* to personify

perspective [pɛrspɛktiv] *f* perspective; outlook; **en perspective** in view

perspicace [pɛrspikas] *adj* perspicacious

persuader [pɛrsɥade] **§97, §99** *tr* to persuade; **persuader q.ch. à qn or persuader qn de q.ch** to persuade s.o. of s.th. ‖ **§98** *intr*—**persuader à qn de** to persuade s.o. to ‖ *ref* to be convinced

persuasion [pɛrsɥazjɔ̃] *f* persuasion

perte [pɛrt] *f* loss; ruin, downfall; **à perte de vue** as far as the eye can see; **en pure perte** uselessly

perti·nent [pɛrtinɑ̃] **-nente** [nɑ̃t] *adj* pertinent

perturba·teur [pɛrtyrbatœr] **-trice** [tris] *adj* disturbing ‖ *mf* troublemaker

perturbation [pɛrtyrbɑsjɔ̃] *f* disruption; perturbation; **perturbation atmosphérique** atmospheric disturbance

perturber [pɛrtyrbe] *tr* to perturb; disturb

péru·vien [peruvjɛ̃] **-vienne** [vjɛn] *adj* Peruvian ‖ (*cap*) *mf* Peruvian

pervenche [pɛrvɑ̃ʃ] *f* periwinkle

per·vers [pɛrvɛr] **-verse** [vɛrs] *adj* perverted ‖ *mf* pervert

perversion [pɛrvɛrsjɔ̃] *f* perversion

perversité [pɛrvɛrsite] *f* perversity, depravity

pervertir [pɛrvɛrtir] *tr* to pervert

pesage [pəzaʒ] *m* weigh-in; paddock

pesamment [pəzamɑ̃] *adv* heavily

pe·sant [pəzɑ̃] **-sante** [zɑ̃t] *adj* heavy ‖ *m*—**valoir son pesant d'or** to be worth one's weight in gold

pesanteur [pəzɑ̃tœr] *f* heaviness; weight; (phys) gravity

pèse-bébé [pɛzbebe] *m* (*pl* **-bébés**) baby scale

pesée [pəze] *f* weighing; leverage

pèse-lettre [pɛzlɛtr] *m* (*pl* **-lettres**) letter scale

pèse-personne [pɛzpɛrsɔn] *m* (*pl* **-personnes**) bathroom scale

peser [pəze] **§2** *tr* to weigh ‖ *intr* to weigh; **peser à** to hang heavy on; **peser sur** to bear down on; lie down on; lie heavy on; stress ‖ *ref* to weigh oneself; weigh in

peson [pəzɔ̃] *m* spring scale

pessimisme [pesimism] *m* pessimism

pessimiste [pesimist] *adj* pessimistic ‖ *mf* pessimist

peste [pɛst] *f* plague; pest, nuisance ‖ *interj* gosh!

pester [pɛste] *intr* to grouse; **pester contre** to rail at

pestifé·ré -rée [pɛstifere] *adj* plague-ridden ‖ *mf* victim of the plague

pestilence [pɛstilɑ̃s] *f* pestilence

pet [pɛ] *m* (slang) scandal; (vulg) wind; **ça ne vaut pas un pet (de lapin)** (coll) it's not worth a wooden nickel ‖ *interj* (coll) look out!

pétale [petal] *m* petal

pétanque [petɑ̃k] *f* petanque

pétarade [petarad] *f* series of explosions; backfire; (vulg) making wind

pétard [petar] *m* firecracker; blast; (slang) gat, revolver; (slang) backside; **faire du pétard** (coll) to kick up a fuss; **lancer un pétard** (coll) to drop a bombshell

pet-de-loup [pɛdlu] *m* (*pl* **pets-de-loup**) absent-minded professor

pet-de-nonne [pɛdnɔn] *m* (*pl* **pets-de-nonne**) fritter

pet-en-l'air [pɛtälɛr] *m invar* short jacket

péter [pete] §10 *tr*—**péter du feu** (coll) to be a live wire ‖ *intr* (coll) to go bang; (vulg) to break wind, fart

pètesec [pɛtsɛk] *adj invar* (coll) bossy, despotic ‖ *m invar* (coll) martinet, bossy fellow

pétil·lant [petijä] **-lante** [jät] *adj* crackling; sparkling

pétiller [petije] *intr* to crackle; to sparkle

pe·tiot [pɔtjo] **-tiote** [tjɔt] *adj* (coll) tiny, wee ‖ *mf* (coll) tot

pe·tit [pɔti] **-tite** [tit] (precedes the noun it modifies) §91 *adj* small, little; short; minor, lower; **en petit** shortened; miniature; **petit à petit** little by little, bit by bit ‖ *mf* youngster; young (*of an animal*); poor little thing ‖ *m* little boy ‖ *f* little girl

petit-beurre [pɔtibœr] *m* (*pl* **petits-beurre**) cookie

petit-cou·sin [pɔtikuzɛ̃] **-sine** [zin] *mf* (*pl* **petits-cousins**) second cousin

petite-fille [pɔtitfij] *f* (*pl* **petites-filles**) granddaughter

petite-nièce [pɔtitnjɛs] *f* (*pl* **petites-nièces**) great-niece

petitesse [pɔtitɛs] *f* smallness

petit-fils [pɔtifis] *m* (*pl* **petits-fils**) grandson; grandchild

petit-gris [pɔtigri] *m* (*pl* **petits-gris**) miniver; snail

pétition [petisjɔ̃] *f* petition; **faire une pétition de principe** to beg the question

petit-lait [pɔtilɛ] *m* (*pl* **petits-laits**) whey

petit-neveu [pɔtinvø] *m* (*pl* **petits-neveux**) great-nephew

petits-enfants [pɔtizäfä] *mpl* grandchildren

petit-suisse [pɔtisɥis] *m* (*pl* **petits-suisses**) cream cheese

peton [pɔtɔ̃] *m* (coll) tiny foot

pétoncle [petɔ̃kl] *m* scallop

Pétrarque [petrark] *m* Petrarch

pétrifier [petrifje] *tr & ref* to petrify

pétrin [petrɛ̃] *m* kneading trough; (coll) mess, jam

pétrir [petrir] *tr* to knead; mold

pétrochimique [petrɔʃimik] *adj* petrochemical

pétrole [petrɔl] *m* petroleum; **à pétrole** kerosene (*lamp*); **pétrole brut** crude oil; **pétrole lampant** kerosene

pétro·lier [petrɔlje] **-lière** [ljɛr] *adj* oil ‖ *m* tanker; oil baron

P et T [peete] *fpl* (letterword) (**Postes et télécommunications**) post office, telephone, and telegraph

pétu·lant [petylä] **-lante** [lät] *adj* lively, frisky

peu [pø] *m* bit, little; **peu de** few; not much; not many; **peu de chose** not much ‖ *adv* §91 little; not very; **à peu près** about, practically; **depuis peu** of late; **peu ou prou** more or less; **peu probable** improbable; **peu s'en faut** very nearly; **pour peu que, si peu que** however little; **quelque peu** somewhat; **sous peu** before long; **tant soit peu** ever so little

peuplade [pœplad] *f* tribe

peuple [pœpl] *adj* plebeian, common ‖ *m* people

peuplement [pœplɔmä] *m* populating; planting; stocking (*e.g., with fish*)

peupler [pœple] *tr* to people; plant; stock ‖ *intr* to multiply, breed

peuplier [pøplje] *m* poplar

peur [pœr] *f* fear; **avoir peur (de)** to be afraid (of); **de peur que** lest, for fear that; **une peur bleue** (coll) an awful fright

peu·reux [pœrø] **-reuse** [røz] *adj* fearful, timid

peux [pø] (*v* **peut, peuvent**) see **pourvoir**

peut-être [pøtɛtr] *adv* perhaps; **peut-être que non** perhaps not

p. ex. *abbr* (**par exemple**) e.g.

phalange [falãʒ] *f* phalanx

phalène [falɛn] *m & f* moth

phallique [falik] *adj* phallic

phallus [falys] *m* phallus, penis

Pharaon [faraɔ̃] *m* Pharaoh

phare [far] *m* lighthouse; beacon; (aut) headlight; **phares code** dimmers

phari·sien [farizjɛ̃] **-sienne** [zjɛn] *adj* pharisaic ‖ *mf* pharisee

pharmaceutique [farmasøtik] *adj* pharmaceutical ‖ *f* pharmaceutics

pharmacie [farmasi] *f* drugstore, pharmacy; medicine chest; drugs

pharma·cien [farmasjɛ̃] **-cienne** [sjɛn] *mf* pharmacist

pharynx [farɛ̃ks] *m* pharynx

phase [faz] *f* phase

Phébé [febe] *f* Phoebe

Phénicie [fenisi] *f* Phoenicia; **la Phénicie** Phoenicia

phéni·cien [fenisjɛ̃] **-cienne** [sjɛn] *adj* Phoenician ‖ (*cap*) *mf* Phoenician

phénix [feniks] *m* phoenix

phénomé·nal **-nale** [fenɔmenal] *adj* (*pl* **-naux** [no]) phenomenal

phénomène [fenɔmɛn] *m* phenomenon; (coll) monster, freak

philanthrope [filätrɔp] *mf* philanthropist

philanthropie [filätrɔpi] *f* philanthropy

philatélie [filateli] *f* philately

philatéliste [filatelist] *mf* philatelist

philip·pin [filipɛ̃] **-pine** [pin] *adj* Philippine ‖ (*cap*) *mf* Filipino

Philippines [filipin] *fpl* Philippines

philistin [filistɛ̃] *adj masc & m* Philistine

philologie [filɔlɔʒi] *f* philology

philologue [filɔlɔg] *mf* philologist

philosophe [filozɔf] *adj* philosophic ‖ *mf* philosopher

philosophie [filɔzɔfi] *f* philosophy
philosophique [filɔzɔfik] *adj* philosophic(al)
philtre [filtr] *m* philter
phlébite [flebit] *f* phlebitis
phobie [fɔbi] *f* phobia
phonétique [fɔnetik] *adj* phonetic ‖ *f* phonetics
phoniatrie [fɔnjatri] *f* speech therapy
phono [fɔno] *m* (coll) phonograph
phonographe [fɔnɔgraf] *m* phonograph
phonologie [fɔnɔlɔʒi] *f* phonology
phonothèque [fɔnɔtɛk] *f* record library
phoque [fɔk] *m* seal
phosphate [fɔsfat] *m* phosphate
phosphore [fɔsfɔr] *m* phosphorus
phosphores·cent [fɔsfɔresɑ̃] **-cente** [sɑ̃t] *adj* phosphorescent
photo [fɔto] *f* photo, snapshot
photocopier [fɔtɔkɔpje] *tr* to photocopy, to photostat
photocopieur [fɔtɔkɔpjœr] *m* photocopier
photogénique [fɔtɔʒenik] *adj* photogenic
photographe [fɔtɔgraf] *mf* photographer
photographie [fɔtɔgrafi] *f* photography; photograph
photographier [fɔtɔgrafje] *tr* to photograph
photogravure [fɔtɔgravyr] *f* photoengraving
photostat [fɔtɔsta] *m* photostat
photothèque [fɔtɔtɛk] *f* photograph library
phrase [fraz] *f* sentence; (mus) phrase; **phrase de choc** punch line
phrénologie [frenɔlɔʒi] *f* phrenology
physi·cien [fizisjɛ̃] **-cienne** [sjɛn] *mf* physicist
physiologie [fizjɔlɔʒi] *f* physiology
physiologique [fizjɔlɔʒik] *adj* physiological
physionomie [fizjɔnɔmi] *f* physiognomy
physique [fizik] *adj* physical; material ‖ *m* physique; appearance ‖ *f* physics
piaffer [pjafe] *intr* to paw the ground; fidget, fume
piailler [pjɑje] *intr* (coll) to cheep; (coll) to squeal
pianiste [pjanist] *mf* pianist
piano [pjano] *m* piano; **piano à queue** grand piano; **piano droit** upright piano ‖ *adv* (coll) quietly
pianoter [pjanɔte] *intr* to strum; to drum, to thrum; to rattle away
piastre [pjastr] *f* (Canad) dollar
piaule [pjol] *f* (slang) pad (*one's home*)
piauler [pjole] *intr* to peep; screech (*said of pulley*); (coll) to whine
pic [pik] *m* peak; (*tool*) pick; (orn) woodpecker; **à pic** sheer, steep; (coll) in the nick of time; **couler à pic** to sink like a stone
picaillons [pikajɔ̃] *mpl* (slang) dough
picaresque [pikarɛsk] *adj* picaresque
piccolo [pikɔlo] *m* piccolo
pichet [piʃɛ] *m* pitcher, jug
pick-up [pikœp] *m invar* pickup; record player; pickup truck
picoler [pikɔle] *intr* (slang) to get pickled
picorer [pikɔre] *tr & intr* to peck

picoter [pikɔte] *tr* to prick; peck at; sting
picotin [pikɔtɛ̃] *m* peck (*measure*)
pictu·ral -rale [piktyral] *adj* (*pl* **-raux** [ro]) pictorial
pie [pi] *adj invar* piebald ‖ *f* magpie
pièce [pjɛs] *f* piece; patch; room; play; document; coin; wine barrel; **à la pièce** separately; **donner la pièce à** to tip; **faire pièce à** to play a trick on; to put a check on; **inventé de toutes pièces** made up out of the whole cloth; **la pièce** apiece; **pièce à conviction** (law) exhibit; **pièce comptable** voucher; **pièce d'eau** ornamental pond; **pièce de rechange, pièce détachée** spare part; **pièce de résistance** pièce de résistance; (culin) entree; **pièce rapportée** in-law; **pièces rendues** change; **reprenez alors votre pièce au retour de monnaies** take your change from the coin return; **tout d'une pièce** in one piece; (coll) rigid; (coll) stiffly ‖ *adv* apiece
pied [pje] *m* foot; foothold; **à pied** on foot; **à pied d'œuvre** on the site, on the spot, where the work is being done; **au pied de la lettre** literally; **au pied levé** offhand; **c'est des pieds!** (slang) that's cool!, that's fresh!; **de pied en cap** from head to toe; **faire le pied de grue** (coll) to cool one's heels, to stand around waiting; **faire les pieds à** (coll) to give what's coming to; **faire un pied de nez** (coll) to thumb one's nose; **lever le pied** to abscond; **mettre à pied** to dismiss, fire; **mettre les pieds dans le plat** (coll) to put one's foot in one's mouth; **mettre pied à terre** to dismount; **mettre qn au pied du mur** to corner s.o.; force s.o. to a showdown; **pied d'athlète** (pathol) athlete's foot; **pied équin** clubfoot; **travailler comme un pied** (coll) to botch one's work; **vous avez pied?** can you touch bottom?
pied-à-terre [pjetatɛr] *m invar* hangout, temporary base
pied-bot [pjebo] *m* (*pl* **pieds-bots**) club-footed person
pied-d'alouette [pjedalwɛt] *m* (*pl* **pieds-d'alouette**) delphinium
pied-de-poule [pjedəpul] *adj invar* hound's-tooth (*design or pattern*)
pied-droit [pjedrwa] *m* (*pl* **pieds-droits**) (archit) pier
piédes·tal -tale [pjedɛstal] *m* (*pl* **-taux** [to]) pedestal
pied-noir [pjenwar] *m* (*pl* **pieds-noirs**) Algerian of European descent
piège [pjɛʒ] *m* trap, snare
piéger [pjeʒe] §1 *tr* to trap, snare; booby-trap
pie-grièche [pigrijɛʃ] *f* (*pl* **pies-grièches**) shrike; shrew
pierraille [pjɛrɑj] *f* rubble
pierre [pjɛr] *f* stone; **faire d'une pierre deux coups** to kill two birds with one stone; **Pierre** Peter; **pierre à aiguiser** whetstone; **pierre à briquet** flint; **pierre à chaux, pierre à plâtre** gypsum; **pierre à feu, pierre à fusil** gunflint;

pierre angulaire cornerstone; **pierre à rasoir** hone; **pierre calcaire** limestone; **pierre d'achoppement** stumbling block; **pierre de gué** stepping stone; **pierre de touche** touchstone; **pierre tombale** tombstone

pierreries [pjɛri] *fpl* precious stones

pier·reux [pjɛrø] **-reuse** [røz] *adj* stony ‖ *f* (coll) streetwalker

pierrot [pjɛro] *m* clown; sparrow; (coll) oddball; (coll) greenhorn

piété [pjete] *f* piety; devotion

piéter [pjete] §10 *intr* to toe the line ‖ *ref* to stand firm

piétiner [pjetine] *tr* to trample on ‖ *intr* to stamp; mark time

piéton [pjetɔ̃] *m* pedestrian

piètre [pjɛtr] *adj* poor, wretched

pieu [pjø] *m* (*pl* **pieux**) post, stake; (archit) pile

pieuvre [pjœvr] *f* octopus; (coll) leech

pieux [pjø] **pieuse** [pjøz] *adj* pious; dutiful; white (*lie*)

pif [pif] *m* (slang) snout (*nose*) ‖ *interj* bang!

pige [piʒ] *f* (slang) year; **à la pige** (journ) so much a line; on a free-lance basis; **faire la pige à** (slang) to outdo

pigeon [piʒɔ̃] *m* pigeon; **pigeon voyageur** homing pigeon

pigeonner [piʒɔne] *tr* (coll) to dupe

pigeonnier [piʒɔnje] *m* dovecote

piger [piʒe] §38 *tr* (slang) to look at; (slang) to get ‖ *intr*—**tu piges?** (slang) do you get it?

pigment [pigmɑ̃] *m* pigment

pignocher [piɲɔʃe] *intr* to pick at one's food

pignon [piɲɔ̃] *m* gable; (mach) pinion; **avoir pignon sur rue** (coll) to have a home of one's own; (coll) to be well off; **pignon de chaîne** sprocket wheel

pile [pil] *f* stack, pile; pier; (elec) battery (*primary cell*); (coll) thrashing; **pile atomique** atomic pile; **pile ou face** heads or tails; **pile sèche** dry cell ‖ *adv* (coll) short; (coll) exactly; **tomber pile** (coll) to happen at the right moment

piler [pile] *tr* to grind, crush

pilier [pilje] *m* pillar; **pilier de cabaret** barfly

pillage [pijaʒ] *m* looting

pil·lard [pijar] **-larde** [jard] *adj* looting ‖ *mf* looter

piller [pije] *tr & intr* to loot; plagiarize

pil·leur [pijœr] **-leuse** [jøz] *mf* pillager

pilon [pilɔ̃] *m* pestle; (coll) drumstick (*of chicken*); (coll) wooden leg; **pilon à vapeur** steam hammer

pilonnage [pilɔnaʒ] *m* crushing; **pilonnage aérien** saturation bombing

pilonner [pilɔne] *tr* to crush; bomb

pilori [pilɔri] *m* pillory

pilot [pilo] *m* pile (*in piling*); rags (*for paper*)

pilotage [pilɔtaʒ] *m* piloting; **pilotage sans visibilité** blind flying

pilote [pilɔt] *m* pilot; **pilote de ligne** airline pilot; **pilote d'émission** (telv) anchor man; **pilote d'essai** test pilot

piloter [pilɔte] *tr* to pilot; guide; drive piles into ‖ *intr* to pilot; be a guide

pilotis [pilɔti] *m* piles

pilule [pilyl] *f* pill; (coll) bitter pill; **dorer la pilule** to gild the lily

piment [pimɑ̃] *m* allspice (*berry*); (fig) spice; **piment doux** sweet pepper; **piment rouge** red or hot pepper

pimenter [pimɑ̃te] *tr* to season with red pepper; (fig) to spice

pim·pant [pɛ̃pɑ̃] **-pante** [pɑ̃t] *adj* smart, spruce

pin [pɛ̃] *m* pine; **pin de Weymouth** (*Pinus strobus*) white pine; **pin sylvestre** (*Pinus sylvestris*) Scotch pine

pinacle [pinakl] *m* pinnacle

pince [pɛ̃s] *f* tongs; pliers; forceps; crowbar; gripper; grip; pleat; claw (*of crab*); **aller à pinces** (slang) to hoof it; **petites pinces, pince à épiler** tweezers; **pince à linge** clothespin; **pince à sucre** sugar tongs; **pince hémostatique** hemostat; **pinces** tongs; pincers; pliers; **pinces de cycliste** bicycle clips; **serrer la pince à** (slang) to shake hands with

pin·cé -cée [pɛ̃se] *adj* prim, tight-lipped; thin, pinched ‖ *f* see **pincée**

pin·ceau [pɛ̃so] *m* (*pl* **-ceaux**) paintbrush; pencil (*of light*)

pincée [pɛ̃se] *f* pinch

pincement [pɛ̃smɑ̃] *m* pinching; plucking

pince-monseigneur [pɛ̃smɔ̃sɛɲœr] *f* (*pl* **pinces-monseigneur**) jimmy

pince-nez [pɛ̃sne] *m invar* nose glasses

pincer [pɛ̃se] §51 *tr* to pinch; grip; nip off; pluck; top (*plants*); purse (*the lips*); pleat; (coll) to nab, to catch ‖ *intr* to bite (*said of cold*); **en pincer pour** (slang) to have a crush on; **pincer de** (mus) to strum on

pince-sans-rire [pɛ̃ssɑ̃rir] *adj invar* deadpan ‖ *mf invar* deadpan comic

pincette [pɛ̃sɛt] *f* tweezers; **pincettes** tweezers; fire tongs

pinçon [pɛ̃sɔ̃] *m* bruise (*from pinch*)

pinède [pinɛd] *f* pine grove

pingouin [pɛ̃gwɛ̃] *m* (*family:* Alcidae) auk

ping-pong [piŋpɔ̃g] *m* table tennis, Ping-Pong

pingre [pɛ̃gr] *adj* (coll) stingy ‖ *mf* (coll) tightwad

pinson [pɛ̃sɔ̃] *m* (orn) finch

pintade [pɛ̃tad] *f* guinea fowl

pin up [pinœp] *f invar* (coll) pinup girl

pioche [pjɔʃ] *f* pickax

piocher [pjɔʃe] *tr & intr* to dig, pick; (coll) to cram

pio·cheur [pjɔʃœr] **-cheuse** [ʃøz] *mf* digger; (coll) grind ‖ *f* (mach) cultivator

piolet [pjɔlɛ] *m* ice ax

pion [pjɔ̃] *m* (checkers) man; (chess & fig) pawn; (slang) proctor; **damer le pion à** (coll) to get the better of

pionnier [pjɔnje] *m* pioneer; young student chess player

pipe [pip] *f* pipe; **casser sa pipe** (slang) to kick the bucket

pi·peau [pipo] *m* (*pl* **-peaux**) bird call; shepherd's pipe; lime twig

piper [pipe] *tr* to snare, catch; load (*the dice*); mark (*the cards*) ‖ *intr*—**ne pipe pas!** (coll) not a peep out of you!

pi·quant [pikɑ̃] **-quante** [kɑ̃t] *adj* piquant, intriguing; racy, spicy ‖ *m* sting; prickle; quill (*of porcupine*); piquancy, pungency; point (*of story*); (fig) bite

pique [pik] *m* (cards) spade; (cards) spades ‖ *f* pike; pique

pi·qué -quée [pike] *adj* stung; sour; (mus) staccato; (coll) batty; **ne pas être piqué des vers** (slang) to be first rate; **piqué de** studded with ‖ *m* quilt; **descendre en piqué** to nose-dive

pique-assiette [pikasjɛt] *mf* (*pl* **-assiettes**) (coll) sponger

pique-feu [pikfø] *m invar* poker

pique-fleurs [pikflœr] *m invar* flower holder

pique-nique [piknik] *m* (*pl* **-niques**) picnic

pique-niquer [piknike] *intr* to picnic

piquer [pike] *tr* to sting; prick; pique; stimulate; quilt; spur; give a shot to; (mus) to play staccato; (slang) to filch; (slang) to pinch, nab ‖ *intr* to turn sour; (aer) to nose-dive ‖ §97 *ref* to be piqued; spot; give oneself a shot; **se piquer de** to take pride in; **se piquer pour** to take a fancy to

piquet [pikɛ] *m* peg, stake; picket; **piquet de grève** picket line

piqueter [pikte] §34 *tr* to stake out; spot, dot

piquette [pikɛt] *f* poor wine; (coll) crushing defeat

pi·queur [pikœr] **-queuse** [køz] *mf* stitcher ‖ *m* huntsman; outrider

piqûre [pikyr] *f* sting, bite; prick; injection, shot; stitching; puncture; **piqûre de ver** moth hole

pirate [pirat] *m* pirate; **pirate de l'air** hijacker

pirater [pirate] *intr* to pirate

piraterie [piratri] *f* piracy; **piraterie aérienne** hijacking

pire [pir] (precedes the noun it modifies) §91 *adj comp & super* worse; worst ‖ *m* (the) worst

pirouette [pirwɛt] *f* pirouette

pirouetter [pirwete] *intr* to pirouette

pis [pi] *adj comp & super* worse; worst ‖ *m* udder; **au pis aller** at worst; **de pis en pis** worse and worse; **(le) pis** (the) worst; **qui pis est** what's worse; **tant pis** so much the worse ‖ *adv comp & super* §91 worse; worst

pis-aller [pizale] *m invar* makeshift

piscine [pisin] *f* swimming pool

pissenlit [pisɑ̃li] *m* dandelion

pisser [pise] *tr* (coll) to spout (*water*); (coll) to leak; (slang) to pass (*e.g., blood*); **pisser de la copie** (slang) to be a hack writer ‖ *intr* (slang) to urinate

pisse-vinaigre [pisvinɛgr] *m invar* (coll) skinflint

pissoir [piswar] *m* (coll) urinal

pissotière [pisɔtjɛr] *f* (coll) street urinal

pistache [pistaʃ] *f* pistachio

pistage [pistaʒ] *m* tracking

piste [pist] *f* track; trail; ring (*of, e.g., circus*); rink; lane (*of highway*); **à double piste** four-lane (*highway*); runway; **piste cavalière** bridle path; **piste cyclable** bicycle path; **piste d'atterrissage** landing strip; **piste de danse** dance floor; **piste d'envol** runway; **piste pour skieurs** ski run; **piste sonore** sound track

pister [piste] *tr* to track, trail

pistolet [pistɔlɛ] *m* pistol; spray gun; (coll) card; **pistolet à bouchon** popgun; **pistolet à souder** welding gun; **pistolet d'arçon** horse pistol; **pistolet mitrailleur** submachine gun

piston [pistɔ̃] *m* piston; (coll) pull

pistonner [pistɔne] *tr* (coll) to push, back

pitance [pitɑ̃s] *f* ration; food

pi·teux [pitø] **-teuse** [tøz] *adj* pitiful, sorry, sad

pitié [pitje] *f* pity; **à faire pitié** (coll) very badly; **par pitié!** for pity's sake!; **quelle pitié!** how awful!

piton [pitɔ̃] *m* screw eye; peak

pitou [pitu] *m* (Canad) dog; (Canad) tyke

pitoyable [pitwajabl] *adj* pitiful

pitre [pitr] *m* clown

pittoresque [pitɔrɛsk] *adj* picturesque

pivoine [pivwan] *f* peony

pivot [pivo] *m* pivot

pivoter [pivɔte] *intr* to pivot

P.J. [peʒi] *f* (letterword) (**police judiciaire**) (coll) police (*dealing with criminal cases*)

placage [plakaʒ] *m* veneering; plating

placard [plakar] *m* cupboard; closet; placard, poster; (typ) galley; **placards de presse** press passes

placarder [plakarde] *tr* to placard; (typ) to print in galleys

place [plas] *f* place; city square; room; seat; job, position; fare; **places debout** standing room; **sur place** on the spot

placement [plasmɑ̃] *m* placement; investment; **de placement** employment (*agency*)

placer [plase] §51 *tr* to place; invest; slip in ‖ *ref* to seat oneself; rank; get a job; take place

pla·ceur [plasœr] **-ceuse** [søz] *mf* employment agent ‖ *m* usher

placide [plasid] *adj* placid

pla·cier [plasje] **-cière** [sjɛr] *mf* agent, representative

placoplâtre [plakɔplɑtr] *m* plasterboard

plafond [plafɔ̃] *m* ceiling

plafonner [plafɔne] *intr*—**plafonner (à)** to hit the top (at)

plafonnier [plafɔnje] *m* ceiling light; (aut) dome light

plage [plaʒ] *f* beach; band (*of record*); (poetic) clime

plagiaire [plaʒjɛr] *mf* plagiarist

plagiat [plaʒja] *m* plagiarism

plagier [plaʒje] *tr & intr* to plagiarize

plagiste [plaʒist] *mf* beach concessionaire

plaider [plede] *tr* to argue (*a case*); plead (*e.g., ignorance*) ‖ *intr* to plead; go to law

plai·deur [plɛdœr] **-deuse** [døz] *mf* litigant

plaidoirie [plɛdwari] *f* pleading

plaidoyer [plɛdwaje] *m* appeal (*of lawyer to judge or jury*)

plaie [plɛ] *f* wound, sore; plague; **plaie en séton** flesh wound

plai·gnant [plɛɲɑ̃] **-gnante** [ɲɑ̃t] *mf* plaintiff

plain [plɛ̃] *m* high tide

plaindre [plɛ̃dr] §15, §97 *tr* to pity ‖ *ref* to complain

plaine [plɛn] *f* plain

plain-pied [plɛ̃pje] *m*—**de plain-pied** on the same floor; (fig) on an equal footing

plainte [plɛ̃t] *f* complaint; moan

plain·tif [plɛ̃tif] **-tive** [tiv] *adj* plaintive

plaire [plɛr] §52 *intr* to please; **plaire à** to be pleasing to, appeal to, e.g., **cette musique leur plaît** that music appeals to them; to inspire liking in, e.g., **le lait lui plaît** he likes milk, **le dîner m'a plu** I liked the dinner; to be suitable for, e.g., **ce plan lui plaît** that plan suits her; **s'il vous plaît** please ‖ §96 *ref* (*pp* **plu** *invar*) to be pleased; enjoy oneself; like one another; **se plaire à** to like it in, e.g., **je me plais à la campagne** I like it in the country

plaisance [plɛzɑ̃s] *f*—**de plaisance** pleasure (*e.g., boat*)

plai·sant [plɛzɑ̃] **-sante** [zɑ̃t] *adj* pleasant; funny ‖ *m*—**mauvais plaisant** practical joker

plaisanter [plɛzɑ̃te] *tr* to poke fun at ‖ *intr* to joke

plaisanterie [plɛzɑ̃tri] *f* joke; joking

plaisantin [plɛzɑ̃tɛ̃] *adj masc* roguish, waggish ‖ *m* wag, kidder

plaisent [plɛz] *v* (**plaisons**) see **plaire**

plaisir [plezir] *m* pleasure; **à plaisir** without cause; at one's pleasure; **au plaisir (de vous revoir)** good-by; **faire plaisir à** to please, give pleasure to

plaît [ple] *v* see **plaire**

plan [plɑ̃] **plane** [plan] *adj* even, flat; plane (*angle*) ‖ *m* plan; design; (geom) plane; **au deuxième plan** in the background; **au premier plan** in the foreground; downstage; **au troisième plan** far in the background; **gros plan** (mov) close-up; **laisser en plan** (coll) to leave stranded; (coll) to put off, delay; **lever un plan** to survey; **plan de paix** peace plan; **plan de travail** work schedule; **plan d'occupation des sols (P.O.S.)** zoning code; **rester en plan** (coll) to remain in suspense; **sur le plan de** from the point of view of ‖ *f* see **plane**

planche [plɑ̃ʃ] *f* board; plank; (hort) bed; (typ) plate; (slang) blackboard; **faire de la planche à voile** to go wind surfing; **faire la planche** to float on one's back; **planche à pain** breadboard; (slang) flat-chested woman; **planche à repasser** iron-

ing board; **planche à roulettes** skateboard; **planche de bord** instrument panel; **planche de débarquement** gangplank; **planche de salut** sheet anchor; last hope; **planche pourrie** (slang) dubious character

planchéier [plɑ̃ʃeje] *tr* to floor; board

plancher [plɑ̃ʃe] *m* floor; **le plancher des vaches** (coll) terra firma

plane [plan] *f* drawknife

planer [plane] *tr* to plane ‖ *intr* to hover; glide; float; **planer sur** to overlook, sweep (*e.g., a landscape with one's eyes*); (fig) to hover over

planète [planɛt] *f* planet

planeur [planœr] *m* glider

planeuse [planøz] *f* planing machine

planification [planifikɑsjɔ̃] *f* planning; **planification des naissances** family planning

planifier [planifje] *tr* to plan

planisme [planism] *m*—**planisme familial** family planning

planning [planiŋ] *m* detailed plan; **planning familial** birth control

plan-plan [plɑ̃plɑ̃] *adv* (coll) quietly, without hurrying

planque [plɑ̃k] *f* (coll) soft job; (slang) hideout

planquer [plɑ̃ke] *tr* to hide ‖ *ref* (mil) to take cover; (slang) to hide out

plant [plɑ̃] *m* planting; bed, patch; seedling, sapling

plantation [plɑ̃tɑsjɔ̃] *f* planting; plantation; **plantation de cheveux** hairline; head of hair

plante [plɑ̃t] *f* plant; sole

plan·té -tée [plɑ̃te] *adj* set, situated

planter [plɑ̃te] *tr* to plant; set; **planter là** to give the slip to ‖ *ref* to stand

planteur [plɑ̃tœr] *m* planter

plantoir [plɑ̃twar] *m* (hort) dibble

planton [plɑ̃tɔ̃] *m* (mil) orderly

plantu·reux [plɑ̃tyrø] **-reuse** [røz] *adj* abundant; fertile; (coll) buxom

plaque [plak] *f* plate; plaque; splotch; **plaque à crêpes** pancake griddle; **plaque croûteuse** scab; **plaque d'immatriculation, plaque minéralogique** (aut) license plate; **plaque tournante** (rr) turntable; (fig) hub (*of a city*)

plaquer [plake] *tr* to plate; veneer; plaster down (*one's hair*); strike (*a chord*); (football) to tackle; (coll) to jilt; **plaquer à l'électricité** to electroplate ‖ *ref* to lie flat; (aer) to pancake

plaquette [plakɛt] *f* plaque; pamphlet; (histology) platelet

plastic [plastik] *m* plastic bomb

plastique [plastik] *adj* plastic ‖ *m* plastics ‖ *f* plastic art

plastron [plastrɔ̃] *m* shirt front; breastplate; hostile contingent (*in war games*)

plastronner [plastrɔne] *intr* (fig) to throw out one's chest

plat [pla] **plate** [plat] *adj* flat; even; smooth (*sea*); dead; (*calm*); corny (*joke*); **à plat**

run-down; flat; **tomber plat** (coll) to fall unluckily ‖ *m* dish; platter; course (*of meal*); flat (*of hand*); blade (*of oar*); face (*of hammer*); **plat cuisiné** platter, short-order meal; **plat de côtes** sparerib; **plat du jour** today's special, chef's special; **plat principal, plat de résistance** entree; **plats** (bb) boards

platane [platan] *m* plane tree; **faux platane** sycamore

pla·teau [plato] *m* (*pl* -teaux) plateau; tray; shelf; platform; plate; pan (*of scale*); (mov, telv) set; (rr) flatcar; (theat) stage; **plateau porte-disque** turntable (*of phonograph*); **pleateau repas congelé** frozen dinner; **plateau tournant** revolving stage; lazy Susan

plate-bande [platbɑ̃d] *f* (*pl* **plates-bandes**) flower bed

plate-forme [platfɔrm] *f* (*pl* **plates-formes**) platform; (rr) flatcar

platine [platin] *m* platinum ‖ *f* plate; platen; lock (*of gun*); place (*of microscope*)

plati·né -née [platine] *adj* platinum-plated; platinum

platitude [platityd] *f* platitude; flatness; obsequiousness

Platon [platɔ̃] *m* Plato

plâtre [plɑtr] *m* plaster; plaster cast; **essuyer les plâtres** to be the first occupant of a new house; **plâtre à mouler** plaster of Paris

plâtrer [plɑtre] *tr* to plaster; put in a cast; fertilize ‖ *ref* (coll) to pile on the make-up or face powder

plausible [plozibl] *adj* plausible

plé·béien [plebejɛ̃] **-béienne** [bejɛn] *adj & mf* plebeian

plein [plɛ̃] **pleine** [plɛn] *adj* full; round, plump; solid (*bar, wheel, wire, etc.*); continuous (*line*); heavy (*heart*); in foal, with calf, etc.; (coll) drunk; **plein aux as** (coll) well-heeled; **plein de** full of; covered with; preoccupied with; **plein de soi** self-centered ‖ (when standing before noun) *adj* full; high (*tide*); **en plein +** *noun* in the midst of the + *noun,* right in the + *noun;* at the height of the (*season*); in the open (*air*); out at (*sea*), on the high (*seas*); in broad (*daylight*); in the dead of (*winter*) ‖ *m* full (*of the moon*); bull's-eye; downstroke; **battre son plein** to be in full swing; **en plein** plumb, plump, squarely; **faire le plein (de)** to fill up the tank (with) ‖ **plein** *adv* full; **tout plein** very much

plein-emploi [plɛ̃ɑ̃plwa] *m* full employment

pleu·rard [plœrar] **-rarde** [rard] *adj* (coll) whimpering ‖ *mf* (coll) whimperer

pleurer [plœre] *tr* to weep over; shed (*tears*); **pleurer misère** to complain of being poor ‖ *intr* to cry, weep; **pleurer à chaudes larmes** to weep bitterly; **pleurer dans le gilet de qn** (coll) to cry on s.o.'s shoulder

pleurésie [plœrezi] *f* pleurisy

pleu·reur [plœrœr] **-reuse** [røz] *adj* weeping ‖ *f* paid mourner

pleurnicher [plœrniʃe] *intr* to whimper, snivel

pleurs [plœr] *mpl* tears

pleutre [pløtr] *adj* (coll) cowardly ‖ *m* (coll) coward

pleuvasser [pløvase] *intr* (coll) to drizzle

pleuvoir [pløvwar] §53 *intr & impers* to rain; **pleuvoir à verse, à flots,** or **à seaux** to rain buckets

pli [pli] *m* fold; pleat; bend (*of arm or leg*); hollow (*of knee*); letter; envelope; undulation (*of ground*); (cards) trick; **faux pli** crease, wrinkle; **petit pli** tuck; **sous ce pli** enclosed, herewith; **sous pli cacheté** in a sealed envelope; **sous pli distinct** or **séparé** under separate cover; **sous pli fermé** in a sealed envelope

pliage [plijaʒ] *m* folding

pliant [plijɑ̃] **pliante** [plijɑ̃t] *adj* folding; collapsible; pliant ‖ *m* campstool, folding chair

plier [plije] *tr* to fold; bend; force; **plier bagage** to leave ‖ *intr* to fold; bend; yield; **ne pas plier, s.v.p.** (*formula on envelope*) please do not bend ‖ §96 *ref* to fold; yield; fall back (*said of army*)

plinthe [plɛ̃t] *f* baseboard

plisser [plise] *tr* to pleat; crease; wrinkle; squint (*the eyes*) ‖ *intr* to fold ‖ *ref* to wrinkle; pucker up (*said of mouth*)

plomb [plɔ̃] *m* lead; shot; seal; plumb; sinker (*of fishline*); (elec) fuse; **à plomb** plumb, vertical; straight down, directly; **faire sauter un plomb** to burn or blow out a fuse

plombage [plɔ̃baʒ] *m* filing (*of tooth*); sealing (*e.g., at customs*)

plombagine [plɔ̃baʒin] *f* graphite

plom·bé -bée [plɔ̃be] *adj* leaden; in bond, sealed; filled (*tooth*); livid (*hue*)

plomber [plɔ̃be] *tr* to cover with lead; seal; plumb; fill (*a tooth*); make livid; roll (*the ground*)

plomberie [plɔ̃bri] *f* plumbing; plumbing-supply store; leadwork

plombeur [plɔ̃bœr] *m* (mach) roller

plombier [plɔ̃bje] *m* plumber; worker in lead

plonge [plɔ̃ʒ] *f* dishwashing

plon·geant [plɔ̃ʒɑ̃] **-geante** [ʒɑ̃t] *adj* plunging; from above

plongée [plɔ̃ʒe] *f* plunge; dive; dip, slope; **en plongée** submerged

plongeoir [plɔ̃ʒwar] *m* diving board

plongeon [plɔ̃ʒɔ̃] *m* plunge; dive; (football) tackle; **plongeon de haut vol** high dive

plonger [plɔ̃ʒe] §38 *tr* to plunge; thrust, stick ‖ *intr* to plunge; dive; (coll) to have a good view; **plonger raide** to crash-dive ‖ *ref*—**se plonger dans** to immerse oneself in; give oneself over to

plon·geur [plɔ̃ʒœr] **-geuse** [ʒøz] *adj* diving ‖ *mf* diver; dishwasher (*in restaurant*) ‖ *m* (mach) plunger; (orn) diver

plot [plo] *m* (elec) contact point

plouc [pluk] *m* (coll) peasant, hick
ployer [plwaje] §47 *tr* & *intr* to bend
plu [ply] *v* see **plaire**; see **pleuvoir**
pluches [plyʃ] *fpl* (mil) K.P.
pluie [plɥi] *f* rain; shower; **pluie acide** acid rain; **pluies radioactives** fallout
plumage [plymaʒ] *m* plumage
plumard [plymar] *m*—**aller au plumard** (slang) to hit the hay
plume [plym] *f* feather; pen; penpoint
plu·meau [plymo] *m* (*pl* **-meaux**) feather duster
plumer [plyme] *tr* to pluck; (coll) to fleece ‖ *intr* to feather one's oar
plumet [plymɛ] *m* plume
plu·meux [plymø] **-meuse** [møz] *adj* feathery
plumier [plymje] *m* pencil box
plupart [plypar] *f*—**la plupart** most; the most; for the most part; **la plupart de** most; the most; most of, the majority of; **la plupart d'entre nous (eux)** most of us (them); **pour la plupart** for the most part
plu·riel **-rielle** [plyrjɛl] *adj* & *m* plural; **au pluriel** in the plural
plus [ply] ([plyz] before vowel; [plys] in final position) *m* plus; **au plus, tout au plus** at the most, at best; at the latest; at the outside; **d'autant plus** all the more so; **de plus** more; moreover, besides; **de plus en plus** more and more; **en plus** extra; **en plus de** in addition to, besides; **le plus, la plus, les plus** (the) most; **le plus de** the most; **le plus que** as much as, as fast as; **ni ... non plus** nor ... either, e.g., **ni moi non plus** nor I either; **ni plus ni moins** neither more nor less; **non plus** neither, not ... either; **plus de** more, e.g., **plus de chaleur** more heat; no more, e.g., **plus de potage** no more soup; **plus est** what is more, moreover ‖ *adv comp* & *super* §91 more; **des plus** + *adj* most + *adj*, extremely + *adj*; **(le) plus ...** (the) most ... , e.g., **ce que j'aime le plus** what I like (the) most; **le** (or **son**, etc.) **plus** + *adj* the (or his, etc.) most; **ne ... plus** §90 no more, no longer; **ne ... plus que** §90 now only, e.g., **il n'y a plus que mon oncle** there is now only my uncle; **on ne peut plus** + *adj* or *adv* extremely + *adj* or *adv*; **plus de** (followed by numeral) more than; **plus jamais** never more; **plus ... plus** (or **moins**) the more ... the more (or the less); **plus que** more than; **plus tôt** sooner ‖ *prep* plus
plusieurs [plyzjœr] *adj* & *pron indef* several
plus-que-parfait [plyskəparfɛ] *m* pluperfect
plus-value [plyvaly] *f* (*pl* **-values**) appreciation; increase; surplus; extra cost; surplus value (*in Marxian economics*)
Plutarque [plytark] *m* Plutarch
Pluton [plytɔ̃] *m* Pluto
plutonium [plytɔnjɔm] *m* plutonium
plutôt [plyto] *adv* rather; instead; **plutôt ... que** rather ... than

pluvier [plyvje] *m* (orn) plover
plu·vieux [plyvjø] **-vieuse** [vjøz] *adj* rainy
P.N.B. [peɛnbe] *m* (letterword) (**produit national brut**) G.N.P. (*gross national product*)
pneu [pnø] *m* (*pl* **pneus**) tire; express letter (*by Parisian tube*); **pneu ballon** or **confort** balloon tire; **pneu de secours** spare tire; **pneu radial** radial tire; **pneus à clous** studded tires; **pneus neiges** snow tires
pneumatique [pnømatik] *adj* pneumatic ‖ *m* tire; express letter (*by Parisian tube*); **pneumatiques à carcasse radiale** radial tires
pneumonie [pnømɔni] *f* pneumonia
pochade [pɔʃad] *f* sketch
po·chard [pɔʃar] **-charde** [ʃard] *mf* (coll) boozer, guzzler
poche [pɔʃ] *f* pocket; bag, pouch; crop (*of bird*)
po·ché **-chée** [pɔʃe] *adj* poached; black (*eye*)
pocher [pɔʃe] *tr* to poach; dash off (*a sketch*)
pochette [pɔʃɛt] *f* folder; book (*of matches*); kit; fancy handkerchief; **pochette à disque** record jacket; **pochette surprise** surprise package
pocheuse [pɔʃøz] *f* egg poacher
pochoir [pɔʃwar] *m* stencil
poêle [pwal] *m* stove; pall; canopy ‖ *f* frying pan
poêlon [pwalɔ̃] *m* saucepan
poème [pɔɛm] *m* poem; **poème symphonique** tone poem
poésie [pɔezi] *f* poetry; poem
poète [pɔɛt] *mf* poet
poétesse [pɔetɛs] *f* poetess
poétique [pɔetik] *adj* poetic(al) ‖ *f* poetics
pogrom [pɔgrɔm] *m* pogrom
poids [pwa], [pwɑ] *m* weight; **deux poids deux mesures** double standard; **poids brut, poids total** gross weight; **poids coq** bantamweight; **poids et haltères** weightlifting; weights; **poids léger** lightweight; **poids lourd** heavy truck; (boxing) heavyweight; **poids mort** (& fig) dead weight; **poids moyen** middleweight; **poids net** net weight; **poids plume, poids mouche** featherweight; **poids welter** welterweight
poi·gnant [pwaɲɑ̃] **-gnante** [ɲɑ̃t] *adj* poignant
poignard [pwaɲar] *m* dagger
poignarder [pwaɲarde] *tr* to stab
poigne [pwaɲ] *f* grip, grasp; **à poigne** strong, energetic
poignée [pwaɲe] *f* handful; handle; grip; hilt; **poignée de main** handshake
poignet [pwaɲɛ] *m* wrist; cuff; **poignet mousquetaire** French cuff
poil [pwal] *m* hair; bristle; nap, pile; coat (*of animals*); **à long poil** shaggy; **à poil** naked; bareback; **au poil** (slang) peachy; **avoir un poil dans la main** (coll) to be lazy; **de mauvais poil** (coll) in a bad mood; **de tout poil** (coll) of every shade

and hue; **poil follet** down; **reprendre du poil de la bête** (coll) to be one's own self again; **se mettre à poil** to strip to the skin

poi·lu -lue [pwaly] *adj* hairy ‖ *m* (mil) doughboy

poinçon [pwɛ̃sɔ̃] *m* punch; stamp; hallmark; **poinçon à glace** ice pick

poinçonner [pwɛ̃sɔne] *tr* to punch; stamp; prick; hallmark

poinçonneuse [pwɛ̃sɔnøz] *f* stamping machine; ticket punch

poindre [pwɛ̃dr] §35 *intr* to dawn; sprout

poing [pwɛ̃] *m* fist; **dormir à poings fermés** to sleep like a log

point [pwɛ̃] *m* point; stitch; period (*used also in French to mark the divisions of whole numbers*); hole (*in a strap*); mark (*on a test*); (aer, naut) position; (typ) point; **à point** at the right moment; to a turn, medium; **à point nommé** in the nick of time; **à tel point que** to such a degree that; **au dernier point** to the utmost degree; **de point en point** exactly to the letter; **de tout point, en tout point** entirely; **deux points** colon; **faire le point** to take stock, get one's bearings; **mettre au point** to focus; adjust, tune up; develop, perfect; **mettre les points sur les i** to dot one's i's; **point d'appui** fulcrum; base of operations; **point de bâti** (sewing) tack; **point de coupure** cut-off; **point de départ** starting point; **point de mire** target; **point de repère** point of reference, guide; (surv) bench mark; (fig) landmark; **point d'estime** dead reckoning; **point de vue** viewpoint; **point d'exclamation** exclamation point; **point d'interrogation** question mark; **point d'orgue** (mus) pause; **point du jour** break of day; **point et virgule** semicolon; **point mort** dead center; (aut) neutral; **point noir** construction (*on highway*); **points et traits** dots and dashes ‖ *adv*—**ne . . . point** §90 not; not at all

pointage [pwɛ̃taʒ] *m* checking; check mark; aiming

pointe [pwɛ̃t] *f* point; tip; peak; head (*of arrow*); nose (*e.g., of bullet*); toe (*of shoe*); twinge (*of pain*); dash (*of, e.g., vanilla*); suggestion, touch; witty phrase, quip; (geog) cape, point; (mil) spearhead; **à pointes** spiked (*shoes*); **de pointe** peak (*e.g., hours*); **discuter sur les pointes d'épingle** to split hairs; **en pointe** tapering; **faire des pointes** to toe-dance; **pointe d'aiguille** needlepoint; **pointe de Paris** wire nail; **pointe de vitesse** spurt; **pointe du jour** daybreak; **sur la pointe des pieds** on tiptoe

poin·teau [pwɛ̃to] *m* (*pl* **-teaux**) checker; needle

pointer [pwɛ̃tœr] *m* pointer (*dog*) ‖ [pwɛ̃te] *tr* to check off; check in; prick up (*the ears*); dot ‖ *intr* to rise, soar skywards; stand out; sprout; **pointer sur** (coll) zero in on ‖ *ref* to check in, show up

poin·teur [pwɛ̃tœr] **-teuse** [tøz] *mf* checker; scorer; timekeeper; gunner; (*dog*) pointer

pointillé [pwɛ̃tije] *m* perforated line

pointil·leux [pwɛ̃tijø] **-leuse** [jøz] *adj* punctilious; touchy; captious

poin·tu -tue [pwɛ̃ty] *adj* pointed; shrill; (fig) touchy

pointure [pwɛ̃tyr] *f* size

poire [pwar] *f* pear; bulb (*of camera, syringe, horn, etc.*); (slang) mug; (slang) sucker, sap; **couper la poire en deux** to split the difference; **garder une poire pour la soif** to put something aside for a rainy day; **poire à poudre** powder flask; **poire électrique** pear-shaped switch

poi·reau [pwaro] *m* (*pl* **-reaux**) (bot) leek; **faire le poireau** (slang) to cool one's heels

poirée [pware] *f* (bot) Swiss chard

poirier [pwarje] *m* pear tree

pois [pwa], [pwɑ] *m* pea; polka dot; **petits pois, pois verts** peas; **petit pois sauteur** jumping bean; **pois cassés** split peas; **pois chiche** chickpea; **pois de senteur** sweet pea

poison [pwazɔ̃] *m* poison

pois·sard [pwasar] **-sarde** [sard] *adj* vulgar ‖ *f* fishwife

poisser [pwase] *tr* to coat with wax or pitch ‖ *intr* to be sticky

pois·seux [pwasø] **-seuse** [søz] *adj* sticky

poisson [pwasɔ̃] *m* fish; **les Poissons** (astr, astrol) Pisces; **poisson d'avril** April Fool (*joke, trick*); **poisson rouge** goldfish

poisson-chat [pwasɔ̃ʃa] *m* (*pl* **poissons-chats**) catfish

poissonnerie [pwasɔnri] *f* fish market

poisson·nier [pwasɔnje] **-nière** [njɛr] *mf* dealer in fish ‖ *f* fishwife; fish kettle

poitrail [pwatraj] *m* breast

poitrinaire [pwatrinɛr] *adj* & *mf* (pathol) consumptive

poitrine [pwatrin] *f* chest; breast; bosom

poivre [pwavr] *m* pepper

poivrer [pwavre] *tr* to pepper

poivrier [pwavrije] *m* pepper plant; pepper shaker

poivrière [pwavrijɛr] *f* pepper shaker; pepper plantation; **en poivrière** bulblike, turreted

poivron [pwavrɔ̃] *m* pepper; sweet pepper plant

poix [pwa], [pwɑ] *f* pitch; **poix sèche** resin

poker [pɔkɛr] *m* poker; four of a kind

polaire [pɔlɛr] *adj* pole, polar

polariser [pɔlarize] *tr* to polarize

pôle [pol] *m* pole

po·li -lie [pɔli] *adj* polished; polite ‖ *m* polish, gloss

police [pɔlis] *f* police; policy; **police d'assurance** insurance policy

policer [pɔlise] §51 *tr* to civilize; (obs) to police

Polichinelle [pɔliʃinɛl] *m* Punch; **de polichinelle** open (*secret*)

poli·cier [pɔlisje] **-cière** [sjɛr] *adj* police (*investigation, dog, etc.*); detective (*e.g., story*) ‖ *m* plain-clothes man, detective

polio [pɔljo] *mf* (coll) polio victim ‖ *f* (coll) polio

polir [pɔlir] *tr* to polish

polissoir [pɔliswar] *m* polisher

polis·son [pɔlisɔ̃] **-sonne** [sɔn] *adj* smutty ‖ *mf* scamp, rascal

politesse [pɔlitɛs] *f* politeness; **politesses** civilities, compliments

politicard [pɔlitikar] *m* unscrupulous politician

politi·cien [pɔlitisjɛ̃] **-cienne** [sjɛn] *adj* short-sighted; insincere ‖ *mf* (often pej) politician

politique [pɔlitik] *adj* political; prudent, wise ‖ *m* politician; statesman ‖ *f* politics; policy; cunning, shrewdness; **politique du place-sous** patronage

pollen [pɔlɛn] *m* pollen

pol·luant [pɔlɥɑ̃] **-luante** [lɥɑ̃t] *adj* polluting

polluer [pɔlɥe] *tr* to pollute

pollution [pɔlysjɔ̃] *f* pollution; **pollutions nocturnes** wet dreams

polo [pɔlo] *m* polo

poloéiste [pɔlɔeist] *mf* polo player

Pologne [pɔlɔɲ] *f* Poland; **la Pologne** Poland

polo·nais [pɔlɔnɛ] **-naise** [nɛz] *adj* Polish ‖ *m* Polish (*language*) ‖ (*cap*) *mf* Pole

polonium [pɔlɔnjɔm] *m* polonium

pol·tron [pɔltrɔ̃] **-tronne** [trɔn] *adj* cowardly ‖ *mf* coward

polycopie [pɔlikɔpi] *f* mimeographing; **tiré à la polycopie** mimeographed

polycopié [pɔlikɔpje] *m* mimeographed university lectures

polycopier [pɔlikɔpje] *tr* to mimeograph

polygame [pɔligam] *adj* polygamous ‖ *mf* polygamist

polyglotte [pɔliglɔt] *adj* polyglot ‖ *mf* polyglot, linguist

polygone [pɔligɔn] *m* polygon; shooting range

polynôme [pɔlinom] *m* polynomial

polype [pɔlip] *m* polyp

polythéiste [pɔliteist] *adj* polytheistic ‖ *mf* polytheist

pom [pɔ̃] *interj* bang!

pommade [pɔmad] *f* pomade; **passer de la pommade à** (coll) to soft-soap

pomme [pɔm] *f* apple; ball, knob; head (*of lettuce*); **pomme à couteau** eating apple; **pomme de discorde** bone of contention; **pomme de pin** pine cone; **pomme de terre** potato; **pommes chips** potato chips; **pommes de terre au four** baked potatoes; scalloped potatoes; **pommes de terre en robe de chambre, en robe des champs,** or **en chemise** potatoes in their jackets; **pommes de terre sautées** fried potatoes; **pommes frites** French fried potatoes; **pommes soufflées** potato puffs; **pommes vapeur** boiled potatoes; steamed potatoes

pom·meau [pɔmo] *m* (*pl* **-meaux**) pommel; butt (*of fishing pole*)

pomme·lé -lée [pɔmle] *adj* dappled; fleecy (*clouds*); mackerel (*sky*)

pommette [pɔmɛt] *f* cheekbone

pommier [pɔmje] *m* apple tree

pompe [pɔ̃p] *f* pomp; pump; **à la pompe** on draught; **aller à toute pompe** (slang) to go lickety-split; **être en dehors de ses pompes** (slang) to be absent-minded; **pompe à incendie** fire engine; **pompe aspirante** suction pump; **pompe à vélo** bicycle pump; **pompe de chaleur** heat pump; **pompes funèbres** funeral

pomper [pɔ̃pe] *tr* to pump; suck in

pompette [pɔ̃pɛt] *adj* (coll) tipsy

pom·peux [pɔ̃pø] **-peuse** [pøz] *adj* pompous; high-flown

pom·pier [pɔ̃pje] **-pière** [pjɛr] *adj* conventional; pretentious ‖ *mf* fitter ‖ *m* fireman

pompiste [pɔ̃pist] *mf* filling-station attendant

pomponner [pɔ̃pɔne] *tr & ref* to dress up

ponçage [pɔ̃saʒ] *m* sandpapering; pumicing

ponce [pɔ̃s] *f* pumice stone

pon·ceau [pɔ̃so] (*pl* **-ceaux**) *adj* poppy-red ‖ *m* rude bridge; culvert

poncer [pɔ̃se] §51 *tr* to sandpaper; pumice

ponceuse [pɔ̃søz] *f* sander

poncho [pɔ̃tʃo] *m* poncho

poncif [pɔ̃sif] *m* banality

ponctualité [pɔ̃ktɥalite] *f* punctuality

ponctuation [pɔ̃ktɥasjɔ̃] *f* punctuation

ponc·tuel -tuelle [pɔ̃ktɥɛl] *adj* punctual

ponctuer [pɔ̃ktɥe] *tr* to punctuate

pondération [pɔ̃derasjɔ̃] *f* balance; weighting

pondé·ré -rée [pɔ̃dere] *adj* moderate, well-balanced; weighted

pondérer [pɔ̃dere] §10 *tr* to balance; weight

pondeuse [pɔ̃døz] *f* layer (*hen*); (coll) prolific woman

pondre [pɔ̃dr] *tr* to lay (*an egg*); (coll) to turn out (*a book*); (slang) to bear (*a child*) ‖ *intr* to lay

poney [pɔnɛ] *m* pony

pongiste [pɔ̃ʒist] *mf* table-tennis player, Ping-Pong player

pont [pɔ̃] *m* bridge; (naut) deck; **faire le pont** (coll) to take the intervening day or days off; **pont aérien** airlift; **pont arrière** (aut) rear-axle assembly; **pont cantilever, pont à consoles** cantilever bridge; **ponts et chaussées** [pɔ̃zeʃose] highway department; **ponts restaurants** turnpike restaurants; **pont suspendu** suspension bridge

ponte [pɔ̃t] *f* egg laying; eggs

pontet [pɔ̃tɛ] *m* trigger guard

pontife [pɔ̃tif] *m* pontiff

pont-levis [pɔ̃lvi] *m* (*pl* **ponts-levis**) drawbridge

ponton [pɔ̃tɔ̃] *m* pontoon; landing stage

pont-promenade [pɔ̃prɔmnad] *m* (*pl* **ponts-promenades**) promenade deck

pool [pul] *m* pool (*combine*)

pope [pɔp] *m* Orthodox priest

popeline [pɔplin] *f* poplin

popote [pɔpɔt] *adj invar* (coll) stay-at-home ‖ *f* (mil) mess; (coll) cooking; **faire la**

popote (coll) to do the cooking oneself
populace [pɔpylas] *f* populace, rabble
populaire [pɔpylɛr] *adj* popular; vulgar, common
populariser [pɔpylarize] *tr* to popularize
popularité [pɔpylarite] *f* popularity
population [pɔpylɑsjɔ̃] *f* population
popu·leux [pɔpylø] **-leuse** [løz] *adj* populous; crowded
populo [pɔpylo] *m* (coll) rabble
porc [pɔr] *m* pig, hog; pork
porcelaine [pɔrsəlɛn] *f* porcelain; china
porcelet [pɔrsəlɛ] *m* piglet
porc-épic [pɔrkepik] *m* (*pl* **porcs-épics** [pɔrkepik] porcupine
porche [pɔrʃ] *m* porch, portico
porcher [pɔrʃe] *m* swineherd
porcherie [pɔrʃəri] *f* pigpen
pore [pɔr] *m* pore
po·reux [pɔrø] **-reuse** [røz] *adj* porous
porno [pɔrno] *m* & *f* (coll) porn
pornographie [pɔrnɔgrafi] *f* pornography
porphyre [pɔrfir] *m* porphyry
port [pɔr] *m* port; carryings; wearing; bearing; shipping charges; **arriver à bon port** to arrive safe; **port d'attache** home port; **port d'escale** port of call; **port franc** duty-free; free port; **port payé** postpaid
portable [pɔrtabl] *adj* portable; wearable
portail [pɔrtaj] *m* portal, gate
por·tant [pɔrtɑ̃] **-tante** [tɑ̃t] *adj* bearing; lifting; **être bien portant** to be in good health ‖ *m* handle
porta·tif [pɔrtatif] **-tive** [tiv] *adj* portable
porte [pɔrt] *f* door; doorway; gate; **fausse porte** blind door; **porte à deux battants** double door; **porte à porte** door to door (*selling*); **porte à tambour** revolving door; **porte battante** swinging door; **porte cochère** covered carriage entrance
porte-à-faux [pɔrtafo] *m invar*—**en porte-à-faux** out of line; (fig) in an untenable position
porte-aiguilles [pɔrtegɥi] *m invar* needle case
porte-allumettes [pɔrtalymɛt] *m invar* matchbox
porte-assiette [pɔrtasjɛt] *m* (*pl* **-assiette** or **-assiettes**) place mat
porte-avions [pɔrtavjɔ̃] *m invar* aircraft carrier
porte-bagages [pɔrtbagaʒ] *m invar* baggage rack
porte-bannière [pɔrtbanjɛr] *mf* (*pl* **-bannière** or **-bannières**) colorbearer
porte-bonheur [pɔrtbɔnœr] *m invar* good-luck charm
porte-carte [pɔrtəkart] *m* (*pl* **-carte** or **-cartes**) card case
porte-chapeaux [pɔrtʃapo] *m invar* hatrack
porte-cigarette [pɔrtsigarɛt] *m invar* cigarette holder
porte-cigarettes [pɔrtsigarɛt] *m invar* cigarette case
porte-clés or **porte-clefs** [pɔrtəkle] *m invar* key ring
porte-disques [pɔrtdisk] *m invar* record case

porte-documents [pɔrtdɔkymɑ̃] *m invar* letter case, portfolio
porte-drapeau [pɔrtdrapo] *m* (*pl* **-drapeau** or **-drapeaux**) standard-bearer
portée [pɔrte] *f* range, reach; import, significance; litter; (mus) staff; **à la portée de** within reach of; **à portée de la voix** within speaking distance; **à portée de l'oreille** within hearing distance; **hors de la portée de** out of reach of
portefaix [pɔrtəfɛ] *m* porter; dock hand
porte-fenêtre [pɔrtfənɛtr], [pɔrtəfnɛtr] *f* (*pl* **portes-fenêtres**) French window, French door
portefeuille [pɔrtəfœj] *m* portfolio; wallet, billfold
porteman·teau [pɔrtmɑ̃to] *m* (*pl* **-teaux**) clothes tree; **en portemanteau** square (*shoulders*)
porte-mine [pɔrtəmin] *m* (*pl* **-mine** or **mines**) mechanical pencil
porte-monnaie [pɔrtmɔnɛ] *m invar* change purse
porte-parapluies [pɔrtparaplɥi] *m invar* umbrella stand
porte-parole [pɔrtparɔl] *m invar* spokesperson, spokesman, mouthpiece
porte-plume [pɔrtəplym] *m invar* penholder; **porte-plume réservoir** fountain pen
porter [pɔrte] §96, §100 *tr* to carry; bear; wear; propose (*a toast*); **être porté à** to be inclined to; **être porté sur** to have a weakness for; **porter à l'écran** (mov) to put on the screen; **porter qn sur son testament** to put s.o. in one's will; **portez . . . arme!** present . . . arms! ‖ *intr* to carry; **porter sur** to bear down on, emphasize; be aimed at ‖ *ref* to be worn; proceed, go; to be, e.g., **comment vous portez-vous?** how are you?; **se porter à** to indulge in; **se porter candidat** to run as a candidate
porte-savon [pɔrtsavɔ̃] *m* (*pl* **-savon** or **-savons**) soap dish
porte-serviettes [pɔrtsɛrvjɛt] *m invar* towel rack
por·teur [pɔrtœr] **-teuse** [tøz] *mf* porter; bearer; holder
porte-vêtement [pɔrtəvɛtmɑ̃] *m invar* clothes hanger
porte-voix [pɔrtəvwa] *m invar* megaphone; **mettre les mains en porte-voix** to cup one's hands
por·tier [pɔrtje] **-tière** [tjɛr] *mf* concierge ‖ *m* doorman ‖ *f* door (*of car*); portiere
portillon [pɔrtijɔ̃] *m* gate; (rr) side gate (*at crossing*); **refouler du portillon** (slang) to have bad breath
portion [pɔrsjɔ̃] *f* portion; share
portique [pɔrtik] *m* portico
porto [pɔrto] *m* port wine
portori·cain [pɔrtorikɛ̃] **-caine** [kɛn] *adj* Puerto Rican ‖ (*cap*) *mf* Puerto Rican
Porto Rico [pɔrtoriko] *f* Puerto Rico
portrait [pɔrtrɛ] *m* portrait; **être tout le portrait de** to be the very image of;

portrait à mi-corps half-length portrait; **portrait de face** full-faced portrait

portraitiste [pɔrtretist] *mf* portrait painter

portu·gais [pɔrtygɛ] **-gaise** [gɛz] *adj* Portuguese ‖ *m* Portuguese (*language*) ‖ (*cap*) *mf* Portuguese (*person*)

Portugal [pɔrtygal] *m*—**le Portugal** Portugal

P.O.S. [peoɛs] *m* (letterword) (**plan d'occupation des sols**) zoning code

pose [poz] *f* pose; laying, setting in place; (phot) exposure

po·sé -sée [poze] *adj* poised, steady; trained (*voice*)

pose-marge [pozmarʒ] *f invar* margin setter (*on a typewriter*)

posément [pozemɑ̃] *adv* calmly, steadily, carefully

posemètre [pozmɛtr] *m* (phot) light meter, exposure meter

poser [poze] *tr* to place; arrange; ask (*a question*); set up (*a principle*) ‖ *intr* to pose ‖ *ref* to pose; alight; land; **se poser en** to set oneself up as

po·seur [pozœr] **-seuse** [zøz] *mf* layer; poseur; phony; **poseur d'affiches** billposter

posi·tif [pozitif] **-tive** [tiv] *adj & m* positive

position [pozisjɔ̃] *f* position

posologie [pozɔlɔʒi] *f* dosage

posséder [pɔsede] §10 *tr* to possess, own; have a command of, know perfectly ‖ *ref* to control oneself

possession [pɔsesjɔ̃] *f* possession

possibilité [pɔsibilite] *f* possibility

possible [pɔsibl] *adj & m* possible

postage [pɔstaʒ] *m* mailing

pos·tal -tale [pɔstal] *adj* (*pl* **-taux** [to]) postal

postalage [pɔstalaʒ] *m* selling by mail

postdate [pɔstdat] *f* postdate

postdater [pɔstdate] *tr* to postdate

poste [pɔst] *m* post; station; set; position, job; **poste de douane** port of entry; **poste d'émetteur** broadcasting station; **poste de pilotage** cockpit; **poste de radio** radio set; **poste de repérage** tracking station; **poste de secours** first-aid station; **poste des malades** (nav) sick bay; **poste d'essence** gas station; **poste d'incendie** fire station; **poste supplémentaire** (telp) extension ‖ *f* post, mail; **mettre à la poste** to mail; **poste restante** general delivery; **postes** post office department

poster [pɔste] *tr* to post ‖ *ref* to lie in wait

postérité [pɔsterite] *f* posterity

posthume [pɔstym] *adj* posthumous

postiche [pɔstiʃ] *adj* false; detachable ‖ *m* toupee; switch, false hair

pos·tier [pɔstje] **-tière** [tjɛr] *mf* postal clerk

postscolaire [pɔstskɔlɛr] *adj* adult (*education*); extension (*courses*)

post-scriptum [pɔstskriptɔm] *m invar* postscript

postu·lant [pɔstylɑ̃] **-lante** [lɑ̃t] *mf* applicant, candidate; postulant

postuler [pɔstyle] *tr* to apply for ‖ *intr* to apply; **postuler pour** to represent (*a client*)

posture [pɔstyr] *f* posture; situation

pot [po] *m* pot; pitcher; jug; jar; can; **avoir du pot** (coll) to be lucky; **découvrir le pot aux roses** (coll) to discover the secret; **payer les pots cassés** (coll) to pay the piper; **pot à bière** beer mug; **pot à fleurs** flowerpot; **pot de café** coffee mug; **pot d'échappement** (aut) muffler; **pot de noir** cloudy weather; **pot d'étain** pewter tankard; **tourner autour du pot** (coll) to beat about the bush

potable [pɔtabl] *adj* drinkable; (coll) acceptable, passable

potache [pɔtaʃ] *m* (coll) schoolboy

potage [pɔtaʒ] *m* soup; **potage de maïs** hominy; **pour tout potage** (lit) all told

pota·ger [pɔtaʒe] **-gère** [ʒɛr] *adj* vegetable ‖ *m* vegetable garden; dinner pail

potasse [pɔtas] *f* potash

potasser [pɔtase] *tr* (coll) to bone up on ‖ *intr* (coll) to grind away

potas·seur [pɔtasœr] **-seuse** [søz] *mf* (coll) grind

potassium [pɔtasjɔm] *m* potassium

pot-au-feu [pɔtofø] *adj invar* (coll) homeloving ‖ *m invar* beef stew

pot-de-vin [podvɛ̃] *m* (*pl* **pots-de-vin**) bribe, money under the table

po·teau [pɔto] *m* (*pl* **-teaux**) post, pole; **franchir le poteau** to reach the goal (*to succeed*); **poteau de but** goal post; **poteau indicateur** signpost

pote·lé -lée [pɔtle] *adj* chubby

potence [pɔtɑ̃s] *f* gallows; bracket

potentat [pɔtɑ̃ta] *m* potentate

poten·tiel -tielle [pɔtɑ̃sjɛl] *adj & m* potential

poterie [pɔtri] *f* pottery; metalware; **poterie mordorée** lusterware

poterne [pɔtɛrn] *f* postern

potiche [pɔtiʃ] *f* large Oriental vase; (fig) figurehead

potin [pɔtɛ̃] *m* piece of gossip; racket; **faire du potin** (coll) to raise a row; **potins** gossip

potiner [pɔtine] *intr* to gossip

potion [posjɔ̃] *f* potion

potiron [pɔtirɔ̃] *m* pumpkin; **potiron lumineux** jack-o'-lantern

pou [pu] *m* (*pl* **poux**) louse

poubelle [pubɛl] *f* garbage can

pouce [pus] *m* thumb; big toe; inch; **manger sur le pouce** (coll) to eat on the run

poudre [pudr] *f* powder; face powder; **en poudre** powdered; granulated (*sugar*); **il n'a pas inventé la poudre** (coll) he's not so smart; **jeter de la poudre aux yeux de** to deceive; **poudre à pâte** baking powder; **poudre dentifrice** tooth powder; **se mettre de la poudre** to powder one's nose

poudrer [pudre] *tr* to powder

poudrerie [pudrəri] *f* powder mill

pou·dreux [pudrø] **-dreuse** [drøz] *adj* powdery; dusty ‖ *f* sugar shaker

poudrier [pudrije] *m* compact
poudrière [pudrijɛr] *f* powder magazine; (fig) powder keg
poudroyer [pudrwaje] §47 *intr* to raise the dust; shine through the dust
pouf [puf] *m* hassock, pouf ‖ *interj* plop!; **faire pouf** (slang) to flop
pouffer [pufe] *intr* to burst out laughing
pouil·leux [pujø] **-leuse** [jøz] *adj* lousy; sordid ‖ *mf* person covered with lice
pouillot [pujo] *m* (orn) warbler
poulailler [pulɑje] *m* henhouse; (theat) peanut gallery
poulain [pulɛ̃] *m* colt, foal
poule [pul] *f* hen; chicken; (*in games*) pool; jackpot; (turf) sweepstakes; (coll) skirt, dame; (slang) tart, mistress; **ma poule** (coll) my pet; **poule au pot** chicken stew; **poule de luxe** (slang) high-class prostitute; call girl; **poule d'Inde** turkey hen; **poule mouillée** (coll) milksop, coward; **tuer la poule aux œufs d'or** to kill the goose that lays the golden eggs
poulet [pulɛ] *m* chicken; (coll) love letter; (slang) cop; **mon petit poulet** (coll) my pet; **poulet d'Inde** turkey cock
poulette [pulɛt] *f* pullet; (coll) gal; **ma poulette** (coll) darling
pouliche [puliʃ] *f* filly
poulie [puli] *f* pulley; block
pou·lot [pulo] **-lotte** [lɔt] *mf* child, kid, lovie, baby (*term of affection*); **attention aux petits poulots** (*public sign*) watch children
poulpe [pulp] *m* octopus
pouls [pu] *m* pulse; **tâter le pouls à** to feel the pulse of
poumon [pumɔ̃] *m* lung
poupe [pup] *f* (naut) stern, poop
poupée [pupe] *f* doll; dummy; sore finger; (mach) headstock
pou·pon [pupɔ̃] **-ponne** [pɔn] *mf* baby; chubby-faced youngster
pouponnière [pupɔnjɛr] *f* nursery
pour [pur] *m*—**le pour et le contre** the pros and the cons ‖ *adv*—**pour lors** then; **pour peu que** however little; **pour que** in order that; **pour . . . que** however, e.g., **pour charmante qu'elle soit** however charming she may be ‖ *prep* for; in order to; **pour ainsi dire** so to speak; **pour cent** per cent
pourboire [purbwar] *m* tip
pour·ceau [purso] *m* (*pl* **-ceaux**) swine, hog, pig
pourcentage [pursɑ̃taʒ] *m* percentage
pourchasser [purʃase] *tr* to hound
pourlécher [purleʃe] §10 *ref* to smack one's lips
pourparlers [purparle] *mpl* talks, parley, conference
pourpoint [purpwɛ̃] *m* doublet
pourpre [purpr] *adj* purple ‖ *m* purple (*violescent*) ‖ *f* purple (*deep red, crimson*)
pourquoi [purkwa] *m* why; **le pourquoi et le comment** the why and the wherefore ‖

adv & conj why; **pourquoi pas?** why not?
pour·ri -rie [puri] *adj* rotten; spoiled ‖ *m* rotten part
pourrir [purir] *tr, intr, & ref* to rot; spoil; corrupt
pourriture [purityr] *f* rot; decay; corruption
poursuite [pursɥit] *f* pursuit; (aer) tracking; (law) action, suit; (coll) spotlight
poursui·vant [pursɥivɑ̃] **-vante** [vɑ̃t] *mf* pursuer; (law) plaintiff
poursuivre [pursɥivr] §67 *tr* to pursue, chase; proceed with; persecute; sue ‖ *intr* to continue ‖ *ref* to be continued
pourtant [purtɑ̃] *adv* however, nevertheless, yet
pourtour [purtur] *m* circumference
pourvoi [purvwa] *m* (law) appeal
pourvoir [purvwar] §54, §95 *tr*—**pourvoir de** to supply with, provide with; favor with ‖ *intr*—**pourvoir à** to provide for, attend to ‖ *ref* (law) to appeal
pour·voyeur [purvwajœr] **-voyeuse** [vwajøz] *mf* provider, supplier; caterer; **pourvoyeurs** gun crew
pourvu que [purvykə] *conj* provided that
pousse [pus] *f* shoot, sprout
pous·sé -sée [puse] *adj* elaborate; searching, exhaustive ‖ *f* push, shove; thrust; rise; pressure; (rok) thrust
pousse-café [puskafe] *m invar* liqueur
pousser [puse] §96, §100 *tr* to push, shove, egg on; urge; utter (*a cry*); heave (*a sigh*); **pousser plus loin** to carry further ‖ *intr* to push, shove; grow; push on ‖ *ref* to push oneself forward
poussette [pusɛt] *f* baby carriage
poussier [pusje] *m* coal dust
poussière [pusjɛr] *f* dust; powder; **poussière d'eau** spray; **une poussière** a trifle; **une poussière de** a lot of
poussié·reux [pusjerø] **-reuse** [røz] *adj* dusty; powdery
pous·sif [pusif] **-sive** [siv] *adj* wheezy
poussin [pusɛ̃] *m* chick
poussoir [puswar] *m* push button
poutre [putr] *f* beam; joist; girder
poutrelle [putrɛl] *f* small girder
pouvoir [puvwar] *m* power; **pouvoir d'achat** purchasing power ‖ §55, §95 *tr* to be able to do; **je n'y puis rien** I can't or cannot help it, I can do nothing about it ‖ *intr* to be able; **on ne peut mieux** couldn't be better; **on ne peut plus** I (we, they, etc.) can do no more; I'm (we're, they're, etc.) all in ‖ *aux* used to express **1)** ability, e.g., **elle peut prédire l'avenir** she is able to predict the future, she can predict the future; **2)** permission, e.g., **vous pouvez partir** you may go; e.g., **puis-je partir?** may I go?; **3)** possibility, e.g., **il peut pleuvoir** it may rain; e.g., **il a pu oublier son parapluie** he may have forgotten his umbrella; **4)** optative, e.g., **puisse-t-il venir!** may he come! ‖ *impers ref*—**il se peut que** it is possible that, e.g., **il se peut qu'il vienne ce soir** it is

possible that he may come this evening, he may come this evening; **il se pourrait bien que** it might well be that, e.g., **il se pourrait bien qu'il vînt ce soir** it might well be that he will come this evening, he might come this evening ‖ *ref* to be possible; **cela ne se peut pas** that is not possible

pragmatique [pragmatik] *adj* pragmatic(al)

prairie [prɛri], [preri] *f* meadow; **les Prairies** the prairie

praticable [pratikabl] *adj* practicable; passable ‖ *m* practicable stage property; (mov, telv) camera platform

prati·cien [pratisjɛ̃] **-cienne** [sjɛn] *mf* practitioner

prati·quant [pratikɑ̃] **-quante** [kɑ̃t] *adj* practicing (*e.g., Catholic*); churchy ‖ *mf* churchgoer

pratique [pratik] *adj* practical ‖ *f* practice; contact, company; customer; **libre pratique** freedom of worship; (naut) freedom from quarantine

pratiquement [pratikmɑ̃] *adv* practically, in practice

pratiquer [pratike] *tr* to practice; cut, make (*e.g., a hole*); frequent; read a great deal of ‖ *intr* to practice (*said, e.g., of doctor*); practice one's religion ‖ *ref* to be practiced, done; rule, prevail (*said of prices*)

pré [pre] *m* meadow; **pré et marée** surf and turf; **sur le pré** on the field of honor (*dueling ground*)

préalable [prealabl] *adj* previous; preliminary ‖ *m* prerequisite; **au préalable** before, in advance

préambule [preɑ̃byl] *m* preamble

préau [preo] *m* (*pl* **préaux**) yard

préavis [preavi] *m* advance warning; **avec préavis** person-to-person (*telephone call*)

précaire [prekɛr] *adj* precarious

précaution [prekosjɔ̃] *f* precaution

précautionner [prekosjone] *tr* to caution ‖ *intr* to be on one's guard

précaution·neux [prekosjɔnø] **-neuse** [nøz] *adj* precautious

précédemment [presedamɑ̃] *adv* before, previously

précé·dent [presedɑ̃] **-dente** [dɑ̃t] *adj* preceding ‖ *m* precedent

précéder [presede] §10 *tr* & *intr* to precede

précepte [presɛpt] *m* precept

précep·teur [presɛptœr] **-trice** [tris] *mf* tutor

prêche [prɛʃ] *m* sermon

prêcher [preʃe] *tr* to preach; preach to ‖ *intr* to preach; **prêcher d'exemple** to practice what one preaches

prê·cheur [prɛʃœr] **-cheuse** [ʃøz] *adj* preaching ‖ *mf* sermonizer

pré·cieux [presjø] **-cieuse** [sjøz] *adj* precious; valuable; affected

préciosité [presjozite] *f* preciosity (*French literary style corresponding to English euphuism*)

précipice [presipis] *m* precipice

précipi·té -tée [presipite] *adj* hurried, precipitious ‖ *m* precipitate

précipiter [presipite] *tr* to hurl ‖ *ref* to hurl oneself; precipitate; hurry, rush

pré·cis [presi] **-cise** [siz] *adj* precise; sharp, e.g., **trois heures précises** three o'clock sharp ‖ *m* abstract, summary

précisément [presizemɑ̃] *adv* precisely, exactly; clearly, accurately

préciser [presize] *tr* to specify ‖ *intr* to be precise ‖ *ref* to become clear; take shape, jell

précision [presizjɔ̃] *f* precision; **précisions** data

préci·té -tée [presite] *adj* aforementioned

précoce [prekɔs] *adj* precocious; (bot) early

précon·çu -çue [prekɔ̃sy] *adj* preconceived

préconiser [prekɔnize] *tr* to advocate, recommend

précurseur [prekyrsœr] *adj masc* precursory ‖ *m* forerunner, harbinger

prédateur [predatœr] *adj masc* predatory ‖ *m* predatory animal

prédécesseur [predesesœr] *m* predecessor

prédicateur [predikatœr] *m* preacher

prédiction [prediksjɔ̃] *f* prediction

prédire [predir] §40 *tr* to predict

prédisposer [predispoze] *tr* to predispose

prédomi·nant [predɔminɑ̃] **-nante** [nɑ̃t] *adj* predominant

préémi·nent [preeminɑ̃] **-nente** [nɑ̃t] *adj* preeminent

préfabri·qué -quée [prefabrike] *adj* prefabricated

préface [prefas] *f* preface

préfacer [prefase] §51 *tr* to preface

préfecture [prefɛktyr] *f* prefecture; **préfecture de police** police headquarters

préférable [preferabl] *adj* preferable

préférence [preferɑ̃s] *f* preference

préférer [prefere] §10, §95 *tr* to prefer

préfet [prefɛ] *m* prefect; **préfet de police** police commissioner

préfixe [prefiks] *m* prefix

préfixer [prefikse] *tr* to prefix

préhistorique [preistorik] *adj* prehistoric

préjudice [preʒydis] *m* prejudice, detriment; **porter préjudice à** to injure, to harm; **sans préjudice de** without affecting

préjudiciable [preʒydisjabl] *adj* detrimental

préjudicier [preʒydisje] *intr*—**préjudicier à** to harm, damage

préjugé [preʒyʒe] *m* prejudice

préjuger [preʒyʒe] §38 *tr* to foresee ‖ *intr*—**préjuger de** to prejudge

prélart [prelar] *m* tarpaulin

prélasser [prelase] *ref* to lounge

prélat [prela] *m* prelate

prélèvement [prelɛvmɑ̃] *m* deduction; sample; levy

prélever [prelve] §2 *tr* to set aside, deduct; take (*a sample*); levy; **prélever à** to take from

préliminaire [preliminɛr] *adj* & *m* preliminary

prélude [prelyd] *m* prelude

préluder [prelyde] *intr* to warm up (*said of singer, musician, etc.*); **préluder à** to prelude

prématu·ré -rée [prematyre] *adj* premature

préméditer [premedite] *tr* to premeditate

prémices [premis] *fpl* first fruits; beginning

pre·mier [prəmje] **-mière** [mjɛr] §92 *adj* first; raw (*materials*); prime (*number*); the First, e.g., **Jean premier** John the First ‖ (when standing before noun) *adj* first; prime (*minister*); maiden (*voyage*); early (*infancy*) ‖ *m* first; **jeune premier** leading man; **premier de cordée** leader ‖ *f* first; first class; (theat) première; **jeune première** leading lady ‖ *pron* (*masc & fem*) first

premièrement [prəmjɛrmɑ̃] *adv* firstly, first, in the first place, to begin with

premier-né [prəmjene] **-née** [ne] (*pl* **premiers-nés**) *adj & mf* first-born

prémisse [premis] *f* premise

prémonition [premɔnisjɔ̃] *f* premonition

prémunir [premynir] *tr* to forewarn ‖ *ref*—**se prémunir contre** to protect oneself against

pre·nant [prənɑ̃] **-nante** [nɑ̃t] *adj* sticky; winning, pleasing

prendre [prɑ̃dr] §56 *tr* to take; take on; take up; catch; get (*to obtain and bring*); steal (*a kiss*); buy (*a ticket*); make (*an appointment*); **à tout prendre** all things considered; **prendre de l'âge** to be getting old; **prendre la mer** to take to sea; **prendre l'eau** to leak; **prendre le large** to take to the open sea; **prendre q.ch. à qn** to take s.th. from s.o.; charge s.o. s.th. (*i.e., a certain sum of money*); **prendre son temps** to take one's time ‖ *intr* to catch (*said of fire*); take root; form (*said of ice*); set (*said of mortar*); stick (*to a pan or dish*); catch on (*said of a style*); to turn (*right or left*); **prendre à droite** to bear to the right; **qu'est-ce qui lui prend?** what's come over him? ‖ §96 *ref* to get caught, catch (*e.g., on a nail*); congeal; clot; curdle; jam; take from each other; **pour qui se prend-il?** who does he think he is?; **s'en prendre à qn de q.ch.** to blame s.o. for s.th.; **se prendre à** to begin to; **se prendre d'amitié** to strike up a friendship; **se prendre de vin** to get drunk; **s'y prendre** to go about it

pre·neur [prənœr] **-neuse** [nøz] *mf* taker; buyer; payee; lessee

prenne [prɛn] *v* (**prennes, prennent**) see **prendre**

prénom [prenɔ̃] *m* first name

prénommer [prenɔme] *tr* to name ‖ *ref*—**il** (**elle**, etc.) **se prénomme** his (her, etc.) first name is

préoccupation [preɔkypɑsjɔ̃] *f* preoccupation

préoccuper [preɔkype] *tr* to preoccupy ‖ *ref*—**se préoccuper de** to pay attention to; be concerned about

prépara·teur [preparatœr] **-trice** [tris] *mf* laboratory assistant

préparatifs [preparatif] *mpl* preparations

préparation [preparɑsjɔ̃] *f* preparation; notice, warning

préparatoire [preparatwar] *adj* preparatory

préparer [prepare] §96, §100 *tr, intr, & ref* to prepare

prépondé·rant [prepɔ̃derɑ̃] **-rante** [rɑ̃t] *adj* preponderant

prépo·sé -sée [prepoze] *mf* employee, clerk; mail carrier, postman; **préposé de la douane** customs officer; **préposée au vestiaire** hatcheck person, hatcheck girl

préposer [prepoze] *tr*—**préposer qn à q.ch.** to put s.o. in charge of s.th.

préposition [prepozisjɔ̃] *f* preposition

prérogative [prerɔgativ] *f* prerogative

près [prɛ] *adv* near; **à beaucoup près** by far; **à cela près** except for that; **à peu d'exceptions près** with few exceptions; **à peu près** about, practically; **à . . . près** except for; within, e.g., **je peux vous dire l'heure à cinq minutes près** I can tell you what time it is within five minutes; **au plus près** to the nearest point; **de près** close; closely; **ici près** near here; **près de** near; nearly, about; alongside, at the side of; **près de + inf** about to + *inf*; **tout près** nearby, right here ‖ *prep* near; to, at

présage [prezaʒ] *m* presage, foreboding

présager [prezaʒe] §38 *tr* to presage, forebode; anticipate

pré-salé [presale] *m* (*pl* **prés-salés**) salt-meadow sheep; salt-meadow mutton

presbyte [prɛsbit] *adj* far-sighted ‖ *mf* far-sighted person

presbytère [prɛsbitɛr] *m* presbytery

presbyté·rien [prɛsbiterjɛ̃] **-rienne** [rjɛn] *adj & mf* Presbyterian

presbytie [prɛsbisi] *f* far-sightedness

prescription [prɛskripsjɔ̃] *f* prescription

prescrire [prɛskrir] §25, §97, §98 *tr* to prescribe ‖ *ref* to be prescribed

préséance [preseɑ̃s] *f* precedence

présélection [preselɛksjɔ̃] *f*—**présélection des candidats** screening of candidates

présence [prezɑ̃s] *f* presence; attendance; **en présence** face to face; under consideration

pré·sent [prezɑ̃] **-sente** [zɑ̃t] *adj* present ‖ *m* present, gift; (gram) present; **les présents** those present

présentable [prezɑ̃tabl] *adj* presentable

présenta·teur [prezɑ̃tatœr] **-trice** [tris] *mf* (rad) announcer; **présentateur de disques** disk jockey

présentateur-tronc [prezɑ̃tatœrtrɔ̃] *m* (telv) anchor man

présentation [prezɑ̃tasjɔ̃] *f* presentation; introduction; appearance; look, form (*of a new product*)

présentement [prezɑ̃tmɑ̃] *adv* right now

présenter [prezɑ̃te] *tr* to present; introduce; offer; pay (*one's respects*) ‖ *ref* to present oneself; present itself; **se présenter à** to be a candidate for

présérie [preseri] *f* (com) trial run, sample run

préservatif [prezɛrvatif] *m* preventive; condom, prophylactic

préserver [prezɛrve] *tr* to preserve

présidence [prezidɑ̃s] *f* presidency; chairmanship; presidential mansion

prési·dent [prezidɑ̃] **-dente** [dɑ̃t] *mf* president; chairperson; chairman; presiding judge ‖ *f* president's wife; chairwoman; **madame la présidente** madam chairman

présiden·tiel -tielle [prezidɑ̃sjɛl] *adj* presidential

présider [prezide] *tr* to preside over ‖ *intr* to preside; **présider à** to preside over

présomp·tif [prezɔ̃ptif] **-tive** [tiv] *adj* presumptive, presumed

présomption [prezɔ̃psjɔ̃] *f* presumption

présomp·tueux [prezɔ̃ptɥø] **-tueuse** [tɥøz] *adj* presumptuous

présonorisation [presɔnɔrizasjɔ̃] *f* playback

presque [prɛsk(ə)] *adv* almost, nearly; **presque jamais** hardly ever; **presque personne** scarcely anybody

presqu'île [prɛskil] *f* peninsula

pres·sant [presɑ̃] **-sante** [sɑ̃t] *adj* pressing, urgent

presse [prɛs] *f* press; hurry, rush; crowd; hand screw, clamp; **mettre sous presse** to go to press

pres·sé -sée [prese] §93 *adj* pressed; pressing, urgent; squeezed

presse-bouton [presbutɔ̃] *adj invar* push-button (*warfare*)

presse-citron [prɛssitrɔ̃] *m invar* lemon squeezer

pressentiment [presɑ̃timɑ̃] *m* presentiment, foreboding

pressentir [presɑ̃tir] §41 *tr* to have a foreboding of; sound out

presse-papiers [prɛspapje] *m invar* paperweight

presse-purée [prɛspyre] *m invar* potato masher

presser [prese], [prɛse] §97 *tr* to press; squeeze; hurry, hasten ‖ *intr* to be urgent ‖ *ref* to hurry; **se presser à** to crowd around

pressing [presiŋ] *m* dry cleaner's

pression [presjɔ̃] *f* pressure; snap fastener; **à la pression** on draught; **pression artérielle** blood pressure

pressoir [preswar] *m* press

pressurer [presyre] *tr* to press, squeeze; bleed white, wring money out of

pressuriser [presyrize] *tr* to pressurize

prestance [prestɑ̃s] *f* commanding appearance, dignified bearing

prestation [prestasjɔ̃] *f* taking (*of oath*); tax; allotment, allowance, benefit

preste [prɛst] *adj* nimble

prestidigita·teur [prestidiʒitatœr] **-trice** [tris] *mf* magician

prestidigitation [prestidiʒitasjɔ̃] *f* sleight of hand, legerdemain

prestige [prestiʒ] *m* prestige; illusion, magic

presti·gieux [prestiʒjø] **-gieuse** [ʒjøz] *adj* prestigious, famous; marvelous

présumer [prezyme] §95, §97 *tr* to presume; presume to be ‖ *intr* to presume; **présumer de** to presume upon

présupposer [presypoze] *tr* to presuppose

présure [prezyr] *f* rennet

prêt [prɛ] **prête** [prɛt] §92 *adj* ready; **prêt à porter** ready-to-wear, ready-made; **prêt à tout** ready for anything ‖ *m* loan

prêt-à-monter [prɛtamɔ̃te] *m* (*pl* **prets-à-monter** [prɛzamɔ̃te]) kit

prêt-à-porter [prɛtapɔrte] *m* (*pl* **prêts-à-porter** [prɛtapɔrte]) ready-to-wear, ready-made clothes

prêt-bail [prɛbaj] *m invar* lend-lease

préten·dant [pretɑ̃dɑ̃] **-dante** [dɑ̃t] *mf* pretender ‖ *m* suitor

prétendre [pretɑ̃dr] §95, §96 *tr* to claim; require ‖ *intr*—**prétendre à** to aspire to; lay claim to

préten·du -due [pretɑ̃dy] *adj* so-called, alleged ‖ *m* fiancé ‖ *f* fiancée

prête-nom [prɛtnɔ̃] *m* (*pl* **-noms**) dummy, figurehead, straw man

prétentaine [pretɑ̃tɛn] *f*—**courir la prétentaine** (coll) to be on the loose; (coll) to have many love affairs

préten·tieux [pretɑ̃sjø] **-tieuse** [sjøz] *adj* pretentious

prétention [pretɑ̃sjɔ̃] *f* pretention, pretense; claim, pretensions

prêter [prete], [prɛte] *tr* to lend; give (*e.g., help*); pay (*attention*); take (*an oath*); impart (*e.g., luster*); attribute, ascribe ‖ *intr* to lend; stretch; **prêter à** to lend itself to ‖ *ref*—**se prêter à** to lend itself to; be a party to; countenance; indulge in

prê·teur [pretœr] **-teuse** [tøz] *mf* lender; **prêteur sur gages** pawnbroker

prétexte [pretɛkst] *m* pretext

prétexter [pretɛkste] *tr* to give as a pretext

prétonique [pretɔnik] *adj* pretonic

prêtre [prɛtr] *m* priest

prêtresse [prɛtres] *f* priestess

prêtrise [pretriz] *f* priesthood

preuve [prœv] *f* proof, evidence

preux [prø] *adj masc* valiant ‖ *m* doughty knight

prévaloir [prevalwar] §71 (*subj* **prévale,** etc.) *intr* to prevail ‖ *ref*—**se prévaloir de** to avail oneself of; pride oneself on

prévarication [prevarikasjɔ̃] *f* breach of trust

prévariquer [prevarike] *intr* to betray one's trust

prévenance [prɛvnɑ̃s] *f* kindness, thoughtfulness

préve·nant [prɛvnɑ̃] **-nante** [nɑ̃t] *adj* attentive, considerate; prepossessing

prévenir [prevnir] §72 *tr* to anticipate; avert, forestall; ward off, prevent; notify, inform; bias, prejudice

préven·tif [prevɑ̃tif] **-tive** [tiv] *adj* preventive; pretrial (*detention*)

prévention [prevɑ̃sjɔ̃] *f* bias, prejudice; predisposition; custody, imprisonment; prevention (*of accidents*); **prévention rou-tière** traffic police; road safety

préve·nu -nue [prɛvny] *adj* biased, preju-diced; forewarned; accused ‖ *mf* prisoner, accused, defendant

prévision [previzjɔ̃] *f* anticipation, estimate; **prévision du temps** weather forecast; **prévisions** expectations

prévoir [prevwar] §57 *tr* to foresee, antici-pate; forecast

prévoyance [prevwajɑ̃s] *f* foresight

pré·voyant [prevwajɑ̃] **-voyante** [vwajɑ̃t] *adj* far-sighted, provident

prie-dieu [pridjø] *m invar* prie-dieu ‖ *f* praying mantis

prier [prije] §96, §97, §99 *tr* to ask, beg; pray (*God*); **je vous en prie!** I beg your pardon!; by all means!; you are welcome!; please have some!; **je vous prie!** please!; **prier qn de** + *inf* to ask, beg s.o. to + *inf* ‖ *intr* to pray

prière [prijɛr] *f* prayer; **prière de . . .** please . . . ; **prière de faire suivre** please for-ward; **prière de garder jusqu'à l'arrivée** please hold until arrival; **prière d'insérer** publisher's insert for reviewers

primaire [primɛr] *adj* primary; first (*offender*); (coll) narrow-minded ‖ *m* (elec) primary; (coll) primitive

primat [prima] *m* (eccl) primate

primate [primat] *m* (zool) primate

primauté [primote] *f* supremacy

prime [prim] *adj* early (*youth*); (math) prime ‖ *f* premium; bonus; free gift; (eccl) prime; **prime de transport** traveling expenses

primer [prime] *tr* to excel; take priority over; award a prize to

primerose [primroz] *f* hollyhock

primesau·tier [primsotje] **-tière** [tjɛr] *adj* impulsive, quick

primeur [primœr] *f* freshness; first fruit; early vegetable; (journ) beat, scoop; **pri-meurs** fruits and vegetables out of season

primevère [primvɛr] *f* primrose

primi·tif [primitif] **-tive** [tiv] *adj* primitive; original, early; primary (*colors; tense*) ‖ *mf* primitive

primo [primo] *adv* firstly

primor·dial -diale [primɔrdjal] *adj* (*pl* **-diaux** [djo]) primordial; fundamental, prime, primary

prince [prɛ̃s] *m* prince; **prince de Galles** Prince of Wales

princesse [prɛ̃sɛs] *f* princess

prin·cier [prɛ̃sje] **-cière** [sjɛr] *adj* princely

princi·pal -pale [prɛ̃sipal] *adj & m* (*pl* **-paux** [po]) principal, chief

principauté [prɛ̃sipote] *f* principality

principe [prɛ̃sip] *m* principle; beginning; source

printa·nier [prɛ̃tanje] **-nière** [njɛr] *adj* spring; springlike

printemps [prɛ̃tɑ̃] *m* spring; springtime; **au printemps** in the spring

priorité [prijɔrite] *f* priority; right of way; **de priorité** preferred (*stock*); main (*road*); **priorité à droite, priorité à gauche**

(*public sign*) yield; **priorité piétons** pe-destrian right of way

pris [pri] **prise** [priz] *adj* set, frozen; **être pris** to be busy; **pris de vin** drunk ‖ *f* capture, seizure; taking; hold; setting; tap, faucet; (med) dose; (naut) prize; **donner prise à** to lay oneself open to; **être aux prises avec** to be struggling with; **hors de prise** out of gear; **lâcher prise** to let go; **mettre en prise** (aut) to put into gear; **prise d'air** ventilator; **prise d'antenne** (rad) lead-in; **prise d'armes** military pa-rade; **prise d'eau** water faucet; hydrant; **prise de bec** (coll) quarrel; **prise de con-science** awakening, awareness; **prise de courant** (elec) plug; (elec) tap, outlet; **prise de position** statement of opinion; **prise de sang** blood specimen; **prise de son** recording; **prise de tabac** pinch of snuff; **prise de terre** (elec) ground con-nection; **prise de vue(s)** (phot) shot, pic-ture taking; **prise de vue directe** (telv) live broadcast; **prise directe** high gear ‖ *v* see **prendre**

prisée [prize] *f* appraisal

priser [prize] *tr* to value; snuff up ‖ *intr* to take snuff

pri·seur [prizœr] **-seuse** [zøz] *mf* snuffer ‖ *m* appraiser

prisme [prism] *m* prism

prison [prizɔ̃] *f* prison

prison·nier [prizɔnje] **-nière** [njɛr] *mf* pris-oner

privautés [privote] *fpl* liberties

pri·vé -vée [prive] *adj* private; tame, pet ‖ *m* private life ‖ *v* see **priver**

priver [prive] §97 *tr* to deprive ‖ *ref* to deprive oneself; **se priver de** to do with-out, abstain from

privilège [privilɛʒ] *m* privilege

privilé·gié -giée [privileʒje] *adj* privileged; preferred (*stock*)

prix [pri] *m* price; prize; value; **à aucun prix** not at any price; by no means; **à tout prix** at all costs; **au prix de** at the price of; at the rate of; compared with; **dans mes prix** within my means; **grand prix** championship race; **hors de prix** at a prohibitive cost; **prix courant** list price; **prix de départ** upset price; **prix de détail** retail price; **prix de fabrique** factory price; **prix de gros** wholesale price; **prix de lancement** introductory offer; **prix de la vie** cost of living; **prix de location** rent; **prix de revient** cost price; **prix de vente** selling price; **prix fixe** table d'hôte; **prix unique** variety store

probabilité [prɔbabilite] *f* probability

probable [prɔbabl] *adj* probable, likely

probablement [prɔbabləmɑ̃] *adv* probably

pro·bant [prɔbɑ̃] **-bante** [bɑ̃t] *adj* convinc-ing; conclusive (*evidence*)

probatoire [prɔbatwar] *adj* experimental, preliminary

probe [prɔb] *adj* honest, upright

problème [prɔblɛm] *m* problem

procédé [prɔsede] *m* process; procedure; tip (*of cue*); **procédés** proceedings; behavior

procéder [prɔsede] §10, §96 *intr* to proceed; **procéder à** to carry out, conduct, undertake, perform; **procéder de** to arise from

procédure [prɔsedyr] *f* procedure; proceedings

procès [prɔsɛ] *m* lawsuit, case; trial; **intenter un procès à** to sue; to prosecute; **sans autre forme de procès** then and there, without appeal

proces·sif [prɔsesif] **-sive** [siv] *adj* litigious

procession [prɔsesjɔ̃] *f* procession

processus [prɔsesys] *m* process

procès-verbal [prɔsɛvɛrbal] *m* (*pl* **-verbaux** [vɛrbo]) report; minutes; ticket (*e.g., for speeding*)

pro·chain [prɔʃɛ̃] **-chaine** [ʃɛn] *adj* next; impending; (lit) nearest, immediate; **la prochaine semaine** the next week; **la semaine prochaine** next week ‖ *m* neighbor, fellow-man ‖ *f*—**à la prochaine!** (coll) so long!

prochainement [prɔʃɛnmɑ̃] *adv* shortly

proche [prɔʃ] *adj* near; nearby; close (*relative*) ‖ **proches** *mpl* close relatives ‖ *adv*—**de proche en proche** little by little

proclamer [prɔklame] *tr* to proclaim

proclitique [prɔklitik] *adj & m* proclitic

procuration [prɔkyrasjɔ̃] *f* power of attorney; **par procuration** by proxy

procurer [prɔkyre] *tr & ref* to procure, get

procureur [prɔkyrœr] *m* attorney; **procureur de la république** district attorney; **procureur général** attorney general

prodige [prɔdiʒ] *m* prodigy; wonder

prodi·gieux [prɔdiʒjø] **-gieuse** [ʒjøz] *adj* prodigious, wonderful; terrific

prodigue [prɔdig] *adj* prodigal, lavish ‖ *mf* prodigal, spendthrift

prodiguer [prɔdige] *tr* to squander, waste; lavish ‖ *ref* to not spare oneself; show off

prodrome [prɔdrom] *m* harbinger; introduction

produc·teur [prɔdyktœr] **-trice** [tris] *adj* productive ‖ *mf* producer

produc·tif [prɔdyktif] **-tive** [tiv] *adj* productive; producing

production [prɔdyksjɔ̃] *f* production

produire [prɔdɥir] §19 *tr* to produce; create; introduce ‖ *ref* to take place; be produced; show up

produit [prɔdɥi] *m* product; proceeds; offspring; **produit de luxe** luxury item; **produit pharmaceutique** patent medicine, drug; **produits agricoles** agricultural produce; **produits de beauté** cosmetics

proémi·nent [prɔeminɑ̃] **-nente** [nɑ̃t] *adj* prominent, protuberant

profane [prɔfan] *adj* profane; lay, uninformed ‖ *mf* profane; layman

profaner [prɔfane] *tr* to profane; (fig) to prostitute

proférer [prɔfere] §10 *tr* to utter

professer [prɔfese] *tr* to profess; teach ‖ *intr* to teach

professeur [prɔfɛsœr] *m* teacher; professor

profession [prɔfɛsjɔ̃] *f* profession; occupation, trade

profession·nel -nelle [prɔfɛsjɔnɛl] *adj & mf* professional

profil [prɔfil] *m* profile; pattern; side face; cross section; skyline (*of city*)

profi·lé -lée [prɔfile] *adj* streamlined, aerodynamic

profiler [prɔfile] *tr* to profile ‖ *ref*—**se profiler sur** to stand out against

profit [prɔfi] *m* profit; **mettre à profit** to take advantage of; **profits et pertes** profit and loss

profitable [prɔfitabl] *adj* profitable

profiter [prɔfite] *intr* to profit; to thrive, grow; **profiter à qn** to benefit s.o.; **profiter de** to profit from, take advantage of

profi·teur [prɔfitœr] **-teuse** [tøz] *mf* profiteer

pro·fond [prɔfɔ̃] **-fonde** [fɔ̃d] *adj* profound; deep; low (*bow; voice*); **peu profond** shallow ‖ *m* depths ‖ *f* (slang) pocket ‖ **profond** *adv* deep

profondément [prɔfɔ̃demɑ̃] *adv* profoundly, deeply; soundly; deep

profondeur [prɔfɔ̃dœr] *f* depth

progéniture [prɔʒenityr] *f* progeny; offspring, child

programma·teur [prɔgramatœr] **-trice** [tris] *mf* (mov, rad, telv) programer

programmation [prɔgramasjɔ̃] *f* programming

programme [prɔgram] *m* program; **programme de prévoyance** retirement program; **programme des études** curriculum

programmer [prɔgrame] *tr* to program

programmerie [prɔgramri] *f* (comp) software

program·meur [prɔgramœr] **-meuse** [møz] *mf* (comp) programer

progrès [prɔgrɛ] *m* progress; **faire des progrès** to make progress

progresser [prɔgrese] *intr* to progress

progres·sif [prɔgresif] **-sive** [siv] *adj* progressive

progressiste [prɔgresist] *adj & mf* progressive

prohiber [prɔibe] *tr* to prohibit

prohibition [prɔibisjɔ̃] *f* prohibition

proie [prwa], [prwɑ] *f* prey; **de proie** predatory; **en proie à** a prey to

projecteur [prɔʒɛktœr] *m* projector; searchlight; (mov) projection machine

projectile [prɔʒɛktil] *m* projectile; **projectile téléguidé** guided missile

projection [prɔʒɛksjɔ̃] *f* projection; **projection en boucle fermée** endless strip

projet [prɔʒɛ] *m* project; draft; sketch, plan; **faire des projets** to make plans; **projet de loi** bill

projeter [prɔʒte] §34, §97 *tr* to project; pour fourth (*smoke*); cast (*a shadow*); plan ‖ *intr* to plan

prolétaire [prɔletɛr] *m* proletarian

prolétariat [prɔletarja] *m* proletariat

proléta·rien [prɔletarjɛ̃] **-rienne** [rjɛn] *adj* proletarian
proliférer [prɔlifere] §10 *intr* to proliferate
prolifique [prɔlifik] *adj* prolific
prolixe [prɔliks] *adj* prolix
prologue [prɔlɔg] *m* prologue; preface
prolongateur [prɔlɔ̃gatœr] *m* extension cord
prolongation [prɔlɔ̃gɑsjɔ̃] *f* extension (*of time*); overtime period
prolonger [prɔlɔ̃ʒe] §38 *tr* to prolong; extend ‖ *ref* to be prolonged; continue, extend
promenade [prɔmnad] *f* promenade; walk; ride; drive; sail; **faire une promenade (en auto, à cheval, à motocyclette, en bateau,** etc.) to take a ride
promener [prɔmne] §2 *tr* to take for a walk; take for a ride; walk (*e.g., a dog*); take along; **envoyer promener qn** (coll) to send s.o. packing; **promener . . . sur** to run (*e.g., one's hand, eyes*) over ‖ *ref* to stroll; go for a walk, ride, drive, or sail; **allez vous promener!** get out of here!
prome·neur [prɔmnœr] **-neuse** [nøz] *mf* walker, stroller
promenoir [prɔmnwar] *m* ambulatory, cloister; (theat) standing room
promesse [prɔmɛs] *f* promise
promettre [prɔmɛtr] §42, §98 *tr* to promise; **promettre q.ch. à qn** to promise s.th. to s.o. ‖ *intr* to look promising; **promettre à qn de** + *inf* to promise s.o. to + *inf* ‖ §97 *ref* to promise oneself; **se promettre de** to resolve to
pro·mis [prɔmi] **-mise** [miz] *adj* promised; **promis à** headed for
promiscuité [prɔmiskɥite] *f* indiscriminate mixture; lack of privacy
promontoire [prɔmɔ̃twar] *m* promontory
promo·teur [prɔmɔtœr] **-trice** [tris] *mf* promoter; originator; **promoteur immobilier** housing developer
promotion [prɔmosjɔ̃] *f* promotion; uplift; class (*in school*)
promouvoir [prɔmuvwar] §45 (*pp* **promu**) *tr* to promote
prompt [prɔ̃] **prompte** [prɔ̃t] *adj* prompt, ready, quick
promptitude [prɔ̃tityd] *f* promptness
promulguer [prɔmylge] *tr* to promulgate
prône [pron] *m* homily
prôner [prone] *tr* to extol
pronom [prɔnɔ̃] *m* pronoun
pronomi·nal **-nale** [prɔnɔminal] *adj* (*pl* **-naux** [no]) pronominal; reflexive (*verb*)
pronon·cé -cée [prɔnɔ̃se] *adj* marked; sharp (*curve*); prominent (*nose*)
prononcer [prɔnɔ̃se] §51 *tr* to pronounce; utter; deliver (*a speech*); pass (*judgment*) ‖ *intr* to decide ‖ *ref* to be pronounced; express an opinion
prononciation [prɔnɔ̃sjɑsjɔ̃] *f* pronunciation
pronostic [prɔnɔstik] *m* prognosis
pronostiquer [prɔnɔstike] *tr* to prognosticate
propagande [prɔpagɑ̃d] *f* propaganda; publicity, advertising

propager [prɔpaʒe] §38 *tr* to propagate; spread ‖ *ref* to be propagated; spread
propédeutique [prɔpedøtik] *f* (educ) preliminary study
propension [prɔpɑ̃sjɔ̃] *f* propensity
prophète [prɔfɛt] *m* prophet
prophétesse [prɔfetɛs] *f* prophetess
prophétie [prɔfesi] *f* prophecy
prophétiser [prɔfetize] *tr* to prophesy
prophylactique [prɔfilaktik] *adj* prophylactic
propice [prɔpis] *adj* propitious; lucky (*star*)
proportion [prɔpɔrsjɔ̃] *f* proportion; **en proportion de** in proportion to
proportion·né -née [prɔpɔrsjɔne] *adj* proportionate
proportion·nel **-nelle** [prɔpɔrsjɔnɛl] *adj* proportional
proportionner [prɔpɔrsjɔne] *tr* to proportion
propos [prɔpo] *m* remark; purpose; **à ce propos** in this connection; **à propos** by the way; timely, fitting; at the right moment; **à propos de** with regard to, concerning; **à tout propos** at every turn; **changer de propos** to change the subject; **de propos délibéré** on purpose; **des propos en l'air** idle talk; **hors de propos** out of place; irrelevant
proposer [prɔpoze] §97, §98 *tr* to propose; nominate; recommend (*s.o.*) ‖ *ref* to have in mind; apply (*for a job*); **se proposer de** to intend to
proposition [prɔpozisjɔ̃] *f* proposition; proposal; clause
propre [prɔpr] *adj* clean, neat; original (*meaning*); proper (*name*); literal (*meaning*); **propre à** fit for, suited to ‖ (when standing before noun) *adj* own ‖ *m* characteristic; **au propre** in the literal sense; **c'est du propre!** (coll) what a dirty trick! **en propre** in one's own right
proprement [prɔprəmɑ̃] *adv* neatly; cleanly; properly; exactly, literally; strictly
pro·pret [prɔprɛ] **-prette** [prɛt] *adj* (coll) clean, bright
propreté [prɔprəte] *f* cleanliness, neatness
propriétaire [prɔprijetɛr] *mf* proprietor, owner; landowner ‖ *m* landlord ‖ *f* propriétress; landlady
propriété [prɔprijete] *f* property; propriety, appropriateness
propulseur [prɔpylsœr] *m* engine, motor; outboard motor; (rok) booster
propulsion [prɔpylsjɔ̃] *f* propulsion; **propulsion à réaction** jet propulsion
prorata [prɔrata] *m invar*—**au prorata de** in proportion to
proroger [prɔrɔʒe] §38 *tr* to postpone; extend; adjourn ‖ *ref* to be adjourned
prosaïque [prozaik] *adj* prosaic
prosateur [prozatœr] *m* prose writer
proscrire [prɔskrir] §25 *tr* to proscribe; banish, outlaw
pros·crit [prɔskri] **-crite** [krit] *adj* banished ‖ *mf* outlaw
prose [proz] *f* prose; (coll) style (*of writing*)

prosélyte [prɔzelit] *mf* proselyte
prosodie [prɔzɔdi] *f* prosody
prospecter [prɔspɛkte] *tr & intr* to prospect
prospec·teur [prɔspɛktœr] **-trice** [tris] *mf* prospector
prospecteur-placier [prɔspɛktœrplasje] *m* head hunter *(for employment)*
prospectus [prɔspɛktys] *m* prospectus; handbill
prospère [prɔspɛr] *adj* prosperous
prospérer [prɔspere] §10 *intr* to prosper, thrive
prospérité [prɔsperite] *f* prosperity
prostate [prɔstat] *f* prostate (gland)
prosternation [prɔstɛrnasjɔ̃] *f* prostration; groveling
prosterner [prɔstɛrne] *tr* to bend over ‖ *ref* to prostrate oneself; grovel
prostituée [prɔstitɥe] *f* prostitute
prostituer [prɔstitɥe] *tr* to prostitute
prostration [prɔstrasjɔ̃] *f* prostration
pros·tré -trée [prɔstre] *adj* prostrate
protagoniste [prɔtagɔnist] *m* protagonist
prote [prɔt] *m* (typ) foreman
protection [prɔtɛksjɔ̃] *f* protection; **protection civile** civil defense
proté·gé -gée [prɔteʒe] *adj* guarded; arterial *(crossing)*; **automatiquement protégé fail-safe** ‖ *mf* protégé, dependent; pet
protège-cahier [prɔtɛʒkaje] *m* (*pl* **-cahiers**) notebook cover
protège-livre [prɔtɛʒlivr] *m* (*pl* **-livres**) dust jacket
protège-slip [prɔtɛʒslip] *m* (*pl* **-slips** [slip]) panty liner
protéger [prɔteʒe] §1 *tr* to protect; be a patron of
protéine [prɔtein] *f* protein
protes·tant [prɔtɛstɑ̃] **-tante** [tɑ̃t] *adj & mf* Protestant; protestant
protestation [prɔtɛstasjɔ̃] *f* protest
protester [prɔtɛste] §97 *tr & intr* to protest; **protester de** to protest
protêt [prɔtɛ] *m* (com) protest
protocole [prɔtɔkɔl] *m* protocol
proton [prɔtɔ̃] *m* proton
protoplasme [prɔtɔplasm] *m* protoplasm
prototype [prɔtɔtip] *m* prototype
protozoaire [prɔtɔzɔɛr] *m* protozoan
protubérance [prɔtyberɑ̃s] *f* protuberance
proue [pru] *f* prow, bow
prouesse [pruɛs] *f* prowess
prouver [pruve] *tr* to prove
provenance [prɔvnɑ̃s] *f* origin; **en provenance de** from
proven·çal -çale [prɔvɑ̃sal] (*pl* **-çaux** [so]) *adj* Provençal ‖ *m* Provençal *(language)* ‖ (*cap*) *mf* Provençal *(person)*
provenir [prɔvnir] §72 *intr* (*aux*: ÊTRE) —**provenir de** to come from
proverbe [prɔvɛrb] *m* proverb
providence [prɔvidɑ̃s] *f* providence
providen·tiel -tielle [prɔvidɑ̃sjɛl] *adj* providential
province [prɔvɛ̃s] *adj invar* (coll) provincial ‖ *f* province; **la province** the provinces *(all of France outside of Paris)*

proviseur [prɔvizœr] *m* headmaster
provision [prɔvizjɔ̃] *f* stock, store; deposit; **aller aux provisions** to go shopping; **faire provision de** to stock up on; **provisions** provisions, foodstuffs; **sans provision** bad *(check)*
provisoire [prɔvizwar] *adj* provisional, temporary; emergency
provo·cant [prɔvɔkɑ̃] **-cante** [kɑ̃t] *adj* provocative
provoquer [prɔvɔke] §96 *tr* to provoke; cause, bring about; arouse
proxénète [prɔksenɛt] *mf* procurer ‖ *m* pimp
proximité [prɔksimite] *f* proximity; **à proximité de** near
prude [pryd] *adj* prudish ‖ *f* prude
prudemment [prydamɑ̃] *adv* carefully, prudently
prudence [prydɑ̃s] *f* prudence
pru·dent [prydɑ̃] **-dente** [dɑ̃t] *adj* prudent
pruderie [prydri] *f* prudery
prud'homme [prydɔm] *m* arbitrator; (obs) solid citizen
prudhommesque [prydɔmɛsk] *adj* pompous
pruine [prɥin] *f* bloom
prune [pryn] *f* plum; **des prunes!** (slang) nuts!; **pour des prunes** (coll) for nothing
pru·neau [pryno] *m* (*pl* **-neaux**) prune; (slang) bullet
prunelle [prynɛl] *f* pupil (*of eye*); sloe; sloe gin; **jouer de la prunelle** (coll) to ogle; **prunelle de ses yeux** apple of his (one's, etc.) eye
prunellier [prynelje] *m* sloe, blackthorn
prunier [prynje] *m* plum tree
prus·sien [prysjɛ̃] **-sienne** [sjɛn] *adj* Prussian ‖ (*cap*) *mf* Prussian
P.-S. [pɛɛs] *m* (letterword) (**post-scriptum**) P.S.
psalmodier [psalmɔdje] *tr & intr* to speak in a singsong
psaume [psom] *m* psalm
psautier [psotje] *m* psalter
pseudonyme [psødɔnim] *adj* pseudonymous ‖ *m* pseudonym; nom de plume
psitt [psit] *interj* (coll) hist!
P.S.V. [peɛsve] *m* (letterword) (**pilotage sans visibilité**) blind flying
psychanalyse [psikanaliz] *f* psychoanalysis
psychanalyser [psikanalize] *tr* to psychoanalyze
psyché [psiʃe] *f* psyche; cheval glass
psychiatre [psikjatr] *mf* psychiatrist
psychiatrie [psikjatri] *f* psychiatry
psychique [psiʃik] *adj* psychic
psychologie [psikɔlɔʒi] *f* psychology
psychologique [psikɔlɔʒik] *adj* psychologic(al)
psychologue [psikɔlɔg] *mf* psychologist
psychopathe [psikɔpat] *mf* psychopath
psychose [psikoz] *f* psychosis
psychotique [psikɔtik] *adj & mf* psychotic
ptomaïne [ptɔmain] *f* ptomaine
P.T.T. [petete] *fpl* (letterword) (**Postes, télégraphes et téléphones**) post office, telephone, and telegraph

pu [py] *v* see **pouvoir**; see **paître**

puant [pɥɑ̃] **puante** [pɥɑ̃t] *adj* stinking

puanteur [pɥɑ̃tœr] *f* stench, stink

pub [pyb] *abbr* (**publicité**) publicity

puberté [pybɛrte] *f* puberty

pu·blic -blique [pyblik] *adj* public; notorious ‖ *m* public; audience

publication [pyblikɑsjɔ̃] *f* publication; proclamation

publiciste [pyblisist] *mf* public-relations expert

publicitaire [pyblisitɛr] *adj* advertising ‖ *m* advertising specialist

publicité [pyblisite] *f* publicity; advertising; **publicité aérienne** skywriting

publier [pyblije] *tr* to publish; publicize, proclaim

puce [pys] *f* flea; (comp) chip; **mettre la puce à l'oreille à qn** (fig) to put a bug in s.o.'s ear

pu·ceau -celle [sɛl] (*pl* -ceaux) *adj & mf* (coll) virgin ‖ *f* maid

puceron [pysrɔ̃] *m* plant louse

pudding [pudiŋ] *m* plum pudding

puddler [pydle] *tr* to puddle

pudeur [pydœr] *f* modesty

pudi·bond -bonde [bɔ̃d] *adj* prudish

pudibonderie [pydibɔ̃dri] *f* false modesty

pudique [pydik] *adj* modest, chaste

puer [pɥe] *tr* to reek of ‖ *intr* to stink

pué·ril -rile [pɥeril] *adj* puerile

puérilité [pɥerilite] *f* puerility

pugilat [pyʒila] *m* fight, brawl

pugiliste [pyʒilist] *m* pugilist

pugnace [pygnas] *adj* pugnacious

pui·né -née [pɥine] *adj* younger ‖ *mf* younger child

puis [pɥi] *adv* then; next; **et puis** besides; **et puis aprés?** (coll) what next? ‖ *v* see **pouvoir**

puisard [pɥizar] *m* drain, cesspool; sump

puisatier [pɥizatje] *m* well digger

puiser [pɥize] *tr* to draw (*water*); **puiser à** or **dans** to draw (*s.th.*) from ‖ *intr*—**puiser à** or **dans** to draw from or on; dip or reach into

puisque [pɥisk(ə)] *conj* since, as, seeing that

puissamment [pɥisamɑ̃] *adv* powerfully; exceedingly

puissance [pɥisɑ̃s] *f* power

puis·sant -sante [pɥisɑ̃] *adj* powerful

puisse [pɥis] *v* (**puisses, puissions,** etc.) see **pouvoir**

puits [pɥi] *m* well; pit; (min) shaft; (naut) locker; **puits absorbant, puits perdu** cesspool; **puits de pétrole** oil well; **puits de science** fountain of knowledge

pull-over [pulɔvœr], [pylɔvɛr] *m* (*pl* -overs) sweater, pullover

pulluler [pylyle] *intr* to swarm, to teem

pulmonaire [pylmɔnɛr] *adj* pulmonary ‖ *f* (bot) lungwort

pulpe [pylp] *f* pulp

pulsation [pylsɑsjɔ̃] *f* pulsation, beat; pulse

pulsion [pylsjɔ̃] *f* (psychoanal) impulse

pulvérisateur [pylverizatœr] *m* spray, atomizer

pulvérisation [pylverisɑsjɔ̃] *f* (med) spray (*for nose or throat*)

pulvériser [pylverize] *tr* to pulverize; spray

punaise [pynɛz] *f* bug; bedbug; thumbtack

punch [pɔ̃ʃ] *m* punch (*drink*) ‖ [pœnʃ] *m* (boxing) punch

punching-ball [pœnʃiŋbol] *m* punching bag

punir [pynir] §97 *tr & intr* to punish

punition [pynisjɔ̃] *f* punishment

pupille [pypil], [pypij] *mf* ward ‖ *f* pupil (*of eye*)

pupitre [pypitr] *m* desk; stand, rack; lectern; console, controls; **pupitre à musique** music stand

pur pure [pyr] *adj* pure ‖ *mf* diehard; **les purs** the pure in heart

purée [pyre] *f* purée; mashed potatoes; (coll) wretch; **être dans la purée** (coll) to be broke; **purée de pois** (culin, fig) pea soup ‖ *interj* (slang) how awful!

pureté [pyrte] *f* purity

purga·tif -tive [pyrgatif] [tiv] *adj & m* purgative

purgatoire [pyrgatwar] *m* purgatory

purge [pyrʒ] *f* purge

purger [pyrʒe] §38 *tr* to purge; pay off (*e.g., a mortgage*); serve (*a sentence*)

purifier [pyrifje] *tr* to purify

puri·tain [pyritɛ̃] **-taine** [tɛn] *adj & mf* puritan; Puritan

pur-sang [pyrsɑ̃] *adj & m invar* thoroughbred

pus [py] *m* pus ‖ *v* (**put, pûmes,** etc.) see **pouvoir**

pusillanime [pyzilanim] *adj* pusillanimous

pustule [pystyl] *f* pimple

putain [pytɛ̃] *adj invar* (coll) amiable, agreeable ‖ *f* (vulg) whore

putois [pytwa] *m* skunk, polecat

putréfier [pytrefje] *tr & ref* to decompose, rot

putride [pytrid] *adj* putrid

puy [pɥi] *m* volcanic peak

puzzle [pœzl] *m* jigsaw puzzle

p.-v. [peve] *m* (letterword) (**procès-verbal**) (coll) ticket, e.g., **attraper un p.-v.** to get a ticket

pygargue [pigarg] *m* osprey, fish hawk

pygmée [pigme] *m* pygmy

pygméen [pigmeɛ̃] **pygméenne** [pigmeɛn] *adj* pygmy

pyjama [piʒama] *m* pajamas; **un pyjama** a pair of pajamas

pylône [pilon] *m* pylon; tower

pyramide [piramid] *f* pyramid

Pyrénées [pirene] *fpl* Pyrenees

pyrite [pirit] *f* pyrites

pyrotechnie [pirɔtɛkni] *f* pyrotechnics

pyrotechnique [pirɔtɛknik] *adj* pyrotechnical

python [pitɔ̃] *m* python

pythonisse [pitɔnis] *f* pythoness

pyxide [piksid] *f* pyx

Q, q [ky] *m invar* seventeenth letter of the French alphabet

Q.I. [kyi] *m* (letterword) (**quotient intellectuel**) I.Q.

quadrant [kwadrɑ̃], [kadrɑ̃] *m* (math) quadrant

quadrilatère [kwadrilatɛr] *m* quadrilateral

quadrupède [kwadrypɛd] *m* quadruped

quadruple [kwadrypl] *adj & m* quadruple

quadrupler [kwadryple] *tr & intr* to quadruple

quadru·plés -plées [kwadryple] *mfpl* quadruplets

quai [ke] *m* quay, wharf; platform (*e.g., in a railroad station*); embankment, levee; **amener à quai** to berth; **le Quai d'Orsay** the French foreign office

qua·ker [kwɛkœr], [kwakɛr], **-keresse** [krɛs] *mf* Quaker

qualifiable [kalifjabl] *adj* describable

quali·fié -fiée [kalifje] *adj* qualified; qualifying; aggravated (*crime*)

qualifier [kalifje] *tr & intr* to qualify

qualité [kalite] *f* quality; title, capacity; **avoir qualité pour** to be authorized to; **en qualité de** in the capacity of

quand [kɑ̃] *adv* when; how soon; **n'importe quand** anytime; **quand même** though, just the same ‖ *conj* when; **quand même** even if

quant [kɑ̃] *adv*—**quant à** as for, as to, as far as; **quant à cela** for that matter

quant-à-soi [kɑ̃taswa] *m* dignity, reserve; **rester** or **se tenir sur son quant-à-soi** to keep one's distance

quantique [kwɑ̃tik] *adj* quantum

quantité [kɑ̃tite] *f* quantity

quan·tum [kwɑ̃tɔm] *m* (*pl* **-ta** [ta]) quantum

quarantaine [karɑ̃tɛn] *f* age of forty, forty mark, forties; quarantine; **une quarantaine de** about forty

quarante [karɑ̃t] §94 *adj, pron, & m* forty; **quarante et un** forty-one; **quarante et unième** forty-first

quarante-deux [karɑ̃tdø] §94 *adj, pron, & m* forty-two

quarante-deuxième [karɑ̃tdøzjɛm] §94 *adj, pron (masc, fem), & m* forty-second

quarantième [karɑ̃tjɛm] §94 *adj, pron (masc, fem), & m* fortieth

quart [kar] *m* quarter; fourth (*in fractions*); quarter of a pound; quarter of a liter; **au quart de tour** immediately; **bon quart!** (naut) all's well!; **passer un mauvais quart d'heure** to have a trying time; **petit quart** (naut) dogwatch; **prendre le quart** (naut) to come on watch; **quart de cercle** quadrant; **quart de soupir** (mus) sixteenth-note rest; **quart d'heure de Rabelais** day of reckoning; **tous les quarts d'heure au quart d'heure juste** every quarter-hour on the quarter-hour; **un petit quart d'heure** a quarter of an hour or so

quarte [kart] *adj* quartan (*fever*) ‖ *f* half-gallon; (escr) quarte; (mus) fourth

quarte·ron [kartərɔ̃] **-ronne** [rɔn] *mf* quadroon ‖ *m* handful (*e.g., of people*)

quartette [kwartɛt] *m* combo (*foursome*)

quartier [kartje] *m* quarter; neighborhood; section (*of orange*); portion; **à quartier** aloof; apart; **avoir quartier libre** (mil) to have a pass; to be off duty; **les beaux quartiers** the upper-class residential district; **mettre en quartiers** to dismember; **quartier d'affaires** business district; **quartier général** (mil) headquarters; **quartier réservé** red-light district; **quartiers** quarters, barracks

quartier-maître [kartjemɛtr] *m* (*pl* **quartiers-maîtres**) quartermaster

quartz [kwarts] *m* quartz

quasar [kwazar], [kazar] *m* quasar

quasi [kazi] *m* butt (*of a loin cut*) ‖ *adv* almost

quasi-collision [kazikɔlisjɔ̃] *f* (aer) near collision, near miss

quasiment [kazimɑ̃] *adv* (coll) almost

quatorze [katɔrz] §94 *adj & pron* fourteen; the Fourteenth, e.g., **Jean quatorze** John the Fourteenth; **c'est parti comme en quatorze** (slang) it's off to a good start ‖ *m* fourteen; fourteenth (*in dates*)

quatorzième [katɔrzjɛm] §94 *adj, pron (mas, fem), & m* fourteenth

quatrain [katrɛ̃] *m* quatrain

quatre [katr] §94 *adj & pron* four; the Fourth, e.g., **Jean quatre** John the Fourth; **quatre à quatre** four at a time; **quatre heures** four o'clock ‖ *m* four; fourth (*in dates*); **se mettre en quatre pour** to fall all over oneself for; **se tenir à quatre** to keep oneself under control

quatre-épices [katrepis] *m & f invar* allspice (*plant*); **des quatre-épices** allspice (*spice*)

quatre-saisons [katrəsɛzɔ̃], [katsɛzɔ̃] *f invar* everbearing small strawberry

quatre-temps [katrətɑ̃] *mpl* Ember days

quatre-vingt-deux [katrəvɛ̃dø] *adj, pron, & m* eighty-two

quatre-vingt-deuxième [katrəvɛ̃døzjɛm] *adj, pron (masc, fem), & m* eighty-second

quatre-vingt-dix [katrəvɛ̃di(s)] §94 *adj, pron, & m* ninety

quatre-vingt-dixième [katrəvɛ̃dizjɛm] §94 *adj, pron (masc, fem), & m* ninetieth

quatre-vingtième [katrəvɛ̃tjɛm] §94 *adj, pron (masc, fem), & m* eightieth

quatre-vingt-onze [katrəvɛ̃ɔ̃z] §94 *adj, pron, & m* ninety-one

quatre-vingt-onzième [katrəvɛ̃ɔ̃zjɛm] §94 *adj, pron (masc, fem), & m* ninety-first

quatre-vingts [katrəvɛ̃] §94 *adj & pron* eighty; **quatre-vingt** eighty, e.g., **page quatre-vingt** page eighty ‖ *m* eighty

quatre-vingt-un [katrəvɛ̃œ̃] §94 *adj, pron, & m* eighty-one

quatre-vingt-unième [katrəvɛ̃ynjɛm] §94 *adj, pron (masc, fem), & m* eighty-first

quatrième [katrijɛm] §94 *adj, pron* (*masc, fem*), & *m* fourth

quatuor [kwatɥɔr] *m* (*mus*) quartet

que [kə] (or **qu'** [k] before a vowel or mute **h**) *pron rel* whom; which, that; **ce que** that which, what ‖ *pron interr* what; **qu'est-ce que** ... ? what (as direct object) ... ?; **qu'est-ce qui** ... ? what (as subject) ... ? ‖ *adv* why, e.g., **qu'avez-vous besoin de tant de livres?** why do you need so many books?; how!, e.g., **que cette femme est belle!** how beautiful that woman is!; **que de** what a lot of, e.g., **que de difficultés!** what a lot of difficulties! ‖ *conj* that; when, e.g., **un jour que je suis allé chez le dentiste** once when I went to the dentist; since, e.g., **il y a trois jours qu'il est arrivé** it is three days since he came; until, e.g., **attendez qu'il vienne** wait until he comes; than, e.g., **plus grand que moi** taller than I; as, e.g., **aussi grand que moi** as tall as I; but, e.g., **personne que vous** no one but you; whether, e.g., **qu'il parte ou qu'il reste** whether he leaves or stays; (in a conditional sentence without **si**, to introduce the conditional in a dependent clause which represents the main clause of the corresponding sentence in English), e.g., **il ferait faillite que cela ne m'étonnerait pas** if he went bankrupt it would not surprise me; (as a repetition of another conjunction), e.g., **si elle chante et que la salle soit comble** if she sings and there is a full house; e.g., **comme il avait soif et que le vin était bon** as he was thirsty and the wine was good; (in a prayer or exhortation), e.g., **que Dieu vous bénisse!** may God bless you!, God bless you!; (in a command), e.g., **qu'il parle (aille, parte,** etc.**)** let him speak (go, leave, etc.); **ne ... que** §90 only, but

quel quelle [kɛl] §80

quelconque [kɛlkɔ̃k] *adj indef* any; any, whatever; any at all, some kind of ‖ (when standing before noun) *adj indef* some, some sort of ‖ *adj* ordinary, non-descript, mediocre

quelque [kɛlkə] *adj indef* some, any; **quelque chose** (always *masc*) something; **quelque chose de bon** something good; **quelque part** somewhere; **quelque ... qui** or **quelque ... que** whatever ... ; whichever ... ; **quelques** a few ‖ *adv* some, about; **quelque peu** somewhat; **quelque** + *adj* or *adv* ... **que** however + *adj* or *adv*

quelquefois [kɛlkəfwa] *adv* sometimes

quel·qu'un [kɛlkœ̃] **-qu'une** [kyn] §81

quémander [kemɑ̃de] *tr* to beg for ‖ *intr* to beg

qu'en-dira-t-on [kɑ̃diratɔ̃] *m invar* what other people will say, gossip

quenotte [kənɔt] *f* (coll) baby tooth

quenouille [kənuj] *f* distaff; distaff side

querelle [kərɛl] *f* quarrel; **chercher querelle à** to pick a quarrel with; **une querelle d'Allemand, une mauvaise querelle** a groundless quarrel

quereller [kərɛle] *tr* to nag, scold ‖ *ref* to quarrel

querel·leur [kərɛlœr] **-leuse** [løz] *adj* quarrelsome ‖ *mf* wrangler ‖ *f* shrew

quérir [kerir] (used only in *inf*) *tr* to go for, to fetch

question [kɛstjɔ̃] *f* question; **question discutable** moot point

questionnaire [kɛstijɔner] *m* questionnaire

questionner [kɛstjɔne] *tr* to question

question·neur [kɛstjɔnœr] **-neuse** [nøz] *adj* inquisitive ‖ *mf* inquisitive person ‖ *m* (rad, telv) quizmaster

quête [kɛt] *f* quest; **faire la quête** to take up the collection

quêter [kete] *tr* to beg or fish for (*votes, praise, etc.*); hunt for (*game*); collect (*contributions*) ‖ *intr* to take up a collection

quetsche [kwɛtʃ] *f* quetsch

queue [kø] *f* tail; queue; billiard cue; train (*of dress*); handle (*of pan*); bottom (*of class*); stem, stalk; **à la queue leu leu** in single file; **en queue** at the back; **faire la queue** to line up, to queue up; **fausse queue** miscue; **queue de cheval** (bot) horsetail; **queue de loup** (bot) purple foxglove; **queue de poisson** (aut) fishtail; **queue de vache** cat's-tail (*cirrus*); **sans queue ni tête** without head or tail; **venir en queue** to bring up the rear

queue-d'aronde [kødarɔ̃d] *f* (*pl* **queues-d'aronde**) dovetail; **assembler à queue-d'aronde** to dovetail

queue-de-cheval [kødʃval] *f* (*pl* **queues-de-cheval**) ponytail

queue-de-morue [kødmɔry] *f* (*pl* **queues-de-morue**) tails, swallow-tailed coat; (painting) flat brush

queue-de-rat [kødəra] *f* (*pl* **queues-de-rat**) rat-tail file; taper

qui [ki] *pron rel* who, whom; which; that; **ce qui** that which, what; **n'importe qui** anyone; **qui que** anyone, no one; whoever, e.g., **qui que vous soyez** whoever you are ‖ *pron interr* who, whom; **qui est-ce que** ... ? whom ... ?; **qui est-ce qui** ... ?

quia [kɥija]—**mettre** or **réduire qn à quia** (obs) to stump or floor s.o.

quiconque [kikɔ̃k] *pron indef* whoever, whosoever; whomever; anyone

quidam [kɥidam], [kidam] *m* individual, person

quiétude [kɥijetyd], [kjetyd] *f* peace of mind; quiet, calm

quignon [kiɲɔ̃] *m* hunk (*of bread*)

quille [kij] *f* keel; pin (*for bowling*); **quilles** ninepins

quincaillerie [kɛ̃kɑjri] *f* hardware; hardware store

quincail·lier [kɛ̃kɑje] **-lière** [jɛr] *mf* hardware dealer

quinconce [kɛ̃kɔ̃s] *m* quincunx; **en quinconce** quincuncially
quinine [kinin] *f* quinine
quinquen·nal -nale [kɥɛ̃kɥɛnal] *adj* (*pl* **-naux** [no]) five-year
quinquet [kɛ̃ke] *m*—**allume tes quinquets!** (slang) open your eyes!
quinquina [kɛ̃kina] *m* cinchona
quin·tal [kɛ̃tal] *m* (*pl* **-taux** [to]) hundredweight; one hundred kilograms
quinte [kɛ̃t] *f* whim; (cards) sequence of five; (mus) fifth; **quinte de toux** fit of coughing
quintessence [kɛ̃tesɑ̃s] *f* quintessence
quintette [kɥɛ̃tɛt], [kɛ̃tɛt] *m* (mus) quintet; (coll) five-piece combo; **quintette à cordes** string quintet
quin·teux [kɛ̃tø] **-teuse** [tøz] *adj* crotchety, fitful, restive
quintu·plés -plées [kɛ̃typle] *mfpl* quintuplets
quinzaine [kɛ̃zɛn] *f* (group of) fifteen; two weeks, fortnight; **une quinzaine de** about fifteen
quinze [kɛ̃z] §94 *adj & pron* fifteen; the Fifteenth, e.g., **Jean quinze** John the Fifteenth ‖ *m* fifteen; fifteenth (*in dates*)
quinzième [kɛ̃zjɛm] §94 *adj, pron* (*masc, fem*), & *m* fifteenth
quiproquo [kiprɔko] *m* mistaken identity, misunderstanding
quiscale [kɥiskal] *m* (orn) purple grackle

quittance [kitɑ̃s] *f* receipt
quitte [kit] *adj* free (*from obligation*); clear (*of debts*); (en) **être quitte pour** to get off with; **être quitte** to be quits; **tenir qn quitte de** to release s.o. from ‖ *m*—**jouer (à) quitte ou double** to play double or nothing ‖ *adv*—**quitte** is even if it means separate
quitter [kite] *tr* to leave; take off (*e.g., a coat*) ‖ *intr* to leave, go away; **ne quittez pas!** (telp) hold the line! ‖ *ref* to part, separate
quitus [kɥitys] *m* discharge, acquittance
qui-vive [kiviv] *m invar*—**sur le quivive** on the qui vive ‖ *interj* (mil) who goes there?
quoi [kwa] *pron indef* what, which; **à quoi bon?** what's the use?; **de quoi** enough; **moyennant quoi** in exchange for which; **n'importe quoi** anything; **quoi que** whatever; **quoi qu'il en soit** be that as it may; **sans quoi** otherwise
quoique [kwakə] *conj* although, though
quolibet [kɔlibɛ] *m* gibe, quip
quorum [kwɔrɔm], [kɔrɔm] *m* quorum
quota [kwɔta], [kɔta] *m* quota
quote-part [kɔtpar] *f invar* quota, share
quoti·dien [kɔtidjɛ̃] **-dienne** [djɛn] *adj* daily ‖ *m* daily newspaper
quotient [kɔsjɑ̃] *m* quotient; **quotient cours-bénéficié** price-earnings ratio; **quotient intellectuel** intelligence quotient
quotité [kɔtite] *f* share, amount

R

R, r [ɛr], *[ɛr] *m invar* eighteenth letter of the French alphabet
rabâcher [rabɑʃe] *tr* to harp on ‖ *intr* to harp on the same thing
rabais [rabɛ] *m* reduction, discount
rabaisser [rabese] *tr* to lower; to disparage
rabat [raba] *m* flap (*vestment*)
rabat-joie [rabaʒwa] *m invar* kill-joy
rabattre [rabatr] §7 *tr* to lower; discount; turn down, fold up; pull down; cut back; flush (*game*) ‖ *intr* to turn; **en rabattre** to come down a peg or two; **rabattre de** to reduce (*a price*) ‖ *ref* to fold; drop down; turn the other way; **se rabattre sur** to fall back on
rabat·tu -tue [rabaty] *adj* turndown
rabbin [rabɛ̃] *m* rabbi
rabibocher [rabibɔʃe] *tr* (coll) to patch up ‖ *ref* (coll) to make up
rabiot [rabjo] *m* overtime; extra bit; (mil) extra service; (coll) graft
rabioter [rabjɔte] *tr & intr* to graft
râ·blé -blée [rɑble] *adj* husky
rabot [rabo] *m* plane
raboter [rabɔte] *tr* to plane

rabo·teux [rabotø] **-teuse** [tøz] *adj* rough, uneven ‖ *f* (mach) planer
rabou·gri -grie [rabugri] *adj* scrub, scrawny
rabrouer [rabrue] *tr* to snub
racaille [rakɑj] *f* riffraff
raccommodage [rakɔmɔdaʒ] *m* mending; darning; patching
raccommodement [rakɔmɔdmɑ̃] *m* (coll) reconciliation
raccommoder [rakɔmɔde] *tr* to mend; darn; patch; (coll) to patch up
raccompagner [rakɔ̃paɲe] *tr* to see back, see home
raccord [rakɔr] *m* connection; coupling; joint; adapter; **faire un raccord à** to touch up
raccordement [rakɔrdəmɑ̃] *m* connecting, linking, joining
raccorder [rakɔrde] *tr & ref* to connect
raccour·ci -cie [rakursi] *adj* shortened; abridged; squat, dumpy; bobbed (*hair*) ‖ *m* abridgment; shortcut, cutoff; foreshortening; **en raccourci** in miniature; in a nutshell

raccourcir [rakursir] *tr* to shorten; abridge; foreshorten ‖ *intr* to grow shorter

raccourcissement [rakursismã] *m* shortening; abridgment; shrinking

raccroc [rakro] *m* (billiards) fluke

raccrocher [rakrɔʃe] *tr* & *intr* to hang up ‖ *ref*—**se raccrocher à** to hang on to

race [ras] *f* race; **de race** thoroughbred

ra·cé -cée [rase] *adj* thoroughbred

rachat [raʃa] *m* repurchase; redemption; ransom

racheter [raʃte] §2 *tr* to buy back; redeem; ransom

rachitique [raʃitik] *adj* rickety

rachitisme [raʃitism] *m* rickets

ra·cial -ciale [rasjal] *adj* (*pl* -**ciaux** [sjo]) race, racial

racine [rasin] *f* root; **racine carrée** square root; **racine cubique** cube root

racisme [rasism] *m* racism

raciste [rasist] *adj* & *mf* racist

racket [rakɛt] *m* (coll) racket

racketter or **racketteur** [rakɛtœr] *m* racketeer

raclée [rakle] *f* beating

racler [rakle] *tr* to scrape

raclette [raklɛt] *f* scraper; hoe; (phot) squeegee

racloir [raklwar] *m* scraper

raclure [raklyr] *f* scrapings

racolage [rakɔlaʒ] *m* soliciting

racoler [rakɔle] *tr* (coll) to solicit; (archaic) to shanghai

raco·leur [rakɔlœr] **-leuse** [løz] *mf* recruiter ‖ *f* (coll) hustler, streetwalker

racontar [rakɔ̃tar] *m* (coll) gossip

raconter [rakɔ̃te] *tr* to tell, narrate; describe

racon·teur [rakɔ̃tœr] **-teuse** [tøz] *mf* storyteller

racornir [rakɔrnir] *tr* & *intr* to harden; shrivel

radar [radar] *m* radar

rade [rad] *f* roadstead; **en rade** (coll) abandoned

ra·deau [rado] *m* (*pl* -**deaux**) raft

ra·diant [radjã] **-diante** [djãt] *adj* (astr, phys) radiant

radiateur [radjatœr] *m* radiator

radiation [radjasjɔ̃] *f* radiation; striking off

radi·cal -cale [radikal] *adj* & *mf* (*pl* -**caux** [ko]) radical ‖ *m* (chem, gram, math) radical

radier [radje] *tr* to cross out, strike out or off

ra·dieux [radjø] **-dieuse** [djøz] *adj* radiant

radin [radɛ̃] *adj masc* & *fem* (slang) stingy

radio [radjo] *m* radiogram; radio operator ‖ *f* radio; radio set; X-ray

radioac·tif [radjɔaktif] **-tive** [tiv] *adj* radioactive

radio-crochet [radjokrɔʃɛ] *m* (*pl* -**crochets**) talent show

radiodiffuser [radjɔdifyze] *tr* to broadcast

radiodiffusion [radjɔdifyzjɔ̃] *f* broadcasting

radiofréquence [radjofrekãs] *f* radiofrequency

radiogramme [radjɔgram] *m* radiogram

radiographier [radjɔgrafje] *tr* to X-ray

radioguidage [radjɔgidaʒ] *m* radio control; radio guidance; **radioguidage d'aérodrome** instrument-landing system

radiogui·dé -dée [radjɔgide] *adj* radiocontrolled; guided (*missile*)

radio-journal [radjɔʒurnal] *m* (*pl* -**journaux** [ʒurno]) radio newscast

radiologie [radjɔlɔʒi] *f* radiology

radiophare [radjofar] *m* radio beacon

radioreportage [radjɔrəpɔrtaʒ] *m* news broadcast; sports broadcast

radioscopie [radjɔskɔpi] *f* radioscopy, fluoroscopy

radio-taxi [radjɔtaksi] *m* (*pl* -**taxis**) radio taxi

radiotéléphone [radjɔtelefɔn] *m* radiophone, car telephone

radiotélévi·sé -sée [radjɔtelevize] *adj* broadcast over radio and television

radis [radi] *m* radish

radium [radjɔm] *m* radium

radius [radjys] *m* (anat) radius

radotage [radɔtaʒ] *m* drivel, twaddle

radoter [radɔte] *intr* to talk nonsense, ramble

radoub [radu] *m* (naut) graving

radouber [radube] *tr* (naut) to grave

radoucir [radusir] *tr* & *ref* to calm down

rafale [rafal] *f* squall, gust; burst of gunfire

raffermir [rafɛrmir] *tr* & *ref* to harden

raffinage [rafinaʒ] *m* refining

raffinement [rafinmã] *m* refinement

raffiner [rafine] *tr* to refine ‖ *intr* to be subtle; **raffiner sur** to overdo

raffinerie [rafinri] *f* refinery

raffoler [rafɔle] *intr*—**raffoler de** to dote on, to be wild about

raffut [rafy] *m* (coll) uproar

rafistolage [rafistɔlaʒ] *m* (coll) patching up

rafistoler [rafistɔle] *tr* (coll) to patch up

rafle [rɑfl] *f* raid, mass arrest; stalk; corncob

rafler [rɑfle] *tr* (coll) to carry away, make a clean sweep of

rafraîchir [rafreʃir] *tr* to cool; refresh; freshen up; trim (*the hair*) ‖ *intr* to cool ‖ *ref* to cool off; refresh oneself

rafraîchissement [rafreʃismã] *m* refreshment; cooling off

ragaillardir [ragajardir] *tr* to cheer up

rage [raʒ] *f* rage; rabies; **à la rage** madly, **faire rage** to rage

rager [raʒe] §38 *intr* (coll) to be enraged

ra·geur [raʒœr] **-geuse** [ʒøz] *adj* badtempered

ragot [rago] *m* (coll) gossip

ragoût [ragu] *m* stew, ragout; (obs) spice, relish

ragoû·tant [ragutã] **-tante** [tãt] *adj* tempting, inviting; pleasing; **peu ragoûtant** not very appetizing

rai [rɛ] *m* ray; spoke

raid [rɛd] *m* raid; air raid; endurance test

raide [rɛd] *adj* stiff; tight, taut, steep; (coll) incredible ‖ *adv* suddenly

raideur [rɛdœr] *f* stiffness

raidillon [rɛdijɔ̃] *m* short steep path

raidir [redir] *tr & ref* to stiffen

raie [rɛ] *f* stripe, streak; stroke; line (*of spectrum*); part (*of hair*); (ichth) ray, skate

raifort [rɛfɔr] *m* horseradish

rail [rɑj] *m* rail; **rail conducteur** third rail; **remettre sur les rails** (fig) to put back on the track; **sortir des rails** to jump the track

railler [rɑje] *tr* to make fun of || *intr* to joke || *ref*—**se railler de** to make fun of

raillerie [rɑjri] *f* raillery, banter

rail·leur [rɑjœr] **-leuse** [jøz] *adj* teasing, bantering || *mf* teaser

rainette [rɛnɛt] *f* tree frog

rainure [renyr] *f* groove

raisin [rɛzɛ̃] *m* grapes; grape; **raisin d'ours** (bot) bearberry; **raisins de Corinthe** currants; **raisins de mer** cuttlefish eggs; **raisins de Smyrne** seedless raisins; **raisins secs** raisins

raisiné [rɛzine] *m* grape jelly; (slang) blood

raison [rɛzɔ̃] *f* reason; ratio, rate; **à raison de** at the rate of; **avoir raison** to be right; **avoir raison de** to get the better of; **donner raison à** to back, support; **en raison de** because of; **raison sociale** trade name; **se faire une raison** to resign oneself

raisonnable [rɛzɔnabl] *adj* reasonable; rational

raison·né **-née** [rɛzɔne] *adj* rational; detailed

raisonnement [rɛzɔnmɑ̃] *m* reasoning; argument

raisonner [rɛzɔne] *tr* to reason out; reason with || *intr* to reason; argue || *ref* to reason with oneself

raison·neur [rɛzɔnœr] **-neuse** [nøz] *adj* rational; argumentative || *mf* reasoner; arguer

rajeunir [raʒœnir] *tr* to rejuvenate || *intr* to grow young again || *ref* to pretend to be younger than one is

rajeunissement [raʒœnismɑ̃] *m* rejuvenation

rajouter [raʒute] *tr* to add again; (coll) to add more

rajuster [raʒyste] *tr* to readjust; adjust || *ref* to adjust one's clothes

râle [rɑl] *m* rale; death rattle; (orn) rail

ralen·ti **-tie** [ralɑ̃ti] *adj* slow || *m* slowdown; **au ralenti** slowdown (*work*); go-slow (*policy*); slow-motion (*moving picture*); idling (*motor*); **tourner au ralenti** (aut) to idle

ralentir [ralɑ̃tir] *tr, intr, & ref* to slow down; **ralentir** (*public sign*) slow

ralliement [ralimɑ̃] *m* rally

rallier [ralje] *tr & ref* to rally

rallonge [ralɔ̃ʒ] *f* extra piece; extension cord; extra (*in building a new house*); (coll) raise (*in pay*); leaf (*of table*); (coll) under-the-table payment; **à rallonges** extension (*table*)

rallonger [ralɔ̃ʒe] §38 *tr & intr* to lengthen || *ref* to grow longer

rallumer [ralyme] *tr* to relight; (fig) to rekindle || *intr* to put on the lights again || *ref* to be rekindled

rallye [rali] *m* rallye

ramage [ramaʒ] *m* floral design; warbling

ramas [ramɑ] *m* heap; pack (*e.g., of thieves*)

ramassage [ramɑsaʒ] *m* gathering; **ramassage scolaire** school-bus service

ramas·sé **-sée** [ramɑse] *adj* stocky; compact (*style*)

ramasse-poussière [ramaspusjɛr] *m invar* dustpan

ramasser [ramɑse] *tr* to gather; gather together; pick up; (coll) to catch (*a scolding; a cold*) || *ref* to gather; gather oneself together

rambarde [rɑ̃bard] *f* handrail

rame [ram] *f* prop, stick; oar, pole; ream (*of paper*); string (*e.g., of barges*); (rr) train, section; **rame de métro** subway train

ra·meau [ramo] *m* (*pl* **-meaux**) branch; sprig

ramée [rame] *f* boughs

ramener [ramne] §2 *tr* to lead back; bring back; reduce; restore

ramer [rame] *tr* to stake (*a plant*) || *intr* to row

ra·meur [ramœr] **-meuse** [møz] *mf* rower

ramier [ramje] *m* wood pigeon

ramifier [ramifje] *tr & ref* to ramify, branch out

ramol·li **-lie** [ramɔli] *adj* sodden; (coll) half-witted || *mf* (coll) half-wit

ramollir [ramɔlir] *tr & ref* to soften

ramoner [ramɔne] *tr* to sweep (*a chimney*)

ramoneur [ramɔnœr] *m* chimney sweep

ram·pant [rɑ̃pɑ̃] **-pante** [pɑ̃t] *adj* crawling, creeping; (hum) ground (*crew*)

rampe [rɑ̃p] *f* ramp; grade, gradient; banister; flight (*of stairs*); (aer) runway lights; (theat) footlights; **rampe de lancement** launching pad

ramper [rɑ̃pe] *intr* to crawl; grovel; (bot) to creep

ramure [ramyr] *f* branches; antlers

rancart [rɑ̃kar] *m* (slang) rendezvous; **mettre au rancart** (coll) to scrap, to shelve

rance [rɑ̃s] *adj* rancid

ranch [rɑ̃tʃ] *m* ranch

rancir [rɑ̃sir] *intr & ref* to turn rancid

rancœur [rɑ̃kœr] *f* rancor

rançon [rɑ̃sɔ̃] *f* ransom; price (*e.g., of fame*); **mettre à rançon** to hold for ransom

rançonner [rɑ̃sɔne] *tr* to ransom, to hold for ransom; extort money from; steal from; to overcharge, e.g., **cet hôtelier rançonne ses clients** that hotel manager overcharges his guests

rancune [rɑ̃kyn] *f* grudge

rancu·nier [rɑ̃kynje] **-nière** [njɛr] *adj* vindictive, spiteful, rancorous

randonnée [rɑ̃dɔne] *f* long walk; long ride

rang [rɑ̃] *m* rank; **au premier rang** in the first row; ranking; **en rang d'oignons** in a line

ran·gé -gée [rɑ̃ʒe] *adj* orderly; pitched (*battle*); steady (*person*)

ranger [rɑ̃ʒe] §38 *tr* to range; rank ‖ *ref* to take one's place; get out of the way; mend one's ways; **se ranger à** to adopt, take (*e.g., a suggestion*)

ranimer [ranime] *tr & ref* to revive

raout [raut] *m* reception

rapace [rapas] *adj* rapacious ‖ *m* bird of prey

rapatriement [rapatrimɑ̃] *m* repatriation

rapatrier [rapatrije] *tr* to repatriate

râpe [rɑp] *f* rasp; grater

râ·pé -pée [rɑpe] *adj* grated; threadbare ‖ *m* (coll) grated cheese

râper [rɑpe] *tr* to rasp, grate

rapetasser [raptase] *tr* (coll) to patch up

rapetisser [raptise] *tr, intr, & ref* to shrink, shorten

râ·peux [rɑpø] **-peuse** [pøz] *adj* raspy, grating

ra·piat [rapja] **-piate** [pjat] *adj* (coll) stingy ‖ *mf* (coll) skinflint

rapide [rapid] *adj* rapid; steep ‖ *m* rapids; (rr) express; **rapides** rapids

rapidement [rapidmɑ̃] *adv* rapidly

rapidité [rapidite] *f* rapidity; steepness

rapiéçage [rapjesaʒ] *m* patching

rapiécer [rapjese] §58 *tr* to patch

rapière [rapjɛr] *f* rapier

rapin [rapɛ̃] *m* dauber; (coll) art student

rapine [rapin] *f* rapine, pillage

rappel [rapɛl] *m* recall; reminder; call-up; recurrence; booster (*shot*); (*public sign*) end of speed limit, resume speed; (theat) curtain call; **battre le rappel** to call to arms; **rappel au règlement** point of order; **rappel de chariot** backspacer

rappeler [raple] §34 *tr* to recall; remind; call back; call up ‖ §95, §97 *ref* to remember

rapport [rapɔr] *m* yield, return; report; connection, bearing; (math) ratio; **avoir de bons rapports avec** to be on good terms with; **en rapport avec** in touch with; in keeping with; **par rapport à** in comparison with; **rapports** relations; sexual relations; **sous le rapport de** from the standpoint of; **sous tous les rapports** in all respects

rapporter [rapɔrte] *tr* to bring back; yield; report; relate; repeal, call off; attach; retrieve (*game*); (bk) to post ‖ *intr* to yield; (coll) to squeal ‖ *ref*—**s'en rapporter à** to leave it up to; **se rapporter à** to be related to, refer to, have to do with

rappor·teur [rapɔrtœr] **-teuse** [tøz] *mf* tattletale ‖ *m* recorder; (geom) protractor

rapprochement [raprɔʃmɑ̃] *m* bringing together; parallel; rapprochement

rapprocher [raprɔʃe] *tr* to bring closer; reconcile; compare ‖ *ref* to draw closer, approach; **se rapprocher de** to approximate, resemble

rapt [rapt] *m* kidnaping

raquette [rakɛt] *f* racket; snowshoe; tennis player; (bot) prickly pear

rare [rar] *adj* rare; scarce; sparse, thin (*hair*)

rarement [rarmɑ̃] *adv* rarely, seldom

rareté [rarte] *f* rarity; scarcity; rareness

R.A.S. [ɛrɑɛs] (letterword) (**rien à signaler**) nothing worth talking about

ras [rɑ] **rase** [rɑz] *adj* short (*hair, nap, etc.*); level; close-cropped; close-shaven; open (*country*) ‖ *m*—**à ras de, au ras de** flush with; **ras d'eau** water line; **ras du cou** crew neck; **voler au ras du sol** to skim along the ground

rasade [rɑzad] *f* bumper, glassful

rasage [rɑzaʒ] *m* shearing; shaving

ra·sant [rɑzɑ̃] **-sante** [zɑ̃t] *adj* level; grazing; close to the ground; (coll) boring

rase-mottes [rɑzmɔt] *m invar* hedgehopper; **faire du rase-mottes** or **voler en rase-mottes** to hedgehop

raser [rɑze] *tr* to shave; raze; graze ‖ *ref* to shave

ra·seur [rɑzœr] **-seuse** [zøz] *adj* (coll) boring ‖ *mf* (coll) bore

rasoir [rɑswar] *adj invar* (slang) boring ‖ *m* razor; (slang) bore; **rasoir à manche** straight razor; **rasoir de sûreté** safety razor

rassasiement [rasazimɑ̃] *m* satiation

rassasier [rasazje] *tr* to satisfy; satiate ‖ *ref* to have one's fill

rassemblement [rasɑ̃bləmɑ̃] *m* assembling; crowd; muster; (*trumpet call*) assembly; **rassemblement!** (mil) fall in!

rassembler [rasɑ̃ble] *tr & ref* to gather together

rasseoir [raswar] §5 *tr* to reseat; set in place again ‖ *ref* to sit down again

rasséréner [raserene] §10 *tr & ref* to calm down

rassir [rasir] *intr & ref* (coll) to get stale

ras·sis [rasi] **-sise** [siz] *adj* level-headed; stale (*bread*)

rassortir [rasɔrtir] *tr* to restock ‖ *ref* to lay in a new stock

rassurer [rasyre] *tr* to reassure ‖ *ref* to be reassured

rastaquouère [rastakwɛr] *m* (coll) flashy stranger

rat [ra] *m* rat; (coll) tightwad; **fait comme un rat** caught like a rat in a trap; **mon rat** (coll) my turtledove; **rat à bourse** gopher; **rat de bibliothèque** bookworm; **rat de cale** stowaway; **rat de cave** thin candle; tax collector; **rat d'égout** sewer rat; **rat des champs** field mouse; **rat d'hôtel** hotel thief; **rat d'Opéra** ballet girl; **rat musqué** muskrat

ratatiner [ratatine] *ref* to shrivel up

ratatouille [ratatuj] *f* ratatouille; (coll) stew; (coll) bad cooking; (coll) blows

rate [rat] *f* spleen; female rat

ra·té -tée [rate] *adj* miscarried; bad (*shot, landing, etc.*) ‖ *mf* failure, dropout

râ·teau [rɑto] *m* (*pl* **-teaux**) rake

râteler [rɑtle] §34 *tr* to rake

râtelier [rɑtəlje] *m* rack; set of false teeth; **manger à deux râteliers** (coll) to play both sides of the street; **râtelier d'armes** gun rack

rater [rate] *tr* to miss ‖ *intr* to miss, misfire; fail

ratiboiser [ratibwaze] *tr* (coll) to take to the cleaners; **ratiboiser q.ch. à qn** (coll) to clean s.o. out of s.th.

ratière [ratjɛr] *f* rattrap

ratifier [ratifje] *tr* to ratify

ration [rɑsjɔ̃] *f* ration

ration·nel -nelle [rasjɔnɛl] *adj* rational

rationnement [rasjɔnmɑ̃] *m* rationing

rationner [rasjɔne] *tr* to ration

ratisser [ratise] *tr* to rake; rake in; search with a fine-tooth comb; (coll) to fleece

ratissoire [ratiswar] *f* hoe

raton [ratɔ̃] *m* little rat; **raton laveur** raccoon

rattacher [rataʃe] *tr* to tie again; link; unite ‖ *ref* to be connected

rattrapage [ratrapaʒ] *m* catch-up; (typ) catchword

rattraper [ratrape] *tr* to catch up to; recover; recapture ‖ *ref* to catch up; **se rattraper à** to catch hold of; **se rattraper de** to make good, recoup

rature [ratyr] *f* erasure

raturer [ratyre] *tr* to cross out

rauque [rok] *adj* hoarse, raucous

ravage [ravaʒ] *m* ravage

ravager [ravaʒe] §38 *tr* to ravage

ravalement [ravalmɑ̃] *m* trimming down; resurfacing; disparagement

ravaler [ravale] *tr* to choke down; disparage; drag down; resurface; eat (*one's words*) ‖ *ref* to lower oneself

ravaudage [ravodaʒ] *m* mending; darning; (fig) patchwork

ravauder [ravode] *tr* to mend; darn

ra·vi -vie [ravi] §93 *adj* delighted, happy, charmed

ravier [ravje] *m* hors-d'oeuvre dish

ravigoter [ravigɔte] *tr* (coll) to revive

ravilir [ravilir] *tr* to debase

ravin [ravɛ̃] *m* ravine

ravine [ravin] *f* mountain torrent

raviner [ravine] *tr* to furrow

ravir [ravir] *tr* to ravish; kidnap, abduct; delight, entrance; **ravir q.ch. à qn** to snatch, take s.th. from s.o. ‖ *intr*—**à ravir** marvelously

raviser [ravize] *ref* to change one's mind

ravis·sant [ravisɑ̃] **-sante** [sɑ̃t] *adj* ravishing, entrancing

ravis·seur [ravisœr] **-seuse** [søz] *mf* kidnaper

ravitaillement [ravitajmɑ̃] *m* supplying; supplies

ravitailler [ravitaje] *tr* to supply; fill up the gas tank of (*a vehicle*) ‖ *ref* to lay in supplies; fill up (*to get gas*)

raviver [ravive] *tr* to revive; brighten up; reopen (*an old wound*) ‖ *ref* to revive; break out again

ravoir [ravwar] (used only in *inf*) *tr* to get back again

rayer [reje] §49 *tr* to cross out, strike out; rule, line; stripe, pinstripe; rifle (*a gun*)

rayon [rɛjɔ̃] *m* ray; radius; spoke; shelf; honeycomb; department (*in a store*); point (*of star*); **ce n'est pas mon rayon** (coll) that's not in my line; **rayon de lune** moonbeam; **rayons X** X rays; **rayon visuel** line of sight

rayonnage [rɛjɔnaʒ] *m* set of shelves, shelving

rayon·nant [rɛjɔnɑ̃] **-nante** [nɑ̃t] *adj* radiant; radiating; radioactive; (rad) transmitting

rayonne [rɛjɔn] *f* rayon

rayonnement [rɛjɔnmɑ̃] *m* radiance; influence, diffusion; (phys) radiation; **rayonnement de faible (grande) énergie** low-level (high-level) radiation; **rayonnement diffusé** scattered radiation; **rayonnement ionisant** ionizing radiation; **rayonnement parasite** stray radiation; **rayonnement solaire** solar radiation

rayonner [rɛjɔne] *intr* to radiate

rayure [rejyr] *f* stripe; scratch; rifling

raz [rɑ] *m* race (*channel and current of water*); **raz de marée** tidal wave; landslide (*in an election*)

razzia [razja] *f* raid

razzier [razje] *tr* to raid

réacteur [reaktœr] *m* reactor; **réacteur nucléaire** nuclear reactor

réactif [reaktif] *m* (chem) reagent

réaction [reaksjɔ̃] *f* reaction; kick (*of rifle*); **à réaction** jet; **réaction en chaîne** chain reaction

réactionnaire [reaksjɔnɛr] *adj & mf* reactionary

réactiver [reaktive] *tr* to reactivate

réadaptation [readaptasjɔ̃] *f* rehabilitation; readjustment; **réadaptation fonctionnelle** occupational therapy

réadapter [readapte] *tr* to rehabilitate; readjust ‖ *ref* to be rehabilitated

réaffirmer [reafirme] *tr* to reaffirm

réagir [reaʒir] *intr* to react

réalisable [realizabl] *adj* feasible; (com) saleable

réalisa·teur [realizatœr] **-trice** [tris] *adj* producing ‖ *mf* achiever; producer ‖ *m* (mov, rad, telv) director

réalisation [realizasjɔ̃] *f* accomplishment; work; (mov, rad, telv) production; (com) liquidation

réaliser [realize] *tr* to accomplish; realize; sell out; (mov) to produce ‖ *ref* to come to pass, be realized

réalisme [realism] *m* realism

réaliste [realist] *adj* realistic ‖ *mf* realist

réalité [realite] *f* reality; **en réalité** in reality, really, in actual fact

réanimer [reanime] *tr* to revive

réapparaître [reaparɛtr] §12 *intr* to reappear

réapparition [reaparisjɔ̃] *f* reappearance

réarmement [rearməmɑ̃] *m* rearmament

réassortir [reasɔrtir] *tr* to restock ‖ *ref* to lay in a new stock

réassurer [reasyre] *tr* to reinsure
rébarba·tif [rebarbatif] -tive [tiv] *adj* forbidding, repulsive
rebâtir [rəbɑtir] *tr* to rebuild
rebattre [rəbatr] §7 *tr* to beat; reshuffle; repeat over and over again
rebat·tu -tue [rəbaty] *adj* hackneyed
rebelle [rəbɛl] *adj* rebellious ‖ *mf* rebel
rebeller [rəbele], [rəbɛlle] *ref* to rebel
rébellion [rebeljɔ̃] *f* rebellion
rebiffer [rɛbife] *ref* to kick over the traces
reboisement [rəbwazmɑ̃] *m* reforestation
rebond [rəbɔ̃] *m* rebound
rebon·di -die [rəbɔ̃di] *adj* plump, buxom; paunchy
rebondir [rəbɔ̃dir] *intr* to bounce; (fig) to come up again
rebord [rəbɔr] *m* edge, border; sill, ledge; hem; brim (*of hat*); rim (*of saucer*); lip (*of cup*)
reboucher [rəbuʃe] *tr* to recork; stop up ‖ *ref* to be stopped up
rebours [rəbur] *m*—à rebours backwards; against the grain; the wrong way; backhanded (*compliment*); à or au rebours de contrary to
rebouter [rəbute] *tr* to set (*a bone*)
rebrousse-poil [rəbruspwal]—à rebrousse-poil against the grain, the wrong way
rebrousser [rəbruse] *tr* to brush up; rebrousser chemin to turn back; rebrousser qn (coll) to rub s.o. the wrong way ‖ *ref* to turn up, bend back
rebuffade [rəbyfad] *f* rebuff; essuyer une rebuffade to be snubbed
rebut [rəby] *m* castoff; waste; scum (*of society*); rebuff; de rebut castoff; waste; unclaimed (*letter*); mettre au rebut to discard
rebu·tant [rəbytɑ̃] -tante [tɑ̃t] *adj* dull, tedious; repugnant
rebuter [rəbyte] *tr* to rebuff; bore; be repulsive to
recaler [rəkale] *tr* (coll) to flunk
récapitulation [rekapitylɑsjɔ̃] *f* recapitulation
recéder [rəsede] §10 *tr* to give back; sell back; resell
recel [rəsɛl] *m* concealment (*of stolen goods; of criminals*)
receler [rəsle] §2 or recéler [rəsele] §10 *tr* to conceal; receive (*stolen goods*); harbor (*a criminal*) ‖ *intr* to hide
rece·leur [rəslœr] -leuse [løz] *mf* fence, receiver of stolen goods
récemment [resamɑ̃] *adv* recently, lately
recensement [rəsɑ̃smɑ̃] *m* census; recensement du contingent draft registration
recenser [rəsɑ̃se] *tr* to take the census of; take a count of
recenseur [rəsɑ̃sœr] *m* census taker
ré·cent [resɑ̃] -cente [sɑ̃t] *adj* recent
récépissé [resepise] *m* receipt; certificate, permit
réceptacle [resɛptakl] *m* receptacle
récep·teur [resɛptœr] -trice [tris] *adj* receiving ‖ *m* receiver

récep·tif [resɛptif] -tive [tiv] *adj* receptive
réception [resɛpsjɔ̃] *f* reception; receipt; approval; admission (*to a club*); registration desk (*of hotel*); landing (*of, e.g., a parachutist*); (sports) catch; accuser réception de to acknowledge receipt of
réceptionnaire [resɛpsjɔnɛr] *mf* consignee; chief receptionist
récession [resesjɔ̃] *f* recession
recette [rəsɛt] *f* receipt; collection (*of debts, taxes, etc.*); (culin) recipe; faire recette to be a box-office attraction; recettes de métier tricks of the trade
recevable [rəsvabl] *adj* acceptable; admissible
rece·veur [rəsvœr] -veuse [vøz] *mf* collector; conductor (*of bus, streetcar, etc.*); blood recipient; receveur des postes postmaster; receveur universel recipient of blood from a universal donor
recevoir [rəsvwar] §59 *tr* to receive; accommodate; admit (*to a school, club, etc.*); être reçu to be admitted; pass ‖ *intr* to receive
rechange [rəʃɑ̃ʒ] *m* replacement, change; de rechange spare (*e.g., parts*)
rechaper [rəʃape] *tr* to recap, retread
réchapper [reʃape] *intr*—en réchapper to get away with it; to get well; réchapper à or de to escape from
recharge [rəʃarʒ] *f* refill; recharging; reloading
recharger [rəʃarʒe] §38 *tr* to recharge; refill; reload; ballast (*a roadbed*)
réchaud [reʃo] *m* hot plate
réchauffer [reʃofe] *tr & ref* to warm up
rêche [rɛʃ] *adj* rough, harsh
recherche [rəʃɛrʃ] *f* search; quest; investigation, piece of research; refinement; recherches research
recher·ché -chée [rəʃɛrʃe] *adj* sought-after, in demand; elaborate; studied, affected
rechercher [rəʃɛrʃe] *tr* to seek, look for
rechigner [rəʃiɲe] *intr*—rechigner à to balk at
rechute [rəʃyt] *f* relapse
rechuter [rəʃyte] *intr* to relapse
récidive [residiv] *f* recurrence; second offense
récidiver [residive] *intr* to recur; relapse
récif [resif] *m* reef
récipiendaire [resipjɑ̃dɛr] *m* new member, inductee; recipient
récipient [resipjɑ̃] *m* container, receptacle, recipient
réciprocité [resiprɔsite] *f* reciprocity
réciproque [resiprɔk] *adj* reciprocal ‖ *f* converse
récit [resi] *m* recital, account
réci·tal [resital] *m* (*pl* -tals) recital
récitation [resitɑsjɔ̃] *f* recitation
réciter [resite] *tr* to recite
récla·mant [reklamɑ̃] -mante [mɑ̃t] *mf* claimant
réclamation [reklamɑsjɔ̃] *f* complaint; demand

réclame [reklam] *f* advertising; advertisement; (theat) cue; (typ) catchword; **faire de la réclame** to advertise, to ballyhoo; **réclame à éclipse** flashing sign; **réclame lumineuse** illuminated sign

réclamer [reklame] *tr* to claim; clamor for; demand ‖ *intr* to lodge a complaint; intercede ‖ *ref*—**se réclamer de** to appeal to; claim kinship with; **se réclamer de qn** to use s.o.'s name as a reference

reclassement [rəklɑsmɑ̃] *m* reclassification

reclasser [rəklɑse] *tr* to reclassify

re·clus [rəkly] **-cluse** [klyz] *adj* & *mf* recluse

recoin [rəkwɛ̃] *m* nook, cranny

récollection [rekɔlɛksjɔ̃] *f* religious meditation

recoller [rəkɔle] *tr* to paste again

récolte [rekɔlt] *f* harvest

récolter [rekɔlte] *tr* to harvest

recommander [rəkɔmɑ̃de] §97, §98 *tr* to recommend; register (*a letter*) ‖ *ref*—**se recommander à** to seek the protection of; **se recommander de** to ask (*s.o.*) for a reference

recommencer [rəkɔmɑ̃se] §51, §96, §97 *tr* & *intr* to begin again

récompense [rekɔ̃pɑ̃s] *f* recompense, reward; award

récompenser [rekɔ̃pɑ̃se] *tr* to recompense

réconcilier [rekɔ̃silje] *tr* to reconcile

reconduction [rəkɔ̃dyksjɔ̃] or **réconduction** [rekɔ̃dyksjɔ̃] *f* continuation; renewal (*of a lease*)

reconduire [rəkɔ̃dɥir] §19 *tr* to escort; (coll) to kick out, to send packing

réconfort [rekɔ̃fɔr] *m* comfort

réconfor·tant [rekɔ̃fɔrtɑ̃] **-tante** [tɑ̃t] *adj* consoling; stimulating

réconforter [rekɔ̃fɔrte] *tr* to comfort; revive ‖ *ref* to recuperate; cheer up

reconnaissance [rəkɔnɛsɑ̃s] *f* recognition; gratitude; (mil) reconnaissance; **aller en reconnaissance** to reconnoiter; **reconnaissance de** or **pour** gratitude for

reconnais·sant [rəkɔnɛsɑ̃] **-sante** [sɑ̃t] *adj* grateful; **être reconnaissant de** + *inf* to be grateful for + *ger;* **être reconnaissant de** or **pour** to be grateful for

reconnaître [rəkɔnɛtr] §12, §95 *tr* to recognize; (mil) to reconnoiter ‖ *ref* to recognize oneself; know where one is; acknowledge oneself (*e.g., guilty*); **s'y reconnaître** to know where one is

reconquérir [rəkɔ̃kerir] §3 *tr* to reconquer

reconquête [rəkɔ̃kɛt] *f* reconquest

reconsidérer [rəkɔ̃sidere] §10 *tr* to reconsider

reconstituant [rəkɔ̃stitɥɑ̃] *m* tonic

reconstituer [rəkɔ̃stitɥe] *tr* to reconstruct; restore

reconstruire [rəkɔ̃strɥir] §19 *tr* to reconstruct

record [rəkɔr] *adj invar* & *m* record

recordman [rəkɔrdman] *m* record holder

recoudre [rəkudr] §13 *tr* to sew up

recoupement [rəkupmɑ̃] *m* cross-check, cross-checking; **faire un recoupement** to cross-check

recouper [rəkupe] *tr* to cut again; blend (*wines*)

recourir [rəkurir] §14 *intr* to run again; **recourir à** to resort to; appeal to

recours [rəkur] *m* recourse; **avoir recours à** to resort to; call on for help; **en dernier recours** as a last resort; **recours en grâce** petition for pardon

recouvrement [rəkuvrəmɑ̃] *m* recovery

recouvrer [rəkuvre] *tr* to recover

recouvrir [rəkuvrir] §65 *tr* to cover; cover up; mask; resurface (*e.g., a road*) ‖ *ref* to overlap

récréation [rekreasjɔ̃] *f* recreation; recess (*at school*)

recréer [rəkree] *tr* to re-create

récréer [rekree] *tr* & *ref* to relax

récrier [rekrije] *ref* to cry out

récrire [rekrir] §25 *tr* to rewrite; write again

recroquevil·lé -lée [rəkrɔkvije] *adj* shriveled up, curled up; huddled up

recroqueviller [rəkrɔkvije] *tr* & *ref* to shrivel up, curl up

re·cru -crue [rəkry] *adj* exhausted

recrue [rəkry] *f* recruit

recruter [rəkryte] *tr* to recruit; **recrutons** (*public sign for job openings*) help wanted ‖ *ref* to be recruited

rectangle [rɛktɑ̃gl] *m* rectangle

rectificateur [rɛktifikatœr] *m* rectifier

rectifier [rɛktifje] *tr* to rectify; true up; grind (*a cylinder*)

rectum [rɛktɔm] *m* rectum

re·çu -cue [rəsy] *adj* received; accepted, recognized; successful ‖ *m* receipt ‖ *v* see recevoir

recueil [rəkœj] *m* collection; compilation

recueillement [rəkœjmɑ̃] *m* meditation

recueillir [rəkœjir] §18 *tr* to collect, gather; take in (*a needy person*); receive (*a legacy*) ‖ *ref* to collect oneself, meditate

recuire [rəkɥir] §19 *tr* to anneal, temper; cook over again ‖ *intr* (fig) to stew

recul [rəkyl] *m* backing, backward movement; kick, recoil; **être en recul** to be losing ground; **prendre du recul** to consider in perspective

reculer [rəkyle] *tr* to move back; put off (*e.g., a decision*) ‖ *intr* to move back; back out; recoil; **reculer devant** to shrink from ‖ *ref* to move back

reculons [rəkylɔ̃]—**à reculons** backwards

récupération [rekyperasjɔ̃] *f* recovery

récupérer [rekypere] §10 *tr* to salvage, recover; recuperate; make up (*e.g., lost hours*); find another job for ‖ *intr* to recuperate

récurer [rekyre] *tr* to scour

récur·rent [rekyrɑ̃] **-rente** [rɑ̃t] *adj* recurrent

récusable [rekyzabl] *adj* (law) untrustworthy, unreliable

récuser [rekyze] *tr* to take exception to ‖ *ref* to refuse to give one's opinion

recyclage [rəsiklaʒ] *m* recycling; retraining, reorientation

recycler [rəsikle] *tr* to recycle; retrain, re-orient

rédac·teur [redaktœr] **-trice** [tris] *mf* editor; **rédacteur en chef** editor in chief; **rédacteur gérant** managing editor; **rédacteur publicitaire** copywriter; **rédacteur sportif** sports editor

rédaction [redaksjɔ̃] *f* editorial staff; editorial office; edition; editing

reddition [redisjɔ̃] *f* surrender

redécouvrir [rədekuvrir] §65 *tr* to rediscover

rédemp·teur [redɑ̃ptœr] **-trice** [tris] *adj* redemptive ‖ *mf* redeemer

rédemption [redɑ̃psjɔ̃] *f* redemption

redevable [rədvabl] *adj* indebted

redevance [rədvɑ̃s] *f* dues, fees; rent; tax (*on radio sets*); royalty

rédiger [rediʒe] §38 *tr* to edit; draft; write up

redingote [rədɛ̃gɔt] *f* frock coat

redire [rədir] §22 *tr* to repeat; give away (*a secret*) ‖ *intr*—**trouver à redire à** to find fault with

redon·dant [redɔ̃dɑ̃] **-dante** [dɑ̃t] *adj* redundant

redoublement [rədubləmɑ̃] *m* redoubling; repeating (*of a course*)

redoutable [rədutabl] *adj* frightening

redoute [rədut] *f* redoubt

redouter [rədute] §97 *tr* to dread

redressement [rədrɛsmɑ̃] *m* straightening out; redress; (elec) rectifying

redresser [rədrese] *tr* to straighten; hold up (*e.g., the head*); redress; (elec) to rectify ‖ *ref* to straighten up

redresseur [rədrɛsœr] *m* (elec) rectifier; **redresseur de torts** knight-errant; (coll) reformer

réduction [redyksjɔ̃] *f* reduction; **réduction des effectifs** reduction in force

réduire [redɥir] §19, §96, §100 *tr* to reduce; set (*a bone*) ‖ §96 *ref* to boil down; **se réduire à** to amount to; **se réduire en** to be reduced to

réduit [redɥi] *m* retreat, nook; redoubt

rééditer [reedite] *tr* to reedit

réel réelle [reɛl] *adj & m* real, actual

réélection [reelɛksjɔ̃] *f* reelection

réellement [reɛlmɑ̃] *adv* really

réémetteur [reemɛtœr] *m* (electron) relay transmitter

réescompte [reɛskɔ̃t] *m* rediscount

réexamen [reɛgzamɛ̃] *m* reexamination

réexpédier [reɛkspedje] *tr* to reship; return to sender

réexpédition [reɛkspedisjɔ̃] *f* reshipment; return

refaire [rəfɛr] §29 *tr* to redo ‖ *intr*—**à refaire** to be done over; be dealt over ‖ *ref* to recover; make good one's losses

réfection [refɛksjɔ̃] *f* repairing, rebuilding, remaking

référence [referɑ̃s] *f* reference

référendum or **referendum** [referɛ̃dɔm] *m* referendum

référer [refere] §10 *intr*—**en référer à** to appeal to ‖ *ref*—**s'en référer à** to leave it up to; **se référer à** to refer to

refermer [rəfɛrme] *tr & ref* to close again, to close

refiler [rəfile] *tr*—**refiler à qn** (slang) to palm off on s.o.

réflé·chi -chie [refleʃi] *adj* thoughtful; well-thought-out; (gram) reflexive ‖ *m* (gram) reflexive

réfléchir [refleʃir] *tr & intr* to reflect; **réfléchir à, réfléchir sur** to think about, ponder ‖ *ref* to be reflected

réflec·teur [reflɛktœr] **-trice** [tris] *adj* reflecting ‖ *m* reflector

reflet [rəflɛ] *m* reflection; glint, gleam

refléter [rəflete] §10 *tr* to reflect, mirror ‖ *ref* to be mirrored

réflexe [reflɛks] *adj & m* reflex

réflexion [reflɛksjɔ̃] *f* reflection

refluer [rəflye] *intr* to ebb

reflux [rəfly] *m* ebb

refonte [rəfɔ̃t] *f* recasting

réforma·teur [reformatœr] **-trice** [tris] *mf* reformer

réformation [reformasjɔ̃] *f* reformation

réforme [reform] *f* reform; **la Réforme** the Reformation

réfor·mé -mée [reforme] *adj* (eccl) Reformed; (mil) disabled

reformer [rəforme] *tr & ref* to regroup

réformer [reforme] *tr* to reform; (mil) to discharge ‖ *ref* to reform

refou·lé -lée [rəfule] *adj* (coll) inhibited

refoulement [rəfulmɑ̃] *m* driving back; (psychoanal) repression

refouler [rəfule] *tr* to drive back; choke back (*a sob*); sail against (*the current*); compress, stem; (psychoanal) to repress ‖ *intr* to flow back

réfractaire [refraktɛr] *adj* refractory; rebellious ‖ *mf* insubordinate; draft dodger

réfraction [refraksjɔ̃] *f* refraction

refrain [rəfrɛ̃] *m* refrain; hum; **le même refrain** the same old tune; **refrain publicitaire** (advertising) jingle

refréner [rəfrene] §10 *tr* to curb

réfrigérateur [refriʒeratœr] *m* refrigerator

réfrigérer [refriʒere] §10 *tr* to refrigerate; (coll) to chill to the bone

refroidir [rəfrwadir] *tr* to cool; (slang) to rub out ‖ *intr* to cool ‖ *ref* to cool; catch cold

refroidissement [rəfrwadismɑ̃] *m* cooling

refuge [rəfyʒ] *m* refuge; shelter; safety zone

réfu·gié -giée [refyʒje] *mf* refugee

réfugier [refyʒje] *ref* to take refuge

refus [rəfy] *m* refusal; **refus seulement** regrets only (*to invitation*)

refuser [rəfyze] §96, §97, §98 *tr* to refuse; recognize; flunk; decline ‖ *intr* to refuse; **refuser de** or **à** to refuse to ‖ §96 *ref* to be refused; **se refuser à** to refuse to accept

réfuter [refyte] *tr* to refute

regagner [rəgaɲe] *tr* to regain
regain [rəgɛ̃] *m* second growth; (fig) aftermath; **regain de** new lease on
ré·gal [regal] *m* (*pl* **-gals**) treat
régaler [regale] *tr* to treat; level ‖ *intr* to treat
regard [rəgar] *m* look, glance; **couver du regard** to gloat over; look fondly at; look greedily at; **en regard** facing, opposite
regar·dant [rəgardɑ̃] **-dante** [dɑ̃t] *adj* (coll) penny-pinching
regarder [rəgarde] §95 *tr* to look at; face; concern ‖ *intr* to look; **regarder à** to pay attention to; watch (*one's money*); mind (*the price*); **y regarder à deux fois** to watch one's step, think twice ‖ *ref* to face each other
régate [regat] *f* regatta
régence [reʒɑ̃s] *f* regency
régénérer [reʒenere] §10 *tr & ref* to regenerate
ré·gent [reʒɑ̃] **-gente** [ʒɑ̃t] *mf* regent
régenter [reʒɑ̃te] *tr & intr* to boss
régicide [reʒisid] *mf* regicide (*person*) ‖ *m* regicide (*act*)
régie [reʒi] *f* commission, administration; excise tax; stage management; **en régie** state-owned or -operated
regimber [rəʒɛ̃be] *intr & ref* to revolt; balk
régime [reʒim] *m* government, form of government; administration; system; diet; performance, working conditions; rate (*of speed; of flow; of charge or discharge of a storage battery*); bunch, cluster; stem (*of bananas*); (gram) complement; (gram) government; **en régime permanent** under steady working conditions
régiment [reʒimɑ̃] *m* regiment
régimentaire [reʒimɑ̃tɛr] *adj* regimental
région [reʒjɔ̃] *f* region, area
régir [reʒir] *tr* to govern
régisseur [reʒisœr] *m* manager; stage manager
registre [rəʒistr] *m* register; damper; throttle valve
réglable [reglabl] *adj* adjustable
réglage [reglaʒ] *m* setting, adjusting; lines (*on paper*); (mach, rad, telv) tuning
règle [rɛgl] *f* rule; ruler; **en règle** in order; **en règle générale** as a general rule; **règle à calcul** slide rule; **règles** menstrual period
ré·glé -glée [regle] *adj* regulated; adjusted, tuned; well-behaved, orderly; ruled (*paper*); finished, decided
règlement [rɛgləmɑ̃] *m* regulation, rule; settlement; **en règlement judiciaire** in bankruptcy proceedings; **règlement intérieur** bylaws
réglementaire [regləmɑ̃tɛr] *adj* regular; regulation
réglementer [regləmɑ̃te] *tr* to regulate, control
régler [regle] §10 *tr* to regulate, put in order; set (*a watch*); settle (*an account*); rule (*paper*); (aut, rad, telv) to tune ‖ *intr* to pay

réglisse [reglis] *m & f* licorice
ré·gnant [reɲɑ̃] **-gnante** [ɲɑ̃t] *adj* reigning; ruling; prevailing, prevalent
règne [rɛɲ] *m* reign; (biol) kingdom
régner [reɲe] §10 *intr* to reign
regorger [rəgɔrʒe] §38 *intr* to overflow; **regorger de** to abound in
regratter [rəgrate] *tr* to scrape ‖ *intr* to pinch pennies
regret [rəgrɛ] *m* regret; **à regret** regretfully
regrettable [rəgrɛtabl] *adj* regrettable
regretter [rəgrete] *tr* to regret; long for, miss; **regretter** + *subj* to be sorry that + *ind* ‖ §97 *intr* to be sorry, regret, e.g., **je regrette d'avoir fait cela** I regret having done that
régulariser [regylarize] *tr* to regularize; adjust, regulate
régularité [regylarite] *f* regularity
régula·teur [regylatœr] **-trice** [tris] *adj* regulating ‖ *m* (mach) governor
régulation [regylasjɔ̃] *f* regulation
régu·lier [regylje] **-lière** [ljɛr] *adj* regular; scheduled; exact, prompt; legitimate; honest, aboveboard, on the level ‖ *m* (mil, rel) regular ‖ *f*—**ma régulière** (slang) my woman
réhabiliter [reabilite] *tr* to rehabilitate
rehausser [rəose] *tr* to heighten; enhance
Reims [rɛ̃s] *m* Rheims
rein [rɛ̃] *m* kidney
réincarnation [reɛ̃karnasjɔ̃] *f* reincarnation
reine [rɛn] *f* queen
reine-claude [rɛnklod] *f* (*pl* **-claudes** or **reines-claudes**) greengage
reine-des-prés [rɛndepre] *f* (*pl* **reines-des-prés**) meadowsweet
reine-marguerite [rɛnmargərit] *f* (*pl* **reines-marguerites**) aster
réintégrer [reɛ̃tegre] §10 *tr* to reinstate; return to
réitérer [reitere] §10 *tr* reiterate
rejaillir [rəʒajir] *intr* to spurt out; bounce; splash; **rejaillir sur** to reflect on
rejet [rəʒɛ] *m* casting up; rejection; enjambment; (bot) shoot
rejeter [rəʒte] §34 *tr* to reject; throw back; throw up; shift (*responsibility*) ‖ *ref* to fall back
rejeton [rəʒtɔ̃] *m* shoot; offshoot, offspring; (coll) child
rejeu [rəʒø] *m* (electron) playback
rejoindre [rəʒwɛ̃dr] §35 *tr* to rejoin; overtake ‖ *ref* to meet
réjouir [reʒwir] *tr* to gladden, cheer ‖ §97 *ref* to rejoice, be delighted
réjouissance [reʒwisɑ̃s] *f* rejoicing; **réjouissances** festivities
réjouis·sant [reʒwisɑ̃] **-sante** [sɑ̃t] *adj* cheery; amusing
relâche [rəlaʃ] *m & f* respite, letup ‖ *f* (naut) stop; **faire relâche** (naut) to make a call; (theat) to close (*for a day or two*); **relâche** (*public sign*) no performance today
relâ·ché -chée [rəlaʃe] *adj* lax; loose

relâchement [rəlɑʃmɑ̃] *m* relaxation; letting up

relâcher [rəlɑʃe] *tr* to loosen; relax; release ‖ *intr* (naut) to make a call ‖ *ref* to loosen; become lax

relais [rəlɛ] *m* relay; shift; **prendre le relais** (slang) to take up the slack; **relais routier** service stop (*on a superhighway*)

relance [rəlɑ̃s] *f* raise (*e.g., in poker*); outbreak

relancer [rəlɑ̃se] §51 *tr* to start up again; harass, hound; return (*the ball*); raise (*the ante*) ‖ *intr* (cards) to raise

re·laps -lapse [rəlaps] *mf* backslider

relater [rəlate] *tr* to relate

rela·tif [rəlatif] **-tive** [tiv] *adj* relative

relation [rəlɑsjɔ̃] *f* relation; **en relation avec, en relations avec** in touch with; **relations** connections

relativité [rəlativite] *f* relativity

relaxation [rəlaksɑsjɔ̃] *f* relaxation

relaxer [rəlakse] *tr* to relax; free ‖ *ref* to relax

relayer [rəleje] §49 *tr* to relay; relieve ‖ *ref* to work in relays or shifts

reléguer [rəlege] §10 *tr* to relegate

relent [rəlɑ̃] *m* musty smell

relève [rəlɛv] *f* relief; change (*of the guard*); **prendre la relève** to take over

rele·vé -vée [rəlve] *adj* lofty, elevated; turned up; graded (*curve*); spicy ‖ *m* check list; tuck (*in dress*); (culin) next course; **faire le relevé de** to survey; to check off; **relevé de compte** bank statement; **relevé de compteur** meter reading; **relevé de notes des écoles** transcript of grades

relèvement [rəlɛvmɑ̃] *m* raising; recovery; improvement; picking up (*e.g., of wounded*); (naut) bearing

relever [rəlve] §2 *tr* to raise; turn up; restore; relieve, enhance; pick out; take a reading of; season; (mil) to relieve ‖ *intr*—**relever de** to recover from; depend on ‖ *ref* to rise; recover; right itself; take turns

re·lié -liée [rəlje] *adj* (bb) hardbound, hardcover; **relié cuir** leather-bound; **relié plein chagrin** entirely bound in grained leather

relief [rəljɛf] *m* relief; **en relief** in relief; **reliefs** leavings

relier [rəlje] *tr* to bind; to link

re·lieur [rəljœr] **-lieuse** [ljøz] *mf* bookbinder

reli·gieux [rəliʒjø] **-gieuse** [ʒjøz] *adj* religious ‖ *m* monk ‖ *f* nun; cream puff

religion [rəliʒjɔ̃] *f* religion

reliquat [rəlika] *m* remainder

relique [rəlik] *f* relic

relire [rəlir] §36 *tr* to read again; read over again

reliure [rəljyr] *f* binding; bookbinding

reloger [rələʒe] §38 *tr* to find a new home for, relocate

reluire [rəlɥir] §37 *intr* to shine, gleam, sparkle

relui·sant [rəlɥizɑ̃] **-sante** [zɑ̃t] *adj* shiny, gleaming; **peu reluisant** unpromising, not brilliant

reluquer [rəlyke] *tr* to have an eye on

remâcher [rəmɑʃe] *tr* (coll) to stew over

remailler [rəmɑje] *tr* to mend the meshes of

remanier [rəmanje] *tr* to revise, revamp; to reshuffle

remarier [rəmarje] *tr* & *ref* to remarry

remarquable [rəmarkabl] *adj* remarkable

remarque [rəmark] *f* remark; **accompagner de remarques** to annotate; **des remarques?** any comments?; **faire une remarque** to make a remark; remark, make a critical observation

remarquer [rəmarke] *tr* & *intr* to remark, notice; **faire remarquer** to point out ‖ *ref*—**se fair remarquer** to make oneself conspicuous

remballer [rɑ̃bale] *tr* to repack

rembarquer [rɑ̃barke] *tr*, *intr*, & *ref* to reembark

rembarrer [rɑ̃bare] *tr* to snub, rebuff

remblai [rɑ̃blɛ] *m* fill; embankment

remblayer [rɑ̃bleje] §49 *tr* to fill; bank up

rembobiner [rɑ̃bɔbine] *tr* to rewind

remboîter [rɑ̃bwate] *tr* to reset (*a bone*); recase (*a book*)

rembourrer [rɑ̃bure] *tr* to upholster; stuff; pad

rembourrure [rɑ̃buryr] *f* stuffing

remboursement [rɑ̃bursəmɑ̃] *m* reimbursement; **contre remboursement** C.O.D.; with cash, e.g., **envoi contre remboursement** cash with order; **remboursement dans le bas de l'appareil** coin return

rembourser [rɑ̃burse] *tr* to reimburse

rembrunir [rɑ̃brynir] *tr* to darken; sadden ‖ *ref* to cloud over

remède [rəmɛd] *m* remedy

remédier [rəmedje] *intr*—**remédier à** to remedy

remembrement [rəmɑ̃brəmɑ̃] *m* regrouping

remémorer [rəmemɔre] *tr*—**remémorer q.ch. à qn** to remind s.o. of s.th. ‖ *ref* to remember

remerciement [rəmɛrsimɑ̃] *m* thanking; **remerciements** thanks; **mille remerciements de** or **pour** a thousand thanks for

remercier [rəmɛrsje] §97 *tr* to thank; dismiss (*an employee*); refuse with thanks; **remercier qn de** + *inf* to thank s.o. for + *ger;* **remercier qn de** or **pour** to thank s.o. for

remettre [rəmɛtr] §42 *tr* to remit, deliver; put back; put back on; give back; put off; reset ‖ *ref* to resume; recover; pull oneself together; (*said of weather*) clear; **s'en remettre à** to leave it up to, depend on

remise [rəmiz] *f* remittance; discount; delivery; postponement; surrender, return; garage; cover (*for game*); **de remise** rented (*car*)

remiser [rəmize] *tr* to put away; park ‖ *ref* to take cover

rémission [remisjɔ̃] *f* remission

remmailler [rɑ̃mɑje] *tr* to darn

remmener [rɑ̃mne] §2 *tr* to take back

remodelage [rəmɔdlaʒ] *m* remodeling; plastic surgery

remon·tant [rəmɔ̃tɑ̃] **-tante** [tɑ̃t] *adj* fortifying; remontant (*rose*) ‖ *m* tonic

remonte [rəmɔ̃t] *f* ascent

remontée [rəmɔ̃te] *f* climb; surfacing; comeback

remonte-pente [rəmɔ̃tpɑ̃t] *m* (*pl* **-pentes**); ski lift

remonter [rəmɔ̃te] *tr* to remount; pull up; wind (*a clock*); pep up; (theat) to put on again ‖ *intr* (*aux:* ÉTRE) to go up again; date back ‖ *ref* to pep up

remontoir [rəmɔ̃twar] *m* knob (*of stemwinder*); key, winder

remontrance [rəmɔ̃trɑ̃s] *f* remonstrance

remontrer [rəmɔ̃tre] *tr* to show again; point out ‖ *intr*—**en remontrer à** to outdo, best

remords [rəmɔr] *m* remorse

remorque [rəmɔrk] *f* tow rope; trailer; **à la remorque** in tow

remorquer [rəmɔrke] *tr* to tow; haul

remorqueur [rəmɔrkœr] *m* tugboat

rémouleur [remulœr] *m* knife grinder, scissors grinder

remous [rəmu] *m* eddy; wash (*of boat*); agitation

rempailler [rɑ̃pɑje] *tr* to cane

rempart [rɑ̃par] *m* rampart

remplaçable [rɑ̃plasabl] *adj* replaceable

rempla·çant [rɑ̃plasɑ̃] **-çante** [sɑ̃t] *mf* replacement, substitute

remplacement [rɑ̃plasmɑ̃] *m* replacement

remplacer [rɑ̃plase] §51 *tr* to replace; take the place of; **remplacer par** to replace with

rem·pli -plie [rɑ̃pli] *adj* full ‖ *m* tuck

remplir [rɑ̃plir] *tr* to fill; fill up; fill out or in; fulfill ‖ *ref* to fill up

remplissage [rɑ̃plisaʒ] *m* filling up

remplumer [rɑ̃plyme] *ref* (coll) to put on flesh again; (coll) to make a comeback

remporter [rɑ̃pɔrte] *tr* to take back; carry off; win

remue-ménage [rəmymenaʒ] *m invar* stir, bustle, to-do

remue-méninges [rəmymenɛ̃ʒ] *f invar* (slang) brainstorming

remuer [rəmɥe] *tr* to move; stir; remove (*e.g., a piece of furniture*) ‖ *intr* to move ‖ *ref* to move; hustle

rémunération [remynerɑsjɔ̃] *f* remuneration

renâcler [rənɑkle] *intr* to snort; **renâcler à** (coll) to shrink from, bridle at

renaissance [rənɛsɑ̃s] *f* renascence, rebirth; renaissance

renais·sant [rənɛsɑ̃] **-sante** [sɑ̃t] *adj* renascent, reviving; Renaissance

renaître [rənɛtr] §46 *tr* to be reborn; revive; grow again

re·nard [rənar] **-narde** [nard] *mf* fox

renché·ri -rie [rɑ̃ʃeri] *adj* fastidious

renchérir [rɑ̃ʃerir] *tr* to make more expensive ‖ *intr* to go up in price; **renchérir sur** to improve on

rencontre [rɑ̃kɔ̃tr] *f* meeting, encounter; clash; collision; **aller à la rencontre de** to go to meet; **de rencontre** chance (*e.g., acquaintance*)

rencontrer [rɑ̃kɔ̃tre] *tr* to meet, encounter ‖ *ref* to meet; collide; occur

rendement [rɑ̃dmɑ̃] *m* yield; (mech) output, efficiency

rendez-vous [rɑ̃devu] *m* appointment, date; rendezvous; **donner (un) rendez-vous à, fixer (un) rendez-vous à** to make an appointment with; **sur rendez-vous** by appointment

rendre [rɑ̃dr] *tr* to render; yield; surrender; make; translate; vomit ‖ *intr* to bring in, yield ‖ *ref* to surrender; **se rendre à** to go to; **se rendre compte de** to realize

ren·du -due [rɑ̃dy] *adj* arrived; translated; all in, exhausted ‖ *m* rendering; returned article

rêne [rɛn] *f* rein

rené·gat [rənega] **-gate** [gat] *mf* renegade

renfer·mé -mée [rɑ̃fɛrme] *adj* closemouthed, stand-offish ‖ *m* close smell; **sentir le renfermé** to smell stuffy

renfermer [rɑ̃fɛrme] *tr* to contain; include ‖ *ref*—**se renfermer dans** to withdraw into; confine oneself to

renfler [rɑ̃fle] *ref* to swell up

renflouer [rɑ̃flue] *tr* to keep afloat; salvage

renfoncement [rɑ̃fɔ̃smɑ̃] *m* recess; hollow; dent

renfoncer [rɑ̃fɔ̃se] §51 *tr* to recess; dent; pull down (*e.g., one's hat*) ‖ *ref* to recede; draw back

renforcement [rɑ̃fɔrsəmɑ̃] *m* reinforcement

renforcer [rɑ̃fɔrse] §51 *tr* to reinforce

renforcir [rɑ̃fɔrsir] *tr* (slang) to strengthen ‖ *intr* (slang) to grow stronger

renfort [rɑ̃fɔr] *m* reinforcement

renfro·gné -gnée [rɑ̃frɔɲe] *adj* sullen, glum

renfrogner [rɑ̃frɔɲe] *ref* to scowl

rengager [rɑ̃gaʒe] §38 *tr* to rehire ‖ *intr* & *ref* to reenlist

rengaine [rɑ̃gɛn] *f*—**la même rengaine** the same old story; **vieille rengaine** old refrain

rengorger [rɑ̃gɔrʒe] §38 *ref* to strut

reniement [rənimɑ̃] *m* denial

renier [rənje] *tr* to deny; repudiate

renifler [rənifle] *tr* & *intr* to sniff

renne [rɛn] *m* reindeer

renom [rənɔ̃] *m* renown, fame

renom·mé -mée [rənɔme] *adj* renowned, well-known ‖ *f* fame; reputation

renommer [rənɔme] *tr* to reelect; reappoint

renoncement [rənɔ̃smɑ̃] *m* renunciation

renoncer [rənɔ̃se] §51, §96 *tr* (lit) to renounce, repudiate ‖ *intr* to give up; (cards) to renege; **renoncer à** to renounce; give up, abandon, e.g., **lui renoncer** to abandon her (or him); **y renoncer** to give it up

renonciation [rənɔ̃sjɑsjɔ̃] *f* renunciation; waiver

renoncule [rənɔ̃kyl] *f* buttercup; **renoncule double** bachelor's-button; **renoncule langue** spearwort

renouer [rǝnwe] *tr* to tie again; resume (*e.g., a conversation*) ‖ *intr* to renew a friendship

renou·veau [rǝnuvo] *m* (*pl* **-veaux**) springtime; revival

renouvelable [rǝnuvlabl] *adj* renewable

renouveler [rǝnuvle] §34 *tr & ref* to renew

renouvellement [rǝnuvɛlmɑ̃] *m* renewal

rénover [renɔve] *tr* to renew; renovate

renseignement [rɑ̃sɛɲmɑ̃] *m* piece of information; **de renseignements** (mil) intelligence; **renseignements** information

renseigner [rɑ̃sɛɲe] *tr* to inform ‖ *ref* to find out; **se renseigner auprès de qn** to inquire of s.o.

rentable [rɑ̃tabl] *adj* profitable

rente [rɑ̃t] *f* revenue, income; annuity; dividend, return; **rente viagère** life annuity

ren·té -tée [rɑ̃te] *adj* well-off

renter [rɑ̃te] *tr* to endow

ren·tier [rɑ̃tje] **-tière** [tjɛr] *mf* person of independent means

ren·tré -trée [rɑ̃tre] *adj* sunken (*eyes*); suppressed (*feelings*) ‖ *f* return; reopening (*of school*); yield, income; (comp) reentry

rentrer [rɑ̃tre] §95 *tr* to bring in or back; put in; hold back (*e.g., one's tears*); draw in (*claws*) ‖ *intr* (*aux:* ÊTRE) to return, reenter; go or come home; be paid or collected; **rentrer dans** to fit into; come back to; get back, recover; **rentrer en soi-même** to take stock of oneself

renverse [rɑ̃vɛrs] *f* shift, turn; **à la renverse** backwards

renversement [rɑ̃vɛrsǝmɑ̃] *m* reversal, shift; upset, overturn; overthrow

renverser [rɑ̃vɛrse] *tr* to reverse; overthrow; bowl over, astonish ‖ *intr & ref* to capsize

renvoi [rɑ̃vwa] *m* dismissal; postponement; reference; return; belch

renvoyer [rɑ̃vwaje] §26 *tr* to dismiss; fire (*an employee*); postpone; refer; send back

réorganiser [reɔrganize] *tr & ref* to reorganize

réouverture [reuvɛrtyr] *f* reopening

repaire [rǝpɛr] *m* den

repaître [rǝpɛtr] §12 *tr* to graze; **repaître de** to feast (*e.g., one's eyes*) on ‖ *ref* to eat one's fill (*said of only animals*); **se repaître de** to indulge in, to wallow in

répandre [repɑ̃dr] *tr* to spread; strew, scatter; spill; shed ‖ *ref* to spread; **se répandre en** to be profuse in

répan·du -due [repɑ̃dy] *adj* widespread; widely known

reparaître [rǝparɛtr] §12 *intr* to reappear

répara·teur [reparatœr] **-trice** [tris] *adj* restorative ‖ *m* repairman

réparation [reparɑsjɔ̃] *f* repair; reparation; restoration

réparer [repare] *tr* to repair, fix; mend, patch; make up (*a loss*); redress (*a wrong*); restore (*one's strength*)

repartie [rǝparti], [reparti] *f* repartee

repartir [rǝpartir] §64 *tr* to retort ‖ *intr* (*aux:* ÊTRE) to start again; leave again; **repartir à zéro** to go back to square one

répartir [repartir] *tr* to distribute

répartiteur [repartitœr] *m* distributor; assessor; dispatcher

répartition [repartisjɔ̃] *f* distribution; apportionment; range (*of words*)

repas [rǝpɑ] *m* meal, repast; **dernier repas** (rel) last supper; **repas champêtre** picnic; **repas de noce** wedding breakfast; **repas froid** cold snack; **repas principal** main meal; **repas sur le pouce** takeout meal; **repas tiré du sac** brown-bag lunch

repassage [rǝpɑsaʒ] *m* recrossing; ironing; stropping; whetting

repasser [rǝpɑse] *tr* to pass again; go over, review; iron; strop; whet ‖ *intr* to pass by again; drop in again

repêcher [rǝpɛʃe] *tr* to fish out; give another chance to; (coll) to get (*s.o.*) out of a scrape

repentance [rǝpɑ̃tɑ̃s] *f* repentance

repen·tant [rǝpɑ̃tɑ̃] **-tante** [tɑ̃t] *adj* repentant

repen·ti -tie [rǝpɑ̃ti] *adj* repentant

repentir [rǝpɑ̃tir] *m* repentance ‖ §41, §97 *ref* to repent; **se repentir de** to be sorry for, to repent

repérage [rǝperaʒ] *m* spotting, locating; tracking; marking with a reference mark; (mov) synchronization

répercussion [repɛrkysjɔ̃] *f* repercussion; reverberation

répercuter [repɛrkyte] *tr* to reflect ‖ *ref* to reverberate; have repercussions

repère [rǝpɛr] *m* mark, reference

repérer [rǝpere] §10 *tr* to locate, spot; mark with a reference mark; (mov) to synchronize

répertoire [repɛrtwar] *m* repertory; index; **répertoire à onglets** thumb index; **répertoire d'adresses** address book; **répertoire vivant** walking encyclopedia

répéter [repete] §10 *tr & ref* to repeat

répéti·teur [repetitœr] **-trice** [tris] *mf* assistant teacher; coach, tutor

répétition [repetisjɔ̃] *f* repetition; private lesson, tutoring; rehearsal; **répétition des couturières** next-to-last dress rehearsal; **répétition générale** final dress rehearsal

repeupler [rǝpœple] *tr* to repeople; restock

repiquer [rǝpike] *tr* to plant out (*seedlings*); repave; restitch; rerecord; (phot) to retouch ‖ *intr*—**repiquer à** (slang) to come back to

répit [repi] *m* respite, letup

replacement [rǝplasmɑ̃] *m* replacement; reinvestment

replacer [rǝplase] §51 *tr* to replace; find a new job for; reinvest ‖ *ref* to find a new job

replâtrage [rǝplɑtraʒ] *m* replastering; makeshift; (fig) patchwork

re·plet [rǝplɛ] **-plète** [plɛt] *adj* fat, plump

repli [rǝpli] *m* crease, fold; dip, depression; (mil) falling back

replier [rǝplije] *tr* to refold; turn up; close (*e.g., an umbrella*) ‖ *ref* to curl up, coil up; (mil) to fall back

réplique [replik] *f* reply, retort; replica; **donner la réplique à qn** to answer s.o.; (theat) to give s.o. his cue; (theat) to play the straight man or stooge for s.o.

répliquer [replike] *tr & intr* to reply

replonger [rəplɔ̃ʒe] §38 *tr* to plunge again ‖ *intr* to dive again ‖ *ref*—**se replonger dans** to get back into

répon·dant [repɔ̃dɑ̃] **-dante** [dɑ̃t] *mf* guarantor; (eccl) server; **avoir du répondant** (coll) to have money behind one

répon·deur [repɔ̃dœr] **-deuse** [døz] *adj* (coll) back-talking ‖ *m*—**répondeur automatique**, **répondeur téléphonique** (telephone) answering machine

répondre [repɔ̃dr] §98 *tr* to answer (*e.g., yes or no*); assure ‖ *intr* to answer, reply; answer back, be saucy; reecho; **répondre à** to answer (*e.g., a question, a letter*); correspond to; **répondre de** to answer for (*a person*); guarantee (*a thing*) ‖ *ref* to answer each other; correspond to each other; be in harmony

réponse [repɔ̃s] *f* answer, response; **réponse normande** evasive answer

report [rəpɔr] *m* carrying forward or over; carry-over

reportage [rəpɔrtaʒ] *m* reporting

reporter [rəpɔrtɛr] *m* reporter; **reporter d'images** news cameraman ‖ [rəpɔrte] *tr* to carry back; to postpone; (math) to carry forward ‖ *intr* (com) to carry stock; **à reporter** carried forward ‖ *ref*—**se reporter à** to be carried back to (*e.g., childhood days*); refer to

reporteur [rəpɔrtœr] *m* broker

repos [rəpo] *m* rest, repose; **au repos** not running, still; **de tout repos** reliable; **en repos** at rest; **repos!** (mil) at ease!

repo·sé -sée [rəpoze] *adj* refreshed, relaxed

reposer [rəpoze] *tr* to rest ‖ *intr* to rest; **ici repose . . .** here lies . . . ‖ *ref* to rest; **s'en reposer sur** to rely on

repous·sant [rəpusɑ̃] **-sante** [sɑ̃t] *adj* repulsive

repousser [rəpuse] *tr* to push, shove; repulse, repel; reject, refuse; postpone; emboss ‖ *intr* to grow again; be offensive; (arti) to recoil

repoussoir [rəpuswar] *m* foil; contrast; (mach) driving bolt

reprendre [rəprɑ̃dr] §56, §97 *tr* to take back; resume; regain (*consciousness*); find fault with; take in (*e.g., a dress*); catch (*one's breath*); (theat) to put on again ‖ *intr* to start again; pick up, improve; criticize ‖ *ref* to pull oneself together; correct oneself in speaking

représailles [rəprezaj] *fpl* reprisal

représen·tant [rəprezɑ̃tɑ̃] **-tante** [tɑ̃t] *adj & mf* representative; **représentant de commerce** traveling salesman

représenta·tif [rəprezɑ̃tatif] **-tive** [tiv] *adj* representative

représentation [rəprezɑ̃tɑsjɔ̃] *f* representation; performance; remonstrance

représenter [rəprezɑ̃te] *tr* to represent; put on, perform ‖ *intr* to make a good showing

répression [represjɔ̃] *f* repression

réprimande [reprimɑ̃d] *f* reprimand

réprimander [reprimɑ̃de] §97 *tr* to reprimand

réprimer [reprime] *tr* to repress

re·pris [rəpri] **-prise** [priz] *adj* recaptured; **être repris de** to suffer from a recurrence of ‖ *m*—**repris de justice** hardened criminal, habitual offender ‖ *f* see **reprise**

reprisage [rəprizaʒ] *m* darning

reprise [rəpriz] *f* recapture; resumption; darning; pickup (*acceleration of motor*); (mov) rerun; (theat) revival; **à plusieurs reprises** several times; **faire une reprise à** to darn; **par reprises** a little at a time

repriser [rəprize] *tr* to darn; mend

réproba·teur [reprɔbatœr] **-trice** [tris] *adj* reproving

reproche [rəprɔʃ] *m* reproach

reprocher [rəprɔʃe] §98 *tr* to reproach; begrudge; (law) to take exception to (*a witness*); **reprocher q.ch. à qn** to reproach s.o. for s.th.; begrudge s.o. s.th.; remind s.o. reproachfully of s.th.

reproduction [rəprɔdyksjɔ̃] *f* reproduction

reproduire [rəprɔdɥir] §19 *tr & ref* to reproduce

reprographieur [rəprɔgrafjœr] *m* copying machine

réprou·vé -vée [repruve] *adj & mf* outcast; damned

réprouver [repruve] *tr* to disapprove

reptile [rɛptil] *m* reptile

re·pu -pue [rəpy] *adj* satiated

républi·cain [repyblikɛ̃] **-caine** [kɛn] *adj & mf* republican

république [repyblik] *f* republic

répudier [repydje] *tr* to repudiate

répu·gnant [repyɲɑ̃] **-gnante** [ɲɑ̃t] *adj* repugnant

répugner [repyɲe] §96, §97 *intr*—**répugner à** to be repugnant to, disgust, repel, e.g., **cette odeur leur répugne** that odor disgusts them; **il me (te, lui,** etc.) **répugne de** it is distasteful for me (you, him, etc.) to; **répugner à** or **de** + *inf* to be reluctant or loath to + *inf*, balk at + *ger*

répul·sif [repylsif] **-sive** [siv] *adj* repulsive

réputation [repytasjɔ̃] *f* reputation

répu·té -tée [repyte] *adj* of high repute; **être réputé** to be reputed to be

requérir [rəkerir] §3 *tr* to demand; ask; require; summon

requête [rəkɛt] *f* petition, appeal

requiem [rekɥijem] *m* requiem

requin [rəkɛ̃] *m* shark

re·quis [rəki] **-quise** [kiz] *adj* required, requisite ‖ *mf* conscript ‖ *v* see **requérir**

réquisition [rekizisjɔ̃] *f* requisition

réquisitionner [rekizisjɔne] *tr* to requisition

réquisitoire [rekizitwar] *m* indictment

res·capé -capée [rɛskape] *adj* rescued ‖ *mf* survivor

rescinder [resɛ̃de] *tr* to rescind

rescousse [rɛskus] *f* rescue

ré·seau [rezo] *m* (*pl* **-seaux**) net; network, system; **réseau de barbelés** barbed wire entanglement

réséda [rezeda] *m* mignonette

réservation [rezɛrvɑsjɔ̃] *f* reservation; booking

réserve [resɛrv] *f* reserve; reservation; reserve room (*in a library*); **de réserve** emergency, reserve (*rations, fund, etc.*); **réserve des imprimés** periodical room (*in a library*); **sous réserve que** on condition that; **sous toutes réserves** without committing oneself

réserver [rezɛrve] §97 *tr* to reserve; set aside ‖ *ref* to set aside·for oneself; wait and see, hold off

réserviste [rezɛrvist] *m* reservist

réservoir [rezɛrvwar] *m* reservoir, tank; **réservoir de bombes** bomb bay

résidanat [rezidana] *m* (med) residency

résidence [rezidɑ̃s] *f* residence

rési·dent [rezidɑ̃] **-dente** [dɑ̃t] *mf* alien, foreigner; (dipl) resident

résiden·tiel -tielle [rezidɑ̃sjɛl] *adj* residential

résider [rezide] *intr* to reside

résidu [rezidy] *m* residue; refuse

resi·duel -duelle [rezidɥɛl] *adj* residual

résignation [reziɲɑsjɔ̃] *f* resignation

résigner [reziɲe] *tr* to resign ‖ §96 *ref* to be or become resigned

résilier [rezilje] *tr* to cancel

résille [rezij] *f* hair net

résine [rezin] *f* resin

résistance [rezistɑ̃s] *f* resistance

résis·tant [rezistɑ̃] **-tante** [tɑ̃t] *adj* resistant; strong; fast (*color*) ‖ *mf* (hist) Resistance fighter

résister [reziste] §96 *intr* to be fast, not run (*said of colors or dyes*); **résister à** to weather (*e.g., a storm*); resist, hold out against, withstand, e.g., **inutile de lui résister** useless to resist him; **résister à** + *inf* to resist + *ger*

réso·lu -lue [rezɔly] §92 *adj* resolute, resolved ‖ *v* see **résoudre**

résolution [rezɔlysjɔ̃] *f* resolution; canceling

résonance [rezɔnɑ̃s] *f* resonance

résonner [rezɔne] *intr* to resound; to re-echo, ring, clank; twang

résorber [rezɔrbe] *tr* to absorb ‖ *ref* to become absorbed

résoudre [rezudr] §60, §96, §97 *tr* to resolve; decide; solve; persuade; cancel; **être résolu à** to be resolved to ‖ *intr*—**résoudre de** to decide to ‖ §96—*ref*—**se résoudre à** to decide to; reconcile oneself to; **se résoudre en** to turn into

résout [rezu] *v* see **résoudre**

respect [rɛspɛ] *m* respect; **présenter ses respects (à)** to pay one's respects (to); **respect de soi** or **soi-même** self-respect; **respect humain** [rɛspɛkymɛ̃] fear of what people might say; **sauf votre (mon,** etc.) **respect** with all due respect; pardon the

language; **tenir en respect** to keep at a respectful distance

respectable [rɛspɛktabl] *adj* respectable

respecter [rɛspɛkte] *tr* to respect; **respecter les fleurs** (*public sign*) keep off the flowers ‖ *ref* to keep one's self-respect

respec·tif [rɛspɛktif] **-tive** [tiv] *adj* respective

respec·tueux [rɛspɛktɥø] **-tueuse** [tɥøz] *adj* respectful

respirer [rɛspire] *tr* to breathe ‖ *intr* to breathe; catch one's breath

resplendis·sant [rɛsplɑ̃disɑ̃] **-sante** [sɑ̃t] *adj* radiant, beaming, shining, aglow, resplendent

responsabilité [rɛspɔ̃sabilite] *f* responsibility

responsable [rɛspɔ̃sabl] *adj* responsible; **responsable de** responsible for; **responsable envers** accountable to; **solidairement responsable** jointly liable ‖ *mf* person responsible, person in charge

resquiller [rɛskije] *tr* (coll) to obtain by fraud ‖ *intr* (coll) to crash the gate

resquil·leur [rɛskijœr] **-leuse** [jøz] *mf* (coll) gate-crasher

ressac [rəsak] *m* surf; undertow

ressaisir [rəsezir] *tr* to recapture ‖ *ref* to regain one's self-control

ressasser [rəsase] *tr* to go over and over again

ressaut [rəso] *m* projection; sharp rise

ressemblance [rəsɑ̃blɑ̃s] *f* resemblance

ressembler [rəsɑ̃ble] *intr*—**ressembler à** to look like, resemble, e.g., **le fils lui ressemble** the son looks like him ‖ *ref* (*pp* **ressemblé** *invar*) to resemble one another; be alike, look alike

ressemeler [rəsəmle] §34 *tr* to resole

ressentiment [rəsɑ̃timɑ̃] *m* resentment

ressentir [rəsɑ̃tir] §41 *tr* to feel keenly, be hurt by (*an insult*); experience (*joy, pain, surprise*) ‖ *ref*—**se ressentir de** to feel the aftereffects of

resserre [rəsɛr] *f* shed, storeroom

resserrer [rəsere] *tr* to tighten; contract; close; lock up (*e.g., valuables*) again ‖ *ref* to tighten; contract

ressort [rəsɔr] *m* spring; springiness; motive; **du ressort de** within the jurisdiction of; **en dernier ressort** without appeal; as a last resort; **ressort à boudin** coil spring; **sans ressort** slack

ressortir [rəsɔrtir] *intr*—**ressortir à** to come under the jurisdiction of; fall under the head of ‖ §64 *intr* (aux: ᴇ̄ᴛʀᴇ) to go out again; stand out, be evident; **faire ressortir** to set off; **il ressort de** it follows from; **il ressort que** it follows that

ressortis·sant [rəsɔrtisɑ̃] **-sante** [sɑ̃t] *adj*—**ressortissant à** under the jurisdiction of ‖ *mf* national

ressource [rəsurs] *f* resource; **de ressource** resourceful; **sans ressources** without resources

ressouvenir [rəsuvnir] §72, §97 *ref* to reminisce; **se ressouvenir de** to recall

ressusciter [resysite] *tr* to resuscitate; to resurrect ‖ *intr* (*aux:* ÉTRE) to rise from the dead; get well

res·tant [rɛstɑ̃] **-tante** [tɑ̃t] *adj* remaining ‖ *m* remainder

restaupouce [rɛstɔpus] *m* fast-food restaurant

restaurant [rɛstɔrɑ̃] *m* restaurant; **restaurant libre-service** self-service restaurant

restauration [rɛstɔrɑsjɔ̃] *f* restoration; restaurant business; **restauration rapide** fast food

restaurer [rɛstɔre] *tr* to restore ‖ *ref* (coll) to take some nourishment

reste [rɛst] *m* rest, remainder; remnant; relic; **au reste, du reste** moreover; **de reste** spare; **restes** remains; leftovers

rester [rɛste] §96 *intr* (*aux:* ÉTRE) to remain, stay; be left over; **en rester** to stop, leave off; **en rester là** to stop right there; **il me** (**te, leur,** etc.) **reste q.ch.** I (you, they, etc.) have s.th. left

restituer [rɛstitɥe] *tr* to restore; give back; (comp) to print out

restitution [rɛstitysjɔ̃] *f* restitution; restoration

restoroute [rɛstɔrut] *m* drive-in restaurant; service stop (*on a superhighway*)

restreindre [rɛstrɛ̃dr] §50 *tr* to restrict; curtail ‖ *ref* to become limited; cut down expenses

res·treint [rɛstrɛ̃] **-treinte** [trɛ̃t] *adj* limited

restriction [rɛstriksjɔ̃] *f* restriction; **restriction mentale** mental reservation

résultat [rezylta] *m* result; **résultat financier** bottom line

résulter [rezylte] *intr* to result; **il en résulte que** it follows that

résumé [rezyme] *m* summary, recapitulation; **en résumé** in short, in a word

résumer [rezyme] *tr* to summarize ‖ *ref* to be summed up

résurrection [rezyrɛksjɔ̃] *f* resurrection

rétablir [retablir] *tr* to restore ‖ *ref* to recover

rétablissement [retablismɑ̃] *m* restoration; recovery

retailler [rətaje] *tr* to resharpen

retape [rətap] *f* (slang) streetwalking

retaper [rətape] *tr* (coll) to straighten up; (coll) to give a lick and a promise to ‖ *ref* (coll) to perk up

retard [rətar] *m* delay; **en retard** late; slow (*clock*); **en retard sur** behind

retardataire [rətardatɛr] *adj* tardy; retarded ‖ *mf* latecomer, straggler

retarder [rətarde] *tr* to delay; put off; set back ‖ *intr* to go slow, be behind

retenir [rətnir] §72 *tr* to hold back, keep back; detain; remember, note; reserve; retain (*a lawyer*); carry (*a number*) ‖ §97 *ref*—**se retenir à** to cling to; **se retenir de** to refrain from

retentir [rətɑ̃tir] *intr* to resound

rete·nu **-nue** [rətny] *adj* reserved; held back ‖ *f* withholding; reserve; **retenue à la source** withholding tax

réticence [retisɑ̃s] *f* evasiveness, concealment; hesitation; reservation, misgiving

réti·cent [retisɑ̃] **-cente** [sɑ̃t] *adj* evasive; hesitant; reserved, withdrawn

réticule [retikyl] *m* handbag

ré·tif [retif] **-tive** [tiv] *adj* restive

rétine [retin] *f* retina

reti·ré **-rée** [rətire] *adj* remote, out-of-the-way; retired

retirement [rətirmɑ̃] *m* contraction

retirer [rətire] *tr* to withdraw; take off; fire again ‖ *intr* to fire again ‖ *ref* to withdraw; retire

retombée [rətɔ̃be] *f* fall; hang (*of cloth*); **retombées radioactives** fallout

retomber [rətɔ̃be] *intr* (*aux:* ÉTRE) to fall again; fall; fall back; hang, hang down; relapse

retordre [rətɔrdrə] *tr* to twist; wring out

rétorquer [retɔrke] *tr* to retort

re·tors [rətɔr] **-torse** [tɔrs] *adj* twisted; wily; curved (*beak*) ‖ *mf* rascal

retouche [rətuʃ] *f* retouch; (phot) retouching; **retouches** alterations

retoucher [rətuʃe] *tr* to retouch; make alterations on

retour [rətur] *m* return; turn, bend; reversal (*e.g., of opinion*); **de retour** in return; **en retour d'équerre** at right angles; **être de retour** to be back; **par retour du courrier** by return mail; **retour à la masse** (elec) ground (*on chassis of auto, radio, etc.*); **retour à la terre** (elec) ground; **retour à l'envoyeur** return to sender (*on letter*); **retour d'âge** change of life; **retour de flamme** backfire; **retour de manivelle** kick (of the crank); (fig) backlash; **retour de monnaie** coin return; **retour en arrière** flashback

retourner [rəturne] §95 *tr* to send back, return; upset; turn over (*e.g., the soil*); turn inside out ‖ *intr* (*aux:* ÉTRE) to go back, return ‖ *ref* to turn around, look back; turn over; (fig) to veer, shift; **s'en retourner** to go back; **se retourner contre** to turn against

retracer [rətrase] §51 *tr* to retrace; bring to mind, recall ‖ *ref* to recall

rétracter [retrakte] *tr* & *ref* to retract

rétraction [retraksjɔ̃] *f* contraction

retrait [rətrɛ] *m* withdrawal; shrinkage; running out (*of tide*); **en retrait** set back, recessed; (typ) indented; **retrait de permis** suspension of driver's license

retraite [rətrɛt] *f* retreat; retirement; pension; **battre en retraite** to retreat; **en retraite** retired; **prendre sa retraite** to retire; **retraite anticipée** early retirement; **toucher sa retraite** to draw one's pension

retrai·té **-tée** [rətrete] *adj* pensioned, retired ‖ *mf* pensioner

retranchement [rətrɑ̃ʃmɑ̃] *m* retrenchment; cutting out

retrancher [rətrɑ̃ʃe] *tr* to cut off or out, retrench ‖ *ref* to become entrenched

retransmettre [rətrɑ̃smɛtr] §42 *tr* to retransmit; rebroadcast

retransmission [rətrɑ̃smisjɔ̃] f retransmission; rebroadcast

rétré·ci -cie [retresi] adj narrow; shrunk

rétrécir [retresir] tr to shrink; take in (a garment) ‖ intr & ref to shrink; narrow

retremper [rətrɑ̃pe] tr to soak again; retemper; give new strength to ‖ ref to take another dip; get new vigor

rétribuer [retribɥe] tr to remunerate

rétribution [retribysjɔ̃] f retribution; salary, fee

rétro [retro] adj invar—**le style rétro** (coll) the style of the twenties ‖ m recoil; rearview mirror

rétroaction [retrɔaksjɔ̃] f feedback; retroaction

rétrofusée [retrɔfyze] f retrorocket

rétrograder [retrɔgrade] intr to retrogress

rétroprojecteur [retrɔprɔʒɛktœr] m overhead projector

rétrospec·tif [retrɔspɛktif] **-tive** [tiv] adj retrospective ‖ m flashback

rétrospection [retrɔspɛksjɔ̃] f restrospection

retrousser [rətruse] tr to roll up, turn up; curl up (one's lip) ‖ ref to turn up or pull up one's clothes

retrouve [rətruv] f (comp) retrieval

retrouver [rətruve] tr to find again; recover ‖ ref to be back again; meet again; get one's bearings

rétroviseur [retrɔvizœr] m rear-view mirror

rets [rɛ] m—**prendre dans des rets** to snare

réunification [reynifikɑsjɔ̃] f reunification

réunion [reynjɔ̃] f reunion; meeting; **réunion de service** staff meeting

réunir [reynir] tr to unite, join; reunite; call together, convene ‖ ref to meet; reunite

réus·si -sie [resyi] adj successful

réussir [resyir] §96 tr to make a success of, be good at; accomplish ‖ intr to succeed; **réussir à** to succeed in; pass (an exam)

réussite [resyit] f success; **faire une réussite** (cards) to play solitaire

réutilisable [reytilizabl] adj reusable

revaloir [rəvalwar] §71 tr—**revaloir q.ch à qn** to pay s.o. back for s.th.

revaloriser [rəvalɔrize] tr to revalue, reassert the value of; raise (a salary)

revan·chard [rəvɑ̃ʃar] **-charde** [ʃard] adj (coll) vengeful ‖ mf (coll) avenger

revanche [rəvɑ̃ʃ] f revenge; return bout or engagement, return match; **en revanche** on the other hand; **prendre sa revanche sur** to get even with

revancher [rəvɑ̃ʃe] ref to get even

rêvasser [rɛvase] intr to daydream

rêvasserie [rɛvasri] f fitful dreaming; daydreaming

rêve [rɛv] m dream

revêche [rəvɛʃ] adj sullen, crabbed

réveil [revɛj] m awakening; recovery; alarm clock; (mil) reveille

réveille-matin [revɛjmatɛ̃] m invar alarm clock

réveiller [reveje] tr & ref to wake up

réveillon [revɛjɔ̃] m Christmas Eve supper; New Year's Eve party

réveillonner [revɛjɔne] intr to celebrate Christmas Eve or New Year's Eve

révéla·teur [revelatœr] **-trice** [tris] adj revealing; telltale ‖ mf informer ‖ m (phot) developer

révélation [revelɑsjɔ̃] f revelation

révéler [revele] §10 tr to reveal; (phot) to develop

revenant [rəvnɑ̃] m ghost

reven·deur [rəvɑ̃dœr] **-deuse** [døz] mf retailer; secondhand dealer

revendication [rəvɑ̃dikɑsjɔ̃] f claim

revendiquer [rəvɑ̃dike] tr to claim; insist upon; assume (a responsibility)

revendre [rəvɑ̃dr] tr to resell

revenez-y [rəvnezi] m invar (coll) return; **un goût de revenez-y** (coll) a taste like more

revenir [rəvnir] §72, §95 intr (aux: ÉTRE) to return, come back; **en revenir** to have a narrow escape; **faire revenir** (culin) to brown; **n'en pas revenir** to not get over it; **revenir à** to come to, amount to; come to (e.g., mind); **revenir à soi** to come to; **revenir bredouille** to come back empty-handed; **revenir de** to recover from; realize (a mistake); **revenir de loin** to have been at death's door; **revenir sur** to go back on (e.g., one's word) ‖ ref —**s'en revenir** to come back

revente [rəvɑ̃t] f resale

revenu [rəvny] m revenue, income

revenue [rəvny] f new growth (of trees)

rêver [rɛve] tr to dream ‖ intr to dream; **rêver à** to dream of (think about); **rêver de** to dream of (in sleep); to long to + inf

réverbère [revɛrbɛr] m streetlight

réverbérer [revɛrbere] §10 tr to reflect (light, heat, etc.); re-echo, reverberate ‖ ref to be reflected

reverdir [rəvɛrdir] tr to make green ‖ intr to grow green; become young again

révérence [reverɑ̃s] f reverence; curtsy; **révérence parler** (coll) pardon the language; **tirer sa révérence** to bow out

révéren·cieux [reverɑ̃sjø] **-cieuse** [sjøz] adj obsequious

révé·rend [reverɑ̃] **-rende** [rɑ̃d] adj & m reverend

révérer [revere] §10 tr to revere

rêverie [rɛvri] f reverie

revers [rəvɛr] m reverse; lapel; (tennis) backhand; **à revers** from behind; **revers de main** slap with the back of the hand

reverser [rəvɛrse] tr to pour back; pour out again

réversible [revɛrsibl] adj reversible

revêtement [rəvɛtmɑ̃] m surfacing; facing; lining; casing

revêtir [rəvɛtir] §73 tr to put on; clothe, dress up; invest; surface; line; face; assume (a form; an aspect)

rê·veur [rɛvœr] **-veuse** [vøz] adj dreamy ‖ mf dreamer; **cela me laisse rêveur** that leaves me puzzled

revirement [rəvirmɑ̃] m sudden reversal; (naut) tack

réviser [revize] *tr* to revise; review; overhaul; recondition

réviseur [revizœr] *m* proofreader

révision [revizjɔ̃] *f* revision; review; overhauling; proofreading

révisionniste [revizjɔnist] *adj* & *mf* revisionist

revivre [rəvivr] §74 *tr* to live again, relive ‖ *intr* to live again

révocation [revɔkɑsjɔ̃] *f* dismissal; revocation

revoici [rəvwasi] *prep*—**me** (**vous,** etc.) **revoici** (coll) here I am (you are, etc.) again

revoilà [rəvwala] *prep*—**le** (**la,** etc.) **voilà** (coll) there it, he (she, etc.) is again

revoir [rəvwar] *m*—**au revoir** good-by ‖ §75 *tr* to see again; review; revise ‖ *ref* to meet again

révol·tant [revɔltɑ̃] -**tante** [tɑ̃t] *adj* revolting

révolte [revɔlt] *f* revolt, rebellion

révol·té -tée [revɔlte] *adj* & *mf* rebel

révolter [revɔlte] *tr* & *ref* to revolt; **se révolter devant** to be revolted by

révo·lu -lue [revɔly] *adj* completed; elapsed; bygone

révolution [revɔlysjɔ̃] *f* revolution

révolutionnaire [revɔlysjɔnɛr] *adj* & *mf* revolutionary

revolver [revɔlvɛr] *m* revolver

révoquer [revɔke] *tr* to revoke; countermand; dismiss; recall

re·vu -vue [rəvy] *adj* revised ‖ *f* see **revue**

revue [rəvy] *f* review; magazine, journal; (theat) revue; **passer en revue** to review (*past events; troops*)

rez-de-chaussée [redʃose] *m invar* first floor, ground floor

R.F. *abbr* (**République Française**) French Republic

rhabiller [rabije] *tr* to repair; dress again; refurbish ‖ *ref* to change one's clothes; **va te rhabiller!** (pej) get out!

rhapsodie [rapsɔdi] *f* rhapsody

Rhénanie [renani] *f* Rhineland

rhéostat [reɔsta] *m* rheostat

rhétorique [retɔrik] *adj* rhetorical ‖ *f* rhetoric

Rhin [rɛ̃] *m* Rhine

rhinocéros [rinɔserɔs] *m* rhinoceros

rhubarbe [rybarb] *f* rhubarb

rhum [rɔm] *m* rum

rhumati·sant [rymatizɑ̃] -**sante** [zɑ̃t] *adj* & *mf* rheumatic

rhumatis·mal -male [rymatismal] *adj* (*pl* -**maux** [mo]) rheumatic

rhumatisme [rymatism] *m* rheumatism

rhume [rym] *m* cold; **rhume des foins** hay fever

ri [ri] *v* see **rire**

riant [rjɑ̃] **riante** [rjɑ̃t] *adj* smiling; cheerful, pleasant

ribambelle [ribɑ̃bɛl] *f* (coll) long string, swarm, lot

ri·baud [ribo] -**baude** [bod] *adj* licentious ‖ *mf* camp follower; debauchee

ricanement [rikanmɑ̃] *m* snicker

ricane [rikane] *intr* to snicker

ri·chard [riʃar] -**charde** [ʃard] *mf* (coll) moneybags

riche [riʃ] *adj* rich ‖ *m* rich man; **nouveaux riches** newly rich

riche·lieu [riʃəljø] *m* (*pl* -**lieu** or -**lieus**) oxford

richesse [riʃɛs] *f* wealth; richness; **richesses** riches; **richesses naturelles** natural resources

ricin [risɛ̃] *m* castor-oil plant; castor bean

ricocher [rikɔʃe] *intr* to ricochet, rebound

ricochet [rikɔʃɛ] *m* ricochet; **faire des ricochets** to play ducks and drakes; **par ricochet** indirectly

rictus [riktys] *m* rictus; grin

ride [rid] *f* wrinkle; ripple

ri·dé -dée [ride] *adj* wrinkled; corrugated

ri·deau [rido] *m* (*pl* -**deaux**) curtain; **rideau d'arbres** line of trees; **rideau de fer** iron curtain; safety blind (*of a store*); (theat) fire curtain; **rideau de feu** (mil) cover of artillery fire; **rideau de fumée** smoke screen

ridectomie [ridɛktɔmi] *f* face-lift

ridelle [ridɛl] *f* rave, side rails (*of wagon*)

rider [ride] *tr* to wrinkle; ripple

ridicule [ridikyl] *adj* ridiculous ‖ *m* ridicule

ridiculiser [ridikylize] *tr* to ridicule

rien [rjɛ̃] *m* trifle; **comme un rien** with no trouble at all; **un rien de** just a little (bit) of; **un rien de temps** no time at all ‖ *pron indef*—**de rien** don't mention it, you're welcome; of no importance; **il n'en est rien** such is not the case; **rien ne** or **ne . . . rien** §90B nothing, not anything; **rien de moins (que)** nothing less (than); **rien que** nothing but

rieur [rjœr] **rieuse** [rjøz] *adj* laughing ‖ *mf* laugher, mocker ‖ *f* (orn) black-headed gull

riflard [riflar] *m* coarse file; jack plane; paring chisel

rigide [riʒid] *adj* rigid; stiff; strict

rigolade [rigɔlad] *f* (coll) good time; fun; (coll) big joke

rigole [rigɔl] *f* drain; ditch

rigoler [rigɔle] *intr* (slang) to laugh, joke

rigo·lo [rigɔlo] -**lote** [lɔt] *adj* (coll) comical; (coll) queer, funny ‖ *mf* (coll) card ‖ *m* (slang) rod, gat

rigou·reux [rigurø] -**reuse** [røz] *adj* rigorous; severe

rigueur [rigœr] *f* rigor, strictness; **à la rigueur** to the letter; as a last resort; **de rigueur** compulsory, de rigueur

rillons [rijɔ̃] *mpl* cracklings

rimail·leur [rimajœr] -**leuse** [jøz] *mf* (coll) rhymester

rime [rim] *f* rhyme; **rimes croisées** alternate rhymes; **rimes plates** couplets of alternate masculine and feminine rhymes

rimer [rime] *tr* & *intr* to rhyme

rimmel [rimɛl] *m* mascara

rinçage [rɛ̃saʒ] *m* rinse

rince-bouche [rɛ̃sbuʃ] *m invar* mouthwash

rince-bouteilles [rɛ̃sbutɛj] *m invar* (mach) bottle-washing machine

rince-doigts [rɛ̃sdwa] *m invar* fingerbowl

rincer [rɛ̃se] §51 *tr* to rinse; (slang) to ruin, take to the cleaners

rinçure [rɛ̃syr] *f* rinsing water

ring [riŋ] *m* ring (*for, e.g., boxing*)

ringard [rɛ̃gar] *m* poker (*for fire*)

ripaille [ripɑj] *f* (coll) blowout; **faire ri-paille** (coll) to carouse

ripe [rip] *f* scraper

riper [ripe] *tr* to scrape; (naut) to slip ‖ *intr* to slip; skid

riposte [ripɔst] *f* riposte, retort

riposter [ripɔste] *tr* to riposte, retort

rire [rir] *m* laugh; laughter; laughing; **fou rire** uncontrollable laughter; **gros rire** guffaw; **rire jaune** forced laugh ‖ §61 (*pp* **ri** *invar*) *intr* to laugh, joke, smile; **pour rire** for fun, in jest; **rire dans sa barbe, rire sous cape** to laugh up one's sleeve; **rire de** to laugh at or over; **rire du bout des lèvres, rire du bout des dents** to titter; **rire jaune** to force a laugh ‖ §97 *ref*—**se rire de** to laugh at

ris [ri] *m* (naut) reef; (obs) laughter; **ris d'agneau** or **de veau** sweetbread

risée [rize] *f* scorn; laughingstock; light squall

risible [rizibl] *adj* laughable

risque [risk] *m* risk

ris·qué -quée [riske] *adj* risky; risqué

risquer [riske] §97 *tr* to risk; hasard (*e.g., a remark*) ‖ *intr*—**risquer de** + *inf* to risk + *ger;* have a good chance of + *ger*

risque-tout [riskətu] *mf invar* daredevil

rissoler [risɔle] *tr* & *intr* to brown

ristourne [risturn] *f* rebate, refund; dividend

ristourner [risturne] *tr* to refund

ritournelle [riturnɛl] *f*—**c'est toujours la même ritournelle** it's always the same old story; **ritournelle publicitaire** advertising jingle or slogan

ri·tuel -tuelle [ritɥɛl] *adj* & *m* ritual

rivage [rivaʒ] *m* shore; bank

ri·val -vale [rival] (*pl* **-vaux** [vo] **-vales**) *adj* & *mf* rival

rivaliser [rivalize] *intr* to compete; **rivaliser avec** to compete with, rival

rivalité [rivalite] *f* rivalry

rive [riv] *f* shore; bank; **rive droite** Right Bank; **rive gauche** Left Bank

river [rive] *tr* to rivet

rive·rain -raine [rivrɛ̃] **-raine** [rɛn] *adj* waterfront; bordering ‖ *mf* riversider; dweller along a street or road

riveraineté [rivrɛnte] *f* riparian rights

rivet [rivɛ] *m* rivet

rivière [rivjɛr] *f* river, stream, tributary; (turf) water jump; **rivière de diamants** diamond necklace

rixe [riks] *f* brawl

riz [ri] *m* rice; **riz au lait** rice pudding; **riz glacé** polished rice; **riz précuit** minute rice

rizière [rizjɛr] *f* rice field

robe [rɔb] *f* dress; gown; robe; wrapper (*of cigar*); skin (*of onion, sausage, etc.*); husk (*of, e.g., bean*); **robe de chambre** dressing gown; **robe de cocktail** cocktail dress; **robe de grossesse** maternity dress; **robe de mariée** wedding dress; **robe d'intérieur** housecoat; **robe du soir** evening gown; **robe tunique** smock

rober [rɔbe] *tr* to husk, skin; wrap (*a cigar*)

roberts [rɔbɛr] *mpl* (slang) breasts

robin [rɔbɛ̃] *m* (coll) judge; (pej) shyster

robinet [rɔbinɛ] *m* faucet, tap; cock; **robi-net d'eau tiède** (coll) bore; **robinet mé-langeur** mixing faucet

robinier [rɔbinje] *m* (bot) locust tree

robot [rɔbo] *m* robot; pilotless (*airplane*); **robot cireur** automatic shoeshiner

robotiser [rɔbɔtize] *tr* to robotize

robre [rɔbr] *m* rubber (*in bridge*)

robuste [rɔbyst] *adj* robust; firm

roc [rɔk] *m* rock

rocade [rɔkad] *f* bypass (*of a road*)

rocaille [rɔkɑj] *adj* rococo ‖ *f* stones; rocky ground; stonework

rocail·leux [rɔkɑjø] **-leuse** [jøz] *adj* rocky, stony; harsh

roche [rɔʃ] *f* rock; boulder

rocher [rɔʃe] *m* rock; crag

rochet [rɔʃɛ] *m* ratchet; bobbin

ro·cheux [rɔʃø] **-cheuse** [ʃøz] *adj* rocky

rodage [rɔdaʒ] *m* grinding; breaking in; **en rodage** being broken in, new

roder [rɔde] *tr* to grind (*a valve*); break in (*a new car*); polish up (*a new play*)

rôder [rɔde] *intr* to prowl

rô·deur [rɔdœr] **-deuse** [døz] *adj* prowling ‖ *mf* prowler

rogatons [rɔgatɔ̃] *mpl* (coll) scraps

rogne [rɔɲ] *f* (coll) anger; **mettre qn èn rogne** (coll) to make s.o. see red

rogner [rɔɲe] *tr* to pare, trim

rognon [rɔɲɔ̃] *m* kidney

rogomme [rɔgɔm] *m*—**de rogomme** (coll) husky, beery (*voice*)

rogue [rɔg] *adj* arrogant

roi [rwa], [rwɑ] *m* king; **tirer les rois** to gather to, eat the Twelfth-night cake

roitelet [rwatlɛ] *m* kinglet; (orn) kinglet

rôle [rol] *m* role; roll, muster

ro·main [rɔmɛ̃] **-maine** [mɛn] *adj* Roman; roman (*type*); romaine (*lettuce*) ‖ *m* (typ) roman ‖ *f* romaine (lettuce); **bon comme la romaine** (slang) done for ‖ (*cap*) *mf* Roman (*person*)

ro·man [rɔmɑ̃] **-mane** [man] *adj* Romance (*language*); (archit) Romanesque ‖ *m* novel; **roman à l'eau de rose** romance; **roman d'anticipation, roman de science fiction** science-fiction novel; **roman de série noire** thriller; **roman noir** who-dunit; Gothic novel; **roman policier** de-tective story

romance [rɔmɑ̃s] *f* ballad

romanche [rɔmɑ̃ʃ] *m* Romansh

roman·cier [rɔmɑ̃sje] **-cière** [sjɛr] *mf* nov-elist; **romancier d'anticipation** science-fiction writer

ro·mand [rɔmɑ̃] **-mande** [mɑ̃d] *adj* French-speaking (*Switzerland*)

romanesque [rɔmanɛsk] *adj* romanesque, romantic, fabulous

roman-feuilleton [rɔmɑ̃fœjtɔ̃] *m* (*pl* **romans-feuilletons**) newspaper serial

roman-fleuve [rɔmɑ̃flœv] *m* (*pl* **romans-fleuves**) saga novel

romani·chel **-chelle** [rɔmaniʃɛl] *mf* gypsy, vagrant

romantique [rɔmɑ̃tik] *adj* & *mf* romantic

romantisme [rɔmɑ̃tism] *m* romanticism

romarin [rɔmarɛ̃] *m* (bot) rosemary

Rome [rɔm] *f* Rome

rompre [rɔ̃pr] (3d *sg pres ind* **rompt** [rɔ̃]) *tr* to break; burst; break in, train; break off ‖ *intr* & *ref* to break

rom·pu **-pue** [rɔ̃py] *adj*—**rompu à** accustomed to, experienced in; **rompu de** tired out from or by, exhausted with

romsteck [rɔmstɛk] *m* rump steak

ronce [rɔ̃s] *f* bramble; curly grain (*of wood*); **en ronces artificielles** barbed-wire (*fence*)

ronchonner [rɔ̃ʃɔne] *intr* (coll) to belly-ache, grumble

rond [rɔ̃] **ronde** [rɔ̃d] *adj* round; rounded; plump; straightforward; (slang) tight, drunk ‖ *m* ring, circle; round slice; (coll) dough, money; **en rond** in a circle; **faire les ronds de jambes** (slang) to bow and scrape; **rond comme une queue de pelle** (slang) soused, stoned, dead drunk; **rond de fumée** smoke ring; **rond de serviette** napkin ring ‖ *f* round; beat, round; round dance; radius; round hand; (mus) whole note; **à la ronde** around; **s'amuser à la ronde**, **faire la ronde** to go ring-around-a-rosy ‖ **rond** *adv*—**tourner rond** to work or go smoothly

rond-de-cuir [rɔ̃dkɥir] *m* (*pl* **ronds-de-cuir**) leather seat; (pej) bureaucrat

ron·deau [rɔ̃do] *m* (*pl* **-deaux**) rondeau; field roller

ronde·let [rɔ̃dlɛ] **-lette** [lɛt] *adj* plump; tidy (*sum*)

rondelle [rɔ̃dɛl] *f* disk; slice; washer (*of faucet, bolt, etc.*)

rondement [rɔ̃dmɑ̃] *adv* briskly; **mener rondement** to make short work of; **parler rondement** to be blunt

rondeur [rɔ̃dœr] *f* roundness; plumpness; frankness

rond-point [rɔ̃pwɛ̃] *m* (*pl* **ronds-points**) intersection, crossroads; traffic circle; circus, roundabout (Brit)

ronéo [rɔneo] *f* Mimeograph machine

ronéotyper [rɔneotipe] *tr* to mimeograph

ron·flant [rɔ̃flɑ̃] **-flante** [flɑ̃t] *adj* snoring; roaring; whirring; humming; (pej) high-sounding, pretentious

ronflement [rɔ̃fləmɑ̃] *m* snore; roar; whirr, hum

ronfler [rɔ̃fle] *intr* to snore; roar; whirr, hum

ron·fleur [rɔ̃flœr] **-fleuse** [fløz] *mf* snorer ‖ *m* vibrator (*replacing bell*)

ronger [rɔ̃ʒe] §38 *tr* to gnaw, nibble; eat away; bite (*one's nails*); corrode; torment ‖ *ref* to be worn away; be eaten away; eat one's heart out, fret

ron·geur [rɔ̃ʒœr] **-geuse** [ʒøz] *adj* gnawing ‖ *m* rodent

ronron [rɔ̃rɔ̃] *m* purr; drone

ronronnement [rɔ̃rɔnmɑ̃] *m* purring

ronronner [rɔ̃rɔne] *intr* to purr

roquer [rɔke] *intr* (chess) to castle

roquet [rɔkɛ] *m* cur, yapper; (*breed of dog*) pug

roquette [rɔkɛt] *f* (*plant; missile*) rocket

rosace [rozas] *f* rose window; (archit) rosette

rosa·cé **-cée** [rozase] *adj* roselike ‖ *f* skin eruption

rosaire [rozɛr] *m* rosary

rosâtre [rozɑtr] *adj* dusty-pink

rosbif [rɔsbif] *m* roast beef

rose [roz] *adj* & *m* rose, pink (*color*) ‖ *f* rose; rose window; **dire la rose** to box the compass; **rose des vents** compass card; **rose d'Inde** (*Tagetes*) marigold

ro·sé **-sée** [roze] *adj* rose, rose-colored ‖ *m* rosé wine ‖ *f* see **rosée**

ro·seau [rozo] *m* (*pl* **-seaux**) reed

rosée [roze] *f* dew

roséole [rozeɔl] *f* rash; rose rash

roseraie [rozrɛ] *f* rose garden

rosette [rozɛt] *f* bowknot; rosette; red ink; red chalk

rosier [rozje] *m* rosebush; **rosier églantier** sweetbrier

rosse [rɔs] *adj* nasty, mean; strict, stern; cynical ‖ *f* (coll) beast, stinker; (coll) nag; **sale rosse** (coll) dirty bitch

rossée [rɔse] *f* (coll) thrashing

rosser [rɔse] *tr* to beat up, thrash; (coll) to beat, best

rossignol [rɔsiɲɔl] *m* skeleton key; (orn) nightingale; (coll) piece of junk, drug on the market

rot [ro] *m* (slang) burp, belch

rota·tif [rɔtatif] **-tive** [tiv] *adj* rotary ‖ *f* rotary press

rotation [rɔtasjɔ̃] *f* rotation; turnover (*of merchandise*)

rotatoire [rɔtatwar] *adj* rotary

roter [rɔte] *intr* (slang) to burp

rô·ti **-tie** [roti] *adj* roasted ‖ *m* roast ‖ *f* piece of toast; **rôtie à l'anglaise** Welsh rarebit

rotin [rɔtɛ̃] *m* rattan; **de** or **en rotin** cane (*chair*); **pas un rotin!** not a penny!

rôtir [rotir] *tr*, *intr*, & *ref* to roast; toast; scorch

rôtisserie [rotisri] *f* rotisserie shop (*where roasted fowl is sold*); grillroom (*restaurant*)

rôtissoire [rotiswar] *f* rotisserie

rotogravure [rɔtɔgravyr] *f* rotogravure

rotonde [rɔtɔ̃d] *f* rotunda; (rr) roundhouse

rotor [rɔtɔr] *m* rotor

rotule [rɔtyl] *f* kneecap

roture [rɔtyr] *f* common people

rotu·rier [rɔtyrje] **-rière** [rjɛr] *adj* plebeian, of the common people ‖ *mf* commoner
rouage [rwaʒ] *m* cog; **rouages** movement (*of a watch*)
rou·blard [rublar] **-blarde** [blard] *adj* (coll) wily ‖ *mf* (coll) schemer
roublardise [rublardiz] *f* (coll) cunning
roucoulement [rukulmɑ̃] *m* cooing; billing and cooing
roucouler [rukule] *tr & intr* to coo
roue [ru] *f* wheel; **faire la roue** to turn cartwheels; to strut; **roue de secours** spare wheel (*with tire*)
roué rouée [rwe] *adj* slick; knocked out ‖ *mf* slicker ‖ *m* rake
rouelle [rwɛl] *f* fillet (*of veal*)
rouer [rwe] *tr* to break upon the wheel; **rouer de coups** to thrash, beat up
rouerie [ruri] *f* trickery; trick
rouet [rwɛ] *m* spinning wheel
rouge [ruʒ] *adj* red ‖ *m* red; rouge; blush; **porter au rouge** to heat red-hot; **rouge à lèvres** lipstick ‖ *adv* red
rou·geaud [ruʒo] **-geaude** [ʒod] *adj* ruddy ‖ *mf* ruddy-faced person
rouge-gorge [ruʒgɔrʒ] *m* (*pl* **rouges-gorges**) robin (*Erithacus rubecula*)
rougeole [ruʒɔl] *f* measles
rougeoyer [ruʒwaje] §47 *intr* to glow red; turn red
rougeur [ruʒœr] *f* redness; blush; **rougeurs** red spots
rougir [ruʒir] §97 *tr* to redden ‖ *intr* to turn red; blush
rouille [ruj] *f* rust
rouil·lé -lée [ruje] *adj* rusty; (*out of practice; blighted*) rusty
rouiller [ruje] *tr, intr, & ref* to rust
roulade [rulad] *f* trill; (mus) run
rou·lant [rulɑ̃] **-lante** [lɑ̃t] *adj* rolling; (coll) funny
rou·leau [rulo] *m* (*pl* **-leaux**) roller; roll; spool; rolling pin; **rouleau compresseur** road roller; **rouleau du printemps** egg roll
roulement [rulmɑ̃] *m* roll; rotation; rattle, clatter; exchange; **par roulement** in rotation; **roulement à billes** ball bearing
rouler [rule] *tr* to roll; (coll) to take in, cheat ‖ *intr* to roll; roll along; **rouler sur** to roll in (*wealth*); turn on ‖ *ref* to roll; roll up; toss and turn; to twiddle (*one's thumbs*); **se les rouler** (coll) to not turn a hand
route-ta-bille [rultabij] *m invar* (coll) rolling stone
roulette [rulɛt] *f* small wheel; castor; roulette; **aller comme sur des roulettes** to go well, to work smoothly
rou·leur [rulœr] **-leuse** [løz] *mf* drifter (*from one job to another*) ‖ *m* freight handler ‖ *f* streetwalker
roulis [ruli] *m* (naut) roll
roulotte [rulɔt] *f* trailer; gypsy wagon
rou·main [rumɛ̃] **-maine** [mɛn] *adj* Rumanian ‖ *m* Rumanian (*language*) ‖ (*cap*) *mf* Rumanian (*person*)

roupiller [rupije] *intr* to take a snooze
rou·quin [rukɛ̃] **-quine** [kin] *adj* (coll) red-headed; ‖ *mf* (coll) redhead ‖ *m* (slang) red wine; **Rouquin** Red (*nickname*)
rouspéter [ruspete] §10 *intr* (coll) to belly-ache, complain, kick
rouspé·teur [ruspetœr] **-teuse** [tøz] *mf* (coll) bellyacher, complainer
roussâtre [rusɑtr] *adj* auburn
rousse [rus] *f* redhead, auburn-haired woman; (slang) cops
rousseur [rusœr] *f* reddishness; freckle
roussir [rusir] *tr* to scorch; singe ‖ *intr* to become brown; **faire roussir** (culin) to brown
route [rut] *f* road; route, itinerary; **bonne route!** happy motoring!; **en route!** let's go!; **faire fausse route** to take the wrong road; (fig) to be on the wrong track; **mettre en route** to start; **route déformée** rough road; **route déviée** detour; **route express** expressway
rou·tier [rutje] **-tière** [tjɛr] *adj* road (*e.g., map*) ‖ *m* trucker; bicycle racer; Explorer, Rover (*boy scout*); (naut) track chart; **vieux routier** veteran, old hand
routine [rutin] *f* routine
routi·nier [rutinje] **-nière** [njɛr] *adj* routine; one-track (*mind*)
rouvieux [ruvjø] *adj masc* mangy ‖ *m* mange
rouvrir [ruvrir] §65 *tr & intr* to reopen
roux [ru] **rousse** [rus] *adj* russet, reddish; red, auburn (*hair*); browned (*butter*) ‖ *mf* redhead ‖ *m* russet, reddish brown, auburn (*color*); brown sauce ‖ *f* see **rousse**
royal royale [rwajal] *adj* (*pl* **royaux** [rwajo]) royal ‖ *f* imperial, goatee
royaliste [rwajalist] *adj & mf* royalist
royaume [rwajom] *m* kingdom
royauté [rwajote] *f* royalty
R.S.V.P. [ɛrɛsvepe] *m* (letterword) (**ré-pondez, s'il vous plaît**) R.S.V.P.
R.T.F. [ɛrteɛf] *f* (letterword) (**radio-diffusion-télévision française**) French radio and television
ruade [ryad] *f* kick, buck
ruban [rybɑ̃] *m* ribbon; tape; **ruban adhésif** adhesive tape; **ruban adhésif transparent** transparent tape; **ruban cache** masking tape; **ruban de chapeau** hatband; **ruban de frein** brake lining; **ruban encreur** typewriter ribbon; **ruban magnétique** recording tape
rubéole [rybeɔl] *f* German measles
rubis [rybi] *m* ruby; jewel (*of watch*); **payer rubis sur l'ongle** to pay down on the nail
rubrique [rybrik] *f* rubric; caption, heading; label (*in a dictionary*)
ruche [ryʃ] *f* beehive
rude [ryd] *adj* rude, rough; rugged; hard; steep; (coll) amazing
rudement [rydmɑ̃] *adv* roughly; (coll) awfully, mighty
rudesse [rydɛs] *f* rudeness, roughness; harshness
rudiment [rydimɑ̃] *m* rudiment

rudoyer [rydwaje] §47 *tr* to bully, browbeat; abuse, treat roughly

rue [ry] *f* street; **rue barrée** (*public sign*) no thoroughfare; (*public sign*) closed for repairs; **rue piétonne** pedestrian mall; **rue sans issue** (*public sign*) no outlet

ruée [rɥe] *f* rush; **ruée vers l'or** gold rush

ruelle [rɥɛl] *f* alley, lane; space between bed and wall

ruer [rɥe] *intr* to kick, buck; **ruer dans les brancards** to kick over the traces ‖ *ref*—**se ruer sur** to rush at

rugir [ryʒir] *intr* to roar, bellow

rugissement [ryʒismɑ̃] *m* roar

rugosité [rygozite] *f* roughness; ruggedness, bumpiness; coarseness

ru·gueux [rygø] **-gueuse** [gøz] *adj* rough, rugged; coarse; gnarled (*tree*)

ruine [rɥin] *f* ruin

ruiner [rɥine] *tr* to ruin ‖ *ref* to ruin oneself; fall into ruins

ruis·seau [rɥiso] *m* (*pl* **-seaux**) stream, brook; (fig) gutter

ruisseler [rɥisle] §34 *intr* to stream; drip, trickle

ruisselet [rɥislɛ] *m* little stream

ruissellement [rɥisɛlmɑ̃] *m* streaming; (*e.g.*, *of light*) flood

rumeur [rymœr] *f* rumor; hum (*e.g.*, *of voices*); roar (*of the sea*); **rumeur publique** public opinion

ruminer [rymine] *tr* & *intr* to ruminate; ruminate on or over

ru·pin [rypɛ̃] **-pine** [pin] *adj* (slang) rich ‖ *mf* (slang) swell

rupiner [rypine] *tr* & *intr* (coll) to do well

rupteur [ryptœr] *m* (elec) contact breaker

rupture [ryptyr] *f* rupture; breach; break; breaking off

ru·ral -rale [ryral] (*pl* **-raux** [ro]) *adj* rural ‖ *mf* farmer; **ruraux** country people

ruse [ryz] *f* ruse

ru·sé -sée [ryze] *adj* cunning, crafty ‖ *mf* sly one

russe [rys] *adj* Russian ‖ *m* Russian (*language*) ‖ (*cap*) *mf* Russian (*person*)

Russie [rysi] *f* Russia; **la Russie** Russia

rus·taud [rysto] **-taude** [tod] *adj* rustic, clumsy ‖ *mf* bumpkin

rustique [rystik] *adj* rustic; hardy

rustre [rystr] *adj* oafish ‖ *m* bumpkin, oaf; (obs) peasant

rut [ryt] *m* (zool) rut

ruti·lant [rytilɑ̃] **-lante** [lɑ̃t] *adj* bright-red; gleaming

rutiler [rytile] *intr* to gleam, glow

rythme [ritm] *m* rhythm; rate (*of production*)

ryth·mé -mée [ritme] *adj* rhythmic(al); cadenced

rythmer [ritme] *tr* to cadence; mark with a rhythm

rythmique [ritmik] *adj* rhythmic(al)

S

S, s [ɛs], *[ɛs] *m invar* nineteenth letter of the French alphabet

S. *abbr* (**saint**) St.

s' = **se** before vowel or mute **h**

sa [sa] §88 his, her, its

S.A. [ɛsɑ] *f* (letterword) (**société anonyme**) Inc.

sabbat [saba] *m* Sabbath; witches' Sabbath; racket, uproarious gaiety; **sabbat des chats** caterwauling

sabir [sabir] *m* pidgin

sable [sɑbl] *m* sand; sable; **sable mouvant** quicksand

sabler [sɑble] *tr* to sandblast; drink in one gulp; toss off (*some champagne*)

sa·bleux [sɑblø] **-bleuse** [bløz] *adj* sandy ‖ *f* sandblast; sandblaster

sablier [sɑblije] *m* hourglass; (*for drying ink*) sandbox; dealer in sand

sablière [sɑblijɛr] *f* sandpit; wall plate; (rr) sandbox

sablon·neux [sɑblɔnø] **-neuse** [nøz] *adj* sandy

sablonnière [sɑblɔnjɛr] *f* sandpit

sabord [sabɔr] *m* porthole

saborder [sabɔrde] *tr* to scuttle

sabot [sabo] *m* wooden shoe; hoof; whipping top; bungled work; ferrule; caster cup; **dormir comme un sabot** to sleep like a top; **sabot de frein** brake shoe; **sabot d'enrayage** wedge, block, scotch

sabotage [sabotaʒ] *m* sabotage

saboter [sabɔte] *tr* to sabotage; bungle ‖ *intr* (coll) to make one's wooden shoes clatter

sabo·teur [sabɔtœr] **-teuse** [tøz] *mf* saboteur; bungler

sabo·tier [sabɔtje] **-tière** [tjɛr] *mf* maker and seller of wooden shoes ‖ *f* clog dance

sabre [sɑbr] *m* saber

sabrer [sɑbre] *tr* to saber; (coll) to botch; (coll) to cut, condense

sac [sak] *m* sack, bag; **être un sac d'os** [dos] to be nothing but skin and bones; **mettre à sac** (coll) to rifle; **sac à main** handbag; **sac à malice** bag of tricks; **sac à provisions** shopping bag; **sac de couchage** sleeping bag; **sac de nœuds** (slang) can of worms; **sac de voyage** traveling bag, overnight suitcase; **vider son sac** (slang) to get something off one's chest

saccade [sakad] *f* jerk

sacca·dé -dée [sakade] *adj* jerky

saccager [sakaʒe] §38 *tr* to sack; (coll) to upset, turn topsy-turvy

saccha·rin [sakarɛ̃] **-rine** [rin] *adj* saccharine ‖ *f* saccharin

saccharose [sakaroz] *m* sucrose

sacerdoce [sasɛrdɔs] *m* priesthood

sacerdo·tal -tale [sasɛrdɔtal] *adj* (*pl* **-taux** [to]) sacerdotal, priestly

sache [saʃ] *v* (**saches, sachions,** etc.) see **savoir**

sachet [saʃɛ] *m* sachet; packet (*of needles, medicine, etc.*); powder charge

sacoche [sakɔʃ] *f* satchel

sacramen·tel -telle [sakramɑ̃tɛl] *adj* sacramental

sacre [sakr] *m* crowning, consecration

sa·cré -crée [sakre] *adj* sacred; (anat) sacral ‖ (when standing before noun) *adj* (coll) darned, blasted

sacrement [sakrəmɑ̃] *m* sacrament

sacrer [sakre] *tr* to crown, consecrate ‖ *intr* to curse

sacrifice [sakrifis] *m* sacrifice

sacrifier [sakrifje] *tr* to sacrifice

sacrilège [sakrilɛʒ] *adj* sacrilegious ‖ *mf* sacrilegious person ‖ *m* sacrilege

sacristain [sakristɛ̃] *m* sexton

sadique [sadik] *adj* sadistic ‖ *mf* sadist

safran [safrɑ̃] *m* saffron

sagace [sagas] *adj* sagacious, shrewd

sage [saʒ] *adj* wise; well-behaved; modest (*woman*); good (*child*); **soyez sage!** be good! ‖ *mf* sage

safe-femme [saʒfam] *f* (*pl* **sages-femmes**) midwife

sagesse [saʒɛs] *f* wisdom; good behavior

Sagittaire [saʒitɛr] *m*—**le Sagittaire** (astr, astrol) Sagittarius

sai·gnant [seɲɑ̃] **-gnante** [ɲɑ̃t] *adj* bleeding; (*wound*) fresh; (*meat*) rare

saignée [seɲe] *f* bloodletting; bend of the arm, small of the arm; (fig) drain on the purse

saignement [seɲmɑ̃] *m* bleeding; **saignement de nez** nosebleed

saigner [seɲe], [seɲe] *tr* & *intr* to bleed; **saigner à blanc, saigner aux quatre veines** to bleed white

sail·lant [sajɑ̃] **-lante** [jɑ̃t] *adj* prominent, salient; projecting; high (*cheekbones*)

saillie [saji] *f* projection; spurt; sally, outburst; **faire saillie** to jut out, project

saillir [sajir] (used only in *inf, ger,* & 3d *sg* & *pl*) *tr* (agr) to cover ‖ §69 *intr* to protrude, project; spurt

sain [sɛ̃] **saine** [sɛn] *adj* healthy; **sain d'esprit** sane; **sain et sauf, saine et sauve** safe and sound

saindoux [sɛ̃du] *m* lard

sainement [sɛnmɑ̃] *adv* soundly

sais [se] *v* (**sait**) see **savoir**

saint [sɛ̃] **sainte** [sɛ̃t] *adj* saintly; sacred, holy ‖ *mf* saint

Saint-Esprit [sɛ̃tɛspri] *m* (rel) Holy Spirit

sainteté [sɛ̃təte] *f* holiness

Saint-Siège [sɛ̃sjɛʒ] *m* Holy See

saisie [sezi] *f* seizure; foreclosure

saisie-arrêt [seziarɛ] *f* (*pl* **-arrêts**) attachment, garnishment

saisir [sezir] *tr* to seize; sear (*meat*); grasp (*to understand*); strike, startle; overcome; **saisir un tribunal de** to lay before a court ‖ *ref*—**se saisir de** to take possession of

saisissement [sezismɑ̃] *m* chill; shock

saison [sɛzɔ̃] *f* season

salace [salas] *adj* salacious

salade [salad] *f* salad; (fig) mess; **raconter des salades** (slang) to tell fish stories; **salade de fruits** fruit salad

saladier [saladje] *m* salad bowl

salaire [salɛr] *m* salary, wage; recompense, punishment

salariat [salarja] *m* salaried workers, employees; salary (*fixed wage*)

sala·rié -riée [salarje] *adj* salaried, hired ‖ *mf* wage earner; employee

sa·laud [salo] **-laude** [lod] *adj* (coll) slovenly ‖ *mf* (slang) skunk, scoundrel

sale [sal] *adj* dirty; dull (*color*) ‖ *mf* dirty person

sa·lé -lée [sale] *adj* salty, salted; dirty (*joke*); padded (*bill*); (slang) exaggerated ‖ *m* salt pork

saler [sale] *tr* to salt

saleté [salte] *f* dirtiness; piece of dirt; (slang) dirty trick; (slang) dirt

saleuse [saløz] *f* road-salting truck

salière [saljɛr] *f* saltcellar

salir [salir] *tr* & *ref* to soil

salive [saliv] *f* saliva

salle [sal] *f* room; hall; auditorium; ward (*in a hospital*); (theat) audience, house; **salle à manger** dining room; **salle d'armes** fencing room; **salle d'attente** waiting room; **salle de bains** bathroom; **salle d'écoute** language laboratory; **salle de détente** rec room; **salle de jeux électroniques** amusement arcade; **salle d'embarquement** (aer) gate; **salle de la réserve** rare-book room; **salle de police** (mil) guardhouse; **salle de réveil, salle de réanimation** (med) recovery room; **salle de rédaction** city room; **salle des accouchées** maternity ward; **salle de séjour** living room; **salle de services du prêt** reserve-book room; **salle des fêtes** hall, auditorium; **salle des machines** engine room; **salle des pas perdus** lobby, waiting room; **salle de spectacle** movie house; **salle des ventes** salesroom, showroom; **salle de travail** delivery room; **salle d'exposition** showroom

salmigondis [salmigɔ̃di] *m* hodgepodge

salon [salɔ̃] *m* living room, parlor; exposition; saloon (*ship's lounge*); **salon de beauté** beauty parlor; **salon de l'automobile** automobile show; **salon de thé** tearoom

salon·nard [salɔnar] **-narde** [nard] *mf* sycophant

saloperie [salɔpri] *f* (slang) trash

salopette [salɔpɛt] *f* coveralls, overalls; bib; smock

salpêtre [salpɛtr] *m* saltpeter
salsepareille [salsəparɛj] *f* sarsaparilla
saltimbanque [saltɛ̃bɑ̃k] *mf* tumbler; mountebank, charlatan
salubre [salybr] *adj* salubrious, healthful
saluer [salɥe] *tr* to salute; greet, bow to, wave to
salut [saly] *m* health; safety; salvation; salute; greeting, bow; nod; **salut!** (coll) hi!, howdy!; **salut les gars!, salut les copains!** hi, fellows!
salutaire [salytɛr] *adj* healthy, salutary, beneficial
salutation [salytɑsjɔ̃] *f* greeting; **salutations distinguées** or **sincères salutations** (complimentary close) yours truly
salve [salv] *f* salvo, salute
samari·tain [samaritɛ̃] **-taine** [tɛn] *adj* Samaritan ‖ (*cap*) *mf* Samaritan
samedi [samdi] *m* Saturday
sanatorium [sanatɔrjɔm] *m* sanitarium
sanctifier [sɑ̃ktifje] *tr* to sanctify
sanction [sɑ̃ksjɔ̃] *f* sanction; penalty
sanctionner [sɑ̃ksjɔne] *tr* to sanction; penalize
sanctuaire [sɑ̃ktɥɛr] *m* sanctuary
sandale [sɑ̃dal] *f* sandal; gym shoe
sandwich [sɑ̃dwitʃ], [sɑ̃dviʃ] *m* (*pl* **sandwiches, sandwichs**) sandwich
sang [sɑ̃] *m* blood; **avoir le sang chaud** (coll) to be a go-getter; **bon sang!** (coll) darn it!; **sang et tripes** blood and guts; **se faire du bon sang** to enjoy oneself; **se faire du mauvais sang** to get all stewed up
sang-froid [sɑ̃frwa] *m* self-control
san·glant [sɑ̃glɑ̃] **-glante** [glɑ̃t] *adj* bloody; cruel
sangle [sɑ̃gl] *f* cinch
sanglier [sɑ̃glije] *m* wild boar; **tirer sur un sanglier de carton** (coll) to tear down a straw man
sanglot [sɑ̃glo] *m* sob
sangloter [sɑ̃glɔte] *intr* to sob
sang-mêlé [sɑ̃mɛle] *m invar* half-breed
sangsue [sɑ̃sy] *f* bloodsucker, leech
san·guin [sɑ̃gɛ̃] **-guine** [gin] *adj* sanguine ‖ *f* (fa) sanguine
sanitaire [sanitɛr] *adj* sanitary; hospital, e.g., **avion sanitaire** hospital plane
sans [sɑ̃] *adv*—**sans que** without; **sans quoi** or else ‖ *prep* without; **sans cesse** ceaselessly; **sans façon** informally; **sans fil** wireless
sans-abri [sɑ̃zabri] *mf invar* homeless person
sans-cœur [sɑ̃kœr] *mf invar* heartless person
sans-filiste [sɑ̃filist] *mf* (*pl* **-filistes**) radio operator; radio amateur
sans-gêne [sɑ̃ʒɛn] *adj invar* offhanded ‖ *mf invar* offhanded person ‖ *m* offhandedness
sansonnet [sɑ̃sɔnɛ] *m* starling; blackbird
sans-travail [sɑ̃travaj] *mf invar* unemployed worker
san·tal [sɑ̃tal] *m* (*pl* **-taux** [to]) (bot) sandalwood

santé [sɑ̃te] *f* health; sanity; **santé publique** public-health service
sape [sap] *f* sap (*undermining*)
saper [sape] *tr* to sap, undermine
sapeur [sapœr] *m* (mil) sapper; **fumer comme un sapeur** (coll) to smoke like a chimney
sapeur-pompier [sapœrpɔ̃pje] *m* (*pl* **sapeurs-pompiers**) fireman; **sapeurs-pompiers** fire department
saphir [safir] *m* sapphire; sapphire needle
sapin [sapɛ̃] *m* fir
sapristi [sapristi] *interj* hang it!
saquer [sake] *tr* (slang) to fire, sack
sarbacane [sarbakan] *f* blowgun
sarcasme [sarkasm] *m* sarcasm
sarcler [sarkle] *tr* to weed, root out
sarcloir [sarklwar] *m* hoe
Sardaigne [sardɛɲ] *f* Sardinia; **la Sardaigne** Sardinia
sarde [sard] *adj* Sardinian ‖ *m* Sardinian (*language*) ‖ (*cap*) *mf* Sardinian (*person*)
sardine [sardin] *f* sardine
S.A.R.L. *abbr* (**société à responsabilité limitée**) corporation
sarment [sarmɑ̃] *m* vine; vine shoot
sarra·sin [sarazɛ̃] **-sine** [zin] *adj* Saracen ‖ *m* buckwheat ‖ *f* portcullis ‖ (*cap*) *mf* Saracen
sar·rau [saro] *m* (*pl* **-raus**) smock
sarriette [sarjɛt] *f* (bot) savory
sas [sɑ], [sɑs] *m* sieve; lock (*of canal, submarine, etc.*); air lock (*of caisson, spaceship, etc.*); **sas d'évacuation** (aer) escape hatch
sasser [sɑse] *tr* to sift, screen; pass through a lock
satanique [satanik] *adj* satanic; fiendish, wicked
satelliser [satelize] *tr* to make a satellite of; (rok) to put into orbit
satellite [satelit] *adj & m* satellite; **satellite de relais** relay satellite
satin [satɛ̃] *m* satin
satinette [satinɛt] *f* sateen
satire [satir] *f* satire
satirique [satirik] *adj* satiric(al)
satiriser [satirize] *tr* to satirize
satisfaction [satisfaksjɔ̃] *f* satisfaction
satisfaire [satisfɛr] §29 *tr* to satisfy ‖ *intr*—**satisfaire à** to satisfy, fulfill, meet, e.g., **avez-vous satisfait à tous les besoins?** have you met all the needs? ‖ *ref* to be satisfied
satisfai·sant [satisfəzɑ̃] **-sante** [zɑ̃t] *adj* satisfactory; satisfying
saturer [satyre] *tr* to saturate
Saturne [satyrn] *m* Saturn
saturnisme [satyrnism] *m* lead poisoning
sauce [sos] *f* sauce; gravy; drawing pencil; (tech) solution
saucer [sose] §51 *tr* to dip in sauce or gravy; (coll) to soak to the skin; (coll) to reprimand severely
saucière [sosjɛr] *f* gravy bowl
saucisse [sosis] *f* sausage; frankfurter
saucisson [sosisɔ̃] *m* bologna, sausage

sauf [sof] **sauve** [sov] *adj* safe ‖ **sauf** *prep* save, except; barring; subject to (*e.g.*, *correction*)

sauf-conduit [sofkɔ̃dɥi] *m* (*pl* **-conduits**) safe-conduct

sauge [soʒ] *f* (bot) sage, salvia

saugre·nu -nue [sogrəny] *adj* absurd, silly

saule [sol] *m* willow

saumâtre [somɑtr] *adj* brackish

saumon [somɔ̃] *m* salmon; pig (*of crude metal*)

saumure [somyr] *f* brine

sauner [sone] *intr* to make salt

saupoudrer [sopudre] *tr* to sprinkle (*with powder, sugar; citations*)

saurai [sɔre] *v* (**sauras, saura, saurons,** etc.) see **savoir**

saurer [sɔre] *tr* to kipper

saut [so] *m* leap, jump; falls, waterfall; **au saut du lit** on getting out of bed; **faire le saut** to take the fatal step; **faire un saut chez** to drop in on; **par sauts et par bonds** by fits and starts; **saut à la perche** pole vault; **saut de carpe** jackknife; **saut de l'ange** swan dive; **saut en chute libre** skydiving; **saut en hauteur** high jump; **saut en longueur** long jump; **saut pé-rilleux** somersault

saut-de-lit [sodli] *m invar* wrap

saut-de-mouton [sodmutɔ̃] *m* (*pl* **sauts-de-mouton**) overpass

saute [sot] *f* change in direction, shift

saute-mouton [sotmutɔ̃] *m* leapfrog

sauter [sote] *tr* to leap over; skip ‖ *intr* to leap, jump; blow up; **faire sauter** to sauté (*a pancake*); fire (*an employee*); **sauter à cloche-pied** to hop on one foot; **sauter à pieds joints** to do a standing jump; **sauter aux nues** to get mad

sauterelle [sotrɛl] *f* grasshopper

sauterie [sotri] *f* (coll) hop (*dancing party*)

sau·teur [sotœr] **-teuse** [tøz] *adj* jumping ‖ *mf* jumper; **sauteur (sauteuse) en hauteur** high jumper; ‖ *m* jumper, jumping horse ‖ *f* frying pan

sautiller [sotije] *intr* to hop

sautoir [sotwar] *m* St. Andrew's cross; **en sautoir** crossways

sauvage [sovaʒ] *adj* savage; wild; shy ‖ *mf* savage

sauvagerie [sovaʒri] *f* savagery; wildness; shyness

sauvegarde [sovgard] *f* safeguard

sauvegarder [sovgarde] *tr* to safeguard

sauve-qui-peut [sovkipø] *m invar* panic, stampede, rout

sauver [sove] *tr* to save; rescue ‖ *intr*—**sauve qui peut!** every man for himself! ‖ *ref* to run away; escape; (theat) to exit; **sauve-toi!** (coll) scram!

sauvetage [sovtaʒ] *m* salvage; lifesaving; rescue

sauveteur [sovtœr] *adj masc* lifesaving ‖ *m* lifesaver

sauveur [sovœr] *adj masc* Saviour ‖ *m* savior; **Le Sauveur** the Saviour

savamment [savamɑ̃] *adv* knowingly; skill-fully

savane [savan] *f* prairie, savanna

sa·vant [savɑ̃] **-vante** [vɑ̃t] *adj* scholarly, learned ‖ *mf* scientist, scholar, savant; **savant atomiste** nuclear physicist

savate [savat] *f* old slipper; foot boxing; (coll) butterfingers; **trainer la savate** to be down at the heel

saveur [savœr] *f* savor, taste

savoir [savwar] *m* learning ‖ §62, §95 *tr* & *intr* to know; know how to; **à savoir** namely, to wit; **à savoir que** with the understanding that; **en savoir long** to know all about it; **pas que je sache** not that I know of

savoir-faire [savwarfɛr] *m invar* know-how

savon [savɔ̃] *m* soap; (slang) sharp repri-mand; **savon à barbe** shaving soap; **passer un savon à** (slang) to shout at; **savon en paillettes** soap flakes

savonnage [savɔnaʒ] *m* soaping

savonner [savɔne] *tr* to soap

savonnerie [savɔnri] *f* soap factory

savonnette [savɔnɛt] *f* toilet soap

savon·neux [savɔnø] **-neuse** [nøz] *adj* soapy

savourer [savure] *tr* to savor

savou·reaux [savurø] **-reuse** [røz] *adj* sa-vory, tasty

saxon [saksɔ̃] **saxonne** [saksɔn] *adj* Saxon ‖ *m* Saxon (*language*) ‖ (*cap*) *mf* Saxon (*person*)

saxophone [saksɔfɔn] *m* saxophone

saynète [sɛnɛt] *f* sketch, playlet

sca·bieux [skabjø] **-bieuse** [bjøz] *adj* scabby ‖ *f* scabious

sca·breux [skɑbrø] **-breuse** [brøz] *adj* rough (*road*); risky (*business*); scabrous (*remark*)

scalpel [skalpɛl] *m* scalpel

scalper [skalpe] *tr* to scalp

scandale [skɑdal] *m* scandal; disturbance

scanda·leux [skɑdalø] **-leuse** [løz] *adj* scandalous

scandaliser [skɑdalize] *tr* to lead astray; scandalize ‖ *ref* to take offense

scander [skɑde] *tr* to scan (*verses*)

scandinave [skɑdinav] *adj* Scandinavian ‖ *m* Scandinavian (*language*) ‖ (*cap*) *mf* Scandinavian (*person*); **Scandinaves** Scandinavian countries

scanographe [skanɔgraf] *m* (med) CAT scanner

scaphandre [skafɑdr] *m* diving suit; space-suit; **scaphandre autonome** aqualung; **scaphandre spatial** spacesuit

scaphandrier [skafɑdrije] *m* diver

scarlatine [skarlatin] *f* scarlet fever

scarole [skarɔl] *f* escarole

sceau [so] *m* (*pl* **-seaux**) seal

scélé·rat [selera] **-rate** [rat] *adj* villainous ‖ *mf* villain

scellé [sɛle] *m* seal

sceller [sɛle] *tr* to seal

scénario [senarjo] *m* scenario

scène [sɛn] *f* scene; stage; theater

scénique [senik] *adj* scenic
scepticisme [sɛptisism] *m* skepticism
sceptique [sɛptik] *adj & mf* skeptic
sceptre [sɛptr] *m* scepter
schah [ʃa] *m* shah
schelem [ʃlɛm] *m* slam (*at bridge*)
schéma [ʃema] *m* diagram, sketch; outline; pattern
schisme [ʃism] *m* schism
schiste [ʃist] *m* schist, shale
schizophrène [skizɔfrɛn] *adj & mf* schizophrenic
schlague [ʃlag] *f* flogging
schooner [skunœr], [ʃunœr] *m* schooner
sciatique [sjatik] *adj* sciatic ‖ *f* (pathol) sciatica
scie [si] *f* saw; (coll) bore, nuisance; scie à découper, scie sauteuse jig saw
sciemment [sjamɑ̃] *adv* knowingly
science [sjɑ̃s] *f* science; learning, knowledge; science de l'information computer science
science-fiction [sjɑ̃sfiksjɔ̃] *f* science fiction
scientifique [sjɑ̃tifik] *adj* scientific ‖ *mf* scientist
scier [sje] *tr* to saw; (coll) to bore ‖ *intr* (naut) to row backwards
scierie [siri] *f* sawmill
scieur [sjœr] *m* sawyer
scinder [sɛ̃de] *tr* to divide ‖ *ref* to be divided
scintil·lant [sɛ̃tijɑ̃] -lante [jɑ̃t] *adj* scintillating; twinkling
scintillation [sɛ̃tijɑ̃sjɔ̃] *f* twinkling, twinkle; (phys) scintillation
scintillement [sɛ̃tijmɑ̃] *m* twinkling
scintiller [sɛ̃tije] *intr* to scintillate; twinkle
scion [sjɔ̃] *m* scion; tip (*of fishing rod*)
scission [sisjɔ̃] *f* schism; (biol & phys) fission
sciure [sjyr] *f* sawdust
sclérose [skleroz] *f* sclerosis
scolaire [skɔlɛr] *adj* school
scolastique [skɔlastik] *adj & m* scholastic ‖ *f* scholasticism
sconse [skɔ̃s] *m* skunk fur; skunk
scories [skɔri] *fpl* slag, dross
scorpion [skɔrpjɔ̃] *m* scorpion; le Scorpion (astr, astrol) Scorpion
scout scoute [skut] *adj & m* scout
scoutisme [skutism] *m* scouting
scribe [skrib] *m* scribe
script [skript] *m* scrip; (typ) script
scripturaire [skriptyrɛr] *adj* Scriptural ‖ *m* fundamentalist
scrofule [skrɔfyl] *f* scrofula
scrotum [skrɔtɔm] *m* scrotum
scrupule [skrypyl] *m* scruple
scrupu·leux [skrypylø] -leuse [løz] *adj* scrupulous
scruter [skryte] *tr* to scrutinize
scrutin [skrytɛ̃] *m* ballot; balloting, voting, poll; dépouiller le scrutin to count the votes; scrutin de ballottage runoff election
scrutiner [skrytine] *intr* to ballot

sculpter [skylte] *tr* to sculpture; carve (*wood*)
sculpteur [skyltœr] *m* sculptor
sculpture [skyltyr] *f* sculpture
s.d. *abbr* (sans date) n.d.
S.D.E.C. [ɛsdeəse] *m* (letterword) (Service de documentation extérieure et de contre-espionnage) foreign-intelligence agency (*equivalent of the C.I.A.*)
S.D.N. [ɛsdeɛn] *f* (letterword) (Société des Nations) League of Nations
se [sə] §87 *ref pron*
séance [seɑ̃s] *f* session, sitting; seat (*in an assembly*); performance, showing; séance; séance tenante on the spot
séant [seɑ̃] séante [seɑ̃t] *adj* fitting, decent; sitting (*as a king or a court in session*) ‖ *m* buttocks, bottom; se mettre sur son séant to sit up (*in bed*)
seau [so] *m* (*pl* seaux) bucket, pail; il pleut à seaux it's raining cats and dogs; seau à charbon coal scuttle
sébile [sebil] *f* wooden bowl; (telp) coin return
sec [sɛk] sèche [sɛʃ] *adj* dry; sharp; rude; unguarded (*card*); total (*loss*); en cinq sec in a jiffy; sec comme un hareng (coll) long and thin; tout sec and nothing more ‖ *m* dryness; à sec dry; (coll) broke ‖ *f see* sèche ‖ sec *adv*—aussi sec (slang) on the spot; boire sec to drink one's liquor straight; frapper sec to land a hard fast punch; parler sec to talk tough
sécession [sesesjɔ̃] *f* secession
sèche [sɛʃ] *f* (slang) fag, cigarette
sèche-cheveux [sɛʃʃəvø] *m invar* hair drier
sèche-linge [sɛʃlɛ̃ʒ] *m invar* clothes drier
sécher [seʃe] §10 *tr* to dry; season; cut (*a class*) ‖ *intr* to become dry
sécheresse [seʃrɛs] *f* dryness; drought; baldness (*of style*); curtness (fig) coldness
séchoir [seʃwar] *m* drier; drying room; clotheshorse
se·cond [səgɔ̃] -conde [gɔ̃d] *adj & pron* second; en second next in rank ‖ *m* second ‖ *f see* seconde
secondaire [səgɔ̃dɛr] *adj & m* secondary
seconde [səgɔ̃d] *f* second (*in time; musical interval; of angle*); second class
seconder [səgɔ̃de] *tr* to help, second
se·coué -couée [səkwe] *adj* (slang) nuts, crazy
secouer [səkwe] *tr* to shake; shake off or down ‖ *ref* to pull oneself together
secourable [səkurabl] *adj* helpful
secourir [səkurir] §14 *tr* to help, aid
secourisme [səkurism] *m* first aid
secouriste [səkurist] *mf* first-aider; first-aid worker
secours [səkur] *m* help, aid; au secours! help!; de secours emergency; spare (*tire*); des secours supplies, relief
secousse [səkus] *f* shake, jolt; (elec) shock
se·cret [səkrɛ] -crète [krɛt] *adj* secret; secretive ‖ *m* secret; secrecy; au secret in solitary confinement ‖ *f see* secrète

secrétaire [səkretɛr] *mf* secretary ‖ *m* secretary (*desk*)
secrète [səkrɛt] *f* central intelligence
sécréter [sekrete] §10 *tr* to secrete
sectaire [sɛktɛr] *adj & mf* sectarian
secte [sɛkt] *f* sect
secteur [sɛktœr] *m* sector; (elec) house current, local supply circuit; **secteur postal** postal zone; (mil) A.P.O. number
section [sɛksjɔ̃] *f* section; cross section
sectionner [sɛksjɔne] *tr* to section; cut ‖ *ref* to break apart
séculaire [sekylɛr] *adj* secular
sécu·lier [sekylje] **-lière** [ljɛr] *adj & m* secular
sécurité [sekyrite] *f* security
séda·tif [sedatif] **-tive** [tiv] *adj & m* sedative
sédation [sedɑsjɔ̃] *f* sedation
sédentaire [sedɑ̃tɛr] *adj* sedentary
sédiment [sedimɑ̃] *m* sediment
sédi·tieux [sedisjø] **-tieuse** [sjøz] *adj* seditious
sédition [sedisjɔ̃] *f* sedition
séduc·teur [sedyktœr] **-trice** [tris] *adj* seducing, bewitching ‖ *mf* seducer ‖ *f* vamp
séduction [sedyksjɔ̃] *f* seduction
séduire [sedɥir] §19 *tr* to seduce; charm, bewitch; bribe
sédui·sant [sedɥizɑ̃] **-sante** [zɑ̃t] *adj* seductive, tempting
segment [sɛgmɑ̃] *m* segment; **segment de piston** piston ring
ségrégation [segregɑsjɔ̃] *f* segregation
ségrégationniste [segregɑsjɔnist] *adj* segregationist
seiche [sɛʃ] *f* cuttlefish; tidal wave; **chasser la seiche** (slang) to look for the end of the rainbow
séide [seid] *m* henchman
seigle [sɛgl] *m* rye
seigneur [sɛɲœr] *m* lord
sein [sɛ̃] *m* breast; bosom; womb; **au sein de** in the heart of
seine [sɛn] *f* dragnet
seing [sɛ̃] *m* signature; **sous seing privé** privately witnessed
seize [sɛz] §94 *adj & pron* sixteen; the Sixteenth, e.g., **Jean seize** John the Sixteenth ‖ *m* sixteen (*in dates*)
seizième [sɛzjɛm] §94 *adj, pron* (*masc, fem*), *& m* sixteenth
séjour [seʒur] *m* stay, visit
séjourner [seʒurne] *intr* to reside; stay, visit
sel [sɛl] *m* salt; **gros sel** coarse salt; (fig) dirty joke; **sel ammoniac** sal ammoniac; **sel fin, sel de table** table salt; **sel gemme** rock salt
sélec·tif [selɛktif] **-tive** [tiv] *adj* selective
sélection [selɛksjɔ̃] *f* selection
sélectionner [selɛksjɔne] *tr* to select
self [sɛlf] *f* (elec) coil, spark coil
self-service [sɛlfsɛrvis] *m* self-service
selle [sɛl] *f* saddle; seat (*of bicycle, motorcycle, etc.*); sculptor's tripod; stool, movement; (culin) saddle; **aller à la selle** to go to the toilet
seller [sɛle] *tr* to saddle

sellier [sɛlje] *m* saddler
selon [səlɔ̃] *adv*—**c'est selon** that depends; **selon que** according as ‖ *prep* according to; after (*e.g., my own heart*)
semailles [səmɑj] *fpl* sowing, seeding
semaine [səmɛn] *f* week; week's wages; set of seven; **à la petite semaine** day-to-day, hand-to-mouth; short-sighted; **de semaine** on duty during the week; **la semaine des quatre jeudis** (coll) never; **semaine anglaise** five-day workweek
semai·nier [səmenje] **-nière** [njɛr] *mf* week worker ‖ *m* highboy; office calendar
sémantique [semɑ̃tik] *adj* semantic ‖ *f* semantics
sémaphore [semafɔr] *m* semaphore
semblable [sɑ̃blabl] *adj* similar, like ‖ *m* fellow-man, equal
semblant [sɑ̃blɑ̃] *m* semblance, appearance; **faire semblant** to pretend
sembler [sɑ̃ble] §95 *intr* to seem; seem to
semelle [səmɛl] *f* sole; foot (*of stocking*); tread (*of tire*); bed (*of concrete*); **battre la semelle** to stamp one's feet
semence [səmɑ̃s] *f* seed; semen; brad; **semence de perles** seed pearls
semer [səme] §2 *tr* to seed, sow; scatter, strew; lay (*mines*); (slang) to outdistance; (slang) to drop (*an acquaintance*)
semestre [səmɛstr] *m* semester; six-month period
semes·triel **-trielle** [səmɛstrijɛl] *adj* six-month; semester
se·meur [səmœr] **-meuse** [møz] *mf* sower; spreader of gossip ‖ *f* seeder, drill
semi-chenillé [səmiʃnije] *m* half-track
semi-conduc·teur [səmikɔ̃dyktœr] **-trice** [tris] *adj* semiconductive ‖ *m* semiconductor
semifi·ni **-nie** [səmifini] *adj* unfinished
sémil·lant [semijɑ̃] **-lante** [jɑ̃t] *adj* sprightly, lively
séminaire [seminɛr] *m* seminary; seminar; conference
semi-remorque [səmirəmɔrk] *f* (*pl* **-remorques**) semitrailer
semis [səmi] *m* sowing; seedling; seedbed
sémite [semit] *adj* Semitic ‖ (*cap*) *mf* Semite
sémitique [semitik] *adj* Semitic
semoir [səmwar] *m* seeder, drill
semonce [səmɔ̃s] *f* reprimand; (naut) order to heave to
semoncer [səmɔ̃se] §51 *tr* to reprimand; (naut) to order to heave to
semoule [səmul] *f* (culin) semolina
sénat [sena] *m* senate
sénateur [senatœr] *m* senator
sénile [senil] *adj* senile
sens [sɑ̃s] *m* sense, meaning; opinion; direction; **à double sens** ambiguous, e.g., **mot à double sens** double entendre; **en sens inverse** in the opposite direction; **sens antihoraire** counterclockwise; **sens dessus dessous** [sɑ̃dəsydəsu] upside down; **sens devant derrière** [sɑ̃dəvɑ̃dɛrjɛr] back to front; **sens interdit** (*public sign*)

no entry; **sens obligatoire** (*public sign*) right way, this way; **sens unique** (*public sign*) one way
sensation [sãsasjɔ̃] *f* sensation
sensation·nel -nelle [sãsasjɔnɛl] *adj* sensational
sen·sé -sée [sãse] *adj* sensible
sensibiliser [sãsibilize] *tr* to sensitize
sensibilité [sãsibilite] *f* sensitivity, sensitiveness; compassion, feeling
sensible [sãsibl] *adj* sensitive; considerable, appreciable; perceptible; (mus) leading (*note*)
sensiblement [sãsibləmã] *adv* approximately; appreciably, noticeably; acutely, keenly
sensi·tif [sãsitif] **-tive** [tiv] *adj* sensory; sensitive, touchy
senso·riel -rielle [sãsɔrjɛl] *adj* sensory
sen·suel -suelle [sãsɥɛl] *adj* sensual
sent-bon [sãbɔ̃] *m invar* odor, perfume
sentence [sãtãs] *f* proverb; (law) sentence
senteur [sãtœr] *f* odor, perfume
sentier [sãtje] *m* path; **hors des sentiers battus** off the beaten track
sentiment [sãtimã] *m* feeling; opinion; **nos meilleurs sentiments** (*formula in letter writing*) our best wishes
sentimen·tal -tale [sãtimãtal] *adj* (*pl* **-taux** [to]) sentimental
sentine [sãtin] *f* bilge
sentinelle [sãtinɛl] *f* sentinel
sentir [sãtir] §41, §95 *tr* to feel; smell; smell like, smell of; taste of; have all the earmarks of; show the effects of; **ne pas pouvoir sentir qn** to be unable to stand s.o. ‖ *intr* to smell; smell bad ‖ *ref* to feel; be felt; **se sentir de** to feel the effects of
seoir [swar] §5A (3d *pl pres ind* **siéent;** used only in 3d *sg & pl* of most simple tenses) *intr*—**seoir à** to be fitting for, proper to; be suitable to, suit, become, e.g., **cette robe lui sied** that dress suits her, that dress becomes her ‖ (*used only in inf and 2d sg & pl and 1st pl impv*) *ref* (coll & poetic) to sit down, have a seat
séparation [separasjɔ̃] *f* separation
séparer [separe] *tr & ref* to separate, divide
sept [sɛt] §94 *adj & pron* seven; the Seventh, e.g., **Jean sept** John the Seventh; **sept heures** seven o'clock ‖ *m* seven; seventh (*in dates*)
septembre [sɛptãbr] *m* September
septentrio·nal -nale [sɛptãtrijɔnal] (*pl* **-naux** [no]) *adj* northern
septième [sɛtjɛm] §94 *adj, pron* (*masc, fem*), & *m* seventh
septique [sɛptik] *adj* septic
sépulcre [sepylkr] *m* sepulcher
sépulture [sepyltyr] *f* grave, tomb, burial place; burial
séquelle [sekɛl] *f* gang; (pathol) complications; **séquelles** aftermath
séquence [sekãs] *f* sequence; (*in poker*) straight
séquestrer [sekɛstre] *tr* to sequester

serai [sɔre], [sre] *v* (**seras, sera, serons,** etc.) see **être**
sérail [seraj] *m* (*pl* **sérails**) seraglio
séraphin [serafɛ̃] *m* seraph; (coll) angel
serbe [sɛrb] *adj* Serb ‖ (*cap*) *mf* Serb
se·rein [sɔrɛ̃] **-reine** [rɛn] *adj* serene ‖ *m* night dew
sérénade [serenad] *f* serenade
sérénité [serenite] *f* serenity
serf [sɛr], [sɛrf] **serve** [sɛrv] *mf* serf
serge [sɛrʒ] *f* serge
sergent [sɛrʒã] *m* sergeant
série [seri] *f* series, string, set; (elec) series; **de série** standard; stock (*car*); **en série** in (a) series; mass, e.g., **fabrication en série** mass production; **hors série** outsize (*wearing apparel*); discontinued (*as an item of manufacture*); custom-built; almost unheard of; **série noire** run of bad luck
sé·rieux [serjø] **-rieuse** [rjøz] *adj* serious
serin [sɔrɛ̃] *m* canary; (coll) simpleton
seringa [sɔrɛ̃ga] *m* mock orange
seringue [sɔrɛ̃g] *f* syringe; (hort) spray gun; **seringue à graisse** grease gun; **seringue à injections** hypodermic syringe; **seringue à instillations** nasal spray
serment [sɛrmã] *m* oath; **prêter serment to** take oath
sermon [sɛrmɔ̃] *m* sermon
sermonner [sɛrmɔne] *tr* to sermonize
serpe [sɛrp] *f* billhook
serpent [sɛrpã] *m* snake, serpent; **serpent à sonnettes** rattlesnake; **serpent caché sous les fleurs** snake in the grass
serpenter [sɛrpãte] *intr* to wind
serpen·tin [sɛrpãtɛ̃] **-tine** [tin] *adj* serpentine ‖ *m* coil; worm (*of still*); paper streamer
serpillière [sɛrpijɛr] *f* floorcloth; sacking, burlap
serpolet [sɛrpɔle] *m* thyme
serre [sɛr] *f* greenhouse; **serres** claws, talons
ser·ré -rée [sɛre] *adj* tight; narrow; compact; close ‖ **serré** *adv* —**jouer serré** to play it close to the vest
serre-fils [sɛrfil] *m invar* (elec) binding post
serre-freins [sɛrfrɛ̃] *m invar* brakeman
serre-livres [sɛrlivr] *m invar* book end
serrement [sɛrmã] *m* squeezing, pressing; (min) partition (*to keep out water*); (pathol) pang; **serrement de cœur** heaviness of heart; **serrement de main** handshake
serrer [sɛre] *tr* to press; squeeze; wring; tighten; close up (*ranks*); clasp, shake, e.g., **serrer la main à** to shake hands with; grit (*one's teeth*); put on (*the brakes*) ‖ *intr*—**serrez à droite** (*public sign*) squeeze to right ‖ *ref* to squeeze together, be close together
serre-tête [sɛrtɛt] *m invar* headband; kerchief; crash helmet; (telp) headset
serrure [sɛryr] *f* lock; **serrure de sûreté** safety lock
serrurier [sɛryrje] *m* locksmith
sers [sɛr] *v* (**sert**) see **servir**

sertir [sɛrtir] *tr* to set (*a stone*)

sérum [serɔm] *m* serum

servage [sɛrvaʒ] *m* serfdom

ser·veur [sɛrvœr] **-veuse** [vøz] *mf* (tennis) server ‖ *m* waiter; barman ‖ *f* waitress; barmaid; extra maid; (mach) coffee maker

serviable [sɛrvjabl] *adj* obliging

service [sɛrvis] *m* service; agency; **service après vente** warranty service; **être de service** to be on duty; **service compris** tip included; **service de déminage** bomb squad; **service de garde** twenty-four-hour service; **service des abonnés absents** telephone answering service; **service des renseignements téléphoniques** information; **service sanitaire** ambulance corps

serviette [sɛrvjɛt] *f* napkin; towel; brief case; **serviette de bain** bath towel; **serviette de table** table napkin; **serviette de toilette en papier** paper towel; **serviette en papier** paper napkin; **serviette éponge** washcloth; Turkish towel; **serviette hygiénique** sanitary napkin

servile [sɛrvil] *adj* servile

servir [sɛrvir] §63, §96 *tr* to serve; deal (*cards*) ‖ *intr* to serve; **servir à** to be useful for, to serve as; **servir à qn de** to serve s.o. as; **servir de** to serve as, to function as ‖ *ref* to help oneself; **se servir chez** to patronize; **se servir de** to use

serviteur [sɛrvitœr] *m* servant

servitude [sɛrvityd] *f* servitude; (law) easement

servofrein [sɛrvɔfrɛ̃] *m* power brake

ses [se] §88

sésame [sezam] *m* sesame

session [sesjɔ̃] *f* session

seuil [sœj] *m* threshold

seul seule [sœl] §92 *adj* alone; lonely ‖ (when standing before noun) *adj* sole, single, only ‖ *pron indef* single one, only one; single person, only person ‖ **seul** *adv* alone

seulement [sœlmɑ̃] *adv* only, even ‖ *conj* but

sève [sɛv] *f* sap; vim

sévère [sevɛr] *adj* severe; stern; strict

sévices [sevis] *mpl* cruelty, brutality

sévir [sevir] *intr* to rage

sevrage [səvraʒ] *m* weaning

sevrer [səvre] §2 *tr* to wean

sexe [sɛks] *m* sex; **le beau sexe** the fair sex; **le sexe fort** the sterner sex

sexisme [sɛksism] *m* sexism

sexiste [sɛksist] *adj & mf* sexist

sextant [sɛkstɑ̃] *m* sextant

sextuor [sɛkstɥɔr] *m* (mus) sextet

sexuel sexuelle [sɛksɥɛl] *adj* sexual

seyant [sɛjɑ̃] **seyante** [sɛjɑ̃t] *adj* becoming

shampooing [ʃɑ̃pwɛ̃] *m* shampoo

shérif [ʃerif] *m* sheriff

shooter [ʃute] *ref* (slang) to shoot up (*intravenously*)

short [ʃɔrt] *m* shorts

si [si] *m invar* if; **des si et des cars** ifs and buts ‖ *adv* so; as; (to contradict a negative statement or question) yes, e.g., **Vous ne le saviez pas. Si!** You didn't know. Yes, I did!; **si bien que** so that, with the result that; **si peu que** so little that; **si peu que ce soit** however little it may be; **si + adj** or *adv* + **que** + *subj* however + *adj* or *adv* + *ind*, e.g., **si vite qu'il s'en aille** however fast he goes away ‖ *conj* if; whether; **si . . . ne** unless, e.g., **si je ne me trompe** unless I am mistaken; **si ce n'est** unless; **si tant est que** if it is true that

sia·mois [sjamwa] **-moise** [mwaz] *adj* Siamese ‖ (*cap*) *mf* Siamese

sibé·rien [siberjɛ̃] **-rienne** [rjɛn] *adj* Siberian ‖ (*cap*) *mf* Siberian

sibylle [sibil] *f* sibyl

Sicile [sisil] *f* Sicily; **la Sicile** Sicily

sici·lien [sisiljɛ̃] **-lienne** [ljɛn] *adj* Sicilian ‖ (*cap*) *mf* Sicilian

SIDA [sida] *m* (acronym) (**syndrome d'immunodéficience acquise**)—**le SIDA** AIDS (*acquired immune-deficiency syndrome*)

sidé·ral -rale [sideral] *adj* (*pl* **-raux** [ro]) sidereal

sidérer [sidere] §10 *tr* (coll) to flabbergast

sidérurgie [sideryrʒi] *f* iron-and-steel industry

sidérurgique [sideryrʒik] *adj* iron-and-steel

siècle [sjɛkl] *m* century; age; (eccl) world

siège [sjɛʒ] *m* seat; headquarters; (eccl) see; (mil) siege; **siège à glissière** glider; **siège arrière** back seat; **siège avant** front seat; **siège baquet** (*pl* **sièges baquets**) bucket seat; **siège billes** bean-bag chair; **siège éjectable** ejection seat

siéger [sjeʒe] §1 *intr* to sit, be in session; (*said of malady*) be seated

sien [sjɛ̃] **sienne** [sjɛn] §89

sieste [sjɛst] *f* siesta; **faire le sieste** to take a siesta; (coll) to be caught napping

sifflement [sifləmɑ̃] *m* whistle; hiss; swish, whiz; wheezing

siffler [sifle] *tr* to whistle (*e.g., a tune*); to hiss, boo; whistle to ‖ *intr* to whistle; hiss; swish, whiz

sifflet [siflɛ] *m* whistle; **sifflet à gaz** protective whistle in a woman's handbag

sif·fleur [siflœr] **-fleuse** [fløz] *mf* whistler

siffloter [siflɔte] *tr & intr* to whistle (a tune)

sigle [sigl] *m* abbreviation; word formed by literation; acronym

si·gnal [siɲal] *m* (*pl* **-gnaux** [ɲo]) signal; sign; (telp) busy signal

signa·lé -lée [siɲale] *adj* signal, noteworthy

signalement [siɲalmɑ̃] *m* description

signaler [siɲale] *tr* to signal; point out ‖ *ref* to distinguish oneself

signalisation [siɲalizasjɔ̃] *f* signs

signataire [siɲatɛr] *adj & mf* signatory

signature [siɲatyr] *f* signature; signing

signe [siɲ] *m* sign; **faire signe à** to motion to, to signal; **signe de ponctuation** punctuation mark; **signe de tête** nod

signer [siɲe] *tr* to sign ‖ *ref* to cross oneself

signet [siɲɛ], [sinɛ] *m* bookmark

significa·tif [siɲifikatif] **-tive** [tiv] *adj* significant

signifier [siɲifje] §97 *tr* to signify; mean

silence [silɑ̃s] *m* silence

silen·cieux [silɑ̃sjø] **-cieuse** [sjøz] *adj* silent ‖ *m* silencer (*of a gun*); (aut) muffler

silex [silɛks] *m* flint

silhouette [silwɛt] *f* silhouette

silhouetter [silwete] *tr* to silhouette

silicium [silisjɔm] *m* silicon

silicone [silikon] *f* silicone

sillage [sijaʒ] *m* wake

sillet [sijɛ] *m* (mus) nut

sillon [sijɔ̃] *m* furrow; groove; **sillon sonore** sound track

sillonner [sijɔne] *tr* to furrow; groove; cross, streak

silo [silo] *m* silo

silure [silyr] *m* catfish

simagrée [simagre] *f* pretense

similaire [similɛr] *adj* similar

similigravure [similigravyr] *f* halftone

similitude [similityd] *f* similarity

similor [similɔr] *m* ormolu

simple [sɛ̃pl] *adj* simple; one-way (*ticket*); **à simple interligne** (typ) single-spaced; **passer en simple police** to go to police court; **simple particulier** private citizen; **simple soldat** private ‖ *mf* simple-minded person ‖ *m* simple (*herb*); (tennis) singles

simplement [sɛ̃pləmɑ̃] *adv* simply, plainly, naturally; simply, merely, just; with a simple mind

sim·plet [sɛ̃plɛ] **-plette** [plɛt] *adj* artless

simplicité [sɛ̃plisite] *f* simplicity; simpleness; simple-mindedness; **en toute simplicité** naturally, without affectation; **venez en toute simplicité** come as you are

simplifier [sɛ̃plifje] *tr* to simplify

simpliste [sɛ̃plist] *adj* oversimple

simulacre [simylakr] *m* sham; **simulacre de combat** sham battle

simuler [simyle] *tr* to simulate

simulta·né -née [simyltane] *adj* simultaneous; **en simultané** simultaneous (*translation*)

sinapisme [sinapism] *m* mustard plaster

sincère [sɛ̃sɛr] *adj* sincere

sincérité [sɛ̃serite] *f* sincerity

sinécure [sinekyr] *f* sinecure

singe [sɛ̃ʒ] *m* monkey; (slang) boss; **grimacer comme un vieux singe** to grin like a Cheshire cat

singer [sɛ̃ʒe] §38 *tr* to ape

singerie [sɛ̃ʒri] *f* monkeyshine; grimace; monkey cage

singulariser [sɛ̃gylarize] *tr* to draw attention to ‖ *ref* to stand out

singu·lier [sɛ̃gylje] **-lière** [ljɛr] *adj & m* singular

sinistre [sinistr] *adj* sinister ‖ *m* disaster

sinis·tré -trée [sinistre] *adj* damaged, ruined; homeless; shipwrecked ‖ *mf* victim

sinon [sinɔ̃] *adv* if not; perhaps even; **sinon que** except for the fact that ‖ *prep* except for, except to ‖ *conj* except, unless; or else, else, otherwise

si·nueux [sinɥø] **-nueuse** [nɥøz] *adj* sinuous, winding

sinus [sinys] *m* sinus; (trig) sine

sionisme [sjɔnism] *m* Zionism

siphon [sifɔ̃] *m* siphon; siphon bottle; trap (*double-curved pipe*)

siphonner [sifɔne] *tr* to siphon

sire [sir] *m* sire; (archaic) sir; **un triste sire** a miserable wretch

sirène [sirɛn] *f* siren; foghorn; mermaid

sirop [siro] *m* syrup; **sirop pectoral** cough syrup

siroter [sirɔte] *tr & intr* (coll) to sip

sis [si] **sise** [siz] *adj* located

sismique [sismik] *adj* seismic

sismographe [sismɔgraf] *m* seismograph

sismologie [sismɔlɔʒi] *f* seismology

site [sit] *m* site; lay of the land

sitôt [sito] *adv* immediately; **sitôt dit, sitôt fait** no sooner said than done; **sitôt que** as soon as

sittelle [sitɛl] *f* (orn) nuthatch

situation [sitɥasjɔ̃] *f* situation; **situation sans issue** deadlock, impasse

situer [sitɥe] *tr* to situate, locate

six [si(s)] §94 *adj & pron* six; the Sixth, e.g., **Jean six** John the Sixth; **six heures** six o'clock ‖ *m* six; sixth (*in dates*)

sixième [sizjɛm] §94 *adj, pron* (*masc, fem*), & *m* sixth

six-quatre-deux [siskatdø]—**à la six-quatre-deux** (coll) slapdash

sizain [sizɛ̃] *m* six-line verse; pack (*of cub scouts*)

sizerin [sizrɛ̃] *m* (orn) redpoll

ski [ski] *m* ski; skiing; **faire du ski** to go skiing; **ski de fond** cross-country ski; **ski nautique** water-skiing

skier [skje] *intr* to ski

skieur [skjœr] **skieuse** [skjøz] *mf* skier

slalom [slalɔm] *m* slalom

slave [slav] *adj* Slav; Slavic ‖ *m* Slavic (*language*) ‖ (*cap*) *mf* Slav (*person*)

slip [slip] *m* supporter; swimming trunks; (women's) panties; **slip de soutien, slip coquille** supporter, jockstrap; **slip minimum** bikini

s.l.n.d. *abbr* (**sans lieu ni date**) n.p. & n.d.

slogan [slɔgɑ̃] *m* (com) slogan

slovaque [slɔvak] *adj* Slovak ‖ *m* Slovak (*language*) ‖ (*cap*) *mf* Slovak (*person*)

smicard [smikar] *m* (coll) minimum-wage earner

smoking [smɔkiŋ] *m* tuxedo

smurf [smyrf] *m* break dancing

snack [snak] *m* snack bar

S.N.C.F. [ɛsɛnseɛf] *f* (letterword) (**Société nationale des chemins de fer français**) French railroad

snob [snɔb] *adj invar* snobbish ‖ *mf* (*pl* **snob** or **snobs**) snob

snober [snɔbe] *tr* to snub

snobisme [snɔbism] *m* snobbery

sobre [sɔbr] *adj* sober, moderate; simple (*ornamentation*)

sobriété [sɔbrijete] *f* sobriety; moderation (*in eating, speaking*)

sobriquet [sɔbrikɛ] *m* nickname
soc [sɔk] *m* plowshare
sociable [sɔsjabl] *adj* sociable, neighborly; social (*creature*)
so·cial -ciale [sɔsjal] *adj* (*pl* **-ciaux** [sjo]) social
sociali·sant [sɔsjalizɑ̃] **-sante** [zɑ̃t] *adj* socialistic ‖ *mf* socialist sympathizer
socialiser [sɔsjalize] *tr* to socialize
socialisme [sɔsjalism] *m* socialism
socialiste [sɔsjalist] *adj & mf* socialist
sociétaire [sɔsjetɛr] *mf* stockholder; member (*e.g., of an acting company*)
société [sɔsjete] *f* society; company; firm, partnership; **société anonyme** stock company, corporation; **société de gardiennage** security-systems company; **société de prévoyance** benefit society; **Société des Nations** League of Nations; **société d'investissement à capital variable** mutual-fund society
sociologie [sɔsjɔlɔʒi] *f* sociology
socle [sɔkl] *m* pedestal; footing, socle; **socle roulant** portable stand (*e.g., for a television set*)
socque [sɔk] *m* clog, sabot; (theat) comedy
socquette [sɔkɛt] *f* anklet
Socrate [sɔkrat] *m* Socrates
soda [sɔda] *m* soda water
sodium [sɔdjɔm] *m* sodium
sodomie [sɔdɔmi] *f* sodomy
sœur [sœr] *f* sister; **et ta sœur!** (slang) knock it off!; **ma sœur** (eccl) sister
sofa [sɔfa] *m* sofa
soi [swa] §85, §85B; **à part soi** to oneself (himself, etc.); **de soi, en soi** in itself
soi-disant [swadizɑ̃] *adj invar* so-called, self-styled ‖ *adv* supposedly
soie [swa] *f* silk; bristle
soierie [swari] *f* silk goods; silk factory
soif [swaf] *f* thirst; **avoir soif** to be thirsty
soi·gné -gnée [swaɲe] *adj* well-groomed, trim; polished (*speech*)
soigner [swaɲe] *tr* to nurse, take care of; groom; polish (*one's style*)
soigneur [swaɲœr] *m* (sports) trainer
soi·gneux [swaɲø] **-gneuse** [ɲøz] *adj* careful, meticulous
soi-même [swamɛm] §86
soin [swɛ̃] *m* care, attention; treatment; **aux bons soins de** in care of (*c/o*); **être aux petits soins auprès de** to wait on (*s.o.*) hand and foot; **premiers soins** first aid; **soins à domicile** home-care nursing; **soins d'urgence** first aid; **soins infirmière** nursing
soir [swar] *m* evening, night; **hier soir** last night; **le soir** in the evening, at night
soirée [sware] *f* evening; evening party; **en soirée** evening (*performance*); **soirée dansante** dance; **soirée-hébergement** pajama party
sois [swa] *v* (**soit, soient**) see **être**
soit [swa], [swat] *conj* take for instance, e.g., **soit quatre multiplié par deux** take for instance four multiplied by two; say, e.g., **bien des hommes étaient perdus,**

soit un million many men were lost, say a million; **soit . . . soit** either . . . or, whether . . . or; **soit que . . . soit que** whether . . . or ‖ [swat] *interj* so be it!, all right!
soixante [swasɑ̃t] §94 *adj, pron, & m* sixty; **soixante et onze** seventy-one; **soixante et onzième** seventy-first; **soixante et un** sixty-one; **soixante et unième** sixty-first
soixante-dix [swasɑ̃tdi(s)] §94 *adj, pron, & m* seventy
soixante-dixième [swasɑ̃tdizjɛm] §94 *adj, pron* (*masc, fem*), *& m* seventieth
soixante-douze [swasɑ̃tduz] §94 *adj, pron, & m* seventy-two
soixante-douzième [swasɑ̃tduzjɛm] §94 *adj, pron* (*masc, fem*), *& m* seventy-second
soixantième [swasɑ̃tjɛm] §94 *adj, pron* (*masc, fem*), *& m* sixtieth
soja [sɔʒa] *m* soybean
sol [sɔl] *m* soil; ground; floor
solaire [sɔlɛr] *adj* solar
soldat [sɔlda] *m* soldier
soldatesque [sɔldatɛsk] *adj* barrack-room (*humor; manners*) ‖ *f* rowdies
solde [sɔld] *m* balance (*of an account*); remnant; clearance sale; **en solde** reduced (*in price*) ‖ *f* (mil) pay
solder [sɔlde] *tr* to settle (*an account*); to sell out; (mil) to pay ‖ *intr* to sell out
sol·deur [sɔldœr] **-deuse** [døz] *mf* dealer in seconds and remnants
sole [sɔl] *f* sole (*fish*); field (*used for crop rotation*)
soleil [sɔlɛj] *m* sun; sunshine, sunlight; sunflower; pinwheel; **il fait (du) soleil** it is sunny
solen·nel -nelle [sɔlanɛl] *adj* solemn
solenniser [sɔlanize] *tr* to solemnize
solénoïde [sɔlenɔid] *m* solenoid
solfège [sɔlfɛʒ] *m* sol-fa
solidage [sɔlidaʒ] *f* goldenrod
solidaire [sɔlidɛr] *adj* interdependent; jointly binding; **solidaire de** responsible for; answerable to; integral with, in one piece with
solidariser [sɔlidarize] *ref* to join together
solidarité [sɔlidarite] *f* solidarity, interdependence
solide [sɔlid] *adj & m* solid
solidité [sɔlidite] *f* solidity; soundness; strength (*e.g., of a fabric*)
soliloque [sɔlilɔk] *m* soliloquy
soliste [sɔlist] *mf* soloist
solitaire [sɔlitɛr] *adj* solitary; lonely ‖ *m* solitary, anchorite; old wild boar; solitaire
solitude [sɔlityd] *f* solitude
solive [sɔliv] *f* joist
soli·veau [sɔlivo] *m* (*pl* **-veaux**) small joist; (coll) nobody
solliciter [sɔllisite] *tr* to solicit; apply for; incite; attract (*attention; iron*); induce ‖ *intr* to seek favors
sollici·teur [sɔllisitœr] **-teuse** [tøz] *mf* solicitor, office seeker, petitioner, lobbyist
solo [sɔlo] *adj invar & m* solo

solstice [sɔlstis] *m* solstice
soluble [sɔlybl] *adj* soluble; solvable
solution [sɔlysjɔ̃] *f* solution
solutionner [sɔlysjɔne] *tr* to solve
solvabilité [sɔlvabilite] *f* solvency
solvable [sɔlvabl] *adj* solvent
solvant [sɔlvɑ̃] *m* solvent
sombre [sɔ̃br] *adj* somber; sullen
sombrer [sɔ̃bre] *intr* to sink; vanish (*as a fortune*)
sommaire [sɔmɛr] *adj & m* summary
sommation [sɔmasjɔ̃] *f* summons; sentry challenge; **faire les trois sommations** to read the riot act
somme [sɔm] *m* nap ‖ *f* sum; **en somme, somme toute** in short, when all is said and done
sommeil [sɔmɛj] *m* sleep; **avoir sommeil** to be sleepy
sommeiller [sɔmeje] *intr* to doze; lie dormant
sommelier [sɔməlje] *m* wine steward
sommer [sɔme] §97 *tr* to add up; summon, issue a legal writ to
sommes [sɔm] *v* see **être**
sommet [sɔme] *m* summit, top; apex (*of a triangle*); vertex (*of an angle*); (fig) acme
sommier [sɔmje] *m* bedspring; ledger; crossbeam; (archaic) pack animal; **sommier élastique** spring mattress
sommité [sɔmite] *f* pinnacle, crest; leader, authority
somnambule [sɔmnɑ̃byl] *adj* sleepwalking ‖ *mf* sleepwalker
somnifère [sɔmnifɛr] *adj* sleep-inducing, soporific ‖ *m* sleeping pill
somnolence [sɔmnɔlɑ̃s] *f* drowsiness; indolence, laziness
somno·lent [sɔmnɔlɑ̃] **-lente** [lɑ̃t] *adj* somnolent, drowsy; indolent
somnoler [sɔmnɔle] *intr* to doze
somptuaire [sɔ̃ptɥɛr] *adj* luxury (*tax*)
somp·tueux [sɔ̃ptɥø] **-tueuse** [tɥøz] *adj* sumptuous
son [sɔ̃] *adj poss* §88 his, her, its ‖ *m* sound; bran
sonal [sɔnal] *m* (advertising) jingle
sonate [sɔnat] *f* sonata
sondage [sɔ̃daʒ] *m* sounding, probing; **sondage de l'opinion** public-opinion poll; **sondage d'exploration** wildcat (*well*); **sondage isoloir** exit poll
sonde [sɔ̃d] *f* lead, probe; borer, drill; **sonde spatiale** space probe
sonder [sɔ̃de] *tr* to sound, probe, bore, fathom; explore, reconnoiter; poll (*e.g., public opinion*); sound out (*s.o.*)
son·deur [sɔ̃dœr] **-deuse** [døz] *mf* prober, sounder
songe [sɔ̃ʒ] *m* dream
songe-creux [sɔ̃ʒkrø] *m invar* visionary, pipe dreamer
songer [sɔ̃ʒe] §38, §96 *tr* to dream up ‖ *intr* to dream; think; intend to; **songer à** to think of; imagine, dream of; **songez-y!** think it over!
songerie [sɔ̃ʒri] *f* reverie, daydreaming

son·geur [sɔ̃ʒœr] **-geuse** [ʒøz] *adj* dreamy, preoccupied ‖ *mf* daydreamer
sonique [sɔnik] *adj* sonic, of sound
sonnaille [sɔnaj] *f* cowbell, sheepbell
sonnailler [sɔnaje] *m* bellwether ‖ *intr* to ring often and without cause
son·nant [sɔnɑ̃] **-nante** [nɑ̃t] *adj* striking (*clock*); metal (*money*); at the stroke of, e.g., **à huit heures sonnantes** at the stroke of eight
son·né -née [sɔne] *adj* past, e.g., **deux heures sonnées** past two o'clock; over, e.g., **il a soixante ans sonnés** he is over sixty; (slang) cuckoo, nuts; (slang) stunned; **être sonné** (slang) to be knocked out
sonner [sɔne] *tr* to ring; ring for; sound ‖ *intr* to ring; strike; sound
sonnerie [sɔnri] *f* chimes, chiming; set of bells, carillon; fanfare; ring (*of a telephone, doorbell, etc.*); alarm or striking mechanism (*of clock*)
sonnet [sɔnɛ] *m* sonnet
sonnette [sɔnɛt] *f* doorbell; pile driver
sonneur [sɔnœr] *m* bellringer; trumpeter
sonore [sɔnɔr] *adj* sonorous; sound (*wave, track*); echoing (*hall, cathedral, etc.*); (phonet) voiced ‖ *f* voiced consonant
sonorisation [sɔnɔrizasjɔ̃] *f* public-address system; (mov) sound track
sonoriser [sɔnɔrize] *tr* to record sound effects on (*a film*); equip (*an auditorium*) with loudspeakers
sonorité [sɔnɔrite] *f* sonority, resonance
sonotone [sɔnɔtɔn] *m* hearing aid
sont [sɔ̃] *v* see **être**
sophistication [sɔfistikasjɔ̃] *f* adulteration
sophisti·qué -quée [sɔfistike] *adj* adulterated; artificial, counterfeit; (comp) sophisticated
sophistiquer [sɔfistike] *tr* to adulterate; subtilize
Sophocle [sɔfɔkl] *m* Sophocles
sopraniste [sɔpranist] *m* male soprano
sopra·no [sɔprano] *mf* (*pl* **-ni** [ni] or **-nos**) soprano ‖ *m* soprano (*voice*)
sorbet [sɔrbɛ] *m* sherbet
sorbetière [sɔrbətjɛr] *f* ice-cream freezer
sorbon·nard [sɔrbɔnar] **-narde** [nard] *mf* (coll) Sorbonne student; (coll) Sorbonne professor
sorcellerie [sɔrsɛlri] *f* sorcery
sor·cier [sɔrsje] **-cière** [sjɛr] *adj* sorcerer's; **cela n'est pas sorcier** there's no trick to that ‖ *m* sorcerer, wizard ‖ *f* sorceress, witch; **vieille sorcière** old hag
sordide [sɔrdid] *adj* sordid
sornette [sɔrnɛt] *f* nonsense
sors [sɔr] *v* (**sort**) see **sortir**
sort [sɔr] *m* fate, destiny; fortune, lot; spell, charm
sortable [sɔrtabl] *adj* suitable, acceptable; presentable
sor·tant [sɔrtɑ̃] **-tante** [tɑ̃t] *adj* retiring (*congressman*); winning (*number*) ‖ *mf* person leaving

sorte [sɔrt] *f* sort, kind; state, condition; way, manner; **de la sorte** this way, thus; **de sorte que** so that, with the result that; **en quelque sorte** in a certain way; **en sorte que** in such a way that

sortie [sɔrti] *f* exit, way out; outing, jaunt; quitting time; outburst, tirade; (mil) sortie; **faire une sortie à** (slang) to bawl out; **sortie de bain** bathrobe; **sortie de bal** evening wrap; **sortie de secours** emergency exit; **sortie de voiture(s)** driveway

sortilège [sɔrtilɛʒ] *m* spell, charm

sortir [sɔrtir] §64 *tr* to take out, bring out; publish ‖ *intr* (*aux:* ÊTRE) to go out, come out; come forth; stand out; **au sortir de** on coming out of; **sortir de** + *inf* (coll) to have just + *pp*

S.O.S. [ɛsoɛs] *m* (letterword) S.O.S.

sosie [sozi] *m* double

sot [so] **sotte** [sɔt] (precedes the noun it modifies) *adj* stupid, silly ‖ *mf* fool, simpleton

sottise [sɔtiz] *f* stupidity, silliness, foolishness

sou [su] *m* sou; (fig) penny, farthing; **sans le sou** penniless; **sou à sou** or **sou par sou** a penny at a time

soubassement [subɑsmɑ̃] *m* subfoundation, infrastructure

soubresaut [subrəso] *m* sudden start, jerk; palpitation, jump (*of the heart*)

soubrette [subrɛt] *f* (theat) soubrette; (coll) attractive chambermaid

souche [suʃ] *f* stump; stock; stack (*of fireplace*); strain (*of virus*); (coll) dolt; **de pure souche** full-blooded

souci [susi] *m* care; marigold; **sans souci** carefree

soucier [susje] §97 *ref* to care, concern oneself

soucieusement [susjøzmɑ̃] *adv* uneasily, anxiously; with concern

sou·cieux [susjø] **-cieuse** [sjøz] *adj* solicitous, concerned; uneasy, anxious

soucoupe [sukup] *f* saucer; **soucoupe volante** flying saucer

soudage [sudaʒ] *m* soldering; welding

sou·dain [sudɛ̃] **-daine** [dɛn] *adj* sudden ‖ **soudain** *adv* suddenly

soudainement [sudɛnmɑ̃] *adv* suddenly

soudaineté [sudɛnte] *f* suddenness

souda·nais [sudanɛ] **-naise** [nɛz] *adj* Sudanic ‖ *m* Sudanic (*language*) ‖ (*cap*) *mf* Sudanese (*person*)

soude [sud] *f* (chem) soda

souder [sude] *tr* to solder; weld ‖ *ref* to knit (*as bones do*)

soudeur [sudœr] *m* welder

soudoyer [sudwaje] §47 *tr* to bribe; hire (*assassins*)

soudure [sudyr] *f* solder; soldering; soldered joint; knitting (*of bones*); **faire la soudure** to bridge the gap; **soudure autogène** welding

soue [su] *f* pigsty

soufflage [suflaʒ] *m* blowing; glass blowing

souf·fert [sufɛr] **-ferte** [fɛrt] *v* see **souffrir**

souffle [sufl] *m* breath; breathing; **second souffle** second wind

souf·flé **-flée** [sufle] *adj* puffed up ‖ *m* soufflé

souffler [sufle] *tr* to blow; blow out (*a candle*); blow up (*a balloon*); prompt (*an actor*); huff (*a checker*); suggest (*an idea*); **ne pas souffler mot** to not breathe a word; **souffler à l'oreille** to whisper; **souffler q.ch. à qn** to take s.th. from s.o. ‖ *intr* to blow; pant, puff; take a breather, catch one's breath

soufflerie [sufləri] *f* bellows; wind tunnel

soufflet [suflɛ] *m* slap in the face; affront, insult; bellows; gore (*of dress*); (rr) flexible cover (*between two cars*)

souffleter [suflətə] §34 *tr* to slap in the face; affront

souf·fleur [suflœr] **-fleuse** [fløz] *mf* (theat) prompter ‖ *m* glass blower ‖ *f* (mach) blower

soufflure [suflyr] *f* blister, bubble

souffrance [sufrɑ̃s] *f* suffering; **en souffrance** unfinished (*business*); outstanding (*bill*); unclaimed (*parcel*); at a standstill, suspended

souf·frant [sufrɑ̃] **-frante** [frɑ̃t] *adj* suffering; sick, ailing

souffre-douleur [sufrədulœr] *m invar* butt (*of a joke*), laughingstock

souffre·teux [sufrətø] **-teuse** [tøz] *adj* sickly; destitute, half-starved

souffrir [sufrir] §65, §96, §97 *tr* to suffer; stand, bear, tolerate; permit ‖ *intr* to suffer ‖ *ref* to put up with each other

soufre [sufr] *m* sulfur

soufrer [sufre] *tr* to sulfurate

souhait [swɛ] *m* wish; **à souhait** to one's liking, to perfection; **à vos souhaits!** (salutation) gesundheit!; **souhaits** good wishes; **souhaits de bonne année** New Year's greetings

souhaitable [swɛtabl] *adj* desirable

souhaiter [swɛte] §95, §97 *tr* to wish; wish for; wish to; **je vous la souhaite bonne et heureuse** I wish you a happy New Year

souille [suj] *f* wallow

souiller [suje] *tr* to dirty, spot, stain, soil, sully

souillon [sujɔ̃] *f* (coll) scullery maid

souillure [sujyr] *f* spot, stain

soûl [su] **soûle** [sul] *adj* drunk; sottish ‖ *m* fill, e.g., **manger son soûl** to eat one's fill

soulagement [sulaʒmɑ̃] *m* relief; comfort

soulager [sulaʒe] §38 *tr* to relieve; comfort

soûler [sule] *tr* (slang) to cram down one's throat; (slang) to get (*s.o.*) drunk ‖ *ref* (fig) to have one's fill; (slang) to get drunk

soulèvement [sulɛvmɑ̃] *m* upheaval; uprising; surge; **soulèvement de cœur** nausea

soulever [sulve] §2 *tr* to raise, heave, lift (up); stir up ‖ *ref* to rise; raise oneself; revolt

soulier [sulje] *m* shoe; **être dans ses petits souliers** (coll) to feel awkward; **souliers à**

talons hauts high-heeled shoes; **souliers bas** low-heeled shoes; **souliers compensés** elevator shoes; **souliers de marche** walking shoes; **souliers montants** boots; **souliers richelieu** oxfords

soulignement [suliɲəmɑ̃] *m* underlining

souligner [suliɲe] *tr* to underline; emphasize

soulte [sult] *f* balance due

soumettre [sumɛtr] §42 *tr* to submit; subject; overcome, subdue ‖ *ref* to submit, surrender

sou·mis [sumi] **-mise** [miz] *adj* submissive, subservient; subject; amenable (*to a law*)

soumission [sumisjɔ̃] *f* submission, surrender; bid (*to perform a service*); guarantee

soumissionnaire [sumisjɔnɛr] *mf* bidder

soupape [supap] *f* valve; **soupape à réglage** or **à papillon** damper; **soupape de sûreté** safety valve; **soupape électrique** rectifier

soupçon [supsɔ̃] *m* suspicion; misgiving; dash, touch (*small amount*)

soupçonner [supsɔne] §97 *tr & intr* to suspect

soupçon·neux [supsɔnø] **-neuse** [nøz] *adj* suspicious

soupe [sup] *f* vegetable soup; sop (*bread*); (mil) mess; **de soupe** on K.P.; **soupe au lait** (coll) mean-tempered person; **soupe populaire** soup kitchen; **trempé comme une soupe** soaking wet

soupente [supɑ̃t] *f* attic

souper [supe] *m* supper ‖ *intr* to have supper

soupeser [supəze] §2 *tr* to heft, weigh (*e.g., a package*) in one's hand

soupière [supjɛr] *f* soup tureen

soupir [supir] *m* sigh; breath; (mus) quarter rest

soupi·rail [supiraj] *m* (*pl* **-raux** [ro]) cellar window

soupirant [supirɑ̃] *m* suitor

soupirer [supire] *intr* to sigh; **soupirer après** or **pour** to long for

souple [supl] *adj* supple; flexible, pliant; versatile, adaptable

souplesse [suplɛs] *f* suppleness, flexibility

souquer [suke] *tr* to haul taut ‖ *intr* to pull hard (*on the oars*)

source [surs] *f* source; spring, fountain; **source de pétrole** oil well; **source jaillissante** gusher

sourcier [sursje] *m* dowser

sourcil [surci] *m* eyebrow

sourciller [sursije] *intr* to knit one's brows; **sans sourciller** without batting an eye

sourcil·leux [sursijø] **-leuse** [jøz] *adj* supercilious

sourd [sur] **sourde** [surd] *adj* deaf; quiet; dull (*sound, color*); deep (*voice*); undeclared (*war*); (phonet) unvoiced; **sourd comme un pot** (coll) stone-deaf ‖ *mf* deaf person ‖ *f* unvoiced consonant

sourdement [surdəmɑ̃] *adv* secretly; heavily; dully

sourdine [surdin] *f* (mus) mute; **à la sourdine** muted; **en sourdine** on the sly

sourd-muet [surmɥɛ] **sourde-muette** [surdəmɥɛt] (*pl* **sourds-muets**) *adj* deaf and dumb, deaf-mute ‖ *mf* deaf-mute

sourdre [surdr] (used in: *inf;* 3d *sg & pl pres ind* **sourd, sourdent**) *intr* to spring, well up

souricier [surisje] *m* mouser

souricière [surisjɛr] *f* mousetrap; (fig) trap

sourire [surir] *m* smile ‖ §61, §97 *intr* to smile; **sourire à** to smile at; smile on; look good to

souris [suri] *m* (obs) smile ‖ *f* mouse

sour·nois [surnwa] **-noise** [nwaz] *adj* sly, cunning, artful

sous [su] *prep* under; on (*a certain day; certain conditions*); **sous caoutchouc** rubber-covered; **sous clef** under lock and key; **sous la main** at hand; **sous les drapeaux** in the army; **sous main** underhandedly; **sous peu** shortly; **sous un certain angle** from a certain point of view

sous-alimentation [suzalimɑ̃tasjɔ̃] *f* undernourishment

sous-bois [subwa] *m* underbrush, undergrowth

sous-chef [suʃɛf] *m* (*pl* **-chefs**) assistant (*to the head person*), deputy, second-in-command

souscripteur [suskriptœr] *m* subscriber (*to a loan or charity*); signer (*of a commercial paper*)

souscription [suskripsjɔ̃] *f* signature; subscription; **souscription de soutien** sustaining membership

souscrire [suskrir] §25 *tr & intr* to subscribe

sous-cuta·né **-née** [sukytane] *adj* subcutaneous

sous-dévelop·pé **-pée** [sudɛvlɔpe] *adj* underdeveloped

sous-diacre [sudjakr] *m* subdeacon

sous-direc·teur [sudirɛktœr] **-trice** [tris] *mf* (*pl* **-directeurs**) second-in-command

sous-entendre [suzɑ̃tɑ̃dr] *tr* to understand (*what is not expressed*); to imply

sous-entendu [suzɑ̃tɑ̃dy] *m* inference, implication, innuendo, double meaning, double entendre

sous-entente [suzɑ̃tɑ̃t] *f* mental reservation; hidden, cryptic meaning

sous-entrepreneur [suzɑ̃trəprənœr] *m* (*pl* **-entrepreneurs**) subcontractor

sous-estimer [suzɛstime] *tr* to underestimate

sous-fifre [sufifr] *m* (*pl* **-fifres**) (coll) underling

sous-garde [sugard] *f* trigger guard

sous-lieutenant [suljøtnɑ̃] *m* (*pl* **-lieutenants**) second lieutenant

sous-location [sulɔkasjɔ̃] *f* sublease

sous-louer [sulwe] *tr* to sublet, sublease

sous-main [sumɛ̃] *m invar* desk blotter; **en sous-main** underhandedly

sous-marin [sumarɛ̃] **-marine** [marin] *adj & m* (*pl* **-marins**) submarine

sous-marinier [sumarinje] *m* (*pl* **-mariniers**) submarine crewman

sous-mentonnière [sumɑ̃tɔnjər] *f* (*pl* **-mentonnières**) chin strap
sous-nappe [sunap] *f* (*pl* **-nappes**) table pad
sous-off [suzɔf] *m* (*pl* **-offs**) noncom
sous-officier [suzɔfisje] *m* (*pl* **-officiers**) noncommissioned officer
sous-ordre [suzɔrdr] *m* (*pl* **-ordres**) underling, subordinate; (biol) suborder; **en sous-ordre** subordinate; subordinately
sous-production [suprɔdyksjɔ̃] *f* underproduction
sous-produit [suprɔdɥi] *m* (*pl* **-produits**) by-product
sous-secrétaire [suskretɛr] *m* (*pl* **-secrétaires**) undersecretary
sous-secrétariat [suskretarja] *m* undersecretaryship
sous-seing [susɛ̃] *m invar* privately witnessed document
soussi·gné -gnée [sisiɲe] *adj* & *mf* undersigned
sous-sol [susɔl] *m* (*pl* **-sols**) subsoil; basement
sous-titre [sutitr] *m* (*pl* **-titres**) subtitle
sous-titrer [sutitre] *tr* to subtitle
soustraction [sustraksjɔ̃] *f* subtraction; (law) purloining
soustraire [sustrɛr] §68 *tr* to remove; take away; subtract; deduct; **soustraire de** to subtract from; **soustraire q.ch. à qn** to take s.th. away from s.o.; steal s.th. from s.o. ‖ *ref* to withdraw; **se soustraire à** to escape from
sous-traitant [sutrɛtɑ̃] *m* (*pl* **-traitants**) subcontractor; sublessee
sous-traité [sutrɛte] *m* (*pl* **-traités**) subcontract
sous-traiter [sutrɛte] *tr* & *intr* to subcontract
sous-ventrière [suvɑ̃trijɛr] *f* (*pl* **-ventrières**) girth
sous-verre [suvɛr] *m invar* passe-partout; coaster
sous-vêtement [suvɛtmɑ̃] *m* (*pl* **-vêtements**) undergarment
soutache [sutaʃ] *f* braid
soutacher [sutaʃe] *tr* to trim with braid
soutane [sutan] *f* soutane, cassock
soutanelle [sutanɛl] *f* frock coat; choir robe
soute [sut] *f* (naut) storeroom; **soute à charbon** coal bunker
soutenable [sutnabl] *adj* supportable, tenable
soutenance [sutnɑ̃s] *f* defense (*of an academic thesis*)
soutènement [sutɛnmɑ̃] *m* support
souteneur [sutnœr] *m* pimp
soutenir [sutnir] §72, §95 *tr* to support, bear; sustain; insist, claim; defend (*a thesis*) ‖ *ref* to stand up; keep afloat
soute·nu -nue [sutny] *adj* sustained; elevated (*style*); steady (*market*); true (*colors*)
souter·rain -raine [sutɛrɛ̃] -raine [rɛn] *adj* subterranean, underground; underhanded ‖ *m* tunnel, subway (*for pedestrians*)
soutien [sutjɛ̃] *m* support; stand-by

soutien-gorge [sutjɛ̃gɔrʒ] *m* (*pl* **soutiens-gorge**) brassiere
soutirage [sutiraʒ] *m* racking
soutirer [sutire] *tr* to rack (*wine*); **soutirer q.ch. à qn** to get s.th. out of s.o., sponge on s.o. for s.th.
souvenir [suvnir] *m* memory, remembrance; souvenir; **en souvenir de** in remembrance of ‖ §72 *intr*—**faire souvenir qn de q.ch.** to remind s.o. of s.th. ‖ §97 *ref* to remember; **se souvenir de** to remember
souvent [suvɑ̃] *adv* often
souve·rain -raine [rɛn] *adj* & *mf* sovereign ‖ *m* sovereign (*coin*)
souveraineté [suvrɛnte] *f* sovereignty
soviet [sɔvjɛt] *m* soviet
soviétique [sɔvjetik] *adj* Soviet ‖ (*cap*) *mf* Soviet Russian
soya [sɔja] *m* soybean
soyeux [swajø] **soyeuse** [swajøz] *adj* silky
soyez [swaje] *v* (**soyons**) see **être**
S.P. *abbr* (**sapeurs-pompiers**) fire department
spa·cieux [sapsjø] **-cieuse** [sjøz] *adj* spacious, roomy
spadassin [spadasɛ̃] *m* hatchet man, hired thug
spaghetti [spageti] *mpl* spaghetti
sparadrap [sparadra] *m* adhesive tape
spartiate [sparsjat] *adj* Spartan ‖ (*cap*) *mf* Spartan
spasme [spasm] *m* spasm
spasmodique [spasmɔdik] *adj* spasmodic; (pathol) spastic
spath [spat] *m* (mineral) spar
spa·tial -tiale [spasjal] *adj* (*pl* **-tiaux** [sjo]) spatial
spatiocarte [spasjɔkart] *f* maps drawn from satellite pictures
spationef [spasjɔnef] *m* space vehicle
spatule [spatyl] *f* spatula; (orn) spoon-bill
spea·ker [spikœr] **-kerine** [krin] *mf* (rad, telv) announcer ‖ *m* speaker (*presiding officer*)
spé·cial -ciale [spesjal] *adj* (*pl* **-ciaux** [sjo]) special, especial, particular; specialized; peculiar, odd
spécialiser [spesjalize] *tr* & *ref* to specialize
spécialiste [spesjalist] *mf* specialist; expert
spécialité [spesjalite] *f* specialty; specialization; patent medicine
spécialement [spesjalmɑ̃] *adv* specially, especially, particularly
spé·cieux [spesjø] **-cieuse** [sjøz] *adj* specious
spécifier [spesifje] *tr* to specify
spécifique [spesifik] *adj* & *m* specific
spécimen [spesimɛn] *m* specimen; sample copy
spectacle [spɛktakl] *m* spectacle, sight; show; play; **à grand spectacle** spectacular (*production*); **spectacle solo** one-man show
specta·teur [spɛktatœr] **-trice** [tris] *mf* spectator
spectre [spɛktr] *m* ghost; spectrum; (fig) specter

spécula·teur [spekylatœr] **-trice** [tris] *mf* speculator
spéculer [spekyle] *tr* to speculate
spéléologie [speleɔlɔʒi] *f* speleology
sperme [spɛrm] *m* sperm
sphère [sfɛr] *f* sphere
sphérique [sferik] *adj* spherical
sphinx [sfɛ̃ks] *m* sphinx
spider [spider] *m* (aut) rumble seat
spi·nal -nale [spinal] *adj* (*pl* **-naux** [no]) spinal
spi·ral -rale [spiral] (*pl* **-raux** [ro]) *adj* spiral ‖ *m* hairspring (*of watch*) ‖ *f* spiral; **en spirale** spiral
spire [spir] *f* turn (*in a wire*); whorl (*of a shell*)
spirée [spire] *f* (bot) spirea
spirite [spirit] *adj* & *mf* spiritualist
spiri·tuel -tuelle [spirityɛl] *adj* spiritual; sacred (*music*); witty ‖ *m* ecclesiastical power
spiri·tueux [spirityø] **-tueuse** [tyøz] *adj* spirituous ‖ *m* spirituous liquor
spleen [splin] *m* boredom, melancholy
splendeur [splɑ̃dœr] *f* splendor
splendide [splɑ̃did] *adj* splendid; bright, brilliant
spolia·teur [spɔljatœr] **-trice** [tris] *adj* despoiling ‖ *mf* despoiler
spolier [spɔlje] *tr* to despoil
spon·gieux [spɔ̃ʒjø] **-gieuse** [ʒjøz] *adj* spongy
sponta·né -née [spɔ̃tane] *adj* spontaneous
sporadique [spɔradik] *adj* sporadic(al)
sport [spɔr] *adj invar* sport, sporting; sportsmanlike ‖ *m* sport
spor·tif -tive [spɔrtif] [tiv] *adj* sport, sporting ‖ *mf* athlete, player ‖ *m* sportsman
spot [spɔt] *m* spotlight; (radar) blip
spoutnik [sputnik] *m* sputnik
spu·meux [spymø] **-meuse** [møz] *adj* frothy, foamy
squale [skwal] *m* (ichth) dogfish
squelette [skəlɛt] *m* skeleton
squelettique [skəletik] *adj* skeletal
S.R. *abbr* (**service de renseignements**) information desk or bureau
stabiliser [stabilize] *tr* to stabilize
stabilité [stabilite] *f* stability
stable [stabl] *adj* stable
stade [stad] *m* stadium; (fig) stage (*of development*)
stage [staʒ] *m* probationary period, apprenticeship; training period
stagiaire [staʒjɛr] *adj* apprentice ‖ *mf* trainee, apprentice; student teacher
stag·nant -nante [stagnɑ̃] [nɑ̃t] *adj* stagnant
stalle [stal] *f* stall; parking spot
stance [stɑ̃s] *f* stanza
stand [stɑ̃d] *m* stands; shooting gallery; pit (*for motor racing*)
standard [stɑ̃dar] *adj invar* standard ‖ *m* standard; switchboard
standardiser [stɑ̃dardize] *tr* to standardize
standardiste [stɑ̃dardist] *mf* switchboard operator, telephone operator

standing [stɑ̃diŋ] *m* status, standing; standard of living; **de grand standing** luxury (*apartments*)
star [star] *f* (mov, theat) star
starter [starter], [startœr] *m* (aut) choke; (sports) starter
station [stasjɔ̃] *f* station; resort; (rr) flag station; **station balnéaire** beach resort; **station d'autobus** bus stop; **station d'écoute** monitoring station; **station d'émission** broadcasting station; **station de repérage** tracking station; **station de taxis** taxi stand; **station libre-service** self-service station; **station orbitale** space station; **stations de la Croix** (rel) Stations of the Cross
stationnaire [stasjɔnɛr] *adj* stationary ‖ *m* gunboat
stationnement [stasjɔnmɑ̃] *m* parking; **stationnement interdit** (*public sign*) no parking
stationner [stasjɔne] *intr* to stop; park
station-service [stasjɔ̃sɛrvis] *f* (*pl* **stations-service**) service station
statique [statik] *adj* static
statisti·cien [statistisjɛ̃] **-cienne** [sjɛn] *mf* statistician
statistique [statistik] *adj* statistical ‖ *f* statistics
statuaire [statyɛr] *adj* statuary ‖ *mf* sculptor ‖ *f* statuary
statue [staty] *f* statue
statuer [statye] *tr* to hand down (*a ruling*) ‖ *intr* to hand down a ruling
statu quo [statykwo], [statuko] *m* status quo
stature [statyr] *f* stature
statut [staty] *m* statute; legal status; **le statut de** the status of
statutaire [statytɛr] *adj* statutory
Ste *abbr* (**Sainte**) St. (*female saint*)
Sté *abbr* (**Société**) Inc.
sténo [steno] *f* stenographer; stenography
sténodactylo [stenɔdaktilo] *f* shorthand typist; shorthand typing
sténogramme [stenɔgram] *m* shorthand notes
sténographe [stenɔgraf] *mf* stenographer
sténographie [stenɔgrafi] *f* stenography
sténographier [stenɔgrafje] *tr* to take down in shorthand
stéréo [stereo] *adj invar* stereo ‖ *f*—**en stéréo** (electron) in stereo
stéréophonie [stereɔfɔni] *f* stereophonic sound system; **en stéréophonie** stereophonic (*e.g.*, *broadcast*)
stéréoscopique [stereɔskɔpik] *adj* stereo, stereoscopic
stéréoty·pé -pée [stereɔtipe] *adj* stereotyped
stérile [steril] *adj* sterile
stériliser [sterilize] *tr* to sterilize
stérilité [sterilite] *f* sterility
sterling [stɛrliŋ] *adj invar* sterling
stéthoscope [stetɔskɔp] *m* stethoscope
stick [stik] *m* walking stick
stigmate [stigmat] *m* stigma
stigmatiser [stigmatize] *tr* to stigmatize

stimu·lant [stimylɑ̃] **-lante** [lɑ̃t] *adj* & *m* stimulant
stimulateur [stimylatœr] *m* pacemaker
stimuler [stimyle] *tr* to stimulate
stimu·lus [stimylys] *m* (*pl* **-li** [li]) (physiol) stimulus
stipendier [stipɑ̃dje] *tr* to hire (*e.g.*, *an assassin*); bribe
stipuler [stipyle] *tr* to stipulate
stock [stɔk] *m* goods, stock; hoard
stocker [stɔke] *tr* & *intr* to stockpile
stockiste [stɔkist] *m* authorized dealer (*carrying parts, motors, etc.*)
stoï·cien [stɔisjɛ̃] **-cienne** [sjɛn] *adj* & *mf* Stoic
stoïque [stɔik] *adj* stoical ‖ *mf* stoic
stop [stɔp] *m* stop; stoplight; **du stop** (coll) hitchhiking ‖ *interj* stop!
stoppage [stɔpaʒ] *m* reweaving, invisible mending
stopper [stɔpe] *tr* to reweave; stop ‖ *intr* to stop
store [stɔr] *m* blind; window awning; outside window shade
strabique [strabik] *adj* squint-eyed
strabisme [strabism] *m* squint
strapontin [strapɔ̃tɛ̃] *m* jump seat; (theat) attached folding seat
strass [stras] *m* paste (*jewelry*)
stratagème [strataʒɛm] *m* stratagem
strate [strat] *f* (geol) stratum
stratège [stratɛʒ] *m* strategist
stratégie [strateʒi] *f* strategy
stratégique [strateʒik] *adj* strategic(al)
stratégiste [strateʒist] *m* strategist
stratifier [stratifje] *tr* & *ref* to stratify
stratosphère [stratɔsfɛr] *f* stratosphere
strict stricte [strikt] *adj* strict
stri·dent [stridɑ̃] **-dente** [dɑ̃t] *adj* strident
strie [stri] *f* streak; stripe
strier [strije] *tr* to streak; score, groove
strip-teaseuse [striptisøz] *f* (*pl* **-teaseuses**) stripteaser
strontium [strɔ̃sjɔm] *m* strontium
strophe [strɔf] *f* verse, stanza; strophe
structu·ral -rale [stryktyral] *adj* (*pl* **-raux** [ro]) structural
structure [stryktyr] *f* structure
strychnine [striknin] *f* strychnine
stuc [styk] *m* stucco; **enduire de stuc** to stucco
stu·dieux [stydjø] **-dieuse** [djøz] *adj* studious
studio [stydjo] *m* studio
stupé·fait [stypefɛ] **-faite** [fɛt] *adj* dumfounded, amazed
stupé·fiant [stypefjɑ̃] **-fiante** [fjɑ̃t] *adj* astounding ‖ *m* drug, narcotic
stupéfier [stypefje] *tr* to astound; stupefy (*as with a drug*)
stupeur [stypœr] *f* stupor; amazement
stupide [stypid] *adj* stupid
stupidité [stypidite] *f* stupidity
stuquer [styke] *tr* to stucco
style [stil] *m* style; stylus
styler [stile] *tr* to train
stylet [stilɛ] *m* stiletto

styliser [stilize] *tr* to stylize
stylo [stilo] *m* pen, fountain pen; **stylo à bille** ball-point pen; **stylo à réservoir** fountain pen
stylo-bille [stilobij] *m* (*pl* **stylos-billes**) ball-point pen
stylo-feutre [stiloføtr] *m* (*pl* **stylos-feutres**) felt-tip pen
styptique [stiptik] *adj* & *m* styptic
suaire [sɥɛr] *m* shroud, winding sheet
suave [sɥav] *adj* sweet (*perfume, music, etc.*); bland (*food*); suave
subcons·cient [sypkɔ̃sjɑ̃] **-ciente** [sjɑ̃t] *adj* & *m* subconscious
subdiviser [sybdivize] *tr* to subdivide
subir [sybir] *tr* to submit to; undergo; feel, experience; take (*an exam*); serve (*a sentence*)
su·bit [sybi] **-bite** [bit] *adj* sudden
subjec·tif [sybʒɛktif] **-tive** [tiv] *adj* subjective
subjonc·tif [sybʒɔ̃ktif] **-tive** [tiv] *adj* & *m* subjunctive
subjuguer [sybʒyge] *tr* to dominate; spellbind
sublime [syblim] *adj* sublime
sublimer [syblime] *tr* to sublimate
submerger [sybmɛrʒe] §38 *tr* to submerge
submersible [sybmɛrsibl] *adj* & *m* submersible
submersion [sybmɛrsjɔ̃] *f* submersion
subodorer [sybɔdɔre] *tr* to scent (*game*); (fig) to scent (*a plot*)
subordon·né -née [sybɔrdɔne] *adj* & *mf* subordinate
subordonner [sybɔrdɔne] *tr* to subordinate
suborner [sybɔrne] *tr* to bribe
subrécargue [sybrekarg] *m* supercargo
subreptice [sybrɛptis] *adj* surreptitious
subsé·quent [sypsekɑ̃] **-quente** [kɑ̃t] *adj* subsequent
subside [sypsid], [sybzid] *m* subsidy
subsidiaire [sypsidjɛr] *adj* subsidiary
subsistance [sybzistɑ̃s], [sypsistɑ̃s] *f* subsistence; (mil) rations
subsister [sybziste], [sypsiste] *intr* to subsist
substance [sypstɑ̃s] *f* substance; **en substance** briefly
substan·tiel -tielle [sypstɑ̃sjɛl] *adj* substantial
substan·tif [sypstɑ̃tif] **-tive** [tiv] *adj* & *m* substantive
substituer [sypstitɥe] *tr*—**substituer qn or q.ch. à** to substitute s.o. or s.th. for, e.g., **une biche fut substituée à Iphigénie** a hind was substituted for Iphigenia ‖ *ref*—**se substituer à** to take the place of
substitut [sypstity] *m* substitute
substitution [sypstitysjɔ̃] *f* substitution
substrat [sypstra] *m* substratum
subterfuge [sypterfyʒ] *m* subterfuge
sub·til -tile [syptil] *adj* subtle; fine (*powder, dust, etc.*); quick (*poison*); delicate (*scent*); clever (*crook*)
subtiliser [syptilize] *tr* to pick (*a purse*) ‖ *intr* to split hairs

subtilité [syptilite] *f* subtlety

subur·bain [sybyrbɛ̃] **-baine** [bɛn] *adj* suburban

subvenir [sybvənir] §72 *intr* to supply, provide, satisfy

subvention [sybvɑ̃sjɔ̃] *f* subsidy, subvention

subventionner [sybvɑ̃sjɔne] *tr* to subsidize

subver·sif [sybvɛrsif] **-sive** [siv] *adj* subversive

subvertir [sybvɛrtir] *tr* to subvert

suc [syk] *m* juice; sap; (fig) essence

succéda·né -née [syksedane] *adj* & *m* substitute

succéder [syksede] §10 *intr* to happen; **succéder à** to succeed, follow, e.g., **son fils lui succédera** his son will succeed him ‖ *ref* (*pp* **succédé** *invar*) to follow one another, follow one after the other

succès [syksɛ] *m* success; outcome; **avoir du succès** to be a success

succes·sif [syksɛsif] **-sive** [siv] *adj* successive

succession [syksɛsjɔ̃] *f* succession; inheritance; heirs

suc·cinct [syksɛ̃] **-cincte** [sɛ̃t] *adj* succinct; scanty; meager

succion [syksjɔ̃] *f* suction

succomber [sykɔ̃be] *intr* to succumb

succursale [sykyrsal] *f* branch

sucer [syse] §51 *tr* to suck

sucette [sysɛt] *f* pacifier; lollipop, sucker

su·ceur [sysœr] **-ceuse** [søz] *adj* sucking ‖ *m* nozzle

suçon [sysɔ̃] *m* (coll) hickie

suçoter [sysɔte] *tr* to suck away at

sucre [sykr] *m* sugar; **sucre brut** brown sugar; **sucre candi** rock candy; **sucre de canne** cane sugar; **sucre d'érable** maple sugar; **sucre en morceaux** cube sugar, lump sugar; **sucre glace** confectioners' sugar; **sucre semoule** granulated sugar

su·cré -crée [sykre] *adj* sugary; with sugar, e.g., **du café sucré** coffee with sugar ‖ *f*—**faire la sucrée** to be mealy-mouthed

sucrer [sykre] *tr* to sugar; (slang) to take away, cut out ‖ *ref* (slang) to grab the lion's share

sucrerie [sykrəri] *f* sugar refinery; **sucreries** candy

su·crier [sykrije] **-crière** [krijɛr] *adj* sugar ‖ *m* sugar bowl

sud [syd] *adj invar* south, southern ‖ *m* south; **du sud** southern; **faire le sud** to steer southward; **vers le sud** southward

sud-améri·cain [sydamerikɛ̃] **-caine** [kɛn] *adj* South American ‖ (*cap*) *mf* (*pl* **Sud-Américains**) South American

sudation [sydɑsjɔ̃] *f* sweating

sud-est [sydɛst] *adj invar* & *m* southeast

sudiste [sydist] *mf* Southerner (*in U.S.A.*)

sud-ouest [sydwɛst] *adj invar* & *m* southwest

suède [sɥɛd] *m* suede ‖ (*cap*) *f* Sweden; **la Suède** Sweden

sué·dois [sɥedwa] **-doise** [dwaz] *adj* Swedish ‖ *m* Swedish (*language*) ‖ (*cap*) *mf* Swede

suée [sɥe] *f* sweating

suer [sɥe] *tr* & *intr* to sweat

sueur [sɥœr] *f* sweat

suffire [syfir] §66, §96 *intr* to suffice; **il suffit de** + *inf* it suffices to + *inf;* **suffire à** to be sufficient for, be adequate to, meet, satisfy, e.g., **suffire à mes besoins** to meet my needs; **suffire à** + *inf* to suffice to + *inf;* **suffit!** enough! ‖ *ref* (*pp* **suffi** *invar*) to be self-sufficient

suffisamment [syfizamɑ̃] *adv* sufficiently, adequately

suffisance [syfizɑ̃s] *f* sufficiency; self-sufficiency, smugness

suffi·sant [syfizɑ̃] **-sante** [zɑ̃t] *adj* sufficient; smug, sophomoric; impudent ‖ *mf* prig

suffixe [syfiks] *m* suffix

suffo·cant [syfɔkɑ̃] **-cante** [kɑ̃t] *adj* suffocating, stifling; astonishing, stunning

suffoquer [syfɔke] *tr* & *intr* to suffocate, choke, stifle, smother

suffrage [syfraʒ] *m* suffrage, vote; public approval; **au suffrage universel** by popular vote; **suffrage capacitaire** suffrage contingent upon literacy tests; **suffrage censitaire** suffrage upon payment of taxes

suggérer [sygʒere] §10, §97, §98 *tr* to suggest

sugges·tif [sygʒɛstif] **-tive** [tiv] *adj* suggestive

suggestion [sygʒɛstjɔ̃] *f* suggestion

suggestionner [sygʒɛstjɔne] *tr* to influence by means of suggestion

suicide [sɥisid] *adj* suicidal ‖ *m* suicide (*act*)

suici·dé -dée [sɥiside] *adj* dead by suicide ‖ *mf* suicide (*person*)

suicider [sɥiside] *ref* to commit suicide

suie [sɥi] *f* soot

suif [sɥif] *m* tallow

suint [sɥɛ̃] *m* wool fat, wool grease

suinter [sɥɛ̃te] *intr* to seep, ooze; sweat (*said of wall*); run (*said of wound*)

suis [sɥi] *v* see **être**; see **suivre**

suisse [sɥis] *adj* Swiss; **faire suisse** to eat or drink by oneself; to go Dutch ‖ *m* Swiss guard; uniformed usher; **petit suisse** cream cheese ‖ (*cap*) *f* Switzerland; **la Suisse** Switzerland ‖ **Suisse Suissesse** [sɥisɛs] *mf* Swiss (*person*)

suite [sɥit] *f* suite; consequence; continuation, sequel (*of literary work*); sequence, series; **à la suite de** after; **de suite** in succession; in a row; **par la suite** later on; **par suite** consequently; **par suite de** because of

sui·vant [sɥivɑ̃] **-vante** [vɑ̃t] *adj* next, following, succeeding ‖ *mf* follower; next (person) ‖ *f* servant, confidante ‖ **suivant** *adv*—**suivant que** according as ‖ **suivant** *prep* according to

sui·veur [sɥivœr] **-veuse** [vøz] *adj* follow-up (*e.g., car*) ‖ *mf* follower

sui·vi -vie [sɥivi] *adj* connected, coherent; popular

suivre [sɥivr] §67 *tr* to follow; take (*a course in school*); **suivre la mode** (fig) to follow suit ‖ *intr* to follow; **à suivre** to be continued ‖ *ref* to follow in succession; follow one after the other

su·jet [syʒɛ] **-jette** [ʒɛt] *adj* subject; apt, liable; inclined ‖ *mf* subject (*of a government*); **mauvais sujet** ne'er-do-well ‖ *m* subject, topic; (*gram*) subject; **au sujet de** about, concerning

sujétion [syʒesjɔ̃] *f* subjection

sulfamide [sylfamid] *m* sulfa drug

sulfate [sylfat] *m* sulphate

sulfure [sylfyr] *m* sulfide

sulfurique [sylfyrik] *adj* sulfuric

sultan [syltɑ̃] *m* sultan

sumac [symak] *m* sumac; **sumac vénéneux** poison ivy

sunlight [sœnlaɪt] *m invar* (mov, telv) projector

super [sypɛr] *m* (coll) high-test gas

superbe [sypɛrb] *adj* superb; proud ‖ *m* proud person ‖ *f* pride

supercarburant [sypɛrkarbyrɑ̃] *m* high-test gasoline

supercherie [sypɛrʃəri] *f* hoax, swindle

superdécrochage [sypɛrdekrɔʃaʒ] *m* (aer) deep stall

superfétatoire [sypɛrfetatwar] *adj* redundant

superficie [sypɛrfisi] *f* surface, area

superfi·ciel -cielle [sypɛrfisjɛl] *adj* superficial

super·flu -flue [sypɛrfly] *adj* superfluous ‖ *m* superfluity, excess

supé·rieur -rieure [syperjœr] *adj* superior; higher; upper (*e.g., story*); **supérieur à** above; more than ‖ *mf* superior

supérieurement [syperjœrmɑ̃] *adv* superlatively, exceptionally

supériorité [syperjɔrite] *f* superiority

superla·tif [sypɛrlatif] **-tive** [tiv] *adj & m* superlative; **au superlatif** superlatively; in the superlative

supermarché [sypɛrmarʃe] *m* supermarket

superposer [sypɛrpoze] *tr* to superimpose ‖ *ref* to intervene

supersonique [sypɛrsɔnik] *adj* supersonic

supersti·tieux [sypɛrstisjø] **-tieuse** [sjøz] *adj* superstitious

superstition [sypɛrstisjɔ̃] *f* superstition

superstrat [sypɛrstra] *m* superstratum

superviser [sypɛrvize] *tr* to inspect; revise; correct; supervise

supplanter [syplɑ̃te] *tr* to supplant

suppléance [sypleɑ̃s] *f* substituting; temporary post

sup·pléant [sypleɑ̃] **-pléante** [pleɑ̃t] *adj* substituting ‖ *mf* substitute (*e.g., a teacher, judge*)

suppléer [syplee] *tr* to supply; take the place of; make up for (*what is lacking*); fill in (*the gaps*); substitute for (*s.o.*); fill (*a vacancy*) ‖ *intr*—**suppléer à** to make up for (*s.th.*)

supplément [syplemɑ̃] *m* supplement; extra charge

supplémentaire [syplemɑ̃tɛr] *adj* supplementary, additional, extra; supplemental

supplé·tif [sypletif] **-tive** [tiv] *adj & m* (mil) auxiliary

sup·pliant [syplijɑ̃] **-pliante** [plijɑ̃t] *adj & mf* suppliant, supplicant

supplice [syplis] *m* torture; punishment; **être au supplice** to be in agony

supplicier [syplisje] *tr* to torture to death; torment

supplier [syplije] §97, §99 *tr* to beseech, implore, supplicate; **je vous en supplie** I beg you; **supplier qn de** to implore s.o. to

supplique [syplik] *f* petition

support [sypɔr] *m* support, prop, pillar, bracket, strut; standard (*e.g., for a lamp*)

support-chaussette [sypɔrʃosɛt] *m* (*pl* **supports-chaussette**) garter (*for men*)

supporter [sypɔrtœr], [sypɔrtɛr] *m* fan, devotee, supporter, partisan ‖ [sypɔrte] *tr* to support, prop up; bear, endure; stand, tolerate, put up with ‖ *intr*—**supporter de** + *inf* to tolerate or stand for + *ger* ‖ *ref* to be tolerated; put up with each other

suppo·sé -sée [sypoze] *adj* supposed, admitted; spurious, assumed ‖ **supposé** *prep* supposing, admitting, granting

supposer [sypoze] §95 *tr* to suppose; imply; **à supposer que . . .** suppose that . . . ; **supposer un testament** to palm off a forged will

supposition [sypozisjɔ̃] *f* supposition; forgery, fraudulent substitution or alteration; **supposition de part** or **supposition d'enfant** false claim of maternity and maternal rights

suppositoire [sypozitwar] *m* suppository

suppôt [sypo] *m* henchman, tool, agitator, hireling; **suppôt de Bacchus** drunkard; **suppôt du diable** imp

suppression [sypresjɔ̃] *f* suppression; elimination (*of a job*); discontinuance (*of a festival*); killing (*of a person*); **suppression de part** or **suppression d'enfant** concealment of a child's birth or death

supprimer [syprime] *tr* to suppress, cancel, abolish; cut out, omit; (slang) to eliminate, liquidate ‖ *ref* to kill oneself

suppurer [sypyre] *intr* to suppurate

supputation [sypytasjɔ̃] *f* calculation, evaluation, reckoning

supputer [sypyte] *tr* to calculate (*e.g., forthcoming profits, expenses*)

suprématie [sypremasi] *f* supremacy

suprême [syprɛm] *adj* supreme; last

sur sure [syr] *adj* sour ‖ **sur** *prep* on, over; about, concerning; with (*on the person of*); out of, in, e.g., **un jour sur quatre** one day out of four, one day in four; after, e.g., **page sur page** page after page; **sur ce, sur quoi** whereupon; **sur le fait** in the act

sûr sûre [syr] §93 *adj* sure; trustworthy; safe; certain; **à coup sûr, pour sûr** for sure, without fail

surabon·dant [syrabɔ̃dɑ̃] **-dante** [dɑ̃t] *adj* superabundant

surabonder [syrabɔ̃de] *intr* to superabound; **surabonder de** or **en** to be glutted with

surajouter [syraʒute] *tr* to add on

suralimentation [syralimɑ̃tasjɔ̃] *f* forced feeding; (aut) supercharging

suran·né -née [syrane] *adj* outmoded, out-of-date, superannuated; expired (*driver's license, passport, etc.*)

surboum [syrbum] *f* (slang) dance, hop

surcharge [syrʃarʒ] *f* surcharge; overwriting; (sports) handicap (*of weight on a horse*); (comp) overload(ing)

surcharger [syrʃarʒe] §38 *tr* to surcharge; write a word over (*another word*); write a word over a crossed-out word on (*a document*)

surchauffe [syrʃof] *f* superheating; overheating (*of the economy*)

surchauffer [syrʃofe] *tr* to superheat (*steam; an oven*); overheat (*an oven, iron, etc.*)

surchoix [syrʃwa] *m* finest quality

surclasser [syrklase] *tr* to outclass

surcompo·sé -sée [syrkɔ̃poze] *adj* (gram) double-compound

surcompression [syrkɔ̃presjɔ̃] *f* pressurization, high compression

surcompri·mé -mée [syrkɔ̃prime] *adj* high-compression (*engine*)

surcomprimer [syrkɔ̃prime] *tr* to supercharge; pressurize

surcontrer [syrkɔ̃tre] *tr* (cards) to redouble

surcouper [syrkupe] *tr* (cards) to overtrump

surcroît [syrkrwa], [syrkrwa] *m* addition, increase; **de surcroît** or **par sucroît** in addition, extra

surdi-mutité [syrdimцtite] *f* deaf-muteness

surdité [syrdite] *f* deafness

surdosage [syrdɔsaʒ] *m* overdose

su·reau [syro] *m* (*pl* **-reaux**) elderberry

surélévation [syrelevasjɔ̃] *f* escalation, excessive increase; extra story (*added to a building*)

surélever [syrelve] §2 *tr* to raise, raise up; drive up; jack up

sûrement [syrmɑ̃] *adv* surely, certainly; safely; steadily, confidently

surenchère [syrɑ̃ʃɛr] *f* higher bid; **surenchère électorale** campaign promise, political outbidding

surenchérir [syrɑ̃ʃerir] *intr* to make a higher bid; **surenchérir sur qn** to outbid s.o.

surestimer [syrɛstime] *tr* to overestimate

su·ret [syrɛ] **-rette** [rɛt] *adj* tart

sûreté [syrte] *f* safety, security; sureness (*of touch; of taste*); surety; **à sûreté intégrée** fail-safe; **en sûreté** out of harm's way; in custody, confined (*e.g., in prison*); **sûreté individuelle** legal protection (*e.g., against arbitrary arrest*); **Sûreté nationale** or **la Sûreté** central intelligence; **sûretés** precautions; guarantees, security (*for a loan*)

surévaluer [syrevalцe] *tr* to overvalue

surexciter [syrɛksite] *tr* to overexcite

surexposer [syrɛkspoze] *tr* (phot) to overexpose

surexposition [syrɛkspozisjɔ̃] *f* (phot) overexposure

surface [syrfas] *f* surface; financial backing; **faire surface** to surface (*said of a submarine*)

surfaire [syrfɛr] §29 *tr* & *intr* to overprice; to overrate

sur·fin [syrfɛ̃] **-fine** [fin] *adj* superfine

surgélation [syrʒelasjɔ̃] *f* deep freezing

surge·lé -lée [syrʒəle] *adj* frozen (*foods*)

surgeon [syrʒɔ̃] *m* offshoot, sucker

surgir [syrʒir] *intr* to spring up; arise, appear; arrive, reach port

surglacer [syrglase] §51 *tr* to glaze; ice (*cake*)

surhaussement [syrosmɑ̃] *m* heightening, raising; banking (*of road*)

surhausser [syrose] *tr* to heighten, raise; force up (*prices*); force up the price of (*s.th.*); bank (*a road*)

surhomme [syrɔm] *m* superman

surhu·main [syrymɛ̃] **-maine** [mɛn] *adj* superhuman

surimpression [syrɛ̃presjɔ̃] *f* superimposition; (mov) montage

surintendant [syrɛ̃tɑ̃dɑ̃] *m* superintendent, administrator

surir [syrir] *intr* to turn sour

surjeu [syrʒə] *m* playback

sur-le-champ [syrlʃɑ̃] *adv* on the spot, immediately

surlendemain [syrlɑ̃dmɛ̃] *m*—**le surlendemain** the second day after, two days later

surlier [syrlje] *tr* to whip (*a rope*)

surliure [syrljyr] *f* whipping (*of rope*)

surmédicaliser [syrmedikalize] *intr* (med) to overprescribe, overmedicate

surmenage [syrmənaʒ] *m* overworking, fatigue

surmener [syrməne] §2 *tr* & *ref* to overwork

sur·moi [syrmwa] *m* superego

surmonter [syrmɔ̃te] *tr* to surmount ‖ *intr* to come to the top (*said of oil in water*)

surmouler [syrmule] *tr* to cast from another mold

surmultiplication [syrmyltiplikasjɔ̃] *f* (aut) overdrive

surnager [syrnaʒe] §38 *intr* to float; survive

surnatu·rel -relle [syrnatyrɛl] *adj* & *m* supernatural

surnom [syrnɔ̃] *m* nickname, sobriquet

surnombre [syrnɔ̃br] *m* excess number; **en surnombre** supernumerary; spare; **rester en surnombre** to be odd man; **surnombre des habitants** overpopulation

surnommer [syrnɔme] *tr* to name, call, nickname

surnuméraire [syrnymerɛr] *adj* supernumerary, extra ‖ *mf* substitute, supernumerary

suroffre [syrɔfr] *f* better or higher offer

suroît [syrwa] *m* southwest wind

surpasser [syrpase] *tr* to surpass; astonish ‖ *ref* to outdo oneself

surpaye [syrpɛj] *f* extra pay

surpayer [syrpɛje] §49 *tr* to pay too much to; pay too much for

surpeu·plé -plée [syrpœple] *adj* overpopulated

surpeuplement [syrpœpləmɑ̃] *m* overpopulation

surplis [syrpli] *m* surplice

surplomber [syrplɔ̃be] *tr* & *intr* to overhang; to look down upon

surplus [syrply] *m* surplus; **au surplus** moreover

surpopulation [syrpɔpylɑsjɔ̃] *f* overpopulation

surprendre [syrprɑ̃dr] §56, §96 *tr* to surprise; come upon by chance; detect; overtake, catch

surprise [syrpriz] *f* surprise

surprise-party or **surprise-partie** [syrprizparti] *f* (*pl* **surprises-parties**) private dancing party

surproduction [syrprɔdyksjɔ̃] *f* overproduction

surréalisme [syrealism] *m* surrealism

surrégénérateur [syreʒeneratœr] **-trice** [tris] *adj* (nucl) breeder (reactor)

surréservation [syresɛrvɑsjɔ̃] *f* overbooking

sursaut [syrso] *m* sudden start; **en sursaut** with a start

sursauter [syrsote] *intr* to give a jump, start, jerk

surseoir [syrswar] §5B (*fut* **surseoirai**, etc.) *intr*—**surseoir à** (law) to defer, postpone, stay, e.g., **surseoir à une exécution** to stay an execution

sursis [syrsi] *m* suspension (*of penalty*); postponement, deferment, stay; **en sursis, avec sursis** suspended (*sentence*)

surtaxe [syrtaks] *f* surtax, surcharge; **surtaxe postale** postage due

surtaxer [syrtakse] *tr* to surtax

surtension [syrtɑ̃sjɔ̃] *f* (elec) surge

surtout [syrtu] *m* topcoat; centerpiece, epergne ‖ *adv* especially, particularly

surveillance [syrvɛjɑ̃s] *f* supervision; (*by the police*) surveillance

surveil·lant [syrvɛjɑ̃] **-lante** [jɑ̃t] *mf* supervisor, superintendent, overseer; **surveillant d'études** study-hall proctor

surveiller [syrvɛje] *tr* to inspect, put under surveillance; supervise, watch over, monitor

survenir [syrvənir] §72 *intr* (*aux:* ÊTRE) to arrive unexpectedly, happen suddenly, crop up

survenue [syrvəny] *f* unexpected arrival

survêtement [syrvɛtmɑ̃] *m* track suit, sweat shirt

survie [syrvi] *f* survival; afterlife; (law) survivorship; **survie du plus apte** survival of the fittest

survivance [syrvivɑ̃s] *f* survival

survi·vant [syrvivɑ̃] **-vante** [vɑ̃t] *adj* surviving ‖ *mf* survivor

survivre [syrvivr] §74 *intr* to survive; **survivre à** to survive, outlive, e.g., **elle lui**

survécut she survived him ‖ *ref* (*pp* **survécu** *invar*) (fig) to outlive one's time; **se survivre dans** to live on in

survoler [syrvɔle] *tr* to fly over; skim over (*e.g., a problem*)

survol·té -tée [syrvɔlte] *adj* electrified, charged with emotion

sus [sys], [sy] *adv*—**en sus de** in addition to ‖ *interj* up and at it (them)!

susceptible [sysɛptibl] *adj* sensitive, touchy; **susceptible de** capable of, liable to, susceptible of

susciter [sysite] *tr* to stir up, evoke, rouse; (lit) to raise up

sus·dit [sysdi] **-dite** [dit] *adj* aforesaid

susmention·né -née [sysmɑ̃sjɔne] *adj* aforementioned

sus·pect [syspɛ], [syspɛkt] **-pecte** [pɛkt] *adj* suspect, suspicious ‖ *mf* suspect

suspecter [syspɛkte] *tr* to suspect

suspendre [syspɑ̃dr] *tr* to suspend; hang, hang up; **être suspendu aux lèvres de qn** to hang on s.o.'s every word ‖ *ref* to be hung; hang on

suspen·du -due [syspɑ̃dy] *adj* suspended; hanging

suspens [syspɑ̃] *m* suspense; **en suspens** suspended; in abeyance; outstanding; in suspense

suspension [syspɑ̃sjɔ̃] *f* suspension

suspi·cieux [syspisjø] **-cieuse** [sjøz] *adj* suspicious

suspicion [syspisjɔ̃] *f* suspicion

sustenter [systɑ̃te] *tr* to sustain ‖ *ref* to sustain oneself

susurrer [sysyre] *tr* & *intr* to murmur, whisper

susvi·sé -sée [sysvize] *adj* above-mentioned

suture [sytyr] *f* suture

suturer [sytyre] *tr* to suture

suze·rain [syzrɛ̃] **-raine** [rɛn] *adj* & *mf* suzerain

svastika [svastika] *m* swastika

svelte [svɛlt] *adj* slender, lithe, willowy

S.V.P. [ɛsvepe] *m* (letterword) (**s'il vous plaît**) if you please, please

sweater [switœr] *m* sweater; **sweater à col roulé** turtleneck sweater

sycophante [sikɔfɑ̃t] *m* informer

syllabe [silab] *f* syllable

syllogisme [silɔʒism] *m* syllogism

sylphe [silf] *m* sylph

sylvestre [silvɛstr] *adj* sylvan

symbole [sɛ̃bɔl] *m* symbol; **Symbole des apôtres** Apostles' Creed

symbolique [sɛ̃bɔlik] *adj* symbolic(al)

symboliser [sɛ̃bɔlize] *tr* to symbolize

symbolisme [sɛ̃bɔlism] *m* symbolism

symétrie [simetri] *f* symmetry

symétrique [simetrik] *adj* symmetric(al)

sympa [sɛ̃pa] *adj* (coll) likable, attractive

sympathie [sɛ̃pati] *f* fondness, liking; sympathy

sympathique [sɛ̃patik] *adj* likable, attractive; sympathetic

sympathi·sant [sɛ̃patizɑ̃] **-sante** [zɑ̃t] *adj* sympathetic ‖ *mf* sympathizer

sympathiser [sɛ̃patize] *intr* to get along well; **sympathiser avec** to be drawn toward; support
symphonie [sɛ̃fɔni] *f* symphony
symptôme [sɛ̃ptom] *m* symptom
synagogue [sinagɔg] *f* synagogue
synchrone [sɛ̃krɔn] *adj* synchronous
synchroniser [sɛ̃krɔnize] *tr* to synchronize
syncope [sɛ̃kɔp] *f* faint, swoon, syncope; syncopation
syndicat [sɛ̃dika] *m* labor union; **syndicat de distribution** (journ) syndicate; **syndicat d'initiative** chamber of commerce; **syndicat patronal** employers' association
syndicats-patrons [sɛ̃dikapatrɔ̃] *adj invar* labor-management
syndi·qué -quée [sɛ̃dike] *adj* union ‖ *mf* union member
syndiquer [sɛ̃dike] *tr & ref* to unionize
syndrome [sɛ̃drom] *m* syndrome; **syndrome de l'usure au travail** burnout; **syndrome d'immunodéficience acquise** acquired immune-deficiency syndrome, AIDS

synonyme [sinɔnim] *adj* synonymous ‖ *m* synonym
synopsis [sinɔpsis] *m & f* (mov) synopsis
syntaxe [sɛ̃taks] *f* syntax
synthèse [sɛ̃tɛz] *f* synthesis
synthétique [sɛ̃tetik] *adj* synthetic
synthétiser [sɛ̃tetize] *tr* to synthesize
syntonisation [sɛ̃tɔnizɑsjɔ̃] *f* tuning (*of radio*)
syntoniser [sɛ̃tɔnize] *tr* to tune in
syphilis [sifilis] *f* syphilis
Syrie [siri] *f* Syria; **la Syrie** Syria
sy·rien [sirjɛ̃] **-rienne** [rjɛn] *adj* Syrian ‖ (*cap*) *mf* Syrian (*person*)
systématique [sistematik] *adj* systematic; routine
systématiser [sistematize] *tr* to systematize
système [sistɛm] *m* system; **courir, porter,** or **taper sur le système à qn** (slang) to get on s.o.'s nerves; **système D** (coll) resourcefulness; **système d'exploitation** (comp) operating system
systole [sistɔl] *f* systole

T

T, t [te] *m invar* twentieth letter of the French alphabet
t. *abbr* (**tome**) vol.
t' = **te** before vowel or mute **h**
ta [ta] §88 your
tabac [taba] *m* tobacco; tobacco shop; **avoir le gros tabac** (slang) to be a hit; **passer qn à tabac** (coll) to give s.o. the third degree; **tabac à chiquer** chewing tobacco; **tabac à priser** snuff
tabagie [tabaʒi] *f* smoke-filled room
tabasser [tabase] *tr* (slang) to give a licking to, shellac
tabatière [tabatjɛr] *f* snuffbox; skylight, dormer window
tabernacle [tabɛrnakl] *m* tabernacle
table [tabl] *f* table; **aimer la table** to like good food; **à table!** dinner is served!; **dresser** or **mettre la table** to set the table; **faire table rase** to make a clean sweep; **sainte table** altar rail; **se mettre à table** (slang) to tell all, to confess, to squeal; **table à abattants** gate-leg table; **table à ouvrage** worktable; **table à rallonges** extension table; **table à salade** salad bar; **table de chevet, table de nuit** bedside table; **table d'écoute** wiretap; **table de jeu** card table; **table de toilette** dressing table; **table d'hôte** table d'hôte; chef's special; **table d'opération** operating table; **table du téléphone** telephone table; **table gigogne** nest of tables; **table interurbaine** long-distance switchboard; **table roulante**

serving cart; **tenir table ouverte** to keep open house
ta·bleau [tablo] *m* (*pl* **-bleaux**) painting, picture; scoreboard; board; table, catalogue; panel (*of jurors*); **former un tableau** (law) to empanel a jury; **jouer sur les deux tableaux** (slang) to play both sides of the street; **tableau d'affichage** bulletin board; **tableau d'avancement** seniority list; **tableau de bord** dashboard; instrument panel; **tableau de distribution** switchboard; **tableau d'honneur** honor roll; **tableau noir** blackboard; **tableau vivant** tableau
tableautier [tablotje] *m* tabulator (*of typewriter*)
tabler [table] *intr*—**tabler sur** to count on; use as a base
tablette [tablɛt] *f* shelf; mantelpiece; bar (*e.g., of chocolate*); **rayez cela de vos tablettes** don't count on it; **tablettes** pocket notebook
table-valise [tabləvaliz] *f* (*pl* **tables-valises**) folding table
tablier [tablije] *m* apron; roadway (*of bridge*); hood (*of chimney*); **tablier de fer** protective shutter (*on store window*)
ta·bou -bou or **-boue** [tabu] *adj & m* taboo
tabouret [taburɛ] *m* stool; footstool
tabulaire [tabylɛr] *adj* tabular
tabulateur [tabylatœr] *m* tabulator
tac [tak] *m* click, clack; **du tac au tac** tit for tat; **tac tac tac!** rat-a-tat-tat!
tache [taʃ] *f* spot, stain; blemish, flaw; blot; smear; speck; **faire tache** to be out of

place; **faire tache d'huile** to spread; **sans tache** spotless, unblemished; **tache de rousseur, tache de son** freckle; **tache de vin** birthmark; **tache originelle** original sin; **tache solaire** sunspot

tâche [taʃ] *f* task, job; **prendre à tâche de** to try to; **travailler à la tâche** to do piecework

tacher [taʃe] *tr & ref* to spot, stain

tâcher [taʃe] §96, §97 *tr*—**tâcher que** to see to it that ‖ *intr*—**tâcher de** to try to; **y tâcher** to try

tâcheron [taʃrɔ̃] *m* small jobber; piece-worker; hard worker; wage slave

tacheter [taʃte] §34 *tr* to spot, speckle

tacite [tasit] *adj* tacit

taciturne [tasityrn] *adj* taciturn

tacot [tako] *m* (coll) jalopy

tact [takt] *m* tact; sense of touch

tacticien [taktisjɛ̃] *m* tactician

tactique [taktik] *adj* tactical ‖ *f* tactics

taffetas [tafta] *m* taffeta; **taffetas gommé** adhesive tape

Tage [taʒ] *m* Tagus

taïaut [tajo] *interj* tallyho!

taie [tɛ] *f* (pathol) leukoma; **avoir une taie sur l'œil** (fig) to be blinded by prejudice; **taie d'oreiller** pillowcase

taillader [tajade] *tr & ref* to slash, cut

taille [taj] *f* cutting (*e.g., of diamond*); trimming (*e.g., of hedge*); height, stature; waist, waistline; size; cut (*of garment*); **à la taille de, de la taille de** to the measure of, suitable for; **avoir la taille fine** to have a slim waist; **de taille** big enough, strong enough; (coll) big; **être de taille à** to be up to, to be big enough to; **taille de guêpe** wasp waist; **taille en dessous** next size smaller; **taille en dessus** next size larger

tail·lé -lée [taje] *adj* cut; trimmed; **bien taillé** well-built; **taillé pour** cut out for

taille-crayon [tajkrɛjɔ̃] *m* (*pl* **-crayon** or **-crayons**) pencil sharpener

taille-douce [tajdus] *f* (*pl* **tailles-douces**) copperplate

taille-haies [taj-ɛ] *m invar* hedge cutter

taille-pain [tajpɛ̃] *m invar* bread knife; bread slicer

tailler [taje] *tr* to cut; sharpen (*a pencil*); prune, trim (*a tree*); carve (*stone*); clip (*hair*) ‖ *intr* (cards) to deal ‖ *ref* to carve out (*a path; a career*); (coll) to beat it

tailleur [tajœr] *m* tailor; woman's suit; (cards) dealer; **en tailleur** squatting (*while tailoring*); **tailleur de diamants** diamond cutter; **tailleur de pierre** stonecutter; **tailleur sur mesure** lady's tailor-made suit

taillis [taji] *m* thicket, copse

tain [tɛ̃] *m* silvering (*of mirror*)

taire [tɛr] §52 (3d *sg pres ind* **tait**) *tr* to hush up, hide; **la tairas-tu?** (slang) will you shut your trap?; **taire q.ch. à qn** to keep s.th. from s.o. ‖ *intr*—**faire taire** to silence ‖ *ref* to keep quiet, keep still; **se taire sur** to say nothing about; **tais-toi!** shut up!

talent [talɑ̃] *m* talent

talen·tueux [talɑ̃tɥø] **-tueuse** [tɥøz] *adj* talented

talkie-walkie [tɔkiwɔki] *m* (*pl* **talkies-walkies**) walkie-talkie

taloche [talɔʃ] *f* plastering trowel; (coll) clout, smack

talon [talɔ̃] *m* heel; stub

talonnage [talɔnaʒ] *m* tailgating

talonner [talɔne] *tr* to tail; tailgate; harass; dig one's spurs into ‖ *intr* to bump

talus [taly] *m* slope; embankment; **talus de neige** snowbank

tambour [tɑ̃bur] *m* drum; drummer; entry-way; spool (*of reel*); **tambour battant** (coll) roughly; (coll) quickly; **tambour cylindrique** revolving door; **tambour de basque** tambourine; **tambour de freins** brake drum; **tambour de ville** town crier

tambouriner [tɑ̃burine] *tr* to drum; broadcast far and wide ‖ *intr* to beat a tattoo; drum

tambour-major [tɑ̃burmaʒɔr] *m* (*pl* **tambours-majors**) drum major

tamis [tami] *m* sieve; **passer au tamis** to sift; **tamis à farine** flour sifter

Tamise [tamiz] *f* Thames

tamiser [tamize] *tr & intr* to sift

tampon [tɑ̃pɔ̃] *m* plug; bung; swab; rubber stamp; buffer; cancellation; postmark; (surg) tampon; **tampon buvard** hand blotter; **tampon encreur** stamp pad

tamponner [tɑ̃pɔne] *tr* to swag, dab; bump, bump into; (surg) to tampon

tan [tɑ̃] *adj invar* tan ‖ *m* tanbark

tancer [tɑ̃se] §51 *tr* to scold

tandem [tɑ̃dɛm] *m* tandem; **en tandem** tandem

tandis que [tɑ̃dika], [tɑ̃diskə] *conj* while; whereas

tangage [tɑ̃gaʒ] *m* (naut) pitching

Tanger [tɑ̃ʒe] *m* Tangier

tangible [tɑ̃ʒibl] *adj* tangible

tanguer [tɑ̃ge] *intr* to pitch (*said of ship*)

tanière [tanjɛr] *f* den, lair

tanker [tɑ̃kɛr] *m* oil tanker

tan·nant [tanɑ̃] **-nante** [nɑ̃t] *adj* (coll) boring

tanne [tan] *f* spot (*on leather*); blackhead

tanner [tane] *tr* to tan; (coll) to pester

tannerie [tanri] *f* tannery

tanneur [tanœr] *m* tanner

tan-sad [tɑ̃sad] *m* (*pl* **-sads**) rear seat (*of motorcycle*)

tant [tɑ̃] *adv* so, so much; so long; **en tant que** in, in so far as; **si tant est que** if it is true that; **tant bien que mal** somehow or other; **tant de** so many; so much; **tant mieux** so much the better; **tant pis** so much the worse; never mind; **tant qu'à faire** while we're (you're, etc.) at it; **tant que** as well as; as long as; **tant s'en faut** far from it; **tant soit peu** ever so little; **vous m'en direz tant** (coll) you've just said a mouthful

tante [tɑ̃t] *f* aunt; (slang) fairy; **ma tante** (coll) the hockshop

tantième [tɑ̃tjɛm] *m* percentage

tantine [tɑ̃tin] *f* (coll) auntie

tantôt [tɑ̃to] *m* (coll) afternoon ‖ *adv* in a little while; a little while ago; (coll) in the afternoon; **à tantôt** see you soon; **tantôt . . . tantôt** sometimes . . . sometimes

taon [tɑ̃] *m* horsefly

tapage [tapaʒ] *m* uproar

tapa·geur [tapaʒœr] **-geuse** [ʒøz] *adj* loud

tape [tap] *f* tap, slap

ta·pé -pée [tape] *adj* dried (*fruit*); rotten in spots; (coll) crazy; (slang) worn (*with age or fatigue*); **bien tapé** (coll) well done; (coll) nicely served; (coll) to the point

tape-à-l'œil [tapalœj] *adj* gaudy, showy ‖ *m invar* mere show

taper [tape] *tr* to tap, slap; type; (coll) to hit (*s.o. for money*) ‖ *intr* to tap, slap; type; (coll) to go to the head (*said of wine*); **ça tape ici** (slang) it hurts here; **taper dans** (coll) to use; **taper dans le mille** (coll) to succeed; **taper dans l'œil de qn** (coll) to make a hit with s.o.; **taper de** to hit (*e.g., 100 m.p.h.*); **taper des pieds** to stamp one's feet; **taper sur** (coll) to get on (*s.o.'s nerves*); **taper sur le ventre de qn** (coll) to give s.o. a poke in the ribs; **taper sur qn** (coll) to run down s.o., give s.o. a going-over

tapette [tapɛt] *f* carpet beater; fly swatter; handball; (slang) homo, fruit (*homosexual*); **avoir une fière tapette** (coll) to be a chatterbox; **tapette tue-mouche** fly swatter

tapin [tapɛ̃] *m* (coll) drummer boy; (slang) solicitation (*by a prostitute*)

tapinois [tapinwa]—**en tapinois** stealthily

tapir [tapir] *ref* to crouch, squat; hide

tapis [tapi] *m* carpet; rug; game of chance; **mettre sur le tapis** to bring up for discussion; **tapis de bain** bath mat; **tapis de sol** ground cloth; **tapis de table** table covering; **tapis d'orient** oriental rug; **tapis mur à mur** wall-to-wall carpeting; **tapis roulant** conveyor belt; moving sidewalk

tapis-brosse [tapibrɔs] *m* (*pl* **-brosses**) doormat

tapisser [tapise] *tr* to upholster; tapestry; wallpaper

tapisserie [tapisri] *f* upholstery; tapestry; **faire tapisserie** to be a wallflower

tapis·sier [tapisje] **-sière** [sjɛr] *mf* upholsterer; tapestry maker; paperhanger

tapoter [tapɔte] *tr & intr* to tap

taquet [takɛ] *m* wedge, peg; (mach) tappet; (naut) cleat; **taquet d'arrêt** (rr) scotch, wedge

ta·quin [takɛ̃] **-quine** [kin] *adj* teasing ‖ *mf* tease

taquiner [takine] *tr* to tease

taquinerie [takinri] *f* teasing

taraud [taro] *m* (mach) tap

tarauder [tarode] *tr* (mach) to tap; (coll) to pester

taraudeuse [tarodøz] *f* tap wrench

tard [tar] *m*—**sur le tard** late in the day; late in life ‖ *adv* late; **pas plus tard que** no later than; **plus tard** later on

tarder [tarde] §96, §97 *intr* to delay; **tarder à** to be long in ‖ *impers*—**il me (te,** etc.**) tarde de** + *inf* **I** (you, etc.) long to + *inf*, e.g., **il lui tarde de vous voir** he longs to see you

tar·dif [tardif] **-dive** [div] *adj* late; backward; tardy

tardivement [tardivmɑ̃] *adv* belatedly

tare [tar] *f* defect, blemish; taint; loss in value; tare (*weight*)

tarer [tare] *tr* to damage; taint; tare ‖ *ref* to spoil

targette [tarʒɛt] *f* latch

targuer [targe] *ref*—**se targuer de** to pride oneself on

tarière [tarjɛr] *f* auger, drill

tarif [tarif] *m* price list; rate, tariff; **plein tarif** full fare; **tarifs postaux** postal rates

tarifaire [tarifɛr] *adj* tariff

tarifer [tarife] *tr* to price; rate

tarir [tarir] *tr* to drain, exhaust, dry up ‖ *intr* to dry up, run dry; **ne pas tarir** to never run out ‖ *ref* to dry up; be exhausted

tarse [tars] *m* tarsus; instep

tartare [tartar] *adj* tartar (*sauce*); Tartar ‖ (*cap*) *mf* Tartar

tarte [tart] *adj* (coll) silly, stupid; (coll) ugly ‖ *f* pie, tart; (slang) slap; **c'est pas de la tarte** (slang) it's no easy matter; **tarte à la crème** custard pie; (slang) slapstick comedy; **tarte mousseline** chiffon pie

tartine [tartin] *f* slice of bread and butter or jam; (coll) long-winded speech; (coll) rambling article

tartiner [tartine] *tr* to spread

tartre [tartr] *m* tartar; scale

tartuferie [tartyfri] *f* hypocrisy

tas [tɑ] *m* heap, pile; **mettre en tas** to pile up; **prendre sur le tas** to catch red-handed; **tas de foin** haystack; **un tas de** (coll) a lot of

tasse [tɑs] *f* cup; **tasse à café** coffee cup; **tasse à thé** teacup; **tasse de café** cup of coffee

tas·sé -sée [tɑse] *adj* squat, dumpy; shrunk; curled up, slumped; complete; well-filled; packed tight; stiff (*drink*)

tas·seau [tɑso] *m* (*pl* **-seaux**) bracket; cleat; lug (*on casting*)

tasser [tɑse] *tr* to cram; tamp, pack down ‖ *intr* to grow thick ‖ *ref* to settle; huddle; (coll) to go back to normal

taste-vin [tastəvɛ̃] *m invar* wine taster (*cup*); sampling tube

tata [tata] *f* (slang) auntie

tâter [tɑte] *tr* to feel, touch; test, feel out; **tâter le pouls à qn** to feel s.o.'s pulse ‖ *intr*—**tâter de** to taste; experience; try one's hand at ‖ *ref* to stop to think, ponder

tâte-vin [tɑtvɛ̃] *m invar* wine taster (*cup*); sampling tube

tatil·lon [tatijɔ̃] **-lonne** [jɔn] *adj* fussy, hairsplitting ‖ *mf* hairsplitter

tâtonner [tɑtɔne] *intr* to grope

tâtons [tɑtɔ̃]—**à tâtons** gropingly

tatouage [tatwaʒ] *m* tattoo

tatouer [tatwe] *tr* to tattoo

taudis [todi] *m* hovel; **taudis** *mpl* slums

taule [tol] *f* (slang) fleabag; (slang) jug, clink; **faire de la taule** (slang) to do a stretch

taupe [top] *f* mole; moleskin

taupin [topɛ̃] *m* (mil) sapper; (coll) engineering student

taupinière [topinjɛr] *f* molehill

tau·reau [toro] *m* (*pl* **-reaux**) bull; **le Taureau** (astr, astrol) Taurus

taux [to] *m* rate; ratio; degree (*of disability*); **taut de base** prime rate; **taux de change** exchange rate; **taux d'escompte** discount rate; **taux d'intérêt** interest rate

taveler [tavle] §34 *tr* to spot ‖ *ref* to become spotted

taverne [tavɛrn] *f* inn, tavern

taxation [taksɑsjɔ̃] *f* fixing (*of prices, wages, etc.*); assessment; taxation

taxe [taks] *f* fixed price; rate; tax; **taxe à la valeur ajoutée** value-added tax; **taxe de luxe** luxury tax; **taxe de séjour** nonresident tax; **taxe directe** sales tax; **taxe perçue** postage paid; **taxe supplémentaire** postage due; **taxe sur les spectacles** entertainment tax

taxer [takse] *tr* to fix the price of; regulate the rate of; assess; tax; **taxer qn de** to tax or charge s.o. with ‖ *ref* to set an offering price; **se taxer de** to accuse oneself of

taxi [taksi] *m* taxi; (coll) cabdriving; **hep taxi!** taxi! ‖ *mf* (coll) cabdriver

taxidermie [taksidɛrmi] *f* taxidermy

taxiphone [taksifɔn] *m* pay phone

Tchécoslovaquie [tʃekɔslɔvaki] *f* Czechoslovakia; **la Tchécoslovaquie** Czechoslovakia

tchèque [tʃɛk] *adj* Czech ‖ *m* Czech (*language*) ‖ (*cap*) *mf* Czech (*person*)

te [ta] §87 you, to you

techni·cien [tɛknisjɛ̃] **-cienne** [sjɛn] *mf* technician; engineer

technique [tɛknik] *adj* technical ‖ *f* technique; engineering

teck [tɛk] *m* teak

teckel [tɛkɛl] *m* dachshund

teigne [tɛɲ] *f* moth; ringworm; (fig) pest, nuisance

teindre [tɛ̃dr] §50 *tr* to dye; tint ‖ *ref* to be tinted; dye or tint (*one's hair*)

teint [tɛ̃] **teinte** [tɛ̃t] *adj* dyed; with dyed hair ‖ *m* dye; complexion; **bon teint** fast color ‖ *f* tint, shade; (fig) tinge

teinter [tɛ̃te] *tr* to tint; tinge

teinture [tɛ̃tyr] *f* dye; dyeing; tincture; (fig) smattering; **teinture d'iode** (pharm) iodine

teinturerie [tɛ̃tyrri] *f* dry cleaner's; dyer's; dyeing

teintu·rier [tɛ̃tyrje] **-rière** [rjɛr] *mf* dry cleaner; dyer

tel telle [tɛl] *adj* such; like, e.g., **tel père tel fils** like father like son; **de telle sorte que** so that; **tel ou tel** such and such a; **tel que** such as, the same as, as; **tel quel** as is ‖ *mf*—**un tel** or **une telle** so-and-so ‖ *pron* such a one, such

télé [tele] *f* (coll) TV; (coll) TV set

télécommander [telekɔmɑ̃de] *tr* to operate by remote control; (fig) to inspire, influence

télécommunications [telekɔmynikɑsjɔ̃] *fpl* telecommunications

téléenseignement [teleɑ̃sɛɲmɑ̃] *m* educational television

téléférique [teleferik] *m* skyride, cableway

télégramme [telegram] *m* telegram

télégraphe [telegraf] *m* telegraph

télégraphier [telegrafje] *tr* & *intr* to telegraph

télégraphiste [telegrafist] *mf* telegrapher

téléguider [telegide] *tr* to guide (*e.g., a missile*); (coll) to influence

téléimprimeur [teleɛ̃primœr] *m* teletype, teleprinter

télémètre [telemɛtr] *m* telemeter; range finder

téléobjectif [teleɔbʒɛktif] *m* telephoto lens

télépathie [telepati] *f* telepathy

téléphérique [teleferik] *m* skyride, cableway

téléphone [telefɔn] *m* telephone; **téléphone à clavier** tone telephone, digital telephone, push-button telephone; **téléphone non sur la liste rouge** unlisted telephone; **téléphone public** public telephone; **téléphone payant** coin telephone; **téléphone rouge** (pol) hot line

téléphoner [telefɔne] *tr* & *intr* to telephone

téléphoniste [telefɔnist] *mf* telephone operator ‖ *m* lineman

télescope [telɛskɔp] *m* telescope

télescoper [telɛskɔpe] *intr* & *ref* to telescope

télescopique [telɛskɔpik] *adj* telescopic

téléscripteur [teleskriptœr] *m* teletype, teletypewriter

télésiège [telesjɛʒ] *m* chair lift

téléski [teleski] *m* ski lift

télésouffleur [telesuflœr] *m* teleprompter

téléspecta·teur [telespɛktatœr] **-trice** [tris] *mf* (television) viewer

télétraitement [teletrɛtmɑ̃] *m* (comp) processing by modem

télétype [teletip] *m* teletype

téléviser [televize] *tr* to televise

téléviseur [televizœr] *m* television set; **téléviseur à servo-réglage** remote-control television set

télévision [televizjɔ̃] *f* television; (coll) television set; **télévision payante** pay television

télévi·suel **-suelle** [televizɥɛl] *adj* television

tellement [tɛlmɑ̃] *adv* so much; so; **tellement de** so much, so many; **tellement que** to such an extent that

téméraire [temerɛr] *adj* rash, reckless, foolhardy

témérité [temerite] *f* temerity, rashness

témoignage [temwaɲaʒ] *m* testimony, witness; **en témoignage de quoi** in witness whereof; **rendre témoignage à** or **pour** to testify in favor of

témoigner [temwaɲe] §95 *tr* to show; testify ‖ *intr* to testify; **témoigner de** to give evidence of; bear witness to

témoin [temwɛ̃] *adj invar* type, model; pilot; sample, model (*home or apartment*) ‖ *m* witness; control (*in scientific experiment*); second (*in duel*); **prendre à témoin** to call to witness; **témoin à charge** witness for the prosecution; **témoin à décharge** witness for the defense; **témoin oculaire** eyewitness; **Témoins de Jéhovah** Jehovah's Witnesses

tempe [tɑ̃p] *f* (anat) temple

tempérament [tɑ̃peramɑ̃] *m* temperament; amorous nature; **à tempérament** on the installment plan

tempérance [tɑ̃perɑ̃s] *f* temperance

tempé·rant [tɑ̃perɑ̃] **-rante** [rɑ̃t] *adj* temperate

température [tɑ̃peratyr] *f* temperature

tempé·ré -rée [tɑ̃pere] *adj* temperate; tempered; restrained

tempérer [tɑ̃pere] §10 *tr* to temper ‖ *ref* to moderate

tempête [tɑ̃pɛt] *f* tempest, storm; **affronter la tempête** (fig) to face the music; **tempête dans un verre d'eau** tempest in a teapot; **tempête de neige** blizzard; **tempête de poussière** dust storm; **tempête de sable** sandstorm

tempêter [tɑ̃pete] *intr* to storm

tempé·tueux [tɑ̃petɥø] **-tueuse** [tɥøz] *adj* tempestuous

temple [tɑ̃pl] *m* temple; chapel; church

tempo [tɛmpo], [tɛ̃po] *m* tempo

temporaire [tɑ̃pɔrɛr] *adj* temporary

tempo·ral -rale [tɑ̃pɔral] *adj* (*pl* **-raux** [ro]) (anat) temporal

tempo·rel -relle [tɑ̃pɔrɛl] *adj* temporal

temporiser [tɑ̃pɔrize] *intr* to temporize, stall

temps [tɑ̃] *m* time; times; cycle (*of internal-combustion engine*); position, movement (*in gymnastics, fencing, carrying of arms*); weather, e.g., **quel temps fait-il?** what is the weather like?; (gram) tense; (mus) beat, measure; **à temps** in time; **au temps de** in the time of; **avoir fait son temps** to have seen better days; **dans le bon vieux temps, en le bon vieux temps** in the good old days; **dans le temps** formerly; **de temps en temps** from time to time; **en même temps** at the same time; **en temps de crise** in the time of crisis; **en temps et lieu** in due course; **en temps partagé** (comp) time-sharing; **en temps utile** in due course; **faire son temps** to do time (*in prison*); **gagner du temps** to save time; **le bon vieux temps** the good old days; **Le Temps** Father Time; **temps atomique** atomic era; **temps d'arrêt** pause, halt; **temps de chien** (slang) lousy weather; **temps mort** (sports) time-out;

temps partagé (comp) time sharing; **temps réel** (comp) real time

tenable [tənabl] *adj*—**pas tenable** untenable; unbearable

tenace [tənas] *adj* tenacious

ténacité [tenasite] *f* tenacity

tenailler [tənaje] *tr* to torture

tenailles [tənaj] *fpl* pliers, pincers

tenan·cier [tənɑ̃sje] **-cière** [sjɛr] *mf* sharecropper; lessee; keeper (*e.g., of a dive*)

te·nant [tənɑ̃] **-nante** [nɑ̃t] *adj* attached (*collar*) ‖ *mf* (sports) holder (*of a title*) ‖ *m* champion, supporter; **connaître les tenants et les aboutissants** to know the ins and outs; **d'un seul tenant** in one piece

tendance [tɑ̃dɑ̃s] *f* tendency

tendan·cieux [tɑ̃dɑ̃sjø] **-cieuse** [sjøz] *adj* tendentious, slanted

ten·deur [tɑ̃dœr] **-deuse** [døz] *mf* paperhanger; layer (*of traps*) ‖ *m* stretcher

tendoir [tɑ̃dwar] *m* clothesline

tendon [tɑ̃dɔ̃] *m* tendon

tendre [tɑ̃dr] *adj* tender ‖ §96 *tr* to stretch; hang; bend (*a bow*); lay (*a trap*); strain (*one's ear*); hold out, reach out ‖ *intr*—**tendre à** to aim at; tend toward ‖ *ref* to become strained

tendresse [tɑ̃drɛs] *f* tenderness, love, affection; (coll) partiality; **mille tendresses** (*closing of letter*) fondly

tendreté [tɑ̃drəte] *f* tenderness

ten·du -due [tɑ̃dy] *adj* tense, taut; strained; stretched out; **tendu de** hung with

ténèbres [tenɛbr] *fpl* darkness

téné·breux [tenebrø] **-breuse** [brøz] *adj* dark; somber (*person*); shady (*deal*); obscure (*style*)

te·neur [tənœr] **-neuse** [nøz] *mf* holder; **teneur de livres** bookkeeper ‖ **teneur** *f* tenor, gist; text; grade (*e.g., of ore*)

ténia [tenja] *m* tapeworm

tenir [tənir] §72, §96 *tr* to hold; keep; take up (*space*); **être tenu à** to be obliged to; **être tenu de** to be responsible for ‖ *intr* to hold; **il ne tient qu'à vous** it's up to you; **tenez!** here!; **tenir à** to insist upon; care for, value; be caused by; **tenir dans** to fit in; **tenir de** to take after, resemble; **tenir debout** (fig) to hold water, ring true; **tenir q.ch. de qn** to have s.th. from s.o., learn s.th. from s.o.; **tiens!** well!, hey! ‖ *ref* to stay, remain; sit up; stand up; behave; contain oneself; **à quoi s'en tenir** what to believe; **s'en tenir à** to limit oneself to; abide by

tennis [tenis] *m* tennis; tennis court; **tennis de table** table tennis, Ping-Pong

ténor [tenɔr] *adj masc* tenor ‖ *m* tenor; star performer

tension [tɑ̃sjɔ̃] *f* tension; blood pressure; pressure; voltage; **avoir de la tension** to have high blood pressure; **haute tension** (elec) high tension; **tension artérielle, tension du sang** blood pressure

tentacule [tɑ̃takyl] *m* tentacle

tenta·teur [tɑ̃tatœr] **-trice** [tris] *mf* tempter

tentation [tɑ̃tasjɔ̃] *f* temptation
tentative [tɑ̃tativ] *f* attempt
tente [tɑ̃t] *f* tent; awning
tente-abri [tɑ̃tabri] *f* (*pl* **tentes-abris** [tɑ̃tabri]) pup tent
tenter [tɑ̃te] §**97** *tr* to tempt; attempt ‖ *intr*—**tenter de** to attempt to
tenture [tɑ̃tyr] *f* drape; hangings; wallpaper
te·nu -nue [təny] §**93** *adj* firm (*securities, market, etc.*); **bien tenu** well-kept ‖ *f* see **tenue** ‖ *v* see **tenir**
té·nu -nue [teny] *adj* tenuous; thin
tenue [təny] *f* holding; managing; upkeep, maintenance; behavior; bearing; dress, costume; uniform; session; (mus) hold; **avoir de la tenue** to have good manners; **avoir une bonne tenue** (equit) to have a good seat; **en bonne tenue physique** in good shape physically; **en tenue** in uniform; **grande tenue** (mil) full dress; **petite tenue** (mil) undress; **tenue des livres** bookkeeping; **tenue de soirée** evening clothes; **tenue de ville** street clothes
térébenthine [terebɑ̃tin] *f* turpentine
tergiverser [terʒiverse] *intr* to duck, equivocate, vacillate
terme [term] *m* term; end, limit; quarterly payment; **avant terme** prematurely; **terme fatal** last day of grace
terminaison [terminɛzɔ̃] *f* ending, termination
termi·nal -nale [terminal] *adj* & *m* (*pl* **-naux** [no]) terminal
terminer [termine] *tr* & *ref* to terminate; **se terminer par** to end with ‖ *interj*—**terminé** over (*in CB language*)
terminus [terminys] *m* terminal ‖ *interj* the end has come!
termite [termit] *m* termite
terne [tern] *adj* dull, drab
ternir [ternir] *tr* & *ref* to tarnish
terrain [terɛ̃] *m* ground; terrain; playing field; dueling field; **ne pas être sur son terrain** to be out of one's depth; **tâter le terrain** to find out the lay of the land; **terrain à bâtir** or **à lotir** building plot; **terrain brûlant** (fig) unsafe ground; **terrain d'atterrissage** landing field; **terrain d'aviation** airfield; **terrain de courses** race track; **terrain de jeux** playground; **terrain de manœuvres** parade ground; **terrain vague** vacant lot; **tout terrain** all-surface (vehicle)
terrasse [teras] *f* terrace; sidewalk café; **terrasse en plein air** outdoor café
terrasser [terase] *tr* to embank; floor, knock down
terre [ter] *f* earth; land; (elec) ground; **descendre à terre** to go ashore; **la Terre Sainte** the Holy Land; **mettre pied à terre** to dismount; **par terre** on the floor; on the ground; **terre cuite** terra cotta; **Terre de Feu** Tierra del Fuego; **terre ferme** terra firma; **terre franche** loam
ter·reau [tero] *m* (*pl* **-reaux**) compost

terre-neuve [ternœv] *m invar* Newfoundland dog ‖ *f*—**Terre-Neuve** Newfoundland
terre-plein [terplɛ̃] *m* (*pl* **-pleins**) median, divider (*of road*); fill, embankment; earthwork, rampart; terrace; (rr) roadbed
terrer [tere] *tr* to earth up (*e.g., a tree*); earth over (*seed*) ‖ *ref* to burrow; entrench oneself
terrestre [terestr] *adj* land; terrestrial
terreur [terœr] *f* terror; **la Terreur** the Reign of Terror
ter·reux -reuse [terø] [røz] *adj* earthy; dirty; sallow (*complexion*)
terrible [teribl] *adj* terrible; terrific
ter·rien -rienne [terjɛ̃] [rjɛn] *adj* landed (*gentry*) ‖ *mf* landowner; landlubber ‖ *m* earthman
terrier [terje] *m* hole, burrow; (*dog*) terrier
terrifier [terifje] *tr* to terrify
terrir [terir] *intr* to come close to shore (*said of fish*)
territoire [teritwar] *m* territory
terroir [terwar] *m* soil; homeland
terroriser [terɔrize] *tr* to terrorize
tertiaire [tersjer] *adj* tertiary
tertre [tertr] *m* mound, knoll
tes [te] §**88** your
tesson [tesɔ̃] *m* shard; broken glass
test [test] *m* test; (zool) shell; **test de capacité intellectuelle** intelligence test; **test de la descendance** paternity test; **test de niveau** placement test; **test d'intelligence pratique, test de talent** aptitude test; **test nucléaire** nuclear test
testament [testamɑ̃] *m* testament; will
testa·teur [testatœr] **-trice** [tris] *mf* testator
tester [teste] *tr* to test ‖ *intr* to make one's will
testicule [testikyl] *m* testicle
tétanos [tetanos] *m* tetanus
têtard [tetar] *m* tadpole; (bot) pollard
tête [tet] *f* head; heading (*e.g., of chapter*); **à la tête de** in charge of, at the head of; **à tête reposée** at (one's) leisure; **avoir la tête près du bonnet** (coll) to be quick-tempered; **avoir une bonne tête** to have a pleasant look or expression; **de tête** in one's mind's eye, mentally; capable, e.g., **une femme de tête** a capable woman; **en avoir par-dessus la tête** (coll) to be fed up with it; **en tête** foremost, at the front, leading; **en tête à tête avec** alone with; **faire la tête à** to frown at, give a dirty look to; **faire une tête** to wear a long face; **forte tête** strong-minded person; **jeter à la tête à qn** (fig) to cast in s.o.'s face; **tête en bas** head downwards, upside down; **la tête la première** headfirst, headlong; **laver la tête à qn** (coll) to give s.o. a dressing down; **mauvaise tête** troublemaker; **monter à la tête de qn** to go to s.o.'s head; **n'en faire qu'à sa tête** to be a law unto oneself; **par tête** per capita, per head; **piquer une tête** to take a header, dive; **saluer de la tête** to nod; **se mettre en tête de** to take it into

one's head to; **se payer la tête de qn** (coll) to pull s.o.'s leg; **tenir tête à** to face up to, to stand up to; **tête baissée** headlong, heedless; **tête bêche** from top to bottom; head to foot; **tête brûlée** daredevil; **tête chercheuse** homing head (*of missile*); **tête d'affiche** (theat) headliner; **tête de bois** blockhead; **tête de cuvée** choice wine; **tête de lecture** (elec) playback head; **tête de ligne** truck terminal; railhead; **tête de linotte** scatterbrain; **tête de pont** (mil) bridgehead, beachhead; **tête de Turc** butt, scapegoat, fall guy; **tête montée** excitable person; **tête morte et tibias** skull and crossbones; **tomber sur la tête** (coll) to be off one's rocker

tête-à-queue [tɛtakø] *m invar* about-face, slue

tétée [tete] *f* sucking; feeding time

téter [tete] §10 *tr & intr* to suck

tétine [tetin] *f* nipple; teat

téton [tetɔ̃] *m* (coll) tit

tétras [tetrɑ] *m* grouse

tette [tɛt] *f* (coll) tit

tê·tu -tue [tety] *adj* stubborn

teuf-teuf [tœftœf] *m* (*pl* **teuf-teuf** or **teufs-teufs**) (coll) jalopy ‖ *interj* chug! chug!

tévé [teve] *f* (acronym) (**télévision**) TV

texte [tɛkst] *m* text; (mov, telv) script; **apprendre son texte** (theat) to learn one's lines

textile [tɛkstil] *adj & m* textile

tex·tuel -tuelle [tɛkstɥɛl] *adj* textual; verbatim

texture [tɛkstyr] *f* texture

thaï [tai] *adj invar & m* Thai

thaïlan·dais [tajlɑ̃dɛ] **-daise** [dɛz] *adj* Thai ‖ (*cap*) *mf* Thai

Thaïlande [tajlɑ̃d] *f* Thailand

thaumaturge [tomatyrʒ] *m* miracle worker, magician

thé [te] *m* tea

théâ·tral -trale [teɑtral] *adj* (*pl* **-traux** [tro]) theatrical

théâtre [teɑtr] *m* theater; stage, boards; scene (*e.g., of the crime*)

théier [teje] **théière** [tejɛr] *adj* tea ‖ *m* tea (*shrub*) ‖ *f* see **théière**

théière [tejɛr] *f* teapot

thème [tɛm] *m* theme; translation (*into a foreign language*)

théologie [teɔlɔʒi] *f* theology

théorème [teɔrɛm] *m* theorem

théorie [teɔri] *f* theory; procession

théorique [teɔrik] *adj* theoretical

thérapeutique [terapøtik] *adj* therapeutic ‖ *f* therapeutics

thérapie [terapi] *f* therapy

Thérèse [terɛz] *f* Theresa

ther·mal -male [tɛrmal] *adj* (*pl* **-maux** [mo]) thermal

thermique [tɛrmik] *adj* thermal

thermocouple [tɛrmɔkupl] *m* thermocouple

thermodynamique [tɛrmɔdinamik] *adj* thermodynamic ‖ *f* thermodynamics

thermomètre [tɛrmɔmɛtr] *m* thermometer

thermonucléaire [tɛrmɔnykleɛr] *adj* thermonuclear

Thermopyles [tɛrmɔpil] *fpl*—**les Thermopyles** Thermopylae

thermos [tɛrmɔs] *f* thermos bottle

thermosiphon [tɛrmɔsifɔ̃] *m* hot-water heater

thermostat [tɛrmɔsta] *m* thermostat

thésauriser [tezorize] *tr & intr* to hoard

thésauri·seur [tezorizœr] **-seuse** [zøz] *mf* hoarder

thèse [tɛz] *f* thesis; viewpoint, idea, position

thon [tɔ̃] *m* tuna

thorax [tɔraks] *m* thorax

thrène [trɛn] *m* threnody

thuriféraire [tyriferɛr] *m* incense bearer; flatterer

thym [tɛ̃] *m* thyme

thyroïde [tiroid] *adj & f* thyroid

tiare [tjar] *f* tiara (*papal miter*); papacy

tibia [tibja] *m* tibia; shin; **tibias croisés et tête de mort** skull and crossbones

tic [tik] *m* (pathol) tic; tic tac ticktock

ticket [tikɛ] *m* ticket (*of bus, subway, etc.*); check (*for article in baggage room*); ration stamp; **sans tickets** unrationed; **ticket de quai** platform ticket

tic-tac [tiktak] *m invar* tick

tiède [tjɛd] *adj* lukewarm; mild

tiédeur [tjedœr] *f* lukewarmness; mildness

tiédir [tjedir] *tr* to take the chill off ‖ *intr* to become lukewarm

tien [tjɛ̃] §89 yours

tiens [tjɛ̃] *interj* well!, hey! ‖ *v* see **tenir**; **un "tiens" vaux mieux que deux "tu l'auras"** a bird in the hand is worth two in the bush

tiers [tjɛr] **tierce** [tjɛrs] *adj* third; tertian (*fever*) ‖ *m* third (*in fractions*); **le tiers a** third; the third party; **le tiers et le quart** (coll) everybody and anybody; **le Tiers Monde** the Third World ‖ *f* (typ) press proof

tige [tiʒ] *f* stem; trunk; shaft; shank; piston rod; leg (*of boot*); stock (*of genealogy*)

tignasse [tiɲas] *f* shock, mop (*of hair*)

tigre [tigr] *m* tiger

ti·gré -grée [tigre] *adj* striped; speckled, spotted

tigresse [tigrɛs] *f* tigress

tillac [tijak] *m* top deck (*of old-time ships*)

tilleul [tijœl] *m* linden

tilt [tilt] *m*—**faire tilt** to give an out-of-order signal; (slang) to strike home

timbale [tɛ̃bal] *f* metal cup, mug; (culin) mold; (mus) kettledrum; **décrocher la timbale** (coll) to carry off the prize

timbalier [tɛ̃balje] *m* kettledrummer

timbrage [tɛ̃braʒ] *m* stamping; cancellation (*of mail*)

timbre [tɛ̃br] *m* bell; doorbell; buzzer; seal, stamp; postage stamp; postmark; snare (*of drum*); (phonet, phys) timbre

tim·bré -brée [tɛ̃bre] *adj* stamped; ringing (*voice*); (coll) cracked, crazy

timbre-poste [tɛ̃brəpɔst] *m* (*pl* **timbres-poste**) postage stamp

timbrer [tɛ̃bre] *tr* to stamp; postmark

timbres-prime [tɛ̃mbrəprim] *mpl* trading stamps

timide [timid] *adj* timid, shy

timon [timɔ̃] *m* pole (*of carriage*); beam (*of plow*); (naut) helm

timonier [timɔnje] *m* helmsman; wheel horse

timo·ré -rée [timɔre] *adj* timorous

tin [tɛ̃] *m* chock

tinette [tinɛt] *f* firkin (*tub*); bucket (*for fecal matter*)

tintamarre [tɛ̃tamar] *m* uproar

tintement [tɛ̃tmɑ̃] *m* tolling (*of bell*); tinkle (*of bell*); ringing (*in ears*)

tinter [tɛ̃te] *tr* to toll ‖ *intr* to toll; tinkle; jingle, clink; ring (*said of ears*)

tintin [tɛ̃tɛ̃] *m*—**faire tintin** (slang) to do without ‖ *interj* (slang) nothing doing!

tintouin [tɛ̃twɛ̃] *m* (coll) trouble

tique [tik] *f* (ent) tick

tiquer [tike] *intr* to twitch; (coll) to wince; **sans tiquer** (coll) without turning a hair

tir [tir] *m* shooting; firing; aim; shooting gallery; **tir à la cible** target practice; **tir à l'arc** archery; **tir au fusil** gunnery; **tir au pigeon** trapshooting

tirade [tirad] *f* (theat) long speech

tirage [tiraʒ] *m* drawing; towing; draft (*of chimney*); printing; circulation (*of newspaper*); (coll) tension, friction; **tirage à part** offprint; **tirage au sort** lottery drawing; **tirage de luxe** deluxe edition

tiraillement [tirɑjmɑ̃] *m* pain, cramp; conflict, tension

tirailler [tirɑje] *tr* to pull about, tug at; pester ‖ *intr* to blaze away; **tirailler sur** to snipe at ‖ *ref* to have a misunderstanding

tirailleur [tirɑjœr] *m* sharpshooter; sniper; (fig) free lance

tirant [tirɑ̃] *m* string; strap; **tirant d'eau** draft (*of ship*)

tire [tir] *f* (heral) row (*of vair*); (slang) car, auto; (Canad) taffy pull

ti·ré -rée [tire] *adj* drawn; printed ‖ *m* shooting preserve; payee; **tiré à part** offprint

tire-au-flanc [tiroflɑ̃] *m invar* (coll) malingerer, shirker, goof-off

tire-botte [tirbɔt] *m* (*pl* **-bottes**) bootjack

tire-bouchon [tirbuʃɔ̃] *m* (*pl* **-bouchons**) corkscrew; corkscrew curl

tire-bouchonner [tirbuʃɔne] *tr* to twist in a spiral

tire-bouton [tirbutɔ̃] *m* (*pl* **-boutons**) buttonhook

tire-clou [tirklu] *m* (*pl* **-clous**) nail puller

tire-d'aile [tirdɛl]—**à tire-d'aile** with wings outspread, swiftly

tire-fond [tirfɔ̃] *m invar* spike; screw eye

tire-larigot [tirlarigo]—**boire à tire-larigot** to drink like a fish

tire-ligne [tirliɲ] *m* (*pl* **-lignes**) ruling pen

tirelire [tirlir] *f* piggy bank; (*face*) (coll) mug; (*head*) (coll) noggin; (slang) belly

tire-l'œil [tirlœj] *m invar* eye catcher

tirer [tire] *tr* to draw; pull, tug; shoot, fire; run off, print; take out; take, get; stick out (*one's tongue*); **tirer au clair** to bring out into the open; **tirer parti de** to turn to account ‖ *intr* to pull; shoot; draw (*e.g., to a close*); draw (*said of chimney*); **tirer à, vers,** or **sur** to border on ‖ *ref* to extricate oneself; **s'en tirer** to manage; get off (*get out of a difficulty*); **se tirer d'affaire** to pull through, get along

tiret [tirɛ] *m* dash; blank (*on an exam*)

tirette [tirɛt] *f* slide (*of desk*); damper (*of chimney*)

tireur [tirœr] *m* marksman; drawer, payer (*of check*); printer; **tireur de bois flotté** log driver; **tireur d'élite** sharpshooter; **tireur d'épée** fencer; **tireur isolé** sniper

tireuse [tirøz] *f* markswoman; **tireuse de cartes** fortuneteller

tiroir [tirwar] *m* drawer; (mach) slide valve; **à tiroirs** episodic (*play, novel, etc.*)

tiroir-caisse [tirwarkɛs] *m* (*pl* **tiroirs-caisses**) cash register

tisane [tizan] *f* tea, infusion; (coll) bad champagne; (slang) slap

tison [tizɔ̃] *m* ember; (fig) firebrand

tisonner [tizɔne] *tr* to poke

tisonnier [tizɔnje] *m* poker

tissage [tisaʒ] *m* weaving

tisser [tise] *tr* & *intr* to weave

tisse·rand [tisrɑ̃] **-rande** [rɑ̃d] *mf* weaver

tis·seur [tisœr] **-seuse** [søz] *mf* weaver

tissu [tisy] *m* tissue; cloth; fabric, material; pack (*of lies*)

tissu-éponge [tisyepɔ̃ʒ] *m* (*pl* **tissus-éponges**) toweling, terry cloth

tissure [tisyr] *f* texture; (fig) framework

titane [titan] *m* titanium

titi [titi] *m* (slang) street urchin

Titien [tisjɛ̃] *m*—**le Titien** Titian

titre [titr] *m* title; title page; heading; headline; fineness (*of coinage*); claim, right; concentration (*of a solution*); **à juste titre** rightly so; **à titre de** in the capacity of; by virtue of; **à titre d'emprunt** as a loan; **à titre d'essai** on trial; **à titre expérimental** as an experiment; **à titre gratuit** or **gracieux** free of charge; **titres** qualifications; (com) securities

titrer [titre] *tr* to title; subtitle (*films*)

tituber [titybe] *intr* to stagger

titulaire [titylɛr] *adj* titular ‖ *mf* incumbent; holder (*of passport, license, degree, post, lock box, etc.*)

titulariser [titylarize] *tr* to confirm the appointment of

toast [tost] *m* toast; **porter un toast à** to toast

toboggan [tɔbɔgɑ̃] *m* toboggan; toboggan run; slide, chute

toc [tɔk] *adj invar* (coll) worthless; (coll) crazy ‖ *m* (mach) chuck; (coll) imitation; **en toc** (coll) worthless; **toc, toc!** knock, knock!

tohu-bohu [tɔybɔy] *m* hubbub

toi [twa] §85, §87 you

toile [twal] *f* cloth; linen; canvas, painting; (theat) curtain; **toile à coton** calico; **toile à laver** dishrag; **toile à matelas** ticking; **toile à voile** sailcloth; **toile cirée** oilcloth; **toile d'araignée** cobweb; **toile de fond** backdrop

toilette [twalɛt] *f* toilet; dressing table; dress, outfit (*of a woman*); **aimer la toilette** to be fond of clothing; **faire la toilette de** to lay out (*a corpse*)

toi-même [twamɛm] §86 yourself

toise [twaz] *f* fathom; **passer à la toise** to measure the height of

toiser [twaze] *tr* to size up

toison [twazɔ̃] *f* fleece; mop (*of hair*); **Toison d'or** Golden Fleece

toit [twa] *m* roof; rooftop; home, house; **crier sur les toits** to shout from the housetops

toiture [twatyr] *f* roofing

tôle [tol] *f* sheet metal; tole (*decorative metalware*); **tôle de blindage** armor plate; **tôle étamée** tin plate; **tôle galvanisée** galvanized iron; **tôle noire** sheet iron; **tôle ondulée** corrugated iron

tolérable [tɔlerabl] *adj* tolerable, bearable

tolérance [tɔlerɑ̃s] *f* tolerance

tolérer [tɔlere] §10 *tr* to tolerate

tôlerie [tolri] *f* sheet metal; rolling mill

tolet [tɔlɛ] *m* oarlock

tollé [tɔle] *m* outcry, protest

tomaison [tɔmɛzɔ̃] *f* volume number

tomate [tɔmat] *f* tomato

tombe [tɔ̃b] *f* tomb; grave; tombstone

tom·beau [tɔ̃bo] *m* (*pl* **-beaux**) tomb; **à tombeau couvert** lickety-split

tombée [tɔ̃be] *f* fall (*of rain, snow, etc.*); **tombée de la nuit** nightfall

tomber [tɔ̃be] *tr* to throw (*a wrestler*); (coll) to remove (*a piece of clothing*); (slang) to seduce (*a woman*) ‖ *intr* (*aux:* ÉTRE) to fall, drop; **tomber amoureux** to fall in love; **tomber bien** to happen just in time; **tomber en panne** to have a breakdown; **tomber sur** to run into, chance upon; turn to (*said of conversation*)

tombe·reau [tɔ̃bro] *m* (*pl* **-reaux**) dump truck; dumpcart; load

tombola [tɔ̃bɔla] *m* raffle

tome [tɔm] *m* tome, volume

ton [tɔ̃] *adj poss* §88 your ‖ *m* tone; (mus) key

to·nal -nale [tɔnal] *adj* (*pl* **-nals**) tonal

tonalité [tɔnalite] *f* tonality; (telp) dial tone; **tonalité continue** dial tone; **tonalité d'appel** ring; **tonalité insolite** warning tone; out-of-order signal

ton·deur [tɔ̃dœr] **-deuse** [døz] *mf* shearer ‖ *f* shears; **tondeuse à cheveux** hair clippers; **tondeuse à gazon** lawn mower; **tondeuse (à gazon) à moteur** power mower; **tondeuse auto-portée** riding mower; **tondeuse électrique** electric clippers; **tondeuse mécanique** cropper; power mower

tondre [tɔ̃dr] *tr* to clip; shear; mow

toni·fiant [tɔnifjɑ̃] **-fiante** [fjɑ̃t] *adj & m* tonic

tonifier [tɔnifje] *tr* to tone up

tonique [tɔnik] *adj & m* tonic

toni·truant [tɔnitryɑ̃] **-truante** [tryɑ̃t] *adj* (coll) thunderous

tonne [tɔn] *f* ton; tun

ton·neau [tɔno] *m* (*pl* **-neaux**) barrel; cart; roll (*of automobile, airplane, etc.*); (naut) ton; **au tonneau** on draught; **tonneau de poudre** powder keg

tonnelet [tɔnlɛ] *m* keg

tonnelier [tɔnəlje] *m* cooper

tonnelle [tɔnɛl] *f* arbor

tonner [tɔne] *intr* to thunder

tonnerre [tɔnɛr] *m* thunder

tonte [tɔ̃t] *f* clipping; shearing; mowing

tonton [tɔ̃tɔ̃] *m* (slang) uncle

top [tɔp] *m* beep

topaze [tɔpaz] *f* topaz

toper [tɔpe] *intr* to shake hands on it; **tope là!** it's a deal!

topinambour [tɔpinɑ̃bur] *m* Jerusalem artichoke

topique [tɔpik] *adj* local, regional

topographie [tɔpɔgrafi] *f* topography

toquade [tɔkad] *f* (coll) infatuation

toquante [tɔkɑ̃t] *f* (coll) ticker (*watch*)

toque [tɔk] *f* toque; cap (*of chef; of judge*)

to·qué -quée [tɔke] *adj* (coll) crazy, cracked ‖ *mf* (coll) nut

toquer [tɔke] *tr* to infatuate ‖ *intr* (coll) to rap, tap ‖ *ref*—**se toquer de** to be infatuated with

torche [tɔrʃ] *f* torch; **se mettre en torche** to fail to open (*said of parachute*); **torche électrique** flashlight

torcher [tɔrʃe] *tr* to wipe clean; rush through, botch; daub with clay and straw; (vulg) **je m'en torche!** to hell with it!

torchère [tɔrʃɛr] *f* candelabrum; floor lamp

torchis [tɔrʃi] *m* adobe

torchon [tɔrʃɔ̃] *m* dishcloth; rag; (coll) scribble; **le torchon brûle** they're squabbling

torchonner [tɔrʃɔne] *tr* (coll) to botch

tor·dant [tɔrdɑ̃] **-dante** [dɑ̃t] *adj* (coll) sidesplitting

tord-boyaux [tɔrbwajo] *m invar* (coll) rotgut

tordeuse [tɔrdøz] *f* moth

tordoir [tɔrdwar] *m* wringer; rope-making machine

tordre [tɔrdr] *tr* to twist; wring ‖ *ref* to twist; writhe; **se tordre de rire** to split one's sides laughing

toréador [tɔreadɔr] *m* (obs) toreador

tornade [tɔrnad] *f* tornado

toron [tɔrɔ̃] *m* strand (*of rope*)

torpédo [tɔrpedo] *f* (archaic) open touring car

torpeur [tɔrpœr] *f* torpor

torpille [tɔrpij] *f* torpedo; (arti) mine

torpiller [tɔrpije] *tr* to torpedo

torpilleur [tɔrpijœr] *m* torpedo boat; torpedoman

torque [tɔrk] *f* coil of wire; twist (*of tobacco*)

torréfaction [tɔrefaksjɔ̃] *f* roasting

torréfier [tɔrefje] *tr* to roast

torrent [tɔrɑ̃] *m* torrent

torride [tɔrid] *adj* torrid

tors [tɔr] **torse** [tɔrs] *adj* twisted; crooked ‖ *m* twist ‖ see **torse** *m*

torsade [tɔrsad] *f* twisted cord; coil (*of hair*); **à torsades** fringed

torsader [tɔrsade] *tr* to twist

torse [tɔrs] *m* torso, trunk

torsion [tɔrsjɔ̃] *f* twisting, torsion

tort [tɔr] *m* wrong; harm; **à tort** wrongly; **à tort et à travers** at random, wildly; carelessly, inconsiderately; **à tort ou à raison** rightly or wrongly; **avoir tort** to be wrong; **donner tort à** to lay the blame on; **faire tort à** to wrong

torticolis [tɔrtikɔli] *m* stiff neck

tortillard [tɔrtijar] *adj masc* knotty ‖ *m* (coll) jerkwater train

tortiller [tɔrtije] *tr* to twist, twirl; (slang) to gulp down ‖ *intr* to wriggle; (coll) to beat about the bush ‖ *ref* to wriggle, squirm; writhe, twist

tor·tu -tue [tɔrty] *adj* crooked ‖ *f* turtle, tortoise

tor·tueux [tɔrtɥø] **-tueuse** [tɥøz] *adj* winding; devious, underhanded

torture [tɔrtyr] *f* torture

torturer [tɔrtyre] *tr* to torture

torve [tɔrv] *adj* menacing

tos·can [tɔskɑ̃] **-cane** [kan] *adj* Tuscan ‖ *m* Tuscan (*dialect*) ‖ (*cap*) *mf* Tuscan (*person*)

tôt [to] *adv* soon; early; **au plus tôt** as soon as possible; at the earliest; **le plus tôt possible** as soon as possible; **pas de si tôt** not soon; **tôt ou tard** sooner or later

to·tal -tale [tɔtal] *adj & m* (*pl* **-taux** [to]) total

totaliser [tɔtalize] *tr* to total

totalitaire [tɔtalitɛr] *adj* totalitarian

totem [tɔtɛm] *m* totem

toton [tɔtɔ̃] *m* teetotum

toubib [tubib] *m* (coll) medical officer; (coll) doctor, physician

tou·chant [tuʃɑ̃] **-chante** [ʃɑ̃t] *adj* touching ‖ **touchant** *prep* touching, concerning

touche [tuʃ] *f* touch; key (*of piano or typewriter*); stop (*of organ*); fret (*of guitar*); fingerboard (*of violin*); hit (*in fencing*); bite (*on fishline*); goad (*for cattle*); tab (*of file index*); thumb index; (elec) contact; (coll) look, appearance; **touche de blocage** shift lock; **touche de manœuvre** shift key; **touche de recul** backspacer; **touche marge libre, touche passe-marge** margin release

touche-à-tout [tuʃatu] *m invar* (coll) busybody

toucher [tuʃe] *m* touch, sense of touch ‖ *tr* to touch; concern; cash (*a check*); draw out (*money*); goad (*cattle*); (mus) to pluck (*the strings*) ‖ *intr* to touch; **toucher à** to touch (*one's food, capital, etc.*); touch

on; call at (*a port*); be about to achieve (*one's aim*); **toucher de** to play (*e.g., the piano*) ‖ *ref* to touch

touer [twe] *tr* to warp, kedge

touffe [tuf] *f* tuft; clump (*of trees*)

touffeur [tufœr] *f* suffocating heat

touf·fu -fue [tufy] *adj* bushy; (fig) dense

touille [tuj] *m* dogfish, shark

touiller [tuje] *tr* (coll) to stir; (coll) to mix; (coll) to shuffle

toujours [tuʒur] *adv* always; still; anyhow; **M. Toujours** (coll) yes man; **pour toujours** forever

toupet [tupɛ] *m* tuft (*of hair*); forelock (*of horse*); (coll) nerve, brass

toupie [tupi] *f* top; molding board; silly woman

tour [tur] *m* turn; tour; trick; lathe; **à tour de bras** with all one's might; **à tour de rôle** in turn; **en un tour de main** in a jiffy, in a flash; **faire le tour de** to tour, to visit; to walk or ride around; **faire un tour de** to take a walk or ride in; **faire un tour de cochon à** (slang) to play a dirty trick on; **fermer à double tour** to double-lock; **tour à tour** by turns; **tour de bâton** (coll) rake-off; killing; **tour de main, tour d'adresse** sleight of hand; **tour de poitrine** chest size; **tour de reins** sudden back pain; **tour de taille** waist measurement; **tour de tête** hat size; **tours et retours** twists and turns; **tours mn.** revolutions per minute ‖ *f* tower; (chess) castle, rook; (mil) turret; **tour de contrôle** control tower; **tour de forage** oil rig, derrick; **tour de guet** lookout tower

tourbe [turb] *f* peat; mob

tourbillon [turbijɔ̃] *m* whirl; whirlpool; whirlwind

tourbillonner [turbijɔne] *intr* to whirl, to swirl

tourelle [turɛl] *f* turret

tourillon [turijɔ̃] *m* axle; trunnion

tourisme [turism] *m* tourism; tourist industry; sightseeing; **de tourisme** tourist; **faire du tourisme** to do some sightseeing

touriste [turist] *adj & mf* tourist

tourment [turmɑ̃] *m* torment

tourmente [turmɑ̃t] *f* storm

tourmenter [turmɑ̃te] *tr* to torment ‖ *ref* to fret

tour·nant [turnɑ̃] **-nante** [nɑ̃t] *adj* turning, revolving ‖ *m* turn; turning point; water wheel

tourne-à-gauche [turnagoʃ] *m invar* wrench; saw set; diestock

tournebroche [turnəbrɔʃ] *m* roasting jack, turnspit

tourne-disque [turnədisk] *m* (*pl* **-disques**) record player

tournedos [turnədo] *m* filet mignon

tournée [turne] *f* round; **en tournée** (theat) on tour; **faire une tournée** to take a trip; **offrir la tournée générale** (coll) to treat everyone to a round of drinks; **tournée électorale** political campaign

tournemain [turnəmɛ̃]—**en un tournemain** in a split second

tourne-pierre [turnɛpjɛr] *m* (*pl* **-pierres**) (orn) turnstone

tourner [turne] *tr* to turn; turn over; shoot (*a moving picture; a scene*); outflank; **tourner et retourner** to turn over and over ‖ *intr* to turn; (mov) to shoot a picture; (theat) to tour; **la tête me (lui,** etc.) **tourne** my (his, etc.) head is turning, I feel (he feels, etc.) dizzy; **silence, on tourne!** quiet on the set!; **tourner à** or **en** to turn into; **tourner autour du pot** (coll) to beat about the bush; **tourner bien** to turn out well; **tourner court** to make a sharp turn; **tourner en rond** to go around in circles, spin; **tourner mal** to go bad ‖ *ref* to turn

tournesol [turnəsɔl] *m* litmus; sunflower

tournevis [turnəvis] *m* screwdriver

tourniquet [turnikɛ] *m* turnstile; revolving door; revolving display stand; (surg) tourniquet; **passer au tourniquet** (slang) to be court-martialed

tournoi [turnwa] *m* tournament

tournoyer [turnwaje] §47 *intr* to turn, wheel; twirl; tourney

tournure [turnyr] *f* turn, course (*of events*); wording, phrasing, turn (*of phrase*); expression; shape, figure; **prendre tournure** to take shape

tourte [turt] *adj* (slang) stupid ‖ *f* (coll) dolt; **tourte à la viande** meat pie

tour·teau [turto] *m* (*pl* **-teaux**) oil cake; crab

tourte·reau [turtəro] *m* (*pl* **-reaux**) turtledove, young lover

tourterelle [turtərɛl] *f* turtledove

tourtière [turtjɛr] *f* pie pan

toussailler [tusaje] *intr* to keep on coughing

Toussaint [tusɛ̃] *f* All Saints' Day; **la Toussaint** All Saints' Day

tousser [tuse] *intr* to cough; clear one's throat

tousserie [tusri] *f* constant coughing

toussotement [tusɔtmɑ̃] *m* slight coughing

toussoter [tusɔte] *intr* to cough slightly

tout [tu] **toute** [tut] (*pl* **tous toutes**) *adj* any, every, all; all, all of, e.g., **tous les hommes** all men, all of the men; whole, entire, e.g., **toute la journeé** the whole day; **à tout coup** every time; **à toute heure** at any time; **tous les deux** both; **tout le monde** everybody, everyone ‖ *m* (*pl* **touts**) whole, all; everything; sum; **du tout** (coll) not at all; **en tout** wholly, in all; **jouer le tout pour le tout** (slang) to shoot the works; **pas du tout** not at all ‖ **tout toute** (*pl* **tous** [tus] **toutes**) *pron* all, everything, anything; **à tout prendre** on the whole; **tout compté** all things considered ‖ **tout** *adv* all, quite, completely; very, e.g., **un des tout premiers** one of the very foremost; **tout à côté de** right next to; **tout à coup** suddenly; **tout à fait** quite; **tout à l'heure** in a little while; a little while ago; **tout au plus** at most; **tout**

de même however, all the same; **tout de suite** at once, immediately; **tout d'un coup** all at once; **tout en** while, e.g., **tout en parlant** while talking; **tout éveillé** wide awake; **tout fait** ready-made; **tout haut** aloud; **tout neuf** brand-new; **tout nu** stark-naked; **tout près** nearby; **tout . . . que** despite the fact that, e.g., **tout vieux qu'il était** despite the fact that he was old ‖ **toute toutes** *adv* (before a feminine word beginning with a consonant or an aspirate **h**) all, quite, completely, e.g., **elles sont toutes seules** they are all (or quite or completely) alone

tout-à-l'égout [tutalegu] *m invar* sewerage

toute-épice [tutepis] *f* (*pl* **toutes-épices** [tutepis]) allspice (*berry*)

toutefois [tutfwa] *adv* however

toute-puissance [tutpɥisɑ̃s] *f* omnipotence

toutou [tutu] *m* (coll) doggie

Tout-Paris [tupari] *m invar* high society, smart set (*in Paris*)

tout-petit [tupəti] *m* (*pl* **-petits**) toddler

tout-puissant [tupɥisɑ̃] **toute-puissante** [tutpɥisɑ̃t] (*pl* **tout-puissants toutes-puissantes**) *adj* almighty ‖ **le Tout-Puissant** the Almighty

tout-venant [tuvnɑ̃] *m invar* all comers; run-of-the-mine coal; run-of-the-mill product; ordinary run of people

toux [tu] *f* cough

toxicomane [tɔksikɔman] *adj* addicted ‖ *mf* drug addict, junkie

toxicomanie [tɔksikɔmani] *f* drug addiction

toxique [tɔksik] *adj* toxic ‖ *m* poison

tph *abbr* (**telephone**) tel.

trac [trak] *m* (coll) stage fright; **avoir le trac** (coll) to lose one's nerve; **tout à trac** without thinking

tracas [traka] *m* worry, trouble

tracasser [trakase] *tr & ref* to worry

tracasserie [trakasri] *f* bother; **tracasseries** interference

tracassin [trakasɛ̃] *m* (coll) worry

trace [tras] *f* trace; track, trail; sketch; footprint; **marcher sur les traces de** to follow in the footsteps of

tracé [trase] *m* tracing; **faire le tracé de** to lay out; (math) to plot

tracer [trase] §51 *tr* to trace, draw

tra·ceur [trasœr] **-ceuse** [søz] *mf* tracer ‖ *m* tracer (*radioactive substance*)

trachée [traʃe] *f* trachea, windpipe

trachée-artère [traʃeartɛr] *f* (*pl* **trachées-artères**) windpipe

tract [trakt] *m* tract

tractation [traktɑsjɔ̃] *f* underhanded deal

tracteur [traktœr] *m* tractor

traction [traksjɔ̃] *f* traction; **faire des tractions** to do chin-ups; **traction avant** front-wheel drive

tradition [tradisjɔ̃] *f* tradition

tradition·nel -nelle [tradisjɔnɛl] *adj* traditional

traduc·teur [tradyktœr] **-trice** [tris] *mf* translator

traduction [tradyksjɔ̃] *f* translation

traduire [tradµir] §19 *tr* to translate; **traduire en justice** to haul into court

trafic [trafik] *m* traffic, trade; **trafic d'influence** influence peddling; **trafic routier** highway traffic

trafi·quant [trafikɑ̃] **-quante** [kɑ̃t] *mf* racketeer; **trafiquant en stupéfiants** dope peddler

trafiquer [trafike] *tr* to traffic in ‖ *intr* to traffic; **trafiquer de** to traffic in or on

trafi·queur [trafikœr] **-queuse** [køz] *mf* racketeer

tragédie [traʒedi] *f* tragedy

tragé·dien [traʒedjɛ̃] **-dienne** [djɛn] *mf* tragedian

tragique [traʒik] *adj* tragic

trahir [trair] *tr* to betray

trahison [traizɔ̃] *f* betrayal; treason

train [trɛ̃] *m* pace, speed; manner, way; series; raft (*of logs*); (rr) train; (coll) row, racket; (slang) hind end; **aller son petit train** to go along nicely; **être en train de** + *inf* to be in the act or process of + *ger*; (translated by a progressive form of the verb), e.g., **je suis en train d'écrire** I am writing; **mettre en train** to start; **se magner le train** (slang) to get a move on; **train arrière** (aut) rear-axle assembly; (rr) rear car; **train avant** (aut) front-axle assembly; **train d'atterrissage** landing gear; **train de banlieue** suburban train; **train de marchandises** freight train; **train d'enfer** furious pace; **train de vie** way of life; standard of living; **train de voyageurs** passenger train; **train direct** express train; **train omnibus** local train; **train sanitaire** military hospital train

traî·nant [trɛnɑ̃] **-nante** [nɑ̃t] *adj* trailing; creeping; drawling; languid

traî·nard [trɛnar] **-narde** [nard] *mf* straggler

traîne [trɛn] *f* train (*of dress*); dragnet; **à la traîne** dragging; straggling; in tow

traî·neau [trɛno] *m* (*pl* **-neaux**) sleigh; sled; sledge; dragnet

traînée [trene] *f* trail, train; streak; (aer) drag; (coll) streetwalker

traîner [trene] *tr* to drag, lug; drawl; shuffle (*the feet*) ‖ *intr* to drag; straggle; lie around ‖ *ref* to crawl; creep; limp

traî·neur [trɛnœr] **-neuse** [nøz] *mf* straggler; loiterer

train-train [trɛ̃trɛ̃] *m* routine

traire [trɛr] §68 *tr* to milk

trait [trɛ] *m* arrow, dart; dash; stroke; feature (*of face*); trait, characteristic; trace (*of harness*); **avoir trait à** to refer to; **de trait** draft (*horse*); **d'un trait** in one gulp; **partir comme un trait** to be off like a shot; **tracer à grands traits** to trace in broad outlines; **trait d'esprit** witticism; **trait d'héroïsme** heroic deed; **trait d'union** hyphen; **trait pour trait** exactly ‖ *f* see **traite** ‖ **trait** [trɛ] **traite** [trɛt] *v* see **traire**

traitable [trɛtabl] *adj* tractable

traite [trɛt] *f* trade, traffic; milking; (com) draft; **tout d'une traite** at a single stretch ‖ *v* see **traire**

traité [trete] *m* treatise; treaty

traitement [trɛtmɑ̃] *m* treatment; salary; (comp) processing; **mauvais traitements** affront, mistreatment; **traitement des données, traitement de l'information** information processing; **traitement de texte** word processing

traiter [trete] *tr* to treat; receive; **traiter qn de** to call s.o. (*a name*) ‖ *intr* to negotiate; **traiter de** to deal with

traiteur [trɛtœr] *m* caterer; (obs) restaurateur

traî·tre [trɛtr] **-tresse** [trɛs] *adj* traitorous; treacherous; (coll) single ‖ *mf* traitor; (theat) villain ‖ *f* traitress

traîtrise [tretriz] *f* treachery

trajectoire [traʒɛktwar] *f* trajectory; **trajectoire d'attente** (aer) holding pattern

trajet [traʒɛ] *m* distance, trip, passage; (aer) flight

tralala [tralala] *m* (coll) fuss

trame [tram] *f* weft; web (*of life*); conspiracy

tramer [trame] *tr* to weave; hatch (*a plot*) ‖ *ref* to be plotted

traminot [tramino] *m* traction-company employee

tramontane [tramɔ̃tan] *f* north wind; **perdre la tramontane** to lose one's bearings

tramp [trɑ̃p] *m* tramp steamer

tramway [tramwɛ] *m* streetcar

tran·chant [trɑ̃ʃɑ̃] **-chante** [ʃɑ̃t] *adj* cutting; glaring; trenchant ‖ *m* cutting edge; knife; side (*of hand*); **à double tranchant** or **à deux tranchants** two-edged

tranche [trɑ̃ʃ] *f* slice; section; portion, installment; group (*of figures*); cross section; tax bracket; **doré sur tranches** (bb) gilt-edged; (coll) gilded (*e.g., youth*); **une tranche de vie** a slice of life

tranchée [trɑ̃ʃe] *f* trench; **tranchées** colic

trancher [trɑ̃ʃe] *tr* to cut off; slice; decide, settle ‖ *intr* to decide once and for all; stand out; **trancher avec** to contrast with; **trancher dans le vif** to cut to the quick; (fig) to take drastic measures; **trancher de** (lit) to affect the manners of

trancheuse [trɑ̃ʃøz] *f* food slicer

tranquille [trɑ̃kil] *adj* quiet, tranquil; **laissez-moi tranquille** leave me alone; **soyez tranquille** don't worry

tranquillement [trɑ̃kilmɑ̃] *adv* quietly, tranquilly

tranquilli·sant [trɑ̃kilizɑ̃] **-sante** [zɑ̃t] *adj* tranquilizing ‖ *m* tranquilizer

tranquilliser [trɑ̃kilize] *tr* to tranquilize; to reassure ‖ *ref* to calm down

tranquillité [trɑ̃kilite] *f* tranquillity

transaction [trɑ̃zaksjɔ̃] *f* transaction; compromise

transat [trɑ̃zat] *m* (coll) transatlantic liner; (coll) deck chair ‖ **la Transat** (coll) the French Line

transatlantique [trɑ̃zatlɑ̃tik] *adj* transatlantic ‖ *m* transatlantic liner; deck chair
transbordement [trɑ̃sbɔrdəmɑ̃] *m* transshipment, transfer
transborder [trɑ̃sbɔrde] *tr* to transship, transfer
transbordeur [trɑ̃sbɔrdœr] *m* transporter bridge
transcender [trɑ̃sɑ̃de] *tr* & *ref* to transcend
transcription [trɑ̃skripsjɔ̃] *f* transcription
transcrire [trɑ̃skrir] §25 *tr* to transcribe; **transcrire en clair** to decode
transe [trɑ̃s] *f* apprehension, anxiety; trance; **être dans des transes** to be quaking in one's boots
transept [trɑ̃sɛpt] *m* transept
transférer [trɑ̃sfere] §10 *tr* to transfer; convey
transfert [trɑ̃sfɛr] *m* transfer, transference
transfo [trɑ̃sfo] *m* (coll) transformer
transforma·teur [trɑ̃sfɔrmatœr] **-trice** [tris] *adj* (elec) transforming ‖ *m* (elec) transformer; **transformateur abaisseur (de tension)** step-down transformer; **transformateur de sonnerie** doorbell transformer; **transformateur élévateur (de tension)** step-up transformer
transformer [trɑ̃sfɔrme] *tr* & *ref* to transform
transfuge [trɑ̃sfyʒ] *m* turncoat
transfuser [trɑ̃sfyze] *tr* to transfuse; instill
transfusion [trɑ̃sfyzjɔ̃] *f* transfusion
transgresser [trɑ̃sgrese] *tr* to transgress
transgression [trɑ̃sgrɛsjɔ̃] *f* transgression
transhumer [trɑ̃zyme] *tr* & *intr* to move from winter to summer pasture
tran·si -sie [trɑ̃zi], [trɑ̃si] *adj* chilled to the bone; numb, transfixed (*with fright*)
transiger [trɑ̃ziʒe] §38 *intr* to compromise
transistor [trɑ̃zistɔr] *m* transistor
transit [trɑ̃zit] *m* transit
transi·tif [trɑ̃zitif] **-tive** [tiv] *adj* transitive
transition [trɑ̃zisjɔ̃] *f* transition
transitoire [trɑ̃zitwar] *adj* transitory; transitional
translation [trɑ̃slɑsjɔ̃] *f* transfer, translation
translitérer [trɑ̃slitere] §10 *tr* to transliterate
translucide [trɑ̃slysid] *adj* translucent
transmetteur [trɑ̃smɛtœr] *adj masc* transmitting ‖ *m* (telg, telp) transmitter; **transmetteur d'ordres** (naut) engine-room telegraph
transmettre [trɑ̃smɛtr] §42 *tr* to transmit; transfer; (sports) to pass
transmission [trɑ̃smisjɔ̃] *f* transmission; broadcast; **transmission en différé** recorded broadcast; **transmission en direct** live broadcast; **transmissions** (mil) signal corps
transmuer [trɑ̃smɥe] *tr* to transmute
transmuter [trɑ̃smyte] *tr* to transmute
transparaître [trɑ̃sparɛtr] §12 *intr* to show through
transparence [trɑ̃sparɑ̃s] *f* transparency; (mov) back projection

transpa·rent [trɑ̃sparɑ̃] **-rente** [rɑ̃t] *adj* transparent ‖ *m* transparent screen; transparency
transpercer [trɑ̃spɛrse] §51 *tr* to transfix
transpiration [trɑ̃spirɑsjɔ̃] *f* perspiration
transpirer [trɑ̃spire] *tr* to sweat ‖ *intr* to sweat, perspire; leak out (*said of news*)
transplanter [trɑ̃splɑ̃te] *tr* to transplant
transport [trɑ̃spɔr] *m* transport; transportation; **transport au cerveau** cerebral hemorrhage; **transport en commun** public transportation
transpor·té -tée [trɑ̃spɔrte] *adj* enraptured, carried away
transporter [trɑ̃spɔrte] *tr* to transport
transposer [trɑ̃spoze] *tr* to transpose
transver·sal -sale [trɑ̃svɛrsal] *adj* (*pl* **-saux** [so]) transversal; cross (*street*)
trapèze [trapɛz] *m* trapeze; trapezoid
trappe [trap] *f* trap door; pitfall, trap; Trappist monastery; **Trappe** Trappist order
trappeur [trapœr] *m* trapper
tra·pu -pue [trapy] *adj* stocky, squat
traque [trak] *f* driving of game
traquenard [traknar] *m* trap, booby trap, pitfall
traquer [trake] *tr* to hem in, bring to bay
traumatique [tromatik] *adj* traumatic
tra·vail [travaj] *m* (*pl* **-vaux** [vo]) work; workmanship; **en travail** in labor; **Travail** Labor; **travail à la pièce, travail à la tâche** piecework; **travail d'équipe** teamwork; **travail de Romain** herculean task; **travaux forcés** hard labor; **travaux ménagers** housework ‖ *m* (*pl* **-vails**) stocks (*for horses*)
travail·lé -lée [travaje] *adj* finely wrought, elaborate; labored
travailler [travaje] §96 *tr* to work; worry ‖ *intr* to work; warp (*said of wood*); **travailler à son compte, travailler pour son compte, travailler à la pige** to freelance; **travailler d'arrache-pied** (coll) to work like a beaver
travail·leur [travajœr] **-leuse** [jøz] *adj* hardworking ‖ *mf* worker, toiler
travailliste [travajist] *adj* & *mf* Labourite (Brit)
travaillomane [travajoman] *mf* (coll) workaholic
travée [trave] *f* span (*of bridge*); row of seats; (archit) bay
traveling [travliŋ] *m* (mov, telv) dolly (*for camera*)
travers [travɛr] *m* breadth; fault, failing; **à travers** across, through; **de travers** awry; **en travers de** across; **par le travers de** abreast of
traverse [travɛrs] *f* crossbeam; cross street; setback; rung (*of ladder*); (rr) tie; **de traverse** cross (*e.g., street*); **mettre à la traverse de** to oppose
traversée [travɛrse] *f* crossing
traverser [travɛrse] *tr* to cross; cut across
traver·sier [travɛrsje] **-sière** [sjɛr] *adj* cross, crossing

traversin [travɛrsɛ̃] *m* bolster (*of bed*)

traves·ti -tie [travɛsti] *adj* disguised; costume (*ball*) ‖ *m* fancy costume, disguise; transvestite; female impersonator

travestir [travɛstir] *tr* to travesty; disguise

travestissement [travɛstismɑ̃] *m* travesty; disguise

trébucher [trebyʃe] *intr* to stumble

tréfiler [trefile] *tr* to wiredraw

trèfle [trɛfl] *m* clover; trefoil; cloverleaf (*intersection*); (cards) club; (cards) clubs

tréfonds [trefɔ̃] *m* secret depths

treillage [trɛjaʒ] *m* trellis

treillager [trɛjaʒe] §38 *tr* to trellis

treille [trɛj] *f* grape arbor

treillis [trɛji] *m* latticework; iron grating; denim; **treillis métallique** wire netting

treilliser [trɛjise] *tr* to trellis

treize [trɛz] §94 *adj & pron* thirteen; the Thirteenth, e.g., **Jean treize** John the Thirteenth ‖ *m* thirteen; thirteenth (*in dates*); **treize à la douzaine** baker's dozen

treizième [trɛzjɛm] §94 *adj, pron* (*masc, fem*), & *m* thirteenth

tréma [trema] *m* dieresis

tremble [trɑ̃bl] *m* aspen (*tree*)

tremblement [trɑ̃bləmɑ̃] *m* trembling; **tremblement de terre** earthquake

trembler [trɑ̃ble] §96, §97 *intr* to tremble

trembleur [trɑ̃blœr] *m* vibrator, buzzer; (rel) Shaker; (rel) Quaker

trembloter [trɑ̃blɔte] *intr* to quiver; quaver

trémie [tremi] *f* hopper

trémolo [tremɔlo] *m* tremolo

trémoussement [tremusmɑ̃] *m* fluttering, flutter; jiggling, jiggle

trémousser [tremuse] *ref* to flutter; jiggle; (coll) to bustle

trempage [trɑ̃paʒ] *m* soaking

trempe [trɑ̃p] *f* temper; soaking; (slang) scolding

trempée [trɑ̃pe] *f* tempering

tremper [trɑ̃pe] *tr* to temper; dilute; dunk ‖ *intr* to soak; become involved (*in, e.g., a crime*)

trempette [trɑ̃pɛt] *f*—**faire la trempette, faire une trempette** to dunk; **faire trempette** to take a dip

tremplin [trɑ̃plɛ̃] *m* springboard, diving board; trampoline; ski jump; (fig) springboard

trentaine [trɑ̃tɛn] *f* age of thirty; **une trentaine de** about thirty

trente [trɑ̃t] §94 *adj & pron* thirty; **sur son trente et un** (coll) all spruced up; **trente et un** thirty-one; **trente et unième** thirty-first ‖ *m* thirty; thirtieth (*in dates*); **trente et un** thirty-one; thirty-first (*in dates*); **trente et unième** thirty-first

trente-deux [trɑ̃tdø] §94 *adj, pron, & m* thirty-two

trente-deuxième [trɑ̃tdøzjɛm] §94 *adj, pron* (*masc, fem*), & *m* thirty-second

trente-six [trɑ̃tsi(s)] §94 *adj, pron, & m* thirty-six; **tous les trente-six du mois** (coll) once in a blue moon

trentième [trɑ̃tjɛm] §94 *adj, pron* (*masc, fem*), & *m* thirtieth

trépas [trepa] *m* (lit) death; **passer de vie à trépas** (lit) to pass away

trépasser [trepase] *intr* (lit) to die

trépied [trepje] *m* tripod

trépigner [trepiɲe] *intr* to stamp one's feet

très [trɛ] *adv* very; **le très honorable** the Right Honorable

trésor [trezɔr] *m* treasure; **Trésor** Treasury

trésorerie [trezɔrri] *f* treasury

tréso·rier [trezɔrje] **-rière** [rjɛr] *mf* treasurer

tressaillement [tresajmɑ̃] *m* start, quiver

tressaillir [tresajir] §69 *intr* to give a start, quiver

tressauter [tresote] *intr* to start

tresse [trɛs] *f* tress

tresser [trɛse] *tr* to braid, plait; weave (*e.g., a basket*)

tré·teau [treto] *m* (*pl* **-teaux**) trestle; **sur les tréteaux** (theat) on the boards

treuil [trœj] *m* windlass; winch

trêve [trɛv] *f* truce; respite; **faire trêve à q.ch.** to interrupt or suspend s.th.; **trêve de . . .** that's enough . . .

tri [tri] *m* sorting

triage [trijaʒ] *m* sorting, selection; classification; (rr) shifting

triangle [trijɑ̃gl] *m* triangle

tribord [tribɔr] *m* starboard

tribu [triby] *f* tribe

tribu·nal [tribynal] *m* (*pl* **-naux** [no]) tribunal, court; **en plein tribunal** in open court; **tribunal de police** police court; **tribunaux pour enfants** juvenile courts

tribune [tribyn] *f* rostrum, tribune; gallery; grandstand; **monter à la tribune** to take the floor; **tribune des journalistes** press box; **tribune d'orgue** organ loft; **tribune libre** open forum; **tribune téléphonique** phone-in show

tribut [triby] *m* tribute

tributaire [tribytɛr] *adj & m* tributary; **être tributaire de** to be dependent upon

tricher [triʃe] *tr & intr* to cheat

tricherie [triʃri] *f* cheating

tri·cheur [triʃœr] **-cheuse** [ʃøz] *mf* cheater; **tricheur professionnel** cardsharper

tricolore [trikɔlɔr] *adj & m* tricolor

tricot [triko] *m* knitting; knitted garment; **tricot de corps, tricot de peau** undershirt

tricotage [trikɔtaʒ] *m* knitting

tricoter [trikɔte] *tr & intr* to knit

trictrac [triktrak] *m* backgammon; backgammon board

trier [trije] *tr* to pick out, screen; **trier sur le volet** to hand-pick

trieur [trijœr] **trieuse** [trijøz] *mf* sorter ‖ *m & f* (mach) sorter

trigonométrie [trigɔnɔmetri] *f* trigonometry

trille [trij] *m* trill

triller [trije] *tr & intr* to trill

trillion [triljɔ̃] *m* quintillion (U.S.A.); trillion (Brit)

trilogie [trilɔʒi] *f* trilogy

trimbaler [trɛ̃bale] *tr* to cart around

trimer [trime] *intr* to slave

trimestre [trimɛstr] *m* quarter (*of a year*); quarter's salary; quarter's rent; (educ) term

tringle [trɛ̃gl] *f* rod; **tringle de rideau** curtain rod

trinité [trinite] *f* trinity

trinquer [trɛ̃ke] *intr* to clink glasses, toast; (slang) to drink; **trinquer avec** to hobnob with

trio [trijo] *m* trio

triom·phant [trijɔ̃fɑ̃] **-phante** [fɑ̃t] *adj* triumphant

triomphe [trijɔ̃f] *m* triumph; **faire triomphe à** to welcome in triumph

tripar·ti -tie [triparti] *adj* tripartite

tripartite [tripartit] *adj* tripartite

tripatouiller [tripatuje] *tr* (coll) to tamper with

tripette [tripɛt] *f*—**ça ne vaut pas tripette** it's not worth a wooden nickel

triple [tripl] *adj & m* triple

tri·plé -plée [triple] *mf* triplet

tripler [triple] *tr & intr* to triple

triplicata [triplikata] *m invar* triplicate

tripot [tripo] *m* gambling den; house of ill repute

tripoter [tripɔte] *tr* to finger, toy with ‖ *intr* to dabble, potter around; rummage

trique [trik] *f* (coll) cudgel

triste [trist] *adj* sad

tristesse [tristɛs] *f* sadness, sorrow

triturer [trityre] *tr* to pulverize, grind ‖ *ref*—**se triturer la cervelle** to rack one's brain

tri·vial -viale [trivjal] *adj* (*pl* **-viaux** [vjo]) trivial; vulgar, coarse

trivialité [trivjalite] *f* triviality; vulgarity, coarseness

tr/mn *abbr* (**tours par minute**) r.p.m.

troc [trɔk] *m* barter; swap; **troc pour troc** even up

troglodyte [trɔglɔdit] *m* cave dweller; (orn) wren

trognon [trɔɲɔ̃] *m* core; (slang) darling, pet

Troie [trwa], [trwa] *f* Troy

trois [trwa] §94 *adj & pron* three; the Third, e.g., **Jean trois** John the Third; **trois heures** three o'clock ‖ *m* three; third (*in dates*)

troisième [trwazjɛm] §94 *adj, pron* (*masc, fem*), & *m* third

trolley [trɔlɛ] *m* trolley

trolleybus [trɔlɛbys] *m* trackless trolley

trombe [trɔ̃b] *f* waterspout; **entrer en trombe** to dash in; **trombe d'eau** deluge

trombone [trɔ̃bɔn] *m* trombone; paper clip

trompe [trɔ̃p] *f* horn; trunk (*of elephant*); beak (*of insect*); **trompe d'Eustache** Eustachian tube

trompe-la-mort [trɔ̃plamɔr] *mf invar* daredevil

trompe-l'œil [trɔ̃plœj] *m invar* dummy effect; (coll) bluff, fake; **en trompe-l'œil** in perspective

tromper [trɔ̃pe] *tr* to deceive, cheat ‖ *ref* to be wrong; **se tromper de** to be mistaken about

tromperie [trɔ̃pri] *f* deceit; fraud; illusion

trompeter [trɔ̃pte] §34 *tr & intr* to trumpet

trompette [trɔ̃pɛt] *m* trumpeter ‖ *f* trumpet; **en trompette** turned up

trom·peur [trɔ̃pœr] **-peuse** [pøz] *adj* false, lying ‖ *mf* deceiver

tronc [trɔ̃] *m* trunk; (slang) head; **tronc des pauvres** poor box

tronche [trɔ̃ʃ] *f* (slang) noodle

tronçon [trɔ̃sɔ̃] *m* stump; section (*e.g., of track*)

tronçonneuse [trɔ̃sɔnøz] *f* chain saw

trône [tron] *m* throne

trôner [trone] *intr* to sit in state ‖ *ref*—**se trôner sur** to lord it over

tronquer [trɔ̃ke] *tr* to truncate, cut off; mutilate

trop [tro] *m* excess; too much; **de trop** too much; to excess; in the way, e.g., **il est de trop ici** he is in the way here; **par trop** altogether, excessively; **trop de . . .** too much . . . ; too many . . . ‖ *adv* too; too much; **trop lourd** overweight

trophée [trɔfe] *m* trophy

tropi·cal -cale [trɔpikal] *adj* (*pl* **-caux** [ko]) tropical

trop-plein [trɔplɛ̃] *m* (*pl* **-pleins**) overflow

troquer [trɔke] *tr* to barter; **troquer contre** to swap for

trot [tro] *m* trot; **au trot** at a trot; (coll) on the double, quickly

trotte [trɔt] *f* (coll) quite a distance to walk

trotter [trɔte] *intr* to trot

trot·teur [trɔtœr] **-teuse** [tøz] *mf* (turf) trotter ‖ *f* second hand; **trotteuse centrale** sweep-second

trottin [trɔtɛ̃] *m* errand girl

trottinette [trɔtinɛt] *f* scooter

trottoir [trɔtwar] *m* sidewalk; **faire le trottoir** to walk the streets (*said of prostitute*); **trottoir roulant** moving walkway, moving sidewalk

trou [tru] *m* hole; pothole; eye (*of needle*); gap; jerkwater town; **boire comme un trou** to drink like a fish; **faire son trou** to feather one's nest; **faire un trou à la lune** to fly the coop; **trou d'air** air pocket; **trou de balle, trou du cul** (vulg) asshole; (fig) asshole; **trou de clef** keyhole (*of clock*); **trou de la serrure** keyhole; **trou de souris** mousehole; **trou d'homme** manhole; **trou d'obus** shell hole; **trou du souffleur** prompter's box; **trou individuel** (mil) foxhole; **trou noir** (astr) black hole

trouble [trubl] *adj* muddy, cloudy, turbid (*liquid*); murky (*sky*); misty (*glass*); blurred (*image; sight*); dim (*light*); vague, disquieting ‖ *m* disquiet; unrest; trouble (*illness*); **troubles dûs au décalage horaire** jet lag

trouble-fête [trubləfɛt] *mf invar* wet blanket, kill-joy

troubler [truble] *tr* to upset, trouble; make muddy; disturb; make cloudy; blur ‖ *ref* to become muddy or cloudy; lose one's composure

trouée [true] *f* gap, breach; (mil) breakthrough

trouille [truj] *f*—**avoir la trouille** (slang) to get cold feet

troupe [trup] *f* troop; band, party; (theat) troupe

trou·peau [trupo] *m* (*pl* -**peaux**) flock; herd; **attention aux troupeaux** (*public sign*) cattle crossing

troupier [trupje] *m* (coll) soldier; **jurer comme un troupier** to swear like a trooper

trousse [trus] *f* case, kit; **avoir qn à ses trousses** to have s.o. at one's heels; **trousse de première urgence** first-aid kit

trous·seau [truso] *m* (*pl* -**seaux**) trousseau; outfit; bunch (*of keys*)

troussequin [truskɛ̃] *m* cantle

trousser [truse] *tr* to turn up; tuck up; polish off; (culin) to truss ‖ *ref* to lift one's skirts

trouvaille [truvɑj] *f* find

trouver [truve] §96 *tr* to find ‖ §95 *ref* to be found; find oneself; to be, e.g., **où se trouve-t-il?** where is he?; **il se trouve que . . .** it happens that . . . ; **se trouver mal** to feel ill

troyen [trwajɛ̃] **troyenne** [trwajɛn] *adj* Trojan ‖ (*cap*) *mf* Trojan

truand [tryɑ̃] **truande** [tryɑ̃d] *adj & m* good-for-nothing

truc [tryk] *m* gadget, device; (coll) trick, gimmick; (coll) thing; (coll) what's-his-name

truchement [tryʃmɑ̃] *m* spokesman; interpreter; **par le truchement de** thanks to, through

trucu·lent [trykylɑ̃] -**lente** [lɑ̃t] *adj* truculent

truelle [tryɛl] *f* trowel

truffe [tryf] *f* truffle

truie [trɥi] *f* sow

truisme [tryism] *m* truism

truite [trɥit] *f* trout; **truite arc-en-ciel** rainbow trout; **truite saumonée** salmon trout

tru·meau [trymo] *m* (*pl* -**meaux**) trumeau (*mirror with painting above in same frame*)

truquage [trykaʒ] *m* faking

truquer [tryke] *tr* to fake; cook (*the accounts*); stack (*the deck*); load (*the dice*); fix (*the outcome of a fight*) ‖ *intr* to resort to fakery

trust [trœst] *m* trust, holding company

T.S.F. [teɛsɛf] *f* (letterword) (**télégraphie sans fil**) wireless; radio

t.s.v.p. *abbr* (**tournez s'il vous plaît**) over (*please turn the page*)

tu [ty] §87 you; **être à tu et à toi avec** to hobnob with

T.U. [tey] *m* (letterword) (**temps universel**) universal time, Greenwich Mean Time

tube [tyb] *m* tube; pipe; (anat) duct; (slang) hit

tubercule [tybɛrkyl] *m* tubercle; tuber

tuberculose [tybɛrkyloz] *f* tuberculosis

tue-mouches [tymuʃ] *m invar* flypaper

tuer [tɥe] *tr* to kill ‖ §96 *ref* to be killed; kill oneself

tuerie [tyri] *f* slaughter

tue-tête [tytɛt]—**à tue-tête** at the top of one's voice

tuile [tɥil] *f* tile; (coll) nasty blow

tuilerie [tɥilri] *f* tileworks

tulipe [tylip] *f* tulip

tumeur [tymœr] *f* tumor

tumulte [tymylt] *m* tumult, hubbub

tungstène [tœkstɛn] *m* tungsten

tunique [tynik] *f* tunic; membrane; (bot) coat, envelope, skin

tunnel [tynɛl] *m* tunnel; **passer sous un tunnel** to go through a tunnel; **tunnel aérodynamique** wind tunnel

turban [tyrbɑ̃] *m* turban

turbine [tyrbin] *f* turbine

turbopropulseur [tyrbɔprɔpylsœr] *m* turboprop

turboréacteur [tyrbɔreaktœr] *m* turbojet

turbu·lent [tyrbylɑ̃] -**lente** [lɑ̃t] *adj* turbulent

turc turque [tyrk] *adj* Turkish ‖ *m* Turkish (*language*) ‖ (*cap*) *mf* Turk (*person*)

turf [tyrf] *m*—**le turf** the turf, the track

turfiste [tyrfist] *m* turfman, racegoer

turlututu [tyrlytyty] *interj* fiddlesticks!, nonsense!

Turquie [tyrki] *f* Turkey; **la Turquie** Turkey

turquoise [tyrkwaz] *m* turquoise (*color*) ‖ *f* turquoise (*stone*)

tutelle [tytɛl] f guardianship, tutelage; trusteeship

tu·teur [tytœr] -**trice** [tris] *mf* guardian ‖ *m* (hort) stake, prop

tutoyer [tytwaje] §47 *tr* to address familiarly; use familiar grammatical forms (**toi, tu,** etc.) in speaking to an intimate, an inferior, or (if a Protestant) to God (*to "thou"*) ‖ *ref* to be on a first-name basis

tuyau [tɥijo], [tyjo] *m* (*pl* **tuyaux**) pipe, tube; fluting; (coll) tip; **tuyau d'arrosage** garden hose; **tuyau d'échappement** exhaust; **tuyau d'incendie** fire hose

tuyauter [tɥijote], [tyjote] *tr* to flute; (coll) to tip off ‖ *intr* (coll) to crib

tuyauterie [tɥijotri] *f* pipe mill; piping; (aut) manifold; **tuyauterie d'admission** intake manifold; **tuyauterie d'échappement** exhaust manifold

tympan [tɛ̃pɑ̃] *m* eardrum; (archit, mus) tympanum

type [tip] *m* type; (coll) fellow, character

typer [tipe] *tr* to type, mark, stamp; characterize

typesse [tipɛs] *f* (slang) dame, broad, gal

typhoïde [tifɔid] *adj & f* typhoid

typhon [tifɔ̃] *m* typhoon

typique [tipik] *adj* typical; South American (*music*)

typographie [tipɔgrafi] *f* typography

typographique [tipɔgrafik] *adj* typograph-ic(al)

typon [tipɔ̃] *m* offset film

tyran [tirɑ̃] *m* tyrant; (orn) kingbird

tyrannie [tirani] *f* tyranny

tyrannique [tiranik] *adj* tyrannic(al)

U

U, u [y], *[y] *m invar* twenty-first letter of the French alphabet

Ukraine [ykrɛn] *f* Ukraine

ukrai·nien [ykrɛnjɛ̃] **-nienne** [njɛn] *adj* Ukrainian ‖ *m* Ukrainian (*language*) ‖ (*cap*) *mf* Ukrainian (*person*)

ulcère [ylsɛr] *m* ulcer, sore

ulcérer [ylsere] §10 *tr* to ulcerate; embitter ‖ *ref* to ulcerate; fester

ulté·rieur -rieure [ylterjœr] *adj* ulterior; subsequent

ultimatum [yltimatɔm] *m* ultimatum

ultime [yltim] *adj* ultimate, final

ultra [yltra] *m* (pol) extremist

ultra-court [yltrakur] **-courte** [kurt] *adj* (electron) ultrashort

ultravio·let [yltravjɔlɛ] **-lette** [lɛt] *adj* & *m* ultraviolet

ululer [ylyle] *intr* to hoot

un [œ̃] **une** [yn] §77 *adj* & *pron* one; **l'un à l'autre** to each other, to one another; **l'un et l'autre** both; **l'un l'autre** each other, one another; **ni l'un ni l'autre** neither, neither one; **un à un** one by one; **une heure** one o'clock ‖ *art indef* a ‖ *m* one ‖ *f*—**il était moins une** it was a narrow escape; **la une** the front page

unanime [ynanim] *adj* unanimous

unanimité [ynanimite] *f* unanimity

Unesco [ynɛsko] *f* (acronym) (**Organisation des Nations Unies pour l'Éducation, la Science et la Culture**)—**l'Unesco UNESCO**

u·ni -nie [yni] *adj* united; smooth; level; uneventful; plain; solid (*color*); together (*said, e.g., of the hands of a clock*) ‖ *m* plain cloth

unicorne [ynikɔrn] *m* unicorn

unième [ynjɛm] *adj* first, e.g., **vingt et unième** twenty-first

unification [ynifikɑsjɔ̃] *f* unification

unifier [ynifje] *tr* to unify ‖ *ref* to consolidate, merge; become unified

uniforme [ynifɔrm] *adj* & *m* uniform

uniformément [ynifɔrmemɑ̃] *adv* uniformly; regularly; steadily

uniformiser [ynifɔrmize] *tr* to make uniform

uniformité [ynifɔrmite] *f* uniformity

unijambiste [yniʒɑ̃bist] *adj* one-legged ‖ *mf* one-legged person

unilaté·ral -rale [ynilateral] *adj* (*pl* **-raux** [ro]) unilateral

union [ynjɔ̃] *f* union; **union libre** common-law marriage

unique [ynik] *adj* only, single; unique

unir [ynir] *tr* & *ref* to unite

unisson [ynisɔ̃] *m* unison

unitaire [ynitɛr] *adj* unit

unité [ynite] *f* unity; unit; battleship; (coll) one million old francs; **unités de valeur** (educ) hours of credit

univers [ynivɛr] *m* universe

univer·sel -selle [ynivɛrsɛl] *adj* & *m* universal

universitaire [ynivɛrsitɛr] *adj* university; academic ‖ *mf* academic

université [ynivɛrsite] *f* university

Untel [œ̃tɛl] *mf* so-and-so, e.g., **Monsieur/Madame Untel** Mr. and Mrs. So-and-so

uranium [yranjɔm] *m* uranium

ur·bain [yrbɛ̃] **-baine** [bɛn] *adj* urban; urbane

urbaniser [yrbanize] *tr* to urbanize

urbanisme [yrbanism] *m* city planning

urbaniste [yrbanist] *adj* zoning (*ordinance*) ‖ *mf* city planner

urbanité [yrbanite] *f* urbanity

urètre [yrɛtr] *m* urethra

urgence [yrʒɑ̃s] *f* urgency; emergency; emergency case; **d'urgence** emergency (*e.g., hospital ward*); right away, without delay

ur·gent [yrʒɑ̃] **-gente** [ʒɑ̃t] *adj* urgent; emergency (*case*); (formula on letter or envelope) rush ‖ *m* urgent matter

urinaire [yrinɛr] *adj* urinary

uri·nal [yrinal] *m* (*pl* **-naux** [no]) urinal (*for use in bed*)

urine [yrin] *f* urine

uriner [yrine] *tr* & *intr* to urinate

urinoir [yrinwar] *m* urinal (*place*)

urne [yrn] *f* urn; ballot box; **aller aux urnes** to go to the polls

urologie [yrɔlɔʒi] *f* urology

U.R.S.S. [yɛrɛsɛs] *f* (letterword) (**Union des Républiques Socialistes Soviétiques**) U.S.S.R.

Ursse [yrs] *f* (acronym) (**Union des Républiques Socialistes Soviétiques**) U.S.S.R.

urticaire [yrtikɛr] *f* hives

urubu [yryby] *m* turkey vulture

us [ys] *mpl*—**les us et (les) coutumes** the manners and customs

U.S. [yɛs] *adj* (letterword) (**United States**) U.S., e.g., **l'aviation U.S.** U.S. aviation

U.S.A. [yɛsa] *mpl* (letterword) (**United States of America**) U.S.A.

usage [yzaʒ] *m* usage; custom; use; **faire de l'usage** to wear well; **hors d'usage** outmoded; (gram) obsolete; **manquer**

d'usage to lack good breeding; **usage du monde** good breeding, savoir-vivre

usa·gé -gée [yzaʒe] *adj* secondhand; worn-out, used

usa·ger [yzaʒe] **-gère** [ʒɛr] *mf* user

usant [yzɑ̃] **usante** [yzɑ̃t] *adj* exhausting, wearing

u·sé -sée [yze] *adj* worn-out; trite, commonplace

user [yze] *tr* to wear out; wear away; ruin (*e.g., health*) ‖ *intr*—**en user bien avec** to treat well; **user de** to use ‖ *ref* to wear out

usine [yzin] *f* factory, mill, plant; **usine à gaz** gasworks

usiner [yzine] *tr* to machine, tool

usi·nier [yzinje] **-nière** [njɛr] *adj* manufacturing; factory (*town*) ‖ *m* manufacturer

usi·té -tée [yzite] *adj* used, in use; **peu usité** out of use, rare

ustensile [ystɑ̃sil] *m* utensil, implement

u·suel -suelle [yzɥɛl] *adj* usual

usure [yzyr] *f* usury; wear and tear

usurper [yzyrpe] *tr* to usurp

utérus [yterys] *m* uterus, womb

utile [ytil] §92 *adj* useful, helpful; **puis-je vous être utile?** can I be of help?

utilisable [ytilazabl] *adj* usable

utilisa·teur [ytilizatœr] **-trice** [tris] *mf* user

utilitaire [ytilitɛr] *adj* utilitarian; utility (*vehicle, goods, etc.*)

utilité [ytilite] *f* utility, usefulness, use; (theat) support; (theat) supporting rôle; **jouer les utilités** (fig) to play second fiddle; **utilités** (theat) small parts

utopique [ytɔpik] *adj* utopian

utopiste [ytɔpist] *mf* utopian

V

V, v [ve] *m invar* twenty-second letter of the French alphabet

v. *abbr* (**voir**) see; (**volume**) vol.

va [va] *v* see **aller**

vacance [vakɑ̃s] *f* vacancy, opening; **vacances** vacation

vacancier [vakɑ̃sje] *m* vacationist

va·cant [vakɑ̃] **-cante** [kɑ̃t] *adj* vacant

vacarme [vakarm] *m* din, racket

vacation [vakɑsjɔ̃] *f* investigation; **vacations** fee; recess

vaccin [vaksɛ̃] *m* vaccine

vaccination [vaksinɑsjɔ̃] *f* vaccination

vaccine [vaksin] *f* cowpox

vacciner [vaksine] *tr* to vaccinate

vache [vaʃ] *adj* embarrassing (*question*); cantankerous (*person*) ‖ *f* cow; cowhide; (*woman*) (slang) bitch; (*man*) (slang) swine, rat; (*policeman*) (slang) flatfoot, bull; **en vache** leather (*e.g., suitcase*); **manger de la vache enragée** (coll) not to have a red cent to one's name; **oh, la vache!** damn it!; **parler français comme une vache espagnole** (coll) to murder the French language; **vache à eau** canvas bucket (*for camping*); **vache à lait** milch cow; (coll) gull, sucker

vachement [vaʃmɑ̃] *adv* (slang) tremendously

va·cher [vaʃe] **-chère** [ʃɛr] *mf* cowherd

vacherie [vaʃri] *f* cowshed; dairy farm; (coll) dirty trick

vachette [vaʃɛt] *f* young calf; calf (*leather*)

vaciller [vasije] *intr* to vacillate, waver; flicker; totter

vacuité [vakɥite] *f* vacuity, emptiness

vacuum [vakɥɔm] *m* vacuum

vade-mecum [vademekɔm] *m invar* handbook, vade mecum

vadrouille [vadruj] *f* (naut) mop, swab; plunger (*plumber's*); (slang) bender, spree

vadrouiller [vadruje] *intr* (slang) to ramble around, gad about

vadrouil·leur [vadrujœr] **-leuse** [jøz] *mf* (slang) rounder

va-et-vient [vaevjɛ̃] *m invar* backward-and-forward motion; hurrying to and fro; comings and goings; ferryboat; (elec) two-way switch

vaga·bond [vagabɔ̃] **-bonde** [bɔ̃d] *adj* vagabond ‖ *mf* vagabond, tramp

vagabondage [vagabɔ̃daʒ] *m* vagrancy; **vagabondage interdit** (*public sign*) no loitering, no begging

vagabonder [vagabɔ̃de] *intr* to wander about, roam, tramp

vagin [vaʒɛ̃] *m* vagina

vagi·nal -nale [vaʒinal] (*pl* **-naux** [no]) *adj* vaginal

vagir [vaʒir] *intr* to cry, wail

vague [vag] *adj* vague; vacant (*look; lot*); waste (*land*) ‖ *m* vagueness; (fig) space, thin air; **vague à l'âme** uneasy sadness ‖ *f* wave; **la nouvelle vague** the wave of the future; **vague de fond** ground swell

vaguemestre [vagmɛstr] *m* (mil, nav) mail clerk

vaguer [vage] *intr* to wander

vaillance [vajɑ̃s] *f* valor

vail·lant [vajɑ̃] **-lante** [jɑ̃t] *adj* valiant; up to scratch

vaille [vaj] *v* (**vailles, vaillent**) see **valoir**

vain [vɛ̃] **vaine** [vɛn] *adj* vein; **en vain** in vain

vaincre [vɛ̃kr] §70 *tr* to defeat, conquer; overcome (*fear, instinct, etc.*) ‖ *intr* to conquer ‖ *ref* to control oneself

vaincs [vɛ̃] *v* (**vainc**) see **vaincre**

vain·cu -cue [vɛ̃ky] *adj* defeated, beaten, conquered ‖ *mf* loser ‖ *v* see **vaincre**

vainquant [vɛ̃kɑ̃] *v* (**vainquez, vainquons**) see **vaincre**

vainqueur [vɛ̃kœr] *adj masc* victorious ‖ *m* victor, winner

vairon [vɛrɔ̃] *adj masc* whitish (*eye*); **vairons** of different colors (*said of eyes*) ‖ *m* (ichth) minnow

vais [vɛ] *v* see **aller**

vais·seau [vɛso] *m* (*pl* **-seaux**) vessel; nave (*of church*); **vaisseau amiral** flagship; **vaisseau sanguin** blood vessel; **vaisseau spatial** spaceship

vaisseau-école [vɛsoekɔl] *m* (*pl* **vaisseaux-écoles**) (nav) training ship

vaisselier [vɛsəlje] *m* china closet

vaisselle [vɛsɛl] *f* dishes; **faire la vaisselle** to wash the dishes; **vaisselle plate** plate (*of gold or silver*)

val [val] *m* (*pl* **vaux** [vo] or **vals**) (obs) valley; **à val** going down the valley; **à val de** (obs) down from

valable [valabl] *adj* valid; worthwhile (*e.g., experience*)

valence [valɑ̃s] *f* (chem) valence

valen·tin [valɑ̃tɛ̃] **-tine** [tin] *mf* valentine (*sweetheart*)

valet [valɛ] *m* valet; holdfast, clamp; (cards) jack; **valet de chambre** valet; **valet de ferme** hired man; **valet de pied** footman

valeur [valœr] *f* value, worth, merit; valor; (*person, thing, or quality worth having*) asset; (com) security, stock; **de valeur** able; valuable; (Canad) too bad, unfortunate; **envoyer en valeur déclarée** to insure (*a package*); **mettre en valeur** to develop (*avenir, a region*); set off, enhance; **valeur d'avenir** growth stock; **valeur de père de famille** blue chips

valeu·reux [valœrø] **-reuse** [røz] *adj* valorous, brave

validation [validɑsjɔ̃] *f* validation

valide [valid] *adj* valid; fit, able-bodied

valider [valide] *tr* to validate

validité [validite] *f* validity

valise [valiz] *f* suitcase; **faire ses valises** to pack, pack one's bags; **valise diplomatique** diplomatic pouch

vallée [vale] *f* valley

vallon [valɔ̃] *m* vale, dell

valoir [valwar] **§71, §95** *tr* to equal; **un service en vaut un autre** one good turn deserves another; **valoir q.ch.** à **qn** to get or bring s.o. s.th., *e.g.,* **cela lui a valu une amélioration** that got him a raise; *e.g.,* **la condamnation lui a valu cinq ans de prison** the verdict brought him five years in prison ‖ *intr* to be worth; **autant vaut y renoncer** might as well give up; **cela ne vaut rien** it's worth nothing; **faire valoir** to set off to advantage; use to advantage; develop (*one's land*); invest (*funds, capital*); put forward (*one's reasons*); **faire valoir que . . .** to argue that . . . ; **vaille que vaille** somehow or other ‖ *impers*—**il vaut mieux** it

would be better to, *e.g.,* **il vaut mieux attendre** it would be better to wait; **mieux vaut tard que jamais** better late than never ‖ *ref*—**les deux se valent** one is as good as the other

valse [vals] *f* waltz

valser [valse] *tr* & *intr* to waltz

va·lu -lue [valy] *v* see **valoir**

valve [valv] *f* (aut, bot, zool) valve; (elec) vacuum tube

valvule [valvyl] *f* valve

vamp [vɑ̃p] *f* vamp

vamper [vɑ̃pe] *tr* (coll) to vamp

vampire [vɑ̃pir] *m* vampire

van [vɑ̃] *m* van (*for moving horses*)

vandale [vɑ̃dal] *adj* vandal; Vandal ‖ *m* vandal ‖ (*cap*) *mf* Vandal

vandalisme [vɑ̃dalism] *m* vandalism

vanille [vanij] *f* vanilla

vani·teux [vanitø] **-teuse** [tøz] *adj* vain, conceited

vanne [van] *f* sluice gate, floodgate; butterfly valve; (slang) gibe

van·neau [vano] *m* (*pl* **-neaux**) (orn) lapwing

vanner [vane] *tr* to winnow; tire out

vannerie [vanri] *f* basketry

vannier [vanje] *m* basket maker

van·tail [vɑ̃taj] *m* (*pl* **-taux** [to]) leaf (*of door, shutter, sluice gate, etc.*)

van·tard [vɑ̃tar] **-tarde** [tard] *adj* bragging, boastful ‖ *mf* braggart

vantardise [vɑ̃tardiz] *f* bragging, boasting

vanter [vɑ̃te] **§97** *tr* to praise; boost, push (*a product on the market*) ‖ *ref* to brag, boast

va-nu-pieds [vanypje] *mf invar* (coll) tramp

vapeur [vapœr] *m* steamship ‖ *f* steam; vapor, mist; **à la vapeur** steamed (*e.g., potatoes*); under steam; (coll) at full speed; **à vapeur** steam (*e.g., engine*); **vapeur d'eau** water vapor; **vapeurs** low spirits

vaporisateur [vapɔrizatœr] *m* atomizer, spray

vaporiser [vapɔrize] *tr* & *ref* to vaporize; spray

vaquer [vake] *intr* to take a recess; **vaquer à** to attend to ‖ *impers*—**il vaque** there is vacant

varappe [varap] *f* cliff; rock climbing

varech [varɛk] *m* wrack, seaweed

vareuse [varøz] *f* (mil) blouse; (nav) peacoat

variable [varjabl] *adj* & *f* variable

va·riant [varjɑ̃] **-riante** [rjɑ̃t] *adj* & *f* variant

variation [varjɑsjɔ̃] *f* variation

varice [varis] *f* varicose veins

varicelle [varisɛl] *f* chicken pox

va·rié -riée [varje] *adj* varied

varier [varje] *tr* & *intr* to vary

variété [varjete] *f* varity; **variétés** selections (*from literary works*); vaudeville

variole [varjɔl] *f* smallpox

vari·queux [varikø] **-queuse** [køz] *adj* varicose

Varsovie [varsɔvi] *f* Warsaw
vase [vɑs] *m* vase; vessel; **en vase clos** shut up; in an airtight chamber; **vase de nuit** chamber pot ‖ *f* mud, slime
vas [va] *v* see **aller**
vaseline [vazlin] *f* petroleum jelly, Vaseline
va·seux [vazø] **-seuse** [zøz] *adj* muddy, slimy; (coll) all in, tired; (coll) fuzzy, obscure
vasistas [vazistɑs] *m* transom
vasouiller [vazuje] *tr* (coll) to make a mess of ‖ *intr* (coll) to go badly
vasque [vask] *f* basin (*of fountain*)
vas·sal -sale [vasal] (*pl* **-saux** [so] **-sales**) *adj* & *mf* vassal
vaste [vast] *adj* vast
vastement [vastəmɑ̃] *adv* (coll) very
Vatican [vatikɑ̃] *m* Vatican
vaticane [vatikan] *adj fem* Vatican
va-tout [vatu] *m*—**jouer son va-tout** to stake one's all, play one's last card
vaudeville [vodvil] *m* vaudeville (*light theatrical piece interspersed with songs*); (obs) satirical song
vaudou [vodu] *adj invar* & *m* voodoo
vaudrai [vodre] *v* (**vaudras, vaudra, vaudrons,** etc.) see **valoir**
vau-l'eau [volo]—**à vau-l'eau** downstream; **s'en aller à vau-l'eau** (fig) to go to pot
vau·rien [vorjɛ̃] **-rienne** [rjɛn] *mf* good-for-nothing
vautour [votur] *m* vulture
vautrer [votre] *ref* to wallow
vaux [vo] *v* (**vaut**) see **valoir**
veau [vo] *m* (*pl* **veaux**) calf; veal; calfskin; (coll) lazybones, dope; **pleurer comme un veau** to cry like a baby; **veau marin** seal
vé·cu -cue [veky] *adj* true to life ‖ *v* see **vivre**
vedette [vədɛt] *f* patrol boat; scout; lead, star; **en vedette** in the limelight; **mettre en vedette** to headline, to highlight; **vedette de l'écran** movie star; **vedette du petit écran** television star
végé·tal -tale [veʒetal] (*pl* **-taux** [to]) *adj* vegetable, vegetal ‖ *m* vegetable
végéta·rien [veʒetarjɛ̃] **-rienne** [rjɛn] *adj* & *mf* vegetarian
végétation [veʒetɑsjɔ̃] *f* vegetation; **végétations** (**adénoïdes**) adenoids
végéter [veʒete] §10 *intr* to vegetate
véhémence [veemɑ̃s] *f* vehemence
véhé·ment [veemɑ̃] **-mente** [mɑ̃t] *adj* vehement
véhicule [veikyl] *m* vehicle
veille [vɛj] *f* watch, vigil; wakefulness; **à la veille de** on the eve of; just before; on the verge or point of; **la veille de** the eve of; the day before; **la Veille de Noël** Christmas Eve; **la Veille du jour de l'An** New Year's Eve; **veilles** sleepless nights, late nights; night work
veillée [veje] *f* evening; social evening; **veillée funèbre, veillée du corps** wake

veiller [veje] *tr* to sit up with, watch over ‖ *intr* to sit up, stay up; keep watch; **veiller à** to look after, see to
veil·leur [vɛjœr] **-leuse** [jøz] *mf* watcher ‖ *m* watchman; **veilleur de nuit** night watchman ‖ *f* see **veilleuse**
veilleuse [vɛjøz] *f* night light; rushlight; pilot light; **mettre en veilleuse** to turn down low; to dim (*the headlights*); to slow down (*production in a factory*)
vei·nard [venar] **-narde** [nard] *adj* (coll) lucky ‖ *mf* (coll) lucky person
veine [vɛn] *f* vein; luck; **veine alors!** (coll) swell!
veiner [vene] *tr* to vein
vei·neux [vɛnø] **-neuse** [nøz] *adj* veined; venous
vélaire [velɛr] *adj* & *f* v‿lar
vêler [vele] *intr* to calve
vélin [velɛ̃] *m* vellum
velléitaire [veleitɛr] *adj* & *mf* erratic
velléité [veleite] *f* stray impulse, fancy; **velléité de sourire** slight smile
vélo [velo] *m* bike; **faire du vélo** to go bicycle riding
vélocité [velɔsite] *f* velocity; speed; agility
vélomoteur [velɔmɔtœr] *m* motorbike
velours [vəlur] *m* velvet; **velours côtelé** corduroy
velou·té -tée [vəlute] *adj* velvety ‖ *m* velvetiness
velouter [vəlute] *tr* to make velvety
ve·lu -lue [vəly] *adj* hairy
vélum [velɔm] *m* awning
velvet [vɛlvɛt] *m* velveteen
venaison [vənɛzɔ̃] *f* venison
ve·nant [vənɑ̃] **-nante** [nɑ̃t] *adj* coming; thriving ‖ *mf* comer; **à tout venant** to all comers
vendange [vɑ̃dɑ̃ʒ] *f* grape harvest; vintage
vendanger [vɑ̃dɑ̃ʒe] §38 *tr* to pick (*the grapes*) ‖ *intr* to harvest grapes
ven·deur [vɑ̃dœr] **-deuse** [døz] *mf* seller; vendor; salesclerk; **vendeur ambulant** peddler ‖ *m* salesman ‖ *f* salesgirl, saleslady
vendre [vɑ̃dr] *tr* to sell; sell out, betray; **à vendre** for sale; **vendre à découvert** to sell short; **vendre au détail** to retail; **vendre aux enchères** to auction off; **vendre en gros** to wholesale ‖ *ref* to sell; sell oneself, sell out
vendredi [vɑ̃drədi] *m* Friday; **vendredi saint** Good Friday
ven·du -due [vɑ̃dy] *adj* sold; corrupt ‖ *mf* traitor
véné·neux [venenø] **-neuse** [nøz] *adj* poisonous
vénérable [venerabl] *adj* venerable
vénérer [venere] §10 *tr* to venerate
véné·rien [venerjɛ̃] **-rienne** [rjɛn] *adj* venereal ‖ *mf* person with venereal disease
vengeance [vɑ̃ʒɑ̃s] *f* vengeance, revenge
venger [vɑ̃ʒe] §38 *tr* to avenge ‖ *ref* to get revenge
ven·geur [vɑ̃ʒœr] **-geuse** [ʒøz] *adj* avenging ‖ *mf* avenger

veni·meux [vənimø] **-meuse** [møz] *adj* venomous

venin [vənɛ̃] *m* venom

venir [vənir] §72, §95, §96, §97 *intr (aux:* ÊTRE) to come; **à venir** forthcoming; **faire venir** to send for; **où voulez-vous en venir?** what are you getting at?; **venez avec** (coll) come along; **venir de** to have just, e.g., **il vient de partir** he has just left ‖ *impers*—**il me (nous,** etc.) **vient à l'esprit que** it occurs to me (to us, etc.) that

Venise [vəniz] *f* Venice

véni·tien [venisjɛ̃] **-tienne** [sjɛn] *adj* Venetian ‖ *(cap) mf* Venetian

vent [vɑ̃] *m* wind; **avoir le vent en poupe** to be in luck; **avoir vent de** to get wind of; **contre vents et marées** through thick and thin; **en plein vent** in the open air; **être dans le vent** to be up to date; **il fait du vent** it is windy; **les vents** (mus) the woodwinds; **vent arrière** tailwind; **vent coulis** draft; **vent debout** headwind; **vent en poupe** (naut) tailwind

vente [vɑ̃t] *f* sale; felling *(of timber)*; **en vente** on sale; **en vente libre** (pharm) on sale without a prescription; **jeunes ventes** new overgrowth; **vente à l'éventaire** sidewalk sale; **vente amiable** private sale; **vente à tempérament** installment selling; **vente à terme** sale on time; **vente au détail** retailing; **vente aux enchères** auction; **vente en gros** wholesaling; **vente par correspondance** mail-order business

ventilateur [vɑ̃tilatœr] *m* ventilator; fan; electric fan

ventiler [vɑ̃tile] *tr* to ventilate; to value separately; (bk) to apportion

ventouse [vɑ̃tuz] *f* sucker; suction cup; suction grip; nozzle *(of vacuum cleaner)*; vent; plunger *(for clogged drain)*

ventre [vɑ̃tr] *m* belly; stomach; womb; **à plat ventre** prostrate; **à ventre déboutonné** (coll) excessively; (coll) with all one's might; **q.ch. dans le ventre** (coll) to have s.th. on the ball; **bas ventre** (fig) genitals; **ventre à terre** (coll) lickety-split

ventricule [vɑ̃trikyl] *m* ventricle

ventriloque [vɑ̃trilɔk] *mf* ventriloquist

ventriloquie [vɑ̃trilɔki] *f* ventriloquism

ventripo·tent [vɑ̃tripɔtɑ̃] **-tente** [tɑ̃t] *adj* (coll) potbellied

ven·tru -true [vɑ̃try] *adj* potbellied

ve·nu -nue [vəny] *adj*—**bien venu** successful; welcome ‖ *mf*—**le premier venu** the first comer; just anyone; **les nouveaux venus** the newcomers ‖ *f* coming, advent ‖ *v* see **venir**

Vénus [venys] *f* Venus

vénusté [venyste] *f* charm, grace

vêpres [vɛpr] *fpl* vespers

ver [vɛr] *m* worm; **tirer les vers du nez à** to worm secrets out of, to pump; **ver à soie** silkworm; **ver de terre** earthworm; **ver luisant** glowworm

véracité [verasite] *f* veracity

véranda [verɑ̃da] *f* veranda

ver·bal -bale [vɛrbal] *adj (pl* **-baux** [bo]) verbal; (gram) verb

verbaliser [vɛrbalize] *intr* to write out a report or summons; **verbaliser contre qn** to give s.o. a ticket *(e.g., for speeding)*

verbe [vɛrb] *m* verb; **avoir le verbe haut** to talk loud; **Verbe** (eccl) Word

ver·beux [vɛrbø] **-beuse** [bøz] *adj* verbose, wordy

verbiage [vɛrbjaʒ] *m* verbiage

verdâtre [vɛrdɑtr] *adj* greenish

verdeur [vɛrdœr] *f* greenness; vigor, spryness; crudeness *(of speech)*

verdict [vɛrdik], [vɛrdikt] *m* verdict

verdir [vɛrdir] *tr & intr* to turn green

verdoyer [vɛrdwaje] §47 *intr* to become green

verdure [vɛrdyr] *f* verdure; greens

vé·reux [verø] **-reuse** [røz] *adj* wormy

verge [vɛrʒ] *f* rod; shank *(of anchor)*; penis

verger [vɛrʒe] *m* orchard

verglas [vɛrgla] *m* glare ice; sleet

vergogne [vɛrgɔɲ] *f*—**sans vergogne** immodest, brazen; immodestly, brazenly

vérifica·teur [verifikatœr] **-trice** [tris] *mf* inspector, examiner; **vérificateur comptable** auditor

vérification [verifikasjɔ̃] *f* verification; auditing; ascertainment

vérifier [verifje] *tr* to verify; audit; ascertain

vérin [verɛ̃] *m* jack; (aer) control; **vérin hydraulique** hydraulic lift, hydraulic jack

véritable [veritabl] *adj* veritable; real, genuine

vérité [verite] *f* truth; **à la vérité** to tell the truth; **dire à qn ses quatre vérités** (coll) to give s.o. a piece of one's mind; **en vérité** truly, in truth

ver·meil -meille [vɛrmɛj] *adj* rosy

vermillon [vɛrmijɔ̃] *adj invar & m* vermillion

vermine [vɛrmin] *f* vermin

vermou·lu -lue [vɛrmuly] *adj* worm-eaten

vermout or **vermouth** [vɛrmut] *m* vermouth

vernaculaire [vɛrnakylɛr] *adj* vernacular

vernir [vɛrnir] *tr* to varnish; **être verni** (coll) to be lucky

vernis [vɛrni] *m* varnish; (fig) veneer

vernissage [vɛrnisaʒ] *m* varnishing; private viewing *(of pictures)*

vernisser [vɛrnise] *tr* to glaze

vérole [verɔl] *f* (slang) syphilis; **petite vérole** smallpox

verrai [vere] *v* (**verras, verra, verrons,** etc.) see **voir**

verre [vɛr] *m* glass; crystal *(of watch)*; **verre à vitre** windowpane; **verre consigné** bottle with deposit; **verre de contact** contact lens; **verre de lampe** lamp chimney; **verre dépoli** frosted glass; **verre perdu** disposable bottle *(no deposit)*; **verres** eyeglasses; **verres de soleil** sunglasses; **verres grossissants** magnifying glasses; **verre taillé** cut glass

verrière [vɛrjɛr] *f* stained-glass window

verrou [vɛru] *m* bolt; **être sous les verrous** to be locked up

verrouiller [vɛruje] *tr* to bolt; lock up ‖ *ref* to lock oneself in

verrue [vɛry] *f* wart

vers [vɛr] *m* verse; **les vers** verse, poetry ‖ *prep* toward; about, e.g., **vers les cinq heures** about five o'clock

Versailles [vɛrsaj] *f* Versailles

versant [vɛrsɑ̃] *m* slope, side

versatile [vɛrsatil] *adj* fickle

verse [vɛrs] *f*—**pleuvoir à verse** to pour

ver·sé -sée [vɛrse] *adj*—**versé dans** versed in

Verseau [vɛrso] *m*—**le Verseau** (astr, astrol) Aquarius

versement [vɛrsəmɑ̃] *m* deposit; installment; **versement anticipé** payment in advance

verser [vɛrse] *tr* to pour; upset; tip over; deposit ‖ *intr* to overturn

verset [vɛrsɛ] *m* (Bib) verse

versification [vɛrsifikɑsjɔ̃] *f* versification

versifier [vɛrsifje] *tr & intr* to versify

version [vɛrsjɔ̃] *f* version; translation from a foreign language

verso [vɛrso] *m* verso; **au verso** on the back

vert [vɛr] **verte** [vɛrt] *adj* green; verdant; vigorous (*person*); new (*wine*); raw (*leather*); sharp (*scolding*); spicy (*story*); **ils sont trop verts!** sour grapes! ‖ *m* green; greenery; **mettre au vert** to put out to pasture; **se mettre au vert** to take a rest in the country

vert-de-gris [vɛrdəgri] *m invar* verdigris

vertèbre [vɛrtɛbr] *f* vertebra

verté·bré -brée [vɛrtebre] *adj & m* vertebrate

verti·cal -cale [vɛrtikal] (*pl* **-caux** [ko] **-cales**) *adj* vertical ‖ *m* (astr) vertical circle ‖ *f* vertical

vertige [vɛrtiʒ] *m* vertigo, dizziness

vertigo [vɛrtigo] *m* staggers (*of horse*); caprice

vertu [vɛrty] *f* virtue

ver·tueux [vɛrtɥø] **-tueuse** [tɥøz] *adj* virtuous

verve [vɛrv] *f* verve

ver·veux [vɛrvø] **-veuse** [vøz] *adj* lively, animated ‖ *m* fishnet

vésanie [vezani] *f* madness

vesce [vɛs] *f* vetch

vésicule [vezikyl] *f* vesicle; blister; **vésicule bilaire** gall bladder

vespasienne [vɛspazjɛn] *f* street urinal

vessie [vesi] *f* bladder; **vessie à glace** ice bag

veste [vɛst] *f* coat, suit coat; **remporter une veste** (coll) to suffer a setback; **retourner sa veste** (coll) to do an about-face; **veste croisée** double-breasted coat; **veste de pyjama** pajama top; **veste de sport** sport coat; **veste d'intérieur, veste d'appartement** lounging robe; **veste droite** single-breasted coat

vestiaire [vɛstjɛr] *m* checkroom, cloakroom; dressing room

vestibule [vɛstibyl] *m* vestibule

vestige [vɛstiʒ] *m* vestige; footprint

veston [vɛstɔ̃] *m* coat

Vésuve [vezyv] *m*—**le Vésuve** Vesuvius

vêtement [vɛtmɑ̃] *m* garment; **vêtements assortis, vêtements coordonnés** mix-and-match clothes; **vêtements de bébé** baby clothes; **vêtements de travail** working clothes

vétéran [veterɑ̃] *m* veteran

vétérinaire [veterinɛr] *adj & mf* veterinary

vétille [vetij] *f* trifle

vétiller [vetije] *intr* to split hairs

vêtir [vɛtir] §73 *tr & ref* to dress

veto [veto] *m* veto; **mettre** or **opposer son veto à** to veto

vê·tu -tue [vɛty] *v* see **vêtir**

vétuste [vetyst] *adj* decrepit, rickety

veuf [vœf] **veuve** [vœv] *adj* widowed ‖ *m* widower ‖ *f* see **veuve**

veuille [vœj] *v* (**veuilles, veuillent**) see **vouloir**

veule [vøl] *adj* (coll) feeble, weak

veuvage [vœvaʒ] *m* widowhood; widowerhood

veuve [vœv] *adv* widow

veux [vø] *v* (**veut**) see **vouloir; en veux-tu en voilà** (slang) as many as you want

vexation [vɛksɑsjɔ̃] *f* vexation

vexer [vɛkse] *tr* to vex

via [vja] *prep* via

viaduc [vjadyk] *m* viaduct

via·ger [vjaʒe] **-gère** [ʒɛr] *adj* life, for life ‖ *m* life annuity

viande [vjɑ̃d] *f* meat; **amène ta viande!** (slang) get over here!

vibration [vibrɑsjɔ̃] *f* vibration

vibrer [vibre] *intr* to vibrate

vicaire [vikɛr] *m* vicar

vice [vis] *m* vice; defect; **vice de conformation** physical defect; **vice de forme** (law) irregularity, flaw; **vice versa** vice versa

vice-amiral [visamiral] *m* (*pl* **-amiraux** (amiro)) vice-admiral

vice-président [visprezidɑ̃] **-présidente** [prezidɑ̃t] *mf* (*pl* **-présidents**) vice-president

vice-roi [visrwa] *m* (*pl* **-rois**) viceroy

vice-versa [visɛvɛrsa], [visvɛrsa] *adv* vice versa

vi·cié -ciée [visje] *adj* foul, polluted; poor, thin (*blood*)

vicier [visje] *tr* to foul, pollute; taint, spoil

vi·cieux [visjø] **-cieuse** [sjøz] *adj* vicious; wrong (*use*); libertine; balky

vici·nal -nale [visinal] *adj* (*pl* **-naux** [no]) local, side (*road*)

vicissitude [visisityd] *f* vicissitude

vicomte [vikɔ̃t] *m* viscount

victime [viktim] *f* victim

victoire [viktwar] *f* victory

victo·rieux [viktɔrjø] **-rieuse** [rjøz] *adj* victorious

victuailles [viktɥaj] *fpl* victuals, foods

vidange [vidɑ̃ʒ] *f* draining; night soil; drain (*of pipe, sink, etc.*)

vidanger [vidɑ̃ʒe] §38 *tr* to drain

vide [vid] *adj* empty; blank; vacant ‖ *m* emptiness, void; vacuum; **emballé sous vide** vacuum packed; **vide d'air** air space

vi·dée [vide] *adj* cleaned (*fish, fowl, etc.*); played out, exhausted

vide-bouteille [vidbutɛj] *m* (*pl* **-bouteilles**) siphon

vide-cave [vidkav] *m invar* sump pump

vide-citron [vidsitrɔ̃] *m* (*pl* **-citrons**) lemon squeezer

vide-gousset [vidgusɛ] *m* (*pl* **-goussets**) (hum) thief

vidéocâble [videokɑbl] *m* cable television

vidéocassette [videokasɛt] *f* videocassette, videotape

vidéogramme [videogram] *m* videorecording, videotape

vide-ordures [vidɔrdyr] *m invar* garbage shoot

vide-poches [vidpɔʃ] *m invar* dresser; pin tray; (aut) glove compartment

vider [vide] *tr* to empty; drain; clean (*fish, fowl, etc.*); settle (*a question*); **se faire vider de** (coll) to get thrown out of; be fired from; be expelled from

vi·deur [vidœr] **-deuse** [døz] *mf* (coll) bouncer (*in a night club*)

viduité [vidɥite] *f* widowhood

vidure [vidyr] *f* guts (*e.g., of cleaned fish*); **vidures de poubelle** garbage

vie [vi] *f* life; livelihood, living; **à vie** for life; **de ma** (**sa,** etc.) **vie** in my (his, etc.) life, e.g., **je ne l'ai jamais vu de ma vie** I have never seen it in my life; **jamais de la vie!** not on your life!; **vie de bâton de chaise** disorderly life; **vie de château** life of ease

vieil [vjɛj] *adj* see **vieux**

vieillard [vjɛjar] *m* old man; **les vieillards** old people

vieille [vjɛj] *f* old woman ‖ *adj* see **vieux**

vieilleries [vjɛjri] *fpl* old things; old ideas

vieillesse [vjɛjɛs] *f* old age

vieil·li -lie [vjeji] *adj* aged; out-of-date, antiquated

vieillir [vjejir] *tr* to age; make (*s.o.*) look older ‖ *intr* to age, grow old ‖ *ref* to make oneself look older

vieil·lot [vjɛjo] **-lotte** [jɔt] *adj* (coll) oldish, quaint

vielle [vjɛl] *f* (hist) hurdy-gurdy

viendrai [vjɛ̃dre] *v* (**viendras, viendra, viendrons,** etc.) see **venir**

Vienne [vjɛn] *f* Vienna; Vienne (*city in France*)

vien·nois [vjɛnwa] **-noise** [nwaz] *adj* Viennese ‖ (*cap*) *mf* Viennese

viens [vjɛ̃] *v* (**vient**) see **venir**

vierge [vjɛrʒ] *adj* virginal; virgin; blank; unexposed (*film*) ‖ *f* virgin; **la Vierge** (astr, astrol) Virgo

Vietnam [vjɛtnam] *m*—**le Vietnam** Vietnam

vietna·mien [vjɛtnamjɛ̃] **-mienne** [mjɛn] *adj* Vietnamese ‖ (*cap*) *mf* Vietnamese

vieux [vjø] (or **vieil** [vjɛj] before vowel or mute **h**) **vieille** [vjɛj] *adj* old (*wine*) ‖ (when standing before noun) *adj* old; old-fashioned; obsolete (*word, meaning, etc.*) ‖ *mf* old person ‖ *m* old man; **les vieux** old people; **mon vieux** (coll) my boy ‖ *f* see **vieille**

vif [vif] **vive** [viv] *adj* alive, living; lively, quick; bright, intense; hearty, heartfelt; sharp (*criticism*); keen (*pleasure*); spring (*water*) ‖ *m* quick; **couper dans le vif** to take drastic measures; **entrer dans le vif de** to get to the heart of; **peindre au vif** to paint from life; **piqué au vif** stung to the quick

vif-argent [vifarʒɑ̃] *m* quicksilver; (*person*) live wire

vigie [viʒi] *f* lookout

vigilance [viʒilɑ̃s] *f* vigilance

vigi·lant [viʒilɑ̃] **-lante** [lɑ̃t] *adj* vigilant ‖ *m* night watchman

vigile [viʒil] *m* night watchman ‖ *f* (eccl) vigil

vigne [viɲ] *f* vine; vineyard; **vigne blanche** clematis; **vigne de Judas** bittersweet; **vigne vierge** Virginia creeper

vigne·ron [viɲrɔ̃] **-ronne** [rɔn] *mf* winegrower; vintner

vignette [viɲɛt] *f* vignette; tax stamp; gummed tab

vignoble [viɲɔbl] *m* vineyard

vigou·reux [vigurø] **-reuse** [røz] *adj* vigorous

vigueur [vigœr] *f* vigor; **entrer en vigueur** to go into effect

vil vile [vil] *adj* vile; cheap

vi·lain [vilɛ̃] **-laine** [lɛn] (precedes the noun it modifies) *adj* nasty; ugly; naughty ‖ *mf* nasty person

vilebrequin [vilbrəkɛ̃] *m* brace (*of brace and bit*); crankshaft

vilenie [vilni] *f* villainy; abuse

villa [villa] *f* villa; cottage, small one-story home

village [vilaʒ] *m* village

villa·geois [vilaʒwa] **-geoise** [ʒwaz] *mf* villager

ville [vil] *f* city; town; **aller en ville** to go downtown; **la Ville Lumière** the City of Light (*Paris*); **ville champignon** boom town; **ville satellite** suburban town; **villes jumelées, villes réunies** twin cities

villégiature [vileʒjatyr] *f* vacation

vin [vɛ̃] *m* wine; **avoir le vin gai** to be hilariously drunk; **être entre deux vins** to be tipsy; **vin d'honneur** reception (*at which toasts are offered*); **vin d'orange** sangaree; **vin mousseux** sparkling wine; **vin ordinaire** table wine

vinaigre [vinɛgr] *m* vinegar

vinaigrette [vinɛgrɛt] *f* French dressing, vinaigrette sauce

vindica·tif [vɛ̃dikatif] **-tive** [tiv] *adj* vindictive

vingt [vɛ̃] §94 *adj & pron* twenty; the Twentieth, e.g., **Jean vingt** John the Twentieth; **vingt et un** [vɛ̃teœ̃] twenty-one; Twenty-first, e.g., **Jean vingt et un** John the Twenty-first; **vingt et unième**

twenty-first ‖ *m* twenty; twentieth (*in dates*); **vingt et un** twenty-one; twenty-first (*in dates*); **vingt et unième** twenty-first

vingtaine [vɛ̃tɛn] *f* score; **une vingtaine de** about twenty

vingt-deux [vɛ̃tdø] §94 *adj & pron* twenty-two; the Twenty-second, e.g., **Jean vingt-deux** John the Twenty-second ‖ *m* twenty-two; twenty-second (*in dates*) ‖ *interj* (slang) watch out!, cheese it!

vingt-deuxième [vɛ̃tdøzjɛm] §94 *adj, pron* (*masc, fem*), & *m* twenty-second

vingt-et-un [vɛ̃teœ̃] *m* (cards) twenty-one

vingtième [vɛ̃tjɛm] §94 *adj, pron* (*masc, fem*), & *m* twentieth

vinyle [vinil] *m* vinyl

viol [vjɔl] *m* rape; **viol collectif** gang rape

violation [vjɔlɑsjɔ̃] *f* violation

violence [vjɔlɑ̃s] *f* violence

vio·lent [vjɔlɑ̃] **-lente** [lɑ̃t] *adj* violent

violenter [vjɔlɑ̃te] *tr* to do violence to

violer [vjɔle] *tr* to violate; break (*the faith*); rape, ravish

vio·let [vjɔlɛ] **-lette** [lɛt] *adj & m* violet (*color*) ‖ *f* (bot) violet

violon [vjɔlɔ̃] *m* violin; (slang) calaboose, jug; **payer les violons** (coll) to pay the piper; **violon d'Ingres** hobby

violoncelle [vjɔlɔ̃sɛl] *m* violoncello

violoniste [vjɔlɔnist] *mf* violinist

vipère [vipɛr] *f* viper

virage [viraʒ] *m* turning; turn, e.g., **pas de virage à gauche** no left turn; (aer) bank; (phot) toning; **virage en épingle à cheveux** hairpin curve; **virages** (*public sign*) winding road; **virage sur place** U-turn

virago [virago] *f* mannish woman

virée [vire] *f* (coll) spin (*in a car*); (coll) round (*of bars*)

virement [virmɑ̃] *m* transfer (*of funds*); (naut) tacking

virer [vire] *tr* to transfer (*funds*); (phot) to tone ‖ *intr* to turn; (aer) to bank; **virer à** to turn (*sour, red, etc.*); **virer de bord** (naut) to tack

virevolte [virvɔlt] *f* turn; about-face

virevolter [virvɔlte] *intr* to make an about-face; go hither and thither

virginité [virʒinite] *f* virginity, maidenhood

virgule [virgyl] *f* (gram) comma; (*used in French to set off the decimal fraction from the integer*) decimal point

virilité [virilite] *f* virility

virole [virɔl] *f* ferrule

virologie [virɔlɔʒi] *f* virology

vir·tuel -tuelle [virtɥɛl] *adj* potential; (mech, opt, phys) virtual

virtuose [virtɥoz] *mf* virtuoso

virtuosité [virtɥozite] *f* virtuosity

virulence [virylɑ̃s] *f* virulence

viru·lent [virylɑ̃] **-lente** [lɑ̃t] *adj* virulent

virus [virys] *m* virus

vis [vis] *f* screw; thread (*of screw*); spiral staircase; **fermer à vis** to screw shut; **serrer la vis à** (fig) to put the screws on; **vis à ailettes** wing nut; **vis à bois** wood

screw; **vis à métaux, vis à tôle** machine screw; **vis à tête plate** flat-headed screw; **vis à tête ronde** round-headed screw; **vis de blocage** setscrew ‖ [vi] *v* (**vit**) see **vivre**; see **voir**

visa [viza] *m* visa; (fig) approval

visage [vizaʒ] *m* face; **à deux visages** two-faced; **faire bon visage à** to pretend to be friendly to; **trouver visage de bois** to find the door closed; **visages pâles** palefaces; **voir qn sous son vrai visage** to see s.o. in his true colors

visagiste [vizaʒist] *mf* beautician

vis-à-vis [vizavi] *adv* vis-à-vis; **vis-à-vis de** vis-à-vis; towards; in the presence of ‖ *m* vis-à-vis; **en vis-à-vis** facing

viscère [visɛr] *m* organ; **viscères** viscera

visée [vize] *f* aim

viser [vize] §96 *tr* to aim; aim at; concern; visa ‖ *intr* to aim; **viser à** to aim at; aim to

viseur [vizœr] *m* viewfinder; sight (*of gun*); **viseur de lancement** bombsight

visibilité [vizibilite] *f* visibility; **sans visibilité** blind (*flying*)

visible [vizibl] *adj* visible; obvious; (coll) at home, free; (coll) open to the public

visière [vizjɛr] *f* visor; sight (*of gun*); **rompre en visière à** to take a stand against

vision [vizjɔ̃] *f* vision

visionnaire [vizjɔnɛr] *adj & mf* visionary

visionner [vizjɔne] *tr* to view, inspect

visionneuse [vizjɔnøz] *f* viewer

visite [vizit] *f* visit; inspection; **en** or **de visite** visiting; **faire** or **rendre visite à** to visit

visiter [vizite] *tr* to visit; inspect

visi·teur [vizitœr] **-teuse** [tøz] *adj* visiting (*e.g., nurse*) ‖ *mf* visitor; inspector

vison [vizɔ̃] *m* mink

vis·queux [viskø] **-queuse** [køz] *adj* viscous

visser [vise] *tr* to screw; screw on; (coll) to put the screws on

visualiser [vizɥalize] *tr* to visualize

vi·suel -suelle [vizɥɛl] *adj* visual

vi·tal -tale [vital] *adj* (*pl* **-taux** [to]) vital

vitaliser [vitalize] *tr* to vitalize

vitalité [vitalite] *f* vitality

vitamine [vitamin] *f* vitamin

vite [vit] *adj* fast, swift ‖ *adv* fast, quickly; **faites vite!** hurry up!

vitesse [vitɛs] *f* speed, velocity; rate; **à toute vitesse** at full speed; **changer de vitesse** (aut) to shift gears; **en grande vitesse** (rr) by express; **en petite vitesse** (rr) by freight; **en première (seconde, etc.) vitesse** (aut) in first (second, etc.) gear; **vitesse acquise** momentum

viticole [vitikɔl] *adj* wine

viticulteur [vitikyltœr] *m* winegrower

vitrage [vitraʒ] *m* glasswork; small window curtain; sash; glazing

vi·trail [vitraj] *m* (*pl* **-traux** [tro]) stained-glass window

vitre [vitr] *f* windowpane, pane; (aut) window; **casser les vitres** (coll) to kick up a fuss

vi·tré -trée [vitre] *adj* glazed; vitreous (*humor*); glassed-in

vi·treux [vitrø] **-treuse** [trøz] *adj* glassy; vitreous

vitrier [vitrije] *m* glazier

vitrine [vitrin] *f* show window; showcase; glass cabinet; **lécher les vitrines** (coll) to go window-shopping

vitupérer [vitypere] §10 *tr* to vituperate, abuse ‖ *intr*—**vitupérer contre** (coll) to vituperate

vivace [vivas] *adj* hardy, vigorous; long-lived; (bot) perennial

vivacité [vivasite] *f* vivacity

vivan·dier [vivɑ̃dje] **-dière** [djɛr] *mf* sutler ‖ *f* camp follower

vi·vant [vivɑ̃] **-vante** [vɑ̃t] *adj* living, alive; lively; modern, spoken (*language*) ‖ *m*—**bon vivant** high liver, jolly companion; **du vivant de** during the lifetime of; **les vivants et les morts** the quick and the dead

vivat [viva] *m* viva ‖ *interj* viva!

vivement [vivmɑ̃] *adv* quickly, warmly; deeply; sharply, briskly

viveur [vivœr] *m* pleasure seeker, rounder

vivier [vivje] *m* fish preserve, fishpond

vivifier [vivifje] *tr* to vivify, vitalize

vivisection [vivisɛksjɔ̃] *f* vivisection

vivoir [vivwar] *m* (Canad) living room

vivoter [vivɔte] *intr* (coll) to live from hand to mouth

vivre [vivr] *m*—**le vivre et le couvert** room and board; **le vivre et le vêtement** food and clothing; **vivres** provisions; (mil) rations, supplies ‖ §74 *tr* to live (*one's life, faith, art*); live through, experience ‖ *intr* to live; **être difficile à vivre** to be difficult to live with; **qui vivra verra** time will tell; **vive!, vivent!** viva!, long live!; **vivre au jour le jour** to live from hand to mouth; **vivre de** to live on

vizir [vizir] *m* vizier

vlan [vlɑ̃] *interj* whack!

vocable [vɔkabl] *m* word

vocabulaire [vɔkabylɛr] *m* vocabulary

vo·cal -cale [vɔkal] *adj* (*pl* **-caux** [ko]) vocal

vocaliser [vɔkalize] *tr, intr,* & *ref* to vocalize

vocatif [vɔkatif] *m* vocative

vocation [vɔkɑsjɔ̃] *f* vocation, calling; **vocation pédagogique** teaching career

vociférer [vɔsifere] §10 *tr* to shout (*e.g., insults*) ‖ *intr* to vociferate

vœu [vø] *m* (*pl* **vœux**) vow; wish; resolution; **meilleurs vœux!** best wishes!; **tous mes vœux!** my best wishes!

vogue [vɔg] *f* vogue, fashion; **en vogue** in vogue, in fashion

voguer [vɔge] *intr* to sail; **vogue la galère!** let's chance it, here goes!

voici [vwasi] *prep* here is, here are; for, e.g., **voici quatre jours qu'elle est partie** she has been gone for four days; **le voici** here he is; **nous voici** here we are; **que voici** here, e.g., **mon frère que voici va vous accompagner** my brother here is going to accompany you

voie [vwa] *f* way; road; lane (*of highway*); (anat) tract; (rr) track; **en voie de** on the road to, nearing; **être en bonne voie** to be doing well; **voie d'eau** leak; **voie de garage** driveway; **voie d'évitement** siding; **voie lactée** Milky Way; **voie maritime** seaway; **voie(s) de fait** (law) assault and battery; **voie surface** surface mail

voilà [vwala] *prep* there is, there are; here is, here are; that's, e.g., **voilà pourquoi** that's why; ago, e.g., **voilà quatre jours qu'elle est partie** she left four days ago; **voilà, monsieur** there you are, sir

voile [vwal] *m* veil; (phot) fog (*on negative*); **voile du palais** soft palate; **voile noir** (pathol) blackout ‖ *f* sail; sailboat; **faire voile sur** to set sail for

voi·lé -lée [vwale] *adj* veiled; overcast; muffled; warped; husky (*voice*); (phot) fogged (*e.g., hint*); **peu voilé** thinly veiled, broad (*e.g., hint*)

voiler [vwale] *tr* to veil; (phot) to fog ‖ *ref* to cloud over; become warped

voi·lier [vwalje] **-lière** [ljɛr] *adj* sailing ‖ *m* sailboat; sailmaker; migratory bird

voilure [vwalyr] *f* sails; warping

voir [vwar] §75, §95 *tr* to see; **faire voir** to show; **voir jouer** to see (*s.o.*) playing, to see (*s.o.*) play; to see (*s.th.*) played; **voir qn qui vient** to see s.o. coming, see s.o. come; **voir venir qn** to see s.o. coming, see s.o. come; (fig) to see through s.o. ‖ *intr* to see; **faites voir!** let's see it!, let me see it!; **j'en ai vu bien d'autres** I have seen worse than that; **n'avoir rien à voir avec, à,** or **dans** to have nothing to do with; **voir à** + *inf* to see that + *ind*, e.g., **voir à nous loger** to see that we are housed; **voir au dos** see other side, turn the page; **voyons!** see here!, come now! ‖ *ref* to see oneself; see one another; be obvious; be seen, be found

voire [vwar] *adv* nay, indeed; **voire même** or even, and even

voirie [vwari] *f* highway department; garbage collection; dump

voi·sé -sée [vwaze] *adj* voiced

voi·sin [vwazɛ̃] **-sine** [zin] *adj* neighboring; adjoining; **voisin de** near ‖ *mf* neighbor

voisinage [vwazinaʒ] *m* neighborhood; neighborliness

voisiner [vwazine] *intr* to visit one's neighbors; **voisiner avec** to be placed next to

voiture [vwatyr] *f* vehicle; carriage; (aut, rr) car; **en voiture!** all aboard!; **petite voiture** (coll) wheelchair; **voiture à bras** handcart; **voiture banalisée** unmarked police car; **voiture de location** rented car; **voiture d'enfant** baby carriage; **voiture de pompier** fire engine; **voiture de remise** rented car; **voiture de ronde** patrol car; **voiture de série** stock car; **voiture de tourisme** pleasure car; **voiture d'infirme** wheelchair; **voiture d'occasion** used car

voiture-bar [vwatyrbar] *f* (*pl* **voitures-bars**) club car

voiturette [vwatyrɛt] *f*—**voiturette de golf** golf cart

voiture-lit [vwatyrli] *f* (*pl* **voitures-lits**) sleeping car

voiturer [vwatyre] *tr* to transport, convey

voiture-restaurant [vwatyrrɛstɔrɑ̃] *f* (*pl* **voitures-restaurants**) dining car

voiture-salon [vwatyrsalɔ̃] *f* (*pl* **voitures-salons**) parlor car

voix [vwa], [vwɑ] *f* voice; vote; **à haute voix** aloud; in a loud voice; **à pleine voix** at the top of one's voice; **avoir voix au chapitre** (coll) to have a say in the matter; **à voix basse** in a low voice; **à voix haute** in a loud voice; **de vive voix** by word of mouth; **voix de tête, voix de fausset** falsetto

vol [vɔl] *m* theft, robbery; flight; flock; **au vol** in flight; in passing; **à vol d'oiseau** as the crow flies; **de haut vol** high-flying; big-time (*crook*); **vol à la demande** charter flight; **vol à la tire** purse snatching; **vol à l'étalage** shoplifting; **vol avec effraction** burglary; **vol à voile** gliding; **vol cosmique** space flight; **vol plané** volplane; **vol sans visibilité** blind flying; **vol sur aile delta, vol libre** hang gliding

volage [vɔlaʒ] *adj* fickle, changeable

volaille [vɔlɑj] *f* fowl; (slang) hens (*women*); (slang) gal

vo·lant [vɔlɑ̃] **-lante** [lɑ̃t] *adj* flying ‖ *m* steering wheel; flywheel; shuttlecock; sail (*of windmill*); flounce (*of dress*); leaf (*attached to stub*); **volant de sécurité** safety margin, reserve

vola·til -tile [vɔlatil] *adj* volatile ‖ *m* bird; fowl

volatiliser [vɔlatilize] *tr & ref* to volatilize

volcan [vɔlkɑ̃] *m* volcano

volcanique [vɔlkanik] *adj* volcanic

vole [vɔl] *f*—**faire la vole** to take all the tricks

volée [vɔle] *f* volley; flight (*of birds; of stairs*); flock; **à la volée** on the wing; at random; **à toute volée** loud and clear; **de haute volée** upper-class; **de la première volée** first-class, crack; **sonner à toute volée** to peal out

voler [vɔle] §95 *tr* to rob; steal; fly at; **ne l'avoir pas volé** to deserve all that is coming; **voler à** to steal from ‖ *intr* to rob; steal; fly

volet [vɔlɛ] *m* shutter; inside flap; end paper; (aer) flap; **trier sur le volet** to choose with care

voleter [vɔlte] §34 *intr* to flutter

vo·leur [vɔlœr] **-leuse** [løz] *adj* thievish ‖ *mf* thief; **au voleur!** stop thief!; **voleur à la tire** pickpocket; **voleur à l'étalage** shoplifter; **voleur de grand chemin** highwayman

volition [vɔlisjɔ̃] *f* volition

volley-ball [vɔlɛbol] *m* volleyball

vol·leyeur [vɔlɛjœr] **-leyeuse** [lɛjøz] *mf* volleyball player

volontaire [vɔlɔ̃tɛr] *adj* voluntary; headstrong, willful; determined (*chin*) ‖ *mf* volunteer

volonté [vɔlɔ̃te] *f* will; wishes; **à volonté** at will; **bonne volonté** good will; **faire ses quatre volontés** (coll) to do just as one pleases; **mauvaise volonté** ill will

volontiers [vɔlɔ̃tje] *adv* gladly, willingly

volt [vɔlt] *m* volt

voltage [vɔltaʒ] *m* voltage

volte-face [vɔltəfas] *f invar* volte-face

voltige [vɔltiʒ] *f* acrobatics

voltiger [vɔltiʒe] §38 *intr* to flit about; flutter

voltmètre [vɔltmɛtr] *m* voltmeter

volubile [vɔlybil] *adj* voluble

volume [vɔlym] *m* volume; **faire du volume** (coll) to put on airs

volumi·neux [vɔlyminø] **-neuse** [nøz] *adj* voluminous

volupté [vɔlypte] *f* voluptuousness, ecstasy

volup·tueux [vɔlyptɥø] **-tueuse** [tɥøz] *adj* voluptuous ‖ *mf* voluptuary

vomir [vɔmir] *tr & intr* to vomit

vomissure [vɔmisyr] *f* vomit

vont [vɔ̃] *v* see **aller**

vorace [vɔras] *adj* voracious

voracité [vɔrasite] *f* voracity

vos [vo] §88 your

vo·tant [vɔtɑ̃] **-tante** [tɑ̃t] *mf* voter

vote [vɔt] *m* vote; **passer au vote** to vote on; **vote affirmatif** yea; **vote négatif** nay; **vote par correspondance** absentee ballot; **vote par procuration** proxy

voter [vɔte] *tr* to vote; vote for ‖ *intr* to vote; **voter à mains levées** to vote by show of hands; **voter par assis et levé** to give one's vote by standing or by remaining seated

vo·tif [vɔtif] **-tive** [tiv] *adj* votive

votre [vɔtr] §88 your

vôtre [votr] §89 yours

voudrai [vudre] *v* (**voudras, voudra, voudrons,** etc.) see **vouloir**

vouer [vwe] *tr* to vow, dedicate; doom, condemn; **voué à** headed for; doomed to ‖ §96 *ref*—**se vouer à** to dedicate oneself to

vouloir [vulwar] *m* will ‖ §76, §95 *tr* to want, wish; require; **je voudrais** I would like; I would like to; **veuillez + inf** please + *inf*; **voulez-vous vous taire?** will you be quiet?; **vouloir bien** to be glad to, be willing to; **vouloir dire** to mean ‖ *intr*—**en vouloir à** to bear a grudge against; **je veux!** (slang) and how!; **je veux bien** I'm quite willing; **si vous voulez bien** if you don't mind ‖ *ref*—**s'en vouloir** to have it in for each other

vou·lu -lue [vuly] *adj* required; deliberate ‖ *v* see **vouloir**

vous [vu] §85, §87 you, to you; **vous autres Américans** you Americans

vous-même [vumɛm] §86 yourself

voussoir [vuswar] *m* (archit) arch stone

voussure [vusyr] *f* arch, arching

voûte [vut] *f* vault; **voûte céleste** canopy of heaven

voûter [vute] *tr* to vault; bend ‖ *ref* to become round-shouldered

vouvoyer [vuvwaje] §47 *tr* to address with formality; use formal grammatical forms (**vous**, etc.) in speaking to a stranger, a superior, or, often (if a Catholic), to God ‖ *ref* to use **vous** and corresponding verbal forms in speaking with one another

voy. *abbr* (**voyez**) see

voyage [vwaja3] *m* trip, journey, voyage; ride (*in car, train, plane, etc.*); **voyage à forfait** all-expense tour; **voyage aller et retour** round trip; **voyage de noces** honeymoon

voyager [vwaja3e] §38 *intr* to travel

voya·geur [vwaja3œr] **-geuse** [3øz] *mf* traveler; passenger

voyance [vwaja͂s] *f* clairvoyance

voyant [vwaja͂] **voyante** [vwaja͂t] *adj* loud, gaudy ‖ *mf* clairvoyant ‖ *m* signal; (aut) gauge ‖ *f* fortuneteller

voyelle [vwajɛl] *f* vowel

voyeur [vwajœr] **voyeuse** [vwajøz] *mf* voyeur ‖ *m* Peeping Tom

voyez [vwaje] *v* (**voyons**) see **voir**

voyou [vwaju] **voyoute** [vwajut] *adj* gutter (*e.g., language*) ‖ *mf* guttersnipe; brat; hoodlum

vrac [vrak]—**en vrac** unpacked, loose; in bulk; in disorder

vrai vraie [vrɛ], [vre] *adj* true, real, genuine ‖ *m* truth; **à vrai dire** to tell the truth; **pour vrai** (coll) for good

vraiment [vrɛma͂] *adv* truly, really

vraisemblable [vrɛsa͂blabl] *adj* probable, likely; true to life, realistic (*play, novel*)

vraisemblance [vrɛsa͂bla͂s] *f* probability, likelihood; realism

vrille [vrij] *f* drill; (aer) spin; (bot) tendril

vriller [vrije] *tr* to bore ‖ *intr* to go into a tailspin

vrombir [vrɔ͂bir] *intr* to throb; buzz; hum, purr (*said of motor*)

vu vue [vy] *adj* seen, regarded; **bien vu de** in favor with; **mal vu de** out of favor with ‖ *m*—au vu de upon presentation of; **au vu et au su de tout le monde** openly ‖ *f* view; sight; eyesight; **avoir à vue** to have in mind; **à vue** in sight; (com) on demand; **à vue de nez** at first sight; at a rough estimate; **à vue d'œil** visibly, quickly; **de vue** by sight; **en vue** in evidence; in sight; **en vue de** in order to; **garder à vue** to keep under observation, keep locked up; **perdre qn de vue** to lose sight of s.o.; get out of touch with s.o.; **vue à vol d'oiseau** bird's-eye view; **vues sur** designs on ‖ *vu prep* considering, in view of; **vu que** whereas ‖ *v* see **voir**

vulcaniser [vylkanize] *tr* to vulcanize

vulgaire [vylgɛr] *adj* common, vulgar; ordinary, everyday; vernacular ‖ *m* common herd; vernacular

vulgariser [vylgarize] *tr* to popularize; make vulgar

vulgarité [vylgarite] *f* vulgarity

vulnérable [vylnerabl] *adj* vulnerable

Vve *abbr* (**veuve**) widow

W

W, w [dublǝve] *m invar* twenty-third letter of the French alphabet

wagon [vag5] *m* (rr) car, coach; (coll) big car; **un wagon** (coll) a lot; **wagon à bagages** baggage car; **wagon à bestiaux** cattle car; **wagon couvert** boxcar; **wagon de marchandises** freight car; **wagon de voyageurs** passenger car; **wagon frigorifique** or **réfrigérant** refrigerator car; **wagon plat** flat car

wagon-bar [vag5bar] *m* (*pl* **wagons-bars**) club car

wagon-citerne [vag5sitɛrn] *m* (*pl* **wagons-citernes**) tank car

wagon-lit [vag5li] *m* (*pl* **wagons-lits**) sleeping car

wagon-poste [vag5pɔst] *m* (*pl* **wagons-poste**) mail car

wagon-réservoir [vag5rezɛrvwar] *m* (*pl* **wagons-réservoirs**) tank car

wagon-restaurant [vag5rɛstɔra͂] *m* (*pl* **wagons-restaurants**) dining car

wagon-salon [vag5sal5] *m* (*pl* **wagons-salons**) parlor car

wagon-tombereau [vag5t5bro] *m* (*pl* **wagons-tombereaux**) dump truck

walkman [wɔkman] *m* walkman (*portable earphones*)

wallace [valas] *f* drinking fountain

wal·lon [val5] **-lonne** [lɔn] *adj* Walloon ‖ *m* Walloon (*dialect*) ‖ (*cap*) *mf* Walloon

warrant [vara͂], [vara͂] *m* receipt

water-polo [watɛrpɔlo] *m* water polo

waterproof [watɛrpruf] *adj invar* waterproof ‖ *m invar* raincoat

waters [watɛr], [vater] *mpl* toilet

watt [wat] *m* watt

watt-heure [watœr] *m* (*pl* **watts-heures**) watt-hour

wattman [watman] *m* motorman

wattmètre [watmɛtr] *m* wattmeter

week-end [wikɛnd] *m* (*pl* **-ends**) weekend

whisky [wiski] *m* whiskey; **whisky écossais** Scotch

wolfram [vɔlfram] *m* wolfram

X

X, x [iks], *[iks] *m invar* twenty-fourth letter of the French alphabet
Xavier [gzavje] *m* Xavier
xénon [ksenɔ̃] *m* xenon
xénophobe [ksenɔfɔb] *adj* xenophobic ‖ *mf* xenophobe

Xérès [kerɛs], [gzerɛs] *m* Jerez; sherry
xérographie [kserɔgrafi] *f* xerography
xérographier [kserɔgrafje] *tr* to xerograph
Xerxès [gzɛrsɛs] *m* Xerxes
xylophone [ksilɔfɔn] *m* xylophone

Y

Y, y [igrɛk], *[igrɛk] *m invar* twenty-fifth letter of the French alphabet
y [i] *pron pers* §87 to it, to them; at it, at them; in it, in them; by it, by them; of it, of them, e.g., **j'y pense** I am thinking of it or them; (untranslated with certain verbs), e.g., **je n'y vois pas** I don't see; e.g., **il s'y connaît** (coll) he's an expert, he knows what he's talking about; him, her, e.g., **je m'y fie** I trust him; **allez-y!** go ahead!, start!; **ça y est!** that's it!; **je n'y suis pour personne** I am not at home for anybody; **je n'y suis pour rien** I have nothing to do with it; **j'y suis!** I've got it! ‖ *adv* there; here, in, e.g., **Monsieur votre père y est-il?** is your father here?, is your father in?
yacht [jɔt], [jak] *m* yacht; **yacht à glace** iceboat

yacht-club [jɔtklœb] *m* yacht club
yankee [jãki] *adj masc* Yankee ‖ (*cap*) *mf* Yankee
yèble [jɛbl] *f* (bot) elder; **l'yèble** the elder
yeoman [jɔman] *m* yeoman
yeuse [jøz] *f* holm oak; **l'yeuse** the holm oak
yeux [jø] *mpl* see œil
yé-yé [jeje] (*pl* -yés) *adj & mf* jitterbug
yi·dich -diche [jidiʃ] *adj & m* Yiddish
yiddish [jidiʃ] *adj invar & m* Yiddish
yogourt [jɔgur] *m* yogurt
yole [jɔl] *f* yawl
Yonne [jɔn] *f* Yonne; **l'Yonne** the Yonne
yougoslave [jugɔslav] *adj* Yugoslav ‖ (*cap*) *mf* Yugoslav
Yougoslavie [jugɔslavi] *f* Yugoslavia; **la Yougoslavie** Yugoslavia
youyou [juju] *m* dinghy

Z

Z, z [sɛd] *m invar* twenty-sixth letter of the French alphabet
za·zou -zoue [zazu] *adj* (coll) jazzy ‖ *m* (coll) zoot suiter
zèbre [zɛbr] *m* zebra; (slang) guy
zébrer [zebre] §10 *tr* to stripe; **le soleil zèbre** the sun casts streaks of light on
zébrure [zebryr] *f* stripe
zéla·teur [zelatœr] **-trice** [tris] *mf* zealot
zèle [zɛl] *m* zeal
zénith [zenit] *m* zenith
zéphyr [zefir] *m* zephyr
zeppelin [zɛplɛ̃] *m* zeppelin
zéro [zero] *m* zero; **les avoir à zéro** (slang) to be scared stiff
zest [zɛst] *m*—**entre le zist et le zest** (coll) betwixt and between ‖ *interj* tush!
zeste [zɛst] *m* peel (*of citrus fruit*); dividing membrane (*of nut*); **pas un zeste** (fig) not a particle of difference
Zeus [zøs] *m* Zeus
zézaiement [zezɛmɑ̃] *m* lisp

zézayer [zezeje] §49 *intr* to lisp
zibeline [ziblin] *f* sable
zieuter [zjøte] *tr* (slang) to get a load of
zigzag [zigzag] *m* zigzag; gypsy moth
zigzaguer [zigzage] *intr* to zigzag
zinc [zɛ̃g] *m* zinc; (coll) bar
zizanie [zizani] *f* wild rice; tare; **semer la zizanie** to sow discord
zodiaque [zɔdjak] *m* zodiac
zonage [zɔnaʒ] *m* zoning
zone [zon] *f* zone; **zone bleue** center city with limited parking; **zone chic** fashionable neighborhood
zoning [zoniŋ] *m* zoning
zoo [zɔo] *m* zoo
zoologie [zɔɔlɔʒi] *f* zoology
zoologique [zɔɔlɔʒik] *adj* zoologic(al)
zoom [zum] *m* zoom; zoom lens
zouave [zwav] *m* Zouave; **faire le zouave** (coll) to play the fool
zut [zyt] *interj* heck!; hang it!
zygote [zigɔt] *m* zygote

ANGLAIS–FRANÇAIS

A

A, a [e] *s* Iière lettre de l'alphabet

a *art indef* un

aback [ə'bæk] *adv* avec le vent dessus; **taken aback** déconcerté

abandon [ə'bændən] *s* abandon *m* ‖ *tr* abandonner

abase [ə'bes] *tr* abaisser, humilier

abasement [ə'besmənt] *s* abaissement *m*

abash [ə'bæʃ] *tr* décontenancer

abashed *adj* confus, confondu

abate [ə'bet] *tr* (*to reduce*) diminuer, réduire; (*part of price*) rabattre ‖ *intr* se calmer; (*said of wind*) tomber

abbess ['æbɪs] *s* abbesse *f*

abbey ['æbi] *s* abbaye *f*

abbot ['æbət] *s* abbé *m*

abbreviate [ə'brivɪ,et] *tr* abréger

abbreviation [ə,brivɪ'eʃən] *s* abréviation *f*

A B C's [,e,bi'siz] *spl* (letterword) a b c *m*

abdicate ['æbdɪ,ket] *tr & intr* abdiquer

abdomen ['æbdəmən], [æb'domən] *s* abdomen *m*

abduct [æb'dʌkt] *tr* enlever, ravir

abet [ə'bet] *v* (*pret & pp* **abetted;** *ger* **abetting**) *tr* encourager

abettor [ə'betər] *s* complice *mf*

abeyance [ə'be·əns] *s* suspension *f;* **in abeyance** en suspens

ab·hor [æb'hɔr] *v* (*pret & pp* **-horred;** *ger* **-horring**) *tr* abhorrer, détester

abhorrent [æb'hɔrənt] *adj* détestable, répugnant

abide [ə'baɪd] *v* (*pret & pp* **abode** or **abided**) *tr* attendre‖ *intr* demeurer, continuer, persister; **to abide by** s'en tenir à; rester fidèle à

abili·ty [ə'bɪlɪti] *s* (*pl* **-ties**) (*power to perform*) capacité *f,* compétence *f;* (*proficiency*) aptitude *f;* (*cleverness*) habileté *f,* talent *m*

abject [æb'dʒɛkt] *adj* abject

ablative ['æblətɪv] *adj & s* ablatif *m*

ablaut ['æblaut] *s* apophonie *f*

ablaze [ə'blez] *adj* (*on fire*) enflammé; (*colorful*) replendissant ‖ *adv* en feu

able ['ebəl] *adj* capable, habile; **to be able to** pouvoir

a'ble-bod'ied *adj* robuste, vigoureux; (*seaman*) breveté

abloom [ə'blum] *adj & adv* en fleur

abnormal [æb'nɔrməl] *adj* anormal

abnormali·ty [,æbnɔr'mælɪti] *s* (*pl* **-ties**) anomalie *f,* irrégularité *f;* (*of body*) difformité *f*

aboard [ə'bord] *adv* à bord; **all aboard!** en voiture!; **to go aboard** s'embarquer ‖ *prep* à bord de

abode [ə'bod] *s* demeure *f,* résidence *f*

abolish [ə'bɑlɪʃ] *tr* abolir

A-bomb ['e,bɑm] *s* bombe *f* atomique

abomination [ə,bɑmɪ'neʃən] *s* abomination *f*

aborigines [,æbə'rɪdʒɪ,niz] *spl* aborigènes *mpl*

abort [ə'bɔrt] *intr* avorter

abortion [ə'bɔrʃən] *s* avortement *m,* I.V.G. *f*

abound [ə'baund] *intr* abonder

about [ə'baut] *adv* (*all round*) à la ronde, tout autour; (*almost*) presque; (*here and there*) çà et là; **to be about to** être sur le point de ‖ *prep* (*around*) autour de, aux environs de; (*approximately*) environ; vers, e.g., **about six o'clock** vers six heures; (*concerning*) au sujet de; **it is about** (*it concerns*) . . . il s'agit de . . .

about'-face' or **about'-face'** *s* volte-face *f;* (mil) demi-tour *m* ‖ **about'-face'** *intr* faire volte-face

above [ə'bʌv] *adv* (*overhead*) en haut, audessus; (*earlier*) ci-dessus ‖ *prep* audessus de; (*more than*) plus que, outre; (*another point on the river*) en amont de; **above all** surtout

above'-men'tioned *adj* susmentionné

abrasive [ə'bresɪv] *adj & s* abrasif *m*

abreast [ə'brɛst] *adj & adv* de front; **three abreast** par rangs de trois; **to be abreast of** or **with** être en ligne avec; **to keep abreast of** se tenir au courant de

abridge [ə'brɪdʒ] *tr* abréger

abridgment [ə'brɪdʒmənt] *s* (*shortened version*) abrégé *m,* résumé *m;* (*shortening*) diminution *f,* réduction *f*

abroad [ə'brɔd] *adv* au loin; (*in foreign parts*) à l'étranger

abrogate ['æbrə,get] *tr* abroger

abrupt [ə'brʌpt] *adj* (*steep; impolite*) abrupt; (*hasty*) brusque, précipité

abscess ['æbsɛs] *s* abcès *m*

abscond [æb'skɑnd] *intr* s'enfuir, déguerpir; **to abscond with** lever le pied avec

absence ['æbsəns] *s* absence *f*

absent ['æbsənt] *adj* absent ‖ [æb'sɛnt] *tr*—**to absent oneself** s'absenter

absentee [,æbsən'ti] *s* absent *m*

ab'sentee bal'lot *s* vote *m* par correspondance

ab'sent-mind'ed *adj* absent, distrait

absolute ['æbsə,lut] *adj & s* absolu *m*

absolutely [,æbsə'lutli] *adv* absolument

absolve [æb'sɑlv] *tr* absoudre

absorb [æb'sɔrb] *tr* absorber; **to be** or **become absorbed in** s'absorber dans

absorbent [æb'sɔrbənt] *adj & s* absorbant; (*cotton*) hydrophile ‖ *s* absorbant *m*

absorbing [æb'sɔbɪŋ] *adj* absorbant

abstain [æb'sten] *intr* s'abstenir

abstemious [æb'stimɪ·əs] *adj* abstinent, sobre

abstinent ['æbstɪnənt] *adj* abstinent

abstract ['æbstrækt] *adj* abstrait ‖ *s* abrégé *m,* résumé *m* ‖ *tr* résumer ‖ [æb'strækt] *tr* abstraire; (*to remove*) soustraire

abstractedly [æb'stræktɪdli] *adv* d'un œil distrait

abstruse [æb'strus] *adj* abstrus

absurd [æb'sʌrd] *adj* absurde

absurdi·ty [æb'sʌrdɪti] *s* (*pl* **-ties**) absurdité *f*

abundance [ə'bʌndəns] s abondance f
abundant [ə'bʌndənt] adj abondant
abuse [ə'bjus] s abus m; (mistreatment) maltraitement m; (insulting words) insultes fpl ‖ [ə'bjuz] tr abuser de; maltraiter; insulter
abusive [ə'bjusɪv] adj (insulting) injurieux; (wrong) abusif
abut [ə'bʌt] v (pret & pp **abutted**; ger **abutting**) intr—**to abut on** border, confiner
abutment [ə'bʌtmənt] s (of wall) contrefort m; (of bridge) culée f; (of arch) pied-droit m
abyss [ə'bɪs] s abîme m
A.C. ['e'si] s (letterword) (**alternating current**) courant m alternatif
academic [,ækə'dɛmɪk] adj (of a college) universitaire; (of an academy) académique; (theoretical) théorique ‖ s étudiant m or professeur m de l'université
academician [ə,kædə'mɪʃən] s académicien m
acade·my [ə'kædəmi] s (pl **-mies**) académie f; (preparatory school) collège m
accede [æk'sid] intr acquiescer; **to accede to** accéder à; (the throne) monter sur
accelerate [æk'sɛlə,ret] tr & intr accélérer
accelerator [æk'sɛlə,retər] s accélérateur m
accent ['æksɛnt] s accent m ‖ ['æksɛnt], [æk'sɛnt] tr accentuer
accentuate [æk'sɛntʃu,et] tr accentuer
accept [æk'sɛpt] tr accepter
acceptable [æk'sɛptəbəl] adj acceptable
acceptance [æk'sɛptəns] s acceptation f; (approval) approbation f
acceptation [,æksɛp'teʃən] s acceptation f; (meaning) acception f
access ['æksɛs] s accès m
accessible [æk'sɛsɪbəl] adj accessible
accession [æk'sɛʃən] s accession f
accesso·ry [æk'sɛsəri] adj accessoire ‖ s (pl **-ries**) accessoire m; (to a crime) complice mf
acc'ess route' s voie f de raccordement, bretelle f
accident ['æksɪdənt] s accident m; **by accident** par accident
accidental [,æksɪ'dɛntəl] adj accidentel ‖ s (mus) accident m
ac'cident-prone' adj prédisposé aux accidents
acclaim [ə'klem] tr acclamer
acclimate ['æklɪ,met] tr acclimater
accommodate [ə'kamə,det] tr accommoder; (to oblige) rendre service à; (to lodge) loger
accommodating [ə'kamə,detɪŋ] adj accommodant, serviable
accommodation [ə,kamə'deʃən] s accommodation f; **accommodations** commodités fpl; (in a train) place f; (in a hotel) chambre f; (room and board) le vivre et le couvert
accompaniment [ə'kʌmpənɪmənt] s accompagnement m

accompanist [ə'kʌmpənist] s accompagnateur m
accompa·ny [ə'kʌmpəni] v (pret & pp **-nied**) tr accompagner
accomplice [ə'kamplɪs] s complice mf
accomplish [ə'kamplɪʃ] tr accomplir
accomplishment [ə'kamplɪʃmənt] s accomplissement m, réalisation f; (thing itself) œuvre f accomplie; **accomplishments** arts mpl d'agrément, talents mpl
accord [ə'kɔrd] s accord m; **in accord** d'accord; **of one's own accord** de son plein gré ‖ tr accorder ‖ intr se mettre d'accord
accordance [ə'kɔrdəns] s accord m; **in accordance with** conformément à
according [ə'kɔrdɪŋ] adj—**according as** selon que; **according to** selon, d'après, suivant; **according to expert advice** au dire d'experts
accordingly [ə'kɔrdɪŋli] adv en conséquence
accordion [ə'kɔrdi·ən] s accordéon m
accost [ə'kɔst] tr accoster
account [ə'kaʊnt] s (calculation; bill; bank account; report) compte m; (benefit) profit m, avantage m; (narration) récit m; (report) compte rendu; (explanation) explication f; **of no account** sans importance; **on account of** à cause de; **on no account** en aucune façon; **to call to account** demander des comptes à ‖ intr—**to account for** expliquer; (money) rendre compte de
accountable [ə'kaʊntəbəl] adj responsable; (explainable) explicable
accountant [ə'kaʊntənt] s comptable mf
account' book' s registre m de comptabilité
accounting [ə'kaʊntɪŋ] s (profession) comptabilité f
accouterments [ə'kutərmənts] spl équipement m
accredit [ə'krɛdɪt] tr accréditer
accretion [ə'kriʃən] s accroissement m
accrue [ə'kru] intr s'accroître; **to accrue from** dériver de; **to accrue to** échoir à
accumulate [ə'kjumjə,let] tr accumuler ‖ intr s'accumuler
accuracy ['ækjərəsi] s exactitude f
accurate ['ækjərɪt] adj exact; (aim) juste; (translation) fidèle
accursed [ə'kʌrsɪd], [ə'kʌrst] adj maudit
accusation [,ækjə'zeʃən] s accusation f
accusative [ə'kjuzətɪv] adj & s accusatif m
accuse [ə'kjuz] tr accuser
accused s accusé m, inculpé m
accustom [ə'kʌstəm] tr accoutumer; **to become accustomed** s'accoutumer
ace [es] s as m; **to have an ace up one's sleeve** avoir un atout dans la manche
acetate ['æsɪ,tet] s acétate m
ace'tic ac'id [ə'sitɪk] s acide m acétique
acetone ['æsɪ,ton] s acétone f
acet'ylene torch' [ə'sɛtɪ,lin] s chalumeau m oxyacétylénique
ache [ek] s douleur f ‖ intr faire mal; **my head aches** j'ai mal à la tête; **to be aching to** (coll) brûler de

achieve [ə'tʃiv] *tr* (*a task*) accomplir; (*an aim*) atteindre; (*success*) obtenir; (*a victory*) remporter

achievement [ə'tʃivmənt] *s* (*completion*) accomplissement *m*, réalisation *f*; (*thing itself*) œuvre *f* remarquable, réussite *f*; (*heroic deed*) exploit *m*

Achil'les' heel' [ə'kɪliz] *s* talon *m* d'Achille

acid ['æsɪd] *adj* & *s* acide *m*

acidi·ty [ə'sɪdɪti] *s* (*pl* **-ties**) acidité *f*

ac'id rain' *s* pluie *f* acide

ac'id test' *s* (fig) épreuve *f* définitive

acknowledge [æk'nɑlɪdʒ] *tr* reconnaître; **to acknowledge receipt of** accuser réception de

acknowledgment [æk'nɑlɪdʒmənt] *s* (*recognition*) reconnaissance *f*; (*of an error*) aveu *m*; (*of a letter*) accusé *m* de réception; (*receipt*) récépissé *m*

acme ['ækmi] *s* comble *m*, sommet *m*

acne ['ækni] *s* acné *f*

acolyte ['ækə,laɪt] *s* enfant *m* de chœur; (*priest*) acolyte *m*; assistant *m*

acorn ['ekɔrn] *s* gland *m*

acoustic [ə'kustɪk] *adj* acoustique ‖ **acoustics** *s* & *spl* acoustique *f*

acquaint [ə'kwent] *tr* informer; **to be acquainted** se connaître; **to be acquainted with** connaître

acquaintance [ə'kwentəns] *s* connaissance *f*

acquiesce [,ækwɪ'ɛs] *intr* acquiescer

acquiescence [,ækwɪ'ɛsəns] *s* acquiescement *m*, contentement *m*

acquire [ə'kwaɪr] *tr* acquérir; (*friends; a reputation*) s'acquérir

acquired' immune'-defi'ciency syn'drome [ə'kwaɪrd] *s* syndrome *m* d'immunodéficience acquise (le SIDA)

acquirement [ə'kwaɪrmənt] *s* acquisition *f*

acquisition [,ækwɪ'zɪʃən] *s* acquisition *f*

acquisitive [ə'kwɪzɪtɪv] *adj* âpre au gain, avide

acquit [ə'kwɪt] *v* (*pret* & *pp* **acquitted;** *ger* **acquitting**) *tr* acquitter; **to acquit oneself** se comporter

acquittal [ə'kwɪtəl] *s* acquittement *m*

acre ['ekər] *s* acre *f*

acrid ['ækrɪd] *adj* âcre

acrimonious [,ækrɪ'moni·əs] *adj* acrimonieux

acrobat ['ækrə,bæt] *s* acrobate *mf*

acrobatic [,ækrə'bætɪk] *adj* acrobatique ‖ **acrobatics** *s* (*profession*) acrobatie *f*; **acrobatics** *spl* (*stunts*) acrobaties

acronym ['ækrənɪm] *s* sigle *m*

acropolis [ə'krɑpəlɪs] *s* acropole *f*

across [ə'krɔs] *adv* en travers, à travers; (*sidewise*) en largeur ‖ *prep* en travers de; (*e.g., the street*) de l'autre côté de; **across country** à travers champs; **to come across** rencontrer par hasard; **to go across** traverser

acrostic [ə'krɔstɪk] *s* acrostiche *m*

acrylic [ə'krɪlɪk] *adj* acrylique

act [ækt] *s* action *f*, acte *m*; (circus, rad, telv) numéro *m*; (govt) loi *f*; (law, theat) acte; (coll) allure *f* affectée, comédie *f*; **in the act** sur le fait, en flagrant délit ‖ *tr* jouer; **to act the fool** faire le pitre ‖ *intr* agir; se conduire; (theat) jouer; **to act as** servir de; **to act on** influer sur

acting ['æktɪŋ] *adj* intérimaire, par intérim ‖ *s* (*actor's art*) jeu *m*; (*profession*) théâtre *m*

action ['ækʃən] *s* action *f*; (law) acte *m*; (mach) jeu *m*; (theat) intrigue *f*; **out of action** hors de service; **to go into action** (mil) aller au feu; **to suit the action to the word** joindre le geste à la parole; **to take action** prendre des mesures

activate ['æktɪ,vet] *tr* activer, actionner

active ['æktɪv] *adj* actif

activi·ty [æk'tɪvɪti] *s* (*pl* **-ties**) activité *f*

actor [æktər] *s* acteur *m*

actress ['æktrɪs] *s* actrice *f*

actual ['æktʃu·əl] *adj* véritable, réel, effectif

actually ['æktʃu·əli] *adv* réellement, en réalité, effectivement

actuar·y ['æktʃu,ɛri] *s* (*pl* **-ies**) actuaire *m*

actuate ['æktʃu,et] *tr* (*to turn on*) actionner; (*to motivate*) animer

acuity [ə'kju·ɪti] *s* acuité *f*

acumen [ə'kjumən] *s* finesse *f*

acupuncture ['ækjupʌnktʃər] *s* acupuncture *f*, acuponcture *f*

acute [ə'kjut] *adj* aigu; (fig) avisé

acutely [ə'kjutli] *adv* profondément

A.D. ['e'di] *adj* (letterword) (**Anno Domini**) ap. **J.-C.**

ad [æd] *s* (coll) annonce *f*

adage ['ædɪdʒ] *s* adage *m*

Adam ['ædəm] *s* Adam *m*; **I don't know him from Adam** (coll) je ne le connais ni d'Ève ni d'Adam

adamant ['ædəmənt] *adj* inflexible

Ad'am's ap'ple *s* pomme *f* d'Adam

adapt [ə'dæpt] *tr* adapter

adaptation [,ædæp'teʃən] *s* adaptation *f*

adapter [ə'dæptər] *s* adaptateur *m*; (phot) bague *f* porte-objectif

add [æd] *tr* ajouter; **to add up** additionner ‖ *intr* additionner; **to add up to** s'élever à

adder ['ædər] *s* (zool) vipère *f*

addict ['ædɪkt] *s* (pathol) toxicomane *mf*; (sports) fanatique *mf* ‖ [ə'dɪkt] *tr* atteindre de toxicomanie; **to be addicted to** (*to enjoy*) s'adonner à

addiction [ə'dɪkʃən] *s* toxicomanie *f*; **addiction to** penchant *m* pour

add'ing machine' *s* machine *f* à calculer, additionneuse *f*, calculatrice *f*

addition [ə'dɪʃən] *s* addition *f*; **in addition to** en plus de

additive ['ædɪtɪv] *adj* & *s* additif *m*

addle ['ædəl] *tr* brouiller

address [ə'drɛs], ['ædrɛs] *s* adresse *f* ‖ [ə'drɛs] *s* discours *m*; **to deliver an address** prononcer un discours ‖ *tr* adresser; s'adresser à; (*an audience*) faire un discours à

address' book' *s* carnet *m* d'adresses

addressee [,ædrɛ'si] *s* destinataire *mf*

adduce [ə'd(j)us] *tr* alléguer; (*proof*) fournir

adenoids ['ædə,nɔɪdz] *spl* végétations *fpl* adénoïdes

adept [ə'dɛpt] *adj* habile ‖ *s* adepte *mf*

adequate ['ædɪkwɪt] *adj* suffisant, adéquat; **adequate to** à la hauteur de, proportionné à

adhere [æd'hɪr] *intr* adhérer

adherence [æd'hɪrəns] *s* adhérence *f*

adherent [æd'hɪrənt] *adj & s* adhérent *m*

adhesion [æd'hiʒən] *s* adhésion *f*; (pathol) adhérence *f*

adhesive [æd'hisɪv] *adj & s* adhésif *m*

adhe'sive hook' *s* piton *m* adhésif

adhe'sive tape' *s* sparadrap *m*

adieu [ə'd(j)u] *s* (*pl* **adieus** or **adieux**) adieu *m* ‖ *interj* adieu!

ad infinitum [,æd,ɪnfɪ'naɪtəm] *adv* sans fin

adjacent [ə'dʒesənt] *adj* adjacent

adjective ['ædʒɪktɪv] *adj & s* adjectif *m*

adjoin [ə'dʒɔɪn] *tr* avoisiner ‖ *intr* être contigus

adjoining [ə'dʒɔɪnɪŋ] *adj* contigu

adjourn [ə'dʒʌrn] *tr* (*to postpone*) remettre, reporter; (*a meeting, a session*) lever; (*sine die; for resumption at another time or place*) ajourner ‖ *intr* s'ajourner; lever la séance

adjournment [ə'dʒʌrnmənt] *s* suspension *f* de séance

adjudge [ə'dʒʌdʒ] *tr* adjuger; (*a criminal*) condamner

adjudicate [ə'dʒudɪ,ket] *tr & intr* juger

adjunct ['ædʒʌŋkt] *adj & s* adjoint *m*; **adjuncts** accessoires *mpl*

adjust [ə'dʒʌst] *tr* ajuster ‖ *intr* s'adapter

adjustable [ə'dʒʌstəbəl] *adj* réglable; (*antenna*) orientable

adjustment [ə'dʒʌstmənt] *s* (*act of adjusting*) ajustage *m*, réglage *m*; (*wages, prices*) rajustement *m*; (*arrangement*) ajustement *m*, règlement *m*; (telv) mise *f* au point

adjutant ['ædʒətənt] *s* adjutant *m*

ad-lib [,æd'lɪb] *adj* improvisé ‖ *v* (*pret & pp* **-libbed;** *ger* **-libbing**) *tr & intr* improviser (en cascade)

administer [æd'mɪnɪstər] *tr* administrer; **to administer an oath** faire prêter serment ‖ *intr*—**to administer to** pourvoir à, aider, assister

administration [æd,mɪnɪs'treʃən] *s* (*management*) administration *f*; (*government*) gouvernement *m*

administrator [æd'mɪnɪs,tretər] *s* administrateur *m*

admiral ['ædmɪrəl] *s* amiral *m*

admiration [,ædmɪ'reʃən] *s* admiration *f*

admire [æd'maɪr] *tr* admirer

admirer [æd'maɪrər] *s* admirateur *m*; (*suitor*) soupirant *m*

admission [æd'mɪʃən] *s* (*entry*) admission *f*; (*price*) entrée *f*; (*confession*) aveu *m*

ad·mit [æd'mɪt] *v* (*pret & pp* **-mitted;** *ger* **-mitting**) *tr* admettre; (*e.g., a mistake*) avouer; **admit bearer** laisser passer

admittance [æd'mɪtəns] *s* entrée *f*

admittedly [æd'mɪtɪdli] *adv* manifestement

admonish [æd'manɪʃ] *tr* admonester

ad nauseam [æd'nɔʃɪ·əm], [æd'nɔsɪ·əm] *adv* jusqu'au dégoût

ado [ə'du] *s* agitation *f*; **much ado about nothing** beaucoup de bruit pour rien; **without further ado** sans plus de façons

adolescence [,ædə'lɛsəns] *s* adolescence *f*

adolescent [,ædə'lɛsənt] *adj & s* adolescent *m*

adopt [ə'dapt] *tr* adopter

adoption [ə'dapʃən] *s* adoption *f*

adoptive [ə'daptɪv] *adj* adoptif

adorable [ə'dorəbəl] *adj* adorable

adoration [,ædə'reʃən] *s* adoration *f*

adore [ə'dor] *tr* adorer

adorn [ə'dɔrn] *tr* orner, parer

adornment [ə'dɔrnmənt] *s* parure *f*

adre'nal glands' [æd'rinəl] *spl* (capsules) surrénales *fpl*

adrenaline [ə'drɛnəlɪn] *s* adrénaline *f*

Adriatic [,edrɪ'ætɪk] *adj & s* Adriatique *f*

adrift [ə'drɪft] *ad & adv* à la dérive

adroit [ə'drɔɪt] *adj* adroit, habile

adulate ['ædʒə,let] *tr* aduler

adult [ə'dʌlt] *adj & s* adulte *mf*

adult' book' shop *s* érotothèque *f*

adulterate [ə'dʌltə,ret] *tr* frelater

adulteration [ə,dʌltə'reʃən] *s* frelatage *m*

adulterer [ə'dʌltərər] *s* adultère *m*

adulteress [ə'dʌltərɪs] *s* adultère *f*

adulterous [ə'dʌltərəs] *adj* adultère

adulter·y [ə'dʌltəri] *s* (*pl* **-ies**) adultère *m*

adumbrate ['ædəm,bret] *tr* ébaucher; (*to foreshadow*) présager

advance [æd'væns] *s* avance *f*; **advances** propositions *fpl*; propositions malhonnêtes; **in advance** d'avance; en avance ‖ *tr* avancer ‖ *intr* avancer, s'avancer; (*said of prices*) augmenter; (*said of stocks*) monter

advancement [æd'vænsmənt] *s* avancement *m*

advance' pay'ment *s* versement *m* anticipé

advantage [æd'væntɪdʒ] *s* avantage *m*; **to take advantage of** profiter de

advent ['ædvɛnt] *s* venue *f*; **Advent** (eccl) Avent *m*

adventitious [,ædvɛn'tɪʃəs] *adj* adventice

adventure [æd'vɛntʃər] *s* aventure *f*

adventurer [æd'vɛntʃərər] *s* aventurier *m*

adventuress [æd'vɛntʃərɪs] *s* aventurière *f*

adventurous [æd'vɛntʃərəs] *adj* aventureux

adverb ['ædvʌrb] *s* adverbe *m*

adversar·y ['ædvər,sɛri] *s* (*pl* **-ies**) adversaire *mf*

adverse [æd'vʌrs] *adj* adverse

adversi·ty [æd'vʌrsɪti] *s* (*pl* **-ties**) adversité *f*

advertise ['ædvər,taɪz] *tr & intr* annoncer

advertisement [æd'vʌrtɪzmənt] *s* annonce *f*

advertiser ['ædvər,taɪzər] *s* annonceur *m*

advertising ['ædvər,taɪzɪŋ] *s* réclame *f*

ad'vertising a'gency *s* agence *f* de publicité

ad'vertising spe'cialist *s* publicitaire *mf*, entrepreneur *m* de publicité

advice [æd'vaɪs] s conseil m; conseils; **a piece of advice** un conseil
advisable [æd'vaɪzəbəl] adj opportun, recommandable
advise [æd'vaɪz] tr (to counsel) conseiller; (to inform) aviser; **to advise against** déconseiller; **to advise s.o. to + inf** conseiller à qn de + inf
advisedly [æd'vaɪzɪdli] adv en connaissance de cause
advisement [æd'vaɪzmənt] s conseils mpl; **to take under advisement** mettre en délibération
adviser [æd'vaɪzər] s conseiller m
advisory [æd'vaɪzəri] adj consultatif
advocacy ['ædvəkəsi] s plaidoyer m
advocate ['ædvə,ket] s partisan m; (lawyer) avocat m ‖ tr préconiser
Aege′an Sea′ [ɪ'dʒi·ən] s mer f Égée, mer de l'Archipel
aegis ['idʒɪs] s égide f
aerate ['ɛret] tr aérer
aerial ['ɛrɪ·əl] adj aérien ‖ s antenne f
aerodynamic [,ɛrodaɪ'næmɪk] adj aérodynamique ‖ **aerodynamics** s aérodynamique f
aeronautic [,ɛro'nɔtɪk] adj aéronautique ‖ **aeronautics** s aéronautique f
aerosol ['ɛrə,sol] s aérosol m
aerospace ['ɛrə,spes] adj aérospatial
Aeschylus ['ɛskɪləs] s Eschyle m
aesthete ['ɛsθit] s esthète mf
aesthetic [ɛs'θɛtɪk] adj esthétique ‖ **aesthetics** s esthétique f
afar [ə'fɑr] adv au loin
affable ['æfəbəl] adj affable
affair [ə'fɛr] s affaire f; (of lovers) affaire de cœur
affect [ə'fɛkt] tr affecter
affectation [,æfɛk'teʃən] s affectation f
affected adj affecté, maniéré
affection [ə'fɛkʃən] s affection f
affectionate [ə'fɛkʃənɪt] adj affectueux
affidavit [,æfɪ'devɪt] s déclaration f sous serment
affiliate [ə'fɪlɪ,et] s (com) société f affiliée ‖ tr affilier ‖ intr s'affilier
affini·ty [ə'fɪnɪti] s (pl -ties) affinité f; (connection, resemblance) rapport m, ressemblance f; (liking) attrait m, attraction f
affirm [ə'fʌrm] tr & intr affirmer
affirmative [ə'fʌrmətɪv] adj affirmatif ‖ s affirmative f
affix ['æfɪks] s affixe m ‖ [ə'fɪks] tr (a signature) apposer; (guilt) attribuer; (a stamp) coller
afflict [ə'flɪkt] tr affliger
affliction [ə'flɪkʃən] s (sorrow) affliction f; (disorder) infirmité f
affluence ['æflu·əns] s affluence f de biens, richesse f
afford [ə'fɔrd] tr (to provide) fournir; (to be able to pay for) se permettre, avoir de quoi payer, avoir les moyens d'acheter
affront [ə'frʌnt] s affront m ‖ tr insulter
Afghanistan [æf'gænɪ,stæn] s l'Afghanistan m

afire [ə'faɪr] adj & adv en feu
aflame [ə'flem] adj & adv en flammes
afloat [ə'flot] adj & adv à flot; (rumor) en circulation; **to keep afloat on the water** se tenir sur l'eau
afoot [ə'fʊt] adj & adv à pied; (underway) en œuvre
aforesaid [ə'for,sɛd] adj susdit, susmentionné, précité
afraid [ə'fred] adj effrayé; **to be afraid** avoir peur
afresh [ə'frɛʃ] adv à nouveau
Africa ['æfrɪkə] s Afrique f; l'Afrique f
African ['æfrɪkən] adj africain ‖ s Africain m
after ['æftər] adj suivant, postérieur ‖ adv après, plus tard ‖ prep après, à la suite de; (in the manner or style of) d'après; (not translated in expressions of time), e.g., **eight minutes after ten** dix heures huit ‖ conj après que
af′ter-din′ner adj d'après dîner
af′ter-effect′ s contrecoup m; **after-effects** (pathol) séquelles fpl
af′ter-glow′ s lueur f du coucher
af′ter-im′age s image f consécutive
af′ter-life′ s survie f
aftermath ['æftər,mæθ] s conséquences fpl sérieuses, suites fpl; (agr) regain m
af′ter-noon′ s après-midi m & f; **good afternoon!** bonjour!
af′ter-shav′ing lo′tion s eau f de Cologne pour la barbe
af′ter-taste′ s arrière-goût m
af′ter-thought′ s réflexion f après coup
afterward ['æftərwərd] adv après, ensuite
again [ə'gɛn] adv encore; (besides, moreover) de plus, d'ailleurs, en outre; (once more) de nouveau, encore une fois; **as much again** deux fois autant; **not again** ne . . . plus, e.g., **I won't do it again** je ne le ferai plus; **now and again** de temps en temps
against [ə'gɛnst] prep contre; **against the grain** à rebrousse-poil; **over against** en face de; par contraste avec
age [edʒ] s âge m; (about a hundred years) siècle m; **for ages** depuis longtemps; **of age** majeur; **to come of age** atteindre sa majorité; **under age** mineur ‖ tr & intr vieillir
age′ brack′et s tranche f d'âge
aged [edʒd] adj (wine, cheese, etc.) vieilli; (of the age of) âgé de ‖ ['edʒɪd] adj âgé, vieux
agen·cy ['edʒənsi] s (pl -cies) agence f; (means) action f
agenda [ə'dʒɛndə] s ordre m du jour
agent ['edʒənt] s agent m; (means) moyen m; (com) commissionnaire m
agglomeration [ə,glɑmə'reʃən] s agglomération f
aggrandizement [ə'grændɪzmənt] f agrandissement m
aggravate ['ægrə,vet] tr aggraver; (coll) exaspérer

aggregate ['ægrɪ,get] *adj* global ‖ *s* agrégat *m* ‖ *tr* rassembler; (coll) s'élever à
aggression [ə'grɛʃən] *s* agression *f*
aggressive [ə'grɛsɪv] *adj* agressif; (*live-wire*) entreprenant
aggressor [ə'grɛsər] *s* agresseur *m*
aghast [ə'gæst] *adj* abasourdi
agile ['ædʒɪl] *adj* agile
agility [ə'dʒɪlɪti] *s* agilité *f*
agitate ['ædʒɪ,tet] *tr* agiter
agitator ['ædʒɪ,tetər] *s* agitateur *m*
aglow [ə'glo] *adj & adv* rougeoyant
agnostic [æg'nɑstɪk] *adj & s* agnostique *mf*
ago [ə'go] *adv* il y a, e.g., **two days ago** il y a deux jours
agog [ə'gɑg] *adj & adv* en émoi
agonizing ['ægə,naɪzɪŋ] *adj* angoissant
ago·ny ['ægəni] *s* (*pl* **-nies**) (*physical pain*) douleur *f* atroce; (*mental pain*) angoisse *f*; (*death struggle*) agonie *f*
agrarian [ə'grɛrɪ·ən] *adj* agraire; (law) agrairien ‖ *s* agrairien *m*
agree [ə'gri] *intr* être d'accord, s'accorder; **agreed!** d'accord!; **to agree to** consentir à
agreeable [ə'gri·əbəl] *adj* agréable, sympathique; (*consenting*) d'accord
agreement [ə'grimənt] *s* accord *m*
agriculture ['ægrɪ,kʌltʃər] *s* agriculture *f*
aground [ə'graʊnd] *adj* (naut) échoué ‖ *adv*—**to run aground** échouer
ahead [ə'hɛd] *adj & adv* en avant; **ahead of** avant; devant; **straight ahead** tout droit; **to get ahead of** devancer
ahem [ə'hɛm] *interj* hum!
ahoy [ə'hɔɪ] *interj*—**ship ahoy!** ohé du navire!
aid [ed] *s* (*assistance*) aide *f*; (*assistant*) aide *mf* ‖ *tr* aider
aide-de-camp ['eddə'kæmp] *s* (*pl* **aides-de-camp**) officier *m* d'ordonnance, aide *m* de camp
AIDS [edz] *s* (acronym) (**acquired immune-deficiency syndrome**) le SIDA (syndrome d'immuno-déficience acquise)
ail [el] *tr* affliger; **what ails you?** qu'avez-vous? ‖ *intr* être souffrant
ailment ['elmənt] *s* indisposition *f*, maladie *f*
aim [em] *s* (*purpose*) but *m*, objectif *m*; (*of gun*) pointage *m* ‖ *tr* diriger; (*a blow*) allonger; (*a telescope, cannon, etc.*) pointer, viser ‖ *intr* viser
air [ɛr] *s* air *m*; **on the air** à la radio, à la télévision, à l'antenne; **to put on airs** prendre des airs; **to put on the air** radiodiffuser; **to walk on air** ne pas toucher terre; **up in the air** confondu, sidéré; (*angry*) très monté ‖ *tr* aérer; (*a question*) ventiler; (*feelings*) donner libre cours à
air' bag' *s* (aut) coussin *m* gonflable
air-borne ['ɛr,born] *adj* aéroporté
air' brake' *s* frein *m* à air comprimé
air'-condi'tion *tr* climatiser
air' condi'tioner *s* climatiseur *m*
air' condi'tioning *s* climatisation *f*
air'craft' *s* aéronef *m*, appareil *m* d'aviation
air'craft car'rier *s* porte-avions *m*

air'drop' *s* parachutage *m* ‖ *tr* parachuter
air'field' *s* terrain *m* d'aviation, aérodrome *m*
air'foil' *s* voilure *f*
air' force' *s* forces *fpl* aériennes
air' freight' *s* (*parcels*) transport *m* par avion, fret *m* par avion; (*company*) messageries *fpl* aériennes
air' gap' *s* (elec) entrefer *m*
air' let'ter *s* aérogramme *m*
air'lift' *s* pont *m* aérien
air'line' *s* ligne *f* aérienne
air'line pi'lot *s* pilote *m* de ligne
air'lin'er *s* avion *m* de transport
air'mail' *adj* aéropostal ‖ *s* poste *f* aérienne; **by airmail** par avion
air' mat'tress *s* matelas *m* pneumatique
air'plane' *s* avion *m*
air' pock'et *s* trou *m* d'air
air' pollu'tion *s* pollution *f* de l'air
air'port' *s* aéroport *m*
air'port police' *s* police *f* de l'air
air' raid' *s* attaque *f* aérienne
air'-raid drill' *s* exercice *m* d'alerte aérienne
air'-raid shel'ter *s* abri *m*
air'-raid ward'en *s* chef *m* d'îlot
air'-raid warn'ing *s* alarme *f* aérienne
air'sick' *adj* atteint du mal de l'air
air'sick'ness *s* mal *m* de l'air
air' sleeve' or **sock'** *s* manche *f* à air
air'strip' *s* piste *f*
air'term'inal *s* aérogare *f*
air'tight' *adj* hermétique
air' (traf'fic) control'ler *s* contrôleur *m* aérien, aiguilleur *m* (du ciel), contrôleur de la navigation aérienne
air'waves' *spl* ondes *fpl* radiophoniques
air'way' *s* route *f* aérienne
air·y ['ɛri] *adj* (*comp* **-ier**; *super* **-iest**) (*room*) bien aéré; (*casual, light*) léger; (*graceful*) gracieux; (coll) maniéré
aisle [aɪl] *s* (*through rows of seats*) passage *m* central, allée *f*; (*in a train*) couloir *m*; (*long passageway in a church*) nef *f* latérale
ajar [ə'dʒɑr] *adj* entrebâillé
akimbo [ə'kɪmbo] *adj & adv*—**with arms akimbo** les poings sur les hanches
akin [ə'kɪn] *adj* apparenté
alabaster ['ælə,bæstər] *s* albâtre *m*
alacrity [ə'lækrɪti] *s* vivacité *f*, empressement *m*
alarm [ə'lɑrm] *s* alarme *f*; (*of clock*) sonnerie *f* ‖ *tr* alarmer
alarm' clock' *s* réveille-matin *m*, réveil *m*
alarming [ə'lɑrmɪŋ] *adj* alarmant
alas [ə'læs] *interj* hélas!
Albanian [æl'benɪ·ən] *adj* albanais ‖ *s* (*language*) albanais *m*; (*person*) Albanais
albatross ['ælbə,trɔs] *s* albatros *m*
albi·no [æl'baɪno] *adj* albinos ‖ *s* (*pl* **-nos**) albinos *m*
album ['ælbəm] *s* album *m*
albumen [æl'bjumən] *s* albumen *m*
alchemy ['ælkɪmi] *s* alchimie *f*
alcohol ['ælkə,hɔl] *s* alcool *m*

alcoholic [ˌælkəˈhɔlɪk] *adj* & *s* alcoolique *mf*

alcove [ˈælkov] *s* niche *f*; (*for a bed*) alcôve *f*

alder [ˈɔldər] *s* aune *m*

alder·man [ˈɔldərmən] *s* (*pl* **-men**) conseiller *m* municipal

ale [el] *s* ale *f*

alembic [əˈlɛmbɪk] *s* alambic *m*; (fig) creuset *m*

alert [əˈlʌrt] *adj* & *s* alerte *f* ‖ *tr* alerter

alfalfa [ælˈfælfə] *s* luzerne *f*

algebra [ˈældʒɪbrə] *s* algèbre *f*

Algeria [ælˈdʒɪrɪ·ə] *s* Algérie *f*

Algerian [ælˈdʒɪrɪ·ən] *adj* (*of Algeria*) algérien; (*of Algiers, the Barbary state*) algérois ‖ *s* Algérien *m*; Algérois *m*

Algiers [ælˈdʒɪrz] *s* Alger *m*

alias [ˈelɪ·əs] *s* nom *m* d'emprunt ‖ *adv* alias, autrement dit

ali·bi [ˈælɪˌbaɪ] *s* (*pl* **-bis**) excuse *f*; (law) alibi *m*

alien [ˈeljən] *adj* & *s* étranger *m*

alienate [ˈeljəˌnet] *tr* aliéner, s'aliéner

alight [əˈlaɪt] *adj* allumé ‖ *v* (*pret* & *pp* **alighted** or **alit** [əˈlɪt]) *intr* descendre, se poser; (aer) (*on land*) atterrir; (aer) (*on sea*) amerrir

align [əˈlaɪn] *tr* aligner ‖ *intr* s'aligner

alike [əˈlaɪk] *adj* pareils, e.g., **these books are alike** ces livres sont pareils; **to look alike** se ressembler ‖ *adv* de la même façon

alimony [ˈælɪˌmoni] *s* pension *f* alimentaire après divorce

alive [əˈlaɪv] *adj* vivant; vif; **alive to** sensible à

alka·li [ˈælkəˌlaɪ] *s* (*pl* **-lis** or **-lies**) alcali *m*

alkaline [ˈælkəˌlaɪn] *adj* alcalin

all [ɔl] *adj indef* tout; tout le ‖ *s* tout *m* ‖ *pron indef* tout; tous; **all of** tout le; **first of all** tout d'abord; **is that all?** c'est tout?; (*ironically*) ce n'est que ça?; **not at all** pas du tout ‖ *adv* tout; **all at once** tout à coup; **all but** presque; **all in** (coll) éreinté; **all in all** à tout prendre; **all off** (slang) abandonné; **all right** bon, ça va, très bien; **all's well!** (naut) bon quart!; **all the better** tant mieux; **all told** en tout; **fifteen (thirty,** etc.) **all** (tennis) égalité à quinze (trente, etc.); **all round**, e.g., **thirty all** trente partout; **to be all for** ne demander mieux que

allay [əˈle] *tr* apaiser

all′-clear′ *s* fin *f* d'alerte

allege [əˈlɛdʒ] *tr* (*to assert*) alléguer; (*to assert without proof*) affirmer sans preuve; (law) déclarer sous serment

alleged *adj* présumé, prétendu, censé

allegedly [əˈlɛdʒɪdli] *adv* prétendument, censément

allegiance [əˈlidʒəns] *s* allégeance *f*

allegoric(al) [ˌælɪˈgɔrɪk(əl)] *adj* allégorique

allego·ry [ˈælɪˌgori] *s* (*pl* **-ries**) allégorie *f*

aller·gy [ˈælərdʒi] *s* (*pl* **-gies**) allergie *f*

alleviate [əˈlivɪˌet] *tr* soulager, alléger

alley [ˈæli] *s* ruelle *f*; **that is up my alley** (slang) cela est dans mes cordes

al′ley cat′ *s* chat *m* de gouttière

alliance [əˈlaɪ·əns] *s* alliance *f*

alligator [ˈælɪˌgetər] *s* alligator *m*

al′ligator clip′ *s* pince *f* crocodile

al′ligator pear′ *s* poire *f* d'avocat

al′ligator wrench′ *s* clef *f* crocodile

alliteration [əˌlɪtəˈreʃən] *s* allitération *f*

all′-know′ing *adj* omniscient

allocate [ˈæləˌket] *tr* allouer, assigner

allot [əˈlɑt] *v* (*pret* & *pp* **allotted;** *ger* **allotting**) *tr* répartir

allotment [əˈlɑtmənt] *s* allocation *f*

all′-out′ *adj* total

allow [əˈlaʊ] *tr* (*to permit*) permettre, tolérer; (*to concede*) admettre; (*as a grant*) allouer, accorder ‖ *intr*—**to allow for** tenir compte de

allowance [əˈlaʊ·əns] *s* (*money*) allocation *f*, indemnité *f*; (com) réduction *f*, rabais *m*, concession *f*; **to make allowances for** tenir compte de

alloy [ˈælɔɪ] *s* alliage *m* ‖ [əˈlɔɪ] *tr* allier

all′ right′ *interj* bon!, très bien!, ça va!; (*agreed!*) c'est entendu!, d'accord!

all′-round′ *adj* (*athlete*) complet; (*man*) universel; total, global

All′ Saints′′ Day′ *s* la Toussaint

All′ Souls′′ Day′ *s* la fête des Morts

all′spice′ *s* (*plant*) quatre-épices *f*; (*berry*) toute-épice *f*; piment *m*

all′-time′ *adj* record

allude [əˈlud] *intr*—**to allude to** faire allusion à

allure [əˈlʊr] *tr* séduire, tenter

allurement [əˈlʊrmənt] *s* charme *m*

alluring [əˈlʊrɪŋ] *adj* séduisant

all′ wet′ *adj* (coll) fichu, erroné

al·ly [ˈælaɪ] *s* (*pl* **-lies**) allié *m* ‖ [əˈlaɪ] *v* (*pret* & *pp* **-lied**) *tr* allier

almanac [ˈɔlməˌnæk] *s* almanach *m*

almighty [ɔlˈmaɪti] *adj* omnipotent

almond [ˈɑmənd], [ˈæmənd] *s* amande *f*

al′mond tree′ *s* amandier *m*

almost [ˈɔlmost] *adv* presque; **I almost fell** j'ai failli tomber

alms [ɑmz] *s* & *spl* aumône *f*

alms′house′ *s* hospice *m*

aloe [ˈælo] *s* aloès *m*

aloft [əˈlɔft] *adv* en l'air, en haut; (aer) en vol; (naut) en haut

alone [əˈlon] *adj* seul, e.g., **my arm alone suffices** mon bras seul suffit; e.g., **the metropolis alone** la seule métropole; **let alone . . .** sans compter . . . ; **to leave alone** laisser tranquille ‖ *adv* seulement

along [əˈlɔŋ] *adv* avec; **all along** tout le temps; **come along!** venez donc!; **to get along** s'en aller; se porter, faire des progrès ‖ *prep* le long de; sur

along′side′ *adv* à côté ‖ *prep* à côté de

aloof [əˈluf] *adj* isolé, peu abordable ‖ *adv* à l'écart, à distance

aloud [əˈlaud] *adv* à haute voix

alpenstock [ˈælpənˌstɑk] *s* bâton *m* ferré

alphabet [ˈælfəˌbɛt] *s* alphabet *m*

alpine [ˈælpaɪn] *adj* alpin

Alps [ælps] *spl*—**the Alps** les Alpes *fpl*

already [ɔlˈrɛdi] *adv* déjà

Alsatian [ælˈseʃən] *adj* alsacien ‖ *s (dialect)* alsacien *m*; *(person)* Alsacien *m*

also [ˈɔlso] *adv* aussi, également

altar [ˈɔltər] *s* autel *m*

al′tar boy′ *s* enfant *m* de chœur

al′tar cloth′ *s* nappe *f* d'autel

al′tar-piece′ *s* rétable *m*

al′tar rail′ *s* grille *f* du chœur, grille de l'autel

alter [ˈɔltər] *tr (to transform)* changer, modifier; *(to date; evidence)* falsifier, fausser; *(a text)* altérer; *(a suit of clothes)* retoucher, faire des retouches à; *(an animal)* châtrer ‖ *intr* changer, se modifier

alteration [ˌɔltəˈreʃən] *s (transformation)* changement *m*; *(falsification)* altération *f*; *(in a building)* modification *f*; **alterations** *(in clothing)* retouches *fpl*

alternate [ˈɔltərnɪt] *adj* alternatif; *(angle)* alterne; *(rhyme)* croisé ‖ [ˈɔltər,net] *tr* faire alternance à ‖ *intr* alterner

al′ternating cur′rent *s* courant *m* alternatif

alternative [ɔlˈtʌrnətɪv] *adj* alternatif ‖ *s* alternative *f*

although [ɔlˈðo] *conj* bien que, quoique

altitude [ˈæltɪ,t(j)ud] *s* altitude *f*

al·to [ˈælto] *s (pl* -tos) alto *m*

altogether [ˌɔltəˈgɛðər] *adv (wholly)* entièrement, tout à fait; *(on the whole)* somme toute, tout compte fait; *(with everything included)* en tout, tout compris

altruist [ˈæltrʊ·ɪst] *adj & s* altruiste *mf*

alum [ˈæləm] *s* alun *m*

aluminum [əˈlumɪnəm] *s* aluminium *m*

alu′minum foil′ *s* papier *m* alu

alum·nus [əˈlʌmnəs] *s (pl* -ni [naɪ]) diplômé *m*, ancien étudiant *m*

alveo·lus [ælˈvi·ələs] *s (pl* -li [,laɪ]) alvéole *m*

always [ˈɔlwɪz], [ˈɔlwez] *adv* toujours

AM [ˈeˈɛm] *s* (letterword) **(amplitude modulation)** modulation *f* d'amplitude

A.M. [ˈeˈɛm] *adv* (letterword) **(ante meridiem)** du matin, a.m.

amalgam [əˈmælgəm] *s* amalgame *m*

amalgamate [əˈmælgə,met] *tr* amalgamer ‖ *intr* s'amalgamer

amass [əˈmæs] *tr* amasser

amateur [ˈæmətʃər] *adj & s* amateur *m*

amaze [əˈmez] *tr* étonner

amazing [əˈmezɪŋ] *adj* étonnant

amazon [ˈæmə,zɑn] *s* amazone *f*; **Amazon** Amazone *f*; *(river)* fleuve *m* des Amazones

ambassador [æmˈbæsədər] *s* ambassadeur *m*

ambassadress [æmˈbæsədrɪs] *s* ambassadrice *f*, ambassadeur *m*

amber [ˈæmbər] *adj* ambré ‖ *s* ambre *m* jaune, ambre succin

ambidextrous [ˌæmbɪˈdɛkstrəs] *adj* ambidextre

ambigui·ty [ˌæmbɪˈgju·ɪti] *s (pl* -ties) ambiguïté *f*

ambition [æmˈbɪʃən] *s* ambition *f*

ambitious [æmˈbɪʃəs] *adj* ambitieux

amble [ˈæmbəl] *s* amble *m* ‖ *intr (to stroll)* déambuler; *(equit)* ambler

ambulance [ˈæmbjələns] *s* ambulance *f*

am′bulance corps′ *s* service *m* sanitaire

am′bulance driv′er *s* ambulancier *m*

ambulatory [ˈæmbjələ,tori] *adj* ambulatoire

ambush [ˈæmbuʃ] *s* embuscade *f* ‖ *tr* embusquer

ameliorate [əˈmiljə,ret] *tr* améliorer ‖ *intr* s'améliorer

amen [ˈeˈmɛn], [ˈɑˈmɛn] *s* amen *m* ‖ *interj* ainsi soit-il!

amenable [əˈminəbəl] *adj* docile; **amenable to** *(a court)* justiciable de; *(a fine)* passible de; *(a law)* soumis à; *(persuasion)* disposé à; *(a superior)* responsable envers

amend [əˈmɛnd] *tr* amender ‖ *intr* s'amender

amendment [əˈmɛndmənt] *s* amendement *m*

amends [əˈmɛndz] *spl* dédommagement *m*; **to make amends to** dédommager

ameni·ty [əˈmɛnɪti] *s (pl* -ties) aménité *f*; **amenities** agréments *mpl*; civilités *fpl*

America [əˈmɛrɪkə] *s* Amérique *f*; l'Amérique

American [əˈmɛrɪkən] *adj* américain ‖ *s* Américain *m*

Amer′ican Eng′lish *s* anglais *m* d'Amérique, américain *m*

Amer′ican In′dian *s* amérindien *m*

Americanism [əˈmɛrɪkə,nɪzəm] *s (word)* américanisme *m*; patriotisme *m* américain

Amer′ican plan′ *s* pension *f* complète

Amer′ican way of life′ *s* mode *m* de vie américain

Amerindian [ˌæməˈrɪndɪ·ən] *adj* amérindien ‖ *s* Amérindien *m*

amethyst [ˈæmɪθɪst] *s* améthyste *f*

amiable [ˈemɪ·əbəl] *adj* aimable

amicable [ˈæmɪkəbəl] *adj* amical

amid [əˈmɪd] *prep* au milieu de

amid′ships *adv* au milieu du navire

amidst [əˈmɪdst] *prep* au milieu de

amiss [əˈmɪs] *adj* détraqué; **not amiss** pas mal; **something amiss** quelque chose qui manque, quelque chose qui cloche ‖ *adv* de travers; **to take amiss** prendre en mauvaise part

ami·ty [ˈæmɪti] *s (pl* -ties) amitié *f*

ammeter [ˈæm,mitər] *s* ampèremètre *m*

ammonia [əˈmonɪ·ə] *s (gas)* ammoniac *m*; *(gas dissolved in water)* ammoniaque *f*

ammunition [ˌæmjəˈnɪʃən] *s* munitions *fpl*

amnesia [æmˈniʒə] *s* amnésie *f*

amnes·ty [ˈæmnɪsti] *s (pl* -ties) amnistie *f* ‖ *v (pret & pp* -tied) *tr* amnistier

amoeba [əˈmibə] *s* amibe *f*

among [əˈmʌŋ] *prep* entre, parmi

amorous [ˈæmərəs] *adj* amoureux

amorphous [əˈmɔrfəs] *adj* amorphe

amortize [ˈæmər,taɪz] *tr* amortir

amount [əˈmaunt] *s* montant *m*, quantité *f* ‖ *intr*—**to amount to** s'élever à

ampere [ˈæmpɪr] *s* ampère *m*

ampersand ['æmpər,sænd] *s* esperluète *f*

amphibian [æm'fɪbɪ-ən] *adj & s* amphibie *mf*; amphibien *m*

amphibious [æm'fɪbɪ-əs] *adj* amphibie

amphitheater ['æmfɪ,θi-ətər] *s* amphithéâtre *m*

ample ['æmpəl] *adj* ample; (*speech*) satisfaisant; (*reward*) suffisant

amplifier ['æmplɪ,faɪ-ər] *s* amplificateur *m*

ampli·fy ['æmplɪ,faɪ] *v* (*pret & pp* **-fied**) *tr* amplifier

amplitude ['æmplɪ,t(j)ud] *s* amplitude *f*

am'plitude modula'tion *s* modulation *f* d'amplitude

amputate ['æmpjə,tet] *tr* amputer

amputee [,æmpjə'ti] *s* amputé *m*

amuck [ə'mʌk] *adv*—**to run amuck** s'emballer

amulet ['æmjəlɪt] *s* amulette *f*

amuse [ə'mjuz] *tr* amuser

amusement [ə'mjuzmənt] *s* amusement *m*

amuse'ment arcade' *s* salle *f* de jeux électroniques

amuse'ment park' *s* parc *m* d'attractions

amusing [ə'mjuzɪŋ] *adj* amusant

an [æn], [ən] *art indef* (devant un son vocalique) un

anachronism [ə'nækrə,nɪzəm] *s* anachronisme *m*

analogous [ə'næləgəs] *adj* analogue

analo·gy [ə'nælədʒi] *s* (*pl* **-gies**) analogie *f*

analy·sis [ə'nælɪsɪs] *s* (*pl* **-ses**) [,siz]) analyse *f*

analyst ['ænəlɪst] *s* analyste *mf*

analytic(al) [,ænə'lɪtɪk(əl)] *adj* analytique

analyze ['ænə,laɪz] *tr* analyser

anarchist ['ænərkɪst] *s* anarchiste *mf*

anarchy ['ænərki] *s* anarchie *f*

anathema [ə'næθɪmə] *s* anathème *m*

anatomic(al) [,ænə'tɑmɪk(əl)] *adj* anatomique

anato·my [ə'nætəmi] *s* (*pl* **-mies**) anatomie *f*

ancestor ['ænsɛstər] *s* ancêtre *m*

ances·try ['ænsɛstri] *s* (*pl* **-tries**) ancêtres *mpl*, aïeux *mpl*; (*line*) ascendance *f*

anchor ['æŋkər] *s* ancre *f*; **anchors aweigh!** ancres levées!; **to cast anchor** jeter l'ancre, mouiller l'ancre; **to weigh anchor** lever l'ancre || *tr & intr* ancrer

an'chor man' *s* (telv) présentateur-tronc *m*, pilote *m* d'émission

ancho·vy ['æntʃovi] *s* (*pl* **-vies**) anchois *m*

ancient ['enʃənt] *adj* ancien

and [ænd] *conj* et; **and/or** et/ou; **and so forth** et ainsi de suite

andiron ['ænd,aɪ-ərn] *s* chenet *m*

anecdote ['ænɪk,dot] *s* anecdote *f*

anemia [ə'nimɪ-ə] *s* anémie *f*

anesthesia [,ænɪs'θiʒə] *s* anesthésie *f*

anesthetic [,ænɪs'θɛtɪk] *adj & s* anesthésique *m*

anesthetist [æ'nɛsθɪtɪst] *s* anesthésiste *mf*

anesthetize [æ'nɛsθɪ,taɪz] *tr* anesthésier

aneurysm ['ænjə,rɪzəm] *s* anévrisme *m*

anew [ə'n(j)u] *adv* à (or de) nouveau

angel ['endʒəl] *s* ange *m* (*financial backer*) (coll) bailleur *m* de fonds

angelic(al) [æn'dʒɛlɪk(əl)] *adj* angélique

anger ['æŋgər] *s* colère *f* || *tr* mettre en colère, fâcher

angina pectoris [æn'dʒaɪnə'pɛktərɪs] *s* angine *f* de poitrine

angle ['æŋgəl] *s* angle *m* || *tr* (journ) présenter sous un certain angle || *intr* pêcher à la ligne; **to angle for** essayer d'attraper; (*a compliment*) quêter

angler ['æŋglər] *s* (*fisherman*) pêcheur *m* à la ligne; (*schemer*) intrigant *m*

an·gry ['æŋgri] *adj* (*comp* **-grier**; *super* **-griest**) fâché; **angry at** fâché de; **angry with** fâché contre; **to become angry** se mettre en colère

anguish ['æŋgwɪʃ] *s* angoisse *f*

angular ['æŋgjələr] *adj* angulaire; (*features*) anguleux

animal ['ænɪməl] *adj & s* animal *m*

animate ['ænɪmɪt] *adj* animé || ['ænɪ,met] *tr* animer

an'imated cartoon' *s* dessins *mpl* animés

animation [,ænɪ'meʃən] *s* animation *f*

animosi·ty [,ænɪ'mɑsɪti] *s* (*pl* **-ties**) animosité *f*

animus ['ænɪməs] *s* animosité *f*; intention *f*

anion ['æn,aɪ-ən] *s* anion *m*

anise ['ænɪs] *s* anis *m*

aniseed ['ænɪ,sid] *s* graine *f* d'anis

ankle ['æŋkəl] *s* cheville *f*

anklet ['æŋklɪt] *s* (*sock*) socquette *f*; (*ornamental circlet*) bracelet *m* de cheville

annals ['ænəlz] *spl* annales *fpl*

anneal [ə'nil] *tr* recuire, détremper

annex ['ænɛks] *s* annexe *f* || [ə'nɛks] *tr* annexer, rattacher

annexation [,ænɛks'eʃən] *s* annexion *f*, rattachement *m*

annihilate [ə'naɪ-ɪ,let] *tr* annihiler

annihilation [ə,naɪ-ɪ'leʃən] *s* anéantissement *m*

anniversa·ry [,ænɪ'vʌrsəri] *adj* anniversaire || *s* (*pl* **-ries**) anniversaire *m*

annotate ['ænə,tet] *tr* annoter

announce [ə'nauns] *tr* annoncer

announcement [ə'naunsmənt] *s* annonce *f*, avis *m*

announcer [ə'naunsər] *s* annonceur *m*; (rad) présentateur *m*, speaker *m*

annoy [ə'nɔɪ] *tr* ennuyer, tourmenter

annoyance [ə'nɔɪ-əns] *s* ennui *m*

annoying [ə'nɔɪ-ɪŋ] *adj* ennuyeux

annual ['ænju-əl] *adj* annuel || *s* annuaire *m*; plante *f* annuelle

annui·ty [ə'n(j)u-ɪti] *s* (*pl* **-ties**) (*annual payment*) annuité *f*; (*of a retired person*) pension *f* de retraite, pension viagère

an·nul [ə'nʌl] *v* (*pret & pp* **-nulled**; *ger* **-nulling**) *tr* annuler; abolir

anode ['ænod] *s* anode *f*

anodyne ['ænə,daɪn] *adj & s* anodin *m*

anoint [ə'nɔɪnt] *tr* oindre

anon [ə'nɑn] *adv* tout à l'heure

anonymity [,ænə'nɪmɪti] *s* anonymat *m*

anonymous [ə'nɑnɪməs] *adj* anonyme

another [ə'nʌðər] *adj & pron indef* un autre; *(an additional)* encore un; **many another** beaucoup d'autres

answer ['ænsər] *s* réponse *f*; (math) solution *f* ‖ *tr (e.g., yes or no)* répondre; *(a question, a letter)* répondre à ‖ *intr* répondre; **to answer for** répondre de

an'swer book' *s* livre *m* du maître

an'swering machine' *s* répondeur *m* automatique

an'swering ser'vice *s* (telp) service *m* des abonnés absents

ant [ænt] *s* fourmi *f*

antagonism [æn'tægə,nɪzəm] *s* antagonisme *m*

antagonize [æn'tægə,naɪz] *tr* contrarier; *(a friend)* s'aliéner

Antarctic [ænt'ɑrktɪk] *adj & s* Antarctique *f*

Antarctica [ænt'ɑrktɪkə] *s* l'Antarctique *f*

Antarc'tic O'cean *s* Océan *m* glacial antarctique

ante ['ænti] *s* mise *f* ‖ *tr* miser ‖ *intr* miser, caver; **ante up!** misez!

anteater ['ænt,itər] *s* fourmilier *m*

antecedent [,ænti'sidənt] *adj & s* antécédent *m*

antechamber ['ænti,tʃembər] *s* antichambre *f*

antelope ['ænti,lop] *s* antilope *f*

anten·na [æn'tɛnə] *s* (*pl* **-nae** [ni]) (ent) antenne *f* ‖ *s* (*pl* **-nas**) (rad) antenne *f*

antepenult [,ænti'pinʌlt] *s* antépénultième *f*

anterior [æn'tɪrɪ·ər] *adj* antérieur

anthem ['ænθəm] *s* hymne *m*; (eccl) antienne *f*, hymne *f*

ant' hill' *s* fourmilière *f*

antholo·gy [æn'θɑlədʒi] *s* (*pl* **-gies**) anthologie *f*

anthropoid ['ænθro,pɔɪd] *adj & s* anthropoïde *m*

antiaircraft [,ænti'ɛr,kræft] *adj* antiaérien, contre-avions

antibiotic [,æntibaɪ'ɑtɪk] *adj & s* antibiotique *m*

antibod·y ['ænti,bɑdi] *s* (*pl* **-ies**) anticorps *m*

anticipate [æn'tɪsɪ,pet] *tr* anticiper; *(to expect)* s'attendre à

anticipation [æn,tɪsɪ'peʃən] *s* anticipation *f*

anticlimax [,ænti'klaɪmæks] *s* chute *f* dans le trivial, désillusion *f*

antics ['æntɪks] *spl* bouffonnerie *f*

antidote ['ænti,dot] *s* antidote *m*

antifreeze [,ænti'friz] *s* antigel *m*

antiglare [,ænti'glɛr] *adj* antiaveuglant

antiknock [,ænti'nɑk] *adj & s* antidétonant *m*

an'timis'sile mis'sile [,ænti'mɪsəl] *s* missile *m* antimissile

antimony ['ænti,moni] *s* antimoine *m*

antipa·thy [æn'tɪpəθi] *s* (*pl* **-thies**) antipathie *f*

antiperspirant [,ænti'pʌrspərənt] *s* antitranspirant *m*

antiphon ['ænti,fɑn] *s* antienne *f*

antiquated ['ænti,kwetɪd] *adj* vieilli, démodé

antique [æn'tik] *adj* antique; ancien ‖ *s* *(piece of furniture)* original *m*; **antiques** meubles *mpl* d'époque

antique' deal'er *s* antiquaire *m*

antique' shop' *s* magasin *m* d'antiquités, maison *f* de meubles d'époque

antiqui·ty [æn'tɪkwɪti] *s* (*pl* **-ties**) antiquité *f*; *(oldness)* ancienneté *f*

anti-Semitic [,æntɪsɪ'mɪtɪk] *adj* antisémite, antisémitique

antiseptic [,ænti'sɛptɪk] *adj & s* antiseptique *m*

an'titank' gun' [,ænti'tæŋk] *s* canon *m* antichar

antithe·sis [æn'tɪθɪsɪs] *s* (*pl* **-ses** [,siz]) antithèse *f*

antitoxin [,ænti'tɑksɪn] *s* antitoxine *f*

antiwar [,ænti'wɔr] *adj* antimilitariste

antler ['æntlər] *s* andouiller *m*

antonym ['æntənɪm] *s* antonyme *m*

anvil ['ænvɪl] *s* enclume *f*

anxie·ty [æŋ'zaɪ·əti] *s* (*pl* **-ties**) anxiété *f*, inquiétude *f*

anxious ['æŋkʃəs] *adj* inquiet, soucieux; **to be anxious to** avoir envie de, tenir beaucoup à

any ['ɛni] *adj indef* quelque; du, e.g., **do you have any butter?** avez-vous du beurre?; aucun, e.g., **he reads more than any other child** il lit plus qu'aucun autre enfant; **any day** n'importe quel jour; **any place** n'importe où; **any time** n'importe quand, à tout moment; **any way** n'importe comment, de toute façon ‖ *pron indef* quiconque; quelques-uns §81; **not . . . any** ne . . . aucun §90; ne . . . en . . . pas, e.g., **I will not give him any** je ne lui en donnerai pas ‖ *adv* un peu

an'y·bod'y *pron indef* quelqu'un §81; n'importe qui; **not . . . anybody** ne . . . personne

an'y·how' *adv* en tout cas

an'y·one' *pron indef* quelqu'un §81; n'importe qui; quiconque; **not . . . anyone** ne . . . personne, e.g., **I don't see anyone** je ne vois personne

an'y·thing' *pron indef* quelque chose; n'importe quoi, e.g., **say anything (at all)** dites n'importe quoi; **anything at all** quoi que se soit, si peu que ce soit; **anything but** rien moins que; **anything else?** et avec ça?, ensuite?; **not . . . anything** ne . . . rien

an'y·way' *adv* en tout cas

an'y·where' *adv* n'importe où; **not . . . anywhere** ne . . . nulle part

aor·ta [e'ɔrtə] *s* (*pl* **-tas** or **-tae** [ti]) aorte *f*

apace [ə'pes] *adv* vite, rapidement

apache [ə'pæʃ] *s* apache *m* ‖ **Apache** [ə'pætʃi] *s* apache *m*

apart [ə'pɑrt] *adj* séparé ‖ *adv* à part, à l'écart; **apart from** en dehors de

apartment [ə'pɑrtmənt] *s* appartement *m*

apart'ment house' *s* maison *f* de rapport, immeuble *m* d'habitation

apathetic [,æpə'θɛtɪk] *adj* apathique, amorphe

apa·thy ['æpəθi] *s* (*pl* **-thies**) apathie *f*

ape [ep] *s* singe *m* ‖ *tr* singer

aperture ['æpərtʃər] *s* ouverture *f*; (phonet) aperture *f*

apex ['epɛks] *s* (*pl* **apexes** or **apices** ['æpɪ,siz]) sommet *m*; (astr) apex *m*

aphid ['æfɪd] *s* puceron *m*

aphorism ['æfə,rɪzəm] *s* aphorisme *m*

aphrodisiac [,æfrə'dɪzɪ,æk] *adj* & *s* aphrodisiaque *f*

apiar·y ['epɪ,ɛri] *s* (*pl* **-ies**) rucher *m*

apiece [ə'pis] *adv* la pièce, chacun

apish ['epɪʃ] *adj* simiesque; (fig) imitateur

aplomb [ə'plɑm] *s* aplomb *m*

apocalyptic(al) [ə,pɑkə'lɪptɪk(əl)] *adj* apocalyptique

Apocrypha [ə'pɑkrɪfə] *s* apocryphes *mpl*

apogee ['æpə,dʒi] *s* apogée *m*

Apollo [ə'pɑlo] *s* Apollon *m*

apologetic [ə,pɑlə'dʒɛtɪk] *adj* prêt à s'excuser, humble, penaud

apologize [ə'pɑlə,dʒaɪz] *intr* faire des excuses, s'excuser

apolo·gy [ə'pɑlədʒi] *s* (*pl* **-gies**) excuse *f*; (*makeshift*) semblant, *m*, prétexte *m*; (*apologia*) apologie *f*

A.P.O. number ['e'pi'ˌnʌmbər] *s* (letterword) (**Army Post Office**) secteur *m* postal

apoplectic [,æpə'plɛktɪk] *adj* & *s* apoplectique *mf*

apoplexy ['æpə,plɛksi] *s* apoplexie *f*

apostle [ə'pɑsəl] *s* apôtre *m*

Apos'tles' Creed' *s* symbole *m* des apôtres

apos'tle·ship' *s* apostolat *m*

apostrophe [ə'pɑstrəfi] *s* apostrophe *f*

apothecar·y [ə'pɑθɪ,kɛri] *s* (*pl* **-ies**) apothicaire *m*

appall [ə'pɔl] *tr* épouvanter, effrayer, consterner

appalling [ə'pɔlɪŋ] *adj* épouvantable

appara·tus [,æpə'rætəs] *s* (*pl* **-tus** or **tuses**) appareil *m*, dispositif *m*

appar·el [ə'pærəl] *s* (*equipment; clothes*) appareil *m*; (*clothes*) habillement *m* ‖ *v* (*pret* & *pp* **-eled** or **-elled**; *ger* **-eling** or **elling**) *tr* habiller, vêtir; parer

apparent [ə'pærənt] *adj* apparent; (*heir*) présomptif

apparition [,æpə'rɪʃən] *s* apparition *f*

appeal [ə'pil] *s* (*call*) appel *m*; (*attraction*) charme *m*, attrait *m*; (law) pourvoi *m*, appel ‖ *tr* (*a case*) faire appeler ‖ *intr* (*to request publicly*) lancer un appel; (*to beg*) faire appel; (law) pouvoir en appel; **to appeal to** (*to attract*) séduire, charmer

appealing [ə'pilɪŋ] *adj* séduisant, attrayant, sympathique

appear [ə'pɪr] *intr* (*to come into view; to be published; to seem*) paraître; (*to come into view*) apparaître

appearance [ə'pɪrəns] *s* (*look*) apparence *f*, aspect *m*; (*act of showing up*) apparition *f*; (*in print*) parution *f*; **to all appearances** selon toute vraisemblance; **to make one's appearance** faire acte de présence

appease [ə'piz] *tr* apaiser

appeasement [ə'pizmənt] *s* apaisement *m*

appeaser [ə'pizər] *s* conciliateur *m*, pacificateur *m*

appel'late court' [ə'pɛlet] *s* tribunal *m* d'appel; **highest appellate court** cour *f* de cassation

append [ə'pɛnd] *tr* apposer, ajouter

appendage [ə'pɛndɪdʒ] *s* dépendance *f*, accessoire *m*

appendecto·my [,æpən'dɛktəmi] *s* (*pl* **-mies**) appendicectomie *f*

appendicitis [ə,pɛndɪ'saɪtɪs] *s* appendicite *f*

appen·dix [ə'pɛndɪks] *s* (*pl* **-dixes** or **dices** (dɪ,siz]) appendice *m*

appertain [,æpər'ten] *intr* se rapporter

appetite ['æpɪ,taɪt] *s* appétit *m*

appetizer ['æpɪ,taɪzər] *s* stimulant *m*, tonique *m*; (culin) premier plat *m*

appetizing ['æpɪ,taɪzɪŋ] *adj* appétissant

applaud [ə'plɔd] *tr* (*to give applause to*) applaudir; (*to approve*) applaudir à; **to applaud s.o. for** applaudir qn de ‖ *intr* applaudir

applause [ə'plɔz] *s* applaudissements *mpl*

apple ['æpəl] *s* pomme *f*; (*tree*) pommier *m*

ap'ple·jack' *s* calvados *m*

ap'ple of the eye' *s* prunelle *f* des yeux

ap'ple or'chard *s* pommeraie *f*, verger *m* à pommes

ap'ple pie' *s* tarte *f* aux pommes

ap'ple pol'isher *s* (coll) chien *m* couchant, flagorneur *m*

ap'ple·sauce' *s* compote *f* de pommes; (slang) balivernes *fpl*

ap'ple tree' *s* pommier *m*

ap'ple turn'over *s* chausson *m* (aux pommes)

appliance [ə'plaɪ·əns] *s* (*machine or instrument*) appareil *m*; (*act of applying*) application *f*; **appliances** accessoires *mpl*

applicable ['æplɪkəbəl] *adj* applicable

applicant ['æplɪkənt] *s* candidat *m*, postulant *m*

application [,æplɪ'keʃən] *s* (*putting into effect*) application *f*; (*for a job*) demande *f*, sollicitation *f*

applica'tion blank' *s* formule *f*

applied' arts' *spl* arts *mpl* industriels

ap·ply [ə'plaɪ] *v* (*pret* & *pp* **-plied**) *tr* appliquer ‖ *intr* s'appliquer; **to apply for** solliciter, postuler; **to apply to s.o.** s'adresser à qn

appoint [ə'pɔɪnt] *tr* nommer, désigner; (obs) équiper

appointed *adj* (*person*) nommé, désigné; (*time*) convenu, dit

appointment [ə'pɔɪntmənt] *s* (*engagement*) rendez-vous *m*; (*to a position*) désignation *f*, nomination *f*; **appointments** (*of a room*) aménagements *mpl*; **by appointment** sur rendez-vous

apportion [ə'porʃən] *tr* répartir; (com) ventiler

appraisal [ə'prezəl] *s* appréciation *f*, estimation *f*, évaluation *f*

appraise [ə'prez] *tr* estimer, évaluer

appraiser [ə'prezər] s estimateur m, évaluateur m

appreciable [ə'priʃɪ·əbəl] adj appréciable, sensible

appreciate [ə'priʃɪ,et] tr (to value, esteem) apprécier; (to be grateful for) reconnaître; (to be aware of) être sensible à, s'apercevoir de ‖ intr augmenter, hausser

appreciation [ə,priʃɪ'eʃən] s (judgment, estimation) appréciation f; (gratitude) reconnaissance f; (rise in value) plus-value f

appreciative [ə'priʃɪ,etɪv] adj reconnaissant

apprehend [,æprɪ'hɛnd] tr (to understand) comprendre; (to seize; fear) apprehender

apprehension [,æprɪ'hɛnʃən] s appréhension f

apprehensive [,æprɪ'hɛnsɪv] adj craintif

apprentice [ə'prɛntɪs] s apprenti m, stagiaire mf

appren'tice·ship' s apprentissage m, stage m

apprise [ə'praɪz] tr prévenir, informer, mettre au courant

approach [ə'protʃ] s approche f; **to make approaches to** faire des avances à ‖ tr approcher, approcher de, s'approcher de ‖ intr approcher, s'approcher

approachable [ə'protʃəbəl] adj abordable, accessible

approbation [,æprə'beʃən] s approbation f

appropriate [ə'propri·ɪt] adj approprié ‖ [ə'propri,et] tr (to take for oneself) s'approprier; (to assign) affecter

appropriation [ə,propri'eʃən] s appropriation f; (assigning) affectation f; (govt) crédit m budgétaire

approval [ə'pruvəl] s approbation f, consentement m; **on approval** à l'essai, à condition

approve [ə'pruv] tr approuver ‖ intr être d'accord; **to approve of** approuver

approximate [ə'praksɪmɪt] adj approximatif ‖ [ə'praksɪ,met] tr se rapprocher de

apricot [æprɪ,kɑt] s abricot m; (tree) abricotier m

April ['eprɪl] s avril m

A'pril fool' s (joke) poisson m d'avril; (victim) dupe f, dindon m

A'pril Fools'' Day' s le jour du poisson d'avril

apron ['eprən] s tablier m; (aer) aire f de manœuvre

apropos [,æprə'po] adj opportun ‖ adv opportunément; **apropos of** quant à, à l'égard de

apse [æps] s abside f

apt [æpt] adj apte; bien à propos; **apt to** enclin à, porté à

aptitude ['æptɪ,t(j)ud] s aptitude f

ap'titude test' s test m d'intelligence pratique, test de talent

aquacade ['ækwə,ked] s féerie f sur l'eau, spectacle m aquatique

aqualung ['ækwə,lʌŋ] s scaphandre m autonome

aquamarine [,ækwəmə'rin] s aiguemarine f

aquaplane ['ækwə,plen] s aquaplane m

aquari·um [ə'kwɛrɪ·əm] s (pl **-ums** or **-a** [ə]) aquarium m

Aquarius [ə'kwɛrɪ·əs] s (astr, astrol) le Verseau

aquatic [ə'kwætɪk] adj aquatique ‖ **aquatics** spl sports mpl nautiques

aqueduct ['ækwə,dʌkt] s aqueduc m

aqueous ['ækwɪ,əs] adj aquilin

Arab ['ærəb] adj arabe ‖ s (horse) arabe m; (person) Arabe mf

Arabian [ə'rebɪ·ən] adj arabe ‖ s Arabe mf

Arabic ['ærəbɪk] adj arabique ‖ s (language) arabe m

Ar'abic nu'meral s chiffre m arabe

arbiter ['ɑrbɪtər] s arbitre m

arbitrary ['ɑrbɪ,trɛri] adj arbitraire

arbitrate ['ɑrbɪ,tret] tr & intr arbitrer

arbitration [,ɑrbɪ'treʃən] s arbitrage m

arbitrator ['ɑrbɪ,tretər] s arbitre m, médiateur m; (law) amiable compositeur m

arbor ['ɑrbər] s (shady recess) berceau m, charmille f; (mach) arbre m

arbore·tum [,ɑrbə'ritəm] s (pl **-tums** or **-ta** [tə]) jardin m botanique d'arbres

arbutus [ɑr'bjutəs] s arbousier m

arc [ɑrk] s (elec, geom) arc m

arcade [ɑr'ked] s (for shopping) galerie f marchande; (archit) arcade f

arcane [ɑr'ken] adj mystérieux

arch [ɑrtʃ] adj insigne; espiègle ‖ s (of a building, cathedral, etc.) arc m; (of bridge) arche f; (of vault) voûte f ‖ tr (the back) arquer; (archit) voûter ‖ intr s'arquer; se voûter

archaic [ɑr'ke·ɪk] adj archaïque

archaism ['ɑrke,ɪzəm] s archaïsme m

archangel ['ɑrk,endʒəl] s archange m

arch'bish'op s archevêque m

arch'duke' s archiduc m

arched [ɑrtʃt] adj voûté, courbé, arqué

archeologist [,ɑrkɪ'ɑlədʒɪst] s archéologue mf

archeology [,ɑrkɪ'ɑlɪdʒi] s archéologie f

archer ['ɑrtʃər] s archer m

archery ['ɑrtʃəri] s tir m à l'arc

archetype ['ɑrkɪ,taɪp] s archétype m

archipela·go [,ɑrkɪ'pɛləgo] s (pl **-gos** or **-goes**) archipel m

architect ['ɑrkɪ,tɛkt] s architecte m

architecture ['ɑrkɪ,tɛktʃər] s architecture f

archives ['ɑrkaɪvz] spl archives fpl

arch'priest' s archiprêtre m

arch'way' s voûte f, arcade f

Arctic ['ɑrktɪk] adj & s (ocean) Arctique m; (region) Arctique f

arc' weld'ing s soudure f à l'arc

ardent ['ɑrdənt] adj ardent

ardor ['ɑdər] s ardeur f

arduous ['ɑrdjʊ·əs] adj ardu, difficile

area ['ɛrɪ·ə] s région f, e.g., **the New York area** la région de New York; (surface measure) aire f, superficie f, e.g., **area of a triangle** aire d'un triangle; (of knowledge; field) domaine m, champ m; (geog; pol) territoire m; (mil) secteur m, zone f; **in this area** (on this subject) à ce propos

arena [ə'rinə] *s* arène *f*

Argentina [ˌɑrdʒən'tinə] *s* Argentine *f*; l'Argentine

argue ['ɑrgju] *tr* (*a question*) discuter; (*a case*) plaider; (*a point*) soutenir; (*to imply*) arguer; **to argue s.o. into** + *ger* persuader à qn de + *inf* ‖ *intr* discuter, argumenter; plaider

argument ['ɑrgjəmənt] *s* (*proof; reason; theme*) argument *m*; (*debate*) discussion *f*, dispute *f*

argumentative [ˌɑrgjə'mɛntətɪv] *adj* disposé à argumenter, raisonneur

aria ['ɑrɪ·ə] *s* aria *f*

arid ['ærɪd] *adj* aride

aridity [ə'rɪdɪti] *s* aridité *f*

Aries ['ɛriz] *s* (astr, astrol) le Bélier

arise [ə'raɪz] *v* (*pret* **arose** [ə'roz]; *pp* **arisen** [ə'rɪzən]) *intr* (*to rise*) se lever; (*to originate*) provenir, prendre naissance; (*to occur*) se produire; (*to be raised, as objections*) s'élever

aristocra·cy [ˌærɪs'tɑkrəsi] *s* (*pl* -**cies**) aristocratie *f*

aristocrat [ə'rɪstə,kræt] *s* aristocrate *mf*

aristocratic [ə,rɪstə'krætɪk] *adj* aristocrate

Aristotle ['ærɪ,stɑtəl] *s* Aristote *m*

arithmetic [ə'rɪθmətɪk] *s* arithmétique *f*

arithmetician [ə,rɪθmə'tɪʃən] *s* arithméticien *m*

ark [ɑrk] *s* arche *f*

arm [ɑrm] *s* bras *m*; (mil) arme *f*; **arm in arm** bras dessus bras dessous; **at arm's length** à bout de bras; **under my (your, etc.) arm** sous mon (ton, etc.) aisselle; **up in arms** en rébellion ouverte ‖ *tr* armer ‖ *intr* s'armer

armada [ɑr'mɑdə] *s* armada *f*, grande flotte *f*

armadil·lo [ˌɑrmə'dɪlo] *s* (*pl* -**los**) tatou *m*

armament ['ɑrməmənt] *s* armement *m*

armature ['ɑrmə,tʃər] *f* (elec) induit *m*

arm'band' *s* brassard *m*

arm'chair' *s* fauteuil *m*, chaise *f* à bras

Armenian [ɑr'minɪ·ən] *adj* arménien ‖ *s* (*language*) arménien *m*; (*person*) Arménien

armful ['ɑrm,fʊl] *s* brassée *f*

arm'hole' *s* emmanchure *f*, entournure *f*

armistice ['ɑrmɪstɪs] *s* armistice *m*

armor ['ɑrmər] *s* (*personal*) armure *f*; (*on ships, tanks, etc.*) cuirasse *f*, blindage *m* ‖ *tr* cuirasser, blinder ‖ *intr* se mettre l'armure

ar'mored car' *s* fourgon *m* blindé

ar'mor plate' *s* plaque *f* de blindage

ar'mor-plate' *tr* cuirasser, blinder

armor·y ['ɑrməri] *s* (*pl* -**ies**) ateliers *mpl* d'armes, salle *f* d'armes

arm'pit' *s* aisselle *f*

arm'rest' *s* appui-bras *m*, accoudoir *m*

arms' race' *s* course *f* aux armements

arms' reduc'tion *s* contrôle *m* des armes

arm'wres'tle *intr* faire le bras de fer

ar·my ['ɑrmi] *adj* militaire ‖ *s* (*pl* -**mies**) armée *f*

aroma [ə'romə] *s* arôme *m*

aromatic [ˌærə'mætɪk] *adj* aromatique

around [ə'raʊnd] *adv* (*nearby*) autour, alentour; **all around** de tous côtés ‖ *prep* autour de; (*approximately*) environ, à peu près; **around 1950** (coll) vers 1950

arouse [ə'raʊz] *tr* éveiller; (*from sleep*) réveiller

arpeg'gio [ɑr'pɛdʒo] *s* (*pl* -**gios**) arpège *m*

arraign [ə'ren] *tr* accuser; (law) mettre en accusation

arrange [ə'rendʒ] *tr* arranger ‖ *intr* s'arranger

arrangement [ə'rendʒmənt] *s* arrangement *m*

array [ə're] *s* (*display*) étalage *m*; (*adornment*) parure *f*; (mil) ordre *m*, rang *m* ‖ *tr* ranger, disposer; (*to adorn*) parer

arrearage [ə'rɪrɪdʒ] *s* arriéré *m*

arrears [ə'rɪrz] *spl* arriéré *m*; **in arrears** arriéré

arrest [ə'rɛst] *s* (*capture*) arrestation *f*; (*halt*) arrêt *m* ‖ *tr* arrêter; fixer; (*attention*) retenir

arrival [ə'raɪvəl] *s* arrivée *f*; (*of goods or ships*) arrivage *m*

arrive [ə'raɪv] *intr* arriver

arrogance ['ærəgəns] *s* arrogance *f*

arrogant ['ærəgənt] *adj* arrogant

arrogate ['ærə,get] *tr*—**to arrogate to oneself** s'arroger

arrow ['æro] *s* flèche *f*

ar'row·head' *s* (*point*) tête *f* de flèche; (bot) sagittaire *m*

arsenal ['ɑrsənəl] *s* (*stock*) arsenal *m*; (*factory*) manufacture *f* d'armes

arsenic ['ɑrsɪnɪk] *s* arsenic *m*

arson ['ɑrsən] *s* incendie *m* volontaire

arsonist ['ɑrsənɪst] *s* incendiaire *mf*

art [ɑrt] *s* art *m*

arterial [ɑr'tɪrɪ·əl] *adj* artériel

arteriosclerotic [ɑr,tɪrɪ·osklɪ'rɑtɪk] *adj* artérioscléreux

arter·y ['ɑrtəri] *s* (*pl* -**ies**) artère *f*

arte'sian well' [ɑr'tiʒən] *s* puits *m* artésien

artful ['ɑrtfəl] *adj* (*skillful*) ingénieux; (*crafty*) artificieux, sournois; artificiel

arthritis [ɑr'θraɪtɪs] *s* arthrite *f*

artichoke ['ɑrtɪ,tʃok] *s* artichaut *m*

article ['ɑrtɪkəl] *s* article; **article of clothing** objet *m* d'habillement

articulate [ɑr'tɪkjəlɪt] *adj* articulé; (*expressing oneself clearly*) clair, expressif; (*speech*) intelligible; (*creature*) doué de la parole ‖ [ɑr'tɪkjə,let] *tr* articuler ‖ *intr* s'articuler

artifact ['ɑrtɪ,fækt] *s* objet *m* fabriqué; (biol) artefact *m*

artifice ['ɑrtɪfɪs] *s* artifice *m*

artificial [ˌɑrtɪ'fɪʃəl] *adj* artificiel

artifi'cial insem'ina'tion *s* fécondation *f* artificielle

artificiali·ty [ˌɑrtɪ,fɪʃɪ'ælɪti] *s* (*pl* -**ties**) manque *m* de naturel

artifi'cial respira'tion *s* respiration *f* artificielle

artillery [ɑr'tɪləri] *s* artillerie *f*

artil'lery·man *s* (*pl* -**men**) artilleur *m*

artisan ['ɑrtɪzən] *s* artisan *m*

artist ['ɑrtɪst] *s* artiste *mf*

artistic [ɑr'tɪstɪk] *adj* artistique, artiste

artistry ['ɑrtɪstri] *s* art *m*, habileté *f*

artless ['ɑrtlɪs] *adj* (*uncontrived*) naturel; (*ingenuous*) ingénu, naïf; (*lacking art*) sans art

arts' and crafts' *spl* arts et métiers *mpl*

Aryan ['ɛrɪ·ən] *adj* aryen ‖ *s* (*person*) Aryen *m*

as [æz], [əz] *pron rel* que, e.g., **the same as** le même que ‖ *adv* aussi, e.g., **as . . . as** aussi . . . que; **as for** quant à; **as is** tel quel; **as of** (*a certain date*) en date du; **as regards** en ce qui concerne; **as soon as** aussitôt que; **as though** comme si; **as yet** jusqu'ici ‖ *prep* comme; (*in the capacity of*) en tant que, en qualité de, à titre de; (*in such a way as*) en manière de; (*such as*) tel que; (*considered as*) considéré comme; (*insofar as*) dans la mesure où; (*at the same time as and to the same degree as*) au fur et à mesure que ‖ *conj* puisque; comme; que

asbestos [æs'bɛstəs] *s* amiante *m*, asbeste *m*

ascend [ə'sɛnd] *tr* (*a ladder*) monter à; (*a mountain*) gravir; (*a river*) remonter ‖ *intr* monter, s'élever

ascendancy [ə'sɛndənsi] *s* supériorité *f*, domination *f*

ascension [ə'sɛnʃən] *s* ascension *f*

Ascen'sion Day' *s* Ascension *f*

ascent [ə'sɛnt] *s* ascension *f*

ascertain [,æsər'ten] *tr* vérifier

ascertainment [,æsər'tenmənt] *s* constatation *f*

ascetic [ə'sɛtɪk] *adj* ascétique ‖ *s* ascéte *mf*

asceticism [ə'sɛtɪ,sɪzəm] *s* ascétisme *m*, ascése *f*

ascor'bic ac'id [ə'skɔrbɪk] *s* acide *m* ascorbique

ascribe [ə'skraɪb] *tr* attribuer, imputer

aseptic [e'sɛptɪk] *adj* aseptique

ash [æʃ] *s* cendre *f*; (*tree*) frêne *m*

ashamed [ə'ʃemd] *adj* honteux; **to be ashamed** avoir honte

ash'can' *s* poubelle *f*

ashen ['æʃən] *adj* cendré

ashore [ə'ʃor] *adv* à terre; **to go ashore** débarquer

ash'tray' *s* cendrier *m*

Ash' Wednes'day *s* le mercredi des Cendres

Asia ['eʒə] *s* Asie *f*; l'Asie

A'sia Mi'nor *s* Asie *f* Mineure; l'Asie Mineure

aside [ə'saɪd] *s* aparté *m* ‖ *adv* de côté, à part; (*aloof, at a distance*) à l'écart; **aside from** en dehors de, à part; **to step aside** s'écarter; (*fig*) quitter la partie

asinine ['æsɪ,naɪn] *adj* stupide

ask [æsk] *tr* (*a favor; one's way*) demander; (*a question*) poser; **to ask s.o. about s.th.** interroger qn au sujet q.ch.; **to ask s.o. for s.th.** demander q.ch. à qn; **to ask s.o. to** + *inf* demander à qn de + *inf*, prier qn de + *inf* ‖ *intr*—**to ask about** s'enquérir

de; **to ask for** (*a package; a porter*) demander; (*to inquire about*) demander après; **you asked for it** (*you're in for it*) (coll) c'est bien fait pour vous

askance [ə'skæns] *adv* de côté; **to look askance at** regarder de travers

askew [ə'skju] *adj & adv* de travers, en biais, de biais

asleep [ə'slip] *adj* endormi; **to fall asleep** s'endormir

asp [æsp] *s* aspic *m*

asparagus [ə'spærəgəs] *s* asperge *f*; (*stalks and tips used as food*) des asperges

aspect ['æspɛkt] *s* aspect *m*

aspen ['æspən] *s* tremble *m*

aspersion [ə'spʌrʒən] *s* (*sprinkling*) aspersion *f*; (*slander*) calomnie *f*

asphalt ['æsfɔlt] *s* asphalte *m*

asphyxiate [æs'fɪksɪ,et] *tr* asphyxier

aspirate ['æspɪrɪt] *adj & s* (phonet) aspiré *m* ‖ ['æspɪ,ret] *tr* aspirer

aspire [ə'spaɪr] *intr*—**to aspire to** aspirer à

aspirin ['æspɪrɪn] *s* aspirine *f*

ass [æs] *s* âne *m*; (anat & vulg) cul *m*; (*person*) (vulg) imbécile *mf*, crétin *m*, âne *m*

assail [ə'sel] *tr* assaillir

assailant [ə'selənt] *s* assaillant *m*

assassin [ə'sæsɪn] *s* assassin *m*

assassinate [ə'sæsɪ,net] *tr* assassiner

assassination [ə,sæsɪ'neʃən] *s* assassinat *m*

assault [ə'sɔlt] *s* (*military attack*) assaut *m*; (*unlawful physical attack*) agression *f*; (*rape*) viol *m*; (law) voie *f* de fait ‖ *tr* assaillir

assault' and bat'tery *s* (law) voies *fpl* de fait

assay [ə'se], ['æse] *s* essai *m*; métal *m* titré ‖ [ə'se] *t* essayer; titrer

assayer [ə'se·ər] *s* essayeur *m*

as'say val'ue *s* teneur *f*

assemblage [ə'sɛmblɪdʒ] *s* assemblage *m*

assemble [ə'sɛmbəl] *tr* assembler ‖ *intr* s'assembler, se réunir

assem·bly [ə'sɛmbli] *s* (*pl* -**blies**) (*meeting*) assemblée *f*, réunion *f*; (*assembling*) assemblage *m*, montage *m*

assemb'ly hall' *s* salle *f* de conférences; (educ) grand amphithéâtre *m*

assem'bly line' *s* chaîne *f* de fabrication, chaîne de montage

assem'bly room' *s* salle *f* de réunion; (mach) atelier *m* de montage

assent [ə'sɛnt] *s* assentiment *m* ‖ *intr* assentir

assert [ə'sʌrt] *tr* affirmer; (*one's rights*) revendiquer; **to assert oneself** imposer le respect, s'imposer

assertion [ə'sʌrʃən] *s* assertion *f*

assess [ə'sɛs] *tr* (*damages, taxes, etc.*) évaluer; (*value of property*) coter; (*property for tax purposes*) grever

assessment [ə'sɛsmənt] *s* (*estimation*) évaluation *f*; (*of real estate*) calcul *m* (de la valeur imposable); (*amount of tax*) charge *f*, taxe *f*

assessor [ə'sɛsər] *s* répartiteur *m* d'impôts

asset ['æsɛt] *s* (*advantage*) avantage *m*, atout *m*; **assets** biens *mpl*, avoirs, *mpl*, actif *m*

ass'hole' *s* (anat, fig, vulg) trou *m* de cul, trou de balle

assiduous [ə'sɪdjʊ·əs] *adj* assidu

assign [ə'saɪn] *tr* (*task, date, etc.*) assigner; (mil) affecter

assignation [,æsɪg'neʃən] *s* attribution *f*, allocation *f*, affectation *f*; (*lovers' tryst*) rendez-vous *m* illicite

assignment [ə'saɪnmənt] *s* (*allocation*) attribution *f*; (*schoolwork*) devoirs *mpl*; (law) assignation *f*, transfer *m*; (mil) affectation *f*

assimilate [ə'sɪmɪ,let] *tr* assimiler ‖ *intr* s'assimiler

assimilation [ə,sɪmɪ'leʃən] *s* assimilation *f*

assist [ə'sɪst] *tr* assister, aider, secourir ‖ *intr* être assistant

assistance [ə'sɪstəns] *s* assistance *f*, aide *f*, secours *m*

assistant [ə'sɪstənt] *adj & s* assistant *m*, adjoint *m*

assizes [ə'saɪzɪz] *spl* assises *fpl*

associate [ə'soʃɪ·ɪt] *adj* associé ‖ *s* associé *m* ‖ [ə'soʃɪ,et] *tr* associer ‖ *intr* s'associer

association [ə,soʃɪ'eʃən] *s* association *f*

assonance ['æsənəns] *s* assonance *f*

assort [ə'sɔrt] *tr* assortir ‖ *intr* s'associer

assorted *adj* assorti

assortment [ə'sɔrtmənt] *s* assortiment *m*

assuage [ə'swedʒ] *tr* assouvir; soulager, apaiser

assume [ə's(j)um] *tr* (*to suppose*) supposer; (*various forms*) affecter; (*a fact*) présumer; (*a name*) emprunter; (*duties*) assumer, se charger de

assumed *adj* (*supposed*) supposé; (*borrowed*) d'emprunt, emprunté; (*feigned*) feint

assumed' name' *s* nom *m* d'emprunt, nom de guerre

assuming [ə's(j)umɪŋ] *adj* prétentieux

assumption [ə'sʌmpʃən] *s* (*supposition*) présomption *f*, hypothèse *f*; (*of virtue*) affectation *f*; (*of power*) appropriation *f*; **Assumption** (eccl) Assomption *f*

assurance [ə'ʃʊrəns] *s* (*certainty; self-confidence*) assurance; (*guarantee*) promesse *f*

assure [ə'ʃʊr] *tr* assurer, garantir

astatine ['æstə,tin] *s* astate *m*

aster ['æstər] *s* aster *m*; (*China aster*) reine-marguerite *f*

asterisk ['æstə,rɪsk] *s* astérisque *m*

astern [ə'stʌrn] *adv* à l'arrière

asthma ['æzmə] *s* asthme *m*

astonish [ə'stanɪʃ] *tr* étonner

astonishing [ə'stanɪʃɪŋ] *adj* étonnant

astonishment [ə'stanɪʃmənt] *s* étonnement *m*

astound [ə'staʊnd] *tr* stupéfier, ahurir, étonner

astounding [ə'staʊndɪŋ] *adj* étonnant, stupéfiant, abasourdissant

astraddle [ə'strædəl] *adv* à califourchon

astray [ə'stre] *adv*—**to go astray** s'égarer; **to lead astray** égarer

astride [ə'straɪd] *adv* à califourchon ‖ *prep* à califourchon sur

astrologer [ə'stralədʒər] *s* astrologue *m*

astrology [ə'stralədʒi] *s* astrologie *f*

astronaut ['æstrə,nɔt] *s* astronaute *mf*

astronautics [,æstrə'nɔtɪks] *s* astronautique *f*

astronomer [ə'stranəmər] *s* astronome *m*

astronomic(al) [,æstrə'namɪk(əl)] *adj* astronomique

as'tronom'ical year' *s* année *f* solaire, année tropique

astronomy [ə'stranəmi] *s* astronomie *f*

astute [ə'st(j)ut] *adj* astucieux, fin

asunder [ə'sʌndər] *adj* séparé ‖ *adv* en deux

asylum [ə'saɪləm] *s* asile *m*

at [æt], [ət] *prep* à, e.g., **at Paris** à Paris; chez, e.g., **at John's** chez Jean; en, e.g., **at the same time** en même temps

atheism ['eθi,ɪzəm] *s* athéisme *m*

atheist ['eθi·ɪst] *s* athée *mf*

atheistic [,eθi'ɪstɪk] *adj* athée

Athens ['æθɪnz] *s* Athènes *f*

athlete ['æθlit] *s* athlète *m*, sportif *m*

ath'lete's foot' *s* pied *m* d'athlète

athletic [æθ'lɛtɪk] *adj* athlétique ‖ **athletics** *s* athlétisme *m*

athwart [ə'θwɔrt] *adv* par le travers

Atlantic [æt'læntɪk] *adj & s* Atlantique *m*

atlas ['ætləs] *s* atlas *m*

atmosphere ['ætməs,fɪr] *s* atmosphère *f*

atmospheric [,ætməs'fɛrɪk] *adj* atmosphérique ‖ **atmospherics** *spl* parasites *mpl* atmosphériques

atom ['ætəm] *s* atome *m*

atomic [ə'tamɪk] *adj* atomique

atom'ic bomb' *s* bombe *f* atomique

atom'ic nuc'leus *s* noyau *m* d'atome

atom'ic pile' *s* pile *f* atomique

atom'ic struc'ture *s* édifice *m* atomique

atom'ic weight' *s* poids *m* atomique, masse *f* atomique

atomize ['ætə,maɪz] *tr* atomiser

atomizer ['ætə,maɪzər] *s* atomiseur *m*, vaporisateur *m*; (e.g., *of hair spray*) bombe *f*

atone [ə'ton] *intr*—**to atone for** expier

atonement [ə'tonmənt] *s* expiation *f*

atrocious [ə'troʃəs] *adj* atroce

atroci·ty [ə'trasɪti] *s* (*pl* **-ties**) atrocité *f*

atro·phy ['ætrəfi] *s* atrophie *f* ‖ *v* (*pret & pp* **-phied**) *tr* atrophier ‖ *intr* s'atrophier

attach [ə'tætʃ] *tr* (*to join; attribute*) attacher; (*property*) saisir; (*salary*) mettre opposition sur; **to be attached to** s'attacher à

attachment [ə'tætʃmənt] *s* (*fastener*) attache *f*; (*of the sentiments*) attachement *m*; (*supplementary device*) accessoire *m*; (law) opposition *f*, saisie-arrêt *f*

attack [ə'tæk] *s* attaque *f* ‖ *tr* attaquer; s'attaquer à ‖ *intr* attaquer

attacker [ə'tækər] *s* assaillant *m*

attain [ə'ten] *tr* atteindre

attainment [ə'tenmənt] *s* acquisition *f*, réalisation *f*; **attainments** connaissances *fpl*

attar ['ætər] *s* essence *f*

attempt [ə'tɛmpt] *s* tentative *f*, effort *m*; (*try*) essai *m*; (*assault*) attentat *m* ‖ *tr* tenter; (*s.o.'s life*) attenter à

attend [ə'tɛnd] *tr* (*a performance*) assister à; (*a sick person*) soigner; (*a person*) servir; **to attend classes** suivre des cours ‖ *intr*—**to attend to** vaquer à, s'occuper de

attendance [ə'tɛndəns] *s* (*number of people present*) assistance *f*; (*being present*) présence *f*; (med) soins *mpl*

attendant [ə'tɛndənt] *adj* concomitant ‖ *s* assistant *m*; (*to royalty*) serviteur *m*; **attendants** suite *f*

attention [ə'tɛnʃən] *s* attention *f*; **attention: Mr. Doe** à l'attention de M. Dupont; **attentions** égards *mpl* ‖ *interj* attention!; (mil) garde à vous!

attentive [ə'tɛntɪv] *adj* attentif

attenuate [ə'tɛnju,et] *tr* (*to make thin*) amincir; (*words; bacteria*) atténuer

attest [ə'tɛst] *tr* attester ‖ *intr*—**to attest to** attester

Attic ['ætɪk] *adj* attique ‖ (*l.c.*) *s* mansarde *f*, grenier *m*, soupente *f*

attire [ə'taɪr] *s* vêtement *m*, parure *f* ‖ *tr* habiller, vêtir, parer

attitude ['ætɪ,t(j)ud] *s* attitude *f*

attorney [ə'tʌrni] *s* avoué *m*, avocat *m*

attor'ney gen'eral *s* procureur *m* général, ministre *m* de la justice

attract [ə'trækt] *tr* attirer

attraction [ə'trækʃən] *s* attraction *f*

attractive [ə'træktɪv] *adj* (*person, manner*) attirant, attrayant; (*said, e.g., of a force*) attractif; (*price, offer; idea*) intéressant

attribute ['ætrɪ,bjut] *s* attribut *m* ‖ [ə'trɪbjut] *tr* attribuer

attrition [ə'trɪʃən] *s* attrition *f*, usure *f*

attune [ə't(j)un] *tr* accorder

auburn ['ɔbərn] *adj* auburn, brun rougeâtre

auction ['ɔkʃən] *s* vente *f* aux enchères ‖ *tr* vendre aux enchères

auctioneer [,ɔkʃən'ɪr] *s* adjudicateur *m*, commissaire-priseur *m* ‖ *tr & intr* vendre aux enchères

audacious [ɔ'deʃəs] *adj* audacieux

audacity [ɔ'dæsɪti] *s* audace *f*

audience ['ɔdɪ·əns] *s* (*hearing; formal interview*) audience *f*; (*assembly of hearers or spectators*) assistance *f*, salle *f*, auditoire *m*; (*those who follow what one says or writes*) public *m*

au'dio fre'quency ['ɔdɪ,o] *s* audio-fréquence *f*

audiometer [,ɔdɪ'ɑmɪtər] *s* audiomètre *m*

audiovisual [,ɔdɪ·o'vɪʒʊ·əl] *adj* audiovisuel

au'dio·visual aids' *spl* support *m* audiovisuel, moyens *mpl* audio-visuels

audit ['ɔdɪt] *s* apurement *m* ‖ *tr* apurer; **to audit a class** assister à la classe en auditeur libre

audition [ɔ'dɪʃən] *s* audition *f* ‖ *tr & intr* auditionner

auditor ['ɔdɪtər] *s* (com) comptable *m* agréé, expert comptable *m*; (educ) auditeur *m* libre

auditorium [,ɔdɪ'tori·əm] *s* auditorium *m*, salle *f*, amphithéâtre *m*

auditory ['ɔdɪ,tori] *adj* auditif

auger ['ɔgər] *s* tarière *f*

aught [ɔt] *s* zéro *m* ‖ *pron indef*—**for aught I know** autant que je sache ‖ *adv* du tout

augment [ɔg'mɛnt] *tr & intr* augmenter

augur ['ɔgər] *s* augure *m* ‖ *tr & intr* augurer; **to augur well** être de bon augure

augu·ry ['ɔgjəri] *s* (*pl* **-ries**) augure *m*

august [ɔ'gʌst] *adj* auguste ‖ **August** ['ɔgəst] *s* août *m*

auk [ɔk] *s* guillemot *m*

aunt [ænt], [ɑnt] *s* tante *f*

aureomycin [,ɔri·o'maisin] *s* (pharm) auréomycine *f*

auricle ['ɔrikəl] *s* auricule *f*, oreillette *f*

aurora [ə'rorə] *s* aurore *f*

auscultate ['ɔskəl,tet] *tr* ausculter

auspices ['ɔspɪsɪz] *spl* auspices *mpl*

auspicious [ɔs'pɪʃəs] *adj* propice, favorable

austere [ɔs'tɪr] *adj* austère

Australia [ɔ'streljə] *s* Australie *f*; l'Australie

Australian [ɔ'streljən] *adj* australien ‖ *s* (*person*) Australien *m*

Austria ['ɔstrɪ·ə] *s* Autriche *f*; l'Autriche

Austrian ['ɔstrɪ·ən] *adj* autrichien ‖ *s* (*person*) Autrichien *m*

authentic [ɔ'θɛntɪk] *adj* authentique

authenticate [ɔ'θɛntɪ,ket] *tr* authentifier, constater l'authenticité de

author ['ɔθər] *s* auteur *m*

authoress ['ɔθərɪs] *s* femme *f* auteur

authoritarian [ɔ,θɑrɪ'tɛrɪ·ən], [ɔ,θɔrɪ'tɛrɪ·ən] *adj* autoritaire ‖ *s* homme *m* autoritaire

authoritative [ɔ'θɔrɪ,tetɪv] *adj* autorisé; (*dictatorial*) autoritaire

authority [ɔ'θɔrɪti] *s* (*pl* **-ties**) autorité *f*; **on good authority** de bonne part

authorize ['ɔθə,raɪz] *tr* autoriser

au'thor·ship' *s* paternité *f*

autistic [ɔ'tɪstɪk] *adj* autistique

au·to ['ɔto] *s* (*pl* **-tos**) (coll) auto *f*, voiture *f*

autobiogra·phy [,ɔtobaɪ'ɑgrəfi] *s* (*pl* **-phies**) autobiographie *f*

autocrat ['ɔtə,kræt] *s* autocrate *mf*

autocratic(al) [,ɔtə'krætɪk(əl)] *adj* autocratique

autograph ['ɔtə,græf] *s* autographe *m* ‖ *tr* écrire l'autographe sur, dédicacer

au'tographed cop'y *s* exemplaire *m* dédicacé

au'to·intox'ica'tion *s* auto-intoxication *f*

automat ['ɔtə,mæt] *s* restaurant *m* libre service

automate ['ɔtə,met] *tr* automatiser

automatic [,ɔtə'mætɪk] *adj* automatique ‖ *s* revolver *m*

automat′ed tell′er *s* (com) machine *f* de télégestion bancaire, guichet *m* libre service

automat′ic transmis′sion *s* changement *m* de vitesse automatique

automation [,ɔtə'meʃən] *s* automatisation *f*, automation *f*

automa·ton [ɔ'tɑmə,tɑn] *s* (*pl* **-tons** or **-ta**) [tə] automate *m*

automobile [,ɔtəmo'bil] *s* automobile *f*

automobile′ show′ *s* salon *m* de l'automobile

automotive [,ɔtə'motɪv] *adj* automobile; automoteur

autonomous [ɔ'tɑnəməs] *adj* autonome

autonomy [ɔ'tɑnəmi] *s* autonomie *f*

autop·sy ['ɔtɑpsi] *s* (*pl* **-sies**) autopsie *f*

autumn ['ɔtəm] *s* automne *m*

autumnal [ɔ'tʌmnəl] *adj* automnal, d'automne

auxilia·ry [ɔg'zɪljəri] *adj* auxiliaire ‖ *s* (*pl* **-ries**) auxiliaire *mf*; **auxiliaries** (mil) troupes *fpl* auxiliaires

avail [ə'vel] *s* utilité *f* ‖ *tr* profiter à; **to avail oneself of** avoir recours à, profiter de ‖ *intr* être utile, servir

available [ə'veləbəl] *adj* disponible; (*e.g.*, *train*) accessible; **to make available to** mettre à la disposition de

avalanche ['ævə,læntʃ] *s* avalanche *f*

avarice ['ævərɪs] *s* avarice *f*

avaricious [,ævə'rɪʃəs] *adj* avaricieux

avenge [ə'vɛndʒ] *tr* venger

avenger [ə'vɛndʒər] *s* vengeur *m*

avenue ['ævə,n(j)u] *s* avenue *f*

aver [ə'vʌr] *v* (*pret* & *pp* **averred;** *ger* **averring**) *tr* avérer, affirmer

average ['ævərɪdʒ] *adj* moyen ‖ *s* moyenne *f*; **on the average** en moyenne ‖ *tr* prendre la moyenne de ‖ *intr* atteindre une moyenne

averse [ə'vʌs] *adj*—**averse to** hostile à, opposé à, ennemi de

aversion [ə'vʌrʒən] *s* aversion *f*

avert [ə'vʌrt] *tr* (*one's eyes; a blow*) détourner, écarter; (*an accident*) éviter

aviar·y ['evɪ,ɛri] *s* (*pl* **-ies**) volière *f*

aviation [,evɪ'eʃən] *s* aviation *f*

aviator ['evɪ,etər] *s* aviateur *m*

avid ['ævɪd] *adj* avide; **avid for** avide de

avidity [ə'vɪdɪti] *s* avidité *f*

avoca·do [,ævo'kɑdo] *s* (*pl* **-dos**) avocat *m*

avocation [,ævə'keʃən] *s* occupation *f*, profession *f*; (*hobby*) distraction *f*

avoid [ə'vɔɪd] *tr* éviter

avoidable [ə'vɔɪdəbəl] *adj* évitable

avoidance [ə'vɔɪdəns] *s* dérobade *f*

avow [ə'vaʊ] *tr* avouer

avowal [ə'vaʊ·əl] *s* aveu *m*

avowedly [ə'vaʊ·ɪdli] *adv* ouvertement, franchement

await [ə'wet] *tr* attendre

awake [ə'wek] *adj* éveillé ‖ *v* (*pret* & *pp* **awoke** [ə'wok] or **awaked**) *tr* éveiller ‖ *intr* s'éveiller

awaken [ə'wekən] *tr* éveiller, réveiller ‖ *intr* se réveiller

awakening [ə'wekənɪŋ] *s* réveil *m*

award [ə'wɔrd] *s* (*prize*) prix *m*; (law) dommages et intérêts *mpl* ‖ *tr* (*a prize*) décerner; (*a sum of money*) allouer; (*damages*) accorder

aware [ə'wɛr] *adj* conscient; **to become aware of** se rendre compte de

awareness [ə'wɛrnɪs] *s* conscience *f*

away [ə'we] *adj* absent ‖ *adv* au loin, loin; **away from** éloigné de, loin de; **to do away with** abolir; **to get away** s'absenter; (*to escape*) échapper; **to go away** s'en aller; **to make away with** (*to steal*) dérober; **to run away** se sauver; **to send away** renvoyer; **to take away** enlever ‖ *interj* hors d'ici!; **away with!** à bas!

awe [ɔ] *s* crainte *f* révérentielle ‖ *tr* inspirer de la crainte à

awesome ['ɔsəm] *adj* impressionnant

awful ['ɔfəl] *adj* terrible; (coll) terrible, affreux

awfully ['ɔfəli] *adv* terriblement; (coll) joliment, rudement

awhile [ə'hwaɪl] *adv* quelque temps, un peu, un moment

awkward ['ɔkwərd] *adj* (*clumsy*) gauche, maladroit; (*moment*) embarrassant; (*problem, situation*) délicat

awl [ɔl] *s* alène *f*

awning ['ɔnɪŋ] *s* (*over a window*) tente *f*; (*in front of store*) banne *f*

A.W.O.L. ['ewɔl] *s* (acronym) (**absent without leave**) absence *f* illégale; **to be A.W.O.L.** être absent sans permission

awry [ə'raɪ] *adv* de travers

ax [æks] *s* hache *f*

axiom ['æksɪ·əm] *s* axiome *m*

axiomatic [,æksɪ·ə'mætɪk] *adj* axiomatique

axis ['æksɪs] *s* (*pl* **axes** ['æksiz]) axe *m*

axle ['æksəl] *s* essieu *m*

ax′le grease′ *s* cambouis *m*

ay or **aye** [aj] *s* oui *m*; **aye, aye, sir!** oui, commandant!, bien, capitaine!; **the ayes have it** les oui l'emportent ‖ [e] *adv* toujours

azalea [ə'zeljə] *s* azalée *f*

azimuth ['æzɪməθ] *s* azimut *m*

Azores [ə'zorz] *spl* Açores *fpl*

Aztecs ['æztɛks] *spl* Aztèques *mpl*

azure ['eʒər] *adj* azuré, d'azur ‖ *s* azur *m* ‖ *tr* azurer

B, b [bi] *s* **II**ᶜ lettre de l'alphabet

babble ['bæbəl] *s* babil *m* ‖ *tr* (*secrets*) dire à tort et à travers ‖ *intr* babiller; (*said of birds*) jaser; (*said of brook*) murmurer

babbling ['bæblɪŋ] *adj* (*gossiper*) babillard; (*brook*) murmurant ‖ *s* babillage *m*

babe [beb] *s* bébé *m*, bambin *m*; (*naive person*) (coll) enfant *mf*; (*pretty girl*) (coll) pépée *f*, môme *f*

babel ['bebəl] *s* brouhaha *m*, vacarme *m*

baboon [bæ'bun] *s* babouin *m*

ba·by ['bebi] *s* (*pl* **-bies**) bébé *m*; (*youngest child*) cadet *m*, benjamin *m*; **baby!** (*honey!*) (coll) ma choute! ‖ *v* (*pret & pp* **-bied**) *tr* traiter en bébé, dorloter; (*e.g., a machine*) traiter avec soin

ba'by car'riage *s* voiture *f* d'enfant, poussette *f*; (*with hood*) landau *m*

ba'by foods' *spl* aliments *mpl* pour bébés premier âge, nourriture *f* pour enfants premier âge, la diététique infantile

ba'by grand' *s* piano *m* demi-queue

ba'by-sit'ter *s* gardienne *f* d'enfants, garde-bébé *mf*

ba'by-sit'ting *s* gardiennage *m* d'enfants

ba·by talk' *s* babil *m* enfantin

ba'by teeth' *spl* dents *fpl* de lait

baccalaureate [,bækə'lɔrɪ·ɪt] *s* baccalauréat *m*

bacchanal ['bækənəl] *adj* bachique ‖ *s* bacchanale *f*; (*person*) noceur *m*

bachelor ['bætʃələr] *s* (*single person*) célibataire *m*; (*graduate*) bachelier *m*

bach'elor apart'ment *s* garçonnière *f*

bach'elor girl *s* garçonne *f*

bach'elor's degree' *s* baccalauréat *m*

bacil·lus [bə'sɪləs]*s* (*pl* **-li** [laɪ]) bacille *m*

back [bæk] *adj* postérieur ‖ *s* (*part of the body; of a living being, hand, tongue, garment, chair, page*) dos *m*; (*of house; of head or body*) derrière *m*; (*of house; of car*) arrière *m*; (*of room*) fond *m*; (*of fabric*) envers *m*; (*of seat*) dossier *m*; (*of medal; of hand*) revers *m*; (*of page*) verso *m*; (sports) arrière *m*; **at the back** en queue; **back to back** dos à dos; **with one's back to the wall** poussé au pied du mur, aux abois ‖ *adv* en arrière, à l'arrière; **as far back as** déjà en, dès, **back and forth** de long en large; **back of** derrière; **back to front** sens devant derrière; **in back** par derrière; **some weeks back** il y a quelques semaines; **to be back** être de retour; **to come back** revenir; **to go back** retourner; **to go back home** rentrer; **to go back on** (coll) abandonner; **to go back to** (*to hark back to*) remonter à; **to make one's way back** s'en retourner ‖ *tr* faire faire marche arrière à; (*e.g., a car*) faire reculer; (*to support*) appuyer, soutenir; (*to reinforce*) renforcer; (*e.g. a racehorse*) parier pour; **to back s.o. up** soutenir qn; **to back water** nager à culer ‖ *intr* reculer; faire marche arrière; **to back down** (fig) se rétracter, se retirer; **to back out of** (*e.g.,*

an agreement) se dédire de, se soustraire à; **to back up** reculer

back'ache' *s* mal *m* de dos

back'bite' *v* (*pret* **-bit**; *pp* **-bitten** or **bit**) *tr* médire de ‖ *intr* médire

back'bit'er *s* médisant *m*

back'bone' *s* (*spinal column*) colonne *f* vertébrale, épine *f* dorsale, échine *f*; (*of a fish*) grande arête *f*; (*of an enterprise*) colonne *f*, appui *m*; (fig) caractère *m*, cran *m*; **to have no backbone** (fig) avoir l'échine souple

back'break'ing *adj* éreintant, dur

back'door' *adj* (fig) secret, clandestin

back' door' *s* porte *f* de derrière; (fig) petite porte

back'down' *s* (coll) palinodie *f*

back'drop' *s* toile *f* de fond

backer ['bækər] *s* (*of team, party, etc.*) supporter *m*; (com) bailleur *m* de fonds, commanditaire *m*

back'fire' *s* retour *m* de flamme, pétarade *f*; (*for firefighting*) contre-feu *m*; (mach) contre-allumage *m* ‖ *intr* donner des retours de flamme; (fig) produire un résultat imprévu

backgammon ['bæk,gæmən] *s* trictrac *m*, jacquet *m*

back'ground' *s* fond *m*; (*of person*) origines *fpl*, éducation *f*; (*music, sound effects, etc.*) fond sonore

back'hand' *s* (tennis) revers *m*

back'hand'ed *adj* de revers; (*compliment*) à rebours, équivoque

backing ['bækɪŋ] *s* (*support*) appui *m*, soutien *m*; (*reinforcement*) renforcement *m*; (*backing up*) recul *m*

back' in'terest *s* arrérages *mpl*

back'lash' *s* contrecoup *m*

back'light'ing *s* contre-jour *m*

back'log' *s* arriéré *m*, accumulation *f*

back' num'ber *s* (*of newspaper, magazine*) vieux numéro *m*; (coll) vieux jeu *m*

back'pain *s* tour *m* de reins

back' pay' *s* salaire *m* arriéré; (mil) arriéré *m* de solde

back' pay'ment *s* arriéré *m*

back' scratch'er *s* gratte-dos *m*; (slang) lèche-bottes *m*

back' seat' *s* banquette *f* arrière; **to take a back seat** (fig) aller au second plan

back'side' *s* derrière *m*, postérieur *m*

back'slide' *intr* récidiver

back'slid'er *s* récidiviste *mf*, relaps *m*

back'spac'er *s* touche *f* d'espace arrière, touche de recul

back'spin' *s* (*of ball*) coup *m* en bas, effet *m*

back'stage' *adv* dans les coulisses

back'stairs' *adj* caché, indirect

back' stairs' *spl* escalier *m* de service

back'stitch' *s* point *m* arrière

back'stop' *s* (*baseball*) attrapeur *m* ‖ *v* (*pret & pp* **-stopped**; *ger* **-stopping**) *tr* (coll) soutenir

back′stroke′ s (*of piston*) course f de retour; (*swimming*) brasse f sur le dos

back′swept wing′ s aile f en flèche

back′ talk′ s réplique f impertinente

back′ tax′es spl impôts mpl arriérés

back′track′ intr rebrousser chemin

back′up′ s appui m, soutien m

back′up light′ s phare m de recul

backward [′bækwərd] adj (*in direction*) en arrière, rétrograde; (*in time*) en retard; (*in development*) arriéré, attardé ‖ adv en arrière; (*opposite to the normal*) à rebours; (*walking*) à reculons; (*flowing*) à contre-courant; (*stroking of the hair*) à contre-poil; **backward and forward** de long en large; **to go backward and forward** aller et venir

back′ward-and-for′ward mo′tion s va-et-vient m

backwardness [′bækwərdnɪs] s retard m, lenteur f

backwards [′bækwərdz] adv var of **backward**

back′wash′ s remous m

back′wa′ter s (*of river*) bras m mort; (*e.g., of water wheel*) remous m; (*fig*) endroit m isolé, trou m

back′ wheel′ s roue f arrière

back′woods′ spl forêts fpl de l'intérieur; (*godforsaken place*) bled m, brousse f

back′woods′man s (*pl* -**men**) défricheur m de forêts, coureur m des bois

back′yard′ s derrière m (de la maison)

bacon [′bekən] s lard m, bacon m; (slang) butin m; **bacon and eggs** œufs au bacon; **to bring home the bacon** (coll) remporter la timbale

bacteria [bæk′tɪrɪ·ə] spl bactéries fpl

bacteriology [bæk,tɪrɪ′ɑlədʒi] s bactériologie f

bacteri·um [bæk′tɪrɪ·əm] s (*pl* -**a** [ə]) bactérie f

bad [bæd] adj mauvais §91; (*wicked*) méchant; (*serious*) grave; **from bad to worse** de mal en pis; **too bad!** c'est dommage!

bad′ breath′ s haleine f forte

bad′ check′ s chèque m en bois, chèque sans provision

bad′ com′pany s mauvaises fréquentations fpl

bad′ debt′ s mauvaise créance f

bad′ egg′ s (slang) mauvais sujet m

bad′ exam′ple s exemple m pernicieux

badge [bædʒ] s insigne m, plaque f

badger [′bædʒər] s blaireau m ‖ tr harceler, ennuyer

bad′ lot′ s voyous mpl, racaille f

badly [′bædli] adv mal §91; (*seriously*) gravement; **to want badly** avoir grande envie de

bad′man′ s (*pl* -**men′**) bandit m

badness [′bædnɪs] s mauvaise qualité f; (*of character*) méchanceté f

bad′-tem′pered adj susceptible, méchant; (*e.g., horse*) vicieux, rétif

bad′ trip′ s (slang) (*on drugs*) voyage m trop poussé

baffle [′bæfəl] s déflecteur m, chicane f ‖ tr déconcerter, confondre

baffling [′bæflɪŋ] adj déconcertant

bag [bæg] s sac m; (*suitcase*) valise f; (*of game*) chasse f; **it's in the bag** (coll) c'est du tout cuit ‖ v (*pret & pp* **bagged;** *ger* **bagging**) tr ensacher, mettre en sac; (*game*) abattre, tuer ‖ intr (*said of clothing*) faire poche

bagful [′bæg,ful] s sachée f

baggage [′bægɪdʒ] s bagage m, bagages

bag′gage car′ s (rr) fourgon m à bagages

bag′gage check′ s (*receipt*) bulletin m de bagages; (*checking*) consigne f ordinaire

bag′gage rack′ s (aer) casier m à bagages; (rr) porte-bagages m invar, filet m

bag′gage room′ s bureau m de gare expéditeur; (*checkroom*) consigne f

bag′gage truck′ s chariot m à bagages; (*hand truck*) diable m

bag·gy [′bægi] adj (*comp* -**gier;** *super* -**giest**) bouffant

bag′ of tricks′ s sac m à malice

bag′pipe′ s cornemuse f

bail [bel] s caution f; **to be out on bail** être libre sous caution; **to put up bail** se porter caution ‖ tr cautionner; **to bail out** se porter caution pour; (*a boat*) écoper ‖ intr—**to bail out** (aer) sauter en parachute

bailiff [′belɪf] s (*of a court*) huissier m, bailli m; (*on a farm*) régisseur m

bailiwick [′belɪwɪk] s bailliage m, rayon m; (*fig*) domaine m

bait [bet] s appât m, amorce f ‖ tr appâter, amorcer; (*to harass*) harceler

bake [bek] tr faire cuire au four; **to bake bread** boulanger, faire le pain ‖ intr cuire au four

baked′ pota′toes spl pommes fpl de terre au four

bakelite [′bekə,laɪt] s bakélite f

baker [′bekər] s boulanger m

bak′er's doz′en s treize m à la douzaine

baker·y [′bekəri] s (*pl* -**ies**) boulangerie f

baking [′bekɪŋ] s cuisson f au four

bak′ing pow′der s levure f anglaise, poudre f à pâte

bak′ing so′da s bicarbonate m de soude

balance [′bæləns] s balance f, équilibre m; (*scales*) balance f; (*what is left*) reste m; (com) solde m, report m ‖ tr balancer; (*an account*) solder ‖ intr se balancer; se solder

bal′ance of pay′ments s balance f des comptes

bal′ance of pow′er s équilibre m politique

bal′ance of trade′ s balance du commerce

bal′ance sheet′ s bilan m

bal′ance wheel′ s balancier m

balancing [′bælənsɪŋ] s (*oscillation*) balancement m; (*evening up*) équilibrage m, ajustement m; (com) règlement m des comptes

balco·ny [′bælkəni] s (*pl* -**nies**) balcon m; (*in a theater*) galerie f

bald [bɔld] adj chauve; (*fact, statement, etc.*) simple, net, carré

baldness ['bɔldnɪs] s calvitie f
bale [bɔl] s balle f ‖ tr emballer
baleful ['belfəl] adj funeste, fatal; triste
balk [bɔk] s (disappointment) déception f, contretemps m; (beam) poutre f; (agr) billon m ‖ tr frustrer ‖ intr regimber
Balkan ['bɔlkən] adj balkanique
balk·y ['bɔki] adj (comp -ier; super -iest) regimbé, rétif
ball [bɔl] s balle f; (in billiards; in bearings) bille f; (spherical body) boule f; (dance) bal m; **balls** (vulg) couilles fpl **to be on the ball** (slang) être toujours là pour le coup; **to have s.th. on the ball** (slang) avoir q.ch. dans le ventre; **to play ball** jouer à la balle, jouer au ballon; (slang) coopérer; (to be in cahoots) (slang) être en tandem ‖ tr—**to ball up** (slang) bousiller, embrouiller
ballad ['bæləd] s (song) romance f, complainte f; (poem) ballade f
ball′ and chain′ s boulet m; (slang) femme f, épouse f
ball′-and-sock′et joint′ s joint m à rotule
ballast ['bæləst] s (aer, naut) lest m; (rr) ballast m ‖ tr lester; ballaster
ball′ bear′ing s bille f, roulement m à billes
ball′ cock′ s robinet m à flotteur
ballerina [,bælə'rinə] s ballerine f
ballet ['bæle] s ballet m
ballistic [bə'lɪstɪk] adj balistique ‖ **ballistics** s balistique f
ballis′tic mis′sile s engin m balistique
balloon [bə'lun] s ballon m ‖ tr ballonner ‖ intr ballonner, se ballonner
ballot ['bælət] s (balloting) scrutin m; (individual ballot) bulletin m (de vote) ‖ intr scrutiner, voter
bal′lot box′ s urne f; **to stuff the ballot boxes** bourrer les urnes
balloting ['bælətɪŋ] s scrutin m
ball′-point pen′ s stylo m à bille, crayon m à bille
ball′room′ s salon m de bal, salle f de danse
ballyhoo ['bælɪ,hu] s publicité f tapageuse ‖ tr faire de la réclame pour
balm [bɑm] s baume m ‖ tr parfumer
balm·y ['bɑmi] adj (comp -ier; super -iest) embaumé; (slang) toqué
baloney [bə'loni] s (culin) mortadelle f; (slang) fadaises fpl
balsam ['bɔlsəm] s baume m
bal′sam fir′ s sapin m baumier
bal′sam pop′lar s peuplier m baumier
Balt [bɔlt] s Balte mf
Bal′timore o′riole ['bɔltɪ,mor] s loriot m de Baltimore
baluster ['bæləstər] s balustre m
balustrade [,bæləs'tred] s balustrade f, rampe f
bamboo [bæm'bu] s bambou m
bamboozle [bæm'buzəl] tr (slang) mystifier
ban [bæn] s ban m, interdiction f; **bans** bans mpl ‖ v (pret & pp **banned**; ger **banning**) tr mettre au ban
banal ['bænəl], [bə'næl] adj banal
banali·ty [bə'nælɪti] s (pl -ties) banalité f

banana [bə'nænə] s banane f
banan′a tree′ s bananier m
band [bænd] s (strap, connection) bande f, lien m; (group) bande, troupe f; (brass band) musique f, fanfare f; (dance band) orchestre m; (strip of color) raie f; **to beat the band** (slang) sans pareille; (hastily) vivement ‖ tr entourer de bandes; (a bird) marquer de bandes ‖ intr—**to band together** se grouper
bandage ['bændɪdʒ] s (dressing) pansement m; (holding the dressing in place) bandage m ‖ tr panser; bander
band′box′ s carton m de modiste
bandit ['bændɪt] s bandit m
band′mas′ter s chef m de musique
band′saw′ s scie f à ruban
band′stand′ s kiosque m
band′wag′on s char m de la victoire; **to jump on the bandwagon** suivre la majorité victorieuse
ban·dy ['bændi] adj tortu ‖ v (pret & pp -died) tr renvoyer, échanger; **to bandy words** se renvoyer des paroles ‖ intr se disputer
ban′dy-leg′ged adj bancal
bane [ben] s poison m; ruine f
baneful 'benfəl] adj funeste, nuisible
bang [bæŋ] s coup m; (of a door) claquement m; (of fireworks; of a gun) détonation f; **bangs** frange f; **to go off with a bang** détoner; (slang) réussir ‖ tr frapper; (a door) faire claquer; **to bang down** (e.g., a lid) abattre violemment; **to bang up** (slang) rosser, cogner ‖ intr claquer avec fracas; **to bang against** cogner; **to bang on** frapper à ‖ interj pan!; pom!
bang′-up′ adj (slang) de premier ordre, à la hauteur
banish ['bænɪʃ] tr bannir, exiler
banishment ['bænɪʃmənt] s bannissement m
banister ['bænɪstər] s balustre m; **banisters** balustrade f, rampe f
bank [bæŋk] s (for money, blood, data, etc.) banque f; (of river) rive f, bord m; (shoal) banc m; (slope) talus m, terrasse f; (in a gambling game) cave f; (aer) virage m incliné; **to break the bank** faire sauter la banque ‖ tr terrasser; (money) déposer; (an airplane) incliner ‖ intr (aer) virer, virer sur l'aile, s'incliner; **to bank on** compter sur
bank′ account′ s compte m en banque
bank′book′ s carnet m de banque
bank′ card′ s carte-retrait f
banked adj incliné
banker ['bæŋkər] s banquier m
banking ['bæŋkɪŋ] adj bancaire
bank′ note′ s billet m de banque
bank′roll′ s paquet m de billets, liasse f de billets
bankrupt ['bæŋkrʌpt] adj & s failli m; (with guilt) banqueroutier m; **to go bankrupt** faire banqueroute ‖ tr mettre en faillite

bankrupt·cy [ˈbæŋkrʌptsi] s (pl **-cies**) faillite f, banqueroute f; (fig) ruine f

bank' vault' s chambre f forte

banner [ˈbænər] s bannière f

ban'ner cry' s cri m de guerre

ban'ner year' s année f record

banquet [ˈbæŋkwɪt] s banquet m ‖ intr banqueter

bantam [ˈbæntəm] adj nain ‖ s poulet m nain, poulet de bantam

ban'tam·weight' s poids m bantam; (boxing) poids bantam, poids coq

banter [ˈbæntər] s badinage m ‖ tr & intr badiner

bantering [ˈbæntərɪŋ] adj railleur, goguenard

baptism [ˈbæptɪzəm] s baptême m

baptismal [bæpˈtizməl] adj baptismal

baptis'mal certif'icate s extrait m de baptême

baptis'mal font' s fonts mpl baptismaux

Baptist [ˈbæptɪst] s baptiste mf

baptister·y [ˈbæptɪstəri] s (pl **-ies**) baptistère m

baptize [ˈbæptaɪz] tr baptiser

bar [bɑr] s barre f, barreau m; (obstacle) barrière f, empêchement m; (barroom; counter) bar m; (profession of law) barreau; (of public opinion) tribunal m; (of chocolate) tablette f, plaquette f; (mus) mesure f; (phys) bar; **behind bars** sous les barreaux ‖ prep—**bar none** sans exception ‖ v (pret & pp **barred**; ger **barring**) tr barrer

barb [bɑrb] s (of a fishhook, arrow, feather) barbillon m; (arrowhead) dent f d'une flèche; (in metalwork) barbe f ‖ tr garnir de barbillons

Barbados [bɑrˈbedoz] s la Barbade

barbarian [bɑrˈbɛrɪ·ən] adj & s barbare mf

barbaric [bɑrˈbærɪk] adj barbare

barbarism [ˈbɑrbəˌrɪzəm] s barbarie f; (in speech or writing) barbarisme m

barbari·ty [bɑrˈbærɪti] s (pl **-ties**) barbarie f

barbarous [ˈbɑrbərəs] adj barbare

barbecue [ˈbɑrbɪˌkju] s grillade f en plein air ‖ tr griller à la sauce piquante et au charbon de bois

bar'becue pit' s rôtisserie f en plein air

barbed adj barbelé, pointu

barbed' wire' s fil m de fer barbelé

barbed'-wire entan'glement s réseau m de barbelés

barber [ˈbɑrbər] s coiffeur m; (who shaves) barbier m

bar'ber pole' s enseigne f de barbier

bar'ber·shop' s salon m de coiffeur

bar'ber·shop quartet' s ensemble m harmonique de chanteurs amateurs

barbiturate [bɑrˈbɪtʃəˌret], [ˌbɑrbɪˈtjuret] adj & s barbiturique m

bard [bɑrd] s barde m

bare [bɛr] adj nu; (uncovered) découvert; (wire) dénudé, à nu; (necessities) simple, strict; (ace, king, queen) sec ‖ tr mettre à nu

bare'back' adv à nu

bare'faced' adj éhonté, effronté

bare'foot' adj nu-pieds

bare'head'ed adj nu-tête

bare'leg'ged adj nu-jambes

barely [ˈbɛrli] adv à peine

bareness [ˈbɛrnɪs] s nudité f, dénuement m; (of style) pauvreté f

bar'fly' s (pl **-flies**) (slang) pilier m de cabaret

bargain [ˈbɑrgɪn] s (deal) marché m, affaire f; (cheap purchase) solde m, occasion f; **into the bargain** par-dessus le marché ‖ tr—**to bargain away** vendre à perte ‖ intr entrer en négociations; **she gave him more than he bargained for** (fig) elle lui a donné du fil à retordre; **to bargain over** marchander; **to bargain with** traiter avec

bar'gain coun'ter s rayon m des soldes

bar'gain sale' s vente f de soldes

barge [bɑrdʒ] s barge f, chaland m, péniche f ‖ intr—**to barge into** entrer sans façons

baritone [ˈbærɪˌton] adj de baryton ‖ s baryton m

barium [ˈbɛˌrɪ·əm] s baryum m

bark [bɑrk] s (of tree) écorce f; (of dog) aboiement m; (boat) trois-mâts m; **his bark is worse than his bite** il fait plus de bruit que de mal ‖ tr—**to bark out** dire d'un ton sec ‖ intr aboyer; **to bark up the wrong tree** suivre une mauvaise piste

bar'keep'er s barman m

barker [ˈbɑrkər] (coll) s bonimenteur m, barnum m

barley [ˈbɑrli] s orge f

bar'maid' s fille f comptoir, demoiselle f de comptoir, serveuse f

barn [bɑrn] s (for grain) grange f; (for horses) écurie f; (for livestock) étable f

barnacle [ˈbɑrnəkəl] s (on a ship) anatife m, patelle f; (goose) bernacle f

barn' owl' s (Tyto alba) effraie f

barn'storm' intr aller en tournée

barn'yard' s basse-cour f

barometer [bəˈrɑmɪtər] s baromètre m

barometric [ˌbærəˈmɛtrɪk] adj barométrique

baron [ˈbærən] s baron m; (of steel, coal, lumber) (coll) magnat m

baroness [ˈbærənɪs] s baronne f

baroque [bəˈrok] adj & s baroque m

barracks [ˈbærəks] spl caserne f

barrage [bəˈrɑʒ] s barrage m

barred adj barré; (excluded) exclu

barrel [ˈbærəl] s tonneau m, fût m; **large barrel** barrique f; **small barrel** baril m, baricaut m, barillet m

bar'rel or'gan s orgue m de Barbarie

barren [ˈbærən] adj stérile; (bare) nu; (of style) aride, sec

barricade [ˌbærɪˈked] s barricade f ‖ tr barricader

barrier [ˈbærɪ·ər] s barrière f

bar'rier reef' s récif-barrière m

barring [ˈbɑrɪŋ] prep sauf

barrister [ˈbærɪstər] s (Brit) avocat m

bar'room' s cabaret m, bar m, bistrot m

bar'tend'er s barman m

barter ['bɑrtər] s échange m, troc m ‖ tr échanger

ba'sal metab'olism ['besəl] s métabolisme m basal

basalt [bə'sɔlt], ['bæsɔlt] s basalte m

base [bes] adj bas, vil ‖ s (main ingredient; starting point; lowest part) base f; (fundamental, principal) fondement m, ligne f d'appui, principe m; (pedestal) socle m ‖ tr baser; fonder

base'ball' s base-ball m

base'board' s plinthe f

basement ['besmənt] s sous-sol m, cave f

base'ment win'dow s soupirail m

bash [bæʃ] tr cogner, assommer

bashful ['bæʃfəl] adj timide

basic ['besɪk] adj fondamental, de base, essentiel; (alkaline) basique

basil ['bæzəl] s basilic m

basilica [bə'sɪlɪkə] s basilique f

basin ['besɪn] s (bowl; pond; dock) bassin m; (washbasin) cuvette f; (bowl) bol m

ba·sis ['besɪs] s (pl -ses [siz]) base f, fondement m; **on the basis of** sur la base de, par suite de

bask [bæsk] intr se chauffer

basket ['bæskɪt] s panier m; (with a handle) corbeille f; (carried on the back) hotte f

bas'ket·ball' s basket-ball m, basket m

bas'ket-ball play'er s basketteur m

bas'ket lunch' s panier-repas m

bas'ket·mak'er s vannier m

bas'ket·work' s vannerie f

Basque [bæsk] adj basque ‖ s (language) basque m; (person) Basque mf

bass [bes] adj grave, bas ‖ s (mus) basse f ‖ [bæs] s (ichth) bar m

bass' clef' s clef f de fa

bass' drum' [bes] s grosse caisse f

bassinet [,bæsɪ'nɛt] s bercelonnette f

bassoon [bə'sun] s bassoon m

bass viol ['bes'vaɪ·əl] s basse f de viole

basswood ['bæs,wʊd] s tilleul m

bastard ['bæstərd] adj bâtard ‖ s bâtard m; (vulg) salaud m, saligaud m

baste [best] tr (to thrash) rosser; (to scold) éreinter; (culin) arroser; (sewing) faufiler, baguer, bâtir

bastion ['bæstʃən] s bastion m

bat [bæt] s (cudgel) bâton m; (for cricket) bat m; (sports) batte f; (zool) chauve-souris f; (blow) (coll) coup m; **right off the bat** sur-le-champ; **to be at bat** tenir la batte; **to go to bat for** (coll) intervenir au profit de; **to have bats in the belfry** (coll) avoir une araignée dans le plafond ‖ v (pret & pp **batted;** ger **batting**) tr battre

batch [bætʃ] s (of papers) liasse f; (comp) paquetage m; (coll) fournée f, lot m

batch' proc'essing (comp) traitement m par lots

bated ['betɪd] adj—**with bated breath** en baissant la voix, dans un souffle

bath [bæθ] s bain m; (bathroom) salle f de bains; **to take a bath** prendre un bain, se baigner

bathe [beð] tr baigner ‖ intr se baigner

bather ['beðər] s baigneur m

bath'house' s établissement m de bains; (at the seashore) cabine f

bath'ing suit' s costume m de bain

bath'ing trunks' s slip m de bain

bath' mat' s tapis m de bain

bath'robe' s peignoir m

bath'room' s salle f de bains

bath'room fix'tures spl appareils mpl sanitaires

bath'room scale' s pèse-personne m

bath' tow'el s serviette f de bain

bath'tub' s baignoire f

baton [bæ'tɑn] s (scepter) bâton m; (mus) baguette f, bâton de chef d'orchestre; (sports) bâton de relais, témoin m

battalion [bə'tæljən] s bataillon m

batten ['bætən] tr—**to batten down the hatches** condamner les panneaux

batter ['bætər] s (culin) pâte f; (sports) batteur m ‖ tr battre

bat'tering ram' s bélier m

batter·y ['bætəri] s (pl -ies) (elec, mil, mus) batterie f; (primary cell) pile f; (secondary cell or cells) accumulateur m, accu m

battle ['bætəl] s bataille f; **to do battle** livrer combat ‖ tr & intr combattre

bat'tle·ax' s hache f d'armes; (shrew) (slang) harpie f, mégère f

bat'tle cruis'er s croiseur m de bataille

bat'tle cry' s cri m de guerre

bat'tle·field' s champ m de bataille

bat'tle·front' s front m de bataille

bat'tle line' s ligne f de feu

battlement ['bætəlmənt] s créneau m; **battlements** parapet m, rempart m

bat'tle roy'al s mêlée f générale

bat'tle·ship' s cuirassé m, navire m de guerre

bat·ty ['bæti] adj (comp -tier; super -tiest) (slang) dingo, maboul, braque

bauble ['bɔbəl] s babiole f, bagatelle f; (of jester) marotte f

Bavaria [bə'vɛrɪ·ə] s la Bavière

Bavarian [bə'vɛrɪ·ən] adj bavarois ‖ s Bavarois m

bawd·y ['bɔdi] adj (comp -ier; super -iest) obscène, impudique

bawl [bɔl] tr—**to bawl out** (slang) faire une sortie à, engueuler ‖ intr gueuler; (to cry) sangloter

bawl'ing out' s (slang) engueulade f

bay [be] adj & s baie f; **at bay** aux abois ‖ intr aboyer, hurler

bay'ber'ry s (pl -ries) baie f

bay'berry tree' s laurier m

bayonet ['be·ənɪt] s baïonnette f ‖ tr percer d'un coup de baïonnette

bayou ['baɪ·u] s anse f

bay' rum' s eau f de toilette au laurier

bay' win'dow s fenêtre f en saillie; (slang) bedaine f, gros ventre m

bazaar [bə'zɑr] s bazar m; (social event) kermesse f

B.C. ['bi'si] adv (letterword) (**before Christ**) av. J.-C.

be [bi] *v* (*pres am* [æm], **is** [ɪz], **are** [ɑr]; *pret* **was** [wɑz] or [wʌz], **were** [wʌr]; *pp* **been** [bɪn]) *intr* être; avoir, e.g., **to be five years old** avoir cinq ans; e.g., **to be ten feet long** avoir dix pieds de long; e.g., **what is the matter with you?** qu'a-vez-vous?; **here is** or **here are** voici; **how are you?** comment allez-vous?, ça va?, comment vous portez-vous?; **how much is that?** combien coûte cela?, c'est com-bien ça?; **so be it** ainsi soit-il; **there is** or **there are** il y a; (in directing the atten-tion) voilà; for expressions like **it is warm** il fait chaud or **I am cold** j'ai froid, see the noun ‖ *aux* (to form the passive voice) être, e.g., **he is loved by everybody** il est aimé de tout le monde; (progressive not expressed in French), e.g., **he is eating** il mange; **to be to** + *inf* devoir + *inf*, e.g., **I am to give a speech** je dois prononcer un discours

beach [bitʃ] *s* plage *f*, bord *m* de la mer; grève *f*, rivage *m* ‖ *tr* & *intr* échouer

beach' ball' *s* ballon *m* de plage

beach' bug'gy *s* buggy *m*

beach'comb'er *s* batteur *m* de grève

beach'head' *s* (mil) tête *f* de pont

beach' resort' *s* station *f* balnéaire

beach' robe' *s* sortie *f* de bain, peignoir *m* de bain

beach' shoe' *s* claquette *f*

beach' umbrel'la *s* parasol *m* de plage

beach' wear' *s* tenue *f* de plage

beacon ['bikən] *s* signal *m*, phare *m* ‖ *tr* éclairer ‖ *intr* briller

bead [bid] *s* perle *f*, grain *m*; (of a gun) guidon *m*; **beads** collier *m*; (of sweat) gouttes *fpl*; (eccl) chapelet *m*; **to draw a bead on** viser; **to tell one's beads** égrener son chapelet

beagle ['bigəl] *s* beagle *m*, briquet *m*

beak [bik] *s* bec *m*; (nose) (slang) pif *m*; grand nez *m* crochu

beaker ['bikər] *s* coupe *f*, vase *m* à bec, verre *m* à expérience

beam [bim] *s* (girder) poutre *f*; (plank) madrier *m*; (of roof) solive *f*; (of ship) bau *m*, barrot *m*; (of light; of hope) rayon *m*; (rad) faisceau *m*; **on the beam** (slang) sur la bonne piste; **to be off the beam** (slang) faire fausse route ‖ *tr* (light, waves, etc.) émettre; **to beam a broadcast** faire une émission ‖ *intr* rayonner

bean [bin] *s* haricot *m*; (broad bean) fève *f*; (slang) caboche *f*; **to spill the beans** (coll) vendre la mèche

bean'-bag chair' *s* siège-billes *m*

bean'pole' *s* perche *f* à fèves; (person) (slang) asperge *f*

bean'stalk' *s* tige *f* de fève, tige de haricot

bear [bɛr] *s* ours *m*; (in the stock market) baissier *m* ‖ *v* (*pret* **bore** [bor]; *pp* **borne** [born]) *tr* porter; (a child) enfanter; (in-terest on money) rapporter; (to put up with) souffrir, supporter; **to bear the market** jouer à la baisse ‖ *intr* porter; **to bear down** appuyer; **to bear up against**

résister à; **to bear upon** avoir du rapport à; **to bring to bear** mettre en jeu

bearable ['bɛrəbəl] *adj* supportable

bear' cub' *s* ourson *m*

beard [bɪrd] *s* barbe *f* ‖ *tr* braver, narguer

bearded *adj* barbu

beardless ['bɪrdlɪs] *adj* imberbe, sans barbe

bearer ['bɛrər] *s* porteur *m*

bearing ['bɛrɪŋ] *s* (posture; behavior) port *m*, maintien *m*; (mach) roulement *m*, coussinet *m*; (naut) relèvement *m*; **to get one's bearings** se retrouver; **to have a bearing on** s'appliquer à; **to take bear-ings** (naut) faire le point

bear' mar'ket *s* marché *m* à la baisse

bear'skin' *s* peau *f* d'ours; colback *m*

beast [bist] *s* bête *f*, animal *m*; (person) brute *f*, animal *m*

beast·ly ['bistli] *adj* (*comp* **-lier;** *super* **-liest**) brutal, bestial; (coll) abominable, détestable

beast' of bur'den *s* bête *f* de somme, bête de charge

beat [bit] *s* (of heart, pulse, drums) batte-ment *m*; (of policeman) ronde *f*; (mus) mesure *f*, temps *m* ‖ *v* (*pret* **beat;** *pp* **beat** or **beaten**) *tr* battre; (to defeat) vaincre, battre; **that beats me!** (slang) ça me dépasse!; **to beat back** or **down** rabattre; **to beat in** enfoncer; **to beat it** (slang) filer, décamper; **to beat s.o. hollow** (coll) battre qn à plate couture; **to beat s.o. out of money** (slang) escroquer qn; **to beat time** battre la mesure; **to beat up** (slang) rosser ‖ *intr* battre; **to beat around the bush** (coll) tourner autour du pot

beater ['bitər] *s* batteur *m*; (culin) fouet *m*

beati·fy [bɪ'ætɪ,faɪ] *v* (*pret* & *pp* **-fied**) *tr* béatifier

beating ['bitɪŋ] *s* (of wings, heart, pulse, drums) battement *m*; (thrashing) correc-tion *f*, rossée *f*, raclée *f*; (defeat) défaite *f*, raclée; **to take a beating** se faire battre à plate couture

beatitude [bɪ'ætɪ,t(j)ud] *s* béatitude *f*

beau [bo] *s* (pl **beaus** or **beaux** [boz]) beau *m*, galant *m*

beautician [bju'tɪʃən] *s* coiffeur *m*, coif-feuse *f*, esthéticienne *f*

beautiful ['bjutɪfəl] *adj* beau

beautifully ['bjutɪfəli] *adv* admirablement

beauti·fy ['bjutɪ,faɪ] *v* (*pret* & *pp* **-fied**) *tr* embellir

beau·ty ['bjuti] *s* (pl **-ties**) beauté *f*

beau'ty con'test *s* concours *m* de beauté

beau'ty par'lor or **beau'ty shop'** *s* salon *m* de beauté, institut *m* de beauté

beau'ty queen' *s* reine *f* de beauté

beau'ty sleep' *s* sommeil *m* avant minuit

beau'ty spot' *s* (place) coin *m* délicieux; (on face) grain *m* de beauté

beaver ['bivər] *s* castor *m*

becalm [bɪ'kɑm] *tr* calmer, apaiser; (naut) abriter

because [bɪ'kɔz] *conj* parce que; **because of** à cause de, par suite de

beck [bɛk] *s*—**to be at s.o.'s beck and call** obéir à qn au doigt et à l'œil

beckon [ˈbɛkən] *tr* faire signe à, appeler ‖ *intr* appeler

be·come [bɪˈkʌm] *v* (*pret* **-came;** *pp* **-come**) *tr* convenir à, aller à, seoir à ‖ *intr* devenir; se faire, e.g., **to become a doctor** se faire médecin; e.g., **to become known** se faire connaître; **to become accustomed** s'accoutumer; **to become old** vieillir; **what has become of him?** qu'est-ce qu'il est devenu?

becoming [bɪˈkʌmɪŋ] *adj* convenable, seyant

bed [bɛd] *s* lit *m*; couche *f*; **to go to bed** se coucher; **to put to bed** coucher

bed' and board' *s* le vivre et le couvert

bed' and break'fast *s* (Brit) chambre *f* avec petit déjeuner

bed'bug' *s* punaise *f* (des lits)

bed'clothes' *spl* couvertures *fpl* et draps *mpl*

bedding [ˈbɛdɪŋ] *s* literie *f*

bedeck [bɪˈdɛk] *tr* parer, orner, chamarrer; **to bedeck oneself** s'attifer

bed'fast' *adj* cloué au lit

bed'fel'low *s* camarade *m* de lit

bed'jack'et *s* liseuse *f*

bedlam [ˈbɛdləm] *s* pétaudière *f*, tumulte *m*

bed'lamp' *s* lampe *f* de chevet

bed' lin'en *s* literie *f*, draps *mpl* en toile de fil

bed'pan' *s* bassin *m* (de lit)

bed'post' *s* pied *m* de lit

bedraggled [bɪˈdrægəld] *adj* crotté, échevelé

bedridden [ˈbɛd,rɪdən] *adj* alité, cloué au lit

bed'rock' *s* roche *f* de fond; (geol) soubassement *m*; (fig) fondement *m*, base *f*

bed'room' *s* chambre *f* à coucher

bed'room lamp' *s* lampe *f* de chevet

bed'side' *s* bord *m* du lit, chevet *m*

bed'side book' *s* livre *m* de chevet

bed'sore' *s* escarre *f*

bed'spread' *s* dessus-de-lit *m invar*

bed'spring' *s* sommier *m*

bed'stead' *s* bois *m* de lit

bed' tick' *s* coutil *m*

bed'time' *s* l'heure *f* du coucher

bed' warm'er *s* chauffe-lit *m*

bed'wet'ting *s* énurésie *f*

bee [bi] *s* abeille *f*; (*get-together*) réunion *f*; (*contest*) concours *m*

beech [bitʃ] *s* hêtre *m*

beech' mar'ten *s* (zool) fouine *f*

beech'nut' *s* faîne *f*

beef [bif] *s* bœuf *m* ‖ *tr*—**to beef up** (coll) renforcer ‖ *intr* (slang) rouspéter

beef' cat'tle *s* bœufs *mpl* de boucherie

beef'steak' *s* bifteck *m*

beef' stew' *s* ragoût *m* de bœuf

bee'hive' *s* ruche *f*

bee'keep'er *s* apiculteur *m*

bee'keep'ing *s* apiculture *f*

bee'line' *s*—**to make a beeline for** aller en droite ligne à

beeper [ˈbipər] *s* bip-bip *m*

beer [bɪr] *s* bière *f*

beer' bot'tle or **beer' can** *s* canette *f* (de bière)

bees'wax' *s* circe *f* d'abeille

beet *s* betterave *f*

beetle [ˈbitəl] *s* scarabée *m*, escarbot *m*

bee'tle-browed' *adj* à sourcils épais, à sourcils fournis

be·fall [bɪˈfɔl] *v* (*pret* **-fell;** *pp* **-fallen**) *tr* arriver à ‖ *intr* arriver

befitting [bɪˈfɪtɪŋ] *adj* convenable, seyant

before [bɪˈfor] *adv* avant, auparavant ‖ *prep* avant; (*in front of*) devant; **before** + *ger* avant de + *inf* ‖ *conj* avant que

before'hand' *adv* d'avance, préalablement, auparavant

befriend [bɪˈfrɛnd] *tr* venir en aide à

befuddle [bɪˈfʌdəl] *tr* embrouiller

beg [bɛg] *v* (*pret & pp* **begged;** *ger* **begging**) *tr* mendier; (*to entreat*) supplier ‖ *intr* mendier; (*said of dog*) faire le beau; **I beg of you** je vous en prie; **to beg for** solliciter; **to beg off** s'excuser; **to beg off from** se faire excuser de; **to go begging** (fig) rester pour compte

be·get [bɪˈgɛt] *v* (*pret* **-got;** *pp* **-gotten** or **-got;** *ger* **-getting**) *tr* engendrer

beggar [ˈbɛgər] *s* mendiant *m*

beggarly [ˈbɛgərli] *adj* chétif, misérable

be·gin [bɪˈgɪn] *v* (*pret* **-gan** [ˈgæn]; *pp* **-gun** [ˈgʌn]; *ger* **-ginning**) *tr & intr* commencer; **beginning with** à partir de; **to begin to** commencer à

beginner [bɪˈgɪnər] *s* débutant *m*, commençant *m*; (*tyro*) blanc-bec *m*, novice *m*, béjaune *m*; (mil) bleu *m*

beginning [bɪˈgɪnɪŋ] *s* commencement *m*, début *m*

begrudge [bɪˈgrʌdʒ] *tr* donner à contre-cœur; **to begrudge s.o. s.th.** envier q.ch. à qn

beguile [bɪˈgaɪl] *tr* charmer, tromper

behalf [bɪˈhæf] *s*—**on behalf of** de la part de, au nom de

behave [bɪˈhev] *intr* se comporter, se conduire; (*to behave well*) se comporter bien

behavior [bɪˈhevjər] *s* comportement *m*, conduite *f*; (mach) fonctionnement *m*

behaviorism [bɪˈhevjərɪzəm] *s* behaviorisme *m*

behead [bɪˈhɛd] *tr* décapiter

beheading [bɪˈhɛdɪŋ] *s* décapitation *f*

behest [bɪˈhɛst] *s* ordre *m*, demande *f*

behind [bɪˈhaɪnd] *s* derrière *m* ‖ *adv* derrière, par derrière; **to be behind** être en retard; **to fall behind** traîner en arrière ‖ *prep* derrière; en arrière de; **behind the back of** dans le dos de; **behind time** en retard

be·hold [bɪˈhold] *v* (*pret & pp* **-held** [ˈhɛld]) *tr* contempler ‖ *interj* voyez!, voici!

behoove [bɪˈhuv] *impers*—**it behooves him to** il lui appartient de; **it does not behoove him to** mal lui sied de

being [ˈbi·ɪŋ] *adj*—**for the time being** pour le moment ‖ *s* être *m*

belabor [bɪˈlebər] *tr* rosser; (fig) trop insister sur

belated [bɪˈletɪd] *adj* attardé, tardif

belch [bɛltʃ] *s* éructation *f*; rot *m* (slang) ‖ *tr & intr* éructer

bel·fry [ˈbɛlfri] *s* (*pl* -**fries**) beffroi *m*, clocher *m*

Belgian [ˈbɛldʒən] *adj* belge ‖ *s* Belge *mf*

Belgium [ˈbɛldʒəm] *s* Belgique *f*; la Belgique

be·lie [bɪˈlaɪ] *v* (*pret & pp* -**lied** [ˈlaɪd]; *ger* -**lying** [ˈlaɪɪŋ]) *tr* démentir

belief [bɪˈlif] *s* croyance *f*

believable [bɪˈlivəbəl] *adj* croyable

believe [bɪˈliv] *tr & intr* croire; **to believe in** croire à or en; **to make believe** faire semblant, feindre

believer [bɪˈlivər] *s* croyant *m*

belittle [bɪˈlɪtəl] *tr* rabaisser

bell [bɛl] *s* (*hollow instrument*) cloche *f*; (*of a clock or gong*) timbre *m*; (*small bell*) sonnette *f*; clochette *f*; (*big bell*) bourdon *m*; (*on animals*) grelot *m*, clarine *f*, sonnaille *f*; (*of a trumpet*) pavillon *m*; **bells** sonnerie *f* ‖ *tr* attacher un grelot à

belladonna [ˌbɛləˈdɑnə] *s* belladone *f*

bell′-bot′tom trou′sers *spl* pantalon *m* à pattes d'éléphant

bell′boy′ *s* chasseur *m*, garçon *m* d'hôtel

bell′ glass′ *s* globe *m*, garde-poussière *m*

bell′hop′ *s* chasseur *m*, garçon *m* d'hôtel

bellicose [ˈbɛlɪˌkos] *adj* belliqueux

belligerent [bəˈlɪdʒərənt] *adj & s* belligérant *m*

bell′ jar′ *s* var of **bell glass**

bellow [ˈbɛlo] *s* mugissement *m*; **bellows** (*of camera; of fireplace*) soufflet *m*; (*of organ; of forge*) soufflerie *f* ‖ *intr* mugir, beugler

bell′ pull′ *s* cordon *m* de sonnette

bell′ ring′er *s* sonneur *m*; carillonneur *m*

bell′-shaped′ *adj* en forme de cloche

bell′ tow′er *s* clocher *m*, campanile *m*

bellwether [ˈbɛlˌwɛðər] *s* sonnailler *m*

bel·ly [ˈbɛli] *s* (*pl* -**lies**) ventre *m* ‖ *v* (*pret & pp* -**lied**) *intr*—**to belly out** s'enfler

bel′ly·ache′ *s* (coll) mal *m* de ventre ‖ *intr* (slang) rouspéter

bel′ly·but′ton *s* (coll) nombril *m*

bel′ly dance′ *s* (coll) danse *f* du ventre

bel′ly flop′ *s* plat ventre *m* (acrobatique)

bellyful [ˈbɛliˌfʊl] *s* (slang) ventrée *f*

bel′ly-land′ *intr* (aer) aterrir sur le ventre

belong [bɪˈlɔŋ] *intr* (*to have the proper qualities*) aller bien; **to belong in** devoir être dans, e.g., **this chair belongs in that corner** cette chaise doit être dans ce coin-là; **to belong to** appartenir à; **to belong together** aller ensemble

belongings [bɪˈlɔŋɪŋz] *spl* biens *mpl*, effets *mpl*

beloved [bɪˈlʌvɪd], [bɪˈlʌvd] *adj & s* bien-aimé *m*

below [bɪˈlo] *adv* dessous, au-dessous, en bas; (*as follows, following*) ci-dessous, ci-après ‖ *prep* sous, au-dessous de; (*another point on the river*) en aval de

belt [bɛlt] *s* (*encircling band or strip*) ceinture *f*; (*tract of land, region*) zone *f*; (*blow*) coup *m*; (*of a machine*) courroie *f*; **to tighten one's belt** se serrer la ceinture ‖ *tr* ceindre; (slang) cogner

belt′ buck′le *s* boucle *f* de ceinturon

belt′ convey′or *s* tapis *m* roulant

belted *adj* à ceinture

belt′way′ *s* route *f* de ceinture, boulevard *m* périphérique

bemoan [bɪˈmon] *tr* déplorer

bemuse [bɪˈmjuz] *tr* stupéfier, hébéter

bench [bɛntʃ] *s* banc *m*; (law) siège *m*

bench′ mark′ *s* repère *m*

bend [bɛnd] *s* (*curvature*) courbure *f*; (*of river, tube, road*) coude *m*; (*of arm, knee*) pli *m*; **bends** mal *m* des caissons ‖ *v* (*pret & pp* **bent** [bɛnt]) *tr* courber; (*the elbow*) a person to one's will) plier; (*the knee*) fléchir ‖ *intr* courber; plier; **do not bend** (label) ne pas plier; **to bend down** se courber

bender [ˈbɛndər] *s*—**to go on a bender** (slang) faire la bombe

beneath [bɪˈniθ] *adv* dessous, au-dessous, en bas ‖ *prep* sous, au-dessous de

benediction [ˌbɛnɪˈdɪkʃən] *s* bénédiction *f*

benefactor [ˈbɛnɪˌfæktər] *s* bienfaiteur *m*

beneficence [bɪˈnɛfɪsəns] *s* bienfaisance *f*

beneficent [bɪˈnɛfɪsənt] *adj* bienfaisant

beneficial [ˌbɛnɪˈfɪʃəl] *adj* profitable, avantageux; (*remedy*) salutaire

beneficiar·y [ˌbɛnɪˈfɪʃɪˌɛri] *s* (*pl* -**ies**) bénéficiaire *mf*, ayant droit *m*

benefit [ˈbɛnɪfɪt] *s* profit *m*; (theat) bénéfice *m*; **benefits** bienfaits *mpl*, avantages *mpl*; **for the benefit of** au profit de ‖ *tr* profiter à ‖ *intr* se trouver bien, gagner

ben′efit soci′ety *s* société *f* de prévoyance

benevolent [bɪˈnɛvələnt] *adj* bienveillant, bienfaisant, bénévole

benign [bɪˈnaɪn] *adj* bénin

bent [bɛnt] *adj* courbé, plié; (*person's back*) voûté; (*determined*) résolu; **bent over** (*shoulders*) voûté; (*figure, person*) courbé; **to be bent on** être acharné à ‖ *s* penchant *m*; **to have a bent for** avoir du goût pour

benzene [bɛnˈzin] *s* (chem) benzène *m*

benzine [bɛnˈzin] *s* benzine *f*

bequeath [bɪˈkwið] *tr* léguer

bequest [bɪˈkwɛst] *s* legs *m*

berate [bɪˈret] *tr* gronder

be·reave [bɪˈriv] *v* (*pret & pp* -**reaved** or -**reft** [ˈrɛft]) *tr* priver; (*to cause sorrow to*) affliger

bereavement [bɪˈrivmənt] *s* (*loss*) privation *f*; (*sorrow*) deuil *m*, affliction *f*

Berlin [bərˈlɪn] *adj* berlinois ‖ *s* Berlin *m*

Berliner [bərˈlɪnər] *s* berlinois *m*

Bermuda [bərˈmjudə] *s* les Bermudes *fpl*

ber·ry [ˈbɛri] *s* (*pl* -**ries**) baie *f*; (*seed*) grain *m*

berserk [bərˈzʌrk] *adv* frénétiquement; **to go berserk** frapper à tort et à travers

berth [bʌrθ] *s* (*sleeping space*) couchette *f*; (*at a dock*) emplacement *m*; (*space to* *move about*) évitage *m*; (*fig*) poste *m*, situation *f* ‖ *tr* (*a ship*) acoster

beryllium [bə'rɪlɪ·əm] *s* béryllium *m*

be·seech [bɪ'sitʃ] *v* (*pret & pp* **-sought** ['sɔt] or **-seeched**) *tr* supplier

be·set [bɪ'sɛt] *v* (*pret & pp* **-set; ger -setting**) *tr* assiéger, assaillir

beside [bɪ'saɪd] *prep* à côté de, auprès de; **to be beside oneself** être hors de soi; **to be beside oneself with** (*e.g., joy*) être transporté de

besides [bɪ'saɪdz] *adv* (*in addition*) en outre, de plus; (*otherwise*) d'ailleurs ‖ *prep* en sus de, en plus de, outre

besiege [bɪ'sidʒ] *tr* assiéger

besmear [bɪ'smɪr] *tr* barbouiller

besmirch [bɪ'smʌrtʃ] *tr* souiller

best [bɛst] *adj super* (le) meilleur §91 ‖ *s* (le) meilleur *m*; **at best** au mieux; **to do one's best** faire de son mieux; **to get the best of it** avoir le dessus; **to make the best of** s'accommoder de ‖ *adv super* (le) mieux §91 ‖ *tr* l'emporter sur

best′ girl′ *s* (coll) petite amie *f*, atitrée *f*

bestial ['bɛstjəl] *adj* bestial, brutal

best′ man′ *s* garçon *m* d'honneur

bestow [bɪ'sto] *tr* accorder, conférer

bestowal bɪ'sto·əl] *s* don *m*, dispensation *f*

best′ sel′ler *s* livre *m* à succès, succès *m* de librairie, champion *m*

bet [bɛt] *s* pari *m*, gageure *f*; **make your bets!** faites vos jeux! ‖ *v* (*pret & pp* **bet** or **betted**; *ger* **betting**) *tr & intr* parier; **you bet!** (slang) je vous crois!, tu parles!

be·take [bɪ'tek] *v* (*pret* **-took**; *pp* **-taken**) *tr*—**to betake oneself** se rendre

betray [bɪ'tre] *tr* trahir

betrayal [bɪ'tre·əl] *s* trahison *f*

betrayer [bɪ'tre·ər] *s* traître *m*

betrothal [bɪ'troðəl] *s* fiançailles *fpl*

better ['bɛtər] *adj comp* meilleur §91; **better than** meilleur que ‖ *adv comp* mieux §91; **better than** mieux que; (*followed by numeral*) plus de; **it is better to** il vaut mieux de; **so much the better** tant mieux; **to be better** (*in better health*) aller mieux; **to be better to** valoir mieux; **to get better** s'améliorer; **to get the better of** l'emporter sur; **to think better** se raviser ‖ *tr* améliorer ‖ *intr* s'améliorer

bet′ter half′ *s* (coll) chère moitié *f*

bet′ting odds′ *spl* cote *f* (des paris)

bettor ['bɛtər] *s* parieur *m*, gageur *m*

between [bɪ'twin] *adv* au milieu, dans l'intervalle ‖ *prep* entre; **between friends** dans l'intimité

between′-decks′ *s* (naut) entrepont *m*

bev·el ['bɛvəl] *adj* biseauté, taillé en biseau ‖ *s* (*instrument*) équerre *f*; (*sloping part*) biseau *m* ‖ *v* (*pret & pp* **-eled** or **-elled**; *ger* **-eling** or **-elling**) *tr* biseauter, chanfreiner, équerrer

beverage ['bɛvərɪdʒ] *s* boisson *f*

bev·y ['bɛvi] *s* (*pl* **-ies**) bande *f*

bewail [bɪ'wel] *tr* lamenter, pleurer

beware [bɪ'wɛr] *tr* se bien garder de ‖ *intr* prendre garde; **to beware of** prendre garde à ‖ *interj* gare!, prenez garde!

bewilder [bɪ'wɪldər] *tr* confondre, ahurir

bewilderment [bɪ'wɪldərmənt] *s* confusion *f*, ahurissement *m*

bewitch [bɪ'wɪtʃ] *tr* ensorceler

bewitching [bɪ'wɪtʃɪŋ] *adj* enchanteur

beyond [bɪ'jɑnd] *s*—**the beyond** l'au-delà *m* ‖ *adv* au-delà ‖ *prep* au-delà de; **beyond a doubt** hors de doute; **it's beyond me** (coll) je n'y comprends rien; **to go beyond** dépasser

biannual [baɪ'ænju·əl] *adj* semi-annuel

bias ['baɪ·əs] *adj* biais *m*; (*fig*) prévention *f*, préjugé *m* ‖ *tr* prédisposer, prévenir, rendre partial

bib [bɪb] *s* bavette *f*

Bible ['baɪbəl] *s* Bible *f*

Biblical ['bɪblɪkəl] *adj* biblique

bibliographer [,bɪblɪ'ɑgrəfər] *s* bibliographe *m*

bibliogra·phy [,bɪblɪ'ɑgrəfi] *s* (*pl* **-phies**) bibliographie *f*

biceps ['baɪsɛps] *s* biceps *m*

bicker ['bɪkər] *intr* se quereller, se chamailler

bickering ['bɪkərɪŋ] *s* bisbille *f*

bicuspid [baɪ'kʌspɪd] *s* prémolaire *f*

bicycle ['baɪsɪkəl] *s* bicyclette *f*, vélo *m* ‖ *intr* faire de la bicyclette, aller à bicyclette

bi′cycle path′ *s* piste *f* cyclable

bi′cycle pump′ *s* pompe *f* à vélo

bicyclist ['baɪsɪklɪst] *s* cycliste *mf*

bid [bɪd] *s* (*offer*) enchère *f*, offre *f*, mise *f*; (*e.g., to build a school*) soumission *f*; (cards) demande *f* ‖ *v* (*pret* **bade** [bæd] or **bid**; *ger* **bidden** ['bɪdən]) *tr* inviter; (*to order*) commander; (cards) demander; **to bid ten thousand on** mettre une enchère de dix mille sur ‖ *intr*—**to bid on** mettre une enchère sur

bidder ['bɪdər] *s* enchérisseur *m*, offrant *m*; (*person who submits an estimate*) soumissionnaire *mf*

bidding ['bɪdɪŋ] *s* enchères *fpl*; **at s.o.'s bidding** aux ordres de qn

bide [baɪd] *tr*—**to bide one's time** attendre l'heure or le bon moment

biennial [baɪ'ɛnɪ·əl] *adj* biennal

bier [bɪr] *s* (*frame or stand*) catafalque *m*; (*coffin*) cercueil *m*

biff [bɪf] *s* (slang) gnon *m*, beigne *f* ‖ *tr* (slang) gifler, cogner

bifocal [baɪ'fokəl] *adj* bifocal ‖ **bifocals** *spl* lunettes *fpl* bifocales

big [bɪg] *adj* (*comp* **bigger**; *super* **biggest**) gros, grand; (*man*) de grande taille ‖ *adv*—**to grow big** grossir, grandir; **to talk big** (slang) se vanter

bigamist ['bɪgəmɪst] *s* bigame *mf*

bigamous ['bɪgəməs] *adj* bigame

bigamy ['bɪgəmi] *s* bigamie *f*

big′boned′ *adj* ossu, à gros os

big′ broth′er *s* grand frère *m*

big′ busi′ness *s* (pej) les grosses affaires *fpl*

Big′ Dip′per s Grand Chariot m
big′ game′ s fauves mpl, gros gibier m
big′-heart′ed adj généreux, cordial
big′ mouth′ s (slang) gueulard m
bigot [′bɪgət] s bigot m
bigoted [′bɪgətɪd] adj bigot
bigot·ry [′bɪgətri] s (pl -ries) bigoterie f
big′ shot′ s (slang) grand manitou m, gros bonnet m, grand caïd m, grosse légume f
big′ sis′ter s grande sœur f
big′ splash′ s (slang) sensation f à tout casser
big′ stiff′ s (slang) personnage m guindé
big′ talk′ s (slang) vantardise f
big′ toe′ s orteil m, gros orteil
big′ top′ s (circus tent) chapiteau m
big′ wheel′ s (slang) gros bonnet m, grand manitou m, grosse légume f
big′wig′ s (coll) gros bonnet m, grand manitou m, grosse légume f
bike [baɪk] s (coll) bécane f, vélo m
bikini [bɪ′kini] s slip m minimum
bile [baɪl] s bile f
bilge [bɪldʒ] s sentine f, cale f
bilge′ wa′ter s eau f de cale
bilingual [baɪ′lɪŋgwəl] adj bilingue
bilious [′bɪljəs] adj bilieux
bilk [bɪlk] s tromperie f, escroquerie f ‖ tr tromper, escroquer
bill [bɪl] s (invoice) facture f, mémoire m; (in a hotel) note f; (in a restaurant) addition f; (currency) billet m; (of a bird) bec m; (posted) affiche f, placard m, écriteau m; (in a legislature) projet m de loi; **post no bills** (public sign) défense d'afficher; **to head the bill** (theat) avoir la vedette ‖ tr facturer
bill′board′ s tableau m d'affichage, panneau m d'affichage
billet [′bɪlɪt] s (order) billet m de logement; (of metal or wood) billette f ‖ tr loger, cantonner
bill′fold′ s portefeuille m
bil′liard ball′ s bille f
billiards [′bɪljərdz] s & spl billard m
bil′liard ta′ble s billard m
billion [′bɪljən] s (U.S.A.) milliard m; (Brit) billion m
billionaire [,bɪljən′ɛr] s milliardaire mf
bill′ of exchange′ s lettre f de change, traite f
bill′ of fare′ s carte f du jour
bill′ of health′ s patente f de santé
bill′ of lad′ing s connaissement m
bill′ of rights′ s déclaration f des droits de l'homme
bill′ of sale′ s acte m de vente
billow [′bɪlo] s flot m, grosse vague f ‖ intr ondoyer
billowy [′bɪlo·i] adj onduleux, ondoyant
bill′post′er s colleur m d'affiches, afficheur m
bil·ly [′bɪli] s (pl -lies) bâton m
bil′ly goat′ s (coll) bouc m
bimonthly [baɪ′mʌnθli] adj bimestriel
bin [bɪn] s huche f, coffre m
binary [′baɪnəri] adj binaire

binaural [baɪ′nɔrəl] adj stéréophonique; à deux oreilles
bind [baɪnd] v (pret & pp **bound** [baʊnd] tr (to fasten) lier, attacher; (a book) relier; (s.o. to an agreement) obliger; **to bind with** (to encircle) entourer de ‖ intr (to be obligatory) être obligatoire; (to cohere) adhérer
binder [′baɪndər] s (person) lieur m; (of books) relieur m; (agreement) conventions fpl; (mach) lieuse f
binder·y [′baɪndəri] s (pl -ies) atelier m de reliure
binding [′baɪndɪŋ] adj obligatoire; (med) astringent; **binding on all concerned** solidaire ‖ s reliure f
bind′ing post′ s (elec) borne f
binge [bɪndʒ] s (coll) noce f, bombe f
bingo [′bɪŋgo] s loto m
binocular [bɪ′nɑkjələr] adj & s binoculaire m; **binoculars** jumelles fpl
binomial [baɪ′nomɪ·əl] adj & s binôme m
biochemistry [,baɪ·o′kɛmɪstri] s biochimie f
biodegradable [′baɪ·odɪ′gredəbəl] adj biodégradable
biographer [baɪ′ɑgrəfər] s biographe mf
biographic(al) [,baɪ·ə′græfɪk(əl)] adj biographique
biogra·phy [baɪ′ɑgrəfi] s (pl -phies) biographie f
biologist [baɪ′ɑlədʒɪst] s biologiste mf
biology [baɪ′ɑlədʒi] s biologie f
biophysics [,baɪ·ə′fɪzɪks] s biophysique f
biop·sy [′baɪ·ɑpsi] s (pl -sies) biopsie f
bipartisan [baɪ′pɑrtɪzən] adj bipartite
bipartite [baɪ′pɑrtaɪt] adj biparti
biped [′baɪpɛd] adj & s bipède m
biplane [′baɪ,plen] s biplan m
birch [bʌrtʃ] s bouleau m; (for whipping) verges fpl ‖ tr battre à coups de verges
birch′ rod′ s verges fpl
bird [bʌrd] s oiseau m; (slang) type m, individu m; **a bird in the hand is worth two in the bush** un ''tiens'' vaut mieux que deux ''tu l'auras''; **to give s.o. the bird** (slang) envoyer qn promener; **to kill two birds with one stone** faire d'une pierre deux coups
bird′ bath′ s bain m pour oiseaux
bird′cage′ s cage f d'oiseau
bird′ call′ s appeau m, pipeau m
bird′ dog′ s chien m pour la plume
bird′ fan′cier s oiselier m
birdie [′bʌrdi] s oiselet m, oisillon m
bird′lime′ s glu f
bird′ of pas′sage s oiseau m de passage
bird′ of prey′ s oiseau m de proie
bird′seed′ s alpiste m, chènevis m
bird's′-eye′ s (pattern) œil-de-perdrix m
bird's′-eye view′ s vue f à vol d'oiseau, tour m d'horizon, vue d'ensemble
biretta [bɪ′rɛtə] s barrette f
birth [bʌrθ] s naissance f; **by birth** de naissance; **to give birth to** donner naissance à

birth′ certif′icate *s* acte *m* de naissance, extrait *m* de naissance, bulletin *m* de naissance

birth′ control′ *s* contrôle *m* des naissances, natalité *f* dirigée

birth′day′ *s* anniversaire *m*; **happy birth-day!** heureux anniversaire!

birth′day cake′ *s* gâteau *m* d'anniversaire

birth′day can′dles *spl* bougies *fpl* de gâteaux d'anniversaire

birth′day pres′ent *s* cadeau *m* d'anniversaire

birth′mark′ *s* tache *f*, envie *f*

birth′place′ *s* lieu *m* de naissance

birth′ rate′ *s* natalité *f*, taux *m* de natalité

birth′right′ *s* droit *m* de naissance

biscuit [′bɪskɪt] *s* petit pain *m*, crêpe *f* au beurre, gâteau *m* feuilleté

bisect [baɪˈsɛkt] *tr* couper en deux, diviser en deux

bisexual [baɪˈsɛkʃ‿ʊ‿əl] *adj* bissexuel

bishop [′bɪʃəp] *s* évêque *m*; (chess) fou *m*

bishopric [′bɪʃəprɪk] *f* évêché *m*

bison [′baɪzən] *s* bison *m*

bisulfate [baɪˈsʌlfet] *s* bisulfate *m*

bisulfite [baɪˈsʌlfaɪt] *s* bisulfite *m*

bit [bɪt] *s* (*morsel*) morceau *m*, bout *m*, brin *m*; (*of a bridle*) mors *m*; (*of a drill*) mèche *f*; (comp) binon *m*, bit *m*; (*of a drill*) **bit by bit** petit à petit

bitch [bɪtʃ] *s* (*dog*) chienne *f*; (*fox*) renarde *f*; (*wolf*) louve *f*; (vulg) vache *f*, salope *f*, ordure *f*

bite [baɪt] *s* (*of food*) bouchée *f*; (*by an animal*) morsure *f*; (*by an insect*) piqûre *f*; (*by a fish on a hook*) touche *f* ‖ *v* (*pret* **bit** [bɪt]; *pp* **bit** *or* **bitten** [′bɪtən]) *tr* mordre; (*said of an insect or snake*) piquer; **to bite off** mordre d'un coup de dent; **to feel like biting off one's tongue because of it** s'en mordre la langue

biting [′baɪtɪŋ] *adj* mordant; (*cold*) piquant; (*wind*) coupant

bit′ play′er *s* figurant *m*

bitter [′bɪtər] *adj* amer; (*cold*) âpre noir, (*flight*) acharné; (*style*) mordant ‖ **bitters** *spl* bitter *m*

bit′ter end′ *s*—**to the bitter end** jusqu'au bout

bit′ter-end′er *s* (coll) intransigeant *m*, jusqu'au-boutiste *mf*

bitterness [′bɪtərnɪs] *s* amertume *f*; (*of winter*) âpreté *f*; (fig) aigreur *f*

bit′ter-sweet′ *adj* aigre-doux ‖ *s* douceamère *f*

bitumen [bɪˈt(j)umən] *s* bitume *m*

bivou·ac [′bɪvu‚æk] *s* bivouac *m*, cantonnement *m* ‖ *v* (*pret & pp* **-acked**; *ger* **-acking**) *intr* bivouaquer

biweekly [baɪˈwikli] *adj* bimensuel ‖ *adv* bimensuellement

biyearly [baɪˈjɪrli] *adj* semestriel ‖ *adv* semestriellement

bizarre [bɪˈzɑr] *adj* bizarre

blab [blæb] *v* (*pret & pp* **blabbed**; *ger* **blabbing**) *tr* ébruiter ‖ *intr* jaser

blabber [′blæbər] *intr* jaser

blab′ber·mouth′ *s* (slang) jaseur *m*

black [blæk] *adj & s* noir *m*; **black is beautiful** nous sommes fiers d'être noirs ‖ *tr* noircir; **to black out** faire le black-out dans

black′-and-blue′ *adj* couvert de bleus

black′-and-white′ *adj* en blanc et noir

black′ball′ *tr* blackbouler

black′ber′ry *s* (*pl* **-ries**) mûre *f*, mûre de ronce

black′bird′ *s* (*Turdus merula*) merle *m*

black′board′ *s* tableau *m* noir

black′board eras′er *s* éponge *f*, chiffon *m*

black′ bod′y *s* (phys) corps *m* noir

black′ box′ *s* (aer) enregistreur *m* d'accident

black′ cur′rant *s* cassis *m*

black′ damp′ *s* mofette *f*

blacken [′blækən] *tr* noircir

black′ eye′ *s* œil *m* poché; (*shiner*) coquart *m*; **to give s.o. a black eye** pocher l'œil à qn; (fig) ruiner la réputation de qn

black′-eyed Su′san [′suzən] *s* marguerite *f* américaine

blackguard [′blægɑrd] *s* vaurien *m*, salaud *m*

black′head′ *s* comédon *m*, tanne *f*

black′-headed gull′ *s* mouette *f* rieuse

black′ hole′ *s* (astr) trou *m* noir

blacking [′blækɪŋ] *s* cirage *m* noir

blackish [′blækɪʃ] *adj* noirâtre

black′jack′ *s* assommoir *m*; (cards) vingt-et-un *m* ‖ *tr* assommer

black′ lead′ [lɛd] *s* mine *f* de plomb

black′ let′ter *s* caractère *m* gothique

black′ list′ *s* liste *f* noire

black′-list′ *tr* mettre à l'index, mettre en quarantaine

black′ lo′cust *s* (bot) faux acacia *m*

black′ mag′ic *s* magie *f* noire

black′mail′ *s* chantage *m* ‖ *tr* faire chanter ‖ *intr* faire du chantage

blackmailer [′blæk‚melər] *s* maître *m* chanteur

black′ mark′ *s* (*of censure*) tache *f*

black′ mar′ket *s* marché *m* noir

black′ marketeer′ [‚mɑrkɪˈtir] *s* trafiquant *m* du marché noir

black′out′ *s* (*accidental*) panne *f* d'électricité; (*planned for protection*) feux *mpl* masqués, black-out *m*; (*of aviator*) cécité *f* temporaire

black′ pep′per *s* poivre *m* noir

black′ sheep′ *s* (fig) brebis *f* galeuse

black′smith′ *s* forgeron *m*, maréchal-ferrant *m*

bladder [′blædər] *s* vessie *f*

bladderwort [′blædər‚wʌrt] *s* utriculaire *f*

blade [bled] *s* (*of knife, tool, weapon, razor*) lame *f*; (*of scissors*) branche *f*; (*of grass*) brin *m*; (*of propeller*) aile *f*, pale *f*; (*of oar; of tongue*) plat *m*; (*of guillotine*) couperet *m*; (*of windshield wiper*) caoutchouc *m*; (*young man*) gaillard *m*; (mach) ailette *f*, palette *f*, aube *f*

blah [blɑ] *s* (slang) sornettes *fpl*, fadaises *fpl*, bêtises *fpl* ‖ *interj* patati-patata!

blah-blah ['blɑ'blɑ] s baratin m

blamable ['bleməbəl] adj blâmable, coupable

blame [blem] s (censure) blâme m, reproches mpl; (responsibility) faute f ‖ tr blâmer; reprocher; s'en prendre à

blameless ['blemlɪs] adj sans reproche

blame'wor'thy adj blâmable

blanch [blæntʃ] tr & intr blanchir

bland [blænd] adj doux, suave; (with dissimulation) narquois

blandish ['blændɪʃ] tr flatter, cajoler

blandishment ['blændɪʃmənt] s flatterie

blank [blæŋk] adj blanc; (check; form) en blanc; (mind) confondu, déconcerté ‖ s (void) blanc m; (gap) trou m, vide m, lacune f; (metal mold) flan m; (form to be filled out) fiche f, formule f, feuille f; (space to be filled in) tiret m ‖ tr—**to blank out** effacer ‖ intr—**to blank out** (coll) s'évanouir

blank' check' s chèque m en blanc; (fig) chèque en blanc

blanket ['blæŋkɪt] adj général ‖ s couverture f ‖ tr envelopper

blank' verse' s vers mpl blancs

blare [blɛr] s bruit m strident; (of trumpet) sonnerie f ‖ tr faire retentir; (like a trumpet) sonner ‖ intr retentir

blarney ['blɑrni] s (coll) flagornerie f ‖ tr (coll) flagorner

blaspheme [blæs'fim] tr & intr blasphémer

blasphemous ['blæsfɪməs] adj blasphématoire, blasphémateur

blasphe·my ['blæsfɪmi] s (pl -mies) blasphème m

blast [blæst] s (gust) rafale f, souffle m; (of bomb) explosion f; (of dynamite) charge f; (of whistle) coup m; (of trumpet) sonnerie f; **at full blast** à toute allure ‖ tr (to blow up) faire sauter; (hopes) ruiner; (a plant) flétrir ‖ intr (said of plant) se faner; **to blast off** (said of rocket) se mettre à feu

blast' fur'nace s haut fourneau m

blasting ['blæstɪŋ] s abattage m à la poudre; (of hopes) anéantissement m; (coll) abattage m, verte semonce f

blast'ing cap' s capsule f fulminante

blast'off' s mise f à feu, lancement m

blatant ['bletənt] adj criard; (injustice) criant

blaze [blez] s (fire) flamme f, flambée f; (e.g., blazing house) incendie m; **to run like blazes** (slang) courir furieusement ‖ tr—**to blaze the trail** frayer la piste ‖ intr flamboyer, s'embraser

blazing ['blezɪŋ] adj (building, etc.) embrasé, en feu; (sun) flamboyant

blazon ['blezən] s (heral) blason m ‖ tr célébrer; exalter; (heral) blasonner

bleach [blitʃ] s (for washing clothes) décolorant m, eau f de Javel; (for hair) eau oxygénée f ‖ tr blanchir, décolorer

bleachers ['blitʃərz] spl grandins mpl, tribune f

bleak [blik] adj froid, morne, nu

blear-eyed ['blɪr'aɪd] adj (teary) chassieux, larmoyant; (dull) d'un esprit épais

blear·y ['blɪri] adj (comp -ier; super -iest) (eyes) chassieux; (prospect) voilé, incertain

bleat [blit] s bêlement m ‖ intr bêler, bégueter

bleed [blid] v (pret & pp bled [blɛd]) tr & intr saigner; **to bleed white** saigner à blanc

bleeding ['blidɪŋ] adj saignant ‖ s saignement m; (bloodletting) saignée f

blemish ['blɛmɪʃ] s défaut m, tache f ‖ tr défigurer; (a reputation) tacher

blench [blɛntʃ] intr (to turn pale) pâlir; (to draw back) broncher

blend [blɛnd] s mélange m ‖ v (pret & pp blended or blent [blɛnt]) tr mêler, mélanger; fondre, marier ‖ intr se fondre, se marier

bless [blɛs] tr bénir

blessed ['blɛsɪd] adj (holy) béni, saint; (happy) bienheureux

blessing ['blɛsɪŋ] s bénédiction f; (at meals) bénédicité m

blight [blaɪt] s (of cereals, plants) rouille f, nielle f; (of peaches) cloque f; (of potatoes; of vines) brunissure f; (fig) flétrissure f ‖ tr rouiller, nieller; (hopes, aspirations) flétrir, frustrer

blimp [blɪmp] s vedette f (aérienne)

blind [blaɪnd] adj aveugle; **blind by birth** aveugle-né; **blind in one eye** borgne; **blind person** aveugle m ‖ s store m; (for hunting) guet-apens m; (fig) feinte f; (cards) talon m ‖ tr aveugler; (by dazzling) éblouir

blind' al'ley s cul-de-sac m, impasse f

blinder ['blaɪndər] s œillère f

blind' flight' s vol m à l'aveuglette

blind' fly'ing s (aer) pilotage m sans visibilité

blind'fold' adj les yeux bandés ‖ s bandeau m ‖ tr bander les yeux de

blindly ['blaɪndli] adv aveuglément

blind' man' s aveugle m

blind'man's bluff' s colin-maillard m

blindness ['blaɪndnɪs] s cécité f; (fig) aveuglement m

blind' spot' s côté m faible

blink [blɪŋk] s clignotement m ‖ tr faire clignoter ‖ intr clignoter

blinker ['blɪŋkər] s (signal) feu m clignotant; (for horses) œillère f; (for signals) projecteur m clignotant

blink'er light' s feu m à éclipses

blinking ['blɪŋkɪŋ] s clignement m

blip [blɪp] s spot m, bip m

bliss [blɪs] s félicité f, béatitude f

blissful ['blɪsfəl] adj bienheureux

blister ['blɪstər] s ampoule f, bulle f ‖ tr couvrir d'ampoules; (paint) boursoufler ‖ intr se couvrir d'ampoules; se boursoufler

blithe [blaɪθ] adj gai, joyeux

blitzkrieg ['blɪts,krig] s guerre f éclair

blizzard 'blɪzərd] s tempête f de neige

bloat [blot] *tr* boursoufler, enfler ‖ *intr* se boursoufler, enfler

blob [blɑb] *s* motte *f*; (*of color*) tache *f*; (*of ink*) pâté *m*

block [blɑk] *s* (*stone*) bloc *m*; (*toy*) cube *m*; (*of shares*) tranche *f*; (*of houses*) pâté *m*, îlot *m* ‖ *tr* (*a project*) contrecarrer; (*a wall*) condamner, murer; **to block up** boucher, bloquer

blockade [blɑˈked] *s* blocus *m*; **to run the blockade** forcer le blocus ‖ *tr* bloquer

block′ and tac′kle *s* palan *m*

block′head′ *s* sot *m*, niais *m*

blond [blɑnd] *adj* & *s* blond *m*

blonde [blɑnd] *adj* & *s* blonde *f*

blood [blʌd] *s* sang *m*; **in cold blood** de sang-froid; **to put new blood into** infuser un sang nouveau à

blood′ and guts′ *spl* sang *m* et tripes

blood′bank′ *s* banque *f* du sang

blood′ count′ *s* numération *f* globulaire

blood′curd′ling *adj* horripilant

blood′ don′or *s* donneur *m* de sang

blood′hound′ *s* limier *m*

bloodless [ˈblʌdlɪs] *adj* (*without blood*) exsangue; (*revolution*) sans effusion de sang

bloodletting [ˈblʌdˌlɛtɪŋ] *s* saignée *f*; (fig) effusion *f* de sang

blood′ plas′ma *s* plasma *m* sanguin

blood′ poi′soning *s* septicémie *f*, empoisonnement *m* du sang

blood′ pres′sure *s* tension *f* artérielle

blood′ sam′ple *s* échantillon *m* de sang

blood′shed′ *s* effusion *f* de sang

blood′shot′ *adj* injecté, éraillé

blood′ spec′imen *s* prise *f* de sang

blood′stained′ *adj* taché de sang

blood′stream′ *s* circulation *f* du sang

blood′suck′er *s* sangsue *f*

blood′ test′ *s* examen *m* du sang, analyse *f* de sang

blood′thirst′y *adj* sanguinaire

blood′ transfu′sion *s* transfusion *f* de sang, transfusion sanguine

blood′ type′ *s* groupe *m* de sang

blood′ ves′sel *s* vaisseau *m* sanguin

blood·y [ˈblʌdi] *adj* (*comp* -**ier**; *super* -**iest**) sanglant

bloom [blum] *s* fleur *f*; (*of a fruit*) velouté *m*, duvet *m*; **in bloom** en fleur; **in full bloom** en pleine floraison ‖ *intr* fleurir

bloomers [ˈblumərz] *spl* culotte *f* de femme

blooper [ˈblupər] *s* (coll) gaffe *f*, bévue *f*; (rad) poste *m* brouilleur

blossom [ˈblɑsəm] *s* fleur *f*; **in blossom** en fleur ‖ *intr* fleurir; **to blossom out** s'épanouir

blot [blɑt] *s* (& fig) tache *f*, pâté *m* ‖ *v* (*pret* & *pp* **blotted**; *ger* **blotting**) *tr* tacher, barbouiller; (*ink*) sécher; **to blot out** rayer ‖ *intr* (*said of ink*) boire

blotch [blɑtʃ] *s* tache *f* ‖ *tr* couvrir de taches; (*the skin*) marbrer

blotch·y [ˈblɑtʃi] *adj* (*comp* -**ier**; *super* -**iest**) brouillé, tacheté

blotter [ˈblɑtər] *s* buvard *m*

blot′ting pa′per *s* papier *m* buvard

blouse [blaʊs] *s* (*women's wear*) corsage *m*; (*children's*) chemise *f*; (mil) vareuse *f*

blow [blo] *s* coup *m*; **to come to blows** en venir aux coups ‖ *v* (*pret* **blew** [blu]; *pp* **blown**) *tr* souffler; **to blow one's nose** se moucher; **to blow out** (*a candle*) éteindre; **to blow up** faire sauter; (*a photograph*) agrandir; (*a balloon*) gonfler ‖ *intr* souffler; (slang) décamper en vitesse; **to blow out** (*said of a tire*) éclater; **to blow over** passer; **to blow up** éclater; (slang) se mettre en colère

blower [ˈblo·ər] *s* soufflerie *f*; (mach) ventilateur *m*

blow′fly′ *s* (*pl* -**flies**) mouche *f* à viande

blow′gun′ *s* sarbacane *f*

blow′hard′ *s* (slang) hâbleur *m*

blow′hole′ *s* (*of tunnel*) ventilateur *m*; (*of whale*) évent *m*

blowing [ˈblo·ɪŋ] *s* soufflage *m*; (*of the wind*) soufflement *m*

blow′out′ *s* (*of a tire*) éclatement *m*; (*of an oil well*) éruption *f*; (*orgy*) (slang) gueuleton *m*

blow′pipe′ *s* chalumeau *m*

blow′torch′ *s* lampe *f* à souder

blubber [ˈblʌbər] *s* graisse *f* de baleine ‖ *tr* bredouiller ‖ *intr* pleurer comme un veau

bludgeon [ˈblʌdʒən] *s* matraque *f* ‖ *tr* assommer

blue [blu] *adj* bleu; **to be blue** (coll) broyer du noir, avoir le cafard ‖ *s* bleu *m*; **from out of the blue** du ciel, à l'improviste; **the blues** le cafard, l'humeur *f* noire ‖ *tr* bleuir

blue′bell′ *s* jacinthe *f* des bois

blue′ber′ry *s* (*pl* -**ries**) myrtille *f*

blue′bird′ *s* oiseau *m* bleu

blue′-black′ *adj* noir tirant sur le bleu

blue′ blood′ *s* sang *m* royal, sang noble

blue′bot′tle *s* bluet *m*, barbeau *m*

blue′cheese′ *s* roquefort *m* américain

blue′ chip′ *s* valeur-vedette *f*, valeur *f* de tout repos, valeur de père de famille

blue′-gray′ *adj* gris bleuté, gris-bleu

blue′jay′ *s* geai *m* bleu

blue′ jeans′ *spl* blue-jean *m*

blue′ moon′ *s*—**once in a blue moon** tous les trente-six du mois

blue′nose′ *s* puritain *m*, collet *m* monté

blue′-pen′cil *v* (*pret* & *pp* -**ciled** or -**cilled**; *ger* -**ciling** or -**cilling**) *tr* (*to make corrections*) corriger au crayon bleu; (*to censure*) couper, censurer

blue′print′ *s* dessin *m* négatif, photocalque *m*; (fig) plan *m*, schéma *m* ‖ *tr* planifier

blue′stock′ing *s* (coll) bas-bleu *m*

bluff [blʌf] *adj* (*steep*) abrupt; (*cliff*) accore, escarpé; (*person*) brusque ‖ *s* (*cliff*) falaise *f*, cap *m* à pic; (*deception*) bluff *m*; **to call s.o.'s bluff** relever un défi ‖ *tr* & *intr* bluffer

bluffer [ˈblʌfər] *s* bluffeur *m*

bluish [ˈblu·ɪʃ] *adj* bleuté, bleuâtre

blunder [ˈblʌndər] *s* bévue *f*, gaffe *f* ‖ *intr* faire une bévue, gaffer; **to blunder into**

se heurter contre; **to blunder upon** découvrir par hasard; tomber sur

blunt [blʌnt] *adj* (*blade*) émoussé; (*point*) épointé; (*person*) brusque ‖ *tr* émousser; épointer

bluntly [ˈblʌntli] *adv* (*rudely*) brusquement, sans façons; (*frankly*) carrément, sans ménagements

blur [blʌr] *s* barbouillage *m* ‖ *v* (*pret & pp* **blurred**; *ger* **blurring**) *tr* embrouiller, voiler

blurb [blʌrb] *s* (*ad*) baratin *m* publicitaire; (*on book cover*) publicité *f* au protège-livre

blurt [blʌrt] *tr*—**to blurt out** laisser échapper, lâcher

blush [blʌʃ] *s* rougeur *f*; **at first blush** au premier abord ‖ *intr* rougir

bluster [ˈblʌstər] *s* rodomontade *f*, fanfaronnade *f* ‖ *intr* (*of wind*) souffler en rafales; (*of person*) faire du fracas

blustery [ˈblʌstəri] *adj* (*wind*) orageux; (*person*) bravache, fanfaron

boar [bor] *s* (*male swine*) verrat *m*; (*wild hog*) sanglier *m*

board [bord] *s* (*piece of wood*) planche *f*; (*e.g., of directors*) conseil *m*, commission *f*; (*meals*) le couvert; **above board** cartes sur table; **on board** à bord ‖ *tr* (*a ship*) monter à bord de; (*paying guests*) nourrir ‖ *intr* monter à bord; (*said of paying guest*) prendre pension

board' and room' *s* pension *f* et chambre *f*

boarder [ˈbordər] *s* pensionnaire *mf*; (*student*) interne *mf*

board'ing·house' *s* pension *f* (de famille)

board' of direc'tors *s* conseil *m* d'administration, gérance *f*

board' of trade' *s* association *f* des industriels et commerçants

board' of trustees' *s* comité *m* administrateur (*e.g., of a university*)

board'walk' *s* promenade *f* planchéiée au bord de la mer; (*over mud*) caillebotis *m*

boast [bost] *s* vanterie *f* ‖ *intr* se vanter

boastful [ˈbostfəl] *adj* vantard

boasting [ˈbostɪŋ] *s* jactance *f*

boat [bot] *s* bateau *m*; (*small boat*) embarcation *f*; **to miss the boat** (coll) manquer le coche

boat' hook' *s* gaffe *f*

boat'house' *s* hangar *m* à bateaux or à canots

boating [ˈbotɪŋ] *s* canotage *m*; **to go boating** faire du canotage

boat'load' *s* batelée *f*

boat'man *s* (*pl* **-men**) batelier *m*

boat' race' *s* régate *f*

boatswain [ˈbosən], [ˈbot,swen] *s* maître *m* d'équipage

bob [bab] *s* (*hair style*) coiffure *f* courte ‖ *v* (*pret & pp* **bobbed**; *ger* **bobbing**) *intr* s'agiter, danser

bobbin [ˈbabɪn] *s* bobine *f*

bob'by pin' *s* épingle *f* à cheveux

bob'by·socks' *spl* (coll) socquettes *fpl*, chaussettes *fpl* basses

bobbysoxer [ˈbabɪ,saksər] *s* (coll) zazou *m*, jeune lycéenne *f*

bob'sled' *s* bobsleigh *m*

bob'tail' *adj* à queue écartée ‖ *tr* couper court

bode [bod] *tr & intr* présager

bodily [ˈbadɪli] *adj* corporel, physique ‖ *adv* corporellement, en corps

bod·y [ˈbadi] *s* (*pl* **-ies**) corps *m*; (*dead body*) cadavre *m*; (*solidity*) consistance *f*; (*flavor of wine*) sève *f*, générosité *f*; (aer) fuselage *m*; (aut) carrosserie *f*; **to come in a body** venir en corps

bod'y·guard' *s* garde *m* du corps; (*group*) garde *f* du corps

bog [bag] *s* marécage *m*, fondrière *f* ‖ *v* (*pret & pp* **bogged**; *ger* **bogging**) *intr*—**to bog down** s'enliser

bogey·man [ˈbogi,mæn] *s* (*pl* **-men**) croquemitaine *m*

bogus [ˈbogəs] *adj* faux, simulé

Bohemia [boˈhimɪ·ə] *s* (*country*) Bohême *f*, la Bohême; (*of artistic world*) la bohème

Bohemian [boˈhimɪ·ən] *adj* (*of Bohemia*) bohémien; (*unconventional, arty*) bohème, de bohème ‖ *s* (*person living in the country of Bohemia*) Bohémien *m*; (*artist*) bohème *mf*

boil [bɔɪl] *s* (*boiling*) ébullition *f*; (*on the skin*) furoncle *m*, clou *m* ‖ *tr* faire bouillir ‖ *intr* bouillir

boiled' din'ner *s* pot-au-feu *m*

boiled' ham' *s* jambon *m* d'York

boiled' pota'toes *spl* pommes *fpl* bouillies, pommes vapeur

boiler [ˈbɔɪlər] *s* chaudière *f*

boi'ler·mak'er *s* chaudronnier *m*

boiling [ˈbɔɪlɪŋ] *adj* bouillonnant ‖ *s* ébullition *f*, bouillonnement *m*

boil'ing point' *s* point *m* d'ébullition

boisterous [ˈbɔɪstərəs] *adj* bruyant

bold [bold] *adj* hardi, osé, intrépide; (*forward*) effronté, impudent; (*cliff*) abrupt

bold'face' *s* (typ) caractères *mpl* gras

bold'-faced' *adj* (*forward*) effronté

boldness [ˈboldnɪs] *s* hardiesse *f*; effronterie *f*

boll' wee'vil [bol] *s* anthonome *m* du cotonnier, charançon *m* du coton

bologna [bəˈlonə], [bəˈlonjə] *s* mortadelle *f*, gros saucisson *m*

bolster [ˈbolstər] *s* traversin *m* ‖ *tr* soutenir

bolt [bolt] *s* (*of door or window*) verrou *m*; (*of lock*) pêne *m*; (*with a thread at one end*) boulon *m*; (*of cloth*) rouleau *m* ‖ *tr* verrouiller; (*food*) gober; (*e.g., a political party*) lâcher ‖ *intr* décamper

bomb [bam] *s* bombe *f* ‖ *tr* bombarder

bombard [bamˈbard] *tr* bombarder

bombardier [,bambərˈdɪr] *s* bombardier *m*

bombardment [bamˈbardmənt] *s* bombardement *m*

bombast [ˈbambæst] *s* boursouflure *f*

bombastic [bamˈbæstɪk] *adj* boursouflé

bomb' bay' *s* (aer) soute *f* à bombes

bomb' cra'ter *s* entonnoir *m*, trou *m* d'obus

bomber [ˈbɑmər] s avion m de bombardement, bombardier m

bombing [ˈbɑmɪŋ] s bombardement m

bomb′proof′ adj à l'épreuve des bombes

bomb′shell′ s obus m; **to fall like a bombshell** tomber comme une bombe

bomb′ shel′ter s abri m à l'épreuve des bombes

bomb′sight′ s viseur m de lancement

bomb′ squad′ s service m de déminage

bona fide [ˈbɑnəˌfaɪdə] adj & adv de bonne foi

bonanza [bəˈnænzə] s aubaine f, filon m

bonbon [ˈbɑnˌbɑn] s bonbon m

bond [bɑnd] s (link) lien m; (com) obligation f; **in bond** en entrepôt ‖ tr (com) entreposer, mettre en entrepôt

bondage [ˈbɑndɪdʒ] s esclavage m

bond′hold′er s obligataire mf

bone [bon] s os m; (of a fish) arête f; **to have a bone to pick** avoir maille à partir ‖ tr (meat or fish) désosser ‖ intr—**to bone up on** (a subject) (slang) potasser, piocher

bone′head′ s (slang) ignorant m

boneless [ˈbonlɪs] adj sans os; sans arêtes

bone′ of conten′tion s pomme f de discorde

boner [ˈbonər] s (coll) bourde f

bonfire [ˈbɑnˌfaɪr] s feu m de joie; (for burning trash) feu m de jardin

bonnet [ˈbɑnɪt] s bonnet m; chapeau m à brides; (fig) chapeau

bonus [ˈbonəs] s boni m, prime f

bon·y [ˈboni] adj (comp -ier; super -iest) osseux; (thin) décharné

boo [bu] s huée f, sifflement m; **not to say boo** ne pas souffler mot ‖ tr & intr huer, siffler

boob [bub] s (coll) emplâtre m

boo·by [ˈbubi] s (pl -bies) (coll) nigaud m

boo′by hatch′ s (slang) asile m d'aliénés; (prison) (slang) violon m

boo′by prize′ s fiche f de consolation

boo′by trap′ s engin m piégé; (fig) attrape-nigaud m, traquenard m

boo′by-trap′ v (pret & pp -trapped; ger -trapping) tr piéger

book [bʊk] s livre m; (of tickets) carnet m; (libretto) livret m; **by the book** d'après le texte, selon les règles; **to make book** (sports) inscrire les paris ‖ tr (a seat or room) retenir, réserver

book′bind′er s relieur m

book′bind′er·y s (pl -ies) atelier m de reliure

book′bind′ing s reliure f

book′case′ s bibliothèque f, étagère f

book′ end′ s serre-livres m, appui-livres m

booking [ˈbʊkɪŋ] s réservation f; (theat) location f

bookish [ˈbʊkɪʃ] adj livresque; (person) studieux

book′keep′er s comptable mf, teneur m de livres

book′keep′ing s comptabilité f

book′ learn′ing s science f livresque

booklet [ˈbʊklɪt] s livret m; (notebook) cahier m; (pamphlet) brochure f

book′lov′er s bibliophile mf

book′mark′ s signet m

bookmobile [ˈbʊkmoˌbil] s bibliobus m

book′plate′ s ex-libris m

book′rack′ s étagère f

book′ review′ s compte m rendu

book′sel′ler s libraire mf

book′shelf′ s (pl -shelves) rayon m, étagère f

books′ in print′ s livres mpl disponibles

book′stand′ s étalage m de livres; (in a station) bibliothèque f

book′store′ s librairie f

book′ val′ue s (com) valeur f comptable

book′worm′ s ciron m; (fig) rat m de bibliothèque

boom [bum] s retentissement m, grondement m; (rapid rise or growth) vague f de prospérité, boom m; (naut) bout-dehors m ‖ intr retentir; (com) prospérer ‖ interj boum!

boomer [ˈbumər] s (electron) boomer m

boomerang [ˈbuməˌræŋ] s boomerang m

boom′ town′ s ville f champignon

boon [bun] s bienfait m, avantage m; (archaic) don m, faveur f

boor [bur] s rustre m, goujat m

boost [bust] s relèvement m; (help) aide f ‖ tr soulever par derrière; (prices) hausser; (to praise) faire la réclame pour

booster [ˈbustər] s (enthusiastic backer) réclamiste mf; (go-getter) homme m d'expédition, lanceur m d'affaires; (aut) suramplificateur m; (elec) survolteur m; (rok) booster m, propulseur m

boost′er rock′et s fusée f de lancement

boost′er rod′ s (nucl) barre f de dopage

boost′er shot′ s piqûre f de rappel

boot [but] s botte f, bottine f; **to boot** en sus; **to lick s.o.'s boots** (coll) lécher les bottes à qn ‖ tr botter

boot′black′ s cireur m de bottes

booth [buθ] s (at fair) baraque f; (e.g., for telephoning) cabine f

boot′leg′ adj (slang) clandestin, de contrebande ‖ v (pret & pp -legged; ger -legging) tr (slang) faire la contrebande de ‖ intr (slang) faire la contrebande

bootlegger [ˈbutˌlɛgər] s (slang) contrebandier m; (slang) contrebandier m d'alcool, bootlegger m

boot′leg′ging s contrebande f

boot′lick′ tr (coll) lécher les bottes à

boo·ty [ˈbuti] s (pl -ties) butin m

booze [buz] s (coll) boisson f alcoolique ‖ intr (coll) s'adonner à la boisson

border [ˈbɔrdər] s (edge) bord m, bordure f; (of field and forest; of a piece of cloth) lisière f; (of a road) marge f; (of a country) frontière f; (edging) galon m, bordé m ‖ tr border; (a handkerchief) lisérer ‖ intr—**to border on** confiner à, toucher à; (a color) tirer sur

bor′der·line′ adj indéterminé ‖ s ligne f de démarcation

bor'der·line case' s cas m limite

bore [bor] s (hole) trou m; (of gun) calibre m; (of cannon) âme f; (of cylinder) alésage m; (nuisance) ennui m; (person) raseur m; **what a bore!** c'est la barbe!, ô rasoir! ‖ tr percer; (a cylinder) aléser; (to annoy) ennuyer

boreal ['borɪ·əl] adj boréal

boredom ['bordəm] s ennui m

boring ['borɪŋ] adj ennuyeux, rasant, rasoir ‖ s perçage m, percement m

born [bɔrn] adj né; **to be born** naître

borrow ['baro], ['bɔro] tr emprunter; **to borrow from** emprunter à

borrower ['baro·ər], ['bɔro·ər] s emprunteur m

bor'rower's card' s bulletin m de prêt

borrowing ['boro·ɪŋ] s emprunt m

borzoi ['bɔrzɔɪ] s lévrier m russe

bosom ['buzəm] s sein m, poitrine f; (of the Church) giron m

boss [bɔs] s patron m, chef m; (foreman) contremaître m ‖ tr mener, régenter

boss·y ['bɔsi] adj (comp -ier; super -iest) autoritaire, tyrannique

botanical [bə'tænɪkəl] adj botanique

botanist ['batənɪst] s botaniste mf

botany ['batəni] s botanique f

botch [batʃ] tr—**to botch up** bousiller, saloper

both [boθ] adj deux, e.g., **with both hands** à deux mains; les deux, e.g., **both books** les deux livres ‖ pron les deux, tous les deux ‖ conj à la fois; **both . . . and** aussi bien . . . que, e.g., **both in England and France** aussi bien en Angleterre qu'en France

bother ['baðər] s ennui m ‖ tr ennuyer, déranger ‖ intr se déranger

bothersome ['baðərsəm] adj importun

bottle ['batəl] s bouteille f ‖ tr mettre en bouteille, embouteiller

bot'tle cap' s capsule f

bot'tle depos'it s consigne f

bot'tled gas' s gaz m en cylindre

bot'tle·neck' s goulot m; (fig) embouteillage m, goulot m d'étranglement

bot'tle o'pener s ouvre-bouteilles m, décapsuleur m

bottler ['batlər] s metteur m en bouteilles

bottling ['batlɪŋ] s mise f en bouteilles

bottom ['batəm] s fond m; **at the bottom of** au fond de; (the page) en bas de; **to reach the bottom of the barrel** (coll) être à fond de cale

bot'tom dol'lar s dernier sou m

bottomless ['batəmlɪs] adj sans fond

bot'tom line' s (com) résultat m financier; (fig) conclusion f; point m essentiel

bough [baʊ] s rameau m

boulder ['boldər] s bloc m, rocher m

boulevard ['bʊlə,vard] s boulevard m

bounce [baʊns] s (elasticity) bond m; (of a ball) rebond m ‖ tr faire rebondir; (slang) flanquer à la porte ‖ intr rebondir

bouncer ['baʊnsər] s (in night club) (coll) videur m, gorille m

bound [baʊnd] adj (tied) lié; (obliged) obligé, tenu; **bound for** en partance pour ‖ s bond m, saut m; **bounds** bornes fpl, limites fpl; **out of bounds** hors jeu; (prohibited) défendu ‖ tr borner, limiter ‖ intr bondir

bounda·ry ['baʊndəri] s (pl -ries) borne f, limite f

boun'dary stone' s borne f

boundless ['baʊndlɪs] adj sans bornes

boun·ty ['baʊnti] s (pl -ties) largesse f; (award) prime f

bouquet [bu'ke] s bouquet m

bout [baʊt] s (time) période f; (of fever) accès m, attaque f; (sports) combat m, rencontre f

bow [baʊ] s (greeting) inclination f, révérence f; (of ship) avant m, proue f ‖ tr incliner, courber ‖ intr s'incliner, se courber; **to bow down** se prosterner; **bow out** se retirer; **to bow to** saluer ‖ [bo] s (weapon) arc m; (bowknot) nœud m; (of violin) archet m ‖ intr (mus) tirer l'archet

bowdlerize ['baʊdlə,raɪz] tr expurger

bowel ['baʊ·əl] s intestin m, boyau m; **bowels** entrailles fpl

bower ['baʊ·ər] s berceau m, tonnelle f

bow'ie knife' ['bo·ɪ] s couteau-poignard m

bowknot ['bo,nat] s nœud m en forme de rose, rosette f

bowl [bol] s (container) bol m, jatte f; (of pipe) fourneau m; (of spoon) cuilleron m; **bowls** (sports) boules fpl ‖ tr rouler, lancer; **to bowl over** (to overturn) (coll) renverser; (slang) déconcerter ‖ intr—**to bowl along** rouler rapidement

bowlegged ['bo,lɛgd], ['bo,lɛgɪd] adj aux jambes arquées

bowler ['bolər] s (hat) chapeau m melon; (in cricket) lanceur m; (in bowling) joueur m de boules

bowling ['bolɪŋ] s bowling m; (lawn bowling) jeu m de boules; (skittles) jeu de quilles

bowl'ing al'ley s boulodrome m, bowling m

bowl'ing green' s boulingrin m

bowl'ing pin' s quille f

bowsprit ['baʊsprɪt] s beaupré m

bow' tie' [bo] s nœud m papillon

box [baks] s boîte f; (in a questionnaire) case f; (law) barre f; (theat) loge f, baignoire f; **box on the ear** claque f ‖ tr emboîter; (to hit) boxer; **to box the compass** réciter la rose des vents ‖ intr (sports) boxer

box'car' s (rr) wagon m couvert

boxer ['baksər] s (person) boxeur m; (dog) boxer m

boxing ['baksɪŋ] s emboîtage m; (sports) boxe f

box' of'fice s bureau m de location

box'-office flop' s (slang) four m

box'-office hit' s pièce f à succès

box' wood' s buis m

boy [bɔɪ] s garçon m; (little boy) garçonnet m

boycott [ˈbɔɪkɑt] s boycottage m ‖ tr boycotter

boy' friend' s ami m, camarade m; (of a girl) bon ami m

boyhood [ˈbɔɪhʊd] s enfance f, jeunesse f, adolescence f

boyish [ˈbɔɪ·ɪʃ] adj de garçon

boy' scout' s boy-scout m

bra [brɑ] (coll) soutien-gorge m

brace [bres] s (support) attache f, lien m; (of game birds) couple f; (of pistols) paire f; (to impart a rotary movement to a bit) vilebrequin m; (aer, aut) entretoise f; (dentistry) appareil m; (med) appareil orthopédique; (mus, typ) accolade f ‖ tr ancrer, entretoiser; (to tone up) fortifier, remonter ‖ intr—**to brace up** prendre courage

brace' and bit' s vilebrequin m

bracelet [ˈbreslɪt] s bracelet m

bracer [ˈbresər] s tonique m

bracing [ˈbresɪŋ] adj tonique, fortifiant

bracket [ˈbrækɪt] s (angled support) support m, console f; (grouping) group m, classe f, tranche f; (level) niveau m; (mach) chaise f; (typ) crochet m ‖ tr grouper; (typ) mettre entre crochets

brackish [ˈbrækɪʃ] adj saumâtre

brad [bræd] s semence f, clou m (sans tête)

brag [bræg] s (pret & pp **bragged**; ger **bragging**) intr se vanter, se targuer

braggadoci·o [ˌbrægəˈdoʃɪ,o] s (pl **-os**) fanfaronnade f; (person) fanfaron m

braggart [ˈbrægərt] s vantard m

bragging [ˈbrægɪŋ] s vanterie f

Brah·man [ˈbrɑmən] s (pl **-mans**) brahmane m

braid [bred] s tresse f, passement m; (mil) galon m; **to trim with braid** soutacher ‖ tr passementer; (the hair) tresser

braille [brel] s braille m

brain [bren] s cerveau m; **brains** cervelle f; (fig) intelligence f, cerveau; **to rack one's brains** se creuser la cervelle ‖ tr casser la tête à

brain' child' s idée f de génie

brain' drain' s évasion f de(s) cerveaux, fuite f de(s) cerveaux

brainless [ˈbrenlɪs] adj sans cervelle

brain'storm' s accès m de folie; (coll) confusion f mentale; (coll) trouvaille f, bonne idée f

brain' storm'ing s remue-méninges m

brain' trust' s cerveauté f, projéticiens mpl

brain'wash' tr faire un lavage de cerveau à

brain'wash'ing s lavage m de cerveau

brain'work' s travail m intellectuel

brain·y [ˈbreni] adj (comp **-ier**; super **-iest**) (coll) intelligent à l'esprit vif

braise [brez] tr braiser, endauber

brais'ing pan' s braisière f

brake [brek] s frein m; **to put on the brakes** serrer les freins ‖ tr & intr freiner

brake' drum' s tambour m de frein

brake' light' s (aut) feu m de freinage

brake' lin'ing s garniture f de frein

brake'man s (pl **-men**) serre-freins m

brake' ped'al s pédale f de frein

brake' shoe' s sabot m de frein

bramble [ˈbræmbəl] s ronce f

bran [bræn] s son m, bran m

branch [bræntʃ] s branche f; (of tree) rameau m, branche; (of a business) succursale, filiale ‖ intr—**to branch off** s'embrancher, se bifurquer; **to branch out** se ramifier

branch' line' s embranchement m

branch' of'fice s succursale f

branch' road' s embranchement m

brand [brænd] s (trademark) marque f; (torch) brandon m; (coal) tison m; (on a criminal) flétrissure f; (on cattle) marque ‖ tr marquer au fer rouge, flétrir

brand'ing i'ron s fer m à flétrir

brandish [ˈbrændɪʃ] tr brandir

brand'-new' adj tout neuf, flambant neuf

bran·dy [ˈbrændi] s (pl **-dies**) eau-de-vie f

brash [bræʃ] adj impertinent

brass [bræs] s (metal) laiton m; (mil) (coll) officiers mpl supérieurs, galonnard m; (slang) toupet m, culot m; **big brass** (slang) grosses légumes fpl; **the brasses** (mus) les cuivres

brass' band' s fanfare f, musique f

brassiere [brəˈzɪr] s soutien-gorge m

brass' knuck'les spl coup-de-poing m

brass' tack' s semence f (de tapissier); **to get down to brass tacks** (coll) en venir aux faits

brat [bræt] s (coll) gamin m, gosse mf

brava·do [brəˈvɑdo] s (pl **-does** or **-dos**) bravade f

brave [brev] adj brave ‖ s guerrier m peaurouge ‖ tr braver

bravery [ˈbrevəri] s bravoure f

bra·vo [ˈbrɑvo] (pl **-vos**) bravo m ‖ interj bravo!

brawl [brɔl] s bagarre f, querelle f ‖ intr se bagarrer, se quereller

brawler [ˈbrɔlər] s bagarreur m

brawn [brɔn] s (strength) muscle m; (muscles) muscles bien développés; (culin) fromage m de cochon

brawn·y [ˈbrɔni] adj (comp **-ier**; super **-iest**) bien découplé, musclé

bray [bre] s braiment m ‖ intr braire

braze [brez] tr braser

brazen [ˈbrezən] adj effronté, hardi ‖ tr—**to brazen through** mener à bonne fin avec une effronterie audacieuse

Brazil [brəˈzɪl] s le Brésil

Brazilian [brəˈzɪljən] adj brésilien ‖ s (person) Brésilien m

Brazil' nut' s noix f du Brésil

breach [britʃ] s (in a wall) brèche f; (violation) infraction f ‖ tr ouvrir une brèche dans

breach' of con'tract s rupture f de contrat

breach' of prom'ise s rupture f de fiançailles

breach' of the peace' s attentat m contre l'ordre public

breach' of trust' s abus m de confiance

bread [brɛd] s pain m ‖ tr paner, gratiner

bread′ and but′ter s (fig) gagne-pain m
bread′bas′ket s corbeille f à pain
bread′board′ s planche f à pain
bread′ crumbs′ spl chapelure f
breaded adj (culin) au gratin
bread′ed veal′ cut′let s escalope f panée de veau
bread′fruit′ s fruit m à pain; (tree) arbre m à pain, jacquier m
bread′ knife′ s couteau m à pain
breadth [brɛdθ] s largeur f
bread′win′ner s soutien m de famille
break [brek] s (fracture) rupture f; (of an object) brisure f, cassure f; (in time or space) trou m, pause f; (slang) chance f || v (pret **broke** [brok]; pp **broken**) tr rompre, briser, casser; (a law) violer; (the heart) fendre; (one's word) manquer à; (a will; a soldier by reducing his rank) casser; **to break bread** rompre le pain; **to break down** (for analysis) analyser; **to break in** (a door) enfoncer; (a new car) roder || intr rompre, briser, se briser; (said of clouds) se dissiper; (said of waves) déferler; **to break down** avoir une panne
breakable [′brekəbəl] adj fragile
breakage [′brekɪdʒ] s casse f
break′ danc′ing s smurf m
break′down′ s (stoppage) arrêt m; (disaster) débâcle f; (of health) effondrement m, dépression f; (of negotiations) rupture f; (for analysis) analyse f, ventilation f; (mach) panne f
breaker [′brekər] s brisant m
breakfast [′brɛkfəst] s petit déjeuner m || intr prendre le petit déjeuner
break′fast food′ s céréales fpl (pour le petit déjeuner)
break′ing point′ s point m limite zéro
break′neck′ adj vertigineux; **at breakneck speed** à tombeau ouvert
break′ of day′ s point m du jour
break′through′ s (mil) percée f; (fig) découverte f sensationnelle
break′up′ s (splitting up) dissolution f; (of ice) débâcle f; (of friendship) rupture f
break′wa′ter s digue f, brise-lames m
breast [brɛst] s sein m; (of cooked chicken) blanc m; **to make a clean breast of it** se déboutonner
breast′bone′ s sternum m; (of fowl) bréchet m
breast′ feed′ing s allaitement m maternel
breast′ opera′tion s remodelage m
breast′plate′ s (of high priest) pectoral m; (of armor) plastron m
breast′stroke′ s brasse f
breast′work′ s (mil) parapet m
breath [brɛθ] s haleine f, souffle m; **last breath** dernier soupir m; **out of breath** hors d'haleine
breathalyzer [′brɛθə,laɪzər] s alcotest m, prise f d'haleine
breathe [brið] tr & intr respirer, souffler; **not to breathe a word** ne pas souffler mot

breathing [′briðɪŋ] s souffle m
breath′ing space′ s répit m
breathless [′brɛθlɪs] adj haletant, hors d'haleine; (silence) ému; (lifeless) inanimé
breath′tak′ing adj émouvant, sensationnel
breech [britʃ] s culasse f
breech′es bu′oy s (naut) bouée-culotte f
breed [brid] s race f || v (pret & pp **bred** [brɛd]) tr engendrer; (e.g., cattle) élever || intr se reproduire
breeder [′bridər] s éleveur m
breed′er reac′tor s (nucl) réacteur m surrégénérateur
breeding [′bridɪŋ] s (of animals) élevage m; **good breeding** savoir-vivre m
breeze [briz] s brise f
breez·y [′brizi] adj (comp **-ier**; super **-iest**) aéré; (coll) désinvolte, dégagé
brethren [′brɛðrɪn] spl frères mpl
Breton [′brɛtən] adj breton || s (language) breton m; (person) Breton m
breviar·y [′brɛvɪ,ɛri] s (pl **-ies**) (eccl) bréviaire m
brevi·ty [′brɛvɪti] s (pl **-ties**) brièveté f
brew [bru] s breuvage m, infusion f || tr infuser; (beer) brasser || intr s'infuser
brewer [′bru·ər] s brasseur m
brew′er's yeast′ s levure f de bière
brewer·y [′bru·əri] s (pl **-ies**) brasserie f
brewing [′bru·ɪŋ] s brassage m
bribe [braɪb] s pot-de-vin m || tr corrompre, suborner, soudoyer
briber·y [′braɪbəri] f (pl **-ies**) corruption f, subornation f
brick [brɪk] s brique f; (of ice cream) bloc m || tr briqueter
brick′bat′ s brocard m; **to hurl brickbats** lancer des brocards
brick′lay′er s briqueteur m
brick′work′ s briquetage m
brick′yard′ s briqueterie f
bridal [′braɪdəl] adj nuptial
bride [braɪd] s (nouvelle) mariée f
bride′groom′ s (nouveau) marié m
brides′maid′ s demoiselle f d'honneur
bride′-to-be′ s future femme f
bridge [brɪdʒ] s pont m; (cards, dentistry) bridge m; (naut) passerelle f; **to burn one's bridges** couper les ponts || tr construire un pont sur; **to bridge a gap** combler une lacune
bridge′head′ s (mil) tête f de pont
bridle [′braɪdəl] s bride f; (fig) frein m || tr brider; (fig) freiner || intr se raidir
bri′dle path′ s piste f cavalière
brief [brif] adj bref || s résumé m; (law) dossier m; **briefs** slip m; **to hold a brief for** plaider pour || tr mettre au courant
brief′ case′ s serviette f
briefing [′brifɪŋ] s briefing m, renseignements mpl tactiques
briefly [′brifli] adv bref, brièvement, en substance
brier [′braɪ·ər] s ronce f
brig [brɪg] s prison f navale; (ship) brick m
brigade [brɪ′ged] s brigade f

brigadier [ˌbrɪgəˈdɪr] *s* général *m* de brigade

brigand [ˈbrɪgənd] *s* brigand *m*

brigantine [ˈbrɪgənˌtin] *s* brigantin *m*

bright [braɪt] *adj* brillant; (*day*) clair; (*color*) vif; (*person*) (fig) brillant

brighten [ˈbraɪtən] *tr* faire briller; égayer, réjouir ‖ *intr* s'éclaircir

bright′ ide′a *s* (coll) idée *f* lumineuse

brightness [ˈbraɪtnɪs] *s* éclat *m*, clarté *f*; (*of mind*) vivacité *f*

brilliance [ˈbrɪljəns] or **brilliancy** [ˈbrɪljənsi] *s* brillant *m*, éclat *m*

brilliant [ˈbrɪljənt] *adj & s* brillant *m*

brim [brɪm] *s* bord *m* ‖ *v* (*pret & pp* **brimmed**; *ger* **brimming**) *intr*—**to brim over (with)** déborder (de)

brimful [ˈbrɪmˌful] *adj* à ras bords

brim′stone′ *s* soufre *m*

brine [braɪn] *s* saumure *f*

bring [brɪŋ] *v* (*pret & pp* **brought** [brɔt]) *tr* apporter; (*a person*) amener, conduire; **to bring back** rapporter; (*a person*) ramener; **to bring down** (*baggage*) descendre; (*with a gun*) abbatre; **to bring in** enterrer, introduire; **to bring out** faire ressortir; (*e.g., a book*) publier; **to bring together** réunir; **to bring to pass** causer, opérer; **to bring up** éduquer, élever; (*baggage*) monter

bring′ing-up′ *s* éducation *f*

brink [brɪŋk] *s* bord *m*

brisk [brɪsk] *adj* vif, actif, animé

brisket [ˈbrɪskɪt] *s* (culin) poitrine *f*

bristle [ˈbrɪsəl] *s* soie *f*; (*of brush*) poil *m* ‖ *tr* hérisser ‖ *intr* se hérisser

bristling [ˈbrɪslɪŋ] *adj* hérissé

Bris′tol board′ [ˈbrɪstəl] *s* bristol *m*

Britain [ˈbrɪtən] *s* Grande-Bretagne *f*; **la Grande-Bretagne**

British [ˈbrɪtɪʃ] *adj* britannique ‖ **the British** les Britanniques

Britisher [ˈbrɪtɪʃər] *s* Britannique *mf*

Briton [ˈbrɪtən] *s* Britannique *mf*

Brittany [ˈbrɪtəni] *s* Bretagne *f*; la Bretagne

brittle [ˈbrɪtəl] *adj* fragile, cassant

broach [brotʃ] *s* (spit) broche *f*; (*for tapping casks*) mèche *f* à percer, perçoir *m*, foret *m* ‖ *tr* (*e.g., a keg of beer*) mettre en perce; (*a subject*) entamer

broad [brɔd] *adj* (*wide*) large; (*immense*) vaste; (*mind, views*) libéral, tolérant; (*accent*) fort, prononcé; (*use, sense*) répandu, général; (*daylight*) plein; (*joke, story*) grossier, salé

broad′-backed′ *adj* d'une belle carrure

broad′brimmed′ *adj* à larges bords

broad′cast′ *adj* diffusé; (rad) radiodiffusé ‖ *s* (rad) radiodiffusion *f*, émission *f* ‖ *v* (*pret & pp* **-cast**) *tr* diffuser, répandre ‖ (*pret & pp* **-cast** or **-casted**) *tr* radiodiffuser ‖ *intr* (rad) émettre

broad′cast′er *s* communicateur *m*

broad′casting sta′tion *s* station *f* d'émission

broad′cloth′ *s* popeline *f*

broaden [ˈbrɔdən] *tr* élargir ‖ *intr* s'élargir

broad′-gauge′ *adj* à voie large

broad′ jump′ *s* saut *m* en longueur

broad′-mind′ed *adj* évolué, à l'esprit large

broad′side′ *s* bordée *f*; (typ) placard *m*

brocade [broˈked] *s* brocart *m* ‖ *tr* brocher

broccoli [ˈbrakəli] *s* brocoli *m*

brochure [broˈʃur] *s* brochure *f*

brogue [brog] *s* accent *m* irlandais; (*shoe*) soulier *m* grossier

broil [brɔil] *s* grillade *f*; (*quarrel*) rixe *f* ‖ *tr & intr* griller

broiler [ˈbrɔilər] *s* gril *m*

broke [brok] *adj* (slang) fauché

broken [ˈbrokən] *adj* brisé, cassé; (*promise; ranks; beam*) rompu

bro′ken-down′ *adj* délabré; en panne

bro′ken-heart′ed *adj* au cœur brisé

broker [ˈbrokər] *s* courtier *m*

brokerage [ˈbrokərɪdʒ] *s* courtage *m*

bro′kerage fee′ *s* (frais *mpl* de) courtage *m*

bromide [ˈbromaɪd] *s* bromure *m*; (coll) platitude *f*

bromine [ˈbromin] *s* brome *m*

bronchial [ˈbraŋkɪ·əl] *adj* bronchique

bron′chial tube′ *s* bronche *f*

bronchitis [braŋˈkaɪtɪs] *s* bronchite *f*

bron·co [ˈbraŋko] *s* (*pl* **-cos**) cheval *m* sauvage

bronze [branz] *adj* bronzé ‖ *s* bronze *m* ‖ *tr* bronzer ‖ *intr* se bronzer

brooch [brotʃ], [brutʃ] *s* broche *f*

brood [brud] *s* couvée *f*; (*of children*) nichée *f* ‖ *intr* couver; (*to sulk*) broyer du noir; **to brood over** songer sombrement à

brood′ hen′ *s* couveuse *f*

brood′mare′ *s* poulinière *f*

brook [bruk] *s* ruisseau *m* ‖ *tr*—**to brook no** ne pas tolérer

brooklet [ˈbruklɪt] *s* ruisseau *m*

broom [brum] *s* balai *m*; (bot) genêt *m*

broom′stick′ *s* manche *m* à balai

broth [brɔθ] *s* bouillon *m*, consommé *m*

brothel [ˈbrɛðəl] *s* bordel *m*

brother [ˈbrʌðər] *s* frère *m*

broth′er·hood′ *s* fraternité *f*

broth′er-in-law′ *s* (*pl* **brothers-in-law**) beau-frère *m*

brotherly [ˈbrʌðərli] *adj* fraternel ‖ *adv* fraternellement

brow [braʊ] *s* (*forehead*) front *m*; (*eyebrow*) sourcil *m*; **to knit one's brow** froncer le sourcil

brow′beat′ *v* (*pret* **-beat**; *pp* **-beaten**) *tr* rabrouer, brusquer

brown [braʊn] *adj* marron; (*eyes*) brun; (*hair*) brun, châtain; (*shoes*) marron; (*ale*) brune; (*bread*) bis; (*sugar*) brun; (*butter*) roux, noir; (*bear*) brun; (*tanned*) bronzé, bruni; (*dark-complexioned*) brun de peau; **brown wrapping paper** papier *m* d'emballage ‖ *s* marron *m*, brun *m* ‖ *tr* (*skin*) bronzer, brunir; (culin) faire dorer, rissoler ‖ *intr* (*sauce; leaves*) roussir; (*skin*) brunir; (culin) dorer, rissoler

brown′ bag′ lunch *s* repas *m* tiré du sac

brownish [ˈbraʊnɪʃ] *adj* brunâtre

brown′ out′ s (*shortage of power*) panne f partielle; (mil) camouflage m partiel des lumières

brown′ stone′ s (*brownstone front*) bâtiment m de grès brun; (mineral) grès m brun

brown′ stud′y s—**in a brown study** absorbé dans des méditations

brown′ sug′ar s cassonade f, sucre m brut

browse [brauz] intr (*said of animals*) brouter; (*said of booklovers*) butiner; (*said of customers for secondhand books*) bouquiner

bruise [bruz] s (*on body or fruit*) meurtrissure f; (*on body*) contusion f || tr meurtrir, contusionner

bruiser [′bruzər] s (coll) costaud m

bruit [brut] tr ébruiter; **to bruit about** répandre

brunette [bru′nɛt] adj & s brune f, brunette f

brunt [brʌnt] s choc m, assaut m; **to bear the brunt of** (fig) faire tous les frais de

brush [brʌʃ] s brosse f; (*countryside*) brousse f; (elec) balai m || tr brosser; **to brush aside** écarter || intr—**to brush against** frôler; **to brush up on** repasser, rafraîchir

brush′-off′ s (slang) affront m; **to give a brush-off to** (slang) expédier avec rudesse

brush′wood′ s broussailles fpl, brindilles fpl

brusque [brʌsk] adj brusque

Brussels [′brʌsəlz] s Bruxelles f

Brus′sels sprouts′ mpl chou m de Bruxelles

brutal [′brutəl] adj brutal

brutali·ty [bru′tælɪti] s (pl -ties) brutalité f

brute [brut] adj brutal || s bête f, animal m; (*person*) brute f, animal m

brutish [′brutɪʃ] adj grossier, brut, brutal

bubble [′bʌbəl] s bulle f || intr bouillonner; (*said of drink*) pétiller; **to bubble over** déborder

bub′ble bath′ s bain m moussant, bain de mousse

bub′ble gum′ s gomme f à claquer

bub·bly [′bʌbli] adj (comp -blier; super -bliest) bouillonnant, gazeux

bubon′ic plague′ [bju′banɪk] s peste f bubonique

buccaneer [,bʌkə′nɪr] s boucanier m

buck [bʌk] s (*red deer*) cerf m; (*fallow deer*) daim m; (*roebuck*) chevreuil m; (slang) dollar m; the male of many animals such as: (*goat*) bouc m; (*rabbit*) lapin m; (*hare*) lièvre m; **to pass the buck** (coll) renvoyer la balle || tr—**to buck off** (*a rider*) désarçonner; **to buck up** (coll) remonter le courage de || intr—**to buck up** (coll) reprendre courage

bucket [′bʌkɪt] s seau m; **to kick the bucket** (slang) casser sa pipe, claquer, crever

buck′et seat′ s siège m baquet

buckle [′bʌkəl] s boucle f || tr boucler || intr arquer, gauchir; **to buckle down** s'appliquer

buck′ pri′vate s simple soldat m

buckram [′bʌkrəm] s bougran m

buck′saw′ s scie f à bûches

buck′shot′ s gros plomb m

buck′tooth′ s (pl -teeth) dent f saillante

buck′wheat′ s sarrasin m

buck′wheat cake′ s crêpe f de sarrasin

bud [bʌd] s bouton m, bourgeon m || v (pret & pp budded; ger budding) intr boutonner, bourgeonner

Buddhism [′budɪzəm] s bouddhisme m

Buddhist [′budɪst] adj & s bouddhiste mf

budding [′bʌdɪŋ] adj en bouton; (*beginning*) en germe, naissant

bud·dy [′bʌdi] s (pl -dies) (coll) copain m

budge [bʌdʒ] tr faire bouger || intr bouger

budget [′bʌdʒɪt] s budget m || tr comptabiliser, inscrire au budget

budgetary [′bʌdʒɪ,tɛrij] adj budgétaire

buff [bʌf] adj (*color*) chamois || s (coll) fanatique mf, enthousiaste mf || tr polir, émeuler

buffa·lo [′bʌfə,lo] s (pl -loes or -los) bison m; (*water buffalo; Cape buffalo*) buffle m

buffer [′bʌfər] s (mach) brunissoir m; (rr) (*on cars*) tampon m; (rr) (*at end of track*) butoir m

buff′er state′ s état m tampon

buf′fer zone′ s zone f tampon

buffet [bu′fe] s buffet m || [′bʌfɪt] tr frapper (violemment)

buffet′ lunch′ [bu′fe] s lunch m

buffet′ sup′per s buffet m

buffoon [bə′fun] s bouffon m

buffooner·y [bə′funəri] s (pl -ies) bouffonnerie f

bug [bʌg] s insecte m; (germ) microbe m; (*in a mechanical device*) vice m, défaut m; (*hidden microphone*) micro m; (comp) bogue f; (coll) idée f fixe, lutin m; (Brit) punaise f; **he's a bug for . . .** (coll) il est fou de . . . || v (pret & pp bugged; ger bugging) tr (slang) installer une table d'écoute dans; installer un microphone dans; (*to annoy*) (slang) embêter, emmerder

bug′bear′ s (*scare*) épouvantail m, croquemitaine m; (*pet peeve*) bête f noire

bug′-eyed′ adj (slang) aux yeux saillants

bug·gy [′bʌgi] adj (comp -gier; super -giest) infesté d'insectes; infesté; (slang) fou || s (pl -gies) buggy m à quatre roues; (*two-wheeled*) buggy m, boguet m

bug′house′ s (slang) cabanon m

bugle [′bjugəl] s (bot) bugle f; (mus) clairon m || tr & intr clletronner

bu′gle call′ s sonnerie f de clairon

bugler [′bjuglər] s clairon m

build [bɪld] s (*of human body*) taille f, charpente f, carrure f || v (pret & pp built [bɪlt]) tr bâtir, construire

builder [′bɪldər] s constructeur m; (*of bridges, roads, etc.*) entrepreneur m

building [′bɪldɪŋ] s immeuble m, bâtiment m, édifice m; (*erection*) construction f

build′ing and loan′ associa′tion s société f de prêt à la construction

build'ing lot' s terrain m à bâtir
build'ing per'mit s permis m de construire
build'ing site' s chantier m de construction; lotissement m à bâtir
build'-up s (of excitement) montée f; (of pressure) intensification f; (of gas) accumulation f; (fig) présentation f publicitaire, battage m
built'-in' adj incorporé, encastré
built'-up' adj aggloméré; (heel) renforcé; (land) bâti, loti
bulb [bʌlb] s bulbe m; (of vaporizer) poire f; (bot) oignon m; (elec) ampoule f
bulbous ['bʌlbəs] adj bulbeux
Bulgaria [bʌl'gɛrɪ·ə] s Bulgarie f; la Bulgarie
Bulgarian [bʌl'gɛrɪ·ən] adj bulgare ‖ s (language) bulgare m; (person) Bulgare mf
bulge [bʌldʒ] s bosse f, bombement m; (mil) saillant m ‖ tr bourrer, gonfler ‖ intr faire une bosse, bomber
bulk [bʌlk] s masse f, volume m; **in bulk** en bloc; (com) en vrac ‖ tr entasser (en vrac) ‖ intr tenir de la place; **to bulk large** devenir important
bulk'head' s (naut) cloison f
bulk·y ['bʌlki] adj (comp **-ier**; super **-iest**) volumineux
bull [bul] s taureau m; (on the stock exchange) haussier m, spéculateur m à la hausse; (eccl) bulle f; (policeman) (slang) flic m, vache f; (exaggeration) (slang) blague f, boniment m, chiqué m; **like a bull in a china shop** comme un éléphant dans un magasin de porcelaine; **to take the bull by the horns** (fig) prendre le taureau par les cornes ‖ tr—**to bull the market** jouer à la hausse
bull'dog' s bouledogue m
bull'doze' tr passer au bulldozer; (coll) intimider
bulldozer ['bul,dozər] s chasse-terre m, bouteur m, bouldozeur m
bullet ['bulɪt] s balle f
bulletin ['bulətɪn] s bulletin m; (e.g., of a university) annuaire m
bul'letin board' s tableau m d'affichage
bul'let·proof' adj à l'épreuve des balles ‖ tr blinder
bul'let·proof vest' s gilet m pare-balles
bull'fight' s course f de taureaux
bull'fight'er s torero m
bull'fight'ing s tauromachie f
bull'finch' s bouvreuil m
bull'frog' s grenouille f d'Amérique
bull'head' s (ichth) chabot m, cabot m; (miller's-thumb) meunier m, cabot
bull'head'ed adj entêté
bullion ['buljən] s (of gold) or m; (of silver) argent m; encaisse f métallique, lingots mpl d'or, lingots d'argent; (on uniform) cordonnet m d'or, cordonnet d'argent
bull' mar'ket s marché m à la hausse
bullock ['bulək] s bœuf m
bull' pen' s toril m; (jail) poste m de détention préventive

bull'ring' s arène f, arène pour les courses de taureaux
bull's'-eye' s mouche f; **to hit the bull's-eye** faire mouche
bull's'-eye win'dow s œil-de-bœuf m
bul·ly ['buli] adj (coll) épatant ‖ s (pl **-lies**) brute f, brutal m; (at school) brimeur m, tyranneau m ‖ v (pret & pp **-lied**) tr brutaliser, malmener; (at school) brimer, tyranniser
bulrush ['bul,rʌʃ] s jonc m des marais
bulwark ['bulwərk] s rempart m; (naut) pavois m ‖ tr garnir de remparts; (fig) protéger
bum [bʌm] adj (slang) moche, de camelote ‖ s (slang) clochard m ‖ v (pret & pp **bummed**; ger **bumming**) tr & intr (slang) écornifler
bumble ['bʌmbəl] tr bâcler ‖ intr (to stumble) trébucher; (in speaking) bafouiller; (said of bee) bourdonner
bum'ble·bee' s bourdon m
bump [bʌmp] s (blow) choc m; (protuberance) bosse f; (of car on rough road) cahot m ‖ tr cogner, tamponner, heurter; **to bump off** (to kill) (slang) buter ‖ intr se cogner; **to bump along** (said of car) cahoter; **to bump into** buter contre, choquer
bumper ['bʌmpər] adj exceptionnel ‖ s (aut) pare-chocs m; (rr) tampon m; **bumper to bumper** pare-chocs contre pare-chocs
bump'er car' s (at a carnival) auto f tamponneuse
bump'er stick'er s autocollant m, macaron m
bumpkin ['bʌmpkɪn] s péquenot m, rustre m
bumptious ['bʌmpʃəs] adj outrecuidant
bump·y ['bʌmpi] adj (comp **-ier**; super **-iest**) bosselé; (road) cahoteux
bun [bʌn] s brioche f, petit pain m; (hair) chignon m
bunch [bʌnʃ] s (of vegetables) botte f; (of bananas) régime m; (of flowers) bouquet m; (of grapes) grappe f; (of keys) trousseau m; (of people) groupe m, bande f; (of ribbons) flot m; (of feathers, hair) touffe f; (of twigs) paquet m; (on body) bosse f ‖ tr grouper ‖ intr se serrer
buncombe ['bʌnkəm] s (coll) balivernes fpl, sornettes fpl
bundle ['bʌndəl] s paquet m; (of banknotes, papers, etc.) liasse f ‖ tr empaqueter, mattre en paquet; **to bundle up** (in warm clothing) emmitoufler ‖ intr—**to bundle up** s'emmitoufler
bung [bʌn] s bonde f ‖ tr mettre une bonde à
bungalow ['bʌngə,lo] s bungalow m
bung'hole' s bonde f
bungle ['bʌngəl] s gâchis m, bousillage m ‖ tr saboter, bousiller ‖ intr saboter
bungler ['bʌnglər] s gâcheur m, bousilleur m

bungling [ˈbʌŋglɪŋ] *adj* gauche, maladroit ‖ *s* maladresse *f*

bunion [ˈbʌnjən] *s* oignon *m* (au pied)

bunk [bʌŋk] *s* (*bed*) couchette *f*; (slang) balivernes *fpl*, sornettes *fpl* ‖ *intr* (coll) se coucher

bunk′ bed′ *s* lit *m* superposé; (naut) cadre *m*

bunker [ˈbʌŋkər] *s* (golf) banquette *f*; (naut) soute *f*; (mil) blockhaus *m*, bunker *m*

bun·ny [ˈbʌni] *s* (*pl* -nies) petit lapin *m*

bunting [ˈbʌntɪŋ] *s* (*flags*) drapeaux *mpl*; (*cloth*) étamine *f*; (orn) bruant *m*

buoy [bɔɪ], [ˈbuˑi] *s* bouée *f* ‖ *tr*—**to buoy up** faire flotter; (fig) soutenir

buoyancy [ˈbɔɪˑənsi] *s* flottabilité *f*

buoyant [ˈbɔɪˑənt] *adj* flottant; (*cheerful*) plein d'allant, plein de ressort

bur [bʌr] *s* (*of chestnut*) bogue *f*; (*ragged metal edge*) bavure *f*, barbe *f*

burble [ˈbʌrbəl] *s* murmure *m* ‖ *intr* murmurer

burden [ˈbʌrdən] *s* fardeau *m*, charge *f*; (mus) refrain *m* ‖ *tr* charger

bur′den of proof′ *s* fardeau *m* de la preuve

burdensome [ˈbʌrdənsəm] *adj* onéreux

burdock [ˈbʌrdɑk] *s* bardane *f*

bureau [ˈbjuro] *s* (*piece of furniture*) commode *f*, chiffonier *m*; (*office*) bureau *m*

bureaucra·cy [bjuˈrɑkrəsi] *s* (*pl* -cies) bureaucratie *f*, énarchie *f*

bureaucrat [ˈbjurəˌkræt] *s* bureaucrate *mf*, rond-de-cuir *m*, énarque *mf*

bureaucratic [ˌbjurəˈkrætɪk] *adj* bureaucratique

bur′eau of vi′tal statis′tics *s* bureau *m* de l'état civil

burglar [ˈbʌrglər] *s* cambrioleur *m*

bur′glar alarm′ *s* signalisateur *m* anti-vol, sonnette *f* d'alarme

burglarize [ˈbʌrgləˌraɪz] *tr* cambrioler

bur′glar·proof′ *adj* incrochetable

burglar·y [ˈbʌrgləri] *s* (*pl* -ies) cambriolage *m*

Burgundian [bərˈgʌndiˑən] *adj* bourguignon ‖ *s* (*dialect*) bourguignon *m*; (*person*) Bourguignon *m*

Burgundy [ˈbʌrgəndi] *s* Bourgogne *f*; la Bourgogne ‖ **burgun·dy** *s* (-dies) (*wine*) bourgogne *m*

burial [ˈbɛrɪˑəl] *s* enterrement *m*, inhumation *f*

bur′ial ground′ *s* cimetière *m*

burlap [ˈbʌrlæp] *s* toile *f* d'emballage, serpillière *f*

burlesque [bərˈlɛsk] *adj* & *s* burlesque *m* ‖ *tr* parodier

burlesque′ show′ *s* strip-tease *m*

bur·ly [ˈbʌrli] *adj* (*comp* -lier; *super* -liest) solide, costaud

Burma [ˈbʌrmə] *s* Birmanie *f*; la Birmanie

Bur·mese [bərˈmiz] *adj* birman ‖ *s* (*pl* -mese) (*language*) birman *m*; (*person*) Birman *m*

burn [bʌrn] *s* brûlure *f* ‖ *v* (*pret* & *pp* **burned** or **burnt** [bʌrnt]) *tr* & *intr* brûler; **to burn out** (elec) griller

burner [ˈbʌrnər] *s* (*on which to cook*) brûleur *m*; (*using gas*) bec *m*; (*of a stove*) feu *m*

burning [ˈbʌrnɪŋ] *adj* brûlant; (*in flames*) en feu ‖ *s* brûlure *f*; (*fire*) incendie *m*

burnish [ˈbʌrnɪʃ] *tr* brunir, polir

burn′-out *s* arrêt *m* par épuisement; (*emotional breakdown*) syndrome *m* de l'usure au travail

burrow [ˈbʌro] *s* terrier *m* ‖ *tr* creuser ‖ *intr* se terrer

bursar [ˈbʌrsər] *s* économe *m*

burst [bʌrst] *s* éclat *m*, explosion *f* ‖ *v* (*pret* & *pp* **burst**) (*of a balloon*) crever; (*a boiler; one's buttons*) faire sauter ‖ *intr* éclater, exploser; (*said of tire*) crever; **to burst into tears** fondre en larmes; **to burst out laughing** éclater de rire

bur·y [ˈbɛri] *v* (*pret* & *pp* -ied) *tr* enterrer, ensevelir; (*e.g., pirate treasure*) enfouir

bus [bʌs] *s* (*pl* **busses** or **buses**) (*city*) autobus *m*, bus *m*; (*interurban or sightseeing*) car *m*, autocar *m*; **to miss the bus** (fig) manquer le coche ‖ *v* (*pret* & *pp* **bused** or **bussed**) *ger* **busing** or **bussing**) *tr* transporter en autobus

bus′boy′ *s* aide-serveur *m*, desserveur *m*, débarasseur *m*

bush [buʃ] *s* (*shrub*) buisson *m*; (*small shrub*) arbuste *m*; (*in Africa and Australia*) brousse *f*; **to beat around the bush** tourner autour du pot, tortiller

bushed [buʃt] *adj* (coll) éreinté

bushel [ˈbuʃəl] *s* boisseau *m*

bushing [ˈbuʃɪŋ] *s* manchon *m*, douille *f*, bague *f*, coussinet *m*

bush·y [ˈbuʃi] *adj* (*comp* -ier; *super* -iest) (*countryside*) buissonneux; (*hair*) touffu; (*eyebrows*) broussailleux

business [ˈbɪznɪs] *adj* commercial ‖ *s* affaires *fpl*, les affaires; (*subject*) sujet *m*; (*store*) commerce *m*; (*company*) établissement *m*; (theat) jeux *mpl* de scène; **it's none of your business** cela ne vous regarde pas; **mind your own business!** occupez-vous de vos affaires!, faites votre métier!; **to mean business** (coll) ne pas plaisanter; **to send about one's business** envoyer paître

busi′ness dis′trict *s* quartier *m* commerçant

busi′ness hours′ *s* heures *fpl* d'ouverture

busi′ness house′ *s* maison *f* de commerce

busi′ness·like′ *adj* pratique; (*manner, transaction*) sérieux

busi′ness lunch′ *s* déjeuner *m* d'affaires, déjeuner de travail

busi′ness·man′ *s* (*pl* -men′) homme *m* d'affaires; **big businessman** grand industriel *m*, chef *m* d'industrie

busi′ness man′ager *s* directeur *m* commercial

busi′ness reply′ card′ *s* carte *f* postale avec réponse payée

busi′ness suit′ *s* complet *m* veston

busi′ness·wom′an *s* (*pl* -wom′en) femme *f* d'affaires

busing [ˈbʌsɪŋ] s busing m, ramassage m scolaire

bus′ shel′ter s abribus m

buskin [ˈbʌskɪn] s brodequin m

bus′ sta′tion s gare f routière

bus′ stop′ s arrêt m d'autobus

bust [bʌst] s (statue) buste m; (of woman) gorge f, buste; (slang) faillite f ‖ tr (mil) limoger; (slang) casser ‖ intr (slang) échouer

busting [ˈbʌstɪŋ] s (mil) cassation f

bustle [ˈbʌsəl] s remue-ménage m, affairement m, branle-bas m ‖ intr se remuer, s'affairer

bustling [ˈbʌslɪŋ] adj affairé

bus·y [ˈbɪzi] adj (comp **-ier**; super **-iest**) occupé ‖ v (pret & pp **-ied**) tr—**to busy oneself with** s'occuper de

bus′y·bod′y s (pl **-ies**) officieux m

bus′y sig′nal s (telp) signal m d'occupation, tonalité f occupée; **there's a busy signal** la ligne est occupée

but [bʌt] adv seulement; ne . . . que, e.g., **to have nothing but trouble** n'avoir que des ennuis; **but for** sans; **but for that** à part cela ‖ prep sauf, excepté; **all but** presque ‖ conj mais

butcher [ˈbʊtʃər] s boucher m ‖ tr (an animal for meat) abattre, dépecer; (to massacre; to bungle) massacrer

butch′er knife′ s couperet m, coutelas m (de boucher)

butch′er shop′ s boucherie f

butler [ˈbʌtlər] s maître m d'hôtel, intendant m

butt [bʌt] s (end) bout m; (cask) futaille f; (of a gun) crosse f; (of a cigarette) mégot m; (of a joke) souffre-douleur m, plastron m; (blow) coup m de tête, coup de corne; (slang) postérieur m, derrière m ‖ tr (like a goat) donner un coup de corne à ‖ intr—**to butt up against** buter contre; **to butt in** (coll) intervenir sans façon

butte [bjut] s butte f, tertre m, puy m

butt′ end′ s gros bout m

butter [ˈbʌtər] s beurre m ‖ tr beurrer; **to butter up** (coll) passer de la pommade à, pateliner

but′ter·cup′ s renoncule f, bouton-d'or m

but′ter dish′ s beurrier m, beurrière f

but′ter·fat′ s crème f

but′ter·fin′gered adj maladroit

but′ter·fin′gers s brise-tout mf

but′ter·fly′ s (pl **-flies**) papillon m

but′ter knife′ s couteau m à beurre

but′ter·milk′ s babeurre m

but′ter·scotch′ s caramel m au beurre

buttocks [ˈbʌtəks] spl fesses fpl

button [ˈbʌtən] s bouton m ‖ tr boutonner

but′ton cell′ s (battery) pile-bouton f

but′ton·hole′ s boutonnière f ‖ tr (coll) retenir (qqn) par le pan de sa veste

but′ton·hook′ s tire-bouton m

buttress [ˈbʌtrɪs] s contrefort m ‖ tr arc-bouter; (fig) étayer

buxom [ˈbʌksəm] adj plantureuse

buy [baɪ] s—**a good buy** (coll) une bonne affaire ‖ v (pret & pp **bought** [bɔt]) tr acheter; (a ticket) prendre; **to buy a drink for** payer un verre à; **to buy back** racheter; **to buy from** acheter à or de; **to buy out** (a partner) désintéresser; **to buy s.o. off** se débarrasser de qn, racheter qn; **to buy up** accaparer

buyer [ˈbaɪ·ər] s acheteur m

buzz [bʌz] s bourdonnement m; **to give s.o. a buzz** (on the telephone) (coll) passer un coup de fil à ‖ tr (aer) survoler à basse altitude ‖ intr bourdonner

buzzard [ˈbʌzərd] s buse f

buzz′ bomb′ s bombe f volante

buzzer [ˈbʌzər] s vibreur m sonore, trembleur m

buzz′ saw′ s scie f circulaire

buzz′ word′ s grand mot m, mot résonnant et emphatique

by [baɪ] adv près, auprès; (aside) de côté; **by and by** tout à l'heure, sous peu; **by and large** généralement parlant ‖ prep par; (near) près de; **by a head** (taller) d'une tête; **by day** pendant la journée; **by far** de beaucoup; **by Monday** d'ici à lundi; **by 1944** déjà en 1944, en 1944 au plus tard; **by profession** de profession; **by the way** à propos; **to be followed (loved,** etc.) **by** être suivi (aimé, etc.) de

by-and-by [ˈbaɪ·ən′baɪ] s proche avenir m; **in the sweet by-and-by** à la Saint-Glinglin

by′gone′ adj d'autrefois, passé

by′law′ s ordonnance f, règlement m

by′-line′ s signature f de journaliste

by′-pass′ s (road) bretelle f de contournement, rocade f; (elec, med) dérivation f ‖ tr éviter, contourner; (mach) amener or placer en dérivation

by′-play′ s (theat) jeu m en aparté

by′-prod′uct s sous-produit m

by′-road′ s chemin m détourné

bystander [ˈbaɪˌstændər] s spectateur m, assistant m

byte [baɪt] s (comp) multiplet m; (of eight bits) octet m

by′way′ s chemin m écarté, voie f indirecte

by′word′ s dicton m, proverbe m; objet m de dérision

Byzantine [ˈbɪzənˌtin] adj & s byzantin m

C

C, c [si] *s* IIIe lettre de l'alphabet
cab [kæb] *s* taxi *m*; (*of locomotive or truck*) cabine *f*; (*hansom*) fiacre *m*, cab *m*
cabaret [,kæbə're] *s* boîte *f* de nuit, cabaret *m*
cabbage ['kæbidʒ] *s* chou *m*
cab'driv'er *s* chauffeur *m* de taxi
cabin ['kæbin] *s* (*hut*) case *f*, cabane *f*; (*of ship or airplane*) cabine *f*
cab'in boy' *s* (naut) mousse *m*
cabinet ['kæbinit] *s* (*small room; room for displaying art; political committee*) cabinet *m*; (*piece of furniture*) meuble *m* à tiroirs, cabinet; (*wall cupboard*) placard *m*, armoire *f* fixe
cab'inet-mak'er *s* ébéniste *m*, menuisier *m*
cab'inet mem'ber *s* ministre *m*
cable ['kebəl] *s* câble *m* ‖ *tr & intr* câbler
ca'ble car' *s* funiculaire *m*, téléférique *m*, tramway *m* funiculaire
ca'ble-gram' *s* câblogramme *m*
ca'ble ship' *s* câblier *m*
ca'ble's length' *s* encablure *f*
ca'ble tel'evision *s* câblodistribution *f*, vidéocâble *m*
caboose [kə'bus] *s* (naut) coquerie *f*; (rr) fourgon *m* de queue, wagon *m* du personnel
cab'stand' *s* station *f* de taxi
cache [kæʃ] *s* cachette *f*, cache *f* ‖ *tr* mettre dans une cachette, cacher
cachet [kæ'ʃe] *s* cachet *m*
cackle ['kækəl] *s* caquet *m* ‖ *intr* caqueter; (*said of goose*) cacarder
cacopho·ny [kə'kɑfəni] *s* (*pl* **-nies**) cacophonie *f*
cac·tus ['kæktəs] *s* (*pl* **-tuses** or **-ti** [taɪ]) cactus *m*
cad [kæd] *s* malotru *m*
cadaver [kə'dævər] *s* cadavre *m*
cad·dy ['kædi] *s* (*pl* **-dies**) boîte *f* à thé; (*person*) cadet *m*, caddie *m*
cadence ['kedəns] *s* cadence *f*
cadet [kə'dɛt] *s* cadet *m*
cadmium ['kædmɪ·əm] *s* cadmium *m*
Caesar'ean opera'tion [sɪ'zɛrɪ·ən] *s* césarienne *f*
café [kæ'fe] *s* cabaret *m*; café-restaurant *m*
ca'fé soci'ety *s* gens *mpl* chic des cabarets à la mode
cafeteria [,kæfə'tɪrɪ·ə] *s* cafétéria *f*, restaurant *m* de libre-service
caffeine [kæ'fin], ['kæfi·in] *s* caféine *f*
cage [kedʒ] *s* cage *f* ‖ *tr* mettre en cage
ca·gey ['kedʒi] *adj* (*comp* **-gier**; *super* **-giest**) prudent, peu communicatif; (*secretive*) dissimulé; (coll) rusé, fin
cahoots [kə'huts] *s*—**in cahoots** (slang) de mèche
CAI ['si'e'aɪ] *s* (letterword) (**computer-assisted instruction**) E.A.O. (enseignement assisté par ordinateur)
Cain [ken] *s* Caïn *m*; **to raise Cain** (coll) faire le diable à quatre
Cairo ['kaɪro] *s* Le Caire

caisson ['kesən] *s* caisson *m*
cais'son disease' *s* maladie *f* des caissons
cajole [kə'dʒol] *tr* cajoler, enjôler
cajoler·y [kə'dʒoləri] *s* (*pl* **-ies**) cajolerie *f*, enjôlement *m*
cake [kek] *s* (*dessert; shaped like a cake*) gâteau *m*; (*one-layer cake*) galette *f*; (*pastry*) pâtisserie *f*; (*of soap, wax*) pain *m*; (*of ice*) bloc *m*; (*crust*) croûte *f*; **to sell like hot cakes** (coll) se vendre comme des petits pains; **to take the cake** (coll) être la fin des haricots ‖ *tr* couvrir d'une croûte ‖ *intr* s'agglutiner, faire croûte
calabash ['kælə,bæʃ] *s* calebasse *f*; (*tree*) calebassier *m*
calaboose ['kælə,bus] *s* (coll) violon *m*, tôle *f*
calamitous [kə'læmɪtəs] *adj* calamiteux
calami·ty [kə'læmɪti] *s* (*pl* **-ties**) calamité *f*
calci·fy ['kælsɪ,faɪ] *v* (*pret & pp* **-fied**) *tr* calcifier ‖ *intr* se calcifer
calcium ['kælsɪ·əm] *s* calcium *m*
calculate ['kælkjə,let] *tr & intr* calculer
calculating ['kælkjə,letɪŋ] *adj* calculateur
calculation [,kælkjə'leʃən] *s* calcul *m*
calcu·lus ['kælkjələs] *s* (*pl* **-luses** or **-li** [,laɪ]) (math, pathol) calcul *m*
caldron ['kɔldrən] *s* (culin) chaudron *m*; (mach) chaudière *f*
calendar ['kæləndər] *s* calendrier *m*
cal'endar year' *s* année *f* civile
calender ['kæləndər] *s* calandre *f* ‖ *tr* calandrer, cylindrer
calf [kæf] *s* (*pl* **calves** [kævz]) veau *m*; (*of leg*) mollet *m*
calf'skin' *s* veau *m*, peau *f* de veau
calf's' liv'er *s* foie *m* de veau
caliber ['kælɪbər] *s* calibre *m*, ‖ graduer, jauger
calibrate ['kælɪ,bret] *tr* calibrer
cali·co ['kælɪ,ko] *s* (*pl* **-coes** or **-cos**) calicot *m*, indienne *f*
California [,kælɪ'fɔrnɪ·ə] *s* Californie *f*; la Californie
calipers ['kælɪpərz] *spl* compas *m* à calibrer
caliph ['kelɪf], ['kælɪf] *s* calife *m*
caliphate ['kælɪfet] *s* califat *m*
calisthenic ['kælɪs'θɛnɪk] *adj* callisthénique ‖ **calisthenics** *spl* callisthénie *f*
calk [kɔk] *s* crampon *m* à glace ‖ *tr* calfater
call [kɔl] *s* (*signal; summons; naming*) appel *m*; (*cry*) cri *m*; (*visit*) visite *f*; (*at a port*) escale *f*; (telp) appel téléphonique; **to have no call to** n'avoir aucune raison de ‖ *tr* appeler; (*e.g., the doctor*) faire venir; (*a meeting*) convoquer; **to call aside** prendre à part; **to call back** rappeler; **to call down** (*from upstairs*) faire descendre; (*the wrath of the gods*) invoquer; (*to scold*) (coll) gronder; **to call off** (*a dog*) rappeler; (coll) annuler, décommander; **to call the roll** faire l'appel; **to call to mind** rappeler; **to call to order** rappeler à l'ordre; **to call up** (coll) passer un coup de fil à; (mil) mobiliser ‖ *intr* appeler, crier; (*to*

visit) faire une visite; (naut) faire escale; **to call upon** faire appel à; **to call upon s.o. to speak** inviter qn à prendre la parole

call′ bell′ *s* sonnette *f*

call′ box′ *s* guérite *f* téléphonique

call′ boy′ *s* (*in a hotel*) chasseur *m*; (theat) avertisseur *m*

caller [ˈkɔlər] *s* visiteur *m*

call′ girl′ *s* call-girl *f*

calling [ˈkɔlɪŋ] *s* (*occupation*) métier *m*, vocation *f*; (*of a meeting*) convocation *f*

call′ing card′ *s* carte *f* de visite

call′ let′ter *s* (telg, rad) indicatif *m* d'appel

call′ mon′ey *s* prêts *mpl* au jour le jour

callous [ˈkæləs] *adj* (*foot, hand, etc.*) calleux; (*unfeeling*) endurci, insensible

callow [ˈkælo] *adj* inexpérimenté, novice

cal′low youth′ *s* blanc-bec *m*

callus [ˈkæləs] *s* (*on skin*) cal *m*, durillon *m*, callosité *f*; (bot) cal *m*

calm [kɑm] *adj & s* calme *m* ‖ *tr* calmer; **to calm down** pacifier ‖ *intr*—**to calm down** se calmer; (*said of wind or sea*) calmir

calorie [ˈkæləri] *s* calorie *f*

calum·ny [ˈkæləmni] *s* (*pl* **-nies**) calomnie *f*

calva·ry [ˈkælvəri] *s* (*pl* **-ries**) calvaire *m*; **Calvary** le Calvaire

calve [kæv], [kɑv] *intr* vêler

cam [kæm] *s* came *f*

cambric [ˈkembrɪk] *s* batiste *f*

camel [ˈkæməl] *s* chameau *m*

camellia [kəˈmiljə] *s* camélia *m*

came·o [ˈkæmi,o] *s* (*pl* **-os**) camée *m*

camera [ˈkæmərə] *s* appareil *m* (photographique)

cam′era bug′ *s* chasseur *m* d'images

cam′era·man′ *s* (*pl* **-men′**) photographe *m*; (mov) cadreur *m*

camomile [ˈkæmə,maɪl] *s* camomille *f*

camouflage [ˈkæmə,flɑʒ] *s* camouflage *m* ‖ *tr* camoufler

camp [kæmp] *s* camp *m* ‖ *intr* camper; **to go camping** faire du camping

campaign [kæmˈpen] *s* campagne *f* ‖ *intr* faire campagne

campaigner [kæmˈpenər] *s* propagandiste *mf*; vétéran *m*

camp′ bed′ *s* lit *m* de camp, lit de sangle

camp′ chair′ *s* chaise *f* pliante

camper [ˈkæmpər] *s* campeur *m*; (aut) camping-car *m*

camp′fire′ *s* feu *m* de camp

camp′ground′ *s* camping *m*

camphor [ˈkæmfər] *s* camphre *m*

camping [ˈkæmpɪŋ] *s* camping *m*

camp′stool′ *s* pliant *m*

campus [ˈkæmpəs] *s* campus *m*, terrain *m* universitaire

cam′shaft′ *s* arbre *m* à cames

can [kæn] *s* (*of food, beer, film, garbage, etc.*) boîte *f*; (*e.g., for gasoline*) bidon *m* ‖ *v* (*pret & pp* **canned**; *ger* **canning**) *tr* mettre en boîte, conserver; (*to dismiss*) (slang) dégommer ‖ *v* (*pret & cond* **could** [kʊd]) *aux*—**Albert can't do it** Albert ne

peut (pas) le faire; **can he swim?** sait-il nager?

Canada [ˈkænədə] *s* le Canada

Canadian [kəˈnedɪ·ən] *adj* canadien ‖ *s* (*person*) Canadien *m*

canal [kəˈnæl] *s* canal *m*

canar·y [kəˈnɛri] *s* (*pl* **-ies**) canari *m*, serin *m*

can·cel [ˈkænsəl] *v* (*pret & pp* **-celed** or **-celled**; *ger* **-celing** or **-celling**) *tr* annuler; (*a word*) biffer, rayer; (*a contract*) résilier; (*a postage stamp*) oblitérer; **to cancel an invitation** décommander les invités; **to cancel each other out** s'annuler, se détruire

cancellation [ˌkænsəˈleʃən] *s* annulation *f*; (*of postage stamp*) oblitération *f*; (*of contract*) résiliation *f*

cancer [ˈkænsər] *s* cancer *m*; **Cancer** (astr, astrol) le Cancer

cancerous [ˈkænsərəs] *adj* cancéreux

candela·brum [ˌkændəˈlebrəm] *s* (*pl* **-bra** [brə] or **-brums**) candélabre *m*

candid [ˈkændɪd] *adj* franc

candida·cy [ˈkændɪdəsi] *s* (*pl* **-cies**) candidature *f*

candidate [ˈkændɪ,det] *s* candidat *m*

can′did cam′era *s* caméra *f* invisible

candied *adj* candi

candied′ fruit′ *s* fruit *m* candi

candle [ˈkændəl] *s* bougie *f*; (*of tallow*) chandelle *f*; (eccl) cierge *m*

can′dle·hold′er *s* bougeoir *m*

can′dle·light′ *s* lumière *f* de bougie

can′dle·pow′er *s* (phys) bougie *f*

can′dle·stick′ *s* chandelier *m*, bougeoir *m*

can′dle ta′ble *s* guéridon *m*

candor [ˈkændər] *s* franchise *f*, loyauté *f*

can·dy [ˈkændi] *s* (*pl* **-dies**) confiserie *f*, bonbons *mpl*; **candies** douceurs *fpl*; **piece of candy** bonbon ‖ *v* (*pret & pp* **-died**) *tr* glacer, faire candir ‖ *intr* se candir

can′dy box′ *s* boîte *f* à bonbons

can′dy corn′ *s* grains *mpl* de maïs soufflés et sucrés

can′dy dish′ *s* bonbonnière

can′dy machine′ *s* distributeur *m* de friandises

can′dy store′ *s* confiserie *f*

cane [ken] *s* canne *f*; (bot) canne ‖ *tr* canner, rempailler

cane′ chair′ *s* chaise *f* cannée

cane′ sug′ar *s* sucre *m* de canne

canine [ˈkenaɪn] *adj* canin ‖ *s* (*tooth*) canine *f*

canister [ˈkænɪstər] *s* boîte *f* métallique; (mil) boîte à mitraille

canker [ˈkæŋkər] *s* chancre *m*; (*in fruit; in society*) ver *m* rongeur ‖ *tr* ronger; (*society*) corrompre

canned [kænd] *adj* (*food*) en boîte, en conserve; (*drunk*) (slang) rétamé, rond; (*fired*) (slang) flanqué à la porte, vidé

canned′ goods′ *spl* conserves *fpl*, aliments *mpl* conservés

canned′ mu′sic *s* (coll) musique *f* enregistrée, musique en conserve

canner·y [ˈkænəri] s (pl **-ies**) conserverie f
cannibal [ˈkænɪbəl] adj & s cannibale mf
canning [ˈkænɪŋ] s conservation f
can′ning fac′tory s conserverie f
cannon [ˈkænən] s canon m
cannonade [,kænəˈned] s canonnade f ‖ tr canonner
can′non·ball′ s boulet m (de canon)
can′non fod′der s chair f à canon
can·ny [ˈkæni] adj (comp **-nier**; super **-niest**) prudent, circonspect; rusé, malin
canoe [kəˈnu] s canoë m
canoeist [kəˈnu·ɪst] s canoéiste mf
canon [ˈkænən] s canon m
canonical [kəˈnɑnɪkəl] adj canonique, canonial ‖ **canonicals** spl vêtements mpl sacerdotaux
canonize [ˈkænə,naɪz] tr canoniser
can′ o′pener s ouvre-boîtes m
canopy [ˈkænəpi] s (pl **-pies**) dais m; (over an entrance) marquise f
cant [kænt] s (insincere conventional expression) l'affectation f de pruderie, des phrases fpl toute faites; (argot) jargon m ‖ tr (to tip) incliner ‖ intr (to tip) s'incliner; (to be hypocritical) papelarder
cantaloupe [ˈkæntə,lop] s cantaloup m
cantankerous [kænˈtæŋkərəs] adj revêche, acariâtre
cantata [kənˈtɑtə] s cantate f
canteen [kænˈtin] s (shop) cantine f; (water flask) bidon m; (service club) foyer m du soldat, du marin, etc.
canter [ˈkæntər] s petit galop m ‖ intr aller au petit galop
canticle [ˈkæntɪkəl] s cantique m, hymne f
cantilever [ˈkæntɪ,livər] adj & s cantilever m
can′tilever bridge′ s pont m cantilever, pont à consoles
canton [ˈkæntɑn] s canton m
canvas [ˈkænvəs] s (cloth) canevas m; (picture) toile f
canvass [ˈkænvəs] s (scrutiny) enquête f; (campaign) tournée f électorale ‖ tr (a voter) solliciter la voix de; (a district) faire une tournée électorale dans; (com) prospecter ‖ intr (com) faire la place; **to canvass for** (a candidate) faire une campagne électorale en faveur de
canyon [ˈkænjən] s cañon m
cap [kæp] s (with visor) casquette f; (without brim) bonnet m; (to wear with academic gown) toque f, mortier m; (of bottle) capsule f; (of cartridge) amorce f, capsule; (of fountain pen) capuchon m, chapeau m; (of valve; to cover photographic lens) chapeau; **to set one's cap for** chercher à captiver ‖ v (pret & pp **capped**; ger **capping**) tr coiffer; (a bottle) capsuler; (a cartridge) amorcer; (a success) couronner; (to outdo) (coll) surpasser
cap. abbr (**capital letter**) maj.
capable [ˈkepəbəl] adj capable
capacious [kəˈpeʃəs] adj spacieux, vaste, ample

capaci·ty [kəˈpæsɪti] s (pl **-ties**) capacité f; **filled to capacity** comble; **in the capacity of** en tant que, en qualité de, à titre de
cap′ and gown′ s costume m académique, toge f et mortier m; **in cap and gown** en toque et en toge
cape [kep] s (clothing) cape f, pèlerine f; (geog) cap m, promontoire m
Cape′ of Good Hope′ s Cap m de Bonne Espérance
caper [ˈkepər] s cabriole f, gambade f; (bot) câpre f ‖ tr cabrioler, gambader
Cape′town′ s Le Cap
capital [ˈkæpɪtəl] adj capital; excellent ‖ s (city) capitale f; (archit) chapiteau m; (com) capital m; (typ) majuscule f, capitale; **small capital** petite capitale
cap′ital and la′bor spl le capital et le travail
capitalism [ˈkæpɪtə,lɪzəm] s capitalisme m
capitalist [ˈkæpɪtəlɪst] adj & s capitaliste mf
capitalize [ˈkæpɪtə,laɪz] tr & intr capitaliser; (typ) écrire avec une majuscule; **to capitalize on** miser sur, tourner à son profit, tirer parti de
cap′ital let′ter s majuscule f
cap′ital pun′ishment s peine f capitale
capitol [ˈkæpɪtəl] s capitole m
capitulate [kəˈpɪtʃə,let] intr capituler
capon [ˈkepɑn] s chapon m
caprice [kəˈpris] s caprice m
capricious [kəˈprɪʃəs] adj capricieux
Capricorn [ˈkæprɪ,kɔrn] s (astr, astrol) le Capricorne
capsize [ˈkæpsaɪz] tr faire chavirer ‖ intr chavirer, capoter
capstan [ˈkæpstən] s cabestan m
capsule [ˈkæpsəl] s capsule f; (bot, rok) capsule
captain [ˈkæptən] s (head) chef m, capitaine m; (mil) capitaine; (naut) commandant m; (sports) chef d'équipe ‖ tr commander, diriger
captain·cy [ˈkæptənsi] s (pl **-cies**) direction f, commandement m; grade m de capitaine
caption [ˈkæpʃən] s légende f; (mov) sous-titre m ‖ tr intituler, donner un sous-titre à
captious [ˈkæpʃəs] adj pointilleux, chicaneux; (insidious) captieux
captivate [ˈkæptɪ,vet] tr captiver
captive [ˈkæptɪv] adj & s captif m
captivi·ty [kæpˈtɪvɪti] s (pl **-ties**) captivité f
captor [ˈkæptər] s ravisseur m; (naut) auteur m d'une prise
capture [ˈkæptʃər] s capture f, prise f ‖ tr capturer
car [kɑr] s (automobile) auto f, voiture f; (of elevator) cabine f; (rr) wagon m, voiture; (for mail, baggage, etc.) (rr) fourgon m
carafe [kəˈræf] s carafe f
caramel [ˈkærəməl] s caramel m
carat [ˈkærət] s carat m
caravan [ˈkærə,væn] s caravane f
caravansa·ry [,kærəˈvænsəri] s (pl **-ries**) caravansérail m
caraway [ˈkærə,we] s carvi m
car′away seed′ s graine f de carvi

car'barn' s dépôt m de tramways

carbide ['kɑrbaɪd] s carbure m

carbine ['kɑrbaɪn] s carabine f

carbol'ic ac'id [kɑr'bɑlɪk] s acide m phénique

car' bomb' s voiture f piégée

carbon ['kɑrbən] s (chemical element) carbone m; (part of arc light or battery) charbon m; (in auto cylinder) calamine f; papier m carbone

car'bonated wa'ter ['kɑrbə,netɪd] s eau f gazeuse, soda m

car'bon cop'y s double m au carbone; (fig) calque m; (person) (fig) sosie m

car'bon diox'ide s gaz m carbonique

car'bon monox'ide s oxyde m de carbone

car'bon monox'ide poi'soning s oxycarbonisme m

car'bon pa'per s papier m carbone

carbuncle ['kɑrbʌŋkəl] s furoncle m

carburetor ['kɑrbə,retər] s carburateur m

carcass ['kɑrkəs] s (dead body) cadavre m; (without offal) carcasse f

carcinogenic [,kɑrsəno'ʒɛnɪk] adj cancérigène, cancérogène

carcinoma ['kɑrsɪ'nomə] s carcinome m

card [kɑrd] s carte f; (for filing) fiche f; (for carding) carde f; (coll) original m, numéro m, type m; **to have a card up one's sleeve** avoir un atout dans sa manche; **to put one's cards on the table** jouer cartes sur table ‖ tr carder, peigner

card'board' s carton m, papier m fort

card' case' s porte-cartes m

card' cat'alogue s fichier m

cardiac ['kɑrdɪ,æk] adj cardiaque ‖ s (patient) (coll) cardiaque mf

cardinal ['kɑrdɪnəl] adj & s cardinal m

card' in'dex s fichier m

cardiogram ['kɑrdɪ,o,græm] s cardiogramme m

card' par'ty s soirée f bridge, soirée poker, soirée whist (etc.)

card'sharp' s tricheur m

card' ta'ble s table f de jeu

card' trick' s tour m de cartes

care [kɛr] s (attention) soin m; (anxiety) souci m; (responsibility) charge f; (upkeep) entretien m; **in care of** aux bons soins de, à l'attention de; **take care!** faites attention!; **to take care not to se** garder de; **to take care of** se charger de; (a sick person) soigner; **to take care to** avoir soin de ‖ intr—**I don't care** ça m'est égal; **to care about** se soucier de, se préoccuper de; **to care for** (s.o.) avoir de la sympathie pour; (s.th.) trouver plaisir à; (a sick person) soigner; **to care to** désirer, vouloir

careen [kə'rin] tr faire coucher sur le côté ‖ intr donner de la bande, s'incliner

career [kə'rɪr] s carrière f

care'free' adj sans souci, insouciant

careful ['kɛrfəl] adj soigneux, attentif; **be careful!** soyez prudent!

careless ['kɛrlɪs] adj (neglectful) négligent; (nonchalant) insouciant

carelessness ['kɛrlɪsnɪs] s négligence f

caress [kə'rɛs] s caresse f ‖ tr caresser

caret ['kærət] s guidon m de renvoi

care'tak'er s concierge mf, gardien m

care'taker gov'ernment s gouvernement m intérimaire

care'worn' adj rongé par les soucis

car'fare' s prix m du trajet, place f; **to pay carfare** payer le parcours

car·go ['kɑrgo] s (pl -goes or -gos) cargaison f

car'go ter'minal s gare f de fret

car' heat'er s chauffage m de voiture

car' hop' s serveur m (qui apporte à manger aux automobilistes dans leur voiture)

Car'ibbe'an Sea [,kærɪ'bi·ən], [kə'rɪbɪ·ən] s Mer f des Caraïbes, Mer des Antilles

caricature ['kærɪkətʃər] s caricature f ‖ tr caricaturer

caricaturist ['kærɪkətʃərɪst] s caricaturiste mf

car'load' s voiturée f

carnage ['kɑrnɪdʒ] s carnage m

carnal ['kɑrnəl] adj charnel; sexuel

car'nal sin' s péché m de la chair

carnation [kɑr'neʃən] s œillet m

carnival ['kɑrnɪvəl] s carnaval m; fête f

car·ol ['kærəl] s chanson f, cantique m; (Christmas carol) noël m ‖ v (pret & pp -oled or -olled; ger -oling or -olling) tr & intr chanter

carom ['kærəm] s carambolage m ‖ intr caramboler

carouse [kə'raʊz] intr faire la bombe

carp [kɑrp] s carpe f ‖ intr se plaindre

carpenter ['kɑrpəntər] s charpentier m; (joiner) menuisier m

carpentry ['kɑrpəntri] s charpenterie f

carpet ['kɑrpɪt] s tapis m ‖ tr recouvrir d'un tapis

car'pet sweep'er s balai m mécanique

car' pool' s co-voiturage m

car'port' s abri m pour auto

car'-rent'al serv'ice s entreprise f de location de voitures

carriage ['kærɪdʒ] s (horse-drawn) voiture f, équipage m; (used to transport royalty) carrosse m; (bearing) port m, maintien m; (cost of transport) frais mpl de port; (of typewriter; of rocket) chariot m; (of gun) affût m

carrier ['kærɪ·ər] s (person) porteur m; (e.g., a teamster) camionneur m, voiturier m; (vehicle) transporteur m

car'rier pig'eon s pigeon m voyageur

car'rier wave' s onde f porteuse

carrion ['kærɪ·ən] s charogne f

carrot ['kærət] s carotte f

carrousel [,kærə'zɛl] s (merry-go-round) manège m de chevaux de bois; (hist) carrousel m

car·ry ['kæri] v (pret & pp -ried) tr porter; (in adding numbers) retenir; **to be carried** (parl) être voté, être adopté; **to be carried**

away (*e.g., with enthusiasm*) être entraîné, s'importer; **to carry away** or **off** emporter, enlever; **to carry back** rapporter; **to carry down** descendre; **to carry forward** avancer; (bk) reporter; **to carry on** continuer; (*e.g., a conversation*) soutenir; **to carry oneself straight** se tenir droit; **to carry out** (*a plan*) exécuter; **to carry over** (bk) reporter; **to carry through** mener à bonne fin; **to carry up** monter; **to carry with one** (*e.g., an audience*) entraîner || *intr* (*said of voice or sound*) porter; **to carry on** continuer; (*in a ridiculous manner*) (coll) faire des espiègleries; (*angrily*) (coll) s'emporter

car′ sick′ness *s* mal *m* de la route

cart [kɑrt] *s* charrette *f*; (*in a supermarket*) poussette *f*; **to put the cart before the horse** mettre la charrue devant les bœufs || *tr* charrier; (*to truck*) camionner

cartel [kɑr′tɛl] *s* cartel *m*

car′ tel′ephone *s* radiotéléphone *m*

cartilage [′kɑrtɪlɪdʒ] *s* cartilage *m*

cartographer [kɑr′tɑgrəfər] *s* cartographe *m*

carton [′kɑrtən] *s* carton *m*, boîte *f*

cartoon [kɑr′tun] *s* dessin *m* humoristique; caricature *f*; (*comic strip*) bande *f* dessinée; (fa) carton *m*; (mov) dessin animé || *tr* caricaturer, ridiculiser

cartoonist [kɑr′tunɪst] *s* caricaturiste *mf*

cartridge [′kɑrtrɪdʒ] *s* cartouche *f*; capsule *f* enregistreuse de pick-up

car′tridge belt′ *s* cartouchière *f*

car′tridge case′ *s* cartouchière *f*

cart′wheel′ *s* roue *f*; **to turn cartwheels** faire la roue

carve [kɑrv] *tr* & *intr* sculpter; (culin) découper

carver [′kɑrvər] *s* sculpteur *m*; (culin) découpeur *m*

carv′ing knife′ *s* couteau *m* à découper

car′wash′ *s* (*place of business*) lave-auto *m*, tunnel *m* de lavage; (*car washing*) lavage *m* de voitures

car′ wax′ *s* crème *f* pour auto

cascade [kæs′ked] *s* cascade *f* || *intr* cascader

case [kes] *s* (*instance, example*) cas *m*; (*for packing; of clock or piano*) caisse *f*; (*for cigarettes, eyeglasses, cartridges*) étui *m*; (*for jewels, silver, etc.*) écrin *m*; (*for watch*) boîtier *m*; (*for pillow*) taie *f*; (*for surgical instruments*) trousse *f*; (*for sausage*) peau *f*; (*showcase*) vitrine *f*; (*covering*) enveloppe *f*, couverture *f*; (*law*) cause *f*; (typ) casse *f*; **as the case may be** selon le cas; **in any case** en tout cas; **in case** au cas où; **in case of emergency** en cas d'imprévu; **in no case** en aucun cas; **just in case** à tout hasard; **to win one's case** avoir gain de cause || *tr* (*to put into a case*) encaisser; (*to package*) envelopper; (*to observe*) (slang) observer, épier

case′hard′en *tr* aciérer, cémenter; (fig) endurcir

casein [′kesi·ɪn] *s* caséine *f*

casement [′kesmənt] *s* croisée *f*

case′ work′ *s* étude *f* sur dossier

cash [kæʃ] *s* espèces *fpl*; **cash down** argent comptant; **cash offer** offre *f* réelle; **cash on delivery** livraison contre remboursement; **cash on hand** fonds *mpl* en caisse; **in cash** en numéraire || *tr* toucher, encaisser || *intr*—**to cash in on** (coll) tirer parti de

cash′ and car′ry *s* achat *m* au comptant et à emporter, paye et prends

cash′ bal′ance *s* solde *m* de caisse

cash′ bar′ *s* bar *m* payant

cash′ dis′count *s* escompte *m* au comptant

cash′ flow′ *s* argent *m* vif, flux *m* de caisse

cashew [′kæʃu] *s* noix *f* d'acajou, anacarde *m*, cajou *m*; (*tree*) anacardier *m*

cash′ew nut′ *s* noix *f* d'acajou, cajou *m*

cashier [kæ′ʃɪr] *s* caissier *m*

cashmere [′kæʃmɪr] *s* cachemire *m*

cash′ reg′ister *s* caisse *f* enregistreuse

casing [′kesɪŋ] *s* enveloppe *f*, chemise *f*, coffrage *m*; (*of door or window*) chambranle *m*

cask [kæsk] *s* tonneau *m*, fût *m*

casket [′kæskɪt] *s* (*for jewels*) écrin *m*, cassette *f*; (*for interment*) cercueil *m*

casserole [′kæsə,rol] *s* terrine *f*

cassette [kə′sɛt] *s* cassette *f*

cassette′ deck′ *s* platine *f* à cassettes

cassette′ play′er *s* lecteur *m* de cassettes

cassock [′kæsək] *s* soutane *f*

cast [kæst] *s* (*mold*) moule *m*; (*of metal*) fonte *f*; (*of fish line*) lancer *m*; (*throw*) jet *m*; (*for broken limb*) plâtre *m*; (*squint*) léger strabisme *m*; (theat) distribution *f* || *v* (*pret* & *pp* **cast**) *tr* fondre, jeter en moule; (*to throw*) lancer; (*a glance*) jeter; (*a play*) distribuer les rôles de; **to be cast in one piece with** venir de fonte avec; **to cast aside** mettre de côté; **to cast lots** tirer au sort; **to cast off** rejeter; **to cast out** mettre à la porte; (*a spell*) exorciser || *intr* (fishing) lancer la canne; **to cast about for** chercher; **to cast off** (naut) larguer les amarres

castanets [,kæstə′nɛts] *spl* castagnettes *fpl*

cast′away′ *adj* & *s* naufragé *m*

caste [kæst] *s* caste *f*

caster [′kæstər] *s* (*wheel*) roulette *f*; (*cruet stand*) huilier *m*; (*shaker*) saupoudreuse *f*

castigate [′kæstɪ,get] *tr* châtier, corriger

Castile [kæs′til] *s* Castille *f*; la Castille

Castilian [kæs′tɪljən] *adj* castillan || *s* (*language*) castillan *m*; (*person*) Castillan *m*

casting [′kæstɪŋ] *s* (*act or process*) fonte *f*; (*thing cast*) pièce *f* fondue; (*act*) lancement *m*; (fishing) pêche *f* au lancer; (theat) distribution *f*

cast′ing rod′ *s* canne *f* à lancer

cast′ i′ron *s* fonte *f*

cast′-i′ron *adj* en fonte

cast′-iron stom′ach *s* estomac *m* d'autruche

castle [′kæsəl] *s* (*palace*) château *m*; (*fortified castle*) château fort; (chess) tour *f* || *tr* & *intr* (chess) roquer

cast′off′ *adj* & *s* rejeté *m*
cas′tor oil′ [′kæstər] *s* huile *f* de ricin
castrate [′kæstret] *tr* castrer
casual [′kæʒʊ·əl] *adj* casuel; (*indifferent*) insouciant, désinvolte
casually [′kæʒʊ·əli] *adv* nonchalamment, avec désinvolture; (*by chance*) fortuitement
casual·ty [′kæʒʊ·əlti] *s* (*pl* -ties) accident *m*; (*person*) accidenté *m*; **casualties** (mil) pertes *fpl*
cas′ualty list′ *s* état *m* des pertes
cat [kæt] *s* (*tomcat*) chat *m*; (*female cat*) chatte *f*; (naut) capon *m*; (*shrew*) (coll) cancanière *f*, chipie *f*; **a cat may look at a queen** un chien regarde bien un évêque; **to let the cat out of the bag** (coll) vendre or éventer la mèche; **to rain cats and dogs** (coll) pleuvoir à seaux
CAT [kæt] *s* (acronym) (**computerized axial tomography**) scanographie *f*
CAT′ scan′ner *s* (med) scanographe *m*
cataclysm [′kætə,klɪzəm] *s* cataclysme *m*
catacombs [′kætə,komz] *spl* catacombes *fpl*
catalogue [′kætə,ləg] *s* catalogue *m*; (*of university*) annuaire *m* ‖ *tr* cataloguer, classer
Catalonia [,kætə′loni·ə] *s* Catalogne *f*; la Catalogne
catalyst [′kætəlɪst] *s* catalyseur *m*
catapult [′kætə,pʌlt] *s* catapulte *f* ‖ *tr* catapulter
cataract [′kætə,rækt] *s* cataracte *f*
catarrh [kə′tɑr] *s* catarrhe *m*
catastrophe [kə′tæstrəfi] *s* catastrophe *f*
cat′call′ *s* huée *f*; (theat) coup *m* de sifflet ‖ *tr* & *intr* (theat) siffler
catch [kætʃ] *s* (*catching and thing caught*) prise *f*, capture *f*; (*on door*) loquet *m*; (*on buckle*) ardillon *m*; (*caught by fisherman*) pêche *f*; (mach) cliquet *m*, chien *m*; **good catch!** (sports) bien rattrapé! **there's a catch to it** (coll) c'est une attrape ‖ *v* (*pret* & *pp* **caught** [kɔt]) *tr* attraper; (*a train; a fish; fire*) prendre; (*a word or sound*) saisir; (*e.g., one's coat*) accrocher; **caught like a rat in a trap** fait comme un rat; **to catch hold of** saisir, s'accrocher à; **to catch s.o. in the act** prendre qn sur le fait; **to catch up** (*in a mistake*) surprendre ‖ *intr* prendre; (*said of fire*) s'allumer, s'enflammer, se prendre; **to catch on** (*a nail, thorn, etc.*) s'accrocher à; (*to understand*) (coll) comprendre; (*to become popular*) (coll) devenir célèbre, devenir populaire; **to catch up** se rattraper; **to catch up with** rattraper
catch′all′ *s* débarras *m*, fourre-tout *m*
catch′ ba′sin *s* bouche *f* d'égout
catching [′kætʃɪŋ] *adj* contagieux; (*e.g., smile*) communicatif
catch′ ques′tion *s* (coll) colle *f*
catch′word′ *s* mot *m* de ralliement, slogan *m*; (*cliché*) rengaine *f*, scie *f*; (*at the bottom of page*) réclame *f*; (theat) réplique *f*; (typ) mot-souche *m*

catch·y [′kætʃi] *adj* (*comp* -ier; *super* -iest) (*tune*) facile à retenir, entraînant; (*question*) insidieux, à traquenard
catechism [′kætɪ,kɪzəm] *s* catéchisme *m*
categorical [,kætɪ′gɔrɪkəl] *adj* catégorique
catego·ry [′kætɪ,gori] *s* (*pl* -ries) catégorie *f*
cater [′ketər] *tr* (*e.g., a wedding*) fournir le buffet de ‖ *intr* être fournisseur; **to cater to** pourvoir à; (*to favor*) entourer de prévenances
cat′er-cor′nered [′kætər,kɔrnərd] *adj* diagonal ‖ *adv* diagonalement
caterer [′ketərər] *s* fournisseur *m*, traiteur *m*
caterpillar [′kætər,pɪlər] *s* chenille *f*
cat′erpillar trac′tor *s* autochenille *f*
cat′fish′ *s* poisson-chat *m*
cat′gut′ *s* boyau *m* de chat; (*string*) corde *f* à boyau, boyau; (surg) catgut *m*
cathedral [kə′θidrəl] *s* cathédrale *f*
catheter [′kæθɪtər] *s* (med) cathéter *m*
catheterization [,kæθɪtərɪ′zeʃən] *s* (surg) cathétérisme *m*
cathode [′kæθod] *s* cathode *m*
catholic [′kæθəlɪk] *adj* (*universal*) catholique; tolérant, large, e.g., **he has a catholic mind** il a l'esprit large, il est fort tolérant ‖ (*cap*) *adj* & *s* catholique *mf*
Catholicism [kə′θɑlɪ,sɪzəm] *s* catholicisme *m*
catholicity [,kæθə′lɪsɪti] *s* catholicité *f*, universalité *f*; (*tolerance*) largeur *f* d'esprit, tolérance *f*
catkin [′kætkɪn] *s* (bot) chaton *m*
cat′nap′ *s* petit somme *m*
cat′nip′ *s* herbe-aux-chats *f*, cataire *f*
cat-o′-nine-tails′ [,kætə′naɪn,telz] *s* chat *m* à neuf queues
cat′s′-paw′ *s* (naut) risée *f*; (coll) dupe *f*
catsup [′kætsəp] *s* = **ketchup**
cattle [′kætəl] *s* bœufs *mpl*; (*including horses*) gros bétail *m*, bestiaux *mpl*
cat′tle car′ *s* fourgon *m* à bestiaux
cat′tle cross′ing *s* passage *m* de troupeaux
cat′tle·man *s* (*pl* -men) éleveur *m* de bétail
cat′tle thief′ *s* voleur *m* de bétail
cat-ty [′kæti] *adj* (*comp* -tier; *super* -tiest) (coll) cancanier, méchant
cat′ty-cor′ner *adj* (coll) diagonal ‖ *adv* (coll) diagonalement
cat′walk′ *s* passerelle *f*
Caucasian [kɔ′keʃən] *adj* caucasien ‖ *s* Caucasien *m*
caucus [′kɔkəs] *s* comité *m* électoral ‖ *intr* se grouper en comité électoral
cauliflower [′kɔlɪ,flau·ər] *s* chou-fleur *m*
caulk [kɔk] *tr* calfater
cause [kɔz] *s* cause *f*; **to have cause to** avoir lieu de ‖ *tr* causer; **to cause to** + *inf* faire + *inf*, e.g., **he caused him to stumble** il l'a fait trébucher
cause′way′ *s* chaussée *f*
caustic [′kɔstɪk] *adj* caustique
cauterize [′kɔtə,raɪz] *tr* cautériser
caution [′kɔʃən] *s* prudence *f*, précaution *f*; (*warning*) avertissement *m* ‖ *tr* mettre en garde, avertir
cautious [′kɔʃəs] *adj* prudent, circonspect

cavalcade [,kævəl'ked] s cavalcade f
cavalier [,kævə'lır] adj & s cavalier m
caval·ry ['kævəlrı] s (pl -ries) cavalerie f
cav′alry·man′ or **cav′alry·man** s (pl -men′ or -men) cavalier m
cave [kev] s caverne f ‖ intr—**to cave in** s'effondrer
cave′-in′ s effondrement m
cave′ man′ s homme m des cavernes; (coll) rustre m, ours m
cavern ['kævərn] s caverne f
caviar ['kævı,ɑr] s caviar m
cav·il ['kævıl] v (pret & pp -iled or -illed; ger -iling or -illing) intr ergoter, chicaner
cavi·ty ['kævıtı] s (pl -ties) cavité f
cavort [kə'vɔrt] intr gambader, caracoler
caw [kɔ] s croassement m ‖ intr croasser, crailler
C.B. ['si'bi] s (letterword) (**citizen band**) bande f publique
C.B. ra′dio s appareil m de radio émetteur-récepteur multicanaux
cease [sis] s cessation f; **without cease** sans cesse ‖ tr & intr cesser; **to cease fire** cesser le feu
cease′-fire′ s cessez-le-feu m
ceaseless ['sislıs] adj incessant, continuel
cedar ['sidər] s cèdre m
cede [sid] tr & intr céder
cedilla [sı'dılə] s cédille f
ceiling ['silıŋ] s plafond m; **to hit the ceiling** (coll) sortir de ses gonds
ceil′ing lamp′ s plafonnier m
ceil′ing price′ s prix m maximum
celebrant ['sɛlıbrənt] s (eccl) célébrant m
celebrate ['sɛlı,bret] tr célébrer
celebrated adj célèbre
celebration [,sɛlı'breʃən] s célébration f, fête f
celebri·ty [sı'lɛbrıtı] s (pl -ties) célébrité f; (e.g., movie star) vedette f
celery ['sɛlərı] m céleri m
celestial [sı'lɛstʃəl] adj céleste
celiba·cy ['sɛlıbəsı] s (pl -cies) célibat m
celibate ['sɛlı,bet] adj & s célibataire mf
cell [sɛl] s cellule f; (of electric battery) élément m
cellar ['sɛlər] s (basement; wine cellar) cave f; (often partly above ground) sous-sol m
cellist or **′cellist** ['tʃɛlıst] s violoncelliste mf
cel·lo or **′cel·lo** ['tʃɛlo] s (pl -los) violoncelle m
cellophane ['sɛlə,fen] s cellophane f
celluloid ['sɛljə,lɔıd] s celluloïd m
Celt [sɛlt], [kɛlt] s Celte mf
Celtic ['sɛltık], ['kɛltık] adj celte, celtique ‖ s celtique m
cement [sı'mɛnt] s ciment m ‖ tr cimenter
cement′ mix′er s bétonnière f
cemeter·y ['sɛmı,tɛrı] s (pl -ies) cimetière m
censer ['sɛnsər] s encensoir m
censor ['sɛnsər] s censeur m ‖ tr censurer
cen′sor·ship′ s censure f
censure ['sɛnʃər] s blâme m ‖ tr blâmer

census ['sɛnsəs] s recensement m, dénombrement m; (in Roman Empire) cens m
cen′sus tak′er s recenseur m; (in ancient Rome) censeur m
cent [sɛnt] s cent m; **not to have a red cent to one's name** n'avoir pas un sou vaillant
centaur ['sɛntɔr] s centaure m
centenarian [,sɛntı'nɛrı·ən] s centenaire mf
centennial [sɛn'tɛnı·əl] adj centennal ‖ s centenaire m
center ['sɛntər] adj central ‖ s centre m; (middle) milieu m ‖ tr centrer ‖ intr—**to center on** concentrer sur
cen′ter cit′y s centre m de (la) ville
cen′ter fold′ s double page f
centering ['sɛntərıŋ] s centrage m; (phot) cadrage m
cen′ter·piece′ s milieu m de table, surtout m
centigrade ['sɛntı,gred] adj & s centigrade m
centimeter ['sɛntı,mitər] s centimètre m
centipede ['sɛntı,pid] s mille-pattes m, myriapodes mpl
central ['sɛntrəl] adj & s central m
Cen′tral Amer′ica s l'Amérique f centrale
Cen′tral Intel′ligence s la Sûreté, la Sûreté nationale
centralize ['sɛntrə,laız] tr centraliser ‖ intr se centraliser
centrifugal [sɛn'trıfjugəl] adj centrifuge
centrifuge ['sɛntrı,fjudʒ] s essoreuse f ‖ tr essorer
centu·ry ['sɛntʃərı] s (pl -ries) siècle m
cen′tury-old′ adj séculaire
ceramic [sı'ræmık] adj céramique ‖ **ceramics** s (art) céramique f; spl (objects) céramiques
cereal ['sırı·əl] adj céréalier ‖ s (grain) céréale f; (oatmeal) flocons mpl d'avoine; (cornflakes) flocons de maïs; (cooked cereal) bouillie f, gruau m
cerebral ['sɛrıbrəl] adj cérébral
ceremonial [,sɛrı'monı·əl] adj cérémonial; (e.g., tribal rites) cérémoniel ‖ s cérémonial m
ceremonious [,sɛrı'monı·əs] adj cérémonieux
ceremo·ny ['sɛrı,monı] s (pl -nies) cérémonie f; **to stand on ceremony** faire des cérémonies
certain ['sʌrtən] adj certain; **a certain** certain; **certain people** certains; **for certain** pour sûr, à coup sûr; **to make certain of** s'assurer de
certainly ['sʌrtənlı] adv certainement
certain·ty ['sʌrtəntı] s (pl -ties) certitude f
certificate [sər'tıfıkıt] s certificat m, acte m; (of birth, of marriage, etc.) bulletin m, acte m, extrait m; (proof) attestation f; (educ) diplôme m
cer′tified cop′y s extrait m; (formula used on documents) pour copie conforme
cer′tified pub′lic account′ant s expert-comptable m, comptable m agréé
certi·fy ['sʌrtı,faı] v (pret & pp -fied) tr certifier

cervix ['sʌrvɪks] *s* (*pl* **cervices** [sər'vaɪsiz]) nuque *f*

cessation [sɛ'seʃən] *s* cessation *f*, cesse *f*

cesspool ['sɛs,pul] *s* fosse *f* d'aisance, cloaque *m*

Ceylon [sɪ'lɑn] *s* Ceylan *m*

Ceylo·nese [,silə'niz] *adj* cingalais ‖ *s* (*pl* **-nese**) Cingalais *m*

chafe [tʃef] *tr* écorcher, irriter ‖ *intr* s'écorcher, s'irriter

chaff [tʃæf] *s* balle *f*; (*banter*) raillerie *f* ‖ *tr* railler, persifler

chaf′ing dish′ *s* réchaud *m* de table, chauffe-plats *m*

chagrin [ʃə'grɪn] *s* mortification *f*, humiliation *f* ‖ *tr* mortifier, humilier

chain [tʃen] *s* chaîne *f* ‖ *tr* enchaîner

chain′ gang′ *s* forçats *mpl* à la chaîne

chain′ reac′tion *s* (phys) réaction *f* en chaîne

chain′ saw′ *s* tronçonneuse *f*

chain′ smok′er *s* fumeur *m* à la file

chain′stitch′ *s* point *m* de chaînette

chain′ store′ *s* magasin *m* à succursales multiples, économat *m*

chair [tʃɛr] *s* (*seat*) chaise *f*; (*held by university professor*) chaire *f*; (*of presiding officer; presiding officer himself*) fauteuil *m*; (*of a committee, department, etc.*) chef *m*; **to take a chair** prendre un siège, s'asseoir; **to take the chair** occuper le fauteuil, présider une assemblée ‖ *tr* présider

chair′ lift′ *s* télésiège *m*

chair′man *s* (*pl* **-men**) président *m*

chair′man·ship′ *s* présidence *f*

chair′wom′an *s* (*pl* **-wom′en**) présidente *f*

chalice ['tʃælɪs] *s* calice *m*

chalk [tʃɔk] *s* craie *f*; **a piece of chalk** une craie, un morceau de craie ‖ *tr* marquer avec de la craie, écrire à la craie

chalk·y ['tʃɔki] *adj* (*comp* **-ier**; *super* **-iest**) crayeux

challenge ['tʃælɪndʒ] *s* (*call, summons*) défi *m*; (*objection*) contestation *f*; (mil) qui-vive *m*; (sports) challenge *m* ‖ *tr* défier; (*to question*) mettre en question, contester; (mil) crier qui-vive à

chamber ['tʃembər] *s* chambre *f*

chamberlain ['tʃembərlɪn] *s* chambellan *m*

cham′ber·maid′ *s* femme *f* de chambre

cham′ber mu′sic *s* musique *f* de chambre

Cham′ber of Com′merce *s* syndicat *m* d'initiative

chameleon [kə'mili·ən] *s* caméléon *m*

chamfer ['tʃæmfər] *s* chanfrein *m* ‖ *tr* chanfreiner

cham·ois ['ʃæmi] *s* (*pl* **-ois**) chamois *m*

champ [tʃæmp] *s* mâchonnement *m* ‖ *tr* mâcher bruyamment; **to champ at the bit** ronger son frein

champagne [ʃæm'pen] *s* champagne *m* ‖ (*cap*) *adj* champenois ‖ (*cap*) *s* Champagne *f*; la Champagne

champion ['tʃæmpɪ·ən] *s* champion *m* ‖ *tr* se faire le champion de, défendre

cham′pion·ship′ *s* championnat *m*

chance [tʃæns] *adj* fortuit, de rencontre ‖ *s* (*luck*) hasard *m*; (*good luck*) chance *f*, coup *m* de chance; (*possibility*) chance, possibilité *f*, e.g., **one chance in four** une chance sur quatre; (*opportunity*) occasion *f*, chance; **by chance** par hasard, fortuitement; **chances** chances *fpl*, sort *m*; **to take a chance** encourir un risque; acheter un billet de loterie; **to take chances** jouer gros jeu ‖ *tr* hasarder, risquer ‖ *intr*—**to chance to** venir à, avoir l'occasion de; **to chance upon** rencontrer par hasard

chance′ acquaint′ance *s* connaissance *f* de rencontre

chancel ['tʃænsəl] *s* chœur *m*, sanctuaire *m*

chanceller·y ['tʃænsələri] *s* (*pl* **-ies**) chancellerie *f*

chancellor ['tʃænsələr] *s* chancelier *m*, ministre *m*

chancre ['ʃæŋkər] *s* chancre *m*

chandelier [,ʃændə'lɪr] *s* lustre *m*

change [tʃendʒ] *s* changement *m*; (*coins*) pièces *fpl* rendues, monnaie *f*; **change in the wind** saute *f* de vent; **change of address** changement de domicile; **change of clothes** vêtements *mpl* de rechange; **for a change** comme distraction; pour changer ‖ *tr* changer; changer de, e.g., **to change religions** changer de culte; **to change sides** tourner casaque ‖ *intr* changer; (*said of voice at puberty*) muer; **to change over** (*e.g., from one system to another*) passer

changeable ['tʃendʒəbəl] *adj* changeable; (*weather*) variable; (*character*) changeant, mobile

changeless ['tʃendʒlɪs] *adj* immuable

change′ of life′ *s* retour *m* d'âge

change′ of voice′ *s* mue *f*

change′o′ver *s* changement *m*, renversement *m*, relève *f*

change′ purse′ *s* porte-monnaie *m*

change′ return′ *s* remboursement *m* dans le bas de l'appareil, retour *m* de monnaies

chan·nel ['tʃænəl] *s* (*body of water joining two others*) canal *m*; (*bed of river*) chenal *m*; (*means of communication*) voie *f*, canal; (*passage*) conduit *m*; (*groove*) cannelure *f*; (*strait*) bras *m* de mer; (*for trade*) débouché *m*; (rad) canal; (rad, telv) chaîne *f*; (telv) canal (Canad); **through channels** par la voie hiérarchique, par la filière ‖ *v* (*pret & pp* **-neled** or **-nelled**; *ger* **-neling** or **-nelling**) *tr* creuser, canneler

Chan′nel Is′lands *spl* îles *fpl* Anglo-Normandes

chant [tʃænt] *s* (*song; singing*) chant *m*; (*monotonous chant*) mélopée *f*; (*chanted by demonstrators*) chant scandé; (mus) psalmodie *f*, plain-chant *m* ‖ *tr & intr* psalmodier

chanter ['tʃæntər] *s* chantre *m*

chantey ['ʃænti] *s* chanson *f* de bord

chaos ['ke·ɑs] *s* chaos *m*

chaotic [ke'ɑtɪk] *adj* chaotique

chap [tʃæp] *s* (*fissure, crack*) crevasse *f*, gerçure *f*; (coll) type *m*, individu *m*; **poor**

chap (coll) pauvre vieux *m*; pauvre garçon *m* ‖ *v* (*pret* & *pp* **chapped**; *ger* **chapping**) *tr* crevasser, gercer ‖ *intr* se crevasser, se gercer

chapel [ˈtʃæpəl] *s* chapelle *f*; (*in a house*) oratoire *m*; (*Protestant chapel*) temple *m*

chaperon [ˈʃæpə,ron] *s* chaperon *m*, duègne *f* ‖ *tr* chaperonner

chaplain [ˈtʃæplɪn] *s* aumônier *m*

chaplet [ˈtʃæplɪt] *s* chapelet *m*

chapter [ˈtʃæptər] *s* chapitre *m*; (*of an association*) bureau *m* régional

char [tʃɑr] *v* (*pret* & *pp* **charred**; *ger* **charring**) *tr* & *intr* charbonner; **to become charred** se charbonner, se carboniser

character [ˈkærɪktər] *s* caractére *m*; (theat) personnage *m*; (typ) signe *m*; (coll) type *m*, sujet *m*, numéro *m*, phénomène *m*

char′acter ac′tor *s* acteur *m* de genre

characteristic [,kærɪktəˈrɪstɪk] *adj* & *s* caractéristique *f*

characterize [ˈkærɪktə,raɪz] *tr* caractériser, typer

char′acter ref′erence *s* certificat *m* de moralité, certificat de bonne vie et mœurs

char′coal′ *s* charbon *m* de bois

char′coal burn′er *s* charbonnier *m*

char′coal pen′cil *s* charbon *m*, crayon *m* de fusain

charge [tʃɑrdʒ] *s* (*responsibility*) charge *f*; (*cost*) prix *m*; (*person cared for*) personne *f* à charge; (*thing cared for*) chose *f* à charge; (*accusing*) accusation *f*; (*against a defendant*) chef *m* d'accusation; (*made to a jury*) résumé *m*; (mil) charge; **on a charge of** sous l'inculpation de; **to reverse the charges** téléphoner en p.c.v.; **to take charge of** se charger de; **without charge** gratis ‖ *tr* charger; **to charge s.o. s.th. for s.th.** prendre or demander q.ch. à qn pour q.ch.; **to charge to s.o.'s account** mettre sur le compte de qn ‖ *intr* (mil) charger; **to charge down on** foncer sur

charge′ account′ *s* compte *m* courant

charger [ˈtʃɑrdʒər] *s* cheval *m* de bataille; (elec) chargeur *m*

chariot [ˈtʃærɪ·ət] *s* char *m*

charisma [kəˈrɪzmə] *s* charme *m*, don *m* de plaire; (theol) charisme *m*

charitable [ˈtʃærɪtəbəl] *adj* charitable

chari·ty [ˈtʃærɪti] *s* (*pl* **-ties**) (*kindness*) charité *f*; (*action*) acte *m* de charité; (*alms*) bienfaisance *f*, aumônes *fpl*, charité; (*institution*) société *f* or œuvre *f* de bienfaisance; **for charity's sake** par charité

charlatan [ˈʃɑrlətən] *s* charlatan *m*

charm [tʃɑrm] *s* charme *m*; (*e.g., on a bracelet*) breloque *f*, porte-bonheur *m* ‖ *tr* charmer

charming [ˈtʃɑrmɪŋ] *adj* charmeur, charmant

charnel [ˈtʃɑrnəl] *adj* de charnier ‖ *s* charnier *m*, ossuaire *m*

chart [tʃɑrt] *s* (*map*) carte *f*; (*graph*) dessin *m* graphique; (*diagram*) diagramme *m*; (*table*) tableau *m* ‖ *tr* inscrire sur un dessin graphique; (naut) porter sur une carte, dresser la carte de

charter [ˈtʃɑrtər] *s* (*document*) charte *f*; (*authorization*) statuts *mpl*; (*of a bank*) privilège; (*chartering of a boat, bus, plane, etc.*) affrètement *m* ‖ *tr* accorder une charte à; (*a ship*) affréter, noliser; (*a bus*) louer

char′ter flight′ *s* vol *m* en charter, vol *m* à la demande

char′ter mem′ber *s* membre *m* fondateur

char′ter plane′ *s* charter *m*, avion *m* affété, avion nolisé

char′wom′an *s* (*pl* **-wom′en**) nettoyeuse *f*

chase [tʃes] *s* chasse *f*, poursuite *f*; (*for printing*) châssis *m* ‖ *tr* chasser; (*a gem*) enchâsser; (*gold*) ciseler; (*metal*) repousser; **to chase away** chasser ‖ *intr*—**to chase after** pourchasser, poursuivre

chaser [ˈtʃesər] *s* chasseur *m*; (*of women*) (coll) coureur *m*; (*taken after an alcoholic drink*) (coll) rince-gueule *m*

chasm [ˈkæzəm] *s* abîme *m*

chas·sis [ˈtʃæsi] *s* (*pl* **-sis** [siz]) châssis *m*

chaste [tʃest] *adj* chaste

chasten [ˈtʃesən] *tr* châtier

chastise [tʃæsˈtaɪz] *tr* châtier, corriger

chastisement [tʃæsˈtaɪzmənt] *s* châtiment *m*

chastity [ˈtʃæstɪti] *s* chasteté *f*

chat [tʃæt] *s* causerie *f*, causette *f* ‖ *v* (*pret* & *pp* **chatted**; *ger* **chatting**) *intr* causer, bavarder

château [ʃæto] *s* château *m*, manoir *m*, castel *m*

chattel [ˈtʃætəl] *s* bien *m* meuble, objet *m* mobiliaire

chatter [ˈtʃætər] *s* bavardage *m*, caquetage *m* ‖ *intr* bavarder, caqueter; (*said of teeth*) claquer

chat′ter·box′ *s* bavard *m*, babillard *m*

chauffeur [ˈʃofər] *s* chauffeur *m*

chauvinistic [,ʃovɪˈnɪstɪk] *adj* chauvin

cheap [tʃip] *adj* bon marché; (coll) honteux; **to get off cheap** (coll) en être quitte à bon compte

cheapen [ˈtʃipən] *tr* baisser le prix de; diminuer la valeur de

cheap′skate′ *s* (slang) rat *m*

cheat [tʃit] *s* tricheur *m*, fraudeur *m* ‖ *tr* tricher, frauder ‖ *intr* (e.g., *at cards*) tricher; (*e.g., in an examination*) frauder

cheating [ˈtʃitɪŋ] *s* tricherie *f*, fraude *f*

check [tʃɛk] *s* (*stopping*) arrêt *m*; (*brake*) frein *m*; (*supervision*) contrôle *m*, vérification *f*; (*in a restaurant*) addition *f*; (*drawn on a bank*) chèque *m*; (e.g., *of a chessboard*) carreau *m*; (*of the king in chess*) échec *m*; (*for baggage*) bulletin *m*; (*pass-out check*) contremarque *f*; (*chip, counter*) jeton *m*; **in check** en échec ‖ *tr* arrêter, freiner; contrôler, vérifier; (*baggage*) faire enregistrer; (e.g., *one's coat*) mettre au vestiaire; (*the king in chess*) faire échec à; **to check off** pointer, cocher ‖ *intr* s'arrêter; **to check in** (*at a hotel*) s'inscrire sur le registre; **to check out** (*of* *a hotel*) régler sa note; **to check up on** contrôler, examiner

check′book′ *s* carnet *m* de chèques, chéquier *m*

checked *adj* (*checkered*) à carreaux; (*syllable*) entravé

checker [ˈtʃɛkər] *s* (*inspector*) contrôleur *m*; (*piece used in game*) pion *m*; (*square of checkerboard*) carreau *m*; **checkers** jeu *m* de dames ‖ *tr* (*to divide in squares*) quadriller; (*to scatter here and there*) diaprer

check′er·board′ *s* damier *m*

checkered *adj* (*divided into squares*) quadrillé, à carreaux; (*varied*) varié, accidenté; (*career, life*) plein de vicissitudes, mouvementé

check′girl′ *s* préposée *f* au vestiaire

check′ing account′ *s* compte *m* en banque

check′ list′ *s* liste *f* de contrôle, liste de vérification

check′ mark′ *s* trait *m* de repère, repère *m*, coche *f*

check′mate′ *s* échec et mat *m*; (fig) échec *m* ‖ *tr* faire échec et mat à, mater ‖ *intr* faire échec et mat, mater ‖ *interj* échec et mat!

check′-out count′er *s* caisse *f* de sortie; (*in supermarket*) caisse de supermarché

check′point′ *s* contrôle *m* de police

check′room′ *s* (*cloakroom*) vestiaire *m*; (*baggage room*) consigne *f*

check′up′ *s* vérification *f*, examen *m* complet; (med) bilan *m* de santé

cheek [tʃik] *s* joue *f*; (coll) aplomb *m*, toupet *m*

cheek′bone′ *s* pommette *f*

cheep [tʃip] *intr* piauler

cheer [tʃɪr] *s* bonne humeur *f*, gaieté *f*; encouragement *m*, e.g., **word of cheer** parole *f* d'encouragement; **cheers** acclamations *fpl*, bravos *mpl*, vivats *mpl*; **three cheers for . . .!** vive . . .!; **to give three cheers** pousser trois hourras ‖ *tr* (*to cheer up*) encourager, égayer; (*to applaud*) acclamer, applaudir ‖ *intr* pousser des vivats, applaudir; **cheer up!** courage!

cheerful [ˈtʃɪrfəl] *adj* de bonne humeur, gai; (*place*) d'aspect agréable

cheerfully [ˈtʃɪrfəli] *adv* gaiement; (*willingly*) de bon cœur

cheer′lead′er *s* chef *m* de claque

cheerless [ˈtʃɪrlɪs] *adj* morne, triste

cheese [tʃiz] *s* fromage *m*

cheese′cake′ *s* (slang) les pin up *fpl*

cheese′ cake′ *s* soufflé *m* au fromage, tarte *f* au fromage

cheese′cloth′ *s* gaze *f*

chees·y [ˈtʃizi] *adj* (*comp* **-ier**; *super* **-iest**) caséeux; (slang) miteux

cheetah [ˈtʃitə] *s* guépard *m*

chef [ʃɛf] *s* chef *m* de cuisine, maître queux *m*

chemical [ˈkɛmɪkəl] *adj* chimique ‖ *s* produit *m* chimique

chemist [ˈkɛmɪst] *s* chimiste *mf*

chemistry [ˈkɛmɪstri] *s* chimie *f*

cherish [ˈtʃɛrɪʃ] *tr* chérir; (*an idea*) nourrir; (*a hope*) caresser

cher·ry [ˈtʃɛri] *s* (*pl* **-ries**) cerise *f*; (*tree*) cerisier *m*

cher′ry or′chard *s* cerisaie *f*

cher′ry tree′ *s* cerisier *m*

cher·ub [ˈtʃɛrəb] *s* (*pl* **-ubim** [əbɪm]) chérubin *m* ‖ *s* (*pl* **-ubs**) (fig) chérubin *m*

chess [tʃɛs] *s* échecs *mpl*; **to play chess** jouer aux échecs

chess′board′ *s* échiquier *m*

chess′ piece′ *s* pièce *f* du jeu d'échecs; (*other than pawn*) figure *f*

chess′ set′ *s* échecs *mpl*

chest [tʃɛst] *s* caisse *f*; (*of drawers*) commode *f*; (anat) poitrine *f*; **to get s.th. off one's chest** (coll) se déboutonner, dire ce qu'on a sur le cœur

chest′ mic′rophone *s* micro-plastron *m*

chestnut [ˈtʃɛsnət] *adj* (*color*) châtain ‖ *s* (*color*) châtain *m*; (*nut*) châtaigne *f*, marron *m*; (*tree*) châtaignier *m*

chest′ of drawers′ *s* commode *f*, chiffonnier *m*

cheval′ glass′ [ʃəˈvæl] *s* psyché *f*

chevron [ˈʃɛvrən] *s* chevron *m*

chew [tʃu] *tr* mâcher; (*tobacco*) chiquer

chewing [ˈtʃu·ɪŋ] *s* mastication *f*

chew′ing gum′ *s* gomme *f* à mâcher, chewing-gum *m*

chicaner·y [ʃɪˈkɛnəri] *s* (*pl* **-ies**) truc *m*, ruse *f*, artifice *m*

chick [tʃɪk] *s* poussin *m*; (*girl*) (slang) tendron *m*, nana *f*

chickadee [ˈtʃɪkə,di] *s* (*Parus atricapillus*) mésange *f* boréale

chicken [ˈtʃɪkən] *s* poulet *m*; **to be chicken** (slang) avoir la frousse ‖ *intr*—**to chicken out** (slang) caner

chick′en coop′ *s* poulailler *m*

chick′en-heart′ed *adj* froussard, poltron

chick′en pox′ *s* varicelle *f*

chick′en stew′ *s* poule-au-pot *m*

chick′en wire′ *s* treillis *m* métallique

chick′pea′ *s* pois *m* chiche

chico·ry [ˈtʃɪkəri] *s* (*pl* **-ries**) chicorée *f*

chide [tʃaɪd] *v* (*pret* **chided** or **chid** [tʃɪd]; *pp* **chided, chid,** or **chidden** [ˈtʃɪdən]) *tr & intr* gronder

chief [tʃif] *adj* principal, en chef ‖ *s* chef *m*; (*boss*) (coll) patron *m*

chief′ exec′utive *s* chef *m* de l'exécutif

chief′ jus′tice *s* président *m* de la Cour suprême

chiefly [ˈtʃifli] *adv* principalement

chief′ of police′ *s* préfet *m* de police

chief′ of staff′ *s* chef *m* d'état-major

chief′ of state′ *s* chef *m* d'État

chieftain [ˈtʃiftən] *s* chef *m*

chiffon [ʃɪˈfan] *s* mousseline *f* de soie

chiffonier [ˌʃɪfəˈnɪr] *s* chiffonnier *m*

chilblain [ˈtʃɪl,blen] *s* engelure *f*

child [tʃaɪld] *s* (*pl* **children** [ˈtʃɪldrən]) enfant *mf*; **with child** enceinte

child′ molest′ing [moˈlɛstɪŋ] *s* détournement *m* de mineur

child′birth′ *s* accouchement *m*

child'hood *s* enfance *f*
childish ['tʃaɪldɪʃ] *adj* enfantin, puéril
child' la'bor *s* travail *m* des enfants
child'like' *adj* enfantin, d'enfant
child's' play' *s* jeu *m* d'enfant; **it's child's play** c'est l'enfance de l'art
child' wel'fare *s* protection *f* de l'enfance
Chile ['tʃɪli] *s* le Chili
chil'i pep'per ['tʃɪli] *s* piment *m*
chill [tʃɪl] *adj & s* froid *m*; **sudden chill** saisissement *m*, coup *m* de froid; **to take the chill off** faire tiédir ‖ *tr* refroidir; (*a person*) transir, faire frisonner; (*wine*) frapper
chill' fac'tor *s* indice *m* de refroidissement
chill·y ['tʃɪli] *adj* (*comp* **-ier**; *super* **-iest**) froid; (*sensitive to cold*) frileux; **it is chilly** il fait frisquet, il fait frais
chime [tʃaɪm] *s* coup *m* de son; **chimes** (*at doorway*) sonnerie *f*; (*in bell tower*) carillon *m* ‖ *tr & intr* carillonner; **to chime in** faire chorus
chimera [kaɪ'mɪrə] *s* chimère *f*
chiming ['tʃaɪmɪŋ] *s* carillonnement *m*, sonnerie *f*
chimney ['tʃɪmni] *s* cheminée *f*; (*of lamp*) verre *m*
chim'ney pot' *s* abat-vent *m*, mitre *f*
chim'ney sweep' *s* ramoneur *m*
chimpanzee [tʃɪm'pænzi] *s* chimpanzé *m*
chin [tʃɪn] *s* menton *m*
china ['tʃaɪnə] *s* porcelaine *f* de Chine; **China** Chine *f*; la Chine
chi'na clos'et *s* vitrine *f*
chi'na·ware' *s* porcelaine *f*
Chi·nese [tʃaɪ'niz] *adj* chinois ‖ *s* (*language*) chinois *m* ‖ *s* (*pl* **-nese**) Chinois *m* (*person*)
Chi'nese lan'tern *s* lanterne *f* vénitienne, lampion *m*
chink [tʃɪŋk] *s* fente *f*, crevasse *f*; **chink in one's armor** (coll) défaut *m* de la cuirasse
chin' strap' *s* sous-mentonnière *f*, jugulaire *f*
chip [tʃɪp] *s* fragment *m*; (*of wood*) copeau *m*, éclat *m*; (*in gambling*) jeton *m*; (electron) microplaquette *f*, pastille *f*, chip *m*; **chips** (*potato chips*) pommes *fpl* chips; (Brit) frites *fpl* ‖ **to be a chip off the old block** (coll) chasser de race, être un rejeton de la vieille souche ‖ *v* (*pret & pp* **chipped**; *ger* **chipping**) *tr* enlever un copeau à ‖ *intr* s'écailler; **to chip in** contribuer
chipmunk ['tʃɪp,mʌŋk] *s* tamias *m* rayé
chipper ['tʃɪpər] *adj* (coll) en forme, guilleret
chiropodist [kaɪ'rɑpədɪst] *s* pédicure *mf*
chiropractor ['kaɪrə,præktər] *s* chiropracteur *m*
chirp [tʃʌrp] *s* gazouillis *m*, pépiement *m* ‖ *intr* gazouiller, pépier
chis·el ['tʃɪzəl] *s* ciseau *m* ‖ *v* (*pret & pp* **-eled** or **-elled**; *ger* **-eling** or **-elling**) *tr* ciseler; (*a person*) (slang) escroquer, carotter; **to chisel s.o. out of s.th.** (slang) escroquer q.ch. à qn

chiseler ['tʃɪzələr] *s* ciseleur *m*; (slang) escroc *m*
chit [tʃɪt] *s* note *f*, ticket *m*; (coll) gamin *m*
chit'-chat' *s* bavardage *m*
chivalrous ['ʃɪvəlrəs] *adj* honorable, courtois; (lit) chevaleresque
chivalry ['ʃɪvəlri] *s* (*of Middle Ages*) chevalerie *f*; (*politeness*) courtoisie *f*, galanterie *f*
chive [tʃaɪv] *s* ciboulette *f*, civette *f*
chloride ['klɔraɪd] *s* chlorure *m*
chlorinate ['klɔrɪ,net] *tr* (*water*) verduniser
chlorination [,klɔrɪ'neʃən] *s* verdunisation *f*
chlorine ['klɔrin] *s* chlore *m*
chloroform ['klɔrə,fɔrm] *s* chloroforme *m* ‖ *tr* chloroformer
chlorophyll ['klɔrəfɪl] *s* chlorophylle *f*
chock [tʃɑk] *s* cale *f*; (naut) poulie *f* ‖ *tr* caler
chock'-full' *adj* bondé, comble, bourré
chocolate ['tʃɔkəlɪt] *adj & s* chocolat *m*
choc'olate bar' *s* tablette *f* de chocolat
choice [tʃɔɪs] *adj* de choix, choisi ‖ *m* choix *m*; **by choice** par goût, volontairement
choir [kwaɪr] *s* chœur *m*
choir'boy' *s* enfant *m* de chœur
choir'mas'ter *s* chef *m* de chœur; (eccl) maître *m* de chapelle
choir' robe' *s* soutanelle *f*
choke [tʃok] *s* (aut) starter *m* ‖ *tr* étouffer; (*to obstruct*) obstruer, boucher; **to choke back, down,** or **off** étouffer; **to choke up** obstruer, engorger ‖ *intr* étouffer; **to choke up** (*e.g., with tears*) étouffer
choke' coil' *s* (elec) bobine *f* de réactance
choker ['tʃokər] *s* (*scarf*) foulard *m*; (*necklace*) collier *m* court
choking ['tʃokɪŋ] *s* étouffement *m*
cholera ['kɑlərə] *s* choléra *m*
choleric ['kɑlərɪk] *adj* coléreux
cholesterol [kə'lɛstə,rol] *s* cholestérol *m*
choose [tʃuz] *v* (*pret* **chose** [tʃoz]; *pp* **chosen** ['tʃozən]) *tr & intr* choisir
choos·y ['tʃuzi] *adj* (*comp* **-ier**; *super* **-iest**) (coll) difficile à plaire, chipoteur
chop [tʃɑp] *s* (*blow*) coup *m* de hache; (culin) côtelette *f*; **to lick one's chops** (coll) se lécher or s'essuyer les babines ‖ *v* (*pret & pp* **chopped**; *ger* **chopping**) *tr* hacher, couper; **to chop down** abattre; **to chop off** trancher, couper; **to chop up** couper en morceaux, hacher ‖ *intr* (*said of waves*) clapoter
chopper ['tʃɑpər] *s* (*of butcher*) couperet *m*; (coll) hélicoptère *m*; **choppers** (slang) les dents *fpl*
chop'ping block' *s* billot *m*, hachoir *m*
chop·py ['tʃɑpi] *adj* (*comp* **-pier**; *ger* **-piest**) agité; (*waves*) clapoteux
chop'stick' *s* baguette *f*, bâtonnet *m*
choral ['kɔrəl] *adj* choral *m*
chorale [ko'rɑl] *s* choral *m*
cho'ral soci'ety *s* chorale *f*
chord [kɔrd] *s* accord *m*; (geom) corde *f*
chore [tʃor] *s* devoir *m*; (*burdensome chore*) corvée *f*, besogne *f*

choreography [ˌkɔrɪˈɑɡrəfi] s chorégraphie f

chorister [ˈkɔrɪstər] s choriste mf

chortle [ˈtʃɔrtəl] intr glousser

chorus [ˈkorəs] s (group) chœur m, chorale f; (of song) refrain m; (of protest) concert m ‖ tr répéter en chœur, faire chorus

cho′rus boy′ s boy m

cho′rus girl′ s girl f

cho′sen few′ [ˈtʃozən] s élite f

chow [tʃaʊ] s (dog) chow-chow m; (mil) boustifaille f, mangeaille f

chow′-chow′ s (culin) macédoine f assaisonnée

chowder [ˈtʃaʊdər] s soupe f au poisson

Christ [kraɪst] s Christ m; le Christ

christen [ˈkrɪsən] tr baptiser

Christendom [ˈkrɪsəndəm] s chrétienté f

christening [ˈkrɪsənɪŋ] s baptême m

Christian [ˈkrɪstʃən] adj & s chrétien m

Christianity [ˌkrɪstʃɪˈænɪti] s christianisme m

Christianize [ˈkrɪstʃəˈnaɪz] tr christianiser

Christ′ian name′ s nom m de baptême

Christmas [ˈkrɪsməs] adj de Noël ‖ s Noël m; **Merry Christmas!** Joyeux Noël!

Christ′mas card′ s carte f de Noël

Christ′mas car′ol s chanson f de Noël, chant m de Noël; (eccl) cantique m de Noël

Christ′mas Day′ s le jour de Noël

Christ′mas Eve′ s la veille de Noël

Christ′mas gift′ s cadeau m de Noël

Christ′mas tree′ s arbre m de Noël

Christ′mas tree lights′ spl guirlandes fpl

chromatic [kroˈmætɪk] adj chromatique

chrome [krom] adj chromé ‖ s acier m chromé; (color) jaune m; (chem) chrome m ‖ tr chromer

chromium [ˈkromɪ‑əm] s chrome m

chromosome [ˈkroməˌsom] s chromosome m

chronic [ˈkranɪk] adj chronique

chronicle [ˈkranɪkəl] s chronique f ‖ tr faire la chronique de

chronicler [ˈkranɪklər] s chroniqueur m

chronologic(al) [ˌkranəˈladʒɪk(əl)] adj chronologique

chronolo‑gy [krəˈnalədʒi] s (pl ‑gies) chronologie f

chronometer [krəˈnamɪtər] s chronomètre m

chrysanthemum [krɪˈsænθɪməm] s chrysanthème m

chub‑by [ˈtʃʌbi] adj (comp ‑bier; super ‑biest) joufflu, potelé, dodu

chuck [tʃʌk] s (tap, blow, etc.) petite tape f; (under the chin) caresse f sous le menton; (of lathe) mandrin m; (bottom chuck and chuck rib) paleron m; (top chuck roast and chuck rib) entrecôte f ‖ tr tapoter; **to chuck away** jeter

chuckle [ˈtʃʌkəl] s gloussement m, petit rire m ‖ intr glousser, rire tout bas

chum [tʃʌm] s (coll) copain m ‖ v (pret & pp **chummed**; ger **chumming**) intr—**to chum around with** (coll) fraterniser avec

chum·my [ˈtʃʌmi] adj (comp ‑mier; super ‑miest) intime, familier

chump [tʃʌmp] s (slang) ballot m, lourdaud m

chunk [tʃʌŋk] s gros morceau m; (e.g., of wood) bloc m

church [tʃʌrtʃ] s église f

church′go′er s pratiquant m

church′man s (pl ‑men) (clergyman) ecclésiastique m; (layman) membre m d'une église, fidèle mf, paroissien m

church′ mem′ber s fidèle mf

church′ ser′vice s office m, culte m

church′yard′ s cimetière m

churlish [ˈtʃʌrlɪʃ] adj rustre, grossier; (out of sorts) grincheux

churn [tʃʌrn] s baratte f ‖ tr (cream) baratter; (e.g., water) agiter; **to churn butter** battre le beurre ‖ intr bouillonner

chute [ʃut] s (inclined channel or trough) glissière f; (of river) rapide m, chute f d'eau; (aer) parachute m

CIA [ˈsiˈaɪˈe] s (letterword) (central intelligence agency) (equivalent French agency) S.D.E.C. (service de documentation extérieure et de contre-espionnage)

Cicero [ˈsisəˌro] s Cicéron m

cider [ˈsaɪdər] s cidre m

cigar [sɪˈɡɑr] s cigare m

cigarette [ˌsɪɡəˈrɛt] s cigarette f

cigarette′ butt′ s mégot m

cigarette′ case′ s étui m à cigarettes

cigarette′ fiend′ s fumeur m enragé

cigarette′ hold′er s fume-cigarette m

cigarette′ light′er s briquet m

cigar′ hold′er s fume-cigare m

cigar′ store′ s bureau m de tabac

cinch [sɪntʃ] s (of saddle) sangle f; **it's a cinch** (coll) c'est couru d'avance ‖ tr sangler; (to make sure of) (slang) assurer

cinder [ˈsɪndər] s cendre f ‖ tr cendrer

Cinderella [ˌsɪndəˈrɛlə] s la Cendrillon f

cin′der track′ s piste f cendrée

cinema [ˈsɪnəmə] s cinéma m

cinnamon [ˈsɪnəmən] s cannelle f

cipher [ˈsaɪfər] s zéro m; (code) chiffre m; **in cipher** en chiffres ‖ tr & intr chiffrer

circle [ˈsʌrkəl] s cercle m; (coterie) milieu m, monde m; **to have circles around the eyes** avoir les yeux cernés ‖ tr ceindre, entourer; (to travel around) faire le tour de

circuit [ˈsʌrkɪt] s circuit m; (of judge) tournée f

cir′cuit break′er s (elec) disjoncteur m

cir′cuit court′ s cour f d'assises

circuitous [sərˈkju·ɪtəs] adj détourné, indirect

circular [ˈsʌrkjələr] adj & s circulaire f

circulate [ˈsʌrkjəˌlet] tr faire circuler ‖ intr circuler

circulation [ˌsʌrkjəˈleʃən] s circulation f; (of newspaper) tirage m

circumcise [ˈsʌrkəmˌsaɪz] tr circoncire

circumcision [ˌsʌrkəmˈsɪʒən] s circoncision f

circumference [sər'kʌmfərəns] *s* circonférence *f*

circumflex ['sʌrkəm,flɛks] *adj* & *s* circonflexe *m*

circumlocution [,sʌrkəmlo'kjuʃən] *s* circonlocution *f*

circumscribe [,sʌrkəm'skraɪb] *tr* circonscrire

circumspect ['sʌrkəm,spɛkt] *adv* circonspect

circumstance ['sʌrkəm,stæns] *s* circonstance *f*; (*pomp*) cérémonie *f*; **in easy circumstances** aisé; **under no circumstance** sous aucun prétexte; **under the circumstances** dans ces conditions

circumstantial [,sʌrkəm'stænʃəl] *adj* (*derived from circumstances*) circonstanciel; (*detailed*) circonstancié

cir'cumstan'tial ev'idence *s* preuves *fpl* indirectes

circumvent [,sʌrkəm'vɛnt] *tr* circonvenir

circus ['sʌrkəs] *s* cirque *m*; (Brit) rond-point *m*

cirrhosis [sɪ'rosɪs] *s* cirrhose *f*

cistern ['sɪstərn] *s* citerne *f*

citadel ['sɪtədəl] *s* citadelle *f*

citation [saɪ'teʃən] *s* citation *f*; (*award*) présentation *f*, mention *f*

cite [saɪt] *tr* citer

cither ['sɪθər] *s* cithare *f*

citified ['sɪtɪ,faɪd] *adj* urbain

citizen ['sɪtɪzən] *s* citoyen *m*

citizen·ry ['sɪtɪzənri] *s* (*pl* **-ries**) citoyens *mpl*

cit'izen·ship' *s* citoyenneté *f*

citric ['sɪtrɪk] *adj* citrique

citron ['sɪtrən] *s* cédrat *m*; (*tree*) cédratier *m*

citronella [,sɪtrə'nɛlə] *s* citronnelle *f*

cit'rus fruit' ['sɪtrəs] *s* agrumes *mpl*

cit·y ['sɪti] *s* (*pl* **-ies**) ville *f*; **the City** (*district within ancient boundaries*) la Cité

cit'y coun'cil *s* conseil *m* municipal

cit'y hall' *s* hôtel *m* de ville

cit'y plan'ner *s* urbaniste *mf*

cit'y plan'ning *s* urbanisme *m*

cit'y room' *s* (journ) salle *f* de rédaction

civ'et cat' ['sɪvɪt] *s* civette *f*

civic ['sɪvɪk] *adj* civique; **civics** instruction *f* civique

civies ['sɪviz] *spl* (coll) vêtements *mpl* civils; **in civies** en civil, en bourgeois

civil ['sɪvɪl] *adj* civil; (*courteous*) poli

civ'il defense' *s* protection *f* civile

civ'il engineer'ing *s* génie *m* civil

civilian [sɪ'vɪljən] *adj* & *s* civil *m*

civil'ian life' *s* vie *f* civile

civili·ty [sɪ'vɪlɪti] *s* (*pl* **-ties**) civilité *f*

civilization [,sɪvɪlɪ'zeʃən] *s* civilisation *f*

civilize ['sɪvɪ,laɪz] *tr* civiliser

civ'il rights' *spl* droits *mpl* civiques, droits politiques

civ'il ser'vant *s* fonctionnaire *mf*

civ'il serv'ice *s* fonction *f* publique

civ'il war' *s* guerre *f* civile; **Civil War** (*of the United States*) Guerre de Sécession

clack [klæk] *s* claquement *m* ‖ *intr* claquer

clad [klæd] *adj* vêtu, habillé

claim [klem] *s* (*request*) demande *f*; (*to a right*) revendication *f*; (*assertion*) affirmation *f*; (*right*) droit *m*, titre *m*; (*insurance claim*) déclaration de sinistre, demande d'indemnité; (*in prospecting*) concession *f* ‖ *tr* (*a right*) réclamer, revendiquer; (*to require*) exiger, demander; **to claim that . . .** prétendre que . . .; **to claim to** prétendre

claimant ['klemənt] *s* prétendant *m*, ayant droit *m*

clairvoyance [klɛr'vɔɪ·əns] *s* voyance *f*, seconde vue *f*; (*keen insight*) clairvoyance *f*

clairvoyant [klɛr'vɔɪ·ənt] *adj* clairvoyant ‖ *s* voyante *f*; voyant *m* ·

clam [klæm] *s* palourde *f* ‖ *v* (*pret* & *pp* **clammed**; *ger* **clamming**) *intr*—**to clam up** (slang) se taire

clam'bake' *s* pique-nique *m* aux palourdes

clamber ['klæmbər] *intr* grimper; **to clamber over** or **up** escalader

clam·my ['klæmi] *adj* (*comp* **-mier**; *super* **-miest**) moite; (*clinging*) collant

clamor ['klæmər] *s* clameur *f* ‖ *intr* vociférer; **to clamor for** réclamer

clamorous ['klæmərəs] *adj* bruyant

clamp [klæmp] *s* crampon *m*, agrafe *f*; (med) clamp *m* ‖ *tr* fixer, attacher; **to clamp together** cramponner ‖ *intr*—**to clamp down on** (coll) visser

clan [klæn] *s* clan *m*

clandestine [klæn'dɛstɪn] *adj* clandestin

clang [klæŋ] *s* bruit *m* métallique, choc *m* retentissant, cliquetis *m* ‖ *tr* faire résonner ‖ *intr* résonner

clank [klæŋk] *s* bruit *m* sec, bruit métallique, cliquetis *m* ‖ *tr* faire résonner ‖ *intr* résonner

clannish ['klænɪʃ] *adj* partisan

clap [klæp] *s* (*sound*) bruit *m* sec, claquement *m*; (*action*) tape *f*; (*with the hands*) battement *m* ‖ *v* (*pret* & *pp* **clapped**; *ger* **clapping**) *tr* battre; (*into jail*) (coll) fourrer; **to clap the hands** claquer or battre les mains ‖ *intr* applaudir, claquer

clapper ['klæpər] *s* (*person*) applaudisseur *m*; (*of bell*) battant *m*

clapping ['klæpɪŋ] *s* (*applause*) applaudissements *mpl*

claque [klæk] *s* (*paid clappers*) claque *f*; (*crush hat*) claque *m*

claret ['klærɪt] *s* bordeaux *m*

clari·fy ['klærɪ,faɪ] *v* (*pret* & *pp* **-fied**) *tr* clarifier

clarinet [,klærɪ'nɛt] *s* clarinette *f*

clarity ['klærɪti] *s* clarté *f*

clash [klæʃ] *s* (*sound*) choc *m* métallique; (*conflict*) dispute *f*, heurt *m*, choc; (*between people; with police*) accrochage *m*; (*of colors*) disparate *f* ‖ *intr* se heurter, s'entre-choquer; (*said of colors*) former une disparate

clasp [klæsp] *s* (*on brooch, necklace, purse*) agrafe *f*, fermoir *m*; (*embrace*) étreinte *f* ‖ *tr* agrafer; (*to embrace*) étreindre

clasp' knife' *s* couteau *m* pliant

class [klæs] *s* classe *f* ‖ *tr* classer

classic ['klæsɪk] *adj* & *s* classique *m*

classical ['klæsɪkəl] *adj* classique

classicism ['klæsɪ‚sɪzəm] *s* classicisme *m*

classicist ['klæsɪsɪst] *s* classique *mf*

classification [‚klæsɪfɪ'keʃən] *s* classification *f*, classement *m*

classified *adj* classifié, classé; (*documents*) secret, confidentiel

clas'sified advertise'ments *spl* petites annonces *fpl*

classi·fy ['klæsɪ‚faɪ] *v* (*pret* & *pp* **-fied**) *tr* classifier

class'mate *s* camarade *mf* de classe

class'room' *s* salle *f* de classe, classe *f*

class·y ['klæsi] *adj* (*comp* **-ier**; *super* **-iest**) (slang) chic

clatter ['klætər] *s* fracas *m* ‖ *intr* faire un fracas

clause [klɔz] *s* clause *f*, article *m*; (gram) proposition *f*

clavicle ['klævɪkəl] *s* clavicule *f*

claw [klɔ] *s* (*of animal*) griffe *f*; (*of crab*) pince *f*; (*of hammer*) panne *f* fendue ‖ *tr* griffer, déchirer

clay [kle] *s* argile *f*, glaise *f*

clay' pig'eon *s* pigeon *m* d'argile, pigeon de tir

clay' pipe' *s* pipe *f* en terre

clay' pit' *s* argilière *f*, glaisière *f*

clean [klin] *adj* propre; (*precise*) net ‖ *adv* net; tout à fait ‖ *tr* nettoyer; (*fish*) vider; (*streets*) balayer; **to clean out** curer; (*a person*) (slang) mettre à sec, décaver; **to clean up** nettoyer ‖ *intr* faire le nettoyage

clean' and jerk' *s* (weightlifting) épaulé-jeté *m*

clean'-cut' *adj* bien délimité, net; (*e.g., athlete*) bien découplé

cleaner ['klinər] *s* (*person*) nettoyeur *m*, dégraisseur *m*; (*cleaning agent*) nettoyant *m*; **to be taken to the cleaners** (slang) se faire rincer

cleaning ['klinɪŋ] *s* nettoyage *m*

clean'ing wom'an *s* femme *f* de ménage

cleanliness ['klɛnlɪnɪs] *s* propreté *f*, netteté *f*

cleanse [klɛnz] *tr* nettoyer, écurer; (*e.g., a wound*) assainir; (*e.g., one's thoughts*) purifier

cleanser ['klɛnzər] *s* produit *m* de nettoyage; (*soap*) détersif *m*

clean'-shav'en *adj* rasé de frais

cleans'ing cream' *s* crème *f* de démaquillage

clean'up' *s* nettoiement *m*

clear [klɪr] *adj* clair; (*sharp*) net; (*free*) dégagé, libre; (*unmortgaged*) franc d'hypothèque; **to become clear** s'éclaircir; **to keep clear of** éviter ‖ *tr* (*to brighten*) éclaircir; (*e.g., a fence*) franchir; (*obstacles*) dégager; (*land*) défricher; (*goods in customs*) dédouaner; (*an account*) solder; **to clear away** écarter, enlever; **to clear oneself** se disculper; **to clear out** (*e.g., a garden*) jardiner; **to clear the table** desservir, enlever le couvert, ôter la nappe; **to clear up** éclaircir ‖ *intr* (*said of weather*) s'éclaircir; **to clear out** (coll) filer, se sauver

clearance ['klɪrəns] *s* (*permission*) permis *m*, laissez-passer *m*, autorisation *f*; (*between two objects*) espace *m* libre; (aer) clairance *f*; (com) compensation *f*; (mach) espace *m* mort, jeu *m*

clear'ance sale' *s* vente *f* de soldes

clear'-cut' *adj* net, tranché; (*case*) absolu

clear'-head'ed *adj* lucide, perspicace

clearing ['klɪrɪŋ] *s* (*in clouds*) éclaircie *f*; (*in forest*) clairière *f*, trouée *f*

clear'ing house' *s* (com) comptoir *m* de règlement, chambre *f* de compensation

clearness ['klɪrnɪs] *s* clarté *f*, netteté *f*

clear'-sight'ed *adj* perspicace, clairvoyant

cleat [klit] *s* taquet *m*

cleavage ['klivɪdʒ] *s* clivage *m*

cleave [kliv] *v* (*pret* & *pp* **cleft** [klɛft] or **cleaved**) *tr* fendre ‖ *intr* se fendre; **to cleave to** s'attacher à, adhérer à

cleaver ['klivər] *s* couperet *m*, hachoir *m*

clef [klɛf] *s* (mus) clef *f*

cleft [klɛft] *adj* fendu ‖ *s* fente *f*, crevasse *f*

cleft' pal'ate *s* palais *m* fendu, fissure *f* palatine

clemen·cy ['klɛmənsi] *s* (*pl* **-cies**) clémence *f*

clement ['klɛmənt] *adj* clément

clench [klɛntʃ] *tr* serrer, crisper

cler·gy ['klʌrdʒi] *s* (*pl* **-gies**) (*members*) clergé *m*; (*profession*) clergie *f*

cler'gy·man (*pl* **-men**) ecclésiastique *m*, clerc *m*

cleric ['klɛrɪk] *s* clerc *m*, ecclésiastique *m*

clerical ['klɛrɪkəl] *adj* clerical; de bureau ‖ *s*—**clericals** habit *m* ecclésiastique

cler'ical er'ror *s* faute *f* de copiste, faute de sténographe

cler'ical work' *s* travail *m* de bureau

clerk [klʌrk] *s* (*clerical worker*) employé *m* de bureau, commis *m*; (*in lawyer's office*) clerc *m*; (*in store*) vendeur *m*; (*in bank*) comptable *mf*; (*of court*) greffier *m*; (eccl) clerc

clever ['klɛvər] *adj* habile, adroit

cliché [kli'ʃe] *s* cliché *m*, expression *f* consacrée

click [klɪk] *s* cliquetis *m*, clic *m*; (*of heels*) bruit *m* sec; (*of tongue*) claquement *m*; (*of a machine*) déclic *m* ‖ *intr* cliqueter, faire un déclic; (*to succeed*) (coll) réussir; (*to get along well*) (coll) s'entendre à merveille

client ['klaɪ·ənt] *s* client *m*

clientele [‚klaɪ·ən'tɛl] *s* clientèle *f*

cliff [klɪf] *s* falaise *f*, talus *m* raide

climate ['klaɪmɪt] *s* climat *m*

climax ['klaɪmæks] *s* point *m* culminant, comble *m*

climb [klaɪm] *s* montée *f*, ascension *f* ‖ *tr* & *intr* monter, gravir; grimper; **to climb down** descendre

climber ['klaɪmər] *s* grimpeur *m*; (bot) plante *f* grimpante; (*social climber*) parvenu *m*, arriviste *mf*

climbing ['klaɪmɪŋ] *s* montée *f*, escalade *f*

clinch [klɪntʃ] s (*act*) rivetage m; (*fastener*) crampon m, rivet m; (boxing) corps-à-corps m ‖ tr (*a nail*) river; (*a bargain*) boucler ‖ intr se prendre corps à corps

clincher ['klɪntʃər] s (coll) argument m sans réplique

cling [klɪŋ] v (pret & pp **clung** [klʌŋ]) intr s'accrocher, se cramponner; **to cling to** (*a person*) se serrer contre; (*a belief*) adhérer à

cling'stone peach' s alberge f

clinic ['klɪnɪk] s clinique f

clinical ['klɪnɪkəl] adj clinique

clinician [klɪ'nɪʃən] s clinicien m

clink [klɪŋk] s cliquetis m; (*e.g., of glasses*) tintement m, choc m; (*jail*) (slang) taule f, bloc m ‖ tr (*glasses, in a toast*) choquer; **to clink glasses with** trinquer avec ‖ intr tinter, cliqueter

clip [klɪp] s (*for papers*) attache f; (*brooch*) agrafe f, clip m; (*of gun*) chargeur m; (*blow*) (coll) taloche f; (*fast pace*) (coll) pas m rapide ‖ v (pret & pp **clipped**; ger **clipping**) tr (*to fasten*) attacher; (*hair*) rafraîchir; (*sheep*) tondre; (*one's words*) avaler

clipper ['klɪpər] s (aer) clipper m; (naut) voilier m de course; **clippers** tondeuse f

clipping ['klɪpɪŋ] s tondage m; (*of sheep*) tonte f; (*of one's hair*) taille f; (*of newspaper*) coupure f (de presse); **clippings** (*cuttings, shavings, etc.*) rognures fpl, chutes fpl

clip'ping ser'vice s argus m

clique [klik] s coterie f, clan m, chapelle f

clitoris ['klɪtərɪs] s clitoris m

cloak [klok] s manteau m ‖ tr masquer

cloak'-and-dag'ger adj (*e.g., story*) de cape et d'épée

cloak'room' s vestiaire m; (rr) consigne f

clock [klɑk] s (*larger type of clock*) horloge f; (*smaller type of clock*) pendule f; (*e.g., in a tower*) horloge; **to turn back the clock** retarder l'horloge; (fig) revenir en arrière ‖ tr chronométrer

clock'mak'er s horloger m

clock'tow'er s tour f de l'horloge

clock'wise' adj & adv dans le sens des aiguilles d'une montre

clock'work' s mouvement m d'horlogerie; **like clockwork** (coll) comme une horloge

clod [klɑd] s motte f; (*person*) rustre mf

clod'hop'per s cul-terreux m; (*shoe*) godillot m

clog [klɑg] s (*shoe*) galoche f, socque m; (*hindrance*) entrave f ‖ v (pret & pp **clogged**; ger **clogging**) tr (*e.g., a pipe*) boucher; (*e.g., traffic*) entraver ‖ intr se boucher

cloister ['klɔɪstər] s cloître m ‖ tr cloîtrer

clone [klon] s clone m ‖ tr faire du clonage à ‖ intr faire du clonage

cloning ['klonɪŋ] s clonage m

close [klos] adj proche, tout près; (*game; weave; formation, order*) serré; (*friend*) intime; (*friendship*) étroit; (*room*) renfermé, étouffant; (*translation*) fidèle; **close**

to près de ‖ adv près, de près ‖ [kloz] s (*enclosure*) clos m; (*end*) fin f; (*closing*) fermeture f ‖ tr fermer; (*to end*) conclure, terminer; (*an account*) régler, clôturer; (*ranks*) serrer, resserrer; (*a meeting*) lever; **close quotes** fermez les guillemets; **to close in** enfermer; **to close out** (com) liquider, solder ‖ intr se fermer; finir, se terminer; (*on certain days*) (theat) faire relâche; **to close in on** (*the enemy*) aborder

close' call' [klos] s—**to have a close call** (coll) l'échapper belle

close-cropped ['klos'krɑpt] adj coupé ras

closed [klozd] adj fermé; (*road*) barré; (*e.g., pipe*) obturé, bouché; (*ranks*) serré; (*public sign in front of theater*) relâche; **with closed eyes** les yeux clos

closed' car' s conduite f intérieure

closed'-cir'cuit tel'evision s télévision f en circuit fermé

closed' sea'son s fermeture f de la chasse, fermeture de la pêche

closefisted ['klos'fɪstəd] adj ladre, avare

close-fitting ['klos'fɪtɪŋ] adj collant, ajusté, qui moule le corps

close-grained ['klos'grend] adj serré

closely ['klosli] adv (*near*) de près, étroitement; (*exactly*) exactement

close-mouthed ['klos'mauðd] adj peu communicatif, économe de mots

closeness ['klosnɪs] s (*nearness*) proximité f; (*accuracy*) exactitude f; (*stinginess*) avarice f; (*of weather*) lourdeur f; (*of air*) manque m d'air

close'out' s fin f de série

close' shave' [klos] s—**to have a close shave** se faire raser de près; (coll) échapper à un cheveu près

closet ['klɑzɪt] s placard m

clos'et dra'ma s spectacle m dans un fauteuil

close-up ['klos,ʌp] s premier plan m, gros plan, plan serré, plan rapproché

closing ['klozɪŋ] adj dernier, final ‖ s fermeture f; (*of account; of meeting*) clôture f

clos'ing-out' sale' s soldes mpl des fins de séries

clos'ing price' s dernier cours m

clot [klɑt] s caillot m ‖ v (pret & pp **clotted**; ger **clotting**) tr cailler ‖ intr se cailler

cloth [klɔθ] s étoffe f; (*fabric*) tissu m; (*of wool*) drap m; (*of cotton or linen*) toile f; **cloths** (*for cleaning*) chiffons mpl, torchons mpl, linge m; **the cloth** le clergé

clothe [kloð] v (pret & pp **clothed** or **clad** [klæd]) tr habiller, vêtir; (*e.g., with authority*) revêtir, investir

clothes [kloz] spl vêtements mpl, habits mpl; (*underclothes, shirts, etc.; wash*) linge m; **in plain clothes** en civil; **to put on one's clothes** s'habiller; **to take off one's clothes** se déshabiller

clothes'bas'ket s panier m à linge

clothes'brush' s brosse f à habits

clothes' clos'et s garde-robe f, penderie f, placard m

clothes′ dry′er *s* séchoir *m* à linge
clothes′ hang′er *s* cintre *m*
clothes′horse′ *s* séchoir-chevalet *m*
clothes′line′ *s* corde *f* à linge, étendoir *m*
clothes′ moth′ *s* gerce *f*
clothes′pin′ *s* pince *f* à linge
clothes′ rack′ *s* patère *f*
clothier [′kloðjər] *s* confectionneur *m*, marchand *m* de confections
clothing [′kloðɪŋ] *s* vêtements *mpl*
cloud [klaʊd] *s* nuage *m*; (*heavy cloud; multitude*) nuée *f*; **in the clouds** dans les nues ‖ *tr* couvrir de nuages; (phot) voiler ‖ *intr* (phot) se voiler; **to cloud over** or **up** se couvrir de nuages
cloud′burst′ *s* averse *f*, rafale *f* de pluie
cloud′ cham′ber *s* (phys) chambre *f* d'ionisation
cloudless [′klaʊdlɪs] *adj* sans nuages
cloud·y [′klaʊdi] *adj* (*comp* **-ier**; *super* **-iest**) nuageux; (phot) voilé
clout [klaʊt] *s* (coll) gifle *f* ‖ *tr* (coll) gifler
clove [klov] *s* (*spice*) clou *m* de girofle, girofle *m*; (*of garlic*) gousse *f*; (bot) giroflier *m*
clove′ hitch′ *s* demi-clef *f* à capeler
clo′ven hoof′ [′klovən] *s* pied *m* fourchu; **to show the cloven hoof** (coll) montrer le bout de l'oreille
clover [′klovər] *s* trèfle *m*; **to be in clover** (coll) être sur le velours
clo′ver·leaf′ *s* (*pl* **-leaves**) (*leaf*) feuille *f* de trèfle; (*intersection*) croisement *m* en trèfle, échangeur *m* en trèfle
clown [klaʊn] *s* clown *m*, pitre *m*, bouffon *m* ‖ *intr* faire le pitre
clownish [′klaʊnɪʃ] *adj* bouffon; (*clumsy*) empoté, rustre
cloy [klɔɪ] *tr* rassasier
club [klʌb] *s* (*weapon*) massue *f*, gourdin *m*, assommoir *m*; (*group*) cercle *m*, amicale *f*, club *m*; (cards) trèfle *m*; (golf) crosse *f*, club *m* ‖ *v* (*pret & pp* **clubbed**; *ger* **clubbing**) *tr* (*to strike*) assommer; (*to pool*) mettre en commun ‖ *intr*—**to club together** s'associer; se cotiser
club′ car′ *s* voiture-salon *f*
club′foot′ *s* (*pl* **-feet**) pied *m* équin, pied bot
club′foot′ed *adj*—**to be clubfooted** avoir le pied bot, être pied-bot
club′house′ *s* club *m*, club-house *m*
club′man *s* (*pl* **-men**) clubman *m*
club′room′ *s* salle *f* de réunion
club′ steak′ *s* aloyau *m* de bœuf
club′wom′an *s* (*pl* **-wom′en**) cercleuse *f*
cluck [klʌk] *s* gloussement *m* ‖ *intr* glousser
clue [klu] *s* indice *m*, indication *f*; **to find the clue** trouver la clef; **to give s.o. a clue** mettre qn sur la piste; **to have the clue** tenir le bout du fil
clump [klʌmp] *s* (*of earth*) bloc *m*, masse *f*; (*of trees*) bouquet *m*; (*of shrubs or flowers*) massif *m*; (*gait*) pas *m* lourd ‖ *intr*—**to clump along** marcher lourdement

clum·sy [′klʌmzi] *adj* (*comp* **-sier**; *super* **-siest**) (*worker*) maladroit, gauche; (*work*) bâclé, grossier
cluster [′klʌstər] *s* (*of people*) groupe *m*, rassemblement *m*; (*of trees*) bouquet *m*; (*of grapes, fruit, blossoms, flowers*) grappe *f*; (*of pears*) glane *f*; (*of bananas*) régime *m*; (*of diamonds*) épi *m*, nœud *m*; (*of stars*) amas *m* ‖ *tr* grouper ‖ *intr*—**to cluster around** se rassembler; **to cluster together** se conglomérer
clutch [klʌtʃ] *s* (*grasp, grip*) griffe *f*, serre *f*; (aut) embrayage *m*; (aut) pédale *f* d'embrayage; **to fall into the clutches of** tomber sous la patte de; **to let in the clutch** embrayer; **to throw out the clutch** débrayer ‖ *tr* saisir, empoigner ‖ *intr*—**to clutch at** se raccrocher à
clutter [′klʌtər] *s* encombrement *m* ‖ *tr*—**to clutter up** encombrer
Co. *abbr* (**Company**) Cie
c/o *abbr* (**in care of**) a/s (aux soins de)
coach [kotʃ] *s* (*drawn by horses*) coche *m*, carrosse *f*; (*bus*) autocar *m*, car *m*; (*two-door sedan*) coche *m*; (rr) voiture *f*; (sports) entraîneur *m*, moniteur *m* ‖ *tr* donner des leçons particulières à; entraîner; (*for an exam*) préparer à un examen, chauffer; (*an actor*) faire répéter
coach′-and-four′ *s* carrosse *f* à quatre chevaux
coach′ box′ *s* siège *m* du cocher
coach′ house′ *s* remise *f*
coaching [′kotʃɪŋ] *s* leçons *fpl* particulières, chauffage *m*, répétitions *fpl*; (sport) entraînement *m*
coach′man *s* (*pl* **-men**) cocher *m*
coagulate [ko′ægjə,let] *tr* coaguler ‖ *intr* se coaguler
coal [kol] *adj* charbonnier, houiller ‖ *s* houille *f*, charbon *m*; **coals** (*embers*) tisons *mpl*, charbons ardents; **to carry coals to Newcastle** porter de l'eau à la rivière
coal′bin′ *s* coffre *m* à charbon
coal′ bunk′er *s* soute *f* à charbon
coal′ car′ *s* wagon-tombereau *m*
coal′deal′er *s* charbonnier *m*
coalesce [,ko·ə′lɛs] *intr* s'unir, se combiner, fusionner
coal′ field′ *s* bassin *m* houiller
coalition [,ko·ə′lɪʃən] *s* coalition *f*; **to form a coalition** se coaliser
coal′ mine′ *s* houillère *f*
coal′ oil′ *s* pétrole *m* lampant
coal′ scut′tle *s* seau *m* à charbon
coal′ tar′ *s* goudron *m* de houille
coal′yard′ *s* charbonnerie *f*
coarse [kors] *adj* (*in manners*) grossier; (*composed of large particles*) gros; (*hair, skin*) rude
coarse′-grained′ *adj* à gros grain; (*wood*) à gros fil
coarseness [′korsnɪs] *s* (*in manners*) grossièreté *f*; (*of hair, skin*) rudesse *f*
coast [kost] *s* côte *f*; **the coast is clear** la route est libre ‖ *intr* caboter; (*said of automobile*) aller au débrayé; (*said of*

bicycle) aller en roue libre; **to coast along** continuer sur sa lancée

coastal [ˈkostəl] *adj* côtier

coaster [ˈkostər] *s (under a glass)* dessous-de-verre *m*, sous-verre *m*; (naut) caboteur *m*

coast′er brake′ *s* frein *m* à contrepédalage

coast′ guard′ *s* service *m* de guet le long des côtes

coast′-guard cut′ter *s* garde-côte *m*

coast′guards′man *s (pl* -men) soldat *m* chargé de la garde des côtes

coasting [ˈkostɪŋ] *s (e.g., on a cycle)* descente *f* en roue libre

coast′ing trade′ *s* cabotage *m*

coast′line′ *s* littoral *m*

coast′wise′ *adj* côtier ‖ *adv* le long de la côte

coat [kot] *s (jacket)* veste *f*; *(suitcoat)* veston *m*; *(topcoat)* manteau *m*; *(of an animal)* robe *f*, pelage *m*, livrée *f*; *(of paint)* couche *f* ‖ *tr* enduire; *(with chocolate)* enrober; *(a pill)* dragéifier

coat′ hang′er *s* cintre *m*, portemanteau *m*

coating [ˈkotɪŋ] *s* enduit *m*, couche *f*

coat′ of arms′ *s* écu *m* armorial; *(bearings)* blason *m*, armoiries *fpl*

coat′ of mail′ *s* cotte *f* de mailles

coat′rack′ *s* portemanteau *m*

coat′room′ *s* vestiaire *m*

coat′tail′ *s* basque *f*

coauthor [koˈɔθər] *s* coauteur *m*

coax [koks] *tr* cajoler, amadouer

cob [kab] *s (of corn)* épi *m* de maïs; *(horse)* cob *m*; *(swan)* cygne *m* mâle

cobalt [ˈkobɔlt] *s* cobalt *m*

cobbler [ˈkablər] *s (shoemaker)* cordonnier *m*; *(cake)* tourte *f* aux fruits; *(drink)* boisson *f* glacée

cobblestone [ˈkabəl,ston] *s* pavé *m*

cob′web′ *s* toile *f* d'araignée

cocaine [koˈken] *s* cocaïne *f*

cock [kak] *s (rooster)* coq *m*; *(faucet)* robinet *m*; *(of gun)* chien *m* ‖ *tr (one′s ears)* dresser, redresser; *(one′s hat)* mettre sur l'oreille, retrousser; *(a rifle)* armer

cockade [kaˈked] *s* cocarde *f*

cock-a-doodle-doo [ˈkakə,dudəlˈdu] *interj* cocorico!

cock′-and-bull′ sto′ry *s* coq-à-l'âne *m*

cock′crow′ *s* cocorico *m*

cocked′ hat′ *s* chapeau *m* à cornes; **to knock into a cocked hat** (slang) démolir, aplatir

cock′er span′iel [ˈkakər] *s* cocker *m*

cock′eyed′ *adj* (coll) de travers, de biais; (slang) insensé

cock′fight′ *s* combat *m* de coqs

cockle [ˈkakəl] *s* (bot) nielle *f*; (zool) bucarde *f*, clovisse *f*

cock′pit′ *s* (aer) cockpit *m*, carlingue *f*, poste *m* de pilotage, habitacle *m*

cock′roach′ *s* blatte *f*, cafard *m*

cockscomb [ˈkaks,kom] *s* crête *f* de coq; (bot) crête-de-coq *f*

cock′sure′ *adj* (coll) sûr et certain

cock′tail′ *s* cocktail *m*

cock′tail dress′ *s* robe *f* de cocktail

cock′tail par′ty *s* cocktail *m*

cock′tail shak′er *s* shaker *m*

cock·y [ˈkaki] *adj (comp* -ier; *super* -iest) (coll) effronté, suffisant

cocoa [ˈkoko] *s* cacao *m*

co′coa bean′ *s* cacao *m*

coconut [ˈkokə,nʌt] *s* noix *f* de coco, coco *m*

co′conut palm′ *s* cocotier *m*

cocoon [kəˈkun] *s* cocon *m*

cod [kad] *s* (ichth) morue *f*

C.O.D. [ˈsiˈoˈdi] *s* (letterword) (**Collect on Delivery**) C.R., contre remboursement, e.g., **send it to me C.O.D.** envoyez-le-moi C.R.

coddle [ˈkadəl] *tr* dorloter, gâter

code [kod] *s* code *m*; *(secret code)* chiffre *m* ‖ *tr* chiffrer

code′ word′ *s* mot *m* convenu

codex [ˈkodɛks] *s (pl* **codices** [ˈkadɪ,siz]) manuscrit *m* ancien

cod′fish′ *s* morue *f*

codger [ˈkadʒər] *s*—**old codger** (coll) vieux bonhomme *m*

codicil [ˈkadɪsɪl] *s (of will)* codicille *m*; *(of contract, treaty, etc.)* avenant *m*

codi·fy [ˈkadɪ,faɪ] *v (pret & pp* -**fied**) *tr* codifier

cod′-liver oil′ *s* huile *f* de foie de morue

coed [ˈko,ɛd] *s* collégienne *f*, étudiante *f* universitaire

coeducation [,ko·ɛdʒəˈkeʃən] *s* coéducation *f*, enseignement *m* mixte

co′educa′tional school′ [,ko·ɛdʒəˈkeʃənəl] *s* école *f* mixte

coefficient [,ko·ɪˈfɪʃənt] *s* coefficient *m*

coerce [koˈʌrs] *tr* contraindre, forcer

coercion [koˈʌrʃən] *s* coercition *f*

coexist [,ko·ɪgˈzɪst] *intr* coexister

coexistence [,ko·ɪgˈzɪstəns] *s* coexistence *f*

coffee [ˈkɔfi] *s* café *m*; **black coffee** café noir, café nature; **ground coffee** café moulu; **roasted coffee** café brûlé, café torréfié

cof′fee and rolls′ *s* café *m* complet

cof′fee bean′ *s* grain *m* de café

cof′fee break′ *s* pause-café *f*, pause café

cof′fee·cake′ *s* gimblette *f* (qui se prend avec le café)

cof′fee cup′ *s* tasse *f* à café

cof′fee grind′er *s* moulin *m* à café

cof′fee grounds′ *spl* marc *m* de café

cof′fee mak′er *s* percolateur *m*

cof′fee mill′ *s* moulin *m* à café

cof′fee mug′ *s* pot *m* de café

cof′fee planta′tion *s* caféière *f*

cof′fee·pot′ *s* cafetière *f*; *(for pouring)* verseuse *f*

cof′fee roast′er *s* brûloir *m*

cof′fee shop′ *s (of hotel)* hôtel-restaurant *m*; *(in station)* buffet *m*

cof′fee tree′ *s* caféier *m*

coffer [ˈkɔfər] *s* coffre *m*, caisse *f*; *(archit)* caisson *m*; **coffers** trésor *m*, fonds *mpl*

cof′fer·dam′ *s* coffre *m*, bâtardeau *m*

coffin [ˈkɔfɪn] *s* cercueil *m*, bière *f*

cog [kɑg] *s* dent *f*; (*cogwheel*) roue *f* dentée; **to slip a cog** (coll) avoir des absences

cogency [ˈkodʒənsi] *s* force *f* (de persuasion)

cogent [ˈkodʒənt] *adj* puissant, convaincant

cogitate [ˈkɑdʒɪ,tet] *tr* & *intr* méditer

cognac [ˈkɒnjæk] *s* cognac *m*

cognate [ˈkɑgnet] *adj* congénère, apparenté ‖ *s* congénère *mf*; (*word*) mot *m* apparenté

cognizance [ˈkɑgnɪzəns] *s* connaissance *f*

cognizant [ˈkɑgnɪzənt] *adj* informé

cog′wheel′ *s* roue *f* dentée

cohabit [koˈhæbɪt] *intr* cohabiter

coheir [koˈɛr] *s* cohéritier

cohere [koˈhɪr] *intr* s'agglomérer, adhérer; (*said of reasoning or style*) se suivre logiquement, correspondre

coherent [koˈhɪrənt] *adj* cohérent

cohesion [koˈhiʒən] *s* cohésion *f*

coiffeur [kwɑˈfʌr] *s* coiffeur *m* pour dames

coiffure [kwɑˈfjʊr] *s* coiffure *f* ‖ *tr* coiffer

coil [kɔɪl] *s* (*something wound in a spiral*) rouleau *m*; (*single turn of spiral*) tour *m*; (*of a still*) serpentin *m*; (*of hair*) boucle *f*; (elec) bobine *f*; **coils** (*of snake*) nœuds *mpl* ‖ *tr* enrouler; (naut) lover, gléner ‖ *intr* s'enrouler; (*said of snake or stream*) serpenter

coil′ spring′ *s* ressort *m* en spirale, ressort à boudin

coin [kɔɪn] *s* monnaie *f*; (*single coin*) pièce *f* de monnaie; (*wedge*) coin *m*; **in coin** en espèces, en numéraire; **to pay back s.o. in his own coin** rendre à qn la monnaie de sa pièce; **to toss a coin** jouer à pile ou face ‖ *tr* (*a new word; a story or lie*) forger, inventer; **to coin money** frapper de la monnaie; (coll) faire des affaires d'or, s'enrichir à vue d'œil

coinage [ˈkɔɪnɪdʒ] *s* monnayage *m*; (fig) invention *f*

coincide [,ko·ɪnˈsaɪd] *intr* coïncider

coincidence [koˈɪnsɪdəns] *s* coïncidence *f*

coin′ lock′er *s* consigne *f* automatique

coin′ return′ *s* retour *m* de monnaie; (*receptacle*) sébile *f*

coin′ tel′ephone *s* téléphone *m* payant

coition [koˈɪʃən] or **coitus** [ˈko·ɪtəs] *s* coït *m*

coke [kok] *s* coke *m* ‖ *tr* cokéfier ‖ *intr* se cokéfier

colander [ˈkʌləndər] *s* passoire *f*

cold [kold] *adj* froid; **it is cold** (*said of weather*) il fait froid; **to be cold** (*said of person*) avoir froid ‖ *s* froid *m*; (*indisposition*) rhume *m*; **to be left out in the cold** (slang) rester en carafe; **to catch a cold** attraper un rhume, s'enrhumer

cold′ blood′ *s*—**in cold blood** de sang-froid

cold′-blood′ed *adj* insensible; (*sensitive to cold*) frileux; (zool) à sang froid

cold′ chis′el *s* ciseau *m* à froid

cold′ com′fort *s* maigre consolation *f*

cold′ cream′ *s* cold-cream *m*

cold′ cuts′ *spl* viandes *fpl* froides, assiette *f* anglaise

cold′ feet′ [fit] *spl*—**to have cold feet** (coll) avoir froid aux yeux

cold′ front′ *s* front *m* froid

cold′-heart′ed *adj* au cœur dur, insensible

coldness [ˈkoldnɪs] *s* froideur *f*; (*in the air*) froidure *f*

cold′ should′er *s*—**to give s.o. the cold shoulder** (coll) battre froid à qn

cold′ snap′ *s* coup *m* de froid

cold′ stor′age *s* entrepôt *m* frigorifique; **in cold storage** en glacière

cold′-stor′age *adj* frigorifique

cold′ war′ *s* guerre *f* froide

cold′ wave′ *s* vague *f* de froid

coleslaw [ˈkol,slɔ] *s* salade *f* de chou

colic [ˈkɑlɪk] *s* colique *f*

coliseum [,kɑlɪˈsi·əm] *s* colisée *m*

colitis [koˈlaɪtɪs] *s* colite *f*

collaborate [kəˈlæbə,ret] *intr* collaborer

collaborationist [kə,læbəˈreʃənɪst] *s* collaborationniste *mf*

collaborator [kəˈlæbə,retər] *s* collaborateur *m*

collapse [kəˈlæps] *s* écroulement *m*, effondrement *m*; (*of prices, of government*) chute *f*; (*of prices; of a beam*) fléchissement *m*; (pathol) collapsus *m* ‖ *intr* s'écrouler, s'effondrer; (*said of government*) tomber; (*said of structure or prices*) s'effondrer; (*said of balloon*) se dégonfler

collapsible [kəˈlæpsɪbəl] *adj* démontable, rabattable, pliant

collar [ˈkɑlər] *s* (*of dress, shirt*) collet *m*, col *m*; (*worn by dog; on pigeon*) collier *m*; (mach) collier ‖ *tr* colleter; (coll) empoigner

col′lar·band′ *s* pied *m* de col (d'une chemise)

col′lar·bone′ *s* clavicule *f*

collate [kəˈlet] *tr* collationner, conférer

collateral [kəˈlætərəl] *adj* (*fact*) correspondant, concomitant; (*parallel*) parallèle; (*subordinate*) accessoire; (*kin*) collatéral ‖ *s* (*kin*) collatéral *m*; (com) nantissement *m*

collation [kəˈleʃən] *s* collation *f*

colleague [ˈkɑlig] *s* collègue *mf*

collect [ˈkɑlɛkt] *s* (eccl) collecte *f* ‖ [kəˈlɛkt] *tr* rassembler; (*taxes*) percevoir, lever; (*stamps, antiques*) collectionner; (*eggs; classroom papers; tickets*) ramasser; (*mail*) faire la levée de; (*debts*) recouvrer; (*gifts, money*) collecter; (*one's thoughts; anecdotes*) recueillir; **to collect oneself** se reprendre, se remettre ‖ *intr* (*for the poor*) quêter; (*to gather together*) se rassembler, se réunir; (*to pile up*) s'amasser ‖ *adv* en p.c.v., e.g., **to telephone collect** téléphoner en p.c.v.

collect′ call′ *s* (telp) communication *f* P.C.V.

collected *adj* recueilli, maître de soi

collection [kəˈlɛkʃən] *s* collection *f*; (*of taxes*) perception *f*, levée *f*, recouvrement *m*; (*of mail*) levée; (*of verses*) recueil *m*

collec′tion a′gency *s* agence *f* de recouvrement

collec′tion plate′ *s* plateau *m* de quête

collective [kəˈlɛktɪv] *adj* collectif
collector [kəˈlɛktər] *s* (*of stamps, antiques*) collectionneur *m*; (*of taxes*) percepteur *m*, receveur *m*, collecteur *m*; (*of tickets*) contrôleur *m*
college [ˈkalɪdʒ] *s* (*of cardinals, electors, etc.*) collège *m*; (*school in a university*) faculté *f*; (U.S.A.) école *f* des arts et sciences
collegian [kəˈlidʒɪ·ən] *s* étudiant *m*
collegiate [kəˈlidʒɪ·ɪt] *adj* collégial, de l'université, universitaire
collide [kəˈlaɪd] *intr* se heurter, se tamponner; **to collide with** se heurter à or contre, heurter contre
collier [ˈkaljər] *s* houilleur *m*; (*ship*) charbonnier *m*
collier·y [ˈkaljəri] *s* (*pl* **-ies**) houillère *f*
collision [kəˈlɪʒən] *s* collision *f*
collocate [ˈkalo͵ket] *tr* disposer en rapport; (*creditors*) colloquer
colloid [ˈkalɔɪd] *adj* colloïdal ‖ *s* colloïde *m*
colloquial [kəˈlokwɪ·əl] *adj* familier
colloquialism [kəˈlokwɪ·ə͵lɪzəm] *s* expression *f* familière
collo·quy [ˈkaləkwi] *s* (*pl* **-quies**) colloque *m*
collusion [kəˈluʒən] *s* collusion *f*; **to be in collusion with** être d'intelligence avec
cologne [kəˈlon] *s* eau *f* de Cologne
Colombia [kəˈlʌmbɪ·ə] *s* Colombie *f*; la Colombie
colon [ˈkolən] *s* (anat) côlon *m*; (gram) deux points *mpl*
colonel [ˈkʌrnəl] *s* colonel *m*
colonial [kəˈlonɪ·əl] *adj & s* colonial *m*
colonist [ˈkalənɪst] *s* colon *m*
colonize [ˈkalə͵naɪz] *tr & intr* coloniser
colonnade [͵kaləˈned] *s* colonnade *f*
colo·ny [ˈkaləni] *s* (*pl* **-nies**) colonie *f*
colophon [ˈkalə͵fan] *s* colophon *m*
color [ˈkʌlər] *s* couleur *f*; **the colors** les couleurs, le drapeau; **to call to the colors** appeler sous les drapeaux; **to give** or **lend color to** colorer; (fig) rendre vraisemblable; **to show one's true colors** se révéler sous son vrai jour; **under color of** sous couleur de; **with flying colors** enseignes déployées ‖ *tr* colorer; (*e.g., a drawing*) colorier; (*to exaggerate*) donner de l'éclat à, imager; (*to dye*) teindre ‖ *intr* se colorer; (*to blush*) rougir
col′or·bear′er *s* porte-drapeau *m*
col′or·blind′ *adj* daltonien, aveugle des couleurs
col′or-cod′ed *adj* (chem) chromocodé
colored *adj* coloré; (*ink*) de couleur; (*person; usually offensive*) de couleur; (*drawing*) colorié
colorful [ˈkʌlərfəl] *adj* (*striking*) coloré; (*unusual*) pittoresque
col′or guard′ *s* garde *f* d'honneur du drapeau
coloring [ˈkʌlərɪŋ] *adj* colorant ‖ *s* colorant *m*; (*of painting, complexion, style*) coloris *m*
colorless [ˈkʌlərlɪs] *adj* incolore

col′or photog′raphy *s* photographie *f* en couleurs
col′or salute′ *s* (mil) salut *m* au drapeau, salut aux couleurs
col′or ser′geant *s* sergent-chef *m*, sergent-major *m*
col′or tel′evision *s* télévision *f* en couleurs
colossal [kəˈlasəl] *adj* colossal
colossus [kəˈlasəs] *s* colosse *m*
colt [kolt] *s* poulain *m*
Columbus [kəˈlʌmbəs] *s* Colomb *m*
column [ˈkaləm] *s* colonne *f*; (journ) rubrique *f*, chronique *f*, courrier *m*; (mil) colonne
columnar [kəˈlʌmnər] *adj* en colonne
columnist [ˈkaləmɪst] *s* chroniqueur *m*, courriériste *m*
coma [ˈkomə] *s* (pathol) coma *m*
comb [kom] *s* (*for hair*) peigne *m*; (*currycomb*) étrille *f*; (*of rooster; of wave*) crête *f*; (*filled with honey*) rayon *m* ‖ *tr* peigner; explorer minutieusement, fouiller; **to comb out** démêler ‖ *intr* (*said of waves*) déferler
com·bat [ˈkambæt] *s* combat *m* ‖ [ˈkambæt], [kəmˈbæt] *v* (*pret & pp* **-bated** or **-batted**; *ger* **-bating** or **-batting**) *tr & intr* combattre
combatant [ˈkambətənt] *adj & s* combattant *m*
com′bat du′ty *s* service *m* de combat, service au front
combination [͵kambɪˈneʃən] *s* combinaison *f*
combine [ˈkambaɪn] *s* (com) trust *m*, combinaison *f* financière, entente *f* industrielle; (agr) moissonneuse-batteuse *f* ‖ [kəmˈbaɪn] *tr* combiner ‖ *intr* se liguer, fusionner; (chem) se combiner
combin′ing form′ *s* élément *m* de composition
combo [ˈkambo] *s* (*of four musicians*) quartette *f*
combustible [kəmˈbʌstɪbəl] *adj & s* combustible *m*
combustion [kəmˈbʌstʃən] *s* combustion *f*
come [kʌm] *v* (*pret* **came** [kem]; *pp* **come**) *intr* venir; **come in!** entrez!; **to come after** succéder à, suivre; (*to come to get*) venir chercher; **to come apart** se séparer, se défaire; **to come around** (*to snap back*) se rétablir; (*to give in*) céder; **to come at** (*to attack*) se jeter sur; **to come back** revenir; (coll) revenir en vogue; **to come before** précéder; (*e.g., a legislature*) se mettre devant; **to come between** s'interposer entre; **to come by** (*to get*) obtenir; (*to pass*) passer; **to come down** descendre; **to come downstairs** descendre (en bas); **to come down with** tomber malade avec; **to come for** venir chercher; **to come from** provenir de, dériver de; (*said of wind*) chasser de; **to come in** entrer; entrer dans; (*said of tide*) monter; (*said of style*) entrer en vogue; **to come in for** avoir part à; (*e.g., an inheritance*) succéder à; (*e.g., sympathy*) s'attirer; **to**

come off se détacher; (*to take place*) avoir lieu; en sortir, e.g., **to come off victorious** en sortir vainqueur; **to come out** sortir; (*said of sun, stars; said of book*) paraître; (*said of buds*) éclore; (*said of news*) se divulguer; (*said of debutante*) débuter; **to come out for** se prononcer pour; **to come over** se laisser persuader; arriver, e.g., **what's come over him?** qu'est-ce qui lui est arrivé?; **to come through** (*e.g., fields*) passer par, passer à travers; (*e.g., a wall*) pénétrer; (*an illness*) surmonter; se tirer indemne; **to come to** revenir à soi; **to come together** s'assembler, se réunir; **to come true** se réaliser; **to come up** monter; (*to occur*) se présenter; **to come upstairs** monter (en haut); **to come up to** monter jusqu'à, venir à; **to come up with** proposer

come′-and-go′ *s* va-et-vient *m*

come′back′ *s* (*of style*) (coll) retour *m* en vogue; (*of statesman*) (coll) retour *m* au pouvoir; (slang) réplique *f*, riposte *f*; **to stage a comeback** (coll) se réhabiliter, faire une belle remontée

comedian [kə′midɪ·ən] *s* (*comic*) comique *m*; (*on the legitimate stage*) comédien *m*; (*author*) auteur *m* comique

comedienne [kə‚midɪ′ɛn] *s* comédienne *f*

come′down′ *s* humiliation *f*, déchéance *f*

come·dy [′kɑmədi] *s* (*pl* **-dies**) comédie *f*

come·ly [′kʌmli] *adj* (*comp* **-lier**; *super* **-liest**) (*attractive*) avenant, gracieux; (*decorous*) convenable, bienséant

come′-on′ *s* (slang) leurre *m*, attrape *f*

comet [′kɑmɪt] *s* comète *f*

comfort [′kʌmfərt] *s* (*well-being*) confort *m*; (*sympathy*) consolation *f*; (*person*) consolateur *m*; **comforts** commodités *fpl*, agréments *mpl* ‖ *tr* consoler, réconforter

comfortable [′kʌmfərtəbəl] *adj* confortable; (*in a state of comfort*) bien; (*well-off*) à l'aise

comforter [′kʌmfərtər] *s* (*person*) consolateur *m*; (*bedcover*) couvre-pieds *m* piqué; (*of wool*) cache-nez *m*; (*for baby*) tétine *f*, sucette *f*

comforting [′kʌmfərtɪŋ] *adj* consolateur, réconfortant

com′fort sta′tion *s* châlet *m* de nécessité, lieux *mpl* d'aisances, toilette *f*

comic [′kɑmɪk] *adj & s* comique *m*; **comics** (*cartoons*) dessins *mpl* humoristiques

com′ic op′era *s* opéra *m* bouffe

com′ic strip′ *s* bande *f* humoristique, bande dessinée

coming [′kʌmɪŋ] *adj* qui vient; (*future*) d'avenir, de demain ‖ *s* arrivée *f*, venue *f*; **comings and goings** allées et venues

com′ing out′ *s* (*of stocks, bonds, etc.*) émission *f*; (*of a book*) parution *f*; (*of a young lady*) début *m*

comma [′kɑmə] *s* virgule *f*; (*in French a period or sometimes a small space is used to mark the divisions of whole numbers*) point *m*

command [kə′mænd] *s* (*leadership*) gouvernement *m*; (*order, direction*) commandement *m*, ordre *m*; (*e.g., of a foreign language*) maîtrise *f*; **to be at s.o.'s command** être aux ordres de qn; **to have a command of** (*a language*) posséder; **to have at one's command** avoir à sa disposition ‖ *tr* commander, ordonner; (*respect*) inspirer; (*to look out over*) dominer; (*a language*) connaître ‖ *intr* (mil) commander, donner les ordres

commandant [‚kɑmən′dænt] *s* commandant *m*

commandeer [‚kɑmən′dɪr] *tr* réquisitionner

commander [kə′mændər] *s* commandant *m*

comman′der in chief′ *s* commandant *m* en chef

commanding [kə′mændɪŋ] *adj* imposant; (*in charge*) d'autorité

commemorate [kə′mɛməret] *tr* commémorer, célébrer

commence [kə′mɛns] *tr & intr* commencer

commencement [kə′mɛnsmənt] *s* commencement *m*; (educ) jour *m* de la distribution des prix, jour de la collation des grades

commence′ment ex′ercise *s* cérémonie *f* de remise des diplômes

commend [kə′mɛnd] *tr* (*to praise*) louer; (*to entrust*) confier, recommander

commendable [kə′mɛndəbəl] *adj* louable

commendation [‚kɑmən′deʃən] *s* louange *f*, éloge *m*; (mil) citation *f*

comment [′kɑmənt] *s* remarque *f*, observation *f*, commentaire *m* ‖ *intr* faire des observations; **to comment on** commenter

commentar·y [′kɑmən‚tɛri] *s* (*pl* **-ies**) commentaire *m*

commentator [′kɑmən‚tetər] *s* commentateur *m*

commerce [′kɑmərs] *s* commerce *m*, négoce *m*

commercial [kə′mʌrʃəl] *adj* commercial, commerçant ‖ *s* annonce *f* publicitaire

commercialize [kə′mʌrʃə‚laɪz] *tr* commercialiser

commiserate [kə′mɪzə‚ret] *intr*—**to commiserate with** compatir aux malheurs de

commiseration [kə‚mɪzə′reʃən] *s* commisération *f*

commissar [‚kɑmɪ′sɑr] *s* commissaire *m*

commissar·y [′kɑmɪ‚sɛri] *s* (*pl* **-ies**) (*person*) commissaire *m*; (*canteen*) cantine *f*

commission [kə′mɪʃən] *s* commission *f*; (*board, council*) conseil *m*; (com) guelte *f*; (mil) brevet *m*; **out of commission** hors de service; (naut) désarmé ‖ *tr* commissionner; (mil) promouvoir

commis′sioned of′ficer *s* breveté *m*

commissioner [kə′mɪʃənər] *s* commissaire *m*

com·mit [kə′mɪt] *v* (*pret & pp* **-mitted**; *ger* **-mitting**) *tr* (*an error, crime, etc.*) commettre; (*one's soul, one's money, etc.*) confier; (*one's word*) engager; (*to a mental hospital*) interner; **to commit to mem-**

ory apprendre par cœur; **to commit to prison** envoyer en prison; **to commit to writing** coucher par écrit

commitment [kə'mɪtmənt] s (*act of committing*) perpétration *f*; (*to a mental institution*) internement *m*; (*to prison*) emprisonnement *m*; (*to a cause*) engagement *m*

committal [kə'mɪtəl] s (*of a crime*) perpétration *f*; (*of a task*) délégation *f*; **committal to prison** mise *f* en prison

commit'tal ser'vice s (eccl) prières *fpl* au bord de la tombe

committee [kə'mɪti] s comité *m*, commission *f*

commode [kə'mod] s (*toilet*) chaise *f* percée; (*dressing table*) grande table *f* de nuit

commodious [kə'modɪ·əs] adj spacieux, confortable

commodi·ty [kə'madɪti] s (*pl* **-ties**) denrée *f*, marchandise *f*

common ['kamən] adj commun ‖ s terrain *m* communal; **commons** communaux *mpl*; (*of school*) réfectoire *m*; **the Commons** (Brit) les communes *fpl*

com'mon car'rier s entreprise *f* de transports en commun

commoner ['kamənər] s homme *m* du peuple, roturier *m*; (Brit) membre *m* de la Chambre des communes

com'mon law' s droit *m* coutumier, coutume *f*

com'mon-law mar'riage s union *f* libre, collage *m*

Com'mon Mar'ket s Marché *m* Commun

com'mon noun' s nom *m* commun

com'mon·place' adj banal ‖ s banalité *f*

com'mon sense' s sens *m* commun

com'mon-sense' adj sensé

com'mon stock' s action *f* ordinaire, actions ordinaires

commonweal ['kamən,wil] s bien *m* public

com'mon·wealth' s état *m*, république *f*

commotion [kə'moʃən] s commotion *f*

commune [kə'mjun] intr s'entretenir; (eccl) communier

communicant [kə'mjunɪkənt] s informateur *m*; (eccl) communiant *m*

communicate [kə'mjunɪ,ket] tr & intr communiquer

communicating [kə'mjunɪ,ketɪŋ] adj communicant

communication [kə,mjunɪ'keʃən] s communication *f*

communica'tions sat'ellite s satellite *m* de transmission

communicative [kə'mjunɪ,ketɪv] adj communicatif

communion [kə'mjunjən] s communion *f*; **to take communion** communier

communism ['kamjə,nɪzəm] s communisme *m*

communist ['kamjənɪst] adj & s communiste *mf*

communi·ty [kə'mjunɪti] s (*pl* **-ties**) (*locality*) voisinage *m*; (*group of people living together*) communauté *f*

commu'nity chest' s caisse *f* de secours

commutation [,kamjə'teʃən] s commutation *f*

commuta'tion tick'et s carte *f* d'abonnement

commutator ['kamjə,tetər] s (elec) collecteur *m*

commute [kə'mjut] tr échanger; (*e.g., a prison term*) commuer ‖ intr s'abonner au chemin de fer; voyager avec carte d'abonnement

commuter [kə'mjutər] s abonné *m* au chemin de fer

commut'er air'line s transporteur *m* d'appoint

compact [kəm'pækt] adj compact ‖ ['kampækt] s (*agreement*) pacte *m*; (*for cosmetics*) poudrier *m*, boîte *f* à poudre

companion [kəm'pænjən] s compagnon *m*; (*female companion*) compagne *f*

companionable [kəm'pænjənəbəl] adj sociable

compan'ion·ship' s camaraderie *f*

compan'ion·way' s escalier *m* des cabines

compa·ny ['kʌmpəni] s (*pl* **-nies**) compagnie *f*; (com) société *f*, compagnie; (naut) équipage *m*; (theat) troupe *f*; **to have company** avoir du monde; **to keep bad company** fréquenter la mauvaise compagnie; **to keep company** sortir ensemble; **to keep s.o. company** tenir compagnie à qn; **to part company** se séparer

comparative [kəm'pærətɪv] adj comparatif; (*anatomy, literature, etc.*) comparé ‖ s comparatif *m*

compare [kəm'pɛr] s—**beyond compare** incomparablement, sans égal ‖ tr comparer; **compared to** en comparaison de; **to be compared to** se comparer à

comparison [kəm'pærɪsən] s comparaison *f*

compartment [kəm'partmənt] s compartiment *m*

compass ['kʌmpəs] s (*for showing direction*) boussole *f*; (*range, reach*) portée *f*; (*for drawing circles*) compas *m*; **to box the compass** réciter la rose des vents ‖ tr—**to compass about** entourer

com'pass card' s rose *f* des vents

compassion [kəm'pæʃən] s compassion *f*

compassionate [kəm'pæʃənɪt] adj compatissant

compatibility [kəm,pætɪ'bɪlɪti] s compatibilité *f*, convenance *f*

com·pel [kəm'pɛl] v (*pret & pp* **-pelled**; *ger* **-pelling**) tr contraindre, obliger; (*respect, silence*) imposer

compelling [kəm'pɛlɪŋ] adj irrésistible; (*motive*) impérieux

compendious [kəm'pɛndɪ·əs] adj abrégé, succinct

compensate ['kampən,set] tr compenser; **to compensate s.o. for** dédommager qn de ‖ intr—**to compensate for** compenser

compensation [,kampən'seʃən] s compensation *f*

compete [kəm'pit] intr concourir

competence ['kampɪtəns] or **competency** ['kampɪtənsi] s compétence *f*

competent [ˈkɑmpɪtənt] *adj* compétent
competition [ˌkɑmpɪˈtɪʃən] *s* concurrence *f*, compétition *f*; (*contest*) concours *m*; (sports) compétition, épreuve *f*
competitive [kəmˈpɛtɪtɪv] *adj* compétitif
compet′itive exam′ination *s* concours *m*
competitiveness [kəmˈpɛtɪtɪvnɪs] *s* compétitivité *f*
competitor [kəmˈpɛtɪtər] *s* concurrent *m*
compilation [ˌkɑmpɪˈleʃən] *s* compilation *f*
compile [kəmˈpaɪl] *tr* compiler
compiler [kəmˈpaɪlər] *s* compilateur *m*, rédacteur *m*; (comp) compilateur
complacency [kəmˈplesənsi] *s* complaisance *f*; (*self-satisfaction*) suffisance *f*
complacent [kəmˈplesənt] *adj* complaisant; content de soi, suffisant
complain [kəmˈplen] *intr* se plaindre
complainant [kəmˈplenənt] *s* plaignant *m*
complaint [kəmˈplent] *s* plainte *f*; (*grievance*) grief *m*; (*illness*) maladie *f*, mal *m*, symptômes *mpl*, doléances *fpl*
complaisant [kəmˈplezənt] *adj* complaisant
complement [ˈkɑmplɪmənt] *s* complément *m*; (mil) effectif *m* ‖ [ˈkɑmplɪˌmɛnt] *tr* compléter
complete [kəmˈplit] *adj* complet ‖ *tr* compléter
complex [kəmˈplɛks] *adj* complexe ‖ [ˈkɑmplɛks] *s* complexe *m*
complexion [kəmˈplɛkʃən] *s* (*texture of skin, especially of face*) teint *m*; (*general aspect*) caractère *m*; (*constitution*) complexion *f*
compliance [kəmˈplaɪ·əns] *s* complaisance *f*; soumission *f*, conformité *f*; **in compliance with** conformément à
complicate [ˈkɑmplɪˌket] *tr* compliquer
complicated *adj* compliqué
complication [ˌkɑmplɪˈkeʃən] *s* complication *f*
complici·ty [kəmˈplɪsɪti] *s* (*pl* -ties) complicité *f*
compliment [ˈkɑmplɪmənt] *s* compliment *m*; **compliments** (*kind regards*) civilités *fpl*; **to pay a compliment to** faire un compliment à; **with the compliments of the author** hommage de l'auteur ‖ *tr* complimenter
com′plimen′tary cop′y [ˌkɑmplɪˈmɛntəri] *s* exemplaire *m* en hommage; **to give a complimentary copy of a book** faire hommage d'un livre
com′plimen′tary tick′et *s* billet *m* de faveur
com·ply [kəmˈplaɪ] *v* (*pret & pp* -plied) *intr*—**to comply with** se conformer à, acquiescer à
component [kəmˈponənt] *adj* composant ‖ *s* (chem) composant *m*; (mech, math) composante *f*
comportment [kəmˈportmənt] *s* comportement *m*
compose [kəmˈpoz] *tr* composer; **to be composed of** se composer de; **to compose oneself** se calmer
composed *adj* paisible, tranquille

composer [kəmˈpozər] *s* compositeur *m*
compos′ing stick′ *s* composteur *m*
composite [kəmˈpazɪt] *adj & s* composé *m*
composition [ˌkɑmpəˈzɪʃən] *s* composition *f*
compositor [kəmˈpazɪtər] *s* compositeur *m*
compost [ˈkɑmpost] *s* compost *m*
composure [kəmˈpoʒər] *s* calme *m*, sang-froid *m*
compote [ˈkɑmpot] *s* (*stewed fruits*) compote *f*; (*dish*) compotier *m*
compound [ˈkɑmpaʊnd] *adj* composé ‖ *s* (*mixture*) composé *m*; (gram) mot *m* composé; (math) complexe *m*; (mil) enceinte *f* ‖ [kɑmˈpaʊnd] *tr* composer, combiner; (*interest*) capitaliser
comprehend [ˌkɑmprɪˈhɛnd] *tr* comprendre
comprehensible [ˌkɑmprɪˈhɛnsɪbəl] *adj* compréhensible
comprehension [ˌkɑmprɪˈhɛnʃən] *s* compréhension *f*
comprehensive [ˌkɑmprɪˈhɛnsɪv] *adj* compréhensif, étendu; (*study, view, measure*) d'ensemble
comprehen′sive insur′ance *s* assurance *f* multirisque
compress [ˈkɑmprɛs] *s* (med) compresse *f* ‖ [kəmˈprɛs] *tr* comprimer
compression [kəmˈprɛʃən] *s* compression *f*
comprise [kəmˈpraɪz] *tr* comprendre, renfermer
compromise [ˈkɑmprəˌmaɪz] *s* compromis *m*; (*with one's conscience*) transaction *f*; **rough compromise** cote *f* mal taillée ‖ *tr* (*e.g., one's honor*) compromettre ‖ *intr* (*to make concessions*) transiger
comptroller [kənˈtrolər] *s* vérificateur *m*, contrôleur *m*
compulsive [kəmˈpʌlsɪv] *adj* obligatoire; (psychol) compulsif
compulsory [kəmˈpʌlsəri] *adj* obligatoire, forcé
compute [kəmˈpjut] *tr* computer, calculer, supputer ‖ *intr* calculer
computer [kəmˈpjutər] *adj* informatique ‖ *s* ordinateur *m*; **to operate a computer** faire de l'informatique
comput′er or composi′tion *s* (typ) composition *f* programmée
computerization [kəmˌpjutəraɪˈzeʃən] *s* informatisation *f*, mise *f* sur ordinateur
computerize [kəmˈpjutəraɪz] *tr* informatiser, mettre sur ordinateur
computerized *adj* fait à l'ordinateur
comput′er lan′guage *s* langage *m* de programmation
comput′er pro′gramer *s* programmeur *m*
comput′er pro′graming *s* programmation *f*
comput′er sci′ence *s* informatique *f*, science *f* de l'information
comrade [ˈkɑmræd] *s* camarade *mf*
com′rade in arms′ *s* compagnon *m* d'armes
com′rade·ship′ *s* camaraderie *f*
con [kɑn] *s* contre *m* ‖ *v* (*pret & pp* **conned**; *ger* **conning**) *tr* étudier; (naut) gouverner; (slang) escroquer
concave [kɑnˈkev] *adj* concave

conceal [kən'sil] *tr* dissimuler
concealment [kən'silmənt] *s* (*hiding*) dissimulation *f*; (*place*) cachette *f*
concede [kən'sid] *tr & intr* concéder
conceit [kən'sit] *s* (*vanity*) vanité *f*; (*witty expression*) saillie *f*, mot *m*; **conceits** concetti *mpl*
conceited *adj* vaniteux, vain
conceivable [kən'sivəbəl] *adj* concevable
conceive [kən'siv] *tr & intr* concevoir
concentrate ['kɑnsən,tret] *tr* concentrer ‖ *intr* se concentrer
concentra'tion camp' [,kɑnsən'treʃən] *s* camp *m* de concentration
concentric [kən'sɛntrɪk] *adj* concentrique
concept ['kɑnsɛpt] *s* concept *m*
conception [kən'sɛpʃən] *s* conception *f*
concern [kən'sʌrn] *s* (*business establishment*) maison *f*, compagnie *f*; (*worry*) inquiétude *f*; (*relation, reference*) intérêt *m*; (*matter*) affaire *f* ‖ *tr* concerner; **as concerns** quant à; **my book concerns . . .** mon livre traite de . . ., il s'agit dans mon livre de . . .; **persons concerned** intéressés *mpl*; **to be concerned** être inquiet; **to be concerned about** se préoccuper de; **to concern oneself with** s'intéresser à; **to whom it may concern** à qui de droit
concerning [kən'sʌrnɪŋ] *prep* concernant, en ce qui concerne, touchant
concert ['kɑnsərt] *s* concert *m*; **in concert** de concert ‖ [kən'sʌrt] *tr* concerter ‖ *intr* se concerter
con'cert·mas'ter *s* premier violon *m* soliste
concer·to [kən'tʃɛrto] *s* (*pl* **-tos** or **-ti** [ti]) concerto *m*
concession [kən'sɛʃən] *s* concession *f*
conciliate [kən'sɪlɪ,et] *tr* concilier
conciliatory [kən'sɪlɪ·ə,tori] *adj* conciliatoire
concise [kən'saɪs] *adj* concis
conclude [kən'klud] *tr & intr* conclure
conclusion [kən'kluʒən] *s* conclusion *f*
conclusive [kən'klusɪv] *adj* concluant
concoct [kən'kɑkt] *tr* confectionner; (*a story*) inventer; (*a plan*) machiner
concoction [kən'kɑkʃən] *s* confection *f*; (*mixture*) mélange *m*; (*pej*) drogue *f*
concomitant [kən'kɑmɪtənt] *adj* concomitant ‖ *s* accompagnement *m*
concord ['kɑŋkɔrd] *s* concorde *f*; (*gram*) concordance *f*; (*mus*) accord *m*
concordance [kən'kɔrdəns] *s* concordance *f*
concourse ['kɑŋkors] *s* (*of people*) concours *m*, foule *f*; (*road*) boulevard *m*; (*of railroad station*) hall *m*, salle *f* des pas perdus
concrete ['kɑnkrit] *adj* concret; de béton ‖ *s* concret *m*; (*for construction*) béton *m* ‖ *tr* (*a sidewalk*) bétonner
con'crete block' *s* parpaing *m*
con'crete mix'er *s* bétonnière *f*
concubine ['kɑŋkjə,baɪn] *s* concubine *f*
con·cur [kən'kʌr] *v* (*pret & pp* **-curred**; *ger* **-curring**) *intr* (*said of events*) concourir; (*said of persons*) s'accorder

concurrence [kən'kʌrəns] *s* concours *m*
concurrent [kən'kʌrənt] *adj* concourant
concussion [kən'kʌʃən] *s* secousse *f*, ébranlement *m*; (*pathol*) commotion *f*
condemn [kən'dɛm] *tr* condamner
condemnation [,kɑndɛm'neʃən] *s* condamnation *f*
condense [kən'dɛns] *tr* condenser ‖ *intr* se condenser
condenser [kən'dɛnsər] *s* condenseur *m*; (*elec*) condensateur *m*
condescend [,kɑndɪ'sɛnd] *intr* condescendre
condescending [,kɑndɪ'sɛndɪŋ] *adj* condescendant
condescension [,kɑndɪ'sɛnʃən] *s* condescendance *f*
condiment ['kɑndɪmənt] *s* condiment *m*
condition [kən'dɪʃən] *s* condition *f*; **on condition that** à condition que ‖ *tr* conditionner
conditional [kən'dɪʃənəl] *adj & s* conditionnel *m*
condi'tioned re'flex *s* réflexe *m* conditionné
conditioning [kən'dɪʃənɪŋ] *s* conditionnement *m*
condo ['kɑndo] *s* (coll) immeuble *m* à copropriété
condole [kən'dol] *intr*—**to condole with** offrir ses condoléances à
condolence [kən'doləns] *s* condoléances *fpl*
condom ['kɑndəm] *s* préservatif *m*, capote *f* anglaise
condominium [,kɑndə'mɪni·əm] *s* immeuble *m* à copropriété
condone [kən'don] *tr* pardonner, tolérer
conducive [kən'd(j)usɪv] *adj* favorable
conduct ['kɑndʌkt] *s* conduite *f*, comportement *m* ‖ [kən'dʌkt] *tr* conduire
conductor [kən'dʌktər] *s* (*on bus or streetcar*) receveur *m*; (*mus*) chef *m* d'orchestre; (*rr*) chef de train; (*elec, phys*) conducteur *m*; (*elec, phys*) (in predicate after **to be**, it may be translated by an adjective) conducteur, e.g., **metals are good conductors of electricity** les métaux sont bons conducteurs de l'électricité
conduit ['kɑndɪt], ['kɑndu·ɪt] *s* (*pipe*) conduit *m*, tuyau *m*; (*elec*) caniveau *m*, tube *m*
cone [kon] *s* cône *m*; (*for popcorn, ice cream*) cornet *m*, plaisir *m*
confection [kən'fɛkʃən] *s* confiserie *f*
confectioner [kən'fɛkʃənər] *s* confiseur *m*
confec'tioners' sug'ar *s* sucre *m* glace
confectioner·y [kən'fɛkʃə,nɛri] *s* (*pl* **-ies**) confiserie *f*
confedera·cy [kən'fɛdərəsi] *s* (*pl* **-cies**) confédération *f*; (*for unlawful purposes*) conspiration *f*, entente *f*
confederate [kən'fɛdərɪt] *adj* confédéré ‖ *s* complice *mf*; **Confederate** (hist) Confédéré *m* ‖ [kən'fɛdə,ret] *tr* conféderer ‖ *intr* se confédérer
con·fer [kən'fʌr] *v* (*pret & pp* **-ferred**; *ger* **-ferring**) *tr & intr* conférer

conference ['kɑnfərəns] *s* conférence *f*; (*interview*) entretien *m*; (*sports*) groupement *m* (d'équipes); **to be in conference** être en conférence
con'ference room' *s* salle *f* de conférences
con'ference ta'ble *s* table *f* de conférence
conferment [kən'fʌrmənt] *s* (*of degrees*) collation *f*
confess [kən'fɛs] *tr* confesser ‖ *intr* se confesser
confession [kən'fɛʃən] *s* confession *f*
confessional [kən'fɛʃənəl] *s* confessional *m*
confessor [kən'fɛsər] *s* confesseur *m*
confidant [,kɑnfɪ'dænt] *s* confident *m*
confide [kən'faɪd] *tr* confier ‖ *intr*—**to confide in** se confier à
confidence ['kɑnfɪdəns] *s* confiance *f*; (*secret*) confidence *f*; **in strict confidence** sous toute réserve; **to have confidence in** se confier à
confident ['kɑnfɪdənt] *adj* confiant ‖ *s* confident *m*
confidential [,kɑnfɪ'dɛnʃəl] *adj* confidentiel
confiden'tial sec'retary *s* secrétaire *m* particulier, secrétaire *f* particulière
confine ['kɑnfaɪn] *s* (*obs*) confinement *m*; **the confines** les confins *mpl* ‖ [kən'faɪn] *tr* confiner, enfermer; (*to keep within limits*) limiter; **to be confined** (*said of woman*) accoucher; **to be confined to bed** être alité
confinement [kən'faɪnmənt] *s* limitation *f*; (*in prison*) emprisonnement *m*; (*in childbirth*) accouchement *m*
confirm [kən'fʌrm] *tr* confirmer
confirmed *adj* (*reassured*) confirmé; (*bachelor*) endurci; (*drunkard*) fieffé; (*drinker*) invétéré; (*smoker*) émérite
confiscate ['kɑnfɪs,ket] *tr* confisquer
conflagration [,kɑnflə'greʃən] *s* conflagration *f*, incendie *m*
conflict ['kɑnflɪkt] *s* conflit *m* ‖ [kən'flɪkt] *intr* être en contradiction, se heurter
conflicting [kən'flɪktɪŋ] *adj* contradictoire; (*events, class hours, etc.*) incompatible
con'flict of in'terest *s* conflit *m* d'intérêts, conflit des intérêts
conform [kən'fɔrm] *tr* conformer ‖ *intr* se conformer, s'accommoder
conformist [kən'fɔrmɪst] *s* conformiste *mf*
conformi·ty [kən'fɔrmɪti] *s* (*pl* **-ties**) conformité *f*; **in conformity with** conformément à
confound [kɑn'faʊnd] *tr* confondre ‖ ['kɑn'faʊnd] *tr* maudire; **confound it!** diable!
confounded *adj* confus; (*damned*) sacré
confrere ['kɑnfrɛr] *s* confrère *m*
confront [kən'frʌnt] *tr* (*to face boldly*) affronter, faire face à; (*witnesses; documents*) confronter; **to be confronted by** se trouver en face de
confuse [kən'fjuz] *tr* confondre
confused *adj* confus, embarrassé
confusing [kən'fjuzɪŋ] *adj* déroutant, embrouillant
confusion [kən'fjuʒən] *s* confusion *f*

confute [kən'fjut] *tr* réfuter
congeal [kən'dʒil] *tr* congeler ‖ *intr* se congeler
congenial [kən'dʒinjəl] *adj* sympathique, agréable; compatible; **congenial to** or **with** apparenté à, conformer au tempérament de
congenital [kən'dʒɛnɪtəl] *adj* congénital
con'ger eel' ['kɑŋgər] *s* congre *m*, anguille *f* de mer
congest [kən'dʒɛst] *tr* congestionner ‖ *intr* se congestionner
congestion [kən'dʒɛstʃən] *s* congestion *f*
conglomeration [kən,glɑmə'reʃən] *s* conglomération *f*
congratulate [kən'grætʃə,let] *tr* féliciter, congratuler; **to congratulate s.o. for** féliciter qn de or pour; **to congratulate s.o. for** + *ger* féliciter qn de + *inf*
congratulations [kən,grætʃə'leʃənz] *spl* félicitations *fpl*
congregate ['kɑŋgrɪ,get] *tr* rassembler ‖ *intr* se rassembler
congregation [,kɑŋgrɪ'geʃən] *s* (*grouping*) rassemblement *m*; (*parishioners*) fidèles *mfpl*; (*Protestant parishioners; committee of Roman Catholic prelates*) congrégation *f*
congress ['kɑŋgrɪs] *s* congrès *m*
congressional [kən'grɛʃənəl] *adj* parlementaire
con'gress·man *s* (*pl* **-men**) congressiste *m*, parlementaire *m*
con'gress·wom'an *s* (*pl* **-wom'en**) congressiste *f*, parlementaire *f*
congruent ['kɑŋgru·ənt] *adj* (*math*) congru
conical ['kɑnɪkəl] *adj* conique
conjecture [kən'dʒɛktʃər] *s* conjecture *f* ‖ *tr & intr* conjecturer
conjugal ['kɑndʒəgəl] *adj* conjugal
conjugate ['kɑndʒə,get] *tr* conjuguer
conjugation [,kɑndʒə'geʃən] *s* conjugaison *f*
conjunction [kən'dʒʌŋkʃən] *s* conjonction *f*
conjuration [,kɑndʒə'reʃən] *s* conjuration *f*
conjure [kən'dʒʊr] *tr* (*to appeal to solemnly*) conjurer ‖ ['kɑndʒər], ['kʌndʒər] *tr* (*to exorcise, drive away*) conjurer; **to conjure up** évoquer ‖ *intr* faire de la sorcellerie
con' man' *s* escroc *m*
connect [kə'nɛkt] *tr* (*to join*) relier, joindre; (*e.g., two parties on the telephone*) mettre en communication; (*a pipe, an electrical device*) brancher, connecter ‖ *intr* se lier, se joindre; **to connect with** (*said of train*) correspondre avec
connected *adj* (*related*) connexe; (*logical*) suivi
connecting [kə'nɛktɪŋ] *adj* de liaison; (*wire*) de connexion; (*pipe*) de raccord; (*street*) communiquant
connect'ing flight' *s* vol *m* en transit
connect'ing rod' *s* bielle *f*
connection [kə'nɛkʃən] *s* connexion *f*, liaison *f*; (*between two causes*) connexité *f*;

(*in families*) parenté *f*, parent *m*; (*by telephone*) communication *f*; (*of trains*) correspondance *f*; (elec) connexion; **connections** (*in the business world*) clientèle *f*, relations *fpl*; (*in families*) alliés *mpl*, consanguins *mpl*; **in connection with** à propos de

con′ning tow′er [ˈkɑnɪŋ] *s* (*e.g., on battleship*) poste *m* or tourelle *f* de commandement; (*on sub*) kiosque *m*

conniption [kəˈnɪpʃən] *s* (*coll*) rogne *f*

connive [kəˈnaɪv] *intr* être de connivence, être complice

connote [kəˈnot] *tr* (*to signify*) signifier, vouloir dire; (*to imply*) suggérer, sousentendre

connubial [kəˈn(j)ubɪ·əl] *adj* conjugal

conquer [ˈkɑŋkər] *tr* conquérir

conqueror [ˈkɑŋkərər] *s* conquérant

conquest [ˈkɑŋkwɛst] *s* conquête *f*

conscience [ˈkɑnʃəns] *s* conscience *f*; **in all conscience** en conscience; **to have on one's conscience** avoir sur la conscience

conscientious [ˌkɑnʃɪˈɛnʃəs] *adj* consciencieux

conscien′tious objec′tor [əbˈdʒɛktər] *s* objecteur *m* de conscience

conscious [ˈkɑnʃəs] *adj* conscient; **to be conscious** (*not unconscious*) avoir connaissance; **to be conscious of** avoir conscience de

consciousness [ˈkɑnʃəsnɪs] *s* (*not sleep or coma*) connaissance *f*; (*awareness*) conscience *f*

conscript [ˈkɑnskrɪpt] *s* (mil) conscrit *m*; (nav) inscrit *m* maritime ‖ [kənˈskrɪpt] *tr* (mil) enrôler; (nav) inscrire

conscription [kənˈskrɪpʃən] *s* conscription *f*

consecrate [ˈkɑnsɪˌkret] *tr* consacrer; (*e.g., bread*) bénir; (*a king or bishop*) sacrer

consecration [ˌkɑnsɪˈkreʃən] *s* consécration *f*; (*to a task*) dévouement *m*; (*of a king or bishop*) sacre *m*

consecutive [kənˈsɛkjətɪv] *adj* de suite, consécutif

consensus [kənˈsɛnsəs] *s* consensus *m*

consent [kənˈsɛnt] *s* consentement *m*; **by common consent** d'un commun accord ‖ *intr* consentir

consequence [ˈkɑnsɪˌkwɛns] *s* conséquence *f*

consequential [ˌkɑnsɪˈkwɛnʃəl] *adj* conséquent, logique

consequently [ˈkɑnsɪˌkwɛntli] *adv* conséquemment, par conséquent

conservation [ˌkɑnsərˈveʃən] *s* conservation *f*

conservatism [kənˈsʌrvəˌtɪzəm] *s* conservatisme *m*

conservative [kənˈsʌrvətɪv] *adj & s* conservateur *m*; **at a conservative estimate** au bas mot, au moins

conservato·ry [kənˈsʌrvəˌtori] *s* (*pl* **-ries**) (*of music*) conservatoire *m*; (*greenhouse*) serre *f*

conserve [kənˈsʌrv] *tr* conserver

consider [kənˈsɪdər] *tr* considérer

considerable [kənˈsɪdərəbəl] *adj* considérable

considerate [kənˈsɪdərɪt] *adj* prévenant, plein d'égards

consideration [kənˌsɪdəˈreʃən] *s* (*thoughtfulness; careful thought; fact*) considération *f*; (*remuneration*) rétribution *f*; (*favor*) indulgence *f*; **to take into consideration** tenir compte de; **under consideration** à l'étude, en ligne de compte, en présence

considering [kənˈsɪdərɪŋ] *prep* eu égard à; **considering that** vu que

consign [kənˈsaɪn] *tr* consigner

consignee [ˌkɑnsaɪˈni] *s* consignataire *m*

consignment [kənˈsaɪnmənt] *s* consignation *f*, livraison *f*

consist [kənˈsɪst] *intr*—**to consist in** consister dans or en; **to consist in** + *ger* consister à + *inf*; **to consist of** consister dans or en

consistency [kənˈsɪstənsi] *s* (*pl* **-cies**) (*logical connection*) conséquence *f*; (*firmness, amount of firmness*) consistance *f*

consistent [kənˈsɪstənt] *adj* (*agreeing with itself or oneself*) conséquent; (*holding firmly together*) consistant; **consistent with** compatible avec

consisto·ry [kənˈsɪstəri] *s* (*pl* **-ries**) consistoire *m*

consolation [ˌkɑnsəˈleʃən] *s* consolation *f*

console [ˈkɑnsol] *s* console *f* ‖ [kənˈsol] *tr* consoler

con′sole ta′ble *s* console *f*

consolidate [kənˈsɑlɪˌdet] *tr* consolider

consonant [ˈkɑnsənənt] *adj* (*in sound*) consonant; **consonant with** d'accord avec ‖ *s* consonne *f*

consort [ˈkɑnsort] *s* (*husband*) conjoint *m*; (*wife*) conjointe *f*; prince *m* consort; (*convoy*) conserve *f* ‖ [kənˈsort] *tr* unir ‖ *intr* s'associer; (*to harmonize*) s'accorder; **to consort with** s'associer à or avec

conspicuous [kənˈspɪkju·əs] *adj* (*difference*) apparent, frappant; (*attracting special attention*) voyant; **to make oneself conspicuous** se faire remarquer

conspira·cy [kənˈspɪrəsi] *s* (*pl* **-cies**) conspiration *f*, conjuration *f*

conspirator [kənˈspɪrətər] *s* conspirateur *m*, conjuré *m*

conspire [kənˈspaɪr] *intr* conspirer

constancy [ˈkɑnstænsi] *s* constance *f*

constant [ˈkɑnstənt] *adj* constant ‖ *s* constante *f*

constantly [ˈkɑnstəntli] *adv* constamment

constellation [ˌkɑnstəˈleʃən] *s* constellation *f*

constipate [ˈkɑnstɪˌpet] *tr* constiper

constipation [ˌkɑnstɪˈpeʃən] *s* constipation *f*

constituen·cy [kənˈstɪtʃu·ənsi] *s* (*pl* **-cies**) (*persons*) électeurs *mpl*, commettants *mpl*; (*place*) circonscription *f* électorale

constituent [kənˈstɪtʃu·ənt] *adj* constituant, constitutif ‖ *s* élément *m*, constituant *m*; (*voter, client*) électeur *m*, commettant *m*

constitute [ˈkɑnstɪˌt(j)ut] *tr* constituer

constitution [ˌkɑnstɪ'tju)uʃən] *s* constitution *f*

constrain [kən'stren] *tr* contraindre

constraint [kən'strent] *s* contrainte *f*; (*restraint*) retenue *f*; (*uneasiness*) gêne *f*

constrict [kən'strɪkt] *tr* resserrer

construct [kən'strʌkt] *tr* construire

construction [kən'strʌkʃən] *s* construction *f*; interprétation *f*

construc'tion per'mit *s* permis *m* de construire

construc'tion start' *s* mise *f* en chantier

constructive [kən'strʌktɪv] *adj* constructif, constructeur

construe [kən'stru] *tr* expliquer, interpréter; (gram) construire

consul ['kɑnsəl] *s* consul *m*

consular ['kɑns(j)ələr] *adj* consulaire

consulate ['kɑns(j)əlɪt] *s* consulat *m*

consult [kən'sʌlt] *tr* consulter ‖ *intr* consulter; se consulter

consultant [kən'sʌltənt] *s* conseiller *m*, consultant *m*

consultation [ˌkɑn,səl'teʃən] *s* consultation *f*; (eccl, law) consulte *f*

consume [kən's(j)um] *tr* (*to make use of, use up*) consommer; (*to use up entirely; to destroy*) consumer, épuiser

consumer [kən's(j)umər] *s* consommateur *m*; (*of gas, electricity, etc.*) abonné *m*

consum'er goods' *spl* denrées *fpl* de consommation

consummate [kən'sʌmɪt] *adj* consommé ‖ ['kɑnsə,met] *tr* consommer

consumption [kən'sʌmpʃən] *s* consommation *f*; (pathol) tuberculose *f* pulmonaire

contact ['kɑntækt] *s* contact *m*; **to put in contact** mettre en contact ‖ *tr* (coll) prendre contact avec, contacter ‖ *intr* prendre contact

con'tact lens' *s* verre *m* de contact, lentille *f* de contact, lentille cornéenne

contagion [kən'tedʒən] *s* contagion *f*

contagious [kən'tedʒəs] *adj* contagieux

contain [kən'ten] *tr* contenir; (*one's sorrow*) apprivoiser

container [kən'tenər] *s* boîte *f*, contenant *m*, récipient *m*; (*to ship goods*) conteneur *m*

containment [kən'tenmənt] *s* refoulement *m*, retenue *f*; (*in a nuclear reactor*) confinement *m*

contaminate [kən'tæmɪ,net] *tr* contaminer

contamination [kən,tæmɪ'neʃən] *s* contamination *f*

contemplate ['kɑntəm,plet] *tr & intr* contempler; (*e.g., a trip*) projeter; **to contemplate** + *ger* penser + *inf*

contemplation [ˌkɑntəm'pleʃən] *s* contemplation *f*

contemporaneous [kən,tɛmpə'renɪ·əs] *adj* contemporain

contemporar·y [kən'tɛmpə,rɛri] *adj* contemporain ‖ *s* (*pl* **-ies**) contemporain *m*

contempt [kən'tɛmpt] *s* mépris *m*, nargue *f*; (law) contumace *f*; **to hold in contempt** mépriser

contemptible [kən'tɛmptɪbəl] *adj* méprisable

contempt' of court' *s* outrage *m* à la justice

contemptuous [kən'tɛmptʃʊ·əs] *adj* méprisant

contend [kən'tɛnd] *tr* prétendre ‖ *intr* combattre; **to contend with** lutter contre

contender [kən'tɛndər] *s* concurrent *m*, compétiteur *m*

content [kən'tɛnt] *adj & s* content *m* ‖ ['kɑntɛnt] *s* contenu *m*; **contents** contenu; (*of table of contents*) matières *fpl* ‖ [kən'tɛnt] *tr* contenter

contented [kən'tɛntɪd] *adj* content, satisfait

contention [kən'tɛnʃən] *s* (*strife*) dispute *f*, différend *m*; (*point argued for*) point *m* discuté, argument *m*; (law) contentieux *m*

contentious [kən'tɛnʃəs] *adj* contentieux

contentment [kən'tɛntmənt] *s* contentement *m*

contest ['kɑntɛst] *s* (*struggle, fight*) lutte *f*, dispute *f*; (*competition*) concours *m*, compétition *f* ‖ [kən'tɛst] *tr & intr* contester

contestant [kən'tɛstənt] *s* concurrent *m*

context ['kɑntɛkst] *s* contexte *m*

contiguous [kən'tɪgju·əs] *adj* contigu

continence ['kɑntɪnəns] *s* continence *f*

continent ['kɑntɪnənt] *adj & s* continent *m*

continental [ˌkɑntɪ'nɛntəl] *adj* continental

contingen·cy [kən'tɪndʒənsi] *s* (*pl* **-cies**) contingence *f*, éventualité *f*

contingent [kən'tɪndʒənt] *adj & s* contingent *m*

continual [kən'tɪnju·əl] *adj* continuel

continuation [kən,tɪnju'eʃən] *s* continuation *f*; (*e.g., of a story*) suite *f*

continue [kən'tɪnju] *tr & intr* continuer; **continued on page two (three, etc.)** suite page deux (trois, etc.); **to be continued** à suivre

continui·ty [ˌkɑntɪ'n(j)u·ɪti] *s* (*pl* **-ties**) continuité *f*; (mov, rad, telv) découpage *m*, scénario *m*

continuous [kən'tɪnju·əs] *adj* continu

contin'uous show'ing *s* (mov) spectacle *m* permanent

contin'uous waves' *spl* ondes *fpl* entretenues

contortion [kən'tɔrʃən] *s* contorsion *f*

contour ['kɑntʊr] *s* contour *m* ‖ *tr* contourner

con'tour line' *s* courbe *f* de niveau

contraband ['kɑntrə,bænd] *adj* contrebandier ‖ *s* contrebande *f*

contrabass ['kɑntrə,bes] *s* contrebasse *f*

contraceptive [ˌkɑntrə'sɛptɪv] *adj & s* contraceptif *m*

contract ['kɑntrækt] *s* contrat *m* ‖ *tr* contracter ‖ *intr* se contracter

contraction [kən'trækʃən] *s* contraction *f*

contractor [kən'træktər], [kɑntræktər] *s* entrepreneur *m* du bâtiment

contradict [ˌkɑntrə'dɪkt] *tr* contredire

contradiction [ˌkɑntrə'dɪkʃən] *s* contradiction *f*

contradictory [ˌkɑntrə'dɪktəri] *adj* contradictoire

contral·to [kən'trælto] *s* (*pl* **-tos**) contralto *m*

contraption [kən'træpʃən] *s* (coll) machin *m*, truc *m*

contra·ry ['kɑntrɛri] *adj* contraire ‖ *adv* contrairement ‖ [kən'trɛri] *adj* (coll) obstiné, têtu ‖ ['kɑntrɛri] *s* (*pl* **-ries**) contraire *m*; **on the contrary** au contraire, par contre

contrast ['kɑntræst] *s* contraste *m* ‖ [kən'træst] *tr* & *intr* contraster

contravene [ˌkɑntrə'vin] *tr* contredire; (*a law*) contrevenir

contribute [kən'trɪbjut] *tr* (*e.g.*, *a sum of money*) contribuer pour ‖ *intr* contribuer; (*to a newspaper, conference, etc.*) collaborer

contribution [ˌkɑntrɪ'bjuʃən] *s* contribution *f*, apport *m*; (*e.g.*, *for charity*) souscription *f*; (*to a newspaper, conference, etc.*) collaboration *f*

contributor [kən'trɪbjutər] *s* (*donor*) donneur *m*; (*e.g.*, *to a charitable cause*) souscripteur *m*; (*to a newspaper, conference, etc.*) collaborateur *m*

contrite [kən'traɪt] *adj* contrit

contrition [kən'trɪʃən] *s* contrition *f*

contrivance [kən'traɪvəns] *s* invention *f*, expédient *m*; (*gadget*) dispositif *m*

contrive [kən'traɪv] *tr* inventer ‖ *intr* s'arranger; **to contrive to** trouver moyen de

con·trol [kən'trol] *s* (*authority*) direction *f*, autorité *f*; (*mastery*) maîtrise *f*; (*surveillance*) contrôle *m*; **controls** commandes *fpl* ‖ *v* (*pret* & *pp* **-trolled**; *ger* **-trolling**) *tr* diriger; maîtriser; (*to give surveillance to*) contrôler; (*to handle the controls of*) commander; **to control oneself** se contrôler

controller [kən'trolər] *s* contrôleur *m*, appareil *m* de contrôle; (elec) controller *m*

control' pan'el *s* (aer) planche *f* de bord, tableau *m* de bord

control' rod' *s* (nucl) barre *f* de contrôle

control' stick' *s* (aer) manche *m* à balai

control' tow'er *s* poste-vigie *m*, tourelle *f* de commandement

controversial [ˌkɑntrə'vʌrʃəl] *adj* controversable

controver·sy ['kɑntrə,vʌrsi] *s* (*pl* **-sies**) controverse *f*; dispute *f*, querelle *f*

controvert ['kɑntrə,vʌrt] *tr* controverser; contredire

contumacious [ˌkɑnt(j)u'meʃəs] *adj* rebelle, récalcitrant

contume·ly ['kɑnt(j)umɪli] *s* (*pl* **-lies**) injure *f*, outrage *m*, mépris *m*

contusion [kən't(j)uʒən] *s* contusion *f*

conundrum [kə'nʌndrəm] *s* devinette *f*, énigme *f*

convalesce [ˌkɑnvə'lɛs] *intr* guérir, se remettre, se rétablir

convalescence [ˌkɑnvə'lɛsəns] *s* convalescence *f*

convalescent [ˌkɑnvə'lɛsənt] *adj* & *s* convalescent *m*

convales'cent home' *s* maison *f* de repos

convene [kən'vin] *tr* assembler, convoquer ‖ *intr* s'assembler

convenience [kən'vinjəns] *s* commodité *f*, confort *m*; **at your convenience** quand cela vous conviendra; **at your earliest convenience** (com) dans les meilleurs délais; **for my own convenience** pour mon utilité personnelle

conven'ience store' *s* centre *m* commercial de quartier, épicerie *f* de dépannage

convent ['kɑnvɛnt] *s* couvent *m* (de religieuses)

convention [kən'vɛnʃən] *s* (*meeting*) assemblée *f*, congrès *m*; (*agreement*) convention *f*; (*accepted usage*) convention sociale; **conventions** convenances *fpl*, bienséances *fpl*

conventional [kən'vɛnʃənəl] *adj* conventionnel; (*in conduct*) respectueux des convenances; (*everyday*) usuel; (*model, type*) traditionnel

converge [kən'vʌrdʒ] *intr* converger

conversant [kən'vʌrsənt] *adj* familier, versé

conversation [ˌkɑnvər'seʃən] *s* conversation *f*

conversational [ˌkɑnvər'seʃənəl] *adj* de conversation; (comp) de dialogue

conversa'tional mode' *s* (comp) mode *m* dialogué

converse ['kɑnvʌrs] *adj* & *s* contraire *m*, inverse *m*, réciproque *f* ‖ [kən'vʌrs] *intr* converser

conversion [kən'vʌrʒən] *s* conversion *f*

convert ['kɑnvʌrt] *s* converti *m* ‖ [kən'vʌrt] *tr* convertir ‖ *intr* se convertir

converter [kən'vʌrtər] *s* convertisseur *m*

convertible [kən'vʌrtɪbəl] *adj* (*person*) convertissable; (*thing; security*) convertible; (*sofa*) transformable; (aut) décapotable ‖ *s* (aut) décapotable *f*

convex [kɑn'vɛks] *adj* convexe, bombé

convey [kən've] *tr* (*goods, passengers*) transporter; (*e.g.*, *a message*) communiquer; (*e.g.*, *property*) transmettre; (law) céder

conveyance [kən've·əns] *s* (*of goods, passengers*) transport *m*; (*vehicle*) moyen *m* de transport, voiture *f*; (*of message*) communication *f*; (*transfer*) transmission *f*; (law) transfert *m*, cession *f*

conveyor [kən've·ər] *s* transporteur *m*, convoyeur *m*

convey'or belt' *s* tapis *m* roulant

convict ['kɑnvɪkt] *s* condamné *m*, forçat *m* ‖ [kən'vɪkt] *tr* condamner, convaincre

conviction [kən'vɪkʃən] *s* (*sentencing*) condamnation *f*; (*certainty*) conviction *f*

convince [kən'vɪns] *tr* convaincre

convincing [kən'vɪnsɪŋ] *adj* convaincant

convivial [kən'vɪvɪ·əl] *adj* jovial, plein d'entrain

convocation [ˌkɑnvə'keʃən] *s* (*calling together*) convocation *f*; (*meeting*) assemblée *f*

convoke [kən'vok] *tr* convoquer

convolution [ˌkɑnvə'luʃən] *s* (*of brain*) circonvolution *f*

convoy ['kɑnvɔɪ] s convoi m, conserve f, e.g., **to sail in convoy** naviguer de conserve ‖ tr convoyer

convulse [kən'vʌls] tr convulsionner, convulser; **to be convulsed with laughter** se tordre de rire

coo [ku] intr roucouler

cooing ['ku·ɪŋ] s roucoulement m

cook [kʊk] s cuisinier m, chef m; (female cook) cuisinière f ‖ tr cuisiner, faire cuire; **to cook up** (a plot) machiner, tramer ‖ intr faire la cuisine, cuisiner; (said of food) cuire

cook'book' s livre m de cuisine

cooker ['kʊkər] s réchaud m, cuisinière f

cookery ['kʊkəri] s cuisine f

cookie ['kʊki] s var of **cooky**

cooking ['kʊkɪŋ] s cuisine f; (e.g., of meat) cuisson f

cook'ing uten'sils spl batterie f de cuisine

cook'stove' s cuisinière f

cook·y ['kʊki] s (pl -ies) biscuit m, gâteau m sec

cool [kul] adj frais; (e.g., to an idea) indifférent; **it is cool out** il fait frais; **to keep cool** tenir au frais; se tenir tranquille ‖ s fraîcheur f ‖ tr rafraîchir, refroidir; **to cool one's heels** (coll) se morfondre ‖ intr se refroidir, se rafraîchir; **to cool down** se calmer; **to cool off** se refroidir

cooler ['kulər] s frigorifique m; (prison) (slang) violon m, tôle f

cool'-head'ed adj imperturbable, de sang-froid

coolness ['kulnɪs] s fraîcheur f; (of disposition) sang-froid m, calme m; (standoffishness) froideur f

coon [kun] s raton m laveur

coop [kup] s poulailler m; **to fly the coop** (slang) débiner, décamper ‖ tr enfermer dans un poulailler; **to coop up** claque-murer

co-op ['ko·ɑp] s entreprise f coopérative

cooper ['kupər] s tonnelier m

cooperate [ko'ɑpə,ret] intr coopérer; (to be helpful) faire preuve de bonne volonté

cooperation [ko,ɑpə'reʃən] s coopération f

cooperative [ko'ɑpə,retɪv] adj coopératif ‖ s coopérative f

coordinate [ko'ɔrdɪnɪt] adj coordonné ‖ s coordonnée f ‖ [ko'ɔrdɪ,net] tr coordonner

coordination [ko,ɔrdə'neʃən] s coordination f

coot [kut] s foulque f; **old coot** (coll) vieille baderne f

cootie ['kuti] s (slang) pou m

cop [kɑp] s (coll) agent m ‖ v (pret & pp copped) ger copping) tr (slang) dérober

copartner [ko'pɑrtnər] s coassocié m, coparticipant m; (in crime) complice mf

cope [kop] intr—**to cope with** faire face à, tenir tête à

cope'stone' s couronnement m

copier ['kɑpɪ·ər] s (person who copies) copiste mf, imitateur m; (apparatus) appareil m à copier; (making photocopies)

machine f à photocopier, reprographieur m

copilot ['ko,paɪlət] s copilote m

coping ['kopɪŋ] s faîte m, comble m; (of bridge) chape f

copious ['kopɪ·əs] adj copieux

cop'-out' s (slang) démission f, dérobade f

copper ['kɑpər] adj de cuivre, en cuivre; (color) cuivré ‖ s cuivre m; (coin) petite monnaie f; (slang) flic m

cop'per·smith' s chaudronnier m

coppery ['kɑpəri] adj cuivreux

coppice ['kɑpɪs] s taillis m

copulate ['kɑpjə,let] intr s'accoupler

copulation [,kɑpjə'leʃən] s copulation f, accouplement m

cop·y ['kɑpi] s (pl -ies) copie f; (of a book) exemplaire m; (of a magazine) numéro m; (for printer) original m; **to make copies** exécuter des doubles ‖ v (pret & pp -ied) tr & intr copier

cop'y·book' s cahier m

cop'y·cat' s (coll) imitateur m, singe m

cop'ying machine' ['kɑpɪ·ɪŋ] s machine f à photocopier, reprographieur m

cop'y·right' s propriété f artistique or littéraire, droit m de l'artiste or de l'auteur, copyright m; (formula on printed matter) dépôt m légal ‖ tr réserver les droits de publication de

cop'y·right'ed adj (formula used on printed material) droits de reproduction réservés

cop'y·writ'er s rédacteur m d'annonces publicitaires

co·quet [ko'kɛt] v (pret & pp -quetted; ger -quetting) intr coqueter

coquet·ry ['kokətri] s (pl -ries) coquetterie f

coquette [ko'kɛt] s coquette f ‖ intr coqueter

coquettish [ko'kɛtɪʃ] adj coquet

coral ['kɔrəl] adj de corail, en corail ‖ s corail m

cor'al reef' s récif m de corail

cord [kɔrd] s corde f; (string) ficelle f; (attached to a bell) cordon m; (elec) fil m ‖ tr corder

cordage ['kɔrdɪdʒ] s cordage m

cordial ['kɔrdʒəl] adj & s cordial m

cordiali·ty [kɔr'dʒælɪti] s (pl -ties) cordialité f

corduroy ['kɔrdə,rɔɪ] s velours m côtelé; **corduroys** pantalon en velours côtelé

core [kor] s (of fruit) trognon m, cœur m; (of magnet, cable, earth, atom) noyau m; (nucl) cœur m; **rotten to the core** pourri à la base ‖ tr vider

corespondent [,korɪs'pɑndənt] s complice mf d'adultère

cork [kɔrk] s liège m; (of bottle) bouchon m; **to take the cork out of** déboucher ‖ tr boucher

corking ['kɔrkɪŋ] adj (coll) épatant

cork' oak' s chêne-liège m

cork'screw' s tire-bouchon m

cork'-tipped' adj à bout de liège

cormorant ['kɔrmərənt] s cormoran m

corn [kɔrn] *s* (*in U.S.A.*) maïs *m*; (*in England*) blé *m*; (*in Scotland*) avoine *f*; (*single seed*) grain *m*; (*on foot*) cor *m*, durillon *m*; (*whiskey*) (coll) eau-de-vie *f* de grain; (slang) platitude *f*, banalité *f*

corn' bread' *s* pain *m* de maïs

corn'cob' *s* épi *m* de maïs; (*without the grain*) rafle *f*

corn'cob pipe' *s* pipe *f* en rafle de maïs

corn'crib' *s* dépôt *m* de maïs

cornea [ˈkɔrnɪ·ə] *s* cornée *f*

corned' beef' *s* bœuf *m* salé

corner [ˈkɔrnər] *adj* cornier ‖ *s* coin *m*, angle *m*; (*of room*) encoignure *f*; (*of lips*) commissure *f*; (*on the market*) prise *f* de contrôle; **around the corner** au tournant; **in a corner** (fig) au pied du mur, à l'accul; **to cut a corner close** prendre un virage à la corde; **to cut corners** (*in spending*) rogner les dépenses; (*in work*) bâcler un travail ‖ *tr* coincer, acculer; (*the market*) accaparer

cor'ner cup'board *s* encoignure *f*

cor'ner room' *s* pièce *f* d'angle

cor'ner·stone' *s* pierre *f* angulaire

cornet [kɔrˈnɛt] *s* cornet *m*; (*headdress*) cornette *f*; (mil) cornette *m*; (mus) cornet à pistons

corn' exchange' *s* bourse *f* des céréales

corn'field' *s* (*in U.S.A.*) champ *m* de maïs; (*in England*) champ de blé; (*in Scotland*) champ d'avoine

corn'flakes' *spl* paillettes *fpl* de maïs

corn' flour' *s* farine *f* de maïs

corn'flow'er *s* bluet *m*, barbeau *m*

corn' frit'ter *s* crêpes *fpl* de maïs

corn'husk' *s* enveloppe *f* de l'épi de maïs

cornice [ˈkɔrnɪs] *s* corniche *f*

corn' meal' *s* farine *f* de maïs

corn' on the cob' *s* maïs *m* en épi

corn' pad' *s* bourrelet *m* coricide

corn' pone' *s* pain *m* de maïs

corn' pop'per *s* appareil *m* pour faire éclater le maïs

corn' remov'er *s* coricide *m*

corn' silk' *s* barbe *f* de maïs

corn'stalk' *s* tige *f* de maïs

corn'starch' *s* fécule *f* de maïs

cornucopia [ˌkɔrnəˈkopɪ·ə] *s* corne *f* d'abondance

Cornwall [ˈkɔrn,wɔl] *s* la Cornouailles

corn·y [ˈkɔrnɪ] *adj* (*comp* **-ier**; *super* **-iest**) (slang) banal, trivial, fade

corollar·y [ˈkɔrə,lɛrɪ] *s* (*pl* **-ies**) corollaire *m*

coronary [ˈkɔrə,nɛrɪ] *adj* coronaire

cor'onary thrombo'sis *s* (pathol) infarctus *m* du myocarde

coronation [ˌkɔrəˈneʃən] *s* couronnement *m*, sacre *m*

cor'oner's in'quest [ˈkɔrənərz] *s* enquête *f* judiciaire par-devant jury (en cas de mort violente ou suspecte)

coronet [ˈkɔrə,nɛt] *s* (*worn by lady*) diadème *m*; (*worn by members of nobility*) couronne *f*; (*worn by earl or baron*) tortil *m*

corporal [ˈkɔrpərəl] *adj* corporel ‖ *s* (mil) caporal *m*

corporate [ˈkɔrpərɪt] *adj* incorporé

corporation [ˌkɔrpəˈreʃən] *s* société *f* anonyme, compagnie *f* anonyme

corporeal [kɔrˈporɪ·əl] *adj* corporel, matériel

corps [kor] *s* (*pl* **corps** [korz]) corps *m*; (mil) corps d'armée

corpse [kɔrps] *s* cadavre *m*

corps'man *s* (*pl* **-men**) (mil) infirmier *m*

corpulent [ˈkɔrpjələnt] *adj* corpulent

corpuscle [ˈkɔrpəsəl] *s* (phys) corpuscule *m*; (physiol) globule *m*

corpus delicti [ˈkɔrpəsdɪˈlɪktaɪ] *s* (law) corps *m* du délit

cor·ral [kəˈræl] *s* corral *m*, enclos *m* ‖ *v* (*pret & pp* **-ralled**; *ger* **-ralling**) *tr* enfermer dans un corral; (fig) saisir

correct [kəˈrɛkt] *adj* correct ‖ *tr* corriger

correction [kəˈrɛkʃən] *s* correction *f*

corrective [kəˈrɛktɪv] *adj & s* correctif *m*

correc'tive lens'es *spl* verres *mpl* correcteurs

correctness [kəˈrɛktnɪs] *s* correction *f*

correlate [ˈkɔrə,let] *tr* mettre en corrélation ‖ *intr* correspondre; **to correlate with** correspondre à

correlation [ˌkɔrɪˈleʃən] *s* corrélation *f*

correspond [ˌkɔrɪˈspɑnd] *intr* correspondre

correspondence [ˌkɔrɪˈspɑndəns] *s* correspondance *f*

correspond'ence course' *s* cours *m* de l'enseignement par correspondance

correspondent [ˌkɔrɪˈspɑndənt] *adj & s* correspondant *m*

corresponding [ˌkɔrɪˈspɑndɪŋ] *adj* correspondant

corridor [ˈkɔrɪdər] *s* corridor *m*, couloir *m*

corroborate [kəˈrɑbə,ret] *tr* corroborer

corrode [kəˈrod] *tr* corroder ‖ *intr* se corroder

corrosion [kəˈroʒən] *s* corrosion *f*

corrosive [kəˈrosɪv] *adj & s* corrosif *m*

corrugated [ˈkɔrə,getɪd] *adj* ondulé

corrupt [kəˈrʌpt] *adj* corrompu ‖ *tr* corrompre

corruption [kəˈrʌpʃən] *s* corruption *f*

corsage [kɔrˈsɑʒ] *s* bouquet *m* porté or fleur *f* portée à l'épaule ou à la ceinture; (*waist*) corsage *m*

corsair [ˈkɔr,sɛr] *s* corsaire *m*

corset [ˈkɔrsɪt] *s* corset *m*

Corsica [ˈkɔrsɪkə] *s* Corse *f*; la Corse

Corsican [ˈkɔrsɪkən] *adj* corse ‖ *s* (*dialect*) corse *m*; (*person*) Corse *mf*

cortege [kɔrˈteʒ] *s* cortège *m*

cor·tex [ˈkɔr,tɛks] *s* (*pl* **-tices** [tɪ,siz]) cortex *m*

cortisone [ˈkɔrtɪ,son] *s* cortisone *f*

coruscate [ˈkɔrəs,ket] *intr* scintiller

cosmetic [kazˈmɛtɪk] *adj & s* cosmétique *m*

cosmic [ˈkazmɪk] *adj* cosmique

cosmonaut [ˈkazmə,nɔt] *s* cosmonaute *mf*

cosmopolitan [ˌkazməˈpalɪtən] *adj & s* cosmopolite *mf*

cosmos [ˈkazməs] *s* cosmos *m*

Cossack ['kɑ,sæk] *adj* cosaque ‖ *s* Cosaque *mf*

cost [kɔst] *s* coût *m*; (*price*) prix *m*; **at all costs** à tout prix, coûte que coûte; **at cost** au prix coûtant; **costs** frais *mpl*; (*law*) dépens *mpl* ‖ *v* (*pret & pp* **cost**) *intr* coûter

cost' account'ing *s* comptabilité *f* industrielle

costliness ['kɔstlɪnɪs] *s* cherté *f*, haut prix *m*

cost·ly ['kɔstli] *adj* (*comp* **-lier**; *super* **-liest**) coûteux, cher

cost' of liv'ing *s* coût *m* de la vie

cost' price' *s* prix *m* coûtant; (*net price*) prix de revient

costume ['kɑst(j)um] *s* costume *m*

cos'tume ball' *s* bal *m* costumé

cos'tume jew'elry *s* bijoux *mpl* en toc

costumer [kɑs't(j)umər] *s* costumier *m*

cot [kɑt] *s* lit *m* de sangle

coterie ['kotəri] *s* coterie *f*

cottage ['kɑtɪdʒ] *s* chalet *m*, cabanon *m*, villa *f*; (*with a thatched roof*) chaumière *f*

cot'tage cheese' *s* lait *m* caillé, caillé *m*, jonchée *f*

cot'ter pin' ['kɑtər] *s* goupille *f* fendue, clavette *f*

cotton ['kɑtən] *adj* cotonnier, de coton ‖ *s* coton *m* ‖ *intr*—**to cotton up to** (coll) éprouver de la sympathie pour

cot'ton bat'ting *s* coton *m* or ouate *f* hydrophile

cot'ton field' *s* cotonnerie *f*

cot'ton gin' *s* égreneuse *f*

cot'ton mill' *s* filature *f* de coton, cotonnerie *f*

cot'ton pick'er *s* cotonnier *m*

cot'ton pick'ing *s* récolte *f* du coton

cot'ton·seed' *s* graine *f* de coton

cot'tonseed oil' *s* huile *f* de coton

cot'ton waste' *s* déchets *mpl* or bourre *f* de coton

cot'ton·wood' *s* peuplier *m* de Virginie

cottony ['kɑtəni] *adj* cotonneux

couch [kautʃ] *s* (*without back*) divan *m*; (*with back*) sofa *m*, canapé *m* ‖ *tr* (*a demand, a letter*) rédiger ‖ *intr* (*to lie in wait*) se tapir

cougar ['kugər] *s* couguar *m*, cougouar *m*

cough [kɔf], [kɑf] *s* toux *f* ‖ *tr*—**to cough up** cracher en toussant; (slang) (*money*) cracher ‖ *intr* tousser

cough' drop' *s* pastille *f* pectorale, pastille pour la toux

cough' syr'up *s* sirop *m* pectoral, sirop contre la toux

could [kud] *aux*—**he could not come** il ne pouvait pas venir; **he couldn't do it** il n'a (pas) pu le faire; **he couldn't do it if he wanted to** il ne pourrait (pas) le faire s'il le voulait, il ne saurait (pas) le faire s'il le voulait

council ['kaunsəl] *s* conseil *m*; (eccl) concile *m*

coun'cil·man *s* (*pl* **-men**) conseiller *m* municipal

councilor ['kaunsələr] *s* conseiller *m*

coun·sel ['kaunsəl] *s* conseil *m*, avis *m*; (*lawyer*) avocat *m* ‖ *v* (*pret & pp* **-seled** or **-selled**; *ger* **-seling** or **-selling**) *tr & intr* conseiller; **to counsel s.o. to** + *inf* conseiller à qn de + *inf*

counselor ['kaunsələr] *s* conseiller *m*, conseil *m*; (*lawyer*) avocat *m*

count [kaunt] *s* (*counting*) compte *m*; (*nobleman*) comte *m* ‖ *tr* compter; **to count the votes** dépouiller le scrutin ‖ *intr* compter; **count off!** (mil) comptez-vous!; **to count for** valoir; **to count on** (*to have confidence in*) compter sur (*s.o. or s.th.*); **to count on** + *ger* compter + *inf*

countable ['kauntəbəl] *adj* comptable

count'down' *s* compte *m* à rebours

countenance ['kauntɪnəns] *s* mine *f*, contenance *f*; **to give countenance to** appuyer; **to keep one's countenance** garder son sérieux; **to lose countenance** perdre contenance ‖ *tr* soutenir, approuver

counter ['kauntər] *adj* contraire ‖ *s* (*counting agent or machine*) compteur *m*; (*piece of wood or metal for keeping score*) jeton *m*; (*board in shop over which business is transacted*) comptoir *m*; (*in a bar or café*) zinc *m*; **over the counter** (com) hors bourse, hors cote; **under the counter** en dessous de table, sous le comptoir, sous cape ‖ *adv* contrairement; **in sens inverse**; **to run counter to** aller à l'encontre de ‖ *tr* contrarier, contrecarrer; (*a move, e.g., in chess*) contrer; (*an opinion*) prendre le contre-pied de ‖ *intr* parer le coup, parer un coup; **to counter with** riposter par

coun'ter·act' *tr* contrebalancer

coun'ter·attack' *s* contre-attaque *f* ‖ **coun'ter·attack'** *tr* contre-attaquer

coun'ter·bal'ance *s* contrepoids *m* ‖ **coun'ter·bal'ance** *tr* contrebalancer

coun'ter·clock'wise' *adj & adv* en sens inverse des aiguilles d'une montre, en sens antihoraire

coun'ter·cul'ture *s* contre-culture *f*

coun'ter·cur'rent *s* contre-courant *m*

coun'ter·es'pionage *s* contre-espionnage *m*

counterfeit ['kauntərfɪt] *adj* contrefait; (*beauty*) sophistiqué ‖ *s* contrefaction *f*, contrefaçon *f*; (*money*) fausse monnaie *f* ‖ *tr* contrefaire; (*e.g., an illness*) feindre

counterfeiter ['kauntər,fɪtər] *s* contrefacteur *m*; (*of money*) faux-monnayeur *m*

coun'terfeit mon'ey *s* fausse monnaie *f*, faux billets *mpl*

coun'ter·ir'ritant *adj & s* révulsif *m*

countermand ['kauntər,mænd] *s* contre-ordre *m* ‖ *tr* contremander

coun'ter·march' *s* contremarche *f* ‖ *intr* faire une contremarche

coun'ter·meas'ure *s* contre-mesure *f*

coun'ter·offen'sive *s* contre-offensive *f*

coun'ter·pane' *s* courtepoint *f*

coun'ter·part' *s* contrepartie *f*, homologue *m*

coun'ter·point' *s* contrepoint *m*

coun'ter·poise' *s* contrepoids *m* ‖ *tr* faire équilibre à

coun'ter·rev'olu'tionar·y *adj* contrerévolutionnaire ‖ *s* (*pl* **-ies**) contrerévolutionnaire *mf*

coun'ter·sign' *s* contremarque *f*; (*signature*) contreseing *m*; (mil) mot *m* d'ordre ‖ *tr* contresigner

coun'ter·sig'nature *s* contreseing *m*

coun'ter·sink' *s* fraise *f*, chasse-clou *m* ‖ *v* (*pret & pp* **-sunk**) *tr* fraiser

coun'ter·spy' *s* (*pl* **-spies**) contre-espion *m*

coun'ter·stroke' *s* contrecoup *m*

coun'ter·weight' *s* contrepoids *m*

countess ['kaʊntɪs] *s* comtesse *f*

countless ['kaʊntlɪs] *adj* innombrable

countrified ['kʌntrɪ,faɪd] *adj* provincial, compagnard

coun·try ['kʌntri] *s* (*pl* **-tries**) (*territory of a nation*) pays *m*; (*land of one's birth*) patrie *f*; (*region*) contrée *f*; (*not the city*) campagne *f*

coun'try club' *s* club *m* privé situé hors des agglomérations

coun'try estate' *s* domaine *m*

coun'try·folk' *s* campagnards *mpl*

coun'try gen'tleman *s* châtelain *m*, propriétaire *m* d'un château

coun'try house' *s* maison *f* de campagne

coun'try·man *s* (*pl* **-men**) (*of the same country*) compatriote *mf*; (*rural*) compagnard *m*

coun'try mu'sic *s* musique *f* rustique

coun'try·side' *s* paysage *m*, campagne *f*

coun'try town' *s* petite ville *f* de province

coun'try·wide *adj* national

coun'try·wom'an *s* (*pl* **-wom'en**) (*of the same country*) compatriote *f*; (*rural*) campagnarde *f*

coun·ty ['kaʊnti] *s* (*pl* **-ties**) comté *m*

coun'ty seat' *s* chef-lieu *m* de comté

coupé [kupe] *s* coupé *m*

couple ['kʌpəl] *s* (*man and wife; male and female; friends*) couple *m*, paire *f*; (*of eggs, cakes, etc.*) couple *f*; (elec, mech) couple *m* ‖ *tr* coupler, accoupler; (mach) embrayer ‖ *intr* s'accoupler

coupler ['kʌplər] *s* (mach) coupleur *m*

coupling ['kʌplɪŋ] *s* accouplement *m*; (mach) couplage *m*

coupon ['k(j)upɑn] *s* coupon *m*, bon *m*

courage ['kʌrɪdʒ] *s* courage *m*

courageous [kə'redʒəs] *adj* courageux

courier ['kʊrɪ·ər] *s* courrier *m*; (*on horseback*) estafette *f*

course [kors] *s* (*duration, process; course in school*) cours *m*; (*of a meal*) service *m*, plat *m*; (*of a stream*) parcours *m*, cours *m*; (*direction*) route *f*, chemin *m*; **course before the main course** (culin) entrée *f*; **first course** (culin) premier plat, entrée en matière *f*; **in due course** en temps voulu; **in the course of time** avec le temps; **main course** (culin) plat principal, pièce *f* de résistance; **of course!** naturellement!, bien entendu!; **to give a course** faire un cours; **to set a course for** (naut) mettre le cap sur; **to take a course** suivre un cours ‖ *tr & intr* courir

court [kort] *s* cour *f*; (*of law*) tribunal *m*, cour; (sports) terrain *m*, court *m*; **out of court** à l'amiable ‖ *tr* courtiser, faire la cour à; (*favor, votes*) briguer, solliciter; (*danger*) aller au-devant de

courteous ['kʌrtɪ·əs] *adj* poli, courtois

courtesan ['kɔrtɪzən] *s* courtisane *f*

courte·sy ['kʌrtɪsi] *s* (*pl* **-sies**) politesse *f*, courtoisie *f*; **through the courtesy of** avec la gracieuse permission de

court'house' *s* palais *m* de justice

courtier ['kortɪ·ər] *s* courtisan *m*

court' jest'er *s* bouffon *m* du roi

court·ly ['kortli] *adj* (*comp* **-lier**; *super* **-liest**) courtois, élégant

court'-mar'tial *s* (*pl* **courts-martial**) conseil *m* de guerre ‖ *v* (*pret & pp* **-tialed** or **-tialled**; *ger* **-tialing** or **-tialling**) *tr* traduire en conseil de guerre; **to be court-martialed** passer en conseil de guerre

court' plas'ter *s* taffetas *m* gommé, sparadrap *m*

court'room' *s* salle *f* du tribunal

court'ship *s* cour *f*

court'yard' *s* cour *f*

cousin ['kʌzɪn] *s* cousin *m*

cove [kov] *s* anse *f*, crique *f*

covenant ['kʌvənənt] *s* contrat *m*, accord *m*, pacte *m*; (Bib) alliance *f*

cover ['kʌvər] *s* (*blanket; military protection; book cover*) couverture *f*; (*lid*) couvercle *m*; (*for furniture*) housse *f*; (*of wild game*) remise *f*, gîte *m*; (com) couverture *f*, provision *f*, marge *f*; (mach) chape *f*; (phila) enveloppe *f*; **from cover to cover** de la première page à la dernière; **to take cover** se mettre à l'abri; **under cover** (*e.g., of trees*) sous les couverts; (*safe from harm*) à couvert; **under cover of** sous le couvert de, dissimulé dans; **under separate cover** sous pli distinct ‖ *tr* couvrir; (*a certain distance*) parcourir; (*a newspaper story*) faire le reportage de; (*one's tracks*) brouiller; (*with, e.g., chocolate*) enrober; **to cover up** recouvrir ‖ *intr* se couvrir; (*to brood*) couver

coverage ['kʌvərɪdʒ] *s* (*amount or space covered*) portée *f*; (*of news*) reportage *m*; (*insurance*) assurance *f*, couverture *f* d'assurance

co'ver·alls' *spl* salopette *f*, bleus *mpl*

cov'er charge' *s* couvert *m*

cov'ered wag'on *s* chariot *m* couvert

cov'er girl' *s* cover-girl *f*, pin up *f*

covering ['kʌvərɪŋ] *s* couverture *f*, recouvrement *m*

covert ['kʌvərt] *adj* couvert, caché

cov'er-up' *s* subterfuge *m*; (*reply*) réponse *f* évasive

covet ['kʌvɪt] *tr* convoiter

covetous ['kʌvɪtɪs] *adj* cupide, avide

covetousness ['kʌvɪtəsnɪs] *s* convoitise *f*, cupidité *f*

covey ['kʌvi] *s* couvée *f*; (*in flight*) volée *f*

cow [kaʊ] *s* vache *f*; (*of seal, elephant*) femelle *f* ‖ *tr* (coll) intimider

coward [ˈkaʊ·ərd] *s* lâche *mf*

cowardice [ˈkaʊ·ərdɪs] *s* lâcheté *f*

cowardly [ˈkaʊ·ərdli] *adj* lâche ‖ *adv* lâchement, peureusement

cow'bell' *s* grelot *m*, clarine *f*

cow'boy' *s* cow-boy *m*

cow'catch'er *s* (rr) chasse-bestiaux *m*

cower [ˈkaʊ·ər] *intr* se tapir

cow'herd' *s* vacher *m*, bouvier *m*

cow'hide' *s* vache *f*, peau *f* de vache; fouet *m* ‖ *tr* fouetter

cowl [kaʊl] *s* (*religious dress*) capuchon *m*, cagoule *f*; (*of chimney*) chapeau *m*; (aer, aut) capot *m*

cow'lick' *s* mèche *f* rebelle

cow'pox' *s* (pathol) vaccine *f*

coxcomb [ˈkɑks,kom] *s* (*conceited person*) petit-maître *m*, fat *m*; (bot) crête-de-coq *f*

coxswain [ˈkɑksən], [ˈkɑk,swen] *s* (naut) patron *m* de chaloupe; (rowing) barreur *m*

coy [kɔɪ] *adj* réservé, modeste

co·zy [ˈkozi] *adj* (*comp* **-zier**; *super* **-ziest**) douillet, intime ‖ *s* (*pl* **-zies**) couvre-théière *m*

C.P.A. [ˈsiˈpiˈe] *s* (letterword) (**certified public accountant**) expert-comptable *m*, comptable *m* agréé

CPI [ˈsiˈpiˈaɪ] *s* (letterword) (**consumer price index**) indexation *f* des traitements sur le coût de la vie

crab [kræb] *s* crabe *m*; (*grouch*) grincheux *m* ‖ *v* (*pret & pp* **crabbed**; *ger* **crabbing**) *intr* (coll) se plaindre

crab' ap'ple *s* pomme *f* sauvage

crabbed [ˈkræbɪd] *adj* acariâtre; (*handwriting*) de chat; (*author*) hermétique; (*style*) entortillé

crab·by [ˈkræbi] *adj* (*comp* **-bier**; *super* **-biest**) (coll) revêche, grognon

crack [kræk] *adj* d'élite; (coll) expert, de premier ordre ‖ *s* (*noise*) bruit *m* sec, craquement *m*; (*of whip*) claquement *m*; (*fissure*) fente *f*; (*e.g., in a dish*) fêlure *f*; (*e.g., in a wall*) lézarde *f*; (*in skin*) gerçure *f*; (*joke*) bon mot *m*; **crack of dawn** pointe *f* du jour ‖ *tr* (*one's fingers; petroleum*) faire craquer; (*a whip*) claquer; (*to split*) fendre; (*e.g., a dish*) fêler; (*e.g., a wall*) lézarder; (*the skin*) gercer; (*nuts*) casser; **to crack a joke** (slang) faire or lâcher une plaisanterie; **to crack up** (*to praise*) (coll) vanter, prôner; (*to crash*) (coll) écraser ‖ *intr* (*to make a noise*) craquer; (*said of whip*) claquer; (*to be split*) se fendre; (*said of dish*) se fêler; (*said of wall*) se lézarder; (*said of skin*) se gercer; **to crack up** (*to crash*) (coll) s'écraser; (*to break down*) (coll) craquer, s'effondrer

crack'-brained' *adj* timbré; **to be crack-brained** avoir le cerveau fêlé

crack'down' *s* (coll) répression *f*

cracked *adj* (*split*) fendu, fêlé; (*foolish*) (coll) timbré, toqué, cinglé

cracker [ˈkrækər] *s* biscuit *m* sec

crack'er-bar'rel *adj* (coll) en chambre, au petit pied

crack'er-jack' *adj* (slang) expérimenté, remarquable ‖ *s* (slang) crack *m*

cracking [ˈkrækɪŋ] *s* (*of petroleum*) cracking *m*

crackle [ˈkrækəl] *s* crépitation *f* ‖ *intr* crépiter, pétiller

crack'le·ware' *s* porcelaine *f* craquelée

crackling [ˈkræklɪŋ] *s* crépitement *m*, pétillement *m*; (culin) couenne *f* rissolée;

cracklings cretons *mpl*

crack'pot' *adj & s* (slang) original *m*, excentrique *mf*

crack' shot' *s* (coll) fin tireur *m*

crack'-up' *s* (*collision*) (coll) écrasement *m*; (*breakdown*) (coll) effondrement *m*

cradle [ˈkredəl] *s* berceau *m* ‖ *tr* bercer

cra'dle·song' *s* berceuse *f*

craft [kræft] *s* (*profession*) métier *m*; (*trickery*) artifice *m*; (naut) embarcation *f*, barque *f*

craftiness [ˈkræftɪnɪs] *s* ruse *f*, astuce *f*

crafts'man *s* (*pl* **-men**) artisan *m*

crafts'man·ship' *s* habileté *f* technique; exécution *f*

craft·y [ˈkræfti] *adj* (*comp* **-ier**; *super* **-iest**) rusé

crag [kræg] *s* rocher *m* escarpé

cram [kræm] *v* (*pret & pp* **crammed**; *ger* **cramming**) *tr* (*with food*) bourrer, gaver; (*with people*) bonder; (*for an exam*) (coll) chauffer ‖ *intr* se bourrer, se gaver; (*for an exam*) (coll) potasser

cramp [kræmp] *s* (*metal bar; clamp*) crampon *m*; (*in a muscle*) crampe *f*; (carpentry) serre-joint *m* ‖ *tr* cramponner, agrafer; presser, serrer; (*one's movements, style, or manner of living*) gêner

cranber·ry [ˈkræn,bɛri] *s* (*pl* **-ries**) (*Vaccinium oxycoccus or V. uliginosum*) canneberge *f*, airelle *f* coussinette

crane [kren] *s* (mach, orn) grue *f* ‖ *tr* (*one's neck*) allonger, tendre ‖ *intr* allonger le cou

crani·um [ˈkreni·əm] *s* (*pl* **-a** [ə]) crâne *m*

crank [kræŋk] *s* (*which turns*) manivelle *f*; (*person*) (coll) excentrique *mf* ‖ *tr* (*a motor*) faire partir à la manivelle

crank'case' *s* carter *m*

crank'shaft' *s* vilebrequin *m*

crank·y [ˈkræŋki] *adj* (*comp* **-ier**; *super* **-iest**) (*person*) revêche, grincheux; (*not working well*) détraqué; (*queer*) excentrique

cran·ny [ˈkræni] *s* (*pl* **-nies**) fente *f*, crevasse *f*; (*corner*) coin *m*

crape [krep] *s* crêpe *m*

crape'hang'er *s* (slang) rabat-joie *m*

craps [kræps] *s* (slang) jeu *m* de dés; **to shoot craps** (slang) jouer aux dés

crash [kræʃ] *s* (*noise*) fracas *m*, écroulement *m*; (*of thunder*) coup *m*; (*e.g., of airplane*) écrasement *m*; (*e.g., on stock market*) krach *m* ‖ *tr* briser, fracasser; (*e.g., an airplane*) écraser ‖ *intr* retentir; (*said of airplane*) s'écraser; (*to fail*)

craquer; **to crash into** emboutir, tamponner; **to crash through** enfoncer
crash′ dive′ s brusque plongée f
crash′ hel′met s casque m
crash′-land′ing s crash m, atterrissage m violent
crash′ record′er s (aer) enregistreur m d'accident
crass [kræs] adj grossier; (ignorance) crasse
crate [kret] s caisse f à claire-voie, cageot m, caisson m ‖ tr emballer dans une caisse à claire-voie
crater [′kretər] s cratère m
cravat [krə′væt] s cravate f
crave [krev] tr (drink, tobacco, etc.) avoir un besoin maladif de; (affection) avoir grand besoin de; (attention) solliciter; **to crave s.o.'s pardon** implorer le pardon de qn ‖ intr—**to crave for** désirer ardemment; implorer
craven [′krevən] adj & s poltron m
craving [′krevɪŋ] s désir m ardent, désir obsédant
craw [krɔ] s jabot m
crawl [krɔl] s (snail's pace) allure f très ralentie; (swimming) crawl m ‖ intr ramper; (to go slowly) avancer au pas; **to be crawling with** fourmiller de, grouiller de; **to crawl along** se traîner; **to crawl on one's hands and knees** aller à quatre pattes; **to crawl over** escalader; **to crawl up** grimper
crayon [′kre·ən] s crayon m de pastel, pastel m ‖ tr crayonner
craze [krez] s manie f, toquade f ‖ tr rendre fou
cra·zy [′krezi] adj (comp -zier; super -ziest) fou; (rickety) délabré; (coll) dingue, fou; **to be crazy about** (coll) être fou de, être toqué de; **to drive crazy** rendre fou, affoler; **to go crazy** perdre la boule
cra′zy bone′ s nerf m du coude
cra′zy quilt′ s courtepointe f multicolore
creak [krik] s cri m, grincement m ‖ intr crier, grincer
creak·y [′kriki] adj (comp -ier; super -iest) criard
cream [krim] s crème f; **creams** (with chocolate coating) chocolats mpl fourrés ‖ tr écrémer; (butter and sugar together) mélanger ‖ intr crémer
cream′ cheese′ s fromage m à la crème, fromage blanc, petit suisse m
creamer·y [′kriməri] s (pl -ies) laiterie f; compagnie f laitière
cream′ of tar′tar s crème f de tartre
cream′ pitch′er s crémière f
cream′ puff′ s chou m à la crème
cream′ sep′arator [′sɛpə,retər] s écrémeuse f
cream·y [′krimi] adj (comp -ier; super -iest) crémeux
crease [kris] s pli m, faux pli m ‖ tr & intr plisser
create [kri′et] tr créer
creation [kri′eʃən] s création f
creative [kri′etɪv] adj créateur, inventif

creator [kri′etər] s créateur m
creature [′kritʃər] s créature f
credence [′kridəns] s créance f, croyance f, foi f
credentials [krɪ′dɛnʃəlz] spl papiers mpl, pièces fpl justificatives, lettres fpl de créance
credibility [,krɛdɪ′bɪlɪti] s crédibilité f
credible [′krɛdɪbəl] adj croyable, digne de foi
credit [′krɛdɪt] s crédit m; **on credit** à crédit; **to be a credit to** faire honneur à; **to take credit for** s'attribuer le mérite de ‖ tr croire, ajouter foi à; (com) créditer, porter au crédit
creditable [′krɛdɪtəbəl] adj estimable, honorable
cred′it card′ s carte f de crédit
creditor [′krɛdɪtər] s créditeur m, créancier m
cre·do [′krido] s (pl -dos) credo m
credulous [′krɛdʒələs] adj crédule
creed [krid] s credo m; (denomination) foi f
creek [krik] s ruisseau m
creep [krip] v (pret & pp crept [krɛpt]) intr (to crawl) ramper; (stealthily) se glisser; (slowly) se traîner, se couler; (to climb) grimper; (with a sensation of insects) fourmiller; **to creep up on s.o.** s'approcher de qn à pas lents
creeper [′kripər] s plante f rampante
creeping [′kripɪŋ] adj (lagging) lent, traînant; (plant) rampant ‖ s rampement m
creep·y [′kripi] adj (comp -ier; super -iest) (coll) mystérieux, terrifiant; **to feel creepy** fourmiller
cremate [′krimet] tr incinérer
cremation [krɪ′meʃən] s crémation f, incinération f
cremato·ry [′krimə,tori] adj crématoire ‖ s (pl -ries) crématoire m, four m crématoire
Creole [′kri·ol] adj créole ‖ s (language) créole m; (person) Créole mf
crepe [krep] s (paper) crêpe m; (pancake) crêpe f
crepe′ pa′per s papier m crêpe
crescent [′krɛsənt] s croissant m
cress [krɛs] s cresson m
crest [krɛst] s crête f
crested [′krɛstɪd] adj à crête; (with feathers) huppé
crest′fall′en adj abattu, découragé
Cretan [′kritən] adj crétois ‖ s Crétois m
Crete [krit] s Crète f; la Crète
cretin [′kritən] s crétin m
crevice [′krɛvɪs] s crevasse f, fente f
crew [kru] s (rowing; group working together) équipe f; (of a ship) équipage m; (group, especially of armed men) bande f, troupe f
crew′ cut′ s cheveux mpl en brosse
crew′ mem′ber s équipier m
crib [krɪb] s lit m d'enfant; (manger) crèche f, mangeoire f; (for grain) coffre m; (student's pony) antisèche m & f ‖ v (pret & pp cribbed; ger cribbing) tr & intr (coll) copier à la dérobée

cricket ['krɪkɪt] *s* (ent) grillon *m*; (sports) cricket *m*; (coll) franc jeu *m*, jeu loyal; **to be cricket** être de bonne guerre
crier ['kraɪ·ər] *s* crieur *m*
crime [kraɪm] *s* crime *m*; (*misdemeanor*) délit *m*
criminal ['krɪmɪnəl] *adj* & *s* criminel *m*
crim'inal code' *s* code *m* pénal
crim'inal court' *s* cour *f* d'assises
crim'inal law' *s* loi *f* pénale
crimp [krɪmp] *s* (*in cloth*) pli *m*; (*in hair*) frisure *f*; (*recruiter*) racoleur *m*; **to put a crimp in** (coll) mettre obstacle à ‖ *tr* (*cloth*) plisser; (*hair*) friser, crêper; (*metal*) onduler
crimson ['krɪmzən] *adj* & *s* cramoisi *m*
cringe [krɪndʒ] *intr* s'humilier, s'abaisser
cringing ['krɪndʒɪŋ] *adj* craintif, servile ‖ *s* crainte *f*, servilité *f*
crinkle ['krɪŋkəl] *s* pli *m*, ride *f* ‖ *tr* froisser, plisser ‖ *intr* se froisser
cripple ['krɪpəl] *s* estropié *m*, boiteux *m*; (*disabled*) infirme, invalide ‖ *tr* estropier; (*a machine*) disloquer; (*business or industry*) paralyser; (*a ship*) désemparer
cri·sis ['kraɪsɪs] *s* (*pl* **-ses** [siz]) crise *f*
crisp [krɪsp] *adj* (*crackers, bread, etc.*) croustillant; (*tone*) tranchant, brusque; (*air*) vif, frais
crisscross ['krɪs,krɔs] *adj* entrecroisé, treillissé ‖ *s* entrecroisement *m*; (*e.g., of wires*) enchevêtrement *m* ‖ *adv* en forme de croix ‖ *tr* entrecroiser ‖ *intr* s'entrecroiser
criteri·on [kraɪ'tɪrɪ·ən] *s* (*pl* **-a** [ə] or **-ons**) critère *m*
critic ['krɪtɪk] *s* (*of books, music, films, etc.*) critique *mf*; (*fault-finder*) critiqueur *m*, désapprobateur *m*
critical ['krɪtɪkəl] *adj* critique
critically ['krɪtɪkəli] *adv* en critique; **critically ill** gravement malade
criticism ['krɪtɪ,sɪzəm] *s* critique *f*
criticize ['krɪtɪ,saɪz] *tr* & *intr* critiquer
croak [krok] *s* (*of raven*) croassement *m*; (*of frog*) coassement *m* ‖ *intr* (*said of raven*) croasser; (*said of frog*) coasser; (*to die*) (slang) mourir
Croat ['kro·æt] *s* (*language*) croate *m*; (*person*) Croate *mf*
Croatian [kro'eʃən] *adj* croate ‖ *s* (*language*) croate *m*; (*person*) Croate *mf*
cro·chet [kro'ʃe] *s* crochet *m* ‖ *v* (*pret* & *pp* **-cheted** ['ʃed]; *ger* **-cheting** ['ʃe·ɪŋ]) *tr* & *intr* tricoter au crochet
crochet' nee'dle *s* crochet *m*
crock [krak] *s* pot *m* de terre
crock'pot *s* mijoteuse *f*
crockery ['krakəri] *s* faïence *f*, poterie *f*
crocodile ['krakə,daɪl] *s* crocodile *m*
croc'odile tears' *spl* larmes *fpl* de crocodile
crocus ['krokəs] *s* crocus *m*
crone [kron] *s* vieille ratatinée *f*, vieille bique *f*
cro·ny ['kroni] *s* (*pl* **-nies**) copain *m*
cronyism ['kroni·ɪzəm] *s* copinisme *m*

crook [kruk] *s* (*hook*) croc *m*; (*of shepherd*) houlette *f*; (*of bishop*) crosse *f*; (*in road*) courbure *f*; (*person*) (coll) escroc *m* ‖ *tr* courber ‖ *intr* se courber
crooked ['krukɪd] *adj* (*stick*) courbé, crochu; (*path; conduct*) tortueux; (*tree; nose; legs*) tortu; (*person*) (coll) malhonnête, fourbe
croon [krun] *intr* chanter des chansons sentimentales
crooner ['krunər] *s* chanteur *m* de charme
crop [krap] *s* (*produce*) produit *m* agricole; (*amount produced*) récolte *f*; (*head of hair*) cheveux *mpl* ras; (*of bird*) jabot *m*; (*whip*) fouet *m*; (*of whip*) manche *m*; (*of appointments, promotions, heroes, discoveries*) moisson *f* ‖ *v* (*pret* & *pp* **cropped**; *ger* **cropping**) *tr* tondre; (*head of hair*) couper, tailler; (*ears of animal*) essoriller ‖ *intr*—**to crop up** (coll) surgir, s'élever brusquement
crop' dust'ing *s* pulvérisation *f* des cultures
croquet [kro'ke] *s* croquet *m*
crosier ['kroʒər] *s* crosse *f*
cross [krɔs] *adj* (*diagonal*) transversal, oblique; (*breed*) croisé; (*ill-humored*) maussade ‖ *s* croix *f*; (*of races or breeds; of roads*) croisement *m* ‖ *tr* (*e.g., one's arms or legs*) croiser; (*the sea; a street*) traverser; (*breeds*) croiser, métisser; (*the threshold*) franchir; (*said of one road with respect to another*) couper; (*the letter t*) barrer; (*e.g., s.o.'s plans*) (coll) contrecarrer; **to cross oneself** (eccl) se signer; **to cross out** biffer, rayer ‖ *intr* se croiser, passer; **to cross over** passer de l'autre côté
cross'bones' *spl* tibias *mpl* croisés
cross'bow' *s* arbalète *f*
cross'breed' *v* (*pret* & *pp* **-bred**) *tr* croiser, métisser
cross'-check' *s* recoupement *m* ‖ *tr* faire un recoupement de
cross'-coun'try *adj* à travers champs
cross'-country ski'ing *s* ski *m* de fonds
cross'cur'rent *s* contre-courant *m*; tendance *f* contraire
cross'-examina'tion *s* contre-interrogatoire *m*
cross'-exam'ine *tr* contre-interroger, contre-examiner
cross'-eyed' *adj* louche
crossing ['krɔsɪŋ], ['krɑsɪŋ] *s* (*road junction*) croisement *m*; (*of ocean*) traversée *f*; (*of river, mountain, etc.*) passage *m*; (rr) passage *m* à niveau; (*for pedestrians*) passage *m* clouté
cross'ing gate' *s* barrière *f* d'un passage à niveau
cross'patch' *s* (coll) grincheux *m*, grognon *m*
cross'piece' *s* entretoise *f*
cross' ref'erence *s* renvoi *m*
cross'road' *s* voie *f* transversale, chemin *m* de traverse; **crossroads** carrefour *m*, croisement *m*

cross′ sec′tion *s* (*cut*) coupe *f* transversale; (*e.g.*, *of building*) section *f*; (*of opinion*) sondage *m*, groupe *m* représentatif, échantillon *m*

cross′-sec′tion *tr* couper transversalement

cross′ street′ *s* rue *f* de traverse, rue transversale

cross′wise′ *adv* en croix, en sautoir

cross′word puz′zle *s* mots *mpl* croisés

crotch [krɑtʃ] *s* (*forked piece*) fourche *f*; (*between legs*) entrejambe *f*, enfourchure *f*

crotchet [′krɑtʃɪt] *s* (mus) noire *f*; (coll) lubie *f*

crotchety [′krɑtʃɪti] *adj* capricieux, fantasque

crouch [kraʊtʃ] *s* accroupissement *m* ‖ *intr* s′accroupir, se blottir

croup [krup] *s* (*of horse*) croupe *f*; (pathol) croup *m*

croupier [′krupɪ·ər] *s* croupier *m*

crouton [′krutɑn] *s* croûton *m*

crow [kro] *s* corbeau *m*; (*rook*) corneille *f*, freux *m*; **as the crow flies** à vol d′oiseau; **to eat crow** (coll) avaler des couleuvres ‖ *intr* (*said of cock*) chanter; (*said of babies*) gazouiller; **to crow over** chanter victoire sur, triompher bruyamment de

crow′bar′ *s* levier *m*; (*for forcing doors*) pince-monseigneur *f*

crowd [kraʊd] *s* foule *f*; (*clique, set*) bande *f*, monde *m*; **a crowd** (*of people*) du monde, beaucoup de monde ‖ *tr* serrer, entasser; (*to push*) pousser; (*a debtor*) presser; **to crowd out** ne pas laisser de place à ‖ *intr* affluer, s′amasser; **to crowd around** se presser autour de; **to crowd in** s′attrouper

crowded *adj* encombré, bondé

crow′foot′ *s* renoncule *f*, bouton *m* d′or

crowing [′kro·ɪŋ] *s* chant *m* de coq, cocorico *m*; (*of babies*) gazouillement *m*

crown [kraʊn] *s* couronne *f*; (*of hat*) calotte *f* ‖ *tr* couronner, sacrer; (checkers) damer; **to crown s.o.** (slang) flanquer un coup sur la tête à qn

crowning [′kraʊnɪŋ] *s* couronnement *m*

crown′ prince′ *s* prince *m* héritier

crown′ prin′cess *s* princesse *f* héritière

crow′s′-foot′ *s* (*pl* **-feet**) patte-d′oie *f*

crow′s′-nest *s* (naut) nid *m* de pie, tonneau *m* de vigie

crucial [′kruʃəl] *adj* crucial

crucible [′krusɪbəl] *s* creuset *m*

crucifix [′krusɪfɪks] *s* crucifix *m*, christ *m*

crucifixion [,krusɪ′fɪkʃən] *s* crucifixion *f*

cruci·fy [′krusɪ,faɪ] *v* (*pret & pp* **-fied**) *tr* crucifier

crude [krud] *adj* (*raw, unrefined*) cru, brut; (*lacking culture*) fruste, grossier; (*unfinished*) informe, grossier, mal développé; (*oil*) brut

crudi·ty [′krudɪti] *s* (*pl* **-ties**) crudité *f*; (*of person*) grossièreté *f*

cruel [′kru·əl] *adj* cruel

cruel·ty [′kru·əlti] *s* (*pl* **-ties**) cruauté *f*

cruet [′kru·ɪt] *s* burette *f*

cru′et stand′ *s* huilier *m*

cruise [kruz] *s* croisière *f* ‖ *intr* croiser

cruiser [′kruzər] *s* croiseur *m*

cruising [′kruzɪŋ] *adj* en croisière; (*taxi*) en maraude

cruis′ing range′ *s* autonomie *f*

cruis′ing speed′ *s* vitesse *f* de route

cruller [′krʌlər] *s* beignet *m*

crumb [krʌm] *s* miette *f*; (*soft part of bread*) mie *f* ‖ *tr* (*cutlets, etc.*) paner

crumble [′krʌmbəl] *tr* émietter, réduire en miettes; (*e.g., stone*) effriter ‖ *intr* s′émietter; s′effriter; (*to fall to pieces*) s′écrouler

crum·my [′krʌmi] *adj* (*comp* **-mier**; *super* **-miest**) (slang) sale, minable

crumple [′krʌmpəl] *tr* friper, froisser; (*a fender*) mettre en accordéon ‖ *intr* se friper, se froisser

crunch [krʌntʃ] *tr* croquer, broyer ‖ *intr* (*said of snow*) craquer

crupper [′krʌpər] *s* croupière *f*

crusade [kru′sed] *s* croisade *f* ‖ *intr* se croiser, prendre part à une croisade

crush [krʌʃ] *s* (*crushing*) écrasement *m*; (*of people*) presse *f*, foule *f*; **to have a crush on** (slang) avoir un béguin pour ‖ *tr* écraser; (*e.g., stone*) broyer, concasser; (*to oppress, grieve*) accabler, aplatir

crush′ hat′ *s* claque *m*, gibus *m*

crust [krʌst] *s* croûte *f*

crustacean [krʌs′teʃən] *s* crustacé *m*

crust·y [′krʌsti] *adj* (*comp* **-ier**; *super* **-iest**) croustillant; (*said of person*) bourru, hargneux

crutch [krʌtʃ] *s* béquille *f*

crux [krʌks] *s* nœud *m*

cry [kraɪ] *s* (*pl* **cries**) (*loud shout*) cri *m*; (*of wolf*) hurlement *m*; (*of bull*) mugissement *m*; **to cry one′s eyes out** pleurer à chaudes larmes; **to have a good cry** donner libre cours aux larmes ‖ *v* (*pret & pp* **cried**) *tr* crier; **to cry out** crier ‖ *intr* crier; (*to weep*) pleurer; **to cry for** à; **to cry for joy** pleurer de joie; **to cry out** pousser des cris, s′écrier; **to cry out against** crier à

cry′ba′by *s* (*pl* **-bies**) pleurard *m*

crying [′kraɪ·ɪŋ] *adj* pleurant; (*need*) pressant; **for crying out loud!** (coll) il ne manquait plus que ça!; **a crying shame** une honte ‖ *s* larmes *fpl*, pleurs *mpl*

crypt [krɪpt] *s* crypte *f*

cryptic(al) [′krɪptɪk(əl)] *adj* secret, occulte; (*silence*) énigmatique

crystal [′krɪstəl] *s* cristal *m*

crys′tal ball′ *s* boule *f* de cristal

crystalline [′krɪstəlɪn] *adj* cristallin

crystallize [′krɪstə,laɪz] *tr* cristalliser; (*sugar*) candir ‖ *intr* cristalliser; (*said of sugar*) se candir; (*said of one′s thoughts*) (fig) se cristalliser

cub [kʌb] *s* (*of animal*) petit *m*; (*of bear*) ourson *m*; (*of fox*) renardeau *m*; (*of lion*) lionceau *m*; (*of wolf*) louveteau *m*

Cuban [′kjuban] *adj* cubain ‖ *s* Cubain *m*

cubbyhole [′kʌbɪ,hol] *s* (*room*) retraite *f*; (*in wall*) placard *m*; (*in furniture*) case *f*

cube [kjub] *adj & s* cube *m*; **in cubes** (*said of sugar*) en morceaux ‖ *tr* cuber
cube' root' *s* racine *f* cubique
cube' sug'ar *s* sucre *m* en morceaux
cubic [ˈkjubɪk] *adj* cubique, cube
cu'bic me'ter *s* mètre *m* cube
cub' report'er *s* reporter *m* débutant
cub' scout' *s* louveteau *m*
cuckold [ˈkʌkəld] *adj & s* cocu *m*, cornard *m* ‖ *tr* cocufier
cuckoo [ˈkuku] *adj* (slang) niais, benêt ‖ *s* coucou *m*
cuck'oo clock' *s* coucou *m*
cucumber [ˈkjukəmbər] *s* concombre *m*
cud [kʌd] *s* bol *m* alimentaire; **to chew the cud** ruminer
cuddle [ˈkʌdəl] *tr* serrer doucement dans les bras ‖ *intr* (*said of lovers*) s'étreindre; **to cuddle up** se pelotonner
cudg·el [ˈkʌdʒəl] *s* gourdin *m*, trique *f*; **to take up the cudgels for** prendre fait et cause pour ‖ *v* (*pret & pp* **-eled** or **-elled**; *ger* **-eling** or **-elling**) *tr* bâtonner, rosser
cue [kju] *s* (*notice*) signal *m*; (*hint*) mot *m*; (*rod used in billiards; persons in line*) queue *f*; (*mus*) indication *f* de rentrée; (*theat*) réclame *f*; **to give s.o. the cue** faire la leçon à qn, donner le mot à qn; **to take one's cue from** se conformer à
cuff [kʌf] *s* (*of shirt*) poignet *m*, manchette *f*; (*of coat or trousers*) parement *m*; (*blow*) taloche *f*, manchette *f* ‖ *tr* talocher, flanquer une taloche à
cuff' link' *s* bouton *m* de manchette
cuirass [kwɪˈræs] *s* cuirasse *f*
cuisine [kwɪˈzin] *s* cuisine *f*
culinary [ˈkjulɪˌnɛri] *adj* culinaire
cull [kʌl] *tr* (*to select*) choisir; (*to gather, pluck*) cueillir; **to cull from** recueillir dans
culm [kʌlm] *s* chaume *m*; (*coal dust*) charbonnaille *f*
culminate [ˈkʌlmɪˌnet] *intr* (astr) culminer; **to culminate in** finir par, se terminer en
culmination [ˌkʌlmɪˈneʃən] *s* point *m* culminant; (astr) culmination *f*
culottes [k(j)uˈlɑts] *spl* pantalon *m* de plage
culpable [ˈkʌlpəbəl] *adj* coupable
culprit [ˈkʌlprɪt] *s* (*guilty one*) coupable *mf*; (*accused*) accusé *m*, prévenu *m*
cult [kʌlt] *s* culte *m*
cultivate [ˈkʌltɪˌvet] *tr* cultiver
cultivation [ˌkʌltɪˈveʃən] *s* culture *f*
cultivator [ˈkʌltɪˌvetər] *s* (*person*) cultivateur *m*, exploitant *m* agricole; (mach) cultivateur *m*, scarificateur *m*
cultural [ˈkʌltʃərəl] *adj* culturel
culture [ˈkʌltʃər] *s* culture *f* ‖ *tr* cultiver
cultured adj (*learned*) cultivé, lettré
cul'tured pearl' *s* perle *f* de culture
culvert [ˈkʌlvərt] *s* ponceau *m*, cassis *m*
cumbersome [ˈkʌmbərsəm] *adj* incommode, encombrant; (*clumsy*) lourd, difficile à manier
cummerbund [ˈkʌmərˌbʌnd] *s* ceinture *f* d'étoffe

cumulative [ˈkjumjəˌlɛtɪv] *adj* croissant, cumulatif
cunning [ˈkʌnɪŋ] *adj* (*sly*) astucieux, rusé; (*clever*) habile, fin; (*attractive*) gentil ‖ *s* (*slyness*) astuce *f*, ruse *f*; (*cleverness*) habileté *f*, finesse *f*
cup [kʌp] *s* (*for coffee or tea; cupful*) tasse *f*; (*of metal*) gobelet *m*, timbale *f*; (bot, eccl) calice *m*; (mach) godet *m* graisseur; (sports) coupe *f* ‖ *v* (*pret & pp* **cupped**; *ger* **cupping**) *tr* (surg) ventouser
cupboard [ˈkʌbərd] *s* armoire *f*; (*in wall*) placard *m*
Cupid [ˈkjupɪd] *s* Cupidon *m*
cupidity [kjuˈpɪdɪti] *s* cupidité *f*
cupola [ˈkjupələ] *s* coupole *f*
cur [kʌr] *s* (*mongrel dog*) chien *m* métis, roquet *m*; (*despicable person*) mufle *m*
curate [ˈkjurɪt] *s* vicaire *m*
curative [ˈkjurətɪv] *adj* curatif
curator [kjuˈretər] *s* conservateur *m*
curb [kʌrb] *s* (*edge of road*) bordure *f* de pavés, bord *m* de trottoir; (*of well*) margelle *f*; (*of bit*) gourmette *f*; (*market*) coulisse *f*; (*check, restraint*) frein *m* ‖ *tr* (*a horse*) gourmer; (*passions, anger, desires*) réprimer, refréner; **curb your dog** (public sign) faites faire votre chien dans le ruisseau
curb' serv'ice *s* restoroute *m*
curb'stone' *s* garde-pavé *m*; **curbstones** bordure *f* de pavés
curd [kʌrd] *s* caillé *m*; **curds** caillebotte *f* ‖ *tr* cailler, caillebotter ‖ *intr* se cailler, se caillebotter
curdle [ˈkʌrdəl] *tr* (*milk*) cailler; (*the blood*) figer ‖ *intr* se cailler; se figer
curds' and whey' *spl* lait *m* caillé sucré
cure [kjur] *s* (*recovery*) guérison *f*; (*treatment*) cure *f*; (*remedy*) remède *m* ‖ *tr* guérir; (*meat; leather*) saler; (*a pipe*) culotter
cure'-all' *s* panacée *f*
curfew [ˈkʌrfju] *s* couvre-feu *m*
curi·o [ˈkjuri,o] *s* (*pl* **-os**) bibelot *m*
curiosi·ty [ˌkjuriˈɑsɪti] *s* (*pl* **-ties**) curiosité *f*
curious [ˈkjuri·əs] *adj* curieux
curl [kʌrl] *s* (*of hair*) boucle *f*, frisure *f*; (*spiral-shaped*) volute *f*; (*of smoke*) spirale *f* ‖ *tr* boucler, friser; (*to coil, to roll up*) enrouler, tire-bouchonner; **to curl one's lip** faire la moue ‖ *intr* boucler, friser; (*said of smoke*) s'élever en spirales; (*said of waves*) onduler, déferler; **to curl up** (*said of leaves, paper, etc.*) se recroqueviller; (*in bed*) se rouler en boule
curlew [ˈkʌrl(j)u] *s* courlis *m*
curlicue [ˈkʌrli,kju] *s* paraphe *m*
curl'ing i'ron *s* fer *m* à friser
curl'pa'per *s* papillote *f*
curl·y [ˈkʌrli] *adj* (*comp* **-ier**; *super* **-iest**) bouclé, frisé
curmudgeon [kərˈmʌdʒən] *s* (*crosspatch*) bourru *m*, sale bougre *m*; (*miser*) ladre *mf*
currant [ˈkʌrənt] *s* groseille *f*

curren·cy [ˈkʌrənsi] s (pl **-cies**) circulation f; (legal tender) monnaie f, devises fpl; **to give currency to** donner cours à

current [ˈkʌrənt] adj (opinion, price, word, etc.) courant; (month) en cours; (accepted) admis, reçu; (present-day) actuel ‖ s courant m; (stream) courant, cours m

cur′rent account′ s compte m courant

cur′rent events′ spl actualités fpl

cur′rent fail′ure s panne f de secteur

cur′rent is′sue s dernier numéro m

curricu·lum [kəˈrɪkjələm] s (pl **-lums** or **-la** [lə]) programme m scolaire, plan m d'études

cur·ry [ˈkʌri] s (pl **-ries**) cari m ‖ v (pret & pp **-ried**) tr (a horse) étriller; (culin) apprêter au cari; **to curry favor with** faire la cour à

cur′ry·comb′ s étrille f ‖ tr étriller

cur′ry pow′der s cari m

curse [kʌrs] s (imprecation) malédiction f; (swearword) juron m; (bane) fléau m, malheur m ‖ tr maudire ‖ intr jurer, sacrer

cursed [ˈkʌrsɪd], [kʌrst] adj maudit, exécrable, sacré

cursive [ˈkʌrsɪv] adj cursif ‖ s cursive f

cursory [ˈkʌrsəri] adj superficiel, précipité

curt [kʌrt] adj brusque, court

curtail [kərˈtel] tr (to reduce) raccourcir, diminuer; (expenses) restreindre; (rights) enlever

curtailment [kʌrˈtelmənt] s (reduction) diminution f; (of expenses) restriction f; (of rights) privation f

curtain [ˈkʌrtən] s rideau m ‖ tr garnir de rideaux; (to hide) cacher sous des rideaux; **to curtain off** séparer par un rideau

cur′tain call′ s rappel m

cur′tain rais′er s (play) lever m de rideau

cur′tain ring′ s anneau m de rideau

cur′tain rod′ s tringle f de rideau

curt·sy [ˈkʌrtsi] s (pl **-sies**) révérence f ‖ v (pret & pp **-sied**) intr faire la révérence

curvature [ˈkʌrvətʃər] s courbure f; (of spine) déviation f

curve [kʌrv] s courbe f; (of road) virage m; (curvature) courbure f ‖ tr courber ‖ intr se courber

curved adj courbe, courbé

cushion [ˈkʊʃən] s coussin m ‖ tr (a chair) rembourrer; (a shock) amortir

cuspidor [ˈkʌspɪˌdɔr] s crachoir m

cuss [kʌs] s (person) (coll) vaurien m, chenapan m ‖ tr (coll) maudire ‖ intr (coll) jurer, sacrer

cuss′word′ s (coll) juron m

custard [ˈkʌstərd] s flan m, œufs mpl au lait, crème f caramel

custodian [kəsˈtodɪ·ən] s gardien m; concierge mf

custo·dy [ˈkʌstədi] s (pl **-dies**) (care) garde f; (imprisonment) emprisonnement m; **in custody** en sûreté; **to take into custody** mettre en état d'arrestation

custom [ˈkʌstəm] s coutume f; (customers) clientèle f; **customs** douane f; (duties) droits mpl de douane

customary [ˈkʌstəˌmɛri] adj coutumier, ordinaire, habituel

custom-built [ˈkʌstəmˈbɪlt] adj hors série, fait sur commande

customer [ˈkʌstəmər] s (buyer) client m, chaland m; (coll) individu m, type m; **customers** clientèle f, achalandage m

cus′tom·house′ adj douanier ‖ s douane f

custom-made [ˈkʌstəmˈmed] adj fait sur commande; (clothes) sur mesure

cus′toms clear′ance s expédition f douanière

cus′toms of′ficer s douanier m

cus′toms un′ion s union f douanière

cus′tom tai′lor s tailleur m à façon

cut [kʌt] adj coupé; **cut out** taillé, e.g., **he is not cut out for that** il n'est pas taillé pour cela; e.g., **your work is cut out for you** voilà votre besogne taillée ‖ s (of a garment; of cards; haircut; act of cutting) coupe f; (piece cut off) tranche f, morceau m; (slash) coupure f; (with knife, whip, etc.) coup m; (in prices, wages, etc.) réduction f, baisse f; (typ) gravure f, planche f; (absence from school) (coll) séchage m; (in winnings, earnings, etc.) (slang) part f; **the cheap cuts** les bas morceaux mpl ‖ v (pret & pp **cut**; ger **cutting**) tr couper; (meat, bread) trancher; (prices) réduire, baisser; (e.g., a hole) pratiquer; (glass, diamonds) tailler; (fingernails) rogner; (an article, play, speech) sabrer, faire des coupures à; (a phonograph record) enregistrer; (a class) (coll) sécher; **to cut down** faucher, abattre; (expenses) réduire; **to cut off, out,** or **up** découper, couper; **to cut short** couper court à ‖ intr couper; trancher; **to cut in** (a conversation) s'immiscer dans; (coll) enlever la danseuse d'un autre; **to cut off** (debate) clore; **to cut up** (slang) faire le pitre

cut′-and-dried′ adj décidé d'avance, tout fait; monotone, rasoir

cutaneous [kjuˈteni·əs] adj cutané

cut′away′ s frac m

cut′back′ s réduction f; (mov) retour m en arrière

cute [kjut] adj (coll) mignon; (shrewd) (coll) rusé

cut′ flowers′ spl fleurs fpl coupées

cut′ glass′ s cristal m taillé

cuticle [ˈkjutɪkəl] s cuticule f

cutlass [ˈkʌtləs] s coutelas m

cutlery [ˈkʌtləri] s coutellerie f

cutlet [ˈkʌtlɪt] s (slice of meat) côtelette f; (without bone) escalope f; (croquette of minced chicken, etc.) croquette f

cut′off′ s point m de coupure; (road) raccourci m; (of river) bras m mort; (of cylinder) obturateur m

cut′out′ s (aut) échappement m libre; (elec) coupe-circuit m; (mov) décor m découpé

cut′-rate′ adj à prix réduit

cutter [ˈkʌtər] s (naut) cotre m

cut′throat′ s coup-jarret m

cutting [ˈkʌtɪŋ] adj tranchant; (tone, remark) mordant, cinglant ‖ s (action)

coupe *f*; (*from a newspaper*) coupure *f*; (*e.g.*, *of prices*) réduction *f*; (hort) bouture *f*; (mov) découpage *m*
cuttlefish [ˈkʌtəlˌfɪʃ] *s* seiche *f*
cut′wa′ter *s* (naut) étrave *f*; (*of bridge*) bec *m*
cyanamide [saɪˈænəˌmaɪd] *s* cyanamide *f*
cyanide [ˈsaɪ·əˌnaɪd] *s* cyanure *m*
cyanosis [ˌsaɪ·əˈnosɪs] *s* cyanose *f*
cycle [ˈsaɪkəl] *s* cycle *m*; (*of internal-combustion engine*) temps *m*; (phys) période *f* ‖ *intr* faire de la bicyclette
cyclic(al) [ˈsɪklɪk(əl)] *adj* cyclique
cyclist [ˈsaɪklɪst] *s* cycliste *mf*
cyclone [ˈsaɪklon] *s* cyclone *m*
cyclops [ˈsaɪklɑps] *s* cyclope *m*
cyclotron [ˈsaɪkloˌtrɑn] *s* cyclotron *m*
cylinder [ˈsɪlɪndər] *s* cylindre *m*; (*of revolver*) barillet *m*
cyl′inder block′ *s* cylindre *m*
cyl′inder bore′ *s* alésage *m*
cyl′inder head′ *s* culasse *f*

cylindric(al) [sɪˈlɪndrɪk(əl)] *adj* cylindrique
cymbal [ˈsɪmbəl] *s* cymbale *f*
cynic [ˈsɪnɪk] *adj* & *s* cynique *m*
cynical [ˈsɪnɪkəl] *adj* cynique
cynicism [ˈsɪnɪˌsɪzəm] *s* cynisme *m*
cynosure [ˈsaɪnəˌʃʊr] *s* guide *m*, exemple *m*, norme *f*; (*center of attention*) clou *m*; (astr) cynosure *f*
cypress [ˈsaɪprəs] *s* cyprès *m*
Cyprus [ˈsaɪprəs] *s* Chypre *f*
Cyrillic [sɪˈrɪlɪk] *adj* cyrillique
cyst [sɪst] *s* kyste *m*; (*on the skin*) vésicule *f*
czar [zɑr] *s* tsar *m*, czar *m*
czarina [zɑˈrinə] *s* tsarine *f*, czarine *f*
Czech [tʃɛk] *adj* tchèque ‖ *s* (*language*) tchèque *m*; (*person*) Tchèque *mf*
Czecho-Slovak [ˈtʃɛkoˈslovæk] *adj* tchécoslovaque ‖ *s* Tchécoslovaque *mf*
Czecho-Slovakia [ˌtʃɛkosloˈvækɪ·ə] *s* Tchécoslovaquie *f*; la Tchécoslovaquie

D

D, d [di] *s* IVe lettre de l'alphabet
dab [dæb] *s* touche *f*; (*of ink*) tache *f*; (*of butter*) petit morceau *m* ‖ *v* (*pret & pp* **dabbed**; *ger* **dabbing**) *tr* essuyer légèrement; (*to pat*) tapoter
dabble [ˈdæbəl] *tr* humecter ‖ *intr* barboter; **to dabble in** se mêler de; **to dabble in the stock market** boursicoter
dachshund [ˈdɑksˌhund] *s* teckel *m*
dad [dæd] *s* (coll) papa *m*
dad·dy [ˈdædi] *s* (*pl* **-dies**) papa *m*
dad′dy-long′legs′ *s* (*pl* **-legs**) faucheux *m*
daffodil [ˈdæfədɪl] *s* jonquille *f* des prés, narcisse *m* des bois
daff·y [ˈdæfi] *adj* (*comp* **-ier**; *super* **-iest**) (coll) timbré, toqué
dagger [ˈdægər] *s* poignard *m*, dague *f*; (typ) croix *f*, obel *m*; **to look daggers at** foudroyer du regard
dahlia [ˈdæljə] *s* dahlia *m*
dai·ly [ˈdeli] *adj* quotidien, journalier ‖ *s* (*pl* **-lies**) quotidien *m* ‖ *adv* journellement
dain·ty [ˈdenti] *adj* (*comp* **-tier**; *super* **-tiest**) délicat ‖ *s* (*pl* **-ties**) friandise *f*
dair·y [ˈdɛri] *s* (*pl* **-ies**) laiterie *f*; (*shop*) crémerie *f*; (*farm*) vacherie *f*
dair′y farm′ *s* vacherie *f*
dair′y·man *s* (*pl* **-men**) laitier *m*
dais [ˈde·ɪs] *s* estrade *f*
dai·sy [ˈdezi] *s* (*pl* **-sies**) marguerite *f*
dal·ly [ˈdæli] *v* (*pret & pp* **-lied**) *intr* (*to tease*) badiner; (*to delay*) s'attarder
dam [dæm] *s* (*obstruction*) barrage *m*; (*female quadruped*) mère *f* ‖ *v* (*pret & pp* **dammed**; *ger* **damming**) *tr* contenir, endiguer

damage [ˈdæmɪdʒ] *s* dommage *m*, dégâts *mpl*; (*to engine, ship, etc.*) avaries *fpl*; (*to one's reputation*) tort *m*; **damages** (law) dommages-intérêts *mpl* ‖ *tr* endommager; (*merchandise; a machine*) avarier; (*a reputation*) faire du tort à
damaging [ˈdæmɪdʒɪŋ] *adj* dommageable, préjudiciable
damascene [ˈdæməˌsin], [ˌdæməˈsin] *adj* damasquiné ‖ *s* damasquinage *m* ‖ *tr* damasquiner
Damascus [dəˈmæskəs] *s* Damas *f*
dame [dem] *s* dame *f*; (coll) jupon *m*, typesse *f*, gonzesse *f*
damn [dæm] *s* juron *m*, gros mot *m*; **I don't give a damn** (slang) je m'en fiche; **that's not worth a damn** (slang) ça ne vaut pas un pet de lapin, ça ne vaut pas chipette ‖ *tr* condamner; (*to criticize harshly*) éreinter; (*to curse*) maudire; **damn him!** qu'il aille au diable!; **damn it!** merde!, nom de Dieu!, oh, la vache!; **I'll be damned if . . .** que le diable m'emporte si . . . ; **to damn with faint praise** assommer avec des fleurs; **well, I'll be damned!** ça c'est trop fort! ‖ *intr* maudire
damnation [dæmˈneʃən] *s* damnation *f*
damned [dæmd] *adj* damné *m* ‖ *s*—**the damned** les damnés ‖ [dæm] *adv* (slang) diablement, bigrement
damp [dæmp] *adj* humide, moite ‖ *s* humidité *f*; (*firedamp*) grisou *m* ‖ *tr* (*to dampen*) humecter, mouiller; (*a furnace*) étouffer; (*sound; electromagnetic waves*) amortir
dampen [ˈdæmpən] *tr* (*to moisten*) hu-

mecter; (*enthusiasm*) refroidir; (*to muffle*) amortir

damper ['dæmpər] *s* (*of chimney*) registre *m*; (*of stovepipe*) soupage *f* de réglage; (*of piano*) étouffoir *m*; **to put a damper on** (fig) jeter un froid sur

damsel ['dæmzəl] *s* demoiselle *f*

dance [dæns] *s* danse *f*; bal *m*, soirée *f* dansante ‖ *tr* & *intr* danser

dance' band' *s* orchestre *m* de danse

dance' floor' *s* piste *f* de danse

dance' hall' *s* dancing *m*, salle *f* de danse

dance' pro'gram *s* carnet *m* de bal

dancer ['dænsər] *s* danseur *m*

danc'ing part'ner *s* danseur *m*

danc'ing wa'ters *spl* fontaines *fpl* vivantes

dandelion ['dændɪ,laɪ·ən] *s* pissenlit *m*

dandruff ['dændrəf] *s* pellicules *fpl*

dan·dy ['dændi] *adj* (*comp* **-dier**; *super* **-diest**) (coll) chic, chouette ‖ *s* (*pl* **-dies**) dandy *m*, élégant *m*

Dane [den] *s* Danois *m*

danger ['dendʒər] *s* danger *m*

dangerous ['dendʒərəs] *adj* dangereux

dangle ['dæŋgəl] *tr* faire pendiller ‖ *intr* pendiller

Danish ['denɪʃ] *adj* & *s* danois *m*

dank [dæŋk] *adj* humide, moite

Danube ['dænjub] *s* Danube *m*

dapper ['dæpər] *adj* fringant, élégant

dappled ['dæpəld] *adj* (*mottled*) tacheté; (*sky*) pommelé; (*horse*) moucheté, miroité

dare [dɛr] *s* défi *m*; **to take a dare** relever un défi ‖ *tr* défier; oser; **to dare s.o. to** + *inf* défier qn de + *inf* ‖ *intr* oser; **to dare** + *inf* oser + *inf*

dare'dev'il *s* risque-tout *mf*

daring ['dɛrɪŋ] *adj* audacieux, hardi ‖ *s* audace *f*, hardiesse *f*

dark [dɑrk] *adj* sombre, obscur; (*color*) foncé; (*complexion*) basané, brun; **it is dark** il fait noir, il fait nuit ‖ *s* obscurité *f*, ténèbres *fpl*

Dark' Ag'es *spl* âge *m* des ténèbres

dark' brown' *adj* brun, brun foncé, chocolat

dark' choc'olate *s* chocolat *m* à croquer

dark'-complex'ioned *adj* brun, basané, brun de peau

darken ['dɑrkən] *tr* assombrir; (*the complexion*) brunir; (*a color*) foncer ‖ *intr* s'assombrir; (*said of forehead*) se rembrunir

dark' glass'es *spl* lunettes *fpl* noires, verres *mpl* fumés

dark' horse' *s* (pol) candidat *m* obscur; (sports) outsider *m*

darkly ['dɑrkli] *adv* obscurément; (*mysteriously*) ténébreusement; (*threateningly*) d'un air menaçant

dark' meat' *s* viande *f* brune; (*of game*) viande noire

darkness ['dɑrknɪs] *s* obscurité *f*

dark'room' *s* (phot) chambre *f* noire

darling ['dɑrlɪŋ] *adj* & *s* chéri *m*, bien-aimé *m*; **my darling** mon chou

darn [dɑrn] *s* reprise *f*, raccommodage *m* ‖ *tr* repriser, raccommoder ‖ *interj* zut!

darn'ing egg' *s* œuf *m* à repriser

darn'ing nee'dle *s* aiguille *f* à repriser

dart [dɑrt] *s* dard *m*; (*small missile used in a game*) fléchette *f* ‖ *intr* se précipiter, aller comme une flèche

dash [dæʃ] *s* (*sudden rush*) mouvement *m* brusque; (*small amount*) soupçon *m*, petit brin *m*; (*of color*) pointe *f*, touche *f*; (*splash*) choc *m*, floc *m*; (*spirit*) élan *m*, fougue *f*; (*in printing, writing*) tiret *m*; (*in telegraphy*) trait *m*, longue *f*; (sports) sprint *m* ‖ *tr* (*quickly*) précipiter; (*violently*) heurter; (*hopes*) abattre; **to dash off** écrire d'un trait, esquisser; **to dash to pieces** fracasser ‖ *intr* se précipiter; **to dash against** se heurter contre; **to dash by** filer à grand train; **to dash in** entrer en trombe; **to dash off** or **out** s'élancer, s'élancer dehors

dash'board' *s* tableau *m* de bord

dashing ['dæʃɪŋ] *adj* impétueux, fougueux; (*elegant*) fringant

dastard ['dæstərd] *adj* & *s* lâche *mf*

data ['detə], ['dætə] *spl* données *fpl*

da'ta bank' *s* banque *f* de données

da'ta base' *s* base *f* de données

da'ta proc'essing *s* analyse *f* des renseignements, étude *f* des données, (l') informatique *f*

date [det] *s* (*time*) date *f*; (*on books, on coins*) millésime *m*; (*palm*) dattier *m*; (*fruit*) datte *f*; (*of note, of loan*) terme *m*, échéance *f*; (*appointment*) rendez-vous *m*; **out of date** suranné, périmé; **to date** à ce jour; **up to date** à la page, au courant ‖ *tr* dater; (*e.g., a work of art*) assigner une date à; (coll) fixer un rendez-vous avec ‖ *intr* (*to be outmoded*) dater; **to date from** dater de, remonter à

date' line' *s* ligne *f* de changement de date

date' palm' *s* dattier *m*

dative ['detɪv] *s* datif *m*

daub [dɔb] *s* barbouillage *m* ‖ *tr* barbouiller

daughter ['dɔtər] *s* fille *f*

daugh'ter-in-law' *s* (*pl* **daughters-in-law**) belle-fille *f*, bru *f*

daunt [dɔnt] *tr* intimider, abattre

dauntless ['dɔntlɪs] *adj* intrépide

dauphin ['dɔfɪn] *s* dauphin *m*

davenport ['dævən,port] *s* canapé-lit *m*

daw [dɔ] *s* choucas *m*

dawdle ['dɔdəl] *intr* flâner, muser

dawn [dɔn] *s* aube *f*, aurore *f* ‖ *intr* poindre; **to dawn on** venir à l'esprit à

day [de] *adj* (*work*) diurne; (*worker*) de journée ‖ *s* jour *m*; (*of travel, work, worry*) journée *f*; (*of the month*) quantième *m*; **a day** (*per day*) par jour; **by the day** à la journée; **day by day** au jour le jour, jour par jour; **every day** tous les jours, chaque jour; **every other day** tous les deux jours; **from day to day** de jour en jour; **good old days** bon vieux temps; **in less than a day** du jour au lendemain; **in these days** de nos jours; **in those days**

à ce moment-là, à cette époque; **one fine day** un beau jour; **the day after** le lendemain; le lendemain de; **the day after tomorrow** après-demain; l'après-demain *m*; **the day before** la veille; la veille de; **the day before yesterday** avant-hier; l'avant-hier *m*; **to have had its day** avoir fait son temps

day′ bed′ *s* canapé-lit *m*, petit lit *m* de repos

day′break′ *s* pointe *f* du jour, lever *m* du jour; **at daybreak** au jour levant

day′ coach′ *s* (rr) voiture *f*

day′dream′ *s* rêvasserie *f*, rêverie *f* ‖ *intr* rêvasser, rêver creux

day′dream′er *s* songe-creux *m*, songeur *m*

day′dream′ing *s* rêvasserie *f*

day′ la′borer *s* journalier *m*

day′light′ *s* jour *m*; **in broad daylight** en plein jour; **to see daylight** (coll) comprendre; (coll) voir la fin d'une tâche difficile

day′light-sav′ing time′ *s* heure *f* d'été

day′ lil′y *s* lis *m* jaune, belle-d'un-jour *f*

day′ nurs′ery *s* garderie *f* d'enfants, crèche *f*

day′ off′ *s* jour *m* de congé, jour chômé

day′ of reck′oning *s* jour *m* de règlement; (*last judgment*) jour d'expiation

day′ shift′ *s* équipe *f* de jour

day′ stu′dent *s* externe *mf*

day′time′ *s* jour *m*, journée *f*

daze [dez] *s* étourdissement *m*; **in a daze** hébété ‖ *tr* étourdir

dazzle [′dæzəl] *s* éblouissement *m* ‖ *tr* éblouir

dazzling [′dæzlɪŋ] *adj* éblouissant

D.C. [′di′si] *s* (letterword) (**District of Columbia**) le district de Columbia; (**direct current**) le courant continu

D′-day′ *s* le jour J

deacon [′dikən] *s* diacre *m*

deaconess [′dikənɪs] *s* diaconesse *f*

dead [dɛd] *adj* mort; (*tired*) épuisé; (*color*) terne; (*business*) stagnant; (*sleep*) profond; (*calm*) plat; (*loss*) sec; (*typewriter key*) immobile; **on a dead level** à franc niveau ‖ *s*—**in the dead of night** au milieu de la nuit—**the dead** les morts; **the dead of winter** le cœur de l'hiver ‖ *adv* absolument; **to stop dead** s'arrêter net

dead′beat′ *s* (slang) écornifleur *m*

dead′ bolt′ *s* pêne *m* dormant

dead′ calm′ *s* calme *m* plat

dead′ cen′ter *s* point *m* mort

dead′-drunk′ *adj* ivre mort

deaden [′dɛdən] *tr* amortir; (*sound*) assourdir

dead′ end′ *s* cul-de-sac *m*, impasse *f*

dead′latch′ *s* pêne *m* dormant

dead′-let′ter of′fice *s* bureau *m* des rebuts

dead′line′ *s* dernier délai *m*, date *f* limite, terme *m* de rigueur

dead′lock′ *s* serrure *f* à pêne dormant; (fig) impasse *f* ‖ *tr* faire aboutir à une impasse

dead·ly [′dɛdli] *adj* (*comp* **-lier**; *super* **-liest**) mortel; (*sin*) capital

dead′ pan′ *s* (slang) visage *m* sans expression

dead′ reck′oning *s* estime *f*; (*position*) point *m* d'estime

dead′ ring′er *s* (coll) portrait *m* vivant

dead′ sol′dier *s* (*bottle*) (slang) cadavre *m*

dead′ weight′ *s* poids *m* mort

dead′wood′ *s* bois *m* mort; (fig) objet *m* or individu *m* inutile

deaf [dɛf] *adj* sourd; **to turn a deaf ear** faire la sourde oreille

deaf′-and-dumb′ *adj* sourd-muet

deafen [′dɛfən] *tr* assourdir

deafening [′dɛfənɪŋ] *adj* assourdissant

deaf′-mute′ *adj* & *s* sourd-muet *m*

deafness [′dɛfnɪs] *s* surdité *f*

deal [dil] *s* (*bargain*) affaire *f*; (cards) main *f*, donne *f*; **a good deal (of)** or **a great deal (of)** beaucoup (de); **to think a great deal of s.o.** estimer qn ‖ *v* (*pret* & *pp* **dealt** [dɛlt]) *tr* (*a blow*) donner, porter; (cards) donner, distribuer; **to deal out** (*e.g., gifts*) distribuer, répartir; (*alms*) dispenser; (*justice*) rendre ‖ *intr* négocier; (cards) faire la donne; **to deal in** faire le commerce de; **to deal with** (*a person*) traiter avec; (*a subject*) traiter de

dealer [′dilər] *s* marchand *m*, négociant *m*, revendeur *m*; (*of cards*) donneur *m*; (*middleman, e.g., in selling automobiles*) concessionnaire *m*, stockiste *m*

deal′er's plate′ *s* (aut) immatriculation *f* de livraison

dean [din] *s* doyen *m*; (educ) chef *m* de branche

dean′ship *s* doyenné *m*, décanat *m*

dear [dɪr] *adj* cher; **dear me!** mon Dieu!; **Dear Sir** (*salutation in a letter*) Monsieur ‖ *s* chéri *m*, chérie *f*

dearie [′dɪri] *s* (coll) chérie *f*, chéri *m*

dearth [dʌrθ] *s* disette *f*, pénurie *f*

death [dɛθ] *s* mort *f*; **at death's door** à deux doigts de la mort; **to bore to death** raser; **to put to death** mettre à mort; **to starve to death** mourir de faim; faire mourir de faim

death′bed′ *s* lit *m* de mort

death′blow′ *s* coup *m* mortel

death′ certif′icate *s* constatation *f* de décès, extrait *m* mortuaire

death′ house′ *s* quartier *m* de la mort

death′ knell′ *s* glas *m* funèbre

deathless [′dɛθlɪs] *adj* immortel

deathly [′dɛθli] *adj* mortel ‖ *adv* mortellement, comme la mort

death′ mask′ *s* masque *m* mortuaire

death′ pen′alty *s* peine *f* capitale, peine de mort

death′ rate′ *s* mortalité *f*, taux *m* de mortalité

death′ rat′tle *s* râle *m* de la mort

death′ row′ *s* couloir *m* de la mort

death′ war′rant *s* ordre *m* d'exécution

death′watch′ *s* veillée *m* funèbre

deb [dɛb] *s* (slang) débutante *f*

debacle [də′bakəl] *s* débâcle *f*

de·bar [dɪ′bar] *v* (*pret* & *pp* **-barred**; *ger* **-barring**) *tr* exclure; empêcher

debark [dɪ′bɑrk] *tr* & *intr* débarquer

debarkation [,dɪbɑr'keʃən] s débarquement *m*

debase [dɪ'bes] *tr* avilir, abaisser; (*e.g., money*) altérer

debatable [dɪ'betəbəl] *adj* discutable

debate [dɪ'bet] s débat *m*; **under debate** en discussion || *tr & intr* discuter

debauch [dɪ'bɔtʃ] s débauche *f* || *tr* débaucher, corrompre

debauchee [,dɛbɔ'ʃi] s débauché *m*

debaucher·y [dɪ'bɔtʃəri] s (*pl* -ies) débauche *f*

debenture [dɪ'bɛntʃər] s (*bond*) obligation *f*; (*voucher*) reçu *m*

debilitate [dɪ'bɪlɪ,tet] *tr* débiliter

debili·ty [dɪ'bɪlɪti] s (*pl* -ties) débilité *f*

debit ['dɛbɪt] s débit *m*; (*entry on debit side*) article *m* au débit || *tr* débiter, porter au débit

deb'it bal'ance s solde *m* débiteur

debonair [,dɛbə'nɛr] *adj* gai, jovial; élégant, charmant

debris [də'bri] s débris *mpl*, détritus *m*; (*from ruined buildings*) décombres *mpl*

debt [dɛt] s dette *f*; **to run into debt** s'endetter

debtor ['dɛtər] s débiteur *m*

debug [di'bʌg] *tr* (*an activity*) enlever les défauts de; (*a room*) enlever des micros de; (*comp*) déboguer

debut [de'bju] s début *m* || *intr* débuter

debutante ['dɛbjə,tænt] s débutante *f*

decade ['dɛked] s décennie *f*, décade *f*

decadence [dɪ'kedəns] s décadence *f*

decadent [dɪ'kedənt] *adj & s* décadent *m*

decaffeinated [di'kæfənetɪd] *adj* décaféiné

decal ['dikæl] s décalcomanie *f*

decamp [dɪ'kæmp] *intr* décamper

decanter [dɪ'kæntər] s carafe *f*

decapitate [dɪ'kæpɪ,tet] *tr* décapiter

decay [dɪ'ke] s (*rotting*) pourriture *f*; (*decline*) décadence *f*; (*falling to pieces*) délabrement *m*; (*of teeth*) carie *f* || *tr* pourrir; (*teeth*) carier || *intr* pourrir, se gâter; (*said of teeth*) se carier; tomber en décadence or ruine; délabrer

decease [dɪ'sis] s décès *m* || *intr* décéder

deceit [dɪ'sit] s tromperie *f*

deceitful [dɪ'sitfəl] *adj* trompeur

deceive [dɪ'siv] *tr & intr* tromper

decelerate [dɪ'sɛlə,ret] *tr & intr* ralentir

December [dɪ'sɛmbər] s décembre *m*

decen·cy ['disənsi] s (*pl* -cies) décence *f*; **decencies** convenances *fpl*

decent ['disənt] *adj* décent

decently ['disəntli] *adv* décemment

decentralize [dɪ'sɛntrə,laɪz] *tr* décentraliser

deception [dɪ'sɛpʃən] s tromperie *f*

deceptive [dɪ'sɛptɪv] *adj* trompeur

decibel ['dɛsəbɛl] s décibel *m*

decide [dɪ'saɪd] *tr* décider; (*the outcome*) décider de || *intr* décider, se décider; **to decide to** + *inf* décider de + *inf*, se décider à + *inf*; **to decide upon a day** fixer un jour

deciduous [dɪ'sɪdʒʊ·əs] *adj* caduc

decimal ['dɛsɪməl] *adj* décimal || s décimale *f*

dec'imal point' s (*in French the comma is used to separate the decimal fraction from the integer*) virgule *f*

decimate ['dɛsɪ,met] *tr* décimer

decipher [dɪ'saɪfər] *tr* déchiffrer

decision [dɪ'sɪʒən] s décision *f*

decisive [dɪ'saɪsɪv] *adj* décisif

deck [dɛk] s (*of cards*) jeu *m*, paquet *m*; (*of ship*) pont *m*; **between decks** (naut) dans l'entrepont || *tr*—**to deck out** parer, orner

deck' chair' s transatlantique *m*, transat *m*, chaise *f* longue de bord

deck' hand' s matelot *m* de pont

deck'-land' *intr* apponter

deck'-land'ing s appontage *m*

deck'le edge' ['dɛkəl] s barbes *fpl*, bords *mpl* baveux

declaim [dɪ'klem] *tr & intr* déclamer

declaration [,dɛklə'reʃən] s déclaration *f*

declarative [dɪ'klærətɪv] *adj* déclaratif

declare [dɪ'klɛr] *tr & intr* déclarer

declension [dɪ'klɛnʃən] s (gram) déclinaison *f*

declination [,dɛklɪ'neʃən] s (astr, geog) déclinaison *f*

decline [dɪ'klaɪn] s déclin *m*, décadence *f*; (*in prices*) baisse *f* || *tr & intr* décliner

declivi·ty [dɪ'klɪvɪti] s (*pl* -ties) déclivité *f*, pente *f*

decode [dɪ'kod] *tr* décoder, déchiffrer

decompose [,dikəm'poz] *tr* décomposer || *intr* se décomposer

decomposition [,dikɑmpə'zɪʃən] s décomposition *f*

decompression [,dikəm'prɛʃən] s décompression *f*

decontamination [,dikən,tæmɪ'neʃən] s décontamination *f*

decontrol [,dikən'trol] *tr* lever les contrôles gouvernementaux de

decorate ['dɛkə,ret] *tr* décorer

decoration [,dɛkə'reʃən] s décoration *f*

decorator ['dɛkə,retər] s décorateur *m*

decorous ['dɛkərəs], [dɪ'korəs] *adj* convenable, correct, bienséant

decorum [dɪ'korəm] s décorum *m*

decoy ['dikɔɪ] s leurre *m*, appât *m*; (*bird*) appeau *m* || *tr* [dɪ'kɔɪ] *tr* leurrer

decrease ['dikris] s diminution *f* || [dɪ'kris] *tr & intr* diminuer

decree [dɪ'kri] s décret *m*, arrêté *m*; (*of divorce*) ordonnance *f* || *tr* décréter, arrêter, ordonner

decrepit [dɪ'krɛpɪt] *adj* décrépit

de·cry [dɪ'kraɪ] *v* (*pret & pp* -cried) *tr* décrier, dénigrer

dedicate ['dɛdɪ,ket] *tr* dédier

dedication [,dɛdɪ'keʃən] s consécration *f*; (*e.g., in a book*) dédicace *f*

dedicatory ['dɛdɪkə,tori] *adj* dédicatoire

deduce [dɪ'd(j)us] *tr* déduire, inférer

deduct [dɪ'dʌkt] *tr* déduire

deduction [dɪ'dʌkʃən] s déduction *f*

deed [did] s action *f*, acte *m*; (law) acte, titre *m*, contrat *m*; **deed of valor** haut fait *m*;

good deed bonne action; **in deed** dans le fait ‖ *tr* transférer par un acte

deem [dim] *tr* estimer, juger, croire ‖ *intr* penser

deep [dip] *adj* profond; (*sound*) grave; (*color*) foncé; de profondeur, e.g., **to be twenty feet deep** avoir vingt pieds de profondeur; **deep in debt** criblé de dettes; **deep in thought** plongé dans la méditation ‖ *adv* profondément; **deep into the night** très avant dans la nuit

deepen ['dipən] *tr* approfondir ‖ *intr* s'approfondir

deep'-freeze' *v* (*pret* **-froze;** *pp* **-frozen** or *pret* & *pp* **-freezed**) *tr* surgeler

deep' freez'er *s* congélateur *m*

deep' freez'ing *s* surgélation *f*

deep'-fry' *v* (*pret* & *pp* **-fried**) *tr* faire frire (en friteuse)

deep' fry'er *s* friteuse *f*

deep'-laid' *adj* habilement ourdi

deep' mourn'ing *s* grand deuil *m*

deep'-root'ed *adj* profondément enraciné, indéracinable

deep'-sea fish'ing *s* grande pêche *f* au large, pêche maritime

deep' space' *s* espace *m* lointain

deep' stall' *s* (aer) superdécrochage *m*

deer [dɪr] *s* (*red deer*) cerf *m*; (*fallow deer*) daim *m*; (*roe deer*) chevreuil *m*

deer'skin' *s* peau *f* de daim

deface [dɪ'fes] *tr* défigurer

de facto [di'fækto] *adv* de fait, de facto

defamation [,dɛfə'meʃən] *s* diffamation *f*, injures *fpl*

defame [dɪ'fem] *tr* diffamer

default [dɪ,fɔlt] *s* manque *m*, défaut *m*; (*on an obligation*) carence *f*; **by default** par défaut; (sports) par forfait; **in default of** à défaut de ‖ *tr* (*a debt*) manquer de s'acquitter de ‖ *intr* ne pas tenir ses engagements; (sports) perdre par forfait

defeat [dɪ'fit] *s* défaite *f*; **unexpected defeat** contre-performance *f* ‖ *tr* vaincre, battre, défaire

defeatism [dɪ'fitɪzəm] *s* défaitisme *m*

defeatist [dɪ'fitɪst] *adj* & *s* défaitiste *mf*

defecate ['dɛfɪ,ket] *intr* déféquer

defect ['difɛkt] *s* défaut *m*, imperfection *f*, vice *m* ‖ [dɪ'fɛkt] *intr* faire défection, déserter

defection [dɪ'fɛkʃən] *s* défection *f*

defective [dɪ'fɛktɪv] *adj* défectueux, vicieux; (gram) défectif

defend [dɪ'fɛnd] *tr* défendre

defendant [dɪ'fɛndənt] *s* (law) défendeur *m*, intimé *m*

defense [dɪ'fɛns] *s* défense *f*

defenseless [dɪ'fɛnslɪs] *adj* sans défense

defensive [dɪ'fɛnsɪv] *adj* défensif ‖ *s* défensive *f*

de·fer [dɪ'fʌr] *v* (*pret* & *pp* **-ferred;** *ger* **-ferring**) *tr* (*to postpone*) différer; (mil) mettre en sursis ‖ *intr*—**to defer to** (*to yield to*) déférer à

deference ['dɛfərəns] *s* déférence *f*

deferential [,dɛfə'rɛnʃəl] *adj* déférent

deferment [dɪ'fʌrmənt] *s* (*postponement*) ajournement *m*, remise *f*; (*extension of time*) délai *m*; (mil) sursis *m* d'appel, sursis d'incorporation

defiance [dɪ'faɪ·əns] *s* défi *m*, provocation *f*, nargue *f*; **in defiance of** au mépris de, en dépit de

defiant [dɪ'faɪ·ənt] *adj* provocant, hostile, de défi

deficien·cy [dɪ'fɪʃənsi] *s* (*pl* **-cies**) déficience *f*, insuffisance *f*; (*of vitamins or minerals*) carence *f*; (com) déficit *m*

deficient [dɪ'fɪʃənt] *adj* déficient, insuffisant

deficit ['dɛfɪsɪt] *adj* déficitaire ‖ *s* déficit *m*

defile [dɪ'faɪl], ['difaɪl] *s* défilé *m* ‖ [dɪ'faɪl] *tr* souiller ‖ *intr* défiler

defilement [dɪ'faɪlmənt] *s* souillure *f*

define [dɪ'faɪn] *tr* définir

definite ['dɛfɪnɪt] *adj* défini; (*opinions, viewpoints*) décidé

definitely ['dɛfɪnɪtli] *adv* décidément, nettement

definition [,dɛfɪ'nɪʃən] *s* définition *f*

definitive [dɪ'fɪnɪtɪv] *adj* définitif

deflate [dɪ'flet] *tr* dégonfler; (*currency*) amener la déflation de ‖ *intr* se dégonfler

deflation [dɪ'fleʃən] *s* dégonflement *m*; (*of prices*) déflation *f*

deflect [dɪ'flɛkt] *tr* & *intr* dévier

deflower [di'flau·ər] *tr* déflorer; (*to strip of flowers*) défleurir

defogging [dɪ'fɔgɪŋ] *s* dénébulation *f*

deforest [di'fɔrɪst] *tr* déboiser

deform [dɪ'fɔrm] *tr* déformer

deformed *adj* contrefait, difforme

deformi·ty [dɪ'fɔrmɪti] *s* (*pl* **-ties**) difformité *f*

defraud [dɪ'frɔd] *tr* frauder

defray [dɪ'fre] *tr* payer, supporter

defrost [dɪ'frɔst] *tr* décongeler, dégivrer

defroster [di'frɔstər] *s* déglaceur *m*, dégivreur *m*

defrosting [di'frɔstɪŋ] *s* dégèlement *m*, dégivrage *m*

deft [dɛft] *adj* adroit, habile; (*hand*) exercé, preste

defunct [dɪ'fʌŋkt] *adj* défunt; (*practice, style, etc.*) tombé en désuétude

de·fy [dɪ'faɪ] *v* (*pret* & *pp* **-fied**) *tr* défier, braver, porter un défi à

degeneracy [dɪ'dʒɛnərəsi] *s* dégénérescence *f*

degenerate [dɪ'dʒɛnərɪt] *adj* & *s* dégénéré *m* ‖ [dɪ'dʒɛnə,ret] *intr* dégénérer

degrade [dɪ'gred] *tr* dégrader

degrading [dɪ'gredɪŋ] *adj* dégradant

degree [dɪ'gri] *s* degré *m*; (*from a university*) grade *m*; (*of humidity*) titre *m*; **to take a degree** obtenir ses diplômes, obtenir ses titres universitaires

dehumidi·fy [,dihju'mɪdɪ,faɪ] *v* (*pret* & *pp* **-fied**) *tr* déshumidifier

dehydrate [di'haɪdret] *tr* déshydrater; (*the body*) dessécher

deice [di'aɪs] *tr* déglacer, dégivrer

deicer [di'aɪsər] *s* dégivreur *m*, antigivrant *m*

dei·fy ['di·ɪ,faɪ] v (pret & pp **-fied**) tr déifier

deign [den] intr—**to deign to** daigner

dei·ty ['di·ɪtɪ] s (pl **-ties**) divinité f; (mythol) déité f; **the Deity** Dieu m

dejected [dɪ'dʒɛktɪd] adj abattu, découragé

dejection [dɪ'dʒɛkʃən] s abattement m

delay [dɪ'le] s retard m; (postponement) sursis m, remise f; **without delay** sans délai; **without further delay** sans plus tarder ‖ tr retarder; (to put off) remettre, différer ‖ intr tarder, s'attarder

delayed'-ac'tion adj à action différée

delayed'-ac'tion switch' s minuterie f d'escalier

delayed' record'ing s différé m

delayed'-time' switch' s coupe-circuit m à action différée

dele ['dili] s (typ) deleatur m

delectable [dɪ'lɛktəbəl] adj délectable

delegate ['dɛlɪ,get] s délégué m; (at a convention) congressiste mf, délégué ‖ tr déléguer

delegation [,dɛlɪ'geʃən] s délégation f

delete [dɪ'lit] tr supprimer

deletion [dɪ'liʃən] s suppression f; (the deleted part) passage m supprimé

deliberate [dɪ'lɪbərɪt] adj (premeditated) délibéré, réfléchi; (cautious) circonspect; (slow) lent ‖ [dɪ'lɪbə,ret] tr & intr délibérer

deliberately [dɪ'lɪbərɪtlɪ] adv (on purpose) exprès, de propos délibéré; (without hurrying) posément, sans hâte

deliberation [dɪ,lɪbə'reʃən] s délibération f; (slowness) lenteur f

delica·cy ['dɛlɪkəsi] s (pl **-cies**) délicatesse f; (choice food) friandise f, gourmandise f

delicate ['dɛlɪkɪt] adj délicat

delicatessen [,dɛlɪkə'tɛsən] s charcuterie f

delicious [dɪ'lɪʃəs] adj délicieux

delight [dɪ'laɪt] s délice m, délices fpl, plaisir m ‖ tr enchanter, ravir ‖ intr—**to delight in** se délecter à

delighted adj enchanté, ravi, content

delightful [dɪ'laɪtfəl] adj délicieux, ravissant, enchanteur

delineate [dɪ'lɪnɪ,et] tr esquisser

delinquen·cy [dɪ'lɪŋkwənsi] s (pl **-cies**) délit m, faute f; (e.g., of juveniles) délinquance f

delinquent [dɪ'lɪŋkwənt] adj négligent, coupable; (in payment) arriéré; (in guilt) délinquant ‖ s délinquant m; créancier m en retard

delirious [dɪ'lɪrɪ·əs] adj délirant

deliri·um [dɪ'lɪrɪ·əm] s (pl **-ums** or **-a** [ə]) délire m

deliver [dɪ'lɪvər] tr délivrer; (e.g., laundry) livrer; (mail) distribuer; (a blow) asséner; (an opinion) exprimer; (a speech) prononcer; (energy) débiter, fournir; **to be delivered of a child** accoucher d'un enfant

deliver·y [dɪ'lɪvəri] s (pl **-ies**) s remise f; (e.g., of a package) livraison f; (of mail) distribution f; (of a speech; of electricity)

débit m; (of a woman in childbirth) accouchement m, délivrance f; **free delivery** livraison franco

deliv'ery·man' s (pl **-men**) livreur m

deliv'ery room' s salle f d'accouchement, salle de travail

deliv'ery truck' s fourgon m à livraison

dell [dɛl] s vallon m

delouse [di'laus] tr épouiller

delphinium [dɛl'fɪnɪ·əm] s dauphinelle f, pied-d'alouette m

delta ['dɛltə] s delta m

delude [dɪ'lud] tr duper, tromper

deluge ['dɛljudʒ] s déluge m ‖ tr inonder

delusion [dɪ'luʒən] s illusion f, tromperie f; **delusions** (psychopathol) hallucinations fpl; **delusions of grandeur** folie f des grandeurs

delusive [dɪ'lusɪv] or **delusory** [dɪ'lusəri] adj trompeur

de luxe [dɪ'lʌks] adj & adv de luxe

delve [dɛlv] intr—**to delve into** fouiller dans, approfondir

demagnetize [di'mægnɪ,taɪz] tr démagnétiser, désaimanter

demagogue ['dɛmə,gɑg] s démagogue mf

demand [dɪ'mænd] s exigence f; (of the buying public) demande f; **demands** exigences; **in great demand** très recherché; **on demand** sur demande ‖ tr exiger

demanding [dɪ'mændɪŋ] adj exigeant

demarcate ['dimɑr,ket] tr délimiter

demean [dɪ'min] tr dégrader; **to demean oneself** se conduire

demeanor [dɪ'minər] s conduite f, tenue f

demented [dɪ'mɛntɪd] adj aliéné, fou

demerit [dɪ'mɛrɪt] s démérite m

demigod ['dɛmɪ,gɑd] s demi-dieu m

demijohn ['dɛmɪ,dʒɑn] s dame-jeanne f

demilitarize [di'mɪlɪtə,raɪz] tr démilitariser

demise [dɪ'maɪz] s décès m

demitasse ['dɛmɪ,tæs] s petite tasse f à café; (contents) café m noir

demobilize [di'mobɪ,laɪz] tr démobiliser

democra·cy [dɪ'mɑkrəsi] s (pl **-cies**) démocratie f

democrat ['dɛmə,kræt] s démocrate mf

democratic [,dɛmə'krætɪk] adj démocratique

demolish [dɪ'mɑlɪʃ] tr démolir

demolition [,dɛmə'lɪʃən] s démolition f

demon ['dimən] s démon m

demoniac [dɪ'monɪ,æk] adj & s démoniaque mf

demonic [dɪ'mɑnɪk] adj démoniaque

demonstrate ['dɛmən,stret] tr démontrer ‖ intr (to show feelings in public gatherings) manifester

demonstration [,dɛmən'streʃən] s démonstration f; (public show of feeling) manifestation f

demonstrative [dɪ'mɑnstrətɪv] adj démonstratif

demonstrator ['dɛmən,stretər] s (salesman) démonstrateur m; (agitator) manifestant m

demoralize [dɪ'mɔrə,laɪz] tr démoraliser

demote [dɪ'mot] tr rétrograder

demotion [dɪ'moʃən] s rétrogradation f

de·mur [dɪ'mʌr] v (pret & pp **-murred**; ger **-murring**) intr faire des objections

demure [dɪ'mjʊr] adj modeste, posé

demurrage [dɪ'mʌrɪdʒ] s (naut) surestarie f

den [dɛn] s (of animals; of thieves) repaire m, retraite f; officine f; (of wild beasts) antre m; (of lions) tanière f; (room in a house) cabinet m de travail, fumoir m, coin m de détente, coin de retraite; (Cub Scouts) sizaine f

denaturalize [di'nætʃərə,laɪz] tr dénaturaliser

denial [dɪ'naɪ·əl] s (contradiction) dénégation f, démenti m; (refusal) refus m, déni m

denim ['dɛnɪm] s coutil m

denizen ['dɛnɪzən] s habitant m

Denmark ['dɛnmark] s le Danemark

denomination [dɪ'nɑmɪ'neʃən] s dénomination f; (of coin or stamp) valeur f; (eccl) secte f, confession f, communion f

denote [dɪ'not] tr dénoter

denounce [dɪ'naʊns] tr dénoncer

dense [dɛns] adj dense; (stupid) bête

densi·ty ['dɛnsɪti] s (pl **-ties**) densité f

dent [dɛnt] s (depression) marque f de coup, creux m; (in a knife; in a fortune) brèche f; **to make a dent in** faire une brèche à ‖ tr ébrécher

dental ['dɛntəl] adj dentaire; (phonet) dental ‖ s dentale f

den'tal brac'es spl appareil m dentaire

den'tal floss' s fil m dentaire, soie f dentaire

den'tal lab'oratory s laboratoire m de prothèse dentaire

den'tal sur'geon s chirurgien-dentiste m

dentifrice ['dɛntɪfrɪs] s dentifrice m

dentist ['dɛntɪst] s dentiste mf

dentistry ['dɛntɪstri] s odontologie f

denture ['dɛntʃər] s (set of teeth) denture f; (set of artificial teeth) dentier m, râtelier m, prothèse f dentaire

denunciation [dɪ,nʌnsɪ'eʃən] s dénonciation f

de·ny [dɪ'naɪ] v (pret & pp **-nied**) tr nier, démentir; **to deny oneself** se refuser, se priver

deodorant [di'odərənt] adj & s désodorisant m

deodorize [di'odə,raɪz] tr désodoriser

depart [dɪ'pɑrt] intr partir; **to depart from** se départir de

departed adj (dead) mort, défunt

department [dɪ'pɑrtmənt] s département m; (of hospital) service m; (of agency) bureau m; (of store) rayon m, comptoir m; (of university) section f

Depart'ment of State' s ministère m des affaires étrangères

depart'ment store' s grands magasins mpl, galerie f

departure [dɪ'pɑrtʃər] s départ m

depend [dɪ'pɛnd] intr dépendre; **to depend on** or **upon** dépendre de

dependable [dɪ'pɛndəbəl] adj sûr; (person) digne de confiance

dependence [dɪ'pɛndəns] s dépendance f; **dependence on** dépendance de; (trust in) confiance en

dependen·cy [dɪ'pɛndənsi] s (pl **-cies**) dépendance f; (country, territory) possession f, colonie f

dependent [dɪ'pɛndənt] adj dépendant; **dependent on** dépendant de; (s.o. for family support) à la charge de ‖ s charge f de famille

depend'ent clause' s proposition f subordonnée

depict [dɪ'pɪkt] tr dépeindre, décrire

depiction [dɪ'pɪkʃən] s peinture f

deplete [dɪ'plit] tr épuiser

depletion [dɪ'pliʃən] s épuisement m

deple'tion allow'ance s déduction f pour remplacement

deplorable [dɪ'plorəbəl] adj déplorable

deplore [dɪ'plor] tr déplorer

deploy [dɪ'plɔɪ] tr (mil) déployer ‖ intr (mil) se déployer

deployment [dɪ'plɔɪmənt] s (mil) déploiement m

depolarize [di'polə,raɪz] tr dépolariser

depopulate [di'pɑpjə,let] tr & intr dépeupler

deport [dɪ'port] tr déporter; **to deport oneself** se comporter

deportation [,dipor'teʃən] s déportation f

deportee [,dipor'ti] s déporté m

deportment [dɪ'portmənt] s comportement m, tenue f, manières fpl

depose [dɪ'poz] tr & intr déposer

deposit [dɪ'pɑzɪt] s dépôt m; (as pledge) cautionnement m, arrhes fpl, gage m; **no deposit** (bottle) perdu; **to pay a deposit** verser une provision, un acompte, or une caution; **with deposit** (on a bottle) consigné ‖ tr déposer; laisser comme provision

depos'it account' s compte m courant

depositor [dɪ'pɑzɪtɔr] s déposant m

deposito·ry [dɪ'pɑzɪ,tori] s (pl **-ries**) dépôt m; (person) dépositaire mf

depot ['dipo] s dépôt m; (rr) gare f

depraved [dɪ'prevd] adj dépravé

depravi·ty [dɪ'prævɪti] s (pl **-ties**) dépravation f

deprecate ['dɛprɪ,ket] tr désapprouver

depreciate [dɪ'priʃɪ,et] tr déprécier ‖ intr se déprécier

depreciation [dɪ,priʃɪ'eʃən] s dépréciation f

depredation [,dɛprɪ'deʃən] s déprédation f

depress [dɪ'prɛs] tr déprimer; (prices) abaisser

depressing [dɪ'prɛsɪŋ] adj attristant

depression [dɪ'prɛʃən] s dépression f

deprive [dɪ'praɪv] tr priver

deprogram [di'progræm] tr déprogrammer

depth [dɛpθ] s profondeur f; (in sound) gravité f; **depths** abîme m; **in the depth of winter** en plein hiver; **to go beyond one's depth** perdre pied; sortir de sa compétence

depth' bomb' s bombe f sous-marine

depth' charge' s grenade f sous-marine

deputation [,dɛpjə'teʃən] s députation f

deputize [ˈdɛpjəˌtaɪz] tr députer
depu·ty [ˈdɛpjəti] s (pl **-ties**) député m
derail [dɪˈrel] tr faire dérailler ‖ intr dérailler
derailment [dɪˈrelmənt] s déraillement m
derange [dɪˈrendʒ] tr déranger
derangement [dɪˈrendʒmənt] s dérangement m; (of mind) aliénation f
der·by [ˈdʌrbi] s (pl **-bies**) (race) derby m; (hat) chapeau m melon
deregulate [dɪˈrɛgjəˌlet] tr déréglementer
derelict [ˈdɛrɪlɪkt] adj abandonné, délaissé; (in one's duty) négligent ‖ s épave f
dereliction [ˌdɛrɪˈlɪkʃən] s abandon m, renoncement m
deride [dɪˈraɪd] tr tourner en dérision, ridiculiser
derision [dɪˈrɪʒən] s dérision f
derisive [dɪˈraɪsɪv] adj dérisoire
derivation [ˌdɛrɪˈveʃən] s dérivation f
derivative [dɪˈrɪvətɪv] adj & s dérivé m
derive [dɪˈraɪv] tr & intr dériver
dermatitis [ˌdɛrməˈtaɪtɪs] s dermatite f, dermite f
dermatology [ˌdʌrməˈtalədʒi] s dermatologie f
derogatory [dɪˈragəˌtori] adj péjoratif
derrick [ˈdɛrɪk] s (crane) grue f; (for extracting oil) derrick m, tour f (de forage)
dervish [ˈdʌrvɪʃ] s derviche m
desalinization [diˌsɛlɪnɪˈzeʃən] s dessalement m
desalt [diˈsɔlt] tr dessaler
descend [dɪˈsɛnd] tr descendre ‖ intr descendre; (said of rain) tomber; **to be descended from** descendre de; **to be directly descended from** (e.g., an idea) être dans le droit-fil de; **to descend on** s'abattre sur
descendant [dɪˈsɛndənt] adj & s descendant m
descendent [dɪˈsɛndənt] adj descendant
descent [dɪˈsɛnt] s descente f; (drop in temperature) chute f; (lineage) descendance f, naissance f; **of German descent** d'extraction allemande
descrambling [diˈskræmblɪŋ] s (electron) désembrouillage m
describe [dɪˈskraɪb] tr décrire
description [dɪˈskrɪpʃən] s description f
descriptive [dɪˈskrɪptɪv] adj descriptif
de·scry [dɪˈskraɪ] v (pret & pp **-scried**) tr découvrir, apercevoir
desecrate [ˈdɛsɪˌkret] tr profaner
desegregate [diˈsɛgrɪˌget] intr supprimer la ségrégation raciale
desegregation [diˌsɛgrɪˈgeʃən] s déségrégation f
desensitize [diˈsɛnsɪˌtaɪz] tr désensibiliser
desert [ˈdɛzərt] adj & s désert m ‖ [dɪˈzʌrt] s mérite m; **to get one's just deserts** recevoir son salaire, recevoir sa juste punition ‖ tr & intr déserter
deserted adj (person) abandonné; (place) désert, nu
deserter [dɪˈzʌrtər] s déserteur m
desertion [dɪˈzʌrʃən] s désertion f

deserve [dɪˈzʌrv] tr & intr mériter
deservedly [dɪˈzʌrvɪdli] adv à juste titre, dignement
deserving [dɪˈzʌrvɪŋ] adj méritoire, digne
design [dɪˈzaɪn] s (combination of details; art of designing; work of art) dessin m; (plan, scheme) dessein m, projet m, plan m; (model, outline) modèle m, type m, grandes lignes fpl; **to have designs on** avoir des desseins sur ‖ tr inventer, projeter; (e.g., a dress) dessiner; (a secret plan) combiner; **designed for** destiné à
designate [ˈdɛzɪgˌnet] tr désigner
designer [dɪˈzaɪnər] s dessinateur m; (com) concepteur-projecteur m; (mov, theat) décorateur m
designing [dɪˈzaɪnɪŋ] adj artificieux, intrigant ‖ s dessin m
desirable [dɪˈzaɪrəbəl] adj désirable
desire [dɪˈzaɪr] s désir m ‖ tr désirer
desirous [dɪˈzaɪrəs] adj désireux
desist [dɪˈzɪst] intr cesser
desk [dɛsk] s (in office) bureau m; (in schoolroom) pupitre m; (of cashier) caisse f
desk' blot'ter s sous-main m
desk' clerk' s réceptionnaire mf, réceptionniste mf
desk' set' s écritoire f
desolate [ˈdɛsəlɪt] adj désert; (sad) désolé; (alone) abandonné ‖ [ˈdɛsəˌlet] tr désoler
desolation [ˌdɛsəˈleʃən] s désolation f
despair [dɪˈspɛr] s désespoir m, désespérance f ‖ intr désespérer
despairing [dɪˈspɛrɪŋ] adj désespéré
despera·do [ˌdɛspəˈrado] s (pl **-does** or **-dos**) hors-la-loi m
desperate [ˈdɛspərɪt] adj capable de tout, poussé à bout; (bitter, excessive) acharné, à outrance; (hopeless) désespéré; (remedy) héroïque
desperation [ˌdɛspəˈreʃən] s (despair) désespoir m; (recklessness) témérité f
despicable [ˈdɛspɪkəbəl] adj méprisable, mesquin
despise [dɪˈspaɪz] tr mépriser, dédaigner
despite [dɪˈspaɪt] prep en dépit de, malgré
despoil [dɪˈspɔɪl] tr dépouiller
desponden·cy [dɪˈspandənsi] s (pl **-cies**) abattement m, accablement m
despondent [dɪˈspandənt] adj abattu, accablé, déprimé
despot [ˈdɛspat] s despote m, tyran m
despotic [dɛsˈpatɪk] adj despotique
despotism [ˈdɛspəˌtɪzəm] s despotisme m
dessert [dɪˈzʌrt] s dessert m
dessert' spoon' s cuiller f à dessert
destination [ˌdɛstɪˈneʃən] s destination f
destine [ˈdɛstɪn] tr destiner
desti·ny [ˈdɛstɪni] s (pl **-nies**) destin m, destinée f
destitute [ˈdɛstɪˌt(j)ut] adj (poverty-stricken) indigent; (lacking) dépourvu, dénué
destitution [ˌdɛstɪˈt(j)uʃən] s dénuement m, indigence f
destroy [dɪˈstrɔɪ] tr détruire

destroyer [dɪ'strɔɪ·ər] *s* destructeur *m*; (nav) destroyer *m*

destruction [dɪ'strʌkʃən] *s* destruction *f*

destructive [dɪ'strʌktɪv] *adj* destructeur, destructif

desultory ['dɛsəl,tori] *adj* décousu, sans suite; (*conversation*) à bâtons rompus

detach [dɪ'tætʃ] *tr* détacher

detachable [dɪ'tætʃəbəl] *adj* détachable, démontable; (*collar*) faux

detached *adj* détaché

detachment [dɪ'tætʃmənt] *s* détachement *m*

detail [dɪ'tel], ['ditel] *s* détail *m*; (mil) extrait *m* de l'ordre du jour; (mil) détachement *m* ‖ [dɪ'tel] *tr* détailler

detailed' state'ment *s* bordereau *m*

detain [dɪ'ten] *tr* retenir, retarder; (*in prison*) détenir

detect [dɪ'tɛkt] *tr* déceler, détecter

detection [dɪ'tɛkʃən] *s* détection *f*

detective [dɪ'tɛktɪv] *adj* (*device*) détecteur; (*film, novel*) policier ‖ *s* détective *m*, agent *m* de la sûreté

detec'tive sto'ry *s* roman *m* policier

detector [dɪ'tɛktər] *s* détecteur *m*

detention [dɪ'tɛnʃən] *s* détention *f*

de·ter [dɪ'tʌr] *v* (*pret & pp* **-terred**; *ger* **-terring**) *tr* dissuader, détourner

detergent [dɪ'tʌrdʒənt] *adj & s* détersif *m*, détergent *m*

deteriorate [dɪ'tɪrɪ·ə,ret] *tr* détériorer ‖ *intr* se détériorer

determination [di,tʌrmɪ'neʃən] *s* détermination *f*

determine [dɪ'tʌrmɪn] *tr* déterminer

determined *adj* déterminé, résolu

deterrent [dɪ'tʌrənt] *adj & s* préventif *m*

detest [dɪ'tɛst] *tr* détester

dethrone [dɪ'θron] *tr* détrôner

detonate ['dɛtə,net] *tr* faire détoner, faire éclater ‖ *intr* détoner

detour ['ditur] *s* déviation *f*; (*indirect manner*) détour *m* ‖ *tr & intr* dévier

detract [dɪ'trækt] *tr* diminuer ‖ *intr*—to **detract from** amoindrir

detractor [dɪ'træktər] *s* détracteur *m*

detriment ['dɛtrɪmənt] *s* détriment *m*

detrimental [,dɛtrɪ'mɛntəl] *adj* préjudiciable, nuisible

deuce [d(j)us] *s* deux *m*; (*score*) égalité *f*; **what the deuce!** (coll) diantre!, que diable!

devaluate [di'vælju,et] *tr* dévaluer

devaluation [di,vælju'eʃən] *s* dévaluation *f*

devastate ['dɛvəs,tet] *tr* dévaster

devastating ['dɛvəs,tetɪŋ] *adj* dévastateur; (coll) écrasant, accablant

devastation [,dɛvəs'teʃən] *s* dévastation *f*

develop [dɪ'vɛləp] *tr* développer; (*a mine*) exploiter; (*to perfect*) mettre au point, réaliser, étudier; (*e.g., a fever*) contracter, être atteint de; (phot) révéler, développer ‖ *intr* se développer; (*to become evident*) se produire, se manifester

developer [dɪ'vɛləpər] *s* entrepreneur *m*, aménager *m*; (*of houses*) promoteur *m* de

construction, lotisseur *m*; (*builder*) maître *m* d'œuvre; (phot) révélateur *m*

development [dɪ'vɛləpmənt] *s* développement *m*; (*event*) événement *m* récent; (*of housing*) aménagement *m*, lotissement *m*, grand ensemble *m*

deviate ['divi,et] *s* perverti *m* ‖ *tr* faire dévier ‖ *intr* dévier

deviation [,divi'eʃən] *s* déviation *f*

device [dɪ'vaɪs] *s* appareil *m*, dispositif *m*; (*trick*) stratagème *m*, ruse *f*; emblème *m*, devise *f*; **to leave s.o. to his own devices** abandonner qn à ses propres moyens

dev·il ['dɛvəl] *s* diable *m*; **speak of the devil!** (coll) je vois un loup!; **to be between the devil and the deep blue sea** (coll) se trouver entre l'enclume et le marteau; **to raise the devil** (slang) faire le diable à quatre ‖ *v* (*pret & pp* **-iled** or **-illed**; *ger* **-iling** or **-illing**) *tr* épicer fortement; (coll) tourmenter

devilish ['dɛvəlɪʃ] *adj* diabolique; (*roguish*) coquin

dev'il-may-care' *adj* insouciant, étourdi

devilment ['dɛvəlmənt] *s* (*mischief*) diablerie *f*; (*evil*) méchanceté *f*

devil·try ['dɛvəltri] *s* (*pl* **-tries**) méchanceté *f*, cruauté *f*; (*mischief*) espièglerie *f*

devious ['divi·əs] *adj* (*straying*) détourné, dévié; (*roundabout; shifty*) tortueux

devise [dɪ'vaɪz] *tr* combiner, inventer; (law) léguer

devoid [dɪ'vɔɪd] *adj* dépourvu, vide, dénué

devolve [dɪ'vɑlv] *intr*—**to devolve on, to,** or **upon** échoir à

devote [dɪ'vot] *tr* consacrer

devoted *adj* dévoué; **devoted to** voué à, dévoué à, attaché à

devotee [,dɛvə'ti] *s* dévot *m*, adepte *mf*; (sports) fervent *m*, fanatique *mf*

devotion [dɪ'voʃən] *s* dévotion *f*; (*to study, work, etc.*) dévouement *m*; **devotions** dévotions, prières *fpl*

devour [dɪ'vaur] *tr* dévorer

devout [dɪ'vaut] *adj* dévot, pieux

dew [d(j)u] *s* rosée *f*

dew'drop' *s* goutte *f* de rosée

dew'lap' *s* fanon *m*, double menton *m*

dew' point' *s* point *m* de rosée

dew·y ['d(j)u·i] *adj* (*comp* **-ier**; *super* **-iest**) couvert de rosée

dexterity [dɛks'tɛrɪti] *s* dextérité *f*, adresse *f*

diabetes [,daɪ·ə'bitiz] *s* diabète *m*

diabetic [,daɪ·ə'bɛtɪk] *adj & s* diabétique *mf*

diabolic(al) [,daɪ·ə'bɑlɪk(əl)] *adj* diabolique

diacritical [,daɪ·ə'krɪtɪkəl] *adj* diacritique

diadem ['daɪ·ə,dɛm] *s* diadème *m*

diaeresis = dieresis

diagnose [,daɪ·əg'nos] *tr* diagnostiquer

diagnosis [,daɪ·əg'nosɪs] *s* (*pl* **-ses** [siz]) diagnostic *m*

diagonal [daɪ'ægənəl] *adj* diagonal ‖ *s* diagonale *f*

dia·gram ['daɪ·ə,græm] *s* diagramme *m*, croquis *m* coté ‖ *v* (*pret & pp* **-gramed** or

-grammed; *ger* -graming or -gramming) *tr* représenter schématiquement

di·al ['daɪ·əl] *s* cadran *m* ‖ *v* (*pret & pp* -aled or -alled; *ger* -aling or -alling) *tr* (*a telephone number*) composer ‖ *intr* faire un numéro

dialect ['daɪ·ə,lɛkt] *s* dialecte *m*

dialing ['daɪ·əlɪŋ] *s* (telp) composition *f* du numéro

dialogue ['daɪ·ə,lɔg] *s* dialogue *m*; **to carry on a dialogue** dialoguer

di·al tel'ephone *s* téléphone *m* automatique, automatique *m*

di·al tone' *s* (telp) tonalité *f*

diameter [daɪ'æmɪtər] *s* diamètre *m*

diametric(al) [,daɪ·ə'mɛtrɪk(əl)] *adj* diamètral

diamond ['daɪmənd] *s* (*gem*) diamant *m*; (*figure of a rhombus*) losange *m*; (baseball) petit champ *m*; (cards) carreau *m*

diaper ['daɪ·əpər] *s* lange *m*, couche *f* ‖ *tr* (*to variegate*) diaprer

diaphanous [daɪ'æfənəs] *adj* diaphane

diaphragm ['daɪ·ə,fræm] *s* diaphragme *m*

diarrhea [,daɪ·ə'ri·ə] *s* diarrhée *f*

dia·ry ['daɪ·əri] *s* (*pl* -ries) journal *m*

diastole [daɪ'æstəli] *s* diastole *f*

diathermy ['daɪ·ə,θʌrmi] *s* diathermie *f*

diatribe ['daɪ·ə,traɪb] *s* diatribe *f*

dice [daɪs] *spl* dés *mpl*; **no dice!** (slang) pas moyen!; **to load the dice** piper les dés ‖ *tr* couper en cubes

dice'box' *s* cornet *m* à dés

dichoto·my [daɪ'kɑtəmi] *s* (*pl* -mies) dichotomie *f*

Dictaphone ['dɪktə,fon] *s* (trademark) dictaphone *m*

dictate ['dɪktet] *s* précepte *m*, règle *f* ‖ *tr & intr* dicter

dictation [dɪk'teʃən] *s* dictée *f*; **to take dictation from** écrire sous la dictée de

dictator [dɪk'tetər] *s* dictateur *m*

dic'tator·ship' *s* dictature *f*

diction ['dɪkʃən] *s* diction *f*

dictionar·y ['dɪkʃən,ɛri] *s* (*pl* -ies) dictionnaire *m*

dic·tum ['dɪktəm] *s* (*pl* -ta [tə]) dicton *m*; (law) opinion *f*, arrêt *m*

didactic(al) [dɪ'dæktɪk(əl)] *adj* didactique

die [daɪ] *s* (*pl* dice [daɪs]) dé *m*; **the die is cast** le dé en est jeté ‖ *s* (*pl* dies) (*for stamping coins, medals, etc.*) coin *m*; (*for cutting threads*) filière *f*; (*key pattern*) jeu *m* ‖ *v* (*pret & pp* died; *ger* dying) *intr* mourir; **to be dying** se mourir; **to be dying to** (coll) mourir d'envie de; **to die away** s'éteindre; **to die laughing** (coll) mourir de rire

die'hard' *adj* intransigeant ‖ *s* intransigeant *m*, jusqu'au-boutiste *mf*

diere·sis ['daɪ'ɛrɪsɪs] *s* (*pl* -ses [,siz]) (*separation*) diérèse *f*; (*mark*) tréma *m*

die'sel en'gine ['dizəl] *s* diesel *m*, moteur *m* diesel

die'sel oil' *s* gas-oil *m*, gasoil *m*, gazole *m*

die'stock' *s* porte-filière *m*

diet ['daɪ·ət] *s* (*food and drink*) nourriture *f*; (*congress; abstention from food*) diète *f*; (*special menu*) régime *m* ‖ *intr* être or se mettre au régime, suivre un régime

dietetic [,daɪ·ə'tɛtɪk] *adj* diététique ‖ **dietetics** *s* diététique *f*

dietician [,daɪ·ə'tɪʃən] *s* diététicien *m*

differ ['dɪfər] *intr* différer; **to differ with** être en désaccord avec

difference [,dɪfərəns] *s* différence *f*; (*controversy*) différend *m*; **to make no difference** ne rien faire; **to split the difference** partager le différend

different [,dɪfərənt] *adj* différent

differential [,dɪfə'rɛnʃəl] *adj* différentiel ‖ *s* (mach) différentiel *m*; (math) différentielle *f*

differentiate [,dɪfə'rɛnʃɪ,et] *tr* différencier ‖ *intr* se différencier

difficult ['dɪfɪ,kʌlt] *adj* difficile

difficul·ty ['dɪfɪ,kʌlti] *s* (*pl* -ties) difficulté *f*

diffident ['dɪfɪdənt] *adj* défiant, timide

diffuse [dɪ'fjus] *adj* diffus ‖ [dɪ'fjuz] *tr* diffuser ‖ *intr* se diffuser

dig [dɪg] *s*—**to give s.o. a dig** (coll) lancer un trait à qn ‖ *v* (*pret & pp* dug [dʌg]; *ger* digging) *tr* bêcher, creuser; **to dig up** déterrer ‖ *intr* bêcher

digest ['daɪdʒɛst] *s* abrégé *m*, résumé *m*; (*publication*) digest *m*, sélection *f*; (law) digeste *m* ‖ [dɪ'dʒɛst] *tr & intr* digérer

digestible [dɪ'dʒɛstɪbəl] *adj* digestible

digestion [dɪ'dʒɛstʃən] *s* digestion *f*

digestive [dɪ'dʒɛstɪv] *adj* digestif

diges'tive tract' *s* appareil *m* digestif

digit ['dɪdʒɪt] *s* (*numeral*) chiffre *m*; (*finger*) doigt *m*; (*toe*) doigt du pied

digital ['dɪdʒɪtəl] *adj* (*numerical*) numérique; (anat) digital

dig'ital comput'er *s* calculateur *m* numérique

digitalis [,dɪdʒɪ'tælɪs] *s* (bot) digitale *f*; (pharm) digitaline *f*

dig'ital watch' *s* montre *f* à affichage numérique

dignified *adj* distingué; (*air*) digne

digni·fy ['dɪgnɪ,faɪ] *v* (*pret & pp* -fied) *tr* glorifier, honorer

dignitar·y ['dɪgnɪ,tɛri] *s* (*pl* -ies) dignitaire *mf*

digni·ty ['dɪgnɪti] *s* (*pl* -ties) dignité *f*; **to stand on one's dignity** rester sur son quant-à-soi, le prendre de haut

digress [dɪ'grɛs] *intr* faire une digression

digression [dɪ'grɛʃən] *s* digression *f*

dihedral [daɪ'hidrəl] *adj & s* dièdre *m*

dike [daɪk] *s* digue *f*

dilapidated [dɪ'læpɪ,detɪd] *adj* délabré, déglingué

dilate [daɪ'let] *tr* dilater ‖ *intr* se dilater

dilatory ['dɪlə,tori] *adj* lent, tardif; (*strategy, answer*) dilatoire

dilemma [dɪ'lɛmə] *s* dilemme *m*

dilettan·te [,dɪlə'tænti] *adj* dilettante ‖ *s* (*pl* -tes or -ti [ti]) dilettante *mf*

diligence ['dɪlɪdʒəns] *s* diligence *f*

diligent ['dɪlɪdʒənt] *adj* diligent

dill [dɪl] *s* fenouil *m* bâtard, aneth *m*

dillydal·ly [ˈdɪlɪ,dælɪ] *v* (*pret & pp* **-lied**) *intr* traînasser

dilute [dɪˈlut] *adj* dilué ‖ *tr* diluer, délayer

dilution [dɪˈluʃən] *s* dilution *f*

dim [dɪm] *adj* faible, indistinct; (*forebodings*) obscur; (*memory*) effacé; (*color*) terne; (*idea of what is going on*) obtus, confus; **to take a dim view of** envisager sans enthousiasme ‖ *v* (*pret & pp* **dimmed**; *ger* **dimming**) *tr* affaiblir, obscurcir; (*beauty*) ternir; (*the headlights*) baisser, mettre en code ‖ *intr* s'affaiblir, s'obscurcir; (*said of color, beauty, etc.*) se ternir

dime [daɪm] *s* monnaie *f* de dix cents américains

dimension [dɪˈmɛnʃən] *s* dimension *f*

diminish [dɪˈmɪnɪʃ] *tr & intr* diminuer

diminutive [dɪˈmɪnjətɪv] *adj & s* diminutif *m*

dimi·ty [ˈdɪmɪtɪ] *s* (*pl* **-ties**) basin *m*, brillanté *m*

dimly [ˈdɪmlɪ] *adv* indistinctement

dimmers [ˈdɪmərz] *spl* (aut) feux *mpl* code, feux de croisement; **to put on the dimmers** se mettre en code

dimple [ˈdɪmpəl] *s* fossette *f*

dim'wit' *s* (slang) sot *m*, niais *m*

din [dɪn] *s* tapage *m*, fracas *m* ‖ *v* (*pret & pp* **dinned**; *ger* **dinning**) *tr* assourdir; répéter sans cesse ‖ *intr* sonner bruyamment

dine [daɪn] *tr* fêter par un dîner ‖ *intr* dîner; **to dine out** dîner en ville

diner [ˈdaɪnər] *s* (*eater*) dîneur *m*; (*short-order restaurant*) plats-cuisinés *m*; (rr) wagon-restaurant *m*

dinette [daɪˈnɛt] *s* coin-repas *m*

ding-dong [ˈdɪŋ,dɔŋ] *s* tintement *m*, digue-din-don *m*

din·ghy [ˈdɪŋgɪ] *s* (*pl* **-ghies**) canot *m*, youyou *m*

din·gy [ˈdɪndʒɪ] *adj* (*comp* **-gier**; *super* **-giest**) défraîchi, terne

din'ing car' *s* wagon-restaurant *m*

din'ing hall' *s* salle *f* à manger; (*of university*) réfectoire *m*

din'ing room' *s* salle *f* à manger

din'ing-room suite' *s* salle *f* à manger

dinner [ˈdɪnər] *s* dîner *m*

din'ner coat' *s* smoking *m*

din'ner dance' *s* dîner *m* suivi de bal

din'ner guest' *s* convive *mf*, invité *m*

din'ner jack'et *s* smoking *m*

din'ner pail' *s* potager *m*

din'ner set' *s* service *m* de table

din'ner time' *s* heure *f* du dîner

dinosaur [ˈdaɪnə,sɔr] *s* dinosaure *m*

dint [dɪnt] *s*—**by dint of** à force de

diocese [ˈdaɪ·ə,sɪs] *s* diocèse *m*

diode [ˈdaɪ·od] *s* diode *f*

dioxide [daɪˈaksaɪd] *s* bioxyde *m*

dip [dɪp] *s* (*immersion*) plongeon *m*; (*swim*) baignade *f*; (*slope*) pente *f*; (*of magnetic needle*) inclinaison *f* ‖ *v* (*pret & pp* **dipped**; *ger* **dipping**) *tr* plonger; (*a flag*) marquer ‖ *intr* plonger; (*said of magnetic*

needle) incliner; (*said of scale*) pencher; **to dip into** (*a book*) feuilleter; (*one's capital*) prendre dans

diphtheria [dɪfˈθɪrɪ·ə] *s* diphtérie *f*

diphthong [ˈdɪfθɔŋ] *s* diphtongue *f*

diphthongize [ˈdɪfθɔŋ,gaɪz] *tr* diphtonguer ‖ *intr* se diphtonguer

diploma [dɪˈplomə] *s* diplôme *m*

diploma·cy [dɪˈploməsɪ] *s* (*pl* **-cies**) diplomatie *f*

diplomat [ˈdɪplə,mæt] *s* diplomate *mf*

diplomatic [,dɪpləˈmætɪk] *adj* diplomatique, diplomate

dip'lomat'ic pouch' *s* valise *f* diplomatique

dipper [ˈdɪpər] *s* louche *f*, cuiller *f* à pot

dip'stick' *s* jauge *f* d'huile, jauge à tige

dire [daɪr] *adj* affreux, terrible

direct [dɪˈrɛkt] *adj* direct; franc, sincère ‖ *tr* diriger; (*to order*) ordonner; (*a letter, question, etc.*) adresser; (*to point out*) indiquer; (theat) mettre en scène

direct' cur'rent *s* courant *m* continu

direct' di'aling *s* (telp) automatique *m* interurbain

direct' hit' *s* coup *m* or tir *m* direct

direction [dɪˈrɛkʃən] *s* direction *f*; (*e.g., of a street*) sens *m*; (theat) mise *f* en scène; **directions** (*orders*) instructions *fpl*; (*for use*) mode *m* d'emploi, instructions

directional [dɪˈrɛkʃənəl] *adj* directionnel

direc'tional sig'nal *s* clignotant *m*

directive [dɪˈrɛktɪv] *s* ordre *m*, avis *m*, directive *f*

direct' ob'ject *s* (gram) complément *m* direct

director [dɪˈrɛktər] *s* directeur *m*, administrateur *m*, chef *m*; (*of a board*) membre *m* du conseil, votant *m*; (theat) metteur *m* en scène

direc'tor·ship' *s* direction *f*, directorat *m*

directo·ry [dɪˈrɛktərɪ] *s* (*pl* **-ries**) (*board of directors*) conseil *m* d'administration; (*e.g., of telephone*) annuaire *m*; (*e.g., of genealogy*) almanach *m*; (eccl) directoire *m*

dirge [dʌrdʒ] *s* hymne *f* or chant *m* funèbre

dirigible [ˈdɪrɪdʒɪbəl] *adj & s* dirigeable *m*

dirt [dʌrt] *s* saleté *f*, ordure *f*; (*on clothes, skin, etc.*) crasse *f*; (*mire*) crotte *f*, boue *f*; (*earth*) terre *f*; **to get the dirt out of** décrasser

dirt'-cheap' *adj* vendu à vil prix

dirt' road' *s* chemin *m* de terre

dirt·y [ˈdʌrtɪ] *adj* (*comp* **-ier**; *super* **-iest**) sale, malpropre; (*clothes, skin, etc.*) crasseux; (*muddy*) crotté, boueux; (*mean*) méchant, vilain

dir'ty lin'en *s* linge *m* sale; **don't wash your dirty linen in public** il faut laver son linge sale en famille

dir'ty trick' *s* (slang) sale tour *m*; **to play a dirty trick on** (slang) faire un tour de cochon à

disabili·ty [,dɪsəˈbɪlɪtɪ] *s* (*pl* **-ties**) incapacité *f*, invalidité *f*

disabil'ity insur'ance *s* assurance *f* invalidité

disabil′ity pen′sion *s* pension *f* d'invalidité
disable [dɪs′ebəl] *tr* rendre incapable, mettre hors de combat; (*to hurt the limbs of*) estropier, mutiler
disabled *adj* (*serviceman*) invalide; (*ship*) désemparé
disa′bled vet′eran *s* invalide *m*, réformé *m*
disabuse [‚dɪsə′bjuz] *tr* désabuser
disadvantage [‚dɪsəd′væntɪdʒ] *s* désavantage *m* ‖ *tr* désavantager
disadvantaged *adj* défavorisé, désavantagé
disadvantageous [dɪs‚ædvən′tedʒəs] *adj* désavantageux
disagree [‚dɪsə′gri] *intr* différer; **to disagree with** (*to cause discomfort to*) ne pas convenir à; (*to dissent from*) donner tort à
disagreeable [‚dɪsə′gri·əbəl] *adj* désagréable; (*mood, weather, etc.*) maussade
disagreement [‚dɪsə′grimənt] *s* désaccord *m*, différend *m*
disallow [‚dɪsə′laʊ] *tr* désapprouver, rejeter
disappear [‚dɪsə′pɪr] *intr* disparaître; (phonet) s'amuïr
disappearance [‚dɪsə′pɪrəns] *s* disparition *f*; (phonet) amuïssement *m*
disappoint [‚dɪsə′pɔɪnt] *tr* décevoir, désappointer
disappointed *adj* déçu
disappointment [‚dɪsə′pɔɪntmənt] *s* déception *f*, désappointement *m*
disapproval [‚dɪsə′pruvəl] *s* désapprobation *f*
disapprove [‚dɪsə′pruv] *tr & intr* désapprouver
disarm [dɪs′arm] *tr & intr* désarmer
disarmament [dɪs′arməmənt] *s* désarmement *m*
disarming [dɪs′armɪŋ] *adj* désarmant
disarray [‚dɪsə′re] *s* désarroi *m*, désordre *m*; **in disarray** (*said of apparel*) à demi vêtu ‖ *tr* mettre en désarroi
disassemble [‚dɪsə′sɛmbəl] *tr* démonter, désassembler
disassociate [‚dɪsə′soʃɪ,et] *tr* dissocier
disaster [dɪ′zæstər] *s* désastre *m*
disas′ter ar′ea *s* région *f* sinistrée
disastrous [dɪ′zæstrəs] *adj* désastreux
disavow [‚dɪsə′vaʊ] *tr* désavouer
disavowal [‚dɪsə′vaʊ·əl] *s* désaveu *m*
disband [dɪs′bænd] *tr* licencier, congédier ‖ *intr* se débander, se disperser
dis-bar [dɪs′bar] *v* (*pret & pp* **-barred**; *ger* **-barring**) *tr* (law) rayer du barreau
disbelief [‚dɪsbɪ′lif] *s* incroyance *f*
disbelieve [‚dɪsbɪ′liv] *tr & intr* ne pas croire
disburse [dɪs′bʌrs] *tr* débourser
disbursement [dɪs′bʌrsmənt] *s* déboursement *m*; **disbursements** débours *mpl*
disc [dɪsk] *s* disque *m*
discard [dɪs′kard] *s* rebut *m*; (cards) écart *m*; **discards** marchandises *fpl* de rebut ‖ *tr* mettre de côté, jeter; (cards) écarter ‖ *intr* (cards) se défausser
discern [dɪ′sʌrn] *tr* discerner, percevoir
discernible [dɪ′sʌrnɪbəl] *adj* discernable
discerning [dɪ′sʌrnɪŋ] *adj* judicieux, pénétrant, éclairé

discernment [dɪ′sʌrnmənt] *s* discernement *m*
discharge [dɪs′tʃardʒ] (*of a gun; of a battery*) décharge *f*; (*of a prisoner*) élargissement *m*; (*from a job*) congé *m*, renvoi *m*; (*from the armed forces*) libération *f*; (*from the armed forces for unfitness*) réforme *f*; (*from a wound*) suppuration *f* ‖ *tr* décharger; (*a prisoner*) élargir; (*an employee*) congédier, renvoyer, licencier; (*a soldier*) libérer, réformer ‖ *intr* se décharger; (pathol) suppurer
disciple [dɪ′saɪpəl] *s* disciple *m*
disciplinarian [‚dɪsɪplɪ′nɛrɪ·ən] *s* partisan *m* d'une forte discipline; personne *f* qui impose une forte discipline
disciplinary [′dɪsɪplɪ‚nɛri] *adj* disciplinaire
discipline [′dɪsɪplɪn] *s* discipline *f* ‖ *tr* discipliner
disclaim [dɪs′klem] *tr* désavouer, renier
disclaimer [dɪs′klemər] *s* désaveu *m*
disclose [dɪs′kloz] *tr* découvrir, révéler
disclosure [dɪs′kloʒər] *s* découverte *f*, révélation *f*
disco [′dɪsko] *s* discothèque *f*
discolor [dɪs′kʌlər] *tr* décolorer ‖ *intr* se décolorer
discoloration [dɪs‚kʌlə′reʃən] *s* décoloration *f*
discomfit [dɪs′kʌmfɪt] *tr* décontenancer, bafouer
discomfiture [dɪs′kʌmfɪtʃər] *s* déconfiture *f*, déconvenue *f*
discomfort [dɪs′kʌmfərt] *s* (*uneasiness, mild pain*) malaise *f*; (*inconvenience*) gêne *f* ‖ *tr* gêner
disconcert [‚dɪskən′sʌrt] *tr* déconcerter
disconnect [‚dɪskə′nɛkt] *tr* (*to separate*) désunir, séparer; (*a mechanism*) débrayer; (*a plug*) débrancher; (*current*) couper
disconsolate [dɪs′kansəlɪt] *adj* désolé, inconsolable
discontent [‚dɪskən′tɛnt] *adj* mécontent ‖ *s* mécontentement *m* ‖ *tr* mécontenter
discontented *adj* mécontent
discontinue [‚dɪskən′tɪnju] *tr* discontinuer
discontinuous [‚dɪskən′tɪnju·əs] *adj* discontinu
discord [′dɪskɔrd] *s* discorde *f*, désaccord *m*; (mus) discordance *f*
discordance [dɪs′kɔrdəns] *s* discordance *f*
discotheque [′dɪsko‚tɛk] *s* discothèque *f*
discount [′dɪskaʊnt] *s* escompte *m*, remise *f*, rabais *m* ‖ [dɪs′kaʊnt] *tr* escompter, rabattre
dis′count rate′ *s* taux *m* d'escompte
dis′count store′ *s* magasin *m* de rabais, minimarge *f*
discourage [dɪs′kʌrɪdʒ] *tr* décourager
discouragement [dɪs′kʌrɪdʒmənt] *s* découragement *m*
discourse [′dɪskors] *s* discours *m* ‖ [dɪs′kors] *intr* discourir
discourteous [dɪs′kʌrtɪ·əs] *adj* impoli, discourtois
discourte·sy [dɪs′kʌrtəsi] *s* (*pl* **-sies**) impolitesse *f*, discourtoisie *f*

discover [dɪs'kʌvər] *tr* découvrir
discoverer [dɪs'kʌvərər] *s* découvreur *m*
discover·y [dɪs'kʌvəri] *s* (*pl* **-ies**) découverte *f*
discredit [dɪs'krɛdɪt] *s* discrédit *m* ‖ *tr* discréditer
discreditable [dɪs'krɛdɪtəbəl] *adj* déshonorant, peu honorable
discreet [dɪs'krit] *adj* discret
discrepan·cy [dɪs'krɛpənsi] *s* (*pl* **-cies**) désaccord *m*, différence *f*
discretion [dɪs'krɛʃən] *s* discrétion *f*
discriminate [dɪs'krɪmɪ,net] *tr & intr* discriminer; **to discriminate against** défavoriser
discrimination [dɪs,krɪmɪ'neʃən] *s* discrimination *f*
discriminatory [dɪs'krɪmɪnə,tori] *adj* discriminatoire
discus ['dɪskəs] *s* (sports) disque, *m*, palet *m*
discuss [dɪs'kʌs] *tr & intr* discuter
discussion [dɪs'kʌʃən] *s* discussion *f*
disdain [dɪs'den] *s* dédain *m* ‖ *tr* dédaigner
disdainful [dɪs'denfəl] *adj* dédaigneux
disease [dɪ'ziz] *s* maladie *f*
diseased *adj* malade
disembark [,dɪsɛm'bark] *tr & intr* débarquer
disembarkation [dɪs,ɛmbar'keʃən] *s* débarquement *m*
disembow·el [,dɪsɛm'bau·əl] *v* (*pret & pp* **-eled** or **-elled**; *ger* **-eling** or **-elling**) *tr* éventrer
disenchant [,dɪsɛn'tʃænt] *tr* désenchanter
disenchantment [,dɪsɛn'tʃæntmənt] *s* désenchantement *m*
disengage [,dɪsɛn'gedʒ] *tr* dégager; (*toothed wheels*) désengrener; (*a motor*) débrayer ‖ *intr* se dégager
disengagement [,dɪsɛn'gedʒmənt] *s* dégagement *m*, détachement *m*
disentangle [,dɪsɛn'tæŋgəl] *tr* démêler, débrouiller
disentanglement [,dɪsɛn'tæŋgəlmənt] *s* démêlage *m*, débrouillement *m*
disestablish [,dɪsɛs'tæblɪʃ] *tr* (*the Church*) séparer de l'État
disfavor [dɪs'fevər] *s* défaveur *f* ‖ *tr* défavoriser
disfigure [dɪs'fɪgjər] *tr* défigurer, enlaidir
disfigurement [dɪs'fɪgjərmənt] *s* défiguration *f*
disfranchise [dɪs'fræntʃaɪz] *tr* priver de ses droits civiques
disgorge [dɪs'gɔrdʒ] *tr & intr* dégorger
disgrace [dɪs'gres] *s* déshonneur *m* ‖ *tr* déshonorer; (*to deprive of favor*) disgracier; **to disgrace oneself** se déshonorer
disgraceful [dɪs'gresfəl] *adj* déshonorant, honteux
disgruntled [dɪs'grʌntəld] *adj* contrarié, de mauvaise humeur
disguise [dɪs'gaɪz] *s* déguisement *m* ‖ *tr* déguiser
disgust [dɪs'gʌst] *s* dégoût *m* ‖ *tr* dégoûter
disgusting [dɪs'gʌstɪŋ] *adj* dégoûtant

dish [dɪʃ] *s* plat *m*; (*food*) mets *m*, plat; **to wash the dishes** faire la vaisselle ‖ *tr*—**to dish up** servir
dish' clos'et *s* étagère *f* à vaisselle
dish'cloth' *s* lavette *f*
dishearten [dɪs'hartən] *tr* décourager
dishev·el [dɪ'ʃɛvəl] *v* (*pret & pp* **-eled** or **-elled**; *ger* **-eling** or **-elling**) *tr* écheveler
dishonest [dɪs'anɪst] *adj* malhonnête, déloyal
dishones·ty [dɪs'anɪsti] *s* (*pl* **-ties**) malhonnêteté *f*, déloyauté *f*, improbité *f*
dishonor [dɪs'anər] *s* déshonneur *m* ‖ *tr* déshonorer
dishonorable [dɪs'anərəbəl] *adj* déshonorant
dish'pan' *s* bassine *f*
dish' rack' *s* égouttoir *m*
dish'rag' *s* lavette *f*
dish'tow'el *s* torchon *m*
dish'wash'er *s* machine *f* à laver la vaisselle, lave-vaisselle *f*; (*person*) plongeur *m*
dish'wa'ter *s* eau *f* de vaisselle
disillusion [,dɪsɪ'luʒən] *s* désillusion *f* ‖ *tr* désillusionner
disillusionment [,dɪsɪ'luʒənmənt] *s* désillusionnement *m*
disinclination [dɪs,ɪnklɪ'neʃən] *s* répugnance *f*, aversion *f*
disinclined [,dɪsɪn'klaɪnd] *adj* indisposé
disinfect [,dɪsɪn'fɛkt] *tr* désinfecter
disinfectant [,dɪsɪn'fɛktənt] *adj & s* désinfectant *m*
disinformation [dɪs,ɪnfər'meʃən] *s* désinformation *f*
disingenuous [,dɪsɪn'dʒɛnju·əs] *adj* insincère, sans franchise
disinherit [,dɪsɪn'hɛrɪt] *tr* déshériter
disintegrate [dɪs'ɪntɪ,gret] *tr* désagréger; (nucl) désintégrer ‖ *intr* se désagréger; (nucl) se désintégrer
disintegration [dɪs,ɪntɪ'greʃən] *s* désagrégation *f*; (nucl) désintégration *f*
disin·ter [,dɪsɪn'tʌr] *v* (*pret & pp* **-terred**; *ger* **-terring**) *tr* déterrer
disinterested [dɪs'ɪntə,rɛstɪd] *adj* désintéressé
disjointed [dɪs'dʒɔɪntɪd] *adj* désarticulé; (*e.g., style*) décousu
disjunctive [dɪs'dʒʌŋktɪv] *adj* disjonctif; (*pronoun*) tonique
disk [dɪsk] *s* disque *m*
diskette [dɪs'kɛt] *s* (comp) disquette *f*
disk' jock'ey *s* présentateur *m* de disques, animateur *m*
dislike [dɪs'laɪk] *s* aversion *f*; **to take a dislike for** prendre en aversion ‖ *tr* ne pas aimer
dislocate ['dɪslo,ket] *tr* disloquer; (*a joint*) luxer
dislodge [dɪs'ladʒ] *tr* déplacer; (*e.g., the enemy*) déloger
disloyal [dɪs'lɔɪ·əl] *adj* déloyal
disloyal·ty [dɪs'lɔɪ·əlti] *s* (*pl* **-ties**) déloyauté *f*
dismal ['dɪzməl] *adj* sombre, triste

dismantle [dɪsˈmæntəl] *tr* démanteler; (*a machine*) démonter; (*a ship*) désarmer

dismay [dɪsˈme] *s* consternation *f* ‖ *tr* consterner

dismember [dɪsˈmɛmbər] *tr* démembrer

dismiss [dɪsˈmɪs] *tr* (*a thought, suggestion, or subject*) écarter; (*an employee*) congédier, renvoyer, licencier; (*an official, an officer*) destituer, casser; terminer; (*an appeal*) (law) rejeter; (*a class in school*) laisser partir, congédier; **class dismissed!** partez!

dismissal [dɪsˈmɪsəl] *s* congédiement *m*, renvoi *m*, destitution *f*; (*of an idea*) abandon *m*; (*of an appeal*) (law) rejet *m*

dismount [dɪsˈmaʊnt] *tr* démonter ‖ *intr* descendre

disobedience [ˌdɪsəˈbidɪ·əns] *s* désobéissance *f*

disobedient [ˌdɪsəˈbidɪ·ənt] *adj* désobéissant

disobey [ˌdɪsəˈbe] *tr* désobéir à; **to be disobeyed** être désobéi ‖ *intr* désobéir

disorder [dɪsˈɔrdər] *s* désordre *m* ‖ *tr* désordonner

disorderly [dɪsˈɔrdərli] *adj* désordonné, déréglé; (*crowd*) turbulent, effervescent

disor'derly con'duct *s* conduite *f* désordonnée

disorganize [dɪsˈɔrgə,naɪz] *tr* désorganiser

disoriented [dɪsˈɔri,ɛntɪd] *adj* désorienté; **to become disoriented** perdre le nord

disown [dɪsˈon] *tr* désavouer, renier

disparage [dɪˈspærɪdʒ] *tr* dénigrer, déprécier

disparagement [dɪˈspærɪdʒmənt] *s* dénigrement *m*, dépréciation *f*

disparate [ˈdɪspərɪt] *adj* disparate

dispari·ty [dɪˈspærɪti] *s* (*pl* -ties) disparité *f*

dispassionate [dɪsˈpæʃənɪt] *adj* calme; impartial

dispatch [dɪˈspætʃ] *s* envoi *m*, expédition *f*; (govt, journ, mil) dépêche *f*; (*promptness*) promptitude *f* ‖ *tr* dépêcher, expédier, envoyer; (coll & fig) expédier

dis·pel [dɪsˈpɛl] *v* (*pret & pp* -**pelled**; *ger* -**pelling**) *tr* dissiper, disperser

dispensa·ry [dɪˈspɛnsəri] *s* (*pl* -ries) dispensaire *m*

dispensation *s* [ˌdɪspɛnˈseʃən] (*dispensing*) dispensation *f*; (*exemption*) dispense *f*

dispense [dɪˈspɛns] *tr* dispenser, distribuer ‖ *intr*—**to dispense with** se passer de; se défaire de

dispenser [dɪˈspɛnsər] *s* dispensateur *m*; (*automatic*) distributeur *m*

disperse [dɪˈspɑrs] *tr* disperser ‖ *intr* se disperser

dispersion [dɪˈspɑrʒən] *s* dispersion *f*

dispirit [dɪˈspɪrɪt] *tr* décourager

displace [dɪsˈples] *tr* déplacer; (*to take the place of*) remplacer

displaced' per'son *s* personne *f* déplacée

displacement [dɪsˈplesmənt] *s* déplacement *m*; (*substitution*) remplacement *m*

display [dɪˈsple] *s* exposition *f*, étalage *m*; (*of emotion*) manifestation *f*; (comp) vi-suel ‖ *tr* exposer, étaler; (*anger, courage, etc.*) manifester; (*ignorance*) révéler; (comp) afficher, visualiser

display' cab'inet *s* vitrine *f*

display' win'dow *s* vitrine *f*, devanture *f*

displease [dɪsˈpliz] *tr* déplaire à

displeasing [dɪsˈplizɪŋ] *adj* déplaisant

displeasure [dɪsˈplɛʒər] *s* déplaisir *m*, mécontentement *m*

disposable [dɪˈspozəbəl] *adj* (*available*) disponible; (*made to be disposed of*) jetable, à jeter; (*container*) perdu, e.g., **disposable bottle** verre perdu

disposal [dɪˈspozəl] *s* disposition *f*; (*of a question*) résolution *f*; (*of trash, garbage, etc.*) destruction *f*

dispos'able tis'sues *spl* mouchoirs *mpl* à jeter

dispose [dɪˈspoz] *tr* disposer ‖ *intr* disposer; **to dispose of** disposer de; (*to get rid of*) se défaire de; (*a question*) résoudre, trancher

disposed *adj*—**to be disposed to** se disposer à, être porté à

disposition [ˌdɪspəˈzɪʃən] *s* disposition *f*; (*mental outlook*) naturel *m*; (mil) dispositif *m*

dispossess [ˌdɪspəˈzɛs] *tr* déposséder; expulser

disproof [dɪsˈpruf] *s* réfutation *f*

disproportionate [ˌdɪsprəˈporʃənɪt] *adj* disproportionné

disprove [dɪsˈpruv] *tr* réfuter

dispute [dɪsˈpjut] *s* dispute *f*; **beyond dispute** incontestable ‖ *tr* disputer ‖ *intr* se disputer

disquali·fy [dɪsˈkwɑlɪ,faɪ] *v* (*pret & pp* -**fied**) *tr* disqualifier

disquiet [dɪsˈkwaɪ·ət] *s* inquiétude *f* ‖ *tr* inquiéter

disquisition [ˌdɪskwɪˈzɪʃən] *s* essai *m*, traité *m* considérable

disregard [ˌdɪsrɪˈgɑrd] *s* indifférence *f*; **disregard for** manque *m* d'égards envers ‖ *tr* ne pas faire cas de, passer sous silence

disrepair [ˌdɪsrɪˈpɛr] *s* délabrement *m*

disreputable [dɪsˈrɛpjətəbəl] *adj* déshonorant, suspect; (*shabby*) débraillé, râpé

disrepute [ˌdɪsrɪˈpjut] *s* discrédit *m*

disrespect [ˌdɪsrɪˈspɛkt] *s* irrévérence *f*; manque *m* de respect, irrespect *m*

disrespectful [ˌdɪsrɪˈspɛktfəl] *adj* irrévérencieux, irrespectueux; **to be disrespectful to** manquer de respect à

disrobe [dɪsˈrob] *tr* déshabiller ‖ *intr* se déshabiller

disrupt [dɪsˈrʌpt] *tr* rompre; (*to throw into disorder*) bouleverser

disruption [dɪsˈrʌpʃən] *s* bouleversement *m*, perturbation *f*, interruption *f*

dissatisfaction [ˌdɪssætɪsˈfækʃən] *s* mécontentement *m*

dissatisfied *adj* mécontent

dissatis·fy [dɪsˈsætɪs,faɪ] *v* (*pret & pp* -**fied**) *tr* mécontenter

dissect [dɪˈsɛkt] *tr* disséquer

dissection [dɪˈsɛkʃən] *s* dissection *f*

dissemble [dɪˈsɛmbəl] *tr & intr* dissimuler
disseminate [dɪˈsɛmɪˌnet] *tr* disséminer
dissension [dɪˈsɛnʃən] *s* dissension *f*
dissent [dɪˈsɛnt] *s* dissentiment *m*; (*nonconformity*) dissidence *f* ‖ *intr* différer
dissenter [dɪˈsɛntər] *s* dissident *m*
dissertation [ˌdɪsərˈteʃən] *s* dissertation *f*; (*for a degree*) thèse *f*; (*speech*) discours *m*
disservice [dɪˈsʌrvɪs] *s* mauvais service *m*, tort *m*
dissidence [ˈdɪsɪdəns] *s* dissidence *f*
dissident [ˈdɪsɪdənt] *adj & s* dissident *m*
dissimilar [dɪˈsɪmɪlər] *adj* dissemblable
dissimilate [dɪˈsɪmɪˌlet] *tr* (phonet) dissimiler
dissimulate [dɪˈsɪmjəˌlet] *tr & intr* dissimuler
dissipate [ˈdɪsɪˌpet] *tr* dissiper; (*energy, heat, etc.*) disperser ‖ *intr* se dissiper
dissipated *adj* dissipé; débauché
dissipation [ˌdɪsɪˈpeʃən] *s* dissipation *f*; (*of energy, heat, etc.*) dispersion *f*
dissociate [dɪˈsoʃɪˌet] *tr* dissocier ‖ *intr* se dissocier
dissolute [ˈdɪsəˌlut] *adj* dissolu
dissolution [ˌdɪsəˈluʃən] *s* dissolution *f*
dissolve [dɪˈzɑlv] *tr* dissoudre ‖ *intr* se dissoudre
dissonance [ˈdɪsənəns] *s* dissonance *f*
dissuade [dɪˈswed] *tr* dissuader
distaff [ˈdɪstæf] *s* quenouille *f*
dis′taff side′ *s* côté *m* maternel
distance [ˈdɪstəns] *s* distance *f*; **at a distance** à distance; **in the distance** au loin, dans le lointain ‖ *tr* distancer
distant [ˈdɪstənt] *adj* distant; (*uncle, cousin, etc.*) éloigné
distaste [dɪsˈtest] *s* dégoût *m*, aversion *f*
distasteful [dɪsˈtestfəl] *adj* dégoûtant, répugnant
distemper [dɪsˈtɛmpər] *s* (*of dog*) roupie *f*; (painting) détrempe *f* ‖ *tr* peindre en détrempe
distend [dɪˈstɛnd] *tr* distendre ‖ *intr* se distendre
distension [dɪˈstɛnʃən] *s* distension *f*
distill [dɪˈstɪl] *tr* distiller
distillation [ˌdɪstɪˈleʃən] *s* distillation *f*
distiller·y [dɪsˈtɪləri] *s* (*pl* -ies) distillerie *f*
distinct [dɪsˈtɪŋkt] *adj* distinct; (*unusual*) insigne
distinction [dɪsˈtɪŋkʃən] *s* distinction *f*
distinctive [dɪsˈtɪŋktɪv] *adj* distinctif
distinguish [dɪsˈtɪŋgwɪʃ] *tr* distinguer; **to distinguish oneself** se distinguer, se faire remarquer
distinguished *adj* distingué
distort [dɪsˈtɔrt] *tr* déformer
distortion [dɪsˈtɔrʃən] *s* déformation *f*; (*of meaning*) sens *m* forcé; (phot, rad) distorsion *f*
distract [dɪsˈtrækt] *tr* (*to amuse*) distraire; (*to bewilder*) bouleverser
distracted *adj* bouleversé, éperdu
distraction [dɪsˈtrækʃən] *s* (*amusement*) distraction *f*; (*madness*) folie *f*
distraught [dɪsˈtrɔt] *adj* bouleversé

distress [dɪˈstrɛs] *s* détresse *f* ‖ *tr* affliger
distress′ call′ *s* signal *m* de détresse
distressing [dɪˈstrɛsɪŋ] *adj* affligeant, pénible
distribute [dɪˈstrɪbjut] *tr* distribuer
distribution [ˌdɪstrəˈbjuʃən] *s* distribution *f*
distributor [dɪˈstrɪbjətər] *s* distributeur *m*; (*for a product*) concessionnaire *mf*
district [ˈdɪstrɪkt] *s* contrée *f*, région *f*; (*of a city*) quartier *m*; (*administrative division*) district *m*, circonscription *f* ‖ *tr* diviser en districts
dis′trict attor′ney *s* procureur *m* de la République, procureur général
distrust [dɪsˈtrʌst] *s* défiance *f*, méfiance *f* ‖ *tr* se défier de, se méfier de
distrustful [dɪsˈtrʌstfəl] *adj* défiant
disturb [dɪsˈtʌrb] *tr* déranger, troubler; (*the peace*) perturber
disturbance [dɪsˈtʌrbəns] *s* dérangement *m*, trouble *m*; (*riot*) bagarre *f*, émeute *f*; (*in the atmosphere or magnetic field*) perturbation *f*
disuse [dɪsˈjus] *s* désuétude *f*
ditch [dɪtʃ] *s* fossé *m*; **to the last ditch** jusqu'à la dernière extrémité ‖ *tr* fossoyer; (slang) se défaire de ‖ *intr* (aer) faire un amerrissage forcé
ditch′ reed′ *s* (bot) laîche *f*
dither [ˈdɪðər] *s* agitation *f*; **to be in a dither** (coll) s'agiter sans but
dit·to [ˈdɪto] *s* (*pl* -tos) le même; (*on a duplicating machine*) copie *f*, duplicata *m* ‖ *adv* dito, de même, idem ‖ *tr* copier, reproduire
dit·ty [ˈdɪti] *s* (*pl* -ties) chansonnette *f*; **old ditty** (coll) vieux refrain *m*
diva [ˈdivə] *s* diva *f*
divan [ˈdaɪvæn], [dɪˈvæn] *s* divan *m*
dive [daɪv] *s* (*of a swimmer*) plongeon *m*; (*of a submarine*) plongée *f*; (aer) piqué *m*; (coll) gargote *f*, cabaret *m* borgne ‖ *v* (*pret & pp* **dived** or **dove** [dov]) *intr* plonger; (*said of submarine*) plonger, effectuer une plongée; (aer) piquer; **to dive for** (*e.g., pearls*) pêcher; **to dive into** (coll) piquer une tête dans
dive′-bomb′ *tr & intr* bombarder en piqué
dive′ bomb′er *s* bombardier *m* à piqué
dive′ bomb′ing *s* bombardement *m* en piqué, piqué *m*
diver [ˈdaɪvər] *s* plongeur *m*; (*person who works under water*) scaphandrier *m*; (orn) plongeon *m*
diverge [dɪˈvʌrdʒ] *intr* diverger
divers [ˈdaɪvərz] or **diverse** [dɪˈvʌrs] *adj* divers
diversi·fy [dɪˈvʌrsɪˌfaɪ] *v* (*pret & pp* **-fied**) *tr* diversifier ‖ *intr* se diversifier
diversion [dɪˈvʌrʒən] *s* (*relaxation*) distraction *f*, dérivatif *m*, diversion *f*; (*of traffic*) déviation *f*; (*rerouting*) dérivation *f*, détournement *m*; (mil) diversion
diversi·ty [dɪˈvʌrsɪti] *s* (*pl* -ties) diversité *f*
divert [dɪˈvʌrt] *tr* détourner; (*to entertain*) distraire, divertir
diverting [dɪˈvʌrtɪŋ] *adj* divertissant

divest [dɪ'vɛst] *tr* dépouiller; **to divest one- self of** se défaire de; (*property, holdings*) se déposséder de

divestment [dɪ'vɛstmənt] *s* dépossession *f*

divide [dɪ'vaɪd] *s* (geog) ligne *f* de partage ‖ *tr* diviser ‖ *intr* se diviser

dividend ['dɪvɪ,dɛnd] *s* dividende *m*

dividers [dɪ'vaɪdərz] *spl* compas *m* de me- sure

dividing [dɪ'vaɪdɪŋ] *s* division *f*; **dividing up** répartition *f*, partage *m*

divination [,dɪvɪ'neʃən] *s* divination *f*

divine [dɪ'vaɪn] *adj* divin ‖ *s* ecclésiastique *mf* ‖ *tr* deviner

diviner [dɪ'vaɪnər] *s* devin *m*

diving ['daɪvɪŋ] *s* plongeon *m*

div'ing bell' *s* cloche *f* à plongeur

div'ing board' *s* plongeoir *m*, tremplin *m*

div'ing suit' *s* scaphandre *m*

divin'ing rod' [dɪ'vaɪnɪŋ] *s* baguette *f* divi- natoire

divini·ty [dɪ'vɪnɪti] *s* (*pl* **-ties**) divinité *f*; (*subject of study*) théologie *f*; **the Divinity** Dieu *m*

divisible [dɪ'vɪzɪbəl] *adj* divisible

division [dɪ'vɪʒən] *s* division *f*

divisor [dɪ'vaɪzər] *s* diviseur *m*

divorce [dɪ'vors] *s* divorce *m*; **to get a divorce** divorcer; **to get a divorce from** (*husband or wife*) divorcer d'avec ‖ *tr* (*the married couple*) divorcer; (*husband or wife*) divorcer d'avec ‖ *intr* divorcer

divorcee [dɪvor'si] *s* divorcée *f*

divulge [dɪ'vʌldʒ] *tr* divulguer

dizziness ['dɪzɪnɪs] *s* vertige *m*

diz·zy ['dɪzi] *adj* (*comp* **-zier**; *super* **-ziest**) vertigineux; (coll) étourdi, farfelu; **to feel dizzy** avoir le vertige; **to make dizzy** étourdir

do [du] *v* (3d *pers* **does** [dʌz]; *pret* **did** [dɪd]; *pp* **done** [dʌn]; *ger* **doing** ['du·ɪŋ]) *tr* faire; (*homage; justice; a good turn*) rendre; **to do over** refaire; **to do up** emballer, envelopper ‖ *intr* faire; **how do you do?** enchanté de faire votre connais- sance; **that will do** c'est bien; en voilà assez; **that will never do** cela n'ira ja- mais; **to do away with** supprimer; **to do without** se passer de; **will I do?** suis-je bien comme ça?; **will it do?** ça va-t-il comme ça? ‖ *aux* used in English but not specifically expressed in French: 1) in questions, e.g., **do you speak French?** parlez-vous français?; 2) in negative sen- tences, e.g., **I do not speak French** je ne parle pas français; 3) as a substitute for another verb in an elliptical question, e.g., **I saw him. Did you?** je l'ai vu. L'avez-vous vu?; 4) for emphasis, e.g., **I do believe what you told me** je crois bien ce que vous m'avez dit; 5) in inversions after certain adverbs, e.g., **hardly did we finish when . . .** à peine avions-nous fini que . . .; 6) in an imperative entreaty, e.g., **do come in!** entrez donc!

do. *abbr* (**ditto**) d°

docile ['dasɪl] *adj* docile

dock [dak] *s* embarcadère *m*, quai *m*; (*area including piers and waterways*) bassin *m*, dock *m*; (bot) oseille *f*, patience *f*; (law) banc *m* des prévenus ‖ *tr* faire entrer au bassin; (*an animal*) couper la queue à; (*s.o.'s salary*) retrancher ‖ *intr* (naut) s'amarrer au quai

docket ['dakɪt] *s* (law) rôle *m*; **on the docket** pendant, non jugé; **to put on the docket** (coll) prendre en main

dock' hand' *s* docker *m*

docking ['dakɪŋ] *s* (rok) arrimage *m*, acco- stage *m*

dock' work'er *s* docker *m*

dock'yard' *s* chantier *m*

doctor ['daktər] *s* docteur *m*; (*woman*) femme *f* docteur; (med) docteur, médecin *m*; (med) doctoresse *f*; **Doctor Curie** (*professor, Ph.D., etc.*) Monsieur Curie; Madame Curie ‖ *tr* soigner; (*e.g., a chipped vase*) réparer; (*e.g., the facts*) falsifier ‖ *intr* pratiquer la médecine; (coll) être en traitement; (coll) prendre des mé- dicaments

doctorate ['daktərɪt] *s* doctorat *m*

Doc'tor of Laws' *s* docteur *m* en droit

doctrine ['daktrɪn] *s* doctrine *f*

document ['dakjəmənt] *s* document *m* ‖ ['dakjə,mɛnt] *tr* documenter

documenta·ry [,dakjə'mɛntəri] *adj* docu- mentaire ‖ *s* (*pl* **-ries**) documentaire *m*

documentation [,dakjəmɛn'teʃən] *s* docu- mentation *f*

doddering ['dadərɪŋ] *adj* tremblotant, gâteux

dodge [dadʒ] *s* écart *m*, esquive *f*; (coll) ruse *f*, truc *m* ‖ *tr* esquiver; (*a question*) éluder ‖ *intr* s'esquiver

dodge' ball' *s* chasse-ballon *m invar*

do·do ['dodo] *s* (*pl* **-dos** or **-does**) (orn) dronte *m*, dodo *m*; (coll) vieux fossile *m*, innocent *m*

doe [do] *s* (*of fallow deer*) daine *f*, (*hind*) biche *f*; (*roe doe*) chevrette *f*; (*of hare*) hase *f*; (*of rabbit*) lapine *f*

doe'skin' *s* peau *f* de daim

doff [daf] *tr* ôter

dog [dɔg] *s* chien *m*; **let sleeping dogs lie** il ne faut pas réveiller le chat qui dort; **to go to the dogs** (coll) se débaucher; (*said of business*) (coll) aller à vau-l'eau; **to put on the dog** (coll) faire de l'épate ‖ *v* (*pret & pp* **dogged**; *ger* **dogging**) *tr* poursuivre

dog'catch'er *s* employé *m* de la fourière

dog' days' *spl* canicule *f*

doge [dodʒ] *s* doge *m*

dog'face' *s* (slang) troufion *m*

dog'fight' *s* (aer) combat *m* aérien tour- noyant et violent; (coll) bagarre *f*

dogged ['dɔgɪd] *adj* tenace, obstiné

doggerel ['dɔgərəl] *s* vers *mpl* de mirliton

dog·gy ['dɔgi] *adj* (*comp* **-gier**; *super* **-giest**) canin, de chien ‖ *s* (*pl* **-gies**) toutou *m*

dog'gy bag' *s* emporte-restes *m*

dog'house' *s* niche *f* à chien; **in the dog- house** (slang) en disgrâce

dog′ in the man′ger s chien m du jardinier
dog′ Lat′in s latin m de cuisine
dogma [′dɔgmə] s dogme m
dogmatic [dɔg′mætɪk] adj dogmatique ‖ **dogmatics** s dogmatique f
dog′ pound′ s fourrière f
dog′ rac′ing s courses fpl de lévriers
dog′ rose′ s rose f des haies
dog's′-ear′ s corne f ‖ tr corner
dog′ show′ s exposition f canine
dog′ sled′ or **dog′ sledge′** s traîneau m à chiens
dog's′ life′ s vie f de chien
Dog′ Star′ s Canicule f
dog′ tag′ s (mil) plaque f d'identité
dog′-tired′ adj éreinté, fourbu
dog′tooth′ s (pl -teeth) dent f de chien, canine f; (archit, bot, mach) dent-de-chien f
dog′tooth vi′olet s dent-de-chien f
dog′trot′ s petit-trot m
dog′watch′ s (naut) petit quart m
dog′wood′ s cornouiller m
doi·ly [′dɔɪli] s (pl -lies) napperon m; (underplate) garde-nappe m
doings [′du·ɪŋz] spl actions fpl, œuvres fpl, faits et gestes mpl
do-it-yourself [,du·ɪt′ʃər′sɛlf] adj de bricolage ‖ s bricolage m
doldrums [′dɔldrəmz] spl marasme m; (naut) zone f des calmes
dole [dol] s aumône f; indemnité f de chômage ‖ tr—**to dole out** distribuer parcimonieusement
doleful [′dolfəl] adj dolent
doll [dɑl] s poupée f ‖ tr—**to be dolled up** (coll) être tiré à quatre épingles ‖ intr—**to doll up** (coll) se parer, s'endimancher
dollar [′dɑlər] s dollar m
dol·ly [′dɑli] s (pl -lies) (low movable frame) chariot m; (hand truck) diable m; (child's doll) poupée f; (mov, telv) travelling m
dolphin [′dɑlfɪn] s dauphin m
dolt [dolt] s nigaud m, lourdaud m
doltish [′doltɪʃ] adj nigaud, lourdaud
domain [do′men] s domaine m; (private estate) terres fpl, propriété f
dome [dom] s dôme m, coupole f
dome′ light′ s (aut) plafonnier m; (aut) (flashing, revolving outside light) gyrophare m
domestic [də′mɛstɪk] adj & s domestique mf
domesticate [də′mɛstɪ,ket] tr domestiquer
domesticity [,domɛs′tɪsɪti] s caractère m casanier; vie f familiale
domicile [′dɑmɪsɪl] s domicile m ‖ tr domicilier
dominance [′dɑmɪnəns] s prédominance f; (genetics) dominance f
dominant [′dɑmɪnənt] adj prédominant, dominant ‖ s (mus) dominante f
dominate [′dɑmɪ,net] tr & intr dominer
dominating [′dɑmɪ,netɪŋ] adj dominateur
domination [,dɑmɪ′neʃən] s domination f

domineer [,dɑmɪ′nɪr] intr se montrer tyrannique
domineering [,dɑmɪ′nɪrɪŋ] adj tyrannique, autoritaire
dominion [də′mɪnjən] s domination f; (of British Commonwealth) dominion m
domi·no [′dɑmɪ,no] s (pl -noes or -nos) domino m; **dominoes** sg (game) les dominos
don [dɑn] s (tutor) précepteur m ‖ v (pret & pp donned; ger donning) tr mettre, enfiler
donate [′donet] tr faire un don de
donation [do′neʃən] s don m, cadeau m
done [dʌn] adj fait; **are you done?** en avez-vous fini?; **it is done** (it is finished) c'en est fait; **to be done** (e.g., beefsteak) être cuit; **to have done with** en finir avec; **well done!** très bien!, bravo!, à la bonne heure!
done′ for′ adj (tired out) (coll) fourbu; (ruined) (coll) abattu; (out of the running) (coll) hors de combat; (dead) (coll) estourbi
donkey [′dɑŋki] s âne m, baudet m
donor [′donər] s donneur m; (law) donateur m
doodle [′dudəl] s (doodling) crayonnages mpl ‖ tr & intr griffonner
doom [dum] s condamnation f; destin m funeste ‖ tr condamner
dooms′day′ s jugement m dernier
door [dor] s porte f; (of a carriage or automobile) portière f; (one part of a double door) battant m; **behind closed doors** à huis clos; **to see to the door** conduire à la porte; **to show s.o. the door** éconduire qn, mettre qn à la porte
door′bell′ s timbre m, sonnette f
door′bell transform′er s transformateur m de sonnerie
door′bell wire′ s fil m sonnerie
door′ check′ s arrêt m de porte
door′frame′ s chambranle m, huisserie f, dormant m
door′head′ s linteau m
door′jamb′ s jambage m
door′knob′ s bouton m de porte
door′knock′er s heurtoir m, marteau m de porte
door′ latch′ s loquet m
door′man′ s (pl -men) portier m
door′mat′ s essuie-pieds m, paillasson m
door′nail′ s clou m de porte; **dead as a doornail** (coll) bien mort
door′post′ s montant m de porte
door′ scrap′er [′skrepər] s décrottoir m, grattepieds m
door′sill′ s seuil m, traverse f
door′step′ s seuil m, pas m
door′stop′ s entrebâilleur m, butoir m
door′-to-door′ adj porte-à-porte
door′-to-door′ sell′ing s démarchage m
door′way′ s porte f, portail m
dope [dop] s (varnish) enduit m; (slang) narcotique m, stupéfiant m; (information) (slang) renseignements mpl; (fool) (slang)

cornichon *m* ‖ *tr* enduire; (slang) doper, stupéfier; **to dope out** (slang) deviner, déchiffrer

dope′ fiend′ *s* (slang) toxicomane *mf*

dope′ ped′dler *s* trafiquant *m* de stupéfiants

dormant [′dɔrmənt] *adj* endormi, assoupi; latent; **to lie dormant** dormir

dor′mer win′dow [′dɔrmər] *s* lucarne *f*

dormito·ry [′dɔrmɪ,tori] *s* (*pl* **-ries**) (*room*) dortoir *m*; (*building*) pavillon *m* des étudiants, maison *f* de résidence, foyer *m* d'étudiants

dor′mitory com′plex *s* cité *f* universitaire

dor·mouse [′dɔr,maʊs] *s* (*pl* **-mice**) loir *m*

dosage [′dosɪdʒ] *s* (*administration*) dosage *m*; (*amount*) dose *f*; (*information on medicine bottle*) posologie *f*

dose [dos] *s* dose *f* ‖ *tr* donner en doses; donner un médicament à

dossier [′dɑsɪ,e] *s* dossier *m*

dot [dɑt] *s* point *m*; **on the dot** (coll) à l'heure tapante; pile, e.g., **at noon on the dot** à midi pile ‖ *v* (*pret & pp* **dotted**; *ger* **dotting**) *tr* (*to make with dots*) pointiller; **to dot one's i's** mettre les points sur les i

dotage [′dotɪdʒ] *s* radotage *m*

dotard [′dotərd] *s* gâteux *m*, gaga *m*

dote [dot] *intr* radoter; **to dote on** raffoler de

doting [′dotɪŋ] *adj* radoteur; (*loving to excess*) qui aime follement

dots′ and dash′es *spl* (telg) points et traits *mpl*

dot′ted line′ *s* ligne *f* pointillée, ligne hachée, pointillé *m*; **to sign on the dotted line** signer en bonne et due forme

double [′dʌbəl] *adj & adv* double, en deux, deux fois ‖ *s* double *m*; (cards) contre *m*; (*stunt man*) (mov) cascadeur *m*; **doubles** (tennis) double; **on the double!** (coll) dare-dare!, au trot!; **to play double or nothing** jouer à quitte ou double ‖ *tr* doubler; (cards) contrer; **to double up** plier en deux ‖ *intr* doubler; (cards) contrer; **to double back** faire un crochet; **to double up** se plier, se tordre

dou′ble-act′ing *adj* à double effet

dou′ble-bar′reled *adj* (*gun*) à deux coups

dou′ble bass′ [bes] *s* contrebasse *f*

dou′ble bed′ *s* grand lit *m*, lit à deux places

dou′ble-broil′er *s* bain-marie *m*

dou′ble-breast′ed *adj* croisé

dou′ble chin′ *s* double menton *m*

dou′ble cross′ *s* (slang) entourloupette *f*, double jeu *m*

dou′ble-cross′ *tr* (coll) doubler, rouler, faire une entourloupette à

dou′ble-cross′er *s* (slang) personne *f* double, faux jeton *m*

Dou′ble-Cros′tic [′krɒstɪk] *s* (trademark) chassé-croisé *m*

dou′ble date′ *s* partie *f* carrée, sortie *f* à quatre

dou′ble-deal′er *s* personne *f* double, homme *m* à deux visages

dou′ble-deal′ing *adj* hypocrite ‖ *s* duplicité *f*

dou′ble-deck′er *s* (*bed*) lits *mpl* superposés, lit gigognes, lit à deux étages; (*bus*) autobus *m* à deux étages; (*sandwich*) double sandwich *m*; (aer, naut) deux-ponts *m*

dou′ble-edged′ *adj* à deux tranchants, à double tranchant

double entendre [′dubəlɑn′tɑndrə] *s* expression *f* à double entente, mot *m* à double sens

dou′ble-en′try *adj* en partie double

dou′ble-faced′ *adj* à double face

dou′ble fea′ture *s* (mov) deux grands films *mpl*, double programme *m*

dou′ble-joint′ed *adj* désarticulé

dou′ble-lock′ *tr* fermer à double tour

dou′ble-park′ *tr* faire stationner en double file ‖ *intr* stationner en double file, se garer en double file

dou′ble room′ *s* chambre *f* à deux lits

dou′ble-spaced′ *adj* à l'interligne double, à double interligne

dou′ble stand′ard *s* code *m* de morale à deux aspects; **to have a double standard** avoir deux poids et deux mesures

doublet [′dʌblɪt] *s* (*close-fitting jacket*) pourpoint *m*; (*counterfeit stone; each of two words having the same origin*) doublet *m*

dou′ble-talk′ *s* (coll) non-sens *m*; (coll) paroles *fpl* creuses or ambiguës, mots *mpl* couverts

dou′ble time′ *s* (*for work*) salaire *m* double; (mil) pas *m* redoublé

doubleton [′dʌbəltən] *s* deux cartes *fpl* d'une couleur

dou′ble track′ *s* double piste *f*

doubling [′dʌblɪŋ] *s* doublement *m*

doubly [′dʌbli] *adv* doublement

doubt [daʊt] *s* doute *m*; **beyond a doubt** à n'en pas douter; **no doubt** sans doute ‖ *tr* douter de; **to doubt that** douter que; **to doubt whether** douter si ‖ *intr* douter

doubter [′daʊtər] *s* douteur *m*

doubtful [′daʊtfəl] *adj* douteux; indécis, hésitant

doubtless [′daʊtlɪs] *adv* sans doute

douche [duʃ] *s* douche *f*; (*instrument*) seringue *f* à lavement ‖ *tr* doucher ‖ *intr* se doucher

dough [do] *s* pâte *f*; (slang) fric *m*, blé *m*, beurre *m*; **big dough** (slang) grosse galette *f*

dough′boy′ *s* (coll) troufion *m*, biffin *m*; (*in the First World War*) poilu *m*

dough′nut′ *s* beignet *m*

dough·ty [′daʊti] *adj* (*comp* **-tier**; *super* **-tiest**) vaillant, preux

dough·y [′do·i] *adj* (*comp* **-ier**; *super* **-iest**) pâteux

dour [daʊr], [dʊr] *adj* (*severe*) austère; (*obstinate*) buté; (*gloomy*) mélancolique

douse [daʊs] *tr* tremper, arroser; (slang) éteindre

dove [dʌv] *s* colombe *f*

dovecote [′dʌv,kot] *s* pigeonnier *m*, colombier *m*

Dover ['dovər] s Douvres

dove'tail' s queue-d'aronde f, adent m ‖ tr assembler à queue-d'aronde, adenter; (fig) raccorder, opérer le raccord entre ‖ intr se raccorder

dove'tailed' adj à queue-d'aronde

dowager ['dɑu·ədʒər] s douairière f

dow·dy ['dɑudi] adj (comp **-dier**; super **-diest**) gauche, fagoté, mal habillé

dow·el ['dɑu·əl] s goujon m ‖ v (pret & pp **-eled** or **-elled**; ger **-eling** or **-elling**) tr goujonner

dower ['dɑu·ər] s (widow's portion) douaire m; (marriage portion) dot f; (natural gift) don m ‖ tr assigner un douaire à; doter

down [dɑun] adj bas; (train) descendant; (storage battery) épuisé; (tire) à plat; (sun) couché; (wind, sea, etc.) calmé; (blinds; prices) baissé; (stocks) en moins-value; (sad) abattu, triste ‖ s (on a bird) duvet m; (sand hill) dune f ‖ adv en bas, au bas, vers les bas; à terre; (south) au sud; **down!** (in elevator) on descend!, pour la descente!; **down from** du haut de; **down there** là-bas; **down to** jusqu'à; **down under** aux antipodes; **down with . . . !** à bas . . . !; for expressions like **to go down** descendre or **to pay down** payer comptant, see the verb ‖ prep en bas de; (along) le long de; (a stream) en descendant ‖ tr descendre, abattre; (to swallow) (coll) avaler

down'-and-out' adj décavé

down'beat' s (mus) temps m fort, frappé m, premier accent m

down'cast' adj abattu, baissé

down'fall' s chute f, ruine f

down'grade' adj (coll) descendant ‖ s descente f; **to be on the downgrade** déchoir ‖ adv en déclin ‖ tr déclasser

down'heart'ed adj abattu, découragé

down'hill' adj descendant ‖ adv—**to go downhill** aller en descendant; (fig) décliner

down' pay'ment s acompte m

down'pour' s déluge m, averse f

down'right' adj absolu, véritable ‖ adv tout à fait, absolument

down'stairs' adj rez-de-chaussée m ‖ adv en bas; **to go downstairs** descendre

down'stream' adv en aval

down'stroke' s (of piston) course f descendante; (in writing) jambage m

down'-to-earth' adj terre-à-terre

down'town' adj du centre ‖ s centre m ‖ adv en ville

down'trend' s tendance f à la baisse

downtrodden ['dɑun,trɑdən] adj opprimé

downward ['dɑunwərd] adj descendant ‖ adv en bas, en descendant

downwards ['dɑunwərdz] adv en bas, en descendant

down'wash' s (aer) air m déplacé

down·y ['dɑuni] adj (comp **-ier**; super **-iest**) duveteux; (velvety) velouté; (soft) mou, moelleux

dow·ry ['dɑuri] s (pl **-ries**) dot f

dowser ['dɑuzər] s sourcier m, hydroscope m

doze [doz] s petit somme m ‖ intr sommeiller; **to doze off** s'assoupir

dozen ['dʌzən] s douzaine f; **a dozen . . .** une douzaine de · · . ; **by the dozen** à la douzaine

D.P. abbr (**displaced person**) personne f déplacée

Dr. abbr (**Doctor**) Dʳ

drab [dræb] adj (comp **drabber**; super **drabbest**) gris ‖ s gris m

drach·ma ['drækmə] s (pl **-mas** or **-mae** [mi]) drachme f

draft [dræft] s (air current) courant m d'air; (pulling; current of air in chimney) tirage m; (sketch, outline) ébauche f; (of a letter, novel, etc.) brouillon m, premier jet m; (of a bill in Congress) projet m; (of a law) avant-projet m; (drink) trait m, gorgée f; (com) mandat m, traite f; (mil) conscription f; (naut) tirant m d'eau; **drafts** (game) dames fpl; **on draft** à la pression; **to be exempted from the draft** être exempté du service militaire ‖ tr (a document) rédiger, faire le brouillon de; (a bill in Congress) dresser; (a recruit) appeler sous les drapeaux; **to be drafted** être appelé sous les drapeaux

draft' beer' s bière f pression

draft' board' s conseil m de révision; commission f locale des conscriptions

draft' call' s appel m sous les drapeaux

draft' dodg'er ['dɑdʒər] s embusqué m, réfractaire mf

draftee [,dræf'ti] s appelé m (sous les drapeaux), conscrit m

draft' horse' s cheval m de trait

drafting ['dræftɪŋ] s dessin m industriel

draft'ing room' s bureau m d'études

drafts'man s (pl **-men**) dessinateur m; (man who draws up documents) rédacteur m

draft·y ['dræfti] adj (comp **-ier**; super **-iest**) plein de courants d'air

drag [dræg] s (net) drège f; (sledge or sled) traîneau m; (stone drag) fardier m; (brake) enrayure f; (impediment) entrave f; (aer) traînée f ‖ v (pret & pp **dragged**; ger **dragging**) tr traîner; (one's feet) traînasser; (a net) draguer; (a field) herser; **to drag down** entraîner; **to drag in** introduire de force; **to drag on** traîner en longueur; **to drag out** faire sortir de force ‖ intr traîner à terre; se traîner

drag'net' s traîneau m, chalut m

dragon ['drægən] s dragon m

drag'on·fly' s (pl **-flies**) demoiselle f, libellule f

dragoon [drə'gun] s dragon m ‖ tr tyranniser; forcer, contraindre

drain [dren] s (sewer) égout m; (pipe) tuyau m d'égout; (ditch) tranchée f d'écoulement; (source of continual expense) saignée f; (med) drain m ‖ tr (wet ground) drainer; (a glass or cup) vider entièrement; (a crankcase) vidanger; (s.o. of strength) épuiser; (med) drainer ‖ *intr* s'égoutter, s'écouler

drainage ['dreɪnɪdʒ] *s* drainage *m*

drain′ board′ *s* égouttoir *m*

drain′ cock′ *s* purgeur *m*

drain′ pipe′ *s* tuyau *m* d'écoulement, drain *m*

drain′ plug′ *s* bouchon *m* de vidange

drake [drek] *s* canard *m* mâle

dram [dræm] *s* (*weight*) drachme *m*; (*drink*) petit verre *f*, goutte *f*

drama ['drɑmə], ['dræmə] *s* drame *m*

dra′ma crit′ic *s* chroniqueur *m* dramatique

dra′ma review′ *s* avant-première *f*

dramatic [drə'mætɪk] *adj* dramatique ‖ **dramatics** *s* dramaturgie *f*, art *m* dramatique

dramatist ['dræmətɪst] *s* auteur *m* dramatique, dramaturge *mf*

dramatize ['dræmə,taɪz] *tr* dramatiser

drape [drep] *s* (*curtain*) rideau *m*; (*hang of a curtain, skirt, etc.*) drapement *m* ‖ *tr* draper, tendre; se draper dans

draper·y ['drepəri] *s* (*pl* **-ies**) draperie *f*; **draperies** rideaux *mpl*, tentures *fpl*

drastic ['dræstɪk] *adj* énergique, radical; (*laxative*) drastique

draught [dræft] *s* (*of fish*) coup *m* de filet; (*drink*) trait *m*, gorgée *f*; (naut) tirant *m* d'eau; **draughts** (*game*) dames *fpl*; **on draught** à la pression

draught′ beer′ *s* bière *f* pression

draught′board′ *s* damier *m*

draw [drɔ] *s* (*taking, drawing, pulling; in a fireplace*) tirage *m*; (*in a game or other contest*) partie *f* nulle, match *m* nul ‖ *v* (*pret* **drew** [dru]; *pp* **drawn** [drɔn]) *tr* tirer; (*a crowd*) attirer; (*a design*) dessiner; (*a card*) tirer; (*trumps*) faire tomber; (*a bow*) bander, tendre; (*water*) puiser; **to draw a conclusion** tirer une conséquence; **to draw aside** prendre à l'écart; **to draw blood** faire saigner; **to draw interest** porter intérêt; **to draw lots** tirer au sort; **to draw off** (*e.g., a liquid*) soutirer; **to draw out** (*a person*) faire parler; (*an activity*) prolonger, traîner; **to draw up** (*a list*) dresser; (*a plan*) rédiger; (naut) jauger ‖ *intr* tirer; dessiner; faire partie nulle, faire match nul; **to draw away** s'éloigner; **to draw back** reculer, se retirer; **to draw near** approcher; s'approcher de

draw′back′ *s* désavantage *m*, inconvénient *m*

draw′bridge′ *s* pont-levis *m*

drawee [,drɔ'i] *s* tiré *m*, accepteur *m*

drawer ['drɔ·ər] *s* dessinateur *m*; (com) tireur *m* ‖ [drɔr] *s* tiroir *m*; **drawers** caleçon *m*

drawing ['drɔ·ɪŋ] *s* (*sketch*) dessin *m*; (*in a lottery*) tirage *m*; **drawing off** tirage *m*

draw′ing board′ *s* planche *f* à dessin

draw′ing card′ *s* attrait *m*, attraction *f*

draw′ing room′ *s* salon *m*

draw′knife′ *s* (*pl* **-knives**) plane *f*

drawl [drɔl] *s* voix *f* traînante ‖ *tr* dire d'une voix traînante ‖ *intr* traîner la voix en parlant

drawn′ but′ter [drɔn] *s* beurre *m* fondu; sauce *f* blanche

drawn′ work′ *s* broderie *f* à fils tirés

dray [dre] *s* haquet *m*, charrette *f*; (*sledge*) fardier *m*, schlitte *f*

drayage ['dre·ɪdʒ] *s* charriage *m*, charroi *m*; frais *mpl* de transport

dray′ horse′ *s* cheval *m* de trait

dray′man *s* (*pl* **-men**) haquetier *m*

dread [drɛd] *adj* redoutable, terrible ‖ *s* terreur *f*, crainte *f* ‖ *tr* & *intr* redouter, craindre

dreadful ['drɛdfəl] *adj* épouvantable

dream [drim] *s* rêve *m*, songe *m*; (*fancy, illusion*) rêverie *f*, songerie *f* ‖ *v* (*pret* & *pp* **dreamed** or **dreamt** [drɛmt]) *tr*—**to dream up** rêver ‖ *intr* rêver, songer; **to dream of** (*future plans*) rêver à; (*s.o.*) rêver de

dreamer ['drimər] *s* rêveur *m*

dream′land′ *s* pays *m* des songes

dream′ world′ *s* monde *m* des rêves

dream·y ['drimi] *adj* (*comp* **-ier**; *super* **-iest**) rêveur; (slang) épatant

drear·y ['drɪri] *adj* (*comp* **-ier**; *super* **-iest**) triste, morne; monotone

dredge [drɛdʒ] *s* drague *f* ‖ *tr* draguer

dredger ['drɛdʒər] *s* dragueur *m*; (mach) drague *f*

dredging ['drɛdʒɪŋ] *s* dragage *m*

dregs [drɛgz] *spl* lie *f*

drench [drɛntʃ] *tr* tremper, inonder

dress [drɛs] *s* habillement *m*, costume *m*; (*woman's attire*) toilette *f*, mise *f*; (*woman's dress*) robe *f* ‖ *tr* habiller, vêtir; (*apply a dressing to*) panser; (culin) garnir; **to dress down** (coll) passer un savon à, chapitrer; **to dress up** parer; (*ranks*) (mil) aligner; **to get dressed** s'habiller ‖ *intr* s'habiller, se vêtir; (mil) s'aligner; **to be dressing** être à sa toilette; **to dress up** se parer

dress′ ball′ *s* bal *m* paré

dress′ cir′cle *s* corbeille *f*, premier balcon *m*

dress′ coat′ *s* frac *m*

dresser ['drɛsər] *s* coiffeuse *f*; commode *f* à miroir; (*sideboard*) dressoir *m*; **to be a good dresser** être recherché dans sa mise

dress′ form′ *s* mannequin *m*

dress′ goods′ *spl* étoffes *fpl* pour costumes

dressing ['drɛsɪŋ] *s* (*providing with clothes*) habillement *m*; (*for food*) assaisonnement *m*, sauce *f*; (*stuffing for fowl*) farce *f*; (*fertilizer*) engrais *m*; (*for a wound*) pansement *m*

dress′ing down′ *s* (coll) savon *m*, verte réprimande *f*, algarade *f*

dress′ing gown′ *s* peignoir *m*, robe *f* de chambre

dress′ing room′ *s* cabinet *m* de toilette, vestiaire *m*; (theat) loge *f*

dress′ing sta′tion *s* poste *m* de secours

dress′ing ta′ble *s* coiffeuse *f*, toilette *f*

dress'mak'er s couturière f
dress'mak'ing s couture f
dress'making estab'lishment s maison f de couture
dress' rehear'sal s répétition f en costume; **final dress rehearsal** répétition générale
dress' shield' s dessous-de-bras m
dress' shirt' s chemise f à plastron
dress' shop' s magasin m de modes
dress' suit' s habit m de cérémonie, tenue f de soirée
dress' tie' s cravate f de smoking, cravate-plastron f
dress' u'niform s (mil) grande tenue f
dress·y ['drɛsi] adj (comp -ier; super -iest) (coll) élégant, chic
dribble ['drɪbəl] s dégouttement m; (of child) bave f; (sports) dribble m || tr (sports) dribbler || intr dégoutter; (said of child) baver; (sports) dribbler
driblet ['drɪblɪt] s chiquet m; **in driblets** au compte-gouttes
dried' ap'ple [draɪd] s pomme f tapée
dried' beef' s viande f boucanée
dried' fig' s figue f sèche
dried' fruit' s fruit m sec
dried' pear' s poire f tapée
drier ['draɪ·ər] s (for clothes) séchoir m, sécheuse f; (for paint) siccatif m; (mach) sécheur m
drift [drɪft] s mouvement m, force f, poussée f; (of sand, snow) amoncellement m; (of meaning) sens m, direction f; (aer & naut) dérive f, dérivation f || intr aller à la dérive; (said of snow) s'amonceler; (aer, naut) dériver; (fig) se laisser aller, flotter
drift' ice' s glaces fpl flottantes
drift'wood' s bois m flotté
drill [drɪl] s (for metal, wood) foret m, mèche f; (machine) perforatrice f; (fabric) coutil m, treillis m; (furrow) sillon m; (agricultural implement) semoir m; (in school; on the drill ground) exercice m || tr instruire; (e.g., students) former, entraîner; (mach) forer; (mil) faire faire l'exercice à; **to drill s.th. into s.o.** seriner q.ch. à qn || intr faire l'exercice; forer
driller ['drɪlər] s foreur m
drill' field' or **drill' ground'** s terrain m d'exercice
drilling ['drɪlɪŋ] s (of metal; of an oil well) forage m; (dentistry) fraisage m
drill'mas'ter s moniteur m; (mil) instructeur m
drill' press' s foreuse f à colonnes
drink [drɪŋk] s boisson f, breuvage m; boire m, e.g., **food and drink** le boire et le manger || v (pret **drank** [dræŋk]; pp **drunk** [drʌŋk]) tr boire; (e.g., with a meal) prendre; **to drink down** boire d'un trait || intr boire; **to drink out of** (a glass) boire dans; (a bottle) boire à; **to drink to the health of** boire à la santé de
drinkable ['drɪŋkəbəl] adj buvable, potable
drinker ['drɪŋkər] s buveur m

drink'ing foun'tain s fontaine f à boire, borne-fontaine f
drink'ing song' s chanson f à boire
drink'ing trough' s abreuvoir m
drink'ing wa'ter s eau f potable
drip [drɪp] s (drop) goutte f; (dripping) égout m, dégouttement m; (person) (slang) cornichon m || v (pret & pp **dripped**; ger **dripping**) intr dégoutter, goutter
drip' cof'fee s café-filtre m
drip' cof'fee mak'er s cafetière f à filtre
drip'-dry' adj à séchage rapide; (label on shirt) repassage inutile
dripolator ['drɪpə,letər] s filtre m à café
drip' pan' s égouttoir m
dripping ['drɪpɪŋ] s ruissellement m; **drippings** graisse f de rôti
drive [draɪv] s (in an automobile) promenade f; (road) chaussée f; (vigor) énergie f, initiative f; (fund-raising) campagne f; (push forward) propulsion f; (aut) (point of power application to roadway) traction f; (golf) crossée f; (mach) transmission f; **to go for a drive** faire une promenade en auto || v (pret **drove** [drov]; pp **driven** ['drɪvən]) tr (an automobile, locomotive, etc.; an animal; a person in an automobile) conduire; (a nail) enfoncer; (a bargain) conclure; (the ball in a game) renvoyer, chasser; (to push, force) pousser, forcer; (to overwork) surmener; **to drive away** chasser; **to drive back** repousser; (e.g., in a car) reconduire; **to drive crazy** rendre fou; **to drive in** enfoncer; **to drive out** chasser; **to drive to despair** conduire au désespoir || intr conduire; **drive slowly** (public sign) marcher au pas; **to drive away** partir, démarrer; **to drive back** rentrer en auto; **to drive on** continuer sa route; **to drive out** sortir
drive'-in' s (motion-picture theater) cinéma m auto, ciné-park m; (restaurant) resto-route m
driv·el ['drɪvəl] s (slobber) bave f; (nonsense) bêtises fpl || v (pret **-eled** or **-elled**; ger **-eling** or **-elling**) intr baver; (to talk nonsense) radoter
driver ['draɪvər] s chauffeur m, conducteur m; (of a carriage) cocher m; (of a locomotive) mécanicien m; (of pack animals) toucheur m
driv'er's li'cense s permis m de conduire
drive' shaft' s arbre m d'entraînement
drive'way' s voie f de garage, sortie f de voiture
drive' wheel' s roue f motrice, roue de transmission
driv'ing school' s auto-école f
drizzle ['drɪzəl] s pluie f fine, bruine f || intr bruiner, brouillasser
droll [drol] adj drôle, drolatique
dromedar·y ['drɑmə,dɛri] s (pl -ies) dromadaire m
drone [dron] s (humming) bourdonnement m; (of plane or engine) vrombissement m, ronron m; (do-nothing) fainéant m; (aer) avion m téléguidé, avion sans pilote; (ent)

faux bourdon *m* ‖ *intr* bourdonner, ronronner

drool [drul] *intr* baver

droop [drup] *s* inclinaison *f* ‖ *intr* se baisser; (*to lose one's pep*) s'alanguir; (bot) languir

drooping ['drupɪŋ] *adj* languissant

drop [drɑp] *s* (*e.g., of water*) goutte *f*; (*fall*) chute *f*; (*slope*) précipice *m*; (*depth of drop*) hauteur *f* de chute; (*in price; in temperature*) baisse *f*; (*lozenge*) pastille *f*; (*of supplies from an airplane*) droppage *m*; **a drop in the bucket** une goutte d'eau dans la mer ‖ *v* (*pret & pp* **dropped**; *ger* **dropping**) *tr* laisser tomber; (*a curtain; the eyes, voice*) baisser; (*from an airplane*) lâcher; (*e.g., a name from a list*) omettre, supprimer; (*a remark*) glisser; (*a conversation; relations; negotiations*) cesser; (*anchor*) jeter, mouiller; (*an idea, a habit, etc.*) renoncer à; **to drop off** déposer ‖ *intr* tomber; se laisser tomber; baisser; cesser; **to drop in** entrer en passant; **to drop in on** faire un saut chez; **to drop off** se détacher; s'endormir; **to drop out of** (*to quit*) renoncer à, abandonner

drop′ cur′tain *s* rideau *m* d'entracte

drop′-cord light′ *s* baladeuse *f*

drop′ ham′mer *s* marteau-pilon *m*

drop′ kick′ *s* coup *m* tombé

drop′ leaf′ *s* abattant *m*

drop′light′ *s* lampe *f* suspendue

drop′out′ *s* raté *m*; **to become a dropout** abandonner les études

dropper ['drɑpər] *s* compte-gouttes *m*

dropsy ['drɑpsi] *s* hydropisie *f*

drop′ ta′ble *s* table *f* à abattants

dross [drɔs] *s* scories *mpl*, écume *f*

drought [draʊt] *s* sécheresse *f*

drove [drov] *s* (*of animals*) troupeau *m*; (*multitude*) foule *f*, flots *mpl*; **in droves** par bandes

drover ['drovər] *s* bouvier *m*

drown [draʊn] *tr* noyer; **to drown out** couvrir ‖ *intr* se noyer

drowse [drauz] *intr* somnoler, s'assoupir

drow·sy ['drauzi] *adj* (*comp* **-sier**; *super* **-siest**) somnolent

drub [drʌb] *v* (*pret & pp* **drubbed**; *ger* **drubbing**) *tr* flanquer une raclée à, rosser

drudge [drʌdʒ] *s* homme *m* de peine, piocheur *m*; **harmless drudge** (*e.g., who compiles dictionaries*) gratte-papier *m* inoffensif

drudger·y ['drʌdʒəri] *s* (*pl* **-ies**) corvée *f*, travail *m* pénible

drug [drʌg] *s* (*medicine*) produit *m* pharmaceutique, drogue *f*; (*narcotic*) stupéfiant *m*, drogue; **drug on the market** rossignol *m* ‖ *v* (*pret & pp* **drugged**; *ger* **drugging**) *tr* (*a person*) donner un stupéfiant à, stupéfier; (*food or drink*) ajouter un stupéfiant à

drug′ ad′dict *s* toxicomane *mf*, drogué *m*, intoxiqué *m*, camé *m*

drug′ addic′tion *s* toxicomanie *f*

drug′ deal′er *s* ravitailleur *m* en drogues; (slang) dealer *m*, vendeur *m* de mort, fourmi *f*

druggist ['drʌgɪst] *s* pharmacien *m*

drug′ hab′it *s* toxicomanie *f*, vice *m* des stupéfiants

drug′ push′er *s* revendeur *m* (de drogues); (slang) dealer *m*, vendeur *m* de mort, fourmi *f*

drug′store′ *s* pharmacie-bazar *f*, pharmacie *f*

drug′ traf′fic *s* trafic *m* des stupéfiants

druid ['dru·ɪd] *s* druide *m*

drum [drʌm] *s* (*cylinder; instrument of percussion*) tambour *m*; (*container for oil, gasoline, etc.*) bidon *m*; **to play the drum** battre du tambour ‖ *v* (*pret & pp* **drummed**; *ger* **drumming**) *tr* (*e.g., a march*) tambouriner; rassembler au son du tambour; **to drum into** fourrer dans; **to drum up customers** racoler des clients ‖ *intr* jouer du tambour; (*with the fingers*) tambouriner; (*on the piano*) pianoter

drum′ and bu′gle corps′ *s* clairons et tambours *mpl*, clique *f*

drum′beat′ *s* coup *m* de tambour

drum′fire′ *s* (mil) tir *m* nourri, feu *m* roulant

drum′head′ *s* peau *f* de tambour; (naut) noix *f*

drum′ ma′jor *s* tambour-major *m*

drummer ['drʌmər] *s* tambour *m*; (*salesman*) (coll) commis *m* voyageur

drum′stick′ *s* baguette *f* de tambour; (*of chicken*) (coll) cuisse *f*, pilon *m*

drunk [drʌŋk] *adj* ivre, soûl; **to get drunk** s'enivrer; **to get s.o. drunk** enivrer qn ‖ *s* (*person*) (coll) ivrogne *m*; (*state*) ivresse *f*; **to go on a drunk** (coll) se soûler

drunkard ['drʌŋkərd] *s* ivrogne *m*

drunken ['drʌŋkən] *adj* enivré

drunk′en driv′er *s* chauffeur *m* en état d'ivresse

drunk′en driv′ing *s* conduite *f* en état d'ivresse, ivresse *f* au volant, alcoolisme *m* au volant

drunkenness ['drʌŋkənnɪs] *s* ivresse *f*

dry [drai] *adj* (*comp* **drier**; *super* **driest**) sec; (*thirsty*) assoiffé; (*boring*) aride ‖ *s* (*pl* **drys**) (*prohibitionist*) antialcoolique *mf* ‖ *v* (*pret & pp* **dried**) *tr* sécher; (*the dishes*) essuyer ‖ *intr* sécher; **to dry up** se dessécher; (slang) se taire

dry′ bat′tery *s* pile *f* sèche; (*number of dry cells*) batterie *f* de piles

dry′ cell′ *s* pile *f* sèche

dry′-clean′ *tr* nettoyer à sec

dry′ clean′er *s* nettoyeur *m* à sec, teinturier *m*

dry′ clean′er's *s* teinturerie *f*

dry′ clean′ing *s* nettoyage *m* à sec

dry′ dock′ *s* cale *f* sèche, bassin *m* de radoub

dry′-eyed′ *adj* d'un œil sec

dry′ goods′ *spl* tissus *mpl*, étoffes *fpl*

dry′ ice′ *s* glace *f* sèche

dry′ land′ *s* terre *f* ferme

dry′ meas′ure *s* mesure *f* à grains

dryness ['draɪnɪs] *s* sécheresse *f*; (*e.g., of a speaker*) aridité *f*

dry′ nurse′ *s* nourrice *f* sèche

dry′ rot′ *s* carie *f* sèche

dry′ run′ *s* exercice *m* simulé, répétition *f*, examen *m* blanc

dry′ sea′son *s* saison *f* sèche

dry′ wash′ *s* blanchissage *m* sans repassage

dual ['d(j)u·əl] *adj* double ‖ *s* duel *m*

dub [dʌb] *s* (slang) balourd *m* ‖ *v* (*pret & pp* **dubbed**; *ger* **dubbing**) *tr* (*to nickname*) donner un sobriquet à; (*to knight*) donner l'accolade à, adouber; (*a tape recording or movie film*) doubler

dubbing ['dʌbɪŋ] *s* (mov) doublage *m*

dubious ['d(j)ubɪ·əs] *adj* (*undecided*) hésitant; (*questionable*) douteux

ducat ['dʌkət] *s* ducat *m*

duchess ['dʌtʃɪs] *s* duchesse *f*

duch·y ['dʌtʃi] *s* (*pl* **-ies**) duché *m*

duck [dʌk] *s* canard *m*; (*female*) cane *f*; (*motion*) esquive *f*; **ducks** (*trousers*) pantalon *m* de coutil ‖ *tr* (*the head*) baisser ‖ *intr* se baisser; **to duck out** (coll) s'esquiver

ducking ['dʌkɪŋ] *s* plongeon *m*, bain *m* forcé

duckling ['dʌklɪŋ] *s* caneton *m*; (*female*) canette *f*

ducks′ and drakes′ *s*—**to play at ducks and drakes** faire des ricochets sur l'eau; (fig) jeter son argent par les fenêtres

duck′-toed′ *adj* qui marche en canard

duct [dʌkt] *s* conduit *m*, canal *m*

duct′less glands′ ['dʌktlɪs] *spl* glandes *fpl* closes

duct′work′ *s* tuyauterie *f*, canalisation *f*

dud [dʌd] *s* (slang) obus *m* qui a raté, fusée *f* mouillée; (slang) raté *m*, navet *m*; **duds** (*clothes*) (coll) frusques *fpl*, nippes *fpl*

dude [d(j)ud] *s* poseur *m*, gommeux *m*

dude′ ranch′ *s* ranch *m* d'opérette

due [d(j)u] *adj* dû; (*note*) échéant; (*bill*) exigible; (*train, bus, person*) attendu; **due to** par suite de; **in due (and proper) form** en bonne forme, en règle, en bonne et due forme; **to fall due** venir à l'échéance; **when is the train due?** à quelle heure doit arriver le train? ‖ *s* dû *m*; **dues** cotisation *f*; **to pay one's dues** cotiser ‖ *adv* droit vers, e.g., **due north** droit vers le nord

due′ date′ *s* échéance *f*

duel ['d(j)u·əl] *s* duel *m*; **to fight a duel** se battre en duel ‖ *v* (*pret & pp* **dueled** or **duelled**; *ger* **dueling** or **duelling**) *intr* se battre en duel

duelist or **duellist** ['d(j)u·əlɪst] *s* duelliste *m*

duenna [d(j)u'ɛnə] *s* duègne *f*

dues′-pay′ing *adj* cotisant

duet [d(j)u'ɛt] *s* duo *m*

duke [d(j)uk] *s* duc *m*

dukedom ['d(j)ukdəm] *s* duché *m*

dull [dʌl] *adj* (*not sharp*) émoussé; (*color*) terne; (*sound; pain*) sourd; (*stupid*) lourd; (*business*) lent; (*boring*) ennuyeux; (*flat*) fade, insipide; **to become dull** s'émousser; (*said of senses*) s'engourdir ‖ *tr* (*a knife*) émousser; (*color*) ternir; (*sound; pain*) amortir; (*spirits*) hébéter, engourdir ‖ *intr* s'émousser; se ternir; s'amortir; s'engourdir

dullard ['dʌlərd] *s* lourdaud *m*, hébété *m*

dullness ['dʌlnɪs] *s* (*of knife*) émoussement *m*; (*e.g., of wits*) lenteur *f*

duly ['d(j)uli] *adv* dûment, justement

dumb [dʌm] *adj* (*lacking the power to speak*) muet; (coll) gourde, imbécile; **completely dumb** (coll) bouché à l'émeri; **to play dumb** (coll) feindre l'innocence

dumb′bell′ *s* (sports) haltère *m*; (slang) gourde *f*, imbécile *mf*

dumb′ crea′ture *s* animal *m*, brute *f*

dumb′wait′er *s* monte-plats *m*; (*serving table*) table *f* roulante

dumfound ['dʌm,faʊnd] *tr* abasourdir, ébahir

dum·my ['dʌmi] *adj* faux, factice ‖ *s* (*pl* **-mies**) (*dress form*) mannequin; (*in card games*) mort *m*; (*figurehead, straw man*) prête-nom *m*, homme *m* de paille; (*skeleton copy of a book or magazine*) maquette *f*; (*object put in place of the real thing*) simulacre *m*; (slang) bêta *m*, ballot *m*

dump [dʌmp] *s* (*pile of rubbish*) amas *m*, tas *m*; (*place*) dépotoir *m*; (mil) dépôt *m*; (slang) taudis *m*; **to be down in the dumps** (coll) avoir le cafard ‖ *tr* décharger, déverser; (*on rubbish pile*) jeter au rebut; (com) vendre en faisant du dumping

dumping ['dʌmpɪŋ] *s* (com) dumping *m*

dumpling ['dʌmplɪŋ] *s* dumpling *m*, boulette *f*

dump′ truck′ *s* tombereau *m*

dump·y ['dʌmpi] *adj* (*comp* **-ier**; *super* **-iest**) (*short and fat*) courtaud, trapu, tassé; (*shabby*) râpé, minable

dun [dʌn] *adj* isabelle ‖ *s* créancier *m* importun; (*demand for payment*) demande *f* pressante ‖ *v* (*pret & pp* **dunned**; *ger* **dunning**) *tr* (*for payment*) importuner, poursuivre

dunce [dʌns] *s* âne *m*, cancre *m*

dunce′ cap′ *s* bonnet *m* d'âne

dune [d(j)un] *s* dune *f*

dune′ bug′gy *s* autosable *m*

dung [dʌŋ] *s* fumier *m*

dungarees [,dʌŋgə'riz] *spl* pantalon *m* de treillis, treillis *m*, bleu *m*

dungeon ['dʌndʒən] *s* cachot *m*, cul-de-basse-fosse *m*; (*keep of castle*) donjon *m*

dung′hill′ *s* tas *m* de fumier

dunk [dʌŋk] *tr & intr* tremper

du·o ['d(j)u·o] *s* (*pl* **-os**) duo *m*

duode·num [,d(j)u·ə'dinəm] *s* (*pl* **-na** [nə]) duodénum *m*

dupe [d(j)up] *s* dupe *f*, dindon *m* de la farce ‖ *tr* duper, flouer, faire marcher

duplex ['d(j)uplɛks] *adj* double, duplex ‖ *s* (*apartment*) appartement *m* sur deux étages, duplex *m*; (*house*) maison *f* double

du′plex house′ *s* maison *f* double

duplicate [′d(j)uplɪkɪt] *adj* double ‖ *s* duplicata *m*, polycopie *f*; **in duplicate** en double, en duplicata ‖ [′d(j)uplɪ,ket] *tr* faire le double de, reproduire; (*on a machine*) polycopier, ronéocopier

du′plicating machine′ *s* duplicateur *m*

duplici·ty [d(j)u′plɪsɪti] *s* (*pl* **-ties**) duplicité *f*

durable [′d(j)ʊrəbəl] *adj* durable

duration [d(j)ʊ′reʃən] *s* durée *f*

duress [d(j)ʊ′rɛs] *s* contrainte *f*; emprisonnement *m*

during [′d(j)ʊrɪŋ] *prep* pendant

dusk [dʌsk] *s* crépuscule *m*; **at dusk** entre chien et loup

dust [dʌst] *s* poussière *f* ‖ *tr* (*to free of dust*) épousseter; (*to sprinkle with dust*) saupoudrer; **to dust off** épousseter

dust′ bowl′ *s* région *f* dénudée

dust′cloth′ *s* chiffon *m* à épousseter

dust′ cloud′ *s* nuage *m* de poussière

duster [′dʌstər] *s* (*made of feathers*) plumeau *m*; (*made of cloth*) chiffon *m*; (*overgarment*) cache-poussière *m*

dust′ jack′et *s* protège-livre *m*, couvre-livre *m*, liseuse *f*

dust′pan′ *s* pelle *f* à poussière, ramasse-poussière *m invar*

dust′ rag′ *s* chiffon *m* à épousseter

dust′ storm′ *s* tempête *f* de poussière

dust·y [′dʌsti] *adj* (*comp* **-ier**; *super* **-iest**) poussiéreux; (*color*) cendré

Dutch [dʌtʃ] *adj* hollandais, néerlandais; (slang) allemand ‖ *s* (*language*) hollandais *m*, néerlandais *m*; (slang) allemand *m*; **in Dutch** (slang) en disgrâce; **the Dutch** les Hollandais *mpl*, les Néerlandais *mpl*; (slang) les Allemands *mpl*; **we will**

go Dutch (coll) chacun paiera son écot

Dutch′man *s* (*pl* **-men**) Hollandais *m*, Néerlandais *m*; (slang) Allemand *m*

Dutch′ treat′ *s* —**to have a Dutch treat** (coll) faire suisse, payer son écot

dutiable [′d(j)utɪ·əbəl] *adj* soumis aux droits de douane

dutiful [′d(j)utɪfəl] *adj* respectueux, soumis, plein d'égards

du·ty [′d(j)uti] *s* (*pl* **-ties**) devoir *m*; **duties** fonctions *fpl*; (*taxes, customs*) droits *mpl*; **to be off duty** ne pas être de service, avoir quartier libre; **to be on duty** être de service, être de garde; **to have the duty to** avoir pour devoir de

du′ty-free′ *adj* exempt de droits

du′ty-free shop′ *s* boutique *f* franche

dwarf [dwɔrf] *adj* & *s* nain *m* ‖ *tr* & *intr* rapetisser

dwell [dwɛl] *v* (*pret* & *pp* **dwelled** or **dwelt** [dwɛlt]) *intr* demeurer; **to dwell on** appuyer sur

dwelling [′dwɛlɪŋ] *s* demeure *f*, habitation *f*

dwell′ing house′ *s* maison *f* d'habitation

dwindle [′dwɪndəl] *intr* diminuer; **to dwindle away** s'affaiblir

dye [daɪ] *s* teinture *f* ‖ *v* (*pret* & *pp* **dyed**; *ger* **dyeing**) *tr* teindre

dyed′-in-the-wool′ *adj* intransigeant

dyeing [′daɪ·ɪŋ] *s* teinture *f*

dyer [′daɪ·ər] *s* teinturier *m*

dying [′daɪ·ɪŋ] *adj* mourant, moribond

dynamic [daɪ′næmɪk], [dɪ′næmɪk] *adj* dynamique ‖ **dynamics** *s* dynamique *f*

dynamite [′daɪnə,maɪt] *s* dynamite *f* ‖ *tr* dynamiter

dyna·mo [′daɪnə,mo] *s* (*pl* **-mos**) dynamo *f*

dynas·ty [′daɪnəsti] *s* (*pl* **-ties**) dynastie *f*

dysentery [′dɪsən,tɛri] *s* dysenterie *f*

dyspepsia [dɪs′pɛpsɪ·ə] *s* dyspepsie *f*

E

E, e [i] *s* V^e lettre de l'alphabet

each [itʃ] *adj indef* chaque ‖ *pron indef* chacun; **each other** nous, se; l'un l'autre; **to each other** l'un à l'autre ‖ *adv* chacun; (*apiece*) pièce, la pièce

eager [′igər] *adj* ardent, empressé; **eager for** avide de; **to be eager to** brûler de, désirer ardemment

ea′ger bea′ver *s* bûcheur *m*, mouche *f* du coche

eagerness [′igərnɪs] *s* ardeur *f*, empressement *m*

eagle [′igəl] *s* aigle *m*

ea′gle-eyed′ *adj* à l'œil d'aigle

ea′gle ray′ *s* (ichth) aigle *m* de mer

eaglet [′iglɪt] *s* aiglon *m*

ear [ɪr] *s* oreille *f*; (*of corn or wheat*) épi *m*; **to box s.o.'s ears** frotter les oreilles à qn;

to prick up one's ears dresser l'oreille; **to turn a deaf ear** faire la sourde oreille ‖ *intr* (*said of grain*) épier

ear′ache′ *s* douleur *m* d'oreille

ear′drop′ *s* pendant *m* d'oreille

ear′drum′ *s* tympan *m*

ear′flap′ *s* lobe *m* de l'oreille; (*on a cap*) protège-oreilles *m*

earl [ʌrl] *s* comte *m*

earldom [′ʌrldəm] *s* comté *m*

ear·ly [′ʌrli] (*comp* **-lier**; *super* **-liest**) *adj* primitif; (*first in a series*) premier; (*occurring in the near future*) prochain; (*in the morning*) matinal; (*ahead of time*) en avance; **at an early age** dès l'enfance ‖ *adv* de bonne heure, tôt; anciennement; **as early as** dès; **earlier** plus tôt, de meilleure heure

ear'ly bird' *s* matinal *m*

ear'ly mass' *s* première messe *f*

ear'ly-morn'ing *adj* matinal

ear'ly retire'ment *s* retraite *f* anticipée

ear'ly ris'er *s* matinal *m*

ear'ly-ris'ing *adj* matineux, matinal

ear'mark' *s* marque *f*, cachet *m* ‖ *tr* (*animals*) marquer à l'oreille; (*e.g., money*) spécialiser; **to earmark for** affecter à, assigner à

ear'muff' *s* couvre-oreille *m*

earn [ʌrn] *tr* gagner; (*to get as one's due*) mériter; (*interest*) rapporter

earnest [ˈʌrnɪst] *adj* sérieux; **in earnest** sérieusement ‖ *s* gage *m*; (com) arrhes *fpl*

earn'ing pow'er *s* (*person*) capacité *f* de gain; (*stock*) rentabilité *f*

earnings [ˈʌrnɪŋz] *spl* (*wages*) gages *mpl*; (*profits*) profit *m*, bénéfices *mpl*

ear'phone' *s* écouteur *m*; **earphones** casque *m*, écouteurs

ear'ring' *s* boucle *f* d'oreille

ear'split'ting *adj* assourdissant

earth [ʌrθ] *s* terre *f*; **to come down to earth** retomber des nues; **where on earth . . .?** où diable . . .?

earthen [ˈʌrθən] *adj* de terre, en terre

ear'then·ware' *s* faïence *f*

earthly [ˈʌrθli] *adj* terrestre

earth'man' *s* (*pl* **men**) terrien *m*

earth'quake' *s* tremblement *m* de terre

earth'work' *s* terrassement *m*

earth'worm' *s* lombric *m*, ver *m* de terre

earth·y [ˈʌrθi] *adj* (*comp* **-ier**; *super* **-iest**) terreux; (*worldly*) mondain; (*unrefined*) grossier, terre à terre

ear'trum'pet *s* cornet *m* acoustique

ease [iz] *s* aise *f*; (*readiness, naturalness*) désinvolture *f*; (*comfort, well-being*) bien-être *m*, tranquillité *f*; **at ease** tranquille; (mil) au repos; **to take one's ease** prendre ses aises; **with ease** facilement ‖ *tr* faciliter; (*a burden*) alléger; (*e.g., one's mind*) calmer, apaiser; (*to let up on*) ralentir ‖ *intr* se calmer, s'apaiser

easel [ˈizəl] *s* chevalet *m*

easement [ˈizmənt] *s* (law) servitude *f*

easily [ˈizɪli] *adv* facilement, aisément; (*certainly*) sans doute

easiness [ˈizɪnɪs] *s* facilité *f*; (*of manner*) désinvolture *f*, insouciance *f*

east [ist] *adj* & *s* est *m* ‖ *adv* à l'est, vers l'est

Easter [ˈistər] *s* Pâques *m*; **Happy Easter!** Joyeuses Pâques!

East'er egg' *s* œuf *m* de Pâques

East'er Mon'day *s* lundi *m* de Pâques

eastern [ˈistərn] *adj* oriental, de l'est

East'ern Stan'dard Time' *s* l'heure *f* de l'Est

East'ern Town'ships *spl* (*in Canada*) Cantons *mpl* de l'Est

eastward [ˈistwərd] *adv* vers l'est

eas·y [ˈizi] *adj* (*comp* **-ier**; *super* **-iest**) facile; (*easygoing*) aisé, désinvolte; **it's not easy to** + *inf* ce n'est pas commode à + *inf* ‖ *adv* (coll) facilement; (coll) lente-

ment; **to take it easy** (coll) en prendre à son aise

eas'y chair' *s* fauteuil *m*, bergère *f*

eas'y·go'ing *adj* insouciant, nonchalant, commode à vivre

eas'y mark' *s* jobard *m*

eas'y pay'ments *spl* facilités *fpl* de paiement

eat [it] *v* (*pret* **ate** [et]; *pp* **eaten** [ˈitən]) *tr* manger; **to eat away** ronger ‖ *intr* manger

eatable [ˈitəbəl] *adj* comestible

eat'ing ap'ple *s* pomme *f* à couteau

eaves [ivz] *spl* avant-toits *mpl*

eaves'drop' *v* (*pret* & *pp* **-dropped**; *ger* **-dropping**) *intr* écouter à la porte

ebb [ɛb] *s* reflux *m*, baisse *f* ‖ *intr* refluer, baisser; **to ebb and flow** monter et baisser, fluer et refluer

ebb' and flow' *s* flux et reflux *m*

ebb' tide' *s* marée *f* descendante, jusant *m*

ebon·y [ˈɛbəni] *s* (*pl* **-ies**) ébène *f*; (*tree*) ébénier *m*

ebullient [ɪˈbʌljənt] *adj* bouillonnant; (fig) enthousiaste, exubérant

eccentric [ɛkˈsɛntrɪk] *adj* excentrique ‖ *s* (*odd person*) excentrique *mf*; (*device*) excentrique *m*

eccentrici·ty [ˌɛksɛnˈtrɪsɪti] *s* (*pl* **-ties**) excentricité *f*

ecclesiastic [ɪˌkliziˈæstɪk] *adj* & *s* ecclésiastique *m*

echelon [ˈɛʃəˌlɑn] *s* échelon *m* ‖ *tr* (mil) échelonner

ech·o [ˈɛko] *s* (*pl* **-oes**) écho *m* ‖ *tr* répéter ‖ *intr* faire écho

eclectic [ɛkˈlɛktɪk] *adj* & *s* éclectique *mf*

eclipse [ɪˈklɪps] *s* éclipse *f* ‖ *tr* éclipser

eclogue [ˈɛklɔg] *s* églogue *f*

ecology [ɪˈkɑlədʒi] *s* écologie *f*

economic [ˌikəˈnɑmɪk] *adj* économique ‖ **economics** *s* économique *f*

economical [ˌikəˈnɑmɪkəl] *adj* économe

economize [ɪˈkɑnəˌmaɪz] *tr* & *intr* économiser

econo·my [ɪˈkɑnəmi] *s* (*pl* **-mies**) économie *f*

ecsta·sy [ˈɛkstəsi] *s* (*pl* **-sies**) extase *f*

ecstatic [ɛkˈstætɪk] *adj* & *s* extatique *mf*

Ecuador [ˈɛkwəˌdɔr] *s* l'Équateur *m*

ecumenic(al) [ˌɛkjəˈmɛnɪk(əl)] *adj* œcuménique

eczema [ˈɛksɪmə] *s* eczéma *m*

edema [ɪˈdimə] *s* (pathol) œdème *m*

ed·dy [ˈɛdi] *s* (*pl* **-dies**) tourbillon *m* ‖ *v* (*pret* & *pp* **-died**) *intr* tourbillonner

edelweiss [ˈedəlˌvaɪs] *s* edelweiss *m*, fleur *f* de neige

Eden [ˈidən] *s* (fig) éden *m*

edge [ɛdʒ] *s* bord *m*; (*of a knife, sword, etc.*) fil *m*, tranchant *m*; (*of a field, forest, etc.; of a strip of cloth*) lisière *f*; (slang) avantage *m*; **on edge** de chant; (*nervous*) énervé, crispé; **to be on edge** avoir les nerfs à fleur de peau; **to have the edge on** (coll) enfoncer; **to set the teeth on edge** agacer les dents ‖ *tr* border; (*to sharpen*) affiler, aiguiser ‖ *intr* s'avancer de biais;

to edge away s'écarter peu à peu; **to edge in** se glisser parmi or dans
edge′ways′ adv de côté, de biais
edging [ˈɛdʒɪŋ] s bordure f
edg·y [ˈɛdʒi] adj (comp **-ier**; super **-iest**) (nervous) crispé, irritable
edible [ˈɛdɪbəl] adj comestible
edict [ˈidɪkt] s édit m
edification [ˌɛdɪfɪˈkeʃən] s édification f
edifice [ˈɛdɪfɪs] s édifice m
edi·fy [ˈɛdɪˌfaɪ] v (pret & pp **-fied**) tr édifier
edifying [ˈɛdɪˌfaɪ·ɪŋ] adj édifiant
edit [ˈɛdɪt] tr préparer la publication de; (e.g., a newspaper) diriger, rédiger; (a text) éditer
edition [ɪˈdɪʃən] s édition f
editor [ˈɛdɪtər] s (of newspaper or magazine) rédacteur m; (of manuscript) éditeur m; (of feature or column) chroniqueur m, courriériste mf
editorial [ˌɛdɪˈtɔrɪ·əl] adj & s éditorial m
edito′rial of′fice s rédaction f
edito′rial pol′icy s ligne f politique
edito′rial staff′ s rédaction f
ed′itor in chief′ s rédacteur m en chef
educate [ˈɛdʒʊˌket] tr instruire, éduquer
educated adj cultivé, instruit
education [ˌɛdʒʊˈkeʃən] s éducation f, instruction f
educational [ˌɛdʒʊˈkeʃənəl] adj éducatif, éducateur
educa′tional tel′evision s télé-enseignement m, télévision f éducative, télévision scolaire
educator [ˈɛdʒʊˌketər] s éducateur m
eel [il] s anguille f
ee·rie or **ee·ry** [ˈiri] adj (comp **-rier**; super **-riest**) mystérieux, spectral
efface [ɪˈfes] tr effacer
effect [ɪˈfɛkt] s effet m; **in effect** en fait, effectivement; **to be in effect** être en vigueur; **to feel the effects of** se ressentir de; **to go into effect, to take effect** prendre effet; (said of law) entrer en vigueur ‖ tr effectuer, mettre à exécution
effective [ɪˈfɛktɪv] adj efficace; (actually in effect) en vigueur; (striking) impressionnant; **to become effective** produire son effet; (to go into effect) entrer en vigueur
effectual [ɪˈfɛktʃʊ·əl] adj efficace
effectuate [ɪˈfɛktʃʊˌet] tr effectuer
effeminacy [ɪˈfɛmɪnəsi] s effémination f
effeminate [ɪˈfɛmɪnɪt] adj efféminé; **to become effeminate** s'efféminer
effervesce [ˌɛfərˈvɛs] intr être en effervescence
effervescent [ˌɛfərˈvɛsənt] adj effervescent
effete [ɪˈfit] adj stérile, épuisé
efficacious [ˌɛfɪˈkeʃəs] adj efficace
efficacy [ˈɛfɪkəsi] s efficacité f
efficien·cy [ɪˈfɪʃənsi] s (pl **-cies**) efficacité f; (of business) efficience f; (of machine) rendement m; (of person) compétence f
effi′ciency ex′pert s ingénieur m en organisation

efficient [ɪˈfɪʃənt] adj efficace; (of machine) efficient, de bon rendement; (of person) efficient, compétent
effi·gy [ˈɛfɪdʒi] s (pl **-gies**) effigie f
effort [ˈɛfərt] s effort m
effronter·y [ɪˈfrʌntəri] s (pl **-ies**) effronterie f
effusion [ɪˈfjuʒən] s effusion f
effusive [ɪˈfjusɪv] adj démonstratif; **to be effusive in** se répandre en
e.g. abbr (Lat: **exempli gratia** for example) par ex., ex.
egg [ɛg] s œuf m; **eggs and bacon** œufs mpl au bacon; **good (bad) egg** (person) (slang) brave (sale) type; **to put all one's eggs in one basket** mettre tous ses œufs dans le même panier ‖ tr—**to egg on** (coll) pousser, inciter
egg′beat′er s fouet m, batteur m à œufs
egg′cup′ s coquetier m
egg′head′ s (slang) intellectuel m
eggnog [ˈɛgˌnɑg] s lait m de poule
egg′plant′ s aubergine f
egg′ poach′er s pocheuse f
egg′shell′ s coquille f d'œuf
egg′ white′ s blanc m d'œuf
egoism [ˈigo͜ɪzəm] s égoïsme m
egoist [ˈigo·ɪst] s égoïste mf
egotism [ˈigotɪzəm] s égotisme m
egotist [ˈigotɪst] s égotiste mf
egregious [ɪˈgridʒəs] adj insigne, notoire
egress [ˈigrɛs] s sortie f, issue f
egret [ˈigrɛt] s aigrette f
Egypt [ˈidʒɪpt] s Égypte f; l'Égypte
Egyptian [ɪˈdʒɪpʃən] adj égyptien ‖ s Égyptien m
ei′der down′ [ˈaɪdər] s édredon m
ei′der duck′ s eider m
eight [et] adj & pron huit ‖ s huit m; (group of eight) huitaine f; **about eight** une huitaine de; **eight o'clock** huit heures
eight′ball′ s—**behind the eightball** (coll) dans le pétrin
eighteen [ˈetˈtin] adj, pron, & s dix-huit m
eighteenth [ˈetˈtinθ] adj & pron dix-huitième (masc, fem); **the Eighteenth** dix-huit, e.g., **John the Eighteenth** Jean dix-huit ‖ s dix-huitième m; **the eighteenth** (in dates) le dix-huit
eighth [etθ] adj & pron huitième (masc, fem); **the Eighth** huit, e.g., **John the Eighth** Jean huit ‖ s huitième m; **the eighth** (in dates) le huit
eightieth [ˈetɪ·ɪθ] adj & pron quatre-vingtième (masc, fem) ‖ s quatre-vingtième m
eigh·ty [ˈeti] adj & pron quatre-vingts ‖ s (pl **-ties**) quatre-vingts m
eight′y-first′ adj & pron quatre-vingt-unième (masc, fem) ‖ s quatre-vingt-unième m
eight′y-one′ adj, pron, & s quatre-vingt-un m
either [ˈiðər], [ˈaɪðər] adj & pron indef l'un ou l'autre; l'un et l'autre; **on either side** de chaque côté ‖ adv—**not either** non plus ‖ conj—**either . . . or** ou

. . . ou, soit . . . soit, ou bien . . . ou bien

ejaculate [ɪ'dʒækjə,let] *tr & intr* crier; (physiol) éjaculer

eject [ɪ'dʒɛkt] *tr* éjecter; (*to evict*) expulser, chasser

ejection [ɪ'dʒɛkʃən] *s* éjection *f*; (*eviction*) expulsion *f*

ejec'tion seat' *s* (aer) siège *m* éjectable

eke [ik] *tr*—**to eke out** gagner avec difficulté

elaborate [ɪ'læbərɪt] *adj* élaboré, soigné; (*ornate*) orné, travaillé; (*involved*) compliqué, recherché ‖ [ɪ'læbə,ret] *tr* élaborer ‖ *intr*—**to elaborate on** or **upon** donner des détails sur

elapse [ɪ'læps] *intr* s'écouler

elastic [ɪ'læstɪk] *adj & s* élastique *m*

elasticity [,ilæs'tɪsɪti] *s* élasticité *f*

elated [ɪ'letɪd] *adj* transporté, exalté

elation [ɪ'leʃən] *s* transport *m*, exultation *f*

elbow ['ɛlbo] *s* coude *m*; **at one's elbow** à portée de la main; **to rub elbows with** coudoyer ‖ *tr* coudoyer; **to elbow one's way** se frayer un chemin à coups de coude ‖ *intr* jouer des coudes

el'bow grease' *s* (coll) huile *f* de coude

el'bow·room' *s* espace *m*; **to have elbow-room** avoir ses coudées franches

elder ['ɛldər] *adj* aîné, plus âgé ‖ *s* aîné *m*; (*senior*) doyen *m*; (bot) sureau *m*; (eccl) ancien *m*

el'der·ber'ry *s* (*pl* **-ries**) sureau *m*; (*berry*) baie *f* de sureau

elderly ['ɛldərli] *adj* vieux, âgé

eld'er states'man *s* vétéran *m* de la politique

eldest ['ɛldɪst] *adj* (l')aîné, (le) plus âgé

elect [ɪ'lɛkt] *adj* élu ‖ *s*—**the elect** les élus *mpl* ‖ *tr* élire

election [ɪ'lɛkʃən] *s* élection *f*

electioneer [ɪ,lɛkʃə'nɪr] *intr* faire la campagne électorale, solliciter des voix

elective [ɪ'lɛktɪv] *adj* électif; (*optional*) facultatif ‖ *s* matière *f* à option

elec'toral col'lege [ɪ'lɛktərəl] *s* collège *m* électoral

electorate [ɪ'lɛktərɪt] *s* corps *m* électoral, électeurs *mpl*, votants *mpl*

electric(al) [ɪ'lɛktrɪk(əl)] *adj* électrique

elec'trical engineer' *s* ingénieur *m* électricien

elec'trical engineer'ing *s* technique *f* électrique

elec'tric blan'ket *s* couverture *f* chauffante

elec'tric chair' *s* chaise *f* électrique

elec'tric clothes' dri'er *s* séchoir *m* électrique

elec'tric eel' *s* gymnote *m*

elec'tric eye' *s* cellule *f* photo-électrique

elec'tric fan' *s* ventilateur *m* électrique

elec'tric heat'er *s* radiateur *m* électrique

electrician [,ɛlɛk'trɪʃən] *s* électricien *m*

electricity [,ɛlɛk'trɪsɪti] *s* électricité *f*

elec'tric light' *s* lampe *f* électrique

elec'tric me'ter *s* compteur *m* de courant

elec'tric mix'er *s* batteur *m* électrique

elec'tric per'colator *s* cafetière *f* électrique

elec'tric range' *s* cuisinière *f* électrique

elec'tric shav'er *s* rasoir *m* électrique

elec'tric shock' treat'ment *s* (med) électrochoc *m*

elec'tric tim'er *s* prise *f* de courant programmatrice

electri·fy [ɪ'lɛktrɪ,faɪ] *v* (*pret & pp* **-fied**) *tr* (*to provide with electric power*) électrifier; (*to communicate electricity to; to thrill*) électriser

elec·tro [ɪ'lɛktro] *s* (*pl* **-tros**) électrotype *m*

electrocute [ɪ'lɛktrə,kjut] *tr* électrocuter

electrode [ɪ'lɛktrod] *s* électrode *f*

electrolysis [,ɛlɛk'trɑlɪsɪs] *s* électrolyse *f*

electrolyte [ɪ'lɛktrə,laɪt] *s* électrolyte *m*

elec'tro·mag'net *s* électro-aimant *m*

elec'tro·magnet'ic *adj* électromagnétique

electron [ɪ'lɛktrɑn] *s* électron *m*

elec'tron gun' *s* canon *m* à électrons

electronic [,ɛlɛk'trɑnɪk] *adj* électronique ‖ **electronics** *s* électronique *f*

elec'tron mi'croscope *s* microscope *m* électronique

electroplate [ɪ'lɛktrə,plet] *tr* galvaniser

elec'tro·type' *s* électrotype *m* ‖ *tr* électrotyper

elegance ['ɛlɪgəns] *s* élégance *f*

elegant ['ɛlɪgənt] *adj* élégant

elegiac [,ɛlɪ'dʒaɪ·æk] *adj* élégiaque

ele·gy ['ɛlɪdʒi] *s* (*pl* **-gies**) élégie *f*

element ['ɛlɪmənt] *s* élément *m*

elementary [,ɛlɪ'mɛntəri] *adj* élémentaire

elephant ['ɛlɪfənt] *s* éléphant *m*

elevate ['ɛlɪ,vet] *tr* élever

elevated *adj* élevé; (*style*) soutenu; (*train, railway, etc*) aérien

el'evated rail'way *s* métro *m* aérien

elevation [,ɛlɪ'veʃən] *s* élévation *f*

elevator ['ɛlɪ,vetər] *s* ascenseur *m*; (*for freight*) monte-charge *m*; (*for hoisting grain*) élévateur *m*; (*warehouse for storing grain*) silo *m* à céréales; (aer) gouvernail *m* d'altitude, gouvernail de profondeur

el'evator shoes' *spl* souliers *mpl* compensés

eleven [ɪ'lɛvən] *adj & pron* onze ‖ *s* onze *m*; **eleven o'clock** onze heures

eleventh [ɪ'lɛvənθ] *adj & pron* onzième (*masc, fem*); **the Eleventh** onze, e.g., **John the Eleventh** Jean onze ‖ *s* onzième *m*; **the eleventh** (*in dates*) le onze

elev'enth hour' *s* dernier moment *m*

elf [ɛlf] *s* (*pl* **elves** [ɛlvz]) elfe *m*

elicit [ɪ'lɪsɪt] *tr* (*e.g., a smile*) provoquer, faire sortir; (*e.g., help*) obtenir

elide [ɪ'laɪd] *tr* élider

eligible ['ɛlɪdʒɪbəl] *adj* éligible; (*e.g., bachelor*) sortable

eliminate [ɪ'lɪmɪ,net] *tr* éliminer

elision [ɪ'lɪʒən] *s* élision *f*

elite [e'lit] *s* élite *f*

elk [ɛlk] *s* élan *m*

ellipse [ɪ'lɪps] *s* (geom) ellipse *f*

ellip·sis [ɪ'lɪpsɪs] *s* (*pl* **-ses** [siz]) ellipse *f*; (*punctuation*) points *mpl* de suspension

elliptic(al) [ɪ'lɪptɪk(əl)] *adj* elliptique

elm [ɛlm] *s* orme *m*

elongate [ɪ'lɔŋget] *tr* allonger, prolonger

elope [ɪ'lop] *intr* s'enfuir avec un amant

elopement [ɪ'lopmənt] *s* enlèvement *m* consenti

eloquence ['ɛləkwəns] *s* éloquence *f*

eloquent ['ɛləkwənt] *adj* éloquent

else [ɛls] *adj*—**nobody else** personne d'autre; **nothing else** rien d'autre; **somebody else** quelqu'un d'autre, un autre; **something else** autre chose; **what else** quoi encore; **who else** qui encore; **who's else** de qui d'autre ‖ *adv* d'une autre façon, autrement; **how(ever) else** de toute autre façon; **nowhere else** nulle part ailleurs; **or else** sinon, ou bien, sans quoi; **somewhere else** ailleurs, autre part; **when else** quand encore; **where else** où encore

else'where' *adv* ailleurs, autre part

elucidate [ɪ'lusɪ,det] *tr* élucider

elude [ɪ'lud] *tr* éluder, se soustraire à; (*a pursuer*) échapper à

elusive [ɪ'lusɪv] *adj* évasif, fuyant; (*baffling*) insaisissable, déconcertant

emaciated [ɪ'meʃɪ,etɪd] *adj* émacié; **to become emaciated** s'émacier

emanate ['ɛmə,net] *intr* émaner

emancipate [ɪ'mænsɪ,pet] *tr* émanciper

embalm [ɛm'bɑm] *tr* embaumer

embalming [ɛm'bɑmɪŋ] *s* embaumement *m*

embankment [ɛm'bæŋkmənt] *s* (*of river*) digue *f*; (*of road*) remblai *m*

embar·go [ɛm'bɑrgo] *s* (*pl* **-goes**) embargo *m* ‖ *tr* mettre un embargo sur

embark [ɛm'bɑrk] *intr* s'embarquer

embarkation [,ɛmbɑr'keʃən] *s* embarquement *m*

embarrass [ɛm'bærəs] *tr* faire honte à; (*to make difficult*) embarrasser

embarrassment [ɛm'bærəsmənt] *s* honte *f*, confusion *f*, gêne *f*; (*difficulty*) embarras *m*

embas·sy ['ɛmbəsi] *s* (*pl* **-sies**) ambassade *f*

em·bed [ɛm'bɛd] *v* (*pret & pp* **-bedded**; *ger* **-bedding**) *tr* encastrer

embellish [ɛm'bɛlɪʃ] *tr* embellir

embellishment [ɛm'bɛlɪʃmənt] *s* embellissement *m*

ember ['ɛmbər] *s* tison *m*; **embers** braise *f*

Em'ber days' *spl* quatre-temps *mpl*

embezzle [ɛm'bɛzəl] *tr* détourner, s'approprier ‖ *intr* commettre des détournements

embezzler [ɛm'bɛzlər] *s* détourneur *m* de fonds

embitter [ɛm'bɪtər] *tr* aigrir

emblazon [ɛm'blezən] *tr* embellir; exalter, célébrer

emblem ['ɛmbləm] *s* emblème *m*

emblematic(al) [,ɛmblə'mætɪk(əl)] *adj* emblématique

embodiment [ɛm'bɑdɪmənt] *s* personnification *f*, incarnation *f*

embod·y [ɛm'bɑdi] *v* (*pret & pp* **-ied**) *tr* personnifier, incarner; (*to include*) incorporer

embolden [ɛm'boldən] *tr* enhardir

embolism ['ɛmbə,lɪzəm] *s* embolie *f*

emboss [ɛm'bɔs] *tr* (*to raise in relief*) graver en relief; (*metal*) bosseler; (*e.g., leather*) gaufrer, repousser

embouchure [,ɑmbu'ʃʊr] *s* embouchure *f*; (*mus*) position *f* des lèvres

embrace [ɛm'bres] *s* étreinte *f*, embrassement *m* ‖ *tr* étreindre, embrasser ‖ *intr* s'étreindre, s'embrasser

embroider [ɛm'brɔɪdər] *tr* broder

embroider·y [ɛm'brɔɪdəri] *s* (*pl* **-ies**) broderie *f*

embroil [ɛm'brɔɪl] *tr* (*to throw into confusion*) embrouiller; (*to involve in contention*) brouiller

embroilment [ɛm'brɔɪlmənt] *s* embrouillage *m*, brouillamini *m*, imbroglio *m*

embry·o ['ɛmbrɪ,o] *s* (*pl* **-os**) embryon *m*

embryology [,ɛmbrɪ'ɑlədʒi] *s* embryologie *f*

embryonic [,ɛmbrɪ'ɑnɪk] *adj* embryonnaire

emend [ɪ'mɛnd] *tr* corriger

emendation [,imɛn'deʃən] *s* correction *f*

emerald ['ɛmərəld] *s* émeraude *f*

emerge [ɪ'mʌrdʒ] *intr* émerger

emergence [ɪ'mʌrdʒəns] *s* émergence *f*

emergen·cy [ɪ'mʌrdʒənsi] *adj* urgent, d'urgence; (*exit*) de secours ‖ *s* (*pl* **-cies**) cas *m* urgent

emer'gency brake' *s* frein *m* de secours

emer'gency ex'it *s* sortie *f* de secours

emer'gency land'ing *s* atterrissage *m* forcé

emer'gency opera'tion *s* (med) opération *f* à chaud

emer'gency ra'tions *spls* vivres *mpl* de réserve

emer'gency shut'down *s* arrêt *m* d'urgence

emer'gency ward' *s* salle *f* d'urgence

emeritus [ɪ'mɛrɪtəs] *adj* honoraire, d'honneur

emersion [ɪ'mʌrʒən] *s* émersion *f*

emery ['ɛməri] *s* émeri *m*

em'ery cloth' *s* toile *f* d'émeri

em'ery wheel' *s* meule *f* en émeri

emetic [ɪ'mɛtɪk] *adj & s* émétique *m*

emigrant ['ɛmɪgrənt] *adj & s* émigrant *m*

emigrate ['ɛmɪ,gret] *intr* émigrer

eminence ['ɛmɪnəns] *s* éminence *f*

eminent ['ɛmɪnənt] *adj* éminent; **most eminent** (eccl) éminentissime

emissar·y ['ɛmɪ,sɛri] *s* (*pl* **-ies**) émissaire *m*

emit [ɪ'mɪt] *v* (*pret & pp* **emitted**; *ger* **emitting**) *tr* émettre; (*a gas, an odor, etc.*) exhaler

emolument [ɪ'mɑljəmənt] *s* émoluments *mpl*

emotion [ɪ'moʃən] *s* émotion *f*

emotional [ɪ'moʃənəl] *adj* émotif, émotionnable

emperor ['ɛmpərər] *s* empereur *m*

empha·sis ['ɛmfəsɪs] *s* (*pl* **-ses** [,siz]) (*on an idea, event, project, etc.*) importance *f* accordée, mise *f* en relief, insistance *f*; (*on a word or phrase*) accent *m* d'insistance, accentuation *f*; **to place emphasis on** insister vivement sur, souligner; (*a word or syllable*) mettre l'accent sur; **with**

emphasis on en insistant particulièrement sur

emphasize [ˈɛmfə,saɪz] *tr* appuyer sur, insister sur, mettre en relief, faire ressortir, souligner; (*a word or syllable*) mettre l'accent sur

emphatic [ɛmˈfætɪk] *adj* accentué, énergique; (*denial*) catégorique

emphysema [,ɛmfɪˈsimə] *s* emphysème *m*

empire [ˈɛmpaɪr] *s* empire *m*

empiric(al) [ɛmˈpɪrɪk(əl)] *adj* empirique

empiricist [ɛmˈpɪrɪsɪst] *s* empirique *m*

emplacement [ɛmˈplesmənt] *s* emplacement *m*

employ [ɛmˈplɔɪ] *s* service *m* ‖ *tr* employer

employee [,ɛmplɔɪˈi] *s* employé *m*

employer [ɛmˈplɔɪ·ər] *s* employeur *m*, patron *m*, chef *m*

employment [ɛmˈplɔɪmənt] *s* emploi *m*

employ′ment a′gency *s* bureau *m* de placement

empower [ɛmˈpaʊ·ər] *tr* autoriser

empress [ˈɛmprɪs] *s* impératrice *f*

emptiness [ˈɛmptɪnɪs] *s* vide *m*

emp·ty [ˈɛmpti] *adj* (*comp* **-tier**; *super* **-tiest**) vide; (*hollow*) creux, vain; (coll) affamé ‖ *v* (*pret & pp* **-tied**) *tr* vider ‖ *intr* se vider; (*said of river*) se jeter; (*said of auditorium*) se dégarnir

emp′ty-hand′ed *adj & adv* les mains vides

emp′ty-head′ed *adj* écervelé

empye·ma [,ɛmpɪˈimə] *s* (*pl* **-mata** [mətə]) empyème *m*

empyrean [,ɛmpɪˈri·ən] *s* empyrée *m*

emu [ˈimju] *s* (zool) émeu *m*

emulate [ˈɛmjə,let] *tr* chercher à égaler, imiter ‖ *intr* rivaliser

emulator [ˈɛmjə,letər] *s* émule *mf*

emulsi·fy [ɪˈmʌlsɪ,faɪ] *v* (*pret & pp* **-fied**) *tr* émulsionner

emulsion [ɪˈmʌlʃən] *s* émulsion *f*

enable [ɛnˈebəl] *tr*—**to enable to** rendre capable de, mettre à même de

enact [ɛnˈækt] *tr* (*to decree*) décréter, arrêter; (theat) représenter

enactment [ɛnˈæktmənt] *s* (*establishing*) établissement *m*; (govt) promulgation *f*; (law) décret *m*, arrêté *m*; (theat) représentation *f*

enam·el [ɪˈnæməl] *s* émail *m* ‖ *v* (*pret & pp* **-eled** or **-elled**; *ger* **-eling** or **-elling**) *tr* émailler

enameling [ɪˈnæməlɪŋ] *s* émaillage *m*

enam′el·ware′ *s* ustensiles *mpl* en fer émaillé

enamor [ɛnˈæmər] *tr* rendre amoureux; **to become enamored with** s'énamourer de

encamp [ɛnˈkæmp] *tr & intr* camper

encampment [ɛnˈkæmpmənt] *s* campement *m*

encase [ɛnˈkes] *tr* mettre en caisse; enfermer, envelopper

encephalitis [ɛn,sɛfəˈlaɪtɪs] *s* encéphalite *f*

enchain [ɛnˈtʃen] *tr* enchaîner

enchant [ɛnˈtʃænt] *tr* enchanter

enchanting [ɛnˈtʃæntɪŋ] *adj* charmant, ravissant; (*casting a spell*) enchanteur

enchantment [ɛnˈtʃæntmənt] *s* enchantement *m*

enchantress [ɛnˈtʃæntrɪs] *s* enchanteresse *f*

encircle [ɛnˈsʌrkəl] *tr* encercler, cerner; (*a word*) entourer d'un cercle

enclitic [ɛnˈklɪtɪk] *adj & s* enclitique *m*

enclose [ɛnˈkloz] *tr* enclore, entourer; (*in a letter*) inclure, joindre

enclosed *adj* (*surrounded*) entouré; (*fenced in*) clôturé; (*covered*) couvert; (*with a letter*) ci-joint, ci-inclus

enclosure [ɛnˈklozər] *s* clôture *f*, enceinte *f*, enclos *m*; (*e.g., in a letter*) pièce *f* jointe, pièce annexée

encomi·um [ɛnˈkomɪ·əm] *s* (*pl* **-ums** or **-a** [ə]) panégyrique *m*, éloge *m*

encompass [ɛnˈkʌmpəs] *tr* entourer, renfermer

encore [ˈɑnkor] *s* rappel *m*, bis *m* ‖ *tr* bisser ‖ *interj* bis!

encounter [ɛnˈkaʊntər] *s* rencontre *f* ‖ *tr* rencontrer ‖ *intr* se rencontrer, combattre

encourage [ɛnˈkʌrɪdʒ] *tr* encourager

encouragement [ɛnˈkʌrɪdʒmənt] *s* encouragement *m*

encroach [ɛnˈkrotʃ] *intr*—**to encroach on** or **upon** empiéter sur; abuser de

encumber [ɛnˈkʌmbər] *tr* encombrer, embarrasser; (*with debts*) grever

encumbrance [ɛnˈkʌmbrəns] *s* encombrement *m*, embarras *m*; (law) charge *f*

encyclical [ɛnˈsɪklɪkəl] *adj & s* encyclique *f*

encyclopedia [ɛn,saɪkləˈpidɪ·ə] *s* encyclopédie *f*

encyclopedic [ɛn,saɪkləˈpidɪk] *adj* encyclopédique

end [ɛnd] *s* (*in time*) fin *f*; (*in space; small piece*) bout *m*; (*purpose*) but *m*; (*end of set period of time*) terme *m*; **at loose ends** en pagaille; **at the end, in the end** à la fin; **to be at the end of one's rope** être au bout de son rouleau; **to bring to an end** mettre fin à; **to come to an end** prendre fin; **to make both ends meet** joindre les deux bouts; **to stand on end** (*said of hair*) se dresser; **to this end** à cet effet ‖ *tr* achever, terminer ‖ *intr* s'achever, se terminer; **to end up by** finir par; **to end with** (or in) se terminer par

endanger [ɛnˈdendʒər] *tr* mettre en danger

endear [ɛnˈdɪr] *tr* faire aimer; **to endear oneself to** se faire aimer de

endeavor [ɛnˈdɛvər] *s* effort *m*, tentative *f* ‖ *intr*—**to endeavor to** s'efforcer de, tâcher de

endemic [ɛnˈdɛmɪk] *adj* endémique

ending [ˈɛndɪŋ] *s* fin *f*, terminaison *f*; (gram) désinence *f*

endive [ˈɛndaɪv] *s* (*blanched type*) endive *f*; (*Cichorium endivia*) chicorée *f* frisée

endless [ˈɛndlɪs] *adj* sans fin

end′most′ *adj* extrême

endocrine [ˈɛndokrɪn] *adj* endocrine

endorse [ɛnˈdɔrs] *tr* endosser; (*a candidate*) appuyer; (*a plan*) souscrire à

endorsement [ɛn'dɔrsmənt] *s* endos *m*, endossement *m*; (*approval*) appui *m*, approbation *f*

endorser [ɛn'dɔrsər] *s* endosseur *m*

endow [ɛn'dau] *tr* doter, fonder

endowment [ɛn'daumənt] *s* dotation *f*, fondation *f*; (*talent*) don *m*

endow'ment fund' *s* caisse *f* de dotation

end' pa'per *s* pages *fpl* de garde

endurance [ɛn'd(j)urəns] *s* endurance *f*

endur'ance test' *s* épreuve *f* d'endurance

endure [ɛn'd(j)ur] *tr* endurer ‖ *intr* durer

enduring [ɛn'd(j)urɪŋ] *adj* durable

enema ['ɛnəmə] *s* lavement *m*

ene·my ['ɛnəmi] *adj* ennemi ‖ *s* (*pl* **-mies**) ennemi *m*

en'emy al'ien *s* étranger *m* ennemi

energetic [,ɛnər'dʒɛtɪk] *adj* énergique

energizing ['ɛnər,dʒaɪzɪŋ] *adj* énergétique

ener·gy ['ɛnərdʒi] *s* (*pl* **-gies**) énergie *f*

en'ergy bal'ance *s* (nucl) bilan *m* énergétique

enervate ['ɛnər,vet] *tr* énerver

enfeeble [ɛn'fibəl] *tr* affaiblir

enfold [ɛn'fold] *tr* envelopper, enrouler; (*to embrace*) embrasser

enforce [ɛn'fors] *tr* (*a law*) faire exécuter, mettre en vigueur; (*one's rights, one's point of view*) faire valoir, appuyer; (*e.g., obedience*) imposer

enforcement [ɛn'forsmənt] *s* contrainte *f*; (*of a law*) exécution *f*, mise *f* en vigueur

enfranchise [ɛn'fræntʃaɪz] *tr* affranchir; donner le droit de vote à

engage [ɛn'gedʒ] *tr* engager; (*to hire*) engager, embaucher; (*to reserve*) retenir, réserver, louer; (*s.o.'s attention*) fixer, attirer; (*the clutch*) embrayer; (*toothed wheels*) engrener; **to be engaged in** s'occuper de; **to be engaged to be married** être fiancé; **to engage s.o. in conversation** entamer une conversation avec qn ‖ *intr* s'engager; (mach) engrener; **to engage in** s'embarquer dans, entrer en or dans

engaged *adj* (*to be married*) fiancé; (*busy*) occupé, pris; (mach) en prise; (mil) aux prises, aux mains

engagement [ɛn'gedʒmənt] *s* engagement *m*; (*betrothal*) fiançailles *fpl*; (*appointment*) rendez-vous *m*; (mach) embrayage *m*, engrenage *m*; (mil) engagement, combat *m*

engage'ment ring' *s* bague *f* or anneau *m* de fiançailles

engaging [ɛn'gedʒɪŋ] *adj* engageant, attirant

engender [ɛn'dʒɛndər] *tr* engendrer

engine ['ɛndʒɪn] *s* machine *f*; (*of automobile*) moteur *m*

engineer [,ɛndʒə'nɪr] *s* ingénieur *m*; (*engine driver*) mécanicien *m* ‖ *tr* diriger or construire en qualité d'ingénieur; (coll) manigancer, machiner

engineer' corps' *s* génie *m*

engineering [,ɛndʒə'nɪrɪŋ] *s* ingénierie *f*

en'gine house' *s* dépôt *m* de pompes à incendie

en'gine·man' *s* (*pl* **-men'**) mécanicien *m*

en'gine room' *s* chambre *f* des machines

en'gine-room tel'egraph *s* (naut) transmetteur *m* d'ordres

en'gine trou'ble *s* panne *f* de moteur

England ['ɪŋglənd] *s* Angleterre *f*; l'Angleterre

English ['ɪŋglɪʃ] *adj* anglais ‖ *s* (*language*) anglais *m*; (billiards) effet *m*; **the English** les Anglais

Eng'lish Chan'nel *s* Manche *f*

Eng'lish dai'sy *s* marguerite *f* des champs

Eng'lish horn' *s* cor *m* anglais

Eng'lish·man *s* (*pl* **-men**) Anglais *m*

Eng'lish-speak'ing *adj* anglophone, d'expression anglaise; (*country*) de langue anglaise

Eng'lish·wom'an *s* (*pl* **-wom'en**) Anglaise *f*

engraft [ɛn'græft] *tr* greffer; (fig) implanter

engrave [ɛn'grev] *tr* graver

engraver [ɛn'grevər] *s* graveur *m*

engraving [ɛn'grevɪŋ] *s* gravure *f*

engross [ɛn'gros] *tr* absorber, occuper; (*a document*) grossoyer

engrossing [ɛn'grosɪŋ] *adj* absorbant

engulf [ɛn'gʌlf] *tr* engouffrer, engloutir

enhance [ɛn'hæns] *tr* rehausser, relever

enhancement [ɛn'hænsmənt] *s* rehaussement *m*

enigma [ɪ'nɪgmə] *s* énigme *f*

enigmatic(al) [,ɪnɪg'mætɪk(əl)] *adj* énigmatique

enjoin [ɛn'dʒɔɪn] *tr* enjoindre; (*to forbid*) interdire

enjoy [ɛn'dʒɔɪ] *tr* jouir de; **to enjoy** + *ger* prendre plaisir à + *inf*; **to enjoy oneself** s'amuser, se divertir

enjoyable [ɛn'dʒɔɪ·əbəl] *adj* agréable, plaisant; (*show, party, etc.*) divertissant

enjoyment [ɛn'dʒɔɪmənt] *s* (*pleasure*) plaisir *m*; (*pleasurable use*) jouissance *f*

enkindle [ɛn'kɪndəl] *tr* allumer

enlarge [ɛn'lɑrdʒ] *tr* agrandir, élargir; (phot) agrandir ‖ *intr* s'agrandir, s'élargir; **to enlarge on** or **upon** discourir longuement sur, amplifier

enlargement [ɛn'lɑrdʒmənt] *s* agrandissement *m*

enlighten [ɛn'laɪtən] *tr* éclairer

enlightenment [ɛn'laɪtənmənt] *s* éclaircissements *mpl*; **the Enlightenment** le siècle des lumières

enlist [ɛn'lɪst] *tr* enrôler ‖ *intr* s'enrôler, s'engager

enlist'ed man' *s* homme *m* de troupe

enlistment [ɛn'lɪstmənt] *s* enrôlement *m*, engagement *m*

enliven [ɛn'laɪvən] *tr* animer, égayer

enmesh [ɛn'mɛʃ] *tr* prendre dans les rets; (*e.g., in an evil design*) empêtrer; (mach) engrener

enmi·ty ['ɛnmɪti] *s* (*pl* **-ties**) inimitié *f*

ennoble [ɛn'nobəl] *tr* ennoblir; (*to confer a title of nobility upon*) anoblir

ennui ['ɑnwi] *s* ennui *m*

enormous [ɪ'nɔrməs] *adj* énorme

enormously [ɪ'nɔrməsli] *adv* énormément

enough [ɪ'nʌf] *adj, s, & adv* assez; **more than enough** plus qu'il n'en faut; **that's enough!** en voilà assez!; **to be intelligent enough** être assez intelligent; **to have enough to live on** avoir de quoi vivre ‖ *interj* assez!, ça suffit!

enounce [ɪ'nɑuns] *tr* énoncer

enrage [ɛn'redʒ] *tr* faire enrager, rendre furieux; **to be enraged** enrager

enrapture [ɛn'ræptʃər] *tr* ravir, transporter

enrich [ɛn'rɪtʃ] *tr* enrichir

enrichment [ɛn'rɪtʃmənt] *s* enrichissement *m*

enroll [ɛn'rol] *tr* enrôler; (*a student*) inscrire; (*to wrap up*) enrouler ‖ *intr* s'enrôler; (*said of student*) prendre ses inscriptions, se faire inscrire

enrollment [ɛn'rolmənt] *s* enrôlement *m*; (*of a student*) inscription *f*; (*wrapping up*) enroulement *m*

ensconce [ɛn'skɑns] *tr* cacher; **to ensconce oneself** s'installer

ensemble [ɑn'sɑmbəl] *s* ensemble *m*

ensign ['ɛnsaɪn] *s* enseigne *f* ‖ ['ɛnsən] *s* (nav) enseigne *m* de deuxième classe

ensilage ['ɛnsɪlɪdʒ] *s* fourrage *m* d'un silo américain ‖ *tr* ensiler

enslave [ɛn'slev] *tr* asservir, réduire en esclavage

enslavement [ɛn'slevmənt] *s* asservissement *m*

ensnare [ɛn'snɛr] *tr* prendre au piège, attraper

ensue [ɛn's(j)u] *intr* s'ensuivre, résulter

ensuing [ɛn's(j)u·ɪŋ] *adj* suivant

ensure [ɛn'ʃur] *tr* assurer, garantir

entail [ɛn'tel] *tr* occasionner, entraîner

entangle [ɛn'tæŋgəl] *tr* embrouiller

entanglement [ɛn'tæŋgəlmənt] *s* embrouillement *m*, embarras *m*

enter ['ɛntər] *tr* (*a room, a house, etc.*) entrer dans; (*a school, the army, etc.*) entrer à; (*e.g., a period of convalescence*) entrer en; (*a highway, a public square, etc.*) déboucher sur; (*e.g., a club*) devenir membre de; (*a request*) enregistrer, consigner par écrit; (*a student, a contestant, etc.*) admettre, faire inscrire; (*in the customhouse*) déclarer; (*to make a record of*) inscrire, porter; **to enter one's name for** se faire inscrire à or pour ‖ *intr* entrer; (theat) entrer en scène; **to enter into** entrer à, dans, or en; (*to be an ingredient of*) entrer pour; **to enter on** or **upon** entreprendre, débuter dans

enterprise ['ɛntər,praɪz] *s* (*undertaking*) entreprise *f*; (*spirit, push*) esprit *m* d'entreprise, allant *m*, entrain *m*

enterprising ['ɛntər,praɪzɪŋ] *adj* entreprenant

entertain [,ɛntər'ten] *tr* (*to distract*) amuser, divertir; (*to show hospitality to*) recevoir; (*at a meal*) régaler; (*a hope*) entretenir,

nourrir; (*an idea*) concevoir ‖ *intr* recevoir

entertainer [,ɛntər'tenər] *s* (*host*) hôte *m*, amphitryon *m*; amuseur *m*; (*comedian*) comique *mf*

entertaining [,ɛntər'tenɪŋ] *adj* amusant, divertissant

entertainment [,ɛntər'tenmənt] *s* (*distraction*) amusement *m*, divertissement *m*; (*show*) spectacle *m*; (*as a guest*) accueil *m*, hospitalité *f*

en'tertain'ment tax' *s* taxe *f* sur les spectacles

enthrall [ɛn'θrɔl] *tr* (*to charm*) captiver, charmer; (*to enslave*) asservir, rendre esclave

enthrone [ɛn'θron] *tr* introniser

enthuse [ɛn'θ(j)uz] *tr* (coll) enthousiasmer ‖ *intr* (coll) s'enthousiasmer

enthusiasm [ɛn'θ(j)uzɪ,æzəm] *s* enthousiasme *m*

enthusiast [ɛn'θ(j)uzɪ,æst] *s* enthousiaste *mf*; (*camera fiend, sports fan, etc.*) fanatique *mf*, enragé *m*

enthusiastic [ɛn,θ(j)uzɪ'æstɪk] *adj* enthousiaste; (*for sports, music, a hobby*) fanatique, enragé

entice [ɛn'taɪs] *tr* attirer, séduire; (*to evil*) tenter, chercher à séduire

enticement [ɛn'taɪsmənt] *s* attrait *m*, appât *m*; tentation *f*, séduction *f*

entire [ɛn'taɪr] *adj* entier

entirely [ɛn'taɪrli] *adv* entièrement, en entier; (*absolutely*) tout à fait, absolument

entire·ty [ɛn'taɪrti] *s* (*pl* **-ties**) totalité *f*, entier *m*; **in its entirety** dans sa totalité

entitle [ɛn'taɪtəl] *tr* (*to name*) intituler; (*to qualify*) donner le droit à; **to be entitled to** avoir droit à

enti·ty ['ɛntɪti] *s* (*pl* **-ties**) entité *f*

entomb [ɛn'tum] *tr* ensevelir

entombment [ɛn'tummənt] *s* ensevelissement *m*

entomology [,ɛntə'mɑlədʒi] *s* entomologie *f*

entourage [,ɑntu'rɑʒ] *s* entourage *m*

entrails ['ɛntrelz] *spl* entrailles *fpl*

entrain [ɛn'tren] *tr* faire prendre le train, embarquer; (*to carry along*) entraîner ‖ *intr* embarquer, s'embarquer

entrance ['ɛntrəns] *s* entrée *f*; (theat) entrée en scène; **entrance to . . .** (public sign) accès à . . . ‖ [ɛn'træns], [ɛn'trɑns] *tr* enchanter, ensorceler; **to be entranced** s'extasier

en'trance examina'tion *s* examen *m* d'entrée

en'trance fee' *s* prix *m* d'entrée, droit *m* d'entrée

entrancing [ɛn'trænsɪŋ] *adj* enchanteur, ensorceleur

entrant ['ɛntrənt] *s* inscrit *m*; (*in a competition*) concurrent *m*, participant *m*

en·trap [ɛn'træp] *v* (*pret & pp* **-trapped**; *ger* **-trapping**) *tr* attraper

entreat [ɛn'trit] *tr* supplier, prier, conjurer

entreat·y [ɛn'triti] *s* (*pl* **-ies**) supplication *f*, prière *f*

entree ['ɑntre] *s* (*entrance; course preceding the roast*) entrée *f*; (*main dish*) plat *m* de résistance

entrench [ɛn'trɛntʃ] *tr* retrancher; **to be entrenched** se retrancher ‖ *intr*—**to entrench on** or **upon** empiéter sur

entrust [ɛn'trʌst] *tr*—**to entrust s.o. with s.th., to entrust s.th. to s.o.** confier q.ch. à qn

en·try ['ɛntri] *s* (*pl* **-tries**) entrée *f*; (*in a dictionary*) article *m*, entrée; (*on a register*) inscription *f*; (*in a competition*) concurrent *m*, participant *m*; (*thing entered for judging in a competition*) objet *m* exposé

en'try blank' *s* feuille *f* d'inscription

en'try vi'sa *s* visa *m* d'entrée

en'try word' *s* (*of a dictionary*) mot *m* d'entrée, mot-souche *m*, entrée *f*, adresse *f*

entwine [ɛn'twaɪn] *tr* entrelacer, enlacer ‖ *intr* s'entrelacer, s'enlacer

enumerate [ɪ'n(j)umə,ret] *tr* énumérer

enunciate [ɪ'nʌnsɪ,et] *tr* énoncer, déclarer; (*to articulate*) articuler, prononcer

envelop [ɛn'vɛləp] *tr* envelopper

envelope ['ɛnvə,lop], ['ɑnvə,lop] *s* enveloppe *f*; **in an envelope** sous enveloppe, sous pli

envenom [ɛn'vɛnəm] *tr* envenimer, empoisonner

enviable ['ɛnvɪ·əbəl] *adj* enviable, digne d'envie

envious ['ɛnvɪ·əs] *adj* envieux

environment [ɛn'vaɪrənmənt] *s* environnement *m*, milieu *m*

environmental [ɛn,vaɪrən'məntəl] *adj* écologique, du milieu

environs [ɛn'vaɪrənz] *spl* environs *mpl*

envisage [ɛn'vɪzɪdʒ] *tr* envisager

envoi ['ɛnvɔɪ] *s* envoi *m*

envoy ['ɛnvɔɪ] *s* envoyé *m*, émissaire *m*; (*of poem*) envoi *m*

en·vy ['ɛnvi] *s* (*pl* **-vies**) envie *f* ‖ *v* (*pret & pp* **-vied**) *tr* envier

enzyme ['ɛnzaɪm] *s* enzyme *m & f*

epaulet ['ɛpə,lɛt] *s* épaulette *f*

epergne [ɪ'pʌrn], [e'pɛrn] *s* surtout *m*

ephemeral [ɪ'fɛmərəl] *adj* éphémère

epic ['ɛpɪk] *adj* épique ‖ *s* épopée *f*

epicure ['ɛpɪ,kjʊr] *s* gourmet *m*, gastronome *m*

epidemic [,ɛpɪ'dɛmɪk] *adj* épidémique ‖ *s* épidémie *f*

epidemiology [,ɛpɪ,dimɪ'ɑlədʒi] *s* épidémiologie *f*

epidermis [,ɛpɪ'dʌrmɪs] *s* épiderme *m*

epiglottis [,ɛpɪ'glɑtɪs] *s* épiglotte *f*

epigram ['ɛpɪ,græm] *s* épigramme *f*

epilepsy ['ɛpɪ,lɛpsi] *s* épilepsie *f*

epileptic [,ɛpɪ'lɛptɪk] *adj & s* épileptique *mf*

epilogue ['ɛpɪ,lɔg] *s* épilogue *m*

episcopal [ɪ'pɪskəpəl] *adj* épiscopal

Episcopalian [ɪ,pɪskə'pelɪ·ən] *adj* épiscopal ‖ *s* épiscopal *m*

episode ['ɛpɪ,sod] *s* épisode *m*

episodic [,ɛpɪ'sɑdɪk] *adj* épisodique

epistle [ɪ'pɪsəl] *s* épître *f*

epitaph ['ɛpɪ,tæf] *s* épitaphe *f*

epithet ['ɛpɪ,θɛt] *s* épithète *f*

epitome [ɪ'pɪtəmi] *s* (*abridgment*) épitomé *m*; (*representative of a class*) modèle *m*, personnification *f*

epitomize [ɪ'pɪtə,maɪz] *tr* abréger; personnifier

epoch ['ipɑk] *s* époque *f*

epochal ['ɛpəkəl] *adj* mémorable

ep'och-mak'ing *adj* qui fait époque

epoxy [ɪ'pɑksi] *s* résine *f* époxyde

Ep'som salts' ['ɛpsəm] *spl* epsomite *f*, sels *mpl* d'Epsom

equable ['ɛkwəbəl], ['ikwəbəl] *adj* uniforme, égal; tranquille

equal ['ikwəl] *adj* égal; **to be equal to** égaler, valoir; (*e.g., the occasion*) être à la hauteur de; **to be equal to** + *ger* être de force à + *inf*, être à même de + *inf*; **to get equal with** (coll) se venger de ‖ *s* égal *m*, pareil *m* ‖ *v* (*pret & pp* **equaled** or **equalled**; *ger* **equaling** or **equalling**) *tr* égaler

equali·ty [ɪ'kwɑlɪti] *s* (*pl* **-ties**) égalité *f*

equalize ['ikwə,laɪz] *tr* égaliser

equally ['ikwəli] *adv* également

e'qual opportu'nity *s* chances *fpl* égales

equanimity [,ikwə'nɪmɪti] *s* équanimité *f*, égalité *f* d'âme

equate [i'kwet] *tr* égaliser, mettre en équation

equation [i'kweʒən] *s* équation *f*

equator [i'kwetər] *s* équateur *m*

equatorial [,ikwə'torɪ·əl] *adj* équatorial

equestrian [ɪ'kwɛstrɪ·ən] *adj* équestre ‖ *s* cavalier *m*, écuyer *m*

equilateral [,ikwɪ'lætərəl] *adj* équilatéral

equilibrium [,ikwɪ'lɪbrɪ·əm] *s* équilibre *m*

equinoctial [,ikwɪ'nɑkʃəl] *adj* équinoxial

equinox ['ikwɪ,nɑks] *s* équinoxe *m*

equip [ɪ'kwɪp] *v* (*pret & pp* **equipped**; *ger* **equipping**) *tr* équiper, outiller; **to equip with** munir de

equipment [ɪ'kwɪpmənt] *s* équipement *m*, matériel *m*, appareillage *m*

equipoise ['ikwɪ,pɔɪz], ['ɛkwɪ,pɔɪz] *s* équilibre *m* ‖ *tr* équilibrer

equitable ['ɛkwɪtəbəl] *adj* équitable

equi·ty ['ɛkwɪti] *s* (*pl* **-ties**) équité *f*; (com) part *f* résiduaire

equivalent [ɪ'kwɪvələnt] *adj & s* équivalent *m*

equivocal [ɪ'kwɪvəkəl] *adj* équivoque

equivocate [ɪ'kwɪvə,ket] *intr* équivoquer

equivocation [ɪ,kwɪvə'keʃən] *s* tergiversation *f*, équivoque *f*

era ['ɪrə] *s* ère *f*, époque *f*

eradicate [ɪ'rædɪ,ket] *tr* déraciner, extirper

erase [ɪ'res] *tr* effacer, biffer

eraser [ɪ'resər] *s* gomme *f* à effacer; brosse *f*

erasure [ɪ'reʃər] *s* effacement *m*, rature *f*

ere [ɛr] *prep* (poetic) avant ‖ *conj* (poetic) avant que

erect [ɪ'rɛkt] *adj* droit, debout ‖ *tr* (*to set in an upright position*) dresser, élever; (*a* *building*) ériger, édifier; (*a machine*) monter

erection [ɪˈrɛkʃən] *s* érection *f*

erg [ʌrg] *s* erg *m*

ermine [ˈʌrmɪn] *s* hermine *f*

erode [ɪˈrod] *tr* éroder

erosion [ɪˈroʒən] *s* érosion *f*

erotic [ɪˈratɪk] *adj* érotique

err [ʌr] *intr* se tromper, faire erreur, errer; (*to do wrong*) s'égarer, pécher

errand [ˈɛrənd] *s* commission *f*, course *f*; **to go on** or **to run an errand** faire une course

er'rand boy' *s* coursier *m*, garçon *m* de courses

erratic [ɪˈrætɪk] *adj* variable; capricieux, excentrique

erroneous [ɪˈronɪ·əs] *adj* erroné

error [ˈɛrər] *s* erreur *f*

erudite [ˈɛr(j)ʊ,daɪt] *adj* érudit

erudition [,ɛr(j)ʊˈdɪʃən] *s* érudition *f*

erupt [ɪˈrʌpt] *intr* faire éruption

eruption [ɪˈrʌpʃən] *s* éruption *f*

escalate [ˈɛskə,let] *tr* escalader

escalation [,ɛskəˈleʃən] *s* escalade *f*

escalator [ˈɛskə,letər] *s* escalator *m*, escalier *m* mécanique or roulant

es'calator clause' *s* clause *f* d'indexation

escallop [ɛsˈkæləp] *s* (*seafood*) coquille *f* Saint-Jacques, peigne *m*, pétoncle *m*; (culin) coquille au gratin ‖ *tr* (culin) gratiner et cuire au four et à la crème; (culin) servir en coquille

escapade [,ɛskəˈped] *s* fredaine *f*, frasque *f*; (*getting away*) escapade *f*

escape [ɛsˈkep] *s* (*getaway*) évasion *f*, fuite *f*; (*from responsibilities, duties, etc.*) évasion, escapade *f*; (*of gas, liquid, etc.*) échappement *m*, fuite *f*; (*of a clock*) échappement; **to have a narrow escape** l'échapper belle; **to make one's escape** se sauver, s'échapper ‖ *tr* échapper à, éviter ‖ *intr* échapper, s'échapper, s'évader; **to escape from** échapper à

escape' clause' *s* échappatoire *f*

escapee [,ɛskəˈpi] *s* évadé *m*, échappé *m*

escape' hatch' *s* (aer) sas *m* d'évacuation

escapement [ɛsˈkepmənt] *s* issue *f*, débouché *m*; (mach) échappement *m*

escape' wheel' *s* roue *f* de rencontre

escarole [ˈɛskə,rol] *s* scarole *f*

escarpment [ɛsˈkɑrpmənt] *s* escarpement *m*

eschew [ɛsˈtʃu] *tr* éviter, s'abstenir de

escort [ˈɛskɔrt] *s* escorte *f*; (*gentleman escort*) cavalier *m* ‖ [ɛsˈkɔrt] *tr* escorter

escutcheon [ɛsˈkʌtʃən] *s* écusson *m*

Eski·mo [ˈɛskɪ,mo] *adj* eskimo, esquimau ‖ *s* (*pl* **-mos** or **-mo**) (*language; dog*) esquimau *m*; (*person*) Eskimo *m*, Esquimau *m*

Es'kimo wom'an *s* Esquimaude *f*, femme *f* esquimau

esopha·gus [iˈsɑfəgəs] *s* (*pl* **-gi** [,dʒaɪ]) œsophage *m*

esoteric [,ɛsoˈtɛrɪk] *adj* ésotérique

especial [ɛsˈpɛʃəl] *adj* spécial

especially [ɛsˈpɛʃəli] *adv* surtout, particulièrement

Esperanto [,ɛspəˈrɑnto] *s* espéranto *m*

espionage [,ɛspɪ·əˈnɑʒ] *s* espionnage *m*

espousal [ɛsˈpauzəl] *s* épousailles *f*; **espousal of** (*a cause*) adoption de, adhésion à

espouse [ɛsˈpauz] *tr* épouser; (*to advocate, adopt*) adopter, embrasser

Esq. *abbr* (**Esquire**)—**John Smith, Esq.** Monsieur Jean Smith

esquire [ˈɛskwaɪr] *s* (hist) écuyer *m*

essay [ˈɛse] *s* essai *m* ‖ *tr* essayer

essayist [ˈɛse·ɪst] *s* essayiste *mf*

essence [ˈɛsəns] *s* essence *f*

essential [ɛˈsɛnʃəl] *adj & s* essentiel *m*

essentially [əˈsɛnʃəli] *adv* essentiellement, avant tout, au premier chef

establish [ɛsˈtæblɪʃ] *tr* établir

establishment [ɛsˈtæblɪʃmənt] *s* établissement *m*; **the Establishment** (pol) les pouvoirs *mpl* établis, les milieux *mpl* dirigeants

estate [ɛsˈtet] *s* (*landed property*) domaine *m*, propriété *f*, terres *fpl*; (*a person's possessions*) biens *mpl*, possessions *fpl*; (*left by a decedent*) héritage *m*, succession *f*; (*social status*) rang *m*, condition *f*; (hist) état *m*

esteem [ɛsˈtim] *s* estime *f* ‖ *tr* estimer

esthete [ˈɛsθit] *s* esthète *mf*

esthetic [ɛsˈθɛtɪk] *adj* esthétique ‖ **esthetics** *s* esthétique *f*

estimable [ˈɛstɪməbəl] *adj* estimable

estimate [ˈɛstɪ,met] *s* évaluation *f*, appréciation *f*; (*appraisal*) estimation *f* ‖ *tr* (*to judge, deem*) apprécier, estimer; (*the cost*) estimer, évaluer

estimation [,ɛstɪˈmeʃən] *s* (*opinion*) jugement *m*; (*esteem*) estime *f*; (*appraisal*) estimation *f*; **in my estimation** à mon avis

estrangement [ɛsˈtrendʒmənt] *s* éloignement *m*; (*a becoming unfriendly*) désaffection *f*

estuar·y [ˈɛstʃu,ɛri] *s* (*pl* **-ies**) estuaire *m*

etc. *abbr* (Lat **et cetera** and so on) et c., et ainsi de suite

etch [ɛtʃ] *tr & intr* graver à l'eau-forte

etcher [ˈɛtʃər] *s* aquafortiste *m*

etching [ˈɛtʃɪŋ] *s* eau-forte *f*

eternal [ɪˈtʌrnəl] *adj* éternel

eterni·ty [ɪˈtʌrnɪti] *s* (*pl* **-ties**) éternité *f*

ether [ˈiθər] *s* éther *m*

ethereal [ɪˈθɪrɪ·əl] *adj* éthéré

ethical [ˈɛθɪkəl] *adj* éthique

ethics [ˈɛθɪks] *s* (*branch of philosophy*) étique *f*, morale *f*; spl (*one's conduct, one's moral principles*) morale

Ethiopia [,iθɪˈopɪ·ə] *s* Éthiopie *f*; l'Éthiopie

Ethiopian [,iθɪˈopɪ·ən] *adj* éthiopien ‖ *s* (*language*) éthiopien *m*; (*person*) Éthiopien *m*

ethnic(al) [ˈɛθnɪk(əl)] *adj* ethnique

ethnography [ɛθˈnɑgrəfi] *s* ethnographie *f*

ethnology [ɛθˈnɑlədʒi] *s* ethnologie *f*

ethyl [ˈɛθɪl] *s* éthyle *m*

ethylene [ˈɛθɪ,lin] *s* éthylène *m*

etiquette [ˈɛtɪˌkɛt] *s* étiquette *f*

etymolo·gy [ˌɛtɪˈmɑlədʒi] *s* (*pl* **-gies**) étymologie *f*

ety·mon [ˈɛtɪˌmɑn] *s* (*pl* **-mons** or **-ma** [mə]) étymon *m*

eucalyp·tus [ˌjukəˈlɪptəs] *s* (*pl* **-tuses** or **-ti** [taɪ]) eucalyptus *m*

Eucharist [ˈjukərɪst] *s* Eucharistie *f*

euchre [ˈjukər] *s* euchre *m* ‖ *tr* (coll) l'emporter sur

eulogize [ˈjuləˌdʒaɪz] *tr* faire l'éloge de

eulo·gy [ˈjulədʒi] *s* (*pl* **-gies**) éloge *m*

eunuch [ˈjunək] *s* eunuque *m*

euphemism [ˈjufɪˌmɪzəm] *s* euphémisme *m*

euphemistic [ˌjufɪˈmɪstɪk] *adj* euphémique

euphonic [juˈfɑnɪk] *adj* euphonique

eupho·ny [ˈjufəni] *s* (*pl* **-nies**) euphonie *f*

euphoria [juˈforɪ·ə] *s* euphorie *f*

euphuism [ˈjufjuˌɪzəm] *s* euphuisme *m*; préciosité *f*

Europe [ˈjurəp] *s* Europe *f*; l'Europe

European [ˌjurəˈpi·ən] *adj* européen ‖ *s* Européen *m*

euthanasia [ˌjuθəˈneʒə] *s* euthanasie *f*

evacuate [ɪˈvækjuˌet] *tr* évacuer ‖ *intr* s'évacuer

evade [ɪˈved] *tr* échapper à, éviter, esquiver ‖ *intr* s'évader

evaluate [ɪˈvæljuˌet] *tr* évaluer

Evangel [ɪˈvændʒəl] *s* évangile *m*

evangelic(al) [ˌɛvənˈdʒɛlɪk(əl)] *adj* évangélique

evangelist [ɪˈvændʒəlɪst] *s* évangéliste *m*

evaporate [ɪˈvæpəˌret] *tr* évaporer ‖ *intr* s'évaporer

evasion [ɪˈveʒən] *s* évasion *f*; subterfuge *m*, détour *m*

evasive [ɪˈvesɪv] *adj* évasif

eve [iv] *s* veille *f*; (poetic) soir *m*; **on the eve of** à la veille de; **Eve** Ève *f*

even [ˈivən] *adj* (*smooth*) uni; (*number*) pair; (*equal, uniform*) égal; (*temperament*) calme, rassis, égal; **even with** à fleur de; **to be even** être quitte; (cards, sports) être manche à manche or point à point; **to get even with** (coll) rendre la pareille à ‖ *adv* même; **even** + *comp* encore + *comp*, e.g., **even better** encore mieux; **even so** quand même ‖ *tr* aplanir, égaliser

evening [ˈivnɪŋ] *adj* du soir ‖ *s* soir *m*; **all evening** toute la soirée; **every evening** tous les soirs; **in the evening** le soir; **the evening before** la veille au soir

eve'ning clothes' *s* tenue *f* de soirée; (*for women*) toilette *f* de soirée; (*for men*) habit *m* de soirée

eve'ning damp' *s* serein *m*

eve'ning gown' *s* robe *f* du soir

eve'ning prim'rose *s* onagraire *f*

eve'ning star' *s* étoile *f* du soir, étoile du berger

eve'ning wrap' *s* sortie *f* de bal

e'ven·song' *s* (eccl) vêpres *fpl*

event [ɪˈvɛnt] *s* événement *m*; **at all events** or **in any event** en tout cas; **in the event that** dans le cas où

eventful [ɪˈvɛntfəl] *adj* mouvementé; mémorable

eventual [ɪˈvɛntʃu·əl] *adj* final

eventuali·ty [ɪˌvɛntʃuˈælɪti] *s* (*pl* **-ties**) éventualité *f*

eventually [ɪˈvɛntʃu·əli] *adv* finalement, à la longue, en fin de compte

eventuate [ɪˈvɛntʃuˌet] *intr*—**to eventuate in** se terminer par, aboutir à

ever [ˈɛvər] *adv* (*at all times*) toujours; (*at any time*) jamais; **ever since** dès lors, depuis; **for ever and ever** à tout jamais; **hardly ever** presque jamais

ev'er·glade' *s* région *f* marécageuse

ev'er·green' *adj* toujours vert ‖ *s* arbre *m* vert; **evergreens** plantes *fpl* vertes, verdure *f* décorative

ev'er·last'ing *adj* éternel; (*continual*) sempiternel, perpétuel

ev'er·more' *adv* toujours; **for evermore** à jamais

every [ˈɛvri] *adj* tous les; (*each*) chaque, tout; (coll) tout, e.g., **every bit as good as** tout aussi bon que; **every man for himself** sauve qui peut; **every now and then** de temps en temps; **every once in a while** de temps à autre; **every other day** tous les deux jours; **every other one** un sur deux; **every which way** (coll) de tous côtés; (coll) en désordre

ev'ery·bod'y *pron indef* tout le monde

ev'ery·day' *adj* de tous les jours

ev'ery·man' *s* Monsieur Tout-le-monde

ev'ery·one' or **ev'ery one'** *pron indef* chacun, tous, tout le monde

ev'ery·thing' *pron indef* tout

ev'ery·where' *adv* partout, de toutes parts; partout où; **everywhere else** partout ailleurs

evict [ɪˈvɪkt] *tr* évincer, expulser

eviction [ɪˈvɪkʃən] *s* éviction *f*

evidence [ˈɛvɪdəns] *s* évidence *f*; (*proof*) preuve *f*, témoignage *m* ‖ *tr* manifester, démontrer

evident [ˈɛvɪdənt] *adj* évident

evidently [ˈɛvɪdəntli] *adv* évidemment

evil [ˈivəl] *adj* mauvais, méchant ‖ *s* mal *m*, méchanceté *f*

evildoer [ˈivəlˌdu·ər] *s* malfaisant *m*, méchant *m*

e'vil·do'ing *s* malfaisance *f*

e'vil eye' *s* mauvais œil *m*

e'vil-mind'ed *adj* malintentionné, malin

E'vil One' *s* Esprit *m* malin

evince [ɪˈvɪns] *tr* montrer, manifester

evocative [ɪˈvakətɪv] *adj* évocateur

evoke [ɪˈvok] *tr* évoquer

evolution [ˌɛvəˈluʃən] *s* évolution *f*

evolve [ɪˈvalv] *tr* développer, élaborer ‖ *intr* évoluer

ewe [ju] *s* brebis *f*

ewer [ˈju·ər] *s* aiguière *f*

exact [ɛgˈzækt] *adj* exact ‖ *tr* exiger

exacting [ɛgˈzæktɪŋ] *adj* exigeant

exactly [ɛgˈzæktli] *adv* exactement; (*sharp, on the dot*) précisément, justement

exactness [ɛgˈzæktnɪs] *s* exactitude *f*

exaggerate [εg'zædʒə,ret] *tr* exagérer

exalt [εg'zɔlt] *tr* exalter

exam [εg'zæm] *s* (coll) examen *m*

examination [εg,zæmɪ'neʃən] *s* examen *m*; **to take an examination** se présenter à, passer, or subir un examen

examine [εg'zæmɪn] *tr* examiner

examiner [εg'zæmɪnər] *s* inspecteur *m*, vérificateur *m*; (*in a school*) examinateur *m*

example [εg'zæmpəl] *s* exemple *m*; **for example** par exemple

exasperate [εg'zæspə,ret] *tr* exaspérer

exasperation [εg,zæspə'reʃən] *s* exaspération *f*

excavate ['εkskə,vet] *tr* excaver

exceed [εk'sid] *tr* excéder

exceedingly [εk'sidɪŋli] *adv* extrêmement

ex·cel [εk'sεl] *v* (*pret & pp* -**celled**; *ger* -**celling**) *tr* surpasser ‖ *intr* exceller; **to excel in** exceller dans; **to excel in** + *ger* exceller à + *inf*

excellence ['εksələns] *s* excellence *f*

excellen·cy ['εksələnsi] *s* (*pl* -**cies**) excellence *f*; **Your Excellency** Votre Excellence

excelsior [εk'sεlsi·ər] *s* copeaux *mpl* d'emballage

except [εk'sεpt] *adv*—**except for** excepté; **except that** excepté que ‖ *prep* excepté ‖ *tr* excepter

exception [εk'sεpʃən] *s* exception *f*; **to take exception to** trouver à redire à; **with the exception of** à l'exception de

exceptional [εk'sεpʃənəl] *adj* exceptionnel

excerpt ['εksʌrpt] *s* extrait *m*, citation *f* ‖ [εk'sʌrpt] *tr* extraire

excess ['εksεs] *adj* excédentaire ‖ [εk'sεs] *s* (*amount or degree*) excédent *m*, excès *m*; (*excessive amount; immoderate indulgence*) excès *m*; **in excess of** en plus de

ex'cess bag'gage *s* excédent *m* de bagages

ex'cess fare' *s* supplément *m*

excessive [εk'sεsɪv] *adj* excessif

ex'cess-prof'its tax' *s* contribution *f* sur les bénéfices extraordinaires

ex'cess weight' *s* excédent *m* de poids

exchange [εks'tʃendʒ] *s* échange *m*; (*barter*) troc *m*; (com) bourse *f*; (telp) central *m*; **in exchange for** en contrepartie de ‖ *tr* échanger; (*to barter*) troquer; **to exchange compliments** échanger des politesses; **to exchange for** échanger contre, échanger pour

exchange' rate' *s* taux *m* de change

exchequer ['εkstʃεkər] *s* trésor *m* public; ministère *m* des finances; (hist) échiquier *m*

excise ['εksaɪz] *s* contributions *fpl* indirectes ‖ *tr* effacer, rayer; (surg) exciser

excitable [εk'saɪtəbəl] *adj* excitable

excite [εk'saɪt] *tr* exciter

excited *adj* agité, surexcité; **don't get excited!** ne vous énervez pas!; **to get excited** s'emballer; **to get excited about** se passionner de or pour

excitement [εk'saɪtmənt] *m* agitation *f*, excitation *f*

exciting [εk'saɪtɪŋ] *adj* émotionnant, entraînant, passionnant

exclaim [εks'klem] *tr* s'écrier, e.g., **"All is lost!" he exclaimed** "Tout est perdu!" s'écria-t-il ‖ *intr* s'exclamer, se récrier

exclamation [,εksklə'meʃən] *s* exclamation *f*

exclama'tion mark' *s* point *m* d'exclamation

exclude [εks'klud] *tr* exclure

excluding [εks'kludɪŋ] *prep* à l'exclusion de, sans compter

exclusion [εks'kluʒən] *s* exclusion *f*

exclusive [εks'klusɪv] *adj* exclusif; (*expensive; fashionable*) (coll) choisi, select; **exclusive of** à l'exclusion de

exclu'sive rights' *spl* exclusivité *f*

exclu'sive show'ing *s* (public sign in front of a theater) en exclusivité

excommunicate [,εkskə'mjunɪ,ket] *tr* excommunier

excommunication [,εkskə,mjunɪ'keʃən] *s* excommunication *f*

excoriate [εks'kori,et] *tr* (fig) vitupérer

excrement ['εkskrəmənt] *s* excrément *m*

excruciating [εks'kruʃɪ,etɪŋ] *adj* affreux, atroce

exculpate ['εkskʌl,pet] *tr* disculper

excursion [εks'kʌrʒən] *s* excursion *f*

excusable [εks'kjuzəbəl] *adj* excusable

excuse [εks'kjus] *s* excuse *f* ‖ [εks'kjuz] *tr* excuser; **excuse me!** pardon!, je m'excuse!, **to excuse oneself** s'excuser

execrate ['εksɪ,kret] *tr* exécrer; (*to curse*) maudire

execute ['εksɪ,kjut] *tr* exécuter

execution [,εksɪ'kjuʃən] *s* exécution *f*

executioner [,εksɪ'kjuʃənər] *s* bourreau *m*

executive [εg'zεkjətɪv] *adj* (*powers*) exécutif; (*position*) administratif ‖ *s* exécutif *m*; (*of school, business, etc.*) directeur *m*, administrateur *m*

Exec'utive Man'sion *s* (U.S.A.) demeure *f* du Président

executor [εg'zεkjətər] *s* exécuteur *m* testamentaire

executrix [εg'zεkjətrɪks] *s* exécutrice *f* testamentaire

exemplary ['εgzəm,plεri] *adj* exemplaire

exempli·fy [εg'zεmplɪ,faɪ] *v* (*pret & pp* -**fied**) *tr* démontrer par des exemples; (*to be a model of*) servir d'exemple à

exempt [εg'zεmpt] *adj* exempt ‖ *tr* exempter

exemption [εg'zεmpʃən] *s* exemption *f*; **exemptions** (*from taxes*) déductions *fpl*

exercise ['εksər,saɪz] *s* exercice *m*; **exercises** cérémonies *fpl* ‖ *tr* exercer ‖ *intr* s'exercer, s'entraîner

ex'ercise bi'cycle *s* bicyclette *f* d'entraînement, home-trainer *m*

exert [εg'zʌrt] *tr* exercer; **to exert oneself** faire des efforts

exertion [εg'zʌrʃən] *s* effort *m*; (*e.g., of power*) exercice *m*

exhalation [,εks·hə'leʃən] *s* (*of air*) expiration *f*; (*of gas, vapors, etc.*) exhalaison *f*

exhale [ɛks'hel] tr (*air from lungs*) expirer; (*gas, vapor*) exhaler ‖ *intr* expirer; s'exhaler

exhaust [ɛg'zɔst] s (*system*) échappement *m*; (*fumes*) gaz *mpl* d'échappement ‖ *tr* épuiser; faire le vide dans

exhaust′ fan′ s ventilateur *m* aspirant

exhaust′ hood′ s hotte *f* aspirante

exhaustion [ɛg'zɔstʃən] s épuisement *m*

exhaustive [ɛg'zɔstɪv] adj exhaustif

exhaust′ man′ifold s tuyauterie *f* or collecteur *m* d'échappement

exhaust′ pipe′ s tuyau *m* d'échappement

exhaust′ valve′ s soupape *f* d'échappement

exhibit [ɛg'zɪbɪt] s exhibition *f*; (*of art*) exposition ′; (law) document *m* à l'appui, pièce *f* à conviction ‖ *tr* exhiber; (*e.g., pictures*) exposer ‖ *intr* faire une exposition

exhibition [,ɛksɪ'bɪʃən] s exhibition *f*

ex′hibi′tion game′ s (sports) match *m* amical

exhibitor [ɛg'zɪbɪtər] s exposant *m*

exhilarate [ɛg'zɪlə,ret] tr égayer, animer

exhort [ɛg'zɔrt] tr exhorter

exhume [ɛks'hjum] tr exhumer

exigen·cy ['ɛksɪdʒənsi] s (*pl* -cies) exigence *f*

exigent ['ɛksɪdʒənt] adj exigeant

exile ['ɛgzaɪl] s exil *m*; (*person*) exilé *m* ‖ *tr* exiler

exist [ɛg'zɪst] intr exister

existence [ɛg'zɪstəns] s existence *f*

exit ['ɛksɪt] s sortie *f* ‖ *intr* sortir

ex′it poll′ s (pol) sondage *m* isoloir

ex′it tax′i·way s (aer) bretelle *f* de liaison

exodus ['ɛksədəs] s exode *m*

exonerate [ɛg'zɑnə,ret] tr (*to free from blame*) disculper; (*to free from an obligation*) exonérer, dispenser

exorbitant [ɛg'zɔrbɪtənt] adj exorbitant

exorcize ['ɛksɔr,saɪz] tr exorciser

exotic [ɛg'zɑtɪk] adj exotique

expand [ɛks'pænd] tr (*a gas, metal, etc.*) dilater; (*to enlarge, develop*) élargir, développer; (*to unfold, stretch out*) étendre, déployer; (*the chest*) gonfler; (math) développer ‖ *intr* se dilater; s'élargir, se développer; s'étendre, se déployer; se gonfler

expanse [ɛks'pæns] s étendue *f*

expansion [ɛks'pænʃən] s expansion *f*

expan′sion joint′ s joint *m* de dilatation thermique

expansive [ɛks'pænsɪv] adj expansif; (*broad*) large, étendu

expatiate [ɛks'peʃɪ,et] intr discourir, s'étendre

expatriate [ɛks'petrɪ·ɪt] adj & s expatrié *m* ‖ [ɛks'petrɪ,et] tr expatrier

expect [ɛks'pɛkt] tr (*to await the coming of*) attendre; (*to look for as likely*) s'attendre à; **to expect it** s'y attendre; **to expect s.o. to** + *inf* s'attendre à ce que qn + *subj*; **to expect to** + *inf* s'attendre à + *inf*

expectan·cy [ɛks'pɛktənsi] s (*pl* -cies) attente *f*, expectative *f*

expect′ant moth′er [ɛks'pɛktənt] s future mère *f*

expectation [,ɛkspɛk,teʃən] s expectative *f*, espérance *f*

expectorate [ɛks'pɛktə,ret] tr & intr expectorer

expedien·cy [ɛks'pidɪ·ənsi] s (*pl* -cies) convenance *f*, opportunité *f*; opportunisme *m*, débrouillage *m*

expedient [ɛks'pidɪ·ənt] adj expédient; (*looking out for oneself*) débrouillard ‖ s expédient *m*

expedite ['ɛkspɪ,daɪt] tr expédier

expedition [,ɛkspɪ'dɪʃən] s expédition *f*; célérité *f*, promptitude *f*

expeditionary [,ɛkspɪ'dɪʃən,ɛri] adj expéditionnaire

expeditious [,ɛkspɪ'dɪʃəs] adj expéditif

ex·pel [ɛks'pɛl] v (*pret & pp* -pelled; *ger* -pelling) tr expulser; (*from school*) renvoyer

expend [ɛks'pɛnd] tr (*to pay out*) dépenser; (*to use up*) consommer

expendable [ɛks'pɛndəbəl] adj non récupérable; (*soldier*) sacrifiable

expenditure [ɛks'pɛndɪtʃər] s dépense *f*, consommation *f*

expense [ɛks'pɛns] s dépense *f*; **at the expense of** aux dépens de; **expenses** frais *mpl*; (*for which a person will be reimbursed*) indemnité *f*; **to meet expenses** faire face aux dépenses

expense′ account′ s état *m* de frais, note *f* de frais

expensive [ɛks'pɛnsɪv] adj cher, couteux; (*tastes*) dispendieux

experience [ɛks'pɪrɪ·əns] s expérience *f* ‖ *tr* éprouver

experienced adj expérimenté

experiment [ɛks'pɛrɪmənt] s expérience *f* ‖ *intr* faire des expériences, expérimenter

experimental [ɪk,spɛrə'mɛntəl] adj expérimental, probatoire

expert ['ɛkspərt] adj & s expert *m*

expertise [,ɛkspər'tiz] s maîtrise *f*

expiate ['ɛkspɪ,et] tr expier

expiration [,ɛkspə'reʃən] s expiration *f*

expire [ɛks'paɪr] tr & intr expirer

expired adj (*lease; passport*) expiré; (*note; permit*) périmé; (*e.g., driver's license*) suranné; (*insurance policy*) déchu

explain [ɛks'plen] tr expliquer; **to explain oneself** s'expliquer ‖ *intr* expliquer

explainable [ɛks'plenəbəl] adj explicable

explanation [,ɛksplə'neʃən] s explication *f*

explanatory [ɛks'plænə,tori] adj explicatif

explicit [ɛks'plɪsɪt] adj explicite

explode [ɛks'plod] tr faire sauter; (*a theory, opinion, etc.*) discréditer ‖ *intr* exploser, éclater, sauter

exploit ['ɛksplɔɪt] s exploit *m* ‖ [ɛks'plɔɪt] tr exploiter

exploitation [,ɛksplɔɪ'teʃən] s exploitation *f*

exploration [,ɛksplə'reʃən] s exploration *f*

explore [ɛks'plor] tr explorer

explorer [ɛks'plorər] s explorateur *m*; (*boy*

scout) routier *m*

explosion [ɛks'ploʒən] *s* explosion *f*

explosive [ɛks'plosɪv] *adj* explosif; (*mixture*) explosible || *s* explosif *m*

exponent [ɛks'ponənt] *s* interprète *mf*; (math) exposant *m*

export ['ɛksport] *s* exportation *f* || *tr & intr* exporter

exportation [,ɛkspor'teʃən] *s* exportation *f*

exporter ['ɛksportər] *s* exportateur *m*

expose [ɛks'poz] *tr* exposer; (*to unmask*) démasquer, dévoiler; (phot) impressionner

exposé [,ɛkspo'ze] *s* dévoilement *m*, révélation *f*, mise *f* en lumière

exposition [,ɛkspə'zɪʃən] *s* exposition *f*

expostulate [ɛks'pɑstʃə,let] *intr* faire des remontrances; **to expostulate with** faire des remontrances à

exposure [ɛks'poʒər] *s* exposition *f*; (*unmasking*) dévoilement *m*; (phot) exposition *f*, prise *f* de vue(s); (phot) durée *f* d'exposition, indice *m* de pose

expound [ɛks'paʊnd] *tr* exposer

express [ɛks'prɛs] *adj* exprès, formel; (*train; gun*) express || *s* (*merchandise*) messagerie *f*, (*train*) express *m*, rapide *m*, train *m* direct; **by express** (rr) en grande vitesse || *adv* (rr) en grande vitesse || *tr* exprimer; (*merchandise*) envoyer en grande vitesse; (*through the express company*) expédier par les messageries; **to express oneself** s'exprimer

express' com'pany *s* messageries *fpl*

express' high'way *s* autoroute *f*

expression [ɛks'prɛʃən] *s* expression *f*

expressive [ɛks'prɛsɪv] *adj* expressif

expressly [ɛks'prɛsli] *adv* expressément

express'man *s* (*pl* **-men**) entrepreneur *m* de messageries; facteur *m*, agent *m* d'un service de messageries

express' train' *s* train *m* express

express'way' *s* autoroute, route *f* express

expropriate [ɛks'propri,et] *tr* exproprier

expulsion [ɛks'pʌlʃən] *s* expulsion *f*; (*from schools*) renvoi *m*

expunge [ɛks'pʌndʒ] *tr* effacer, supprimer, rayer

expurgate ['ɛkspər,get] *tr* expurger

exquisite ['ɛkskwɪzɪt] *adj* exquis

ex-service-man [,ɛks'sʌrvɪs,mæn] *s* (*pl* **-men'**) ancien combattant *m*

extant ['ɛkstənt], [ɛks'tænt] *adj* existant, subsistant

extemporaneous [ɛks,tɛmpə'reni·əs] *adj* improvisé, impromptu

extemporaneously [ɛks,tɛmpə'reni·əsli] *adv* à l'impromptu, d'abondance

extempore [ɛks'tɛmpəri] *adj* improvisé || *adv* d'abondance, à l'impromptu

extemporize [ɛks'tɛmpə,raɪz] *tr & intr* improviser

extend [ɛks'tɛnd] *tr* (*to stretch out*) étendre; (*a period of time; a street; a line*) prolonger; (*a treaty; a session; a right; a due date*) proroger; (*a helping hand*) tendre || *intr* s'étendre

extended *adj* étendu, prolongé

extend'ed fam'ily *s* communauté *f* familiale, famille *f* étendue

extension [ɛks'tɛnʃən] *s* extension *f*; prolongation *f*; (*board for a table*) rallonge *f*; (*to building*) annexe *f*; (telp) poste *m*

exten'sion cord' *s* cordon *m* prolongateur, prolongateur *m*, rallonge *f*

exten'sion lad'der *s* échelle *f* à coulisse

exten'sion ta'ble *s* table *f* à rallonges

extensive [ɛks'tɛnsɪv] *adj* vaste, étendu

extent [ɛks'tɛnt] *s* étendue *f*; **to a certain extent** dans une certaine mesure; **to a great extent** en grande partie, considérablement; **to the full extent** dans toute la mesure

extenuate [ɛks'tɛnju,et] *tr* atténuer; minimiser

exterior [ɛks'tɪrɪ·ər] *adj & s* extérieur *m*

exterminate [ɛks'tʌrmɪ,net] *tr* exterminer

external [ɛks'tʌrnəl] *adj* extérieur; (pharm, med) externe || **externals** *spl* dehors *mpl*, apparences *fpl*; (*superficialities*) choses *fpl* secondaires

extinct [ɛks'tɪŋkt] *adj* (*volcano*) éteint; disparu; tombé en désuétude

extinction [ɛks'tɪŋkʃən] *s* extinction *f*

extinguish [ɛks'tɪŋgwɪʃ] *tr* éteindre

extinguisher [ɛks'tɪŋgwɪʃər] *s* (*for candles*) éteignoir *m*; (*for fires*) extincteur *m*

extirpate ['ɛkstər,pet] *tr* extirper

ex·tol [ɛks'tol] *v* (*pret & pp* **-tolled**; *ger* **-tolling**) *tr* exalter, vanter

extort [ɛks'tort] *tr* extorquer

extortion [ɛks'torʃən] *s* extorsion *f*

extortionist [ɛks'torʃənɪst] *s* extorqueur *m*

extra ['ɛkstrə] *adj* supplémentaire; (*of high quality*) extra, extra-fin; (*spare*) de rechange || *s* extra *m*; (*of a newspaper*) édition *f* spéciale; (*in building a new house*) rallonge *f*; (mov, theat) figurant *m* || *adv* en plus, en sus; (*not on the bill*) non compris

ex'tra board' *s* (*for extension table*) rallonge *f*

ex'tra charge' *s* supplément *m*

extract ['ɛkstrækt] *s* extrait *m* || [ɛks'trækt] *tr* extraire

extraction [ɛks'trækʃən] *s* extraction *f*

extracurricular [,ɛkstrəkə'rɪkjələr] *adj* extrascolaire

extradite ['ɛkstrə,daɪt] *tr* extrader

extradition [,ɛkstrə'dɪʃən] *s* extradition *f*

ex'tra-dry' *adj* (*champagne*) très sec

ex'tra fare' *s* supplément *m* de billet

ex'tra·galac'tic *adj* extragalactique

ex'tra·mu'ral *adj* à l'extérieur de la ville; à l'extérieur de l'université

extraneous [ɛks'treni·əs] *adj* étranger

extraordinary [ɛks'trordɪ,nɛri] *adj* extraordinaire

extrapolate [ɛks'træpə,let] *tr & intr* extrapoler

ex'tra·sen'sory *adj* extrasensoriel

ex'tra-spe'cial *adj* extra

ex'tra·terres'trial *adj* extraterrestre

extravagance [ɛks'trævəgəns] *s* (*lavishness*)

prodigalité *f*, gaspillage *m*; (*folly*) extravagance *f*

extravagant [ɛks'trævəgənt] *adj* (*person*) dépensier, prodigue; (*price*) exorbitant; (*e.g., praise*) outré; (*e.g., claims*) exagéré, extravagant

extreme [ɛks'trim] *adj & s* extrême *m*; **in the extreme, to extremes** à l'extrême

extremely [ɛks'trimli] *adv* extrêmement

extreme' unc'tion *s* extrême-onction *f*

extremist [ɛks'trimɪst] *adj & s* extrémiste *mf*, ultra *mf*

extremi·ty [ɛks'trɛmɪti] *s* (*pl* **-ties**) extrémité *f*; **extremities** extrémités

extricate ['ɛkstrɪ,ket] *tr* dégager; (*a gas*) libérer; **to extricate oneself from** se tirer de, se dépêtrer de

extrinsic [ɛks'trɪnsɪk] *adj* extrinsèque

extrovert ['ɛkstrə,vʌrt] *adj & s* extraverti *m*

extrude [ɛks'trud] *intr* faire saillie, dépasser

exuberant [ɛg'z(j)ubərənt] *adj* exubérant

exude [ɛg'zud] *tr & intr* exsuder

exult [ɛg'zʌlt] *intr* exulter

exultant [ɛg'zʌltənt] *adj* triomphant

eye [aɪ] *s* œil *m*; (*of needle*) chas *m*, trou *m*; (*of hook and eye*) porte *f*; **eyes** *pl* yeux *mpl*; **to catch s.o.'s eye** tirer l'œil à qn; **to lay eyes on** jeter les yeux sur; **to make eyes at** (coll) faire les yeux doux à; **to see eye to eye with s.o.** voir les choses du même œil que qn; **with an eye to** en vue de; **without batting an eye** (coll) sans sourciller ‖ *v* (*pret & pp* **eyed**; *ger* **eying** or **eyeing**) *tr* toiser, reluquer

eye'ball' *s* globe *m* oculaire

eye' bank' *s* banque *f* des yeux

eye'bolt' *s* boulon *m* à œil

eye'brow' *s* sourcil *m*

eye'cup' *s* œillère *f*

eye' drops' *spl* collyre *m*

eye,' ear,' nose,' and throat' (*public sign*) yeux, nez, gorge, oreilles

eyeful ['aɪfʊl] *s* vue *f*, coup *m* d'œil; **to get an eyeful** (coll) s'en mettre plein la vue, se rincer l'œil

eye'glass' *s* (*of optical instrument*) oculaire *m*; (*eyecup*) œillère *f*; **eyeglasses** lunettes *fpl*

eye'lash' *s* cil *m*; (*fringe of hair*) cils

eyelet ['aɪlɪt] *s* œillet *m*; (*of sail*) œil *m* de pie

eye'lid' *s* paupière *f*

eye' of the morn'ing *s* astre *m* du jour

eye' o'pener ['opənər] *s* révélation *f*; (coll) goutte *f* de bonne heure

eye'piece' *s* oculaire *m*

eye' shade' *s* visière *f*, abat-jour *m*

eye' shad'ow *s* fard *m* à paupières

eye'shot' *s* portée *f* de la vue

eye'sight' *s* vue *f*; (*eyeshot*) portée *f* de la vue

eye' sock'et *s* orbite *f* de l'œil

eye'sore' *s* objet *m* déplaisant

eye'strain' *s* fatigue *f* des yeux; **to suffer from eyestrain** avoir les yeux fatigués

eye' test' *s* examen *m* de la vision

eye'-test chart' *s* tableau *m* de lecture pour la vision

eye'tooth' *s* (*pl* **-teeth**) dent *f* œillère or canine; **to cut one's eyeteeth** (coll) ne pas être un blanc-bec; **to give one's eyeteeth for** (coll) donner la prunelle de ses yeux pour

eye'wash' *s* collyre *m*; (slang) de l'eau bénite de cour, de la poudre aux yeux

eye'wit'ness *s* témoin *m* oculaire

ey·rie or **ey·ry** ['ɛri] *s* (*pl* **-ries**) aire *f* (de l'aigle); (fig) nid *m* d'aigle

F

F, f [ɛf] *s* VIe lettre de l'alphabet

fable ['febəl] *s* fable *f*

fabric ['fæbrɪk] *s* tissu *m*, étoffe *f*

fabricate ['fæbrɪ,ket] *tr* fabriquer

fabrication [,fæbrɪ'keʃən] *s* fabrication *f*; (*lie*) mensonge *m*

fabulous ['fæbjələs] *adj* fabuleux

façade [fə'sɑd] *s* façade *f*

face [fes] *s* visage *m*, figure *f*; (*side*) face *f*; (*of the earth*) surface *f*; (*appearance, expression*) mine *f*, physionomie *f*; **about face!** (mil) demi-tour! **to keep a straight face** montrer un front sérieux; **to lose face** perdre la face; **to make a face** faire une grimace; **to set one's face against** faire front à ‖ *tr* faire face à; (*a wall*) revêtir; (*a garment*) mettre un revers à ‖ *intr*—**to face about** faire demi-tour; **to face up to** faire face à, affronter

face' card' *s* figure *f*

face' lift' or **face' lift'ing** *s* ridectomie *f*, déridage *m*, lissage *m*

face' pow'der *s* poudre *f* de riz

facet ['fæsɪt] *s* facette *f*

facetious [fə'siʃəs] *adj* plaisant

face' tow'el *s* serviette *f* de toilette

face' val'ue *s* valeur *f* faciale, valeur nominale

facial ['feʃəl] *adj* facial ‖ *s* massage *m* esthétique

fa'cial tis'sue *s* serviette *f* à démaquiller

facilitate [fə'sɪlɪ,tet] *tr* faciliter

facili·ty [fə'sɪlɪti] *s* (*pl* **-ties**) facilité *f*; **facilities** installations *fpl*

facing ['fesɪŋ] *s* revêtement *m*; (*of garment*) revers *m*

facsimile [fæk'sɪmɪli] *s* fac-similé *m*

fact [fækt] s fait m; **in fact** en fait, de fait; **the fact is that** c'est que

faction ['fækʃən] s faction f; (strife) discorde f

factor ['fæktər] s facteur m || tr résoudre or décomposer en facteurs

facto·ry ['fæktəri] s (pl -ries) usine f, fabrique f

fac'tory price' s prix m de facture, prix usine

factual ['fæktʃu·əl] adj vrai, réel

facul·ty ['fækəlti] s (pl -ties) faculté f; (teaching staff) corps m enseignant

fad [fæd] s mode f, marotte f, lubie f; **latest fad** dernier cri m

fade [fed] tr déteindre, décolorer || intr déteindre, se décolorer; (to lose vigor, freshness) se faner; **to fade in** apparaître graduellement; **to fade out** disparaître graduellement

fade'-in' s (mov) apparition f en fondu

fade'-out' s (mov) fondu m

fag [fæg] s (slang) cibiche f || v (pret & pp fagged; ger fagging) tr—**to fag out** éreinter

fagot ['fægət] s fagot m; (for filling up trenches) fascine f || tr fagoter

fail [fel] s—**without fail** sans faute || tr manquer à; (a student) refuser; (an examination) échouer à or dans || intr manquer, faire défaut; (to not succeed) échouer, rater; (said of motor) tomber en panne; (to weaken) baisser, faiblir; **to fail completely** faire chou blanc; **to fail in** faillir à; **to fail to** manquer de, faillir à; **to fail to do** or **to keep** faillir à

failing ['felɪŋ] adj défaillant || s défaut m || prep à défaut de

fail'-safe' adj automatiquement protégé, à sûreté intégrée

failure ['feljər] s insuccès m, échec m; (lack) manque m, défaut m; (person) raté m; (com) faillite f

faint [fent] adj faible; **to feel faint** se sentir mal || s évanouissement m || intr s'-évanouir

faint'-heart'ed adj timide, peureux

fair [fɛr] adj juste, équitable; (honest) loyal, honnête; (average) moyen, passable; (clear) clair; (beautiful) beau; (pleasing) agréable, plaisant; (of hair) blond; (complexion) blanc; **to be fair** (to be just) être de bonne guerre || s foire f, fête f; (bazaar) kermesse f || adv impartialement; **to bid fair to** avoir des chances de; **to play fair** jouer franc jeu

fair' cop'y s copie f au net

fair'ground' s champ m de foire

fairly ['fɛrli] adv impartialement, loyalement; assez

fair'-mind'ed adj impartial

fairness ['fɛrnɪs] s impartialité f, justice f; (of complexion) clarté f

fair' play' s franc jeu m

fair' sex' s beau sexe m

fair'way' s (golf) parcours m normal; (naut) chenal m

fair'-weath'er adj (e.g., friend) des beaux jours

fair·y ['fɛri] adj féerique || s (pl -ies) fée f; (homosexual) (pej) tapette f, tante f

fair'y god'mother s marraine f fée; (coll) marraine gâteau

fair'y·land' s royaume m des fées

fair'y tale' s conte m de fées

faith [feθ] s foi f; **to break faith with** manquer de foi à; **to keep faith with** tenir ses engagements envers; **to pin one's faith on** mettre tout son espoir en

faithful ['feθfəl] adj fidèle || s—**the faithful** les fidèles mpl

faithless ['feθlɪs] adj infidèle

fake [fek] adj (coll) faux || s faux m, article m truqué || tr truquer

faker ['fekər] s truqueur m

falcon ['fɔkən], ['fɔlkən] s faucon m

falconer ['fɔkənər] s fauconnier m

fall [fɔl] adj automnal || s chute f; (of prices) baisse f; (season) automne m & f; **falls** chute d'eau f || v (pret **fell** [fɛl]; pp **fallen** ['fɔlən]) intr tomber; (said of prices) baisser; **fall in!** (mil) rassemblement!; **fall out!** (mil) rompez les rangs!; **to fall down** (said of person) tomber par terre; (said of building) s'écrouler; **to fall for** (coll) se laisser prendre à; (to fall in love with) (coll) tomber amoureux de; **to fall in** s'effondrer; (mil) former des rangs; **to fall into the trap** donner dans le piège; **to fall off** tomber de; (to decline) baisser, diminuer; **to fall out** (to disagree) se brouiller; **to fall over oneself to** (coll) se mettre en quatre pour

fallacious [fə'leʃəs] adj fallacieux

falla·cy ['fæləsi] s (pl -cies) erreur f, fausseté f

fall' guy' s (slang) tête f de Turc

fallible ['fælɪbəl] adj faillible

fall'ing star' s étoile f filante

fall'out' s pluies fpl radioactives, retombées fpl radioactives

fall'out shel'ter s abri m antiatomique

fallow ['fælo] adj en friche, en jachère || s friche f, jachère f || tr laisser en friche or en jachère

false [fɔls] adj faux; artificiel, simulé; (hair) postiche || adv faussement; **to play false** tromper

false' alarm' s fausse alerte f

false' bot'tom s double fond m

false' cog'nate s faux ami m

false' eye'lashes spl cils mpl postiches

false' face' s masque m

false'-heart'ed adj perfide, traître

false'hood s mensonge m

false' pretens'es spl faux-semblants mpl

false' return' s fausse déclaration f d'impôts

false' step' s faux-pas m

false' teeth' ['tiθ] spl fausses dents fpl

falset·to [fɔl'sɛto] s (pl -tos) fausset m, voix f de tête; (person) fausset m

falsi·fy ['fɔlsɪ,faɪ] v (pret & pp -fied) tr falsifier, fausser

falsi·ty ['fɔlsɪti] *s* (*pl* **-ties**) fausseté *f*
falter ['fɔltər] *s* vacillation *f*, hésitation *f*; (*of speech*) balbutiement *m* ‖ *intr* vaciller, hésiter; balbutier
fame [fem] *s* renom *m*, renommée *f*
famed *adj* renommé, célèbre
familiar [fə'mɪljər] *adj* & *s* familier *m*; **to become familiar with** se familiariser avec
familiari·ty [fə,mɪlɪ'ærɪti] *s* (*pl* **-ties**) familiarité *f*
familiarize [fə'mɪljə,raɪz] *tr* familiariser
fami·ly ['fæmɪli] *adj* familial; **in a** or **the family way** (coll) dans une position intéressante; (coll) en famille (Canad) ‖ *s* (*pl* **-lies**) famille *f*
fam'ily man' *s* (*pl* **men'**) père *m* de famille; (*stay-at-home*) homme *m* casanier, pantouflard *m*
fam'ily name' *s* nom *m* de famille
fam'ily physi'cian *s* médecin *m* de famille
fam'ily plan'ning *s* planisme *m* familial
fam'ily tree' *s* arbre *m* généalogique
famine ['fæmɪn] *s* famine *f*
famish ['fæmɪʃ] *tr* affamer, priver de vivres ‖ *intr* souffrir de la faim
famished *adj* affamé, famélique; **to be famished** (coll) mourir de faim
famous ['feməs] *adj* renommé, célèbre
fan [fæn] *s* éventail *m*; (mach) ventilateur *m*; (coll) fanatique *mf*, enragé *m* ‖ *v* (*pret* & *pp* **fanned**; *ger* **fanning**) *tr* éventer; (*to winnow*) vanner; (*e.g., passions*) exciter ‖ *intr*—**to fan out** se déployer en éventail
fanatic [fə'nætɪk] *adj* & *s* fanatique *mf*
fanatical [fə'nætɪkəl] *adj* fanatique
fanaticism [fə'nætɪ,sɪzəm] *s* fanatisme *m*
fan' belt' *s* (aut) courroie *f* de ventilateur
fancied *adj* imaginaire, supposé
fanciful ['fænsɪfəl] *adj* fantaisiste, capricieux
fan·cy ['fænsi] *adj* (*comp* **-cier**; *super* **-ciest**) ornemental; (*goods, clothes, bread*) de fantaisie; (*high-quality*) fin, extra, de luxe ‖ *s* (*pl* **-cies**) fantaisie *f*, caprice *m*; **to take a fancy to** prendre du goût pour; (*a loved one*) prendre en affection ‖ *v* (*pret* & *pp* **-cied**) *tr* s'imaginer, se figurer; **to fancy oneself** s'imaginer; **to fancy that** imaginer que
fan'cy dress' *s* costume *m* de fantaisie, travesti *m*
fan'cy dress' ball' *s* bal *m* costumé, bal travesti
fan'cy foods' *spl* comestibles *mpl* de fantaisie
fan'cy-free' *adj* libre, gai, sans amour
fan'cy jew'elry *s* bijouterie *f* de fantaisie
fan'cy skat'ing *s* patinage *m* de fantaisie
fan'cy·work' *s* broderie *f*, ouvrage *m* d'agrément
fanfare ['fænfɛr] *s* fanfare *f*
fang [fæŋ] *s* croc *m*; (*of snake*) crochet *m*
fantastic(al) [fæn'tæstɪk(əl)] *adj* fantastique
fanta·sy ['fæntəsi] *s* (*pl* **-sies**) fantaisie *f*
far [fɑr] *adj* lointain; **on the far side of** à l'autre côté de ‖ *adv* loin; **as far as** autant que; (*up to*) jusqu'à; **as far as I am**

concerned quant à moi; **as far as I know** pour autant que je sache; **by far** de beaucoup; **far and wide** partout; **far away** au loin; **far from** loin de; **far from it** tant s'en faut; **far into the night** fort avant dans la nuit; **far into the woods** avant dans le bois; **far off** au loin; **how far? far off? how far is it from . . .?** jusqu'où?; **how far is it from . . .?** combien y a-t-il de . . .?; **in so far as** dans la mesure où; **so far** or **thus far** jusqu'ici; **to go far** contribuer pour beaucoup à
far'away' *adj* éloigné, distant
farce [fɑrs] *s* farce *f*
farcical ['fɑrsɪkəl] *adj* grotesque, ridicule
fare [fɛr] *s* prix *m*, tarif *m*; (*cost of taxi*) course *f*; (*passenger in taxi*) client *m*; (*passenger in bus*) voyageur *m*; (culin) chère *f*, ordinaire *m*; **fares, please!** vos places, s'il vous plaît! ‖ *intr* se porter; **how did you fare?** comment ça s'est-il passé?
Far' East' *s* Extrême-Orient *m*
fare'well' *s* adieu *m*; **to bid s.o. farewell** dire adieu à qn
far'-fetched' *adj* tiré par les cheveux
far-flung ['fɑr'flʌŋ] *adj* étendu, vaste, d'une grande envergure
farm [fɑrm] *s* ferme *f*; (*sharecropper's farm*) métairie *f* ‖ *tr* cultiver, exploiter; **to farm out** donner à ferme; (*work*) donner en exploitation à l'extérieur ‖ *intr* faire de la culture
farmer ['fɑrmər] *s* fermier *m*
farm' hand' *s* valet *m* de ferme
farm'house' *s* ferme *f*, maison *f* de ferme
farming ['fɑrmɪŋ] *s* agriculture *f*, exploitation *f* agricole
farm'yard' *s* cour *f* de ferme
Far' North' *s* Grand Nord *m*
far'-off' *adj* lointain, éloigné
far'-reach'ing *adj* à longue portée
far'sight'ed *adj* prévoyant; (physiol) presbyte
farther ['fɑrðər] *adj* plus éloigné ‖ *adv* plus loin
farthest ['fɑrðɪst] *adj* (le) plus éloigné ‖ *adv* le plus loin; au plus
farthing ['fɑrðɪŋ] *s* liard *m*
fascinate ['fæsɪ,net] *tr* fasciner
fascinating ['fæsɪ,netɪŋ] *adj* fascinateur, fascinant
fascism ['fæʃɪzəm] *s* fascisme *m*
fascist ['fæʃɪst] *adj* & *s* fasciste *mf*
fashion ['fæʃən] *s* mode *f*, vogue *f*; (*manner*) façon *f*, manière *f*; **after a fashion** tant bien que mal; **in fashion** à la mode, en vogue; **out of fashion** démodé ‖ *tr* façonner
fashionable ['fæʃənəbəl] *adj* à la mode, élégant, chic
fash'ion design'ing *s* haute couture *f*
fash'ion parade' *s* défilé *m* de modes
fash'ion plate' *s* gravure *f* de mode; (*person*) (coll) élégant *m*
fash'ion show' *s* présentation *f* de collection, présentation de modèles

fast [fæst], [fɑst] *adj* rapide; (*fixed*) solide, fixe; (*clock*) en avance; (*friend*) fidèle; (*color*) grand, bon, e.g., **fast color** grand teint, bon teint; (*person*) (slang) dévergondé; **to make fast** fixer, fermer ‖ *s* jeûne *m*; **to break one's fast** rompre le jeûne ‖ *adv* vite, rapidement; (*firmly*) solidement, ferme; (*asleep*) profondément; **to hold fast** tenir bon; **to live fast** (coll) faire la noce, mener la vie à grandes guides; **to stand fast against** tenir tête à ‖ *intr* jeûner

fast′ day′ *s* jour *m* de jeûne, jour maigre

fasten [ˈfæsən] *tr* attacher, fixer; (*e.g., a belt*) ajuster ‖ *intr* s'attacher, se fixer

fastener [ˈfæsənər] *s* attache *f*, agrafe *f*

fast′ food′ *s* or **fast foods** *spl* fast food *m*; (*type of business*) restauration *f* rapide

fast′-food res′taurant *s* restaupouce *m*

fastidious [fæsˈtɪdɪ·əs] *adj* délicat, dégoûté, difficile

fasting [ˈfæstɪŋ] *s* jeûne *m*

fat [fæt] *adj* (*comp* **fatter**; *super* **fattest**) (*plump; greasy*) gras; (*large*) gros; (*soil*) riche; (*spark*) nourri; **to get fat** engraisser ‖ *s* graisse *f*; (*of meat*) gras *m*

fatal [ˈfetəl] *adj* fatal

fatalism [ˈfetə,lɪzəm] *s* fatalisme *m*

fatalist [ˈfetəlɪst] *s* fataliste *mf*

fatali·ty [fəˈtælɪti] *s* (*pl* **-ties**) fatalité *f*; (*in accidents, war, etc.*) mort *f*, accident *m* mortel

fate [fet] *s* sort *m*, destin *m*; **the Fates** les Parques *fpl*

fated *adj* destiné, voué

fateful [ˈfetfəl] *adj* fatal; (*prophetic*) fatidique

fat′head′ *s* (coll) crétin *m*, sot *m*

father [ˈfɑðər] *s* père *m*; **Father** (*salutation given a priest*) Monsieur l'abbé ‖ *tr* servir de père à; (*to beget*) engendrer; (*an idea, project*) inventer

fa′ther·hood′ *s* paternité *f*

fa′ther-in-law′ *s* (*pl* **fathers-in-law**) beaupère *m*

fa′ther·land′ *s* patrie *f*

fatherless [ˈfɑðərlɪs] *adj* sans père, orphelin de père

fatherly [ˈfɑðərli] *adj* paternel

Fa′ther Time′ *s* le Temps

fathom [ˈfæðəm] *s* brasse *f* ‖ *tr* sonder

fathomless [ˈfæðəmlɪs] *adj* insondable

fatigue [fəˈtig] *s* fatigue *f*; **fatigues** (mil) bleus *mpl*

fatigue′ clothes′ *spl* tenue *f* de corvée

fatigue′ du′ty *s* (mil) corvée *f*

fatten [ˈfætən] *tr & intr* engraisser

fat·ty [ˈfæti] *adj* (*comp* **-tier**; *super* **-tiest**) gras, grassieux; (*tissue*) adipeux; (*chubby*) (coll) potelé, dodu ‖ *s* (*pl* **-ties**) (coll) bon gros *m*

fatuous [ˈfætʃʊ·əs] *adj* sot, idiot

faucet [ˈfɔsɪt] *s* robinet *m*

fault [fɔlt] *s* faute *f*; (geol) faille *f*; **to a fault** à l'excès; **to find fault with** trouver à redire à

fault′find′er *s* critiqueur *m*, éplucheur *m*

fault′find′ing *adj* chicaneur ‖ *s* chicanerie *f*, critique *f*

faultless [ˈfɔltlɪs] *adj* sans défaut

fault·y [ˈfɔlti] *adj* (*comp* **-ier**; *super* **-iest**) fautif, défectueux

faun [fɔn] *s* faune *m*

fauna [ˈfɔnə] *s* faune *f*

favor [ˈfevər] *s* faveur *f*; **do me the favor to** faites-moi le plaisir de; **to be in favor of** être partisan de; **to be in favor with** jouir de la faveur de; **to decide in s.o.'s favor** donner gain de cause à qn; **to do a favor in return** renvoyer l'ascenseur ‖ *tr* favoriser; (*to look like*) (coll) tenir de; (*e.g., a sore leg*) (coll) ménager

favorable [ˈfevərəbəl] *adj* favorable

favorite [ˈfevərɪt] *adj & s* favori *m*

fawn [fɔn] *adj* (*color*) fauve ‖ *s* faon *m* ‖ *intr*—**to fawn upon** (*said of dog*) faire des caresses à; (*said of person*) faire le chien couchant auprès de

faze [fez] *tr* (coll) affecter, troubler

FBI [ˌɛf,biˈaɪ] *s* (letterword) (**Federal Bureau of Investigation**) Sûreté *f* nationale, Sûreté (*the French equivalent*)

fear [fɪr] *s* crainte *f*, peur *f* ‖ *tr* craindre, avoir peur de ‖ *intr* craindre, avoir peur

fearful [ˈfɪrfəl] *adj* (*frightened*) peureux, effrayé; (*frightful*) effrayant; (coll) énorme, effrayant

fearless [ˈfɪrlɪs] *adj* sans peur

feasible [ˈfɪzɪbəl] *adj* faisable

feast [fist] *s* festin *m*, régal *m* ‖ *tr* régaler ‖ *intr* faire bonne chère; **to feast on** se régaler de

feast′ day′ *s* fête *f*, jour *m* de fête

feat [fit] *s* exploit *m*, haut fait *m*

feather [ˈfɛðər] *s* plume *f*; **feather in one's cap** (coll) fleuron *m* à sa couronne; **in fine feather** (coll) plein d'entrain ‖ *tr* emplumer; (*an oar*) ramener à plat; **to feather one's nest** (coll) faire son beurre

feath′er bed′ *s* lit *m* de plumes, couette *f*

feath′er·bed′ding *s* emploi *m* de plus d'ouvriers qu'il n'en faut

feath′er·brained′ *adj* braque, étourdi

feath′er dust′er *s* plumeau *m*

feath′er·edge′ *s* (*of board*) biseau *m*; (*of tool*) morfil *m*

feath′er·weight′ *s* (boxing) poids *m* plume, poids mouche

feathery [ˈfɛðəri] *adj* plumeux

feature [ˈfitʃər] *s* trait *m*, caractéristique *f*; (mov) long métrage *m*, grand film *m* ‖ *tr* caractériser; offrir comme attraction principale

fea′ture writ′er *s* rédacteur *m*

February [ˈfɛbru,ɛri] *s* février *m*

feces [ˈfisiz] *spl* fèces *fpl*

feckless [ˈfɛklɪs] *adj* veule, faible

federal [ˈfɛdərəl] *adj & s* fédéral *m*

federate [ˈfɛdə,ret] *adj* fédéré ‖ *tr* fédérer ‖ *intr* se fédérer

federation [ˌfɛdəˈreʃən] *s* fédération *f*

fedora [fɪˈdorə] *s* chapeau *m* mou

fed′ up′ [fɛd] *adj*—**to be fed up** (coll) en avoir marre; **to be fed up with** (coll) avoir plein le dos de

fee [fi] *s* honoraires *mpl*, cachet *m*; **for a nominal fee** pour une somme symbolique

feeble [′fibəl] *adj* faible

fee′ble·mind′ed *adj* imbécile; obtus, à l'esprit lourd

feed [fid] *s* nourriture *f*, pâture *f*; (mach) alimentation *f*; (slang) grand repas *m* ‖ *v* (*pret & pp* **fed** [fɛd]) *tr* nourrir, donner à manger à; (*a machine*) alimenter ‖ *intr* manger; **to feed upon** se nourrir de

feed′back′ *s* réalimentation *f*, régénération *f*, contre-réaction *f*, réaction *f*

feed′ bag′ *s* musette-mangeoire *f*; **to put on the feed bag** (slang) casser la croûte

feeder [′fidər] *s* alimenteur *m*; (elec) canal *m* d'amenée

feed′ pump′ *s* pompe *f* d'alimentation

feed′ trough′ *s* mangeoire *f*, auge *f*

feed′ wire′ *s* (elec) fil *m* d'amenée

feel [fil] *s* sensation *f* ‖ *v* (*pret & pp* **felt** [fɛlt]) *tr* sentir, éprouver; (*the pulse*) tâter; (*to examine*) palper; **to feel one's way** avancer à tâtons ‖ *intr* (*sick, tired, etc.*) se sentir; **I feel as if . . .** il me semble que . . .; **not to feel well** être mal en point; **to feel for** tâtonner, chercher à tâtons; (*to sympathize with*) (coll) être plein de pitié pour; **to feel like** avoir envie de

feeler [′filər] *s* (ent) antenne *f*; **to put out a feeler** (coll) tâter le terrain

feeling [′filɪŋ] *s* (*with senses*) toucher *m*, tact *m*; (*with hands*) tâtage *m*; (*impression, emotion*) sentiment *m*; **feelings** sensibilité *f*

feign [fen] *tr & intr* feindre

feint [fent] *s* feinte *f* ‖ *intr* feinter

feldspar [′fɛld,spar] *s* feldspath *m*

felicitate [fə′lɪsɪ,tet] *tr* féliciter

felicitous [fə′lɪsɪtəs] *adj* heureux, à propos

fell [fɛl] *adj* cruel, féroce ‖ *tr* abattre

felloe [′fɛlo] *s* jante *f*

fellow [′fɛlo] *s* (*of a society*) membre *m*; (*holder of a fellowship*) boursier *m*; (*friend, neighbor, etc.*) homme *m*, compagnon *m*; (coll) type *m*, bonhomme *m*, gars *m*; **poor fellow!** (coll) pauvre garçon!

fel′low cit′izen *s* concitoyen *m*

fel′low coun′tryman *s* compatriote *mf*

fel′low crea′ture *s* semblable *mf*

fel′low-man′ *s* (*pl* **-men′**) semblable *m*, prochain *m*

fel′low mem′ber *s* confrère *m*

fel′low·ship *s* camaraderie *f*; (*scholarship*) bourse *f*; (*organization*) association *f*

fel′low stu′dent *s* condisciple *m*

fel′low trav′eler *s* compagnon *m* de voyage; (pol) compagnon de route

felon [′fɛlən] *s* criminel *m*; (pathol) panaris *m*

felo·ny [′fɛləni] *s* (*pl* **-nies**) crime *m*

felt [fɛlt] *s* feutre *m* ‖ *tr* feutrer

felt′-tip pen′ *s* stylo-feutre *m*

female [′fimel] *adj* (*sex*) féminin *m*; (*animal, plant, piece of a device*) femelle ‖ *s* (*person*) femme *f*; (*plant, animal*) femelle *f*

feminine [′fɛmɪnɪn] *adj & s* féminin *m*

feminism [′fɛmɪ,nɪzəm] *s* féminisme *m*

fen [fɛn] *s* marécage *m*

fence [fɛns] *s* barrière *f*, clôture *f*; palissade *f*; (*for stolen goods*) receleur *m*, marchand *m* clandestin; **on the fence** (coll) indécis, en balance ‖ *tr* clôturer ‖ *intr* faire de l'escrime

fencing [′fɛnsɪŋ] *s* (*enclosure*) clôture *f*; (sports) escrime *f*

fenc′ing acad′emy *s* salle *f* d'armes

fenc′ing mas′ter *s* maître *m* d'armes

fenc′ing match′ *s* assaut *m* d'armes

fend [fɛnd] *tr*—**to fend off** parer ‖ *intr*—**to fend for oneself** (coll) se débrouiller, se tirer d'affaire

fender [′fɛndər] *s* (*mudguard*) aile *f*, garde-boue *m*; (*of locomotive*) chasse-pierres *m*; (*of fireplace*) garde-feu *m*

fennel [′fɛnəl] *s* fenouil *m*

ferment [′fʌrmɛnt] *s* ferment *m* ‖ [fər′mɛnt] *tr* faire fermenter; (*wine*) cuver ‖ *intr* fermenter

fern [fʌrn] *s* fougère *f*

ferocious [fə′roʃəs] *adj* féroce

feroci·ty [fə′rasɪti] *s* (*pl* **-ties**) férocité *f*

ferret [′fɛrɪt] *s* furet *m* ‖ *tr*—**to ferret out** dénicher ‖ *intr* fureter

Fer′ris wheel′ [′fɛrɪs] *s* grande roue *f*

fer·ry [′fɛri] *s* (*pl* **-ries**) bac *m*; (*to transport trains*) ferry-boat *m* ‖ *v* (*pret & pp* **-ried**) *tr & intr* passer en bac

fer′ry·boat′ *s* bac *m*; (*to transport trains*) ferry-boat *m*

fer′ry·man *s* (*pl* **-men**) passeur *m*

fertile [′fʌrtɪl] *adj* fertile, fécond

fertilize [′fʌrtɪ,laɪz] *tr* fertiliser; (*to impregnate*) féconder

fertilizer [′fʌrtɪ,laɪzər] *s* engrais *m*, amendement *m;* (bot) fécondateur *m*

fervent [′fʌrvənt] *adj* fervent

fervid [′fʌrvɪd] *adj* fervent

fervor [′fʌrvər] *s* ferveur *f*

fester [′fɛstər] *s* ulcère *m* ‖ *tr* ulcérer ‖ *intr* s'ulcérer

festival [′fɛstɪvəl] *adj* de fête ‖ *s* fête *f*; (mov, mus) festival *m*

festive [′fɛstɪv] *adj* de fête, gai

festivi·ty [fɛs′tɪvɪti] *s* (*pl* **-ties**) festivité *f*

festoon [fɛs′tun] *s* feston *m* ‖ *tr* festonner

fetch [fɛtʃ] *tr* aller chercher; (*a certain price*) se vendre à

fetching [′fɛtʃɪŋ] *adj* (coll) séduisant

fete [fet] *s* fête *f* ‖ *tr* fêter

fetish [′fɛtɪʃ] *s* fétiche *m*

fetlock [′fɛtlak] *s* boulet *m*; (*tuft of hair*) fanon *m*

fetter [′fɛtər] *s* lien *m*; **fetters** fers *mpl*, chaînes *fpl* ‖ *tr* enchaîner, entraver

fettle [′fɛtəl] *s* condition *f*, état *m*; **in fine fettle** en pleine forme

fetus [′fitəs] *s* fœtus *m*

feud [fjud] *s* querelle *f*, vendetta *f* ‖ *intr* se quereller, être à couteaux tirés

feudal [′fjudəl] *adj* féodal

feudalism ['fjudǝ,lɪzǝm] s féodalisme m

fever ['fivǝr] s fièvre f

fe'ver blis'ter s bouton m de fièvre

feverish ['fivǝrɪʃ] adj fiévreux

few [fju] adj peu de; **a few . . .** quelques
. . .; **quite a few** pas mal de; **the few . . .**
les rares . . . ‖ pron indef peu; **a few**
quelques-uns §81; **quite a few** beaucoup

ff. abbr et seq., et suivantes; **see p. 21 ff.**
voir à partir de la page 21

fiancé [,fi·ɑn'se] s fiancé m

fiancée [,fi·ɑn'se] s fiancée f

fias·co [fɪ'æsko] s (pl **-cos** or **-coes**) fiasco
m, échec m

fiat ['faɪ·æt] s ordonnance f, autorisation f

fib [fɪb] s (coll) petit mensonge m, blague f
‖ v (pret & pp **fibbed**; ger **fibbing**) intr
(coll) blaguer

fiber ['faɪbǝr] s fibre f

fibrous ['faɪbrǝs] adj fibreux

fickle ['fɪkǝl] adj inconstant, volage

fiction ['fɪkʃǝn] s fiction f; (branch of literature) ouvrages mpl d'imagination, ro-
mans mpl

fictional ['fɪkʃǝnǝl] adj romanesque, d'imagination

fictionalize ['fɪkʃǝnǝ,laɪz] tr romancer

fictitious [fɪk'tɪʃǝs] adj fictif

fiddle ['fɪdǝl] s violon m ‖ tr—**to fiddle
away** (coll) gaspiller ‖ intr jouer du violon; **to fiddle around** or **with** (coll) tripoter

fiddler ['fɪdlǝr] s (coll) violoneux m

fid'dle·stick' s (coll) archet m; **fiddlesticks!**
(coll) quelle blague!

fiddling ['fɪdlɪŋ] adj (coll) musard

fideli·ty [fɪ'dɛlɪti] s (pl **-ties**) fidélité f

fidget ['fɪdʒɪt] intr se trémousser; **to fidget
with** tripoter

fidgety ['fɪdʒɪti] adj nerveux

fiduciar·y [fɪ'd(j)uʃɪ,ɛri] adj fiduciaire ‖ s
(pl **-ies**) fiduciaire m

fie [faɪ] interj fi!; **fie on . . .!** nargue
de . . .!

field [fild] s (piece of land) champ m; (area,
activity) domaine m, aire f; (aer, sports)
terrain m; (elec) champ; (of motor or
dynamo) (elec) inducteur m; (mil) aire f,
théâtre m

field' day' s (cleanup) (mil) manœuvres fpl
de garnison; (sports) manifestation f sportive

fielder ['fildǝr] s (baseball) chasseur m,
homme m de champ

field' glass'es spl jumelles fpl

field' hock'ey s hockey m sur gazon

field' hos'pital s ambulance f, formation f
sanitaire

field' house' s complexe m sportif

field' mag'net s aimant m inducteur

field' mar'shal s maréchal m

field' mouse' s mulot m

field'piece' s pièce f de campagne

fiend [find] s démon m; (mischiefmaker)
(coll) espiègle mf; (enthusiast) (coll)
mordu m; (addict) (coll) toxicomane mf

fiendish ['findɪʃ] adj diabolique

fierce [fɪrs] adj féroce, farouche; (wind)
furieux; (coll) très mauvais

fierceness ['fɪrsnɪs] s férocité f

fier·y ['faɪri] adj (comp **-ier**; super **-iest**)
(coals, sun) ardent; (heat, sand) brûlant;
(speech) fougueux, enflammé; (horse,
person, etc.) fougueux, ardent

fife [faɪf] s fifre m

fifteen ['fɪf'tin] adj, pron, & s quinze m;
about fifteen une quinzaine de

fifteenth ['fɪf'tinθ] adj & pron quinzième
(masc, fem); **the Fifteenth** quinze, e.g.,
John the Fifteenth Jean quinze ‖ s quinzième m; **the fifteenth** (in dates) le quinze

fifth [fɪfθ] adj & pron cinquième (masc,
fem); **the Fifth** cinq, e.g., **John the Fifth**
Jean cinq ‖ s cinquième; (mus) quinte f;
the fifth (in dates) le cinq

fifth' col'umn s cinquième colonne f

fiftieth ['fɪftɪ·ɪθ] adj & pron cinquantième
(masc, fem) ‖ s cinquantième m

fif·ty ['fɪfti] adj & pron cinquante ‖ s (pl
-ties) cinquante m; **about fifty** une cinquantaine f; **fifties** (years of the decade)
années fpl cinquante

fif'ty-fif'ty adv—**to go fifty-fifty** (coll) être
de moitié, être en compte à demi

fig [fɪg] s figue f; (tree) figuier m; **a fig for
. . .!** (coll) nargue de . . .!

fight [faɪt] s combat m, bataille f; (spirit)
cœur m; **to pick a fight with** chercher
querelle à ‖ v (pret & pp **fought** [fɔt]) tr
combattre, se battre contre; **to fight off**
repousser ‖ intr combattre, se battre; **to
fight shy of** se défier de

fighter ['faɪtǝr] s combattant m; (game person) batailleur m; (aer) chasseur m, avion
m de chasse

fight'er pi'lot s chasseur m

fig' leaf' s feuille f de figuier; (on statues)
feuille de vigne

figment ['fɪgmǝnt] s fiction f, invention f

figurative ['fɪgjǝrǝtɪv] adj figuratif; (meaning) figuré

figure ['fɪgjǝr] s (diagram, drawing, image;
important person; in skating, dancing)
figure f; (silhouette) forme f; (bodily form)
taille f; (math) chiffre m; **to be good at
figures** être bon en calcul; **to have a good
figure** avoir de la ligne; **to keep one's
figure** garder sa ligne ‖ tr figurer; (to
embellish) orner de motifs; (to imagine)
se figurer, s'imaginer; **to figure out** calculer; (coll) déchiffrer ‖ intr figurer; **to
figure on** compter sur

fig'ured bass' [bes] s (mus) basse f chiffrée

fig'ured silk' s soie f à dessin

fig'ure·head' s prête-nom m, homme m de
paille; (naut) figure f de proue

fig'ure of speech' s figure f de rhétorique;
(fig) façon f de parler

fig'ure skat'ing s patinage m de fantaisie

filament ['fɪlǝmǝnt] s filament m

filbert ['fɪlbǝrt] s noisette f, aveline f; (tree)
noisetier m, avelinier m

filch [fɪltʃ] tr chaparder, chiper

file [faɪl] *s* (*tool*) lime *f*; (*for papers*) classeur *m*; (*for cards*) fichier *m*; (*personal record*) dossier *m*; (*line*) file *f*; **in single file** en file indienne, à la queue leu leu; **to form single file** dédoubler les rangs ‖ *tr* limer; classer, ranger; (*a petition*) déposer; **to file down** enlever à la lime ‖ *intr*—**to file off** défiler; **to file out** sortir un à un

file′ case′ *s* fichier *m*

file′ clerk′ *s* employé *m*, commis *m*

file′ film′ *s* images *fpl* d'archives

file′ num′ber *s* (*e.g.*, *used in answering a letter*) référence *f*

filial [ˈfɪlɪ·əl] *adj* filial

filiation [ˌfɪlɪˈeʃən] *s* filiation *f*

filibuster [ˈfɪlɪˌbʌstər] *s* (*use of delaying tactics*) obstruction *f*; (*legislator*) obstructionniste *mf*; (*pirate*) flibustier *m* ‖ *tr* (*legislation*) obstruer ‖ *intr* faire de l'obstruction

filigree [ˈfɪlɪˌgri] *adj* filigrané ‖ *s* filigrane *m* ‖ *tr* filigraner

filing [ˈfaɪlɪŋ] *s* (*of documents*) classement *m*; (*with a tool*) limage *m*; **filings** limaille *f*, grains *mpl* de limaille

fil′ing cab′inet *s* classeur *m*

fil′ing card′ *s* fiche *f*

Filipi·no [ˌfɪlɪˈpino] *adj* philippin ‖ *s* (*pl* -nos) Philippin *m*

fill [fɪl] *s* (*earth, stones, etc.*) remblai *m*; **I've had my fill!** j'en ai assez!; **to eat one's fill** manger à sa faim, manger tout son content; **to have one's fill of** avoir tout son soûl de ‖ *tr* remplir; (*a prescription*) exécuter; (*a tooth*) plomber; (*a cylinder with gas*) charger; (*a hollow or gap*) combler; (*a job*) occuper; **to fill in** remblayer, combler; **to fill out** (*a questionnaire*) remplir ‖ *intr* se remplir; **to fill out** se gonfler; (*said of sail*) s'enfler; **to fill up** se combler; (*to fill the tank full*) faire le plein

filler [ˈfɪlər] *s* remplissage *m*; (*of cigar*) tripe *f*; (*sizing*) apprêt *m*, mastic *m*; (*in notebook*) papier *m*; (*journ*) pesée *f*

fillet [ˈfɪlɪt] *s* bande *f*; (*for hair*) bandeau *m*; (*archit*) moulure *f* ‖ [ˈfɪle], [ˈfɪlɪt] *s* (*culin*) filet *m* ‖ *tr* couper en filets

filling [ˈfɪlɪŋ] *adj* (*food*) rassasiant ‖ *s* (*of job*) occupation *f*; (*of tooth*) plombage *m*; (*e.g., of turkey*) farce *f*; (*of cigar*) tripe *f*

fill′ing sta′tion *s* poste *m* d'essence

fill′ing-station attend′ant *s* pompiste *mf*

fillip [ˈfɪlɪp] *s* tonique *m*, stimulant *m*; (*with finger*) chiquenaude *f* ‖ *tr* donner une chiquenaude à

fil·ly [ˈfɪli] *s* (*pl* -lies) pouliche *f*; (*coll*) fillette *f*

film [fɪlm] *s* film *m*; (*in a roll*) pellicule *f*, film *m* ‖ *tr* filmer

film′ clip′ *s* bande-annonce *f*

filming [ˈfɪlmɪŋ] *s* filmage *m*

film′ li′brary *s* cinémathèque *f*

film′ mak′er *s* cinéaste *mf*

film′ star′ *s* vedette *f* du cinéma

film′strip′ *s* film *m* fixe

film·y [ˈfɪlmi] *adj* (*comp* -ier; *super* -iest) diaphane, voilé

filter [ˈfɪltər] *s* filtre *m* ‖ *tr & intr* filtrer

filtering [ˈfɪltərɪŋ] *s* filtrage *m*; (*of water*) filtration *f*

fil′ter pa′per *s* papier-filtre *m*

fil′ter tip′ *adj* à bout-filtre ‖ *s* bout-filtre *m*, bout-filtrant *m*

filth [fɪlθ] *s* saleté *f*, ordure *f*; (fig) obscénité *f*

filth·y [ˈfɪlθi] *adj* (*comp* -ier; *super* -iest) sale, immonde

filth′y lu′cre [ˈlukər] *s* (coll) lucre *m*

fin [fɪn] *s* nageoire *f*; **fins** (*for swimming*) palmes *fpl*

final [ˈfaɪnəl] *adj* final; (*last in a series*) ultime, définitif ‖ *s* examen *m* final; (sports) finale *f*

finale [fɪˈnɑli] *s* (mus) final *m*

finalist [ˈfaɪnəlɪst] *s* finaliste *mf*

finally [ˈfaɪnəli] *adv* finalement, enfin

fi′nal touch′ *s* coup *m* de pouce

finance [ˈfaɪnæns] *s* finance *f* ‖ *tr* financer *f*

fi′nance com′pany *s* entreprise *f* de prêt, caisse *f* de prévoyance

financial [faɪˈnænʃəl] *adj* financier; (*interest; distress*) pécuniaire

financier [ˌfaɪnənˈsɪr] *s* financier *m*

financing [ˈfaɪnænsɪŋ] *s* financement *m*

finch [fɪntʃ] *s* pinson *m*

find [faɪnd] *s* trouvaille *f* ‖ *v* (*pret & pp* found [faʊnd]) *tr* trouver; **to find out** apprendre ‖ *intr* (law) déclarer; **to find out (about)** se renseigner (sur), se mettre au courant (de); **find out!** à vous de trouver!

finder [ˈfaɪndər] *s* (*of camera*) viseur *m*; (*of optical instrument*) chercheur *m*

finding [ˈfaɪndɪŋ] *s* découverte *f*; (law) décision *f*; **findings** conclusions *fpl*

fine [faɪn] *adj* fin; (*weather*) beau; (*person, manners, etc.*) distingué, excellent; **that's fine!** bien!, parfait! ‖ *s* amende *f* ‖ *tr* mettre à l'amende

fine′ arts′ *spl* beaux-arts *mpl*

fineness [ˈfaɪnnɪs] *s* finesse *f*; (*of metal*) titre *m*

fine′ print′ *s* petits caractères *mpl*; (*of a contract*) petites lignes *fpl* (illisibles)

finer·y [ˈfaɪnəri] *s* (*pl* -ies) parure *f*

finespun [ˈfaɪnˌspʌn] *adj* ténu; (fig) subtil

finesse [fɪˈnɛs] *s* finesse *f*; (*in bridge*) impasse *f*; **to use finesse** finasser ‖ *tr* faire l'impasse à

fine′-toothed comb′ *s* peigne *m* aux dents fines, peigne fin

finger [ˈfɪŋgər] *s* doigt *m*; (slang) mouchard *m*, indicateur *m*; **not to lift a finger** (fig) ne pas remuer le petit doigt; **to burn one's fingers** (fig) se faire échauder; **to put one's finger on the spot** (fig) mettre le doigt dessus; **to slip between the fingers** glisser entre les doigts; **to snap one's fingers at** (fig) faire la figue à, narguer; **to twist around one's little finger** (coll) mener par le bout du nez, faire tourner comme un toton ‖ *tr* toucher du doigt, manier; (mus) doigter; (slang) espionner; (slang) identifier

fin′ger board′ s (of guitar) touche f; (of piano) clavier m

fin′ger bowl′ s rince-doigts m

fin′ger dexter′ity s (mus) doigté m

fingering [′fɪŋgərɪŋ] s maniement m; (mus) doigté m

fin′ger·nail′ s ongle m

fin′gernail pol′ish s brillant m

fin′ger·print′ s empreinte f digitale ‖ tr prendre les empreintes digitales de

fin′ger·tip′ s bout m du doigt; **to have at one's fingertips** tenir sur le bout du doigt

finicky [′fɪnɪki] adj méticuleux

finish [′fɪnɪʃ] s (perfection) achevé m, fini m; (elegance) finesse f; (conclusion) fin f; (gloss, coating, etc.) fini m ‖ tr & intr finir; **to finish** + ger finir de + inf; **to finish by** + ger finir par + inf

fin′ishing touch′ s dernière main f

finite [′faɪnaɪt] adj & s fini m

Finland [′fɪnlənd] s Finlande f; la Finlande

Finlander [′fɪnləndər] s Finlandais m

Finn [fɪn] s (member of a Finnish-speaking group of people) Finnois m; (native or inhabitant of Finland) Finlandais m

Finnish [′fɪnɪʃ] adj & s finnois m

fir [fʌr] s sapin m

fire [faɪr] s feu m; (destructive burning) incendie m; **to catch fire** prendre feu; **to set on fire** mettre le feu à ‖ tr mettre le feu à; (e.g., passions) enflammer; (a weapon) tirer; (a rocket) lancer; (an employee) (coll) renvoyer ‖ interj (warning) au feu!; (command to fire) feu!

fire′ alarm′ s avertisseur m d'incendie; (box) poste m avertisseur d'incendie

fire′arm′ s arme f à feu

fire′ball′ s globe m de feu; (mil) grenade f incendiaire

fire′bird′ s loriot m d'Amérique

fire′boat′ s bateau-pompe m

fire′box′ s boîte f à feu; (rr) foyer m

fire′brand′ s tison m; (coll) brandon m de discorde

fire′break′ s tranchée f garde-feu, pare-feu m

fire′brick′ s brique f réfractaire

fire′ brigade′ s corps m de sapeurs-pompiers

fire′bug′ s (coll) incendiaire mf

fire′ chief′ s capitaine m des pompiers

fire′ com′pany s corps m de sapeurs-pompiers; (insurance company) compagnie f d'assurance contre l'incendie

fire′crack′er s pétard m

fire′damp′ s grisou m

fire′ depart′ment s service m des incendies, sapeurs-pompiers mpl

fire′dog′ s chenet m, landier m

fire′ drill′ s exercices mpl de sauvetage en cas d'incendie

fire′ en′gine s pompe f à incendie

fire′ escape′ s échelle f de sauvetage, escalier m de secours

fire′ extin′guisher s extincteur m

fire′fly′ s (pl -flies) luciole f

fire′guard′ s (before hearth) pare-étincelles m; (in forest) pare-feu m

fire′ hose′ s manche f d'incendie

fire′house′ s caserne f de pompiers, poste m de pompiers

fire′ hy′drant s bouche f d'incendie

fire′ insur′ance s assurance f contre l'incendie

fire′ i′rons spl garniture f de foyer

fire′ lad′der s échelle f d'incendie

fire′less cook′er [′faɪrlɪs] s marmite f norvégienne

fire′man s (pl -men) (man who stokes fires) chauffeur m; (man who extinguishes fires) sapeur-pompier m, pompier m

fire′place′ s cheminée f, foyer m

fire′plug′ s bouche f d'incendie

fire′ pow′er s puissance f de feu

fire′proof′ adj ignifuge; (dish) apyre ‖ tr ignifuger

fire′ sale′ s vente f après incendie

fire′ screen′ s écran m de cheminée, garde-feu m

fire′ ship′ s brûlot m

fire′ shov′el s pelle f à feu

fire′side′ s coin m du feu

fire′side chat′ s (pol) causerie f télévisée au coin du feu

fire′trap′ s nid-à-feu m

fire′ wall′ s coupe-feu m

fire′ward′en s garde m forestier, vigie f

fire′ wa′ter s (slang) gnole f, whisky m

fire′wood′ s bois m de chauffage

fire′works′ spl feu m d'artifice

firing [′faɪrɪŋ] s (of furnace) chauffe f; (of bricks, ceramics, etc.) cuite f; (of gun) tir m, feu m; (by a group of soldiers) fusillade f; (of an internal-combustion engine) allumage m; (of an employee) (coll) renvoi m

fir′ing line′ s ligne f de feu, chaîne f de combat

fir′ing or′der s rythme m d'allumage

fir′ing pin′ s percuteur m, aiguille f

fir′ing squad′ s peloton m d'exécution; (for ceremonies) piquet m d'honneurs funèbres

firm [fʌrm] adj & adv ferme; **to stand firm** tenir bon ‖ s maison f de commerce, firme f

firmament [′fʌrməmənt] s firmament m

firm′ name′ s nom m commercial

firmness [′fʌrmnɪs] s fermeté f

firm′ware′ s (comp) programmerie f particulière

first [fʌrst] adj, pron, & s premier m; **a first** (a record) une première; **at first** au commencement, au début; **first come first served** les premiers vont devant; **from the first** depuis le premier jour; **John the First** Jean premier ‖ adv premièrement, d'abord; **first and last** en tout et pour tout; **first of all, first off** tout d'abord, de prime abord, premièrement

first′ aid′ s premiers soins mpl, premiers secours mpl

first'-aid' kit' s boîte f à pansements, trousse f de première urgence

first'-aid' sta'tion s poste m de secours

first'-born' adj & s premier-né m

first'-class' adj de première classe, de premier ordre ‖ adv en première classe

first' cous'in s cousin m germain

first' draft' s brouillon m, premier jet m

first' fin'ger s index m

first' floor' s rez-de-chaussée m; (first floor above the ground floor) (Brit) premier étage m

first' fruits' spl prémices fpl

first'hand' adj & adv de première main

first' lieuten'ant s lieutenant m en premier

firstly ['fʌrstli] adv en premier lieu, d'abord

first' mate' s (naut) second m

first' name' s prénom m, petit nom m

first' night' s (theat) première f

first-nighter [,fʌrst'naɪtər] s (theat) habitué m des premières

first' offend'er s délinquant m primaire

first' of'ficer s (naut) officier m en second

first' prize' s (in a lottery) gros lot m; **to win first prize** remporter le prix

first' quar'ter s (of the moon) premier quartier m

first'-rate' adj de premier ordre, de première qualité; (coll) excellent ‖ adv (coll) très bien, à merveille

first'-run mov'ie s film m en exclusivité

first' try' s coup m d'essai

fiscal ['fɪskəl] adj fiscal

fis'cal year' s exercice m budgétaire

fish [fɪʃ] s poisson m; **to be like a fish out of water** être comme un poisson sur la paille; **to be neither fish nor fowl** être ni chair ni poisson; **to drink like a fish** boire comme un trou; **to have other fish to fry** avoir d'autres chiens à fouetter ‖ tr pêcher; (rr) éclisser; **to fish out** or **up** repêcher ‖ intr pêcher; **to fish for compliments** quêter des compliments; **to go fishing** aller à la pêche; **to take fishing** emmener à la pêche

fish'bone' s arête f

fish'bowl' s bocal m

fisher ['fɪʃər] s pêcheur m; (zool) martre f

fish'er·man s (pl -men) pêcheur m

fisher·y ['fɪʃəri] s (pl -ies) (activity; business) pêche f; (grounds) pêcherie f

fish' hawk' s aigle m pêcheur

fish'hook' s hameçon m

fishing ['fɪʃɪŋ] adj pêcheur, de pêche ‖ s pêche f

fish'ing ground' s pêcherie f

fish'ing reel' s moulinet m

fish'ing rod' s canne f à pêche

fish'ing tack'le s attirail m de pêche

fish'line' s ligne f de pêche

fish' mar'ket s poissonnerie f

fish'net stock'ings spl bas mpl en résille

fish'plate' s (rr) éclisse f

fish'pool' s vivier m

fish' spear' s foëne f, fouëne f

fish' sto'ry s hâblerie f, blague f

fish'tail' s queue f de poisson; (aer) embardée f ‖ intr (aer) embarder

fish'wife' s (pl -wives') poissonnière f; (foul-mouthed woman) poissarde f

fish'worm' s asticot m

fish·y ['fɪʃi] adj (comp -ier; super -iest) (eyes) (coll) vitreux; (coll) véreux, louche, pas franc du collier

fission ['fɪʃən] s (biol) scission f; (nucl) fission f

fissionable ['fɪʃənəbəl] adj fissible, fissile

fissure ['fɪʃər] s fissure f, fente f ‖ tr fissurer ‖ intr se fissurer

fist [fɪst] s poing m; (typ) petite main f; **to shake one's fist at** menacer du poing

fist'fight' s combat m à coup de poings

fistful ['fɪstful] s poignée f

fisticuffs ['fɪstɪ,kʌfs] spl empoignade f or rixe f à coups de poing; (sports) boxe f

fit [fɪt] adj (comp fitter; super fittest) bon, convenable; capable, digne; (in good health) en forme, sain; **fit to be tied** (coll) en colère; **fit to drink** buvable; **fit to eat** mangeable; **to feel fit** être frais et dispos ‖ s ajustement m; (of clothes) coupe f, façon f; (of fever, rage, coughing) accès m; **by fits and starts** par accès; **fit of coughing** quinte f de toux ‖ v (pret & pp fitted; ger fitting) tr ajuster; (s.th. in s.th.) emboîter; **to fit for** (e.g., a task) préparer à; **to fit out** or **up** aménager; **to fit out with** garnir de ‖ intr s'emboîter; **to fit in** tenir dans; **to fit in with** s'accorder avec, convenir à

fitful ['fɪtfəl] adj intermittent

fitness ['fɪtnɪs] s convenance f; (for a task) aptitude f; (good shape) bonne forme f

fitter ['fɪtər] s ajusteur m; (of machinery) monteur m; (of clothing) essayeur m

fitting ['fɪtɪŋ] adj convenable, approprié, à propos ‖ s ajustage m; (of a garment) essayage m; **fittings** aménagements mpl; (of metal) ferrures fpl

five [faɪv] adj & pron cinq ‖ s cinq m; **five o'clock** cinq heures

five'-year plan' s plan m quinquennal

fix [fɪks] s (aer, naut) position f; (coll) mauvais pas m; (injection) (slang) piqûre f, piquouse f, dose f; **to be in a fix** (coll) être dans le pétrin; **to give oneself a fix** (slang) se shooter, se piquer ‖ tr réparer; (e.g., a date; a photographic image; prices; one's eyes) fixer; (slang) donner son compte à

fixed' as'sets spl capital m fixe

fixedly ['fɪksɪdli] adv fixement

fixed'-price' con'tract s marché m à forfait

fixing ['fɪksɪŋ] s fixation f; (phot) fixage m; **fixings** (slang) collation f, des mets mpl

fix'ing bath' s bain m de fixage, fixateur m

fixture ['fɪkstʃər] s accessoire m, garniture f; **fixtures** meubles mpl à demeure

fizz [fɪz] s pétillement m ‖ intr pétiller

fizzle ['fɪzəl] s (coll) avortement m ‖ intr (coll) avorter; **to fizzle out** (coll) tomber à l'eau, échouer

flabbergasted ['flæbər,gæstɪd] adj (coll) éberlué, épaté

flab·by ['flæbi] adj (comp **-bier**; super **-biest**) mou, flasque; **to become flabby** s'avachir

flag [flæg] s drapeau m ‖ v (pret & pp **flagged**; ger **flagging**) tr—**to flag s.o.** transmettre des signaux à qn en agitant un fanion ‖ intr faiblir, se relâcher

flag' cap'tain s (nav) capitaine m de pavillon

flag'man s (pl **-men**) signaleur m; (rr) garde-voie m

flag' of truce' s drapeau m parlementaire

flag'pole' s hampe f de drapeau; (naut) mât m de pavillon; (surv) jalon m

flagrant ['flegrənt] adj scandaleux; (e.g., injustice) flagrant

flag'ship' s (nav) vaisseau m amiral

flag'staff' s hampe f de drapeau

flag'stone' s dalle f

flag' stop' s (rr) halte f, arrêt m facultatif

flag'-wav'ing adj cocardier ‖ s patriotisme m de façade

flail [flel] s fléau m ‖ tr (agr) battre au fléau; (fig) éreinter

flair [flɛr] s flair m; aptitude f

flak [flæk] s tir m contre-avions

flake [flek] s (of snow; of cereal) flocon m; (of soap; of mica) paillette f; (of paint) écaille f ‖ intr tomber en flocons; **to flake off** s'écailler

flak·y ['fleki] adj (comp **-ier**; super **-iest**) floconneux, lamelleux

flamboyant [flæm'bɔɪ·ənt] adj fleuri, orné, coloré; (archit) flamboyant

flame [flem] s flamme f; (coll) amant m, amante f ‖ tr flamber ‖ intr flamber, flamboyer

flamethrower ['flem,θro·ər] s lance-flammes m

flaming ['flemɪŋ] adj flambant

flamin·go [flə'mɪŋgo] s (pl **-gos** or **-goes**) flamant m

flammable ['flæməbəl] adj inflammable

Flanders ['flændərz] s Flandre f; la Flandre

flange [flændʒ] s rebord m, saillie f; (of wheel) jante f; (of rail) patin m

flank [flæŋk] s flanc m ‖ tr flanquer

flannel ['flænəl] s flanelle f

flap [flæp] s (part that can be folded under) rabat m; (fold in clothing) pan m; (of a cap) couvre-nuque m; (of a pocket; of an envelope) patte f; (of wings) coup m, battement m; (of a table) battant m; (of a sail, flag, etc.) claquement m; (slap) tape f; (aer) volet m ‖ v (pret & pp **flapped**; ger **flapping**) tr (wings, arms, etc.) battre; (to slap) taper ‖ intr battre; (said of sail, flag, etc.) claquer; (said of curtain) voltiger; (to hang down) pendre

flap'jack' s (coll) crêpe f

flare [flɛr] s (of light or fire) éclat m vif; (e.g., of skirt; of pipe or funnel) évasement m; (for signaling) fusée f éclairante ‖ tr évaser ‖ intr flamboyer; (to spread outward) s'évaser; **to flare up** s'enflammer; (to reappear) se produire de nouveau; (to become angry) s'emporter

flare'-up' s flambée f soudaine; (of illness) recrudescence f; (of anger) accès m de colère

flash [flæʃ] s (of lightning) éclair m; (of flame, jewels) éclat m; (of hope) lueur f, rayon m; (of wit) trait m; (of genius) éclair; (brief moment) instant m; (phot) flash m; (ostentation) (coll) tape-à-l'œil m; (last-minute news) (coll) nouvelle f éclair; **flash in the pan** (coll) feu m de paille; **in a flash** en un clin d'œil ‖ tr projeter; (a gem) faire étinceler; (to show off) faire parade de; (a message) répandre, transmettre ‖ intr jeter des éclairs; (said of gem, eyes, etc.) étinceler; **to flash by** passer comme un éclair

flash'back' s (mov) retour m en arrière, rappel m, rétrospectif m

flash'bulb' s ampoule f flash, flash m

flash' flood' s crue f subite

flashing ['flæʃɪŋ] adj éclatant; (light) à éclats; (signal) clignotant ‖ s bande f de solin

flash'light' s lampe f torche, lampe de poche; (phot) lampe éclair

flash'light bat'tery s pile f torche

flash·y ['flæʃi] adj (comp **-ier**; super **-iest**) (coll) tapageur, criard

flask [flæsk] s flacon m, gourde f; (in lab) ballon m, flacon

flat [flæt] adj (comp **flatter**; super **flattest**) (level) plat, uni; (nose) aplati; (refusal) net; (beer) éventé; (tire) dégonflé; (dull, tasteless) fade, terne; (mus) bémol ‖ s appartement m; (flat tire) crevaison f; (of sword) plat m; (mus) bémol m; (theat) châssis m ‖ adv (outright) (coll) nettement, carrément; **to fall flat** tomber à plat; (fig) manquer son effet; **to sing flat** chanter faux

flat'boat' s plate f

flat-broke ['flæt'brok] adj (coll) complètement fauché, à la côte

flat'car' s plate-forme f

flat'foot' s (police) (slang) flic m, vache f

flat'-foot'ed adj aux pieds plats; (coll) franc, brutal

flat'i'ron s fer m à repasser

flatly ['flætli] adv net, platement

flat'-nosed' adj camard, camus

flatten ['flætən] tr aplatir, aplanir; (metallurgy) laminer ‖ intr s'aplatir, s'aplanir; **to flatten out** (aer) se redresser

flatter ['flætər] tr & intr flatter

flatterer ['flætərər] s flatteur m

flattering ['flætərɪŋ] adj flatteur

flatter·y ['flætəri] s (pl **-ies**) flatterie f

flat' tire' s pneu m dégonflé, à plat, or crevé, crevaison f

flat'top' s (nav) porte-avions m

flatulence ['flætʃələns] s boursouflure f; (pathol) flatulence f

flat'ware' s couverts mpl; (plates) assiettes fpl

flaunt [flɔnt] tr faire étalage de

flautist ['flɔtɪst] s flûtiste mf

flavor [ˈflevər] s saveur f, goût m; (of ice cream) parfum m ‖ tr assaisonner, parfumer

flavoring [ˈflevərɪŋ] s assaisonnement m; (lemon, rum, etc.) parfum m

flaw [flɔ] s (defect) défaut m, tache f, vice m; (crack) fêlure f; (in metal) paille f; (in diamond) crapaud m

flawless [ˈflɔlɪs] adj sans défaut, sans tache

flax [flæks] s lin m

flaxen [ˈflæksən] adj de lin, blond

flax′seed′ s graine f de lin

flay [fle] tr écorcher; (to criticize) rosser, fustiger

flea [fli] s puce f

flea′ and tick′ col′lar s collier m antiparasitaire

flea′bite′ s piqûre f de puce; (trifle) vétille f

fleck [flɛk] s tache f; (particle) particule f ‖ tr tacheter

fledgling [ˈflɛdʒlɪŋ] adj (lawyer, teacher) en herbe, débutant ‖ s oisillon m; (novice) débutant m, béjaune m

flee [fli] v (pret & pp fled [flɛd]) tr & intr fuir

fleece [flis] s toison f ‖ tr tondre; (to strip of money) (coll) écorcher, plumer

fleec·y [ˈflisi] adj (comp -ier; super -iest) laineux; (snow, wool) floconneux; (hair) moutonneux; (clouds) moutonné

fleet [flit] adj rapide ‖ s flotte f

fleet′-foot′ed adj au pied léger

fleeting [ˈflitɪŋ] adj passager, fugitif

Fleming [ˈflɛmɪŋ] s Flamand m

Flemish [ˈflɛmɪʃ] adj & s flamand m

flesh [flɛʃ] s chair f; **in the flesh** en chair et en os; **to lose flesh** perdre de l'embonpoint; **to put on flesh** prendre de l'embonpoint, s'empâter

flesh′ and blood′ s nature f humaine; (relatives) famille f, parenté f

flesh′-col′ored adj couleur f de chair, carné, incarnat

flesh′pot′ s (pot for cooking meat) potau-feu m; **fleshpots** (high living) luxe m, grande chère f; (evil places) maisons fpl de débauche, mauvais lieux mpl

flesh′ wound′ [wund] s blessure f en séton, blessure superficielle

flesh·y [ˈflɛʃi] adj (comp -ier; super -iest) charnu

flex [flɛks] tr & intr fléchir

flexible [ˈflɛksɪbəl] adj flexible

flex(i)time [ˈflɛks(ə)ˌtaɪm] s horaire m flottant

flick [flɪk] s (with finger) chiquenaude f; (with whip) petit coup m; **flicks** (coll) ciné m ‖ tr faire une chiquenaude à; (a whip) faire claquer

flicker [ˈflɪkər] s petite lueur f vacillante; (of eyelids) battement m; (of emotion) frisson m ‖ intr trembloter, vaciller; (said of eyelids) ciller

flier [ˈflaɪ·ər] s aviateur m; (coll) spéculation f au hasard; (rr) rapide m; (handbill) (coll) prospectus m

flight [flaɪt] s fuite f; (of airplane) vol m; (of birds) volée f; (of stairs) volée; (of fancy) élan m; **to put to flight** mettre en fuite; **to take flight** prendre la fuite

flight′ attend′ant s membre m d'un service de vol, stewart m; (air hostess) stewardess f, hôtesse f de l'aire

flight′ controls′ spl commandes fpl de vol

flight′ deck′ s (nav) pont m d'envol

flight′ record′er s enregistreur m de vol

flight·y [ˈflaɪti] adj (comp -ier; super -iest) volage, léger; braque, écervelé

flim·flam [ˈflɪmˌflæm] s (coll) baliverne f; (fraud) (coll) escroquerie f ‖ v (pret & pp -flammed; ger -flamming) tr (coll) escroquer

flim·sy [ˈflɪmzi] adj (comp -sier; super -siest) léger; (e.g., cloth) fragile; (e.g., excuse) frivole

flinch [flɪntʃ] intr reculer, fléchir; **without flinching** sans broncher, sans hésiter

fling [flɪŋ] s jet m; **to go on a fling** faire la noce; **to have a fling at** tenter; **to have one's fling** jeter sa gourme ‖ v (pret & pp flung [flʌŋ]) tr lancer; (on the floor, out the window; in jail) jeter; **to fling open** ouvrir brusquement

flint [flɪnt] s silex m; (of lighter) pierre f

flint′lock′ s fusil m à pierre

flint·y [ˈflɪnti] adj (comp -ier; super -iest) siliceux; (heart) de pierre, insensible

flip [flɪp] adj (comp flipper; super flippest) (coll) mutin, moqueur ‖ s (flick) chiquenaude f; (somersault) culbute f; (aer) petit tour m de vol ‖ v (pret & pp flipped; ger flipping) tr donner une chiquenaude à; (a page) tourner rapidement; **to flip a coin** jouer à pile ou face; **to flip over** (a phonograph record) retourner

flippancy [ˈflɪpənsi] s désinvolture f

flippant [ˈflɪpənt] adj désinvolte

flipper [ˈflɪpər] s nageoire f

flip′ side′ s autre face f (d'un disque)

flirt [flʌrt] s flirteur m, flirt m ‖ intr flirter; (said only of a man) conter fleurette

flit [flɪt] v (pret & pp flitted; ger flitting) intr voleter; **to flit away** passer rapidement; **to flit here and there** voltiger

float [flot] s (raft) radeau m; (on fish line; in carburetor; on seaplane) flotteur m; (on fish line or net) flotte f; (of mason) aplanissoire f; (in parade) char m de cavalcade, char de Carnaval ‖ tr faire flotter; (a loan) émettre, contracter ‖ intr flotter, nager; (on one's back) faire la planche

floater [ˈflotər] s (tramp) vagabond m; (illegal voter) faux électeur m

floating [ˈflotɪŋ] adj flottant; (free) libre ‖ s flottement m; (of loan) émission f

float′ing is′land s (culin) œufs mpl à la neige

flock [flɑk] s (of birds) volée f; (of sheep) troupeau m; (of people) foule f, bande f; (of nonsense) tas m; (of faithful) ouailles fpl ‖ intr s'assembler; **to flock in** entrer en foule; **to flock together** s'attrouper

floe [flo] *s* banquise *f*; (*floating piece of ice*) glaçon *m* flottant

flog [flɑg] *v* (*pret* & *pp* **flogged**; *ger* **flogging**) *tr* fouetter, flageller

flogging [ˈflɑgɪŋ] *s* fouet *m*

flood [flʌd] *s* inondation *f*; (*caused by heavy rain*) déluge *m*; (*sudden rise of river*) crue *f*; (*of tide*) flot *m*; (*of words, tears, light*) flots *mpl*, déluge ‖ *tr* inonder; (*to overwhelm*) submerger, inonder; (*a carburetor*) noyer ‖ *intr* (*said of river*) déborder; (*aut*) se noyer

flood'gate' *s* (*of a dam*) vanne *f*; (*of a canal*) porte *f* d'écluse

flood'light' *s* phare *m* d'éclairage, projecteur *m* de lumière ‖ *tr* illuminer par projecteurs

flood'tide' *s* marée *f* montante, flux *m*

floor [flor] *s* (*inside bottom surface of room*) plancher *m*, parquet *m*; (*story of building*) étage *m*; (*of swimming pool, the sea, etc.*) fond *m*; (*of assembly hall*) enceinte *f*, parquet; (*of the court*) prétoire *m*, parquet; (naut) varangue *f*; **to ask for the floor** réclamer la parole; **to give s.o. the floor** donner la parole à qn; **to have the floor** avoir la parole; **to take the floor** prendre la parole ‖ *tr* parqueter; (*an opponent*) terrasser; (*to disconcert*) (coll) désarçonner

flooring [ˈflorɪŋ] *s* planchéiage *m*, parquetage *m*

floor' lamp' *s* lampe *f* à pied, lampadaire *m*

floor' mop' *s* brosse *f* à parquet

floor' sam'ple *s* article *m* de démonstration, article de montre

floor' show' *s* spectacle *m* de cabaret

floor' tim'ber *s* (naut) varangue *f*

floor'walk'er *s* chef *m* de rayon

floor' wax' *s* cire *f* à parquet, encaustique *f*

flop [flɑp] *s* (coll) insuccès *m*, échec *m*; (*literary work or painting*) (coll) navet *m*; (*play*) (coll) four *m*; **to take a flop** (coll) faire patapouf ‖ *v* (*pret* & *pp* **flopped**; *ger* **flopping**) *intr* tomber lourdement; (*to fail*) (coll) échouer, rater

floppy [ˈflɑpi] *adj* lâche, flottant

flop'py disk' *s* (comp) disquette *f*

flora [ˈflorə] *s* flore *f*

floral [ˈflorəl] *adj* floral

florescence [floˈrɛsəns] *s* floraison *f*

florid [ˈflorɪd] *adj* fleuri, flamboyant; (*complexion*) rubicond

Florida [ˈflorɪdə] *s* Floride *f*; la Floride

Flor'ida Keys' *spl* Cayes *fpl* de la Floride

floss [flos] *s* bourre *f*; (*of corn*) barbe *f*

floss' silk' *s* bourre *f* de soie, filoselle *f*

floss·y [ˈflosi] *adj* (*comp* **-ier**; *super* **-iest**) soyeux; (slang) pimpant, tapageur

flotsam [ˈflɑtsəm] *s* épave *f*

flot'sam and jet'sam *s* choses *fpl* de flot et de mer, épaves *fpl*

flounce [flauns] *s* volant *m* ‖ *tr* garnir de volants ‖ *intr* s'élancer avec emportement

flounder [ˈflaundər] *s* flet *m*; (*plaice*) carrelet *m*, plie *f* ‖ *intr* patauger

flour [flaur] *s* farine *f* ‖ *tr* fariner

flourish [ˈflʌrɪʃ] *s* fioriture *f*; (*on a signature*) paraphe *m*; (*of trumpets*) fanfare *m*; (*brandishing*) brandissement *m* ‖ *tr* brandir; (*to wave*) agiter ‖ *intr* fleurir, prospérer

flourishing [ˈflʌrɪʃɪŋ] *adj* florissant

flour' mill' *s* moulin *m*, minoterie *f*

floury [ˈflauri] *adj* farineux

flout [flaut] *tr* se moquer de, narguer ‖ *intr* se moquer

flow [flo] *s* (*running*) écoulement *m*; (*of tide, blood, words*) flot *m*, flux *m*; (*of blood to the head*) afflux *m*; (*rate of flow*) débit *m*; (*current*) courant *m* ‖ *intr* écouler; (*said of tide*) monter; (*said of blood in the body*) circuler; (fig) couler; **to flow into** déboucher dans, se verser dans; **to flow over** déborder

flow'chart' *s* organigramme *m*, ordinogramme *m*

flower [ˈflau·ər] *s* fleur *f* ‖ *tr* & *intr* fleurir

flow'er bed' *s* plate-bande *f*, parterre *m*; (*round flower bed*) corbeille *f*

flow'er gar'den *s* jardin *m* de fleurs, jardin d'agrément

flow'er girl' *s* bouquetière *f*; (*at a wedding*) fille *f* d'honneur

flow'er·pot' *s* pot *m* à fleurs

flow'er shop' *s* boutique *f* de fleuriste

flow'er show' *s* exposition *f* horticole, floralies *fpl*

flow'er stand' *s* jardinière *f*

flowery [ˈflau·əri] *adj* fleuri

flu [flu] *s* (coll) grippe *f*

fluctuate [ˈflʌktʃu,et] *intr* fluctuer

flue [flu] *s* tuyau *m*

fluency [ˈflu·ənsi] *s* facilité *f*

fluent [ˈflu·ənt] *adj* disert, facile; (*flowing*) coulant

fluently [ˈflu·əntli] *adv* couramment

fluff [flʌf] *s* (*velvety cloth*) peluche *f*; (*tuft of fur, dust, etc.*) duvet *m*; (*boner made by actor*) (coll) loup *m* ‖ *tr* lainer, rendre pelucheux; (*one's entrance*) (coll) louper; (*one's lines*) (coll) bouler ‖ *intr* pelucher

fluff·y [ˈflʌfi] *adj* (*comp* **-ier**; *super* **-iest**) duveteux; (*hair*) flou

fluid [ˈflu·ɪd] *adj* & *s* fluide *m*

fluke [fluk] *s* (*of anchor*) patte *f*; (billiards) raccroc *m*, coup *m* de veine

flume [flum] *s* canalisation *f*, ravin *m*

flunk [flʌŋk] *tr* (*a student*) (coll) recaler, coller; (*an exam*) rater ‖ *intr* être recalé, se faire coller

flunk·y [ˈflʌŋki] *s* (*pl* **-ies**) laquais *m*

fluorescent [,flu·əˈrɛsənt] *adj* fluorescent

fluoridate [ˈflorɪ,det] *tr* & *intr* fluorider

fluoridation [,florɪˈdeʃən] *s* fluoridation *f*

fluoride [ˈflu·ə,raɪd] *s* fluorure *m*

fluorine [ˈflu·ə,rin] *s* fluor *m*

fluoroscopy [,flu·əˈraskəpi] *s* radioscopie *f*

fluorspar [ˈflu·ər,spar] *s* spath *m* fluor

flur·ry [ˈflʌri] *s* (*pl* **-ries**) agitation *f*; (*of wind, snow, etc.*) rafale *f* ‖ *v* (*pret* & *pp* **-ried**) *tr* agiter

flush [flʌʃ] *adj* (*level*) à ras; (*well-provided*) bien pourvu; (*healthy*) vigoureux; **flush**

with au ras de, au niveau de ‖ *s* (*of light*) éclat *m*; (*in the cheeks*) rougeur *f*; (*of joy*) transport *m*; (*of toilet*) chasse *f* d'eau; (*in poker*) flush *m*; **in the first flush of** dans l'ivresse or le premier éclat de ‖ *adv* à ras, de niveau; (*directly*) droit ‖ *tr* (*a bird*) lever; **to flush a toilet** tirer la chasse d'eau; **to flush out** (*e.g., a drain*) laver à grande eau ‖ *intr* (*to blush*) rougir

flush′ switch′ *s* interrupteur *m* encastré

flush′ tank′ *s* réservoir *m* de chasse

flush′ toi′let *s* water-closet *m* à chasse d'eau

fluster [′flʌstər] *s* agitation *f*; **in a fluster** en émoi ‖ *tr* agiter

flute [flut] *s* flûte *f* ‖ *tr* (*a column*) canneler; (*a dress*) tuyauter

flutist [′flutɪst] *s* flûtiste *mf*

flutter [′flʌtər] *s* battement *m*; **all of a flutter** (coll) tout agité ‖ *intr* voleter; (*said of pulse*) battre fébrilement; (*said of heart*) palpiter

flux [flʌks] *s* flux *m*; (*for fusing metals*) acide *m* à souder; **to be in flux** être dans un état indécis

fly [flaɪ] *s* (*pl* **-flies**) mouche *f*; (*for fishing*) mouche artificielle; (*of trousers*) braguette *f*; (*of tent*) auvent *m*; **flies** (theat) cintres *mpl*; **fly in the ointment** (fig) ombre *f* au tableau; **on the fly** au vol ‖ *v* (*pret* **flew** [flu]; *pp* **flown** [flon]) *tr* (*a kite*) faire voler; (*an airplane*) piloter; (*freight or passengers*) transporter en avion; (*e.g., the Atlantic*) survoler; (*to flee from*) fuir ‖ *intr* voler; (*to flee*) fuir; (*said of flag*) flotter; **to fly blind** voler à l'aveuglette; **to fly by** voler; **to fly in the face of** porter un défi à; **to fly off** s'envoler; **to fly off the handle** (coll) sortir de ses gonds; **to fly open** s'ouvrir brusquement; **to fly over** survoler

fly′blow′ *s* œufs *mpl* de mouche

fly′-by-night′ *adj* mal financé, indigne de confiance ‖ *s* financier *m* qui lève le pied

fly′ cast′ing *s* pêche *f* à la mouche noyée

fly′catch′er *s* attrape-mouches *m*; (bot) dionée *f*, attrape-mouches; (orn) gobe-mouches *m*

fly′-fish′ *intr* pêcher à la mouche

flying [′flaɪ·ɪŋ] *adj* volant; rapide; court, passager ‖ *s* aviation *f*; vol *m*

fly′ing but′tress *s* arc-boutant *m*

fly′ing col′ors—with flying colors drapeau *m* déployé; brillamment

fly′ing field′ *s* champ *m* d'aviation

fly′ing-fish′ *s* poisson *m* volant

fly′ing sau′cer *s* soucoupe *f* volante

fly′ing start′ *s* départ *m* lancé

fly′ing time′ *s* heures *fpl* de vol

fly′leaf′ *s* (*pl* **-leaves**) feuille *f* de garde, garde *f*

fly′ net′ *s* (*for a bed*) moustiquaire *f*; (*for a horse*) chasse-mouches *m*

fly′pa′per *s* papier *m* tue-mouches

fly′rod′ *s* canne *f* à mouche

fly′speck′ *s* chiure *f*, chiasse *f*

fly′ swat′ter [,swɑtər] *s* chasse-mouches *m*, émouchoir *m*, tapette *f* tue-mouche

fly′trap′ *s* attrape-mouches *m*

fly′wheel′ *s* volant *m*

FM [′ɛf′ɛm] *s* (letterword) (**frequency modulation**) modulation *f* de fréquence

foal [fol] *s* poulain *m* ‖ *intr* mettre bas

foam [fom] *s* écume *f*; (*on beer*) mousse *f* ‖ *intr* écumer, mousser

foam′ rub′ber *s* caoutchouc *m* mousse

foam·y [′fomi] *adj* (*comp* **-ier**; *super* **-iest**) écumeux, mousseux

fob [fɑb] *s* (*pocket*) gousset *m*; (*ornament*) breloque *f* ‖ *v* (*pret & pp* **fobbed**; *ger* **fobbing**) *tr*—**to fob off s.th. on s.o.** refiler q.ch. à qn

f.o.b. or **F.O.B.** [,ɛf,o′bi] *adv* (letterword) (**free on board**) franco de bord, départ usine

focal [′fokəl] *adj* focal

fo·cus [′fokəs] *s* (*pl* **-cuses** or **-ci** [saɪ]) foyer *m*; **in focus** au point; **out of focus** non réglé, hors du point focal ‖ *v* (*pret & pp* **-cused** or **-cussed**; *ger* **-cusing** or **-cussing**) *tr* mettre au point, faire converger; (*a beam of electrons*) focaliser; (*e.g., attention*) concentrer ‖ *intr* converger; **to focus on** se concentrer sur

fodder [′fɑdər] *s* fourrage *m*

foe [fo] *s* ennemi *m*, adversaire *mf*

fog [fɔg] *s* brouillard *m*; (naut) brume *f*; (phot) voile *m* ‖ *v* (*pret & pp* **fogged**; *ger* **fogging**) *tr* embrumer; (phot) voiler ‖ *intr* s'embrumer; (phot) se voiler

fog′ bank′ *s* banc *m* de brume

fog′ bell′ *s* cloche *f* de brume

fog′bound′ *adj* arrêté par le brouillard, pris dans le brouillard

fog·gy [′fɔgi] *adj* (*comp* **-gier**; *super* **-giest**) brumeux; (phot) voilé; (fig) confus, flou; **it is foggy** il fait du brouillard

fog′horn′ *s* sirène *f*, corne *f*, or trompe *f* de brume

fogy [′fogi] *s* (slang) croulant *m*

foible [′fɔɪbəl] *s* faible *m*, marotte *f*

foil [fɔɪl] *s* (*thin sheet of metal*) feuille *f*, lame *f*; (*of mirror*) tain *m*; (*sword*) fleuret *m*; (*person whose personality sets off another's*) repoussoir *m* ‖ *tr* déjouer, frustrer

foil′-wrapped′ *adj* ceint de papier d'argent

foist [fɔɪst] *tr*—**to foist oneself upon** s'imposer chez; **to foist s.th. on s.o.** imposer q.ch. à qn

fold [fold] *s* (*crease*) pli *m*, repli *m*; (*for sheep*) parc *m*, bergerie *f*; (*of fat*) bourrelet *m*; (*of the faithful*) bercail *m* ‖ *tr* plier, replier; (*one's arms*) se croiser; **to fold in** (culin) incorporer; **to fold up** replier ‖ *intr* se replier; **to fold up** (theat) faire four; (coll) s'effondrer

folder [′foldər] *s* (*covers for holding papers*) chemise *f*, chemise classeur; (*pamphlet*) dépliant *m*; (*person folding newspapers*) plieur *m*

folderol [′fɑldə,rɑl] *s* sottise *f*; (*piece of foolishness*) bagatelle *f*

folding ['foldɪŋ] *adj* pliant, repliant, rabattable

fold′ing cam′era *s* appareil *m* pliant

fold′ing chair′ *s* chaise *f* pliante, chaise brisée

fold′ing cot′ *s* lit *m* pliant or escamotable

fold′ing door′ *s* porte *f* à deux battants

fold′ing rule′ *s* mètre *m* pliant

fold′ing screen′ *s* paravent *m*

fold′ing seat′ *s* strapontin *m*

foliage ['folɪ·ɪdʒ] *s* feuillage *m*, feuillu *m*

foli·o ['folɪ‚o] *adj* in-folio ‖ *s* (*pl* **-os**) (*sheet*) folio *m*; (*book*) in-folio *m* ‖ *tr* folioter, paginer

folk [fok] *adj* populaire, traditionnel, du peuple ‖ *s* (*pl* **folk** or **folks**) peuple *m*, race *f*; **folks** (coll) gens *mpl*, personnes *fpl*; **my folks** (coll) les miens *mpl*, ma famille

folk′ dance′ *s* danse *f* folklorique

folk′lore′ *s* folklore *m*

folk′ mu′sic *s* musique *f* populaire

folk′ song′ *s* chanson *f* du terroir

folk·sy ['foksi] *adj* (*comp* **-sier**; *super* **-siest**) (coll) sociable, liant; (*like common people*) (coll) du terroir

folk′ways′ *spl* coutumes *fpl* traditionnelles

follicle ['falɪkəl] *s* follicule *m*

follow ['falo] *tr* suivre; (*to come after*) succéder; (*to understand*) comprendre; (*a profession*) embrasser; **to follow up** poursuivre; (*e.g., a success*) exploiter ‖ *intr* suivre; (*one after the other*) se suivre; **as follows** comme suit; **it follows that** il s'ensuit que

follower ['falo·ər] *s* suivant *m*; partisan *m*, disciple *m*, épigone *m*

following ['falo·ɪŋ] *adj* suivant ‖ *s* (*of a prince*) suite *f*; (*followers*) partisans *mpl*, disciples *mpl*

fol′low the lead′er *s* jeu *m* de la queue leu leu

fol′low-up′ *adj* de continuation, complémentaire; (*car*) suiveur ‖ *s* soins *mpl* post-hospitaliers

fol·ly ['fali] *s* (*pl* **-lies**) sottise *f*; (*madness*) folie *f*; **follies** spectacle *m* de music-hall, folies *fpl*

foment [fo'mɛnt] *tr* fomenter

fond [fand] *adj* affectueux, tendre; **to become fond of** s'attacher à

fondle ['fandəl] *tr* caresser

fondness ['fandnɪs] *s* affection *f*, tendresse *f*; (*appetite*) goût *m*, penchant *m*

font [fant] *s* source *f*; (*for holy water*) bénitier *m*; (*for baptism*) fonts *mpl*; (typ) fonte *f*

food [fud] *adj* alimentaire ‖ *s* nourriture *f*, aliments *mpl*; **food for thought** matière *f* à réflexion; **good food** bonne cuisine *f*

food′ and cloth′ing *s* le vivre et le vêtement

food′ and drink′ *s* le boire et le manger

food′ proc′essor *s* robot *m* multifonctions

food′ slic′er *s* trancheuse *f*

food′stuffs′ *spl* denrées *fpl* alimentaires, vivres *mpl*

fool [ful] *s* sot *m*; (*jester*) fou *m*; (*person imposed on*) innocent *m*, niais *m*; **to make a fool of** se moquer de; **to play the fool** faire le pitre ‖ *tr* mystifier, abuser; **to fool away** gaspiller sottement ‖ *intr* faire la bête; **to fool around** (coll) gâcher son temps; **to fool with** (coll) tripoter

fooler·y ['fuləri] *s* (*pl* **-ies**) sottise *f*, ânerie *f*

fool′har′dy *adj* (*comp* **-dier**; *super* **-diest**) téméraire

fooling ['fulɪŋ] *s* tromperie *f*; **no fooling!** sans blague!

foolish ['fulɪʃ] *adj* sot, niais; ridicule, absurde

fool′proof′ *adj* à toute épreuve; infaillible

fools′cap′ *s* papier *m* ministre

fool's′ er′rand *s*—**to go on a fool's errand** y aller pour des prunes

foot [fʊt] *s* (*pl* **feet** [fit]) pied *m*; (*of cat, dog, bird*) patte *f*; **on foot** à pied; **to drag one's feet** aller à pas de tortue; **to have one foot in the grave** avoir un pied dans la tombe; **to put one's best foot forward** (coll) partir du bon pied; **to put one's foot down** faire acte d'autorité; **to put one's foot in one's mouth** (coll) mettre les pieds dans le plat; **to stand on one's own feet** voler de ses propres ailes; **to tread under foot** fouler aux pieds ‖ *tr* (*the bill*) payer; **to foot it** aller à pied

footage ['fʊtɪdʒ] *s* (mov, telv) (*in French* métrage *m*, *i.e., length of film in meters*) longueur *f* d'un film en pieds

foot′-and-mouth′ disease′ *s* (vet) fièvre *f* aphteuse

foot′ball′ *s* football *m* américain; (*ball*) ballon *m*

foot′ brake′ *s* frein *m* à pédale

foot′bridge′ *s* passerelle *f*

foot′fall′ *s* pas *m* léger, bruit *m* de pas

foot′hills′ *spl* contreforts *mpl*, collines *fpl* basses

foot′hold′ *s*—**to gain a foothold** prendre pied

footing ['fʊtɪŋ] *s* équilibre *m*; (archit) empattement *m*, base *f*, socle *m*; **to be on a friendly footing** être en bons termes; **to be on an equal footing** être sur un pied d'égalité; **to lose one's footing** perdre pied

foot′lights′ *spl* (theat) rampe *f*

foot′lock′er *s* (mil) cantine *f*

foot′loose′ *adj* libre, sans entraves

foot′man *s* (*pl* **-men**) valet *m* de pied

foot′mark′ *s* empreinte *f* de pied

foot′note′ *s* note *f* au bas de la page

foot′pad′ *s* voleur *m* de grand chemin

foot′path′ *s* sentier *m* pour piétons

foot′print′ *s* empreinte *f* de pas, trace *f*

foot′ race′ *s* course *f* à pied

foot′rest′ *s* cale-pied *m*, repose-pied *m*

foot′ sol′dier *s* fantassin *m*

foot′sore′ *adj* aux pieds endoloris, éclopé

foot′step′ *s* pas *m*; **to follow in s.o.'s footsteps** suivre les traces de qn

foot′stone′ *s* pierre *f* tumulaire (au pied d'une tombe); (archit) première pierre

foot'stool' s tabouret m

foot' warm'er s chauffe-pieds m

foot'wear' s chaussures fpl

foot'work' s jeu m de jambes

foot'worn' adj usé; (person) aux pieds endoloris

fop [fɑp] s petit-maître m, bellâtre m

for [fɔr], [fər] prep pour; de, e.g., **to thank s.o. for** remercier qn de; e.g., **time for dinner** l'heure du dîner; e.g., **to cry for joy** pleurer de joie; e.g., **request for money** demande d'argent; à, e.g., **for sale** à vendre; e.g., **to sell for a high price** vendre à un prix élevé; e.g., **it is for you to decide** c'est à vous de décider; par, e.g., **famous for** célèbre par; e.g., **for example** par exemple; e.g., **for pity's sake** par pitié; contre, e.g., **a remedy for** un remède contre; **as for** quant à; **for** + ger pour + perf inf, e.g., **he was punished for stealing** il fut puni pour avoir volé; **for all that** malgré tout cela; **for short** en abrégé; **he has been in Paris for a week** il est à Paris depuis une semaine, il y a une semaine qu'il est à Paris; **he was in Paris for a week** il était à Paris pendant une semaine; **to be for** (to be in favor of) être en faveur de, être partisan de or pour; **to use s.th. for s.th.** employer q.ch. comme q.ch.; e.g., **to use coal for fuel** employer le charbon comme combustible ‖ conj car, parce que

forage [ˈfɔrɪdʒ] s fourrage m ‖ tr & intr fourrager

foray [ˈfɔre] s incursion f ‖ tr saccager, fourrager ‖ intr faire une incursion

for·bear [fɔrˈbɛr] s (pret -bore; pp -borne) tr s'abstenir de ‖ intr se montrer patient

forbearance [fɔrˈbɛrəns] s abstention f; patience f

for·bid [fɔrˈbɪd] v (pret -bade or -bad [ˈbæd]; pp -bidden; ger -bidding) tr défendre, interdire; **God forbid!** qu'à Dieu ne plaise!; **to forbid s.o. s.th.** défendre q.ch. à qn; **to forbid s.o. to** défendre à qn de

forbidden [fɔrˈbɪdən] adj défendu

forbidding [fɔrˈbɪdɪŋ] adj rebutant, rébarbatif, sinistre

force [fɔrs] s force f; (of a word) signification f, valeur f; **in force** en vigueur; **in full force** en force; **the allied forces** les puissances alliées ‖ tr forcer; **to force back** repousser; (air; water) refouler; **to force in** (e.g., a door) enfoncer; **to force one's way into** (e.g., a house) pénétrer de force dans; **to force s.o.'s hand** forcer la main à qn; **to force s.o. to** + inf forcer qn à or de + inf; **to force s.th. into s.th.** faire entrer q.ch. dans q.ch.; **to force up** (e.g., prices) faire monter

forced' draft' s tirage m forcé

forced' land'ing s atterrissage m forcé

forced' march' s marche f forcée

force'-feed' tr (pret & pp -fed) gaver, suralimenter

force'-feed'ing s suralimentation f

forceful [ˈfɔrsfəl] adj énergique

for·ceps [ˈfɔrsɛps] s (pl -ceps or -cipes [sɪˌpiz]) (dent, surg) pince f; (obstet) forceps m

force' pump' s pompe f foulante

forcible [ˈfɔrsɪbəl] adj énergique, vigoureux; (convincing) convaincant; (imposed) forcé

ford [fɔrd] s gué m ‖ tr franchir à gué

fore [fɔr] adj antérieur; (naut) de l'avant ‖ s (naut) avant m; **to the fore** en vue, en vedette ‖ adv à l'avant ‖ interj (golf) gare devant!

fore' and aft' adv de l'avant à l'arrière

fore'arm' s avant-bras m ‖ **fore·arm'** tr prémunir; (to warn) avertir

fore'bear' s ancêtre m

foreboding [fɔrˈbodɪŋ] s (sign) présage m; (feeling) pressentiment m

fore'cast' s prévision f ‖ v (pret & pp -cast or -casted) tr pronostiquer

forecastle [ˈfoksəl], [ˈfɔrˌkæsəl] s gaillard m d'avant

fore·close' tr exclure; (law) forclore; **to foreclose the mortgage** saisir l'immeuble hypothéqué

foreclosure [fɔrˈkloʒər] s saisie f, forclusion f

fore·doom' tr condamner par avance

fore' edge' s (bb) tranche f

fore'fa'ther s aïeul m, ancêtre m

fore'fin'ger s index m

fore'foot' s (pl -feet) patte f de devant

fore'front' s premier rang m; **in the forefront** en première ligne

fore·go' v (pret -went; pp -gone) tr (to give up) renoncer à

foregoing [fɔrˈgo·ɪŋ] adj précédent, antérieur; (facts, text, etc., already cited) déjà cité, ci-dessus

fore'gone' adj inévitable; (anticipated) décidé d'avance, prévu

fore'ground' s premier plan m

fore'hand'ed adj prévoyant; (thrifty) ménager

forehead [ˈfɔrɪd] s front m

foreign [ˈfɔrɪn] adj étranger

for'eign affairs' spl affaires fpl étrangères

foreigner [ˈfɔrɪnər] s étranger m

for'eign exchange' s change m étranger; (currency) devises fpl

for'eign min'ister s ministre m des affaires étrangères

for'eign of'fice s ministère m des affaires étrangères

for'eign serv'ice s (dipl) service m diplomatique; (mil) service m à l'étranger

for'eign trade' s commerce m extérieur

fore'leg' s jambe f de devant

fore'lock' s mèche f sur le front; (of horse) toupet m; **to take time by the forelock** saisir l'occasion par les cheveux

fore'man s (pl -men) chef m d'équipe; (in machine shop, factory) contremaître m; (of jury) premier juré m

foremast [ˈfɔrməst], [ˈfɔrˌmæst] s mât m de misaine

fore′most′ *adj* premier, principal ‖ *adv* au premier rang

fore′noon′ *s* matinée *f*

fore′part′ *s* avant *m*, devant *m*, partie *f* avant

fore′paw′ *s* patte *f* de devant

fore′quar′ter *s* quartier *m* de devant

fore′run′ner *s* précurseur *m*, avant-coureur *m*; (*sign*) signe *m* avant-coureur

foresail [′fɔrsəl], [′fɔr,sel] *s* misaine *f*, voile *f* de misaine

fore·see′ *v* (*pret* -saw; *pp* -seen) *tr* prévoir

foreseeable [for′si·əbəl] *adj* prévisible

fore·shad′ow *tr* présager, préfigurer

fore·short′en *tr* dessiner en raccourci

fore·short′ening *s* raccourci *m*

fore′sight′ *s* prévision *f*, prévoyance *f*

fore′sight′ed *adj* prévoyant

fore′skin′ *s* prépuce *m*

forest [′fɔrɪst] *adj* forestier ‖ *s* forêt *f*

fore′stage′ *s* (theat) avant-scène *f*

fore·stall′ *tr* anticiper, devancer

for′est rang′er *s* garde *m* forestier

forestry [′fɔrɪstri] *s* sylviculture *f*

fore′taste′ *s* avant-goût *m*

fore·tell′ *v* (*pret & pp* -told) *tr* prédire

fore′thought′ *s* prévoyance *f*; (law) préméditation *f*

for·ev′er *adv* pour toujours, à jamais

fore·warn′ *tr* avertir, prévenir

fore′word′ *s* avant-propos *m*, avis *m* au lecteur

forfeit [′fɔrfɪt] *adj* perdu ‖ *s* (*pledge*) dédit *m*, gage *m*; (*fine*) amende *f*; **to play at forfeits** jouer aux gages ‖ *tr* être déchu de, être privé de

forfeiture [′fɔrfɪtʃər] *s* perte *f*; (*fine*) amende *f*, confiscation *f*

forge [fɔrdʒ] *s* forge *f* ‖ *tr* forger; (*e.g., documents*) contrefaire, falsifier

forger [′fɔrdʒər] *s* forgeur *m*; (*e.g., of documents*) faussaire *mf*

forger·y [′fɔrdʒəri] *s* (*pl* -ies) contrefaçon *f*; (*of a document, a painting, etc.*) faux *m*

for·get [fɔr′gɛt] *v* (*pret* -got; *pp* -got or -gotten; *ger* -getting) *tr & intr* oublier; **forget it!** n'y pensez plus!; **to forget to** + *inf* oublier de + *inf*

forgetful [fɔr′gɛtfəl] *adj* oublieux

forget′-me-not′ *s* myosotis *m*, ne-m'oubliez-pas *m*

forgivable [fɔr′gɪvəbəl] *adj* pardonnable

for·give [fɔr′gɪv] *v* (*pret* -gave; *pp* -given) *tr & intr* pardonner

forgiveness [fɔr′gɪvnɪs] *s* pardon *m*

forgiving [fɔr′gɪvɪŋ] *adj* indulgent, miséricordieux

for·go [fɔr′go] *v* (*pret* -went; *pp* -gone) *tr* renoncer à, s'abstenir de

fork [fɔrk] *s* fourche *f*; (*of road, tree, stem*) fourche *f*, bifurcation *f*; (*at table*) fourchette *f* ‖ *tr & intr* fourcher, bifurquer

forked *adj* fourchu

forked′ light′ning *s* éclairs *mpl* en zigzag

fork′lift truck′ *s* chariot *m* élévateur

forlorn [fɔr′lɔrn] *adj* (*destitute*) abandonné; (*hopeless*) désespéré; (*wretched*) misérable

forlorn′ hope′ *s* tentative *f* désespérée

form [fɔrm] *s* forme *f*; (*paper to be filled out*) formule *f*, fiche *f*, feuille f; (*construction to give shape to cement*) coffrage *m* ‖ *tr* former ‖ *intr* se former

formal [′fɔrməl] *adj* cérémonieux, officiel; (*formalistic*) formaliste; (*superficial*) formel, de pure forme

for′mal attire′ *s* tenue *f* de cérémonie

for′mal call′ *s* visite *f* de politesse

formaldehyde [fɔr′mældə,haɪd] *s* formaldéhyde

for′mal din′ner *s* dîner *m* de cérémonie, dîner prié

formali·ty [fɔr′mælɪti] *s* (*pl* -ties) formalité *f*; (*stiffness*) raideur *f*; (*polite conventions*) cérémonie *f*, étiquette *f*

for′mal par′ty *s* soirée *f* de gala

for′mal speech′ *s* discours *m* d'apparat

format [′fɔrmæt] *s* format *m*

formation [fɔr′meʃən] *s* formation *f*

former [′fɔrmər] *adj* antérieur, précédent; (*long past*) ancien; (*first of two things mentioned*) premier ‖ *pron*—**the former** celui-là §84; le premier

formerly [′fɔrmərli] *adv* autrefois, anciennement, jadis

form′fit′ting *adj* ajusté, moulant

formidable [′fɔrmɪdəbəl] *adj* formidable

formless [′fɔrmlɪs] *adj* informe

form′ let′ter *s* lettre *f* circulaire

formu·la [′fɔrmjələ] *s* (*pl* -las or -lae [,li]) formule *f*

formulate [′fɔrmjə,let] *tr* formuler

for·sake [fɔr′sek] *v* (*pret* -sook [′sʊk]; *pp* -saken [′sekən]) *tr* abandonner, délaisser

fort [fɔrt] *s* fort *m*, forteresse *f*; **hold the fort!** (coll) je vous confie la maison!

forte [fɔrt] *s* fort *m*

forth [fɔrθ] *adv* en avant; **and so forth** et ainsi de suite; **from this day forth** à partir de ce jour; **to go forth** sortir, se mettre en route

forth′com′ing *adj* à venir, à paraître, prochain

forth′right′ *adj* net, direct ‖ *adv* droit, carrément; (*immediately*) tout de suite

forth′with′ *adv* sur-le-champ

fortieth [′fɔrtɪ·ɪθ] *adj & pron* quarantième (*masc, fem*) ‖ *s* quarantième *m*

fortification [,fɔrtɪfɪ′keʃən] *s* fortification *f*

forti·fy [′fɔrtɪ,faɪ] *v* (*pret & pp* -fied) *tr* fortifier; (*wine*) viner

fortitude [′fɔrtɪ,t(j)ud] *s* force *f* d'âme

fortnight [′fɔrt,naɪt] *s* quinze jours *mpl*, quinzaine *f*

fortress [′fɔrtrɪs] *s* forteresse *f*

fortuitous [fɔr′t(j)u·ɪtəs] *adj* (*accidental*) fortuit; (*lucky*) fortuné

fortunate [′fɔrtʃənɪt] *adj* heureux

fortune [′fɔrtʃən] *s* fortune *f*; **to cost a fortune** coûter les yeux de la tête; **to make a fortune** faire fortune; **to tell s.o. his fortune** dire la bonne aventure à qn

for'tune hunt'er *s* coureur *m* de dots

for'tune·tel'ler *s* diseuse *f* de bonne aventure

for·ty ['fɔrti] *adj & pron* quarante ‖ *s* (*pl* **-ties**) quarante *m*; **about forty** une quarantaine

fo·rum ['forəm] *s* (*pl* **-rums** or **-ra** [rə]) forum *m*; (*e.g., of public opinion*) tribunal *m*; **open forum** tribune *f* libre

forward ['fɔrwərd] *adj* de devant; (*precocious*) avancé, précoce; (*bold*) audacieux, effronté ‖ *s* (sports) avant *m* ‖ *adv* en avant; **to bring forward** (bk) reporter; **to come forward** s'avancer; **to look forward to** compter sur, se faire une fête de ‖ *tr* envoyer, expédier; (*a letter*) faire suivre; (*a project*) avancer, favoriser; **please forward** prière de faire suivre

for'warding address' *s* adresse *f* d'expédition, adresse d'envoi

fossil ['fɑsɪl] *adj & s* fossile *m*

foster ['fɔstər] *adj* de lait, nourricier ‖ *tr* encourager, entretenir

fos'ter fa'ther *s* père *m* adoptif

fos'ter moth'er *s* mère *f* adoptive

fos'ter par'enting *s* fosterage *m*

foul [faʊl] *adj* immonde; (*air*) vicié; (*wind*) contraire; (*weather*) gros, sale; (*breath*) fétide; (*language*) ordurier; (*water*) bourbeux; (*ball*) hors jeu ‖ *s* (baseball) faute *f*; (boxing) coup *m* bas ‖ *adv* déloyalement ‖ *tr* (sports) commettre une faute contre ‖ *intr* (said of anchor, propeller, rope, etc.) s'engager

foul-mouthed ['faʊl'maʊðd] *adj* mal embouché

foul' play' *s* malveillance *f*; (sports) jeu *m* déloyal

found [faʊnd] *tr* fonder, établir; (*metal*) fondre

foundation [faʊn'deʃən] *s* (*basis; masonry support*) fondement *m*; (*act of endowing*) dotation *f*; (*endowment*) fondation *f*

founder ['faʊndər] *s* fondateur *m*; (*in foundry*) fondeur *m* ‖ *intr* (*said of horse*) boiter bas; (*said of building*) s'effondrer; (naut) sombrer

foundling ['faʊndlɪŋ] *s* enfant *m* trouvé

found'ling hos'pital *s* hospice *m* des enfants trouvés

found·ry ['faʊndri] *s* (*pl* **-ries**) fonderie *f*

found·ry·man *s* (*pl* **-men**) fondeur *m*

fount [faʊnt] *s* source *f*

fountain ['faʊntən] *s* fontaine *f*

foun'tain·head' *s* source *f*, origine *f*

Foun'tain of Youth' *s* fontaine *f* de Jouvence

foun'tain pen' *s* stylo *m* (à réservoir)

four [for] *adj & pron* quatre ‖ *s* quatre *m*; **four o'clock** quatre heures; **on all fours** à quatre pattes

four'-cy'cle *adj* (mach) à quatre temps

four'-cyl'inder *adj* (mach) à quatre cylindres

four'-flush' *intr* (coll) bluffer, faire le fanfaron

fourflusher ['for,flʌʃər] *s* (coll) bluffeur *m*

four'-foot'ed *adj* quadrupède

four' hun'dred *adj & pron* quatre cents ‖ *s* quatre cents *m*; **the Four Hundred** la haute société; le Tout Paris

four'-in-hand' *s* (*tie*) cravate-plastron *f*; (*team*) attelage *m* à quatre

four'-lane' *adj* à quatre voies

four'-leaf clo'ver *s* trèfle *m* à quatre feuilles

four'-motor plane' *s* quadrimoteur *m*

four'-o'clock' *s* (*Mirabilis jalapa*) belle-de-nuit *f*

four' of a kind' *s* (cards) un carré

four'-post'er *s* lit *m* à colonnes

four'score' *adj* quatre-vingts

foursome ['forsəm] *s* partie *f* double

fourteen ['for'tin] *adj, pron, & s* quatorze *m*

fourteenth ['for'tinθ] *adj & pron* quatorzième (*masc, fem*); **the Fourteenth** quatorze, e.g., **John the Fourteenth** Jean quatorze ‖ *s* quatorze *m*; **the fourteenth** (*in dates*) le quatorze

fourth [forθ] *adj & pron* quatrième (*masc, fem*); **the Fourth** quatre, e.g., **John the Fourth** Jean quatre ‖ *s* quatrième *m*; (*in fractions*) quart *m*; **the fourth** (*in dates*) le quatre

fourth' estate' *s* quatrième pouvoir *m*

fowl [faʊl] *s* volaille *f*

fox [fɑks] *s* renard *m* ‖ *tr* (coll) mystifier

fox'glove' *s* digitale *f*

fox'hole' *s* renardière *f*; (mil) gourbi *m*, abri *m* de tranchée

fox'hound' *s* fox-hound *m*

fox' hunt' *s* chasse *f* au renard

fox' ter'rier *s* fox-terrier *m*

fox' trot' *s* (*of animal*) petit trot *m*; (*dance*) fox-trot *m*

fox·y ['fɑksi] *adj* (*comp* **-ier**; *super* **-iest**) rusé, madré

foyer ['fɔɪ·ər] *s* (*lobby*) foyer *m*; (*entrance hall*) vestibule *m*

fracas ['frekəs] *s* bagarre *f*, rixe *f*

fraction ['frækʃən] *s* fraction *f*

fractional ['frækʃənəl] *adj* fractionnaire

frac'tional cur'rency *s* monnaie *f* divisionnaire

fracture ['fræktʃər] *s* fracture *f*; **to set a fracture** réduire une fracture ‖ *tr* fracturer

fragile ['frædʒɪl] *adj* fragile

fragment ['frægmənt] *s* fragment *m* ‖ *tr* fragmenter

fragrance ['fregrəns] *s* parfum *m*

fragrant ['fregrənt] *adj* parfumé

frail [frel] *adj* frêle; (*e.g., virtue*) fragile, faible ‖ *s* (*basket*) couffe *f*

frail·ty ['frelti] *s* (*pl* **-ties**) fragilité *f*; (*weakness*) faiblesse *f*

frame [frem] *s* (*of picture, mirror*) cadre *m*; (*of glasses*) monture *f*; (*of window, car*) châssis *m*; (*of window, motor*) bâti *m*; (*support, stand*) armature *f*; (*structure*) charpente *f*; (*of embroidering*) métier *m*; (*of comic strip*) cadre, dessin *m*; (mov, telv) image *f* ‖ *tr* former, charpenter; (*a picture*) encadrer; (*film*) cadrer; (*an answer*) formuler; (slang) monter une accusation contre

frame′ house′ s maison f en bois
frame′ of mind′ s disposition f d'esprit
frame′-up′ s (slang) coup m monté
frame′work′ s charpente f, squelette m
framing [′fremɪŋ] s (mov, phot) cadrage m
France [fræns] s France f; la France
franchise [′fræntʃaɪz] s concession f, privilège m; (com) chaîne f volontaire; (pol) droit m de vote
frank [fræŋk] adj franc ‖ s franchise f postale; **Frank** (medieval German person) Franc m; (masculine name) François m ‖ tr affranchir
frankfurter [′fræŋkfərtər] s saucisse f de Francfort
frankincense [′fræŋkɪn,sɛns] s oliban m
Frankish [′fræŋkɪʃ] adj franc ‖ s francique m
frankness [′fræŋknɪs] s franchise f
frantic [′fræntɪk] adj frénétique
fraternal [frə′tʌrnəl] adj fraternel
fraterni·ty [frə′tʌrnɪti] s (pl -ties) fraternité f; (association) confrérie f; (at a university) club m d'étudiants, amicale f estudiantine
fraternize [′frætər,naɪz] intr fraterniser
fraud [frɔd] s fraude f; (person) imposteur m, fourbe mf
fraudulent [′frɔdjələnt] adj frauduleux, en fraude
fraught [frɔt] adj—**fraught with** chargé de
fray [fre] s bagarre f ‖ tr érailler ‖ intr s'érailler
freak [frik] s (sudden fancy) caprice m; (anomaly) curiosité f; (person, animal) monstre m
freakish [′frikɪʃ] adj capricieux; bizarre; (grotesque) monstrueux
freckle [′frɛkəl] s tache f de rousseur, éphélide f
freckly [′frɛkli] adj couvert de taches de rousseur
free [fri] adj (comp **freer** [′fri·ər]; super **freest** [′fri·ɪst]) libre; (without charge) gratuit; (without extra charge) franc, exempt; (e.g., end of a rope) dégagé; (with money, advice, etc.) libéral, généreux; (manner, speech, etc.) franc, ouvert; **to set free** libérer, affranchir ‖ adv franco, gratis, gratuitement; (naut) largue, e.g., **running free** courant largue ‖ v (pret & pp **freed** [frid]; ger **freeing** [′fri·ɪŋ]) tr libérer; (a prisoner) affranchir, élargir; (to disengage) dégager; (from an obligation) exempter
free′ admis′sion s entrée f libre, entrée gratuite
free′ and eas′y adj désinvolte, dégagé
freebooter [′fri,butər] s flibustier m, maraudeur m
free′ com′peti′tion s libre concurrence f
freedom [′fridəm] s liberté f
free′dom of speech′ s liberté f de la parole
free′dom of the press′ s liberté f de la presse
free′dom of the seas′ s liberté f des mers

free′dom of thought′ s liberté f de la pensée
free′dom of wor′ship s liberté f du culte, libre pratique f
free′-for-all′ s foire f d'empoigne, mêlée f
free′ hand′ s carte f blanche
free′-hand draw′ing s dessin m à main levée
free′hand′ed adj libéral, généreux
free′hold′ s (law) propriété f foncière perpétuelle; (hist) franc-alleu m
free′ lance′ s franc-tireur m
free′-lance′ intr travailler à la pige, travailler à (or pour) son compte
free′man s (pl -men) homme m libre; (citizen) citoyen m
Free′ma′son s franc-maçon m
Free′ma′sonry s franc-maçonnerie f
free′ of charge′ adj & adv gratis, exempt de frais, gratuit, bénévolement
free′ on board′ adv franco de bord, départ usine
free′ port′ s port m franc
free′ speech′ s liberté f de la parole
free′-spo′ken adj franc; **to be free-spoken** avoir son franc-parler
free′stone′ adj (bot) à noyau non-adhérent ‖ s (mas) pierre f de taille
free′think′er s libre penseur m
free′ thought′ s libre pensée f
free′ throw′ s (sports) lancer m franc
free′ tick′et s billet m de faveur
free′ trade′ s libre-échange m
free′way′ s autoroute f
free′will′ adj volontaire, de plein gré
free′ will′ s libre arbitre m; **of one's own free will** de son propre gré
freeze [friz] s congélation f ‖ v (pret **froze** [froz]; pp **frozen**) tr geler, congeler; (e.g., wages) geler, bloquer; (foods) surgeler ‖ intr geler; **it is freezing** il gèle
freeze′-dry′ v (pret & pp -dried) tr lyophiliser
freeze′ dry′ing s lyophilisation f
freezer [′frizər] s (for making ice cream) sorbetière f; (for foods) congélateur m
freez′er bag′ s sac m congélateur
freight [fret] s fret m, chargement m; (cost) fret, prix m du transport; **by freight** (rr) en petite vitesse ‖ tr transporter; (a ship, truck, etc.) charger
freight′ car′ s wagon m de marchandises, wagon à caisse
freighter [′fretər] s cargo m
freight′ plat′form s quai m de déchargement
freight′ sta′tion s gare f de marchandises
freight′ train′ s train m de marchandises
freight′ yard′ s (rr) cour f de marchandises
French [frɛntʃ] adj français ‖ s (language) français m; **the French** les Français
French′ Cana′dian s Franco-Canadien m
French′-Cana′dian adj franco-canadien
French′ chalk′ s craie f de tailleur, stéatite f
French′ cuff′ s poignet m mousquetaire
French′ door′ s porte-fenêtre f

French' dress'ing s vinaigrette f
French' fries' spl frites fpl
French' horn' s (mus) cor m d'harmonie
French' horse'power s (735 watts) cheval-vapeur m, cheval m
French' leave' s—**to take French leave** filer à l'anglaise
French'man s (pl -men) Français m
French' roll' s petit pain m
French'-speak'ing adj francophone; (country) de langue française
French' tel'ephone s combiné m
French' toast' s pain m perdu
French' win'dow s porte-fenêtre f
French'wom'an s (pl -wom'en) Française f
frenzied ['frɛnzɪd] adj frénétique
fren·zy ['frɛnzi] s (pl -zies) frénésie f
frequen·cy ['frikwənsi] s (pl -cies) fréquence f
fre'quency modula'tion s modulation f de fréquence
frequent ['frikwənt] adj fréquent ‖ [frɪ'kwɛnt] tr fréquenter
frequently ['frikwəntli] adv fréquemment
fres·co ['frɛsko] s (pl -coes or -cos) fresque f ‖ tr peindre à fresque
fresh [frɛʃ] adj frais; (water) doux; (e.g., idea) nouveau; (wound) saignant; (cheeky) (coll) osé, impertinent; **fresh paint!** (public sign) attention, peinture fraîche! ‖ adv nouvellement; **fresh in** (coll) récemment arrivé; **fresh out** (coll) récemment épuisé
freshen ['frɛʃən] tr rafraîchir ‖ intr se rafraîchir; (said of wind) fraîchir
freshet ['frɛʃɪt] s crue f
fresh'man s (pl -men) étudiant m de première année, bizut m
freshness ['frɛʃnɪs] s fraîcheur f; (sauciness) impudence f, impertinence f
fresh'-wa'ter adj d'eau douce
fret [frɛt] s (interlaced design) frette f; (uneasiness) inquiétude f; (mus) touchette f ‖ v (pret & pp **fretted**; ger **fretting**) tr ajourer ‖ intr s'inquiéter, geindre
fretful ['frɛtfəl] adj irritable, boudeur
fret'work' s ajour m, ornementation f ajourée
Freudianism ['frɔɪdɪ·ə,nɪzəm] s freudisme m
friar ['fraɪ·ər] s moine m
fricassee [,frɪkə'si] s fricassé f
friction ['frɪkʃən] s friction f
fric'tion tape' s chatterton m, ruban m isolant
Friday ['fraɪdi] s vendredi m
fried [fraɪd] adj frit
fried' egg' s œuf m sur le plat
friend [frɛnd] s ami m; **to make friends with** se lier d'amitié avec
friend·ly ['frɛndli] adj (comp -lier; super -liest) amical, sympathique
friendship ['frɛndʃɪp] s amitié f
frieze [friz] s (archit) frise f
frigate ['frɪgɪt] s frégate f

fright [fraɪt] s frayeur f, effroi m; (grotesque or ridiculous person) (coll) épouvantail m; **to take fright at** s'effrayer de
frighten ['fraɪtən] tr effrayer; **to frighten away** effaroucher, faire fuir
frightful ['fraɪtfəl] adj effroyable; (coll) affreux; (huge) (coll) énorme
frigid ['frɪdʒɪd] adj frigide; (zone) glacial
frigidity [frɪ'dʒɪdɪti] s frigidité f
frill [frɪl] s (on shirt front) jabot m; (frippery) falbala m
fringe [frɪndʒ] s frange f; (border) bordure f; (opt) frange; **on the fringe of** en marge de ‖ tr franger
fringe' ben'efits spl supplément m de solde, bénéfices mpl marginaux, avantages mpl sociaux
fripper·y ['frɪpəri] s (pl -ies) (flashiness) clinquant m; (inferior goods) camelote f
Frisbee ['frɪzbi] s (trademark) disque m volant
frisk [frɪsk] tr (slang) fouiller, palper ‖ intr—**to frisk about** gambader, folâtrer
frisk·y ['frɪski] adj (comp -ier; super -iest) vif, folâtre; (horse) fringant
fritter ['frɪtər] s beignet m ‖ tr—**to fritter away** gaspiller
frivolous ['frɪvələs] adj frivole
frizzle ['frɪzəl] s frisure f ‖ tr frisotter; (culin) faire frire ‖ intr frisotter; (culin) grésiller
friz·zly ['frɪzli] adj (comp -zlier; super -zliest) crépu, crépelu
fro [fro] adv—**to and fro** de long en large; **to go to and fro** aller et venir
frock [frɑk] s robe f; (overalls, smock) blouse f; (eccl) froc m
frock' coat' s redingote f
frog [frɑg], [frɔg] s grenouille f; (in throat) chat m
frog'man' s (pl -men') homme-grenouille m
frogs'' legs' spl cuisses fpl de grenouille
frol·ic ['frɑlɪk] s gaieté f, ébats mpl ‖ v (pret & pp -icked; ger -icking) intr s'ébattre, folâtrer
frolicsome ['frɑlɪksəm] adj folâtre
from [frʌm], [frɑm], [frəm] prep de; de la part de, e.g., **greetings from your friend** compliments de la part de votre ami; contre, e.g., **a shelter from the rain** un abri contre la pluie; **from a certain angle** sous un certain angle; **from . . . to** depuis . . . jusqu'à; **from what I hear** d'après ce que j'apprends; **the flight from** le vol en provenance de; **to drink from** (a glass) boire dans; (a bottle) boire à; **to learn from a book** apprendre dans un livre; **to steal from** voler à
front [frʌnt] adj antérieur, de devant ‖ s devant m; (first place) premier rang m; (aut) avant m; (geog, mil, pol) front m; (figurehead) (coll) prête-nom m; **in front** par devant; **in front of** en face de, devant; **to put up a bold front** (coll) faire bonne contenance ‖ tr (to face) donner sur; (to

confront) affronter ‖ *intr*—**to front on** donner sur

frontage ['frʌntɪdʒ] *s* façade *f*; (*along a street, lake, etc.*) largeur *f*

front' door' *s* porte *f* d'entrée

front' drive' *s* (aut) traction *f* avant

frontier [frʌn'tɪr] *adj* frontalier ‖ *s* frontière *f*; (hist) front *m* de colonisation, front pionnier

frontiers'man *s* (*pl* **-men**) frontalier *m*, broussard *m*

frontispiece ['frʌntɪs,pis] *s* frontispice *m*; (archit) façade *f* principale

front' lines' *spl* avant-postes *mpl*

front' mat'ter *s* (*of book*) feuilles *fpl* liminaires

front' of'fice *s* direction *f*

front' page' *s*—**the front page** la première page, la une

front' porch' *s* porche *m*

front' room' *s* chambre *f* sur la rue

front' row' *s* premier rang *m*

front' seat' *s* siège *m* avant; (aut) banquette *f* avant

front' steps' *spl* perron *m*

front' view' *s* vue *f* de face

front'-wheel drive' *s* traction *f* avant

front'yard' *s* devant *m* de la maison

frost [frɔst] *s* (*freezing*) gelée *f*; (*frozen dew*) givre *m* ‖ *tr* (*to freeze*) geler; (*to cover with frost*) givrer; (culin) glacer

frost'bite' *s* engelure *f*

frost'ed glass' *s* verre *m* dépoli

frosting ['frɔstɪŋ] *s* (*on glass*) dépolissage *m*; (culin) fondant *m*

frost·y ['frɔsti] *adj* (*comp* **-ier**; *super* **-iest**) couvert de givre; (*reception, welcome*) glacé, glacial

froth [frɔθ] *s* écume *f*; (*on soap, beer, chocolate*) mousse *f*; (*frivolity*) futilité *f* ‖ *intr* mousser; (*at the mouth*) écumer

froth·y ['frɔθi] *adj* (*comp* **-ier**; *super* **-iest**) écumeux; (*soap, beer, chocolate*) mousseux; (*frivolous*) creux, futile

froward ['frowərd] *adj* obstiné, revêche

frown [fraun] *s* froncement *m* de sourcils ‖ *intr* froncer les sourcils; **to frown at** or **on** être contraire à, désapprouver

frows·y or **frowz·y** ['frauzi] *adj* (*comp* **-ier**; *super* **-iest**) malpropre, négligé, peu soigné; (*smelling bad*) malodorant

fro'zen as'sets ['frozən] *spl* fonds *mpl* gelés

fro'zen din'ner *s* plateau *m* repas congelé

fro'zen foods' *spl* aliments *mpl* surgelés

frugal ['frugəl] *adj* sobre, modéré; (*meal*) frugal

fruit [frut] *adj* fruitier ‖ *s* fruit *m*; les fruits, e.g., **I like fruit** j'aime les fruits; (*homosexual*) (pej) tapette *f*, pédé *m*

fruit' cake' *s* cake *m*

fruit' cup' *s* coupe *f* de fruits

fruit' fly' *s* mouche *f* du vinaigre

fruitful ['frutfəl] *adj* fructueux, fécond

fruition [fru'ɪʃən] *s* réalisation *f*; **to come to fruition** fructifier

fruit' juice' *s* jus *m* de fruits

fruitless ['frutlɪs] *adj* stérile, vain

fruit' sal'ad *s* macédoine *f* de fruits, salade *f* de fruits

fruit' stand' *s* étalage *m* de fruits

fruit' store' *s* fruiterie *f*

frumpish ['frʌmpɪʃ] *adj* fagoté, négligé

frustrate ['frʌstret] *tr* frustrer

fry [fraɪ] *s* (*pl* **-fries**) (culin) friture *f*; (ichth) fretin *m* ‖ *v* (*pret & pp* **fried**) *tr* faire frire; (*to sauté*) faire sauter ‖ *intr* frire

fry'ing pan' *s* poêle *f* à frire; **to jump from the frying pan into the fire** sauter de la poêle dans le feu

fudge [fʌdʒ] *s* fondant *m* de chocolat; (*humbug*) blague *f*

fuel ['fju·əl] *s* combustible *m*; (aut) carburant *m*; (fig) aliment *m* ‖ *v* (*pret & pp* **fueled** or **fuelled**; *ger* **fueling** or **fuelling**) *tr* pourvoir en combustible

fu'el gauge' *s* jauge *f* de combustible

fu'el line' *s* conduite *f* de combustible

fu'el oil' *s* mazout *m*, fuel-oil *m*, fuel *m*

fu'el tank' *s* réservoir *m* de carburant; (aut) réservoir *m* à essence

fu'el truck' *s* camion *m* citerne

fugitive ['fjudʒɪtɪv] *adj* & *s* fugitif *m*

ful·crum ['fʌlkrəm] *s* (*pl* **-crums** or **-cra** [krə]) point *m* d'appui

fulfill [ful'fɪl] *tr* accomplir; (*an obligation*) s'acquitter de, remplir

fulfillment [ful'fɪlmənt] *s* accomplissement *m*

full [ful] *adj* plein; (*dress, garment*) ample, bouffant; (*schedule*) chargé; (*lips*) gros, fort; (*brother, sister*) germain; (*having no more room*) complet; **full to overflowing** plein à déborder ‖ *s* plein *m*; **in full** intégralement, entièrement; (*to spell in full*) en toutes lettres; **to the full** complètement ‖ *adv* complètement; **full in the face** en pleine figure; **full many a** bien des; **full well** parfaitement ‖ *tr* (*cloth*) fouler

full' blast' *adv* (coll) en pleine activité

full'-blood'ed *adj* robuste; (*thoroughbred*) pur sang, de pure souche

full-blown ['ful'blon] *adj* achevé, développé; en pleine fleur

full'-bod'ied *adj* (*e.g., wine*) corsé

full' dress' *s* grande tenue *f*

full'-dress coat' *s* frac *m*

full'-faced' *adj* (*portrait*) de face

full-fledged ['ful'flɛdʒd] *adj* véritable, rien moins que

full-grown ['ful'gron] *adj* (*plant*) mûr; (*tree*) de haute futaie; (*person*) adulte

full' house' *s* (poker) main *f* pleine; (theat) salle *f* comble

full'-length' *adj* (*portrait*) en pied

full'-length mir'ror *s* psyché *f*

full'-length mov'ie *s* long métrage *m*

full' load' *s* plein chargement *m*

full' meas'ure *s* mesure *f* comble

full' moon' *s* pleine lune *f*

full' name' *s* nom *m* et prénoms *mpl*

full' pow'ers *spl* pleins pouvoirs *mpl*

full' rest' *s* (mus) pause *f*

full' sail' *adv* toutes voiles dehors

full' ses'sion *s* assemblée *f* plénière

full′-sized′ *adj* de grandeur nature
full′ speed′ *s* toute vitesse *f*
full′ stop′ *s* (gram) point *m* final; **to come to a full stop** s'arrêter net
full′ swing′ *s*—**in full swing** en pleine activité, en train
full′ tilt′ *adv* à toute vitesse
full′ time′ *adv* à pleines journées
full′-time′ *adj* à temps plein
full′ view′ *s*—**in full view** à la vue de tous
full′ weight′ *s* poids *m* juste
fully ['fʊli] *adv* entièrement, pleinement
fulsome ['fʊlsəm] *adj* écœurant, bas, servile
fumble ['fʌmbəl] *tr* manier maladroitement; (*the ball*) ne pas attraper, laisser tomber ‖ *intr* tâtonner
fume [fjum] *s* (*bad humor*) rage *f*; **fumes** fumées *fpl*, vapeurs *fpl* ‖ *tr & intr* fumer
fumigate ['fjumɪ,get] *tr* fumiger
fun [fʌn] *s* amusement *m*, gaieté *f*; (*badinage*) plaisanterie *f*; **in fun** pour rire; **to have fun** s'amuser; **to make fun of** se moquer de
function ['fʌŋkʃən] *s* fonction *f*; (*meeting*) cérémonie *f* ‖ *intr* fonctionner; **to function as** faire fonction de
functional ['fʌŋkʃənəl] *adj* fonctionnel
functionar·y ['fʌŋkʃə,nɛri] *s* (*pl* **-ies**) fonctionnaire *mf*
fund [fʌnd] *s* fonds *m*; **funds** fonds *mpl* ‖ *tr* (*a debt*) consolider
fundamental [,fʌndə'mɛntəl] *adj* fondamental ‖ *s* principe *m*, base *f*
fundamentalist [,fʌndə'mɛntəlɪst] *s* (rel) scripturaire *m*
funeral ['fjunərəl] *adj* (*march, procession, ceremony*) funèbre; (*expenses*) funéraire ‖ *s* funérailles *fpl*
fu′neral direc′tor *s* entrepreneur *m* de pompes funèbres
fu′neral home′ or **par′lor** *s* chapelle *f* mortuaire; salon *m* mortuaire (Canad); (*business*) entreprise *f* de pompes funèbres
fu′neral proces′sion *s* convoi *m* funèbre, enterrement *m*, deuil *m*
fu′neral serv′ice *s* office *m* des morts
funereal [fju'nɪrɪ·əl] *adj* funèbre
fungicide ['fʌndʒɪ,saɪd] *s* fongicide *m*
fungus ['fʌŋgəs] *s* (*pl* **funguses** or **fungi** ['fʌndʒaɪ]) (bot) champignon *m*; (pathol) fongus *m*
funicular [fju'nɪkjələr] *adj & s* funiculaire *m*
funk [fʌŋk] *s* (coll) frousse *f*
fun·nel ['fʌnəl] *s* (*for pouring through*) entonnoir *m*; (*smokestack*) cheminée *f*; (*tube for ventilation*) tuyau *m* ‖ *v* (*pret & pp* **-neled** or **-nelled**; *ger* **-neling** or **-nelling**) *tr* verser avec un entonnoir; (*to channel*) concentrer
funnies ['fʌniz] *spl* pages *fpl* comiques
fun·ny ['fʌni] *adj* (*comp* **-nier**; *super* **-niest**) comique; amusant, drôle; (coll) bizarre, curieux; **to strike s.o. as funny** paraître drôle à qn
fun′ny pa′per *s* pages *fpl* comiques

fur [fʌr] *s* fourrure *f*; (*on tongue*) empâtement *m*; **furs** pelleteries *fpl*
furbish ['fʌrbɪʃ] *tr* fourbir; **to furbish up** remettre à neuf
furious ['fjʊrɪ·əs] *adj* furieux
furl [fʌrl] *tr* (naut) ferler
fur′-lined′ *adj* doublé de fourrure
furlough ['fʌrlo] *s* permission *f*; **on furlough** en permission ‖ *tr* donner une permission à
furnace ['fʌrnɪs] *s* (*to heat a house*) calorifère *m*; (*to produce steam*) chaudière *f*; (*e.g., to smelt ores*) fourneau *m*; (rr) foyer *m*; (fig) fournaise *f*
furnish ['fʌrnɪʃ] *tr* fournir; (*a house*) meubler
fur′nished apart′ment *s* garni *m*, appartement *m* meublé
furnishings ['fʌrnɪʃɪŋz] *spl* (*of a house*) ameublement *m*; (*things to wear*) articles *mpl* d'habillement
furniture ['fʌrnɪtʃər] *s* meubles *mpl*; **a piece of furniture** un meuble; **a suite of furniture** un mobilier
fur′niture deal′er *s* marchand *m* de meubles
fur′niture pol′ish *s* encaustique *f*
fur′niture store′ *s* maison *f* d'ameublement
fur′niture ware′house *s* garde-meuble *m*
furor ['fjʊrɔr] *s* fureur *f*
furrier ['fʌrɪ·ər] *s* fourreur *m*, pelletier *m*
furrow ['fʌro] *s* sillon *m* ‖ *tr* sillonner
fur·ry ['fʌri] *adj* (*comp* **-rier**; *super* **-riest**) fourré, à fourrure
further ['fʌrðər] *adj* additional, supplémentaire ‖ *adv* plus loin; (*besides*) en outre, de plus ‖ *tr* avancer, favoriser
furtherance ['fʌrðərəns] *s* avancement *m*
fur′ther·more′ *adv* de plus, d'ailleurs
furthest ['fʌrðɪst] *adj* (le) plus éloigné ‖ *adv* le plus loin
furtive ['fʌrtɪv] *adj* furtif
fu·ry ['fjʊri] *s* (*pl* **-ries**) furie *f*
furze [fʌrz] *s* genêt *m* épineux, ajonc *m* d'Europe
fuse [fjuz] *s* (*tube or wick filled with explosive material*) étoupille *f*, mèche *f*; (*device for exploding a bomb or projectile*) fusée *f*; (elec) fusible *m*, plomb *m* de sûreté, plomb fusible; **to burn** or **blow out a fuse** faire sauter un plomb ‖ *tr* fondre; étoupiller ‖ *intr* se fondre
fuse′ box′ *s* boîte *f* à fusibles
fuselage ['fjuzəlɪdʒ] *s* fuselage *m*
fusible ['fjuzɪbəl] *adj* fusible
fusillade [,fjuzɪ'led] *s* fusillade *f*
fusion ['fjuʒən] *s* fusion *f*
fuss [fʌs] *s* (*excitement*) tapage *m*, agitation *f*; (*attention*) façons *fpl*, chichi *m*; (*dispute*) bagarre *f*; **to kick up a fuss** (coll) faire un tas d'histoires; **to make a fuss over** faire grand cas de ‖ *intr* faire des embarras, simagrées, or chichis; **to fuss over** être aux petits soins auprès de
fuss·y ['fʌsi] *adj* (*comp* **-ier**; *super* **-iest**) tracassier, tatillon; (*in dress*) pomponné

fustian ['fʌstʃən] s (*cloth*) futaine *f*; (*bombast*) grandiloquence *f*
futile ['fjutɪl] *adj* futile
future ['fjutʃər] *adj* futur, d'avenir ‖ *s* avenir *m*; (*gram*) futur *m*; **futures** (com) valeurs *fpl* négociées à terme; **in the**

future à l'avenir; **in the near future** à brève échéance
fuzz [fʌz] *s* (*on a peach*) duvet *m*; (*on a blanket*) peluche *f*; (*in pockets and corners*) bourre *f*
fuzz·y ['fʌzi] *adj* (*comp* **-ier**; *super* **-iest**) pelucheux; (*hair*) crêpelu; (*indistinct*) flou

G

G, g [dʒi] *s* VII⁰ lettre de l'alphabet
gab [gæb] *s* (coll) bavardage *m*, langue *f* ‖ *v* (*pret & pp* **gabbed**; *ger* **gabbing**) *intr* (coll) bavarder
gabardine ['gæbər,din] *s* gabardine *f*
gabble ['gæbəl] *s* jacasserie *f* ‖ *intr* jacasser
gable ['gebəl] *s* (*of roof*) pignon *m*; (*over a door or window*) gable *m*
ga'ble end' *s* pignon *m*
ga'ble roof' *s* comble *m* sur pignon, toit *m* à deux pentes
gad [gæd] *v* (*pret & pp* **gadded**; *ger* **gadding**) *intr*—**to gad about** courir la prétantaine, vadrouiller
gad'about' *s* vadrouilleur *m*
gad'fly' *s* (*pl* **-flies**) taon *m*
gadget ['gædʒɪt] *s* dispositif *m*; (*unnamed article*) machin *m*, truc *m*, gimmick *m*
Gaelic ['gelɪk] *adj & s* gaélique *m*
gaff [gæf] *s* gaffe *f*; **to stand the gaff** (slang) ne pas broncher
gaffer ['gæfər] *s* (coll) vieux bonhomme *m*
gag [gæg] *s* bâillon *m*; (*interpolation by an actor*) gag *m*; (*joke*) blague *f* ‖ *v* (*pret & pp* **gagged**; *ger* **gagging**) *tr* bâillonner ‖ *intr* avoir des haut-le-cœur
gage [gedʒ] *s* (*pledge*) gage *m*; (*challenge*) défi *m*
gaie·ty ['ge·ɪti] *s* (*pl* **-ties**) gaieté *f*
gaily ['geli] *adv* gaiement
gain [gen] *s* gain *m*; (*increase*) accroissement *m* ‖ *tr* gagner; (*to reach*) atteindre, gagner ‖ *intr* gagner du terrain; (*said of invalid*) s'améliorer; (*said of watch*) avancer; **to gain on** prendre de l'avance sur
gainful ['genfəl] *adj* profitable
gainsay' *v* (*pret & pp* **-said** [,sed], [,sɛd]) *tr* (*to deny*) nier; (*to contradict*) contredire; **not to gainsay** ne pas disconvenir de
gait [get] *s* démarche *f*, allure *f*
gaiter ['getər] *s* guêtre *f*
gala ['gælə] *adj* de gala ‖ *s* gala *m*
galax·y ['gæləksi] *s* (*pl* **-ies**) galaxie *f*
gale [gel] *s* gros vent *m*; **gales of laughter** éclats *mpl* de rire; **to weather a gale** étaler un coup de vent
gall [gɔl] *s* bile *f*, fiel *m*; (*something bitter*) (fig) fiel *m*, amertume *f*; (*audacity*) (coll) toupet *m* ‖ *tr* écorcher par le frottement; (fig) irriter

gallant ['gælənt] *adj* (*spirited, daring*) vaillant, brave; (*stately, grand*) fier, noble; (*showy, gay*) élégant, superbe, de fête ‖ *adj* galant ‖ *s* galant *m*; vaillant *m* ‖ [gə'lænt] *intr* faire le galant
gallant·ry ['gæləntri] *s* (*pl* **-ries**) galanterie *f*; (*bravery*) vaillance *f*
gall' blad'der *s* vésicule *f* biliaire
gall' duct' *s* conduit *m* biliaire
galleon ['gælɪ·ən] *s* (naut) galion *m*
galler·y ['gæləri] *s* (*pl* **-ies**) galerie *f*; (*cheapest seats in theater*) poulailler *m*; **to play to the gallery** poser pour la galerie
galley ['gæli] *s* (*ship*) galère *f*; (*ship's kitchen*) coquerie *f*; (typ) galée *f*, placard *m*
gal'ley proof' *s* épreuve *f* en placard, épreuve sous le galet
gal'ley slave' *s* galérien *m*
Gallic ['gælɪk] *adj* gaulois
Gal'lic wit' *s* esprit *m* gaulois
galling ['gɔlɪŋ] *adj* irritant, blessant
gallivant ['gælɪ,vænt] *intr* courailler
gall'nut' *s* noix *f* de galle
gallon ['gælən] *s* gallon *m* américain
galloon [gə'lun] *s* galon *m*
gallop ['gæləp] *s* galop *m* ‖ *tr* faire galoper ‖ *intr* galoper
gal·lows ['gæloz] *s* (*pl* **-lows** or **-lowses**) gibet *m*, potence *f*
gal'lows bird' *s* (coll) gibier *m* de potence
gall'stone' *s* calcul *m* biliaire
galore [gə'lor] *adv* à foison, à gogo
galoshes [gə'lɑʃɪz] *spl* caoutchoucs *mpl*
galvanize ['gælvə,naɪz] *tr* galvaniser
gal'vanized i'ron *s* tôle *f* galvanisée
gambit ['gæmbɪt] *s* gambit *m*
gamble ['gæmbəl] *s* risque *m*, affaire *f* de chance ‖ *tr* jouer; **to gamble away** perdre au jeu ‖ *intr* jouer; jouer à la Bourse; (fig) prendre des risques
gambler ['gæmblər] *s* joueur *m*
gambling ['gæmblɪŋ] *s* jeu *m*
gam'bling den' *s* tripot *m*
gam'bling house' *s* maison *f* de jeu
gam'bling ta'ble *s* table *f* de jeu
gam·bol ['gæmbəl] *s* gambade *f* ‖ *v* (*pret & pp* **-boled** or **-bolled**; *ger* **-boling** or **-bolling**) *intr* gambader
gambrel ['gæmbrəl] *s* (*hock*) jarret *m*; (*in butcher shop*) jambier *m*
gam'brel roof' *s* toit *m* en croupe

game [gem] *adj* (*plucky*) crâne, résolu; (*leg*) boiteux ‖ *s* jeu *m*; (*contest*) match *m*; (*score necessary to win*) partie *f*; (*animal or bird*) gibier *m*; **to make game of** tourner en dérision

game′bag′ *s* carnassière *f*, gibecière *f*

game′ bird′ *s* oiseau *m* que l'on chasse

game′cock′ *s* coq *m* de combat

game′keep′er *s* garde-chasse *m*

game′ of chance′ *s* jeu *m* de hasard

game′ preserve′ *s* chasse *f* gardée

game′ war′den *s* garde-chasse *m*

gamut [′gæmət] *s* gamme *f*

gam·y [′gemi] *adj* (*comp* **-ier**; *super* **-iest**) (*having flavor of uncooked game*) faisandé; (*plucky*) crâne

gander [′gændər] *s* jars *m*

gang [gæŋ] *adj* multiple ‖ *s* (*of workmen*) équipe *f*, brigade *f*; (*of thugs*) bande *f*; (*of wrongdoers*) séquelle *f*, clique *f* ‖ *intr*—**to gang up** se concerter; **to gang up on** se liguer contre

gangling [′gæŋglɪŋ] *adj* dégingandé

gangli·on [′gæŋglɪ·ən] *s* (*pl* **-ons** or **-a** [ə]) ganglion *m*

gang′plank′ *s* passerelle *f*, planche *f* de débarquement

gang′ rape′ *s* viol *m* collectif

gangrene [′gæŋgrin] *s* gangrène *f* ‖ *tr* gangrener ‖ *intr* se gangrener

gangster [′gæŋstər] *s* bandit *m*, gangster *m*

gang′way′ *s* (*passageway*) passage *m*, coursive *f*; (*gangplank*) planche *f* de débarquement; (*in ship's side*) coupée *f* ‖ *interj* rangez-vous!, dégagez!

gan·try [′gæntri] *s* (*pl* **-tries**) (*for barrels*) chantier *m*; (*for crane*) portique *m*; (rr) pont *m* à signaux

gan′try crane′ *s* grue *f* à portique

gap [gæp] *s* (*blank*) lacune *f*; (*in wall*) brèche *f*; (*between mountains*) col *m*, gorge *f*; (*between two points of view*) abîme *m*, gouffre *m*

gape [gep] *s* (*gap*) ouverture *f*, brèche *f*; (*yawn*) bâillement *m*; (*look of astonishment*) badauderie *f* ‖ *intr* (*to yawn*) bâiller; (*to look with astonishment*) badauder; **to gape at** regarder bouche bée

garage [gə′rɑʒ] *s* garage *m*

garage′ sale′ *s* braderie *f*, vente *f* bric-à-brac

garb [gɑrb] *s* costume *m* ‖ *tr* vêtir

garbage [′gɑrbɪdʒ] *s* ordures *fpl*

gar′bage can′ *s* poubelle *f*, dépotoir *m* (d'ordures)

gar′bage collec′tion *s* voirie *f*

gar′bage collec′tor *s* boueur *m*

gar′bage dispos′al *s* broyeur *m* d'ordures

gar′bage truck′ *s* benne *f* à ordures

garble [′gɑrbəl] *tr* mutiler, tronquer

garden [′gɑrdən] *s* jardin *m*; (*of vegetables*) potager *m*; (*of flowers*) parterre *m* ‖ *intr* jardiner

gar′den cit′y *s* cité-jardin *f*

gardener [′gɑrdnər] *s* jardinier *m*

gardening [′gɑrdnɪŋ] *s* jardinage *m*

gar′den par′ty *s* garden-party *f*

gargle [′gɑrgəl] *s* gargarisme *m* ‖ *intr* se gargariser

gargoyle [′gɑrgɔɪl] *s* gargouille *f*

garish [′gærɪʃ] *adj* cru, rutilant, criard

garland [′gɑrlənd] *s* guirlande *f* ‖ *tr* guirlander

garlic [′gɑrlɪk] *s* ail *m*

garment [′gɑrmənt] *s* vêtement *m*

gar′ment bag′ *s* housse *f* à vêtements

garner [′gɑrnər] *tr* (*to gather, collect*) amasser; (*cereals*) engranger

garnet [′gɑrnɪt] *adj* & *s* grenat *m*

garnish [′gɑrnɪʃ] *s* garniture *f* ‖ *tr* garnir; (law) effectuer une saisie-arrêt sur

garret [′gærɪt] *s* grenier *m*; (*dormer room*) mansarde *f*

garrison [′gærɪsən] *s* garnison *f* ‖ *tr* (*troops*) mettre en garnison; (*a city*) mettre des troupes en garnison dans

garrote [gə′rɑt], [gə′rot] *s* (*method of execution*) garrotte *f*; (*iron collar used for such an execution*) garrot *m* ‖ *tr* garrotter

garrulous [′gær(j)ələs] *adj* bavard

garter [′gɑrtər] *s* jarretelle *f*, jarretière *f*; (*for men's socks*) support-chaussette *m*, fixe-chaussette *m*

garth [gɑrθ] *s* cour *f* intérieure d'un cloître

gas [gæs] *s* gaz *m*; (coll) essence *f*; (*empty talk*) (coll) bavardage *m*; **out of gas** en panne sèche; **to step on the gas** (coll) appuyer sur le champignon ‖ *v* (*pret & pp* **gassed**; *ger* **gassing**) *tr* gazer, asphyxier ‖ *intr* dégager des gaz; (mil) gazer; (*to talk nonsense*) (coll) bavarder

gas′bag′ *s* enveloppe *f* à gaz; (coll) blagueur *m*, baratineur *m*

gas′ burn′er *s* bec *m* de gaz

gas′ cham′ber *s* chambre *f* à gaz

Gascony [′gæskəni] *s* Gascogne *f*; la Gascogne

gas′ en′gine *s* moteur *m* à gaz

gaseous [′gæsɪ·əs] *adj* gazeux

gas′ gen′erator *s* gazogène *m*

gash [gæʃ] *s* entaille *f*; (*on face*) balafre *f* ‖ *tr* entailler; balafrer

gas′ heat′ *s* chauffage *m* au gaz

gas′ heat′er *s* (*for hot water*) chauffe-eau *m* à gaz; (*for house heat*) calorifère *m* à gaz

gas′hold′er *s* gazomètre *m*

gasi·fy [′gæsɪ,faɪ] *v* (*pret & pp* **-fied**) *tr* gazéifier ‖ *intr* se gazéifier

gas′ jet′ *s* bec *m* de gaz

gasket [′gæskɪt] *s* joint *m*

gas′light′ *s* éclairage *m* au gaz

gas′ main′ *s* conduite *f* de gaz

gas′ mask′ *s* masque *m* à gaz

gas′ me′ter *s* compteur *m* à gaz

gasoline [′gæsə,lin] *s* essence *f*

gas′oline can′ *s* bidon *m* d'essence

gas′oline gauge′ *s* voyant *m* d'essence

gas′oline pump′ *s* pompe *f* à essence

gasp [gæsp] *s* halètement *m*; (*of surprise; of death*) hoquet *m* ‖ *tr*—**to gasp out** (*a word*) dire dans un souffle ‖ *intr* haleter

gas′ pipe′ *s* conduite *f* de gaz

gas′ produc′er *s* gazogène *m*

gas′ range′ *s* fourneau *m* à gaz, cuisinière *f* à gaz

gassed *adj* (*in warfare*) gasé

gas′ sta′tion *s* poste *m* d'essence

gas′ stove′ *s* cuisinière *f* à gaz, réchaud *m* à gaz

gas′ tank′ *s* gazomètre *m*; (aut) réservoir *m* d'essence

gastric [′gæstrɪk] *adj* gastrique

gastronomy [gæs′trɑnəmi] *s* gastronomie *f*

gas′works′ *spl* usine *f* à gaz

gat [gæt] *s* (gun) (slang) flingue *f*

gate [get] *s* porte *f*; (*in fence or wall*) grille *f*; (*main gate*) portail *f*; (*of sluice*) vanne *f*; (*number paying admission; amount paid*) entrée *f*; (*waiting area*) (aer) salle *f* d'embarquement; (rr) barrière *f*; **to crash the gate** resquiller

gate-crasher [′get,kræʃər] *s* (coll) resquilleur *m*

gate′keep′er *s* portier *m*; (rr) garde-barrière *mf*

gate′-leg ta′ble *s* table *f* à abattants

gate′post′ *s* montant *m*

gate′way′ *s* passage *m*, entrée *f*; (*main entrance*) portail *m*

gather [′gæðər] *tr* amasser, rassembler; (*the harvest*) rentrer; (*fruits, flowers, etc.*) cueillir, ramasser; (*one's thoughts*) recueillir; (bb) rassembler; (sewing) froncer; (*to deduce*) (fig) conclure; **to gather dust** s'encrasser; **to gather oneself together** se ramasser ‖ *intr* se réunir, s'assembler; (*said of clouds*) s'amonceler

gathering [′gæðərɪŋ] *s* réunion *m*, rassemblement *m*; (*of harvest*) récolte *f*; (*of fruits, flowers, etc.*) cueillette *f*; (bb) assemblage *m*, cahier *m* (d'imprimerie); (sewing) froncis *m*

gaud·y [′gɔdi] *adj* (*comp* -ier; *super* -iest) criard, voyant

gauge [gedʒ] *s* jauge *f*, calibre *m*; (*of liquid in a container*) niveau *m*; (*of gasoline, oil, etc.*) indicateur *m*; (*of carpenter*) trusquin *m*; (rr) écartement *m* ‖ *tr* jauger, calibrer; (*a person; s.o.'s capacities; a distance*) juger de, jauger

gauge′ glass′ *s* indicateur *m* de niveau

Gaul [gɔl] *s* Gaule *f*; la Gaule

Gaulish [′gɔlɪʃ] *adj* & *s* gaulois *m*

gaunt [gɔnt] *adj* décharné, étique, efflanqué

gauntlet [′gɔntlɪt] *s* gantelet *m*; **to run the gauntlet** passer par les baguettes; **to take up the gauntlet** relever le gant; **to throw down the gauntlet** jeter le gant

gauze [gɔz] *s* gaze *f*

gavel [′gævəl] *s* marteau *m*

gawk [gɔk] *s* (coll) godiche *mf* ‖ *intr* (coll) bayer aux corneilles; **to gawk at** (coll) regarder bouche bée

gawk·y [′gɔki] *adj* (*comp* -ier; *super* -iest) godiche

gay [ge] *adj* de la pédale, homosexuel; (obs) gai

gay′ blade′ *s* (coll) joyeux drille *m*

gaze [gez] *s* regard *m* fixe ‖ *intr* regarder fixement

gazelle [gə′zɛl] *s* gazelle *f*

gazette [gə′zɛt] *s* gazette *f*; journal *m* officiel

gazetteer [,gæzə′tɪr] *s* dictionnaire *m* géographique

gear [gɪr] *s* (*paraphernalia*) attirail *m*, appareil *m*; (*of transmission, steering, etc.*) mécanisme *m*; (*adjustment of automobile transmission*) marche *f*, vitesse *f*; (*two or more toothed wheels meshed together*) engrenage *m*; **out of gear** débrayé; **to throw into gear** embrayer; **to throw out of gear** débrayer; (fig) disloquer ‖ *tr* & *intr* engrener

gear′box′ *s* (aut) boîte *f* de vitesses

gear′shift′ *s* changement *m* de vitesse

gear′shift lev′er *s* levier *m* de changement de vitesse

gear′wheel′ roue *f* d'engrenage

gee [dʒi] *interj* sapristi!; (*to the right*) hue!; **gee up!** hue!

Gei′ger count′er [′gaɪgər] *s* compteur *m* de Geiger

gel [dʒɛl] *s* (chem) gel *m*

gelatine [′dʒɛlətɪn] *s* gélatine *f*

geld [gɛld] *v* (*pret* & *pp* **gelded** or **gelt** [gɛlt]) *tr* châtrer

gelding [′gɛldɪŋ] *s* hongre *m*

gem [dʒɛm] *s* gemme *f*; (fig) bijou *m*

Gemini [′dʒɛmə,naɪ] *s* (astr, astrol) les Gémeaux *mpl*

gender [′dʒɛndər] *s* (gram) genre *m*; (coll) sexe *m*

gene [dʒin] *s* (biol) gène *m*

genealo·gy [,dʒɛnɪ′ælədʒi] *s* (*pl* -gies) généalogie *f*

general [′dʒɛnərəl] *adj* & *s* général *m*; **in general** en général

gen′eral deliv′ery *s* poste *f* restante

generalissi·mo [,dʒɛnərə′lɪsɪmo] *s* (*pl* -mos) généralissime *m*

generali·ty [,dʒɛnə′ræliti] *s* (*pl* -ties) généralité *f*

generalize [′dʒɛnərə,laɪz] *tr* & *intr* généraliser

generally [′dʒɛnərəli] *adj* généralement

gen′eral practi′tioner *s* (med) généraliste *m*

gen′eral·ship′ *s* tactique *f*; (*office*) généralat *m*

gen′eral staff′ *s* état-major *m*

generate [′dʒɛnə,ret] *tr* générer; (*to beget*) engendrer; (geom) engendrer

gen′erating sta′tion *s* usine *f* génératrice, centrale *f*

generation [,dʒɛnə′reʃən] *s* génération *f*

genera′tion gap′ *s* fossé *m* des générations

generator [′dʒɛnə,retər] *s* (chem) gazogène *m*; (elec) génératrice *f*

generic [dʒɪ′nɛrɪk] *adj* générique

generosi·ty [,dʒɛnə′rɑsiti] *s* (*pl* -ties) générosité *f*

generous [′dʒɛnərəs] *adj* (*action, quantity*) généreux; (*supply; harvest*) abondant; (*size*) ample

gene·sis [′dʒɛnɪsɪs] *s* (*pl* -ses [,siz]) genèse *f*; **Genesis** (Bib) La Genèse

genetic [dʒɪˈnɛtɪk] *adj* génétique ‖ **genetics** *s* génétique *f*

genet′ic en′gineer′ing *s* sélection *f* eugénique

Geneva [dʒɪˈnivə] *s* Genève *f*

genial [ˈdʒini·əl] *adj* affable

genie [ˈdʒini] *s* génie *m*

genital [ˈdʒɛnɪtəl] *adj* génital ‖ **genitals** *spl* organes *mpl* génitaux

genitive [ˈdʒɛnɪtɪv] *s* génitif *m*

genius [ˈdʒinjəs] *s* (*pl* **geniuses**) génie *m* ‖ *s* (*pl* **genii** [ˈdʒini,aɪ]) génie *m*

Genoa [ˈdʒɛno·ə] *s* Gênes *f*

genocide [ˈdʒɛnə,saɪd] *s* génocide *m*

genteel [dʒɛnˈtil] *adj* distingué, de bon ton, élégant

gentian [ˈdʒɛnʃən] *s* gentiane *f*

gentile [ˈdʒɛntaɪl] *s* non-juif *m*, chrétien *m*

gentili·ty [dʒɛnˈtɪlɪti] *s* (*pl* **-ties**) (*birth*) naissance *f* distinguée; (*breeding*) politesse *f*

gentle [ˈdʒɛntəl] *adj* doux; (*in birth*) noble, bien né; (*e.g., tap on the shoulder*) léger

gen′tle·folk′ *s* gens *mpl* de bonne naissance

gen′tle·man *s* (*pl* **-men**) monsieur *m*; (*polite person*) homme *m* bien élevé; (*man of independent means*) rentier *m*; (hist) gentilhomme *m*

gentlemanly [ˈdʒɛntəlmənli] *adj* bien élevé, de bon ton

gen′tleman′s agree′ment *s* engagement *m* sur parole, contrat *m* verbal

gen′tle sex′ *s* sexe *m* faible

gentry [ˈdʒɛntri] *s* gens *mpl* de bonne naissance; (Brit) petite noblesse *f*

genuine [ˈdʒɛnju·ɪn] *adj* véritable, authentique; (*person*) sincère, franc

genus [ˈdʒinəs] *s* (*pl* **genera** [ˈdʒɛnərə] or **genuses**) genre *m*

geogra·phy [dʒɪˈɑgrəfi] *s* (*pl* **-phies**) géographie *f*

geologic(al) [,dʒi·əˈlɑdʒɪk(əl)] *adj* géologique

geolo·gy [dʒɪˈɑlədʒi] *s* (*pl* **-gies**) géologie *f*

geometric(al) [,dʒi·əˈmɛtrɪk(əl)] *adj* géométrique

geome·try [dʒɪˈɑmɪtri] *s* (*pl* **-tries**) géométrie *f*

geophysics [,dʒi·əˈfɪzɪks] *s* géophysique *f*

geopolitics [,dʒi·əˈpɑlɪtɪks] *s* géopolitique *f*

George [dʒɔrdʒ] *s* Georges *m*

geranium [dʒɪˈreni·əm] *s* géranium *m*

geriatrics [,dʒɛriˈætrɪks] *s* gériatrie *f*

germ [dʒʌrm] *s* germe *m*

German [ˈdʒʌrmən] *adj* allemand ‖ *s* (*language*) allemand *m*; (*person*) Allemand *m*

germane [dʒɛrˈmen] *adj* à propos, pertinent; **germane to** se rapportant à

Ger′man mea′sles *s* rubéole *f*

Ger′man sil′ver *s* maillechort *m*, argentan *m*

Germa·ny [ˈdʒʌrməni] *s* (*pl* **-nies**) Allemagne *f*; l'Allemagne

germ′-free′ *adj* axénique

germicidal [,dʒʌrmɪˈsaɪdəl] *adj* germicide

germicide [ˈdʒʌrmɪ,saɪd] *s* germicide *m*

germinate [ˈdʒʌrmɪ,net] *intr* germer

germ′ war′fare *s* guerre *f* bactériologique

gerontology [,dʒɛrɑnˈtɑlədʒi] *s* gérontologie *f*

gerrymander [ˈgɛrɪ,mændər] *s* découpage *m* des circonscriptions électorales

gerund [ˈdʒɛrənd] *s* gérondif *m*

gestation [dʒɛsˈteʃən] *s* gestation *f*

gesticulate [dʒɛsˈtɪkjə,let] *intr* gesticuler

gesture [ˈdʒɛstʃər] *s* geste *m* ‖ *intr* faire des gestes; **to gesture to** faire signe à

get [gɛt] *v* (*pret* **got** [gɑt]; *pp* **got** or **gotten** [ˈgɑtən]; *ger* **getting**) *tr* obtenir, procurer; (*to receive*) avoir, recevoir; (*to catch*) attraper; (*to seek*) chercher, aller chercher; (*to reach*) atteindre; (*to find*) trouver, rencontrer; (*to obtain and bring*) prendre; (*e.g., dinner*) faire; (rad) avoir, prendre, accrocher; (*to understand*) (coll) comprendre; **to get across** faire accepter; faire comprendre; **to get a kick out of** (coll) prendre plaisir à; **to get back** ravoir, se faire rendre; **to get down** descendre; (*to swallow*) avaler; **to get in** rentrer; **to get out the trump** purger les atouts; **to get s.o. to** + *inf* persuader à qn de + *inf*; **to get s.th. done** faire faire q.ch. ‖ *intr* (*to become*) devenir, se faire; (*to arrive*) arriver, parvenir; **get up!** (*said to an animal*) hue!; **to get about** (*said of news*) se répandre; (*said of convalescent*) être de nouveau sur pied; (*to move about*) circuler; **to get accustomed to** se faire à; **to get across** traverser; **to get along** circuler; (*to succeed*) se tirer d'affaire; **to get along with** faire bon ménage avec; **to get along without** se passer de; **to get angry** se fâcher; **to get away** s'évader; **to get away with** s'en aller avec; (coll) s'en tirer avec; **to get back** reculer; (*to return*) rentrer; **to get back at** (coll) rendre la pareille à, se venger sur; **to get by** passer; (*to manage, to shift*) (coll) s'en tirer sans peine; **to get dark** faire nuit; **to get down** descendre; **to get going** se mettre en marche; **to get in** or **into** entrer dans; **to get off** (*to go free*) s'en tirer; **to get off (of)** (*a bus, a horse, etc.*) descendre de; (*a chair, the floor*) se lever de; **to get off with** en être quitte pour; **to get on** monter sur; (*a car*) monter dans; continuer; (*to succeed*) faire des progrès; **to get out** sortir; **to get rid of** se défaire de; **to get to** arriver à; (*to have an opportunity to*) avoir l'occasion de; **to get up** se lever; **to not get over it** (coll) ne pas en revenir

get′away′ *s* démarrage *m*; (*flight*) fuite *f*

get′-togeth′er *s* réunion *f*

get′up′ *s* (*style*) (coll) présentation *f*; (*outfit*) (coll) affublement *m*

geyser [ˈgaɪzər] *s* geyser *m*

ghast·ly [ˈgæstli] *adj* (*comp* **-lier**; *super* **-liest**) livide, blême; horrible, affreux

Ghent [gɛnt] *s* Gand *m*

gherkin [ˈgʌrkɪn] *s* cornichon *m*

ghet·to [ˈgɛto] *s* (*pl* **-tos**) ghetto *m*

ghost [gost] *s* revenant *m*, spectre *m*; (*shade, semblance*) ombre *f*; **not the ghost of a**

chance pas la moindre chance; **to give up the ghost** rendre l'âme, rendre l'esprit

ghost' im'age *s* filage *m*

ghost·ly ['gostli] *adj* (*comp* **-lier**; *super* **-liest**) spectral, fantomatique

ghost' sto'ry *s* histoire *f* de revenants

ghost' town' *s* ville *f* morte

ghost' writ'er *s* rédacteur *m* anonyme

ghoul [gul] *s* goule *f*; (*body snatcher*) déterreur *m* de cadavres

ghoulish ['gulɪʃ] *adj* vampirique

GI ['dʒi'aɪ] (letterword) (**General Issue**) *adj* fourni par l'armée ‖ *s* (*pl* **GI's**) soldat *m* américain, simple soldat

giant ['dʒaɪ·ənt] *adj* & *s* géant *m*

giantess ['dʒaɪ·əntɪs] *s* géante *f*

gibberish ['dʒɪbərɪʃ] *s* baragouin *m*

gibbet ['dʒɪbɪt] *s* gibet *m*, potence *f*

gibe [dʒaɪb] *s* raillerie *f*, moquerie *f* ‖ *tr* & *intr* railler; **to gibe at** se moquer de, railler

giblets ['dʒɪblɪts] *spl* abattis *m*, abats *mpl*

gid·dy ['gɪdi] *adj* (*comp* **-dier**; *super* **-diest**) étourdi; (*height*) vertigineux; (*foolish*) léger, frivole

Gideon ['gɪdɪ·ən] *s* (Bib) Gédéon *m*

gift [gɪft] *s* cadeau *m*; (*natural ability*) don *m*, talent *m* ‖ *tr* douer

gifted *adj* doué

gift' horse' *s*—**never look a gift horse in the mouth** à cheval donné on ne regarde pas à la bride

gift' of gab' *s* (coll) bagou *m*, faconde *f*

gift' shop' *s* boutique *f* de souvenirs, magasin *m* de nouveautés

gift'-wrap *v* (*pret* & *pp* **-wrapped**; *ger* **-wrapping**) *tr* faire un paquet cadeau de

gigantic [dʒaɪ'gæntɪk] *adj* gigantesque

giggle ['gɪgəl] *s* petit rire *m* ‖ *intr* pousser des petits rires, glousser

gigo·lo ['dʒɪgə,lo] *s* (*pl* **-los**) gigolo *m*

GI Joe [,dʒi,aɪ'dʒo] *s* le troufion

gild [gɪld] *v* (*pret* & *pp* **gilded** or **gilt** [gɪlt]) *tr* dorer

gilding ['gɪldɪŋ] *s* dorure *f*

gill [gɪl] *s* (*of cock*) fanon *m*; **gills** (*of fish*) ouïes *fpl*, branchies *fpl*

gilt [gɪlt] *adj* & *s* doré *m*

gilt'-edged' *adj* (*e.g.*, *book*) doré sur tranche; (*securities*) de premier ordre, de tout repos

gimcrack ['dʒɪm,kræk] *adj* de pacotille, de camelote ‖ *s* babiole *f*

gimlet ['gɪmlɪt] *s* vrille *f*, perçoir *m*

gimmick ['gɪmɪk] *s* (coll) truc *m*, machin *m*; (*trick*) tour *m*

gin [dʒɪn] *s* (*alcoholic liquor*) gin *m*, genièvre *m*; (*for cotton, corn, etc.*) égreneuse *f*; (*snare*) trébuchet *m* ‖ *v* (*pret* & *pp* **ginned**; *ger* **ginning**) *tr* égrener

ginger ['dʒɪndʒər] *s* gingembre *m*; (fig) entrain *m*, allant *m*

gin'ger ale' *s* boisson *f* gazeuse au gingembre

gin'ger·bread' *s* pain *m* d'épice; ornement *m* de mauvais goût

gingerly ['dʒɪndʒərli] *adj* précautionneux ‖ *adv* tout doux, avec précaution

gin'ger·snap' *s* gâteau *m* sec au gingembre

gingham ['gɪŋəm] *s* guingan *m*

giraffe [dʒɪ'ræf] *s* girafe *f*

gird [gʌrd] *v* (*pret* & *pp* **girt** [gʌrt] or **girded**) *tr* ceindre; **to gird on** se ceindre de; **to gird oneself for** se préparer à

girder ['gʌrdər] *s* poutre *f*

girdle ['gʌrdəl] *s* ceinture *f* ‖ *tr* ceindre, entourer

girl [gʌrl] *s* jeune fille *f*; (*little girl*) petite fille; (*servant*) bonne *f*

girl' friend' *s* (*sweetheart*) petite amie *f*, bonne amie *f*; (*female friend*) amie *f*, camarade *f*

girl'hood *s* enfance *f*, jeunesse *f* d'une femme

girlish ['gʌrlɪʃ] *adj* de jeune fille, de petite fille

girl' scout' *s* éclaireuse *f*, guide *f*

girls'' school' *s* école *f* de filles

girth [gʌrθ] *s* (*band*) sangle *f*; (*measure around*) circonférence *f*; (*of person*) tour *m* de taille

gist [dʒɪst] *s* fond *m*, essence *f*

give [gɪv] *s* élasticité *f* ‖ *v* (*pret* **gave** [gev]; *pp* **given** ['gɪvən]) *tr* donner; (*a speech, a lecture, a class; a smile*) faire; **to give away** donner, distribuer; révéler; **to give back** rendre, remettre; **to give forth** or **off** émettre; **to give oneself up** se rendre; **to give up** renoncer à, abandonner ‖ *intr* donner; **to give in** se rendre; **to give out** manquer; (*to become exhausted*) s'épuiser; **to give way** faire place, reculer

give'-and-take' *s* compromis *m*; échange *m* de propos plaisants

give'away' *s* (coll) révélation *f* involontaire; (coll) trahison *f*; **to play giveaway** jouer à qui perd gagne

given ['gɪvən] *adj* donné; **given that** vu que, étant donné que

giv'en name' *s* prénom *m*

giver ['gɪvər] *s* donneur *m*, donateur *m*

gizzard ['gɪzərd] *s* gésier *m*

glacial ['gleʃəl] *adj* glacial; (chem) en cristaux; (geol) glaciaire

glacier ['gleʃər] *s* glacier *m*

glad [glæd] *adj* (*comp* **gladder**; *super* **gladdest**) content, heureux; **to be glad to** être content or heureux de

gladden ['glædən] *tr* réjouir

glade [gled] *s* clairière *f*, éclaircie *f*, percée *f*

glad' hand' *s* (coll) accueil *m* chaleureux

gladiator ['glædɪ,etər] *s* gladiateur *m*

gladiola [,glædɪ'olə] *s* glaïeul *m*

gladly ['glædli] *adv* volontiers, avec plaisir

gladness ['glædnɪs] *s* joie *f*, plaisir *m*

glad' rags' *spl* (slang) frusques *fpl* des grands jours

glamorous ['glæmərəs] *adj* ravissant, éclatant

glamour ['glæmər] *s* charme *m*, éclat *m*

glam'our girl' *s* ensorceleuse *f*

glance [glæns] *s* coup *m* d'œil; **at a glance** d'un seul coup d'œil; **at first glance** à première vue ‖ *intr* jeter un regard; **to glance at** jeter un coup d'œil sur; **to glance off** ricocher, dévier; **to glance through a book** feuilleter un livre; **to glance up** lever les yeux

gland [glænd] *s* glande *f*

glanders ['glændərz] *spl* (vet) morve *f*

glare [glɛr] *s* (*light*) lumière *f* éblouissante; (*look*) regard *m* irrité ‖ *intr* éblouir, briller; **to glare at** lancer un regard méchant à, foudroyer du regard

glare' ice' *s* verglas *m*

glaring ['glɛrɪŋ] *adj* (*shining*) éblouissant; (*mistake, fact*) évident, qui saute aux yeux; (*blunder, abuse*) grossier, scandaleux

glasnost ['glas,nast] *s* transparence *f*, glasnost *m*

glass [glæs] *s* verre *m*; (*mirror*) glace *f*; **glasses** lunettes *fpl*

glass' blow'er ['blo·ər] *s* verrier-souffleur *m*

glass' case' *s* vitrine *f*

glass' cut'ter *s* (*tool*) diamant *m*; (*workman*) vitrier *m*

glass' door' *s* porte *f* vitrée

glassful ['glæsful] *s* verre *m*

glass' house' *s* serre *f*; (fig) maison *f* de verre

glass'ware' *s* verrerie *f*

glass' wool' *s* laine *f* de verre

glass'works' *s* verrerie *f*, glacerie *f*

glass·y ['glæsi] *adj* (*comp* **-ier**; *super* **-iest**) vitreux; (*smooth*) lisse

glaze [glez] *s* (*ceramics*) vernis *m*; (culin) glace *f*; (tex) lustre *m* ‖ *tr* (*to cover with a glossy coating*) glacer; (*to fit with glass*) vitrer

glazier ['gleʒər] *s* vitrier *m*

gleam [glim] *s* rayon *m*; (*of hope*) lueur *f* ‖ *intr* rayonner, reluire

glean [glin] *tr* glaner

glee [gli] *s* allégresse *f*, joie *f*

glee' club' *s* orphéon *m*, société *f* chorale

glen [glɛn] *s* vallon *m*, ravin *m*

glib [glɪb] *adj* (*comp* **glibber**; *super* **glibbest**) facile; (*tongue*) délié

glide [glaɪd] *s* glissement *m*; (aer) vol *m* plané; (mus) port *m* de voix; (phonet) son *m* transitoire ‖ *intr* glisser, se glisser; (aer) planer

glider ['glaɪdər] *s* (*porch seat*) siège *m* à glissière; (aer) planeur *m*

gliding ['glaɪdɪŋ] *s* vol *m* à voile

glimmer ['glɪmər] *s* faible lueur *f* ‖ *intr* jeter une faible lueur

glimmering ['glɪmərɪŋ] *adj* faible, vacillant ‖ *s* faible lueur *f*, miroitement *m*; soupçon *m*, indice *m*

glimpse [glɪmps] *s* aperçu *m*; **to catch a glimpse of** entrevoir, aviser ‖ *tr* entrevoir

glint [glɪnt] *s* reflet *m*, éclair *m* ‖ *intr* jeter un reflet, étinceler

glisten ['glɪsən] *s* scintillement *m* ‖ *intr* scintiller

glitter ['glɪtər] *s* éclat *m*, étincellement *m* ‖ *intr* étinceler

gloaming ['glomɪŋ] *s* crépuscule *m*, jour *m* crépusculaire

gloat [glot] *intr* éprouver un malin plaisir; **to gloat over** faire des gorges chaudes de; (*e.g., one's victim*) couver du regard

global ['globəl] *adj* sphérique; mondial

globe [glob] *s* globe *m*

globe'-trot'ter *s* globe-trotter *m*

globule ['globjul] *s* globule *m*

gloom [glum] *s* obscurité *f*, ténèbres *fpl*; tristesse *f*

gloom·y ['glumi] *adj* (*comp* **-ier**; *super* **-iest**) sombre, lugubre; (*ideas*) noir

glori·fy ['glorɪ,faɪ] *v* (*pret & pp* **-fied**) *tr* glorifier

glorious ['glorɪ·əs] *adj* glorieux

glo·ry ['glori] *s* (*pl* **-ries**) gloire *f*; **to be in one's glory** être aux anges; **to go to glory** (slang) aller à la ruine ‖ *v* (*pret & pp* **-ried**) *intr*—**to glory in** se glorifier de

gloss [glɔs] *s* lustre *m*; (*on cloth*) cati *m*; (*on floor*) brillant *m*; (*note, commentary*) glose *f*; **to take off the gloss from** décatir ‖ *tr* lustrer; **to gloss over** maquiller, farder

glossa·ry ['glɑsəri] *s* (*pl* **-ries**) glossaire *m*

gloss·y ['glɑsi] *adj* (*comp* **-ier**; *super* **-iest**) lustré, brillant

glot'tal stop' ['glɑtəl] *s* coup *m* de glotte

glottis ['glɑtɪs] *s* glotte *f*

glove [glʌv] *s* gant *m* ‖ *tr* ganter

glove' compart'ment *s* boîte *f* à gants

glove' wash'cloth *s* gant *m* à laver

glow [glo] *s* rougeoiement *m* ‖ *intr* rougeoyer

glower ['glau·ər] *s* grise mine *f* ‖ *intr* avoir l'air renfrogné

glowing ['glo·ɪŋ] *adj* rougeoyant, incandescent; (*healthy*) rayonnant; (*cheeks*) vermeil; (*reports*) enthousiaste, élogieux

glow'worm' *s* ver *m* luisant

glucose ['glukos] *s* glucose *m*

glue [glu] *s* colle *f* ‖ *tr* coller

glue'pot' *s* pot *m* à colle

gluey ['glu·i] *adj* (*comp* **gluier**; *super* **gluiest**) gluant

glum [glʌm] *adj* (*comp* **glummer**; *super* **glummest**) maussade, renfrogné

glut [glʌt] *s* (*excess*) surabondance *f*, excès *m*; (*on the market*) engorgement *m*, surplus *m* ‖ *v* (*pret & pp* **glutted**; *ger* **glutting**) *tr* (*with food*) rassasier; (*the market*) inonder, engorger

glutton ['glʌtən] *s* glouton *m*

gluttonous ['glʌtənəs] *adj* glouton

glutton·y ['glʌtəni] *s* (*pl* **-ies**) gloutonnerie *f*

glycerine ['glɪsərɪn] *s* glycérine *f*

G.M.T. *abbr* (**Greenwich mean time** temps moyen de Greenwich) T.U., temps *m* universel

gnarl [nɑrl] *s* (bot) nœud *m* ‖ *tr* tordre ‖ *intr* grogner

gnarled *adj* noueux

gnash [næʃ] *tr*—**to gnash the teeth** grincer des dents or les dents

gnat [næt] *s* moucheron *m*, moustique *m*

gnaw [nɔ] *tr* ronger

gnome [nom] *s* gnome *m*

G.N.P. [ˈdʒiˈɛnˈpi] *s* (letterword) (**gross national product**) R.N.P. (revenu national brut), P.N.B. (produit national brut)

go [go] *s* (*pl* **goes**) aller *m*; **a lot of go** (slang) beaucoup d'allant; **it's no go** (coll) ça ne marche pas, pas mèche; **to have a go at** (coll) essayer; **to make a go of** (coll) réussir à ‖ *v* (*pret* **went** [wɛnt]; *pp* **gone** [gɔn], [gɑn]) *tr*—**to go it alone** le faire tout seul, faire cavalier seul ‖ *intr* aller; (*to work, operate*) marcher; y aller, e.g., **did you go?** y êtes-vous allé?; devenir, e.g., **to go crazy** devenir fou; faire, e.g., **to go quack-quack** faire couin-couin; **going, going, gone!** une fois, deux fois, adjugé!; **go to it!** allez-y!; **to be going to** or **to go to** + *inf* aller + *inf*, e.g., **I am going to the store to buy some shoes** je vais au magasin acheter des souliers; (to express futurity from the point of view of the present or past) aller + *inf*, e.g., **he is going to get married** il va se marier; e.g., **he was going to get married** il allait se marier; **to go** (*to take out*) (coll) à emporter; **to go against** contrarier; **to go ahead of** dépasser; **to go away** s'en aller; **to go back** retourner; (*to return home*) rentrer; (*to back up*) reculer; (*to date back*) remonter; **to go by** passer; (*a rule, model, etc.*) agir selon; **to go down** descendre; (*said of sun*) se coucher; (*said of ship*) sombrer; (cards) chuter; **to go fishing** aller à la pêche; **to go for** or **to go get** aller chercher; **to go in** entrer; entrer dans; (*to fit into*) tenir dans; **to go in for** se consacrer à; **to go in with** s'associer à or avec, se joindre à; **to go off** (*said of bomb, gun, etc.*) partir; **to go on** + *ger* continuer à + *inf*; **to go out** sortir; (*said of light, fire, etc.*) s'éteindre; **to go over** (*to examine*) parcourir, repasser; **to go through** (*e.g., a door*) passer par; (*e.g., a city*) traverser; (*a fortune*) dissiper, dilapider; **to go together** (*said, e.g., of colors*) s'assortir; (*said of lovers*) être très liés; **to go under** succomber; (*said, e.g., of submarine*) plonger; (*a false name*) être connu sous; **to go up** monter; **to go with** accompagner; (*a color, dress, etc.*) s'assortir avec; **to go without** se passer de; **to let go of** lâcher

goad [god] *s* aiguillon *m* ‖ *tr* aiguillonner

go′-ahead′ *adj* (coll) entreprenant ‖ *s* (coll) signal *m* d'aller en avant

goal [gol] *s* but *m*

goal′keep′er *s* goal *m*, gardien *m* de but

goal′ line′ *s* ligne *f* de but

goal′ post′ *s* montant *m*, poteau *m* de but

goat [got] *s* chèvre *f*; (*male goat*) bouc *m*; (coll) dindon *m*; **to get the goat of** (slang) exaspérer, irriter

goatee [goˈti] *s* barbiche *f*

goat′herd′ *s* chevrier *m*

goat′skin′ *s* peau *f* de chèvre

goat′suck′er *s* (orn) engoulevent *m*

gob [gɑb] *s* (*lump*) (coll) grumeau *m*; (*sailor*) (slang) mataf *m*

gobble [ˈgɑbəl] *s* glouglou *m* ‖ *tr* engloutir, bâfrer ‖ *intr* bâfrer; (*said of turkey*) glouglouter

gobbledegook [ˈgɑbəldɪˌgʊk] *s* (coll) palabre *m* & *f*, charabia *m*

go′-between′ *s* intermédiaire *mf*; (*in shady love affairs*) entremetteur *m*

goblet [ˈgɑblɪt] *s* verre *m* à pied

goblin [ˈgɑblɪn] *s* lutin *m*

go′-by′ *s* (coll) affront *m*; **to give s.o. the go-by** (coll) brûler la politesse à qn

go′cart′ *s* chariot *m*; (*baby carriage*) poussette *f*; (*handcart*) charrette *f* à bras

god [gɑd] *s* dieu *m*; **God damn!** (pej) nom *m* de Dieu!, nom de nom!; **God forbid** qu'à Dieu ne plaise; **God grant** plût à Dieu; **my God!** bon Dieu!; **God willing** s'il plaît à Dieu

god′child′ *s* (*pl* **-chil′dren**) filleul *m*

god′damn′it *interj* nom d'une pipe!, nom d'un chien!, nom d'un petit bonhomme!, cré nom de Dieu!

god′daugh′ter *s* filleule *f*

goddess [ˈgɑdɪs] *s* déesse *f*

god′fa′ther *s* parrain *m*

God′-fear′ing *adj* dévot, pieux

God′forsak′en *adj* abandonné de Dieu; (coll) perdu, misérable

god′head′ *s* divinité *f*; **Godhead** Dieu *m*

godless [ˈgɑdlɪs] *adj* athée, impie

god·ly [ˈgɑdli] *adj* (*comp* **-lier**; *super* **-liest**) dévot, pieux

god′moth′er *s* marraine *f*

God's′ a′cre *s* le champ de repos

god′send′ *s* aubaine *f*

god′son′ *s* filleul *m*

God′speed′ *s* bonne chance *f*, bon voyage *m*

go-getter [ˈgoˌgɛtər] *s* (coll) homme *m* d'expédition, lanceur *m* d'affaires

goggle [ˈgɑgəl] *intr* (*to open the eyes wide*) écarquiller les yeux, rouler de gros yeux ronds

gog′gle-eyed′ *adj* aux yeux saillants

goggles [ˈgɑgəlz] *spl* lunettes *fpl* protectrices

going [ˈgoˌɪŋ] *adj* en marche; **going on two o'clock** presque deux heures ‖ *s* départ *m*; **good going!** bien joué!

go′ing concern′ *s* maison *f* en pleine activité

go′ings on′ *spl* (coll) chahut *m*, tapage *m*; (coll) événements *mpl*

goiter [ˈgɔɪtər] *s* goitre *m*

gold [gold] *adj* d'or, en or ‖ *s* or *m*

gold′beat′er *s* batteur *m* d'or

gold′beater's skin′ *s* baudruche *f*

gold′crest′ *s* roitelet *m* à tête dorée

golden [ˈgoldən] *adj* d'or; (*gilt*) doré; (*hair*) d'or, d'un blond doré; (*opportunity*) favorable, magnifique

gold′en age′ *s* âge *m* d'or

gold′en calf′ *s* veau *m* d'or

Gold′en Fleece′ *s* Toison *f* d'or

gold′en mean′ *s* juste-milieu *m*

gold′en plov′er s pluvier m doré
gold′en·rod′ s solidage f, gerbe f d'or
gold′en rule′ s règle f de la charité chrétienne
gold′en wed′ding s noces fpl d'or, jubilé m
gold′-filled′ adj (tooth) aurifié
gold′finch′ s chardonneret m
gold′fish′ s poisson m rouge
goldilocks [ˈɡoldɪˌlɑks] s jeune fille f aux cheveux d'or
gold′ leaf′ s feuille f d'or
gold′ mine′ s mine f d'or; **to strike a gold mine** (fig) dénicher le bon filon, faire des affaires d'or
gold′ plate′ s vaisselle f d'or
gold′-plate′ tr plaquer d'or
gold′ rush′ s ruée f vers l'or
gold′smith′ s orfèvre m
gold′ stan′dard s étalon-or m
golf [ɡalf] s golf m ‖ intr jouer au golf
golf′ ball′ s balle f de golf
golf′ cart′ s voiturette f de golf
golf′ club′ s crosse f de golf, club m; (association) club m de golf
golfer [ˈɡalfər] s joueur m de golf, golfeur m
golf′ links′ spl terrain m de golf
gondola [ˈɡandələ] s gondole f
gondolier [ˌɡandəˈlɪr] s gondolier m
gone [ɡan] adj parti, disparu; (used up) épuisé; (ruined) ruiné, fichu; (dead) mort; **far gone** avancé; **gone on** (in love with) (coll) entiché de, épris de
gong [ɡɔŋ] s gong m
gonorrhea [ˌɡanəˈriˑə] s blennorragie f, gonococcie f
goo [ɡu] s (slang) matière f collante
good [ɡud] adj (comp **better**; super **best**) bon §91; (child) sage; (meals) soigné; **good for you!** bien joué!; **to be good at** être fort en, être expert à; **to make good** prospérer; (a loss) compenser; (a promise) tenir; **will you be good enough to** voulez-vous être assez aimable de ‖ s bien m; **for good** pour de bon, définitivement; **goods** biens mpl; (com) marchandises fpl; **to catch with the goods** (slang) prendre la main dans le sac; **to the good** de gagné, e.g., **all** or **so much to the good** autant de gagné ‖ interj bon!, bien!, à la bonne heure!; **very good!** parfait!
good′ afternoon′ s bonjour m
good′-by or **good′-bye′** s adieu m ‖ interj au revoir!; (before a long journey) adieu!
good′ cit′izenship s civisme m
good′ day′ s bonjour m
good′ deed′ s bonne action f
good′ egg′ s (slang) chic type m
good′ eve′ning s bonsoir m
good′ faith′ s la bonne volonté
good′ fel′low s brave garçon m, brave type m
good′ fel′lowship s camaraderie f
good′-for-noth′ing adj inutile m ‖ s bon m à rien
Good′ Fri′day s le Vendredi saint
good′ grac′es spl bonnes grâces fpl

good′-heart′ed adj au cœur généreux
good′-hu′mored adj de bonne humeur
good′-look′ing adj beau, joli
good′ looks′ spl belle mine f
good′ luck′ s bonne chance f
good·ly [ˈɡudli] adj (comp **-lier**; super **-liest**) considérable, important; (quality) bon; (appearance) beau
good′ morn′ing s bonjour m
good′-na′tured adj aimable, accommodant
goodness [ˈɡudnɪs] s bonté f; **for goodness' sake!** pour l'amour de Dieu!; **goodness knows** Dieu seul sait ‖ interj mon Dieu!
good′ night′ s bonne nuit f
good′ sense′ s bon sens m
good′-sized′ adj de grandeur moyenne, assez grand
good′ speed′ s succès m, bonne chance f
good′-tem′pered adj de caractère facile, d'humeur égale
good′ time′ s bon temps m; **to have a good time** prendre du bon temps, bien s'amuser; **to make good time** arriver en peu de temps
good′ turn′ s bienfait m, service m
good′ will′ s bonne volonté f; (com) achalandage m
good′ works′ spl bonnes œuvres fpl
good·y [ˈɡudi] adj (coll) d'une piété affectée ‖ s (pl **-ies**) (coll) petit saint m; **goodies** friandises fpl ‖ interj chouette!; chic!
gooey [ˈɡuˑi] adj (comp **gooier**; super **gooiest**) (slang) gluant; (sentimental) (slang) à l'eau de rose
goof [ɡuf] s (slang) toqué m ‖ intr—**to goof off** (slang) tirer au flanc
goof·y [ˈɡufi] adj (comp **-ier**; super **-iest**) (slang) toqué, maboul
goon [ɡun] s (roughneck) (coll) dur m; (coll) terroriste m professionnel; (slang) niais m
goose [ɡus] s (pl **geese** [ɡis]) oie f; **to kill the goose that lays the golden eggs** tuer la poule aux œufs d'or ‖ s (pl **gooses**) (of tailor) carreau m
goose′ber′ry s (pl **-ries**) groseille f verte
goose′ egg′ s œuf m d'oie; (slang) zéro m
goose′ flesh′ s chair f de poule
goose′neck′ s col m de cygne
goose′ pim′ples spl chair f de poule
goose′ step′ s (mil) pas m de l'oie
goose′-step′ v (pret & pp **-stepped**; ger **-stepping**) intr marcher au pas de l'oie
gopher [ˈɡofər] s citelle m
gore [ɡor] s (blood) sang m caillé; (sewing) soufflet m ‖ tr percer d'un coup de corne; (sewing) tailler en pointe
gorge [ɡɔrdʒ] s gorge f ‖ tr gorger ‖ intr se gorger
gorgeous [ˈɡɔrdʒəs] adj magnifique
gorilla [ɡəˈrɪlə] s gorille m
gorse [ɡɔrs] s (bot) genêt m épineux
gor·y [ˈɡori] adj (comp **-ier**; super **-iest**) ensanglanté, sanglant
gosh [ɡaʃ] interj (coll) sapristi!, mon Dieu!
goshawk [ˈɡasˌhɔk] s autour m

gospel ['gɑspəl] *s* évangile *m*; **Gospel** Evangile

gos'pel truth' *s* parole *f* d'Evangile

gossamer ['gɑsəmər] *adj* ténu ‖ *s* toile *f* d'araignée, fils *mpl* de la Vierge; (*gauze*) gaze *f*

gossip ['gɑsɪp] *s* commérage *m*, cancan *m*; (*person*) commère *f*; **piece of gossip** potin *m*, racontar *m* ‖ *intr* cancaner

gos'sip col'umnist *s* échotier *m*

Gothic ['gɑθɪk] *adj* & *s* gothique *m*

gouge [gaʊdʒ] *s* gouge *f* ‖ *tr* gouger; (*to swindle*) empiler

goulash ['gulɑʃ] *s* goulasch *m* & *f*

gourd [gʊrd] *s* gourde *f*

gourmand ['gʊrmənd] *s* gourmand *m*; (*glutton*) glouton *m*

gourmet ['gʊrme] *s* gourmet *m*

gout [gaʊt] *s* goutte *f*

govern ['gʌvərn] *tr* gouverner; (gram) régir ‖ *intr* gouverner

governess ['gʌvərnɪs] *s* institutrice *f*, gouvernante *f*

government ['gʌvərnmənt] *s* gouvernement *m*

governmental [ˌgʌvərn'mɛntəl] *adj* gouvernemental

governor ['gʌvərnər] *s* gouverneur *m*; (mach) régulateur *m*

gown [gaʊn] *s* robe *f*

grab [græb] *s* prise *f*; (coll) vol *m*, coup *m* ‖ *v* (*pret* & *pp* **grabbed**; *ger* **grabbing**) *tr* empoigner, saisir ‖ *intr*—**to grab at** s'agripper à

grab' bag' *s* sac *m* à surprises

grace [gres] *s* grâce *f*; (*prayer at table before meals*) bénédicité *m*; (*prayer at table after meals*) grâces; (*extension of time*) délai *m* de grâce; **in someone's good graces** en odeur de sainteté auprès de qn, dans les petits papiers de qn ‖ *tr* orner; honorer

graceful ['gresfəl] *adj* gracieux

grace' note' *s* note *f* d'agrément, appogiature *f*

gracious ['greʃəs] *adj* gracieux; (*compassionate*) miséricordieux

grackle ['grækəl] *s* (*myna*) mainate *m*; (*purple grackle*) quiscale *m*

gradation [gre'deʃən] *s* gradation *f*

grade [gred] *s* (*rank*) grade *m*; (*of oil*) grade; qualité *f*; (*school class*) classe *f*, année *f*; (*mark in school*) note *f*; (*slope*) pente *f*; **to make the grade** réussir ‖ *tr* classer; (*a school paper*) noter; (*land*) niveler

grade' cross'ing *s* (rr) passage *m* à niveau

grade' school' *s* école *f* primaire

gradient ['gredɪ·ənt] *adj* montant ‖ *s* pente *f*; (phys) gradient *m*

gradual ['grædʒʊ·əl] *adj* & *s* graduel *m*

gradually ['grædʒʊ·əli] *adv* graduellement, peu à peu, par paliers

graduate ['grædʒʊ·ɪt] *s* diplômé *m* ‖ ['grædʒʊ,et] *tr* conférer un diplôme à, décerner des diplômes à; (*to mark with degrees*) graduer ‖ *intr* recevoir son diplôme

grad'uate school' *s* faculté *f* des hautes études

grad'uate stu'dent *s* étudiant *m* avancé, étudiant de maîtrise, de doctorat

grad'uate work' *s* études *fpl* avancées

grad'uat'ing class' *s* classe *f* sortante

graduation [ˌgrædʒʊ'eʃən] *s* collation *f* des grades; (*e.g., marking on beaker*) graduation *f*

graft [græft] *s* (hort, surg) greffe *f*; (*stealing*) (coll) gratte *f*, grattage *m*, magouille *f* ‖ *tr* & *intr* (hort, surg) greffer; (coll) gratter

grafter ['græftər] *s* (hort) greffeur *m*; (coll) homme *m* véreux, concussionnaire *mf*

gra'ham bread' ['gre·əm] *s* pain *m* entier

gra'ham flour' *s* farine *f* entière

grain [gren] *s* (*small seed; tiny particle of sand, etc.; small unit of weight; small amount*) grain *m*; (*cereal seeds*) grains *mpl*, céréales *fpl*; (*in stone*) fil *m*; (*in wood*) fibres *fpl*; **against the grain** à rebours, à contre-fil, à rebrousse-poil ‖ *tr* grener; (*wood, etc.*) veiner

grain' el'evator *s* dépôt *m* et élévateur *m* à grains

grain'field' *s* champ *m* de blé

graining ['grenɪŋ] *s* grenage *m*; (*of painting*) veinage *m*

gram [græm] *s* gramme *m*

grammar ['græmər] *s* grammaire *f*

grammarian [grə'mɛrɪ·ən] *s* grammairien *m*

gram'mar school' *s* école *f* primaire

grammatical [grə'mætɪkəl] *adj* grammatical

grana·ry ['grænəri] *s* (*pl* **-ries**) grenier *m*

grand [grænd] *adj* magnifique; (*person*) grand; (coll) formidable

grand'aunt' *s* grand-tante *f*

grand'child' *s* (*pl* **-chil'dren**) petit-fils *m*; petite-fille *f*; **grandchildren** petits-enfants *mpl*

grand'daugh'ter *s* petite-fille *f*

grand' duch'ess *s* grande-duchesse *f*

grand' duch'y *s* grand-duché *m*

grand' duke' *s* grand-duc *m*

grandee [græn'di] *s* grand *m* d'Espagne

grand'fa'ther *s* grand-père *m*

grand'father clause' *s* clause *f* des droits aquis

grand'father's clock' *s* pendule *f* à gaine, horloge *f* comtoise, horloge normande

grandiose ['grændɪ,os] *adj* grandiose; pompeux

grand' ju'ry *s* jury *m* d'accusation

grand' lar'ceny *s* grand larcin *m*

grand' lodge' *s* grand orient *m*

grandma ['grænd,mɑ], ['græmə] *s* (coll) grand-maman *f*

grand'moth'er *s* grand-mère *f*

grand'neph'ew *s* petit-neveu *m*

grand'niece' *s* petite-nièce *f*

grand' op'era *s* grand opéra *m*

grandpa ['grænd,pɑ], ['græmpə] *s* (coll) grand-papa *m*; (*gramps*) pépé *m*

grand'par'ent *s* grand-père *m*; grand-mère *f*; **grandparents** grands-parents *mpl*

grand′ pian′o *s* piano *m* à queue
grand′ slam′ *s* grand chelem *m*
grand′son′ *s* petit-fils *m*
grand′stand′ *s* tribune *f*, gradins *mpl*
grand′ to′tal *s* total *m* global
grand′un′cle *s* grand-oncle *m*
grand′ vizier′ *s* grand vizir *m*
grange [grendʒ] *s* ferme *f*; syndicat *m* d'agri-
culteurs
granite [′grænɪt] *s* granite *m*, granit *m*
gran·ny [′græni] *s* (*pl* **-nies**) (coll) grand-
mère *f*, mémé *f*
gran′ny knot′ *s* nœud *m* de vache
grant [grænt] *s* (*of land*) concession *f*; (*subsidy*) subvention *f*; (*scholarship*) bourse *f*
∥ *tr* concéder, accorder; (*a wish*) exaucer;
(*e.g., a charter*) octroyer; (*a degree*) décerner; **to take for granted** escompter,
tenir pour évident; traiter avec indifférence
grantee [græn′ti] *s* donataire *mf*
grantor [græn′tɔr] *s* donateur *m*
granular [′grænjələr] *adj* granulaire
granulate [′grænjə,let] *tr* granuler ∥ *intr* se
granuler
gran′ulated sug′ar *s* sucre *m* cristallisé
granule [′grænjul] *s* granule *m*, granulé *m*
grape [grep] *s* (*fruit*) raisin *m*; (*vine*) vigne
f; (*single grape*) grain *m* de raisin
grape′ ar′bor *s* treille *f*
grape′fruit′ *s* (*fruit*) pamplemousse *m* & *f*;
(*tree*) pamplemoussier *m*
grape′ juice′ *s* jus *m* de raisin
grape′shot′ *s* mitraille *f*
grape′vine′ *s* vigne *f*; (*chain of gossip*)
source *f* de canards; téléphone *m* arabe,
téléphone chinois
graph [græf] *s* graphique *m*; (gram) graphie
f
graphic(al) [′græfɪk(əl)] *adj* graphique; (fig)
vivant, net
graphite [′græfaɪt] *s* graphite *m*
graph′ pa′per *s* papier *m* quadrillé
grapnel [′græpnəl] *s* grappin *m*
grapple [′græpəl] *s* (*tool*) grappin *m*; (*fight*)
corps à corps *m* ∥ *tr* (*with a grappling
iron*) saisir au grappin; (*a person*) empoigner à bras le corps ∥ *intr* (*to fight*)
lutter corps à corps; **to grapple with** en
venir aux prises avec, s'attaquer à
grap′pling i′ron *s* grappin *m*
grasp [græsp] *s* prise *f*; **to have a good
grasp of** avoir une profonde connaissance
de; **within one's grasp** à sa portée ∥ *tr*
saisir ∥ *intr*—**to grasp at** tâcher de saisir;
saisir avidement
grasping [′græspɪŋ] *adj* avide, rapace
grass [græs] *s* herbe *f*; (*pasture*) herbage *m*;
(*lawn*) gazon *m*; **keep off the grass**
(*public sign*) ne marchez pas sur le gazon;
to go to grass (fig) s'étaler par terre
grass′hop′per *s* sauterelle *f*
grass′-roots′ *adj* populaire, du peuple
grass′ seed′ *s* graine *f* fourragère; (*for
lawns*) graine *f* pour gazon
grass′ snake′ *s* (*Tropidonotus natrix*) couleuvre *f* à collier
grass′ wid′ow *s* demi-veuve *f*

grass·y [′græsi] *adj* (*comp* **-ier**; *super* **-iest**)
herbeux
grate [gret] *s* grille *f*, grillage *m* ∥ *tr* (*to put
a grate on*) griller; (*e.g., cheese*) râper; **to
grate the teeth** grincer des dents ∥ *intr*
grincer; **to grate on** écorcher
grateful [′gretfəl] *adj* reconnaissant; **to be
grateful for** être reconnaissant de or pour
grater [′gretər] *s* râpe *f*
grati·fy [′grætɪ,faɪ] *v* (*pret* & *pp* **-fied**) *tr*
faire plaisir à, satisfaire
gratifying [′grætɪ,faɪ·ɪŋ] *adj* agréable, satisfaisant
grating [′gretɪŋ] *adj* grinçant ∥ *s* grillage *m*,
grille *f*
gratis [′grætɪs] *adj* gratuit, gracieux ∥ *adv*
gratis, gratuitement
gratitude [′grætɪ,t(j)ud] *s* gratitude *f*, reconnaissance *f*; **gratitude for** reconnaissance de or pour
gratuitous [grə′t(j)u·ɪtəs] *adj* gratuit
gratui·ty [grə′t(j)u·ɪti] *s* (*pl* **-ties**) gratification *f*, pourboire *m*
grave [grev] *adj* grave ∥ *s* fosse *f*, tombe *f*
gravedigger [′grev,dɪgər] *s* fossoyeur *m*
gravel [′grævəl] *s* (*on roadway*) gravier *m*,
gravillons *mpl*; (geol) gravier, (pathol)
gravelle *f*
grav′en im′age [′grevən] *s* image *f* taillée
grave′stone′ *s* pierre *f* tombale
grave′yard′ *s* cimetière *m*
gravitate [′grævɪ,tet] *intr* graviter
gravitation [,grævɪ′teʃən] *s* gravitation *f*
gravi·ty [′grævɪti] *s* (*pl* **-ties**) gravité *f*;
(phys) pesanteur *f*, gravité
gra·vy [′grevi] *s* (*pl* **-vies**) (*juice from
cooking meat*) jus *m*; (*sauce made with
this juice*) sauce *f*; (slang) profit *m* facile,
profit supplémentaire
gra′vy boat′ *s* saucière *f*
gra′vy train′ *s* (slang) assiette *f* au beurre
gray [gre] *adj* gris; (*gray-haired*) gris,
chenu; **to turn gray** grisonner ∥ *s* gris *m* ∥
intr grisonner
gray′beard′ *s* barbon *m*, ancien *m*
gray′-haired′ *adj* gris, chenu
gray′hound′ *s* lévrier *m*; (*female*) levrette *f*
grayish [′gre·ɪʃ] *adj* grisâtre
gray′ mat′ter *s* substance *f* grise
graze [grez] *tr* (*to touch lightly*) frôler,
effleurer; (*to scratch lightly in passing*)
érafler; (*to pasture*) faire paître ∥ *intr*
paître
grease [gris] *s* graisse *f* ∥ [griz] *tr* graisser
grease′ cup′ [gris] *s* godet *m* graisseur
grease′ gun′ [gris] *s* graisseur *m*, seringue *f*
à graisse
grease′ paint′ [gris] *s* fard *m*, grimage *m*
greas·y [′grisi] *adj* (*comp* **-ier**; *super* **-iest**)
graisseux, gras
great [gret] *adj* grand; (coll) excellent, formidable; **a great deal, a great many**
beaucoup
great′-aunt′ *s* grand-tante *f*
Great′ Bear′ *s* Grande Ourse *f*
Great′ Brit′ain *s* Grande Bretagne *f*; la
Grande Bretagne

great′coat′ s capote f
Great′ Dane′ s danois m
Great′er New′ York′ s le Grand New York
great′-grand′child′ s (pl **-chil′dren**) arrière-petit-fils m; arrière-petite-fille f; **great-grandchildren** arrière-petits-enfants mpl
great′-grand′daugh′ter s arrière-petite-fille f
great′-grand′fa′ther s arrière-grand-père m, bisaïeul m
great′-grand′moth′er s arrière-grand-mère f, bisaïeule f
great′-grand′par′ents spl arrière-grands-parents mpl
great′-grand′son s arrière-petit-fils m
greatly [′gretli] adv grandement, fort, beaucoup
great′-neph′ew s petit-neveu m
greatness [′gretnɪs] s grandeur f
great′-niece′ s petite-nièce f
great′-un′cle s grand-oncle m
Grecian [′griʃən] adj grec ‖ s (person) Grec m
Greece [gris] s Grèce f; la Grèce
greed [grid] s avidité f
greed·y [′gridi] adj (comp **-ier**; super **-iest**) avide
Greek [grik] adj grec ‖ s (language) grec m; (unintelligible language) (coll) hébreu m, e.g., **it's Greek to me** (coll) c'est de l'hébreu pour moi; (person) Grec m
Greek′ fire′ s feu m grégeois
green [grin] adj vert; inexpérimenté, novice ‖ s vert m; (lawn) gazon m; (golf) pelouse f d'arrivée; **greens** légumes mpl verts
green′back′ s (U.S.A.) billet m de banque
greener·y [′grinəri] s (pl **-ies**) verdure f
green′-eyed′ adj aux yeux verts; (envious) jaloux
green′gage′ s (bot) reine-claude f
green′gro′cer·y s (pl **-ies**) fruiterie f
green′horn′ s blanc-bec m, bleu m
green′house′ s serre f
green′house effect′ s effet m de serre
greenish [′grinɪʃ] adj verdâtre
Greenland [′grinlənd] s le Groënland
green′ light′ s feu m vert, voie f libre
greenness [′grinnɪs] s verdure f; (unripeness) verdeur f; inexpérience f, naïveté f
green′ pep′per s poivron m vert
green′room′ s (theat) foyer m
greensward [′grin,swɔrd] s pelouse f
green′ thumb′ s—**to have a green thumb** avoir la main verte
greet [grit] tr saluer; (to welcome) accueillir
greeting [′gritɪŋ] s salutation f; (welcome) accueil m; **greetings** (on greeting card) vœux mpl ‖ **greetings** interj salut!
greet′ing card′ s carte f de vœux
gregarious [grɪ′gɛrɪ·əs] adj grégaire
Gregorian [grɪ′gorɪ·ən] adj grégorien
grenade [grɪ′ned] s grenade f
grey [gre] adj, s, & intr var of **gray**
grey′hound′ s var of **grayhound**
grid [grid] s (of storage battery and vacuum tube) grille f; (on map) quadrillage m; (culin) gril m

griddle [′grɪdəl] s plaque f chauffante
grid′dle·cake′ s crêpe f
grid′i′ron s gril m; (sports) terrain m de football
grid′ leak′ s résistance f de fuite de la grille
grid′ line′ s ligne f de quadrillage
grief [grif] s chagrin m, affliction f; **to come to grief** finir mal
grief′-strick′en adj affligé, navré
grievance [′grivəns] s grief m
grieve [griv] tr chagriner, affliger ‖ intr se chagriner, s'affliger
grievous [′grivəs] adj grave, douloureux
griffin [′grifɪn] s griffon m
grill [grɪl] s gril m; (grating) grille f ‖ tr griller; (an accused person) (coll) cuisiner
grille [grɪl] s grille f; (aut) calandre f
grilled′ beef′steak′ s châteaubriand m
grill′room′ s grill-room m
grim [grɪm] adj (comp **grimmer**; super **grimmest**) (fierce) menaçant; (repellent) macabre; (unyielding) implacable; (stern-looking) lugubre
grimace [′grɪməs] s grimace f ‖ intr grimacer
grime [graɪm] s crasse f, saleté f
grim·y [′graɪmi] adj (comp **-ier**; super **-iest**) crasseux, sale
grin [grɪn] s (smile) large sourire m ‖ v (pret & pp **grinned**; ger **grinning**) intr avoir un large sourire, rire à belles dents; (in pain) grimacer
grind [graɪnd] s (of coffee) moulure f; (job) (coll) boulot m, collier m; (student) (coll) bûcheur m, fort-en-thème m; **daily grind** (coll) train-train m quotidien ‖ v (pret & pp **ground** [graʊnd]) tr (coffee, flour) moudre; (food) broyer; (meat) hacher; (a knife) aiguiser; (the teeth) grincer; (valves) roder ‖ intr grincer; **to grind away at** (coll) bûcher
grinder [′graɪndər] s (for coffee, pepper, etc.) moulin m, broyeur m; (for meat) hachoir m; (for tools) repasseur m; (back tooth) molaire f
grind′stone′ s meule f, pierre f à aiguiser
grip [grɪp] s (hold) prise f; (with hand) poigne f; (handle) poignée f; (handbag) sac m de voyage; (understanding) compréhension f; **to come to grips** en venir aux prises; **to lose one's grip** lâcher prise ‖ v (pret & pp **gripped**; ger **gripping**) tr serrer, saisir fortement; (e.g., a theater audience) empoigner
gripe [graɪp] s (coll) rouspétance f ‖ intr (coll) rouspéter, ronchonner
grippe [grɪp] s grippe f
gripping [′grɪpɪŋ] adj passionnant
gris·ly [′grɪzli] adj (comp **-lier**; super **-liest**) horrible, macabre
grist [grɪst] s blé m à moudre
gristle [′grɪsəl] s cartilage m
gris·tly [′grɪsli] adj (comp **-tlier**; super **-tliest**) cartilagineux
grist′mill′ s moulin m à blé
grit [grɪt] s (sand) grès m, sable m; (courage) cran m; **grits** gruau m ‖ v (pret

& *pp* **gritted**; *ger* **gritting**) *tr* (*one's teeth*) grincer

grit·ty ['grɪti] *adj* (*comp* **-tier**; *super* **-tiest**) sablonneux; (fig) plein de cran

griz·zly ['grɪzli] *adj* (*comp* **-zlier**; *super* **-zliest**) grisonnant ‖ *s* (*pl* **-zlies**) ours *m* gris

griz'zly bear' *s* ours *m* gris

groan [gron] *s* gémissement *m* ‖ *intr* gémir

grocer ['grosər] *s* épicier *m*

grocer·y ['grosəri] *s* (*pl* **-ies**) épicerie *f*; **groceries** denrées *fpl*

gro'cery store' *s* épicerie *f*

grog [grɑg] *s* grog *m*

grog·gy ['grɑgi] *adj* (*comp* **-gier**; *super* **-giest**) (coll) vacillant; (*shaky, e.g., from a blow*) (coll) étourdi; (*drunk*) (coll) gris, ivre

groin [grɔɪn] *s* (anat) aine *f*; (archit) arête *f*

groom [grum] *s* (*bridegroom*) marié *m*; (*stableboy*) palefrenier *m* ‖ *tr* soigner, astiquer; (*horses*) panser; (*a politician, a starlet, etc.*) dresser, préparer

grooms'man *s* (*pl* **-men**) garçon *m* d'honneur

groove [gruv] *s* (*for sliding door, etc.*) rainure *f*; (*of pulley*) gorge *f*; (*of phonograph record*) sillon *m*; (*mark left by wheel*) ornière *f*; (*of window, door, etc.*) feuillure *f*; **in the groove** (coll) comme sur des roulettes; **to get into a groove** (coll) devenir routinier ‖ *tr* rainer, canneler

grope [grop] *intr* tâtonner; **to grope for** chercher à tâtons

gropingly ['gropɪŋli] *adv* à tâtons

grosbeak ['gros‚bik] *s* gros-bec *m*

gross [gros] *adj* (*flagrant*) flagrant, choquant; (*error*) gros, lourd; (*fat, burly*) gras, épais; (*crass, vulgar*) grossier; (*weight; receipts*) brut; (*displacement*) global ‖ *s invar* recette *f* brute; (*twelve dozen*) grosse *f* ‖ *tr* produire en recette brute, produire brut, e.g., **the business grossed a million dollars** l'entreprise a produit un million de dollars, brut

gross' na'tional prod'uct *s* revenu *m* national brut (R.N.B.), produit *m* national brut

gross' weight' *s* poids *m* brut, poids total

grotesque [gro'tɛsk] *adj* grotesque ‖ *s* grotesque *m*; (*ornament*) grotesque *f*

grot·to ['grɑto] *s* (*pl* **-toes** or **-tos**) grotte *f*

grouch [graʊtʃ] *s* (coll) humeur *f* grognon; (*person*) (coll) grognon *m* ‖ *intr* (coll) grogner

grouch·y ['graʊtʃi] *adj* (*comp* **-ier**; *super* **-iest**) (coll) grognon, maussade

ground [graʊnd] *s* terre *f*; (*piece of land*) terrain *m*; (*basis, foundation*) fondement *m*, base *f*; (*reason*) motif *m*, cause *f*; (elec) terre *f*; (*body of automobile corresponding to ground*) (elec) masse *f*; **ground for complaint** grief *m*; **grounds** parc *m*, terrain; fondement, cause; (*of coffee*) marc *m*; **on the ground of** pour raison de, sous prétexte de; **to be losing**

ground être en recul; **to break ground** donner le premier coup de pioche; **to have grounds for** avoir matière à; **to stand one's ground** tenir bon or ferme; **to yield ground** lâcher pied ‖ *tr* fonder, baser; (elec) mettre à terre; **grounded** (aer) interdit de vol, gardé au sol; **to ground s.o. in s.th.** enseigner à fond q.ch. à qn

ground' connec'tion *s* prise *f* de terre

ground' crew' *s* équipe *f* au sol, personnel *m* rampant

ground' floor' *s* rez-de-chaussée *m*

ground' glass' *s* verre *m* dépoli

ground' hog' *s* marmotte *f* d'Amérique

grounding ['graʊndɪŋ] *s* (aer) interdiction *f* de vol; (elec) mise *f* à la masse

ground' installa'tions *spl* (aer) infrastructure *f*

ground' lead' [lid] *s* (elec) conduite *f* à terre

groundless ['graʊndlɪs] *adj* sans fondement

ground' meat' *s* viande *f* hachée

ground' plan' *s* plan *m* de base; (archit) plan horizontal

ground' speed' *s* (aer) vitesse *f* par rapport au sol

ground' swell' *s* lame *f* de fond

ground' troops' *spl* (mil) effectifs *mpl* terrestres

ground' wire' *s* (elec) fil *m* de terre, fil de masse

ground'work' *s* fondement *m*, fond *m*

group [grup] *s* groupe *m* ‖ *tr* grouper ‖ *intr* se grouper

grouse [graʊs] *s* coq *m* de bruyère ‖ *intr* (slang) grogner

grove [grov] *s* bocage *m*, bosquet *m*

grov·el ['grʌvəl] *v* (*pret* & *pp* **-eled** or **-elled**; *ger* **-eling** or **-elling**) *intr* se vautrer; (*before s.o.*) ramper

grow [gro] *v* (*pret* **grew** [gru]; *pp* **grown** [gron]) *tr* cultiver, faire pousser; (*a beard*) laisser pousser ‖ *intr* croître; (*said of plants*) pousser; (*said of seeds*) germer; (*to become*) devenir; **to grow angry** se mettre en colère; **to grow old** vieillir; **to grow out of** se développer de; (*e.g., a suit of clothes*) devenir trop grand pour; **to grow up** grandir, profiter

growl [graʊl] *s* grondement *m*, grognement *m* ‖ *tr* & *intr* gronder, grogner

grown'-up' *adj* adulte ‖ *s* (*pl* **grown-ups**) adulte *mf*; **grown-ups** grandes personnes *fpl*

growth [groθ] *s* croissance *f*, développement *m*; (*increase*) accroissement *m*; (*of trees, grass, etc.*) pousse *f*; (pathol) excroissance *f*, grosseur *f*

growth' stock' *s* valeur *f* d'avenir

grub [grʌb] *s* asticot *m*; (*person*) homme *m* de peine; (*food*) (coll) boustifaille *f* ‖ *v* (*pret* & *pp* **grubbed**; *ger* **grubbing**) *tr* défricher ‖ *intr* fouiller

grub·by ['grʌbi] *adj* (*comp* **-bier**; *super* **-biest**) sale, malpropre

grudge [grʌdʒ] *s* rancune *f*; **to have a grudge against** garder rancune à ‖ *tr* donner à contre-cœur

grudgingly [ˈgrʌdʒɪŋli] *adv* à contre-cœur

gruel [ˈgru·əl] *s* gruau *m*, bouillie *f*

grueling [ˈgru·əlɪŋ] *adj* éreintant

gruesome [ˈgrusəm] *adj* macabre

gruff [grʌf] *adj* bourru, brusque; (*voice*) rauque, gros

grumble [ˈgrʌmbəl] *s* grognement *m* ‖ *intr* grogner, grommeler

grump·y [ˈgrʌmpi] *adj* (*comp* **-ier**; *super* **-iest**) maussade, grognon

grunt [grʌnt] *s* grognement *m* ‖ *intr* grogner

G'-string' *s* (*loincloth*) pagne *m*; (*worn by women entertainers*) cache-sexe *m*; (*mus*) corde *f* de sol

guarantee [ˌgærənˈti] *s* garantie *f*; (*guarantor*) garant *m*, répondant *m*; (*security*) caution *f* ‖ *tr* garantir

guarantor [ˈgærənˌtɔr] *s* garant *m*

guaran·ty [ˈgærənti] *s* (*pl* **-ties**) garantie *f* ‖ *v* (*pret & pp* **-tied**) *tr* garantir

guard [gɑrd] *s* garde *f*; (*person*) garde *m*; **on guard** en garde; (*on duty*) de garde; (mil) en faction, de faction; **on one's guard** sur ses gardes; **to mount guard** monter la garde; **under guard** gardé à vue ‖ *tr* garder ‖ *intr* être de faction; **to guard against** se garder de

guard' du'ty *s* service *m* de garde

guarded *adj* (*remark*) prudent

guard'house' *s* guérite *f*, corps-de-garde *m*; (mil) salle *f* de police, prison *f* militaire

guardian [ˈgɑrdɪ·ən] *adj* gardien ‖ *s* gardien *m*; (*of a ward*) tuteur *m*

guard'ian an'gel *s* ange *m* gardien, ange tutélaire

guard'ian·ship' *s* garde *f*; (law) tutelle *f*

guard'rail' *s* garde-fou *m*, parapet *m*, glissière *f* de sécurité

guard'room' *s* corps-de-garde *m*, salle *f* de police; (*prison*) bloc *m*, tôle *f*

guards'man *s* (*pl* **-men**) garde *m*

Guatemalan [ˌgwɑtɪˈmɑlən] *adj* guatémaltèque ‖ *s* Guatémaltèque *mf*

guava [ˈgwɑvə] *s* goyave *f*, (*tree*) goyavier *m*

guerrilla [gəˈrɪlə] *s* guérillero *m*; **guerrillas** (*band*) guérilla *f*

guerril'la war'fare *s* guérilla *f*

guess [gɛs] *s* conjecture *f* ‖ *tr & intr* conjecturer; (*a secret, riddle, etc.*) deviner; (coll) supposer, penser; **I guess so** je crois que oui; **to guess right** bien deviner

guess'work' *s* supposition *f*; **by guesswork** au jugé

guest [gɛst] *s* invité *m*, hôte *mf*; (*in a hotel*) client *m*, hôte

guest' book' *s* livre *m* d'or

guest' room' *s* chambre *f* d'ami

guest' speak'er *s* orateur *m* de circonstance

guffaw [gəˈfɔ] *s* gros rire *m* ‖ *tr* dire avec un gros rire ‖ *intr* rire bruyamment

guidance [ˈgaɪdəns] *s* (*advice*) conseils *mpl*; (*guiding*) conduite *f*; (*in choosing a career*) orientation *f*; (*of rocket*) guidage *m*;

for your guidance pour votre gouverne

guid'ance coun'selor *s* orienteur *m*

guide [gaɪd] *s* guide *m* ‖ *tr* guider

guide'book' *s* guide *m*

guid'ed mis'sile *s* engin *m* téléguidé

guide' dog' *s* chien *m* d'aveugle

guid'ed tour' *s* visite *f* commentée, visite guidée

guide' line' *s* (fig) norme *f*, règle *f*; **guide lines** (*for writing straight lines*) transparent *m*, guide-âne *m*

guide'post' *s* poteau *m* indicateur

guide' word' *s* lettrine *f*

guild [gɪld] *s* association *f*, corporation *f*; (eccl) confrérie *f*; (hist) guilde *f*

guild'hall' *s* hôtel *m* de ville

guile [gaɪl] *s* astuce *f*, artifice *m*

guileful [ˈgaɪlfəl] *adj* astucieux, artificieux

guileless [ˈgaɪllɪs] *adj* candide, innocent

guillotine [ˈgɪləˌtin] *s* guillotine *f* ‖ *tr* guillotiner

guilt [gɪlt] *s* culpabilité *f*

guiltless [ˈgɪltlɪs] *adj* innocent

guilt·y [ˈgɪlti] *adj* (*comp* **-ier**; *super* **-iest**) coupable; **found guilty** reconnu coupable

guinea [ˈgɪni] *s* guinée *f*; **Guinea** Guinée; **la Guinée**

guin'ea fowl' or **hen'** *s* poule *f* de Guinée, pintade *f*

guin'ea pig' *s* cobaye *m*

guise [gaɪz] *s* apparences *fpl*, déguisement *m*; **under the guise of** sous un semblant de, sous le masque de

guitar [gɪˈtɑr] *s* guitare *f*

guitarist [gɪˈtɑrɪst] *s* guitariste *mf*

gulch [gʌltʃ] *s* ravin *m*

gulf [gʌlf] *s* golfe *m*; (fig) gouffre *m*

Gulf' of Mex'ico *s* Golfe *m* du Mexique

Gulf' Stream' *s* Courant *m* du Golfe

gull [gʌl] *s* mouette *f*, goéland *m*; (coll) gogo *m*, jobard *m* ‖ *tr* escroquer, duper

gullet [ˈgʌlɪt] *s* gosier *m*

gullible [ˈgʌlɪbəl] *adj* crédule, naïf

gul·ly [ˈgʌli] *s* (*pl* **-lies**) ravin *m*; (*channel*) rigole *f*

gulp [gʌlp] *s* gorgée *f*, lampée *f*; **at one gulp** d'un trait ‖ *tr*—**to gulp down** avaler à grandes bouchées, lamper; (*e.g., tears*) ravaler, refouler ‖ *intr* avoir la gorge serrée

gum [gʌm] *s* gomme *f*; (*on eyelids*) chassie *f*; (anat) gencive *f* ‖ *v* (*pret & pp* **gummed**; *ger* **gumming**) *tr* gommer; **to gum up** encrasser; (coll) bousiller

gum' ar'abic *s* gomme *f* arabique

gum'boil' *s* phlegmon *m*, fluxion *f*

gum' boot' *s* botte *f* de caoutchouc

gum'drop' *s* boule *f* de gomme, pâte *f* de fruits

gum·my [ˈgʌmi] *adj* (*comp* **-mier**; *super* **-miest**) gommeux; (*eyelids*) chassieux

gumption [ˈgʌmpʃən] *s* (coll) initiative *f*, cran *m*

gum'shoe' *s* caoutchouc *m*; (coll) détective *m* ‖ *intr* rôder en tapinois, marcher furtivement

gun [gʌn] s fusil m; (for spraying) pistolet m; **to stick to one's guns** (coll) ne pas en démordre ‖ v (pret & pp **gunned**; ger **gunning**) tr—**to gun down** tuer d'un coup de fusil; **to gun the engine** (slang) appuyer sur le champignon ‖ intr—**to gun for** (game) chasser; (an enemy) pourchasser

gun′ bar′rel s canon m

gun′boat′ s cannonière f

gun′ car′riage s affût m de canon

gun′cot′ton s fulmicoton m

gun′ crew′ s peloton m de pièce, servants mpl de canon

gun′fire′ s canonnade f, coups mpl de feu

gun′ laws′ spl réglementation f du port d'armes

gun′ lob′by s lobby m des marchands de revolvers

gun′man s (pl -men) s bandit m

gun′ met′al s métal m bleui

gunner ['gʌnər] s canonnier m, artilleur m; (aer) mitrailleur m

gunnery ['gʌnəri] s tir m, canonnage m

gunnysack ['gʌni,sæk] s sac m de serpillière

gun′point′ s—**at gunpoint** à main armée

gun′pow′der s poudre f à canon

gun′run′ning s contrebande f d'armes

gun′shot′ s coup m de feu, coup de fusil

gun′shot wound′ s blessure f par balle

gun′smith′ s armurier m

gun′stock′ s fût m

gunwale ['gʌnəl] s (naut) plat-bord m

gup·py ['gʌpi] s (pl -pies) guppy m

gurgle ['gʌrgəl] s glouglou m, gargouillement m ‖ intr glouglouter, gargouiller

gush [gʌʃ] s jaillissement m ‖ intr jaillir; **to gush over** (coll) s'attendrir sur

gusher ['gʌʃər] s puits m jaillissant

gush·y ['gʌʃi] adj (comp -ier; super -iest) (coll) démonstratif, expansif

gusset ['gʌsɪt] s (in garment) soufflet m; (mach) gousset m

gust [gʌst] s bouffée f, coup m

gusto ['gʌsto] s goût m, entrain m

gust·y ['gʌsti] adj (comp -ier; super -iest) venteux; (wind) à rafales

gut [gʌt] s boyau m; **guts** (coll) cran m; **he has a lot of guts** (pej) il est vachement gonflé ‖ v (pret & pp **gutted**; ger **gutting**) tr raser à l'intérieur; (to take out the guts of) vider

gutter ['gʌtər] s (on side of road) caniveau m; (in street) ruisseau m; (of roof) gouttière f; (ditch formed by rain water) rigole f

gut′ter·snipe′ s (coll) voyou m

guttural ['gʌtərəl] adj guttural ‖ s gutturale f

guy [gaɪ] s (supporting cable) câble m tenseur; (naut) hauban m; (coll) type m, gars m ‖ tr haubaner; (coll) se moquer de

Guyana [gaɪ'ænə] s Guyane f; la Guyane

guy′ rope′ s corde f de tente

guy′ wire′ s câble m tenseur, (naut) hauban m

guzzle ['gʌzəl] tr & intr boire avidement

guzzler ['gʌzlər] s soiffard m

gym [dʒɪm] s (coll) gymnase m

gymnasi·um [dʒɪm'nezɪ·əm] s (pl -ums or -a [ə]) gymnase m

gymnast ['dʒɪmnæst] s gymnaste mf

gynecology [,gaɪnə'kɑlədʒi] s gynécologie f

gyp [dʒɪp] s (slang) escroquerie f; (person) (slang) aigrefin m ‖ v (pret & pp **gypped**; ger **gypping**) tr (slang) tirer une carotte à, refaire, gruger, chiper, chaparder

gypsum ['dʒɪpsəm] s gypse m

gyp·sy ['dʒɪpsi] adj bohémien ‖ s (pl -sies) bohémien m; **Gypsy** (language) tsigane m, romanichel m; (person) gitan m, tsigane mf, romanichel m

gyp′sy moth′ s zigzag m

gyrate ['dʒaɪret] intr tournoyer

gyrocompass ['dʒaɪro,kʌmpəs] s gyrocompas m

gyroscope ['dʒaɪrə,skop] s gyroscope m

H

H, h [etʃ] s VIIIe lettre de l'alphabet

haberdasher ['hæbər,dæʃ ər] s chemisier m

haberdasher·y ['hæbər,dæʃəri] s (pl -ies) chemiserie f, confection f pour hommes

habit ['hæbɪt] s habitude f; (dress) habit m, costume m; **to get into the habit of** s'habituer à

habitual [hə'bɪtʃʊ·əl] adj habituel

habituate [hə'bɪtʃʊ,et] tr habituer

hack [hæk] s (notch) entaille f; (cough) toux f sèche; (hackney) voiture f de louage; (old nag) rosse f; (writer) écrivassier m ‖ tr hacher

hackney ['hækni] s voiture f de louage

hackneyed ['hæknid] adj banal, battu

hack′saw′ s scie f à métaux

haddock ['hædək] s églefin m

hag [hæg] s (ugly woman) guenon f; (witch) sorcière f; **old hag** vieille fée f

haggard ['hægərd] adj décharné, hâve; (wild-looking) hagard, farouche

haggle ['hægəl] intr marchander; **to haggle over** marchander

Hague [heg] s—**The Hague** La Haye

hail [hel] s (frozen rain) grêle f; **within hail** à portée de la voix ‖ tr saluer; (a ship, taxi, etc.) héler ‖ intr grêler; **to hail from** venir de ‖ interj salut!

Hail′ Mar′y s Ave Maria m

hail′stone′ s grêlon m

hail′storm′ s tempête f de grêle
hair [hɛr] s poil m; (of person) cheveu m; (head of human hair) cheveux mpl; **against the hair** à rebrousse-poil, à contrepoil; **hairs** cheveux; **to a hair** à un cheveu près; **to get in s.o.'s hair** (slang) porter sur les nerfs à qn; **to let one's hair down** (slang) en prendre la plus à son aise; **to make s.o.'s hair stand on end** faire dresser les cheveux à qn; **to not turn a hair** ne pas tiquer; **to split hairs** fendre or couper les cheveux en quatre
hair′breadth′ s épaisseur f d'un cheveu; **to escape by a hairbreadth** l'échapper belle
hair′brush′ s brosse f à cheveux
hair′cloth′ s thibaude f; (for furniture) tissu-crin m
hair′cream′ s fixateur m
hair′curl′er [ˌkʌrlər] s frisoir m; (pin) bigoudi m
hair′cut′ s coupe f de cheveux; **to get a haircut** se faire couper les cheveux
hair′do′ s (pl -dos) coiffure f
hair′dress′er s coiffeur m pour dames; coiffeuse f
hair′dress′ing s cosmétique m
hair′dri′er s sèche-cheveux m, séchoir m à cheveux
hair′ dye′ s teinture f des cheveux
hair′line′ s (on face of type) délié m; (along the upper forehead) naissance f des cheveux, plantation f des cheveux
hair′net′ s résille f
hair′pin′ s épingle f à cheveux
hair′pin turn′ s lacet m
hair′-rais′ing adj (coll) horripilant
hair′ rib′bon s ruban m à cheveux
hair′ set′ s mise f en plis
hair′ shirt′ s haire f, cilice m
hair′split′ting adj vétilleux, trop subtil ‖ s ergotage m
hair′ spray′ s (for setting hair) laque f, fixatif m
hair′spring′ s spiral m
hair′ style′ s coiffure f
hair′ ton′ic s lotion f capillaire
hair′ trig′ger s détente f douce
hair·y [ˈhɛri] adj (comp -ier; super -iest) poilu, velu; (on head) chevelu
Haiti [ˈheti] s Haïti f; **the Republic of Haiti** la république d'Haïti
Haitian [ˈheʃən] adj haïtien ‖ s Haïtien m
halberd [ˈhælbərd] s hallebarde f
hal′cyon days′ [ˈhælsɪ-ən] spl jours mpl alcyoniens, jours sereins
hale [hel] adj vigoureux, sain; **hale and hearty** frais et gaillard ‖ tr haler
half [hæf] adj demi ‖ s (pl halves [hævz]) moitié f, la moitié; (of the hour) demi m; **by half** de moitié; (of the hour) demi m; **half an hour** une demi-heure; **in half** en deux; **to go halves** être de moitié ‖ adv moitié, à moitié; **half . . . half** moitié . . . moitié; **half past** et demie, e.g., **half past three** trois heures et demie
half′-and-half′ adj & adv moitié l'un moitié l'autre, en parties égales ‖ s (for coffee)

mélange m de lait et de crème; (beer) mélange de bière et de porter
half′back′ s (football) demi-arrière m, demi m
half′-baked′ adj à moitié cuit; (person) inexpérimenté; (plan) prématuré, incomplet
half′ bind′ing s (bb) demi-reliure f à petits coins
half′-blood′ s métis m; demi-frère m
half′ boot′ s demi-botte f
half′-bound′ adj (bb) en demi-reliure à coins
half′-breed′ s métis m, sang-mêlé m; (e.g., horse) demi-sang m
half′ broth′er s demi-frère m
half′-cocked′ adv (coll) avec trop de hâte
half′-day′ s demi-journée f
half′-doz′en s demi-douzaine f
half′ fare′ s demi-tarif m, demi-place f
half′-full′ adj à moitié plein
half′-heart′ed adj sans entrain, hésitant
half′-hol′iday s demi-congé m
half′ hose′ s chaussettes fpl
half′-hour′ s demi-heure f; **every half-hour on the half-hour** toutes les demi-heures à la demi-heure juste; **on the half-hour** à la demie
half′ leath′er s (bb) demi-reliure f à petits coins
half′-length′ s demi-longueur f
half′-length por′trait s portrait m en buste
half′-life′ s (phys) période f
half′-light′ s demi-jour m
half′-line space′ s (on typewriter) demi-interligne m de base
half′-mast′ s—**at half-mast** en berne, à mi-mât
half′-moon′ s demi-lune f
half′ mourn′ing s demi-deuil m
half′ note′ s (mus) blanche f
half′ pay′ s demi-solde f
halfpen·ny [ˈhepəni], [ˈhepni] s (pl -nies) demi-penny m; (fig) sou m
half′ pint′ s demi-pinte f; (little runt) (slang) petit culot m
half′-seas o′ver adj—**to be half-seas over** avoir du vent dans les voiles
half′ shell′ s (either half of a bivalve) écaille f; **on the half shell** dans sa coquille
half′ sis′ter s demi-sœur f
half′ sole′ s demi-semelle f
half′-staff′ s—**at half-staff** à mi-mât
half′-tim′bered adj à demi-boisage
half′ time′ s (sports) mi-temps m
half′-time′ adj à demi-journée
half′ ti′tle s faux titre m, avant-titre m
half′tone′ s (painting, phot) demi-teinte f; (typ) similigravure f
half′ tone′ s (mus) demi-ton m
half′-track′ s semi-chenillé m
half′-truth′ s demi-vérité f
half′turn′ s demi-tour m; (of wheel) demi-révolution f
half′way′ adj & adv à mi-chemin; **halfway through** à moitié de; **halfway up** à mi-

côte; **to meet s.o. halfway** couper la poire en deux avec qn
half′-wit′ted *adj* à moitié idiot
halibut [ˈhælɪbət] *s* flétan *m*
halitosis [ˌhælɪˈtosɪs] *s* mauvaise haleine *f*
hall [hɔl] *s* (*passageway*) corridor *m*, couloir *m*; (*entranceway*) entrée *f*, vestibule *m*; (*large meeting room*) salle *f*, hall *m*, salle des fêtes; (*assembly room of a university*) amphithéâtre *m*; (*building of a university*) bâtiment *m*
halleluiah or **hallelujah** [ˌhælɪˈlujə] *s* alléluia *m* ‖ *interj* alléluia!
hall′mark′ *s* estampille *f*, poinçon *m*; (fig) cachet *m*, marque *f*
hal·lo [həˈlo] *s* (*pl* **-los**) holà *m* ‖ *intr* huer ‖ *interj* holà!, ohé!; (hunting) taïaut!
hallow [ˈhælo] *tr* sanctifier
hallowed *adj* sanctifié, saint
Halloween or **Hallowe'en** [ˌhæloˈin] *s* la veille de la Toussaint
hallucinate [həˈlusɪnet] *intr* avoir des hallucinations
hallucination [həˌlusɪˈneʃən] *s* hallucination *f*
hallucinogenic [həˌlusənoˈdʒɛnɪk] *adj* hallucinogène
hall′way′ *s* corridor *m*, couloir *m*
ha·lo [ˈhelo] *s* (*pl* **-los** or **-loes**) (meteo) auréole *f*, halo *m*; (*around a head*) auréole *f*
halogen [ˈhælədʒən] *s* halogène *m*
halt [hɔlt] *adj* boiteux, estropié ‖ *s* halte *f*, arrêt *m*; **to come to a halt** faire halte ‖ *tr* faire faire halte à ‖ *intr* faire halte ‖ *interj* halte!; (mil) halte-là!
halter [ˈhɔltər] *s* licou *m*; (*noose*) corde *f*
halting [ˈhɔltɪŋ] *adj* boiteux; hésitant
halve [hæv] *tr* diviser or partager en deux; réduire de moitié
halyard [ˈhæljərd] *s* (naut) drisse *f*
ham [hæm] *s* (*part of leg behind knee*) jarret *m*; (*thigh and buttock*) fesse *f*; (culin) cuisse *f*; (*cured*) (culin) jambon *m*; (rad) radio amateur *m*; (theat) cabotin *m*; **hams** fesses
hamburger [ˈhæmˌbʌrgər] *s* sandwich *m* à la hambourgeoise, hamburger *m*; (*Hamburg steak*) biftek *m* haché
hamlet [ˈhæmlɪt] *s* hameau *m*
hammer [ˈhæmər] *s* marteau *m*; (*of gun*) chien *m*, percuteur *m* ‖ *tr* marteler; **to hammer out** étendre au marteau; (*to resolve*) résoudre ‖ *intr*—**to hammer away at** (*e.g., a job*) travailler d'arrache-pied à
hammock [ˈhæmək] *s* hamac *m*
hamper [ˈhæmpər] *s* manne *f* ‖ *tr* embarrasser, gêner, empêcher
hamster [ˈhæmstər] *s* hamster *m*
ham′string′ *v* (*pret & pp* **-strung**) *tr* couper le jarret à; (fig) couper les moyens à
hand [hænd] *adj* à main, à la main, manuel ‖ *s* main *f*; (*workman*) manœuvre *m*, ouvrier *m*; (*way of writing*) écriture *f*; (*clapping of hands*) applaudissements *mpl*; (*of clock or watch*) aiguille *f*; (*a round of play*) coup *m*, partie *f*, main; (*of God*) doigt *m*; (*measure*) palme *m*; (cards)

jeu *m*; **at hand** sous la main; (*said of approaching event*) proche, prochain; **by hand** à la main; **hand in hand** main dans la main; **hands up!** haut les mains!; **hand to hand** corps à corps; **on every hand** de toutes parts, de tous côtés; **on the one hand . . . on the other hand** d'une part . . . d'autre part; **to live from hand to mouth** vivre au jour le jour; **to rule with a firm hand** avoir de la poigne; **to shake hands with** serrer la main à; **to wait on hand and foot** être aux petits soins pour; **to win hands down** gagner dans un fauteuil; **under the hand and seal of** signé et scellé de ‖ *tr* donner, présenter; (*e.g., food at table*) passer; **to hand down** (*e.g., property*) léguer; (*a verdict*) prononcer; **to hand in** remettre; **to hand on** transmettre; **to hand out** distribuer; **to hand over** céder, livrer
hand′bag′ *s* sac *m* à main
hand′ bag′gage *s* menus bagages *mpl*, bagages à main
hand′ball′ *s* pelote *f*; (*game*) handball *m*
hand′bill′ *s* prospectus *m*
hand′book′ *s* manuel *m*
hand′ brake′ *s* frein *m* à main
hand′car′ *s* (rr) draisine *f*
hand′cart′ *s* voiture *f* à bras
hand′clasp′ *s* poignée *f* de main
hand′ control′ *s* commande *f* à la main
hand′cuff′ *s* menotte *f* ‖ *tr* mettre les menottes à
handful [ˈhændˌful] *s* poignée *f*
hand′ glass′ *s* miroir *m* à main; (*magnifying glass*) loupe *f* à main
hand′ grenade′ *s* grenade *f* à main
handi·cap [ˈhændɪˌkæp] *s* handicap *m* ‖ *v* (*pret & pp* **-capped**; *ger* **-capping**) *tr* handicaper
handicraft [ˈhændɪˌkræft] *s* habileté *f* manuelle; métier *m*; **handicrafts** produits *mpl* d'artisanat
handiwork [ˈhændɪˌwʌrk] *s* ouvrage *m*, travail *m* manuel; (fig) œuvre *f*
handkerchief [ˈhæŋkərtʃɪf] *s* mouchoir *m*
handle [ˈhændəl] *s* (*of basket, crock, pitcher*) anse *f*; (*of shovel, broom, knife*) manche *m*; (*of umbrella, sword, door*) poignée *f*, (*of frying pan*) queue *f*; (*of pump*) brimbale *f*; (*of handcart*) brancard *m*; (*of wheelbarrow*) bras *m*; (*opportunity, pretext*) prétexte *m*; (mach) manivelle *f*, manette *f*; **to fly off the handle** (coll) sortir de ses gonds ‖ *tr* manier; (*with one's hands*) palper, tâter; **handle with care** (*shipping label*) fragile; **to handle roughly** malmener ‖ *intr*—**to handle well** (mach) avoir de bonnes réactions
han′dle·bars′ *spl* guidon *m*
handler [ˈhændlər] *s* (sports) entraîneur *m*
handling [ˈhændlɪŋ] *s* (*e.g., of tool*) maniement *m*; (*e.g., of person*) traitement *m*; (*of merchandise*) manutention *f*
hand′made′ *adj* fait à la main

hand′maid′ or **hand′maid′en** *s* servante *f*;
(fig) auxiliaire *mf*

hand′-me-down′ *s* (coll) décrochez-moi-ça
m

hand′ or′gan *s* orgue *m* de Barbarie

hand′out′ *s* (*notes*) (coll) documentation *f*;
(slang) aumône *f*

hand′-picked′ *adj* trié sur le volet

hand′rail′ *s* main *f* courante, rampe *f*

hand′saw′ *s* égoïne *f*, scie *f* à main

hand′set′ *s* combiné *m*

hand′shake′ *s* poignée *f* de main

handsome [ˈhænsəm] *adj* beau; (*e.g., fortune*) considérable

hand′spring′ *s*—**to do a handspring** prendre appui sur les mains pour faire la
culbute

hand′-to-hand′ *adj* corps-à-corps

hand′-to-mouth′ *adj*—**to lead a hand-
to-mouth existence** vivre au jour le jour

hand′ truck′ *s* bard *m*, diable *m*

hand′work′ *s* travail *m* à la main

hand′writ′ing *s* écriture *f*

handwritten [ˈhænd,rɪtən] *adj* manuscrit,
autographe

hand·y [ˈhændi] *adj* (*comp* **-ier**; *super* **-iest**)
(*easy to handle*) maniable; (*within easy
reach*) accessible, sous la main; (*skillful*)
adroit, habile; **to come in handy** être très
à propos

hand′y·man *s* (*pl* **-men′**) homme *m* à tout
faire, bricoleur *m*

hang [hæŋ] *s* (*of dress, curtain, etc.*) retombée *f*, drapé *m*; (*skill; insight*) adresse
f, sens *m*; **I don't give a hang!** (coll) je
m'en moque pas mal!; **to get the hang**
(coll) saisir le truc, attraper le chic ‖ *v*
(*pret & pp* **hung** [hʌŋ]) *tr* pendre;
(*laundry*) étendre; (*wallpaper*) coller;
(*one's head*) baisser; **hang it all!** zut
alors!; **to hang up** suspendre, accrocher;
(telp) raccrocher ‖ *intr* pendre, être ac-
croché; **to hang around** flâner, rôder; **to
hang on** se cramponner à, s'accrocher à;
(*to depend on*) dépendre de; (*to stay put*)
tenir bon; **to hang out** pendre dehors;
(slang) percher, loger; **to hang over** (*to
threaten*) peser sur, menacer; **to hang
together** rester unis; **to hang up** (telp)
raccrocher ‖ *v* (*pret & pp* **hung** or
hanged) *tr* (*to execute by hanging*) pendre
‖ *intr* se pendre

hangar [ˈhæŋər], [ˈhæŋgɑr] *s* hangar *m*

hang′dog′ *adj* (*look*) patibulaire

hanger [ˈhæŋər] *s* crochet *m*; (*coathanger*)
cintre *m*, portemanteau *m*

hang′er-on′ *s* (*pl* **hangers-on**) parasite *m*,
pique-assiette *m*

hang′ glid′er *s* deltaplane *m*

hang′ glid′ing *s* vol *m* à libre, vol sur aile
delta

hanging [ˈhæŋɪŋ] *adj* pendant, suspendu ‖ *s*
pendaison *f*; **hangings** tentures *fpl*

hang′man *s* (*pl* **-men**) bourreau *m*

hang′nail′ *s* envie *f*

hang′out′ *s* (coll) repaire *m*

hang′o′ver *s* (coll) gueule *f* de bois

hank [hæŋk] *s* écheveau *m*

hanker [ˈhæŋkər] *intr*—**to hanker after** or
for désirer vivement, être affamé de

Hannibal [ˈhænɪbəl] *s* Annibal *m*

haphazard [,hæpˈhæzərd] *adj* fortuit,
imprévu; au petit bonheur ‖ *adv* à l'aventure, au hasard

hapless [ˈhæplɪs] *adj* malheureux, malchanceux

happen [ˈhæpən] *intr* arriver, se passer; (*to
be the case by chance*) survenir; **happen
what may** advienne que pourra; **how does
it happen that . . . ?** comment se fait-il
que . . . ?, d'où vient-il que . . . ?; **to
happen at the right moment** tomber
pile; **to happen on** tomber sur; **to happen
to** + *inf* se trouver + *inf*, venir à + *inf*

happening [ˈhæpənɪŋ] *s* événement *m*

happily [ˈhæpɪli] *adv* heureusement

happiness [ˈhæpɪnɪs] *s* bonheur *m*

hap·py [ˈhæpi] *adj* (*comp* **-pier**; *super*
-piest) heureux; (*pleased*) content; (*hour*)
propice; **to be happy to** être heureux or
content de

hap′py-go-luck′y *adj* sans souci, insouciant ‖ *adv* (archaic) à l'aventure

hap′py me′dium *s* juste-milieu *m*

Hap′py New′ Year′ *interj* bonne année!

harangue [həˈræŋ] *s* harangue *f* ‖ *tr & intr*
haranguer

harass [həˈræs] *tr* harceler; tourmenter

harbinger [ˈhɑrbɪndʒər] *s* avant-coureur *m*,
précurseur *m*

harbor [ˈhɑrbər] *s* port *m* ‖ *tr* héberger,
donner asile à; (*a criminal, stolen goods,
etc.*) receler; (*suspicions; a hope*) entretenir, nourrir; (*a grudge*) garder

har′bor mas′ter *s* capitaine *m* de port

hard [hɑrd] *adj* dur; (*difficult*) difficile;
(*water*) cru, calcaire; (*work*) assidu, dur;
to be hard on (*to treat severely*) être dur
or sévère envers; (*to wear out fast*) user ‖
adv dur, fort; (*firmly*) ferme; **hard upon**
de près, tout contre; **to rain hard** pleuvoir fort; **to try hard** bien essayer

hard′-and-fast′ *adj* strict, inflexible, établi

hard-bitten [ˈhɑrdˈbɪtən] *adj* tenace, dur à
cuire

hard′-boiled′ *adj* (*egg*) dur; (coll) dur,
inflexible

hard′bound edi′tion *s* édition *f* reliée

hard′ can′dy *s* bonbons *mpl*; **piece of hard
candy** bonbon *m*

hard′ cash′ *s* espèces *fpl* sonnantes

hard′ ci′der *s* cidre *m*

hard′ coal′ *s* houille *f* éclatante, anthracite
m

hard′ cop′y *s* (comp) fac-sim *m*

hard′ core′ *s* (*of supporters, opponents,
resistance*) noyau *m*, cercle *m*, centre *m*

hard′-core′ *adj* (*support, opposition*) inconditionnel

hard′-core′ pornog′raphy *s* pornographie *f*
(dite) dure

hard′cov′er *adj* (*hardbound*) relié ‖ *s* livre
m relié

hard′ drink′ s boissons fpl alcooliques, liqueurs fpl fortes

hard′ drink′er s grand buveur m

hard′-earned′ adj péniblement gagné

harden [′hɑrdən] tr durcir, endurcir ‖ intr se durcir, s'endurcir

hardening [′hɑrdənɪŋ] s durcissement m; (fig) endurcissement m

hard′ fact′ s fait m brutal; **hard facts** réalités fpl

hard-fought [′hɑrd′fɔt] adj acharné, chaudement disputé

hard′-head′ed adj positif, à la tête froide

hard′-heart′ed adj dur, sans compassion

hardihood [′hɑrdɪ,hʊd] s endurance f; courage m; audace f

hardiness [′hɑrdɪnɪs] s vigueur f

hard′ la′bor s travaux mpl forcés

hard′ land′ing s atterrissage m dur

hard′ luck′ s guigne f, malchance f

hardly [′hɑrdli] adv guère, à peine, ne . . . guère, e.g., **he hardly thinks of anything else** à peine pense-t-il à autre chose, il ne pense guère à autre chose; **hardly ever** presque jamais

hardness [′hɑrdnɪs] s dureté f

hard′ of hear′ing adj dur d'oreille; **the hard of hearing** les malentendants

hard′-pressed′ adj aux abois, gêné

hard′ rub′ber s caoutchouc m durci, ébonite f

hard′ sell′ s (coll) vente f à l'arraché

hard′-shell′ adj (clam) à carapace dure; (coll) opiniâtre

hard′ship′ s peine f; **hardships** privations fpl; fatigues fpl

hard′tack′ s biscuit m, biscotin m

hard′ times′ spl difficultés fpl, temps mpl difficiles

hard′ to please′ adj difficile à contenter, exigeant

hard′ up′ adj (coll) à court d'argent; **to be hard up for** (coll) être à court de

hard′ware′ s quincaillerie f; (trimmings) ferrure f; (comp) matériel m

hard′ware′man s (pl -men) quincaillier m

hard′ware store′ s quincaillerie f

hard-won [′hɑrd,wʌn] adj chèrement disputé, conquis de haute lutte

hard′wood′ s bois m dur; arbre m de bois dur

hard′wood floor′ s parquet m

har·dy [′hɑrdi] adj (comp -dier; super -diest) vigoureux, robuste; (rash) hardi; (hort) résistant

hare [hɛr] s lièvre m

hare′brained′ adj écervelé, farfelu

hare′lip′ s bec-de-lièvre m

harem [′hɛrəm] s harem m

hark [hɑrk] intr écouter; **to hark back to** en revenir à ‖ interj écoutez!

harken [′hɑrkən] intr—**to harken to** écouter

harlequin [′hɑrləkwɪn] s arlequin m

harlot [′hɑrlət] s prostituée f, fille f publique

harm [hɑrm] s mal m, dommage m ‖ tr nuire à, faire du mal à

harmful [′hɑrmfəl] adj nuisible

harmless [′hɑrmlɪs] adj inoffensif

harmonic [hɑr′mɑnɪk] adj harmonique

harmonica [hɑr′mɑnɪkə] s harmonica m

harmonious [hɑr′monɪ·əs] adj harmonieux

harmonize [′hɑrmə,naɪz] tr harmoniser ‖ intr s'harmoniser

harmo·ny [′hɑrməni] s (pl -nies) harmonie f

harness [′hɑrnɪs] s harnais m, harnachement m; **to die in the harness** (coll) mourir sous le harnais, mourir debout; **to get back in the harness** (coll) reprendre le collier ‖ tr harnacher; (e.g., a river) aménager, capter

har′ness mak′er s bourrelier m, harnacheur m

har′ness race′ s course f attelée

harp [hɑrp] s harpe f ‖ intr—**to harp on** rabâcher

harpist [′hɑrpɪst] s harpiste mf

harpoon [hɑr′pun] s harpon m ‖ tr harponner

harpsichord [′hɑrpsɪ,kɔrd] s clavecin m

har·py [′hɑrpi] s (pl -pies) harpie f

harrow [′hæro] s (agr) herse f ‖ tr tourmenter; (agr) herser

harrowing [′hæro·ɪŋ] adj horripilant

har·ry [′hæri] v (pret & pp -ried) tr harceler; (to devastate) ravager

harsh [hɑrʃ] adj (life, treatment, etc.) sévère, dur; (to the touch) rude; (to the taste) âpre; (to the ear) discordant

harshness [′hɑrʃnɪs] s dureté f, rudesse f; âpreté f

hart [hɑrt] s cerf m

harum-scarum [′hɛrəm′skɛrəm] adj & s écervelé ‖ adv en casse-cou

harvest [′hɑrvɪst] s récolte f; (of grain) moisson f ‖ tr récolter, moissonner ‖ intr faire la récolte or moisson

harvester [′hɑrvɪstər] s moissonneur m; (mach) moissonneuse f

har′vest home′ s fin f de la moisson; fête f de la moisson

har′vest moon′ s lune f des moissons

has-been [′hæz,bɪn] s (coll) vieille croûte f

hash [hæʃ] s hachis m ‖ tr hacher

hash′house′ s (slang) gargote f

hashish [′hæʃiʃ] s hachisch m

hasp [hæsp], [hɑsp] s moraillon m

hassle [′hæsəl] s (coll) querelle f, accrochage m

hassock [′hæsək] s pouf m

haste [hest] s hâte f; **in haste** à la hâte; **to make haste** se hâter

hasten [′hesən] tr hâter ‖ intr se hâter

hast·y [′hesti] adj (comp -ier; super -iest) hâtif, précipité; (rash) inconsidéré, emporté

hat [hæt] s chapeau m; **hat in hand** chapeau bas; **hats off to . . . !** chapeau bas devant . . . !; **to keep under one's hat** (coll) garder strictement pour soi; **to talk through one's hat** (coll) parler à tort et à travers; **to throw one's hat in the ring** (coll) descendre dans l'arène

hat′band′ s ruban m de chapeau

hat′ block′ s forme f à chapeaux

hat′box′ s carton m à chapeaux

hatch [hætʃ] s (brood) éclosion f; (trap door) trappe f; (lower half of door) demi-porte f; (opening in ship's deck) écoutille f; (hood over hatchway) capot m; (lid for opening in ship's deck) panneau m de descente; **down the hatch!** (bottoms up!) derrière la cravate! ‖ tr (eggs) couver, faire éclore; (a plot) ourdir, manigancer; (to hachure) hachurer ‖ intr éclore; (said of chicks) sortir de la coquille

hatch′back′ s (aut) hayon m

hat′check girl′ s préposée f au vestiaire

hatchet [′hætʃɪt] s hachette f; **to bury the hatchet** faire la paix

hatch′way′ s écoutille f

hate [het] s haine f ‖ tr haïr, détester; **to hate to** haïr de

hateful [′hetfəl] adj haïssable

hat′pin′ s épingle f à chapeau

hat′rack′ s porte-chapeaux m

hatred [′hetrɪd] s haine f

hat′shop′ s chapellerie f

hatter [′hætər] s chapelier m

haughtiness [′hɔtɪnɪs] s hauteur f

haugh·ty [′hɔti] adj (comp **-tier**; super **-tiest**) hautain, altier

haul [hɔl] s (pull, tug) effort m; (amount caught) coup m de filet, prise f; (distance covered) parcours m, distance f de transport ‖ tr (to tug) tirer; (com) transporter

haulage [′hɔlɪdʒ] s transport m; (cost) frais m de transport

haunch [hɔntʃ] s (hip) hanche f; (hind quarter of an animal) quartier m; (leg of animal used for food) cuissot m

haunt [hɔnt], [hɑnt] s lieu m fréquenté, rendez-vous m; (e.g., of criminals) repaire m ‖ tr (to obsess) hanter; (to frequent) fréquenter

haunt′ed house′ s maison f hantée par les fantômes

Havana [hə′vænə] s La Havane

have [hæv] s—**the haves and the have-nots** les riches et les pauvres ‖ v (3d pers **has** [hæz]; pret & pp **had** [hæd]) tr avoir; **to have** + inf faire + inf, e.g., **I shall have him go** je le ferai aller; **to have** + pp faire + inf, e.g., **I am going to have a suit made** je vais faire faire un complet; **to have it in for someone** garder un chien de sa chienne; **to have nothing to do with** n'avoir rien à voir avec; **to have on** (clothing) porter; **to have s.th. to** + inf avoir q.ch. à + inf, e.g., **I have a lot of work to do** j'ai beaucoup de travail à faire ‖ intr—**to have to** avoir à; devoir; falloir, e.g., **I have to go** il me faut aller; falloir que, e.g., **I have to read him the letter** il faut que je lui lise la lettre ‖ aux (to form compound past tenses) avoir, e.g., **I have run too fast** j'ai couru trop vite; (to form compound past tenses with

some intransitive verbs and all reflexive verbs) être, e.g., **they have arrived** elles sont arrivées; **to have just** + pp venir de + inf, e.g., **they have just returned** ils viennent de rentrer; e.g., **they had just returned** ils venaient de rentrer

have′lock s couvre-nuque m

haven [′hevən] s havre m, asile m

haversack [′hævər,sæk] s havresac m

havoc [′hævək] s ravage m; **to play havoc with** causer des dégâts à

haw [hɔ] s (bot) cenelle f ‖ tr & intr tourner à gauche ‖ interj dia!, à gauche!

Hawaiian [hə′waɪjən] adj hawaïen ‖ s Hawaïen m

Hawai′ian Is′lands spl îles fpl Hawaii

haw′-haw′ s rire m bête ‖ intr rire bêtement ‖ interj heu!

hawk [hɔk] s faucon m; (mortarboard) taloche f; (pol & fig) épervier m; (sharper) (coll) vautour m ‖ tr colporter; **to hawk up** expectorer ‖ intr chasser au faucon; (to hawk up phlegm) graillonner

hawker [′hɔkər] s colporteur m

hawk′ owl′ s chouette f épervière

hawks′bill tur′tle s caret m, caouane f

hawse [hɔz] s (hole) écubier m; (prow) nez m; (distance) évitage m

hawse′hole′ s écubier m

hawser [′hɔzər] s haussière f

haw′thorn′ s aubépine f

hay [he] s foin m; **to hit the hay** (slang) aller au plumard; **to make hay** faire les foins

hay′ fe′ver s rhume m des foins

hay′field′ s pré m à foin

hay′fork′ s fourche f à foin

hay′loft′ s fenil m, grenier m à foin

hay′mak′er s (boxing) coup m de poing en assommoir

haymow [′he,mau] s fenil m; approvisionnement m de foin

hay′rack′ s râtelier m

hay′ride′ s promenade f en charrette de foin

hay′seed′ s graine f de foin; (coll) culterreux m

hay′stack′ s meule f de foin

hay′wire′ adj (slang) en pagaille; **to go haywire** (slang) perdre la boussole ‖ s fil m de fer à lier le foin

hazard [′hæzərd] s risque m, danger m; (golf) obstacle m; **at all hazards** à tout hasard ‖ tr hasarder, risquer

hazardous [′hæzərdəs] adj hasardé

haze [hez] s brume f; (fig) obscurité f ‖ tr brimer

hazel [′hezəl] adj couleur de noisette, brun clair ‖ s (tree) noisetier m, avelinier m

ha′zel·nut′ s noisette f, aveline f

hazing [′hezɪŋ] s brimade f; (of university freshmen) bizutage m

ha·zy [′hezi] adj (comp **-zier**; super **-ziest**) brumeux; (notion) nébuleux, vague

H′-bomb′ s bombe f H

he [hi] pron pers il §87; lui §85; ce §82B; **he who** celui qui §83

head [hɛd] s tête f; (of bed) chevet m; (of boil) tête; (on glass of beer) mousse f; (of drum) peau f; (of cane) pomme f; (of coin) face f; (of barrel, cylinder, etc.) fond m; (of cylinder of automobile engine) culasse f; (of celery) pied m; (of ship) avant m; (of spear, ax, etc.) fer m; (of arrow) pointe f; (of business, department, etc.) chef m, directeur m; (of school) directeur, principal m; (of stream) source f; (of lake) tête; (of the table) bout m, haut bout; (of a match) bout; (caption) titre m; (decisive point) point m culminant, crise f; **at the head of** à la tête de; **from head to foot** des pieds à la tête; **head downwards** la tête en bas; **head of a pin** tête d'épingle; **head of cattle** bœuf m; **head over heels in love (with)** éperdument amoureux (de); **heads or tails** pile ou face; **over one's head** (beyond reach) hors de la portée de qn; (going to a higher authority) sans tenir compte de qn; **to be out of one's head** (coll) être timbré ou fou; **to go to one's head** monter à la tête de qn; **to keep one's head** garder son sang-froid; **to keep one's head above water** se tenir à flot; **to not make head or tail of it** n'y comprendre rien; **to put heads together** prendre conseil; **to take it into one's head to** avoir l'idée de, se mettre en tête de; **to win by a head** gagner d'une tête ‖ tr (to direct) diriger; (a procession) conduire, mener; (an organization; a class in school) être en tête de; (a list) venir en tête de; **to head off** détourner ‖ intr (said of grain) épier; **to head for** or **toward** se diriger vers

head′ache′ s mal m de tête
head′band′ s bandeau m
head′board′ s panneau m de tête
head′cheese′ s fromage m de tête
head′ cold′ s rhume m de cerveau
head′dress′ s coiffure f
head′first′ adv la tête la première; (impetuously) précipitamment
head′frame′ s (min) chevalement m
head′gear′ s garniture f de tête, couvre-chef m; (for protection) casque m
head′hunt′er s chasseur m de têtes; (for employment) prospecteur-placier m
heading [ˈhɛdɪŋ] s titre m; (of letter) en-tête m; (of chapter) tête f
headland [ˈhɛdlənd] s promontoire m
headless [ˈhɛdlɪs] adj sans tête; (leaderless) sans chef
head′light′ s (aut) phare m; (naut) fanal m; (rr) feu m d'avant
head′line′ s (of newspaper) manchette f; (of article) titre m; **to make the headlines** apparaître aux premières pages des journaux ‖ tr mettre en vedette
head′lin′er s (slang) tête f d'affiche
head′long′ adj précipité ‖ adv précipitamment
head′man′ s (pl -men′) chef m
head′mas′ter s principal m, directeur m
head′most′ adj de tête, premier

head′ of′fice s bureau m central; (director's office) direction f; (of a corporation) siège m social
head′ of hair′ s chevelure f
head′-on′ adj & adv de front, face à face
head′phones′ spl écouteurs mpl, casque m
head′piece′ s (any covering for head) casque m; (headset) écouteur m; (brains, judgment) tête f, caboche f; (typ) vignette f, en-tête m
head′quar′ters s bureau m central, siège m principal; (police station) commissariat m de police; (mil) quartier m général; (staff headquarters) (mil) état-major m
head′rest′ s appui-tête m
head′set′ s casque m, écouteurs mpl
heads′man s (pl -men) bourreau m
head′stone′ s pierre f tumulaire (à la tête d'une tombe); (cornerstone) pierre angulaire
head′strong′ adj têtu, entêté
head′wait′er s maître m d'hôtel
head′wa′ters spl cours m supérieur d'une rivière
head′way′ s progrès m, marche f avant; (between buses) intervalle m; (naut) erre f; **to make headway** progresser, aller de l'avant
head′wear′ s garniture f de tête
headwind [ˈhɛd,wɪnd] s vent m contraire, vent debout
head′word′ s (of a dictionary) mot m d'entrée, mot-souche m, entrée f, adresse f
head′work′ s travail m mental, travail de tête
head·y [ˈhɛdi] adj (comp -ier; super -iest) (wine) capiteux; (conduct) emporté; (news) excitant; (perfume) entêtant
heal [hil] tr guérir; (a wound) cicatriser ‖ intr guérir
healer [ˈhilər] s guérisseur m
healing [ˈhilɪŋ] s guérison f
health [hɛlθ] s santé f; **to be in good health** se porter bien, être en bonne santé; **to be in poor health** se porter mal, être en mauvaise santé; **to drink to the health of** boire à la santé de; **to enjoy radiant health** avoir une santé florissante; **to your health!** à votre santé!
health′-food store′ s magasin m diététique
healthful [ˈhɛlfəl] adj sain; (air, climate, etc.) salubre; (recreation, work, etc.) salutaire
health′ insur′ance s assurance f maladie-securité
health·y [ˈhɛlθi] adj (comp -ier; super -iest) sain; (air, climate, etc.) salubre; (person) bien portant; (appetite) robuste
heap [hip] s tas m, amas m ‖ tr entasser, amasser; **to heap** (honors, praise, etc.) **on s.o.** combler qn de; **to heap** (insults) **on s.o.** accabler qn de
hear [hɪr] v (pret & pp **heard** [hʌrd]) tr entendre, ouïr; **to hear it said** l'entendre dire; **to hear s.o. sing, to hear s.o. singing** entendre chanter qn, entendre qn qui chante; **to hear s.th. sung** entendre

chanter q.ch. ‖ *intr* entendre; **hear! hear!** très bien!, bravo!; **hear ye!** oyez!; **to hear about** entendre parler de; **to hear from** avoir des nouvelles de; **to hear of** entendre parler de; **to hear tell of** (coll) entendre parler de; **to hear that** entendre dire que

hearer [`hɪrər] *s* auditeur *m*; **hearers** auditoire *m*

hearing [`hɪrɪŋ] *s* (*sense*) l'ouïe *f*; (*act; opportunity to be heard*) audition *f*; (law) audience *f*; **in the hearing of** en la présence de, devant; **within hearing** à portée de la voix

hear'ing aid' *s* sonotone *m*, microvibrateur *m*, appareil *m* de correction auditive, appareil auditif; aide *f* auditive; (*fitted as part of eyeglasses*) lunettes *fpl* auditives

hear'say' *s* ouï-dire *m*

hear'say ev'idence *s* simples ouï-dire *mpl*

hearse [hʌrs] *s* corbillard *m*, char *m* funèbre

heart [hɑrt] *s* cœur *m*; (cards) cœur; **after one's heart** selon son cœur; **at heart** au fond; **by heart** par cœur; **heart and soul** corps et âme; **lift up your hearts!** haut les cœurs!; **to break the heart of** fendre le cœur à; **to die of a broken heart** mourir de chagrin; **to eat one's heart out** se ronger le cœur; **to eat to one's heart's content** manger tout son soûl; **to get to the heart of the matter** entrer dans le vif de la question; **to have one's heart in one's work** avoir le cœur à l'ouvrage; **to have one's heart in the right place** avoir le cœur bien placé; **to lose heart** perdre courage; **to open one's heart to** épancher son cœur à; **to take heart** prendre courage; **to take to heart** prendre à cœur; **to wear one's heart on one's sleeve** avoir le cœur sur les lèvres; **with a heavy heart** le cœur gros; **with all one's heart** de tout son cœur; **with one's heart in one's mouth** le gosier serré

heart'ache' *s* peine *f* de cœur

heart' attack' *s* crise *f* cardiaque

heart'beat' *s* battement *m* du cœur

heart'break' *s* crève-cœur *m*

heartbroken [`hɑrt,brokən] *adj* navré, chagriné

heart'burn' *s* pyrosis *m*

heart' cher'ry *s* guigne *f*

heart' disease' *s* maladie *f* de cœur

hearten [`hɑrtən] *tr* encourager

heart' fail'ure *s* arrêt *m* du cœur

heartfelt [`hɑrt,fɛlt] *adj* sincère, cordial, bien senti

hearth [hɑrθ] *s* foyer *m*, âtre *m*

hearth'stone' *s* pierre *f* de cheminée

heartily [`hɑrtɪli] *adv* de bon cœur, sincèrement

heartless [`hɑrtlɪs] *adj* sans cœur

heart' of stone' *s* (fig) cœur *m* de bronze

heart'-rend'ing *adj* désolant, navrant

heart'sick' *adj* désolé, chagrin

heart'strings' *spl* fibres *fpl*, replis *mpl* du cœur

heart'-to-heart' *adj* franc, ouvert; sérieux ‖ *adv* à cœur ouvert

heart' trans'plant *s* greffe *f* du cœur, transplantation *f* cardiaque

heart' trou'ble *s* maladie *f* de cœur

heart'wood' *s* bois *m* de cœur

heart·y [`hɑrti] *adj* (*comp* **-ier**; *super* **-iest**) cordial, sincère; (*meal*) copieux; (*laugh*) sonore; (*eater*) gros

heat [hit] *s* chaleur *f*; (*heating*) chauffage *m*; (*rut of animals*) rut *m*; (*in horse racing*) éliminatoire *f*; **in heat** en rut ‖ *tr* échauffer; (*e.g., a house*) chauffer ‖ *intr* s'échauffer; **to heat up** chauffer

heated *adj* chauffé; (fig) chaud, échauffé

heater [`hitər] *s* (*for food*) réchaud *m*; (*for heating house*) calorifère *m*

heath [hiθ] *s* bruyère *f*

hea·then [`hiðən] *adj* païen ‖ *s* (*pl* **-then** or **-thens**) païen *m*

heathendom [`hiðəndəm] *s* paganisme *m*

heather [`hɛðər] *s* bruyère *f*

heating [`hitɪŋ] *adj* échauffant ‖ *s* chauffage *m*

heat'ing oil' *s* fuel *m*

heat' light'ning *s* éclairs *mpl* de chaleur

heat' pump' *s* pompe *f* de chaleur

heat' shield' *s* (rok) bouclier *m* contre la chaleur, bouclier antithermique

heat'stroke' *s* insolation *f*, coup *m* de chaleur

heat' wave' *s* vague *f* de chaleur; (phys) onde *f* calorifique

heave [hiv] *s* soulèvement *m*; **heaves** (vet) pousse *f* ‖ *v* (*pret & pp* **heaved** or **hove** [hov]) *tr* soulever; (*to throw*) lancer; (*a sigh*) pousser; (*the anchor*) lever ‖ *intr* se soulever; faire des efforts pour vomir; (*said of bosom*) palpiter

heaven [`hɛvən] *s* ciel *m*; **for heaven's sake** pour l'amour de Dieu; **Heaven** le ciel; **heavens** cieux *mpl*, ciel

heavenly [`hɛvənli] *adj* céleste

heav'enly bod'y *s* corps *m* céleste

heav·y [`hɛvi] *adj* (*comp* **-ier**; *super* **-iest**) lourd, pesant; (*heart; crop; eater; baggage; rain, sea, weather*) gros; (*meal*) copieux; (*sleep*) profond; (*work*) pénible; (*book, reading, etc.*) indigeste; (*parts*) (theat) tragique, sombre ‖ *adv* lourd, lourdement; **to hang heavy on** peser sur

heav'y drink'er *s* fort buveur *m*

heav'y·du'ty *adj* extra-fort, à grand rendement

heav'y-heart'ed *adj* au cœur lourd

heav'y·set' *adj* de forte carrure, costaud

heav'y wa'ter *s* eau *f* lourde

heav'y·weight' *s* (boxing) poids *m* lourd

Hebraist [`hibre·ɪst] *s* hébraïsant *m*

Hebrew [`hibru] *adj* hébreu, hébraïque ‖ *s* (*language*) hébreu *m*, langue *f* hébraïque; (*man*) Hébreu *m*, Juif *m*; (*woman*) Juive *f*

hecatomb [`hɛkə,tom] *s* hécatombe *f*

heckle [`hɛkəl] *tr* interrompre bruyamment, chahuter; (*on account of trifles*) asticoter, harceler

heckler [ˈhɛklər] s interrupteur m impertinent, interpellateur m

hectic [ˈhɛktɪk] adj fou, bouleversant

hedge [hɛdʒ] s haie f ‖ tr entourer d'une haie; **to hedge in** entourer de tous côtés ‖ intr chercher des échappatoires, hésiter; (com) faire la contrepartie

hedge′ cut′ter s taille-haies m invar

hedge′hog′ s hérisson m; (porcupine) porc-épic m

hedge′hop′ v (pret & pp -hopped; ger -hopping) intr (aer) voler en rasemottes

hedge′hop′per s rase-mottes m invar

hedgerow [ˈhɛdʒ‚ro] s bordure f de haies, haie f vive

heed [hid] s attention f, soin m; **to take heed** prendre garde ‖ tr faire attention à, prendre garde à ‖ intr faire attention, prendre garde

heedful [ˈhidfəl] adj attentif

heedless [ˈhidlɪs] adj inattentif

heehaw [ˈhi‚hɔ] s hi-han m ‖ intr pousser des hi-hans

heel [hil] s talon m; (slang) goujat m; **to be down at the heel** traîner la savate; **to cool one's heels** (coll) croquer le marmot, faire le pied de grue, faire le poireau

heft·y [ˈhɛfti] adj (comp -ier; super -iest) costaud; (heavy) pesant

hegira [hɪˈdʒaɪrə] s fuite f précipitée, hégire f; **Hegira** (rel) hégire

heifer [ˈhɛfər] s génisse f

height [haɪt] s hauteur f; (e.g., of folly) comble m

heighten [ˈhaɪtən] tr rehausser; (to increase the amount of) augmenter; (to set off, bring out) relever ‖ intr se rehausser; augmenter

heinous [ˈhenəs] adj odieux, atroce

heir [ɛr] s héritier m; **to become the heir of** hériter de

heir′ appar′ent s (pl **heirs apparent**) héritier m présomptif

heiress [ˈɛrɪs] s héritière f

heir′loom′ s meuble m, bijou m, or souvenir m de famille

Helen [ˈhɛlən] s Hélène f

helicopter [ˈhɛlɪ‚kɑptər] s hélicoptère m

hel′icopter land′ing s hélistation f

heliport [ˈhɛlɪ‚pɔrt] s héliport m

helium [ˈhilɪ·əm] s hélium m

helix [ˈhilɪks] s (pl **helixes** or **helices** [ˈhɛlɪ‚siz]) hélice f; (anat) hélix m

hell [hɛl] s enfer m; **a hell of a lot of** tout un tas de; **come hell or high water** en dépit de tout, quoiqu'il arrive; **go to hell!** va te faire voir!, la barbe!; **to give s.o. hell** passer une engueulade à qn; **to raise hell** faire la foire

hell′bent′ adj (slang) hardi; **hellbent on** (slang) acharné en diable à

hell′cat′ s (bad-tempered woman) harpie f; (witch) sorcière f

Hellenic [ˈhɛlin] s Hellène mf

Hellenic [hɛˈlɛnɪk], [hɛˈlinɪk] adj hellène

hell′fire′ s feu m de l'enfer

hellish [ˈhɛlɪʃ] adj infernal

hel·lo [hɛˈlo] s (pl -los) bonjour m ‖ interj bonjour!; (on telephone) allô!

helm [hɛlm] s gouvernail m

helmet [ˈhɛlmɪt] s casque m

helms′man s (pl -men) homme m de barre

help [hɛlp] s aide f, secours m; (workers) main-d'œuvre f; (office workers) employés mpl; (domestic servants) domestiques mfpl; **help wanted** (public sign) offres d'emploi, on embauche, recrutons; **there's no help for it** il n'y a pas de remède ‖ tr aider, secourir; **so help me God!** que Dieu me juge!; **to help down** aider à descendre; **to help oneself** se défendre; (to food) se servir; **to not be able to help** ne pouvoir s'empêcher de ‖ intr aider ‖ interj au secours!

helper [ˈhɛlpər] s aide mf, assistant m

helpful [ˈhɛlpfəl] adj utile; (person) serviable, secourable

helping [ˈhɛlpɪŋ] s (of food) portion f

helpless [ˈhɛlplɪs] adj (weak) faible; (powerless) impuissant; (penniless) sans ressource; (confused) désemparé; (situation) sans recours

helter-skelter [ˈhɛltərˈskɛltər] adj désordonné ‖ s débandade f ‖ adv pêle-mêle

hem [hɛm] s ourlet m, bord m ‖ v (pret & pp hemmed; ger hemming) tr ourler, border; **to hem in** entourer; cerner ‖ intr faire un ourlet; **to hem and haw** ânonner; (fig) tourner autour du pot ‖ interj hum!

hemisphere [ˈhɛmɪ‚sfɪr] s hémisphère m

hemistich [ˈhɛmɪ‚stɪk] s hémistiche m

hem′line′ s ourlet m de la jupe

hem′lock′ s (Tsuga canadensis) sapin m du Canada, pruche f; (herb and poison) ciguë f

hemoglobin [‚hɛməˈglobɪn] s hémoglobine f

hemophilia [‚hɛməˈfɪlɪ·ə] s hémophilie f

hemophiliac [‚hɛməˈfɪlɪ·æk] s hémophile mf

hemorrhage [ˈhɛmərɪdʒ] s hémorragie f

hemorrhoids [ˈhɛmə‚rɔɪdz] spl hémorroïdes fpl

hemostat [ˈhɛmə‚stæt] s hémostatique m

hemp [hɛmp] s chanvre m

hem′stitch′ s ourlet m à jour ‖ tr ourler à jour ‖ intr faire un ourlet à jour

hen [hɛn] s poule f

hence [hɛns] adv d'ici; (therefore) d'où, donc

hence′forth′ adv désormais, dorénavant

hench·man [ˈhɛntʃmən] s (pl -men) partisan m, acolyte m, complice mf

hen′coop′ s cage f à poules, épinette f

hen′house′ s poulailler m

henna [ˈhɛnə] s henné m ‖ tr teindre au henné

hen′peck′ tr mener par le bout du nez

hep [hɛp] adj (slang) à la page, dans le train; **to be hep to** (slang) être au courant de

hepatitis [‚hɛpəˈtaɪtɪs] s (pathol) hépatite f

her [hʌr] adj poss son §88 ‖ pron pers elle §85; la §87; lui §87

herald ['hɛrəld] s héraut m; (fig) avant-coureur m ‖ tr annoncer; **to herald in** introduire

herald·ry ['hɛrəldri] s (pl **-ries**) héraldique f, blason m

herb [ʌrb], [hʌrb] s herbe f; (pharm) herbe médicinale or officinale; **herbs for seasoning** fines herbes

herbicide ['hʌrbɪ,saɪd] s herbicide m

herculean [hʌr'kjulɪ·ən] adj herculéen

herd [hʌrd] s troupeau m ‖ tr rassembler en troupeau ‖ intr—**to herd together** s'attrouper

herds′man s (pl **-men**) pâtre m; (of sheep) berger m; (of cattle) bouvier m

here [hɪr] adv ici; **from here to there** d'ici là; **here and there** çà et là, par-ci par-là; **here below** ici-bas; **here is** or **here are** voici; **here lies** ci-gît; **that′s neither here nor there** ça n'a rien à y voir ‖ interj tenez!; (answering roll call) présent!

hereabouts ['hɪrə,bauts] adv près d'ici

here·af′ter s—**the hereafter** l'autre monde ‖ adv désormais, à l'avenir; (farther along) ci-après

here·by′ adv par ce moyen, par ceci; (in legal language) par les présentes

hereditary [hɪ'rɛdɪ,tɛri] adj héréditaire

heredi·ty [hɪ'rɛdɪti] s (pl **-ties**) hérédité f

here·in′ adv ici; (on this point) en ceci; (in this writing) ci-inclus

here·of′ adv de ceci, à ce sujet

here·on′ adv là-dessus

here·sy ['hɛrəsi] s (pl **-sies**) hérésie f

heretic ['hɛrətɪk] adj & s hérétique mf

heretical [hɪ'rɛtɪkəl] adj hérétique

heretofore [,hɪrtu'for] adv jusqu'ici

here·upon′ adv là-dessus

here·with′ adv ci-joint, avec ceci

heritage ['hɛrɪtɪdʒ] s héritage m

hermetic(al) [hʌr'mɛtɪk(əl)] adj hermétique

hermit ['hʌrmɪt] s ermite m

hermitage ['hʌrmɪtɪdʒ] s ermitage m

herni·a ['hʌrnɪ·ə] s (pl **-as** or **-ae** [,i]) hernie f

he·ro ['hɪro] s (pl **-roes**) héros m

heroic [hɪ'ro·ɪk] adj héroïque ‖ **heroics** spl (verse) vers m héroïque; (language) grandiloquence f

heroin ['hɛro·ɪn] s héroïne f

her′oin ad′dict s héroïnomane mf

heroine ['hɛro·ɪn] s héroïne f

heroism ['hɛro,ɪzəm] s héroïsme m

heron ['hɛrən] s héron m

herpes ['hʌr,piz] s (pathol) herpès m

herring ['hɛrɪŋ] s hareng m

her′ring·bone′ s (in fabrics) point m de chausson; (in hardwood floors) parquet m à batons rompus; (in design) arête f de hareng

hers [hʌrz] pron poss le sien §89

her·self′ pron pers elle §85; soi §85; elle-même §86; se §87

hesitan·cy ['hɛzɪtənsi] s (pl **-cies**) hésitation f

hesitant ['hɛzɪtənt] adj hésitant

hesitate ['hɛzɪ,tet] intr hésiter

hesitation [,hɛzɪ'teʃən] s hésitation f

heterodox ['hɛtərə,daks] adj hétérodoxe

heterodyne ['hɛtərə,daɪn] adj hétérodyne

heterogeneous [,hɛtərə'dʒɪnɪ·əs] adj hétérogène

hew [hju] v (pret **hewed**; pp **hewed** or **hewn**) tr tailler, couper; **to hew down** abattre ‖ intr—**to hew close to the line** (coll) agir dans les règles, être très méticuleux

hex [hɛks] s porte-guigne m ‖ tr porter la guigne à

hey [he] interj hé!; attention!

hey′day′ s meilleure période f, fleur f

hi [haɪ] interj salut!

hia·tus [haɪ'etəs] s (pl **-tuses** or **-tus**) (gap) lacune f; (in a text; in verse) hiatus m

hibernate ['haɪbər,net] intr hiberner

hibiscus [hɪ'bɪskəs] s hibiscus m, ketmie f

hiccough or **hiccup** ['hɪkəp] s hoquet m ‖ intr hoqueter

hick [hɪk] adj (pej) péquenaud ‖ s (pej) péquenaud m, plouc m

hicko·ry ['hɪkəri] s (pl **-ries**) hickory m

hidden ['hɪdən] adj caché, dérobée; (mysterious) occulte

hide [haɪd] s peau f, cuir m ‖ v (pret **hid** [hɪd]; pp **hid** or **hidden** ['hɪdən]) tr cacher; **to hide s.th. from** cacher q.ch. à ‖ intr se cacher; **to hide from** se cacher à

hide′-and-seek′ s cache-cache m

hide′bound′ adj à l'esprit étroit

hideous ['hɪdɪ·əs] adj hideux

hide′-out′ s (coll) repaire m, planque f

hiding ['haɪdɪŋ] s dissimulation f; (punishment) (coll) raclée f, rossée f; **in hiding** caché

hid′ing place′ s cachette f

hierar·chy ['haɪ·ə,rɑrki] s (pl **-chies**) hiérarchie f

hieroglyphic [,haɪ·ərə'glɪfɪk] adj hiéroglyphique ‖ s hiéroglyphe m

hi-fi ['haɪ'faɪ] adj (coll) de haute fidélité ‖ s (coll) haute fidélité f

hi′-fi′ fan′ s (coll) fanatique mf de la haute fidélité

high [haɪ] adj haut; (river, price, rate, temperature, opinion) élevé; (fever, wind) fort; (sea, wind) gros; (cheekbones) saillant; (sound) aigu; (coll) gris; (culin) avancé; **high and dry** à sec; **high and mighty** prétentieux; **to be high** (coll) avoir son pompon ‖ s (aut) prise f directe; **on high** en haut, dans le ciel ‖ adv haut; à un prix élevé; **high and low** partout; **to aim high** viser haut; **to come high** se vendre cher

high′ al′tar s maître-autel m

high′ball′ s whisky m à l'eau

high′ blood′ pres′sure s hypertension f

high′born′ adj de haute naissance

high′boy′ s chiffonnier m semainier

high′brow′ adj & s (slang) intellectuel m

high′ chair′ s chaise f d'enfant

high′ command′ s haut commandement m

high′ cost of liv′ing s cherté f de la vie

high′er educa′tion [ˈhaɪ·ər] s enseignement m supérieur

high′er-up′ s (coll) supérieur m hiérarchique

high′est bid′der [ˈhaɪ·ɪst] s dernier enchérisseur m

high′ explo′sive s haut explosif m, explosif puissant

highfalutin [ˌhaɪfəˈlutən] adj (coll) pompeux, ampoulé

high′ fidel′ity s haute fidélité f

high′ fre′quency s haute fréquence f

high′ gear′ s (aut) prise f directe

high′-grade′ adj de qualité supérieure

high′-hand′ed adj autoritaire, arbitraire

high′ hat′ s chapeau m haut de forme

high′-hat′ adj (coll) snob, poseur ‖ **high′-hat′** v (pret & pp **-hatted**; ger **-hatting**) tr (coll) traiter de haut en bas

high′-heeled′ adj à talons hauts

high′ horse′ s raideur f hautaine; **to get up on one's high horse** monter sur ses grands chevaux

high′ jinks′ [ˌdʒɪŋks] s (slang) clownerie f, drôlerie f

high′ jump′ s saut m en hauteur

high′-key′ adj (phot) lumineux

highland [ˈhaɪlənd] s pays m de montagne; **highlands** hautes terres fpl

high′-level lan′guage s (comp) langage m évolué

high′ life′ s grand monde m

high′ light′ s (big moment) clou m, instant m le plus marquant, point m culminant; (of a career) grand succès m; **highlights** (in a picture) clairs mpl ‖ tr mettre en vedette

highly [ˈhaɪli] adv hautement; (very) extrêmement, fort; haut, e.g., **highly colored** haut en couleur; **to think highly of** avoir une bonne opinion de

High′ Mass′ s grand-messe f

high′-mind′ed adj magnanime, noble

highness [ˈhaɪnɪs] s hauteur f; **Highness** Altesse f

high′ noon′ s plein midi m

high′-oc′tane adj à indice d'octane élevé

high′-pitched′ adj aigu; (roof) à forte pente

high′-powered′ adj de haute puissance

high′-pres′sure adj à haute pression; (fig) dynamique, persuasif ‖ tr (coll) gonfler à bloc

high′-priced′ adj de prix élevé

high′ priest′ s grand prêtre m; (fig) pontife m

high′road′ s grand-route f; (fig) bonne voie f

high′ school′ s école f secondaire publique; (in France) lycée m

high′-school stu′dent s lycéen m; collégien m

high′ sea′ s houle f, grosse mer f; **high seas** haute mer

high′ soci′ety s la haute société, le beau monde

high′-sound′ing adj pompeux, prétentieux

high′-speed′ adj à grande vitesse, en accéléré

high′-spir′ited adj fougueux, plein d'entrain

high′ spir′its spl gaieté f, entrain m

high′ stakes′ spl—**to play for high stakes** jouer gros jeu

high-strung [ˈhaɪˈstrʌŋ] adj tendu, nerveux

high′-test′ gas′oline s supercarburant m

high′ tide′ s marée f haute, haute marée

high′ time′ s heure f, e.g., **it is high time for you to go** c'est certainement l'heure de votre départ; (slang) bombance f, bombe f

high′ trea′son s haute trahison f

high′ volt′age s haute tension f

high wa′ter s marée f haute, hautes eaux fpl

high′way′ s grand-route f

high′way commis′sion s administration f des ponts et chaussées

high′way′man s (pl **-men**) voleur m de grand chemin

high′way map′ s carte f routière

hijack [ˈhaɪˌdʒæk] tr (coll) arrêter et voler sur la route; (coll) saisir de force; (an airplane) (coll) détourner

hijacker [ˈhaɪˌdʒækər] s (coll) bandit m, bandit de grand chemin; (coll) pirate m de l'air, pirate aérien

hijacking [ˈhaɪˌdʒækɪŋ] s (coll) piraterie f aérienne, détournement m

hike [haɪk] s excursion f à pied, voyage m pédestre; (e.g., in rent) hausse f ‖ tr hausser, faire monter ‖ intr faire de longues promenades à pied

hiker [ˈhaɪkər] s excursionniste mf à pied, touriste mf pédestre

hilarious [hɪˈlɛrɪ·əs], [haɪˈlɛrɪ·əs] adj hilare, gai; (joke) hilarant

hill [hɪl] s colline f, coteau m; (incline) côte f; (mil) cote f; **over hill and dale** par monts et par vaux ‖ tr (a plant) butter, chausser

hill′bil′ly s (pl **-lies**) montagnard m rustique

hillock [ˈhɪlək] s tertre m, butte f

hill′side′ s versant m, coteau m

hill·y [ˈhɪli] adj (comp **-ier**; super **-iest**) montueux, accidenté; (steep) en pente, à fortes pentes

hilt [hɪlt] s poignée f; **up to the hilt** jusqu'à la garde

him [hɪm] pron pers lui §85, §87; le §87

him·self′ pron lui §85; soi §85; lui-même §86; se §87

hind [haɪnd] adj postérieur, de derrière ‖ s biche f

hind′ end′ s (slang) train m

hinder [ˈhɪndər] tr empêcher

hind′ legs′ spl pattes fpl de derrière

hind′most adj dernier, ultime

hind′quar′ter s arrière-train m, train m de derrière; (of horse) arrière-main m

hindrance [ˈhɪndrəns] s empêchement m

hind′sight′ s (of firearm) hausse f; compréhension f tardive

Hindu [ˈhɪndu] adj hindou ‖ s Hindou m

hinge [hɪndʒ] s charnière f, gond m; (of mollusk) charnière; (bb) onglet m ‖ intr—**to hinge on** axer sur, dépendre de

hin·ny [ˈhɪni] s (pl **-nies**) bardot m

hint [hɪnt] s insinuation f; (small quantity) soupçon m; **to take the hint** comprendre à demi-mot, accepter le conseil ‖ tr insinuer ‖ intr procéder par insinuation; **to hint at** laisser entendre

hinterland [ˈhɪntərˌlænd] s arrière-pays m

hip [hɪp] adj (slang) à la page, dans le train; **to be hip to** (slang) être au courant de ‖ s hanche f; (of roof) arête f

hip′bone′ s os m coxal, os de la hanche

hip′ boots′ spl cuissardes fpl

hipped adj—**to be hipped on** (coll) avoir la manie de

hippety-hop [ˈhɪpɪtɪˈhɑp] adv (coll) en sautillant

hip·po [ˈhɪpo] s (pl **-pos**) (coll) hippopotame m

hippopota·mus [ˌhɪpəˈpɑtəməs] s (pl **-muses** or **-mi** [ˌmaɪ]) hippopotame m

hip′ roof′ s toit m en croupe

hire [haɪr] s (salary) gages mpl; (renting) louage m; **for hire** à louer; (public sign) libre; **in the hire of** aux gages de ‖ tr (a person) engager, embaucher; (to rent) louer, prendre en location ‖ intr—**to hire out** (said of person) se louer, entrer en service

hired′ man′ s (pl **men′**) s (coll) valet m de ferme, garçon m de ferme

hireling [ˈhaɪrlɪŋ] adj & s mercenaire m

hiring [ˈhaɪrɪŋ] s embauchage m

his [hɪz] adj poss son §88 ‖ pron poss le sien §89

Hispanic [hɪsˈpænɪk] adj hispanique

hiss [hɪs] s sifflement m ‖ tr & intr siffler

hist [hɪst] interj psitt!, pst!

histology [hɪsˈtɑlədʒi] s histologie f

historian [hɪsˈtɔri·ən] s historien m

historic(al) [hɪsˈtɔrɪk(əl)] adj historique

histo·ry [ˈhɪstəri] s (pl **-ries**) histoire f

histrionic [ˌhɪstrɪˈɑnɪk] adj théâtral ‖ **histrionics** s art m du théâtre; (fig) attitude f spectaculaire

hit [hɪt] s coup m; (blow that hits its mark) coup au but, coup heureux; (sarcastic remark) coup de patte, trait m satirique; (on the hit parade) tube m; (baseball) coup de batte; (theat) succès m, spectacle m très couru; (coll) réussite f; **to make a hit** (coll) faire sensation ‖ v (pret & pp **hit**; ger **hitting**) tr frapper; (the mark) atteindre; (e.g., a car) heurter, heurter contre; (to move the emotions of) toucher; **to hit it off** (coll) s'entendre, se trouver d'accord ‖ intr frapper; **to hit on** tomber sur, trouver

hit′-and-run′ driv′er s chauffard m qui abandonne la scène d'un accident, qui prend la fuite

hitch [hɪtʃ] s saccade f, secousse f; obstacle m, difficulté f; (knot) nœud m, e.g., **timber hitch** nœud de bois; **without a hitch**

sans accroc ‖ tr accrocher; (naut) nouer; **to hitch up** (e.g., a horse) atteler

hitch′hike′ intr (coll) faire de l'auto-stop

hitch′hik′er s auto-stoppeur m

hitch′hik′ing s auto-stop m

hitch′ing post′ s poteau m d'attache

hither [ˈhɪðər] adv ici; **hither and thither** çà et là

hith′er·to′ adv jusqu'ici, jusqu'à présent

hit′-or-miss′ adj capricieux, éventuel

hit′ parade′ s (coll) chansons fpl populaires du moment, palmarès m

hit′ rec′ord s (coll) disque m à succès

hive [haɪv] s ruche f; **hives** (pathol) urticaire f

hoard [hord] s entassement m, trésor m ‖ tr accumuler secrètement, thésauriser ‖ intr accumuler, entasser, thésauriser

hoarding [ˈhordɪŋ] s accumulation f secrète, thésaurisation f

hoarfrost [ˈhorˌfrɔst] s givre m, gelée f blanche

hoarse [hors] adj enroué, rauque

hoarseness [ˈhorsnɪs] s enrouement m

hoar·y [ˈhori] adj (comp **-ier**; super **-iest**) chenu, blanchi

hoax [hoks] s mystification f, canard m ‖ tr mystifier

hob [hɑb] s (of fireplace) plaque f; **to play hob** (coll) causer des ennuis; **to play hob with** (coll) bouleverser

hobble [ˈhɑbəl] s (limp) boitillement m; (rope used to tie legs of animal) entrave f ‖ tr faire boiter; (e.g., a horse) entraver ‖ intr boiter, clocher

hob·by [ˈhɑbi] s (pl **-bies**) distraction f, violon m d'Ingres; (orn) hobereau m; **to ride one's hobby** enfourcher son dada

hob′by·horse′ s cheval m de bois

hob′gob′lin s lutin m; (bogy) épouvantail m

hob′nail′ s caboche f

hob·nob [ˈhɑbˌnɑb] v (pret & pp **-nobbed**; ger **-nobbing**) intr trinquer ensemble; **to hobnob with** être à tu et à toi avec

ho·bo [ˈhobo] s (pl **-bos** or **-boes**) chemineau m, vagabond m

hock [hɑk] s (of horse) jarret m; (wine) vin m du Rhin; (pawn) (coll) gage m; **in hock** (coll) au clou; (in prison) (coll) au bloc ‖ tr couper le jarret à; (to pawn) (coll) mettre en gage, mettre au clou

hockey [ˈhɑki] s hockey m

hock′ey play′er s hockeyeur m

hock′shop′ s (slang) mont-de-piété m, clou m

hocus-pocus [ˈhokəsˈpokəs] s tour m de passe-passe; (meaningless formula) abracadabra m

hod [hɑd] s oiseau m, auge f

hod′ car′rier s aide-maçon m

hodgepodge [ˈhɑdʒˌpɑdʒ] s salmigondis m, méli-mélo m

hoe [ho] s houe f, binette f ‖ tr houer, biner

hog [hɔg] s pourceau m, porc m; (pig) cochon ‖ v (pret & pp **hogged**; ger **hogging**) tr (slang) s'emparer de, saisir avidement

hog′back′ *s* dos *m* d'âne
hoggish [`hɔgɪʃ] *adj* glouton
hogs′head′ *s* barrique *f*
hog′wash′ *s* eaux *fpl* grasses; vinasse *f*; (fig) boniments *mpl* à la noix de coco
hoist [hɔɪst] *s* monte-charge *m*, grue *f*; (*shove*) poussée *f* vers le haut ‖ *tr* lever, guinder; (*a flag, sail, boat, etc.*) hisser
hoity-toity [`hɔɪti`tɔɪti] *adj* hautain; **to be hoity-toity** le prendre de haut
hokum [`hokəm] *s* (coll) boniments *mpl*, fumisterie *f*
hold [hold] *s* (*grasp*) prise *f*; (*handle*) poignée *f*, manche *m*; (*domination*) pouvoir *m*, autorité *f*; (mus) point *m* d'orgue; (naut) cale *f*; **hold for arrival** (*formula on envelope*) garder jusqu'à l'arrivée; **to be on hold** (telp) être en ligne, attendre; **to get hold of** (*s.th.*) trouver; (*s.o.*) contacter; **to take hold of** empoigner, saisir ‖ *v* (*pret & pp* held [hɛld]) *tr* tenir; (*one's breath; s.o.'s attention*) retenir; (*to contain*) contenir; (*a job; a title*) avoir, posséder; (*e.g., a university chair*) occuper; (*a fort*) défendre; (*a note*) (mus) tenir, prolonger; **to be held to be** . . . passer pour . . . ; **to hold** (telp) rester en ligne, attendre; **to hold back** or **in** retenir; **to hold one's own** rivaliser, se défendre; **to hold out** tendre, offrir; **to hold over** continuer, remettre; **to hold s.o. to be** . . . tenir qn pour . . . ; **to hold s.o. to his word** obliger qn à tenir sa promesse; **to hold up** (*to delay*) retarder; (*to keep from falling*) retenir, soutenir; (*to rob*) (coll) voler à main armée ‖ *intr* (*to hold good*) rester valable, rester en vigueur; **hold on!** (telp) restez en ligne!; **to hold back** se retenir, hésiter; **to hold forth** disserter; **to hold off** se tenir à distance; **to hold on** or **out** tenir bon; **to hold on to** s'accrocher à, se cramponner à; **to hold out for** insister pour
holder [`holdər] *s* possesseur *m*; (*of stock*) porteur *m*; (*of stock; of a record*) détenteur *m*; (*of degree, fellowship, etc.*) impétrant *m*; (*for a cigarette*) porte-cigarettes *m*; (*of a post, a right, etc.*) titulaire *mf*; (*for holding, e.g., a hot dish*) poignée *f*
holding [`holdɪŋ] *s* possession *f*; **holdings** valeurs *fpl*; (*of an investor*) portefeuille *m*; (*of a landlord*) propriétés *fpl*
hold′ing bay′ *s* (aer) aire *f* d'attente
hold′ing com′pany *s* holding trust *m*, holding *m*, société *f* d'unigestion
hold′ing pat′tern *s* (aer) trajectoire *f* d'attente
hold′up′ *s* (*stop, delay*) arrêt *m*; (coll) attaque *f* à main armée, hold-up *m*; **what's the holdup?** (coll) qu'est-ce qu'on attend?
hole [hol] *s* trou *m*; **in the hole** (coll) dans l'embarras; **to burn a hole in s.o.'s pocket** (coll) brûler la poche à qn; **to get s.o. out of a hole** (coll) tirer qn d'un mauvais pas; **to pick holes in** (coll)

trouver à redire à, démolir; **to wear holes in** (*e.g., a garment*) trouer ‖ *intr*—**to hole up** se terrer
holiday [`hɑlɪ,de] *s* jour *m* de fête, jour férié; (*vacation*) vacances *fpl*
holiness [`holɪnɪs] *s* sainteté *f*; **His Holiness** Sa Sainteté
holla [`hɑlə], [hə`lɑ] *interj* holà!
Holland [`hɑlənd] *s* Hollande *f*; la Hollande
Hollander [`hɑləndər] *s* Hollandais *m*
hollow [`hɑlo] *adj & s* creux *m* ‖ *adv*—**to beat all hollow** (coll) battre à plate couture ‖ *tr* creuser
hol·ly [`hɑli] *s* (*pl* -**lies**) houx *m*
hol′ly·hock′ *s* primerose *f*, rose *f* trémière
holm′ oak′ [hom] *s* yeuse *f*
holocaust [`hɑlə,kɔst] *s* (*sacrifice*) holocauste *m*; (*disaster*) sinistre *m*
holster [`holstər] *s* étui *m*; (*on saddle*) fonte *f*
ho·ly [`holi] *adj* (*comp* -**lier**; *super* -**liest**) saint; (*e.g., water*) bénit
Ho′ly Ghost′ *s* Saint-Esprit *m*
Ho′ly or′ders *spl* ordres *mpl* sacrés
Ho′ly Scrip′ture *s* l'Écriture *f* Sainte
Ho′ly See′ *s* Saint-Siège *m*
Ho′ly Sep′ulcher *s* Saint Sépulcre *m*
Ho′ly Spir′it *s* Saint-Esprit *m*
ho′ly wa′ter *s* eau *f* bénite
Ho′ly Writ′ *s* l'Écriture *f* Sainte
homage [`hɑmɪdʒ] *s* hommage *m*
home [hom] *adj* (*family*) domestique, de famille; (econ, pol) national, du pays ‖ *s* foyer *m*, chez-soi *m*, domicile *m*; (*house*) maison *f*; (*of the arts; native land*) patrie *f*; (*for the sick, poor, etc.*) asile *m*, foyer, hospice *m*; **at home** à la maison; (*at ease*) à l'aise; **make yourself at home** faites comme chez vous ‖ *adv* à la maison; **to see s.o. home** raccompagner qn jusqu'à chez lui; **to strike home** frapper juste, toucher au vif
home′ address′ *s* adresse *f* personnelle; (*on a form*) domicile *m* (permanent)
home′-baked′ *adj* fait à la maison
home′bod′y *s* (*pl* -**ies**) casanier *m*, pantouflard *m*
homebred [`hom,brɛd] *adj* élevé à la maison; du pays, indigène
home′-brew′ *s* boisson *f* faite à la maison
home′-care nurs′ing *s* soins *mpl* à domicile
home′com′ing *s* retour *m* au foyer; (*at university, church, etc.*) journée *f* or semaine *f* des anciens
home′ comput′er *s* ordinateur *m* domestique, ordinateur familial, ordinateur maison
home′ coun′try *s* pays *m* natal
home′ deliv′ery *s* livraison *f* à domicile
home′ econom′ics *s* économie *f* domestique; (*instruction*) enseignement *m* ménager
home′ front′ *s* théâtre *m* d'opérations à l'intérieur du pays
home′ ground′ *s* domaine *m*, terrain *m*

home'-grown' *adj* (*e.g., vegetables*) du jardin

home'land' *s* patrie *f*, pays *m* natal

homeless [ˈhomlɪs] *adj* sans foyer

home' life' *s* vie *f* familiale

home'like' *adj* familial, comme chez soi

home'-lov'ing *adj* casanier

home·ly [ˈhomli] *adj* (*comp* **-lier**; *super* **-liest**) (*not good-looking*) laid, vilain; (*not elegant*) sans façons

home'made' *adj* fait à la maison, de ménage

home'mak'er *s* maîtresse *f* de maison, ménagère *f*

home' of'fice *s* siège *m* social

homeopathy [ˌhomiˈɑpəθi] *s* homéopathie *f*

home'own'er *s* propriétaire *mf*

home' plate' *s* (baseball) marbre *m* (Canad)

home' port' *s* port *m* d'attache

home' rule' *s* autonomie *f*, gouvernement *m* autonome

home'sick' *adj* nostalgique; **to be homesick** avoir le mal du pays

home'sick'ness *s* mal *m* du pays, nostalgie *f*

homespun [ˈhom‚spʌn] *adj* filé à la maison; (fig) simple, sans apprêt

home'stead *s* bien *m* de famille, ferme *f*

home'stretch' *s* fin *f* de course, dernière étape *f*

home' team' *s* locaux *mpl*, équipe *f* qui reçoit

home'town' *s* ville *f* natale

homeward [ˈhomwərd] *adj* de retour ‖ *adv* vers la maison; vers son pays

home'work' *s* travail *m* à la maison; devoirs *mpl*

homey [ˈhomi] *adj* (*comp* **homier**; *super* **homiest**) (coll) familial, intime

homicidal [ˌhɑmɪˈsaɪdəl] *adj* homicide

homicide [ˈhɑmɪˌsaɪd] *s* (*act*) homicide *m*; (*person*) homicide *mf*

homi·ly [ˈhɑmɪli] *s* (*pl* **-lies**) homélie *f*

hom'ing head' *s* (*of missile*) tête *f* chercheuse

hom'ing pi'geon *s* pigeon *m* voyageur

hominy [ˈhɑmɪni] *s* semoule *f* de maïs

homo [ˈhomo] *s* (slang, pej) (*homosexual*) tapette *f*, tante *f*

homogeneous [ˌhomoˈdʒini·əs], [ˌhɑməˈdʒɪni·əs] *adj* homogène

homogenize [hɑˈmɑdʒəˌnaɪz] *tr* homogénéiser

homonym [ˈhɑmənɪm] *s* homonyme *m*

homonymous [həˈmɑnɪməs] *adj* homonyme

homosexual [ˌhomoˈsɛkʃʊ·əl] *adj & s* homosexuel *m*

homosexuality [ˌhomoˌsɛkʃʊˈælɪti] *s* homosexualité *f*

hone [hon] *s* pierre *f* à aiguiser ‖ *tr* aiguiser, affiler

honest [ˈɑnɪst] *adj* honnête; (*money*) honnêtement acquis

honesty [ˈɑnɪsti] *s* honnêteté *f*; (bot) monnaie *f* du pape

hon·ey [ˈhʌni] *s* miel *m* ‖ *v* (*pret & pp* **-eyed** or **-ied**) *tr* emmieller

hon'ey·bee' *s* abeille *f* à miel

hon'ey·comb' *s* rayon *m*, gâteau *m* de cire; (*anything like a honeycomb*) nid *m* d'abeilles ‖ *tr* cribler

honeyed *adj* emmiellé

hon'ey·moon' *s* lune *f* de miel; voyage *m* de noces ‖ *intr* passer la lune de miel

hon'ey·suck'le *s* chèvrefeuille *m*

honk [hɔŋk] *s* (aut) klaxon *m* ‖ *tr* (*the horn*) sonner ‖ *intr* klaxonner

honkytonk [ˈhɔŋkiˌtɔŋk] *s* (slang) boui-boui *m*

honor [ˈɑnər] *s* honneur *m*; (*award*) distinction *f*; **honors** honneurs ‖ *tr* honorer; **in honor of** en l'honneur de

honorable [ˈɑnərəbəl] *adj* honorable

hon'orable dis'charge *s* (mil) démobilisation *f* honorable

honorari·um [ˌɑnəˈrɛri·əm] *s* (*pl* **-ums** or **-a** [ə]) *s* honoraires *mpl*

honorary [ˈɑnəˌrɛri] *adj* honoraire

honorific [ˌɑnəˈrɪfɪk] *adj* honorifique ‖ *s* formule *f* de politesse

hood [hʊd] *s* capuchon *m*, chaperon *m*; (*of chimney*) hotte *f*; (*academic hood*) capuce *m*; (aut) capot *m*; (slang) gangster *m*, loubard *m* ‖ *tr* capoter

hoodlum [ˈhʊdləm] *s* (coll) chenapan *m*

hoodoo [ˈhʊdu] *s* (*bad luck*) guigne *f*; (*rites*) vaudou *m* ‖ *tr* porter la guigne à

hood'wink' *tr* tromper, abuser, anarquer

hooey [ˈhu·i] *s* (slang) blague *f*

hoof [hʊf] *s* sabot *m*; **on the hoof** sur pied ‖ *tr*—**to hoof it** (coll) aller à pied

hoof'beat' *s* pas *m* de cheval

hook [hʊk] *s* crochet *m*; (*for fishing*) hameçon *m*; (*to join two things*) croc *m*; (*boxing*) crochet *m*; **by hook or by crook** (coll) de bric ou de broc, coûte que coûte; **hook line and sinker** (coll) tout à fait, avec tout le bataclan; **to get one's hooks on to** (coll) mettre le grappin sur; **to take off the hook** décrocher ‖ *tr* accrocher; (*e.g., a dress*) agrafer; (*e.g., a boat*) crocher, gaffer; (slang) amorcer, attraper; **to hook up** agrafer; (*e.g., a loudspeaking system*) monter ‖ *intr* s'accrocher

hookah [ˈhʊkə] *s* narguilé *m*

hook' and eye' *s* agrafe *f* et porte *f*

hook' and lad'der *s* camion *m* équipé d'une échelle d'incendie

hooked' rug' *s* tapis *m* à points noués

hook' shot' *s* (sports) bras *m* roulé

hook'up' *s* (*diagram*) (rad, telv) montage *m*; (*network*) (rad, telv) chaîne *f*

hook'worm' *s* ankylostome *m*

hooky [ˈhʊki] *s*—**to play hooky** (coll) faire l'école buissonnière

hooligan [ˈhulɪgən] *s* voyou *m*

hooliganism [ˈhulɪgənˌɪzəm] *s* voyouterie *f*

hoop [hup] *s* cerceau *m*; (*of cask*) cercle *m* ‖ *tr* cercler, entourer

hoop' skirt' *s* crinoline *f*

hoot [hut] *s* huée *f*; (*of owl*) ululement *m*; **I don't care a hoot** (slang) je m'en bats l'œil, je m'en fiche ‖ *tr* huer ‖ *intr* huer; (*said of owl*) ululer; **to hoot at** huer

hoot′ owl′ *s* chat-huant *m*, hulotte *f*
hop [hɑp] *s* saut *m*; (*dance*) (coll) sauterie *f*;
surboum *m*; (coll) vol *m* en avion, étape *f*;
hops (bot) houblon *m* ‖ *v* (*pret & pp*
hopped; *ger* **hopping**) *tr* sauter, franchir;
(*e.g., a taxi*) (coll) prendre ‖ *intr* sauter,
sautiller; **to hop on one foot** sauter à
cloche-pied; **to hop over** sauter
hope [hop] *s* (*feeling of hope*) espérance *f*;
(*instance of hope*) espoir *m*; (*person or
thing one puts one's hope in*) espérance,
espoir ‖ *tr & intr* espérer; **to hope for**
espérer; **to hope to** + *inf* espérer + *inf*
hope′ chest′ *s* trousseau *m*
hopeful [ˈhopfəl] *adj* (*feeling hope*) plein
d'espoir; (*giving hope*) prometteur
hopeless [ˈhoplɪs] *adj* sans espoir
hopper [ˈhɑpər] *s* (*funnel-shaped container*)
trémie *f*; (*of blast furnace*) gueulard *m*
hop′per car′ *s* wagon-trémie *m*
hop′scotch′ *s* marelle *f*
horde [hord] *s* horde *f*
horehound [ˈhor,haʊnd] *s* (bot) marrube *m*
horizon [həˈraɪzən] *s* horizon *m*
horizontal [,hɔrɪˈzɑntəl] *adj* horizontal ‖ *s*
horizontale *f*
hor′izon′tal hold′ *s* (telv) commande *f* de
stabilité horizontale, molette *f* horizontale
hormone [ˈhɔrmon] *s* hormone *f*
horn [hɔrn] *s* (*bony projection on head of
certain animals*) corne *f*; (*of anvil*) bigorne *f*; (*of auto*) klaxon *m*; (*of snail; of
insect*) antenne *f*; (mus) cor *m*; (*French
horn*) (mus) cor d'harmonie; **horns** (*of
deer*) bois *m*; **to blow one's own horn**
(coll) se vanter, exalter son propre mérite;
to draw in one's horns (fig) rentrer les
cornes; **to toot the horn** corner ‖ *intr*—**to
horn in** (slang) intervenir sans façon
horn′beam′ *s* (bot) charme *m*
horned *adj* cornu
horned′ owl′ *s* duc *m*
hornet [ˈhɔrnɪt] *s* frelon *m*; **to stir up a
hornet's nest** mettre le feu aux poudres
hor′net's nest′ *s* guêpier *m*
horn′ of plen′ty *s* corne *f* d'abondance
horn′pipe′ *s* chalumeau *m*; (*dance*) matelote *f*
horn′rimmed glas′ses *spl* lunettes *fpl* à
monture en corne
horn·y [ˈhɔrni] *adj* (*comp* -ier; *super* -iest)
(*like horn*) corné; (*hands*) calleux; (*sexually aroused*) (slang) en rut, excité
horoscope [ˈhɔrə,skop] *s* horoscope *m*; **to
cast s.o.'s horoscope** tirer l'horoscope de
qn
horrible [ˈhɔrɪbəl] *adj* horrible; (coll) horrible, détestable
horrid [ˈhɔrɪd] *adj* affreux; (coll) affreux,
très désagréable
horri·fy [ˈhɔrɪ,faɪ] *v* (*pret & pp* -fied) *tr*
horrifier
horror [ˈhɔrər] *s* horreur *f*; **to have a
horror of** avoir horreur de
hors d'oeuvre [ɔrˈdʌrv] *s* (*pl* **hors
d'oeuvres** [ɔrˈdʌrvz]) hors-d'œuvre *m invar*

horse [hɔrs] *s* cheval *m*; (*of carpenter*)
chevalet *m*; **hold your horses!** (coll) ar-
rêtez un moment!; **to back the wrong
horse** (coll) miser sur le mauvais cheval;
to be a horse of another color (coll) être
une autre paire de manches; **to eat like a
horse** (coll) manger comme un ogre; **to
ride a horse** monter à cheval ‖ *intr*—**to
horse around** (slang) muser, se baguenauder
horse′back′ *s*—**on horseback** à cheval ‖
adv—**to ride horseback** monter à cheval
horse′back rid′ing *s* équitation *f*, exercice
m à cheval
horse′ blan′ket *s* couverture *f* de cheval
horse′ break′er *s* dompteur *m* de chevaux
horse′car′ *s* tramway *m* à chevaux
horse′ chest′nut *s* (*tree*) marronnier *m*
d'Inde; (*nut*) marron *m* d'Inde
horse′cloth′ *s* housse *f*
horse′ coll′ar *s* collier *m* de cheval
horse′ deal′er *s* marchand *m* de chevaux
horse′ doc′tor *s* (coll) vétérinaire *m*
horse′ fly′ *s* (*pl* **flies**) taon *m*
horse′hair′ *s* crin *m*
horse′hide′ *s* peau *f* or cuir *m* de cheval
horse′laugh′ *s* gros rire *m* bruyant
horse′less car′riage [ˈhɔrslɪs] *s* voiture *f*
sans chevaux
horse′man *s* (*pl* -men) cavalier *m*; (*at race
track*) turfiste *m*
horsemanship [ˈhɔrsmən,ʃɪp] *s* équitation *f*
horse′ meat′ *s* viande *f* de cheval
horse′ op′era *s* (coll) western *m*
horse′ pis′tol *s* pistolet *m* d'arçon
horse′play′ *s* jeu *m* de mains, clownerie *f*
horse′pow′er *s* (*746 watts*) cheval-vapeur
m anglais
horse′ race′ *s* course *f* de chevaux
horse′rad′ish *s* raifort *m*
horse′ sense′ *s* (coll) gros bon sens *m*
horse′shoe′ *s* fer *m* à cheval
horse′shoe′ing *s* ferrure *f*, ferrage *m*
horse′shoe mag′net *s* aimant *m* en fer à
cheval
horse′ show′ *s* exposition *f* de chevaux,
concours *m* hippique
horse′tail′ *s* queue *f* de cheval; (bot) prèle *f*
horse′ thief′ *s* voleur *m* de chevaux
horse′ trad′er *s* maquignon *m*
horse′ trad′ing *s* maquignonnage *m*
horse′whip′ *s* cravache *f* ‖ *v* (*pret & pp*
-whipped; *ger* -whipping) *tr* cravacher
horse′wom′an *s* (*pl* -wom′en) *s* cavalière *f*,
amazone *f*
hors·y [ˈhɔrsi] *adj* (*comp* -ier; *super* -iest)
chevalin; (coll) hippomane; (*awkward in
appearance*) (coll) maladroit
horticultural [,hɔrtɪˈkʌltʃərəl] *adj* horticole
horticulture [ˈhɔrtɪ,kʌltʃər] *s* horticulture *f*
hose [hoz] *s* (*flexible tube*) tuyau *m* ‖ *s* (*pl
hose*) (*stocking*) bas *m*; (*sock*) chaussette *f*
hosier [ˈhoʒər] *s* bonnetier *m*
hosiery [ˈhoʒəri] *s* la bonneterie; (*stockings*) les bas *mpl*
hospice [ˈhɑspɪs] *s* hospice *m*

hospitable [ˈhɑspɪtəbəl] *adj* hospitalier

hospital [ˈhɑspɪtəl] *s* hôpital *m*, clinique *f*, maison *f* de santé

hospitali·ty [ˌhɑspɪˈtælɪti] *s* (*pl* -ties) hospitalité *f*

hospitalize [ˈhɑspɪtəˌlaɪz] *tr* hospitaliser

hos′pital plane′ *s* avion *m* sanitaire

hos′pital ship′ *s* navire-hôpital *m*

hos′pital train′ *s* train *m* sanitaire

hos′pital ward′ *s* pavillon *m*

host [host] *s* hôte *m*; (*who entertains dinner guests*) amphitryon *m*; (*multitude*) foule *f*, légion *f*; (*army*) armée *f*; **Host** (eccl) hostie *f*

hostage [ˈhɑstɪdʒ] *s* otage *m*

hostel [ˈhɑstəl] *s* hôtellerie *f*; (*youth hostel*) auberge *f* de la jeunesse

hostel·ry [ˈhɑstəlri] *s* (*pl* -ries) hôtellerie *f*

hostess [ˈhostɪs] *s* hôtesse *f*; (*taxi dancer*) entraîneuse *f*

hostile [ˈhɑstɪl] *adj* hostile

hostili·ty [hɑsˈtɪlɪti] *s* (*pl* -ties) hostilité *f*

hostler [ˈhɑslər], [ˈɑslər] *s* palefrenier *m*, valet *m* d'écurie

hot [hɑt] *adj* (*comp* **hotter**; *super* **hottest**) chaud; (*spicy*) piquant; (*fight, pursuit, etc.*) acharné; (*in rut*) en chaleur; (*radioactive*) (coll) fortement radioactif; **hot off** (*e.g., the press*) (coll) sortant tout droit de; **to be hot** (*said of person*) avoir chaud; (*said of weather*) faire chaud; **to get hot under the collar** (coll) s'emporter; **to make it hot for** (coll) rendre la vie intenable à, harceler

hot′ air′ *s* (slang) hâblerie *f*, discours *mpl* vides

hot′-air′ fur′nace *s* calorifère *m* à air chaud

hot′ and cold′ run′ning wa′ter *s* eau *f* courante chaude et froide

hot′bed′ *s* (hort) couche *f*, couche de fumier; (*e.g., of vice*) foyer *m*; (*e.g., of intrigue*) officine *f*

hot′-blood′ed *adj* au sang fougueux

hot′box′ *s* (rr) coussinet *m* échauffé

hot′ cake′ *s* crêpe *f*; **to sell like hot cakes** (coll) se vendre comme des petits pains

hot′ dog′ *s* saucisse *f* de Francfort, saucisse chaude, hot-dog *m*

hotel [hoˈtɛl] *adj* hôtelier ‖ *s* hôtel *m*

hotel′keep′er *s* hôtelier *m*

hot′foot′ *adv* (coll) à toute vitesse ‖ *tr*—**to hotfoot it after** (coll) s'élancer à la poursuite de

hot′head′ed *adj* exalté, fougueux

hot′house′ *s* serre *f* chaude

hot′ line′ *s* (pol) téléphone *m* rouge

hot′ mon′ey *s* (slang) capitaux *mpl* fébriles

hot′ pad′ *s* (*for plates at table*) garde-nappe *m*, dessous-de-plat *m*

hot′ pep′per *s* piment *m* rouge

hot′ plate′ *s* réchaud *m*

hot′ rod′ *s* (slang) bolide *m*

hot′ rod′der [ˌrɑdər] *s* (slang) bolide *m*, casse-cou *m*

hot′ springs′ *spl* sources *fpl* thermales

hot′-temp′ered *adj* coléreux, irascible

hot′ wa′ter *s* (coll) mauvaise passe *f*; **to be in hot water** (coll) être dans le pétrin

hot′-wa′ter boil′er *s* chaudière *f* à eau chaude

hot′-wa′ter bot′tle *s* bouillotte *f*

hot′-wa′ter heat′er *s* calorifère *m* à eau chaude; (*with instantaneous delivery of hot water*) chauffe-eau *m*

hot′-wa′ter heat′ing *s* chauffage *m* par eau chaude

hot′-wa′ter tank′ *s* réservoir *m* d'eau chaude, bâche *f*

hound [haʊnd] *s* chien *m* de chasse, chien courant; **to follow the hounds** or **to ride to hounds** chasser à courre ‖ *tr* poursuivre avec ardeur, pourchasser

hound's′-tooth′ *adj* pied-de-poule

hour [aʊr] *s* heure *f*; **by the hour** à l'heure; **hours of credit** (educ) unités *fpl* de valeur; **on the hour** à l'heure sonnante; **to keep late hours** se coucher tard

hour′glass′ *s* sablier *m*, horloge *f* à sable

hour′-glass fig′ure *s* taille *f* de guêpe

hour′ hand′ *s* petite aiguille *f*, aiguille *f* des heures

hourly [ˈaʊrli] *adj* à l'heure, horaire ‖ *adv* toutes les heures; (*hour by hour*) d'heure en heure

house [haʊs] *s* (*pl* **houses** [ˈhaʊzɪz]) maison *f*; (*legislative body*) chambre *f*; (theat) salle *f*, e.g., **full house** salle comble; **to be on the house** (coll) être au frais du patron; **to bring down the house** (theat) faire crouler la salle sous les applaudissements; **to keep house for** tenir la maison de; **to put one's house in order** (fig) mettre de l'ordre dans ses affaires ‖ [haʊz] *tr* loger, abriter

house′ arrest′ *s*—**under house arrest** en résidence surveillée

house′boat′ *s* péniche *f*, bateau-maison *m*

house′boy′ *s* boy *m*

house′break′er *s* cambrioleur *m*

house′break′ing *s* effraction *f*, cambriolage *m*

housebroken [ˈhaʊsˌbrokən] *adj* (*dog or cat*) dressé à la propreté

house′ clean′ing *s* grand nettoyage *m* de la maison

house′coat′ *s* peignoir *m*

house′ cur′rent *s* courant *m* de secteur, secteur *m*

house′fly′ *s* (*pl* -**flies**) mouche *f* domestique

houseful [ˈhaʊsˌful] *s* pleine maison *f*

house′ fur′nishings *spl* ménage *m*

house′hold′ *adj* domestique, du ménage ‖ *s* ménage *m*, maisonnée *f*

house′hold′er *s* chef *m* de famille, maître *m* de maison

house′ hunt′ing *s* chasse *f* aux appartements

house′keep′er *s* ménagère *f*; (*employee*) femme *f* de charge; (*for a bachelor*) gouvernante *f*

house′keep′ing *s* le ménage, l'économie *f* domestique; **to set up housekeeping** se mettre en ménage

house'maid' s bonne f
house'moth'er s maîtresse f d'internat
house' of cards' s château m de cartes
House' of Com'mons s Chambre f des communes
house' of ill' repute' s maison f mal famée, maison borgne
House' of Represen'tatives s Chambre f des Représentants
house' paint'er s peintre m en bâtiments
house' physi'cian s (in hospital) interne m; (e.g., in hotel) médecin m
house'top' s toit m; **to shout from the housetops** (coll) crier sur les toits
house' trail'er s caravane f
house'warm'ing s—**to have a house-warming** pendre la crémaillère
house'wife' s (pl -wives') maîtresse f de maison, ménagère f
house'work' s travaux mpl ménagers; **to do the housework** faire le ménage
housing ['hauzɪŋ] s logement m, habitation f; (horsecloth) housse f; (mach) enchâssure f, carter m
hous'ing devel'oper s promoteur m immobilier
hous'ing devel'opment s grand ensemble m, habitations fpl neuves, ensemble immobilier, lotissement m, complexe m résidentiel
hous'ing pro'ject s (apartments) projet m immobilier, cité f
hous'ing short'age s crise f du logement
hovel ['hʌvəl] s bicoque f, masure f; (shed for cattle, tools, etc.) appentis m, cabane f
hover ['hʌvər] intr planer, voltiger; (to move to and fro near a person) papillonner; (to hang around threateningly) rôder; (said of smile on lips) errer; hésiter
Hovercraft ['hʌvər,kræft] s (trademark) aéroglisseur m
how [hau] s comment m; **the how, the when, and the wherefore** (coll) tous les détails || adv comment; **how + adj** quel + adj, e.g., **how beautiful a morning!** quelle belle matinée!; comme + c'est + adj, e.g., **how beautiful it is!** comme c'est beau!; que + c'est + adj, e.g., **how beautiful it is!** que c'est beau!; **how are you?** comment allez-vous?, ça va?' **how early** quand, à quelle heure; **how else** de quelle autre manière; **how far** jusqu'où; à quelle distance, e.g., **how far is it?** à quelle distance est-ce?; **how long** (in time) jusqu'à quand, combien de temps; **how long is the stick?** quelle est la longueur du bâton?; **how many** combien; **how much** combien; (at what price) à combien; **how often** combien de fois; **how old are you?** quel âge avez-vous?; **how soon** quand, à quelle heure; **how to** mode m de commande; **to know how to** savoir
how-do-you-do ['haudəjə'du] s—**that's a fine how-do-you-do!** (coll) en voilà une affaire!

how·ev'er adv cependant, pourtant, toutefois; **however little it may be** si peu que ce soit; **however much** or **many it may be** autant que ce soit; **however pretty she may be** quelque jolie qu'elle soit; **however that may be** quoi qu'il en soit || conj comme, e.g., **do it however you want** faites-le comme vous voudrez
howitzer ['hau·ɪtsər] s obusier m
howl [haul] s hurlement m || tr hurler; **to howl down** faire taire en poussant des huées || intr hurler; (said of wind) mugir
howler ['haulər] s hurleur m; (coll) grosse gaffe f, bourde f, bévue f
hoyden ['hɔɪdən] s petite coquine f
H.P. or **hp** abbr (horsepower) CV
hub [hʌb] s moyeu m; (fig) centre m
hubbub ['hʌbəb] s vacarme m, tumulte m
hub'cap' s enjoliveur m, chapeau m de roue
huckster ['hʌkstər] s (peddler) camelot m; (adman) publicitaire mf
huddle ['hʌdəl] s (coll) conférence f secrète; **to go into a huddle** (coll) entrer en conclave || intr s'entasser, se presser
hue [hju] s teinte f, nuance f
hue' and cry' s clameur f de haro; **with hue and cry** et à cri
huff [hʌf] s accès m de colère; **in a huff** vexé, offensé
hug [hʌg] s étreinte f || v (pret & pp hugged; ger hugging) tr étreindre; (e.g., the coast) serrer; (e.g., the wall) raser || intr s'étreindre
huge [hjudʒ] adj énorme, immense
huh [hʌ] interj hein!, hé!
hulk [hʌlk] s (body of an old ship) carcasse f; (old ship used as warehouse, prison, etc.) ponton m; (heavy, unwieldy person) mastodonte m
hull [hʌl] s (of certain vegetables) cosse f; (of nuts) écale f; (of ship or hydroplane) coque f || tr (e.g., peas) écosser; (e.g., almonds) écaler
hullabaloo ['hʌləbə,lu] s (coll) boucan m, brouhaha m
hum [hʌm] s (e.g., of bee) bourdonnement m; (e.g., of motor) vrombissement m; (of singer) fredonnement m || v (pret & pp hummed; ger humming) tr (a melody) fredonner, chantonner || intr (said of bee) bourdonner; (said of machine) vrombir; (said of singer) fredonner, chantonner; (to be active) (coll) aller rondement || interj hum!
human ['hjumən] adj humain
hu'man be'ing s être m humain
humane [hju'men] adj humain, compatissant
humanist ['hjumənɪst] adj & s humaniste m
humanitarian [hju,mænɪ'tɛrɪ·ən] adj & s humanitaire mf
humani·ty [hju'mænɪti] s (pl -ties) humanité f; **humanities** (Greek and Latin classics) humanités classiques; (belles-lettres) humanités modernes
hu'man·kind' s genre m humain

humble [ˈhʌmbəl], [ˈʌmbəl] *adj* humble ‖ *tr* humilier; **to humble oneself** s'humilier
hum′ble pie′ *s*—**to eat humble pie** faire amende honorable, s'humilier
hum′bug′ *s* blague *f*; (*person*) imposteur *m* ‖ *v* (*pret & pp* -**bugged**; *ger* -**bugging**) *tr* mystifier
hum′drum′ *adj* monotone, banal
humer·us [ˈhjumərəs] *s* (*pl* -**i** [ˌaɪ]) humérus *m*
humid [ˈhjumɪd] *adj* humide, moite
humidifier [hjuˈmɪdɪˌfaɪ·ər] *s* humidificateur *m*
humidi·fy [hjuˈmɪdɪˌfaɪ] *v* (*pret & pp* -**fied**) *tr* humidifier
humidity [hjuˈmɪdɪti] *s* humidité *f*
humiliate [hjuˈmɪlɪˌet] *tr* humilier
humiliating [hjuˈmɪlɪˌetɪŋ] *adj* humiliant
humili·ty [hjuˈmɪlɪti] *s* (*pl* -**ties**) humilité *f*
hum′ming·bird′ *s* oiseau-mouche *m*, colibri *m*
humor [ˈhjumər], [ˈjumər] *s* (*comic quality*) humour *m*; (*frame of mind; fluid*) humeur *f*; **out of humour** maussade, grognon; **to be in the humor to** être d'humeur à ‖ *tr* ménager, satisfaire; (*s.o.'s fancies*) se plier à, accéder à
humorist [ˈhjumərɪst], [ˈjumərɪst] *s* humoriste *mf*, comique *mf*
humorous [ˈhjumərəs], [ˈjumərəs] *adj* humoristique; (*writer*) humoriste
hump [hʌmp] *s* bosse *f*
hump′back′ *s* bossu *m*; (*whale*) mégaptère *m*
humus [ˈhjuməs] *s* humus *m*
hunch [hʌntʃ] *s* (*hump*) bosse *f*; (*premonition*) (coll) pressentiment *m* ‖ *tr* arrondir, voûter ‖ *intr* s'accroupir
hunch′back′ *s* bossu *m*
hundred [ˈhʌndrəd] *adj* cent ‖ *s* cent *m*, centaine *f*; **about a hundred** une centaine; **a hundred** or **one hundred** cent; une centaine; **by the hundreds** par centaines
hun′dred·fold′ *adj & s* centuple *m*; **to increase a hundredfold** centupler ‖ *adv* au centuple
hundredth [ˈhʌndrədθ] *adj, pron, & s* centième *m*
Hungarian [hʌŋˈgɛrɪ·ən] *adj* hongrois ‖ *s* (*language*) hongrois *m*; (*person*) Hongrois *m*
Hungary [ˈhʌŋgəri] *s* Hongrie *f*; la Hongrie
hunger [ˈhʌŋgər] *s* faim *f* ‖ *intr* avoir faim; **to hunger for** être affamé de
hun′ger march′ *s* marche *f* de la faim
hun′ger strike′ *s* grève *f* de la faim
hun·gry [ˈhʌŋgri] *adj* (*comp* -**grier**; *super* -**griest**) affamé; **to be hungry** avoir faim
hunk [hʌŋk] *s* gros morceau *m*
hunt [hʌnt] *s* (*act of hunting*) chasse *f*; (*hunting party*) équipage *m* de chasse; **on the hunt for** à la recherche de; **to use the hunt-and-peck system** taper à tâtons ‖ *tr* chasser; (*to seek, look for*) chercher; **to hunt down** donner la chasse à, traquer; **to**

hunt out faire la chasse à ‖ *intr* chasser; (*with dogs*) chasser à courre; **to go hunting** aller à la chasse; **to hunt for** chercher; **to take hunting** emmener à la chasse
hunter [ˈhʌntər] *s* chasseur *m*
hunting [ˈhʌntɪŋ] *adj* de chasse ‖ *s* chasse *f*
hunt′ing dog′ *s* chien *m* de chasse
hunt′ing ground′ *s* terrain *m* de chasse, chasse *f*
hunt′ing horn′ *s* cor *m* de chasse
hunt′ing jack′et *s* paletot *m* de chasse
hunt′ing knife′ *s* couteau *m* de chasse
hunt′ing li′cense *s* permis *m* de chasse
hunt′ing lodge′ *s* pavillon *m* de chasse
hunt′ing sea′son *s* saison *f* de la chasse
huntress [ˈhʌntrɪs] *s* chasseuse *f*
hunts′man *s* (*pl* -**men**) chasseur *m*
hurdle [ˈhʌrdəl] *s* (*hedge over which horses jump*) haie *f*; (*wooden frame over which runners jump*) barrière *f*; (fig) obstacle *m*; **hurdles** course *f* d'obstacles ‖ *tr* sauter
hur′dle race′ *s* course *f* d'obstacles; (turf) course de haies
hurdy-gur·dy [ˈhʌrdiˈgʌrdi] *s* (*pl* -**dies**) orgue *m* de Barbarie
hurl [hʌrl] *s* lancée *f* ‖ *tr* lancer; **to hurl back** repousser, refouler
hurrah [haˈrɑ] or **hurray** [hʊˈre] *s* hourra *m* ‖ *interj* hourra!; **hurrah for . . . !** vive . . . !
hurricane [ˈhʌrɪˌken] *s* ouragan *m*, hurricane *m*
hurried [ˈhʌrid] *adj* pressé, précipité; (*hasty*) hâtif, fait à la hâte
hur·ry [ˈhʌri] *s* (*pl* -**ries**) hâte *f*; **to be in a hurry** être pressé ‖ *v* (*pret & pp* -**ried**) *tr* hâter, presser ‖ *intr* se hâter, se presser; **to hurry after** courir après; **to hurry away** s'en aller bien vite; **to hurry back** revenir vite; **to hurry over** venir vite; **to hurry up** se dépêcher
hurt [hʌrt] *adj* blessé ‖ *s* blessure *f*; (*pain*) douleur *f* ‖ *v* (*pret & pp* **hurt**) *tr* faire mal à ‖ *intr* faire mal, e.g., **does that hurt?** ça fait mal?; avoir mal, e.g., **my head hurts** j'ai mal à la tête
hurtful [ˈhʌrtfəl] *adj* nuisible
hurtle [ˈhʌrtəl] *intr* se précipiter
husband [ˈhʌzbənd] *s* mari *m*, époux *m* ‖ *tr* ménager, économiser
hus′band·man *s* (*pl* -**men**) cultivateur *m*
husbandry [ˈhʌzbəndri] *s* agriculture *f*; (*raising of livestock*) élevage *m*
hush [hʌʃ] *s* silence *m*, calme *m* ‖ *tr* faire taire; **to hush up** (*e.g., a scandal*) étouffer ‖ *intr* se taire ‖ *interj* chut!
hushaby [ˈhʌʃəˌbaɪ] *interj* fais dodo!
hush′-hush′ *adj* très secret
hush′ mon′ey *s* prix *m* du silence
husk [hʌsk] *s* (*of certain vegetables*) cosse *f*, gousse *f*; (*of nuts*) écale *f*; (*of corn*) enveloppe *f*; (*of oats*) balle *f*; (*of onion*) pelure *f* ‖ *tr* (*grain*) vanner; (*vegetables*) éplucher; (*peas*) écosser; (*nuts*) écaler
husk′ing bee′ *s* réunion *f* pour l'épluchage du maïs

husk·y [ˈhʌski] *adj* (*comp* -ier; *super* -iest) (*burly*) costaud; (*hoarse*) enroué ‖ *s* (*pl* -ies) (*dog*) chien *m* esquimau
hus·sy [ˈhʌsi] *s* (*pl* -sies) (coll) coquine *f*, mâtine *f*; (pej) garce *f*, traînée *f*
hustle [ˈhʌsəl] *s* (coll) bousculade *f*, énergie *f*, allant *m* ‖ *tr* pousser, bousculer ‖ *intr* se dépêcher, se presser; (*to work hard*) (coll) se démener, s'activer
hustler [ˈhʌslər] *s* (*go-getter*) homme *m* d'action; (*swindler*) (slang) filou *m*; (*streetwalker*) (slang) traînée *f*, grue *f*
hut [hʌt] *s* hutte *f*, cabane *f*; (mil) baraque *f*
hutch [hʌtʃ] *s* (*for rabbits*) clapier *m*; (*used by baker*) huche *f*, pétrin *m*
hyacinth [ˈhaɪ·əsɪnθ] *s* (*stone*) hyacinthe *f*; (*flower*) jacinthe *f*
hybrid [ˈhaɪbrɪd] *adj* & *s* hybride *m*
hy·dra [ˈhaɪdrə] *s* (*pl* -dras or -drae [dri]) hydre *f*
hydrant [ˈhaɪdrənt] *s* prise *f* d'eau; (*faucet*) robinet *m*; (*fire hydrant*) bouche *f* d'incendie
hydrate [ˈhaɪdret] *s* hydrate *m* ‖ *tr* hydrater ‖ *intr* s'hydrater
hydraulic [haɪˈdrɔlɪk] *adj* hydraulique ‖ **hydraulics** *s* hydraulique *f*
hydrau'lic lift' *s* vérin *m* hydraulique
hydrau'lic ram' *s* bélier *m* hydraulique
hydrocarbon [ˌhaɪdrəˈkɑrbən] *s* hydrocarbure *m*
hy'drochlo'ric ac'id [ˌhaɪdrəˈklorɪk] *s* acide *m* chlorhydrique
hydroelectric [ˌhaɪdro·ɪˈlɛktrɪk] *adj* hydroélectrique
hydrofoil [ˈhaɪdrə,fɔɪl] *s* hydrofoil *m*, hydroptère *m*
hydrogen [ˈhaɪdrədʒən] *s* hydrogène *m*
hy'drogen bomb' *s* bombe *f* à hydrogène
hy'drogen perox'ide *s* eau *f* oxygénée
hy'drogen sul'fide *s* hydrogène *m* sulfuré
hydrometer [haɪˈdrɑmɪtər] *s* aréomètre *m*, hydromètre *m*
hydrophobia [ˌhaɪdrəˈfobɪ·ə] *s* hydrophobie *f*
hydroplane [ˈhaɪdrə,plen] *s* hydravion *m*

hydroxide [haɪˈdrɑksaɪd] *s* hydroxyde *m*
hyena [haɪˈinə] *s* hyène *f*
hygiene [ˈhaɪdʒin] *s* hygiène *f*
hygienic [ˌhaɪdʒɪˈɛnɪk] *adj* hygiénique
hymn [hɪm] *s* hymne *m*; (eccl) hymne *f*, cantique *m*
hymnal [ˈhɪmnəl] *s* livre *m* d'hymnes
hyperacidity [ˌhaɪpərəˈsɪdɪti] *s* hyperacidité *f*
hyperactivity [ˌhaɪpərækˈtɪvəti] *s* suractivité *f*
hyperbola [haɪˈpʌrbələ] *s* hyperbole *f*
hyperbole [haɪˈpʌrbəli] *s* hyperbole *f*
hypersensitive [ˌhaɪpərˈsɛnsɪtɪv] *adj* hypersensible, hypersensitif
hypertension [ˌhaɪpərˈtɛnʃən] *s* hypertension *f*
hyphen [ˈhaɪfən] *s* trait *m* d'union
hyphenate [ˈhaɪfə,net] *tr* joindre avec un trait d'union
hypno·sis [hɪpˈnosɪs] *s* (*pl* -ses [siz]) hypnose *f*
hypnotic [hɪpˈnɑtɪk] *adj* & *s* hypnotique *m*
hypnotism [ˈhɪpnə,tɪzəm] *s* hypnotisme *m*
hypnotist [ˈhɪpnətɪst] *s* hypnotiseur *m*
hypnotize [ˈhɪpnə,taɪz] *tr* hypnotiser
hypochondriac [ˌhaɪpəˈkɑndrɪ,æk] *adj* & *s* hypocondriaque *mf*
hypocri·sy [hɪˈpɑkrəsi] *s* (*pl* -sies) hypocrisie *f*
hypocrite [ˈhɪpəkrɪt] *s* hypocrite *mf*
hypocritical [ˌhɪpəˈkrɪtɪkəl] *adj* hypocrite
hypodermic [ˌhaɪpəˈdʌrmɪk] *adj* hypodermique
hyposulfite [ˌhaɪpəˈsʌlfaɪt] *s* hyposulfite *m*
hypotenuse [haɪˈpɑtɪ,n(j)us] *s* hypoténuse *f*
hypothe·sis [haɪˈpɑθɪsɪs] *s* (*pl* -ses [,siz]) hypothèse *f*
hypothetic(al) [ˌhaɪpəˈθɛtɪk(əl)] *adj* hypothétique
hysteria [hɪsˈtɪrɪ·ə] *s* agitation *f*, frénésie *f*; (pathol) hystérie *f*
hysteric [hɪsˈtɛrɪk] *adj* hystérique ‖ **hysterics** *spl* crise *f* de nerfs, crise de larmes, fou rire *m*
hysterical [hɪsˈtɛrɪkəl] *adj* hystérique

I

I, i [aɪ] *s* IXe lettre de l'alphabet
I *pron* je §87; moi §85
iambic [aɪˈæmbɪk] *adj* ïambique
Iberian [aɪˈbɪrɪ·ən] *adj* ibérien, ibérique ‖ *s* Ibérien *m*
ibex [ˈaɪbɛks] *s* (*pl* ibexes or ibices [ˈɪbɪ,siz] bouquetin *m*
ice [aɪs] *s* glace *f*; **to break the ice** (fig) rompre la glace; **to cut no ice** (coll) ne rien casser, ne pas prendre; **to skate on thin ice** (coll) s'engager sur un terrain dangereux ‖ *tr* glacer; (*e.g., champagne*)

frapper; (*e.g., melon*) rafraîchir ‖ *intr* geler; **to ice up** (*said of windshield, airplane wings, etc.*) se givrer
ice' age' *s* époque *f* glaciaire
ice' bag' *s* sac *m* à glace
ice' bank' *s* banquise *f*
iceberg [ˈaɪs,bʌrg] *s* banquise *f*, iceberg *m*; (*person*) (coll) glaçon *m*
ice'boat' *s* (*icebreaker*) brise-glace *m*; (*for sport*) bateau *m* à patins
icebound [ˈaɪs,baʊnd] *adj* pris dans les glaces

ice'box' s glacière f
ice'break'er s brise-glace m
ice'cap' s calotte f glaciaire
ice' cream' s glace f
ice'-cream' cone' s cornet m de glace, glace f en cornet
ice'-cream' freez'er s sorbetière f
ice' crush'er s broyeur m de glace
ice' cube' s glaçon m
ice'-cube' tray' s bac m à glaçons
iced' tea' s thé m glacé
ice' floe' s banquise f
ice' hock'ey s hockey m sur glace
ice' jam' s embâcle m
Iceland ['aɪslənd] s Islande f; l'Islande
Icelander ['aɪs,lændər] s Islandais m
Icelandic [aɪs'lændɪk] adj & s islandais m
ice'man' s (pl -men') glacier m
ice' pack' s (pack ice) embâcle m; (med) vessie f de glace
ice' pail' s seau m à glace
ice' pick' s poinçon m à glace; (of mountain climber) piolet m
ice' skate' s patin m à glace
ice' wa'ter s eau f glacée f
ichthyology [,ɪkθɪ'ɑlədʒi] s ichtyologie f
icicle ['aɪsɪkəl] s glaçon m, chandelle f de glace
icing ['aɪsɪŋ] s (on cake) glaçage m; (aer) givrage m
icon ['aɪkɑn] s icône f
iconoclast [aɪ'kɑnə,klæst] s iconoclaste mf
iconoclastic [aɪ,kɑnə'klæstɪk] adj iconoclaste
Iconoscope [aɪ'kɑnə,skop] s (trademark) iconoscope m
icy ['aɪsi] adj (comp icier; super iciest) glacé; (slippery) glissant; (fig) froid, glacial
idea [aɪ'di·ə] s idée f; the very idea! par exemple!
ideal [aɪ'di·əl] adj & s idéal m
idealist [aɪ'di·əlɪst] adj & s idéaliste mf
idealistic [aɪ,di·əl'ɪstɪk] adj idéaliste
idealize [aɪ'di·ə,laɪz] tr idéaliser
identic(al) [aɪ'dɛntɪk(əl)] adj identique
identification [aɪ,dɛntɪfɪ'keʃen] s identification f
identifica'tion card' s carte f d'identité
identifica'tion tag' s plaque f d'identité
identi·fy [aɪ'dɛntɪ,faɪ] v (pret & pp -fied) tr identifier
identi·ty [aɪ'dɛntɪti] s (pl -ties) identité f
ideolo·gy [,aɪdɪ'ɑlədʒi] s (pl -gies) idéologie f
ides [aɪdz] spl ides fpl
idio·cy ['ɪdɪ·əsi] s (pl -cies) idiotie f
idiom ['ɪdɪ·əm] s (phrase, expression) idiotisme m; (language, style) idiome m
idiomatic [,ɪdɪ·ə'mætɪk] adj idiomatique
idiosyncra·sy [,ɪdɪ·ə'sɪnkrəsi] s (pl -sies) idiosyncrasie f
idiot ['ɪdɪ·ət] s idiot m
idiotic [,ɪdɪ'ɑtɪk] adj idiot
idle ['aɪdəl] adj oisif, désœuvré; (futile) oiseux; to run idle marcher au ralenti ‖ tr—to idle away (time) passer à ne rien

faire ‖ intr fainéanter; (mach) tourner au ralenti
idleness ['aɪdəlnɪs] s oisiveté f
idler ['aɪdlər] s oisif m
idling ['aɪdlɪŋ] s (of motor) ralenti m
idol ['aɪdəl] s idole f
idola·try [aɪ'dɑlətri] s (pl -tries) idolâtrie f
idolize ['aɪdə,laɪz] tr idolâtrer
idyll ['aɪdəl] s idylle f
idyllic [aɪ'dɪlɪk] adj idyllique
i.e. abbr (Lat id est that is) c.-à-d., à savoir
if [ɪf] s—ifs and buts des si et des mais ‖ conj si; even if quand même; if it is true that si tant est que; if not sinon; if so dans ce cas, s'il en est ainsi
ignis fatuus ['ɪgnɪs'fætʃu·əs] s (pl ignes fatui ['ɪgniz'fætʃu,aɪ]) feu m follet
ignite [ɪg'naɪt] tr allumer ‖ intr prendre feu
ignition [ɪg'nɪʃən] s ignition f; (aut) allumage m; to switch on the ignition mettre le contact
igni'tion coil' s (aut) bobine f d'allumage
igni'tion key' s clef m de contact, clef d'allumage
igni'tion switch' s (aut) contact m
ignoble [ɪg'nobəl] adj ignoble
ignominious [,ɪgnə'mɪnɪ·əs] adj ignominieux
ignoramus [,ɪgnə'reməs] s ignorant m
ignorance ['ɪgnərəns] s ignorance f
ignorant ['ɪgnərənt] adj ignorant; to be ignorant of ignorer
ignore [ɪg'nor] tr ne pas tenir compte de, ne pas faire attention à; (a suggestion) passer outre à; (to snub) faire semblant de ne pas voir, ignorer à dessein
ilk [ɪlk] s espèce f; of that ilk de cet acabit
ill [ɪl] adj (comp worse [wʌrs]; super worst [wʌrst] malade, souffrant ‖ adv mal; to take ill prendre en mauvaise part; (to get sick) tomber malade
ill'-advised' adj (person) malavisé; (action) peu judicieux
ill' at ease' adj mal à l'aise, gêné
ill-bred ['ɪl'brɛd] adj mal élevé
ill'-consid'ered adj peu réfléchi, hâtif
ill'-disposed' adj mal disposé, malintentionné
illegal [ɪ'ligəl] adj illégal
illegible [ɪ'lɛdʒɪbəl] adj illisible
illegitimate [,ɪlɪ'dʒɪtɪmɪt] adj illégitime
ill'-famed' adj mal famé
ill'-fat'ed adj malheureux, infortuné
ill'-gotten ['ɪl'gɑtən] adj mal acquis
ill' health' s mauvaise santé f
ill'-hu'mored adj de mauvaise humeur, maussade
illicit [ɪ'lɪsɪt] adj illicite
illitera·cy [ɪ'lɪtərəsi] s (pl -cies) ignorance f; analphabétisme m
illiterate [ɪ'lɪtərɪt] adj (uneducated) ignorant, illettré; (unable to read or write) analphabète ‖ s analphabète mf
ill'-man'nered adj malappris, mal élevé
ill'-na'tured adj désagréable, méchant
illness ['ɪlnɪs] s maladie f
illogical [ɪ'lɑdʒɪkəl] adj illogique

ill-spent [ˈɪlˈspɛnt] *adj* gaspillé

ill´-starred´ *adj* néfaste, de mauvais augure

ill´-tem´pered *adj* désagréable, de mauvais caractère

ill´-timed´ *adj* intempestif, mal à propos

ill´-treat´ *tr* maltraiter, rudoyer

illuminate [ɪˈlumɪˌnet] *tr* illuminer; (*a manuscript*) enluminer

illu´minating gas´ *s* gaz *m* d'éclairage

illumination [ɪˈlumɪˈneʃən] *s* illumination *f*; (*in manuscript*) enluminure *f*

illusion [ɪˈluʒən] *s* illusion *f*

illusive [ɪˈlusɪv] *adj* illusoire, trompeur

illusory [ɪˈlusəri] *adj* illusoire

illustrate [ˈɪləsˌtret] *tr* illustrer

illustration *s* [ˌɪləsˈtreʃən] *s* illustration *f*; (*explanation*) explication *f*, éclaircissement *m*

illustrative [ɪˈlʌstrətɪv] *adj* explicatif, éclairant

illustrator [ˈɪləsˌtretər] *s* illustrateur *m*, dessinateur *m*

illustrious [ɪˈlʌstrɪ·əs] *adj* illustre

ill´ will´ *s* rancune *f*

image [ˈɪmɪdʒ] *s* image *f*

image·ry [ˈɪmɪdʒri] *s* (*pl* **-ries**) images *fpl*

imaginary [ɪˈmædʒɪˌnɛri] *adj* imaginaire

imagination [ɪˌmædʒɪˈneʃən] *s* imagination *f*

imagine [ɪˈmædʒɪn] *tr* imaginer, s'imaginer || *intr* imaginer; **imagine!** figurez-vous!

imbecile [ˈɪmbɪsɪl] *adj* & *s* imbécile *mf*

imbecili·ty [ˌɪmbɪˈsɪlɪti] *s* (*pl* **-ties**) imbécillité *f*

imbibe [ɪmˈbaɪb] *tr* absorber || *intr* boire, lever le coude

imbue [ɪmˈbju] *tr* imprégner, pénétrer; **imbued with** imbu de

imitate [ˈɪmɪˌtet] *tr* imiter

imitation [ˌɪmɪˈteʃən] *adj* d'imitation || *s* imitation *f*

imitator [ˈɪmɪˌtetər] *s* imitateur *m*

immaculate [ɪˈmækjəlɪt] *adj* immaculé

Immac´ulate Concep´tion *s* (rel) Immaculée Conception *f*

immaterial [ˌɪməˈtɪrɪ·əl] *adj* immatériel; (*pointless*) sans conséquence; **it's immaterial to me** cela m'est égal

immature [ˌɪməˈtjʊr] *adj* pas mûr, peu mûr; pas adulte

immeasurable [ɪˈmɛʒərəbəl] *adj* immensurable

immediacy [ɪˈmidɪ·əsi] *s* caractère *m* immédiat, imminence *f*

immediate [ɪˈmidɪ·ɪt] *adj* immédiat

immediately [ɪˈmidɪ·ɪtli] *adv* immédiatement

immemorial [ˌɪmɪˈmorɪ·əl] *adj* immémorial

immense [ɪˈmɛns] *adj* immense

immerse [ɪˈmʌrs] *tr* immerger, plonger

immersion [ɪˈmʌrʒən] *s* immersion *f*

immigrant [ˈɪmɪɡrənt] *adj* & *s* immigrant *m*

immigrate [ˈɪmɪˌɡret] *intr* immigrer

immigration [ˌɪmɪˈɡreʃən] *s* immigration *f*

imminent [ˈɪmɪnənt] *adj* imminent, très prochain

immobile [ɪˈmobɪl] *adj* immobile

immobilize [ɪˈmobɪˌlaɪz] *tr* immobiliser

immoderate [ɪˈmɑdərɪt] *adj* immodéré

immodest [ɪˈmɑdɪst] *adj* impudique

immoral [ɪˈmɔrəl] *adj* immoral

immortal [ɪˈmɔrtəl] *adj* & *s* immortel *m*

immortalize [ɪˈmɔrtəˌlaɪz] *tr* immortaliser

immune [ɪˈmjun] *adj* dispensé, exempt; (med) immunisé

immune´ sys´tem *s* système *m* immunitaire

immunize [ˈɪmjəˌnaɪz] *tr* immuniser

imp [ɪmp] *s* suppôt *m* du diable; (*child*) diablotin *m*, polisson *m*

impact [ˈɪmpækt] *s* impact *m*

impair [ɪmˈpɛr] *tr* endommager, affaiblir; (*health, digestion*) délabrer

impan·el [ɪmˈpænəl] *v* (*pret* & *pp* **-eled** or **-elled**; *ger* **-eling** or **-elling**) *tr* appeler à faire partie de; (*a jury*) dresser la liste de

impart [ɪmˈpɑrt] *tr* imprimer, communiquer; (*to make known*) communiquer

impartial [ɪmˈpɑrʃəl] *adj* impartial

impassable [ɪmˈpæsəbəl] *adj* (*road*) impraticable; (*mountain*) infranchissable

impassible [ɪmˈpæsɪbəl] *adj* impassible

impassioned [ɪmˈpæʃənd] *adj* passionné

impassive [ɪmˈpæsɪv] *adj* insensible; (*look, face*) impassible, composé

impatience [ɪmˈpeʃəns] *s* impatience *f*

impatient [ɪmˈpeʃənt] *adj* impatient

impeach [ɪmˈpitʃ] *tr* accuser; (*s.o.'s honor, veracity*) attaquer; (pol) entamer la procédure d'impeachment contre

impeachment [ɪmˈpitʃmənt] *s* accusation *f*; (*of honor, veracity*) attaque *f*; (pol) procédure *f* d'impeachment, mise *f* en accusation devant le Sénat, destitution *f*

impeccable [ɪmˈpɛkəbəl] *adj* impeccable

impecunious [ˌɪmpɪˈkjunɪ·əs] *adj* besogneux, impécunieux

impede [ɪmˈpid] *tr* entraver, empêcher

impediment [ɪmˈpɛdɪmənt] *s* obstacle *m*, empêchement *m*

im·pel [ɪmˈpɛl] *v* (*pret* & *pp* **-pelled**; *ger* **-pelling**) *tr* pousser, forcer

impending [ɪmˈpɛndɪŋ] *adj* imminent

impenetrable [ɪmˈpɛnətrəbəl] *adj* impénétrable

impenitent [ɪmˈpɛnɪtənt] *adj* impénitent *m*

imperative [ɪˈpɛrɪtɪv] *adj* & *s* impératif *m*

imperceptible [ˌɪmpərˈsɛptɪbəl] *adj* imperceptible

imperfect [ɪmˈpʌrfɪkt] *adj* & *s* imparfait *m*

imperfection [ˌɪmpərˈfɛkʃən] *s* imperfection *f*

imperial [ɪmˈpɪrɪ·əl] *adj* impérial

imperialist [ɪmˈpɪrɪ·əlɪst] *adj* & *s* impérialiste *mf*

imper·il [ɪmˈpɛrɪl] *v* (*pret* & *pp* **-iled** or **-illed**; *ger* **-iling** or **illing**) *tr* mettre en péril, exposer au danger

imperious [ɪmˈpɪrɪ·əs] *adj* impérieux

imperishable [ɪmˈpɛrɪʃəbəl] *adj* impérissable

impersonal [ɪmˈpʌrsənəl] *adj* impersonnel

impersonate [ɪmˈpʌrsəˌnet] *tr* contrefaire, singer; jouer le rôle de

impertinent [ɪmˈpʌrtinənt] *adj* impertinent

impetuous [ɪmˈpɛtʃu·əs] *adj* impétueux

impetus [ˈɪmpɪtəs] *s* impulsion *f*; (mech) force *f* impulsive; (fig) élan *m*

impie·ty [ɪmˈpaɪ·əti] *s* (*pl* **-ties**) impiété *f*

impinge [ɪmˈpɪndʒ] *intr*—**to impinge on** or **upon** empiéter sur; (*to violate*) enfreindre

impious [ˈɪmpɪ·əs] *adj* impie

impish [ˈɪmpɪʃ] *adj* espiègle

implacable [ɪmˈplekəbəl] *adj* implacable

implant [ɪmˈplænt] *tr* implanter

implement [ˈɪmplɪmənt] *s* outil *m*, ustensile *m* ‖ *tr* mettre en œuvre, réaliser; (*to provide with implements*) outiller

implicate [ˈɪmplɪ,ket] *tr* impliquer

implicit [ɪmˈplɪsɪt] *adj* implicite

implied [ɪmˈplaɪd] *adj* implicite, sous-entendu

implore [ɪmˈplor] *tr* implorer, supplier, solliciter

im·ply [ɪmˈplaɪ] *v* (*pret* & *pp* **-plied**) *tr* impliquer

impolite [,ɪmpəˈlaɪt] *adj* impoli

import [ˈɪmport] *s* importance *f*; (*meaning*) sens *m*, signification *f*; (*extent*) portée *f*; (com) article *m* d'importation; **imports** importations *fpl* ‖ *tr* importer; (*to mean*) signifier, vouloir dire

importance [ɪmˈpɔrtəns] *s* importance *f*

important [ɪmˈpɔrtənt] *adj* important

importer [ɪmˈpɔrtər] *s* importateur *m*

importune [,ɪmpɔrˈt(j)un] *tr* importuner, harceler

impose [ɪmˈpoz] *tr* imposer ‖ *intr*—**to impose on** or **upon** en imposer à, abuser de

imposing [ɪmˈpozɪŋ] *adj* imposant

imposition [,ɪmpəˈzɪʃən] *s* (*laying on of a burden or obligation*) imposition *f*; (*rudeness, taking unfair advantage*) abus *m*

impossible [ɪmˈpɑsɪbəl] *adj* impossible

impostor [ɪmˈpɑstər] *s* imposteur *m*

imposture [ɪmˈpɑstjər] *s* imposture *f*

impotence [ˈɪmpətəns] *s* impuissance *f*

impotent [ˈɪmpətənt] *adj* impuissant

impound [ɪmˈpaʊnd] *tr* confisquer, saisir; (*a dog, an auto, etc.*) mettre en fourrière

impoverish [ɪmˈpɑvərɪʃ] *tr* appauvrir

impracticable [ɪmˈpræktɪkəbəl] *adj* impraticable, inexécutable

impractical [ɪmˈpræktɪkəl] *adj* peu pratique; (*plan*) impraticable

impregnable [ɪmˈprɛgnəbəl] *adj* imprenable, inexpugnable

impregnate [ɪmˈprɛgnet] *tr* imprégner; (*to make pregnant*) féconder

impresari·o [,ɪmprɪˈsɑri,o] *s* (*pl* **-os**) imprésario *m*

impress [ɪmˈprɛs] *tr* (*to have an effect on the mind or emotions of*) impressionner; (*to mark by using pressure*) imprimer; (*on the memory*) graver; (mil) enrôler de force; **to impress s.o. with** pénétrer qn de

impression [ɪmˈprɛʃən] *s* impression *f*

impressive [ɪmˈprɛsɪv] *adj* impressionnant

imprint [ˈɪmprɪnt] *s* empreinte *f*; (typ) rubrique *f*, griffe *f* ‖ [ɪmˈprɪnt] *tr* imprimer

imprison [ɪmˈprɪzən] *tr* emprisonner

imprisonment [ɪmˈprɪzənmənt] *s* emprisonnement *m*

improbable [ɪmˈprɑbəbəl] *adj* improbable

impromptu [ɪmˈprɑmpt(j)u] *adj* & *adv* impromptu ‖ *s* (mus) impromptu *m*

impromp′tu speech′ *s* improvisation *f*, discours *m* improvisé

improper [ɪmˈprɑpər] *adj* (*not the right*) impropre; (*contrary to good taste or decency*) inconvenant, incorrect

improve [ɪmˈpruv] *tr* améliorer, perfectionner ‖ *intr* s'améliorer, se perfectionner

improvement [ɪmˈpruvmənt] *s* amélioration *f*, perfectionnement *m*; (*of a building site*) viabilité *f*

improvident [ɪmˈprɑvɪdənt] *adj* imprévoyant

improvise [ˈɪmprə,vaɪz] *tr* & *intr* improviser

imprudent [ɪmˈprudənt] *adj* imprudent

impudent [ˈɪmpjədənt] *adj* impudent, effronté

impugn [ɪmˈpjun] *tr* contester, mettre en doute

impulse [ˈɪmpʌls] *s* impulsion *f*

impulsive [ɪmˈpʌlsɪv] *adj* impulsif

impunity [ɪmˈpjunɪti] *s* impunité *f*

impure [ɪmˈpjʊr] *adj* impur

impuri·ty [ɪmˈpjurɪti] *s* (*pl* **-ties**) impureté *f*

impute [ɪmˈpjut] *tr* imputer

in [ɪn] *adv* en dedans, à l'intérieur; (*at home*) à la maison, chez soi; (pol) au pouvoir; **all in** (*tired*) (coll) éreinté; **in here** ici, par ici; **in there** là-dedans, là ‖ *prep* dans; en; (*inside*) en dedans de, à l'intérieur de; (*in ratios*) sur, e.g., **one in a hundred** un sur cent; **in that** du fait que; **in one's life** de sa vie ‖ *s* (coll) entrée *f*, e.g., **to have an in with** avoir ses entrées chez

inability [,ɪnəˈbɪlɪti] *s* incapacité *f*, impuissance *f*

inaccessible [,ɪnækˈsɛsɪbəl] *adj* inaccessible, inabordable

inaccura·cy [ɪnˈækjərəsi] *s* (*pl* **-cies**) inexactitude *f*, infidélité *f*

inaccurate [ɪnˈækjərɪt] *adj* inexact, infidèle

inaction [ɪnˈækʃən] *s* inaction *f*

inactive [ɪnˈæktɪv] *adj* inactif

inactivity [,ɪnækˈtɪvɪti] *s* inactivité *f*

inadequate [ɪnˈædɪkwɪt] *adj* insuffisant

inadvertent [,ɪnədˈvʌrtənt] *adj* distrait, étourdi; commis par inadvertance

inadvisable [,ɪnədˈvaɪzəbəl] *adj* imprudent, peu sage

inane [ɪnˈen] *adj* inepte, absurde

inanimate [ɪnˈænɪmɪt] *adj* inanimé

inappropriate [,ɪnəˈpropri·ɪt] *adj* inapproprié; (*word*) impropre

inarticulate [,ɪnɑrˈtɪkjəlɪt] *adj* inarticulé; (*person*) muet, incapable de s'exprimer

inartistic [,ɪnɑrˈtɪstɪk] *adj* peu artistique; (*person*) peu artiste

inasmuch as [,ɪnəzˈmʌtʃ ,æz] *conj* attendu que, vu que

inattentive [,ɪnəˈtɛntɪv] *adj* inattentif

inaudible [ɪnˈɔdɪbəl] *adj* inaudible

inaugural [ɪn'ɔgjərəl] *adj* inaugural ‖ *s* discours *m* d'inauguration
inaugurate [ɪn'ɔgjəˌret] *tr* inaugurer
inauguration [ɪnˌɔgjə'reʃən] *s* inauguration *f*; (*investiture*) installation *f*
inborn ['ɪnˌbɔrn] *adj* inné, infus
in'breed'ing *s* croisement *m* consanguin
Inc. *abbr* (**Incorporated**) S.A. (société anonyme)
incandescent [ˌɪnkən'dɛsənt] *adj* incandescent
incapable [ɪn'kepəbəl] *adj* incapable
incapacitate [ˌɪnkə'pæsɪˌtet] *tr* rendre incapable
incarcerate [ɪn'karsəˌret] *tr* incarcérer
incarnate [ɪn'karnet] *adj* incarné ‖ *tr* incarner
incarnation [ˌɪnkar'neʃən] *s* incarnation *f*
incendiar·y [ɪn'sɛndɪˌɛri] *adj* incendiaire ‖ *s* (*pl* **-ies**) incendiaire *mf*
incense ['ɪnsɛns] *s* encens *m* ‖ *tr* (*to burn incense before*) encenser ‖ [ɪn'sɛns] *tr* exaspérer, irriter
in'cense burn'er *s* brûle-parfum *m*
incentive [ɪn'sɛntɪv] *adj* & *s* stimulant *m*
inception [ɪn'sɛpʃən] *s* début *m*
incessant [ɪn'sɛsənt] *adj* incessant
incest ['ɪnsɛst] *s* inceste *m*
incestuous [ɪn'sɛstʃ u·əs] *adj* incestueux
inch [ɪntʃ] *s* pouce *m*; **by inches** peu à peu, petit à petit; **not to give way an inch** ne pas reculer d'une semelle; **within an inch of** à deux doigts de ‖ *intr*—**to inch along** se déplacer imperceptiblement; **to inch forward** avancer peu à peu
incidence ['ɪnsɪdəns] *s* incidence *f*; (*range of occurrence*) portée *f*
incident ['ɪnsɪdənt] *adj* & *s* incident *m*
incidental [ˌɪnsɪ'dɛntəl] *adj* accidentel, fortuit; (*expenses*) accessoire ‖ **incidentals** *spl* faux frais *mpl*
incidentally [ˌɪnsɪ'dɛntəli] *adv* incidemment, à propos
incinerate [ɪn'sɪnəˌret] *tr* incinérer
incipient [ɪn'sɪpɪ·ənt] *adj* naissant
incision [ɪn'sɪʒən] *s* incision *f*
incisive [ɪn'saɪsɪv] *adj* incisif
incisor [ɪn'saɪzər] *s* incisive *f*
incite [ɪn'saɪt] *tr* inciter
inclement [ɪn'klɛmənt] *adj* inclément
inclination [ˌɪnklɪ'neʃən] *s* inclination *f*; (*slope*) inclinaison *f*
incline ['ɪnklaɪn] *s* inclinaison *f*, pente *f* ‖ [ɪn'klaɪn] *tr* incliner ‖ *intr* s'incliner
include [ɪn'klud] *tr* comprendre, comporter; (*to contain*) renfermer; (*e.g., in a letter*) inclure
including [ɪn'kludɪŋ] *prep* y compris; **up to and including page ten** jusqu'à la page dix incluse
inclusive [ɪn'klusɪv] *adj* global; (*including everything*) tout compris; **from Wednesday to Saturday inclusive** de mercredi à samedi inclus; **inclusive of . . .** qui comprend . . . ‖ *adv* inclusivement
incogni·to [ɪn'kagnɪˌto] *adj* & *adv* incognito ‖ *s* (*pl* **-tos**) incognito *m*

incoherent [ˌɪnko'hɪrənt] *adj* incohérent
incombustible [ˌɪnkəm'bʌstɪbəl] *adj* incombustible
income ['ɪnkʌm] *s* revenu *m*, revenus; (*annual income*) rentes *fpl*, rentrée *f*
in'come tax' *s* impôt *m* sur le revenu
in'come-tax' blank' *s* feuille *f* d'impôt
in'come-tax return' *s* déclaration *f* de revenus
in'com'ing *adj* entrant, rentrant; (*tide*) montant ‖ *s* arrivée *f*
incomparable [ɪn'kampərəbəl] *adj* incomparable
incompatible [ˌɪnkəm'pætɪbəl] *adj* incompatible
incompetent [ɪn'kampɪtənt] *adj* & *s* incompétent *m*, incapable *mf*
incomplete [ˌɪnkəm'plit] *adj* incomplet
incomprehensible [ˌɪnkamprɪ'hɛnsɪbəl] *adj* incompréhensible
inconceivable [ˌɪnkən'sivəbəl] *adj* inconcevable
inconclusive [ˌɪnkən'klusɪv] *adj* peu concluant, non concluant
incongruous [ɪn'kaŋgru·əs] *adj* incongru, impropre; disparate
inconsequential [ɪnˌkansɪ'kwɛnʃəl] *adj* sans importance
inconsiderate [ˌɪnkən'sɪdərɪt] *adj* inconsidéré
inconsisten·cy [ˌɪnkən'sɪstənsi] *s* (*pl* **-cies**) (*lack of coherence; instability*) inconsistance *f*; (*lack of logical connection or uniformity*) inconséquence *f*
inconsistent [ˌɪnkən'sɪstənt] *adj* (*lacking coherence of parts; unstable*) inconsistant; (*not agreeing with itself or oneself*) inconséquent
inconspicuous [ˌɪnkən'spɪkju·əs] *adj* peu apparent, peu impressionnant
inconstant [ɪn'kanstənt] *adj* inconstant
incontinent [ɪn'kantɪnənt] *adj* incontinent
incontrovertible [ˌɪnkantrə'vʌtɪbəl] *adj* incontestable
inconvenience [ˌɪnkən'vini·əns] *s* incommodité *f* ‖ *tr* incommoder, gêner
inconvenient [ˌɪnkən'vini·ənt] *adj* incommode, gênant; (*time*) inopportun
incorporate [ɪn'kɔrpəˌret] *tr* incorporer; (*com*) constituer en société anonyme ‖ *intr* s'incorporer; (*com*) se constituer en société anonyme
incorporation [ɪnˌkɔrpə'reʃən] *s* incorporation *f*; (*of company*) constitution *f* en société anonyme; (*of town*) érection *f* en municipalité
incorrect [ˌɪnkə'rɛkt] *adj* incorrect
increase ['ɪnkris] *s* augmentation *f*; **on the increase** en voie d'accroissement ‖ [ɪn'kris] *tr* & *intr* augmenter
increasingly [ɪn'krisɪŋli] *adv* de plus en plus
incredible [ɪn'krɛdɪbəl] *adj* incroyable
incredulous [ɪn'krɛdʒələs] *adj* incrédule
increment ['ɪnkrɪmənt] *s* augmentation *f*; (comp, econ, math, pol) incrément *m* ‖ *tr* (comp) incrémenter

incriminate [ɪn'krɪmɪ,net] *tr* incriminer
incrust [ɪn'krʌst] *tr* incruster
incubate ['ɪnkjə,bet] *tr* incuber, couver ‖ *intr* couver
incubator ['ɪnkjə,betər] *s* incubateur *m*
inculcate [ɪn'kʌlket] *tr* inculquer
incumben·cy [ɪn'kʌmbənsi] *s* (*pl* -cies) charge *f*; période *f* d'exercice
incumbent [ɪn'kʌmbənt] *adj*—**to be incumbent on** incomber à ‖ *s* titulaire *mf*; (pol) sortant *m*
incunabula [,ɪnkju'næbjələ] *spl* origines *fpl*; (*books*) incunables *mpl*
in·cur [ɪn'kʌr] *v* (*pret & pp* -**curred**; *ger* -**curring**) *tr* encourir, s'attirer; (*a debt*) contracter
incurable [ɪn'kjʊrəbəl] *adj & s* incurable *mf*, inguérissable *mf*
incursion [ɪn'kʌrʒən] *s* incursion *f*
indebted [ɪn'dɛtɪd] *adj* endetté; **indebted to s.o. for** redevable à qn de
indecen·cy [ɪn'disənsi] *s* (*pl* -cies) indécence *f*, impudeur *f*, incorrection *f*
indecent [ɪn'disənt] *adj* indécent, impudique, incorrect
inde'cent expo'sure *s* attentat *m* à la pudeur
indecisive [,ɪndɪ'saɪsɪv] *adj* indécis
indeclinable [,ɪndɪ'klaɪnəbəl] *adj* (gram) indéclinable
indeed [ɪn'did] *adv* en effet, vraiment, en vérité; (as an intensifier) effectivement, extrêmement, infiniment; **is it indeed!** vraiment?, c'est vrai?; **yes indeed!** bien sûr!, certainement!
indefatigable [,ɪndɪ'fætɪgəbəl] *adj* infatigable
indefensible [,ɪndɪ'fɛnsɪbəl] *adj* indéfendable
indefinable [,ɪndɪ'faɪnəbəl] *adj* indéfinissable
indefinite [ɪn'dɛfɪnɪt] *adj* indéfini
indelible [ɪn'dɛlɪbəl] *adj* indélébile
indelicate [ɪn'dɛlɪkɪt] *adj* indélicat
indemnification [ɪn,dɛmnɪfɪ'keʃən] *s* indemnisation *f*
indemni·fy [ɪn'dɛmnɪ,faɪ] *v* (*pret & pp* -**fied**) *tr* indemniser
indemni·ty [ɪn'dɛmnɪti] *s* (*pl* -**ties**) indemnité *f*
indent [ɪn'dɛnt] *tr* denteler; (*to make a dent in*) laisser une empreinte sur; (*a sheet of metal*) bosseler; (*to recess*) renfoncer; (typ) mettre en alinéa, rentrer ‖ *intr* (typ) faire un alinéa
indentation [,ɪndɛn'teʃən] *s* (*notched edge*) dentelure *f*, découpure *f*; (*act*) découpage *m*; (*hollow mark*) empreinte *f*; (*in metal*) bosse *f*; (*recess*) renfoncement *m*; (typ) alinéa *m*
indented *adj* (typ) en alinéa
indenture [ɪn'dɛntʃər] *s* contrat *m* d'apprentissage ‖ *tr* mettre en apprentissage
independence [,ɪndɪ'pɛndəns] *s* indépendance *f*
independen·cy [,ɪndɪ'pɛndənsi] *s* (*pl* -cies) indépendance *f*; nation *f* indépendante

independent [,ɪndɪ'pɛndənt] *adj & s* indépendant *m*
indescribable [,ɪndɪ'skraɪbəbəl] *adj* indescriptible, indicible
indestructible [,ɪndɪ'strʌktɪbəl] *adj* indestructible
index ['ɪndɛks] *s* (*pl* **indexes** or **indices** ['ɪndɪ,siz]) index *m*; (*of prices*) indice *m*; (typ) main *f*; **Index** Index ‖ *tr* répertorier; (*a book*) faire un index à
in'dex card' *s* fiche *f*
in'dex fin'ger *s* index *m*
in'dex tab' *s* onglet *m*
India ['ɪndɪ·ə] *s* Inde *f*; l'Inde
In'dia ink' *s* encre *f* de Chine
Indian ['ɪndɪ·ən] *adj* indien ‖ *s* Indien *m*
In'dian club' *s* mil *m*, massue *f*
In'dian corn' *s* maïs *m*
In'dian file' *s* file *f* indienne ‖ *adv* en file indienne, à la queue leu leu
In'dian O'cean *s* mer *f* des Indes, océan *m* Indien
In'dian sum'mer *s* l'été *m* de la Saint-Martin
In'dia rub'ber *s* caoutchouc *m*, gomme *f*
indicate ['ɪndɪ,ket] *tr* indiquer
indication ['ɪndɪ'keʃən] *s* indication *f*
indicative [ɪn'dɪkətɪv] *adj & s* indicatif *m*
indicator ['ɪndɪ,ketər] *s* indicateur *m*
indict [ɪn'daɪt] *tr* (law) inculper
indictment [ɪn'daɪtmənt] *s* inculpation *f*, mise *f* en accusation
indifferent [ɪn'dɪfərənt] *adj* indifférent; (*poor*) médiocre
indigenous [ɪn'dɪdʒɪnəs] *adj* indigène
indigent ['ɪndɪdʒənt] *adj* indigent
indigestible [,ɪndɪ'dʒɛstɪbəl] *adj* indigeste
indigestion [,ɪndɪ'dʒɛstʃən] *s* indigestion *f*
indignant [ɪn'dɪgnənt] *adj* indigné
indignation [,ɪndɪg'neʃən] *s* indignation *f*
indigni·ty [ɪn'dɪgnɪti] *s* (*pl* -**ties**) indignité *f*
indi·go ['ɪndɪ,go] *adj* indigo ‖ *s* (*pl* -**gos** or -**goes**) indigo *m*
indirect [,ɪndɪ'rɛkt] *adj* indirect
in'direct dis'course *s* discours *m* indirect, style *m* indirect
indiscreet [,ɪndɪs'krit] *adj* indiscret
indispensable [,ɪndɪs'pɛnsəbəl] *adj* indispensable
indispose [,ɪndɪs'poz] *tr* indisposer
indisposed *adj* indisposé; (*disinclined*) peu enclin, peu disposé
indisputable [,ɪndɪ'spjutəbəl] *adj* incontestable, indiscutable
indissoluble [,ɪndɪ'saljəbəl] *adj* indissoluble
indistinct [,ɪndɪ'stɪŋkt] *adj* indistinct
individual [,ɪndɪ'vɪdʒʊ·əl] *adj* individuel ‖ *s* individu *m*
individuali·ty [,ɪndɪ,vɪdʒʊ'ælɪti] *s* (*pl* -**ties**) individualité *f*
indivisible [,ɪndɪ'vɪzɪbəl] *adj* indivisible
Indochina ['ɪndo·'tʃaɪnə] *s* Indochine *f*; l'Indochine
indoctrinate [ɪn'daktrɪ,net] *tr* endoctriner, catéchiser

Indo-European [ˈɪndo‚jʊrəˈpi·ən] *adj* indo-européen ‖ *s* (*language*) indo-européen *m*; (*person*) Indo-Européen *m*

indolent [ˈɪndələnt] *adj* indolent

Indonesia [‚ɪndoˈniʒə] *s* Indonésie *f*; l'Indonésie

Indonesian [‚ɪndoˈniʒən] *adj* indonésien ‖ *s* (*language*) indonésien *m*; (*person*) Indonésien *m*

indoor [ˈɪn‚dor] *adj* d'intérieur; (*home-loving*) casanier; (*tennis*) couvert; (*swimming pool*) fermé

indoors [ˈɪnˈdorz] *adv* à l'intérieur

indubitable [ɪnˈd(j)ubɪtəbəl] *adj* indubitable

induce [ɪnˈd(j)us] *tr* induire; (*to bring about*) provoquer; **to induce s.o. to** porter qn à

induced *adj* provoqué; (elec) induit

inducement [ɪnˈd(j)usmənt] *s* encouragement *m*, mobile *m*, invite *f*

induct [ɪnˈdʌkt] *tr* installer; (mil) incorporer

inductee [‚ɪnˈdʌkti] *s* appelé *m*

induction [ɪnˈdʌkʃən] *s* installation *f*; (elec, logic) induction *f*; (mil) incorporation *f*

induc′tion coil′ *s* bobine *f* d'induction

indulge [ɪnˈdʌldʒ] *tr* favoriser; (*s.o.'s desires*) donner libre cours à; (*a child*) tout passer à ‖ *intr* (coll) boire; (coll) fumer; **to indulge in** se livrer à

indulgence [ɪnˈdʌldʒəns] *s* indulgence *f*; **indulgence in** jouissance de

indulgent [ɪnˈdʌldʒənt] *adj* indulgent

industrial [ɪnˈdʌstrɪ·əl] *adj* industriel

industrialist [ɪnˈdʌstrɪ·əlɪst] *s* industriel *m*

industrialize [ɪnˈdʌstrɪ·ə‚laɪz] *tr* industrialiser

industrious [ɪnˈdʌstrɪ·əs] *adj* industrieux, appliqué, assidu

indus·try [ˈɪndəstri] *s* (*pl* **-tries**) industrie *f*; (*zeal*) assiduité *f*

inebriation [ɪn‚ibrɪˈeʃən] *s* ébriété *f*

inedible [ɪnˈɛdɪbəl] *adj* incomestible

ineffable [ɪnˈɛfəbəl] *adj* ineffable

ineffective [‚ɪnɪˈfɛktɪv] *adj* inefficace; (*person*) incapable

ineffectual [‚ɪnɪˈfɛktʃu·əl] *adj* inefficace

inefficiency [‚ɪnəˈfɪʃənsi] *s* (*action, machine*) inefficacité *f*; (*person*) incapacité *f*, incompétence *f*

inefficient [‚ɪnɪˈfɪʃənt] *adj* (*action, machine*) inefficace; (*person*) incapable, incompétent

ineligible [ɪnˈɛlɪdʒɪbəl] *adj* inéligible

inept [ɪnˈɛpt] *adj* inepte

inequali·ty [‚ɪnɪˈkwɑlɪti] *s* (*pl* **-ties**) inégalité *f*

inequi·ty [ɪnˈɛkwɪti] *s* (*pl* **-ties**) injustice *f*

inertia [ɪnˈʌrʃə] *s* inertie *f*

inescapable [‚ɪnɛsˈkepəbəl] *adj* inéluctable

inevitable [ɪnˈɛvɪtəbəl] *adj* inévitable

inexact [‚ɪnɛgˈzækt] *adj* inexact

inexcusable [‚ɪnɛksˈkjuzəbəl] *adj* inexcusable

inexhaustible [‚ɪnɛgˈzɔstɪbəl] *adj* inexhaustible, inépuisable

inexorable [ɪnˈɛksərəbəl] *adj* inexorable

inexpedient [‚ɪnɛkˈspidɪ·ənt] *adj* inopportun, peu expédient

inexpensive [‚ɪnɛkˈspɛnsɪv] *adj* pas cher, bon marché

inexperience [‚ɪnɛkˈspɪrɪ·əns] *s* inexpérience *f*

inexperienced *adj* inexpérimenté

inexplicable [ɪnˈɛksplɪkəbəl] *adj* inexplicable

inexpressible [‚ɪnɛkˈsprɛsɪbəl] *adj* inexprimable, indicible

I.N.F. [ˈaɪˈɛnˈɛf] *spl* (letterword) (**intermediate-range nuclear forces**) F.N.I. *fpl* (forces nucléaires intermédiaires)

infallible [ɪnˈfælɪbəl] *adj* infaillible

infamous [ˈɪnfəməs] *adj* infâme

infa·my [ˈɪnfəmi] *s* (*pl* **-mies**) infamie *f*

infan·cy [ˈɪnfənsi] *s* (*pl* **-cies**) première enfance *f*; (fig) enfance

infant [ˈɪnfənt] *adj* infantile; (*in the earliest stage*) (fig) débutant ‖ *s* nourrisson *m*, bébé *m*; enfant *mf* en bas âge

infantile [ˈɪnfən‚taɪl], [ˈɪnfəntɪl] *adj* infantile; (*childish*) enfantin

in′fantile paral′ysis *s* paralysie *f* infantile

infan·try [ˈɪnfəntri] *s* (*pl* **-tries**) infanterie *f*

in′fantry·man *s* (*pl* **-men**) militaire *m* de l'infanterie, fantassin *m*

infatuated [ɪnˈfætʃu‚etɪd] *adj* entiché, épris; **infatuated with oneself** infatué; **to be infatuated** s'engouer

infect [ɪnˈfɛkt] *tr* infecter

infection [ɪnˈfɛkʃən] *s* infection *f*

infectious [ɪnˈfɛkʃəs] *adj* infectieux; (*laughter*) communicatif, contagieux

in·fer [ɪnˈfʌr] *v* (*pret & pp* **-ferred**) *ger* **-ferring**) *tr* inférer

inferior [ɪnˈfɪrɪ·ər] *adj & s* inférieur *m*

inferiority [ɪn‚fɪrɪˈɑriti] *s* infériorité *f*

inferior′ity com′plex *s* complexe *m* d'infériorité

infernal [ɪnˈfʌrnəl] *adj* infernal

infest [ɪnˈfɛst] *tr* infester

infidel [ˈɪnfɪdəl] *adj & s* infidèle *mf*

infideli·ty [‚ɪnfɪˈdɛlɪti] *s* (*pl* **-ties**) infidélité *f*

in′field′ *s* (baseball) petit champ *m*

infiltrate [ˈɪnfɪl‚tret] *tr* s'infiltrer dans, pénétrer; (*with conspirators*) noyauter ‖ *intr* s'infiltrer

infinite [ˈɪnfɪnɪt] *adj & s* infini *m*

infinitely [ˈɪnfɪnɪtli] *adv* infiniment

infinitive [ɪnˈfɪnɪtɪv] *adj & s* infinitif *m*

infini·ty [ɪnˈfɪnɪti] *s* (*pl* **-ties**) infinité *f*; (math) infini *m*

infirm [ɪnˈfʌrm] *adj* infirme, maladif

infirma·ry [ɪnˈfʌrməri] *s* (*pl* **-ries**) infirmerie *f*

infirmi·ty [ɪnˈfʌrmɪti] *s* (*pl* **-ties**) infirmité *f*

in′fix *s* infixe *m*

inflame [ɪnˈflem] *tr* enflammer ‖ *intr* s'enflammer

inflammable [ɪnˈflæməbəl] *adj* inflammable

inflammation [‚ɪnfləˈmeʃən] *s* inflammation *f*

inflammatory [ɪn'flæmə,tori] *adj* incendiaire, provocateur; (pathol) inflammatoire

inflate [ɪn'flet] *tr* gonfler ‖ *intr* se gonfler

inflation [ɪn'fleʃən] *s* gonflement *m*; (com) inflation *f*

inflationary [ɪn'fleʃən,ɛri] *adj* inflationniste

inflect [ɪn'flɛkt] *tr* infléchir; (*e.g., a noun*) décliner; (*a verb*) conjuguer; (*the voice*) moduler

inflection [ɪn'flɛkʃən] *s* inflexion *f*

inflexible [ɪn'flɛksɪbəl] *adj* inflexible

inflict [ɪn'flɪkt] *tr* infliger

influence ['ɪnflu·əns] *s* influence *f* ‖ *tr* influencer, influer sur

in'fluence ped'dling *s* trafic *m* d'influence

influential [,ɪnflu'ɛnʃəl] *adj* influent

influenza [,ɪnflu'ɛnzə] *s* influenza *f*

in'flux' *s* afflux *m*

inform [ɪn'fɔrm] *tr* informer, renseigner; **keep me informed** tenez-moi au courant ‖ *intr*—**to inform on** informer contre, dénoncer

informal [ɪn'fɔrməl] *adj* sans cérémonie; (*person; manners*) familier; (*unoff.cial*) officieux

infor'mal dance' *s* sauterie *f*

informant [ɪn'fɔrmənt] *s* informateur *m*; (*in, e.g., language study*) source *f* d'informations

information [,ɪnfər'meʃən] *s* information *f*, renseignements *mpl*; (telp) service *m* des renseignements téléphoniques; **piece of information** information, renseignement

informational [,ɪnfər'meʃənəl] *adj* instructif, documentaire; (comp) informatique

informa'tion bu'reau *s* bureau *m* de renseignements

informa'tion desk' *s* comptoir *m* informations

informa'tion proc'essing *s* (comp) traitement *m* des données, traitement de l'information

informative [ɪn'fɔrmətɪv] *adj* instructif, édifiant

informed' sour'ces *spl* sources *fpl* bien informées

informer [ɪn'fɔrmər] *s* délateur *m*, dénonciateur *m*; (*police spy*) indicateur *m*, mouchard *m*

infraction [ɪn'frækʃən] *s* infraction *f*

infrared [,ɪnfrə'rɛd] *adj & s* infrarouge *m*

infrastructure ['ɪnfrə,strʌktʃər] *s* infrastructure *f*

infrequent [ɪn'frikwənt] *adj* peu fréquent, rare

infringe [ɪn'frɪndʒ] *tr* enfreindre; (*a patent*) contrefaire ‖ *intr*—**to infringe on** empiéter sur, enfreindre

infringement [ɪn'frɪndʒmənt] *s* infraction *f*; (*on patent rights*) contrefaçon *f*

infuriate [ɪn'fjʊri,et] *tr* rendre furieux

infuse [ɪn'fjuz] *tr* infuser

infusion [ɪn'fjuʒən] *s* infusion *f*

ingenious [ɪn'dʒinjəs] *adj* ingénieux

ingenui·ty [,ɪndʒɪ'n(j)u·ɪti] *s* (*pl* -ties) ingéniosité *f*

ingenuous [ɪn'dʒɛnju·əs] *adj* ingénu, naïf

ingenuousness [ɪn'dʒɛnju·əsnɪs] *s* ingénuité *f*, naïveté *f*

ingest [ɪn'dʒɛst] *tr* ingérer

ingot ['ɪŋgət] *s* lingot *m*

in·grained' *adj* imprégné; (*habit*) invétéré; (*prejudice*) enraciné

ingrate ['ɪngret] *adj & s* ingrat *m*

ingratiate [ɪn'greʃi,et] *tr*—**to ingratiate oneself (with)** se faire bien voir (de)

ingratiating [ɪn'greʃi,etɪŋ] *adj* insinuant, persuasif

ingratitude [ɪn'grætɪ,t(j)ud] *adj* ingratitude *f*

ingredient [ɪn'gridɪ·ənt] *s* ingrédient *m*

in'growing nail' *s* ongle *m* incarné

ingulf [ɪn'gʌlf] *tr* engouffrer

inhabit [ɪn'hæbɪt] *tr* habiter

inhabitant [ɪn'hæbɪtənt] *s* habitant *m*

inhale [ɪn'hel] *tr* inhaler, aspirer; (*smoke*) avaler ‖ *intr* (*while smoking*) avaler

inherent [ɪn'hɪrənt] *adj* inhérent

inherit [ɪn'hɛrɪt] *tr* (*e.g., money*) hériter; (*e.g., money to become the heir or successor of*) hériter de; **to inherit s.th. from s.o.** hériter q.ch. de qn

inheritance [ɪn'hɛrɪtəns] *s* héritage *m*

inher'itance tax' *s* droits *mpl* de succession

inheritor [ɪn'hɛrɪtər] *s* héritier *m*

inhibit [ɪn'hɪbɪt] *tr* inhiber

inhibition [,ɪnɪ'bɪʃən] *s* inhibition *f*

inhospitable [ɪn'hɑspɪtəbəl] *adj* inhospitalier

inhuman [ɪn'hjumən] *adj* inhumain

inhumane [,ɪnhju'men] *adj* inhumain, insensible

inhumani·ty [,ɪnhju'mænɪti] *s* (*pl* -ties) inhumanité *f*

inimical [ɪ'nɪmɪkəl] *adj* inamical

iniqui·ty [ɪ'nɪkwɪti] *s* (*pl* -ties) iniquité *f*; (*wickedness*) méchanceté *f*

ini·tial [ɪ'nɪʃəl] *adj* initial ‖ *s* initiale *f*; **initials** parafe *m*, initiales ‖ *v* (*pret* **-tialed** or **-tialled**; *ger* **-tialing** or **-tialling**) *tr* signer de ses initiales, parapher

initiate [ɪ'nɪʃi,et] *s* initié *m* ‖ *tr* initier; (*a project*) commencer

initiation [ɪ,nɪʃi'eʃən] *s* initiation *f*

initiative [ɪ'nɪʃi·ətɪv] *s* initiative *f*

inject [ɪn'dʒɛkt] *tr* injecter; (*a remark or suggestion*) introduire

injection [ɪn'dʒɛkʃən] *s* injection *f*

injudicious [,ɪndʒu'dɪʃəs] *adj* peu judicieux

injunction [ɪn'dʒʌŋkʃən] *s* injonction *f*; (law) mise *f* en demeure

injure ['ɪndʒər] *tr* (*to harm*) nuire à; (*to wound*) blesser; (*to offend*) faire tort à, léser

injurious [ɪn'dʒʊri·əs] *adj* nuisible, préjudiciable; (*offensive*) blessant, injurieux

inju·ry ['ɪndʒəri] *s* (*pl* -ries) blessure *f*, lésion *f*; (*harm*) tort *m*; injure *f*, offense *f*

injustice [ɪn'dʒʌstɪs] *s* injustice *f*

ink [ɪŋk] *s* encre *f* ‖ *tr* encrer

ink' blot' *s* pâté *m*, macule *f*

inkling [ˈɪŋklɪŋ] s soupçon m, pressentiment m

ink′ pad′ s tampon m encreur

ink′stand′ s encrier m

ink′well′ s encrier m de bureau

ink·y [ˈɪŋki] adj (comp **-ier**; super **-iest**) noir foncé; taché d'encre

inlaid [ˈɪnˌled], [ˌɪnˈled] adj incrusté

inland [ˈɪnlənd] adj & s intérieur m ‖ adv à l'intérieur, vers l'intérieur

in′-law′ s (coll) parent m par alliance, pièce f rapportée; **the in-laws** (coll) la belle-famille, les beaux-parents mpl

in·lay [ˈɪnˌle] s incrustation f ‖ [ˈɪnˌle] v (pret & pp **-laid**) tr incruster

in′let s bras m de mer, crique f; (e.g., of air) arrivée f

in′mate s habitant m; (of an institution) pensionnaire mf

inn [ɪn] s auberge f

innate [ɪˈnet] adj inné, infus

inner [ˈɪnər] adj intérieur; (e.g., ear) interne; intime, secret

in′ner core′ s noyau m (de la cité)

in′ner·spring′ mat′tress s sommier m à ressorts internes

in′ner tube′ s chambre f à air

inning [ˈɪnɪŋ] s manche f, tour m

inn′keep′er s aubergiste mf

innocence [ˈɪnəsəns] s innocence f

innocent [ˈɪnəsənt] adj & s innocent m

innocuous [ɪˈnɑkju·əs] adj inoffensif

innovate [ˈɪnəˌvet] tr & intr innover

innovation [ˌɪnəˈveʃən] s innovation f

innuen·do [ˌɪnjuˈɛndo] s (pl **-does**) allusion f, sous-entendu m

innumerable [ɪˈn(j)umərəbəl] adj innombrable

inoculate [ɪnˈɑkjəˌlet] tr inoculer

inoculation [ɪnˌɑkjəˈleʃən] s inoculation f

inoffensive [ˌɪnəˈfɛnsɪv] adj inoffensif

inoperative [ɪnˈɑpərətɪv] adj inopérant

inopportune [ɪnˌɑpərˈt(j)un] adj inopportun, mal choisi

inordinate [ɪnˈɔrdɪnɪt] adj désordonné, déréglé; (unrestrained) démesuré

inorganic [ˌɪnɔrˈgænɪk] adj inorganique

in′put′ s (comp) information f fournie, données fpl; (elec) prise f, entrée f, énergie f; (mach) consommation f

inquest [ˈɪnkwɛst] s enquête f

inquire [ɪnˈkwaɪr] tr s'informer de, e.g., **to inquire the price of** s'informer du prix de ‖ intr s'enquérir; **to inquire about** s'enquérir de, se renseigner sur; **to inquire into** faire des recherches sur

inquir·y [ˈɪnkwɪri] s (pl **-ies**) investigation f, enquête f; (question) demande f; **to make inquiries** s'informer

inquisition [ˌɪnkwɪˈzɪʃən] s inquisition f

inquisitive [ɪnˈkwɪzɪtɪv] adj curieux, questionneur

in′road′ s incursion f, empiètement m

ins′ and outs′ spl tours et détours mpl

insane [ɪnˈsen] adj dément, fou; (unreasonable) insensé, insane

insane′ asy′lum s asile m d'aliénés

insani·ty [ɪnˈsænɪti] s (pl **-ties**) démence f, aliénation f

insatiable [ɪnˈseʃəbəl] adj insatiable

inscribe [ɪnˈskraɪb] tr inscrire; (a book) dédier

inscription [ɪnˈskrɪpʃən] s inscription f; (of a book) dédicace f; (on a medal) exergue m, inscription

inscrutable [ɪnˈskrutəbəl] adj impénétrable, fermé

insect [ˈɪnsɛkt] s insecte m

insecticide [ɪnˈsɛktɪˌsaɪd] adj & s insecticide m

insecure [ˌɪnsɪˈkjʊr] adj peu sûr; (nervous) inquiet

insensitive [ɪnˈsɛnsɪtɪv] adj insensible

inseparable [ɪnˈsɛpərəbəl] adj inséparable

insert [ˈɪnsʌrt] s (sewing) incrustation f; (typ) hors-texte m, encart m ‖ [ɪnˈsʌrt] tr insérer, introduire; (typ) encarter

insertion [ɪnˈsʌrʃən] s insertion f; (sewing) incrustation f

in·set [ˈɪnˌsɛt] s (map, picture, etc.) médaillon m, cartouche m; (sewing) incrustation f; (typ) hors-texte m, encart m ‖ [ɪnˈsɛt], [ˈɪnˌsɛt] v (pret & pp **-set**; ger **-setting**) tr insérer; (a page or pages) encarter

in′shore′ adj côtier ‖ adv près de la côte

in′side′ adj d'intérieur, interne; (information) secret, à la source ‖ s intérieur m, dedans m; **insides** (coll) entrailles fpl ‖ adv à l'intérieur; **inside and out** au-dedans et au-dehors; **inside of** à l'intérieur de; **inside out** à l'envers; **to turn inside out** (e.g., a coat) retourner ‖ prep à l'intérieur de, dans

in′side informa′tion s tuyau m, tuyaux m

insider [ˌɪnˈsaɪdər] s initié m

in′side track′ s—**to have the inside track** prendre à la corde; (fig) avoir un avantage

insidious [ɪnˈsɪdi·əs] adj insidieux

in′sight′ s pénétration f; (psychol) défoulement m

insigni·a [ɪnˈsɪgni·ə] s (pl **-a** or **-as**) insigne m

insignificant [ˌɪnsɪgˈnɪfɪkənt] adj insignifiant

insincere [ˌɪnsɪnˈsɪr] adj insincère, peu sincère

insinuate [ɪnˈsɪnjuˌet] tr insinuer

insipid [ɪnˈsɪpɪd] adj insipide

insist [ɪnˈsɪst] intr insister; **to insist on** insister sur; **to insist on** + ger insister pour + inf

insofar as [ˌɪnsoˈfɑrəz] conj pour autant que, dans la mesure où

insolence [ˈɪnsələns] s insolence f

insolent [ˈɪnsələnt] adj insolent

insoluble [ɪnˈsɑljəbəl] adj insoluble

insolven·cy [ɪnˈsɑlvənsi] s (pl **-cies**) insolvabilité f

insolvent [ɪnˈsɑlvənt] adj insolvable

insomnia [ɪnˈsɑmnɪ·ə] s insomnie f

insomuch [ˌɪnsoˈmʌtʃ] adv—**insomuch as** vu que; **insomuch that** à tel point que

inspect [ɪnˈspɛkt] tr inspecter

inspection [ɪn`spɛkʃən] *s* inspection *f*
inspector [ɪn`spɛktər] *s* inspecteur *m*
inspiration [ˌɪnspɪ`reʃən] *s* inspiration *f*
inspire [ɪn`spaɪr] *tr* inspirer
inspiring [ɪn`spaɪrɪŋ] *adj* inspirant
install [ɪn`stɔl] *tr* installer
installment [ɪn`stɔlmənt] *s* installation *f*; (*delivery*) livraison *f*; (*serial story*) feuilleton *m*; (*partial payment*) acompte *m*, versement *m*; **in installments** par acomptes, par tranches
install'ment buy'ing *s* achat *m* à tempérament
install'ment plan' *s* vente *f* à tempérament or à crédit; **on the installment plan** avec facilités de paiement
instance [`ɪnstəns] *s* cas *m*, exemple *m*; **for instance** par exemple
instant [`ɪnstənt] *adj* imminent, immédiat; **on the fifth instant** le cinq courant ‖ *s* instant *m*, moment *m*
instantaneous [ˌɪnstən`tenɪ·əs] *adj* instantané
in'stant cof'fee *s* café *m* en poudre, café instantané
instantly [`ɪnstəntli] *adv* à l'instant
instead [ɪn`stɛd] *adv* plutôt, au contraire; à ma (votre, sa, etc.) place; **instead of** au lieu de
in'step' *s* cou-de-pied *m*
instigate [`ɪnstɪˌget] *tr* inciter
instigation [ˌɪnstɪ`geʃən] *s* instigation *f*
instill [ɪn`stɪl] *tr* instiller
instinct [`ɪnstɪŋkt] *s* instinct *m*
instinctive [ɪn`stɪŋktɪv] *adj* instinctif
institute [`ɪnstɪˌt(j)ut] *s* institut *m* ‖ *tr* instituer
institution [ˌɪnstɪ`t(j)uʃən] *s* institution *f*
instruct [ɪn`strʌkt] *tr* instruire
instruction [ɪn`strʌkʃən] *s* instruction *f*; (comp) instructions
instruc'tional soft'ware [ɪn`strʌkʃənəl] *s* (comp) didacticiel *m*
instruc'tion man'ual *s* livret *m* d'instruction
instructive [ɪn`strʌktɪv] *adj* instructif
instructor [ɪn`strʌktər] *s* instructeur *m*
instrument [`ɪnstrəmənt] *s* instrument *m* ‖ [`ɪnstrəˌmɛnt] *tr* instrumenter
instrumental [ˌɪnstrə`mɛntəl] *adj* instrumental; **to be instrumental in** contribuer à
instrumentalist [ˌɪnstrə`mɛntəlɪst] *s* instrumentiste *mf*
instrumentali·ty [ˌɪnstrəmən`tælɪti] *s* (*pl* **-ties**) intermédiaire *m*, intervention *f*
in'strument board' *s* tableau *m* de bord
in'strument fly'ing *s* radio-navigation *f*, vol *m* aux instruments
in'strument land'ing *s* atterrissage *m* aux instruments, aide *f* à la navigation
in'strument pan'el *s* tableau *m* de bord
insubordinate [ˌɪnsə`bɔrdɪnɪt] *adj* insubordonné
insufferable [ɪn`sʌfərəbəl] *adj* insupportable, intolérable, imbuvable
insufficient [ˌɪnsə`fɪʃənt] *adj* insuffisant

insuffi'cient ev'idence *s* insuffisance *f* de preuves
insular [`ɪnsələr], [`ɪnsjʊlər] *adj* insulaire
insulate [`ɪnsəˌlet] *tr* insoler
in'sulating tape' *s* ruban *m* isolant, chatterton *m*
insulation [ˌɪnsə`leʃən] *s* isolation *f*
insulator [`ɪnsəˌletər] *s* isolant *m*
insulin [`ɪnsəlɪn] *s* insuline *f*
insult [`ɪnsʌlt] *s* insulte *f* ‖ [ɪn`sʌlt] *tr* insulter
insulting [ɪn`sʌltɪŋ] *adj* insultant, injurieux
insurable [ɪn`ʃʊrəbəl] *adj* assurable
insurance [ɪn`ʃʊrəns] *s* assurance *f*
insure [ɪn`ʃʊr] *tr* assurer
insurer [ɪn`ʃʊrər] *s* assureur *m*
insurgent [ɪn`sʌrdʒənt] *adj & s* insurgé *m*
insurmountable [ˌɪnsər`maʊntəbəl] *adj* insurmontable
insurrection [ˌɪnsə`rɛkʃən] *s* insurrection *f*
intact [ɪn`tækt] *adj* intact
in'take' *s* (*place*) entrée *f*; (*act or amount*) prise *f*; (mach) admission *f*
in'take man'ifold *s* tubulure *f* d'admission, collecteur *m* d'admission
in'take valve' *s* soupape *f* d'admission
intangible [ɪn`tændʒɪbəl] *adj* intangible
intan'gible as'sets *spl* actif *m* incorporel
integer [`ɪntɪdʒər] *s* nombre *m* entier
integral [`ɪntɪɡrəl] *adj* intégral (*part*) intégrant; **integral with** solidaire de ‖ *s* intégrale *f*
intergrate [`ɪntɪˌɡret] *tr* intégrer
integration [ˌɪntɪ`ɡreʃən] *s* intégration *f*
integrity [ɪn`tɛɡrɪti] *s* intégrité *f*
intellect [`ɪntəˌlɛkt] *s* intellect *m*; (*person*) intelligence *f*
intellectual [ˌɪntə`lɛktʃu·əl] *adj & s* intellectuel *m*
intelligence [ɪn`tɛlɪdʒəns] *s* intelligence *f*
intel'ligence bu'reau *s* deuxième bureau *m*, service *m* de renseignements
intel'ligence quo'tient *s* quotient *m* intellectuel
intel'ligence test' *s* test *m* d'habileté mentale, test de capacité intellectuelle
intelligent [ɪn`tɛlɪdʒənt] *adj* intelligent
intelligible [ɪn`tɛlɪdʒɪbəl] *adj* intelligible
intemperate [ɪn`tɛmpərɪt] *adj* intempérant
intend [ɪn`tɛnd] *tr* destiner; signifier; vouloir dire; **to intend to** avoir l'intention de, penser; **to intend to become** se destiner à
intended *adj & s* (coll) futur *m*
intense [ɪn`tɛns] *adj* intense
intensi·fy [ɪn`tɛnsɪˌfaɪ] *v* (*pret & pp* **-fied**) *tr* intensifier ‖ *intr* s'intensifier
intensi·ty [ɪn`tɛnsɪti] *s* (*pl* **-ties**) intensité *f*
intensive [ɪn`tɛnsɪv] *adj* intensif
intent [ɪn`tɛnt] *adj* attentif; (*look, gaze*) fixe, intense; **intent on** résolu à ‖ *s* intention *f*; **to all intents and purposes** en fait, pratiquement
intention [ɪn`tɛnʃən] *s* intention *f*
intentional [ɪn`tɛnʃənəl] *adj* intentionnel, délibéré
intentionally [ɪn`tɛnʃənəli] *adv* exprès, à dessein

in·ter [ɪn'tʌr] *v* (*pret* & *pp* **-terred;** *ger* **-terring**) *tr* enterrer

interact [,ɪntər'ækt] *intr* agir réciproquement

interaction [,ɪntər'ækʃən] *s* interaction *f*

inter·breed [,ɪntər'brid] *v* (*pret* & *pp* **-bred**) *tr* croiser ‖ *intr* se croiser

intercalate [ɪn'tʌrkə,let] *tr* intercaler

intercede [,ɪntər'sid] *intr* intercéder

intercept [,ɪntər'sɛpt] *tr* intercepter

interceptor [,ɪntər'sɛptər] *s* intercepteur *m*

interchange ['ɪntər,tʃendʒ] *s* échange *m*, permutation *f*; (*transfer point*) correspondance *f*; (*on highway*) échangeur *m* ‖ [,ɪntər'tʃendʒ] *tr* échanger, permuter ‖ *intr* permuter

intercollegiate [,ɪntərkə'lidʒɪ·ɪt] *adj* interuniversitaire, entre universités

intercom ['ɪntər,kɑm] *s* (coll) interphone *m*, intervox *m*

intercourse ['ɪntər,kors] *s* relations *fpl*, rapports *mpl*; (*copulation*) copulation *f*, coït *m*

intercross [,ɪntər'krɔs], [,ɪntər'krɑs] *tr* entrecroiser ‖ *intr* s'entrecroiser

interdict ['ɪntər,dɪkt] *s* interdit *m* ‖ [,ɪntər'dɪkt] *tr* interdire; **to interdict s.o. from** + *ger* interdire à qn de + *inf*

interdisciplinary [,ɪntər'dɪsəplənɛri] *adj* interdisciplinaire

interest ['ɪntərɪst] *s* intérêt *m* ‖ ['ɪntə,rɛst] *tr* intéresser

interested *adj* intéressé; **to be interested in** s'intéresser à or dans

interesting ['ɪntrɪstɪŋ] *adj* intéressant

in'terest rate' *s* taux *m* d'intérêt

interface ['ɪntər,fes] *s* interface *f*

interfere [,ɪntər'fɪr] *intr* (*to meddle*) s'ingérer, s'immiscer; (phys) interférer; **to interfere with** intervenir dans, se mêler de; (*e.g., one's plans*) entraver, contrecarrer; **to interfere with each other** interférer (entre eux)

interference [,ɪntər'fɪrəns] *s* ingérence *f*, immixtion *f*; (phys) interférence *f*; (*static*) (rad) parasites *mpl*; (*jamming*) (rad) brouillage *m*; **interference with** immixtion dans

interim ['ɪntərɪm] *adj* provisoire, par intérim ‖ *s* intérim *m*

interior [ɪn'tɪrɪ·ər] *adj* & *s* intérieur *m*

inte'rior dec'orator *s* décorateur *m* d'intérieurs

interject [,ɪntər'dʒɛkt] *tr* interposer; (*questions*) lancer

interjection [,ɪntər'dʒɛkʃən] *s* intervention *f*; (gram) interjection *f*

interlard [,ɪntər'lɑrd] *tr* entrelarder

in'terli'brary loan' *s* le prêt interbibliothèque, le service des prêts entre bibliothèques

interline [,ɪntər'laɪn] *tr* interligner

interlining ['ɪntər,laɪnɪŋ] *s* doublure *f* intermédiaire

interlock [,ɪntər'lɑk] *tr* emboîter, engager ‖ *intr* s'emboîter, s'engager

interloper [,ɪntər'lopər] *s* intrus *m*

interlude ['ɪntər,lud] *s* (mov, mus, telv) interlude *m*; (theat, fig) intermède *m*

intermediar·y [,ɪntər'midɪ,ɛri] *adj* intermédiaire ‖ *s* (*pl* **-ies**) intermédiaire *mf*, interprète *mf*

intermediate [,ɪntər'midɪ·ɪt] *adj* intermédiaire

interme'diate-range' mis'sile *s* missile *m* à portée intermédiaire

interment [ɪn'tʌrmənt] *s* enterrement *m*, sépulture *f*

interminable [ɪn'tʌrmɪnəbəl] *adj* interminable

intermingle [,ɪntər'mɪŋgəl] *tr* entremêler ‖ *intr* s'entremêler

intermission [,ɪntər'mɪʃən] *s* relâche *m*, pause *f*; (theat) entracte *m*

intermittent [,ɪntər'mɪtənt] *adj* intermittent

intermix [,ɪntər'mɪks] *tr* entremêler ‖ *intr* s'entremêler

intern ['ɪntʌrn] *s* interne *mf* ‖ [ɪn'tʌrn] *tr* interner

internal [ɪn'tʌrnəl] *adj* interne

inter'nal-combus'tion en'gine *s* moteur *m* à explosion

inter'nal rev'enue *s* recettes *fpl* fiscales

international [,ɪntər'næʃənəl] *adj* international; (*exposition*) universel

in'terna'tional date' line' *s* ligne *f* de changement de date

in'terna'tional time' zone' *s* fuseau *m* horaire international

internecine [,ɪntər'nisɪn] *adj* domestique, intestin; (*war*) sanguinaire, d'extermination

internee [,ɪntʌr'ni] *s* interné *m*

internment [ɪn'tʌrnmənt] *s* internement *m*

in'tern·ship' *s* internat *m*

interpellate [,ɪntər'pɛlet] *tr* interpeller

interplanetary [,ɪntər'plænə,tɛri] *adj* interplanétaire

interplan'etary trav'el *s* voyages *mpl* interplanétaires

interplay ['ɪntər,ple] *s* interaction *f*

interpolate [ɪn'tʌrpə,let] *tr* interpoler

interpose [,ɪntər'poz] *tr* interposer

interpret [ɪn'tʌrprɪt] *tr* interpréter

interpretation [ɪn,tʌrprɪ'teʃən] *s* interprétation *f*

interpreter [ɪn'tʌrprɪtər] *s* interprète *mf*

interrogate [ɪn'tɛrə,get] *tr* interroger

interrogation [ɪn,tɛrə'geʃən] *s* interrogation *f*

interroga'tion mark' *s* point *m* d'interrogation

interrupt [,ɪntə'rʌpt] *tr* interrompre

interruption [,ɪntə'rʌpʃən] *s* interruption *f*

intersect [,ɪntər'sɛkt] *tr* entrecouper ‖ *intr* s'entrecouper

intersection [,ɪntər'sɛkʃən] *s* intersection *f*

intersperse [,ɪntər'spʌrs] *tr* entremêler

interstellar [,ɪntər'stɛlər] *adj* interstellaire

interstice [ɪn'tʌrstɪs] *s* interstice *m*

intertwine [,ɪntər'twaɪn] *tr* entrelacer ‖ *intr* s'entrelacer

interval ['ɪntərvəl] *s* intervalle *m*

intervene [,ɪntər'vin] *intr* intervenir

intervening [,ɪntər'vinɪŋ] *adj* (*period*) inter-médiaire; (*party*) intervenant

intervention [,ɪntər'vɛnʃən] *s* intervention *f*

interview ['ɪntər,vju] *s* entrevue *f*; (journ) interview *f* ‖ *tr* avoir une entrevue avec; (journ) interviewer

inter·weave [,ɪntər'wiv] *v* (*pret* **-wove** or **-weaved**; *pp* **-wove, woven** or **weaved**) *tr* entrelacer; (*to intermingle*) entremêler

intestate [ɪn'tɛstet] *adj* & *s* intestat *m*

intestine [ɪn'tɛstɪn] *adj* & *s* intestin *m*

intima·cy ['ɪntɪməsi] *s* (*pl* **-cies**) intimité *f*; rapports *mpl* sexuels

intimate ['ɪntɪmɪt] *adj* & *s* intime *mf* ‖ ['ɪntɪ,met] *tr* donner à entendre

intimation [,ɪntɪ'meʃən] *s* suggestion *f*, insinuation *f*

intimidate [ɪn'tɪmɪ,det] *tr* intimider

into ['ɪntʊ] *prep* dans, en

intolerant [ɪn'tɑlərənt] *adj* intolérant

intonation [,ɪnto'neʃən] *s* intonation *f*

intone [ɪn'ton] *tr* (*to begin to sing*) entonner; (*to sing or recite in a monotone*) psalmodier ‖ *intr* psalmodier

intoxicant [ɪn'tɑksɪkənt] *s* boisson *f* alcoolique

intoxicate [ɪn'tɑksɪ,ket] *tr* enivrer; (*to poison*) intoxiquer

intoxication [ɪn,tɑksɪ'keʃən] *s* ivresse *f*; (*poisoning*) intoxication *f*; (fig) enivrement *m*

intractable [ɪn'træktəbəl] *adj* intraitable

intransigent [ɪn'trænsɪdʒənt] *adj* intransigeant

intransitive [ɪn'trænsɪtɪv] *adj* intransitif

intravenous [,ɪntrə'vinəs] *adj* intraveineux

intrave'nous drip' *s* goutte-à-goutte *m* in-var

intrepid [ɪn'trɛpɪd] *adj* intrépide

intricate ['ɪntrɪkɪt] *adj* compliqué

intrigue [ɪn'trig] *s* intrigue *f* ‖ *tr* & *intr* intriguer

intrinsic(al) [ɪn'trɪnsɪk(əl)] *adj* intrinsèque

introduce [,ɪntrə'd(j)us] *tr* introduire; (*to make acquainted*) présenter

introduction [,ɪntrə'dʌkʃən] *s* introduction *f*; (*the beginning part*) entrée en matière, exorde *m* (*of one person to another or others*) présentation *f*

introductory [,ɪntrə'dʌktəri] *adj* préliminaire; (*text*) liminaire; (*speech, letter, etc.*) de présentation

introduc'tory of'fer *s* offre *f* de présentation, prix *m* de lancement

introspective [,ɪntrə'spɛktɪv] *adj* introspectif; (*person*) méditatif

introvert ['ɪntrə,vʌrt] *adj* & *s* introverti *m*

intrude [ɪn'trud] *intr* s'ingérer, s'immiscer; **to intrude on s.o.** déranger qn

intruder [ɪn'trudər] *s* intrus *m*

intrusion [ɪn'truʒən] *s* intrusion; (*upon privacy*) immixtions *fpl*, ingérences *fpl*

intrusive [ɪn'trusɪv] *adj* importun

intuition [,ɪnt(j)u'ɪʃən] *s* intuition *f*

inundate ['ɪnən,det] *tr* inonder

inundation [,ɪnən'deʃən] *s* inondation *f*

inure [ɪn'jʊr] *tr* aguerrir, endurcir ‖ *intr* entrer en vigueur; **to inure to** rejaillir sur

invade [ɪn'ved] *tr* envahir

invader [ɪn'vedər] *s* envahisseur *m*

invalid [ɪn'vælɪd] *adj* invalide, nul ‖ ['ɪnvəlɪd] *adj* & *s* malade *mf*, invalide *mf*

invalidate [ɪn'vælɪ,det] *tr* invalider

invalidity [,ɪnvə'lɪdɪti] *s* invalidité *f*, nullité *f*

invaluable [ɪn'væljʊ·əbəl] *adj* inappréciable, inestimable

invariable [ɪn'vɛrɪ·əbəl] *adj* invariable

invasion [ɪn'veʒən] *s* invasion *f*

invective [ɪn'vɛktɪv] *s* invective *f*

inveigh [ɪn've] *intr*—**to inveigh against** invectiver contre

inveigle [ɪn'vegəl] *tr* séduire, enjôler; **to inveigle s.o. into** + *ger* entraîner qn à + *inf*

invent [ɪn'vɛnt] *tr* inventer

invention [ɪn'vɛnʃən] *s* invention *f*

inventive [ɪn'vɛntɪv] *adj* inventif

inventiveness [ɪn'vɛntɪvnɪs] *s* esprit *m* inventif

inventor [ɪn'vɛntər] *s* inventeur *m*

invento·ry ['ɪnvən,tori] *s* (*pl* **-ries**) inventaire *m*; **beginning inventory** (com) stock *m* d'ouverture; **ending inventory** (com) stock de fermeture ‖ *v* (*pret* & *pp* **-ried**) *tr* inventorier

inverse [ɪn'vʌrs] *adj* & *s* inverse *m*

inversion [ɪn'vʌrʒən] *s* interversion *f*, inversion *f*

invert ['ɪnvʌrt] *adj* & *s* inverti *m* ‖ [ɪn'vʌrt] *tr* inverser; (*an image*) invertir

invertebrate [ɪn'vʌrtɪ,bret] *adj* & *s* invertébré *m*

invest [ɪn'vɛst] *tr* investir; (*money*) investir, placer; **to invest with** investir de ‖ *intr* investir or placer de l'argent

investigate [ɪn'vɛstɪ,get] *tr* examiner, rechercher

investigation [ɪn,vɛstɪ'geʃən] *s* investigation *f*

investigator [ɪn'vɛstɪ,getər] *s* investigateur *m*, chercheur *m*

investment [ɪn'vɛstmənt] *s* investissement *m*, placement *m*; (*with an office or dignity*) investiture *f*; (*siege*) investissement *m*

invest'ment trust' *s* fonds *m* de placement fermé

investor [ɪn'vɛstər] *s* capitaliste *mf*

inveterate [ɪn'vɛtərɪt] *adj* invétéré

invidious [ɪn'vɪdɪ·əs] *adj* odieux

invigorate [ɪn'vɪgə,ret] *tr* vivifier, fortifier

invigorating [ɪn'vɪgə,retɪŋ] *adj* vivifiant, fortifiant

invincible [ɪn'vɪnsɪbəl] *adj* invincible

invisible [ɪn'vɪzɪbəl] *adj* invisible

invis'ible ink' *s* encre *f* sympathique

invitation [,ɪnvɪ'teʃən] *s* invitation *f*

invite [ɪn'vaɪt] *tr* inviter

inviting [ɪn'vaɪtɪŋ] *adj* invitant

invoice ['ɪnvɔɪs] *s* facture *f*; **as per invoice** suivant facture ‖ *tr* facturer

invoke [ɪn'vok] *tr* invoquer

involuntary [ɪn'vɑlən,tɛri] *adj* involontaire

involve [ɪn'vɑlv] *tr* impliquer, entraîner, engager

invulnerable [ɪn'vʌlnərəbəl] *adj* invulnérable

inward ['ɪnwərd] *adj* intérieur ‖ *adv* intérieurement, en dedans

iodide ['aɪ·ə,daɪd] *s* iodure *m*

iodine ['aɪ·ə,dɪn] *s* (chem) iode *m* ‖ ['aɪ·ə,daɪn] *s* (pharm) teinture *f* d'iode

ion ['aɪ·ən], ['aɪ·ɑn] *s* ion *m*

ionize [['aɪ·ə,naɪz] *tr* ioniser

ionosphere [aɪ'ɑnə,sfɪr] *s* ionosphère *f*

I.O.U. ['aɪ,o'ju] *s* (letterword) (**I owe you**) reconnaissance *f* de dette

I.Q. ['aɪ'kju] *s* (letterword) (**intelligence quotient**) quotient *m* intellectuel

Iran [ɪ'rɑn], [aɪ'ræn] *s* l'Iran *m*

Iranian [aɪ'renɪ·ən] *adj* iranien ‖ *s* (*language*) iranien *m*; (*person*) Iranien *m*

Iraq [ɪ'rɑk] *s* l'Irak *m*

Ira·qi [ɪ'rɑki] *adj* irakien ‖ *s* (*pl* -**qis**) Irakien *m*

irate ['aɪret], [aɪ'ret] *adj* irrité

ire [aɪr] *s* courroux *m*, colère *f*

Ireland ['aɪrlənd] *s* Irlande *f*; l'Irlande

iris ['aɪrɪs] *s* iris *m*

Irish ['aɪrɪʃ] *adj* irlandais ‖ *s* (*language*) irlandais *m*, **the Irish** les Irlandais

I′rish·man *s* (*pl* -**men**) Irlandais *m*

I′rish stew′ *s* ragoût *m* irlandais

I′rish·wom′an *s* (*pl* -**wom′en**) Irlandaise *f*

irk [ʌrk] *tr* ennuyer, fâcher

irksome ['ʌrksəm] *adj* ennuyeux

iron ['aɪ·ərn] *s* fer *m*; (*for pressing clothes*) fer à repasser; **irons** (*fetters*) fers; **to have too many irons in the fire** courir deux lièvres à la fois; **to strike while the iron is hot** battre le fer tant qu'il est chaud ‖ *tr* (*clothes*) repasser; **to iron out** (*a difficulty*) aplanir

i′ron and steel′ in′dustry *s* sidérurgie *f*

i′ron-bound′ *adj* cerclé de fer; (*unyielding*) inflexible; (*rock-bound*) plein de récifs

ironclad ['aɪ·ərn,klæd] *adj* blindé, ferré, cuirassé; (*e.g., contract*) infrangible

i′ron cur′tain *s* rideau *m* de fer

i′ron diges′tion *s* estomac *m* d'autruche

i′ron gate′ *s* grille *f* d'entrée

i′ron horse′ *s* coursier *m* de fer

ironic(al) [aɪ'rɑnɪk(əl)] *adj* ironique

ironing ['aɪ,ərnɪŋ] *s* repassage *m*

i′roning board′ *s* planche *f* à repasser

i′ron lung′ *s* poumon *m* d'acier

i′ron ore′ *s* minerai *m* de fer

i′ron-tipped′ *adj* ferré

i′ron·ware′ *s* quincaillerie *f*, ferblanterie *f*

i′ron will′ *s* volonté *f* inflexible

i′ron·work′ *s* ferrure *f*, ferronnerie *f*

i′ron·work′er *s* ferronnier *m*

iro·ny ['aɪrəni] *s* (*pl* -**nies**) ironie *f*

irradiate [ɪ'redɪ,et] *tr* & *intr* irradier

irrational [ɪ'ræʃənəl] *adj* irrationnel

irredeemable [,ɪrɪ'diməbəl] *adj* irrémédiable; (*bonds*) non remboursable

irrefutable [,ɪrɪ'fjutəbəl] *adj* irréfutable

irregular [ɪ'rɛgjələr] *adj* & *s* irrégulier *m*

irrelevant [ɪ'rɛləvənt] *adj* non pertinent, hors de propos

irreligious [,ɪrɪ'lɪdʒəs] *adj* irréligieux

irremediable [,ɪrɪ'midɪ·əbəl] *adj* irrémédiable

irreparable [ɪ'rɛpərəbəl] *adj* irréparable

irreplaceable [,ɪrɪ'plesəbəl] *adj* irremplaçable

irrepressible [,ɪrɪ'prɛsɪbəl] *adj* irrépressible, irrésistible

irreproachable [,ɪrɪ'protʃəbəl] *adj* irréprochable

irresistible [,ɪrɪ'zɪstɪbəl] *adj* irrésistible

irrespective [,ɪrɪ'spɛktɪv] *adj*—**irrespective of** indépendant de

irresponsible [,ɪrɪ'spɑnsɪbəl] *adj* irresponsable

irretrievable [,ɪrɪ'trivəbəl] *adj* irréparable; (*lost*) irrécupérable

irreverent [ɪ'rɛvərənt] *adj* irrévérencieux

irrevocable [ɪ'rɛvəkəbəl] *adj* irrévocable

irrigate ['ɪrɪ,get] *tr* irriguer

irrigation [,ɪrɪ'geʃən] *s* irrigation *f*

irritant ['ɪrɪtənt] *adj* & *s* irritant *m*

irritate ['ɪrɪ,tet] *tr* irriter

irritation [,ɪrɪ'teʃən] *s* irritation *f*

irruption [ɪ'rʌpʃən] *s* irruption *f*

Isaiah [aɪ'ze·ə] *s* Isaïe *m*

isinglass ['aɪzɪŋ,glæs] *s* gélatine *f*, colle *f* de poisson; (mineral) mica *m*

Islam ['ɪsləm], [ɪs'lɑm] *s* l'Islam *m*

Islamic [ɪs'lɑmɪk] *adj* islamique

island ['aɪlənd] *s* insulaire ‖ *s* île *f*

islander ['aɪləndər] *s* insulaire *mf*

isle [aɪl] *s* îlot *m*; (poetic) île *f*

isolate ['aɪsə,let] *tr* isoler

isolation [,aɪsə'leʃən] *s* isolement *m*

isolationist [,aɪsə'leʃənɪst] *adj* & *s* isolationniste *mf*

isosceles [aɪ'sɑsə,liz] *adj* isocèle

isotope ['aɪsə,top] *s* isotope *m*

Israel ['ɪzrɪ·əl] *s* Israël *m*; **in Israel** en Israël; **of Israel** d'Israël, e.g., **the state of Israel** l'état d'Israël; **to Israel** (*to give to*) à Israël; (*to go to*) en Israël

Israe·li [ɪz'reli] *adj* israélien ‖ *s* (*pl* -**lis** [liz]) Israélien *m*

Israelite ['ɪzrɪ·ə,laɪt] *adj* israélite ‖ *s* Israélite *mf*

issuance ['ɪʃu·əns] *s* émission *f*

issue ['ɪʃu] *s* (*way out*) sortie *f*, issue *f*; (*outcome*) issue; (*of a magazine*) numéro *m*; (*offspring*) descendance *f*; (*of banknotes, stamps, etc.*) émission *f*; (*under discussion*) point *m* à discuter; (pathol) écoulement *m*; **at issue** en jeu, en litige; **to take issue with** être en désaccord avec; **without issue** sans enfants ‖ *tr* (*a book, a magazine*) publier; (*banknotes, stamps, etc.*) émettre; (*a summons*) lancer; (*an order*) donner; (*a proclamation*) faire; (*a verdict*) rendre ‖ *intr* sortir, déboucher

isthmus ['ɪsməs] *s* isthme *m*

it [ɪt] *pron pers* ce §82B, §85; lui §85; il §87; le §87; y §87; en §87

Italian [ɪ'tæljən] *adj* italien ‖ *s* (*language*) italien *m*; (*person*) Italien *m*

italic [ɪˈtælɪk] *adj* (typ) italique; **Italic** italique ‖ **italics** *spl* caractères *mpl* penchés, italique *m*; **italics mine** c'est moi qui souligne

italicize [ɪˈtælɪˌsaɪz] *tr* mettre en italique

Italy [ˈɪtəli] *s* Italie *f*; l'Italie

itch [ɪtʃ] *s* démangeaison *f*; (pathol) gale *f* ‖ *tr* démanger à ‖ *intr* (*said of part of body*) démanger; (*said of person*) avoir une démangeaison; **to itch to** (fig) avoir une démangeaison de

itch·y [ˈɪtʃi] *adj* (*comp* **-ier**; *super* **-iest**) piquant; (pathol) galeux

item [ˈaɪtəm] *s* article *m*; (*in a list*) point *m*; (*piece of news*) nouvelle *f*

itemize [ˈaɪtəˌmaɪz] *tr* spécifier, énumérer

itinerant [aɪˈtɪnərənt] *adj* & *s* itinérant *m*

itinerar·y [aɪˈtɪnəˌrɛri] *adj* itinéraire ‖ *s* (*pl* **-ies**) itinéraire *m*

its [ɪts] *adj poss* son §88 ‖ *pron poss* le sien §89

it's = **it is** c'est; il est, elle est

it'self' *pron pers* soi §85; lui-même §86; se §87

ivied [ˈaɪvid] *adj* couvert de lierre

ivo·ry [ˈaɪvəri] *adj* d'ivoire, en ivoire ‖ *s* (*pl* **-ries**) ivoire *m*; **to tickle the ivories** (slang) taquiner l'ivoire

i'vory tow'er *s* (fig) tour *f* d'ivoire

I.V. stand [ˌaɪˈviˈstænd] *s* (med) goutte-à-goutte *m invar*

ivy [ˈaɪvi] *s* (*pl* **ivies**) lierre *m*

J

J, j [dʒe] *s* Xᵉ lettre de l'alphabet

jab [dʒæb] *s* (*with a sharp point; with a penknife; with the elbow*) coup m; (*with a needle*) piqûre *f*; (*with the fist*) coup sec ‖ *v* (*pret & pp* **jabbed**; *ger* **jabbing**) *tr* donner un coup de coude à; piquer; donner un coup sec à; (*a knife*) enfoncer

jabber [ˈdʒæbər] *tr* & *intr* jaboter

jack [dʒæk] *s* (aut) cric *m*, vérin *m*; (cards) valet *m*; (elec) jack *m*, prise *f*; (coll) fric *m*; **Jack** Jeannot *m* ‖ *tr*—**to jack up** soulever au cric; (*prices*) faire monter

jackal [ˈdʒækəl] *s* chacal *m*

jack'ass' *s* baudet *m*

jack'daw' *s* choucas *m*

jacket [ˈdʒækɪt] *s* (*of a woman; of a book*) jaquette *f*; (*of a man's suit*) veston *m*; (*metal casing*) chemise *f*

Jack' Frost' *s* le Bonhomme Hiver

jack'-in-the-box' *s* diable *m* à ressort, boîte *f* à surprise

jack'knife' *s* (*pl* **-knives**) couteau *m* de poche, couteau pliant; (*fancy dive*) saut *m* de carpe

jack'-of-all'-trades' *s* bricoleur *m*

jack-o'-lantern [ˈdʒækə ˌlæntərn] *s* potiron *m* lumineux

jack'pot' *s* gros lot *m*, poule *f*; **to hit the jackpot** décrocher la timbale

jack' rab'bit *s* lièvre *m* des prairies

Jacob [ˈdʒekəb] *s* Jacques *m*

jade [dʒed] *s* (*stone; color*) jade *m*; (*horse*) haridelle *f*; (*woman*) coquine *f*, friponne *f*

jaded *adj* éreinté, excédé; blasé

jag [dʒæg] *s* dentelure *f*; **to have a jag on** (slang) être paf

jagged [ˈdʒægɪd] *adj* dentelé

jaguar [ˈdʒægwɑr] *s* jaguar *m*

jail [dʒel] *s* prison *f* ‖ *tr* emprisonner

jail'bird' *s* cheval *m* de retour

jailer [ˈdʒelər] *s* geôlier *m*

jalop·y [dʒəˈlɑpi] *s* (*pl* **-ies**) bagnole *f*, tacot *m*, guimbarde *f*, clou *m*

jam [dʒæm] *s* confiture *f*; **to be in a jam** (coll) être dans le pétrin ‖ *v* (*pret & pp* **jammed**; *ger* **jamming**) *tr* coincer ‖ *intr* se coincer

jamboree [ˌdʒæmbəˈri] *s* (*of boy scouts*) jamboree *m*; (slang) bombance *f*

James [dʒemz] *s* Jacques *m*

jamming [ˈdʒæmɪŋ] *s* (rad) brouillage *m*

Jane [dʒen] *s* Jeanne *f*

jangle [ˈdʒæŋgəl] *s* cliquetis *m* ‖ *tr* faire cliqueter; (*nerves*) mettre en boule ‖ *intr* cliqueter

janitor [ˈdʒænitər] *s* concierge *m*

janitress [ˈdʒænɪtrɪs] *s* concierge *f*

January [ˈdʒænjuˌɛri] *s* janvier *m*

ja·pan [dʒəˈpæn] *s* laque *m* du Japon; **Japan** le Japon ‖ *v* (*pret & pp* **-panned**; *ger* **-panning**) *tr* laquer

Japa·nese [ˌdʒæpəˈniz] *adj* japonais ‖ *s* (*language*) japonais *m* ‖ *s* (*pl* **-nese**) (*person*) Japonais *m*

Jap'anese bee'tle *s* cétoine *f*

Jap'anese lan'tern *s* lanterne *f* vénitienne

jar [dʒɑr] *s* (*container*) pot *m*, bocal *m*; (*jolt*) secousse *f* ‖ *v* (*pret & pp* **jarred**; *ger* **jarring**) *tr* ébranler, secouer ‖ *intr* trembler, vibrer; (*said of sounds, colors, opinions*) disorder; **to jar on the nerves** taper sur les nerfs

jargon [ˈdʒɑrgən] *s* jargon *m*

jasmine [ˈdʒæsmɪn] *s* jasmin *m*

jasper [ˈdʒæspər] *s* jaspe *m*

jaundice [ˈdʒɔndɪs] *s* jaunisse *f*, ictère *m*

jaundiced *adj* ictérique; (fig) amer

jaunt [dʒɔnt] *s* excursion *f*

jaun·ty [ˈdʒɔnti] *adj* (*comp* **-tier**; *super* **-tiest**) vif, dégagé; (*smart*) chic

javelin [ˈdʒævlɪn] *s* javelot *m*

jaw [dʒɔ] *s* mâchoire *f*; (*of animal*) gueule *f*; **jaws** (*e.g., of death*) griffes *fpl* ‖ *tr* (slang) engueuler ‖ *intr* (*to gossip*) (slang) bavarder

jaw′bone′ *s* mâchoire *f*, maxillaire *m*

jay [dʒe] *s* geai *m*

jay′walk′ *intr* traverser la rue en dehors des clous

jaw′walk′er *s* piéton *m* distrait

jazz [dʒæz] *s* jazz *m* ‖ *tr*—**to jazz up** (coll) animer, égayer

jazz′ band′ *s* orchestre *m* de jazz

jazz′ sing′er *s* chanteur *m* de rythme

jealous [ˈdʒɛləs] *adj* jaloux

jealous·y [ˈdʒɛləsi] *s* (*pl* **-ies**) jalousie *f*

jean [dʒin] *s* treillis *m*; **Jean** Jeanne *f*; **jeans** pantalon *m* de treillis

jeep [dʒip] *s* jeep *f*

jeer [dʒɪr] *s* raillerie *f* ‖ *intr* railler; **to jeer at** se moquer de

Jehovah [dʒɪˈhovə] *s* Jéhovah *m*

jell [dʒɛl] *s* gelée *f* ‖ *intr* se convertir en gelée; (*to take hold*) prendre forme, se préciser

jel·ly [ˈdʒɛli] *s* (*pl* **-lies**) gelée *f* ‖ *v* (*pret & pp* **-lied**) *tr* convertir en gelée ‖ *intr* se convertir en gelée

jel′ly·fish′ *s* méduse *f*; (*person*) chiffe *f*

jeopardize [ˈdʒɛpərˌdaɪz] *tr* mettre en danger, compromettre

jeopardy [ˈdʒɛpərdi] *s* danger *m*

jerk [dʒʌrk] *s* saccade *f*, secousse *f*; (slang) mufle *m* ‖ *tr* tirer brusquement, secouer ‖ *intr* se mouvoir brusquement

jerk′water town′ *s* trou *m*, petite ville *f* de province

jerk′water train′ *s* tortillard *m*

jerk·y [ˈdʒʌrki] *adj* (*comp* **-ier;** *super* **-iest**) saccadé

Jerome [dʒəˈrom] *s* Jérôme *m*

jersey [ˈdʒʌrzi] *s* jersey *m*

Jerusalem [dʒɪˈrusələm] *s* Jérusalem *f*

jest [dʒɛst] *s* plaisanterie *f*; **in jest** en plaisantant ‖ *intr* plaisanter

jester [ˈdʒɛstər] *s* plaisantin *m*; (*medieval clown*) bouffon *m*

Jesuit [ˈdʒɛʒʊ·ɪt] *adj* jésuite, jésuitique ‖ *s* Jésuite *m*

Jesus [ˈdʒizəs] *s* Jésus *m*

Je′sus Christ′ *s* Jésus-Christ *m*

jet [dʒɛt] *s* (*color; mineral*) jais *m*; (*of water, gas, etc.*) jet *m*; avion *m* à réaction ‖ *v* (*pret & pp* **jetted**) *ger* **jetting**) *intr* gicler, jaillir; voyager en jet

jet′-black′ *adj* noir de jais

jet′ en′gine *s* moteur *m* à réaction

jet′ fight′er *s* chasseur *m* à réaction

jet′ fu′el *s* carburéacteur *m*, kérosène *m* aviation

jet′ lag′ *s* troubles *mpl* dûs au décalage horaire

jet′ lin′er *s* avion *m* de ligne à réaction

jet′ plane′ *s* avion *m* à réaction

jet′ propul′sion *s* propulsion *f* par réaction

jetsam [ˈdʒɛtsəm] *s* marchandise *f* jetée à la mer

jet′ set′ *s* monde *m* des playboys

jet′ stream′ *s* (meteo) courant-jet *m*

jettison [ˈdʒɛtɪsən] *s* jet *m* à la mer ‖ *tr* jeter à la mer; (fig) mettre au rebut, rejeter

jet·ty [ˈdʒɛti] *s* (*pl* **-ties**) (*wharf*) appontement *m*; (*breakwater*) jetée *f*

Jew [dʒu] *s* Juif *m*; (rel) juif *m*

jewel [ˈdʒu·əl] *s* joyau *m*, bijou *m*; (*of a watch*) rubis *m*; (*of a clock*) pierre *f*; (*person*) bijou

jew′el case′ *s* écrin *m*

jeweler or **jeweller** [ˈdʒu·ələr] *s* horloger-bijoutier *m*, bijoutier *m*

jewelry [ˈdʒu·əlri] *s* joaillerie *f*

jew′elry store′ *s* bijouterie *f*; (*for watches*) horlogerie *f*

Jewess [ˈdʒu·ɪs] *s* Juive *f*; (rel) juive *f*

Jewish [ˈdʒj·ɪʃ] *adj* juif, judaïque

jews′-harp or **jew′s-harp** [ˈdjuzˌharp] *s* guimbarde *f*

jib [dʒɪb] *s* (mach) flèche *f*; (naut) foc *m*

jibe [dʒaɪb] *s* moquerie *f* ‖ *intr* (coll) concorder; **to jibe at** se moquer de

jif·fy [ˈdʒɪfi] *s* (*pl* **-fies**)—**in a jiffy** (coll) en un clin d′œil

jig [dʒɪg] *s* (*dance*) gigue *f*; **the jig is up** (slang) il n′y a pas mèche, tout est dans le lac

jigger [ˈdʒɪgər] *s* mesure *f* qui contient une once et demie; (*for fishing*) leurre *m*; (*tackle*) palan *m*; (*flea*) puce *f*; (*for separating ore*) crible *m*; (naut) tapecul *m*; (*gadget*) (coll) machin *m*

jiggle [ˈdʒɪgəl] *s* petite secousse *f* ‖ *tr* agiter, secouer ‖ *intr* se trémousser

jig′saw′ *s* chantourner, scie à découper, scie sauteuse

jig′ saw′ *s* scie *f* à chantourner

jig′saw puz′zle *s* casse-tête *m* chinois, puzzle *m*

jilt [dʒɪlt] *tr* lâcher, repousser

jim·my [ˈdʒɪmi] *s* (*pl* **-mies**) pince-monseigneur *f* ‖ *v* (*pret & pp* **-mied**) *tr* forcer à l′aide d′une pince-monseigneur

jingle [ˈdʒɪngəl] *s* (*small bell*) grelot *m*; (*sound*) grelottement *m*, tintement *m*, cliquetis *m*; (*poem*) rimes *fpl* enfantines; (*catchy verse*) petit couplet, slogan *m* à rimes; **advertising jingle** couplet *m* publicitaire, refrain *m* publicitaire, réclame *f* chantée, sonal *m* ‖ *tr* faire grelotter ‖ *intr* grelotter

jin·go [ˈdʒɪngo] *adj* chauvin ‖ *s* (*pl* **-goes**) chauvin *m*; **by jingo!** (coll) sapristi!

jingoism [ˈdʒɪngoˌɪzəm] *s* chauvinisme *m*

jinx [dʒɪnks] *s* guigne *f* ‖ *tr* (coll) porter la guigne à

jitters [ˈdʒɪtərz] *spl* (coll) frousse *f*, trouille *f*; **to give the jitters to** (coll) flanquer la trouille à

jittery [ˈdʒɪtəri] *adj* froussard

Joan′ of Arc′ *s* Jeanne *f* d′Arc

job [dʒab] *s* (*piece of work*) travail *m*; (*chore*) besogne *f*, tâche *f*; (*employment*) emploi *m*; (*work done by contract*) travail à forfait; (slang) vol *m*; **bad job** (fig) mauvaise affaire *f*; **by the job** à la pièce; **on the job** faisant un stage; (slang) attentif; **soft job** (coll) filon *m*, fromage *m*; **to**

be out of a job être en chômage; **to lie down on the job** (slang) tirer au flanc

job′ ac′tion s grève f du zèle

jobber [′dʒɑbər] s grossiste m; (*pieceworker*) ouvrier m à la tâche; (*dishonest official*) agioteur m

job′ descrip′tion s définition f de fonction

job′ hold′er s employé m; (*in the government*) fonctionnaire m

job′ lot′ s solde m de marchandises

job′ print′ing s bilboquet m

job′ secur′ity s sécurité f de l'emploi

job′ va′cancy s poste m à pourvoir

jockey [′dʒɑki] s jockey m ‖ tr (coll) manœuvrer

jockstrap [′dʒɑk,stræp] s suspensoir m, slip m de soutien

jocose [dʒo′kos] adj jovial, joyeux

jocular [′dʒɑkjələr] adj facétieux

jog [dʒɑg] s saccade f ‖ v (*pret & pp* **jogged**; *ger* **jogging**) tr secouer; (*the memory*) rafraîchir ‖ intr—**to jog along** aller au petit trot

jogging [′dʒɔgɪŋ] s jogging m

John [dʒɑn] s Jean m; **john** (slang) toilettes fpl; (*prostitute's customer*) (slang) micheton m

John′ Bull′ s l'Anglais m typique

John′ Doe′ s M. Dupont, M. Durand

Johnny [′dʒɑni] s (coll) Jeannot m

john′ny·cake′ s galette f de farine de maïs

John′ny-come′-late′ly s (coll) nouveau venu m

join [dʒɔɪn] tr joindre; (*to meet*) rejoindre; (*a club, a church*) se joindre à, entrer dans; (*a political party*) s'affilier à; (*the army*) s'engager dans; **to join s.o. in** + ger se joindre à qn pour + inf ‖ intr se joindre

joiner [′dʒɔɪnər] s menuisier m; (coll) clubiste mf

joint [dʒɔɪnt] adj commun, conjugué, joint, réuni ‖ s (*articulation*) joint m; (culin) rôti m; (*place*) (slang) boîte f; (*notorious drinking place*) (slang) bistrot m mal famé; (*gambling den*) (slang) tripot m; (*reefer*) (slang) joint m; **out of joint** disloqué; (fig) de travers

joint′ account′ s compte m indivis

joint′ commit′tee s commission f mixte

joint′ estate′ s (*of husband and wife*) communauté f

joint′ own′er s copropriétaire mf

joint′-stock′ com′pany s société f par actions

joist [dʒɔɪst] s solive f, poutre f

joke [dʒok] s plaisanterie f; **to play a joke on** faire une attrape à ‖ intr plaisanter

joker [′dʒokər] s farceur m, blagueur m; (cards) joker m, fou m; (coll) clause f ambiguë

jol·ly [′dʒɑli] adj (*comp* **-lier**; *super* **-liest**) joyeux, enjoué ‖ adv (coll) rudement

Jol′ly Rog′er [′rɑdʒər] s pavillon m noir

jolt [dʒolt] s cahot m, secousse f ‖ tr cahoter, secouer ‖ intr cahoter

Jonah [′dʒonə] s Jonas m

jonquil [′dʒɑŋkwɪl] s jonquille f

Jordan [′dʒɔrdən] s (*country*) Jordanie f; la Jordanie; (*river*) Jourdain m

josh [dʒɑʃ] tr & intr (coll) blaguer

jostle [′dʒɑsəl] tr bousculer ‖ intr se bousculer

jot [dʒɑt] s—**not a jot** pas un iota ‖ v (*pret & pp* **jotted**; *ger* **jotting**) tr—**to jot down** prendre note de

journal [′dʒʌrnəl] s journal m; (*magazine*) revue f; (mach) tourillon m; (naut) journal de bord

jour′nal box′ s boîte f d'essieu

journalism [′dʒʌrnə,lɪzəm] s journalisme m

journalist [′dʒʌrnəlɪst] s journaliste mf

journey [′dʒʌrni] s voyage m; trajet m, parcours m ‖ intr voyager

jour′ney·man s (*pl* **-men**) compagnon m

joust [dʒaʊst] s joute f ‖ intr jouter

Jove [dʒov] s Jupiter m; **by Jove!** parbleu!

jovial [′dʒovɪ·əl] adj jovial

jowl [dʒaʊl] s bajoue f

joy [dʒɔɪ] s joie f

joyful [′dʒɔɪfəl] adj joyeux

joyless [′dʒɔɪlɪs] adj sans joie

joyous [′dʒɔɪ·əs] adj joyeux

joy′ ride′ s (coll) balade f en auto

joy′ stick′ s manche m à balai

Jr. abbr (**junior**) fils, e.g., **Mr. Martin, Jr.** M. Martin fils

jubilant [′dʒubɪlənt] adj jubilant

jubilee [′dʒubɪ,li] s jubilé m

Judaism [′dʒude,ɪzəm] s judaïsme m

judge [dʒʌdʒ] s juge m ‖ tr & intr juger; **judging by** à en juger par

judge′ ad′vocate s commissaire m du gouvernement

judgment [′dʒʌdʒmənt] s jugement m

judg′ment day′ s jour m du jugement dernier

judicial [dʒu′dɪʃəl] adj judiciaire; (*legal*) juridique

judiciar·y [dʒu′dɪʃɪ,ɛri] adj judiciaire ‖ s (*pl* **-ies**) pouvoir m judiciaire; (*judges*) judicature f

judicious [dʒu′dɪʃəs] s judicieux

jug [dʒʌg] s (*of earthenware*) cruche f; (*of metal*) broc m; (*jail*) (slang) bloc m, taule f

juggle [′dʒʌgəl] tr jongler avec; **to juggle away** escamoter ‖ intr jongler

juggler [′dʒʌglər] s jongleur m; imposteur m, mystificateur m

juggling [′dʒʌglɪŋ] s jonglerie f; (*trickery*) passe-passe m

Jugoslavia [′jugo′slɑvɪ·ə] s Yougoslavie f; la Yougoslavie

jugular [′dʒʌgjələr] adj & s jugulaire f

juice [dʒus] s jus m; (coll) courant m électrique

juic·y [′dʒusi] adj (*comp* **-ier**; *super* **-iest**) juteux; (fig) savoureux

jukebox [′dʒuk,bɑks] s pick-up m électrique à sous, distributeur m de musique

July [dʒu′laɪ] s juillet m

jumble [ˈdʒʌmbəl] s fouillis m, enchevêtrement m ‖ tr brouiller

jumbo [ˈdʒʌmbo] adj (coll) géant

jum′bo jet′ s avion-géant m, gros-porteur m

jump [dʒʌmp] s saut m, bond m; (nervous start) sursaut m; (sports) saut m; (sports) obstacle m ‖ tr sauter; **to jump ship** tirer une bordée; **to jump the gun** démarrer trop tôt; **to jump the track** dérailler ‖ intr sauter, bondir; **to jump at the chance** sauter sur l'occasion

jump′ ball′ s (sports) entre-deux m, chandelle f d'arbitre

jumper [ˈdʒʌmpər] s sauteur m, sauteuse f; (dress) robe-chasuble f

jump′er ca′ble s câble m de démarrage

jump′ing bean′ s petit pois m sauteur

jump′ing jack′ s pantin m

jump′ rope′ s corde f à sauter

jump′ seat′ s strapontin m

jump′ suit′ s (aer) combinaison f de saut

jump·y [ˈdʒʌmpi] adj (comp **-ier**; super **-iest**) nerveux

junction [ˈdʒʌŋkʃən] s jonction f; (of railroads, roads) embranchement m

juncture [ˈdʒʌŋktʃər] s jointure f; (occasion) conjoncture f; **at this juncture** en cette occasion

June [dʒun] s juin m

jungle [ˈdʒʌŋgəl] s jungle f

jun′gle war′fare s guerre f de la brousse

junior [ˈdʒunjər] adj cadet; **Bobby Watson, Junior** le jeune Bobby Watson; **Martin, Junior** Martin fils ‖ s cadet m; (educ) étudiant m de troisième année

jun′ior of′ficer s officier m subalterne

juniper [ˈdʒunɪpər] s genévrier m

ju′niper ber′ry s genièvre m

junk [dʒʌŋk] s (old metal) ferraille f; (worthless objects) bric-à-brac m; (cheap merchandise) camelote f, pacotille f; (coll)

gnognote f; (naut) jonque f ‖ tr mettre au rebut

junk′ deal′er s fripier m; marchand m de ferraille

junket [ˈdʒʌŋkɪt] s excursion f; voyage m officiel aux frais de la princesse

junk′ food′ s camelote f alimentaire

junkie [ˈdʒʌŋki] s (slang) camé m, drogué m

junk′ man′ s (pl **-men′**) ferrailleur m; chiffonnier m

junk′ shop′ s boutique f de bric-à-brac et friperie; bric-à-brac m

junk′ yard′ s cimetière m de ferraille

jurisdiction [ˌdʒʊrɪsˈdɪkʃən] s juridiction f; **within the jurisdiction of** du ressort de

jurist [ˈdʒʊrɪst] s légiste m

juror [ˈdʒʊrər] s juré m

ju·ry [ˈdʒʊri] s (pl **-ries**) jury m

just [dʒʌst] adj juste ‖ adv seulement; justement; **just as** à l'instant où; (in the same way that) de même que; **just as it is** tel quel; **just out** vient de paraître; **to have just** venir de

justice [ˈdʒʌstɪs] s justice f; (judge) juge m

jus′tice of the peace′ s juge m de paix

justi·fy [ˈdʒʌstɪˌfaɪ] v (pret & pp **-fied**) tr justifier

justly [ˈdʒʌstli] adv justement

jut [dʒʌt] v (pret & pp **jutted**; ger **jutting**) intr—**to jut out** faire saillie

jute [dʒut] s jute m

juvenile [ˈdʒuvəˌnaɪl] adj juvénile, adolescent; (e.g., books) pour la jeunesse ‖ s adolescent m

ju′venile delin′quency s délinquance f juvénile

ju′venile delin′quent s délinquant m juvénile; **juvenile delinquents** jeunes délinquants mpl

juxtapose [ˌdʒʌkstəˈpoz] tr juxtaposer

K

K, k [ke] s XIᵉ lettre de l'alphabet

kale [kel] s chou m frisé

kaleidoscope [kəˈlaɪdəˌskop] s kaléidoscope m

kamikaze [ˌkɑməˈkɑzi] s kamikaze m

kangaroo [ˌkæŋgəˈru] s kangourou m

kan′garoo court′ s tribunal m bidon

karate [kəˈrɑti] s karaté m

Kashmir [ˈkæʃmɪr] s le Cachemire

kash′mir shawl′ s châle m de cachemire

kayak [ˈkaɪæk] s kayak m

keel [kil] s quille f ‖ intr—**to keel over** (naut) chavirer; (coll) tomber dans les pommes

keen [kin] adj (having a sharp edge) aiguisé, affilé; (sharp, cutting) mordant, pénétrant; (sharp-witted) perçant, perspi-

cace; (eager, much interested) enthousiaste, vif; (slang) formidable; **keen on** engoué de, passionné de

keep [kip] s (of medieval castle) donjon m; **for keeps** (for good) (coll) pour de bon; (forever) (coll) à tout jamais; **to earn one's keep** (coll) gagner sa nourriture, gagner sa vie; **to play for keeps** (coll) jouer le tout pour le tout ‖ v (pret & pp **kept** [kɛpt]) tr garder, conserver; (one's word or promise; accounts, a diary) tenir; (animals) élever; (a garden) cultiver; (a hotel, a school, etc.) diriger; (an appointment) ne pas manquer à; (a holiday) observer; (a person) avoir à sa charge, entretenir; **keep it up!** ne flanchez pas!, continuez!; **keep off the flowers** (public *sign)* respecter les fleurs; **keep out of the bushes** (*public sign*) il est interdit de pénétrer dans le bosquet; **to keep away** éloigner; **to keep back** retenir; **to keep down** baisser; (*prices*) maintenir bas; (*a revolt*) réprimer; **to keep in** retenir; (*a student after school*) garder en retenue; (*dust, fire, etc.*) entretenir; **to keep off** éloigner; **to keep out** tenir éloigné, empêcher d'entrer; **to keep quiet** faire taire; **to keep running** laisser marcher; **to keep score** marquer les points; **to keep servants** avoir des domestiques; **to keep s.o. busy** occuper qn; **to keep s.o. clean (cool, warm, etc.)** tenir qn propre (au frais, au chaud, etc.); **to keep s.o. or s.th. from** + *ger* empêcher qn or q.ch. de + *inf*; **to keep s.o. informed about** mettre or tenir qn au courant de; **to keep s.o. waiting** faire attendre qn; **to keep up** maintenir; (*e.g., all night*) faire veiller ‖ *intr* rester, se tenir; (*in good shape*) demeurer, se conserver; (*e.g., from rotting*) se garder; **keep out** (public sign) entrée interdite; **that can keep** (coll) ça peut attendre; **to keep** + *ger* continuer à + *inf*; **to keep away** s'éloigner, se tenir à l'écart; **to keep from** + *ger* s'abstenir de + *inf*; **to keep in with** rester en bons termes avec; **to keep on** + *ger* continuer à + *inf*; **to keep out** rester dehors; **to keep out of** ne pas se mêler de; **to keep quiet** rester tranquille, se taire; **to keep to** (*e.g., the right*) garder (*e.g., la droite*); **to keep up** tenir bon, tenir ferme; **to keep up with** aller de pair avec

keeper [ˈkipər] *s* gardien *m*, garde *m*; (*of a game preserve*) garde forestier; (*of a horseshoe magnet*) armature *f*

keeping [ˈkipɪŋ] *s* garde *f*, surveillance *f*; (*of a holiday*) observance *f*; **in keeping with** en accord avec; **in safe keeping** sous bonne garde; **out of keeping with** en désaccord avec

keep′sake′ *s* souvenir *m*, gage *m* d'amitié

keg [kɛg] *s* tonnelet *m*; (*of herring*) caque *f*

ken [kɛn] *s*—**beyond the ken of** hors de la portée de

kennel [ˈkɛnəl] *s* chenil *m*

kep·i [ˈkɛpi] *s* (*pl* **-is**) képi *m*

kept′ wom′an [kɛpt] *s* (*pl* **wom′en**) femme *f* entretenue

kerchief [ˈkʌrtʃɪf] *s* fichu *m*

kernel [ˈkʌrnəl] *s* (*inner part of a nut or fruit stone*) amande *f*; (*of wheat or corn*) grain *m*; (fig) noyau *m*, cœur *m*

kerosene [ˈkɛrəˌsin] *s* kérosène *m*, pétrole *m* lampant

ker′osene lamp′ *s* lampe *f* à pétrole

kerplunk [ˌkʌrˈpluŋk] *interj* patatras!

ketchup [ˈkɛtʃəp] *s* ketchup *m*

kettle [ˈkɛtəl] *s* chaudron *m*, marmite *f*; (*teakettle*) bouilloire *m*; **that's not my kettle of fish** (coll) ça n'est pas mes oignons

ket′tle·drum′ *s* timbale *f*

key [ki] *adj* clef, clé ‖ *s* clef *f*, clé *f*; (*of piano, typewriter, etc.*) touche *f*; (*wedge or cotter used to lock parts together*) cheville *f*, clavette *f*; (*reef or low island*) caye *f*; (*answer book*) livre *m* du maître; (*tone of voice*) ton *m*; (*to a map*) légende *f*; (bot) samare *f*; (mus) tonalité *f*; (telg) manipulateur *m*; **key to the city** droit *m* de cité; **off key** faux; **on key** juste ‖ *tr* claveter, coincer; **to be keyed up** être surexcité, être tendu

key′board′ *s* clavier *m*

key′hole′ *s* trou *m* de la serrure; (*of clock*) trou de clef

key′man′ *s* (*pl* **-men′**) pivot *m*, homme *m* indispensable

key′ mon′ey *s* pas *m* de porte

key′note′ *s* (mus) tonique *f*; (fig) dominante *f*

key′note speech′ *s* discours *m* d'ouverture

key′punch′ *s* (mach) perforatrice *f*

key′punch op′erator *s* perforeur *m*

key′ ring′ *s* porte-clefs *m*

key′ sig′nature *s* (mus) armature *f* de la clé

key′stone′ *s* clef *f* de voûte

key′ word′ *s* mot-clé *m*

kha·ki [ˈkɑki], [ˈkæki] *adj* kaki ‖ *s* (*pl* **-kis**) kaki *m*

khan [kɑn] *s* khan *m*

kibitz [ˈkɪbɪts] *intr* (coll) faire la mouche du coche

kibitzer [ˈkɪbɪtsər] *s* (coll) casse-pieds *mf*, curieux *m*

kick [kɪk] *s* coup *m* de pied; (*e.g., of a horse*) ruade *f*; (*of a gun*) recul *m*; (*complaint*) (slang) plainte *f*; (*thrill*) (slang) effet *m*, frisson *m*; **to get a kick out of** (slang) s'en payer une tranche de ‖ *tr* donner un coup de pied à; (*a ball*) botter; **to kick out** (coll) chasser à coups de pied; **to kick s.o. in the pants** (coll) botter le derrière à qn; **to kick the bucket** (coll) casser sa pipe, passer l'arme à gauche; **to kick up a row** (slang) déclencher un chahut ‖ *intr* donner un coup de pied; (*said of gun*) reculer; (*said of horse*) ruer; (sports) botter; **to kick against** regimber contre; **to kick off** (football) donner le coup d'envoi

kick′back′ *s* contrecoup *m*; (slang) ristourne *f*

kicker [ˈkɪkər] *s* (sports) botteur *m*

kick′off′ *s* (sports) coup *m* d'envoi

kid [kɪd] *s* chevreau *m*; (*child*) (coll) gosse *mf*; mioche *mf*; poulot *m* ‖ *v* (*pret & pp* **kidded**; *ger* **kidding**) *tr & intr* (slang) blaguer; **to kid oneself** (slang) se faire des illusions

kidder [ˈkɪdər] *s* (slang) blagueur *m*, plaisantin *m*

kidding [ˈkɪdɪŋ] *s* (slang) blague *f*; **no kidding!** (slang) sans blague!; **you're kidding!** (slang) tu galèges!

kid′ gloves′ *spl* gants *mpl* de chevreau; **to handle with kid gloves** traiter avec douceur, ménager

kid′nap v (pret & pp **-naped** or **-napped**; ger **-naping** or **-napping**) tr kidnapper
kidnaper or **kidnapper** [ˈkɪdnæpər] s kidnappeur m
kidnaping or **kidnapping** [ˈkɪdnæpɪŋ] s kidnappage m, enlèvement m
kidney [ˈkɪdni] s rein m; (culin) rognon m
kid′ney bean′ s haricot m de Soissons
kid′ney-shaped′ adj réniforme
kid′ney stone′ s calcul m rénal
kid′ney trans′plant s greffe f du rein
kill [kɪl] s mise f à mort; (bag of game) gibier m tué ‖ tr tuer; (an animal) abattre; (a bill, amendment, etc.) mettre son veto à, faire échouer
killer [ˈkɪlər] s assassin m
kill′er whale′ s épaulard m, orque f
killing [ˈkɪlɪŋ] adj meurtrier; (exhausting; ridiculous) crevant ‖ s tuerie f; **to make a killing** (coll) réussir un beau coup
kill′-joy′ s rabat-joie m, trouble-fête mf
kiln [kɪl], [kɪln] s four m
kil-o [ˈkilo] s (pl **-os**) kilo m, kilogramme m; kilomètre m
kilocycle [ˈkɪlə,saɪkəl] s kilocycle m
kilogram [ˈkɪlə,græm] s kilogramme m
kilometer [ˈkɪlə,mitər] s kilomètre m
kilowatt [ˈkɪlə,wɑt] s kilowatt m
kilowatt-hour [ˈkɪlə,wɑtˈaʊr] s (pl **-hours**) kilowatt-heure m
kilt [kɪlt] s kilt m
kilter [ˈkɪltər] s—**to be out of kilter** (coll) être détraqué
kimo-no [kɪˈmono] s (pl **-nos**) kimono m
kin [kɪn] s (family relationship) parenté f; (relatives) les parents mpl; **of kin** apparenté; **the next of kin** le plus proche parent, les plus proches parents
kind [kaɪnd] adj bon, bienveillant; **kind to** bon pour; **to be so kind as to** être assez aimable que ‖ s espèce f, genre m, sorte f, classe f; **all kinds of** (coll) quantité de; **kind of** (coll) plutôt, en quelque sorte; **of a kind** semblable, de même nature; **to pay in kind** payer en nature
kindergarten [ˈkɪndər,gɑrtən] s jardin m d'enfants
kindergartner [ˈkɪndər,gɑrtnər] s élève mf de jardin d'enfants; (teacher) jardinière f
kind′-heart′ed adj bon, bienveillant
kindle [ˈkɪndəl] tr allumer ‖ intr s'allumer
kindling [ˈkɪndlɪŋ] s allumage m; (wood) bois m d'allumage
kin′dling wood′ s bois m d'allumage
kind·ly [ˈkaɪndli] adj (comp **-lier**; super **-liest**) (kind-hearted) bon, bienveillant; (e.g., climate) doux; (e.g., terrain) favorable ‖ adv avec bonté, avec bienveillance; **to take kindly** prendre en bonne part; **to take kindly to** prendre en amitié
kindness [ˈkaɪndnɪs] s bonté f, obligeance f
kindred [ˈkɪndrɪd] adj apparenté, de même nature ‖ s parenté f, famille f; parenté, ressemblance f
Kinescope [ˈkɪnɪ,skop] s (trademark) kinescope m

kinetic [kɪˈnɛtɪk] adj cinétique ‖ **kinetics** s cinétique f
kinet′ic en′ergy s énergie f cinétique
king [kɪŋ] s roi m; (cards, chess, & fig) roi; (checkers) pion m doublé, dame f ‖ tr (checkers) damer
king′bolt′ s cheville f maîtresse
kingdom [ˈkɪŋdəm] s royaume m; (one of three divisions of nature) règne m
king′fish′er s martin-pêcheur m
king·ly [ˈkɪŋli] adj (comp **-lier**; super **-liest**) royal, de roi, digne d'un roi ‖ adv en roi, de roi, comme un roi
king′pin′ s cheville f ouvrière; (bowling) quille f du milieu; (coll) ponte m, pontife m
king′ post′ s poinçon m
kingship [ˈkɪŋʃɪp] s royauté f
king′-size′ adj grand format, géant
king′s′ ran′som s rançon f de roi
kink [kɪŋk] s (twist, e.g., in a rope) nœud m; (in a wire) faux pli m; (in hair) frisette f, bouclette f; (soreness in neck) torticolis m; (flaw, difficulty) point m faible; (mental twist) lubie f; (naut) coque f ‖ tr nouer, entortiller ‖ intr se nouer, s'entortiller
kink·y [ˈkɪŋki] adj (comp **-ier**; super **-iest**) crépu, bouclé
kinsfolk [ˈkɪnz,fok] spl parents mpl
kin′ship s parenté f
kins·man [ˈkɪnzmən] s (pl **-men**) parent m
kins·woman [ˈkɪnz,wʊmən] s (pl **-wom′en**) parente f
kipper [ˈkɪpər] s kipper m ‖ tr saurer
kiss [kɪs] s baiser m ‖ tr embrasser, donner un baiser à ‖ intr s'embrasser
kit [kɪt] s nécessaire m; (tub) tonnelet m; (to put together) prêt-à-monter m; (of traveler) trousse f de voyage; (mil) équipement m, sac m; **the whole kit and caboodle** (coll) tout le saint-frusquin
kitchen [ˈkɪtʃən] s cuisine f
kitch′en cup′board s vaisselier m
kitchenette [,kɪtʃəˈnɛt] s petite cuisine f, cuisinette f
kitch′en gar′den s jardin m potager
kitch′en·maid′ s fille f de cuisine
kitch′en police′ s (mil) corvée f de cuisine
kitch′en range′ s cuisinière f
kitch′en sink′ s évier m; **everything but the kitchen sink** tout sauf les murs
kitch′en·ware′ s ustensiles mpl de cuisine
kite [kaɪt] s cerf-volant m; (orn) milan m; **to fly a kite** lancer or enlever un cerf-volant
kith′ and kin′ [kɪθ] spl amis et parents mpl, cousinage m
kitten [ˈkɪtən] s chaton m, petit chat m
kittenish [ˈkɪtənɪʃ] adj enjoué, folâtre; (woman) coquette, chatte
kit·ty [ˈkɪti] s (pl **-ties**) minet m, minou m; (in card games) cagnotte f, poule f; **kitty, kitty, kitty!** minet, minet, minet!
kleptomaniac [,klɛptəˈmeni,æk] adj & s kleptomane mf
knack [næk] s adresse f, chic m
knapsack [ˈnæp,sæk] s sac m à dos, havresac m

knave [nev] s fripon m; (cards) valet m

knaver·y ['nevəri] s (pl **-ies**) friponnerie f

knead [nid] tr pétrir; (to massage) masser

knee [ni] s genou m; **to bring s.o. to his knees** mettre qn à genoux; **to go down on one's knees** se mettre à genoux

knee' breech'es spl culotte f courte

knee'cap' s rotule f; (protective covering) genouillère f

knee'-deep' adj jusqu'aux genoux

knee'-high' adj à la hauteur du genou

knee'hole' s trou m, évidement m pour l'entrée des genoux

knee' jerk' s réflexe m rotulien

kneel [nil] v (pret & pp **knelt** [nɛlt] or **kneeled**) intr s'agenouiller, se mettre à genoux

knee'pad' s genouillère f

knee'pan' s rotule f

knee' swell' s (of organ) genouillère f

knell [nɛl] s glas m; **to toll the knell of** sonner le glas de ‖ intr sonner le glas

knickers ['nɪkərz] spl pantalons mpl de golf, knickerbockers mpl

knickknack ['nɪk,næk] s colifichet m

knife [naɪf] s (pl **knives** [naɪvz] couteau m; (of paper cutter or other instrument) couperet m, lame f; **to go under the knife** (coll) monter or passer sur le billard ‖ tr poignarder

knife' sharp'ener s fusil m, affiloir m

knife' switch' s (elect) interrupteur m à couteau

knight [naɪt] s chevalier m; (chess) cavalier m ‖ tr créer or faire chevalier

knight-errant ['naɪt'ɛrənt] s (pl **knights-errant**) chevalier m errant

knighthood ['naɪthʊd] s chevalerie f

knightly ['naɪtli] adj chevaleresque

knit [nɪt] v (pret & pp **knitted** or **knit**; ger **knitting**) tr tricoter; (one's brows) froncer; **to knit together** lier, unir ‖ intr tricoter; (said of bones) se souder

knit' goods' spl tricot m, bonneterie f

knitting ['nɪtɪŋ] s (action) tricotage m; (product) tricot m

knit'ting machine' s tricoteuse f

knit'ting nee'dle s aiguille f à tricoter

knit'wear' s tricot m

knob [nɑb] s (lump) bosse f; (of a door, drawer, etc.) bouton m, poignée f; (of a radio) bouton

knock [nɑk] s coup m, heurt m; (of an internal-combustion engine) cognement m; (slang) éreintement m, dénigrement m ‖ tr frapper; (repeatedly) cogner à, contre, or sur; (slang) éreinter, dénigrer; **to knock about** bousculer; **to knock against** heurter contre; **to knock down** (with a blow, punch, etc.) renverser; (to the highest bidder) adjuger; **to knock in** enfoncer; **to knock off** faire tomber; **to knock out** faire sortir en cognant; (boxing) mettre knock-out; (to fatigue) (coll) claquer, fatiguer; **to knock up** (slang) engrosser ‖ intr frapper; (said of internal-combustion engine) cogner; **to knock about** vaga-

bonder, se balader; **to knock against** se heurter contre; **to knock at** or **on** (e.g., a door) heurter à, frapper à; **to knock off** (to stop working) (coll) débrayer

knock'down' adj (dismountable) démontable ‖ s (blow) coup m d'assommoir; (discount) escompte m

knocked' out' adj éreinté, sonné; (boxing) knock-out

knocker ['nɑkər] s (on a door) heurtoir m, marteau m; (critic) (coll) éreinteur m

knock-kneed ['nɑk,nid] adj cagneux

knock'out' s (boxing) knock-out m; (person) (coll) type m renversant; (thing) (coll) chose f sensationnelle

knock'out drops' spl (slang) narcotique m

knoll [nol] s mamelon m, tertre m

knot [nɑt] s nœud m; (e.g. of people) groupe m; (naut) nœud m, mille m marin à l'heure; (loosely) (naut) mille marin; **to tie a knot** faire un nœud; **to tie the knot** (coll) prononcer le conjungo ‖ v (pret & pp **knotted**; ger **knotting**) tr nouer; **to knot one's brow** froncer le sourcil ‖ intr se nouer

knot'hole' f trou m de nœud

knot·ty ['nɑti] adj (comp **-tier**; super **-tiest**) noueux; (e.g., question) épineux

know [no] s—**to be in the know** (coll) être au courant, être à la page, être au parfum ‖ v (pret **knew** [n(j)u]; pp **known**) tr & intr (by reasoning or learning) savoir; (by the senses or by perception; through acquaintance or recognition) connaître; **as far as I know** autant que je sache; **to know about** être informé de, savoir; **to know best** être le meilleur juge; **to know how to** + inf savoir + inf; **to let s.o. know about** faire part à qn de; **you ought to know better** vous devriez avoir honte; **you ought to know better than to . . .** vous devriez vous bien garder de . . .; **you wouldn't know s.o. from . . .** on prendrait qn pour . . .

knowable ['no·əbəl] adj connaissable

know'-how' s technique f, savoir-faire m

knowing ['no·ɪŋ] adj avisé; (look, smile) entendu

knowingly ['no·ɪŋli] adv sciemment, en connaissance de cause; (on purpose) exprès

know'-it-all' adj (coll) omniscient ‖ s (coll) Monsieur Je-sais-tout m

knowledge ['nɑlɪdʒ] s (faculty) science f, connaissances fpl, savoir m; (awareness, familiarity) connaissance f; **not to my knowledge** pas que je sache; **to have a thorough knowledge of** posséder une connaissance approfondie de; **to my knowledge, to the best of my knowledge** à ma connaissance, autant que je sache; **without my knowledge** à mon insu

knowledgeable ['nɑlɪdʒəbəl] adj (coll) intelligent, bien informé

know'-noth'ing s ignorant m

knuckle ['nʌkəl] s jointure f or articulation f du doigt; (of a quadruped) jarret m;

(mach) joint *m* en charnière; **knuckle of ham** jambonneau *m*; **to rap s.o. over the knuckles** donner sur les doigts or ongles à qn ‖ *intr*—**to knuckle down** se soumettre; (*to work hard*) s'y mettre sérieusement
knurl [nʌrl] *s* molette *f* ‖ *tr* moleter
k.o. [ˈkeˈo] (letterword) (**knockout**) *s* k.o. *m* ‖ *tr* mettre k.o.
Koran [koˈrɑn], [koˈræn] *s* Coran *m*
Korea [koˈri·ə] *s* Corée *f*; la Corée
Korean [koˈri·ən] *adj* coréen ‖ *s* (*language*) coréen; (*person*) Coréen *m*

kosher [ˈkoʃər] *adj* casher, kasher, kascher; (coll) convenable; **it's kosher** c'est kascher
kowtow [ˈkauˈtau] *intr* se prosterner à la chinoise; **to kowtow to** faire des courbettes à or devant
K.P. [ˈkeˈpi] *s* (letterword) (**kitchen police**) (mil) corvée *f* de cuisine; **to be on K.P. duty** (mil) être de soupe
Kremlin [ˈkrɛmlɪn] *s*—**the Kremlin** le Kremlin
kudos [ˈk(j)udɑs] *s* (coll) gloire *f*, éloges *mpl*, flatteries *fpl*

L

L, l [ɛl] *s* XIIe lettre de l'alphabet
la·bel [ˈlebəl] *s* étiquette *f*; (*brand*) marque *f*; (*in a dictionary*) rubrique *f*, référence *f* ‖ *v* (*pret & pp* **-beled** or **-belled**; *ger* **-beling** or **-belling**) *tr* étiqueter
labeling [ˈlebəlɪŋ] *s* étiquetage *m*; **labeling and sealing** habillage *m*
labial [ˈlebɪ·əl] *adj* labial ‖ *s* labiale *f*
labor [ˈlebər] *adj* ouvrier ‖ *s* travail *m*; (*toil*) labeur *m*, peine *f*; (*job, task*) tâche *f*, besogne *f*; (*manual work involved in an undertaking; the wages for such work*) main-d'œuvre *f*; (*wage-earning worker as contrasted with capital and management*) le salariat, le travail; (*childbirth*) couches *fpl*, travail; **to be in labor** être en couches ‖ *tr* (*a point, subject, etc.*) insister sur; (*one's style*) travailler, élaborer ‖ *intr* travailler; (*to toil*) travailler dur, peiner; (*to exert oneself*) s'efforcer; (*said of ship*) fatiguer, bourlinguer; **to labor under** être victime de; **to labor up** (*a hill, slope, etc.*) gravir; **to labor uphill** peiner en côte; **to labor with child** être en travail d'enfant
la'bor and man'agement *spl* la classe ouvrière et le patronat
laborato·ry [ˈlæbərə,tori] *s* (*pl* **-ries**) laboratoire *m*
lab'oratory class' *s* classe *f* de travaux pratiques
labored [ˈlebərd] *adj* travaillé, trop élaboré; (*e.g., breathing*) pénible
laborer [ˈlebərər] *s* travailleur *m*, ouvrier *m*; (*unskilled worker*) journalier *m*, manœuvre *m*
laborious [ləˈborɪ·əs] *adj* laborieux
la'bor move'ment *s* mouvement *m* syndicaliste
la'bor un'ion *s* syndicat *m*, syndicat ouvrier
Labourite [ˈleba,raɪt] *adj & s* (Brit) travailliste *mf*
La'bour Par'ty [ˈlebər] *adj* (Brit) travailliste ‖ *s* parti *m* travailliste
Labrador [ˈlæbrə,dɔr] *s* le Labrador

laburnum [ləˈbʌrnəm] *s* cytise *m*
labyrinth [ˈlæbɪrɪnθ] *s* labyrinthe *m*
lace [les] *s* dentelle *f*; (*string to tie shoe, corset, etc.*) lacet *m*, cordon *m*; (*braid*) broderies *fpl* ‖ *tr* garnir or border de dentelles; (*shoes, corset, etc.*) lacer; (*to braid*) entrelacer; (coll) flanquer une rossée à rosser
lace' trim'ming *s* p. .ssementerie *f*
lace'work' *s* dentelles *fpl*, passementerie *f*
lachrymose [ˈlækrɪ,mos] *adj* larmoyant
lacing [ˈlesɪŋ] *s* lacet *m*, cordon *m*; (*trimming*) galon *m*, passement *m*; (coll) rossée *f*
lack [læk] *s* manque *m*, défaut *m*; (*lack of necessities*) pénurie *f*, faute *f* ‖ *tr* manquer de, être dépourvu de ‖ *intr* (*to be lacking*) manquer, faire défaut
lackadaisical [,lækəˈdezɪkəl] *adj* languissant, apathique
lackey [ˈlæki] *s* laquais *m*
lacking [ˈlækɪŋ] *prep* dépourvu de, dénué de
lack'lus'ter *adj* terne, fade
laconic [ləˈkɑnɪk] *adj* laconique
lacquer [ˈlækər] *s* laque *m & f* ‖ *tr* laquer
lac'quer ware' *s* laques *mpl*, objets *mpl* d'art en laque
lacrosse [ləˈkrɔs] *s* crosse *f*, jeu *m* de crosse; **to play lacrosse** jouer à la crosse
lacu·na [ləˈkjunə] *s* (*pl* **-nas** or **-nae** [ni]) lacune *f*
lac·y [ˈlesi] *adj* (*comp* **-ier**; *super* **-iest**) de dentelle; (fig) fin, léger
lad [læd] *s* garçon *m*, gars *m*
ladder [ˈlædər] *s* échelle *f*; (*stepping stone*) (fig) marchepied *m*, échelon *m*; (*stepladder*) marchepied, escabeau *m*; (*run in stocking*) (Brit) démaillage *m*; (*stairway*) (naut) escalier *m*
lad'der truck' *s* fourgon-pompe *m* à échelle
la'dies' room' *s* toilettes *fpl* pour dames, lavabos *mpl* pour dames
ladle [ˈledəl] *s* louche *f* ‖ *tr* servir à la louche

la·dy ['ledi] s (pl **-dies**) dame f; **ladies** (public sign) dames; **ladies and gentlemen!** (formula used in addressing an audience) mesdames, mesdemoiselles, messieurs!; messieurs dames! (coll)

la'dy·bird' or **la'dy·bug'** s cocinelle f, bête f à bon Dieu

la'dy·fin'ger s biscuit m à la cuiller

la'dy-in-wait'ing s (pl **ladies-in-waiting**) demoiselle f d'honneur

la'dy-kil'ler s bourreau m des cœurs, tombeur m de femmes

la'dy·like' adj de bon ton, de dame

la'dy·love' s bien-aimée f, dulcinée f

la'dy of the house' s maîtresse f de maison

la'dy's maid' s camériste f

la'dy's man' s homme m à succès

lag [læg] s retard m ‖ v (pret & pp **lagged**; ger **lagging**) intr traîner; **to lag behind** rester en arrière

la'ger beer' ['lɑgər] s bière f de fermentation basse, lager m

laggard ['lægərd] adj tardif ‖ s traînard m

lagoon [lə'gun] s lagune f

laid' pa'per [led] s papier m vergé

laid' up' adj mis en réserve; (naut) mis en rade; (coll) alité, au lit

lair [lɛr] s tanière f; (fig) repaire m

laity ['le·ɪti] s profanes mfpl; (eccl) laïques mfpl

lake [lek] adj lacustre ‖ s lac m

lamb [læm] s agneau m

lambaste [læm'best] tr (to thrash) (coll) flanquer une rossée à; (to reprimand harshly) (coll) passer un savon à

lamb' chop' s côtelette f d'agneau

lambkin ['læmkɪn] s agnelet m

lamb'skin' s peau f d'agneau; (dressed with its wool) mouton m, agnelin m

lame [lem] adj boiteux; (sore) endolori; (e.g., excuse) faible, piètre ‖ tr estropier, rendre boiteux

lament [lə'mɛnt] s lamentation f; (dirge) complainte f ‖ tr déplorer ‖ intr lamenter, se lamenter

lamentable ['læməntəbəl] adj lamentable

lamentation [,læmən'teʃən] s lamentation f

laminate ['læmɪ,net] tr laminer

lamp [læmp] s lampe f

lamp'black' s noir m de fumée

lamp' chim'ney s verre m de lampe

lamp'light' s lumière f de lampe

lamp'light'er s allumeur m de réverbères

lampoon [læm'pun] s libelle m, pasquinade f ‖ tr faire des libelles contre

lamp'post' s réverbère m, poteau m de réverbère

lamprey ['læmpri] s lamproie f

lamp'shade' s abat-jour m

lamp'wick' s mèche f de lampe

lance [læns] s lance f; (surg) lancette f, bistouri m ‖ tr percer d'un coup de lance; (surg) donner un coup de lancette or bistouri à

lancet ['lænsɪt] s (surg) lancette f, bistouri m

land [lænd] adj terrestre, de terre ‖ s terre f; **land of milk and honey** pays de cocagne;

to make land toucher terre; **to see how the land lies** sonder or tâter le terrain ‖ tr débarquer, mettre à terre; (an airplane) atterrir; (a fish) amener à terre; (e.g., a job) (coll) décrocher; (a blow) (coll) flanquer ‖ intr débarquer, descendre à terre; (said of airplane) atterrir; **to land on one's feet** retomber sur ses pieds; **to land on the moon** alunir; **to land on the water** amerrir

land' breeze' s brise f de terre

landed adj (owning land) terrien; (real estate) immobilier

land'ed prop'erty s propriété f foncière

land'fall' s (sighting land) abordage m; (landing of ship or plane) atterrissage m; (landslide) glissement m de terrain

land'fill' s dépotoir m

landing ['lændɪŋ] s (of plane) atterrissage m; (of ship) mise f à terre, débarquement m; (place where passengers and goods are landed) débarcadère m; (of stairway) palier m; (on the moon) alunissage m

land'ing bea'con s (aer) radiophare m d'atterrissage

land'ing craft' s (nav) péniche f de débarquement

land'ing field' s (aer) terrain m d'atterrissage

land'ing force' s (nav) détachement m de débarquement

land'ing gear' s (aer) train m d'atterrissage

land'ing par'ty s (nav) détachement m de débarquement

land'ing stage' s débarcadère m

land'ing strip' s (aer) piste f d'atterrissage, aire f d'atterrissage

land'la'dy s (pl **-dies**) (e.g., of an apartment) logeuse f, propriétaire f; (of a lodging house) patronne f; (of an inn) aubergiste f

land'locked' adj entouré de terre

land'lord' s (e.g., of an apartment) logeur m, propriétaire m; (of a lodging house) patron m; (of an inn) aubergiste m

landlubber ['lænd,lʌbər] s marin m d'eau douce

land'mark' s point m de repère, borne f; (important event) étape f importante; (naut) amer m

land' of'fice s bureau m du cadastre

land'own'er s propriétaire m foncier

landscape ['lænd,skep] s paysage m ‖ tr aménager en jardins

land'scape ar'chitect s architecte m paysagiste

land'scape gar'dener s jardinier m paysagiste

land'scape paint'er s paysagiste mf

landscapist ['lænd,skepɪst]·s paysagiste mf

land'slide' s glissement m de terrain, éboulement m; (in an election) raz m de marée, majorité f écrasante

landward ['lændwərd] adv du côté de la terre, vers la terre

land' wind' [wɪnd] s vent m de terre

lane [len] *s* (*narrow street or passage*) ruelle *f*; (*in the country*) sentier *m*; (*of an automobile highway*) voie *f*; (*line of cars*) file *f*; (*of an air. or ocean route*) route *f* de navigation

langsyne [ˈlæŋˈsaɪn] *s* (Scotch) le temps jadis ‖ *adv* (Scotch) au temps jadis

language [ˈlæŋgwɪdʒ] *s* langage *m*; (*e.g., of a nation*) langue *f*

lan′guage lab′oratory *s* laboratoire *m* de langues

languid [ˈlæŋgwɪd] *adj* languissant

languish [ˈlæŋgwɪʃ] *intr* languir

languor [ˈlæŋgər] *s* langueur *f*

languorous [ˈlæŋgərəs] *adj* langoureux

lank [læŋk] *adj* efflanqué, maigre; (*hair*) plat, e.g., **lank hair** cheveux plats

lank·y [ˈlæŋki] *adj* (*comp* **-ier;** *super* **-iest**) grand et maigre

lanolin [ˈlænəlɪn] *s* lanoline *f*

lantern [ˈlæntərn] *s* lanterne *f*

lan′tern slide′ *s* diapositive *f*

lanyard [ˈlænjərd] *s* (*around the neck*) cordon *m*; (*arti*) tire-feu *m*; (*naut*) ride *f*

lap [læp] *s* (*of human body or clothing*) genoux *mpl*, giron *m*; (*of garment*) genoux, pan *m*; (*with the tongue*) coup *m* de langue; (*of the waves*) clapotis *m*; (*in a race*) (sports) tour *m*; **last lap** dernière étape *f* ‖ *v* (*pret & pp* **lapped;** *ger* **lapping**) *tr* (*with the tongue*) laper; **to lap up** laper; (coll) gober ‖ *intr* laper; (*said of waves*) clapoter; **to lap over** déborder

lap′ dog′ *s* bichon *m*, chien *m* de manchon

lapel [ləˈpɛl] *s* revers *m*

Lap′land′ *s* Laponie *f*; la Laponie

Laplander [ˈlæpˌlændər] *s* Lapon *m*

Lapp [læp] *s* (*language*) lapon *m*; (*person*) Lapon *m*

lap′ robe′ *s* couverture *f* de voyage

lapse [læps] *s* intervalle *m*; (*slipping into guilt or error*) faute *f* légère, écart *m*; (*fall, decline*) disparition *f*, oubli *m*, déchéance *f*; (*e.g., of an insurance policy*) expiration *f*, échéance *f*; (*of memory*) trou *m*, absence *f*; **a lapse of time** un laps de temps ‖ *intr* (*to elapse*) s'écouler, passer; (*to err*) manquer à ses devoirs; (*to decline*) déchoir; (*said, e.g., of a right*) périmer, tomber en désuétude; (*said, e.g., of a legacy*) devenir caduc; (*said, e.g., of an insurance policy*) cesser d'être en vigueur

lap′wing′ *s* (orn) vanneau *m* huppé

larce·ny [ˈlɑrsəni] *s* (*pl* **-nies**) larcin *m*, vol *m*

larch [lɑrtʃ] *s* (bot) mélèze *m*

lard [lɑrd] *s* saindoux *m* ‖ *tr* larder

larder [ˈlɑrdər] *s* garde-manger *m*

large [lɑrdʒ] *adj* grand; **at large** en liberté

large′ intes′tine *s* gros intestin *m*

largely [ˈlɑrdʒli] *adv* principalement

largeness [ˈlɑrdʒnɪs] *s* grandeur *f*

large′-scale′ *adj* sur une large échelle, de grande envergure

lariat [ˈlærɪ·ət] *s* (*for catching animals*) lasso *m*; (*for tying grazing animals*) longe *f*

lark [lɑrk] *s* alouette *f*; (*prank*) espièglerie *f*; **to go on a lark** (coll) faire la bombe

lark′spur′ *s* (*rocket larkspur*) pied-d'alouette *m*; (*field larkspur*) consoude *f* royale

lar·va [ˈlɑrvə] *s* (*pl* **-vae** [vi]) larve *f*

laryngeal [ˌlærɪnˈdʒi·əl] *adj* laryngé, laryngien

laryngitis [ˌlærɪnˈdʒaɪtɪs] *s* laryngite *f*

laryngoscope [ləˈrɪŋgəˌskop] *s* laryngoscope *m*

larynx [ˈlærɪŋks] *s* (*pl* **larynxes** or **larynges** [ləˈrɪndʒiz]) larynx *m*

lascivious [ləˈsɪvɪ·əs] *adj* lascif

lasciviousness [ləˈsɪvɪ·əsnɪs] *s* lasciveté *f*

laser [ˈlezər] *s* (acronym) (**light amplification by stimulated emission of radiation**) laser *m*

lash [læʃ] *s* (*cord on end of whip*) mèche *f*; coup *m*; (*splatter of rain on window*) fouettement *m*; (*eyelash*) cil *m* ‖ *tr* fouetter, cingler; (*to bind, tie*) lier; (naut) amarrer ‖ *intr* fouetter; **to lash out at** cingler

lashing [ˈlæʃɪŋ] *s* fouettée *f*; (*rope*) amarre *f*; (naut) amarrage *m*

lass [læs] *s* jeune fille *f*, jeunesse *f*; bonne amie *f*

lassitude [ˈlæsɪˌt(j)ud] *s* lassitude *f*

las·so [ˈlæso] *s* (*pl* **-sos** or **-soes**) lasso *m*

last [læst] *adj* (*in a series*) dernier (before noun), e.g., **the last week of the war** la dernière semaine de la guerre; (*just elapsed*) dernier (after noun), e.g., **last week** la semaine dernière; **before last** avant-dernier, e.g., **the time before last** l'avant-dernière fois; **the last two** les deux derniers ‖ *s* dernier *m*; (*the end*) fin *f*, bout *m*; (*for holding shoe*) forme *f*; **at last** enfin, à la fin; **at long last** à la fin des fins; **the last of the month** la fin du mois; **to the last** jusqu'à la fin, jusqu'au bout ‖ *intr* durer; (*to hold out*) tenir

last′ eve′ning *adv* hier soir

lasting [ˈlæstɪŋ] *adj* durable

lastly [ˈlæstli] *adv* pour finir, en dernier lieu, enfin

last′-minute news′ *s* nouvelles *fpl* de dernière heure

last′ name′ *s* nom *m*, nom de famille

last′ night′ *adv* hier soir; cette nuit

last′ quar′ter *s* dernier quartier *m*

last′ sleep′ *s* sommeil *m* de la mort

last′ straw′ *s*—**that's the last straw!** c'est le comble!

Last′ Sup′per *s* (eccl) Cène *f*

last′ will′ and tes′tament *s* testament *m*, acte *m* de dernière volonté

last′ word′ *s* dernier mot *m*; (*latest style*) (coll) dernier cri *m*

latch [lætʃ] *s* loquet *m* ‖ *tr* fermer au loquet

latch′key′ *s* clef *f* de porte d'entrée

latch′string′ *s* cordon *m* de loquet

late [let] *adj* (*happening after the usual time*) tardif; (*person; train, bus, etc.*) en retard; (*e.g., art*) de la dernière époque; (*events*) dernier, récent; (*news*) de la dernière heure; (*incumbent of an office*) ancien; (*deceased*) défunt, feu; **at a late hour in** (*the night, the day*) bien avant dans, à une heure avancée de; **in the late seventeenth century (eighteenth century, etc.)** vers la fin du dix-septième siècle (dix-huitième siècle, etc.); **it is late** il est tard; **of late** dernièrement, récemment, depuis peu; **to be late** être en retard; **to be late in** + *ger* tarder à + *inf* ‖ *adv* tard, tardivement; (*after the appointed time*) en retard; **better late than never** mieux vaut tard que jamais; **late in** (*the afternoon, the season, the week, the month*) vers la fin de; **late in life** sur le tard; **very late in** (*the night, the day*) bien avant dans, à une heure avancée de

late-comer ['let,kʌmər] *s* (*newcomer*) nouveau venu *m*; (*one who arrives late*) retardataire *mf*

lateen' sail' [læ'tin] *s* voile *f* latine

lateen' yard' *s* antenne *f*

lately ['letli] *adv* dernièrement, récemment, depuis peu

latency ['letənsi] *s* latence *f*

latent ['letənt] *adj* latent

later ['letər] *adj comp* plus tard, plus tardif; (*event*) subséquent, plus récent; (*kings, luminaries, etc.*) derniers en date; **later than** postérieur à ‖ *adv comp* plus tard; **later on** plus tard, par la suite; **see you later** (coll) à tout à l'heure

lateral ['lætərəl] *adj* latéral

lath [læθ] *s* latte *f* ‖ *tr* latter

lathe [leð] *s* (mach) tour *m*; **to turn on a lathe** façonner au tour

lather ['læðər] *s* (*of soap*) mousee *f*; (*of horse*) écume *f* ‖ *tr* savonner ‖ *intr* (*said of soap*) mousser; (*said of horse*) être couvert d'écume

lathing ['læθɪŋ] *s* lattage *m*

Latin ['lætən] *adj* latin ‖ *s* (*language*) latin *m*; (*person*) Latin *m*

Lat'in Amer'ica *s* l'Amérique *f* latine

Lat'in-Amer'ican *adj* latino-américain ‖ *s* Latino-américain *m*

latitude ['lætɪ,t(j)ud] *s* latitude *f*

latrine [lə'trin] *s* latrines *fpl*

latter ['lætər] *adj* dernier; **the latter part of** (*e.g., a century*) la fin de ‖ *pron*—**the latter** celui-ci §84; le dernier

lattice ['lætɪs] *adj* treillissé ‖ *s* treillis *m* ‖ *tr* treillisser

lat'tice gird'er *s* poutre *f* à croisillons

lat'tice-work' *s* treillis *m*, grillage *m*

laud [lɔd] *tr* louer

laudable ['lɔdəbəl] *adj* louable

laudanum ['lɔdənəm] *s* laudanum *m*

laudatory ['lɔdə,tori] *adj* laudatif, élogieux

laugh [læf] *s* rire *m* ‖ *tr*—**to laugh away** chasser en riant; **to laugh off** tourner en plaisanterie ‖ *intr* rire; **to laugh at** rire de

laughable ['læfəbəl] *adj* risible

laughing ['læfɪŋ] *adj* riant, rieur; **it's no laughing matter** il n'y a pas de quoi rire ‖ *s* rire *m*

laugh'ing gas' *s* gaz *m* hilarant

laugh'ing·stock' *s* risée *f*, fable *f*

laughter ['læftər] *s* rire *m*

launch [lɔntʃ] *s* (*open motorboat*) canot *m* automobile, vedette *f*; (naut) chaloupe *f* ‖ *tr* lancer; (*an attack*) déclencher ‖ *intr*—**to launch into, to launch out on** se lancer dans

launching ['lɔntʃɪŋ] *s* lancement *m*

launch'ing pad' *s* rampe *f* de lancement, aire *f* de lancement

launder ['lɔndər] *tr* blanchir

launderer ['lɔndərər] *s* blanchisseur *m*, buandier *m*

laundering ['lɔndərɪŋ] *s* blanchissage *m*

laundress ['lɔndrɪs] *s* blanchisseuse *f*; buandière *f*

Laundromat ['lɔndrə,mæt] *s* (trademark) laverie *f* automatique, laverie libre-service, lavromat *m*

laun·dry ['lɔndri] *s* (*pl* -**dries**) linge *m* à blanchir, lessive *f*; (*room*) buanderie *f*; (*business*) blanchisserie *f*

laun'dry·man *s* (*pl* -**men**) blanchisseur *m*, buandier *m*

laun'dry room' *s* buanderie *f*

laun'dry·wom'an *s* (*pl* -**wom'en**) blanchisseuse *f*, buandière *f*

laureate ['lɔrɪ·ɪt] *adj & s* lauréat *m*

lau·rel ['lɔrəl] *s* laurier *m*; **to rest on one's laurels** s'endormir sur ses lauriers ‖ *v* (*pret & pp* -**reled** or -**relled**; *ger* -**reling** or -**relling**) *tr* couronner de lauriers

lava ['lɑvə] *s* lave *f*

lavaliere [,lævə'lɪr] *s* pendentif *m*

lavato·ry ['lævə,tori] *s* (*pl* -**ries**) (*room equipped for washing hands and face; bowl with running water*) lavabo *m*; (*toilet*) lavabos

lavender ['lævəndər] *s* lavande *f*

lav'ender wa'ter *s* eau *f* de lavande

lavish ['lævɪʃ] *adj* prodigue; (*reception, dinner, etc.*) somptueux, magnifique ‖ *tr* prodiguer

law [lɔ] *s* (*of man, of nature, of science*) loi *f*; (*branch of knowledge concerned with law; body of laws; study of law, profession of law*) droit *m*; **to go to law** recourir à la justice; **to go to law with s.o.** citer qn en justice; **to lay down the law** faire la loi; **to practice law** exercer le droit; **to read law** étudier le droit, faire son droit

law'-abid'ing *adj* soumis aux lois, respectueux des lois

law' and or'der *s* ordre *m* public; **to maintain law and order** maintenir or faire régner l'ordre

law'break'er *s* transgresseur *m* de la loi

law' court' *s* cour *f* de justice, tribunal *m*

lawful ['lɔfəl] *adj* légal, légitime

lawless ['lɔlɪs] *adj* sans loi; (*unbridled*) sans frein, déréglé

law'mak'er *s* législateur *m*

lawn [lɔn] *s* pelouse *f*, gazon *m*; (*fabric*) batiste *f*, linon *m*
lawn′ mow′er *s* tondeuse *f* de gazon
law′ of′fice *s* étude *f* (d'avocat)
law′ of na′tions *s* loi *f* des nations
law′ of the jun′gle *s* loi *f* de la jungle
law′ stu′dent *s* étudiant *m* en droit
law′suit′ *s* procès *m*
lawyer ['lɔjər] *s* avocat *m*
lax [læks] *adj* (*in morals, discipline, etc.*) relâché, négligent; (*loose, not tense*) lâche; (*vague*) vague, flou
laxative ['læksətɪv] *adj & s* laxatif *m*
lay [le] *adj* (*not belonging to clergy*) laïc or laïque; (*not having special training*) profane ‖ *s* situation *f*; (*poem*) lai *m* ‖ *v* (*pret & pp* **laid** [led]) *tr* poser, mettre; (*a trap*) tendre; (*eggs*) pondre; (*e.g., bricks*) ranger; (*a foundation*) jeter, établir; (*a cable*) poser; (*a mine*) (naut) mouiller; **to be laid in Rome (in France, etc.)** (*said, e.g., of scene*) se passer à Rome (en France, etc.); **to lay aside, away,** or **by** mettre de côté; **to lay down** (*one's life*) sacrifier; (*one's weapons*) déposer; (*conditions*) imposer; **to lay down the law to s.o.** (coll) rappeler qn à l'ordre; **to lay in** (*supplies*) faire provision de; **to lay into s.o.** (coll) sauter dessus qn; **to lay it on thick** (coll) y aller fort; **to lay low** (*to overwhelm*) abattre, terrasser; **to lay off** (*an employee*) congédier; (*to mark the boundaries of*) tracer; (*to stop bothering*) (coll) laisser tranquille; **to lay on** (*paint*) appliquer; (*hands; taxes*) imposer; **to lay open** mettre à nu; **to lay out** arranger; (*to display*) étaler; (*to outline*) tracer; (*money*) débourser; (*a corpse*) faire la toilette de; (*a garden*) aménager; **to lay up** (*to stock up on*) amasser; (*to injure*) aliter; (*a boat*) mettre en rade ‖ *intr* (*said of hen*) pondre; **to lay about** frapper de tous côtés; **to lay for** être à l'affût de, guetter; **to lay into** (slang) rosser, battre; **to lay off** (coll) cesser; **to lay off smoking** (coll) renoncer au tabac; **to lay over** faire escale; **to lay to** (naut) se mettre à la cape
lay′ broth′er *s* frère *m* lai, frère convers
layer ['le·ər] *s* couche *f*; (*hen*) pondeuse *f* ‖ *tr* (hort) marcotter
lay′er cake′ *s* gâteau *m* sandwich
layette [le'ɛt] *s* layette *f*
lay′ fig′ure *s* mannequin *m*
laying ['le·ɪŋ] *s* (*of carpet*) pose *f*; (*of foundation*) assise *f*; (*of eggs*) ponte *f*
lay′man *s* (*pl* **-men**) (*person who is not a clergyman*) laïc *m* or laïque *mf*; (*person who has no special training*) profane *mf*
lay′off′ *s* (*discharge*) renvoi *m*; (*unemployment*) chômage *m*
lay′ of the land′ *s* configuration *f* du terrain; (fig) aspect *m* de l'affaire
lay′out′ *s* plan *m*, dessin *m*, tracé *m*; (*of tools*) montage *m*; (*organization*) disposition *f*; (*banquet*) (coll) festin *m*
lay′o′ver *s* arrêt *m* en cours de route
lay′ sis′ter *s* sœur *f* laie, sœur converse

laziness ['lezɪnɪs] *s* paresse *f*
la·zy ['lezi] *adj* (*comp* **-zier**; *super* **-ziest**) paresseux
la′zy·bones′ *s* (coll) flemmard *m*, fainéant *m*
la′zy Su′san *s* plateau *m* tournant
lb. *abbr* (**pound**) livre *f*
lea [li] *s* (*meadow*) pâturage *m*, prairie *f*
lead [lɛd] *adj* en plomb, de plomb ‖ [lɛd] *s* plomb *m*; (*of lead pencil*) mine *f* (de plombagine); (*for sounding depth*) (naut) sonde *f*; (typ) interligne *f* ‖ [lɛd] *v* (*pret & pp* **leaded**; *ger* **leading**) *tr* plomber; (typ) interligner ‖ [lid] *s* (*foremost place*) avance *f*; (*guidance*) direction *f*, conduite *f*; (*leash*) laisse *f*; (*of a newspaper article*) article *m* de fond; (*leading role*) premier rôle *m*; (*leading man*) jeune premier *m*; (elec) câble *m* de canalisation, conducteur *m*; (elec, mach) avance *f*; (min) filon *m*; **to follow s.o.'s lead** suivre l'exemple de qn; **to have the lead** (cards) avoir la main; **to return the lead** (cards) rejouer la couleur; **to take the lead** prendre le pas ‖ [lid] *v* (*pret & pp* **led** [lɛd]) *tr* conduire, mener; (*to command*) commander, diriger; (*to be foremost in*) être à la tête de; (*e.g., an orchestra*) diriger; (*a good or bad life*) mener; (*a certain card*) attaquer de; (*a certain card suit*) attaquer; (elec, mach) canaliser; **to lead away** or **off** emmener; **to lead off** (*to start*) commencer; **to lead on** encourager; **to lead s.o. to believe** mener qn à croire ‖ *intr* aller devant, tenir la tête; (cards) avoir la main; **to lead to** conduire à, mener à; (*another street, a certain result, etc.*) aboutir à; **to lead up to** (*a great work*) préluder à (*un grand ouvrage*); (*a subject*) amener (*un sujet*)
leaden ['lɛdən] *adj* (*of lead; like lead*) de plomb, en plomb; (*heavy as lead*) pesant; (*sluggish*) alangui; (*complexion*) plombé
leader ['lidər] *s* chef *m*, guide *mf*; (*ringleader*) tête *f*; chef d'orchestre; (*in a dance; among animals*) meneur *m*; (*in a newspaper*) article *m* de fond; (*of a reel of tape or film*) amorce *f*; (*bargain*) article réclame; (*vein of ore*) filon *m*
leadership ['lidər‚ʃɪp] *s* direction *f*; don *m* de commandement
leading ['lidɪŋ] *adj* principal, premier
lead′ing edge′ *s* (aer) bord *m* d'attaque
lead′ing la′dy *s* vedette *f*, étoile *f*, jeune première *f*
lead′ing man′ *s* (*pl* **men′**) jeune premier *m*
lead′ing ques′tion *s* question *f* tendancieuse
lead′-in wire′ ['lid‚ɪn] *s* (rad, telv) fil *m* d'amenée
lead′ pen′cil [lɛd] *s* crayon *m* (à mine de graphite)
lead′ poi′soning [lɛd] *s* saturnisme *m*
leaf [lif] *s* (*pl* **leaves** [livz]) feuille *f*; (*inserted leaf of table*) rallonge *f*; (*hinged leaf of door or table top*) battant *m*; **to shake like a leaf** trembler comme une feuille; **to turn over a new leaf** tourner la page, faire peau neuve ‖ *intr*—**to leaf through** feuilleter

leafless ['liflɪs] *adj* sans feuilles, dénudé
leaflet ['liflɪt] *s* dépliant *m*, papillon *m*, feuillet *m*; (bot) foliole *f*
leaf′stalk′ *s* (bot) pétiole *m*
leaf·y ['lifi] *adj* (*comp* **-ier**; *super* **-iest**) feuillu, touffu
league [lig] *s* (*unit of distance*) lieue *f*; (*association, alliance*) ligue *f* ‖ *tr* liguer ‖ *intr* se liguer
League′ of Na′tions *s* Société *f* des Nations
leak [lik] *s* fuite *f*; (*in a ship*) voie *f* d'eau; (*of electricity, heat, etc.*) perte *f*, fuite; (*of news, secrets, money, etc.*) fuite; **to spring a leak** avoir une fuite; (naut) faire une voie d'eau ‖ *tr* faire couler; (*gas, steam; secrets, news*) laisser échapper ‖ *intr* fuire, s'écouler; (naut) faire eau; **to leak away** se perdre; **to leak out** (*said of news, secrets, etc.*) transpirer, s'ébruiter
leakage ['likɪdʒ] *s* fuite *f*; (elec) perte *f*
leak·y ['liki] *adj* (*comp* **-ier**; *super* **-iest**) percé, troué; qui a des fuites; (*shoes*) qui prennent l'eau; (coll) indiscret
lean [lin] *adj* maigre; (*gasoline mixture*) pauvre ‖ *s* (*leaning*) inclinaison *f*; (*of meat*) maigre *m* ‖ *v* (*pret & pp* **leaned** or **leant** [lɛnt]) *tr* incliner; **to lean s.th. against s.th.** appuyer q.ch. contre q.ch. ‖ *intr* s'incliner, pencher; **to lean against** s'appuyer contre; **to lean forward** s'incliner or se pencher en avant; **to lean out of** (*e.g., a window*) se pencher par; **to lean over** se pencher; (*e.g., s.o.'s shoulder*) se pencher sur; **to lean toward** (fig) incliner à or vers, pencher pour or vers
leaning ['linɪŋ] *adj* penché ‖ *s* inclinaison *f*; (fig) inclination *f*, penchant *m*
lean′-to′ *s* (*pl* **-tos**) appentis *m*
lean′ years′ *spl* années *fpl* maigres
leap [lip] *s* saut *m*, bond *m*; **by leaps and bounds** par sauts et par bonds; **leap in the dark** saut *m* à l'aveuglette ‖ *v* (*pret & pp* **leaped** or **leapt** [lɛpt]) *tr* sauter, franchir ‖ *intr* sauter, bondir; **to leap across** or **over** sauter; **to leap up** sursauter; (*said, e.g., of flame*) jaillir
leap′ day′ *s* jour *m* intercalaire
leap′frog′ *s* saute-mouton *m*
leap′ year′ *s* année *f* bissextile
learn [lʌrn] *v* (*pret & pp* **learned** [lʌrnd] or **learnt** [lʌrnt]) *tr* apprendre ‖ *intr* apprendre; **to learn to** apprendre à
learned ['lʌrnɪd] *adj* savant, érudit
learn′ed jour′nal *s* revue *f* d'une société savante
learn′ed profes′sion *s* profession *f* libérale
learn′ed soci′ety *s* société *f* savante
learn′ed word′ *s* mot *m* savant
learner ['lʌrnər] *s* élève *mf*; (*beginner*) débutant *m*, apprenti *m*
learn′er's per′mit *s* (aut) permis *m* de conduire (*d'un élève chauffeur*)
learning ['lʌrnɪŋ] *s* (*act and time devoted*) étude *f*; (*scholarship*) savoir *m*, érudition *f*, science *f*
lease [lis] *s* bail *m*; **to give a new lease on life** donner un regain de vie ‖ *tr* (*in the role of landlord*) donner or louer à bail; (*in the role of tenant*) prendre à bail
lease′hold′ *adj* tenu à bail ‖ *s* tenure *f* à bail
leash [liʃ] *s* laisse *f*; **on the leash** en laisse, à l'attache; **to strain at the leash** (fig) ruer dans les brancards ‖ *tr* tenir en laisse
leasing ['lisɪŋ] *s* crédit-bail *m*
least [list] *adj super* (le) moindre §91 ‖ *s* (le) moins *m*; **at least** du moins; **at the very least** tout au moins; **it's the least of my worries** c'est le cadet de mes soucis; **not in the least** pas le moins du monde, nullement; **to say the least** pour ne pas dire plus ‖ *adv super* (le) moins §91
leather ['lɛðər] *s* cuir *m*
leath′er·back tur′tle *s* luth *m*
leath′er-bound′ *adj* relié cuir
leath′er·neck′ *s* (slang) fusilier *m* marin
leathery ['lɛðəri] *adj* (*e.g., steak*) (coll) coriace
leave [liv] *s* permission *f*; (mil) permission de détente; **by your leave** ne vous en déplaise; **on leave** en congé; (mil) en permission; **to give leave to s.o.** to permettre or accorder à qn de; **to take leave (of)** prendre congé (de), faire ses adieux (à) ‖ *v* (*pret & pp* **left** [lɛft]) *tr* (*to let stay; to stop, give up; to disregard*) laisser; (*to go away from*) partir de, quitter; (*to bequeath*) léguer, laisser; (*a wife*) quitter, abandonner; **to be left** rester, e.g., **the letter was left unanswered** la lettre est restée sans réponse; e.g., **there are three dollars left** il reste trois dollars; **to be left for s.o.** to être à qn de; **to be left over** rester; **to leave about** (*without putting away*) laisser traîner; **to leave alone** laisser tranquille; **to leave it up to** s'en remettre à, s'en rapporter à; **to leave no stone unturned** faire flèche de tout bois, mettre tout en œuvre; **to leave off** (*a piece of clothing*) ne pas mettre; (*a passenger*) déposer; **to leave off** + *inf* cesser de + *inf*, renoncer à + *inf*; **to leave out** omettre ‖ *intr* partir, s'en aller; **where did we leave off?** où en sommes-nous restés?
leaven ['lɛvən] *s* levain *m* ‖ *tr* faire lever; (fig) transformer, modifier
leavening ['lɛvənɪŋ] *adj* transformateur ‖ *s* levain *m*
leave′ of ab′sence *s* congé *m*
leave′-tak′ing *s* congé *m*, adieux *mpl*
leavings ['livɪŋz] *spl* restes *mpl*, reliefs *mpl*
Leba·nese [,lɛbə'niz] *adj* libanais ‖ *s* (*pl* **-nese**) Libanais *m*
Lebanon ['lɛbənən] *s* le Liban
lecher ['lɛtʃər] *s* débauché *m*, libertin *m* ‖ *intr* vivre dans la débauche
lecherous ['lɛtʃərəs] *adj* lubrique, lascif
lechery ['lɛtʃəri] *s* lubricité *f*, lasciveté *f*
lectern ['lɛktərn] *s* lutrin *m*
lecture ['lɛktʃər] *s* conférence *f*; (*tedious reprimand*) sermon *m* ‖ *tr* faire une conférence à; (*to rebuke*) sermonner ‖ *intr* faire une conférence or des conférences
lecturer ['lɛktʃərər] *s* conférencier *m*

ledge [lɛdʒ] saillie *f*, corniche *f*; (*projection in a wall*) corniche *f*

ledger [ˈlɛdʒər] *s* (*slab*) pierre *f* tombale; (com) grand livre *m*

ledg′er line′ *s* (mus) ligne *f* supplémentaire

lee [li] *s* (*shelter*) (naut) abri *m*; (*quarter toward which wind blows*) côté *m* sous le vent; **lees** lie *f*

leech [litʃ] *s* sangsue *f*; **to stick like a leech to s.o.** s'accrocher à qn

leek [lik] *s* poireau *m*

leer [lɪr] *s* regard *m* lubrique, œillade *f* ‖ *intr* lancer or jeter une œillade; **to leer at** lorgner

leer·y [ˈlɪri] *adj* (*comp* **-ier**; *super* **-iest**) (coll) soupçonneux, méfiant

leeward [ˈliwərd], [ˈluˑərd] *adj & adv* sous le vent ‖ *s* côté *m* sous le vent; **to pass to leeward of** passer sous le vent de

Lee′ward Is′lands [ˈliwərd] *spl* îles *fpl* Sous-le-Vent

lee′way′ *s* (aer, naut) dérive *f*; (*of time, money*) (coll) marge *f*; (*for action*) (coll) champ *m*, liberté *f*

left [lɛft] *adj* gauche; (*left over*) de surplus ‖ *s* (*left hand*) gauche *f*; (boxing) gauche *m*; **on the left, to the left** à gauche; **the Left** (pol) la gauche; **to make a left** tourner à gauche ‖ *adv* à gauche

left′ field′ *s* (baseball) gauche *f* du grand champ

left′-hand′ drive′ *s* conduite *f* à gauche

left′-hand′ed *adj* gaucher; (*clumsy*) gauche; (*counterclockwise*) à gauche, en sens inverse des aiguilles d'une montre; (*e.g., compliment*) douteux, ambigu

leftish [ˈlɛftɪʃ] *adj* gauchisant

leftism [ˈlɛftɪzəm] *s* gauchisme *m*

leftist [ˈlɛftɪst] *adj & s* gauchiste *mf*

left′o′ver *adj* de surplus, restant ‖ **leftovers** *spl* restes *mpl*

left′-wing′ *adj* gauchiste, gauchisant

left′-winger [ˈlɛftˈwɪŋər] *s* (coll) gauchiste *mf*

left·y [ˈlɛfti] *adj* (coll) gaucher ‖ *s* (*pl* **-ies**) (coll) gaucher *m*

leg [lɛg] *s* jambe *f*; (*of boot or stocking*) tige *f*; (*of fowl; of frogs*) cuisse *f*; (*of journey*) étape *f*; **to be on one's last legs** n'avoir plus de jambes; **to pull the leg of** (coll) se payer la tête de, faire marcher

lega·cy [ˈlɛgəsi] *s* (*pl* **-cies**) legs *m*

legal [ˈligəl] *adj* légal; (*practice*) juridique

le′gal flaw′ *s* vice *m* de forme

le′gal hol′iday *s* jour *m* férié

legali·ty [lɪˈgælɪti] *s* (*pl* **-ties**) légalité *f*

legalize [ˈligəˌlaɪz] *tr* légaliser

le′gal ten′der *s* cours *m* légal, monnaie *f* libératoire

legate [ˈlɛgɪt] *s* ambassadeur *m*, envoyé *m*; (eccl) légat *m*

legatee [ˌlɛgəˈti] *s* légataire *mf*

legation [lɪˈgeʃən] *s* légation *f*

legend [ˈlɛdʒənd] *s* légende *f*

legendary [ˈlɛdʒənˌdɛri] *adj* légendaire

legerdemain [ˌlɛdʒərdɪˈmen] *s* escamotage *m*, passe-passe *m*

leggings [ˈlɛgɪŋz] *spl* jambières *fpl*, guêtres *fpl*, leggings *fpl*

leg·gy [ˈlɛgi] *adj* (*comp* **-gier**; *super* **-giest**) (*awkward*) dégingandé; (*attractive*) aux longues jambes élégantes

leg′horn′ *s* (*hat*) chapeau *m* de paille d'Italie; (*chicken*) leghorn *f*; **Leghorn** Livourne *f*

legibility [ˌlɛdʒɪˈbɪlɪti] *s* lisibilité *f*

legible [ˈlɛdʒɪbəl] *adj* lisible

legion [ˈlidʒən] *s* légion *f*

le′gionnaire′s′ disease′ [ˈlidʒəˌnɛrz] *s* (pathol) maladie *f* du légionnaire

legislate [ˈlɛdʒɪsˌlet] *tr* imposer à force de loi ‖ *intr* faire des lois, légiférer

legislation [ˌlɛdʒɪsˈleʃən] *s* législation *f*

legislative [ˈlɛdʒɪsˌletɪv] *adj* législatif

legislator [ˈlɛdʒɪsˌletər] *s* législateur *m*

legislature [ˈlɛdʒɪsˌletʃər] *s* assemblée *f* législative, législature *f*

legitimacy [lɪˈdʒɪtɪməsi] *s* légitimité *f*

legitimate [lɪˈdʒɪtɪmɪt] *adj* légitime ‖ [lɪˈdʒɪtɪˌmet] *tr* légitimer

legit′imate dra′ma *s* théâtre *m* régulier

legitimize [lɪˈdʒɪtɪˌmaɪz] *tr* légitimer

leg′ of lamb′ *s* gigot *m* d'agneau

leg′ of mut′ton *s* gigot *m*

leg′-of-mut′ton sleeve′ *s* manche *f* gigot

legume [ˈlɛgjum], [lɪˈgjum] *s* (*pod*) légume *m*; (bot) légumineuse *f*

leisure [ˈliʒər], [ˈlɛʒər] *s* loisir *m*; **at leisure** à loisir; **in leisure moments** à temps perdu; **leisure activities** loisirs *mpl*

lei′sure class′ *s* désœuvrés *mpl*, rentiers *mpl*

lei′sure hours′ *spl* heures *fpl* de loisir

leisurely [ˈliʒərli] *adj* tranquille, posé ‖ *adv* posément, sans hâte

lemon [ˈlɛmən] *s* citron *m*; (*e.g., worthless car*) (coll) clou *m*

lemonade [ˌlɛməˈned] *s* citronnade *f*

lem′on squeez′er *s* presse-citron *m*

lem′on tree′ *s* citronnier *m*

lem′on verbe′na [vərˈbinə] *s* verveine *f* citronnelle

lend [lɛnd] *v* (*pret & pp* **lent** [lɛnt]) *tr* prêter

lender [ˈlɛndər] *s* prêteur *m*

lend′ing li′brary *s* bibliothèque *f* de prêt

length [lɛŋ θ] *s* longueur *f*; (*e.g., of string*) bout *m*, morceau *m*; (*of time*) durée *f*; **at length** longuement, en détail; (*finally*) enfin, à la fin; **in length** de longueur; **to go to any length to** ne reculer devant rien pour; **to keep at arm's length** tenir à distance

lengthen [ˈlɛŋ θən] *tr* allonger, rallonger ‖ *intr* s'allonger

length′wise′ *adj* longitudinal ‖ *adv* en longueur, dans le sens de la longueur

length·y [ˈlɛŋ θi] *adj* (*comp* **-ier**; *super* **-iest**) prolongé, assez long

leniency [ˈlini·ənsi] *s* douceur *f*, clémence *f*

lenient [ˈlini·ənt] *adj* doux, clément

lens [lɛnz] *s* lentille *f*; (anat) cristallin *m*

Lent [lɛnt] *s* le Carême

Lenten [ˈlɛntən] *adj* de carême

lentil [ˈlɛntəl] *s* lentille *f*

Leo ['li·o] s (astr, astrol) le Lion
leopard ['lɛpərd] s léopard m
leper ['lɛpər] s lépreux m
lep'er house' s léproserie f
leprosy ['lɛprəsi] s lèpre f
leprous ['lɛprəs] adj lépreux
lesbian ['lɛzbɪ·ən] adj érotique; **Lesbian** lesbien [l]; s (female homosexual) lesbienne f; **Lesbian** Lesbien m
lesbianism ['lɛzbɪ·ə,nɪzəm] s saphisme m
lese majesty ['liz'mædʒɪsti] s crime m de lèse-majesté
lesion ['liʒən] s lésion f
less [lɛs] adj comp moindre §91 [l] s moins m [l] adv comp moins §91; **less and less** de moins en moins; **less than** moins que; (followed by numeral) moins de; **the less . . . the less** (or **the more**) moins . . . moins (or plus)
lessee [lɛs'i] s preneur m; (e.g., of house) locataire mf; (e.g., of gasoline station) concessionnaire mf
lessen ['lɛsən] tr diminuer, amoindrir [l] intr se diminuer, s'amoindrir
lesser ['lɛsər] adj comp moindre §91; **the lesser of two evils** le moindre de deux maux
lesson ['lɛsən] s leçon f
lessor ['lɛsər] s bailleur m
lest [lɛst] conj de peur que, de crainte que
let [lɛt] v (pret & pp let; ger letting) tr laisser; (to rent) louer; **let + inf** que + subj, e.g., **let him come in** qu'il entre; **let alone** sans parler de, sans compter; **let well enough alone** le mieux est souvent l'ennemi du bien; **let us eat, work, etc.** mangeons, travaillons, etc.; **to be let off with** en être quitte pour; e.g., **house to let** maison à louer; **let alone, to let be** laisser tranquille; **to let by** laisser passer; **to let down** baisser, descendre; (one's hair) dénouer, défaire; (e.g., a garment) allonger; (to leave in the lurch) laisser en panne, faire faux bond à; **to let fly** décocher; **to let go** laisser partir; **to let have** laisser, e.g., **he let Robert have it for three dollars** il l'a laissé à Robert pour trois dollars; **to let in** laisser entrer; **to let in the clutch** (aut) embrayer; **to let into** admettre dans; **to let loose** lâcher; **to let off** laisser partir; (e.g., steam from a boiler) laisser échapper, lâcher; (e.g., a culprit) pardonner à; **to let oneself go** se laisser aller; **to let on that** (coll) faire croire que; **to let out** faire or laisser sortir; (e.g., a dress) élargir; (a cry; a secret; a prisoner) laisser échapper; (to reveal) révéler, divulguer; **to let out on bail** relâcher sous caution; **to let out the clutch** débrayer; **to let slip** laisser tomber; **to let s.o. + inf** permettre à qn de + inf; laisser qn + inf, e.g., **he let Mary go to the theater** il a laissé Marie aller au théâtre; **to let s.o. in on** (a secret) (coll) confier à qn; (e.g., a racing tip) (coll) tuyauter qn sur; **to let s.o. know s.th.** faire savoir q.ch. à qn, mettre qn au courant de q.ch.; **to let s.o. off with** faire grâce à qn de; **to let stand** laisser, e.g., **he let the errors stand** il a laissé les fautes; **to let s.th. go for** (a low price) laisser q.ch. pour; **to let through** laisser passer; **to let up** laisser monter [l] intr (said of house, apartment, etc.) se louer; **to let down** (coll) ralentir; **to let go of** lâcher prise de; **to let out** (said of class, school, etc.) finir, se terminer; **to let up** (coll) ralentir, diminuer; (on discipline; on a person) devenir moins sévère
let'down' s diminution f; (disappointment) déception f
lethal ['liθəl] adj mortel; (weapon) meurtrier
lethargic [lɪ'θɑrdʒɪk] adj léthargique
lethar·gy ['lɛθərdʒi] s (pl -gies) léthargie f
letter ['lɛtər] s lettre f; **letters** (literature) lettres; **to the letter** à la lettre, au pied de la lettre [l] tr marquer avec des lettres
let'ter box' s boîte f aux lettres
let'ter car'rier s facteur m
let'ter drop' s passe-lettres m, fente f (dans la porte pour le courrier)
lettered adj (person) lettré
let'ter file' s classeur m de lettres
let'ter·head' s en-tête m
lettering ['lɛtərɪŋ] s (action) lettrage m; (title) inscription f
let'ter of cred'it s lettre f de crédit
let'ter o'pener s coupe-papier m
let'ter pa'per s papier m à lettres
let'ter·per'fect adj correct; sûr
let'ter press' s presse f à copier
let'ter·press' s impression f typographique; (in distinction to illustrations) texte m
let'ter scales' spl pèse-lettre m
let'ter·word' s sigle m
lettuce ['lɛtɪs] s laitue f
let'up' s accalmie f, pause f; **without letup** sans relâche
leucorrhea [,lukə'ri·ə] s leucorrhée f
leukemia [lu'kimɪ·ə] s leucémie f
Levant [lɪ'vænt] s Levant m
Levantine ['lɛvən,tin], [lɪ'væntin] adj levantin [l] s Levantin m
levee ['lɛvi] s (embankment) levée f, digue f; réception f royale
lev·el ['lɛvəl] adj de niveau; (flat) égal, uni; (spoonful) arasé; **level with** de niveau avec, à fleur de [l] s niveau m; **on a level with** au niveau de; **to be on the level** (coll) être de bonne foi; **to find one's level** trouver son niveau [l] v (pret & pp -eled or -elled; ger -eling or -elling) tr niveler; (to smooth, flatten out) aplanir, araser; (to bring down) raser; (a gun) braquer; (accusations, sarcasm) lancer, diriger; **to level out** égaliser; **to level up** (aer) redresser [l] intr (aer) redresser; **to level with** (coll) parler franchement à
lev'el·head'ed adj équilibré, pondéré
lev'eling rod' s (surv) jalon-mire m, jalon m d'arpentage
lever ['livər] s levier m [l] tr soulever or ouvrir au moyen d'un levier

leverage ['lɛvərɪdʒ] s puissance f or force f de levier; (fig) influence f, avantage m
leviathan [lɪ'vaɪ·əθən] s léviathan m
levitation [,lɛvɪ'teʃən] s lévitation f
levi·ty ['lɛvɪti] s (pl -ties) légèreté f
lev·y ['lɛvi] s (pl -ies) levée f ‖ v (pret & pp -ied) tr lever; (a fine) imposer
lewd [lud] adj luxurieux, lubrique
lewdness ['ludnɪs] s luxure f, lubricité f
lexical ['lɛksɪkəl] adj lexical
lexicographer [,lɛksɪ'kɑgrəfər] s lexicographe mf
lexicographic(al) [,lɛksɪkə'græfɪk(əl)] adj lexicographique
lexicography [,lɛksɪ'kɑgrəfi] s lexicographie f
lexicology [,lɛksɪ'kɑlədʒi] s lexicologie f
lexicon ['lɛksɪkən] s lexique m
liabili·ty [,laɪ·ə'bɪlɪti] s (pl -ties) responsabilité f; (e.g., to disease) prédisposition f; **liabilities** obligations fpl, dettes fpl
liabil′ity insur′ance s assurance f tous risques
liable ['laɪ·əbəl] adj sujet; **liable for** (a debt, fine, etc.) passible de, responsable de; **we (you, etc.) are liable to** + inf (coll) il se peut que nous (vous, etc.) + pres subj; (coll) il est probable que nous (vous, etc.) + pres ind
liaison [li'ezən] s liaison f
liar ['laɪ·ər] s menteur m
libation [laɪ'beʃən] s libation f
li·bel ['laɪbəl] s diffamation f, calomnie f; (in writing) écrit m diffamatoire ‖ v (pret & pp -beled or -belled; ger -beling or -belling) tr diffamer, calomnier
libelous ['laɪbələs] adj diffamatoire, calomnieux
liberal ['lɪbərəl] adj libéral; (share, supply, etc.) libéral, généreux, copieux; (ideas) large ‖ s libéral m
liberali·ty [,lɪbə'rælɪti] s (pl -ties) libéralité f; (breadth of mind) largeur f de vues
lib′eral·mind′ed adj tolérant
liberate ['lɪbə,ret] tr libérer
liberation [,lɪbə'reʃən] s libération f
liberator ['lɪbə,retər] s libérateur m
libertine ['lɪbər,tin] adj & s libertin m
liber·ty ['lɪbərti] s (pl -ties) liberté f; (mil) permission f exceptionnelle; **at liberty** en liberté; **at liberty to** libre de; **to take the liberty to** se permettre de, prendre la liberté de
libidinous [lɪ'bɪdɪnəs] adj libidineux
libido [lɪ'bido], [lɪ'baɪdo] s libido f
Libra ['lɪbrə] s (astr, astrol) la Balance
librarian [laɪ'brɛrɪ·ən] s bibliothécaire mf
librar·y ['laɪ,brɛri] s (pl -ies) bibliothèque f
li·brary num′ber s cote f
libret·to [lɪ'brɛto] s (pl -tos) livret m, libretto m
license ['laɪsəns] s permis m, licence f; (to drive) permis de conduire ‖ tr accorder un permis à, autoriser
li′cense num′ber s numéro m d'immatriculation; (aut) numéro minéralogique

li′cense plate′ or **tag′** s plaque f d'immatriculation, plaque minéralogique
licentious [laɪ'sɛnʃəs] adj licencieux
lichen ['laɪkən] s lichen m
lick [lɪk] s (with the tongue) coup m de langue; (salt lick) terrain m salifère; (blow) (coll) coup m; **at full lick** (coll) à plein gaz; **to give a lick and a promise to** (coll) nettoyer à la six-quatre-deux; (coll) faire un brin de toilette à ‖ tr lécher; (e.g., the fingers) se lécher; (to beat, thrash) (coll) enfoncer les côtes à, rosser; (to beat, surpass, e.g., in a sporting event) (coll) battre, enfoncer; (e.g., a problem) (coll) venir à bout de; **to lick into shape** (coll) dégrossir; **to lick up** lécher
licking ['lɪkɪŋ] s léchage m; (drubbing) (coll) raclée f
licorice ['lɪkərɪs] s réglisse f
lid [lɪd] s (on a dish, kettle, etc.) couvercle m; (eyelid) paupière f; (hat) (slang) couvre-chef m
lie [laɪ] s mensonge m; **to give the lie to** donner le démenti à ‖ v (pret & pp lied; ger lying) tr—**to lie one's way out** se tirer d'affaire par des mensonges ‖ intr mentir ‖ v (pret lay; pp lain [lɛn]; ger lying) intr être couché; (to be located) se trouver; (e.g., in the grave) gésir, e.g., **here lies** ci-gît; **to lie down** se coucher
lie′ detec′tor s détecteur m de mensonges, polygraphe m
lien [lin] s privilège m, droit m de rétention
lieu [lu] s—**in lieu of** au lieu de
lieutenant [lu'tɛnənt] s lieutenant m; (nav) lieutenant m de vaisseau
lieuten′ant colo′nel s lieutenant-colonel m
lieuten′ant comman′der s (nav) capitaine m de corvette
lieuten′ant gov′ernor s (U.S.A.) vice-gouverneur m; (Brit) lieutenant-gouverneur m
lieuten′ant jun′ior grade′ s (nav) enseigne m de première classe
life [laɪf] s (pl lives [laɪvz]) vie f; (of light bulb, lease, insurance policy) durée f; **bigger than life** plus grand que nature; **for dear life** de toutes ses forces; **for life** à vie, pour la vie, à perpétuité; **for the life of me!** (coll) de ma vie!; **lives lost** morts mpl; **long life** longévité f; **never in my life!, not on your life!** jamais de la vie!; **run for your life!** sauve qui peut!; **such is life!** c'est la vie!; **taken from life** pris sur le vif; **to come to life** revenir à la vie; **to depart this life** quitter ce monde; **to risk life and limb** risquer sa peau
life′ annu′ity s viagère f
life′ belt′ s ceinture f de sauvetage
life′blood′ s sang m; (fig) vie f
life′boat′ s chaloupe f de sauvetage; (for shore-based rescue services) canot m de sauvetage
life′ buoy′ s bouée f de sauvetage
life′ expect′ancy s espérance f de vie
life′ float′ s radeau m de sauvetage

life′ guard′ s (mil) garde f du corps
life′guard′ s sauveteur m, maître nageur m
life′ impris′onment s emprisonnement m à vie, détention f perpétuelle
life′ insur′ance s assurance f sur la vie, assurance-vie f
life′ jack′et s gilet m de sauvetage
lifeless [ˈlaɪflɪs] adj sans vie, inanimé; (colors) embu, terne
life′like′ adj vivant, ressemblant
life′ line′ s ligne f or corde f de sauvetage, planche f de salut
life′long′ adj de toute la vie, perpétuel
life′ mem′ber s membre m à vie, membre perpétuel
life′ of lei′sure s vie f de château
life′ of Ri′ley [ˈraɪli] s (slang) joyeuse vie f, vie oisive
life′ of the par′ty s (coll) boute-en-train m
life′ preserv′er [prɪˈzʌrvər] s appareil m de sauvetage
lifer [ˈlaɪfər] s (slang) condamné m à perpétuité
life′ raft′ s radeau m de sauvetage
lifesaver [ˈlaɪfˌsevər] s sauveteur m; (fig) planche f de salut
life′sav′ing s sauvetage m
life′ sen′tence s condamnation f à perpétuité
life′-size′ adj de grandeur nature
life′ span′ s durée f de vie, espérance f de vie
life′time′ adj à vie ‖ s vie f, toute une vie; **in his lifetime** de son vivant
life′work′ s travail m de toute une vie
lift [lɪft] s haussement m, levée f; (aer) poussée f, portance f; (Brit) ascenseur m; (of dumbbell or weight) (sports) arraché m; **to give a lift to** (by offering a ride) conduire d'un coup de voiture, faire monter dans la voiture; (to aid) donner un coup de main à; (to raise the morale of) remonter le moral de, ranimer ‖ tr lever, soulever; (heart, mind, etc.) élever, ranimer; (a sail) soulager; (an embargo) lever; (e.g., passages from a book) démarquer, plagier; (to rob) (slang) dérober; **to lift up** (the hands) lever; (the head) relever; (the voice) élever ‖ intr se lever, se soulever; (said of clouds, fog, etc.) se lever, se dissiper
lift′ bridge′ s pont m levant, pont-levis m
lift′off′ s (rok) montée verticale, chandelle f
lift′ truck′ s chariot m élévateur
ligament [ˈlɪɡəmənt] s ligament m
ligature [ˈlɪɡətʃər] s ligature f
light [laɪt] adj léger; (having illumination) éclairé; (color, complexion, hair) clair; (beer) blond; (wine) léger; **to make light of** faire peu de cas de ‖ s lumière f; (to control traffic) feu m; (window or other opening in a wall) jour m; (example, shining figure) lumière f; (headlight of automobile) phare m; du feu, e.g., **do you have a light?** (e.g., to light a cigarette) avez-vous du feu?; **according to one's lights** selon ses lumières, dans la mesure

de son intelligence; **against the light** à contre-jour; **in a false light** sous un faux jour; **in a new light** sous un jour nouveau; **in the same light** sous le même aspect; **it is light (out)** il fait jour; **lights** (navigation lights; parking lights) feux mpl; (of sheep, calf, etc.) mou m; **lights out** (mil) l'extinction f des feux; **to bring to light** mettre au jour; **to come to light** se révéler; **to shed** or **throw light on** éclairer; **to strike a light** allumer ‖ adv à vide; **to run light** (said of engine) aller haut le pied ‖ v (pret & pp **lighted** or **lit** [lɪt]) tr (to furnish with illumination) éclairer, illuminer; (to set afire, ignite) allumer; **to light the way for** éclairer; **to light up** illuminer ‖ intr s'éclairer, s'illuminer; allumer; (to perch) se poser; **to light from** or **off** (an auto, carriage, etc.) descendre de; **to light into** (to attack; to berate) (slang) tomber sur; **to light out** (to skedaddle) (slang) décamper; **to light up** s'éclairer, s'illuminer; **to light upon** (by happenstance) tomber sur, trouver par hasard
light′ bulb′ s ampoule f électrique, lampe f électrique
light′ complex′ion s teint m clair
lighten [ˈlaɪtən] tr (to make lighter in weight) alléger, soulager; (to provide more light) éclairer, illuminer; (to give a lighter or brighter hue to) éclaircir; (grief, punishment, etc.) adoucir ‖ intr (to become less dark or sorrowful) s'éclairer; (to give off flashes of lightning) faire des éclairs; (to become less weighty) s'alléger
lighter [ˈlaɪtər] s (to light cigarette) briquet m; (flat-bottomed barge) chaland m, péniche f
light′-fin′gered adj à doigts agiles
light′-foot′ed adj au pied léger
light′-head′ed adj étourdi
light′-heart′ed adj joyeux, allègre, au cœur léger
light′house′ s phare m
lighting [ˈlaɪtɪŋ] s allumage m, éclairage m
light′ing fix′tures spl appareils mpl d'éclairage
light′ me′ter s posemètre m
lightness [ˈlaɪtnɪs] s (in weight) légèreté f; (in illumination; of complexion) clarté f
light′ning [ˈlaɪtnɪŋ] s (electric discharge) foudre f; (light produced by this discharge) éclairs mpl ‖ v (ger **-ning**) intr faire des éclairs
light′ning arrest′er [əˌrɛstər] f parafoudre m
light′ning bug′ s luciole f
light′ning rod′ s paratonnerre m
light′ op′era s opérette f
light′ pen′ s (comp) photostyle m
light′ read′ing s livres mpl d'agrément; lecture f légère or amusante
light′ship′ s bateau-feu m
light-struck [ˈlaɪtˌstrʌk] adj (phot) voilé
light′ wave′ s onde f lumineuse

light′weight′ *adj* léger ‖ *s* (sports) poids *m* léger

light′weight coat′ *s* surtout *m* de demisaison

light′-year′ *s* année-lumière *f*

likable [′laɪkəbəl] *adj* sympathique, agréable

like [laɪk] *adj* (*alike*) pareils, semblables; pareil à, semblable à; (*typical of*) caractéristique de; (*poles of a magnet*) (elec) de même nom; **like father like son** tel père tel fils; **that is like him** il n'en fait pas d'autres ‖ *s* pareil *m*, semblable *m*; **likes** (*desires*) goût *m*, inclinations *fpl*; **the likes of him** son pareil ‖ *adv*—**like enough** probablement; **like mad** comme un fou ‖ *prep* comme; **like that** de la sorte ‖ *conj* (coll) de la même manière que, comme ‖ *tr* aimer, aimer bien, trouver bon; plaire à, e.g., **I like milk** le lait me plaît; se plaire, e.g., **I like it in the country** je me plais à la campagne ‖ *intr* vouloir; **as you like** comme vous voudrez; **if you like** si vous voulez

likelihood [′laɪklɪ,hʊd] *s* probabilité *f*, vraisemblance *f*

like·ly [′laɪkli] *adj* (*comp* **-lier**; *super* **-liest**) probable, vraisemblable; **to be likely to** + *inf* être probable que + *ind*, e.g., **Mary is likely to come to see us tomorrow** il est probable que Marie viendra nous voir demain ‖ *adv* probablement, vraisemblablement

like′-mind′ed *adj* du même avis

liken [′laɪkən] *tr* comparer, assimiler

likeness [′laɪknɪs] *s* (*picture or image*) portrait *m*; (*similarity*) ressemblance *f*

like′wise′ *adv* également, de même; **to do likewise** en faire autant

liking [′laɪkɪŋ] *s* sympathie *f*, penchant *m*; **to one's liking** à souhait; **to take a liking to** (*a thing*) accueillir avec sympathie; (*a person*) montrer de la sympathie à, se prendre d'amitié pour

lilac [′laɪlək] *adj & s* lilas *m*

Lilliputian [,lɪlɪ′pjuʃən] *adj & s* lilliputien *m*

lilt [lɪlt] *s* cadence *f*

lil·y [′lɪli] *s* (*pl* **-ies**) lis *m*, lis blanc; (*royal arms of France*) fleur *f* de lis; **to gild the lily** orner la beauté même

lil′y of the val′ley *s* muguet *m*

lil′y pad′ *s* feuille *f* de nénuphar

lil′y-white′ *adj* blanc comme le lis, lilial

Li′ma bean′ [′laɪmə] *s* (*Phaseolus limensis*) haricot *m* de Lima

limb [lɪm] *s* (*arm or leg*) membre *m*; (*of a tree*) branche *f*; (*of a cross; of the sea*) bras *m*; (astr, bot) limbe *m*; **to be out on a limb** (coll) être sur la corde raide

limber [′lɪmbər] *adj* souple, flexible ‖ *intr*—**to limber up** se dégourdir

lim·bo [′lɪmbo] *s* (*pl* **-bos**) limbes *mpl*

lime [laɪm] *s* (*calcium oxide*) chaux *f*; (*linden tree*) tilleul *m*; (*Citrus aurantifolia*) citron *m*; **sweet lime** (*Citrus limetta*) lime *f*

lime′kiln′ *s* four *m* à chaux

lime′light′ *s*—**to be in the limelight** être sous les feux de la rampe

limerick [′lɪmərɪk] *s* poème *m* humoristique en cinq vers

lime′stone′ *adj* calcaire ‖ *s* calcaire *m*, pierre *f* à chaux

limit [′lɪmɪt] *s* limite *f*, borne *f*; **to be the limit** (*to be exasperating*) (coll) être le comble; (*to be bizarre*) (coll) être impayable; **to go the limit** aller jusqu'au bout ‖ *tr* limiter, borner

limitation [,lɪmɪ′teʃən] *s* limitation *f*

lim′ited-ac′cess high′way *s* autoroute *f*

lim′ited mon′archy *s* monarchie *f* constitutionnelle

limitless [′lɪmɪtlɪs] *adj* sans bornes, illimité

limousine [,lɪmə′zin] *s* (aut) limousine *f*

limp [lɪmp] *adj* mou, flasque, souple ‖ *s* boiterie *f* ‖ *intr* boiter

limpid [′lɪmpɪd] *adj* limpide

linchpin [′lɪntʃ,pɪn] *s* cheville *f* d'essieu, esse *f*

linden [′lɪndən] *s* tilleul *m*

line [laɪn] *s* ligne *f*; (*of poetry*) vers *m*; (*rope, string*) cordage *m*, corde *f*; (*wrinkle*) ride *f*; (*dash*) trait *m*; (*bar*) barre *f*; (*lineage*) lignée *f*; (*trade*) métier *m*; (*of merchandise*) article *m*; (*of traffic*) file *f*; (mil) rang *m*; (*of the spectrum*) (phys) raie *f*; **fault line** ligne de faille; **hold the line!** (telp) ne quittez pas!; **in line** aligné, en rang; **in line with** conforme à, d'accord avec; **off line** (comp) autonome; **on line** (comp) en ligne; **on the line** (telp) au bout du fil; **out of line** désaligné; en désaccord; **straight line** ligne droite; **the line is busy** (telp) la ligne est occupée; **to bring into line with** mettre d'accord avec; **to drop s.o. a line** envoyer un mot à qn; **to fall into line** se mettre en ligne, s'aligner; **to hand s.o. a line** (slang) faire du baratin à qn, bourrer le crâne de qn; **to have a line on** (coll) se tuyauter sur; **to learn one's lines** apprendre son texte or rôle; **to read between the lines** lire entre les lignes; **to stand or wait in line** faire la queue; **to toe the line** se mettre au pas ‖ *tr* aligner; (*a face*) rider; (*a suit, coat, etc.*) doubler; (*brakes*) fourrer; **to be lined with** (*e.g., trees*) être bordé de ‖ *intr*—**to line up** s'aligner, se mettre en ligne; faire la queue

lineage [′lɪnɪ·ɪdʒ] *s* lignée *f*, race *f*, lignage *m*

lineal [′lɪnɪ·əl] *adj* linéal; (*succession*) en ligne directe

lineaments [′lɪnɪ·əmənts] *spl* linéaments *mpl*

linear [′lɪnɪ·ər] *adj* linéaire

lined′ pa′per *s* papier *m* rayé

line′man *s* (*pl* **-men**) (elec) poseur *m* de lignes; (rr) garde-ligne *m*

linen [′lɪnən] *adj* de lin ‖ *s* (*fabric*) toile *f* de lin; (*yarn*) fil *m* de lin; (*sheets, cloths, underclothes, etc.*) linge *m*, lingerie *f*; **don't wash your dirty linen in public** il faut laver son linge sale en famille; il ne faut pas laver en public un linge sanglant; **pure linen** pur fil

lin'en clos'et s lingerie f

line' of fire' s (mil) ligne f de tir

line' of sight' s ligne f de mire, ligne de visée

liner ['laɪnər] s (naut) paquebot m

line'-up' s (row) file f, mise f en rang; (arrangement) disposition f; (of suspects) séance f d'identification d'un suspect; (pol) front m; (sports) composition f de l'équipe

linger ['lɪŋgər] intr s'attarder; (said of hope, doubt, etc.) persister; **to linger on** traîner; **to linger over** s'attarder sur

lingerie [,lænʒə'ri] s lingerie f fine pour dames, lingerie f de dame

lingering ['lɪŋgərɪŋ] adj prolongé, lent

lingual ['lɪŋgwəl] adj lingual ‖ s (consonant) linguale f

linguist ['lɪŋgwɪst] s (person skilled in several languages) polyglotte mf; (specialist in linguistics) linguiste mf

linguistic [lɪŋ'gwɪstɪk] adj linguistique ‖ **linguistics** s linguistique f

liniment ['lɪnɪmənt] s liniment m

lining ['laɪnɪŋ] s (of a coat) doublure f; (of a hat) coiffe f; (of auto brake) garniture f; (of furnace, wall, etc.) revêtement m

link [lɪŋk] s maillon m, chaînon m; (fig) lien m; **links** terrain m de golf ‖ tr enchaîner; lier ‖ intr—**to link in, on,** or **up** se lier

link'up s (rok) arrimage m

linnet ['lɪnɪt] s (orn) linotte f

linoleum [lɪ'nolɪ·əm] s linoléum m

linotype ['laɪnə,taɪp] (trademark) s linotype f ‖ tr & intr composer à la lino

lin'otype op'erator s linotypiste mf

lin'otype slug' s ligne-bloc m

linseed ['lɪn,sid] s linette f, graine f de lin

lin'seed oil' s huile f de lin

lint [lɪnt] s (minute shreds) petites parcelles fpl de fil; (fluff) peluches fpl; (used to dress wounds) charpie f; tissu m ouaté

lintel ['lɪntəl] s linteau m

lion ['laɪ·ən] s lion m; (fig) lion; **to put one's head in the lion's mouth** se fourrer dans la gueule du loup ou du lion

lioness ['laɪ·ənɪs] s lionne f

li'on-heart'ed adj au cœur de lion

lionize ['laɪ·ə,naɪz] tr faire une célébrité de, traiter en vedette

li'ons' den' s (Bib) fosse f aux lions

li'on's share' s part f du lion

lip [lɪp] s lèvre f; (edge) bord m; (slang) impertinence f; **to hang on the lips of** être suspendu aux lèvres de; **to smack one's lips** se lécher les babines

lip'read' v (pret & pp **-read** [,rɛd]) tr & intr lire sur les lèvres

lip' read'ing s lecture f sur les lèvres

lip' serv'ice s dévotion f des lèvres

lip'stick' s bâton m de rouge à lèvres

lique·fy ['lɪkwɪ,faɪ] v (pret & pp **-fied**) tr liquéfier

liqueur [lɪ'kʌr] s liqueur f

liquid ['lɪkwɪd] adj liquide ‖ s liquide m; (consonant) liquide f

liq'uid as'sets spl valeurs fpl disponibles

liquidate ['lɪkwɪ,det] tr & intr liquider

liquidity [lɪ'kwɪdɪti] s liquidité f

liquor ['lɪkər] s boisson f alcoolique, spiritueux m; (culin) jus m, bouillon m

Lisbon ['lɪzbən] s Lisbonne f

lisle [laɪl] s fil m d'Écosse, fil retors de coton

lisp [lɪsp] s zézayement m, blésement m ‖ intr zézayer, bléser

lissome ['lɪsəm] adj souple, flexible; (nimble) agile, leste

list [lɪst] s liste f; (selvage) lisière f; (naut) bande f, inclinaison f; **to enter the lists** entrer en lice; **to have a list** (naut) donner de la bande ‖ tr cataloguer, enregistrer; (comp) lister ‖ intr (naut) donner de la bande

listen ['lɪsən] intr écouter; **to listen in** rester à l'écoute; **to listen to** écouter; **to listen to reason** entendre raison

listener ['lɪsənər] s auditeur m; (educ) auditeur libre

listening ['lɪsənɪŋ] s écoute f

lis'tening post' s poste m d'écoute

listing ['lɪstɪŋ] s énumération f, compte m; (comp) listage m

listless ['lɪstlɪs] adj apathique, inattentif

list' price' s prix m courant, cote f

lita·ny ['lɪtəni] s (pl **-nies**) litanie f

liter ['litər] s litre m

literal ['lɪtərəl] adj littéral; (person) prosaïque

literally ['lɪtərəli] adv littéralement, mot à mot, au sens propre; (without interpretation) au pied de la lettre, à la lettre; (really) réellement; (absolutely) (coll) littéralement

literary ['lɪtə,rɛri] adj littéraire

literate ['lɪtərɪt] adj qui sait lire et écrire; (well-read) lettré ‖ s personne f qui sait lire et écrire; lettré m, érudit m

literati [,lɪtə'rati] spl littérateurs mpl

literature ['lɪtərətʃər] s littérature f; (com) documentation f

lithe [laɪð] adj souple, flexible

lithia ['lɪθɪ·ə] s (chem) lithine f

lithium ['lɪθɪ·əm] s (chem) lithium m

lithograph ['lɪθə,græf] s lithographie f ‖ tr lithographier

lithographer [lɪ'θagrəfər] s lithographe mf

lithography [lɪ'θagrəfi] s lithographie f

litigant ['lɪtɪgənt] adj plaidant ‖ s plaideur m

litigate ['lɪtɪ,get] tr mettre en litige ‖ intr plaider

litigation [,lɪtɪ'geʃən] s litige m

lit'mus pa'per ['lɪtməs] s papier m de tournesol

litter ['lɪtər] s (disorder) fouillis m; (things strewn about) jonchee f; (scattered rubbish) ordures fpl; (young brought forth at one birth) portée f; (bedding for animals) litière f; (vehicle carried by men or animals) palanquin m; (stretcher) civière f ‖ tr joncher ‖ intr (to bring forth young) mettre bas

lit′ter·bug′ s souillon m, malpropre m, personne f qui dépose des ordures et des papiers dans la rue

littering [ˈlɪtərɪŋ] s—**no littering** (*public sign*) défense de déposer des ordures

little [ˈlɪtəl] adj petit; (*in amount*) peu de, e.g., **little money** peu d'argent; **a little** peu de, e.g., **a little money** un peu d'argent ‖ s peu m; **a little** un peu; **to make little of,** **to think little of** faire peu de cas de; **wait a little** attendez un petit moment, attendez quelques instants ‖ adv peu §91; ne . . . guère §90, e.g., **she little thinks that** elle ne se doute guère que; **little by little** peu à peu, petit à petit

Lit′tle Bear′ s Petite Ourse f

Lit′tle Dip′per s Petit Chariot m

lit′tle fin′ger s petit doigt m, auriculaire m; **to twist around one's little finger** mener par le bout du nez

lit′tle·neck′ s coque f de Vénus

littleness [ˈlɪtəlnɪs] s petitesse f

lit′tle owl′ s (*Athene noctua*) chouette f chevêche, chevêche f

lit′tle peo′ple spl (*fairies*) fées fpl; (*common people*) menu peuple m

Lit′tle Red Rid′ing·hood′ s le Petit Chaperon rouge

lit′tle slam′ s (bridge) petit chelem m

liturgic(al) [lɪˈtʌrdʒɪk(əl)] adj liturgique

litur·gy [ˈlɪtərdʒi] s (*pl* **-gies**) liturgie f

livable [ˈlɪvəbəl] adj (*house*) habitable; (*life, person*) supportable

live [laɪv] adj vivant, vif; (*coals; flame*) ardent; (*microphone*) actif; (elec) sous tension; (telv) en direct ‖ [lɪv] tr vivre; **to live down** faire oublier ‖ intr vivre; (*in a certain locality*) demeurer, habiter; **live and learn** qui vivra verra; **to live high** mener grand train; **to live in** (e.g., *a city*) habiter; **to live on** continuer à vivre; (e.g., *meat*) vivre de; (*a benefactor*) vivre aux crochets de; (*one's capital*) manger; **to live up to** (e.g., *one's reputation*) faire honneur à

live′ coal′ [laɪv] s charbon m ardent

livelihood [ˈlaɪvlɪ,hʊd] s vie f; **to earn one's livelihood** gagner sa vie

livelong [ˈlɪv,lɔŋ] adj—**all the livelong day** toute la sainte journée

live·ly [ˈlaɪvli] adj (*comp* **-lier;** *super* **-liest**) animé, vivant, plein d'entrain; (*merry*) enjoué, gai; (*active, keen*) vif; (*resilient*) élastique

liven [ˈlaɪvən] tr animer ‖ intr s'animer

liver [ˈlɪvər] s vivant m; (e.g., *in cities*) habitant m; (anat) foie m

liver·y [ˈlɪvəri] s (*pl* **-ies**) livrée f

liv′ery·man s (*pl* **-men**) loueur m de chevaux

liv′ery sta′ble s écurie f de louage

live′ show′ [laɪv] s (telv) prise f de vues en direct

live′stock′ s bétail m, bestiaux mpl, cheptel m

live′ tel′evision broad′cast s prise f de vues en direct

live′ wire′ s fil m sous tension; (slang) type m dynamique, boute-en-train m invar

livid [ˈlɪvɪd] adj livide

living [ˈlɪvɪŋ] adj vivant, en vie ‖ s vie f; **to earn** or **to make a living** gagner sa vie

liv′ing quar′ters spl appartements mpl, habitations fpl

liv′ing room′ s salle f de séjour, salon m; (*in a studio apartment*) living m

liv′ing space′ s espace m vital

liv′ing wage′ s salaire m suffisant pour vivre, salaire de base

lizard [ˈlɪzərd] s lézard m

load [lod] s charge f; **loads (of)** (coll) énormément (de); **to get a load of** (slang) observer, écouter; **to have a load on** (slang) avoir son compte ‖ tr charger ‖ intr charger; se charger

loaded adj chargé; (*very drunk*) (slang) soûl; (*very rich*) (slang) huppé

load′ed dice′ spl dés mpl pipés

load′stone′ s pierre f d'aimant; (fig) aimant m

loaf [lof] s (*pl* **loaves** [lovz]) pain m ‖ intr flâner

loafer [ˈlofər] s flâneur m

loam [lom] s terre f franche, glaise f; (*mixture used in making molds*) potée f

loamy [ˈlomi] adj franc, glaiseux

loan [lon] s prêt m, emprunt m ‖ tr prêter

loan′ of′fice s entreprise f de prêt, caisse f de prévoyance

loan′ shark′ s usurier m

loan′ word′ s mot m d'emprunt

loath [loθ] adj—**loath to** peu enclin à

loathe [loð] tr détester

loathing [ˈloðɪŋ] s dégoût m

loathsome [ˈloðsəm] adj dégoûtant

lob [lab] s (tennis) lob m ‖ v (*pret & pp* **lobbed;** *ger* **lobbing**) tr frapper en hauteur, lober

lob·by [ˈlabi] s (*pl* **-bies**) vestibule m; (e.g., *in a theater*) foyer m; (*pressure group*) groupe m de pression, lobby m ‖ v (*pret & pp* **-bied**) intr faire les couloirs

lobbying [ˈlabɪ·ɪŋ] s intrigues fpl de couloir

lobbyist [ˈlabɪ·ɪst] s intrigant m de couloir

lobe [lob] s lobe m

lobster [ˈlabstər] s (*spiny lobster*) langouste f; (*Homarus*) homard m

lob′ster pot′ s casier m à homards

local [ˈlokəl] adj local ‖ s (*of labor union*) succursale f; (journ) informations fpl régionales; (rr) train m omnibus

locale [loˈkæl] s lieu m, milieu m; scène f

locali·ty [loˈkælɪti] s (*pl* **-ties**) localité f

localize [ˈlokə,laɪz] tr localiser

lo′cal supply′ cir′cuit s secteur m

locate [ˈloket] tr (*to discover the location of*) localiser; (*to place, to settle*) placer, installer; (*to ascribe a particular location to*) situer; **to be located** se trouver ‖ intr se fixer, s'établir

location [loˈkeʃən] s (*place, position*) situation f, emplacement m; (*act of placing*) établissement m; (*act of finding*) localisation f, détermination f; (*of a railroad line*) tracé m; **on location** (mov) en extérieur

loca′tion shot′ s (mov) extérieur m

lock [lɑk] s serrure f; (of a canal) écluse f; (of hair) mèche f, boucle f; (of a firearm) platine f; (wrestling) clef f; **lock, stock, and barrel** tout le bataclan, tout le fourbi; **under lock and key** sous clé ‖ tr fermer à clef; (to key) caler, bloquer; (a boat) écluser, sasser; (a switch) (rr) verrouiller; **to be locked in each other's arms** être enlacés; **to lock in** enfermer à clef; **to lock out** fermer la porte à or sur; (workers) fermer les ateliers contre; **to lock up** fermer à clef, mettre sous clé; (e.g., a prisoner) boucler, enfermer; (a form) (typ) serrer ‖ intr (said of door) fermer à clef; (said of brake, wheel, etc.) se bloquer; **to lock into** s'engrener dans

locker [′lɑkər] s armoire f, coffre m de sûreté; (in a station or airport) casier m; (for keeping clothes) vestiaire m, placard m individuel; (locker room) vestiaire m

lock′er room′ s vestiaire m, vestiaire à placards individuels

locket [′lɑkɪt] s médaillon m

lock′jaw′ s trisme m

lock′ nut′ s contre-écrou m

lock′out′ s lock-out m

lock′smith′ s serrurier m

lock′ step′ s —**to march in lock step** emboîter le pas

lock′ stitch′ s point m indécousable

lock′ten′der s éclusier m

lock′up′ s (prison) (coll) bloc m, violon m

lock′ wash′er s rondelle à ressort

locomotive [,lokə′motɪv] s locomotive f

lo·cus [′lokəs] s (pl -ci [saɪ]) lieu m; (math) lieu géométrique

locust [′lokəst] s (Pachytylus) (ent) criquet m migrateur, locuste f; (Cicada) (ent) cigale f; (bot) faux acacia m

lode [lod] s filon m, veine f

lode′star′ s (astr) étoile f polaire; (fig) pôle m d'attraction

lodge [lɑdʒ] s (of gatekeeper; of animal; of Mason) loge f; (residence, e.g., for hunting) pavillon m; (hotel) relais m, hostellerie f ‖ tr loger; **to lodge a complaint with** porter plainte auprès de ‖ intr loger; (said of arrow, bullet) se loger

lodger [′lɑdʒər] s locataire mf, pensionnaire mf

lodging [′lɑdʒɪŋ] s logement m; (of a complaint) déposition f

loft [lɔft] s (attic) grenier m, soupente f; (hayloft) fenil m; (in theater or church) tribune f; (in store or office building) atelier m

loft·y [′lɔfti] adj (comp -ier; super -iest) (towering; sublime) élevé, exalté; (haughty) hautain

log [lɔg] s (of wood) bûche f, rondin m; (record book) registre m de travail; (aer) livre m de vol; (record book) (naut) journal m de bord; (chip log) (naut) loch m; (rad) carnet m d'écoute; **to sleep like a log** dormir comme une souche ‖ v (pret & pp logged; ger logging) tr (wood) tron-

çonner; (an event) porter au journal; (a certain distance) (naut) filer ‖ intr (to cut wood) couper des rondins

logarithm [′lɔgə,rɪðəm] s logarithme m

log′book′ s (aer) livre m de vol; (naut) journal m de bord, livre de loch

log′ cab′in s cabane f en rondins

log′ chip′ s (naut) flotteur m de loch

log′ driv′er s flotteur m

log′ driv′ing s flottage m

logger [′lɔgər] s bûcheron m; (loader) (mach) grue f de chargement; (mach) tracteur m

log′ger·head′ s tête f de bois; **at loggerheads** en bisbille, aux prises

logic [′lɑdʒɪk] s logique f

logical [′lɑdʒɪkəl] adj logique

logician [lo′dʒɪʃən] s logicien m

logistic(al) [lo′dʒɪstɪk(əl)] adj logistique

logistics [lo′dʒɪstɪks] s logistique f

log′jam′ s embâcle m de bûches; (fig) bouchon m, embouteillage m

log′ line′ s (naut) ligne f de loch

log′roll′ intr faire trafic de faveurs politiques

log′wood′ s bois m de campêche; (tree) campêche m

loin [lɔɪn] s (of beef) aloyau m; (of veal) longe f; (of pork) échine f; **to gird up one's loins** se ceindre les reins

loin′cloth′ s pagne m

loiter [′lɔɪtər] tr—**to loiter away** perdre en flânant ‖ intr flâner

loiterer [′lɔɪtərər] s flâneur m

loll [lɑll] intr se prélasser, s'allonger, s'affaler

lollipop [′lɑli,pɑp] s sucette f

Lom′bardy pop′lar [′lɑmbərdi] s peuplier m noir

London [′lʌndən] adj londonien ‖ s Londres m

Londoner [′lʌndənər] s Londonien m

lone [lon] adj (alone) solitaire, seul; (sole, single) unique

loneliness [′lonlinɪs] s solitude f

lone·ly [′lonli] adj (comp -lier; super -liest) solitaire, isolé

lonesome [′lonsəm] adj solitaire, seul

lone′ wolf′ s (fig) solitaire mf, ours m

long [lɔŋ] (comp **longer** [′lɔŋgər]; super **longest** [′lɔŋgɪst]) adj long; de long, de longueur, e.g., **two meters long** deux mètres de long or de longueur ‖ adv longtemps; **as long as** aussi longtemps que; (provided that) tant que; **before long** sous peu; **how long?** combien de temps?, depuis combien de temps?, depuis quand?; **long ago** il y a longtemps; **long before** longtemps avant; **longer** plus long; **long since** depuis longtemps; **no longer** ne . . . plus longtemps; ne . . . plus, e.g., **I could no longer see him** je ne pouvais plus le voir; **so long!** (coll) à bientôt!; **so long as** tant que; **to be long in** tarder à ‖ intr—**to long for** soupirer pour or après

long′boat′ s chaloupe f

long′ dis′tance *s* (telp) l'interurbain *m*; **to call s.o. long distance** appeler qn par l'interurbain

long′-dis′tance call′ *s* (telp) appel *m* interurbain

long′-dis′tance flight′ *s* (aer) vol *m* au long cours, raid *m* aérien

long′-drawn′-out′ *adj* prolongé; (*story*) délayé

longevity [lɑn′dʒɛvɪti] *s* longévité *f*

long′ face′ *s* (coll) triste figure *f*

long′ hair′ *adj & s* intellectuel *m*; fanatique *mf* de la musique classique

long′-haired′ *adj* à cheveux longs

long′hand′ *s* écriture *f* ordinaire; **in longhand** à la main

longing [′lɔŋɪŋ] *adj* ardent ‖ *s* désir *m* ardent

longitude [′lɑndʒɪ,t(j)ud] *s* longitude *f*

long′ jump′ *s* saut *m* en longueur

long-lived [′lɔŋ′laɪvd], [′lɔŋ′lɪvd] *adj* à longue vie; persistant

long′-play′ing rec′ord *s* disque *m* de longue durée

long′ prim′er [′prɪmər] *s* (typ) philosophie *f*

long′-range′ *adj* à longue portée; (*e.g., plan*) à long terme

long′-range plane′ *s* long-courrier *m*

long′shore′man *s* (*pl* **-men**) arrimeur *m*, débardeur *m*

long′ shot′ *s* (turf) outsider *m*

long′-stand′ing *adj* de longue date

long′-suf′fering *adj* patient, endurant

long′ suit′ *s* (cards) couleur *f* longue, longue *f*; (fig) fort *m*

long′-term′ *adj* à longue échéance

long′-wind′ed [′wɪndɪd] *adj* interminable; (*person*) intarissable

look [lʊk] *s* (*appearance*) aspect *m*; (*glance*) regard *m*; **looks** apparence *f*, mine *f*; **to take a look at** jeter un coup d'œil sur or à ‖ *tr* regarder; (*e.g., one's age*) paraître; **to look daggers at** lancer un regard furieux à; **to look the part** avoir le physique de l'emploi; **to look up** (*e.g., in a dictionary*) chercher, rechercher; (*to visit*) aller voir, venir voir ‖ *intr* regarder; (*to seek*) chercher; **it looks like rain** le temps est à la pluie; **look here!** dites donc!; **look out!** gare!, attention!; **to look after** s'occuper de; (*e.g., an invalid*) soigner; **to look at** regarder; **to look away** détourner les yeux; **to look back** regarder en arrière; **to look down on** mépriser; **to look for** chercher; (*to expect*) s'attendre à; **to look forward to** s'attendre à, attendre avec impatience; **to look ill** avoir mauvaise mine; **to look in on** passer voir; **to look into** examiner, vérifier; **to look like** (*s.o. or s.th.*) ressembler à; (*to give promise of*) avoir l'air de; **to look out** faire attention; (*e.g., the window*) regarder par; **to look out on** donner sur; **to look through** (*a window*) regarder par; (*a telescope*) regarder dans; (*a book*) feuilleter; **to look toward** regarder du côté de; **to look up** lever les yeux; **to look up to** respecter; **to look well** avoir bonne mine

looker-on [,lʊkər′ɑn] *s* (*pl* **lookers-on**) spectateur *m*, assistant *m*

look′ing glass′ *s* miroir *m*

look′out′ *s* (*observation*) guet *m*, surveillance *f*; (*person*) guetteur *m*; (*place*) poste *m* d'observation; (*person or place*) (naut) vigie *f*; **that's his lookout** (coll) ça, c'est son affaire; **to be on the lookout for** être à l'affût de

loom [lum] *s* métier *m* ‖ *intr* (*to appear*) apparaître indistinctement; (*to threaten*) menacer, paraître imminent; **to loom up** surgir, s'élever

loon [lun] *s* lourdaud *m*, sot *m*; (orn) plongeon *m*

loon·y [′luni] *adj* (*comp* **-ier**; *super* **-iest**) (slang) toqué ‖ *s* (*pl* **-ies**) (slang) toqué *m*

loop [lup] *s* boucle *f*; (*for fastening a button*) bride *f*; (*circular route*) boulevard *m* périphérique; (*in skating*) croisé *m*; **to loop the loop** (aer) boucler la boucle ‖ *tr & intr* boucler

loop′hole′ *s* meurtrière *f*; (fig) échappatoire *f*

loop′-the-loop′ *s* looping *m*

loose [lus] *adj* lâche; (*stone, tooth*) branlant; (*screw*) desserré; (*pulley, wheel*) fou; (*rope*) mou, détendu; (*coat, dress*) vague, ample; (*earth, soil*) meuble, friable; (*bowels*) relâché; (*style*) décousu; (*translation*) libre, peu exact; (*life, morals*) relâché, dissolu; (*woman*) facile; (*unpackaged*) en vrac; (*unbound, e.g., pages*) détaché; **to become loose** se détacher; **to break loose** (*from captivity*) s'évader; (fig) se déchaîner; **to let loose** lâcher, lâcher la bride à ‖ *s*—**to be on the loose** (*to debauch*) (coll) courir la prétentaine; (*to be out of work*) (coll) être sans occupation ‖ *tr* lâcher; (*to untie*) détacher

loose′ end′ *s* (fig) affaire *f* pendante; **at loose ends** désœuvré, indécis

loose′-leaf note′book *s* cahier *m* à feuilles mobiles

loosen [′lusən] *tr* lâcher, relâcher; (*a screw*) desserrer ‖ *intr* se relâcher

looseness [′lusnɪs] *s* relâchement *m*; (*of garment*) ampleur *f*; (*play of screw*) jeu *m*, desserrage *m*

loose′strife′ *s* (*common yellow type*) chassebosse *f*, grande lysimaque *f*; (*spiked-purple type*) salicaire *f*

loose′-tongued′ *adj*—**to be loose-tongued** avoir la langue déliée

loot [lut] *s* butin *m*, pillage *m* ‖ *tr* piller, saccager

lop [lɑp] *v* (*pret & pp* **lopped**; *ger* **lopping**) *tr*—**to lop off** abattre, trancher; (*a tree, a branch*) élaguer ‖ *intr* pendre

lope [lop] *s* galop *m* lent ‖ *intr*—**to lope along** aller doucement

lop′sid′ed *adj* déjeté, bancal

loquacious [lo′kweʃəs] *adj* loquace

lord [lɔrd] *s* seigneur *m*; (hum & poetic) époux *m*; (Brit) lord *m* ‖ *tr*—**to lord it over** dominer despotiquement, traiter avec arrogance

lord·ly ['lɔrdli] *adj* (*comp* **-lier**; *super* **-liest**) de grand seigneur, majestueux; (*arrogant*) hautain, altier

Lord's' Day' *s* jour *m* du Seigneur

lordship ['lɔrdʃɪp] *s* seigneurie *f*

Lord's' Prayer' *s* oraison *f* dominicale

Lord's Sup'per *s* communion *f*, cène *f*; Cène

lore [lor] *s* savoir *m*, science *f*; tradition *f* populaire

lorgnette [lɔrn'jɛt] *s* (*eyeglasses*) face-à-main *m*; (*opera glasses*) lorgnette *f*

lor·ry ['lɔri] *s* (*pl* **-ries**) lorry *m*, wagonnet *m*; (*truck*) (Brit) camion *m*; (*wagon*) (Brit) fardier *m*

lose [luz] *v* (*pret & pp* **lost** [lɔst] *tr* perdre; (*a patient who dies*) ne pas réussir à sauver; (*several minutes, as a timepiece does*) retarder de; **to lose oneself in** s'absorber dans; **to lose one's way** s'égarer ‖ *intr* perdre; (*said of timepiece*) retarder

loser ['luzər] *s* perdant *m*

losing ['luzɪŋ] *adj* perdant ‖ **losings** *spl* pertes *fpl*

loss [lɔs] *s* perte *f*; **to be at a loss** ne savoir que faire; **to be at a loss** to avoir de la peine à, être bien embarrassé pour; **to sell at a loss** vendre à perte

loss' of face' *s* perte *f* de prestige

lost [lɔst] *adj* perdu; **lost in thought** perdu or absorbé dans ses pensées; **lost to** perdu pour

lost'-and-found' depart'ment *s* bureau *m* des objets trouvés

lost' sheep' *s* brebis *f* perdue, brebis égarée

lot [lɑt] *s* lot *m*; (*for building*) lotissement *m*, lot; (*fate*) sort *m*, lot; **a bad lot** (coll) un mauvais sujet, de la mauvaise graine; **a lot of** or **lots of** (coll) un tas de; **a queer lot** (coll) un drôle de numéro; **in a lot** en bloc; **to cast** or **to throw in one's lot with** tenter la fortune avec; **to draw** or **to cast lots** tirer au sort; **such a lot of** tellement de; **what a lot of . . . !** que de . . . !

lotion ['loʃən] *s* lotion *f*

lotter·y ['lɑtəri] *s* (*pl* **-ies**) loterie *f*

lotto ['lɑto] *s* loto *m*

lotus ['lotəs] *s* lotus *m*

loud [lɑud] *adj* (*volume*) haut, fort; (*noisy*) bruyant; (*voice*) fort; (*showy*) voyant ‖ *adv* fort; (*noisily*) bruyamment; **out loud** à haute voix

loud·mouthed ['lɑud,mɑuθt] *adj* au verbe haut, gueulard

loud'speak'er *s* haut-parleur *m*

Louisiana [lu,izɪ'ænə] *s* Louisiane *f*; la Louisiane

lounge [lɑundʒ] *s* divan *m*, sofa *m*; (*room*) petit salon *m*, salle *f* de repos; (*in a hotel*) hall *m* ‖ *intr* flâner; (*e.g., in a chair*) se vautrer

lounge' liz'ard *s* (slang) gigolo *m*

louse [lɑus] *s* (*pl* **lice** [lɑis]) pou *m*; (slang) salaud *m* ‖ *tr*—**to louse up** (slang) bâcler

lous·y ['lɑuzi] *adj* (*comp* **-ier**; *super* **-iest**) pouilleux; (*mean; ugly*) (coll) moche;

(*bungling*) (coll) maladroit, gauche; **lousy with** (slang) chargé de

lout [lɑut] *s* lourdaud *m*, balourd *m*

louver ['luvər] *s* abat-vent *m*; (aut) auvent *m*

lovable ['lʌvəbəl] *adj* aimable, sympathique

love [lʌv] *s* amour *m*; (*ending a letter*) affectueusement, bons baisers, je t'embrasse; passion *f*, e.g., **the theater was her great love** le théâtre était sa grande passion; (tennis) zéro *m*; **in love with** amoureux de; **love at first sight** le coup de foudre; **love to all!** vives amitiés à tous!; **not for love or money** pour rien au monde, à aucun prix; **to make love to** faire la cour à; **with much love!** avec mes affectueuses pensées! ‖ *tr & intr* aimer

love' affair' *s* affaire *f* de cœur

love'birds' *spl* (orn) perruches *fpl* inséparables; (*persons*) (fig) tourtereaux *mpl*

love' child' *s* enfant *mf* de l'amour

love' feast' *s* (eccl) agape *f*

love' game' *s* (tennis) jeu *m* blanc

love' knot' *s* lacs *m* d'amour

loveless ['lʌvlɪs] *adj* sans amour; (*feeling no love*) insensible à l'amour

love' let'ter *s* billet *m* doux

lovelorn ['lʌv,lɔrn] *adj* délaissé d'amour; éperdu d'amour

love·ly ['lʌvli] *adj* (*comp* **-lier**; *super* **-liest**) beau; (*adorable*) charmant, gracieux; (*enjoyable*) (coll) agréable, aimable

love' match' *s* mariage *m* d'amour

love' nest' *s* nid *m* d'amoureux

love' po'tion *s* philtre *m* d'amour

lover ['lʌvər] *s* amoureux *m*, amant *m*; (*of hunting, sports, music, etc.*) amateur *m*, fanatique *mf*

love' seat' *s* causeuse *f*

love'sick' *adj* féru d'amour

love'sick'ness *s* mal *m* d'amour

love' song' *s* romance *f*, chanson *f* d'amour

love' sto'ry *s* histoire *f* d'amour

loving ['lʌvɪŋ] *adj* aimant, affectueux; affectionné, e.g., **your loving daughter** votre fille affectionnée

lov'ing cup' *s* coupe *f* de l'amitié; trophée *m*

lov'ing-kind'ness *s* bonté *f* d'âme

low [lo] *adj* bas; (*speed; price*) bas; (*speed; price; number; light*) faible; (*opinion*) défavorable; (*dress*) décolleté; (*sound, note*) bas, grave; (*fever*) lent; (*bow*) profond; **to lay low** étendre, terrasser; **to lie low** se tenir coi ‖ *s* bas *m*; (*moo of cow*) meuglement *m*; (aut) première vitesse *f*; (meteo) dépression *f* ‖ *adv* bas; **to speak low** parler à voix basse ‖ *intr* (*said of cow*) meugler

low'born' *adj* de basse naissance

low'boy' *s* commode *f* basse

low'brow' *adj* (coll) peu intellectuel ‖ *s* (coll) ignorant *m*

low'-cost' hous'ing *s* habitations *fpl* à loyer modéré or à bon marché

Low' Coun'tries *spl* Pays-Bas *mpl*

low'-down' *adj* (coll) bas, vil ‖ **low'-down'** *s* (slang) faits *mpl* véritables; **to**

give s.o. the low-down on (slang) tuyauter qn sur

lower ['loˑər] *adj* inférieur, bas ‖ *tr & intr* baisser ‖ ['lauˑər] *intr* se renfrogner, regarder de travers

low′er berth′ *s* couchette *f* inférieure

low′er case′ *s* (typ) bas *m* de casse

low′er mid′dle class′ *s* petite bourgeoisie *f*

lowermost ['loˑər,most] *adj* (le) plus bas

low′-fre′quency *adj* à basse fréquence

low′ gear′ *s* première vitesse *f*

low′-in′come hous′ing *s* habitations *fpl* à bon marché (HBM)

lowland ['loland] *s* plaine *f*, basse; **Lowlands** (*in Scotland*) Basse-Écosse *f*

low·ly ['loli] *adj* (*comp* -**lier**; *super* -**liest**) humble, modeste; (*in growth or position*) bas, infime

Low′ Mass′ *s* messe basse *f*, petite messe

low′-mind′ed *adj* d'esprit vulgaire

low′ neck′ *s* décolleté *m*

low′-necked′ *adj* décolleté

low′-pitched′ *adj* (*sound*) grave; (*roof*) à faible inclinaison

low′-pres′sure *adj* à basse pression

low′-priced′ *adj* à bas prix

low′ shoe′ *s* soulier *m* bas

low′-speed′ *adj* à petite vitesse

low′-spir′ited *adj* abattu

low′ spir′its *spl* abattement *m*, accablement *m*

low′ tide′ *s* marée *f* basse

low′ vis′ibil′ity *s* (aer) mauvaise visibilité *f*

low′-warp′ *adj* (tex) de basse lice

low′ wa′ter *s* (*of river*) étiage *m*; (*of sea*) niveau *m* des basses eaux); marée *f* basse

loyal ['lɔɪˑəl] *adj* loyal

loyalist ['lɔɪˑəlɪst] *s* loyaliste *mf*

loyal·ty ['lɔɪˑəlti] *s* (*pl* -**ties**) loyauté *f*

lozenge ['lɑzɪndʒ] *s* (*candy cough drop*) pastille *f*; (geom) losange *m*

LP ['ɛl'pi] *s* (letterword) (trademark) (**long-playing**) disque *m* de longue durée

lubricant ['lubrɪkənt] *adj & s* lubrifiant *m*

lubricate ['lubrɪ,ket] *tr* lubrifier

lubricous ['lubrɪkəs] *adj* (*slippery*) glissant; (*lewd*) lubrique; inconstant

lucerne [lu'sʌrn] *s* luzerne *f*

lucid ['lusɪd] *adj* lucide

luck [lʌk] *s* (*good or bad*) chance *f*; (*good*) chance, bonne chance; **to be down on one's luck**, **to be out of luck** avoir de la malchance, être dans la déveine; **to be in luck** avoir de la chance, avoir de la veine; **to bring luck** porter bonheur; **to try one's luck** tenter la fortune, tenter l'aventure; **worse luck!** tant pis!, pas de chance!

luckily ['lʌkɪli] *adv* heureusement, par bonheur

luckless ['lʌklɪs] *adj* malheureux, malchanceux

luck·y ['lʌki] *adj* (*comp* -**ier**; *super* -**iest**) heureux, fortuné; (*supposed to bring luck*) porte-bonheur; **how lucky!** quelle chance!; **to be lucky** avoir de la chance, être verni, avoir du pot

luck′y charm′ *s* porte-bonheur *m*

luck′y dog′ *s* (coll) veinard *m*

luck′y find′ *s* (coll) trouvaille *f*

luck′y hit′ *s* (coll) coup *m* de bonheur, coup de chance

lucrative ['lukrətɪv] *adj* lucratif

ludicrous ['ludɪkrəs] *adj* ridicule, risible

lug [lʌg] *s* oreille *f*; (*pull, tug*) saccade *f* ‖ *v* (*pret & pp* **lugged**; *ger* **lugging**) *tr* traîner, tirer; (*to bring up irrelevantly*) (coll) ressortir, amener de force

luggage ['lʌgɪdʒ] *s* bagages *mpl*

lug′gage car′rier *s* porte-bagages *m*

lugubrious [lu'g(j)ubrɪˑəs] *adj* lugubre

lukewarm ['luk'wɔrm] *adj* tiède

lull [lʌl] *s* accalmie *f* ‖ *tr* bercer, endormir, calmer

lulla·by ['lʌlə,baɪ] *s* (*pl* -**bies**) berceuse *f*

lumbago [lʌm'bego] *s* lumbago *m*

lumber ['lʌmbər] *s* bois *m* de charpente, bois de construction ‖ *intr* se traîner lourdement

lum′ber·jack′ *s* bûcheron *m*

lum′ber·jack′et *s* canadienne *f*

lum′ber·man *s* (*pl* -**men**) (*dealer*) exploitant *m* forestier, propriétaire *m* forestier; (*man who cuts down lumber*) bûcheron *m*

lum′ber raft′ *s* train *m* de flottage

lum′ber room′ *s* fourre-tout *m*, débarras *m*

lum′ber·yard′ *s* chantier *m* de bois, dépôt *m* de bois de charpente

luminar·y ['lumɪ,nɛri] *s* (*pl* -**ies**) corps *m* lumineux; (astr) luminaire *m*; (*person*) (fig) lumière *f*

luminescent [,lumi'nɛsənt] *adj* luminescent

luminous ['lumɪnəs] *adj* lumineux

lummox ['lʌməks] *s* (coll) lourdaud *m*

lump [lʌmp] *s* masse *f*; (*of earth*) motte *f*; (*of sugar*) morceau *m*; (*of salt, flour, porridge, etc.*) grumeau *m*; (*swelling*) bosse *f*; (*of ice, stone, etc.*) bloc *m*; **in the lump** en bloc; **to get a lump in one's throat** avoir un serrement de gorge ‖ *tr* réunir; **to lump together** prendre en bloc, englober ‖ *intr*—**to lump along** marcher d'un pas lourd

lumpish ['lʌmpɪʃ] *adj* balourd

lump′ sug′ar *s* sucre *m* en morceaux

lump′ sum′ *s* somme *f* globale

lump·y ['lʌmpi] *adj* (*comp* -**ier**; *super* -**iest**) grumeleux; (*covered with lumps*) couvert de bosses; (sea) clapoteux

luna·cy ['lunəsi] *s* (*pl* -**cies**) folie *f*

lu′nar land′er ['lunər] *s* alunisseur *m*

lu′nar land′ing *s* alunissage *m*

lu′nar mod′ule *s* (rok) module *m* lunaire

lunatic ['lunətɪk] *adj & s* fou *m*

lu′natic asy′lum *s* maison *f* de fous

lu′natic fringe′ *s* minorité *f* fanatique, frange *f* des dingues

lunch [lʌntʃ] *s* (*midday meal*) déjeuner *m*; (*light meal*) collation *f*, petit repas *m* ‖ *intr* déjeuner; (*to snack*) casser la croûte, manger sur le pouce

lunch′ bas′ket *s* panier *m* à provisions

lunch′ cloth′ *s* napperon *f* à thé

lunch′ coun′ter *s* snack *m*, buffet *m*

luncheon ['lʌntʃən] *s* déjeuner *m*

luncheonette [,lʌntʃə'nɛt] *s* brasserie *f*, café-restaurant *m*

lunch'room' *s* brasserie *f*, café-restaurant *m*

lunch' time' *s* heure *f* du déjeuner

lung [lʌŋ] *s* poumon *m*

lung' can'cer *s* cancer *m* du poumon

lunge [lʌndʒ] *s* mouvement *m* en avant; (*with a sword*) botte *f* ‖ *intr* se précipiter en avant; (*with a sword*) se fendre; **to lunge at** porter une botte à

lurch [lʌrtʃ] *s* embardée *f*; (*of person*) secousse *f*; **to leave in the lurch** laisser en plan ‖ *intr* faire une embardée; (*said of person*) vaciller

lure [lʊr] *s* (*decoy*) leurre *m*, amorce *f*; (fig) attrait *m* ‖ *tr* leurrer; **to lure away** détourner

lurid ['lʊrɪd] *adj* sensationnel; (*gruesome*) terrible, macabre; (*fiery*) rougeoyant; (*livid*) blafard

lurk [lʌrk] *intr* se cacher; (*to prowl*) rôder

luscious ['lʌʃəs] *adj* délicieux, succulent; luxueux, somptueux

lush [lʌʃ] *adj* plein de sève; (*abundant*) luxuriant; opulent, luxueux

lust [lʌst] *f* désir *m* ardent; (*greed*) convoitise *f*, soif *f*; (*strong sexual appetite*) luxure *f*

luster ['lʌstər] *s* lustre *m*

lus'ter·ware' *s* poterie *f* lustrée, poterie à reflets métalliques

lustful ['lʌstfəl] *adj* luxurieux, lascif, lubrique

lustrous ['lʌstrəs] *adj* lustré, chatoyant

lust·y ['lʌsti] *adj* (*comp* **-ier**; *super* **-iest**) robuste, vigoureux

lute [lut] *s* (mus) luth *m*; (*substance used to close or seal a joint*) (chem) lut *m*

Lutheran ['luθərən] *adj* luthérien ‖ *s* Luthérien *m*

Luxemburg ['lʌksəm,bʌrg] *s* le Luxembourg

luxuriant [lʌg'ʒʊrɪ·ənt] *adj* luxuriant; (*overornamented*) surchargé

luxurious [lʌg'ʒʊrɪ·əs] *adj* luxueux, somptueux

luxu·ry ['lʌgʒəri] *s* (*pl* **-ries**) luxe *m*

lux'ury i'tem *s* produit *m* de luxe

lux'ury tax' *s* impôt *m* somptuaire

lyceum [laɪ'si·əm] *s* lycée *m*

lye [laɪ] *s* lessive *f*

lying ['laɪ·ɪŋ] *adj* menteur ‖ *s* le mensonge

ly'ing-in' hos'pital *s* maternité *f*, clinique *f* d'accouchement

lymph [lɪmf] *s* lymphe *f*

lymphatic [lɪm'fætɪk] *adj* lymphatique

lynch [lɪntʃ] *tr* lyncher

lynching ['lɪntʃɪŋ] *s* lynchage *m*

lynx [lɪŋks] *s* lynx *m*

Lyons ['laɪ·ənz] *s* Lyon *m*

lyre [laɪr] *s* (mus) lyre *f*

lyric ['lɪrɪk] *adj* lyrique ‖ *s* poème *m* lyrique; **lyrics** (*of song*) paroles *fpl*; (theat) chansons *fpl* du livret

lyrical ['lɪrɪkəl] *adj* lyrique

lyricism ['lɪrɪ,sɪzəm] *s* lyrisme *m*

lyricist ['lɪrɪsɪst] *s* poète *m* lyrique; (*writer of words for songs*) parolier *m*

M

M, m [ɛm] XIIIe lettre de l'alphabet

ma'am [mæm], [mɑm] *s* (coll) madame *f*

macadam [mə'kædəm] *s* macadam *m*

macadamize [mə'kædə,maɪz] *tr* macadamiser

macaroon [,mækə'run] *s* macaron *m*

macaw [mə'kɔ] *s* (orn) ara *m*

mace [mes] *s* masse *f*

mace'bear'er *s* massier *m*

machination [,mækɪ'neʃən] *s* machination *f*

machine [mə'ʃin] *s* machine *f*; (*of a political party*) noyau *m* directeur, leviers *mpl* de commande ‖ *tr* usiner, façonner

machine'gun' *s* mitrailleuse *f*

ma·chine'-gun' *v* (*pret & pp* **-gunned**; *ger* **-gunning**) *tr* mitrailler

ma·chine'-made' *adj* fait à la machine

machiner·y [mə'ʃinəri] *s* (*pl* **-ies**) machinerie *f*, machines *fpl*; (*of a watch; of government*) mécanisme *m*; (*in literature*) merveilleux *m*

machine' screw' *s* vis *f* à métaux; vis à tôle

machine' shop' *s* atelier *m* d'usinage

machine' tool' *s* machine-outil *f*

machine' transla'tion *s* traduction *f* automatique

machinist [mə'ʃinɪst] *s* mécanicien *m*

mackerel ['mækərəl] *s* maquereau *m*

mack'erel sky' *s* ciel *m* pommelé or moutonné

mad [mæd] *adj* (*comp* **madder**; *super* **maddest**) fou; (*dog*) enragé; (coll) fâché, irrité; **as mad as a hatter** fou à lier; **like mad** (coll) comme un fou, éperdument; **to be mad about** (coll) être fou or passionné de; **to drive mad** rendre fou

madam ['mædəm] *s* madame *f*; (*of a brothel*) (slang) tenancière *f*

mad'cap' *adj* & *s* écervelé *m*, étourdi *m*

madden ['mædən] *tr* rendre fou ‖ *intr* devenir fou

made-to-order ['medtə'ɔrdər] *adj* fait sur demande; (*clothing*) fait sur mesure

made'-up' *adj* inventé; (*artificial*) postiche; (*face*) maquillé

mad'house' *s* maison *f* de fous

mad′man′ s (pl **-men′**) fou m
madness [′mædnɪs] s folie f; (of dog) rage f
Madonna [mə′dɑnə] s madone f; (eccl) Madone
maelstrom [′melstrəm] s maelstrom m, tourbillon m
Mafia or **Maffia** [′mɑfɪ·ə] s mafia f, maffia f
magazine [′mægə,zin], [,mægə′zin] s (periodical) revue f, magazine m; (warehouse; for cartridges of gun or camera; for munitions or powder) magasin m; (naut) soute f
mag′azine′ rack′ s casier m à revues
Magdalen [′mægdələn] s Madeleine f
Maggie [′mægi] s (coll) Margot f
maggot [′mægət] s asticot m
Magi [′medʒaɪ] spl mages mpl
magic [′mædʒɪk] adj magique ‖ s magie f; **as if by magic** comme par enchantement
magician [mə′dʒɪʃən] s magicien m
mag′ic mark′er pen′ s crayon-feutre m
magisterial [,mædʒɪs′tɪrɪ·əl] adj magistral
magistrate [′mædʒɪs,tret] s magistrat m
Magna Charta [′mægnə′kɑrtə] s la Grande Charte f
magnanimous [mæg′nænɪməs] adj magnanime
magnate [′mægnet] s magnat m
magnesium [mæg′niʃɪ·əm] s magnésium m
magnet [′mægnɪt] s aimant m
magnetic [mæg′nɛtɪk] adj magnétique; (fig) attrayant, séduisant
magnetism [′mægnɪ,tizəm] s magétisme m
magnetize [′mægnɪ,taɪz] tr aimanter
magne·to [mæg′nito] s (pl **-tos**) magnéto f
magnificent [mæg′nɪfɪsənt] adj magnifique
magni·fy [′mægnɪ,faɪ] v (pret & pp **-fied**) tr grossir; (opt) grossir
mag′nifying glass′ s loupe f
magnitude [′mægnɪ,t(j)ud] s grandeur f; (astr) magnitude f
magpie [′mæg,paɪ] s (orn, fig) pie f
mahlstick [′mɑl,stɪk] s appui-main m
mahoga·ny [mə′hɑgəni] s (pl **-nies**) acajou m
mahout [mə′haut] s cornac m
maid [med] s (servant) bonne f; (young woman) jeune fille f, demoiselle f
maiden [′medən] s jeune fille f, demoiselle f
maid′en·hair′ s (bot) capillaire m
maid′en·head′ s hymen m
maid′en·hood′ s virginité f
maid′en la′dy s demoiselle f, célibataire f
maidenly [′medənli] adj virginal, de jeune fille
maid′en name′ s nom m de jeune fille
maid′en voy′age s premier voyage m
maid′-in-wait′ing s (pl **maids-in-waiting**) fille f d'honneur, dame f d'honneur
maid′ of hon′or s demoiselle f d'honneur
maid′serv′ant s fille f de service, servante f
mail [mel] adj postal ‖ s courrier m; (system) poste f; (armor) mailles fpl, cotte f de mailles; **by return mail** par retour du courrier; **mails** poste ‖ tr mettre à la poste, envoyer par la poste

mail′bag′ s sac m postal
mail′boat′ s paquebot m, bateau-poste m
mail′box′ s boîte f aux lettres
mail′ car′ s fourgon m postal, bureau m ambulant, wagon-poste m
mail′ car′rier s facteur m, préposé m
mail′ clerk′ s postier m; (mil, nav) vaguemestre m; (rr) convoyeur m des postes
mailing [′melɪŋ] s envoi m; (preparation) adressage m
mail′ing list′ s liste f d'adresses, (of subscribers) liste d'abonnés
mail′ing per′mit s (label on envelopes) dispensé du timbrage
mail′man′ s (pl **-men′**) facteur m
mail′ or′der s commande f par la poste
mail′-order house′ s établissement m de vente par correspondance or de vente sur catalogue; comptoir m postal (Canad)
mail′-order sell′ing s vente f par correspondance
mail′plane′ s avion m postal
mail′ train′ s train-poste m
maim [mem] tr mutiler, estropier
main [men] adj principal ‖ s (sewer) égout m collecteur, canalisation f or conduite f principale; **in the main** en général, pour la plupart
main′ clause′ s proposition f principale
main′ course′ s (culin) plat m principal, pièce f de résistance
main′ deck′ s pont m principal
main′ en′trance s entrée f principale
main′ floor′ s rez-de-chaussée m
mainland [′men,lænd], [′menlənd] s terre f ferme, continent m
main′ line′ s (rr) grande ligne f
mainly [′menli] adv principalement
mainmast [′menməst] s grand mât m
mainsail [′mensəl] s grand-voile f
main′spring′ s (of watch) ressort m moteur, grand ressort; (fig) mobile m essentiel, principe m
main′stay′ s (naut) étai m de grand mât; (fig) point m d'appui
main′ street′ s rue f principale
maintain [men′ten] tr maintenir; (e.g., a family) entretenir, faire subsister
maintenance [′mentɪnəns] s entretien m, maintien m; (department entrusted with upkeep) services mpl d'entretien, maintenance f
maître d'hôtel [,metərdo′tɛl] s maître m d'hôtel
maize [mez] s maïs m
majestic [mə′dʒɛstɪk] adj majestueux
majes·ty [′mædʒɪsti] s (pl **-ties**) majesté f
major [′medʒər] adj majeur ‖ s (person of full legal age) majeur m; (educ) spécialisation f; (mil) commandant m ‖ intr (educ) se spécialiser
Majorca [mə′dʒɔrkə] s Majorque f; île f de Majorque
Majorcan [mə′dʒɔrkən] adj majorquin ‖ s Majorquin m
ma′jor gen′eral s général m de division

majori·ty [mə'dʒɑrɪti], [mə'dʒɔrɪti] *adj* majoritaire ‖ *s* (*pl* **-ties**) majorité *f*; (mil) grade *m* de commandant; **the majority of** la plupart de

major'ity vote' *s* scrutin *m* majoritaire

make [mek] *s* (*brand name*) marque *f*; (*production*) fabrication *f*; **on the make** (coll) prêt à tout pour faire fortune ‖ *v* (*pret & pp* **made** [med]) *tr* faire; rendre, e.g., **to make sick** rendre malade; (*money*) gagner; (*the cards*) battre; (*a train*) attraper; **to make into** transformer en; **to make known** faire savoir; **to make out** déchiffrer, distinguer; (*a bill, receipt, check*) écrire; (*a list*) dresser; **to make s.o.** + *inf* faire + *inf* + qn, e.g., **I will make my uncle talk** je ferai parler mon oncle ‖ *intr* être, e.g., **to make sure** être sûr; **to make believe** feindre; **to make good** réussir; **to make off** filer, décamper

make'-believe' *adj* simulé ‖ *s* faux-semblant *m*, feinte *f*

maker ['mekər] *s* fabricant *m*

make'shift' *adj* de fortune, de circonstance ‖ *s* expédient *m*; (*person*) bouche-trou *m*

make'-up' *s* arrangement *m*, composition *f*; (*cosmetic*) maquillage *m*; (typ) mise *f* en pages, imposition *f*

make'-up man' *s* (theat) maquilleur *m*; (typ) metteur *m* en pages, imposeur *m*

make'weight' *s* complément *m* de poids

making ['mekɪŋ] *s* fabrication *f*; (*of a dress, of a cooked dish*) confection *f*; **makings** éléments *mpl* constitutifs; (*money*) recettes *fpl*; **to have the makings of** avoir l'étoffe de

maladjusted [,mælə'dʒʌstɪd] *adj* inadapté

maladjustment [,mælə'dʒʌstmənt] *s* inadaptation *f*

mala·dy ['mælədi] *s* (*pl* **-dies**) maladie *f*

malaise [mæ'lez] *s* malaise *m*

malaria [mə'lɛrɪ·ə] *s* malaria *f*, paludisme *m*

Malay ['mele], [mə'le] *adj* malais ‖ *s* (*language*) malais *m*; (*person*) Malais *m*

Malaya [mə'le·ə] *s* Mallaisie *f*; la Malaisie

malcontent ['mælkən,tɛnt] *adj & s* mécontent *m*

male [mel] *adj & s* mâle *m*

malediction [,mælɪ'dɪkʃən] *s* malédiction *f*

malefactor ['mælɪ,fæktər] *s* malfaiteur *m*

male' nurse' *s* infirmier *m*

malevolent [mə'lɛvələnt] *adj* malveillant

malfeasance [,mæl'fizəns] *s* prévarication *f*, trafic *m*

malice ['mælɪs] *s* méchanceté *f*, malice *f*

malicious [mə'lɪʃəs] *adj* méchant

malign [mə'laɪn] *adj* pernicieux; malveillant ‖ *tr* calomnier

malignan·cy [mə'lɪgnənsi] *s* (*pl* **-cies**) malignité *f*

malignant [mə'lɪgnənt] *adj* méchant, malin

malinger [mə'lɪŋgər] *intr* faire le malade

malingerer [mə'lɪŋgərər] *s* simulateur *m*

mall [mɔl], [mæl] *s* (*tree-lined walk*) mail *m*, allée *f*; (*shopping mall*) galerie *f* marchande

mallard ['mælərd] *s* (orn) col-vert *m*

malleable ['mælɪ·əbəl] *adj* malléable

mallet ['mælɪt] *s* maillet *m*

mallow ['mælo] *s* (bot) mauve *f*

malnutrition [,mæln(j)u'trɪʃən] *s* sous-alimentation *f*, malnutrition *f*

malodorous [mæl'odərəs] *adj* malodorant

malpractice [mæl'præktɪs] *s* incurie *f*, méfait *m*; (med) incurie professionnelle, négligence *f*, faute *f* professionnelle

malt [mɔlt] *s* malt *m*

maltreat [mæl'trit] *tr* maltraiter

mamma ['mɑmə], [mə'mɑ] *s* maman *f*

mammal ['mæməl] *s* mammifère *m*

mammalian [mæ'melɪ·ən] *adj & s* mammifère *m*

mammoth ['mæməθ] *adj* énorme, colossal ‖ *s* mammouth *m*

man [mæn] *s* (*pl* **men** [mɛn]) *s* homme *m*; (*servant*) domestique *m*; (*worker*) ouvrier *m*, employé *m* (checkers) pion *m*; (chess) pièce *f*; **a man on**, e.g., **what can a man do?** qu'est-ce qu'on peut faire?; **every man for himself!** sauve qui peut!; **man alive!** (coll) tiens!; fichtre!; **man and wife** mari et femme; **men at work** (public sign) travaux en cours ‖ *v* (*pret & pp* **manned**; *ger* **manning**) *tr* (*a ship*) équiper; (*a fort*) garnir; (*a cannon, the pumps, etc.*) armer; (*a battery*) servir

man' about town' *s* boulevardier *m*, coureur *m* de cabarets

manacle ['mænəkəl] *s* manilla *f*; **manacles** menottes *fpl* ‖ *tr* mettre les menottes à

manage ['mænɪdʒ] *tr* gérer, diriger; (*to handle*) manier ‖ *intr* se débrouiller; **how did you manage to . . . ?** comment avez-vous fait pour . . . ?; **to manage to** s'arranger pour

manageable ['mænɪdʒəbəl] *adj* maniable

management ['mænɪdʒmənt] *s* direction *f*, gérance *f*; (*group who manage*) direction, administration *f*; (*in contrast to labor*) patronat *m*; **under new management** (public sign) changement de propriétaire

manager [mænədʒər] *s* directeur *m*, gérant *m*; (*e.g., of a department*) chef *m*; (*impresario*) manager *m*

managerial [,mænə'dʒɪrɪ·əl] *adj* patronal

man'aging ed'itor *s* rédacteur *m* gérant

Manchuria [mæn'turɪə] *s* Mandchourie *f*; la Mandchourie

man'darin or'ange ['mændərɪn] *s* mandarine *f*

mandate ['mændet] *s* mandat *m* ‖ *tr* placer sous le mandat de

mandatory ['mændə,tori] *adj* obligatoire

mandolin ['mændəlɪn] *s* mandoline *f*

mandrake ['mændrek] *s* mandragore *f*

mane [men] *s* crinière *f*

maneuver [mə'nuvər] *s* manœuvre *m* ‖ *tr & intr* manœuvrer

manful ['mænfəl] *adj* viril, hardi

manganese ['mæŋgə,nis] *s* manganèse *m*

mange [mendʒ] *s* gale *f*

manger ['mendʒər] *s* mangeoire *f*, crèche *f*

mangle ['mæŋgəl] s calandre f ‖ tr lacérer, mutiler; (to press) calandrer

man·gy ['mendʒi] adj (comp -gier; super -giest) galeux; (dirty, squalid) miteux

man'han'dle tr malmener

man'hole' s trou m d'homme, regard m

manhood ['mænhʊd] s virilité f; humanité f

man'hunt' s chasse f à l'homme; chasse au mari

mania ['menɪ·ə] s manie f

maniac ['menɪ,æk] adj & s maniaque mf

maniacal [mə'naɪ·əkəl] adj maniaque

manicure [mænɪ,kjʊr] s soins mpl esthétiques des mains et des ongles; (person) manucure mf ‖ tr manucurer

manicurist ['mænɪ,kjʊrɪst] s manucure mf

manifest ['mænɪ,fɛst] adj manifeste ‖ s (naut) manifeste m ‖ tr & intr manifester

manifestation [,mænɪfɛs'teʃən] s manifestation f

manifes·to [,mænɪ'fɛsto] s (pl -toes) manifeste m

manifold ['mænɪ,fold] adj multiple, nombreux ‖ s (aut) tuyauterie f, collecteur m

manikin ['mænɪkɪn] s mannequin m; (dwarf) nabot m

man' in the moon' s homme m dans la lune

man' in the street' s homme m de la rue

manipulate [mə'nɪpjə,let] tr manipuler

man'kind' s le genre humain, l'humanité f ‖ **man'kind'** s le sexe fort, les hommes mpl

manliness ['mænlɪnɪs] s virilité f

man·ly ['mænli] adj (comp -lier; super -liest) viril, masculin

manna ['mænə] s manne f

manned' space'craft s vaisseau m spatial habité

mannequin ['mænɪkɪn] s mannequin m

manner ['mænər] s manière f; **by all manner of means** certainement; **by no manner of means** en aucune manière; **in a manner of speaking** pour ainsi dire; **in the manner of** à la, e.g., **in the manner of the French, in the French manner** à la manière française, à la française; **manners** manières; **manners of the time** mœurs fpl de l'époque; **to the manner born** créé et mis au monde pour ça

mannerism ['mænə,rɪzm] s maniérisme m

mannish ['mænɪʃ] adj hommasse

man' of let'ters s homme m de lettres, bel esprit m

man' of parts' s homme m de talent

man' of straw' s homme m de paille

man' of the world' s homme m du monde

man-of-war [,mænəv'wɔr] s (pl **men-of-war**) navire m de guerre

manor ['mænər] s seigneurie f

man'or house' s château m, manoir m

man' o'verboard' interj un homme à la mer!

man'pow'er s main-d'œuvre f; (mil) effectifs mpl

manse [mæns] s maison f du pasteur

man'serv'ant s (pl -men'serv'ants) valet m

mansion ['mænʃən] s hôtel m particulier; château m, manoir m

man'slaugh'ter s (law) homicide m involontaire

mantel ['mæntəl] s manteau m de cheminée

man'tel·piece' s manteau m de cheminée; dessus m de cheminée

mantilla [mæn'tɪlə] s mantille f

mantle ['mæntəl] s manteau m, mante f; (of gaslight) manchon m ‖ tr envelopper d'une mante; couvrir, revêtir; (to hide) voiler ‖ intr (said of face) rougir

manual ['mænjʊ·əl] adj manuel ‖ s (book) manuel m; (of arms) (mil) maniement m; (mus) clavier m d'orgue

man'ual dexter'ity s habileté f manuelle

man'ual train'ing s apprentissage m manuel

manufacture [,mænjə'fæktʃər] s fabrication f; (thing manufactured) produit m fabriqué ‖ tr fabriquer

manufacturer [,mænjə'fæktʃərər] s fabricant m

manure [mə'n(j)ʊr] s fumier m ‖ tr fumer

manuscript ['mænjə,skrɪpt] adj & s manuscrit m

many ['mɛni] adj beaucoup de; **a good many** bien des, maintes; **how many** combien de; **many another** bien d'autres; **many more** beaucoup d'autres; **so many** tant de; **too many** trop de; **twice as many** deux fois autant de ‖ pron beaucoup; **as many as** autant de; jusqu'à, e.g., **as many as twenty** jusqu'à vingt; **how many** combien; **many a** maint; **many another** bien d'autres; **many more** beaucoup d'autres; **so many** tant; **too many** trop; **twice as many** deux fois autant

man'y-sid'ed adj polygonal; (having many interests or capabilities) complexe

map [mæp] s carte f; (of a city) plan m ‖ v (pret & pp **mapped**; ger **mapping**) tr faire la carte de; **to map out** tracer le plan de; **to put on the map** (coll) faire connaître, mettre en vedette

maple ['mepəl] s érable m

ma'ple sug'ar s sucre m d'érable

mar [mar] v (pret & pp **marred**; ger **marring**) tr défigurer, gâcher

marathon ['mærə,θan] s marathon m

maraud [mə'rɔd] tr piller ‖ intr marauder

marauder [mə'rɔdər] s maraudeur m

marauding [mə'rɔdɪŋ] adj maraudeur ‖ s maraude f

marble ['marbəl] s marbre m; (little ball of glass) bille f; **marbles** (game) jeu m de billes ‖ tr marbrer; (the edge of a book) jasper

march [martʃ] s marche f; **March** mars m; **to steal a march on** prendre de l'avance sur ‖ tr faire marcher ‖ intr marcher

marchioness ['marʃənɪs] s marquise f

mare [mɛr] s (female horse) jument m; (female donkey) ânesse f

Margaret ['margərɪt] s Marguerite f

margarine ['mardʒərɪn] s margarine f

margin [`mɑrdʒɪn] s marge f; (border) bord m; (com) acompte m

mar′gin account′ s (com) compte m de couverture

marginal [`mɑrdʒɪnəl] adj marginal

mar′gin release′ s déclenche-marge f, touche f marge libre, touche passe-marge

mar′gin set′ter s pose-marge f

mar′gin stop′ s margeur m

marigold [`mærɪ,gold] s (Calendula) souci m; (Tagetes) illet m d'Inde

marihuana or **marijuana** [,mɑrɪ`hwɑnə] s marihuana f or marijuana f

marinate [`mærɪ,net] tr mariner

marine [mə`rin] adj marin, maritime ‖ s flotte f; (nav) fusilier m marin; **tell it to the marines!** (coll) à d'autres!

Marine′ Corps′ s infanterie f de marine

mariner [`mærɪnər] s marin m

marionette [,mærɪ·ə`nɛt] s marionette f

marital [`mærɪtəl] adj matrimonial

mar′ital sta′tus s état m civil

maritime [`mærɪ,taɪm] adj maritime

marjoram [`mɑrdʒərəm] s marjolaine f; origan m

mark [mɑrk] s marque f, signe m; (of punctuation) point m; (in an examination) note f; (spot, stain) tache f, marque; (monetary unit) mark m; (starting point in a race) ligne f de départ; **as a mark of** en témoignage de; **Mark** Marc m; **on your mark!** à vos marques!; **to hit the mark** mettre dans le mille, atteindre le but; **to leave one's mark** laisser son empreinte; **to make one's mark** se faire un nom, marquer; **to miss the mark** manquer le but; **to toe the mark** se conformer au mot d'ordre ‖ tr marquer; (a student; an exam) donner une note à; (e.g., one's approval) témoigner; **to mark down** noter; (com) démarquer; **to mark off** distinguer; **to mark up** (com) majorer

mark′down′ s rabais m

marker [`mɑrkər] s marqueur m; (of boundary) borne f; (landmark) repère m

market [`mɑrkɪt] s marché m; **to bear the market** jouer à la baisse; **to bull the market** jouer à la hausse; **to play the market** jouer à la bourse; **to put on the market** lancer, vendre, or mettre sur le marché ‖ tr commercialiser

marketable [`mɑrkɪtəbəl] adj vendable

mar′ket bas′ket s panier m à provisions

marketing [`mɑrkɪtɪŋ] s marché m; (of a product) commercialisation f, exploitation f

mar′ket·place′ s place f du marché

mar′ket price′ s cours m du marché, prix m courant

mark′ing gauge′ s trusquin m

marks·man [`mɑrksmən] s (pl -men) tireur m

marks′man·ship′ s habileté f au tir, adresse f au tir

mark′up′ s (profit) marge f bénéficiaire; (price increase) majoration f de prix

marl [mɑrl] s marne f ‖ tr marner

marmalade [`mɑrmə,led] s marmelade f

maroon [mə`run] adj & s (color) lie f de vin, rouge m violacé, bordeaux ‖ tr abandonner, isoler

marquee [mɑr`ki] s marquise f

marquis [`mɑrkwɪs] s marquis m

marquise [mɑr`kiz] s marquise f

marriage [`mærɪdʒ] s mariage m

marriageable [`mærɪdʒəbəl] adj mariable

mar′riage certif′icate s acte m de mariage

mar′riage por′tion s dot f

mar′riage rate′ s taux m de nuptialité

mar′ried life′ [`mærɪd] s vie f conjugale

marrow [`mæro] s moelle f

mar·ry [`mæri] v (pret & pp -ried) tr (to join in wedlock) marier; (to take in marriage) se marier avec; **to get married to** se marier avec; **to marry off** marier ‖ intr se marier

Mars [mɑrz] s Mars m

Marseilles [mɑr`selz] s Marseille f

marsh [mɑrʃ] s marais m, marécage m

mar·shal [`mɑrʃəl] s maître m des cérémonies; (policeman) shérif m; (mil) maréchal m ‖ v (pret & pp -shaled or -shalled; ger -shaling or -shalling) tr conduire; (one's reasons, arguments, etc.) ranger, rassembler

marsh′ mal′low s (bot) guimauve f

marsh′mal′low s (sweetened paste) pâte f de guimauve; (candy) bonbon m à la guimauve

marsh·y [`mɑrʃi] adj (comp -ier; super -iest) marécageux

mart [mɑrt]s marché m, foire f

marten [`mɑrtən] s (pine marten) martre f; (beech marten) fouine f

Martha [`mɑrθə] s Marthe f

martial [`mɑrʃəl] adj martial

mar′tial law′ s loi f martiale

martin [`mɑrtɪn] s (orn) martinet m

martinet [,mɑrtɪ`nɛt] s pètesec m

martyr [`mɑrtər] s martyr m ‖ tr martyriser

martyrdom [`mɑrtərdəm] s martyre m

mar·vel [`mɑrvəl] s merveille f ‖ v (pret & pp -veled or -velled; ger -veling or -velling) intr s'émerveiller; **to marvel at** s'émerveiller de

marvelous [`mɑrvələs] adj merveilleux

Marxist [`mɑrksɪst] adj & s marxiste mf

Maryland [`mɛrələnd] s le Maryland

marzipan [`mɑrzɪ,pæn] s massepain m

mascara [mæs`kærə] s rimmel m

mascot [`mæskɑt] s mascotte f

masculine [`mæskjəlɪn] adj & s masculin m

mash [mæʃ] s (crushed mass) bouillie f; (to form wort) fardeau m ‖ tr écraser; (malt, in brewing) brasser

mashed′ pota′toes spl purée f de pommes de terre

masher [`mæʃər] s (device) broyeur m; (slang) tombeur m

mask [mæsk] s masque m; (phot) cache m ‖ tr masquer; (phot) poser un cache à ‖ intr se masquer

masked′ ball′ s bal m masqué

mask′ing tape′ s ruban m cache

mason ['mesən] *s* maçon *m*; **Mason** Maçon

mason·ry ['mesənri] *s* (*pl* **-ries**) maçonnerie *f*; **Masonry** Maçonnerie

masquerade [,mæskə'red] *s* mascarade *f* ‖ *intr* se déguiser; **to masquerade as** se faire passer pour

mass [mæs] *s* masse *f*; (eccl) messe *f* ‖ *tr* masser ‖ *intr* se masser

massacre ['mæsəkər] *s* massacre *m* ‖ *tr* massacrer

massage [mə'saʒ] *s* massage *m* ‖ *tr* masser

mass' arrest' *s* rafle *f*

masseur [mə'sʌr] *s* masseur *m*

masseuse [mə'suz] *s* masseuse *f*

massive ['mæsɪv] *adj* massif

mass' me'dia ['midɪ·ə] *spl* communication *f* de masse, media *mpl*; journalistes *mfpl*; presse *f*, radio *f*, télé *f*

mass' meet'ing *s* meeting *m* monstre, rassemblement *m*

mass' produc'tion *s* fabrication *f* en série

mast [mæst] *s* mât *m*; (*food for swine*) gland *m*, faîne *f*; **before the mast** comme simple matelot

master ['mæstər] *s* maître *m*; (*employer*) chef *m*, patron *m*; (*male head of household*) maître de maison; (*title of respect*) Monsieur *m*; (naut) commandant *m* ‖ *tr* maîtriser; (*a subject*) connaître à fond, posséder

mas'ter bed'room *s* chambre *f* du maître

mas'ter build'er *s* entrepreneur *m* de bâtiments

masterful ['mæstərfəl] *adj* magistral, expert; impérieux, en maître

mas'ter key' *s* passe-partout *m*

masterly ['mæstərli] *adj* magistral, de maître ‖ *adv* magistralement

mas'ter mechan'ic *s* maître *m* mécanicien

mas'ter·mind *s* organisateur *m*, cerveau *m* ‖ *tr* organiser, diriger

mas'ter of cer'emonies *s* maître *m* des cérémonies; (*in a night club, on television, etc.*) animateur *m*

mas'ter·piece *s* chef-d'œuvre *m*

mas'ter stroke' *s* coup *m* de maître

mas'ter tape' *s* bande *f* génératrice, bande mère, bande souche

mas'ter·work *s* chef-d'œuvre *m*

master·y ['mæstəri] *s* (*pl* **-ies**) maîtrise *f*

mast'head *s* (*of a newspaper*) en-tête *m*; (naut) tête *f* de mât

masticate ['mæstɪ,ket] *tr* mastiquer

mastiff ['mæstɪf] *s* mâtin *m*

masturbate ['mæstər,bet] *tr* masturber ‖ *intr* se masturber

mat [mæt] *s* (*for floor*) natte *f*; (*for a cup, vase, etc.*) dessous *m* de plat; (*before a door*) paillasson *m* ‖ *v* (*pret & pp* **matted;** *ger* **matting**) *tr* (*to cover with matting*) couvrir de nattes; (*hair*) emmêler; (*with blood*) coller ‖ *intr* s'emmêler

match [mætʃ] *s* (*producing fire*) allumette *f*; (*wick*) mèche *f*; (*counterpart*) égal *m*, pair *m*; (*suitable partner in marriage*) parti *m*; (*suitably associated pair*) assortiment *m*; (*game, contest*) match *m*, partie *f*; **to be a**

match for être de la force de, être à la hauteur de; **to meet one's match** trouver son pareil ‖ *tr* égaler; (*objects*) faire pendant à, assortir ‖ *intr* s'assortir

match'box' *s* boîte *f* d'allumettes, porte-allumettes *m*

matchless ['mætʃlɪs] *adj* incomparable, sans pareil

match'mak'er *s* marieur *m*

mate [met] *s* (*husband*) conjoint *m*; (*wife*) conjointe *f*; (*to a female*) mâle *m*; (*to a male*) femelle *f*; (*fellow worker*) camarade *mf*; (*one of a pair*) l'autre gant *m*, l'autre soulier *m*, l'autre chaussure *f* (*etc.*); (*checkmate*) mat *m*; (naut) officier *m* en second, second maître *m* ‖ *tr* marier; (zool) accoupler ‖ *intr* se marier; s'accoupler

material [mə'tɪrɪ·əl] *adj* matériel; important ‖ *s* matériel *m*; (*what a thing is made of*) matière *f*; (*cloth, fabric*) étoffe *f*; (archit) matériau *m*; **materials** matériaux *mpl*

materialist [mə'tɪrɪ·əlɪst] *s* matérialiste *mf*

materialistic [mə'tɪrɪ·ə'lɪstɪk] *adj* matérialiste, matériel

materialize [mə'tɪrɪə,laɪz] *intr* se matérialiser; (*to be realized*) se réaliser

matériel [mə,tɪrɪ'ɛl] *s* matériel *m*

maternal [mə'tʌrnəl] *adj* maternel

maternity [mə'tʌrnɪti] *s* maternité *f*

mater'nity dress' *s* robe *f* de grossesse

mater'nity hos'pital *s* maternité *f*

mater'nity room' *s* salle *f* d'accouchement

mater'nity ward' *s* salle *f* des accouchées

math [mæθ] *s* (coll) math *fpl*

mathematical [,mæθɪ'mætɪkəl] *adj* mathématique

mathematician [,mæθɪmə'tɪʃən] *s* mathématicien *m*

mathematics [,mæθɪ'mætɪks] *s* mathématiques *fpl*

matinée [,mætɪ'ne] *s* matinée *f*

mat'ing sea'son *s* saison *f* des amours

matins ['mætɪnz] *spl* matines *fpl*

matriarch ['metrɪ,ark] *s* matrone *f*

matriar·chy ['metrɪ,arki] *s* (*pl* **-chies**) matriarcat *m*

matricide ['mætrɪ,saɪd] *s* (*person*) matricide *mf*; (*action*) matricide *m*

matriculate [mə'trɪkjə,let] *tr* immatriculer ‖ *intr* s'inscrire à l'université, prendre ses inscriptions

matriculation [mə,trɪkjə'leʃən] *s* inscription *f*; immatriculation *f*

matrimonial [,mætrɪ'monɪ·əl] *adj* matrimonial

matrimo·ny ['mætrɪ,moni] *s* (*pl* **-nies**) mariage *m*, vie *f* conjugale

ma·trix ['metrɪks] *s* (*pl* **-trices** [trɪ,siz] or **-trixes**) matrice *f*

matron ['metrən] *s* (*woman no longer young, and of good standing*) matrone *f*; intendante *f*, surveillante *f*

matronly ['metrənli] *adj* de matrone, digne, respectable

matter [ˈmætər] s matière f; (pathol) pus m; **a matter of** affaire de, une question de; **for that matter** à vrai dire; **no matter** n'importe, pas d'importance; **no matter when** n'importe quand; **no matter where** n'importe où; **no matter who** n'importe qui; **what is the matter? what is the matter with you?** qu'avez-vous? ‖ intr importer; **it doesn't matter** cela ne fait rien

mat′ter of course′ s chose f qui va de soi

mat′ter of fact′ s—**as a matter of fact** en réalité, effectivement, de fait

matter-of-fact [ˈmætərəv‚fækt] adj prosaïque, terre à terre

mattock [ˈmætək] s pioche f

mattress [ˈmætrɪs] s matelas m

mat′tress cov′er s alèze f

mature [məˈtʃʊr], [məˈtʊr] adj mûr; (due) échu ‖ tr faire mûrir ‖ intr mûrir; (to become due) échoir

maturity [məˈtʃʊrɪti], [məˈtʊrɪti] s maturité f; (com) échéance f

maudlin [ˈmɔdlɪn] adj larmoyant

maul [mɔl] tr malmener; (to split) fendre au coin

maulstick [ˈmɔl‚stɪk] s appui-main m

Maun′dy Thurs′day [mɔndi] s jeudi m saint

mausole·um [‚mɔsəˈli·əm] s (pl **-ums** or **-a** [ə]) mausolée m

maw [mɔ] s (of birds) jabot m; (of fish) poche f d'air

mawkish [ˈmɔkɪʃ] adj à l'eau de rose; (sickening) écœurant

maxim [ˈmæksɪm] s maxime f

maximum [ˈmæksɪməm] adj & s maximum m

May [me] s mai m ‖ (l.c.) v (pret & cond **might** [maɪt]) aux—**it may be** il ne peut; **may I?** vous permettez?; **may I** + inf puis-je + inf, est-ce que je peux + inf; **may I** (may we, etc.) + inf peut-on + inf; **may you be happy!** puissiez-vous être heureux!

maybe [ˈmebi] adv peut-être

May′ Day′ s le premier mai m

mayhem [ˈmehɛm] s mutilation f

mayonnaise [‚me·əˈnez] s mayonnaise f

mayor [ˈme·ər], [mɛr] s maire m

May′pole′ s mai m

May′ queen′ s reine f du premier mai

maze [mez] s labyrinthe m, dédale m

me [mi] pron moi §85, §87; me §87

meadow [ˈmɛdo] s prairie f, pré m

mead′ow·land′ s herbage m, prairie f

meager [ˈmigər] adj maigre

meal· [mil] s (dinner, lunch, etc.) repas m; (grain) farine f; **to miss a meal** serrer la ceinture d'un cran

meal′ tick′et s ticket-repas m; (job) gagne-pain m

meal′time′ s heure f du repas

meal·y [ˈmili] adj (comp **-ier;** super **-iest**) farineux

mean [min] adj (intermediate) moyen; (low in station or rank) bas, humble; (shabby) vil, misérable; (stingy) mesquin; (small-minded) bas, vilain, méprisable; (vicious) sauvage, mal intentionné; **no mean** fameux, excellent ‖ s milieu m, moyen terme m; (math) moyenne f; **by all means** de toute façon, je vous en prie; **by means of** au moyen de; **by no means** en aucune façon; **means** ressources fpl, fortune f; (agency) moyen m; **means to an end** moyens d'arriver à ses fins; **not by any means!** jamais de la vie! ‖ v (pret & pp **meant** [mɛnt]) tr vouloir dire, signifier; (to intend) entendre; (to entail) entraîner; **to mean s.th. for s.o.** destiner q.ch à qn; **to mean to** avoir l'intention de, compter ‖ intr—**to mean well** avoir de bonnes intentions

meander [mɪˈændər] s méandre m ‖ intr faire des méandres

meaning [ˈminɪŋ] s signification f, sens m; intention f

meaningful [ˈminɪŋfəl] adj significatif

meaningless [ˈminɪŋlɪs] adj sans signification, dénué de sens

meanness [ˈminnɪs] s bassesse f, vilenie f; (stinginess) mesquinerie f

mean′time′ s—**in the meantime** dans l'intervalle, sur ces entrefaites ‖ adv entre-temps, en attendant

mean′while′ s & adv var of **meantime**

measles [ˈmizəlz] s rougeole f; (German measles) rubéole f

mea·sly [ˈmizli] adj (comp **-slier;** super **-sliest**) rougeoleux; (slang) piètre, insignifiant

measurable [ˈmɛʒərəbəl] adj mesurable

measure [ˈmɛʒər] s mesure f; (step, procedure) mesure, démarche f; (legislative bill) projet m de loi; (mus, poetic) mesure; **in a large measure** en grande partie; **in a measure** dans une certaine mesure; **to take measures to** prendre des mesures pour; **to take s.o.'s measure** (fig) prendre la mesure de qn ‖ tr mesurer; **to measure out** mesurer, distribuer ‖ intr mesurer

measurement [ˈmɛʒərmənt] s mesure f; **to take s.o.'s measurements** prendre les mesures de qn

meas′uring cup′ s verre m gradué

meat [mit] s viande f; (food in general) nourriture f; (gist) moelle f, substance f

meat′ball′ s boulette f de viande

meat′hook′ s croc m, allonge f

meat′ mar′ket s boucherie f

meat′ pie′ s tourte f à la viande, pâté m en croûte

meat·y [ˈmiti] adj (comp **-ier;** super **-iest**) charnu; (fig) plein de substance, étoffé

Mecca [ˈmɛkə] s La Mecque

mechanic [məˈkænɪk] s mécanicien m; **mechanics** mécanique f

mechanical [məˈkænɪkəl] adj mécanique; (fig) mécanique, machinal

mechan′ical draw′ing s dessin m industriel

mechan′ical engineer′ s ingénieur m mécanicien

mechan'ical toy' *s* jouet *m* mécanique
mechanics [mɪˈkænɪks] *s* mécanique *f*
mechanism [ˈmɛkə,nɪzəm] *s* mécanisme *m*
mechanize [ˈmɛkə,naɪz] *tr* mécaniser
medal [ˈmɛdəl] *s* médaille *f*
medallion [mɪˈdæljən] *s* médaillon *m*
meddle [ˈmɛdəl] *intr* s'ingérer; **to meddle in** or **with** se mêler de, s'immiscer dans
meddler [ˈmɛdlər] *s* intrigant *m*, touche-à-tout *m*
meddlesome [ˈmɛdəlsəm] *adj* intrigant
media [ˈmidɪ·ə] *s* (journ, rad, telv) journalistes *mfpl*; presse *f*, radio *f*, télé *f*; **the media** les media *mpl*
median [ˈmidɪ·ən] *adj* médian ‖ *s* médiane *f*
me'dian strip' *s* bande *f* médiane
mediate [ˈmidɪ,et] *tr* procurer par médiation, négocier ‖ *intr* s'entremettre, s'interposer
mediation [,midɪˈeʃən] *s* médiation *f*
mediator [ˈmidɪ,etər] *s* médiateur *m*
medical [ˈmɛdɪkəl] *adj* médical
med'ical stu'dent *s* étudiant *m* en médecine
medicinal [məˈdɪsɪnəl] *adj* médicinal
medicine [ˈmɛdɪsɪn] *s* (*science and art*) médecine *f*; (pharm) médicament *m*
med'icine cab'inet *s* armoire *f* à pharmacie, armoire de toilette
med'icine kit' *s* pharmacie *f* portative
med'icine man' *s* (*pl* **men'**) sorcier *m* indien; (*mountebank*) charlatan *m*
medi·co [ˈmɛdɪ,ko] *s* (*pl* **-cos**) (slang) carabin *m*, morticole *m*
medieval [,midɪˈivəl], [,mɛdɪˈivəl] *adj* médiéval, moyenâgeux; (pej) périmé, funeste
medievalist [,mɛdɪˈivəlɪst] *s* médiéviste *mf*
mediocre [ˈmidɪˈokər] *adj* médiocre
mediocri·ty [,midɪˈɑkrɪti] *s* (*pl* **-ties**) médiocrité *f*
meditate [ˈmɛdɪ,tet] *tr* & *intr* méditer
meditation [,mɛdɪˈteʃən] *s* méditation *f*
Mediterranean [,mɛdɪtəˈreni·ən] *adj* méditerranéen ‖ *s* Méditerranée *f*
medi·um [ˈmidɪ·əm] *adj* moyen; (culin) à point ‖ *s* (*pl* **-ums** or **-a** [ə]) milieu *m*; (*means*) moyen *m*; (*in spiritualism*) médium *m*; (journ) organe *m*; **through the medium of** par l'intermédiaire de
me'dium of exchange' *s* agent *m* monétaire
me'dium-range' *adj* à portée moyenne
me'dium-sized' *adj* de grandeur moyenne
medlar [ˈmɛdlər] *s* (*fruit*) nèfle *f*; (*tree*) néflier *m*
medley [ˈmɛdli] *s* mélange *m*; (mus) potpourri *m*
medul·la [mɪˈdʌlə] *s* (*pl* **-lae** [li]) moelle *f*
Medusa [məˈduzə] *s* Méduse *f*
meek [mik] *adj* doux, humble
meekness [ˈmiknɪs] *s* douceur *f*, humilité *f*
meerschaum [ˈmɪrʃəm] *s* écume *f* de mer; pipe *f* d'écume de mer
meet [mit] *adj*—**it is meet that** il convient que ‖ *s* (sports) meeting *m* ‖ *v* (*pret & pp* **met** [mɛt]) *tr* rencontrer; (*to make the acquaintance of*) faire la connaissance de; (*to go to meet*) aller au-devant de; (*a car in the street; a person on the sidewalk*) croiser; (*by appointment*) retrouver, rejoindre; (*difficulties; expenses*) faire face à; (*one's debts*) honorer; (*one's death*) trouver; (*a need*) satisfaire à; (*an objection*) réfuter; (*the ear*) frapper; **meet my wife (my friend, etc.)** je vous présente ma femme (mon ami, etc.) ‖ *intr* se rencontrer; (*for an appointment*) se retrouver, se rejoindre; (*to assemble*) se réunir; (*to join, touch*) se joindre, se toucher; (*said of rivers*) confluer; (*said of roads; said of cars, persons, etc.*) croiser; **till we meet again** au revoir; **to meet with** se rencontrer avec, rencontrer; (*difficulties, an affront, etc.*) subir
meeting [ˈmitɪŋ] *s* rencontre *f*; (*session*) séance *f*; (*assemblage*) réunion *f*, assemblée *f*; (*of an association*) congrès *m*; (*of two rivers*) confluent *m*; (*of two cars; of two roads*) croisement *m*; (pol) meeting *m*
meet'ing of the minds' *s* bonne entente *f*
meet'ing place' *s* rendez-vous *m*
megacycle [ˈmɛgə,saɪkəl] *s* mégacycle *m*
megaphone [ˈmɛgə,fon] *s* mégaphone *m*, porte-voix *m*
megohm [ˈmɛg,om] *s* mégohm *m*
melancholia [,mɛlənˈkoli·ə] *s* mélancolie *f*
melanchol·y [ˈmɛlən,kɑli] *adj* mélancolique ‖ *s* (*pl* **-ies**) mélancolie *f*
melee [ˈmele] *s* mêlée *f*
mellow [ˈmɛlo] *adj* moelleux; enjoué, débonnaire; (*ripe*) mûr ‖ *tr* rendre moelleux, mûrir
melodic [mɪˈlɑdɪk] *adj* mélodique
melodious [,mɪˈlodɪ·əs] *adj* mélodieux
melodramatic [,mɛlədrəˈmætɪk] *adj* mélodramatique
melo·dy [ˈmɛlədi] *s* (*pl* **-dies**) mélodie *f*
melon [ˈmɛlən] *s* melon *m*
melt [mɛlt] *tr* & *intr* fondre; **to melt into** (*e.g., tears*) fondre en
melt'ing pot' *s* creuset *m*
member [ˈmɛmbər] *s* membre *m*
mem'ber·ship' *s* membres *mpl*; (*in a club, etc.*) association *f*; (*belonging*) appartenance *f*
mem'bership blank' *s* bulletin *m* d'adhésion
membrane [ˈmɛmbren] *s* membrane *f*
memen·to [mɪˈmɛnto] *s* (*pl* **-tos** or **-toes**) mémento *m*
mem·o [ˈmɛmo] *s* (*pl* **-os**) (coll) note *f*, rappel *m*
mem'o book' *s* calepin *m*, mémento *m*
memoir [ˈmɛmwɑr] *s* biographie *f*; **memoirs** mémoires *mpl*
mem'o pad' *s* bloc-notes *m*, bloc *m*
memoran·dum [,mɛməˈrændəm] *s* (*pl* **-dums** or **-da** [də]) memorandum *m*; note *f*, rappel *m*
memorial [mɪˈmorɪ·əl] *adj* commémoratif ‖ *s* mémorial *m*; pétition *f*, mémoire *f*
memo'rial arch' *s* arc *m* de triomphe
Memo'rial Day' *s* la journée du Souvenir
memorialize [mɪˈmorɪ·ə,laɪz] *tr* commémorer

memorize [ˈmɛməˌraɪz] *tr* apprendre par cœur

memo·ry [ˈmɛməri] *s* (*pl* **-ries**) mémoire *f*; **from memory** de mémoire; **in memory of** en souvenir de, à la mémoire de

menace [ˈmɛnɪs] *s* menace *f* ‖ *tr* & *intr* menacer

menagerie [məˈnæʒəri] *s* ménagerie *f*

mend [mɛnd] *s* raccommodage *m*, reprise *f* ‖ *tr* réparer; (*to patch*) raccommoder; (*stockings*) repriser; (*to reform*) améliorer ‖ *intr* s'améliorer, s'amender

mendacious [mɛnˈdeʃəs] *adj* mensonger

mendicant [ˈmɛndɪkənt] *adj* & *s* mendiant *m*

mending [ˈmɛndɪŋ] *s* raccommodage *m*; (*of stockings*) reprisage *m*

menfolk [ˈmɛnˌfok] *spl* hommes *mpl*

menial [ˈminɪ·əl] *adj* servile ‖ *s* domestique *mf*

menses [ˈmɛnsiz] *spl* menstrues *fpl*

men's' fur'nishings *spl* confection *f* pour hommes

men's' room' *s* toilettes *fpl* pour hommes, lavabos *mpl* pour messieurs

menstrual [ˈmɛnstrʊ·əl] *adj* menstruel

menstruate [ˈmɛnstrʊˌet] *intr* avoir ses règles

menstruation [ˌmɛnstrʊˈeʃən] *s* menstruation *f*

mental [ˈmɛntəl] *adj* mental

men'tal arith'metic *s* calcul *m* mental

men'tal case' *s* cas *m* mental

men'tal defec'tive *s* débile *mf*

men'tal ill'ness *s* maladie *f* mentale

mentali·ty [mɛnˈtælɪti] *s* (*pl* **-ties**) mentalité *f*

men'tal reserva'tion *s* arrière-pensée *f*, restriction *f* mentale

men'tal test' *s* test *m* psychologique

mention [ˈmɛnʃən] *s* mention *f* ‖ *tr* mentionner; **don't mention it** il n'y a pas de quoi, je vous en prie

menu [ˈmɛnju] *s* menu *m*, carte *f*

meow [mɪˈaʊ] *s* miaou *m* ‖ *intr* miauler

Mephistophelian [ˌmɛfɪstəˈfiliˌən] *adj* méphistophélique

mercantile [ˈmʌrkənˌtaɪl] *adj* commercial, commerçant

mercenar·y [ˈmʌrsəˌnɛri] *adj* mercenaire ‖ *s* (*pl* **-ies**) mercenaire *mf*

merchandise [ˈmʌrtʃənˌdaɪz] *s* marchandise *f*

merchandizing [ˈmʌrtʃənˌdaɪzɪŋ] marchandisage *m*

merchant [ˈmʌrtʃənt] *adj* & *s* marchand *m*

mer'chant·man *s* (*pl* **-men**) navire *m* marchand

mer'chant marine' *s* marine *f* marchande

mer'chant ves'sel *s* navire *m* marchand

merciful [ˈmʌrsɪfəl] *adj* miséricordieux

merciless [ˈmʌrsɪlɪs] *adj* impitoyable

mercurial [mɛrˈkjʊrɪ·əl] *adj* inconstant, versatile; (*lively*) vif

mercu·ry [ˈmʌrkjəri] *s* (*pl* **-ries**) mercure *m*

mer·cy [ˈmʌrsi] *s* (*pl* **-cies**) miséricorde *f*, pitié *f*; **at the mercy of** à la merci de

mere [mɪr] *adj* simple, pur; seul, e.g., **at the mere thought of it** à la seule pensée de cela; rien que, e.g., **to shudder at the mere thought of it** frissoner rien que d'y penser

meretricious [ˌmɛrɪˈtrɪʃəs] *adj* factice, postiche; de courtisane

merge [mʌrdʒ] *tr* fusionner ‖ *intr* fusionner; (*said of two roads*) converger; **to merge into** se fondre dans

merger [ˈmʌrdʒər] *s* fusion *f*

meridian [məˈrɪdɪ·ən] *adj* & *s* méridien *m*

meringue [məˈræŋ] *s* meringue *f*

merit [ˈmɛrɪt] *s* mérite *m* ‖ *tr* mériter

meritorious [ˌmɛrɪˈtɔrɪ·əs] *adj* méritoire; (*person*) méritant

merlin [ˈmʌrlɪn] *s* (orn) émerillon *m*

mermaid [ˈmʌrˌmed] *s* sirène *f*

merriment [ˈmɛrɪmənt] *s* gaieté *f*, réjouissance *f*

mer·ry [ˈmɛri] *adj* (*comp* **-rier**; *super* **-riest**) gai, joyeux; **to make merry** se divertir

Mer'ry Christ'mas *s* Joyeux Noël *m*

mer'ry-go-round' *s* chevaux *mpl* de bois, manège *m* forain

mer'ry·mak'er *s* noceur *m*, fêtard *m*

mesh [mɛʃ] *s* (*network*) réseau *m*; (*each open space of net*) maille *f*; (*net*) filet *m*; (*engagement of gears*) engrenage *m*; **meshes** rets *m*, filets *mpl* ‖ *tr* (mach) engrener ‖ *intr* s'engrener

mesmerize [ˈmɛsməˌraɪz] *tr* magnétiser

mess [mɛs] *s* (*disorder*) gâchis *m*; (*refuse*) saleté *f*; (*meal*) (mil) ordinaire *m*; (*for officers*) (mil) mess *m*; **to get into a mess** se mettre dans le pétrin; **to make a mess of** gâcher ‖ *tr*—**to mess up** (*to botch*) gâcher; (*to dirty*) salir ‖ *intr*—**to mess around** (*to putter*) (coll) bricoler; (*to waste time*) (coll) lambiner

message [ˈmɛsɪdʒ] *s* message *m*

messenger [ˈmɛsəndʒər] *s* messager *m*; (*one who goes on errands*) commissionnaire *m*

mess' hall' *s* cantine *f*; (*for officers*) mess *m*

Messiah [məˈsaɪ·ə] *s* Messie *m*

mess' kit' *s* gamelle *f*

mess'mate' *s* camarade *mf* de table; (nav) camarade de plat

mess' of pot'tage [ˈpɑtɪdʒ] *s* (Bib) plat *m* de lentilles

Messrs. [ˈmɛsərz] *pl* of **Mr.**

mess·y [ˈmɛsi] *adj* (*comp* **-ier**; *super* **-iest**) en désordre; (*dirty*) sale, poisseux

metal [ˈmɛtəl] *s* métal *m*

metallic [mɪˈtælɪk] *adj* métallique

metallurgy [ˈmɛtəˌlʌrdʒi] *s* métallurgie *f*

met'al pol'ish *s* brillant *m* à métaux

met'al·work' *s* serrurerie *f*, travail *m* des métaux

metamorpho·sis [ˌmɛtəˈmɔrfəsɪs] *s* (*pl* **-ses** [ˌsiz]) métamorphose *f*

metaphony [məˈtæfəni] *s* métaphonie *f*, inflexion *f*

metaphor [ˈmɛtəˌfɔr] *s* métaphore *f*

metaphorical [ˌmɛtəˈfɔrɪkəl] *adj* métaphorique

metathe·sis [mɪ'tæθɪsɪs] s (pl -ses [,siz]) métathèse f

mete [mit] tr—**to mete out** distribuer

meteor ['mitɪ·ər] s étoile f filante; (atmospheric phenomenon) météore m

meteoric [,mitɪ'ɔrɪk] adj météorique; (fig) fulgurant

meteorite ['mitɪ·ə,raɪt] s météorite m & f

meteorology [,mitɪ·ə'ralədʒi] s météorologie f

meter ['mitər] s (unit of measurement; verse) mètre m; (instrument for measuring gas, electricity, water) compteur m; (mus) mesure f

me'ter maid' s contractuelle f, aubergine f

me'ter read'er s releveur m de compteurs

methane ['mɛθen] s méthane m

method ['mɛθəd] s méthode f

methodic(al) [mɪ'θɑdɪk(əl)] adj & s méthodique

Methodist ['mɛθədɪst] adj & s méthodiste mf

Methuselah [mɪ'θuzələ] s Mathusalem m

meticulous [mɪ'tɪkjələs] adj méticuleux

metric(al) ['mɛtrɪk(əl)] adj métrique

metrics ['mɛtrɪks] s métrique f

metronome ['mɛtrə,nom] s métronome m

metropolis [mɪ'trɑpəlɪs] s métropole f

metropolitan [,mɛtrə'palɪtən] adj & s métropolitain m

mettle ['mɛtəl] s ardeur f, fougue f; **to be on one's mettle** se piquer au jeu

mettlesome ['mɛtəlsəm] adj ardent, vif, fougueux

mew [mju] s miaulement m ‖ intr miauler

Mexican ['mɛksɪkən] adj mexicain ‖ s Mexicain m

Mexico ['mɛksɪ,ko] s le Mexique

Mex'ico Cit'y s Mexico

mezzanine ['mɛzə,nin] s entresol m; (theat) mezzanine m & f, corbeille f

mica ['maɪkə] s mica m

microbe ['maɪkrob] s microbe m

microbiology [,maɪkrəbaɪ'alədʒi] s microbiologie f

microcomputer ['maɪkrəkəm,pjutər] s micro-ordinateur m

microfilm ['maɪkrə,fɪlm] s microfilm m ‖ tr microfilmer

microgroove ['maɪkrə,gruv] adj & s microsillon m

mi'crogroove rec'ord s disque m à microsillons

microphone ['maɪkrə,fon] s microphone m

microprocesser ['maɪkrə'prɑsəsər] s microprocesseur m

microscope ['maɪkrə,skop] s microscope m

microscopic [,maɪkrə'skɑpɪk] adj microscopique

microwave ['maɪkrə,wev] s micro-onde f

mid [mɪd] adj—**in mid course** à mi-chemin

mid'day' s midi m

middle ['mɪdəl] adj moyen, du milieu ‖ s milieu m; **in the middle of** au milieu de

mid'dle age' s âge m moyen; **Middle Ages** moyen-âge m

middle-aged ['mɪdəl,edʒd] adj d'un âge moyen

mid'dle class' s classe f moyenne, bourgeoisie f

mid'dle-class' adj bourgeois

Mid'dle East' s Moyen-Orient m

Mid'dle Eng'lish s moyen anglais m

mid'dle fin'ger s majeur m, doigt m du milieu

mid'dle·man' s (pl -men') intermédiaire mf

mid'dle·weight' s (boxing) poids m moyen

middling ['mɪdlɪŋ] adj moyen, assez bien, passable ‖ adv (coll) assez bien, passablement

mid·dy ['mɪdi] s (pl -dies) (coll) aspirant m

mid'dy blouse' s marinière f

midget ['mɪdʒɪt] s nain m, nabot m

midland ['mɪdlənd] adj de l'intérieur ‖ s centre m du pays

mid'night' s minuit; **to burn the midnight oil** pâlir sur les livres, se crever les livres ‖ s minuit m

midriff ['mɪdrɪf] s diaphragme m

mid'ship'man s (pl -men) aspirant m

midst [mɪdst] s centre m; **in our (your, etc.)** midst parmi nous (vous, etc.); **in the midst of** au milieu de

mid'stream' s—**in midstream** au milieu du courant

mid'sum'mer s milieu m de l'été

mid'way' adj & adv à mi-chemin ‖ **mid'way'** s fête f foraine

mid'week' s milieu m de la semaine

mid'wife' s (pl -wives') sage-femme f

mid'win'ter s milieu m de l'hiver

mid'year' s mi-année f

mien [min] s mine f, aspect m

miff [mɪf] s (coll) fâcherie f ‖ tr (coll) fâcher

might [maɪt] s puissance f, force f; **with might and main, with all one's might** de toute sa force ‖ aux used to form the potential mood, e.g., **she might not be able to come** il se pourrait qu'elle ne puisse pas venir

mightily ['maɪtɪli] adv puissamment; (coll) énormément

might·y ['maɪti] adj (comp -ier; super -iest) puissant; (of great size) grand, vaste ‖ adv (coll) rudement, diablement

mignonette [,mɪnjə'nɛt] s réséda m

migraine ['maɪgren] s migraine f

migrant ['maɪgrənt] adj & s (animal) migrateur m; (person) nomade mf; **migrant worker** travailleur m, migrant m; (seasonal) travailleur saisonnier

migrate ['maɪgret] intr émigrer

migratory ['maɪgrə,tori] adj migratoire

milch [mɪltʃ] adj laitier

mild [maɪld] adj doux

mildew ['mɪl,d(j)u] s moisissure f; (on vine) mildiou m, blanc m

mildness ['maɪldnɪs] s douceur f

mile [maɪl] s mille m

mileage ['maɪlɪdʒ] s distance f en milles; (charge) tarif m au mille

mile'post' s borne f milliaire

mile'stone' s borne f milliaire; (fig) jalon m
militancy ['mɪlɪtənsi] s esprit m militant
militant ['mɪlɪtənt] adj & s militant m
militarism ['mɪlɪtə,rɪzəm] s militarisme m
militarize ['mɪlɪtə,raɪz] tr militariser
military ['mɪlɪ,tɛri] adj & s militaire m
mil'itary police'man s (pl -men) agent m de la police militaire
militate ['mɪlɪ,tet] intr militer
militia [mɪ'lɪʃə] s milice f
mili'tia·man s (pl -men) milicien m
milk [mɪlk] adj laitier ‖ s lait m ‖ tr traire; abuser de, exploiter; **to milk s.th. from s.o.** soutirer q.ch. à qn
milk' can' s pot m à lait, berthe f
milk' car'ton s boîte f de lait, berlingot m
milk' choc'olate s chocolat m au lait
milk' di'et s régime m lacté
milk'maid' s laitière f
milk'man' s (pl -men') laitier m, crémier m
milk' pail' s seau m à lait
milk'sop' s poule f mouillée
milk' tooth' s dent f de lait
milk'weed' s laiteron m
milk·y ['mɪlki] adj (comp -ier; super -iest) laiteux
Milk'y Way' s Voie f Lactée
mill [mɪl] s moulin m; (factory) fabrique f, usine f; millième m de dollar; **to put through the mill** (coll) faire passer au laminoir ‖ tr moudre, broyer; (a coin) créneler; (gears) fraiser; (steel) laminer; (ore) bocarder; (chocolate) faire mousser ‖ intr—**to mill around** circuler
millennial [mɪ'lɛnɪ·əl] adj millénaire
millenni·um [mɪ'lɛnɪ·əm] s (pl -ums or -a [ə]) millénaire m
miller ['mɪlər] s meunier m
millet ['mɪlɪt] s millet m
milligram ['mɪlɪ,græm] s milligramme m
millimeter ['mɪlɪ,mitər] s millimètre m
milliner ['mɪlɪnər] s modiste f
mil'linery shop' ['mɪlɪ,nɛri] s boutique f de modiste
milling ['mɪlɪŋ] s (of grain) mouture f
mill'ing machine' s fraiseuse f
million ['mɪljən] adj million de ‖ s million m
millionaire [,mɪljən'ɛr] s millionnaire mf
millionth ['mɪljənθ] adj & pron millionième (masc, fem) ‖ s millionième m
mill'pond' s retenue f, réservoir m
mill'race' s bief m
mill'stone' s meule f; (fig) boulet m
mill' wheel' s roue f de moulin
mill'work' s ouvrage m de menuiserie
mime [maɪm] s mime mf ‖ tr & intr mimer
mimeograph ['mɪmɪ·ə,græf] s ronéo f ‖ tr ronéocopier, ronéotyper
mim·ic ['mɪmɪk] s mime mf, imitateur m ‖ v (pret & pp -icked; ger -icking) tr mimer, imiter
mimic·ry ['mɪmɪkri] s (pl -ries) mimique f, imitation f
minaret [,mɪnə'rɛt] s minaret m
mince [mɪns] tr (meat) hacher menu ‖ intr minauder

mince'meat' s hachis m de viande et de fruits aromatisés; **to make mincemeat of** (coll) mettre en marmelade
mind [maɪnd] s esprit m; **to be of one mind** être d'accord; **to change one's mind** changer d'avis; **to have a mind to** avoir envie de; **to have in mind** avoir en vue; **to lose one's mind** perdre la raison; **to make up one's mind to** prendre le parti de; **to slip one's mind** échapper à qn; **to speak one's mind** donner son avis ‖ tr (to take care of) garder; (to obey) obéir à; (to be troubled by) s'inquiéter de; (e.g., one's manners) faire attention à; (e.g., a dangerous step) prendre garde à; **mind your own business!** occupez-vous de vous affaires! ‖ intr—**do you mind?** cela ne vous ennuie pas?, cela ne vous gêne pas?; **if you don't mind** si cela ne vous fait rien, si cela vous est égal; **never mind!** n'importe!
mind'-bend'ing s renversant
mind'-blow'ing s hallucinant
mindful ['maɪndfəl] adj attentif; **mindful of** attentif à, soigneux de
mind' read'er s liseur m de la pensée
mind' read'ing s lecture f de la pensée
mine [maɪn] s mine f ‖ pron poss le mien §89; à moi §85 A, 10 ‖ tr (coal, minerals, etc.) extraire; (to undermine; to lay mines in) miner
mine'field' s champ m de mines
mine'lay'er s poseur m de mines
miner ['maɪnər] s mineur m
mineral ['mɪnərəl] adj & s minéral m
mineralogy [,mɪnə'rɑlədʒi] s minéralogie f
min'eral wool' s laine f minérale, laine de scories
mine'sweep'er s dragueur m de mines
mingle ['mɪŋgəl] tr mêler, mélanger ‖ intr se mêler, se mélanger
miniature ['mɪnɪ·ətʃər] s miniature f; **in miniature** en abrégé
miniaturization [,mɪnɪ·ətʃərɪ'zeʃən] s miniaturisation f
miniaturize ['mɪnɪ·ətʃə,raɪz] tr miniaturiser
minimal ['mɪnɪməl] adj minimum
minimize ['mɪnə,maɪz] tr minimiser
minimum ['mɪnɪməm] adj minimum; (temperature) minimal ‖ s minimum m
min'imum wage' s salaire m minimum, minimum m vital
min'imum-wage' earn'er s smicard m
mining ['maɪnɪŋ] adj minier ‖ s exploitation f des mines; (nav) pose f de mines
minion ['mɪnjən] s favori m; (henchman) séide m
miniskirt ['mɪnɪ,skʌrt] s minijupe f
minister ['mɪnɪstər] s ministre m; (eccl) pasteur m ‖ intr—**to minister to** (the needs of) subvenir à; (a person) soigner; (a parish) desservir
ministerial [,mɪnɪs'tɪrɪ·əl] adj ministériel
minis·try ['mɪnɪstri] s (pl -tries) ministère m; (eccl) clergé m; (eccl) pastorat m
mink [mɪŋk] s vison m

minnow ['mɪno] s vairon m

minor ['maɪnər] adj & s mineur m

Minorca [mɪ'nɔrkə] s Minorque f; île f de Minorque

minori·ty [mɪ'nɔrɪti] adj minoritaire ‖ s (pl -ties) minorité f

minstrel ['mɪnstrəl] s (in a minstrel show) interprète m de chants nègres; (hist) ménestrel m

mint [mɪnt] s hôtel m des Monnaies, Monnaie f; (bot) menthe f; (fig) mine f ‖ tr frapper, monnayer; (fig) forger

minuet [,mɪnju'ɛt] s menuet m

minus ['maɪnəs] adj négatif ‖ s moins m ‖ prep moins; (coll) sans, dépourvu de

minute [maɪ'n(j)ut] adj (tiny) minime; (meticulous) minutieux ‖ ['mɪnɪt] s minute f; **minutes** compte m rendu, procès-verbal m de séance; (often omitted in expressions of time), e.g., **ten after two, ten minutes after two** deux heures dix; **up to the minute** de la dernière heure; à la dernière mode; au courant

min′ute hand′ ['mɪnɪt] s grande aiguille f

min′ute rice′ s riz m précuit

min′ute steak′ s entrecôte f minute

minutiae [mɪ'n(j)uʃɪ,i] spl minuties fpl

minx [mɪŋks] s effrontée f

miracle ['mɪrəkəl] s miracle m

mir′acle play′ s miracle m

miraculous [mɪ'rækjələs] adj miraculeux

mirage [mɪ'rɑʒ] s mirage m

mire [maɪr] s fange f

mirror ['mɪrər] s miroir m, glace f ‖ tr refléter

mirth [mʌrθ] s joie f, gaieté f

mir·y ['maɪri] adj (comp -ier; super -iest) fangeux

misadventure [,mɪsəd'vɛntʃər] s mésaventure f

misanthrope ['mɪsən,θrop] s misanthrope mf

misapprehension [,mɪsæprɪ'hɛnʃən] s fausse idée f, malentendu m

misappropriation [,mɪsə,proprɪ'eʃən] s détournement m de fonds

misbehave [,mɪsbɪ'hev] intr se conduire mal

misbehavior [,mɪsbɪ'hevɪ·ər] s mauvaise conduite f

miscalculation [,mɪskælkjə'leʃən] s mécompte m

miscarriage [mɪs'kærɪdʒ] s fausse couche f; (e.g., of letter) perte f; (of justice) déni m, mal-jugé m; (fig) avortement m, insuccès m

miscar·ry [mɪs'kæri] v (pret & pp -ried) intr faire une fausse couche; (said, e.g., of letter) s'égarer; (fig) avorter, échouer

miscellaneous [,mɪsə'lenɪ·əs] adj divers, mélangé

miscella·ny ['mɪsə,leni] s (pl -nies) miscellanées fpl

mischief ['mɪstʃɪf] s (harm) tort m; (disposition to annoy) méchanceté f; (prankishness) espièglerie f

mis′chief-mak′er s brandon m de discorde

mischievous ['mɪstʃɪvəs] adj (harmful) nuisible; (mean) méchant; (prankish) espiègle

misconception [,mɪskən'sɛpʃən] s conception f erronée

misconduct [mɪs'kɑndʌkt] s inconduite f; (e.g., of a business) mauvaise administration f ‖ [,mɪskən'dʌkt] tr mal administrer; **to misconduct oneself** se conduire mal

misconstrue [,mɪskən'stru], [mɪs'kɑnstru] tr mal interpréter

miscount [mɪs'kaunt] s erreur f de calcul ‖ tr & intr mal compter

miscue [mɪs'kju] s fausse queue f; (blunder) bévue f ‖ intr faire fausse queue; (theat) se tromper de réplique

mis·deal ['mɪs,dil] s maldonne f, mauvaise donne f ‖ [mɪs'dil] v (pret & pp -dealt) tr mal distribuer ‖ intr faire maldonne

misdeed ['mɪs,did] s méfait m

misdemeanor [,mɪsdɪ'minər] s mauvaise conduite f; (law) délit m correctionnel

misdirect [,mɪsdɪ'rɛkt] tr mal diriger

misdoing [mɪs'du·ɪŋ] s méfait m

miser ['maɪzər] s avare mf

miserable ['mɪzərəbəl] adj misérable

miserly ['maɪzərli] adj avare

miser·y ['mɪzəri] s (pl -ies) misère f, détresse f

misfeasance [mɪs'fizəns] s (law) abus m de pouvoir

misfire [mɪs'faɪr] s raté m ‖ intr rater

mis·fit ['mɪs,fɪt] s (clothing) vêtement m manqué; (thing) laissé-pour-compte m; (person) (fig) inadapté m

misfortune [mɪs'fɔrtʃən] s infortune f, malheur m; **misfortunes** misères fpl

misgiving [mɪs'gɪvɪŋ] s pressentiment m, appréhension f, soupçon m

misgovern [mɪs'gʌvərn] tr mal gouverner

misguidance [mɪs'gaɪdəns] s mauvais conseils mpl

misguided [mɪs'gaɪdɪd] adj mal placé, hors de propos; (e.g., youth) dévoyé

mishap ['mɪshæp] s contretemps m, mésaventure f

mishmash ['mɪʃ,mæʃ] s méli-mélo m

misinform [,mɪsɪn'fɔrm] tr mal renseigner

misinterpret [,mɪsɪn'tʌrprɪt] tr mal interpréter

misjudge [mɪs'dʒʌdʒ] tr & intr mal juger

mis·lay [mɪs'le] v (pret & pp -laid) tr égarer, perdre

mis·lead [mɪs'lid] v (pret & pp -led) tr égarer; corrompre

misleading [mɪs'lidɪŋ] adj trompeur

mismanagement [mɪs'mænɪdʒmənt] s mauvaise administration f

misnomer [mɪs'nomər] s faux nom m

misplace [mɪs'ples] tr mal placer; (to mislay) (coll) égarer, perdre

misprint ['mɪs,prɪnt] s erreur f typographique, coquille f ‖ [mɪs'prɪnt] tr imprimer incorrectement

mispronounce [,mɪsprə'nauns] tr mal prononcer

misquote [mɪsˈkwot] *tr* citer à faux, citer inexactement

misrepresent [ˌmɪsrɛprɪˈzɛnt] *tr* représenter sous un faux jour; (*e.g., facts*) dénaturer, travestir

miss [mɪs] *s* coup *m* manqué; **a miss!** à côté!; **Miss** Mademoiselle *f*, Mlle; (*winner of beauty contest*) Miss *f* ‖ *tr* manquer; (*to feel the absence of*) regretter; (*not to run into*) ne pas voir, ne pas rencontrer; (*e.g., one's way*) se tromper de; **he misses you very much** vous lui manquez beaucoup ‖ *intr* manquer

missal [ˈmɪsəl] *s* missel *m*

misshapen [mɪsˈʃepən] *adj* difforme, contrefait

missile [ˈmɪsɪl] *s* projectile *m*; (*guided missile*) missile *m*

mis′sile gap′ *s* déséquilibre *m* (de missiles)

mis′sile launch′er *s* lance-fusées *m*

missing [ˈmɪsɪŋ] *adj* manquant, absent; perdu; **missing in action** (mil) porté disparu; **to be missing** manquer, e.g., **three are missing** il en manque trois

miss′ing per′sons *spl* disparus *mpl*

mission [ˈmɪʃən] *s* mission *f*

missionar·y [ˈmɪʃənˌɛri] *adj* missionnaire ‖ *s* (*pl* -ies) missionnaire *m*

missis [ˈmɪsɪz] *s*—**the missis** (coll) votre femme *f*

missive [ˈmɪsɪv] *adj & s* missive *f*

mis·spell [mɪsˈspɛl] *v* (*pret & pp* -spelled or -spelt) *tr & intr* écrire incorrectement

misspelling [mɪsˈspɛlɪŋ] *s* faute *f* d'orthographe

misspent [mɪsˈspɛnt] *adj* gaspillé; dissipé

misstatement [mɪsˈstetmənt] *s* rapport *m* inexact, erreur *f* de fait

misstep [mɪsˈstɛp] *s* faux pas *m*

miss·y [ˈmɪsi] *s* (*pl* -ies) (coll) mademoiselle *f*

mist [mɪst] *s* brume *f*, buée *f*; (*fine spray*) vapeur *f*; (*of tears*) voile *m*

mis·take [mɪsˈtek] *s* faute *f*; **by mistake** par erreur, par méprise; **to make a mistake** se tromper ‖ *v* (*pret* -took; *pp* -taken) *tr* (*to misunderstand*) mal comprendre; (*to be wrong about*) se tromper de; **to mistake s.o. for s.o. else** prendre qn pour qn d'autre

mistaken [mɪsˈtekən] *adj* erroné, faux; (*person*) dans l'erreur

mistak′en iden′tity *s* erreur *f* d'identité, erreur sur la personne

mistakenly [mɪsˈtekənli] *adv* par erreur

mister [ˈmɪstər] *s*—**the mister** (coll) votre mari *m* ‖ *interj* (slang & pej) Jules!, mon petit bonhomme!

mistletoe [ˈmɪsəlˌto] *s* gui *m*

mistreat [mɪsˈtrit] *tr* maltraiter

mistreatment [mɪsˈtritmənt] *s* mauvais traitement *m*

mistress [ˈmɪstrɪs] *s* maîtresse *f*

mistrial [mɪsˈtraɪ·əl] *s* (law) procès *m* entaché de nullité

mistrust [mɪsˈtrʌst] *s* méfiance *f* ‖ *tr* se méfier de ‖ *intr* se méfier

mistrustful [mɪsˈtrʌstfəl] *adj* méfiant

mist·y [ˈmɪsti] *adj* (*comp* -ier; *super* -iest) brumeux; vague, indistinct

misunder·stand [ˌmɪsʌndərˈstænd] *v* (*pret & pp* -stood) *tr* mal comprendre

misunderstanding [ˌmɪsʌndərˈstændɪŋ] *s* malentendu *m*

misuse [mɪsˈjus] *s* mauvais usage *m*, abus *m*; (*of words*) emploi *m* abusif ‖ [mɪsˈjuz] *tr* faire mauvais usage de, abuser de; (*a person*) maltraiter

misword [mɪsˈwʌrd] *tr* mal rédiger, mal exprimer

mite [maɪt] *s* (*small contribution*) obole *f*; (*small amount*) brin *m*, bagatelle *f*; (ent) mite *f*

miter [ˈmaɪtər] *s* (*carpentry*) onglet *m*; (eccl) mitre *f* ‖ *tr* tailler à onglet

mi′ter box′ *s* boîte *f* à onglets

mitigate [ˈmɪtɪˌget] *tr* adoucir, atténuer

mitt [mɪt] *s* (*fingerless glove*) mitaine *f*; (*mitten*) moufle *f*; (baseball) gant *m* de prise; (*hand*) (slang) main *f*

mitten [ˈmɪtən] *s* moufle *f*

mix [mɪks] *tr* mélanger, mêler; (*cement; a cake*) malaxer; (*the cards; the salad*) touiller; **to mix up** (*to confuse*) confondre ‖ *intr* se mélanger, se mêler; **to mix with** s'associer à or avec

mixed *adj* mélangé; (*races; style; colors*) mêlé; (*feelings; marriage; school; doubles*) mixte; (*candy*) assorti; (*salad, vegetables, etc.*) panaché; (*number*) fractionnaire; **to be all mixed up** (*facts, account*) être embrouillé; (*person*) être déboussolé, pédaler dans la choucroute

mixed′ drink′ *s* boisson *f* mélangée

mixer [ˈmɪksər] *s* (*device*) mélangeur *m*; (*for, e.g., concrete*) malaxeur *m*; **to be a good mixer** (coll) avoir le don de plaire

mix′ing fau′cet *s* robinet *m* mélangeur

mixture [ˈmɪkstʃər] *s* mélange *m*

mix′-up′ *s* embrouillage *m*

mizzen [ˈmɪzən] *s* artimon *m*

moan [mon] *s* gémissement *m* ‖ *intr* gémir

moat [mot] *s* fossé *m*

mob [mab] *s* (*mass of common people*) foule *f*, masse *f*; (*crush of people*) cohue *f* grouillante; (*crowd bent on violence*) foule en colère; (*criminal gang*) bande *f*, gang *m*; (pej) populace *f* ‖ *v* (*pret & pp* mobbed; *ger* mobbing) *tr* s'attrouper autour de; (*to attack*) fondre sur, assaillir

mobile [ˈmobɪl], [ˈmobil] *adj & s* mobile *m*

mobility [moˈbɪlɪti] *s* mobilité *f*

mobilization [ˌmobɪlɪˈzeʃən] *s* mobilisation *f*

mobilize [ˈmobɪˌlaɪz] *tr & intr* mobiliser

mob′ rule′ *s* loi *f* de la populace

mobster [ˈmabstər] *s* (slang) gangster *m*

moccasin [ˈmakəsɪn] *s* mocassin *m*

Mo′cha cof′fee [ˈmokə] *s* moka *m*

mock [mak] *adj* simulé, contrefait ‖ *s* moquerie *f* ‖ *tr* se moquer de, moquer; (*to imitate*) contrefaire, singer; (*to deceive*) tromper ‖ *intr* se moquer; **to mock at** se moquer de; **to mock up** construire une maquette de

mock′ elec′tion *s* élection *f* blanche

mocker·y ['mɑkəri] *s* (*pl* **-ies**) moquerie *f*; (*subject of derision*) objet *m* de risée; (*poor imitation*) parodie *f*; (*e.g., of justice*) simulacre *m*

mockingbird ['mɑkɪŋ ,bʌrd] *s* moqueur *m*, oiseau *m* moqueur

mock′ or′ange *s* seringa *m*

mock′ tur′tle soup′ *s* potage *m* à la tête de veau

mock′-up′ *s* maquette *f*

mode [mod] *s* (*kind*) mode *m*; (*fashion*) mode *f*; (gram, mus) mode *m*

mod·el ['mɑdəl] *adj* modèle ‖ *s* modèle *m*; (*for dressmaker or artist; at a fashion show*) mannequin *m*; (*of a statue*) maquette *f* ‖ *v* (*pret & pp* **-eled** or **-elled**; *ger* **-eling** or **-elling**) *tr* modeler ‖ *intr* dessiner des modèles; servir de modèle, poser

mod′el air′plane *s* aéromodèle *m*

mod′el-air′plane build′er *s* aéromodéliste *mf*

mod′el-air′plane build′ing *s* aéromodélisme *m*

mod′el home′ *s* (*sample home*) maison *f* exposition, pavillon *m* témoin, villa *f* modèle

moderate ['mɑdərɪt] *adj* modéré ‖ ['mɑdə,ret] *tr* modérer; (*a meeting*) présider ‖ *intr* se modérer; présider

moderator ['mɑdə ,retər] *s* (*over an assembly*) président *m*; (*mediator; substance used for slowing down neutrons*) modérateur *m*

modern ['mɑdərn] *adj* moderne

modernize ['mɑdər,naɪz] *tr* moderniser

mod′ern lan′guages *spl* langues *fpl* vivantes

modest ['mɑdɪst] *adj* modeste

modes·ty ['mɑdɪsti] *s* (*pl* **-ties**) modestie *f*

modicum ['mɑdɪkəm] *s* petite quantité *f*

modifier ['mɑdɪ,faɪ·ər] *s* (gram) modificateur *m*

modi·fy ['mɑdɪ,faɪ] *v* (*pret & pp* **-fied**) *tr* modifier

modish ['modɪʃ] *adj* à la mode, élégant

modulate ['mɑdʒə,let] *tr & intr* moduler

modulation [,mɑdʒə'leʃən] *s* modulation *f*

mohair ['mo,hɛr] *s* mohair *m*

Mohammad [mo'hæməd] *s* Mahomet *m*

Mohammedan [mo'hæmɪdən] *adj* mahométan *s* mahométan *m*

Mohammedanism [mo'hæmɪdə,nɪzəm] *s* mahométisme *m*

moist [mɔɪst] *adj* humide; (*e.g., skin*) moite

moisten ['mɔɪsən] *tr* humecter ‖ *intr* s'humecter

moisture ['mɔɪstʃər] *s* humidité *f*

molar ['molər] *adj & s* molaire *f*

molasses [mə'læsɪz] *s* mélasse *f*

mold [mold] *s* moule *m*; (*fungus*) moisi *m*, moisissure *f*; (agr) humus *m*, terreau *m*; (fig) trempe *f* ‖ *tr* mouler; (*to make moldy*) moisir ‖ *intr* moisir, se moisir

molder ['moldər] *s* mouleur *m* ‖ *intr* tomber en poussière

molding ['moldɪŋ] *s* moulage *m*; (*cornice, shaped strip of wood, etc.*) moulure *f*

mold·y ['moldi] *adj* (*comp* **-ier**; *super* **-iest**) moisi

mole [mol] *s* (*breakwater*) môle *m*; (*inner harbor*) bassin *m*; (*spot on skin*) grain *m* de beauté; (*small mammal*) taupe *f*

molec′ular phys′ics [mə'lɛkjələr] *s* physique *f* moléculaire

molecule ['mɑlɪ,kjul] *s* molécule *f*

mole′hill′ *s* taupinière *f*

mole′skin′ *s* (*fur*) taupe *f*; (*fabric*) moleskine *f*

molest [mə'lɛst] *tr* déranger, inquiéter; molester, rudoyer

moll [mɑl] *s* (slang) femme *f* du Milieu

molli·fy ['mɑlɪ,faɪ] *v* (*pret & pp* **-fied**) *tr* apaiser, adoucir

mollusk ['mɑləsk] *s* mollusque *m*

mollycoddle ['mɑlɪ,kɑdəl] *s* poule *f* mouillée ‖ *tr* dorloter

molt [molt] *s* mue *f* ‖ *intr* muer

molten ['moltən] *adj* fondu

molybdenum [mə'lɪbdɪnəm] *s* molybdène *m*

moment ['momənt] *s* moment *m*; **at any moment** d'un moment à l'autre; **at that moment** à ce moment-là; **at this moment** en ce moment; **in a moment** dans un instant; **of great moment** d'une grande importance; **one moment please!** (telp) ne quittez pas!

momentary ['momən,tɛri] *adj* momentané

momentous [mo'mɛntəs] *adj* important, d'importance

momen·tum [mo'mɛntəm] *s* (*pl* **-tums** or **-ta** [tə]) élan *m*; (mech) force *f* d'impulsion, quantité *f* de mouvement

monarch ['mɑnərk] *s* monarque *m*

monarchic(al) [mə'nɑrkɪk(əl)] *adj* monarchique

monar·chy ['mɑnərki] *s* (*pl* **-chies**) monarchie *f*

monaster·y ['mɑnɛs,tɛri] *s* (*pl* **-ies**) monastère *m*

monastic [mə'næstɪk] *adj* monastique

monasticism [mə'næstɪ,sɪzəm] *s* monachisme *m*

Monday ['mʌndi] *s* lundi *m*

monetary ['mɑnɪ,tɛri] *adj* (*pertaining to coinage*) monétaire; (*pertaining to money*) pécuniaire

money ['mʌni] *s* argent *m*; (*legal tender of a country*) monnaie *f*; **to get one's money's worth** en avoir pour son argent; **to make money** gagner de l'argent

mon′ey·bag′ *s* sacoche *f*; **moneybags** (*wealth*) (coll) sac *m*; (*wealthy person*) (coll) richard *m*

mon′ey belt′ *s* ceinture *f* porte-monnaie

moneychanger ['mʌni,tʃendʒər] *s* changeur *m*, cambiste *m*

moneyed ['mʌnid] *adj* possédant

mon′ey·lend′er *s* bailleur *m* de fonds

mon′ey·mak′er *s* amasseur *m* d'argent; (fig) source *f* de gain

mon′ey or′der *s* mandat *m* postal

Mongol [ˈmɑŋgəl] *adj* mongol ‖ *s* (*language*) mongol *m*; (*person*) Mongol *m*

mon·goose [ˈmɑŋgus] *s* (*pl* **-gooses**) mangouste *f*

mongrel [ˈmʌŋgrəl] *adj* & *s* métis *m*

monitor [ˈmɑnɪtər] *s* contrôleur *m*; (*at school*) pion *m*, moniteur *m*; (comp) moniteur *m* ‖ *tr* contrôler; (rad) écouter

monk [mʌŋk] *s* moine *m*

monkey [ˈmʌŋki] *s* singe *m*; (*female*) guenon *f*; **to make a monkey of** tourner en ridicule ‖ *intr*—**to monkey around** tripoter; **to monkey around with** tripoter; **to monkey with** (*to tamper with*) tripatouiller

mon′key·shine′ *s* (slang) singerie *f*

mon′key wrench′ *s* clé *f* anglaise

monks′hood *s* (bot) napel *m*

monocle [ˈmɑnəkəl] *s* monocle *m*

monogamy [məˈnɑgəmi] *s* monogamie *f*

monogram [ˈmɑnəˌgræm] *s* monogramme *m*

monograph [ˈmɑnəˌgræf] *s* monographie *f*

monolingual [ˌmɑnəˈlɪŋgwəl] *adj* monolingue

monolithic [ˌmɑnəˈlɪθɪk] *adj* monolithique

monologue [ˈmɑnəˌlɔg] *s* monologue *m*

monomania [ˌmɑnəˈmɛnɪ·ə] *s* monomanie *f*

monomial [məˈnomɪ·əl] *s* monôme *m*

monoplane [ˈmɑnəˌplen] *s* monoplan *m*

monopolize [məˈnɑpəˌlaɪz] *tr* monopoliser

monopo·ly [məˈnɑpəli] *s* (*pl* **-lies**) monopole *m*

monorail [ˈmɑnəˌrel] *s* monorail *m*

monosyllable [ˈmɑnəˌsɪləbəl] *s* monosyllabe *m*

monotheist [ˈmɑnəˌθi·ɪst] *adj* & *s* monothéiste *mf*

monotonous [məˈnɑtənəs] *adj* monotone

monotony [məˈnɑtəni] *s* monotonie *f*

monotype [ˈmɑnəˌtaɪp] *s* monotype *m*; (*machine to set type*) monotype *f*

monoxide [məˈnɑksaɪd] *s* oxyde *m*, e.g., **carbon monoxide** oxyde *m* de carbone

monsignor [mɑnˈsinjər] *s* (*pl* **monsignors** or **monsignori**) [ˌmɑnsiˈnjori]) (eccl) monseigneur *m*

monsoon [mɑnˈsun] *s* mousson *f*

monster [ˈmɑnstər] *adj* & *s* monstre *m*

monstrance [ˈmɑnstrəns] *s* ostensoir *m*

monstrous [ˈmɑnstrəs] *adj* monstrueux

month [mʌnθ] *s* mois *m*

month·ly [ˈmʌnθli] *adj* mensuel ‖ *s* (*pl* **-lies**) revue *f* mensuelle; **monthlies** (coll) règles *fpl* ‖ *adv* mensuellement

monument [ˈmɑnjəmənt] *s* monument *m*

moo [mu] *s* meuglement *m* ‖ *intr* meugler ‖ *interj* meuh! meuh!

mood [mud] *s* humeur *f*, disposition *f*; (gram) mode *m*; **moods** accès *mpl* de mauvaise humeur

mood·y [ˈmudi] *adj* (*comp* **-ier**; *super* **-iest**) d'humeur changeante; (*melancholy*) maussade

moon [mun] *s* lune *f* ‖ *intr*—**to moon about** musarder; (*to daydream about*) rêver à

moon′beam′ *s* rayon *m* de lune

moon′light′ *s* clair *m* de lune ‖ *intr* cumuler

moon′light′ing *s* travail *m* noir

moon′lighting job′ *s* accessoire *m*, deuxième emploi *m*

moon′shine′ *s* clair *m* de lune; (*idle talk*) baliverne *f*; (coll) alcool *m* de contrebande

moon′ shot′ *s* tir *m* à la lune

moor [mur] *s* lande *f*, bruyère *f*; **Moor** Maure *m* ‖ *tr* amarrer ‖ *intr* s'amarrer

Moorish [ˈmurɪʃ] *adj* mauresque

moose [mus] *s* (*pl* **moose**) élan *m* du Canada, orignal *m*; (*European elk*) élan *m*

moot [mut] *adj* discutable

moot′ point′ question *f* discutable

mop [mɑp] *s* balai *m* à franges; (*of hair*) tignasse *f* ‖ *v* (*pret* & *pp* **mopped;** *ger* **mopping**) *tr* nettoyer avec un balai à franges; (*e.g., one's brow*) s'essuyer; **to mop up** (mil) nettoyer

mope [mop] *intr* avoir le cafard

moral [ˈmɔrəl] *adj* moral ‖ *s* (*of a fable*) morale *f*; **morals** mœurs *fpl*

morale [məˈræl] *s* moral *m*

morali·ty [məˈrælɪti] *s* (*pl* **-ties**) moralité *f*

morass [məˈræs] *s* marais *m*

moratori·um [ˌmɔrəˈtɔri·əm] *s* (*pl* **-ums** or **-a** [ə]) moratoire *m*, moratorium *m*

morbid [ˈmɔrbɪd] *adj* morbide

mordacious [mɔrˈdeʃəs] *adj* mordant

mordant [ˈmɔrdənt] *adj* & *s* mordant *m*

more [mɔr] *adj comp* plus de §91; plus nombreux; de plus, e.g., **one minute more** une minute de plus; **more than** plus que; (followed by numeral) plus de ‖ *s* plus *m*; **all the more so** d'autant plus; **what is more** qui plus est; **what more do you need?** que vous faut-il de plus? ‖ *pron indef* plus, davantage ‖ *adv comp* plus §91; davantage; **more and more** de plus en plus; **more or less** plus ou moins; **more than** plus que, davantage que; (followed by numeral) plus de; **neither more nor less** ni plus ni moins; **never more** jamais plus, plus jamais; **no more** ne . . . plus §90; **once more** une fois de plus; **the more . . . the more** (or **the less**) plus . . . plus (or moins)

more·o′ver *adv* de plus, du reste

Moresque [moˈrɛsk] *adj* mauresque

morgue [mɔrg] *s* institut *m* médico-légal, morgue *f*; (journ) archives *fpl*

Mormon [ˈmɔrmən] *adj* & *s* mormon *m*

morning [ˈmɔrnɪŋ] *adj* matinal, du matin ‖ *s* matin *m*; (*time between sunrise and noon*) matinée *f*, matin; **in the morning** le matin; **the morning after** le lendemain matin; (coll) le lendemain de bombe

morn′ing coat′ *s* jaquette *f*

morn′ing-glo′ry *s* (*pl* **-ries**) belle-de-jour *f*

morn′ing sick′ness *s* des nausées *fpl*

morn′ing star′ *s* étoile *f* du matin

Moroccan [məˈrɑkən] *adj* marocain ‖ *s* Marocain *m*

morocco [mə'rɑko] s (leather) maroquin m; **Morocco** le Maroc

moron ['morɑn] s arriéré m; (coll) minus mf, minus habens mf

morose [mə'ros] adj morose

morphine ['mɔrfin] s morphine f

morphology [mɔr'fɑlədʒi] s morphologie f

morrow ['mɔro] s—**on the morrow (of)** le lendemain (de)

Morse' code' [mɔrs] s alphabet m morse

morsel ['mɔrsəl] s morceau m

mortal ['mɔrtəl] adj & s mortel m

mortality [mɔr'tælɪti] s mortalité f

mortar ['mɔrtər] s mortier m

mor'tar·board' s bonnet m carré; (of mason) taloche f

mortgage ['mɔrgɪdʒ] s hypothèque f ‖ tr hypothéquer

mortgagee [,mɔrgɪ'dʒi] s créancier m hypothécaire

mortgagor ['mɔrgɪdʒər] s débiteur m hypothécaire

mortician [mɔr'tɪʃən] s entrepreneur m de pompes funèbres

morti·fy ['mɔrtɪ,faɪ] v (pret & pp -**fied**) tr mortifier

mortise ['mɔrtɪs] s mortaise f ‖ tr mortaiser

mortuar·y ['mɔrtʃu,ɛri] adj mortuaire ‖ s (pl -**ies**) morgue f; chapelle f mortuaire

mosaic [mo'ze·ɪk] adj & s mosaïque f

Moscow ['mɑskaʊ] s Moscou m

Moses ['moziz] s Moïse m

Mos·lem ['mɑzləm] adj & s var of **Muslim**

mosque [mɑsk] s mosquée f

mosqui·to [məs'kito] s (pl -**toes** or -**tos**) moustique m

mosqui'to control' s démoustication f

mosqui'to net' s moustiquaire f

moss [mɔs] s mousse f

moss·y ['mɔsi] adj (comp -**ier**; super -**iest**) moussu

most [most] adj super (le) plus de §91, (la) plupart de; **for the most part** pour la plupart ‖ s (le) plus, (la) plupart; **at the most** au plus, tout au plus; **most of** la plupart de; **to make the most of** tirer le meilleur parti possible de ‖ pron indef la plupart ‖ adv super (le) plus §91, e.g., **what I like (the) most** ce que j'aime le plus; **the** (or **his, etc.) most** + adj le (or son, etc.) plus + adj ‖ adv très, bien, fort, des plus

mostly ['mostli] adv pour la plupart, principalement

motel [mo'tɛl] s motel m

moth [mɔθ] s teigne f, papillon m nocturne; (clothes moth) mite f

moth'ball' s boule f antimite, boule de naphtaline

moth-eaten ['mɔθ,itən] adj mité

mother ['mʌðər] s mère f ‖ tr servir de mère à; (to coddle) dorloter

moth'er coun'try s mère patrie f

Moth'er Goos'e's Nurs'ery Rhymes' spl les Contes de ma mère l'oie

moth'er·hood' s maternité f

mothering ['mʌðərɪŋ] s maternage m

moth'er-in-law' s (pl **mothers-in-law**) belle-mère f

motherless ['mʌðərlɪs] adj orphelin de mère

motherly ['mʌðərli] adj maternel

mother-of-pearl ['mʌðərəv'pʌrl] adj de nacre, en nacre ‖ s nacre f

Moth'er's Day' s fête f des mères

moth'er supe'rior s mère f supérieure

moth'er tongue' s langue f maternelle

moth'er wit' s bon sens m, esprit m

moth' hole' s trou m de mite

moth'proof' adj antimite ‖ tr rendre antimite

moth·y ['mɔθi] adj (comp -**ier**; super -**iest**) mité, plein de mites

motif [mo'tif] s motif m

motion ['moʃən] s mouvement m; (gesture) geste m; (in a deliberative assembly) motion f, proposition f ‖ intr—**to motion to** faire signe à

motionless ['moʃənlɪs] adj immobile

mo'tion pic'ture s film m; **motion pictures** cinéma m

mo'tion-pic'ture adj cinématographique

mo'tion-pic'ture the'ater s cinéma m

motivate ['motɪ,vet] tr animer, inciter, pousser; (to provide with a motive) motiver

motive ['motɪv] adj moteur ‖ s mobile m, motif m

mo'tive pow'er s force f motrice

motley ['mɑtli] adj bigarré; (mixed) mélangé

motor ['motər] adj & s moteur m ‖ intr aller en voiture

mo'tor·bike' s vélomoteur m

mo'tor·boat' s canot m automobile

mo'tor·bus' s autocar m

motorcade ['motər,ked] s défilé m de voitures

mo'tor·car' s automobile f

mo'tor·cy'cle s moto f

motorist ['motərɪst] s automobiliste mf

motorize ['motə,raɪz] tr motoriser

mo'tor launch' s chaloupe f à moteur

mo'tor·man s (pl -**men**) conducteur m, wattman m

mo'tor pool' s parc m automobile

mo'tor scoot'er s scooter m

mo'tor ship' s navire m à moteurs

mo'tor truck' s camion m automobile

mo'tor ve'hicle s véhicule m automobile

mottle ['mɑtəl] tr marbrer, tacheter

mot·to ['mɑto] s (pl -**toes** or -**tos**) devise f

mound [maʊnd] s monticule m

mount [maʊnt] s montage m; (hill, mountain) mont m; (horse for riding) monture f ‖ tr & intr monter

mountain ['maʊntən] s montagne f

moun'tain climb'ing s alpinisme m

mountaineer [,maʊntə'nɪr] s montagnard m; (climber) alpiniste mf

mountainous ['maʊntənəs] adj montagneux

moun'tain range' s chaîne f de montagnes

mountebank ['maʊntɪ,bæŋk] s saltimbanque mf

mounting ['maʊntɪŋ] s montage m

mourn [morn] *tr* & *intr* pleurer

mourner [ˈmornər] *s* affligé *m*; *(woman hired as mourner)* pleureuse *f*; pénitent *m*; **mourners** *(funeral procession)* cortège *m* funèbre, deuil *m*

mourn'er's bench' *s* banc *m* des pénitents

mournful [ˈmornfəl] *adj* lugubre

mourning [ˈmornɪŋ] *s* deuil *m*

mouse [maʊs] *s* *(pl* **mice** [maɪs]) souris *f*

mouse'hole' *s* trou *m* de souris

mouser [ˈmaʊzər] *s* souricier *m*

mouse'trap' *s* souricière *f*

moustache [məsˈtæʃ] *s* moustache *f*

mouth [maʊθ] *s* *(pl* **mouths** [maʊðz]) bouche *f*; *(of gun; of, e.g., wolf)* gueule *f*; *(of river)* embouchure *f*; **by mouth** par voie buccale; **to make s.o.'s mouth water** faire venir l'eau à la bouche à qn

mouthful [ˈmaʊθ,fʊl] *s* bouchée *f*

mouth' or'gan *s* harmonica *m*

mouth'piece' *s* embouchure *f*; *(person)* porte-parole *m*

mouth'-to-mouth' resus'cita'tion *s* méthode *f* insufflatoire bouche à bouche

mouth'wash' *s* rince-bouche *m*, eau *f* dentifrice

movable [ˈmuvəbəl] *adj* mobile

move [muv] *s* mouvement *m*; *(from one house to another)* déménagement *m*; *(player's turn)* tour *m*; *(in chess and checkers)* coup *m*; *(maneuver)* démarche *f*; **knight's move** marche *f* du cavalier; **on the move** en mouvement ‖ *tr* remuer; *(to excite the feelings of)* émouvoir; **to move that** (parl) proposer que; **to move up** *(a date)* avancer ‖ *intr* remuer; *(to stir)* se remuer; *(said of traffic, crowd, etc.)* circuler; *(e.g., to another city)* déménager; **don't move!** ne bougez pas!; **to move away** or **off** s'éloigner; **to move back** reculer; **to move in** emménager

movement [ˈmuvmənt] *s* mouvement *m*

movie [ˈmuvi] *s* (coll) film *m*; **movies** (coll) cinéma *m*

mov'ie cam'era *s* caméra *f*

movie-goer [ˈmuvi,go·ər] *s* (coll) amateur *m* de cinéma

mov'ie house' *s* (coll) cinéma *m*, salle *f* de spectacles

moving [ˈmuvɪŋ] *adj* mouvant, en marche; *(touching)* émouvant; *(force)* moteur ‖ *s* mouvement *m*; *(from one house to another)* déménagement *m*

mov'ing pic'ture *s* film *m*; **moving pictures** cinéma *m*

mov'ing-pic'ture the'ater *s* cinéma *m*

mov'ing side'walk *s* trottoir *m* roulant

mov'ing spir'it *s* âme *f*

mov'ing stair'way *s* escalier *m* mécanique, escalier roulant

mov'ing van' *s* voiture *f* de déménagement, camion *m* de déménagement

mow [mo] *v* *(pret* **mowed**; *pp* **mowed** or **mown**) *tr* faucher; *(a lawn)* tondre; **to mow down** faucher

mower [ˈmo·ər] *s* faucheur *m*; (mach) faucheuse *f*; *(for lawns)* (mach) tondeuse *f*

m.p.h. [ˈɛmˈpiˈetʃ] *spl* (letterword) **(miles per hour—***six tenths of a mile equaling approximately one kilometer)* km/h

Mr. [ˈmɪstər] *s* Monsieur *m*, M.

Mrs. [ˈmɪsɪz] *s* Madame *f*, Mme

much [mʌtʃ] *adj* beaucoup de, e.g., **much time** beaucoup de temps; bien de + *art*, e.g., **much trouble** bien du mal ‖ *pron indef* beaucoup; **too much** trop ‖ *adv* beaucoup, bien §91; **however much** pour autant que; **how much** combien; **much less** encore moins; **too much** trop; **very much** beaucoup

mucilage [ˈmjusɪlɪdʒ] *s* colle *f* de bureau; *(gummy secretion in plants)* mucilage *m*

muck [mʌk] *s* fange *f*

muck'rake' *intr* (coll) dévoiler des scandales

mucous [ˈmjukəs] *adj* muqueux

mu'cous lin'ing *s* (anat) muqueuse *f*

mucus [ˈmjukəs] *s* mucus *m*, mucosité *f*

mud [mʌd] *s* boue *f*; **to sling mud at** couvrir de boue

muddle [ˈmʌdəl] *s* confusion *f*, fouillis *m* ‖ *tr* embrouiller ‖ *intr*—**to muddle through** se débrouiller

mud'dle·head' *s* brouillon *m*

mud·dy [ˈmʌdi] *adj* *(comp* **-dier**; *super* **-diest**) boueux; *(clothes)* crotté ‖ *v* *(pret* & *pp* **-died**) *tr* salir; *(clothes)* crotter; *(a liquid)* troubler; (fig) embrouiller

mud'guard' *s* garde-boue *m*

mud'hole' *s* bourbier *m*

mudslinger [ˈmʌd,slɪŋər] *s* (fig) calomniateur *m*

muff [mʌf] *s* manchon *m*; *(failure)* coup *m* raté ‖ *tr* rater, louper

muffin [ˈmʌfɪn] *s* petit pain *m* rond, muffin *m*

muffle [ˈmʌfəl] *tr* *(a sound)* assourdir; *(the face)* emmitoufler

muffler [ˈmʌflər] *s* *(scarf)* cache-nez *m*; *(aut)* pot *m* d'échappement, silencieux *m*

mufti [ˈmʌfti] *s* vêtement *m* civil; **in mufti** en civil, en pékin, en bourgeois

mug [mʌg] *s* timbale *f*, gobelet *m*; *(tankard)* chope *f*; (slang) gueule *f*, museau *m* ‖ *v* *(pret* & *pp* **mugged**; *ger* **mugging**) *tr* *(e.g., a suspect)* (slang) photographier; *(a victim)* (slang) saisir à la gorge ‖ *intr* (slang) faire des grimaces

mugger [ˈmʌgər] *s* agresseur *m*

mug·gy [ˈmʌgi] *adj* *(comp* **-gier**; *super* **-giest**) lourd, étouffant

mulat·to [məˈlæto] *s* *(pl* **-toes**) mulâtre *m*

mulber·ry [ˈmʌl,bɛri] *s* *(pl* **-ries**) mûre *f*; *(tree)* mûrier *m*

mulct [mʌlkt] *tr* *(a person)* priver, dépouiller; *(money)* carotter, extorquer

mule [mjul] *s* *(female mule; slipper)* mule *f*; *(male mule)* mulet *m*

muleteer [,mjulə'tɪr] *s* muletier *m*

mulish [ˈmjulɪʃ] *adj* têtu, entêté

mull [mʌl] *tr* chauffer avec des épices; *(to muddle)* embrouiller ‖ *intr*—**to mull over** réflécher sur, remâcher

mullion [ˈmʌljən] *s* meneau *m*

multigraph ['mʌltɪ,græf] *s* (trademark) ronéo *f* ‖ *tr* ronéotyper, polycopier
multilateral [,mʌltɪ'lætərəl] *adj* multilatéral
multinational [,mʌltɪ'næʃənəl] *adj* multinational ‖ **multinationals** *spl* (*corporations*) mégagroupes *mpl* mondiaux
multiple ['mʌltɪpəl] *adj & s* multiple *m*
mul'tiple sclero'sis *s* (pathol) sclérose *f* en plaques
multiplici·ty [,mʌltɪ'plɪsɪti] *s* (*pl* -ties) multiplicité *f*
multi·ply ['mʌltɪ,plaɪ] *v* (*pret & pp* -plied) *tr* multiplier ‖ *intr* se multiplier
multiprocessing [,mʌltɪ'prɑsɛsɪŋ] *s* (comp) multitraitement *m*
multiprocessor [,mʌltɪ'prɑsɛsər] *s* (comp) multiprocesseur *m*
multitude ['mʌltɪ,t(j)ud] *s* multitude *f*
mum [mʌm] *adj* silencieux; **mum's the word!** motus!, bouche cousue!; **to keep mum about** ne souffler mot de
mumble ['mʌmbəl] *tr & intr* marmotter
mummer·y ['mʌməri] *s* (*pl* -ies) momerie *f*
mum·my ['mʌmi] *s* (*pl* -mies) momie *f*; (slang) maman *f*
mumps [mʌmps] *s* oreillons *mpl*
munch [mʌntʃ] *tr* mâchonner
mundane ['mʌnden] *adj* mondain
municipal [mju'nɪsɪpəl] *adj* municipal
municipali·ty [mju,nɪsɪ'pælɪti] *s* (*pl* -ties) municipalité *f*
munificent [mju'nɪfɪsənt] *adj* munificent
munition [mju'nɪʃən] *s* munition *f* ‖ *tr* approvisionner de munitions
mural ['mjurəl] *adj* mural ‖ *s* peinture *f* murale
murder ['mʌrdər] *s* assassinat *m*, meurtre *m* ‖ *tr* assassiner; (*a language, proper names, etc.*) (coll) estropier, écorcher
murderer ['mʌrdərər] *s* meurtrier *m*, assassin *m*
murderess ['mʌrdərɪs] *s* meurtrière *f*
murderous ['mʌrdərəs] *adj* meurtrier
murk·y ['mʌrki] *adj* (*comp* -ier; *super* -iest) ténébreux, nébuleux
murmur ['mʌrmər] *s* murmure *m* ‖ *tr & intr* murmurer
Mur'phy bed' *s* (trademark) lit *m* escamotable
muscle ['mʌsəl] *s* muscle *m*
muscular ['mʌskjələr] *adj* musclé, musculeux; (*system, tissue, etc.*) musculaire
muse [mjuz] *s* muse *f*; **the Muses** les Muses ‖ *intr* méditer; **to muse on** méditer
museum [mju'zi·əm] *s* musée *m*
muse'um piece' *s* pièce *f* de musée
mush [mʌʃ] *s* bouillie *f*; (coll) sentimentalité *f* de guimauve
mush'room' *s* champignon *m* ‖ *intr* pousser comme un champignon
mush'room cloud' *s* champignon *m* atomique
mush·y ['mʌʃi] *adj* (*comp* -ier; *super* -iest) mou; (*ground*) détrempé; (coll) à la guimauve, sentimental

music ['mjuzɪk] *s* musique *f*; **to face the music** (coll) affronter les opposants; **to set to music** mettre en musique
musical ['mjuzɪkəl] *adj* musical
mu'sical com'edy *s* comédie *f* musicale
musicale [,mjuzɪ'kæl] *s* soirée *f* musicale; matinée *f* musicale
mu'sic box' *s* boîte *f* à musique
mu'sic cab'inet *s* casier *m* à musique
mu'sic hall' *s* salle *f* de musique; (Brit) music-hall *m*
musician [mju'zɪʃən] *s* musicien *m*
mu'sic lov'er *s* mélomane *mf*
musicology [,mjuzɪ'kɑlədʒi] *s* musicologie *f*
mu'sic rack' or **mu'sic stand'** *s* pupitre *m* à musique
musk [mʌsk] *s* musc *m*
musk' deer' *s* porte-musc *m*
musketeer [,mʌskɪ'tɪr] *s* mousquetaire *m*
musk'mel'on *s* melon *m*; cantaloup *m*
musk'rat' *s* rat *m* musqué, ondatra *m*
mus·lim ['mʌzlɪm] *adj* musulman ‖ *s* (*pl* -lims or -lim) musulman *m*
muslin ['mʌzlɪn] *s* mousseline *f*
muss [mʌs] *tr* (*the hair*) ébouriffer; (*the clothing*) froisser
muss·y ['mʌsi] *adj* (*comp* -ier; *super* -iest) en désordre, froissé
must [mʌst] *s* moût *m*; nécessité *f* absolue ‖ *aux* used to express 1) necessity, e.g., **he must go away** il doit s'en aller; 2) conjecture, e.g., **he must be ill** il doit être malade; **he must have been ill** il a dû être malade
mustache [məs'tæʃ] *s* moustache *f*
mustard ['mʌstərd] *s* moutarde *f*
mus'tard plas'ter *s* sinapisme *m*
muster ['mʌstər] *s* rassemblement *m*; (mil) revue *f*; **to pass muster** être porté à l'appel; (fig) être acceptable ‖ *tr* rassembler; **to muster in** enrôler; **to muster out** démobiliser; **to muster up courage** prendre son courage à deux mains
mus'ter roll' *s* feuille *f* d'appel
mus·ty ['mʌsti] *adj* (*comp* -tier; *super* -tiest) (*moldy*) moist; (*stale*) renfermé; (*antiquated*) désuet
mutation [mju'teʃən] *s* mutation *f*
mute [mjut] *adj* muet ‖ *s* muet *m*; (mus) sourdine *f* ‖ *tr* amortir; (mus) mettre une sourdine à
mutilate ['mjutɪ,let] *tr* mutiler
mutineer [,mjutɪ'nɪr] *s* mutin *m*
mutinous ['mjutɪnəs] *adj* mutiné
muti·ny ['mjutɪni] *s* (*pl* -nies) mutinerie *f* ‖ *v* (*pret & pp* -nied) *intr* se mutiner
mutt [mʌt] *s* (*dog*) (slang) cabot *m*, clebs *m*; (*person*) (slang) nigaud *m*
mutter ['mʌtər] *tr & intr* marmonner
mutton ['mʌtən] *s* mouton *m*
mut'ton·chop' *s* côtelette *f* de mouton; **muttonchops** favoris *mpl* en côtelette
mutual ['mjutʃu·əl] *adj* mutuel
mu'tual aid' *s* entraide *f*
mu'tual fund' *s* société *f* d'investissement à capital variable

mu′tual insur′ance com′pany s mutuelle f

muzzle [ˈmʌzəl] s (projecting part of head of animal) museau m; (device to keep animal from biting) muselière f; (of firearm) gueule f ‖ tr museler

my [maɪ] adj poss mon §88

myriad [ˈmɪrɪ·əd] adj innombrable ‖ s myriade f

myrrh [mɪr] s myrrhe f

myrtle [ˈmʌrtəl] s myrte m; (periwinkle) pervenche f

my·self′ pron pers moi §85; moi-même §86; me §87

mysterious [mɪsˈtɪrɪ·əs] adj mystérieux

myster·y [ˈmɪstəri] s (pl -ies) mystère m

mystic [ˈmɪstɪk] adj & s mystique mf

mystical [ˈmɪstɪkəl] adj mystique

mysticism [ˈmɪstɪˌsɪzəm] s mysticisme m

mystification [ˌmɪstɪfɪˈkeʃən] s mystification f

mysti·fy [ˈmɪstɪˌfaɪ] v (pret & pp -fied) tr mystifier

myth [mɪθ] s mythe m

mythical [ˈmɪθɪkəl] adj mythique

mythological [ˌmɪθəˈlɑdʒɪkəl] adj mythologique

mytholo·gy [mɪˈθɑlədʒi] s (pl -gies) mythologie f

N

N, n [ɛn] s XIVᵉ lettre de l'alphabet

nab [næb] v (pret & pp nabbed; ger nabbing) tr (slang) happer; (to arrest) (slang) pincer, harponner

nag [næg] s bidet m ‖ v (pret & pp nagged; ger nagging) tr & intr gronder constamment; **to nag at** gronder constamment

nail [nel] s (of finger) ongle m; (to be hammered) clou m; **to bite one's nails** se ronger les ongles; **to hit the nail on the head** mettre le doigt dessus, frapper juste ‖ tr clouer; (a lie) mettre à découvert; (coll) saisir, attraper

nail′ brush′ s brosse f à ongles

nail′ clip′pers spl coupe-ongles m

nail′ file′ s lime f à ongles

nail′ pol′ish s vernis m à ongles

nail′ scis′sors s & spl ciseaux mpl à ongles

nail′ set′ s chasse-clou m

naïve [nɑˈiv] adj naïf

naked [ˈnekɪd] adj nu; **to be naked** être au poil; **to strip naked** se mettre tout nu; mettre tout nu; **with the naked eye** à l'œil nu

namby-pamby [ˈnæmbiˈpæmbi] adj minaudier

name [nem] s nom m; (reputation) renom m; **by name** de nom; **by the name of** sous le nom de; **to call names** traiter de tous les noms; **what is your name?** comment vous appelez-vous? ‖ tr nommer; (a price) fixer, indiquer

name′ brand′ s image f de marque

name′ day′ s fête f

nameless [ˈnemlɪs] adj sans nom, anonyme; (horrid) odieux

namely [ˈnemli] adv à savoir, nommément

name′sake′ s homonyme m

name′ tag′ s insigne m d'identité, barrette f

nan·ny [ˈnæni] s (pl -nies) nounou f

nan′ny goat′ s (coll) chèvre f, bique f

nap [næp] s (short sleep) somme m, sieste f; (of cloth) poil m, duvet m; **to take a nap** faire un petit somme ‖ v (pret & pp napped; ger napping) intr faire un somme; manquer de vigilance; **to catch napping** prendre au dépourvu

napalm [ˈnerpɑm] s (mil) napalm m

nape [nep] s nuque f

naphtha [ˈnæfθə] s naphte m

napkin [ˈnæpkɪn] s serviette f

nap′kin ring′ s rond m de serviette

Napoleonic [nəˌpolɪˈɑnɪk] adj napoléonien

narcissus [nɑrˈsɪsəs] s narcisse m; **Narcissus** Narcisse

narcotic [nɑrˈkɑtɪk] adj & s narcotique m

narrate [næˈret] tr narrer, raconter

narration [næˈreʃən] s narration f

narrative [ˈnærətɪv] adj narratif ‖ s narration f, récit m

narrator [næˈretər] s narrateur m

narrow [ˈnæro] adj étroit; (e.g., margin of votes) faible ‖ **narrows** spl détroit m, goulet m ‖ tr rétrécir ‖ intr se rétrécir

nar′row escape′ s—**it was a narrow escape** il était moins une; **to have a narrow escape** l'échapper belle

nar′row gauge′ s voie f étroite

nar′row-mind′ed adj à l'esprit étroit, intolérant

nasal [ˈnezəl] adj nasal; (sound, voice) nasillard ‖ s (phonet) nasale f

nasalize [ˈnezəˌlaɪz] tr & intr nasaliser

nasturtium [nəˈstɑrʃəm] s capucine f

nas·ty [ˈnæsti] adj (comp -tier; super -tiest) mauvais, sale, dégoûtant; féroce, farouche; désagréable

nation [ˈneʃən] s nation f

national [ˈnæʃənəl] adj national ‖ s national m, ressortissant m

na′tional an′them s hymne m national

nationalism [ˈnæʃənəˌlɪzəm] s nationalisme m

nationali·ty [ˌnæʃənˈælɪti] s (pl -ties) nationalité f

nationalize [ˈnæʃənəˌlaɪz] tr nationaliser, étatiser, fonctionnariser

na′tion·wide′ adj de toute la nation

native [ˈnetɪv] *adj* natif; (*land, language*) natal; **native of** originaire de ‖ *s* natif *m*; (*original inhabitant*) naturel *m*, indigène *mf*, autochtone *mf*

na′tive land′ *s* pays *m* natal

nativi·ty [nəˈtɪvɪti] *s* (*pl* **-ties**) naissance *f*; (astrol) nativité *f*; **Nativity** Nativité *f*

NATO [ˈneto] *s* (acronym) (**North Atlantic Treaty Organization**) l'O.T.A.N. *f*, l'OTAN *f*

nat·ty [ˈnæti] *adj* (*comp* **-tier**; *super* **-tiest**) coquet, élégant, soigné

natural [ˈnætʃərəl] *adj* naturel ‖ *s* (mus) bécarre *m*; (mus) touche *f* blanche; **a natural** (coll) juste ce qu'il faut

naturalism [ˈnætʃərə‚lɪzəm] *s* naturalisme *m*

naturalist [ˈnætʃərəlɪst] *s* naturaliste *mf*

naturalization [‚nætʃərəlɪˈzeʃən] *s* naturalisation *f*

naturaliza′tion pa′pers *spl* déclaration *f* de naturalisation

naturalize [ˈnætʃərə‚laɪz] *tr* naturaliser

nature [ˈnetʃər] *s* nature *f*

naught [nɔt] *s* zéro *m*; rien *m*; **to come to naught** n'aboutir à rien

naugh·ty [ˈnɔti] *adj* (*comp* **-tier**; *super* **-tiest**) méchant, vilain; (*story*) risqué

nausea [ˈnɔʃɪ·ə], [ˈnɔsɪ·ə] *s* nausée *f*

nauseate [ˈnɔʃɪ‚et], [ˈnɔsɪ‚et] *tr* donner la nausée à ‖ *intr* avoir des nausées

nauseating [ˈnɔʃɪ‚etɪŋ], [ˈnɔsɪ‚etɪŋ] *adj* nauséabond

nauseous [ˈnɔʃɪ·əs], [ˈnɔsɪ·əs] *adj* nauséeux

nautical [ˈnɔtɪkəl] *adj* nautique; naval, marin

naval [ˈnevəl] *adj* naval

na′val acad′emy *s* école *f* navale

na′val of′ficer *s* officier *m* de marine

na′val sta′tion *s* station *f* navale

nave [nev] *s* (*of a church*) nef *f*, vaisseau *m*; (*of a wheel*) moyeu *m*

navel [ˈnevəl] *s* nombril *m*

na′vel or′ange *s* orange *f* navel

navigable [ˈnævɪɡəbəl] *adj* (*river*) navigable; (*aircraft*) dirigeable; (*ship*) bon marcheur

navigate [ˈnævɪ‚ɡet] *tr* gouverner, conduire; (*the sea*) naviguer sur ‖ *intr* naviguer

navigation [‚nævɪˈɡeʃən] *s* navigation *f*

navigator [ˈnævɪ‚ɡetər] *s* navigateur *m*

na·vy [ˈnevi] *adj* bleu marine ‖ *s* (*pl* **-vies**) marine *f* militaire, marine de guerre; (*color*) bleu *m* marine

na′vy bean′ *s* haricot *m* blanc

na′vy blue′ *s* bleu *m* marine

na′vy yard′ *s* chantier *m* naval

nay [ne] *adv* non; voire, même ‖ *s* non *m*; (parl) vote *m* négatif

Nazarene [‚næzəˈrin] *adj* nazaréen ‖ *s* (*person*) Nazaréen *m*

Nazi [ˈnatsi] *adj* & *s* nazi *m*

n.d. *abbr* (**no date**) s.d.

Ne′apol′itan ice′ cream′ [‚ni·əˈpɑlɪtən] *s* glace *f* panachée

neap′ tide′ [nip] *s* morte-eau *f*

near [nɪr] *adj* proche, prochain; **near at hand** tout près; **near side** (*of horse*) côté *m* de montoir ‖ *adv* près, de près; (*nearly*) presque; **to come near** s'approcher ‖ *prep* près de ‖ *tr* s'approcher de

near′by′ *adj* proche ‖ *adv* tout près

Near′ East′ *s*—**the Near East** le Proche Orient

nearly [ˈnɪrli] *adv* presque, de près; faillir, manquer de, e.g., **I nearly fell** j'ai failli tomber

near′ miss′ *s* (*near collision*) (aer) collision *f* manquée, quasi-collision *f*

near′-sight′ed *adj* myope

near′-sight′edness *s* myopie *f*

neat [nit] *adj* soigné, rangé; concis; (*clever*) adroit; (*liquor*) nature; (slang) chouette

neat′s′-foot oil′ *s* huile *f* de pied de bœuf

nebu·la [ˈnɛbjələ] *s* (*pl* **-lae** [‚li] or **-las**) nébuleuse *f*

nebulous [ˈnɛbjələs] *adj* nébuleux

necessarily [‚nɛsɪˈsɛrɪli] *adv* nécessairement, forcément

necessary [ˈnɛsɪ‚sɛri] *adj* nécessaire; **if necessary** si besoin est

necessitate [nɪˈsɛsɪ‚tet] *tr* nécessiter, exiger

necessi·ty [nɪˈsɛsɪti] *s* (*pl* **-ties**) nécessité *f*

neck [nɛk] *s* cou *m*; (*of bottle*) col *m*, goulot *m*; (*of land*) cap *m*; (*of tooth*) collet *m*; collet; (*of violin*) manche *m*, (*strait*) étroit *m*; **neck and neck** manche à manche; **to break one's neck** (coll) se rompre le cou; **to stick one's neck out** prêter le flanc; **to win by a neck** gagner par une encolure ‖ *intr* (slang) se peloter

neck′band′ *s* tour *m* de cou

neckerchief [ˈnɛkərtʃɪf] *s* foulard *m*

necking [ˈnɛkɪŋ] *s* (slang) pelotage *m*, bécotage *m*

necklace [ˈnɛklɪs] *s* collier *m*

neck′piece′ *s* col *m* de fourrure

neck′tie′ *s* cravate *f*

neck′tie pin′ *s* épingle *f* de cravate

necrolo·gy [nɛˈkrɑlədʒi] *s* (*pl* **-gies**) nécrologie *f*

nectar [ˈnɛktər] *s* nectar *m*

nectarine [‚nɛktəˈrin] *s* brugnon *m*

nee [ne] *adj* née

need [nid] *s* besoin *m*; (*want, poverty*) besoin, indigence *f*, nécessité *f*; **if need be** au besoin, s'il le faut ‖ *tr* avoir besoin de, falloir, e.g., **he needs money** il a besoin d'argent, il lui faut de l'argent; demander, e.g., **the motor needs oil** le moteur demande de l'huile ‖ *aux* devoir

needful [ˈnidfəl] *adj* nécessaire

needle [ˈnidəl] *s* aiguille *f*; **to look for a needle in a haystack** chercher une aiguille dans une botte de foin ‖ *tr* (*to prod*) aiguillonner; (coll) taquiner; (*a drink*) (coll) corser

nee′dle·point′ *s* broderie *f* sur canevas; (*lace*) dentelle *f* à l'aiguille

needless [ˈnidlɪs] *adj* inutile

nee′dle·work′ *s* ouvrage *m* à l'aiguille

need·y [ˈnidɪ] *adj* (*comp* **-ier**; *super* **-iest**) nécessiteux ‖ *s*—**the needy** les nécessiteux

ne'er-do-well [ˈnɛrdu,wɛl] *adj* propre à rien ‖ *s* vaurien *m*

nefarious [nɪˈfɛrɪ·əs] *adj* scélérat

negate [nɪˈget] *tr* invalider; nier

negation [nɪˈgeʃən] *s* négation *f*

negative [ˈnɛgətɪv] *adj* négatif ‖ *s* (*opinion*) négative *f*; (gram) négation *f*; (phot) négatif *m*

neglect [nɪˈglɛkt] *s* négligence *f* ‖ *tr* négliger; **to neglect to** négliger de

négligée or **negligee** [,nɛglɪˈʒe] *s* négligé *m*, robe *f* de chambre

negligence [ˈnɛglɪdʒəns] *s* négligence *f*

negligent [ˈnɛglɪdʒənt] *adj* négligent

negligible [ˈnɛglɪdʒɪbəl] *adj* négligeable

negotiable [nɪˈgoʃɪ·əbəl] *adj* négociable

negotiate [nɪˈgoʃɪ·et] *tr* & *intr* négocier

negotiation [nɪ,goʃɪˈeʃən] *s* négociation *f*

negotiator [nɪ,goʃɪ,etər] *s* négociateur *m*

Ne·gro [ˈnigro] *adj* (usually offensive) noir, nègre ‖ *s* (*pl* **-groes**) (usually offensive) noir *m*, nègre *m*

neigh [ne] *s* hennissement *m* ‖ *intr* hennir

neighbor [ˈnebər] *adj* voisin ‖ *s* voisin *m*; (fig) prochain *m* ‖ *tr* avoisiner ‖ *intr* être voisin

neigh'bor·hood' *s* voisinage *m*; **in the neighborhood of** aux environs de; (*approximately, about*) (coll) environ

neighborliness [ˈnebərlɪnɪs] *s* bon voisinage *m*

neighborly [ˈnebərlɪ] *adj* bon voisin

neither [ˈniðər], [ˈnaɪðər] *adj indef* ni, e.g., **neither one of us** ni l'un ni l'autre ‖ *pron indef* ni, e.g., **neither** ni l'un ni l'autre ‖ *conj* ni; ni . . . non plus, e.g., **neither do I** ni moi non plus; **neither . . . nor** ni . . . ni

neme·sis [ˈnɛmɪsɪs] *s* (*pl* **-ses** [,sɪz]) juste châtiment *m*; **Nemesis** Némésis *f*

neologism [niˈɑlə,dʒɪzəm] *s* néologisme *m*

neon [ˈni·ɑn] *s* néon *m*

ne'on lamp' *s* lampe *f* au néon

ne'on sign' *s* réclame *f* lumineuse

neophyte [ˈni·ə,faɪt] *s* néophyte *mf*

nephew [ˈnɛfju], [ˈnɛvju] *s* neveu *m*

neptunium [nɛpˈt(j)unɪ·əm] *s* neptunium *m*

Nero [ˈnɪro] *s* Néron *m*

nerve [nʌrv] *adj* nerveux ‖ *s* nerf *m*; (*self-confidence*) assurance *f*, courage *m*; **to get on s.o.'s nerves** porter sur les nerfs à qn; **to have a lot of nerve** (*to have a lot of cheek*) avoir du toupet; **to have nerves of steel** avoir du nerf; **to lose one's nerve** avoir le trac

nerve' cen'ter *s* (anat) centre *m* nerveux; (fig) centre *m* opérations, nœud *m* vital

nerve' end'ing *s* terminaison *f* nerveuse

nerve' gas' *s* gaz *m* asphyxiant

nerve'-rack'ing [ˈrækɪŋ] *adj* énervant, agaçant

nervous [ˈnʌrvəs] *adj* nerveux

ner'vous break'down *s* épuisement *m* nerveux, dépression *f* nerveuse

nerv·y [ˈnʌrvɪ] *adj* (*comp* **-ier**; *super* **-iest**) nerveux, musclé; (coll) audacieux, culotté; (slang) dévergondé

nest [nɛst] *s* nid *m*; (*set of things fitting together*) jeu *m* ‖ *intr* se nicher

nest' egg' *s* nichet *m*; (fig) boursicot *m*, bas *m* de laine

nestle [ˈnɛsəl] *intr* se blottir, se nicher

nest' of ta'bles *s* table *f* gigogne

net [nɛt] *adj* net ‖ *s* filet *m*; (*for fishing; for catching birds*) nappe *f*; (tex) tulle *m* ‖ *v* (*pret* & *pp* **netted**; *ger* **netting**) *tr* (*a profit*) réaliser

Netherlander [ˈneðər,lændər] *s* Néerlandais *m*

Netherlands [ˈneðərləndz] *s*—**The Netherlands** les Pays-Bas *mpl*

net' prof'it *s* bénéfice *m* net

nettle [ˈnɛtəl] *s* ortie *f* ‖ *tr* piquer au vif

net' weight' *s* poids *m* net

net'work' *s* réseau *m*; (rad, telv) chaîne *f*, réseau

neuralgia [n(j)ʊˈrældʒə] *s* névralgie *f*

neuron [ˈn(j)ʊrɑn] *s* neurone *m*

neuro·sis [n(j)ʊˈrosɪs] *s* (*pl* **-ses** [siz]) névrose *f*

neurotic [n(j)ʊˈrɑtɪk] *adj* & *s* névrosé *m*

neuter [ˈn(j)utər] *adj* & *s* neutre *m*

neutral [ˈn(j)utrəl] *adj* neutre ‖ *s* neutre *m*; (*gear*) point *m* mort

neutrality [n(j)uˈtrælɪtɪ] *s* neutralité *f*

neutralize [ˈn(j)utrə,laɪz] *tr* neutraliser

neutron [ˈn(j)utrɑn] *s* neutron *m*

neu'tron bomb' *s* bombe *f* à neutrons

never [ˈnɛvər] *adv* jamais §90B; ne . . . jamais §90, e.g., **he never talks** il ne parle jamais

nev'er·more' *adv* ne . . . plus jamais ‖ *interj* jamais plus!, plus jamais!

nev'er·the·less' *adv* néanmoins

new [n(j)u] *adj* (*unused*) neuf; (*other, additional, different*) nouveau (before noun); (*recent*) nouveau (after noun); (*inexperienced*) novice; (*wine*) jeune; **what's new?** quoi de nouveau?, quoi de neuf?

new'born' *adj* nouveau-né

new'born child' *s* nouveau-né *m*

New'cas'tle *s*—**to carry coals to Newcastle** porter de l'eau à la rivière

newcomer [ˈn(j)u,kʌmər] *s* nouveau venu *m*

New' Cov'enant *s* (Bib) nouvelle alliance *f*

newel [ˈn(j)u·əl] *s* (*of winding stairs*) noyau *m*; (*post at end of stair rail*) pilastre *m*

New' Eng'land *s* Nouvelle-Angleterre *f*; la Nouvelle-Angleterre

newfangled [ˈn(j)u,fæŋgəld] *adj* à la dernière mode, du dernier cri

Newfoundland [ˈn(j)ufənd,lænd] *s* Terre-Neuve *f*; **in** or **to Newfoundland** à Terre-Neuve ‖ [n(j)uˈfaʊndlənd] *s* (*dog*) terre-neuve *m*

newly [ˈn(j)ulɪ] *adv* nouvellement

new'ly·wed' *s* nouveau marié *m*

new' moon' *s* nouvelle lune *f*

newness [ˈn(j)unɪs] *s* nouveauté *f*

New' Or'leans [ˈɔrlɪ·ənz] *s* la Nouvelle-Orléans

news [n(j)uz] *s* nouvelles *fpl;* **a news item** un fait-divers; **a piece of news** une nouvelle

news′ a′gency *s* agence *f* d'information, agence de presse; (com) agence à journaux

news′beat′ *s* exclusivité *f*

news′boy′ *s* vendeur *m* de journaux

news′ bul′letin *s* bulletin *m* d'actualités

news′ cam′era·man *s* reporter *m* d'images

news′cast′ *s* journal *m* parlé; journal télévisé

news′cast′er *s* reporter *m* de la radio

news′ con′ference *s* conférence *f* de presse

news′ cov′erage *s* reportage *m*

news′deal′er *s* marchand *m* de journaux

news′ ed′itor *s* rédacteur *m* des actualités, rédacteur de la chronique du jour

news′let′ter *s* (*of a company, organization, etc.*) bulletin *m* (de . . .) (*de la compagnie, etc.*)

news′man′ *s* (*pl* **-men′**) journaliste *m*; (*dealer*) marchand *m* de journaux

New′ South′ Wales′ *s* la Nouvelle-Galles du Sud

news′pa′per *adj* journalistique ‖ *s* journal *m*

news′paper clip′ping *s* coupure *f* de presse

news′paper·man′ *s* (*pl* **-men′**) journaliste *m*; (*dealer*) marchand *m* de journaux

news′paper rack′ *s* casier *m* à journaux

news′paper route′ *s* tournée *f* de distribution de journaux

news′paper se′rial *s* feuilleton *m*

news′print′ *s* papier *m* journal

news′reel′ *s* actualités *fpl* (filmées)

news′room′ *s* salle *f* de rédaction

news′stand′ *s* kiosque *m*

news′week′ly *s* (*pl* **-lies**) hebdomadaire *m*

news′wor′thy *adj* d'actualité

New′ Tes′tament *s* Nouveau Testament *m*

New′ Year's′ Day′ *s* le jour de l'an, le nouvel an

New′ Year's′ Eve′ *s* la Saint-Sylvestre

New′ Year's′ greet′ings *spl* souhaits *mpl* de nouvel An

New′ Year's′ resolu′tion *s* résolution *f* de nouvel An

New′ York′ [jɔrk] *adj* newyorkais ‖ *s* New York *m*

New′ York′er [′jɔrkər] *s* newyorkais *m*

next [nɛkst] *adj* (*in time*) prochain, suivant; (*in place*) voisin; (*first in the period which follows*) prochain (before noun), e.g., **the next time** la prochaine fois; (*following the present time*) prochain (after noun), e.g., **next week** la semaine prochaine; **next to** à côté de ‖ *adv* après, ensuite; la prochaine fois; **who comes next?** à qui le tour? ‖ *interj* au premier de ces messieurs!, au suivant!

next′-door′ *adj* d'à côté, voisin ‖ **next′-door′** *adv* à côté; **next-door to** à côté de; à côté de chez

next′ of kin′ *s* (*pl* **next of kin**) proche parent *m*

Niag′ara Falls′ [naɪ′ægərə] *s* les chutes *fpl* du Niagara

nib [nɪb] *s* pointe *f*; (*of pen*) bec *m*

nibble [′nɪbəl] *s* grignotement *m*; (*on fish line*) touche *f*; (fig) morceau *m* ‖ *tr & intr* grignoter

nice [naɪs] *adj* agréable, gentil, aimable; (*distinction*) subtil, fin; (*weather*) beau; **nice and . . .** (coll) très; **not nice** (coll) vilain

nicely [′naɪsli] *adv* bien; avec délicatesse

nice·ty [′naɪsəti] *s* (*pl* **-ties**) précision *f*; (*subtlety*) finesse *f*

niche [nɪtʃ] *s* niche *f*; (*job, position*) place *f*, poste *m*

nick [nɪk] *s* (*e.g., on china*) brèche *f*; **in the nick of time** à point nommé, à pic ‖ *tr* ébrécher; (*for money, favors*) (slang) cramponner

nickel [′nɪkəl] *s* (*metal*) nickel *m*; (*coin*) pièce *f* de cinq sous ‖ *tr* nickeler

nick′el plate′ *s* nickelure *f*

nick′el-plate′ *tr* nickeler

nicknack [′nɪk,næk] *s* colifichet *m*

nick′name′ *s* sobriquet *m*, surnom *m* ‖ *tr* donner un sobriquet à, surnommer

nicotine [′nɪkə,tin] *s* nicotine *f*

niece [nis] *s* nièce *f*

nif·ty [′nɪfti] *adj* (*comp* **-tier;** *super* **-tiest**) (slang) coquet, pimpant

niggard [′nɪgərd] *adj & s* avare *mf*

night [naɪt] *s* nuit *f*; (*evening*) soir *m*; **last night** (*night that has just passed*) cette nuit; (*last evening*) hier soir; **night before last** avant-hier soir

night′cap′ *s* bonnet *m* de nuit, casque *m* à mèche; (*drink*) posset *m*

night′ club′ *s* boîte *f* de nuit

night′fall′ *s* tombée *f* de la nuit

night′gown′ *s* chemise *f* de nuit

night′hawk′ *s* noctambule *mf;* (orn) engoulevent *m*

nightingale [′naɪtən,gel] *s* rossignol *m*

night′latch′ *s* serrure *f* à ressort

night′ light′ *s* veilleuse *f*

night′long′ *adj* de toute la nuit ‖ *adv* pendant toute la nuit

nightly [′naɪtli] *adj* nocturne; de chaque nuit ‖ *adv* nocturnement; chaque nuit

night′mare′ *s* cauchemar *m*

nightmarish [′naɪt,mɛrɪʃ] *adj* (coll) cauchemardesque, cauchemardeux

night′owl′ *s* (coll) noctambule *mf*

night′ school′ *s* cours *mpl* du soir

night′shade′ *s* morelle *f*

night′ shift′ *s* équipe *f* de nuit

night′ ta′ble *s* table *f* de chevet

night′ watch′man *s* (*pl* **-men**) veilleur *m* de nuit

nihilism [′naɪ·ɪ,lɪzəm] *s* nihilisme *m*

nil [nɪl] *s* rien *m*

Nile [naɪl] *s* Nil *m*

nimble [′nɪmbəl] *adj* agile, leste; (*mind*) délié

nim·bus [′nɪmbəs] *s* (*pl* **-buses** or **-bi** [baɪ]) nimbe *m*, auréole *f*; (meteo) nimbus *m*

nincompoop [′nɪnkəm,pup] *s* nigaud *m*

nine [naɪn] *adj & pron* neuf ‖ *s* neuf *m*; **nine o'clock** neuf heures

nine'pins' *s* quilles *fpl*

nineteen ['naɪn'tin] *adj, pron, & s* dix-neuf *m*

nineteenth ['naɪn'tinθ] *adj & pron* dix-neuvième (*masc, fem*); **the Nineteenth** dix-neuf, e.g., **John the Nineteenth** Jean dix-neuf ‖ *s* dix-neuvième *m*; **the nineteenth** (*in dates*) le dix-neuf

ninetieth ['naɪntɪ·ɪθ] *adj & pron* quatre-vingt-dixième (*masc, fem*) ‖ *s* quatre-vingt-dixième *m*

nine·ty ['naɪntɪ] *adj & pron* quatre-vingt-dix ‖ *s* (*pl* **-ties**) quatre-vingt-dix *m*

nine'ty-first' *adj & pron* quatre-vingt-onzième (*masc, fem*) ‖ *s* quatre-vingt-onzième *m*

nine'ty-one' *adj, pron, & s* quatre-vingt-onze *m*

ninth [naɪnθ] *adj & pron* neuvième (*masc, fem*); **the Ninth** neuf, e.g., **John the Ninth** Jean neuf ‖ *s* neuvième *m*; **the ninth** (*in dates*) le neuf

nip [nɪp] *s* pincement *m*, petite morsure *f*; (*of cold weather*) morsure; (*of liquor*) goutte *f* ‖ *v* (*pret & pp* **nipped**; *ger* **nipping**) *tr* pincer, donner une petite morsure à; **to nip in the bud** tuer dans l'œuf ‖ *intr* (coll) biberonner, picoler

nipple ['nɪpəl] *s* mamelon *m*; (*of nursing bottle*) tétine *f*; (mach) raccord *m*

nip·py ['nɪpi] *adj* (*comp* **-pier**; *super* **-piest**) piquant; (*cold*) vif; (Brit) leste, rapide

nirvana [nɪr'vanə] *s* le nirvâna

nit [nɪt] *s* pou *m*; (*egg*) lente *f*

nit'pick' *intr* chercher la petite bête

niter ['naɪtər] *s* nitrate *m* de potasse; nitrate de soude

nitrate ['naɪtret] *s* azotate *m*, nitrate *m*; (*fertilizer*) engrais *m* nitraté ‖ *tr* nitrater

nitric ['naɪtrɪk] *adj* azotique, nitrique

nitrogen ['naɪtrədʒən] *s* azote *m*

nitroglycerin [,naɪtrə'glɪsərɪn] *s* nitroglycérine *f*

nitrous ['naɪtrəs] *adj* azoteux

ni'trous ox'ide *s* oxyde *m* azoteux, protoxyde *m* d'azote

nit'wit' *s* (coll) imbécile *mf*

no [no] *adj indef* aucun, nul, pas de §90B; **no admittance** entrée *f* interdite; **no answer** pas de réponse; **no comment!** rien à dire!; **no go** or **no soap** (coll) pas mèche *f*; **no kidding** (coll) blague *f* à part; **no littering** défense *f* de déposer des ordures; **no loitering** vagabondage *m* interdit; **no parking** stationnement *m* interdit; **no place** nulle part; **no place else** nulle part ailleurs; **no shooting** chasse *f* réservée; **no smoking** défense de fumer; **no thoroughfare** circulation *f* interdite, passage *m* interdit; **no use** inutile; **with no** sans ‖ *s* non *m* ‖ *adv* non; **no good** vil; **no longer** ne . . . plus §90, e.g., **he no longer works here** il ne travaille plus ici; **no more** ne . . . plus §90, e.g., **he has no more** il n'en a plus; **no more . . .** (or *comp* in **-er**) **than** ne . . . pas plus . . . que, e.g.,

she is no happier than he elle n'est pas plus heureuse que lui

No'ah's Ark' ['no·əz] *s* l'arche *f* de Noé

nobili·ty [no'bɪlɪti] *s* (*pl* **-ties**) noblesse *f*

noble ['nobəl] *adj & s* noble *mf*

no'ble·man *s* (*pl* **-men**) noble *m*

nobleness ['nobəlnɪs] *s* noblesse *f*

nobod·y ['no,badi] *s* (*pl* **-ies**) nullité *f* ‖ *pron indef* personne; ne . . . personne §90, e.g., **I see nobody there** je n'y vois personne; personne ne, nul ne §90, e.g., **nobody knows it** personne ne le sait, nul ne le sait

nocturnal [nak'tʌrnəl] *adj* nocturne

nocturne ['naktʌrn] *s* nocturne *m*

nod [nad] *s* signe *m* de tête; (*greeting*) inclination *f* de tête ‖ *v* (*pret & pp* **nodded**; *ger* **nodding**) *tr* (*the head*) incliner; **to nod assent** faire un signe d'assentiment ‖ *intr* (*with sleep*) dodeliner de la tête; (*to greet*) incliner la tête

node [nod] *s* nœud *m*

noise [nɔɪz] *s* bruit *m* ‖ *tr* (*a rumor*) ébruiter

noiseless ['nɔɪzlɪs] *adj* silencieux

nois·y ['nɔɪzi] *adj* (*comp* **-ier**; *super* **-iest**) bruyant

nomad ['nomæd] *adj & s* nomade *mf*

no' man's' land' *s* région *f* désolée; (mil) zone *f* neutre

nominal ['namɪnəl] *adj* nominal

nominate ['namɪ,net] *tr* désigner; (*to appoint*) nommer

nomination [,namɪ'neʃən] *s* désignation *f*, investiture *f*

nominative ['namɪnətɪv] *adj & s* nominatif *m*

nominee [,namɪ'ni] *s* désigné *m*, candidat *m*

nonbelligerent [,nanbə'lɪdʒərənt] *adj & s* non-belligérant *m*

nonbreakable [nan'brekəbəl] *adj* incassable

nonchalant ['nanʃələnt] *adj* nonchalant

noncom ['nan,kam] *s* (coll) sous-off *m*

noncombatant [nan'kambətənt *adj & s* non-combattant *m*

noncommissioned [,nankə'mɪʃənd] *adj* non-breveté

non'commis'sioned of'ficer *s* sous-officier *m*

noncommittal [,nankə'mɪtəl] *adj* évasif, réticent

nonconductor [,nankən'dʌktər] *s* non-conducteur *m*, mauvais conducteur *m*

nonconformist [,nankən'fɔrmɪst] *adj & s* non-conformiste *mf*

nondenominational [,nandɪ,namɪ'neʃənəl] *adj* indépendant, qui ne fait partie d'aucune secte religieuse; (*school*) laïque

nondescript ['nandɪ,skrɪpt] *adj* indéfinissable, inclassable

nondiscriminating [,nandɪs'krɪmɪ,netɪŋ] *adj* (*employment, etc.*) égalitaire

none [nʌn] *pron indef* aucun §90B; (*nobody*) personne, nul §90B; ne . . . aucun, ne . . . nul §90; n'en . . . pas, e.g., **I have none** je n'en ai pas; (*as a response on the blank of an official form*) néant ‖

adv—**to be none the wiser** ne pas en être plus sage

nonenti·ty [nɑnˈɛntɪtɪ] *s* (*pl* **-ties**) nullité *f*

none'such' *s* nonpareil *m*; (*apple*) nonpareille *f*; (bot) lupuline *f*, minette *f*

nonfiction [nɑnˈfɪkʃən] *s* littérature *f* autre que le roman

nonfulfillment [ˌnɑnfʊlˈfɪlmənt] *s* inaccomplissement *m*

nonintervention [ˌnɑnɪntərˈvɛnʃən] *s* nonintervention *f*, non-ingérence *f*

nonmetal [ˈnɑnˌmɛtəl] *s* métalloïde *m*

nonpartisan [nɑnˈpɑrtɪzən] *adj* neutre, indépendant

nonpayment [nɑnˈpemənt] *s* non-paiement *m*

non·plus [nɑnˈplʌs] *s* perplexité *f* ‖ *v* (*pret* & *pp* **-plused** or **-plussed**; *ger* **-plusing** or **-plussing**) *tr* déconcerter, dérouter

nonprof'it or'ganization *s* organisation *f* sans but lucratif

nonresident [nɑnˈrɛzɪdənt] *adj* & *s* nonrésident *m*

nonresidential [nɑnˌrɛzɪˈdɛnʃəl] *adj* commercial

nonreturnable [ˌnɑnrɪˈtʌrnəbəl] *adj* (*bottle*) perdu

nonscientific [nɑnˌsaɪ·ənˈtɪfɪk] *adj* antiscientifique

nonsectarian [ˌnɑnsəkˈtɛrɪ·ən] *adj* nonsectaire; qui ne fait partie d'aucune secte religieuse; (*education*) laïque

nonsense [ˈnɑnsɛns] *s* bêtise *f*, nonsens *m*

nonskid [ˈnɑnˈskɪd] *adj* antidérapant

nonstop [ˈnɑnˈstɑp] *adj* & *adv* sans arrêt, continu; (*without landing*) sans escale

nonviolence [nɑnˈvaɪ·ələns] *s* nonviolence *f*

noodle [ˈnudəl] *s* nouille *f*; (*fool*) (slang) niais *m*; (*head*) (slang) tronche *f*

nook [nʊk] *s* coin *m*, recoin *m*

noon [nun] *s* midi *m*

no' one' or **no'-one'** *pron indef* personne §90B; ne . . . personne §90, e.g., **I see no one there** je n'y vois personne; personne ne, nul ne §90B, e.g., **no one knows it** personne ne le sait, nul ne le sait; **no one else** personne d'autre

noon'time' *s* midi *m*

noose [nus] *s* nœud *m* coulant; (*for hanging*) corde *f*, hart *f*

nor [nɔr] *conj* ni

norm [nɔrm] *s* norme *f*

normal [ˈnɔrməl] *adj* normal

Norman [ˈnɔrmən] *adj* normand ‖ *s* (*dialect*) normand *m*; (*person*) Normand *m*

Normandy [ˈnɔrməndi] *s* Normandie *f*; la Normandie

Norse [nɔrs] *adj* & *s* norrois *m*

Norse'man *s* (*pl* **-men**) Norrois *m*

north [nɔrθ] *adj* & *s* nord *m* ‖ *adv* au nord, vers le nord

North' Af'rican *adj* nord-africain ‖ *s* Nord-Africain *m*

north'east' *adj* & *s* nord-est *m*

north'east'er *s* vent *m* du nord-est

northern [ˈnɔrðərn] *adj* septentrional, du nord

North' Kore'a *s* Corée *f* du Nord; la Corée du Nord

North' Kore'an *adj* nord-coréen ‖ *s* (*person*) Nord-Coréen *m*

North' Pole' *s* pôle *m* Nord

northward [ˈnɔrθwərd] *adv* vers le nord

north'west' *adj* & *s* nord-ouest *m*

north' wind' *s* bise *f*

Norway [ˈnɔrwe] *s* Norvège *f*; la Norvège

Norwegian [nɔrˈwidʒən] *adj* norvégien ‖ *s* (*language*) norvégien *m*; (*person*) Norvégien *m*

nose [noz] *s* nez *m*; (*of certain animals*) museau *m*; **to blow one's nose** se moucher; **to have a nose for** avoir le flair de; **to keep one's nose to the grindstone** travailler sans relâche, buriner; **to lead by the nose** mener par le bout du nez; **to look down one's nose at** faire un nez à; **to talk through one's nose** parler du nez; **to thumb one's nose at** faire un pied de nez à; **to turn up one's nose at** faire la nique à; **under the nose of** à la barbe de ‖ *tr* flairer, sentir; **to nose out** flairer, dépister ‖ *intr*—**to nose about** fouiner; **to nose over** capoter

nose'bag' *s* musette *f*

nose'bleed' *s* saignement *m* de nez

nose' cone' *s* ogive *f*

nose' dive' *s* piqué *m*

nose'-dive' *intr* descendre en piqué

nose' drops' *spl* instillations *fpl* nasales

nose'gay' *s* bouquet *m*

nose' glass'es *spl* pince-nez *m*, binocle *m*

nostalgia [nɑˈstældʒə] *s* nostalgie *f*

nostalgic [nɑˈstældʒɪk] *adj* nostalgique

nostril [ˈnɑstrɪl] *s* narine *f*; (*of horse, cow, etc.*) naseau *m*

nostrum [ˈnɑstrəm] *s* (*quack and his medicine*) orviétan *m*; panacée *f*

nos·y [ˈnozi] *adj* (*comp* **-ier**; *super* **-iest**) fureteur, indiscret

not [nɑt] *adv* ne §87, §90C; ne . . . pas §90, e.g., **he is not here** il n'est pas ici; non, non pas; **not at all** pas du tout; **not much** peu de chose; **not one** pas un; **not that** non pas que; **not yet** pas encore; **to think not** croire que non

notable [ˈnotəbəl] *adj* & *s* notable *m*

notarize [ˈnotəˌraɪz] *tr* authentiquer

notarized *adj* authentique

nota·ry [ˈnotəri] *s* (*pl* **-ries**) notaire *m*

notation [noˈteʃən] *s* notation *f*

notch [nɑtʃ] *s* coche *f*, entaille *f*; (*of a belt*) cran *m*; (*of a wheel*) dent *f*; (*gap in a mountain*) brèche *f* ‖ *tr* encocher, entailler

note [not] *s* note *f*; (*short letter*) billet *m*; **notes** commentaires *mpl*; (*of a speech*) feuillets *mpl*; **note to the reader** avis *m* au lecteur; **to hit a wrong note** faire un canard ‖ *tr* noter; **to note down** prendre note de

note'book' *s* cahier *m*; (*bill book, memo pad, etc.*) carnet *m*, calepin *m*

note'book cov'er *s* protège-cahier *m*

noted [ˈnotɪd] *adj* éminent, distingué, connu

note' pad' *s* bloc-notes *m*

note′wor′thy *s* notable, remarquable

nothing [′nʌθɪŋ] *s* rien *m*; **nothing of importance** rien à signaler; **to count for nothing** compter pour du beurre ‖ *pron indef* rien §90B; ne . . . rien §90, e.g., **I have nothing** je n'ai rien; **nothing at all** rien du tout; **nothing doing!** (slang) pas mèche! ‖ *adv*—**nothing less than** rien moins que

nothingness [′nʌθɪŋnɪs] *s* néant *m*

notice [′notɪs] *s* (*warning; advertisement*) avis *m*; (*in a newspaper*) annonce *f*; (*observation*) attention *f*; (*of dismissal*) congé *m*; **at short notice** à bref délai; **to take notice of** faire attention à; **until further notice** jusqu'à nouvel ordre ‖ *tr* s'apercevoir de, remarquer

noticeable [′notɪsəbəl] *adj* apparent, perceptible

notification [,notɪfɪ′keʃən] *s* notification *f*, avertissement *m*

noti·fy [′notɪ,faɪ] *v* (*pret & pp* **-fied**) *tr* aviser, avertir

notion [′noʃən] *s* notion *f*; intention *f*; **notions** mercerie *f*; **to have a notion to** avoir dans l'idée, avoir envie de

notorie·ty [,notə′raɪ·ɪti] *s* (*pl* **-ties**) renom *m* déshonorant, triste notoriété *f*

notorious [no′torɪ·əs] *adj* insigne, mal famé; (*person*) d'une triste notoriété

no′-trump′ *adj & s* sans-atout *m*

notwithstanding [,nɑtwɪθ′stændɪŋ] *adv* non-obstant, néanmoins ‖ *prep* malgré ‖ *conj* quoique

nought [nɔt] *s* var of **naught**

noun [naʊn] *s* nom *m*

nourish [′nʌrɪʃ] *tr* nourrir

nourishment [′nʌrɪʃmənt] *s* nourriture *f*, alimentation *f*

Nova Scotia [′novə′skoʃə] *s* Nouvelle-Écosse *f*; la Nouvelle-Écosse

novel [′nɑvəl] *adj* nouveau; original, bizarre ‖ *s* roman *m*

novelette [,nɑvəl′ɛt] *s* nouvelle *f*, bluette *f*

novelist [′nɑvəlɪst] *s* romancier *m*

novel·ty [′nɑvəlti] *s* (*pl* **-ties**) nouveauté *f*; **novelties** bibelots, *mpl*, souvenirs *mpl*

November [no′vɛmbər] *s* novembre *m*

novice [′nɑvɪs] *s* novice *mf*

novitiate [no′vɪʃɪ·ɪt] *s* noviciat *m*

novocaine [′novə,ken] *s* novocaïne *f*

now [naʊ] *adv* maintenant; **just now** tout à l'heure, naguère; **now and again** de temps en temps ‖ *interj* allez-y!

nowadays [′naʊ·ə,dez] *adv* de nos jours

no′way′ or **no′ways′** *adv* en aucune façon

no′where′ *adv* nulle part; ne . . . nulle part; **nowhere else** nulle autre part, nulle part ailleurs

noxious [′nɑkʃəs] *adj* nocif

nozzle [′nɑzəl] *s* (*of hose*) ajutage *m*; (*of fire hose*) lance *f*; (*of sprinkling can*) pomme *f*; (*of candlestick*) douille *f*; (*of pitcher; of gas burner*) bec *m*; (*of carburetor*) buse *f*; (*of vacuum cleaner*) suceur *m*; (*nose*) (slang) museau *m*

nth [ɛnθ] *adj* énième, nième; **for the nth time** pour la énième fois; **the nth power** la énième puissance

nuance [nju′ɑns], [′nju·ɑns] *s* nuance *f*

nub [nʌb] *s* protubérance *f*; (*piece*) petit morceau *m*; (slang) nœud *m*

nuclear [′n(j)uklɪ·ər] *adj* nucléaire

nu′clear ac′cident *s* accident *m* nucléaire

nu′clear pow′er plant′ *s* centrale *f* nucléaire

nu′clear reac′tor *s* réacteur *m* nucléaire

nu′clear re′search lab′oratory *m* laboratoire *m* nucléaire

nu′clear test′ *s* test *m* nucléaire, essai *m* nucléaire

nu′clear test′ ban′ *s* interdiction *f* des essais nucléaires

nucleolus [n(j)u′kli·ələs] *s* nucléole *m*

nucleon [′n(j)ukli·ɑn] *s* nucléon *m*

nucle·us [′n(j)ukli·əs] *s* (*pl* **-i** [,aɪ] or **-uses**) noyau *m*

nude [n(j)ud] *adj* nu ‖ *s* nu *m*; **in the nude** nu, sans vêtements

nudge [nʌdʒ] *s* coup *m* de coude ‖ *tr* pousser du coude

nudist [′n(j)udɪst] *adj & s* nudiste *mf*

nudity [′n(j)uditi] *s* nudité *f*

nugget [′nʌgɪt] *s* pépite *f*

nuisance [′n(j)usəns] *s* ennui *m*; (*person*) peste *f*

null [nʌl] *adj indef* nul

null′ and void′ *adj* nul et non avenu

nulli·fy [′nʌlɪ,faɪ] *v* (*pret & pp* **-fied**) *tr* annuler

numb [nʌm] *adj* engourdi; **to grow numb** s'engourdir ‖ *tr* engourdir

number [′nʌmbər] *s* (*quantity*) nombre *m*; (*figure, numeral, digit*) chiffre *m*; (*house, page, registration, telephone, magazine*) numéro *m*; (*circus or vaudeville act*) numéro; (*car, manufactured goods, clothes*) modèle *m*; **even (odd, whole, cardinal, ordinal) number** nombre pair (impair, entier, cardinal, ordinal); **round number** chiffre rond; **wrong number** faux numéro ‖ *tr* numéroter; nombrer; (*to amount to*) s'élever à, compter; **to number among** compter parmi

numberless [′nʌmbərlɪs] *adj* innombrable

numbness [′nʌmnɪs] *s* engourdissement *m*

numeral [′n(j)umərəl] *adj* numéral ‖ *s* numéro *m*, chiffre *m*; **Arabic numeral** chiffre arabe; **Roman numeral** chiffre romain

numeration [,n(j)umə′reʃən] *s* numération *f*

numerical [n(j)u′mɛrɪkəl] *adj* numérique

numerous [′n(j)umərəs] *adj* nombreux

numismatic [,n(j)umɪz′mætɪk] *adj* numismatique ‖ **numismatics** *s* numismatique *f*

numskull [′nʌm,skʌl] *s* (coll) sot *m*

nun [nʌn] *s* religieuse *f*, nonne *f*

nunci·o [′nʌnʃɪ,o] *s* (*pl* **-os**) nonce *m*

nuptial [′nʌpʃəl] *adj* nuptial ‖ **nuptials** *spl* noces *fpl*

nurse [nʌrs] *s* (*female nurse*) infirmière *f*; (*male nurse*) infirmier *m*; (*wet nurse*) nourrice *f*; (*practical nurse*) garde-malade mf; (*children's nurse*) bonne *f* d'enfant, nurse *f* ‖ *tr* soigner; (*hopes; plants; a baby*) nourrir

nurse′maid′ *s* bonne *f* d'enfant

nurser·y [′nʌrsəri] *s* (*pl* **-ies**) chambre *f* des enfants; (*for day care*) crèche *f*, pouponnière *f*; (*hort*) pépinière *f*

nurs′ery·man *s* (*pl* **-men**) pépiniériste *m*

nurs′ery school′ *s* maternelle *f*, école *f* maternelle

nurs′e's aid′ *s* aide-soignante *f*

nursing [′nʌrsɪŋ] *s* (*care of invalids*) soins *mpl* infirmière; (*profession*) métier *m or* profession *f* d'infirmière; (*suckling*) allaitement *m*; (*mothering*) maternage *m*

nurs′ing bot′tle *s* biberon *m*

nurs′ing home′ *s* maison *f* de repos, maison de santé

nursling [′nʌrslɪŋ] *s* nourrisson *m*

nurture [′nʌrtʃər] *s* (*training*) éducation *f*; (*food*) nourriture *f* ‖ *tr* élever; (*to nurse*) nourrir

nut [nʌt] *s* noix *f*, e.g., **Brazil nut** noix du Brésil; (*of walnut tree*) noix; (*of filbert*) noisette *f*; (*to screw on a bolt*) écrou *m*; (slang) extravagant *m*; **to be nuts about** (slang) être follement épris de

nut′crack′er *s* casse-noisettes *m*, casse-noix *m*; (orn) casse-noix

nut′hatch′ *s* sittelle *f*

nut′meat′ *s* graine *f* de fruit sec, graine de noix

nutmeg [′nʌt‚mɛg] *s* (*seed or spice*) noix *f* muscade, muscade *f*; (*tree*) muscadier *m*

nutriment [′n(j)utrɪmənt] *s* nourriture *f*

nutrition [n(j)u′trɪʃən] *s* nutrition *f*

nutritious [n(j)u′trɪʃəs] *adj* nutritif

nuts [nʌts] *adj* (coll) dingue, cinglé, toqué; **to be nuts about** être emballé par ‖ *interj* la barbe!, je m'en fiche!

nut′shell′ *s* coquille *f* de noix; **in a nutshell** en un mot

nut·ty [′nʌti] *adj* (*comp* **-tier**; *super* **-tiest**) à goût de noisette, à goût de noix; (slang) cinglé, dingue

nuzzle [′nʌzəl] *tr* fouiller du groin ‖ *intr* fouiller du groin; s'envelopper chaudement; **to nuzzle up to** se pelotonner contre

nylon [′naɪlɑn] *s* nylon *m*; **nylons** bas *mpl* de nylon, bas nylon

nymph [nɪmf] *s* nymphe *f*

O

O, o [o] *s* XVᵉ lettre de l'alphabet

oaf [of] *s* lourdaud *m*, rustre *m*

oak [ok] *s* chêne *m*

oaken [′okən] *adj* de chêne, en chêne

oakum [′okəm] *s* étoupe *f*

oar [or], [ɔr] *s* rame *f*, aviron *m*

oar′lock′ *s* tolet *m*

oars′man′ *s* (*pl* **-men′**) rameur *m*

oa·sis [o′esɪs] *s* (*pl* **-ses** [siz]) oasis *f*

oat [ot] *s* avoine *f*; **oats** (*edible grain*) avoine; **to feel one's oats** être imbu de sa personne; **to sow one's wild oats** (coll) jeter sa gourme

oath [oθ] *s* (*pl* **oaths** [oðz]) serment *m*; (*swearword*) juron *m*; **to administer an oath to** (law) faire prêter serment à; **to take an oath** prêter serment

oat′meal′ *s* farine *f* d'avoine; (*breakfast food*) flocons *mpl* d'avoine

obbligato [‚ɑblɪ′gɑto] *s* accompagnement *m* à volonté

obdurate [′ɑbdjərɪt] *adj* obstiné, endurci

obedience [o′bidɪ·əns] *s* obéissance *f*

obedient [o′bidɪ·ənt] *adj* obéissant

obeisance [o′besəns] *s* hommage *m*; (*greeting*) révérance *f*

obelisk [′ɑbəlɪsk] *s* obélisque *m*

obese [o′bis] *adj* obèse

obesity [o′bisɪti] *s* obésité *f*

obey [ə′be] *tr* obéir à; **to be obeyed** être obéi ‖ *intr* obéir

obfuscate [′ɑbfəs‚ket] *tr* offusquer

obituar·y [o′bɪtʃu‚ɛri] *adj* nécrologique ‖ *s* (*pl* **-ies**) nécrologie *f*

object [′ɑbdʒɪkt] *s* objet *m* ‖ [ɑb′dʒɛkt] *tr* objecter, rétorquer ‖ *intr* faire des objections; **to object to** s'opposer à, avoir des objections contre

objection [ɑb′dʒɛkʃən] *s* objection *f*

objectionable [ɑb′dʒɛkʃənəbəl] *adj* répréhensible; répugnant, désagréable

objective [ɑb′dʒɛktɪv] *adj* & *s* objectif *m*

obligate [′ɑblɪ‚get] *tr* obliger

obligation [‚ɑblɪ′geʃən] *s* obligation *f*

obligatory [ə′blɪgə‚tori] *adj* obligatoire

oblige [ə′blaɪdʒ] *tr* obliger; **much obliged** bien obligé, très reconnaissant; **to be obliged to** être obligé de

obliging [ə′blaɪdʒɪŋ] *adj* accommodant, obligeant

oblique [ə′blik] *adj* oblique

obliterate [ə′blɪtə‚ret] *tr* effacer, oblitérer

oblivion [ə′blɪvɪ·ən] *s* oubli *m*

oblivious [ə′blɪvɪ·əs] *adj* oublieux

oblong [′ɑblɔŋ] *adj* oblong

obnoxious [əb′nɑkʃəs] *adj* odieux, désagréable

oboe [′obo] *s* hautbois *m*

oboist [′obo·ɪst] *s* hautboïste *mf*

obscene [ɑb′sin] *adj* obscène

obsceni·ty [ɑb′sɛnɪti] *s* (*pl* **-ties**) obscénité *f*

obscure [əb′skjur] *adj* obscur; (*vowel*) relâché, neutre

obscuri·ty [əb'skjurıti] s (pl **-ties**) obscurité f

obsequies ['absıkwiz] spl obsèques fpl

obsequious [əb'sikwı·əs] adj obséquieux

observance [əb'zʌrvəns] s observance f

observant [əb'zʌrvənt] adj observateur

observation [,abzər've∫ən] s observation f

observato·ry [əb'zʌrvə,tori] s (pl **-ries**) observatoire m

observe [əb'zʌrv] tr observer; (silence) garder; (a holiday) célébrer; dire, remarquer

observer [əb'zʌrvər] s observateur m

obsess [əb'sɛs] tr obséder

obsession [əb'sɛ∫ən] s obsession f

obsolescent [,absə'lɛsənt] adj vieillissant

obsolete ['absəlit] adj désuet, vieilli, (gram) obsolète

obstacle ['abstəkəl] s obstacle m

ob'stacle course' s champ m d'obstacles, piste f d'obstacles

obstetrical [ab'stɛtrıkəl] adj obstétrique

obstetrics [ab'stɛtrıks] spl obstétrique f

obstina·cy ['abstınəsi] s (pl **-cies**) obstination f, entêtement m

obstinate ['abstınıt] adj obstiné

obstreperous [əb'strɛpərəs] adj turbulent

obstruct [əb'strʌkt] tr obstruer; (movements) empêcher, entraver

obstruction [əb'strʌk∫ən] s obstruction f; (on railroad tracks) obstacle m; (to movement) empêchement m, entrave f

obtain [əb'ten] tr obtenir, se procurer ‖ intr prévaloir

obtrusive [əb'trusıv] adj importun, intrus

obtuse [əb't(j)us] adj obtus

obviate ['abvı,et] tr obvier à

obvious ['abvı·əs] adj évident

occasion [ə'keʒən] s occasion f; **on occasion** en de différentes occasions ‖ tr occasionner

occasional [ə'keʒənəl] adj fortuit, occasionnel; (verses) de circonstance; (showers) épars; (chair) volant

occasionally [ə'keʒənəli] adv de temps en temps, occasionnellement

occident ['aksıdənt] s occident m

occidental [,aksə'dɛntəl] adj & s occidental m

occlusion [ə'kluʒən] s occlusion f

occlusive [ə'klusıv] adj occlusif ‖ s occlusive f

occult [ə'kʌlt], ['akʌlt] adj occulte

occupancy ['akjəpənsi] s occupation f, habitation f

occupant ['akjəpənt] s occupant m

occupation [,akjə'pe∫ən] s occupation f

occupational [,akjə'pe∫ənəl] adj professionnel; de métier

oc'cupa'tional ther'apy s thérapie f rééducative, réadaptation f fonctionnelle

occu·py ['akjə,paı] v (pret & pp **-pied**) tr occuper; **to be occupied with** s'occuper de

oc·cur [ə'kʌr] v (pret & pp **-curred**; ger **-curring**) intr arriver, avoir lieu; (to be found; to come to mind) se présenter; **it**

occurs to me that il me vient à l'esprit que

occurrence [ə'kʌrəns] s événement m; cas m, exemple m; **everyday occurrence** fait m journalier

ocean ['o∫ən] s océan m

oceanic [,o∫ı'ænık] adj océanique

o'cean lin'er s paquebot m transocéanique

ocher ['okər] s ocre f

o'clock [ə'klak] **—it is one o'clock** il est une heure; **it is two o'clock** il est deux heures

octane ['akten] s octane m

oc'tane num'ber s indice m d'octane

octave ['aktıv], ['aktev] s octave f

October [ak'tobər] s octobre m

octo·pus ['aktəpəs] s (pl **-puses** or **-pi** [,paı]) pieuvre f, poulpe m

octoroon ['aktə'run] s octavon m

ocular ['akjələr] adj & s oculaire m

oculist ['akjəlıst] s oculiste mf

odd [ad] adj (number) impair; (that doesn't match) dépareillé, déparié; (queer) bizarre, étrange; (occasional) divers; quelque, e.g., **three hundred odd horses** quelque trois cents chevaux; et quelques ‖ **odds** spl chances fpl; (disparity) inégalité f; (on a horse) cote f; **at odds** en désaccord, en bisbille; **by all odds** sans aucun doute; **to be at odds with** être mal avec; **to give odds to** donner de l'avance à; **to set at odds** brouiller

oddi·ty ['adıti] s (pl **-ties**) bizarrerie f

odd' jobs' spl bricolage m, petits travaux mpl

odd' man' out' s—**to be odd man out** être en trop

odds' and ends' spl petits bouts mpl, bribes fpl; (trinkets) bibelots mpl; (food) restes mpl

ode [od] s ode f

odious ['odı·əs] adj odieux

odor ['odər] s odeur f; **to be in bad odor** être mal vu

odorless ['odərlıs] adj inodore

Odyssey ['adısi] s Odyssée f

Œdipus ['ɛdıpəs], ['idəpəs] s Œdipe m

of [av], [ʌv], [əv] prep de; à, e.g., **to think of** penser à; e.g., **to ask s.th. of s.o.** demander q.ch. à qn; en, e.g., **a doctor of medicine** un docteur en médecine; moins, e.g., **a quarter of two** deux heures moins le quart; entre, e.g., **he of all people** lui entre tous; d'entre, e.g., **five of them** cinq d'entre eux; par, e.g., **of necessity** par nécessité; (made of) en, de, e.g., **made of wood** en bois, de bois; (not translated), e.g., **the fifth of March** le cinq mars; e.g., **we often see her of a morning** nous la voyons souvent le matin

off [ɔf], [af] adj mauvais, e.g., **off day** (bad day) mauvaise journée; libre, e.g., **off day** journée libre; de congé, e.g., **off day** jour de congé; (account, sum) inexact; (meat) avancé; (electric current) coupé; (light) éteint; (radio; faucet) fermé; (street) secondaire, transversal; (distant) éloigné, écarté || *adv* loin; à . . . de distance, e.g., **three kilometers off** à trois kilomètres de distance; parti, e.g., **they're off!** les voilà partis!; bas, e.g., **hats off!** chapeaux bas!; (naut) au large; (theat) à la cantonade || *prep* de; (*at a distance from*) éloigné de, écarté de; (naut) au large de, à la hauteur de; **from off** de dessous de; **off line** (comp) autonome

offal ['ɔfəl] *s* (*of butchered meat*) abats *mpl*; (*refuse*) ordures *fpl*

off′ and on′ *adv* de temps en temps, par intervalles

off′beat′ *adj* (slang) insolite, rare

off′ chance′ *s* chance *f* improbable

off′-col′or *adj* décoloré; (*e.g., story*) grivois, vert

offend [ə'fɛnd] *tr* offenser; **to be offended** s'offenser || *intr*—**to offend against** enfreindre

offender [ə'fɛndər] *s* offenseur *m*; (*criminal*) délinquant *m*, coupable *mf*

offense [ə'fɛns] *s* offense *f*; (law) délit *m*; **to take offense (at)** s'offenser (de)

offensive [ə'fɛnsɪv] *adj* offensant, blessant; (mil) offensif || *s* offensive *f*

offer ['ɔfər] *s* offre *f* || *tr* offrir; (*excuses; best wishes*) présenter; (*prayers*) adresser || *intr*—**to offer to** faire l'offre de; faire mine de, e.g., **he offered to fight** il a fait mine de se battre

offering ['ɔfərɪŋ] *s* offre *f*; (eccl) offrande *f*

off′hand′ *adj* improvisé; brusque || *adv* au pied levé; brusquement

office ['ɔfɪs] *s* (*function*) charge *f*, fonction *f*, office *m*; (*in business, school, government*) bureau *m*; (*national agency*) office *m*; (*of lawyer*) étude *f*; (*of doctor*) cabinet *m*; **elective office** poste *m* électif; **good offices** bons offices; **to run for office** se présenter aux élections

of′fice boy′ *s* coursier *m*, commissionaire *m* de bureau

of′fice desk′ *s* bureau *m* ministre

of′fice·hold′er *s* fonctionnaire *mf*

of′fice hours′ *spl* heures *fpl* de bureau; (*of doctor, counselor, etc.*) heures de consultation

officer ['ɔfɪsər] *s* (*of a company*) administrateur *m*, dirigeant *m*; (*of army, an order, a society, etc.*) officier *m*; (*police officer*) agent *m* de police, officier de police; **officer of the day** (mil) officier de service

of′ficer can′didate *s* élève-officier *m*

of′fice seek′er *s* solliciteur *m*

of′fice supplies′ *spl* fournitures *fpl* de bureau, articles *mpl* de bureau

of′fice-supply′ store′ *s* papeterie *f*

of′fice work′ *s* travail *m* de bureau

official [ə'fɪʃəl] *adj* officiel; (*e.g., stationery*) réglementaire || *s* fonctionnaire *mf*, officiel *m*; **officials** cadres *mpl*; (*executives*) dirigeants *mpl*

offi′cial board′ *s* comité *m* directeur

offi′cial chan′nels *spl* filière *f* administrative

officialese [ə,fɪʃə'liz] *s* jargon *m* administratif

officiate [ə'fɪʃɪ,et] *intr* (eccl) officier; **to officiate as** exercer les fonctions de

officious [ə'fɪʃəs] *adj* trop empressé; **to be officious** faire l'officieux

offing ['ɔfɪŋ] *s*—**in the offing** au large; (fig) en perspective

off′-lim′its *adj* défendu; (public sign) défense d'entrer, entrée interdite; (mil) interdit aux troupes

off′-peak heat′er *s* thermosiphon *m* à accumulation

off′print′ *s* tiré *m* à part

off′-seas′on *s adj* hors-saison || *s* morte-saison *f*; **in the off season** à la morte-saison

off′set′ *s* compensation *f*; (typ) offset *m* || **off′set′** *v* (*pret & pp* **-set;** *ger* **-setting**) *tr* compenser

off′shoot′ *s* rejeton *m*

off′shore′ *adj* éloigné de la côte, du côté de la terre; (*wind*) de terre || *adv* au large, vers la haute mer

off′side′ *adv* (sports) hors jeu

off′spring′ *s* descendance *f*; (*descendant*) rejeton *m*, enfant *mf*; (*result*) conséquence *f*

off′stage′ *adj* dans les coulisses || *adv* à la cantonade

off′-the-cuff′ *adj* (coll) impromptu

off′-the-rec′ord *adj* confidentiel

off′-white′ *adj* blanc cassé

often ['ɔfən], ['ɑfən] *adv* souvent; **how often?** combien de fois?; **tous les combien?;** **not often** rarement; **once too often** une fois de trop

ogive ['odʒaɪv], [o'dʒaɪv] *s* ogive *f*

ogle ['ogəl] *tr* lancer une œillade à; (*to stare at*) dévisager

ogre ['ogər] *s* ogre *m*

ohm [om] *s* ohm *m*

oil [ɔɪl] *s* huile *f*; (*painting*) huile, peinture *f* à l'huile; **holy oil** huile sainte, saintes huiles; **to pour oil on troubled waters** calmer la tempête, verser de l'huile sur les plaies de qn; **to smell of midnight oil** sentir l'huile; **to strike oil** atteindre une nappe pétrolifère; (fig) trouver le filon || *tr* huiler; (*to bribe*) graisser la patte à || *intr* (naut) faire le plein de mazout

oil′-and-vin′egar cru′et *s* huilier *m*

oil′ burn′er *s* réchaud *m* à pétrole

oil′can′ *s* bidon *m* d'huile, burette *f* d'huile

oil′cloth′ *s* toile *f* cirée

oil′ com′pany *s* société *f* pétrolière

oil′cup′ *s* (mach) godet *m* graisseur

oil′ drum′ *s* bidon *m* d'huile

oil′ field′ *s* gisement *m* pétrolifère

oil′ gauge′ *s* jauge *f* de niveau d'huile

oil′ lamp′ *s* lampe *f* à huile, lampe à pétrole

oil′man′ *s* (*pl* **-men′**) (*retailer*) huilier *m*; (*operator*) pétrolier *m*

oil′ pipe′line *s* oléoduc *m*

oil′ pump′ *s* pompe *f* à huile

oil′ rig′ *s* derrick *m*, tour *f* de forage; (*in water*) plate-forme *f* pétrolière

oil′ short′age *s* pénurie *f* de pétrole

oil′ stove′ *s* poêle *m* à mazout, fourneau *m* à pétrole

oil′ tank′er *s* pétrolier *m*, tanker *m*

oil′ well′ *s* puits *m* à pétrole

oil·y [′ɔɪli] *adj* (*comp* -ier; *super* -iest) huileux, oléagineux; (fig) onctueux

ointment [′ɔɪntmənt] *s* onguent *m*, pommade *f*

O.K. [′o′ke] (letterword) *adj* (coll) très bien, parfait ‖ *s* (coll) approbation *f* ‖ *adv* (coll) très bien ‖ *v* (*pret* & *pp* **O.K.′d**; *ger* **O.K.′ing**) *tr* (coll) approuver ‖ *interj* **O.K.!** ça colle!, d'accord!

okra [′okrə] *s* gombo *m*, ketmie *f* comestible

old [old] *adj* vieux; (*of former times*) ancien; (*wine*) vieux; **any old** n'importe, e.g., **any old time** n'importe quand; quelconque, e.g., **any old book** un livre quelconque; **at . . . years old** à . . . ans; **how old is . . . ?** quel âge a . . . ?; **of old** d'autrefois, de jadis; **to be . . . years old** avoir . . . ans

old′ age′ *s* vieillesse *f*, âge *m* avancé

old′-clothes′man *s* (*pl* -men′) fripier *m*

old′ coun′try *s* mère patrie *f*

Old′ Cov′enant *s* (Bib) ancienne alliance *f*

old′-fash′ioned *adj* démodé, suranné, vieux jeu; (*literary style*) vieillot

old′ fo′gey or **old′ fo′gy** [′fogi] *s* (*pl* -gies) vieux bonhomme *m*, grime *m*

Old′ French′ *s* ancien français *m*

Old′ Glo′ry *s* le drapeau des Etats-Unis

old′ hag′ *s* vieille fée *f*

old′ hand′ *s* vieux routier *m*

old′ lad′y *s* vieille dame *f*; (coll) grand-mère *f*

old′ maid′ *s* vieille fille *f*

old′ mas′ter *s* grand maître *m*; œuvre *f* d'un grand maître

old′ moon′ *s* lune *f* à son décours

old′ peo′ple's home′ *s* hospice *m* de vieillards

old′ salt′ *s* loup *m* de mer

old′ school′ *s* vieille école *f*, vieille roche *f*

oldster [′oldstər] *s* vieillard *m*, vieux *m*

Old′ Tes′tament *s* Ancien Testament *m*

old′-time′ *adj* du temps jadis, d'autrefois

old′-tim′er *s* (coll) vieux *m* de la vieille, vieux routier *m*

old′ wives′′ tale′ *s* conte *m* de bonne femme

Old Wom′an who lived′ in a shoe′ *s* mère *f* Gigogne

Old′ World′ *s* vieux monde *m*

old′-world′ *adj* de l'ancien monde; du vieux monde

oleander [,olɪ′ændər] *s* laurier-rose *m*

olfactory [al′fæktɔri] *adj* olfactif

oligar·chy [′alɪ,garki] *s* (*pl* -chies) oligarchie *f*

olive [′alɪv] *adj* olive; (*complexion*) olivâtre ‖ *s* olive *f*; (*tree*) olivier *m*

ol′ive branch′ *s* rameau *m* d'olivier

ol′ive grove′ *s* olivaie *f*

ol′ive oil′ *s* huile *f* d'olive

Oliver [′alɪvər] *s* Olivier *m*

ol′ive tree′ *s* olivier *m*

olympiad [o′lɪmpɪ,æd] *s* olympiade *f*

Olympian [o′lɪmpɪ·ən] *adj* olympien

Olympic [o′lɪmpɪk] *adj* olympique ‖ **Olympics** *spl* jeux *mpl* olympiques

ombudsman [′ambʌdz,mæn] *s* intercesseur *m*, médiateur *m*

omelet [′amlɪt] *s* omelette *f*

omen [′omən] *s* augure *m*, présage *m*

ominous [′amɪnəs] *adj* de mauvais augure

omission [o′mɪʃən] *s* omission *f*

omit [o′mɪt] *v* (*pret* & *pp* **omitted**; *ger* **omitting**) *tr* omettre

omnibus [′amnɪbəs] *adj* & *s* omnibus *m*

omnipotent [am′nɪpətənt] *adj* omnipotent

omniscient [am′nɪʃənt] *adj* omniscient

omnivorous [am′nɪvərəs] *adj* omnivore

on [an], [ɔn] *adj* (*light, radio*) allumé; (*faucet*) ouvert; (*machine, motor*) en marche; (*electrical appliance*) branché; (*brake*) serré; (*steak, chops, etc.*) dans la poêle; (*game, program, etc.*) commencé ‖ *adv*—**and so on** et ainsi de suite; **come on!** (coll) allons donc!; **farther on** plus loin; **from this day on** à dater de ce jour; **later on** plus tard; **move on!** circulez!; **to be on** (theat) être en scène; **to be on to s.o.** (coll) voir clair dans le jeu de qn; **to have on** être vêtu de, porter; **to . . . on** continuer à + *inf*, e.g., **to sing on** continuer à chanter; **well on** avancé, e.g., **well on in years** d'un âge avancé ‖ *prep* sur; (*at the time of*) lors de; à, e.g., **on foot** à pied; e.g., **on my arrival** à mon arrivée; e.g., **on page three** à la page trois; e.g., **on the first floor** au rez-de-chaussée; e.g., **on the right** à droite; en, e.g., **on a journey** en voyage; e.g., **on arriving** en arrivant; e.g., **on fire** en feu; e.g., **on sale** en vente; e.g., **on the** or **an average** en moyenne; e.g., **on the top of** en dessus de; dans, e.g., **on a farm** dans une ferme; e.g., **on the jury** dans le jury; e.g., **on the street** dans la rue; e.g., **on the train** dans le train; par, e.g., **he came on the train** il est venu par le train; e.g., **on a fine day** par un beau jour; de, e.g., **on good authority** de source certaine, de bonne part; e.g., **on the north** du côté du nord; e.g., **on the one hand . . . on the other hand** d'une part . . . d'autre part; e.g., **on this side** de ce côté-ci; e.g., **to have pity on** avoir pitié de; **to live on bread and water** vivre de pain et d'eau; sous, e.g., **on a charge of** sous l'inculpation de; e.g., **on pain of death** sous peine de mort; (not translated), e.g., **on Tuesday** mardi; e.g., **on Tuesdays** le mardi, tous les mardis; e.g., **on July fourteenth** le quatorze juillet; contre, e.g., **an attack on** une attaque contre; **it's on me** (*it's my turn to pay*) (coll) c'est ma tournée; **it's on the house** (coll) c'est la tournée du patron; **on examination** après

examen; **on it y,** e.g., **there is the shelf; put the book on it** voilà l'étagère; mettez-y le livre; **on line** (comp) en ligne; **on or about** (*a certain date*) aux environs de; **on or after** (*a certain date*) à partir de; **on tap** en perce, à la pression; **on the spot** (*immediately*) sur-le-champ; (*there*) sur place; (slang) en danger imminent; **to be on the committee** faire partie du comité; **to march on a city** marcher sur une ville
on' and on' *adv* continuellement, sans fin
once [wʌns] *s*—**this once** pour cette fois-ci || *adv* une fois; (*formerly*) autrefois; **all at once** (*all together*) tous à la fois; (*suddenly*) tout à coup; **at once** tout de suite, sur-le-champ; (*at the same time*) à la fois, en même temps; **for once** pour une fois; **once and for all** une bonne fois, une fois pour toutes; **once in a while** de temps en temps; **once more** encore une fois; **once or twice** une ou deux fois; **once upon a time there was** il était une fois || *conj* une fois que, dès que
once'-o'ver *s* (slang) examen *m* rapide; travail *m* hâtif; **to give the once-over to** (slang) jeter un coup d'œil à
one [wʌn] *adj* & *pron* un §77; un certain, e.g., **one Dupont** un certain Dupont; un seul, e.g., **with one voice** d'une seule voix; unique, e.g., **one price** prix unique; (not translated when preceded by an adjective), e.g., **the red pencil and the blue one** le crayon rouge et le bleu; **not one** pas un; **one and all** tous; **one and only one** the **one and only closet in the house** l'armoire unique de la maison; seul et unique, e.g., **my one and only umbrella** mon seul et unique parapluie; **one another** l'un l'autre; les uns les autres; **one by one** un à un; **one on one** en tête-à-tête, discussion *f* en tête-à-tête; **that one** celui-là; **the one that** celui que, celui qui; **this one** celui-ci; **to become one** s'unir, se marier || *s* un *m*; **one o'clock** une heure || *pron indef* on §87, e.g., **one cannot go there alone** on ne peut pas y aller seul; **one's** son, e.g., **one's son** son fils
one'-horse' *adj* à un cheval; (coll) provincial, insignifiant
one'-horse town' *s* (coll) trou *m*
one'-man band' *s* homme-orchestre *m*
one'-man show' *s* spectacle *m* solo
onerous ['ɑnərəs] *adj* onéreux
one·self' *pron* soi §85; soi-même §86; se §87, e.g., **to cut oneself** se couper; **to be oneself** se conduire sans affectation
one'-sid'ed *adj* à un côté, à une face; (*e.g., decision*) unilatéral; (*unfair*) partial, injuste
one'-track' *adj* à une voie; (coll) routinier
one'-way' *adj* à sens unique
one'-way tick'et *s* billet *m* d'aller, billet simple
onion ['ʌnjən] *s* oignon *m*; **to know one's onions** (coll) connaître son affaire

on'ion·skin' *s* papier *m* pelure
on'look'er *s* assistant *m*, spectateur *m*
only ['onli] *adj* seul, unique; (*child*) unique || *adv* seulement; ne . . . que, e.g., **I have only two** je n'en ai que deux; réservé, e.g., **staff only** (public sign) réservé au personnel || *conj* mais, si ce n'était que
on'rush' *s* ruée *f*
on'set' *s* attaque *f*; **at the onset** de prime abord, au premier abord
onslaught ['ɑn,slɔt] *s* assaut *m*
on'-the-job' *adj* (*training*) en stage; (coll) alerte
onus ['onəs] *s* charge *f*, fardeau *m*
onward ['ɑnwərd] or **onwards** ['ɑnwərdz] *adv* en avant
onyx ['ɑnɪks] *s* onyx *m*
ooze [uz] *s* suintement *m*; (*mud*) vase *f*, limon *m* || *tr* filtrer || *intr* suinter, filtrer; **to ooze out** s'écouler
opal ['opəl] *s* opale *f*
opaque [o'pek] *adj* opaque; (*style*) obscur
OPEC ['opɛk] *s* (acronym) (**organization of petroleum-exporting countries**) OPEP (organisation des pays exportateurs de pétrole)
open ['opən] *adj* ouvert; (*personality*) franc, sincère; (*job, position*) vacant; (*hour*) libre; (*automobile*) découvert; (*market, trial*) public; (*question*) pendant, indécis; (*wound*) béant; (*to attack, to criticism, etc.*) exposé; (sports) international; **to break** or **crack open** éventrer; **to throw open the door** ouvrir la porte toute grande || *s* ouverture *f*; (*in the woods*) clairière *f*; **in the open** au grand air, à ciel ouvert; (*in the open country*) en rase campagne; (*in the open sea*) en pleine mer; (*without being hidden*) découvert; (*openly*) ouvertement || *tr* ouvrir; (*a canal lock*) lâcher; **to open fire** déclencher le feu || *intr* ouvrir, s'ouvrir; (*said, e.g., of a play*) commencer, débuter; **to open into** aboutir à, déboucher sur; **to open on** donner sur; **to open up** s'épanouir, s'ouvrir
o'pen-air' *adj* en plein air, au grand air
o'pen-eyed' *adj* les yeux écarquillés
o'pen-hand'ed *adj* libéral, la main ouverte
o'pen-heart'ed *adj* ouvert, franc
o'pen-heart' sur'gery *s* chirurgie *f* à cœur ouvert
o'pen house' *s* journée *f* d'accueil; **to keep open house** tenir table ouverte
opening ['opənɪŋ] *s* ouverture *f*; (*in the woods*) clairière *f*, percée *f*; (*vacancy*) vacance *f*, poste *m* vacant; (*chance to say something*) occasion *f* favorable
o'pening night' *s* première *f*
o'pening num'ber *s* ouverture *f*
o'pening price' *s* cours *m* de début
o'pen-mind'ed *adj* à l'esprit ouvert, sans parti pris
o'pen se'cret *s* secret *m* de Polichinelle
o'pen shop' *s* atelier *m* ouvert aux nonsyndiqués
o'pen tick'et *s* coupon *m* date libre
o'pen·work' *s* ouvrage *m* à jour, ajours *mpl*

opera [ˈɑpərə] s opéra m
op′era glass′es spl jumelles fpl de spectacle
op′era hat′ s claque m, gibus m
op′era house′ s opéra m
operate [ˈɑpəˌret] tr actionner, faire marcher; exploiter ‖ intr fonctionner; s'opérer; (surg) opérer; **to operate on** (surg) opérer
operatic [ˌɑpəˈrætɪk] adj d'opéra
opera′ting expen′ses spl (overhead) frais mpl généraux, frais d'exploitation
op′erating room′ s salle f d'opération
opera′ting sys′tem s (comp) système m d'exploitation
op′erating ta′ble s table f d'opération, billard m
operation [ˌɑpəˈreʃən] s opération f; (of a business, of a machine, etc.) fonctionnement m; (med) intervention f chirurgicale, opération; **to have an operation (for)** se faire opérer (de); passer sur le billard (coll)
operative [ˈɑpərətɪv] adj opératif; (surg) opératoire ‖ s (workman) ouvrier m; (spy) agent m, espion m
operator [ˈɑpəˌretər] s opérateur m; (e.g., of a mine) propriétaire m exploitant; (of an automobile) conducteur m; (telp) téléphoniste mf, standardiste mf; (slang) chevalier m d'industrie, aigrefin m; **operator on duty** opérateur de permanence
operetta [ˌɑpəˈretə] s opérette f
opiate [ˈopiˌet] adj opiacé ‖ s médicament m opiacé; (coll) narcotique m
opinion [əˈpɪnjən] s opinion f; **in my opinion** à mon avis
opinionated [əˈpɪnjəˌnetɪd] adj fier de ses opinions, dogmatique
opin′ion poll′ s sondage m d'opinion
opium [ˈopiˌəm] s opium m
o′pium den′ s fumerie f
o′pium pop′py s œillette f
opossum [əˈpɑsəm] s opossum m, sarigue f
opponent [əˈponənt] s adversaire mf, opposant m
opportune [ˌɑpərˈt(j)un] adj opportun, convenable
opportunist [ˌɑpərˈt(j)unɪst] s opportuniste mf
opportuni·ty [ˌɑpərˈt(j)unɪti] s (pl -ties) (appropriate time) occasion f; (favorable condition or good chance for advancement) chance f; **at your first** (or **earliest**) **opportunity** à votre première occasion
oppose [əˈpoz] tr s'opposer à
opposite [ˈɑpəsɪt] adj opposé, contraire; d'en face, e.g., **the house opposite** la maison d'en face ‖ s opposé m, contraire m ‖ adv en face, vis-à-vis ‖ prep en face de, à l'opposite de
op′posite num′ber s (fig) homologue mf
opposition [ˌɑpəˈzɪʃən] s opposition f
oppress [əˈprɛs] tr opprimer; (to weigh heavily upon) oppresser
oppression [əˈprɛʃən] s oppression f
oppressive [əˈprɛsɪv] adj oppressif; (stifling) étouffant, accablant

oppressor [əˈprɛsər] s oppresseur m
opprobrious [əˈprobri·əs] adj infamant, injurieux, honteux
opprobrium [əˈprobri·əm] s opprobre m
optic [ˈɑptɪk] adj optique ‖ **optics** s optique f
optical [ˈɑptɪkəl] adj optique
op′tical illu′sion s illusion f d'optique
optician [ɑpˈtɪʃən] s opticien m
optimism [ˈɑptɪˌmɪzəm] s optimisme m
optimist [ˈɑptɪmɪst] s optimiste mf
optimistic [ˌɑptɪˈmɪstɪk] adj optimiste
optimize [ˈɑptɪˌmaɪz] tr optimiser
option [ˈɑpʃən] s option f
optional [ˈɑpʃənəl] adj facultatif
optometrist [ɑpˈtɑmɪtrɪst] s opticien m; optométriste mf (Canad)
opulent [ˈɑpjələnt] adj opulent
or [ɔr] conj ou
oracle [ˈɔrəkəl] s oracle m
oracular [oˈrækjələr] adj d'oracle; dogmatique, sentencieux; (ambiguous) équivoque
oral [ˈorəl] adj oral
orange [ˈɔrɪndʒ] adj orangé, orange ‖ s (color) orangé m, orange m; (fruit) orange f
orangeade [ˌɔrɪndʒˈed] s orangeade f
or′ange blos′som s fleur f d'oranger
or′ange grove′ s orangeraie f
or′ange juice′ s jus m d'orange
or′ange squeez′er s presse-fruits m
or′ange tree′ s oranger m
orang-outang [oˈræŋuˌtæŋ] s orang-outan m
oration [oˈreʃən] s discours m
orator [ˈɔrətər] s orateur m
oratorical [ˌɔrəˈtɔrɪkəl] adj oratoire
oratori·o [ˌɔrəˈtɔri,o] s (pl -os) oratorio m
orato·ry [ˈɔrəˌtori] s (pl -ries) art m oratoire; (eccl) oratoire m
orb [ɔrb] s orbe m
orbit [ˈɔrbɪt] s orbite f; **in orbit** sur orbite ‖ tr (e.g., the sun) tourner autour de; (e.g., a rocket) mettre en orbite, satelliser ‖ intr se mettre en orbite
orchard [ˈɔrtʃərd] s verger m
orchestra [ˈɔrkɪstrə] s orchestre m; (pit for musicians) fosse f d'orchestre; (for spectators) fauteuils mpl d'orchestre
orchestrate [ˈɔrkɪˌstret] tr orchestrer
orchid [ˈɔrkɪd] s orchidée f
ordain [ɔrˈden] tr destiner; (eccl) ordonner; **to be ordained** (eccl) recevoir les ordres
ordeal [ɔrˈdi·əl] s épreuve f; (hist) ordalie f
order [ˈɔrdər] s ordre m; (of words) ordonnance f; (for merchandise, a meal, etc.) commande f; (military formation) ordre; (law) arrêt m, arrêté m; **in order** en ordre; **in order of appearance** (theat) dans l'ordre d'entrée en scène; **in order that** pour que, afin que; **in order to** + inf pour + inf, afin de + inf; **on order** en commande, commandé; **order!** à l'ordre!; **orders** (eccl) les ordres; (mil) la consigne; **pay to the order of** (com) payez à l'ordre de; **to get s.th. out of order** détraquer q.ch.; **to put in order** mettre en règle ‖ tr ordonner; (com) commander; **to order**

around faire aller et venir; **to order s.o. to** + *inf* ordonner à qn de + *inf*

or′der blank′ *s* bon *m* de commande, bulletin *m* de commande

order·ly [′ɔrdərli] *adj* ordonné; (*life*) réglé; **to be orderly** avoir de l′ordre ‖ *s* (*pl* **-lies**) (med) ambulancier *m*, infirmier *m*; (mil) planton *m*

ordinal [′ɔrdɪnəl] *adj & s* ordinal *m*

ordinance [′ɔrdɪnəns] *s* ordonnance *f*

ordinary [′ɔrdɪn‚ɛri] *adj* ordinaire; **out of the ordinary** exceptionnel

ordination [‚ɔrdɪ′eʃən] *s* ordination *f*

ordnance [′ɔrdnəns] *s* artillerie *f*; (*branch of an army*) service *m* du matériel

ore [or] *s* minerai *m*

oregano [ə′rɛgə‚no] *s* origan *m*

organ [′ɔrgən] *s* (anat, journ) organe *m*; (mus) orgue *m*

organdy [′ɔrgəndi] *s* organdi *m*

or′gan grind′er *s* joueur *m* d′orgue

organic [ɔr′gænɪk] *adj* organique

organism [′ɔrgə‚nɪzəm] *s* organisme *m*

organist [′ɔrgənɪst] *s* organiste *mf*

organization [‚ɔrgənɪ′zeʃən] *s* organisation *f*

organize [′ɔrgə‚naɪz] *tr* organiser

organizer [′ɔrgə‚naɪzər] *s* organisateur *m*

or′gan loft′ *s* tribune *f* d′orgue

orgasm [′ɔrgæzəm] *s* orgasme *m*

or·gy [′ɔrdʒi] *s* (*pl* **-gies**) orgie *f*

orient [′ɔri·ənt] *s* orient *m*; **Orient** Orient ‖ [′ɔri‚ɛnt] *tr* orienter

oriental [‚ɔri′ɛntəl] *adj* oriental ‖ (*cap*) *s* Oriental *m*

orien′tal rug′ *s* tapis *m* d′orient

orientate [′ɔri·ɛn‚tet] *tr* orienter

orientation [‚ɔri·ɛn′teʃən] *s* orientation *f*

orifice [′ɔrɪfɪs] *s* orifice *m*

origin [′ɔfədʒɪn] *s* origine *f*

original [ə′rɪdʒɪnəl] *adj* (*new, not copied; inventive*) original; (*earliest*) originel, primitif; (*first*) originaire, premier ‖ *s* original *m*

originality [ə‚rɪdʒɪ′næliti] *s* originalité *f*

originate [ə′rɪdʒə‚net] *tr* faire naître, créer ‖ *intr* prendre naissance; **to originate from** provenir de

oriole [′ɔri‚ol] *s* loriot *m*

ormolu [′ɔrmə‚lu] *s* bronze *m* doré; (*powdered gold for gilding*) or *m* moulu; (*alloy of zinc and copper*) similor *m*

ornament [′ɔrnəmənt] *s* ornement *m* ‖ [′ɔrnə‚mɛnt] *tr* ornementer, orner

ornamental [‚ɔrnə′mɛntəl] *adj* ornemental

ornate [ɔr′net], [′ɔrnet] *adj* orné, fleuri

ornery [′ɔrnəri] *adj* (coll) acariâtre, intraitable

ornithology [‚ɔrnɪ′θɑlədʒi] *s* ornithologie *f*

orphan [′ɔrfən] *adj & s* orphelin *m*

orphanage [′ɔrfənɪdʒ] *s* (*asylum*) orphelinat *m*; (*orphanhood*) orphelinage *m*

Orpheus [′ɔrfi·əs] *s* Orphée *m*

orthodontics [‚ɔrθə′dɑntɪks] *s* orthodontie *f*

orthodox [′ɔrθə‚dɑks] *adj* orthodoxe

orthogra·phy [ɔr′θɑgrəfi] *s* (*pl* **-phies**) orthographe *f*

oscillate [′ɑsɪ‚let] *intr* osciller

osier [′oʒər] *s* osier *m*

osmosis [ɑz′mosɪs] *s* osmose *f*

osprey [′ɑspri] *s* aigle *m* pêcheur

ossi·fy [′ɑsɪ‚faɪ] *v* (*pret & pp* **-fied**) *tr* ossifier ‖ *intr* s′ossifier

ostensible [ɑs′tɛnsɪbəl] *adj* prétendu, apparent, soi-disant

ostentatious [‚ɑstɛn′teʃəs] *adj* ostentatoire, fastueux

osteopathy [‚ɑstɪ′ɑpəθi] *s* ostéopathie *f*

ostracism [′ɑstrə‚sɪzəm] *s* ostracisme *m*

ostracize [′ɑstrə‚saɪz] *tr* frapper d′ostracisme

ostrich [′ɑstrɪtʃ] *s* autruche *f*

other [′ʌðər] *adj* autre; **every other day** tous les deux jours; **every other one** un sur deux ‖ *pron indef* autre ‖ *adv*—**other than** autrement que

otherwise [′ʌðər‚waɪz] *adv* autrement, à part cela ‖ *conj* sinon, e.g., **come at once, otherwise it will be too late** venez tout de suite, sinon il sera trop tard; sans cela, e.g., **thanks, otherwise I′d have forgotten** merci, sans cela j′aurais oublié

oth′er·world′ly *adj* détaché des contingences de ce monde

otter [′ɑtər] *s* loutre *f*

Ottoman [′ɑtəmən] *adj* ottoman ‖ (*l.c.*) *s* (*corded fabric*) ottoman *m*; (*divan*) ottomane *f*; (*footstool*) pouf *m*; **Ottoman** (*person*) Ottoman *m*

ouch [autʃ] *interj* aïe!

ought [ɔt] *s* zéro *m*; **for ought I know** pour autant que je sache ‖ *aux* used to express obligation, e.g., **he ought to go away** il devrait s′en aller; e.g., **he ought to have gone away** il aurait dû s′en aller

ounce [auns] *s* once *f*

our [aur] *adj poss* notre §88

ours [aurz] *pron poss* le nôtre §89

our·selves′ *pron pers* nous-mêmes §86; nous §85, §87

oust [aust] *tr* évincer, chasser

out [aut] *adj* extérieur; absent; (*fire*) éteint; (*secret*) divulgé; (*tide*) bas; (*flower*) épanoui; (*rope*) filé; (*lease*) expiré; (*gear*) débrayé; (*unconscious person*) évanoui; (*boxer*) knockouté; (*book, magazine, etc.*) paru, publié; (*out of print, out of stock*) épuisé; (*a ball*) (sports) hors jeu; (*a player*) (sports) éliminé ‖ *s* (*pretext*) échappatoire *f*; **to be on the outs with** être brouillé avec ‖ *adv* dehors, au dehors; (*outdoors*) en plein air; **out and out** complètement; **out for** en quête de; **out for lunch** parti déjeuner; **out of** (*cash*) démuni de; (*a glass, cup, etc.*) dans; (*a bottle*) à; (*the window; curiosity, friendship, respect, etc.*) par; (*range, sight*) hors de; de, e.g., **to cry out of joy** pleurer de joie; e.g., **made out of** fait de, sur, e.g., **nine times out of ten** neuf fois sur dix; **out of sight, out of mind** loin des yeux, loin du cœur; **out with it!** allez, dites-le!; **to be out** (*to be absent*) être sorti; faire, e.g., **the sun is out** il fait du soleil;

to be out of bounds (sports) être hors jeu ‖ *prep* par ‖ *interj* hors d'ici!, ouste!

out′ and away′ *adv* de beaucoup, de loin

out′-and-out′ *adj* vrai; (*fanatic*) intransigeant; (*liar*) achevé

out′-and-out′er *s* (coll) intransigeant *m*

out′bid′ *v* (*pret* **-bid**; *pp* **-bid** or **-bidden**; *ger* **-bidding**) *tr* enchérir sur; (fig) renchérir sur ‖ *intr* surenchérir

out′board mo′tor *s* moteur *m* hors-bord, motogodille *f*

out′break′ *s* déchaînement *m*; (*of hives; of anger; etc.*) éruption *f*; (*of epidemic*) manifestation *f*; (*insurrection*) révolte *f*

out′build′ing *s* annexe *f*, dépendance *f*

out′burst′ *s* explosion *f*; (*of anger*) accès *m*; (*of laughter*) éclat *m*; (*e.g., of generosity*) élan *m*

out′cast′ *adj* & *s* banni *m*, proscrit *m*

out′caste′ *adj* hors caste ‖ *s* hors-caste *mf*

out′come′ *s* résultat *m*, dénouement *m*

out′cry′ *s* (*pl* **-cries**) clameur *f*; (*of indignation*) levée *f* de boucliers, tollé *m*

out·dat′ed *adj* démodé, suranné

out′dis′tance *tr* dépasser; (sports) distancer

out′do′ *v* (*pret* **-did**; *pp* **-done**) *tr* surpasser, l'emporter sur; **to outdo oneself** se surpasser

out′door′ *adj* au grand air; (sports) de plein air

out′door grill′ *s* rôtisserie *f* en plein air

out′doors′ *s* rase campagne *f*, plein air *m* ‖ *adv* au grand air, en plein air; en plein air; (*outside of the house*) hors de la maison; (*at night*) à la belle étoile

out′door swim′ming pool′ *s* piscine *f* à ciel ouvert

outer [′aʊtər] *adj* extérieur, externe

out′er space′ *s* cosmos *m*, espace *m* cosmique

out′field′ *s* (*baseball*) grand champ *m*

out′fit′ *s* équipement *m*, attirail *m*; (*caseful of implements*) trousse *f*, nécessaire *m*; (*ensemble*) costume et accessoires *mpl*; (*of a bride*) trousseau *m*; (*team*) équipe *f*; (*group of soldiers*) unité *f*, (com) compagnie *f* ‖ *v* (*pret* & *pp* **-fitted**; *ger* **-fitting**) *tr* équiper

out′go′ing *adj* en partance, partant; (*officeholder*) sortant; (*friendly*) communicatif, sympathique

out′grow′ *v* (*pret* **-grew**; *pp* **-grown**) *tr* devenir plus grand que; (*e.g., childhood clothes, activities, etc.*) devenir trop grand pour; abandonner, se défaire de

out′growth′ *s* excroissance *f*; (fig) résultat *m*, conséquence *f*

outing [′aʊtɪŋ] *s* excursion *f*, sortie *f*

outlandish [aʊt′lændɪʃ] *adj* bizarre, baroque

out′last′ *tr* durer plus longtemps que; survivre (with *dat*)

out′law′ *s* hors-la-loi *m*, proscrit *m* ‖ *tr* mettre hors la loi, proscrire

out′lay′ *s* débours *mpl*, dépenses *fpl* ‖ **out′lay′** *v* (*pret* & *pp* **-laid**) *tr* débourser, dépenser

out′let′ *s* (*for water, etc.*) sortie *f*, issue *f*; (*escape valve*) deversoir *m*; (*for, e.g., pent-up emotions*) exutoire *m*; (com) débouché *m*; (elec) prise *f* de courant, prise électrique; **no outlet** (public sign) rue sans issue

out′line′ *s* (*profile*) contour *m*; (*sketch*) esquisse *f*; (*summary*) aperçu *m*; (*of a work in preparation*) plan *m*; (*main points*) grandes lignes *fpl* ‖ *tr* esquisser; (*a work in preparation*) ébaucher

out′live′ *tr* survivre (with *dat*)

out′lived′ *adj* caduc, désuet

out′look′ *s* perspective *f*, point *m* de vue

out′ly′ing *adj* éloigné, écarté, isolé

outmoded [,aʊt′moʊdɪd] *adj* démodé

out′num′ber *tr* surpasser en nombre

out′ of bounds′ *adj* hors jeu

out′-of-date′ *adj* démodé, suranné; (*document*) périmé

out′-of-door′ *adj* au grand air

out′-of-doors′ *adj* au grand air ‖ *s* rase campagne *f*, plein air *m* ‖ *adv* au grand air, hors de la maison

out′ of or′der *adj* en panne, en dérangement; **to be out of order** (*to be out of sequence*) ne pas être dans l'ordre

out′ of print′ *adj* épuisé

out′ of step′ *s*—**to be out of step** ne pas être au pas; **to be out of step with** marcher à contre-pas de; **to get out of step** perdre le pas

out′ of tune′ *adj* désaccordé ‖ *adv* faux, e.g., **to sing out of tune** chanter faux

out′ of work′ *adj* en chômage

out′pa′tient *s* malade *mf* de consultation externe

out′patient clin′ic *s* consultation *f* externe

out′post′ *s* avant-poste *m*, antenne *f*

out′put′ *s* rendement *m*, débit *m*; (*of a mine; of a worker*) production *f*

out′rage *s* outrage *m*; (*wanton violence*) atrocité *f*, attentat *m* honteux ‖ *tr* faire outrage à, outrager; (*a woman*) violer

outrageous [aʊt′reʤəs] *adj* outrageux; (*intolerable*) insupportable

out′rank′ *tr* dépasser en grade, dépasser en rang

out′rid′er *s* explorateur *m*; cow-boy *m*; (*mounted attendant*) piqueur *m*

outrigger [′aʊt,rɪgər] *s* (*outboard framework*) balancier *m*; (*oar support*) porte-en-dehors *m*

out′right′ *adj* pur, absolu; (*e.g., manner*) franc, direct ‖ **out′right′** *adv* complètement; (*frankly*) franchement; (*at once*) sur le coup

out′set′ *s* début *m*, commencement *m*

out′side′ *adj* du dehors, d'extérieur ‖ **out′side′** *s* dehors *m*, extérieur *m*; surface *f*; **at the outside** tout au plus, au maximum ‖ **out′side′** *adv* dehors, à l'extérieur; (*outdoors*) en plein air; **outside of** en dehors de, à l'extérieur de; (*except for*) sauf ‖ **out′side′** or **out′side′** *prep* en dehors de, à l'extérieur de

outsider [ˌaʊt'saɪdər] *s* étranger *m*; (*intruder*) intrus *m*; (*uninitiated*) profane *mf*; (*dark horse*) outsider *m*

out'size' *adj* hors série

out'skirts' *spl* approches *fpl*, périphérie *f*

out'spo'ken *adj* franc; **to be outspoken** avoir son franc-parler

out'stand'ing *adj* saillant; (*eminent*) hors pair, hors ligne; (*debts*) à recouvrer, impayé

outward ['aʊtwərd] *adj* extérieur; (*apparent*) superficiel; (*direction*) en dehors ‖ *adv* au dehors, vers le dehors

out'weigh' *tr* peser plus que; (*in value*) l'emporter en valeur sur

out'wit' *v* (*pret & pp* **-witted;** *ger* **-witting**) *tr* duper, déjouer; (*a pursuer*) dépister

oval ['ovəl] *adj & s* ovale *m*

ova·ry ['ovəri] *s* (*pl* **-ries**) ovaire *m*

ovation [o've∫ən] *s* ovation *f*

oven ['ʌvən] *s* four *m*; (fig) fournaise *f*

over ['ovər] *adj* fini, passé; (*additional*) en plus; (*excessive*) en excès; plus, e.g., **eight and over** huit et plus ‖ *adv* au-dessus, dessus; (*on the other side*) de l'autre côté; (*again*) de nouveau; (*on the reverse side of sheet of paper*) au verso; (*finished*) passé, achevé; **all over** (*everywhere*) partout; (*finished*) fini; (*completely*) jusqu'au bout des ongles; **I'll be right over** (coll) j'arrive tout de suite; **over!** (*turn the page!*) voir au verso!, tournez!; (rad) à vous!; **over again** de nouveau, encore une fois; **over against** en face de; (*compared to*) auprès de; **over and above** en plus de; **over and out!** (rad) terminé!; **over and over** à coups répétés, à plusieurs reprises; **over here** ici, de ce côté; **over there** là-bas; **to be over** (*an illness*) s'être remis de; **to hand over** remettre ‖ *prep* au-dessus de; (*on top of*) sur, par-dessus; (*with motion*) par-dessus, e.g., **to jump over a fence** sauter par-dessus une barrière; (*a period of time*) pendant, au cours de; (*near*) près de; (*a certain number or amount*) plus de, au-dessus de; (*concerning*) à propos de, au sujet de; (*on the other side of*) au delà de, de l'autre côté de; à, e.g., **over the telephone** au téléphone; (*while doing s.th.*) tout en prenant, e.g., **over a cup of coffee** tout en prenant une tasse de café; **all over** répandu sur; **over and above** en sus de, en plus de; **to fall over** (*e.g., a cliff*) tomber du haut de; **to reign over** régner sur ‖ *interj* (CB language) terminé!

o'ver·all' *adj* hors tout, complet; général, total ‖ **overalls** *spl* combinaison *f* d'homme, cotte *f*, salopette *f*

o'ver·awe' *tr* impressionner, intimider

o'ver·bear'ing *adj* impérieux, tranchant, autoritaire

o'ver·board' *adv* par-dessus bord; **man overboard!** un homme à la mer!; **to throw overboard** jeter par-dessus le bord; (fig) abandonner

o'ver·book'ing *s* surréservation *f*

o'ver·cast' *adj* obscurci, nuageux ‖ *s* ciel *m* couvert ‖ *v* (*pret & pp* **-cast**) *tr* obscurcir, couvrir

o'ver·charge' *s* prix *m* excessif, majoration *f* excessive; (elec) surcharge *f* ‖ **o'ver·charge'** *tr* (*a customer*) rançonner; (elec) surcharger; **to overcharge s.o. for s.th.** faire payer trop cher q.ch. à qn ‖ *intr* demander un prix excessif

o'ver·coat' *s* pardessus *m*

o'ver·come' *v* (*pret* **-came;** *pp* **-come**) *tr* vaincre; (*difficulties*) surmonter

o'ver·con'fidence *s* témérité *f*, confiance *f* exagérée

o'ver·con'fident *adj* téméraire, excessivement confiant

o'ver·cooked' *adj* trop cuit

o'ver·crowd' *tr* bonder; (*a town, region, etc.*) surpeupler

o'ver·do' *v* (*pret* **-did;** *pp* **-done**) *tr* exagérer; **overdone** (culin) trop cuit ‖ *intr* se surmener

o'ver·dose' *s* dose *f* excessive, surdosage *m*

o'ver·draft' *s* découvert *m*, solde *m* débiteur

o'ver·draw' *v* (*pret* **-drew;** *pp* **-drawn**) *tr* tirer à découvert ‖ *intr* excéder son crédit

o'ver·drive' *s* (aut) surmultiplication *f*

o'ver·due' *adj* en retard; (com) échu, arriéré

o'ver·eat' *v* (*pret* **-ate;** *pp* **-eaten**) *tr & intr* trop manger

o'ver·exer'tion *s* surmenage *m*

o'ver·expose' *tr* surexposer

o'ver·expo'sure *s* surexposition *f*

o'ver·flow' *s* débordement *m*; (*pipe*) trop-plein *m* ‖ **o'ver·flow'** *tr & intr* déborder

o'ver·fly' *v* (*pret* **-flew;** *pp* **-flown**) *tr* survoler

o'ver·grown' *adj* démesuré; (*e.g., child*) trop grand pour son âge; **overgrown with** (*e.g., weeds*) envahi par, recouvert de

o'ver·hang' *v* (*pret & pp* **-hung**) *tr* surplomber, faire saillie au-dessus de; (*to threaten*) menacer ‖ *intr* (*to jut out*) faire saillie

o'ver·haul' *s* remise *f* en état ‖ **o'ver·haul'** *tr* remettre en état; (*to catch up to*) rattraper

o'ver·head' *adj* élevé; aérien, surélevé ‖ *s* (*overpass*) pont-route *m*; (com) frais *mpl* généraux ‖ **o'ver·head'** *adv* au-dessus de la tête, en haut

o'ver·head projec'tor *s* rétroprojecteur *m*

o'ver·head valve' *s* soupape *f* en tête

o'ver·hear' *v* (*pret & pp* **-heard**) *tr* entendre par hasard; (*a conversation*) surprendre

o'ver·heat' *tr* surchauffer

overjoyed [ˌovər'dʒɔɪd] *adj* ravi, transporté de joie

overland ['ovərˌlænd] *adj & adv* par terre, par voie de terre

o'ver·lap' *v* (*pret & pp* **-lapped;** *ger* **-lapping**) *tr* enchevaucher, imbriquer ‖ *intr* chevaucher

o'ver·lap'ping *s* recouvrement *m*, chevauchement *m*, imbrication *f*; (*of functions, offices, etc.*) double emploi *m*

o'ver·load' *s* surcharge *f*; (comp) surcharge; **sudden overload** (elec) coup *m* de collier ‖ **o'ver·load'** *tr* surcharger

o'ver·look' *tr* (*to survey*) donner sur, avoir vue sur; (*to ignore*) fermer les yeux sur, passer sous silence; (*to neglect*) oublier, négliger

o'ver·lord' *s* suzerain *m* ‖ **o'ver·lord'** *tr* dominer, tyranniser

overly ['ovərli] *adv* (coll) trop, à l'excès

o'ver·med'icate *intr* (med) surmédicaliser

o'ver·night' *adv* toute la nuit; du jour au lendemain; **to stay overnight** passer la nuit

o'ver·night' bag' *s* sac *m* de nuit

o'ver·pass' *s* passage *m* supérieur, pont-route *m*, saut-de-mouton *m*

o'ver·pay'ment *s* surpaye *f*, rétribution *f* excessive

o'ver·pop'ula'tion *s* surpeuplement *m*, surpopulation *f*

o'ver·pow'er *tr* maîtriser; **overpowered with grief** accablé de douleur

o'ver·pow'ering *adj* accablant, irrésistible

o'ver·produc'tion *s* surproduction *f*

o'ver·rate' *tr* surestimer

o'ver·reach' *tr* dépasser

o'ver·ripe' *adj* blet, trop mûr

o'ver·rule' *tr* décider contre; (*to set aside*) annuler, casser

o'ver·run' *v* (*pret* **-ran;** *pp* **-run;** *ger* **-running**) *tr* envahir; (*to flood*) inonder; (*limits, boundaries, etc.*) dépasser ‖ *intr* déborder

o'ver·sea' or **o'ver·seas'** *adj* d'outre-mer ‖ **o'ver·sea'** or **o'ver·seas'** *adv* outre-mer

o'ver·see' *v* (*pret* **-saw;** *pp* **-seen**) *tr* surveiller

o'ver·se'er *s* surveillant *m*, inspecteur *m*

o'ver·sexed' *adj* hypersexué

o'ver·shad'ow *tr* ombrager; (fig) éclipser

o'ver·shoes' *spl* caoutchoucs *mpl*

o'ver·sight' *s* inadvertance *f*, étourderie *f*

o'ver·sleep' *v* (*pret & pp* **-slept**) *intr* dormir trop longtemps

o'ver·step' *v* (*pret & pp* **-stepped;** *ger* **-stepping**) *tr* dépasser, outrepasser

o'ver·stock' *tr* surapprovisionner

o'ver·stuffed' *adj* rembourré

o'ver·sup·ply' *s* (*pl* **-plies**) excédent *m*, abondance *f* ‖ **o'ver·sup·ply'** *v* (*pret & pp* **-plied**) *tr* approvisionner avec excès

overt ['ovərt], [o'vʌrt] *adj* ouvert, manifeste; (*intentional*) prémédité

o'ver·take' *v* (*pret* **-took;** *pp* **-taken**) *tr* rattraper; (*a runner*) dépasser; (*an automobile*) doubler; (*to surprise*) surprendre

o'ver·tax' *tr* surtaxer; (*to tire*) surmener, excéder

o'ver-the-coun'ter *adj* vendu directement à l'acheteur

o'ver·throw' *s* renversement *m* ‖ **o'ver·throw'** *v* (*pret* **-threw;** *pp* **-thrown**) *tr* renverser

o'ver·time' *adj & adv* en heures supplémentaires ‖ *s* heures *fpl* supplémentaires

o'ver·time pe'riod *s* prolongation *f*

o'ver·tone' *s* (mus) harmonique *m*; (fig) signification *f*, sous-entendue *m*

o'ver·trump' *tr* surcouper

overture ['ovərtʃər] *s* ouverture *f*

o'ver·turn' *tr* renverser, chavirer ‖ *intr* chavirer; (aer, aut) capoter

overweening [,ovər'winɪŋ] *adj* arrogant, outrecuidant

o'ver·weight' *adj* au-dessus du poids normal; (*fat*) obèse ‖ *s* excédent *m* de poids

overwhelm [,ovər'hwɛlm] *tr* accabler, écraser; (*with favors, gifts, etc.*) combler

o'ver·work' *s* surmenage *m*, excès *m* de travail ‖ **o'ver·work'** *tr* surmener, surcharger; abuser de, trop employer ‖ *intr* se surmener

Ovid ['ɑvɪd] *s* Ovide *m*

ow [au] *interj* aïe!

owe [o] *tr* devoir ‖ *intr* avoir des dettes; **to owe for** avoir à payer, devoir

owing ['o·ɪŋ] *adj* dû, redû; **owing to** à cause de, en raison de

owl [aul] *s* (*Asio*) hibou *m*; (*Strix*) chouette *f*, hulotte *f*; (*Tyto alba*) effraie *f*

own [on] *adj* propre, e.g., **my own brother** mon propre frère ‖ *s*—**all its own** spécial, authentique, e.g., **an aroma all its own** un parfum spécial, un parfum authentique; **my own (your own, etc.)** le mien (le vôtre, etc.) §89; **of my own (of their own, etc.)** bien à moi (bien à eux, etc.); **on one's own** à son propre compte, de son propre chef; **to come into one's own** entrer en possession de son bien; (*to win out*) obtenir de succès; (*to receive due praise*) recevoir les honneurs qu'on mérite; **to hold one's own** se maintenir, se défendre ‖ *tr* posséder; être propriétaire de; (*to acknowledge*) reconnaître ‖ *intr*—**to own to** convenir de, reconnaître; **to own up** (coll) faire des aveux; **to own up to** (coll) faire l'aveu de, avouer

owner ['onər] *s* propriétaire *mf*, possesseur *m*

ownership ['onər,ʃɪp] *s* propriété *f*, possession *f*

own'er's li'cense *s* carte *f* grise

ox [ɑks] *s* (*pl* **oxen** ['ɑksən**]**) bœuf *m*

ox'cart' *s* char *m* à bœufs

oxfords ['ɑksfərdz] *spl* richelieus *mpl*

oxide ['ɑksaɪd] *s* oxyde *m*

oxidize ['ɑksɪ,daɪz] *tr* oxyder ‖ *intr* s'oxyder

oxygen ['ɑksɪdʒən] *s* oxygène *m*

oxygenate ['ɑksɪdʒə,net] *tr* oxygéner

ox'ygen tent' *s* tente *f* à oxygène

oxytone ['ɑksɪ,ton] *adj & s* oxyton *m*

oyster ['ɔɪstər] *adj* huîtrier ‖ *s* huître *f*

oys'ter bed' *s* huîtrière *f*, banc *m* d'huîtres

oys'ter cock'tail *s* huîtres *fpl* écaillées aux condiments

oys'ter farm' *s* parc *m* à huîtres, clayère *f*

oys'ter fork' *s* fourchette *f* à huîtres

oys'ter knife' *s* couteau *m* à huîtres

oys'ter·man *s* (*pl* **-men**) écailler *m*

oys′ter o′pener *s* (*person*) écailler *m*; (*implement*) ouvre-huîtres *m*
oys′ter plant′ *s* salsifis *m*

oys′ter shell′ *s* coquille *f* d'huître
oys′ter stew′ *s* soupe *f* à huîtres
ozone [ˈozon] *s* ozone *m*; (coll) air *m* frais

P

P, p [pi] *s* XVIe lettre de l'alphabet
pace [pes] *s* pas *m*; **to keep pace with** marcher de pair avec; **to put through one's paces** mettre à l'épreuve; **to set the pace** mener le train ‖ *tr* arpenter; **to pace off** mesurer au pas ‖ *intr* aller au pas; (equit) ambler
pace′mak′er *s* meneur *m* de train; (med) stimulateur *m* (cardiaque)
pacific [pəˈsɪfɪk] *adj* pacifique ‖ **Pacific** *adj* & *s* Pacifique *m*
pacifier [ˈpæsɪˌfaɪər] *s* pacificateur *m*; (*teething ring*) sucette *f*
pacifism [ˈpæsɪˌfɪzəm] *s* pacifisme *m*
pacifist [ˈpæsɪfɪst] *adj* & *s* pacifiste *mf*
paci·fy [ˈpæsɪˌfaɪ] *v* (*pret* & *pp* **-fied**) *tr* pacifier
pack [pæk] *s* (*of peddler*) ballot *m*; (*of soldier*) paquetage *m*, sac *m*; (*of beast of burden*) bât *m*; (*of hounds*) meute *f*; (*of evildoers; of wolves*) bande *f*; (*of lies*) tissu *m*; (*of playing cards*) jeu *m*; (*of cigarettes*) paquet *m*; (*of floating ice*) banquise *f*; (*of troubles*) foule *f*; (*of fools*) tas *m*; (med) enveloppement *m* ‖ *tr* emballer, empaqueter; mettre en boîte; (*e.g., earth*) tasser; (*to stuff*) bourrer; **to send packing** (coll) envoyer promener ‖ *intr* faire ses bagages
package [ˈpækɪdʒ] *s* paquet *m* ‖ *tr* empaqueter
pack′age deal′ *s* accord *m* global, achat *m* forfaitaire
pack′age plan′ *s* voyage *m* à forfait
pack′aging *s* conditionnement *m*
pack′aging and prepara′tion *s* habillage *m*
pack′ an′imal *s* bête *f* de somme
packet [ˈpækɪt] *s* paquet *m*; (naut) paquebot *m*; (pharm) sachet *m*
pack′ horse′ *s* cheval *m* de bât
pack′ing box′ or **case′** *s* caisse *f* d'emballage
pack′ing house′ *s* conserverie *f*
pack′sad′dle *s* bât *m*
pack′thread′ *s* ficelle *f*
pack′train′ *s* convoi *m* de bêtes de somme
pact [pækt] *s* pacte *m*
pad [pæd] *s* (*to prevent friction or damage*) bourrelet *m*; (*of writing paper*) bloc *m*; (*for inking*) tampon *m*; (*of an aquatic plant*) feuille *f*; (*for launching a rocket*) rampe *f*; (*sound of footsteps*) pas *m*; (*one's home*) (slang) piaule *f*, turne *f*, baraque *f* ‖ *v* (*pret* & *pp* **padded**; *ger* **padding**) *tr* rembourrer; (*to expand unnecessarily*) délayer ‖ *intr* aller à pied

pad′ded cell′ *s* cellule *f* matelassée, cabanon *m*
paddle [ˈpædəl] *s* (*of a canoe*) pagaie *f*; (*for table tennis*) raquette *f*; (*of a wheel*) aube *f*; (*for beating*) palette *f* ‖ *tr* pagayer; (*to spank*) fesser ‖ *intr* pagayer; (*to splash*) barboter
pad′dle wheel′ *s* roue *f* à aubes
paddock [ˈpædək] *s* enclos *m*; (*at race track*) paddock *m*
pad′dy wag′on [ˈpædi] *s* (slang) panier *m* à salade
pad′lock′ *s* cadenas *m* ‖ *tr* cadenasser
pagan [ˈpagən] *adj* & *s* païen *m*
paganism [ˈpegəˌnɪzəm] *s* paganisme *m*
page [pedʒ] *s* (*of a book*) page *f*; (*boy attendant*) page *m*; (*in a hotel or club*) chasseur *m* ‖ *tr* (*a book*) paginer; appeler, demander, e.g., **you are being paged** on vous demande
pageant [ˈpædʒənt] *s* parade *f* à grand spectacle
pageant·ry [ˈpædʒəntri] *s* (*pl* **-ries**) grand apparat *m*; vaines pompes *fpl*
page′ proof′ *s* épreuve *f* de pages, seconde épreuve; (journ) morasse *f*
paginate [ˈpædʒɪˌnet] *tr* paginer
paging [ˈpedʒɪŋ] *s* mise *f* en pages
paid′ in full′ [ped] *adj* (*formula stamped on bill*) pour acquit
paid′ vaca′tion *s* congé *m* payé
pail [pel] *s* seau *m*
pain [pen] *s* douleur *f*; **on pain of** sous peine de; **pain in the neck** (fig) casse-pieds *m*; **to take pains** se donner de la peine ‖ *tr* faire mal à; **it pains me to** il me coûte de ‖ *intr* faire mal
painful [ˈpenfəl] *adj* douloureux
pain′kil′ler *s* (coll) calmant *m*
painless [ˈpenlɪs] *adj* sans douleur
pains′tak′ing *adj* soigneux; (*work*) soigné
paint [pent] *s* peinture *f*; **wet paint** peinture fraîche; (*public sign*) attention à la peinture! ‖ *tr* & *intr* peindre
paint′box′ *s* boîte *f* de couleurs
paint′brush′ *s* pinceau *m*
paint′ buck′et *s* camion *m*
painter [ˈpentər] *s* peintre *mf*
painting [ˈpentɪŋ] *s* peinture *f*
paint′ remov′er *s* décapant *m*
pair [pɛr] *s* paire *f*; (*of people*) couple *m* ‖ *tr* accoupler ‖ *intr* s'accoupler
pair′ of scis′sors *s* ciseaux *mpl*
pair′ of trou′sers *s* pantalon *m*
pajam′a par′ty [pəˈdʒamə] *s* soirée-hébergement *f*

pajamas *spl* pyjama *m*, pyjamas
Pakistan [‚pɑkɪˈstɑn] *s* le Pakistan
Pakista·ni [‚pɑkɪˈstɑni] *adj* pakistanais ‖ *s* (*pl* -**nis**) Pakistanais *m*
pal [pæl] *s* copain *m* ‖ *v* (*pret & pp* **palled**; *ger* **palling**) *intr* (coll) être de bons copains; **to pal with** être copain de
palace [ˈpælɪs] *s* palais *m*
palatable [ˈpælətəbəl] *adj* savoureux; (*acceptable*) agréable
palatal [ˈpælətəl] *adj* palatal ‖ *s* palatale *f*
palate [ˈpælɪt] *s* palais *m*
pale [pel] *adj* pâle ‖ *s* (*stake*) pieu *m*; **beyond the pale** au-delà de la limite permise ‖ *intr* pâlir
pale′face′ *s* visage *m* pâle
palette [ˈpælɪt] *s* palette *f*
palfrey [ˈpɔlfri] *s* palefroi *m*
palisade [‚pælɪˈsed] *s* palissade *f*; (*line of cliffs*) falaise *f*
pall [pɔl] *s* (*over a casket*) poêle *m*, drap *m* mortuaire; (*coffin*) cercueil *m*, poêle; (*to cover chalice*) pale *f*; (*vestment*) pallium *m* ‖ *intr* devenir fade; **to pall on** rassasier
pall′bear′er *s* porteur *m* d'un cordon du poêle; **to be a pallbearer** tenir les cordons du poêle
pallet [ˈpælɪt] *s* grabat *m*
palliate [ˈpælɪˌet] *tr* pallier
pallid [ˈpælɪd] *adj* pâle, blême
pallor [ˈpælər] *s* pâleur *f*
palm [pɑm] *s* (*of the hand*) paume *f*; (*measure*) palme *m*; (*leaf*) palme *f*; (*tree*) palmier *m*; **to carry off the palm** remporter la palme; **to grease the palm of** (slang) graisser la patte à ‖ *tr* (*a card*) escamoter; **to palm off s.th. on s.o.** refiler q.ch. à qn
palmet·to [pælˈmɛto] *s* (*pl* -**tos** or -**toes**) palmier *m* nain
palmist [ˈpɑmɪst] *s* chiromancien *m*
palmistry [ˈpɑmɪstri] *s* chiromancie *f*
palm′ leaf′ *s* palme *f*
palm′ oil′ *s* huile *f* de palme
Palm′ Sun′day *s* le dimanche des Rameaux
palm′ tree′ *s* palmier *m*
palpable [ˈpælpəbəl] *adj* palpable
palpitate [ˈpælpɪˌtet] *intr* palpiter
pal·sy [ˈpɔlzi] *s* (*pl* -**sies**) paralysie *f* ‖ *v* (*pret & pp* -**sied**) *tr* paralyser
pal·try [ˈpɔltri] *adj* (*comp* -**trier**; *super* -**triest**) misérable
pamper [ˈpæmpər] *tr* choyer, gâter
pamphlet [ˈpæmflɪt] *s* brochure *f*
pan [pæn] *s* (*for cooking*) casserole *f*; (*basin*; *scale of a balance*) bassin *m*; (slang) binette *f*; **Pan** Pan *m* ‖ *v* (*pret & pp* **panned**; *ger* **panning**) *tr* (*gold*) laver à la batée; (coll) débiner, éreinter ‖ *intr* laver à la batée; (mov) panoramiquer; **to pan out well** (coll) réussir
panacea [‚pænəˈsi·ə] *s* panacée *f*
Panama [ˈpænəˌmɑ] *s* le Panama
Pan′ama Canal′ *s* canal *m* de Panama
Pan′ama Canal′ Zone′ *s* zone *f* canal du Panama
Pan′ama hat′ *s* panama *m*

Pan-American [‚pænəˈmɛrɪkən] *adj* panaméricain
pan′cake′ *s* crêpe *f* ‖ *intr* (aer) descendre à plat, se plaquer
pan′cake land′ing *s* atterrissage *m* plaque, sur le ventre, or à plat
panchromatic [‚pænkroˈmætɪk] *adj* panchromatique
pancreas [ˈpænkrɪ·əs] *s* pancréas *m*
panda [ˈpændə] *s* panda *m*
pander [ˈpændər] *s* entremetteur *m* ‖ *intr* servir d'entremetteur; **to pander to** se prêter à; encourager
pane [pen] *s* carreau *m*, vitre *f*
pan·el [ˈpænəl] *s* panneau *m*; (*on wall*) lambris *m*; (*door, wall*) panneau *m*; (*ceiling*) caisson *m*; (*discussion group*) groupe *m* de discussion; (law) liste *f*, tableau *m* ‖ *v* (*pret & pp* -**eled** or -**elled**; *ger* -**eling** or -**elling**) *tr* (*a room*) garnir de boiseries; (*a wall*) lambrisser
pan′el discus′sion *s* colloque *m*
panelist [ˈpænəlɪst] *s* membre *m* d'un groupe de discussion
pang [pæŋ] *s* élancement *m*, angoisse *f*
pan′han′dle *s* queue *f* de la poêle; (geog) projection *f* d'un territoire dans un autre ‖ *intr* (slang) mendigoter
pan′han′dler *s* (slang) mendigot *m*
pan·ic [ˈpænɪk] *adj & s* panique *f* ‖ *v* (*pret & pp* -**icked**; *ger* -**icking**) *tr* semer la panique dans ‖ *intr* être pris de panique
pan′ic-strick′en *adj* pris de panique
pano·ply [ˈpænəpli] *s* (*pl* -**plies**) panoplie *f*
panorama [‚pænəˈrɑmə] *s* panorama *m*
pan·sy [ˈpænzi] *s* (*pl* -**sies**) pensée *f*; (slang) tapette *f*
pant [pænt] *s* halètement *m*; **pants** pantalon *m*; **to wear the pants** (coll) porter la culotte ‖ *intr* haleter, panteler
pantheism [ˈpænθɪˌɪzəm] *s* panthéisme *m*
pantheon [ˈpænθɪˌɑn] *s* panthéon *m*
panther [ˈpænθər] *s* panthère *f*
panties [ˈpæntiz] *spl* culotte *f*, slip *m* de femme
pantomime [ˈpæntəˌmaɪm] *s* pantomime *f*
pan·try [ˈpæntri] *s* (*pl* -**tries**) office *m & f*, dépense *f*
pant′y hose′ [ˈpænti] *s* collant *m*
pant′y lin′er *s* protège-slip *m*
pap [pæp] *s* bouillie *f*
papa [ˈpɑpə], [pəˈpɑ] *s* papa *m*
papa·cy [ˈpepəsi] *s* (*pl* -**cies**) papauté *f*
paper [ˈpepər] *s* papier *m*; (*newspaper*) journal *m*; (*of needles*) carte *f* ‖ *tr* tapisser
pa′per·back′ *s* livre *m* broché; (*pocketbook*) livre de poche
pa′per·boy′ *s* vendeur *m* de journaux
pa′per clip′ *s* attache *f*, trombone *m*
pa′per cone′ *s* cornet *m* de papier
pa′per cup′ *s* verre *m* en carton, gobelet *m* de papier
pa′per cut′ter *s* coupe-papier *m*
pa′per hand′kerchief *s* mouchoir *m* à jeter, mouchoir en papier
pa′per·hang′er *s* tapissier *m*
pa′per knife′ *s* coupe-papier *m*

pa′per mill′ *s* papeterie *f*
pa′per mon′ey *s* papier-monnaie *m*
pa′per nap′kin *s* serviette *f* en papier
pa′per plate′ *s* assiette *f* en carton, assiette de papier
pa′per tape′ *s* bande *f* de papier
pa′per tow′el *s* serviette *f* de toilette en papier
pa′per tow′eling *s* essuie-mains *m invar* en papier
pa′per·weight′ *s* presse-papiers *m*
pa′per work′ *s* travail *m* de bureau
papier-mâché [,pepərmə`ʃe] *s* papier-pierre *m*, papier *m* mâché
paprika [pæ`prikə] *s* paprika *m*
papy·rus [pə`paɪrəs] *s* (*pl* **ri** [raɪ]) papyrus *m*
par [pɑr] *s* pair *m*; (golf) normale *f* du parcours; **at par** au pair; **to be on a par with** aller de pair avec
parable [`pærəbəl] *s* parabole *f*
parabola [pə`ræbələ] *s* parabole *f*
parachute [`pærə,ʃut] *s* parachute *m* ‖ *tr* & *intr* parachuter
par′achute jump′ *s* saut *m* en parachute
parachutist [`pærə,ʃutɪst] *s* parachutiste *mf*
parade [pə`red] *s* défilé *m*; (*ostentation*) parade *f*; (mil) parade ‖ *tr* faire parade de ‖ *intr* défiler; parader
paradise [`pærə,daɪs] *s* paradis *m*
paradox [`pærə,dɑks] *s* paradoxe *m*
paradoxical [,pærə`dɑksɪkəl] *adj* paradoxal
paraffin [`pærəfɪn] *s* paraffine *f* ‖ *tr* paraffiner
paragon [`pærə,gɑn] *s* parangon *m*
paragraph [`pærə,græf] *s* paragraphe *m*
Paraguay [`pærə,gwaɪ] *s* le Paraguay
Paraguayan [,pærə`gwaɪ·ən] *adj* paraguayen ‖ *s* Paraguayen *m*
parakeet [`pærə,kit] *s* perruche *f*
paral·lel [`pærə,lɛl] *adj* parallèle ‖ *s* (*line*) parallèle *f*; (*latitude; declination; comparison*) parallèle *m*; **parallels** (typ) barres *fpl*; **without parallel** sans pareil ‖ *v* (*pret* & *pp* **-leled** or **-lelled;** *ger* **-leling** or **-lelling**) *tr* mettre en parallèle; entrer en parallèle avec, égaler
par′allel bars′ *spl* barres *fpl* parallèles
paraly·sis [pə`rælɪsɪs] *s* (*pl* **-ses** [,siz]) paralysie *f*
paralytic [,pærə`lɪtɪk] *adj* & *s* paralytique *mf*
paralyze [`pærə,laɪz] *tr* paralyser
paramount [`pærə,maunt] *adj* suprême, capital
paranoiac [,pærə`nɔɪ·æk] *adj* & *s* paranoïaque *mf*
parapet [`pærə,pɛt] *s* parapet *m*
paraphernalia [,pærəfər`nelɪ·ə] *spl* effets *mpl* personnels; attirail *m*
paraphrase [`pærə,frez] *s* remaniement *m* ‖ *tr* remanier
paraplegic [,pærə`plidʒɪk] *adj* & *s* paraplégique *mf*
parasite [`pærə,saɪt] *s* parasite *m*
parasitic(al) [,pærə`sɪtɪk(əl)] *adj* parasite
parasol [`pærə,sɔl] *s* parasol *m*, ombrelle *f*

paratrooper [`pærə,trupər] *s* parachutiste *m*
parboil [`pɑr,bɔɪl] *tr* faire cuire légèrement; (*vegetables*) blanchir
par·cel [`pɑrsəl] *s* colis *m*, paquet *m* ‖ *v* (*pret* & *pp* **-celed** or **-celled;** *ger* **-celing** or **-celling**) *tr* morceler; **to parcel out** répartir
par′cel post′ *s* colis *mpl* postaux
parch [pɑrtʃ] *tr* dessécher; (*beans, grain, etc.*) griller
parchment [`pɑrtʃmənt] *s* parchemin *m*
pardon [`pɑrdən] *s* pardon *m*; (*remission of penalty by the state*) grâce *f*; **I beg your pardon** je vous demande pardon ‖ *tr* pardonner; pardonner à; (*a criminal*) gràcier; **to pardon s.o. for s.th.** pardonner q.ch. à qn
pardonable [`pɑrdənəbəl] *adj* pardonnable
pare [pɛr] *tr* (*potatoes, fruit, etc.*) éplucher; (*the nails*) rogner; (*costs*) réduire
parent [`pɛrənt] *s* père *m or* mère *f*; origine *f*, base *f*; **parents** parents *mpl*, père et mère
parentage [`pɛrəntɪdʒ] *s* paternité *f* or maternité *f*; naissance *f*, origine *f*
parenthe·sis [pə`rɛnθɪsɪs] *s* (*pl* **-ses** [,siz]) parenthèse *f*; **in parentheses** entre parenthèses
parenthood [`pɛrənt,hud] *s* paternité *f* or maternité *f*
pariah [pə`raɪ·ə], [`pɑrɪ·ə] *s* paria *m*
par′ing knife′ *s* couteau *m* à éplucher
Paris [`pærɪs] *s* Paris *m*
parish [`pærɪʃ] *adj* paroissien ‖ *s* paroisse *f*
parishioner [pə`rɪʃənər] *s* paroissien *m*
Parisian [pə`riʒən] *adj* & *s* parisien *m*
parity [`pærɪti] *s* parité *f*
park [pɑrk] *s* parc *m* ‖ *tr* garer, parquer ‖ *intr* stationner
parked *adj* en stationnement
parking [`pɑrkɪŋ] *s* parcage *m*; (*e.g., in a city street*) stationnement *m*; **no parking** (*public sign*) stationnement interdit
park′ing ar′ea *s* aire *f* de stationnement
park′ing lights′ *spl* (aut) feux *mpl* de stationnement, feux de position
park′ing lot′ *s* parking *m*, parc *m* à autos
park′ing me′ter *s* parcomètre *m*, compteur *m* de stationnement
park′ing spot′ *s* stalle *f*
park′ing tick′et *s* contravention *f*, papillon *m*
park′way′ *s* route *f* panoramique; (*turnpike*) autoroute *f*
parley [`pɑrli] *s* pourparlers *mpl* ‖ *intr* parlementer
parliament [`pɑrlɪmənt] *s* parlement *m*
parliamentarian [,pɑrlɪmɛn`tɛrɪ·ən] *s* expert *m* en usages parlementaires
parlor [`pɑrlər] *s* salon *m*; (*in an institution*) parloir *m*
par′lor car′ *s* (rr) wagon-salon *m*
par′lor game′ *s* jeu *m* de société
Parnassus [pɑr`næsəs] *s* le Parnasse
parochial [pə`roki·əl] *adj* paroissial; (*attitude*) provincial

paro′chial school′ s école f confessionnelle, école libre

paro·dy [′pærədi] s (pl **-dies**) parodie f ‖ v (pret & pp **-died**) tr parodier

parole [pə′rol] s parole f d'honneur; liberté f sur parole ‖ tr libérer sur parole

par·quet [par′ke], [par′kɛt] s parquet m; (theat) premiers rangs mpl du parterre ‖ v (pret & pp **-queted** [′ked], [′kɛtɪd]; ger **-queting** [′ke·ɪŋ], [′kɛtɪŋ]) tr parqueter

parricide [′pærɪ,saɪd] s (act) parricide m; (person) parricide mf

parrot [′pærət] s perroquet m ‖ tr répéter or imiter comme un perroquet

par·ry [′pæri] s (pl **-ries**) parade f ‖ v (pret & pp **-ried**) tr parer; (a question) éluder

parse [pars] tr faire l'analyse grammaticale de

parsimonious [,parsɪ′moni·əs] adj parcimonieux, regardant

parsley [′parsli] s persil m

parsnip [′parsnɪp] s panais m

parson [′parsən] s curé m; pasteur m protestant

parsonage [′parsənɪdʒ] s presbytère m

part [part] s (section, division) partie f; (share) part f; (of a machine) organe m, pièce f; (of the hair) raie f; (theat) rôle m; **for my part** pour ma part; **for the most part** pour la plupart; **in part** en partie; **in these parts** dans ces parages; **on the part of** de la part de; **parts** (personal qualities) talent m; (anat) parties (génitales); (geog) région(s) f(pl); **to be** or **form part of** faire partie de; **to be part and parcel of** faire partie intégrante de; **to do one's part** faire son devoir; **to live a part** (theat) entrer dans la peau d'un personnage; **to look the part** avoir le physique de l'emploi; **to take part in** prendre part à; **to take the part of** prendre parti pour; jouer le rôle de ‖ adv partiellement, en partie; **part . . . part** moitié . . . moitié ‖ tr séparer; **to part the hair** se faire une raie ‖ intr se séparer; (said, e.g., of road) diverger; (to break) rompre; **to part with** se défaire de; se dessaisir de

par·take [par′tek] v (pret **-took**; pp **-taken**) intr—**to partake in** participer à; **to partake of** (e.g., a meal) prendre; (e.g., joy) participer de

partial [′parʃəl] adj partiel; (prejudiced) partial

participant [par′tɪsɪpənt] adj & s participant m

participate [par′tɪsɪ,pet] intr participer

participation [par,tɪsɪ′peʃən] s participation f

participle [′partɪ,sɪpəl] s participe m

particle [′partɪkəl] s particule f; **a particle of truth** un grain de vérité; **not a particle of evidence** pas l'ombre d'une preuve

particular [pər′tɪkjələr] adj particulier; difficile, exigeant; méticuleux; **a particular . . .** un certain . . . ‖ s détail m

particularize [pər′tɪkjələ,raɪz] tr & intr individualiser, particulariser

parting [′partɪŋ] s séparation f

partisan [′partɪzən] adj & s partisan m

partition [par′tɪʃən] s (dividing) partage m, division f; (of land) morcellement m; (wall) paroi f, cloison f ‖ tr partager; **to partition off** séparer par des cloisons

partner [′partnər] s partenaire mf; (husband) conjoint m; (wife) conjointe f; (in a dance) cavalier m; (in business) associé m

part′ner·ship′ s association f; (com) société f

part′ of speech′ s partie f du discours

part′ own′er s copropriétaire mf

partridge [′partrɪdʒ] s perdrix m

part′-time′ adj & adv à mi-temps

par·ty [′parti] adj de gala ‖ s (pl **-ties**) fête f, soirée f; (diversion of a group of persons; individual named in contract or lawsuit) partie f; (with whom one is conversing) interlocuteur m; (mil) détachement m, peloton m; (pol) parti m; (telp) correspondant m; (coll) individu m; **to be a party to** être complice de

party-goer [′parti,go·ər] s invité m; (nightlifer) noceur m

par′ty hack′ s politicien m à la petite semaine

par′ty line′ s (between two properties) limite f; (telp) ligne f à postes groupés ‖ **par′ty line′** s ligne du parti; (of communist party) directives fpl du parti

par′ty pol′itics s politique f de parti

par′ty wall′ s mur m mitoyen

pass [pæs] s (navigable channel; movement of hands of magician; in sports) passe f; (straits) pas m; (in mountains) col m, passage m; (document) laissez-passer m; difficulté f; (mil) permission f; (rr) permis m de circulation; (theat) billet m de faveur ‖ tr passer; (an exam) réussir à; (e.g., a student) recevoir; (a law) adopter, voter; (a red light) brûler; (to get ahead of) dépasser; (a car going in the same direction) doubler; (s.o. or s.th. coming toward one) croiser; (a certain place) passer devant; **to pass around** faire circuler; **to pass oneself off as** se faire passer pour; **to pass out** distribuer; **to pass over** passer sous silence; (to hand over) transmettre; **to pass s.th. off on s.o.** repasser or refiler q.ch. à qn ‖ intr passer; (educ) être reçu; **to bring to pass** réaliser; **to come to pass** se passer; **to pass as** or **for** passer pour; **to pass away** disparaître; (to die out) s'éteindre; (to die) mourir; **to pass by** passer devant; **to pass out** sortir; (slang) s'évanouir; **to pass over** passer sur; (an obstacle) franchir; (said of storm) s'éloigner; (to pass through) traverser; **to pass over to** (e.g., the enemy) passer à

passable [′pæsəbəl] adj passable; (road, river, etc.) franchissable

passage [′pæsɪdʒ] s passage m; (of time) cours m; (of a law) adoption f

pass′book′ s carnet m de banque

passenger [ˈpæsəndʒər] *adj* (*e.g.*, *train*) de voyageurs; (*e.g.*, *pigeon*) de passage ‖ *s* voyageur *m*, passager *m*

passer-by [ˈpæsərˈbaɪ] *s* (*pl* **passers-by**) passant *m*

passing [ˈpæsɪŋ] *adj* passager ‖ *s* passage *m* (*act of passing*) dépassement *m*; (*death*) trépas *m*; (*of time*) écoulement *m*; (*of a law*) adoption *f*; (*in an examination*) la moyenne; une mention passable; **in passing** (*in parenthesis*) du passage

passion [ˈpæʃən] *s* passion *f*

passionate [ˈpæʃənɪt] *adj* passionné

passive [ˈpæsɪv] *adj & s* passif *m*

pass'key' *s* passe-partout *m*

pass'-out' check' *s* contremarque *f*

Pass'o'ver *s* Pâque *f*

pass'port' *s* passeport *m*

pass'word' *s* mot *m* de passe

past [pæst] *adj* passé, dernier; (*e.g.*, *president*) ancien ‖ *s* passé *m* ‖ *prep* au-delà de, passé, plus de; hors de, e.g., **past all understanding** hors de toute compréhension; **it's twenty past five** il est cinq heures vingt; **it's past three o'clock** il est trois heures passées

paste [pest] *s* (*glue*) colle *f* de pâte; (*jewelry*) strass *m*; (culin) pâte *f* ‖ *tr* coller

paste'board' *s* carton *m*

pastel [pæsˈtɛl] *adj & s* pastel *m*

pasteurize [ˈpæstə,raɪz] *tr* pasteuriser

pastime [ˈpæs,taɪm] *s* passe-temps *m*

past' mas'ter *s* expert *m* en la matière, passé maître

pastor [ˈpæstər] *s* pasteur *m*

pastoral [ˈpæstərəl] *adj* pastoral ‖ *s* pastorale *f*

pastorate [ˈpæstərɪt] *s* pastorat *m*

pas·try [ˈpestri] *s* (*pl* **-tries**) pâtisserie *f*

pas'try cook' *s* pâtissier *m*

pas'try shop' *s* pâtisserie *f*

pasture [ˈpæstʃər] *s* pâturage *m*, pâture *f* ‖ *tr* faire paître ‖ *intr* paître

past·y [ˈpesti] *adj* (*comp* **-ier**; *super* **-iest**) pâteux; (*face*) terreux

pat [pæt] *adj* à propos; (*e.g.*, *excuse*) tout prêt ‖ *s* (*light stroke*) petite tape *f*; (*on an animal*) caresse *f*; (*of butter*) coquille *f* ‖ *v* (*pret & pp* **patted**; *ger* **patting**) *tr* tapoter; caresser; **to pat on the back** encourager, complimenter

patch [pætʃ] *s* (*e.g.*, *of cloth*) pièce *f*, raccommodage *m*; (*of land*) parcelle *f*; (*of ice*) plaque *f*; (*of inner tube*) rustine *f*; (*e.g.*, *of color*) tache *f*; (*beauty spot*) mouche *f* ‖ *tr* rapiécer; **to patch up** rapetasser; (*e.g.*, *a quarrel*) arranger, raccommoder

patent [ˈpetənt] *adj* patent ‖ [ˈpætənt] *adj* breveté ‖ *s* brevet *m* d'invention; **patent applied for** une demande de brevet a été déposée ‖ *tr* breveter

pat'ent leath'er [ˈpætənt] *s* cuir *m* verni

pat'ent med'icine *s* specialité *f* pharmaceutique

pat'ent rights' *spl* propriété *f* industrielle

paternal [pəˈtʌrnəl] *adj* paternel

paternity [pəˈtʌrnɪti] *s* paternité *f*

path [pæθ] *s* (*way*) sentier *m*; (*in garden*) allée *f*; (*of bullet, heavenly body, etc.*) trajectoire *f*; (*for, e.g., riding horses*) piste *f*; (*course*) route *f*; **to beat a path** frayer un chemin

pathetic [pəˈθɛtɪk] *adj* pathétique

path'find'er *s* pionnier *m*

pathology [pəˈθɑlədʒi] *s* pathologie *f*

pathol'ogy lab'oratory *s* laboratoire *m* d'analyses

pathos [ˈpeθɑs] *s* pathétique *m*

path'way' *s* sentier *m*; (fig) voie *f*

patience [ˈpeʃəns] *s* patience *f*

patient [ˈpeʃənt] *adj* patient ‖ *s* malade *mf*; (*undergoing surgery*) patient *m*

pati·o [ˈpɑtɪ,o] *s* (*pl* **-os**) patio *m*

patriarch [ˈpetrɪ,ɑrk] *s* patriarche *m*

patrician [pəˈtrɪʃən] *adj & s* patricien *m*

patricide [ˈpætrɪ,saɪd] *s* (*act*) parricide *m*; (*person*) parricide *mf*

patrimo·ny [ˈpætrɪ,moni] *s* (*pl* **-nies**) patrimoine *m*

patriot [ˈpetrɪ·ət] *s* patriote *mf*

patriotic [,petrɪˈɑtɪk] *adj* patriotique, patriote

patriotism [ˈpetrɪ·ə,tɪzəm] *s* patriotisme *m*

pa·trol [pəˈtrol] *s* patrouille *f* ‖ *v* (*pret & pp* **-trolled**; *ger* **-trolling**) *tr* faire la patrouille dans ‖ *intr* patrouiller

patrol' car' *s* voiture *f* de ronde

patrol'man *s* (*pl* **-men**) *s* agent *m* de police

patrol' wag'on *s* voiture *f* cellulaire

patron [ˈpetrən] *adj* patron ‖ *s* protecteur *m*; (com) client *m*

patronage [ˈpetrənɪdʒ] *s* patronage *m*, clientèle *f*; (pol) politique *f* du place-sous

patronize [ˈpetrə,naɪz] *tr* patronner, protéger; traiter avec condescendance; (com) acheter chez

pa'tron saint' *s* patron *m*

patter [ˈpætər] *s* (*sounds*) petit bruit *m*; (*of rain*) fouettement *m*; (*of magician, peddler, etc.*) boniment *m* ‖ *intr* (*said of rain*) fouetter; (*said of little feet*) trottiner

pattern [ˈpætərn] *s* (*design*) dessin *m*, motif *m*; (*salient characteristics*) profil *m*; (*model*) modèle *m*, exemple *m*; (sewing) patron *m*; **behavior pattern** type *m* de comportement ‖ *tr* (*to decorate*) orner de motifs; **to pattern s.th. on** modeler q.ch. sur

pat'tern book' *s* album *m* d'échantillons; (sewing) album de modes

pat·ty [ˈpæti] *s* (*pl* **-ties**) petit pâté *m*

paucity [ˈpɔsɪti] *s* rareté *f*; manque *m*, disette *f*

paunch [pɔntʃ] *s* panse *f*

paunch·y [ˈpɔntʃi] *adj* (*comp* **-ier**; *super* **-iest**) ventru

pauper [ˈpɔpər] *s* indigent *m*

pause [pɔz] *s* (*rest*) pause *f*; (mus) point *m* d'orgue; **to give pause to** faire hésiter ‖ *intr* faire une pause; hésiter

pave [pev] *tr* paver

pavement [ˈpevmənt] *s* pavé *m*; (*surface*) chaussée *f*

pavilion [pə'vɪljən] s pavillon m
paw [pɔ] s patte f; (coll) main f ‖ tr donner un coup de patte à ‖ intr (said of horse) piaffer
pawl [pɔl] s cliquet m d'arrêt
pawn [pɔn] s (in chess) pion m; (security, pledge) gage m; (tool of another person) jouet m ‖ tr mettre en gage; **to pawn s.th. off on s.o.** (coll) refiler q.ch. à qn
pawn'bro'ker s prêteur m sur gages
pawn'shop' s mont-de-piété m, crédit m municipal
pawn' tick'et s reconnaissance f du mont-de-piété
pay [pe] s paye f; (mil) solde f ‖ v (pret & pp **paid** [ped]) tr payer; (mil) solder; (a compliment; a visit; attention) faire; **to pay back** payer de retour; **to pay down** payer comptant; **to pay off** (a debt) acquitter; (a mortgage) purger; (a creditor) rembourser; **to pay s.o. for s.th.** payer qn de q.ch., payer q.ch. à qn ‖ intr payer, rapporter; **to pay for** payer; **to pay off** (coll) avoir du succès; **to pay up** se libérer par un paiement
payable ['pe·əbəl] adj payable
pay' boost' s augmentation f
pay'check' s paye f
pay'day' s jour m de paye
pay'dirt' s alluvion f exploitable; (coll) source f d'argent
payee [pe'i] s bénéficiaire mf
pay' en'velope s sachet m de paye; paye f
payer ['pe·ər] s payeur m
pay'load' s charge f payante, charge utile; (aer) poids m utile
pay'mas'ter s payeur m
payment ['pemənt] m paiement m; (install-ment, deposit, etc.) versement m
pay' phone' s taxiphone m
pay'roll' s bulletin m de paye; (for officers) état m de solde; (for enlisted men) feuille f de prêt
pay' sta'tion s téléphone m public
pay' tel'evision s télévision f payante
pea [pi] s pois m; **green peas** petits pois
peace [pis] s paix f
peaceable ['pisəbəl] adj pacifique
peaceful ['pisfəl] adj paisible, pacifique
peace'mak'er s pacificateur m
peace' of mind' s tranquillité f d'esprit
peace' pipe' s calumet m de paix
peach [pitʃ] s pêche f; (slang) bijou m
peach' tree' s pêcher m
peach·y ['pitʃi] adj (comp -ier; super -iest) (slang) chouette
pea'coat' s (naut) caban m
pea'cock' s paon m
pea'hen' s paonne f
peak [pik] s cime f, sommet m; (mountain; mountain top) pic m; (of beard) pointe f; (of a cap) visière f; (elec) pointe
peak' hour' s heure f de pointe
peak' load' s (elec) charge f de point
peak' vol'tage s tension f de crête
peal [pil] s retentissement m; (of bells) carillon m ‖ intr carillonner

peal' of laugh'ter s éclat m de rire
peal' of thun'der s coup m de tonnerre
pea'nut' s cacahuète f; (bot) arachide f
pea'nut but'ter s beurre m de cacahuètes or d'arachide
pear [pɛr] s poire f
pearl [pʌrl] s perle f
pearl' oys'ter s huître f perlière
pear' tree' s poirier m
peasant ['pɛzənt] adj & s paysan m
pea'shoot'er s sarbacane f
pea' soup' s (culin, fig) purée f de pois
peat [pit] s tourbe f
pebble ['pɛbəl] s caillou m; (on seashore) galet m
pebbled adj (leather) grenu
peck [pɛk] s (pecking) coup m de bec; (eight quarts) picotin m; (kiss) (coll) baiser m d'oiseau, bécot m; (coll) tas m ‖ tr becqueter ‖ intr picorer; **to peck at** picorer; (food) pignocher
peculation [,pɛkjə'ləʃən] s péculat m, détournement m de fonds
peculiar [pɪ'kjuljər] adj particulier; (strange) bizarre
pedagogue ['pɛdə,gag] s pédagogue mf
pedagogy ['pɛdə,gadʒi] s pédagogie f
ped·al ['pɛdəl] s pédale f ‖ v (pret & pp **-aled** or **-alled**; ger **-aling** or **-alling**) tr actionner les pédales de ‖ intr pédaler
pe'dal push'ers spl pantalon m corsaire
pedant ['pɛdənt] s pédant m
pedantic [pɪ'dæntɪk] adj pédant
pedant·ry ['pɛdəntri] s (pl -ries) pédanterie f
peddle ['pɛdəl] tr & intr colporter
peddler ['pɛdlər] s colporteur m
pederast ['pɛdə,ræst] s pédéraste m
pedestal ['pɛdɪstəl] s piédestal m
pedestrian [pɪ'dɛstrɪ·ən] adj (style) prosaïque ‖ s piéton m; **pedestrian right of way** (public sign) priorité piétons
pedes'trian mall' s rue f piétonne
pediatrics [,pidɪ'ætrɪks] s pédiatrie f
pedigree ['pɛdɪ,gri] s généalogie f; (table) arbre m généalogique; (of animal) pedigree m
pediment ['pɛdɪmənt] s fronton m
peek [pik] s coup m d'œil furtif ‖ intr—**to peek at** regarder furtivement
peel [pil] s pelure f; (of lemon) zeste m ‖ tr peler; **to peel off** enlever ‖ intr se peler; (said of paint) s'écailler
peep [pip] s regard m furtif; (of, e.g., chick-ens) piaulement m ‖ intr piauler; **to peep at** regarder furtivement
peep'hole' s judas m
peer [pɪr] s pair m ‖ intr regarder avec attention; **to peer at** or **into** scruter
peerless ['pɪrlɪs] adj sans pareil
peeve [piv] s (coll) embêtement m ‖ tr (coll) irriter, embêter, fâcher
peevish ['pivɪʃ] adj maussade
peg [pɛg] s (of wood) cheville f; (of metal) fiche f; (for coat and hat) patère f; (for tent) piquet m; **to take down a peg** (coll) rabattre le caquet de ‖ v (pret & pp

pegged; *ger* **pegging)** *tr* cheviller; (*e.g.*, *prices*) indexer, fixer; (*points*) marquer ‖ *intr* piocher; **to peg away at** travailler ferme à

Pegasus ['pɛgəsəs] *s* Pégase *m*

peg' leg' *s* jambe *f* de bois

peg' top' *s* toupie *f*; **peg tops** pantalon *m* fuseau

Pekin·ese [,pikɪ'niz] *adj* pékinois ‖ *s* (*pl* **-ese**) Pékinois *m*

Peking ['pi'kɪŋ] *s* Pékin *m*

pelf [pɛlf] *s* (pej) lucre *m*

pelican ['pɛlɪkən] *s* pélican *m*

pellet ['pɛlɪt] *s* (*of paper or bread*) boulette *f*; (*bullet*) grain *m* de plomb; (pharm) pilule *f*

pell-mell ['pɛl'mɛl] *adj* confus ‖ *adv* pêle-mêle

pelt [pɛlt] *s* (*hide*) peau *m*; (*whack*) coup *m* violent; (*of stones, insults, etc.*) grêle *f* ‖ *tr* cribler; (*e.g., stones*) lancer ‖ *intr* tomber à verse

pen [pɛn] *s* (*for writing*) plume *f*; (*fountain pen*) stylo *m*; (*corral*) enclos *m*; (fig) plume; (*prison*) (slang) bloc *m* ‖ *v* (*pret & pp* **penned;** *ger* **penning**) *tr* écrire ‖ *v* (*pret & pp* **penned** or **pent** [pɛnt]; *ger* **penning**) *tr* parquer

penalize ['pinə,laɪz] *tr* (*an action*) sanctionner; (*a person*) punir; (sports) pénaliser

penal·ty ['pɛnəlti] *s* (*pl* **-ties**) peine *f*; (*for late payment; in a game*) pénalité *f*; **under penalty of** sous peine de

penance ['pɛnəns] *s* pénitence *f*

penchant ['pɛnʃənt] *s* penchant *m*

pen·cil ['pɛnsəl] *s* crayon *m*; (*of light*) faisceau *m* ‖ *v* (*pret & pp* **-ciled** or **-cilled;** *ger* **-ciling** or **-cilling**) *tr* crayonner

pen'cil sharp'ener *s* taille-crayon *m*

pendent ['pɛndɛnt] *adj* pendant ‖ *s* pendant *m*, pendentif *m*; (*of chandelier*) pendeloque *f*

pending ['pɛndɪŋ] *adj* pendant ‖ *prep* en attendant

pendulum ['pɛndʒələm] *s* pendule *m*

pen'dulum bob' *s* lentille *f*

penetrate ['pɛnɪ,tret] *tr & intr* pénétrer

penguin ['pɛŋgwɪn] *s* manchot *m*

pen'hold'er *s* porte-plume *m*; (*rack*) pose-plumes *m*

penicillin [,pɛnɪ'sɪlɪn] *s* pénicilline *f*

peninsula [pə'nɪnsələ] *s* presqu'île *f*; (*large peninsula like Spain or Italy*) péninsule *f*

peninsular [pə'nɪnsələr] *adj* péninsulaire

penis ['pinɪs] *s* pénis *m*

penitence ['pɛnɪtəns] *s* pénitence *f*

penitent ['pɛnɪtənt] *adj & s* pénitent *m*

pen'knife' *s* (*pl* **-knives**) canif *m*

penmanship ['pɛnmən,ʃɪp] *s* calligraphie *f*; (*person's handwriting*) écriture *f*

pen' name' *s* pseudonyme *m*

pennant ['pɛnənt] *s* flamme *f*; (sports) banderole *f* du championnat

penniless ['pɛnɪlɪs] *adj* sans le sou

pen·ny ['pɛni] *s* (*pl* **-nies**) (U.S.A.) centime *m*; **not a penny** pas un sou ‖ *s* (*pl* **pence** [pɛns]) (Brit) penny *m*

pen'ny-pinch'ing *adj* regardant

pen'ny·weight' *s* poids *m* de 24 grains

pen' pal' *s* (coll) correspondant *m*

pen'point' *s* bec *m* de plume

pension ['pɛnʃən] *s* pension *f* ‖ *tr* pensionner

pensioner ['pɛnʃənər] *s* pensionné *m*

pensive ['pɛnsɪv] *adj* pensif

Pentagon ['pɛntə,gɑn] *s* Pentagone *m*

Pentecost ['pɛntɪ,kɔst] *s* la Pentecôte

penthouse ['pɛnt,haʊs] *s* toit *m* en auvent, appentis *m*; appartement *m* sur toit, maison *f* à terrasse

pent-up ['pɛnt,ʌp] *adj* renfermé, refoulé

penult ['pinʌlt] *s* pénultième *f*

penum·bra [pɪ'nʌmbrə] *s* (*pl* **-brae** [bri] or **-bras**) pénombre *f*

penurious [pɪ'nʊrɪ·əs] *adj* (*stingy*) mesquin, parcimonieux; (*poor*) pauvre

penury ['pɛnjəri] *s* indigence *f*, misère *f*

pen'wip'er *s* essuie-plume *m*

peo·ny ['pi·əni] *s* (*pl* **-nies**) pivoine *f*

people ['pipəl] *spl* gens *mpl*, personnes *fpl*; **many people** beaucoup de monde; **my people** ma famille, mes parents; **people say** on dit ‖ *s* (*pl* **peoples**) peuple *m*, nation *f* ‖ *tr* peupler

pep [pɛp] *s* (coll) allant *m* ‖ *v* (*pret & pp* **pepped;** *ger* **pepping**) *tr*—**to pep up** (coll) animer

pepper ['pɛpər] *s* (*spice*) poivre *m*; (*fruit*) grain *m* de poivre; (*plant*) poivrier *m*; (*plant or fruit of the hot or red pepper*) piment *m* rouge; (*plant or fruit of the sweet or green pepper*) piment doux, poivron *m* vert ‖ *tr* poivrer; (*e.g., with bullets*) cribler

pep'per·box' *s* poivrière *f*

pep'per mill' *s* moulin *m* à poivre

pep'per·mint' *s* menthe *f* poivrée; (*lozenge*) pastille *f* de menthe

per [pʌr] *prep* par; **as per** suivant

perambulator [pər'æmbjə,letər] *s* voiture *f* d'enfant

per capita [pər'kæpɪtə] par tête, par personne

perceive [pər'siv] *tr* (*by the senses*) apercevoir; (*by understanding*) percevoir

per cent or **percent** [pər'sɛnt] pour cent

percentage [pər'sɛntɪdʒ] *s* pourcentage *m*; **to get a percentage** (slang) avoir part au gâteau

perceptible [pər'sɛptəbəl] *adj* perceptible, sensible, appréciable

perception [pər'sɛpʃən] *s* perception *f*; compréhension *f*, pénétration *f*

perch [pʌrtʃ] *s* (*vantage point*) perchoir *m*; (ichth) perche *f* ‖ *tr* percher ‖ *intr* percher, se percher

percolate ['pʌrkə,let] *tr & intr* filtrer

percolator ['pʌrkə,letər] *s* cafetière *f* à filtre

percussion [pər'kʌʃən] *s* percussion *f*

percus'sion cap' *s* capsule *f* fulminante

per diem [pər'daɪ·əm] par jour

perdition [pər'dɪʃən] s perdition f
peremptory [pə'rɛmptəri] adj péremptoire
perennial [pə'rɛnɪ·əl] adj perpétuel; (bot) vivace ‖ s plante f vivace
perfect ['pʌrfɪkt] adj & s parfait m ‖ [pər'fɛkt] tr perfectionner
perfidious [pər'fɪdɪ·əs] adj perfide
perfi·dy ['pʌrfɪdi] s (pl -dies) perfidie f
perforate ['pʌrfə,ret] tr perforer
per'forated line' s pointillé m
perforation [,pʌrfə'reʃən] s perforation f; (of postage stamp) dentelure f
perforce [pər'fors] adv forcément
perform [pər'fɔrm] tr exécuter; (surg) faire; (theat) représenter ‖ intr jouer; (said of machine) fonctionner
performance [pər'fɔrməns] s (accomplishing) exécution f; (production) rendement m; (of a machine) fonctionnement m; (of actor, singer, dancer) interprétation f; (sports) performance f; (theat) représentation f; **in the performance of his duties** dans l'exercice de ses fonctions
performer [pər'fɔrmər] s artiste mf, interprète mf
perform'ing arts' spl arts mpl du spectacle
perfume ['pʌrfjum] s parfum m ‖ [pər'fjum] tr parfumer
perfunctory [pər'fʌŋktəri] adj superficiel; négligent
perhaps [pər'hæps] adv peut-être; **perhaps not** peut-être que non
per hour' à l'heure
peril ['pɛrəl] s péril m
perilous ['pɛrɪləs] adj périlleux
period ['pɪrɪ·əd] s période f; (in school) heure f de cours; (gram) point m; (sports) division f
pe'riod cos'tume s costume m d'époque
pe'riod fur'niture s meubles m d'époque
periodic [,pɪrɪ'ɑdɪk] adj périodique
periodical [,pɪrɪ'ɑdɪkəl] adj périodique ‖ s publication f périodique
period'ical room' s (in a library) salle f des imprimés
peripheral [pə'rɪfərəl] adj périphérique
peripher·y [pə'rɪfəri] s (pl -ies) périphérie f
periscope ['pɛrɪ,skop] s périscope m; (of a tank) épiscope m
perish ['pɛrɪʃ] intr périr
perishable ['pɛrɪʃəbəl] adj périssable
perjure ['pʌrdʒər] tr—**to perjure oneself** se parjurer
perju·ry ['pʌrdʒəri] s (pl -ries) parjure m
perk [pʌrk] tr—**to perk up** (the head) redresser; (the ears) dresser; (the appetite) ravigoter ‖ intr—**to perk up** se ranimer
permafrost ['pʌrmə,frɔst] s pergélisol m
permanence ['pʌrmənəns] s permanence f
permanent ['pʌrmənənt] adj permanent ‖ s permanente f
per'manent address' s domicile m fixe
per'manent ten'ure s inamovibilité f
per'manent wave' s ondulation f permanente
permeate ['pʌrmɪ,et] tr & intr pénétrer
permissible [pər'mɪsɪbəl] adj permis

permission [pər'mɪʃən] s permission f
permissive [pər'mɪsɪv] adj tolérant; (morals, law) laxiste; (society) de tolérance; (pej) trop tolérant
permissiveness [pər'mɪsɪvnɪs] s tolérance f; (pej) excès m de tolérance, mollesse f, laxisme m
per·mit ['pʌrmɪt] s permis m; (com) passavant m ‖ [pər'mɪt] v (pret & pp -mitted; ger -mitting) tr permettre; **to permit s.o. to** permettre à qn de
permute [pər'mjut] tr permuter
pernicious [pər'nɪʃəs] adj pernicieux
pernickety [pər'nɪkɪti] adj (coll) pointilleux
perox'ide blonde' [pər'ɑksaɪd] s blonde f décolorée
perpendicular [,pʌrpən'dɪkjələr] adj & s perpendiculaire f
perpetrate ['pʌrpɪ,tret] tr perpétrer
perpetual [pər'pɛtʃʊ·əl] adj perpétuel
perpetuate [pər'pɛtʃʊ,et] tr perpétuer
perplex [pər'plɛks] tr rendre perplexe
perplexed [pər'plɛkst] adj perplexe
perplexi·ty [pər'plɛksɪti] s (pl -ties) perplexité f
persecute ['pʌrsɪ,kjut] tr persécuter
persecution [,pʌrsɪ'kjuʃən] s persécution f
persevere [,pʌrsɪ'vɪr] intr persévérer
Persian ['pʌrʒən] adj persan ‖ s (language) persan m; (person) Persan m
Per'sian blind' s persienne f
Per'sian Gulf' s Golfe m Persique
Per'sian rug' s tapis m de Perse
persimmon [pər'sɪmən] s plaquemine f; (tree) plaqueminier m
persist [pər'sɪst] intr persister; **to persist in** persister dans; + ger persister à + inf
persistent [pər'sɪstənt] adj persistant
person ['pʌrsən] s personne f; **no person** personne; **per person** par personne, chacun
personage ['pʌrsənɪdʒ] s personnage m
personal ['pʌrsənəl] adj personnel ‖ s (journ) note f dans la chronique mondaine
personali·ty [,pʌrsə'nælɪti] s (pl -ties) personnalité f
per'sonal prop'erty s biens mpl mobiliers
personi·fy [pər'sɑnɪ,faɪ] v (pret & pp -fied) tr personnifier
personnel [,pʌrsə'nɛl] s personnel m
per'son-to-per'son tel'ephone call' s communication f avec préavis
perspective [pər'spɛktɪv] s perspective f
perspicacious [,pʌrspɪ'keʃəs] adj perspicace
perspiration [,pʌrspɪ'reʃən] s transpiration f
perspire [pər'spaɪr] intr transpirer
persuade [pər'swed] tr persuader; **to persuade s.o. of s.th.** persuader q.ch. à qn, persuader qn de q.ch.; **to persuade s.o. to** persuader à qn de
persuasion [pər'sweʒən] s persuasion f; (faith) (coll) croyance f
pert [pʌrt] adj effronté; (sprightly) animé
pertain [pər'ten] intr—**to pertain to** avoir rapport à

pertinacious [,pʌrtɪ'neʃəs] *adj* obstiné, persévérant

pertinent ['pʌrtɪnənt] *adj* pertinent

perturb [pər'tʌrb] *tr* perturber

Peru [pə'ru] *s* le Pérou

peruse [pə'ruz] *tr* lire; lire attentivement

Peruvian [pə'ruvɪ·ən] *adj* péruvien ‖ *s* Péruvien *m*

pervade [pər'ved] *tr* pénétrer, s'infiltrer dans

perverse [pər'vʌrs] *adj* pervers; obstiné; capricieux

perversion [pər'vʌrʒən] *s* perversion *f*

perversi·ty [pər'vʌrsɪti] *s* (*pl* **-ties**) perversité *f*; obstination *f*

pervert ['pʌrvərt] *s* pervers *m*, perverti *m* ‖ [pər'vʌrt] *tr* pervertir

pes·ky ['pɛski] *adj* (*comp* **-kier**; *super* **-kiest**) (coll) importun

pessimism ['pɛsɪ,mɪzəm] *s* pessimisme *m*

pessimist ['pɛsɪmɪst] *s* pessimiste *mf*

pessimistic [,pɛsɪ'mɪstɪk] *adj* pessimiste

pest [pɛst] *s* insecte *m* nuisible; (*pestilence*) peste *f*; (*annoying person*) raseur *m*

pester ['pɛstər] *tr* casser la tête à, importuner

pest′house′ *s* lazaret *m*

pesticide ['pɛstɪ,saɪd] *s* pesticide *m*

pestiferous [pɛs'tɪfərəs] *adj* pestiféré; (coll) ennuyeux

pestilence ['pɛstɪləns] *s* pestilence *f*

pestle ['pɛsəl] *s* pilon *m*

pet [pɛt] *s* animal *m* favori, animal familial; (*child*) enfant *m* gâté; (*anger*) accès *m* de mauvaise humeur; **teacher's pet** chouchou *m* (*or* chouchoute *f*) du professeur ‖ *v* (*pret & pp* **petted**; *ger* **petting**) *tr* choyer; (*e.g., an animal's fur*) caresser ‖ *intr* (slang) se bécoter

petal ['pɛtəl] *s* pétale *m*

pet′cock′ *s* robinet *m* de purge

Peter ['pitər] *s* Pierre *m*; **to rob Peter to pay Paul** découvrir saint Pierre pour habiller saint Paul ‖ (*l.c.*) *intr*—**to peter out** (coll) s'épuiser, s'en aller en fumée

petition [pɪ'tɪʃən] *s* pétition *f* ‖ *tr* adresser or présenter une pétition à

pet′ name′ *s* mot *m* doux, nom *m* d'amitié

Petrarch ['pitrɑrk] *s* Pétrarque *m*

petri·fy ['pɛtrɪ,faɪ] *v* (*pret & pp* **-fied**) *tr* pétrifier ‖ *intr* se pétrifier

petrochemical [,pɛtro'kɛmɪkəl] *adj* pétrochimique

petrol ['pɛtrəl] *s* (Brit) essence *f*

petroleum [pɪ'trolɪ·əm] *s* pétrole *m*

pet′ shop′ *s* boutique *f* aux petites bêtes; (*for birds*) oisellerie *f*

petticoat ['pɛtɪ,kot] *s* jupon *m*

pet·ty ['pɛti] *adj* (*comp* **-tier**; *super* **-tiest**) insignifiant, petit; (*narrow*) mesquin; intolérant

pet′ty cash′ *s* petite caisse *f*

pet′ty expen′ses *s* menus frais *mpl*

pet′ty lar′ceny *s* vol *m* simple

pet′ty of′ficer *s* (naut) officier *m* marinier

petulant ['pɛtjələnt] *adj* irritable, boudeur

pew [pju] *s* banc *m* d'église

pewter ['pjutər] *s* étain *m*

Pfc. ['pi'ɛf'si] *s* (letterword) (**private first class**) soldat *m* de première

phalanx ['felæŋks] *s* phalange *f*

phallic ['fælɪk] *adj* phallique

phallus ['fæləs] *s* phallus *m*, pénis *m*

phantasm ['fæntæzəm] *s* fantasme *m*

phantom ['fæntəm] *s* fantôme *m*

Pharaoh ['fɛro] *s* Pharaon *m*

pharisee ['færɪ,si] *s* pharisien *m*; **Pharisee** Pharisien *m*

pharmaceutical [,fɑrmə'sutɪkəl] *adj* pharmaceutique

pharmacist ['fɑrməsɪst] *s* pharmacien *m*

pharma·cy ['fɑrməsi] *s* (*pl* **-cies**) pharmacie *f*

pharynx ['færɪŋks] *s* pharynx *m*

phase [fez] *s* phase *f*; **out of phase** (*said of motor*) décalé ‖ *tr* mettre en phase; développer en phases successives; (coll) inquiéter; **to phase out** faire disparaître peu à peu

pheasant ['fɛzənt] *s* faisan *m*

phenobarbital [,finobɑrbɪ,tæl] *s* phénobarbital *m*

phenomenal [fɪ'nɑmɪ,nəl] *adj* phénoménal

phenome·non [fɪ'nɑmɪ,nɑn] *s* (*pl* **-na** [nə]) phénomène *m*

phial ['faɪ·əl] *s* fiole *f*

philanderer [fɪ'lændərər] *s* coureur *m*, galant *m*

philanthropist [fɪ'lænθrəpɪst] *s* philanthrope *mf*

philanthro·py [fɪ'lænθrəpi] *s* (*pl* **-pies**) philanthropie *f*

philatelist [fɪ'lætəlɪst] *s* philatéliste *mf*

philately [fɪ'lætəli] *s* philatélie *f*

Philippine ['fɪlɪ,pin] *adj* philippin ‖ **Philippines** *spl* Philippines *fpl*

Philistine ['fɪlɪ,stin] *adj* & *s* philistin *m*

philologist [fɪ'lɑlədʒɪst] *s* philologue *mf*

philology [fɪ'lɑlədʒi] *s* philologie *f*

philosopher [fɪ'lɑsəfər] *s* philosophe *mf*

philosophic(al) [,fɪlə'sɑfɪk(əl)] *adj* philosophique

philoso·phy [fɪ'lɑsəfi] *s* (*pl* **-phies**) philosophie *f*

philter ['fɪltər] *s* philtre *m*

phlebitis [flɪ'baɪtɪs] *s* phlébite *f*

phlegm [flɛm] *s* flegme *m*; **to cough up phlegm** cracher des glaires, tousser gras

phlegmatic(al) [flɛg'mætɪk(əl)] *adj* flegmatique

phobia ['fobɪ·ə] *s* phobie *f*

Phoebe ['fibi] *s* Phébé *f*

Phoenicia [fɪ'nɪʃə] *s* Phénicie *f*; la Phénicie

Phoenician [fɪ'nɪʃən] *adj* phénicien ‖ *s* Phénicien *m*

phoenix ['finɪks] *s* phénix *m*

phone [fon] *s* (coll) téléphone *m* ‖ *tr & intr* (coll) téléphoner

phone′ call′ *s* coup *m* de téléphone, coup de fil

phonetic [fo'nɛtɪk] *adj* phonétique ‖ **phonetics** *s* phonétique *f*

phone-in′ show′ *s* (rad, telv) tribune *f* téléphonique

phonograph ['fonə,græf] s phonographe m
phonology [fə'nalədʒi] s phonologie f
pho·ny ['foni] adj (comp -nier; super -niest) faux, truqué ‖ s (pl -nies) charlatan m
pho'ny war' s drôle f de guerre
phosphate ['fasfet] s phosphate m
phosphorescent [,fasfə'rɛsənt] adj phosphorescent
phospho·rus ['fasfərəs] s (pl -ri [,raɪ]) phosphore m
pho·to [foto] s (pl -tos) (coll) photo f
pho'to·cop'ier s photocopieur m
pho'to·cop'y s photocopie f
pho'to·engrav'ing s photogravure f
pho'to fin'ish s photo-finish f
photogenic [,foto'dʒɛnɪk] adj photogénique
pho'to·graph' s photographie f ‖ tr photographier ‖ intr—**to photograph well** être photogénique
photographer [fə'tagrəfər] s photographe mf
pho'to·graph li'brary s photothèque f
photography [fə'tagrəfi] s photographie f
Photostat ['fotə,stæt] s (trademark) photostat m ‖ tr & intr photocopier
phrase [frez] s locution f, expression f; (mus) phrase f ‖ tr exprimer, rédiger; (mus) phraser
phrenology [frɪ'nalədʒi] s phrénologie f
phys·ic ['fɪzɪk] s médicament m; (laxative) purgatif m ‖ v (pret & pp -icked; ger -icking) tr purger
physical ['fɪzɪkəl] adj physique
phys'ical de'fect s vice m de conformation
physician [fɪ'zɪʃən] s médecin m
physicist ['fɪzɪsɪst] s physicien m
physics ['fɪzɪks] s physique f
physiogno·my [,fɪzɪ'agnəmi] s (pl -mies) physionomie f
physiological [,fɪzɪ·ə'ladʒɪkəl] adj physiologique
physiology [,fɪzɪ'alədʒi] s physiologie f
physique [fɪ'zik] s physique m
pi [paɪ] s (math) pi m; (typ) pâté m ‖ v (pret & pp pied; ger piing) tr (typ) mettre en pâte
pianist ['pi·ənɪst] s pianiste mf
pian·o [pɪ'æno] s (pl -os) piano m
pian'o stool' s tabouret m de piano
pian'o tun'er s accordeur m (de piano)
pian'o wire' s corde f à piano
picayune [,pɪkə'jun] adj mesquin
picco·lo ['pɪkəlo] s (pl -los) piccolo m
pick [pɪk] s (tool) pic m, pioche f; (choice) choix m; (choicest) élite f, fleur f ‖ tr choisir; (flowers) cueillir; (fibers) effiler; (one's teeth, nose, etc.) se curer; (a scab) gratter; (a fowl) plumer; (a bone) ronger; (a lock) crocheter; (the ground) piocher; (e.g., guitar strings) toucher; (a quarrel; flaws) chercher; **to pick off** enlever; (to shoot) descendre; **to pick out** trier; **to pick pockets** voler à la tire; **to pick to pieces** (coll) éplucher; **to pick up** ramasser; (one's strength) reprendre; (speed) accroître; (a passenger) prendre; (a man overboard) recueillir; (an anchor;

a stitch; a fallen child) relever; (information; a language) apprendre; (the scent) retrouver; (rad) capter ‖ intr (said of birds) picorer; **to pick at** (to scold) (coll) gronder; **to pick at one's food** manger du bout des dents; **to pick on** choisir; (coll) gronder; **to pick up** (coll) se rétablir
pick'ax s pioche f
picket ['pɪkɪt] s (stake, pale) pieu m; (of strikers; of soldiers) piquet m ‖ tr entourer de piquets de grève ‖ intr faire le piquet
pick'et fence' s palis m
pick'et line' s piquet m de grève
pickle ['pɪkəl] s (gherkin) cornichon m; (brine) marinade f, saumure f; (coll) gâchis m ‖ tr conserver dans du vinaigre
pick'lock' s crochet m; (person) crocheteur m
pick'-me-up' s (coll) remontant m
pick'pock'et s voleur m à la tire
pick'up' s (passenger) passager m; (of a motor) reprise f; (truck; phonograph cartridge) pick-up m; (restorative) remontant m; (casual lover) partenaire mf de rencontre
pick'up arm' s bras m de pick-up
pick'up truck' s camionnette f; pick-up m invar
pic·nic ['pɪknɪk] s pique-nique m ‖ v (pret & pp -nicked; ger -nicking) intr pique-niquer
pictorial [pɪk'torɪ·əl] adj & s illustré m
picture ['pɪktʃər] s tableau m, image f; (photograph) photographie f; (painting) peinture f; (engraving) gravure f; (mov) film m; (screen) (mov, telv) écran m; **a picture is worth a thousand words** une image vaut mieux que dix mille mots; **the very picture of** le portrait de, l'image de; **to receive the picture** (telv) capter l'image ‖ tr dépeindre, représenter; **to picture to oneself** s'imaginer
pic'ture gal'lery s musée m de peinture
pic'ture post' card' s carte f postale illustrée
pic'ture show' s exhibition f de peinture; (mov) cinéma m
pic'ture sig'nal s signal m vidéo
picturesque [,pɪktʃə'rɛsk] adj pittoresque
pic'ture tube' s tube m de l'image
pic'ture win'dow s fenêtre f panoramique
piddling ['pɪdlɪŋ] adj insignifiant
pie [paɪ] s pâté m; (dessert) tarte f; (bird) pie f
piece [pis] s (of music; of bread) morceau m; (cannon, coin, chessman, pastry, clothing) pièce f; (of land) parcelle f; (e.g., of glass) éclat m; **a piece of advice** un conseil; **a piece of furniture** un meuble; **to break into pieces** mettre en pièces, mettre en morceaux; **to give s.o. a piece of one's mind** (coll) dire son fait à qn; **to go to pieces** se désagréger; (to be hysterical) avoir ses nerfs; **to pick to**

pieces (coll) éplucher ‖ *tr* rapiécer; **to piece together** rassembler, coordonner

piece′meal′ *adv* pièce à pièce

piece′work′ *s* travail *m* à la tâche

piece′work′er *s* ouvrier *m* à la tâche

pied [paɪd] *adj* bigarré, panaché; (typ) tombé en pâté

pier [pɪr] *s* (*with amusements*) jetée *f*; (*breakwater*) brise-lames *m*; (*of a bridge*) pile *f*; (*of a harbor*) jetée *f*; (*wall between two openings*) (archit) trumeau *m*

pierce [pɪrs] *tr & intr* percer

piercing [′pɪrsɪŋ] *adj* perçant; (*sharp*) aigu

pier′ glass′ *s* grand miroir *m*

pie·ty [′paɪ·ətɪ] *s* (*pl* **-ties**) piété *f*

piffle [′pɪfəl] *s* (coll) futilités *fpl*, sottises *fpl*

pig [pɪg] *s* cochon *m*, porc *m*

pigeon [′pɪdʒən] *s* pigeon *m*

pi′geon·hole′ *s* boulin *m*; (*in desk*) case *f* ‖ *tr* caser; mettre au rancart

pi′geon house′ *s* pigeonnier *m*

piggish [′pɪgɪʃ] *adj* goinfre

piggyback [′pɪgɪ,bæk] *adv* sur le dos, sur les epaules; (rr) en auto-couchette

pig′gy bank′ [′pɪgɪ] *s* tirelire *f*, grenouille *f*

pig′-head′ed *adj* cabochard, têtu

pig′ i′ron *s* gueuse *f*

piglet [′pɪglɪt] *s* cochonnet *m*

pigment [′pɪgmənt] *s* pigment *m*

pig′pen′ *s* porcherie *f*

pig′skin′ *s* peau *f* de porc; (coll) ballon *m* du football

pig′sty′ *s* (*pl* **-sties**) porcherie *f*

pig′tail′ *s* queue *f*, natte *f*; (*of tobacco*) carotte *f*

pike [paɪk] *s* pique *f*; autoroute *f* à péage; (*fish*) brochet *m*

piker [′paɪkər] *s* (slang) rat *m*

pile [paɪl] *s* (*heap*) tas *m*; (*stake*) pieu *m*; (*of rug*) poil *m*; (*of building*) masse *f*; (elec, phys) pile *f*; (coll) fortune *f*; **piles** (pathol) hémorroïdes *fpl* ‖ *tr* empiler ‖ *intr* s'empiler

pile′ dri′ver *s* batteur *m* de pieux; sonnette *f*

pile′up′ *s* (aut) carambolage *m*

pilfer [′pɪlfər] *tr & intr* chaparder

pilgrim [′pɪlgrɪm] *s* pèlerin *m*

pilgrimage [′pɪlgrɪmɪdʒ] *s* pèlerinage *m*

pill [pɪl] *s* pilule *f*; (*something unpleasant*) pilule; (coll) casse-pieds *m*

pillage [′pɪlɪdʒ] *s* pillage *m* ‖ *tr & intr* piller

pillar [′pɪlər] *s* pilier *m*

pillo·ry [′pɪlərɪ] *s* (*pl* **-ries**) pilori *m* ‖ *v* (*pret & pp* **-ried**) *tr* clouer au pilori

pillow [′pɪlo] *s* oreiller *m*

pil′low·case′ or **pil′low·slip′** *s* taie *f* d'oreiller

pilot [′paɪlət] *s* pilote *m*; (*of gas range*) veilleuse *f* ‖ *tr* piloter

pi′lot en′gine *s* locomotive-pilote *f*

pi′lot light′ *s* veilleuse *f*

pimp [pɪmp] *s* entremetteur *m*

pimple [′pɪmpəl] *s* bouton *m*

pim·ply [′pɪmplɪ] *adj* (*comp* **-plier;** *super* **-pliest**) boutonneux

pin [pɪn] *s* épingle *f*; (*of wearing apparel*) agrafe *f*; (*bowling*) quille *f*; (mach) cla-vette *f*, cheville *f*, goupille *f*; **to be on pins and needles** être sur les chardons ardents ‖ *v* (*pret & pp* **pinned;** *ger* **pinning**) *tr* épingler; (mach) cheviller, goupiller; **to pin down** fixer, clouer

pinafore [′pɪnə,for] *s* tablier *m* d'enfant

pin′ball′ *s* billard *m* américain

pin′ball machine′ *s* flipper *m*

pincers [′pɪnsərz] *s & spl* pinces *fpl*

pinch [pɪntʃ] *s* (*pinching*) pincement *m*; (*of salt*) pincée *f*; (*of tobacco*) prise *f*; (*of hunger*) morsure *f*; (*trying time*) moment *m* critique; (slang) arrestation *f*; **in a pinch** au besoin ‖ *tr* pincer; (*to press tightly on*) serrer; (*e.g., one's finger in a door*) se prendre; (*to arrest*) (slang) pincer; (*to steal*) (slang) chiper ‖ *intr* (*said, e.g., of shoe*) gêner; (*to save*) lésiner

pinchers [′pɪntʃərz] *s & spl* pinces *fpl*

pin′cush′ion *s* pelote *f* d'épingles

pine [paɪn] *s* pin *m* ‖ *intr* languire; **to pine for** soupirer après

pine′ap′ple *s* ananas *m*

pine′ cone′ *s* pomme *f* de pin

pine′ nee′dle *s* aiguille *f* de pin

ping [pɪŋ] *s* sifflement *m*; (*in a motor*) cognement *m* ‖ *intr* siffler; cogner

Ping-Pong [′pɪŋ,pɔŋ] *s* (trademark) ping-pong *m*, tennis *m* de table

Ping′-Pong play′er *s* pongiste *mf*

pin′head′ *s* tête *f* d'épingle; (pej) crétin *m*

pink [pɪŋk] *adj* rose ‖ *s* rose *m*; (bot) œillet *m*; **to be in the pink** se porter à merveille

pin′ mon′ey *s* argent *m* de poche

pinnacle [′pɪnəkəl] *s* pinacle *m*

pin′point′ *adj* exact ‖ *s* (fig) point *m* critique ‖ *tr* situer avec précision

pin′prick′ *s* piqûre *f* d'épingle

pin′-striped′ *adj* rayé

pint [paɪnt] *s* chopine *f*

pin′up girl′ *s* pin up *f*

pin′wheel′ *s* (*fireworks*) soleil *m*; (*child's toy*) moulinet *m*

pioneer [,paɪ·ə′nɪr] *s* pionnier *m* ‖ *tr* défricher ‖ *intr* faire œuvre de pionnier

pious [′paɪ·əs] *adj* pieux, dévot

pip [pɪp] *s* (*in fruit*) pépin *m*; (*on cards, dice, etc.*) point *m*; (rad) top *m*; (vet) pépie *f*

pipe [paɪp] *s* tuyau *m*, tube *m*, conduit *m*; (*to smoke tobacco*) pipe *f*; (*of an organ*) tuyau *m*; (mus) chalumeau *m* ‖ *tr* canaliser ‖ *intr* jouer du chalumeau; **pipe down!** (slang) boucle-la!

pipe′ clean′er *s* cure-pipe *m*

pipe′ dream′ *s* rêve *m*, projet *m* illusoire

pipe′ line′ *s* pipe-line *m*; (*of information*) tuyau *m*

pipe′ or′gan *s* grandes orgues *fpl*

piper [′paɪpər] *s* joueur *m* de chalumeau; (*bagpiper*) cornemuseur *m*; **to pay the piper** payer les violons

pipe′ wrench′ *s* clef *f* à tubes

piping [′paɪpɪŋ] *s* tuyauterie *f*; (sewing) passepoil *m*

pippin [′pɪpɪn] *s* (*apple*) reinette *f*; (*highly admired person or thing*) bijou *m*

piquancy [ˈpikənsi] s piquant m

piquant [ˈpikənt] adj piquant

pique [pik] s pique f ‖ tr piquer; **to pique oneself on** se piquer de

pira·cy [ˈpairəsi] s (pl -cies) piraterie f

Piraeus [paiˈri·əs] s Le Pirée

pirate [ˈpairit] s pirate m ‖ tr piller ‖ intr pirater

pirouette [ˌpiruˈɛt] s pirouette f ‖ intr pirouetter

Pisces [ˈpaisiz] s (astr, astrol) les Poissons mpl

pistol [ˈpistəl] s pistolet m

piston [ˈpistən] s piston m

pis′ton ring′ s segment m de piston

pis′ton rod′ s tige f de piston

pis′ton stroke′ s course f de piston

pit [pit] s fosse f, trou m; (in the skin) marque f; (of certain fruit) noyau m; (for cockfights, etc.) arène f; (of the stomach) creux m; (min) puits m; (theat) fauteuils mpl d'orchestre derrière les musiciens ‖ v (pret & pp pitted; ger pitting) tr trouer; (the face) grêler; (fruit) dénoyauter; **to pit oneself against** se mesurer contre

pitch [pitʃ] s (black sticky substance) poix f; (throw) lancement m, jet m; (of a boat) tangage m; (of a roof) degré m de pente; (of, e.g., a screw) pas m; (of a tone, of the voice, etc.) hauteur f; (coll) boniment m, tamtam m; **to such a pitch that** à tel point que ‖ tr lancer, jeter; (hay) faircher; (a tent) dresser; enduire de poix; (mus) donner le ton de ‖ intr (said of boat) tanguer; **to pitch in** (coll) se mettre à la besogne; (coll) commencer à manger; **to pitch into** s'attaquer à

pitch′ ac′cent s accent m de hauteur

pitcher [ˈpitʃər] s broc m, cruche f; (baseball) lanceur m

pitch′fork′ s fourche f; **to rain pitchforks** pleuvoir à torrents

pitch′ pipe′ s diapason m de bouche

pit′fall′ s trappe f; (fig) écueil m, pierre f d'écueil

pith [piθ] s moelle f; (fig) suc m

pith·y [ˈpiθi] adj (comp -ier; super -iest) moelleux; (fig) plein de suc

pitiful [ˈpitifəl] adj pitoyable

pitiless [ˈpitilis] adj impitoyable

pit·y [ˈpiti] s (pl -ies) pitié f; **for pity's sake!** par pitié!; **what a pity!** quel dommage! ‖ v (pret & pp -ied) tr avoir pitié de, plaindre

pivot [ˈpivət] s pivot m ‖ tr faire pivoter ‖ intr pivoter

placard [ˈplækɑrd] s placard m, affiche f ‖ tr placarder

placate [ˈpleket] tr apaiser

place [ples] s (location) endroit m, lieu m; (job) poste m, emploi m; (seat) place f; (rank) rang m; **everything in its place** chaque chose à sa place; **in no place** nulle part; **in place of** au lieu de; **in your place** à votre place; **out of place** déplacé; **to change places** changer de place; **to keep one's place** (fig) tenir ses distances; **to**

take place avoir lieu ‖ tr mettre, placer; (to find a job for; to invest) placer; (to recall) remettre, se rappeler; (to set down) poser ‖ intr (turf) finir placé

place·bo [pləˈsibo] s (pl -bos or -boes) remède m factice

place′ card′ s marque-place f, carton m marque-place

place′ mat′ s garde-nappe m

placement [ˈplesmənt] s placement m; (location) emplacement m

place′ment exam′ s examen m probatoire

place′-name′ s nom m de lieu, toponyme m

placid [ˈplæsid] adj placide

plagiarism [ˈpledʒəˌrizəm] s plagiat m

plagiarist [ˈpledʒərist] s plagiaire mf

plagiarize [ˈpledʒəˌraiz] tr plagier

plague [pleg] s peste f; (great public calamity) fléau m ‖ tr tourmenter

plaid [plæd] s plaid m

plain [plen] adj (manifest) clair, évident; (unambiguous) clair, franc; (talk) sans équivoque; (dress, style, diet, food) simple; (sheer, utter) pur, tout pur; (color) uni; (ugly) sans attraits ‖ s plaine f

plain′ clothes′ spl—**in plain clothes** en civil, en bourgeois

plain′clothes′man s (pl -men′) agent m en civil

plain′ cook′ing s cuisine f bourgeoise

plain′ om′elet s omelette f nature

plain′ speech′ s franc-parler m

plaintiff [ˈplentif] s (law) demandeur m, plaignant m

plaintive [ˈplentiv] adj plaintif

plan [plæn] s plan m, projet m; (drawing, diagram) plan, dessein m ‖ v (pret & pp planned; ger planning) tr projeter; **to plan to** se proposer de ‖ intr faire des projets

plane [plen] adj plan, plat ‖ s (aer) avion m; (bot) platane m; (carpentry) rabot m; (geom) plan m ‖ tr raboter

plane′ sick′ness s mal m de l'air

planet [ˈplænit] s planète f

plane′ tree′ s platane m

plan′ing mill′ s atelier m de rabotage

plank [plæŋk] s planche f; (pol) article m d'une plate-forme électorale

planning [ˈplæniŋ] s planification f, planning m

plant [plænt] s (factory) usine f; (building and equipment) installation f; (bot) plante f ‖ tr planter

plantation [plænˈteʃən] s plantation f

planter [ˈplæntər] s planteur m

plant′ louse′ s puceron m

plasma [ˈplæzmə] s plasma m

plaster [ˈplæstər] s plâtre m; (poultice) emplâtre m ‖ tr plâtrer; (a bill, poster) coller; (slang) griser

plas′ter·board′ s placoplâtre m

plas′ter cast′ s plâtre m

plas′ter of Par′is s plâtre m à mouler

plastic [ˈplæstik] adj & s plastique m

plas′tic bomb′ s plastic m

plas'tic sur'gery s chirurgie f esthétique, chirurgie plastique

plate [plet] s (dish) assiette f; (platter) plateau m; (sheet of metal) tôle f, plaque f; vaisselle f d'or or d'argent; (anat, elec, phot, rad, zool) plaque; (typ) planche f || tr plaquer; (elec) galvaniser; (typ) clicher

plateau [plæ'to] s plateau m, massif m

plate' glass' s verre m cylindré

platen ['plætən] s rouleau m

platform ['plæt,fɔrm] s plate-forme f; (for arrivals and departures) quai m; (of a speaker) estrade f; (political program) plate-forme

plat'form car' s (rr) plate-forme f

platinum ['plætɪnəm] s platine m

plat'inum blonde' s blonde f platinée

platitude ['plætɪ,t(j)ud] s platitude f

Plato ['pleto] s Platon m

platoon [plə'tun] s section f

platter ['plætər] s plat m; (slang) disque m

plausible ['plɔzɪbəl] adj plausible

play [ple] s jeu m; (drama) pièce f; (mach) jeu; to give full play to donner libre cours à || tr jouer; (e.g., the fool) faire; (cards; e.g., football) jouer à; (an instrument) jouer de; to play back (a tape) faire repasser; to play down diminuer; to play hooky faire l'école buissonnière; to play off (sports) rejouer; to play up accentuer || intr jouer; to play out s'épuiser; to play safe prendre des précautions; to play sick faire semblant d'être malade; to play up to passer de la pommade à

play'back' s (device) lecteur m; (reproduction) lecture f, réécoute f, surjeu m; (act) présonorisation f

play'back head' s tête f de lecture

play'bill' s programme m; (poster) affiche f

player ['ple·ər] s joueur m; (mus) musicien m, joueur, exécutant m; (theat) acteur m, interprète mf

play'er pian'o s piano m mécanique

playful ['plefəl] adj enjoué, badin

playgoer ['ple,go·ər] s amateur m de théâtre

play'ground' s terrain m de jeu

play'house' s théâtre m; (dollhouse) maison f de poupée

play'ing card' s carte f à jouer

play'ing field' s terrain m de sports

play'mate' s compagnon m de jeu

play'-off' s finale f, match m d'appui

play' on words' s jeu m de mots

play'pen' s parc m d'enfants

play'room' s salle f de jeux

play'thing' s jouet m

play'time' s recréation f

playwright ['ple,raɪt] s auteur m dramatique, dramaturge mf

play'writ'ing s dramaturgie f

plea [pli] s requête f, appel m; prétexte m; (law) défense f

plead [plid] v (pret & pp pleaded or pled [pled]) tr & intr plaider; to plead not guilty plaider non coupable

pleasant ['plɛzənt] adj agréable

pleasant·ry ['plɛzəntri] s (pl -ries) plaisanterie f

please [pliz] tr plaire à; it pleases him to il lui plaît de; please + inf veuillez + inf; to be pleased with être content or satisfait de || intr plaire; as you please comme vous voulez; if you please s'il vous plaît

pleasing ['plizɪŋ] adj agréable

pleasure ['plɛʒər] s plaisir m; at the pleasure of au gré de; what is your pleasure? qu'y a-t-il pour votre service?, que puis-je faire pour vous?

pleas'ure car' s voiture f de tourisme

pleas'ure trip' s voyage m d'agrément

pleat [plit] s pli m || tr plisser

plebe [plib] s élève m de première année

plebeian [plɪ'bi·ən] adj & s plébéien m

plebiscite ['plɛbɪ,saɪt] s plébiscite m

pledge [plɛdʒ] s (security) gage m; (promise) engagement m d'honneur, promesse f || tr mettre en gage; (one's word) engager

plentiful ['plɛntɪfəl] adj abondant

plenty ['plɛnti] s abondance f; plenty of beaucoup de || adv (coll) largement

pleurisy ['plʊrɪsi] s pleurésie f

pliable ['plaɪ·əbəl] adj (substance) pliable, flexible; (character) docile, souple, malléable

pliers ['plaɪ·ərz] s & spl pinces fpl, tenailles fpl

plight [plaɪt] s embarras m; (promise) engagement m || tr engager; to plight one's troth promettre fidélité

PLO ['pi'ɛl'o] s (letterword) (Palestine Liberation Organization) O.L.P. (Organisation de la libération de la Palestine)

plod [plɑd] v (pret & pp plodded; ger plodding) tr parcourir lourdement et péniblement || intr cheminer; travailler laborieusement

plot [plɑt] s (conspiracy) complot m; (of a play or novel) intrigue f; (of ground) lopin m, parcelle f; (map) tracé m, plan m; (of vegetables) caré m || v (pret & pp plotted; ger plotting) tr comploter, tramer; (a tract of land) faire le plan de; (a point) relever; (lines) tracer || intr comploter; to plot to + inf comploter de + inf

plough [plaʊ] s, tr, & intr var of **plow**

plover ['plʌvər], ['plovər] s pluvier m

plow [plaʊ] s charrue f; (for snow) chasseneige m || tr labourer; (the sea; the forehead) sillonner; (snow) déblayer; to plow back (com) affecter aux investissements || intr labourer; to plow through avancer péniblement dans

plow'man s (pl -men) laboureur m

plow'share' s soc m de charrue

pluck [plʌk] s courage m, cran m; (tug) petit coup m || tr arracher; (flowers) cueillir; (a fowl) plumer; (one's eyebrows) épiler; (e.g., the strings of a guitar) pincer; to pluck off or out arracher; to pluck up the courage to trouver le courage de || intr—to pluck at arracher d'un coup sec; to pluck up reprendre courage

pluck·y [ˈplʌki] *adj* (*comp* **-ier;** *super* **-iest**) courageux, crâne

plug [plʌɡ] *s* (*stopper*) tampon *m*, bouchon *m*; (*of sink, bathtub, etc.*) bonde *f*; (*of tobacco*) chique *f*; (aut) bougie *f*; (*on wall*) (elec) prise *f*; (*prongs*) (elec) fiche *f*, prise; (*old horse*) (coll) rosse *f*; (*hat*) (slang) haut-de-forme *m*; (slang) annonce *f* publicitaire ‖ *v* (*pret & pp* **plugged;** *ger* **plugging**) *tr* boucher; (*a melon*) entamer; **to plug in** (elec) brancher ‖ *intr*—**to plug away** (coll) persévérer

plum [plʌm] *s* prune *f*; (*tree*) prunier *m*; (slang) fromage *m*

plumage [ˈplumɪdʒ] *s* plumage *m*

plumb [plʌm] *adj* d'aplomb; (coll) pur ‖ *s* plomb *m*; **out of plumb** hors d'aplomb ‖ *adv* d'aplomb; (coll) en plein; (coll) complètement ‖ *tr* sonder

plumb′ bob′ *s* plomb *m*

plumber [ˈplʌmər] *s* plombier *m*

plumbing [ˈplʌmɪŋ] *s* plomberie *f*

plumb′ line′ *s* fil *m* à plomb

plume [plum] *s* (*cluster of feathers*) plumes *fpl*; (*small plume on hat*) plumet *m*; (*of a hat, of smoke, etc.*) panache *m* ‖ *tr* orner de plumes; (*feathers*) lisser; **to plume oneself on** se piquer de

plummet [ˈplʌmɪt] *s* plomb *m* ‖ *intr* tomber d'aplomb, se précipiter

plump [plʌmp] *adj* grassouillet, potelé, dodu ‖ *s* (coll) chute *f* lourde; (coll) bruit *m* sourd ‖ *adv* en plein; brusquement ‖ *tr* jeter brusquement; **to plump oneself down** s'affaler ‖ *intr* tomber lourdement

plum′ toma′to *s* olivette *f*

plunder [ˈplʌndər] *s* pillage *m*; (*booty*) butin *m* ‖ *tr* piller

plunge [plʌndʒ] *s* (*dive*) plongeon *m*; (*steep fall*) chute *f*; (*pitching movement*) tangage *m* ‖ *tr* plonger ‖ *intr* plonger; se précipiter; (fig) se plonger; (naut) tanguer; (slang) risquer de grosses sommes

plunger [ˈplʌndʒər] *s* (*for blocked drain*) ventouse *f*, débouchoir *m*; (*gambler*) (slang) risque-tout *m*

plunk [plʌŋk] *adv* d'un coup sec; (*squarely*) carrément ‖ *tr* jeter bruyamment ‖ *intr* tomber raide

plural [ˈplurəl] *adj & s* pluriel *m*

plus [plʌs] *adj* positif ‖ *s* (*sign*) plus *m*; quantité *f* positive ‖ *prep* plus

plush [plʌʃ] *adj* en peluche; (coll) rupin ‖ *s* peluche *f*

plush·y [ˈplʌʃi] *adj* (*comp* **-ier;** *super* **-iest**) pelucheux; (coll) rupin

plus′ sign′ *s* signe *m* plus

Plutarch [ˈplutɑrk] *s* Plutarque *m*

Pluto [ˈpluto] *s* Pluton *m*

plutonium [pluˈtonɪ·əm] *s* plutonium *m*

ply [plaɪ] *s* (*pl* **plies**) (*e.g., of a cloth*) pli *m*; (*of rope, wool, etc.*) brin *m* ‖ *v* (*pret & pp* **plied**) *tr* manier; (*a trade*) exercer; **to ply s.o. with** presser qn de ‖ *intr* faire la navette

ply′wood′ *s* bois *m* de placage, contreplaqué *m*

P.M. [ˈpiˈɛm] *adv* (letterword) (**post meridiem**) de l'après-midi, du soir

pneumatic [n(j)uˈmætɪk] *adj* pneumatique

pneumat′ic drill′ *s* foreuse *f* à air comprimé, marteau-piqueur *m*

pneumonia [n(j)uˈmonɪ·ə] *s* pneumonie *f*

P.O. [ˈpiˈo] *s* (letterword) (**post office**) poste *f*

poach [potʃ] *tr* (*eggs*) pocher ‖ *intr* (hunting) braconner

poached′ egg′ *s* œuf *m* poché

poacher [ˈpotʃər] *s* braconnier *m*

pock [pɑk] *s* pustule *f*

pocket [ˈpɑkɪt] *s* poche *f*; (billiards) blouse *f*; (aer) trou *m* d'air ‖ *tr* empocher; (*a billiard ball*) blouser; (*insults*) avaler

pock′et·book′ *s* portefeuille *m*; (*small book*) livre *m* de poche

pock′et cal′culator *s* calculatrice *f* de poche, calculette *f*

pock′et comput′er *s* ordinateur *m* de poche

pock′et hand′kerchief *s* mouchoir *m* de poche

pock′et·knife′ *s* (*pl* **-knives**) couteau *m* de poche, canif *m*

pock′et mon′ey *s* argent *m* de poche

pock′mark′ *s* marque *f* de la petite vérole

pock′marked′ *adj* grêlé

pod [pɑd] *s* cosse *f*, gousse *f*

poem [ˈpo·ɪm] *s* poème *m*

poet [ˈpo·ɪt] *s* poète *m*, poétesse *f*

poetess [ˈpo·ɪtɪs] *s* poétesse *f*

poetic [poˈɛtɪk] *adj* poétique ‖ **poetics** *s* poétique *f*

poetry [ˈpo·ɪtri] *s* poésie *f*

pogrom [ˈpogrəm] *s* pogrom *m*

poignancy [ˈpɔɪnənsi] *s* piquant *m*

poignant [ˈpɔɪnənt] *adj* poignant

point [pɔɪnt] *s* (*spot, dot, score, etc.*) point *m*; (*tip*) pointe *f*; (*of pen*) bec *m*; (*of conscience*) cas *m*; (*of a star*) rayon *m*; (*of a joke*) piquant *m*; (*of, e.g., grammar*) question *f*; (geog, naut) pointe; (typ) point; **beside the point, off the point** hors de propos; **on the point of** sur le point de; (*death*) à l'article de; **on this point** à cet égard, à ce propos; **point of a compass** aire *f* de vent; **point of order** rappel *m* au règlement; **point of view** point de vue; **points** (aut) vis *f* platinées; **to carry one's point** avoir gain de cause; **to come to the point** venir au fait; **to have one's good points** avoir ses qualités; **to make a point of** se faire un devoir de ‖ *tr* (*a gun, telescope, etc.*) braquer, pointer; (*a finger*) tendre; (*the way*) indiquer; (*a wall*) jointoyer; (*to sharpen*) tailler en point; **to point out** signaler, faire remarquer ‖ *intr* pointer; (*said of hunting dog*) tomber en arrêt; **to point at** montrer du doigt

point′-blank′ *adj & adv* (*fired straight at the mark*) à bout portant; (*straight forward*) à brûle-pourpoint

pointed *adj* pointu; (*remark*) mordant

pointer [ˈpɔɪntər] *s* (*stick*) baguette *f*; (*of a dial*) aiguille *f*; (*dog*) chien *m* d'arrêt, pointeur *m*

poise [pɔɪz] *s* équilibre *m*; (*assurance*) aplomb *m* ‖ *tr* tenir en équilibre ‖ *intr* être en équilibre; (*in the air*) planer

poison [ˈpɔɪzən] *s* poison *m* ‖ *tr* empoisonner

poi′son gas′ *s* gaz *m* asphyxiant

poi′son i′vy *s* sumac *m* vénéneux

poisonous [ˈpɔɪzənəs] *adj* toxique; (*plant*) vénéneux; (*snake*) venimeux

poke [pok] *s* poussée *f*; (*with elbow*) coup *m* de coude; (coll) traînard *m* ‖ *tr* pousser; (*the fire*) tisonner; **to poke fun at** se moquer de; **to poke one's nose into** (coll) fourrer son nez dans; **to poke s.th. into** fourrer q.ch. dans ‖ *intr* aller sans se presser; **to poke about** fureter

poker [ˈpokər] *s* tisonnier *m*; (cards) poker *m*

pok′er face′ *s* visage *m* impassible

pok·y [ˈpoki] *adj* (*comp* **-ier;** *super* **-iest**) (coll) lambin, lent

Poland [ˈpolənd] *s* Pologne *f*; la Pologne

polar [ˈpolər] *adj* polaire

po′lar bear′ *s* ours *m* blanc

polarize [ˈpoləˌraɪz] *tr* polariser

pole [pol] *s* (*long rod or staff*) perche *f*; (*of flag*) hampe *f*; (*upright support*) poteau *m*; (astr, biol, elec, geog, math) pôle *m*; **Pole** (*person*) Polonais *m* ‖ *tr* pousser à la perche

pole′cat′ *s* putois *m*

pole′star′ *s* étoile *f* polaire

pole′ vault′ *s* saut *m* à la perche

police [pəˈlis] *s* police *f* ‖ *tr* maintenir l'ordre dans

police′ brutal′ity *s* brutalité *f* policière

police′ commis′sioner *s* préfet *m* de police

police′man *s* (*pl* **-men**) agent *m* de police

police′ pre′cinct *s* commissariat *m* de police

police′ state′ *s* régime *m* policier

police′ sta′tion *s* poste *m* de police, commissariat *m*

police′wom′an *s* (*pl* **-wom′en**) femme *f* agent

poli·cy [ˈpalɪsi] *s* (*pl* **-cies**) politique *f*; (ins) police *f*

polio [ˈpolɪˌo] *s* (coll) polio *f*

polish [ˈpalɪʃ] *s* (*shine*) poli *m*; (*for household uses*) cire *f*; (*for shoes*) cirage *m*; (fig) politesse *f*, vernis *m* ‖ *tr* polir; (*shoes, floor, etc.*) cirer; (*one's nails*) vernir; **to polish off** (coll) expédier; (*e.g., a meal*) (slang) engloutir ‖ **Polish** [ˈpolɪʃ] *adj* & *s* polonais *m*

polite [pəˈlaɪt] *adj* poli

politeness [pəˈlaɪtnɪs] *s* politesse *f*

politic [ˈpalɪtɪk] *adj* (*prudent*) diplomatique, politique; (*shrewd*) rusé

political [pəˈlɪtɪkəl] *adj* politique

politician [ˌpalɪˈtɪʃən] *s* politicien *m*

politics [ˈpalɪtɪks] *s* & *spl* politique *f*

poll [pol] *s* (*list of voters*) liste *f* électorale; (*vote*) scrutin *m*; (*head*) tête *f*; (*opinion survey*) sondage *m* d'opinion; **to go to the polls** aller aux urnes; **to take a poll** faire une enquête par sondage ‖ *tr* (*e.g., a delegation*) dépouiller le scrutin de; (*a certain number of votes*) recevoir

pollen [ˈpalən] *s* pollen *m*

poll′ing booth′ [ˈpolɪŋ] *s* isoloir *m*

polliwog [ˈpalɪˌwag] *s* têtard *m*

pol′liwog initia′tion *s* baptême *m* de la ligne

pollster [ˈpolstər] *s* sondeur *m*, enquêteur *m*

poll′ tax′ *s* taxe *f* par tête

pollute [pəˈlut] *tr* polluer

polluting [pəˈlutɪŋ] *adj* polluant

pollution [pəˈluʃən] *s* pollution *f*

polo [ˈpolo] *s* polo *m*

polonium [pəˈlonɪ·əm] *s* polonium *m*

polo shirt′ *s* chemise *f* polo

polygamist [pəˈlɪgəmɪst] *s* polygame *mf*

polygamous [pəˈlɪgəməs] *adj* polygame

polyglot [ˈpalɪˌglat] *adj* & *s* polyglotte *mf*

polygon [ˈpalɪˌgan] *s* polygone *m*

polynomial [ˌpalɪˈnomɪ·əl] *s* polynôme *m*

polyp [ˈpalɪp] *s* polype *m*

polytheist [ˈpalɪˌθi·ɪst] *s* polythéiste *mf*

polytheistic [ˌpalɪθiˈɪstɪk] *adj* polythéiste

polyvalent [palɪˈvelənt] *adj* polyvalent

pomade [pəˈmed] *s* pommade *f*

pomegranate [ˈpamˌgrænɪt] *s* (*shrub*) grenadier *m*; (*fruit*) grenade *f*

pom·mel [ˈpʌməl] *s* pommeau *m* ‖ *v* (*pret* & *pp* **-meled** or **-melled;** *ger* **-meling** or **-melling**) *tr* rosser

pomp [pamp] *s* pompe *f*

pompous [ˈpampəs] *adj* pompeux

pon·cho [ˈpantʃo] *s* (*pl* **-chos**) poncho *m*

pond [pand] *s* étang *m*, mare *f*

ponder [ˈpandər] *tr* peser ‖ *intr* méditer; **to ponder over** réfléchir sur

ponderous [ˈpandərəs] *adj* pesant

poniard [ˈpanjərd] *s* poignard *m* ‖ *tr* poignarder

pontiff [ˈpantɪf] *s* pontife *m*

pontifical [panˈtɪfɪkəl] *adj* (*e.g., air*) de pontife

pontoon [panˈtun] *s* ponton *m*

po·ny [ˈponi] *s* (*pl* **-nies**) poney *m*; (*for drinking liquor*) petit verre *m*; (coll) aide-mémoire *m* illicite

po′ny·tail′ *s* queue-de-cheval *f*

poodle [ˈpudəl] *s* caniche *m*

pool [pul] *s* (*small puddle*) mare *f*; (*for swimming*) piscine *f*; (*game*) billard *m*; (*in certain games*) poule *f*; (*of workers*) équipe *f*; (*combine*) pool *m*; (com) fonds *m* commun ‖ *tr* mettre en commun

pool′room′ *s* salle *f* de billard

pool′ ta′ble *s* table *f* de billard

poop [pup] *s* (naut) dunette *f* ‖ *tr* (slang) casser la tête à

pooped *adj* (slang) vanné, à plat, flagada

poor [pur] *adj* pauvre; (*mediocre*) piètre; (*unfortunate*) pauvre (before noun); (*without money*) pauvre (after noun)

poor′ box′ *s* tronc *m* des pauvres

poor′house′ *s* asile *m* des indigents

poorly [ˈpurli] *adj* souffrant ‖ *adv* mal

pop [pap] *s* bruit *m* sec; (*soda*) boisson *f* gazeuse ‖ *v* (*pret* & *pp* **popped;** *ger* **popping**) *tr* (*corn*) faire éclater ‖ *intr* *(said, e.g., of balloon)* crever; *(said of cork)* sauter

pop′corn′ *s* maïs *m* éclaté, maïs explosé; grains *mpl* de maïs soufflés, pop-corn *m*

pope [pop] *s* pape *m*

pop′eyed′ *adj* aux yeux saillants

pop′gun′ *s* canonnière *f*

poplar [′pɑplər] *s* peuplier *m*

pop·py [′pɑpi] *s* (*pl* **-pies**) pavot *m*; *(corn poppy)* coquelicot *m*

pop′py·cock′ *s* (coll) fadaises *fpl*

populace [′pɑpjəlɪs] *s* peuple *m*, populace *f*

popular [′pɑpjələr] *adj* populaire

popularize [′pɑpjələ,raɪz] *tr* populariser, vulgariser

populate [′pɑpjə,let] *tr* peupler

population [,pɑpjə′leʃən] *s* population *f*

populous [′pɑpjələs] *adj* populeux

porcelain [′pɔrslɪn] *s* porcelaine *f*

porch [pɔrtʃ] *s* *(portico)* porche *m*; *(enclosed)* véranda *f*

porcupine [′pɔrkjə,paɪn] *s* porc-épic *m*

pore [por] *s* pore *m* ‖ *intr*—**to pore over** examiner avec attention, s'absorber dans

pork [pork] *s* porc *m*

pork′ and beans′ *spl* fèves *fpl* au lard

pork′chop′ *s* côtelette *f* de porc

porn [pɔrn] *s* (coll) porno *m* & *adj*

pornography [pɔr′nɑgrəfi] *s* pornographie *f*

porous [′porəs] *adj* poreux

porphy·ry [′pɔrfɪri] *s* (*pl* **-ries**) porphyre *m*

porpoise [′pɔrpəs] *s* marsouin *m*

porridge [′pɔrɪdʒ] *s* bouillie *f*, porridge *m*

port [port] *s* port *m*; *(opening in ship's side)* hublot *m*, sabord *m*; *(left side of ship or airplane)* bâbord *m*; *(wine)* porto *m*; (mach) orifice *m*

portable [′portəbəl] *adj* portatif

port′able stand′ *s* *(for a television set)* socle *m* roulant

port′able type′writer *s* machine *f* à écrire portative

portage [′portɪdʒ] *s* transport *m*; portage *m*

portal [′portəl] *s* portail *m*

portcullis [port′kʌlɪs] *s* herse *f*

portend [por′tɛnd] *tr* présager

portent [′portɛnt] *s* présage *m*

portentous [por′tɛntəs] *adj* extraordinaire; de mauvais augure

porter [′portər] *s* *(doorkeeper)* portier *m*, concierge *m*; *(in hotels and trains)* porteur *m*

portfoli·o [port′foli,o] *s* (*pl* **-os**) portefeuille *m*

port′hole′ *s* hublot *m*

porti·co [′portɪ,ko] *s* (*pl* **-coes** or **-cos**) portique *m*

portion [′porʃən] *s* portion *f*; *(dowry)* dot *f* ‖ *tr*—**to portion out** partager, répartir

port·ly [′portli] *adj* (*comp* **-lier**; *super* **-liest**) corpulent

port′ of call′ *s* port *m* d'escale

portrait [′portret] *s* portrait *m*; **to sit for one's portrait** se faire faire son portrait

portray [por′tre] *tr* faire le portrait de; dépeindre, décrire; (theat) jouer le rôle de

portrayal [por′tre·əl] *s* représentation *f*; description *f*

Portugal [′portʃəgəl] *s* le Portugal

Portu·guese [′portʃə,giz] *adj* portugais ‖ *s* *(language)* portugais *m* ‖ *s* (*pl* **-guese**) *(person)* Portugais *m*

port′ wine′ *s* porto *m*

pose [poz] *s* pose *f* ‖ *tr* & *intr* poser; **to pose as** se poser comme

posh [pɑʃ] *adj* (slang) chic, élégant

position [pə′zɪʃən] *s* position *f*; *(job)* poste *m*; **in position** en place; **in your position** à votre place

positive [′pɑzɪtɪv] *adj* & *s* positif *m*

possess [pə′zɛs] *tr* posséder

possession [pə′zɛʃən] *s* possession *f*; **to take possession of** s'emparer de

possible [′pɑsɪbəl] *adj* possible

possum [′pɑsəm] *s* opossum *m*; **to play possum** (coll) faire le mort

post [post] *s* *(upright)* poteau *m*; *(job, position)* poste *m*; *(post office)* poste *f*; (mil) poste *m* ‖ *tr* *(a notice, placard, etc.)* afficher, placarder; *(a letter)* poster, mettre à la poste; *(a sentinel)* poster; *(with news)* tenir au courant; **post no bills** *(public sign)* défense d'afficher

postage [′postɪdʒ] *s* port *m*, affranchissement *m*

post′age due′ *s* port *m* dû, affranchissement *m* insuffisant

post′age me′ter *s* affranchisseuse *f* à compteur

post′age stamp′ *s* timbre-poste *m*

postal [′postəl] *adj* postal

post′al card′ *s* carte *f* postale

post′al clerk′ *s* postier *m*

post′al mon′ey or′der *s* mandat-poste *m*

post′al per′mit *s* franchise *f* postale, dispensé *m* du timbrage

post′al sav′ings bank′ *s* caisse *f* d'épargne postale

post′ card′ *s* carte *f* postale

post′date′ *s* postdate *f* ‖ **post′date′** *tr* postdater

poster [′postər] *s* affiche *f*

posterity [pɑs′tɛrɪti] *s* postérité *f*

postern [′postərn] *s* poterne *f*

post′haste′ *adv* en toute hâte

posthumous [′pɑstʃuməs] *adj* posthume

post′man *s* (*pl* **-men**) facteur *m*, préposé *m*

post′mark′ *s* cachet *m* d'oblitération, timbre *m* ‖ *tr* timbrer

post′mas′ter *s* receveur *m* des postes, administrateur *m* du bureau de postes

post′master gen′eral *s* ministre *m* des Postes et Télécommunications

post-mortem [,post′mortəm] *adj* après décès; (fig) après le fait ‖ *s* autopsie *f*; discussion *f* après le fait

post′ of′fice *s* bureau *m* de poste

post′-office box′ *s* case *f* postale, boîte *f* postale

post′paid′ *adv* port payé, franc de port, franco de port

postpone [post′pon] *tr* remettre, différer; *(a meeting)* ajourner

postponement [post'ponmənt] *s* remise *f*, ajournement *m*

postscript ['post,skript] *s* post-scriptum *m*

posture ['pɑstʃər] *s* posture *f* ‖ *intr* prendre une posture

post'war' *adj* d'après-guerre

po·sy ['pozi] *s* (*pl* **-sies**) fleur *f*; bouquet *m*

pot [pɑt] *s* pot *m*; (*in gambling*) mise *f*; (*culin*) marmite *f*, pot; (*marijuana*) (slang) kif *m*, marie-jeanne *f*; **to go to pot** (slang) s'en aller à vau-l'eau

potash ['pɑt,æʃ] *s* potasse *f*

potassium [pə'tæsɪ·əm] *s* potassium *m*

pota·to [pə'teto] *s* (*pl* **-toes**) pomme *f* de terre; (*sweet potato*) patate *f*

pota'to chips' *spl* pommes *fpl* chips; croustelle *f* (Canad)

potbellied ['pɑt,belɪd] *adj* ventru

poten·cy ['potənsi] *s* (*pl* **-cies**) puissance *f*; virilité *f*

potent ['potənt] *adj* puissant, fort; (*effective*) efficace

potentate ['potən,tet] *s* potentat *m*

potential [pə'tɛnʃəl] *adj* & *s* potentiel *m*

pot'hang'er *s* crémaillère *f*

pot'herb' *s* herbe *f* potagère

pot'hold'er *s* poignée *f*

pot'hole' *s* nid *m* de poule

pot'hook' *s* croc *m*

potion ['poʃən] *s* potion *f*

pot'luck' *s*—**to take potluck** manger à la fortune du pot

pot' shot' *s* coup *m* tiré à courte distance

potter ['pɑtər] *s* potier *m* ‖ *intr*—**to potter around** s'occuper de bagatelles, bricoler

pot'ter's clay' *s* terre *f* à potier

pot'ter's field' *s* fosse *f* commune

pot'ter's wheel' *s* roue *f* or tour *m* de potier

potter·y ['pɑtəri] *s* (*pl* **-ies**) poterie *f*

pouch [pautʃ] *s* poche *f*, petit sac *m*; (*of kangaroo*) poche *f* ventrale; (*for tobacco*) blague *f*

poultice ['poltɪs] *s* cataplasme *m*

poultry ['poltri] *s* volaille *f*

poul'try·man *s* (*pl* **-men**) éleveur *m* de volailles; (*dealer*) volailleur *m*

pounce [pauns] *intr*—**to pounce on** fondre sur, s'abattre sur

pound [paund] *s* (*weight*) livre *f*; (*for automobiles, stray animals, etc.*) fourrière *f* ‖ *tr* battre; (*to pulversize*) piler, broyer; (*to bombard*) pilonner; (*e.g., an animal*) mettre en fourrière; (*e.g., the sidewalk*) (fig) battre ‖ *intr* battre

pound' ster'ling *s* livre *f* sterling

pour [por] *tr* verser; (*tea*) servir; **to pour off** décanter ‖ *intr* écouler; (*said of rain*) tomber à verse; **to pour out of** sortir à flots

pout [paut] *s* moue *f* ‖ *intr* faire la moue

poverty ['pɑvərti] *s* pauvreté *f*

POW ['pi'o'dʌbl,ju] *s* (letterword) (**prisoner of war**) P.G.

powder ['paudər] *s* poudre *f* ‖ *tr* réduire en poudre; (*to sprinkle with powder*) poudrer ‖ *intr* se poudrer

pow'dered cof'fee *s* café *m* soluble

pow'dered sug'ar *s* sucre *m* de confiseur, sucre en poudre, sucre glace

pow'der puff' *s* houppe *f*

pow'der room' *s* toilettes *fpl* pour dames

powdery ['paudəri] *adj* (*like powder*) poudreux; (*sprinkled with powder*) poussiéreux; (*crumbly*) friable

power ['pau·ər] *s* (*authority; capacity*) pourvoir *m*; (*influential nation; energy, force, strength; of a machine, microscope, number*) puissance *f*; (*talent, capacity, etc.*) faculté *f*; **the powers that be** les autorités *fpl*; **to seize power** saisir le pouvoir ‖ *tr* actionner

pow'er brake' *s* (aut) servo-frein *m*

pow'er dive' *s* piqué *m* à plein gaz

pow'er-dive' *intr* piquer à plein gaz

powerful ['pau·ərfəl] *adj* puissant

pow'er·house' *s* usine *f* centrale; (coll) foyer *m* d'énergie

pow'er lawn' mower *s* tondeuse *f* à gazon à moteur

powerless ['pau·ərlɪs] *adj* impuissant

pow'er line' *s* secteur *m* de distribution

pow'er mow'er *s* tondeuse *f* à gazon à moteur; motofaucheuse *f*

pow'er of attorn'ey *s* procuration *f*, mandat *m*

pow'er pack' *s* (rad) unité *f* d'alimentation

pow'er plant' *s* (*powerhouse*) centrale *f* électrique; (aer, aut) groupe *m* motopropulseur

pow'er saw' *s* tronçonneuse *f*

pow'er steer'ing *s* (aut) servo-direction *f*

practicable ['præktɪkəbəl] *adj* praticable

practical ['præktɪkəl] *adj* pratique

prac'tical joke' *s* farce *f*, attrape *f*

prac'tical jok'er *s* fumiste *m*

practically ['præktɪkəli] *adv* pratiquement; (*more or less*) à peu près

prac'tical nurse' *s* garde-malade *mf*

practice ['præktɪs] *s* (*habit, usage*) pratique *f*; (*of a profession*) exercice *m*; (*of a doctor*) clientèle *f*; (*exercise, training*) entraînement *m*; (*rehearsal*) répétition *f*; **in practice** en pratique, pratiquement; (*well-trained*) en forme; **out of practice** rouillé ‖ *tr* pratiquer; (*a profession*) exercer, pratiquer; (*e.g., the violin*) s'exercer à; **to practice what one preaches** prêcher d'exemple ‖ *intr* faire des exercices, s'exercer; (*said of doctor, lawyer, etc.*) exercer

practiced *adj* expert

practitioner [præk'tɪʃənər] *s* praticien *m*

prairie ['prɛri] *s* steppes *fpl*; **the prairie** les Prairies *fpl*

praise [prez] *s* louange *f* ‖ *tr* louer

praise'wor'thy *adj* louable, digne d'éloges

pram [præm] *s* voiture *f* d'enfant

prance [præns] *intr* caracoler, cabrioler

prank [præŋk] *s* espièglerie *f*

prate [pret] *intr* bavarder, papoter

prattle ['prætəl] *s* bavardage *m*, papotage *m* ‖ *intr* bavarder, papoter; (*said of children*) babiller

prawn [prɔn] *s* crevette *f* rose, bouquet *m*

pray [pre] *tr & intr* prier
prayer [prɛr] *s* prière *f*
prayer' book' *s* livre *m* de prières
pray'ing man'tis [ˈmæntɪs] *s* mante *f* religieuse
preach [pritʃ] *tr & intr* prêcher
preacher [ˈpritʃər] *s* prédicateur *m*
preamble [ˈpri,æmbəl] *s* préambule *m*
precarious [prɪˈkɛrɪ·əs] *adj* précaire
precaution [prɪˈkɔʃən] *s* précaution *f*
precede [prɪˈsid] *tr & intr* précéder
precedent [ˈprɛsɪdənt] *s* précédent *m*
precept [ˈprisɛpt] *s* précepte *m*
precinct [ˈprisɪŋkt] *s* enceinte *f*; circonscription *f* électorale
precious [ˈprɛʃəs] *adj* précieux ‖ *adv*—**precious little** (coll) très peu
precipice [ˈprɛsɪpɪs] *s* précipice *m*
precipitate [prɪˈsɪpɪ,tet] *adj & s* précipité *m* ‖ *tr* précipiter ‖ *intr* se précipiter
precipitous [prɪˈsɪpɪtəs] *adj* escarpé; (*hurried*) précipité
precise [prɪˈsais] *adj* précis
precision [prɪˈsɪʒən] *s* précision *f*
preclude [prɪˈklud] *tr* empêcher
precocious [prɪˈkoʃəs] *adj* précoce
preconceived [,prikənˈsivd] *adj* préconçu
predatory [ˈprɛdə,tori] *adj* rapace; (zool) prédateur
predecessor [,prɛdɪˈsɛsər] *s* prédécesseur *m*, devancier *m*
predicament [prɪˈdɪkəmənt] *s* situation *f* difficile
predict [prɪˈdɪkt] *tr* prédire
prediction [prɪˈdɪkʃən] *s* prédiction *f*
predispose [,pridɪsˈpoz] *tr* prédisposer
predominant [prɪˈdɑmɪnənt] *adj* prédominant
preeminent [priˈɛmɪnənt] *adj* prééminent
preempt [priˈɛmpt] *tr* s'approprier
preen [prin] *tr* lisser; **to preen oneself** bichonner; être fier, se piquer
prefabricated [priˈfæbrɪ,ketɪd] *adj* préfabriqué
preface [ˈprɛfɪs] *s* préface *f* ‖ *tr* préfacer
pre·fer [prɪˈfʌr] *v* (*pret & pp* **-ferred;** *ger* **-ferring**) *tr* préférer
preferable [ˈprɛfərəbəl] *adj* préférable
preference [ˈprɛfərəns] *s* préférence *f*
preferred' stock' *s* action *f* privilégiée, actions privilégiées
prefix [ˈprifɪks] *s* préfixe *m* ‖ *tr* préfixer
pregnan·cy [ˈprɛgnənsi] *s* (*pl* **-cies**) grossesse *f*
pregnant [ˈprɛgnənt] *adj* enceinte, grosse; (fig) gros
prehistoric [,prihɪsˈtɔrɪk] *adj* préhistorique
prejudice [ˈprɛdʒədɪs] *s* préjugé *m*; (*detriment*) préjudice *m* ‖ *tr* prévenir, prédisposer; (*to harm*) porter préjudice à
prejudicial [,prɛdʒəˈdɪʃəl] *adj* préjudiciable
prelate [ˈprɛlɪt] *s* prélat *m*
prelim [ˈprilɪm] *s* (educ) examen *m* préliminaire; (sports) épreuve *f* éliminatoire
preliminar·y [prɪˈlɪmɪ,nɛri] *adj* préliminaire ‖ *s* (*pl* **-ies**) préliminaire *m*

prelude [ˈprɛljud] *s* prélude *m* ‖ *tr* introduire; préluder à; (*a piece of music*) préluder par
premature [,priməˈt(j)ʊr] *adj* prématuré; (*plant*) hâtif
premeditate [priˈmɛdɪ,tet] *tr* préméditer
premier [prɪˈmɪr] *s* premier ministre *m*
première [prəˈmjɛr], [prɪˈmɪr] *s* première *f*; (*actress*) vedette *f*
premise [ˈprɛmɪs] *s* prémisse *f*; **on the premises** sur les lieux; **premises** local *m*, locaux *mpl*
premium [ˈprimɪ·əm] *s* prime *f*; **to be at a premium** faire prime
premonition [,priməˈnɪʃən] *s* prémonition *f*
preoccupation [pri,ɑkjəˈpeʃən] *s* préoccupation *f*
preoccu·py [priˈɑkjə,pai] *v* (*pret & pp* **-pied**) *tr* préoccuper
prepaid [priˈped] *adj* payé d'avance; (*letter*) affranchi
preparation [,prɛpəˈreʃən] *s* préparation *f*; **preparations** (*for a trip; for war*) préparatifs *mpl*
preparatory [prɪˈpærə,tori] *adj* préparatoire
prepare [prɪˈpɛr] *tr* préparer ‖ *intr* se préparer
preparedness [prɪˈpɛrdnɪs] *s* préparation *f*; armement *m* préventif
pre·pay [priˈpe] *v* (*pret & pp* **-paid**) *tr* payer d'avance
preponderant [prɪˈpɑndərənt] *adj* prépondérant
preposition [,prɛpəˈzɪʃən] *s* préposition *f*
prepossessing [,pripəˈzɛsɪŋ] *adj* avenant, agréable
preposterous [prɪˈpɑstərəs] *adj* absurde, extravagant
preppie [ˈprɛpi] *s* (slang) bon chic bon genre *m* (B.C.B.G.)
prep' school' [prɛp] *s* école *f* préparatoire
prerecorded [,prirɪˈkɔrdɪd] *adj* (rad, telv) différé, en différé
prerequisite [priˈrɛkwɪzɪt] *s* préalable *m*; (educ) cours *m* préalable
prerogative [prɪˈrɑgətɪv] *s* prérogative *f*
presage [ˈprɛsɪdʒ] *s* présage *m*; (*foreboding*) pressentiment *m* ‖ [prɪˈsedʒ] *tr* présager; pressentir
Presbyterian [,prɛzbɪˈtɪrɪ·ən] *adj & s* presbytérien *m*
prescribe [prɪˈskraɪb] *tr* prescrire ‖ *intr* faire une ordonnance
prescription [prɪˈskrɪpʃən] *s* prescription *f*; (*pharm*) ordonnance *f*
presence [ˈprɛzəns] *s* présence *f*
present [ˈprɛzənt] *adj* (*at this time*) actuel; (*at this place or time*) présent; **to be present at** assister à ‖ *s* cadeau *m*, présent *m*; (*present time or tense*) présent; **at present** à présent ‖ [prɪˈzɛnt] *tr* présenter
presentable [prɪˈzɛntəbəl] *adj* présentable, sortable
presentation [,prɛzənˈteʃən] *s* présentation *f*
presenta'tion cop'y *s* exemplaire *m* offert à titre d'hommage

presentiment [prɪˈzɛntɪmənt] s pressentiment m

presently [ˈprɛzəntli] adv tout à l'heure; (now) à présent

preserve [prɪˈzʌrv] s confiture f; (for game) chasse f gardée ‖ tr préserver, conserver; (to can) conserver

pre-shrunk [priˈʃʌŋk] adj irrétrécissable

preside [prɪˈzaɪd] intr présider; **to preside over** présider

presiden·cy [ˈprɛzɪdənsi] s (pl -cies) présidence f

president [ˈprɛzɪdənt] s président m; (of a university) recteur m

pres'ident-elect' s président m désigné

presidential [ˌprɛzɪˈdɛnʃəl] adj présidentiel

press [prɛs] s presse f; (e.g., for wine) pressoir m; (pressure) pression f; (for clothes) armoire f; (in weight lifting) développé m; **in press** (said of clothes) lisse et net; (said of book being published) sous presse; **to go to press** être mis sous presse ‖ tr presser; (e.g., a button) appuyer sur, presser; (clothes) donner un coup de fer à, repasser ‖ intr presser; **to press against** se serrer contre; **to press forward, to press on** presser le pas

press' a'gent s agent m de publicité

press' box' s tribune f des journalistes

press' card' s coupe-file m d'un journaliste

press' con'ference s conférence f de presse

pressing [ˈprɛsɪŋ] adj pressé, pressant

press' pass' s placard m de presse

press' release' s communiqué m de presse

pressure [ˈprɛʃər] s pression f

pres'sure cook'er s autocuiseur m, cocotte f minute

pressurize [ˈprɛʃəˌraɪz] tr pressuriser

prestige [prɛsˈtiʒ] s prestige m

pre'stressed con'crete [ˈpriˌstrɛst] s béton m précontraint

presumably [prɪˈz(j)uməbli] adv probablement

presume [prɪˈz(j)um] tr présumer; **to presume to** présumer ‖ intr présumer; **to presume on** or **upon** abuser de

presumption [prɪˈzʌmpʃən] s présomption f

presumptuous [prɪˈzʌmptʃʊ·əs] adj présomptueux

presuppose [ˌprisəˈpoz] tr présupposer

pretend [prɪˈtɛnd] tr feindre; **to pretend to** + inf feindre de + inf; (to claim) prétendre, e.g., **I don't pretend to know everything** je ne prétends pas tout savoir; (to imagine) se dire, e.g., **I am going to pretend to be sitting at an outdoor café** je vais me dire que je m'assieds à une terrace de café ‖ intr feindre; **let's pretend!** (let's imagine that it's true) imaginons-nous!; **to pretend to** (e.g., the throne) prétendre à

pretender [prɪˈtɛndər] s prétendant m; (imposter) simulateur m

pretense [prɪˈtɛns], [ˈpritɛns] s prétention f; feinte f; **under false pretenses** par des moyens frauduleux; **under pretense of** sous prétexte de

pretension [prɪˈtɛnʃən] s prétention f

pretentious [prɪˈtɛnʃəs] adj prétentieux

pretext [ˈpritɛkst] s prétexte m

pretonic [prɪˈtɑnɪk] adj prétonique

pret·ty [ˈprɪti] adj (comp -tier; super -tiest) joli; (coll) considérable ‖ adv assez; très

prevail [prɪˈvel] intr prévaloir, régner; **to prevail on** or **upon** persuader

prevailing [prɪˈvelɪŋ] adj (opinion) prédominant, courant; (conditions) actuel; (wind) dominant; (fashion) en vogue

prevalent [ˈprɛvələnt] adj commun, courant, regnant

prevaricate [prɪˈværɪˌket] intr mentir

prevent [prɪˈvɛnt] tr empêcher

prevention [prɪˈvɛnʃən] s empêchement m; (e.g., of accidents) prévention f

preventive [prɪˈvɛntɪv] adj & s préventif m

preview [ˈpriˌvju] s (of something to come) amorce f; (private showing) (mov) avant-première f; (show of brief scenes for advertising) film m annonce

previous [ˈprivɪ·əs] adj précédent, antérieur; (notice) préalable; (coll) pressé ‖ adv—**previous to** antérieurement à

prewar [ˈpriˌwɔr] adj d'avant-guerre

prey [pre] s proie f; **to be a prey to** être en proie à ‖ intr—**to prey on** or **upon** faire sa proie de; (e.g., a seacoast) piller; (e.g., the mind) ronger, miner

price [praɪs] s prix m ‖ tr mettre un prix à, tarifer; s'informer du prix de

price' control' s contrôle m des prix

price' cut'ting s rabais m, remise f

price'-earn'ings ra'tio s quotient m cours-bénéficie

price' fix'ing s stabilisation f des prix

price' freez'ing s blocage m des prix

priceless [ˈpraɪslɪs] adj sans prix, inestimable; (very funny) (coll) impayable, absurde

price' list' s liste f de prix, tarif m

price' war' s guerre f des prix

prick [prɪk] s piqûre f; (spur; sting of conscience) aiguillon m ‖ tr piquer; **to prick up** (the ears) dresser

prick·ly [ˈprɪkli] adj (comp -lier; super -liest) épineux

prick'ly heat' s lichen m vésiculaire, miliaire f

prick'ly pear' s figue f de Barbarie; (plant) figuier m de Barbarie

pride [praɪd] s (self-respect) orgueil m; (satisfaction) fierté f; (pej) arrogance f, orgueil; **to take pride in** être fier de ‖ tr—**to pride oneself on** or **upon** s'enorgueillir de

priest [prist] s prêtre m

priestess [ˈpristɪs] s prêtresse f

priesthood [ˈpristˌhʊd] s sacerdoce m

priest·ly [ˈpristli] adj (comp -lier; super -liest) sacerdotal

prig [prɪg] s poseur m, pédant m

prim [prɪm] adj (comp primmer; super primmest) compassé, guindé

prima·ry ['praɪməri] *adj* primaire ‖ *s* (*pl* -ries) élection *f* primaire; (elec) primaire *m*

primate ['praɪmet] *s* (eccl) primat *m*; (zool) primate *m*

prime [praɪm] *adj* (*first*) premier, principal; (*of the best quality*) de première qualité, (le) meilleur; (math) prime ‖ *s* fleur *f*, perfection *f*; commencement *m*, premiers jours *mpl*; **prime of life** fleur or force de l'âge ‖ *tr* amorcer; (*a surface to be painted*) appliquer une couche de fond à; (*to supply with information*) mettre au courant

prime' min'ister *s* premier ministre *m*

primer ['prɪmər] *s* premier livre *m* de lecture, manuel *m* élémentaire ‖ ['praɪmər] *s* (*for paint*) couche *f* de fond, impression, *f*; (mach) amorce *f*

prime' rate' *s* (com) taux *m* de base

primeval [praɪ'mivəl] *adj* primitif

primitive ['prɪmɪtɪv] *adj* & *s* primitif *m*

primordial [praɪ'mɔrdɪ·əl] *adj* primordial

primp [prɪmp] *tr* bichonner, pomponner ‖ *intr* se bichonner, se pomponner

prim'rose *s* primevère *f*

prim'rose path' *s* chemin *m* de velours

prince [prɪns] *s* prince *m*

prince·ly ['prɪnsli] *adj* (*comp* -lier; *super* -liest) princier

Prince' of Wales' *s* prince *m* de Galles

princess ['prɪnsɪs] *s* princesse *f*

principal ['prɪnsɪpəl] *adj* & *s* principal *m*

principali·ty [,prɪnsɪ'pælɪti] *s* (*pl* -ties) principauté *f*

principle ['prɪnsɪpəl] *s* principe *m*

print [prɪnt] *s* (*mark*) empreinte *f*; (*printed cloth*) imprimé *m*; (*design in printed cloth*) estampe *f*; (*lettering*) lettres *fpl* moulées; (*act of printing*) impression *f*; (phot) épreuve *f*; **out of print** épuisé; **small print** petits caractères *mpl* ‖ *tr* imprimer; écrire en lettres moulées; publier; (*an edition; a photographic negative*) tirer; **to print out** (comp) imprimer, restituer

print'ed cir'cuit *s* circuit *m* imprimé

print'ed mat'ter *s* imprimés *mpl*

printer ['prɪntər] *s* imprimeur *m*; (comp) imprimante *f*

prin'ter's dev'il *s* apprenti *m* imprimeur

prin'ter's er'ror *s* faute *f* d'impression, coquille *f*

prin'ter's ink' *s* encre *f* d'imprimerie

prin'ter's mark' *s* nom *m* de l'imprimeur

printing ['prɪntɪŋ] *s* imprimerie *f*; (*act*) impression *f*; (*by hand*) écriture *f* en caractères d'imprimerie; édition *f*; tirage *m*; (phot) tirage

print'ing frame' *s* (phot) châssis-presse *m*

print'ing of'fice *s* imprimerie *f*

print'out' *s* (comp) tapuscrit *m*, listage *m*

prior ['praɪ·ər] *adj* antérieur ‖ *s* prieur *m* ‖ *adv* antérieurement; **prior to** avant; avant de

priori·ty [praɪ'ɔriti] *s* (*pl* -ties) priorité *f*

prism ['prɪzəm] *s* prisme *m*

prison ['prɪzən] *s* prison *f* ‖ *tr* emprisonner

prisoner ['prɪznər] *s* prisonnier *m*

pris'on van' *s* voiture *f* cellulaire

pris·sy ['prɪsi] *adj* (*comp* -sier; *super* -siest) (coll) bégueule

priva·cy ['praɪvəsi] *s* (*pl* -cies) intimité *f*; secret *m*

private ['praɪvɪt] *adj* privé, particulier; confidentiel, secret; (*public sign*) défense d'entrer ‖ *s* simple soldat *m*; **in private** dans l'intimité, en particulier; **privates** parties *fpl*

pri'vate cit'izen *s* simple particulier *m*, simple citoyen *m*

pri'vate first' class' *s* soldat *m* de première

pri'vate hos'pital *s* clinique *f*

pri'vate sec'retary *s* secrétaire *m* particulier

pri'vate sid'ing *s* embranchement *m* particulier

privet ['prɪvɪt] *s* troène *m*

privilege ['prɪvɪlɪdʒ] *s* privilège *m*

priv·y ['prɪvi] *adj* privé; **privy to** averti de ‖ *s* (*pl* -ies) cabinets *mpl* au fond du jardin

prize [praɪz] *s* prix *m*; (*something captured*) prise *f* ‖ *tr* faire cas de, estimer

prize' fight' *s* match *m* de boxe

prize' fight'er *s* boxeur *m* professionnel

prize' ring' *s* ring *m*

prize'win'ner *s* lauréat *m*; **prizewinners** (*list*) palmarès *m*

pro [pro] *s* (*pl* pros) vote *m* affirmatif; (*professional*) (coll) pro *m*; **the pros and the cons** le pour et le contre ‖ *prep* en faveur de

probabili·ty [,prabə'bɪlɪti] *s* (*pl* -ties) probabilité *f*

probable ['prabəbəl] *adj* probable

probably ['prabəbli] *adv* probablement

probate ['probet] *s* homologation *f* ‖ *tr* homologuer

probation [pro'beʃən] *s* liberté *f* surveillée; (*on a job*) stage *m*

probe [prob] *s* sondage *m*; (*instrument*) sonde *f*; (rok) échos *mpl*; (rok) engin *m* exploratoire ‖ *tr* sonder

problem ['prabləm] *s* problème *m*

probl'em child' *s* enfant *mf* terrible

procedure [pro'sidʒər] *s* procédé *m*

proceed ['prosid] *s*—**proceeds** produit *m*, bénéfices *mpl* ‖ [pro'sid] *intr* avancer, continuer; continuer à parler; **to proceed from** procéder de; **to proceed to** se mettre à; (*to go to*) se diriger à

proceeding [pro'sidɪŋ] *s* procédé *m*; **proceedings** actes *mpl*

process ['prasɛs] *s* (*technique*) procédé *m*; (*development*) processus *m*; **in the process of** en train de ‖ *tr* soumettre à un procédé, traiter

processing ['prasɛsɪŋ] *s* (comp) traitement *m*, façonnage *m*; **processing by modem** (comp) télétraitement *m*

procession [pro'sɛʃən] *s* cortège *m*, défilé *m*, procession *f*

pro'cess serv'er *s* huissier *m* exploitant

proclaim [pro'klem] *tr* proclamer

proclitic [pro'klɪtɪk] *adj* & *s* proclitique *m*

procrastinate [pro'kræstɪ,net] *tr* différer ‖ *intr* remettre les affaires à plus tard

proctor ['prɑktər] *s* surveillant *m*

procure [pro'kjʊr] *tr* obtenir, se procurer; (*a woman*) entraîner à la prostitution ‖ *intr* faire du proxénétisme

procurement [pro'kjʊrmənt] *s* obtention *f*, acquisition *f*

procurer [pro'kjʊrər] *s* proxénète *mf*

prod [prɑd] *s* poussée *f*; (*stick*) aiguillon *m* ‖ *v* (*pret* & *pp* **prodded**; *ger* **prodding**) *tr* aiguillonner

prodigal ['prɑdɪgəl] *adj* & *s* prodigue *mf*

prodigious [pro'dɪdʒəs] *adj* prodigieux

prodi·gy ['prɑdɪdʒi] *s* (*pl* **-gies**) prodige *m*

produce ['prɑd(j)us] *s* produit *m*; (*eatables*) denrées *fpl* ‖ [pro'd(j)us] *tr* produire; (*a play*) mettre en scène; (geom) prolonger

producer [pro'd(j)usər] *s* producteur *m*

product ['prɑdəkt] *s* produit *m*

production [pro'dʌkʃən] *s* production *f*

profane [pro'fen] *adj* profane; (*language*) impie, blasphématoire ‖ *s* profane *mf*; impie *mf* ‖ *tr* profaner

profani·ty [pro'fænɪti] *s* (*pl* **-ties**) blasphème *m*

profess [pro'fɛs] *tr* professer

profession [pro'fɛʃən] *s* profession *f*

professor [pro'fɛsər] *s* professeur *m*

proffer ['prɑfər] *s* offre *f* ‖ *tr* offrir, tendre

proficient [pro'fɪʃənt] *adj* compétent, expert

profile ['profaɪl] *s* profil *m*; courte biographie *f* ‖ *tr* profiler; **to be profiled against** se profiler sur

profit ['prɑfɪt] *s* bénéfice *m*, profit *m* ‖ *tr* profiter à ‖ *intr* profiter; **to profit from** profiter à, de, or en

profitable ['prɑfɪtəbəl] *adj* profitable

prof'it-and-loss' account' *s* compte *m* de profits et pertes

profiteer [,prɑfɪ'tɪr] *s* profiteur *m* ‖ *intr* faire des bénéfices excessifs

prof'it mar'gin *s* marge *f* bénéficiaire

prof'it tak'ing *s* prise *f* de bénéfices

profligate ['prɑflɪgɪt] *adj* & *s* débauché *m*

pro' for'ma in'voice [,pro'fɔrmə] *s* facture *f* simulée

profound [pro'faʊnd] *adj* profond

pro-French' *adj* francophile

profuse [prə'fjuz] *adj* abondant; (*extravagant*) prodigue

proge·ny ['prɑdʒəni] *s* (*pl* **-nies**) progéniture *f*

progno·sis [prɑg'nosɪs] *s* (*pl* **-ses** [siz]) pronostic *m*

prognosticate [prɑg'nɑstɪ,ket] *tr* pronostiquer

pro·gram ['progræm] *s* programme *m* ‖ *v* (*pret* & *pp* **-gramed**; *ger* **-graming**) *tr* programmer

pro'gramed learn'ing *s* enseignement *m* séquentiel

programer ['progræmər] *s* (comp) programmeur *m*; (mov, rad, telv) programmateur *m*

programing ['progræmɪŋ] *s* programmation

pro'gram pack'aging *s* (rad, telv) groupage *m* d'émissions

progress ['prɑgrɛs] *s* progrès *m*; cours *m*, e.g., **work in progress** travaux en cours; **to make progress** faire des progrès ‖ [prə'grɛs] *intr* progresser

progressive [prə'grɛsɪv] *adj* progressif; (pol) progressiste ‖ *s* (pol) progressiste *mf*

prohibit [pro'hɪbɪt] *tr* prohiber, interdire

prohibition [,pro·ə'bɪʃən] *s* prohibition *f*

project ['prɑdʒɛkt] *s* projet *m* ‖ [prə'dʒɛkt] *tr* projeter ‖ *intr* (*to jut out*) saillir; (theat) passer la rampe

projectile [prə'dʒɛktɪl] *s* projectile *m*

projection [prə'dʒɛkʃən] *s* projection *f*; (*something jutting out*) saillie *f*

projec'tion booth' *s* (mov) cabine *f* de projection

projector [prə'dʒɛktər] *s* projecteur *m*; (mov, telv) sunlight *m invar*

proletarian [,proli'tɛri·ən] *adj* prolétarien ‖ *s* prolétaire *m*

proletariat [,proli'tɛri·ət] *s* prolétariat *m*

proliferate [prə'lifə,ret] *intr* proliférer

prolific [prə'lɪfɪk] *adj* prolifique

prolix ['proliks] *adj* prolixe

prologue ['prolɔg] *s* prologue *m*

prolong [pro'lɔŋ] *tr* prolonger

promenade [,prɑmɪ'ned] *s* promenade *f*; bal *m* d'apparat; (theat) promenoir *m* ‖ *intr* se promener

prom'enade' deck' *s* (naut) pont-promenade *m*

prominent ['prɑmɪnənt] *adj* proéminent; (*well-known*) éminent

promiscuity [,prɑmɪs'kju·əti] *s* promiscuité *f* sexuelle

promiscuous [prə'mɪskju,əs] *adj* (*in sexual matters*) de mœurs faciles, de mœurs légères, immoral; (*disorderly*) confus

promise ['prɑmɪs] *s* promesse *f* ‖ *tr* & *intr* promettre; **to promise s.o. to** promettre à qn de; **to promise s.th. to s.o.** promettre q.ch. à qn

prom'issory note' ['prɑmɪ,sori] *m* billet *m* à ordre

promonto·ry ['prɑmən,tori] *s* (*pl* **-ries**) promontoire *m*

promote [prə'mot] *tr* promouvoir

promoter [prə'motər] *s* promoteur *m*

promotion [prə'moʃən] *s* promotion *f*

prompt [prɑmpt] *adj* prompt; ponctuel ‖ *tr* inciter; (theat) souffler son rôle à

prompter ['prɑmptər] *s* (theat) souffleur *m*

promp'ter's box' *s* (theat) trou *m* du souffleur

promptness ['prɑmptnɪs] *s* promptitude *f*

promulgate ['prɑməl,get] *tr* promulguer

prone [pron] *adj* à plat ventre, prostré; **prone to** enclin à

prong [prɔŋ], [prɑŋ] *s* dent *f*

pronoun ['pronaʊn] *s* pronom *m*

pronounce [prə'naʊns] *tr* prononcer

pronouncement [prə'naʊnsmənt] *s* déclaration *f*

pronunciation [prə,nʌnsi'eʃən] *s* prononciation *f*

proof [pruf] *adj*—**proof against** à l'épreuve de, résistant à ‖ *s* preuve *f*; (phot, typ) épreuve *f*; **to read proof** corriger les épreuves

proof′read′er *s* correcteur *m*

prop [prɑp] *s* appui *m*; (*to hold up a plant*) tuteur *m*; **props** (theat) accessoires *mpl* ‖ *v* (*pret & pp* **propped;** *ger* **propping**) *tr* appuyer; (hort) tuteurer

propaganda [ˌprɑpə'gændə] *s* propagande *f*

propagate ['prɑpə,get] *tr* propager

pro·pel [prə'pɛl] *s* (*pret & pp* **-pelled;** *ger* **-pelling**) *tr* propulser

propellant [prə'pɛlənt] *s* (rok) ergol *m*

propeller [prə'pɛlər] *s* hélice *f*

propensi·ty [prə'pɛnsɪti] *s* (*pl* **-ties**) propension *f*

proper ['prɑpər] *adj* (*fitting, correct*) convenable, correct; (*person*) comme il faut; (*name*) propre

proper·ty ['prɑpərti] *s* (*pl* **-ties**) propriété *f*; **properties** (theat) accessoires *mpl*

prop′erty own′er *s* propriétaire *mf*

prop′erty tax′ *s* impôt *m* foncier

prophe·cy ['prɑfɪsi] *s* (*pl* **-cies**) prophétie *f*

prophe·sy ['prɑfɪ,saɪ] *v* (*pret & pp* **-sied**) *tr* prophétiser

prophet ['prɑfɪt] *s* prophète *m*

prophetess ['prɑfɪtɪs] *s* prophétesse *f*

prophylactic [ˌprofɪ'læktɪk] *adj* prophylactique ‖ *s* (*preventive*) prophylactique *m*; (*contraceptive*) préservatif *m*, capote *f* anglaise

propitiate [prə'pɪʃɪ,et] *tr* apaiser

propitious [prə'pɪʃəs] *adj* propice

prop′jet′ *s* turbopropulseur *m*

proportion [prə'pɔrʃən] *s* proportion *f*; **in proportion as** à mesure que; **in proportion to** en proportion de, en raison de; **out of proportion** hors de proportion ‖ *tr* proportionner

proportionate [prə'pɔrʃənɪt] *adj* proportionné

proposal [prə'pozəl] *s* proposition *f*; demande *f* en mariage

propose [prə'poz] *tr* proposer ‖ *intr* faire sa déclaration; **to propose to** demander sa main à; (*to decide to*) se proposer de

proposition [ˌprɑpə'zɪʃən] *s* proposition *f* ‖ *tr* faire des propositions malhonnêtes à

propound [prə'paund] *tr* proposer

proprietor [prə'praɪ·ətər] *s* propriétaire *mf*

proprietress [prə'praɪ·ətrɪs] *s* propriétaire *f*

proprie·ty [prə'praɪ·əti] *s* (*pl* **-ties**) propriété *f*; (*of conduct*) bienséance *f*; **proprieties** convenances *fpl*

propulsion [prə'pʌlʃən] *s* propulsion *f*

prorate [pro'ret] *tr* partager au prorata

prosaic [pro'ze·ɪk] *adj* prosaïque

proscenium [pro'sɪnɪ·əm] *s* avant-scène *f*

proscribe [pro'skraɪb] *tr* proscrire

prose [proz] *adj* en prose ‖ *s* prose *f*

prosecute ['prɑsɪ,kjut] *tr* poursuivre

prosecutor ['prɑsɪ,kjutər] *s* (*lawyer*) procureur *m*; (*plaintiff*) plaignant *m*

proselyte ['prɑsɪ,laɪt] *s* prosélyte *mf*

prose′ writ′er *s* prosateur *m*

prosody ['prɑsədi] *s* prosodie *f*

prospect ['prɑspɛkt] *s* (*outlook*) perspective *f*; (*future*) avenir *m*; (com) client *m* éventuel ‖ *tr & intr* prospecter; **to prospect for** (*e.g., gold*) chercher

prospector ['prɑspɛktər] *s* prospecteur *m*

prospectus [prə'spɛktəs] *s* prospectus *m*

prosper ['prɑspər] *intr* prospérer

prosperity [prɑs'pɛrɪti] *s* prospérité *f*

prosperous ['prɑspərəs] *adj* prospère

prostate (gland′) ['prɑstet] *s* prostate *f*

prostitute ['prɑstɪ,t(j)ut] *s* prostituée *f* ‖ *tr* prostituer

prostrate ['prɑstret] *adj* prosterné; (*exhausted*) prostré ‖ *tr* abattre; **to prostrate oneself** se prosterner

prostration [prɑs'treʃən] *s* prostration *f*; (*abasement*) prosternation *f*

protagonist [pro'tægənɪst] *s* protagoniste *m*

protect [prə'tɛkt] *tr* protéger

protection [prə'tɛkʃən] *s* protection *f*

protein ['protɪ·ɪn] *s* protéine *f*

pro-tempore [pro'tɛmpə,ri] *adj* intérimaire, par intérim

protest ['protɛst] *s* protestation *f* ‖ [pro'tɛst] *tr* protester de; protester ‖ *intr* protester

Protestant ['prɑtɪstənt] *adj & s* protestant *m*

protocol ['protə,kɑl] *s* protocole *m*

proton ['protɑn] *s* proton *m*

protoplasm ['protə,plæzəm] *s* protoplasme *m*

prototype ['protə,taɪp] *s* prototype *m*

protozoan [ˌprotə'zo·ən] *s* protozoaire *m*

protract [pro'trækt] *tr* prolonger

protrude [pro'trud] *intr* saillir

protuberance [pro't(j)ubərəns] *s* protubérance *f*

proud [praud] *adj* fier; (*vain*) orgueilleux

proud′ flesh′ *s* chair *f* fongueuse

prove [pruv] *v* (*pret* **proved;** *pp* **proved** or **proven** ['pruvən]) *tr* prouver; (*to put to the test*) éprouver ‖ *intr* se montrer, se trouver; **to prove to be** se révéler, s'avérer

proverb ['prɑvərb] *s* proverbe *m*

provide [prə'vaɪd] *tr* pourvoir, fournir; **to provide s.th. for s.o.** fournir q.ch. à qn ‖ *intr*—**to provide for** pourvoir à; (*e.g., future needs*) parer à

provided *conj* pourvu que, à condition que

providence ['prɑvɪdəns] *s* providence *f*; (*prudence*) prévoyance *f*

providential [ˌprɑvɪ'dɛnʃəl] *adj* providentiel

providing [prə'vaɪdɪŋ] *conj* pourvu que, à condition que

province ['prɑvɪns] *s* province *f*; (*sphere*) compétence *f*

prov′ing ground′ *s* terrain *m* d'essai

provision [prə'vɪʒən] *s* (*supplying*) fourniture *f*; clause *f*; **provisions** provisions *fpl*

provi·so [prə'vaɪzo] *s* (*pl* **-sos** or **-soes**) condition *f*, stipulation *f*

provocative [prə'vɑkətɪv] *adj* provocant

provoke [prə'vok] *tr* provoquer; fâcher, contrarier

provoking [prə'vokɪŋ] *adj* contrariant

prow [praʊ] s proue f
prowess ['praʊ·ɪs] s prouesse f
prowl [praʊl] intr rôder
prowler ['praʊlər] s rôdeur m
proximity [prɑk'sɪmɪti] s proximité f
prox·y ['prɑksi] s (pl -ies) mandat m; (agent) mandataire mf; **by proxy** par procuration
prude [prud] s prude mf
prudence ['prudəns] s prudence f
prudent ['prudənt] adj prudent
pruder·y ['prudəri] s (pl -ies) pruderie f
prudish ['prudɪʃ] adj prude
prune [prun] s pruneau m ‖ tr élaguer
pruning ['prunɪŋ] s taille f, émondage m, cisaillement m
prun'ing shears' spl cisailles fpl
Prussian ['prʌʃən] adj prussien ‖ s Prussien m
pry [praɪ] v (pret & pp pried) tr—**to pry open** forcer avec un levier; **to pry s.th. out of s.o.** extorquer, soutirer q.ch. à qn ‖ intr fureter; **to pry into** fourrer son nez dans
P.S. ['pi'ɛs] s (letterword) (postscript) P.-S.
psalm [sɑm] s psaume m
Psalter ['sɔltər] s psautier m
pseudo ['s(j)udo] adj faux, supposé, feint, factice
pseudonym ['s(j)udənɪm] s pseudonyme m
psyche ['saɪki] s psyché f
psychedelic [,saɪkɪ'dɛlɪk] adj psychédélique
psychiatrist [saɪ'kaɪ·ətrɪst] s psychiatre mf
psychiatry [saɪ'kaɪ·ətri] s psychiatrie f
psychic ['saɪkɪk] adj psychique; médiumnique ‖ s médium m
psycho ['saɪko] adj & s (slang) fou m, dingue mf, cinglé m, agité m
psychoanalysis [,saɪko·ə'nælɪsɪs] s psychanalyse f
psychoanalyze [,saɪko'ænə,laɪz] tr psychanalyser
psychologic(al) [,saɪko'lɑdʒɪk(əl)] adj psychologique
psychologist [saɪ'kɑlədʒɪst] s psychologue mf
psychology [saɪ'kɑlədʒi] s psychologie f
psychopath ['saɪkə,pæθ] s psychopathe mf
psycho·sis [saɪ'kosɪs] s (pl -ses [siz]) psychose f
psy'cho·ther'apy s psychothérapie f
psychotic [saɪ'kɑtɪk] adj & s psychotique mf
ptomaine ['tomen] s ptomaïne f
pub [pʌb] s (Brit) bistrot m, café m
puberty ['pjubərti] s puberté f
public ['pʌblɪk] adj & s public m
pub'lic-address' sys'tem s sonorisation f
publication [,pʌblɪ'keʃən] s publication f
pub'lic educa'tion s enseignement m public
publicity [pʌb'lɪsɪti] s publicité f
public'ity stunt' s canard m publicitaire
publicize ['pʌblɪ,saɪz] tr publier
pub'lic li'brary s bibliothèque f municipale

pub'lic-opin'ion poll' s sondage m de l'opinion, enquête f par sondage
pub'lic rela'tions spl relations fmpl publiques
pub'lic-rela'tions ex'pert s publiciste mf, publicitaire mf
pub'lic school' s (U.S.A.) école f primaire; (Brit) école privée
pub'lic serv'ant s fonctionnaire mf
pub'lic speak'ing s art m oratoire, éloquence f
pub'lic tel'ephone s téléphone m public
pub'lic toi'let s chalet m de nécessité
pub'lic transporta'tion s transport m en commun
pub'lic util'ity s entreprise f de service public; **public utilities** actions fpl émises par les entreprises de service public
publish ['pʌblɪʃ] tr publier
publisher ['pʌblɪʃər] s éditeur m
pub'lishing house' s maison f d'édition
puck [pʌk] s palet m
pucker ['pʌkər] s fronce m, faux pli m ‖ tr froncer ‖ intr se froncer
pudding ['pʊdɪŋ] s entremets m sucré au lait, crème f
puddle ['pʌdəl] s flaque f ‖ tr puddler
pudg·y ['pʌdʒi] adj (comp -ier; super -iest) bouffi, rondouillard
puerile ['pju·əɪl] adj puéril
puerili·ty [,pju·ə'rɪlɪti] s (pl -ties) puérilité f
Puerto Rican ['pwɛrto'rikən] adj portoricain ‖ s Portoricain m
puff [pʌf] s (of air) souffle m; (of smoke) bouffée f; (in clothing) bouillon m; (in sleeve) bouffant m; (for powder) houppette f; (swelling) boursouflure f; (praise) battage m; (culin) moule m de pâte feuilletée fourré à la crème, à la confiture, etc. ‖ tr lancer des bouffées de; **to puff oneself up** se rengorger; **to puff out** souffler; **to puff up** gonfler ‖ intr souffler; (to swell) gonfler, se gonfler; **to puff at** or **on** (a pipe) tirer sur
puff'paste' s pâte f feuilletée
pugilism ['pjudʒɪ,lɪzəm] s science f pugilistique, boxe f
pugilist ['pjudʒɪlɪst] s pugiliste m
pugnacious [pʌg'neʃəs] adj pugnance
pug'-nosed' adj camus
puke [pjuk] s (slang) dégobillage m ‖ tr & intr (slang) dégobiller
pull [pʊl] s (tug) traction f, secousse f, coup m; (handle of door) poignée f; (of the moon) attraction f; (slang) piston m, appuis mpl ‖ tr tirer; (a muscle) tordre; (the trigger) appuyer sur; (a proof) (typ) tirer; **to pull about** tirailler; **to pull away** arracher; **to pull down** baisser; (e.g., a house) abattre; (to degrade) abaisser; **to pull in** rentrer; **to pull off** enlever; (fig) réussir; **to pull on** (a garment) mettre; **to pull oneself together** se ressaisir; **to pull out** sortir; (a tooth) arracher ‖ intr tirer; bouger lentement, bouger avec effort; **to pull at** tirer sur; **to pull for** (slang) plaider en faveur de; **to pull in** rentrer; (said of

train) entrer en gare; **to pull out** partir; (*said of train*) sortir de la gare; **to pull through** se tirer d'affaire; (*to get well*) se remettre

pull′ chain′ *s* chasse *f* d'eau

pullet [′pʊlɪt] *s* poulette *f*

pulley [′pʊli] *s* poulie *f*

pulmonary [′pʌlmə,nɛri] *adj* pulmonaire

pulp [pʌlp] *s* pulpe *f*; (*to make paper*) pâte *f*; (*of tooth*) bulbe *m*; **to beat to a pulp** (coll) mettre en bouillie

pulp′ fic′tion *s* romans *mpl* à sensation; le roman de la concierge

pulpit [′pʊlpɪt] *s* chaire *f*

pulsate [′pʌlset] *intr* palpiter; vibrer

pulsation pʌl′se∫ən] *s* pulsation *f*

pulse [pʌls] *s* pouls *m*; **to feel** or **take the pulse of** tâter le pouls à

pulverize [′pʌlvə,raɪz] *tr* pulvériser

pu′mice stone′ [′pʌmɪs] *s* pierre *f* ponce

pum·mel [′pʌməl] *v* (*pret & pp* **-meled** or **-melled;** *ger* **-meling** or **-melling**) *tr* bourrer de coups

pump [pʌmp] *s* pompe *f*; (*slipperlike shoe*) escarpin *m* ‖ *tr* pomper; (coll) tirer les vers du nez à; **to pump up** pomper; (*a tire*) gonfler ‖ *intr* pomper

pump′han′dle *s* bras *m* de pompe

pumpkin [′pʌmpkɪn] *s* citrouille *f*, potiron *m*

pun [pʌn] *s* calembour *m*, jeu *m* de mots ‖ *v* (*pret & pp* **punned;** *ger* **punning**) *intr* faire des jeux de mots

punch [pʌnt∫] *s* (*blow*) coup *m* de poing; (*to pierce metal*) mandrin *m*; (*to drive a nail or bolt*) poinçon *m*; (*for tickets*) pince *f*, emporte-pièce *m*; (*drink; blow*) punch *m*; (mach) poinçonneuse *f*; (*energy*) (coll) allant *m*, punch: **to pull no punches** parler carrément ‖ *tr* donner un coup de poing à; poinçonner

punch′ bowl′ *s* bol *m* à punch

punch′ card′ *s* carte *f* perforée

punch′ clock′ *s* horloge *f* de pointage

punch′-drunk′ *adj* abruti de coups; (coll) abruti, étourdi

punched′ tape′ *s* bande *f* enregistreuse perforée

punch′ing bag′ *s* punching-ball *m*; (fig) tête *f* de Turc, souffre-douleur *m invar*

punch′ line′ *s* point *m* final, phrase *f* clé

punctilious [pʌŋk′tɪlɪ·əs] *adj* pointilleux, minutieux

punctual [′pʌŋkt∫ʊ·əl] *adj* ponctuel

punctuate [′pʌŋkt∫ʊ,et] *tr & intr* ponctuer

punctuation [,pʌŋkt∫ʊ′e∫ən] *s* ponctuation *f*

punctua′tion mark′ *s* signe *m* de ponctuation

puncture [′pʌŋkt∫ər] *s* (*in skin, paper, leather*) piqûre *f*; (*of a tire*) crevaison *f*; (med) ponction *f* ‖ *tr* perforer; (*a tire*) crever; (med) ponctionner

punc′ture-proof′ *adj* increvable

pundit [′pʌndɪt] *s* pandit *m*; (*savant*) mandarin *m*; (pej) pontife *m*

pungent [′pʌndʒənt] *adj* piquant

punish [′pʌnɪ∫] *tr & intr* punir

punishment [′pʌnɪ∫mənt] *s* punition *f*; (*for a crime*) peine *f*; (*severe handling*) mauvais traitements *mpl*

punk [pʌŋk] *adj* (slang) moche, fichu; **to feel punk** (slang) être mal fichu ‖ *s* amadou *m*; mèche *f* d'amadou; (*decayed wood*) bois *m* pourri; (slang) voyou *m*, mauvais sujet *m*, loubard *m*

punster [′pʌnstər] *s* faiseur *m* de calembours

pu·ny [′pjuni] *adj* (*comp* **-nier;** *super* **-niest**) chétif, malingre

pup [pʌp] *s* chiot *m*

pupil [′pjupəl] *s* élève *mf*; (*of the eye*) pupille *f*, prunelle *f*

puppet [′pʌpɪt] *s* marionnette *f*; (*person controlled by another*) fantoche *m*, pantin *m*

pup′pet gov′ernment *s* gouvernement *m* fantoche

pup′pet show′ *s* spectacle *m* de marionnettes, marionnettes *fpl*

pup·py [′pʌpi] *s* (*pl* **-pies**) petit chien *m*

pup′py love′ *s* premières amours *fpl*

pup′ tent′ *s* tente-abri *f*

purchase [′pʌrt∫əs] *s* achat *m*; (*leverage*) point *m* d'appui, prise *f* ‖ *tr* acheter

pur′chasing pow′er *s* pouvoir *m* d'achat

pure [pjʊr] *adj* pur

purgative [′pʌrgətɪv] *adj & s* purgatif *m*

purgato·ry [′pʌrgə,tori] *s* (*pl* **-ries**) purgatoire *m*

purge [pʌrdʒ] *s* purge *f* ‖ *tr* purger

puri·fy [′pjʊrɪ,faɪ] *v* (*pret & pp* **-fied**) *tr* purifier

puritan [′pjʊrɪtən] *adj & s* puritain *m*; **Puritan** puritain

purity [′pjʊrɪti] *s* pureté *f*

purloin [pər′lɔɪn] *tr & intr* voler

purple [′pʌrpəl] *adj* pourpre ‖ *s* (*violescent*) pourpre *m*; (*deep red, crimson*) pourpre *f*; **born to the purple** né dans la pourpre

purport [′pʌrport] *s* sens *m*, teneur *f*; (*intention*) but *m*, objet *m* ‖ [pər′port] *tr* signifier, vouloir dire

purpose [′pʌrpəs] *s* intention *f*, dessein *m*; (*goal*) but *m*, objet *m*, fin *f*; **for all purposes** à tous usages; pratiquement; **for the purpose of, with the purpose of** dans le dessein de, dans le but de; **for this purpose** à cet effet; **for what purpose?** à quoi bon? à quelle fin?; **on purpose** exprès, à dessein; **to good purpose, to some purpose** utilement; **to no purpose** vainement; **to serve the purpose** faire l'affaire

purposely [′pʌrpəsli] *adv* exprès, à dessein, de propos délibéré

purr [pʌr] *s* ronron *m* ‖ *intr* ronronner ‖ *interj* miam! miam!

purse [pʌrs] *s* bourse *f*, porte-monnaie *m*; (*handbag*) sac *m* à main ‖ *tr* (*one's lips*) pincer

purser [′pʌrsər] *s* commissaire *m*

purse′ snatch′er [′snæt∫ər] *s* voleur *m* à la tire

purse′ strings′ *spl* cordons *mpl* de bourse

pursue [pər's(j)u] *tr* poursuivre; (*a profession*) suivre

pursuit [pər's(j)ut] *s* poursuite *f*; profession *f*

pursuit' plane' *s* chasseur *m*, avion *m* de chasse

purvey [pər've] *tr* fournir

pus [pʌs] *s* pus *m*

push [pʊʃ] *s* poussée *f* ‖ *tr* pousser; (*a button*) appuyer sur, presser; **to push around** (coll) rudoyer; **to push aside** écarter; **to push away** or **back** repousser; **to push in** enfoncer; **to push over** faire tomber; **to push through** amener à bonne fin; (*a resolution, bill, etc.*) faire adopter ‖ *intr* pousser; **to push forward** or **on** avancer; **to push off** se mettre en route; (naut) pousser au large

push' but'ton *s* bouton *m* électrique, poussoir *m*

push'-button tel'ephone *s* téléphone *m* à clavier

push'-but'ton war'fare *s* guerre *f* presse-bouton

push'cart' *s* voiture *f* à bras

pusher ['pʊʃər] *s* (*drug dealer*) revendeur *m* (de drogues); (slang) dealer *m*, vendeur *m* de mort, fourmi *f*

pushing ['pʊʃɪŋ] *adj* entreprenant; indiscret; agressif

pusillanimous [,pjusɪ'lænɪməs] *adj* pusillanime

puss [pʊs] *s* minet *m*; (slang) gueule *f*; **sly puss** (*girl*) (coll) futée *f* ‖ *interj* minet!

Puss' in Boots' *s* Chat *m* botté

puss' in the cor'ner *s* les quatre coins *mpl*

puss·y ['pʊsi] *s* (*pl* **-ies**) *s* minet *m* ‖ *interj* minet!

puss'y wil'low *s* saule *m* nord-américain aux chatons très soyeux

put [pʊt] *v* (*pret & pp* **put**; *ger* **putting**) *tr* mettre, placer; (*to throw*) lancer; (*a question*) poser; **to put across** passer; faire accepter; **to put aside** mettre de côté; **to put away** ranger; (*to jail*) mettre en prison; **to put back** remettre; retarder; **to put down** poser; (*e.g., a name*) noter; (*a revolution*) réprimer; (*to lower*) baisser; **to put off** renvoyer; (*to mislead*) dérouter; **to put on** (*clothes*) mettre; (*a play*) mettre en scène, monter; (*a brake*) serrer; (*a light, radio, etc.*) allumer; (*to feign*) feindre, simuler; **to put oneself out** se déranger; **to put on sale** mettre en vente; mettre en solde; **to put out** (*the hand*) étendre; (*the fire, light, etc.*) éteindre; (*s.o.'s eyes*) crever; (*e.g., a book*) publier; (*to show to the door*) mettre dehors; (*to vex*) contrarier; **to put over** (coll) faire accepter; **to put s.o. through s.th.** faire subir q.ch. à qn; **to put through** passer; (*a resolution, bill, etc.*) faire adopter; **to put up** lever; (*a house*) construire, faire construire; (*one's collar, hair, etc.*) relever; (*a picture*) accrocher; (*a notice*) afficher; (*a tent*) dresser; (*an umbrella*) ouvrir; (*the price*) augmenter; (*money as an investment*) fournir; (*resistance*) offrir; (*an overnight guest*) loger; (*fruit, vegetables, etc.*) conserver; (coll) pousser, inciter ‖ *intr* se diriger; **to put on** feindre; **to put up** loger; **to put up with** tolérer, s'accommoder de

put'-out' *adj* ennuyeux, fâcheux

putrid ['pjutrɪd] *adj* putride

putter ['pʌtər] *intr*—**to putter around** s'occuper de bagatelles

put·ty ['pʌti] *s* (*pl* **-ties**) mastic *m* ‖ *v* (*pret & pp* **-tied**) *tr* mastiquer

put'ty knife' *s* (*pl* **knives**) couteau *m* à mastiquer

put'-up' *adj* (coll) machiné à l'avance, monté

put'-up job' *s* (slang) coup *m* monté, micmac *m*

puzzle ['pʌzəl] *s* énigme *f* ‖ *tr* intriguer; **to puzzle out** déchiffrer ‖ *intr*—**to puzzle over** se creuser la tête pour comprendre

puzzler ['pʌzlər] *s* énigme *f*, colle *f*

puzzling ['pʌzlɪŋ] *adj* énigmatique

PW ['pi'dʌbəl,ju] *s* (letterword) (**prisoner of war**) P.G.

pyg·my ['pɪgmi] *adj* pygméen ‖ *s* (*pl* **-mies**) pygmée *m*

pylon ['paɪlɑn] *s* pylône *m*

pyramid ['pɪrəmɪd] *s* pyramide *f* ‖ *tr* augmenter graduellement ‖ *intr* pyramider

pyre [paɪr] *s* bûcher *m* funéraire

Pyrenees ['pɪrɪ,niz] *spl* Pyrénées *fpl*

pyrites ['paɪraɪts] *s* pyrite *f*

pyrotechnical [,paɪrə'tɛknɪkəl] *adj* pyrotechnique

pyrotechnics [,paɪrə'tɛknɪks] *spl* pyrotechnie *f*

python ['paɪθən] *s* python *m*

pythoness ['paɪθənɪs] *s* pythonisse *f*

pyx [pɪks] *s* (eccl) ciboire *m*; (*for carrying Eucharist to sick*) (eccl) pyxide *f*; (*at a mint*) boîte *f* des monnaies

Q

Q,q [kju] *s* XVIIe lettre de l'alphabet

quack [kwæk] *adj* frauduleux, de charlatan ‖ *s* charlatan *m* ‖ *intr* cancaner, faire couin-couin

quacker·y ['kwækəri] *s* (*pl* **-ies**) charlatanisme *m*

quadrangle ['kwɑd,ræŋgəl] *s* plan *m* quadrangulaire; cour *f* carrée

quadrant ['kwɑdrənt] *s* (*instrument*) quart *m* de cercle, secteur *m*; (math) quadrant *m*

quadroon [kwɑd'run] *s* quarteron *m*

quadruped [ˈkwɑdrəˌpɛd] *adj* & *s* quadrupède *m*

quadruple [ˈkwɑdrupəl] *adj* & *s* quadruple *m* ‖ *tr* & *intr* quadrupler

quadruplets [ˈkwɑdruˌplɛts] *spl* quadruplés *mpl*

quaff [kwɑf], [kwæf] *s* lampée *f* ‖ *tr* & *intr* boire à longs traits

quagmire [ˈkwægˌmaɪr] *s* bourbier *m*, fondrière *f*

quail [kwel] *s* caille *f* ‖ *intr* fléchir

quaint [kwent] *adj* pittoresque, bizarre

quake [kwek] *s* tremblement *m*; (*earthquake*) tremblement de terre ‖ *intr* trembler

Quaker [ˈkwekər] *adj* & *s* quaker *m*

Quak'er meet'ing *s* réunion *f* de quakers; (coll) réunion où il y a très peu de conversation

quali·fy [ˈkwɑlɪˌfaɪ] *v* (*pret* & *pp* **-fied**) *tr* qualifier; (*e.g., a recommendation*) apporter des réserves à, modifier; **to qualify oneself for** se préparer à, se rendre apte à ‖ *intr* se qualifier

quali·ty [ˈkwɑlɪti] *s* (*pl* **-ties**) qualité *f*; (*of a sound*) timbre *m*; **of good quality** de bonne facture; **quality of life** qualité de la vie

qualm [kwɑm] *s* scrupule *m*; (*remorse*) remords *m*; (*nausea*) soulèvement *m* de cœur

quanda·ry [ˈkwɑndəri] *s* (*pl* **-ries**) incertitude *f*, impasse *f*

quanti·ty [ˈkwɑntɪti] *s* (*pl* **-ties**) quantité *f*

quan·tum [ˈkwɑntəm] *adj* quantique ‖ *s* (*pl* **-ta** [tə]) quantum *m*

quan'tum the'ory *s* théorie *f* des quanta

quarantine [ˈkwɑrənˌtin] *s* quarantaine *f* ‖ *tr* mettre en quarantaine

quar·rel [ˈkwɑrəl] *s* querelle *f*, dispute *f*; **to have no quarrel with** n'avoir rien à redire à; **to pick a quarrel with** chercher querelle à ‖ *v* (*pret* & *pp* **-reled** or **-relled**; *ger* **-reling** or **-relling**) *intr* se quereller, se disputer; **to quarrel over** contester sur, se disputer

quarrelsome [ˈkwɑrəlsəm] *adj* querelleur

quar·ry [ˈkwɑri] *s* (*pl* **-ries**) carrière *f*; (*hunted animal*) proie *f* ‖ *v* (*pret* & *pp* **-ried**) *tr* extraire ‖ *intr* exploiter une carrière

quart [kwɔrt] *s* quart *m* de gallon, pinte *f*

quarter [ˈkwɔrtər] *s* quart *m*; (*American coin*) vingt-cinq cents *mpl*; (*of a year*) trimestre *m*; (*of town; of beef; of moon; of shield*) quartier *m*; **a quarter after one** une heure et quart; **a quarter of an hour** un quart d'heure; **a quarter to one** une heure moins le quart; **at close quarters** corps à corps; **quarters** (mil) quartiers *mpl*, cantonnement *m* ‖ *tr* & *intr* (mil) loger, cantonner

quar'ter·deck' *s* gaillard *m* d'arrière

quar'ter-hour' *s* quart *m* d'heure; **every quarter-hour on the quarter-hour** tous les quarts d'heure au quart d'heure juste

quarter·ly [ˈkwɔrtərli] *adj* trimestriel ‖ *s* (*pl* **-lies**) publication *f* or revue *f* trimestrielle ‖ *adv* trimestriellement, par trimestre

quar'ter·mas'ter *s* (mil) quartier-maître *m*, intendant *m* militaire

Quar'ter·master Corps' *s* Intendance *f*, service *m* d l'Intendance

quar'ter note' *s* (mus) noire *f*

quar'ter rest' *s* (mus) soupir *m*

quar'ter tone' *s* (mus) quart *m* de ton

quartet [kwɔrˈtɛt] *s* quatuor *m*

quartz [kwɔrts] *s* quartz *m*

quartz' watch' *s* montre *f* à quartz

quasar [ˈkwesɑr] *s* (astr) quasar *m*

quash [kwɑʃ] *tr* étouffer; (*to set aside*) annuler, invalider

quatrain [ˈkwɑtren] *s* quatrain *m*

quaver [ˈkwevər] *s* tremblement *m*; (*in the singing voice*) trémolo *m*; (mus) croche *f* ‖ *intr* trembloter

quay [ki] *s* quai *m*, débarcadère *m*

queen [kwin] *s* reine *f*; (cards, chess) reine *f*

queen' bee' *s* reine *f* des abeilles

queen' dow'ager *s* reine *f* douairière

queen·ly [ˈkwinli] *adj* (*comp* **-lier**; *super* **-liest**) de reine, digne d'une reine

queen' moth'er *s* reine *f* mère

queen' post' *s* faux poinçon *m*

queer [kwɪr] *adj* bizarre, drôle; (*suspicious*) (coll) suspect; (*perverted*) pervers, inverti; (*homosexual*) (pej) de la pédale; **to feel queer** (coll) se sentir indisposé ‖ *s* excentrique *mf*; (*pervert*) pervers *m*, inverti *m*; (*homosexual male*) (pej) pédale *f*, pédé *m*; (*homosexual female*) (pej) gouine *f*, lesbienne *f* ‖ *tr* (slang) faire échouer, déranger

quell [kwɛl] *tr* étouffer, réprimer; (*pain, sorrow, etc.*) calmer

quench [kwɛntʃ] *tr* (*the thirst*) étancher; (*a rebellion*) étouffer; (*a fire*) éteindre

que·ry [ˈkwɪri] *s* (*pl* **-ries**) question *f*; doute *m*; (*question mark*) point *m* d'interrogation ‖ *v* (*pret* & *pp* **-ried**) *tr* questionner, mettre en doute; (*to affix a question mark*) marquer d'un point d'interrogation

quest [kwɛst] *s* quête *f*; **in quest of** en quête de

question [ˈkwɛstʃən] *s* question *f*; (*doubt*) doute *m*; **beyond question** indiscutable, incontestable; **it is a question of** il s'agit de; **out of the question** impossible, impensable; **to ask s.o. a question** poser une question à qn; **to beg the question** faire une pétition de principe; **to call into question** mettre en question; **to move the previous question** (parl) demander la question préalable; **without question** sans aucun doute ‖ *tr* interroger, questionner; (*to cast doubt upon*) douter de, contester

questionable [ˈkwɛstʃənəbəl] *adj* discutable, douteux

ques'tion mark' *s* point *m* d'interrogation

questionnaire [ˌkwɛstʃənˈɛr] *s* questionnaire *m*

queue [kju] *s* queue *f* ‖ *intr*—**to queue up** faire la queue

quibble [ˈkwɪbəl] *intr* chicaner, ergoter

quibbling [ˈkwɪblɪŋ] *s* chicane *f*

quick [kwɪk] *adj* rapide, vif ‖ *s*—**the quick and the dead** les vivants et les morts; **to cut to the quick** piquer au vif

quicken [ˈkwɪkən] *tr* accélérer; (*e.g., the imagination*) animer ‖ *intr* s'accélérer; s'animer

quick′lime′ *s* chaux *f* vive

quick′ lunch′ *s* casse-croûte *m*, repas *m* léger

quickly [ˈkwɪkli] *adj* vite, rapidement

quick′sand′ *s* sable *m* mouvant

quick′sil′ver *s* vif-argent *m*, mercure *m*

quick′-tem′pered *adj* coléreux

quiet [ˈkwaɪ·ət] *adj* (*still*) tranquille, silencieux; (*person*) modeste, discret; (*market*) (com) calme; **be quiet!** taisez-vous!; **to keep quiet** rester tranquille; (*to not speak*) se taire ‖ *s* tranquillité *f*; (*rest*) repos *m*; **on the quiet** en douce, à la dérobée ‖ *tr* calmer, tranquilliser; (*a child*) faire taire ‖ *intr*—**to quiet down** se calmer

quill [kwɪl] *s* plume *f* d'oie; (*hollow part*) tuyau *m* (de plume); (*of hedgehog, porcupine*) piquant *m*

quilt [kwɪlt] *s* courtepointe *f* ‖ *tr* piquer

quince [kwɪns] *s* coing *m*; (*tree*) cognassier *m*

quinine [ˈkwaɪnaɪn] *s* quinine *f*

quinsy [ˈkwɪnzi] *s* angine *f*

quintessence [kwɪnˈtɛsəns] *s* quintessence *f*

quintet [kwɪnˈtɛt] *s* quintette *m*

quintuplets [kwɪnˈtʌplɛts] *spl* quintuplés *mpl*

quip [kwɪp] *s* raillerie *f*, quolibet *m* ‖ *v* (*pret & pp* **quipped;** *ger* **quipping**) *tr* dire sur un ton railleur ‖ *intr* railler

quire [kwaɪr] *s* main *f*

quirk [kwʌrk] *s* excentricité *f*; (*subterfuge*) faux-fuyant *m*; **quirk of fate** caprice *m* du sort

quit [kwɪt] *adj* quitte; **to be quits** être quitte; **to call it quits** cesser, s'y renoncer; **we are quits** nous voilà quittes ‖ *v* (*pret & pp* **quit** or **quitted;** *ger* **quitting**) *tr* (*e.g., a city*) quitter; (*one's work, a pursuit, etc.*) cesser, **I quit!** j'abandonne!; **to quit** + *ger* s'arrêter de + *inf* ‖ *intr* partir; (coll) lâcher la partie

quite [kwaɪt] *adv* tout à fait; **quite a story** (coll) toute une histoire

quitter [ˈkwɪtər] *s* défaitiste *m*, lâcheur *m*

quiver [ˈkwɪvər] *s* tremblement *m*; (*to hold arrows*) carquois *m* ‖ *intr* trembler

quixotic [kwɪksˈɑtɪk] *adj* de don Quichotte; visionnaire, exalté

quiz [kwɪz] *s* (*pl* **quizzes**) interrogation *f*, colle *f* ‖ *v* (*pret & pp* **quizzed;** *ger* **quizzing**) *tr* examiner, interroger

quiz′ sec′tion *s* classe *f* d'exercices

quiz′ show′ *s* émission-questionnaire *f*

quizzical [ˈkwɪzɪkəl] *adj* curieux; (*laughable*) risible; (*mocking*) railleur

quoin [kɔɪn] *s* angle *m*; (*cornerstone*) pierre *f* d'angle; (*wedge*) coin *m*, cale *f* ‖ *tr* coincer, caler

quoit [kwɔɪt] *s* palet *m*; **to play quoits** jouer au palet

quondam [ˈkwɑndæm] *adj* ci-devant, d'autre-fois

quorum [ˈkworəm] *s* quorum *m*

quota [ˈkwotə] *s* quote-part *f*; (*e.g., of immigration*) quota *m*, contingent *m*

quotation [kwoˈteʃən] *s* (*from a book*) citation *f*; (*of prices*) cours *m*, cote *f*

quota′tion marks′ *spl* guillements *mpl*

quote [kwot] *s* (*from a book*) citation *f*; (*of prices*) cours *m*, cote *f*; **in quotes** (coll) entre guillemets ‖ *tr* (*from a book*) citer; (*values*) coter ‖ *intr* tirer des citations; **to quote out of context** citer hors contexte ‖ *interj* je cite

quotient [ˈkwoʃənt] *s* quotient *m*

R

R, r [ɑr] *s* XVIIIᵉ lettre de l'alphabet

rabbet [ˈræbɪt] *s* feuillure *f* ‖ *tr* feuiller

rab·bi [ˈræbaɪ] *s* (*pl* -**bis** or -**bies**) rabbin *m*

rabbit [ˈræbɪt] *s* lapin *m*

rab′bit stew′ *s* lapin *m* en civet

rabble [ˈræbəl] *s* canaille *f*

rab′ble-rous′er *s* fomentateur *m*, agitateur *m*

rabies [ˈrebiz] *s* rage *f*

raccoon [ræˈkun] *s* raton *m* laveur

race [res] *s* (*ethnic background*) race *f*; (*contest*) course *f*; (*channel to lead water*) bief *m*; (*rapid current*) raz *m* ‖ *tr* lutter de vitesse avec; (*e.g., a horse*) faire courir;

(*a motor*) emballer ‖ *intr* faire une course, courir; (*said of motor*) s'emballer

race′horse′ *s* cheval *m* de course

race′ ri′ot *s* émeute *f* raciale

race′ track′ *s* champ *m* de courses, hippodrome *m*

racial [ˈreʃəl] *adj* racial

rac′ing car′ *s* automobile *f* de course

rac′ing odds′ *spl* cote *f*

racism [ˈresɪzəm] *s* racisme *m*

racist [ˈresɪst] *s* raciste *mf*

rack [ræk] *s* (*shelf*) étagère *f*; (*to hang clothes*) portemanteau *m*; (*for baggage*) porte-bagages *m*; (*for guns; for fodder*) râtelier *m*; (*for torture*) chevalet *m*; (*bar made to gear with a pinion*) crémaillère *f*; **to go to rack and ruin** aller à vau-l'eau ‖ *tr* (*with hunger, remorse, etc.*) tenailler; (*one's brains*) se creuser

racket ['rækɪt] *s* (*noise*) vacarme *m*; (sports) raquette *f*; (slang) racket *m*; **to make a racket** faire du tapage

racketeer [,rækɪ'tɪr] *s* racketter *m* ‖ *intr* pratiquer l'escroquerie

rack' rail'way *s* chemin *m* de fer à crémaillère

rac·y ['resɪ] *adj* (*comp* **-ier;** *super* **-iest**) plein de verve, vigoureux; parfumé; (*off-color*) sale, grivois

radar ['redɑr] *s* (acronym) (**radio detecting and ranging**) radar *m*

ra'dar sta'tion *s* poste *m* radar

ra'dial tire' ['redɪ·əl] *s* pneu *m* radial, pneumatique *m* à carcasse radiale

radiant ['redɪ·ənt] *adj* radieux, rayonnant; (*astr, phys*) radiant

radiate ['redɪ,et] *tr* rayonner; (*e.g., happiness*) répandre ‖ *intr* rayonner

radiation [,redɪ'eʃən] *s* rayonnement *m*, radiation *f*

radia'tion sick'ness *s* mal *m* des rayons

radiator ['redɪ,etər] *s* radiateur *m*

ra'diator cap' *s* bouchon *m* de radiateur

radical ['rædɪkəl] *adj* & *s* radical *m*

radi·o ['redɪ,o] (*pl* **-os**) radio *f* ‖ *tr* radiodiffuser

ra'dio·ac'tive *adj* radioactif

ra'dio·ac'tive fall'out *s* retombées *fpl* radioactives

ra'dio·ac'tive waste' *s* déchets *mpl* radioactifs

ra'dio am'ateur *s* sans-filiste *mf*

ra'dio announ'cer *s* speaker *m*

ra'dio·broad'cast'ing *s* radiodiffusion *f*

ra'dio control' *s* (rok) radioguidage *m*

ra'dio·fre'quency *s* radiofréquence *f*

ra'dio·gram' *s* radiogramme *m*

ra'dio lis'tener *s* auditeur *m* de la radio

radiology [,redɪ'ɑlədʒɪ] *s* radiologie *f*

ra'dio net'work *s* chaîne *f* de radiodiffusion

ra'dio news'cast *s* journal *m* parlé, radio-journal *m*

ra'dio·phone' *s* radiotéléphone *m*

ra'dio receiv'er *s* récepteur *m* de radio

radioscopy [,redɪ'ɑskəpi] *s* radioscopie *f*

ra'dio set' *s* poste *m* de radio

ra'dio sta'tion *s* poste *m* émetteur

ra'dio tax'i *s* radio-taxi *m*

ra'dio·ther'apy *s* radiothérapie *f*

ra'dio tube' *s* lampe *f* de radio

radish ['rædɪʃ] *s* radis *m*

radium ['redɪ·əm] *s* radium *m*

radi·us ['redɪ·əs] *s* (*pl* **-i** [,aɪ] or **-uses**) rayon *m*; (anat) radius *m*; **within a radius of** dans un rayon de, à . . . à la ronde

raffish ['ræfɪʃ] *adj* bravache; (*flashy*) criard

raffle ['ræfəl] *s* tombola *f* ‖ *tr* mettre en tombola

raft [ræft] *s* (*floating on water*) radeau *m*; **a raft of** (*a lot of*) (coll) un tas de

rafter ['ræftər] *s* chevron *m*

rag [ræg] *s* chiffon *m*; **in rags** en haillons; **to chew the rag** (slang) tailler une bavette

ragamuffin ['rægə,mʌfɪn] *s* gueux *m*, va-nu-pieds *m*; (*urchin*) gamin *m*

rag' doll' *s* poupée *f* de chiffon

rage [redʒ] *s* rage *f*; **to be all the rage** faire fureur; **to fly into a rage** entrer en fureur ‖ *intr* faire rage

rag' fair' *s* marché *m* aux puces

ragged ['rægɪd] *adj* en haillons; (*edge*) hérissé

ragpicker ['ræg,pɪkər] *s* chiffonnier *m*

rag'time' *s* rythme *m* syncopé du jazz; musique *f* syncopée du jazz

rag'weed' *s* ambrosie *f*

ragwort ['ræg,wʌrt] *s* (*Senecio vulgaris*) séneçon *m*; (*S. jacobaea*) jacobée *f*

raid [red] *s* incursion *f*, razzia *f*; (*by police*) descente *f*; (mil) raid *m* ‖ *tr* razzier; faire une descente dans

rail [rel] *s* rail *m*; (*railing*) balustrade *f*; (*of stairway*) rampe *f*; (*of, e.g., a bridge*) garde-fou *m*; (orn) râle *m*; **by rail** par chemin de fer ‖ *intr* invectiver; **to rail at** invectiver

rail' fence' *s* palissade *f* à claire-voie

rail'head' *s* tête *f* de ligne

railing ['relɪŋ] *s* balustrade *f*

rail'road' *adj* ferroviaire ‖ *s* chemin *m* de fer ‖ *tr* (*a bill*) faire voter en vitesse; (coll) emprisonner à tort

rail'road cros'sing *s* passage *m* à niveau

railroader ['rel,rodər] *s* cheminot *m*

rail'road sta'tion *s* gare *f*

rail'way' *adj* ferroviaire ‖ *s* chemin *m* de fer

raiment ['remənt] *s* habillement *m*

rain [ren] *s* pluie *f*; **in the rain** sous la pluie ‖ *tr* faire pleuvoir ‖ *intr* pleuvoir; **it is raining cats and dogs** il pleut à seaux

rainbow ['ren,bo] *s* arc-en-ciel *m*

rain'bow trout' *s* truite *f* arc-en-ciel

rain'coat' *s* imperméable *m*

rain'fall' *s* chute *f* de pluie

rain'proof' *adj* imperméable

rain' wa'ter *s* eau *f* de pluie

rain·y ['reni] *adj* (*comp* **-ier;** *super* **-iest**) pluvieux

raise [rez] *s* augmentation *f*, rallonge *f*; (*in poker*) relance *f* ‖ *tr* augmenter; (*plants, animals, children; one's voice; a number to a certain power*) élever; (*an army, a camp, a siege; anchor; game*) lever; (*an objection, questions, etc.*) soulever; (*doubts; a hope; a storm*) faire naître; (*a window*) relever; (*one's head, one's voice; prices; the land*) hausser; (*a flag*) arborer; (*the dead*) ressusciter; (*money*) se procurer; (*the ante*) relancer; **to raise up** soulever, dresser

raisin ['rezən] *s* raisin *m* sec, grain *m* de raisin sec

rake [rek] *s* râteau *m*; (*person*) débauché *m* ‖ *tr* ratisser; **to rake together** râteler

rake'-off' *s* (coll) gratte *f*

rakish ['rekɪʃ] *adj* gaillard; dissolu

ral·ly ['ræli] *s* (*pl* **-lies**) ralliement *m*; (pol) réunion *f* politique; (*in a game*) reprise *f*; (*auto race*) rallye *m* ‖ *v* (*pret & pp* **-lied**) *tr* rallier ‖ *intr* se rallier; (*from illness*) se remettre; (sports) se reprendre; **to rally to the side of** se rallier à

ram [ræm] *s* bélier *m* ‖ *v* (*pret & pp* **rammed**; *ger* **ramming**) *tr* tamponner; **to ram down** or **in** enfoncer ‖ *intr* se tamponner; **to ram into** tamponner

RAM ['ɑr'e'ɛm] *s* (letterword) (**random access memory**) mémoire *f* vive

ramble ['ræmbəl] *s* flânerie *f* ‖ *intr* flâner, errer à l'aventure; (*to talk aimlessly*) divaguer

rami·fy ['ræmɪ,faɪ] *v* (*pret & pp* **-fied**) *tr* ramifier ‖ *intr* se ramifier

ramp [ræmp] *s* rampe *f*, bretelle *f*

rampage ['ræmpedʒ] *s* tempête *f*; **to go on a rampage** se déchaîner

rampart ['ræmpɑrt] *s* rempart *m*

ram'rod' *s* écouvillon *m*

ram'shack'le *adj* délabré

ranch [rænt∫] *s* ranch *m*, rancho *m*

rancid ['rænsɪd] *adj* rance

rancor ['ræŋkər] *s* rancæur *f*

random ['rændəm] *adj* fortuit; **at random** au hasard

ran'dom ac'cess *s* (comp) accès *m* aléatoire, accès direct

ran'dom-ac'cess mem'ory *s* (comp) mémoire *f* vive, mémoire à accès sélectif

range [rendʒ] *s* (*row*) rangée *f*; (*scope*) portée *f*; (*mountains*) chaîne *f*; (*stove*) cuisinière *f*; (*for rifle practice*) champ *m* de tir; (*of colors, musical notes, prices, speeds, etc.*) gamme *f*; (*or words*) répartition *f*; (*of voice*) tessiture *f*; (*of vision, of activity, etc.*) champ *m*; (*for pasture*) grand pâturage *m*; **within range of** à portée de ‖ *tr* ranger ‖ *intr* se ranger; **to range from** s'échelonner entre, varier entre; **to range over** parcourir

range' find'er *s* télémètre *m*

rank [ræŋk] *adj* fétide, rance; (*injustice*) criant; (*vegetation*) luxuriant ‖ *s* rang *m* ‖ *tr* ranger ‖ *intr* occuper le premier rang; **to rank above** être supérieur à; **to rank with** aller de pair avec

rank' and file' *s* hommes *mpl* de troupe; commun *m* des mortels; (*of the party, union, etc.*) commun *m*

rankle ['ræŋkəl] *tr* ulcérer; irriter ‖ *intr* s'ulcérer

ransack ['rænsæk] *tr* fouiller, fouiller dans; mettre à sac

ransom ['rænsəm] *s* rançon *f*; **to hold for ransom** mettre à rançon ‖ *tr* rançonner

rant [rænt] *intr* tempêter

rap [ræp] *s* (*blow*) tape *f*; (*noise*) petit coup *m* sec; (slang) éreintement *m*; **to not care a rap** (slang) s'en ficher; **to take the rap** (slang) se laisser châtier ‖ *v* (*pret & pp* **rapped**; *ger* **rapping**) *tr & intr* frapper d'un coup sec

rapacious [rə'pe∫əs] *adj* rapace

rape [rep] *s* viol *m* ‖ *tr* violer

rapid ['ræpɪd] *adj* rapide ‖ **rapids** *spl* rapides *mpl*

rap'id-fire' *adj* à tir rapide

rapidity [rə'pɪdəti] *s* rapidité *f*

rapier ['repɪ·ər] *s* rapière *f*

rapt [ræpt] *adj* ravi; absorbé

rapture ['ræpt∫ər] *s* ravissement *m*

rare [rɛr] *adj* rare; (*meat*) saignant; (*amusing*) (coll) impayable

rare' bird' *s* merle *m* blanc

rare'-book' room' *s* salle *f* de la réserve

rarely ['rɛrli] *adv* rarement

rascal ['ræskəl] *s* coquin *m*

rash [ræ∫] *adj* téméraire ‖ *s* éruption *f*

rasp [ræsp] *s* crissement *m*; (*tool*) râpe *f* ‖ *tr* râper ‖ *intr* crisser

raspber·ry ['ræz,bɛri] *s* (*pl* **-ries**) framboise *f*

rasp'berry bush' *s* framboisier *m*

rat [ræt] *s* rat *m*; (*false hair*) (coll) postiche *m*; (*deserter*) (slang) lâcheur *m*; (*informer*) (slang) mouchard *m*; (*scoundrel*) (slang) cochon *m*; **rats!** zut!; **to smell a rat** (coll) soupçonner anguille sous roche

ratchet ['ræt∫ɪt] *s* encliquetage *m*

rate [ret] *s* taux *m*; (*for freight, mail, a subscription*) tarif *m*; **at any rate** en tout cas; **at the rate of** à raison de ‖ *tr* évaluer; mériter ‖ *intr* (coll) être favori

rate' of exchange' *s* cours *m*

rather ['ræðər], ['rɑðər] *adv* plutôt; (*fairly*) assez; **rather than** plutôt que ‖ *interj* je vous crois!

rathskeller ['ræts,kɛlər] *s* caveau *m*

rati·fy ['rætɪ,faɪ] *v* (*pret & pp* **-fied**) *tr* ratifier

rating ['retɪŋ] *s* classement *m*, cote *f*

ra·tio ['re∫o] *s* (*pl* **-tios**) raison *f*, rapport *m*

ration ['ræ∫ən] *s* ration *f* ‖ *tr* rationner

rational ['ræ∫ənəl] *adj* rationnel

ra'tion book' *s* tickets *mpl* de rationnement

ra'tion card' *s* carte *f* de ravitaillement

rat' poi'son *s* mort *m* aux rats

rat' race' *s* foire *f* d'empoigne

rat'-tail file' *s* queue-de-rat *f*

rattan [ræ'tæn] *s* rotin *m*

rattle ['rætəl] *s* (*number of short, sharp sounds*) bruit *m* de ferraille, cliquetis *m*; (*noisemaking device*) crécelle *f*; (*child's toy*) hochet *m*; (*in the throat*) râle *m* ‖ *tr* agiter; (*to confuse*) (coll) affoler; **to rattle off** débiter comme un moulin ‖ *intr* cliqueter; (*said of windows*) trembler

rat'tle·snake' *s* serpent *m* à sonnettes

rat'trap' *s* ratière *f*

raucous ['rɔkəs] *adj* rauque

ravage ['rævɪdʒ] *s* ravage *m*; **ravages** (*of time*) injure *f* ‖ *tr* ravager

rave [rev] *s* (coll) éloge *m* enthousiaste ‖ *intr* délirer; **to rave about** or **over** s'extasier devant or sur

raven ['revən] *s* corbeau *m*

ravenous ['rævənəs] *adj* vorace

rave' review' *s* article *m* dithyrambique

ravine [rə'vin] *s* ravin *m*

ravish ['rævɪ∫] *tr* ravir

ravishing ['rævɪ∫ɪŋ] *adj* ravissant

raw [rɔ] *adj* (*uncooked*) cru; (*sugar, metal*) brut; (*silk*) grège; (*wound*) vif; (*wind*) aigre; (*weather*) humide et froid; novice, inexpérimenté

raw′boned′ *adj* décharné

raw′ deal′ *s* (slang) mauvais tour *m*

raw′hide′ *s* cuir *m* vert

raw′ mate′rial *s* matière *f* première, matières premières, matière brute

ray [re] *s* (*of light*) rayon *m*; (*fish*) raie *f*

rayon [′re·ɑn] *s* rayonne *f*

raze [rez] *tr* raser

razor [′rezər] *s* rasoir *m*

ra′zor blade′ *s* lame *f* de rasoir

ra′zor strop′ *s* cuir *m* à rasoir

razz [ræz] *tr* (slang) mettre en boîte

reach [ritʃ] *s* portée *f*; (*of a boxer*) allonge *f*; **out of reach (of)** hors d'atteinte (de), hors de portée (de); **within reach of** à portée de ‖ *tr* atteindre; arriver à; **to reach out** (*a hand*) tendre; (*an arm*) allonger ‖ *intr* s'étendre

react [rɪ′ækt] *intr* réagir

reaction [rɪ′ækʃən] *s* réaction *f*

reactionar·y [rɪ′ækʃən‚ɛri] *adj* réactionnaire ‖ *s* (*pl* **-ies**) réactionnaire *mf*

reactivate [rɪ′æktə‚vet] *tr* réactiver

reactor [rɪ′æktər] *s* réacteur *m*

read [rid] *v* (*pret & pp* **read** [rɛd]) *tr* lire; **to read over** parcourir ‖ *intr* lire; (*said of passage, description, etc.*) se lire; (*said, e.g., of thermometer*) marquer; **to read on** continuer à lire; **to read up on** étudier

reader [′ridər] *s* lecteur *m*; livre *m* de lecture

read′head′ *s* (comp) lecteur *m* de disquette

readily [′rɛdɪli] *adv* (*willingly*) volontiers; (*easily*) facilement

reading [′ridɪŋ] *s* lecture *f*

read′ing desk′ *s* pupitre *m*

read′ing glass′ *s* loupe *f*; **reading glasses** lunettes *fpl* pour lire

read′ing lamp′ *s* lampe *f* de bureau

read′ing room′ *s* salle *f* de lecture

readjust [‚ri·ə′dʒʌst] *tr* réadapter; (*to correct*) rectifier; (*salaries*) rajuster

read′-on′ly mem′ory *s* (comp) mémoire *f* morte

read·y [′rɛdi] *adj* (*comp* **-ier**; *super* **-iest**) prêt; (*quick*) vif; (*money*) comptant ‖ *v* (*pret & pp* **-ied**) *tr* préparer ‖ *intr* se préparer

read′y cash′ *s* argent *m* comptant

read′y-made′ suit′ *s* (*for men*) complet *m* de confection; (*for women*) costume *m* de confection

ready-to-eat [′rɛditə′it] *adj* prêt à servir

ready-to-wear [′rɛditə′wɛr] *adj* prêt à porter ‖ *s* prêt-à-porter *m*

reaffirm [‚ri·ə′fʌrm] *tr* réaffirmer

reagent [rɪ′edʒənt] *s* (chem) réactif *m*

real [′ri·əl] *adj* vrai, réel

re′al estate′ *s* biens *mpl* immobiliers

re′al-estate′ *adj* immobilier

re′al-estate a′gent *s* agent *m* immobilier, agent de location

realism [′ri·ə‚lɪzəm] *s* réalisme *m*

realist [′ri·əlɪst] *s* réaliste *mf*

realistic [‚ri·ə′lɪstɪk] *adj* réaliste

reali·ty [rɪ′ælɪti] *s* (*pl* **-ties**) réalité *f*

realize [′ri·ə‚laɪz] *tr* se rendre compte de, s'apercevoir de; (*hopes, profits, etc.*) réaliser

really [′ri·əli] *adv* vraiment réellement, en réalité

realm [rɛlm] *s* royaume *m*; (*field*) domaine *m*

re′al time′ *s* (comp) temps *m* réel

Realtor [′ri·əltər] *s* (*official member*) (U.S.A.) agent *m* immobilier, agent de location

ream [rim] *s* rame *f*; **reams** (coll) masses *fpl* ‖ *tr* aléser

reap [rip] *tr* moissonner; (*to gather*) recueillir

reaper [′ripər] *s* moissonneur *m*; (mach) moissonneuse *f*

reappear [‚ri·ə′pɪr] *intr* réapparaître

reappearance [‚ri·ə′pɪrəns] *s* réapparition *f*

reapportionment [‚ri·ə′porʃənmənt] *s* nouvelle répartition *f*

rear [rɪr] *adj* arrière, d'arrière, de derrière ‖ *s* derrière *m*; (*of a car, ship, etc.; of an army*) arrière *m*; (*of a row*) queue *f*; **to the rear!** (mil) demitour à droite! ‖ *tr* élever ‖ *intr* (*said of animal*) se cabrer

rear′ ad′miral *s* contre-amiral *m*

rear′-axle assem′bly *s* (*pl* **-blies**) pont *m* arrière

rear′ drive′ *s* traction *f* arrière

rearmament [rɪ′ɑrməmənt] *s* réarmement *m*

rearrange [‚ri·ə′rendʒ] *tr* arranger de nouveau

rear′-view mir′ror *s* rétroviseur *m*

rear′ win′dow *s* (aut) lunette *f* arrière

reason [′rizən] *s* raison *f*; **by reason of** à cause de; **for good reason** pour cause; **to listen to reason** entendre raison; **to stand to reason** être de toute évidence ‖ *tr & intr* raisonner

reasonable [′rizənəbəl] *adj* raisonnable

reassessment [‚ri·ə′sɛsmənt] *s* réévaluation *f*

reassure [‚ri·ə′ʃur] *tr* rassurer

reawaken [‚ri·ə′wekən] *tr* réveiller ‖ *intr* se réveiller

rebate [′ribet] *s* (*discount*) rabais *m*, escompte *m*, ristourne *f*; (*money back*) remboursement *m*, ristourne *f* ‖ [rɪ′bet] *tr* faire un rabais sur

rebel [′rɛbəl] *adj & s* rebelle *mf* ‖ **re·bel** [rɪ′bɛl] *v* (*pret & pp* **-belled**; *ger* **-belling**) *intr* se rebeller

rebellion [rɪ′bɛljən] *s* rébellion *f*

rebellious [rɪ′bɛljəs] *adj* rebelle

re·bind [ri′baɪnd] *v* (*pret & pp* **-bound**) *tr* (bb) relier à neuf

rebirth [′ribʌrθ] *s* renaissance *f*

rebore [ri′bor] *tr* rectifier

rebound [′ri‚baund] *s* rebondissement *m* ‖ [ri′baund] *intr* rebondir

rebroad·cast [ri′brɔd‚kæst] *s* retransmission *f* ‖ *v* (*pret & pp* **-cast** or **-casted**) *tr* retransmettre

rebuff [rɪ′bʌf] *s* rebuffade *f* ‖ *tr* mal accueillir

re·build [ri'bɪld] *v* (*pret & pp* -built) *tr* reconstruire

rebuke [rɪ'bjuk] *s* réprimande *f* ‖ *tr* réprimander

re·but [rɪ'bʌt] *v* (*pret & pp* -butted; *ger* -butting) *tr* réfuter, repousser

rebuttal [rɪ'bʌtəl] *s* réfutation *f*

recall ['rikɔl] *s* rappel *m* ‖ [rɪ'kɔl] *tr* rappeler; se rappeler de

recant [rɪ'kænt] *tr* rétracter ‖ *intr* se rétracter

re·cap ['ri,kæp] *v* (*pret & pp* -capped; *ger* -capping) *tr* rechaper

recapitulation [,rikə,pɪtʃə'leʃən] *s* récapitulation *f*

re·cast ['ri,kæst] *s* refonte *f* ‖ [ri'kæst] *v* (*pret & pp* -cast) *tr* (*metal; a play, novel, etc.*) refondre; (*the actors of a play*) redistribuer

recede [rɪ'sid] *intr* reculer; (*said of forehead, chin, etc.*) fuir; (*said of sea*) se retirer

receipt [rɪ'sit] *s* (*for goods*) récépissé *m*; (*for money*) récépissé, reçu *m*; (*recipe*) recette *f*; **receipts** recettes; **to acknowledge receipt of** accuser réception de ‖ *tr* acquitter

receive [rɪ'siv] *tr* recevoir; (*stolen goods*) recéler; (*a station*) (rad) capter; **received payment** pour acquit ‖ *intr* recevoir

receiver [rɪ'sivər] *s* (*of letter*) destinataire *mf*; (*in bankruptcy*) syndic *m*, liquidateur *m*; (telp) récepteur *m*

receiv'ing set' *s* poste *m* récepteur

recent ['risənt] *adj* récent

recently ['risəntli] *adv* récemment

receptacle [rɪ'sɛptəkəl] *s* récipient *m*; (*in a coin phone*) sébile *f*; (elec) prise *f* femelle

reception [rɪ'sɛpʃən] *s* réception *f*; (*welcome*) accueil *m*

recep'tion desk' *s* réception *f*

receptionist [rɪ'sɛpʃənɪst] *s* préposé *m* à la réception

receptive [rɪ'sɛptɪv] *adj* réceptif

recess ['risɛs] *s* (*of court, legislature, etc.*) ajournement *m*; (*at school*) récréation *f*; (*in a wall*) niche *f* ‖ [rɪ'sɛs] *tr* ajourner; (*s.th., e.g., in a wall*) encastrer ‖ *intr* s'adjourner

recession [rɪ'sɛʃən] *s* récession *f*

rechargeable [ri'tʃardʒəbəl] *adj* rechargeable

recipe ['rɛsɪ,pi] *s* recette *f*

recipient [rɪ'sɪpɪ·ənt] *s* (*person*) bénéficiaire *mf*; (*of a degree, honor, etc.*) récipiendaire *m*; (*of blood*) receveur *m*; (*container*) récipient *m*

reciprocal [rɪ'sɪprəkəl] *adj* réciproque

reciprocity [,rɛsɪ'prɑsɪti] *s* réciprocité *f*

recital [rɪ'saɪtəl] *s* récit *m*; (*of music or poetry*) récital *m*

recite [rɪ'saɪt] *tr* réciter; narrer

reckless ['rɛklɪs] *adj* téméraire, imprudent, insouciant

reckon ['rɛkən] *tr* calculer; considérer; (coll) supposer, imaginer ‖ *intr* calculer; **to reckon on** compter sur; **to reckon with** tenir compte de

reclaim [rɪ'klem] *tr* récupérer; (*e.g., waste land*) mettre en valeur; (*a person*) réformer

reclamation [,rɛklə'meʃən] *s* récupération *f*; (*e.g., of waste land*) mise *f* en valeur; (*of a person*) réforme *f*

recline [rɪ'klaɪn] *tr* appuyer, reposer ‖ *intr* s'appuyer, se reposer

reclin'ing seat' *s* siège *m* à dossier réglable

recluse ['rɛklus] *adj & s* reclus *m*

recognition [,rɛkəg'nɪʃən] *s* reconnaissance *f*

recognize ['rɛkəg,naɪz] *tr* reconnaître; (parl) donner la parole à

recoil [rɪ'kɔɪl] *s* répugnance *f*; (*of, e.g., firearm*) recul *m* ‖ *intr* reculer

recollect [,rɛkə'lɛkt] *tr* se rappeler

recollection [,rɛkə'lɛkʃən] *s* souvenir *m*

recommend [,rɛkə'mɛnd] *tr* recommander

recommendation [,rɛkəmɛn'daʃən] *s* recommandation *f*; (*written*) certificat *m*

recompense ['rɛkəm,pɛns] *s* récompense *f* ‖ *tr* récompenser

reconcile ['rɛkən,saɪl] *tr* réconcilier; **to reconcile oneself** to se résigner à

reconnaissance [rɪ'kɑnɪsəns] *s* reconnaissance *f*

reconnoiter [,rɛkə'nɔɪtər] *tr & intr* reconnaître

reconquer [ri'kɑŋkər] *tr* reconquérir

reconquest [ri'kɑŋkwɛst] *s* reconquête *f*

reconsider [,rikən'sɪdər] *tr* reconsidérer

reconstruct [,rikən'strʌkt] *tr* reconstruire; (*a crime*) reconstituer

reconversion [,rikən'vʌrʒən] *s* reconversion *f*

record ['rɛkərd] *s* enregistrement *m*, registre *m*; (*to play on the phonograph*) disque *m*; (mil) état *m* de service; (sports) record *m*; **off the record** en confidence; **records** archives *fpl*; **to break the record** battre le record; **to have a good record** être bien noté; (*at school*) avoir de bonnes notes ‖ [rɪ'kɔrd] *tr* enregistrer

rec'ord chang'er *s* tourne-disque *m* automatique

recorder [rɪ'kɔrdər] *s* (electron) appareil *m* enregistreur; (law) greffier *m*; (mus) flûte *f* à bec

rec'ord hold'er *s* recordman *m*

recording [rɪ'kɔrdɪŋ] *adj* enregistreur ‖ *s* enregistrement *m*

record'ing tape' *s* ruban *m* magnétique

rec'ord li'brary *s* discothèque *f*

rec'ord play'er *s* électrophone *m*

recount ['ri,kaunt] *s* nouveau dépouillement *m* du scrutin ‖ [ri'kaunt] *tr* (*to count again*) recompter ‖ [rɪ'kaunt] *tr* (*to tell*) raconter

recoup [rɪ'kup] *tr* recouvrer; **to recoup s.o. for** dédommager qn de

recourse [ri'kors], ['rikors] *s* recours *m*; **to have recourse to** recourir à

recover [rɪ'kʌvər] *tr (to get back)* recouvrer; *(to cover again)* recouvrir ‖ *intr (to get well)* se rétablir

recov'er·y [rɪ'kʌvəri] *s (pl -ies)* récupération *f*, recouvrement *m*; *(e.g., of health)* rétablissement *m*

recov'ery room' *s* (med) salle *f* de reveil, salle de réanimation

recreant ['rɛkrɪ·ənt] *adj & s* lâche *mf*; traître *m*; apostat *m*

recreation [,rɛkrɪ'eʃən] *s* récréation *f*

rec' room' [rɛk] *s* salle *f* de détente

recruit [rɪ'krut] *s* recrue *f* ‖ *tr* recruter; **to be recuited** se recruter

rectangle ['rɛk,tæŋgəl] *s* rectangle *m*

rectifier ['rɛktə,faɪ·ər] *s* rectificateur *m*; (elec) redresseur *m*

recti·fy ['rɛktɪ,faɪ] *v (pret & pp -fied) tr* rectifier; (elec) redresser

rec·tum ['rɛktəm] *s (pl -ta* [tə]) rectum *m*

recumbent [rɪ'kʌmbənt] *adj* couché

recuperate [rɪ'kjupə,ret] *tr & intr* récupérer

re·cur [rɪ'kʌr] *v (pret & pp -curred; ger -curring) intr* revenir, se reproduire; revenir à la mémoire de

recurrent [rɪ'kʌrənt] *adj* récurrent

recycle [ri'saɪkəl] *tr* recycler

recycling [ri'saɪklɪŋ] *s* recyclage *m*

red [rɛd] *adj (comp* **redder**; *super* **reddest**) rouge ‖ *s (color)* rouge *m*; **in the red** en déficit; **Red** *(communist)* rouge *mf*; *(nickname)* Rouquin *m*; **to glow** or **turn red** rougeoyer

red'bait' *tr* taxer de communiste

red'bird' *s* cardinal *m* d'Amérique, tangara *m*

red'-blood'ed *adj* vigoureux

red'breast' *s* rouge-gorge *m*

red'cap' *s* porteur *m*; (Brit) soldat *m* de la police militaire

red' cell' *s* globule *m* rouge

Red' Cross' *s* Croix-Rouge *f*

redden ['rɛdən] *tr & intr* rougir

redeem [rɪ'dim] *tr* racheter; *(a pawned article)* dégager; *(a promise)* remplir; *(a debt)* s'acquitter de, acquitter

redeemer [rɪ'dimər] *s* rédempteur *m*

redemption [rɪ'dɛmpʃən] *s* rachat *m*; (rel) rédemption *f*

red'-haired' *adj* roux

red'hand'ed *adj & adv* sur le fait, en flagrant délit

red'head' *s (woman)* rousse *f*

red' her'ring *s* hareng *m* saur; (fig) fauxfuyant *m*

red'-hot' *adj* chauffé au rouge; ardent; *(news)* tout frais

rediscount [ri'dɪskaʊnt] *s* réescompte *m*; ‖ *tr* réescompter

rediscover [,ridɪs'kʌvər] *tr* redécouvrir

red'-let'ter day' *s* jour *m* mémorable

red' light' *s* feu *m* rouge; **to go through a red light** brûler feu rouge

red'-light' dis'trict *s* quartier *m* réservé

red' man' *s (pl* **men'**) Peau-Rouge *m*

re·do ['ri'du] *v (pret* **-did**; *pp* **-done**) *tr* refaire

redolent ['rɛdələnt] *adj* parfumé; **redolent of** exhalant une senteur de; qui fait penser à

redouble [ri'dʌbəl] *s* (bridge) surcontre *m* ‖ *tr & intr* redoubler; (bridge) surcontrer

redoubt [rɪ'daʊt] *s* redoute *f*

redound [rɪ'daʊnd] *intr* contribuer; **to redound** to tourner à

red' pep'per *s* piment *m* rouge

redress ['ridrəs] *s* redressement *m* ‖ [rɪ'drɛs] *tr* redresser

Red' Rid'ing·hood' *s* Chaperon rouge *m*

red'skin' *s* Peau-Rouge *mf*

red' tape' *s* paperasserie *f*, chinoiseries *fpl* administratives

reduce [rɪ'd(j)us] *tr* réduire, diminuer ‖ *intr* maigrir

reduc'ing ex'ercises *spl* exercises *mpl* amaigrissants

reduction [rɪ'dʌkʃən] *s* réduction *f*, diminution *f*

redundant [rɪ'dʌndənt] *adj* redondant

red' wine' *s* vin *m* rouge

red'wing' *s* (orn) mauvis *m*

red'wood' *s* séquoia *m*

reed [rid] *s (of instrument)* anche *f*; (bot) roseau *m*; **reeds** (mus) instruments *mpl* à anche

reedit [ri'ɛdɪt] *tr* rééditer

reef [rif] *s* récif *m*; *(of sail)* ris *m* ‖ *tr* (naut) prendre un ris dans

reefer ['rifər] *s* (slang) joint *m*, cigarette *f* de marijuana

reek [rik] *intr* fumer; **to reek of** or **with** empester, puer

reel [ril] *s (cylinder)* bobine *f*; *(of film)* rouleau *m*, bobine, bande *f*; *(of fishing rod)* moulinet *m*; *(sway)* balancement *m*; **off the reel** (coll) d'affilée ‖ *tr* bobiner; **to reel off** dévider; (coll) réciter d'un trait ‖ *intr* chanceler

reelection [,ri·ɪ'lɛkʃən] *s* réélection *f*

reenlist [,ri·ɛn'lɪst] *tr* rengager ‖ *intr* rengager, se rengager

reenlistment [,ri·ɛn'lɪstmənt] *s* rengagement *m*; *(person)* rengagé *m*

reen·try [ri'ɛntri] *s (pl* **-tries**) rentrée *f*; (rok) retour *m* à la terre

reexamination [,ri·ɛg,zæmɪ'neʃən] *s* réexamen *m*

re·fer [rɪ'fʌr] *v (pret & pp -ferred; ger -ferring) tr* renvoyer ‖ *intr*—**to refer to** se référer à

referee [,rɛfə'ri] *s* arbitre *m*, directeur *m* de jeu ‖ *tr & intr* arbitrer

reference ['rɛfərəns] *s* référence *f*

ref'erence room' *s* bibliothèque *f* de consultation

referen·dum [,rɛfə'rɛndəm] *s (pl* **-da** [də]) référendum *m*

refill ['rifɪl] *s* recharge *f* ‖ [ri'fɪl] *tr* remplir à nouveau

refine [rɪ'faɪn] *tr* raffiner

refinement [rɪ'faɪnmənt] *s* raffinage *m*; *(e.g., of manners)* raffinement *m*

refiner·y [rɪ'faɪnəri] *s (pl* **-ies**) raffinerie *f*

reflect [rɪˈflɛkt] *tr* réfléchir, refléter ‖ *intr* (*to be reflected*) se refléter; (*to meditate*) réfléchir; **to reflect on** or **upon** réfléchir à or sur; (*to harm*) nuire à la réputation de

reflection [rɪˈflɛkʃən] *s* (*e.g., of light; thought*) réflexion *f*; (*reflected light; image*) reflet *m*; **to cast reflections on** faire des réflexions à

reflector [rɪˈflɛktər] *s* réflecteur *m*

reflex [ˈriflɛks] *adj* & *s* réflexe *m*

reflexive [rɪˈflɛksɪv] *adj* & *s* réflechi *m*

reforestation [ˌrifɔrɪsˈteʃən] *s* reboisement *m*

reform [rɪˈfɔrm] *s* réforme *f* ‖ *tr* réformer ‖ *intr* se réformer

reformation [ˌrɛfərˈmeʃən] *s* réformation *f*; **the Reformation** la Réforme

reformato·ry [rɪˈfɔrməˌtori] *s* (*pl* **-ries**) maison *f* de correction

reformer [rɪˈfɔrmər] *s* réformateur *m*

reform' school' *s* maison *f* de correction

refraction [rɪˈfrækʃən] *s* réfraction *f*

refrain [rɪˈfren] *s* refrain *m* ‖ *intr* s'abstenir

refresh [rɪˈfrɛʃ] *tr* rafraîchir ‖ *intr* se rafraîchir

refreshing [rɪˈfrɛʃɪŋ] *adj* rafraîchissant

refreshment [rɪˈfrɛʃmənt] *s* rafraîchissement *m*

refresh'ment bar' *s* buvette *f*

refrigerate [rɪˈfrɪdʒəˌret] *tr* réfrigérer

refrigerator [rɪˈfrɪdʒəˌretər] *s* (*icebox*) glacière; réfrigérateur *m*; (*condenser*) congélateur *m*

refrig'erator car' *s* (rr) wagon *m* frigorifique

re·fuel [riˈfjul] *v* (*pret* & *pp* **-fueled** or **-fuelled;** *ger* **-fueling** or **-fuelling**) *tr* ravitailler en carburant ‖ *intr* se ravitailler en carburant

refuge [ˈrɛfjudʒ] *s* refuge *m*; **to take refuge (in)** se réfugier (dans)

refugee [ˌrɛfjuˈdʒi] *s* réfugié *m*

refund [ˈrifʌnd] *s* remboursement *m* ‖ [ˈrifʌnd] *tr* (*to pay back*) rembourser ‖ [rɪˈfʌnd] *tr* (*to fund again*) consolider

refurnish [riˈfʌrnɪʃ] *tr* remeubler

refusal [rɪˈfjuzəl] *s* refus *m*

refuse [ˈrɛfjus] *s* ordures *fpl*, détritus *mpl* ‖ [rɪˈfjuz] *tr* & *intr* refuser

refute [rɪˈfjut] *tr* réfuter

regain [rɪˈgen] *tr* regagner; (*consciousness*) reprendre

regal [ˈrigəl] *adj* royal

regale [rɪˈgel] *tr* régaler

regalia [rɪˈgelɪ·ə] *spl* atours *mpl*, ornements *mpl*; (*of an office*) insignes *mpl*

regard [rɪˈgɑrd] *s* considération *f*; (*esteem*) respect *m*; (*look*) regard *m*; **in** or **with regard to** à l'égard de; **regards** sincères amitiés *fpl* ‖ *tr* considérer, estimer; **as regards** quant à

regarding [rɪˈgɑrdɪŋ] *prep* au sujet de, touchant

regardless [rɪˈgɑrdlɪs] *adj* inattentif ‖ *adv* (coll) coûte que coûte; **regardless of** sans tenir compte de

regatta [rɪˈgætə] *s* régates *fpl*

regen·cy [ˈridʒənsi] *s* (*pl* **-cies**) régence *f*

regenerate [rɪˈdʒɛnəˌret] *tr* régénérer ‖ *intr* se régénérer

regent [ˈridʒənt] *s* régent *m*

regicide [ˈrɛdʒɪˌsaɪd] *s* (*act*) régicide *m*; (*person*) régicide *mf*

regime [reˈʒim] *s* régime *m*

regiment [ˈrɛdʒɪmənt] *s* régiment *m* ‖ [ˈrɛdʒɪˌmɛnt] *tr* enrégimenter, régenter

regimental [ˌrɛdʒɪˈmɛntəl] *adj* régimentaire ‖ **regimentals** *spl* tenue *f* militaire

region [ˈridʒən] *s* région *f*

register [ˈrɛdʒɪstər] *s* registre *m* ‖ *tr* enregistrer; (*a student; an automobile*) immatriculer; (*a letter*) recommander ‖ *intr* s'inscrire

reg'istered let'ter *s* lettre *f* recommandée

reg'istered mail' *s* envoi *m* en recommandé

reg'istered nurse' *s* infirmière *f* diplômée

registrar [ˈrɛdʒɪsˌtrɑr] *s* archiviste *mf*, secrétaire *mf*

registration [ˌrɛdʒɪsˈtreʃən] *s* enregistrement *m*; immatriculation *f*, inscription *f*; (*of mail*) recommandation *f*

registra'tion blank' *s* fiche *f* d'inscription

registra'tion fee' *s* frais *mpl* d'inscription, droit *m* d'inscription

registra'tion num'ber *s* (*of soldier or student*) numéro *m* matricule

re·gret [rɪˈgrɛt] *s* regret *m*; **regrets** excuses *fpl* ‖ *v* (*pret* & *pp* **-gretted;** *ger* **-gretting**) *tr* regretter

regrettable [rɪˈgrɛtəbəl] *adj* regrettable

regular [ˈrɛgjələr] *adj* & *s* régulier *m*

reg'ular fel'low *s* (coll) chic type *m*

regularity [ˌrɛgjəˈlærɪti] *s* régularité *f*

regularize [ˈrɛgjələˌraɪz] *tr* régulariser

regulate [ˈrɛgjəˌlet] *tr* régler; (*to control*) réglementer

regulation [ˌrɛgjəˈleʃən] *s* régulation *f*; (*rule*) règlement *m*

rehabilitate [ˌrihəˈbɪlɪˌtet] *tr* réadapter; (*in reputation, standing, etc.*) réhabiliter

rehearsal [rɪˈhʌrsəl] *s* répétition *f*

rehearse [rɪˈhʌrs] *tr* & *intr* répéter

reign [ren] *s* règne *m* ‖ *intr* régner

reimburse [ˌri·ɪmˈbʌrs] *tr* rembourser

rein [ren] *s* rêne *f*; **to give free rein to** donner libre cours à ‖ *tr* contenir, freiner

reincarnation [ˌri·ɪnkɑrˈneʃən] *s* réincarnation *f*

rein'deer' *s* renne *m*

reinforce [ˌri·ɪnˈfors] *tr* renforcer; (*concrete*) armer

reinforcement [ˌri·ɪnˈforsmənt] *s* renforcement *m*

reinstate [ˌri·ɪnˈstet] *tr* rétablir

reiterate [rɪˈɪtəˌret] *tr* réitérer

reject [ˈridʒɛkt] *s* pièce *f* or article *m* de rebut; **rejects** rebuts *mpl* ‖ [rɪˈdʒɛkt] *tr* rejeter

rejection [rɪˈdʒɛkʃən] *s* rejet *m*, refus *m*

rejoice [rɪˈdʒɔɪs] *intr* se réjouir

rejoin [rɪˈdʒɔɪn] *tr* rejoindre

rejoinder [rɪˈdʒɔɪndər] *s* réplique *f*; (law) réponse *f* à une réplique

rejuvenation [rɪ,dʒuvɪ'neʃən] s rajeunissement m

rekindle [ri'kɪndəl] tr rallumer

relapse [rɪ'læps] s rechute f ‖ intr rechuter

relate [rɪ'let] tr (to narrate) relater; (e.g., two events) établir un rapport entre; **to be related** être apparenté

relation [rɪ'leʃən] s (relationship) relation f, rapport m; (telling) récit m, relation; (relative) parent m; (kinship) parenté f; **in relation to or with** par rapport à; **relations** (of a sexual nature) rapports mpl; (diplomatic) relations fpl

relationship [rɪ'leʃən,ʃɪp] s (connection) rapport m; (kinship) parenté f

relative ['rɛlətɪv] adj relatif ‖ s parent m

relativity [,rɛlə'tɪvəti] s relativité f

relax [rɪ'læks] tr détendre; **to be relaxed** être décontracté or détendu ‖ intr se détendre, décompresser

relaxation [,rilæks'eʃən] s détente f, délassement m

relaxing [rɪ'læksɪŋ] adj tranquillisant, apaisant; (diverting) délassant

relay ['rile] s relais m ‖ v (pret & pp **-layed**) tr relayer; (rad, telg, telp, telv) retransmettre ‖ [rɪ'le] v (pret & pp **-laid**) tr tendre de nouveau

re′lay race′ s course f de relais

re′lay sat′ellite s satellite m de relais

re′lay transmit′ter s (electron) réémetteur m

release [rɪ'lis] s (from jail) mise f en liberté, libération f; (permission) autorisation f; (exemption) dérogation f; (aer) lâchage m; (mach) déclenchement m; **release on bail** libération f sous caution; **release on parole** libération conditionnelle ‖ tr délivrer; (from jail) mettre en liberté; autoriser; (a bomb) lâcher

relegate ['rɛli,get] tr reléguer

relent [rɪ'lɛnt] intr se laisser attendrir, s'adoucir

relentless [rɪ'lɛntlɪs] adj implacable

relevant ['rɛlɪvənt] adj pertinent

reliable [rɪ'laɪ·əbəl] adj digne de confiance, digne de foi, fiable

reliance [rɪ'laɪ·əns] s confiance f

relic ['rɛlɪk] s (rel) relique f; (fig) vestige m

relief [rɪ'lif] s (from pain, anxiety) soulagement m; (projection of figures; elevation) relief m; (aid) secours m; (welfare program) aide f sociale; (mil) relève f; **in relief** en relief

relieve [rɪ'liv] tr soulager; (to aid) secourir; (to release from a post; to give variety to) relever; (mil) relever

religion [rɪ'lɪdʒən] s religion f

religious [rɪ'lɪdʒəs] adj religieux

relinquish [rɪ'lɪŋkwɪʃ] tr abandonner

relish ['rɛlɪʃ] s (enjoyment) goût m; (condiment) assaisonnement m; **relish for** penchant pour ‖ tr goûter, apprécier

reluctance [rɪ'lʌktəns] s répugnance f; **with reluctance** à contrecœur

reluctant [rɪ'lʌktənt] adj hésitant, peu disposé

re·ly [rɪ'laɪ] v (pret & pp **-lied**) intr—**to rely on** compter sur, se fier à

remain [rɪ'men] s—**remains** restes mpl; œuvres fpl posthumes ‖ intr rester

remainder [rɪ'mendər] s reste m; **remainders** bouillons mpl ‖ tr solder

re·make [ri'mek] v (pret & pp **-made**) tr refaire

remark [rɪ'mɑrk] s remarque f, observation f ‖ tr & intr remarquer, observer; **to remark on** faire des remarques sur

remarkable [rɪ'mɑrkəbəl] adj remarquable

remar·ry [rɪ'mæri] v (pret & pp **-ried**) tr remarier; se remarier avec ‖ intr se remarier

reme·dy ['rɛmɪdi] s (pl **-dies**) remède m ‖ v (pret & pp **-died**) tr remédier à

remember [rɪ'mɛmbər] tr se souvenir de, se rappeler; **remember me to** rappelez-moi au bon souvenir de ‖ intr se souvenir, se rappeler

remembrance [rɪ'mɛmbrəns] s souvenir m; **in remembrance of** en souvenir de

remind [rɪ'maɪnd] tr rappeler

reminder [rɪ'maɪndər] s note f de rappel, mémento m, pense-bête f

reminisce [,rɛmɪ'nɪs] intr se livrer au souvenirs, raconter ses souvenirs

remiss [rɪ'mɪs] adj négligent

remission [rɪ'mɪʃən] s rémission f

re·mit [rɪ'mɪt] v (pret & pp **-mitted;** ger **-mitting**) tr remettre ‖ intr se calmer

remittance [rɪ'mɪtəns] s remise f, envoi m

remnant ['rɛmnənt] s (remainder) reste m; (of cloth) coupon m; (at reduced price) solde m

remod·el [ri'mɑdəl] v (pret & pp **-eled** or **-elled;** ger **-eling** or **-elling**) tr modeler de nouveau, remanier; (a house) transformer

remonstrance [rɪ'mɑnstrəns] s remontrance f

remonstrate [rɪ'mɑnstret] intr protester; **to remonstrate with** faire des remontrances à

remorse [rɪ'mɔrs] s remords m

remorseful [rɪ'mɔrsfəl] adj contrit, repentant, plein de remords

remote′ [rɪ'mot] adj loigné, retiré

remote′ control′ s commande f à distance, télécommande f

removable [rɪ'muvəbəl] adj amovible

removal [rɪ'muvəl] s enlèvement m; (from house) déménagement m; (dismissal) révocation f

remove [rɪ'muv] tr enlever, ôter; éloigner; (furniture) déménager; (to dismiss) révoquer ‖ intr se déplacer; déménager

remuneration [rɪ,mjunə'reʃən] s rémunération f

renaissance [,rɛnə'sɑns] s renaissance f

rend [rɛnd] v (pret & pp **-rent** [rɛnt]) tr déchirer; (to split) fendre; (the air; the heart) fendre

render ['rɛndər] tr rendre; (a piece of music) interpréter; (lard) fondre

rendez·vous ['rɑndə,vu] s (pl **-vous** [,vuz]) rendez-vous m ‖ v (pret & pp **-voused**

[‚vud]; *ger* **-vousing** [‚vuɪŋ]) *intr* se rencontrer

rendition [rɛnˈdɪʃən] *s* (*translation*) traduction *f*; (mus) interprétation *f*

renegade [ˈrɛnɪ‚ged] *s* renégat *m*

renege [rɪˈnɪg] *s* renonce *f* ‖ *intr* renoncer; (coll) se dédire, ne pas tenir sa parole

renew [rɪˈn(j)u] *tr* renouveler ‖ *intr* se renouveler

renewable [rɪˈn(j)u·əbəl] *adj* renouvelable

renewal [rɪˈn(j)u·əl] *s* renouvellement *m*; (*of strength*) regain *m*; (*of a lease*) reconduction *f*

renounce [rɪˈnauns] *s* renonce *f* ‖ *tr* renoncer à ‖ *intr* renoncer

renovate [ˈrɛnə‚vet] *tr* renouveler; (*a room, a house, etc.*) mettre à neuf, rénover, transformer

renown [rɪˈnaun] *s* renom *m*

renowned [rɪˈnaund] *adj* renommé

rent [rɛnt] *adj* déchiré ‖ *s* loyer *m*, location *f*; (*tear, slit*) déchirure *f*; **for rent** à louer ‖ *tr* louer ‖ *intr* se louer

rental [ˈrɛntəl] *s* loyer *m*, location *f*

rent'al a'gen·cy *s* (*pl* **-cies**) agence *f* de location

rent'ed car' *s* voiture *f* de louage, voiture de location; (*chauffeur-driven limousine*) voiture de grande remise

renter [ˈrɛntər] *s* locataire *mf*

renunciation [rɪ‚nʌnsɪˈeʃən] *s* renonciation *f*

reopen [riˈopən] *tr & intr* rouvrir

reopening [riˈopənɪŋ] *s* réouverture *f*; (*of school*) rentrée *f*

reorganize [riˈɔrgə‚naɪz] *tr* réorganiser ‖ *intr* se réorganiser

repair [rɪˈpɛr] *s* réparation *f*; **in good repair** en bon état ‖ *tr* réparer ‖ *intr* se rendre

repair'man' *s* (rad, telv) agent *m* de dépannage

repaper [riˈpepər] *tr* retapisser

reparation [‚rɛpəˈreʃən] *s* réparation *f*

repartee [‚rɛpɑrˈti] *s* repartie *f*

repast [rɪˈpæst] *s* repas *m*

repatriate [riˈpetrɪ‚et] *tr* rapatrier

re·pay [rɪˈpe] *v* (*pret & pp* **-paid**) *tr* rembourser; récompenser

repayment [rɪˈpemənt] *s* remboursement *m*; récompense *f*

repeal [rɪˈpil] *s* révocation *f*, abrogation *f* ‖ *tr* révoquer, abroger

repeat [rɪˈpit] *s* répétition *f* ‖ *tr & intr* répéter

re·pel [rɪˈpɛl] *v* (*pret & pp* **-pelled;** *ger* **-pelling**) *tr* repousser; dégoûter

repent [rɪˈpɛnt] *tr* se repentir de ‖ *intr* se repentir

repentance [rɪˈpɛntəns] *s* repentir *m*

repentant [rɪˈpɛntənt] *adj* repentant

repercussion [‚ripərˈkʌʃən] *s* répercussion *f*, contrecoup *m*

reperto·ry [ˈrɛpər‚tori] *s* (*pl* **-ries**) répertoire *m*

repetition [‚rɛpɪˈtɪʃən] *s* répétition *f*

replace [rɪˈples] *tr* (*to put back*) remettre en place; (*to take the place of*) remplacer

replaceable [rɪˈplesəbəl] *adj* remplaçable, amovible

replacement [rɪˈplesmənt] *s* (*putting back*) remise *f* en place, replacement *m*; (*substitution*) remplacement *m*; (*substitute part*) pièce *f* de rechange; (*person*) remplaçant *m*

replay [ˈriple] *s* match *m* rejoué; (telv) action *f* replay ‖ [riˈple] *tr* rejouer

replenish [rɪˈplɛnɪʃ] *tr* réapprovisionner; remplir

replete [rɪˈplit] *adj* rempli, plein

replica [ˈrɛplɪkə] *s* reproduction *f*, réplique *f*

re·ply [rɪˈplaɪ] *s* (*pl* **-plies**) réponse *f*, réplique *f* ‖ *v* (*pret & pp* **-plied**) *tr & intr* répondre, répliquer

reply' cou'pon *s* coupon-réponse *m*

report [rɪˈport] *s* (*account, statement*) rapport *m*; (*rumor*) bruit *m*; (*e.g., of firearm*) détonation *f* ‖ *tr* rapporter; dénoncer; **it is reported that** le bruit court que; **reported missing** porté manquant ‖ *intr* faire un rapport; (*to show up*) se présenter

report' card' *s* bulletin *m* scolaire

reportedly [rɪˈportɪdli] *adv* au dire de tout le monde

reporter [rɪˈportər] *s* reporter *m*

reporting [rɪˈportɪŋ] *s* reportage *m*

repose [rɪˈpoz] *s* repos *m* ‖ *tr* reposer; (*confidence*) placer ‖ *intr* reposer

reprehend [‚rɛprɪˈhɛnd] *tr* reprendre

represent [‚rɛprɪˈzɛnt] *tr* représenter

representation [‚rɛprɪzɛnˈteʃən] *s* représentation *f*

representative [‚rɛprɪˈzɛntətɪv] *adj* représentatif ‖ *s* représentant *m*

repress [rɪˈprɛs] *tr* réprimer; (psychoanal) refouler

repression [rɪˈprɛʃən] *s* répression *f*; (psychoanal) refoulement *m*

reprieve [rɪˈpriv] *s* sursis *m* ‖ *tr* surseoir à l'exécution de

reprimand [ˈrɛprɪ‚mænd] *s* réprimande *f* ‖ *tr* réprimander

reprint [ˈri‚prɪnt] *s* (*book*) réimpression *f*; (*offprint*) tiré *m* à part ‖ [riˈprɪnt] *tr* réimprimer

reprisal [rɪˈpraɪzəl] *s* représailles *fpl*

reproach [rɪˈprotʃ] *s* (*rebuke*) reproche *m*; (*discredit*) opprobre *m* ‖ *tr* reprocher; couvrir d'opprobre; **to reproach s.o. for s.th.** reprocher q.ch. à qn

reproduce [‚riprəˈd(j)us] *tr* reproduire ‖ *intr* se reproduire

reproduction [‚riprəˈdʌkʃən] *s* reproduction *f*

reproof [rɪˈpruf] *s* reproche *m*

reprove [rɪˈpruv] *tr* réprimander

reptile [ˈrɛtɪl] *s* reptile *m*

republic [rɪˈpʌblɪk] *s* république *f*

republican [rɪˈpʌblɪkən] *adj & s* républicain *m*

repudiate [rɪˈpjudɪ‚et] *tr* répudier

repugnant [rɪˈpʌgnənt] *adj* répugnant

repulse [rɪˈpʌls] *s* refus *m*; (*setback*) échec *m* ‖ *tr* repousser

repulsive [rɪˈpʌlsɪv] *adj* répulsif

reputation [‚rɛpjəˈteʃən] *s* réputation *f*

repute [rɪ'pjut] s réputation f; **of ill repute** mal famé ‖ tr—**to be reputed to be** être réputé

reputedly [rɪ'pjutɪdli] adv suivant l'opinion commune

request [rɪ'kwɛst] s demande f; **on request** sur demande ‖ tr demander

Requiem ['rɛkwɪ,ɛm] s Requiem m

require [rɪ'kwaɪr] tr exiger

requirement [rɪ'kwaɪrmənt] s exigence f; besoin m

requisite ['rɛkwɪzɪt] adj requis ‖ s chose f nécessaire; condition f nécessaire

requisition [,rɛkwɪ'zɪʃən] s réquisition f ‖ tr réquisitionner

requital [rɪ'kwaɪtəl] s récompense f; (retaliation) revanche f

requite [rɪ'kwaɪt] tr récompenser; (to avenge) venger

re·read [ri'rid] v (pret & pp **-read** ['rɛd]) tr relire

rerun ['ri,rʌn] s reprise f ‖ [ri'rʌn] tr (film, tape) passer de nouveau; (race) courir de nouveau

resale ['ri,sel], [ri'sel] s revente f

rescind [rɪ'sɪnd] tr abroger

rescue ['rɛskju] s sauvetage m; **to the rescue** au secours, à la rescousse ‖ tr sauver, secourir

res'cue par'ty s équipe f de secours

research [rɪ'sʌrtʃ], ['risʌrtʃ] s recherche f ‖ intr faire des recherches

re·sell [ri'sɛl] v (pret & pp **-sold**) tr revendre; (to sell back) recéder

resemblance [rɪ'zɛmbləns] s ressemblance f

resemble [rɪ'zɛmbəl] tr ressembler à; **to resemble one another** se ressembler

resent [rɪ'zɛnt] tr s'offenser de

resentful [rɪ'zɛntfəl] adj offensé

resentment [rɪ'zɛntmənt] s ressentiment m

reservation [,rɛzər'veʃən] s (booking) location f, réservation f; (Indian land) réserve f; **without reservation** sans réserve

reserve [rɪ'zʌrv] s réserve f ‖ tr réserver

reserve' room' s (in a library) réserve f, salle f de services du prêt

reservist [rɪ'zʌrvɪst] s réserviste m

reservoir ['rɛzər,vwɑr] s réservoir m

re·set [ri'sɛt] v (pret & pp **-set**; ger **-setting**) tr remettre; (a gem) remonter

re·ship [ri'ʃɪp] v (pret & pp **-shipped**; ger **-shipping**) tr réexpédier; (on a ship) rembarquer ‖ intr se rembarquer

reshipment [ri'ʃɪpmənt] s réexpédition f; (on a ship) rembarquement m

reside [rɪ'zaɪd] intr résider, demeurer

residence ['rɛzɪdəns] s résidence f, domicile m

residency ['rɛzɪdənsi] s (med) résidanat m

resident ['rɛzɪdənt] adj & s habitant m

residential [,rɛzɪ'dɛnʃəl] adj résidentiel

residue ['rɛzɪ,d(j)u] s résidu m

resign [rɪ'zaɪn] tr démissionner de, résigner; **to resign oneself to** se résigner à ‖ intr démissionner; se résigner; **to resign from** démissionner de

resignation [,rɛzɪg'neʃən] s (from a job, etc.) démission f; (submissive state) résignation f

resin ['rɛzɪn] s résine f

resist [rɪ'zɪst] tr résister à; **to resist +** ger s'empêcher de + inf ‖ intr résister

resistance [rɪ'zɪstəns] s résistance f

resole [ri'sol] tr ressemeler

resolute ['rɛzə,lut] adj résolu

resolution [rɛzə'luʃən] s résolution f

resolve [rɪ'zɑlv] s résolution f ‖ tr résoudre ‖ intr résoudre, se résoudre

resonance ['rɛzənəns] s résonance f

resort [rɪ'zɔrt] s station f, e.g., **health resort** station climatique; (summer resort) camp m de vacances; (for help or support) recours m; **as a last resort** en dernier ressort ‖ intr—**to resort to** recourir à, avoir recours à

resound [rɪ'zaʊnd] intr résonner

resource [rɪ'sors], ['risors] s ressource f

resourceful [rɪ'sorsfəl] adj débrouillard, de ressource

respect [rɪ'spɛkt] s respect m; **in many respects** à bien des égards; **in this respect** sous ce rapport; **to pay one's respects (to)** présenter ses respects (à); **with respect to** par rapport à ‖ tr respecter

respectable [rɪ'spɛktəbəl] adj respectable; considérable

respectful [rɪ'spɛktfəl] adj respectueux

respectfully [rɪ'spɛktfəli] adv respectueusement; **respectfully yours** (complimentary close) veuillez agréer l'assurance de mes sentiments très respectueux

respective [rɪ'spɛktɪv] adj respectif

res'piratory tract' ['rɛspɪrə,tori] s appareil m respiratoire

respite ['rɛspɪt] s répit m; **without respite** sans relâche

resplendent [rɪ'splɛndənt] adj resplendissant

respond [rɪ'spɑnd] intr répondre

response [rɪ'spɑns] s réponse f

responsibili·ty [rɪ,spɑnsɪ'bɪlɪti] s (pl **-ties**) responsabilité f

responsible [rɪ'spɑnsɪbəl] adj responsable; (person) digne de confiance; (job, position) de confiance; **responsible for** responsable de; **responsible to** responsable envers

responsive [rɪ'spɑnsɪv] adj sensible, réceptif; prompt à sympathiser

rest [rɛst] s (repose) repos m; (lack of motion) pause f; (what remains) reste m; (mus) silence m; **at rest** en repos; (dead) mort; **the rest** les autres; (the remainder) le restant; **the rest of us** nous autres; **to come to rest** s'immobiliser; **to lay to rest** enterrer ‖ tr reposer ‖ intr reposer, se reposer; **to rest on** reposer sur, s'appuyer sur

restaurant ['rɛstərənt] s restaurant m

rest' cure' s cure f de repos

restful ['rɛstfəl] adj reposant; (calm) tranquille, paisible

rest' home' s maison f de repos

rest′ing place′ *s* lieu *m* de repos, gîte *m*; (*of the dead*) dernière demeure *f*

restitution [,rɛstɪ't(j)uʃən] *s* restitution *f*

restive ['rɛstɪv] *adj* rétif

restless ['rɛstlɪs] *adj* agité, inquiet; sans repos

restock [ri'stɑk] *tr* réapprovisionner; (*with fish or game*) repeupler

restoration [,rɛstə'reʃən] *s* restauration *f*

restore [rɪ'stor] *tr* restaurer; (*health*) rétablir; (*to give back*) restituer

restrain [rɪ'stren] *tr* retenir, contenir

restraint [rɪ'strent] *s* restriction *f*, contrainte *f*

restrict [rɪ'strɪkt] *tr* restreindre

restriction [rɪ'strɪkʃən] *s* restriction *f*

rest′ room′ *s* cabinet *m* d'aisance

rest′ stop′ *s* (*turnpike restaurant*) restoroute *m*

result [rɪ'zʌlt] *s* résultat *m*; **as a result of** par suite de ‖ *intr* résulter; **to result in** aboutir à

resume [rɪ'z(j)um] *tr & intr* reprendre

résumé [,rez(j)ʊ'me] *s* résumé *m*

resumption [rɪ'zʌmpʃən] *s* reprise *f*

resurface [ri'sʌrfɪs] *tr* refaire le revêtement de ‖ *intr* (*said of submarine*) faire surface

resurrect [,rezə'rɛkt] *tr & intr* ressusciter

resurrection [,rezə'rɛkʃən] *s* résurrection *f*

resuscitate [rɪ'sʌsɪ,tet] *tr & intr* ressusciter

retail ['ritel] *adj & adv* au détail ‖ *s* vente *f* au détail ‖ *tr* vendre au détail, détailler ‖ *intr* se vendre au détail

retailer ['ritelər] *s* détaillant *m*

retain [rɪ'ten] *tr* retenir; engager

retaliate [rɪ'tælɪ,et] *intr* prendre sa revanche, user de représailles

retaliation [rɪ,tælɪ'eʃən] *s* représailles *fpl*

retard [rɪ'tɑrd] *s* retard *m* ‖ *tr* retarder

retarded *adj* (pathol) retardé, arriéré; (pej) demeuré

retch [rɛtʃ] *tr* vomir ‖ *intr* avoir un haut-le-cœur

retching ['rɛtʃɪŋ] *s* haut-le-cœur *m*

reticence ['rɛtɪsəns] *s* réserve *f*

reticent ['rɛtɪsənt] *adj* réservé

retina ['rɛtɪnə] *s* rétine *f*

retinue ['rɛtɪ,n(j)u] *s* suite *f*, cortège *m*

retire [rɪ'taɪr] *tr* mettre à la retraite ‖ *intr* se retirer

retired *adj* en retraite, retiré

retirement [rɪ'taɪrmənt] *s* retraite *f*

retire′ment pro′gram *s* programme *m* de prévoyance

retire′ment vil′lage *s* cité *f* retraite

retiring [rɪ'taɪrɪŋ] *adj* (*shy*) effacé; (*e.g., congressman*) sortant

retort [rɪ'tɔrt] *s* riposte *f*, réplique *f*; (chem) cornue *f* ‖ *tr & intr* riposter

retouch [rɪ'tʌtʃ] *tr* retoucher

retrace [rɪ'tres] *tr* retracer; (*one's steps*) revenir sur

retract [rɪ'trækt] *tr* rétracter ‖ *intr* se rétracter

retractable [rɪ'træktəbəl] *adj* (aer) escamotable

retraining [ri'trenɪŋ] *s* recyclage *m*

re·tread ['ri,trɛd] *s* pneu *m* rechapé ‖ [ri'trɛd] *v* (*pret & pp* **-treaded**) *tr* rechaper ‖ *v* (*pret* **-trod;** *pp* **-trod** or **-trodden**) *tr & intr* repasser

retreat [rɪ'trit] *s* retraite *f*; **to beat a retreat** battre en retraite ‖ *intr* se retirer

retrench [rɪ'trɛntʃ] *tr* restreindre ‖ *intr* faire des économies

retribution [,rɛtrɪ'bjuʃən] *s* rétribution *f*

retrieval [rɪ'trivəl] *s* récupération *f*; (comp) retrouve *f*

retrieve [rɪ'triv] *tr* retrouver, recouvrer; (*a fortune, a reputation, etc.*) rétablir; (*game*) rapporter ‖ *intr* (*said of hunting dog*) rapporter

retriever [rɪ'trivər] *s* retriever *m*

retroactive [,rɛtro'æktɪv] *adj* rétroactif

retrogress ['rɛtrə,grɛs] *intr* rétrograder

retrorocket ['rɛtro,rɑkɪt] *s* rétrofusée *f*

retrospect ['rɛtrə,spɛkt] *s*—**to consider in retrospect** jeter un coup d'œil rétrospectif à

retrospective [,rɛtrə'spɛktɪv] *adj* rétrospectif

re·try [ri'traɪ] *v* (*pret & pp* **-tried**) *tr* essayer de nouveau; (law) juger à nouveau

return [rɪ'tʌrn] *adj* de retour; **by return mail** par retour du courrier ‖ *s* retour *m*; (*profit*) bénéfice *m*; (*yield*) rendement *m*; (*unwanted merchandise*) rendu *m*; (*of ball*) renvoi *m*; (*of income tax*) déclaration *f*; (*typewriter key*) touche *f* de rappel de chariot, touche retour arrière; **in return** de retour; **in return for** en récompense de; **returns** (*profits*) recettes *fpl*; (*of an election*) résultats *mpl*; **many happy returns of the day!** bon anniversaire! ‖ *tr* rendre; (*to put back*) remettre; (*to bring back*) rapporter; (*e.g., a letter*) retourner ‖ *intr* (*to go back*) retourner; (*to come back*) revenir; (*to get back home*) rentrer; **return to sender** (*on letter*) retour à l'expéditeur; **to return empty-handed** revenir bredouille

return′able bot′tle *s* [rɪ'tərnəbəl] emballage *m* consigné

return′ address′ *s* adresse *f* de l'expéditeur

return′ bout′ *s* revanche *f*

return′ game′ or **match′** *s* match *m* retour

return′ tick′et *s* aller et retour *m*

return′ trip′ *s* voyage *m* de retour

reunification [ri,junɪfɪ'keʃən] *s* réunification *f*

reunion [ri'junjən] *s* réunion *f*

reunite [,riju'naɪt] *tr* réunir ‖ *intr* se réunir

reusable [ri'juzəbəl] *adj* réutilisable

rev [rɛv] *s* (coll) tour *m* ‖ *v* (*pret & pp* **revved;** *ger* **revving**) *tr* (coll) accélérer; (*to race*) (coll) emballer ‖ *intr* (coll) s'accélérer

revalue [ri'vælju] *tr* révaloriser

revamp [ri'væmp] *tr* refaire

reveal [rɪ'vil] *tr* révéler

reveille [rɪ'vɛli] *s* réveil *m*

rev·el ['rɛvəl] *s* fête *f*; **revels** ébats *mpl*, orgie *f* ‖ *v* (*pret & pp* **-eled** or **-elled;** *ger*

-eling or **-elling**) *intr* faire la fête, faire la bombe; **to revel in** se délecter à

revelation [,rɛvəˈleʃən] *s* révélation *f*; **Revelation** (Bib) Apocalypse *f*

revel·ry [ˈrɛvəlri] *s* (*pl* **-ries**) réjouissances *fpl*, orgie *f*

revenge [rɪˈvɛndʒ] *s* vengeance *f*; **to take revenge on s.o. for s.th.** se venger de q.ch. sur qn ‖ *tr* venger

revengeful [rɪˈvɛndʒfəl] *adj* vindicatif

revenue [ˈrɛvə,n(j)u] *s* revenu *m*

rev′enue cut′ter *s* garde-côte *m*, vedette *f*

rev′enue stamp′ *s* timbre *m* fiscal

reverberate [rɪˈvʌrbə,ret] *intr* résonner, réverbérer

revere [rɪˈvɪr] *tr* révérer

reverence [ˈrɛvərəns] *s* révérence *f* ‖ *tr* révérer

reverend [ˈrɛvərənd] *adj* & *s* révérend *m*

reverent [ˈrɛvərənt] *adj* révérenciel

reverie [ˈrɛvəri] *s* rêverie *f*

reversal [rɪˈvʌrsəl] *s* renversement *m*

reverse [rɪˈvʌrs] *adj* contraire ‖ *s* (*opposite*) contraire *m*; (*of medal; of fortune*) revers *m*; (*of page*) verso *m*; (aut) marche *f* arrière ‖ *tr* renverser; (*a sentence*) (law) révoquer ‖ *intr* renverser; (*said of motor*) faire machine arrière; (aut) faire marche arrière

reverse′ lev′er *s* levier *m* de renvoi

reverse′ side′ *s* revers *m*, dos *m*

reversible [rɪˈvʌrsɪbəl] *adj* réversible

revert [rɪˈvʌrt] *intr* revenir, faire retour

review [rɪˈvju] *s* (*inspection*) revue *f*; (*of a book*) compte *m* rendu; (*of a lesson*) révision *f* ‖ *tr* revoir; (*a book*) faire la critique de; (*a lesson*) réviser, revoir; (*past events; troops*) passer en revue ‖ *intr* faire des révisions

revile [rɪˈvaɪl] *tr* injurier, outrager

revise [rɪˈvaɪz] *s* (typ) épreuve *f* de révision ‖ *tr* réviser, revoir

revised′ edi′tion *s* édition *f* revue et corrigée

revision [rɪˈvɪʒən] *s* révision *f*

revisionist [rɪˈvɪʒənɪst] *adj* & *s* révisionniste *mf*

revival [rɪˈvaɪvəl] *s* retour *m* à la vie; (*of learning*) renaissance *f*; (rel) réveil *m*; (theat) reprise *f*

reviv′al meet′ings *spl* (rel) réveils *mpl*

revive [rɪˈvaɪv] *tr* ranimer; (*a victim*) ressusciter; (*a memory*) réveiller; (*a play*) reprendre; (*hopes*) faire renaître; ‖ *intr* reprendre; se ranimer

revoke [rɪˈvok] *tr* révoquer

revolt [rɪˈvolt] *s* révolte *f* ‖ *tr* révolter ‖ *intr* se révolter

revolting [rɪˈvoltɪŋ] *adj* dégoûtant, repoussant; rebelle, révolté

revolution [,rɛvəˈluʃən] *s* révolution *f*

revolutionar·y [,rɛvəˈluʃə,nɛri] *adj* révolutionnaire ‖ *s* (*pl* **-ies**) révolutionnaire *mf*

revolve [rɪˈvalv] *tr* faire tourner; (*in one′s mind*) retourner ‖ *intr* tourner

revolver [rɪˈvalvər] *s* revolver *m*

revolv′ing book′case *s* bibliothèque *f* tournante

revolv′ing door′ *s* porte *f* à tambour, tambour *m* cylindrique

revolv′ing fund′ *s* fonds *m* de roulement

revolv′ing stage′ *s* scène *f* tournante

revue [rɪˈvju] *s* (theat) revue *f*

revulsion [rɪˈvʌlʃən] *s* aversion *f*, répugnance *f*; (*change of feeling*) revirement *m*

reward [rɪˈwɔrd] *s* récompense *f* ‖ *tr* récompenser

rewarding [rɪˈwɔrdɪŋ] *adj* rémunérateur; (*experience*) enrichissant

re·wind [riˈwaɪnd] *v* (*pret & pp* **-wound**) *tr* (*film, tape, etc.*) renverser la marche de; (*a typewriter ribbon*) embobiner de nouveau; (*a clock*) remonter

rewire [riˈwaɪr] *tr* (*a building*) refaire l'installation électrique dans

re·write [riˈraɪt] *v* (*pret* **-wrote;** *pp* **-written**) *tr* récrire

rhapso·dy [ˈræpsədi] *s* (*pl* **-dies**) *s* rhapsodie *f*

rheostat [ˈri·ə,stæt] *s* rhéostat *m*

rhetoric [ˈrɛtərɪk] *s* rhétorique *f*

rhetorical [rɪˈtɔrɪkəl] *adj* rhétorique

rheumatic [ruˈmætɪk] *adj* rhumatismal; (*person*) rhumatisant ‖ *s* rhumatisant *m*

rheumatism [ˈrumə,tɪzəm] *s* rhumatisme *m*

Rhine [raɪn] *s* Rhin *m*

Rhineland [ˈraɪn,lænd] *s* Rhénanie *f*

rhine′stone′ *s* faux diamant *m*

rhinoceros [raɪˈnɑsərəs] *s* rhinocéros *m*

rhubarb [ˈrubarb] *s* rhubarbe *f*

rhyme [raɪm] *s* rime *f*; **in rhyme** en vers ‖ *tr & intr* rimer

rhythm [ˈrɪðəm] *s* rythme *m*

rhythmic(al) [ˈrɪðmɪk(əl)] *adj* rythmique

rib [rɪb] *s* côte *f*; (*of umbrella*) baleine *f*; (*archit, biol, mach*) nervure *f* ‖ *v* (*pret & pp* **ribbed;** *ger* **ribbing**) *tr* garnir de nervures; (slang) taquiner

ribald [ˈrɪbəld] *adj* grivois

ribbon [ˈrɪbən] *s* ruban *m*

rice [raɪs] *s* riz *m*

rice′ field′ *s* rizière *f*

rice′ pud′ding *s* riz *m* au lait

rich [rɪtʃ] *adj* riche; (*voice*) sonore; (*wine*) généreux; (*funny*) (coll) impayable; (coll) ridicule; **to get rich** s'enrichir; **to strike it rich** trouver le bon filon ‖ **riches** *spl* richesses *fpl*

rickets [ˈrɪkɪts] *s* rachitisme *m*

rickety [ˈrɪkɪti] *adj* (*object*) boiteux, délabré; (*person*) chancelant: (*suffering from rickets*) rachitique

rickshaw [ˈrɪk,ʃɔ] *s* pousse-pousse *m*

rid [rɪd] *v* (*pret & pp* **rid;** *ger* **ridding**) *tr* débarrasser; **to get rid of** se débarrasser de, débarquer

riddance [ˈrɪdəns] *s* débarras *m*; **good riddance!** bon débarras!

riddle [ˈrɪdəl] *s* devinette *f*, énigme *f* ‖ *tr*—**to riddle with** cribler de

ride [raɪd] *s* promenade *f*; **to take a ride** faire une promenade (en auto, à cheval, à motocyclette, etc.); **to take s.o. for a**

ride (*to dupe s.o.*) (slang) faire marcher qn; (*to murder s.o.*) (slang) descendre qn ‖ *v* (*pret* **rode** [rod]; *pp* **ridden** [ˈrɪdən]) *tr* monter à; (coll) se moquer de; **ridden** dominé; **to ride out** (*e.g., a storm*) étaler ‖ *intr* monter à cheval (à bicyclette, etc.); **to let ride** (coll) laisser courir

rider [ˈraɪdər] *s* (*on horseback*) cavalier *m*; (*on a bicycle*) cycliste *mf*; (*in a vehicle*) voyageur *m*; (*to a document*) annexe *f*

ridge [rɪdʒ] *s* arête *f*, crête *f*; (*of a fabric*) grain *m*

ridge′pole′ *s* faîtage *m*

ridicule [ˈrɪdɪˌkjul] *s* ridicule *m* ‖ *tr* ridiculiser

ridiculous [rɪˈdɪkjələs] *adj* ridicule

rid′ing acad′emy *s* école *f* d'équitation

rid′ing boot′ *s* botte *f* de cheval, botte à l'écuyère

rid′ing hab′it *s* habit *m* d'amazone

rid′ing mow′er *s* tondeuse *f* auto-portée

rife [raɪf] *adj* répandu; **rife with** abondant en

riffraff [ˈrɪfˌræf] *s* racaille *f*

rifle [ˈraɪfəl] *s* fusil *m*; (*spiral groove*) rayure *f* ‖ *tr* piller, mettre à sac; (*a gun barrel*) rayer

rift [rɪft] *s* fente *f*, crevasse *f*; (*disagreement*) désaccord *m*

rig [rɪg] *s* équipement *m*; (*carriage*) équipage *m*; (naut) gréement *m*; (*getup*) (coll) accoutrement *m* ‖ *v* (*pret & pp* **rigged;** *ger* **rigging**) *tr* équiper; (*to falsify*) truquer; (naut) gréer; **to rig out with** (coll) accoutrer de

rigging [ˈrɪgɪŋ] *s* gréement *m*; (*fraud*) truquage *m*

right [raɪt] *adj* droit; (*change, time, etc.*) exact; (*statement, answer, etc.*) correct; (*conclusion, word, etc.*) juste; (*name*) vrai; (*moment, house, road, etc.*) bon, e.g., **it's not the right road** ce n'est pas la bonne route; **qu'il faut,** e.g., **it's not the right village** (**spot, boy,** etc.) ce n'est pas le village (endroit, garçon, etc.) qu'il faut; **to be all right** aller très bien; **to be right** avoir raison ‖ *s* (*justice*) droit *m*; (*reason*) raison *f*; (*right hand*) droite *f*; (*fist or blow in boxing*) droit; **all rights reserved** tous droits réservés; **by right of** à titre de; **by rights** de plein droit; **by the right!** (mil) guide à droite!; **on the right** à droite; **right and wrong** le bien et le mal; **rights** droits; **to be in the right** avoir raison ‖ *adv* directement; correctement; complètement; bien, en bon état; (*to the right*) à droite; (coll) très, même, e.g., **right here** ici même; **all right!** d'accord!; **right and left** à droite et à gauche; **right away** tout de suite; **to put right** mettre bon ordre à, mettre en état ‖ *tr* faire droit à; (*to correct*) corriger; (*to set upright*) redresser ‖ *intr* se redresser ‖ *interj* parfait!

right′ about′ face′ *s* volte-face *f* ‖ *interj* (mil) demi-tour à droite!

righteous [ˈraɪtʃəs] *adj* juste; vertueux

right′ field′ *s* (baseball) champ *m* droit

rightful [ˈraɪtfəl] *adj* légitime

right′-hand drive′ *s* conduite *f* à droite

right-hander [ˈraɪtˈhændər] *s* droitier *m*

right′-hand man′ *s* bras *m* droit

rightist [ˈraɪtɪst] *adj* & *s* droitier *m*

rightly [ˈraɪtli] *adv* à bon droit, à juste titre; correctement, avec sagesse; **rightly or wrongly** à tort ou à raison

right′ of assem′bly *s* liberté *f* de réunion

right′ of way′ *s* droit *m* de passage; **to yield the right of way** céder le pas

rights′ of man′ *spl* droits *mpl* de l'homme

right′-to-lif′er *s* (coll) nataliste *mf*

right to work [ˈraɪtəˈwʌrk] *s* liberté *f* du travail des ouvriers non syndiqués

right′-wing′ *adj* de droite

right-winger [ˈraɪtˈwɪŋər] *s* (coll) droitier *m*

rigid [ˈrɪdʒɪd] *adj* rigide

rigmarole [ˈrɪgməˌrol] *s* galimatias *m*

rigor [ˈrɪgər] *s* rigueur *f*; (pathol) rigidité *f*

rigorous [ˈrɪgərəs] *adj* rigoureux

rile [raɪl] *tr* (coll) exaspérer

rill [rɪl] *s* ruisselet *m*

rim [rɪm] *s* bord *m*, rebord *m*; (*of spectacles*) monture *f*; (*of wheel*) jante *f*

rind [raɪnd] *s* écorce *f*; (*of cheese*) croûte *f*; (*of bacon*) couenne *f*

ring [rɪŋ] *s* anneau *m*; (*for the finger*) bague *f*, anneau *m*; (*for some sport or exhibition*) piste *f*; (*for boxing*) ring *m*; (*for bullfight*) arène *f*; (*of a group of people*) cercle *m*; (*of evildoers*) gang *m*; (*under the eyes*) cerne *m*; (*sound*) son *m*; (*of bell, clock, telephone, etc.*) sonnerie *f*; (*of a small bell; in the ears; of the glass of glassware*) tintement *m*; (*to summon a person*) coup *m* de sonnette; (*quality*) timbre *m*; (telp) coup de téléphone ‖ *v* (*pret & pp* **ringed**) *tr* cerner ‖ *intr* décrire des cercles ‖ *v* (*pret* **rang** [ræŋ]; *pp*; **rung** [rʌŋ]) *tr* sonner; **to ring up** (telp) donner un coup de téléphone à ‖ *intr* sonner; (*said, e.g., of ears*) tinter; **to ring out** résonner

ring′bolt′ *s* piton *m*

ring′dove′ *s* (orn) ramier *m*

ring′ fin′ger *s* annulaire *m*

ringing [ˈrɪŋɪŋ] *adj* résonnant, retentissant ‖ *s* sonnerie *f*; (*in the ears*) tintement *m*

ring′lead′er *s* meneur *m*

ringlet [ˈrɪŋlɪt] *s* bouclette *f*

ring′mas′ter *s* maître *m* de manège, chef *m* de piste

ring′side′ *s* premier rang *m*

ring′snake′ *s* (*Tropidonotus natrix*) couleuvre *f* à collier

ring′worm′ *s* teigne *f*

rink [rɪŋk] *s* patinoire *f*

rinse [rɪns] *s* rinçage *m* ‖ *tr* rincer

riot [ˈraɪ·ət] *s* émeute *f*; (*of colors*) orgie *f*; **to run riot** se déchaîner; (*said of plants or vines*) pulluler ‖ *intr* émeuter

rioter [ˈraɪ·ətər] *s* émeutier *m*

ri′ot squad′ unité *f* antimanifestation

rip [rɪp] *s* déchirure *f* ‖ *v* (*pret & pp* **ripped;** *ger* **ripping**) *tr* déchirer; **to rip away or off** arracher; **to rip off** (slang) arnaquer, braquer; **to rip open** or **up** découdre; (*a letter, package, etc.*) ouvrir en le déchirant ‖ *intr* se déchirer

rip′ cord′ *s* (*of parachute*) cordelette *f* de déclenchement

ripe [raɪp] *adj* mûr; (*cheese*) fait; (*olive*) noir

ripen [′raɪpən] *tr & intr* mûrir

rip′off *s* (slang) arnaque *f*, vol *m* à main armée

ripple [′rɪpəl] *s* ride *f*; (*sound*) murmure *m* ‖ *tr* rider ‖ *intr* se rider; murmurer

rise [raɪz] *s* hausse *f*, augmentation *f*; (*of ground; of the voice*) élévation *f*; (*of a heavenly body; of the curtain*) lever *m*; (*in one's employment, in one's fortunes*) ascension *f*; (*of water*) montée *f*; (*of a source of water*) naissance *f*; **to get a rise out of** (slang) se payer la tête de; **give rise to** donner naissance à ‖ *v* (*pret* **rose** [roz]; *pp* **risen** [′rɪzən]) *intr* s'élever, monter; (*to get out of bed; to stand up; to ascend in the heavens*) se lever; (*to revolt*) se soulever; (*said, e.g., of a danger*) se montrer; (*said of a fluid*) jaillir; (*in someone's esteem*) grandir; (*said of river*) prendre sa source; **to rise above** dépasser; (*unfortunate events, insults, etc.*) se montrer supérieur à; **to rise to** (*e.g., the occasion*) se montrer à la hauteur de

riser [′raɪzər] *s* (*of staircase*) contremarche *f*; (*of gas or water*) colonne montante; **to be a late riser** faire la grasse matinée; **to be an early riser** être matinal

risk [rɪsk] *s* risque *m* ‖ *tr* risquer

risk·y [′rɪski] *adj* (*comp* **-ier**; *super* **-iest**) dangereux, hasardeux, risqué

risqué [rɪs′ke] *adj* risqué, osé

rite [raɪt] *s* rite *m*; **last rites** derniers sacrements *mpl*

ritual [′rɪtʃʊ·əl] *adj & s* rituel *m*

ri·val [′raɪvəl] *adj & s* rival *m* ‖ *v* (*pret & pp* **-valed** or **-valled**; *ger* **-valing** or **-valling**) *tr* rivaliser avec

rival·ry [′raɪvəlri] *s* (*pl* **-ries**) rivalité *f*

river [′rɪvər] *adj* fluvial ‖ *s* fleuve *m*; (*tributary*) rivière *f*; (*stream*) cours *m* d'eau; **down the river** en aval; **up the river** en amont

riv′er bas′in *s* bassin *m* fluvial

riv′er·bed′ *s* lit *m* de rivière

riv′er·front′ *s* rive *f* d'un fleuve

riv′er·side′ *adj* riverain ‖ *s* rive *f*

rivet [′rɪvɪt] *s* rivet *m* ‖ *tr* river

riv′et gun′ *s* riveuse *f* pneumatique

rivulet [′rɪvjəlɪt] *s* ruisselet *m*

R.N. [′ɑr′ɛn] *s* (letterword) (**registered nurse**) infirmière *f* diplômée

roach [rotʃ] *s* (ent) blatte *f*, cafard *m*; (ichth) gardon *m*

road [rod] *s* route *f*, chemin *m*; (naut) rade *f*; **road under construction** (*public sign*) travaux

road′bed′ *s* assiette *f*; (rr) infrastructure *f*

road′block′ *s* barrage *m*

road′ divid′er *s* séparateur *m*

road′ hog′ *s* écraseur *m*, chauffard *m*

road′house′ *s* guinguette *f* au bord de la route

road′ map′ *s* carte *f* routière

road′-salt′ing truck′ *s* saleuse *f*

road′ ser′vice *s* secours *m* routier

road′side′ *s* bord *m* de la route

road′ sign′ *s* poteau *m* indicateur

road′stead′ *s* rade *f*

road′way′ *s* chaussée *f*

roam [rom] *tr* parcourir; (*the seas*) sillonner ‖ *intr* errer, rôder

roar [ror] *s* (*of a lion*) rugissement *m*; (*of cannon, engine, etc.*) grondement *m*; (*of crowd*) hurlement *m*; (*of laughter*) éclat *m* ‖ *intr* rugir; gronder; hurler

roast [rost] *s* rôti *m*; (*of coffee*) torréfaction *f* ‖ *tr* rôtir; (*coffee*) torréfier; (*chestnuts*) griller ‖ *intr* se rôtir; se torréfier

roast′ beef′ *s* rosbif *m*, rôti *m* de bœuf

roaster [′rostər] *s* (*appliance*) rôtissoire *f*; (*for coffee*) brûloir *m*; (*fowl*) volaille *f* à rôtir

roast′ pork′ *s* porc *m* rôti

rob [rɑb] *v* (*pret & pp* **robbed;** *ger* **robbing**) *tr & intr* voler; **to rob s.o. of s.th.** voler q.ch. à qn

robber [′rɑbər] *s* voleur *m*

robber·y [′rɑbəri] *s* (*pl* **-ies**) vol *m*

robe [rob] *s* (*of a judge*) robe *f*; (*of a professor, judge, etc.*) toge *f*; (*dressing gown*) robe *f* de chambre; (*for lap in a carriage*) couverture *f* ‖ *tr* revêtir d'une robe ‖ *intr* revêtir sa robe

robin [′rɑbɪn] *s* (*Erithacus rubecula*) rouge-gorge *m*; (*Turdus migratorius*) grive *f* migratoire

robot [′robɑt] *s* robot *m*

robotize [′robətaɪz] *tr* robotiser

robust [ro′bʌst] *adj* robuste

rock [rɑk] *s* roche *f*; (*eminence*) roc *m*, rocher *m*; (*sticking out of water*) rocher; (*one that is thrown*) pierre *f*; (slang) diamant *m*; **on the rocks** (coll) fauché, à sec; (*said of liquor*) (coll) sur glace ‖ *tr* balancer; (*to rock to sleep*) bercer ‖ *intr* se balancer; se bercer

rock′-bot′tom *adj* (le) plus bas ‖ *s* (le) fin fond *m*

rock′ can′dy *s* candi *m*

rock′ crys′tal *s* cristal *m* de roche

rocker [′rɑkər] *s* bascule *f*; (*chair*) chaise *f* à bascule; **to go off one's rocker** (slang) perdre la boussole

rock′er arm′ *s* culbuteur *m*

rocket [′rɑkɪt] *s* fusée *f*; (arti, bot) roquette *f* ‖ *intr* monter en chandelle; (*said of prices*) monter en flèche

rock′et bomb′ *s* bombe *f* volante, fusée *f*

rock′et fu′el *s* kérosène *m* aviation

rock′et launch′er *s* lance-fuses *m*; (arti) lance-roquettes *m*

rock′et ship′ *s* fusée *f* interplanétaire, fusée interstellaire

rock′ gar′den *s* jardin *m* de rocaille

rock′ing chair′ *s* fauteuil *m* à bascule

rock′ing horse′ *s* cheval *m* à bascule

Rock′ of Gibral′tar [dʒɪ‵brɔltər] *s* rocher *m* de Gibraltar

rock′ salt′ *s* sel *m* gemme

rock′ sing′er *s* chanteur *m* de rock

rock′ wool′ *s* laine *f* minérale, laine de verre

rock·y [‵rɑki] *adj* (*comp* **-ier**; *super* **-iest**) rocheux, rocailleux

Rock′y Moun′tains *spl* Montagnes *fpl* Rocheuses

rod [rɑd] *s* (*wooden stick*) baguette *f*; (*for punishment*) verge *f*; (*of the retina; elongated microorganism*) bâtonnet *m*; (*of authority*) main *f*; (*of curtain*) tringle *f*; (*for fishing*) canne *f*; (Bib) lignée *f*, race *f*; (mach) bielle *f*; (surv) jalon *m*; (*revolver*) (slang) pétard *m*, flingot *m*, flingue *m*; **rod and gun** la chasse et la pêche

rodent [‵rodənt] *adj & s* rongeur *m*

roe [ro] *s* (*deer*) chevreuil *m*; (*of fish*) œufs *mpl*

roger [‵rɑdʒər] *interj* O.K.!; (rad) message reçu!

rogue [rog] *s* coquin *m*

rogues′′ gal′lery *s* fichier *m* de la police de portraits de criminels

roguish [‵rogɪʃ] *adj* espiègle, coquin

roister [‵rɔɪstər] *intr* faire du tapage

role or **rôle** [rol] *s* rôle *m*

roll [rol] *s* (*of paper, cloth, netting, wire, hair, etc.*) rouleau *m*; (*of thunder, drums, etc.*) roulement *m*; (*roll call*) appel *m*; (*list*) rôle *m*; (*of film*) rouleau; (*of paper money*) liasse *f*; (*of dice*) coup *m*; (*of a boat*) roulis *m*; (*of fat*) bourrelet *m*; (culin) petit pain *m*; **to call the roll** faire l'appel ‖ *tr* rouler; (*to rob*) (slang) entôler; **to roll over** retourner; **to roll up** enrouler ‖ *intr* rouler; (*said of thunder*) gronder; (*to sway*) se balancer; (*to overturn*) faire panache; (*said of ship*) rouler; **to roll over** se retourner; **to roll up** se rouler

roll′back′ *s* repoussement *m*; (com) baisse *f* de prix

roll′ call′ *s* appel *m*; (*vote*) appel nominal

roller [‵rolər] *s* rouleau *m*; (*of a skate*) roulette *f*; (*wave*) lame *f* de houle

roll′er bear′ing *s* coussinet *m* à rouleaux

roll′er coast′er *s* montagnes *fpl* russes

roll′er skate′ *s* patin *m* à roulettes

roll′er-skate′ *intr* patiner sur des roulettes

roll′er-skating rink′ *s* skating *m*

roll′er tow′el *s* essuie-mains *m* à rouleau, serviette *f* sans fin

roll′ing mill′ *s* usine *f* de laminage; (*set of rollers*) laminoir *m*

roll′ing pin′ *s* rouleau *m*

roll′ing stock′ *s* (rr) matériel *m* roulant

roll′-top desk′ *s* bureau *m* à cylindre

roly-poly [‵roli‵poli] *adj* rondelet

ROM [‵ɑr‵o‵ɛm] *s* (letterword) (**read-only memory**) mémoire *f* morte

romaine [ro‵men] *s* romaine *f*

roman [‵romən] *adj & s* (typ) romain *m*; **Roman** Romain *m*

Ro′man can′dle *s* chandelle *f* romaine

Ro′man Cath′olic *adj & s* catholique *mf*

Romance [‵romæns], [ro‵mæns] *adj* roman ‖ (*l.c.*) [ro‵mæns], [‵romæns] *s* (*chivalric narrative*) roman *m* de chevalerie; (*love story*) roman à l'eau de rose; (*made-up story*) conte *m* bleu; (*love affair*) idylle *f*; (mus) romance *f* ‖ (*l.c.*) [ro‵mæns] *intr* exagérer, broder

Romanesque [‚romən‵ɛsk] *adj & s* roman *m*

Ro′man nose′ *s* nez *m* aguilin

Ro′man nu′meral *s* chiffre *m* romain

romantic [ro‵mæntɪk] *adj* (*genre; literature; scenery*) romantique; (*imagination*) romanesque

romanticism [ro‵mæntɪ,sɪzəm] *s* romantisme *m*

romanticist [ro‵mæntɪsɪst] *s* romantique *mf*

romp [rɑmp] *intr* s'ébattre

rompers [‵rɑmpərz] *spl* barboteuse *f*

roof [ruf] *s* toit *m*; (*of the mouth*) palais *m*; **to raise the roof** (slang) faire un boucan de tous les diables

roofer [‵rufər] *s* couvreur *m*

roof′ gar′den *s* terrasse *f* avec jardin, pergola *f*

rook [ruk] *s* (chess) tour *f*; (orn) freux *m*, corneille *f* ‖ *tr* (coll) rouler; **to rook s.o. out of s.th.** (coll) filouter q.ch. à qn

rookie [‵ruki] *s* (slang) bleu *m*

room [rum], [rum] *s* pièce *f*; (*especially bedroom*) chambre *f*; (*where people congregate*) salle *f*; (*space*) place *f*; **rooms** appartement *m*; **to make room for** faire place à ‖ *intr* vivre en garni; **to room with** partager une chambre avec

room′ and board′ *s* le vivre et le couvert, pension *f*; **for room and board** au pair

room′ clerk′ *s* employé *m* à la réception

roomer [‵rumər] *s* locataire *mf*

roomette [ru‵mɛt] *s* chambrette *f* de sleeping

room′ing house′ *s* maison *f* de rapport, immeuble *m* de rapport

room′mate′ *s* camarade *mf* de chambre

room·y [‵rumi] *adj* (*comp* **-ier**; *super* **-iest**) spacieux, ample; (*clothes*) large, ample

roost [rust] *s* perchoir *m*; (coll) logis *m*, demeure *f*; **to rule the roost** (coll) faire la loi ‖ *intr* se percher, percher

rooster [‵rustər] *s* coq *m*

root [rut] *s* racine *f*; **to get to the root of** approfondir; **to take root** prendre racine ‖ *tr* fouiller; **to root out** déraciner ‖ *intr* s'enraciner; **to root around in** fouiller dans; **to root for** (coll) applaudir, encourager

rooter [‵rutər] *s* (coll) fanatique *mf*, fana *mf*

rope [rop] *s* corde *f*; (*lasso*) corde à nœud coulant; **to jump rope** sauter à la corde; **to know the ropes** (slang) connaître les ficelles ‖ *tr* corder; (*cattle*) prendre au lasso; **to rope in** (slang) entraîner

rope′ lad′der *s* échelle *f* de corde

rope′ walk′er *s* funambule *mf*, danseur *m* de corde

rosa·ry [‵rozəri] *s* (*pl* **-ries**) rosaire *m*

rose [roz] *adj* rose ‖ *s* (*color*) rose *m*; (bot) rose *f*

rose′ bee′tle s cétoine f dorée

rose′bud′ s bouton m de rose

rose′bush′ s rosier m

rose′-col′ored adj rosé, couleur de rose; **to see everything through rose-colored glasses** voir tout en rose

rose′ gar′den s roseraie f

rosemar·y [ˈrozˌmɛri] s (pl -ies) romarin m

rose′ of Shar′on [ˈʃɛrən] s rose f de Saron

rosette [roˈzɛt] s rosette f; (archit, elec) rosace f

rose′ win′dow s rosace f, rose f

rose′wood′ s bois m de rose, palissandre m

rosin [ˈrazɪn] s colophane f

roster [ˈrɑstər] s liste f, appel m; (educ) heures fpl de classe; (mil) tableau m de service; (naut) ôle m

rostrum [ˈrɑstrəm] s tribune f

ros·y [ˈrozi] adj (comp -ier; super -iest) rosé; (complexion) vermeil; (fig) riant

rot [rɑt] s pourriture f; (slang) sottise f ‖ v (pret & pp rotted; ger rotting) tr & intr pourrir

ro′tary press′ [ˈrotəri] s rotative f

rotate [ˈrotet] tr & intr tourner; (agr) alterner

rotation [roˈteʃən] s rotation f; **in rotation** à tour de rôle

rote [rot] s routine f; **by rote** par cœur, machinalement

rot′gut′ s (slang) tord-boyaux m

rotisserie [roˈtɪsəri] s rôtissoire f

rotogravure [ˌrotəɡrəˈvjur] s rotogravure f

rotten [ˈrɑtən] adj pourri

rotund [roˈtʌnd] adj rond, arrondi; (e.g., language) ampoulé

rotunda [roˈtʌndə] s rotonde f

rouge [ruʒ] s fard m, rouge m ‖ tr farder ‖ intr se farder, se mettre du rouge

rough [rʌf] adj (sound, voice, speech) rude; (uneven) inégal; (coarse) grossier; (unfinished) brut; (road) raboteux; (game) brutal; (sea) agité; (guess) approximatif ‖ tr—**to rough it** faire du camping, coucher sur la dure; **to rough up** malmener

roughage [ˈrʌfɪdʒ] s fibres fpl alimentaires

rough′ draft′ s ébauche f, avant-projet m, brouillon m

rough′house′ s boucan m, chahut m ‖ intr faire du boucan, chahuter

rough′ ide′a s aperçu m

roughly [ˈrʌfli] adv grossièrement; brutalement; approximativement

rough′neck′ s (coll) canaille f

roulette [ruˈlɛt] s roulette f

round [raund] adj rond; (rounded) arrondi, rond; (e.g., shoulders) voûté; **three (four, etc.) feet round** trois (quatre, etc.) pieds de tour ‖ s rond m; (inspection) ronde f; (of golf; of drinks; of postman, doctor, etc.) tournée f; (of applause) salve f; (of ammunition) cartouche f; (of veal) noix f; (in a game) manche f; (boxing) round m; **to go the rounds** faire le tour ‖ adv à la ronde; **round about** aux alentours; **the year round** pendant toute l'année; **to pass round** faire circuler, passer à la ronde ‖ prep autour de ‖ tr (to make round) arrondir; (e.g., a corner) tourner, prendre; (a cape) doubler; **to round off** or **out** arrondir; (to finish) achever; **to round up** rassembler; (suspects) cueillir ‖ intr s'arrondir

roundabout [ˈraundəˌbaut] adj indirect ‖ s détour m; (carrousel) (Brit) manège m; (traffic circle) (Brit) rond-point m

rounder [ˈraundər] s (coll) fêtard m

round′-headed screw′ s vis f à tête ronde

round′house′ s (rr) rotonde f

round′-shoul′dered adj voûté

round′ steak′ s gîte m à la noix

round′ ta′ble s table f ronde; **Round Table** Table ronde

round′-trip′ tick′et s billet m d'aller et retour

round′up′ s (of cattle) rassemblement m; (of suspects) rafle f

rouse [rauz] tr réveiller ‖ intr se réveiller

rout [raut] s déroute f ‖ tr mettre en déroute

route [rut] s route f; (of, e.g., bus) ligne f, parcours m ‖ tr acheminer

routine [ruˈtin] adj routinier, systématique ‖ s routine f

routine′ examina′tion s examen m de routine

rove [rov] intr errer, vagabonder

rover [ˈrovər] s vagabond m

row [rau] s (coll) altercation f, prise f de bec; **to raise a row** (coll) faire du boucan ‖ [ro] s rang m; (of, e.g., houses) rangée f; (boat ride) promenade f en barque; **in a row** à la file; (without interruption) de suite; **in rows** par rangs ‖ intr ramer

rowboat [ˈroˌbot] s bateau m à rames, canot m

row·dy [ˈraudi] adj (comp -dier; super -diest) tapageur ‖ s (pl -dies) tapageur m

rower [ˈroˌər] s rameur m

rowing [ˈroˌɪŋ] s nage f, canotage m, sport m de l'aviron

royal [ˈrɔɪəl] adj royal

royalist [ˈrɔɪəlɪst] adj & s royaliste mf

royal·ty [ˈrɔɪəlti] s (pl -ties) royauté f; (remuneration) droit m d'auteur; redevance f, droit d'inventeur

r.p.m. [ˈɑrˈpiˈɛm] spl (letterword) (**revolutions per minute**) tr/mn, tours mpl à la minute

rub [rʌb] s frottement m; **there's the rub** (coll) voilà le hic ‖ v (pret & pp rubbed; ger rubbing) tr frotter; **to rub elbows with** coudoyer; **to rub out** effacer; (slang) descendre, liquider ‖ intr se frotter; (said, e.g., of moving parts) frotter; **to rub off** s'enlever, disparaître

rubber [ˈrʌbər] s caoutchouc m; (eraser) gomme f à effacer; (in bridge) robre m; (condom) préservatif m; **rubbers** (overshoes) caoutchoucs

rub′ber ball′ s balle f élastique

rub′ber band′ s élastique m

rubberize [ˈrʌbəˌraɪz] tr caoutchouter

rub′ber·neck′ s (coll) badaud m ‖ intr (coll) badauder

rub'ber plant' s figuier m élastique, caout-choutier m; (*tree*) arbre m à caoutchouc, hévéa m

rub'ber stamp' s tampon m; (coll) béni-oui-oui m

rub'ber-stamp' tr apposer le tampon sur; (*with a person's signature*) estampiller; (coll) approuver à tort et à travers

rub'bing al'cohol s alcool m pour les frictions

rubbish ['rʌbɪʃ] s détritus m, rebut m; (coll) imbécillités fpl

rubble ['rʌbəl] s (*broken stone*) décombres mpl; (*used in masonry*) moellons mpl

rub'down' s friction f

rubric ['rubrɪk] s rubrique f

ru·by ['rubi] adj (*lips*) vermeil ‖ s (pl -bies) rubis m

rucksack ['rʌk,sæk] s sac-à-dos m

rudder ['rʌdər] s gouvernail m

rud·dy ['rʌdi] adj (comp **-dier;** super **-diest**) rougeaud, coloré

rude [rud] adj (*rough, rugged*) rude; (*discourteous*) impoli, grossier

rudeness ['rudnɪs] s rudesse f; impolitesse f

rudiment ['rudɪmənt] s rudiment m

rue [ru] tr regretter amèrement

rueful ['rufəl] adj lamentable; triste

ruffian ['rʌfɪən] s brute f

ruffle ['rʌfəl] s (*in water*) rides fpl; (*of drum*) roulement m; (sewing) jabot m plissé ‖ tr (*to crease; to vex*) froisser; (*the water*) rider; (*its feathers*) hérisser; (*one's hair*) ébouriffer

rug [rʌg] s tapis m, carpette f

rugged ['rʌgɪd] adj (*manners, person, features*) rude, sévère; (*ground, landscape*) accidenté; (*coast*) déchiqueté; (*road, country, etc.*) raboteux; (*husky*) robuste; (*e.g., machine*) résistant à toute épreuve

ruin ['ru·ɪn] s ruine f; **to fall into ruins** se ruiner ‖ tr ruiner

rule [rul] s règle f; (*regulation*) règlement m; (*custom*) coutume f, habitude f; (*authority*) autorité f; (*reign*) règne m; (law) décision f; **as a rule** en général; **by rule of thumb** empiriquement, à vue de nez ‖ tr gouverner; (*to lead*) diriger, guider; (*one's passions*) contenir; (*with lines*) régler; (law) décider; **to rule out** écarter, éliminer ‖ intr gouverner; (*to be the rule*) prévaloir; **to rule over** régner sur

ruler ['rulər] s dirigeant m; souverain m; (*for ruling lines*) règle f

ruling ['rulɪŋ] adj actuel; (*e.g., classes*) dirigeant; (*quality, trait, etc.*) dominant ‖ s (*of paper*) réglage m; (law) décision f

rum [rʌm] s rhum m

Rumanian [ru'menɪ·ən] adj roumain ‖ s (*language*) roumain m; (*person*) Roumain m

rumble ['rʌmbəl] s (*of thunder*) grondement m; (*of a cart*) roulement m; (*of intestines*) gargouillement m; (*gang war*) (slang) baroud m, rixe f entre gangs ‖ intr gronder, rouler

ruminate ['rumɪ,net] tr & intr ruminer

rummage ['rʌmɪdʒ] intr fouiller

rum'mage sale' s vente f d'objets usagés

rumor ['rumər] s rumeur f ‖ tr—**it is rumored that** le bruit court que

rump [rʌmp] s (*of animal*) croupe f; (*of bird*) croupion m; (*cut of meat*) culotte f; (*buttocks*) postérieur m

rumple ['rʌmpəl] s faux pli m ‖ tr (*paper, cloth, etc.*) froisser, chiffonner; (*one's hair*) ébouriffer

rump' steak' s romsteck m

rumpus ['rʌmpəs] s (coll) chahut m; (*argument*) (coll) prise f de bec; **to raise a rumpus** (coll) déclencher un chahut; faire une scène violente

rum'pus room' s salle f de jeux

run [rʌn] s (*act of running*) course f; (*e.g., of good or bad luck*) suite f; (*on a bank by depositors*) descente f; (*of salmon*) remonte f; (*of, e.g., a bus*) parcours m; (*in a stocking*) échelle f, démaillage m; (*cards*) séquence f; (*mus*) roulade f; **in the long run** à la longue; **on the run** à la débandade, en fuite; **run of bad luck** série f noire; **the general run** la généralité; **to give free run to** donner libre carrière à; **to give s.o. a run for his money** en donner à qn pour son argent; **to have a long run** (theat) tenir longtemps l'affiche; **to have the run of** avoir libre accès à ou dans; **to keep s.o. on the run** ne laisser aucun répit à qn; **to make a run in** (*a stocking*) démailler ‖ v (pret **ran** [ræn]; pp **run**; ger **running**) tr (*the streets; a race; a risk*) courir; (*a motor, machine, etc.*) faire marcher; (*an organization, project, etc.*) diriger; (*a business, factory, etc.*) exploiter; (*a blockade*) forcer; (*a line*) tracer; (*turf*) faire courir; **to run aground** échouer; **to run down** (*to knock down*) renverser; (*to find*) dépister; (*game*) mettre aux abois; (*to disparage*) (coll) dénigrer; **to run in** (*a motor*) roder; **to run off** (*a liquid*) faire écouler; (*copies, pages, etc.*) tirer; **to run through** (*e.g., with a sword*) transpercer; **to run up** (*a flag*) hisser; (*a debt*) (coll) laisser accumuler ‖ intr courir; (*said, e.g., of water; said of fountain pen, nose, etc.*) couler; (*said of stockings*) se démailler; (*said of salmon*) faire la montaison; (*said of colors*) s'étaler, se déteindre; (*said of sore*) suppurer; (*said of rumor, news, etc.*) circuler, courir; (*for office*) se présenter; (mach) fonctionner, marcher; (theat) rester à l'affiche, se jouer; **run along!** filez!; **to run across** (*to meet by chance*) rencontrer par hasard; **to run along** border, longer; (*to go*) s'en aller; **to run at** se jeter sur; **to run away** se sauver, s'enfuir; (*said of horse*) s'emballer, s'emporter; **to run away with** enlever; **to run down** (*e.g., a hill*) descendre en courant; (*said of spring*) se détendre; (*said of watch*) s'arrêter (faute d'être remonté); (*said of storage battery*) se décharger, s'épuiser; **to run for** (*an office*) poser sa candidature pour; **to run in the family** tenir de famille; **to run into** heurter; (*to meet*) (coll) rencontrer; **to run off** se sauver, s'enfuir; (*said of liquid*) s'écouler; **to run out** (*said of passport, lease, etc.*) expirer; **to run out of** être à court de; **to run over** (*said of a liquid*) déborder; (*an article, a text, etc.*) parcourir; (*s.th. in the road*) passer sur; (*e.g., a pedestrian*) écraser; **to run through** (*an article, text, etc.*) parcourir; (*a fortune*) gaspiller

run′away′ *adj* fugitif; (*horse*) emballé ‖ *s* fugitif *m*; cheval *m* emballé

run′down′ *s* compte rundu *m*, récit *m*

run′-down′ *adj* délabré; (*person; battery*) épuisé, à plat; (*clock spring*) détendu

rung [rʌŋ] *s* (*of ladder or chair*) barreau *m*; (*of wheel*) rayon *m*

runner [′rʌnər] *s* (*person*) coureur *m*; (*messenger*) courrier *m*; (*of ice skate or sleigh*) patin *m*; (*narrow rug*) rampe *f* d'escalier; (*strip of cloth for table top*) chemin *m* de table; (*in stockings*) démaillage *m*; (bot) coulant *m*

run′ner-up′ *s* (*pl* **runners-up**) bon second *m*, premier accessit *m*

running [′rʌnɪŋ] *adj* (*person; water; expenses*) courant; (*stream; knot; style*) coulant; (*sore*) suppurant; (*e.g., motor*) en marche ‖ *s* (*of man or animal*) course *f*; (*of water*) écoulement *m*; (*of machine*) fonctionnement *m*, marche *f*; (*of business*) direction *f*

run′ning board′ *s* marchepied *m*

run′ning com′mentar′y *s* (*pl* **-ies**) reportage *m* en direct (rad, telv)

run′ning head′ *s* titre *m* courant

run′ning mate′ *s* (pol) coéquipier *m*, co-listier *m*

run′ning start′ *s* départ *m* lancé

run′off′ elec′tion *s* scrutin *m* de ballottage

run′proof′ *adj* indémaillable

runt [rʌnt] *s* avorton *m*

run′way′ *s* piste *f*, rampe *f*

rupture [′rʌptʃər] *s* rupture *f*; (pathol) hernie *f* ‖ *tr* rompre; (*a ligament, blood vessel, etc.*) se rompre ‖ *intr* se rompre

rural [′rʊrəl] *adj* rural

ru′ral free′ deliv′ery *s* distribution *f* gratuite par le facteur rural

ru′ral police′man *s* garde *m* champêtre

ruse [ruz] *s* ruse *f*

rush [rʌʃ] *adj* urgent ‖ *s* (*rapid movement*) course *f* précipitée, ruée *f*; (*haste*) hâte *f*, précipitation *f*; (bot) jonc *m*; (*formula on envelope or letterhead*) urgent; **rushes** (mov) épreuves *fpl*; **to be in a rush to** être pressé de ‖ *tr* pousser vivement; (*e.g., to the hospital*) transporter d'urgence; (*a piece of work*) exécuter d'urgence; (*e.g., a girl*) (slang) insister auprès de; **to rush through** (*e.g., a law*) faire passer à la hâte ‖ *intr* se précipiter, se ruer; **to rush about** courir çà et là; **to rush headlong** foncer tête baissée; **to rush into** (*e.g., a room*) faire irruption dans; (*an affair*) se jeter dans; **to rush out** sortir précipitamment; **to rush through** (*one's lessons, prayers, etc.*) expédier; (*e.g., a town*) traverser à toute vitesse; (*a tourist attraction*) visiter au pas de course; (*a book*) lire à la hâte; **to rush to** s'empresser de; **to rush to one's face** (*said of blood*) monter au visage à qn; **to rush up to** accourir à *or* vers

rush′-bot′tomed chair′ *s* chaise *f* à fond de paille

rush′ hours′ *spl* heures *fpl* d'affluence or de pointe

rush′ or′der *s* commande *f* urgente

russet [′rʌsɪt] *adj* roussâtre, roux

Russia [′rʌʃə] *s* Russie *f*; la Russie

Russian [′rʌʃən] *adj* russe ‖ *s* (*language*) russe *m*; (*person*) Russe *mf*

rust [rʌst] *s* rouille *f* ‖ *tr* rouiller ‖ *intr* se rouiller

rustic [′rʌstɪk] *adj* rustique; simple, net; (pej) rustaud ‖ *s* paysan *m*, villageois *m*

rustle [′rʌsəl] *s* (*of leaves*) bruissement *m*; (*of a dress*) froufrou *m*, bruissement; (*of papers*) froissement *m* ‖ *tr* faire bruire; (*cattle*) (coll) voler ‖ *intr* bruire; (*said, e.g., of a dress*) froufrouter; **to rustle around** (coll) se démener

rust′proof′ *adj* inoxydable

rust·y [′rʌsti] *adj* (*comp* **-ier**; *super* **-iest**) rouillé

rut [rʌt] *s* ornière *f*; (zool) rut *m*

ruthless [′ruθlɪs] *adj* impitoyable

rye [raɪ] *s* seigle *m*; whisky *m* de seigle

S

S, s [ɛs] *s* XIVᵉ lettre de l'alphabet

Sabbath [′sæbəθ] *s* sabbat *m;* dimanche *m*

sabbat′ical year′ [sə′bætɪkəl] *s* année *f* de congé

saber [′sebər] *s* sabre *m* ‖ *tr* sabrer

sable [′sebəl] *adj* noir ‖ *s* (*animal, fur*) zibeline *f*; noir *m*; **sables** vêtements *mpl* de deuil

sabotage [′sæbə,taʒ] *s* sabotage *m* ‖ *tr* & *intr* saboter

saccharin [′sækərɪn] *s* saccharine *f*

sachet [sæ′ʃe] *s* sachet *m* (à parfums)

sack [sæk] *s* sac *m*; (*wine*) xérès *m* ‖ *tr* mettre en sac; (mil) saccager; (coll) saquer, congédier

sack′cloth′ *s* grosse toile *f* d'emballage,

serpillière *f*; (*worn for penitence*) cilice *m*; **in sackcloth and ashes** sous le sac et la cendre

sacrament ['sækrəmənt] *s* sacrement *m*

sacramental [,sækrə'mɛntəl] *adj* sacramentel

sacred ['sekrəd] *adj* sacré

sa′cred cow′ *s* (fig) monstre *m* sacré

sacrifice ['sækrɪ,faɪs] *s* sacrifice *m*; **at a sacrifice** à perte ‖ *tr & intr* sacrifier

sacrilege ['sækrəlɪdʒ] *s* sacrilège *m*

sacrilegious [,sækrɪ'lɪdʒəs] *adj* sacrilège

sacristan ['sækrɪstən] *s* sacristain *m*

sad [sæd] *adj* (*comp* **sadder;** *super* **saddest**) triste

sadden ['sædən] *tr* attrister ‖ *intr* s'attrister

saddle ['sædəl] *s* selle *f* ‖ *tr* seller; **to saddle with** charger de, encombrer de

sad′dle·bag′ *s* sacoche *f* (de selle)

saddlebow ['sædəl,bo] *s* arçon *m* de devant

saddler ['sædlər] *s* sellier *m*

sad′dle·tree′ *s* arçon *m*

sadist ['sedɪst] *s* sadique *mf*

sadistic [sæ'dɪstɪk] *adj* sadique

sadness ['sædnɪs] *s* tristesse *f*

sad′ sack′ *s* (slang) bidasse *mf*

safe [sef] *adj* (*from danger*) sûr; (*unhurt*) sauf; (*margin*) certain; **safe and sound** sain et sauf; **safe from** à l'abri de ‖ *s* coffre-fort *m*, caisse *f*

safe′-con′duct *s* sauf-conduit *m*

safe′-depos′it box′ *s* coffre *m* à la banque; coffret de sûreté (Canad)

safe′guard′ *s* sauvegarde *f* ‖ *tr* sauvegarder

safe′keep′ing *s* bonne garde *f*

safe·ty ['sefti] *adj* de sûreté ‖ *s* (*pl* **-ties**) (*state of being safe*) sécurité *f*, sûreté *f*; (*avoidance of danger*) salut *m*

safe′ty belt′ *s* ceinture *f* de sécurité

safe′ty fac′tor *s* (aer) coefficient *m* de sécurité

safe′ty match′ *s* allumette *f* de sûreté

safe′ty pin′ *s* épingle *f* de sûreté

saf′ty ra′zor *s* rasoir *m* de sûreté

safe′ty valve′ *s* soupape *f* de sûreté

safe′ty zone′ *s* zone *f* protégée pour piétons

saffron ['sæfrən] *adj* safrane ‖ *s* safran *m*

sag [sæg] *s* affaissement *m* ‖ *v* (*pret & pp* **sagged;** *ger* **sagging**) *intr* s'affaisser

sagacious [sə'geʃəs] *adj* sagace

sage [sedʒ] *adj* sage ‖ *s* sage *mf*; (*plant*) sauge *f*

sage′brush′ *s* armoise *f*

Sagittarius [,sædʒɪ'tɛrɪ·əs] *s* (astr, astrol) le Sagittaire

sail [sel] *s* voile *f*; (*sails*) voilure *f*; (*of windmill*) aile *f*; **full sail** toutes voiles dehors; **to set sail** mettre les voiles; **to take a sail** faire une promenade à la voile; **to take in sail** baisser pavillon ‖ *tr* (*a ship*) gouverner, commander; (*to travel over*) naviguer sur ‖ *intr* naviguer; **to sail along the coast** côtoyer; **to sail into** (coll) assaillir

sail′boat′ *s* bateau *m* à voiles

sail′cloth′ *s* toile *f* à voile

sailing ['selɪŋ] *s* navigation *f*; (*working of ship*) manœuvre *f*; (*of pleasure craft*) voile *f*

sail′ing ves′sel *s* voilier *m*

sail′mak′er *s* voilier *m*

sailor ['selər] *s* marin *m*; (*simple crewman*) matelot *m*

saint [sent] *adj & s* saint *m*

saint′hood *s* sainteté *f*

saintliness ['sentlɪnɪs] *s* sainteté *f*

Saint′ Vi′tus's dance′ ['vaɪtəsəz] *s* (pathol) danse *f* de Saint-Guy

sake [sek] *s*—**for the sake of** pour l'amour de, dans l'intérêt de; **for your sake** pour vous

salable ['seləbəl] *adj* vendable

salacious [sə'leʃəs] *adj* lubrique

salad ['sæləd] *s* salade *f*

sal′ad bar′ *s* buffet *m* de salades, table *f* à salade

sal′ad bowl′ *s* saladier *m*

sala·ry ['sæləri] *s* (*pl* **-ries**) salaire *m*

sale [sel] *s* vente *f*; **for sale** en vente; **on sale** en solde, en réclame

sales′ clerk′ *s* vendeur *m*

sales′la′dy *s* (*pl* **-dies**) vendeuse *f*, demoiselle *f* de magasin

sales′man *s* (*pl* **-men**) vendeur *m*, commis *m*

sales′man·ship′ *s* l'art *m* de vendre

sales′ promo′tion *s* stimulation *f* de la vente

sales′room′ *s* salle *f* de vente

sales′ talk′ *s* raisonnements *mpl* destinés à convaincre le client

sales′ tax′ *s* taxe *f* sur les ventes, impôt *m* indirect

saliva [sə'laɪvə] *s* salive *f*

sallow ['sælo] *adj* olivâtre

sal·ly ['sæli] *s* (*pl* **-lies**) saillie *f*; (mil) sortie *f* ‖ *v* (*pret & pp* **-lied**) *intr* faire une sortie

salmon ['sæmən] *adj & s* saumon *m*

salm′on trout′ *s* truite *f* saumonée

saloon [sə'lun] *s* cabaret *m*, estaminet *m*, bistrot *m*; (naut) salon *m*

salt [sɔlt] *s* sel *m* ‖ *tr* saler; **to salt away** (coll) économiser, mettre de côté

salt′cel′lar *s* salière *f*

salt′ lick′ *s* terrain *m* salifère

salt′pe′ter *s* (*potassium nitrate*) salpêtre *m*; (*sodium nitrate*) nitrate *m* du Chili

salt′ pork′ *s* salé *m*

salt′sha′ker *s* salière *f*

salt·y ['sɔlti] *adj* (*comp* **-ier;** *super* **-iest**) salé

salute [sə'lut] *s* salut *m* ‖ *tr* saluer

salvage ['sælvɪdʒ] *s* sauvetage *m*; biens *mpl* sauvés *f* ‖ *tr* sauver; récupérer

salvation [sæl'veʃən] *s* salut *m*

Salva′tion Ar′my *s* Armée *f* du Salut

salve [sæv] *s* onguent *m*, pommade *f*; (fig) baume *m* ‖ *tr* appliquer un onguent sur; (fig) apaiser

sal·vo ['sælvo] *s* (*pl* **-vos** or **-voes**) salve *f*

Samaritan [sə'mærɪtən] *adj* samaritain ‖ *s* Samaritain *m*

same [sem] *adj & pron indef* même (before noun); **at the same time** en même temps, au même moment, à la fois; **it's all the**

same to me ça m'est égal; **just the same, all the same** malgré tout, quand même; **the same . . . as** le même . . . que

sameness ['semnɪs] s monotonie f

sample ['sæmpəl] s échantillon m ‖ tr échantillonner; essayer

sam'ple cop'y s (pl -ies) numéro m spécimen, spécimen m

sam'ple home' s villa f modèle, maison f exposition, pavillon m témoin

sancti·fy ['sæŋktɪ,faɪ] v (pret & pp -fied) tr sanctifier

sanctimonious [,sæŋktɪ'monɪ·əs] adj papelard, bigot

sanction ['sæŋkʃən] s sanction f ‖ tr sanctionner

sanctuar·y ['sæŋktʃu,ɛri] s (pl -ies) sanctuaire m; refuge m, asile m

sand [sænd] s sable m ‖ tr sablonner

sandal ['sændəl] s sandale f

san'dal·wood' s santal m

sand'bag' s sac m de sable

sand' bar' s banc m de sable

sand'blast' s jet m de sable; (apparatus) sableuse f ‖ tr sabler

sand'box' s (rr) sablière f

sander ['sændər] s (mach) ponceuse f

sand'glass' s sablier m

sand'pa'per s papier m de verre ‖ tr polir au papier de verre

sand'pi'per s bécasseau m

sand'stone' s grès m

sand'storm' s tempête f de sable

sandwich ['sændwɪtʃ] s sandwich m ‖ tr intercaler

sand'wich man' s homme-affiche m

sand·y ['sændi] adj (comp -ier; super -iest) sablonneux; (hair) blond roux

sane [sen] adj sain, équilibré; (principles) raisonnable

sanguine ['sæŋgwɪn] adj confiant, optimiste; (countenance) sanguin

sanitary ['sænɪ,tɛri] adj sanitaire

san'itary nap'kin s serviette f hygiénique

sanitation [,sænɪ'teʃən] s hygiène f, salubrité f; (drainage) assainissement m

sanity ['sænɪti] s santé f mentale; bon sens m

Santa Claus ['sæntə,klɔz] s le père Noël

sap [sæp] s sève f; (mil) sape f; (coll) poire f, nigaud m ‖ v (pret & pp sapped; ger sapping) tr tirer la sève de; (to weaken) affaiblir; (mil) saper

sapling ['sæplɪŋ] s jeune arbre m; jeune homme m

sapphire ['sæfaɪr] s saphir m

Saracen ['særəsən] adj sarrasin ‖ s Sarrasin m

sarcasm ['sɑrkæzəm] s sarcasme m

sardine [sɑr'din] s sardine f; **packed in like sardines** serrés comme des harengs

Sardinia [sɑr'dɪnɪ·ə] s Sardaigne; la Sardaigne

Sardinian [sɑr'dɪnɪ·ən] adj sarde ‖ s (language) sarde m; (person) Sarde mf

sarsaparilla [,sɑrsəpə'rɪlə] s salsepareille f

sash [sæʃ] s ceinture f; (of window) châssis m

sash' win'dow s fenêtre f à guillotine

sas·sy ['sæsi] adj (comp -sier; super -siest) (coll) impudent, effronté

satchel ['sætʃəl] s sacoche f; (of schoolboy) carton m

sate [set] tr soûler

sateen [sæ'tin] s satinette f

satellite ['sætə,laɪt] adj & s satellite m

sat'ellite coun'try s pays m satellite

sat'ellite dish' s (telv) disque m de satellite

satiate ['seʃɪ,et] adj rassasié ‖ tr rassasier

satin ['sætɪn] s satin m

satire ['sætaɪr] s satire f

satiric(al) [sə'tɪrɪk(əl)] adj satirique

satirize ['sætɪ,raɪz] tr satiriser

satisfaction [,sætɪs'fækʃən] s satisfaction f

satisfactory [,sætɪs'fæktəri] adj satisfaisant

satis·fy ['sætɪs,faɪ] v (pret & pp -fied) tr satisfaire; (a requirement, need, etc.) satisfaire à ‖ intr satisfaire

saturate ['sætʃə,ret] tr saturer

satura'tion bom'ing [,sætʃə'reʃən] s bombardement m en tapis, tactique f de saturation

Saturday ['sætərdi] s samedi m

Saturn ['sætərn] s Saturne m

sauce [sɔs] s sauce f; (coll) insolence f, toupet m ‖ tr assaisonner ‖ tr (coll) parler avec impudence à

sauce'pan' s casserole f

saucer ['sɔsər] s soucoupe f

sau·cy ['sɔsi] adj (comp -cier; super -ciest) impudent, effronté

sauerkraut ['saur,kraut] s choucroute f

saunter ['sɔntər] s flânerie f ‖ intr flâner

sausage ['sɔsɪdʒ] s saucisse f, saucisson m

sauté [so'te] tr sauter, faire sauter

savage ['sævɪdʒ] adj & s sauvage mf

savant ['sævənt] s savant m, érudit m

save [sev] prep sauf, excepté ‖ tr sauver; (money) épargner; (time) gagner ‖ intr économiser

saving ['sevɪŋ] adj économe ‖ **savings** spl épargne f, économies fpl

sav'ings account' s dépôt m d'épargne

sav'ings and loan' associa'tion s caisse f d'épargne et de prêt

sav'ings bank' s caisse f d'épargne

sav'ings book' s livret m de caisse d'épargne

savior ['sevjər] s sauveur m

Saviour ['sevjər] s Sauveur m

savor ['sevər] s saveur f ‖ tr savourer ‖ intr—**to savor of** avoir un goût de

savor·y ['sevəri] adj (comp -ier; super -iest) (taste) savoureux; (smell) odorant ‖ s (pl -ies) (bot) sariette f

saw [sɔ] s scie f; (proverb) dicton m ‖ tr scier

saw'dust' s sciure f de bois

sawed'-off shot'gun s fusil m à canon scié

saw'horse' s chevalet m

saw'mill' s scierie f

Saxon ['sæksən] adj saxon ‖ s (language) saxon m; (person) Saxon m

saxophone ['sæksə,fon] s saxophone m

say [se] *s*—**to have one's say** avoir son mot à dire, avoir voix au chapitre ‖ *v* (*pret & pp* **said** [sɛd]) *tr* dire; **I should say not!** absolument pas!; **I should say so!** je crois bien!; **it is said** on dit; **no sooner said than done** sitôt dit, sitôt fait; **that is to say** c'est-à-dire; **to go without saying** aller sans dire; **what will the neighbors say?** qu'en dira-t-on?; **you don't say!** tu parles Charles!; **you said it!** (coll) et comment!, tu parles!

saying [ˈse·ɪŋ] *s* proverbe *m*

scab [skæb] *s* croûte *f*; (*strikebreaker*) jaune *m*; canaille *f*

scabbard [ˈskæbərd] *s* fourreau *m*

scab·by [ˈskæbi] *adj* (*comp* **-bier**; *super* **-biest**) croûteux; (coll) vil

scabrous [ˈskæbrəs] *adj* scabreux; (*uneven*) rugueux

scads [skædz] *spl* (slang) des tas *mpl*

scaffold [ˈskæfəld] *s* échafaud *m*; (*used in construction*) échafaudage *m*

scaffolding [ˈskæfəldɪŋ] *s* échafaudage *m*

scald [skɔld] *tr* échauder

scale [skel] *s* (*of thermometer, map, salaries, etc.*) échelle *f*; (*for weighing*) plateau *m*; (*incrustation*) tartre *m*; (bot, zool) écaille *f*; (mus) échelle; **on a large scale** sur une grande échelle; **scales** balance *f*; **to tip the scales** faire pencher la balance ‖ *tr* escalader; **to scale down** réduire l'échelle de

scallion [ˈskælɪ·ən] *s* échalote *f*, ciboule *f*

scallop [ˈskæləp] *s* (*seafood*) coquille *f* Saint-Jacques, peigne *m*, pétoncle *m*; (*thin slice of meat*) escalope *f*; (*on edge of cloth*) feston *m* ‖ *tr* (*the edges*) denteler, découper; (culin) gratiner et cuire au four et à la crème

scalp [skælp] *s* cuir *m* chevelu; (*trophy*) scalp *m* ‖ *tr* scalper; (*tickets*) (coll) faire le trafic de; (*too hoodwink*) (slang) abuser de

scalpel [ˈskælpəl] *s* scalpel *m*

scal·y [ˈskeli] *adj* (*comp* **-ier**; *super* **-iest**) écailleux

scamp [skæmp] *s* garnement *m*

scamper [ˈskæmpər] *intr* courir allégrement; **to scamper away** or **off** détaler

scan [skæn] *v* (*pret & pp* **scanned**; *ger* **scanning**) *tr* scruter; (*e.g., a page*) jeter un coup d'œil sur; (*verses*) scander; (telv) balayer

scandal [ˈskændəl] *s* scandale *m*

scandalize [ˈskændə‚laɪz] *tr* scandaliser

scandalous [ˈskændələs] *adj* scandaleux

Scandinavian [‚skændɪˈnevɪ·ən] *adj* scandinave ‖ *s* (*language*) scandinave *m*; (*person*) Scandinave *mf*

scanning [ˈskænɪŋ] *s* (telv) balayage *m*

scant [skænt] *adj* maigre; (*attire*) léger, sommaire ‖ *tr* réduire; lésiner sur

scant·y [ˈskænti] *adj* (*comp* **-ier**; *super* **-iest**) rare, maigre; léger

scapegoat [ˈskep‚got] *s* bouc *m* émissaire, tête *f* de Turc

scar [skɑr] *s* cicatrice *f*; (*on face*) balafre *f* ‖ *v* (*pret & pp* **scarred**; *ger* **scarring**) *tr* balafrer

scarce [skɛrs] *adj* rare, peu abondant

scarcely [ˈskɛrsli] *adv* à peine, presque pas; ne . . . guère §90; **scarcely ever** rarement

scarci·ty [ˈskɛrsɪti] *s* (*pl* **-ties**) manque *m*, pénurie *f*

scare [skɛr] *s* panique *f*, effroi *m* ‖ *tr* épouvanter, effrayer; **to scare away** or **off** effaroucher; **to scare up** (coll) procurer ‖ *intr* s'effaroucher

scare·crow *s* épouvantail *m*

scarf [skɑrf] *s* (*pl* **scarfs** or **scarves** [skɑrvz]) foulard *m*, écharpe *f*

scarlet [ˈskɑrlɪt] *adj & s* écarlate *f*

scar·let fe·ver *s* scarlatine *f*

scar·y [ˈskɛri] *adj* (*comp* **-ier**; *super* **-iest**) (*easily frightened*) (coll) peureux, ombrageux; (*causing fright*) (coll) effrayant

scathing [ˈskeðɪŋ] *adj* cinglant

scatter [ˈskætər] *tr* éparpiller; (*a mob*) disperser ‖ *intr* se disperser

scat·ter·brained *adj* (coll) étourdi

scenari·o [sɪˈnɛrɪ‚o] *s* (*pl* **-os**) scénario *m*

scene [sin] *s* scène *f*; (*landscape*) paysage *m*; **behind the scenes** dans les coulisses; **to make a scene** faire une scène

scener·y [ˈsinəri] *s* (*pl* **-ies**) paysage *m*; (theat) décor *m*, décors

sceneshifter [ˈsin‚ʃɪftər] *s* (theat) machiniste *m*

scenic [ˈsinɪk] *adj* pittoresque; spectaculaire; (theat) scénique

sce·nic rail·way *s* chemin *m* de fer en miniature des parcs d'attraction

scent [sɛnt] *s* odeur *f*; parfum *m*; (*trail*) piste *f* ‖ *tr* parfumer; (*an odor*) renifler; (*game as a dog does; a trap*) flairer

scepter [ˈsɛptər] *s* sceptre *m*

sceptio [ˈskɛptɪk] *adj & s* sceptique *mf*

sceptical [ˈskɛptɪkəl] *adj* sceptique

scepticism [ˈskɛptɪ‚sɪzəm] *s* scepticisme *m*

schedule [ˈskɛdjul] *s* (*of work*) plan *m*, programme *m*; (*of things to do*) emploi *m* du temps; (*of prices*) barème *m*; (rr) horaire *m*; **on schedule** selon l'horaire; selon les prévisions ‖ *tr* classer; inscrire au programme, à l'horaire, etc.; **scheduled to speak** prévu comme orateur

scheduled *adj* prévu, indiqué; (*train, bus, plane*) régulier

sched·uled air·line *s* compagnie *f* aérienne de transport régulier

scheme [skim] *s* projet *m*; machination *f*, truc *m* ‖ *tr* projeter ‖ *intr* ruser

schemer [ˈskimər] *s* faiseur *m* de projets; intrigant *m*

schism [ˈsɪzəm] *s* schisme *m*, scisson *f*

schizophrenia [‚skɪtsəˈfrini·ə] *s* schizophrénie *f*

scholar [ˈskɑlər] *s* (*pupil*) écolier *m*; (*learned person*) érudit *m*, savant *m*; (*holder of scholarship*) boursier *m*

scholarly [ˈskɑlərli] *adj* érudit, savant ‖ *adv* savamment

schol·ar·ship *s* érudition *f*; (*award*) bourse *f*

scholasticism [skə'læstɪ,sɪzəm] s scolastique f
school [skul] adj scolaire ‖ s école f; (of a university) faculté f; (of fish) banc m ‖ tr instruire, discipliner
school' board' s conseil m de l'instruction publique
school'book' s livre m de classe, livre scolaire
school'boy' s écolier m
school' bus' s voiture f école
school'girl' s écolière f
school'house' s maison f d'école
schooling ['skulɪŋ] s instruction f, études fpl; (teaching) enseignement m
schoolmarm ['skul,mɑrm] s maîtresse f d'école, institutrice f
school'mas'ter s maître m d'école, instituteur m
school'mate' s camarade mf d'école, condisciple m
school'room' s classe f, salle f de classe
school'teach'er s enseignant m, instituteur m
school'yard' s cour f de récréation
school' year' s année f scolaire
school' zone' s (public sign) ralentir école
schooner ['skunər] s schooner m, goélette f
sciatica [saɪ'ætɪkə] s (pathol) sciatique f
science ['saɪ·əns] s science f
sci'ence fic'tion s science-fiction f
scientific [,saɪ·ən'tɪfɪk] adj scientifique
scientist ['saɪ·əntɪst] s homme m de science, savant m
scimitar ['sɪmɪtər] s cimeterre m
scintillate ['sɪntɪ,let] intr scintiller, étinceler
scion ['saɪ·ən] s héritier m; (hort) scion m
scissors ['sɪzərz] s & spl ciseaux mpl
scis'sors-grind'er s rémouleur m; (orn) engoulevent m
scoff [skɔf] s raillerie f ‖ intr—to scoff at se moquer de
scold [skold] s harpie f ‖ tr & intr gronder
scolding ['skoldɪŋ] s gronderie f
scoop [skup] s (for flour, sugar, etc.) pelle f à main; (for ice cream) cuiller f à glace; (kitchen utensil) louche f; (of dredge) godet m; (for coal) seau m; (journ) nouvelle f à sensation, nouvelle en exclusivité, scoop m; (mach) benne f preneuse; (naut) écope f ‖ tr creuser; to scoop out excaver à la pelle; (water) écoper
scoot [skut] intr (coll) détaler
scooter ['skutər] s trottinette f, patinette f
scope [skop] s (field) domaine m, étendue f; (reach) portée f, envergure f; to give free scope to donner libre carrière à
scorch [skɔrtʃ] tr roussir; flétrir, dessécher
scorched'-earth' pol'icy s politique f de la terre brûlée
scorching ['skɔrtʃɪŋ] adj brûlant; caustique, mordant
score [skor] s (debt) compte m; (twenty) vingtaine f; (notch) entaille f; (on metal) rayure f, éraflure f; (mus) partition f; (sports) score m, marque f; on that score à cet égard; to keep score compter les

points; to settle a score with s.o. régler son compte à qn ‖ tr (to notch) entailler; (to criticize) blâmer; (metal) rayer, érafler; (a success) remporter; (e.g., a goal) marquer; (mus) orchestrer
score'board' s tableau m
score'keep'er s marqueur m
scorn [skɔrn] s mépris m, dédain m ‖ tr mépriser, dédaigner ‖ intr—to scorn to dédaigner de
Scorpio ['skɔrpɪ,o] s (astr, astrol) le Scorpion
scorpion ['skɔrpɪ·ən] s scorpion m
Scot [skɑt] s Écossais m
Scotch [skɑtʃ] adj écossais; (slang) avare, chiche ‖ s (dialect) écossais m; whiskey m écossais; the Scotch les Écossais ‖ (l.c.) s (wedge) cale f; (notch) entaille f ‖ tr caler; entailler; (a rumor) étouffer
Scotch'man s (pl -men) Écossais m
Scotch' pine' s pin m sylvestre
Scotch' tape' s (trademark) ruban m cellulosique, adhésif m scotch
Scotland ['skɑtlənd] s Écosse f; l'Écosse
Scottish ['skɑtɪʃ] adj écossais ‖ s (dialect) écossais m; the Scottish les Écossais
scoundrel ['skaundrəl] s coquin m, fripon m, canaille f
scour [skaur] tr récurer; (e.g., the countryside) parcourir
scourge [skʌrdʒ] s nerf m de bœuf, discipline f; (fig) fléau m ‖ tr fouetter, flageller
scout [skaut] adj scout ‖ s éclaireur m; (boy scout) scout m, éclaireur; a good scout (coll) un brave gars ‖ tr reconnaître; (to scoff at) repousser avec dédain ‖ intr aller en reconnaissance
scouting ['skautɪŋ] s scoutisme m
scout'ing par'ty s (pl -ties) (mil) détachement m de reconnaissance
scout'mas'ter s chef m de troupe
scowl [skaul] s renfrognement m ‖ intr se renfrogner
scram [skræm] v (pret & pp scrammed; ger scramming) intr (coll) ficher le camp; scram! (coll) fiche-moi le camp!
scramble ['skræmbəl] s bousculade f ‖ tr brouiller ‖ intr se disputer; grimper à quatre pattes
scram'bled eggs' spl œufs mpl brouillés
scrambling ['skræmblɪŋ] s (electron) embrouillage m
scrap [skræp] s (metal) ferraille f; (little bit) bout m, petit morceau m; (fight) (coll) chamaillerie f ‖ v (pret & pp scrapped; ger scrapping) tr mettre au rebut ‖ intr (coll) se chamailler
scrap'book' s album m de découpures
scrape [skrep] s grincement m; (coll) mauvaise affaire f ‖ tr gratter, râcler
scrap' heap' s tas m de rebut
scrap' i'ron s ferraille f
scrap' pa'per s bloc-notes m; (refuse) papier m de rebut
scratch [skrætʃ] s égratignure f; to start from scratch partir de rien ‖ tr gratter,

égratigner; (*to eliminate from an event*) déclarer forfait

scratch′ pad′ *s* bloc-notes *m*, brouillon *m*

scratch′ pa′per *s* bloc-notes *m*

scrawl [skrɔl] *s* griffonnage *m* ‖ *tr & intr* griffonner

scraw·ny [ˈskrɔni] *adj* (*comp* **-nier;** *super* **-niest**) décharné, mince

scream [skrim] *s* cri *m* perçant; (slang) personne *f* ridicule; (slang) chose *f* ridicule ‖ *tr & intr* pousser des cris, crier

screech [skritʃ] *s* cri *m* perçant ‖ *intr* jeter des cris perçants

screech′ owl′ *s* chat-huant *m*; (*barn owl*) effraie *f*

screen [skrin] *s* écran *m*; grillage *m* en fil de fer, treillis *m* métallique; (*for sifting*) crible *m* ‖ *tr* abriter; (*candidates*) trier; (mov) porter à l'écran

screen′ grid′ *s* (electron) grille *f* blindée

screening [ˈskrinɪŋ] *s* présélection *f*; (med) dépistage *m*

screen′ play′ *s* scénario *m*; drame *m* filmé

screen′ test′ *s* bout *m* d'essai

screw [skru] *s* vis *f*; (naut) hélice *f*; **to have a screw loose** (coll) être toqué ‖ *tr* visser; **to screw off** dévisser; **to screw tight** visser à bloc; **to screw up** (*one's courage*) rassembler ‖ *intr* se visser

screw′ball′ *adj & s* (slang) extravagant *m*, loufoque *m*

screw′driv′er *s* tournevis *m*

screw′ eye′ *s* vis *f* à œil

screw′ press′ *s* cric *m* à vis

screw′ propel′ler *s* hélice *f*

screw·y [ˈskru·i] *adj* (*comp* **-ier;** *super* **-iest**) (slang) loufoque

scrib′al er′ror [ˈskraɪbəl] *s* faute *f* de copiste

scribble [ˈskrɪbəl] *s* griffonnage *m* ‖ *tr & intr* griffonner

scribe [skraɪb] *s* scribe *m*

scrimmage [ˈskrɪmɪdʒ] *s* mêlée *f*

scrimp [skrɪmp] *tr* lésiner sur ‖ *intr* lésiner

scrip [skrɪp] *s* monnaie *f* scriptural, script *m*

script [skrɪpt] *s* manuscrit *m*, original *m*; (*handwriting*) écriture *f*; (mov) scénario *m*; (typ) script *m*; (mov, telv) texte *m*

scriptural [ˈskrɪptʃərəl] *adj* biblique

scripture [ˈskrɪptʃər] *s* citation *f* tirée de l'Écriture; **Scripture** l'Ecriture *f*; **the Scriptures** les Ecritures

script′writ′er *s* scénariste *mf*

scrofula [ˈskrɑfjələ] *s* scrofule *f*

scroll [skrol] *s* rouleau *m*; (archit) volute *f*

scroll′work′ *s* ornementation *f* en volute

scro·tum [ˈskrotəm] *s* (*pl* **-ta** [tə] or **-tums**) scrotum *m*, bourses *fpl*

scrub [skrʌb] *adj* rabougri ‖ *s* (*scrubbing*) nettoyage *m* à la brosse; (*underbrush*) broussailles *fpl*; (rok) vol *m* annulé; (sports) joueur *m* novice ‖ *v* (*pret & pp* **scrubbed;** *ger* **scrubbing**) *tr* frotter, nettoyer, récurer; (*to cancel*) (rok) annuler

scrub′bing brush′ *s* brosse *f* de chiendent

scrub′wom′an *s* (*pl* **-wom′en**) nettoyeuse *f*

scruff [skrʌf] *s* nuque *f*

scruple [ˈskrupəl] *s* scrupule *f*

scrupulous [ˈskrupjələs] *adj* scrupuleux

scrutinize [ˈskrutɪˌnaɪz] *tr* scruter

scruti·ny [ˈskrutɪni] *s* (*pl* **-nies**) examen *m* minutieux

scuff [skʌf] *s* usure *f* ‖ *tr* érafler

scuffle [ˈskʌfəl] *s* bagarre *f* ‖ *intr* se bagarrer

scull [skʌl] *s* (*stern oar*) godille *f*; aviron *m* de couple ‖ *tr* godiller ‖ *intr* ramer en couple

sculler·y [ˈskʌləri] *s* (*pl* **-ies**) arrière-cuisine *f*

scul′lery maid′ *s* laveuse *f* de vaisselle

scullion [ˈskʌljən] *s* marmiton *m*

sculptor [ˈskʌlptər] *s* sculpteur *m*

sculptress [ˈskʌlptrɪs] *s* femme *f* sculpteur

sculpture [ˈskʌlptʃər] *s* sculpture *f* ‖ *tr & intr* sculpter

scum [skʌm] *s* écume *f*; (*of society*) canaille *f* ‖ *v* (*pret & pp* **scummed;** *ger* **scumming**) *tr & intr* écumer

scum·my [ˈskʌmi] *adj* (*comp* **-mier;** *super* **-miest**) écumeux; (fig) vil

scurrilous [ˈskʌrɪləs] *adj* injurieux, grossier, outrageant

scur·ry [ˈskʌri] *v* (*pret & pp* **-ried**) *intr*—**to scurry around** galoper; **to scurry away** or **off** déguerpir

scur·vy [ˈskʌrvi] *adj* (*comp* **-vier;** *super* **-viest**) méprisable, vil ‖ *s* scorbut *m*

scuttle [ˈskʌtəl] *s* (*bucket for coal*) seau *m* à charbon; (*trap door*) trappe *f*; (*run*) course *f* précipitée; (naut) écoutillon *m* ‖ *tr* saborder ‖ *intr* filer, déguerpir

scut′tle·butt′ *s* (coll) on-dit *m*

scythe [saɪð] *s* faux *f*

sea [si] *s* mer *f*; **at sea** en mer; (fig) désorienté; **by the sea** au bord de la mer; **to put to sea** prendre le large

sea′board′ *s* littoral *m*

sea′ breeze′ *s* brise *f* de mer

sea′ coast′ *s* côte *f*, littoral *m*

seafarer [ˈsiˌfɛrər] *s* marin *m*; voyageur *m* par mer

sea′food′ *s* fruits *mpl* de mer, marée *f*

seagoing [ˈsiˌgo·ɪŋ] *adj* de haute mer, au long cours

sea′ gull′ *s* mouette *f*, goéland *m*

seal [sil] *s* (*on a document*) sceau *m*; (zool) phoque *m* ‖ *tr* sceller; **in a sealed envelope** sous pli fermé

sea′ legs′ *spl* pied *m* marin

sea′ lev′el *s* niveau *m* de la mer

seal′ing wax′ *s* cire *f* à cacheter

sea′ li′on *s* otarie *f*

seal′skin′ *s* peau *f* de phoque

seam [sim] *s* couture *f*; (*of metal*) joint *m*; (geol) fissure *f*; (min) couche *f*

sea′man *s* (*pl* **-men**) marin *m*

sea′ mile′ *s* mille *m* marin

seamless [ˈsimlɪs] *adj* sans couture; (mach) sans soudure

seamstress [ˈsimstrɪs] *s* couturière *f*

seam·y [ˈsimi] *adj* (*comp* **-ier;** *super* **-iest**) plein de coutures; vil, vilain

séance [ˈse·ɑns] *s* séance *f* de spiritisme

sea′plane′ *s* hydravion *m*

sea'port' *s* port *m* de mer
sea' pow'er *s* puissance *f* maritime
sear [sɪr] *adj* desséché ‖ *s* cicatrice *f* de brûlure ‖ *tr* dessécher; marquer au fer rouge
search [sʌrtʃ] *s* recherche *f*; **in search of** à la recherche de ‖ *tr & intr* fouiller; **to search for** chercher
searching ['sʌrtʃɪŋ] *adj* pénétrant, scrutateur
search'light' *s* projecteur *m*
search' war'rant *s* mandat *m* de perquisition
seascape ['si,skep] *s* panorama *m* marin; (*painting*) marine *f*
sea' shell' *s* coquille *f* de mer
sea'shore' *s* bord *m* de la mer
sea'sick' *adj*—**to be seasick** avoir le mal de mer
sea'sick'ness *s* mal *m* de mer
season ['sizən] *s* saison *f* ‖ *tr* assaisonner; (*troops*) aguerrir; (*wood*) sécher
seasonal ['sizənəl] *adj* saisonnier
seasoning ['sizənɪŋ] *s* assaisonnement *m*
sea'son's greet'ings *spl* meilleurs souhaits *mpl*, tous mes vœux *mpl*
sea'son tick'et *s* carte *f* d'abonnement
seat [sit] *s* siège *m*; (*place or right*) place *f*; (*in theater*) fauteuil *m*; (*on bus or train*) banquette *f*; (*on cycle*) selle *f*; (*of trousers*) fond *m*; **have a seat** asseyez-vous donc; **keep your seat** restez assis; **to have a good seat** (*equit*) avoir une bonne assiette ‖ *tr* asseoir; (*a number of persons*) contenir; **to be seated** (*to sit down*) s'asseoir; (*to be in sitting posture*) être assis
seat' belt' *s* ceinture *f* de sécurité
seat' cov'er *s* (aut) housse *f*
SEATO ['sito] *s* (acronym) (**Southeast Asia Treaty Organization**) OTASE *f*
sea' wall' *s* digue *f*
sea'way' *s* voie *f* maritime; (*of ship*) sillage *m*; (*rough sea*) mer *f* dure
sea'weed' *s* algue *f* marine; plante *f* marine
sea'wor'thy *adj* en état de naviguer
secede [sɪ'sid] *intr* se séparer, faire sécession
secession [sɪ'sɛʃən] *s* sécession *f*
seclude [sɪ'klud] *tr* tenir éloigné; (*to shut up*) enfermer
secluded *adj* retiré, écarté
seclusion [sɪ'kluʒən] *s* retraite *f*
second ['sɛkənd] *adj & pron* deuxième (*masc, fem*), second; **the Second** deux, e.g., **John the Second** Jean deux; **to be second in command** commander en second; **to be second to none** ne le céder à personne ‖ *s* deuxième *m*, second *m*; (*in time; musical interval; of angle*) seconde *f*; (*in a duel*) témoin *m*, second *m*; (com) article *m* de deuxième qualité; **the second** (*in dates*) deux ‖ *adv* en second lieu ‖ *tr* affirmer; (*to back up*) seconder
secondar·y ['sɛkən,dɛri] *adj* secondaire ‖ *s* (*pl* -**ies**) (elec) secondaire *m*
sec'ondary educa'tion *s* enseignement *m* secondaire
sec'ond best' *s* pis-aller *m*

sec'ond-best' *adj* (*everyday*) de tous les jours; **to come off second-best** être battu
sec'ond-class' *adj* de second ordre; (rr) de seconde classe
sec'ond floor' *s* premier étage *m*; (*second floor above the ground floor* = *American third floor*) (Brit) deuxième étage
sec'ond hand' *s* trotteuse *f*
sec'ond·hand' *adj* d'occasion, de seconde main
sec'ond·hand book'dealer *s* bouquiniste *mf*
sec'ond lieuten'ant *s* sous-lieutenant *m*
sec'ond mate' *s* (naut) second maître *m*
sec'ond-rate' *adj* de second ordre
sec'ond sight' *s* seconde vue *f*
sec'ond wind' *s* second souffle *m*; **to get one's second wind** reprendre haleine
secre·cy ['sikrəsi] *s* (*pl* -**cies**) secret *m*; **in secrecy** en secret
secret ['sikrɪt] *adj & s* secret *m*; **in secret** en secret
secretar·y ['sɛkrɪ,tɛri] *s* (*pl* -**ies**) secrétaire *mf*; (*desk*) secrétaire *m*
se'cret bal'lot *s* scrutin *m* secret
secrete [sɪ'krit] *tr* cacher; (physiol) sécréter
secretive [sɪ'kritɪv] *adj* cachottier
se'cret serv'ice *s* deuxième bureau *m*
sect [sɛkt] *s* secte *f*
sectarian [sɛk'tɛri·ən] *adj* sectaire; (*school*) confessionnel ‖ sectaire *mf*
section ['sɛkʃən] *s* section *f*
sectionalism ['sɛkʃənə,lɪzəm] *s* régionalisme *m*
sec'tion hand' *s* cantonnier *m*
sector ['sɛktər] *s* secteur *m*; (*instrument*) compas *m* de proportion
secular ['sɛkjələr] *adj* (*worldly, of this world*) séculier; (*century-old*) séculaire ‖ *s* séculier *m*
secularism ['sɛkjələ,rɪzəm] *s* laïcisme *m*, mondanité *f*
secure [sɪ'kjʊr] *adj* sûr ‖ *tr* obtenir; (*to make fast*) fixer
securi·ty [sɪ'jʊrɪti] *s* (*pl* -**ties**) sécurité *f*; (*pledge*) garantie *f*; (*person*) garant *m*; **securities** valeurs *fpl*
secu'rity-sys'tems com'pany *s* société *f* de gardiennage
sedan [sɪ'dæn] *s* (aut) conduite *f* intérieure
sedan' chair' *s* chaise *f* à porteurs
sedate [sɪ'det] *adj* calme, discret
sedation [sɪ'deʃən] *s* sédation *f*
sedative ['sɛdətɪv] *adj & s* sédatif *m*
sedentary ['sɛdən,tɛri] *adj* sédentaire
sedge [sɛdʒ] *s* (*Carex*) laîche *f*
sediment ['sɛdɪmənt] *s* sédiment *m*
sedition [sɪ'dɪʃən] *s* sédition *f*
seditious [sɪ'dɪʃəs] *adj* séditieux
seduce [sɪ'd(j)us] *tr* séduire
seducer [sɪ'd(j)usər] *s* séducteur *m*
seduction [sɪ'dʌkʃən] *s* séduction *f*
seductive [sɪ'dʌktɪv] *adj* séduisant
sedulous ['sɛdʒələs] *adj* assidu
see [si] *s* (eccl) siège *m* ‖ *v* (*pret* **saw** [sɔ]; *pp* **seen** [sin]) *tr* voir; **see other side** (*turn the page*) voir au dos; **to see s.o. play, to**

see s.o. playing voir jouer qn, voir qn qui joue; to see s.th. played voir jouer q.ch. ‖ *intr* voir; to see through s.o. (fig) voir venir qn

seed [sid] *s* graine *f*, semence *f*; sperme *m*; (*in fruit*) pépin *m*; (fig) germe *m*; to go to seed monter en graine ‖ *intr* semer, ensemencer

seed'bed' *s* semis *m*

seeder ['sidər] *s* (mach) semeuse *f*

seedling ['sidlɪŋ] *s* semis *m*

seed·y ['sidi] *adj* (*comp* -ier; *super* -iest) (coll) râpé, miteux

seeing ['si·ɪŋ] *adj* voyant ‖ *s* vue *f* ‖ *conj* vu que

See'ing Eye' dog' *s* (trademark) chien *m* d'aveugle

seek [sik] *v* (*pret* & *pp* sought [sɔt]) *tr* chercher ‖ *intr* chercher; to seek after rechercher; to seek to chercher à

seem [sim] *intr* sembler

seemingly ['simɪŋli] *adv* en apparence

seem·ly ['simli] *adj* (*comp* -lier; *super* -liest) gracieux; (*correct*) bienséant

seep [sip] *intr* suinter

seer [sɪr] *s* prophète *m*, voyant *m*

see'saw' *s* balançoire *f*, bascule *f*; (*motion*) va-et-vient *m* ‖ *intr* basculer, balancer

seethe [sið] *intr* bouillonner

segment ['sɛgmənt] *s* segment *m*

segregate ['sɛgrɪ,get] *tr* mettre à part, isoler

segregation [,sɛgrɪ'geʃən] *s* ségrégation *f*

segregationist [,sɛgrɪ'geʃənɪst] *s* ségrégationniste *mf*

seismic ['saɪzmɪk] *adj* sismique

seismograph ['saɪzmə,græf] *s* sismographe *m*

seismology [saɪz'mɑlədʒi] *s* sismologie *f*

seize [siz] *tr* saisir

seizure ['siʒər] *s* prise *f*; (law) saisie *f*; (pathol) attaque *f*

seldom ['sɛldəm] *adv* rarement

select [sɪ'lɛkt] *adj* choisi ‖ *tr* choisir, sélectionner

selection [sɪ'lɛkʃən] *s* sélection *f*

selective [sɪ'lɛktɪv] *adj* sélectif

self [sɛlf] *adj* de même ‖ *s* (*pl* selves [sɛlvz]) moi *m*, être *m*; all by one's self tout seul; one's better self notre meilleur côté ‖ *pron*—payable to self payable à moi-même

self'-addressed en'velope *s* enveloppe *f* adressée à l'envoyeur

self'-cen'tered *adj* égocentrique

self'-clean'ing ov'en *s* four *m* auto-nettoyant

self'-con'fidence *s* confiance *f* en soi

self'-con'fident *adj* sûr de soi

self'-con'scious *adj* gêné, embarrassé, emprunté

self'-control' *s* sang-froid *m*, maîtrise *f* de soi

self'-defense' *s* autodéfense *f*; in self-defense en légitime défense

self'-deni'al *s* abnégation *f*

self'-deter'mina'tion *s* autodétermination *f*

self'-dis'cipline *s* discipline *f* personnelle

self'-ed'ucated *adj* autodidacte

self'-employed' *adj* indépendant

self'-esteem' *s* amour-propre *m*

self'-ev'ident *adj* évident aux yeux de tout le monde

self'-explan'ator'y *adj* qui s'explique de soi-même

self'-gov'ernment *s* autonomie *f*; maîtrise *f* de soi

self'-impor'tant *adj* suffisant, présomptueux

self'-indul'gence *s* faiblesse *f* envers soi-même, intempérance *f*

self'-in'terest *s* intérêt *m* personnel

selfish ['sɛlfɪʃ] *adj* égoïste

selfishness ['sɛlfɪʃnɪs] *s* égoïsme *m*

selfless ['sɛlflɪs] *adj* désintéressé

self'-love' *s* égoïsme *m*

self'-made man' *s* (*pl* -men') fils *m* de ses œuvres

self'-por'trait *s* autoportrait *m*

self'-possessed' *adj* maître de soi

self'-pres'erva'tion *s* conservation *f* de soi-même

self'-reli'ant *adj* sûr de soi, assuré

self'-respect'ing *adj* correct, honorable

self'-right'eous *adj* pharisaïque

self'-sac'rifice' *s* abnégation *f*

self'same' *adj* identique

self'-sat'isfied' *adj* content de soi

self'-seal'ing *adj* (*envelope*) autocollant, auto-adhésif; (*container*) à obturation automatique

self'-seek'ing *adj* égoïste, intéressé

self'-serv'ice *s* libre-service *m*

self'-serv'ice laun'dry *s* (*pl* -dries) laverie *f* libre-service, laverie automatique, lavromat *m*

self'-serv'ice sta'tion *s* station *f* libre-service

self'-start'er *s* démarreur *m* automatique

self'-styled' *adj* soi-disant

self'-taught' *adj* autodidacte

self'-tim'er *s* (phot) retardateur *m*

self'-willed' *adj* obstiné, entêté

self'-wind'ing *adj* à remontage automatique

sell [sɛl] *v* (*pret* & *pp* sold [sold]) *tr* vendre; to sell back récéder; to sell out solder; (*to betray*) vendre ‖ *intr* vendre; to sell for (e.g., *ten dollars*) se vendre à

seller ['sɛlər] *s* vendeur *m*

selling ['sɛlɪŋ] *s* vente *f*; selling by mail postalage *m*; selling price prix *m* de vente

Selt'zer wa'ter ['sɛltsər] *s* eau *f* de Seltz

selvage ['sɛlvɪdʒ] *s* (*of fabric*) lisière *f*; (*of lock*) gâche *f*

semantic [sɪ'mæntɪk] *adj* sémantique ‖ semantics *s* sémantique *f*

semaphore ['sɛmə,for] *s* sémaphore *m*

semblance ['sɛmbləns] *s* semblant *m*

semen ['simɛn] *s* sperme *m*, semence *f*

semester [sɪ'mɛstər] *adj* semstriel ‖ *s* semestre *m*

semes'ter hour' *s* (educ) heure *f* semestrielle

semicircle ['sɛmɪ,sʌrkəl] *s* demi-cercle *m*

semicolon ['sɛmɪ,kolən] *s* point-virgule *m*

semiconductor [,sɛmɪkən'dʌktər] s semi-conducteur m

semiconscious [,sɛmɪ'kanʃəs] adj à demi conscient

semifinal [,sɛmɪ'faɪnəl] adj avant-dernière ‖ s demi-finale f

semilearned [,sɛmɪ'lʌrnɪd] adj à moitié savant

seminar ['sɛmɪ,nɑr] s séminaire m

seminar·y ['sɛmɪ,nɛri] s (pl -ies) séminaire m

semiprecious [,sɛmɪ'prɛʃəs] adj fin, semi-précieux

Semite ['sɛmaɪt] s Sémite mf

Semitic [sɪ'mɪtɪk] adj (e.g., language) sémitique; (person) sémite

semitrailer ['sɛmɪ,trelər] s semi-remorque f

senate ['sɛnɪt] s sénat m

senator ['sɛnətər] s sénateur m

send [sɛnd] v (pret & pp sent [sɛnt]) tr envoyer; (rad, telv) émettre; **to send back** renvoyer; **to send out** envoyer; **to send s.o. for s.th. or s.o.** envoyer q.ch. or qn; **to send s.o. to** + inf envoyer qn + inf ‖ intr (rad, telv) émettre; **to send for** envoyer chercher

sender ['sɛndər] s expéditeur m; (telg) transmetteur m

send'-off' s manifestation f d'adieu

senile ['sinaɪl] adj sénile

senility [sɪ'nɪlɪti] s sénilité f

senior ['sinjər] adj aîné; (clerk, partner, etc.) principal; (rank) supérieur; père, e.g., **Maurice Laporte, Senior** Maurice Laporte père ‖ s aîné m, doyen m; (U.S. upperclassman) étudiant m de dernière année

sen'ior cit'izens spl les vieilles gens fpl

seniority [sin'jɔrɪti] s ancienneté f, doyenneté f

sen'ior staff' s personnel m hors classe

sensation [sɛn'seʃən] s sensation f

sensational [sɛn'seʃənəl] adj sensationnel

sense [sɛns] s sens m; (wisdom) bon sens; (e.g., of pain) sensation f; **to make sense out of** arriver à comprendre ‖ tr percevoir, sentir

senseless ['sɛnslɪs] adj (lacking perception) insensible; (unconscious) sans connaissance; (unreasonable) insensé

sense' of guilt' s remords m

sense' or'gans spl organes mpl des sens

sensibili·ty [,sɛnsɪ'bɪlɪti] s (pl -ties) sensibilité f; susceptibilité f

sensible ['sɛnsɪbəl] adj sensible; (endowed with good sense) sensé, raisonnable

sensitive ['sɛnsɪtɪv] adj sensible; (touchy) susceptible, sensitif

sensitize ['sɛnsɪ,taɪz] tr sensibiliser

sensor ['sɛn,sɔr] s (rok) capteur m

sensory ['sɛnsəri] adj sensoriel

sensual ['sɛnʃu·əl] adj sensuel

sensuous ['sɛnʃu·əs] adj sensuel

sentence ['sɛntəns] s (gram) phrase f; (law) sentence f ‖ tr condamner

sentiment ['sɛntɪmənt] s sentiment m

sentimental [,sɛntɪ'mɛntəl] adj sentimental

sentinel ['sɛntɪnəl] s sentinelle f; **to stand sentinel** être en sentinelle

sen·try ['sɛntri] s (pl -tries) sentinelle f

sen'try box' s guérite f

separate ['sɛpərɪt] adj séparé ‖ ['sɛpə,ret] tr séparer ‖ intr se séparer

separation [,sɛpə'reʃən] s séparation f

September [sɛp'tɛmbər] s septembre m

septic ['sɛptɪk] adj septique

sepulcher ['sɛpəlkər] s sépulcre m

sequel ['sikwəl] s conséquence f; (something following) suite f

sequence ['sikwəns] s succession f, ordre m; (cards, mov) séquence f; (of tenses) (gram) concordance f

sequester [sɪ'kwɛstər] tr séquestrer

sequin ['sikwɪn] s paillette f

ser·aph ['sɛrəf] s (pl -aphs or -aphim [əfɪm]) séraphin m

Serb [sʌrb] adj serbe ‖ s Serbe mf

sere [sɪr] adj sec, desséché

serenade [,sɛrə'ned] s sérénade f ‖ tr donner une sérénade à ‖ intr donner des sérénades

serene [sɪ'rin] adj serein

serenity [sɪ'rɛnɪti] s sérénité f

serf [sʌrf] s serf m

serfdom ['sʌrfdəm] s servage m

serge [sʌrdʒ] s serge f

sergeant ['sɑrdʒənt] s sergent m

ser'geant-at-arms' s (pl sergeants-at-arms) huissier m, sergent m d'armes

ser'geant ma'jor s (pl sergeant majors) sergent-major m

serial ['sɪrɪ·əl] adj de série ‖ s roman-feuilleton m

serially ['sɪrɪ·əli] adv en série; (in installments) en feuilleton

se'rial num'ber s numéro m d'ordre; (mil) numéro m matricule

se·ries ['sɪriz] s (pl -ries) série f; **in series** en série

serious ['sɪrɪ·əs] adj (illness, injury, mistake, tone, attitude, smile, look) grave, sérieux; (damage) important, considérable

seriousness ['sɪrɪ·əsnɪs] s sérieux m, gravité f

sermon ['sʌrmən] s sermon m

sermonize ['sʌrmə,naɪz] tr & intr sermonner

serpent ['sʌrpənt] s serpent m

se·rum ['sɪrəm] s (pl -rums or -ra [rə]) sérum m

servant ['sʌrvənt] s domestique mf; (civil servant) fonctionnaire mf; (housemaid) bonne f; (humble servant) (fig) serviteur m

serv'ant girl' s servante f

serv'ant prob'lem s crise f domestique

serve [sʌrv] tr servir; **to serve s.o. as** servir à qn de; **to serve time** purger une peine ‖ intr servir; **to serve as** (to function as) servir de; (to be useful for) servir à

service ['sʌrvɪs] s service m; (eccl) office m; **the services** (mil) les forces fpl armées ‖ tr entretenir, réparer

serviceable ['sʌrvɪsəbəl] adj utile, pratique; résistant

serv'ice club' s foyer m du soldat
serv'ice·man' s (pl -men') réparateur m; (mil) militaire m
serv'ice rec'ord s état m de service
serv'ice sta'tion s station-service f
ser'vice stop' s (on a superhighway) relais m routier
serv'ice stripe' s chevron m, galon m
servicing ['sʌrvɪsɪŋ] s entretien m courant
servile ['sʌrvɪl] adj servile
servitude ['sʌrvɪ,t(j)ud] s servitude f
sesame ['sɛsəmi] s sésame m; **open sesame!** sésame, ouvre-toi!
session ['sɛʃən] s session f; **to be in session** siéger
set [sɛt] adj (rule) établi; (price) fixe; (time) fixé; (smile; locution) figé ‖ s ensemble m; (of dishes, linen, etc.) assortiment m; (of dishes) service m; (of kitchen utensils) batterie f (of pans; of weights; of tickets) série f; (of tools, chessmen, oars, etc.) jeu m; (of books) collection f; (of diamonds) parure f; (of tennis) set m; (of cement) prise f; (of a garment) tournure f; (group of persons) coterie f; (mov) plateau m; (rad) poste m; (theat) mise f en scène; **set of false teeth** dentier m; **set of teeth** denture f ‖ v (pret & pp set; ger setting) tr mettre, placer, poser; (a date, price, etc.) fixer; (a gem) monter; (a trap) tendre; (a timepiece) mettre à l'heure, régler; (the hair) mettre en plis; (a bone) remettre; to set aside mettre de côté; annuler; **to set going** mettre en marche; **to set off** mettre en valeur; (e.g., a rocket) lancer, tirer ‖ intr se figer; (said of sun, moon, etc.) se coucher; (said of hen) couver; (said of garment) tomber; **to set about, to set out to** se mettre à; **to set upon** attaquer
set'back' s revers m, échec m
set'screw' s vis f de pression
settee [sɛ'ti] s canapé m; (for two) canapé à deux places, causeuse f
setting ['sɛtɪŋ] s (surroundings) cadre m; (of a gem) monture f; (of cement) prise f; (of sun) coucher m; (of a bone) recollement m; (of a watch) réglage m; (adjustment) ajustage m; (theat) mise f en scène
set'ting-up' ex'ercises spl gymnastique f rhythmique, gymnastique suédoise
settle ['sɛtəl] tr (a region) coloniser; (a dispute, account, debt, etc.) régler; (a problem) résoudre; (doubts, fears, etc.) calmer; (to stop wobbling) stabiliser ‖ intr se coloniser; se calmer; (said of weather) se mettre au beau; (said of building) se tasser; (said of sediment, dust, etc.) se déposer; (said of liquid) se clarifier; **to settle down** s'établir; (to be less wild) se ranger; **to settle down to** (a task) s'appliquer à; **to settle on** se décider pour
settlement ['sɛtəlmənt] s établissement m, colonie f; (of an account, dispute, etc.) règlement m; (of a debt) liquidation f; (settlement house) œuvre f sociale
settler ['sɛtlər] s colon m

set'up' s port m, maintien m; (of the parts of a machine) installation f; (coll) organisation f
seven ['sɛvən] adj & pron sept ‖ s sept m; **seven o'clock** sept heures
seventeen ['sɛvən'tin] adj, pron, & s dix-sept m
seventeenth ['sɛvən'tinθ] adj & pron dix-septième (masc, fem); **the Seventeenth** dix-sept, e.g., **John the Seventeenth** Jean dix-sept ‖ s dix-septième m; **the seventeenth** (in dates) le dix-sept
seventh ['sɛvənθ] adj & pron septième (masc, fem); **the Seventh** sept, e.g., **John the Seventh** Jean sept ‖ s septième m; **the seventh** (in dates) le sept
seventieth ['sɛvəntɪ·ɪθ] adj & pron soixante-dixième (masc, fem) ‖ s soixante-dixième m
seven·ty ['sɛvənti] adj & pron soixante-dix ‖ s (pl -ties) soixante-dix m
sev'enty-first' adj & pron soixante et onzième (masc, fem) ‖ s soixante et onzième m
sev'enty-one' adj, pron, & s soixante et onze m
sever ['sɛvər] tr séparer; (relations) rompre ‖ intr se séparer
several ['sɛvərəl] adj & pron indef plusieurs
severance ['sɛvərəns] s séparation f; (of relations) rupture f; (of communications) interruption f
sev'erance pay' s indemnité f pour cause de renvoi
severe [sɪ'vɪr] adj sévère; (weather) rigoureux; (pain) aigu; (illness) grave
sew [so] v (pret sewed; pp sewed or sewn) tr & intr coudre
sewage ['s(j)u·ɪdʒ] s eaux fpl d'égouts
sewer ['s(j)u·ər] s égout m ‖ ['so·ər] s (one who sews) couseur m
sewerage ['s(j)u·ərɪdʒ] s (removal) vidange f; (system) système m d'égouts; (sewage) eaux fpl d'égouts
sew'ing bas'ket s nécessaire m de couture
sew'ing machine' s machine f à coudre
sew'ing ta'ble s chiffonnière f
sex [sɛks] s sexe m; **the fair sex** le beau sexe; **the sterner sex** le sexe fort; **to have sex with** (coll) avoir des rapport avec
sex' appeal' s sex-appeal m
sexism ['sɛksɪzəm] s sexisme m
sexist ['sɛksɪst] adj & s sexiste mf
sextant ['sɛkstənt] s sextant m
sextet [sɛks'tɛt] s sextuor m
sexton ['sɛkstən] s sacristain m
sexual ['sɛkʃu·əl] adj sexuel
sex·y ['sɛksi] adj (comp -ier; super -iest) (slang) aguichant, grivois; (story) érotique; **to be sexy** avoir du chien
sh [ʃ] interj chut!
shab·by ['ʃæbi] adj (comp -bier; super -biest) râpé, usé; (mean) mesquin; (house) délabré
shack [ʃæk] s cabane f, case f
shackle ['ʃækəl] s boucle f; **shackles** entraves fpl ‖ tr entraver

shad [ʃæd] *s* alose *f*

shade [ʃed] *s* (*shadow*) ombre *f*; (*of lamp*) abat-jour *m*; (*of window*) store *m*; (*hue; slight difference*) nuance *f*; (*little bit*) soupçon *m* ‖ *tr* ombrager; (*to make gradual changes in*) nuancer

shadow [ʃædo] *s* ombre *f* ‖ *tr* ombrager; (*to spy on*) filer, pister

shad′ow gov′ernment *s* gouvernement *m* fantôme

shadowy [ʃædo·i] *adj* ombreux, sombre; (fig) vague, obscur

shad·y [ʃedi] *adj* (*comp* **-ier;** *super* **-iest**) ombreux, ombragé; (coll) louche

shaft [ʃæft] *s* (*of mine; of elevator*) puits *m*; (*of feather*) tige *f*; (*of arrow*) bois *m*; (*of column*) fût *m*, tige; (*of flag*) mât *m*; (*of wagon*) brancard *m*, limon *m*; (*of motor*) arbre *m*; (*of light*) rayon *m*; (*to make fun of s.o.*) trait *m*

shag·gy [ʃægi] *adj* (*comp* **-gier;** *super* **-giest**) poilu, à longs poils

shag′gy dog′ sto′ry *s* (*pl* **-ries**) histoire *f* sans queue ni tête

shagreen [ʃə′grin] *s* peau *f* de chagrin

shake [ʃek] *s* secousse *f* ‖ *v* (*pret* **shook** [ʃʊk]; *pp* **shaken**) *tr* secouer; (*the head*) hocher, secouer; (*one's hand*) serrer; **to shake down** faire tomber; (*a thermometer*) secouer; (slang) escroquer; **to shake off** secouer; (*to get rid of*) se débarrasser de; **to shake up** (*a liquid*) agiter; (fig) ébranler ‖ *intr* trembler

shake′down′ *adj* (*cruise*) préparatoire, préliminaire ‖ *s* (*search*) fouille *f*; (*extortion*) extorsion *f*, chantage *m*

shaker [ʃekər] *s* (*for salt*) salière *f*; (*for cocktails*) shaker *m*

shake′up′ *s* bouleversement *m*; (*reorganization*) remaniement *m*

shak·y [ʃeki] *adj* (*comp* **-ier;** *super* **-iest**) tremblant, chancelant; (*hand; writing*) tremblé; (*voice*) tremblotant

shale [ʃel] *s* schiste *m* (argileux)

shall [ʃæl] *v* (*cond* **should** [ʃʊd]) *aux* used to express 1) the future indicative, e.g., **I shall arrive** j'arriverai; 2) the future perfect indicative, e.g., **I shall have arrived** je serai arrivé; 3) the potential mood, e.g., **what shall he do?** que doit-il faire?

shallow [ʃælo] *adj* peu profond; (*dish*) plat; (fig) creux, superficiel ‖ **shallows** *spl* haut-fond *m*

sham [ʃæm] *adj* feint, simulé ‖ *s* feinte *f*, simulacre *m*; (*person*) imposteur *m* ‖ *v* (*pret* & *pp* **shammed;** *ger* **shamming**) *tr* & *intr* feindre, simuler

sham′ bat′tle *s* combat *m* simulé

shambles [ʃæmbəlz] *spl* boucherie *f*; ravage *m*, ruine *f*; (*disorder*) pagaille *f*

shame [ʃem] *s* honte *f*; **shame on you!, for shame!** quelle honte!; **what a shame!** quel dommage! ‖ *tr* faire honte à

shame′faced′ *adj* penaud, honteux

shameful [ʃemfəl] *adj* honteux

shameless [ʃemlɪs] *adj* éhonté

shampoo [ʃæm′pu] *s* shampooing *m* ‖ *tr* (*the hair*) laver; (*a person*) faire un shampooing à

shamrock [ʃæmrɑk] *s* trèfle *m* d'Irlande

Shanghai [ʃæŋhaɪ] *s* Changhaï ‖ (*l.c.*) *tr* (coll) racoler

Shangri-la [,ʃæŋgrɪ′lɑ] *s* le pays de Cocagne

shank [ʃæŋk] *s* jambe *f*, tibia *m*; (*of horse*) canon *m*; (*of anchor*) verge *f*; (culin) manche *m*; (*of a column*) fût *m*

shan·ty [ʃænti] *s* (*pl* **-ties**) masure *f*, bicoque *f*

shan′ty·town′ *s* bidonville *m*

shape [ʃep] *s* forme *f*; **in bad shape** (coll) mal en point; **in good shape** (*physically*) en bonne tenue; **out of shape** déformé; **to take shape** prendre tournure; ‖ *tr* former ‖ *intr* se former; **to shape up** prendre forme; avancer

shapeless [ʃeplɪs] *adj* informe

shape·ly [ʃepli] *adj* (*comp* **-lier;** *super* **-liest**) bien proportionné, bien fait, svelte

share [ʃɛr] *s* part *f*; (*of stock in a company*) action *f* ‖ *tr* partager ‖ *intr*—**to share in** prendre part à, participer à

sharecropper [ʃɛr,krɑpər] *s* métayer *m*

share′hold′er *s* actionnaire *mf*

shark [ʃɑrk] *s* requin *m*; (*swindler*) escroc *m*; (slang) as *m*, expert *m*

sharp [ʃɑrp] *adj* (*point; pain; intelligence; voice, sound*) aigu; (*wind, cold, pain, fight, criticism, edge, trot; person, mind*) vif; (*knife*) tranchant; (*point; needle, pin, nail; tongue*) acéré; (*slope*) raide; (*curve*) prononcé; (*turn*) brusque; (*photograph*) net; (*hearing*) fin; (*step, gait*) rapide; (*eyesight*) perçant; (*taste*) piquant; (*reprimand*) vert; (*keen*) éveillé; (*cunning*) rusé, fin; (mus) dièse; (*stylish*) (coll) chic; **sharp features** traits *mpl* accentués ‖ *adv* vivement; brusquement; précis, sonnant, tapant, e.g., **at four o'clock sharp** à quatre heures précises, sonnantes, or tapantes; **to stop short** s'arrêter net or pile ‖ *s* (mus) dièse *m* ‖ *tr* (mus) diéser

sharpen [ʃɑrpən] *tr* aiguiser; (*a pencil*) tailler ‖ *intr* s'aiguiser

sharpener [ʃɑrpənər] *s* aiguisoir *m*

sharper [ʃɑrpər] *s* filou *m*, tricheur *m*

sharp′shoot′er *s* tireur *m* d'élite

shatter [ʃætər] *tr* fracasser, briser ‖ *intr* se fracasser, se briser

shat′ter·proof′ *adj* de sécurité

shave [ʃev] *s*—**to get a shave** se faire raser, se faire faire la barbe; **to have a close shave** (coll) l'échapper belle ‖ *tr* (*hair, beard, etc.*) raser; (*a person*) faire la barbe à, raser; (*e.g., wood*) doler; (*e.g., expenses*) rogner ‖ *intr* se raser, se faire la barbe

shaving [ʃevɪŋ] *s* rasage *m*; **shavings** rognures *fpl*, copeaux *mpl*

shav′ing brush′ *s* blaireau *m*

shav′ing soap′ *s* savon *m* à barbe, savonnade *f*

shawl [ʃɔl] *s* châle *m*, fichu *m*

she [ʃi] s femelle f ‖ pron pers elle §85, §87; ce §82B; **she who** celle qui §83

sheaf [ʃif] s (pl **sheaves** [ʃivz]) gerbe f; (of papers) liasse f

shear [ʃIr] s lame f de ciseau; **shears** ciseaux mpl; (to cut metal) cisaille f ‖ v (pret **sheared**; pp **sheared** or **shorn** [ʃorn]) tr (sheep) tondre; (velvet) ciseler; (metal) cisailler; **to shear off** couper

sheath [ʃiθ] s (pl **sheaths** [ʃiðz]) gaine f, fourreau m

sheathe [ʃið] tr envelopper; (a sword) rengainer

shed [ʃɛd] s (warehouse; engine shed; barn) hangar m; (for, e.g., tools) remise f; (rough shelter) hutte f, cabane f; (for cattle) étable f; (line from which water flows in two directions) ligne f de faîte ‖ v (pret & pp **shed**; ger **shedding**) tr répandre, verser; (e.g., leaves) perdre; (e.g., light; skin) jeter

sheen [ʃin] s lustre m, brilliant m

sheep [ʃip] s (pl **sheep**) mouton m; (ewe) brebis f

sheep′dog′ s chien m de berger

sheep′fold′ s bergerie f

sheepish [ʃipiʃ] adj penaud, honteux

sheep′skin′ s (undressed) peau f de mouton; (dressed) basane f; (diploma) (coll) peau d'âne

sheep′skin jack′et s canadienne f

sheer [ʃIr] adj (stocking) extra-fin; (steep) à pic; (impossibility; necessity; waste of time) absolu; (utter) pur; (fig) vif, e.g., **by sheer force** de vive force ‖ intr faire une embardée

sheet [ʃit] s (e.g., for the bed) drap m; (of paper) feuille f; (of metal) tôle f, lame f; (of water) nappe f; (of ice) couche f; (naut) écoute f; **white as a sheet** blanc comme un linge

sheet′ light′ning s fulguration f, éclairs mpl en nappe

sheet′ met′al s tôle f

sheet′ mu′sic s morceaux mpl de musique

sheik [ʃik] s cheik m; (coll) tombeur m de femmes

shelf [ʃɛlf] s (pl **shelves** [ʃɛlvz]) tablette f, planche f; (of cupboard; of library) rayon m; (geog) plateau m; **on the shelf** (inactive) (coll) au rancart, laissé à l'écart; **shelves** rayonnages mpl

shell [ʃɛl] s (of egg, nut, oyster, snail, etc.) coque f, coquille f; (of nut) écale f, coque; (of pea) cosse f; (of oyster, clam, etc.) écaille f; (of tortoise, lobster, crab) carapace f; (of building, ship, etc.) carcasse f; (cartridge) cartouche f; (projectile) obus m; (long, narrow racing boat) yole f, outrigger m ‖ tr écaler, écosser; (mil) bombarder, pilonner; **to shell out** (coll) débourser ‖ intr—**to shell out** (coll) casquer

shel·lac [ʃə'læk] s laque f, gomme f laque ‖ v (pret & pp **-lacked**; ger **-lacking**) tr laquer; (slang) tabasser

shell′fish′ s fruits mpl de mer, coquillages mpl

shell′ hole′ s entonnoir m, trou m d'obus

shell′ shock′ s commotion f cérébrale

shelter ['ʃɛltər] s abri m ‖ tr abriter

shelve [ʃɛlv] tr (a book) ranger; (merchandise) entreposer; (a project, a question, etc., by putting it aside) enterrer, classer; (to provide with shelves) garnir de tablettes, rayons, ou planches

shelving ['ʃɛlvɪŋ] s rayonnage m, étagères fpl

shepherd ['ʃɛpərd] s berger m; (fig) pasteur m ‖ tr veiller sur, guider

shep′herd dog′ s berger m, chien m de berger

shepherdess ['ʃɛpərdɪs] s bergère f

sherbet ['ʃʌrbət] s sorbet m

sheriff ['ʃɛrɪf] s shérif m

sher·ry ['ʃɛri] s (pl **-ries**) xérès m

shield [ʃild] s bouclier m; (elec) blindage m; (heral, hist) écu m, écusson m ‖ tr protéger; (elec) blinder

shift [ʃɪft] s (change) changement m; (in wind, temperature, etc.) saute f; (group of workmen) équipe f de relais; (fig) expédient m ‖ tr changer; (the blame, the guilt, etc.) rejeter; **to shift gears** changer de vitesse ‖ intr changer; changer de place; changer de direction; **to shift for oneself** se débrouiller tout seul

shift′ key′ s touche f majuscules

shiftless ['ʃɪftlɪs] adj mollasse, peu débrouillard

shift′-lock′ key′ s fixe-majuscules m

shift·y ['ʃɪfti] adj (comp **-ier**; super **-iest**) roublard; (look) chafouin; (eye) fuyant

shimmer ['ʃɪmər] s chatoiement m, miroitement m ‖ intr chatoyer, miroiter

shin [ʃɪn] s tibia m; (culin) jarret m ‖ v (pret & pp **shinned**; ger **shinning**) intr—**to shin up** grimper

shin′bone′ s tibia m

shine [ʃaɪn] s (shining) éclat m, brillant m; (of cloth, clothing, etc.) luisant m; (on shoes) coup m de cirage; **to take a shine to** (slang) s'enticher de ‖ v (pret & pp **shined**) tr faire briller, faire reluire; (shoes) cirer ‖ v (pret & pp **shone** [ʃon]) intr briller, reluire

shiner ['ʃaɪnər] s (slang) œil m poché

shingle ['ʃɪŋgəl] s bardeau m; (of doctor, laywer, etc.) (coll) enseigne f; **shingles** (pathol) zona m

shining ['ʃaɪnɪŋ] adj brillant, luisant

shin·y ['ʃaɪni] adj (comp **-ier**; super **-iest**) brillant, reluisant; (from much wear) lustré

ship [ʃɪp] s navire m; (steamer, liner) paquebot m; (aer) appareil m; (nav) bâtiment m ‖ v (pret & pp **shipped**; ger **shipping**) tr expédier; (a cargo; water) embarquer; (oars) armer, rentrer ‖ intr s'embarquer

ship′board′ s bord m; **on shipboard** à bord

ship′build′er s constructeur m de navires

ship′build′ing s construction f navale

ship′mate′ s compagnon m de bord

shipment ['ʃɪpmənt] s expédition f; (*goods shipped*) chargement m
ship'own'er s armateur m
shipper ['ʃɪpər] s expéditeur m
shipping ['ʃɪpɪŋ] s embarquement m, expédition f; (naut) transport m maritime
ship'ping clerk' s expéditionnaire mf
ship'ping mem'o s connaissement m
ship'ping room' s salle f d'expédition
ship'shape' adj & adv en bon ordre
ship's' pa'pers spl papiers mpl de bord
ship's' time' s heure f locale du navire
ship'-to-shore' ra'di·o ['ʃɪptə'ʃor] s (pl -os) liaison f radio maritime
ship'wreck' s naufrage m ‖ tr faire naufrager ‖ intr faire naufrage
ship'yard' s chantier m de construction navale or maritime
shirk [ʃʌrk] tr manquer à, esquiver ‖ intr négliger son devoir
shirred' eggs' [ʃʌrd] spl œufs mpl pochés à la crème
shirt [ʃʌrt] s chemise f; **keep your shirt on!** (slang) ne vous emballez pas!; **to lose one's shirt** perdre jusqu'à son dernier sou
shirt'band' s encolure f
shirt' front' s plastron m de chemise
shirt' sleeve' s manche f de chemise; **in shirt sleeves** en bras de chemise
shirt'tails' spl pans mpl de chemise
shirt'waist' s chemisier m
shiver ['ʃɪvər] s frisson m ‖ intr frissonner
shoal [ʃol] s banc m, bas-fond m
shock [ʃak] s (*bump, clash*) choc m, heurt m; (*upset, misfortune; earthquake tremor*) secousse f; (*of grain*) gerbe f, moyette f; (*of hair*) tignasse f; (elec) commotion f, choc; **to die of shock** mourir de saisissement ‖ tr choquer; (elec) commotionner, choquer
shock' absorb'er [æb,sɔrbər] s amortisseur m
shocking ['ʃakɪŋ] adj choquant, scandaleux
shock' troops' spl troupes fpl de choc
shod·dy ['ʃadi] adj (comp -dier; super -diest) inférieur, de pacotille
shoe [ʃu] s soulier m; **to be in the shoes of** être dans la peau de; **to put one's shoes on** se chausser; **to take one's shoes off** se déchausser ‖ v (pret & pp shod [ʃad]) tr chausser; (*a horse*) ferrer
shoe'black' s cireur m de bottes
shoe'horn' s chausse-pied m
shoe'lace' s lacet m, cordon m de soulier
shoe'mak'er s cordonnier m
shoe' pol'ish s cirage m de chaussures
shoe'shine' s cirage m
shoe' store' s magasin m de chaussures
shoe'string' s lacet m, cordon m de soulier; **on a shoestring** avec de minces capitaux
shoe'tree' s embauchoir m, forme f
shoo [ʃu] tr chasser ‖ interj ich!, filez!
shoot [ʃut] s (*sprout, twig*) rejeton m, pousse f; (*for grain, sand, etc.*) goulotte f; (*contest*) concours m de tir; (*hunting party*) partie f de chasse ‖ v (pret & pp shot [ʃat]) tr tirer; (*a person*) tuer d'un coup

de fusil; (*to execute with a discharge of rifles*) fusiller; (*with a camera*) photographier; (*a scene; a motion picture*) tourner, roder; (*the sun*) prendre la hauteur de; (*dice*) jeter; **to shoot down** abattre; **to shoot up** (slang) cribler de balles ‖ intr tirer; s'élancer, se précipiter; (*said of pain*) lanciner; (*said of star*) filer; **to shoot at** faire feu sur; (*to strive for*) viser; **to shoot up** (*said of plant*) pousser; (*said of flame*) jaillir; (*said of prices*) augmenter; (*intravenously*) (slang) se shooter
shooting ['ʃutɪŋ] s tir m; (phot) prise f de vues
shoot'ing gal'ler·y s (pl -ies) stand m de tir, tir m
shoot'ing match' s concours m de tir
shoot'ing script' s découpage m
shoot'ing star' s étoile f filante
shop [ʃap] s (*store*) boutique f; (*workshop*) atelier m; **to talk shop** parler boutique, parler affaires ‖ v (pret & pp shopped; ger shopping) intr faire des emplettes, faire des courses; magasiner (Canad); **to go shopping** faire des emplettes, faire des courses; **to shop around** être à l'affût de bonnes occasions; **to shop for** chercher à acheter
shop'girl' s vendeuse f
shop'keep'er s boutiquier m
shoplifter ['ʃap,lɪftər] s voleur m à l'étalage
shopper ['ʃapər] s acheteur m
shopping ['ʃapɪŋ] s achat m; (*purchases*) achats mpl, emplettes fpl
shop'ping bag' s sac m à provisions, cabas m
shop'ping cen'ter s centre m commercial
shop'ping dis'trict s quartier m commerçant
shop'ping mall' s galerie f marchande
shop'stew'ard s délégué m d'atelier
shop'win'dow s vitrine f, devanture f
shop'worn' adj défraîchi
shore [ʃor] s rivage m, rive f, bord m; (*sandy beach*) plage f; **shores** (poetic) pays m ‖ tr—**to shore up** étayer
shore' din'ner s dîner m de marée
shore' leave' s (nav) descente f à terre
shore'line' s ligne f de côte
shore' patrol' s patrouille f de garde-côte; (*police*) (nav) police f militaire de la marine
short [ʃort] adj court; (*person*) petit; (*temper*) brusque; (phonet) bref; **in short** en somme; **short of breath** poussif; **to be short for** (coll) être le diminutif de; **to be short of** être à court de ‖ s (elec) court-circuit m; (mov) court-métrage m; **shorts** culotte f courte, culotte de sport ‖ adv court, de court; **to run short of** être à court de, manquer de; **to sell short** (com) vendre à découvert; **to stop short** s'arrêter net ‖ tr (elec) court-circuiter ‖ intr (elec) se mettre en court-circuit
shortage ['ʃortɪdʒ] s manque m, pénurie f; crise f, e.g., **housing shortage** crise du logement; (com) déficit m; **shortages** manquants mpl

short'cake' *s* gâteau *m* recouvert de fruits frais *m*

short'-change' *tr* ne pas rendre assez de monnaie à; (*to cheat*) (coll) rouler

short' cir'cuit *s* court-circuit *m*

short'-cir'cuit *tr* court-circuiter

short'com'ing *s* défaut *m*

short'cut' *s* raccourci *m*

shorten ['ʃɔrtən] *tr* raccourcir ‖ *intr* se raccourcir

shortening ['ʃɔrtənɪŋ] *s* raccourcissement *m*; (culin) saindoux *m*

short'hand' *adj* sténographique ‖ *s* sténographie *f*; **to take down in shorthand** sténographier

short'hand notes' *spl* sténogramme *m*

short'hand typ'ist *s* sténodactylo *mf*

short-lived ['ʃɔrt'laɪvd], ['ʃɔrt'lɪvd] *adj* de courte durée, bref

shortly ['ʃɔrtli] *adv* tantôt, sous peu; brièvement; (*curtly*) sèchement; **shortly after** peu après

short'-range' *adj* à courte portée

short'-range plane' *s* court-courrier *m*

short' sale' *s* vente *f* à découvert

short'-sight'ed *adj* myope; **to be short-sighted** (fig) avoir la vue courte

short' sto'ry *s* nouvelle *f*, conte *m*

short'-tem'pered *adj* vif, emporté

short'-term' *adj* à court terme

short'wave' *adj* aux petites ondes, aux ondes courtes ‖ *s* petite onde *f*, onde courte

short' weight' *s* poids *m* insuffisant

shot [ʃɑt] *adj* (*silk*) changeant; (*e.g., chances*) (coll) réduit à zéro; (*drunk*) (slang) paf ‖ *s* coup *m* de feu, décharge *f*; (*marksman*) tireur *m*; (*pellets*) petits plombs *mpl*; (*of a rocket into space*) lancement *m*, tir *m*; (*in certain games*) shoot *m*; (*snapshot*) instantané *m*; (mov) plan *m*; (*hypodermic injection*) (coll) piqûre *f*; (*drink of liquor*) (slang) verre *m* d'alcool; **a long shot** un gros risque, une chance sur mille; **to fire a shot at** tirer sur; **to start like a shot** partir comme un trait

shot'gun' *s* fusil *m* de chasse

shot'-put' *s* (sports) lancement *m* du poids

should [ʃud] *aux* used to express 1) the present conditional, e.g., **if I waited for him, I should miss the train** si je l'attendais, je manquerais le train; 2) the past conditional, e.g., **if I had waited for him, I should have missed the train** si je l'avais attendu, j'aurais manqué le train; 3) the potential mood, e.g., **he should go at once** il devrait aller aussitôt; e.g., **he should have gone at once** il aurait dû aller aussitôt; 4) a softened affirmation, e.g., **I should like a drink** je prendrais bien quelque chose à boire; e.g., **I should have thought that you would have known better** j'aurais cru que vous auriez été plus avisé

shoulder ['ʃoldər] *s* épaule *f*; (*of a road*) accotement *m*; **across the shoulder** en bandoulière, en écharpe; **shoulders** (*of a garment*) carrure *f*; **to cry on someone's shoulder** pleurer dans le gilet de qn ‖ *tr* (*a gun*) mettre sur l'épaule; **to shoulder aside** pousser de l'épaule

shoul'der blade' *s* omoplate *f*

shoul'der strap' *s* (*of underwear*) épaulette *f*; (mil) bandoulière *f*

shout [ʃaut] *s* cri *m* ‖ *tr* crier; **to shout down** huer ‖ *intr* crier

shove [ʃʌv] *s* poussée *f*, bourrade *f* ‖ *tr* pousser, bousculer ‖ *intr* pousser; **to shove off** pousser au large; (slang) filer, décamper

shov·el ['ʃʌvəl] *s* pelle *f* ‖ *v* (*pret & pp* -eled *or* -elled; *ger* -eling *or* -elling) *tr* pelleter; (*e.g., snow*) balayer

show [ʃo] *s* (*of hatred or affection*) démonstration *f*; (*semblance*) apparence *f*; (*exhibition*) exposition *f*; (*display*) étalage *m*, parade *f*; (*of hands*) levée *f*; (*each performance*) séance *f*; (mov) film *m*; (theat) spectacle *m*; **by show of hands** à main levée; **to make a show of** faire parade de ‖ *v* (*pret* **showed**; *pp* **shown** [ʃon] *or* **showed**) *tr* montrer; (*one's passport*) présenter; (*a film*) projeter; (*e.g., to the door*) conduire; **to show off** faire étalage de; **to show up** (coll) démasquer ‖ *intr* se montrer; **to show through** transparaître; **to show up** (*against a background*) ressortir; (coll) faire son apparition

show'bill' *s* affiche *f*

show'boat' *s* bateau-théâtre *m*

show' busi'ness *s* l'industrie *f* du spectacle

show'case' *s* vitrine *f*

show'down' *s* cartes *fpl* sur table, moment *m* critique; **to come to a showdown** en venir au fait; **to force a showdown** mettre au pied du mur

shower ['ʃau·ər] *s* averse *f*, ondée *f*; (*of blows, bullets, kisses, etc.*) pluie *f*; (*bath*) douche *f* ‖ *tr* faire pleuvoir; **to shower with** combler de ‖ *intr* pleuvoir à verse

show' girl' *s* girl *f*

show'man *s* (*pl* -**men**) impresario *m*; **he's a great showman** c'est un as pour la mise en scène

show'-off' *s* (coll) m'as-tu-vu *m*

show'piece' *s* pièce *f* maîtresse

show'place' *s* lieu *m* célèbre

show'room' *s* salon *m* d'exposition

show' win'dow *s* vitrine *f*

show·y ['ʃo·i] *adj* (*comp* -**ier**; *super* -**iest**) fastueux; (*gaudy*) voyant

shrapnel ['ʃræpnəl] *s* shrapnel *m*, obus *m* à mitraille; éclat *m* d'obus

shred [ʃrɛd] *s* morceau *m*, lambeau *m*; **not a shred of** pas l'ombre de; **to tear to shreds** mettre en lambeaux ‖ *v* (*pret & pp* **shredded** *or* **shred**; *ger* **shredding**) *tr* mettre en lambeaux, déchiqueter

shrew [ʃru] *s* (*nagging woman*) mégère *f*; (zool) musaraigne *f*

shrewd [ʃrud] *adj* sagace, fin

shriek [ʃrik] *s* cri *m* perçant ‖ *intr* pousser un cri perçant

shrike [ʃraɪk] *s* pie-grièche *f*

shrill [ʃrɪl] *adj* aigu, perçant

shrimp [ʃrɪmp] *s* crevette *f*; (*insignificant person*) gringalet *m*

shrine [ʃraɪn] *s* tombeau *m* de saint; (*reliquary*) châsse *f*; (*holy place*) lieu *m* saint, sanctuaire *m*

shrink [ʃrɪŋk] *v* (*pret* **shrank** [ʃræŋk] or **shrunk** [ʃrʌŋk]; *pp* **shrunk** or **shrunken**) *tr* rétrécir ‖ *intr* se rétrécir; **to shrink away** or **back from** reculer devant

shrinkage [ˈʃrɪŋkɪdʒ] *s* rétrécissement *m*

shriv·el [ˈʃrɪvəl] *v* (*pret & pp* **-eled** or **-elled**; *ger* **-eling** or **-elling**) *tr* ratatiner, recroqueviller ‖ *intr* se ratatiner, se recroqueviller

shroud [ʃraʊd] *s* linceul *m*; (*veil*) voile *m*; **shrouds** (naut) haubans *mpl* ‖ *tr* ensevelir; voiler

Shrove' Tues'day [ʃrov] *s* mardi *m* gras

shrub [ʃrʌb] *s* arbuste *m*

shrubber·y [ˈʃrʌbəri] *s* (*pl* **-ies**) bosquet *m*

shrug [ʃrʌg] *s* haussement *m* d'épaules ‖ *v* (*pret & pp* **shrugged**; *ger* **shrugging**) *tr* (*one's shoulders*) hausser; **to shrug off** minimiser; ne tenir aucun compte de ‖ *intr* hausser les épaules

shudder [ˈʃʌdər] *s* frisson *m*, frémissement *m* ‖ *intr* frissonner, frémir

shuffle [ˈʃʌfəl] *s* (*of cards*) battement *m*, mélange *m*; (*of feet*) frottement *m*; (*change of place*) déplacement *m* ‖ *tr* (*cards*) battre; (*the feet*) traîner; (*to mix up*) mêler, brouiller ‖ *intr* battre les cartes; traîner les pieds

shuf'fle·board' *s* jeu *m* de palets

shun [ʃʌn] *v* (*pret & pp* **shunned**; *ger* **shunning**) *tr* éviter, fuir

shunt [ʃʌnt] *tr* garer, manœuvrer; (elec) shunter, dériver

shut [ʃʌt] *adj* fermé ‖ *v* (*pret & pp* **shut**; *ger* **shutting**) *tr* fermer; **to shut in** enfermer; **to shut off** couper; **to shut up** enfermer; (coll) faire taire, clouer le bec à ‖ *intr* se fermer; **shut up!** (slang) tais-toi!, ferme-la!

shut'down' *s* fermeture *f*

shutter [ˈʃʌtər] *s* volet *m*, contrevent *m*; (*over store window*) rideau *m*; (phot) obturateur *m*

shuttle [ˈʃʌtəl] *s* navette *f* ‖ *intr* faire la navette

shut'tle train' *s* navette *f*

shy [ʃaɪ] *adj* (*comp* **shyer** or **shier**; *super* **shyest** or **shiest**) timide, sauvage; (*said of horse*) ombrageux; **I am shy a dollar** il me faut un dollar; **to be shy of** se méfier de ‖ *v* (*pret & pp* **shied**) *intr* (*said of horse*) faire un écart; **to shy away from** éviter

shyster [ˈʃaɪstər] *s* (coll) avocat *m* marron

Sia·mese [ˌsaɪ·əˈmiz] *adj* siamois ‖ *s* (*pl* **-mese**) Siamois *m*

Si'amese twins' *spl* frères *mpl* siamois

Siberian [saɪˈbɪrɪ·ən] *adj* sibérien ‖ *s* Sibérien *m*

sibyl [ˈsɪbɪl] *s* sibylle *f*

sic [sɪk] *adv* sic ‖ [sɪk] *v* (*pret & pp* **sicked**; *ger* **sicking**) *tr*—**sic 'em!** (coll) pille!; **to sic on** lancer après

Sicilian [sɪˈsɪljən] *adj* sicilien ‖ *s* Sicilien *m*

Sicily [ˈsɪsɪli] *s* Sicile *f*; la Sicile

sick [sɪk] *adj* malade; **to be sick and tired of** (coll) en avoir plein le dos de, en avoir marre de; **to be sick at** or **to one's stomach** avoir mal au cœur, avoir des nausées; **to take sick** tomber malade

sick'bed' *s* lit *m* de malade

sicken [ˈsɪkən] *tr* rendre malade ‖ *intr* tomber malade; (*to be disgusted*) être écœuré

sickening [ˈsɪkənɪŋ] *adj* écœurant, dégoûtant

sick' head'ache *s* migraine *f* avec nausées

sickle [ˈsɪkəl] *s* faucille *f*

sick' leave' *s* congé *m* de maladie

sick'le cell' ane'mia *s* (pathol) drépanocytose *f*

sick·ly [ˈsɪkli] *adj* (*comp* **-lier**; *super* **-liest**) maladif, débile

sickness [ˈsɪknɪs] *s* maladie *f*; nausée *f*

side [saɪd] *adj* latéral, de côté ‖ *s* côté *m*; (*of phonograph*) face *f*; (*of team, government, etc.*) camp *m*, parti *m*, côté; **this side up** (*on package*) haut ‖ *intr*—**to side with** prendre le parti de

side' arms' *spl* armes *fpl* de ceinturon

side'board' *s* buffet *m*, desserte *f*

side'burns' *spl* favoris *mpl*

side' dish' *s* plat *m* d'accompagnement

side' door' *s* porte *f* latérale, porte *f* de service

side' effect' *s* effet *m* secondaire

side' en'trance *s* entrée *f* latérale

side' glance' *s* regard *m* de côté

side' is'sue *s* question *f* d'intérêt secondaire

side'line' *s* occupation *f* secondaire; **on the sidelines** sans y prendre part

sidereal [saɪˈdɪrɪ·əl] *adj* sidéral

side' road' *s* chemin *m* de traverse

side'sad'dle *adv* en amazone

side' show' *s* spectacle *m* forain; (fig) événement *m* secondaire

side'slip' *s* glissade *f* sur l'aile

side' split'ting *adj* désopilant

side' step' *s* écart *m*

side'-step' *v* (*pret & pp* **-stepped**; *ger* **-stepping**) *tr* éviter ‖ *intr* faire un pas de côté

side' stroke' *s* nage *f* sur le côté

side' ta'ble *s* console *f*

side'track' *s* voie *f* de garage ‖ *tr* écarter, dévier; (rr) aiguiller sur une voie de garage

side' view' *s* vue *f* de profil

side'walk' *s* trottoir *m*

side'walk café' *s* terrasse *f* de café

side'walk sale' *s* vente *f* à l'éventaire

sideward [ˈsaɪdwərd] *adj* latéral ‖ *adv* latéralement, de côté

side'ways' *adj* latéral ‖ *adv* latéralement, de côté

side' whisk'ers *spl* favoris *mpl*

side′wise′ adj latéral ‖ adv latéralement, de côté

siding [′saɪdɪŋ] s (on a house) bardage m; (rr) voie f d'évitement, voie de garage

sidle [′saɪdəl] intr avancer de biais; **to sidle up to** se couler auprès de

siege [sidʒ] s siège m; **to lay siege to** mettre le siège devant

siesta [si′estə] s sieste f; **to take a siesta** faire la sieste

sieve [sɪv] s crible m, tamis m ‖ tr passer au crible, passer au tamis

sift [sɪft] tr passer au crible, passer au tamis; (flour) tamiser; (fig) examiner soigneusement

sigh [saɪ] s soupir m ‖ intr soupirer

sight [saɪt] s vue f; (of firearm) mire f; (of telescope, camera, etc.) viseur m; chose f digne d'être vue; **a sight of** (coll) énormément de; **at sight** à vue; **à livre ouvert**; **by sight** de vue; **in sight of** à la vue de; **sad sight** spectacle m navrant; **sights** curiosités fpl; **to catch sight of** apercevoir; **what a sight you are!** comme vous voilà fait! ‖ tr & intr viser

sight′ draft′ s (com) effet m à vue

sight′-read′ v (pret & pp **read** [‚rɛd]) tr & intr lire à livre ouvert; (mus) déchiffrer

sight′ read′er s déchiffreur m

sight′see′ing s tourisme m; **to go sightseeing** visiter les curiosités

sightseer [′saɪt‚si·ər] s touriste mf, excursionniste mf

sign [saɪn] s signe m; (on a store) enseigne f ‖ tr signer; **to sign up** engager, embaucher ‖ intr signer; **to sign off** (rad) terminer l'émission; **to sign up for** (coll) s'inscrire à

sig·nal [′sɪɡnəl] adj signalé, insigne ‖ s signal m ‖ v (pret & pp **-naled** or **-nalled**; ger **-naling** or **-nalling**) tr faire signe à, signaler ‖ intr faire des signaux

sig′nal tow′er s tour f de signalisation

signature [′sɪɡnətʃər] s signature f; (bb) cahier m (d'imprimerie); (mus) armature f; (rad) indicatif m

sign′board′ s panneau m d'affichage

signer [′saɪnər] s signataire mf

sig′net ring′ [′sɪɡnɪt] s chevalière f

significance [sɪɡ′nɪfɪkəns] s importance f; (meaning) signification f

significant [sɪɡ′nɪfəkənt] adj important; significatif

signi·fy [′sɪɡnɪ‚faɪ] v (pret & pp **-fied**) tr signifier

sign′post′ s poteau m indicateur

silence [′saɪləns] s silence m ‖ tr faire taire, réduire au silence

silencer [′saɪlənsər] s (of a gun) silencieux m

silent [′saɪlənt] adj silencieux

si′lent major′ity s majorité f silencieuse

si′lent mov′ie s film m muet

silhouette [‚sɪlu′ɛt] s silhouette f ‖ tr silhouetter

silicon [′sɪlɪkən] s silicium m

silicone [′sɪlɪ‚kon] s silicone f

silk [sɪlk] s soie f

silk′-cotton tree′ s fromager m

silken [′sɪlkən] adj soyeux

silk′ hat′ s haut-de-forme m

silk′-stock′ing adj aristocratique ‖ s aristocrate mf

silk′worm′ s ver m à soie

silk·y [′sɪlki] adj (comp **-ier**; super **-iest**) soyeux

sill [sɪl] s (of window) rebord m; (of door) seuil m; (of walls) sablière f

sil·ly [′sɪli] adj (comp **-lier**; super **-liest**) sot, niais

si·lo [′saɪlo] s (pl **-los**) silo m ‖ tr ensiler

silt [sɪlt] s vase f

silver [′sɪlvər] s argent m ‖ tr argenter; (a mirror) étamer

sil′ver·fish′ s (ent) poisson m d'argent

sil′ver foil′ s feuille f d'argent

sil′ver lin′ing s beau côté m, côté brillant

sil′ver plate′ s argenterie f

sil′ver screen′ s écran m

sil′ver·smith′ s orfèvre m

sil′ver spoon′ s—**born with a silver spoon in one's mouth** né coiffé

sil′ver-tongued′ adj à la langue dorée, éloquent

sil′ver·ware′ s argenterie f

similar [′sɪmɪlər] adj semblable

similari·ty [‚sɪmɪ′lærɪti] s (pl **-ties**) ressemblance f, similitude f

simile [′sɪmɪli] s comparaison f

simmer [′sɪmər] tr mijoter ‖ intr mijoter; **to simmer down** s'apaiser

Simon [′saɪmən] s Simon m; **Simon says . . .** (game) Caporal a dit . . .

simper [′sɪmpər] s sourire m niais ‖ intr sourire bêtement

simple [′sɪmpəl] adj & s simple m

sim′ple-mind′ed adj simple, naïf; niais

simpleton [′sɪmpəltən] s niais m

simpli·fy [′sɪmplɪ‚faɪ] v (pret & pp **-fied**) tr simplifier

simulate [′sɪmjə‚let] tr simuler

simultaneous [‚saɪməl′teni·əs] adj simultané

si′multa′neous transla′tion s traduction f en simultanée

sin [sɪn] s péché m ‖ v (pret & pp **sinned**; ger **sinning**) intr pécher

since [sɪns] adv & prep depuis ‖ conj depuis que; (inasmuch as) puisque

sincere [sɪn′sɪr] adj sincère

sincerity [sɪn′sɛrɪti] s sincérité f

sine [saɪn] s (trig) sinus m

sinecure [′saɪnɪ‚kjʊr] s sinécure f

sinew [′sɪnju] s tendon m; (fig) nerf m, force f

sinful [′sɪnfəl] adj (person) pécheur; (act, intention) coupable

sing [sɪŋ] v (pret **sang** [sæŋ] or **sung** [sʌŋ]; pp **sung**) tr & intr chanter

singe [sɪndʒ] v (ger **singeing**) tr roussir; (poultry) flamber

singer [′sɪŋər] s chanteur m

single [′sɪŋɡəl] adj seul, unique; (unmarried) célibataire; (e.g., room in a hotel) à un lit; (bed) à une place; (e.g., devotion) simple, honnête ‖ *tr*—**to single out** distinguer, choisir

sin′gle bless′edness [ˈblɛsɪdnɪs] *s* le bonheur *m* du célibat

sin′gle·breast′ed *adj* droit

sin′gle-en′try *adj* (bk) en partie simple

sin′gle-en′try book′keeping *s* comptabilité *f* simple

sin′gle file′ *s*—**in single file** en file indienne, à la file

sin′gle-hand′ed *adj* sans aide, tout seul

sin′gle life′ *s* vie *f* de célibataire

sin′gle room′ *s* chambre *f* à un lit

sin′gle-spaced′ *s* à simple interligne

sin′gle-track′ *adj* (rr) à voie unique; (coll) d'une portée limitée

sing′song′ *adj* monotone ‖ *s* mélopée *f*

singular [ˈsɪŋɡjələr] *adj & s* singulier *m*

sinister [ˈsɪnɪstər] *adj* sinistre

sink [sɪŋk] *s* (*in kitchen or laundry*) évier *m*; (*in bathroom*) lavabo *m*; (*drain*) égout *m* ‖ *v* (*pret* **sank** [sæŋk] *or* **sunk** [sʌŋk]; *pp* **sunk**) *tr* enfoncer; (*a ship*) couler, faire sombrer; (*a well*) creuser; (*money*) immobiliser ‖ *intr* s'enfoncer, s'affaisser; (*under the water*) couler, sombrer; (*said of heart*) se serrer; (*said of health, prices, sun, etc.*) baisser; **to sink into** plonger dans; (*an armchair*) s'effondrer dans

sink′ing fund′ *s* caisse *f* d'amortissement

sink′hole′ *s* (fig) cloaque *m* de vice

sinless [ˈsɪnlɪs] *adj* sans péché

sinner [ˈsɪnər] *s* pécheur *m*

sintering [ˈsɪntərɪŋ] *s* (metallurgy) frittage *m*

sinuous [ˈsɪnjʊ·əs] *adj* sinueux

sinus [ˈsaɪnəs] *s* sinus *m*

sip [sɪp] *s* petite gorgée *f*, petit coup *m* ‖ *v* (*pret & pp* **sipped;** *ger* **sipping**) *tr* boire à petit coups, siroter

siphon [ˈsaɪfən] *s* siphon *m* ‖ *tr* siphonner

si′phon bot′tle *s* siphon *m*

sir [sʌr] *s* monsieur *m*; (*British title*) Sir *m*; **Dear Sir** Monsieur

sire [saɪr] *s* sire *m*; (*of a quadruped*) père *m* ‖ *tr* engendrer

siren [ˈsaɪrən] *s* sirène *f*

sirloin [ˈsʌrlɔɪn] *s* aloyau *m*

sirup [ˈsɪrəp], [ˈsʌrəp] *s* sirop *m*

sis·sy [ˈsɪsi] *s* (*pl* **-sies**) efféminé *m*; fillette *f*; (*cowardly fellow*) poule *f* mouillée

sister [ˈsɪstər] *adj* (fig) jumeau ‖ *s* sœur *f*

sis′ter-in-law′ *s* (*pl* **sisters-in-law**) belle-sœur *f*

sit [sɪt] *v* (*pret & pp* **sat** [sæt]; *ger* **sitting**) *intr* s'asseoir; être assis; (*said of hen on eggs*) couver; (*for a portrait*) poser; (*said of legislature, court, etc.*) siéger; **to sit down** s'asseoir; **to sit still** ne pas bouger; **to sit up** se redresser; se tenir droit; **to sit up and beg** (*said of dog*) faire le beau

sitcom [ˈsɪt,kɑm] *s* (rad, telv) comédie *f* de situation

sit′-down strike′ *s* grève *f* sur le tas

site [saɪt] *s* site *m*

sit′-in′ *s* occupation *f* sauvage

sitting [ˈsɪtɪŋ] *s* séance *f*

sit′ting duck′ *s* (coll) cible *f* facile

sit′ting room′ *s* salon *m*

situate [ˈsɪtʃʊ,et] *tr* situer

situation [,sɪtʃʊˈeʃən] *s* situation *f*; poste *m*, emploi *m*

sit′up′ *s* (*exercise*) redressement *m* assis

sitz′ bath′ [sɪts] *s* bain *m* de siège

six [sɪks] *adj & pron* six ‖ *s* six *m*; **at sixes and sevens** de travers, en désaccord; **six o′clock** six heures

sixteen [ˈsɪksˈtin] *adj & pron* seize *m*

sixteenth [ˈsɪksˈtinθ] *adj & pron* seizième (*masc, fem*); **the Sixteenth** seize, e.g., **John the Sixteenth** Jean seize ‖ *s* seizième *m*; **the sixteenth** (*in dates*) le seize

sixth [sɪksθ] *adj & pron* sixième (*masc, fem*); **the Sixth** six, e.g., **John the Sixth** Jean six ‖ *s* sixième *m*; **the sixth** (*in dates*) le six

sixtieth [ˈsɪkstɪ·ɪθ] *adj & pron* soixantième (*masc, fem*) ‖ *s* soixantième *m*

six·ty [ˈsɪksti] *adj & pron* soixante; **about sixty** une soixantaine de ‖ *s* (*pl* **-ties**) soixante *m*; (*age of*) soixantaine *f*

sizable [ˈsaɪzəbəl] *adj* assez grand, considérable

size [saɪz] *s* grandeur *f*, dimensions *fpl*; (*of a person or garment*) taille *f*; (*of a shoe, glove, or hat*) pointure *f*; (*of a shirt collar*) encolure *f*; (*of a book or box*) format *m*; (*to fill a porous surface*) apprêt *m*; **what size hat do you wear?** du combien coiffez-vous?; **what size shoes do you wear?** du combien chaussez-vous? ‖ *tr* classer; (*wood to be painted*) coller; **to size up** juger

sizzle [ˈsɪzəl] *s* grésillement *m* ‖ *intr* grésiller

skate [sket] *s* patin *m*; (ichth) raie *f*; **good skate** (slang) brave homme *m* ‖ *intr* patiner; **to go skating** faire du patin

skate′board′ *s* planche *f* à roulettes

skat′ing rink′ *s* patinoire *f*

skein [sken] *s* écheveau *m*

skeleton [ˈskɛlɪtən] *s* squelette *m*; **skeleton in the closet** squelette *m* dans un placard

skel′eton key′ *s* fausse clé *f*, passe-partout *m*

skeptic [ˈskɛptɪk] *adj & s* sceptique *mf*

skeptical [ˈskɛptɪkəl] *adj* sceptique

skepticism [ˈskɛptɪ,sɪzəm] *s* scepticisme *m*

sketch [skɛtʃ] *s* esquisse *f*; (*pen or pencil drawing*) croquis *m*, esquisse; (lit) aperçu *m*; (theat) sketch *m* ‖ *tr* esquisser ‖ *intr* croquer

sketch′book′ *s* album *m* de croquis

skew [skju] *adj & s* biais *m* ‖ *intr* biaiser

skewer [ˈskju·ər] *s* brochette *f* ‖ *tr* embrocher

ski [ski] *s* ski *m* ‖ *intr* skier; **to go skiing** faire du ski

ski′ boots′ *spl* chaussures *fpl* de ski

skid [skɪd] *s* (*sidewise*) dérapage *m*; (*forward*) patinage *m*; (*of wheel*) sabot *m*, patin *m* ‖ *v* (*pret & pp* **skidded;** *ger* **skidding**) *tr* enrayer, bloquer ‖ *intr* (*side wise*) déraper; (*forward*) patiner

skid′ row′ [ro] *s* quartier *m* mal famé

skier [ˈski·ər] *s* skieur *m*

skiff [skɪf] *s* skiff *m*, esquif *m*

skiing [ˈski·ɪŋ] *s* ski *m*

ski′ jack′et *s* anorak *m*

ski′ jump′ *s* (*place to jump*) tremplin *m*; (*act of jumping*) saut *m* en skis

ski′ lift′ *s* remonte-pente *m*, téléski *m*

skill [skɪl] *s* habilité *f*, adresse *f*; (*job*) métier *m*

skilled *adj* habile, adroit

skillet [ˈskɪlɪt] *s* casserole *f*; (*frying pan*) poêle *f*

skillful [ˈskɪlfəl] *adj* habile, expert

skim [skɪm] *v* (*pret & pp* **skimmed;** *ger* **skimming**) *tr* (*milk*) écrémer; (*molten metal*) écumer; (*to graze*) raser ‖ *intr*—to skim over passer légèrement sur

ski′ mask′ *s* passe-montagne *m*

skimmer [ˈskɪmər] *s* écumoire *f*; (*straw hat*) canotier *m*

skim′ milk′ *s* lait *m* écrémé

skimp [skɪmp] *tr* bâcler ‖ *intr* lésiner; to skimp on lésiner sur

skimp·y [ˈskɪmpi] *adj* (*comp* -ier; *super* -iest) maigre; (*garment*) étriqué; avare, mesquin

skin [skɪn] *s* peau *f*; by the skin of one's teeth de justesse, par un cheveu; soaked to the skin trempé jusqu'aux os; to strip to the skin se mettre à poil ‖ *v* (*pret & pp* **skinned;** *ger* **skinning**) *tr* écorcher, dépouiller; (*e.g., an elbow*) s'écorcher; to skin alive (coll) écorcher vif

skin′-deep′ *adj* superficiel; (*beauty*) à fleur de peau

skin′ div′er *s* plongeur *m* autonome

skin′flint′ *s* grippe-sou *m*

skin′ game′ *s* (slang) escroquerie *f*

skin′ graft′ing *s* greffe *f* cutanée, autoplastie *f*

skin·ny [ˈskɪni] *adj* (*comp* -nier; *super* -niest) maigre, décharné

skin′ test′ *s* (med) cuti-réaction *f*

skin′tight′ *adj* collant, ajusté

skip [skɪp] *s* saut *m* ‖ *v* (*pret & pp* **skipped;** *ger* **skipping**) *tr* sauter; skip it! ça suffit!, laisse tomber!; to skip rope sauter à la corde ‖ *intr* sauter; to skip out or off filer

ski′ pole′ *s* bâton *m* de skis

skipper [ˈskɪpər] *s* patron *m* ‖ *tr* commander, conduire

skirmish [ˈskʌrmɪʃ] *s* escarmouche *f* ‖ *intr* escarmoucher

skirt [skʌrt] *s* jupe *f*; (*woman*) (slang) jupe ‖ *tr* côtoyer, longer; éviter

ski′ run′ *s* descente *f* en skis

ski′ stick′ *s* bâton *m* de skis

skit [skɪt] *s* sketch *m*

skittish [ˈskɪtɪʃ] *adj* capricieux; timide; (*e.g., horse*) ombrageux

ski′ wax′ *s* fart *m*

skulduggery [skʌlˈdʌgəri] *s* (coll) fourberie *f*, ruse *f*, cuisine *f*

skull [skʌl] *s* crâne *m*

skull′ and cross′bones *s* tibias *mpl* croisés et tête *f* de mort

skull′cap′ *s* calotte *f*

skunk [skʌŋk] *s* mouffette *f*; (*person*) (coll) salaud *m*

sky [skaɪ] *s* (*pl* skies) ciel *m*; to praise to the skies porter aux nues

sky′div′er *s* parachutiste *mf*

sky′div′ing *s* parachutisme *m*, saut *m* en chute libre

Sky′lab′ *s* laboratoire *m* du ciel

sky′lark′ *s* (*Alauda arvensis*) alouette *f*, alouette des champs ‖ *intr* (coll) batifoler

sky′light′ *s* lucarne *f*

sky′line′ *s* ligne *m* d'horizon; (*of city*) profil *m*

sky′rock′et *s* fusée *f* volante ‖ *intr* monter en flèche

sky′scrap′er *s* gratte-ciel *m*

slab [slæb] *s* (*of stone*) dalle *f*; (*slice*) tranche *f*

slack [slæk] *adj* (*loose*) lâche, mou; (*careless*) négligent ‖ *s* mou *m*; (*slowdown*) ralentissement *m*; **slacks** pantalon *m*; to take up the slack (coll) prendre le relais ‖ *tr* relâcher; (*lime*) éteindre; to slack off larguer ‖ *intr*—to slack off or up se relâcher

slacken [ˈslækən] *tr* relâcher; (*to slow down*) ralentir ‖ *intr* se relâcher; se ralentir

slacker [ˈslækər] *s* flemmard *m*; (mil) tire-au-flanc *m*, embusqué *m*

slack′ hours′ *spl* heures *fpl* creuses

slag [slæg] *s* scorie *f*

slake [slek] *tr* apaiser, étancher; (*lime*) éteindre

slalom [ˈslɑləm] *s* slalom *m*

slam [slæm] *s* claquement *m*; (cards) chelem *m*; (coll) critique *f* sévère ‖ *v* (*pret & pp* **slammed;** *ger* **slamming**) *tr* claquer; (coll) éreinter; to slam down on flanquer sur ‖ *intr* claquer

slander [ˈslændər] *s* calomnie *f* ‖ *tr* calomnier

slanderous [ˈslændərəs] *adj* calomnieux

slang [slæŋ] *s* argot *m*; (*e.g., of the underworld*) langue *f* verte

slant [slænt] *s* pente *f*; (*bias*) point *m* de vue ‖ *tr* mettre en pente, incliner; donner un biais spécial à ‖ *intr* être en pente, s'incliner

slap [slæp] *s* tape *f*, claque *f*; (*in the face*) soufflet *m*, gifle *f* ‖ *v* (*pret & pp* **slapped;** *ger* **slapping**) *tr* taper, gifler

slap′dash′ *adj*—in a slapdash manner à la va-comme-je-te-pousse ‖ *adv* à la six-quatre-deux

slap′stick′ *adj* bouffon ‖ *s* bouffonnerie *f*

slash [slæʃ] *s* entaille *f* ‖ *tr* taillader; (*e.g., prices*) réduire beaucoup

slat [slæt] *s* latte *f*

slate [slet] *s* ardoise *f*; (*of candidates*) liste *f* ‖ *tr* couvrir d'ardoises; inscrire sur la liste, désigner

slate′ pen′cil *s* crayon *m* d'ardoise

slate′ roof′ *s* toit *m* d'ardoises

slattern [ˈslætərn] *s* (*slovenly woman*) marie-salope *f*; (*slut*) voyoute *f*, gueuse *f*

slaughter [ˈslɔtər] *s* boucherie *f* ‖ *tr* abattre; massacrer

slaught′er·house′ s abattoir m
Slav [slɑv], [slæv] adj slave ‖ s (language) slave m; (person) Slave mf
slave [slev] adj & s esclave mf ‖ intr besogner, trimer
slave′ driv′er s (hist, fig) négrier m
slavery [′slevəri] s esclavage m; (institution of keeping slaves) esclavagisme m
slave′ ship′ s négrier m
slave′ trade′ s traite f des noirs
Slavic [′slævɪk] adj & s slave m
slavish [′slevɪʃ] adj servile
slay [sle] v (pret **slew** [slu]; pp **slain** [slen]) tr tuer, massacrer
slayer [′sle·ər] s meurtrier m
sled [slɛd] s luge f ‖ v (pret & pp **sledded**; ger **sledding**) intr faire de la luge, luger
sled′ dog′ s chien m de traîneau
sledge′ ham′mer [slɛdʒ] s massette f, masse f
sleek [slik] adj lisse, luisant ‖ tr lisser
sleep [slip] s sommeil m; **to go to sleep** s'endormir; **to put to sleep** endormir ‖ v (pret & pp **slept** [slɛpt]) tr—**to sleep it over, to sleep on it** prendre conseil de son oreiller; **to sleep off** (a hangover, headache, etc.) faire passer en dormant ‖ intr dormir; (e.g., with a woman) coucher; **to sleep late** faire la grasse matinée; **to sleep like a log** dormir comme un loir
sleeper [′slipər] s dormeur m; (girder) poutre f horizontale; (tie) (rr) traverse f
sleep′ing bag′ s sac m de couchage
sleep′ing car′ s wagon-lit m
sleep′ing pill′ s somnifère m
sleepless [′sliplɪs] adj sans sommeil
sleep′less night′ s nuit f blanche
sleep′walk′er s somnambule mf
sleep·y [′slipi] adj (comp **-ier**; super **-iest**) endormi, somnolent; **to be sleepy** avoir sommeil
sleep′y·head′ s endormi m, grand dormeur m
sleet [slit] s grésil m; (frozen coating on ground) verglas m ‖ intr grésiller
sleet·y [′sliti] adj (comp **-tier**; super **-tiest**) de grésil; (iced-over) verglacé
sleeve [sliv] s manche f; (mach) manchon m, douille f; **to laugh in** or **up one's sleeve** rire sous cape
sleigh [sle] s traîneau m ‖ intr aller en traîneau
sleigh′ bell′ s grelot m
sleigh′ ride′ s promenade f en traîneau
sleight′ of hand′ [slaɪt] s prestidigitation f, tours mpl de passe-passe
slender [′slɛndər] adj svelte, mince, élancé; (resources) maigre
sleuth [sluθ] s limier m, détective m
slew [slu] s (coll) tas m, floppée f
slice [slaɪs] s tranche f ‖ tr trancher
slick [slɪk] adj lisse; (appearance) élégant; (coll) rusé ‖ s tache f, e.g., **oil slick** tache d'huile ‖ tr lisser; **to slick up** (coll) mettre en ordre
slicker [′slɪkər] s ciré m, imper m; (coll) enjôleur m

slide [slaɪd] s (sliding) glissade f, glissement m; (sliding place) glissoire m; (of microscope) plaque f; (of trombone) coulisse f; (on a slide rule) curseur m; (piece that slides) glissière f; (phot) diapositive f, diapo f ‖ v (pret & pp **slid** [slɪd]) tr glisser ‖ intr glisser; **to let slide** ne faire aucun cas de, laisser aller
slide′ fas′tener s fermeture f éclair
slide′ projec′tor s projecteur m de diapositives
slide′ rule′ s règle f à calcul
slide′ valve′ s soupape f à tiroir
slid′ing con′tact s curseur m
slid′ing door′ s porte f à coulisse
slid′ing scale′ s échelle f mobile
slight [slaɪt] adj (small) léger; (slender) mince; (insignificant) faible; (e.g., effort) faible ‖ s affront m ‖ tr faire peu de cas de, dédaigner; (a person) méconnaître
slim [slɪm] adj (comp **slimmer**; super **slimmest**) mince, svelte; (chance, excuse) mauvais; (resources) maigre
slime [slaɪm] s limon m, vase f; (of snakes, fish, etc.) bave f
slim·y [′slaɪmi] adj (comp **-ier**; super **-iest**) limoneux, vaseux
sling [slɪŋ] s (to shoot stones) fronde f; (to hold up a broken arm) écharpe f; (shoulder strap) bretelle f, bandoulière f ‖ v (pret & pp **slung** [slʌŋ]) tr lancer; passer en bandoulière
sling′shot′ s fronde f
slink [slɪŋk] v (pret & pp **slunk** [slʌŋk]) intr—**to slink away** s'esquiver
slip [slɪp] s (slide) dérapage m, glissade f, glissement m; (small sheet) bout m de papier; (for indexing, filing, etc.) fiche f; (cutting from plant) bouture f; (piece of underclothing) combinaison f; (blunder) faux pas m, bévue f; (naut) cale f; **to give the slip to** échapper à ‖ v (pret & pp **slipped**; ger **slipping**) tr glisser; **to slip off** (a garment) enlever, ôter; **to slip on** (a garment, shoes, etc.) enfiler; **to slip one's mind** sortir de l'esprit, échapper à qn ‖ intr glisser; (to blunder) faire un faux pas; **to let slip** laisser échapper; **to slip away** or **off** s'échapper, se dérober; **to slip by** s'échapper; (said of time) s'écouler; **to slip up** se tromper
slip′cov′er s housse f
slipper [′slɪpər] s pantoufle f
slippery [′slɪpəri] adj glissant; (deceitful) rusé
slip′-up′ s (coll) erreur f, bévue f
slit [slɪt] s fente f, fissure f ‖ v (pret & pp **slit**; ger **slitting**) tr fendre; (e.g., pages) couper; **to slit the throat of** égorger
sliver [′slɪvər] s écharde f, éclat m
slob [slɑb] s (slang) rustaud m
slobber [′slɑbər] s bave f; (fig) sentimentalité f ‖ intr baver
sloe [slo] s (shrub) prunellier m; (fruit) prunelle f
slogan [′slogən] s mot m d'ordre, devise f; (com) slogan m

sloop [slup] *s* sloop *m*

slop [slɑp] *s* lavure *f*, rinçure *f* ‖ *v* (*pret & pp* **slopped**; *ger* **slopping**) *tr* répandre ‖ *intr* se répandre; **to slop over** déborder

slope [slop] *s* pente *f*; (*of a roof*) inclinaison *f*; (*of a region, mountain, etc.*) versant *m* ‖ *tr* pencher, incliner ‖ *intr* se pencher, s'incliner

slop·py [slɑpi] *adj* (*comp* **-pier**; *super* **-piest**) mouillé; (*dress*) négligé, mal ajusté; (*work*) bâclé

slot [slɑt] *s* entaille *f*, rainure *f*; (*e.g., in a coin telephone*) fente *f*

sloth [sloθ] *s* paresse *f*; (zool) paresseux *m*

slot′ machine′ *s* (*for gambling*) appareil *m* à sous; (*for vending*) distributeur *m* automatique

slouch [slautʃ] *s* démarche *f* lourde; (*person*) lourdaud *m* ‖ *intr* ne pas se tenir droit; (*e.g., in a chair*) se vautrer; **to slouch along** traîner le pas

slouch′ hat′ *s* chapeau *m* mou

slough [slau] *s* bourbier *m* ‖ [slʌf] *s* (*of snake*) dépouille *f*; (pathol) escarre *f* ‖ *tr*—**to slough off** se débarrasser de ‖ *intr* muer, se dépouiller

Slovak [`slovæk] *adj* slovaque ‖ *s* (*language*) slovaque *m*; (*person*) Slovaque *mf*

sloven·ly [`slʌvənli] *adj* (*comp* **-lier**; *super* **-liest**) négligé, malpropre

slow [slo] *adj* lent; (*sluggish*) traînard; (*clock, watch*) en retard; (*in understanding*) lourdaud ‖ *adv* lentement ‖ *tr & intr* ralentir; **SLOW** (*public sign*) ralentir; **to slow down** ralentir

slow′down′ *s* grève *f* perlée

slow′ mo′tion *s* ralenti *m*; **in slow motion** au ralenti, en ralenti

slow′poke′ *s* (coll) lambin *m*, traînard *m*

slug [slʌg] *s* (*used as coin*) jeton *m*; (*of linotype*) ligne-bloc *f*; (zool) limace *f*; (*blow*) (coll) bon coup *m*; (*drink*) (coll) gorgée *f* ‖ *v* (*pret & pp* **slugged**; *ger* **slugging**) *tr* (coll) flanquer un coup à

sluggard [`slʌgərd] *s* paresseux *m*

sluggish [`slʌgɪʃ] *adj* traînard

sluice [slus] *s* canal *m*; (*floodgate*) écluse *f*; (*dam; flume*) bief *m*

sluice′ gate′ *s* vanne *f*

slum [slʌm] *s* bas quartiers *mpl* ‖ *v* (*pret & pp* **slummed**; *ger* **slumming**) *intr*—**to go slumming** aller visiter les taudis

slumber [`slʌmbər] *s* sommeil *m*, assoupissement *m* ‖ *intr* sommeiller

slum′ber par′ty *s* soirée-hébergement *f*

slum′ dwell′ing *s* taudis *m*

slump [slʌmp] *s* affaissement *m*; (com) crise *f*, baisse *f* ‖ *intr* s'affaisser; (*said of prices, stocks, etc.*) dégringoler, s'effondrer

slur [slʌr] *s* (*in pronunciation*) mauvaise articulation *f*; (*insult*) affront *m*; (mus) liaison *f*; **to cast a slur on** porter atteinte à ‖ *v* (*pret & pp* **slurred**; *ger* **slurring**) *tr* (*a sound, a syllable*) mal articuler; (*a person*) déprécier; (mus) lier; **to slur over** glisser sur

slush [slʌʃ] *s* névasse *f*, fange *f*, boue *f* liquide; (*gush*) sensiblerie *f*

slut [slʌt] *s* chienne *f*; (*slovenly woman*) marie-salope *f*

sly [slaɪ] *adj* (*comp* **slyer** or **slier**; *super* **slyest** or **sliest**) rusé, sournois; (*mischievous*) espiègle, futé; **on the sly** furtivement, en cachette

smack [smæk] *s* (*sound*) claquement *m*; (*with the hand*) gifle *f*, claque *f*; (*trace, touch*) soupçon *m*; (*kiss*) (coll) gros baiser *m* ‖ *adv* en plein ‖ *tr* claquer ‖ *intr*—**to smack of** sentir; avoir un goût de

small [smɔl] *adj* petit §91; (*income*) modique; (*short in stature*) court; (*petty*) mesquin; (typ) minuscule

small′ arms′ *spl* armes *fpl* portatives

small′ beer′ *s* petite bière *f*; (slang) petite bière

small′ busi′ness *s* petite industrie *f*

small′ cap′ital *s* (typ) petite capitale *f*

small′ change′ *s* petite monnaie *f*, menue monnaie

small′ fry′ *s* menu fretin *m*

small′ intes′tine *s* intestin *m* grêle

small′-mind′ed *adj* mesquin, étriqué, étroit

small′ of the back′ *s* chute *f* des reins, bas *m* du dos

smallpox [`smɔl,pɑks] *s* variole *f*

small′ print′ *s* petits caractères *mpl*

small′ talk′ *s* ragots *mpl*, papotage *m*

small′-time′ *adj* de troisième ordre, insignifiant, petit

small′-town′ *adj* provincial

smart [smɑrt] *adj* intelligent, éveillé; (*pace*) vif; (*person, clothes*) élégant, chic; (*pain*) cuisant; (*saucy*) impertinent ‖ *s* douleur *f* cuisante ‖ *intr* brûler, cuire; (*said of person with hurt feelings*) être cinglé

smart′ al′eck [,ælɪk] *s* (coll) fat *m*, présomptueux *m*

smart′ set′ *s* monde *m* élégant, gens *mpl* chic

smash [smæʃ] *s* fracassement *m*, fracas *m*; (coll) succès *m* ‖ *tr* fracasser ‖ *intr* se fracasser; **to smash into** emboutir, écraser

smash′ hit′ *s* (coll) succès *m*, succès fou; (coll) pièce *f* à succès

smash′-up′ *s* collision *f*; débâcle *f*, culbute *f*

smattering [`smætərɪŋ] *s* légère connaissance *f*, teinture *f*

smear [smɪr] *s* tache *f*; (*vilification*) calomnie *f*; (med) frottis *m* ‖ *tr* tacher; calomnier; (*to coat*) enduire

smear′ campaign′ *s* campagne *f* de calomnies

smell [smɛl] *s* odeur *f*; (*aroma*) parfum *m*, senteur *f*; (*sense*) odorat *m* ‖ *v* (*pret & pp* **smelled** or **smelt** [smɛlt]) *tr & intr* sentir; **to smell of** sentir

smell′ing salts′ *spl* sels *mpl* volatils

smell·y [`smɛli] *adj* (*comp* **-ier**; *super* **-iest**) malodorant, puant

smelt [smɛlt] *s* (*fish*) éperlan *m* ‖ *tr & intr* fondre

smile [smaɪl] *s* sourire *m* ‖ *intr* sourire; **to smile at** sourire à

smirk [smʌrk] *s* minauderie *f* ‖ *intr* minauder

smite [smaɪt] *v* (*pret* **smote** [smot]; *pp* **smitten** [ˈsmɪtən] *or* **smit** [smɪt]) *tr* frapper; **to smite down** abattre

smith [smɪθ] *s* forgeron *m*

smith·y [ˈsmɪθi] *s* (*pl* **-ies**) forge *f*

smitten [ˈsmɪtən] *adj* frappé, affligé; (coll) épris, amoureux

smock [smɑk] *s* blouse *f*; (*of artists*) sarrau *m*; (*buttoned in back*) tablier *m*

smock′ frock′ *s* sarrau *m*

smog [smɑg] *s* (coll) brouillard *m* fumeux, fumillard *m*

smoke [smok] *s* fumée *f*; (coll) cigarette *f*; **to go up in smoke** s'en aller en fumée ‖ *tr & intr* fumer

smoked′ glass′es *spl* verres *mpl* fumés

smoke′-filled room′ *s* tabagie *f*

smoke′less pow′der [ˈsmoklɪs] *s* poudre *f* sans fumée

smoker [ˈsmokər] *s* fumeur *m*; (*room*) fumoir *m*; (*meeting*) réunion *f* de fumeurs; (rr) compartiment *m* pour fumeurs

smoke′ rings′ *spl* ronds *mpl* de fumée

smoke′ screen′ *s* rideau *m* de fumée

smoke′stack′ *s* cheminée *f*

smoking [ˈsmokɪŋ] *s* le fumer *m*; **no smoking** (*public sign*) défense de fumer

smok′ing car′ *s* voiture *f* de fumeurs

smok′ing jack′et *s* veston *m* d'intérieur

smok′ing room′ *s* fumoir *m*

smok·y [ˈsmoki] *adj* (*comp* **-ier**; *super* **-iest**) fumeux, enfumé

smolder [ˈsmoldər] *s* (*dense smoke*) fumée *f* épaisse; (*smoldering fire*) feu *m* qui couve ‖ *intr* brûler sans flamme; (*said of fire, anger, rebellion, etc.*) couver

smooch [smutʃ] *intr* (coll) se bécoter

smooth [smuð] *adj* uni, lisse; (*gentle, mellow*) doux, moelleux; (*operation*) doux, régulier; (*style*) facile ‖ *tr* unir, lisser; **to smooth away** (*e.g., obstacles*) aplanir, enlever; **to smooth down** (*to calm*) apaiser, calmer; **to smooth out** défroisser

smooth′-faced′ *adj* imberbe

smooth-shaven [ˈsmuðˈʃevən] *adj* rasé de près

smooth·y [ˈsmuði] *s* (*pl* **-ies**) (coll) chattemite *f*, flagorneur *m*

smother [ˈsmʌðər] *tr* suffoquer, étouffer; (culin) recouvrir

smudge [smʌdʒ] *s* tache *f*; (*smoke*) fumée *f* épaisse ‖ *tr* tacher; (agr) fumiger

smudge′ pot′ *s* fumigène *m*

smug [smʌg] *adj* (*comp* **smugger**; *super* **smuggest**) fat, suffisant

smuggle [ˈsmʌgəl] *tr* introduire en contrebande, faire la contrebande de ‖ *intr* faire la contrebande

smuggler [ˈsmʌglər] *s* contrebandier *m*

smuggling [ˈsmʌglɪŋ] *s* contrebande *f*

smut [smʌt] *s* tache *f* de suie; (*obscenity*) ordure *f*; (agr) nielle *f*

smut·ty [ˈsmʌti] *adj* (*comp* **-tier**; *super* **-tiest**) taché de suie, noirci; (*obscene*) ordurier; (agr) niellé

snack [snæk] *s* casse-croûte *m*; **to have a snack** casser la croûte

snack′ bar′ *s* snack-bar *m*, snack *m*

snag [snæg] *s* (*of tree; of tooth*) chicot *m*; **to hit a snag** se heurter à un obstacle, tomber sur un bec ‖ *v* (*pret & pp* **snagged**; *ger* **snagging**) *tr* (*a stocking*) faire un accroc à

snail [snel] *s* escargot *m*; **at a snail's pace** à pas de tortue, comme un escargot

snake [snek] *s* serpent *m* ‖ *intr* serpenter

snake′ in the grass′ *s* serpent *m* caché sous les fleurs; ami *m* perfide, traître *m*, individu *m* louche

snap [snæp] *s* (*breaking*) cassure *f*; (*crackling sound*) bruit *m* sec; (*of the fingers*) chiquenaude *f*; (*bite*) coup *m* de dents; (*cookie*) biscuit *m* croquant; (*catch or fastener*) bouton-pression *m*, fermoir *m*; (phot) instantané *m*; (slang) jeu *m* d'enfant, coup facile; **cold snap** coup *m* de froid; **it's a snap!** (slang) c'est du tout cuit! ‖ *v* (*pret & pp* **snapped**; *ger* **snapping**) *tr* casser net; (*one's fingers, a whip, etc.*) faire claquer; (*a picture, a scene*) prendre un instantané de; **snap it up!** (*hurry!*) (slang) grouille-toi!; **to snap up** happer, saisir ‖ *intr* casser net; faire un bruit sec; (*from fatigue*) s'effondrer; **to snap at** donner un coup de dents à; (*to speak sharply to*) rembarrer; (*an opportunity*) saisir; **to snap out of it** (slang) secouer; **to snap shut** se fermer avec un bruit sec

snap′ course′ *s* (slang) cours *m* tout mâché

snap′drag′on *s* (bot) gueule-de-loup *f*

snap′ fas′tener *s* bouton-pression *m*

snap′ judg′ment *s* décision *f* prise sans réflexion

snap·py [ˈsnæpi] *adj* (*comp* **-pier**; *super* **-piest**) mordant, acariâtre; (*quick, sudden*) vif; **make it snappy!** (slang) grouillez-vous!

snap′shot′ *s* instantané *m*

snare [snɛr] *s* collet *m*; (*trap*) piège *m*; (*of a drum*) timbre *m*, corde *f* de timbre ‖ *tr* prendre au collet, prendre au piège

snare′ drum′ *s* caisse *f* claire

snarl [snɑrl] *s* (*sound*) grognement *m*; (*intertwining*) enchevêtrement *m* ‖ *tr* dire en grognant; enchevêtrer ‖ *intr* grogner; s'enchevêtrer

snatch [snætʃ] *s* (*action*) geste *m* vif (pour saisir), arrachement *m*; (*theft*) vol *m* (à l'arraché); (*bit, scrap*) fragment *m*; (*in weight lifting*) arraché *m* ‖ *tr* saisir brusquement, arracher; **to snatch from** arracher à; **to snatch up** ramasser vivement ‖ *intr*—**to snatch at** saisir au vol

sneak [snik] *adj* furtif ‖ *s* chipeur *m*, mauvais type *m* ‖ *tr* (*e.g., a drink*) prendre à la dérobée; glisser furtivement; (coll) chiper ‖ *intr* se glisser furtivement; **to sneak into** se faufiler dans; **to sneak out** s'esquiver

sneaker [ˈsnikər] *s* espadrille *f*

sneak′ thief′ *s* chipeur *m*, voleur *m* à la tire

sneak·y [`sniki] *adj* (*comp* **-ier;** *super* **-iest**) furtif, sournois

sneer [snɪr] *s* ricanement *m* ‖ *intr* ricaner; **to sneer at** se moquer de

sneeze [sniz] *s* éternuement *m* ‖ *intr* éternuer; **it's not to be sneezed at** (coll) il ne faut pas cracher dessus

snicker [`snɪkər] *s* rire *m* bête; (*sneer*) rire narquois; (*in response to smut*) petit rire grivois ‖ *intr* rire bêtement; **to snicker at** se moquer de

sniff [snɪf] *s* reniflement *m*; (*odor*) parfum *m*; (*e.g., of air*) bouffée *f* ‖ *tr* renifler; (*e.g., fresh air*) humer; (*e.g., a scandal*) flairer; **to sniff up** renifler ‖ *intr* renifler; **to sniff at** flairer; (*to disdain*) cracher sur

sniffle [`snɪfəl] *s* reniflement *m*; **to have the sniffles** être enchifrené ‖ *intr* renifler

snip [snɪp] *s* (*e.g., of cloth*) petit bout *m*; (*cut*) coup *m* de ciseaux; (coll) personne *f* insignifiante ‖ *v* (*pret & pp* **snipped;** *ger* **snipping**) *tr* couper; **to snip off** enlever, détacher

snipe [snaɪp] *s* (orn) bécassine *f* ‖ *intr*—**to snipe at** canarder

sniper [`snaɪpər] *s* tireur *m* embusqué, tireur isolé

snippet [`snɪpɪt] *s* petit bout *m*, bribe *f*; personne *f* insignifiante

snip·py [`snɪpi] *adj* (*comp* **-pier;** *super* **-piest**) hautain, brusque

snitch [snɪtʃ] *tr* (coll) chaparder ‖ *intr* (coll) moucharder; **to snitch on** (coll) moucharder

sniv·el [`snɪvəl] *s* pleurnicherie *f*; (*mucus*) morve *f* ‖ *v* (*pret & pp* **-eled** or **-elled;** *ger* **-eling** or **-elling**) *intr* pleurnicher; (*to have a runny nose*) être morveux

snob [snɑb] *s* snob *m*

snobbery [`snɑbəri] *s* snobisme *m*

snobbish [`snɑbɪʃ] *adj* snob

snoop [snup] *s* (coll) curieux *m* ‖ *intr* (coll) fouiner, fureter

snoop·y [`snupi] *adj* (*comp* **-ier;** *super* **-iest**) (coll) curieux

snoot [snut] *s* (slang) nez *m*

snoot·y [`snuti] *adj* (*comp* **-ier;** *super* **-iest**) (slang) snob, hautain

snooze [snuz] *s* (coll) petit somme *m* ‖ *intr* (coll) sommeiller

snore [snor] *s* ronflement *m* ‖ *intr* ronfler

snort [snɔrt] *s* ébrouement *m*; (*of person, horse, etc.*) *tr* dire en reniflant, grogner ‖ *intr* s'ébrouer, renifler bruyamment

snot [snɑt] *s* (slang) morve *f*

snot·ty [`snɑti] *adj* (*comp* **-tier;** *super* **-tiest**) (coll) morveux; (slang) snob, hautain

snout [snaut] *s* museau *m*; (*of pig*) groin *m*; (*of bull*) mufle *m*; (*something shaped like the snout of an animal*) bec *m*, tuyère *f*

snow [sno] *s* neige *f* ‖ *intr* neiger; **it is snowing** il neige; **to shovel snow** balayer la neige

snow'ball' *s* boule *f* de neige ‖ *tr* lancer des boules de neige à ‖ *intr* faire boule de neige

snow'bank' *s* talus *m* de neige, banc *m* de neige

snow' blind'ness *s* cécité *f* des neiges

snow' blow'er *s* chasse-neige *m*

snow'-capped' *adj* couronné de neige

snow'-clad' *adj* enneigé

snow'drift' *s* congère *f*

snow'fall' *s* chute *f* de neige; (*amount*) enneigement *m*

snow'flake' *s* flocon *m* de neige

snow' flur'ry *s* (*pl* **-ries**) bouffée *f* de neige

snow' line' *s* limite *f* des neiges éternelles

snow'mak'ing *s* enneigement *m* artificiel

snow'man' *s* (*pl* **-men'**) bonhomme *m* de neige

snowmobile [`snoməˌbil] *s* motoneige *f*

snow'plow' *s* chasse-neige *m*

snow' remov'al *s* déneigement *m*

snow'shoe' *s* raquette *f*

snow'slide' *s* avalanche *f*

snow'storm' *s* tempête *f* de neige

snow' tire' *s* pneu *m* à neige

snow'white' *adj* blanc comme la neige ‖ **Snowwhite** *s* Blanche-Neige *f*

snow·y [`sno·i] *adj* (*comp* **-ier;** *super* **-iest**) neigeux

snow'y owl' *s* chouette *f* blanche

snub [snʌb] *s* affront *m*, rebuffade *f* ‖ *v* (*pret & pp* **snubbed;** *ger* **snubbing**) *tr* traiter avec froideur, rabrouer

snub·by [`snʌbi] *adj* (*comp* **-bier;** *super* **-biest**) trapu; (*nose*) camus

snub'-nosed' *adj* camard

snuff [snʌf] *s* tabac *m* à priser; (*of a candlewick*) mouchure *f*; **to be up to snuff** (*to be shrewd*) (slang) être dessalé; (*to be up to par*) (slang) être dégourdi ‖ *tr* priser; (*a candle*) moucher; **to snuff out** éteindre

snuff'box' *s* tabatière *f*

snuffers [`snʌfərs] *spl* mouchettes *fpl*

snug [snʌg] *adj* (*comp* **snugger;** *super* **snuggest**) confortable; (*garment*) bien ajusté; (*bed*) douillet; (*sheltered*) abrité; (*hidden*) caché; **snug and warm** bien au chaud; **snug as a bug in a rug** comme un poisson dans l'eau

snuggle [`snʌgəl] *tr* serrer dans ses bras ‖ *intr* se pelotonner; **to snuggle up to** se serrer tout près de

so [so] *adv* si, tellement; ainsi; donc, par conséquent, aussi; **or so** plus ou moins; **so as to** afin de, pour; **so far** jusqu'ici; **so long!** (coll) à bientôt!; **so many** tant; tant de; **so much** tant; tant de; **so that** pour que, afin que; de sorte que; **so to speak** pour ainsi dire; **so what?** (slang) et alors?; **to hope so** espérer bien; **to think so** croire que oui ‖ *conj* (coll) de sorte que

soak [sok] *s* trempage *m*; (slang) sac *m* à vin, soûlard *m* ‖ *tr* tremper; (*to swindle*) (slang) estamper; **to soak to the skin** tremper jusqu'aux os ‖ *intr* tremper

so'-and-so' s (pl **-sos**) (pej) triste individu m, mauvais sujet m; **Mr. So-and-so** Monsieur Untel

soap [sop] s savon m ‖ tr savonner

soap'box' s caisse f à savon; (fig) plate-forme f

soap'box or'ator s orateur m de carrefour

soap' bub'ble s bulle f de savon

soap' dish' s plateau m à savon

soap' fac'to·ry s (pl **-ries**) savonnerie f

soap' flakes' spl savon m en paillettes

soap' op'era s mélo m

soap' pow'der s savon m en poudre

soap'stone' s pierre f de savon; craie f de tailleur

soap'suds' spl mousse f de savon, eau f de savon

soap·y ['sopi] adj (comp **-ier**; super **-iest**) savonneux

soar [sor] intr planer dans les airs; prendre l'essor, monter subitement

sob [sɑb] s sanglot m ‖ v (pret & pp **sobbed**; ger **sobbing**) intr sangloter

sober ['sobər] adj sobre; (expression) grave; (truth) simple; (not drunk) pas ivre; (no longer drunk) dégrisé ‖ tr calmer; **to sober up** dégriser ‖ intr—**to sober up** se dégriser

sobriety [so'braɪ·əti] s sobriété f

sob' sis'ter s (slang) journaliste f larmoyante

sob' sto'ry s (pl **-ries**) histoire f larmoyante, histoire d'un pathétique facile, histoire à vous fendre la cœur

so'-called' adj dit; soi-disant, prétendu; ainsi nommé

soccer ['sɑkər] s football m

sociable ['soʃəbəl] adj sociable

social ['soʃəl] adj social ‖ s réunion f sans cérémonie

so'cial climb'er s parvenu m, arriviste mf

so'cial events' spl mondanités fpl

socialism ['soʃə,lɪzəm] s socialisme m

socialist ['soʃəlɪst] s socialiste mf

socialite ['soʃə,laɪt] s (coll) membre m de la haute société

so'cial reg'ister s annuaire m de la haute société

so'cial secu'rity s sécurité f sociale, assistance f familiale

so'cial serv'ice s assistance f sociale, aide f sociale, aide familiale

so'cial stra'ta [,strætə] spl couches fpl sociales

so'cial work'er s assistant m social, travailleuse f familiale

socie·ty [sə'saɪ·əti] s (pl **-ties**) société f

soci'ety col'umn s carnet m mondain

soci'ety ed'itor s chroniqueur m mondain

sociology [,sosɪ'ɑlədʒi] s sociologie f

sock [sɑk] s chaussette f; (slang) coup m de poing ‖ tr (slang) donner un coup de poing à

socket ['sɑkɪt] s (of bone) cavité f, glène f; (of candlestick) tube m; (of caster) sabot m; (of eye) orbite f; (of tooth) alvéole m; (elec) douille f

sock'et joint' s joint m à rotule

sock'et wrench' s clé f à tube

sod [sɑd] s gazon m; motte f de gazon ‖ v (pret & pp **sodded**; ger **sodding**) tr gazonner

soda ['sodə] s (soda water) soda m; (chem) soude f

so'da crack'er s biscuit m soda

so'da wa'ter s soda m

sodium ['sodɪ·əm] s sodium m

sodomy ['sɑdəmi] s sodomie f

sofa ['sofə] s canapé m, sofa m

so'fa bed' s lit-canapé m

soft [sɔft] adj (yielding) mou; (mild) doux; (weak in character) faible; **to go soft** (coll) perdre la boule

soft'-boiled egg' s œuf m à la coque

soft' coal' s houille f grasse

soft' drink' s boisson f non-alcoolisée

soften ['sɔfən] tr amollir; (e.g., noise) atténuer; (one's voice) adoucir; (one's moral fiber) affaiblir; **to soften up** amollir ‖ intr s'amollir; s'adoucir; s'affaiblir

soft' land'ing s (rok) arrivée f en douceur

soft' ped'al s (mus) pédale f sourde

soft'-ped'al v (pret & pp **-aled** or **-alled**; ger **-aling** or **-alling**) tr (coll) atténuer, modérer

soft' shoul'der s (aut) accotement m non-stabilisé

soft' soap' s savon m mou, savon noir; (coll) pommade f

soft'-soap' tr (coll) passer de la pommade à

soft'ware' s (comp) logiciel m, programme-rie f

soft'ware engineer'ing s genie m logiciel

sog·gy ['sɑgi] adj (comp **-gier**; super **-giest**) saturé, détrempé

soil [sɔɪl] s sol m, terroir m ‖ tr salir, souiller ‖ intr se salir

soil' pipe' s tuyau m de descente

sojourn ['sodʒʌrn] s séjour m ‖ intr séjourner

solace ['sɑlɪs] s consolation f ‖ tr consoler

solar ['solər] adj solaire

so'lar bat'tery s photopile f

so'lar heat'er s insolateur m

so'lar radia'tion s rayonnement m solaire

sold [sold] adj—**sold out** (no more room) complet; (no more merchandise) épuisé; **to be sold on** (coll) raffoler de ‖ interj (to the highest bidder) adjugé!

solder ['sɑdər] s soudure f ‖ tr souder

sol'dering i'ron s fer m à souder

soldier ['soldʒər] s soldat m

sole [sol] adj seul, unique ‖ s (of shoe) semelle f; (of foot) plante f; (fish) sole f ‖ tr ressemeler

solemn ['sɑləm] adj sérieux, grave; (ceremony) solennel

solemnize ['sɑləm,naɪz] tr solenniser

solenoid ['solə,nɔɪd] s solénoïde m

solicit [sə'lɪsɪt] tr solliciter ‖ intr quêter; (with immoral intentions) racoler

solicitor [sə'lɪsɪtər] s (for contributions) solliciteur m; (for trade) agent m, représentant *m*; (com) démarcheur *m*; (law) procureur *m*; (Brit) avoué *m*

solicitous [səˈlɪsɪtəs] *adj* soucieux

solid [ˈsɑlɪd] *adj* solide; (*clouds*) dense; (*gold*) massif; (*opinion*) unanime; (*color*) uni; (*hour, day, week*) entier; (*e.g., three days*) d'affilée ‖ *s* solide *m*

sol´id geom´etry *s* géométrie *f* dans l'espace

solidity [səˈlɪdɪti] *s* solidité *f*, consistance *f*

sol´id-state´ *adj* (electron) en état solide

solilo·quy [səˈlɪləkwi] *s* (*pl* **-quies**) soliloque *m*

solitaire [ˈsɑlɪˌtɛr] *s* solitaire *m*; (cards) patience *f*, réussite *f*; **to play solitaire** faire une réussite

solitar·y [ˈsɑlɪˌtɛri] *adj* solitaire ‖ *s* (*pl* **-ies**) solitaire *m*

sol´itary confine´ment *s* régime *m* cellulaire

solitude [ˈsɑlɪˌt(j)ud] *s* solitude *f*

so·lo [ˈsolo] *adj* solo ‖ *s* (*pl* **-los**) solo *m*

soloist [ˈsolo·ɪst] *s* soliste *mf*

solstice [ˈsɑlstɪs] *s* solstice *m*

soluble [ˈsɑljəbəl] *adj* soluble

solution [səˈluʃən] *s* solution *f*

solvable [ˈsɑlvəbəl] *adj* soluble

solve [sɑlv] *tr* résoudre

solvency [ˈsɑlvənsi] *s* solvabilité *f*

solvent [ˈsɑlvənt] *adj* (*substance*) solubilisant; (*person or business*) solvable ‖ *s* (*of a substance*) solvant *m*

somber [ˈsɑmbər] *adj* sombre

some [sʌm] *adj indef* quelque, du; **some way or other** d'une manière ou d'une autre ‖ *pron indef* certains, quelques-uns §81; en §87 ‖ *adv* un peu, passablement, assez; environ; quelque, e.g., **some two hundred soldiers** quelque deux cents soldats

some´bod´y *pron indef* quelqu'un §81; **somebody else** quelqu'un d'autre ‖ *s* (*pl* **-ies**) (coll) quelqu'un *m*

some´day´ *adv* un jour

some´how´ *adv* dans un sens, je ne sais comment; **somehow or other** d'une manière ou d'une autre, vaille que vaille

some´one´ *pron indef* quelqu'un §81; **someone else** quelqu'un d'autre

somersault [ˈsʌmərˌsɔlt] *s* saut *m* périlleux

some´thing *s* (coll) quelque chose *m* ‖ *pron indef* quelque chose (*masc*) ‖ *adv* quelque peu, un peu

some´time´ *adj* ancien, ci-devant ‖ *adv* un jour; un de ces jours

some´times´ *adv* quelquefois, de temps en temps; **sometimes . . . sometimes** tantôt . . . tantôt

some´way´ *adv* d'une manière ou d'une autre

some´what´ *adv* un peu, assez

some´where´ *adv* quelque part; **somewhere else** ailleurs, autre part

somnambulist [sɑmˈnæmbjəlɪst] *s* somnambule *mf*

somnolent [ˈsɑmnələnt] *adj* somnolent

son [sʌn] *s* fils *m*

sonata [səˈnɑtə] *s* sonate *f*

song [sɔŋ] *s* chanson *f*; (*of praise*) hymne *m*; **to buy for a song** (coll) acheter pour une bouchée de pain

song´bird´ *s* oiseau *m* chanteur

song´ book´ *s* recueil *m* de chansons

Song´ of Songs´ *s* (Bib) Cantique *m* des Cantiques

song´thrush´ *s* grive *f* musicienne

song´writ´er *s* chansonnier *m*

sonic [ˈsɑnɪk] *adj* sonique

son´ic boom´ *s* double bang *m*

son´-in-law´ *s* (*pl* **sons-in-law**) gendre *m*, beau fils *m*

sonnet [ˈsɑnɪt] *s* sonnet *m*

son·ny [ˈsʌni] *s* (*pl* **-nies**) fiston *m*

soon [sun] *adv* bientôt; (*early*) tôt; **as soon as** aussitôt que, dès que, sitôt que; **as soon as possible** le plus tôt possible; **how soon** quand; **no sooner said than done** sitôt dit sitôt fait; **soon after** tôt après; **sooner** plus tôt; (*rather*) (coll) plutôt; **sooner or later** tôt ou tard; **so soon** si tôt; **too soon** trop tôt

soot [sʊt] *s* suie *f* ‖ *tr*—**to soot up** encrasser de suie ‖ *intr* s'encrasser

soothe [suð] *tr* calmer, apaiser; flatter

soothsayer [ˈsuθˌse·ər] *s* devin *m*

soot·y [ˈsʊti] *adj* (*comp* **-ier**; *super* **-iest**) (*color; flame*) fuligineux; couvert de suie

sop [sɑp] *s* morceaux *m* trempé; (fig) os *m* à ronger, cadeau *m* ‖ *v* (*pret & pp* **sopped**), *ger* **sopping**) *tr* tremper, faire tremper; **to sop up** absorber

sophisticated [səˈfɪstɪˌketɪd] *adj* mondain, sceptique; complexe; (comp) sophistiqué

sophistication [səˌfɪstɪˈkeʃən] *s* mondanité *f*

sophomore [ˈsɑfəˌmor] *s* étudiant *m* de deuxième année

sophomoric [ˌsɑfəˈmɔrɪk] *adj* naïf, suffisant, présomptueux

sopping [ˈsɑpɪŋ] *adj* détrempé, trempé ‖ *adv*—**sopping wet** trempé comme une soupe

sopran·o [səˈpræno] *adj* de soprano ‖ *s* (*pl* **-os**) soprano *f*; (*boy*) soprano *m*

sorcerer [ˈsɔrsərər] *s* sorcier *m*

sorceress [ˈsɔrsərɪs] *s* sorcière *f*

sorcer·y [ˈsɔrsəri] *s* (*pl* **-ies**) sorcellerie *f*

sordid [ˈsɔrdɪd] *adj* sordide

sore [sor] *adj* douloureux, enflammé; (coll) fâché ‖ *s* plaie *f*, ulcère *m*

sore´head´ *s* (coll) rouspéteur *m*, grincheux *m*

sorely [ˈsorli] *adv* gravement, grièvement; cruellement

soreness [ˈsornɪs] *s* douleur *f*, sensibilité *f*

sore´ throat´ *s*—**to have a sore throat** avoir mal à la gorge

sorori·ty [səˈrɔriti] *s* (*pl* **-ties**) club *m* d'étudiantes universitaires

sorrow [ˈsɔro] *s* chagrin *m*, peine *f*, affliction *f*, tristesse *f* ‖ *intr* s'affliger, avoir du chagrin; être en deuil; **to sorrow for** s'affliger de

sorrowful [ˈsɔrəfəl] *adj* (*person*) affligé, attristé; (*news*) affligeant

sor·ry ['sɔrɪ] *adj* (*comp* **-rier;** *super* **-riest**) désolé, navré, fâché; (*appearance*) piteux, misérable; (*situation*) triste; **to be** or **feel sorry** regretter; **to be** or **feel sorry for** regretter (*q.ch.*); plaindre (*qn*); **to be sorry to** + *inf* regretter de + *inf* ‖ *interj* pardon!

sort [sɔrt] *s* sorte *f*, espèce *f*, genre *m*; **a sort of** une espèce de; **to be out of sorts** être de mauvaise humeur, ne pas être dans son assiette ‖ *tr* classer; **to sort out** trier

so'-so' *adj* (coll) assez bon, passable, supportable ‖ *adv* assez bien, comme ci comme ça

sot [sɑt] *s* ivrogne *mf*

soul [sol] *s* âme *f*; **not a soul** (coll) pas un chat; **upon my soul!** par ma foi!

sound [saʊnd] *adj* (*body, fruit, tree*) sain; (*structure, floor, bridge*) solide, en bon état; (*healthy, robust*) en bonne santé, bien portant; (*sleep*) profond ‖ *s* son *m*; (*probe*) sonde *f*; (geog) goulet *m*, détroit *m*, bras *m* de mer ‖ *adv* (*asleep*) profondément ‖ *tr* sonner; (*to take a sounding of*) sonder; **to sound out** sonder; **to sound the horn** klaxonner, corner ‖ *intr* sonner; **to sound off** parler haut; **to sound strange** sembler bizarre

sound' bar'rier *s* mur *m* du son

sound' film' *s* film *m* sonore

sound' hole' *s* (*of a violin*) ouïe *f*

soundly ['saʊndlɪ] *adj* sainement; profondément; (*hard*) bien

sound' post' *s* (*of a violin*) âme *f*

sound'proof' *adj* insonorisé, insonore ‖ *tr* insonoriser

sound'proof(ed) room' *s* chambre *f* sourde

sound' track' *s* piste *f* sonore, sonorisation *f*

sound' wave' *s* onde *f* sonore

soup [sup] *s* potage *m*, bouillon *m*; (*with vegetables*) soupe *f*; **in the soup** (coll) dans le pétrin ou la mélasse

soup' kitch'en *s* soupe *f* populaire

soup' spoon' *s* cuiller *f* à soupe

soup' tureen' *s* soupière *f*

sour [saʊr] *adj* aigre; (*grapes*) vert; (*apples*) sur; (*milk*) tourné ‖ *tr* rendre aigre ‖ *intr* tourner, s'aigrir

source [sors] *s* source *f*

source' lan'guage *s* langue *f* source, langue de départ

source' mate'rial *s* sources *fpl* originales

sour' cher'ry *s* (*pl* **-ries**) griotte *f*; (*tree*) griottier *m*

sour' grapes' *interj* ils sont trop verts!

sour'puss' *s* (slang) grincheux *m*

south [saʊθ] *adj* & *s* sud *m*; **the South** (*of France, Italy, etc.*) le Midi; (*of U.S.A.*) le Sud ‖ *adv* au sud, vers le sud

South' Af'rica *s* la République sud-africaine

South' Amer'ica *s* Amérique *f* du Sud; l'Amérique du Sud

South' Amer'ican *adj* sud-américain ‖ *s* (*person*) Sud-Américain *m*

south'east' *adj* & *s* sud-est *m*

southern ['sʌðərn] *adj* du sud, méridional

southerner ['sʌðərnər] *s* Méridional *m*; (U.S.A.) sudiste *mf*

South' Kore'a *s* Corée *f* du Sud; la Corée du Sud

South' Kore'an *adj* sud-coréen ‖ *s* (*person*) Sud-Coréen *m*

south'paw' *adj* & *s* (coll) gaucher *m*

South' Pole' *s* pôle *m* Sud

southward ['saʊθwərd] *adv* vers le sud

south'west' *adj* & *s* sud-ouest *m*

souvenir [ˌsuvə'nɪr] *s* souvenir *m*

sovereign ['sɑvrɪn] *adj* souverain ‖ *s* (*king, coin*) souverain *m*; (*queen*) souveraine *f*

sovereign·ty ['sɑvrɪntɪ], *s* (*pl* **-ties**) souveraineté *f*

soviet ['sovɪˌɛt] *adj* soviétique ‖ *s* soviet *m*; **Soviet** (*person*) Soviétique *mf*

So'viet Rus'sia *s* la Russie *f* soviétique

So'viet Un'ion *s* Union *f* soviétique

sow [saʊ] *s* truie *f* ‖ [so] *v* (*pret* **sowed;** *pp* **sown** or **sowed**) *tr* (*seed; a field*) semer; (*a field*) ensemencer

soybean ['sɔɪˌbin] *s* soya *m*, soja *m*

spa [spɑ] *s* ville *f* d'eau, station *f* thermale, bains *mpl*

space [spes] *s* espace *m*; (*in typing*) frappe *f*; (typ) espace *f* ‖ *tr* espacer

space' age' *s* âge *m* de l'exploration spatiale

space' bar' *s* barre *f* d'espacement

space' cap'sule *s* capsule *f* spatiale

space'craft' *s* astronef *m*

space' flight' *s* voyage *m* spatial, vol *m* spatial

space' heat'er *s* chaufferette *f*

space' hel'met *s* casque *m* de cosmonaute

space'man or **space'man** *s* (*pl* **-men** or **-men**) homme *m* de l'espace, astronaute *m*, cosmonaute *m*

space' probe' *s* sonde *m* spatiale, coup *m* de sonde dans l'espace; (*rocket*) fusée *f* sonde

spacer ['spesər] *s* (*of typewriter*) barre *f* d'espacement

space'ship' *s* vaisseau *m* spatial, astronef *m*

space' shut'tle *s* navette *f* spatiale

space' sta'tion *s* station *f* orbitale

space' suit' *s* (rok) scaphandre *m* des cosmonautes, scaphandre spatial, combinaison *f* spatiale

space' ve'hicle *s* spationef *m*

space' walk' *s* promenade *f* dans l'espace

spacious ['speʃəs] *adj* spacieux

spade [sped] *s* bêche *f*; (cards) pique *m*; **to call a spade a spade** (coll) appeler un chat un chat

spade'work' *s* gros travail *m*, défrichage *m*

spaghetti [spə'gɛti] *s* spaghetti *mpl*

Spain [spen] *s* Espagne *f*; l'Espagne

span [spæn] *s* portée *f*; (*of time*) durée *f*; (*of hand*) empan *m*; (*of wing*) envergure *f*; (*of bridge*) travée *f* ‖ *v* (*pret* & *pp* **spanned;** *ger* **spanning**) *tr* couvrir, traverser

spangle ['spæŋgəl] *s* paillette *f* ‖ *tr* orner de paillettes

Spaniard ['spænjərd] *s* Espagnol *m*

spaniel ['spænjəl] *s* épagneul *m*

Spanish ['spænɪʃ] *adj* espagnol ‖ *s* (*language*) espagnol *m*; **the Spanish** (*persons*) les Espagnols *mpl*

Span'ish-Amer'ican *adj* hispano-américain ‖ *s* Hispano-Américain *m*

Span'ish broom' *s* genêt *m* d'Espagne

Span'ish fly' *s* cantharide *f*

Span'ish Main' *s* Terre *f* ferme; mer *f* des Antilles

Span'ish moss' *s* tillandsie *f*

spank [spæŋk] *tr* fesser

spanking ['spæŋkɪŋ] *adj* (Brit) de premier ordre; **at a spanking pace** à toute vitesse ‖ *s* fessée *f*

spar [spɑr] *s* (mineral) spath *m*; (naut) espar *m* ‖ *v* (*pret* & *pp* **sparred**; *ger* **sparring**) *intr* s'entraîner à la boxe; se battre

spare [spɛr] *adj* (*thin*) maigre; (*available*) disponible; (*interchangeable*) de rechange; (*left over*) en surnombre ‖ *tr* (*to save*) épargner, économiser; (*one's efforts*) ménager; (*a person*) faire grâce à, traiter avec indulgence; (*time, money, etc.*) disposer de; (*something*) se passer de

spare' parts' *spl* pièces *fpl* détachées, pièces de rechange

spare'rib' *s* côte *f* découverte de porc, plat *m* de côtes

spare' room' *s* chambre *f* d'ami

spare' tire' *s* pneu *m* de rechange

spare' wheel' *s* roue *f* de secours

sparing ['spɛrɪŋ] *adj* économe, frugal

spark [spɑrk] *s* étincelle *f*

spark' coil' *s* bobine *f* d'allumage

spark' gap' *s* (*of induction coil*) éclateur *m*; (*of spark plug*) entrefer *m*

sparkle ['spɑrkəl] *s* étincellement *m*, éclat *m* ‖ *intr* étinceler

sparkling ['spɑrklɪŋ] *adj* étincelant; (*wine*) mousseux; (*soft drink*) gazeux

spark' plug' *s* bougie *f*

sparrow ['spæro] *s* moineau *m*

spar'row hawk' *s* épervier *m*

sparse [spɑrs] *adj* clairsemé, rare; peu nombreux

Spartan ['spɑrtən] *adj* spartiate ‖ *s* Spartiate *mf*

spasm ['spæzəm] *s* spasme *m*

spasmodic [spæz'mɑdɪk] *adj* intermittent, irrégulier; (pathol) spasmodique

spastic ['spæstɪk] *adj* spasmodique

spat [spæt] *s* (coll) dispute *f*, prise *f* de bec; **spats** demi-guêtres *fpl* ‖ *v* (*pret* & *pp* **spatted**; *ger* **spatting**) *intr* se disputer

spatial ['speʃəl] *adj* spatial, de l'espace

spatter ['spætər] *s* éclaboussure *f* ‖ *tr* éclabousser

spatula ['spætʃələ] *s* spatule *f*

spawn [spɔn] *s* frai *m* ‖ *tr* engendrer ‖ *intr* frayer

spay [spe] *tr* châtrer

speak [spik] *v* (*pret* **spoke** [spok]; *pp* **spoken**) *tr* (*a word, one's mind, the truth*) dire; (*a language*) parler ‖ *intr* parler; **so to speak** pour ainsi dire; **speaking!** à l'appareil!; **to speak out** or **up** parler plus haut, élever la voix; (fig) parler franc

speak'-eas'y *s* (*pl* **-ies**) bar *m* clandestin

speaker ['spikər] *s* parleur *m*; (*person addressing a group*) conférencier *m*; (*presiding officer*) speaker *m*, président *m*; (rad) haut-parleur *m*

spear [spɪr] *s* lance *f* ‖ *tr* percer d'un coup de lance

spear'head' *s* fer *m* de lance; (mil) pointe *f*, avancée *f* ‖ *tr* (*e.g., a campaign*) diriger

spear'mint' *s* menthe *f* verte

special ['spɛʃəl] *adj* spécial, particulier ‖ *s* train *m* spécial

spe'cial-deliv'ery let'ter *s* lettre *f* exprès

specialist ['spɛʃəlɪst] *s* spécialiste *mf*

specialize ['spɛʃə,laɪz] *tr* spécialiser ‖ *intr* se spécialiser

special·ty ['spɛʃəlti] *s* (*pl* **-ties**) spécialité *f*

specie ['spisi] *s*—**in specie** en espèces, en numéraire

spe·cies ['spisiz] *s* (*pl* **-cies**) espèce *f*

specific [spɪ'sɪfɪk] *adj* & *s* spécifique *m*

specif'ic grav'ity *s* poids *m* spécifique

speci·fy ['spɛsɪ,faɪ] *v* (*pret* & *pp* **-fied**) *tr* spécifier

specimen ['spɛsɪmən] *s* spécimen *m*; (coll) drôle *m* de type

specious ['spiʃəs] *adj* spécieux

speck [spɛk] *s* (*on fruit, face, etc.*) tache *f*; (*in the distance*) point *m*; (*small quantity*) brin *m*, grain *m*, atome *m* ‖ *tr* tacheter

speckle ['spɛkəl] *s* petite tache *f* ‖ *tr* tacheter, moucheter

spectacle ['spɛktəkəl] *s* spectacle *m*; **spectacles** lunettes *fpl*

spec'tacle case' *s* étui *m* à lunettes

spectator ['spɛktetər] *s* spectateur *m*

specter ['spɛktər] *s* spectre *m*

spec·trum ['spɛktrəm] *s* (*pl* **-tra** [trə] or **-trums**) spectre *m*

speculate ['spɛkjə,let] *intr* spéculer

speculator ['spɛkjə,letər] *s* spéculateur *m*, boursicotier *m*

speech [spitʃ] *s* (*faculty*) parole *f*; (*language*) langage *m*; (*of a people or region*) parler *m*; (*manner of speaking*) façon *f* de parler; (*enunciation*) articulation *f*, élocution *f*; (*formal address*) discours *m*; (theat) tirade *f*; **to make a speech** prononcer un discours

speech' clin'ic *s* centre *m* de rééducation de la parole

speech' correc'tion *s* rééducation *f* de la parole

speech' de'fect *s* défaut *m* d'élocution

speechless ['spitʃlɪs] *adj* sans parole, muet; (fig) sidéré, stupéfié

speech' ther'apy *s* phoniatrie *f*

speed [spid] *s* vitesse *f*; **at full speed** à toute vitesse ‖ *v* (*pret* & *pp* **speeded** or **sped** [spɛd]) *tr* dépêcher, hâter ‖ *intr* se dépêcher; **to speed up** aller plus vite

speed' bump' *s* dos *m* d'âne

speeding ['spidɪŋ] *s* excès *m* de vitesse

speed' king' *s* as *m* du volant

speed' lim'it *s* vitesse *f* maximum

speedometer [spi'dɑmɪtər] *s* indicateur *m* de vitesse

speed′ rec′ord *s* record *m* de vitesse

speed′-up′ *s* accélération *f*

speed′way′ *s* (*racetrack*) piste *f* d'autos; (*highway*) autoroute *f*

speed·y [′spidi] *adj* (*comp* **-ier;** *super* **-iest**) rapide, vite, prompt

speed′ zone′ *s* zone *f* de vitesse surveillée

spell [spɛl] *s* (*magic power*) sortilège *m*, charme *m*; (*brief period*) intervalle *m*; (*turn*) tour *m*; (*magic words*) formule *f* magique; (*attack*) accès *m* ‖ *v* (*pret & pp* **spelled** or **spelt** [spɛlt]) *tr* (*orally*) épeler; (*in writing*) orthographier, écrire; **to spell out** (coll) expliquer en détail ‖ *v* (*pret & pp* **spelled**) *tr* (*to relieve*) remplacer, relever, relayer

spell′bind′er *s* orateur *m* fascinant, orateur entraînant

spell′bound′ *adj* fasciné

spelling [′spɛlɪŋ] *s* orthographe *f*

spell′ing bee′ *s* concours *m* d'orthographe

spelunker [spɪ′lʌŋkər] *s* spéléo *m*

spend [spɛnd] *v* (*pret & pp* **spent** [spɛnt]) *tr* dépenser; (*a period of time*) passer

spender [′spɛndər] *s* dépensier *m*

spend′ing mon′ey *s* argent *m* de poche pour les menues dépenses

spend′thrift′ *s* prodigue *mf*, grand dépensier *m*

sperm [spʌrm] *s* sperme *m*

sperm′ bank′ *s* banque *f* de sperme

sperm′ whale′ *s* cachalot *m*

spew [spju] *tr & intr* vomir

sphere [sfɪr] *s* sphère *f*; corps *m* céleste

spherical [′sfɛrɪkəl] *adj* sphérique

sphinx [sfɪŋks] *s* (*pl* **sphinxes** or **sphinges** [′sfɪndʒiz]) sphinx *m*

spice [spaɪs] *s* épice *f*; (fig) sel *m*, piquant *m* ‖ *tr* épicer

spick-and-span [′spɪkənd′spæn] *adj* (*room*) brillant comme un sou neuf; (*person*) tiré à quatre épingles

spic·y [′spaɪsi] *adj* (*comp* **-ier;** *super* **-iest**) épicé, aromatique; (*e.g., gravy*) relevé; (*conversation, story, etc.*) épicé, salé, piquant, grivois

spider [′spaɪdər] *s* araignée *f*

spi′der·web′ *s* toile *f* d'araignée

spiff·y [′spɪfi] *adj* (*comp* **-ier;** *super* **-iest**) (slang) épatant, élégant

spigot [′spɪgət] *s* robinet *m*

spike [spaɪk] *s* pointe *f*; (*nail*) clou *m* à large tête; (bot) épi *m*; (rr) crampon *m* ‖ *tr* clouer; ruiner, supprimer; (*a drink*) (coll) corser à l'alcool ‖ *intr* (bot) former des épis

spill [spɪl] *s* chute *f*, culbute *f* ‖ *v* (*pret & pp* **spilled** or **spilt** [spɪlt]) *tr* renverser; (*a liquid*) répandre; (*a rider*) désarçonner; (*passengers*) verser ‖ *intr* se répandre, s'écouler

spill′way′ *s* déversoir *m*

spin [spɪn] *s* (*turning motion*) tournoiement *m*, rotation *f*; (*on a ball*) effet *m*; (aer) vrille *f*; **to go for a spin** (coll) se balader en voiture; **to go into a spin** (aer) descendre en vrille ‖ *v* (*pret & pp* **spun** [spʌn];

ger **spinning**) *tr* filer; faire tournoyer ‖ *intr* filer; tournoyer

spinach [′spɪnɪtʃ] *s* épinard *m*; (*leaves used as food*) des épinards

spinal [′spaɪnəl] *adj* spinal

spi′nal col′umn *s* colonne *f* vertébrale

spi′nal cord′ *s* moelle *f* épinière

spindle [′spɪndəl] *s* fuseau *m*

spin′-dri′er *s* essoreuse *f*

spin′-dry′ *v* (*pret & pp* **-dried**) *tr* essorer

spine [spaɪn] *s* (*in body*) épine *f* dorsale, échine *f*; (*quill, fin*) épine; (*ridge*) arête *f*; (*of book*) dos *m*; (fig) courage *m*

spineless [′spaɪnlɪs] *adj* sans épines; (*weak*) mou; **to be spineless** (fig) avoir l'échine souple

spinet [′spɪnɪt] *s* épinette *f*

spinner [′spɪnər] *s* fileur *m*; machine *f* à filer

spinning [′spɪnɪŋ] *adj* tournoyant ‖ *s* (*act*) filage *m*; (*art*) filature *f*

spin′ning wheel′ *s* rouet *m*

spin′-off′ *s* avantage *m* inattendu; (com) sous-produit *m*, application *f* secondaire; **to be a spin-off from** (telv) être tiré de, être issu de

spinster [′spɪnstər] *s* (usually offensive) célibataire *f*, vieille fille *f*

spiraea [spaɪ′ri·ə] *s* spirée *f*

spi·ral [′spaɪrəl] *adj* spiral, en spirale ‖ *s* spirale *f* ‖ *v* (*pret & pp* **-raled** or **-ralled;** *ger* **-raling** or **-ralling**) *intr* tourner en spirale; (aer) vriller

spi′ral stair′case *s* escalier *m* en colimaçon

spire [spaɪr] *s* aiguille *f*; (*of clock tower*) flèche *f*

spirit [′spɪrɪt] *s* esprit *m*; (*enthusiasm*) feu *m*; (*temper, genius*) génie *m*; (*ghost*) esprit, revenant *m*; **high spirits** joie *f*, abandon *m*; **spirits** (*alcoholic liquor*) esprit *m*, spiritueux *m*; **to raise the spirits of** remonter le courage de ‖ *tr*—**to spirit away** enlever, faire disparaître mystérieusement

spirited *adj* animé, vigoureux

spiritless [′spɪrɪtlɪs] *adj* sans force, abattu, déprimé

spir′it lev′el *s* niveau *m* à bulle

spiritual [′spɪrɪtʃu·əl] *adj* spirituel ‖ *s* chant *m* religieux populaire

spiritualism [′spɪrɪtʃu·ə,lɪzəm] *s* spiritisme *m*

spiritualist [′spɪrɪtʃu·əlɪst] *s* spirite *mf*; (philos) spiritualiste *mf*

spir′ituous bev′erages [′spɪrɪtʃu·əs] *spl* boissons *fpl* spiritueuses

spit [spɪt] *s* salive *f*; (culin) broche *f* ‖ *v* (*pret & pp* **spat** [spæt] or **spit;** *ger* **spitting**) *tr & intr* cracher

spit′ curl′ *s* rouflaquette *f*

spite [spaɪt] *s* dépit *m*, rancune *f*; **in spite of** en dépit de, malgré ‖ *tr* dépiter, contrarier

spiteful [′spaɪtfəl] *adj* rancunier

spit′fire′ *s* mégère *f*

spit′ting im′age *s* (coll) portrait *m* craché

spittoon [spɪ′tun] *s* crachoir *m*

splash [splæʃ] *s* éclaboussure *f*; (*of waves*) clapotis *m*; **to make a splash** (coll) faire

sensation ‖ *tr* & *intr* éclabousser ‖ *interj* flic flac!

splash'down' *s* (rok) amerrissage *m*

spleen [splin] *s* (anat) rate *f*; (fig) maussaderie *f*, mauvaise humeur *f*; **to vent one's spleen on** décharger sa bile sur

splendid ['splɛndɪd] *adj* splendide; (coll) admirable, superbe

splendor ['splɛndər] *s* splendeur *f*

splice [splaɪs] *s* (*in rope*) épissure *f*; (*in wood*) enture *f* ‖ *tr* (*rope*) épisser; (*wood*) enter; (*film*) réparer, coller; (slang) marier

splint [splɪnt] *s* éclisse *f* ‖ *tr* éclisser

splinter ['splɪntər] *s* éclat *m*, éclisse *f*; (*lodged under the skin*) écharde *f* ‖ *tr* briser en éclats ‖ *intr* voler en éclats

splin'ter group' *s* minorité *f* dissidente, groupe *m* fragmentaire

split [splɪt] *adj* fendu; (*pea*) cassé; (*skirt*) déchiré ‖ *s* fente *f*, fissure *f*; (*quarrel*) rupture *f*; (*one's share*) part *f*; (*bottle*) quart *m*, demi *m*; (gymnastics) grand écart *m* ‖ *v* (*pret* & *pp* **split**; *ger* **splitting**) *tr* fendre; (*money; work; ticket*) partager; (*in two*) couper; (*a hide*) dédoubler; **to split hairs** couper les cheveux en quatre; **to split one's sides laughing** se tenir les côtes de rire; **to split the difference** couper la poire en deux ‖ *intr* se fendre; **to split away (from)** se séparer (de)

split' fee' *s* (*between doctors*) dichotomie *f*

split' person'al'ity *s* personnalité *f* dédoublée

split' skirt' *s* jupe-culotte *f*

split' tick'et *s* (pol) panachage *m*

splitting ['splɪtɪŋ] *adj* violent; (*headache*) atroce ‖ *s* fendage *m*; (*of the atom*) désintégration *f*; (*of the personality*) dédoublement *m*

splotch [splɑtʃ] *s* tache *f* ‖ *tr* tacher, barbouiller

splurge [splʌrdʒ] *s* (coll) épate *f* ‖ *intr* (coll) se payer une fête; (*to show off*) (coll) faire de l'épate

splutter ['splʌtər] *s* crachement *m* ‖ *tr*—**splutter out** bredouiller ‖ *intr* crachoter; (*said of candle, grease, etc.*) grésiller

spoil [spɔɪl] *s* (*object of plunder*) prise *f*, proie *f*; **spoils** (*booty*) butin *m*, dépouilles *fpl*; (*emoluments, especially of public office*) assiette *f* au beurre, part *f* du gâteau ‖ *v* (*pret* & *pp* **spoiled** or **spoilt** [spɔɪlt]) *tr* gâter, abîmer ‖ *intr* se gâter, s'abîmer; **to be spoiling for** (coll) brûler du désir de

spoilage ['spɔɪlɪdʒ] *s* déchet *m*

spoiled *adj* gâté

spoil'sport' *s* rabat-joie *m*

spoils' sys'tem *s* système *m* des postes aux petits copains

spoke [spok] *s* rai *m*, rayon *m*; (*of a ladder*) échelon *m*; (*of an umbrella*) baleine *f*

spokes'man *s* (*pl* -**men**) porte-parole *m*, interprète *mf*

sponge [spʌndʒ] *s* éponge *f* ‖ *tr* éponger; (*a meal*) (coll) écornifler ‖ *intr* (coll) écornifler; **to sponge on** (coll) vivre aux crochets de

sponge' cake' *s* gâteau *m* de Savoie, gâteau mousseline, génoise *f*

sponger ['spʌndʒər] *s* écornifleur *m*, pique assiette *mf*

sponge' rub'ber *s* caoutchouc *m* mousse

spon·gy ['spʌndʒi] *adj* (*comp* -**gier**, *supe* -**giest**) spongieux

sponsor ['spɑnsər] *s* patron *m*; (*godfather*, parrain *m*; (*godmother*) marraine *f*; (law) garant *m*; (rad, telv) commanditaire *m* ‖ *tr* patronner, parrainer; (law) se porter garant de; (rad, telv) commanditer

spon'sor·ship' *s* patronnage *m*

spontaneous [spɑn'teni·əs] *adj* spontané

spoof [spuf] *s* (slang) mystification *f*; (slang) parodie *f* ‖ *tr* (slang) mystifier; (slang) blaguer ‖ *intr* (slang) blaguer

spook [spuk] *s* (coll) revenant *m*, spectre *m*

spool [spul] *s* bobine *f*

spoon [spun] *s* cuiller *f*; **to be born with a silver spoon in one's mouth** (coll) être né coiffé ‖ *tr* prendre dans une cuiller; **to spoon off** enlever avec la cuiller ‖ *intr* (coll) se faire des mamours

spooner ['spunər] *s* (coll) peloteur *m*

spoonerism ['spunə‚rɪzəm] *s* contrepètrerie *f*

spoon'-feed' *v* (*pret* & *pp* -**fed**) *tr* nourrir à la cuiller; (*an industry*) subventionner; (coll) mâcher la besogne à

spoonful ['spun‚ful] *s* cuillerée *f*

spoon·y ['spuni] *adj* (*comp* -**ier**; *super* -**iest**) (coll) peloteur

sporadic(al) [spə'rædɪk(əl)] *adj* sporadique

spore [spor] *s* spore *f*

sport [sport] *adj* sportif, de sport ‖ *s* sport *m*; amusement *m*, jeu *m*; (biol) mutation *f*; (coll) chic type *m*; **a good sport** un bon copain; (*a good loser*) un beau joueur; **in sport** par plaisanterie; **to make sport of** tourner en ridicule ‖ *tr* faire parade de, arborer ‖ *intr* s'amuser, jouer

sport' clothes' *spl* vêtements *mpl* de sport

sport'ing goods' *spl* articles *mpl* de sport

sports'cast'er *s* radioreporteur *m* sportif

sports' ed'itor *s* rédacteur *m* sportif

sports' fan' *s* fanatique *mf*, enragé *m* des sports

sports'man *s* (*pl* -**men**) sportif *m*

sports'man·like' *adj* sportif

sports'man·ship' *s* sportivité *f*

sports'wear' *s* vêtements *mpl* sport

sports'writ'er *s* reporter *m* sportif

sport·y ['sporti] *adj* (*comp* -**ier**; *super* -**iest**) (coll) sportif; (*smart in dress*) (coll) chic; (*flashy*) (coll) criard, voyant; (coll) dissolu, libertin

spot [spat] *s* (*stain*) tache *f*; (*place*) endroit *m*, lieu *m*; **on the spot** sur place, à pied d'œuvre; (slang) dans le pétrin; **spots** (*before eyes*) mouches *fpl* ‖ *v* (*pret* & *pp* **spotted**; *ger* **spotting**) *tr* tacher; (coll) repérer, détecter ‖ *intr* se tacher

spot' cash' *s* argent *m* comptant

spot' check' *s* échantillonnage *m*

spot'-check' *tr* échantillonner

spotless ['spatlɪs] *adj* sans tache

spot′light′ *s* spot *m*; (aut) projecteur *m* auxiliaire orientable; **to hold the spotlight** (fig) être en vedette ‖ *tr* diriger les projecteurs sur; (fig) mettre en vedette

spot′ remov′er [rɪ,muvər] *s* détachant *m*

spot′ weld′ing *s* soudage *m* par points

spouse [spaʊz], [spaʊs] *s* (*man*) époux *m*, conjoint *m*; (*woman*) épouse *f*, conjointe *f*

spout [spaʊt] *s* (*discharge pipe or tube*) tuyau *m* de décharge; (*e.g., of teapot*) bec *m*; (*of sprinkling can*) col *m*, queue *f*; (*of water*) jet *m* ‖ *tr* faire jaillir; (*e.g., insults*) (coll) déclamer ‖ *intr* jaillir; **to spout off** (coll) déclamer

sprain [spren] *s* foulure *f*, entorse *f* ‖ *tr* fouler, se fouler

sprawl [sprɔl] *intr* s'étaler, se carrer

spray [spre] *s* (*of ocean*) embruns *mpl*; (*branch*) rameau *m*; (*for insects*) liquide *m* insecticide; (*for weeds*) produit *m* herbicide; (*for spraying insects or weeds*) pulvérisateur *m*; (*for spraying perfume*) vaporisateur *m*, atomiseur *m*; (med) pulvérisation *f* ‖ *tr* pulvériser; (*with a vaporizer*) vaporiser; (hort) désinfecter par pulvérisation d'insecticide; **to spray paint on** peindre au pistolet ‖ *intr*—**to spray out** gicler

sprayer [′spre·ər] *s* vaporisateur *m*, pulvérisateur *m*

spray′ gun′ *s* pulvérisateur *m*; (*for paint*) pistolet *m*; (hort) seringue *f*

spread [sprɛd] *adj* étendu, écarté, ouvert ‖ *s* (*extent, expanse*) étendue *f*, rayonnement *m*; (*of disease, fire*) propagation *f*, progression *f*; (*of wings*) envergure *f*; (*on bed*) dessus-de-lit *m*, couvre-lit *m*; (*on sandwich*) pâte *f*; (*buffet lunch*) collation *f* ‖ *v* (*pret & pp* **spread**) *tr* étendre, étaler; (*news*) répandre; (*disease*) propager; (*the wings*) déployer; (*a piece of bread*) tartiner ‖ *intr* s'étendre, s'étaler; se répandre, rayonner

spree [spri] *s* bombance *f*, orgie *f*; **to go on a spree** (coll) faire la bombe

sprig [sprɪg] *s* brin *m*, brindille *f*

spright·ly [′spraɪtli] *adj* (*comp* **-lier;** *super* **-liest**) vif, enjoué

spring [sprɪŋ] *adj* printanier ‖ *s* (*of water*) source *f*; (*season*) printemps *m*; (*jump*) saut *m*, bond *m*; (*elastic device*) ressort *m*; (*quality*) élasticité *f* ‖ *v* (*pret* **sprang** [spræŋ] or **sprung** [sprʌŋ]; *pp* **sprung**) *tr* (*the frame of a car*) faire déjeter; (*a lock*) faire jouer; (*a leak*) contracter; (*a question*) proposer à l'improviste; (*a prisoner*) (coll) faire sortir de prison ‖ *intr* sauter, bondir; (*said of oil, water, etc.*) jaillir; **to spring up** se lever; naître

spring′-and-fall′ *adj* (*coat*) de demi-saison

spring′board′ *s* tremplin *m*

spring′ fe′ver *s* (hum) malaise *m* des premières chaleurs, flemme *f*

spring′like′ *adj* printanier

spring′time′ *s* printemps *m*

sprinkle [′sprɪŋkəl] *s* pluie *f* fine; (culin) pincée *f* ‖ *tr* (*with water*) asperger, ar-

roser; (*with powder*) saupoudrer; (*to strew*) parsemer ‖ *intr* tomber en pluie fine

sprinkler [′sprɪŋklər] *s* arrosoir *m*

sprinkling [′sprɪŋklɪŋ] *s* aspersion *f*, arrosage *m*; (*with holy water*) aspersion; (*with powder*) saupoudrage *m*; (*of knowledge*) bribes *fpl*, notions *fpl*; (*of persons*) petit nombre *m*

sprin′kling can′ *s* arrosoir *m*

sprint [sprɪnt] *s* course *f* de vitesse, sprint *m* ‖ *intr* faire une course de vitesse, courir à toute vitesse

sprite [spraɪt] *s* lutin *m*

sprocket [′sprɑkɪt] *s* dent *f* de pignon; (*wheel*) pignon *m* de chaîne

sprock′et wheel′ *s* pignon *m* de chaîne

sprout [spraʊt] *s* pousse *f*, rejeton *m*; (*of seed*) germe *m* ‖ *intr* (*said of plant*) pousser, pointer; (*said of seed*) germer

spruce [sprus] *adj* pimpant, tiré à quatre épingles ‖ *s* sapin *m*; (*Norway spruce*) épicéa *m* commun ‖ *intr*—**to spruce up** se faire beau, se pomponner

spry [spraɪ] *adj* (*comp* **spryer** or **sprier;** *super* **spryest** or **spriest**) vif, alerte

spud [spʌd] *s* (*chisel*) bédane *f*; (agr) arrache-racines *m*; (coll) pomme *f* de terre, patate *f*

spun′ glass′ [spʌn] *s* coton *m* de verre

spunk [spʌŋk] *s* (coll) cran *m*, courage *m*

spur [spʌr] *s* éperon *m*; (*of rooster*) ergot *m*; (*stimulant*) aiguillon *m*, stimulant *m*; (rr) embranchement *m*; **on the spur of the moment** sous l'impulsion du moment ‖ *v* (*pret & pp* **spurred;** *ger* **spurring**) *tr* éperonner; **to spur on** aiguillonner, stimuler

spurious [′spjʊrɪ·əs] *adj* faux; (*sentiments*) simulé, feint; (*document*) apocryphe

spurn [spʌrn] *tr* repousser avec mépris, faire fi de

spurt [spʌrt] *s* jaillissement *m*, giclée *f*, jet *m*; (*of enthusiasm*) élan *m*; effort *m* soudain ‖ *intr* jaillir; **to spurt out** gicler

sputnik [′sputnɪk] *s* spoutnik *m*

sputter [′spʌtər] *s* (*manner of speaking*) bredouillement *m*; (*of candle*) grésillement *m*; (*of fire*) crachement *m* ‖ *tr* (*words*) débiter en lançant des postillons ‖ *intr* postillonner; (*said of candle*) grésiller; (*said of fire*) cracher, pétiller

spu·tum [′spjutəm] *s* (*pl* **-ta** [tə]) crachat *m*

spy [spaɪ] *s* (*pl* **spies**) espion *m* ‖ *v* (*pret & pp* **spied**) *tr* (*to catch sight of*) entrevoir; **to spy out** découvrir par ruse ‖ *intr* espionner; **to spy on** épier, guetter

spy′glass′ *s* longue-vue *f*

spying [′spaɪ·ɪŋ] *s* espionnage *m*

spy′ plane′ *s* avion *m* fugitif

spy′ ring′ *s* réseau *m* d'espionnage

spy′ sat′ellite *s* satellite *m* d'espionnage

squabble [′skwɑbəl] *s* chamaillerie *f* ‖ *intr* se chamailler

squad [skwɑd] *s* escouade *f*, peloton *m*; (*of detectives*) brigade *f*

squadron ['skwadrən] s (aer) escadrille f; (mil) escadron m; (nav) escadre f

squalid ['skwalɪd] adj sordide

squall [skwɑl] s (of rain) bourrasque f, rafale f; (cry) braillement m ; (coll) grabuge m ‖ intr souffler en bourrasque; brailler

squalor ['skwalər] s saleté f; misère f

squander ['skwandər] tr gaspiller

square [skwɛr] adj carré; (honest) loyal, franc; (real) véritable; (conventional) (slang) formaliste; **nine (ten, etc.) inches square** de neuf (dix, etc.) pouces en carré; **nine (ten, etc.) square inches** neuf (dix, etc.) pouces carrés; **to get square with** (coll) régler ses comptes avec; **we'll call it square** (coll) nous sommes quittes ‖ s carré m; (of checkerboard or chessboard) case f; (city block) pâté m de maisons; (open area in town or city) place f; (of carpenter) équerre f; **to be on the square** (coll) jouer franc jeu; **to go back to square one** (slang) se retrouver à la case départ, repartir à zéro ‖ adv carrément ‖ tr carrer; (a number) élever au carré; (wood, marble, etc.) équarrir; (a debt) régler; (bk) balancer ‖ intr—**to square off** (coll) se mettre en posture de combat; **to square with** (to tally with) s'accorder avec; régler ses comptes avec

square′ dance′ s quadrille m américain

square′ deal′ s (coll) procédé m loyal

square′ meal′ s repas m copieux

square′ root′ s racine f carrée

squash [skwɑʃ] s écrasement m; (bot) courge f; (sports) squash m ‖ tr écraser ‖ intr s'écraser

squash·y ['skwɑʃi] adj (comp -ier; super -iest) mou et humide; (fruit) à pulpe molle

squat [skwɑt] adj (heavyset) tassé, trapu, ramassé ‖ s position f accroupie ‖ v (pret & pp squatted; ger squatting) intr s'accroupir; (to settle) s'installer sans titre légal

squatter ['skwɑtər] s squatter m

squatting ['skwɑtɪŋ] adj (person) accroupi; (animal) tapi, ramassé

squaw [skwɔ] s femme f peau-rouge

squawk [skwɔk] s cri m rauque; (slang) protestation f, piaillerie f ‖ intr pousser un cri rauque; (slang) protester, piailler

squeak [skwik] s grincement m; (of living being) couic m, petit cri m ‖ intr grincer; pousser des petits cris, couiner

squeal [skwil] s cri m aigu ‖ intr piailler; (slang) manger le morceau; **to squeal on** (slang) moucharder

squealer ['skwilər] s (coll) cafard m

squeamish ['skwimɪʃ] adj trop scrupuleux; prude; sujet aux nausées

squeeze [skwiz] s pression f; (coll) extorsion f; **it's a tight squeeze** (coll) ça tient tout juste ‖ tr serrer; (fruit) presser; **to squeeze from** (coll) extorquer à; **to squeeze into** faire entrer de force dans ‖ intr se blottir; **to squeeze through** se frayer un passage à travers

squeezer ['skwizər] s presse f, presse-fruits m

squelch [skwɛltʃ] s (coll) remarque f écrasante ‖ tr écraser, réprimer

squid [skwɪd] s calmar m

squill [skwɪl] s (bot) scille f; (zool) squille f

squint [skwɪnt] s coup m d'œil furtif; (pathol) strabisme m ‖ tr fermer à moitié ‖ intr loucher; **to squint at** regarder furtivement

squint′-eyed′ adj bigle, strabique; malveillant

squire [skwaɪr] s (knight's attendant) écuyer m; (lady's escort) cavalier m servant; (property owner) propriétaire m terrien; (law) juge m de paix ‖ tr escorter

squirm [skwʌrm] s tortillement m ‖ intr se tortiller; **to squirm out of** se tirer de

squirrel ['skwʌrəl] s écureuil m

squirt [skwʌrt] s giclée f, jet m; (syringe) seringue f; (coll) morveux m ‖ tr faire gicler ‖ intr gicler, jaillir

stab [stæb] s coup m de poignard, de couteau; (wound) estafilade f; (coll) coup d'essai; **to make a stab at** (coll) s'essayer à ‖ v (pret & pp stabbed; ger stabbing) tr poignarder

stabilize ['stebəl,aɪz] tr stabiliser

stab′ in the back′ s coup m de Jarnac, coup de traître

stable ['stebəl] adj stable ‖ s (for cows) étable f; (for horses) écurie f

stack [stæk] s (of wood, books, papers) tas m, pile f; (of hay, straw, etc.) meule f; (of sheaves) gerbier m; (e.g., of rifles) faisceau m; (of ship or locomotive) cheminée f; (of fireplace) souche f; (airplanes in a holding pattern) file f d'attente, pile f d'attente, manège m d'avions; **stacks** (in library) rayons mpl ‖ tr entasser, empiler; mettre en meule, en gerbier, or en faisceau; (a deck of cards) truquer, donner un coup de pouce à; (aer) faire attendre (sur niveaux différents); **to be stacked** (aer) s'échelonner; **to stack arms** former les faisceaux

stadi·um ['stedɪ·əm] s (pl -ums or -a [ə]) stade m

staff [stæf] s (rod, pole) bâton m; (of pilgrim) bourdon m; (of flag) hampe f; (of newspaper) rédaction f; (employees) personnel m; (servants) domestiques mfpl; (support) soutien m; (mil) état-major m; (mus) portée f ‖ tr fournir, pourvoir de personnel; nommer le personnel pour

staff′ head′quarters spl (mil) état-major m

staff′ meet′ing s réunion f de service

staff′ of′ficer s officier m d'état-major

stag [stæg] adj exclusivement masculin; **to go stag** aller sans compagne ‖ s homme m; (male deer) cerf m

stage [stedʒ] s (point in time, section, process) stade m, étape f, phase f; (of rocket) étage m; (stagecoach) diligence f; (scene) champ m d'action, scène f; (staging) échafaudage m; (platform) estrade f; (of microscope) platine f; (theat) scène; **by**

easy stages par petites étapes; **by successive stages** par échelons; **to go on the stage** monter sur les planches ‖ *tr* (*a play, demonstration, riot, etc.*) monter; (*a play*) mettre en scène
stage′coach′ *s* diligence *f*, coche *m*
stage′craft′ *s* technique *f* de la scène
stage′ door′ *s* entrée *f* des artistes
stage′-door John′ny *s* (*pl* -nies) coureur *m* de girls
stage′ effect′ *s* effet *m* scénique
stage′ fright′ *s* trac *m*
stage′hand′ *s* machiniste *m*
stage′ left′ *s* côté *m* jardin
stage′ man′ager *s* régisseur *m*
stage′ name′ *s* nom *m* de théâtre
stage′ prop′erties *spl* accessoires *mpl*
stage′ right′ *s* côté *m* cour
stage′-struck′ [strʌk] *adj* entiché de théâtre
stage′ whis′per *s* aparté *m*
stagger [′stægər] *tr* faire chanceler, faire tituber; (*to upset*) atterrer, bouleverser; (*to surprise*) étonner; (*to arrange*) disposer en chicane, en zigzag; (*hours of work, train schedules, etc.*) échelonner ‖ *intr* chanceler, tituber
staggering [′stægərɪŋ] *adj* (*swaying*) chancelant; (*amazing*) étonnant, faramineux, hallucinant
staging [′stedʒɪŋ] *s* échafaudage *m*; (theat) mise *f* en scène
stagnant [′stægnənt] *adj* stagnant
stag′ par′ty (*pl* -ties) (coll) réunion *f* entre hommes, réunion d'hommes seuls
staid [sted] *adj* posé, sérieux
stain [sten] *s* tache *f*, souillure *f* ‖ *tr* tacher, souiller; (*to tint*) teindre ‖ *intr* se tacher
stained′ glass′ *s* vitre *f* de couleur
stained′-glass win′dow *s* vitrail *m*
stain′less steel′ [′stenlɪs] *s* acier *m* inoxydable
stair [stɛr] *s* escalier *m*; (*step of a series*) marche *f*, degré *m*; **stairs** escalier *m*
stair′case′ or **stair′way′** *s* escalier *m*
stair′well′ *s* cage *f* d'escalier
stake [stek] *s* (*hammered in the ground*) pieu *m*, poteau *m*; (*of tent*) piquet *m*; (*marker*) jalon *m*; (*for burning condemned persons*) bûcher *m*; (*in a game of chance*) mise *f*, enjeu *m*; **at stake** en jeu; **to pull up stakes** (coll) déménager ‖ *tr* (*a road*) bornoyer; (*plants*) échalasser, ramer; (*money*) risquer; (*to back financially*) (slang) fournir aux besoins de; **to stake all** mettre tout en jeu; **to stake off** or **out** jalonner, piqueter
stale [stel] *adj* (*bread*) rassis; (*wine or beer*) éventé; (*air*) confiné; (*joke*) vieux; (*check*) proscrit; (*subject*) rabattu; (*news*) défloré, défraîchi; **to smell stale** (*said of room*) sentir le renfermé
stale′mate′ *s* (chess) pat *m*; (fig) impasse *f*; **in stalemate** pat ‖ *tr* (chess) faire pat; (fig) paralyser
stalk [stɔk] *s* tige *f*; (*of flower or leaf*) queue *f* ‖ *tr* traquer, suivre à la piste ‖ *intr*

marcher fièrement, marcher à grandes enjambées
stall [stɔl] *s* (*for a horse*) stalle *f*; (*at a market*) étal *m*, échoppe *f*; (aer) décrochage *m*; (sports) anti-jeu *m*; (slang) prétexte *m* ‖ *tr* mettre dans une stalle; (*a car*) caler; (*an airplane*) mettre en perte de vitesse; **to stall off** (coll) différer sous prétexte ‖ *intr* (*said of motor*) se bloquer; **to stall for time** (slang) temporiser
stallion [′stæljən] *s* étalon *m*
stalwart [′stɔlwərt] *adj* robuste; vaillant ‖ *s* partisan *m* loyal
stamen [′stemən] *s* étamine *f*
stamina [′stæmɪnə] *s* vigueur *f*, résistance *f*
stammer [′stæmər] *s* bégaiement *m*, balbutiement *m* ‖ *tr* & *intr* bégayer, balbutier
stammerer [′stæmərər] *s* bègue *mf*
stamp [stæmp] *s* (*mark, impression*) empreinte *f*; (*for postage*) timbre *m*; (*for stamping*) poinçon *m* ‖ *tr* (*mail*) affranchir; (*money; leather; a medal*) frapper, estamper; (*a document*) timbrer; (*a passport*) viser; **to stamp one's feet** trépigner; **to stamp one's foot** frapper du pied; **to stamp out** (*e.g., a rebellion*) écraser, étouffer
stampede [stæm′pid] *s* (*of animals or people*) débandade *f*; (*rush*) ruée *f*; (*of people*) sauve-qui-peut *m* ‖ *tr* provoquer la ruée de ‖ *intr* se débander
stamped′ self′-addressed′ en′velope *s* enveloppe *f* timbrée par l'expéditeur
stamp′ing grounds′ *spl*—**to be on one's stamping grounds** (slang) être sur son terrain, être dans son domaine
stamp′ pad′ *s* tampon *m* encreur
stamp′-vend′ing machine′ *s* distributeur *m* automatique de timbres-poste
stance [stæns] *s* attitude *f*, posture *f*
stanch [stɑntʃ] *adj* ferme, solide; vrai, loyal; (*watertight*) étanche ‖ *tr* étancher
stand [stænd] *s* (*place, attitude*) position *f*; (*opposition*) résistance *f*; (*of a merchant*) étal *m*, éventaire *m*; (*of a speaker*) tribune *f*, estrade *f*; (*of a horse*) aplombs *mpl*; (*piece of furniture*) guéridon *m*, console *f*; (*to hold music, papers*) pupitre *m*; **stands** tribune *f*, stand *m* ‖ *v* (*pret* & *pp* **stood** [stud]) *tr* mettre, placer, poser; (*the cold*) supporter; (*a shock; an attack*) soutenir; (*a round of drinks*) (coll) payer; **to stand off** repousser; **to stand up** (*to keep waiting*) (coll) poser un lapin à ‖ *intr* se lever, se mettre debout; se tenir debout, être debout; en être, e.g., **how does it stand?** où en est-il?; **stand by!** en attente!; **to stand aloof** or **aside** se tenir à l'écart; **to stand by** se tenir prêt; (*e.g., a friend*) rester fidèle à; **to stand fast** tenir bon; **to stand for** (*to mean*) signifier; (*to affirm*) soutenir; (*to allow*) tolérer; **to stand in for** doubler, remplacer; **to stand in line** faire la queue; **to stand out** sortir, saillir; **to stand up** se lever, se mettre debout; se tenir debout, être debout; **to stand up**

against or **to** tenir tête à; **to stand up for** prendre fait et cause pour

standard ['stændərd] *adj* (*product, part, unit*) standard, de série, normal; (*current*) courant; (*author, book, work*) classique; (*edition*) définitif; (*keyboard of typewriter*) universel; (*coinage*) au titre ‖ *s* norme *f*, mesure *f*, règle *f*, pratique *f*; (*of quantity, weight, value*) standard *m*; (*banner*) étendard *m*; (*of lamp*) support *m*; (*of wires*) pylône *m*; (*of coinage*) titre *m*; (*for a monetary system*) étalon *m*; (fig) degré *m*, niveau *m*; **standards** critères *mpl*; **up to standard** suivant la norme

stand'ard·bear'er *s* porte-drapeau *m*

stand'ard gauge' *s* voie *f* normale

standardize ['stændər,daɪz] *tr* standardiser

stand'ard of liv'ing *s* niveau *m* de vie

stand'ard time' *s* heure *f* légale

standee [stæn'di] *s* voyageur *m* debout; (theat) spectateur *m* debout

stand'-in' *s* (mov, theat) doublure *f*, remplaçant *m*; (coll) appuis *mpl*, piston *m*

standing ['stændɪŋ] *adj* (*upright*) debout; (*statue*) en pied; (*water*) stagnant; (*army; committee*) permanent; (*price; rule; rope*) fixe; (*custom*) établi, courant; (*jump*) à pieds joints ‖ *s* standing *m*, position *f*, importance *f*; **in good standing** estimé, accrédité; **of long standing** de longue date

stand'ing ar'my *s* armée *f* permanente

stand'ing room' *s* places *fpl* debout

stand'ing vote' *s* vote *m* par assis et levé

stand'pat' *adj* & *s* (coll) immobiliste *mf*

stand'pat'ter *s* (coll) immobiliste *mf*

stand'point' *s* point *m* de vue; **from the standpoint of** sous le rapport de

stand'still' *s* arrêt *m*, immobilisation *f*; **at a standstill** au point mort; **to come to a standstill** s'arrêter court

stand'-up come'dian *s* monologuiste *mf* comique

stanza ['stænzə] *s* strophe *f*

staple ['stepəl] *adj* principal ‖ *s* (*product*) produit *m* principal; (*for holding papers together*) agrafe *f*; (bb) broche *f*; **staples** denrées *fpl* principales ‖ *tr* agrafer; (*books*) brocher

stapler ['steplər] *s* agrafeuse *f*; (bb) brocheuse *f*

star [stɑr] *s* astre *m*; (*heavenly body except sun and moon; figure that represents a star*) étoile *f*; (*of stage or screen*) vedette *f* ‖ *v* (*pret & pp* **starred**; *ger* **starring**) *tr* étoiler, consteller; (mov, rad, telv, theat) mettre en vedette; (typ) marquer d'un astérisque ‖ *intr* apparaître comme vedette

starboard ['stɑr,bord] *adj* de tribord ‖ *s* tribord *m* ‖ *adv* à tribord

star' board'er *s* (coll) pensionnaire *mf* de prédilection

starch [stɑrtʃ] *s* amidon *m*; (*for fabrics*) empois *m*; (*formality*) raideur *f*; (bot, culin) fécule *f*; (coll) force *f*, vigueur *f* ‖ *tr* empeser

starch·y ['stɑrtʃi] *adj* (*comp* **-ier;** *super* **-iest**) empesé; (*foods*) féculent; (*manner*) raide, guindé

stare [stɛr] *s* regard *m* fixe ‖ *tr*—**to stare s.o. in the face** dévisager qn; (*to be obvious to s.o.*) sauter aux yeux de qn ‖ *intr* regarder fixement; **to stare at** regarder fixement, dévisager

star'fish' *s* étoile *f* de mer

star'gaze' *intr* regarder les étoiles; rêvasser, être dans la lune

stark [stɑrk] *adj* pur; rigide; désert, solitaire ‖ *adv* entièrement

stark'-na'ked *adj* tout nu

star'light' *s* lumière *f* des étoiles

starling ['stɑrlɪŋ] *s* étourneau *m*

star·ry ['stɑri] *adj* (*comp* **-rier;** *super* **-riest**) étoilé

Stars' and Stripes' *spl* or **Star'-Spangled Ban'ner** *s* bannière *f* étoilée

start [stɑrt] *s* (*beginning*) commencement *m*, début *m*; (*sudden start*) sursaut *m*, haut-le-corps *m* ‖ *tr* commencer; (*a car, a motor, etc.*) mettre en marche, démarrer; (*a conversation*) entamer; (*a hare*) lever; (*a deer*) lancer; **to start** + *ger* se mettre à + *inf* ‖ *intr* commencer, débuter; démarrer; (*to be startled*) sursauter; **starting from** or **with** à partir de; **to start after** sortir à la recherche de; **to start out** se mettre en route

starter ['stɑrtər] *s* initiateur *m*; (aut) démarreur *m*; (sports) starter *m*

start'ing point' *s* point *m* de départ

startle ['stɑrtəl] *tr* faire tressaillir ‖ *intr* tressaillir

startling ['stɑrtlɪŋ] *adj* effrayant; (*event*) sensationnel; (*resemblance*) saisissant

starvation [stɑr'veʃən] *s* inanition *f*, famine *f*

starva'tion di'et *s* diète *f* absolue

starva'tion wag'es *spl* salaire *m* de famine

starve [stɑrv] *tr* affamer; faire mourir de faim; **to starve out** réduire par la faim ‖ *intr* être affamé; être dans la misère; mourir de faim; (coll) mourir de faim

state [stet] *s* état *m*; (*pomp*) apparat *m;* **to lie in state** être exposé solennellement ‖ *tr* affirmer, déclarer; (*an hour or date*) régler, fixer; (*a problem*) poser

stateless ['stetlɪs] *adj* apatride

state·ly ['stetli] *adj* (*comp* **-lier;** *super* **-liest**) majestueux, imposant

statement ['stetmənt] *s* énoncé *m*, exposé *m*; (*account, report*) compte rendu *m*, rapport *m*; (*of an account*) (com) relevé *m*; (comp) instruction *f*

state' of mind' *s* état *m* d'esprit, état d'âme

state' of the art' *s* état *m* or dernier cri *m* de la technique, état présent

state'room' *s* (naut) cabine *f*; (rr) compartiment *m*

states'man *s* (*pl* **-men**) homme *m* d'État

static ['stætɪk] *adj* statique; (rad) parasite ‖ *s* (rad) parasites *mpl*

station ['steʃən] *s* station *f*; (*for police; for selling gasoline; for broadcasting*) poste *m*; (*of bus, subway, rail line, taxi; for observation*) station; (rr) gare *f* ‖ *tr* poster, placer

sta'tion a'gent *s* chef *m* de gare

stationary ['steʃən,ɛri] *adj* stationnaire

sta'tion break' *s* (rad) pause *f*

stationer ['steʃənər] *s* papetier *m*

stationery ['steʃən,ɛri] *s* papeterie *f*, fournitures *fpl* de bureau

sta'tionery store' *s* papeterie *f*

sta'tion house' *s* commissariat *m* de police

sta'tion identifica'tion *s* (rad) indicatif *m*

sta'tion·mas'ter *s* chef *m* de gare

Sta'tions of the Cross' *s* (rel) stations *fpl* de la Croix

sta'tion wag'on *s* familiale *f*, break *m*

statistical [stə'tıstıkəl] *adj* statistique

statistician [,stætıs'tıʃən] *s* statisticien *m*

statistics [stə'tıstıks] *s* (*science*) statistique *f* ‖ *spl* (*data*) statistique, statistiques

statue ['stætʃʊ] *s* statue *f*

Stat'ue of Lib'erty *s* Liberté *f* éclairant le monde, Statue *f* de la Liberté

statuesque [,stætʃʊ'ɛsk] *adj* sculptural

stature ['stætʃər] *s* stature *f*, taille *f*; caractère *m*, stature

status ['stetəs] *s* condition *f*; rang *m*, standing *m*; **the status of** le statut de

sta'tus quo' [kwo] *s* statu quo *m*

sta'tus seek'er *s* obsédé *m* du standing

sta'tus sym'bol *s* symbole *m* du rang social

statute ['stætʃʊt] *s* statut *m*

stat'ute of limita'tions *s* loi *f* concernant la prescription

statutory ['stætʃʊ,tori] *adj* statutaire

staunch [stɔntʃ] *adj* & *tr* var of **stanch**

stave [stev] *s* (*of barrel*) douve *f*; (*of ladder*) échelon *m*; (mus) portée *f* ‖ *v* (*pret* & *pp* **staved** or **stove** [stov]) *tr*—**to stave in** défoncer, crever; **to stave off** détourner, éloigner

stay [ste] *s* (*visit*) séjour *m*; (*prop*) étai *m*; (*of a corset*) baleine *f*; (*of execution*) sursis *m*; (fig) soutien *m* ‖ *tr* arrêter ‖ *intr* rester; séjourner; (*at a hotel*) descendre; **to stay put** ne pas bouger; **to stay up** veiller

stay'-at-home' *adj* & *s* casanier *m*

STD ['ɛs'ti'di] *s* (letterword) (**sexually transmitted disease**) MST (maladie sexuellement transmissible)

stead [stɛd] *s*—**in s.o.'s stead** à la place de qn; **to stand s.o. in good stead** être fort utile à qn

stead'fast' *adj* ferme; constant

stead·y ['stɛdi] *adj* (*comp* **-ier**; *super* **-iest**) ferme, solide; régulier; (*market*) soutenu ‖ *v* (*pret* & *pp* **-ied**) *tr* raffermir ‖ *intr* se raffermir

steak [stek] *s* (*slice*) tranche *f*; bifteck *m*

steal [stil] *s* (coll) vol *m*; (*bargain*) (coll) occasion *f* ‖ *v* (*pret* **stole** [stol]; *pp* **stolen**) *tr* voler; **to steal s.th. from s.o.** voler q.ch. à qn ‖ *intr* voler; **to steal away** se dérober; **to steal into** se glisser dans; **to steal upon** s'approcher en tapinois de

stealth [stɛlθ] *s*—**by stealth** en tapinois, à la dérobée

steam [stim] *s* vapeur *f*; (*e.g., on a window*) buée *f*; **full steam ahead!** en avant à toute vapeur!; **to get up steam** faire monter la pression; **to let off steam** lâcher la vapeur; (fig) s'épancher ‖ *tr* passer à la vapeur; (culin) cuire à la vapeur; **to steam up** (*e.g., a window*) embuer ‖ *intr* dégager de la vapeur, fumer; s'évaporer; **to steam ahead** avancer à la vapeur; (fig) faire des progrès rapides; **to steam up** s'embuer

steam'boat' *s* vapeur *m*

steam' chest' *s* boîte *f* à vapeur

steam' en'gine *s* machine *f* à vapeur

steamer ['stimər] *s* vapeur *m*

steam' heat' *s* chauffage *m* à la vapeur

steam' roll'er *s* rouleau *m* compresseur; (fig) force *f* irrésistible

steam'ship' *s* vapeur *m*

steam' shov'el *s* pelle *f* à vapeur

steam' ta'ble *s* table *f* à compartiments chauffés à la vapeur

steed [stid] *s* coursier *m*

steel [stil] *adj* (*industry*) sidérurgique ‖ *s* acier *m*; (*for striking fire from flint*) briquet *m*; (*for sharpening knives*) fusil *m* ‖ *tr* aciérer; **to steel oneself against** se cuirasser contre

steel' wool' *s* laine *f* d'acier, paille *f* de fer, jex *m*

steel'works' *spl* aciérie *f*

steelyard ['stil,jɑrd] *s* romaine *f*

steep [stip] *adj* raide, abrupt; (*cliff*) escarpé; (*price*) (coll) exorbitant ‖ *tr* tremper; (*e.g., tea*) infuser; **steeped in** saturé de; (*ignorance*) pétri de; (*the classics*) nourri de

steeple ['stipəl] *s* clocher *m*; (*spire*) flèche *f*

stee'ple·chase' *s* course *f* d'obstacles

steer [stır] *s* bouvillon *m* ‖ *tr* diriger, conduire; (naut) gouverner ‖ *intr* se diriger; (naut) se gouverner; **to steer clear of** (coll) éviter

steerage ['stırıdʒ] *s* entrepont *m*

steer'age pas'senger *s* passager *m* d'entrepont

steer'ing commit'tee *s* comité *m* d'organisation

steer'ing wheel' *s* volant *m*; (naut) roue *f* de gouvernail

stellar ['stɛlər] *adj* stellaire; (*rôle*) de vedette

stem [stɛm] *s* (*of plant; of key*) tige *f*; (*of column; of tree*) fût *m*, tige; (*of fruit*) queue *f*; (*of pipe; of feather*) tuyau *m*; (*of goblet*) pied *m*; (*of watch*) remontoir *m*; (*of word*) radical *m*, thème *m*; (naut) étrave *f*; **from stem to stern** de l'étrave à l'étambot, d'un bout à l'autre ‖ *v* (*pret* & *pp* **stemmed**; *ger* **stemming**) *tr* (*e.g., grapes*) égrapper; (*e.g., the flow of blood*) étancher; (*the tide*) lutter contre, refouler; (*to check*) arrêter, endiguer ‖ *intr*—**to stem from** provenir de

stem'-wind'er *s* montre *f* à remontoir

stench [stɛntʃ] s puanteur f

sten·cil ['stɛnsəl] s (of metal, cardboard) pochoir m; (of paper) poncif m; (work produced by it) travail m au pochoir; (for reproducing typewriting) stencil m ‖ v (pret & pp -ciled or -cilled; ger -ciling or -cilling) tr passer au pochoir; tirer au stencil

stenographer [stə'nɑgrəfər] s sténo f, sténographe mf

stenography [stə'nɑgrəfi] s sténographie f

step [stɛp] s pas m; (of staircase) marche f, degré m; (footprint) trace f; (of carriage) marchepied m; (of ladder) échelon m; (procedure) démarche f; **in step with** au pas avec; **step by step** pas à pas; **to march in step** marcher en cadence; **watch your step!** prenez garde de tomber!; (fig) évitez tout faux pas! ‖ v (pret & pp stepped; ger stepping) tr échelonner; **to step off** mesurer au pas ‖ intr faire un pas; marcher; (coll) aller en toute hâte; **to step aside** s'écarter; **to step back** reculer; **to step in** entrer; **to step on it** (coll) mettre tous les gaz; **to step on the starter** appuyer sur le démarreur

step'broth'er s demi-frère m

step'child' s (pl -child'ren) beau-fils m; belle-fille f

step'daugh'ter s belle-fille f

step'fa'ther s beau-père m

step'lad'der s échelle f double, marche-pied m, escabeau m

step'moth'er s belle-mère f

steppe [stɛp] s steppe f

step'ping stone' s pierre f de passage; (fig) marchepied m

step'sis'ter s demi-sœur f

step'son' s beau-fils m

stere·o ['stɛrɪ,o] adj (coll) stéréo, stéréophonique; (coll) stéréoscopique ‖ s (pl -os) (coll) disque m stéréo; (coll) émission f en stéréophonique; (coll) photographie f stéréoscopique

stereotyped ['stɛrɪ·ə,taɪpt] adj stéréotypé

sterile ['stɛrɪl] adj stérile

sterilize ['stɛrɪ,laɪz] tr stériliser

sterling ['stʌrlɪŋ] adj de bon aloi ‖ s livres fpl sterling; (sterling silver) argent m fin, argent de bon aloi

stern [stʌrn] adj sévère, austère; (look) rébarbatif ‖ s poupe f

stethoscope ['stɛθə,skop] s stéthoscope m

stevedore ['stivə,dor] s arrimeur m

stew [st(j)u] s ragoût m ‖ tr mettre en ragoût ‖ intr être dans tous ses états

steward ['st(j)u·ərd] s (on estate, etc.) régisseur m, intendant m; (in a restaurant) maître m d'hôtel; (aer) flight attendant; (naut) steward m

stewardess ['st(j)u·ərdɪs] s (aer) hôtesse f de l'air; (naut) stewardesse f

stewed' fruit' s compote f

stewed' toma'toes spl purée f de tomates

stick [stɪk] s bâtonnet m, bâton m; (rod) verge f; (wand; drumstick) baguette f; (of chewing gum; of dynamite) bâton;

(firewood) bois m sec; (walking stick) canne f; (naut) mât m; (typ) composteur m ‖ v (pret & pp stuck [stʌk]) tr piquer, enfoncer; (to fasten in position) clouer, ficher, planter; (to glue) coller; (a pig) saigner; (coll) confondre; **stick 'em up!** (slang) haut les mains!; **to be stuck** être pris; (e.g., in the mud) s'enliser; (to be unable to continue) (coll) être en panne; **to stick it out** (coll) tenir jusqu'au bout; **to stick out** (one's tongue) tirer; (one's head) passer; (one's chest) bomber; **to stick up** (in order to rob) (slang) voler à main armée ‖ intr se piquer, s'enfoncer; se ficher, se planter; (to be jammed) être pris, se coincer; (to adhere) coller; (to remain) continuer, rester; **to stick out** saillir, dépasser; (to be evident) sauter aux yeux; **to stick up for** (coll) prendre la défense de

sticker ['stɪkər] s (label) étiquette f gommée; (difficult question) (coll) colle f

stick'pin' s épingle f de cravate

stick'-up' s (slang) attaque f à main armée, hold-up m

stick·y ['stɪki] adj (comp -ier; super -iest) gluant, collant; (hands) poisseux; (weather) étouffant; (question) épineux; (unaccommodating) tatillon

stiff [stɪf] adj raide, difficile, ardu; (joint) ankylosé; (brush; batter) dur; (style, manner) guindé, empesé; (drink) fort; (price) (coll) salé, exagéré; **to be scared stiff** (slang) les avoir à zéro ‖ s (corpse) (slang) macchabée m

stiff' col'lar s col m empesé

stiffen ['stɪfən] tr raidir, tendre; (culin) épaisser ‖ intr se raidir

stiff' neck' s torticolis m

stiff'-necked' adj obstiné, entêté

stiff' shirt' s chemise f empesée, chemise à plastron

stifle ['staɪfəl] tr & intr étouffer

stig·ma ['stɪgmə] s (pl -mas or -mata [mətə]) stigmate m

stigmatize ['stɪgmə,taɪz] tr stigmatiser

stilet·to [stɪ'lɛto] s (pl -tos) stylet m

still [stɪl] adj (peaceful, quiet) tranquille, calme, silencieux; (motionless) immobile; (water) dormant; (wine) non mousseux ‖ s (for distilling) alambic m; (phot) image f; (mov) photogramme m; (poetic) silence m ‖ adv (yet) encore, toujours ‖ conj cependant, pourtant ‖ tr calmer, apaiser; (to silence) faire taire ‖ intr se calmer, s'apaiser; se taire

still'born' adj mort-né

still' life' s (pl still lifes or still lives) nature f morte

stilt [stɪlt] s échasse f; (in the water) pilotis m

stilted adj guindé; (archit) surhaussé

stimulant ['stɪmjələnt] adj & s stimulant m

stimulate ['stɪmjə,let] tr stimuler

stimu·lus ['stɪmjələs] s (pl -li [,laɪ]) stimulant m, aiguillon m; (physiol) stimulus m

sting [stɪŋ] *s* piqûre *f*; (*stinging organ*) aiguillon *m*, dard *m* ‖ *v* (*pret & pp* **stung** [stʌŋ]) *tr & intr* piquer

stin·gy [ˈstɪndʒi] *adj* (*comp* **-gier;** *super* **-giest**) avare, pingre

stink [stɪŋk] *s* puanteur *f* ‖ *v* (*pret* **stank** [stæŋk]; *pp* **stunk** [stʌŋk]) *tr*—**to stink up** empester, empuantir ‖ *intr* puer, empester; **to stink of** puer, empester

stinker [ˈstɪŋkər] *s* (slang) peau *f* de vache, chameau *m*

stint [stɪnt] *s* tâche *f*, besogne *f*; **without stint** sans réserve, sans limite ‖ *tr* limiter, réduire; **to stint oneself** se priver ‖ *intr* lésiner, être chiche

stipend [ˈstaɪpənd] *s* traitement *m*, honoraires *mpl*

stipulate [ˈstɪpjə‚let] *tr* stipuler

stir [stʌr] *s* remuement *m*, agitation *f*; (*prison*) (slang) bloc *m*; **to create a stir** faire sensation ‖ *v* (*pret & pp* **stirred;** *ger* **stirring**) *tr* remuer, agiter; **to stir up** (*trouble*) fomenter ‖ *intr* remuer, s'agiter, bouger

stirring [ˈstʌrɪŋ] *adj* entraînant

stirrup [ˈstʌrəp], [ˈstɪrəp] *s* étrier *m*

stitch [stɪtʃ] *s* (*in sewing*) point *m*; (*in knitting*) maille *f*, (surg) point de suture; **not a stitch of** (coll) pas un brin de; **stitch in the side** point de côté; **to be in stitches** (coll) se tenir les côtes ‖ *tr* coudre; (bb) brocher; (surg) suturer ‖ *intr* coudre

stock [stɑk] *s* (*supply*) réserve *f*, provision *f*, stock *m*; (*assortment*) assortiment *m*; capital *m*, fonds *m*; (*shares*) valeurs *fpl*, actions *fpl*; (*of meat*) bouillon *m*; (*of a tree*) tronc *m*; (*of an anvil*) billot *m*; (*of a rifle*) crosse *f*; (*of a tree; of a family*) souche *f*; (*livestock*) bétail *m*, bestiaux *mpl*; (*handle*) poignée *f*; (*for dies*) tourne-à-gauche *m*; (hort) ente *f*; **in stock** en magasin; **on the stocks** (fig) sur le métier; **out of stock** épuisé; **stocks** (*for punishment*) pilori *m*; (naut) chantier *m*; **to take stock** (com) faire l'inventaire; (fig) faire le point; **to take stock in** (coll) faire grand cas de; **to take stock of** faire l'inventaire de ‖ *tr* approvisionner; garder en magasin; (*a forest or lake*) peupler; (*a farm*) monter en bétail; (*a pool*) empoissonner

stockade [stɑˈked] *s* palanque *f*, palissade *f* ‖ *tr* palissader

stock′breed′er *s* éleveur *m* de bestiaux

stock′breed′ing *s* élevage *m*

stock′bro′ker *s* agent *m* de change, courtier *m* de bourse

stock′ car′ *s* (aut) voiture *f* de série; (rr) wagon *m* à bestiaux

stock′-car race′ *s* course *f* de bolides

stock′ com′pany *s* (com) société *f* anonyme; (theat) troupe *f* à demeure

stock′ div′idend *s* action *f* gratuite

stock′ exchange′ *s* bourse *f*

stock′hold′er *s* actionnaire *mf*

stocking [ˈstɑkɪŋ] *s* bas *m*

stock′ mar′ket *s* bourse *f*, marché *m* des valeurs; **to play the stock market** jouer à la bourse

stock′pile′ *s* stocks *mpl* de réserve ‖ *tr & intr* stocker

stock′ rais′ing *s* élevage *m*

stock′room′ *s* magasin *m*

stock·y [ˈstɑki] *adj* (*comp* **-ier;** *super* **-iest**) trapu, costaud

stock′yard′ *s* parc *m* à bétail

stoic [ˈsto·ɪk] *adj & s* stoïque; **Stoic** stoïcien *m*

stoke [stok] *tr* (*a fire*) attiser; (*a furnace*) alimenter, charger

stoker [ˈstokər] *s* chauffeur *m*; (mach) stoker *m*

stolid [ˈstɑlɪd] *adj* flegmatique, impassible, lourd

stomach [ˈstʌmək] *s* estomac *m* ‖ *tr* digérer; (coll) digérer, avaler

stom′ach ache′ *s* mal *m* d'estomac

stom′ach pump′ *s* pompe *f* stomacale

stone [ston] *s* pierre *f*; (*of fruit*) noyau *m*; (pathol) calcul *m*; (typ) marbre *m* ‖ *tr* lapider; (*fruit*) dénoyauter

stone′-broke′ *adj* (coll) complètement fauché, raide

stone′-deaf′ *adj* sourd comme un pot

stone′ma′son *s* maçon *m*

stone′ quar′ry *s* (*pl* **-ries**) carrière *f*

stone's′ throw′ *s*—**within a stone's throw** à un jet de pierre

stone′wall′ *intr* donner des réponses évasives

ston·y [ˈstoni] *adj* (*comp* **-ier;** *super* **-iest**) pierreux; (fig) dur, endurci

stooge [studʒ] *s* (theat) compère *m*; (slang) homme *f* de paille, acolyte *m*

stool [stul] *s* tabouret *m*, escabeau *m*; (*bowel movement*) selles *fpl*

stool′ pi′geon *s* appeau *m*; (slang) mouchard *m*, mouton *m*

stoop [stup] *s* courbure *f*, inclinaison *f*; (*porch*) véranda *f* ‖ *intr* se pencher; se tenir voûté; (*to debase oneself*) s'abaisser

stoop′-shoul′dered *adj* voûté

stop [stɑp] *s* arrêt *m*; (*in telegrams*) stop *m*; (*full stop*) point *m*; (*of a guitar*) touche *f*; (mus) jeu *m* d'orgue; (*public sign*) stop; **to pull out all the stops** (coll) mettre le paquet; **to put a stop to** mettre fin à ‖ *v* (*pret & pp* **stopped;** *ger* **stopping**) *tr* arrêter; (*a check*) faire opposition à; **to stop up** boucher ‖ *intr* s'arrêter, arrêter; **to stop** + *ger*, cesser de + *inf*, s'arrêter de + *inf*; **to stop off** descendre en passant; **to stop off at** s'arrêter un moment à; **to stop over** (aer, naut) faire escale

stop′cock′ *s* robinet *m* d'arrêt

stop′gap′ *adj* provisoire ‖ *s* bouche-trou *m*

stop′light′ *s* signal *m* lumineux; (aut) feu *m* stop, stop *m*

stop′o′ver *s* arrêt *m* en cours de route, étape *f*

stoppage [ˈstɑpɪdʒ] *s* arrêt *m*; (*of payments*) suspension *f*; (*of wages*) retenue *f*; obstruction *f*; (pathol) occlusion *f*

stopper ['stɑpər] s bouchon m, tampon m
stop'ping for unload'ing s manutention f
stop' sign' s signal m d'arrêt
stop' thief' interj au voleur!
stop'watch' s chronomètre m à déclic, compte-secondes m
storage ['stɔrɪdʒ] s emmagasinage m, entreposage m; **to put in storage** entreposer
stor'age bat'ter·y s (pl -ies) (elec) accumulateur m, accu m
store [stɔr] s (where goods are sold) magasin m; (shop) boutique f; (supply) provision f, réserve f, stock m; (of learning, information) fonds m; (warehouse) (Brit) entrepôt m; **stores** (materials) matériel m; (provisions) vivres mpl; **to set great store by** faire grand cas de ‖ tr emmagasiner; (to warehouse) entreposer; (to supply or stock) approvisionner; **to store away** or **up** accumuler
store'house' s magasin m, entrepôt m; (of information) mine f
store'keep'er s boutiquier m
store'room' s dépense f, office f; (for furniture) garde-meuble m; (naut) soute f
stork [stɔrk] s cigogne f
storm [stɔrm] s orage m; (mil) assaut m; (fig) tempête f; **to take by storm** prendre d'assaut ‖ tr livrer l'assaut à ‖ intr faire de l'orage; (fig) tempêter
storm' cloud' s nuage m orageux; (fig) nuage noir
storm' door' s contre-porte f
storm' pet'rel ['pɛtrəl] s oiseau m des tempêtes
storm' sash' s contre-fenêtre f
storm' sew'er s évacuateur m pluvial
storm' troops' spl troupes fpl d'assaut
storm' win'dow s contre-fenêtre f, double fenêtre f
storm·y ['stɔrmi] adj (comp -ier; super -iest) orageux
sto·ry ['stɔri] s (pl -ries) (narration) histoire f; (tale) conte m; (plot) intrigue f; (floor) étage m; (coll) mensonge m, histoire
sto'ry·tel'ler s conteur m; (fibber) menteur m
stout [staut] adj (fat) corpulent, gros; (courageous) vaillant; (determined) ferme, résolu; (strong) fort ‖ s stout m
stout'-heart'ed adj au cœur vaillant
stove [stov] s (for heating a house or room) poêle m; (for cooking) fourneau m de cuisine, cuisinière f
stove'pipe' s tuyau m de poêle; (hat) (coll) huit-reflets m, tuyau de poêle
stow [sto] tr mettre en place, ranger; (naut) arrimer; **to stow with** remplir de ‖ intr—**to stow away** s'embarquer clandestinement
stowage ['sto·ɪdʒ] s arrimage m; (costs) frais mpl d'arrimage
stow'away' s passager m clandestin
straddle ['strædəl] tr enfourcher, chevaucher ‖ intr se mettre à califourchon; (coll) répondre en normand

strafe [strɑf], [stref] s (slang) bombardement m, marmitage m ‖ tr (slang) bombarder, marmiter
straggle ['strægəl] intr traîner; (to be scattered) s'éparpiller; **to straggle along** marcher sans ordre
straggler ['stræglər] s traînard m
straight [stret] adj (not curved) droit; (shortest route) direct; (honest) loyal, honnête; (in order) correct, en ordre; (chair) à dossier droit; (hair) raide; (whiskey) sec; (candid) franc; (hanging straight) d'aplomb; (part in a play) sérieux; (not homosexual) qui n'est pas homosexuel; (not a drug addict) qui ne se drogue pas; (not a criminal) qui n'est pas véreux; **to set s.o. straight** faire la leçon à qn ‖ s (poker) séquence f ‖ adv droit; directement; loyalement, honnêtement; (without interruption) de suite; **straight ahead** tout droit; **straight out** franchement, sans détours; **straight through** de part en part; d'un bout à l'autre; **to go straight** (coll) vivre honnêtement
straighten ['stretən] tr redresser; mettre en ordre ‖ intr se redresser
straight' face' s—**to keep a straight face** montrer un front sérieux
straight'for'ward adj franc, direct; loyal
straight' off' adv sur-le-champ, d'emblée
straight' ra'zor s rasoir m à main
straight'way' adv sur-le-champ, d'emblée
strain [stren] s tension f, effort m, pression f; (of a muscle) foulure f; (descendants) lignée f; (ancestry; type of virus) souche f; (trait) héritage m, tendance f; (vein) ton m, sens m; (bit) trace f; (coll) grand effort m; **mental strain** surmenage m intellectuel; **strains** (of, e.g., the Marseillaise) accents mpl; **sweet strains** doux accords mpl ‖ tr forcer; (e.g., a wrist) se fouler; (e.g., one's eyes) se fatiguer; (e.g., part of a machine) déformer; (e.g., a liquid) filtrer, tamiser; **to strain oneself** se surmener ‖ intr s'efforcer; filtrer, tamiser; (to trickle) suinter; (said of beam, ship, motor, etc.) fatiguer; **to strain at** (a leash, rope, etc.) tirer sur; (to balk at) reculer devant
strained adj (smile) forcé; (friendship) tendu; (nervous) crispé
strainer ['strenər] s passoire f, filtre m
strait [stret] s détroit m; **straits** détroit m; **to be in dire straits** être dans la plus grande gêne
strait' jack'et s camisole de force
strait'-laced' adj prude, collet monté, puritain
Straits' of Do'ver spl Pas m de Calais
strand [strænd] s (beach) plage f, grève f; (of rope or cable) toron m; (of thread) brin m; (of pearls) collier m; (of hair) cheveu m ‖ tr toronner; (to undo strands of) décorder; (a ship) échouer
stranded adj abandonné; (lost) égaré; (ship) échoué; (rope or cable) à torons; **to leave s.o. stranded** laisser qn en plan

strange [strendʒ] *adj* étrange; (*unfamiliar*) inconnu, étranger; (*unaccustomed*) inhabituel

stranger ['strendʒər] *s* étranger *m*; visiteur *m*

strangle ['stræŋgəl] *tr* étrangler, étouffer ‖ *intr* s'étrangler

strap [stræp] *s* (*of leather, rubber, etc.*) courroie *f*; (*of cloth, metal, leather, etc.*) bande *f*; (*to sharpen a razor*) cuir *m* à rasoir; (*of, e.g., a harness*) sangle *f* ‖ *tr* (*pret & pp* **strapped;** *ger* **strapping**) *tr* attacher avec une courroie, sangler; (*a razor*) repasser sur le cuir

strap'hang'er *s* (coll) voyageur *m* debout

strapping ['stræpɪŋ] *adj* bien découplé, robuste; (coll) énorme, gros

stratagem ['strætədʒəm] *s* stratagème *m*

strategic(al) [strə'tidʒɪk(əl)] *adj* stratégique

strategist ['strætɪdʒɪst] *s* stratège *m*

strate·gy ['strætɪdʒi] *s* (*pl* **-gies**) stratégie *f*

strati·fy ['strætɪ,faɪ] *v* (*pret & pp* **-fied**) *tr* stratifier ‖ *intr* se stratifier

stratosphere ['strætə,sfɪr] *s* stratosphère *f*

stra·tum ['strætəm] *s* (*pl* **-ta** [tə] or **-tums**) couche *f*; (*e.g., of society*) classe *f*, couche

straw [strɔ] *s* paille *f*; (*for drinking*) chalumeau *m*, paille; **it's the last straw!** c'est le bouquet!, il ne manquait plus que cela!, c'est la fin des haricots!

straw'ber'ry *s* (*pl* **-ries**) fraise *f*; (*plant*) fraisier *m*

straw'hat' *s* chapeau *m* de paille; (*skimmer*) canotier *m*

straw' man' *s* (*pl* **-men'**) (*figurehead*) homme *m* de paille, sanglier *m* de carton; (*scarecrow*) épouvantail *m*; (*red herring*) canard *m*, diversion *f*

straw' mat'tress *s* paillasse *f*

straw' vote' *s* vote *m* d'essai

stray [stre] *adj* égaré; (*bullet*) perdu; (*scattered*) épars ‖ *s* animal *m* égaré ‖ *intr* s'égarer

streak [strik] *s* raie *f*, rayure *f*, bande *f*; (*of light*) trait *m*, filet *m*; (*of lightning*) éclair *m*; (*layer*) veine *f*; (*bit*) trace *f*; **like a streak** comme un éclair; **streak of luck** filon *m* ‖ *tr* rayer, strier, zébrer ‖ *intr* faire des raies; passer comme un éclair

stream [strim] *s* (*brook*) ruisseau *m*; (*steady flow of current*) courant *m*; (*of people, abuse, light, etc.*) flot *m*; (*of, e.g., automobiles*) défilé *m* ‖ *intr* couler; (*said of blood*) ruisseler; (*said of light*) jaillir; (*said of flag*) flotter; **to stream out** sortir à flots

streamer ['strimər] *s* banderole *f*

stream'lined' *adj* aérodynamique, caréné; (fig) abrégé, concis

stream'lin'er *s* train *m* caréné de luxe

street [strit] *s* rue *f*; (*surface of the street*) chaussée *f*

street'car' *s* tramway *m*

street' clean'er *s* balayeur *m*; (mach) balayeuse *f*

street' clothes' *spl* vêtements *mpl* de ville

street' floor' *s* rez-de-chaussée *m*

street'light' *s* réverbère *m*

street' sprink'ler *s* arroseuse *f*

street' u'rinal *s* vespasienne *f*, édicule *m*, urinoir *m*

street'walk'er *s* racoleuse *f*, fille *f* des rues

street'wise' *adj* démerdard

strength [strɛŋθ] *s* force *f*, puissance *f*; (*of a fabric*) solidité *f*; (*of spirituous liquors*) degré *m*, titre *m*; (com) tendance *f* à la hausse; (mil) effectif(s) *m(pl)*; **on the strength of** sur la foi de

strengthen ['strɛŋθən] *tr* fortifier, renforcer ‖ *intr* se fortifier, se renforcer

strenuous ['strɛnju·əs] *adj* actif, énergique; (*work*) ardu; (*effort*) acharné; (*objection*) vigoureux

stress [strɛs] *s* tension *f*, force *f*; (mach) stress *m*, tension; (phonet) accent *m* d'intensité; **to lay stress on** insister sur ‖ *tr* (*e.g., a beam*) charger; (*a syllable*) accentuer; (*a point*) insister sur, appuyer sur

stress' ac'cent *s* accent *m* d'intensité

stretch [strɛtʃ] *s* (*act, gesture*) étirement *m*; (*span*) envergure *f*; (*of the arm; of the meaning*) extension *f*; (*of the imagination*) effort *m*; (*distance in time or space*) intervalle *m*, période *f*; (*section of road*) section *f*; (*section of country, water, etc.*) étendue *f*; **at a stretch** d'un trait; **in one stretch** d'une seule traite; **to do a stretch** (slang) faire de la taule ‖ *tr* tendre; (*the sense of a word*) forcer; (*a sauce*) allonger; **to stretch oneself** s'étirer; **to stretch out** allonger, étendre; (*the hand*) tendre ‖ *intr* s'étirer; (*said of shoes, gloves, etc.*) s'élargir; **to stretch out** s'allonger, s'étendre

stretcher ['strɛtʃər] *s* (*for gloves, trousers, etc.*) tendeur *m*; (*for a painting*) châssis *m*; (*to carry sick or wounded*) civière *f*, brancard *m*

stretch'er·bear'er *s* brancardier *m*

strew [stru] *v* (*pret* **strewed;** *pp* **strewed** or **strewn**) *tr* semer, éparpiller; (*e.g., with flowers*) joncher, parsemer

stricken ['strɪkən] *adj* frappé; (*e.g., with grief*) affligé; (*crossed out*) rayé; **stricken with** atteint de

strict [strɪkt] *adj* strict; (*exacting*) sévère

stricture ['strɪktʃər] *s* critique *f* sévère; (pathol) rétrécissement *m*

stride [straɪd] *s* enjambée *f*; **to hit one's stride** attraper la cadence; **to make great** (or **rapid**) **strides** avancer à grands pas; **to take in one's stride** faire sans le moindre effort ‖ *v* (*pret* **strode** [strod]; *pp* **stridden** ['strɪdən]) *tr* parcourir à grandes enjambées; (*to straddle*) enfourcher ‖ *intr*—**to stride across** or **over** enjamber; **to stride along** marcher à grandes enjambées

strident ['straɪdənt] *adj* strident

strife [straɪf] *s* lutte *f*

strike [straɪk] *s* (*blow*) coup *m*; (*stopping of work*) grève *f*; (*discovery of ore, oil, etc.*) rencontre *f*; (baseball) coup du batteur; **to go on strike** se mettre en grève ‖ *v* (*pret & pp* **struck** [strʌk]) *tr* frapper; (*coins*) frapper; (*a match*) frotter; (*a bargain*) conclure; (*camp*) lever; (*the sails; the colors*) amener; (*the hour*) sonner; (*root; a pose*) prendre; **how does he strike you?** quelle impression vous fait-il?; **to strike it rich** trouver le filon; **to strike out** or **off** rayer; **to strike up** (*a song, piece of music, etc.*) attaquer, entonner; (*an acquaintance, conversation, etc.*) lier ‖ *intr* frapper; (*said of clock*) sonner; (*said of workers*) faire la grève; (*mil*) donner l'assaut; **to strike out** se mettre en route

strike′break′er *s* briseur *m* de grève, jaune *m*

strike′ pay′ *s* salaire *m* de gréviste

striker [′straɪkər] *s* frappeur *m*; (*on door*) marteau *m*; (*worker on strike*) gréviste *mf*

striking [′straɪkɪŋ] *adj* frappant, saisissant; (*workers*) en grève

strik′ing pow′er *s* force *f* de frappe

string [strɪŋ] *s* ficelle *f*; (*of onions or garlic; of islands; of pearls; of abuse*) chapelet *m*; (*of words, insults*) enfilade *f*, kyrielle *f*; (*e.g., of cars*) file *f*; (*of beans*) fil *m*; (*for shoes*) lacet *m*; (*mus*) corde *f*; **strings** instruments *mpl* à cordes; **to pull strings** (fig) tirer les ficelles; **with no strings attached** (coll) sans restriction ‖ *v* (*pret & pp* **strung** [strʌŋ]) *tr* mettre une ficelle à, garnir de cordes; (*e.g., a violin*) mettre les cordes à; (*a bow*) bander; (*a tennis racket*) corder; (*beads, sentences, etc.*) enfiler; (*a cord, a thread, a wire, etc.*) tendre; (*to tune*) moner; **to string along** (slang) lanterner, faire marcher; **to string up** (coll) pendre ‖ *intr*—**to string along with** (slang) collaborer avec, suivre

string′ bean′ *s* haricot *m* vert

stringed′ in′strument *s* instrument *m* à cordes

stringent [′strɪndʒənt] *adj* rigoureux; (*tight*) tendu; (*convincing*) convaincant

string′ quartet′ *s* quatuor *m* à cordes

string·y [′strɪŋi] *adj* (*comp* **-ier;** *super* **-iest**) fibreux, filandreux

strip [strɪp] *s* (*of paper, cloth, land, stamps*) bande *f*; (*of metal*) lame *f*, ruban *m* ‖ *v* (*pret & pp* **stripped;** *ger* **stripping**) *tr* dépouiller; (*to strip bare*) mettre à nu; (*the bed*) défaire; (*a screw*) arracher le filet de, faire foirer; (*tobacco*) écoter; **to strip down** (*e.g., a motor*) démonter; **to strip off** enlever; (*e.g., bark*) écorcer ‖ *intr* se déshabiller

stripe [straɪp] *s* raie *f*, bande *f*; (*on cloth*) rayure *f*; (*flesh wound*) marque *f*; (mil, nav) chevron *m*, galon *m*; **of any stripe** de tous poils; **to win one's stripes** gagner ses galons ‖ *tr* rayer

strip′ min′ing *s* exploitation *f* minière à ciel ouvert

strip′tease′ *s* strip-tease *m*, déshabillage *m* suggestif

stripteaser [′strɪp,tizər] *s* effeuilleuse *f*, strip-teaseuse *f*

strive [straɪv] *v* (*pret* **strove** [strov]; *pp* **striven** [′strɪvən]) *intr* s'efforcer; **to strive after** rechercher; **to strive against** lutter

contre; **to strive to** s'efforcer à, s'évertuer à

stroke [strok] *s* coup *m*; (*of pen; of wit*) trait *m*; (*of arms in swimming*) brassée *f*; (*caress with hand*) caresse *f* de la main; (*of a piston*) course *f*; (*of lightning*) foudre *f*; (pathol) attaque *f* d'apoplexie; **at the stroke of** sonnant, e.g., **at the stroke of five** à cinq heures sonnantes; **to not do a stroke of work** ne pas en ficher une ramée ‖ *tr* caresser de la main

stroll [strol] *s* promenade *f*; **to take a stroll** aller faire un tour ‖ *intr* se promener

stroller [′strolər] *s* promeneur *m*; (*for babies*) poussette *f*

strong [strɔŋ] *adj* (*comp* **stronger** [′strɔŋgər]; *super* **strongest** [′strɔŋgɪst]) fort; (*stock market*) ferme; (*musical beat*) marqué; (*spicy*) piquant; (*rancid*) rance

strong′box′ *s* coffre-fort *m*

strong′ drink′ *s* boissons *fpl* spiritueuses

strong′hold′ *s* place *f* forte

strong′ man′ *s* (*pl* **-men′**) (*e.g., in a circus*) hercule *m* forain; (*leader, good planner*) animateur *m*; (*dictator*) chef *m* autoritaire

strong′-mind′ed *adj* résolu, décidé; (*woman*) hommasse

strontium [′strɑnʃɪ·əm] *s* strontium *m*

strop [strɑp] *s* cuir *m* à rasoir ‖ *v* (*pret & pp* **stropped;** *ger* **stropping**) *tr* repasser sur le cuir

strophe [′strofi] *s* strophe *f*

structure [′strʌktʃər] *s* structure *f*; (*building*) édifice *m*

struggle [′strʌgəl] *s* lutte *f* ‖ *intr* lutter; **to struggle along** avancer péniblement

strug′gle for exist′ence *s* lutte *f* pour la vie

strum [strʌm] *v* (*pret & pp* **strummed;** *ger* **strumming**) *tr* (*an instrument*) gratter de; (*a tune*) tapoter ‖ *intr* jouailler; **to strum on** plaquer des arpèges sur

strumpet [′strʌmpɪt] *s* putain *f*

strut [strʌt] *s* (*brace, prop*) étai *m*, support *m*, entretoise *f*; démarche *f* orgueilleuse ‖ *v* (*pret & pp* **strutted;** *ger* **strutting**) *intr* se pavaner

strychnine [′strɪknaɪn] *s* strychnine *f*

stub [stʌb] *s* (*fragment*) tronçon *m*; (*of a tree*) souche *f*; (*of a pencil; of a cigar, cigarette*) bout *m*; (*of a check*) talon *m*, souche ‖ *v* (*pret & pp* **stubbed;** *ger* **stubbing**) *tr*—**to stub one's toe** se cogner le bout du pied

stubble [′stʌbəl] *s* éteule *f*, chaume *m*; (*of beard*) poil *m* court et raide

stubborn [′stʌbərn] *adj* obstiné; (*headstrong*) têtu; (*resolute*) acharné; (*fever*) rebelle; (*soil*) ingrat

stuc·co [′stʌko] *s* (*pl* **-coes** or **-cos**) stuc *m* ‖ *tr* stuquer

stuck [stʌk] *adj* coincé, pris; (*glued*) collé; (*unable to continue*) en panne; **stuck on** (coll) entiché de

stuck′-up′ *adj* (coll) hautain, prétentieux

stud [stʌd] *s* (*nail, knob*) clou *m* à grosse tête; (*ornament*) clou doré; (*on shirt*) bouton *m*; (*studhorse*) étalon *m*; (*horse farm*) haras *m*; (*bolt*) goujon *m*; (*archit*) montant *m* ‖ *v* (*pret & pp* **studded;** *ger* **studding**) *tr* clouter; **studded with** jonché de, parsemé de

stud′ bolt′ *s* goujon *m*

stud′ded tire′ *s* pneu *m* à clou

student [′st(j)udənt] *adj* estudiantin ‖ *s* étudiant *m*; (*researcher*) chercheur *m*

stu′dent bod′y *s* étudiants *mpl*

stu′dent cen′ter *s* foyer *m* d'étudiants, centre *m* social des étudiants

stu′dent nurse′ *s* élève *f* infirmière

stu′dent teach′er *s* stagiaire *mf*

stud′ farm′ *s* haras *m*

stud′horse′ *s* étalon *m*

studied [′stʌdid] *adj* prémédité; recherché

studi·o [′st(j)udɪ‚o] *s* (*pl* **-os**) studio *m*, atelier *m*

studious [′st(j)udɪ·əs] *adj* studieux, appliqué

stud·y [′stʌdi] *s* (*pl* **-ies**) étude *f*; rêverie *f*; cabinet *m* ‖ *v* (*pret & pp* **-ied**) *tr & intr* étudier

stuff [stʌf] *s* chose *f*, truc *m*; (*miscellaneous objects*) choses *fpl*, fatras *m*; (*possessions*) affaires *fpl*; **to know one's stuff** (coll) s'y connaître ‖ *tr* bourrer; (*with food*) gaver; (*furniture*) rembourrer; (*an animal*) empailler; (culin) farcir; **to stuff up** boucher ‖ *intr* se gaver

stuffed′ shirt′ *s* collet *m* monté

stuffing [′stʌfɪŋ] *s* rembourrage *m*; (culin) farce *f*

stuff·y [′stʌfi] *adj* (*comp* **-ier;** *super* **-iest**) (*room*) mal ventilé; (*tedious*) ennuyeux; (*pompous*) collet monté; **to smell stuffy** sentir le renfermé

stumble [′stʌmbəl] *intr* trébucher; (*in speaking*) hésiter

stum′bling block′ *s* pierre *f* d'achoppement

stump [stʌmp] *s* (*of tree*) souche *f*; (*e.g., of arm*) moignon *m*; (*of tooth*) chicot *m* ‖ *tr* (*a design*) estomper; (coll) embarrasser, coller; (*a state, district, region*) (coll) faire une tournée électorale en, dans, or à ‖ *intr* clopiner

stump′ speak′er *s* orateur *m* de carrefour

stump′ speech′ *s* harangue *f* électorale improvisée

stun [stʌn] *v* (*pret & pp* **stunned;** *ger* **stunning**) *tr* étourdir

stunning [′stʌnɪŋ] *adj* (coll) étourdissant, épatant

stunt [stʌnt] *s* (*underdeveloped creature*) avorton *m*; (*feat*) tour *m* de force, acrobatie *f*; (*trick*) truc *m*; **to do a stunt** (mov) faire une cascade ‖ *tr* atrophier ‖ *intr* (coll) faire des acrobaties

stunted *adj* rabougri

stunt′ fly′ing *s* vol *m* de virtuosité, acrobatie *f* aérienne

stunt′ man′ *s* (*pl* **men′**) cascadeur *m*, doublure *f*

stupe·fy [′st(j)upɪ‚faɪ] *v* (*pret & pp* **-fied**) *tr* stupéfier

stupendous [st(j)u′pɛndəs] *adj* prodigieux, formidable

stupid [′st(j)upɪd] *adj* stupide

stupor [′st(j)upər] *s* stupeur *f*

stur·dy [′stʌrdi] *adj* (*comp* **-dier;** *super* **-diest**) robuste, vigoureux; (*resolute*) ferme, hardi

sturgeon [′stʌrdʒən] *s* esturgeon *m*

stutter [′stʌtər] *s* bégaiement *m* ‖ *tr & intr* bégayer

sty [staɪ] *s* (*pl* **sties**) porcherie *f*; (pathol) orgelet *m*

style [staɪl] *s* style *m*; (*fashion*) mode *f*; (*elegance*) ton *m*, chic *m*; **to live in great style** mener grand train ‖ *tr* appeler, dénommer; **to style oneself** s'intituler

stylish [′staɪlɪʃ] *adj* à la mode, élégant, chic

sty·mie [′staɪmi] *v* (*pret & pp* **-mied;** *ger* **-mieing**) *tr* contrecarrer

styp′tic pen′cil [′stɪptɪk] *s* crayon *m* styptique

suave [swɑv] *adj* suave; (*person*) affable; (*manners*) doucereux

sub [sʌb] *s* (coll) sous-marin *m*

subconscious [səb′kɑnʃəs] *adj & s* subconscient *m*

sub′contrac′tor *s* sous-traitant *m*

sub′divide′ or **sub′divide′** *tr* subdiviser ‖ *intr* se subdiviser

subdue [səb′d(j)u] *tr* subjuguer, vaincre, asservir; (*color, light, sound*) adoucir, amortir; (*passions, feelings*) dompter

sub′head′ *s* sous-titre *m*

subject [′sʌbdʒɪkt] *adj* sujet, assujetti, soumis ‖ *s* sujet *m*; (*e.g., in school*) matière *f* ‖ [səb′dʒɛkt] *tr* assujettir, soumettre

subjection [səb′dʒɛkʃən] *s* sujétion *f*, soumission *f*

subjective [səb′dʒɛktɪv] *adj* subjectif

sub′ject mat′ter *s* matière *f*

subjugate [′sʌbdʒə‚get] *tr* subjuguer

subjunctive [səb′dʒʌŋktɪv] *adj & s* subjonctif *m*

sub′lease′ *s* sous-location *f* ‖ **sub′lease′** *tr* sous-louer

sub·let [səb′lɛt], [′sʌb‚lɛt] *v* (*pret & pp* **-let;** *ger* **-letting**) *tr* sous-louer

sub′machine′ gun′ *s* mitraillette *f*

sub′marine′ *adj & s* sous-marin *m*

sub′marine chas′er *s* chasseur *m* de sous-marins

submerge [səb′mʌrdʒ] *tr* submerger ‖ *intr* (*said of submarine*) plonger

submersion [səb′mʌrʒən] *s* submersion *f*

submission [səb′mɪʃən] *s* soumission *f*; (*delivery*) présentation *f*

submissive [səb′mɪsɪv] *adj* soumis

sub·mit [səb′mɪt] *v* (*pret & pp* **-mitted;** *ger* **-mitting**) *tr* soumettre ‖ *intr* se soumettre

subordinate [səb′ɔrdɪnɪt] *adj & s* subordonné *m* ‖ [səb′ɔrdɪ‚net] *tr* subordonner

subpoena [sə′pinə] *s* assignation *f*, citation *f* ‖ *tr* citer

subscribe [səb′skraɪb] *tr* souscrire ‖ *intr*—**to subscribe to** (*an opinion; a charity; a loan; a newspaper*) souscrire à; (*a newspaper*) s'abonner à

subscriber [səb′skraɪbər] *s* abonné *m*

subscription [səb'skrɪpʃən] s souscription f; (to newspaper or magazine) abonnement m; (to club) cotisation f; **to take out a subscription for** s.o. abonner qn; **to take out a subscription to** s'abonner à

subsequent ['sʌbsɪkwənt] adj subséquent, suivant

subservient [səb'sʌrvɪ·ənt] adj asservi, subordonné

subside [səb'saɪd] intr (said of water, ground, etc.) s'abaisser; (said of storm, excitement, etc.) s'apaiser

subsidiar·y [səb'sɪdɪ,ɛri] adj subsidiaire ‖ s (pl -ies) filiale f

subsidize ['sʌbsɪ,daɪz] tr subventionner; suborner

subsi·dy ['sʌbsɪdi] s (pl -dies) subside m, subvention f

subsist [səb'sɪst] intr subsister

subsistence [səb'sɪstəns] s (supplies) subsistance f; existence f

sub'soil' s sous-sol m

subsonic [,sʌb'sɑnɪk] adj subsonique

substance ['sʌbstəns] s substance f

sub·stand'ard adj inférieur au niveau normal

substantial [səb'stænʃəl] adj substantiel; (wealthy) aisé, cossu

substantiate [səb'stænʃɪ,et] tr établir, vérifier

substantive ['sʌbstəntɪv] adj & s substantif m

sub'sta'tion s (of post office) bureau m auxiliaire; (elec) sous-station f

substitute ['sʌbstɪ,t(j)ut] s (person) remplaçant m, suppléant m, substitut m; (for coffee) succédané m ‖ tr remplacer, e.g., they substituted copper for silver ils ont remplacé l'argent par le cuivre; substituer, e.g., a hind was substituted for Iphigenia une biche fut substituée à Iphigénie ‖ intr servir de remplaçant; **to substitute for** remplacer, suppléer

substitution [,sʌbstɪ't(j)uʃən] s substitution f

sub'stra'tum s (pl -ta [tə] or -tums) substrat m

subterfuge ['sʌbtər,fjudʒ] s subterfuge m, faux-fuyant m

subterranean [,sʌbtə'reni·ən] adj souterrain

sub'ti'tle s sous-titre m

subtle ['sʌtəl] adj subtil

subtle·ty ['sʌtəlti] s (pl -ties) subtilité f

subtract [səb'trækt] tr soustraire

subtraction [səb'trækʃən] s soustraction f

suburb ['sʌbʌrb] s ville f de la banlieue; **the suburbs** la banlieue

suburban [sə'bʌrbən] adj suburbain

suburbanite [sə'bʌrbə,naɪt] s banlieusard m

subvention [səb'vɛnʃən] s subvention f ‖ tr subventionner

subversive [səb'vʌrsɪv] adj subversif ‖ s factieux m

subvert [səb'vʌrt] tr corrompre; renverser

sub'way' s métro m; (tunnel for pedestrians) souterrain m

sub'way car' s voiture f de métro

sub'way sta'tion s station f de métro

succeed [sək'sid] tr succéder à; **to succeed one another** se succéder ‖ intr réussir; **to succeed in** + ger réussir à + inf; **to succeed to** (the throne; a fortune) succéder à

success [sək'sɛs] s succès m, réussite f; **to be a howling success** (theat) faire un malheur; **to be a success** avoir du succès

successful [sək'sɛsfəl] adj réussi; heureux, prospère

succession [sək'sɛʃən] s succession f; **in succession** de suite

successive [sək'sɛsɪv] adj successif

succor ['sʌkər] s secours m ‖ tr secourir

succotash ['sʌkə,tæʃ] s plat m de fèves et de maïs

succumb [sə'kʌm] intr succomber

such [sʌtʃ] adj & pron indef tel, pareil, semblable; **such a** un tel; **such and such** tel et tel; **such as** tel que

suck [sʌk] s—**to give suck to** allaiter ‖ tr sucer; (a nipple) téter; **to suck in** aspirer; (to absorb) sucer ‖ intr sucer; téter

sucker ['sʌkər] s suceur m; (sucking organ) suçoir m, ventouse f; (bot) drageon m; (ichth) rémora m; (gullible person) (coll) gogo m; (lollipop) (coll) sucette f

suckle ['sʌkəl] tr allaiter

suck'ling pig' s cochon m de lait

suction ['sʌkʃən] s succion f

suc'tion cup' s ventouse f

suc'tion pump' s pompe f aspirante

sudden ['sʌdən] adj brusque, soudain; **all of a sudden** tout à coup

suddenly ['sʌdənli] adv tout à coup

suds [sʌdz] spl eau f savonneuse; mousse f de savon

sue [s(j)u] tr poursuivre en justice ‖ intr intenter un procès

suede [swed] s suède m; (for shoes) daim m

suet ['s(j)u·ɪt] s graisse f de rognon

suffer ['sʌfər] tr souffrir; (to allow) permettre; (a defeat) essuyer, subir ‖ intr souffrir

sufferance ['sʌfərəns] s tolérance f

suffering ['sʌfərɪŋ] adj souffrant ‖ s souffrance f

suffice [sə'faɪs] tr suffire à ‖ intr suffire; **it suffices to** + inf il suffit de + inf

sufficient [sə'fɪʃənt] adj suffisant

suffix ['sʌfɪks] s suffixe m

suffocate ['sʌfə,ket] tr & intr suffoquer, étouffer

suffrage ['sʌfrɪdʒ] s suffrage m

suffragist ['sʌfrədʒɪst] s partisan m du droit de vote des femmes

suffuse [sə'fjuz] tr baigner, saturer

sugar ['ʃugər] s sucre m ‖ tr sucrer; (a cake) saupoudrer de sucre; (a pill) recouvrir de sucre ‖ intr former du sucre

sug'ar beet' s betterave f sucrière, betterave à sucre

sug'ar bowl' s sucrier m

sug'ar cane' s canne f à sucre

sug'ar-coat' tr dragéifier; (fig) dorer

sug'ar dad'dy s (pl -dies) papa m gâteau

sug'ar ma'ple s érable m à sucre

sug′ar pea′ s mange-tout m
sug′ar tongs′ spl pince f à sucre
sugary [′ʃugəri] adj sucré; (fig) doucereux
suggest [səg′dʒɛst] tr suggérer
suggestion [səg′dʒɛstʃən] s suggestion f; nuance f, pointe f, soupçon m
suggestive [səg′dʒɛstɪv] adj suggestif
suicidal [‚s(j)u·ɪ′saɪdəl] adj suicidaire
suicide [′s(j)u·ɪ‚saɪd] s (act) suicide m; (person) suicidé m; **to commit suicide** se suicider
suit [s(j)ut] s (men′s) complet m, costume m; (women′s) costume tailleur, tailleur m; (lawsuit) procès m; (plea) requête f; (cards) couleur f; **to follow suit** jouer la couleur; (fig) en faire autant ‖ tr adapter; convenir à, e.g., **does that suit him?** cela lui convient?; aller à, seoir à, e.g., **the dress suits her well** la robe lui va bien, la robe lui sied bien ‖ intr convenir, aller
suitable [′s(j)utəbəl] adj convenable, à propos; compétent
suit′case′ s valise f
suite [swit] s suite f ‖ [s(j)ut] s (of furniture) ameublement m, mobilier m
suiting [′s(j)utɪŋ] s étoffe f pour complets
suit′ of clothes′ s complet-veston m
suitor [′s(j)utər] s prétendant m, soupirant m
sul′fa drugs′ [′sʌlfə] spl sulfamides mpl
sulfide [′sʌlfaɪd] s sulfure m
sulfur [′sʌlfər] adj soufré ‖ s soufre m ‖ tr soufrer
sulfuric [sʌl′fjurɪk] adj sulfurique
sul′fur mine′ s soufrière f
sulk [sʌlk] s bouderie f ‖ intr bouder
sulk·y [′sʌlki] adj (comp **-ier;** super **-iest**) boudeur, maussade
sullen [′sʌlən] adj maussade, rébarbatif
sul·ly [′sʌli] v (pret & pp **-lied**) tr souiller
sulphate [′sʌlfet] s sulfate m
sulphur [′sʌlfər] adj, s & tr var of **sulfur**
sultan [′sʌltən] s sultan m
sul·try [′sʌltri] adj (comp **-trier;** super **-triest**) étouffant, suffocant
sum [sʌm] s somme f; tout m, total m; **in sum** somme toute ‖ v (pret & pp **summed;** ger **summing**) tr—**to sum up** résumer
sumac or **sumach** [′sumæk] s sumac m
summarize [′sʌmə‚raɪz] tr résumer
summa·ry [′sʌməri] adj sommaire ‖ s (pl **-ries**) sommaire m
summer [′sʌmər] adj estival ‖ s été m ‖ intr passer l′été
sum′mer resort′ s station f estivale
sum′mer school′ s cours m d′été, cours de vacances
summery [′sʌməri] adj estival, d′été
summit [′sʌmɪt] s sommet m
sum′mit con′ference s conférence f au sommet
summon [′sʌmən] tr appeler, convoquer; (law) sommer, citer, assigner
summons [′sʌmənz] s appel m; (law) mandat m d′amener, citation f, assignation f, exploit m
sumptuous [′sʌmptʃu·əs] adj somptueux

sun [sʌn] s soleil m ‖ v (pret & pp **sunned;** ger **sunning**) tr exposer au soleil ‖ intr prendre le soleil
sun′ bath′ s bain m de soleil
sun′beam′ s rayon m de soleil
sun′bon′net s capeline f
sun′burn′ s coup m de soleil ‖ v (pret & pp **-burned** or **-burnt**) tr hâler, basaner ‖ intr se basaner
sun′burned′ adj brûlé par le soleil
sundae [′sʌndi] s coupe f de glace garnie de fruits, sundae m
Sunday [′sʌndi] adj dominical ‖ s diman-che m
Sun′day best′ s (coll) habits mpl du diman-che
Sun′day driv′er s chauffeur m du diman-che
Sun′day school′ s école f du dimanche
sunder [′sʌndər] tr séparer, rompre
sun′di′al s cadran m solaire, gnomon m, horloge f solaire
sun′down′ s coucher m du soleil
sundries [′sʌndriz] spl articles mpl divers
sundry [′sʌndri] adj divers
sun′fish′ s poisson-lune m
sun′flow′er s soleil m, tournesol m
sun′glass′es spl lunettes fpl de soleil, verres mpl fumés
sunken [′sʌŋkən] adj creux, enfoncé; (rock) noyé; (ship) sous-marin
sun′ lamp′ s lampe f à rayons ultraviolets
sun′light′ s lumière f du soleil
sun·ny [′sʌni] adj (comp **-nier;** super **-niest**) ensoleillé; (happy) enjoué; **it is sunny** il fait du soleil
sun′ny side′ s côté m exposé au soleil; (fig) bon côté
sun′ par′lor s véranda f
sun′rise′ s lever m du soleil
sun′set′ s coucher m du soleil
sun′shade′ s (over door) banne f; parasol m; abat-jour m, visière f
sun′shine′ s clarté f du soleil, soleil m; (fig) gaieté f rayonnante; **in the sunshine** en plein soleil
sun′spot′ s tache f solaire
sun′stroke′ s insolation f
sun′ tan′ s hâle m
sun′-tan oil′ s huile f solaire
sun′up′ s lever m du soleil
sun′ vi′sor s abat-jour m
sup [sʌp] v (pret & pp **supped;** ger **sup-ping**) intr souper
super [′supər] adj (slang) superbe, formida-ble ‖ s (theat) figurant m; (slang) con-cierge mf
su′per·abun′dant adj surabondant
superannuated [‚supər′ænju‚etɪd] adj (per-son) retraité; (thing) suranné
superb [su′pʌrb] adj superbe
su′per·car′go s (pl **-goes** or **-gos**) subré-cargue m
su′per·charge′ s surcompression f ‖ tr sur-comprimer
supercilious [‚supər′sɪlɪ·əs] adj sourcilleux, hautain, arrogant

superficial [,supər'fɪʃəl] *adj* superficiel
superfluous [su'pʌrflu·əs] *adj* superflu
su'per·high'way *s* autoroute *f*
su'per·hu'man *adj* surhumain
su'per·impose' *tr* superposer
su'per·intend' *tr* surveiller; diriger
superintendent [,supərɪn'tɛndənt] *s* directeur *m*, directeur en chef; (*of a building*)
concierge *mf*
superior [sə'pɪrɪ·ər] *adj* & *s* supérieur *m*
superiority [sə,pɪrɪ'arɪti] *s* supériorité *f*
superlative [sə'pʌrlətɪv] *adj* & *s* superlatif *m*
su'per·man' *s* (*pl* -men') surhomme *m*
su'per·mar'ket *s* supermarché *m*
su'per·nat'ural *adj* & *s* surnaturel *m*
supersede [,supər'sid] *tr* remplacer
su'per·sen'sitive *adj* hypersensible
su'per·son'ic *adj* supersonique
superstition [,supər'stɪʃən] *s* superstition *f*
superstitious [,supər'stɪʃəs] *adj* supersti-
tieux
su'per·tank'er *s* pétrolier *m* géant, tanker
m géant
supervene [,supər'vin] *intr* survenir
supervise ['supər,vaɪz] *tr* surveiller; diriger
su'per·vi'sion *s* surveillance *f*; direction *f*
su'per·vi'sor *s* surveillant *m*, inspecteur *m*;
directeur *m*
supper ['sʌpər] *s* souper *m*
sup'per·time' *s* heure *f* du souper
supplant [sə'plænt] *tr* supplanter
supple ['sʌpəl] *adj* souple, flexible
supplement ['sʌplɪmənt] *s* supplément *m* ‖
tr ajouter à
supplementary [,sʌplə'mɛntəri] *adj* supplémentaire
suppliant ['sʌplɪ·ənt] *adj* & *s* suppliant *m*
supplicant ['sʌplɪkənt] *s* suppliant *m*
supplicate ['sʌplɪ,ket] *tr* supplier
supplier [sə'plaɪ·ər] *s* fournisseur *m*, pour-
voyeur *m*
sup·ply [sə'plaɪ] *s* (*pl* -plies) (*action*) fourniture *f*, provision *f*, approvisionnement
m; (*store*) provision *f*, réserve *f*, stock *m*;
supplies fournitures, approvisionnements;
(*of food*) vivres *mpl* ‖ *v* (*pret* & *pp* -plied)
tr fournir; (*a person, a city, a fort*) pourvoir, munir; (*a need*) répondre à; (*what is
lacking*) suppléer; (mil) approvisionner
supply' and demand' *spl* l'offre *f* et la
demande
support [sə'port] *tr* soutien *m*, appui *m*;
(*living expenses*) ressources *fpl*, de quoi
vivre *m*; (*pillar*) support *m* ‖ *tr* soutenir,
appuyer; (*e.g., a wife*) entretenir, soutenir; (*to hold up; to corroborate; to tolerate*) supporter; **to support oneself** gagner
sa vie
supporter [sə'portər] *s* partisan *m*, supporter *m*; (*for part of body*) suspensoir *m*,
slip *m* de soutien
suppose [sə'poz] *tr* supposer; **I suppose so**
probablement; **suppose that . . .** à supposer que . . . ; **suppose we take a walk?**
si nous faisions une promenade?; **to be
supposed to** + *inf* devoir + *inf*; (*to be
considered to be*) être censé + *inf*

supposedly [sə'pozɪdli] *adv* censément
supposition [,sʌpə'zɪʃən] *s* supposition *f*
supposito·ry [sə'pazɪ,tori] *s* (*pl* -ries) suppositoire *m*
suppress [sə'prɛs] *tr* supprimer; (*rebellion;
anger*) réprimer, contenir; (*a yawn*)
étouffer, empêcher
suppression [sə'prɛʃən] *s* suppression *f*; (*of
a rebellion*) subjugation *f*, répression *f*; (*of
a yawn*) empêchement *m*
suppurate ['sʌpjə,ret] *intr* suppurer
supremacy [sə'prɛməsi] *s* suprématie *f*
supreme [sə'prim], [su'prim] *adj* suprême
supreme' court' *s* cour *f* de cassation
surcharge ['sʌr,tʃardʒ] *s* surcharge *f* ‖ *tr*
surcharger
sure [ʃur] *adj* sûr, certain; (*e.g., hand*)
ferme; **for sure** à coup sûr, pour sûr; **to
be sure to** + *inf* ne pas manquer de + *inf;*
to make sure s'assurer ‖ *adv* (coll) certainement; **sure enough** (coll) effectivement, assurément ‖ *interj* (slang) mais
oui!, bien sûr!, entendu!
sure'-foot'ed *adj* au pied sûr
sure·ty ['ʃurti] *s* (*pl* -ties) sûreté *f*
surf [sʌrf] *s* barre *f*, ressac *m*, brisants *mpl*
surface ['sʌrfɪs] *adj* superficiel ‖ *s* surface *f*;
(*area*) superficie *f*; **on the surface** à la
surface, en apparence; **to float under the
surface** nager entre deux eaux ‖ *tr* polir la
surface de; (*a road*) recouvrir, revêtir ‖
intr (*said of submarine*) faire surface
sur'face mail' *s* courrier *m* par voie ordinaire
surf' and turf' *s* (culin) pré *m* et marée
surf'board' *s* planche *f* pour le surf, surf-
board *m*
surfeit ['sʌrfɪt] *s* satiété *f* ‖ *tr* rassasier ‖ *intr*
se rassasier
surf'rid'ing *s* surfing *m*, planking *m*
surge [sʌrdʒ] *s* houle *f*; (elec) surtension *f* ‖
intr être houleux; se répandre; **to surge
up** s'enfler, s'élever
surgeon ['sʌrdʒən] *s* chirurgien *m*
surger·y ['sʌrdʒəri] *s* (*pl* -ies) chirurgie *f*;
salle *f* d'opération
surgical ['sʌrdʒɪkəl] *adj* chirurgical
sur·ly ['sʌrli] *adj* (*comp* -lier; *super* -liest)
hargneux, maussade, bourru
surmise [sər'maɪz] *s* conjecture *f* ‖ *tr* & *intr*
conjecturer
surmount [sər'maunt] *tr* surmonter
surname ['sʌr,nɛm] *s* nom *m* de famille;
surnom *m* ‖ *tr* donner un nom de famille
à; surnommer
surpass [sər'pæs], [sər'pɑs] *tr* surpasser
surplice ['sʌrplɪs] *s* surplis *m*
surplus ['sʌrplʌs] *adj* excédent, excédentaire, en excédent ‖ *s* surplus *m*, excédent *m*
sur'plus bag'gage *s* excédent *m* de bagages
surprise [sər'praɪz] *adj* à l'improviste,
brusqué, inopiné ‖ *s* surprise *f*; **to take by
surprise** prendre à l'improviste, prendre
au dépourvu ‖ *tr* surprendre; **to be surprised at** être surpris de
surprise' attack' *s* attaque *f* brusquée

surprise′ pack′age *s* surprise *f*, pochette *f* surprise

surprise′ par′ty *s* (*pl* **-ties**) réunion *f* à l'improviste

surprising [sər′praɪzɪŋ] *adj* surprenant

surrealism [sə′ri·ə,lɪzəm] *s* surréalisme *m*

surrender [sə′rɛndər] *s* reddition *f*, soumission *f*; (*e.g.*, *of prisoners, goods*) remise *f*; (*e.g.*, *of rights, property*) cession *f* ‖ *tr* rendre, céder ‖ *intr* se rendre

surren′der val′ue *s* valeur *f* de rachat

surreptitious [,sʌrɛp′tɪʃəs] *adj* subreptice

surrogate [′sʌrə,get] *s* substitut *m*

sur′rogate moth′er *s* femme *f* porteuse

surround [sə′raʊnd] *tr* entourer

surrounding [sə′raʊndɪŋ] *adj* entourant, environnant ‖ **surroundings** *spl* environs *mpl*, alentours *mpl*; entourage *m*, milieu *m*

surtax [′sʌr,tæks] *s* surtaxe *f* ‖ *tr* surtaxer

surveillance [sər′vel(j)əns] *s* surveillance *f*

survey [′sʌrve] *s* (*for verification*) contrôle *m*; (*for evaluation*) appréciation *f*, évaluation *f*; (*report*) expertise *f*, aperçu *m*; (*of a whole*) vue *f* d'ensemble, tour *m* d'horizon; (*measured plan or drawing*) levé *m*, plan *m*; (*surv*) lever *m* or levé des plans; **to make a survey** (*to map out*) lever un plan; (*to poll*) effectuer un contrôle par sondage ‖ [sʌr′ve], [′sʌrve] *tr* contrôler; apprécier, évaluer, faire l'expertise de; (*as a whole*) jeter un coup d'œil sur; (*to poll*) sonder; (*e.g.*, *a farm*) arpenter, faire l'arpentage de; (*e.g.*, *a city*) faire le levé de

sur′vey course′ *s* cours *m* général

surveying [sʌr′ve·ɪŋ] *s* arpentage *m*, géodésie *f*, levé *m* des plans

surveyor [sər′ve·ər] *s* arpenteur *m*

survival [sər′vaɪvəl] *s* survivance *f*; (*after death*) survie *f*; **survival of the fittest** loi *f* sélective du plus fort, survie *f* du plus apte

surviv′al kit′ *s* équipement *m* de survie

survive [sər′vaɪv] *tr* survivre à ‖ *intr* survivre

surviving [sər′vaɪvɪŋ] *adj* survivant

survivor [sər′vaɪvər] *s* survivant *m*

survivorship [sər′vaɪvər,ʃɪp] *s* (law) survie *f*

susceptible [sə′sɛptɪbəl] *adj* (*capable*) susceptible; (*liable, subject*) sensible; (*to love*) facilement amoureux

suspect [′sʌspɛkt], [səs′pɛkt] *adj & s* suspect *m* ‖ [səs′pɛkt] *tr* soupçonner ‖ *intr* s'en douter

suspend [səs′pɛnd] *tr* suspendre

suspenders [səs′pɛndərz] *spl* bretelles *fpl*

suspense [səs′pɛns] *s* suspens *m*

suspension [səs′pɛnʃən] *s* suspension *f*; **suspension of driver's license** retrait *m* de permis

suspen′sion bridge′ *s* pont *m* suspendu

suspicion [səs′pɪʃən] *s* soupçon *m*

suspicious [səs′pɪʃəs] *adj* (*inclined to suspect*) soupçonneux; (*subject to suspicion*) suspect

sustain [səs′ten] *tr* soutenir; (*a loss, injury, etc.*) éprouver

sustenance [′sʌstɪnəns] *s* subsistance *f*; (*food*) nourriture *f*

sustain′ing mem′ber [səs′tenɪŋ] *s* membre *m* bienfaiteur

swab [swɑb] *s* écouvillon *m*; (naut) faubert *m*; (surg) tampon *m* ‖ *v* (*pret & pp* **swabbed**; *ger* **swabbing**) *tr* écouvillonner

swaddle [′swɑdəl] *tr* emmailloter

swad′dling clothes′ *spl* maillot *m*

swagger [′swægər] *s* fanfaronnade *f* ‖ *intr* faire des fanfaronnades

swain [swen] *s* garçon *m*; jeune berger *m*; soupirant *m*

swallow [′swɑlo] *s* gorgée *f*; (orn) hirondelle *f* ‖ *tr & intr* avaler

swal′low-tailed coat′ *s* frac *m*

swamp [swɑmp] *s* marécage *m* ‖ *tr* submerger, inonder

swamp·y [′swɑmpi] *adj* (*comp* **-ier**; *super* **-iest**) marécageux

swan [swɑn] *s* cygne *m*

swan′ dive′ *s* saut *m* de l'ange

swank [swæŋk] *adj* (slang) élégant, chic

swan′ knight′ *s* chevalier *m* au cygne

swan's′-down′ *s* cygne *m*, duvet *m* de cygne

swan′ song′ *s* chant *m* du cygne

swap [swɑp] *s* (coll) troc *m* ‖ *v* (*pret & pp* **swapped**; *ger* **swapping**) *tr & intr* troquer

swarm [swɔrm] *s* essaim *m* ‖ *intr* essaimer; (fig) fourmiller

swarth·y [′swɔrði] *adj* (*comp* **-ier**; *super* **-iest**) basané, brun, noiraud

swashbuckler [′swɑʃ,bʌklər] *s* rodomont *m*, bretteur *m*

swat [swɑt] *s* (coll) coup *m* violent ‖ *v* (*pret & pp* **swatted**; *ger* **swatting**) *tr* (coll) frapper; (*a fly*) (coll) écraser

sway [swe] *s* balancement *m*; (*domination*) empire *m* ‖ *tr* balancer ‖ *intr* se balancer; (*to hesitate*) balancer

swear [swɛr] *v* (*pret* **swore** [swor]; *pp* **sworn** [sworn]) *tr* jurer; **to swear in** faire prêter serment à; **to swear off** jurer de renoncer à ‖ *intr* jurer; **to swear at** injurier; **to swear by** (*e.g.*, *a remedy*) préconiser; **to swear to** déclarer sous serment; jurer de + *inf*

swear′ words′ *spl* gros mots *mpl*

sweat [swɛt] *s* sueur *f* ‖ *v* (*pret & pp* **sweat** or **sweated**) *tr* (*e.g.*, *blood*) suer; (slang) faire suer; **to sweat it out** (slang) en baver jusqu'à la fin ‖ *intr* suer

sweater [′swɛtər] *s* chandail *m*

sweat′ shirt′ *s* maillot *m* de sport

sweat·y [′swɛti] *adj* (*comp* **-ier**; *super* **-iest**) suant

Swede [swid] *s* Suédois *m*

Sweden [′swidən] *s* Suède *f*; la Suède

Swedish [′swidɪʃ] *adj & s* suédois *m*

sweep [swip] *s* (*sweeping*) balayage *m*; (*range*) champ *m*, étendue *f*; (*movement of the arm*) grand geste *m*; (*curve*) courbe *f*; (*of wind*) souffle *m*; (*of well*) chadouf *m*; **at one sweep** d'un seul coup; **to make a clean sweep of** faire table rase de; (*to win all of*) rafler ‖ *v* (*pret & pp* **swept** [swɛpt]) *tr* balayer; (*the chimney*) ramoner; (*for* mines) draguer ‖ *intr* balayer; s'étendre

sweeper ['swipər] *s* balayeur *m*; (mach) balai *m* mécanique

sweeping ['swipɪŋ] *adj* (*movement*) vigoureux; (*statement*) catégorique ‖ *s* balayage *m*; **sweepings** balayures *fpl*

sweep'-sec'ond *s* trotteuse *f* centrale

sweep'stakes' *s* or *spl* loterie *f*; (turf) sweepstake *m*

sweet [swit] *adj* doux; (*sugared*) sucré; (*perfume, music, etc.*) suave; (*sound*) mélodieux; (*milk*) frais; (*person*) charmant, gentil; (*dear*) cher; **to be sweet on** (coll) avoir un béguin pour; **to smell sweet** sentir bon ‖ **sweets** *spl* sucreries *fpl*

sweet'bread' *s* ris *m* de veau

sweet'bri'er *s* églantier *m*

sweeten ['switən] *tr* sucrer; purifier; (fig) adoucir ‖ *intr* s'adoucir

sweet'heart' *s* petite amie *f*, chérie *f*; **sweethearts** amoureux *mpl*

sweet' mar'joram *s* marjolaine *f*

sweet'meats' *spl* sucreries *fpl*

sweet' pea' *s* gesse *f* odorante, pois *m* de senteur

sweet' pep'per *s* piment *m* doux, poivron *m*

sweet' pota'to *s* patate *f* douce

sweet'-scent'ed *adj* parfumé

sweet'-talk' *tr* (coll) baratiner

sweet'-toothed' *adj* friand de sucreries

sweet' wil'liam *s* œillet *m* de poète

swell [swɛl] *adj* (coll) élégant; (slang) épatant ‖ *s* (*swelling*) gonflement *m*; (*of sea*) houle *f*; (mus) crescendo *m*; (pathol) enflure *f*; (*dandy*) (coll) rupin *m* ‖ *v* (*pret* **swelled**; *pp* **swelled** or **swollen** ['swolən]) *tr* gonfler, enfler ‖ *intr* se gonfler, s'enfler; (*said of sea*) se soulever; (fig) augmenter

swell'head'ed *adj* suffisant, vaniteux

swelter ['swɛltər] *intr* étouffer de chaleur

swept'back wing' *s* aile *f* en flèche

swerve [swʌrv] *s* écart *m*, déviation *f*; (aut) embardée *f* ‖ *tr* faire dévier ‖ *intr* écarter, dévier; (aut) faire une embardée

swift [swɪft] *adj* rapide ‖ *adv* vite ‖ *s* (orn) martinet *m*

swig [swɪg] *s* (coll) lampée *f*, trait *m* ‖ *v* (*pret & pp* **swigged**; *ger* **swigging**) *tr & intr* lamper

swill [swɪl] *s* eaux *fpl* grasses, ordures *fpl*; (*drink*) lampée *f* ‖ *tr & intr* lamper

swim [swɪm] *s* nage *f*; **to be in the swim** (coll) être dans le train ‖ *v* (*pret* **swam** [swæm]; *pp* **swum** [swʌm]; *ger* **swimming**) *tr* nager ‖ *intr* nager; (*said of head*) tourner; **to swim across** traverser à la nage; **to swim under water** nager entre deux eaux

swimmer ['swɪmər] *s* nageur *m*

swimming ['swɪmɪŋ] *s* natation *f*, nage *f*

swim'ming pool' *s* piscine *f*

swim'ming suit' *s* maillot *m* de bain

swim'ming trunks' *spl* slip *m* de bain

swindle ['swɪndəl] *s* escroquerie *f* ‖ *tr* escroquer

swine [swaɪn] *s* (*pl* **swine**) cochon *m*, pourceau *m*, porc *m*

swing [swɪŋ] *s* balancement *m*, oscillation *f*; (*device used for recreation*) escarpolette *f*; (*trip*) tournée *f*; (boxing, mus) swing *m*; **in full swing** en pleine marche ‖ *v* (*pret & pp* **swung** [swʌŋ]) *tr* balancer, faire osciller; (*the arms*) agiter; (*a sword*) brandir; (*e.g., an election*) mener à bien ‖ *intr* se balancer; (*said of pendulum*) osciller; (*said of door*) pivoter; (*said of bell*) branler; **to swing open** s'ouvrir tout d'un coup

swing'ing door' *s* porte *f* va-et-vient

swinish ['swaɪnɪʃ] *adj* cochon

swipe [swaɪp] *s* (coll) coup *m* à toute volée ‖ *tr* (coll) frapper à toute volée; (*to steal*) (slang) chiper

swirl [swʌrl] *s* remous *m*, tourbillon *m* ‖ *tr* faire tourbillonner ‖ *intr* tourbillonner

swish [swɪʃ] *s* (*e.g., of a whip*) sifflement *m*; (*of a dress*) froufrou *m*; (*e.g., of water*) susurrement *m* ‖ *tr* (*a whip*) faire siffler; (*its tail*) battre ‖ *intr* siffler; froufrouter; susurrer

Swiss [swɪs] *adj* suisse ‖ *s* Suisse *m*; **the Swiss** les Suisses *mpl*

Swiss' chard' [tʃɑrd] *s* bette *f*, poirée *f*

Swiss' cheese' *s* emmenthal *m*, gruyère *m*

Swiss' Guard' *s* suisse *m*

switch [swɪtʃ] *s* (*stick*) badine *f*; (*exchange*) échange *m*; (*hairpiece*) postiche *m*; (elec) interrupteur *m*; (rr) aiguille *f* ‖ *tr* cingler; (*places*) échanger; (rr) aiguiller; **to switch off** couper; (*a light*) éteindre; **to switch on** mettre en circuit; (*a light*) allumer ‖ *intr* changer de place

switch'back' *s* chemin *m* en lacet

switch'blade knife' *s* couteau *m* à cran d'arrêt

switch'board' *s* tableau *m* de distribution; standard *m* téléphonique

switch'board op'erator *s* standardiste *mf*

switch'ing en'gine *s* locomotive *f* de manœuvre

switch'man *s* (*pl* **-men**) aiguilleur *m*

switch' tow'er *s* poste *m* d'aiguillage

switch'yard' *s* gare *f* de triage

Switzerland ['swɪtsərlənd] *s* Suisse *f*; la Suisse

swiv·el ['swɪvəl] *s* pivot *m*; (*link*) émerillon *m* ‖ *v* (*pret & pp* **-eled** or **-elled**; *ger* **-eling** or **-elling**) *tr* faire pivoter ‖ *intr* pivoter

swiv'el chair' *s* fauteuil *m* tournant, chaise *f* pivotante

swiz'zle stick *s* agitateur *m*

swoon [swun] *s* évanouissement *m* ‖ *intr* s'évanouir

swoop [swup] *s* attaque *f* brusque; **at one fell swoop** d'un seul coup ‖ *intr* foncer, fondre; **to swoop down on** s'abattre sur

sword [sord] *s* épée *f*; **to cross swords with** croiser le fer avec; **to put to the sword** passer au fil de l'épée

sword' belt' *s* ceinturon *m*

sword'fish' *s* espadon *m*

swords'man *s* (*pl* **-men**) épéiste *m*

sword′ swal′lower [′swɑlo·ər] *s* avaleur *m* de sabres

sword′ thrust′ *s* coup *m* de pointe, coup d'épée

sworn [sworn] *adj* (*enemy*) juré; **sworn in** assermenté

sycophant [′sɪkəfənt] *s* flagorneur *m*

syllable [′sɪləbəl] *s* syllabe *f*

sylla·bus [′sɪləbəs] *s* (*pl* **-bi** [,baɪ] or **-buses**) programme *m*

syllogism [′sɪlə,dʒɪzəm] *s* syllogisme *m*

sylph [sɪlf] *s* sylphe *m*

sylvan [′sɪlvən] *adj* sylvestre

symbol [′sɪmbəl] *s* symbole *m*

symbolic(al) [′sɪm′bɑlɪk(əl)] *adj* symbolique

symbolism [′sɪmbə,lɪzm] *s* symbolisme *m*

symbolize [′sɪmbə,laɪz] *tr* symboliser

symmetric(al) [sɪ′mɛtrɪk(əl)] *adj* symétrique

symme·try [′sɪmɪtri] *s* (*pl* **-tries**) symétrie *f*

sympathetic [,sɪmpə′θɛtɪk] *adj* (*kind*) compatissant; (*favoring*) bien disposé; (anat, physiol) sympathique

sympathize [′sɪmpə,θaɪz] *intr*—**to sympathize with** compatir à; comprendre

sympa·thy [′sɪmpəθi] *s* (*pl* **-thies**) (*pity*) compassion *f*; (*fellow feeling*) solidarité *f*; sympathie *f*, e.g., **expressions of sympathy** témoignages de sympathie; **to be in sympathy with** être en sympathie avec; **to extend one's sympathy to** offrir ses condoléances à

sym′pathy strike′ *s* grève *f* de solidarité

sympho·ny [′sɪmfəni] *s* (*pl* **-nies**) symphonie *f*

symposi·um [sɪm′pozɪ·əm] *s* (*pl* **-a** [ə]) colloque *m*, symposium *m*

symptom [′sɪmptəm] *s* symptôme *m*

synagogue [′sɪnə,gɔg] *s* synagogue *f*

synchronize [′sɪŋkrə,naɪz] *tr* synchroniser

synchronous [′sɪŋkrənəs] *adj* synchrone

syncopation [,sɪŋkə′peʃən] *s* syncope *f*

syncope [′sɪŋkə,pi] *s* syncope *f*

syndicate [′sɪndɪkɪt] *s* (journ) syndicat *m* (de distribution) ‖ [′sɪndɪ,ket] *tr* syndiquer ‖ *intr* se syndiquer

syndrome [′sɪndrom] *s* syndrome *m*

synonym [′sɪnənɪm] *s* synonyme *m*

synonymous [sɪ′nɑnɪməs] *adj* synonyme

synop·sis [sɪ′nɑpsɪs] *s* (*pl* **-ses** [siz]) abrégé *m*, résumé *m*; (mov) synopsis *m* & *f*

syntax [′sɪntæks] *s* syntaxe *f*

synthe·sis [′sɪnθɪsɪs] *s* (*pl* **-ses** [,siz]) synthèse *f*

synthesize [′sɪnθɪ,saɪz] *tr* synthétiser

synthetic(al) [sɪn′θɛtɪk(əl)] *adj* synthétique

syphilis [′sɪfɪlɪs] *s* syphilis *f*

Syria [′sɪrɪ·ə] *s* Syrie *f*; la Syrie

Syrian [′sɪrɪ·ən] *adj* syrien ‖ *s* (*language*) syrien *m*; (*person*) Syrien *m*

syringe [′sɪrɪndʒ] *s* seringue *f* ‖ *tr* seringuer

syrup [′sɪrəp], [′sʌrəp] *s* sirop *m*

system [′sɪstəm] *s* système *m*; (*of lines, wires, pipes, roads*) réseau *m*

systematic(al) [,sɪstə′mætɪk(əl)] *adj* systématique

systematize [′sɪstəmə,taɪz] *tr* systématiser

systole [′sɪstəli] *s* systole *f*

T

T, t [ti] *s* XXᵉ lettre de l'alphabet

tab [tæb] *s* patte *f*; (*label*) étiquette *f*; (*dinner check*) (coll) note *f*; **to keep tab on** (coll) garder à l'œil; **to pick up the tab** (coll) payer l'addition

tab·by [′tæbi] *s* (*pl* **-bies**) chat *m* moucheté; (*female cat*) chatte *f*; (*old maid*) vieille fille *f*; (*spiteful female*) vieille chipie *f*

tabernacle [′tæbər,nækəl] *s* tabernacle *m*

table [′tebəl] *s* table *f*; (*tableland*) plateau *m*; (*list, chart*) tableau *m*, table; **to clear the table** ôter le couvert; **to set the table** mettre le couvert ‖ *tr* ajourner la discussion de

tab·leau [′tæblo] *s* (*pl* **-leaus** or **leaux** [loz]) tableau *m* vivant

ta′ble·cloth′ *s* nappe f

table d'hôte [′tɑbəl′dot] *s* repas *m* à prix fixe

ta′ble·land′ *s* plateau *m*

ta′ble lin′en *s* nappage *m*, linge *m* de table

ta′ble man′ners *spl*—**to have good table manners** bien se tenir à table

tab′le·mate′ *s* commensal *m*

ta′ble nap′kin *s* serviette *f* de table

ta′ble of con′tents *s* table *f* des matières

ta′ble salt′ *s* sel *m* fin, sel de table

ta′ble·spoon′ *s* cuiller *f* à soupe

tablespoonful [′tebəl,spun,fʊl] *s* cuillerée *f* à soupe or à bouche

tablet [′tæblɪt] *s* (*writing pad*) bloc-notes *m*, bloc *m*; (*lozenge*) pastille *f*, comprimé *m*; plaque *f* commémorative

ta′ble talk′ *s* propos *mpl* de table

ta′ble ten′nis *s* ping-pong *m*, tennis *m* de table

ta′ble-ten′nis play′er *s* pongiste *mf*

ta′ble-top′ *s* dessus *m* de table

ta′ble·ware′ *s* ustensiles *mpl* de table

ta′ble wine′ *s* vin *m* ordinaire

tabloid [′tæblɔɪd] *adj* (*press, article, etc.*) à sensation ‖ *s* journal *m* de petit format à l'affût du sensationnel, tableautier *m*

taboo [tə′bu] *adj* & *s* tabou *m* ‖ *tr* déclarer tabou

tabular [′tæbjələr] *adj* tabulaire

tabulate ['tæbjə,let] *tr* disposer en forme de table or en tableaux, dresser un tableau de, aligner en colonnes

tabulator ['tæbjə,letər] *s* tabulateur *m*

tab'ulator set'ting *s* arrêt *m* de tabulateur

tacit ['tæsɪt] *adj* tacite

taciturn ['tæsɪtərn] *adj* taciturne

tack [tæk] *s* (*nail*) semence *f*; (*plan*) voie *f*, tactique *f*; (*of sail*) amure *f*; (naut) bordée *f*; (sewing) point *m* de bâti ‖ *tr* clouer; (sewing) bâtir ‖ *intr* louvoyer

tackle ['tækəl] *s* (*for lifting*) treuil *m*; (football) plaquage *m*; (naut) palan *m* ‖ *tr* empoigner, saisir; (*a problem, job, etc.*) chercher à résoudre, attaquer; (football) plaquer

tack·y ['tæki] *adj* (*comp* -ier; *super* -iest) collant; (coll) râpé, minable

tact [tækt] *s* tact *m*

tactful ['tæktfəl] *adj* plein de tact; **to be tactful** avoir du tact

tactical ['tæktɪkəl] *adj* tactique

tactician [tæk'tɪʃən] *s* tacticien *m*

tactics ['tæktɪks] *spl* tactique *f*

tactless ['tæktlɪs] *adj* sans tact

tadpole ['tæd,pol] *s* têtard *m*

taffeta ['tæfɪtə] *s* taffetas *m*

taffy ['tæfi] *s* pâte *f* à berlingots; (coll) flagornerie *f*

tag [tæg] *s* (*label*) étiquette *f*; (*of shoelace*) ferret *m*; (*game*) chat *m* perché ‖ *v* (*pret & pp* **tagged**; *ger* **tagging**) *tr* étiqueter; (*in the game of tag*) attraper ‖ *intr* (coll) suivre de près; **to tag along behind s.o.** (coll) traîner derrière qn

tag' day' *s* jour *m* de collecte publique

tag' end' *s* queue *f*; (*remnant*) coupon *m*

Tagus ['tegəs] *s* Tage *m*

tail [tel] *s* queue *f*; (*of shirt*) pan *m*; **tails** (*of a coin*) pile *f*; (*formal dress*) (coll) frac *m*, queue-de-morue *f*; **to turn tail** tourner les talons ‖ *tr* (coll) suivre de tout près ‖ *intr*—**to tail after** marcher sur les talons de; **to tail off** s'éteindre, disparaître

tail' assem'bly *s* (*pl* -blies) (aer) empennage *m*

tail' end' *s* queue *f*, fin *f*

tail' gate' *tr & intr* (aut) talonner

tail'gat'ing *s* (aut) talonnage *m*; (sports) pique-nique *m* à l'occasion d'un match

tail' light' *s* feu *m* arrière

tailor ['telər] *s* tailleur *m* ‖ *tr* (*a suit*) faire ‖ *intr* être tailleur

tailoring ['telərɪŋ] *s* métier *m* de tailleur

tai'lor-made suit' *s* (*men's*) costume *m* sur mesure, complet *m* sur mesure; (*women's*) costume tailleur, tailleur *m*

tai'lor shop' *s* boutique *f* de tailleur

tail'piece' *s* queue *f*; (*of stringed instrument*) cordier *m*

tail'race' *s* canal *m* du fuite

tail'spin' *s* chute *f* en vrille

tail'wind' *s* (aer) vent *m* arrière; (naut) vent en poupe

taint [tent] *s* tache *f* ‖ *tr* tacher; (*food*) gâter

take [tek] *s* prise *f*; (mov) prise *m* de vues; (slang) recette *f* ‖ *v* (*pret* **took** [tʊk]; *pp*

taken) *tr* prendre; (*a walk; a trip*) faire; (*a course; advice*) suivre; (*an examination*) passer; (*a person on a trip*) emmener; (*the occasion*) profiter de; (*a photograph*) prendre; (*a newspaper*) être abonné à; (*a purchase*) garder; (*a certain amount of time*) falloir, e.g., **it takes an hour to walk there** il faut une heure pour y aller à pied; (*to lead*) conduire, mener; (*to tolerate, stand*) supporter; (*a seat*) prendre, occuper, e.g., **this seat is taken** cette place est prise ou occupée; **do you take that to be important?** tenez-vous cela pour important?; **I take it that** je suppose que; **take it easy!** (coll) allez-y doucement!; **to be taken ill** tomber malade; **to take amiss** prendre mal; **to take away** enlever; emmener; (*to subtract*) soustraire, retrancher; **to take down** descendre; (*a building*) démolir; (*in writing*) noter; **to take in** (*a roomer*) recevoir; (*laundry*) prendre à faire à la maison; (*the harvest*) rentrer; (*a seam*) reprendre; (*to include*) embrasser; (*to deceive*) (coll) duper; **to take off** ôter, enlever; (*from the price*) rabattre; (*to imitate*) (coll) singer; **to take on** (*passengers*) prendre; (*a responsibility*) prendre sur soi; (*workers*) embaucher, prendre; **to take out** sortir; (*a bullet from a wound; a passage from a text; an element from a compound*) extraire; (public sign) à emporter; **to take over** (*to escort across*) transporter; (*to assume responsibility for*) reprendre, prendre à sa charge; **to take place** avoir lieu; **to take s.th. from s.o.** enlever, ôter, or prendre q.ch. à qn; **to take up** (*to carry up*) monter; (*to remove*) enlever; (*a dress*) raccourcir; (*an idea, method, etc.*) adopter; (*a profession*) embrasser, prendre; (*a question, a study, etc.*) aborder ‖ *intr* prendre; **to not take to** (*a person*) prendre en grippe; **to take after** ressembler à; (*to chase*) poursuivre; **to take off** s'en aller; (aer) décoller; **to take over** (pol) prendre le pouvoir; **to take over from s.o.** prendre la relève (*or* le relais) de qn; **to take to** (*flight; the woods*) prendre; (*a bad habit*) se livrer à; (*a person*) se prendre d'amitié avec; (*to like*) s'adonner à; **to take to** + *ger* se mettre à + *inf*; **to take up with s.o.** (coll) se lier avec qn

take'-home pay' *s* salaire *m* net

take'-off' *s* (aer) décollage *m*; (coll) caricature *f*

take'o'ver *s* (*of a corporation*) rachat *m*

take'over bid' *s* offre *f* publique d'achat (O.P.A.)

tal'cum pow'der ['tælkəm] *s* poudre *f* de talc

tale [tel] *s* conte *m*; mensonge *m*; (*gossip*) raconter *m*, histoire *f*

tale'bear'er *s* rapporteur *m*

talent ['tælənt] *s* (*ability*) talent *m*; (*persons*) gens *mpl* de talent

talented ['tæləntɪd] *adj* doué, talentueux

tal′ent scout′ s dénicheur m de vedettes

tal′ent show′ s crochet m radiophonique, radio-crochet m

talk [tɔk] s paroles fpl; (gossip) racontars mpl, dires mpl; (lecture) conférence f, causerie f; **to cause talk** défrayer la chronique; **to have a talk with** s'entretenir avec ‖ tr parler; **to talk over** discuter; **to talk up** vanter ‖ intr parler; (to chatter, gossip, etc.) bavarder, jaser; **to talk back** répliquer; **to talk on** continuer à parler

talkative [′tɔkətɪv] adj bavard

talker [′tɔkər] s parleur m; **a great talker** (coll) un causeur, un hâbleur

talkie [′tɔki] s (coll) film m parlant

talk′ing doll′ [′tɔkɪŋ] s poupée f parlante

talk′ show′ s (rad, telv) causerie f (radiodiffusée or télévisée), tête-à-tête m invar or entretien m (radiodiffusé or télévisé)

tall [tɔl] adj haut, élevé; (person) grand; (coll) exagéré

tallow [′tælo] s suif m

tal·ly [′tæli] s (pl -lies) compte m, pointage m ‖ v (pret & pp -lied) tr pointer, contrôler ‖ intr s'accorder

tallyho [′tælɪ,ho] interj taïaut!

tal′ly sheet′ s feuille f de pointage, bordereau m

talon [′tælən] s serre f

tamarack [′tæmə,ræk] s mélèze m d'Amérique

tambourine [,tæmbə′rin] s tambour m de basque

tame [tem] adj apprivoisé; (e.g., lion) dompté; (e.g., style) fade, terne ‖ tr apprivoiser; (e.g., a lion) dompter

tamp [tæmp] tr bourrer; (e.g., a hole in the ground) damer

tamper [′tæmpər] intr—**to tamper with** se mêler de; (a lock) fausser; (a document) falsifier; (a witness) suborner

tampon [′tæmpɑn] s (surg) tampon m ‖ tr (surg) tamponner

tan [tæn] adj jaune; (e.g., skin) bronzé, hâlé ‖ v (pret & pp **tanned**; ger **tanning**) tr tanner; (e.g., the skin) bronzer, hâler ‖ intr se hâler

tandem [′tændəm] adj & adv en tandem, en flèche ‖ s tandem m

tang [tæŋ] s goût m vif, saveur f; (ringing sound) tintement m

tangent [′tændʒənt] adj tangent ‖ s tangente f; **to fly off at** or **on a tangent** changer brusquement de sujet

tangerine [,tændʒə′rin] s mandarine f

tangible [′tændʒɪbəl] adj tangible

tan′gible as′sets spl actifs mpl corporels

Tangier [tæn′dʒɪr] s Tanger m

tangle [′tæŋgəl] s enchevêtrement m ‖ tr enchevêtrer ‖ intr s'enchevêtrer

tank [tæŋk] s réservoir m; (mil) char m

tank′ car′ s (rr) wagon-citerne m

tanker [′tæŋkər] s (ship) bateau-citerne m, pétrolier m; (truck) camion-citerne m; (plane) ravitailleur m

tank′ truck′ s camion-citerne m

tanner [′tænər] s tanneur m

tanner·y [′tænəri] s (pl -ies) tannerie f

tantalize [′tæntə,laɪz] tr tenter, allécher

tantamount [′tæntə,maʊnt] adj équivalent

tantrum [′tæntrəm] s accès m de colère; **in a tantrum** en rogne

tap [tæp] s (light blow) petit coup m; (faucet) robinet m; (elec) prise f; (mach) taraud m; **on tap** au tonneau, en perce; (available) (coll) disponible; **taps** (mil) l'extinction f des feux ‖ v (pret & pp **tapped**; ger **tapping**) tr taper; (a cask) mettre en perce; (a tree) entailler; (a telephone) passer à la table d'écoute; (a nut) tarauder; (resources, talent, etc.) drainer; (elec) brancher sur ‖ intr taper

tap′ dance′ s danse f à claquettes

tap′-dance′ intr danser les claquettes, faire les claquettes

tap′ dan′cer s danseur m à claquettes

tape [tep] s ruban m ‖ tr (an electric wire) guiper; (land) mesurer au cordeau; (to tape-record) enregistrer sur ruban

tape′ meas′ure s mètre-ruban m, centimètre m

taper [′tepər] s (for lighting candles) allumette-bougie f; (eccl) cierge m ‖ tr effiler ‖ intr s'effiler

tape′-record′ tr enregistrer sur ruban magnétique or au magnétophone

tape′ record′er s magnétophone m

tapes·try [′tæpɪstri] s (pl -tries) tapisserie f ‖ v (pret & pp -tried) tr tapisser

tape′worm′ s ver m solitaire

tappet [′tæpɪt] s (mach) taquet m

tap′room′ s débit m de boissons, buvette f

tap′ wa′ter s eau f du robinet

tap′ wrench′ s taraudeuse f

tar [tɑr] s goudron m; (coll) marin m ‖ v (pret & pp **tarred**; ger **tarring**) tr goudronner; **to tar and feather** enduire de goudron et de plumes

tar·dy [′tɑrdi] adj (comp -dier; super -diest) lent; retardataire, en retard

tare [ter] s (weight) tare f; (Bib) ivraie f ‖ tr tarer

target [′tɑrgɪt] s cible f, point m de mire; (goal) but m; (mil) objectif m; (butt) (fig) cible

tar′get ar′ea s zone f de tir

tar′get lan′guage s langue f cible, langue d'arrivée

tar′get prac′tice s tir m à la cible

tariff [′tærɪf] s (duties) droits mpl de douane; (rates in general) tarif m

tarnish [′tɑrnɪʃ] s ternissure f ‖ tr ternir ‖ intr se ternir

tar′ pa′per s papier m goudronné

tarpaulin [tɑr′pɔlɪn] s bâche f, prélart m

tarragon [′tærəgən] s estragon m

tar·ry [′tɑri] adj (comp -rier; super -riest) goudronneux ‖ [′tæri] v (pret & pp -ried) intr tarder, rester, demeurer; (to stay) rester, demeurer

tart [tɑrt] adj (taste) aigrelet; (reply) mordant ‖ s tarte f; (slang) grue f, poule f

tartar [′tɑrtər] adj (sauce) tartare; **Tartar** tartare ‖ s (on teeth) tartre m; **Tartar** Tartare mf

task [tæsk] s tâche f; **to bring** or **take to task** prendre à partie

task' force' s (mil) groupement m stratégique mixte

task'mas'ter s chef m de corvée; (fig) tyran m

tassel ['tæsəl] s gland m; (on corn) barbe f; (on nightcap) mèche f; (bot) aigrette f

taste [test] s goût m, saveur f; (sense of what is fitting) goût, bon goût ‖ tr goûter; (to sample) goûter à; (to try out) goûter de ‖ intr goûter; **to taste like** avoir le goût de; **to taste of** avoir un goût de

taste' bud' s papille f gustative

tasteless ['testlɪs] adj sans saveur, fade; (in bad taste) de mauvais goût

tast·y ['testi] adj (comp -ier; super -iest) (coll) savoureux; (coll) de bon goût

tatter ['tætər] s lambeau m ‖ tr mettre en lambeaux

tatterdemalion [,tætərdɪ'meljen] s loqueteux m

tattered adj en lambeaux, en loques

tattle ['tætəl] s bavardage m; (gossip) cancan m ‖ intr bavarder; cancaner

tat'tle·tale' adj révélateur ‖ s rapporteur m, cancanier m

tattoo [tæ'tu] s tatouage m; (mil) retraite f ‖ tr tatouer

taunt [tɔnt] s sarcasme m ‖ tr bafouer

Taurus ['tɔrəs] s (astr, astrol) le Taureau

taut [tɔt] adj tendu

tavern ['tævərn] s café m, bar m, bistrot m; (inn) taverne f

taw·dry ['tɔdri] adj (comp -drier; super -driest) criard, voyant

taw·ny ['tɔni] adj (comp -nier; super -niest) fauve; (skin) basané

tax [tæks] s impôt m; **to reduce the tax on** dégrever ‖ tr imposer; (e.g., one's patience) mettre à l'épreuve; **to tax s.o. with** (e.g., laziness) taxer qn de

taxable ['tæksəbəl] adj imposable

taxation [tæk'seʃən] s imposition f; charges fpl fiscales, impôts mpl

tax' ba'sis m assiette f fiscale

tax' brack'et s niveau m d'imposition, tranche f

tax' collec'tor s percepteur m

tax' cut' s dégrèvement m d'impôt

tax' deduc'tion s dégrèvement m

tax' eva'sion s fraude f fiscale

tax'-exempt' adj net d'impôt, exempt d'impôts

tax' ha'ven s refuge m fiscal

tax·i ['tæksi] s (pl -is) taxi m ‖ v (pret & pp -ied; ger -iing or -ying) tr (aer) rouler au sol ‖ intr aller en taxi; (aer) rouler au sol ‖ interj hep taxi!

tax'i·cab' s taxi m

tax'i danc'er s taxi-girl f

taxidermy ['tæksɪ,dʌrmi] s taxidermie f

tax'i driv'er s chauffeur m de taxi

tax'i·plane' s avion-taxi m

tax'i stand' s station f de taxis

tax'i·way' s (aer) chemin m de roulement

tax'pay'er s contribuable mf

tax' rate' s taux m de l'impôt

tax' return' s déclaration f de revenus, déclaration d'impôts; (blank) feuille f de déclaration de revenus

tea [ti] s thé m; (medicinal infusion) tisane f

tea' bag' s sachet m de thé

tea' ball' s boule f à thé

tea'cart' s table f roulante

teach [titʃ] v (pret & pp -taught [tɔt]) tr enseigner; **to teach s.o. s.th.** enseigner q.ch à qn; **to teach s.o. to** + inf enseigner à qn à + inf ‖ intr enseigner

teacher ['titʃər] s instituteur m, enseignant m; (such as adversity) (fig) maître m

teach'er's pet' s élève m gâté

teaching ['titʃɪŋ] s enseignement m

teach'ing aids' spl matériel m auxiliaire d'enseignement

teach'ing staff' s corps m enseignant

tea'cup' s tasse f à thé

tea' dance' s thé m dansant

teak [tik] s teck m

tea'ket'tle s bouilloire f

team [tim] s (of horses, oxen, etc.) attelage m; (sports) équipe f ‖ tr atteler ‖ intr—**to team up with** faire équipe avec

team'mate' s équipier m

teamster ['timstər] s (of horses) charretier m; (of a truck) camionneur m

team'work' s travail m en équipe; (spirit) esprit m d'équipe

tea'pot' s théière f

tear [tɪr] s larme f; **to burst into tears** fondre en larmes ‖ [tɛr] s déchirure f ‖ [tɛr] v (pret **tore** [tor]; pp **torn** [torn] tr déchirer; **to tear away, down, off** or **out** arracher; **to tear up** (e.g., a letter) déchirer ‖ intr se déchirer; **to tear along** filer précipitamment, aller à fond de train

tear' bomb' [tɪr] s bombe f lacrymogène

tear' duct' [tɪr] s conduit m lacrymal

tearful ['tɪrfəl] adj larmoyant, éploré

tear' gas' [tɪr] s gaz m lacrymogène

tear·jerker ['tɪr,dʒʌrkər] s (slang) comédie f larmoyante

tea'room' s salon m de thé

tease [tiz] tr taquiner

tea'spoon' s cuiller f à café

teaspoonful ['ti,spun,fʊl] s cuillerée f à café

teat [tit] s tétine f

tea'time' s l'heure f du thé

technical ['tɛknɪkəl] adj technique

technicali·ty [,tɛknɪ'kælɪti] s (pl -ties) technicité f; (fine point) subtilité f

technician [tɛk'nɪʃən] s technicien m

technique [tɛk'nik] s technique f

ted'dy bear' ['tɛdi] s ours m en peluche

tedious ['tidɪ·əs] adj ennuyeux, fatigant

teem [tim] intr fourmiller; **to teem with** abonder en, fourmiller de

teeming ['timɪŋ] adj fourmillant; (rain) torrentiel

teen·ager ['tin,edʒər] s adolescent m de 13 à 19 ans

teens [tinz] spl numéros anglais qui se terminent en -teen (de 13 à 19); adolescence *f* de 13 à 19 ans; **to be in one's teens** être adolescent

tee·ny ['tini] *adj* (*comp* **-nier**; *super* **-niest**) (coll) minuscule, tout petit

teeter ['titər] *s* branlement *m*; balançoire *f* ‖ *intr* se balancer, chanceler

teethe [tið] *intr* faire ses dents

teething ['tiðɪŋ] *s* dentition *f*

teeth'ing ring' *s* sucette *f*

teetotaler [ti'totələr] *s* antialcoolique *mf* (*qui s'abstient totalement de boissons alcooliques*)

tele·cast ['tɛlɪ,kæst] *s* émission *f* télévisée ‖ *v* (*pret & pp* **-cast** or **-casted**) *tr & intr* téléviser

telecommunications ['tɛləkə,mjunə'keʃənz] *s* télécommunications *fpl*

telegram ['tɛlɪ,græm] *s* télégramme *m*

telegraph ['tɛlɪ,græf] *s* télégraphe *m* ‖ *tr & intr* télégraphier

telegrapher [tɪ'lɛgrəfər] *s* télégraphiste *mf*

tel'egraph pole' *s* poteau *m* télégraphique

telemeter [tɪ'lɛmɪtər] *s* télémètre *m*

telepathy [tɪ'lɛpəθi] *s* télépathie *f*

telephone ['tɛlɪ'fon] *s* téléphone *m* ‖ *tr & intr* téléphoner

tel'ephone booth' *s* cabine *f* téléphonique

tel'ephone call' *s* appel *m* téléphonique

tel'ephone direc'tory *s* annuaire *m* du téléphone

tel'ephone exchange' *s* central *m* téléphonique

tel'ephone num'ber *s* numéro *m* d'appel

tel'ephone op'erator *s* standardiste *mf*, téléphoniste *mf*

tel'ephone receiv'er *s* récepteur *m* de téléphone

tel'ephone ta'ble *s* table *f* du téléphone

tel'ephoto lens' ['tɛlɪ,foto] *s* téléobjectif *m*

teleprinter ['tɛlɪ,prɪntər] *s* téléimprimeur *m*

teleprocessing ['tɛlə,prɑsɛsɪŋ] *s* télétraitement *m*

teleprompter ['tɛlə,prɑmptər] *s* télésouffleur *m*

telescope ['tɛlɪ,skop] *s* télescope *m* ‖ *tr* télescoper ‖ *intr* se télescoper

telescopic [,tɛlɪ,skɑpɪk] *adj* télescopique

Teletype ['tɛlɪ,taɪp] *s* (trademark) télétype *m*

tel'etype'writ'er *s* téléscripteur *m*

televangelism ['tɛlɪ'vændʒəlɪzəm] *s* télévangélisme *m*

televangelist ['tɛlɪ'vændʒəlɪst] *s* télévangéliste *m*

teleview ['tɛlɪ,vju] *tr & intr* voir à la télévision

televiewer ['tɛlɪ,vju·ər] *s* téléspectateur *m*

televise ['tɛlɪ,vaɪz] *tr* téléviser

television ['tɛlɪ,vɪʒən] *adj* télévisuel ‖ *s* télévision *f*

tel'evision screen' *s* écran *m* de télévision, petit écran

tel'evision set' *s* téléviseur *m*

telex ['tɛlɛks] *s* télex *m* ‖ *tr* envoyer par télex

tell [tɛl] *v* (*pret & pp* **told** [told]) *tr* dire; (*a story*) raconter; (*to count*) compter; (*to*

recognize as distinct) distinguer; **tell me another!** (coll) à d'autres!; **to tell off** compter; (coll) dire son fait à; **to tell s.o. to** + *inf* dire à qn de + *inf* ‖ *intr* produire un effet; **do tell!** (coll) vraiment!; **to tell on** influer sur; (coll) dénoncer; **who can tell?** qui sait?

teller ['tɛlər] *s* narrateur *m*; (*of a bank*) caissier *m*; (*of votes*) scrutateur *m*

temper ['tɛmpər] *s* humeur *f*, caractère *m*; (*of steel, glass, etc.*) trempe *f*; **to keep one's temper** retenir sa colère; **to lose one's temper** se mettre en colère ‖ *tr* tremper ‖ *intr* se tremper

temperament ['tɛmpərəmənt] *s* tempérament *m*

temperamental [,tɛmpərə'mɛntəl] *adj* constitutionnel; capricieux, instable

temperance ['tɛmpərəns] *s* tempérance *f*

temperate ['tɛmpərɪt] *adj* tempéré; (*in food or drink*) tempérant

temperature ['tɛmpərətʃər] *s* température *f*

tempest ['tɛmpɪst] *s* tempête *f*; **tempest in a teapot** tempête dans un verre d'eau

tempestuous [tɛm'pɛstʃu·əs] *adj* tempétueux

temple ['tɛmpəl] *s* temple *m*; (*side of forehead*) tempe *f*; (*of spectacles*) branche *f*

templet ['tɛmplɪt] *s* gabarit *m*

tem·po ['tɛmpo] *s* (*pl* **-pos** or **-pi** [pi]) tempo *m*

temporal ['tɛmpərəl] *adj* temporel; (anat) temporal

temporary ['tɛmpə,rɛri] *adj* temporaire

temporize ['tɛmpə,raɪz] *intr* temporiser

tempt [tɛmpt] *tr* tenter

temptation [tɛmp'teʃən] *s* tentation *f*

tempter ['tɛmptər] *s* tentateur *m*

tempting ['tɛmptɪŋ] *adj* tentant

ten [tɛn] *adj & pron* dix; **about ten** une dizaine de ‖ *s* dix *m*; **ten o'clock** dix heures

tenable ['tɛnəbəl] *adj* soutenable

tenacious [tɪ'neʃəs] *adj* tenace

tenacity [tɪ'næsɪti] *s* ténacité *f*

tenant ['tɛnənt] *s* locataire *mf*

ten'ant farm'er *s* métayer *m*

tend [tɛnd] *tr* soigner; (*sheep*) garder; (*a machine*) surveiller ‖ *intr*—**to tend to** (*to be disposed to*) tendre à; (*to attend to*) vaquer à; **to tend towards** tendre vers or à

tenden·cy ['tɛndənsi] *s* (*pl* **-cies**) tendance *f*

tender ['tɛndər] *adj* tendre *s* offre *f*; (aer, naut) ravitailleur *m*; (rr) tender *m* ‖ *tr* offrir

ten'der-heart'ed *adj* au cœur tendre

ten'der-loin' *s* filet *m*

tenderness ['tɛndərnɪs] *s* tendresse *f*; (*of, e.g., the skin*) sensibilité *f*; (*of, e.g., meat*) tendreté *f*

tendon ['tɛndən] *s* tendon *m*

tendril ['tɛndrɪl] *s* vrille *f*

tenement ['tɛnɪmənt] *s* maison *f* d'habitation; (*slum tenement house*) taudis *m*

ten'ement house' *s* maison *f* de rapport; (*in the slums*) taudis *m*

tenet ['tɛnɪt] *s* doctrine *f*, principe *m*

tennis [ˈtɛnɪs] *s* tennis *m*
ten′nis ball′ *s* balle *f* de tennis
ten′nis court′ *s* court *m* de tennis
tenor [ˈtɛnər] *s* teneur *f*, cours *m*; (mus) ténor *m*
ten′or clef′ *s* clef *f* d'ut
tense [tɛns] *adj* tendu ‖ *s* (gram) temps *m*
tension [ˈtɛnʃən] *s* tension *f*
tent [tɛnt] *s* tente *f*
tentacle [ˈtɛntəkəl] *s* tentacule *m*
tentative [ˈtɛntətɪv] *adj* provisoire; (*hesitant*) timide
tenth [tɛnθ] *adj* & *pron* dixième (*masc, fem*); **the Tenth** dix, e.g., **John the Tenth** Jean dix ‖ *s* dixième *m*; **the tenth** (*in dates*) le dix
tent′ pole′ *s* montant *m* de tente
tenuous [ˈtɛnju·əs] *adj* ténu
tenure [ˈtɛnjər] *s* (*possession*) tenure *f*; (*of an office*) occupation *f*; (*protection from dismissal*) inamovibilité *f*
tepid [ˈtɛpɪd] *adj* tiède
term [tʌrm] *s* terme *m*; (*of imprisonment*) temps *m*; (*of office*) mandat *m*; (*of the school year*) semestre *m*; **terms** conditions *fpl*; **to be on good terms with** avoir de bons rapports avec ‖ *tr* appeler, qualifier
termagant [ˈtʌrməgənt] *s* mégère *f*
terminal [ˈtʌrmɪnəl] *adj* terminal ‖ *s* (comp) terminal *m*; (elec) borne *f*; (rr) terminus *m*
terminate [ˈtʌrmɪˌnet] *tr* terminer ‖ *intr* se terminer
termination [ˌtʌrmɪˈneʃən] *s* conclusion *f*; (*extremity*) bout *m*; (*of word*) désinence *f*; (*of a treaty*) extinction *f*
terminus [ˈtʌrmɪnəs] *s* bout *m*, extrémité *f*; (*boundary*) borne *f*; (rr) terminus *m*
termite [ˈtʌrmaɪt] *s* termite *m*
term′ pa′per *s* dissertation *f*
terrace [ˈtɛrəs] *s* terrasse *f* ‖ *tr* disposer en terrasse
terra firma [ˈtɛrəˈfʌrmə] *s* terre *f* ferme
terrain [tɛˈren] *s* terrain *m*
terrestrial [təˈrɛstrɪ·əl] *adj* terrestre
terrible [ˈtɛrɪbəl] *adj* terrible; (*extremely bad*) atroce
terrific [təˈrɪfɪk] *adj* terrible, terrifiant; (coll) formidable, dynamite
terri·fy [ˈtɛrɪˌfaɪ] *v* (*pret* & *pp* **-fied**) *tr* terrifier
territo·ry [ˈtɛrɪˌtori] *s* (*pl* **-ries**) territoire *m*
terror [ˈtɛrər] *s* terreur *f*
terrorize [ˈtɛrəˌraɪz] *tr* terroriser
ter′ry cloth′ [ˈtɛri] *s* tissu-éponge *m*
terse [tʌrs] *adj* concis, succinct
tertiary [ˈtʌrʃəri] *adj* tertiaire
test [tɛst] *s* (*physical, mental, moral*) épreuve *f*; (*exam*) examen *m*; (*trial*) essai *m*; (*e.g., of intelligence*) test *m* ‖ *tr* éprouver, mettre à l'épreuve; examiner, tester
testament [ˈtɛstəmənt] *s* testament *m*
test′ ban′ *s* interdiction *f* des essais nucléaires
test′ flight′ *s* vol *m* d'essai
testicle [ˈtɛstɪkəl] *s* testicule *m*

testi·fy [ˈtɛstɪˌfaɪ] *v* (*pret* & *pp* **-fied**) *tr* déclarer ‖ *intr* déposer; **to testify to** témoigner de
testimonial [ˌtɛstɪˈmoni·əl] *s* attestation *m*
testimo·ny [ˈtɛstɪˌmoni] *s* (*pl* **-nies**) témoignage *m*
test′ing ground′ *s* terrain *m* d'essai
test′ pat′tern *s* (telv) mire *f*
test′ pi′lot *s* pilote *m* d'essai
test′ tube′ *s* éprouvette *f*
test′-tube ba′by *s* bébé *m* éprouvette
tes·ty [ˈtɛsti] *adj* (*comp* **-tier**; *super* **-tiest**) susceptible
tetanus [ˈtɛtənəs] *s* tétanos *m*
tether [ˈtɛðər] *s* attache *f*; **at the end of one's tether** à bout de ressources ‖ *tr* mettre à l'attache
tetter [ˈtɛtər] *s* (pathol) dartre *f*
text [tɛkst] *s* texte *m*
text′book′ *s* manuel *m* scolaire, livre *m* de classe
textile [ˈtɛkstaɪl] *adj* & *s* textile *m*
textual [ˈtɛkstʃu·əl] *adj* textuel
texture [ˈtɛkstʃər] *s* texture *f*; (*woven fabric*) tissu *m*
Thai [tɑ·i], [taɪ] *adj* thaï, thaïlandais ‖ *s* (*language*) thaï *m*; (*person*) Thaïlandais *m*; **the Thai** les Thaïlandais
Thailand [ˈtaɪlənd] *s* Thaïlande *f*; la Thaïlande
Thames [tɛmz] *s* Tamise *f*
than [ðæn] *conj* que; (*before a numeral*) de, e.g., **more than three** plus de trois
thank [θæŋk] *adj* (e.g., *offering*) de reconnaissance ‖ **thanks** *spl* remerciements *mpl*; **thanks to** grâce à ‖ **thanks** *interj* merci!; **no thanks!** merci! ‖ **thank** *tr* remercier; **thank you** je vous remercie; **thank you for** merci de or pour; **thank you for** + *ger* merci de + *inf*; **to thank s.o. for** remercier qn de or pour; **to thank s.o. for** + *ger* remercier qn de + *inf*
thankful [ˈθæŋkfəl] *adj* reconnaissant
thankless [ˈθæŋklɪs] *adj* ingrat
Thanksgiv′ing Day′ *s* le jour d'action de grâces
that [ðæt] *adj dem* (*pl* **those**) ce §82; **that one** celui-là §84 ‖ *pron dem* (*pl* **those**) celui §83; celui-là §84 ‖ *pron rel* qui; que ‖ *pron neut* cela, ça; **that is** c'est-à-dire; **that's all** voilà tout; **that will do** cela suffit ‖ *adv* tellement, si, aussi; **that far** si loin, aussi loin; **that much, that many** tant ‖ *conj* que; (*in order that*) pour que, afin que; in that en ce que
thatch [θætʃ] *s* chaume *m* ‖ *tr* couvrir de chaume
thatched′ cot′tage *s* chaumière *f*
thaw [θɔ] *s* dégel *m* ‖ *tr* & *intr* dégeler
the [ðə], [ðɪ], [ði] *art def* le §77 ‖ *adv* d'autant plus, e.g., **she will be the happier for it** elle en sera d'autant plus heureuse; **the more . . . the more** plus . . . plus
theater [ˈθi·ətər] *s* théâtre *m*
the′ater club′ *s* association *f* des spectateurs
the′ater·go′er *s* habitué *m* du théâtre

the'ater page' *s* chronique *f* théâtrale
theatrical [θɪ'ætrɪkəl] *adj* théâtral
thee [ði] *pron pers* (archaic, poetic, Bib) toi §85; te §87
theft [θɛft] *s* vol *m*
their [ðɛr] *adj poss* leur §88
theirs [ðɛrz] *pron poss* le leur §89
them [ðɛm] *pron pers* eux §85; les §87; leur §87; **of them** en §87; **to them** leur §87; y §87
theme [θim] *s* thème *m*; (*essay*) composition *f*; (mus) thème
theme' song' *s* leitmotiv *m*; (rad) indicatif *m*
them·selves' *pron pers* soi §85; eux-mêmes §86; se §87; eux §85
then [ðɛn] *adv* alors; (*next*) ensuite, puis; (*therefore*) donc; **by then** d'ici là; **from then on, since then** depuis lors, dès lors; **then and there** séance tenante; **till then** jusque-là; **what then?** et après?
thence [ðɛns] *adv* de là; (*from that fact*) pour cette raison
thence'forth' *adv* dès lors
theolo·gy [θi'ɑlədʒi] *s* (*pl* -gies) théologie *f*
theorem ['θi·ərəm] *s* théorème *m*
theoretical [,θi·ə'rɛtɪkəl] *adj* théorique
theo·ry ['θi·əri] *s* (*pl* -ries) théorie *f*
therapeutic [,θɛrə'pjutɪk] *adj* thérapeutique || **therapeutics** *spl* thérapeutique *f*
thera·py ['θɛrəpi] *s* (*pl* -pies) thérapie *f*
there [ðɛr] *adv* là; y §87; **down there, over there** là-bas; **from there** de là; en §87; **in there** là-dedans; **on there** là-dessus; **there is** or **there are** il y a; (*pointing out*) voilà; **under there** là-dessous; **up there** là-haut
there'abouts' *adv* aux environs, près de là; (*approximately*) à peu près
there'af'ter *adv* par la suite
there'by' *adv* par là; de cette manière
therefore ['ðɛr,for] *adv* par conséquent, donc
there'in' *adv* dedans, là-dedans
there'of' *adv* de cela; en §87
there'upon' *adv* là-dessus §85A; sur ce
there'with' *adv* avec cela
thermal ['θʌrməl] *adj* (*waters*) thermal; (*capacity*) thermique
ther'mal cone' *s* bouclier *m* thermique
thermocouple ['θʌrmo,kʌpəl] *s* thermocouple *m*
thermodynamic [,θʌrmodaɪ'næmɪk] *adj* thermodynamique || **thermodynamics** *spl* thermodynamique *f*
thermometer [θər'mɑmɪtər] *s* thermomètre *m*
thermonuclear [,θʌrmo'n(j)ukli·ər] *adj* thermonucléaire
Thermopylae [θər'mɑpɪ,li] *s* les Thermopyles *fpl*
ther'mos bot'tle ['θʌrməs] *s* thermos *m* & *f*, bouteille *f* thermos
thermostat ['θʌrmə,stæt] *s* thermostat *m*
thesau·rus [θɪ'sɔrəs] *s* (*pl* -ruses [rəsəs] or -ri [raɪ]) trésor *m*; (*dictionary*) dictionnaire *m* analogique; (*treasury*) trésor *m*; (comp) thesaurus *m*

these [ðiz] *adj dem pl* ces §82 || *pron dem pl* ceux §83; ceux-ci §84
the·sis ['θisɪs] *s* (*pl* -ses [siz]) thèse *f*
they [ðe] *pron pers* ils §87; eux §85; on §87, e.g., **they say** on dit; ce §82B
thick [θɪk] *adj* épais; (*pipe, rod, etc.*) gros; (*forest, eyebrows, etc.*) touffu; (*grass, grain, etc.*) dru; (*voice*) pâteux; (*gravy*) court; (coll) stupide, obtus; (coll) intime || *s* (*of thumb, leg, etc.*) gras *m*; **the thick of** (e.g., *a crowd*) le milieu de; (e.g., *a battle*) le fort de; **through thick and thin** contre vents et marées
thicken ['θɪkən] *tr* épaissir || *intr* s'épaissir; (*said, e.g., of plot*) se corser
thicket ['θɪkɪt] *s* fourré *m*, maquis *m*
thick'-head'ed *adj* à la tête dure
thick'-lipped' *adj* lippu
thick'-set' *adj* trapu
thief [θif] *s* (*pl* thieves [θivz]) voleur *m*
thieve [θiv] *intr* voler
thiever·y ['θivəri] *s* (*pl* -ies) volerie *f*
thigh [θaɪ] *s* cuisse *f*
thigh'bone' *s* fémur *m*
thimble ['θɪmbəl] *s* dé *m*
thin [θɪn] *adj* (*comp* thinner; *super* thinnest) mince; (*person*) élancé, maigre; (*hair*) rare; (*soup*) clair; (*gravy*) long; (*voice*) grêle; (*excuse*) faible || *v* (*pret & pp* thinned; *ger* thinning) *tr* amincir; (*colors*) délayer; **to thin out** éclaircir || *intr* s'amincir; **to thin out** s'éclaircir
thine [ðaɪn] *adj poss* (archaic, poetic, Bib) ton §88 || *pron poss* (archaic, poetic, Bib) le tien §89
thing [θɪŋ] *s* chose *f*; **for another thing** d'autre part; **for one thing** en premier lieu; **of all things!** par exemple!; **to be the thing** être le dernier cri; **to see things** avoir des hallucinations
thingamajig ['θɪŋəmə,dʒɪg] *s* (coll) truc *m*, machin *m*, bidule *f*
think [θɪŋk] *v* (*pret & pp* thought [θɔt]) *tr* penser; (*to deem, consider*) estimer; **to think of** (*to have as an opinion of*) penser de, e.g., **what do you think of your uncle?** que pensez-vous de votre oncle? || *intr* penser, songer; **to think fast** avoir l'esprit alerte; **to think of** (*to direct one's thoughts toward*) penser à, songer à, e.g., **do you ever think of your uncle?** pensez-vous jamais à votre oncle?; **to think of it** or **them** y penser, y songer; **to think so** croire que oui
thinker ['θɪŋkər] *s* penseur *m*
third [θʌrd] *adj & pron* troisième (*masc, fem*); **the Third** trois, e.g., **John the Third** Jean trois || *s* troisième *m*; (*in fractions*) tiers *m*; **the third** (*in dates*) le trois
third' degree' *s* (coll) passage *m* à tabac, cuisinage *m*
third' fin'ger *s* annulaire *m*
third' rail' *s* (rr) rail *m* de contact; rail conducteur
third'-rate' *adj* de troisième ordre
Third' World' *s* Tiers Monde *m*

thirst [θʌrst] *s* soif *f* ‖ *intr* avoir soif; **to thirst for** avoir soif de

thirst'-quench'ing *adj* désaltérant

thirst·y ['θʌrsti] *adj* (*comp* -ier; *super* -iest) altéré, assoiffé; **to be thirsty** avoir soif

thirteen ['θʌr'tin] *adj, pron, & s* treize *m*

thirteenth ['θʌr'tinθ] *adj & pron* treizième (*masc, fem*); **the Thirteenth** treize, e.g., **John the Thirteenth** Jean treize ‖ *s* treizième *m*; **the thirteenth** (*in dates*) le treize

thirtieth ['θʌrtɪ·ɪθ] *adj & pron* trentième (*masc, fem*) ‖ *s* trentième *m*; **the thirtieth** (*in dates*) trente

thir·ty ['θʌrti] *adj & pron* trente; **about thirty** une trentaine de ‖ *s* (*pl* -ties) trente *m*; **the thirties** les années *fpl* trente

this [ðɪs] *adj dem* (*pl* these) ce §82; **this one** celui-ci §84 ‖ *pron dem* (*pl* these) celui §83; celui-ci §84 ‖ *pron neut* ceci ‖ *adv* tellement, si, aussi; **this far** si loin, aussi loin; **this much, this many** tant

thistle ['θɪsəl] *s* chardon *m*

thither ['θɪðər] *adv* là, de ce côté là

thong [θɔŋ] *s* courroie *f*

tho·rax ['θoræks] *s* (*pl* -raxes or -races [rə,siz]) thorax *m*

thorn [θɔrn] *s* épine *f*

thorn·y ['θɔrni] *adj* (*comp* -ier; *super* -iest) épineux

thorough ['θʌro] *adj* approfondi, complet; consciencieux, minutieux

thor'ough·bred' *adj* de race, racé; (*horse*) pur sang ‖ *s* personne *f* racée; (*horse*) pur-sang *m*

thor'ough·fare' *s* voie *f* de communication; **no thoroughfare** (*public sign*) rue barrée

thor'ough·go'ing *adj* parfait; consciencieux

thoroughly ['θʌroli] *adv* à fond

those [ðoz] *adj dem pl* ces §82 ‖ *pron dem pl* ceux §83; ceux-là §84

thou [ðau] *pron pers* (archaic, poetic, Bib) tu §87 ‖ *tr & intr* tutoyer

though [ðo] *adv* cependant ‖ *conj* (*although*) bien que, quoique; (*even if*) même si; **as though** comme si

thought [θɔt] *s* pensée *f*

thought' control' *s* asservissement *m* des consciences

thoughtful ['θɔtfəl] *adj* pensif; (*considerate*) prévenant, attentif; (*serious*) profond

thoughtless ['θɔtlɪs] *adj* étourdi, négligent; inconsidéré

thousand ['θauzənd] *adj & pron* mille; mil, e.g., **the year one thousand nineteen hundred and eighty-one** l'an mil neuf cent quatre-vingt-un ‖ *s* mille *m*; **a thousand** un millier de, mille

thousandth ['θauzəndθ] *adj & pron* millième (*masc, fem*) ‖ *s* millième *m*

thrash [θræʃ] *tr* rosser; (agr) battre; **to thrash out** débattre ‖ *intr* s'agiter; (agr) battre le blé

thread [θrɛd] *s* fil *m*; (bot) filament *m*; (mach) filet *m*; **to hang by a thread** ne tenir qu'à un fil; **to lose the thread of** perdre le fil de ‖ *tr* enfiler; (mach) fileter

thread'bare' *adj* élimé, râpé; (*tire*) usé jusqu'à la corde

threat [θrɛt] *s* menace *f*

threaten ['θrɛtən] *tr & intr* menacer

threatening ['θrɛtənɪŋ] *adj* menaçant

three [θri] *adj & pron* trois ‖ *s* trois *m*; **three o'clock** trois heures; **three of a kind** (cards) un fredon

three'-cor'nered *adj* triangulaire; (*hat*) tricorne

three'-ply' *adj* à trois épaisseurs; (e.g., *wool*) à trois fils

three' R's' [arz] *spl* la lecture, l'écriture et l'arithmétique, premières notions *fpl*

three'score' *adj* soixante

threno·dy ['θrɛnədi] *s* (*pl* -dies) thrène *m*

thresh [θrɛʃ] *tr* (agr) battre; **to thresh out** (*a problem*) débattre ‖ *intr* s'agiter; (agr) battre le blé

thresh'ing floor' *s* aire *f*

thresh'ing machine' *s* batteuse *f*

threshold ['θrɛʃold] *s* seuil *m*; **to cross the threshold** franchir le seuil

thrice [θrais] *adv* trois fois

thrift [θrɪft] *s* économie *f*, épargne *f*

thrift·y ['θrɪfti] *adj* (*comp* -ier; *super* -iest) économe, ménager, frugal; prospère

thrill [θrɪl] *s* frisson *m* ‖ *tr* faire frémir ‖ *intr* frémir

thriller ['θrɪlər] *s* roman *m*, film *m*, or pièce *f* à sensation; (*novel*) roman de série noire

thrilling ['θrɪlɪŋ] *adj* émouvant, passionnant

thrive [θraiv] *v* (*pret* **thrived** or **throve** [θrov]; *pp* **thrived** or **thriven** ['θrɪvən]) *intr* prospérer; (*said of child, plant, etc.*) croître, se développer

throat [θrot] *s* gorge *f*; **to clear one's throat** s'éclaircir le gosier; **to have a sore throat** avoir mal à la gorge

throb [θrab] *s* palpitation *f*, battement *m*; (*of motor*) vrombissement *m* ‖ *v* (*pret & pp* **throbbed**; *ger* **throbbing**) *intr* palpiter, battre fort; (*said of motor*) vrombir

throes [θroz] *spl* (*of childbirth*) douleurs *fpl*; (*of death*) affres *fpl*; **in the throes of** luttant avec

throne [θron] *s* trône *m*

throng [θrɔŋ] *s* foule *f*, affluence *f* ‖ *intr* affluer

throttle ['θratəl] *s* (*of steam engine*) régulateur *m*; (aut) étrangleur *m* ‖ *tr* régler; étrangler

through [θru] *adj* direct; (*finished*) fini; (*traffic*) prioritaire ‖ *adv* à travers; complètement ‖ *prep* au travers de, par; grâce à, par le canal de

through·out' *adv* d'un bout à l'autre ‖ *prep* d'un bout à l'autre de; (*during*) pendant tout

through' street' *s* rue *f* à circulation prioritaire

through'way' *s* autoroute *f*

throw [θro] *s* jet *m*, lancement *m*; (*scarf*) châle *m* ‖ *v* (*pret* **threw** [θru]; *pp* **thrown**) *tr* jeter, lancer; (*a glance; the dice*) jeter; (*e.g., a baseball*) lancer; (*e.g., a shadow*) projeter; (*blame; responsibility*) rejeter; (*a rider*) désarçonner; (*a game, career, etc.*) perdre à dessein; **to throw away** jeter; **to throw back** renvoyer; **to throw in** ajouter; **to throw out** expulser, chasser; (*e.g., an odor*) répandre; (*one's chest*) bomber; **to throw over** abandonner; **to throw up** jeter en l'air; vomir; (*one's hands*) lever; (*e.g., one's claims*) renoncer à ‖ *intr* jeter, lancer; jeter des dés; **to throw up** vomir

throw′back′ *s* recul *m*; (*setback*) échec *m*; (*reversion*) retour *m* atavique

thrum [θrʌm] *v* (*pret & pp* **thrummed**; *ger* **thrumming**) *intr* pianoter

thrush [θrʌʃ] *s* grive *f*

thrust [θrʌst] *s* poussée *f*; (*with a weapon*) coup *m* de pointe; (*with a sword*) coup d'estoc; (*jibe*) trait *m*; (rok) poussée *f*; **thrust and parry** la botte et la parade ‖ *v* (*pret & pp* **thrust**) *tr* pousser; (*e.g., a dagger*) enfoncer; **to thrust oneself on** s'imposer à

thud [θʌd] *s* bruit *m* sourd ‖ *v* (*pret & pp* **thudded**; *ger* **thudding**) *tr & intr* frapper avec un son mat

thug [θʌg] *s* bandit *m*, assassin *m*

thumb [θʌm] *s* pouce *m*; **all thumbs** (coll) maladroit; **to twiddle one's thumbs** se tourner les pouces; **under the thumb of** sous la coupe de ‖ *tr* tripoter; (*a book*) feuilleter; **to thumb a ride** faire de l'auto-stop; **to thumb one's nose at** (coll) faire un pied de nez à

thumb′ in′dex *s* onglet *m*, encoche *f*

thumb′print′ *s* marque *f* de pouce

thumb′screw′ *s* papillon *m*, vis *f* à ailettes

thumb′tack′ *s* punaise *f* ‖ *tr* punaiser

thump [θʌmp] *s* coup *m* violent ‖ *tr* cogner ‖ *intr* tomber avec un bruit sourd; (*said, e.g., of marching feet*) sonner lourdement; (*said of heart*) battre fort

thumping [′θʌmpɪŋ] *adj* (coll) énorme

thunder [′θʌndər] *s* tonnerre *m* ‖ *tr* fulminer ‖ *intr* tonner; **to thunder at** tonner contre, tempêter contre

thun′der·bolt′ *s* foudre *f*; (*disaster*) coup *m* de foudre

thun′der·clap′ *s* coup *m* de tonnerre

thunderous [′θʌndərəs] *adj* orageux; (*voice; applause*) tonnant

thun′der·show′er *s* pluie *f* d'orage

thun′der·storm′ *s* orage *m*

thunderstruck [′θʌndər‚strʌk] *adj* foudroyé, pantois

Thursday [′θʌrzdi] *s* jeudi *m*

thus [ðʌs] *adv* ainsi; (*therefore*) donc; **thus far** jusqu'ici

thwack [θwæk] *s* coup *m* ‖ *tr* flanquer un coup à

thwart [θwɔrt] *adj* transversal ‖ *adv* en travers ‖ *tr* déjouer, frustrer

thy [ðaɪ] *adj poss* (archaic, poetic, Bib) ton §88

thyme [taɪm] *s* thym *m*

thyroid [′θaɪrɔɪd] *s* thyroïde *f*; (pharm) extrait *m* thyroïde

thyself [ðaɪ′sɛlf] *pron* (archaic, poetic, Bib) toi-même §86; te §87

tiara [taɪ′ɑrə], [taɪ′ɛrə] *s* tiare *f*; (*woman's headdress*) diadème *m*

tic [tɪk] *s* (pathol) tic *m*

tick [tɪk] *s* (*ticking*) tic-tac *m*; (*e.g., of pillow*) taie *f*; (*e.g., of mattress*) housse *f* de coutil; (ent) tique *f*; **on tick** à crédit ‖ *tr*—**to tick off** (*to check off*) pointer ‖ *intr* tictaquer; (*said of heart*) battre

ticker [′tɪkər] *s* téléimprimeur *m*; (*watch*) (slang) toquante *f*; (*heart*) (slang) cœur *m*

tick′er tape′ *s* bande *f* de téléimprimeur

ticket [′tɪkɪt] *s* billet *m*; (*of bus, subway, etc.*) ticket *m*; (*of baggage, checkroom*) bulletin *m*; (*of cloakroom*) numéro *m*; (*for boat trip*) passage *m*; (*of a political party*) liste *f* électorale; (*for violation*) (coll) papillon *m* de procès-verbal, contravention *f*; **that's the ticket** (coll) c'est bien ça, à la bonne heure; **tickets, please!** vos places, s'il vous plaît!

tick′et a′gent *s* guichetier *m*

tick′et collec′tor *s* contrôleur *m*

ticketing [′tɪkɪtɪŋ] *s* billetterie *f*

tick′et of′fice *s* guichet *m*; (theat) bureau *m* de location

tick′et scalp′er [‚skælpər] *s* trafiquant *m* de billets de théâtre

tick′et win′dow *s* guichet *m*

ticking [′tɪkɪŋ] *s* (*of a clock*) tic-tac *m*; (tex) coutil *m*

tickle [′tɪkəl] *s* chatouillement *m* ‖ *tr* chatouiller; (*to amuse*) amuser; (*to please*) plaire à ‖ *intr* chatouiller

ticklish [′tɪklɪʃ] *adj* chatouilleux; (*touchy*) susceptible; (*subject, question*) épineux, délicat

tick′-tack-toe′ *s* morpion *m*

ticktock [′tɪk‚tɑk] *s* tic-tac *m* ‖ *intr* faire tic-tac

tid′al ba′sin *s* bassin *m* à flot

tid′al wave′ [′taɪdəl] *s* raz *m* de marée; (*e.g., of popular indignation*) vague *f*

tidbit [′tɪd‚bɪt] *s* bon morceau *m*

tiddlywinks [′tɪdli‚wɪŋks] *s* jeu *m* de puce

tide [taɪd] *s* marée *f*; **against the tide** à contre-marée; **to go with the tide** suivre le courant ‖ *tr*—**to tide over** dépanner, remettre à flot; (*a difficulty*) venir à bout de

tide′land′ *s* terres *fpl* inondées aux grandes marées

tide′wa′ter *s* eaux *fpl* de marée; bord *m* de la mer

tide′water pow′er plant′ *s* usine *f* marémotrice

tidings [′taɪdɪŋz] *spl* nouvelles *fpl*

ti·dy [′taɪdi] *adj* (*comp* **-dier**; *super* **-diest**) propre, net, bien tenu; (*considerable*) (coll) joli, fameux ‖ *s* (*pl* **-dies**) voile *m* de fauteuil ‖ *v* (*pret & pp* **-died**) *tr* mettre en ordre, nettoyer ‖ *intr*—**to tidy up** faire un brin de toilette

tie [taɪ] *s* (*connection*) lien *m*, attache *f*; (*knot*) nœud *m*; (*necktie*) cravate *f*; (*in games*) match *m* nul; (mus) liaison *f*; (rr)

traverse f ‖ v (*pret & pp* **tied**; *ger* **tying**) *tr* lier; (*a knot, a necktie, etc.*) nouer; (*shoelaces; a knot; one's apron*) attacher; (*an artery*) ligaturer; (*a competitor*) être à égalité avec; (mus) lier; **tied up** (*busy*) occupé; **to tie down** assujettir; **to tie up** attacher; (*a package*) ficeler; (*a person*) ligoter; (*a wound*) bander; (*funds*) immobiliser; (*traffic, a telephone line*) embouteiller ‖ *intr* (sports) faire match nul, égaliser

tie′back′ s embrasse f

tie′ game′ s match m nul

tie′pin′ s épingle f de cravate

tier [tɪr] s étage m; (*of stadium*) gradin m

tiger [′taɪgər] s tigre m

ti′ger lil′y s lis m tigré

tight [taɪt] *adj* serré, juste; (*e.g., rope*) tendu; (*clothes*) ajusté; (*container*) étanche; (*game*) serré; (*money*) rare; (*miserly*) (coll) chiche; (*drunk*) (coll) rond, noir ‖ **tights** *spl* collant m, maillot m ‖ *adv* fermement, bien; **to hold tight** tenir serré; se tenir, se cramponner; **to sit tight** (coll) tenir bon

tighten [′taɪtən] *tr* (*a knot, a bolt*) serrer, resserrer; (*e.g., a rope*) tendre ‖ *intr* se serrer; se tendre

tight-fisted [′taɪt′fɪstɪd] *adj* dur à la détente, serré

tight′-fit′ting *adj* collant, ajusté

tight′rope′ s corde f raide

tight′rope walk′er s funambule mf

tight′ squeeze′ s (coll) situation f difficile, embarras m

tight′wad′ s (coll) grippe-sou m

tigress [′taɪgrɪs] s tigresse f

tile [taɪl] s (*for roof*) tuile f; (*for floor*) carreau m ‖ *tr* (*e.g., a house*) couvrir de tuiles; (*a floor*) carreler

tile′ roof′ s toit m de tuiles

till [tɪl] s tiroir-caisse m ‖ *prep* jusqu'à ‖ *conj* jusqu'à ce que ‖ *tr* labourer

tilt [tɪlt] s (*slant*) pente f, inclinaison f; (*contest*) joute f; **full tilt** à fond de train ‖ *tr* pencher, incliner; **to tilt back** renverser en arrière; **to tilt up** redresser ‖ *intr* se pencher, s'incliner; (*with lance*) jouter; (naut) donner de la bande; **to tilt at** attaquer, critiquer; **to tilt back** se renverser en arrière

timber [′tɪmbər] s bois m de construction; (*trees*) bois de haute futaie; (*rafter*) poutre f

tim′ber·land′ s bois m pour exploitation forestière

tim′ber line′ s limite f de la végétation forestière, ligne f des arbres

timbre [′tɪmbər] s (phonet, phys) timbre m

time [taɪm] s temps m; heure f, e.g., **what time is it?** quelle heure est-il?; fois, e.g., **five times** cinq fois; e.g., **five times two is ten** cinq fois deux font dix; (*period of payment*) délai m; (phot) temps d'exposition; **at that time** à ce moment-là; à cette époque; **at the present time** à l'heure actuelle; **at the same time** en même

temps; **at times** parfois; **behind the times** en retard sur son époque; **between times** entre-temps; **full time** plein temps; **in due time** en temps et lieu; **in no time** en moins de rien; **in the time of** au temps de; **on time** à l'heure, à temps; **several times** à plusieurs reprises; **time and time again** maintes fois; **to beat time** (mus) battre la mesure; **to do time** (coll) faire son temps; **to have a good time** s'amuser bien, se divertir; **to lose time** (*said of timepiece*) retarder; **to mark time** marquer le pas; **to play for time** (coll) chercher à gagner du temps ‖ *tr* mesurer la durée de; (sports) chronométrer

time′ bomb′ s bombe f à retardement

time′ card′ s registre m de présence

time′ clock′ s horloge f enregistreuse

time′ expo′sure s (phot) pose f

time′ fuse′ s fusée f fusante

time′-hon′ored *adj* consacré par l'usage

time′keep′er s pointeur m, chronométreur m; (*clock*) pendule f; (*watch*) montre f

timeless [′taɪmlɪs] *adj* sans fin, éternel

time·ly [′taɪmli] *adj* (*comp* **-lier**; *super* **-liest**) opportun, à propos

time′-out′ s (sports) temps m mort

time′piece′ s (*clock*) pendule f; (*watch*) montre f

timer [′taɪmər] s (*person*) chronométreur m; (*of an electrical appliance*) minuterie f, compte-minutes m invar

time′-release medica′tion s médicament m à action prolongée, médication f retard

time′-shar′ing *adj* (comp) en temps partagé

time′ shar′ing s (comp) temps m partagé, partage m du temps

time′ sheet′ s feuille f de présence

time′ sig′nal s signal m horaire

time′ slot′ s créneau m temporel

time′ta′ble s horaire m; (rr) indicateur m

time′work′ s travail m à l'heure

time′worn′ *adj* usé par le temps; (*venerable*) séculaire

time′ zone′ s fuseau m horaire

timid [′tɪmɪd] *adj* timide

timing [′taɪmɪŋ] s (*recording of time*) chronométrage m; (*selecting the right time*) choix m du moment propice; (*of an electrical appliance*) minuterie f; (aut, mach) réglage m; (sports) chronométrage; (theat) tempo m, minutage m

tim′ing gears′ *spl* engrenage m de distribution

timorous [′tɪmərəs] *adj* timoré, peureux

tin [tɪn] s (*element*) étain m; (*tin plate*) fer-blanc m; (*cup, box, etc.*) boîte f ‖ v (*pret & pp* **tinned**; *ger* **tinning**) *tr* étamer; (*to can*) (Brit) mettre en boîte

tin′can′ s boîte f en fer-blanc, boîte de conserve

tincture [′tɪŋktʃər] s teinture f

tin′ cup′ s timbale f

tinder [′tɪndər] s amadou m

tin′der·box′ s briquet m à amadou; (fig) foyer m de l'effervescence

tin′ foil′ s feuille f d'étain, papier m d'argent

ting-a-ling [ˈtɪŋəˌlɪŋ] s drelin m
tinge [tɪndʒ] s teinte f, nuance f ‖ v (ger **tingeing** or **tinging**) tr teinter, nuancer
tingle [ˈtɪŋgəl] s picotement m, fourmillement m ‖ intr picoter, fourmiller; (e.g., with enthusiasm) tressaillir
tin′ hat′ s (coll) casque m en acier
tinker [ˈtɪŋkər] s chaudronnier m ambulant; (bungler) bousilleur m ‖ intr bricoler; **to tinker with** tripatouiller
tinkle [ˈtɪŋkəl] s tintement m ‖ tr faire tinter ‖ intr tinter
tin′ plate′ s fer-blanc m
tin′-plate′ tr étamer
tin′ roof′ s toit m de fer-blanc
tinsel [ˈtɪnsəl] s clinquant m; (for a Christmas tree) paillettes fpl, guirlandes fpl clinquantes
tin′smith′ s ferblantier m
tin′ sol′dier s soldat m de plomb
tint [tɪnt] s teinte f ‖ tr teinter
tin′type′ s ferrotypie f
tin′ware′ s ferblanterie f
ti·ny [ˈtaɪni] adj (comp **-nier;** super **-niest**) minuscule
tip [tɪp] s (end) bout m, pointe f; (slant) inclinaison f; (fee to a waiter) pourboire m; (secret information) (slang) tuyau m ‖ v (pret & pp **tipped;** ger **tipping**) tr incliner; (the scales) faire pencher; (a waiter) donner un pourboire à, donner la pièce à; **to tip off** (slang) tuyauter; **to tip over** renverser ‖ intr se renverser; donner un pourboire
tip′cart′ s tombereau m
tip′-in′ s (bb) hors-texte m
tip′-off′ s (coll) tuyau m
tipped′-in′ adj (bb) hors texte
tipple [ˈtɪpəl] intr biberonner
tip′staff′ s verge f d'huissier; huissier m à verge
tip·sy [ˈtɪpsi] adj (comp **-sier;** super **-siest**) gris, grisé
tip′toe′ s pointe f des pieds ‖ v (pret & pp **-toed;** ger **toeing**) intr marcher sur la pointe des pieds
tirade [ˈtaɪred] s diatribe f
tire [taɪr] s pneu m ‖ tr fatiguer ‖ intr se fatiguer
tire′ chain′ s chaîne f antidérapante
tired [taɪrd] adj fatigué, las
tire′ gauge′ s manomètre m
tire′ i′ron s démonte-pneu m
tireless [ˈtaɪrlɪs] adj infatigable
tire′ pres′sure s pression f des pneus
tire′ pump′ s gonfleur m pour pneus
tiresome [ˈtaɪrsəm] adj fatigant, ennuyeux
tissue [ˈtɪʃu] s (thin paper) papier m de soie; (toilet tissue) papier hygiénique; (paper handkerchief) mouchoir m en papier; (tex) tissu m, étoffe f; (web, mesh) (fig) tissu, enchevêtrement m
tis′sue pa′per s papier m de soie
tit [tɪt] s téton m; (orn) mésange f; **tit for tat** à bon chat bon rat
titanium [taɪˈteni·əm] s titane m

tithe [taɪð] s dixième m; (rel) dîme f ‖ tr soumettre à la dîme; payer la dîme sur
Titian [ˈtɪʃən] s le Titien m
Ti′tian red′ s blond m vénitien
title [ˈtaɪtəl] s titre m; (of an automobile) carte f grise ‖ tr intituler
ti′tle deed′ s titre m de propriété
ti′tle-hold′er s tenant m du titre
ti′tle page′ s page f de titre
ti′tle role′ s rôle m principal
tit′mouse′ s (pl **-mice**) (orn) mésange f
titter [ˈtɪtər] s rire m étouffé ‖ intr rire en catimini
titular [ˈtɪtʃələr] adj titulaire
to [tu], [tu], [tə] adv—**to and fro** de long en large ‖ prep à; (towards) vers; (in order to) afin de, pour; envers, pour, e.g., **good to her** bon envers elle, bon pour elle; jusqu'à, e.g., **to this day** jusqu'à ce jour; e.g., **to count to a hundred** compter jusqu'à cent; moins, e.g., **a quarter to eight** huit heures moins le quart; contre, e.g., **seven to one** sept contre un; dans, e.g., **to a certain extent** dans une certaine mesure; en, e.g., **from door to door** de porte en porte; e.g., **I am going to France** je vais en France; de, e.g., **to try to** + inf essayer de + inf; **to him** lui §87
toad [tod] s crapaud m
toad′stool′ s agaric m; champignon m vénéneux
to-and-fro [ˈtu·ənd′fro] adj de va-et-vient
toast [tost] s pain m grillé; (with a drink) toast m ‖ tr griller; porter un toast à, boire à la santé de
toaster [ˈtostər] s grille-pain m
toast′er ov′en s grille-pain-four m
toast′mas′ter s préposé m aux toasts
tobac·co [təˈbæko] s (pl **-cos**) tabac m
tobac′co pouch′ s blague f
toboggan [təˈbagən] s toboggan m
tocsin [ˈtaksɪn] s tocsin m; (bell) cloche f qui sonne le tocsin
today [tuˈde] s & adv aujourd'hui m
toddle [ˈtadəl] s allure f chancelante ‖ intr marcher à petits pas chancelants
toddler [ˈtadlər] s tout-petit m
tod·dy [ˈtadi] s (pl **-dies**) grog m
to-do [təˈdu] s (pl **-dos**) embarras mpl, chichis mpl, façons fpl
toe [to] s doigt m du pied, orteil m; (of shoe, of stocking) bout m ‖ v (pret & pp **toed;** ger **toeing**) tr—**to toe the line** or **the mark** s'aligner, se mettre au pas
toe′nail′ s ongle m du pied
tog [tag] v (pret & pp **togged;** ger **togging**) tr—**to tog out** or **up** attifer, fringuer ‖ **togs** spl fringues fpl
together [tuˈgeðər] adv ensemble; (at the same time) en même temps, à la fois
tog′gle switch′ [ˈtagəl] s (elec) interrupteur m à culbuteur or à bascule
toil [tɔɪl] s travail m dur; **toils** filet m, piège m ‖ intr travailler dur
toilet [ˈtɔɪlɪt] s toilette f; (rest room) cabinet m de toilette

toi′let ar′ticles *spl* objets *mpl* de toilette
toi′let bowl′ *s* cuvette *f*
toi′let pa′per *s* papier *m* hygiénique
toi′let seat′ *s* siège *m* des toilettes, abattant *m*
toi′let set′ *s* nécessaire *m* de toilette
toi′let soap′ *s* savonnette *f*
toi′let wa′ter *s* eaux *fpl* de toilette
token [′tokən] *adj* symbolique ‖ *s* (*symbol*) signe *m*, marque *f*; (*keepsake*) souvenir *m*; (*used as money*) jeton *m*; **by the same token** de plus; **in token of** en témoignage de
tolerance [′talərəns] *s* tolérance *f*
tolerate [′talə,ret] *tr* tolérer
toll [tol] *s* (*of bells*) glas *m*; (*payment*) droit *m* de passage, péage *m*; (*number of victims*) mortalité *f*; (telp) tarif *m* ‖ *tr* tinter; (*to ring the knell for*) sonner le glas de ‖ *intr* sonner le glas
toll′ bridge′ *s* pont *m* à péage
toll′ call′ *s* appel *m* interurbain
toll′gate′ *s* barrière *f* à péage
toll′ road′ *s* autoroute *f* à péage
toma·to [tə′meto], [tə′mɑto] *s* (*pl* **-toes**) tomate *f*
tomb [tum] *s* tombeau *m*
tomboy [′tam,bɔɪ] *s* garçon *m* manqué
tomb′stone′ *s* pierre *f* tombale
tomcat [′tam,kæt] *s* matou *m*
tome [tom] *s* tome *m*
tomorrow [tu′mɔro] *adj*, *s*, & *adv* demain *m*; **tomorrow morning** demain matin; **until tomorrow** à demain
tom-tom [′tam,tam] *s* tam-tam *m*
ton [tʌn] *s* tonne *f*
tone [ton] *s* ton *m* ‖ *tr* accorder; **to tone down** atténuer; **to tone up** renforcer; (*e.g., the muscles*) tonifier ‖ *intr*—**to tone down** se modérer
tone′ po′em *s* poème *m* symphonique
tone′ tel′ephone *s* téléphone *m* à clavier
tongs [tɔŋz] *spl* pincettes *fpl*; (*e.g., for sugar*) pince *f*; (*of blacksmith*) tenailles *fpl*
tongue [tʌŋ] *s* (*language; part of body*) langue *f*; (*of wagon*) timon *m*; (*of buckle*) ardillon *m*; (*of shoe*) languette *f*; (*neck or narrow strip of land*) langue de terre; **to hold one's tongue** se mordre la langue
tongue-tied [′tʌŋ,taɪd] *adj* bouche cousue
tongue′ twist′er *s* phrase *f* à décrocher la mâchoire, casse-langue *m invar*
tonic [′tanɪk] *adj* & *s* tonique *m*
tonight [tu′naɪt] *adj* & *adv* ce soir
tonsil [′tansəl] *s* amygdale *f*
tonsillitis [,tansɪ′laɪtɪs] *s* amygdalite *f*
ton·y [′toni] *adj* (*comp* **-ier**; *super* **-iest**) (slang) élégant, chic
too [tu] *adv* (*also*) aussi; (*more than enough*) trop; (*moreover*) d'ailleurs; **I did too!** mais si!; **too bad!** c'est dommage!; **too many, too much** trop, trop de
tool [tul] *s* outil ‖ *tr* (*a piece of metal*) usiner; (*leather*) repousser; (bb) dorer ‖ *intr*—**to tool along** rouler; **to tool up** s'outiller
tool′box′ *s* trousse *f* à outils
tool′mak′er *s* taillandier *m*

toot [tut] *s* (*sound of tooting*) son *m* du cor; (*of auto*) coup *m* de klaxon; (*of locomotive*) coup de sifflet ‖ *tr* sonner ‖ *intr* corner; (aut) klaxonner
tooth [tuθ] *s* (*pl* **teeth** [tiθ]) dent *f*; **to grit, grind,** or **gnash the teeth** grincer des dents, crisser des dents
tooth′ache′ *s* mal *m* de dents
tooth′brush′ *s* brosse *f* à dents
toothless [′tuθlɪs] *adj* édenté
tooth′paste′ *s* pâte *f* dentifrice
tooth′pick′ *s* cure-dent *m*
tooth′ pow′der *s* poudre *f* dentifrice
top [tap] *adj* premier, de tête ‖ *s* sommet *m*, cime *f*, faîte *m*; (*of a barrel, table, etc.*) dessus *m*; (*of a page*) haut *m*; (*of a box*) couvercle *m*; (*of a carriage or auto*) capote *f*; (*toy*) toupie *f*; (naut) hune *f*; **at the top of** en haut de; (*e.g., one's class*) à la tête de; **at the top of one's voice** à tue-tête; **from top to bottom** de haut en bas, de fond en comble; **on top of** sur; (*in addition to*) en plus de; **tops** (*e.g., of carrots*) fanes *fpl*; **to sleep like a top** dormir comme un sabot ‖ *v* (*pret* & *pp* **topped;** *ger* **topping**) *tr* couronner, surmonter; (*to surpass*) dépasser; (*a tree, plant, etc.*) écimer
topaz [′topæz] *s* topaze *f*
top′ bill′ing *s* tête *f* d'affiche
top′coat′ *s* surtout *m* de demi-saison
toper [′topər] *s* soiffard *m*
top′ hat′ *s* haut-de-forme *m*
top′-heav′y *adj* trop lourd du haut
topic [′tapɪk] *s* sujet *m*
top′knot′ *s* chignon *m*
top′less swim′suit *s* monokini *m*
top′mast′ *s* mât *m* de hune
top′most′ *adj* (le) plus haut
top′notch′ *adj* (coll) d'élite
top′-of-the-line′ *adj* haut de gamme
topography [tə′pagrəfi] *s* (*pl* **-phies**) topographie *f*
topple [′tapəl] *tr* & *intr* culbuter
top′ prior′ity *s* priorité *f* absolue, priorité numéro un
topsail [′tapsəl], [′tap,sel] *s* (naut) hunier *m*
top′-se′cret *adj* ultra-secret
top′soil′ *s* couche *f* arable
topsy-turvy [′tapsɪ′tʌrvi] *adj* & *adv* sens dessus dessous
torch [tɔrtʃ] *s* torche *f*, flambeau *m*; (Brit) lampe *f* torche; **to carry the torch for** (slang) avoir un amour sans retour pour
torch′bear′er *s* porte-flambeau *m*; (fig) défenseur *m*
torch′light′ *s* lueur *f* des flambeaux
torch′light proces′sion *s* défilé *m* aux flambeaux
torch′ song′ *s* chanson *f* de l'amour non partagé
torment [′tɔrmɛnt] *s* tourment *m* ‖ [tɔr′mɛnt] *tr* tourmenter
torna·do [tɔr′nedo] *s* (*pl* **-does** or **-dos**) tornade *f*
torpe·do [tɔr′pido] *s* (*pl* **-does**) torpille *f* ‖ *tr* torpiller

torpe′do-boat destroy′er *s* contre-torpilleur *m*

torpid [′tɔrpɪd] *adj* engourdi

torque [tɔrk] *s* effort *m* de torsion, couple *m* de torsion

torrent [′tɔrənt] *s* torrent *m*

torrid [′tɔrɪd] *adj* torride

tor·so [′tɔrso] *s* (*pl* **-sos**) torse *m*

tort [tɔrt] *s* (law) acte *m* dommageable sauf rupture de contrat ou abus de confiance

tortoise [′tɔrtəs] *s* tortue *f*

tor′toise shell′ *s* écaille *f*

torture [′tɔrʃər] *s* torture *f* ‖ *tr* torturer

toss [tɔs] *s* (*throw*) lancement *m*; (*of the head*) mouvement *m* dédaigneux ‖ *tr* lancer; (*one's head*) relever dédaigneusement; (*a rider*) démonter; (*a coin*) jouer à pile et face avec; **to toss about** agiter, ballotter; **to toss off** (*e.g., work*) expédier; (*in one gulp*) lamper; **to toss up** jeter en l'air ‖ *intr* s'agiter; **to toss and turn** se tourner et retourner

toss′up′ *s* (*flip of a coin*) (coll) coup *m* de pile ou face; (*fifty-fifty chance*) (coll) chances *fpl* égales

tot [tɑt] *s* bambin *m*, tout petit *m* ‖ *v* (*pret & pp* **totted**; *ger* **totting**) *tr*—**to tot up** additionner

to·tal [′totəl] *adj & s* total *m*; **as a total** au total ‖ *v* (*pret & pp* **-taled** or **-talled**; *ger* **-taling** or **-talling**) *tr* additionner, totaliser; (*to amount to*) s'élever à

totalitarian [to,tælɪ′tɛrɪ·ən] *adj & mf* totalitaire

totem [′totəm] *s* totem *m*

totter [′tɑtər] *intr* chanceler

touch [tʌtʃ] *s* (*act*) attouchement *m*; (*e.g., of color; with a brush*) touche *f*; (*sense; of pianist*) toucher *m*; (*of typist*) frappe *f*; (*little bit*) pointe *f*, brin *m*; **in touch** en communication; **to get in touch with** prendre contact avec ‖ *tr* toucher; (*for a loan*) (slang) taper; **to touch off** déclencher; **to touch up** retoucher ‖ *intr* se toucher; **to touch on** toucher à

touched *adj* touché; (*crazy*) timbré

touching [′tʌtʃɪŋ] *adj* touchant, émouvant ‖ *prep* touchant, concernant

touch·y [′tʌtʃi] *adj* (*comp* **-ier**; *super* **-iest**) susceptible, irritable

tough [tʌf] *adj* dur, coriace; (*tenacious*) résistant; (*task*) difficile ‖ *s* voyou *m*

toughen [′tʌfən] *tr* endurcir ‖ *intr* s'endurcir

tough′ luck′ *s* déveine *f*

tour [tʊr] *s* tour *m*; (*e.g., of inspection*) tournée *f*; **on tour** en tournée ‖ *tr* faire le tour de; (*e.g., a country*) voyager en; (theat) faire une tournée de, en, or dans ‖ *intr* voyager

tour′ing car′ *s* voiture *f* de tourisme

tourist [′tʊrɪst] *adj & s* touriste *mf*

tour′ist in′dustry *s* tourisme *m*

tournament [′tʊrnəmənt], [′tʌrnəmənt] *s* tournoi *m*

tourney [′tʊrni] *s* tournoi *m* ‖ *intr* tournoyer

tourniquet [′tʊrnɪˌkɛt] *s* (surg) garrot *m*, tourniquet *m*

tousle [′tauzəl] *tr* (*to dishevel*) ébouriffer; (*to handle roughly*) tirailler, maltraiter

tow [to] *s* (*towing*) remorque *f*; (*e.g., of hemp*) filasse *f*; **to take in tow** prendre en remorque; (fig) se charger de ‖ *tr* remorquer

towage [′to·ɪdʒ] *s* remorquage *m*; (*fee*) droits *mpl* de remorquage

toward(s) [tord(z)], [tə′wɔrd(z)] *prep* vers; (*in regard to*) envers

tow′boat′ *s* remorqueur *m*

tow·el [′tau·əl] *s* serviette *f*, essuie-main *m* ‖ *v* (*pret & pp* **-eled** or **-elled**; *ger* **-eling** or **elling**) *tr* essuyer avec une serviette

tow′el rack′ *s* porte-serviettes *m*

tower [′tau·ər] *s* tour *f* ‖ *intr* s'élever

towering [′tau·ərɪŋ] *adj* élevé, géant; (*e.g , ambition*) sans bornes

tow′er·man *s* (*pl* **-men**) (aer, rr) aiguilleur *m*

tow′ing serv′ice [′to·ɪŋ] *s* service *m* de dépannage

tow′line′ *s* câble *m* de remorque

town [taʊn] *s* ville *f*; **in town** en ville

town′ clerk′ *s* secrétaire *m* de mairie

town′ coun′cil *s* conseil *m* municipal

town′ cri′er *s* crieur *m* public

town′ hall′ *s* hôtel *m* de ville

town′ plan′ning *s* urbanisme *m*

towns′folk′ *spl* citadins *mpl*

town′ship *s* commune *f*; (U.S.A.) circonscription *f* administrative de six milles carrée

towns′man [′taʊnzmən] *s* (*pl* **-men**) citadin *m*

towns′peo′ple *spl* citadins *mpl*

town′ talk′ *s* sujet *m* du jour

tow′path′ *s* chemin *m* de halage

tow′rope′ *s* corde *f* de remorque

tow′ truck′ *s* dépanneuse *f*, voiture *f* de dépannage, camion *m* de remorquage

toxic [′tɑksɪk] *adj & s* toxique *m*

toy [tɔɪ] *adj* (*small*) petit; (*child's*) d'enfant ‖ *s* jouet *m*; (*trifle*) bagatelle *f* ‖ *intr* jouer, s'amuser; **to toy with** (*a person*) badiner avec; (*an idea*) caresser

toy′ dog′ *s* chien *m* de manchon

toy′ sol′dier *s* soldat *m* de plomb

trace [tres] *s* trace *f*; (*of harness*) trait *m* ‖ *tr* tracer; (*the whereabouts of s.o. or s.th.*) pister; (*e.g., an influence*) retrouver les traces de; (*a design seen through thin paper*) calquer; **to trace back** remonter jusqu'à l'origine de

trace′ el′ement *s* oligo-élément *m*

tracer [′tresər] *s* traceur *m*

trac′er bul′let *s* balle *f* traçante

trache·a [′trekɪ·ə] *s* (*pl* **-ae** [ˌi]) trachée *f*

tracing [′tresɪŋ] *s* tracé *m*

trac′ing tape′ *s* cordeau *m*

track [træk] *s* (*of foot or vehicle*) trace *f*; (*of an animal; in a stadium*) piste *f*; (*of a boat*) sillage *m*; (*of a railroad*) voie *f*; (*of an airplane, or a hurricane*) trajet *m*; (*of a tractor*) chenille *f*; (*course followed*) chemin *m* tracé; (sports) la course et le saut de barrières; (sports) athlétisme *m*; **off the beaten track** hors des sentiers battus; **on the right track** sur la bonne voie; **to be on the wrong track** faire fausse route; **to have an inside track** tenir la corde; **to keep track of** ne pas perdre de vue; **to make tracks** (coll) filer ‖ *tr* traquer; laisser des traces de pas dans; **to track down** dépister

tracking [ˈtrækɪŋ] *s* pistage *m*; (*of spaceship*) repérage *m*; (aer) poursuite *f*

track′ing sta′tion *s* poste *m* de repérage

track′less trol′ley *s* trolleybus *m*

track′ meet′ *s* concours *m* de courses et de sauts, épreuve *f* d'athlétisme

track′walk′er *s* garde-voie *m*

tract [trækt] *s* (*of land*) étendue *f*; (*leaflet*) tract *m*; (anat) voie *f*

traction [ˈtrækʃən] *s* traction *f*

trac′tion com′pany *s* entreprise *f* de transports urbains

tractor [ˈtræktər] *s* tracteur *m*

trade [tred] *s* (*business*) commerce *m*, négoce *m*; (*customers*) clientèle *f*; (*calling, job*) métier *m*; (*exchange*) échange *m*; (*in slaves*) traite *f*; **to take in trade** reprendre en compte ‖ *tr* échanger; **to trade in** (*e.g., a used car*) donner en reprise ‖ *intr* commercer; **to trade in** faire le commerce de; **to trade on** exploiter

trade′-in′ *s* reprise *f*

trade′mark′ *s* marque *f* déposée

trade′ name′ *s* raison *f* sociale

trader [ˈtredər] *s* commerçant *m*

trade′ school′ *s* école *f* des arts et métiers

trade′ show′ *s* exposition *f* interprofessionnelle

trades′man *s* (*pl* -men) commerçant *m*; (*shopkeeper*) boutiquier *m*; (Brit) artisan *m*

trades′ un′ion or **trade′ un′ion** *s* syndicat *m* ouvrier

trade′ winds′ *spl* vents *mpl* alizés

trad′ing post′ [ˈtredɪŋ] *s* factorerie *f*

trad′ing stamp′ *s* timbre-prime *m*

tradition [trəˈdɪʃən] *s* tradition *f*

traditional [trəˈdɪʃənəl] *adj* traditionnel

traf·fic [ˈtræfɪk] *s* (*commerce*) négoce *m*; (*in the street*) circulation *f*; (*illegal*) trafic *m*; (*in, e.g, slaves*) traite *f*; (naut, rr) trafic ‖ *v* (*pret & pp* **-ficked**; *ger* **-ficking**) *intr* trafiquer

traf′fic cir′cle *s* rond-point *m*

traf′fic cop′ *s* agent *m* de la circulation

traf′fic court′ *s* tribunal *m* de simple police (pour les contraventions au code de la route)

traf′fic jam′ *s* embouteillage *m*

traf′fic light′ *s* feu *m* de circulation

traf′fic sign′ *s* panneau *m* de signalisation, poteau *m* indicateur

traf′fic sig′nal *s* signal *m* routier

traf′fic tick′et *s* contravention *f*

traf′fic vi′olator *s* contrevenant *m*

tragedian [trəˈdʒidɪ·ən] *s* tragédien *m*

trage·dy [ˈtrædʒɪdi] *s* (*pl* -dies) tragédie *f*

tragic [ˈtrædʒɪk] *adj* tragique

trail [trel] *s* trace *f*, piste *f*; (*e.g., of smoke*) traînée *f* ‖ *tr* traîner; (*to look for*) pister ‖ *intr* traîner; (*said of a plant*) grimper; **to trail off** se perdre

trailer [ˈtrelər] *s* remorque *f*; (*for vacationing*) remorque de plaisance, caravane *f*; (mov) film-annonce *m*

trail′er court′ *s* camp *m* pour caravanes

trail′er home′ *s* caravane *f*

train [tren] *s* (*of railway cars*) train *m*; (*of dress*) traîne *f*; (*of thought*) enchaînement *m*; (*streak*) traînée *f* ‖ *tr* entraîner, former; (*plants*) palisser; (*a gun; a telescope*) pointer ‖ *intr* s'entraîner

train′ crew′ *s* (rr) personnel de route

trained′ an′imals *spl* animaux *mpl* savants

trained′ nurse′ *s* infirmière *f* diplômée

trainee [treˈni] *s* stagiaire *mf*, apprenti *m*

trainer [ˈtrenər] *s* (*of animals*) dresseur *m*; (sports) entraîneur *m*

training [ˈtrenɪŋ] *s* entraînement *m*, formation *f*, instruction *f*; (*of animals*) dressage *m*

train′ing school′ *s* école *f* technique; (*reformatory*) maison *f* de correction

train′ing ship′ *s* navire-école *m*

trait [tret] *s* trait *m*

traitor [ˈtretər] *s* traître *m*

traitress [ˈtretrɪs] *s* traîtresse *f*

trajecto·ry [trəˈdʒɛktəri] *s* (*pl* -ries) trajectoire *f*

tramp [træmp] *s* (*hobo*) vagabond *m*; (*sound of steps*) bruit *m* de pas lourds ‖ *tr* parcourir à pied; (*the street*) battre ‖ *intr* vagabonder; marcher lourdement; **to tramp on** marcher sur

trample [ˈtræmpəl] *tr* fouler, piétiner ‖ *intr*—**to trample on** or **upon** fouler, piétiner

trampoline [ˈtræmpə,lin] *s* tremplin *m* de gymnase

tramp′ steam′er *s* tramp *m*

trance [træns] *s* transe *f*; **in a trance** en transe

tranquil [ˈtræŋkwɪl] *adj* tranquille

tranquilize [ˈtræŋkwɪ,laɪz] *tr* tranquilliser

tranquilizer [ˈtræŋkwɪ,laɪzər] *s* tranquillisant *m*

tranquillity [trænˈkwɪlɪti] *s* tranquillité *f*

transact [trænˈzækt] *tr* traiter, négocier ‖ *intr* faire des affaires

transaction [trænˈzækʃən] *s* transaction *f*; (*of business*) conduite *f*; **transactions** (*of a society*) actes *mpl*

transatlantic [,trænsətˈlæntɪk] *adj & s* transatlantique *m*

transcend [trænˈsɛnd] *tr* transcender ‖ *intr* se transcender

transcribe [trænˈskraɪb] *tr* transcrire

transcript [ˈtrænskrɪpt] *s* copie *f*; (*of a meeting*) procès-verbal *m*; (educ) livret *m* scolaire

transcription [trænˈskrɪpʃən] *s* transcription *f*

transept [ˈtrænsɛpt] *s* transept *m*

trans·fer [ˈtrænsfər] *s* (*e.g., of stock, property, etc.*) transfert *m*; (*from one place to the other*) translation *f*; (*from one job to* the *other*) mutation *f*; (*of a design*) décalque *m*; (*for bus or subway*) billet *m* de correspondance; (public sign) correspondance ‖ [træns'fʌr], ['trænsfər] *v* (*pret & pp* **-ferred**; *ger* **-ferring**) *tr* transférer; transporter; (*e.g.*, *a civil servant*) déplacer; (*a design*) décalquer ‖ *intr* se déplacer; changer de train (de l'autobus, etc.)

transfix [træns'fɪks] *tr* transpercer

transform [træns'fɔrm] *tr* transformer ‖ *intr* se transformer

transformer [træns'fɔrmər] *s* transformateur *m*

transfusion [træns'fjuʒən] *s* transfusion *f*

transgress [træns'grɛs] *tr & intr* transgresser

transgression [træns'grɛʃən] *s* transgression *f*

transient ['trænʃənt] *adj* transitoire, passager; (*e.g.*, *guest*) de passage ‖ *s* hôte *mf* de passage

transistor [træn'sɪstər] *s* transistor *m*

transistorize [træn'zɪstə,raɪz] *tr* transistoriser

transistorized *adj* transistorisé, à transistors

transit ['trænsɪt], ['trænzɪt] *s* transit *m*

transition [træn'zɪʃən] *s* transition *f*

transitional [træn'zɪʃənəl] *adj* transitoire, de transition

transitive ['trænsɪtɪv] *adj* transitif ‖ *s* verbe *m* transitif

transitory ['trænsɪ,tori] *adj* transitoire

translate ['trænslet] *tr* traduire

translation [træns'leʃən] *s* traduction *f*; (*transfer*) translation *f*

translator [træns'letər] *s* traducteur *m*

transliterate [træns'lɪtə,ret] *tr* translitérer

translucent [træns'lusənt] *adj* translucide, diaphane

transmission [træns'mɪʃən] *s* transmission *f*; (*gear change*) changement *m* de vitesse; (*housing for gears*) boîte *f* de vitesses

transmis'sion-gear' box' *s* boîte *f* de vitesses

trans·mit [træns'mɪt] *v* (*pret & pp* **-mitted**; *ger* **-mitting**) *tr & intr* transmettre; (rad) émettre

transmitter [træns'mɪtər] *s* (telg, telp) transmetteur *m*; (rad) émetteur *m*

transmit'ting sta'tion *s* poste *m* émetteur

transmute [træns'mjut] *tr* transmuer

transom ['trænsəm] *s* (*crosspiece*) linteau *m*; (*window over door*) imposte *f*, vasistas *m*; (*of ship*) barre *f* d'arcasse

transparen·cy [træns'pɛrənsi] *s* (*pl* **-cies**) transparence *f*; (phot) diapositive *f*

transparent [træns'pɛrənt] *adj* transparent

transpire [træns'paɪr] *intr* se passer; (*to leak out*) transpirer

transplant ['træns,plænt] *s* (*organ or tissue*) greffon *m*; (*operation*) greffe *f* ‖ [træns'plænt] *tr* transplanter; (*e.g.*, *a heart*) greffer

transport ['trænsport] *s* transport *m* ‖ [træns'port] *tr* transporter

transportation [,trænspor'teʃən] *s* transport *m*; billet *m* de train, de bateau, or d'avion; (*deportation*) transportation *f*

transport'er bridge' [træns'portər] *s* transbordeur *m*

trans'port work'er *s* employé *m* des entreprises de transport

transpose [træns'poz] *tr* transposer

trans·ship [træns'ʃɪp] *v* (*pret & pp* **-shipped**; *ger* **-shipping**) *tr* transborder

transshipment [træns'ʃɪpmənt] *s* transbordement *m*

transvestism [træns'vɛstɪzəm] *s* travestisme *m*

transvestite [træns'vɛstaɪt] *s* travesti *m*, travestie *f*

trap [træp] *s* piège *m*; (*pitfall*) trappe *f*; (*double-curved pipe*) siphon *m*; **traps** (mus) batterie *f* de jazz ‖ *v* (*pret & pp* **trapped**; *ger* **trapping**) *tr* prendre au piège, attraper

trap' door' *s* trappe *f*

trapeze [trə'piz] *s* trapèze *m*

trapezoid ['træpɪ,zɔɪd] *s* trapèze *m*

trapper ['træpər] *s* trappeur *m*

trappings ['træpɪŋz] *spl* (*adornments*) atours *mpl*; (*of horse's harness*) harnachement *m*

trap'shoot'ing *s* tir *m* au pigeon

trash [træʃ] *s* déchets *mpl*, rebuts *mpl*; (*junk*) camelote *f*; (*nonsense*) ineptie *f*; (*worthless people*) racaille *f*

trash' bag' *s* sac *m* poubelle

trash' can' *s* poubelle *f*

travail [trə'vel] *s* labeur *m*; douleur *f* de l'enfantement

trav·el ['trævəl] *s* voyages *mpl*; (mach) course *f* ‖ *v* (*pret & pp* **-eled** or **-elled**; *ger* **-eling** or **-elling**) *tr* parcourir ‖ *intr* voyager; (mach) se déplacer

trav'el bur'eau *s* agence *f* de voyages

traveler ['trævələr] *s* voyageur *m*

trav'eler's check' *s* chèque *m* de voyage

trav'eling bag' *s* sac *m* de voyage

trav'eling expen'ses *spl* frais *mpl* de voyage

trav'eling sales'man *s* (*pl* **-men**) commis *m* voyageur

traverse [trə'vʌrs] *tr* parcourir, traverser

traves·ty ['trævɪsti] *s* (*pl* **-ties**) *s* travestissement *m* ‖ *v* (*pret & pp* **-tied**) *tr* travestir

trawl [trɔl] *s* chalut *m* ‖ *tr* traîner ‖ *intr* pêcher au chalut

trawler ['trɔlər] *s* chalutier *m*

tray [tre] *s* plateau *m*; (*of refrigerator*) bac *f*; (chem, phot) cuvette *f*

treacherous ['trɛtʃərəs] *adj* traître

treacher·y ['trɛtʃəri] *s* (*pl* **-ies**) trahison *f*

tread [trɛd] *s* (*step; sound of steps*) pas *m*; (*gait*) allure *f*; (*of stairs*) giron *m*; (*of tire*) chape *f*; (*of shoe*) semelle *f*; (*of egg*) cicatricule *f* ‖ *v* (*pret* **trod** [trɑd]; *pp* **trodden** ['trɑdən] or **trod**) *tr* marcher sur, piétiner ‖ *intr* marcher

treadle ['trɛdəl] *s* pédale *f*

tread'mill' *s* trépigneuse *f*; (*futile drudgery*) besogne *f* ingrate

treason ['trizən] *s* trahison *f*

treasonable ['trizənəbəl] *adj* traître

treasure ['trɛʒər] *s* trésor *m* ‖ *tr* garder soigneusement; *(to prize)* tenir beaucoup à

treasurer ['trɛʒərər] *s* trésorier *m*

treasur·y ['trɛʒəri] *s (pl* **-ies)** trésorerie *f*; trésor *m*

treat [trit] *s* régal *m*, plaisir *m* ‖ *tr* traiter; régaler; *(to a drink)* payer à boire à; **to treat everyone to a round of drinks** offrir la tournée générale ‖ *intr* traiter

treatise ['tritɪs] *s* traité *m*

treatment ['tritmənt] *s* traitement *m*

trea·ty ['triti] *s (pl* **-ies)** traité *m*

treble ['trɛbəl] *adj (threefold)* triple; *(mus)* de soprano ‖ *s* soprano *mf*; *(voice)* soprano *m* ‖ *tr & intr* tripler

tre′ble clef′ [klɛf] *s* clef *f* de sol

tree [tri] *s* arbre *m*

tree′ farm′ *s* taillis *m*

treeless ['trilɪs] *adj* sans arbres

tree′top′ *s* cime *f* d'un arbre

trellis ['trɛlɪs] *s* treillis *m*, treillage *m*; *(summerhouse)* tonnelle *f* ‖ *tr* treillager

tremble ['trɛmbəl] *s* tremblement *m* ‖ *intr* trembler

tremendous [trɪ'mɛndəs] *adj* terrible; (coll) formidable

tremolo ['trɛmə,lo] *s* trémolo *m*

tremor ['trɛmər] *s* tremblement *m*

trench [trɛntʃ] *s* tranché *f*

trenchant ['trɛntʃənt] *adj* tranchant

trench′ mor′tar *s* lance-bombes *m*

trend [trɛnd] *s* tendance *f*, cours *m*

trendy ['trɛndi] *adj* dernier cri, dans le vent, à la dernière mode

trespass ['trɛspəs] *s (illegal entry)* entrée *f* sans permission; (rel) offense *f* ‖ *intr* entrer sans permission; **no trespassing** *(public sign)* défense d'entrer; **to trespass against** offenser; **to trespass on** empiéter sur; *(s.o.'s patience)* abuser de

trespasser ['trɛspəsər] *s* intrus *m*

tress [trɛs] *s* tresse *f*; **tresses** chevelure *f*

trestle ['trɛsəl] *s* tréteau *m*; *(bridge)* pont *m* en treillis

trial ['traɪ·əl] *s* essai *m*; *(difficulty)* épreuve *f*; (law) procès *m*; **on trial** à titre d'essai; (law) en jugement; **to bring to trial** faire passer en jugement

tri′al and er′ror *s*—**by trial and error** par tâtonnements

tri′al balloon′ *s* ballon *m* d'essai

tri′al by jur′y *s* jugement *m* par jury

tri′al ju′ry *s* jury *m* de jugement

tri′al or′der *s* commande *f* d'essai

tri′al run′ *s* course *f* d'essai

triangle ['traɪ,æŋgəl] *s* triangle *m*

tribe [traɪb] *s* tribu *f*

tribunal [trɪ'bjunəl] *s* tribunal *m*

tribune ['trɪbjun] *s* tribune *f*

tributar·y ['trɪbjə,tɛri] *adj* tributaire ‖ *s (pl* **-ies)** tributaire *m*

tribute ['trɪbjut] *s (homage; payment)* tribut *m*; **to pay tribute to** *(e.g., merit)* rendre hommage à

trice [traɪs] *s*—**in a trice** en un clin d'œil

trichinosis [,trɪkə'nosɪs] *s* (pathol) trichinose *f*

trick [trɪk] *s (prank, joke)* tour *m*, farce *f*, blague *f*; *(artifice)* ruse *f*; *(cards in one round)* levée *f*; *(habit)* manie *f*; *(girl)* (coll) belle *f*; **to be up to one's old tricks again** faire encore des siennes; **to play a dirty trick on** faire un vilain tour à, faire un tour de cochon à; **tricks of the trade** trucs *mpl* du métier ‖ *tr* duper

tricker·y ['trɪkəri] *s (pl* **-ies)** tromperie *f*

trickle ['trɪkəl] *s* filet *m* ‖ *intr* dégoutter

trickster ['trɪkstər] *s* fourbe *mf*

trick·y ['trɪki] *adj (comp* **-ier;** *super* **-iest)** rusé; *(difficult)* compliqué, délicat

tricolor ['traɪ,kʌlər] *adj & s* tricolore *m*

tried [traɪd] *adj* loyal, éprouvé

trifle ['traɪfəl] *s* bagatelle *f*; *(article of little value)* bricole *f* ‖ *tr*—**to trifle away** gaspiller ‖ *intr* badiner

trifling ['traɪflɪŋ] *adj* frivole; insignifiant

trifocals [traɪ'fokəlz] *spl* lunettes *fpl* à trois foyers

trigger ['trɪgər] *s (of gun)* détente *f*; *(of any device)* déclencheur *m*; **to pull the trigger** appuyer sur la détente ‖ *tr* déclencher

trig′ger-hap′py *adj*—**to be trigger-happy** (coll) avoir la gâchette facile

trigonometry [,trɪgə'namɪtri] *s* trigonométrie *f*

trill [trɪl] *s* trille *m* ‖ *tr & intr* triller

trillion ['trɪljən] *s* (U.S.A.) billion *m*; (Brit) trillion *m*

trilo·gy ['trɪlədʒi] *s (pl* **-gies)** trilogie *f*

trim [trɪm] *adj (comp* **trimmer;** *super* **trimmest)** ordonné, coquet ‖ *s (condition)* état *m*; *(adornment)* ornement *m*; *(of sails)* orientation *f*; *(around doors and windows)* moulures *fpl*; **in good trim** (sports) en bonne forme ‖ *v (pret & pp* **trimmed;** *ger* **trimming)** *tr* enguirlander; *(a Christmas tree)* orner; *(hat, dress, etc.)* garnir; *(the hair)* rafraîchir; *(a candle or lamp)* moucher; *(trees, plants)* tailler; *(the edges of a book)* rogner; *(the sails)* orienter; (coll) battre

trimming ['trɪmɪŋ] *s (of clothes, hat, etc.)* garniture *f*; *(of hedges)* taille *f*; *(of sails)* orientation *f*; **to get a trimming** (coll) essuyer une défaite

trini·ty ['trɪnɪti] *s (pl* **-ties)** trinité *f*; **Trinity** Trinité

trinket ['trɪŋkɪt] *s* colifichet *m*; *(trifle)* babiole *f*

tri·o ['tri·o] *s (pl* **-os)** trio *m*

trip [trɪp] *s (journey)* voyage *m*; *(distance covered)* trajet *m*, parcours *m*; *(stumble; blunder)* faux pas *m*; *(act of causing a person to stumble)* croc-en-jambe *m*; *(on drugs)* (slang) trip *m*, défonce *f* ‖ *v (pret & pp* **tripped;** *ger* **tripping)** *tr* faire trébucher; **to trip up** donner un croc-en-jambe à; prendre en défaut ‖ *intr* trébucher

tripartite [traɪ'partaɪt] *adj* tripartite

tripe [traɪp] *s* tripe *f*; (slang) fatras *m*

trip′ham′mer *s* marteau *m* à bascule

triple ['trɪpəl] *adj & s* triple *m* ‖ *tr & intr* tripler

triplet ['trɪplɪt] *s* (*offspring*) triplet *m*; (*stanza*) tercet *m*; (*mus*) triolet *m*; **triplets** (*offspring*) triplés *mpl*

triplicate ['trɪplɪkɪt] *adj* triple ‖ *s* triplicata *m*; **in triplicate** en trois exemplaires

tripod ['traɪpod] *s* trépied *m*

triptych ['trɪptɪk] *s* triptyque *m*

trite [traɪt] *adj* banal, rebattu

triumph ['traɪ·əmf] *s* triomphe *m* ‖ *intr* triompher; **to triumph over** triompher de

trium′phal arch′ [traɪ′ʌmfəl] *s* arc *m* de triomphe

triumphant [traɪ′ʌmfənt] *adj* triomphant

trivia ['trɪvɪ·ə] *spl* vétilles *fpl*

trivial ['trɪvɪ·əl] *adj* trivial, insignifiant

triviali‧ty [‚trɪvɪ′ælɪti] *s* (*pl* **-ties**) trivialité *f*, insignifiance *f*

Trojan ['trodʒən] *adj* troyen ‖ *s* Troyen *m*

Tro′jan Horse′ *s* cheval *m* de Troie

Tro′jan war′ *s* guerre *f* de Troie

troll [trol] *tr & intr* pêcher à la cuiller

trolley ['trali] *s* trolley *m*; (*streetcar*) tramway *m*

trol′ley car′ *s* tramway *m*

trol′ley pole′ *s* perche *f*

trolling ['trolɪŋ] *s* pêche *f* à la cuiller

trollop ['traləp] *s* souillon *f*; (*prostitute*) traînée *f*

trombone ['trambon] *s* trombone *m*

troop [trup] *s* troupe *f*; **troops** (mil) troupes *fpl* ‖ *tr* (*the colors*) présenter ‖ *intr* s'attrouper

trooper ['trupər] *s* membre *m* de la police montée; (*state trooper*) agent *m* de police; (mil) soldat *m* de cavalerie; **to swear like a trooper** jurer comme un charretier

tro‧phy ['trofi] *s* (*pl* **-phies**) trophée *m*; (sports) coupe *f*

tropic ['trapɪk] *adj & s* tropique *m*; **tropics** tropiques, zone *f* tropicale

tropical ['trapɪkəl] *adj* tropical

trot [trat] *s* trot *m* ‖ *v* (*pret & pp* **trotted**; *ger* **trotting**) *tr* faire trotter; **to trot out** (slang) exhiber ‖ *intr* trotter

troth [troθ] *s* foi *f*; **in troth** en vérité; **to plight one's troth** promettre fidélité; donner sa promesse de mariage

trouble ['trʌbəl] *s* (*unpleasantness*) ennuis *mpl*, dérangement *m*; (*problem*) difficulté *f*, problème *m*; (*bother, effort*) mal *m*, peine *f*; (*social unrest*) troubles *mpl*; **that's not worth the trouble** cela ne vaut pas la peine; **that's the trouble** voilà le hic; **the trouble is that . . .** la difficulté c'est que . . . ; **to be in trouble** avoir des ennuis; (*said of a woman*) (coll) faire Pâques avant les Rameaux; **to be looking for trouble** chercher querelle; **to get into trouble** se créer des ennuis, s'attirer une mauvaise affaire; **to take the trouble to** se donner la peine de; **with very little trouble** à peu de frais ‖ *tr* (*to disturb*) déranger; (*to grieve*) affliger; **to be troubled about** se tourmenter au sujet de; **to trouble oneself** s'inquiéter ‖ *intr* se dé-

ranger; **to trouble to** se donner la peine de

trou′ble light′ *s* lampe *f* de secours

trou′ble‧mak′er *s* fomentateur *m*, perturbateur *m*

troubleshooter ['trʌbəl‚ʃutər] *s* dépanneur *m*; (*in disputes*) arbitre *m*

trou′ble‧shoot′ing *s* dépannage *m*; (*of disputes*) composition *f*, arbitrage *m*

troublesome ['trʌbəlsəm] *adj* ennuyeux

trou′ble spot′ *s* foyer *m* de conflit

trough [trɔf] *s* (*e.g., to knead bread*) pétrin *m*; (*for water for animals*) abreuvoir *m*; (*for feeding animals*) auge *f*; (*under the eaves*) chéneau *m*; (*between two waves*) creux *m*

troupe [trup] *s* troupe *f*

trouper ['trupər] *s* membre *m* de la troupe; vieil acteur *m*; vieux routier *m*

trousers ['trauzərz] *spl* pantalon *m*

trous‧seau [tru′so], ['truso] *s* (*pl* **-seaux** or **-seaus**) trousseau *m*

trout [traut] *s* truite *f*

trowel ['trau·əl] *s* truelle *f*; (*for gardening*) déplantoir *m*

Troy [trɔɪ] *s* Troie *f*

truant ['tru·ənt] *adj* —**to play truant** faire l'école buissonnière

truce [trus] *s* trêve *f*

truck [trʌk] *s* camion *m*, poids *m* lourd; (*for baggage*) diable *m*; (*vegetables*) produits *mpl* maraîchers; **to have no truck with** (coll) refuser d'avoir affaire à ‖ *tr* camionner

truck′driv′er *s* camionneur *m*

truck′ farm′ing *s* culture *f* maraîchère

truck′ gar′den *s* jardin *m* maraîcher

trucking ['trʌkɪŋ] *s* camionnage *m*

truculent ['trʌkjələnt] *adj* truculent

trudge [trʌdʒ] *intr* cheminer

true [tru] *adj* vrai; loyal; (*exact*) juste; (*copy*) conforme; **to come true** se réaliser ‖ *tr* rectifier, dégauchir

true′ cop′y *s* (*pl* **-ies**) copie *f* conforme

true′-heart′ed *adj* au cœur sincère

true′love *s* bien-aimé *m*

truffle ['trʌfəl] *s* truffe *f*

truism ['tru·ɪzm] *s* truisme *m*

truly ['truli] *adv* vraiment; sincèrement; **yours truly** (complimentary close) veuillez agréer, Monsieur (Madame, etc.), l'assurance de mes sentiments distingués

trump [trʌmp] *s* atout *m*; brave garçon *m*, brave fille *f*; **no trump** sans atout ‖ *tr* couper; **to trump up** inventer ‖ *intr* couper

trumpet ['trʌmpɪt] *s* trompette *f* ‖ *tr & intr* trompeter

trumpeter ['trʌmpətər] *s* trompette *m*

truncheon ['trʌntʃən] *s* matraque *f*; (*of policeman*) bâton *m*

trunk [trʌŋk] *s* (*chest for clothes*) malle *f*; (*of elephant*) trompe *f*; (anat, bot) tronc *m*; (aut) coffre *m*; **trunks** slip *m*

truss [trʌs] *s* (*framework*) armature *f*; (med) bandage *m* herniaire ‖ *tr* armer; (culin) trousser

trust [trʌst] s confiance f; (hope) espoir m; (duty) charge f; (safekeeping) dépôt m; (com) trust m, cartel m ‖ tr se fier à; (to entrust) confier; (com) faire crédit à ‖ intr espérer; **to trust in** avoir confiance en
trust′ com′pany s crédit m, société f de banque
trustee [trʌs′ti] s administrateur m; (of a university) régent m; (of an estate) fidéi-commissaire mf
trusteeship [trʌs′tiʃɪp] s tutelle f
trustful [′trʌstfəl] adj confiant
trust′wor′thy adj digne de confiance
trust·y [′trʌsti] adj (comp -ier; super -iest) sûr, loyal ‖ s (pl -ies) forçat m bien noté
truth [truθ] s vérité f; **in truth** en vérité
truthful [′truθfəl] adj véridique
try [traɪ] s (pl tries) essai m ‖ v (pret & pp tried) tr mettre à l'épreuve; (law) juger; **to try on** or **out** essayer ‖ intr essayer; **to try to** essayer de
trying [′traɪ·ɪŋ] adj pénible
tryst [trɪst], [traɪst] s rendez-vous m
T′-shirt′ s gilet m de peau avec manches
tub [tʌb] s cuvier m, baquet m; (clumsy boat) (coll) rafiot m
tube [t(j)ub] s tube m; (aut) chambre f à air; (subway) (Brit) métro m
tuber [′t(j)ubər] s tubercule m
tubercle [′t(j)ubərkəl] s tubercule m
tuberculosis [t(j)u,bʌrkjə′losɪs] s tuberculose f
tuck [tʌk] s pli m, rempli m ‖ tr plisser; remplier; **to tuck away** reléguer; **to tuck in** rentrer; **to tuck in bed** border; **to tuck up** retrousser
tucker [′tʌkər] tr—**to tucker out** (coll) fatiguer
Tuesday [′t(j)uzdi] s mardi m
tuft [tʌft] s touffe f ‖ tr garnir de touffes ‖ intr former une touffe
tug [tʌg] s tiraillement m, effort m; (boat) remorqueur m ‖ v (pret & pp tugged; ger tugging) tr tirer fort; (a boat) remorquer ‖ intr tirer fort
tug′boat′ s remorqueur m
tug′ of war′ s lutte f à la corde (de traction)
tuition [t(j)u′ɪʃən] s enseignement m; (fees) frais mpl de scolarité
tulip [′t(j)ulɪp] s tulipe f
tumble [′tʌmbəl] s chute f; (sports) culbute f ‖ tr culbuter ‖ intr tomber, culbuter; (sports) faire des culbutes; (to catch on) (slang) comprendre; **to tumble down** dégringoler
tum′ble·down′ adj croulant, délabré
tumbler [′tʌmblər] s gobelet m, verre m; acrobate m; (self-righting toy) poussah m, ramponneau m
tummy [′tʌmi] s (coll) bide f
tumor [′t(j)umər] s tumeur f
tumult [′t(j)umʌlt] s tumulte m
tun [tʌn] s tonne f
tuna [′tunə] s thon m
tune [t(j)un] s air m; (manner of acting or speaking) ton m; **in tune** (mus) accordé; (rad) en syntonie; **out of tune** (mus) dés-

accordé; **to change one's tune** (coll) changer de disque ‖ tr accorder; (a radio or television set) régler; **to tune in** (rad) syntoniser; **to tune up** régler
tungsten [′tʌŋstən] s tungstène m
tunic [′t(j)unɪk] s tunique f
tuning [′t(j)unɪŋ] s réglage m; (rad) syntonisation f
tun′ing coil′ s bobine f de syntonisation
tun′ing fork′ s diapason m
tun·nel [′tʌnəl] s tunnel m; (min) galerie f ‖ v (pret & pp -neled or nelled; ger -neling or -nelling) tr percer un tunnel dans or sous
turban [′tʌrbən] s turban m
turbid [′tʌrbɪd] adj trouble
turbine [′tʌrbɪn] s turbine f
turbojet [′tʌrbo,dʒet] s turboréacteur m; avion m à turboréacteur
turboprop [′tʌrbo,prɑp] s turbopropulseur m; avion m à turbopropulseur
turbosupercharger [′tʌrbo′supər′tʃɑrdʒər] s turbocompresseur m de suralimentation
turbulent [′tʌrbjələnt] adj turbulent
tureen [t(j)u′rin] s soupière f
turf [tʌrf] s gazon m; (sod) motte f de gazon; (peat) tourbe f; **the turf** le turf
turf′man s (pl -men) turfiste mf
Turk [tʌrk] s Turc m
turkey [′tʌrki] s dindon m; (culin) dinde f; (flop) (slang) four m; **Turkey** Turquie f, la Turquie
tur′key vul′ture s urubu m
Turkish [′tʌrkɪʃ] adj & s turc m
Turk′ish delight′ s loukoum m
Turk′ish tow′el s serviette f éponge
turmoil [′tʌrmɔɪl] s agitation f
turn [tʌrn] s tour m; (change of direction) virage m; (bend) tournant m; (of events, of an expression) tournure f; (in a wire) spire f; (coll) coup m, choc m; **at every turn** à tout propos; **by turns** tour à tour; **in turn** à tour de rôle; **to a turn** (culin) à point; **to do a good turn** rendre un service; **to take turns** alterner; **to wait one's turn** prendre son tour; **whose turn is it?** à qui le tour? ‖ tr tourner; **to turn about** or **around** retourner; **to turn aside** or **away** détourner; **to turn back** renvoyer; (an attack) repousser; (a clock) retarder; **to turn down** (a collar) rabattre; (e.g., the gas) baisser; (an offer) refuser; **to turn from** détourner de; **to turn in** replier; (a wrong-doer) dénoncer; **to turn into** changer en; **to turn off** (the water, the gas, etc.) fermer; (the light, the radio, etc.) éteindre; (a road) quitter; **to turn on** (the water, the gas, etc.) ouvrir; (the light, the radio, the gas, etc.) allumer; **to turn out** mettre dehors; (to manufacture) produire; (e.g., the light) éteindre; **to turn over and over** tourner et retourner; **to turn up** (a collar) relever; (one's sleeves) retrousser; (to unearth) déterrer ‖ intr tourner, se tourner; (said of milk) tourner; (to toss and turn) se retourner; (to be dizzy) tourner, e.g., **his head is turning**

la tête lui tourne; **to turn about** or **around** se retourner, se tourner; **to turn aside** or **away** se détourner; **to turn back** rebrousser chemin; **to turn down** se rabattre; **to turn in** (coll) aller se coucher; **to turn into** tourner à or en; **to turn on** se jeter sur; (*to depend on*) dépendre de; **to turn out to be** se trouver être; **to turn out well** tourner bien; **to turn over** se retourner; (*said of auto*) capoter; **to turn up** (*to increase*) se relever; (*to appear*) se présenter, arriver

turn′coat′ s transfuge m
turn′down′ adj rabattu ‖ s refus m
turn′ing point′ s moment m décisif
turnip [′tʌrnɪp] s navet m; (*big watch*) (slang) bassinoire f; (slang) tête f de bois
turn′key′ s geôlier m
turn′ of life′ s retour m d'âge
turn′ of mind′ s inclination f naturelle
turn′out′ s (*gathering*) assistance f; (*output*) rendement m; (*equipment*) attelage m
turn′o′ver s renversement m; (com) chiffre m d'affaires
turn′pike′ s autoroute f à péage
turn′pike res′taurants spl ponts mpl restaurants
turn′spit′ s tournebroche m
turnstile [′tʌrn‚staɪl] s tourniquet m
turn′stone′ s (orn) tourne-pierre m
turn′ta′ble s (*of phonograph*) plateau m porte-disque; (rr) plaque f tournante
turpentine [′tʌrpən‚taɪn] s térébenthine f
turpitude [′tʌrpɪ‚t(j)ud] s turpitude f
turquoise [′tʌrkɔɪz] s turquoise f
turret [′tʌrɪt] s tourelle f
turreted adj en poivrière
turtle [′tʌrtəl] s tortue f
tur′tle‧dove′ s tourterelle f
tur′tle‧neck′ s col m roulé
tur′tle‧neck sweat′er s sweater m or chandail m à col roulé
Tuscan [′tʌskən] adj & s toscan m
Tuscany [′tʌskəni] s Toscane f; la Toscane
tusk [tʌsk] s défense f
tussle [′tʌsəl] s bagarre f ‖ intr se bagarrer
tutor [′t(j)utər] s précepteur m, répétiteur m ‖ tr donner des leçons particulières à ‖ intr donner des leçons particulières
tuxe‧do [tʌk′sido] s (pl **-dos**) smoking m
TV [′ti′vi] s (letterword) (**television**) tévé f, télé f
T′V′ din′ner s plateau-repas m congelé
twaddle [′twɑdəl] s fadaises fpl ‖ intr dire des fadaises
twang [twæŋ] s (*of musical instrument*) son m vibrant; (*of voice*) ton m nasillard ‖ tr faire résonner; dire en nasillant ‖ intr nasiller
twang‧y [′twæŋi] adj (comp **-ier**; super **-iest**) (*nasal*) nasillard; (*resonant*) vibrant
tweed [twid] s tweed m
tweet [twit] s pépiement m ‖ intr pépier
tweeter [′twitər] s (rad) tweeter m
tweezers [′twizərz] spl brucelles fpl; pince f à épiler

twelfth [twɛlfθ] adj & pron douzième (masc, fem); **the Twelfth** douze, e.g., **John the Twelfth** Jean douze ‖ s douzième m; **the twelfth** (*in dates*) le douze
twelve [twɛlv] adj & pron douze; **about twelve** une douzaine de ‖ s douze m; **twelve o'clock** (*noon*) midi m; (*midnight*) minuit m
twentieth [′twɛntɪ‧ɪθ] adj & pron vingtième (masc, fem); **the Twentieth** vingt, e.g., **John the Twentieth** Jean vingt ‖ s vingt m; **the twentieth** (*in dates*) le vingt
twen‧ty [′twɛnti] adj & pron vingt; **about twenty** une vingtaine de ‖ s (pl **-ties**) vingt m; **the twenties** les années fpl vingt
twen′ty-first′ adj & pron vingt et unième (masc, fem); **the Twenty-first** vingt et un, e.g., **John the Twenty-first** Jean vingt et un ‖ s vingt et unième m; **the twenty-first** (*in dates*) le vingt et un
twen′ty-one′ adj & pron vingt et un ‖ s vingt et un m; (cards) vingt-et-un
twen′ty-sec′ond adj & pron vingt-deuxième (masc, fem); **the Twenty-second** vingt-deux, e.g., **John the Twenty-second** Jean vingt-deux ‖ s vingt-deuxième m; **the twenty-second** (*in dates*) le vingt-deux
twen′ty-two′ adj, pron, & s vingt-deux m
twice [twaɪs] adv deux fois; **twice over** à deux reprises
twiddle [′twɪdəl] tr tourner, jouer avec; (*e.g., one's moustache*) tortiller
twig [twɪg] s brindille f
twilight [′twaɪ‚laɪt] adj crépusculaire ‖ s crépuscule m
twill [twɪl] s croisé m ‖ tr croiser
twin [twɪn] adj & s jumeau m ‖ v (pret & pp **twinned**; ger **twinning**) tr jumeler
twin′ beds′ spl lits mpl jumeaux
twine [twaɪn] s ficelle f ‖ tr enrouler ‖ intr s'enrouler
twinge [twɪndʒ] s élancement m ‖ intr élancer
twin′jet′ plane′ s biréacteur m
twinkle [′twɪŋkəl] s scintillement m; (*of the eye*) clignotement m ‖ intr scintiller; clignoter
twin′-screw′ adj à hélices jumelles
twirl [twʌrl] s tournoiement m ‖ tr faire tournoyer; (*e.g., a cane*) faire des moulinets avec ‖ intr tournoyer
twist [twɪst] s (*action*) torsion f; (*strand*) cordon m; (*of the wrist, of rope, etc.*) tour m; (*of the road, river, etc.*) coude m; (*of tobacco*) rouleau m; (*of the ankle*) entorse f; (*of mind or disposition*) prédisposition f ‖ tr tordre, tortiller ‖ intr se tordre, se tortiller; **to twist and turn** (*said, e.g., of road*) serpenter; (*said of sleeper*) se tourner et se retourner
twister [′twɪstər] s (coll) tornade f
twit [twɪt] v (pret & pp **twitted**; ger **twitting**) tr taquiner
twitch [twɪtʃ] s crispation f ‖ intr se crisper
twitter [′twɪtər] s gazouillement m ‖ intr gazouiller

two [tu] *adj & pron* deux ‖ *s* deux *m*; **to put two and two together** raisonner juste; **two o'clock** deux heures

two'-cy'cle *adj* (mach) à deux temps

two'-cyl'inder *adj* (mach) à deux cylindres

two'-edged' *adj* à deux tranchants

two' hun'dred *adj, pron, & s* deux cents *m*

twosome ['tusəm] *s* paire *f*; jeu *m* à deux joueurs

two'-time' *tr* (slang) tromper

tycoon [taɪ'kun] *s* (coll) magnat *m*

type [taɪp] *s* type *m* ‖ *tr* typer; (*to typewrite*) taper; (*a sample of blood*) chercher le groupe sanguin sur ‖ *intr* taper

type'face' *s* œil *m*

type'script' *s* manuscrit *m* dactylographié

typesetter ['taɪp,sɛtər] *s* compositeur *m*, typographe *mf*; machine *f* à composer

type'write' *v* (*pret* **-wrote**; *pp* **-written**) *tr & intr* taper à la machine

type'writ'er *s* machine *f* à écrire

type'writer rib'bon *s* ruban *m* encreur

type'writ'ing *s* dactylographie *f*

ty'phoid fe'ver ['taɪfɔɪd] *s* fièvre *f* typhoïde

typhoon [taɪ'fun] *s* typhon *m*

typical ['tɪpɪkəl] *adj* typique

typi·fy ['tɪpɪ,faɪ] *v* (*pret & pp* **-fied**) *tr* symboliser; être le type de

typ'ing er'ror *s* faute *f* de frappe

typist ['taɪpɪst] *s* dactylo *f*

typographic(al) [,taɪpə'græfɪk(əl)] *adj* typographique

typograph'ical er'ror *s* erreur *f* typographique

typography [taɪ'pɑgrəfi] *s* typographie *f*

tyrannic(al) [tɪ'rænɪk(əl)] *adj* tyrannique

tyran·ny ['tɪrəni] *s* (*pl* **-nies**) tyrannie *f*

tyrant ['taɪrənt] *s* tyran *m*

ty·ro ['taɪro] *s* (*pl* **-ros**) novice *mf*

U

U, u [ju] *s* XXIe lettre de l'alphabet

ubiquitous [ju'bɪkwɪtəs] *adj* ubiquiste, omniprésent

udder ['ʌdər] *s* pis *m*

UFO ['ju'ɛf'o] *s* (letterword) (**unidentified flying object**) O.V.N.I. (objet volant non-identifié)

UFOlogy [ju'fɑlədzi] *s* étude *f* des ovnis

ugliness ['ʌglɪnɪs] *s* laideur *f*

ug·ly ['ʌgli] *adj* (*comp* **-lier**; *super* **-liest**) laid; (*disagreeable; mean*) vilain

Ukraine ['jukren], [ju'kren] *s* Ukraine *f*; l'Ukraine

Ukrainian [ju'krenɪ·ən] *adj* ukrainien ‖ *s* (*language*) ukrainien *m*; (*person*) Ukrainien *m*

ulcer ['ʌlsər] *s* ulcère *m*

ulcerate ['ʌlsə,ret] *tr* ulcérer ‖ *intr* s'ulcérer

ulterior [ʌl'tɪrɪ·ər] *adj* ultérieur; secret, inavoué

ultimate ['ʌltɪmɪt] *adj* ultime, final, définitif

ultima·tum [,ʌltɪ'metəm] *s* (*pl* **-tums** or **-ta** [tə]) ultimatum *m*

ultrashort [,ʌltrə'ʃɔrt] *adj* (electron) ultra-court

ultraviolet [,ʌltrə'vaɪ·əlɪt] *adj & s* ultra-violet *m*

ul'travi'olet light' *s* lumière *f* ultraviolette

umbil'ical cord' [ʌm'bɪlɪkəl] *s* cordon *m* ombilical

umbrage ['ʌmbrɪdʒ] *s*—**to take umbrage at** prendre ombrage de

umbrella [ʌm'brɛlə] *s* parapluie *m*; (mil) ombrelle *f* de protection

umbrel'la stand' *s* porte-parapluies *m*

umlaut ['umlaut] *s* métaphonie *f*, inflexion *f* vocalique; (*mark*) tréma *m* ‖ *tr* changer le timbre de; écrire avec un tréma

umpire ['ʌmpaɪr] *s* arbitre *m*, juge *m* arbitre ‖ *tr & intr* arbitrer

UN ['ju'ɛn] (letterword) (**United Nations**) ONU *f*

unable [ʌn'ebəl] *adj* incapable; **to be unable to** être incapable de

unabridged [,ʌnə'brɪdʒd] *adj* intégral

unaccented [,ʌnæk'sɛntɪd] *adj* inaccentué

unacceptable [,ʌnək'sɛptəbəl] *adj* inacceptable, irrecevable

unaccountable [,ʌnə'kaʊntəbəl] *adj* inexplicable; irresponsable

unaccounted-for [,ʌnə'kaʊntɪd,fɔr] *adj* inexpliqué, pas retrouvé

unaccustomed [,ʌnə'kʌstəmd] *adj* inaccoutumé

unafraid [,ʌnə'fred] *adj* sans peur

unaligned [,ʌnə'laɪnd] *adj* non-engagé

unanimity [,junə'nɪmɪti] *s* unanimité *f*

unanimous [ju'nænɪməs] *adj* unanime

unanswerable [ʌn'ænsərəbəl] *adj* incontestable, sans réplique; (*argument*) irréfutable

unappreciative [,ʌnə'priʃɪ,etɪv] *adj* ingrat, peu reconnaissant

unapproachable [,ʌnə'protʃəbəl] *adj* inabordable; (fig) incomparable

unarmed [ʌn'ɑrmd] *adj* sans armes

unascertainable [ʌn,æsər'tenəbəl] *adj* non vérifiable

unasked [ʌn'æskt] *adj* non invité; **to do s.th. unasked** faire q.ch. spontanément

unassembled [,ʌnə'sɛmbəld] *adj* démonté

unassuming [,ʌnə's(j)umɪŋ] *adj* modeste, sans prétentions

unattached [,ʌnə'tætʃt] *adj* indépendant; (*loose*) détaché; (*not engaged to be married*) seul; (mil, nav) en disponibilité

unattainable [ˌʌnəˈtenəbəl] adj inaccessible

unattractive [ˌʌnəˈtræktɪv] adj peu attrayant, peu séduisant

unavailable [ˌʌnəˈveləbəl] adj non disponible

unavailing [ˌʌnəˈveliŋ] adj inutile

unavoidable [ˌʌnəˈvɔidəbəl] adj inévitable

unaware [ˌʌnəˈwɛr] adj ignorant; **to be unaware of** ignorer ‖ adv à l'improviste; à mon (son, etc.) insu

unawares [ˌʌnəˈwɛrz] adv (*unexpectedly*) à l'improviste; (*unknowingly*) à mon (son, etc.) insu

unbalanced [ʌnˈbælənst] adj non équilibré; (*mind*) déséquilibré; (*bank account*) non soldé

unbandage [ʌnˈbændɪdʒ] tr débander

un·bar [ʌnˈbɑr] v (*pret & pp* **-barred;** *ger* **-barring**) tr débarrer

unbearable [ʌnˈbɛrəbəl] adj insupportable, imbuvable

unbeatable [ʌnˈbitəbəl] adj imbattable

unbecoming [ˌʌnbɪˈkʌmɪŋ] adj déplacé, inconvenant; (*dress*) peu seyant

unbelievable [ˌʌnbɪˈlivəbəl] adj incroyable

unbeliever [ˌʌbnɪˈlivər] s incroyant m

unbending [ʌnˈbɛndɪŋ] adj inflexible

unbiased [ʌnˈbaɪ·əst] adj impartial

un·bind [ʌnˈbaind] v (*pret & pp* **-bound**) tr délier

unbleached [ʌnˈblitʃt] adj écru

unbolt [ʌnˈbolt] tr (*a gun; a door*) déverrouiller; (*a machine*) déboulonner

unborn [ʌnˈbɔrn] adj à naître, futur

unbosom [ʌnˈbuzəm] tr découvrir; **to unbosom oneself** ouvrir son cœur

unbound [ʌnˈbaund] adj non relié

unbreakable [ʌnˈbrekəbəl] adj incassable; (*e.g., glasses*) impact résistant

unbroken [ʌnˈbrokən] adj intact; (ininterrompu; (*spirit*) indompté; (*horse*) non rompu

unbuckle [ʌnˈbʌkəl] tr déboucler

unburden [ʌnˈbʌrdən] tr alléger; **to unburden oneself of** se soulager de

unburied [ʌnˈbɛrid] adj non enseveli

unbutton [ʌnˈbʌtən] tr déboutonner

uncalled-for [ʌnˈkɔld,fɔr] adj déplacé; (*e.g., insult*) gratuit

uncanny [ʌnˈkæni] adj inquiétant, mystérieux; rare, remarquable

uncared-for [ʌnˈkɛrd,fɔr] adj négligé; peu soignée

unceasing [ʌnˈsisɪŋ] adj incessant

unceremonious [ˌʌnsɛrɪˈmoni·əs] adj sans façon

uncertain [ʌnˈsʌrtən] adj incertain

uncertain·ty [ʌnˈsʌrtənti] s (*pl* **-ties**) incertitude f

unchain [ʌnˈtʃen] tr désenchaîner

unchangeable [ʌnˈtʃendʒəbəl] adj immuable

uncharted [ʌnˈtʃɑrtɪd] adj inexploré

unchecked [ʌnˈtʃɛkt] adj sans frein, non contenu; non vérifié

uncivilized [ʌnˈsɪvɪ,laɪzd] adj incivilisé

unclad [ʌnˈklæd] adj déshabillé

unclaimed [ʌnˈklemd] adj non réclamé; (*mail*) au rebut

unclasp [ʌnˈklæsp] tr dégrafer; (*one's hands*) desserrer

unclassified [ʌnˈklæsɪ,faɪd] adj non classé; (*documents, information, etc.*) pas secret

uncle [ˈʌŋkəl] s oncle m

unclean [ʌnˈklin] adj sale, immonde

un·clog [ʌnˈklɑg] v (*pret & pp* **-clogged;** *ger* **-clogging**) tr dégager, désobstruer

unclouded [ʌnˈklaudɪd] adj clair, dégagé

uncollectible [ˌʌnkəˈlɛktɪbəl] adj irrécouvrable

uncomfortable [ʌnˈkʌmfərtəbəl] adj (*causing discomfort*) inconfortable; (*feeling discomfort*) mal à l'aise

uncommitted [ˌʌnkəˈmɪtɪd] adj non-engagé

uncommon [ʌnˈkɑmən] adj peu commun

uncompromising [ʌnˈkɑmprə,maɪzɪŋ] adj intransigeant

unconcerned [ˌʌnkənˈsʌrnd] adj indifférent

unconditional [ˌʌnkənˈdɪʃənəl] adj inconditionnel

uncongenial [ˌʌnkənˈdʒini·əl] adj peu sympathique; incompatible; désagréable

unconquerable [ʌnˈkɑŋkərəbəl] adj invincible

unconquered [ʌnˈkɑŋkərd] adj invaincu, indompté

unconscious [ʌnˈkɑnʃəs] adj inconscient; (*temporarily deprived of consciousness*) sans connaissance ‖ s—**the unconscious** l'inconscient m

unconsciousness [ʌnˈkɑnʃəsnɪs] s inconscience f; perte f de connaissance, évanouissement m

unconstitutional [ˌʌnkɑnstɪˈt(j)uʃənəl] adj inconstitutionnel

uncontrollable [ˌʌnkənˈtroləbəl] adj ingouvernable; (*e.g., desires*) irrésistible; (*e.g., laughter*) inextinguible

unconventional [ˌʌnkənˈvɛnʃənəl] adj original, peu conventionnel; (*person*) non-conformiste

uncork [ʌnˈkɔrk] tr déboucher

uncouple [ʌnˈkʌpəl] tr désaccoupler

uncouth [ʌnˈkuθ] adj gauche, sauvage; (*language*) grossier

uncover [ʌnˈkʌvər] tr découvrir

unction [ˈʌŋkʃən] s onction f

unctuous [ˈʌŋktʃu·əs] adj onctueux

uncultivated [ʌnˈkʌltɪ,vetɪd] adj inculte

uncultured [ʌnˈkʌltʃərd] adj inculte, sans culture

uncut [ʌnˈkʌt] adj non coupé; (*stone, diamond*) brut; (*crops*) sur pied; (*book*) non rogné

undamaged [ʌnˈdæmɪdʒd] adj indemne

undaunted [ʌnˈdɔntɪd] adj pas découragé; sans peur

undecided [ˌʌndɪˈsaidɪd] adj indécis

undefeated [ˌʌndɪˈfitɪd] adj invaincu

undefended [ˌʌndɪˈfɛndɪd] adj sans défense

undefiled [ˌʌndɪˈfaild] adj sans tache

undeniable [ˌʌndɪˈnaɪ·əbəl] adj indéniable

under [ˈʌndər] *adj* (*lower*) inférieur; (*underneath*) de dessous ‖ *adv* dessous; **to go under** sombrer; **to keep under** tenir dans la soumission ‖ *prep* sous, au-dessous de, dessous; moins de, e.g., **under forty** moins de quarante ans; dans, e.g., **under the circumstances** dans les circonstances; en, e.g., **under treatment** en traitement; e.g., **under repair** en voie de réparation; à, e.g., **under the microscope** au microscope; e.g., **under examination** à l'examen; e.g., **under the terms of** aux termes de; e.g., **under the word** (*in dictionary*) au mot; **to serve under** servir sous les ordres de

un'der·age' *adj* mineur

un'der·arm pad' *s* dessous-de-bras *m*

un'der·bid' *v* (*pret & pp* **-bid**; *ger* **-bidding**) *tr* offrir moins que

un'der·brush' *s* broussailles *fpl*

un'der·car'riage *s* (aer) train *m* d'atterrissage; (aut) dessous *m*

un'der·clothes' *spl* sous-vêtements *mpl*

un'der·consump'tion *s* sous-consommation *f*

un'der·cov'er *adj* secret

un'der·cur'rent *s* courant *m* de fond; (fig) vague *f* de fond

un'der·devel·oped *adj* sous-développé

un'der·dog' *s* opprimé *m*; (sports) parti *m* non favori, outsider *m*

underdone [ˈʌndərˌdʌn] *adj* pas assez cuit

un'der·es'timate *tr* sous-estimer

un'der·gar'ment *s* sous-vêtement *m*

un'der·go' *v* (*pret* **-went**; *pp* **-gone**) *tr* subir, éprouver, souffrir

un'der·grad'uate *adj & s* non diplômé *m*

un'der·ground' *adj* souterrain; (fig) clandestin ‖ *s* (*subway*) métro *m*; (pol) résistance *f*, maquis *m* ‖ *adv* sous terre; **to go underground** (fig) entrer dans la clandestinité, prendre le maquis

un'der·growth' *s* sous-bois *m*; (*underbrush*) broussailles *fpl*

un'der·hand'ed *adj* sournois, dissimulé

un'der·line' or **un'der·line'** *tr* souligner

underling [ˈʌndərlɪŋ] *s* sous-ordre *m*, sousfifre *m*

un'der·mine' *tr* miner, saper

underneath [ˌʌndərˈniθ] *adj* de dessous; (*lower*) inférieur ‖ *s* dessous *m* ‖ *adv* dessous, en dessous ‖ *prep* sous, au-dessous de

un'der·nour'ished *adj* sous-alimenté

un'der·nour'ishment *s* sous-alimentation *f*

underpaid [ˌʌndərˈped] *adj* mal rétribué

un'der·pass' *s* passage *m* souterrain

un'der·pin' *v* (*pret & pp* **-pinned**; *ger* **-pinning**) *tr* étayer

un'der·priv'ileged *adj* déshérité, défavorisé, déshérité; (econ) économiquement faible

un'der·rate' *tr* sous-estimer

un'der·score' *tr* souligner

un'der·sea' *adj* sous-marin ‖ **un'der·sea'** *adv* sous la surface de la mer

un'der·sec'retar'y *s* (*pl* **-ies**) sous-secrétaire *m*

un'der·sell' *v* (*pret & pp* **-sold**) *tr* vendre à meilleur marché que; (*for less than the actual value*) solder

un'der·shirt' *s* gilet *m*, maillot *m* de corps, tricot *m* de corps, tricot de peau

un'der·signed' *adj* soussigné

un'der·skirt' *s* jupon *m*

un'der·stand' *v* (*pret & pp* **-stood**) *tr & intr* comprendre, entendre

understandable [ˌʌndərˈstændəbəl] *adj* compréhensible; **that's understandable** cela se comprend

un'der·stand'ing *adj* compréhensif ‖ *s* compréhension *f*; (*intellectual faculty, mind*) entendement *m*; (*agreement*) accord *m*, entente *f*; **on the understanding that** à condition que; **to come to an understanding** arriver à un accord

un'der·stud'y *s* (*pl* **-ies**) doublure *f* ‖ *v* (*pret & pp* **-ied**) *tr* (*an actor*) doubler

un'der·take' *v* (*pret* **-took**; *pp* **-taken**) *tr* entreprendre; (*to agree to perform*) s'engager à faire; **to undertake to** s'engager à

undertaker [ˈʌndərˌtekər] *s* (*mortician*) entrepreneur *m* de pompes funèbres

undertaking [ˌʌndərˈtekɪŋ] *s* entreprise *f*; (*commitment*) engagement *m* ‖ [ˈʌndərˌtekɪŋ] *s* service *m* des pompes funèbres

un'der·tone' *s* ton *m* atténué; (*background sound*) fond *m* obscur; **in an undertone** à voix basse

un'der·tow' *s* (*countercurrent below surface*) courant *m* de fond; (*on beach*) ressac *m*

un'der·wear' *s* sous-vêtements *mpl*

un'der·world' *s* (*criminal world*) bas-fonds *mpl*, pègre *f*; (*pagan world of the dead*) enfers *mpl*

un'der·write' or **un'der·write'** *v* (*pret* **-wrote**; *pp* **-written**) *tr* souscrire; (ins) assurer

un'der·writ'er *s* souscripteur *m*; (ins) assureur *m*

undeserved [ˌʌndɪˈzʌrvd] *adj* immérité

undesirable [ˌʌndɪˈzaɪrəbəl] *adj* peu désirable; (*e.g., alien*) indésirable ‖ *s* indésirable *mf*

undetachable [ˌʌndɪˈtætʃəbəl] *adj* inséparable

undeveloped [ˌʌndɪˈvɛləpt] *adj* (*land*) inexploité; (*country*) sous-développé

undigested [ˌʌndɪˈdʒɛstɪd] *adj* indigeste

undignified [ʌnˈdɪgnɪˌfaɪd] *adj* sans dignité, peu digne

undiscernible [ˌʌndɪˈzʌrnɪbəl], [ˌʌndɪˈsʌrnəbəl] *adj* imperceptible

undisputed [ˌʌndɪsˈpjutɪd] *adj* incontesté

undo [ʌnˈdu] *v* (*pret* **-did**; *pp* **-done**) *tr* défaire; (fig) ruiner

undoing [ʌnˈduɪŋ] *s* perte *f*, ruine *f*

undone [ʌnˈdʌn] *adj* défait; (*omitted*) inaccompli; **to come undone** se défaire; **to leave nothing undone** ne rien négliger

undoubtedly [ʌnˈdaʊtɪdli] *adv* sans aucun doute, incontestablement

undramatic [ˌʌndrəˈmætɪk] *adj* peu dramatique

undress [ʌnˈdrɛs] *s* déshabillé *m*; (*scanty dress*) petite tenue *f* ‖ *tr* déshabiller ‖ *intr* se déshabiller

undressing [ʌnˈdrɛsɪŋ] *s* déshabillage *m*, déculottage *m*

undrinkable [ʌnˈdrɪŋkəbəl] *adj* imbuvable

undue [ʌnˈd(j)u] *adj* indu

undulate [ˈʌndjə‚let] *intr* onduler

unduly [ʌnˈd(j)uli] *adv* indûment

undying [ʌnˈdaɪ‚ɪŋ] *adj* impérissable

un′earned in′come [ˈʌnʌrnd] *s* rente *f*, revenu *m* d'un bien

un′earned in′crement *s* plus-value *f*

unearth [ʌnˈʌrθ] *tr* déterrer

unearthly [ʌnˈʌrθli] *adj* surnaturel, spectral; bizarre; (*hour*) indu

uneasy [ʌnˈizi] *adj* inquiet; contraint, gêné

uneatable [ʌnˈitəbəl] *adj* immanageable

uneconomic(al) [ˌʌnikəˈnɑmɪk(əl)] *adj* peu économique; (*person*) peu économe

uneducated [ʌnˈɛdjə‚ketɪd] *adj* ignorant, sans instruction

unemployed [ˌʌnɛmˈplɔɪd] *adj* en chômage, sans travail ‖ *spl* chômeurs *mpl*, sans-travail *mfpl*

unemployment [ˌʌnɛmˈplɔɪmənt] *s* chômage *m*

un′employ′ment insur′ance *s* assurance-chômage *f*, allocation *f* de chômage

unending [ʌnˈɛndɪŋ] *adj* interminable

unequal [ʌnˈikwəl] *adj* inégal; **to be unequal to** (*a task*) ne pas être à la hauteur de

unequaled or **unequalled** [ʌnˈikwəld] *adj* sans égal, sans pareil

unerring [ʌnˈʌrɪŋ] *adj* infaillible

UNESCO [juˈnɛsko] *s* (acronym) (**United Nations Educational, Scientific, and Cultural Organization**) l'Unesco *f*

unessential [ˌʌnɛˈsɛnʃəl] *adj* non essentiel

uneven [ʌnˈivən] *adj* inégal; (*number*) impair

uneventful [ˌʌnɪˈvɛntfəl] *adj* sans incident, peu mouvementé

unexceptionable [ˌʌnɛkˈsɛpʃənəbəl] *adj* irréprochable

unexpected [ˌʌnɛkˈspɛktɪd] *adj* inattendu, imprévu

unexplained [ˌʌnɛkˈsplend] *adj* inexpliqué

unexplored [ˌʌnɛkˈsplord] *adj* inexploré

unexposed [ˌʌnɛkˈspozd] *adj* (phot) vierge

unfading [ʌnˈfedɪŋ] *adj* immarcescible

unfailing [ʌnˈfelɪŋ] *adj* infaillible; (*inexhaustible*) intarissable

unfair [ʌnˈfɛr] *adj* injuste, déloyal

unfaithful [ʌnˈfeθfəl] *adj* infidèle

unfamiliar [ˌʌnfəˈmɪljər] *adj* étranger, peu familier

unfasten [ʌnˈfæsən] *tr* défaire, détacher

unfathomable [ʌnˈfæðəməbəl] *adj* insondable

unfavorable [ʌnˈfevərəbəl] *adj* défavorable

unfeeling [ʌnˈfilɪŋ] *adj* insensible

unfilled [ʌnˈfɪld] *adj* vide; (*post*) vacant

unfinished [ʌnˈfɪnɪʃt] *adj* inachevé

unfit [ʌnˈfɪt] *adj* impropre, inapte

unfitted *adj* inapte, inhabile

unfold [ʌnˈfold] *tr* déplier ‖ *intr* se déplier

unforeseeable [ˌʌnforˈsi‚əbəl] *adj* imprévisible

unforeseen [ˌʌnforˈsin] *adj* imprévu

unforgettable [ˌʌnfərˈgɛtəbəl] *adj* inoubliable

unforgivable [ˌʌnfərˈgɪvəbəl] *adj* impardonnable

unfortunate [ʌnˈfɔrtjənɪt] *adj* & *s* malheureux *m*

un‑freeze [ʌnˈfriz] *v* (*pret* **-froze**; *pp* **-frozen**) *tr* dégeler

unfriendly [ʌnˈfrɛndli] *adj* (*comp* **-lier**; *super* **-liest**) inamical

unfruitful [ʌnˈfrutfəl] *adj* infructueux

unfulfilled [ˌʌnfəlˈfɪld] *adj* inaccompli

unfurl [ʌnˈfʌrl] *tr* déployer

unfurnished [ʌnˈfʌrnɪʃt] *adj* non meublé

ungain‑ly [ʌnˈgenli] *adj* gauche, disgracieux

ungentlemanly [ʌnˈdʒɛntəlmənli] *adj* mal élevé, impoli

ungird [ʌnˈgʌrd] *tr* déceindre

ungodly [ʌnˈgɑdli] *adj* impie; (*dreadful*) (coll) atroce

ungracious [ʌnˈgreʃəs] *adj* malgracieux

ungrammatical [ˌʌngrəˈmætɪkəl] *adj* peu grammatical

ungrateful [ʌnˈgretfəl] *adj* ingrat

ungrudgingly [ʌnˈgrʌdʒɪŋli] *adj* de bon cœur, libéralement

unguarded [ʌnˈgɑrdɪd] *adj* sans défense; (*moment*) d'inattention; (*card*) sec

unguent [ˈʌŋgwənt] *s* onguent *m*

unhandy [ʌnˈhændi] *adj* maladroit; (*e.g., tool*) incommode, pas maniable

unhap‑py [ʌnˈhæpi] *adj* (*comp* **-pier**; *super* **-piest**) malheureux, triste; (*unlucky*) malheureux, malencontreux; (*fateful*) funeste

unharmed [ʌnˈhɑrmd] *adj* indemne

unharness [ʌnˈhɑrnɪs] *tr* dételer

unheal‑thy [ʌnˈhɛlθi] *adj* (*comp* **-thier**, *super* **-thiest**) malsain; (*person*) maladif

unheard-of [ʌnˈhʌrd‚ɑv] *adj* inouï

unhinge [ʌnˈhɪndʒ] *tr* (fig) détraquer

unhitch [ʌnˈhɪtʃ] *tr* décrocher; (*e.g., a horse*) dételer

unho‑ly [ʌnˈholi] *adj* (*comp* **-lier**; *super* **-liest**) profane; (coll) affreux

unhook [ʌnˈhʊk] *tr* décrocher; (*e.g., a dress*) dégrafer

unhoped-for [ʌnˈhopt‚fɔr] *adj* inespéré

unhorse [ʌnˈhɔrs] *tr* désarçonner

unhurt [ʌnˈhʌrt] *adj* indemne

unicorn [ˈjuni‚kɔrn] *s* unicorne *m*

un′iden′tified fly′ing ob′ject [ˌʌnaɪˈdɛntə‚faɪd] *s* objet *m* volant non identifié (O.V.N.I.)

unification [ˌjunɪfɪˈkeʃən] *s* unification *f*

uniform [ˈjuni‚fɔrm] *adj* & *s* uniforme *m* ‖ *tr* uniformiser; vêtir d'un uniforme

uniformi‑ty [ˌjuniˈfɔrmɪti] *s* (*pl* **-ties**) uniformité *f*

uni·fy [ˈjunɪˌfaɪ] *v* (*pret* & *pp* **-fied**) unifier
unilateral [ˌjunɪˈlætərəl] *adj* unilatéral
unimpeachable [ˌʌnɪmˈpitʃəbəl] *adj* irrécusable
unimportant [ˌʌnɪmˈpɔrtənt] *adj* peu important, sans importance
uninhabited [ˌʌnɪnˈhæbɪtɪd] *adj* inhabité
uninspired [ˌʌnɪnˈspaɪrd] *adj* sans inspiration, sans vigueur
unintelligent [ˌʌnɪnˈtɛlɪdʒənt] *adj* inintelligent
unintelligible [ˌʌnɪnˈtɛlɪdʒɪbəl] *adj* inintelligible
uninterested [ʌnˈɪntrɪstɪd], [ʌnˈɪntəˌrɛstɪd] *adj* indifférent
uninteresting [ʌnˈɪntrɪstɪŋ], [ʌnˈɪntəˌrɛstɪŋ] *adj* peu intéressant
uninterrupted [ˌʌnɪntəˈrʌptɪd] *adj* ininterrompu
union [ˈjunjən] *adj* (*leader, scale, card, etc.*) syndical ‖ *s* union *f*; (*of workmen*) syndicat *m*
unionize [ˈjunjəˌnaɪz] *tr* syndiquer ‖ *intr* se syndiquer
un'ion shop' *s* atelier *m* syndical
un'ion suit' *s* sous-vêtement *m* d'une seule pièce
unique [juˈnik] *adj* unique
unisex [ˈjuniˌsɛks] *adj* unisex, unisexué
unison [ˈjunɪsən] *s* unisson *m*; **in unison (with)** à l'unisson (de)
unit [ˈjunɪt] *adj* unitaire ‖ *s* unité *f*; (elec, mach) groupe *m*
unite [juˈnaɪt] *tr* unir ‖ *intr* s'unir
united [juˈnaɪtɪd] *adj* uni
Unit'ed King'dom *s* Royaume-Uni *m*
Unit'ed Na'tions *spl* Nations *fpl* Unies
Unit'ed States' *adj* des États-Unis, américain ‖ *s*—**the United States** les États-Unis *mpl*
uni·ty [ˈjunɪti] *s* (*pl* **-ties**) unité *f*
universal [ˌjunɪˈvʌrsəl] *adj* & *s* universel *m*
u'niversal joint' *s* joint *m* articulé, cardan *m*
universe [ˈjunɪˌvʌrs] *s* univers *m*
universi·ty [ˌjunɪˈvʌrsɪti] *adj* universitaire ‖ *s* (*pl* **-ties**) université *f*
unjust [ʌnˈdʒʌst] *adj* injuste
unjustified [ʌnˈdʒʌstɪˌfaɪd] *adj* injustifié
unkempt [ʌnˈkɛmpt] *adj* dépeigné; mal tenu, négligé
unkind [ʌnˈkaɪnd] *adj* désobligeant; (*pitiless*) impitoyable, dur
unknowable [ʌnˈnoˑəbəl] *adj* inconnaissable
unknowingly [ʌnˈnoˑɪŋli] *adv* inconsciemment
unknown [ʌnˈnon] *adj* inconnu; (*not yet revealed*) inédit; **unknown to** à l'insu de ‖ *s* inconnu *m*; (*math*) inconnue *f*
un'known quan'tity *s* (math, fig) inconnue *f*
Un'known Sol'dier *s* Soldat *m* inconnu
unlace [ʌnˈles] *tr* délacer
unlatch [ʌnˈlætʃ] *tr* lever le loquet de
unlawful [ʌnˈlɔfəl] *adj* illégal, illicite
unleash [ʌnˈliʃ] *tr* lâcher
unleavened [ʌnˈlɛvənd] *adj* azyme

unless [ʌnˈlɛs] *prep* sauf ‖ *conj* à moins que
unlettered [ʌnˈlɛtərd] *adj* illettré
unlike [ʌnˈlaɪk] *adj* (*not alike*) dissemblables; différent de; (*not typical of*) pas caractéristique de; (*poles of a magnet*) (elec) de noms contraires ‖ *prep* (*contrary to*) à la différence de
unlikely [ʌnˈlaɪkli] *adj* peu probable
unlimited [ʌnˈlɪmɪtɪd] *adj* illimité
unlined [ʌnˈlaɪnd] *adj* (*coat*) non fourré; (*paper*) non rayé; (*face*) sans rides
unlist'ed tel'ephone num'ber [ʌnˈlɪstɪd] *s* téléphone *m* non sur la liste rouge
unload [ʌnˈlod] *tr* décharger; (*a gun*) désarmer; (coll) se décharger de ‖ *intr* décharger
unloading [ʌnˈlodɪŋ] *s* déchargement *m*; (*stopping for unloading*) manutention *f*
unlock [ʌnˈlɑk] *tr* ouvrir; (*a bolted door*) déverrouiller; (*the jaws*) desserrer
unloose [ʌnˈlus] *tr* lâcher; (*to undo*) délier; (*a mighty force*) déchaîner
unloved [ʌnˈlʌvd] *adj* peu aimé, haï
unlovely [ʌnˈlʌvli] *adj* disgracieux
unluck·y [ʌnˈlʌki] *adj* (*comp* **-ier; super -iest**) malchanceux, malheureux
un·make [ʌnˈmek] *v* (*pret* & *pp* **-made**) *tr* défaire
unmanageable [ʌnˈmænɪdʒəbəl] *adj* difficile à manier, ingouvernable
unmanly [ʌnˈmænli] *adj* indigne d'un homme, poltron; efféminé
unmannerly [ʌnˈmænərli] *adj* impoli, mal élevé
unmarketable [ʌnˈmɑrkɪtəbəl] *adj* invendable
unmarriageable [ʌnˈmærɪdʒəbəl] *adj* non mariable
unmarried [ʌnˈmærɪd] *adj* célibataire
unmask [ʌnˈmæsk] *tr* démasquer ‖ *intr* se démasquer
unmatched [ʌnˈmætʃt] *adj* sans égal, incomparable; (*unpaired*) désassorti, dépareillé
unmerciful [ʌnˈmʌrsɪfəl] *adj* impitoyable
unmesh [ʌnˈmɛʃ] *tr* (mach) désengrener ‖ *intr* (mach) se désengrener
unmindful [ʌnˈmaɪndfəl] *adj* oublieux
unmistakable [ˌʌnmɪsˈtekəbəl] *adj* évident, facilement reconnaissable
unmitigated [ʌnˈmɪtɪˌgetɪd] *adj* parfait, fieffé
unmixed [ʌnˈmɪkst] *adj* sans mélange
unmoor [ʌnˈmʊr] *tr* désamarrer
unmovable [ʌnˈmuvəbəl] *adj* inamovible
unmoved [ʌnˈmuvd] *adj* impassible
unmuzzle [ʌnˈmʌzəl] *tr* démuseler
unnatural [ʌnˈnætʃərəl] *adj* anormal, dénaturé; maniéré; artificiel
unnecessary [ʌnˈnɛsəˌsɛri] *adj* inutile
unnerve [ʌnˈnʌrv] *tr* démonter, décontenancer, bouleverser
unnoticeable [ʌnˈnotisəbəl] *adj* imperceptible
unnoticed [ʌnˈnotɪst] *adj* inaperçu
unobserved [ˌʌnəbˈzʌrvd] *adj* inobservé, inaperçu

unobtainable [ˌʌnəbˈtenəbəl] *adj* introuvable

unobtrusive [ˌʌnəbˈtrusɪv] *adj* discret, effacé

unoccupied [ʌnˈɑkjəˌpaɪd] *adj* libre, inoccupé

unofficial [ˌʌnəˈfɪʃəl] *adj* officieux, non officiel

unopened [ʌnˈopənd] *adj* fermé; (*letter*) non décacheté

unopposed [ˌʌnəˈpozd] *adj* sans opposition; (*candidate*) unique

unorthodox [ʌnˈɔrθəˌdɑks] *adj* peu orthodox

unpack [ʌnˈpæk] *tr* déballer

unpaid [ʌnˈped] *adj* impayé

unpalatable [ʌnˈpælətəbəl] *adj* fade, insipide

unparalleled [ʌnˈpærəˌlɛld] *adj* sans précédent, sans pareil

unpardonable [ʌnˈpɑrdənəbəl] *adj* impardonnable

unpatriotic [ˌʌnpetrɪˈɑtɪk] *adj* antipatriotique

unperceived [ˌʌnpərˈsivd] *adj* inaperçu

unperturbable [ˌʌnpərˈtʌrbəbəl] *adj* imperturbable

unpleasant [ʌnˈplɛzənt] *adj* désagréable, déplaisant

unpopular [ʌnˈpɑpjələr] *adj* impopulaire

unpopularity [ʌnˌpɑpjəˈlærɪti] *s* impopularité *f*

unprecedented [ʌnˈprɛsɪˌdɛntɪd] *adj* sans précédent, inédit

unprejudiced [ʌnˈprɛdʒədɪst] *adj* sans préjugés, impartial

unpremeditated [ˌʌnprɪˈmɛdɪˌtetɪd] *adj* non prémédité

unprepared [ˌʌnprɪˈpɛrd] *adj* sans préparation; (*e.g., speech*) improvisé

unprepossessing [ˌʌnpriprəˈzɛsɪŋ] *adj* peu engageant

unpresentable [ˌʌnprɪˈzɛntəbəl] *adj* peu présentable

unpretentious [ˌʌnprɪˈtɛnʃəs] *adj* sans prétentions, modeste

unprincipled [ʌnˈprɪnsɪpəld] *adj* sans principes, sans scrupules

unproductive [ˌʌnprəˈdʌktɪv] *adj* improductif

unprofitable [ʌnˈprɑfɪtəbəl] *adj* peu profitable, inutile

unpronounceable [ˌʌnprəˈnaʊnsəbəl] *adj* imprononçable

unpropitious [ˌʌnprəˈpɪʃəs] *adj* défavorable

unpublished [ʌnˈpʌblɪʃt] *adj* inédit

unpunished [ʌnˈpʌnɪʃt] *adj* impuni

unqualified [ʌnˈkwɑləˌfaɪd] *adj* incompétent; parfait, fieffé

unquenchable [ʌnˈkwɛntʃəbəl] *adj* inextinguible

unquestionable [ʌnˈkwɛstʃənəbəl] *adj* indiscutable

unrav·el [ʌnˈrævəl] *v* (*pret & pp* **-eled** or **-elled**; *ger* **-eling** or **-elling**) *tr* effiler; (fig)

débrouiller ‖ *intr* s'effiler; (fig) se débrouiller

unreachable [ʌnˈritʃəbəl] *adj* inaccessible

unreal [ʌnˈri·əl] *adj* irréel

unreali·ty [ˌʌnrɪˈælɪti] *s* (*pl* **-ties**) irréalité *f*

unreasonable [ʌnˈrizənəbəl] *adj* déraisonnable

unrecognizable [ʌnˈrɛkəgˌnaɪzəbəl] *adj* méconnaissable

unreel [ʌnˈril] *tr* dérouler ‖ *intr* se dérouler

unrelenting [ˌʌnrɪˈlɛntɪŋ] *adj* implacable

unreliable [ˌʌnrɪˈlaɪ·əbəl] *adj* peu fidéle, instable, sujet à caution

unremitting [ˌʌnrɪˈmɪtɪŋ] *adj* incessant, infatigable

unrented [ʌnˈrɛntɪd] *adj* libre, sans locataires

unrepentant [ˌʌnrɪˈpɛntənt] *adj* impénitent

un'requit'ed love' [ˌʌnrɪˈkwaɪtɪd] *s* amour *m* non partagé

unresponsive [ˌʌnrɪˈspɑnsɪv] *adj* peu sensible, froid, détaché

unrest [ʌnˈrɛst] *s* agitation *f*, trouble *m*; inquiétude *f*

un·rig [ʌnˈrɪg] *v* (*pret & pp* **-rigged;** *ger* **-rigging**) *tr* (naut) dégréer

unrighteous [ʌnˈraɪtʃəs] *adj* inique, injuste

unripe [ʌnˈraɪp] *adj* vert, pas mûr; précoce

unrivaled or **unrivalled** [ʌnˈraɪvəld] *adj* sans rival

unroll [ʌnˈrol] *tr* dérouler ‖ *intr* se dérouler

unromantic [ˌʌnroˈmæntɪk] *adj* peu romanesque, terre à terre

unruffled [ʌnˈrʌfəld] *adj* calme, serein

unruly [ʌnˈruli] *adj* indiscipliné, ingouvernable

unsaddle [ʌnˈsædəl] *tr* (*a horse*) desseller; (*a horseman*) désarçonner

unsafe [ʌnˈsef] *adj* dangereux

unsaid [ʌnˈsɛd] *adj*—**to leave unsaid** passer sous silence

unsalable [ʌnˈseləbəl] *adj* invendable

unsanitary [ʌnˈsænɪˌtɛri] *adj* peu hygiénique

unsatisfactory [ʌnˌsætɪsˈfæktəri] *adj* peu satisfaisant

unsatisfied [ʌnˈsætɪsˌfaɪd] *adj* insatisfait, inassouvi

unsavory [ʌnˈsevəri] *adj* désagréable; (fig) équivoque, louche

unscathed [ʌnˈskeðd] *adj* indemne

unscientific [ˌʌnsaɪ·ənˈtɪfɪk] *adj* antiscientifique

unscrew [ʌnˈskru] *tr* dévisser

unscrupulous [ʌnˈskrupjələs] *adj* sans scrupules

unseal [ʌnˈsil] *tr* desceller

unsealed *adj* (*mail*) non clos

unseasonable [ʌnˈsizənəbəl] *adj* hors de saison; (*untimely*) inopportun

unseemly [ʌnˈsimli] *adj* inconvenant

unseen [ʌnˈsin] *adj* invisible

unselfish [ʌnˈsɛlfɪʃ] *adj* désintéressé

unsettled [ʌnˈsɛtəld] *adj* instable; (*region*) non colonisé; (*question*) en suspens; (*weather*) variable; (*bills*) non réglé; **to be**

unsettled (*to be uneasy*) avoir du vague à l'âme

unshackle [ʌn'ʃækəl] *tr* désentraver

unshaken [ʌn'ʃekən] *adj* inébranlé

unshapely [ʌn'ʃepli] *adj* difforme, informe

unshaven [ʌn'ʃevən] *adj* non rasé

unsheathe [ʌn'ʃið] *tr* dégainer

unshod [ʌn'ʃɑd] *adj* déchaussé; (*horse*) déferré

unshrinkable [ʌn'ʃrɪŋkəbəl] *adj* irrétrécissable

unsightly [ʌn'saɪtli] *adj* laid, hideux

unsinkable [ʌn'sɪŋkəbəl] *adj* insubmersible

unskilled [ʌn'skɪld] *adj* inexpérimenté; de manœuvre

un'skilled la'borer *s* manœuvre *m*

unskillful [ʌn'skɪlfəl] *adj* maladroit

unsnarl [ʌn'snɑrl] *tr* débrouiller

unsociable [ʌn'soʃəbəl] *adj* insociable

unsold [ʌn'sold] *adj* invendu

unsolder [ʌn'sɑdər] *tr* dessouder

unsophisticated [ˌʌnsə'fɪstɪˌketɪd] *adj* ingénu, naïf, simple

unsound [ʌn'saʊnd] *adj* peu solide; (*false*) faux; (*decayed*) gâté; (*mind*) dérangé; (*sleep*) léger

unspeakable [ʌn'spikəbəl] *adj* indicible; (*disgusting*) sans nom

unsportsmanlike [ʌn'sportsmən‚laɪk] *adj* antisportif

unstable [ʌn'stebəl] *adj* instable

unsteady [ʌn'stɛdi] *adj* chancelant, tremblant, vacillant

unstinted [ʌn'stɪntɪd] *adj* abondant, sans bornes

unstitch [ʌn'stɪtʃ] *tr* découdre

un·stop [ʌn'stɑp] *v* (*pret & pp* **-stopped**; *ger* **-stopping**) *tr* déboucher

unstressed [ʌn'strɛst] *adj* inaccentué

unstrung [ʌn'strʌŋ] *adj* détraqué; (*necklace*) défilé; (*mus*) sans cordes

unsuccessful [ˌʌnsək'sɛsfəl] *adj* non réussi; **to be unsuccessful** ne pas réussir

unsuitable [ʌn's(j)utəbəl] *adj* impropre; (*time*) inopportun; **unsuitable for** peu fait pour, inapte à

unsuspected [ˌʌnsəs'pɛktɪd] *adj* insoupçonné

unswerving [ʌn'swʌrvɪŋ] *adj* ferme, inébranlable

unsympathetic [ˌʌnsɪmpə'θɛtɪk] *adj* peu compatissant

unsystematic(al) [ˌʌnsɪstə'mætɪk(əl)] *adj* non systématique, sans méthode

untactful [ʌn'tæktfəl] *adj* indiscret, indélicat

untamed [ʌn'temd] *adj* indompté

untangle [ʌn'tæŋgəl] *tr* démêler, débrouiller

untenable [ʌn'tɛnəbəl] *adj* insoutenable

unthankful [ʌn'θæŋkfəl] *adj* ingrat

unthinkable [ʌn'θɪŋkəbəl] *adj* impensable

unthinking [ʌn'θɪŋkɪŋ] *adj* irréfléchi

untidy [ʌn'taɪdi] *adj* désordonné, débraillé

un·tie [ʌn'taɪ] *v* (*pret & pp* **-tied**; *ger* **-tying**) *tr* délier, dénouer

until [ʌn'tɪl] *prep* jusqu'à ‖ *conj* jusqu'à ce que, en attendant que

untimely [ʌn'taɪmli] *adj* inopportun; (*premature*) prématuré; (*excessive*) intempestif

untiring [ʌn'taɪrɪŋ] *adj* infatigable

untold [ʌn'told] *adj* incalculable; (*suffering*) inouï; (*joy*) indicible; (*tale*) non raconté

untouchable [ʌn'tʌtʃəbəl] *adj & s* intouchable *mf*

untouched [ʌn'tʌtʃt] *adj* intact; indifférent; non mentionné

untoward [ʌn'tord] *adj* malencontreux

untrained [ʌn'trend] *adj* inexpérimenté; (*animal*) non dressé

untrammeled or **untrammelled** [ʌn'træməld] *adj* sans entraves

untried [ʌn'traɪd] *adj* inéprouvé

untroubled [ʌn'trʌbəld] *adj* calme, insoucieux

untrue [ʌn'tru] *adj* faux; infidèle

untrustworthy [ʌn'trʌst‚wʌrði] *adj* indigne de confiance

untruth [ʌn'truθ] *s* mensonge *m*

untruthful [ʌn'truθfəl] *adj* mensonger

untwist [ʌn'twɪst] *tr* détordre ‖ *intr* se détordre

unused [ʌn'juzd] *adj* inutilisé, inemployé; **unused to** peu accoutumé à, inaccoutumé à

unusual [ʌn'juʒu·əl] *adj* insolite, inusité, inhabituel

unutterable [ʌn'ʌtərəbəl] *adj* indicible, inexprimable

unvanquished [ʌn'væŋkwɪʃt] *adj* invaincu

unvarnished [ʌn'vɑrnɪʃt] *adj* non verni; (fig) sans fard, simple

unveil [ʌn'vel] *tr* dévoiler; (*e.g., a statue*) inaugurer ‖ *intr* se dévoiler

unveiling [ʌn'velɪŋ] *s* dévoilement *m*

unventilated [ʌn'vɛntɪ‚letɪd] *adj* sans aération

unvoice [ʌn'vɔɪs] *tr* dévoiser, assourdir

unwanted [ʌn'wɑntɪd] *adj* non voulu

unwarranted [ʌn'wɑrəntɪd] *adj* injustifié; sans garantie

unwary [ʌn'wɛri] *adj* imprudent

unwavering [ʌn'wevərɪŋ] *adj* constant, ferme, résolu

unwelcome [ʌn'wɛlkəm] *adj* (*e.g., visitor*) importun; (*e.g., news*) fâcheux

unwell [ʌn'wɛl] *adj* indisposé, souffrant; (*menstruating*) indisposée

unwholesome [ʌn'holsəm] *adj* malsain, insalubre

unwieldy [ʌn'wildi] *adj* peu maniable

unwilling [ʌn'wɪlɪŋ] *adj* peu disposé

unwillingly [ʌn'wɪlɪŋli] *adv* à contrecœur

un·wind [ʌn'waɪnd] *v* (*pret & pp* **-wound**) *tr* dérouler ‖ *intr* se dérouler

unwise [ʌn'waɪz] *adj* peu judicieux, malavisé

unwished-for [ʌn'wɪʃt‚fɔr] *adj* non souhaité

unwittingly [ʌn'wɪtɪŋli] *adv* inconsciemment, sans le savoir

unwonted [ʌn'wʌntɪd] *adj* inaccoutumé, peu commun

unworldly [ʌn'wʌrldli] *adj* peu mondain; simple, naïf

unworthy [ʌn'wʌrði] *adj* indigne

un·wrap [ʌn'ræp] *v* (*pret* & *pp* **-wrapped;** *ger* **-wrapping**) *tr* dépaqueter, désenvelopper

unwrinkled [ʌn'rɪŋkəld] *adj* uni, lisse, sans rides

unwritten [ʌn'rɪtən] *adj* non écrit; oral; (*blank*) vierge, blanc

unwrit'ten law' *s* droit *m* coutumier

unyielding [ʌn'jildɪŋ] *adj* ferme, solide; inébranlable

unyoke [ʌn'jok] *tr* dételer

up [ʌp] *adj* montant, ascendant; (*raised*) levé; (*standing*) debout; (*time*) expiré; (*blinds*) relevé; **up in arms** soulevé, indigné ‖ *adv* haut, en haut; **to be up against** se heurter à; **to be up against it** avoir la déveine; **to be up to** être capable de, être à la hauteur de; être à, e.g., **to be up to you (me, etc.)** être à vous (moi, etc.); **up and down** de haut en bas; (*back and forth*) de long en large; **up there** là-haut; **up to** jusqu'à; (*at the level of*) au niveau de, à la hauteur de; **up to and including** jusques et y compris; **what's up?** qu'est-ce qui se passe?; for expressions like **to go up** monter and **to get up** se lever, see the verb ‖ *prep* en haut de, vers le haut de; (*a stream*) en montant ‖ *v* (*pret* & *pp* **-upped;** *ger* **upping**) *tr* (coll) faire monter; (*prices, wages*) (coll) élever ‖ *interj* debout!

up-and-coming ['ʌpən'kʌmɪŋ] *adj* (coll) entreprenant

up-and-doing ['ʌpən'du·ɪŋ] *adj* (coll) entreprenant, alerte, énergique

up-and-up ['ʌpən'ʌp] *s*—**to be on the up-and-up** (coll) être en bonne voie; (coll) être honnête

up-braid' *tr* réprimander, reprendre

upbringing ['ʌp,brɪŋɪŋ] *s* éducation *f*

up'coun'try *adv* (coll) à l'intérieur du pays ‖ *s* (coll) intérieur *m* du pays

up-date' *tr* mettre à jour

upheaval [ʌp'hivəl] *s* soulèvement *m*

up'hill' *adj* montant; difficile, pénible ‖ **up'hill'** *adv* en montant

up-hold' *v* (*pret* & *pp* **-held**) *tr* soutenir, maintenir

upholster [ʌp'holstər] *tr* tapisser

upholsterer [ʌp'holstərər] *s* tapissier *m*

upholster·y [ʌp'holstəri] *s* (*pl* **-ies**) tapisserie *f*

up'keep' *s* entretien *m*; (*expenses*) frais *mpl* d'entretien

upland ['ʌp,lænd] *adj* élevé ‖ *s* région *f* montagneuse; **uplands** hautes terres *fpl*

up'lift' *s* élévation *f*; (*moral improvement*) édification *f* ‖ **up-lift'** *tr* soulever, élever

upon [ə'pɑn] *prep* sur; à, e.g., **upon my arrival** à mon arrivée; **upon** + *ger* en + *ger*, e.g., **upon arriving** en arrivant

upper ['ʌpər] *adj* supérieur; haut; (*first*) premier ‖ *s* (*of shoe*) empeigne *f*

up'per berth' *s* couchette *f* du haut, couchette supérieure

up'per-case' *adj* (typ) du haut de casse

up'per clas'ses *spl* hautes classes *fpl*

up'per hand' *s* dessus *m*, haute main *f*

up'per mid'dle class' *s* haute bourgeoisie *f*

up'per·most' *adj* (le) plus haut, (le) plus élevé; (le) premier ‖ *adv* en dessus

Up'per Room' *s* (eccl) cénacle *m*

uppish ['ʌpɪʃ] *adj* (coll) suffisant, arrogant

up·raise' *tr* lever

up'right' *adj* & *adv* droit ‖ *s* montant *m*

uprising ['ʌp,raɪzɪŋ] *s* soulèvement *m*, insurrection *f*

up'roar' *s* tumulte *m*, vacarme *m*

uproarious [ʌp'rorɪ·əs] *adj* tumultueux; (*funny*) comique, impayable

up·root' *tr* déraciner

ups' and downs' *spl* vicissitudes *fpl*

up·set' or **up'set'** *adj* (*overturned*) renversé; (*disturbed*) bouleversé; (*stomach*) dérangé ‖ **up'set'** *s* (*overturn*) renversement *m*; (*of emotions*) bouleversement *m* ‖ **up·set'** *v* (*pret* & *pp* **-set;** *ger* **-setting**) *tr* renverser; bouleverser ‖ *intr* se renverser

up'set price' *s* prix *m* de départ

upsetting [ʌp'sɛtɪŋ] *adj* bouleversant, inquiétant

up'shot' *s* résultat *m*; point *m* essentiel

up'side down' *adv* sense dessus dessous; **to turn upside down** renverser; se renverser; (*said of carriage*) verser

up'stage' *adj* & *adv* au second plan, à l'arrière-plan; **to go upstage** remonter ‖ *s* arrière-plan *m* ‖ **up'stage'** *tr* (coll) prendre un air dédaigneux envers

up'stairs' *adj* d'en haut ‖ *s* l'étage *m* supérieur ‖ *adv* en haut; **to go upstairs** monter, monter en haut

up·stand'ing *adj* droit; (*vigorous*) gaillard; (*sincere*) honnête, probe

up'start' *adj* & *s* parvenu *m*

up'stream' *adj* d'amont ‖ *adv* en amont

up'stroke' *s* (*in writing*) délié *m*; (mach) course *f* ascendante

up'surge' *s* poussée *f*

up'swing' *s* mouvement *m* de montée; (com) amélioration *f*

up'tight' *adj* (coll) inquiet, soucieux

up-to-date ['ʌptə'det] *adj* à la page; (*e.g., account books*) mis à jour

up-to-the-minute ['ʌptəðə'mɪnɪt] *adj* de la dernière heure

up'trend' *s* tendance *f* à la hausse

up'turn' *s* hausse *f*, amélioration *f*

up·turned' *adj* (*e.g., eyes*) levé; (*part of clothing*) relevé; (*nose*) retroussé

upward ['ʌpwərd] *adj* ascendant ‖ *adv* vers le haut; **upward of** plus de

Ural ['jurəl] *adj* Ouralien ‖ *s* Oural *m*; **Urals** Oural

uranium [ju'renɪ·əm] *s* uranium *m*

urban ['ʌrbən] *adj* urbain

urbane [ʌr'ben] *adj* urbain, courtois

ur'ban guer'rilla *s* guérillero *m* urbain
urbanite [`ʌrbə,naɪt] *s* citadin *m*, habitant *m* d'une ville
urbanity [ʌr`bænɪti] *s* urbanité *f*
urbanize [`ʌrbə,naɪz] *tr* urbaniser
ur'ban renew'al *s* renouveau *m* urbain
urchin [`ʌrtʃɪn] *s* gamin *m*, galopin *m*
ure·thra [jʊ`riθrə] *s* (*pl* **-thras** or **-thrae** [θri]) urètre *m*
urge [ʌrdʒ] *s* impulsion *f* ‖ *tr* & *intr* presser
urgen·cy [`ʌrdʒənsi] *s* (*pl* **-cies**) urgence *f*; insistance *f*, sollicitation *f*
urgent [`ʌrdʒənt] *adj* urgent, pressant; (*insistent*) pressant, importun
urinal [`jʊrɪnəl] *s* (*small building or convenience for men*) urinoir *m*, vespasienne *f*; (*for bed*) urinal *m*
urinary [`jʊrɪ,nɛri] *adj* urinaire
urinate [`jʊrɪ,net] *tr* & *intr* uriner; pisser (coll)
urine [`jʊrɪn] *s* urine *f*
urn [ʌrn] *s* urne *f*; (*for tea, coffee, etc.*) fontaine *f*
urology [jʊ`ralədʒi] *s* urologie *f*
us [ʌs] *pron pers* nous §85, §87
U.S.A. [`ju`ɛs`e] *s* (letterword) (**United States of America**) E.-U.A. *mpl* or U.S.A. *mpl*
usable [`juzəbəl] *adj* utilisable
usage [`juzɪdʒ] *s* usage *m*
use [jus] *s* emploi *m*, usage *m*; (*usefulness*) utilité *f*; **in use** occupé; **of what use is it?** à quoi cela sert-il?; **not in use** libre; **out of use** hors de service; **to be of no use** servir à rien; **to have no use for s.o.** tenir qn en mauvaise estime; **to make use of** se servir de; **what's the use?** à quoi bon? ‖ [juz] *tr* employer, se servir de, user de; **to use up** épuiser, user ‖ *intr*—**I used to visit my friend every evening** je visitais mon ami tous les soirs
used [juzd] *adj* usagé, usé; d'occasion, e.g., **used car** voiture *f* d'occasion; **to be used** (*to be put into use*) être usité, être

employé; **to be used as** servir de; **to be used to** (*to be useful for*) servir à; **used to** [`justʊ] accoutumé à; **used up** épuisé
useful [`jusfəl] *adj* utile
usefulness [`jusfəlnɪs] *s* utilité *f*
useless [`juslɪs] *adj* inutile
user [`juzər] *s* usager *m*; (*of a machine, of a computer, of gas, etc.*) utilisateur *m*
usher [`ʌʃər] *s* placeur *m*; ouvreuse *f*; (*doorkeeper*) huissier *m* ‖ *tr*—**to usher in** inaugurer; (*a person*) introduire
U.S.S.R. [`ju`ɛs`ɛs`ɑr] *s* (letterword) (**Union of Soviet Socialist Republics**) U.R.S.S. *f*
usual [`juʒʊ·əl] *adj* usuel; **as usual** comme d'habitude
usually [`juʒʊ·əli] *adv* usuellement, d'habitude, d'ordinaire
usurp [ju`zʌrp] *tr* usurper
usu·ry [`juʒəri] *s* (*pl* **-ries**) usure *f*
utensil [jʊ`tɛnsɪl] *s* ustensile *m*
uter·us [`jutərəs] *s* (*pl* **-i** [,aɪ] utérus *m*
utilitarian [,jutɪlɪ`tɛrɪ·ən] *adj* utilitaire
utili·ty [jʊ`tɪlɪti] *s* (*pl* **-ties**) utilité *f*; service *m* public; **utilities** services en commun (*gaz, transports, etc.*)
utilize [`jutɪ,laɪz] *tr* utiliser
utmost [`ʌt,most] *adj* extrême; (*larger*) plus grand; (*further away*) plus éloigné ‖ *s*—**the utmost** l'extrême *m*, le comble *m*; **to do one's utmost** faire tout son possible; **to the utmost** jusqu'au dernier point
utopia [ju`topɪ·ə] *s* utopie *f*
utopian [ju`topɪ·ən] *adj* utopique ‖ *s* utopiste *mf*
utter [`ʌtər] *adj* complet, total, absolu ‖ *tr* proférer, émettre; (*a cry*) pousser
utterance [`ʌtərəns] *s* expression *f*, émission *f*; (gram) énoncé *m*; **to give utterance to** exprimer
utterly [`ʌtərli] *adv* complètement, tout à fait, totalement
U-turn [`ju,tʌrn] *s* demi-volte *f*

V

V, v [vi] *s* XXIIᵉ lettre de l'alphabet
vacan·cy [`vekənsi] *s* (*pl* **-cies**) (*emptiness; gap, opening*) vide *m*; (*unfilled position or job*) vacance *f*; (*in a building*) appartement *m* disponible; (*in a hotel*) chambre *f* de libre; **no vacancy** (public sign) complet
vacant [`vekənt] *adj* (*empty*) vide; (*having no occupant; untenanted*) vacant, libre, disponible; (*expression, look*) distrait, vague
va'cant lot' *s* terrain *m* vague
vacate [`veket] *tr* quitter, évacuer ‖ *intr* (*to move out*) déménager
vacation [ve`keʃən] *s* vacances *fpl*; **on va-**

cation en vacances ‖ *intr* prendre ses vacances, passer les vacances
vacationist [ve`keʃənɪst] *s* vacancier *m*
vaca'tion with pay' *s* congé *m* payé
vaccinate [`væksɪ,net] *tr* vacciner
vaccination [,væksɪ`neʃən] *s* vaccination *f*
vaccine [væk`sin] *s* vaccin *m*
vacillate [`væsɪ,let] *intr* vaciller
vacui·ty [væ`kju·ɪti] *s* (*pl* **-ties**) vacuité *f*
vacu·um [`vækju·əm] *s* (*pl* **-ums** or **-a** [ə]) vacuum *m*, vide *m* ‖ *tr* passer à l'aspirateur, dépoussiérer
vac'uum clean'er *s* aspirateur *m*
vac'uum pump' *s* pompe *f* à vide
vac'uum tube' *s* tube *m* à vide

vagabond [ˋvægə,bɑnd] *adj & s* vagabond *m*
vagar·y [vəˋgɛri] *s* (*pl* **-ies**) caprice *m*
vagina [vəˋdʒaɪnə] *s* vagin *m*
vagran·cy [ˋvegrənsi] *s* (*pl* **-cies**) vagabondage *m*
vague [veg] *adj* vague
vain [ven] *adj* vain; **in vain** en vain
vainglorious [venˋglorɪ·əs] *adj* vaniteux
valance [ˋvæləns] *s* cantonnière *f*, lambrequin *m*
vale [vel] *s* vallon *m*
valedicto·ry [,vælɪˋdɪktəri] *s* (*pl* **-ries**) discours *m* d'adieu
valence [ˋveləns] *s* (chem) valence *f*
valentine [ˋvælən,taɪn] *s* (*sweetheart*) valentin *m*; (*card*) carte *f* de la Saint-Valentin
Val′entine Day′ *s* la Saint-Valentin
vale′ of tears′ *s* vallée *f* de larmes
valet [ˋvælɪt], [ˋvæle] *s* valet *m*
valiant [ˋvæljənt] *adj* vaillant
valid [ˋvælɪd] *adj* valable, valide
validate [ˋvælɪ,det] *tr* valider; (sports) homologuer
validation [,vælɪˋdeʃən] *s* validation *f*; (sports) homologation *f*
validi·ty [vəˋlɪdɪti] *s* (*pl* **-ties**) validité *f*
valise [vəˋlis] *s* mallette *f*
valley [ˋvæli] *s* vallée *f*, vallon *m*; (*of roof*) cornière *f*
valor [ˋvælər] *s* valeur *f*, vaillance *f*
valorous [ˋvælərəs] *adj* valeureux
valuable [ˋvæljʊ·əbəl], [ˋvæljəbəl] *adj* précieux, de valeur ‖ **valuables** *spl* objets *mpl* de valeur
value [ˋvæljʊ] *s* valeur *f*; (*bargain*) affaire *f*, occasion *f*; **to set a value on** estimer, évaluer ‖ *tr* (*to think highly of*) priser, estimer; (*to set a price for*) estimer, évaluer; **if you value your life** si vous tenez à la vie
val′ue-added tax′ *s* taxe *f* à la valeur ajoutée, T.V.A.
valueless [ˋvæljʊlɪs] *adj* sans valeur
valve [vælv] *s* soupape *f*; (*of mollusk; of fruit; of tire*) valve *f*; (*of heart*) valvule *f*; (mus) clé *f*
valve′ cap′ *s* chapeau *m*, bouchon *m*
valve′ gears′ *spl* (*of gas engine*) engrenages *mpl* de distribution; (*of steam engine*) mécanisme *m* de distribution
valve′-in-head′ en′gine *s* moteur *m* à soupapes en tête, moteur à culbuteurs
valve′ seat′ *s* siège *m* de soupape
valve′ spring′ *s* ressort *m* de soupape
valve′ stem′ *s* tige *f* de soupape
vamp [væmp] *s* (*of shoe*) empeigne *f*; (*patchwork*) rapiéçage *m*; (*woman who preys on man*) (coll) femme *f* fatale, vamp *f* ‖ *tr* (*a shoe*) mettre une empeigne à; (*to piece together*) rapiécer; (*a susceptible man*) (coll) vamper; (*an accompaniment*) (coll) improviser
vampire [ˋvæmpaɪr] *s* vampire *m*; femme *f* fatale, vamp *f*
van [væn] *s* camion *m*, voiture *f* de déménagement; (mil, fig) avant-garde *f*; (*railway car*) (Brit) fourgon *m*
vandal [ˋvændəl] *adj & s* vandale *m* ‖ (*cap*) *adj* vandale ‖ (*cap*) *s* Vandale *mf*
vandalism [ˋvændə,lɪzəm] *s* vandalisme *m*
vane [ven] *s* (*weathervane*) girouette *f*; (*of windmill*) aile *f*; (*of propeller or turbine*) ailette *f*; (*of feather*) lame *f*; (*of a wheel*) aube *f*
vanguard [ˋvæn,gɑrd] *s* (mil, fig) avant-garde *f*; **in the vanguard** à l'avant-garde
vanilla [vəˋnɪlə] *s* vanille *f*
vanish [ˋvænɪʃ] *intr* s'évanouir, disparaître
van′ishing cream′ *s* crème *f* de jour
vani·ty [ˋvænɪti] *s* (*pl* **-ties**) vanité *f*; (*dressing table*) table *f* de toilette, coiffeuse *f*; (*vanity case*) poudrier *m*
van′ity case′ *s* poudrier *m*, nécessaire *m* de toilette
vanquish [ˋvæŋkwɪʃ] *tr* vaincre
van′tage point′ [ˋvæntɪdʒ] *s* position *f* avantageuse
vapid [ˋvæpɪd] *adj* insipide
vapor [ˋvepər] *s* vapeur *f*
vaporize [ˋvepə,raɪz] *tr* vaporiser ‖ *intr* se vaporiser
va′por lock′ *s* bouchon *m* de vapeur
va′por trail′ *s* (aer) sillage *m* de fumée
variable [ˋvɛrɪ·əbl] *adj & s* variable *f*
variance [ˋvɛrɪ·əns] *s* différence *f*, variation *f*; **at variance with** en désaccord avec
variant [ˋvɛrɪ·ənt] *adj* variant ‖ *s* variante *f*
variation [,vɛrɪˋeʃən] *s* variation *f*
varicose [ˋværɪ,kos] *adj* variqueux
var′icose veins′ *spl* (pathol) varice *f*
varied [ˋvɛrid] *adj* varié
variegated [ˋvɛrɪ·ə,getɪd] *adj* varié; (*spotted*) bigarré, bariolé
varie·ty [vəˋraɪ·ɪti] *s* (*pl* **-ties**) variété *f*
vari′ety show′ *s* spectacle *m* de variétés
vari′ety store′ *s* magasin *m* à prix unique
various [ˋvɛrɪ·əs] *adj* divers, différent; (*several*) plusieurs; (*variegated*) bigarré
varnish [ˋvɑrnɪʃ] *s* vernis *m* ‖ *tr* vernir; (*e.g., the truth*) farder, embellir
varsi·ty [ˋvɑrsɪti] *adj* (sports) universitaire ‖ *s* (*pl* **-ties**) (sports) équipe *f* universitaire principale
var·y [ˋvɛri] *v* (*pret & pp* **-ied**) *tr & intr* varier
vase [ves], [vez] *s* vase *m*
Vaseline [ˋvæsə,lin] *s* (trademark) vaseline *f*
vassal [ˋvæsəl] *adj & s* vassal *m*
vast [væst] *adj* vaste
vastness [ˋvæstnɪs] *s* vaste étendue *f*, immensité *f*
vat [væt] *s* cuve *f*, bac *m*
Vatican [ˋvætɪkən] *adj* vaticane ‖ *s* Vatican *m*
vaudeville [ˋvodvɪl] *s* spectacle *m* de variétés, music-hall *m*; (*light theatrical piece interspersed with songs*) vaudeville *m*
vault [vɔlt] *s* (*underground chamber*) souterrain *m*; (*of a bank*) chambre *f* forte;

(*burial chamber*) caveau *m*; (*leap*) saut *m*; (anat, archit) voûte *f* || *tr & intr* sauter
vaunt [vɔnt], [vɑnt] *s* vantardise *f* || *tr* vanter || *intr* se vanter
VCR [ˋviˋsiˋɑr] *s* (letterword) (**videocassette recorder**) magnétoscope *m*
VD [ˋviˋdi] *s* (letterword) (**venereal disease**) maladie *f* vénérienne
veal [vil] *s* veau *m*
veal′ chop′ *s* côtelette *f* de veau
veal′ cut′let *s* escalope *f* de veau
veer [vɪr] *s* virage *m* || *tr* faire virer || *intr* virer
vegetable [ˋvɛdʒɪtəbəl] *adj* végétal || *s* (*plant*) végétal *m*; (*edible part of plant*) légume *m*
veg′etable gar′den *s* potager *m*
veg′etable soup′ *s* potage *m* aux légumes
vegetarian [,vɛdʒɪˋtɛrɪ·ən] *adj & s* végétarien *m*
vegetate [ˋvɛdʒɪ,tet] *intr* végéter
vehemence [ˋvi·ɪməns] *s* véhémence *f*
vehement [ˋvi·ɪmənt] *adj* véhément
vehicle [ˋvi·ɪkəl] *s* véhicule *m*
veil [vel] *s* voile *m*; **to take the veil** prendre le voile || *tr* voiler || *intr* se voiler
vein [ven] *s* veine *f* || *tr* veiner
velar [ˋvilər] *adj & s* vélaire *f*
vellum [ˋvɛləm] *s* vélin *m*; papier *m* vélin
veloci·ty [vɪˋlɑsɪti] *s* (*pl* **-ties**) vitesse *f*
velvet [ˋvɛlvɪt] *s* velours *m*
velveteen [,vɛlvɪˋtin] *s* velvet *m*
velvety [ˋvɛlvɪti] *adj* velouté
vend [vɛnd] *tr* vendre, colporter
vend′ing machine′ *s* distributeur *m* automatique
vendor [ˋvɛndər] *s* vendeur *m*
veneer [vəˋnɪr] *s* placage *m*; (fig) vernis *m* || *tr* plaquer
venerable [ˋvɛnərəbəl] *adj* vénérable
venerate [ˋvɛnə,ret] *tr* vénérer
venereal [vɪˋnɪrɪ·əl] *adj* vénérien
Venetian [vɪˋniʃən] *adj* vénitien || *s* Vénitien *m*
Vene′tian blind′ *s* jalousie *f*, store *m* vénitien
vengeance [ˋvɛndʒəns] *s* vengeance *f*; **with a vengeance** furieusement, à outrance; (*to the utmost limit*) tant que ça peut
vengeful [ˋvɛndʒfəl] *adj* vengeur
Venice [ˋvɛnɪs] *s* Venise *f*
venison [ˋvɛnɪsən] *s* venaison *f*
venom [ˋvɛnəm] *s* venin *m*
venomous [ˋvɛnəməs] *adj* venimeux
vent [vɛnt] *s* orifice *m*; (*for air*) ventouse *f*; **to give vent to** donner libre cours à || *tr* décharger
ventilate [ˋvɛntɪ,let] *tr* ventiler
ventilator [ˋvɛntɪ,letər] *s* ventilateur *m*
ventricle [ˋvɛntrɪkəl] *s* ventricule *m*
ventriloquism [vɛnˋtrɪlə,kwɪzəm] *s* ventriloquie *f*
ventriloquist [vɛnˋtrɪləkwɪst] *s* ventriloque *mf*
venture [ˋvɛntʃər] *s* entreprise *f* risquée; **at a venture** à l'aventure || *tr* aventurer || *intr* s'aventurer; **to venture on** hasarder
venturesome [ˋvɛntʃərsəm] *adj* aventureux
venturous [ˋvɛntʃərəs] *adj* aventureux
vent′ win′dow *s* (aut) déflecteur *m*
venue [ˋvɛnju] *s* (law) lieu *m* du jugement; **change of venue** (law) renvoi *m*
Venus [ˋvinəs] *s* Vénus *f*
veracious [vɪˋreʃəs] *adj* véridique
veraci·ty [vɪˋræsɪti] *s* (*pl* **-ties**) véracité *f*
veranda or **verandah** [vəˋrændə] *s* véranda *f*
verb [vʌrb] *adj* verbal || *s* verbe *m*
verbalize [ˋvʌrbə,laɪz] *tr* exprimer par des mots; (gram) changer en verbe || *intr* être verbeux
verbatim [vərˋbetɪm] *adj* textuel || *adv* textuellement
verbiage [ˋvʌrbɪ·ɪdʒ] *s* verbiage *m*
verbose [vərˋbos] *adj* verbeux
verdant [ˋvʌrdənt] *adj* vert; naïf, candide
verdict [ˋvʌrdɪkt] *s* verdict *m*
verdigris [ˋvʌrdɪ,gris] *s* vert-de-gris *m*
verdure [vʌrdʒər] *s* verdure *f*
verge [vʌrdʒ] *s* bord *m*, limite *f*; **on the verge of** sur le point de || *intr*—**to verge on** or **upon** toucher à; (*bad faith; the age of forty; etc.*) friser
verification [,vɛrɪfɪˋkeʃən] *s* vérification *f*
veri·fy [ˋvɛrɪ,faɪ] *v* (*pret & pp* **-fied**) *tr* vérifier
verily [ˋvɛrɪli] *adv* en vérité
veritable [ˋvɛrɪtəbəl] *adj* véritable
vermilion [vərˋmɪljən] *adj & s* vermillon *m*
vermin [ˋvʌrmɪn] *s* (*objectionable person*) vermine *f* || *spl* (*objectionable animals or persons*) vermine
vermouth [vərˋmuθ], [ˋvʌrmuθ] *s* vermout *m*
vernacular [vərˋnækjələr] *adj* vernaculaire || *s* langue *f* vernaculaire; (*everyday language*) langage *m* vulgaire; (*language peculiar to a class or profession*) jargon *m*
versatile [ˋvʌrsətɪl] *adj* aux talents variés; (*e.g., mind*) universel, souple
verse [vʌrs] *s* vers *mpl*; (*stanza*) strophe *f*; (Bib) verset *m*
versed [vʌrst] *adj*—**versed in** versé dans; spécialiste de
versification [,vʌrsɪfɪˋkeʃən] *s* versification *f*
versi·fy [ˋvʌrsɪ,faɪ] *v* (*pret & pp* **-fied**) *tr & intr* versifier
version [ˋvʌrʒən] *s* version *f*
ver·so [ˋvʌrso] *s* (*pl* **-sos**) (*e.g., of a coin*) revers *m*; (typ) verso *m*
versus [ˋvʌrsəs] *prep* contre
verte·bra [ˋvʌrtɪbrə] *s* (*pl* **-brae** [,bri] or **-bras**) vertèbre *f*
vertebrate [ˋvʌrtɪ,bret] *adj & s* vertébré *m*
ver·tex [ˋvʌrtɛks] *s* (*pl* **-texes** or **-tices** [tɪ,siz]) sommet *m*
vertical [ˋvʌrtɪkəl] *adj* vertical || *s* verticale *f*
ver′tical hold′ *s* (telv) commande *f* de stabilité verticale
ver′tical rud′der *s* gouvernail *m* de direction
ver′tical take′-off *s* décollage *m* vertical

verti·go [ˈvʌrtɪˌgo] s (pl -gos or -goes) vertige m

very [ˈvɛri] adj véritable; même, e.g., **at this very moment** à cet instant même ‖ adv très, e.g., **I am very hungry** j'ai très faim; bien, e.g., **you are very nice** vous êtes bien gentil; tout, e.g., **the very first** le tout premier; e.g., **my very best** tout mon possible; **for my very own** pour moi tout seul; **very much** beaucoup

vesicle [ˈvɛsɪkəl] s vésicule f

vespers [ˈvɛspərz] spl vêpres fpl

vessel [ˈvɛsəl] s bâtiment m, navire m; (container) vase m; (anat, bot, zool) vaisseau m

vest [vɛst] s gilet m; **to play it close to the vest** (coll) jouer serré ‖ tr revêtir; **to vest with** investir de, revêtir de

vest·ed in·terests spl classes fpl dirigeantes

vestibule [ˈvɛstɪˌbjul] s vestibule m

ves·tibule car' s (rr) wagon m à soufflets

vestige [ˈvɛstɪdʒ] s vestige m

vestment [ˈvɛstmənt] s vêtement m sacerdotal

vest'-pock'et adj de poche, de petit format

ves·try [ˈvɛstri] s (pl -tries) sacristie f; (committee) conseil m paroissial

ves'try·man s (pl -men) marguillier m

Vesuvius [vɪˈs(j)uvɪ·əs] s le Vésuve

vetch [vɛtʃ] s vesce f; (Lathyrus sativus) gesse f

veteran [ˈvɛtərən] s vétéran m

veterinarian [ˌvɛtərɪˈnɛri·ən] s vétérinaire mf

veterinar·y [ˈvɛtəriˌnɛri] adj vétérinaire ‖ s (pl -ies) vétérinaire mf

ve·to [ˈvito] s (pl -toes) veto m ‖ tr mettre son veto à

vex [vɛks] tr vexer, contrarier

vexation [vɛkˈseʃən] s vexation f

via [ˈvaɪ·ə] prep via

viaduct [ˈvaɪ·əˌdʌkt] s viaduc m

vial [ˈvaɪ·əl] s fiole f

viand [ˈvaɪ·ənd] s mets m

vibrate [ˈvaɪbret] intr vibrer

vibration [vaɪˈbreʃən] s vibration f

vicar [ˈvɪkər] s vicaire m; (in Church of England) curé m

vicarage [ˈvɪkərɪdʒ] s presbytère m; (duties of vicar) cure f

vicarious [vaɪˈkɛri·əs] adj substitut; (punishment) souffert pour autrui; (power, authority) délégué; (enjoyment) partagé

vice [vaɪs] s vice m; (device) étau m

vice'-ad'miral s vice-amiral m

vice'-pres'ident s vice-président m

viceroy [ˈvaɪsrɔɪ] s vice-roi m

vice' squad' s brigade f des mœurs

vice versa [ˈvaɪsəˈvʌrsə] adv vice versa

vicini·ty [vɪˈsɪnɪti] s (pl -ties) voisinage m; environs mpl, e.g., **New York and vicinity** New York et ses environs

vicious [ˈvɪʃəs] adj vicieux; (mean) méchant; (ferocious) féroce

vicissitude [vɪˈsɪsɪˌt(j)ud] s vicissitude f

victim [ˈvɪktɪm] s victime f; (e.g., of a collision, fire) accidenté m

victimize [ˈvɪktɪˌmaɪz] tr prendre pour victime; (to swindle) duper

victor [ˈvɪktər] s vainqueur m

victorious [vɪkˈtori·əs] adj victorieux

victo·ry [ˈvɪktəri] s (pl -ries) victoire f

victuals [ˈvɪtəlz] spl victuailles fpl

video [ˈvɪdɪ·o] s télévision f

vid'eo·cassette' s vidéocassette f

vid'eo·cassette' record'er s magnétoscope m

vid'eo·cassette' record'ing s magnétoscopie f

vid'eo·record'er s magnétoscope m

vid'eo·record'ing s vidéogramme m, magnétoscopie f

vid'eo·sig'nal s signal m d'image

vid'eo·tape' s bande f vidéo; (in a cassette) vidéocassette f, vidéogramme m

vid'eo·tape' record'er s magnétoscope m

vid'eo·tape' record'ing s magnétoscopie f

vie [vaɪ] v (pret & pp vied; ger vying) intr rivaliser, lutter

Vienna [vɪˈɛnə] s Vienne f

Vien·nese [ˌvi·əˈniz] adj viennois ‖ s (pl -nese) Viennois m

Vietnam [ˌvɪ·ɛtˈnɑm] s le Vietnam

Vietnam·ese [vɪˌɛtnəˈmiz] adj vietnamien ‖ s (pl -ese) Vietnamien m

view [vju] s vue f; **in my view** à mon avis, selon mon opinion; **in view** en vue; **in view of** étant donné, vu; **on view** exposé; **with a view to** en vue de ‖ tr voir, regarder; considérer, examiner

viewer [ˈvju·ər] s spectateur m; (for film, slides, etc.) visionneuse f; (telv) téléspectateur m

view'find'er s viseur m

view'point' s point m de vue

vigil [ˈvɪdʒɪl] s veille f; (eccl) vigile f; **to keep a vigil** veiller

vigilance [ˈvɪdʒɪləns] s vigilance f

vigilant [ˈvɪdʒɪlənt] adj vigilant

vignette [vɪnˈjɛt] s vignette f

vigor [ˈvɪgər] s vigueur f

vigorous [ˈvɪgərəs] adj vigoureux

vile [vaɪl] adj vil; (smell) infect; (weather) sale; (disgusting) détestable

vili·fy [ˈvɪliˌfaɪ] v (pret & pp -fied) tr diffamer, dénigrer

villa [ˈvɪlə] s villa f

village [ˈvɪlɪdʒ] s village m

villager [ˈvɪlɪdʒər] s villageois m

villain [ˈvɪlən] s scélérat m; (of a play) traître m

villainous [ˈvɪlənəs] adj vil, infame

villain·y [ˈvɪləni] s (pl -ies) vilenie f, infamie f

vim [vɪm] s énergie f, vigueur f

vinaigrette' sauce' [ˌvɪnəˈgrɛt] s vinaigrette f

vindicate [ˈvɪndɪˌket] tr justifier, défendre

vindictive [vɪnˈdɪktɪv] adj vindicatif

vine [vaɪn] s plante f grimpante; (grape plant) vigne f

vinegar [ˈvɪnɪgər] s vinaigre m

vinegary [ˈvɪnɪgəri] adj aigre, acide; (ill-tempered) acariâtre

vine' stock' *s* cep *m*

vineyard [ˈvɪnjərd] *s* vignoble *m*, vigne *f*

vintage [ˈvɪntɪdʒ] *s* vendange *f*; (*year*) année *f*, cru *m*; (coll) classe *f*, catégorie *f*

vin'tage wine' *s* bon cru *m*

vin'tage year' *s* grande année *f*

vintner [ˈvɪntnər] *s* négociant *m* en vins; (*person who makes wine*) vigneron *m*

vinyl [ˈvaɪnɪl] *s* vinyle *m*

viola [vaɪˈolə], [vɪˈolə] *s* alto *m*

violate [ˈvaɪ·ə,let] *tr* violer

violation [,vaɪ·əˈleʃən] *s* violation *f*

violence [ˈvaɪ·ələns] *s* violence *f*

violent [ˈvaɪ·ələnt] *adj* violent

violet [ˈvaɪ·əlɪt] *adj* violet ‖ *s* (*color*) violet *m*; (bot) violette *f*

violin [,vaɪ·əˈlɪn] *s* violon *m*

violinist [,vaɪ·əˈlɪnɪst] *s* violoniste *mf*

violoncel·lo [,vaɪ·ələnˈtʃɛlo] *s* (*pl* **-los**) violoncelle *m*

viper [ˈvaɪpər] *s* vipère *f*

vira·go [vɪˈrego] *s* (*pl* **-goes** or **-gos**) mégère *f*

virgin [ˈvʌrdʒɪn] *adj* vierge ‖ *s* vierge *f*; (*male virgin*) puceau *m*

Virgin'ia creep'er [vərˈdʒɪnɪ·ə] *s* vigne *f* vierge

virginity [vərˈdʒɪnɪti] *s* virginité *f*

Virgo [ˈvʌrgo] *s* (astr, astrol) la Vièrge

virility [vɪˈrɪlɪti] *s* virilité *f*

virology [vaɪˈralədʒi] *s* virologie *f*

virtual [ˈvʌrtʃʊ·əl] *adj* véritable, effectif; (mech, opt, phys) virtuel

virtue [ˈvʌrtʃʊ] *s* vertu *f*; mérite *m*, avantage *m*

virtuosi·ty [,vʌrtʃʊˈɑsɪti] *s* (*pl* **-ties**) virtuosité *f*

virtuo·so [,vʌrtʃʊˈoso] *s* (*pl* **-sos** or **-si** [si]) virtuose *mf*

virtuous [ˈvʌrtʃʊ·əs] *adj* vertueux

virulence [ˈvɪrjələns] *s* virulence *f*

virulent [ˈvɪrjələnt] *adj* virulent

virus [ˈvaɪrəs] *s* virus *m*

visa [ˈvizə] *s* visa *m* ‖ *tr* viser

visage [ˈvɪzɪdʒ] *s* visage *m*

vis-à-vis [,vizəˈvi] *adj* face à face ‖ *s & adv* vis-à-vis *m* ‖ *prep* vis-à-vis de

viscera [ˈvɪsərə] *spl* viscères *mpl*

viscount [ˈvaɪkaʊnt] *s* vicomte *m*

viscountess [ˈvaɪkaʊntɪs] *s* vicomtesse *f*

viscous [ˈvɪskəs] *adj* visqueux

vise [vaɪs] *s* étau *m*

visible [ˈvɪzɪbəl] *adj* visible

vision [ˈvɪʒən] *s* vision *f*

visionar·y [ˈvɪʒə,nɛri] *adj* visionnaire ‖ *s* (*pl* **-ies**) visionnaire *mf*

visit [ˈvɪzɪt] *s* visite *f* ‖ *tr* visiter; (*e.g., a person*) rendre visite à ‖ *intr* faire des visites

visitation [,vɪzɪˈteʃən] *s* visite *f*; justice *f* du ciel; clémence *f* du ciel; (*e.g., in a séance*) apparition *f*; **Visitation** (eccl) Visitation *f*

vis'iting card' *s* carte *f* de visite

vis'iting hours' *spl* heures *fpl* de visite

vis'iting nurse' *s* infirmière *f* visiteuse

vis'iting profes'sor *s* visiting *m*

visitor [ˈvɪzɪtər] *s* visiteur *m*

visor [ˈvaɪzər] *s* visière *f*

vista [ˈvɪstə] *s* perspective *f*

visual [ˈvɪʒʊ·əl] *adj* visuel

visualize [ˈvɪʒʊ·ə,laɪz] *tr* (*in one's mind*) se faire une image mentale de, se représenter; (*to make visible*) visualiser

vital [ˈvaɪtəl] *adj* vital ‖ **vitals** *spl* organes *mpl* vitaux

vitality [vaɪˈtælɪti] *s* vitalité *f*

vitalize [ˈvaɪtə,laɪz] *tr* vitaliser

vitamin [ˈvaɪtəmɪn] *s* vitamine *f*

vitiate [ˈvɪʃɪ,et] *tr* vicier

vitreous [ˈvɪtrɪ·əs] *adj* vitreux

vitriolic [,vɪtrɪˈɑlɪk] *adj* (chem) vitriolique; (fig) trempé dans du vitriol

vituperate [vaɪˈt(j)upə,ret] *tr* vitupérer

viva [ˈvivə] *s* vivat *m* ‖ *interj* vive!

vivacious [vaɪˈveʃəs] *adj* vif, animé

vivaci·ty [vaɪˈvæsɪti] *s* (*pl* **-ties**) vivacité *f*

viva voce [ˈvaɪvəˈvosi] *adj* de vive voix

vivid [ˈvɪvɪd] *adj* vif; (*description*) vivant; (*recollection*) vivace

vivi·fy [ˈvɪvɪ,faɪ] *v* (*pret & pp* **-fied**) *tr* vivifier

vivisection [,vɪvɪˈsɛkʃən] *s* vivisection *f*

vixen [ˈvɪksən] *s* mégère *f*; (zool) renarde *f*

viz. *abbr* (Lat: **videlicet** namely, to wit) c.-à-d., à savoir

vizier [vɪˈzɪr], [ˈvɪzjər] *s* vizir *m*

vocabular·y [voˈkæbjə,lɛri] *s* (*pl* **-ies**) vocabulaire *m*

vocal [ˈvokəl] *adj* vocal; (*inclined to express oneself freely*) communicatif, démonstratif

vocalist [ˈvokəlɪst] *s* chanteur *m*

vocalize [ˈvokə,laɪz] *tr* vocaliser ‖ *intr* vocaliser; (phonet) se vocaliser

vocation [voˈkeʃən] *s* vocation *f*; profession *f*, métier *m*

voca'tional guid'ance [voˈkeʃənəl] *s* orientation *f* professionnelle

voca'tional school' *s* école *f* professionnelle

vocative [ˈvokətɪv] *s* vocatif *m*

vociferate [voˈsɪfə,ret] *intr* vociférer

vociferous [voˈsɪfərəs] *adj* vociférant, criard

vogue [vog] *s* vogue *f*; **in vogue** en vogue

voice [vɔɪs] *s* voix *f*; **in a loud voice** à voix haute; **in a low voice** à voix basse; **with one voice** unanimement ‖ *tr* exprimer; (*a consonant*) voiser, sonoriser ‖ *intr* se voiser

voiced *adj* (phonet) voisé, sonore

voiceless [ˈvɔɪslɪs] *adj* sans voix, aphone; (*consonant*) dévoisée, sourde

void [vɔɪd] *adj* vide; (law) nul; **void of** dénué de ‖ *s* vide *m* ‖ *tr* vider; (*the bowels*) évacuer; (law) rendre nul ‖ *intr* évacuer, excréter

voile [vɔɪl] *s* voile *m*

volatile [ˈvɑlətɪl] *adj* (*solvent*) volatil; (*disposition*) volage; (*temper*) vif

volatilize [ˈvɑlətə,laɪz] *tr* volatiliser ‖ *intr* se volatiliser

volcanic [vɑlˈkænɪk] *adj* volcanique

volca·no [vɑlˈkeno] *s* (*pl* **-noes** or **-nos**) volcan *m*

volition [vəˈlɪʃən] s volition f, volonté f; **of one's own volition** de son propre gré
volley [ˈvɑlɪ] s volée f ‖ tr lancer à la volée; (sports) reprendre de volée ‖ intr lancer une volée
vol'ley·ball' s volley-ball m
volplane [ˈvɑl,plen] s vol m plané ‖ intr descendre en vol plané
volt [volt] s volt m
voltage [ˈvoltɪdʒ] s voltage m, tension f; **high voltage** haute tension f
volt'age drop' s perte f de charge
volte-face [ˈvɔltˈfɑs] s volte-face f
volt'me'ter s voltmètre m
voluble [ˈvɑljəbəl] adj volubile
volume [ˈvɑljəm] s volume m; **to speak volumes** en dire long
vol'ume num'ber s tomaison f
voluminous [vəˈluminəs] adj volumineux
voluntar·y [ˈvɑlən,tɛri] adj volontaire ‖ s (pl -ies) (mus) morceau m d'orgue improvisé
volunteer [,vɑlənˈtɪr] adj & s volontaire mf ‖ tr offrir volontairement ‖ intr (mil) s'engager; **to volunteer to** + inf s'offrir à + inf
voluptuar·y [vəˈlʌptʃu,ɛri] adj voluptuaire ‖ s (pl -ies) voluptueux m
voluptuous [vəˈlʌptʃu·əs] adj voluptueux
vomit [ˈvɑmɪt] s vomissure f ‖ tr & intr vomir
voodoo [ˈvudu] adj & s vaudou m
voracious [vəˈreʃəs] adj vorace
voraci·ty [vəˈræsɪti] s (pl -ties) voracité f
vor·tex [ˈvɔrtɛks] s (pl -texes or -tices [tɪ,siz]) vortex m, tourbillon m
vota·ry [ˈvotəri] s (pl -ries) fidèle mf

vote [vot] s vote m; **by popular vote** au suffrage universel; **to put to the vote** mettre aux voix; **to tally the votes** dépouiller le scrutin; **vote by show of hands** vote à main levée ‖ tr voter; **to vote down** repousser; **to vote in** élire ‖ intr voter; **to vote for** voter; **to vote on** passer au vote
voter [ˈvotər] s votant m, électeur m
vot'ing booth' s isoloir m
vot'ing machine' s machine f électorale
votive [ˈvotɪv] adj votif
vouch [vautʃ] tr affirmer, garantir ‖ intr—**to vouch for** répondre de
voucher [ˈvautʃər] s garant m; (certificate) récépissé m, pièce f comptable, bon m de change
vouch·safe' tr octroyer ‖ intr—**to vouchsafe to** + inf daigner + inf
vow [vau] s vœu m; **to take vows** entrer en religion ‖ tr (e.g., revenge) jurer ‖ intr faire un vœu; **to vow to** faire vœu de
vowel [ˈvau·əl] s voyelle f
voyage [ˈvɔɪ·ɪdʒ] s (by air or sea) traversée f; (any journey) voyage m ‖ tr traverser ‖ intr voyager
voyager [ˈvɔɪ·ɪdʒər] s voyageur m
vs. abbr (**versus**) contre
vulcanize [ˈvʌlkə,naɪz] tr vulcaniser
vulgar [ˈvʌlgər] adj grossier; (popular, common; vernacular) vulgaire
vulgari·ty [vʌlˈgærɪti] s (pl -ties) grossièreté f, vulgarité f
Vul'gar Lat'in s latin m vulgaire
vulnerable [ˈvʌlnərəbəl] adj vulnérable
vulture [ˈvʌltʃər] s vautour m

W

W, w [ˈdʌbəl,ju] s XXIIIᵉ lettre de l'alphabet
wad [wɑd] s (of cotton) tampon m; (of papers) liasse f; (in a gun) bourre f ‖ v (pret & pp **wadded**; ger **wadding**) tr bourrer
waddle [ˈwɑdəl] s dandinement m ‖ intr se dandiner
wade [wed] tr traverser à gué ‖ intr marcher dans l'eau, patauger; **to wade into** (coll) s'attaquer à; **to wade through** (coll) avancer péniblement dans
wad'ing bird' s (orn) échassier m
wad'ing pool' s pataugeoire f
wafer [ˈwefər] s (thin, crisp cake) gaufrette f; (pill) cachet m; (for sealing letters) pain m à cacheter; (eccl) hostie f
waffle [ˈwɑfəl] s gaufre f
waf'fle i'ron s gaufrier m, moule m à gaufre
waft [wæt], [wɑft] tr porter; (a kiss) envoyer ‖ intr flotter

wag [wæg] s (of head) hochement m; (of tail) frétillement m; (jester) farceur m ‖ v (pret & pp **wagged**; ger **wagging**) tr (the head) hocher; (the tail) remuer ‖ intr frétiller
wage [wedʒ] s salaire m; **wages** gages mpl, salaire m; (fig) salaire, récompense f ‖ tr—**to wage war** faire la guerre
wage' earn'er [,ʌrnər] s salarié m
wage'-price' freeze' s blocage m des prix et des salaires
wager [ˈwedʒər] s pari m; **to lay a wager** faire un pari ‖ tr & intr parier
wage'work'er s salarié m
waggish [ˈwægɪʃ] adj plaisant, facétieux
wagon [ˈwægən] s charrette f, (Conestoga wagon; plaything) chariot m; (mil) fourgon m; **to be on the wagon** (slang) s'abstenir de boissons alcooliques
wag'tail' s hochequeue m, bergeronnette f
waif [wef] s (founding) enfant m trouvé;

animal *m* égaré or abandonné; (*stray child*) voyou *m*

wail [wel] *s* lamentation *f*, plainte *f* ‖ *intr* se lamenter, gémir

wain·scot ['wenskət] *s* lambris *m* ‖ *v* (*pret & pp* **-scoted** or **-scotted;** *ger* **-scoting or -scotting**) *tr* lambrisser

waist [west] *s* (*of human body; corresponding part of garment*) taille *f*, ceinture *f*; (*garment*) corsage *m*, blouse *f*

waist′band′ *s* ceinture *f*

waist′cloth′ *s* pagne *m*

waistcoat ['west,kot] *s* gilet *m*

waist′-deep′ *adj* jusqu'à la ceinture

waist′line′ *s* taille *f*, ceinture *f*; **to keep or watch one's waistline** garder or soigner sa ligne

wait [wet] *s* attente *f*; **to lie in wait for** guetter ‖ *tr*—**to wait one's turn** attendre son tour ‖ *intr* attendre; **to wait for** attendre; **to wait on** (*customers; dinner guests*) servir

wait′-and-see′ pol′icy *s* attentisme *m*

waiter ['wetər] *s* garçon *m*; (*tray*) plateau *m*

wait′ing list′ *s* liste *f* d'attente

wait′ing room′ *s* salle *f* d'attente; (*of a doctor*) antichambre *f*

waitress ['wetrɪs] *s* serveuse *f*; **waitress!** mademoiselle!

waive [wev] *tr* renoncer à; (*to defer*) différer

waiver ['wevər] *s* renonciation *f*, abandon *m*

wake [wek] *s* (*watch by the body of a dead person*) veillée *f* mortuaire; (*of a boat or other moving object*) silage *m*; **in the wake of** dans le sillage de, à la suite de ‖ *v* (*pret* **waked** or **woke** [wok]; *pp* **waked**) *tr* réveiller ‖ *intr*—**to wake to** se rendre compte de; **to wake up** se réveiller

wakeful ['wekfəl] *adj* éveillé

wakefulness ['wekfəlnɪs] *s* veille *f*

waken ['wekən] *tr* éveiller, réveiller ‖ *intr* s'éveiller, se réveiller

wale [wel] *s* zébrure *f* ‖ *tr* zébrer

Wales [welz] *s* le pays de Galles

walk [wɔk] *s* (*act*) promenade *f*; (*distance*) marche *f*; (*way of walking, bearing*) démarche *f*; (*of a garden*) allée *f*; (*calling*) métier *m*; **to fall into a walk** (*said of horse*) se mettre au pas; **to go for a walk** faire une promenade ‖ *tr* promener; (*a horse*) promener au pas ‖ *intr* aller à pied, marcher; (*to stroll*) se promener; **to walk away** s'en aller à pied; **to walk off with** (*a prize*) gagner; (*a stolen object*) décamper avec; **to walk out** sortir, partir subitement; (*to go on strike*) se mettre en grève; **to walk out on** abandonner; quitter en colère

walk′away′ *s* (coll) victoire *f* facile

walker ['wɔkər] *s* marcheur *m*, promeneur *m*; (*pedestrian*) piéton *m*; (*go-cart*) chariot *m* d'enfant; (*used by an infirm person*) déambulateur *m*

walkie-talkie ['wɔki'tɔki] *s* (rad) talkie-walkie *m*, émetteur-récepteur *m* portatif, parle-en-marche *m*

walk′ing pa′pers *spl*—**to give s.o. his walking papers** (coll) congédier qn

walk′ing shoes′ *spl* souliers *mpl* de marche

walk′ing stick′ *s* canne *f*

walk′man′ *s* (rad) baladeur *m*, walkman *m*, somnambule *m*

walk′-on′ *s* (*actor*) figurant *m*, comparse *mf*; (*role*) figuration *f*

walk′out′ *s* (coll) grève *f* improvisée

walk′o′ver *s* (coll) victoire *f* dans un fauteuil

walk′-up′ *s* appartement *m* sans ascenseur

wall [wɔl] *s* mur *m*; (*between rooms; of a pipe, boiler, etc.*) paroi *f*; (*of a fortification*) muraille *f*; **to go to the wall** succomber; perdre la partie ‖ *tr* entourer de murs; **to wall up** murer

wall′board′ *s* panneau *m* or carreau *m* de revêtement

wall′ clock′ *s* pendule *f* murale

wallet ['wɑlɪt] *s* portefeuille *m*

wall′flow′er *s* (bot) ravenelle *f*, giroflée *f*; **to be a wallflower** (coll) faire tapisserie

wall′ lamp′ *s* applique *f*

wall′ map′ *s* carte *f* murale

Walloon [wɑ'lun] *adj* wallon ‖ *s* (*dialect*) wallon *m*; (*person*) Wallon *m*

wallop ['wɑləp] *s* (coll) coup *m*, gnon *m*; **with a wallop** (fig) à grand fracas ‖ *tr* (coll) tanner le cuir à, rosser; (*a ball*) (coll) frapper raide; (*to defeat*) (coll) battre

wallow ['wɑlo] *s* souille *f* ‖ *intr* se vautrer; (*e.g., in wealth*) nager

wall′pa′per *s* papier *m* peint ‖ *tr* tapisser

wall′-to-wall′ car′peting *s* tapis *m* mur à mur

walnut ['wɔlnət] *s* noix *f*; (*tree and wood*) noyer *m*

walrus ['wɔlrəs], [wɑlrəs] *s* morse *m*

Walter ['wɔltər] *s* Gautier *m*

waltz [wɔlts] *s* valse *f* ‖ *tr & intr* valser

wan [wɑn] *adj* (*comp* **wanner;** *super* **wannest**) pâle blême; (*weak*) faible

wand [wɑnd] *s* baguette *f*; (*emblem of authority*) bâton *m*, verge *f*

wander ['wɑndər] *tr* vagabonder sur, parcourir ‖ *intr* errer, vaguer; (*said of one's mind*) vagabonder

wanderer ['wɑndərər] *s* vagabond *m*

wan′der·lust′ *s* manie *f* des voyages, bougeotte *f*

wane [wen] *s* déclin *m*; (*of moon*) décours *m* ‖ *intr* décliner; (*said of moon*) décroître

wangle ['wæŋgəl] *tr* (*to obtain by scheming*) (coll) resquiller; (*accounts*) (coll) cuisiner; (*e.g., a leave of absence*) (coll) carotter; **to wangle one's way out of** (coll) se débrouiller de ‖ *intr* (coll) pratiquer le système D

want [wɔnt] *s* (*need; misery*) besoin *m*; (*lack*) manque *m*; **for want of** faute de, à défaut de; **to be in want** être dans la gêne ‖ *tr* vouloir; (*to need*) avoir besoin de; **want s.o. to** + *inf* vouloir que qn + *subj*; **to want to** + *inf* avoir envie de + *inf*, vouloir + *inf* ‖ *intr* être dans le besoin; **to be wanting** manquer

want′ ads′ *spl* petites annonces *fpl*

wanton [′wɑntən] *adj* déréglé; (*e.g., cruelty*) gratuit; (*e.g., child*) espiègle; (*e.g., woman*) impudique

war [wɔr] *s* guerre *f*; **to go to war** se mettre en guerre; (*as a soldier*) aller à la guerre; **to wage war** faire la guerre ‖ *v* (*pret & pp* **warred;** *ger* **warring**) *intr* faire la guerre; **to war on** faire la guerre contre

warble [′wɔrbəl] *s* gazouillement *m* ‖ *intr* gazouiller

warbler [′wɔrblər] *s* (orn) fauvette *f*

war′ cloud′ *s* menace *f* de guerre

war′ correspon′dent *s* correspondant *m* de guerre

war′ cry′ *s* (*pl* **cries**) cri *m* de guerre

ward [wɔrd] *s* (*person, usually a minor under protection of another*) pupille *mf*; (*guardianship*) tutelle *f*; (*of a city*) circonscription *f* électorale, quartier *m*; (*of a hospital*) salle *f*; (*of a lock*) gardes *fpl* ‖ *tr*—**to ward off** parer

war′ dance′ *s* danse *f* guerrière

warden [′wɔrdən] *s* gardien *m*; (*of a jail*) directeur *m*; (*of a church*) marguillier *m*; (*gamekeeper*) garde-chasse *m*

ward′ heel′er *s* politicailleur *m* servile

ward′robe′ *s* garde-robe *f*

ward′robe trunk′ *s* malle-armoire *f*

ward′room′ *s* (nav) carré *m* des officiers

ware [wɛr] *s* faïence *f*; **wares** articles *mpl* de vente, marchandises *fpl*

ware′house′ *s* entrepôt *m*

ware′house′man *s* (*pl* **-men**) garde-magasin *m*, magasinier *m*

war′fare′ *s* guerre *f*

war′head′ *s* charge *f* creuse

war′-horse′ *s* cheval *m* de bataille; (coll) vétéran *m*

warily [′wɛrɪli] *adv* prudemment

war′like′ *adj* guerrier

war′ loan′ *s* emprunt *m* de guerre

war′ lord′ *s* seigneur *m* de la guerre

warm [wɔrm] *adj* chaud; (*welcome, thanks, friend, etc.*) chaleureux; (*heart*) généreux; **it is warm** (*said of weather*) il fait chaud; **to be warm** (*said of person*) avoir chaud; **to keep s.th. warm** tenir q.ch. au chaud; **you′re getting warm!** (*you′ve almost found it!*) vous brûlez! ‖ *tr* chauffer, faire chauffer; **to warm up** réchauffer ‖ *intr* se réchauffer; **to warm up** se réchauffer, chauffer, se chauffer; (*said of speaker, discussion, etc.*) s′animer s′échauffer

warm′-blood′ed *adj* passionné, ardent; (*animals*) à sang chaud

war′ memor′ial *s* monument *m* aux morts de la guerre

warmer [′wɔrmər] *s* (culin) réchaud *m*

warm′-heart′ed *adj* au cœur généreux

warm′ing pan′ *s* bassinoire *f*

warmonger [′wɔr,mʌŋgər] *s* belliciste *mf*

war′ moth′er *s* marraine *f* de guerre

warmth [wɔrmθ] *s* chaleur *f*

warm′-up′ *s* exercises *mpl* d′assouplissement; mise *f* en condition

warn [wɔrn] *tr* prévenir; **to warn s.o. to** avertir qn de

warning [′wɔrnɪŋ] *s* avertissement *m*; **without warning** par surprise

warn′ing shot′ *s* coup *m* de semonce

war′ of attri′tion *s* guerre *f* d′usure

warp [wɔrp] *s* (*of a fabric*) chaîne *f*; (*of a board*) gauchissement *m*; (naut) touée *f* ‖ *tr* gauchir; (*the mind, judgment, etc.*) fausser; (naut) touer ‖ *intr* se gauchir; (naut) se touer

war′path′ *s*—**to be on the warpath** être sur le sentier de la guerre; (*to be out of sorts*) (coll) être d′une humeur de dogue

war′plane′ *s* avion *m* de guerre

warrant [′wɔrənt] *s* (*guarantee*) garantie *f*; (*attestation*) certificat *m*; (*right*) justification *f*; (*for arrest*) mandat *m* d′arrêt ‖ *tr* garantir; certifier; justifier

war′rant of′ficer *s* (mil) sous-officier *m* breveté; (nav) premier maître *m*

warran·ty [′wɔrənti] *s* (*pl* **-ties**) garantie *f*; autorisation *f*

war′ranty ser′vice *s* service *m* après vente

warren [′wɔrən] *s* garenne *f*

warrior [′wɔrjər] *s* guerrier *m*

Warsaw [′wɔrsɔ] *s* Varsovie *f*

war′ship′ *s* navire *m* de guerre

wart [wɔrt] *s* verrue *f*

war′time′ *s* temps *m* de guerre

war′-torn′ *adj* dévasté par la guerre

war·y [′wɛri] *adj* (*comp* **-ier;** *super* **-iest**) prudent, avisé

wash [wɔʃ] *s* (*washing*) lavage *m*; (*clothes washed or to be washed*) lessive *f*; (*dirty water*) lavure *f*; (*place where the surf breaks; broken water behind a moving ship*) remous *m*; (aer) souffle *m* ‖ *tr* laver; (*one′s hands, face, etc.*) se laver; (*dishes, laundry, etc.*) faire; (*e.g., a seacoast*) baigner; **to wash away** enlever; (*e.g., a bank*) affouiller, ronger ‖ *intr* se laver; (*to do the laundry*) faire la lessive

washable [′wɔʃəbəl] *adj* lavable

wash′-and-wear′ *adj* de repassage superflu de séchage rapide

wash′ba′sin *s* (*basin*) cuvette *f*; (*fixture*) lavabo *m*

wash′bas′ket *s* corbeille *f* à linge

wash′board′ *s* planche *f* à laver

wash′bowl′ *s* (*basin*) cuvette *f*; (*fixture*) lavabo *m*

wash′cloth′ *s* gant *m* de toilette

wash′day′ *s* jour *m* de lessive

washed′-out′ *adj* délavé, déteint; (coll) flapi, vanné, à plat, vaseux

washed′-up′ *adj* (coll) hors de combat, ruiné

washer [′wɔʃər] *s* (*person*) laveur *m*; (*machine*) laveuse *f*, lessiveuse *f*; (*ring of metal*) rondelle *f*; (*ring of rubber*) rondelle de robinet

wash′er·wom′an *s* (*pl* **-wom′en**) blanchisseuse *f*

wash′ goods′ *spl* tissus *mpl* grand teint

washing ['wɔʃɪŋ] *s* lavage *m*; (*act of washing clothes*) blanchissage *m*; (*clothes washed or to be washed*) lessive *f*; **washings** lavures *fpl*

wash′ing machine′ *s* machine *f* à laver, laveuse *f* automatique

wash′ing so′da *s* cristaux *mpl* de soude

wash′out′ *s* affouillement *m*; (*person*) (coll) raté *m*; **to be a washout** (coll) faire fiasco, faire four

wash′rag′ *s* gant *m* de toilette, torchon *m*

wash′room′ *s* cabinet *m* de toilette, lavabo *m*

wash′ sale′ *s* (com) lavage *m* des titres

wash′stand′ *s* lavabo *m*

wash′tub′ *s* baquet *m*, cuvier *m*

wash′ wa′ter *s* lavure *f*

wasp [wɑsp] *s* guêpe *f*

wasp′ waist′ *s* taille *f* de guêpe

waste [west] *adj* (*land*) inculte; (*material*) de rebut ‖ *s* (*loss*) gaspillage *m*; (*garbage*) déchets *mpl*; (*wild region*) région *f* inculte; (*of time*) perte *f*; (*for wiping machinery*) chiffons *mpl* de nettoyage, effiloche *f* de coton; **to lay waste** dévaster; **wastes** déchets; excrément *m* ‖ *tr* gaspiller, perdre ‖ *intr*—**to waste away** dépérir, maigrir

waste′bas′ket *s* corbeille *f* à papier

wasteful ['westfəl] *adj* gaspilleur

waste′pa′per *s* papier *m* de rebut; (*public sign*) papers

waste′ pipe′ *s* tuyau *m* d'écoulement, vidange *f*

waste′ prod′ucts *spl* déchets *mpl*

wastrel ['westrəl] *s* gaspilleur *m*, prodigue *mf*

watch [wɑtʃ] *s* (*for telling time*) montre *f*; (*lookout*) garde *f*, guet *m*; (naut) quart *m*; **to be on the watch for** guetter; **to be on watch** (naut) être de quart; **to keep watch over** surveiller ‖ *tr* (*to look at*) observer; (*to oversee*) surveiller ‖ *intr* être aux aguets; (*to keep awake*) veiller; **to watch for** guetter; **to watch out** faire attention; **to watch out for** faire attention à; **to watch over** surveiller; **watch out!** attention! gare!

watch′case′ *s* boîtier *m* de montre

watch′ chain′ *s* chaîne *f* de montre

watch′ charm′ *s* breloque *f*

watch′ crys′tal *s* verre *m* de montre

watch′dog′ *s* chien *m* de garde; gardien *m* vigilant

watch′dog′ commit′tee *s* comité *m* de surveillance

watchful ['wɑtʃfəl] *adj* vigilant

watchfulness ['wɑtʃfəlnɪs] *s* vigilance *f*

watch′mak′er *s* horloger *m*

watch′man *s* (*pl* -men) gardien *m*

watch′ night′ *s* réveillon *m* du jour de l'an

watch′ pock′et *s* gousset *m*

watch′ strap′ *s* bracelet *m* d'une montre

watch′tow′er *s* tour *f* de guet

watch′word′ *s* (*password*) mot *m* d'ordre, mot de passe; (*slogan*) devise *f*

water ['wɔtər] *s* eau *f*; **of the first water** de premier ordre; (*diamond*) de première eau; **to back water** (naut) culer; reculer; **to be**

in hot water (coll) être dans le pétrin; **to fish in troubled waters** pêcher en eau trouble; **to hold water** (coll) tenir debout, être bien fondé; **to make water** (*to urinate*) uriner; (naut) faire eau; **to pour** or **throw cold water on** (fig) jeter une douche froide sur, refroidir; **to swim under water** nager entre deux eaux; **to tread water** nager debout ‖ *tr* (*e.g., plants*) arroser; (*horses, cattle, etc.*) abreuver; (*wine*) couper; **to water down** atténuer ‖ *intr* (*said of horses, cattle, etc.*) s'abreuver; (*said of locomotive, ship, etc.*) faire de l'eau; (*said of eyes*) se mouiller, larmoyer

wa′ter bed′ *s* matelas *m* à eau

wa′ter buf′fa·lo *s* (*pl* -loes or -los) buffle *m*

wa′ter car′rier *s* porteur *m* d'eau

wa′ter clock′ *s* horloge *f* à eau, horloge d'eau

wa′ter clos′et *s* water-closet *m*, waters *mpl*

wa′ter·col′or *s* aquarelle *f*

wa′ter-cooled′ *adj* à refroidissement d'eau

wa′ter·course′ *s* cours *m* d'eau; (*of a stream*) lit *m*

wa′ter·cress′ *s* cresson *m* de fontaine

wa′ter cure′ *s* cure *f* des eaux

wa′ter·fall′ *s* chute *f* d'eau

wa′ter·front′ *s* terrain *m* sur la rive

wa′ter gap′ *s* percée *f*, trouée *f*, gorge *f*

wa′ter ham′mer *s* (*in pipe*) coup *m* de bélier

wa′ter heat′er *s* chauffe-eau *m*, chauffe-bain *m*

wa′ter ice′ *s* boisson *f* à demi glacée

wa′ter·ing can′ *s* arrosoir *m*

wa′ter·ing place′ *s* (*for cattle*) abreuvoir *m*; (*for tourists*) ville *f* d'eau

wa′ter·ing pot′ *s* arrosoir *m*

wa′ter·ing trough′ *s* abreuvoir *m*

wa′ter jack′et *s* chemise *f* d'eau

wa′ter lil′y *s* nénuphar *m*

wa′ter line′ *s* ligne *f* de flottaison; niveau *m* d'eau

wa′ter·logged′ *adj* détrempé

wa′ter main′ *s* conduite *f* principale

wa′ter·mark′ *s* (*in paper*) filigrane *m*; (naut) laisse *f*

wa′ter·mel′on *s* pastèque *f*, melon *m* d'eau

wa′ter me′ter *s* compteur *m* à eau

wa′ter pick′ *s* (dentistry) jet *m* dentaire

wa′ter pipe′ *s* conduite *f* d'eau

wa′ter po′lo *s* water-polo *m*

wa′ter pow′er *s* force *f* hydraulique, houille *f* blanche

wa′ter·proof′ *adj* & *s* imperméable *m*

wa′ter·proof′ing *s* imperméabilisation *f*

wa′ter rights′ *spl* droits *mpl* de captation d'eau, droits d'irrigation

wa′ter·shed′ *s* ligne *f* de partage des eaux, ligne de faîte

wa′ter ski′er *s* skieur *m* nautique

wa′ter ski′ing *s* ski *m* nautique

wa′ter sof′tener *s* assouplisseur *m*

wa′ter span′iel *s* (zool) barbet *m*

wa′ter·spout′ *s* descente *f* d'eau, gouttière *f*; (*funnel of wet air*) trombe *f*

whir [hwʌr] *s* ronflement *m* ‖ *v* (*pret & pp* **whirred;** *ger* **whipping**) *intr* ronfler

whirl [hwʌrl] *s* tourbillon *m*; (*of events, parties, etc.*) succession *f* ininterrompue ‖ *tr* faire tourbillonner ‖ *intr* tourbillonner; **his head whirls** la tête lui tourne

whirligig [ˈhwʌrlɪˌgɪg] *s* tourniquet *m*; (ent) gyrin *m*, tourniquet

whirl′pool′ *s* tourbillon *m*, remous *m*

whirl′wind′ *s* tourbillon *m*

whirlybird [ˈhwʌrliˌbʌrd] *s* (coll) hélicoptère *m*

whisk [hwɪsk] *s* (*rapid, sweeping stroke*) coup *m* léger; (*broom*) époussette *f*; (culin) fouet *m* ‖ *tr* balayer; (culin) fouetter; **to whisk out of sight** escamoter ‖ *intr* aller comme un trait

whisk′ broom′ *s* époussette *f*

whiskers [ˈhwɪskərz] *spl* barbe *f*, poils *mpl* de barbe; (*on side of face*) favoris *mpl*; (*of cat*) moustaches *fpl*

whiskey [ˈhwɪski] *s* whisky *m*

whisper [ˈhwɪspər] *s* chuchotement *m* ‖ *tr* chuchoter, dire à l'oreille ‖ *intr* chuchoter

whispering [ˈhwɪspərɪŋ] *s* chuchotement *m*

whist [hwɪst] *s* whist *m*

whistle [ˈhwɪsəl] *s* (*sound*) sifflement *m*; (*device*) sifflet *m*; **to wet one's whistle** (coll) s'humecter le gosier ‖ *tr* siffler, siffloter ‖ *intr* siffler; **to whistle for** siffler; attendre en vain, se voir obligé de se passer de

whis′tle stop′ *s* arrêt *m* facultatif

whit [hwɪt] *s*—**not a whit** pas un brin; **to not care a whit** s'en moquer

white [hwaɪt] *adj* blanc ‖ *s* blanc *m*; blanc d'œuf; **whites** (pathol) pertes *fpl* blanches

white′ caps′ *spl* moutons *mpl*

white′ coal′ *s* houille *f* blanche

white′ cof′fee *s* café *m* crème

white′-col′lar *adj* de bureau

white′-col′lar work′er *s* col *m* blanc

white′ feath′er *s*—**to show the white feather** lâcher pied, flancher, caner

white′fish′ *s* poisson *m* blanc, merlan *m*

white′ goods′ *spl* vêtements *mpl* blancs; tissus *mpl* de coton, cotonnade *f*; (*appliances*) appareils *mpl* électroménagers

white′-haired′ *adj* aux cheveux blancs, chenu; (coll) favori

white′-hot′ *adj* chauffé à blanc

White′ House′ *s*—**the White House** la Maison Blanche

white′ lead′ [led] *s* céruse *f*, blanc *m* de céruse

white′ lie′ *s* mensonge *m* pieux

white′ meat′ *s* blanc *m*

whiten [ˈhwaɪtən] *tr & intr* blanchir

whiteness [ˈhwaɪtnɪs] *s* blancheur *f*

white′ slav′ery *s* traite *f* des blanches

white′ tie′ *s* cravate *f* blanche; tenue *f* de soirée

white′wash′ *s* blanc *m* de chaux, badigeon *m*; (*cover-up*) couverture *f* ‖ *tr* blanchir à la chaux; (*e.g., a guilty person, a scandal*) blanchir

whither [ˈhwɪðər] *adv & conj* où, là où

whitish [ˈhwaɪtɪʃ] *adj* blanchâtre

whitlow [ˈhwɪtlo] *s* panaris *m*

Whitsuntide [ˈhwɪtsənˌtaɪd] *s* saison *f* de la Pentecôte

whittle [ˈhwɪtəl] *tr* tailler au couteau; **to whittle away** or **down** amenuiser

whiz or **whizz** [hwɪz] *s* sifflement *m*; (slang) prodige *m* ‖ *v* (*pret & pp* **whizzed;** *ger* **whizzing**) *intr*—**to whiz by** passer en sifflant, passer comme le vent

who [hu] *pron interr* qui; quel §80; **who else?** qui d'autre?; qui encore?; **who is there?** (mil) qui vive? ‖ *pron rel* qui; celui qui §83

whoa [hwo] *interj* holà!, doucement!

whodunit [huˈdʌnɪt] *s* roman *m* noir

who·ev′er *pron rel* quiconque; celui qui §83; qui que, e.g., **whoever you are** qui que vous soyez

whole [hol] *adj* entier ‖ *s* tout *m*, totalité *f*, ensemble *m*; **on the whole** somme toute, à tout prendre

whole′heart′ed *adj* sincère, de bon cœur

whole′ note′ *s* (mus) ronde *f*

whole′ rest′ *s* (mus) pause *f*

whole′sale′ *adj & adv* en gros; (*e.g., slaughter*) en masse ‖ *s* gros *m*, vente *f* en gros ‖ *tr & intr* vendre en gros

whole′sale price′ *s* prix *m* de gros

wholesaler [ˈholˌselər] *s* commerçant *m* en gros, grossiste *mf*

whole′sale trade′ *s* commerce *m* de gros

wholesome [ˈholsəm] *adj* sain

wholly [ˈholi] *adv* entièrement

whom [hum] *pron interr* qui ‖ *pron rel* que; lequel §78; celui que §83; **of whom** dont, de qui §79

whom·ev′er *pron rel* celui que §83; tous ceux que; (with a preposition) quiconque

whoop [hup], [hwup] *s* huée *f*; (*cough*) quinte *f* ‖ *tr*—**to whoop it up** (slang) pousser des cris ‖ *intr* huer

whoop′ing cough′ [ˈhupɪŋ] *s* coqueluche *f*

whopper [ˈhwɑpər] *s* (coll) chose *f* énorme; (*lie*) (coll) gros mensonge *m*

whopping [ˈhwɑpɪŋ] *adj* (coll) énorme

whore [hor] *s* putain *f* ‖ *intr*—**to whore around** courir la gueuse

whore′house′ *s* maison *f* de débauche, maison publique, maison borgne, boxon *m*

whose [huz] *pron interr* à qui, e.g., **whose pen is that?** à qui est ce stylo? ‖ *pron rel* dont, de qui §79; duquel §78

why [hwaɪ] *s* (*pl* **whys** [hwaɪz]) pourquoi *m*; **the why and the wherefore** le pourquoi et le comment ‖ *adv* pourquoi; **why not?** pourquoi pas? ‖ *interj* tiens!; **why, certainly!** mais bien sûr!; **why, yes!** mais oui!

wick [wɪk] *s* mèche *f*

wicked [ˈwɪkɪd] *adj* méchant, mauvais

wicker [ˈwɪkər] *adj* en osier ‖ *s* osier *m*

wicket [ˈwɪkɪt] *s* guichet *m*; (croquet) arceau *m*

wide [waɪd] *adj* large; (*range*) vaste, étendu; (*spread, angle, etc.*) grand; large de, e.g.,

eight feet wide large de huit pieds ‖ *adv* loin, partout; **open wide!** ouvrez bien!

wide′-an′gle *adj* grand-angulaire

wide′-awake′ *adj* bien éveillé

widen [′waɪdən] *tr* élargir ‖ *intr* s'élargir

wide′-o′pen *adj* grand ouvert

wide′spread′ *adj* (*arms, wings*) étendu; répandu; universel

widow [′wɪdo] *s* veuve *f* ‖ *tr*—**to be widowed** devenir veuf

widower [′wɪdo·ər] *s* veuf *m*

widowhood [′wɪdo,hʊd] *s* veuvage *m*

wid′ow's mite′ *s* obole *f*

wid′ow's weeds′ *spl* deuil *m* de veuve

width [wɪdθ] *s* largeur *f*; (*of cloth*) lé *m*

wield [wild] *tr* (*sword, pen*) manier; (*power*) exercer

wife [waɪf] *s* (*pl* **wives** [waɪvz]) femme *f*, épouse *f*

wig [wɪg] *s* perruque *f*

wiggle [′wɪgəl] *s* tortillement *m* ‖ *tr* agiter ‖ *intr* tortiller, se tortiller

wig′wag′ *s* télégraphie *f* optique ‖ *v* (*pret & pp* **-wagged;** *ger* **-wagging**) *tr* transmettre à bras avec fanions ‖ *intr* signaler à bras avec fanions

wigwam [′wɪgwɑm] *s* wigwam *m*

wild [waɪld] *adj* sauvage; (*untamed*) sauvage, fauve; (*frantic, mad*) frénétique; (*hair; dance; dream*) échevelé; (*passion; torrent; night*) tumultueux; (*idea, plan*) insensé, extravagant; (*life*) déréglé; (*blows, bullet, shot*) perdu; **wild about** or **for** fou de ‖ **wilds** *spl* régions *fpl* sauvages ‖ *adv*—**to run wild** dépasser toutes les bornes; (*said of plants*) pousser librement

wild′ boar′ *s* sanglier *m*

wild′ card′ *s* mistigri *m*

wild′cat′ *s* chat *m* sauvage; lynx *m*, (*well*) sondage *m* d'exploration

wild′cat strike′ *s* grève *f* sauvage, grève spontanée

wild′ cher′ry *s* (*pl* **-ries**) merise *f*; (*tree*) merisier *m*

wilderness [′wɪldərnɪs] *s* désert *m*

wil′derness camp′ing *s* camping *m* sauvage

wild′fire′ *s* feu *m* grégeois; feu *m* follet; éclairs *mpl* en nappe; **like wildfire** comme une traînée de poudre

wild′ flow′er *s* fleur *f* des champs

wild′ goose′ *s* oie *f* sauvage

wild′-goose′ chase′ *s*—**to go on a wild-goose chase** faire buisson creux

wild′life′ *s* animaux *mpl* sauvages

wild′ oats′ *spl*—**to sow one's wild oats** jeter sa gourme

wile [waɪl] *s* ruse *f* ‖ *tr*—**to while away** tuer, faire passer

will [wɪl] *s* volonté *f*; (law) testament *m*; **against one's will** à contre-cœur; **at will** à volonté; **to put s.o. in one's will** porter qn sur son testament; **with a will** de bon cœur ‖ *tr* vouloir; (*to bequeath*) léguer ‖ *intr* vouloir; **do as you will** faites comme vous voudrez ‖ (*pret & cond* **would** [wʊd]) *aux* used to express 1) the future

indicative, e.g., **he will arrive early** il arrivera de bonne heure; 2) the future perfect indicative, e.g., **he will have arrived before I leave** il sera arrivé avant que je parte; 3) the present indicative denoting habit or custom, e.g., **after breakfast he will go out for a walk every morning** après le petit déjeuner il fait une promenade tous les matins

willful [′wɪlfəl] *adj* volontaire; (*stubborn*) obstiné

willfulness [′wɪlfəlnɪs] *s* entêtement *m*

William [′wɪljəm] *s* Guillaume *m*

willing [′wɪlɪŋ] *adj* disposé, prêt; **to be willing to** vouloir bien; **willing or unwilling** bon gré mal gré

willingly [′wɪlɪŋli] *adv* volontiers

willingness [′wɪlɪŋnɪs] *s* bonne volonté *f*, consentement *m*

will-o′-the-wisp [′wɪləðə′wɪsp] *s* feu *m* follet; (fig) chimère *f*

willow [′wɪlo] *s* saule *m*

willowy [′wɪlo·i] *adj* souple, agile; svelte, élancé; couvert de saules

will′ pow′er *s* force *f* de volonté

willy-nilly [′wɪli′nɪli] *adv* bon gré mal gré

wilt [wɪlt] *tr* flétrir ‖ *intr* se flétrir

wil·y [′waɪli] *adj* (*comp* **-ier;** *super* **-iest**) rusé, astucieux

wimp [wɪmp] *s* poule *f* mouillée

wimple [′wɪmpəl] *s* guimpe *f*

win [wɪn] *s* (coll) victoire *f* ‖ *v* (*pret & pp* **won** [wʌn];* ger* **winning**) *tr* gagner; (*a victory, a prize*) remporter; **to win back** regagner; **to win over** gagner, convaincre ‖ *intr* gagner; convaincre; **to win out** (coll) réussir

wince [wɪns] *s*—**without a wince** sans sourciller ‖ *intr* tressaillir

winch [wɪntʃ] *s* treuil *m*; (*handle, crank*) manivelle *f*

wind [wɪnd] *s* vent *m*; (*breath*) haleine *f*, souffle *m*; **to break wind** lâcher un vent, faire un pet; **to get wind of** avoir vent de; **to sail close to the wind** courir au plus près; **to sail into the wind** aller au lof, venir au lof ‖ *tr* faire perdre le souffle à ‖ *intr* flairer le gibier ‖ [waɪnd] *v* (*pret & pp* **wound** [waʊnd]) *tr* enrouler; (*a timepiece*) remonter; (*yarn, thread, etc.*) pelotonner; **to wind up** enrouler; remonter; (*to finish*) (coll) terminer, régler ‖ *intr* serpenter

windbag [′wɪnd,bæg] *s* (*of bagpipe*) outre *f*; (coll) moulin *m* à paroles

wind′break′ *s* abrivent *m*

wind′break′er *s* (*jacket*) blouson *m*

wind′ -chill fac′tor *s* déperdition *f* de chaleur due au vent

wind′ cone′ *s* (aer) manche *f* à air

winded [′wɪndɪd] *adj* essoufflé

wind′fall *s* (fig) aubaine *f*

wind′ing road′ [′waɪndɪŋ] *s* route *f* en lacet

wind′ing sheet′ *s* linceul *m*

wind′ing stairs′ *spl* escalier *m* en colimaçon

wind′ in′strument [wɪnd] s (mus) instrument m à vent

windlass [′wɪndləs] s treuil m

wind′mill′ s moulin m à vent; (on a modern farm) aéromoteur m; **to tilt at windmills** se battre contre des moulins à vent

window [′wɪndo] s fenêtre f; (of ticket office) guichet m; (of store) vitrine f; (aut) glace f

win′dow dress′er s étalagiste mf

win′dow dress′ing s art m de l'étalage; (coll) façade f

win′dow en′velope s enveloppe f à fenêtre

win′dow frame′ s châssis m, dormant m

win′dow·pane′ s vitre f, carreau m

win′dow screen′ s grillage m, écran m en fil de fer

win′dow shade′ s store m

win′dow-shop′ v (pret & pp -shopped; ger -shopping) intr faire du lèche-vitrines, lécher les vitrines

win′dow shut′ter s volet m

win′dow sill′ s rebord m de fenêtre

wind′pipe′ s trachée-artère f

wind′ shear′ s cisaillement m du vent

wind′shield′ s pare-brise m

wind′shield wash′er s lave-glace m

wind′shield wip′er s essuie-glace m

wind′sock′ s manche f à air

wind′storm′ s tempête f de vent

wind′ surf′ing s planche f à voile

wind′ tun′nel s tunnel m aérodynamique

wind-up [′waɪnd,ʌp] s conclusion f, fin f

windward [′wɪndwərd] adj & adv au vent ‖ s côté m du vent; **to turn to windward** louvoyer

wind·y [′wɪndi] adj (comp -ier; super -iest) venteux; (verbose) verbeux; **it is windy** il fait du vent

wine [waɪn] s vin m ‖ tr—**to wine and dine s.o.** fêter qn

wine′ cel′lar s cave f

wine′glass′ s verre m à vin

winegrower [′waɪn,gro·ər] s viticulteur m, vigneron m

winegrowing [′waɪn,gro·ɪŋ] s viticulture f

wine′ list′ s carte f des vins

wine′ press′ s pressoir m

winer·y [′waɪnəri] s (pl -ies) pressoir m

wine′skin′ s outre f à vin

wine′ stew′ard s sommelier m; (of prince, king) bouteiller m

winetaster [′waɪn,testər] s (person) dégustateur m; (pipette) taste-vin m

wing [wɪŋ] s aile f; (e.g., of hospital) pavillon m; (pol) parti m, faction f; **in the wings** (theat) dans la coulisse; **on the wing** au vol; **to take wing** prendre son essor ‖ tr (to wound) blesser; **to wing one's way** voler

wing′ chair′ s fauteuil m à oreilles

wing′ col′lar s col m rabattu

wing′ load′ s (aer) charge f alaire

wing′ nut′ s écrou m ailé, vis f à ailettes

wing′spread′ s envergure f

wink [wɪŋk] s clin m d'œil; **to not sleep a wink** ne pas fermer l'œil; **to take forty winks** (coll) piquer un roupillon ‖ tr cligner ‖ intr cligner des yeux; **to wink at** cligner de l'œil à; (e.g., an abuse) fermer les yeux sur

winner [′wɪnər] s gagnant m, vainqueur m

winning [′wɪnɪŋ] adj gagnant; (attractive) séduisant ‖ **winnings** spl gains mpl

winnow [′wɪno] tr vanner, sasser; (e.g., the evidence) passer au crible

winsome [′wɪnsəm] adj séduisant, engageant

winter [′wɪntər] s hiver m ‖ intr passer l'hiver; (said of animals, troops, etc.) hiverner

win′ter-green′ s (oil) wintergreen m; (bot) gaulthérie f

winterize [′wɪntəraɪz] tr hivériser

win·try [′wɪntri] adj (comp -trier; super -triest) hivernal, froid

wipe [waɪp] tr essuyer; **to wipe away** essuyer; **to wipe off** or **out** effacer; (to annihilate) anéantir; **to wipe up** nettoyer

wiper [′waɪpər] s torchon m; (elec) contact m glissant; (mach) came f

wire [waɪr] s fil m; télégramme m; **hold the wire!** (telp) restez à l'écoute!; **on the wire** (telp) au bout du fil; **reply by wire** réponse f télégraphique; **to get in under the wire** arriver juste à temps; terminer juste à temps; **to pull wires** (coll) tirer les ficelles ‖ tr attacher avec du fil de fer; (a message) télégraphier; (a house) canaliser ‖ intr télégraphier

wire′ cut′ter s coupe-fil m

wire′draw′ v (pret -drew; pp -drawn) tr tréfiler

wire′ entan′glement s réseau m de barbelés

wire′ gauge′ s calibre m or jauge f pour fils métalliques

wire′-haired′ adj à poil dur

wireless [′waɪrlɪs] adj sans fil

wire′ nail′ s clou m de Paris

Wire′pho′to s (pl -tos) (trademark) (device) bélinographe m; (photo) bélinogramme m

wire′ pull′ing s (coll) influences fpl secrètes, piston m

wire′ record′er s magnétophone m à fil d'acier

wire′tap′ s (device) table f d'écoute ‖ v (pret & pp -tapped; ger -tapping) tr passer à la table d'écoute

wiring [′waɪrɪŋ] s (e.g., of house) canalisation f; (e.g., of radio) montage m

wir·y [′waɪri] adj (comp -ier; super -iest) nerveux; (hair) raide

wisdom [′wɪzdəm] s sagesse f

wis′dom tooth′ s dent f de sagesse

wise [waɪz] adj sage; (step, decision) judicieux, prudent; **to be wise to** (slang) voir clair dans le jeu de, percer le jeu de; **to get wise** (coll) se mettre au courant ‖ s—**in no wise** en aucune manière ‖ tr—**to wise up** (slang) avertir, désabuser

wiseacre [′waɪz,ekər] s fat m, fierot m

wise′crack′ s (coll) blague f, plaisanterie f ‖ intr (coll) blaguer, plaisanter

wise′ guy′ s (slang) type m goguenard, fier-à-bras m

wish [wɪʃ] s souhait m, désir m; **best wishes** meilleurs vœux mpl; (formula used to close a letter) amitiés; **last wishes** dernières volontés fpl; **our best wishes** (formula in letter writing) nos meilleurs sentiments; **to make a wish** faire un vœu ‖ tr souhaiter, désirer; **to wish s.o. s.th.** souhaiter q.ch. à qn; **to wish s.o. to** + inf souhaiter que qn + subj; **to wish to** + inf vouloir + inf

wish′bone′ s fourchette f

wishful [ˈwɪʃfəl] adj désireux

wish′ful think′ing s optimisme m à outrance; **to indulge in wishful thinking** se forger des chimères

wish′ing well′ s puits m aux souhaits

wistful [ˈwɪstfəl] adj pensif, rêveur

wit [wɪt] s esprit m; (person) homme m d'esprit; **to be at one's wits' end** ne plus savoir que faire; **to keep one's wits about one** conserver toute sa présence d'esprit; **to live by one's wits** vivre d'expédients

witch [wɪtʃ] s sorcière f

witch′craft′ s sorcellerie f

witch′ doc′tor s sorcier m guérisseur

witch′es′ Sab′bath s sabbat m

witch′ ha′zel s teinture f d'hamamélis; (bot) hamamélis m

witch′ hunt′ s chasse f aux sorcières

with [wɪð], [wɪθ] prep avec; (at the home of; in the case of) chez; (in spite of) malgré; à, e.g., **the girl with the blue eyes** la jeune fille aux yeux bleus; e.g., **coffee with milk** café au lait; e.g., **with open arms** à bras ouverts; e.g., **with these words . . .** à ces mots . . . ; de, e.g., **with a loud voice** d'une voix forte; e.g., **with all his strength** de toutes ses forces; e.g., **to be satisfied with** être satisfait de; e.g., **to fill with** remplir de

with·draw′ v (pret **-drew;** pp **-drawn**) tr retirer ‖ intr se retirer

withdrawal [wɪðˈdrɔ·əl] s retrait m

withdraw′al symp′tom s symptôme m de l'état de manque

wither [ˈwɪðər] tr faner ‖ intr se faner

with·hold′ v (pret & pp **-held**) tr (money, taxes, etc.) retenir; (permission) refuser; (the truth) cacher

with·hold′ing tax′ s impôt m retenu à la source

with·in′ adv à l'intérieur; là-dedans §85A ‖ prep à l'intérieur de; (in less than) en moins de; (within the limits of) dans; (in the bosom of) au sein de; (not exceeding a margin of error of) à . . . près, e.g., **I can tell you what time it is within five minutes** je peux vous dire l'heure à cinq minutes près; à portée de, e.g., **within reach** à portée de la main

with·out′ adv au-dehors, dehors ‖ prep au dehors de; (lacking, not with) sans; **to do without** se passer de; **without** + ger sans + inf, e.g., **he left without seeing me** il est parti sans me voir; sans que + subj,

e.g., **he left without anyone seeing him** il est parti sans que personne ne le voie

with·stand′ v (pret & pp **-stood**) tr résister à

witness [ˈwɪtnɪs] s témoin m; **in witness whereof** en foi de quoi; **to bear witness** rendre témoignage ‖ tr (to be present at) être témoin de, assister à; (to attest) témoigner; (e.g., a contract) signer

wit′ness stand′ s barre f des témoins

witticism [ˈwɪtɪˌsɪzəm] s trait m d'esprit

wittingly [ˈwɪtɪŋli] adv sciemment

wit·ty [ˈwɪti] adj (comp **-tier;** super **-tiest**) spirituel

wizard [ˈwɪzərd] s sorcier m

wizardry [ˈwɪzərdri] s sorcellerie f

wizened [ˈwɪzənd] adj desséché

woad [wod] s guède f

wobble [ˈwɑbəl] intr chanceler; (said of table) branler; (said of voice) chevroter; vaciller

wob·bly [ˈwɑbli] adj (comp **-blier;** super **-bliest**) vacillant

woe [wo] s malheur m, affliction f; **woe is me!** pauvre de moi!; **woes** misères fpl

woebegone [ˈwobɪˌgɔn] adj navré, abattu, désolé

woeful [ˈwofəl] adj triste, désolé; très mauvais

wolf [wʊlf] s (pl **wolves** [wʊlvz]) loup m; galant m, tombeur m de femmes; **to cry wolf** crier au loup; **to keep the wolf from the door** se mettre à l'abri du besoin, joindre les deux bouts ‖ tr & intr engloutir

wolf′ cub′ s louveteau m

wolf′hound′ s chien-loup m

wolf′ pack′ s bande f de loups

wolfram [ˈwʊlfrəm] s (element) tungstène m; (mineral) wolfram m

wolf's′-bane′ or **wolfs′bane′** s tue-loup m, aconit m, napel m

woman [ˈwʊmən] s (pl **women** [ˈwɪmɪn]) femme f

wom′an doc′tor s femme f médecin, doctoresse f

womanhood [ˈwʊmənˌhʊd] s le sexe féminin; les femmes fpl

womanish [ˈwʊmənɪʃ] adj féminin; (effeminate) efféminé

wom′an·kind′ s le sexe féminin

wom′an la′borer s femme f manœuvre

woman·ly [ˈwʊmənli] adj (comp **-lier;** super **-liest**) féminin, femme

wom′an preach′er s femme f pasteur

womb [wum] s utérus m, matrice f; (fig) sein m

wom′en's libera′tion move′ment m mouvement m de la libération de la femme (M.L.F.)

wonder [ˈwʌndər] s merveille f; (feeling of surprise) émerveillement m; (something strange) miracle m; **for a wonder** chose étonnante; **no wonder that . . .** rien d'étonnant que . . . ; **to work wonders** faire des merveilles ‖ tr—**to wonder that** s'étonner que; **to wonder why, if, whether**

se demander pourquoi, si || *intr*—**to won-der at** s'émerveiller de, s'étonner de

won′der drug′ *s* remède *m* miracle, médi-cament *m* miracle, drogue-miracle *f*

wonderful [′wʌndərfəl] *adj* merveilleux, étonnant

won′der·land′ *s* pays *m* des merveilles

wonderment [′wʌndərmənt] *s* étonnement *m*

wont [wɔnt] *adj*—**to be wont to** avoir l'ha-bitude de || *s*—**his wont** son habitude

wonted *adj* habituel, accoutumé

woo [wu] *tr* courtiser

wood [wʊd] *s* bois *m*; (*for wine*) fût *m*; **out of the woods** (coll) hors de danger, hors d'affaire; **to take to the woods** se sauver dans la nature; **woods** bois *m* or *mpl*

woodbine [′wʊd,baɪn] *s* (*honeysuckle*) chèv-refeuille *m*; (*Virginia creeper*) vigne *f* vierge

wood′ carv′ing *s* sculpture *f* sur bois

wood′chuck′ *s* marmotte *f* d'Amérique

wood′cock′ *s* bécasse *f*

wood′cut′ *s* (typ) gravure *f* sur bois

wood′cut′ter *s* bûcheron *m*

wooded [′wʊdɪd] *adj* boisé

wooden [′wʊdən] *adj* en bois; (*style, man-ners*) guindé, raide

wood′ engrav′ing *s* (typ) gravure *f* sur bois

wood′en-head′ed *adj* (coll) stupide, obtus

wood′en leg′ *s* jambe *f* en bois

wood′en shoe′ *s* sabot *m*

wood′ grouse′ *s* grand tétras *m*, grand coq *m* de bruyère

woodland [′wʊdlənd] *adj* sylvestre || *s* pays *m* boisé

wood′land scene′ *s* (painting) paysage *m* boisé

wood′man *s* (*pl* **-men**) bûcheron *m*

woodpecker [′wʊd,pɛkər] *s* pic *m*; (*green woodpecker*) pivert *m*, pic-vert *m*

wood′ pig′eon *s* (orn) ramier *m*

wood′pile′ *s* tas *m* de bois

wood′ screw′ *s* vis *f* à bois

wood′shed′ *s* bûcher *m*

woods′man *s* (*pl* **-men**) bûcheron *m*; (*trapper*) trappeur *m*, chasseur *m*

wood′ tick′ *s* vrillette *f*

wood′winds′ *spl* (mus) bois *mpl*

wood′work′ *s* (*working in wood*) menuise-rie *f*; (*things made of wood*) boiseries *fpl*

wood′work′er *s* menuisier *m*

wood′worm′ *s* (ent) artison *m*

wood·y [′wʊdi] *adj* (*comp* **-ier;** *super* **-iest**) boisé; (*like wood*) ligneux

wooer [′wu·ər] *s* prétendant *m*

woof [wuf] *s* trame *f*; (*fabric*) tissu *m*

woofer [′wʊfər] *s* (rad) boomer *m*, woofer *m*

wool [wʊl] *s* laine *f*

woolen [′wʊlən] *adj* de laine || *s* tissu *m* de laine; **woolens** lainage *m*

wool′gath′ering *s* rêvasserie *f*

woolgrower [′wʊl,gro·ər] *s* éleveur *m* des bêtes à laine

wool·ly [′wʊli] *adj* (*comp* **-lier;** *super* **-liest**) laineux

word [wʌrd] *s* mot *m*; (*promise, assurance*) parole *f*; **in other words** autrement dit; **in your own words** en vous propres termes; **my word!** ça alors!; **not a word!** motus!; **the Word** (eccl) le Verbe; **to break one's word** manquer à sa parole; **to have words with** échanger des propos désagréables avec; **to make s.o. eat his words** faire ravaler ses paroles à qn; **to put in a word** placer un mot; **to take s.o. at his word** prendre qn au mot, croire qn sur parole; **upon my word!** ma foi!; **without a word** sans mot dire; **words** (*e.g., of song*) pa-roles || *tr* formuler, rédiger

word′ forma′tion *s* formation *f* des mots

wording [′wʌrdɪŋ] *s* langage *m*

word′ or′der *s* ordre *m* des mots

word′ proc′essing *s* traitement *m* des mots

word′-stock′ *s* vocabulaire *m*

word·y [′wʌrdi] *adj* (*comp* **-ier;** *super* **-iest**) verbeux

work [wʌrk] *s* travail *m*; (*production, book*) œuvre *f*, ouvrage *m*; **at work** en œuvre; (*not at home*) au travail, au bureau, à l'usine; **out of work** sans travail, en chômage; **to shoot the works** (slang) mettre le paquet, jouer le tout pour le tout; **works** œuvres; mécanisme *m*; (*of clock*) mouvement *m* || *tr* faire travailler; (*to operate*) faire fonctionner, faire marcher; (*wood, iron*) travailler; (*mine*) exploiter; **to work out** élaborer, résoudre; **to work up** préparer; stimuler || *intr* travailler; (*said of motor, machine, etc.*) fonc-tionner, marcher; (*said of remedy*) faire de l'effet; (*said of wine, beer*) fermenter; **how will things work out!** à quoi tout cela aboutira-t-il?; **to work hard** travailler dur; **to work loose** se desserrer; **to work out** (sports) s'entraîner; **to work too hard** se surmener

workable [′wʌrkəbəl] *adj* (*feasible*) réa-lisable; (*that can be worked*) ouvrable

workaholic [′wʌrkə′hɔlɪk] *s* bourreau *m* de travail, drogué *m* du travail, travaillo-mane *mf*

work′bas′ket *s* corbeille *f* à ouvrage

work′bench′ *s* établi *m*

work′book′ *s* manuel *m*; (*notebook*) carnet *m*; (*for student*) cahier *m* de devoirs

work′box′ *s* boîte *f* à ouvrage; (*for needle-work*) coffret *m* de travail

work′day′ *adj* de tous les jours; prosaïque, ordinaire || *s* jour *m* ouvrable; (*part of day devoted to work*) journée *f*

worked′-up′ *adj* préparé, ouvré; (*excited*) agité, emballé

worker [′wʌrkər] *s* travailleur *m*, ouvrier *m*, employé *m*

work′ flow′ *s* déroulement *m* des opérations

work′ force′ *s* main-d'œuvre *f*, personnel *m*

work′horse′ *s* cheval *m* de charge; (*tireless worker*) vrai cheval *m* de labour

work′house′ *s* maison *f* de correction; (Brit) asile *m* des pauvres

work′ing class′ *s* classe *f* ouvrière

work′ing day′ s jour m ouvrable; (daily hours for work) journée f

work′ing hours′ spl heures fpl de travail

work′ing·man′ s (pl -men′) travailleur m

work′ing·wom′an s (pl -wom′en) ouvrière f

work′man s (pl -men) ouvrier m

workmanship [ˈwʌrkmənˌʃɪp] s habileté f professionnelle, facture f; (work executed) travail m

work′ of art′ s œuvre f d'art

work′ or′der s bon m de travail

work′out′ s essai m, épreuve f; (physical exercise) séance f d'entraînement

work′room′ s atelier m; (for study) cabinet m de travail, cabinet d'études

work′shop′ s atelier m

work′ stop′page s arrêt m du travail

world [wʌrld] adj mondial ‖ s monde m; **a world of** énormément de; **for all the world** à tous les égards, exactement; **not for all the world** pour rien au monde; **since the world began** depuis que le monde est monde; **the other world** l'autre monde; **to bring into the world** mettre au monde; **to go around the world** faire le tour du monde; **to see the world** voir du pays; **to think the world of** estimer énormément, avoir une très haute opinion de

world′ affairs′ spl affaires fpl internationales

world′-fa′mous adj de renommée mondiale

world′ his′tory s histoire f universelle

world·ly [ˈwʌrldli] adj (comp -lier; super -liest) mondain

world′ly-wise′ adj—**to be worldy-wise** savoir ce que c'est que la vie

world′ map′ s mappemonde f

World′ Se′ries s championnat m mondial

world′s′ fair′ s exposition f universelle

world′ war′ s guerre f mondiale

world′-wide′ adj mondial, universel

worm [wʌrm] s ver m ‖ tr enlever les vers de; (a secret, money, etc.) soutirer; **to worm it out of him** lui tirer les vers du nez ‖ intr se faufiler

worm-eaten [ˈwʌrmˌitən] adj vermoulu

worm′ gear′ s engrenage m à vis sans fin

worm′wood′ s (Artemisia) armoise f; (Artemisia absinthium) armoise absinthe; (something grievous) (fig) absinthe f

worm·y [ˈwʌrmi] adj (comp -ier; super -iest) véreux

worn [worn] adj usé, fatigué

worn′-out′ adj épuisé, usé; éreinté

worrisome [ˈwʌrisəm] adj inquiétant; inquiet, anxieux

wor·ry [ˈwʌri] s (pl -ries) souci m, inquiétude f; (cause of anxiety) ennui m, tracas m ‖ v (pret & pp -ried) tr inquiéter; (to harass, pester) ennuyer, tracasser; **to be worried** s'inquiéter ‖ intr s'inquiéter; **don't worry!** ne vous en faites pas!

worse [wʌrs] adj comp pire, plus mauvais §91; **and to make matters worse** et par surcroît de malheur; **so much the worse** tant pis; **to make** or **get worse** empirer; **what's worse** qui pis est; **worse and** worse de pis en pis ‖ adv comp pis, plus mal §91

worsen [ˈwʌrsən] tr & intr empirer

wor·ship [ˈwʌrʃɪp] s culte m, adoration f ‖ v (pret & pp -shiped or -shipped; ger -shiping or -shipping) tr adorer ‖ intr prier; (to go to church) aller au culte

worshiper or **worshipper** [ˈwʌrʃɪpər] s adorateur m, fidèle mf

worst [wʌrst] adj super pire §91; pis ‖ s (le) pire, (le) pis; **to be hurt the worst** être le plus gravement atteint (blessé, etc.); **to get the worst of it** avoir le dessous ‖ adv super pis §91

worsted [ˈwʊstɪd] adj de laine peignée ‖ s peigné m, tissu m de laine peignée

wort [wʌrt] s (of beer) moût m

worth [wʌrθ] adj digne de; valant, e.g., **book worth three dollars** livre valant trois dollars; **to be worth** valoir; avoir une fortune de; **to be worth +** ger valoir la peine de **+** inf; **to be worth while** valoir la peine ‖ s valeur f; **a dollar's worth of** pour un dollar de

worthless [ˈwʌrθlɪs] adj sans valeur; (person) bon à rien, indigne

worth′while′ adj utile, de valeur

wor·thy [ˈwʌrði] adj (comp -thier; super -thiest) digne ‖ s (pl -thies) notable mf; (hum, ironical) personnage m

would [wʊd] aux used to express 1) the past future, e.g., **he said he would come** il a dit qu'il viendrait; 2) the present conditional, e.g., **he would come if he could** il viendrait s'il pouvait; 3) the past conditional, e.g., **he would have come if he had been able (to)** il serait venu s'il avait pu; 4) the potential mood, e.g., **would that I knew it!** plût à Dieu que je le sache!, je voudrais le savoir!; 5) the past indicative denoting habit or custom in the past, e.g., **he would visit us every day** il nous visitait tous les jours

would′-be′ adj prétendu

wound [wund] s blessure f ‖ tr blesser

wounded [ˈwundɪd] adj blessé ‖ s—**the wounded** les blessés mpl

wow [waʊ] s (e.g., of phonograph record) distorsion f; (slang) succès m formidable ‖ tr (slang) enthousiasmer ‖ interj (slang) formidable!

wrack [ræk] s vestige m; (ruin) naufrage m; (bot) varech m

wraith [reθ] s apparition f

wrangle [ˈræŋgəl] s querelle f ‖ intr se quereller

wrap [ræp] s couverture f; (coat) manteau m ‖ v (pret & pp wrapped; ger wrapping) tr envelopper, emballer

wrap′around skirt′ s jupe f portefeuille

wrap′around wind′shield s pare-brise m panoramique

wrapper [ˈræpər] s saut-de-lit m; (of newspaper or magazine) bande f; (of tobacco) robe f

wrap′ping pa′per s papier m d'emballage

wrath [ræθ] s colère f

wrathful [ˈræθfəl] *adj* courroucé, en colère

wreak [rik] *tr* assouvir

wreath [riθ] *s* (*pl* **wreaths** [riðz]) couronne *f*; (*of smoke*) volute *f*, panache *m*

wreathe [rið] *tr* enguirlander; (*e.g., flowers*) entrelacer ‖ *intr* (*said of smoke*) s'élever en volutes

wreck [rɛk] *s* (*shipwreck*) naufrage *m*; (*debris at sea or elsewhere*) épave *f*; (*of train*) déraillement *m*; (*of airplane*) écrasement *m*; (*of auto*) accident *m*; (*of one's hopes*) naufrage; **to be a wreck** être une ruine ‖ *tr* (*a ship, one's hopes*) faire échouer; (*a train*) faire dérailler; (*one's health*) ruiner

wreckage [ˈrɛkɪdʒ] *s* débris *mpl*, décombres *mpl*, ruines *fpl*

wrecker [ˈrɛkər] *s* (*tow truck*) dépanneuse *f*; (*person*) dépanneur *m*

wreck'ing car' *s* voiture *f* de dépannage

wreck'ing crane' *s* grue *f* de dépannage

wren [rɛn] *s* (*orn*) troglodyte *m*; (*kinglet*) (*orn*) roitelet *m*

wrench [rɛntʃ] *s* (*tool*) clef *f*; (*pull*) secousse *f*; (*twist of a joint*) foulure *f* ‖ *tr* (*e.g., one's ankle*) se fouler; (*to twist*) tordre

wrest [rɛst] *tr* arracher violemment

wrestle [ˈrɛsəl] *s* lutte *f* ‖ *intr* lutter

wrestling [ˈrɛslɪŋ] *s* (sports) lutte *f*, catch *m*

wres'tling match' *s* rencontre *f* de catch

wretch [rɛtʃ] *s* misérable *mf*

wretched [ˈrɛtʃɪd] *adj* misérable

wriggle [ˈrɪgəl] *s* tortillement *m* ‖ *tr* tortiller ‖ *intr* se tortiller; **to wriggle out of** esquiver adroitement

wrig·gly [ˈrɪgli] *adj* (*comp* **-glier;** *super* **-gliest**) frétillant; évasif

wring [rɪŋ] *v* (*pret & pp* **wrung** [rʌŋ]) *tr* tordre; (*one's hands*) se tordre; (*s.o.'s hand*) serrer fortement; **to wring out** (*clothes*) essorer; (*money, a secret, etc.*) arracher

wringer [ˈrɪŋər] *s* essoreuse *f*

wrinkle [ˈrɪŋkəl] *s* (*in skin*) ride *f*; (*in clothes*) pli *m*, faux pli; (*clever idea or trick*) (coll) truc *m* ‖ *tr* plisser ‖ *intr* se plisser

wrin·kly [ˈrɪŋkli] *adj* (*comp* **-klier;** *super* **-kliest**) ridé, chiffonné

wrist [rɪst] *s* poignet *m*

wrist'band' *s* poignet *m*

wrist' watch' *s* montre-bracelet *f*

writ [rɪt] *s* (eccl) écriture *f*; (law) acte *m* judiciaire

write [raɪt] *v* (*pret* **wrote** [rot]; *pp* **written** [ˈrɪtən]) *tr* écrire; **to write down** con-

signer par écrit; baisser le prix de; **to write in** insérer; **to write off** (*a debt*) passer aux profits et pertes; **to write up** rédiger un compte rendu de; (*to ballyhoo*) faire l'éloge de ‖ *intr* écrire; **to write back** répondre par écrit

writer [ˈraɪtər] *s* écrivain *m*

writ'er's cramp' *s* crampe *f* des écrivains

write'-up' *s* compte *m* rendu; (*ballyhoo*) battage *m*; (com) surestimation *f*

writhe [raɪð] *intr* se tordre

writing [ˈraɪtɪŋ] *s* l'écriture *f*; (*something written*) écrit *m*, œuvre *f*; (*profession*) métier *m* d'écrivain; **at this writing** au moment où j'écris; **to put in writing** mettre par écrit

writ'ing desk' *s* bureau *m*, écritoire *f*; (*in schoolroom*) pupitre *m*

writ'ing pa'per *s* papier *m* à lettres

wrong [rɔŋ] *adj* (*unjust*) injuste; (*incorrect*) erroné; (*road, address, side, place, etc.*) mauvais; ne pas . . . qu'il faut, e.g., **I arrived at the wrong city** je ne suis pas arrivé à la ville qu'il fallait; (*word*) impropre; qui ne marche pas, e.g., **something is wrong with the motor** il y a quelque chose qui ne marche pas dans le moteur; **to be wrong** (*i.e., in error*) avoir tort; (*i.e., to blame*) être le coupable ‖ *s* mal *m*; injustice *f*; **to be in the wrong** être dans son tort, avoir tort; **to do wrong** faire du mal, faire du tort ‖ *adv* mal; **to go wrong** faire fausse route; (*said, e.g., of a plan*) ne pas marcher; (*said of one falling into evil ways*) se dévoyer; **to guess wrong** se tromper ‖ *tr* faire du tort à, être injuste envers

wrongdoer [ˈrɔŋˌduˌər] *s* malfaiteur *m*

wrong'do'ing *s* mal *m*, tort *m*; (*misdeeds*) méfaits *mpl*

wrong' num'ber *s* (telp) mauvais numéro *m*; **you have the wrong number** vous vous trompez de numéro

wrong' side' *s* (*e.g., of material*) revers *m*, envers *m*; (*of the street*) mauvais côté *m*; **to drive on the wrong side** circuler à contre-voie; **to get out of bed on the wrong side** se lever du pied gauche; **wrong side out** à l'envers; **wrong side up** sens dessus dessous

wrought' i'ron [rɔt] *s* fer *m* forgé

wrought'-up' *adj* excité, agité

wry [raɪ] *adj* (*comp* **wrier;** *super* **wriest**) tordu, de travers; forcé, ironique

wry'neck' *s* (orn) torcol *m*; (pathol) torticolis *m*

X

X, x [ɛks] s XXIVᵉ lettre de l'alphabet
Xavier [ˈzevɪ-ər] s Xavier m
xenophobe [ˈzɛnə,fob] s xénophobe mf
xerography [ziˈrɑgrəfi] s xérographie f
Xerxes [ˈzʌrksiz] s Xerxès m
Xmas [ˈkrɪsməs] adj de Noël ‖ s Noël m

X′ ray′ s (photograph) radiographie f; **to have an X ray** passer à la radio; **X rays** rayons mpl X
X′-ray′ adj radiographique ‖ **X′-ray′** tr radiographier
X′-ray treat′ment s radiothérapie f
xylophone [ˈzaɪlə,fon] s xylophone m

Y

Y, y [waɪ] s XXVᵉ lettre de l'alphabet
yacht [jɑt] s yacht m
yacht′club′ s yacht-club m
yah [jɑ] interj (in disgust) pouah!; (in derision) oh là là!
yam [jæm] s igname f; (sweet potato) patate f douce
yank [jæŋk] s (coll) secousse f ‖ tr (coll) tirer d'un coup sec
Yankee [ˈjæŋki] adj & s yankee mf
yap [jæp] s jappement m; (slang) criaillerie f ‖ v (pret & pp **yapped**; ger **yapping**) intr japper; (slang) criailler; (slang) dégoiser
yard [jɑrd] s cour f, (for lumber, for repairs, etc.) chantier m; (measure) yard m; (naut) vergue f, (rr) gare f de triage
yard′arm′ s (naut) bout de vergue
yard′mas′ter s (rr) chef m de dépôt
yard′stick′ s yard m en bois (en métal, etc.); (fig) unité f de comparaison
yarn [jɑrn] s fil m, filé m; (coll) histoire f
yarrow [ˈjæro] s mille-feuille f
yaw [jɔ] s (naut) embardée f; **yaws** (pathol) pian m ‖ intr faire des embardées
yawl [jɔl] s yole f
yawn [jɔn] s bâillement m ‖ intr bâiller; être béant
ye (old spelling of the [ðə]) art le, e.g., **ye olde shoppe** la vieille boutique ‖ [ji] pron pl (obs) vous (pl)
yea [je] s oui m; vote m affirmatif ‖ adv oui, voire
yeah [je] adv (coll) oui; **oh yeah?** (coll) de quoi?; **oh yeah!** (coll) ouais!
yean [jin] intr (said of ewe) agneler; (said of goat) chevreter
year [jɪr] s an m, année f;(of issue; vintage) millésime m; **six-year-old, seven-year-old,** etc. de six ans, de sept ans, etc.; **to be . . . years old** avoir . . . ans; **year in year out** bon an mal an
year′book′ s annuaire m
yearling [ˈjɪrlɪŋ] s animal m d'un an; (horse) yearling m
yearly [ˈjɪrli] adj annuel ‖ adv annuellement
yearn [jʌrn] intr—**to yearn for** soupirer après; **to yearn to** brûler de
yearning [ˈjʌrnɪŋ] s désir m ardent
yeast [jist] s levure f

yell [jɛl] s hurlement m; (school yell) cri m de ralliement ‖ tr & intr hurler
yellow [ˈjɛlo] adj jaune; (cowardly) (coll) froussard; (e.g., press) à sensation; **to turn yellow** jaunir; (coll) avoir la frousse ‖ s jaune m ‖ tr & intr jaunir
yel′low fe′ver s fièvre f jaune
yel′low·ham′mer s (orn) bruant m jaune
yellowish [ˈjɛlo·ɪʃ] adj jaunâtre
yel′low·jack′et s (ent) frelon m
yel′low streak′ s (coll) trait m de lâcheté
yelp [jɛlp] s glapissement m, jappement m ‖ intr glapir, japper
yen [jɛn] s—**to have a yen to** or **for** (coll) avoir envie de
yeo·man [ˈjomən] s (pl -**men**) yeoman m; (clerical worker) (nav) commis m aux écritures
yeo′man of the guard′ s (Brit) hallebardier m de la garde du corps
yeo′man's serv′ice s effort m précieux
yes [jɛs] s oui m ‖ adv oui; (to contradict a negative statement or question) si or pardon, e.g., **"You didn't know." "Yes, I did!"** "Vous ne le saviez pas." "Si!" ‖ v (pret & pp **yessed**; ger **yessing**) tr dire oui à ‖ intr dire oui
yes′ man′ s (pl **men′**) (coll) M. Toujours; **to be a yes man** opiner du bonnet; **yes men** (coll) béni-oui-oui mpl
yesterday [ˈjɛstər,de] adj, s, & adv hier m; **yesterday morning** hier matin
yet [jɛt] adv encore; déjà, e.g., **has he arrived yet?** est-il déjà arrivé?; **as yet** jusqu'à présent; **not yet** pas encore ‖ conj cependant
yew′tree′ [ju] s if m
Yiddish [ˈjɪdɪʃ] adj & s yiddish m invar, yidich m
yield [jild] s rendement m; (crop) produit m; (income produced) rapport m, revenu m ‖ tr rendre, produire; (a profit; a crop) rapporter; (to surrender) céder ‖ intr (to produce) produire, rapporter; (to give way) céder, se rendre; (public sign) priorité (à droite; à gauche)
yo·del [ˈjodəl] s tyrolienne f ‖ v (pret & pp -**deled** or -**delled**; ger -**deling** or -**delling**) tr & intr jodler
yogurt [ˈjogʊrt] s yogourt m

yoke [jok] *s* (*pair of draft animals*) paire *f*; (*device to join a pair of draft animals*) joug *m*; (*of a shirt*) empiècement *m*; (elec) culasse *f*; (fig) joug; **to throw off the yoke** secouer le joug ‖ *tr* accoupler

yokel [ˈjokəl] *s* rustaud *m*, manant *m*

yolk [jok] *s* jaune *m* d'œuf

yonder [ˈjɑndər] *adj* ce . . . -là là-bas, e.g., **that tree yonder** cet arbre-là là-bas ‖ *adv* là-bas

yore [jor] *s*—**of yore** d'antan

you [ju] *pron pers* vous, toi §85; vous, tu §87; vous, te §87 ‖ *pron indef* (coll) on §87, e.g., **you go in this way** on entre par ici

young [jʌŋ] *adj* (*comp* **younger** [ˈjʌŋgər]; *super* **youngest** [ˈjʌŋgɪst]) jeune ‖ **the young** les jeunes; (*of animal*) les petits *mpl*; **to be with young** (*said of animal*) être pleine; **young and old** les grands et les petits

young′ la′dy *s* (*pl* **-dies**) jeune fille *f*; (*married*) jeune femme *f*; **young ladies** jeunes personnes *fpl*

young′ man′ *s* (*pl* **men′**) jeune homme *m*; **young men** jeunes gens *mpl*

young′ peo′ple *spl* jeunes gens *mpl*

youngster [ˈjʌŋstər] *s* gosse *mf*

your [jʊr] *adj poss* votre, ton §88

yours [jʊrz] *pron poss* le vôtre, le tien §89; **a friend of yours** un de vos amis; **cordially yours** (complimentary close) amitiés; **yours truly** or **sincerely yours** (complimentary close) veuillez agréer, Monsieur, l'expression de mes sentiments distingués

your·self [jʊrˈsɛlf] *pron pers* (*pl* **-selves** [ˈsɛlvz]) vous-même, toi-même §86; vous, te §87; vous, toi §85

youth [juθ] *s* (*pl* **youths** [juðs], [juðz]) jeunesse *f*; (*person*) jeune homme *m*; **youths** jeunes *mpl*

youthful [ˈjuθfəl] *adj* jeune, juvénile

youth′ hos′tel *s* auberge *f* de jeunesse

yowl [jaʊl] *s* hurlement *m* ‖ *intr* hurler

Yugoslav [ˈjugoˌslɑv] *adj* yougoslave ‖ *s* Yougoslave *mf*

Yugoslavia [ˌjugoˈslɑvɪ·ə] *s* Yougoslavie *f*; la Yougoslavie

Yule′log′ [jul] *s* bûche *f* de Noël

Yule′tide′ *s* les fêtes *fpl* de Noël

yummy [ˈjʌmi] *adj* délicieux

yum yum [ˈjʌm ˈjʌm] *interj* miam! miam!

Z

Z, z [zi] or [zɛd] (Brit) *s* XXVIe lettre de l'alphabet

za·ny [ˈzeni] *adj* (*comp* **-nier**; *super* **-niest**) bouffon, toqué ‖ *s* (*pl* **-nies**) bouffon *m*

zeal [zil] *s* zèle *m*

zealot [ˈzɛlət] *s* zélateur *m*, adepte *mf*

zealotry [ˈzɛlətri] *s* fanatisme *m*

zealous [ˈzɛləs] *adj* zélé

zebra [ˈzibrə] *s* zèbre *m*

zenith [ˈzinɪθ] *s* zénith *m*

zephyr [ˈzɛfər] *s* zéphyr *m*

zeppelin [ˈzɛpəlin] *s* zeppelin *m*

ze·ro [ˈziro] *s* (*pl* **-ros** or **-roes**) zéro *m* ‖ *intr*—**to zero in** (mil) régler la ligne de mire; **to zero in on** (coll) pointer sur

ze′ro grav′ity *s* apesanteur *f*

ze′ro growth′ *s* croissance *f* zéro

ze′ro hour′ *s* heure *f* H

ze′ro op′tion *s* option *f* nulle

zest [zɛst] *s* enthousiasme *m*; (*agreeable and piquant flavor*) saveur *f*, piquant *m*

Zeus [zus] *s* Zeus *m*

zig·zag [ˈzigˌzæg] *adj* & *adv* en zigzag ‖ *s* zigzag *m* ‖ *v* (*pret* & *pp* **-zagged**; *ger* **-zagging**) *intr* zigzaguer

zinc [zɪŋk] *s* zinc *m*

Zionism [ˈzaɪ·əˌnɪzəm] *s* sionisme *m*

zip [zɪp] *s* (coll) sifflement *m*; (coll) énergie *f* ‖ *v* (*pret* & *pp* **zipped**; *ger* **zipping**) *tr* fermer à fermeture éclair ‖ *intr* siffler; **to zip by** (coll) passer comme un éclair

Zip′ code′ *s* indicatif *m* postal

zipper [ˈzɪpər] *s* fermeture *f* éclair, fermeture *f* à glissière

zither [ˈzɪθər] *s* cithare *f*

zodiac [ˈzodɪˌæk] *s* zodiaque *m*

zone [zon] *s* zone *f*

zoning [ˈzonɪŋ] *s* zonage *m*, zoning *m*

zon′ing code′ *s* plan *m* d'occupation des sols (P.O.S.)

zon′ing or′dinance *s* réglementation *f* urbaine

zon′ing per′mit *s* certificat *m* d'urbanisation

zoo [zu] *s* zoo *m*

zoo·logic(al) [ˌzo·əˈlɑdʒɪk(əl)] *adj* zoologique

zoology [zoˈɑlədʒi] *s* zoologie *f*

zoom [zum] *s* vrombissement *m*; (aer) montée *f* en chandelle ‖ *intr* vrombir; **to zoom up** monter en chandelle

zoom′ lens′ *s* zoom *m*

zoot′ suit′ [zut] *s* costume *m* zazou

Zu·lu [ˈzulu] *adj* zoulou ‖ *s* (*pl* **-lus**) Zoulou *m*

zygote [ˈzaɪgot] *s* zygote *m*

CONVERSION TABLES

American Measurements and the Metric System*

	AMERICAN UNIT	METRIC EQUIVA-LENT	METRIC UNIT	AMERICAN EQUIVA-LENT
Length	one mile (mi.)	1.6 kilometers	un kilomètre (km)	.6 mile
	one yard (yd.)	.9 meter	un mètre (m)	39.34 inches
	one foot (ft.)	30 centimeters	un centimètre (cm)	or 3.28 feet
				.39 inch
	one inch (in.)	25.4 millime-ters	un millimètre (mm)	.039 inch
Surface	one acre (a.)	.4 hectare	un hectare (ha)	2.5 acres
	one square mile (sq. mi.)	259 hectares	un kilomètre carré (km²)	.39 square mile
Volume	one cubic foot (cu. ft.)	.028 cubic meter	un mètre cube (m³)	35.314 cubic feet
Capacity	one liquid quart (qt.)	.95 liter	un litre (l)	1.057 quarts or .26 gal-lon
	one gallon (gal.)	3.8 liters		
Weight	one pound (lb.)	.45 kilogram	un kilogram (kg) (un kilo)	2.2 pounds
	one ounce (oz.)	28.35 grams	100 grammes	3.5 ounces
	one ton (2,000 pounds)	907.2 kilo-grams	un gramme (g)	15.432 grains

* International System of Units—Le système international d'unités (SI).

Approximate Comparison of Fahrenheit and Centigrade (Celsius) Temperatures

FAHRENHEIT			CENTIGRADE
Boiling point ▶	212	100 ◀	*Point d'ébullition*
	140	60	
	104	40	
	100	38	
Normal body temperature ▶ (physiol)	98.6	37 ◀	*Température normale (physiol)*
	97	36	
	88	31	
	77	25	
	68	20	
	59	15	
	50	10	
	41	5	
Freezing point ▶	32	0 ◀	*Point de congélation*
	23	−5	
	14	−10	
	5	−15	
	0	−18	
	−13	−25	
	−22	−30	
	−40	−40	

For exact conversion, use the following:

(a) To convert Fahrenheit into centigrade, subtract 32, multiply by 5, and divide by 9.

(b) To convert centigrade into Fahrenheit, multiply by 9, divide by 5, and add 32.

Tire Pressure

Pounds per square inch *Livres par pouce carré*	Kilograms per square centimeter *Kilogrammes par centimètre carré*	Pounds per square inch *Livres par pouce carré*	Kilograms per square centimeter *Kilogrammes par centimètre carré*
16	1,12	30	2,10
18	1,26	32	2,24
20	1,40	36	2,52
22	1,54	40	2,80
24	1,68	50	3,50
26	1,82	60	4,20
28	1,96	70	4,90

Sizes of Clothing in the United States and France

LADIES—*DAMES*

Size of coats, dresses—*Taille de manteaux, de robes*

American	8	10	12	14	16	18	20
French	38	40	42	44	46	48	50

Size of blouses, sweaters, and slips—*Taille de chemisiers (corsages), de chandails et de combinaisons*

American	32	34	36	38	40	42
French	38	40	42	44	46	48

Size of shoes, slippers—*Pointure de chaussures, de pantoufles*

American	4	5	6	7	8	9
French	36	37	38	39	40	41

MEN—*MESSIEURS*

Size of topcoats, suits—*Taille de pardessus, de costumes*

American	30	32	34	36	38	40	42	44	46
French	40	42	44	46	48	50	52	54	56

Size (neck size) of shirts—*Taille (encolure) de chemises*

American	14	14½	15	15½	16	16½
French	37	38	39	40	41	42

Size of shoes, slippers—*Pointure de chaussures, de pantoufles*

American	8	8½	9	9½	10	10½	11
French	41	42	43	44	45	46	47

Size of hats—*Pointure (tours de la tête en centimètres) de chapeaux*

American	6⅝	6¾	6⅞	7	7⅛	7¼	7⅜	7½	7⅝
French	53	54	55	56	57	58	59	60	61

ROGER J. STEINER is Senior Professor of Languages and Linguistics, University of Delaware. He is the author of numerous articles on lexicography and language.

The New College Series

Edwin B. Williams, General Editor

The New College French & English Dictionary
by Roger J. Steiner
The New College German & English Dictionary
by John C. Traupman
The New College Italian & English Dictionary
by Robert C. Melzi
The New College Latin & English Dictionary
by John C. Traupman
The New College Spanish & English Dictionary
by Edwin B. Williams

Amsco School Publications, Inc.

Perim Island in the Red Sea, off the Aden coast. But lack of water forced the British to abandon the craggy offshore spot and withdraw to Aden proper, then part of the sultanate of Lahej (see chapter 4). Great Britain then forced the sultan of Lahej to cede Aden and to become a British vassal. For nearly a century after its capture in 1839, Aden was administered by the British India government. Finally, in 1937, it became a crown colony, ruled by a governor directly responsible to the Colonial Office in London. From then until the early 1960s Aden's British governor was the final governmental authority, responsible only to London. A Legislative Council, with advisory powers only, was established in 1947. British rule brought such material benefits as roads, schools, and health facilities. Nevertheless, Arab nationalism was strong and anti-British riots were frequent.

The British made Aden into a commercial and trading city of over 100,000 people. Within Aden's crowded eighty square miles, more than three-quarters of the population were Arabs, including several thousand from Yemen. The relatively high living standards created by employment opportunities in British naval and other installations and by the town's trade also attracted several thousand Indians, Pakistanis, and Somalis.

Aden colony was only a small enclave on the tip of Aden protectorate, a long arid belt stretching along the southern Arabian seacoast of the peninsula. Its approximately 112,000 square miles were divided into eastern and western protectorates, containing some twenty-three Arab sultanates, amirates, sheikhdoms, and minor tribal units varying in size from a few hundred people and a dozen square miles to large stretches of several hundred miles square populated by thousands. The extent of British authority exercised in each area differed, although all were subject to the governor in Aden, who appointed the local British agents. The *de jure* relationship with Great Britain was usually a treaty granting protection to the local state and giving Britain control of its foreign affairs. Most of the approximately 800,000 people of the region were Bedouin tribesmen whom even the local chiefs found difficulty in governing. The whole region was policed by the Aden Protectorate Levies, local Arab troops with British officers. The most important principality was the sultanate of Lahej, whose ruler was given the title "His Highness" by the British and was authorized to maintain a small regular army commanded by British officers.

Great Britain invited five, then ten, local rulers to form a federation, the United Arab Sultanates, renamed the Federation of South Arabia in 1962, as a device to counteract growing Arab nationalist fervor. When a third of the Lahej regular army deserted to Yemen in June 1958, in protest against British domination, Great Britain removed the sultan, who then requested help from President Nasser. A Southern Arabian League led by several Lahej officials was formed to oppose the federation formed by Great Britain. Its purpose was to create a new South Arabian state, including Aden colony and the protectorates, which then was to join Yemen and the UAR in the United Arab States.

When British officials attempted in 1962 to associate Aden colony with the South Arabian Federation, there were riots and demonstrations against the union because it was dominated by old-style sheikhs. Britain's hold over the region became increasingly precarious. Disputes were no longer merely petty inter-tribal skirmishes, but international in scope because of their involvement in the Arab nationalist movement.

The Republic of Yemen renewed traditional claims to all of southern Yemen, and border warfare broke out between the republic and British forces along the frontiers. In Aden militant nationalist groups supported by the UAR opened guerrilla warfare against the British, demanding immediate independence and rejecting authority of the "reactionary" South Arabian sheikhs. Despite stepped-up measures to grant Aden self-government, natinalist groups such as the Front for the Liberation of South Yemen (FLOSY) and the National Liberation Front (NLF) continued their attacks on British forces. After several conferences between the British and nationalist groups and after investigation by a United Nations mission, the London government in 1967 declared its intention of withdrawing from all South Arabia. Authority of the sultans also began to crumble until the whole South Arabian Federation collapsed, leaving FLOSY and NLF face to face. After several months of fighting, the two groups tried unsuccessfully to resolve their differences at a conference in Cairo. When the high command of the South Arabian army threw in its lot with the NLF, FLOSY withdrew from competition for control of the area. The NLF, supported by the army, now opened negotiations with the British to take over Aden and South Arabia. As the last British troops were leaving in November 1967, the NLF proclaimed the People's Republic of South Yemen.

Independence left the country with a depleted treasury, loss of much income from the British Base in Aden, continued internal strife, and a severe shortage of technicians and administrators to continue normal government operations. Within the fifteen-member high command of the NLF, the only political party, moderates and leftists clashed. The latter purged the armed forces and police, demanding political commissars for all military units, and establishment of a militia of "popular guards."

In two of the republic's six governorates, leftists seized control in 1968, establishing popular councils of their own choice, ignoring central government authority, ousting the police and armed forces, and taking over oil installations. Similar rebellions also threatened in other areas. In addition to internal instability, there were attacks across the border by units of FLOSY from Yemen, by deposed sheikhs and sultans from Saudi Arabia, and by neighboring sheikhs in Muscat and Oman.

Unable to cope with the situation, the leftist president resigned in June 1969, turning the government over to an even more leftist five-man presidential council headed by a former guerrilla leader. Extensive nationalization of banks, industry, and other business in November 1969 failed to improve the rapidly deteriorating economic situation, leaving the country, especially Aden, with large unemployment and many economic problems.

Since independence political stability in South Yemen was tenuous because the country lacked an integrated state structure. The 23 states or sheikdoms that existed under the British were never really unified. In addition to sectional differences, war with North Yemen, continued forays across the border by FLOSY, and clashes between nationalists and leftists in the NLF have been disruptive. The basic ideological cleavage divided NLF into two groups. The Nasserites wanted a traditional government with political and adminstrative institutions, rather than the party apparatus control of the country. The Radicals wanted the NLF apparatus, its people's organizations and trade unions to be supreme. They were zealous Marxists who called for appointment of political commissars in all army units, strengthening the people's militia, and creation of "popular guards." At times the leftists controlled parts of the east while the Nasserites ruled in Aden. In the 1975 Congress of the NLF statutes were adopted unifying activities of three organizations, the NLF, the People's Avant Garde Party of former Ba'athists, and the Communist oriented Popular Democratic Union. Rhetoric of the republic was Marxist oriented, with goals of the NLF providing for establishment of an "alliance embracing the working class, peasants, intellectuals, and petite bourgeoisie with a view to implementing the democratic and national tasks indispensable for the transformation into a socialist state." Leftist orientation was emphasized in 1970 when the new constitution changed the country's name to the People's Democratic Republic of Yemen. In 1978 the NLF was replaced by the Yemen Socialist Party, modeled on the Communist Party of the USSR. The sole legal party, it proclaimed itself a Marxist-Leninist "vanguard party" headed by a Central Committee, Secretariat, and Politburo. Since the 1970s, most of the economy was government controlled and much of its agricultural output was produced by state farms and cooperatives.

The country's many foreign involvements have been obstacles to deep social change or implementation of Marxist programs. The war with North Yemen in 1972 and participation in the Dhofar rebellion against the sultan of Oman have absorbed much of the Arab Marxist republic's resources and energies.

KUWAIT

Kuwait's strategic location, at the head of the Persian Gulf, attracted British road builders in 1850, but their plans were never carried out. When Kaiser Wilhelm II sought to use Kuwait as a terminus for his Middle Eastern railroad schemes in the 1890s, Great Britain intervened and established a protectorate over the sheikhdom. From 1899 until 1961, the protective treaty authorized British control over all Kuwait's foreign affairs and the country's sheikhs took no important action without first consulting the local British resident.

Nearly all Kuwait's 6000 square miles are waterless, barren desert. Consequently, most of the 500,000 inhabitants live in the old fortress town, also called Kuwait. (The name may be derived from the *kut* (fort) built by the Portuguese during the sixteenth century.) Before oil was discovered, the sparse population lived from pearling, sailing, boat building, and trading. Water was so scarce that it was brought in barrels on boats from the Shatt el-Arab sixty miles away. Thus agriculture was impossible and the population was severely limited in its economic activities.

Because of its great oil revenues and small population, Kuwait has one of the highest per capita incomes in the world (over $18,000 by 1980). Its oil reserves then represented about 10 percent of the Middle Eastern total. By 1961, Kuwait had become the world's fourth largest oil producer, with revenues estimated at 450 million dollars per year and nearly ten billion dollars in 1977.

Until oil was discovered in 1932 by the Kuwait Oil Company (half British Petroleum and half American Gulf Oil), Kuwait was an impoverished sand lot. After World War II, Sheikh Sir Abdullah al-Salim al-Sabah undertook major public works and economic development programs, attracting thousands of outsiders. Now the principal problem was to find something to develop. Until recently, the largest project was a plant to purify water. When operation of the plant became successful, Kuwait was freed from its continued dependence on outside water sources. Large free public hospitals have been built; public education and health programs have been expanded; and electric power plants have been constructed. And roads, airports, a sewage system, and new harbors have been laid out. In effect, Sheikh Abdullah converted his desert patrimony into a welfare sheikhdom.

The principal obstacle to continued economic development has been shortage of technical, administrative, and supervisory personnel. Consequently, many non-Kuwaitis, a total larger than the local population, have been attracted to the country to work as technicians. The sheikh had such a large surplus of money that he was unable to use most of it at home. Instead, he invested hundreds of millions of pounds on the London stock market, becoming the market's largest individual investor during the 1970s.

Kuwait has also been swept into the Arab nationalist movement and, in 1961, Great Britain decided to terminate its protectorate status. Immediately after the British government announced its decision to give Kuwait full freedom, Iraq's Prime Minister Kassim claimed the territory as an integral part of his country. The Iraqi claim was based on an assertion that the 1899 treaty with Great Britain had been forged and that Kuwait, in recent history, had been part of the Ottoman administrative region which included Iraq. No other Arab state supported Iraq's claims, and in July 1961, the Arab League voted to admit Kuwait as a full member state. However, when Kuwait applied for admission to the United Nations late in 1961, its application was vetoed by the Soviet Union, although all Arab states, except Iraq, supported Kuwait's application. Two years later Iraq gave up its claims, and the amirate, as Kuwait was now called, joined the U.N.

The influence of nationalism was evident in the constitutional crisis between the paternalistic royal family and the independent-minded National Assembly during 1965. Arab unity nationalists opposed the amir's government because of its domination by wealthy "reactionary" merchants. The amir responded by opening his cabinet for the first time to the new middle class. However, the constitutional changes were in reality more of a facade since real power remained in the hands of the royal family, which filled all principal cabinet posts including the prime ministry.

The large influx of foreigners also was beginning to create concern, since their number had increased to over half the population. Indeed, by the 1970s the country's population had increased nearly sixfold from about 206,000 in 1968 to 1,600,000 by 1982. Although many outsiders prospered in Kuwait, achieving high living standards, they were barred from high office, from suffrage, and from free use of the many welfare services available to Kuwaitis. Among the most activist were the more than 250,000 Palestinians who provided much of the support for the Arab guerrilla movements fighting Israel.

Kuwait maintained its Arab credentials through the extensive economic assistance it provided to other Arab states. In 1961 it established the Kuwait Fund for Arab Economic Development to provide capital to other developing Arab states. It also became a principal contributor to the fund established for defeated Egypt and Jordan at the 1967 Khartoum Conference. With ever-increasing wealth and so small a population base, Kuwait's material wellbeing was assured, although, as in other revolutionary situations, material wellbeing was no guarantee against political instability. This became clear in 1976 when the ruling family dissolved the National Assembly, suspended civil rights, and imposed press censorship. Until then Kuwait had been, with Lebanon, the only Arab country enjoying relative press freedom. These acts were taken to still opposition to the government because of its support for Syrian intervention in the Lebanese civil war. The royal family feared that the quarrels in Lebanon might spill over into Kuwait where Palestinians constituted nearly one in four of the inhabitants. On the other hand, Kuwait strongly supported the Palestinians in international forums such as the United Nations, the Arab League, and in Third World conferences. Along with Saudi Arabia, Kuwait was the principal financier of the 1967 and 1973 wars against

Israel and of conservative factions among the Palestine guerrilla organizations. In 1981 the regime felt secure enough to permit new elections for the assembly. Fewer than 10 of the 50 members elected represented leftist or Islamic radicalism despite growing apprehension that the religious fervor from Iran would infect Kuwait's own Shi'ite minority. As a precaution to ensure Gulf stability, Kuwait joined other Arab Gulf states to form the Gulf Cooperation Council in 1981. The dilemma facing Kuwait was how to tread the narrow line between support for militant Arab causes and maintenance of its own distinctive identity based chiefly on its immense oil reserves and its traditional sheikly families.

BAHRAIN

The Bahrain archipelago, a small Persian Gulf group of 35 largely desert islands (213 square miles) with some 280,000 people, off the Saudi Arabian coast, would also be totally unknown were it not for its oil resources. Bahrain has been a naval base for powers desiring to dominate the gulf since the fifteenth century. Portugal controlled it during that century, until it was seized by Iran. Arabs drove the Iranians out at the end of the eighteenth century and used Bahrain for gun running, the slave trade, and piracy. In 1820, Great Britain imposed a treaty on the ruling sheikh in an attempt to ban slavery and piracy. Later treaties, in 1880 and 1892, forced the island's rulers to permit British control of its relations with other countries. Because Bahrain was the headquarters of British Persian Gulf activities, the reins were tightly held. The British Royal Navy Persian Gulf headquarters was until recently in Bahrain, and British political agents, who advised other coastal sheikhs, were responsible to the British political resident at Bahrain. The ruling al-Khalifa family made no important decision without consulting its British adviser. After independence in 1971, a United States small base replaced the British naval presence.

Great Britain developed a competent civil administration for the islands, despite the preoil poverty. After the Bahrain Petroleum Company (a subsidiary of the California Standard and Texas Oil Companies) began to produce in 1932, the economy was so revolutionized that the island could offer its inhabitants free medical care and education. Because of closer British supervision, workers there had a higher standard of living than in Kuwait.

Iran claimed Bahrain until 1969. In November 1957 the shah's government declared the islands his fourteenth province. However, in 1969 the shah declared his willingness to recognize an independent Bahrain, provided there was a U.N.-sponsored plebiscite. During the 1950s, proposals were put forward for a union of Saudi Arabia, Kuwait, and Bahrain, but no action was taken to implement them.

After Great Britain announced its intention of ending its military role in all areas east of Suez after 1971, plans were proposed to include Bahrain in a Persian Gulf Federation. However, other potential members of the proposed Federation objected because of Bahrain's considerably greater wealth, population, and consequent influence. Iran also objected to incorporation of the island in a larger Arab political entity. A U.N. mission sent to the island reported that "The overwhelming majority... wish to gain recognition of their identity in a fully independent and sovereign state."[3]

Treaty arrangements with Great Britain were terminated and full independence was proclaimed in 1971. Sheikh Isa of the Khalifa family took the title of Amir. In 1972–1973 an elected Constituent Assembly drafted a constitution which established a National Assembly. Since independence political life on the island has centered on the struggle for the Assembly's 42 seats (30 elected and 12 appointed) between the Popular List and the Religious List. Victory for the leftist popular list created contentious relations with the Amir's government. Delay in granting permission for organization of trade unions also sparked unrest. Leftist trends were represented by the Popular Front, an offshoot of the Popular Front for the Liberation of Oman and the Arab Gulf, and the Bahraini National Liberation Organization. Their demands for nationalization of large companies and for termination of the American presence in Bahrain precipitated a showdown in 1974. The Emir promulgated a new state security law authorizing him to arrest and detain opponents of the regime. The arrests were followed by a decree in 1975 dissolving the National Assembly and suspending the constitution. The 1979 revolution in Iran intensified political unrest in Bahrain where more than half the population is Shi'ite, many of whom sympathized with the Shi'ite revolutionaries in Teheran. This, and the fact that there were nearly twice as many foreign as Bahrain workers, many of them associated with the poorer Shi'ites, led Bahrain's rulers to join in the formation of the Gulf Cooperation Council as a way to combat subversion of the Gulf.

Like the other Gulf states undergoing rapid political and social change, Bahrain was faced with the dilemma of extending popular participation which would lead to intensified clashes between right and left, or imposing strict controls on the political system which would concentrate power in the hands of the royal family.

QATAR, UNITED ARAB EMIRATES, AND OMAN

Qatar, Trucial Oman, and Oman were all until recently small British-controlled desert principalities with sparse population, almost no natural resources except oil, and no effectively organized systems of government. The population of all consisted mostly of Bedouin who lived at subsistence level from grazing and camel raising. There are no large cities among them, and the few small towns are concentrated along the Persian Gulf coast where the Arab population lived from pearling, fishing, or trading.

After the British decision to leave the area by the end of 1971, Qatar Bahrain and the seven Trucial Oman states decided to form the Federation of Gulf Emirates for protection against the rivalries of Saudi Arabia and Iran, and against the revolutionary aspirations of the Arab left. The Federation was launched in October 1969, when it elected the Sheikh of Abu Dhabi as its first president. All states would have equal membership in the Federation's Assembly: thus tiny Fujaira, with only 3000 inhabitants would have equal representation with Bahrain's 200,000 inhabitants. Later, Bahrain and Oman left the Federation after its government decided in favor of independence. With the proclamation of independence in 1971 the Federation became the United Arab Emirates.

Qatar

Qatar is a remote peninsula whose only land frontier, shared with Saudi Arabia, has never been clearly demarcated, a fact that has led to frequent disputes. England controlled the territory's 4000 square miles through a political officer residing in Doha, the capital, after it signed a treaty with Qatar's sheikh in 1882. Before World War II, Qatar was a poor and desolate outpost whose 20,000 inhabitants scratched a meagre living from goat grazing or the Gulf seafaring trades—pearling, fishing, and trading.

With the beginning of oil production during and after World War II, the country began an economic upswing. The population doubled as some 20,000 immigrants, including many Palestine refugees, Indians, Pakistanis, Iranians, and Somalis, were attracted by new employment opportunities. Doha grew from a double row of mud huts strung along the shore to a large city with shops full of imported goods, large and luxurious homes, and a modern free hospital. In the prewar era, there were only a half dozen automobiles. By the 1970s more than 150,000 of Qatar's 200,000 residents lived in Doha.

When wealth first came to Qatar, both the ruling family and the people were austere Wahabi tribesmen. But as oil royalties grew, reaching fifty million dollars per year by 1960, royal spending became wasteful. The ruler disbursed about a quarter of the income among his 400 relatives who squandered it on high-priced Western commodities, such as automobiles, and other mechanical devices. The government began to clamp down, insisting that a third of the royalties be used for economic development. Some eighty million dollars was spent on sixty schools, a 120-bed hospital, roads, and other public services. When public services reached the saturation point, the usual problem arose of how to spend the surpluses.

Like its other Arab neighbors, Qatar has been troubled by growing internal unrest and the threat of external subversion (about half the population is foreign, attracted by the oil boom). The royal family has been reluctant to give up any of its authority, although a provisional constitution in 1970 did establish an advisory council. Since becoming independent it has kept close ties with Saudi Arabia and generally follows the Saudi foreign policy line.

United Arab Emirates

The U.A.E., formerly Trucial Oman, once known as the Pirate Coast, has a long and colorful history, although today its seven sheikhdoms—Abu Dhabi, Dubai, Sharjah, Fujaira, Ras al-Khaima, Umm al-Kuwain, and Ajman—are relatively tame. Until the British quelled the coastal brigands early in the nineteenth century, it was infamous as a pirate-infested refuge (see chapter 4). The Roman historian Pliny and the Italian merchant Marco Polo both wrote of the dangers. Buccaneering was so profitable that pirates were attracted from the world over, including the famous Captain Kidd. Raids on ships sailing out of India convinced Great Britain of the need to end piracy. In 1820, the British imposed a treaty on the local sheikhs forbidding them to raid ships from outside the area. A Treaty of Peace in Perpetuity, or Permanent Truce (thus Trucial states), outlawing all piracy was signed with Great Britain in 1853.

Until recently, Bedouin, who lived in the sheikhdoms, were a law unto themselves. Their love of fighting led them to hire out to feuding sheikhs. Thus the principalities were in constant turmoil. In 1951, the British organized the Trucial Oman Scouts to impose order. When two or more sheikhs threatened to fight each other, a few dozen Arab scouts under a British officer would arrive, buy a sheep, and invite the hostile sheikhs to camp for a friendly feast. All parted friends—until the next time.

After establishment of the Federation of United Arab Emirates (UAE) in 1971, oil development greatly increased its importance. Abu Dhabi, by far the most populous and richest of the seven emirates dominated by the UAE. It contained nearly a third of the more than 650,000 inhabitants, and its ruler was designated president of the UAE Supreme Council. Each of the seven ruling sheikhs retain control over internal policy and local administration in his emirate, but foreign affairs, defense, education, and development policies are decided by the Council. Cabinet seats are allocated according to the size and strength of the members. The 40 seats in the National Federal Assembly are similarly allocated. A Union Defense Force created in 1971 replaced the British-officered Trucial Oman Scouts. There are no political parties or elections and the authorities maintain a tight rein on illegal immigration lest the country become swamped with foreign laborers like many of its neighbors. The UAE also maintains a cautiously conservative foreign policy close to that of Saudi Arabia and its associates in the Gulf Cooperation Council.

Sparse population and immense oil revenues gave the UAE the world's highest per capita income in 1977, about $14,000 per person. It also added prestige and international influence. The Abu Dhabi Fund for Arab Economic Development has extended loans totaling billions of dollars for development to several Arab and other Third World countries. After the oil boom, UAE played a prominent role in financing the 1973 war and in inter-Arab parleys about the postwar situation.

Oman

The sultanate of Oman recently attracted world attention because of the dispute with Saudi Arabia over the Buraimi oasis on the border between the two countries. During the first half of the nineteenth century, the sultanate was powerful enough to possess overseas colonies. The ruling al-Abu Said dynasty then moved its headquarters to Zanzibar island, off the East African coast. After the patriarch Sultan Said Ibn Sultan died, his kingdom was divided between two sons. One established the dynasty that ruled Zanzibar island until it was overthrown and Zanzibar united with Tanzania in 1964, and the other became sultan of Muscat. The British established control in 1891, through a treaty similar to those with the other Persian Gulf Sheikhdoms. However, in 1913 Bedouin tribes in the interior rebelled and elected their own chief, called imam. Ever since, the British have supported the sultan's authority, but it was limited to the coastal regions where order was maintained by the British-officered Muscat and Oman Field Force. After 1953, when there began to be speculation about the oil potential of the Buraimi oasis, the imam and sultan disputed its ownership. Great Britain backed the sultan with troops and military equipment, while Saudi Arabia and the Arab nationalists supported the imam. Claims of a third party, the Trucial Oman sheikh of Abu Dhabi, made the dispute even more complicated, and he, too, was supported against Saudi Arabia by the British. Ten Arab countries pressed the cause of the imam against the sultan in the U.N., charging that the British controlled the sultanate and that it was therefore under colonial domination. After establishment of the People's Republic of South Yemen, hostilities broke out between the two neighboring states. The People's Republic became a base for the insurgent "Popular Front for the Liberation of the Arabian Gulf," an organization established to undermine the royal emirates. With large-scale oil production beginning in the 1960s the sultan promised to initiate several development projects. However he, like other traditional royal chiefs of state in the area, faced the prospect of growing nationalism, along with the benefits of increasing oil revenues and therefore attempted to cut off all contact by his subjects with the outside world. He forbade them to leave the country or even to own agricultural machinery. His feeble efforts at development failed to prevent his overthrow in August 1970 by a "progressive"-minded son who had been educated in England. The new young sultan promised to abolish many of the restrictions imposed by his father to prevent contact with the outside world. One of his first acts was to change the country's name to the Sultanate of Oman as a step to emphasize unity of all the country. He also formally incorporated the Dhofar region into his kingdom. Formerly it had been a separate sultanate joined to Muscat through the person of the ruler.

The new sultan at first asked the Dhofar rebels to cooperate in his development efforts, but only the Dhofar Liberation Front accepted. The Popular Front for the Liberation of the Occupied Arabian Gulf, a leftist group which controlled much of Dhofar continued its efforts to overthrow the monarchy or at least to liberate Dhofar. The Dhofar rebellion became a focal point of the struggle between traditional conservative forces and nationalist "progressives" for control of the Gulf and of South Arabia. Because he perceived the war in Dhofar as crucial, the shah of Iran sent several thousand troops to the aid of the sultan. PFLOAG claimed that there was a secret agreement between the shah and the sultan to repress leftist movements in south Arabia. Iran's large air force received its first combat experience in Dhofar. Jordan also began to assist the Sultan in 1972 with troops and aircraft and by training Omani pilots at the Jordanian Royal Air Academy. PFLOAG has also received foreign aid through the Yemen People's Democratic Republic, including equipment from Communist China. The sultan claimed a complete victory over the rebels late in 1975 and a cease-fire with South Yemen was negotiated by Saudi Arabia. However, reports continued to come from the area indicating that the rebellion continued. By 1982 there were still no representative political institutions and the sultan ruled with total authority under Koranic law.

Oman figured prominently in U.S. plans for establishment of a rapid deployment force in the region during 1982. A special strategic relationship was developed with Oman, and it, along with Somalia and Egypt, participated in military exercises within the new American military command organized to protect U.S. interests in the Gulf.

NOTES

1. Cited in George Lipsky, ed., *Saudi Arabia,* New Haven, 1959, p. 120.
2. H. St. John Philby, *Sa'udi Arabia,* London, 1955, p. 343.
3. *New York Times,* May 3, 1970.

17   Iran

Although the history of Iran (Persia) dates back to the sixth century before Christ and its continuity is longer than any other Middle Eastern nation, it is still not a nation-state in the modern sense. While 90 percent of the people are Shi'ite Muslims who share a history whose roots reach back into the pre-Islamic era, among them still flouishes a variety of ethnic, racial, and linguistic groups who live in relative isolation from each other, hindering unification of the country.

SOCIAL STRATA

Until the massive economic and social changes of the 1960s, the 80 to 85 percent of Iran's population that constituted the peasantry lived in some 50,000 villages similar to those of their Arab and Turkish neighbors; their conditions had changed little over the past 2000 years. Iranian village organization also resembled that of Arab lands where, until recent revolutions, powerful landlords owned not only the soil, but the villages and, for all practical purposes, the peasants. Until the recent land reform in Iran only 15 percent of most of the cultivated land was peasant owned. At least half the land was owned by absentee landlords, another quarter by wakf or religious endowments—such as schools, mosques, and other Muslim institutions—and about 10 percent was state domain. Because of Iran's extensive mountains and deserts, agricultural land is scarce, only 10 percent being truly arable.

496

Village headmen, who were feared by the peasants, usually were the estate managers of the richest landlords. Since the headmen carried out the landlord's will, collected taxes, and controlled the gendarmerie, they were regarded with deep suspicion. A common Iranian saying was: "First see the headman—then fleece the village." In a few regions where there were peasant proprietors, headmen were selected by the villagers from their own wealthier members. Other important village figures included the religious leader (*mullah*), schoolteacher, and elders. The latter, representing heads of leading families, could or could not form a council that the headman consulted should he want to. Some mullahs were politically active and organized the peasants; others were themselves illiterate and ignorant of life beyond the village. The Shi'ite clergy, led by the Ayatollah Ruhollah Khomeini, were the group which galvanized opposition to the shah during the 1960s and 1970s; they led the 1979 Revolution which overthrew the monarchy and established the Islamic Republic which followed. Teachers, many under the influence of the Communist Tudeh party, were government appointed and paid. Hence, as state officials, they also had much influence.

In larger villages along the main roads, the teahouse was the center of social life. Remote from the main thoroughfares, where there was no teahouse, villagers congregated at the home of the headman or schoolteacher, where they heard of national events from the radio or from recent visitors to the large towns. The public bath and mosque were other village institutions where the latest gossip and public events were discussed.

Social organization in the towns was patriarchal, like that in village and tribe. Life was little better for the townsman than for the villager. Both lived in dire poverty. The real distinction between Iranian towns and villages was the existence of bazaars in the former. Most bazaar towns seemed to fit a pattern: they averaged about 40,000 inhabitants; were situated along main highways; and contained quite varied social and ethnic groups and numerous minorities, such as Jews, Arabs, Assyrians, and Armenians. Since nearly all social contact took place within the family circle, the various ethnic and social groups had little contact with each other.

Within the towns resided the small but powerful group of between 200 and 1000 landowning families who occupied or controlled all key positions in the army, police, judiciary, higher clergy, and government. Mobility upward into this class was unusual, although it was possible by accumulation and manipulation of wealth, or the right connections. Because of Iran's strong tradition of a socially graded society, there was much less social mobility than in other Middle Eastern societies. Although considered equal before Allah, all Iranians were not considered equal before man. So great was the reverence for social prestige that any title indicating some kind of upward differentiation was clung to.

Another peculiarly Iranian phenomenon was the bazaar merchant. His social rank was immediately below the landowner, but he was not nearly so powerful. The bazaar merchant (including artisans, shopkeepers, and small traders) was more influential than his counterpart in other Middle Eastern Muslim lands. The bazaar in Iran was much more than a place to exchange goods; it was also a market place for ideas and opinions to which the country's rulers were especially attentive. Before modern communications, the bazaar provided the quickest means of sending news, and it was there that public reaction to the government could be most readily observed. Even Reza Shah slowed down some of his plans when he discovered opposition in the bazaar. The revolution in 1906, discussed below, was a direct result of a bazaar uprising in Tehran. With the growing influence of other institutions such as the bureaucracy, the university, and the working class, the relative influence of the bazaar declined.

Small industrialists, bankers, and businessmen, who came recently into contact with the West and were learning its techniques of operation and management, belonged to the upper-middle class. Many of the *nouveau riche* invested their money in land, hoping thereby to become members of the governing elite. In Tehran and a few other large towns, there was also a new intellectual middle class of doctors, lawyers, engineers, and government employees.

The lower-middle class were generally skilled factory laborers and white-collar workers. They too were becoming acquainted with Western ideas, tastes, and ideologies. The wide social range between the upper- and lower-middle class prevented formation of any strong middle-class consciousness. Some Iranians of this group favored more rapid progress toward reform and Westernization. Others regarded moderate ideas and methods as evil and irreligious, and strenuously opposed them. Generally speaking, however, the middle classes, collaborating with some of the more progressive landed aristocrats and clergy, gave great impetus to social change in Iran.

At the bottom of the social scale were the peasant laborers, servants, and menials. They lacked the initiative to form an effective political force, although they could be rather readily instigated into becoming violent mobs by politicians. They were often organized into a striking force, trained and paid by the politically conscious bazaar merchants, and could be induced to demonstrate for or against any issue.

THE TRIBES

Even among the 90 percent of the Iranians who are Shi'ites (8 percent are Sunnis), there is no common language spoken by a majority. Less than a third of the population speak the Persian dialect of the capital (Pahlavi), and more than two-thirds speak some other Persian tongue. In the densely settled northwestern province of Azerbaijan, where a fifth of the people live, the language is a Turkish dialect called Azari. In addition, there are a number of tribal languages and dialects spoken by the Kurds, Lurs, Bakhtiari, Kashkai, Khamseh, Shahsevans, Arabs, and Baluchis.

An important tribe is the Bakhtiaris, concentrated in their Zagors mountain homeland. They speak a dialect of Persian, although many have also absorbed Arabic or Turkish elements into their speech. Until 1924 they were politically autonomous, fostering their unity on legends of common ancestry. According to one legend, their origin can be traced to a Mongol noble, Bakhtiar, whose descendants were conquered by the Sassanids. Many ruling Bakhtiari families were wealthy landownders who lived in the capital, sent their children to American and European universities, and participated fully in Iranian national life. The second wife of Shah Muhammad Reza Pahlavi was a daughter of a leading Bakhtiari whom he married to strengthen relations with this powerful group. But he divorced her because she bore him no son.

The Kurds are more numerous than the Bakhtiari, but they have never been as influential in Tehran. They tended to remain outside the mainstream of national life, preferring to maintain their own customs and traditions free from contact with other groups. Like Persian, Kurdish is one of the Indo-European family of languages. The Kurds comprise most of the country's Sunni Muslims. Thus they are both an ethnic and a religious minority. After World War II, pro-Communist Kurdish leaders established the Republic of Mahabad with Soviet support (see chapter 5). But their revolt was crushed when Iranian troops overran the region and hanged some twenty leaders in 1947. Kurdish nationalism is still a strong centrifugal force, and the tight kinship uniting hundreds of families constantly undermines Tehran's authority in Kurdish regions.

The Lurs, who resemble the Bakhtiari, live south of the Kurds. Most Lurs still maintain a tribal organization and have a reputation for being a wild, proud people.

The Persian-speaking Kashgai occupy the southwestern province of Fars, in which they established virtual autonomy for several months after World War II. Periodical military expeditions against them failed to suppress their resistance to the central government, and they continued their independent ways with little chance of, or desire for, integration with the rest of the country.

Other tribes, like the Arabs and Baluchi, are politically less significant and have created fewer problems for the central government. A principal dilemma for Tehran is how to create among them a feeling of national identity.

Although they would probably help to defend the country from a foreign invasion, there were few ardent supporters of the central government among them.

Iranian tribes, like those of the Arabs, were organized in federations subdivided into clans and family groups. Reza Shah (see below) used the Iranian army in attempts to impose Tehran's authority on these tribes, but the army's ruthlessness only alientated them further from the government, and strengthened their allegiance to their own tribal leaders, or khans. Even today they remain a law unto themselves, often raiding caravans passing through their territory. A principal activity of the Iranian army was to control these tribes and to subdue those whose independence offered too much threat.

IRANIAN ATTITUDES TOWARD GOVERNMENT

Traditional Iranian attitudes have been unfavorable to development of democratic institutions because all society is organized in an authoritarian fashion. Sons expect to be severely punished if they disobey their fathers. The authoritarian attitudes learned in the family are applied to other areas of society, with the result that little individual initiative develops. Unless ordered to do so by a superior, the individual is usually reluctant to take action on matters which have not been charged to his direct responsibility. Power, rank, and age have been the attributes of traditionally accepted authority. The orientation upward of Iranians leads them to respect the strong leader, who is both feared and obeyed. These attitudes are reflected in Persian literature and in the practice of Shi'ite Islam in the country.

Iranians generally viewed government with fear and suspicion. They regarded it as an agent of the landlord, represented by the army, police, and tax collectors. Government was often considered an institution to be protected from, rather than as the protector of the citizen. Even the idea of popular participation in government was unknown until 1906. Until then, few disputed the shah's role as an absolute despot, responsible only to the religious hierarchy that kept an eye on the morality of his actions. Iranian tradition established the shah's position as "the shadow of God upon earth," the ultimate authority subject only to Shi'ite principles. According to pre-Islamic tradition, the land and all its subjects were his property and any rights of the shah's subjects were received only by good grace, not by divine or natural law.

NATIONAL ORIGINS

Ancient Iran
Since Iran's pre-Islamic origins play such an important role in shaping the contemporary era, it is necessary to examine them, if only briefly. The

ancient Aryans gave Iran its name (meaning, land of the Aryans). They include the Medes, Persians, Parthians, Scythians, and the Achaemenid clan, closely related to and vassals of the Medes. Iran's first great ancient empire was established by the Achaemenid clan, descended from Indo-European-speaking peoples who invaded the region about 2000 B.C., possibly from the plains of what today is south central Russia. The most illustrious Achaemenian was Cyrus the Great, who established his empire 500 years before Christ. Under his leadership the ancient Iranians crushed the rival Babylonians and swept through the Levant, and his successors extended the kingdom from what today is Asia Minor and Central Asia southward to the Red and Arabian seas and from North Africa to the Punjab in northern India.

The Achaemenid Empire (500–331 B.C.) developed a noteworthy system of public works, a distinctive architecture, and an excellent governmental administration. After two centuries of domination, the empire was conquered by Alexander the Great of Macedonia. Seleucus, a successor to Alexander, introduced Greek culture to Iran, and the term "Hellenistic" is used to indicate the blend of these two civilizations. Under Hellenistic influence, Iran had become a cosmopolitan center of arts, literature, and science by the time another northern Aryan tribe, the Parthians, ended the Seleucid regime in 129 B.C.

The Parthians had nothing notable to add to Hellenistic civilization, but they did defend Iran from incursion by the Roman Empire. Some scholars suggest, however, that there success was not so much a result of their military prowess, but rather a result of Roman diversions elsewhere. By A.D. 224, Parthian strength had been dissipated, and they were unable to fight off another Aryan group, the Sassanids (from *sassan,* the ancient Iranian for "commander.."), who were descendants of the Achaemenids. A dynasty of some forty Sassanid kings revived a strong, prosperous Iran modeled on that of Cyrus the Great. While dominating the regions immediately neighboring on Iran, they were unable to wrest the bulk of the Middle East from the Eastern Roman (or Byzantine) Empire, although they seriously challenged it. The Sassanids failed to expand their empire or rival the accomplishments of Cyrus the Great because, even then, it lacked the strength of unity. Imperial authority was at times divided among six or seven great noble families who provided imperial governors, generals, and other officials, but who competed with each other for the ultimate power. The religious establishment of Zoroastrianism and the punishment of heretical groups that resulted also weakened the country.

Zoroastrianism

A major religion founded by the ancient Iranians was the Zoroastrianism, which prevailed—more or less—from early Achaemenid times until the Islamic conquest in 641. The founder of this religion, Zarathustra (Zoroaster), was born sometime in either the seventh or sixth century B.C. in northwestern

Iran. His tenets emerged as a dominant influence during the rule of the Achaemenids. Central to Zoroastrianism was the concept of continuous struggle between the powers of good—led by Ahura Mazda (Ormazd)—and those of evil—led by Ahriman. Religious rites, defined in the holy book *Zend Avesta,* concerned not only the fate of the human soul, but such agricultural matters as the proper cultivation of crops and care of domestic animals. Earth, air, fire, and water in their pure form were considered representations of Ahura Mazda, and their care in Zoroastrian ritual was the responsibility of the priests. A man's fate was determined by the balance between his good and bad deeds recorded in the *Book of Life.* After death, he was to pass over a bridge no wider than a thread. If his good outweighed his evil, his path widened and he reached the realm of light; otherwise, he tumbled into the dark realm of Ahriman. The Sassanids gave new impetus to the religion as part of their efforts to revive the ancient Achaemenid culture.

THE ISLAMIC ERA

After the Islamic conquest of 641, Zoroastrian influence in Iran was such that many practices of Islam in Iran today differ from those of other countries. Many ancient Iranian concepts connected with Zoroastrianism were adopted by Shi'ite Islam in Iran. The Iranian conception of life as a continuous struggle between good and evil is evidence of Zoroastrian influence. Because of their contribution to the Abbasid victory over the Ummayads in 750 (see chapter 2), Iranians acquired great influence in the eastern Muslim empire. Their higher level of cultural development and administrative experience led to the adoption of Iranian dress and manners in the Abbasid caliph's Baghdad court. Persian art motifs (royal hunts, royal audiences, and battle scenes) were later adopted by the Arabs. Persian language and literature played an important role in the development of Arabic culture and to be truly cultivated, the Arab was expected to know the Iranian classics. Later, in the tenth century, when the Islamic empire began to dissolve, local Iranian Samanid and Buwayhid kingdoms arose. Although both were Muslim, they emphasized their claim to descent from the Sassanids; in both, Persian culture was revived and developed. Iran's great poet, Firdausi (c. 940—c. 1020), composed the great epic *Shahnama (Book of Kings),* a saga of 60,000 rhyming couplets about four ancient dynasties. Two of them were legendary, drawn from the *Avesta,* and the other two were the Parthian and Sassanid lines of kings. The *Shahnama* became Iran's folk literature, memorized to the present day by the peasants, even those who cannot read. During this era, many Iranian authors wrote in Arabic script, far simpler than the complicated ancient Pahlavi lettering, which was unrelated to Arabic. While Iranians used the Arabic script, many Iranian words were absorbed into the Arabic language and vice versa.

Iran's independent existence was brought to an end by two more great invasions from Central Asia. About 1050, Seljuk Turkish tribes invaded, and two centuries later, the great Mongol waves swept over the land (see chapter 3). The former not only permitted but even encouraged Iranian culture. Poetry, philosophy, religion, and architecture continued to develop under Seljuk rule. But the thirteenth-century Mongol invasion, led by Genghiz Khan, was wholly destructive. His deeds and those of his grandson Hulagu are still blamed for the decline of civilization in both Iran and Iraq. No less destructive were later invasions led by Timur the Lame (Tamerlane), a Central Asian Turk who sacked, plundered, and terrorized his way to victory. Yet it would be unfair to lay only death and destruction to the Mongols and Timurids, for they began to patronize the arts after consolidating their conquests.

THE MODERN ERA

The Safavids (c. 1500–1736), who took Iran from the Timurids in the sixteenth century, are usually thought of as initiating the modern era. Shah Ismail, their founder and first ruler, led seven Turkish Shi'ite tribes into Azerbaijan, attempting to prove the legitimacy of his power by claims of direct descent from the Sassanids through marriage of 'Ali's son Husain to the last Sassanid princess after the Arab conquest. His dynasty thus claimed to have inherited both the divine right of Sassanid rulers descended from Cyrus the Great and the mantle of Islam through Muhammad's son-in-law 'Ali.

For the first time in eight centuries, under the Safavids Iran was unified and a measure of national consciousness aroused. Success lay in an appeal to Iranians on both the levels of ancient Aryan folklore and a distinctively Iranian form of Shi'ite Islam. Iranian shahs claimed to be the descendants of Cyrus and the offspring of the seventh imam, one of the eleven sinless descendants of 'Ali (see chapter 2). Shah Ismail tried to unify the conglomeration of loosely united tribes scattered through the land by their conversion to Shi'ism as the state religion. During this era theologians laid the basis of Shi'ite theology as now accepted in Iran.

The dominant Safavid figure, whose importance to Iran is second to none, was Shah Abbas (1587–1628). He replaced the haphazard tribal levies with a regular army organized by two hired Englishmen. Unruly tribes were either suppressed or moved to areas where they could be controlled. At Isfahan, a new capital—considered one of the architectural wonders of the world—was built. Roads, canals, and caravansaries were extended throughout the country, making possible the growth of trade and commerce. The Portuguese were driven from the Persian Gulf and extensive commercial alliances were signed with England and Holland.

Renewed conflict among rival tribes toppled the Safavid dynasty in 1722 when an Afghan army captured the capital at Isfahan. They in turn were defeated in 1736, when a Turkish officer who had served under the Safavids established his rule. After a partially successful attempt to expand east and north, he too was overthrown by his own amry. The government of his successor lasted only his own lifetime; at his death, the Kajars (1794–1925), a Turkish tribe, asserted its authority. Unity of a more stable kind was re-established, and from their new capital at Tehran, the Kajars ruled until they were ousted by Reza Shah in 1925. This period in Iranian history constituted a century and a quarter of foreign machinations, wars, and occupations and an internal factional struggle. After Napoleon unsuccessfully attempted to win over the Kajars, Russia began its push down to the Caspian Sea, seizing one northern province after another (see chapter 4). British fear of tsarist ambitions in the Persian Gulf and India kept Iran from being totally overrun by Russia, for Great Britain made it her policy to maintain Iran as a buffer state between the two contending empires. After they reached a compromise of their differences in an entente in 1907, the British and tsarist empires divided up the country north and south into spheres of influences, leaving a "neutral" strip between them.

During the Kajar regime in the nineteenth century, increasing contact with the West made Persia aware of its relatively backward position in the world; and there began an awakening to the need for change. In the 1860s and 1870s the first telegraph lines were set up with British assistance, establishing direct communications with foreign countries and ending Persia's virtual isolation. Under Russian direction a military unit called the Cossack Brigade was organized to keep law and order in and around the capital. Concessions were granted to foreigners to build railroads and to develop the country's rivers and its raw materials. The first modern banks were opened, again by foreign capitalists. However, the Kajar shahs often overextended the country's budget in their attempts to modernize, soon leading to foreign indebtedness and outright intervention, principally by Russia and Great Britain.

As a result of foreign pressures and the collapse of strong central authority within the country, a modern nationalist movement brought about the 1906 revolution. The movement had been growing with the increase of knowledge among Iranian intellectuals, students, merchants, and religious leaders about such Western concepts as the rights of man, self-determination, and popular government. Shi'ite *mujtahids* (doctors of divine law), mullahs, dervishes, and Tehran bazaar merchants had become disenchanted with corruption in the royal court, with the shah's inability to maintain order, with his surrender to Russian influence, and above all, with his confiscation of much clerical property. Under direction of the Shi'ite clergy, protesting masses demonstrated in the capital and bazaar merchants closed their shops, paralyzing economic life. When threatened by the shah's troops, some ten thousand Iranians, including many prominent merchants, sought sanctuary in the British legation grounds. After mediation by the British ambassador, who was sympathetic to the aims of the demonstrators, the shah was forced to convene a constituent assembly. Within a year the assembly issued Iran's first constitution.

Until the 1906 revolution, there was no separation between civil and religious institutions. Sharia law administered by the Shi'ite divines covered all problems. The shah's private purse and the national treasury were one and the same. No division separated executive, judicial, and legislative power. Laws were simply enacted by imperial decree. In effect, religion, philosophy, government, and law—as in the pre-nineteenth-century Ottoman Empire— were part of a single institution.

The 1906 constitution was inspired by the French 1875 model. It established a National Consultative Assembly, or Majlis, and a Senate. Majlis members were to be elected by constituencies divided roughly according to population, although minorities such as Armenians, Zoroastrians, Assyrian Christians, and Jews were granted special representatives. Numbers of members and their terms of office have varied. Originally, there were 162 members elected for two-year terms. The number was raised to 200, 198 elected and 2 designated as minority representatives. Because of parliamentary immunity, the Majlis became another place where opponents of the government found sanctuary.

Neither the constitution nor the resulting parliament fared well. The National Assembly (*Majlis*) represented only the nobility, the merchants, and the religious leaders, men who lived primarily in Tehran and who had little concern for the welfare of the country's nomads and peasants. Because it challenged his exclusive authority, parliament was suppressed by the shah in 1908 with Russian help. Later that year nationalists, with the aid of Bakhtiari tribesmen, rose in defense of the constitution, deposed the shah, and placed his young son on the throne. Russia, however, was determined to keep the country from becoming unified. Continued tsarist intervention in Tehran and Russian control of northern Iran blocked any further nationalist progress.

When World War I broke out, Russia and Great Britain occupied the country and divided it between them. After the Bolshevik revolution in 1917, however, Iran was left completely in British hands. The British attempt to turn the country into a virtual protectorate, the continued corruption of the Iranian government, and the young shah's incompetence stimulated another nationalist uprising in Tehran in 1921. It was led by Sayyid Zia ed-Din Tabatabay, a newspaper editor turned political reformer. Tabatabay relied on the Russian-founded Cossack Brigade to back his authority. Making himself prime minister he named the brigade's commander, Reza, minister of war.

REZA SHAH

For the next two decades, Iran's history is the story of Reza Shah. After being invited to occupy the capital, he ousted Zia ed-Din, seized power, became prime minister in 1923, and was crowned shah in 1925. In some respects, Reza's life resembled Ataturk's. Of a military family, he had distinguished himself in the Cossack Brigade, rising through the ranks despite lack of any formal education. Like Ataturk, too, he was infatuated with the material aspects of Western civilization and sought to introduce them into his country. Factories, railroads, and hospitals were set up with little concern about the availability of natural resources or markets and with very little understanding of the long process required to develop the techniques for operating modern institutions.

Reza Shah attempted to create a united national sentiment by emphasizing Iran's pre-Islamic glories. The lion and the sun, symbols of the Achaemenid and Sassanid empires, came into use; and in an unsuccessful attempt to counteract Muslim clerical influence, Zoroastrianism was reestablished together with Shi'ism as a state religion, although there were few who practiced the pre-Islamic faith. The new dyansty was called Pahlavi, a Sassanian name borrowed from the Parthians. Streets and public places were renamed, honoring pre-Islamic folk heroes, and a new Iranian calendar was adopted based on the Gregorian one of Europe. Reza Shah frequently reminded the Iranians of the glories of their past and especially of Cyrus the Great.

Much was hoped for from this renaissance; only some of it was realized. New schools, including the University of Tehran, and a national conscript army were created. Communications were improved by extending the country's roads and telegraph lines and installing wireless stations. A trans-Iranian railroad, from the Persian Gulf to the Caspian Sea, was begun, financed by the state monopolies of the country's business and industry. State industries were built for refining sugar, manufacturing textiles, and processing food and chemicals.

Reza Shah attempted to modernize the major towns by physical reconstruction. Between 1925 and 1940, he cut wide avenues through many old residential quarters, built branches of the National Bank of Iran, hospitals, and government offices. A 1929 law required Iranians to replace their traditional costumes with more Western clothing. After 1935, European hats were required; after 1936, the veil was to be discarded and the head left uncovered. Since Reza Shah's demise, there has been a reversion to the traditional woman's *chadar* (veil), a length of black cloth covering the whole figure, including the head and face except for the eyes, so that modern and traditional dress now exist side by side.

The dictator's ruthless tactics, however, undermined much of the effectiveness of his program. He did not engender the great *élan* that Ataturk inspired in Turkey. By the mid-1930s, it had become evident that Reza Shah too often surrendered to his own passion for power, wealth, and absolute domination, and his opponents were too often murdered. The aristocracy was victimized by a reign of terror. Reza seized their fortunes, villages, and lands, adding them to his own estates.

While Ataturk sought to encourage individual initiative, Reza Shah so intimidated his subordinates that they avoided any direct responsibility and gave only optimistic, but often false, reports of their activities. With no freedom of speech or press, and without strong or capable administrative and political leaders, there was complete absence of self-criticism. Moral degeneration and a sense of hopeless resignation and helplessness began to pervade the regime.

It is true that Iran was historically much less prepared for extensive reforms than Turkey. Fewer Iranians had been trained in Western educational institutions or attuned to European thought and outlook, and the country had had relatively much less contact with the West than was the case in Turkey on the eve of Ataturk's revolution. Nor was Iran as unified as Turkey, the latter being a much more homogeneous nation in which 90 percent of the population were religiously, linguistically, and ethnically related.

With Hitler's rise to power after 1933, Reza Shah saw in the German dictator a potential ally. Nazi efficiency and regimentation appealed to the Iranian, and he invited the German government to send experts and advisers to assist him. In part, his motivation was to find in Germany a strong ally against the Soviet Union. Reza Shah's commitments to the Nazis finally ensnared him in the web of the great power conflict that led to World War II and ended in the Russian and British reoccupation of Iran in August 1941. Reza Shah was forced to abdicate and leave Iran (see chapter 5).

EVENTS DURING WORLD WAR II

The sudden loosening of Reza Shah's grip on political life resulted in a succession of weak prime ministers, each of whom resigned after finding that he could do nothing about the serious inflation and shortage of goods. Both right- and left-wing extremist movements suddenly emerged, and the tribes began to demand autonomy.

During the first four years of the reign of Reza Shah's son, Shah Muhammad Reza Pahlavi, Iran was occupied by British, American, and Russian troops. Independence was lost; the allies took over or otherwise controlled most governmental functions. In the Russian-controlled northern part of Iran, the Communist Tudeh party was encouraged. To counteract its effect, the British supported a nationalist party, the National Will, led by former Prime Minister Zia ed-Din, who had returned from exile.

Only the 1942 agreement between Iran, Great Britain, and the Soviet Union calling for a withdrawal of foreign troops six months after the war prevented complete partition of the country. And even that agreement was implemented with great difficulty, for Russia was reluctant to leave. During 1945, a separatist pro-Soviet regime was set up in Azerbaijan, headed by a seasoned Communist leader of the Tudeh party. Under Russian auspices, the Kurds also established an "independent" republic in the north. Only after pressure was exerted by the U.N. Security Council and President Truman did Russia evacuate the area (see chapter 5).

MOSADDEQ

Both Russia and Great Britain showed great interest in controlling Iran's rich oil deposits after the war. When the Russians finally left the northern provinces, they did so on condition that favorable consideration be given to a Soviet oil concession. When the bill establishing a joint Soviet-Iranian Oil Company was presented to the Iranian parliament in October 1947, however, it was defeated 100 to 2. At the same time, parliament banned new concessions to any foreigner or to companies in which foreigners held shares and called for re-examination of the Anglo-Iranian Oil Company concession in the south. Between 1908, when Iranian oil was first produced in commercial quantities, and the late 1940s, Iran had become one of the world's largest oil producers and the principal source of Great Britain's oil. During these forty years, the British-owned Anglo-Persian (later Iranian) Oil Company had become a power within Iran, influencing the course of and the conduct of many of the tribes in the oil-producing areas of the country. Iranian nationalists consequently resented the foreign company's presence, and the government which protected it.

A rising storm of anti-British sentiment forced the government to approve a bill nationalizing the Anglo-Iranian Oil Company in March 1951 (see chapter 5). The leader of the new nationalist wave was Dr. Muhammad Mosaddeq, next to Reza Shah and his son Muhammad Pahlavi one of the most forceful individuals who shaped Iran's contemporary history.

In the prewar years, Mosaddeq, who had been a conservative but not an important political figure, was arrested by Reza Shah and exiled to a quiet out-of-the-way village for his criticism of the shah's dictatorship. Mosaddeq now returned to politics as a government official, parliamentary deputy, and cabinet minister. In parliament, he continually hammered away at the theme that Iran must free itself from foreign domination and influences. In a notable speech, lasting over two days in October 1944, he led the attack against the Anglo-Iranian Oil Company. The debate culminated in rejection of the Soviet demand for a concession and instigated the investigation that led up to the 1951 nationalization of that company.

Mosaddeq rallied supporters from half a dozen parliamentary splinter groups into a National Front. With its backing, he became chairman of the strategic parliamentary oil committee that drafted the 1951 nationalization law. After the bill passed, his political influence could no longer be curbed and he was made prime minister. To Iran's masses, intellectuals, middle class, and youth, he had become a messianic leader of the forces of "good" against the evil of foreign domination.

During the period in which Dr. Mosaddeq was prime minister between 1951 and 1953, rumors of a British invasion were frequent. When the oil issue was brought to the United Nations and the World Court, Dr. Mosaddeq personally presented Iran's case. President Truman sent a personal representative to Iran but he too failed to effect any compromise. Mosaddeq and his coalition of religious zealots and fervent nationalists were adamant. They would not surrender Iran's rights to its oil.

Between 1951 and 1953, Great Britain and the West boycotted Iran's oil and the industry was forced to shut down. Since the oil revenues were Iran's principal source of income, the boycott created an economic crisis and discontent in the country. By June 1953, Mosaddeq's coalition had disintegrated. The Tehran press and businessmen complained of deteriorating economic conditions caused by continued lack of oil revenues. Taking advantage of disruption in the nationalist camp, the shah attempted to dismiss Mosaddeq in August. When Mosaddeq refused to leave, street mobs turned out to support him and the shah fled from the country. It looked as though Iran might become a republic: even the capital street names were being changed from "Reza Shah" to "Republic" and from "Pahlavi" to "People."

Mosaddeq, however, had failed to win support from the army. Troops supporting the shah took over the capital, and by the end of August an army general had deposed Mosaddeq and had made himself prime minister. Involvement of the U.S. Central Intelligence Agency in overthrowing Mosaddeq alienated nationalists and the left in the country. When the shah returned from his six-day exile, he was greeted with a tumultuous welcome by the same Teheran street mobs, now paid by pro-shah supporters and organized with C.I.A. help, that only a few days earlier had demanded a republic.

The Mosaddeq phenomenon was of more than passing significance, however. He was one of the few individuals who could rally mass support for a national cause. He symbolized the nation for all classes and for all ethnic and social groups.

EARLY POLITICAL PARTIES

Until World War I, there were no political parties because there was no organized political life. The interwar era was dominated by Reza Shah's dictatorship. Thus until 1941 the constitution and the institutions of parliamentary democracy were ineffective for all practical purposes. Immediately after Reza Shah's forced abdication in 1941, several political groups sprang up, of which only two had a genuine program, a stable organization, and a permanent mass following. The Communist-supported Tudeh party was one, and will be examined below. The other was the National Will, encouraged by Great Britain and led by Zia ed-Din. Despite his program for social and economic reform, he and his followers were attacked by the left as Fascist British agents. Within three years, Zia ed-Din was arrested and disappeared from the political scene, although several of his supporters remained politically active and gave their backing to reforms later proposed by the shah.

Prime Minister Ahmad Qavam attempted to counteract the National Will party by forming the Iranian Democrats in 1946 with government financial support. After winning a parliamentary majority in 1946, Qavam's party was torn by internal dissension and disappeared. Various other so-called parties suffered similar fates in the postwar decades, and the only truly effective group other than the Tudeh was the National Front gathered around Dr. Muhammad Mosaddeq.

When Mosaddeq became prime minister in 1951, he received unprecedented popular support because of his reputation for honest and sincere patriotism. During the preceding two years, the National Front coalition formed groups representing every political viewpoint. Mosaddeq's followers included liberal-minded intellectuals, professionals, merchants, a significant number of landowners, prominent religious divines, some labor leaders, and a few tribal chiefs. Several already existing political groups identified with the National Front. They included the Iran party, a mildly nondoctrinaire group of socialist professionals and intellectuals; the Toilers party, which had made not overly successful attempts at organizing industrial workers under the leadership of Dr. Mozaffar Bakai; Pan-Iranism, an extreme nationalist body; and a band of Shi'ite zealots called Warriors of Islam (*Fidayan-i Islam*) led by Mullah Kashani. Kashani's followers threw their support from group to group, at times backing the Tudeh party, Mosaddeq, or the shah. The Warriors threatened death to all who followed Western customs and assassinated several politicians, including Prime Minister Razmara in 1951. They supported Mosaddeq during the oil crisis because of his determined and forceful opposition to foreign control of and or intervention in the country's internal affairs.

The National Front fell apart after the oil crisis created serious economic dislocations, for which Mosaddeq was blamed. Many conservatives also felt that he had overreached himself when he attempted to place himself above the shah, thus violating Iranian tradition of the shah's supremacy. Within two years, the great nationalist enthusiasm that Mosaddeq had personified had been dissipated, and politics returned to the hands of the court and the landowners. Some Mosaddeq followers organized a small but ineffective National Resistance Movement. He himself could no longer participate in politics, having been exiled to a remote village after serving a three-year prison term for high treason. Mullah Kashani, the second brightest star in the Mosaddeq constellation, also faded into obscurity as merely another Shi'ite cleric. Both men died during the 1960s, leaving behind only memories of their once powerful political influence.

The leaders of the National Front supported constitutionalism, avowed loyalty to the throne, emphasized freedom, promised honest administration, and denounced communism. But these admirable principles were not accompanied by much evidence of political realism or practicality, or by any specific program that would give thoughtful people, in or out of government, a basis for confidence in supporting the organization. As a coalition, the National Front apparently could not agree on such a program, arguing that this is the task of individual parties. Although, according to T. Cuyler Young, there was little doubt that the overwhelming majority of the politically concerned and aware among the people were back of the National Front, the masses, peasants, tribesmen, and laborers were not included. "[T]hey damn the régime, but blame the Shah's advisers and entourage. In a negative sense, the wide support of the National Front is underlined by the fact that recent governments have had to maintain stability and themselves in power by force...."[1]

Officially sponsored "parties" were organized in 1957 and 1958 to give the country a façade of democracy. An experimental "loyal opposition" was chosen by the shah to become the People's party in 1957, and a few months later a progovernment majority, the Nation party, was organized to create a synthetic two-party system. Both groups were formed by friends of the shah who were high-ranking loyal officials. Neither the Nation nor People's parties nor the subsequently organized Independents offered the country more than the same traditional coalitions of landowners, merchants, and tribal leaders. None acquired a popular following and none could offer a program that could arouse popular enthusiasm.

Even this facade of parliamentary democracy was too much for the shah. In 1975 both the government Nation party and the loyal opposition, the People's party, were dissolved. In their place a single party system was decreed. A new Iran National Resurgence party (*Rastakhiz*) was formed to weld together all those who supported the shah's White Revolution with Iran's prime minister as secretary general.

The Tudeh. Although banned from overt political activity in 1949, the Tudeh (Masses) party formed in 1942 remains a potent political force. It was established by the leaders of the old Iranian Communist party whom Reza Shah had imprisoned. When released after the Allied occupation in 1941, they again seized the opportunity to participate in political life. Since northern Iran was occupied by the Soviet Union during the war, it was easy for the party to function there. Its strongly centralized organization and discipline gave the Tudeh a decided advantage over all other political groups. To avoid the impression of foreign control or revolutionary aims, Tudeh couched its official platform in liberal, rather than Communist, terms. Party influence reached the working class, clergy, minorities, and intelligentsia through numerous front groups disguised to serve the special interests of each. For a short period, most newspapers were controlled by the Tudeh through the Freedom Front, a coalition of periodicals created in 1943 that advocated liberal reform and support for the Soviet Union.

The Tudeh party was responsible for reviving the small remnants of the labor movement, which Reza Shah had banned, and in 1942 it united all labor unions. By 1945, the Tudeh-controlled Central United Council of Trade Unions claimed over a quarter of a million members and was able to organize the first effective petroleum strikes. Successful manipulation of several unions and front groups enabled the Tudeh to obtain three cabinet posts in 1946, but when Soviet attempts to seize Azerbaijan failed, the Tudeh party was discredited. After being implicated in a plot to assassinate the shah in 1949, the party and all its organs were banned—although Dr. Mosaddeq quietly continued to cooperate with its members. In 1954, investigations revealed that Communists were placed in several government departments and that 400 military officers were organized in a clandestine, Communist-led network. The Tudeh's greatest weakness is close affinity with the Soviet Union, a country most Iranians regard with more fear than respect because of repeated attempts during the past two centuries, under tsar and Communists alike, to take over all or parts of Iran.

After 1962 Iran became less of a constitutional monarchy and more of a one-man government under the shah. The Majlis was theoretically the people's voice, since any individual could submit to its special Petition Department criticism or complaints that had to be answered. However, with creation of the *Rastakhiz* in 1975, the Majlis lost even the token powers it had before.

Although the 1906 constitution authorized a Senate, it was never convened until 1950, when it became a device to strengthen the shah by weighting parliamentary influence in his favor. Half the 60-member Senate was elected by popular vote and the other half appointed by the shah from the "well-informed, discerning, pious, and respected persons of the realm." Tehran, the capital, supplied half the total number of senators, thus receiving a higher proportion of representatives than actually warranted by its population.

There were constitutional provisions limiting the shah's powers, but little question about his predominant position. He controlled the armed forces, selected half the Senate, and chose the prime minister. His friends and relatives occupied high positions throughout the administration. In national emergencies, the shah suspended the constitutional guarantees of individual rights and freedom of the press and information, or as was frequently the case, he merely ignored them. In constitutional theory, the shah reigned, but did not rule. After 1956, however, he chose to rule. Freedom was curtailed by the shah's secret police, the State Organization for Intelligence and Security (SAVAK), and government decisions were often personal and arbitrary.

SAVAK's activities became of major importance in consolidating the Shah's powers and in the decline of any seriously competitive political or social institutions. The Organization even operated abroad, against dissidents considered a threat to the regime. Its extensive arrests and use of torture aroused international concern. In 1974–75 Amnesty International estimated that there were between 25,000 and 100,000 political pironers in Iran. The secretary general of Amnesty International observed that: "The Shah of Iran retains his benevolent image despite the highest rate of death penalities in the world, no valid system of civilian courts and a history of torture which is beyond belief."

Even though the constitution has had little effect on the life of the average Iranian, it was constantly referred to in public speeches and in bazaar debates as a symbol of Westernization, and Constitution Day became one of the important national holidays. Its influence, however, was limited to the Westernized landowning aristocracy, the bazaar merchants, the urban intelligentsia, and a handful of religious leaders. The illiterate 90 percent of the population had not even a theoretical knowledge of their "rights." Peasant contact with the political process was the vote they cast for their landlord, the only candidate they ever knew of. While members of large tribes were in a somewhat better position, their vote also automatically went to the chief or his representative.

Political power was divided among the royal court, the landed aristocracy, the wealthy merchants, the religious leaders, and the army, with the shah as keystone in the whole structure. He became virtually omnipotent over potential rivals. Each group was a check to the others and each constantly shifted its support to suit its own convenience. The landed aristocrats, for example, successfully managed to block effective implementation of modest land reform legislation by controlling two thirds of the Majlis and virtually all of the Senate until the 1960s. After World War II, the growing middle class became considerably more influential on the political scene and was in large measure responsible for the modest reforms that were made.

ISLAM IN MODERN IRAN

Late in the nineteenth century, the Shi'ite hierarchy led opposition to the shah's money-raising scheme to turn Iran's tobacco industry over to European capitalists, and a boycott organized by the most revered Shi'ite leader forced thousands to give up smoking. The boycott demonstrated to Iranians the effectiveness of passive resistance as a political weapon. It is also noteworthy that without clerical backing, the 1906 constitutional movement would probably not have succeeded.

As a result of their role in the 1906 revolution, the clergy received special parliamentary representation and the constitution authorized the ulema to determine whether or not legislation was in accord with Islamic principles. A special committee of *mujtahids* (Shi'ite clergy) and theologians was appointed to consider all matters brought before the Majlis.

Reza Shah curtailed their authority during the 1920s and 1930s, although he was not antireligious, merely anticlerical. His aim was to curb their political power rather than to end the practice and social institutions of Islam. At one time, Reza Shah was reported to be considering establishment of a republic, but he abandoned the idea in deference to the Shi'ite divines. At the same time, however, Reza Shah permitted no outright clerical interference and forcefully resisted religious opposition to many of his measures, such as universal military training.

Nonetheless Reza Shah was compelled to pay deference to many of the mystical aspects of Shi'ism, a religion in which: "The natural union between religious mysticism and ritual—natural because everything irrational asks for expression in sign, symbol, and ceremony—throws down quite different roots into the souls of men than a faith consisting of a rationalistic conviction practiced only in the inner forum."[2] Although Reza Shah did not desire to destroy religion, he did not hesitate to attack systematically its forms of expression and symbolism in an effort to undermine clerical influence. For example, Dervishes (Muslim monks, see chapter 2), for centuries part of Iranian life, were ordered from the streets and country roads. Pilgrimages to Najaf and Karbala in Iraq, Shi'ism's two most holy shrines, were discouraged. Pressure was brought to bear on the mullahs, the Shi'ite religious teachers, to change to European dress. The flagellations accompanying the fanatic Shi'ite demonstration commemorating Husain's ('Ali's son) death were first banned, then outlawed. The demonstrations were at first replaced by public recitals of the tragedy, but a year later, recitals too were forbidden. All that remained was the custom of *rosekhaneh*, in which a black flag is hung from a home announcing that inside a priest will recite the "Passion of 'Ali and His House."

An indication of Shi'ism's changing status was the initial marriage between Crown Prince Muhammad Pahlavi and the Sunni sister of Egypt's King Farouk (although they were later divorced). Fifteen years earlier, the marriage would have been unthinkable, for it conflicted with a strict interpretation of the constitutional requirement demanding that the shah "must profess and propagate this [Shi'ite] faith." Some interpreted the marriage as a demonstration that the ancient barrier which cut off Shi'ite Iran from the Sunni world was being removed.

A blow to clerical power was confiscation of all pious foundations (awkaf), which were turned over to the Ministry of Education. (Shah Nadir, 1736–1760, had attempted to secularize ecclesiastical property, but the measures were reversed after his death.) Reza Shah used the confiscated revenue to create a new school system and to improve other public services. Depriving the clerics of their wakf possessions limited their political power and means of influencing the population, for they now had no income except that which they received from the government as state functionaries. The state also took from the mullahs the task of educating the clergy, and a government theological school was established at Tehran University, and modern studies and teaching methods were adopted.

A more fundamental change was the adoption of the French legal system in 1927. The trend toward secular law had begun after the 1906 constitutional reform, but there still existed a judicial dualism, dividing legal matters between secular and religious authorities. Initially, the constitution turned jurisdiction over family matters and religious property to the Sharia courts. But Reza Shah restricted the religious courts to a mere advisory role. Clerical judges were to have authority only in cases referred to them by civil courts. While Iranian law no longer required a citizen to be a Muslim, Shi'ism was in actual practice, still the "law of the land," and to be acceptable for high public office, it was necessary to be a member of that faith.

Reza Shah also removed ordinary education from clerical control and used the school system to undermine clerical influence by teaching secularism. Despite the influence of French and British military missions and Christian missionaries during the nineteenth century, clerical influence was still the strongest force in the school system. Neither the French, British, American, German, nor Russian educational institutions opened before World War I, nor the information collected by Iranian military missions in Europe, nor the military school opened at Tehran in 1852 greatly affected the tenor of the educational system. Most Iranians never received the opportunity to attend school, and those who did were taught in institutions where only religious subjects were taught.

Religious nationalism, linking loyalty to Iran with loyalty to Shi'ite Islam, was expressed in the zealotry of Mullah Kashani's partisans and was briefly revived during the Mosaddeq era from 1951 to 1953. Kashani forced the prime minister to authorize Muslim divines to scrutinize all bills according to a constitutional requirement. Finally Kashani's demands became so overbearing that Mosaddeq broke with him. No popular uprising followed and soon after Kashani passed into political obscurity.

To help balance off the strong undercurrents of Islamic influence and tradition, the shah played up the theme of Iran's pre-Islamic greatness. In 1971 (supposedly the 2,500th anniversary of the Persian monarchy), an international festival of sumptuous dimensions was staged. Costs of the celebrations were estimated between $50 million and $300 million. A statement of the kingdom's Persianness was made in 1975 when Iran's calendar was changed from the Muslim date based on the flight of Muhammad from Mecca, to the time when Cyrus the Great established the first Persian empire 1,180 years earlier. Thus the year became 2535 instead of 1355. All of these measures so alienated the Shi'ite clergy and popular consciousness that opinion rapidly rose against the shah, and he in turn intensified repression of dissidence, bringing matters to a head in 1979 (see following).

THE PROBLEMS OF ECONOMIC DEVELOPMENT

Agriculture

Iran, like its neighboring countries in the Middle East, is still today and will remain for decades an underdeveloped country. The prevailing poverty is a product of both natural and social forces. Except for the vast oil reserves, Iran has few natural resources. (In 1967 Iran was the second largest producer of oil in the Middle East and the fourth largest in the world.) Despite the country's great income from oil, however, little has changed in the life of the average Iranian.

The most serious problem is the inadequate supply of arable land and water, the two requirements for building a basic economy. Only a tenth of the area (the total being about a fifth that of the continental United States) is arable. Seven-tenths is mountain or desert and two-tenths forest and grazing land. Mountain ranges, with peaks reaching over 18,000 feet, crisscross the country, making communications and transport difficult.

There are no great rivers. Water shortages and poor soil result in up to two thirds of the cultivable land lying fallow each year. Water is so scarce that it is a source of capital and often considered more important property than soil. Since most land is useless unless irrigated, ownership usually means control of the water supply and frequently farmers have fought over its use. There are also the problems of land tenure, insects and pests, primitive methods and implements, poor health undermining the population's vitality, and the heavy hand of tradition that binds the peasant to outmoded and unscientific farming techniques. The net result is low productivity, a high rate of rural underemployment and the massive influx of peasants to the cities.

Between 1960 and 1980 urban population increased from about a third to more than half, and agricultural production decreased so that Iran had to import much of its food.

Of the 40 percent of the population remaining in agriculture by 1979, less than half owned their own farms. The rest were tenant sharecroppers who lived in perpetual debt at a subsistence level. In theory, agricultural income was divided into five parts: land, water, seed, animals or power, and labor. The supplier of each part received a fifth of the crop. Since most peasants could supply only labor, they received but a fifth of the crop and borrowed at usurious rates to pay for the other four-fifths. Few landlords took direct responsibility for managing their estates and villages. Frequently they sold rent-collecting rights to the highest bidder, who then took as much as he could from tenants. Peasant insecurity discouraged any long-term agricultural investments or major efforts to improve land.

Industry

Since oil has been discovered, there has been a shift of rural population to urban centers. But only about a third of the population is employed in industry. Half these work in small shops and homecrafts, such as carpet-making and handloom weaving. Reza Shah began an all-out effort to industrialize the country's economy in 1930. He called upon the Majlis to make the 1930 session renowned in history as the "economic parliament." A National Economy Ministry was established to direct the drive and regulate national economic life. Since no private capital was readily available, most of it being invested in land, the government itself capitalized various projects, such as textile industries, sugar-refining plants, and monopolies on the import and export of products ranging from matches and animal products to motor vehicles. By the late 1930s, the government controlled a third of all imports and 44 percent of all exports, investing its profits in new plant construction.

Reza Shah's economic schemes were undermined by the world depression and by the failure of Iranian society to cope successfully with modern industry. Nepotism, overstaffing, reluctance to take responsibility or to show initiative, and lack of administrative and technical competence led to collapse of the modernization efforts.

The prevailing tax and administrative system actually discouraged private initiative. Subordinate clerks mismanaged the Finance Ministry despite the honesty of higher officials, and graft and tax evasion were commonplace. The amount government received from a taxpayer depended less on ability to pay then upon bargaining powers with the collector who could assess property at 100 to 200 percent of the actual value. Some rich merchants kept three sets of books, one each for the tax collector, business acquaintances, and themselves. Family connections and political influence often exempted the aristocracy from payment. A list of tax delinquents, including members of the royal family, cabinet, and Senate, was published in

1949 but then totally ignored, becoming a national joke. This system not only discouraged foreign investment but drove local capital out of the country.

Reform

Attempts to reform and develop the economy and to utilize the great oil revenues lagged far behind national requirements. A major obstacle was the reluctance of the landed aristocracy to make the required sacrifices. Until the 1962 land reform the shah had made only a modest beginning by selling royal lands at a fifth of their value to peasant occupants. Even this minimum program required no great sacrifice, since the imperial estates, estimated to cover 750,000 acres, including over 1670 villages with nearly a million occupants, were seized by Reza Shah from the aristocracy. After World War II, when the courts began to examine the legality of ownership, hearings proved so embarassing to the royal family that they were suspended.

The strongest advocates of reform were the landless middle class and the bazaar merchants. Despite extensive parliamentary discussion, the many new resolutions, regulations, and statutes were not enforced and there was no serious land-reform legislation until 1962. Since landlords controlled parliament, they blocked even token projects, fearing that once the door was opened a crack, it would be forced all the way. In January 1962, a land reform law termed "revolutionary," was adopted by the cabinet. It restricted the ownership of each landlord to only one village. The rest was to be sold to landless peasants on long-term installments, and the landlord was to be "equitably" compensated by the government. At first, the government announced, the law would be applied to landlords who owned more than five villages. This would affect some 10,000 of Iran's 45,000 to 50,000 villages. Later the law would apply to the 7000 villages belonging to landlords with more than one or less than five villages.

To achieve the reforms proposed in his "White Revolution," the shah appointed as prime minister one of his chief critics, Dr. Ali Amini. Because many of the envisaged policies were calculated to arouse the conservatives' wrath, the country was placed under martial law, and parliament was dissolved in 1961, so that royal decrees became law backed only by the shah's signature and enforced by the security establishment.

In broad outline the reforms, or "White Revolution," emphasized twelve points for economic and social development of the country: 1) land reform, 2) nationalization of forests and pastures, 3) public sale of state-owned factories to finance land reform, 4) profit sharing in industry, 5) revision of the electoral law to include women, 6) establishment of a literacy corps, 7) a health corps, 8) and a reconstruction and development corps, 9) rural courts of justice, 10) nationalization of the waterways, 11) national reconstruction, 12) educational and administrative revolution.

The new prime minister took stern measures against the widespread political corruption and economic chaos in the country. Several former high government officials and top army officers were brought to trial to account for their mismanagement or misuse of funds. Restrictions were placed on government expenditures and on import of luxury goods.

The body of measures known as the "White Revolution" was systematized in 1963 to "become the creed of the Shah and the Iranian political elite. By 1970 it stood as an important ideology against which the Shah justified his activities and his rule. It is anathema and dangerous to criticize or question the principles of the White Revolution; the most serious accusation that can be made against someone, other than portraying him as an enemy of the Shah, is to present him as an enemy of the White Revolution. This situation has seriously impeded detailed and objective analysis of the implementation of the reform."[3]

The land reform measures aroused the most opposition among the traditionalist estate owners, and the conservative clergy who feared loss of wakf lands. By 1964 it was estimated that about a fifth of the rural population had received some land which was allocated from 12,000 to 13,000 villages (out of some 50,000) that had been redistributed. A second phase of the reform permitted owners to retain a maximum of 30 to 150 hectares of nonmechanized lands. The rest could be disposed of by renting, selling, forming joint stock companies with peasants, or by other means prescribed in the law. Because of the great variety of ways in which the reform was carried out and the diverse quality of land distributed, it was difficult to estimate the effect of the land reform on the peasants. According to a United Nations survey, probably not more than 15 percent of the country's peasants got enough land to support themselves or to increase their living standards substantially. Only a third of these became actual owners. The others became leaseholders or share-owners.

Accompanying the land reform were other measures intended to raise peasant living standards. A Literacy Corps, later renamed the Education Corps, of several thousands students was organized to work with villagers. Its goal was to cut the rate of illiteracy from 80 to 50 percent within the decade. Since nearly half the country's children were receiving no schooling, this was a major priority. The corpsmen were recruited from students of military draft age, and those eligible for the army were released from army service to work in the villages. Likewise, a Health Corps and a Rural Extension Development Corps were sent to rural areas to assist in achieving development goals. In Khuzistan province several experimental programs were planned, including establishment of agro-businesses based on huge irrigated farms, petrochemical industries to utilize the country's oil, and steel plants based on coal and iron deposits believed to exist in the country.

A new innovation, intended to compete with agricultural cooperatives, was the farm-corporation, in which the farmer became a shareholder but lost management rights. In Khuzistan the agricultural corporations met resistance from conservative farmers who were reluctant to sell their traditional family plots to an agrobusiness.

Division of the shah's estates was not very successful. Peasants who acquired shares of the former royal estates knew little about the most fundamental agricultural techniques, such as crop rotation or planting times. Without extensive government programs for education, credit, and cooperative development, surrender of large estates did little to improve the peasant lot. The village moneylender and others who controlled village life continued to do so.

The Iranian Plan Organization was established to utilize 60 percent of oil revenues for national development in 1948. But its seven- and five-year plans concentrated more on great engineering schemes than on social change. It successfully completed dams, hydroelectric plants, irrigation systems in arid regions, and drainage in swamp areas. West German and American experts also lent assistance, and a five-year contract was signed in March 1956 with the American Development and Resources Corporation (Clapp-Lilienthal) to develop Khuzistan in southern Iran.

Long before the 1979 Revolution Coyler Young observed that the aristocracy, the top stratum of society, was still reluctant to share power with the urban middle class, which was becoming increasingly frustrated and angered by what they considered to be betrayal of Iran to the traditional vested interests. In short, the aristocracy feared that partnership with the middle class

> might involve its own "toppling"—that to share its prestige and power might endanger the nation's stability and security. In short, society's top does not trust the bottom, and even less the awakened and aware middle. The heart of Iran's problem is the need for revolutionary *and* responsible leadership; how to traverse the distance from a traditional paternalism to modern industrialism, how to bridge the gulf of mistrust that has developed between modern tinkerers with tradition and rebels against that tradition, how to transmit power from the small, habitual élite to the substantial, untested middle sector of society, and how to effect this in a disturbed and dynamic world in which the country's integrity and independence are ever in peril.[4]

IRAN AS A REGIONAL POWER

At the root of Iranian politics, both domestic and foreign, was the Shah's overriding ambition to make his country the dominant regional power. This required not only the position of primacy in the Gulf, but in areas beyond—by sea into the Indian Ocean and by land into the Middle East and southwest Asia. On more than one occasion he spoke of his goal to achieve status, both economic and political, equal to that of France and Germany by the 1980s and perhaps equal to the world's most advanced powers by the end of the century. In one statement he described two nations as the most important for the "Free World" in Asia—Japan in the Far East and Iran in the Middle East.

He shaped the country's internal economic development and its political institutions with these ambitions in mind. Iran's major resources, including a substantial part of oil revenues, were devoted to these aspirations. Through the "White Revolution," the "Great Iranian Civilization" would be revived. The shah's far-reaching foreign policies reflected his belief that he was "chosen by God" to perform the task of replacing European empires that once dominated the region.

Grandiose ambitions led the shah into a semialliance with Israel involving exchange of technical information, military equipment and training, with Iranian oil shipped directly to the Jewish state. The shah perceived Israel as an obstacle to Soviet subversion and expansion in the Middle East and to the militant leftist Arab regimes with which Iran has feuded.

Relations with the Arab states varied from the brink of war with Iraq, to a cool friendship with Saudi Arabia. The more radical an Arab regime, the more it was perceived as a threat. Thus Saudi Arabia, with its conservative monarchy was an acceptable junior partner in policing the Gulf and its approaches. But in OPEC meetings during the 1970s Iran strongly urged a rapid escalation in prices whereas Saudi Arabia urged only modest increases.

Iran's policies in the Gulf caused apprehension for even the conservative Arab regimes. Threats to take over Bahrain based on nineteenth-century claims were dissipated in 1970 when the shah announced that he would accept a United Nations report stating that the overwhelming majority of Bahrainis favored independence. But all the region's Arab states were incensed when Iran occupied three tiny strategic islands in the Straits of Hormuz between the Persian Gulf and the Gulf of Oman during 1970. Fears of leftist engulfment led to direct intervention by Iranian troops in Oman where they assisted the monarch to suppress the Dhofar rebellion by leftist tribal groups.

The most serious confrontation was with Iraq, the only Arab country with which Iran has a common border. After nearly erupting into war, the series of territorial, water, boundary, and ideological disputes were resolved or suspended in an agreement signed by the shah and Iraq during an OPEC meeting held in Algiers during 1975. The Algiers agreement lasted only five years, until after overthrow of the shah, when Iraq's leader, Saddain Husain, decided to renew the historic conflict. Taking advantage of turmoil in Iran, he invaded in 1980 with the intent to establish Iraqi supremacy in the Gulf, but his plans were thwarted by Iran's military resistance.

By 1975 Iran had become the largest single purchaser of U.S. military equipment with sales totaling over $15 billion between 1972 and 1978. The purchases were made possible by the fivefold increase in oil prices after 1973. The oil boom also extended the shah's global outreach by facilitating major arms and economic deals with the large countries of Western Europe, including acquisition by Iran of a 25 percent interest in Krupp, Germany's largest steel plant.

These foreign relationships and their domestic effects often created the illusion that Iran had already become a power. However, according to a study by the U.S. Senate in 1976, the appearance was deceptive. Iran had not become more independent or powerful, rather, it had increased its long term dependence on the United States. The Senate report observed that Iran "lacks the technical, educational, and industrial base to provide the necessary trained personnel and management capabilities to operate such...[military] establishment effectively."[5]

THE 1979 REVOLUTION

By the late 1970s it was becoming increasingly evident to the shah and his entourage that neither the reforms of the "White Revolution" nor the repression of SAVAK could stem the rising tide of discontent. A first overt acknowledgement of the situation was the shah's replacement during 1977 of Prime Minister Amir Abbas Hoveida, who had held the post since 1965. However, events were moving more rapidly than superficial change could cope with. Labor troubles were spreading, student protests erupted at the universities, and the clergy was more openly flouting the authorities. By 1978 the strikes and unrest slashed oil production and crippled the economy causing sharp cutbacks in government expenditures. Although the shah had already decreased his military budget to make money available to increase the salaries of civil servants and to expand public housing, the oil shutdown undermined these plans. In a desperate effort to save the regime, the shah changed prime ministers four times between mid-1977 and the end of 1978, to no avail.

Opposition to the regime broke out in mass urban demonstrations during 1978 leading to frequent clashes between security forces and protesters with thousands of casualties. Diverse groups openly showed their disapproval of the government. Workers in the cities and oil fields, although better off than a decade earlier, resented the growing gap between their living standards and the ostentatious luxury of the upper class, especially of the royal family whose imperial life style was flaunted openly. The shah's ban on labor unions only intensified hostility and resentment. Students and intellectuals objected to suppression of the press and scholarly journals; to the exile or imprisonment of many prominent Iranian writers, artists, and film makers; and to control of the universities by SAVAK. Remnants of the old nationalist movement felt humiliated by Iran's growing dependence on tens of thousands of foreign technicians and advisors and to their growing visibility in major urban centers. To many it seemed that, despite the shah's grandiose schemes for regional supremacy, Iran was becoming a satellite of the United States. The middle class bazaar merchants suffered both economic decline and psychological trauma because of the so-called reforms. Many were undermined by competition from the new state enterprises created to "modernize" the economy. Furthermore, as traditionalists, many in the bazaar felt disgraced by the influx of Westerners and their life styles introduced by the country's leaders. Their opposition was stimulated by nationalist and religious, as well as by economic resentments. The old aristocracy, whose lands were seized by the shah's father, Reza Shah, still waited for revenge against the Pahlavis, and many would eagerly support opposition to the upstart regime.

The most important center of unrest was the Shi'ite clergy, which became the focal point of opposition; its leader, the Ayatollah Khomeini, living in exile since 1963, became the symbol of opposition and the chief instigator of the movement that toppled the shah in 1979. Although the Pahlavis had successfully undercut the power of the clergy, they had failed to destroy its links to the rural and urban masses or to end the moral and financial support it received from traditionalists in the middle and lower middle classes. Despite Khomeini's exile and repression of many other leading clerics, their influence remained strong (Khomeini's leadership continued from abroad through taped sermons and politico-religious discourses smuggled into the country). He, like most of the clerical leadership was perceived as a personality of great learning, integrity, and simply life style in contrast to the irreligious, spendthrift, cruel shah. The clergy represented the grass roots while the shah personified foreign corruption. Within the religious establishment there was an extensive social welfare system providing for the needy; its managers were regarded as the guardians of social justice and morality. This network provided the informal organizations for opposition to the shah; its prayer meetings in mosques and private homes were the centers of subversion, attended, not only by the pious, but by ever-increasing numbers of other politically disaffected.

Clerical leadership against the regime was not a new phenomenon. In modern times the Shi'ite clergy was known for opposition to secular tyranny. It had played a leading role in opposition to foreign economic concessions during the Kajar dynasty in the nineteenth century and in the constitutional movement at the beginning of the twentieth. During the 1960s it was Khomeini's open denunciation of the shah's economic agreements with the

U.S. that led to his exile. By 1978 when the shah began to retreat in his war against the clergy it was too late; too many clerics had been tortured, exiled, and killed for its establishment to compromise.

By the beginning of 1979 even Shahpur Bakhtiar, a former National Front leader and longtime foe of the monarch appointed prime minister by the shah as a major concession to his opponents, was unacceptable to the clergy. The fact that he was an appointee of the hated monarch was enough to disqualify Bakhtiar in the eyes of the mullahs and their allies. At this juncture, in January 1979, the Shah decided to leave Iran for an extended "vacation." Although not a formal abdication, his departure brought to an end 37 years of his rule and for all practical purposes ended the Pahlavi dynasty in Iran.

Several days after the shah's departure, Ayatollah Khomeini returned from exile in France where he had formed the Council of the Islamic Revolution. Khomeini was received with wild enthusiasm and quickly established his personal absolute authority in the capital and in many other parts of the country. A first political act was to appoint Mehdi Bazargan as a provisional prime minister, parallel to the official Bakhtiar government which Khomeini refused to recognize. Bakhtiar resigned in less than a week, leaving Khomeini and his associates in full command of the government. On April 1, Khomeini formally proclaimed the Islamic Republic of Iran under jurisdiction of his Islamic Council for the Revolution. For the next half-year Bazargan's government was forced to share power with the Revolutionary Council, but as the clerics arrogated increasing authority, the anti-shah coalition began to fall apart. Tension increased between the civil government and the clerical Revolutionary Council until Bazargan's government fell in November and the Council assumed full command.

Even before the civil government collapsed in November, the Revolutionary Council had established a Revolutionary Tribunal in Tehran to conduct secret trials and executions of former officials, military officers, and SAVAK agents in the shah's regime. Elsewhere in the country Revolutionary Guards organized *Komitehs* (local security organizations) to carry out local purges and to impose authority of the new regime. Many harsh measures taken against those who contravened Islamic law and the severity and precipitousness of the revolutionary trials aroused wide opposition among many former Khomeini supporters. One minister in Bazargan's cabinet resigned in protest against the Revolutionary Council's "despotism," and a leading Ayatollah charged Khomeini with "dictatorship." Opposition groups, formerly allies of Khomeini, organized underground death squads to assassinate members of the Revolutionary Council. In the more distant parts of Iran there was a resurgence of ethnic rebellion among the Kurds, Turkomen, and Azerbaijanis. Although Khomeini's authority was entrenched in Tehran and in several other large cities, much of the country was in turmoil and unresponsive to the new Islamic regime.

A major change was introduction of a new Islamic constitution, approved by a 60 to 1 margin in a December 1979 referendum. The constitution emphasized Iran's Islamic character and gave priority to Shi'ite law and institutions. It established a 12-member Council of Guardians, or Leadership Council, headed by a religious leader with supreme authority over all branches of government to assure that all legislation comply with Shi'ite Islamic principles. The supreme leader, called *Faghi* (trustee or guardian) was to act in place of the twelfth Shi'ite imam who disappeared 1,100 years ago and who Shi'ites believe will return one day. According to the new constitution: "During the absence of the Glorious Lord of the Age, the twelfth imam...he will be represented in the Islamic Republic of Iran as religious leader and imam of the people by an honest, virtuous, well-informed, courageous, efficient administrator and religious jurist, enjoying the confidence of the majority of the people as a leader." The first Faghi under the republic was Ayatollah Khomeini, already in his eighties.

The Faghi was endowed with almost absolute powers, above the president or any of the legislative and judicial authorities; he was to command the armed forces, appoint and dismiss heads of the army and Islamic Revolutionary Guards Corps; he had power to declare war and mobilize the armed forces, to improve all presidential candidates, to formalize the president's election, and to dismiss the president at will.

The army, according to the constitution "...must be an Islamic army. It must be a popular and religiously educated army and it must accept worthy people who will be faithful to the goals of the Islamic Revolution and will be self-sacrificing in the attainment of these goals."

Emphasizing the Koranic injunction that followers of the Prophet conduct communal business by "consultation among themselves," the new Majlis was called the National Consultative Assembly or *Majlis ash-shura,* to carry out Islamic law. However the document did reserve several seats for non-Muslim minorities including Zoroastrians, Jews, and Assyrian, Chaldean, and Armenian Christians. Bahais, considered a heretical sect, were given no representation. Instead they were ruthlessly persecuted; many were executed and hundreds imprisoned.

Elections were held for Iran's first president and the new Majlis during 1980 to further legitimize the new regime and its Islamic constitution. However, the results only caused more political fragmentation and intensified the civil war between pro- and anti-Khomeini forces. Abdol Hasan Bani-Sadr, an intellectual who had been close to Khomeini in exile, was elected with more than 75 percent of the vote, but his rather broad world-views and liberal interpretation of Islamic doctrines soon led to confrontation with the conservative Shi'ite clerics, now organized in the Islamic Republican Party (IRP) established in 1979. Bani-Sadr represented the educated civil servants, university faculties, and army officers in contrast to the IRP, which rallied the hard line traditionalists, the bazaar establishment, the lower-middle-class and the poorest, formerly disenfranchised sectors of society.

Tensions developed between Bani-Sadr and the traditionalists over internal and foreign policy, symbolized by disagreements concerning seizure of the U.S. embassy in Tehran by a throng of zealous young students during November 1979. Although not officially approved, the event became a touchstone of Iran's new-won "independence from American imperialism." Moderates in the regime represented by Bani-Sadr finally negotiated release of the 66 American hostages after 444 days, but the affair helped to undermine his status as a staunch supporter of Khomeini.

Bani-Sadr was a disciple of Ali Shariati, considered by many to be the major influence on young intellectuals in the revolutionary movement. Shariati was both an ardent Shi'ite and a modernist who blended traditionalism with progressive economic and social concepts. He believed that Iran's culture was subverted by Western ideas—the malady of "Westoxication." Neither capitalist liberalism nor Marxist or socialist doctrines, but Muhammad's ideal society should serve as the model for Iran. Shi'ite influence was manifest in his belief that the Ummayads began the decadance of Islam. Shariati distinguished between "Alid Shi'ism" (from Muhammad's son-in-law Ali, the first Imam) and "Safavid Shi'ism." The Islam of Ali, the original Islam, represented progress and revolution; it was the Islam of the people. The Safavids who made Shi'ism the state religion politicized and degraded the religion (the latter day heir of "Safavid Shi'ism" was "Pahlavi Shi'ism"). Western democracy, he asserted, was rotten and decadent, divested of humanism, therefore no model for Islamic peoples. Only "Alid Shi'ism" and the ideal community of Muhammad could save Iran.

Bani-Sadr attempted to introduce his own refinements in the form of an Islamic economic system emphasizing social justice, but the short period of his presidency was so full of turmoil and chaos that he lost power before implementing his program. The showdown came in a constitutional crisis during 1981 when Bani-Sadr refused to sign legislation passed by the Majlis. Although at first neutral in the confrontation, Khomeini finally sided with the zealots in parliament against Bani-Sadr whom he denounced as a "corrupt person on earth." The president was first deprived of his authority over the armed forces, a post in which he gained popularity as a result of the war with Iraq. Then in July 1981 after parliament declared Bani-Sadr politically incompetent, Khomeini dismissed him from the presidency. Already in hiding, Bani-Sadr soon reappeared in Paris where he became a leader of the new anti-Kohomeini and anti-IRP coalition of republican, royalist, and other groups.

The fall of Bani-Sadr further polarized Iran's revolutionary movements between the IRP and its supporters versus several of the old anti-shah nationalists and socialist-oriented Islamic factions. Despite propagation of the most fundamentalist Shi'ite radical doctrines, the IRP maintained a working relationship with the Tudeh until 1980, although hundreds of leftists were purged from government because of their "atheism." During the 1979 Majlis elections, only the IRP, Tudeh, Fedayeen al-Khalq, and Mujaheddin al-Khalq participated while the National Front, National Democratic Front, Muslim People's Republican Party, and Arab and Kurdish parties boycotted the balloting. By 1982 the new regime had replaced SAVAK with its own security apparatus, SAVAMA, and was cited by Amnesty International for more official executions during the preceeding three years than in all other countries combined.

There was little economic progress during the first years of the revolution because of cutbacks in oil production to about a tenth of that during the peak years under the shah. Revolutionary ideology strongly militated against the import of foreign machines, luxuries, technicians, and advisors. Rather, the ideal was to strive for self-sufficiency, to cut Iran's dependence on Western goods, methods, and personnel, even if it meant a sharp decline in living standards for the few who had benefited under the shah. After all, only a relatively small number of Iranians had profited from the "White Revolution" and the shah's modernization programs. Whereas the aristocracy and the old elites under the shah were shorn of power and affluence after 1979, a whole new substratum that had been invisible before the revolution emerged from the hovels on the outskirts of Tehran, Shiraz, Izfahan, and other urban centers. Both in large cities and in many rural areas this formerly disenfranchised "non-class," so poor that it was not even called "working-class," emerged as *vox populi,* the backbone of IRP support, of Khomeini zealotry, and of revolutionary Shi'ite folk Islam.

The importance of this phenomenon reached beyond Iran, for Khomeini's message appealed not only to Shi'ites but to Muslim lower classes throughout the area. It appealed especially to the imported workers in oil rich neighbors like Saudi Arabia, Kuwait, and Bahrain. The Ayatollah's call in 1979 to "all oppressed Muslim peoples" to "overthrow the corrupt and tyrannical governments in the Islamic world" and for Islam "to rise against the great powers to annihilate their agents" was worrisome to the conservative neighboring regimes. Thus Jordan's King Husain and the Saud dynasty gave eager support to Iraq in its war with Iran after 1980. Furthermore, the war split the Arab world between the conservatives who backed Iraq, despite its secular-socialist orientations, and the Arab radicals like Syria, Libya, and South Yemen who supported fundamentalist Shi'ite Iran. Khomeini and the IRP replaced the grandiose vision of the shah for a secular empire in the region with the vision of an Islamic revival that would destroy the "corrupt and wicked" and lift up the "poor and oppressed."

NOTES

1. Cuyler Young, "Iran in Continuing Crisis," *Foreign Affairs,* vol. 40, no. 2 (January 1962), pp. 286–287.

2. William S. Haas, *Iran,* New York, 1946, p. 154.

3. James A. Bill & Carl Leiden, *The Middle East Politics and Power,* Allyn and Bacon, Boston, 1974, p. 138.

4. Young, *op. cit.,* pp. 284–285.

5. *U.S. Military Sales to Iran,* 1976, U.S. Senate, 94th Congress, 2nd session, U.S. Government Printing Office, Washington, D.C.

18   Epilogue

Throughout the preceding chapters we have seen that within the Middle East there are many unifying factors that have shaped its historical and political development; yet there is a diversity within the area, a diversity of geography, languages, religions, cultures, and racial and ethnic groups, which also has greatly influenced the area's contemporary image. While the unifying factors, principally the Islamic and Iranian-Ottoman past, have been responsible for many common characteristics of these countries, the diversity within the region has created quite distinctive characteristics that separate them from each other.

Since the end of the nineteenth century, all of these countries have been strongly influenced by the Western world, yet few have successfully adapted themselves to Western political and social systems, and today several are moving away from development of Western institutions. The reasons for this trend and the factors that are significant in the Middle East today should be explored.

The common Islamic heritage of all Middle Eastern countries remains the most influential factor in contemporary society. Even in the most Western and certainly least Muslim nation, Israel, matters of family status (divorce, marriage, inheritance) are still strongly influenced by Muslim institutions inherited by the new state from the Ottoman past and preserved for the most part by the British mandate. Strangely enough, other, no-so-Westernized nations such as Egypt and Turkey have abandoned religious controls over these matters; but in these nations Islam pervades the consciousness and attitudes of their citizenry.

The centuries-old rift beteen Sunni and Shi'ite Muslims still affects political life in the region. In Iraq, Lebanon, and Syria, this antagonism is a strong divisive force.

When Napoleon appeared in Egypt at the beginning of the nineteenth century, Islam was the dominant political and social force throughout the Middle East. The concept of separation between church and state was still unknown in the region, and all governmental institutions were Islamic institutions at one and the same time. With the exception of Iran and the remoter areas of Arabia, all of the countries with which this book has dealt were formally governed by the Ottoman sultan-caliph, although the extent of his authority varied from region to region. Iran was also governed by a Shi'ite Islamic hierarchy headed by a shah, the titular descendant of 'Ali. In central Arabia, the Wahabi religious revival was stirring the Sauds to re-establish a purified Islamic fundamentalist society.

In the more advanced Iranian and Ottoman territories there were superimposed upon and blended with the Islamic society, Ottoman and Persian administrative institutions, many of which still remain. For example, many of the territorial administrative boundaries within the Middle East today are vestiges of the former Ottoman hegemony. Remnants of Ottoman millet law still prevail in Lebanon, Israel, and Iraq. Ottoman legal terminology is still characteristic of the codes of many Middle Eastern nations that were at one time under Ottoman rule.

When Napoleon established his military administration in Egypt, he introduced modifications and revisions into the prevailing Islamic-Iranian-Ottoman system that were to prove of long-term significance. His innovations were followed by increasing Western contacts and gradual adoption of European law, constitutions, parliamentary institutions, and administrative apparatus throughout the area. Motivation for the changes reflected both internal and external situations. To begin with, the Muslim Middle East gradually lost its former self-confidence and sense of superiority toward the "effete" Christian West, for the area found it increasingly difficult to ward off Western intrusions. In fact, many Middle Easterns came to believe the continued existence of their traditional ways of life depended upon the good graces of those Western nations they had formerly regarded with contempt. In their search for an answer to this dilemma, Middle Eastern leaders thought that they found the solution in the adoption of Western governmental institutions, in the introduction of Western administration, and in the use of Western military equipment and organization. Perhaps, it was thought, if they too could make use of these innovations by which the West had overcome and defeated Islamic society, that society could save itself from further disintegration and degradation.

Initial attempts to use Western military devices and tactics soon led the ruling elite to discover that the effective use of Western military apparatus required the adoption of many elements of Western civil organization. Thus, adoption of Western education, hospitals, health services, fiscal reforms, and administrative systems, soon followed, replacing bit by bit aspects of the old Islamic-Iranian-Ottoman society. In Turkey, the Tanzimat era blossomed from initial attempts to reform the army, resulting in extensive legal, administrative, and parliamentary changes. Similarly, the schemes of Muhammad 'Ali and later Ismail the Magnificent to revolutionize Egypt grew from seeds already planted by early military reforms.

External pressures also played a prominent role in changing Middle Eastern society, especially in the Ottoman Empire. Western European nations, seeking to keep the tottering empire intact, also sponsored administrative and parliamentary changes, hoping to revitalize the foundering Ottoman regime. It was believed that Westernizing the government would curtail, if not eliminate, the traditional corruption, nepotism, and intrigue that had sapped the strength of Eastern governments. Therefore, during the mid-nineteenth century the West put increasing pressures upon the Ottoman sultans to "modernize." In this way pressure from within, on the part of indigenous liberals, and from without, fostered by the West, brought about the adoption of various reforms. These measures included laws equalizing the status of Muslims and non-Muslims, financial and legal changes, and new tax systems.

By the beginning of the twentieth century, a superficial kind of Westernization was well on the way. In the more advanced countries of the region, like Egypt, Turkey, and Lebanon, there already were liberal infusions of Western-type laws and administrative practices. However, the effects of these reforms reached only a handful of people, and traditional Oriental society remained unchanged at its roots. The sultan-caliph and age-old Sunni-Ottoman institutions were still supreme in Turkey, and the shah and Shi'ite ulema still dominated Iran.

Changes that occurred as a result of attempts at Westernization did little to alter the relationships between the landowning class and the peasant masses, or to increase the distribution of profits from the nation's resources. Those who ruled Middle Eastern society had never intended that the nineteenth- and early twentieth-century reforms should alter these relationships. Indeed their motivation in introducing such reforms had been to help them preserve their society and the basic relationship between those at the top and the masses below. At most, the power concentrated in the hands of the chief-of-state was to be shared with the elite, not extended to the middle and lower classes. Until the end of World War I, only the elite were represented in the growing government bureaucracies, parliaments, and cabinets of the Westernizing regimes, and they consciously used their new governmental systems to help preserve the existing social system. Tenant-landowner relationships were not disturbed: education was retricted to the well-to-do (extending learning to the peasants would only cultivate insurrection); and the religious organization of the village remained as it had been for centuries. Throughout the Middle East, village life—the life of some four out of five of its population—continued at its traditional pace and in its traditional forms, unaffected by Westernization in the larger towns and cities.

Concentration of the Western reform movement at the top of society meant that much of the reform was rootless, even artificial. Of what value could parliamentary systems be with no effective political parties or meaningful electoral laws? Often Western legal codes were adopted without lawyers or judges to administer them, and courts were opened to which the vast majority had no access. Progress was most genuine and effective in the use of modern administrative techniques and in government reorganization. In Egypt, for example, the British built up an extensive and relatively efficient civil service.

Even reforms that affected only the top level of society were not accepted without a struggle. Many fought each new innovation as though it was a matter of life and death. Conservatives often sabotaged what they could of the new measures; they wished to continue their traditional rule in their traditional way.

However, the greatest obstacle to Westernization was not created in a calculated effort by a specific group. The greatest obstacle was Oriental society itself. There did not as yet exist in the Middle East a national consciousness as had developed in the various European nations. There was yet no strong Egyptian, Iranian, Turkish, or Arab national feeling. The ideas of modern nationalism and the nation-state were familiar only to a handful of Western-educated intellectuals. For most Middle Easterners the basis of society was the family, and family or clan loyalty was the highest ideal. Nepotism, bribery, and intrigue were accepted forms of behavior in government. Traditional authority, centralized in the family, was the basis of discipline, not the state or society at large.

Beyond the settled regions, which at the beginning of this century comprised only a fraction of the Middle East, law and order were little known. Cutting across the pattern of family loyalties were intergroup hostilities such as those between Muslim and Christian, Shi'ite and Sunni, nomad tribes and urban areas.

The incipient national movements that emerged by the end of World War I in Egypt, Iran, Turkey, and the Arab countries represented only a tiny urban minority, composed primarily of those who came from the upper strata of society. Their chief aim was to rid their countries or districts of foreigners and to share power among themselves. Few showed any concern for the economic and social ills that burdened the countryside and the city slums.

After World War I the newly developing middle classes often became an important element in the burgeoning national movements, for they felt that only by ridding themselves of foreign economic domination could they prosper. Those army officers and civil servants who were frustrated by the lack of opportunity for advancement under foreign rule or students aroused by promises of a better life under their own leaders also became active nationalists.

Few leaders had any well-worked-out program for achieving national status or for developing indigenous political institutions. Most of them hoped to superimpose upon their governments copies of institutions with which they had become familiar as students in Western schools. They gave little consideration to whether or not these institutions were indeed serviceable in the Middle East.

During the interwar era, clashes developed between the new generation of Western-educated, middle-class nationalists and their conservative elders. The younger generation was more eager to emulate "modern" techniques and to abandon traditional forms of society. Few of the post-World War I nationalist leaders had intimate ties with the old religious hierarchy. The new nationalism tended to be secular, although it frequently used old Islamic symbols to rally mass approval. The Wafd party in Egypt and the People's Republican party (PRP) in Turkey avoided religious appeals, the former because it desired to include Egyptian Christians and the latter because of a conviction that Islamic institutions were "reactionary."

Although the new nationalist leaders were eager to use Western political forms—often perhaps because they indicated a "modern" approach—few desired to alter fundamental social relationships. Thus Western-type parliaments, political parties, and other institutions were adopted not only to increase the power of the rising middle class, but also to keep political power from the hands of the peasantry and urban proletariat.

In the French and British mandated territories (French Syria and Lebanon; British Iraq, Palestine, and Transjordan) constitutional and administrative forms were introduced in accord with the League of Nations requirement that self-government be extended to native peoples, and because of the growing demands of the nationalists. In Syria and Lebanon, France introduced French systems of government and administration; and in Iraq and Transjordan, Great Britain set up systems modeled on those of England or of British colonies.

Great Britain and France were concerned less with extending democracy, however, than with preserving their respective spheres of influence. Prevailing opinion among both French and British mandatory officials was that preservation of society's *status quo* would best preserve French and British influence. To alter the *status quo,* by substantially enlarging the electorate or by depriving those who were at the top of society of their authority, might create upheaval and jeopardize foreign influence. France and Great Britain carefully avoided that danger: special provisions were introduced in the Syrian, Lebanese, and Iraqi constitutions ensuring continued non-Muslim and tribal representation in parliament; and land legislation introduced in Syria and Iraq gave great power to tribal leaders to ensure their continued support for the foreign powers.

In Iraq, Transjordan, and Egypt, constitutional systems divided power among a strong monarch, the nationalist middle class, and the British. In Syria and Lebanon, France fragmented political power among diverse ethnic, religious, and linguistic groups. French and British parliamentary and constitutional forms gave the appearance, but not the substance, of democracy. To the extent that such systems adopted free speech, permitted opposition parties to exist, and allowed parliamentary discussion of legislation, they resembled Western institutions. However, they lacked those fundamentals that give life and vitality to Western democracy. Parliaments existed without an informed or literate electorate. Political parties, except the Wafd in Egypt and the PRP in Turkey, were small cliques representing minority interests. The press discussed primarily those issues that concerned the upper and middle classes. Without extending education to rural areas, there could be little increase in literacy and no informed electorate. But parliaments made little effort to provide budgets to expand educational facilities. Without an informed population there was little possibility of organizing mass movements among the peasants and urban lower classes. Existing peasant organizations and trade-union movements were regarded by those in power as subversive, and every effort was made to crush them.

Leftist attempts during the interwar era to organize mass movements all failed, usually because the organizers used terms that had no mass appeal. Most individuals who attempted to organize workers and peasants were alien to the feelings and emotions of the classes they sought to organize. Before World War II, Communists agitated for "international solidarity of the working classes," an appeal that was meaningless to most Middle Easterners. By the late 1940s the Communists had abandoned their conventional appeals and slogans and turned to nationalism as their rallying call.

Until defeat of the Axis powers in World War II, rightist ideologies rather than those of the left were popular with Middle East nationalists. The PRP in Turkey and the National Brotherhood and its successor, the Istiqlal in Iraq were more influenced by Fascist corporate-state programs than by socialist ideology. Ataturk, Bakr Sidki, and Reza Shah all found Fascist ideology more appealing because of its apparent dynamism. To these Middle Eastern leaders strongly centralized authority and an emphasis on work, discipline, and glorification of the state were all doctrines that seemed ready-made for their own national purposes. The only influential political group in the Middle East that eschewed Fascist doctrine, aside from the Jewish parties in Palestine was the Wafd party, many of whose leaders admired instead the British liberal tradition. In Iraq, the Ahali, which later became the National Democratic party, was strongly influenced by British socialism, but the group never became a potent national force.

By the end of World War II fascism was thoroughly discredited. Germany and Italy, utterly defeated, had shown that the corporate state was not invincible and that social-democratic nations were not as weak as they had appeared. By the 1950s socialism became *the* popular political ideology in the Middle East, just as it had become so elsewhere in Asia. Numerous Socialist parties flourished in the Arab East, and many political groups that were not really socialist, adopted socialist slogans to compete for popular favor. Indicative of the trend was conversion of Ahmed Husein's one-time Egyptian Fascist party to socialism, although the party never carried great weight in either guise.

After World war II the military also began to feel its political oats. Before the war, army officers had played prominent roles in Turkey, Iraq, and Iran, but they had been an effective political force only in Turkey. Even there, once they entered the political stage, they abandoned their military identity. Although both Ataturk and his successor, Inonu, were former generals, both put off their uniforms after becoming president and insisted that officers in politics surrender their army commissions and that those on active duty refrain from political activity. Reza Shah was also a former army officer who used his position to attain political power, but once he attained power he subordinated Iranian army officers to his will as shah, not as an army general. Iraq's series of military coups, beginning in 1936, soon degenerated from an idealistic reform movement into a naked power struggle among various army cliques. By the early 1940s they were thoroughly discredited and regarded as no better than the country's civilian politicians who also squabbled over personalities, not issues.

Within the Arab officer groups, the upper ranks usually represented the conservative upper levels of society, that element which desired to preserve the social *status quo.* Junior grades were more often held by men from middle- and lower-middle-class families. Many of the latter were converted to an active nationalism by their resentment of the British or French domination. Defeat of the Arab armies by a relatively small, foreign Jewish force during the Palestine war in 1947–1948 was an overwhelming blow to Arab national pride, particularly to the officer group. Many junior officers as well as younger Arab intellectuals were stirred to action by the Palestine debacle and decided that the shame must be wiped away, that the weakness in Arab society that could produce such a disaster must be removed. Initially, those who wanted reform tried the familiar approach of reforming the military machine.

The first series of post-Palestine military coups occurred in Syria. But the officers who seized power there proved to be no better than those who had ruled Iraq after 1936. After attaining power they did little to alter the country's economic, political, or social structure. So burdensome did General Shishakli's military dictatorship become that he was overthrown by a coalition of civilian forces recruited from every political faction from Communists to the conservative landowners.

But Syrian politics again degenerated into the old pattern of control by a small group of wealthy individuals, who were now pressured by the rising middle class and a new, youthful leftist group to make fundamental reforms. However, a stalemate emerged among the old guard, the middle class, and the young leftists. Although the leftists began to rally a mass following among peasants and urban labor groups, most machinery of government remained in the hands of the old guard, who used it to prevent any real social change.

The only Syrian party of consequence to put forward a program advocating fundamental socioeconomic change was the Ba'ath, a socialist group which ascended to power during the 1950s, lost power after Syria was unified with Egypt in 1958, and again in the 1960s seized control of governments in Syria and in Iraq. But the Ba'ath, like other Arab political groups, split into diverse factions, each contending with the other, with the result that no faction succeeded in accomplishing effective changes in Arab society.

The young officer group which seized power in Egypt after 1952 was far more effective. Disillusioned with their national leadership after the Palestine debacle, the group also initially sought to reform the military machine. After seizing power, the officers not only revamped the army, they also imposed fundamental reforms that altered Egypt's basic social relationships. They not only refused to collaborate with the old guard, they completely destroyed its political, economic, and social influence. All other potential sources of political competition were similarly eliminated. The Communists were driven underground, the once powerful Muslim Brotherhood was liquidated, and the Wafd party was shorn of its influence when the army seized its press and absorbed its village branches.

Egypt's revolutionary regime was the first in the Middle East not only to challenge, but drastically to alter the existing complex of social, economic, and political institutions—both those indigenous to the country's culture and those imported from the West. The criterion for accepting new political forms in revolutionary Egypt was no longer whether or not they were Western or Muslim, but how effective they were and whether the revolutionary government could use them to change society fundamentally as it desired. The first victim of the revolution was the old political machine. The European-type monarchy was abolished and the Western-style constitution discarded. At first, there were attempts to adapt the existing parliamentary system to the new regime. But when it became obvious that an effective parliamentary form of government could not work without effective political parties and an informed electorate, the attempts were abandoned. The only real political party was the Wafd, which, despite wide membership, was manipulated by a small group of politicians representing the wealthy. Neither the peasants nor the laboring class was represented in the party hierarchy, or in the governments that it formed when in office. Furthermore, the party had become thoroughly discredited because of the dishonesty of its leaders. Consequently, the revolutionary military regime that seized power in 1952 decided to abolish all political parties and resisted all attempts to reinstitute a system that would return control to the old political groups.

Because it mistrusted all who were not from the same background as themselves, Egypt's new Revolutionary Command Council turned over most responsible state positions to fellow army officers. Thus, a new officer group, representing the lower-middle class, now ascended to power. Because it had no experience in government or in administration, no clearly formulated policy, it attempted to devise new approaches, many borrowed from other political systems. The country's new leader, Gamal Abdel Nasser, had his staff systematically reviewed the programs and accomplishments of other revolutionary regimes, hoping to cull from their successes what would be of value to revolutionary Egypt.

Democratic guarantees, such as free press, free speech, and free political organization were sacrificed, since, Nasser explained, the vast majority of the population had never benefited from them anyhow. Under the old regime the depressed four-fifths of society had been unable to improve their living conditions despite the theoretical existence of democratic freedoms. Before the population could really benefit from democratic freedoms, it would have to become economically secure, literate, and free from the burdens of economic oppression. Democratic institutions imported from the West would serve no use in an Oriental society suffering from traditional Oriental poverty, disease, illiteracy, and gross inequality—so argued the young Egyptian revolutionists. Only after their country's population had attained a material standard of life resembling that in the West could it effectively use Western political institutions.

Various new political forms were tried in revolutionary Egypt to maintain contact between the new officer elite and the masses. At first a Liberation Rally, then a National Union were organized to enlist popular participation in the revolution. Both failed to sustain mass interest in the revolutionary goals; in 1962 political life was again reorganized around a congress of popular forces representing occupational groups and an Arab socialist union with the hope that they would rally the population. While national policy was formulated by the handful of army officers at the top echelon of government, attempts were made to decentralize local decisions and to give greater authority to provincial and subprovincial officials. The dilemma in Egypt, as in Ataturk's republican Turkey, was how to enlist popular support for and participation in national life while retaining control over and direction of the revolution. Nasser, like Ataturk, tried to induce participation of villagers in the national cause through extension of party organization to numerous rural centers. One difference between Ataturk and Nasser is that the Turkish president gave authority to peasants or workers only on one or two occasions, whereas the Egyptian deliberately sought to foster peasant and worker participation in the national parliament, but without great success.

Other Middle Eastern countries were still strugging with European parliamentary forms of government. None has yet found them satisfactory to meet the pressure of economic and social development, with the possible exception of "Western" Israel. In Israel, Western political forms work more or less successfully because the country's origin is European and it has a high rate of literacy, a wide divergence of political and social groups, and an unusually high percentage of popular participation in national political life. Political leaders and opinion-makers in Israel are by and large Westerners, have brought their ideologies and political system with them from Europe, or are Western educated and acculturated.

In Turkey, Iran, Lebanon, Syria, and Jordan, experiments with Western-type parliamentary institutions and constitutional systems can hardly be called successful. In none of these countries are there effective political organizations that represent peasants and laborers on a wide scale. Parliamentary life, where it exists, is controlled by the upper and upper-middle classes. The rulers of most countries so dominate the political scene that opposition is rendered totally ineffective. Lebanon's whole structure of government is distorted by the system of allocating administrative offices, parliamentary seats, and government posts according to the strength of the various religious groups in the country. In Jordan, the monarch is the pivot of political life and maintains a precarious balance between the army, landowners, merchant middle class, and nationalists, constantly fearing that some combination of these forces will topple his regime. Thus in Middle Eastern nations other than Israel, where parliamentary systems do work, such institutions are merely used by the upper stratum of society to maintain its entrenched position.

After Egypt's defeat in the 1967 war with Israel, President Nasser attempted to revitalize his country's parliamentary institutions by cutting back on the influence of the army, by allocating more responsibility to the country's single political party, the Arab Socialist Union, and by permitting greater self-criticism in parliament. Efforts were made to encourage greater and more extensive peasant and village participation in the country's elected institutions, but the low level of literacy and the great poverty inhibited effective spread of popular participation. As part of his "liberalization" measures, Nasser's successor, Anwar Sadat, permitted formation of political parties and greatly diminished the role of the ASU. These steps were seen as a return to Western type political institutions, and a move away from Nasser's revolution, although Sadat and his successor, Husni Mubarak, maintained their government control of the political system.

The Arabian peninsula has not yet been seriously affected by the impact of Western political institutions, although the first tremors of change have already been felt. Until the 1962 resolution, Yemen was ruled by an Oriental potentate, who aimed at no separation of church and state. The imam was still an absolute monarch dominating national civil and religious life, and traditional religious law determined legislation. Until the early 1950s much the same situation existed in Saudi Arabia, although there was a more extensive tribal force of democracy forcing the monarch to consider opinions of tribal chieftains with whom he was allied. Since 1950 a constitutional system has begun to emerge in Saudi Arabia. Extensive legislation has been adopted to supplement Koranic law, and the monarch's powers have been considerably trimmed as he has been forced to consult his ministers. The new oil industry has given birth to a small middle class which is rapidly expanding and insisting on greater representation in government. In other Arabian principalities the sheikhs rule, although the oil industry has awakened a new middle class not only to the material assets of the West, but also to its diverse political ideologies. However in several of these oil rich countries there is growing concern about the huge proportion of imported labor which forms a potentially restive working class.

The spread of radical nationalist ideologies was evident in establishment of the Republic of Yemen, in the new People's Republic of South Yemen, and in unrest in the Persian Gulf emirates. With impending departure of the British from the region, radical nationalist groups backed by Arab socialist regimes began to undermine the authority of traditional rulers who had governed with British support for the last century or two.

There was hope in 1950 that one-party rule in Turkey had ended when the PRP surrendered power to the Democrats, who were victorious in the country's first free elections. Although democracy, including a free press and free speech and unrestricted party activity, seemed to flourish for a year or so, the new Democratic regime soon proved to be even more authoritarian than its PRP predecessor. Parliament was converted by Democratic Prime Minister Adnan Menderes into a tool of his party, over which he held absolute control. The high-handed tactics used by Menderes soon created considerable unrest among the country's intellectuals. His regime became so oppressive that it created a popular uprising in the capital led by the army which resented the prime minister's use of its services to suppress political opponents. In rural areas, however, the many peasants who had benefited from Menderes's economic policies—especially from his protection of them against increased taxation—were not at all enthusiastic about the revolution that destroyed Menderes in 1960.

A period of coalition government followed reinstitution of the parliamentary system by the army until the Justice party won, first one majority in 1965, and then an even larger one in 1969, assuring it control of the government. Victory by the Justice party, successor to the Democratic party of Menderes, showed how strong peasant conservatism was in Turkey, but it also widened the cleavage between the urban lower class and the governing elite, since the latter was unprepared to carry out structural reforms necessary to meet the country's growing problems. Once again in 1971 the army sought to restore the balance and reinstitute a "law and order" regime when it deposed the Justice party and put a coalition government in power. By 1973 martial law was terminated and Turkey returned to multiparty democracy. The dilemma facing the country was that no party seemed able to win a majority. Thus governments were coalitions, often ineffective and unable to cope with the increasing problems. The result was the spread of political instability and tension and another army takeover in 1980.

Most of the countries of the area have resources that still await development while their peoples live in great poverty. Egypt is a notable exception, for its limited resources can not hope to provide for the expanding population under the best of conditions. Recent discovery of oil in Egypt may radically alter that country's position. A crucial problem facing contemporary Middle Eastern society is what form of government can best bring about and direct the social and economic reforms so drastically needed. The use of money and technical competence is not enough to develop national resources, as we have seen in the case of Iraq. Construction of large dams and irrigation systems and the development of land, water, and mineral reserves does not guarantee improvement in the life of the average Middle Easterner. Without extensive social and political change, the majority of the population can not really benefit from economic development. Social and political systems must be devised that can guarantee equitable distribution of the profits from national economic improvements. National resources may be exploited and expanded, but their concentration in the hands of the few individuals at the top of the social pyramid will bring little benefit to society as a whole. Under political systems today prevailing, there is little likelihood that the legislation required for a more equitable distribution of national resources is possible. Effective land reform will continue to be difficult in governments controlled by landowners or wealthy states. Nor will such governments take adequate measures to educate the peasant, organize cooperatives, and extend government services to underdeveloped rural areas.

Even political revolution is not enough. Mere confiscation of wealthy landowners' property will not guarantee an equitable social system or higher living standards. In Egypt, Syria, Yemen, and Iraq, there have been revolutions that have considerably curbed the landowners' political power. But in Egypt the rapidly expanding population still outstrips national resources, and political change alone can not alter the situation. The problem is a social one; it is a question of peasant attitudes toward the family. Technological improvements in agriculture, irrigation, the use of power, and development of industry can improve, but they can not solve the dilemma of Egypt's population explosion.

Most Middle Eastern nations are not yet ready for technological revolution. There are not enough technicians to set up and operate industrial plants, too few economic planners to determine what industries are best suited to development of available national resources, a shortage of managerial talent to direct these operations, and a lack of capital and markets required for industrial expansion. In Egypt confiscatory measures (that is, nationalization of capital) have been inadequate to develop industry, so that the country has again turned to foreign economic and technical assistance—both American and Russian. Concomitant with industrial development are the problems of social uprootedness caused when peasants flock to large cities, where, after they have lost their family and religious ties, they easily become victims of extremist agitators. The large new industrial slums add to the already existing problems of sanitation, health, educaiton, and security.

Growing impatience with the failures of Western political institutions and technolgoical innovations to improve life for the masses in the Middle East became increasingly overt by the late 1970s and early 1980s; it was manifest in the phenomenon described in the West as "Islamic resurgence," i.e., the attraction to fundamentalist Islam of many students, intellectuals, and middle class former adherents of radical secular ideologies. Many of the disenfranchised among the working classes and peasantry openly expressed their disillusionment with Western ways and techniques through their political support for Islamic zealots who entered the political arena like the Muslim Brothers in Egypt and Syria or the Ayatollah Khomeini in Iran. Toppling the shah in the 1979 Islamic Revolution was more than an Iranian happening. It stimulated interest and stirred fundamentalist fervor among the Muslim lower-middle class and proletariat throughout the region and aroused deep apprehension in established regimes.

The economic and social problems of developing nations become international problems when they are the focal points of competition in the world power struggle. Both the United States and the Soviet Union are competing to assist developing Middle Eastern, as well as other nations. Each of the great powers hopes to use influence gained through economic and technical assistance to persuade developing nations of the value of its own political, social, and economic institutions. This power struggle in the Middle Eastern context is closely related to the contest for power between the Soviet Union and the United States in the larger global context. Its effects upon each nation in the region, from an internal point of view, have yet to be resolved.

The intensity of great power competition in the area has greatly increased since the June 1967 war between Israel and Egypt, Jordan, and Syria. The disastrous Arab defeat has led to greater radicalization of politics, with the USSR giving all-out political support and military assistance to revolutionary Arab governments. On the other hand, the ties between Israel and the United States have become closer. Countries in the middle, such as Jordan and

Lebanon, are increasingly threatened by revolutionary movements, especially by the Palestinian Arab commandos. As fighting escalates and each side, the U.S. and the USSR, escalates assistance to its protégés, the danger of big power confrontation becomes greater.

Growing awareness by both superpowers of the dangers in escalating the conflict between their Middle East protégés was evident in their agreements during 1967, 1970, and 1973 to support cease-fires in the Arab-Israeli wars. However, success of the cease-fire depends on willingness of Israel and the Arab states to negotiate their differences, and on an agreement by the United States and the Soviet Union to halt the dangerous supply of even more sophisticated military equipment to the combatants. These were difficult and at times contradictory goals. Each of the wars was followed by an extended series of peace negotiations through the United Nations, bilaterally between the United States and the Soviet Union, through involvement of the middle powers such as Great Britain and France, and even through indirect talks involving Israel and some Arab states. The October 1973 war was followed by the first formal peace talks involving the combatants at Geneva. But after two meetings the Geneva Middle East Peace Conference was suspended for several more years until Egyptian President Anwar Sadat's peace initiative in 1977 which led to the Egyptian-Israeli peace treaty in 1979.

A major obstacle to an overall settlement was the Palestine problem. The Israeli government refused to attend any talks at which the PLO, the official representative body of the Palestinians, attended. The Palestinians, at first ambivalent about representation in peace talks, later insisted that the PLO be given official recognition by the United States and Israel. By 1982 issues of mutual Israeli-Palestinian recognition, Israeli occupation of the territories it had seized in the 1967 war, and doubts about formal recognition of Israel by the Arabs continued to stymie progress.

Throughout these extended parleys, the dangers of renewed war greatly intensified. All parties escalated the quantity and quality of their arms supplies to a level never imagined before. By 1977 Middle East countries, including Iran which was not involved in the Arab-Israeli conflict, were purchasing billions of dollars worth of military equipment yearly. Both in quantity and sophistication, the arms levels of Middle East countries had reached the levels of European NATO members. The world's major arms suppliers, the United States, the Soviet Union, and France, were sending the great bulk of their shipments to the Middle East. This was a threat, not only to Middle Eastern and to world peace, but a substantial drain on the area's resources undermining progress toward economic and social development. Instead of becoming secure and stable, the Middle East had become one of the most volatile regions in the international political system. Even Egyptian President Anwar Sadat's dramatic and surprise peace initiatives in 1977 raised as much apprehension about the future as it stimulated hope. His efforts to unilaterally end the thirty-year war with Israel divided the Arab world and intensified the competition in the region between the superpowers. Only a few Arab states supported his peace offensive at first; most were either reluctant to become involved in direct negotiations with the Jewish state or adamantly opposed them. The United States supported his efforts after initial reserve, but the Soviet Union condemned Sadat for acting without the other Arab states.

By the beginning of the 1980s, the inventory of Middle East problems, both internal and foreign, was far greater than the region could cope with itself, or than any single outside power could manage. No regional constellation of countries, not the U.S. nor the USSR, alone could resolve the Arab-Israeli conflict, settle the Palestinians, end the Iraq-Iran war, terminate the strife in Lebanon, bring stability to the countries torn by civil war, or improve economic and social conditions. Not only did these problems require physical resources beyond the means of any single nation, they required insight, planning, and understanding on a large scale, a scale that would require cooperation among the nations of the Middle East as well as among the powers outside the region for whom the Middle East would be an area of vital importance during decades to come.

Selected Bibliography

Bibliographical, Periodical, and Reference Works

Atiyeh, George N. *The Contemporary Middle East 1948–1973*. Boston, 1975. A massive and comprehensive bibliography of books, articles, and studies.

Bodurgil, Abraham. *Turkey, Politics and Government: A Bibliography 1938–1975*. Washington, D.C., 1978.

Grimwood-Jones, Diana; Hopwood, Derek; and Pearson, J.D. *Arab Islamic Bibliography*. Sussex, 1977. Extensive coverage.

Guclu, Meral. *Turkey*. Santa Barbara, 1981. Part of World Bibliographical Series, vol. 27. Detailed bibliography of all aspects of Turkey.

International Journal of Middle East Studies. A quarterly published by the Middle East Studies Association of North America.

Journal of Palestine Studies. Beirut. Quarterly on Palestinians and the Arab-Israel conflict published by the Institute for Palestine Studies; includes excellent bibliographic references, chronology, and documentation.

Khalidi, Walid, and Khadduri, Jill. *Palestine and the Arab-Israel Conflict*. Beirut, 1974. The most extensive bibliography on the conflict to date with 4,580 listings.

Legum, Colin, and Shaked, Haim, eds. *Middle East Contemporary Survey*. Vols. 1–4, 1976–1980. A series of essays and detailed country reviews with excellent references, diagrams, tables, etc.

MERIP Reports. Washington, D.C. Monthly periodical with Marxian analysis published by the Middle East Research and Information Project.

The Middle East and North Africa. London, latest edition. An annual survey and directory with historical, economic, and geographic background. (1st ed., 1948.)

The Middle East Journal. Washington, D.C. The Middle East Institute. Contains the best English-language bibliography on contemporary affairs, including periodical literature and recent books, with reviews of important works. It is published quarterly.

Middle East Record. Jerusalem. Annual published from 1962 by Shiloah Institute covering political and economic events of the region and its individual countries. Replaced by *Middle East Contemporary Survey* after 1970.

Middle Eastern Studies. London. Quarterly scholarly magazine with historical emphasis.

New Outlook. Monthly published in Tel Aviv, Israel. Contains articles on Israel and its neighbors directed toward Arab-Jewish rapprochement.

Partington, David, ed. *The Middle East Annual: Issues and Events.* Vol. 1, 1981. Boston, 1982. Series of scholarly articles covering principal events with excellent annotated bibliography.

Schultz, Ann. *International and Regional Politics in the Middle East and North Africa: A Guide to Information Sources.* Detroit, 1977. Major emphasis on bibliographic material related to international relations.

Sherman, John, ed. *The Arab-Israeli Conflict, 1945–1971: A Bibliography.* New York, 1978. 419 pages of items.

Atlases

Atlas of the Arab World and the Middle East. New York, 1960. A good presentation of physical characteristics, resources, population, and climate.

Atlas of Islamic History. Compiled by Harry W. Hazard and H. Lester Cooke, Jr. Princeton, N.J., 1951. Traces the history of Islam with helpful commentary.

Gilbert, Martin. *The Arab-Israeli Conflict, Its History in Maps.* 2nd ed. London, 1976.

Historical Atlas of the Muslim Peoples. Compiled by R. Roolvink, *et al.* Cambridge, Mass., 1957. A detailed historical atlas.

The Middle East and North Africa. London, 1960. An economic atlas showing resources, population, industry, and agricultural developments.

Pounds, Norman J.G., and Kingsbury, Robert C. *An Atlas of Middle Eastern Affairs.* New York, 1963. A geopolitical historical atlas from the ancient to modern periods.

Geographical Studies

Beaumont, P.; Blake, G.; and Wagstaff, J. *The Middle East: A Geographical Study.* New York, 1976. Brings up to date older studies.

Fisher, W.B. *The Middle East: A Physical, Social, and Regional Geography.* London, 1950. 7th ed., 1978. Treats the area by geographical regions and in great detail.

Collections of Writings by Middle Easterners and Interpretive Essays

Dessfosses, H., and Levesque, J. *Socialism in the Third World.* New York, 1975. A reader with essays including Syria, Iraq, Libya, and Algeria.

Gardner, George H., and Hanna, Sami A. *Arab Socialism: A Documentary Survey.* Leiden, 1969. Socialist authors and documents.

Gendzier, Irene L. *A Middle East Reader.* New York, 1969. A collection of Middle East and other authors, strongly emphasizing nationalism.

Haim, Sylvia G., ed. *Arab-Nationalism: An Anthology.* Berkeley and Los Angeles, 1976. A selection of writings by Arab authors.

Hamalian, Leo, and Yohannan, John D., eds. *New Writing from the Middle East.* New York, 1978. A collection of fiction, poetry and drama from Arabic, Armenian, Persian, Israeli and Turkish authors.

Hammond, Paul Y. and Alexander, Sidney S. *Political Dynamics in the Middle East.* New York, 1972. Extensive collection of essays on contemporary Middle East political problems including international relations.

Karpat, Kemal, ed. *Political and Social Thought in the Contemporary Middle East.* Rev. ed. New York, 1982. A collection of political writings and statements of all Middle East countries with extensive commentary.

Landen, Robert G. *The Emergence of the Modern Middle East,* New York, 1970. A collection of documents and observations from medieval to modern times.

Peretz, Don. *The Middle East: Selected Readings.* Rev. ed. Boston, 1973. A compilation of writings by Europeans and Middle Easterners from early times to the present.

Anthropological and Sociological Studies

Baer, Gabriel. *Population and Society in the Arab East.* London, 1964. An introduction to the area by an Israeli scholar.

Beck, Lois and Keddie, Nikki, eds. *Women in the Muslim World.* Cambridge, Mass., 1978. A useful series of studies on women.

Berger, Morroe. *The Arab World Today.* New York, 1962. An excellent study of contemporary Arab social organization and institutions, including an examination of attitudes, personality, relationships between men and women, and political life.

Eickelman, Dale F. *The Middle East: An Anthropological Approach.* Englewood Cliffs, N.J., 1981.

Hourani, Albert H. *Minorities in the Arab World.* London, 1947. An account of minority groups and their backgrounds in each of the Arab countries.

El-Saadawi, Nawal. *The Hidden Face of Eve: Women in the Arab World.* Boston, 1982. An account by a woman physician of taboo subjects and oppressive beliefs and practices.

Sweet, Louise E. *Peoples and Cultures of the Middle East.* 2 vols. Garden City, 1970. Collection of essays by anthropologists and sociologists on life in the desert, towns, and cities.

Van Nieuwenhuijze, Christoffel, A.O. *Sociology of the Middle East: A Stocktaking and Interpretation.* Leiden, 1971. Social structure and change in the Middle East region and by country.

———. *Commoners, Climbers and Notables: A Sampler of Studies on Social Ranking in the Middle East.* Leiden, 1977.

Economic Studies of the Region

Cooper, Charles A., and Alexander, Sidney S. *Economic Development and Population Growth in the Middle East.* New York, 1972. Studies of growth and development in several countries and in the region as a whole.

Issawi, Charles P., ed. *The Economic History of the Middle East: 1800–1914.* Chicago, 1966. A documentary collection dealing with economic life.

Lloyd, Edward M.H. *Food and Inflation in the Middle East, 1940–1945.* Stanford, 1956. Describes Middle East economics and planning during and after World War II.

Sayigh, Yusuf. *The Economics of the Arab World.* New York, 1978. Basic and comprehensive study from Morocco to Iraq.

Warriner, Doreen. *Land Reform and Development in the Middle East, A Study of Egypt, Syria, and Iraq.* London, 1957. Critically analyzes agrarian reform, private enterprise, and the flow of oil royalties into three Arab countries.

Economic Developments in the Middle East 1959–1961. Supplement to World Economic Survey, 1961. New York, 1962. Compilation of economic statistics on the region as a whole. Part of a United Nations series begun in 1949–1950.

Final Report of the United Nations Economic Survey Mission for the Middle East. 2 vols. New York, 1949. A critical analysis of economic development possibilities in Israel and the Arab East.

Middle Eastern Oil

Anderson, Irvine H. *Aramco, The United States and Saudi Arabia: A Study of the Dynamics of Foreign Oil Policy, 1933–1950.* Princeton, 1981.

Blair, John M. *The Control of Oil.* New York, 1976. A critical account of oil company policy.

Conant, Melvin A. *The Oil Factor in U.S. Foreign Policy, 1980–1990.* Lexington, Mass., 1982. An overview of the global problem.

Engler, Robert. *The Brotherhood of Oil: Energy Policy and The Public Interest.* Chicago, 1977. A critical account of the oil companies and government policy.

Issawi, Charles, and Yeganeh, Mohammed. *The Economics of Middle Eastern Oil.* New York, 1962. An account of oil investment, production, and the world market.

Lenczowski, George. *Oil and State in the Middle East.* Ithaca, 1960. Examines economic and legal aspects of relations between the oil companies and their host countries.

Longrigg, Stephen H. *Oil in the Middle East, Its Discovery and Development.* London, 1954. 3rd ed., 1968. Factual history of oil in the Middle East.

Mosley, Leonard. *Power Play—Oil in the Middle East.* New York, 1973. History of oil and politics in the Middle East.

Rustow, Dankwart A. *Oil and Turmoil: America Faces OPEC and the Middle East.* New York, 1982. A critical account.

Sampson, Anthony. *The Seven Sisters.* New York, 1975. History of the international oil cartel and its relationships with the Middle East.

Shwadran, Benjamin. *The Middle East, Oil and the Great Powers.* New York, 1955. 2d ed., 1959. A study of oil politics and maneuvers among the great powers.

Tetreault, Mary Ann. *The Organization of Arab Petroleum Exporting Countries: History, Policies, and Prospects.* Westport, Conn., 1981.

Annotated Documents

Alexander, Yonah, and Nanes, Alton, eds. *The United States and Iran: A Documentary History.* Frederick, Md, 1980. A collection of mostly U.S. documents.

Eayrs, James. *The Commonwealth and Suez: A Documentary Study, 1956–57.* New York, 1963. Documentation on the Suez crises and its background.

Fraser, T.G. *The Middle East, 1914–1979.* New York, 1980. Compendium from Husain-McMahon correspondence in 1914 to Camp David, with commentary.

Higgins, Rosalyn, ed. *United Nations Peacekeeping: Documents and Commentary. The Middle East.* Vol. 1. New York, 1969. Documents on UN Middle East forces.

Hurewitz, J.C. *The Middle East and North Africa in World Politics.* Vol. 1. *European Expansion, 1535–1914.* New Haven, 1975. Vol. 2. *British-French Supremacy, 1914–1945.* New Haven, 1979. Well annotated.

Moore, John Norton. *The Arab-Israeli Conflict: Readings and Documents.* Princeton, 1977. Includes materials from 1897 to 1975, official and unofficial.

Department of State. *Foreign Relations of the United States,* Vol. 5, part 1, *1947.* Washington, D.C., 1971; Vol. 5, part 2, *1948.* Washington, D.C., 1976; Vol. 6, *1949.* Washington, D.C., 1977. Extensive documentation on American policy making in the Middle East.

Islam and the Arabs

Of the hundreds of books on Islam and the Arabs, the following few may be particularly helpful as background works for the beginning student of the contemporary Middle East:

Ajami, Fouad. *The Arab Predicament: Arab Political Thought and Practice Since 1967.* Cambridge, 1981. A critical analysis of Arab radicals, Muslim fundamentalists, and conservatives.

Anderson, J.N.D. *Islamic Law in the Modern World.* New York, 1959. A brief study of Islamic law and modern life, including marriage, divorce, and inheritance.

Andrae, Tor. *Mohammed, the Man and His Faith.* New York, 1936. One of the best volumes on the founder of Islam.

Arberry, A.J., ed. *Religion in the Middle East.* 2 vols. Cambridge, England, 1969. Extensive treatment by various authors of Judaism, Christianity, and various Muslim groups.

Bill, James and Leiden, Carl. *Politics in the Middle East.* Boston and Toronto, 1979. A theoretical and analytical study of modernization and politics.

Cragg, Kenneth. *The Call of the Minaret.* New York, 1956. A sympathetic treatment of Islam by a Christian who attempts to understand the religion and its problems in the modern world.

Esposito, John L., ed. *Islam and Development: Religion and Sociopolitical Change.*

Syracuse, 1980. A survey of contemporary Islamic thought and practice in Egypt, Saudi Arabia, Iran, Pakistan, Nigeria, Senegal, and Malaysia.

Esposito, John L., and Donahue, John J. *Islam in Transition: Muslim Perspectives.* New York, 1982. Writings of modern Muslim thinkers; significant documents, with commentary.

Fisher, Sydney N. *The Middle East: A History.* 3rd ed. New York, 1979. Good historical background on Islam from early periods to the present.

Gibb, Hamilton A.R. *Mohammedanism, An Historical Survey.* New York, 1949. 2d ed., 1968. An excellent history of the rise of Islam, its development, and its situation in the modern world.

Gibb, H.A.R., and Kramers, J.H., eds. *Shorter Encyclopedia of Islam.* Ithaca, 1965. Extensive and detailed compilation of Islamic terminology.

Guillaume, Afred. *Islam.* Toronto, 1954. 2d ed., 1956. A brief history of Islam's rise, its sects, philosophies, and contemporary beliefs.

Von Grunebaum, G.E. *Medieval Islam.* Chicago, 1946. An interesting study of Islamic developments during the "Golden Age" of Islam.

Keddie, Nikki R., ed. *Scholars, Saints and Sufis: Muslim Religious Institutions since 1500.* Berkeley and Los Angeles, 1972. A very useful collection of studies on Islam's influence up to the present.

Khaldun, Ibn. *The Muqaddimah: An Introduction to History.* Translated by Franz Rosenthal. 3 vols. New York, 1958. An early Islamic philosophy on the rise and fall of dynasties.

Kritzeck, James, ed. *Anthology of Islamic Literature from the Rise of Islam to Modern Times.* New York, 1963. A useful compilation illustrating Islamic life.

Levy, Reuben. *The Social Structure of Islam.* Cambridge, 1957. Examines social status in the Muslim world, the status of women, children, and slaves, and the religion's fundamental institutions.

Lewis, Bernard. *The Arabs in History.* London, 1950. 3d ed., 1956. The best-written brief history of the Arabs and the rise of Islam.

Lewis, Bernard, ed. *Islam.* Vol. 1, *Politics and War;* Vol. 2, *Religion and Society.* New York, 1974. Collection of translated documents from era of Mohammed to the fall of Constantinople.

Long, David E. *The Hajj Today: A Survey of the Contemporary Pilgrimmage to Makkah.* Albany, 1979. How the Hajj works.

Mortimer, Edward. *Faith and Power: The Politics of Islam.* New York, 1982. The rise, spread, variety, and complexity of Islam in a dozen countries.

Pickthall, Mohammed Marmaduke. *The Meaning of the Glorious Koran.* New York, 1953. 7th ed., 1959. One of the better translations of the Koran with explanatory comments by an English convert to the religion.

Rahman, Fazlur. *Islam.* New York, 1966. An interpretation of Islam from a sympathetic but critical Muslim viewpoint.

Said, Edward. *Orientalism.* New York, 1978. A sharp critique by an American-Arab scholar of Western scholarship about the Middle East.

Schroeder, Eric. *Muhammad's People: A Tale by Anthology.* Portland, Maine, 1945. An anthology of early Islamic writing.

Southern, R.W.. *Western Views of Islam in the Middle Ages.* Cambridge, Mass., 1962. European misconceptions of Islam.

The Ottomans

Until recently, useful English language works on the Ottoman era were few. The following are among the best for supplying an historical background to the contemporary scene:

Brockelmann, Carl. *History of the Islamic Peoples.* New York, 1960. Contains detailed information on the Ottomans in part 3.

Creasy, Edward S. *History of the Ottoman Turks: From the Beginning of their Empire to the Present Time.* London, 1878, reprint, Beirut, 1961. One of the most extensive works tracing Ottoman history from its origins in 1876.

Davison, Roderic H. *Reform in the Ottoman Empire, 1865–1876.* Princeton, 1963. An authoritative study of the Tanzimat era.

Eliot, Charles N.E. *Turkey in Europe.* London, 1908. Reprint, London, 1965. One of the most interesting and best-written accounts of the Ottoman Empire during the nineteenth century, with historical background.

Fisher, Sydney. *The Middle East: A History.* Cited above. Has good historical survey of the rise and fall of the Ottomans.

Gibb, Hamilton A.R. and Bowen, Harold. *Islamic Society and the West, A Study of the Impact of Western Civilization on Modern Culture in the Near East.* Vol. I, *Islamic Society in the Eighteenth Century,* London, 1950 (part 1) and 1957 (part 2). A comprehensive study of Islamic political and social institutions and their evolution from early times.

Gokalp, Ziya. *Turkish Nationalism and Western Civilization.* Translated and edited, with an introduction, by Niyazi Berkes. New York, 1959. A collection of Gokalp's essays on nationalism, religion, and society.

Heyd, Uriel. *Foundations of Turkish Nationalism: The Life and Teachings of Ziya Gokalp.* London, 1950. Biography of the first modern Turkish nationalist philosopher.

Itzkowitz, Norman. *Ottoman Empire and Islamic Tradition.* New York, 1972. Useful text on history of Ottomans and their institutions.

Kushner, David. *The Rise of Turkish Nationalism, 1876–1908.* London, 1977. The era of Abdul Hamid II.

Lewis, Bernard. *Istanbul and the Civilisation of the Ottoman Empire.* Norman, Okla., 1963. A colorful account of the Ottoman capital at its glory.

Mardin, Serif. *The Genesis of Young Ottoman Thought.* Princeton, 1962. Describes the origin of modern political thought in the Ottoman Empire.

Ramsaur, Ernest E., Jr. *The Young Turks.* Princeton, N.J., 1957. The best account of the Young Turks and their era.

Shaw, Stanford H., and Shaw, Kural Ezel. *History of the Ottoman Empire and Modern Turkey.* Vol. 2, *Reform, Revolution and Republic: The Rise of Modern Turkey 1808–1975.* New York and London, 1977. Deals primarily with the era leading up to establishment of the Republic.

Stavrianos, L.S. *The Balkans Since 1453.* Parts 2 and 3. New York, 1958. Gives an excellent account of the rise and fall of the Ottoman Empire.

Vucinich, Wayne S. *The Ottoman Empire: Its Record and Legacy.* Princeton, 1965. Collection of readings with commentary.

Modern History of the Middle East and Its Relations with the West

The number of books on relations between the Middle East and the West is legion. The subject is covered in part by several of the previously mentioned volumes, particularly those dealing with the region as a whole, and it will be covered in part by books to be listed later under specific countries. Detailed bibliographies dealing with relations during the nineteenth and twentieth centuries can be found in several of the following books.

Bromberger, M. and S. *Secrets of Suez*. London, 1957. Purports to reveal secrets of the French government concerning background of the 1956 attack on Suez.

Dawisha, Karen. *Soviet Foreign Policy Towards Egypt*. New York, 1979. A discussion of Soviet policy objectives, mostly during the Nasser era.

Dekmekian, Richard Hrair. *Patterns of Political Leadership: Egypt, Israel and Lebanon*. Albany, 1975. Study of political elites in three countries.

De Novo, John A. *American Interests and Policies in the Middle East, 1900–1939*. Minneapolis, 1963. A history of American commercial and other interests in the area.

Finer, Herman. *Dulles over Suez: The Theory and Practice of His Diplomacy*. Chicago, 1964. A highly critical account of American and Egyptian policies.

Hallberg, Charles W. *The Suez Canal: Its History and Diplomatic Importance*. New York, 1931. Examines the history of the canal and Anglo-French rivalry over its control.

Halliday, Fred. *Soviet Policy in the Arc of Crisis*. Washington, D.C., 1981. Refutes theory that all problems in the region come from Soviet instigation.

Heikel, Mohammed H. *The Road to Ramadan*. Glasgow, 1976. Account of the 1973 war by an Egyptian official close to Nasser.

———. *The Sphinx and the Commissar: The Rise and Fall of Soviet Influence in the Middle East*. New York, 1978. An account by a direct participant in Egypt's negotiations with the USSR.

Hourani, Albert. *Arabic Thought in the Liberal Arts, 1798–1939*. New York and London, 1962. A history and interpretation of modern Arab thought.

Howard, Harry N. *The King-Crane Commission: An American Inquiry in the Middle East*. Beirut, 1963. A study of post World War I American Investigation Commission.

———. *The Partition of Turkey: A Diplomatic History, 1913–1923*. Norman, Okla., 1931. The best work on the postwar manipulations leading to dismemberment of the Ottoman Empire.

Kedourie, Elie. *England and the Middle East*. London, 1956. Presents a critical study of British policy during and after World War I.

Lord Kinross (Patrick Balfour). *Between Two Seas: The Creation of the Suez Canal*. London, 1968. An account by a British diplomat.

Kirk, George. *The Middle East in the War*. London, 1952.

———. *The Middle East, 1945–1950*. London, 1954. This volume, like the one that preceded it, was issued under the auspices of the Royal Institute of International Affairs as part of the Survey of International Affairs; both are very well documented, although the author's pro-British point of view is fully evident.

Lacquer, Walter. *Confrontation: The Middle East and World Politics.* New York, 1974. Account of the 1973 Arab-Israeli war and its impact on world politics, including the oil crisis.

Lenczowski, George, ed. *Political Elites in the Middle East.* Washington, D.C., 1975. Collected essays on elites in various Middle Eastern countries.

———. *The Middle East in World Affairs.* Ithaca, 1952. 4th ed., 1980. Useful diplomatic history of the area since World War I.

Lewis, Bernard. *The Middle East and the West.* Bloomington, 1964. An extensive historical essay on relations with the West.

Long, David E., and Reich, Bernard. *The Government and Politics of the Middle East and North Africa.* Boulder, 1980. A good introduction, with emphasis on the 1970s.

Love, Kennett. *Suez: The Twice Fought War.* New York, 1969. A voluminous study of the 1956 and 1967 wars.

Mangold, Peter. *Superpower Intervention in the Middle East.* New York, 1978. A compendium of superpower activities, largely since 1970.

Marriott, J.A.R. *The Eastern Question: An Historical Study in European Diplomacy.* Oxford, 1917. A classic study of diplomacy in the area during the nineteenth century.

Meade, Edward Earle. *Turkey, the Great Powers, and the Baghdad Railway: A Study in Imperialism.* New York, 1923. A standard work on the Baghdad railroad and the diplomacy surrounding it in the quarter century before World War I.

Monroe, Elizabeth. *Britain's Moment in the Middle East, 1914–1956.* Baltimore, 1963. Britain's role as a dominant power in the Middle East.

Quandt, William B. *Decade of Decisions: American Policy Toward the Arab-Israeli Conflict, 1967–1976.* Berkeley and Los Angeles, 1977. Survey by an informed ex-insider.

Rubenstein, Alvin Z. *Red Star on the Nile: The Soviet-Egyptian Relationship Since the June (1967) War.* Princeton, 1977.

Sachar, Howard M. *Europe Leaves the Middle East, 1936–1954.* New York, 1972. Comprehensive history of Western involvements in the Middle East.

Schonfield, Hugh J. *The Suez Canal in World Affairs.* New York, 1953. A useful history of the canal and the problems surrounding it.

Shotwell, James T., and Deak, Francis. *Turkey at the Straits: A Short History.* New York, 1940. A diplomatic history of the Straits question.

Sousa, Nasim. *The Capitulatory Regime of Turkey, Its History, Origin, and Nature.* Baltimore, 1933. Survey of the capitulations from the sixteenth through twentieth centuries.

Spector, Ivar. *The Soviet Union and the Muslim World, 1917–1958.* Seattle, 1959. A useful survey based on Soviet sources.

Thomas, Hugh. *The Suez Affair.* New York, 1967. A critical analysis.

Tillman, Seth P. *The United States and the Middle East.* Bloomington, 1982. U.S. policy with a focus on the Arab-Israeli problem.

Toynbee, Arnold J. *Survey of International Affairs, 1925.* Vol. I: *The Islamic World since the Peace Settlement.* A classic analysis of the post World War I Middle East.

Wilson, Arnold. *The Suez Canal.* London, 1933. A useful history.

Arab Nationalism

Books in English on Arab nationalism began to appear in large numbers only after World War II. There is an overlap between the subject of Arab nationalism and others treated in this text, and many of the above-mentioned volumes have excellent sections on the subject, as do many of those later listed under specific countries. The following are a few of the best volumes available in English devoted wholly to the subject:

Abu-Lughod, Ibrahim, ed. *The Transformation of Palestine: Essays on the Origin and Development of the Arab-Israeli Conflict.* Evanston, Illinois, 1971. Land, population and other problems in pre-Israel Palestine from an Arab perspective.

Antonius, George. *The Arab Awakening: The Story of the Arab National Movement.* Philadelphia, 1939; New York, 1965. The classic account, giving an Arab's point of view of the rise of the nationalist movement.

Be'eri, Eliezer. *Army Officers in Arab Politics and Society.* London, 1970. A history and analysis of the role of the military in modern Arab life.

Dawn, Ernest C. *From Ottomanism to Arabism: Essays on the Origins of Arab Nationalism.* Urbana, 1973.

Hassouna, Hussein A. *The League of Arab States and Regional Disputes: A Study of Middle East Conflicts.* Dobbs Ferry, New York, 1975. Covers Arab League activities related to regional disputes between 1945 and 1975.

Hudson, Michael C. *Arab Politics: The Search for Legitimacy.* New Haven and London, 1977. A discussion of political modernization and its dilemmas in the Arab world.

Kerr, Malcolm. *The Arab Cold War, 1958–1967: A Study of Ideology in Politics.* 3d ed., New York, 1971. A critical analysis of inter-Arab politics.

Khadduri, Majid. *Political Trends in the Arab World: The Role of Ideas and Ideals in Politics.* Baltimore, 1970. A critical analysis.

———. *Arab Personalities in Politics.* Washington, D.C., 1981. Case studies of monarchs in Jordan, Saudi Arabia, Oman, UAE, Sadat in Egypt, and Assad in Syria.

Khalidi, Walid, ed. *From Haven to Conquest, Readings in Zionism and the Palestine Problem Until 1948.* Beirut, 1971. An excellent collection from diverse perspectives.

Khalil, Khalid Muhamad. *From Here We Start.* Washington, D.C., 1953. A translation from the Arabic of a work stressing the social and economic aspects of nationalism.

Nuseibeh, Hazem Z. *The Ideas of Arab Nationalism.* Ithaca, 1956. A philosophic study of Arab nationalism by a man who became foreign minister of Jordan in 1961–1962.

Saab, Hassan. *The Arab Federalists of the Ottoman Empire.* Amsterdam, 1958. A detailed treatise on the philosophic origins of the Arab nationalist movement.

Sayegh, Fayez A. *Arab Unity: Hope and Fulfillment.* New York, 1958. Studies the attempts at Arab unity and gives an evaluation of their successes and failures.

Sharabi, Hisham. *Arab Intellectuals and the West: The Formative Years, 1875–1914.* Baltimore, 1970. Origins of an Arab ideology.

Zeine, Zeine N. *Arab-Turkish Relations and the Emergence of Arab Nationalism.* Beirut, 1958. 3d ed. Delmar, N.Y., 1976. An excellent account of the origins of the Arab nationalist movement and its early relations with Ottoman authorities from a fresh viewpoint.

————. *The Struggle for Arab Independence.* Beirut, 1960. An account of the Arab Nationalist movement during and immediately after World War I.

Modern Turkey and the Cyprus Conflict

Books listed above under the "Ottomans" and those dealing with Turkey under "The West and the Middle East" provide background for the coming of the Turkish republic. The following are only a few of the many worthwhile volumes published on the subject since World War I:

Ahmad, Feroz. *The Turkish Experiment in Democracy—1950–1975.* London, 1977. Comprehensive and clear study of Turkish politics since World War II.

Berkes, Niyazi. *The Development of Secularism in Turkey.* Montreal, 1964. A study of secularism from the Ottoman to the modern era.

Crawshaw, Nancy. *The Cyprus Revolt: An Account of the Struggle for Union with Greece.* London, 1978. A comprehensive historical account of the Cypriot-Greek revolt against Great Britain.

Dodd, C.H. *Democracy and Development in Turkey.* North Humberside, U.K., 1979. An examination of Turkey's history, society, and government.

Hale, William. *The Political and Economic Development of Modern Turkey.* New York and London, 1981. A useful introduction to Turkish economic problems.

Iz, Fahir, ed. *An Anthology of Modern Turkish Short Stories.* Chicago, 1978. 37 stories published from 1900 to 1975.

Karpat, Kemal, and contributors. *Social Change and Politics in Turkey: A Structural-Historical Analysis.* Leiden, 1973. Study of Turkish politics and society.

Karpat, Kemal. *The Gecekondu: Rural Migration and Urbanization.* New York, 1976. Detailed study of urban slum expansion in modern Turkey.

Lord Kinross (Patrick Balfour). *Ataturk: A Biography of Mustafa Kemal, Father of Modern Turkey.* New York, 1965. An extensive and colorful biography.

Landau, Jacob M. *Radical Politics in Modern Turkey.* Leiden, 1974. A detailed study of both right and left political factions.

Lewis, Geoffrey L. *Turkey.* New York, 1955. 4th ed., 1974. A concise, factual, excellent volume on present-day political and social life in Turkey and the background leading up to developments in 1962.

Makal, Mahmut. *A Village in Anatolia.* London, 1954. An account by a teacher of life in a traditional village.

Özbunden, Ergun. *Social Change and Political Participation in Turkey.* Princeton, 1976. An analysis of the effect of social change on Turkish politics.

Salih, Halil Ibrahim. *Cyprus: The Impact of Diverse Nationalism on a State.* Alabama, 1978. A well-documented account of events leading up to the 1974 Turkish intervention.

Stirling, Arthur P. *Turkish Village.* New York, 1966. A study of tradition and change in a Turkish village.

Toynbee, Arnold J., and Kirkwood, Kenneth P. *Turkey.* New York, 1927. An excellent account of transformation of the Ottoman Empire to the Turkish republic.

Ward, Robert E., and Rustow, Dankwart. *Political Modernization in Japan and Turkey.* Princeton, 1968. A collection of essays by various authors on comparative modernization.

Webster, Donald E. *The Turkey of Ataturk: Social Process in the Turkish Reformation.* Philadelphia, 1939. A detailed and sympathetic survey of political and social change in Turkey up to 1938.

Weiker, Walter F. *The Turkish Revolution, 1960–1961: Aspects of Military Policies.* Washington, 1963. A study of the 1960 coup.

——— *The Modernization of Turkey: From Ataturk to the Present Day.* New York and London, 1981. An overall evaluation of political and social development.

Egypt

Since the 1952 revolution in Egypt the number of books in English on that country has greatly increased, partly as a result of its predominant role in the Arab world today. Books dealing primarily with the Suez Canal problem have been listed above. The following references deal with the country as a whole.

Ahmed, Jamal M. *Intellectual Origins of Egyptian Nationalism.* London, 1960. Contains an excellent study of philosophic origins of the nationalist movement.

Ayrout, Henri H. *The Fellaheen, Cairo, 1945.* Reissue, Boston, 1968. The best account of Egyptian peasant life by a priest who has spent most of his life among the fellaheen.

Baer, Gabriel. *A History of Landownership in Modern Egypt, 1800–1950.* London, 1962. A survey of prerevolutionary landholding.

Binder, Leonard. *In a Moment of Enthusiasm: Political Power and the Second Stratum.* Chicago, 1978. An analysis of second level or local politics in Egypt.

Cooper, Mark N. *The Transformation of Egypt.* Baltimore, 1982. An analysis of the internal problems from 1967 to 1977.

Critchfield, Richard. *Shahhati: An Egyptian.* Syracuse, 1978. A narrative account of the life of an Egyptian peasant from an anthropolgical perspective.

Cromer, Evelyn Baring, Earl. *Modern Egypt.* 2 vols. London, 1908. Presents a British ruler's account of his regime and its social background.

Dekmejian, Richard Hrair. *Egypt Under Nasser: A Study in Political Dynamics.* Albany, 1971. Analysis of the revolutionary leadership and its background.

Harris, Christina Phelps. *Nationalism and Revolution in Egypt: the Role of the Muslim Brotherhood.* The Hague, 1964. Historical account of the Brotherhood.

Holt, P.M., ed. *Political and Social Change in Modern Egypt: Historical Studies from the Ottoman Conquest to the United Arab Republic.* New York, 1967. Three-part anthology: part 1, source material; part 2, 1517–1798; part 3, nineteenth and twentieth centuries.

Hopwood, Derek. *Egypt: Politics and Society: 1945–1981.* Winchester, Mass., 1982. Survey of the Nasser and Sadat regimes.

Issawi, Charles. *Egypt at Mid-Century*. New York, 1954. A fundamental economic analysis.

———. *Egypt in Revolution: An Economic Analysis*. London, 1963. Egypt's economy since the 1952 revolution.

Lacouture, Jean and Simone. *Egypt in Transition*. New York, 1958. A translation from the French of revolutionary Egypt and its background.

Lacouture, Jean. *Nasser: A Biography*. New York, 1973. One of the best on Nasser.

Lane, E.W. *Manners and Customs of the Modern Egyptians*. New York, 1923. A good survey of rural and city life along the Nile.

Lloyd, George Ambrose. *Egypt Since Cromer*. New York, 1933–1934. A former British high commissioner's account of events after Cromer.

Marlowe, John. *A History of Modern Egypt and Anglo-Egyptian Relations, 1800–1953*. New York, 1954. A useful survey of relations with Great Britain.

el Messini, Sawsan. *Ibn Al-Balad: A Concept of Egyptian Identity*. Leiden, 1978. A sociological study of the lower middle class in Cairo.

Mitchell, Richard P. *The Society of Muslim Brothers*. London, 1969. Background, origins, structure, and ideology of the Brotherhood.

Nasser, Gamal Abdel. *Egypt's Liberation: The Philosophy of the Revolution*. Washington, D.C., 1955. The late president's early views on the revolution, which differ from his later ones.

Neguib, Mohammed. *Egypt's Destiny*. New York, 1955. An account of the revolution by the Egyptian republic's first president.

O'Brien, Patrick. *The Revolution in Egypt's Economic System: From Private Enterprise to Socialism, 1952–1965*. London and New York, 1966. Economic change since Nasser.

Richmond, John C.B. *Egypt, 1798–1952—Her Advance toward a Modern Identity*. New York, 1977. An introductory survey.

Rivlin, Helen Anne B. *The Agricultural Policy of Muhammad 'Ali in Egypt*. Cambridge, Mass., 1961. An excellent analysis of Muhammad 'Ali's attempts to create a modern economy.

Sadat, Anwar. *In Search of Identity: An Autobiography*. New York, 1978.

Safran, Nadav. *Egypt in Search of Political Community, An Analysis of the Intellectual and Political Evolution of Egypt, 1804–1952*. Cambridge, Mass., 1961. A valuable survey.

El-Shamy, Hasan M., ed. *Folktales of Egypt*. Chicago, 1980. A collection and analysis of folklore.

Vatikiotis, P.J. *The Egyptian Army in Politics, Pattern for New Nations?* Bloomington, Ind., 1961. Useful analysis of the officers' backgrounds and their attempts at reform.

———. *Nasser and His Generation*. New York, 1978. A psychopolitical portrait of Nasser and his milieu.

Waterbury, John. *Egypt: Burdens of the Past, Options for the Future*. Bloomington, 1978. A series of essays on diverse economic, social, and political problems by a long-time observer.

———. *Hydropolitics in the Nile Valley*. Syracuse, 1979. A study and analysis of political and economic development plans in Egypt and Sudan.

Israel

So great is the amount of material published on Israel and the Palestine problem that it probably exceeds that published on all the other countries covered in this book. The following are but a few of the more useful items:

Begin, Menachem. *The Revolt.* New York, 1978. Revised edition of the Israeli prime minister's early years in Palestine-Israel.

Ben-Dor, Gabriel. *The Druses in Israel, A Political Study: Political Innovation and Integration in a Middle East Minority.* Jerusalem and Boulder, 1979. A study of socio-political change from the local and national perspective.

Ben Gurion, David. *Rebirth and Destiny of Israel.* New York, 1954. Contains a collection of essays on Israel's role by its first prime minister.

Benvenisti, Meron. *Jerusalem: The Torn City.* Minneapolis, 1976. Discusses pros and cons of nearly 50 solutions for the Jerusalem problem.

Brecher, Michael. *The Foreign Policy System of Israel: Setting, Images, Process.* New Haven, 1972. Comprehensive study of organization and context of Israeli foreign policy.

El-Asmar, Fouzi. *To Be an Arab in Israel.* London, 1975. Experiences of an Israeli Arab.

Elon, Amos. *The Israelis Founders and Sons.* New York, 1971. Reissue, 1983. An Israeli's insights into the old and new generations of Israelis.

Fabian, Larry L., and Schiff, Ze'ev. *Israelis Speak: About Themselves and the Palestinians.* Washington, D.C., 1977. In-depth discussion by Israelis of diverse orientations about Arab-Israel and other problems.

Friedlander, Dov, and Goldscheider, Calvin. *The Population of Israel.* New York, 1979. A detailed and scholarly analysis.

Granott, A. *The Land System in Palestine: History and Structure.* London, 1952. History of Arab, Jewish, and government landholdings and laws before 1948.

Halabi, Rafik. *The West Bank Story: An Israeli Arab's View of a Tangled Conflict.* New York, 1982.

Halperin, Samuel. *The Political World of American Zionism.* Detroit, 1961. Contains a good account of the role played by Zionist groups in shaping American policy.

Halpern, Ben. *The Idea of the Jewish State.* Cambridge, Mass., 1961. Detailed and thorough analysis of the concept of Jewish sovereignty.

Herzl, Theodor. *The Jewish State: An Attempt at a Modern Solution of the Jewish Question.* London, 1934. Translation from the German of Herzl's original views.

Hurewitz, J.C. *The Struggle for Palestine.* New York, 1950. A good factual account of the Arab-Jewish-British conflict in Palestine.

Kanofsky, Eliahu. *The Economy of the Israeli Kibbutz.* Cambridge, 1966. A critical analysis.

Laqueur, Walter. *A History of Zionism.* New York, 1972. A comprehensive, in-depth history.

Lilienthal, Alfred. *The Zionist Connection: What Price Peace?* New York, 1978. An anti-Zionist study of Israel–U.S. relations.

Lustick, Ian. *Arabs in the Jewish State: Israel's Control of a National Minority.* Austin, 1980. Discussion of Israel's Arab minority in a new theoretical context.

Penniman, Howard R., ed. *Israel at the Polls: The Knesset Elections of 1977.* Washington, D.C., 1979. Collection of essays on many aspects of the election.

Peretz, Don. *The Government and Politics of Israel.* Boulder, 1979. Discussion of the origins and operation of Israel's government.

Perlmutter, Amos. *Military and Politics in Israel: Nation Building and Role Expansion.* London, 1969. Examines the influence of Israel's military establishment.

———. *Politics and the Military in Israel, 1967–77.* Cambridge, Mass., 1978.

Sachar, Howard M. *A History of Israel from the Rise of Zionism to Our Time.* New York, 1976. Excellent and comprehensive history of modern Israel.

Safran, Nadav. *Israel: The Embattled Ally.* Cambridge and London, 1978. A comprehensive survey of both internal and foreign developments.

Schiff, Gary S. *Tradition and Politics: The Religious Parties of Israel.* Detroit, 1977. An account of the National Religious and Aguda Israel parties.

Schnall, David J. *Radical Dissent in Contemporary Israeli Politics: Cracks in the Wall.* New York, 1979. An examination of several smaller, but important left and right factions.

Segre, Dan V. *A Crisis of Identity: Israel and Zionism.* Oxford and New York, 1980. A discussion of whether or not traditional Jewish culture can adapt to Israel.

Shimshoni, Daniel. *Israeli Democracy: The Middle of the Journey.* New York, 1982. A discussion of diverse problems in policy making.

Smooha, Sammy. *Israel: Pluralism and Conflict.* Berkeley and Los Angeles, 1978. A comprehensive survey of the situation of Israeli Arabs, Oriental and Religious Jews.

Weizmann, Chaim. *Trial and Error: The Autobiography of Chaim Weizmann.* New York, 1949. Relates the trials of Israel's first president up to the time of statehood.

Willner, Dorothy. *Nation-Building and Community in Israel.* Princeton, 1969. A study of Oriental-Jewish community life in Israel.

The Palestinians and the Arab-Israeli Conflict

Amos, John W. *Palestinian Resistance: Organization of a Nationalism Movement.* New York, 1980. An extensive study of all aspects of the Palestinian movement.

Aronson, Sholomo. *Conflict and Bargaining in the Middle East: An Israeli Perspective.* Baltimore, 1978. A heavily documented history of negotiations from Kissinger on.

Brecher, Michael. *Decisions in Crisis: Israel 1967 and 1973.* Berkeley, 1980. A detailed study of decisions by Israeli policy makers leading to the 1967 and 1973 wars.

Brown, William R. *The Last Crusade: A Negotiator's Middle East Handbook.* Chicago, 1980. An examination of the importance of mutual perceptions in negotiations.

Cohen, Aaron. *Israel and the Arab World.* New York, 1970. Excellent study of Arab-Jewish relations in Palestine. Translated from Hebrew.

Dayan, Moshe. *Breakthrough: A Personal Account of Egypt-Israel Peace Negotiations.* London and New York, 1981.

ESCO Foundation for Palestine, Inc. *Palestine: A Study of Jewish, Arab, and British Policies.* 2 vols. New Haven, 1947. A collection of articles on Palestine during the mandate era.

Flapan, Simha. *Zionism and the Palestinians.* New York, 1978. A study of some lost opportunities for peace.

Herzog, Chaim. *The Arab-Israeli Wars.* New York, 1982. A popular but professional military history.

Hirst, David. *The Gun and The Olive Branch: The Roots of Violence in the Middle East.* London, 1977. A sympathetic but not uncritical discussion of the Palestinian movement.

Kerr, Malcolm H., ed. *The Elusive Peace in the Middle East.* Albany, 1975. A collection of articles on Arab-Israel relations and efforts to attain a peace settlement.

Khouri, Fred. *The Arab Israel Dilemma.* Syracuse, 1968. 2d ed., 1976. An extensive study based mostly on UN sources.

Lesch, Ann Mosley. *Arab Politics in Palestine, 1917–1939: The Frustration of a Nationalist Movement.* Ithaca and London, 1979. A scholarly study.

Migdal, Joel S. *Palestinian Society and Politics.* Princeton, 1980. Collection of essays on history and social structure of the Palestinians.

Nakleh, Khalil, and Zureik, Elia, eds. *The Sociology of the Palestinians.* New York, 1980. A collection of articles in social structure and society.

O'Ballance, Edgar. *No Victor, No Vanquished: The Yom Kippur War.* San Rafael, California and London, 1978. An interesting and well-written account.

Polk, William R.; Stamler, D.; and Asfour, E. *Backdrop to Tragedy: The Struggle for Palestine.* Boston, 1957. The best study available of the emotions involved in the Palestine conflict.

Said, Edward. *The Question of Palestine.* New York, 1979. A forceful presentation of the Palestinian case by a Palestinian-American.

Sid-Ahmed, Mohamed. *After the Guns Fall Silent: Peace or Armageddon in the Middle East.* London and New York, 1976. A leftist analysis of the Arab-Israeli conflict and the role of the great powers.

Sykes, Christopher. *Crossroads to Israel.* New York, 1965. Story of Anglo-Jewish Arab relations, 1919–1948.

Weizmann, Ezer. *The Battle for Peace.* New York, Toronto, London, 1981. A former general and defense minister's critique of Begin's peace negotiations.

Wilson, Evan M. *Decision on Palestine: How the U.S. Came to Recognize Israel.* Stanford, 1979. A veteran diplomat's insight into American policy making.

Zurayk, Constantine N. *Palestine: The Meaning of the Disaster.* Beirut, 1956. An analysis of the Arab defeat by a noted scholar, translated from the Arabic.

Lebanon

Because Syria and Lebanon had many aspects of a single administration until their independence at the end of World War II, some authors have treated them in a single volume. The following lists contain a few more useful specific items:

Barakat, Halim. *Lebanon in Strife: Student Preludes to the Civil War.* Austin and London, 1977. A survey and analysis of Lebanese student attitudes.

Deeb, Marius. *The Lebanese Civil War.* New York, 1980. A topical account.

Gabriel, Philip Louis. *In the Ashes: A Story of Lebanon.* Ardmore, Penn., 1978. An account of the social origins of the civil war.

Gordon, David C. *Lebanon: The Fragmented Nation.* Stanford and London, 1980. A personal account of the civil war by an American.

Gulick, John. *Social Structure and Culture Change in a Lebanese Village.* New York, 1955. An anthropologist's study of changing ideas and values.

Hudson, Michael. *The Precarious Republic: Political Modernization in Lebanon.* New York, 1969. A critical political analysis.

Khalidi, Walid. *Conflict and Violence in Lebanon: Confrontation in the Middle East.* Cambridge, Mass., 1980. Background of the civil war by an informed insider.

Owen, Roger, ed. *Essays on the Crisis in Lebanon.* London, 1976. Essays by diverse authors tracing the conflict to its nineteenth century roots.

Polk, William R. *The Opening of South Lebanon, 1788–1840.* Cambridge, 1963. A study of change in nineteenth century rural Lebanon.

Salibi, Kamal S. *Crossroads to Civil War, Lebanon 1958–1976.* Delmar, N.Y., 1976. An account of the 1975–76 war explaining the diverse groups, trends, events, military faces, and personalities.

———. *The Modern History of Lebanon.* New York, 1965. Major emphasis on the nineteenth century.

Suleiman, Michael W. *Political Parties in Lebanon: The Challenge of a Fragmented Political Culture.* Ithaca, 1967. A socio-political study.

Syria

Abu Jaber, Kamal S. *The Arab Ba'ath Socialist Party: History, Ideology, and Organization.* Syracuse, 1966. First major study of the Ba'ath party in English.

Devlin, John F. *The Ba'ath Party: A History From Its Origins to 1966.* Stanford, 1976. Origins during the French mandate to evolution in Jordan and Iraq.

Hourani, Albert H. *Syria and Lebanon.* London, 1946. The best account and analysis of the Levant up to the end of World War II.

Longrigg, Stephen H. *Syria and Lebanon Under French Mandate.* London, 1958. A scholarly history of the Levant from Ottoman times to independence.

Rabinovitch, Itamar. *Syria Under the Ba'ath 1963–1966: The Army-Party Symbiosis.* New York, 1972.

Seale, Patrick. *The Struggle for Syria: A Study of Post-War Arab Politics, 1945–1958.* New York, 1965.

Torrey, Gordon H. *Syrian Politics and the Military, 1945–1958.* Columbus, 1964. A study of the manuevers leading to union with Egypt.

Jordan

In addition to previously mentioned general works, the following books are recommended:

Abdullah Ibn Husayn. *Memoirs of King Abdullah.* New York, 1950. An autobiography, translated from Arabic by G. Khuri.

Antoun, Richard. *Low-Key Politics: Local-Level Leadership and Change in the Middle East.* Albany, 1979. An anthropologist's account of politics at the village level in Jordan.

———. *Arab Village: A Social Structural Study of a Transjordanian Peasant Community.* Bloomington, Illinois, 1972. An anthropological study.

Glubb, J.B. *A Soldier with the Arab.* New York, 1957. Glubb's account of Jordan's role in the 1948 Arab-Israeli War.

———. *The Story of the Arab Legion.* New York, 1957. Personal account of Arab Legion commander.

Harris, George L. *Jordan: Its People, Its Society, Its Culture.* New York, 1958. A composite study by several authors.

Hussein of Jordan. *My "War" With Israel.* New York, 1969. King Hussein's account of the Six-Day War.

———. *Uneasy Lies the Head: The Autobiography of His Majesty King Hussein of the Hashemite Kingdom of Jordan.* New York, 1962.

Lutfiya, Abdullah M. *Baytin: A Jordanian Village: A Study of Social Institutions and Social Change on a Folk Community.* The Hague, 1966.

Shwadran, Benjamin. *Jordan: A State of Tension.* New York, 1959. A history and background of Jordan.

Vatikiotis, Panayotis, J. *Politics and the Military in Jordan: A Study of the Arab Legion, 1921–1957.* New York, 1967.

Iraq

Arfa, Hassan. *The Kurds: An Historical and Political Study.* London, 1966. Kurdish history from early times to the present.

Birdwood, Christopher. *Nuri as-Said: A Study in Arab Leadership.* London, 1960. Eulogistic biography of the former Iraqi prime minister.

Caractacus. *Revolution in Iraq.* London, 1959. An anonymous Englishman's favorable story of the 1958 Iraqi revolution and a critique of Western Middle East policy.

Dann, Uriel. *Iraq Under Qassem: A Political History, 1958–1963.* New York, 1969. The early revolutionary period.

Foster, Henry A. *The Making of Modern Iraq.* Norman, Okla., 1953. A scholarly account of the early history of Iraq.

Gabbay, Rony. *Communism and Agrarian Reform in Iraq.* London, 1978. A historical focus.

Ghareeb, Edmund. *The Kurdish Question in Iraq.* Syracuse, 1981. The Kurds in Iraq with primary focus on the Ba'ath government's approach.

Khadduri, Majid. *Independent Iraq: A Study in Iraqi Politics from 1932 to 1958.* London, 1960. 1st ed., 1951. A thorough study of Iraqi politics and parties.

———. *Republican Iraq: A Study in Iraqi Politics Since the Revolution of 1958.* New York, 1969.

———. *Socialist Iraq: A Study in Iraqi Politics Since 1968.* Washington, D.C., 1978.

Ireland, Philip W. *Iraq: A Study in Political Development.* London, 1937. An excellent account by an American diplomat of Iraq's early history and political progress.

Longrigg, Stephen, and Stoakes, Frank. *Iraq.* New York, 1958. A comprehensive history.

O'Ballance, Edgar. *The Kurdish Revolt, 1961–1970.* London, 1973. Military account of the Kurdish war.

Shwadran, Benjamin. *The Power Struggle in Iraq.* New York, 1960. Analyzes the 1958 revolution and the subsequent political turmoil.

Arabian Peninsula

In addition to the previously mentioned books on oil, which deal primarily with the Arabian peninsula, the following were also recommended:

Anthony, John Duke. *Arab States of the Lower Gulf: People, Politics, Petroleum.* Washington, D.C., 1975. Study of the nine Gulf states.

Clements, F.A. *Oman: The Reborn Land.* New York, 1980. A laudatory account of the Qabus regime.

Doughty, Charles M. *Travels in Arabia Deserta.* New York, 1955. Represents the classic study of an English traveler through the Arabian desert.

Halliday, Fred. *Arabia Without Sultans.* New York, 1975. Survey of revolutionary change in south Arabia and the Gulf from a left perspective.

Holden, David, and Johns, Richard. *The House of Saud: The Rise and Rule of the Most Powerful Dynasty in the Arab World.* London and New York, 1981. A critical account.

Hogarth, David. *The Desert King: The Life of Ibn Saud.* London, 1968. An authoritative biography.

al-Ibrahim, Hasan A. *Kuwayt: A Political Study.* Kuwait, 1975. Covers the political development of Kuwait from 1896 through the 1960s.

Khalifa, Ali Mohammed. *The United Arab Emirates: Unity in Fragmentation.* Boulder, 1979. Treatise on formation and problems of the U.A.E.

Lackner, Helen. *A House Built on Sand: A Political Economy of Saudi Arabia.* London, 1978. A socialist critique of Saudi life and economy.

Long, David E. *The Persian Gulf: An Introduction to Its Peoples, Politics and Economies.* Boulder, Col., 1976. Good short introduction.

Morris, James. *Sultan in Oman.* New York, 1957. A British journalist's story of his adventures in Muscat and Oman.

Nakhleh, Emile. *Bahrein: Political Development in a Modernizing Society.* Lexington, Mass., 1976.

Peterson, John E. *Yemen: The Search for a Modern State.* Baltimore, 1982. The dynamic of political change in Yemen.

Philby, H. St. John, B. *Arabian Jubilee.* London, 1951. The story of the Saud dynasty by a British former close associate and advisor of the king.

———. *Saudi Arabia.* New York, 1955. Philby's history of the kingdom.

Quandt, William B. *Saudi Arabia in the 1980s.* Washington, D.C., 1981. An overview of current Saudi foreign and domestic policies with emphasis on the U.S. connection.

Salibi, Kamal. *A History of Arabia.* Delmar, N.Y., 1980. A detailed history of the Peninsula from 3000 B.C. to the present.

Shaw, John A., and Long, David E. *Saudi Arabian Modernization: The Impact of Change on Stability.* Washington, D.C., 1982. Analysis of problems and potential of economic development and its socio-political impact.

Stookey, Robert W. *Yemen: The Politics of the Yemen Arab Republic.* Boulder, Col., 1978. An insightful work on a little known country.

Thesiger, Wilfred. *Arabian Sands.* New York, 1959. Another account of a British traveler's experiences in the deserts of southern Arabia.

Townsend, John. *Oman: The Making of a Modern State.* New York, 1977. Critique of administrative development and institution building in Oman.

Van der Meulen, Daniel. *The Wells of Ibn Saud.* New York, 1957. Experiences of a Dutch diplomat who lived in Saudi Arabia over ten years.

Zahlan, Rosemarie Said. *The Origins of the United Arab Emirates: A Political and Social History of the Trucial States.* New York, 1978. A critical account of British rule.

Iran

In addition to the general works previously listed, the following are recommended:

Abrahamian, Ervand. *Iran: Between Two Revolutions.* Princeton, 1982. An account from 1905 to 1979 with focus on the Tudeh Party.

Ahmed, Eqbal, ed. *The Iranian Revolution.* London, 1979. A special issue of the British journal, *Race and Class,* vol. 21, no. 1, Summer 1979. Containing a comprehensive group of informative articles.

Akhavi, Shahrough. *Religion and Politics in Contemporary Iran: Clergy-State Relations in the Pahlavi Period.* Albany, 1980. An informed study of the religious background on the 1979 Revolution.

Bill, James A. *The Politics of Iran: Groups, Classes, and Modernization.* Columbus, Ohio, 1972. Study of elites and the power structure.

Browne, Edward G. *The Persian Revolution of 1905-1909.* Cambridge, 1910, republished London, 1966. The best account available of that revolution.

Cottam, Richard W. *Nationalism in Iran.* Pittsburgh, 1964. An analysis of various contending group interests.

Elwell-Sutton, Lawrence P. *Persian Oil: A Study in Power Politics.* London, 1955. The Persian point of view of the oil dispute with Great Britain.

Halliday, Fred. *Iran: Dictatorship and Development.* New York, 1979. A social and economic analysis.

Heikal, Mohamed. *Iran: The Untold Story: An Insider's Account of America's Iranian Adventure and Its Consequences for the Future.* New York, 1981.

Hooglund, Eric J. *Land and Revolution in Iran, 1960-1980.* Austin, 1982. A critique of the Shah's "White Revolution."

Issawi, Charles, ed. *The Economic History of Iran 1800-1914.* Chicago, 1971. Documentary economic history.

Keddie, Nikki R. *Roots of Revolution: An Interpretive History of Modern Iran.* New Haven and London, 1981. The 19th and 20th century origins of the 1979 Revolution.

Kedourie, Elie, and Haim, Sylvia, eds. *Towards a Modern Iran: Politics and Society.* London, 1980. A series of useful essays on background of the 1979 Revolution including some personality sketches.

Lambton, A.K.S. *Landlord and Peasant in Persia: A Study of Land Tenure and Land Reserve Administration.* London, 1953.

———. *Islamic Society in Persia.* London, 1954.

Ledeen, Michael, and Lewis, William. *Debacle: The American Failure in Iran.* New York, 1981. A critique of American policy.

Lenczowski, George. *Russian and the West in Iran, 1918–1948.* Ithaca, 1949. An excellent study by a former Polish diplomat in Iran.

Millspaugh, Arthur C. *Americans in Persia.* Washington, D.C., 1946. The experiences of an American adviser to the Shah.

Pahlavi, Mohammed Reza. *Answer to History.* New York, 1980. The late Shah's account for his regime and its fall.

Ramazani, Rouhollah, K. *Iran's Foreign Policy, 1941–1973: A Study of Foreign Policy in Modernizing Nations.* Charlottesville, Va., 1975.

Rubin, Barry. *Paved With Good Intentions: The American Experience in Iran.* London and New York, 1981. Post World War II relations between the U.S. and Iran.

Saikal, Amin. *The Rise and Fall of the Shah.* Princeton, 1980. History and analysis of the Pahlavi dynasty.

Shuster, Morgan W. *The Strangling of Persia.* New York, 1912. Observations of an American financial adviser to Persia before World War I.

Sykes, Percy M. *A History of Persia.* London, 1915. 3d ed., 1930. 2 vols. Lengthy and detailed history of Persia from ancient times to 1930.

Wilson, Arnold T. *Persia.* New York, 1933. Primarily a historical survey.

Zonis, Marvin. *The Political Elite of Iran.* Princeton, 1971. Relations between Shah and elite.

Index

About the Author

Don Peretz has been professor of political science at the State University of New York in Binghamton, New York since 1967. He was the director of the university's program in South West Asian and North African studies from 1967 to 1977. From 1962 to 1967 he was associate director of the Center for Comparative Programs and Services of the New York State Education Department—University of the State of New York. Other books he has written or co-authored include: *Government and Politics of Israel; Israel and the Palestine Arabs; The Middle East—Selected Readings; Middle East Foreign Policy; Islam—Legacy of the Past, Promise of the Future*. His articles have appeared in *Foreign Affairs, Orbis, Middle East Journal, Wilson Quarterly, Jewish Social Studies, Christianity and Crisis, Progressive, Commonweal, Christian Century, Annals of the Academy of Political and Social Sciences*, and others. He is a member of the Editorial Advisory Board of the *Middle East Journal* and has been a member of the Board of Directors of the Middle East Studies Association of North America.